W9-BOB-976

wwnorton.com/nawol

The StudySpace site that accompanies *The Norton
Anthology of World Literature* is FREE, but you will need
the code below to register for a password that will allow you
to access the copyrighted materials on the site.

ZNVB-LCRJ

THE NORTON ANTHOLOGY OF

WORLD LITERATURE

SHORTER THIRD EDITION

VOLUME 2

THE NORTON ANTHOLOGY OF

WORLD LITERATURE

SHORTER THIRD EDITION

MARTIN PUCHNER, *General Editor*
HARVARD UNIVERSITY

SUZANNE AKBARI
UNIVERSITY OF TORONTO

WIEBKE DENECKE
BOSTON UNIVERSITY

VINAY DHARWADKER
UNIVERSITY OF WISCONSIN, MADISON

BARBARA FUCHS
UNIVERSITY OF CALIFORNIA, LOS ANGELES

CAROLINE LEVINE
UNIVERSITY OF WISCONSIN, MADISON

PERICLES LEWIS
YALE UNIVERSITY

EMILY WILSON
UNIVERSITY OF PENNSYLVANIA

VOLUME 2

W. W. NORTON & COMPANY | New York · London

W. W. Norton & Company has been independent since its founding in 1923, when William Warder Norton and Mary D. Herter Norton first published lectures delivered at the People's Institute, the adult education division of New York City's Cooper Union. The firm soon expanded its program beyond the Institute, publishing books by celebrated academics from America and abroad. By midcentury, the two major pillars of Norton's publishing program—trade books and college texts—were firmly established. In the 1950s, the Norton family transferred control of the company to its employees, and today—with a staff of four hundred and a comparable number of trade, college, and professional titles published each year—W. W. Norton & Company stands as the largest and oldest publishing house owned wholly by its employees.

Editor: Peter Simon
Assistant Editor: Conor Sullivan
Editorial Assistant: Quynh Do
Managing Editor, College: Marian Johnson
Manuscript Editors: Barney Latimer, Alice Falk, Katharine Ings, Michael Fleming, Susan Joseph, Pamela Lawson
Project Editor: Diane Cipollone
Electronic Media Editor: Eileen Connell
Print Ancillary Editor: Laura Musich
Editorial Assistant, Media: Jennifer Barnhardt
Marketing Manager, Literature: Kimberly Bowers
Production Manager, College: Sean Mintus
Photo Editor: Patricia Marx
Permissions Manager: Megan Jackson
Permissions Clearing: Margaret Gorenstein
Text Design: Jo Anne Metsch
Art Director: Rubina Yeh
Cartographer: Adrian Kitzinger
Composition: Jouve North America, Brattleboro, VT
Manufacturing: R. R. Donnelley & Sons—Crawfordsville, IN

The text of this book is composed in Fairfield Medium with the display set in Aperto.

Library of Congress Cataloging-in-Publication Data has been applied for.

ISBN: 978-0-393-91961-5 (pbk.)

W. W. Norton & Company, Inc., 500 Fifth Avenue, New York, NY 10110-0017
wwnorton.com
W. W. Norton & Company Ltd., Castle House, 75/76 Wells Street, London W1T 3QT

1 2 3 4 5 6 7 8 9 0

Contents

V. REALISM ACROSS THE GLOBE   697

VII. POSTWAR AND POSTCOLONIAL LITERATURE, 1945–1968

Preface

In 1665, a Turkish nobleman traveled from his native Istanbul to Europe and recorded with disarming honesty his encounter with an alien civilization. Over the course of his life, Evliya Çelebi would crisscross the Ottoman Empire from Egypt all the way to inner Asia, filling volume after volume with his reports of the cities, peoples, and legends he came across. This was his first journey to Vienna, a longtime foe of the Ottoman Empire. Full of confidence about the superiority of his own culture, Evliya was nevertheless impressed by Vienna's technical and cultural achievements. One episode from his *Travels,* a charming moment of self-deprecation, tells us how, during his tour of Vienna's inner city, Evliya sees what he believes to be "captives from the nation of Muhammad" sitting in front of various shops, toiling away at mind-numbing, repetitive tasks. Feeling pity for them, he offers them some coins, only to find that they are in fact mechanical automatons. Embarrassed and amazed at the same time, Evliya ends this tale by embracing the pleasure of seeing something new: "This was a marvelous and wonderful adventure indeed!"

Throughout his travels, Evliya remained good-humored about such disorienting experiences, and he maintained an open mind as he compared the cultural achievements of his home with those of Vienna. The crowning achievement of Vienna is the cathedral, which towers over the rest of the city. But Evliya found that it couldn't compare with the architectural wonders of Istanbul's great mosques. As soon as he was taken to the library, however, he was awestruck: "There are God knows how many books in the mosques of Sultan Barqūq and Sultan Faraj in Cairo, and in the mosques of [Sultan Meḥmed] The Conqueror and Sultan Süleymān and Sultan Bāyezīd and the New Mosque, but in this St. Stephen's Monastery in Vienna there are even more." He admired the sheer diversity and volume of books: "As many nations and different languages as there are, of all their authors and writers in their languages there are many times a hundred thousand books here." He was drawn, naturally enough, to the books that make visible the contours and riches of the world: atlases, maps, and illustrated books. An experienced travel writer, he nonetheless struggled to keep his equilibrium, saying finally that he was simply "stunned."

Opening *The Norton Anthology of World Literature* for the first time, a reader may feel as overwhelmed by its selection of authors and works (from "as many different languages as there are") as Evliya was by the cathedral library. For most students, the world literature course is a semester- or year-long encounter with the unknown—a challenging and rewarding journey, not a stroll down familiar, well-worn paths. Secure in their knowledge of the culture of their upbringing, and perhaps even proud of its accomplishments, most students will discover in world literature a bewildering variety of similarly rich and admirable cultures about which they know little, or nothing. Setting off on an imaginative journey in an unfamiliar text, readers may ask themselves questions similar to those a traveler in a strange land might ponder: How should I orient myself in this unfamiliar culture? What am I not seeing that someone raised in this culture would recognize right away? What can I learn here? How can I relate to the people I meet? Students might imagine the perils of the encounter, wondering if they will embarrass themselves in the process, or simply find themselves "stunned" by the sheer number of things they do not know.

But as much as they may feel anxiety at the prospect of world literature, students may also feel, as Evliya did, excitement at the discovery of something new, the exhilaration of having their horizons expanded. This, after all, is why Evliya traveled in the first place. Travel, for him, became almost an addiction. He sought again and again the rush of the unknown, the experience of being stunned, the feeling of marveling over cultural achievements from across the world. Clearly Evliya would have liked to linger in the cathedral library and immerse himself in its treasures. This experience is precisely what *The Norton Anthology of World Literature* offers to you and your students.

As editors of the Shorter Third Edition, we celebrate the excitement of world literature, but we also acknowledge that the encounter with the literary unknown is a source of anxiety. From the beginning of our collaboration, we have set out to make the journey more enticing and less intimidating for our readers.

First, we have made the introductory matter clearer and more informative by shortening headnotes and by following a consistent pattern of presentation, beginning with the author's biography, then moving to the cultural context, and ending with a brief introduction to the work itself. The goal of this approach is to provide students with just enough information to prepare them for their own reading of the work, but not so much information that their sense of discovery is numbed.

The mere presentation of an anthology—page after page of unbroken text— can feel overwhelming to anyone, but especially to an inexperienced student of literature. To alleviate this feeling, and to provide contextual information that words might not be able to convey, we have added hundreds of images and other forms of visual support to the anthology. Most of these images are integrated into the introductions to each major section of the anthology, providing context and visual interest. More than fifty of these images are featured in two newly conceived color inserts that offer pictures of various media, utensils, tools, technologies, and types of writing, as well as scenes of writing and reading from different epochs. The result is a rich visual overview of the material and cultural importance of writing and texts. Recognizing the importance of geography to many of the works in the anthology, the editors have revised the map program so that it complements the literature more directly. Each of the twenty-six maps has been redrawn to help readers orient themselves in the many corners of the world to which this anthology will take them. Finally, newly redesigned timelines at the end of each volume help students see at a glance the temporal relationships among literary works and historical events. Taken together, all of these visual elements make the anthology not only more inviting but also more informative than ever before.

The goal of making world literature a pleasurable adventure also guided our selection of translations. World literature gained its power from the way it reflected and shaped the imagination of peoples, and from the way it circulated outside its original context. For this, it depends on translation. While purists sometimes insist on studying literature only in the original language, a dogma that radically shrinks what one can read, world literature not only relies on translation but actually thrives on it. Translation is a necessity, the only thing that enables a worldwide circulation of literature. It also is an art. One need only think of the way in which translations of the Bible shaped the history of Latin or English. Translations are re-creations of works for new readers. Our edition pays keen attention to translation, and we feature dozens of new translations that make classical texts newly readable and capture the originals in compelling ways. With each choice of translation, we sought a version that would spark a sense of wonder while still being accessible to a contemporary reader. Many of the anthology's most fundamental classics—from *Gilgamesh*, Homer's epics, the Greek dramatists, Virgil, the Bible, the *Bhagavad-gītā*, and the Qur'an to *The Canterbury Tales*, *The Tale of Genji*, Goethe's *Faust*, Ibsen's *Hedda Gabler*, and Kafka's *Metamorphosis*—are presented in new translations that are both exciting works in English and skillful echoes of the spirit and flavor of the original. In some cases, we commissioned new translations—for instance, for the work of the South Asian poet Kabir, rendered beautifully by our South Asian editor and prize-winning translator Vinay Dharwadker, and for a portion of Çelebi's travels to Vienna by our Ottoman expert Gottfried Hagen that has never before been translated into English.

Finally, the editors decided to make some of the guiding themes of the world literature course, and this anthology, more visible. Experienced teachers know about these major themes and use them to create linked reading assignments, and the anthology has long touched on these topics, but with the Shorter Third Edition, these themes rise to the surface, giving all readers a clearer sense of the ties that bind diverse works together. Following is a discussion of each of these organizing themes.

Contact and Culture

Again and again, literature evokes journeys away from home and out into the world, bringing its protagonists—and thus its readers—into contact with peoples who are different from them. Such contact, and the cross-pollination it fosters, was crucial for the formation of cultures. The earliest civilizations—the civilizations that invented writing and hence literature—sprang up where they did because they were located along strategic trading and migration routes. Contact was not just something that happened between fully formed cultures, but something that made these cultures possible in the first place.

Committed to presenting the anthology's riches in a way that conveys this central fact of world literature, we have created new sections that encompass broad contact zones—areas of intense trade in peoples, goods, art, and ideas. The largest such zone is centered on the Mediterranean basin and reaches as far as the Fertile Crescent. It is in this large area that the earliest literatures emerged and intermingled. For the Mediterranean Sea was not just a hostile environment that could derail a journey home, as it did for Odysseus, who took ten years to find his way back to Greece from the Trojan War in Asia Minor; it was a connecting tissue as well, allowing for intense contact around its harbors. Medieval maps of the Mediterranean pay tribute to this fact: so-called portolan charts show a veritable mesh of lines connecting hundreds of ports. In the reorganized Mediterranean sections, we have placed together texts from this broad region, the location of intense conflict as well as friendly exchange, rather than isolating them from each other.

One of the many ways that human beings have bound themselves to each other and have attempted to bridge cultural and geographic distances is through religion. As a form of cultural exchange, and an inspiration for cultural conflict, religion is an important part of the deep history of contact and encounter presented in the anthology, and the editors have taken every opportunity to call attention to this fact. This is nowhere more visible than in a new section in volume 1 called "Encounters with Islam," which follows the cultural influence of Islam beyond its point of origin in Arabia and Persia. Here we draw together works from western Africa, Asia Minor, and South Asia, each of them blending the ideas and values of Islam with indigenous folk traditions to create new forms of cultural expression. The original oral stories of the extraordinary Mali epic *Sunjata* (in a newly established version and translation) incorporate elements of Islam much the way the Anglo-Saxon epic *Beowulf* incorporates elements of Christianity. In a different way, the encounter of Islam with other cultures emerges at the eastern end of its sphere of influence, in South Asia, where a multireligious culture absorbs and transforms Islamic material, as in the philosophical poems of Tukaram and Kabir (both presented in new selections and translations). Evliya Çelebi, with his journey to Vienna, belongs to this larger history as well, giving us another lens through which to view the encounter of Islam and Christianity that is dramatized by so many writers elsewhere in the anthology (most notably, in the *Song of Roland*).

The greatest story of encounter between peoples to be told in the first half of the anthology is the encounter of Europe (and thus of Eurasia) with the Americas. To tell this story properly, the editors decided to eliminate the old dividing line between the European Renaissance and the New World that had prevailed in previous editions and instead created one broad cultural sphere that combines the two. A (newly expanded) cluster within this section gathers texts immediately relevant to this encounter, vividly chronicling all of its willful violence and its unintended consequences in the "New" World. This section also reveals the ways in which the European discovery of the Americas wrought violence in Europe. Old certainties and authorities overthrown, new worlds imagined, the very concept of being human revised—nothing that happened in the European Renaissance was untouched by the New World. Rarely had contact between two geographic zones had more consequences: henceforth, the Americas would be an important part of the story of Europe.

In Volume 2, another new section, "Realism across the Globe," traces perhaps the first truly global artistic movement, one that found expression in France, Britain, Russia, Brazil, and Japan.

In the twentieth century, the pace of cultural exchange and contact, so much swifter than in preceding centuries, transformed most literary movements, from modernism to postcolonialism, into truly global phenomena. At the end of the second volume, we encounter Elizabeth Costello, the title character in J. M. Coetzee's novel. A writer herself, Costello has been asked to give lectures on a cruise ship; mobile and deracinated, she and a colleague deliver lectures on the novel in Africa, including the role of geography and oral literature. The scene captures many themes of world literature—and serves as an image of our present stage of globalization. World literature is a story about the relation between the world and literature, and we tell this story partly by paying attention to this geographic dimension.

Worlds of the Imagination

Literature not only moves us to remote corners of the world and across landscapes; it also presents us with whole imagined worlds to which we as readers can travel. The construction of literary, clearly made-up worlds has always been a theme of world literature, which has suggested answers to fundamental questions, including how the world came into being. The Mayan epic *Popol Vuh,* featured in volume 1, develops one of the most elaborate creation myths, including several attempts at creating humans (only the fourth is successful). Other texts underline this theme, including the newly added Babylonian creation epic, the *Enuma Elish*, at the very beginning of the anthology. The myths in this epic and other texts in the first section of the anthology resonate throughout the history of world literature, providing imaginative touchstones for later authors (such as Virgil, Dante, and Goethe) to adapt and use in their own imaginative world-creation.

But world-creation not only operates on a grand scale. It also occurs at moments when literature restricts itself to small, enclosed universes that are observed with minute attention. The great eighteenth-century Chinese novel *The Story of the Stone* by Cao Xueqin (presented in a new selection) withdraws to a family compound, whose walls it almost never leaves, to depict life in all its subtlety within this restricted space for several thousand pages. Sometimes we are invited into the even more circumscribed space of the narrator's own head, where we encounter strange and surreal worlds, as in the great modernist and postmodernist fictions from Franz Kafka and Jorge Luis Borges. By providing a thematic through-line, the new edition of the anthology reveals the myriad ways in which authors not only seek to explain our world but also compete with it by imagining new and different ones.

Genres

Over the millennia, literature has developed a set of rules and conventions that authors work with and against as they make decisions about subject matter, style, and form. These rules help us distinguish between different types of literature—that is, different genres. The broad view of literature afforded by the anthology, across both space and time, is particularly capable of showing how genres emerge and are transformed as they are used by different writers and for different purposes. The new edition of the anthology underscores this crucial dimension of literature by tracking the movement of genres—of, for example, the frame-tale narration from South Asia to northern Europe. To help readers recognize this theme, we have created ways of making genre visible. Lyric poetry is found everywhere in the anthology, and it is the focus of specially designed sections that cast light on classical Sanskrit lyric; China's T'ang poetry; Japan's classical poetry anthologies, the *Kokinshū* and *Man'yōshū* (as well as one of the world's most successful poetic genres, the haiku); and on the poetry of modernism. By the same token, a cluster on manifestos highlights modernism's most characteristic invention, with its shrill demands and aggressive layout. Among the genres, drama is perhaps the most difficult to grapple with because it is so closely entangled with theatrical performance. You don't understand a play unless you understand what kind of theater it was intended for, how it was performed, and how audiences watched it. To capture this dimension, we have grouped one of the most prominent regional drama traditions—Athenian drama of the 5th century B.C.E.—in its own section.

Oral Literature

The relation of the spoken word to literature is perhaps the most important theme that emerges from these pages. All literature goes back to oral storytelling—all the foundational epics, from South Asia via Greece and Africa to Central America, are deeply rooted in oral storytelling; poetry's rhythms are best appreciated when heard; and drama, a form that comes alive in performance, continues to be engaged with an oral tradition. Throughout the anthology, we connect works to the oral traditions from which they sprang and remind readers that writing has coexisted with oral storytelling since the invention of the former. A new and important cluster in volume 2 on oral literature foregrounds this theme and showcases the nineteenth-century interest in oral traditions such as fairy and folk tales and slave stories. At the same time, this cluster, and the anthology as a whole, shows the importance of gaining literacy.

Varieties of Literature

In presenting everything from the earliest literatures to a (much-expanded) selection of contemporary literature reaching to the early twenty-first century, and from oral storytelling to literary experiments of the avant-garde, the anthology confronts us with the question not just of world literature, but of literature as such. The world of Greek myth, for example, is seen by almost everyone as literary, even though it arose from ritual practices that are different from what we associate with literature. But this is even more the case with other texts, such as the Qur'an or the Bible, which still function as religious texts for many, while others appreciate them primarily or exclusively as literature. Some texts, such as the *Daodejing* or *Bhagavad-gītā* belong in philosophy. Our modern conception of literature as imaginative literature, as fiction, is very recent, about two hundred years old. *The Norton Anthology of World Literature* offers a much-expanded conception of literature that includes creation myths, wisdom literature, religious texts, philosophy, and fairy tales in addition to plays, poems, and narrative fiction. This answers to an older definition of literature as writing of high quality.

This brings us to the last and perhaps most important question: When we study the world, why study it through its literature? Hasn't literature lost some of its luster for us, we who are faced with so many competing media and art forms? Like no other art form or medium, literature offers us a deep history of human thinking. As our illustration program shows, writing was invented not for the composition of literature, but for much more mundane purposes, such as the recording of ownership, contracts, or astronomical observations. But literature is writing's most glorious side-product. Because language expresses human consciousness, no other art form can capture the human past with the precision and scope of literature. Language shapes our thinking, and literature, the highest expression of language, plays an important role in that process, pushing the boundaries of what we can think, and how we think it. The other great advantage of literature is that it can be reactivated with each reading. The great architectural monuments of the past are now in ruins. Literature, too, often has to be excavated, as with many classical texts. But once a text has been found or reconstructed it can be experienced as if for the first time by new readers. Even though many of the literary texts collected in this anthology are at first strange, because they originated so very long ago, they still speak to today's readers with great eloquence and freshness.

Because works of world literature are alive today, they continue to elicit strong emotions and investments. The epic *Rāmāyana*, for example, plays an important role in the politics of India, where it has been used to bolster Hindu nationalism, just as the *Bhagavad-gītā*, here in a new translation, continues to be a moral touchstone in the ethical deliberation about war. And the three religions of the book, Judaism, Christianity, and Islam, make our selections from their scriptures a more than historical exercise. China has recently elevated the sayings of Confucius, whose influence on Chinese attitudes about the state had waned in the twentieth century, creating Confucius Institutes all over the world to promote Chinese culture in what is now called New Confucianism. The debates about the role of the church and secularism, which we highlight through a new cluster and selections in all volumes, have become newly important in current deliberations on the relation between church and state. World literature is never neutral. We know its relevance precisely by the controversies it inspires.

Going back to the earliest moments of cultural contact and moving forward to the global flows of the twenty-first century, *The Norton Anthology of World Literature* attempts to provide a deep history. But it is a special type of history: a literary one. World literature is grounded in the history of the world, but it is also the history of imagining this world; it is a history not just of what happened, but also of how humans imagined their place in the midst of history. We, the editors of this Shorter Third Edition, can think of no better way to prepare young people for a global future than through a deep and meaningful exploration of world literature. Evliya Çelebi sums up his exploration of Vienna as a "marvelous and wonderful adventure"—we hope that readers will feel the same about the adventure in reading made possible by this anthology and will return to it for the rest of their lives.

About the Shorter Third Edition

New Selections and Translations

This Shorter Third Edition represents a thoroughgoing, top-to-bottom revision of the anthology that altered nearly every section in important ways. Following is a list of the new sections and works, in order:

VOLUME I

New translations of Egyptian love poems • Benjamin R. Foster's translation of *Gilgamesh* • Selections from chapters 12, 17, 28, 29, 31, 32, and 33 of Genesis, and from chapters 19 and 20 of Exodus • All selections from Genesis, Exodus, and Job are newly featured in Robert Alter's translation, and chapter 25 of Genesis (Esau spurning his birthright) is presented in a graphic visualization by R. Crumb based on Alter's translation • Homer's *Iliad* and *Odyssey* are now featured in Stanley Lombardo's highly regarded translations • A new selection and a new translation of Sappho's lyrics • New translations of *Oedipus the King* (by Robert Bagg), and *Medea* (by Diane Arnson Svarlien) • A new selection of Catullus's poems, in a new translation by Peter Green • *The Aeneid* is now featured in Robert Fagles's career-topping translation, and book II is newly added • New selections from book 1 of Ovid's *Metamorphoses* join the previous selection, now featured in Charles Martin's recent translation • New selections from the Chinese *Classic of Poetry* • Confucius's *Analects* now in a new translation by Simon Leys • The *Daodejing* is newly added • Selections from the Christian Bible now featured in a new translation by Richmond Lattimore • Selections from the Qur'an now featured in M. A. S. Abdel Haleem's translation • A new selection from Abolqasem Ferdowsi's *Shahnameh*, in a new translation by Dick Davis • Additional material from Marie de France's *Lais*, in a translation by Robert Hanning and Joan Ferrante • Dante's *Divine Comedy* now featured in Mark Musa's translation • A new translation by Sheila Fisher of Chaucer's *Canterbury Tales* and "The Wife of Bath's Tale" newly included • New selections in fresh translations of classical Tamil and Sanskrit lyric poetry • New selections and translations of Chinese lyric poetry• Refreshed selections and new translations of lyric poetry in "Japan's Classical Age" • A new, expanded selection from, and a new translation of, Murasaki Shikibu's *The Tale of Genji* • A new translation by David C. Conrad of the West African epic *Sunjata* • A new selection from Evliya Çelebi's *The Book of Travels*, never before translated into English, now in Gottfried Hagen's translation • New selection of Indian lyric poetry by Kabir, Mīrabāī, and Tukaram, in fresh new translations • new selections from, and a new translation of, Michiavelli's *The Prince* • Marguerite de Navarre, *Heptameron*, newly included • A new cluster, "The Encounter of Europe and the New World."

VOLUME 2

Molière's *Tartuffe* now featured in a new translation by Constance Congdon and Virginia Scott • New selections by Sor Juana Inés de la Cruz, in a new translation by Electa Arenal and Amanda Powell • Alexander Pope's "An Essay on Man" • Mary Wollstonecraft's *A Vindication of the Rights of Woman*, newly included • Wu Cheng'en's *The Journey to the West* in a new translation by Anthony Yu • An expanded, refreshed selection from Cao Xueqin's *The Story of the Stone*, part of which is now featured in John Minford's translation • A new cluster, "The World of Haiku," features work by Kitamura Kigin, Matsuo Bashō, Morikawa Kyoriku, Yosa Buson, and Chikamatsu Monzaemon • New selection from book 2 of Rousseau's *Confessions* • A new grouping, "Lyric Poetry in the Long Nineteenth Century," features a generous sampling of lyric poetry from the period, including new poems by William Wordsworth, Anna Bunina, Andrés Bello, John Keats, Heinrich Heine, Elizabeth Barrett Browning, Tennyson, Walt Whitman, and José Martí, as well as an exciting new translation of Arthur Rimbaud's *Illuminations* by John Ashbery • A new selection and all new translations of Ghalib's poetry by Vinay Dharwadker • Flaubert's *A Simple Heart* • Ibsen's *Hedda Gabler*, now featured in a new translation by Rick Davis and Brian Johnston • Machado de Assis's *The Rod of Justice* • Chekhov's *The Cherry Orchard*, now featured in a new translation by Paul Schmidt • Higuchi Ichiyō's *Separate Ways* • A new cluster, "Orature," with a German folktale; Anansi stories from Ghana, Jamaica, and the United States; as well as slave songs, stories, and spirituals, Malagasy wisdom poetry, and the Navajo Night Chant • Thomas Mann's *Death in Venice*, complete • Selection from Marcel Proust's *Remembrance of Things Past*, featured in Lydia Davis's critically acclaimed translation • James Joyce's "The Dead" • Franz Kafka's *The Metamorphosis* now featured in Michael Hofmann's translation • Akutagawa's *In a Bamboo Grove* • Premchand's "The Road to Salvation" • Chapter 1 of Woolf's *A Room of One's Own* newly added to the selection from chapter 3 • Zhang Ailing's *Sealed Off* • Constantine Cavafy • Pablo Neruda • Octavio Paz • Léopold Sédar Senghor • Tadeusz Borowski's *This Way for the Gas, Ladies and Gentlemen* • Paul Celan • Doris Lessing • Saadat Hasan Manto • James Baldwin • Samuel Beckett's *Endgame* • Clarice Lispector's "The Daydreams of a Drunk Woman" • Chinua Achebe's *Chike's School Days* • Alexander Solzhenitsyn's "Matryona's Home" • Mahmoud Darwish • Yehuda Amichai • Derek Walcott • Seamus Heaney • V. S. Naipaul • Ngugi Wa Thiong'o • Bessie Head • Salman Rushdie • Jamaica Kincaid • Hanan Al-Shaykh • Isabel Allende • Chu T'ien-Hsin • J. M. Coetzee.

Supplements for Instructors and Students

Norton is pleased to provide instructors and students with several supplements to make the study and teaching of world literature an even more interesting and rewarding experience:

Instructor Resource Folder

A new Instructor Resource Folder features images and video clips that allow instructors to enhance their lectures with some of the sights and sounds of world literature and its contexts.

Instructor Course Guide

Teaching with The Norton Anthology of World Literature: *A Guide for Instructors* provides teaching plans, suggestions for in-class activities, discussion topics and writing projects, and extensive lists of scholarly and media resources.

Coursepacks

Available in a variety of formats, Norton coursepacks bring digital resources into a new or existing online course. Coursepacks are free to instructors, easy to download and install, and available in a variety of formats, including Blackboard, Desire2Learn, Angel, and Moodle.

StudySpace (wwnorton.com/nawol)

This free student companion site features a variety of complementary materials to help students read and study world literature. Among them are reading-comprehension quizzes, quick-reference summaries of the anthology's introductions, review quizzes, an audio glossary to help students pronounce names and terms, tours of some of the world's important cultural landmarks, timelines, maps, and other contextual materials.

Writing about World Literature

Written by Karen Gocsik, Executive Director of the Writing Program at Dartmouth College, in collaboration with faculty in the world literature program at the University of Nevada, Las Vegas, *Writing about World Literature* provides course-specific guidance for writing papers and essay exams in the world literature course.

For more information about any of these supplements, instructors should contact their local Norton representative.

Acknowledgments

The editors would like to thank the following people, who have provided invaluable assistance by giving us sage advice, important encouragement, and help with the preparation of the manuscript: Sara Akbari, Alannah de Barra, Wendy Belcher, Jodi Bilinkoff, Freya Brackett, Psyche Brackett, Michaela Bronstein, Amanda Claybaugh, Rachel Carroll, Lewis Cook, David Damrosch, Dick Davis, Amanda Detry, Anthony Domestico, Merve Emre, Maria Fackler, Guillermina de Ferrari, Karina Galperín, Stanton B. Garner, Kimberly Dara Gordon, Elyse Graham, Stephen Greenblatt, Sara Guyer, Langdon Hammer, Iain Higgins, Mohja Kahf, Peter Kornicki, Paul Kroll, Lydia Liu, Bala Venkat Mani, Ann Matter, Barry McCrea, Alexandra McCullough-Garcia, Rachel McGuiness, Jon McKenzie, Mary Mullen, Djibril Tamsir Niane, Felicity Nussbaum, Andy Orchard, John Peters, Daniel Taro Poch, Daniel Potts, Megan Quigley, Imogen Roth, Catherine de Rose, Ellen Sapega, Jesse Schotter, Stephen Scully, Brian Stock, Tomi Suzuki, Joshua Taft, Sara Torres, Lisa Voigt, Kristen Wanner, and Emily Weissbourd.

All the editors would like to thank the wonderful people at Norton, principally our editor Pete Simon, the driving force behind this whole undertaking, as well as Marian Johnson (Managing Editor, College), Alice Falk, Michael Fleming, Katharine Ings, Susan Joseph, and Barney Latimer (Copyeditors), Conor Sullivan (Assistant Editor), Quynh Do (Editorial Assistant), Diane Cipollone (Copyeditor and Project Editor), Megan Jackson (College Permissions Manager), Margaret Gorenstein (Permissions), Patricia Marx (Art Research Director), Debra Morton Hoyt (Art Director; cover design), Rubina Yeh (Design Director), Jo Anne Metsch (Designer; interior text design), Adrian Kitzinger (cartography), Agnieszka Gasparska (timeline design), Eileen Connell, (Media Editor), Jennifer Barnhardt (Editorial Assistant, Media), Laura Musich (Associate Editor; Instructor's Guide), Benjamin Reynolds (Production Manager), and Kim Bowers (Marketing Manager, Literature) and Ashley Cain (Humanities Sales Specialist).

This anthology represents a collaboration not only among the editors and their close advisors, but also among the thousands of instructors who teach from the anthology and provide valuable and constructive guidance to the publisher and editors. *The Norton Anthology of World Literature* is as much their book as it is ours, and we are grateful to everyone who has cared enough about this anthology to help make it better. We're especially grateful to the more than five hundred professors of world literature who responded to an online survey in early 2008, whom we have listed below. Thank you all.

Michel Aaij (Auburn University Montgomery); Sandra Acres (Mississippi Gulf Coast Community College); Larry Adams (University of North Alabama);

Mary Adams (Western Carolina University); Stephen Adams (Westfield State College); Roberta Adams (Roger Williams University); Kirk Adams (Tarrant County College); Kathleen Aguero (Pine Manor College); Richard Albright (Harrisburg Area Community College); Deborah Albritton (Jefferson Davis Community College); Todd Aldridge (Auburn University); Judith Allen-Leventhal (College of Southern Maryland); Carolyn Amory (Binghamton University); Kenneth Anania (Massasoit Community College); Phillip Anderson (University of Central Arkansas); Walter Anderson (University of Arkansas at Little Rock); Vivienne Anderson (North Carolina Wesleyan College); Susan Andrade (University of Pittsburgh); Kit Andrews (Western Oregon University); Joe Antinarella (Tidewater Community College); Nancy Applegate (Georgia Highlands College); Sona Aronian (University of Rhode Island); Sona Aronian (University of Rhode Island); Eugene Arva (University of Miami); M. G. Aune (California University of Pennsylvania); Carolyn Ayers (Saint Mary's University of Minnesota); Diana Badur (Black Hawk College); Susan Bagby (Longwood University); Maryam Barrie (Washtenaw Community College); Maria Baskin (Alamance Community College); Samantha Batten (Auburn University); Charles Beach (Nyack College); Michael Beard (University of North Dakota); Bridget Beaver (Connors State College); James Bednarz (C. W. Post College); Khani Begum (Bowling Green State University); Albert Bekus (Austin Peay State University); Lynne Belcher (Southern Arkansas University); Karen Bell (Delta State University); Elisabeth Ly Bell (University of Rhode Island); Angela Belli (St. John's University); Leo Benardo (Baruch College); Paula Berggren (Baruch College, CUNY); Frank Bergmann (Utica College); Nancy Blomgren (Volunteer State Community College); Scott Boltwood (Emory & Henry College); Ashley Bonds (Copiah-Lincoln Community College); Thomas Bonner (Xavier University of Louisiana); Debbie Boyd (East Central Community College); Norman Boyer (Saint Xavier University); Nodya Boyko (Auburn University); Robert Brandon (Rockingham Community College); Alan Brasher (East Georgia College); Harry Brent (Baruch College); Charles Bressler (Indiana Wesleyan University); Katherine Brewer; Mary Ruth Brindley (Mississippi Delta Community College); Mamye Britt (Georgia Perimeter College); Gloria Brooks (Tyler Junior College); Monika Brown (University of North Carolina–Pembroke); Greg Bryant (Highland Community College); Austin Busch (SUNY Brockport); Barbara Cade (Texas College); Karen Caig (University of Arkansas Community College at Morrilton); Jonizo Cain-Calloway (Del Mar College); Mark Calkins (San Francisco State University); Catherine Calloway (Arkansas State University); Mechel Camp (Jackson State Community College); Robert Canary (University of Wisconsin–Parkside); Stephen Canham (University of Hawaii at Manoa); Marian Carcache (Auburn University); Alfred Carson (Kennesaw State University); Farrah Cato (University of Central Florida); Biling Chen (University of Central Arkansas); Larry Chilton (Blinn College); Eric Chock (University of Hawaii at West Oahu); Cheryl Clark (Miami Dade College–Wolfson Campus); Sarah Beth Clark (Holmes Community College); Jim Cody (Brookdale Community College); Carol Colatrella (Georgia Institute of Technology); Janelle Collins (Arkansas State University); Theresa Collins (St. John's University); Susan Comfort (Indiana University of Pennsylvania); Kenneth Cook (National Park Community College); Angie Cook (Cisco Junior College); Yvonne Cooper (Pierce College); Brenda Cornell (Central Texas College); Judith Cortelloni (Lincoln College); Robert

Cosgrove (Saddleback College); Rosemary Cox (Georgia Perimeter College); Daniel Cozart (Georgia Perimeter College); Brenda Craven (Fort Hays State University); Susan Crisafulli (Franklin College); Janice Crosby (Southern University); Randall Crump (Kennesaw State University); Catherine Cucinella (California State University San Marcos); T. Allen Culpepper (Manatee Community College–Venice); Rodger Cunningham (Alice Lloyd College); Lynne Dahmen (Purdue University); Patsy J. Daniels (Jackson State University); James Davis (Troy University); Evan Davis (Southwestern Oregon Community College); Margaret Dean (Eastern Kentucky University); JoEllen DeLucia (John Jay College, CUNY); Hivren Demir-Atay (Binghamton University); Rae Ann DeRosse (University of North Carolina–Greensboro); Anna Crowe Dewart (College of Coastal Georgia); Joan Digby (C. W. Post Campus Long Island University); Diana Dominguez (University of Texas at Brownsville); Dee Douglas-Jones (Winston-Salem State University); Jeremy Downes (Auburn University); Denell Downum (Suffolk University); Sharon Drake (Texarkana College); Damian Dressick (Robert Morris University); Clyburn Duder (Concordia University Texas); Dawn Duncan (Concordia College); Kendall Dunkelberg (Mississippi University for Women); Janet Eber (County College of Morris); Emmanuel Egar (University of Arkansas at Pine Bluff); David Eggebrecht (Concordia University of Wisconsin); Sarah Eichelman (Walters State Community College); Hank Eidson (Georgia Perimeter College); Monia Eisenbraun (Oglala Lakota College/Cheyenne-Eagle Butte High School); Dave Elias (Eastern Kentucky University); Chris Ellery (Angelo State University); Christina Elvidge (Marywood University); Ernest Enchelmayer (Arkansas Tech University); Niko Endres (Western Kentucky University); Kathrynn Engberg (Alabama A&M University); Chad Engbers (Calvin College); Edward Eriksson (Suffolk Community College); Donna Estill (Alabama Southern Community College); Andrew Ettin (Wake Forest University); Jim Everett (Mississippi College); Gene Fant (Union University); Nathan Faries (University of Dubuque); Martin Fashbaugh (Auburn University); Donald J. Fay (Kennesaw State University); Meribeth Fell (College of Coastal Georgia); David Fell (Carroll Community College); Jill Ferguson (San Francisco Conservatory of Music); Susan French Ferguson (Mountain View Comumunity College); Robyn Ferret (Cascadia Community College); Colin Fewer (Purdue Calumet); Hannah Fischthal (St. John's University); Jim Fisher (Peninsula College); Gene Fitzgerald (University of Utah); Monika Fleming (Edgecombe Community College); Phyllis Fleming (Patrick Henry Community College); Francis Fletcher (Folsom Lake College); Denise Folwell (Montgomery College); Ulanda Forbess (North Lake College); Robert Forman (St. John's University); Suzanne Forster (University of Alaska–Anchorage); Patricia Fountain (Coastal Carolina Community College); Kathleen Fowler (Surry Community College); Sheela Free (San Bernardino Valley College); Lea Fridman (Kingsborough Community College); David Galef (Montclair State University); Paul Gallipeo (Adirondack Community College); Jan Gane (University of North Carolina–Pembroke); Jennifer Garlen (University of Alabama–Huntsville); Anita Garner (University of North Alabama); Elizabeth Gassel (Darton College); Patricia Gaston (West Virginia University, Parkersburg); Marge Geiger (Cuyahoga Community College); Laura Getty (North Georgia College & State University); Amy Getty (Grand View College); Leah Ghiradella (Middlesex County College); Dick Gibson (Jacksonville University); Teresa

Gibson (University of Texas–Brownsville); Wayne Gilbert (Community College of Aurora); Sandra Giles (Abraham Baldwin Agricultural College); Pamela Gist (Cedar Valley College); Suzanne Gitonga (North Lake College); James Glickman (Community College of Rhode Island); R. James Goldstein (Auburn University); Jennifer Golz (Tennessee Tech University); Marian Goodin (North Central Missouri College); Susan Gorman (Massachusetts College of Pharmacy and Health Sciences); Anissa Graham (University of North Alabama); Eric Gray (St. Gregory's University); Geoffrey Green (San Francisco State University); Russell Greer (Texas Woman's University); Charles Grey (Albany State University); Frank Gruber (Bergen Community College); Alfonso Guerriero Jr. (Baruch College, CUNY); Letizia Guglielmo (Kennesaw State University); Nira Gupta-Casale (Kean University); Gary Gutchess (SUNY Tompkins Cortland Community College); William Hagen (Oklahoma Baptist University); John Hagge (Iowa State University); Julia Hall (Henderson State University); Margaret Hallissy (C. W. Post Campus Long Island University); Laura Hammons (Hinds Community College); Nancy Hancock (Austin Peay State University); Carol Harding (Western Oregon University); Cynthia Hardy (University of Alaska–Fairbanks); Steven Harthorn (Williams Baptist College); Stanley Hauer (University of Southern Mississippi); Leean Hawkins (National Park Community College); Kayla Haynie (Harding University); Maysa Hayward (Ocean County College); Karen Head (Georgia Institute of Technology); Sandra Kay Heck (Walters State Community College); Frances Helphinstine (Morehead State University); Karen Henck (Eastern Nazarene College); Betty Fleming Hendricks (University of Arkansas); Yndaleci Hinojosa (Northwest Vista College); Richard Hishmeh (Palomar College); Ruth Hoberman (Eastern Illinois University); Rebecca Hogan (University of Wisconsin–Whitewater); Mark Holland (East Tennessee State University); John Holmes (Virginia State University); Sandra Holstein (Southern Oregon University); Fran Holt (Georgia Perimeter College–Clarkston); William Hood (North Central Texas College); Glenn Hopp (Howard Payne University); George Horneker (Arkansas State University); Barbara Howard (Central Bible College); Pamela Howell (Midland College); Melissa Hull (Tennessee State University); Barbara Hunt (Columbus State University); Leeann Hunter (University of South Florida); Gill Hunter (Eastern Kentucky University); Helen Huntley (California Baptist University); Luis Iglesias (University of Southern Mississippi); Judith Irvine (Georgia State University); Miglena Ivanova (Coastal Carolina University); Kern Jackson (University of South Alabama); Kenneth Jackson (Yale University); M. W. Jackson (St. Bonaventure University); Robb Jackson (Texas A&M University–Corpus Christi); Karen Jacobsen (Valdosta State University); Maggie Jaffe (San Diego State University); Robert Jakubovic (Raymond Walters College); Stokes James (University of Wisconsin–Stevens Point); Beverly Jamison (South Carolina State University); Ymitri Jayasundera-Mathison (Prairie View A&M University); Katarzyna Jerzak (University of Georgia); Alice Jewell (Harding University); Elizabeth Jones (Auburn University); Jeff Jones (University of Idaho); Dan Jones (Walters State Community College); Mary Kaiser (Jefferson State Community College); James Keller (Middlesex County College); Jill Keller (Middlesex Community College); Tim Kelley (Northwest-Shoals Community College); Andrew Kelley (Jackson State Community College); Hans Kellner (North Carolina State); Brian Kennedy (Pasadena City College); Shirin Khanmohamadi

(San Francisco State University); Jeremy Kiene (McDaniel College); Mary Catherine Kiliany (Robert Morris University); Sue Kim (University of Alabama–Birmingham); Pam Kingsbury (University of North Alabama); Sharon Kinoshita (University of California, Santa Cruz); Lydia Kualapai (Schreiner University); Rita Kumar (University of Cincinnati); Roger Ladd (University of North Carolina–Pembroke); Daniel Lane (Norwich University); Erica Lara (Southwest Texas Junior College); Leah Larson (Our Lady of the Lake University); Dana Lauro (Ocean County College); Shanon Lawson (Pikes Peak Community College); Michael Leddy (Eastern Illinois University); Eric Leuschner (Fort Hays State University); Patricia Licklider (John Jay College, CUNY); Pamela Light (Rochester College); Alison Ligon (Morehouse College); Linda Linzey (Southeastern University); Thomas Lisk (North Carolina State University); Matthew Livesey (University of Wisconsin–Stout); Vickie Lloyd (University of Arkansas Community College at Hope); Judy Lloyd (Southside Virginia Community College); Mary Long (Ouachita Baptist University); Rick Lott (Arkansas State University); Scott Lucas (The Citadel); Katrine Lvovskaya (Rutgers University); Carolin Lynn (Mercyhurst College); Susan Lyons (University of Connecticut—Avery Point); William Thomas MacCary (Hofstra University); Richard Mace (Pace University); Peter Marbais (Mount Olive College); Lacy Marschalk (Auburn University); Seth Martin (Harrisburg Area Community College–Lancaster); Carter Mathes (Rutgers University); Rebecca Mathews (University of Connecticut); Marsha Mathews (Dalton State College); Darren Mathews (Grambling State University); Corine Mathis (Auburn University); Ken McAferty (Pensacola State College); Jeff McAlpine (Clackamas Community College); Kelli McBride (Seminole State College); Kay McClellan (South Plains College); Michael McClung (Northwest-Shoals Community College); Michael McClure (Virginia State University); Jennifer McCune (University of Central Arkansas); Kathleen McDonald (Norwich University); Charles McDonnell (Piedmont Technical College); Nancy McGee (Macomb Community College); Gregory McNamara (Clayton State University); Abby Mendelson (Point Park University); Ken Meyers (Wilson Community College); Barbara Mezeske (Hope College); Brett Millan (South Texas College); Sheila Miller (Hinds Community College); David Miller (Mississippi College); Matt Miller (University of South Carolina–Aiken); Yvonne Milspaw (Harrisburg Area Community College); Ruth Misheloff (Baruch College); Lamata Mitchell (Rock Valley College); D'Juana Montgomery (Southwestern Assemblies of God University); Lorne Mook (Taylor University); Renee Moore (Mississippi Delta Community College); Dan Morgan (Scott Community College); Samantha Morgan-Curtis (Tennessee State University); Beth Morley (Collin College); Vicki Moulson (College of the Albemarle); L. Carl Nadeau (University of Saint Francis); Wayne Narey (Arkansas State University); LeAnn Nash (Texas A&M University–Commerce); Leanne Nayden (University of Evansville); Jim Neilson (Wake Technical Community College); Jeff Nelson (University of Alabama–Huntsville); Mary Nelson (Dallas Baptist University); Deborah Nester (Northwest Florida State College); William Netherton (Amarillo College); William Newman (Perimeter College); Adele Newson-Horst (Missouri State University); George Nicholas (Benedictine College); Dana Nichols (Gainesville State College); Mark Nicoll-Johnson (Merced College); John Mark Nielsen (Dana College); Michael Nifong (Georgia College & State University); Laura Noell (North Virginia Community College);

Bonnie Noonan (Xavier University of Louisiana); Patricia Noone (College of Mount Saint Vincent); Paralee Norman (Northwestern State University–Leesville); Frank Novak (Pepperdine University); Kevin O'Brien (Chapman University); Sarah Odishoo (Columbia College Chicago); Samuel Olorounto (New River Community College); Jamili Omar (Lone Star College–CyFair); Michael Orlofsky (Troy University); Priscilla Orr (Sussex County Community College); Jim Owen (Columbus State University); Darlene Pagan (Pacific University); Yolanda Page (University of Arkansas–Pine Bluff); Lori Paige (Westfield State College); Linda Palumbo (Cerritos College); Joseph Parry (Brigham Young University); Carla Patterson (Georgia Highlands College); Andra Pavuls (Davenport University); Sunita Peacock (Slippery Rock University); Velvet Pearson (Long Beach City College); Joe Pellegrino (Georgia Southern University); Sonali Perera (Rutgers University); Clem Perez (St. Philip's College); Caesar Perkowski (Gordon College); Gerald Perkus (Collin College); John Peters (University of North Texas); Lesley Peterson (University of North Alabama); Judy Peterson (John Tyler Community College); Sandra Petree (Northwestern Oklahoma State University); Angela Pettit (Tarrant County College NE); Michell Phifer (University of Texas–Arlington); Ziva Piltch (Rockland Community College); Nancy Popkin (Harris-Stowe State University); Marlana Portolano (Towson University); Rhonda Powers (Auburn University); Lisa Propst (University of West Georgia); Melody Pugh (Wheaton College); Jonathan Purkiss (Pulaski Technical College); Patrick Quinn (College of Southern Nevada); Peter Rabinowitz (Hamilton College); Evan Radcliffe (Villanova University); Jody Ragsdale (Northeast Alabama Community College); Ken Raines (Eastern Arizona College); Gita Rajan (Fairfield University); Elizabeth Rambo (Campbell University); Richard Ramsey (Indiana University–Purdue University Fort Wayne); Jonathan Randle (Mississippi College); Amy Randolph (Waynesburg University); Rodney Rather (Tarrant County College Northwest); Helaine Razovsky (Northwestern State University); Rachel Reed (Auburn University); Karin Rhodes (Salem State College); Donald R. Riccomini (Santa Clara University); Christina Roberts (Otero Junior College); Paula Robison (Temple University); Jean Roelke (University of North Texas); Barrie Rosen (St. John's University); James Rosenberg (Point Park University); Sherry Rosenthal (College of Southern Nevada); Daniel Ross (Columbus State University); Maria Rouphail (North Carolina State University); Lance Rubin (Arapahoe Community College); Mary Ann Rygiel (Auburn University); Geoffrey Sadock (Bergen Community College); Allen Salerno (Auburn University); Mike Sanders (Kent State University); Deborah Scally (Richland College); Margaret Scanlan (Indiana University South Bend); Michael Schaefer (University of Central Arkansas); Tracy Schaelen (Southwestern College); Daniel Schenker (University of Alabama–Huntsville); Robyn Schiffman (Fairleigh Dickinson University); Roger Schmidt (Idaho State University); Robert Schmidt (Tarrant County College–Northwest Campus); Adrianne Schot (Weatherford College); Pamela Schuman (Brookhaven College); Sharon Seals (Ouachita Technical College); Su Senapati (Abraham Baldwin Agricultural College); Phyllis Senfleben (North Shore Community College); Theda Shapiro (University of California–Riverside); Mary Sheldon (Washburn University); Donald Shull (Freed-Hardeman University); Ellen Shull (Palo Alto College); Conrad Shumaker (University of Central Arkansas); Sara Shumaker (University of Central Arkansas); Dave Shuping (Spartanburg Methodist College);

Horacio Sierra (University of Florida); Scott Simkins (Auburn University); Bruce Simon (SUNY Fredonia); LaRue Sloan (University of Louisiana–Monroe); Peter Smeraldo (Caldwell College); Renee Smith (Lamar University); Victoria Smith (Texas State University); Connie Smith (College of St. Joseph); Grant Smith (Eastern Washington University); Mary Karen Solomon (Coloardo NW Community College); Micheline Soong (Hawaii Pacific University); Leah Souffrant (Baruch College, CUNY); Cindy Spangler (Faulkner University); Charlotte Speer (Bevill State Community College); John Staines (John Jay College, CUNY); Tanja Stampfl (Louisiana State University); Scott Starbuck (San Diego Mesa College); Kathryn Stasio (Saint Leo University); Joyce Stavick (North Georgia College & State University); Judith Steele (Mid-America Christian University); Stephanie Stephens (Howard College); Rachel Sternberg (Case Western Reserve University); Holly Sterner (College of Coastal Georgia); Karen Stewart (Norwich University); Sioux Stoeckle (Palo Verde College); Ron Stormer (Culver-Stockton College); Frank Stringfellow (University of Miami); Ayse Stromsdorfer (Soldan I. S. H. S.); Ashley Strong-Green (Paine College); James Sullivan (Illinois Central College); Zohreh Sullivan (University of Illinois); Richard Sullivan (Worcester State College); Duke Sutherland (Mississippi Gulf Coast Community College/Jackson County Campus); Maureen Sutton (Kean University); Marianne Szlyk (Montgomery College); Rebecca Taksel (Point Park University); Robert Tally (Texas State University); Tim Tarkington (Georgia Perimeter College); Patricia Taylor (Western Kentucky University); Mary Ann Taylor (Mountain View College); Susan Tekulve (Converse College); Stephen Teller (Pittsburgh State University); Stephen Thomas (Community College of Denver); Freddy Thomas (Virginia State University); Andy Thomason (Lindenwood University); Diane Thompson (Northern Virginia Community College); C. H. Thornton (Northwest-Shoals Community College); Elizabeth Thornton (Georgia Perimeter); Burt Thorp (University of North Dakota); Willie Todd (Clark Atlanta University); Martin Trapp (Northwestern Michigan College); Brenda Tuberville (University of Texas–Tyler); William Tucker (Olney Central College); Martha Turner (Troy University); Joya Uraizee (Saint Louis University); Randal Urwiller (Texas College); Emily Uzendoski (Central Community College–Columbus Campus); Kenneth Van Dover (Lincoln University); Kay Walter (University of Arkansas–Monticello); Cassandra Ward-Shah (West Chester University); Gina Weaver (Southern Nazarene University); Cathy Webb (Meridian Community College); Eric Weil (Elizabeth City State University); Marian Wernicke (Pensacola Junior College); Robert West (Mississippi State University); Cindy Wheeler (Georgia Highlands College); Chuck Whitchurch (Golden West College); Julianne White (Arizona State University); Denise White (Kennesaw State University); Amy White (Lee University); Patricia White (Norwich University); Gwen Whitehead (Lamar State College–Orange); Terri Whitney (North Shore Community College); Tamora Whitney (Creighton University); Stewart Whittemore (Auburn University); Johannes Wich-Schwarz (Maryville University); Charles Wilkinson (Southwest Tennessee Community College); Donald Williams (Toccoa Falls College); Rick Williams (Rogue Community College); Lea Williams (Norwich University); Susan Willis (Auburn University–Montgomery); Sharon Wilson (University of Northern Colorado); J. D. Wireman (Indiana State University); Rachel Wiren (Baptist Bible College); Bertha Wise (Oklahoma City Community College); Sallie Wolf (Arapahoe

Community College); Rebecca Wong (James Madison University); Donna Woodford-Gormley (New Mexico Highlands University); Paul Woodruff (University of Texas–Austin); William Woods (Wichita State University); Marjorie Woods (University of Texas–Austin); Valorie Worthy (Ohio University); Wei Yan (Darton College); Teresa Young (Philander Smith College); Darcy Zabel (Friends University); Michelle Zenor (Lon Morris College); and Jacqueline Zubeck (College of Mount Saint Vincent).

THE NORTON ANTHOLOGY OF

WORLD LITERATURE

SHORTER THIRD EDITION

VOLUME 2

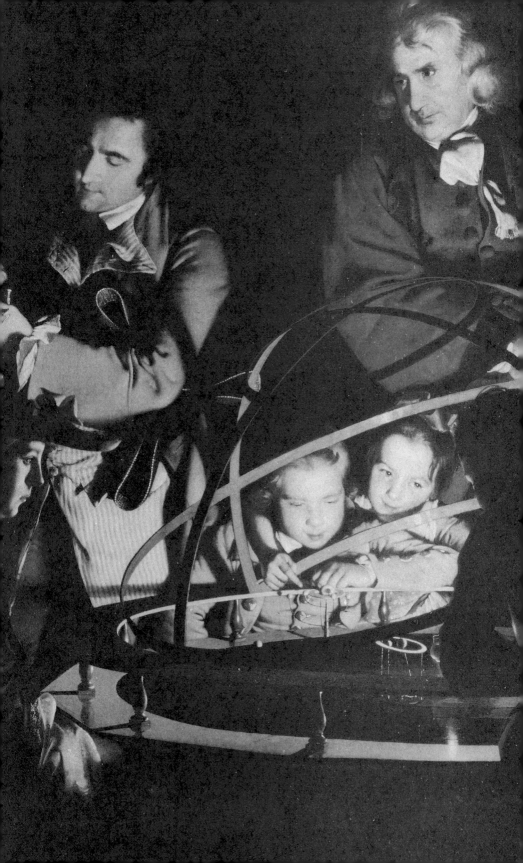

I

The Enlightenment in Europe and the Americas

I s the latest thing always the best? On the whole, our society assumes that progress is likely and desirable. We move and communicate ever faster; we pursue the newest and shiniest things— our appetite for the modern knows no bounds. Yet we also indulge in moments of nostalgia, worrying that things are no longer what they used to be, that something has been lost in our tremendous rush. Before, we tell ourselves, there were standards; now all is confusion. Although the pace of change is now swifter, this ambivalence is nothing new.

The quarrel between "ancients" and "moderns"— those who believed, respectively, that old ideas or new ones were likely to prove superior to any alternatives—proved especially virulent in France and England during the late seventeenth and eighteenth centuries. Those who espoused the cause of the ancients feared—understandably—that the new commitment to individualism promoted by the moderns might lead to social alienation, unscrupulous self-seeking, and lack of moral responsibility. Believing in the universality of truth, they wished to uphold established values, not to invent new ones. On the other side, the moderns upheld the importance of individual autonomy, broad education for

A Philosopher Giving a Lecture in the Orrery, 1766, by Joseph Wright of Derby.

3

This engraving by J. Zucchi, a copy of a painting by Angelica Kauffmann, depicts Urania, the classical muse of astronomy.

women, and intellectual and geographical exploration. They stood for the new and are the recognizable forebears of what we even now call "modernity."

On both sides of the ancient/modern divide, thinkers believed in reason as a dependable guide. Both sides insisted that one should not take any assertion of truth on faith, blindly following the authority of others; instead, one should think skeptically about causes and effects, subjecting all truth-claims to logic and rational inquiry. Dr. Samuel Johnson's famous *Dictionary* defined reason as "the power by which man deduces one proposition from another, or proceeds from premises to consequences." By this definition, illumination occurs not by divine inspiration or by order of kings but by the reasoning powers of the ordinary human mind. Reason, some people argued, would lead human beings back to eternal truths. For others, reason provided a means for discovering fresh solutions to scientific, philosophical, and political questions.

In the realm of philosophy, thinkers turned their attention to defining what it meant to be human. "I think, therefore I am," René Descartes pronounced, declaring the mind the source of truth and meaning. But this idea proved less reassuring than it initially seemed. Subsequent philosophers, exploring the concept's implications, realized the possibility of the mind's isolation in its own constructions. Perhaps, Wilhelm Leibniz suggested, no real communication can take place between one consciousness and another. Possibly, according to David Hume, the idea of individual identity is a fiction constructed by our minds to make discontinuous experiences and memories seem continuous and whole. Philosophers pointed out the impossibility of knowing for sure even the reality of the external world: the only certainty is that we think it exists.

If contemplating the nature of human reason led philosophic skeptics to doubt our ability to know anything with certainty, other thinkers insisted on the existence, beyond ourselves, of an entirely rational physical and moral universe. Isaac Newton's demonstrations of the order of natural law greatly encouraged this line of thought, leading many to believe that the fullness and complexity of the perceived physical world testified to the sublime rationality of a divine plan. The Planner, however, did not necessarily supervise the day-to-day operations of His arrangements; He might rather, as a popular analogy had it, resemble the watchmaker who winds the watch and leaves it running.

God as a watchmaker was the central image for thinkers known as deists, who justified evil in the world by arguing that God never interfered with nature or with human action. Deism encouraged the separation of ethics from religion, as ethics was increas-

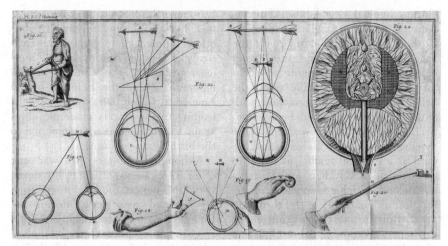

An illustration from an early eighteenth-century edition of the French philosopher René Descartes's unfinished book on the human body. Descartes saw the body as a machine whose operations could be understood mathematically.

ingly understood as a matter of reason. Human beings, Enlightenment thinkers argued, could rely on their own authority—rather than looking to priests or princes—to decide how to act well in the world. Yet no one could fail to recognize that men and women embodied a capacity for passion as well as reason: "On life's vast ocean diversely we sail, / Reason the card, but Passion is the gale," **Alexander Pope's** *Essay on Man* (1733) pointed out. One could hope to steer with reason as guide, but one had to face the omnipresence of unreasonable passions. Life could be understood as a struggle between rationality and emotion, with feeling frequently exercising controlling force. Those who believed in the desirability of reason's governance often worried that it rarely prevailed over feelings of greed, lust, or the desire for power. For them as for us, the gap between the ideal and the actual caused frustration and often despair.

The questions raised by Enlightenment thinkers about human powers and limitations have left a legacy so lasting that it is hard to imagine our world without the Enlightenment. They are the ones who urged us to trust our own judgments and our own senses—while insisting on the need to think skeptically and critically—and they were the ones who shifted the dominant model of truth from divine revelation to human forms of knowledge: science, statistics, history, literature. They imagined conquering nature with ever-increasing knowledge—allowing humans to control their environment and harness nature's power for their own gain. And they ushered in a new sense of the equality of all human beings, launching the demand for universal human rights.

SOCIETY

The late seventeenth century, when the Enlightenment began, was a period of great turmoil, which persisted at intervals throughout the succeeding century. Reason had led many thinkers to the conclusion that kings and queens were ordinary mortals, and that conclusion implied new kinds of uncertainty. Civil war in England had ended in the king's execution in 1649; the French would guillotine their ruler before the end of the eighteenth century. The notion of divine right, the belief that monarchs governed with authority from God, had been effectively destroyed. God seemed to be moving further away. Religion still figured as a political reality, as it did in the struggle of Cavaliers and Puritans in England, which ended with the restoration of Charles II to the throne in 1660. But the most significant social divisions were now those of class and of political conviction—divisions no less powerful for lacking any claim of God-given authority. To England, the eighteenth century brought two unsuccessful but bitter rebellions on behalf of the deposed Stuart monarchs as well as the cataclysmic American Revolution. Throughout the eighteenth century, wars erupted over succession to

European thrones and over nationalistic claims. In Europe, internal divisions often assumed greater importance than struggles between nations. In the Americas, meanwhile, the ideas of the Enlightenment and the example of the American Revolution spread widely, leading to the revolts of creole elites against their European masters and to the birth of new nations.

Although revolution, civil war, and other forms of social instability dominated this period, the idea of civil society retained great power during the Enlightenment. Seventeenth-century English philosopher Thomas Hobbes, who believed that human life before the formation of societies was inevitably "nasty, mean, brutish, and short," thought that men and women had originally banded together for the sake of preservation and progress. By the late seventeenth century in Europe as in the Americas, social organization had evolved into elaborate hierarchical

The Topsy-Turvy World, 1663, by the Dutch genre painter Jan Steen, presents a satirical picture of the disarray in the household of a newly wealthy middle-class family.

structures with the aristocracy at the top. Just below the aristocrats were the educated gentry—clergymen, lawyers, men of leisure with landed property. Below them were masses of workers of various kinds, many of them illiterate, and, in the Americas, the large populations of indigenous or *mestizo* (mixed-race) peoples, as well as slaves of African descent. Although literacy rates grew dramatically during the eighteenth century, those who wrote (and, for a long time, those who read) belonged almost entirely to the two upper classes. As new forms of commerce generated new wealth, and with it, newly wealthy people who felt entitled to their share of social power, the traditional social order faced increasing challenges. In the Americas, white creoles chafed at European entitlements while insisting on their own privilege over other races. By the eighteenth century, the abolitionist movement would begin to question whether slavery could be ethical, a challenge anticipated by Aphra Behn's *Oroonoko*, the story of an African prince tricked into slavery and spirited to the New World.

Among the privileged classes, men had many opportunities: for education, for service in government or diplomacy, for the exercise of political and economic power. Both men and women generally accepted as necessary the subordination of women, who, even in the upper classes, had few opportunities for education and occupation beyond the household. But the increasing value attached to individualism had implications for women as well as men. In the late seventeenth century, **Sor Juana Inés de la Cruz**, a Mexican nun, articulated her own passion for thought and reading, and became an eloquent advocate of the right of women to education and a life of the mind. During the next century, a number of women and an occasional man made the same case. It became increasingly common to argue that limiting women solely to childbearing and childrearing might not conform to the dictates of reason. If God had given all human beings reason, then women were just as entitled to develop and exercise their minds as their male counterparts. The emphasis on education in virtually all of the period's tracts about women provides proof that the concept of rational progress offered a device that could be used to gain at least some rights for women—if not civil rights, which were long in coming, at least the right to thought and knowledge.

Women of the upper classes occupied an important place in Enlightenment society, presiding over "salons," gatherings whose participants engaged in intellectual as well as frivolous conversation. In France as in England, by the late seventeenth century women also began writing novels, their books widely read by men and women alike. Although novels by women often focused attention on the domestic scene, they also ranged further. Women published translations from the Greek as well as volumes of literary criticism, and were the most prolific writers in certain genres, such as Gothic fiction. Even if society as a whole did not acknowledge their full intellectual and moral capacities, individual women were beginning to claim for themselves more rights than those of motherhood.

Society in this period operated, as societies always do, by means of well-defined codes of behavior. Commentators at the time frequently showed themselves troubled by the possibility of sharp discrepancies between social appearance and the "truth" of human nature: **Molière's *Tartuffe*** provides a vivid example, with its exposé of religious sham. Jonathan Swift, lashing the English for institutionalized hypocrisy; Pope, calling attention to ambiguous sexual mores; **Voltaire** and Johnson, sending naive fictional protagonists to find that moralists don't always practice

Molière reading Tartuffe *at the home of Ninon de L'Enclos*, by Nicolas Andre Monsiau.
This eighteenth-century painting of the seventeenth-century playwright is a tribute both to
Molière and to L'Enclos, an author, courtesan, and patron of the arts who was host to some
of the era's most celebrated literary salons.

what they preach—all of these writers call attention to the deceptiveness and the possible misuses of social norms as well as to their necessity. While the social codes may themselves not be at fault, people fail to live up to what they profess. The world would be a better place, these writers suggest, if people examined not only their standards of behavior but also their tendency to hide behind them.

In fiction, drama, poetry, and prose satire, writers of the Enlightenment in one way or another make society their subject. On occasion, they use domestic situations to provide microcosms of a wider social universe. Molière focuses on a private family to suggest how professed sentiment can obscure the operations of ambition; marriage comes to represent a society in miniature, not merely a structure for the fulfillment of personal desire. Marriage, an institution at once social and personal, provides a useful image for human re-

lationship as social and emotional fact. The developing eighteenth-century novel would assume marriage as the normal goal for men and women.

Other writers focus on a broader panorama. In *The Rape of the Lock*, Pope pokes fun at social structures by treating petty social squabbles in an epic form. Voltaire's world travelers witness and participate in a vast range of sobering experiences. In general, women fill subordinate roles in the harsh social environments evoked by these satiric works: erotic love plays a less important part and the position of women becomes increasingly insignificant as the public life is privileged over the home. It is perhaps relevant to note that no literary work in this section describes or evokes children, an omission that the generation of writers to follow—the Romantics—were eager to correct. But for the thinkers of the Enlightenment, it was only in adulthood that people assumed social responsibility; and so it was only then that they could provide interesting substance for social commentary.

HUMANITY AND NATURE

If the subject of human beings' relation to society occupied many writers, the problem of humankind's relation to the universe also perplexed them. Deism assumed the existence of a God who provided evidence of Himself only in His created works. Studying the natural world, therefore, might be seen as a religious act; the powers of reason would enable fruitful study. But how, exactly, should humanity's position in the created universe be understood? Alexander Pope, who in *An Essay on Man* investigates his subject in relation both to society and to the universe, understood creation as a great continuum, with man at the apex of the animal world. This view, sometimes described as belief in a Great Chain of Being, was widely shared. But if one turned the eye of reason on generic man himself, his dominance might seem questionable. Pope describes the inner life of human beings as a "Chaos of Thought and Passion, all confused," and sums up man as "the glory, jest, and riddle of the world." Glory? Perhaps. But when one adds jest and riddle, human preeminence seems less obvious.

Yet the natural order—however incomplete our grasp of it—remains a comfort. It suggests a *system*, a structure of relationships that makes sense at least in theory; rationality thus lies below all apparently irrational experience. It supplies a means of evaluating the natural world: every flower, every minnow, has meaning beyond itself as part of the great pattern. The passion with which the period's thinkers cling to belief in such a system suggests anxiety about what human reason could not do.

The notion of a permanent natural order corresponds to the notion of a permanent human nature, as conceived in the eighteenth century. It was generally believed that human nature remains in all times and places the same: all people hope and fear, are envious and lustful, and possess the capacity to reason. All suffer loss, all face death. Thinkers of the Enlightenment emphasized these common aspects of humanity far more than they considered cultural dissimilarities. Readers and writers alike could draw on this conviction about universality. It provided a test of excellence: if an author's imagining of character failed to conform to what eighteenth-century readers understood as human nature, a work might be securely judged inadequate. Conversely, the idea of a constant human nature held out the hope of longevity for writers who successfully evoked it. Moral philosophers could define human obligation and possibility, convinced that they, too, wrote for all time; ethical standards would never change. Like the vision of order in the physical universe, the notion of constancy in human nature provided bedrock.

CONVENTION AND AUTHORITY

Guides to manners proliferated in the eighteenth century, emphasizing the idea that commitment to decorum helped preserve society's standards. Literary conventions—agreed-on systems of verbal behavior—served comparable purposes in their own sphere, providing continuity between present and past. While these conventions may strike modern readers as antiquated and artificial, to contemporary readers they seemed both natural and proper, much as the plaintive lyrics of current country music or the extravagances of rap operate within restrictive conventions that appear "natural" only because they are familiar to us. Eighteenth-century writers had at their disposal an established set of conventions for every traditional literary genre. As the repetitive rhythms of the country ballad tell listeners what to expect, these literary conventions provided readers with clues about the kind of experience they could anticipate in a given poem or play.

Underlying all the conventions of this era was the classical assumption that literature existed to delight and instruct its readers. The various genres of this period embody such belief in literature's dual function. Stage comedy and tragedy, the early novel, satire in prose and verse, didactic poetry, the philosophical tale: each form developed its own set of devices for creating pleasure as well as for involving audiences and readers in situations requiring moral choice. The insistence in drama on unity of time and place (stage action occupying no more time than its representation, with no change of scene) exemplifies one such set of conventions, intended to produce in their audiences the maximum emotional and moral effect. The elevated diction of the *Essay on Man* ("Mark how it mounts, to Man's imperial race, / From the green myriads in the peopled grass"), and the two-dimensional characters of Johnson's and Voltaire's tales all provide clues about whether the author intends us to read "straight" or to recognize a satirical intention.

One dominant convention of twenty-first-century poetry and prose is something we call "realism." In fiction, verse, and drama, writers often attempt to convey the literal feel of experience, the shape in which events actually occur in the world, the way people really talk. Pope and Voltaire pursued no such goal. Despite their concern with permanent patterns of thought and feeling, they employed deliberate and obvious forms of artifice as modes of emphasis and of indirection. Artistic transformation of life, the period's writers believed, involves the imposition of

Chiswick House in London, an early eighteenth-century villa modeled on the Renaissance architect Palladio's Villa Rotunda outside Vicenza. The Villa Rotunda itself was designed to hearken back to classical ideals.

formal order on the endless flux of event and feeling. The formalities of this literature constitute part of its meaning: its statement that what experience shows as unstable, art makes stable.

By relying on convention, eighteenth-century writers attempted to control an unstable world. The classical past, for many, provided an emblem of that stability, a standard of permanence. But some felt that overvaluing the past was problematic, the problem epitomized by the quarrel of ancients versus moderns in England and France. At stake in this controversy was, among other things, the value of permanence as opposed to the value of change. Proponents of the ancients believed that the giants of Greece and Rome had not only established standards applicable to all future works but had provided models of achievement never to be excelled. Homer wrote the first great epics; subsequent epics could only imitate him. When innovation came, it came by making the old new, as Pope makes a woman's dressing for conquest new by comparing it to the arming of Achilles. Moderns who valued originality for its own sake, who claimed significance for worthless publications that time had not tested, thereby testified to their own inadequacies and their foolish pride.

Those proud to be moderns, on the other hand, held that men (possibly even women) standing on the shoulders of the ancients could see further than their predecessors. The new was conceivably more valuable than the old. One might discover flaws even in revered figures of the classic past, and not everything had yet been accom-plished. This view, of course, corresponds to one widely current since the eighteenth century, but it did not triumph easily: many powerful thinkers of the late seventeenth and early eighteenth centuries adhered to the more conservative position.

Also at issue in this debate was the question of authority, which was to prove so perilous in the political sphere. What position should be assumed by one who hoped to write and be read? Did authority reside only in tradition? If so, must one write in classical forms, rely on classical allusions? Until late in the eighteenth century, virtually all important writers attempted to ally themselves with the authority of tradition, declaring themselves part of a community extending through time as well as space. The problems of authority became particularly important in connection with satire, a popular Enlightenment form. Satire involves criticism of vice and folly; Molière, Pope, and Voltaire at least on occasion wrote in the satiric mode. The fact that satire flourished so richly in this period suggests another version of the central conflict between reason and passion: that of the forces of stability and of instability. In its heightened description of the world (people eating babies, young women initiating epic battles over the loss of a lock of hair), satire calls attention to the powerful presence of the irrational, opposing that presence with the clarity of the satirist's own claim to reason and tradition. As it chastises human beings for their eruptions of passion, urging resistance and control, satire reminds its readers of the universality of the irrational as well as of opposition to it.

MOLIÈRE
(JEAN-BAPTISTE POQUELIN)
1622–1673

Jean-Baptiste Molière, one of the great comic dramatists in the Western tradition, wrote both broad farce and comedies of character in which he caricatured some form of vice or folly by embodying it in a single figure. His targets included the miser, the aspiring but vulgar middle class, female would-be intellectuals, the hypochondriac, and, in *Tartuffe*, the religious hypocrite. Yet Molière's questioning goes far beyond witty farce: his works suggest not only the fallibility of specific types, but also the foolishness of trusting reason to arrange human affairs.

LIFE AND TIMES

Son of a prosperous Paris merchant, Molière (originally named Poquelin) devoted his entire adult life to the creation of stage illusion, as playwright and as actor. He was educated at a prestigious Jesuit school and seems to have studied law for some time, though without taking a degree. At about the age of twenty-five, he took his stage name and abandoned the comfortable life of a bourgeois to join the Illustre Théâtre, a company of traveling players established by the Béjart family. With them he toured the provinces for about twelve years, and, in 1662, he married Armande Béjart. Molière's lengthy experience as an actor doubtless honed his dramatic writing skills, although he first became known not for the tragedies that he preferred but for the short farces that he appended to them. Molière's particular talents, it would soon become clear, lay in satirizing an overly sophisticated society that was heavily invested in fashion, appearances, and proper behavior. Molière's skepticism about religious devotion, which he exposed as hypocrisy, would prove hugely controversial in a France that had recently been led by the powerful Cardinal Mazarin, chief minister while Louis XIV was a young boy, and where the Catholic Church still wielded considerable power.

Over the course of his long reign, Louis XIV, the "Sun King," consolidated royal power by upholding the divine right of kings, and became an important patron of the visual and literary arts. In Louis's France, the true measure of cultural worth was the approval of the court and the Paris stage. After years of courting noble patrons, in 1658 Molière's theatrical company was finally ordered to perform for the king in Paris; a year later, the playwright's first great success, *The High-Brow Ladies* (*Les Précieuses ridicules*), was produced. The company, now patronized by the king, became increasingly successful, developing finally (1680) into the Comédie Française. With success came opposition: the *parti des Devots* (party of the faithful) banded together to protest Molière's irreverence, as he took on more and more of his society's sacred cows. Yet the king continued to protect him, granting him a pension and allowing Molière to evade the censorship often demanded by the Church or the more conservative voices in society.

Molière became increasingly famous—and infamous—as his works met with increasing resistance, culminating in the furor over *Tartuffe*, discussed below. Over the course of his years in Paris, Molière wrote over thirty plays and produced many more on his stage. Ever the man of the theater, he died a few hours after performing in the lead role of his own play *The Imaginary Invalid*.

TARTUFFE

In *Tartuffe* (1664), as in his other plays, Molière employs classic comic devices of plot and character—here, a foolish, stubborn father blocking the course of young love; an impudent servant commenting on her superiors' actions; a happy ending involving a marriage facilitated by implausible means. He often uses such devices, however, to comment on his own immediate social scene, imagining how universal patterns play themselves out in a specific historical context. *Tartuffe* targeted the hypocrisy of piety so directly and transparently that the Catholic Church forced the king to ban it, although Molière managed to have it published and produced once more by 1669.

The play's emotional energy derives not from the simple discrepancy of man and mask in Tartuffe ("Is not a face quite different from a mask?" inquires Cléante, who has no trouble making such distinctions) but from the struggle for erotic, psychic, and economic power in which people employ their masks. Orgon, an aging man with grown children, seeks ways to preserve control and instead falls for the ploys of the hypocritical Tartuffe. A domestic tyrant, Orgon insists on submission from the women in the play, even when they prove far more perceptive than he about Tartuffe's deceptions. Tartuffe's lust, one of those passions forever eluding human mastery, disturbs Orgon's arrangements; in the end, the will of the offstage king resolves everything, as though a benevolent god had intervened.

To make Tartuffe a specifically religious hypocrite is an act of inventive daring. Although one may easily accept Molière's defense of his intentions (not to mock faith but to attack its misuse), it is not hard to see why the play might trouble religious authorities. Molière suggests how readily religious faith lends itself to misuse, how high-sounding pieties allow men and women to evade self-examination and immediate responsibilities. Tartuffe deceives others by his grand gestures of mortification ("Hang up my hair shirt") and charity; he encourages his victims in their own grandiosities. Religion offers ready justification for a course as destructive as it is self-seeking.

Throughout the play, Orgon's brother-in-law Cléante speaks in the voice of wisdom, counseling moderation, common sense, and self-control, calling attention to folly. More important, he emphasizes how the issues Molière examines in this comedy relate to dominant late seventeenth-century themes:

> Ah, Brother, man's a strangely
> fashioned creature
> Who seldom is content to follow
> Nature,
> But recklessly pursues his inclination
> Beyond the narrow bounds of
> moderation,
> And often, by transgressing Reason's
> laws,
> Perverts a lofty aim or noble cause.

To follow Nature means to act appropriately to the human situation in the created universe, recognizing the limitations inherent in the human condition. As Cléante's observations suggest, "to follow Nature," given the rationality of the universe, implies adherence to "Reason's laws." All transgression involves failure to submit to reason's dictates, a point that Molière's stylized comic plot makes insistently.

Although the comedy suggests a social world in which women exist in utter subordination to fathers and husbands, in the plot, two women bring about the unmasking of the villain. The virtuous wife, Elmire, object of Tartuffe's lust, and the clever servant girl, Dorine, confront the immediate situation with pragmatic inventiveness. Both women have a clear sense of right and wrong, although they express it in less resounding terms than does Cléante. Their concrete insistence on facing what is really going on, cutting through all obfuscation, rescues the men from entanglement in their own abstract formulations.

Molière achieves comic effects above all through style and language. Devoted to exposing the follies of his society, his plays use a number of devices that have become the gold standard of comic writing. His characters are often in the grip of a fixed idea, rigidly following a single principle of action, such as extreme religious devotion or sexual rejuvenation. These fixed ideas also manifest themselves in the characters' speech patterns, which are full of ticks and repetitions. Adhering to single abstractions, Molière's comic protagonists often seem like marionettes, whose rigid bearing, behavior and language is controlled by an outside force as if by a puppet master. Yet despite their singlemindedness, his characters are also recognizable portraits of human folly, closely observed and humorously rendered.

Comedies conventionally end in the restoration of order, declaring that good inevitably triumphs; rationality renews itself despite the temporary deviations of the foolish and the vicious. Although at the end of *Tartuffe* order is restored, the arbitrary intervention of the king leaves a disturbing emotional residue. The play has demonstrated that Tartuffe's corrupt will to power can ruthlessly aggrandize itself. Money speaks, in this society as in ours; possession of wealth implies total control over others. In the benign world of comedy, the play reminds its readers of the extreme precariousness with which reason finally triumphs. Tartuffe's monstrous lust, for women, money, power, genuinely endangers the social structure. The play forces us to recognize the constant threats to rationality, and how much we have at stake in trying to use reason as a principle of action.

Tartuffe[1]

CHARACTERS

MADAME PERNELLE, *mother of Orgon*
ORGON, *husband of Elmire*
ELMIRE, *wife of Orgon*
DAMIS, *son of Orgon*
MARIANE, *daughter of Orgon*
VALÈRE, *fiancé of Mariane*
CLÉANTE, *brother-in-law of Orgon*

TARTUFFE,[2] *a religious hypocrite*
DORINE, *lady's maid to Mariane*
MONSIEUR LOYAL, *a bailiff*
THE EXEMPT, *an officer of the king*
FLIPOTE, *lady's maid to Madame Pernelle*
LAURENT, *a servant of Tartuffe*

The scene is Paris, in ORGON's *house.*

1. Versification by Constance Congdon, from a translation by Virginia Scott.
2. The name Tartuffe is similar both to the Italian word *tartufo*, meaning "truffle," and to the French word for truffle, *truffe*, from which is derived the French verb *truffer*—one meaning of which in Molière's day was "to deceive or cheat."

1.1

[MADAME PERNELLE, FLIPOTE, ELMIRE,
MARIANE, DORINE, DAMIS, CLÉANTE]

MADAME PERNELLE[3]   Flipote, come on! My visit here is through!
ELMIRE   You walk so fast I can't keep up with you!
MADAME PERNELLE   Then stop! That's your last step! Don't take another.
  After all, I'm just your husband's mother.
ELMIRE   And, as his wife, I have to see you out—   5
  Agreed? Now, what is this about?
MADAME PERNELLE   I cannot bear the way this house is run—
  As if I don't know how things should be done!
  No one even thinks about my pleasure,
  And, if I ask, I'm served at someone's leisure.   10
  It's obvious—the values here aren't good
  Or everyone would treat me as they should.
  The Lord of Misrule here has his dominion—
DORINE   But—
MADAME PERNELLE   See? A servant with an opinion.
  You're the former nanny, nothing more.   15
  Were I in charge here, you'd be out the door.
DAMIS   If—
MADAME PERNELLE   —You—be quiet. Now let Grandma spell
  Her special word for you: "F-O-O-L."
  Oh yes! Your dear grandmother tells you that,
  Just as I told my son, "Your son's a brat.   20
  He won't become a drunkard or a thief,
  And yet, he'll be a lifetime full of grief."
MARIANE   I think—
MADAME PERNELLE   —Oh, don't do that, my dear grandchild.
  You'll hurt your brain. You think that we're beguiled
  By your quietude, you fragile flower,   25
  But as they say, still waters do run sour.
ELMIRE   But Mother—
MADAME PERNELLE   —Daughter-in-law, please take this well—
  Behavior such as yours leads straight to hell.
  You spend money like it grows on trees
  Then wear it on your back in clothes like these.   30
  Are you a princess? No? You're dressed like one!
  One wonders whom you dress for—not my son.
  Look to these children whom you have corrupted
  When their mama's life was interrupted.
  She spun in her grave when you were wed;   35
  She's still a better mother, even dead.
CLÉANTE   Madame, I do insist—
MADAME PERNELLE   —You do? On what?
  That we live life as you do, caring not

---

3. The role of Madame Pernelle was originally played by a male actor, a practice that was already a comic convention in Molière's time.

For morals? I hear each time you give that speech
Your sister memorizing what you teach. 40
I'd slam the door on you. Forgive my frankness.
That is how I am! And it is thankless.

DAMIS Tartuffe would, from the bottom of his heart,
If he had one, thank you.

MADAME PERNELLE Oh, now you start.
Grandson, it's "Monsieur Tartuffe" to you. 45
And he's a man who should be listened to.
If you provoke him with ungodly chat,
I will not tolerate it, and that's that.

DAMIS Yet I should tolerate this trickster who
Has become the voice we answer to. 50
And I'm to be as quiet as a mouse
About this tyrant's power in our house?
All the fun things lately we have planned,
We couldn't do. And why? Because they're banned—

DORINE By him! Anything we take pleasure in 55
Suddenly becomes a mortal sin.

MADAME PERNELLE Then "he's here just in time" is what I say!
Don't you see? He's showing you the way
To heaven! Yes! So follow where he leads!
My son knows he is just what this house needs. 60

DAMIS Now Grandmother, listen. Not Father, not you,
No one can make me follow this man who
Rules this house, yet came here as a peasant.
I'll put him in his place. It won't be pleasant.

DORINE When he came here he wasn't wearing shoes. 65
But he's no village saint—it's all a ruse.
There was no vow of poverty—he's poor!
And he was just some beggar at the door
Whom we should have tossed. He's a disaster!
To think this street bum now plays the master. 70

MADAME PERNELLE May God have mercy on me. You're
all blind.
A nobler, kinder man you'll never find.

DORINE So you think he's a saint. That's what he wants.
But he's a hypocrite and merely flaunts
This so-called godliness. 75

MADAME PERNELLE Will you be quiet!?

DORINE And that man of his—I just don't buy it—
He's supposed to be his servant? No.
They're in cahoots, I bet.

MADAME PERNELLE How would you know?
When, clearly, you don't understand, in fact,
How a servant is supposed to act? 80
This holy man you think of as uncouth,
Tries to help by telling you the truth
About yourself. But you can't hear it.
He knows what heaven wants and that you fear it.

DORINE   So "heaven" hates these visits by our friends?   85
   I see! And that's why Tartuffe's gone to any ends
   To ruin our fun? But it is he who's zealous
   About "privacy"—and why? He's jealous.
   You can't miss it, whenever men come near—
   He's lusting for our own Madame Elmire.   90
MADAME PERNELLE   Since you, Dorine, have never understood
   Your place, or the concepts of "should"
   And "should not," one can't expect you to see
   Tartuffe's awareness of propriety.
   When these men visit, they bring noise and more—   95
   Valets and servants planted at the door,
   Carriages and horses, constant chatter.
   What must the neighbors think? These things matter.
   Is something going on? Well, I hope not.
   You know you're being talked about a lot.   100
CLÉANTE   Really, Madame, you think you can prevent
   Gossip? When most human beings are bent
   On rumormongering and defamation,
   And gathering or faking information
   To make us all look bad—what can we do?   105
   The fools who gossip don't care what is true.
   You would force the whole world to be quiet?
   Impossible! And each new lie—deny it?
   Who in the world would want to live that way?
   Let's live our lives. Let gossips have their say.   110
DORINE   It's our neighbor, Daphne. I just know it.
   They don't like us. It's obvious—they show it
   In the way they watch us—she and her mate.
   I've seen them squinting at us, through their gate.
   It's true—those whose private conduct is the worst   115
   Will mow each other down to be the first
   To weave some tale of lust, so hearts are broken
   Out of a simple kiss that's just a token
   Between friends—just friends and nothing more.
   See—those whose trysts are kept behind a door   120
   Yet everyone finds out? Well, then, they need
   New stories for the gossip mill to feed
   To all who'll listen. So they must repaint
   The deeds of others, hoping that a taint
   Will color others' lives in darker tone   125
   And, by this process, lighten up their own.
MADAME PERNELLE   Daphne and her mate are not the point.
   But when Orante says things are out of joint,
   There's a problem. She's a person who
   Prays every day and should be listened to.   130
   She condemns the mob that visits here.
DORINE   This good woman shouldn't live so near
   Those, like us, who run a bawdy house.
   I hear she lives as quiet as a mouse—

Devout, though. Everyone applauds her zeal.   135
She needed that when age stole her appeal.
Her passion is policing—it's her duty.
And compensation for her loss of beauty.
She's a reluctant prude. And now, her art,
Once used so well to win a lover's heart,   140
Is gone. Her eyes, that used to flash with lust,
Are steely from her piety. She must
Have seen that it's too late to be a wife,
And so she lives a plain and pious life.
This is a strategy of old coquettes.   145
It's how they manage once the world forgets
Them. First, they wallow in a dark depression,
Then see no recourse but in the profession
Of a prude. They criticize the lives of everyone.
They censure everything, and pardon none.   150
It's envy. Pleasures that they are denied
By time and age, now, they just can't abide.
MADAME PERNELLE You do go on and on. [*To* ELMIRE] My dear Elmire,
This is all your doing. It's so clear
Because you let a servant give advice.   155
Just be aware—I'm tired of being nice.
It's obvious to anyone with eyes
That what my son has done is more than wise
In welcoming this man who's so devout;
His very presence casts the devils out.   160
Or most of them—that's why I hope you hear him.
And I advise all of you to stay near him.
You need his protection and advice.
Your casual attention won't suffice.
It's heaven sent him here to fill a need,   165
To save you from yourselves—oh yes, indeed.
These visits from your friends you seem to want—
Listen to yourselves! So nonchalant!
As if no evil lurks in these events.
As if you're blind to what Satan invents.   170
And dances! What are those but food for slander!
It's to the worst desires these parties pander.
I ask you now, what purpose do they serve?
Where gossip's passed around like an hors-d'oeuvre.
A thousand cackling hens, busy with what?   175
It takes a lot of noise to cover smut.
It truly is the tower of Babylon,[4]
Where people babble on and on and on.
Ah! Case in point—there stands Monsieur Cléante,

4. That is, the biblical Tower of Babel (the Hebrew equivalent of the Akkadian Bab-ilu, or Babylon—a name explained by the similar sounding but unrelated Hebrew verb *balal*, "confuse"), described in Genesis 11.1–9; to prevent it from being constructed and reaching heaven, God scattered all the people and confused their language, creating many tongues where there had been only one.

Sniggering and eyeing me askant,   180
As if this has nothing to do with him,
And nothing that he does would God condemn.
And so, Elmire, my dear, I say farewell.
Till when? When it is a fine day in hell.
Farewell, all of you. When I pass through that door,   185
You won't have me to laugh at anymore.
Flipote! Wake up! Have you heard nothing I have said?
I'll march you home and beat you till you're dead.
March, slut, march.

1.2[5]

[DORINE, CLÉANTE]

CLÉANTE   I'm staying here. She's scary,
    That old lady—
DORINE   I know why you're wary.
    Shall I call her back to hear you say,
    "That *old* lady"? That would make her day.
CLÉANTE   She's lost her mind, she's—now we have the proof—   5
    Head over heels in love with whom? Tartuffe.
DORINE   So here's what's worse and weird—so is her son.
    What's more—it's obvious to everyone.
    Before Tartuffe and he became entwined,
    Orgon once ruled this house in his right mind.   10
    In the troubled times,[6] he backed the prince,
    And that took courage. We haven't seen it since.
    He is intoxicated with Tartuffe—
    A potion that exceeds a hundred proof.
    It's put him in a trance, this devil's brew.   15
    And so he worships this imposter who
    He calls "brother" and loves more than one—
    This charlatan—more than daughter, wife, son.
    This charlatan hears all our master's dreams,
    And all his secrets. Every thought, it seems,   20
    Is poured out to Tartuffe, like he's his priest!
    You'd think they'd see the heresy, at least.
    Orgon caresses him, embraces him, and shows
    More love for him than any mistress knows.
    Come for a meal and who has the best seat?   25
    Whose preferences determine what we eat?
    Tartuffe consumes enough for six, is praised,
    And to his health is every goblet raised,

---

5. In classical French drama, a new scene begins whenever a character enters or leaves the stage, even if the action continues without interruption; this convention has become known as "French scenes." Characters remaining on-stage are listed; others from the previous scene can be assumed to have exited.

6. That is, during the Fronde (literally, "sling"; 1648–53), a civil war that took place while France was being ruled by a regent for Louis XIV—"the prince" whom Orgon supported—as various factions of the nobility sought to limit the growing authority of the monarchy.

While on his plate are piled the choicest bites.
Then when he belches, our master delights   30
In that and shouts, "God bless you!" to the beast,
As if Tartuffe's the reason for the feast.
Did I mention the quoting of each word,
As if it's the most brilliant thing we've heard?
And, oh, the miracles Tartuffe creates!   35
The prophecies! We write while he dictates.
All that's ridiculous. But what's evil
Is seeing the deception and upheaval
Of the master and everything he owns.
He hands him money. They're not even loans—   40
He's giving it away. It's gone too far.
To watch Tartuffe play him like a guitar!
And this Laurent, his man, found some lace.
Shredded it and threw it in my face.
He'd found it pressed inside *The Lives of Saints*,[7]   45
I thought we'd have to put him in restraints.
"To put the devil's finery beside
The words and lives of saintly souls who died—
Is action of satanical transgression!"
And so, of course, I hurried to confession.   50

1.3

[ELMIRE, MARIANE, DAMIS, CLÉANTE, DORINE]

ELMIRE [*to* CLÉANTE]   Lucky you, you stayed. Yes, there was more,
And more preaching from Grandma, at the door.
My husband's coming! I didn't catch his eye.
I'll wait for him upstairs. Cléante, good-bye.
CLÉANTE   I'll see you soon. I'll wait here below,   5
Take just a second for a brief hello.
DAMIS   While you have him, say something for me?
My sister needs for Father to agree
To her marriage with Valère, as planned.
Tartuffe opposes it and will demand   10
That Father break his word, and that's not fair;
Then I can't wed the sister of Valère.
Listening only to Tartuffe's voice,
He'd break four hearts at once—
DORINE   He's here.

7. A text (*Flos Sanctorum*, 1599–1601) by the Spanish Jesuit Pedro de Ribadeneyra, available in
French translation by 1646.

1.4

[ORGON, CLÉANTE, DORINE]

ORGON   Rejoice!
  I'm back.
CLÉANTE   I'm glad to see you, but I'm on my way.
  Just stayed to say hello.
ORGON   No more to say?
  Dorine! Come back! And Cléante, why the hurry?
  Indulge me for a moment. You know I worry.   5
  I've been gone two days! There's news to tell.
  Now don't hold back. Has everyone been well?
DORINE   Not quite. There was that headache Madame had
  The day you left. Well, it got really bad.
  She had a fever—   10
ORGON   And Tartuffe?
DORINE   He's fine—
  Rosy-nosed and red-cheeked, drinking your wine.
ORGON   Poor man!
DORINE   And then, Madame became unable
  To eat a single morsel at the table.
ORGON   Ah, and Tartuffe?
DORINE   He sat within her sight,
  Not holding back, he ate with great delight,   15
  A brace of partridge, and a leg of mutton.
  In fact, he ate so much, he popped a button.
ORGON   Poor man!
DORINE   That night until the next sunrise,
  Your poor wife couldn't even close her eyes.
  What a fever! Oh, how she did suffer!   20
  I don't see how that night could have been rougher.
  We watched her all night long, worried and weepy.
ORGON   Ah, and Tartuffe?
DORINE   At dinner he grew sleepy.
  After such a meal, it's not surprising.
  He slept through the night, not once arising.   25
ORGON   Poor man!
DORINE   At last won over by our pleading,
  Madame agreed to undergo a bleeding.[8]
  And this, we think, has saved her from the grave.
ORGON   Ah, and Tartuffe?
DORINE   Oh, he was very brave.
  To make up for the blood Madame had lost   30
  Tartuffe slurped down red wine, all at your cost.
ORGON   Poor man!
DORINE   Since then, they've both been fine, although

---

8. Bloodletting (whether by leeches or other means), for centuries a standard medical treatment for a wide range of diseases.

Madame needs me. I'll go and let her know
How anxious you have been about her health,
And that you prize it more than all your wealth.   35

1.5

[ORGON, CLÉANTE]

CLÉANTE   You know that girl was laughing in your face.
   I fear I'll make you angry, but in case
   There is a chance you'll listen, I will try
   To say that you are laughable and why.
   I've never known of something so capricious   5
   As letting this man do just as he wishes
   In your home and to your family.
   You brought him here, relieved his poverty,
   And, in return—
ORGON   Now you listen to me!
   You're just my brother-in-law, Cléante. Quite!   10
   You don't know this man. And don't deny it!
CLÉANTE   I don't know him, yes, that may be so,
   But men like him are not so rare, you know.
ORGON   If you only could know him as I do,
   You would be his true disciple, too.   15
   The universe, your ecstasy would span.
   This is a man . . . who . . . ha! . . . well, such a man.
   Behold him. Let him teach you profound peace.
   When first we met, I felt my troubles cease.
   Yes, I was changed after I talked with him.   20
   I saw my wants and needs as just a whim!
   Everything that's written, all that's sung,
   The world, and you and me, well, it's all dung!
   Yes, it's crap! And isn't that a wonder!
   The real world—it's just some spell we're under!   25
   He's taught me to love nothing and no one!
   Mother, father, wife, daughter, son—
   They could die right now, I'd feel no pain.
CLÉANTE   What feelings you've developed, how humane.
ORGON   You just don't see him in the way I do,   30
   But if you did, you'd feel what I feel, too.
   Every day he came to church and knelt,
   And from his groans, I knew just what he felt.
   Those sounds he made from deep inside his soul,
   Were fed by piety he could not control.   35
   Of the congregation, who could ignore
   The way he humbly bowed and kissed the floor?
   And when they tried to turn away their eyes,
   His fervent prayers to heaven and deep sighs
   Made them witness his deep spiritual pain.   40
   Then something happened I can't quite explain.

I rose to leave—he quickly went before
To give me holy water at the door.
He knew what I needed, so he blessed me.
I found his acolyte, he'd so impressed me,   45
To ask who he was and there I learned
About his poverty and how he spurned
The riches of this world. And when I tried
To give him gifts, in modesty, he cried,
"That is too much," he'd say, "A half would do."   50
Then gave a portion back, with much ado.
"I am not worthy. I do not deserve
Your gifts or pity. I am here to serve
The will of heaven, that and nothing more."
Then takes the gift and shares it with the poor.   55
So heaven spoke to me inside my head.
"Just bring him home with you" is what it said
And so I did. And ever since he came,
My home's a happy one. I also claim
A moral home, a house that's free of sin,   60
Tartuffe's on watch—he won't let any in.
His interest in my wife is reassuring,
She's innocent of course, but so alluring,
He tells me whom she sees and what she does.
He's more jealous than I ever was.   65
It's for my honor that he's so concerned.
His righteous anger's all for me, I've learned,
To the point that just the other day,
A flea annoyed him as he tried to pray,
Then he rebuked himself, as if he'd willed it—   70
His excessive anger when he killed it.
CLÉANTE   Orgon, listen. You're out of your mind.
Or you're mocking me. Or both combined.
How can you speak such nonsense without blinking?
ORGON   I smell an atheist! It's that freethinking!   75
Such nonsense is the bane of your existence.
And that explains your damnable resistance.
Ten times over, I've tried to save your soul
From your corrupted mind. That's still my goal.
CLÉANTE   You have been corrupted by your friends,   80
You know of whom I speak. Your thought depends
On people who are blind and want to spread it
Like some horrid flu, and, yes, I dread it.
I'm no atheist. I see things clearly.
And what I see is loud lip service, merely,   85
To make exhibitionists seem devout.
Forgive me, but a prayer is not a shout.
Yet those who don't adore these charlatans
Are seen as faithless heathens by your friends.
It's as if you think you'd never find   90
Reason and the sacred intertwined.

You think I'm afraid of retribution?
Heaven sees my heart and their pollution.
So we should be the slaves of sanctimony?
Monkey see, monkey do, monkey phony.   95
The true believers we should emulate
Are not the ones who groan and lay prostrate.
And yet you see no problem in the notion
Of hypocrisy as deep devotion.
You see as one the genuine and the spurious.   100
You'd extend this to your money? I'm just curious.
In your business dealings, I'd submit,
You'd not confuse the gold with counterfeit.
Men are strangely made, I'd have to say.
They're burdened with their reason, till one day,   105
They free themselves with such force that they spoil
The noblest of things for which they toil.
Because they must go to extremes. It's a flaw.
Just a word in passing, Brother-in-law.

ORGON   Oh, you are the wisest man alive, so   110
You know everything there is to know.
You are the one enlightened man, the sage.
You are Cato the Elder[9] of our age.
Next to you, all men are dumb as cows.

CLÉANTE   I'm not the wisest man, as you espouse,   115
Nor do I know—what—all there is to know?
But I do know, Orgon, that quid pro quo
Does not apply at all to "false" and "true,"
And I would never trust a person who
Cannot tell them apart. See, I revere   120
Everyone whose worship is sincere.
Nothing is more noble or more beautiful
Than fervor that is holy, not just dutiful.
So nothing is more odious to me
Than the display of specious piety   125
Which I see in every charlatan
Who tries to pass for a true holy man.
Religious passion worn as a facade
Abuses what's sacred and mocks God.
These men who take what's sacred and most holy   130
And use it as their trade, for money, solely,
With downcast looks and great affected cries,
Who suck in true believers with their lies,
Who ceaselessly will preach and then demand
"Give up the world!" and then, by sleight of hand,   135
End up sitting pretty at the court,
The best in lodging and new clothes to sport.
If you're their enemy, then heaven hates you.

9. Roman statesman and author (234–149 B.C.E.), famous as a stern moralist devoted to traditional Roman ideals of honor, courage, and simplicity.

That's their claim when one of them berates you.
They'll say you've sinned. You'll find yourself removed   140
And wondering if you'll be approved
For anything, at all, ever again.
Because so heinous was this fictional "sin."
When these men are angry, they're the worst,
There's no place to hide, you're really cursed.   145
They use what we call righteous as their sword,
To coldly murder in the name of the Lord.
But next to these imposters faking belief,
The devotion of the true is a relief.
Our century has put before our eyes   150
Glorious examples we can prize.
Look at Ariston, and look at Periandre,
Oronte, Alcidamas, Polydore, Clitandre:[1]
Not one points out his own morality,
Instead they speak of their mortality.   155
They don't form cabals,[2] they don't have factions,
They don't censure other people's actions.
They see the flagrant pride in such correction
And know that humans can't achieve perfection.
They know this of themselves and yet their lives   160
Good faith, good works, all good, epitomize.
They don't exhibit zeal that's more intense
Than heaven shows us in its own defense.
They'd never claim a knowledge that's divine
And yet they live in virtue's own design.   165
They concentrate their hatred on the sin,
And when the sinner grieves, invite him in.
They leave to others the arrogance of speech.
Instead they practice what others only preach.
These are the men who show us how to live.   170
Their lives, the best example I can give.
These are my men, the ones whom I would follow.
Your man and his life, honestly, are hollow.
I believe you praise him quite sincerely,
I also think you'll pay for this quite dearly.   175
He's a fraud, this man whom you adore.
ORGON   Oh, you've stopped talking. Is there any more?
CLÉANTE   No.
ORGON   I am your servant, sir.
CLÉANTE   No! wait!
There's one more thing—no more debate—
I want to change the subject, if I might.   180
I heard that you said the other night,
To Valère, he'd be your son-in-law.

---

1. Made-up names.
2. A possible allusion to the Compagnie de Saint-Sacrement, a tightly knit group of prom-inent French citizens known for public works as well as strict morality; they were pejora-tively referred to as the *cabale*.

ORGON I did.
CLÉANTE   And set the date?
ORGON   Yes.
CLÉANTE   Did you withdraw?
ORGON I did.
CLÉANTE   You're putting off the wedding? Why?
ORGON Don't know.   185
CLÉANTE   There's more?
ORGON   Perhaps.
CLÉANTE   Again I'll try:
  You would break your word?
ORGON   I couldn't say.
CLÉANTE Then, Orgon, why did you change the day?
ORGON Who knows?
CLÉANTE   But we need to know, don't we now?
  Is there a reason you would break your vow?
ORGON That depends.   190
CLÉANTE   On what? Orgon, what is it?
  Valère was the reason for my visit.
ORGON Who knows? Who knows?
CLÉANTE   So there's some mystery there?
ORGON Heaven knows.
CLÉANTE   It does? And now, Valère—
  May he know, too?
ORGON   Can't say.
CLÉANTE   But, dear Orgon,
  We have no information to go on.   195
  We need to know—
ORGON   What heaven wants, I'll do.
CLÉANTE Is that your final answer? Then I'm through.
  But your pledge to Valère? You'll stand by it?
ORGON Good-bye.

                              [ORGON exits.]
CLÉANTE   More patience, yes, I should try it.
  I let him get to me. Now I confess   200
  I fear the worst for Valère's happiness.

                              2.1

                        [ORGON, MARIANE]

ORGON Mariane.
MARIANE   Father.
ORGON   Come. Now. Talk with me.
MARIANE Why are you looking everywhere?
ORGON   To see
  If everyone is minding their own business.
  So, Child, I've always loved your gentleness.
MARIANE And for your love, I'm grateful, Father dear.   5
ORGON Well said. And so to prove that you're sincere,

And worthy of my love, you have the task
Of doing for me anything I ask.
MARIANE   Then my obedience will be my proof.
ORGON   Good. What do you think of our guest, Tartuffe?   10
MARIANE   Who, me?
ORGON   Yes, you. Watch what you say right now.
MARIANE   Then, Father, I will say what you allow.
ORGON   Wise words, Daughter. So this is what you say:
    "He is a perfect man in every way;
    In body and soul, I find him divine."   15
    And then you say, "Please Father, make him mine."
    Huh?
MARIANE   Huh?
ORGON   Yes?
MARIANE   I heard . . .
ORGON   Yes.
MARIANE   What did you say?
    Who is this perfect man in every way,
    Whom in body and soul I find divine
    And ask of you, "Please, Father, make him mine?"   20
ORGON   Tartuffe.
MARIANE   All that I've said, I now amend
    Because you wouldn't want me to pretend.
ORGON   Absolutely not—that's so misguided.
    Have it be the truth, then. It's decided.
MARIANE   What?! Father, you want—   25
ORGON   Yes, my dear, I do—
    To join in marriage my Tartuffe and you.
    And since I have—

2.2

[DORINE, ORGON, MARIANE]

ORGON   Dorine, I know you're there!
    Any secrets in this house you don't share?
DORINE   "Marriage"—I think, yes, I heard a rumor,
    Someone's failed attempt at grotesque humor,
    So when I heard the story, I said, "No!   5
    Preposterous! Absurd! It can't be so."
ORGON   Oh, you find it preposterous? And why?
DORINE   It's so outrageous, it must be a lie.
ORGON   Yet it's the truth and you will believe it.
DORINE   Yet as a joke is how I must receive it.   10
ORGON   But it's a story that will soon come true.
DORINE   A fantasy!
ORGON   I'm getting tired of you.
    Mariane, it's not a joke—
DORINE   Says he,
    Laughing up his sleeve for all to see.

ORGON   I'm telling you—   15
DORINE   —more make-believe for fun.
  It's very good—you're fooling everyone.
ORGON   You have made me really angry now.
DORINE   I see the awful truth across your brow.
  How can a man who looks as wise as you
  Be such a fool to want—   20
ORGON   What can I do
  About a servant with a mouth like that?
  The liberties you take! Decorum you laugh at!
  I'm not happy with you—
DORINE   Oh sir, don't frown.
  A smile is just a frown turned upside down.
  Be happy, sir, because you've shared your scheme,   25
  Even though it's just a crazy dream.
  Because, dear sir, your daughter is not meant
  For this zealot—she's too innocent.
  She'd be alarmed by his robust desire
  And question heaven's sanction of this fire   30
  And then the gossip! Your friends will talk a lot,
  Because you're a man of wealth and he is not.
  Could it be your reasoning has a flaw—
  Choosing a beggar for a son-in-law?
ORGON   You, shut up! If he has nothing now   35
  Admire that, as if it were his vow,
  This poverty. His property was lost
  Because he would not pay the deadly cost
  Of daily duties nibbling life away,
  Leaving him with hardly time to pray.   40
  The grandeur in his life comes from devotion
  To the eternal, thus his great emotion.
  And at those moments, I can plainly see
  What my special task has come to be:
  To end the embarrassment he feels   45
  And the sorrow he so nobly conceals
  Of the loss of his ancestral domain.
  With my money, I can end his pain.
  I'll raise him up to be, because I can,
  With my help, again, a gentleman.   50
DORINE   So he's a gentleman. Does that seem vain?
  Then what about this piety and pain?
  Those with "domains" are those of noble birth.
  A holy man's domain is not on earth.
  It seems to me a holy man of merit   55
  Wouldn't brag of what he might inherit—
  Even gifts in heaven, he won't mention.
  To live a humble life is his intention.
  Yet he wants something back? That's just ambition
  To feed his pride. Is that a holy mission?   60
  You seem upset. Is it something I said?

I'll shut up. We'll talk of her instead.
Look at this girl, your daughter, your own blood.
How will her honor fare covered with mud?
Think of his age. So from the night they're wed,   65
Bliss, if there is any, leaves the marriage bed,
And she'll be tied unto this elderly person.
Her dedication to fidelity will worsen
And soon he will sprout horns,[3] your holy man,
And no one will be happy. If I can   70
Have another word, I'd like to say
Old men and young girls are married every day,
And the young girls stray, but who's to blame
For the loss of honor and good name?
The father, who proceeds to pick a mate,   75
Blindly, though it's someone she may hate,
Bears the sins the daughter may commit,
Imperiling his soul because of it.
If you do this, I vow you'll hear the bell,
As you die, summoning you to hell.   80
ORGON   You think that you can teach me how to live.
DORINE   If you'd just heed the lessons that I give.
ORGON   Can heaven tell me why I still endure
This woman's ramblings? Yet, of this I'm sure,
I know what's best for you—I'm your father.   85
I gave you to Valère, without a bother.
But I hear he gambles and what's more,
He thinks things that a Christian would abhor.
It's from free thinking that all evils stem.
No wonder, then, at church, I don't see him.   90
DORINE   Should he race there, if he only knew
Which Mass you might attend, and be on view?
He could wait at the door with holy water.
ORGON   Go away. I'm talking to my daughter.
Think, my child, he is heaven's favorite!   95
And age in marriage? It can flavor it,
A sweet comfit suffused with deep, deep pleasure.
You will be loving, faithful, and will treasure
Every single moment—two turtledoves—
Next to heaven, the only thing he loves.   100
And he will be the only one for you.
No arguments or quarrels. You'll be true,
Like two innocent children, you will thrive,
In heaven's light, thrilled to be alive.
And as a woman, surely you must know   105
Wives mold husbands, like making pies from dough.
DORINE   Four and twenty cuckolds baked in a pie.
ORGON   Ugh! What a thing to say!
DORINE   Oh, really, why?

---

3. The traditional sign of the cuckold.

He's destined to be cheated on, it's true.
You know he'd always question her virtue.   110
ORGON   Quiet! Just be quiet. I command it!
DORINE   I'll do just that, because you do demand it!
But your best interests—I will protect them.
ORGON   Too kind of you. Be quiet and neglect them.
DORINE   If I weren't fond of you—   115
ORGON   —Don't want you to
DORINE   I will be fond of you in spite of you.
ORGON   Don't!
DORINE   But your honor is so dear to me,
How can you expose yourself to mockery?
ORGON   Will you never be quiet!
DORINE   Oh, dear sir,
I can't let you do this thing to her,   120
It's against my conscience—
ORGON   You vicious asp!
DORINE   Sometimes the things you call me make me gasp.
And anger, sir, is not a pious trait.
ORGON   It's your fault, girl! You make me irate!
I am livid! Why won't you be quiet!   125
DORINE   I will. For you, I'm going to try it.
But I'll be thinking.
ORGON   Fine. Now, Mariane,
You have to trust—your father's a wise man.
I have thought a lot about this mating.
I've weighed the options—   130
DORINE   It's infuriating
Not to be able to speak.
ORGON   And so
I'll say this. Of up and coming men I know,
He's not one of them, no money in the bank,
Not handsome.
DORINE   That's the truth. Arf! Arf! Be frank.
He's a dog!   135
ORGON   He has manly traits.
And other gifts.
DORINE   And who will blame the fates
For failure of this marriage made in hell?
And whose fault will it be? Not hard to tell.
Since everyone you know will see the truth:
You gave away your daughter to Tartuffe.   140
If I were in her place, I'd guarantee
No man would live the night who dared force me
Into a marriage that I didn't want.
There would be war with no hope of détente.
ORGON   I asked for silence. This is what I get?   145
DORINE   You said not to talk to *you*. Did you forget?
ORGON   What do you call what you are doing now?
DORINE   Talking to myself.

ORGON   You insolent cow!
   I'll wait for you to say just one more word.
   I'm waiting . . .   150
         [ORGON *prepares to give* DORINE *a smack but each time he looks*
         over at her, she stands silent and still.]
                     Just ignore her. Look at me.
   I've chosen you a husband who would be,
   If rated, placed among the highest ranks.
   [*To* DORINE]   Why don't you talk?
DORINE   Don't feel like it, thanks.
ORGON   I'm watching you.
DORINE   Do you think I'm a fool?
ORGON   I realize that you may think me cruel.   155
   But here's the thing, child, I will be obeyed,
   And this marriage, child, will not be delayed.
DORINE [*running from* ORGON, DORINE *throws a line to* MARIANE]
   You'll be a joke with Tartuffe as a spouse.
         [ORGON *tries to slap her but misses.*]
ORGON   What we have is a plague in our own house!   160
   It's her fault that I'm in the state I'm in,
   So furious, I might commit a sin.
   She'll drive me to murder. Or to curse.
   I need fresh air before my mood gets worse.   [ORGON *exits.*]

                          2.3

                  [DORINE, MARIANE]

DORINE   Tell me, have you lost the power of speech?
   I'm forced to play your role and it's a reach.
   How can you sit there with nothing to say
   Watching him tossing your whole life away?
MARIANE   Against my father, what am I to do?   5
DORINE   You want out of this marriage scheme, don't you?
MARIANE   Yes.
DORINE   Tell him no one can command a heart.
   That when you marry, you will have no part
   Of anyone unless he pleases you.
   And tell your father, with no more ado,   10
   That you will marry for yourself, not him,
   And that you won't obey his iron whim.
   Since he finds Tartuffe to be such a catch,
   He can marry him himself. There's a match.
MARIANE   You know that fathers have such sway   15
   Over our lives that I've nothing to say.
   I've never had the strength.
DORINE   Let's think. All right?
   Didn't Valère propose the other night?
   Do you or don't you love Valère?

MARIANE   You know the answer, Dorine—that's unfair.   20
  Just talking about it tears me apart.
  I've said a hundred times, he has my heart.
  I'm wild about him. I know. And I've told you.
DORINE   But how am I to know, for sure, that's true?
MARIANE   Because I told you. And yet you doubt it?   25
  See me blushing when I speak about it?
DORINE   So you do love him?
MARIANE   Yes, with all my might.
DORINE   He loves you just as much?
MARIANE   I think that's right.
DORINE   And it's to the altar you're both heading?
MARIANE   Yes.   30
DORINE   So what about this other wedding?
MARIANE   I'll kill myself. That's what I've decided.
DORINE   What a great solution you've provided!
  To get out of trouble, you plan to die!
  Immediately? Or sometime, by and by?
MARIANE   Oh, really, Dorine, you're not my friend,   35
  Unsympathetic—
DORINE   I'm at my wit's end,
  Talking to you whose answer is dying,
  Who, in a crisis, just gives up trying.
MARIANE   What do you want of me, then?
DORINE   Come alive!
  Love needs a resolute heart to survive.   40
MARIANE   In my love for Valère, I'm resolute.
  But the next step is his.
DORINE   And so, you're mute?
MARIANE   What can I say? It's the job of Valère,
  His duty, before I go anywhere,
  To deal with my father—   45
DORINE   —Then, you'll stay.
  "Orgon was born bizarre" is what some say.
  If there were doubts before, we have this proof—
  He is head over heels for his Tartuffe,
  And breaks off a marriage that he arranged.
  Valère's at fault if your father's deranged?   50
MARIANE   But my refusal will be seen as pride
  And, worse, contempt. And I have to hide
  My feelings for Valère, I must not show
  That I'm in love at all. If people know,
  Then all the modesty my sex is heir to   55
  Will be gone. There's more: how can I bear to
  Not be a proper daughter to my father?
DORINE   No, no, of course not. God forbid we bother
  The way the world sees you. What people see,
  What other people think of us, should be   60
  Our first concern. Besides, I see the truth:

You really want to be Madame Tartuffe.
What was I thinking, urging opposition
To Monsieur Tartuffe! This proposition,
To merge with him—he's such a catch! 65
In fact, for you, he's just the perfect match.
He's much respected, everywhere he goes,
And his ruddy complexion nearly glows.
And as his wife, imagine the delight
Of being near him, every day and night. 70
And vital? Oh, my dear, you won't want more.

MARIANE   Oh, heaven help me!

DORINE   How your soul will soar,
Savoring this marriage down to the last drop,
With such a handsome—

MARIANE   All right! You can stop!
Just help me. Please. And tell me there's a way 75
To save me. I'll do whatever you say.

DORINE   Each daughter must choose always to say yes
To what her father wants, no more and no less.
If he wants to give her an ape to marry,
Then she must do it, without a query. 80
But it's a happy fate! What is this frown?
You'll go by wagon to his little town,
Eager cousins, uncles, aunts will greet you
And will call you "sister" when they meet you,
Because you're family now. Don't look so grim. 85
You will so adore chatting with them.
Welcomed by the local high society,
You'll be expected to maintain propriety
And sit straight, or try to, in the folding chair
They offer you, and never, ever stare 90
At the wardrobe of the bailiff's wife
Because you'll see her every day for life.[4]
Let's not forget the village carnival!
Where you'll be dancing at a lavish ball
To a bagpipe orchestra of locals, 95
An organ grinder's monkey doing vocals—
And your husband—

MARIANE   —Dorine, I beg you, please,
Help me. Should I get down here on my knees?

DORINE   Can't help you.

MARIANE   Please, Dorine, I'm begging you!

DORINE   And you deserve this man. 100

MARIANE   That just not true!

DORINE   Oh yes? What changed?

MARIANE   My darling Dorine . . .

---

4. Dorine's description reflects the stereotypes associated with rural pretensions to culture.

DORINE No.
MARIANE   You can't be this mean.
  I love Valère. I told you and it's true.
DORINE Who's that? Oh. No, Tartuffe's the one for you.
MARIANE   You've always been completely on my side.   105
DORINE   No more. I sentence you to be Tartuffified!
MARIANE   It seems my fate has not the power to move you,
  So I'll seek my solace and remove to
  A private place for me in my despair.
  To end the misery that brought me here.   110
     [MARIANE *starts to exit.*]
DORINE   Wait! Wait! Come back! Please don't go out that door.
  I'll help you. I'm not angry anymore.
MARIANE   If I am forced into this martyrdom,
  You see, I'll have to die, Dorine.
DORINE   Oh come,
  Give up this torment. Look at me—I swear.   115
  We'll find a way. Look, here's your love, Valère.
     [DORINE *moves to the side of the stage.*]

2.4

[VALÈRE, MARIANE, DORINE]

VALÈRE   So I've just heard some news that's news to me,
  And very fine news it is, do you agree?
MARIANE   What?
VALÈRE   You have plans for marriage I didn't know.
  You're going to marry Tartuffe. Is this so?
MARIANE   My father has that notion, it is true.   5
VALÈRE   Madame, your father promised—
MARIANE   —me to you?
  He changed his mind, announced this change to me,
  Just minutes ago . . .
VALÈRE   Quite seriously?
MARIANE   It's his wish that I should marry this man.
VALÈRE   And what do you think of your father's plan?   10
MARIANE   I don't know.
VALÈRE   Honest words—better than lies.
  You don't know?
MARIANE   No.
VALÈRE   No?
MARIANE   What do you advise?
VALÈRE   I advise you to . . . marry Tartuffe. Tonight.
MARIANE   You advise me to . . .
VALÈRE   Yes.
MARIANE   Really?
VALÈRE   That's right.
  Consider it. It's an obvious choice.   15

MARIANE   I'll follow your suggestion and rejoice.
VALÈRE   I'm sure that you can follow it with ease.
MARIANE   Just as you gave it. It will be a breeze.
VALÈRE   Just to please you was my sole intent.
MARIANE   To please you, I'll do it and be content.   20
DORINE   I can't wait to see what happens next.
VALÈRE   And this is love to you? I am perplexed.
  Was it a sham when you—
MARIANE   That's in the past
  Because you said so honestly and fast
  That I should take the one bestowed on me.   25
  I'm nothing but obedient, you see,
  So, yes, I'll take him. That's my declaration,
  Since that's your advice and expectation.
VALÈRE   I see, you're using me as an excuse,
  Any pretext, so you can cut me loose.   30
  You didn't think I'd notice—I'd be blind
  To the fact that you'd made up your mind?
MARINE   How true. Well said.
VALÈRE   And so it's plain to see,
  Your heart never felt a true love for me.
MARIANE   If you want to, you may think that is true.   35
  It's clear this thought has great appeal for you.
VALÈRE   If I want? I will, but I'm offended
  To my very soul. But your turn's ended,
  And I can win this game we're playing at:
  I've someone else in mind.   40
MARIANE   I don't doubt that.
  Your good points—
VALÈRE   Oh, let's leave them out of this.
  I've very few—in fact, I am remiss.
  I must be. Right? You've made that clear to me.
  But I know someone, hearing that I'm free,
  To make up for my loss, will eagerly consent.   45
MARIANE   The loss is not that bad. You'll be content
  With your new choice, replacement, if you will.
VALÈRE   I will. And I'll remain contented still,
  In knowing you're as happy as I am.
  A woman tells a man her love's a sham.   50
  The man's been fooled and his honor blighted.
  He can't deny his love is unrequited,
  Then he forgets this woman totally,
  And if he can't, pretends, because, you see,
  It is ignoble conduct and weak, too,   55
  Loving someone who does not love you.
MARIANE   What a fine, noble sentiment to heed.
VALÈRE   And every man upholds it as his creed.
  What? You expect me to keep on forever
  Loving you after you blithely sever   60

The bond between us, watching as you go
Into another's arms and not bestow
This heart you've cast away upon someone
Who might welcome—
MARIANE   I wish it were done.
That's exactly what I want, you see.   65
VALÈRE   That's what you want?
MARIANE   Yes.
VALÈRE   Then let it be.
I'll grant your wish.
MARIANE   Please do.
VALÈRE   Just don't forget,
Whose fault it was when you, filled with regret,
Realize that you forced me out the door.
MARIANE   True.   70
VALÈRE   You've set the example and what's more,
I'll match you with my own hardness of heart.
You won't see me again, if I depart.
MARIANE   That's good!
        [VALÈRE goes to exit, but when he gets to the door, he returns.]
VALÈRE   What?
MARIANE   What?
VALÈRE   You said . . . ?
MARIANE   Nothing at all.
VALÈRE   Well, I'll be on my way, then.
        [He goes, stops.]
                              Did you call?
MARIANE   Me? You must be dreaming.   75
VALÈRE   I'll go away.
Good-bye, then.
MARIANE   Good-bye.
DORINE   I am here to say,
You both are idiots! What's this about?
I left you two alone to fight it out,
To see how far you'd go. You're quite a pair
In matching tit for tat—Hold on, Valère!   80
Where are you going?
VALÈRE   What, Dorine? You spoke?
DORINE   Come here.
VALÈRE   I'm upset and will not provoke
This lady. Do not try to change my mind.
I'm doing what she wants.
DORINE   You are so blind.
Just stop.   85
VALÈRE   No. It's settled.
DORINE   Oh, is that so?
MARIANE   He can't stand to look at me, I know.
He wants to go away, so please let him.
No, I shall leave so I can forget him.

DORINE   Where are you going?
MARIANE   Leave me alone.
DORINE   Come back here at once.   90
MARIANE   No. Even that tone
   Won't bring me. I'm not a child, you see.
VALÈRE   She's tortured by the very sight of me.
   It's better that I free her from her pain.
DORINE   What more proof do you need? You are insane!
   Now stop this nonsense! Come here both of you.   95
VALÈRE   To what purpose?
MARIANE   What are you trying to do?
DORINE   Bring you two together! And end this fight.
   It's so stupid! Yes?
VALÈRE   No. It wasn't right
   The way she spoke to me. Didn't you hear?
DORINE   Your voices are still ringing in my ear.   100
MARIANE   The way he treated me—you didn't see?
DORINE   Saw and heard it all. Now listen to me.
   The only thing she wants, Valère, is you.
   I can attest to that right now. It's true.
   And Mariane, he wants you for his wife,   105
   And only you. On that I'll stake my life.
MARIANE   He told me to be someone else's bride!
VALÈRE   She asked for my advice and I replied!
DORINE   You're both impossible. What can I do?
   Give your hand—   110
VALÈRE   What for?
DORINE   Come on, you.
   Now yours, Mariane—don't make me shout.
   Come on!
MARIANE   All right. But what is this about?
DORINE   Here. Take each other's hand and make a link.
   You love each other better than you think.
VALÈRE   Mademoiselle, this is your hand I took,   115
   You think you could give me a friendly look?
        [MARIANE peeks at VALÈRE and smiles.]
DORINE   It's true. Lovers are not completely sane.
VALÈRE   Mariane, haven't I good reason to complain?
   Be honest. Wasn't it a wicked ploy?
   To say—   120
MARIANE   You think I told you that with joy?
   And you confronted me.
DORINE   Another time.
   This marriage to Tartuffe would be a crime,
   We have to stop it.
MARIANE   So, what can we do?
   Tell us.
DORINE   All sorts of things involving you.   125
   It's all nonsense and your father's joking.

But if you play along, say, without choking,
And give your consent, for the time being,
He'll take the pressure off, thereby freeing
All of us to find a workable plan   130
To keep you from a marriage with this man.
Then you can find a reason every day
To postpone the wedding, in this way;
One day you're sick and that can take a week.
Another day you're better but can't speak,   135
And we all know you have to say "I do,"
Or the marriage isn't legal. And that's true.
Now bad omens—would he have his daughter
Married when she's dreamt of stagnant water,
Or broken a mirror or seen the dead?   140
He may not care and say it's in your head,
But you will be distraught in your delusion,
And require bed rest and seclusion.
I do know this—if we want to succeed,
You can't be seen together. [To VALÈRE] With all speed,   145
Go, and gather all your friends right now,
Have them insist that Orgon keep his vow.
Social pressure helps. Then to her brother.
All of us will work on her stepmother.
Let's go.   150
VALÈRE   Whatever happens, can you see?
My greatest hope is in your love for me.
MARIANE   Though I don't know just what Father will do,
I do know I belong only to you.
VALÈRE   You put my heart at ease! I swear I will . . .
DORINE   It seems that lovers' tongues are never still.   155
Out, I tell you.
VALÈRE [taking a step and returning]   One last—
DORINE   No more chat!
You go out this way, yes, and you go that.

3.1

[DAMIS, DORINE]

DAMIS   May lightning strike me dead, right here and now,
Call me a villain, if I break this vow:
Forces of heaven or earth won't make me sway
From this my—
DORINE   Let's not get carried away.
Your father only said what he intends   5
To happen. The real event depends
On many things and something's bound to slip,
Between this horrid cup and his tight lip.
DAMIS   That this conceited fool Father brought here
Has plans? Well, they'll be ended—do not fear.   10

DORINE   Now stop that! Forget him. Leave him alone.
   Leave him to your stepmother. He is prone,
   This Tartuffe, to indulge her every whim.
   So let her use her power over him.
   It does seem pretty clear he's soft on her,   15
   Pray God that's true. And if he will concur
   That this wedding your father wants is bad,
   That's good. But he might want it, too, the cad.
   She's sent for him so she can sound him out
   On this marriage you're furious about,   20
   Discover what he feels and tell him clearly
   If he persists that it will cost him dearly.
   It seems he can't be seen while he's at prayers,
   So I have my own vigil by the stairs
   Where his valet says he will soon appear.   25
   Do leave right now, and I'll wait for him here.
DAMIS   I'll stay to vouch for what was seen and heard.
DORINE   They must be alone.
DAMIS   I won't say a word.
DORINE   Oh, right. I know what you are like. Just go.
   You'll spoil everything, believe me, I know.   30
   Out!
DAMIS   I promise I won't get upset.
        [DORINE *pinches* DAMIS *as she used to do when he was a child.*]
                        Ow!
DORINE   Do as I say. Get out of here right *now!*

                        3.2

                [TARTUFFE, LAURENT, DORINE]

TARTUFFE [*noticing* DORINE]   Laurent, lock up my scourge and
      hair shirt,[5] too.
   And pray that our Lord's grace will shine on you.
   If anyone wants me, I've gone to share
   My alms at prison with the inmates there.
DORINE   What a fake! What an imposter! What a sleaze!   5
TARTUFFE   What do you want?
DORINE   To say—
TARTUFFE [*taking a handkerchief from his pocket*]   Good heavens, please,
   Do take this handkerchief before you speak.
DORINE   What for?
TARTUFFE   Cover your bust. The flesh is weak.
   Souls are forever damaged by such sights,
   When sinful thoughts begin their evil flights.   10
DORINE   It seems temptation makes a meal of you—
   To turn you on, a glimpse of flesh will do.

---

5. Implements to mortify his flesh (penitential practices of religious ascetics).

Inside your heart, a furnace must be housed.
For me, I'm not so easily aroused.
I could see you naked, head to toe—   15
Never be tempted once, and this I know.
TARTUFFE   Please! Stop! And if you're planning to resume
This kind of talk, I'll leave the room.
DORINE   If someone is to go, let it be me.
Yes, I can't wait to leave your company.   20
Madame is coming down from her salon,
And wants to talk to you, if you'll hang on.
TARTUFFE   Of course. Most willingly.
DORINE [aside]   Look at him melt.
I'm right. I always knew that's how he felt.
TARTUFFE   Is she coming soon?   25
DORINE   You want me to leave?
Yes, here she is in person, I believe.

3.3

[ELMIRE, TARTUFFE]

TARTUFFE   Ah, may heaven in all its goodness give
Eternal health to you each day you live,
Bless your soul and body, and may it grant
The prayerful wishes of this supplicant.
ELMIRE   Yes, thank you for that godly wish, and please,   5
Let's sit down so we can talk with ease.
TARTUFFE   Are you recovered from your illness now?
ELMIRE   My fever disappeared, I don't know how.
TARTUFFE   My small prayers, I'm sure, had not the power,
Though I was on my knees many an hour.   10
Each fervent prayer wrenched from my simple soul
Was made with your recovery as its goal.
ELMIRE   I find your zeal a little disconcerting.
TARTUFFE   I can't enjoy my health if you are hurting,
Your health's true worth, I can't begin to tell.   15
I'd give mine up, in fact, to make you well.
ELMIRE   Though you stretch Christian charity too far,
Your thoughts are kind, however strange they are.
TARTUFFE   You merit more, that's in my humble view.
ELMIRE   I need a private space to talk to you.
I think that this will do—what do you say?   20
TARTUFFE   Excellent choice. And this is a sweet day,
To find myself here tête-à-tête with you,
That I've begged heaven for this, yes, is true,
And now it's granted to my great relief.   25
ELMIRE   Although our conversation will be brief,
Please open up your heart and tell me all.
You must hide nothing now, however small.

TARTUFFE   I long to show you my entire soul,
  My need for truth I can barely control.   30
  I'll take this time, also, to clear the air—
  The criticisms I have brought to bear
  Around the visits that your charms attract,
  Were never aimed at you or how you act,
  But rather were my own transports of zeal,   35
  Which carried me away with how I feel,
  Consumed by impulses, though always pure,
  Nevertheless, intense in how—
ELMIRE   I'm sure
  That my salvation is your only care.
TARTUFFE [*grasping her fingertips*]   Yes, you're right, and   40
  so my fervor there—
ELMIRE   Ouch! You're squeezing too hard.
TARTUFFE   —comes from this zeal . . .
  I didn't mean to squeeze. How does this feel?
  [*He puts his hand on* ELMIRE'*s knee.*]
ELMIRE   Your hand—what is it doing . . . ?
TARTUFFE   So tender,
  The fabric of your dress, a sweet surrender
  Under my hand—   45
ELMIRE   I'm quite ticklish. Please, don't.
  [*She moves her chair back, and* TARTUFFE *moves his forward.*]
TARTUFFE   I want to touch this lace—don't fret, I won't,
  It's marvelous! I so admire the trade
  Of making lace. Don't tell me you're afraid.
ELMIRE   What? No. But getting back to business now,
  It seems my husband plans to break a vow   50
  And offer you his daughter. Is this true?
TARTUFFE   He mentioned it, but I must say to you,
  The wondrous gifts that catch my zealous eye,
  I see quite near in bounteous supply.
ELMIRE   Not earthly things for which you would atone.   55
TARTUFFE   My chest does not contain a heart of stone.
ELMIRE   Well, I believe your eyes follow your soul,
  And your desires have heaven as their goal.
TARTUFFE   The love that to eternal beauty binds us
  Doesn't stint when temporal beauty finds us.   60
  Our senses can as easily be charmed
  When by an earthly work we are disarmed.
  You are a rare beauty, without a flaw,
  And in your presence, I'm aroused with awe
  But for the Author of All Nature, so,   65
  My heart has ardent feelings, even though
  I feared them at first, questioning their source.
  Had I been ambushed by some evil force?
  I felt that I must hide from this temptation:
  You. My feelings threatened my salvation.   70

Yes, I found this sinful and distressing,
Until I saw your beauty as a blessing!
So now my passion never can be wrong,
And, thus, my virtue stays intact and strong.
That is how I'm here in supplication,   75
Offering my heart in celebration
Of the audacious truth that I love you,
That only you can make this wish come true,
That through your grace, my offering's received,
And accepted, and that I have achieved   80
Salvation of a sort, and by your grace,
I could be content in this low place.
It all depends on you, at your behest—
Am I to be tormented or be blest?
You are my welfare, solace, and my hope,   85
But, whatever your decision, I will cope.
Will I be happy? I'll rely on you.
If you want me to be wretched, that's fine, too.

ELMIRE   Well, what a declaration! How gallant!
But I'm surprised you want the things you want.   90
It seems your heart could use a talking to—
It's living in the chest of someone who
Proclaims to be pious—

TARTUFFE   —And so I am.
My piety's a true thing—not a sham,
But I'm no less a man, so when I find   95
Myself with you, I quickly lose my mind.
My heart is captured and, with it, my thought.
Yet since I know the cause, I'm not distraught.
Words like these from me must be alarming,
But it is your beauty that's so charming,   100
I cannot help myself, I am undone.
And I'm no angel, nor could I be one.
If my confession earns your condemnation,
Then blame your glance for the annihilation
Of my command of this: my inmost being.   105
A surrender of my soul is what you're seeing.
Your eyes blaze with more than human splendor,
And that first look had the effect to render
Powerless the bastions of my heart.
No fasting, tears or prayers, no pious art   110
Could shield my soul from your celestial gaze
Which I will worship till the End of Days.[6]
A thousand times my eyes, my sighs have told
The truth that's in my heart. Now I am bold,
Encouraged by your presence, so I say,   115

---

6. That is, the final days before human history ends and the Kingdom of God is established.

With my true voice, will this be the day
You condescend to my poor supplication,
Offered up with devout admiration,
And save my soul by granting this request:
Accept this love I've lovingly confessed?   120
Your honor has, of course, all my protection,
And you can trust my absolute discretion.
For those men that all the women die for,
Love's a game whose object is a high score.
Although they promise not to talk, they will.   125
They need to boast of their superior skill,
Receive no favors not as soon revealed,
Exposing what they vowed would be concealed.
And in the end, this love is overpriced,
When a woman's honor's sacrificed.   130
But men like me burn with a silent flame,
Our secrets safe, our loves we never name,
Because our reputations are our wealth,
When we transgress, it's with the utmost stealth.
Your honor's safe as my hand in a glove,   135
So I can offer, free from scandal, love,
And pleasure without fear of intervention.
ELMIRE   Your sophistry does not hide your intention.
In fact, you know, it makes it all too clear.
What if, through me, my husband were to hear   140
About this love for me you now confess
Which shatters the ideals you profess?
How would your friendship fare, then, I wonder?
TARTUFFE   It's your beauty cast this spell I suffer under.
I'm made of flesh, like you, like all mankind.   145
And since your soul is pure, you will be kind,
And not judge me harshly for my brashness
In speaking of my love in all its rashness.
I beg you to forgive me my offense,
I plead your perfect face as my defense.   150
ELMIRE   Some might take offense at your confession,
But I will show a definite discretion,
And keep my husband in the dark about
These sinful feelings for me that you spout.
But I want something from you in return: 155
There's a promised marriage, you will learn,
That supersedes my husband's recent plan—
The marriage of Valère and Mariane.
This marriage you will openly support,
Without a single quibble, and, in short,   160
Renounce the unjust power of a man
Who'd give his own daughter, Mariane,
To another when she's promised to Valère.
In return, my silence—

3.4

[ELMIRE, DAMIS, TARTUFFE]

DAMIS [*jumping out from where he had been hiding*]
             —Hold it right there!
  No, no! You're done. All this will be revealed.
  I heard each word. And as I was concealed,
  Something besides your infamy came clear:
  Heaven in its great wisdom brought me here,   5
  To witness and then give my father proof
  Of the hypocrisy of his Tartuffe,
  This so-called saint anointed from above,
  Speaking to my father's wife of love!
ELMIRE Damis, there is a lesson to be learned,   10
  And there is my forgiveness to be earned.
  I promised him. Don't make me take it back.
  It's not my nature to see as an attack
  Such foolishness as this, or see the need
  To tell my husband of the trivial deed.   15
DAMIS So, you have your reasons, but I have mine.
  To grant this fool forgiveness? I decline.
  To want to spare him is a mockery,
  Because he's more than foolish, can't you see?
  This fanatic in his insolent pride,   20
  Brought chaos to my house, and would divide
  Me and my father—unforgivable!
  What's more, he's made my life unlivable,
  As he undermines two true love affairs,
  Mine and Valère's sister, my sister and Valère's!   25
  Father must hear the truth about this man.
  Heaven helped me—I must do what I can
  To use this chance. I'd deserve to lose it,
  If I dropped it now and didn't use it.
ELMIRE Damis—   30
DAMIS   No, please, I have to follow through.
  I've never felt as happy as I do
  Right now. And don't try to dissuade me—
  I'll have my revenge. If you forbade me,
  I'd still do it, so you don't have to bother.
  I'll finish this for good. Here comes my father.   35

3.5

[ORGON, DAMIS, TARTUFFE, ELMIRE]

DAMIS Father! You have arrived. Let's celebrate!
  I have a tale that I'd like to relate.
  It happened here and right before my eyes,
  I offer it to you—as a surprise!

For all your love, you have been repaid   5
With duplicity. You have been betrayed
By your dear friend here, whom I just surprised
Making verbal love, I quickly surmised,
To your wife. Yes, this is how he shows you
How he honors you—he thinks he knows you.   10
But as your son, I know you much better—
You demand respect down to the letter.
Madame, unflappable and so discreet,
Would keep this secret, never to repeat.
But, as your son, my feelings are too strong,   15
And to be silent is to do you wrong.
ELMIRE   One learns to spurn without being unkind,
And how to spare a husband's peace of mind.
Although I understood just what he meant,
My honor wasn't touched by this event.   20
That's how I feel. And you would have, Damis,
Said nothing, if you had listened to me.

3.6

[ORGON, DAMIS, TARTUFFE]

ORGON   Good heavens! What he said? Can it be true?
TARTUFFE   Yes, my brother, I'm wicked through and through.
The most miserable of sinners, I.
Filled with iniquity, I should just die.
Each moment of my life's so dirty, soiled,   5
Whatever I come near is quickly spoiled.
I'm nothing but a heap of filth and crime.
I'd name my sins, but we don't have the time.
And I see that heaven, to punish me,
Has mortified my soul quite publicly.   10
What punishment I get, however great,
I well deserve so I'll accept my fate.
Defend myself? I'd face my own contempt,
If I thought that were something I'd attempt.
What you've heard here, surely, you abhor,   15
So chase me like a criminal from your door.
Don't hold back your rage, please, let it flame,
For I deserve to burn, in my great shame.
ORGON [to DAMIS]   Traitor! And how dare you even try
To tarnish this man's virtue with a lie?   20
DAMIS   What? This hypocrite pretends to be contrite
And you believe him over me?
ORGON   That's spite!
And shut your mouth!
TARTUFFE   No, let him have his say.
And don't accuse him. Don't send him away.
Believe his story—why be on my side?   25

You don't know what motives I may hide.
Why give me so much loyalty and love?
Do you know what I am capable of?
My brother, you have total trust in me,
And think I'm good because of what you see?   30
No, no, by my appearance you're deceived,
And what I say you think must be believed.
Well, believe this—I have no worth at all.
The world sees me as worthy, yet I fall
Far below. Sin is so insidious.   35
[To DAMIS] Dear son, do treat me as perfidious,
Infamous, lost, a murderer, a thief.
Speak on, because my sins, beyond belief,
Can bring this shameful sinner to his knees,
In humble, paltry effort to appease.   40
ORGON [to TARTUFFE]   Brother, there is no need . . .

                                  [To DAMIS] Will you
    relent?
DAMIS   He has seduced you!
ORGON   Can't you take a hint?
   Be quiet! [To TARTUFFE] Brother, please get up. [To DAMIS] Ingrate!
DAMIS   But father, this man
ORGON   —whom you denigrate.
DAMIS   But you should—   45
ORGON   Quiet!
DAMIS   But I saw and heard—
ORGON   I'll slap you if you say another word.
TARTUFFE   In the name of God, don't be that way.
   Brother, I'd rather suffer, come what may,
   Than have this boy receive what's meant for me.
ORGON [to DAMIS]   Heathen!   50
TARTUFFE   Please! I beg of you on bended knee.
ORGON [to DAMIS]   Wretch! See his goodness?!
DAMIS   But—
ORGON   No!
DAMIS   But—
ORGON   Be still!
   And not another word from you until
   You admit the truth. It's plain to see
   Although you thought that I would never be
   Aware and know your motives, yet I do.   55
   You all hate him. And I saw today, you,
   Wife, servants—everyone beneath my roof—
   Are trying everything to force Tartuffe
   Out of my house—this holy man, my friend.
   The more you try to banish him and end   60
   Our sacred brotherhood, the more secure
   His place is. I have never been more sure
   Of anyone. I give him as his bride

My daughter. If that hurts the family pride,
Then good. It needs humbling. You understand? 65
DAMIS You're going to force her to accept his hand?
ORGON Yes, traitor, and this evening. You know why?
To infuriate you. Yes, I defy
You all. I am master and you'll obey.
And you, you ingrate, now I'll make you pay 70
For your abuse of him—kneel on the floor,
And beg his pardon, or go out the door.
DAMIS Me? Kneel and ask the pardon of this fraud?
ORGON What? You refuse? Someone get me a rod!
A stick! Something! [*To* TARTUFFE] Don't hold me. 75
[*To* DAMIS] Here's your whack!
Out of my house and don't ever come back!
DAMIS Yes, I'll leave, but—
ORGON   Get out of my sight!
I disinherit you, you traitor, you're a blight
On this house. And you'll get nothing now
From me, except my curse! 80

3.7

[ORGON, TARTUFFE]

ORGON   You have my vow,
He'll never more question your honesty.
TARTUFFE [*to heaven*] Forgive him for the pain he's given me.
[*To* ORGON] How I suffer. If you could only see
What I go through when they disparage me. 5
ORGON Oh no!
TARTUFFE   The ingratitude, even in thought,
Tortures my soul so much, it leaves me fraught
With inner pain. My heart's stopped. I'm near death,
I can barely speak now. Where is my breath?
ORGON [*running in tears to the door through which he chased* DAMIS]
You demon! I held back, you little snot 10
I should have struck you dead right on the spot!
[*To* TARTUFFE] Get up, Brother. Don't worry anymore.
TARTUFFE Let us end these troubles, Brother, I implore.
For the discord I have caused, I deeply grieve,
So for the good of all, I'll take my leave. 15
ORGON What? Are you joking? No!
TARTUFFE   They hate me here.
It pains me when I see them fill your ear
With suspicions.
ORGON   But that doesn't matter.
I don't listen.
TARTUFFE   That persistent chatter
You now ignore, one day you'll listen to. 20

Repetition of a lie can make it true.
ORGON   No, my brother. Never.
TARTUFFE   A man's wife
Can so mislead his soul and ruin his life.
ORGON   No, no.
TARTUFFE   Brother, let me, by leaving here,
Remove any cause for doubt or fear.   25
ORGON   No, no. You will stay. My soul is at stake.
TARTUFFE   Well, then, a hefty penance I must make.
I'll mortify myself, unless . . .
ORGON   No need!
TARTUFFE   Then we will never speak of it, agreed?
But the question of your honor still remains,   30
And with that I'll take particular pains
To prevent rumors. My absence, my defense—
I'll never see your wife again, and hence—
ORGON   No. You spend every hour with her you want,
And be seen with her. I want you to flaunt,   35
In front of them, this friendship with my wife.
And I know how to really turn the knife
I'll make you my heir, my only one,
Yes, you will be my son-in-law and son.[7]
A good and faithful friend means more to me   40
Than any member of my family.
Will you accept this gift that I propose?
TARTUFFE   Whatever heaven wants I can't oppose.
ORGON   Poor man! A contract's what we need to write.
And let all the envious burst with spite.   45

4.1

[CLÉANTE, TARTUFFE]

CLÉANTE   Yes, everyone is talking and each word
Diminishes your glory, rest assured.
Though your name's tainted with scandal and shame,
I'm glad I ran across you, all the same,
Because I need to share with you my view   5
On this disaster clearly caused by you.
Damis, let's say for now, was so misguided,
He spoke before he thought. But you decided
To just sit back and watch him be exiled
From his own father's house. Were he a child,   10
Then, really, would you dare to treat him so?
Shouldn't you forgive him, not make him go?
However, if there's vengeance in your heart,

---

7. In fact, French laws governing inheritance would have made such a change extremely difficult to accomplish.

And you act on it, tell me what's the part
That's Christian in that? And are you so base,   15
You'd let a son fall from his father's grace?
Give God your anger as an offering,
Bring peace and forgive all for everything.
TARTUFFE   I'd do just that, if it were up to me.
I blame him for nothing, don't you see?   20
I've pardoned him already. That's my way.
And I'm not bitter, but have this to say:
Heaven's best interests will have been served,
When wrongdoers have got what they deserved.
In fact, if he returns here, I would leave,   25
Because God knows what people might believe.
Faking forgiveness to manipulate
My accuser, silencing the hate
He has for me could be seen as my goal,
When I would only wish to save his soul.   30
What he said to me, though unforgivable,
I give unto God to make life livable.
CLÉANTE   To this conclusion, sir, I have arrived:
Your excuses could not be more contrived.
Just how did you come by the opinion   35
Heaven's business is in your dominion,
Judging who is guilty and who is not?
Taking revenge is heaven's task, I thought.
And if you're under heaven's sovereignty,
What human verdict would you ever be   40
The least bit moved by. No, you wouldn't care—
Judging other's lives is so unfair.
Heaven seems to say "live and let live,"
And our task, I believe, is to forgive.
TARTUFFE   I said I've pardoned him. I take such pains   45
To do exactly what heaven ordains.
But after his attack on me, it's clear,
Heaven does not ordain that he live here.
CLÉANTE   Does it ordain, sir, that you nod and smile,
When taking what is not yours, all the while?   50
On this inheritance you have no claim
And yet you think it's yours. Have you no shame?
TARTUFFE   That this gift was, in any way, received
Out of self-interest, would not be believed
By anyone who knows me well. They'd say,   55
"The world's wealth, to him, holds no sway."
I am not dazzled by gold nor its glitter,
So lack of wealth has never made me bitter.
If I take this present from the father,
The source of all this folderol and bother,   60
I am saving, so everyone understands,
This wealth from falling into the wrong hands,

Waste of wealth and property's a crime,
And that is what would happen at this time.
But I would use it as part of my plan: 65
For glory of heaven, and the good of man.
CLÉANTE   Well, sir, I think these small fears that plague you,
In fact, may cause the rightful heir to sue.
Why trouble yourself, sir—couldn't you just
Let him own his property, if he must?   70
Let others say his property's misused
By him, rather than have yourself accused
Of taking it from its rightful owner.
Wouldn't a pious man be a donor
Of property? Unless there is a verse   75
Or proverb about how you fill your purse
With what's not yours, at all, in any part.
And if heaven has put into your heart
This obstacle to living with Damis,
The honorable thing, you must agree,   80
As well as, certainly, the most discreet,
Is pack your bags and, quickly, just retreat.
To have the son of the house chased away,
Because a guest objects, is a sad day.
Leaving now would show your decency,   85
Sir . . .
TARTUFFE   Yes. Well, it is half after three;
Pious duties consume this time of day,
You will excuse my hurrying away.
CLÉANTE   Ah!

4.2

[ELMIRE, MARIANE, DORINE, CLÉANTE]

DORINE   Please, come to the aid of Mariane.
She's suffering because her father's plan
To force this marriage, impossible to bear,
Has pushed her from distress into despair.
Her father's on his way here. Do your best,   5
Turn him around. Use subtlety, protest,
Whatever way will work to change his mind.

4.3

[ORGON, ELMIRE, MARIANE, CLÉANTE, DORINE]

ORGON   Ah! Here's everyone I wanted to find!
[To MARIANE] This document I have here in my hand
Will make you very happy, understand?
MARIANE   Father, in the name of heaven, I plead

To all that's good and kind in you, concede 5
Paternal power, just in this sense:
Free me from my vows of obedience.
Enforcing that inflexible law today
Will force me to confess each time I pray
My deep resentment of my obligation. 10
I know, father, that I am your creation,
That you're the one who's given life to me.
Why would you now fill it with misery?
If you destroy my hopes for the one man
I've dared to love by trying now to ban 15
Our union, then I'm kneeling to implore,
Don't give me to a man whom I abhor.
To you, Father, I make this supplication:
Don't drive me to some act of desperation,
By ruling me simply because you can. 20
ORGON [*feeling himself touched*]   Be strong! Human weakness
    shames a man!
MARIANE   Your affection for him doesn't bother me—
    Let it erupt, give him your property,
    And if that's not enough, then give him mine.
    Any claim on it, I do now decline. 25
    But in this gifting, don't give him my life.
    If I must wed, then I will be God's wife,
    In a convent, until my days are done.
ORGON   Ah! So you will be a holy, cloistered nun,
    Because your father thwarts your love affair. 30
    Get up! The more disgust you have to bear,
    The more of heaven's treasure you will earn,
    And the heaven will bless you in return.
    Through this marriage, you'll mortify your senses.
    Don't bother me with any more pretenses. 35
DORINE   But . . . !
ORGON   Quiet, you! I see you standing there.
    Don't speak a single word! don't even dare!
CLÉANTE   If you permit, I'd like to say a word . . .
ORGON   Brother, the best advice the world has heard
    Is yours—its reasoning, hard to ignore. 40
    But I refuse to hear it anymore.
ELMIRE [*to* ORGON]   And now, I wonder, have you lost your mind?
    Your love for this one man has made you blind.
    Can you stand there and say you don't believe
    A word we've said? That we're here to deceive? 45
ORGON   Excuse me—I believe in what I see.
    You, indulging my bad son, agree
    To back him up in this terrible prank,
    Accusing my dear friend of something rank.
    You should be livid if what you claim took place, 50
    And yet this look of calm is on your face.

ELMIRE   Because a man says he's in love with me,
　　I'm to respond with heavy artillery?
　　I laugh at these unwanted propositions.
　　Mirth will quell most ardent ambitions.　　　　　　　　　55
　　Why make a fuss over an indiscretion?
　　My honor's safe and in my possession.
　　You say I'm calm? Well, that's my constancy—
　　It won't need a defense, or clemency.
　　I know I'll never be a vicious prude　　　　　　　　　　60
　　Who always seems to hear men being rude,
　　And then defends her honor tooth and claw,
　　Still snarling, even as the men withdraw.
　　From honor like that heaven preserve me,
　　If that's what you want, you don't deserve me,　　　　　65
　　Besides, you're the one who has been betrayed.
ORGON   I see through this trick that's being played.
ELMIRE   How can you be so dim? I am amazed
　　How you can hear these sins and stay unfazed.
　　But what if I could show you what he does?　　　　　　70
ORGON   Show?
ELMIRE　　　　　Yes.
ORGON　　　　　　　　A fiction!
ELMIRE　　　　　　　　　　　No, the truth because
　　I am quite certain I can find a way
　　To show you in the fullest light of day . . .
ORGON   Fairy tales!
ELMIRE　　　　　　　Come on, at least answer me.
　　I've given up expecting you to be　　　　　　　　　　75
　　My advocate. What have you got to lose,
　　By hiding somewhere, anyplace you choose,
　　And see for yourself. And then we can
　　Hear what you say about your holy man.
ORGON   Then I'll say nothing because it cannot be.　　　80
ELMIRE   Enough. I'm tired. You'll see what you see.
　　I'm not a liar, though I've been accused.
　　The time is now and I won't be refused.
　　You'll be a witness. And we can stop our rants.
ORGON   All right! I call your bluff, Miss Smarty Pants.　　85
ELMIRE [to DORINE]   Tell Tartuffe to come.
DORINE　　　　　　　　　　　Watch out. He's clever.
　　Men like him are caught, well, almost never.
ELMIRE   Narcissism is a great deceiver,
　　And he has lots of that. He's a believer
　　In his charisma. [To CLÉANTE and MARIANE] Leave us for a bit.　　90

4.4

[ELMIRE, ORGON]

ELMIRE   See this table? Good. Get under it.
ORGON   What!

ELMIRE   You are hiding. Get under there and stay.
ORGON   Under the table?
ELMIRE: Just do as I say.
   I have a plan, but for it to succeed,
   You must be hidden. So are we agreed?   5
   You want to know? I'm ready to divulge it.
ORGON   This fantasy of yours—I'll indulge it.
   But then I want to lay this thing to rest.
ELMIRE   Oh, that'll happen. Because he'll fail the test.
   You see, I'm going to have a conversation   10
   I'd never have—just as an illustration
   Of how this hypocrite behaved with me.
   So don't be scandalized. I must be free
   To flirt. Clearly, that's what it's going to take
   To prove to you your holy man's a fake.   15
   I'm going to lead him on, to lift his mask,
   Seem to agree to anything he'll ask,
   Pretend to respond to his advances.
   It's for you I'm taking all these chances.
   I'll stop as soon as you have seen enough;   20
   I hope that comes before he calls my bluff.
   His plans for me must be circumvented,
   His passion's strong enough to be demented,
   So the moment you're convinced, you let me know
   That I've revealed the fraud I said I'd show.   25
   Stop him so I won't have a minute more
   Exposure to your friend, this lecherous boor.
   You're in control. I'm sure I'll be all right.
   And . . . here he comes—so hush, stay out of sight.

4.5

[TARTUFFE, ELMIRE, ORGON (*under the table*)]

TARTUFFE   I'm told you want to have a word with me.
ELMIRE   Yes. I have a secret but I'm not free
   To speak. Close that door, have a look around,
   We certainly do not want to be found
   The way we were just as Damis appeared.   5
   I was terrified for you and as I feared,
   He was irate. You saw how hard I tried
   To calm him down and keep him pacified.
   I was so upset; I never had the thought
   "Deny it all," which might have helped a lot,   10
   But as it turns out, we've nothing to fear,
   My husband's not upset, it would appear.
   Things are good, to heaven I defer,
   Because they're even better than they were.
   I have to say I'm quite amazed, in fact,   15
   His good opinion of you is intact.

To clear the air and quiet every tongue,
And to kill any gossip that's begun—
You could've pushed me over with a feather—
He wants us to spend all our time together!   20
That's why, with no fear of a critical stare,
I can be here with you or anywhere.
Most important, I am completely free
To show my ardor for you, finally.

TARTUFFE   Ardor? This is a sudden change of tone   25
From the last time we found ourselves alone.

ELMIRE   If thinking I was turning you away
Has made you angry, all that I can say
Is that you do not know a woman's heart!
Protecting our virtue keeps us apart,   30
And makes us seem aloof, and even cold.
But cooler outside, inside the more bold.
When love overcomes us, we are ashamed,
Because we fear that we might be defamed.
We must protect our honor—not allow   35
Our love to show. I fear that even now,
In this confession, you'll think ill of me.
But now I've spoken, and I hope you see
My ardor that is there. Why would I sit
And listen to you? Why would I permit   40
Your talk of love, unless I had a notion
Just like yours, and with the same emotion?
And when Damis found us, didn't I try
To quiet him? And did you wonder why,
In speaking of Mariane's marriage deal,   45
I not only asked you, I made an appeal
That you turn it down? What was I doing?
Making sure I'd be the one you'd be wooing.

TARTUFFE   It is extremely sweet, without a doubt,
To watch your lips as loving words spill out.   50
Abundant honey there for me to drink,
But I have doubts. I cannot help but think,
"Does she tell the truth, or does she lie,
To get me to break off this marriage tie?
Is all this ardor something she could fake,   55
And just an act for her stepdaughter's sake?"
So many questions, yet I want to trust,
But need to know the truth, in fact, I must.
Pleasing you, Elmire, is my main task,
And happiness, and so I have to ask   60
To sample this deep ardor felt for me
Right here and now, in blissful ecstasy.

ELMIRE [coughing to alert ORGON]
You want to spend this passion instantly?
I've been opening my heart consistently,
But for you, it's not enough, this sharing.   65

Yet for a woman, it is very daring.
So why can't you be happy with a taste,
Instead of the whole meal consumed in haste?
TARTUFFE   We dare not hope, all those of us who don't
  Deserve a thing. And so it is I won't   70
  Be satisfied with words. I'll always doubt,
  Assume my fortune's taken the wrong route
  On its way to me. And that is why
  I don't believe in anything till I
  Have touched, partaken until satisfied.   75
ELMIRE   So suddenly, your love can't be denied.
  It wants complete dominion over me,
  And what it wants, it wants violently.
  I know I'm flustered, I know I'm out of breath—
  Your power over me could be the death   80
  Of my reason. Does this seem right to you?
  To use my weakness against me, just to
  Conquer? No one's gallant anymore.
  I invite you in. You break down the door.
TARTUFFE   If your passion for me isn't a pretense,   85
  Then why deny me its best evidence?
ELMIRE   But, heaven, sir, that place that you address
  So often, would judge us both if we transgress.
TARTUFFE   That's all that's in the way of my desires?
  These judgments heaven makes of what transpires?   90
  All you fear is heaven's bad opinion.
ELMIRE   But I am made to fear its dominion.
TARTUFFE   And I know how to exorcise these fears.
  To sin is not as bad as it appears
  If, and stay with me on this, one can think   95
  That in some cases, heaven gives a wink
      [*It is a scoundrel speaking.*][8]
  When it comes to certain needs of men
  Who can remain upright but only when
  There is a pure intention. So you see,
  If you just let yourself be led by me,   100
  You'll have no worries, and I can enjoy
  You. And you, me. Because we will employ
  This way of thinking—a real science
  And a secret, thus, with your compliance,
  Fulfilling my desires without fear,   105
  Is easy now, so let it happen here.
      [ELMIRE *coughs.*]
  That cough, Madame, is bad.
ELMIRE   I'm in such pain.
TARTUFFE   A piece of licorice might ease the strain.

---

8. This stage direction, inserted by Molière himself, supports the playwright's assertion that he took pains to demonstrate Tartuffe's true nature.

ELMIRE [*directed to* ORGON]   This cold I have is very obstinate.
  It stubbornly holds on. I can't shake it.   110
TARTUFFE   That's most annoying.
ELMIRE   More than I can say.
TARTUFFE   Let's get back to finding you a way,
  Finally, to get around your scruples:
  Secrecy—I'm one of its best pupils
  And practitioners. Responsibility   115
  For any evil—you can put on me,
  I will answer up to heaven if I must,
  And give a good accounting you can trust.
  There'll be no sins for which we must atone,
  'Cause evil exists only when it's known.   120
  Adam and Eve were public in their fall.
  To sin in private is not to sin at all.
ELMIRE [*after coughing again*]   Obviously, I must give in to you,
  Because, it seems, you are a person who
  Refuses to believe anything I say.   125
  Live testimony only can convey
  The truth of passion here, no more, no less.
  That it should go that far, I must confess,
  Is such a pity. But I'll cross the line,
  And give myself to you. I won't decline   130
  Your offer, sir, to vanquish me right here.
  But let me make one point extremely clear:
  If there's a moral judgment to be made,
  If anyone here feels the least betrayed,
  Then none of that will be my fault. Instead,   135
  The sin weighs twice as heavy on your head.
  You forced me to this brash extremity.
TARTUFFE   Yes, yes, I will take all the sin on me.
ELMIRE   Open the door and check because I fear
  My husband—just look—might be somewhere near.   140
TARTUFFE   What does it matter if he comes or goes?
  The secret is, I lead him by the nose.
  He's urged me to spend all my time with you.
  So let him see—he won't believe it's true.
ELMIRE   Go out and look around. Indulge my whim.   145
  Look everywhere and carefully for him.

4.6

[ORGON, ELMIRE]

ORGON [*coming out from under the table*]
  I swear that is the most abominable man!
  How will I bear this? I don't think I can.
  I'm stupefied!
ELMIRE   What? Out so soon? No, no.
  You can't be serious. There's more to go.

Get back under there. You can't be too sure.   5
It's never good relying on conjecture.
ORGON   That kind of wickedness comes straight from hell.
ELMIRE   You've turned against this man you know so well?
Good lord, be sure the evidence is strong
Before you are convinced. You might be wrong.
[*She steps in front of* ORGON.]

4.7

[TARTUFFE, ELMIRE, ORGON]

TARTUFFE   Yes, all is well; there's no one to be found,
And I was thorough when I looked around.
To my delight, my rapture, at last . . .
ORGON [*stopping him*]   Just stop a minute there! You move too fast!
Delight and rapture? Fulfilling desire?   5
Ah! Ah! You are a traitor and a liar!
Some holy man you are, to wreck my life,
Marry my daughter? Lust after my wife?
I've had my doubts about you, but kept quiet,
Waiting for you to slip and then deny it.   10
Well, now it's happened and I'm so relieved,
To stop pretending that I am deceived.
ELMIRE [*to* TARTUFFE]   I don't approve of what I've done today,
But I needed to do it, anyway.
TARTUFFE   What? You can't think . . .   15
ORGON   No more words from you.
Get out of here, you. . . . . You and I are through.
TARTUFFE   But my intentions . . .
ORGON   You still think I'm a dunce?
You shut your mouth and leave this house at once!
TARTUFFE   You're the one to leave, you, acting like the master.
Now I'll make it known, the full disaster: 20
This house belongs to me, yes, all of it,
And I'll decide what's true, as I see fit.
You can't entrap me with demeaning tricks,
Yes, here's a situation you can't fix.
Here nothing happens without my consent.   25
You've offended heaven. You must repent.
But I know how to really punish you.
Those who harm me, they know not what they do.

4.8

[ELMIRE, ORGON]

ELMIRE   What was that about? I mean, the latter.
ORGON   I'm not sure, but it's no laughing matter.
ELMIRE   Why?

ORGON   I've made a mistake I now can see,
  The deed I gave him is what troubles me.
ELMIRE The deed?   5
ORGON   And something else. I am undone.
  I think my troubles may have just begun.
ELMIRE What else?
ORGON   You'll know it all. I have to race,
  To see if a strongbox is in its place.

5.1

[ORGON, CLÉANTE]

CLÉANTE Where are you running to?
ORGON   Who knows.
CLÉANTE   Then wait.
  It seems to me we should deliberate,
  Meet, plan, and have some family talks.
ORGON I can't stop thinking about the damned box
  More than anything, that's the loss I fear.   5
CLÉANTE What about this box makes it so dear?
ORGON I have a friend whom I felt sorry for,
  Because he chose the wrong side in the war;[9]
  Before he fled, he brought it to me,
  This locked box. He didn't leave a key.   10
  He told me it has papers, this doomed friend,
  On which his life and property depend.
CLÉANTE Are you saying you gave the box away?
ORGON Yes, that's true, that's what I'm trying to say.
  I was afraid that I would have to lie,   15
  If I were confronted. That is why
  I went to my betrayer and confessed
  And he, in turn, told me it would be best
  If I gave him the box, to keep, in case
  Someone were to ask me to my face   20
  About it all, and I might lie and then,
  In doing so, commit a venial sin.[1]
CLÉANTE As far as I can see, this is a mess,
  And with a lot of damage to assess.
  This secret that you told, this deed you gave,   25
  Make the situation hard to save.
  He's holding all the cards, your holy man,
  Because you gave them to him. If you can,

9. That is, he opposed Louis in the Fronde (see 1.2.11 and note). Although Orgon supported the king, this act left him open to the charge of being a traitor to the throne—a capital offense.

1. A "pardonable" or relatively minor sin. Because Tartuffe had possession of the box, Orgon could deny that he had it without lying.

Restrain yourself a bit and stay away.
That would be best. And do watch what you say. 30
ORGON   What? With his wicked heart and corrupt soul,
Yet I'm to keep my rage under control?
Yes, me who took him in, right off the street?
Damn all holy men! They're filled with deceit!
I now renounce them all, down to the man, 35
And I'll treat them worse than Satan can.
CLÉANTE   Listen to yourself! You're over the top,
Getting carried away again. Just stop.
"Moderation." Is that a word you know?
I think you've learned it, but then off you go. 40
Always ignoring the strength in reason,
Flinging yourself from loyalty to treason.
Why can't you just admit that you were swayed
By the fake piety that man displayed?
But no. Rather than change your ways, you turned 45
Like that. [Snaps fingers] Attacking holy men who've earned
The right to stand among the true believers.
So now all holy men are base deceivers?
Instead of just admitting your delusion,
"They're all like that!" you say—brilliant conclusion. 50
Why trust reason, when you have emotion?
You've implied there is no true devotion.
Freethinkers are the ones who hold that view,
And yet, you don't agree with them, do you?
You judge a man as good without real proof. 55
Appearances can lie—witness: Tartuffe.
If your respect is something to be prized,
Don't toss it away to those disguised
In a cloak of piety and virtue.
Don't you see how deeply they can hurt you? 60
Look for simple goodness—it does exist.
And just watch for imposters in our midst,
With this in mind, try not to be unjust
To true believers, sin on the side of trust.

5.2

[DAMIS, ORGON, CLÉANTE]

DAMIS   Father, what? I can't believe it's true,
That scoundrel has the gall to threaten you?
And use the things you gave him in his case
'Gainst you? To throw you out? I'll break his face.
ORGON   My son, I'm in more pain than you can see. 5
DAMIS   I'll break both his legs. Leave it to me.
We must not bend under his insolence.
I'll finish this business, punish his offense,

I'll murder him and do it with such joy.

CLÉANTE   Damis, you're talking like a little boy.   10
Tantrums head the list of your main flaws.
We live in modern times, with things called "laws."
Murder is illegal. At least for us.

5.3

[MADAME PERNELLE, MARIANE, ELMIRE, DORINE,
DAMIS, ORGON, CLÉANTE]

MADAME PERNELLE   It's unbelievable! Preposterous!
ORGON   Believe it. I've seen it with my own eyes.
He returned kindness with deceit and lies.
I took in a man, miserable and poor,
Brought him home, gave him the key to my door,   5
I loaded him with favors every day,
To him, my daughter, I just gave away,
My house, my wealth, a locked box from a friend.
But to what depths this devil would descend.
This betrayer, this abomination,   10
Who had the gall to preach about temptation,
And know in his black heart he'd woo my wife.
Seduce her! Yes! And then to steal my life.
Using my property, which I transferred to him,
I know, I know—it was a stupid whim.   15
He wants to ruin me, chase me from my door,
He wants me as he was, abject and poor.
DORINE   Poor man!
MADAME PERNELLE   I don't believe a word, my son,
This isn't something that he could have done.
ORGON   What?   20
MADAME PERNELLE   Holy men always arouse envy.
ORGON   Mother, what are you trying to say to me?
MADAME PERNELLE   That you live rather strangely in this house;
He's hated here, especially by your spouse.
ORGON   What has this got to do with what I said?
MADAME PERNELLE   Heaven knows, I've beat into your head: 25
"In this world, virtue is mocked forever;
Envious men may die, but envy never."
ORGON   How does that apply to what's happened here?
MADAME PERNELLE   Someone made up some lies; it's all too clear.
ORGON   But I saw it myself, you understand.   30
MADAME PERNELLE   "Whoever spreads slander has a soiled hand."
ORGON   You'll make me, Mother, say something not nice.
I saw it for myself; I've told you twice.
MADAME PERNELLE   "No one can trust what gossips have to say,
Yet they'll be with us until Judgment Day."   35
ORGON   You're talking total nonsense, Mother!

I said I saw him, this man I called Brother!
I saw him with my wife, with these two eyes.
The word is "saw," past tense of "see." These "lies"
That you misnamed are just the truth.   40
I saw my wife almost beneath Tartuffe.
MADAME PERNELLE   Oh, is that all? Appearances deceive.
  What we think we see, we then believe.
ORGON   I'm getting angry.
MADAME PERNELLE   False suspicions, see?
  We are subject to them, occasionally,   45
  Good deeds can be seen as something other.
ORGON   So I'm to see this as a good thing, Mother,
  A man trying to kiss my wife?
MADAME PERNELLE   You must.
  Because, to be quite certain you are just,
  You should wait until you're very, very sure   50
  And not rely on faulty conjecture.
ORGON   Goddammit! You would have me wait until . . . ?
  And just be quiet while he has his fill,
  Right before my very eyes, Mother, he'd—
MADAME PERNELLE   I can't believe that he would do this "deed"   55
  Of which he's been accused. There is no way.
  His soul is pure.
ORGON   I don't know what to say!
  Mother!
DORINE   Just deserts, for what you put us through.
  You thought we lied, now she thinks that of you.
CLÉANTE   Why are we wasting time with all of this?   60
  We're standing on the edge of the abyss.
  This man is dangerous! He has a plan!
DAMIS   How could he hurt us? I don't think he can.
ELMIRE   He won't get far, complaining to the law—
  You'll tell the truth, and he'll have to withdraw.   65
CLÉANTE   Don't count on it; trust me, he'll find a way
  To use these weapons you gave him today.
  He has legal documents, and the deed.
  To kick us out, just what else does he need?
  And if he's doubted, there are many ways   70
  To trap you in a wicked legal maze.
  You give a snake his venom, nice and quick,
  And after that you poke him with a stick?
ORGON   I know. But what was I supposed to do?
  Emotions got the best of me, it's true.   75
CLÉANTE   If we could placate him, just for a while,
  And somehow get the deed back with a smile.
ELMIRE   Had I known we had all this to lose,
  I never would have gone through with my ruse.
  I would've—   80
     [A knock on the door.]

ORGON   What does that man want? You go find out.
But I don't want to know what it's about.

5.4

[MONSIEUR LOYAL, MADAME PERNELLE, ORGON,
DAMIS, MARIANE, DORINE, ELMIRE, CLÉANTE]

MONSIEUR LOYAL [to DORINE]   Dear sister, hello. Please, I beg of you,
Your master is the one I must speak to.
DORINE   He's not receiving visitors today.
MONSIEUR LOYAL   I bring good news so don't send me away.
My goal in coming is not to displease;   5
I'm here to put your master's mind at ease.
DORINE   And you are . . . who?
MONSIEUR LOYAL   Just say that I have come
For his own good and with a message from
Monsieur Tartuffe.
DORINE [to ORGON]   It's a soft-spoken man,
Who says he's here to do just what he can   10
To ease your mind. Tartuffe sent him.
CLÉANTE   Let's see
What he might want.
ORGON   Oh, what's my strategy?
He's come to reconcile us, I just know.
CLÉANTE   Your strategy? Don't let your anger show,
For heaven's sake. And listen for a truce.   15
MONSIEUR LOYAL   My greetings, sir. I'm here to be of use.
ORGON   Just what I thought. His language is benign.
For the prospect of peace, a hopeful sign.
MONSIEUR LOYAL   Your family's dear to me, I hope
    you know.
I served your father many years ago.   20
ORGON   I humbly beg your pardon, to my shame,
I don't know you, nor do I know your name.
MONSIEUR LOYAL   My name's Loyal. I'm Norman by descent.
My job of bailiff is what pays my rent.
Thanks be to heaven, it's been forty years   25
I've done my duty free of doubts or fear.
That you invited me in, I can report,
When I serve you with this writ from the court.
ORGON   What? You're here . . .
MONSIEUR LOYAL   No upsetting outbursts,
    please.
It's just a warrant saying we can seize,   30
Not me, of course, but this Monsieur Tartuffe—
Your house and land as his. Here is the proof.
I have the contract here. You must vacate
These premises. Please, now, don't be irate.

Just gather up your things now, and make way   35
   For this man, without hindrance or delay.
ORGON   Me? Leave my house?
MONSIEUR LOYAL   That's right, sir, out the door.
   This house, at present, as I've said before,
   Belongs to good Monsieur Tartuffe, you see,
   He's lord and master of this property   40
   By virtue of this contract I hold right here.
   Is that not your signature? It's quite clear.
DAMIS   He's so rude, I do almost admire him.
MONSIEUR LOYAL   Excuse me. Is it possible to fire him?
   My business is with you, a man of reason,   45
   Who knows resisting would be seen as treason.
   You understand that I must be permitted
   To execute the orders as committed.
DAMIS   I'll execute him, Father, to be sure.
   His long black nightgown won't make him secure.   50
MONSIEUR LOYAL   He's your son! I thought he was a servant.
   Control the boy. His attitude's too fervent,
   His anger is a bone of contention—
   Throw him out, or I will have to mention
   His name in this, my official report.   55
DORINE   "Loyal" is loyal only to the court.
MONSIEUR LOYAL   I have respect for all God-fearing men,
   So instantly I knew I'd come here when
   I heard your name attached to this assignment.
   I knew you'd want a bailiff with refinement.   60
   I'm here for you, just to accommodate,
   To make removal something you won't hate.
   Now, if I hadn't come, then you would find
   You got a bailiff who would be less kind.
ORGON   I'm sorry, I don't see the kindness in   65
   An eviction order.
MONSIEUR LOYAL   Let me begin:
   I'm giving you time. I won't carry out
   This order you are so upset about.
   I've come only to spend the night with you,
   With my men, who will be coming through.   70
   All ten of them, as quiet as a mouse,
   Oh, you must give me the keys to the house.
   We won't disturb you. You will have your rest—
   You need a full night's sleep—that's always best.
   There'll be no scandal, secrets won't be bared;   75
   Tomorrow morning you must be prepared,
   To pack your things, down to the smallest plate,
   And cup, and then these premises vacate.
   You'll have helpers; the men I chose are strong,
   And they'll have this house empty before long.   80
   I can't think of who would treat you better

And still enforce the law down to the letter,
Just later with the letter is my gift.
So, no resistance. And there'll be no rift.

ORGON   From that which I still have, I'd give this hour,   85
One hundred coins of gold to have the power
To sock this bailiff with a punch as great
As any man in this world could create.

CLÉANTE   That's enough. Let's not make it worse.

DAMIS   The nerve
Of him. Let's see what my right fist can serve.   90

DORINE   Mister Loyal, you have a fine, broad back,
And if I had a stick, you'd hear it crack.

MONSIEUR LOYAL   Words like that are punishable, my love—
Be careful when a push becomes a shove.

CLÉANTE   Oh, come on, there's no reason to postpone.   95
Just serve your writ and then leave us alone.

MONSIEUR LOYAL   May heaven keep you, till we meet again!

ORGON   And strangle you, and him who sent you in!

5.5

[ORGON, CLÉANTE, MARIANE, ELMIRE, MADAME
PERNELLE, DORINE, DAMIS]

ORGON   Well, Mother, look at this writ. Here is proof
Of treachery supreme by your Tartuffe.
Don't jump to judgment—that's what you admonished.

MADAME PERNELLE   I'm overwhelmed, I'm utterly astonished.

DORINE   I hear you blaming him and that's just wrong.   5
You'll see his good intentions before long.
"Just love thy neighbor" is here on this writ,
Between the lines, you see him saying it.
Because men are corrupted by their wealth,
Out of concern for your spiritual health.   10
He's taking, with a pure motivation,
Everything that keeps you from salvation.

ORGON   Aren't you sick of hearing "Quiet!" from me?

CLÉANTE   Thoughts of what to do now? And quickly?

ELMIRE   Once we show the plans of that ingrate,   15
His trickery can't get him this estate.
As soon as they see his disloyalty,
He'll be denied, I hope, this property.

5.6

[VALÈRE, ORGON, CLÉANTE, ELMIRE, MARIANE, etc.]

VALÈRE   I hate to ruin your day—I have bad news.
Danger's coming. There's no time to lose.
A good friend, quite good, as it turns out,

Discovered something you must know about,
Something at the court that's happening now.   5
That swindler—sorry, if you will allow,
That holy faker—has gone to the king,
Accusing you of almost everything.
But here's the worst: he says that you have failed
Your duty as a subject, which entailed   10
The keeping of a strongbox so well hidden,
That you could deny knowledge, if bidden,
Of a traitor's whereabouts. What's more,
That holy fraud will come right through that door,
Accusing you. You can't do anything.   15
He had this box and gave it to the king.
So there's an order out for your arrest!
And evidently, it's the king's behest,
That Tartuffe come, so justice can be done.
CLÉANTE   Well, there it is, at last, the smoking gun.   20
He can claim this house, at the very least.
ORGON   The man is nothing but a vicious beast.
VALÈRE   You must leave now, and I will help you hide.
Here's ten thousand in gold. My carriage is outside.
When a storm is bearing down on you   25
Running is the best thing one can do.
I have a place where both of us can stay.
ORGON   My boy, I owe you more than I can say.
I pray to heaven that, before too long,
I can pay you back and right the wrong   30
I've done to you. [*To* ELMIRE] Good-bye. Take care, my dear.
CLÉANTE   We'll plan. You go while the way is still clear.

5.7

[THE EXEMPT, TARTUFFE, VALÈRE, ORGON, ELMIRE,
MARIANE, DORINE, *etc.*[2]]

TARTUFFE   Easy, just a minute, you move too fast.
Your cowardice, dear sir, is unsurpassed.
What I have to say is uncontested.
Simply put, I'm having you arrested.
ORGON   You villain, you traitor, your lechery   5
Is second only to your treachery.
And you arrest me—that's the crowning blow.
TARTUFFE   Suffering for heaven is all I know,
So revile me. It's all for heaven's sake.
CLÉANTE   Why does he persist when we know it's fake?   10
DAMIS   He's mocking heaven. What a loathsome beast.

---

2. Molière himself added "etc." to the list of speaking characters. Thus Laurent and Flipote may return to the stage for this final scene.

TARTUFFE   Get mad—I'm not bothered in the least.
  It is my duty, what I'm doing here.
MARIANE   You really think that if you persevere
  In this lie, you'll keep your reputation?   15
TARTUFFE   My honor is safeguarded by my station,
  As I am on a mission from the king.
ORGON   You dog, have you forgotten everything?
  Who picked you up from total poverty?
TARTUFFE   I know that there were things you did for me.   20
  My duty to our monarch is what stifles
  Memory, so your past gifts are trifles.
  My obligations to him are so rife,
  That I would give up family, friends, and life.
ELMIRE   Fraud!   25
DORINE   Now there's a lie that beats everything,
  His pretended reverence for our king!
CLÉANTE   This "duty to our monarch," as you say,
  Why didn't it come up before today?
  You had the box, you lived here for some time,
  To say the least, and yet this crime   30
  That you reported—why then did you wait?
  Orgon caught you about to desecrate
  The holy bonds of marriage with his wife.
  Suddenly, your obligations are so "rife"
  To our dear king, that you're here to turn in   35
  Your former friend and "brother" and begin
  To move into his house, a gift, but look,
  Why would you accept gifts from a crook?
TARTUFFE [to THE EXEMPT]   Save me from this whining! I have had my fill!
  Do execute your orders, if you will.   40
THE EXEMPT   I will. I've waited much too long for that.
  I had to let you have your little chat.
  It confirmed the facts our monarch knew,
  That's why, Tartuffe, I am arresting you.[3]
TARTUFFE   Who, me?   45
THE EXEMPT   Yes, you.
TARTUFFE   You're putting me in jail?
THE EXEMPT   Immediately. And there will be no bail.
  [To ORGON] You may compose yourself now, sir, because
  We're fortunate in leadership and laws.
  We have a king who sees into men's hearts,
  And cannot be deceived, so he imparts   50
  Great wisdom, and a talent for discernment,
  Thus frauds are guaranteed a quick internment.
  Our Prince of Reason sees things as they are,

---

3. In his capacity as officer of the king, The Exempt becomes both Louis's representative and his surrogate.

So hypocrites do not get very far.
But saintly men and the truly devout,   55
He cherishes and has no doubts about.
This man could not begin to fool the king
Who can defend himself against the sting
Of much more subtle predators. And thus,
When this craven pretender came to us,   60
Demanding justice and accusing you,
He betrayed himself. Our king could view
The baseness lurking in his coward's heart.
Evil like that can set a man apart,
And so divine justice nodded her head,   65
The king did not believe a word he said.
It was soon confirmed, he has a crime
For every sin, but why squander the time
To list them or the aliases he used.
For the king, it's enough that he abused   70
Your friendship and your faith. And though we knew
Each accusation of his was untrue,
Our monarch himself, wanting to know
Just how far this imposter planned to go,
Had me wait to find this out, then pounce,   75
Arrest this criminal, quickly denounce
The man and all his lies. And now, the king
Orders delivered to you, everything
This scoundrel took, the deed, all documents,
This locked box of yours and all its contents,   80
And nullifies the contract giving away
Your property, effective today.
And finally, our monarch wants to end
Your worries about aiding your old friend
Before he went into exile because,   85
In that same way, and in spite of the laws,
You openly defended our king's right
To his throne. And you were prepared to fight.
From his heart, and because it makes good sense
That a good deed deserves a recompense,   90
He pardons you. And wanted me to add:
He remembers good longer than the bad.
DORINE   May heaven be praised!
MADAME PERNELLE   I am so relieved.
ELMIRE   A happy ending!
MARIANE   Can it be believed?
ORGON [*to* TARTUFFE]   Now then, you traitor . . .   95
CLÉANTE   Stop that, Brother, please.
You're sinking to his level. Don't appease
His expectations of mankind. His fate
Is misery. But it's never too late
To take another path, and feel remorse.

So let's wish, rather, he will change his course,   100
And turn his back upon his life of vice,
Embrace the good and know it will suffice.
We've all seen the wisdom of this great king,
Whom we should go and thank for everything.
ORGON   Yes, and well said. So come along with me,   105
To thank him for his generosity.
And then once that glorious task is done,
We'll come back here for yet another one—
I mean a wedding for which we'll prepare,
To give my daughter to the good Valère.   110

SOR JUANA INÉS DE LA CRUZ
1648–1695

Sor (Sister) Juana, a nun from New Spain (colonial Mexico), was one of the most famous writers of her time, celebrated as the "Tenth Muse" in Europe and the Americas. She is best known for her spirited defense of women's intellectual rights in *The Poet's Answer to the Most Illustrious Sor Filotea de la Cruz*. While ostensibly declaring her humility and her religious subordination in this text, Sor Juana also manages to advance claims for her sex that are more far-reaching and profound than any previously offered. At the same time, she paints a passionate yet nuanced picture of the life of the mind that combines rhetorical precision and intense emotion.

Born illegitimate to an upper-class creole woman and a Spanish captain, Sor Juana learned to read in her grandfather's library. Despite ongoing tensions among Spaniards, creoles, and the indigenous population, Sor Juana's Mexico was a huge metropole with a lively artistic and intellectual scene centered around the viceregal court. As a young girl, Juana served as lady-in-waiting at the court before entering the Convent of Saint Jerome when she was eighteen. Her *Answer* suggests that she became a nun in search of a safe environment in which to pursue her intellectual interests, and her religious vocation did not prevent her from writing in secular forms—lyric poetry and drama—for which she became known throughout the Spanish-speaking world. She wrote sixty-five sonnets, over sixty *romances* (ballads), and a profusion of poems in other metrical forms. She also wrote for the stage, producing everything from comedies and farces to *autos sacramentales*, religious plays that marked Catholic holidays.

Because her religious superiors rebuked her worldly interests, however, she struggled to continue writing secular literature without abandoning her faith. The natural disturbances and disasters that plagued Mexico City in the 1690s—a solar eclipse, storms, and famine—and the departure of some of her key supporters rekindled her religious passions and led her in 1694 to formally reaffirm her faith in a statement that she signed in her own blood with the words, "I, Sor Juana Inés de la Cruz, the worst of all." She died soon after, while nursing the convent sick during an epidemic.

The *Answer* stems directly from Sor Juana's venture into theological polemic. In 1690 she wrote a commentary on a sermon delivered forty years earlier, on the nature of Christ's love toward humanity. Her commentary, in the form of a letter, was published without her consent by the bishop of Puebla. The bishop provided the title, *Athenagoric Letter*, or "letter worthy of the wisdom of Athena," and also prefixed his own letter to Sor Juana, signed with the pseudonym "Filotea de la Cruz." In the letter, one "nun" advises the other to focus her attention and her talents on religious matters. In her *Answer* (1691), Sor Juana nominally accepts the bishop's rebuke; the smooth surface of her elegant prose, however, conceals both rage and determination to assert her right—and that of other women—to a fully realized life of the mind.

The artistry of this piece of self-defense demonstrates Sor Juana's powers and thus constitutes part of her justification. While asserting her own unimportance, she illustrates the range of her knowledge and of her rhetorical skill. The sheer abundance of her biblical allusions and quotations from theological texts, for instance, proves that she has mastered a large body of religious material and that she has not sacrificed religious for secular study. Her elaborate protestations of deference, her vocabulary of insignificance, and her narrative of subservience all show the verbal dexterity that enables her to achieve her own rhetorical ends even as she denies her commitment to purely personal goals. No matter how often Sor Juana admits that her intellectual longings amount to a form of "vice," she embodies in her prose the energy and the vividness that they generate.

Sor Juana's larger argument depends on her utter denial that intelligence or a thirst for knowledge should be attributed to only one gender. While she draws on history for evidence of female intellectual power, even more forceful is the testimony of her own experience: her account of how, deprived of books, she finds matter for intellectual inquiry everywhere—in the yolk of an egg, the spinning of a top, the reading of the Bible. If she makes us uneasy when she implicitly equates herself, as object of persecution, with Christ, she also makes us feel directly the horror of women's official exclusion, in the past, from intellectual pursuits.

Sor Juana's sonnets offer a different perspective on this versatile writer. By turns playful and passionate, they often have a satiric edge that recalls the artful arguments of the *Answer*. In poem 145, she takes up the Spanish Baroque tradition of *desengaño* or disillusion, in which the poet finds behind the surface of things the emptiness and vanity of earthly existence. But instead of revealing the impermanence of a person or a building, as her models often do, Sor Juana writes about a portrait, so that her sonnet dismantles one piece of art as it makes another. Poem 164 is a passionate, intimate plea to end a lover's quarrel, reminding us of the remarkable poetic range available to this scholarly nun. In "Philosophical Satire," perhaps her most famous poem, Sor Juana methodically analyzes the contradictions in men's expectations of women, in a devastating anatomy of sexual hypocrisy that reverberates far beyond her own sophisticated milieu.

From The Poet's Answer to the Most Illustrious
Sor Filotea de la Cruz[1]

Most illustrious Lady, my Lady:

It has not been my will, but my scant health and a rightful fear that have delayed my reply for so many days. Is it to be wondered that, at the very first step, I should meet with two obstacles that sent my dull pen stumbling? The first (and to me the most insuperable) is the question of how to respond to your immensely learned, prudent, devout, and loving letter. For when I consider how the Angelic Doctor, St. Thomas Aquinas, on being asked of his silence before his teacher Albertus Magnus,[2] responded that he kept quiet because he could say nothing worthy of Albertus, then how much more fitting it is that I should keep quiet—not like the Saint from modesty, but rather because, in truth, I am unable to say anything worthy of you. The second obstacle is the question of how to render my thanks for the favor, as excessive as it was unexpected, of giving my drafts and scratches to the press[3] a favor so far beyond all measure as to surpass the most ambitious hopes or the most fantastic desires, so that as a rational being I simply could not house it in my thoughts. In short, this was a favor of such magnitude that it cannot be bounded by the confines of speech and indeed exceeds all powers of gratitude, as much because it was so large as because it was so unexpected. In the words of Quintilian:[4] *"They produce less glory through hopes, more glory through benefits conferred."* And so much so, that the recipient is struck dumb.

When the mother of [John] the Baptist—felicitously barren, so as to become miraculously fertile—saw under her roof so exceedingly great a guest as the Mother of the Word, her powers of mind were dulled and her speech was halted; and thus, instead of thanks, she burst out with doubts and questions: *"And whence is this to me . . . ?"* The same occurred with Saul when he was chosen and anointed[5] King of Israel: *"Am not I a son of Jemini of the least tribe of Israel, and my kindred the last among all the families of the tribe of Benjamin? Why then hast thou spoken this word to me?"*[6] Just so, I too must say: Whence, O venerable Lady, whence comes such a favor to me? By chance, am I something more than a poor nun, the slightest creature on earth and the least worthy of drawing your attention? Well, *why then hast thou spoken this word to me? And whence is this to me?*

I can answer nothing more to the first obstacle than that I am entirely unworthy of your gaze. To the second, I can offer nothing more than amazement, instead of thanks, declaring that I am unable to thank you for the slightest part of what I owe you. It is not false humility, my Lady, but the candid truth of my very soul, to say that when the printed letter reached my hands—

---

1. Translated by Electa Arenal and Amanda Powell.
2. Thomas Aquinas (1225–1274), scholastic philosopher and theologian who held that faith and reason existed in harmony. The great thinker Albertus Magnus (ca. 1206?–1280) defended his student Thomas from criticisms.
3. "Sor Filotea" (from the Greek, lover of God) was the pseudonym used by Manuel Fernández de Santa Cruz, bishop of Puebla, who had published Sor Juana's commentary on a sermon without her consent.
4. Marcus Fabius Quintilianus (35–100), Roman orator and rhetorician from Hispania.
5. Luke 1.43.
6. I Samuel 9.21.

that letter you were pleased to dub "Worthy of Athena"[7]—I burst into tears (a thing that does not come easily to me), tears of confusion. For it seemed to me that your great favor was nothing other than God's reproof aimed at my failure to return His favors, and while He corrects others with punishments, He wished to chide me through benefits. A special favor, this, for which I acknowledge myself His debtor, as I am indebted for infinitely many favors given by His immense goodness; but this is also a special way of shaming and confounding me. For it is the choicest form of punishment to cause me to serve, knowingly, as the judge who condemns and sentences my own ingratitude. And so when I consider this fully, here in solitude, it is my custom to say: Blessed are you, my Lord God, for not only did you forbear to give another creature the power to judge me, nor have you placed that power in my hands. Rather, you have kept that power for yourself and have freed me of myself and of the sentence I would pass on myself, which, forced by my own conscience, could be no less than condemnation. Instead you have reserved that sentence for your great mercy to declare, because you love me more than I can love myself.

My Lady, forgive the digression wrested from me by the power of truth; yet if I must make a full confession of it, this digression is at the same time a way of seeking evasions so as to flee the difficulty of making my answer. And therefore I had nearly resolved to leave the matter in silence; yet although silence explains much by the emphasis of leaving all unexplained, because it is a negative thing, one must name the silence, so that what it signifies may be understood. Failing that, silence will say nothing, for that is its proper function: to say nothing. The holy Chosen Vessel was carried off to the third Heaven and, having seen the arcane secrets of God, he says: *That he was caught up into paradise, and heard secret words, which it is not granted to man to utter.*[8] He does not say what he saw, but he says that he cannot say it. In this way, of those things that cannot be spoken, it must be said that they cannot be spoken, so that it may be known that silence is kept not for lack of things to say, but because the many things there are to say cannot be contained in mere words. St. John says that if he were to write all of the wonders wrought by Our Redeemer, the whole world could not contain all the books.[9] Vieira says of this passage that in this one phrase the Evangelist says more than in all his other writings; and indeed how well the Lusitanian Phoenix[1] speaks (but when is he not well-spoken, even when he speaks ill?), for herein St. John says all that he failed to say and expresses all that he failed to express. And so I, my Lady, shall answer only that I know not how to answer; I shall thank you only by saying that I know not how to give thanks; and I shall say, by way of the brief label placed on what I leave to silence, that only with the confidence of one so

7. Fernández had entitled Sor Juana's commentary "Athenagoric Letter," letter worthy of Athena, after the Greek goddess of wisdom.
8. 2 Corinthians 12.4. "Chosen Vessel": in Acts 9.15, Christ describes St. Paul as his "chosen vessel" to carry his message to the Gentiles.
9. John 21.25.
1. Lusitania is the Roman name for Portugal; the phoenix was a mythical bird reborn from its own ashes, used as a term of praise for writers in the period. Sor Juana was herself called the Mexican Phoenix. Antonio Vieira (1608–1697), author of the sermon that Sor Juana had criticized in her commentary, was a Jesuit Portuguese priest, diplomat, and orator who served as a missionary in Brazil.

favored and with the advantages granted one so honored, do I dare speak to your magnificence. If this be folly, please forgive it; for folly sparkles in good fortune's crown, and through it I shall supply further occasion for your good-will, and you shall better arrange the expression of my gratitude.

Moses, because he was a stutterer,[2] thought himself unworthy to speak to Pharaoh. Yet later, finding himself greatly favored by God, he was so imbued with courage that not only did he speak to God Himself, but he dared to ask of Him the impossible: "*Shew me thy face.*"[3] And so it is with me, my Lady, for in view of the favor you show me, the obstacles I described at the outset no longer seem entirely insuperable. For one who had the letter printed, unbeknownst to me, who titled it and underwrote its cost, and who thus honored it (unworthy as it was of all this, on its own account and on account of its author), what will such a one not do? What not forgive? Or what fail to do or fail to forgive? Thus, sheltered by the assumption that I speak with the safe-conduct granted by your favors and with the warrant bestowed by your goodwill, and by the fact that, like a second Ahasuerus,[4] you have allowed me to kiss the top of the golden scepter of your affection as a sign that you grant me kind license to speak and to plead my case in your venerable presence, I declare that I receive in my very soul your most holy admonition to apply my study to Holy Scripture; for although it arrives in the guise of counsel, it shall have for me the weight of law. And I take no small consolation from the fact that it seems my obedience, as if at your direction, anticipated your pastoral insinuation, as may be inferred from the subject matter and arguments of that very Letter. I recognize full well that your most prudent warning touches not on the letter, but on the many writings of mine on humane matters that you have seen.[5] And thus, all that I have said can do no more than offer that letter to you in recompense for the failure to apply myself which you must have inferred (and reasonably so) from my other writings. And to speak more specifically, I confess, with all the candor due to you and with the truth and frankness that are always at once natural and customary for me, that my having written little on sacred matters has sprung from no dislike, nor from lack of application, but rather from a surfeit of awe and reverence toward those sacred letters, which I know myself to be so incapable of understanding and which I am so unworthy of handling. For there always resounds in my ears the Lord's warning and prohibition to sinners like me, bringing with it no small terror: "*Why does thou declare my justices, and take my convenant in thy mouth?*"[6] With this question comes the reflection that even learned men were forbidden to read the Song of Songs, and indeed Genesis[7] before they reached the age of thirty: the latter text because of its difficulty, and the former so that with the sweetness of those epithalamiums, imprudent youth might not be stirred to carnal feelings. My great father

---

2. In Exodus 4.10, Moses complains to God that he lacks the eloquence to approach Pharaoh.
3. Exodus 33.13.
4. King Xerxes of Persia, 486–465 B.C.E. In Esther 5.2–3, Ahasuerus holds out his scepter to his queen, Esther, and promises to grant her whatever she wishes, an opportunity that the wise queen uses to save the Jews from destruction.
5. Sor Juana had published secular poetry and drama.
6. Psalms 50.16.
7. First book of the Old Testament. "Song of Songs": Old Testament praise poem, uses erotic imagery.

St. Jerome confirms this, ordering the Song of Songs to be the last text studied, for the same reason: "*Then at last she may safely read the Song of Songs: if she were to read it at the beginning, she might be harmed by not perceiving that it was the song of a spiritual bridal expressed in fleshly language.*"[8] And Seneca[9] says, "*In early years, faith is not yet manifest.*" Then how should I dare take these up in my unworthy hands, when sex, and age, and above all our customs oppose it? And thus I confess that often this very fear has snatched the pen from my hand and has made the subject matter retreat back toward that intellect from which it wished to flow; an impediment I did not stumble across with profane subjects, for a heresy against art is not punished by the Holy Office[1] but rather by wits with their laughter and critics with their censure. And this, "*just or unjust, is not to be feared,*" for one is still permitted to take Communion and hear Mass, so that it troubles me little if at all. For in such matters, according to the judgment of the very ones who slander me, I have no obligation to know how nor the skill to hit the mark, and thus if I miss it is neither sin nor discredit. No sin, because I had no obligation; no discredit, because I had no possibility of hitting the mark, and "*no one is obliged to do the impossible.*" And truth to tell, I have never written save when pressed and forced and solely to give pleasure to others, not only without taking satisfaction but with downright aversion, because I have never judged myself to possess the rich trove of learning and wit that is perforce the obligation of one who writes. This, then, is my usual reply to those who urge me to write, and the more so in the case of a sacred subject: What understanding do I possess, what studies, what subject matter, or what instruction, save four profundities of a superficial scholar? They can leave such things to those who understand them; as for me, I want no trouble with the Holy Office, for I am but ignorant and tremble lest I utter some ill-sounding proposition or twist the true meaning of some passage. I do not study in order to write, nor far less in order to teach (which would be boundless arrogance in me), but simply to see whether by studying I may become less ignorant. This is my answer, and these are my feelings.

My writing has never proceeded from any dictate of my own, but a force beyond me; I can in truth say, "*You have compelled me.*"[2] One thing, however, is true, so that I shall not deny it (first because it is already well known to all, and second because God has shown me His favor in giving me the greatest possible love of truth, even when it might count against me). For ever since the light of reason first dawned in me, my inclination to letters was marked by such passion and vehemence that neither the reprimands of others (for I have received many) nor reflections of my own (there have been more than a few) have sufficed to make me abandon my pursuit of this native impulse that God Himself bestowed on me. His Majesty knows why and to what end He did so, and He knows that I have prayed that He snuff out the light of my intellect,

---

8. St. Jerome (ca. 342–420), ascetic and scholar, learned Church Father, and founder of the Jeronymite order. He wrote this advice for the education of the Roman girl Paula, who would eventually collaborate with Jerome and become a saint in her own right. Sor Juana's convent, St. Paula's of the Order of St. Jerome, was named after both figures.

9. Roman playwright, philosopher, and orator (ca. 3 B.C.E.–63 C.E.).
1. The Holy Office of the Inquisition, founded by the papacy in the 13th century to root out heresy and suppress challenges to religious orthodoxy.
2. 1 Corinthians 12.11.

leaving only enough to keep His Law. For more than that is too much, some would say, in a woman; and there are even those who say that it is harmful. His Majesty knows too that, not achieving this, I have attempted to entomb my intellect together with my name and to sacrifice it to the One who gave it to me; and that no other motive brought me to the life of religion, despite the fact that the exercises and companionship of a community were quite opposed to the tranquillity and freedom from disturbance required by my studious bent. And once in the community, the Lord knows—and in this world only he who needs must know it, does[3]—what I did to try to conceal my name and renown from the public; he did not, however, allow me to do this, telling me it was temptation, and so it would have been. If I could repay any part of my debt to you, my Lady, I believe I might do so merely by informing you of this, for these words have never left my mouth save to that one to whom they must be said. But having thrown wide the doors of my heart and revealed to you what is there under seal of secrecy, I want you to know that this confidence does not gainsay the respect I owe to your venerable person and excessive favors.

To go on with the narration of this inclination of mine, of which I wish to give you a full account: I declare I was not yet three years old when my mother sent off one of my sisters, older than I, to learn to read in one of those girls' schools that they call *Amigas*.[4] Affection and mischief carried me after her; and when I saw that they were giving her lessons, I so caught fire with the desire to learn that, deceiving the teacher (or so I thought), I told her that my mother wanted her to teach me also. She did not believe this, for it was not to be believed; but to humor my whim she gave me lessons. I continued to go and she continued to teach me, though no longer in make-believe, for the experience undeceived her. I learned to read in such a short time that I already knew how by the time my mother heard of it. My teacher had kept it from my mother to give delight with a thing all done and to receive a prize for a thing done well. And I had kept still, thinking I would be whipped for having done this without permission. The woman who taught me (may God keep her) is still living, and she can vouch for what I say.

I remember that in those days, though I was as greedy for treats as children usually are at that age, I would abstain from eating cheese, because I heard tell that it made people stupid, and the desire to learn was stronger for me than the desire to eat—powerful as this is in children. Later, when I was six or seven years old and already knew how to read and write, along with all the other skills like embroidery and sewing that women learn, I heard that in Mexico City there were a University and Schools where they studied the sciences. As soon as I heard this I began to slay my poor mother with insistent and annoying pleas, begging her to dress me in men's clothes and send me to the capital, to the home of some relatives she had there, so that I could enter the University and study. She refused, and was right in doing so; but I quenched my desire by reading a great variety of books that belonged to my grandfather, and neither punishments nor scoldings could prevent me. And so when I did go to Mexico City, people marveled not so much at my intelligence

3. Presumably her confessor, Father Antonio Núñez.
4. Informal schools set up by cultured women in their homes to teach girls.

as at my memory and the facts I knew at an age when it seemed I had scarcely had time to learn to speak.

I began to study Latin, in which I believe I took fewer than twenty lessons. And my interest was so intense, that although in women (and especially in the very bloom of youth) the natural adornment of the hair is so esteemed, I would cut off four to six fingerlengths of my hair, measuring how long it had been before. And I made myself a rule that if by the time it had grown back to the same length I did not know such and such a thing that I intended to study, then I would cut my hair off again to punish my dull-wittedness. And so my hair grew, but I did not yet know what I had resolved to learn, for it grew quickly and I learned slowly. Then I cut my hair right off to punish my dull-wittedness, for I did not think it reasonable that hair should cover a head that was so bare of facts—the more desirable adornment. I took the veil because, although I knew I would find in religious life many things that would be quite opposed to my character (I speak of accessory rather than essential matters), it would, given my absolute unwillingness to enter into marriage, be the least unfitting and the most decent state I could choose, with regard to the assurance I desired of my salvation. For before this first concern (which is, at the last, the most important), all the impertinent little follies of my character gave way and bowed to the yoke. These were wanting to live alone and not wanting to have either obligations that would disturb my freedom to study or the noise of a community that would interrupt the tranquil silence of my books. These things made me waver somewhat in my decision until, being enlightened by learned people as to my temptation, I vanquished it with divine favor and took the state I so unworthily hold. I thought I was fleeing myself, but—woe is me!—I brought myself with me, and brought my greatest enemy in my inclination to study, which I know not whether to take as a Heaven-sent favor or as a punishment. For when snuffed out or hindered with every [spiritual] exercise known to Religion, it exploded like gunpowder; and in my case the saying "*privation gives rise to appetite*" was proven true.

I went back (no, I spoke incorrectly, for I never stopped)—I went on, I mean, with my studious task (which to me was peace and rest in every moment left over when my duties were done) of reading and still more reading, study and still more study, with no teacher besides my books themselves. What a hardship it is to learn from those lifeless letters, deprived of the sound of a teacher's voice and explanations; yet I suffered all these trials most gladly for the love of learning. Oh, if only this had been done for the love of God, as was rightful, think what I should have merited! Nevertheless I did my best to elevate these studies and direct them to His service, for the goal to which I aspired was the study of Theology. Being a Catholic, I thought it an abject failing not to know everything that can in this life be achieved, through earthly methods, concerning the divine mysteries. And being a nun and not a laywoman, I thought I should, because I was in religious life, profess the study of letters—the more so as the daughter of such as St. Jerome and St. Paula: for it would be a degeneracy for an idiot daughter to proceed from such learned parents. I argued in this way to myself, and I thought my own argument quite reasonable. However, the fact may have been (and this seems most likely) that I was merely flattering and encouraging my own inclination, by arguing that its own pleasure was an obligation.

I went on in this way, always directing each step of my studies, as I have said, toward the summit of Holy Theology; but it seemed to me necessary to ascend by the ladder of the humane arts and sciences in order to reach it; for who could fathom the style of the Queen of Sciences without knowing that of her handmaidens? Without Logic, how should I know the general and specific methods by which Holy Scripture is written? Without Rhetoric, how should I understand its figures, tropes, and locutions? Or how, without Physics or Natural Science, understand all the questions that naturally arise concerning the varied natures of those animals offered in sacrifice, in which a great many things already made manifest are symbolized, and many more besides? How should I know whether Saul's cure at the sound of David's harp was owing to a virtue and power that is natural in Music or owing, instead, to a supernatural power that God saw fit to bestow on David?[5] How without Arithmetic might one understand all those mysterious reckonings of years and days and months and hours and weeks that are found in Daniel[6] and elsewhere, which can be comprehended only by knowing the natures, concordances, and properties of numbers? Without Geometry, how could we take the measure of the Holy Ark of the Covenant or the Holy City of Jerusalem, each of whose mysterious measurements forms a perfect cube uniting their dimensions, and each displaying that most marvelous distribution of the proportions of every part?

Without the science of Architecture, how understand the mighty Temple of Solomon—where God Himself was the Draftsman who set forth His arrangement and plan, and the Wise King was but the overseer who carried it out; where there was no foundation without its mystery, nor column without its symbol, nor cornice without its allusion, nor architrave without its meaning, and likewise for every other part, so that even the very least fillet served not only for the support and enhancement of Art, but to symbolize greater things? How, without a thorough knowledge of the order and divisions by which History is composed, is one to understand the Historical Books[7]—as in those summaries, for example, which often postpone in the narration what happened first in fact? How, without command of the two branches of Law, should one understand the Books of Law?[8] Without considerable erudition, how should we understand the great many matters of profane history that are mentioned by Holy Scripture: all the diverse customs of the Gentiles, all their rituals, all their manners of speech? Without knowing many precepts and reading widely in the Fathers of the Church, how could one understand the obscure sayings of the Prophets? Well then, and without being expert in Music, how might one understand those musical intervals and their perfections that occur in a great many passages—especially in Abraham's petitions to God on behalf of the Cities,[9] beseeching God to spare them if there were found fifty righteous people within? And the number fifty Abraham reduced to forty-five, which is sesquinonal [10 to 9] or like the interval from mi to re; this in turn he reduced to

---

5. 1 Samuel 16.23.
6. The book of Daniel includes the numerical interpretation of complex visions (Daniel 9.21–27).
7. The sections of the Old Testament that recount history rather than law or prophecies.

8. The sections of the Old Testament that give laws. "Two branches of law": canon and civil laws, or the codes for church and state.
9. Sodom and Gomorrah. Abraham beseeches God to save Sodom from destruction for the sake of its just inhabitants (Genesis 18.22–23).

forty, which is the sesquioctave [9 to 8] or like the interval from re to mi; thence he went down to thirty, which is sesquitertia, or the interval of the diatessaron [the perfect fourth]; thence to twenty, the sesquialtera or the diapente [the fifth]; thence to ten, the duple, which is the diapason [the interval and consonance of the octave]; and because there are no more harmonic intervals, Abraham went no further. How could all this be understood without knowledge of music?[1] Why, in the very Book of Job, God says to him: "*Shalt thou be able to join together the shining stars the Pleiades, or canst thou stop the turning about of Arcturus? Canst thou bring forth the day star in its time, and make the evening star to rise upon the children of the earth?*"[2] Without knowledge of Astronomy, these terms would be impossible to understand. Nor are these noble sciences alone represented; indeed, not one of the mechanical arts escapes mention. In sum, we see how this Book contains all books, and this Science[3] includes all sciences, all of which serve that She may be understood. And once each science is mastered (which we see is not easy, or even possible), She demands still another condition beyond all I have yet said, which is continual prayer and purity of life, to entreat God for that cleansing of the spirit and illumination of the mind required for an understanding of such high things. And if this be lacking, all the rest is useless.

The Church says these words of the Angelic Doctor, St. Thomas Aquinas: "*At the difficult passages of Holy Scripture, he added fasting to prayer. And he used to say to his companion Brother Reginald that he owed all his knowledge not so much to study or hard work, but rather he had received it from God.*" How then should I, so far from either virtue or learning, find the courage to write? And so, to acquire a few basic principles of knowledge, I studied constantly in a variety of subjects, having no inclination toward any one of them in particular but being drawn rather to all of them generally. Therefore, if I have studied some things more than others it has not been by my choice, but because by chance the books on certain subjects came more readily to hand, and this gave preference to those topics, without my passing judgment in the matter. I held no particular interest to spur me, nor had I any limit to my time compelling me to reduce the continuous study of one subject, as is required in taking a degree. Thus almost at one sitting I would study diverse things or leave off some to take up others. Yet even in this I maintained a certain order, for some subjects I called my study and others my diversion, and with the latter I would take my rest from the former. Hence, I have studied many things but know nothing, for one subject has interfered with another. What I say is true regarding the practical element of those subjects that require practice, for clearly the compass must rest while the pen is moving, and while the harp is playing the organ is still, *and likewise with all things.* Much bodily repetition is needed to form a habit, and therefore a person whose time is divided among several exercises will never develop one perfectly. But in formal and speculative arts the opposite is true, and I wish I might persuade everyone with my own experience: to wit, that far from interfering, these subjects help one another, shedding light and opening a path from one to the next, by way of divergences and

1. Sor Juana refers here to the intervals of classical music theory.
2. Job 38.31–32. "Pleiades": a constellation.

"Arcturus": a star in the Great Bear.
3. Theology, here feminized. "This Book": the Bible.

hidden links—for they were set in place so as to form this universal chain by the wisdom of their great Author.

* * *

I confess that I am far indeed from the terms of Knowledge and that I have wished to follow it, though "*afar off.*" But all this has merely led me closer to the flames of persecution, the crucible of affliction; and to such extremes that some have even sought to prohibit me from study.

They achieved this once, with a very saintly and simple mother superior who believed that study was an affair for the Inquisition and ordered that I should not read. I obeyed her (for the three months or so that her authority over us lasted) in that I did not pick up a book. But with regard to avoiding study absolutely, as such a thing does not lie within my power, I could not do it. For although I did not study in books, I studied all the things that God created, taking them for my letters, and for my book all the intricate structures of this world. Nothing could I see without reflecting upon it, nothing could I hear without pondering it, even to the most minute, material things. For there is no creature, however lowly, in which one cannot recognize the great "*God made me*"; there is not one that does not stagger the mind if it receives due consideration. And so, I repeat, I looked and marveled at all things, so that from the very persons with whom I spoke and from what they said to me, a thousand speculations leapt to my mind: Whence could spring this diversity of character and intelligence among individuals all composing one single species? What temperaments, what hidden qualities could give rise to each? When I noticed a shape, I would set about combining the proportions of its lines and measuring it in my mind and converting it to other proportions. I sometimes walked back and forth along the forewall of one of our dormitories (which is a very large room), and I began to observe that although the lines of its two sides were parallel and the ceiling was flat, yet the eye falsely perceived these lines as though they approached each other and the ceiling as though it were lower in the distance than close by; from this I inferred that visual lines run straight, but not parallel, and that they form a pyramidal figure. And I conjectured whether this might be the reason the ancients were obliged to question whether the world is spherical or not. Because even though it seems so, this could be a delusion of the eye, displaying concavities where there were none.

This kind of observation has been continual in me and is so to this day, without my having control over it; rather, I tend to find it annoying, because it tires my head. Yet I believed this happened to everyone, as with thinking in verse, until experience taught me otherwise. This trait, whether a matter of nature or custom, is such that nothing do I see without a second thought. Two little girls were playing with a top in front of me, and no sooner had I seen the motion and shape than I began, with this madness of mine, to observe the easy movement of the spherical form and how the momentum lasted, now fixed and set free of its cause; for even far from its first cause, which was the hand of the girl, the little top went on dancing. Yet not content with this, I ordered flour to be brought and sifted on the floor, so that as the top danced over it, we could know whether its movement described perfect circles or no. I found they were not circular, but rather spiral lines that lost their circularity as the top lost its momentum. Other girls were playing at spillikins (the most frivolous of all childhood games). I drew near to observe the shapes they made, and when I saw three of the straws by chance fall in a triangle, I fell to intertwining one with another, recalling that this was said to be the very shape of Solomon's mysterious ring[4] where distantly there shone bright traces and representations of the Most Blessed Trinity, by virtue of which it worked great prodigies and marvels. And they say David's harp had the same shape, and thus was Saul cured by its sound; to this day, harps have almost the same form.

Well, and what then shall I tell you, my Lady, of the secrets of nature that I have learned while cooking? I observe that an egg becomes solid and cooks in butter or oil, and on the contrary that it dissolves in sugar syrup. Or again, to ensure that sugar flow freely one need only add the slightest bit of water that has held quince or some other sour fruit. The yolk and white of the very same egg are of such a contrary nature that when eggs are used with sugar, each part separately may be used perfectly well, yet they cannot be mixed together. I shall not weary you with such inanities, which I relate simply to give you a full account of my nature, and I believe this will make you laugh. But in truth, my Lady, what can we women know, save philosophies of the kitchen? It was well put by Lupercio Leonardo [sic][5] that one can philosophize quite well while preparing supper. I often say, when I make these little observations, "Had Aristotle[6] cooked, he would have written a great deal more." And so to go on with the mode of my cogitations: I declare that all this is so continual in me that I have no need of books. On one occasion, because of a severe stomach ailment, the doctors forbade me to study. I spent several days in that state, and then quickly proposed to them that it would be less harmful to allow me my books, for my cogitations were so strenuous and vehement that they consumed more vitality in a quarter of an hour than the reading of books could in four days. And so the doctors were compelled to let me read. What is more, my Lady, not even my sleep has been free of this ceaseless movement of my imagination. Rather, my mind operates in sleep still more freely and unobstructedly, ordering with greater clarity and ease the events it has preserved from the day, presenting arguments and composing verses. I could give you a very long catalogue of these, as I could of certain reasonings and subtle turns I have reached far better in my sleep than while awake; but I leave them out in order not to weary you. I have said enough for your judgment and your surpassing eminence to comprehend my nature with clarity and full understanding, together with the beginnings, the methods, and the present state of my studies.

If studies, my Lady, be merits (for indeed I see them extolled as such in men), in me they are no such thing: I study because I must. If they be a failing, I believe for the same reason that the fault is none of mine. Yet withal, I live always so wary of myself that neither in this nor in anything else do I trust my own judgment. And so I entrust the decision to your supreme skill and straightway submit to whatever sentence you may pass, posing no objection or reluctance, for this has been no more than a simple account of my inclination to letters.

4. It may, like Solomon's seal, have contained a Star of David, composed of triangles.
5. Sor Juana actually refers to his brother, Bernardo Leonardo de Argensola, Spanish poet and satirist (1562–1631).
6. Greek philosopher (384–322 B.C.E.) who studied with Plato and wrote on logic, politics, ethics, natural science, and poetics.

I confess also that, while in truth this inclination has been such that, as I said before, I had no need of exemplars, nevertheless the many books that I have read have not failed to help me, both in sacred as well as secular letters. For there I see a Deborah[7] issuing laws, military as well as political, and governing the people among whom there were so many learned men. I see the exceedingly knowledgeable Queen of Sheba[8] so learned she dares to test the wisdom of the wisest of all wise men with riddles, without being rebuked for it; indeed, on this very account she is to become judge of the unbelievers. I see so many and such significant women: some adorned with the gift of prophecy, like an Abigail; others, of persuasion, like Esther; others, of piety, like Rahab; others, of perseverance, like Anna [Hannah] the mother of Samuel;[9] and others, infinitely more, with other kinds of qualities and virtues.

If I consider the Gentiles, the first I meet are the Sibyls,[1] chosen by God to prophesy the essential mysteries of our Faith in such learned and elegant verses that they stupefy the imagination. I see a woman such as Minerva,[2] daughter of great Jupiter and mistress of all the wisdom of Athens, adored as goddess of the sciences. I see one Polla Argentaria, who helped Lucan, her husband, to write the *Battle of Pharsalia*.[3] I see the daughter of the divine Tiresias,[4] more learned still than her father. I see, too, such a woman as Zenobia,[5] queen of the Palmyrians, as wise as she was courageous. Again, I see an Arete,[6] daughter of Aristippus, most learned. A Nicostrata,[7] inventor of Latin letters and most erudite in the Greek. An Aspasia Miletia,[8] who taught philosophy and rhetoric and was the teacher of the philosopher Pericles. An Hypatia, who taught astrology and lectured for many years in Alexandria. A Leontium, who won over the philosopher Theophrastus and proved him wrong. A Julia, a Corinna, a Cornelia;[9] and, in sum, the vast throng of women who merited titles and earned renown: now as Greeks, again as Muses, and yet again as Pythonesses.[1] For what were they all but learned women, who were considered, celebrated, and indeed venerated as such in Antiquity? Without mentioning still others, of whom the books are full; for I see the Egyptian Catherine,[2] lecturing and refuting all the learning of the most learned men of Egypt. I see a Gertrude[3] read, write, and teach. And seek-

7. Prophetess who judged the Israelites (Judges 4.4–14).
8. Sheba tested King Solomon with her questions (1 Kings 10.1–3).
9. Abigail saved her husband's life by prophesying for King David (1 Samuel 25.2–35). Esther persuaded King Ahasuerus to protect the Jews (Esther 5–9). The harlot Rahab protected two Israelites from the King of Jericho (Joshua 2.1–7). Anna persevered in her prayers until granted the birth of her son (1 Samuel 1.1–20).
1. Female prophets of the ancient world.
2. Roman name for Athena, goddess of wisdom.
3. Epic poem on the civil war between Caesar and Pompey.
4. A blind seer in ancient Thebes, whose daughter Manto was known for her skill in divination.
5. Matriarchal warrior queen of Palmyra (ruled

266–72 C.E.), much admired for her learning.
6. Founder of a Greek school of philosophy (4th century B.C.E.).
7. Mythical healer and teacher who adapted Greek characters into the Roman alphabet.
8. Reputed teacher of eloquence in ancient Athens.
9. Julia Domna (second century C.E.), wife of the Roman emperor Septimius Severus, known for her learning as Julia the Philosopher. Corinna (ca. 500? B.C.E.), a lyric poet of Tanagra who wrote for a female audience. Cornelia (2nd century B.C.E.), noted for her devotion to her children's education.
1. Seers.
2. St. Catherine of Alexandria (4th century?), allegedly so wise she could refute fifty philosophers at once.
3. St. Gertrude (d. 1302), Benedictine nun and mystic.

ing no more examples far from home, I see my own most holy mother Paula, learned in the Hebrew, Greek, and Latin tongues and most expert in the interpretation of the Scriptures. What wonder then can it be that, though her chronicler was no less than the unequaled Jerome, the Saint found himself scarcely worthy of the task, for with that lively gravity and energetic effectiveness with which only he can express himself, he says: "If all the parts of my body were tongues, they would not suffice to proclaim the learning and virtues of Paula." Blessilla, a widow, earned the same praises, as did the luminous virgin Eustochium, both of them daughters of the Saint herself [Paula][4] and indeed Eustochium was such that for her knowledge she was hailed as a World Prodigy. Fabiola,[5] also a Roman, was another most learned in Holy Scripture. Proba Falconia, a Roman woman, wrote an elegant book of centos[6] joining together verses from Virgil, on the mysteries of our holy Faith. Our Queen Isabella,[7] wife of Alfonso X, is known to have written on astrology—without mentioning others, whom I omit so as not merely to copy what others have said (which is a vice I have always detested): Well then, in our own day there thrive the great Christina Alexandra, Queen of Sweden,[8] as learned as she is brave and generous; and too those most excellent ladies, the Duchess of Aveyro and the Countess of Villaumbrosa.

* * *

My Lady, I have not wished to reply, though others have done so without my knowledge. It is enough that I have seen certain papers, among them one I send to you because it is learned, and because reading it will restore to you a portion of your time that I have wasted with what I am writing. If by your wisdom and sense, my Lady, you should be pleased for me to do other than what I propose, then as is only right, to the slightest motion of your pleasure I shall cede my own decision, which was as I have told you to keep still. For although St. John Chrysostom[9] says, "*One's slanderers must be proven wrong, and one's questioners must be taught,*" I see too that St. Gregory[1] says, "*It is no less a victory to tolerate one's enemies than to defeat them,*" and that patience defeats by tolerance and triumphs by suffering. Indeed, it was the custom among the Roman Gentiles, for their captains at the very height of glory—when they entered triumphing over other nations, clothed in purple and crowned with laurel; with their carts drawn by the crowned brows of vanquished kings rather than by beasts of burden; accompanied by the spoils of the riches of all the world, before a conquering army decorated with the emblems of its feats; hearing the crowd's acclaim in such honorable titles and epithets as Fathers of the Fatherland, Pillars of the Empire, Ramparts of Rome, Refuge of the Republic, and other glorious names— it was the custom, at this supreme apex of pride and human felicity, that a common soldier should cry aloud to the conqueror, as if from his own feeling and at the order of the Senate: "Behold, how you are mortal; behold, for you have such and such a failing." Nor were the most shameful excused; as at the triumph of

---

4. Blessilla and Eustochium, daughters of St. Paula, also taught by St. Jerome.
5. Another member of St. Jerome's circle.
6. Poems made up of verses from other authors.
7. Wife of Alfonso X of Spain (1221–1284), also known as Alfonso the Wise.

8. She attracted many scholars and writers to her court (1626–1689).
9. Syrian prelate (ca. 347–407), known as a great orator.
1. Gregory the Great (ca. 540–604), pope from 590.

Caesar, when the most contemptible soldiers shouted in his ears, *"Beware, Romans, for we bring before you the bald adulterer."* All of this was done so that in the midst of great honor the conqueror might not puff up with pride, and that the ballast of these affronts might prove a counterweight to the sails of so much praise, so that the ship of sound judgment should not founder in the winds of acclaim. If, as I say, all this was done by mere Gentiles, guided only by the light of Natural Law, then for us as Catholics, who are commanded to *love* our enemies, is it any great matter for us to tolerate them? For my part, I can testify that these detractions have at times been a mortification to me, but they have never done me harm. For I think that man very foolish who, having the opportunity to earn due merit, undertakes the labor and then forfeits the reward. This is like people who do not want to resign themselves to death. In the end they die all the same, with their resistance serving not to exempt them from dying, but only to deprive them of the merit of conformity to God's will, and thus to give them an evil death when it could have been blessed. And so, my Lady, I think these detractions do more good than harm. I maintain that a greater risk to human frailty is worked by praise, which usually seizes what does not belong to it, so that one must proceed with great care and have inscribed in one's heart these words of the Apostle: *"Or what hast thou that thou hast not received? And if thou hast received, why dost thou glory, as if thou hadst not received it?"*[2] For these words should serve as a shield to deflect the prongs of praises, which are spears that, when not attributed to God to whom they belong, take our very lives and make us thieves of God's honor and usurpers of the talents that He bestowed on us, and of the gifts He lent us, for which we must one day render Him a most detailed account. And so, good Lady, I fear applause far more than slander. For the slander, with just one simple act of patience, is turned to a benefit, whereas praise requires many acts of reflection and humility and self-knowledge if it is not to cause harm. And so, for myself I know and own that this knowledge is a special favor from God, enabling me to conduct myself in the face of one as in the other, following that dictum of St. Augustine.[3] *One must believe neither the friend who speaks praises nor the enemy who reviles."* Although I am such a one as most times must either let the opportunity go to waste, or mix it with such failings and flaws that I spoil what left to itself would have been good. And so, with the few things of mine that have been printed, the appearance of my name—and, indeed, permission for the printing itself—have not followed my own decision, but another's liberty that does not lie under my control, as was the case with the "Letter Worthy of Athena." So you see, only some little *Exercises for the Annunciation* and certain *Offerings for the Sorrows* were printed at my pleasure for the prayers of the public, but my name did not appear. I submit to you a few copies of the same, so that you may distribute them (if you think it seemly) among our sisters the nuns of your blessed community and others in this City. Only one copy remains of the *Sorrows*, because they have all been given away and I could find no more. I made them only for the prayers of my sisters, many years ago, and then they became more widely known. Their subjects are as disproportionate to my lukewarm ability as to my ignorance, and I was helped in writing them only by the fact

2. Corinthians 11.4.
3. North African philosopher and theologian, one of the Latin Church Fathers (354–430).

that they dealt with matters of our great Queen; I know not why it is that in speaking of the Most Blessed Mary, the most icy heart is set aflame. It would please me greatly, my venerable Lady, to send you works worthy of your virtue and wisdom, but as the Poet[4] remarked:

Even when strength is lacking, still the intention must be praised.
I surmise the gods would be content with that.

If ever I write any more little trifles, they shall always seek haven at your feet and the safety of your correction, for I have no other jewel with which to repay you. And in the opinion of Seneca, he who has once commenced to confer benefits becomes obliged to continue them. Thus you must be repaid by your own generosity, for only in that way can I be honorably cleared of my debt to you, lest another statement, again Seneca's, be leveled against me: "*It is shameful to be outdone in acts of kindness.*" For it is magnanimous for the generous creditor to grant a poor debtor some means of satisfying the debt. Thus God behaved toward the world, which could not possibly repay Him: He gave His own Son, that He might offer Himself as a worthy amends.

If the style of this letter, my venerable Lady, has been less than your due, I beg your pardon for its household familiarity or the lack of seemly respect. For in addressing you, my sister, as a nun of the veil, I have forgotten the distance between myself and your most distinguished person, which should not occur were I to see you unveiled. But you, with your prudence and benevolence, will substitute or emend my terms; and if you think unsuitable the familiar terms of address I have employed—because it seems to me that given all the reverence I owe you, "Your Reverence" is very little reverence indeed—please alter it to whatever you think suitable. For I have not been so bold as to exceed the limits set by the style of your letter to me, nor to cross the border of your modesty.

And hold me in your own good grace, so as to entreat divine grace on my behalf; of the same, may the Lord grant you great increase, and may He keep you, as I beg of Him and as I am needful. Written at the Convent of our Father St. Jerome in Mexico City, this first day of March of the year 1691. Receive the embrace of your most greatly favored,

Sor Juana Inés de la Cruz

Poem 145

[She endeavors to expose the praises recorded in a portrait of the poetess by truth, which she calls passion.]

This object which you see—a painted snare
exhibiting the subtleties of art
with clever arguments of tone and hue—
is but a cunning trap to snare your sense;
this object, in which flattery has tried   5

---

4. Generally used to refer to Virgil, but this citation is from Ovid.

to overlook the horrors of the years
and, conquering the ravages of time,
to overcome oblivion and age:
   this is an empty artifice of care,
a flower, fragile, set out in the wind,   10
a letter of safe-conduct sent to Fate;
   it is a foolish, erring diligence,
a palsied will to please which, clearly seen,
is a corpse, is dust, is shadow, and is gone.

Poem 164

[*In which she answers a suspicion with the eloquence of tears.*]

   This afternoon, my darling, when we spoke,
and in your face and gestures I could see
that I was not persuading you with words,
I wished you might look straight into my heart;
   and Love, who was assisting my designs,   5
succeeded in what seemed impossible:
for in the stream of tears which anguish loosed
my heart itself, dissolved, dropped slowly down.
   Enough unkindness now, my love, enough;
don't let these tyrant jealousies torment you   10
nor base suspicions shatter your repose
   with foolish shadows, empty evidence:
in liquid humor you have seen and touched
my heart undone and passing through your hands.

Philosophical Satire

Poem 92

[*The poet proves illogical both the whim and the censure of men who accuse, in women, that which they cause.*]

   You foolish and unreasoning men
who cast all blame on women,
not seeing you yourselves are cause
of the same faults you accuse:

   if, with eagerness unequaled,   5
you plead against women's disdain,
why require them to do well
when you inspire them to fall?

   You combat their firm resistance,
and then solemnly pronounce   10

that what you've won through diligence
is proof of women's flightiness.

What do we see, when we see you
madly determined to see us so,
but the child who makes a monster appear   15
and then goes trembling with fear?

With ridiculous conceit
you insist that woman be
a sultry Thais while you woo her;
a true Lucretia[1] once she's won.   20

Whose behavior could be odder
than that of a stubborn man
who himself breathes on the mirror,
and then laments it is not clear?

Women's good favor, women's scorn   25
you hold in equal disregard:
complaining, if they treat you badly;
mocking, if they love you well.

Not one can gain your good opinion,
for she who modestly withdraws   30
and fails to admit you is ungrateful;
yet if she admits you, too easily won.

So downright foolish are you all
that your injurious justice claims
to blame one woman's cruelty   35
and fault the other's laxity.

How then can she be moderate
to whom your suit aspires,
if, ingrate, she makes you displeased,
or, easy, prompts your ire?   40

Between such ire and such anguish
—the tales your fancy tells—
lucky is she who does not love you;
complain then, as you will!

Your doting anguish feathers the wings   45
of liberties that women take,
and once you've caused them to be bad,
you want to find them as good as saints.

1. A noble Roman woman (d. ca. 508 B.C.E.) who killed herself after being raped; a symbol of
chastity. "Thais": a celebrated courtesan in ancient Greece.

But who has carried greater blame
in a passion gone astray: 50
she who falls to constant pleading,
or he who pleads with her to fall?

Or which more greatly must be faulted,
though either may commit a wrong:
she who sins for need of payment,   55
or he who pays for his enjoyment?

Why then are you so alarmed
by the fault that is your own?
Wish women to be what you make them,
or make them what you wish they were.   60

Leave off soliciting her fall
and then indeed, more justified,
that eagerness you might accuse
of the woman who besieges you.

Thus I prove with all my forces   65
the ways your arrogance does battle:
for in your offers and your demands
we have devil, flesh, and world: a man.

ALEXANDER POPE
1688–1744

Socially marginal and physically disabled, Alexander Pope might seem an unlikely candidate for celebrity, but he won great wealth and fame through his writing. Crowds parted when he entered a room, and people rushed to shake his hand. In 1741, the renowned actor David Garrick heard that Pope was in the audience: "I instantaneously felt a palpitation at my heart. . . . His look shot, and thrilled, like lightning through my frame; and I had some hesitation in proceeding, from anxiety, and from joy." What made Pope so celebrated in his own time? His writing did not strive to be innovative; he proudly turned backward to ancient Greek and Roman traditions of literature and morality—especially Homer, Virgil, and Horace—and borrowed from them to make critical and satirical commentaries on his own society. But his witty, graceful, often bitingly comic poetic lines, coupled with his deep sense of moral and philosophical authority, marked him as both the most respected and the most popular poet of his time.

LIFE

Born to Roman Catholic parents in a year when the last Catholic king of England, James II, was deposed in favor of the Protestant regime of William and Mary, Pope lived when repressive measures against Catholics restricted his freedom. He could not attend a university or hold public office. He was even forbidden to live within ten miles of London. Sickly and undersized in childhood, he never reached more than four feet six inches tall, and had a hunchback for his whole life. In his youth, he was educated sporadically at illegal Catholic schools and at home, learning Latin, Greek, French, and Italian. He began to write epic poetry at the age of twelve. He taught himself a great deal, and developed his understanding of the world through literary friendships that remained important to him throughout his career.

Pope first came to the attention of the literary world with his *Essay on Criticism*, an ambitious piece of writing for a twenty-three year old, since it offered advice to rising writers when he had not yet established himself. This work earned him as many attackers as defenders, and he entered into a lively, sometimes acrimonious, literary debate about whether the ancient writers could be surpassed by modern innovations. *The Rape of the Lock*, Pope's most popular work from his time to ours, appeared in 1714. It sold three thousand copies in the first week of its publication. Then, in the ten years that followed, he produced little new poetry of his own, instead translating Homer's *Iliad* and *Odyssey*, and editing the works of Shakespeare to make both newly accessible to English readers. A rival translation of Homer appeared around the same time, and debate about the two versions reached a fever pitch, with newspapers reporting on both sides. But Pope's translations soon won the field, establishing him as a literary representative of the whole nation. They also earned him substantial sums of money, making him perhaps the first English writer to make a fortune from his work.

Pope never married, but he had some notable friendships with women. For some time he was on close terms with Lady Mary Wortley Montagu, a fellow writer, but they fell out, and she satirized him in print. His closest relationship was with a woman named Martha Blount, whom he had known since adolescence. He wrote her serious letters and for a period saw her every day, giving rise to some scandalous gossip about the pair. When he died he left her his estate.

In his later years, Pope was best known for two works: a philosophical poem that reflects on the role of human beings in the universe, called *The Essay on Man* (1733–34) and *The Dunciad* (completed in 1742), a satirical poem he wrote in response to criticisms of his edition of Shakespeare. Here he condemned almost all of his intellectual contemporaries, scientists, critics, and writers—with the notable exception of his friend Jonathan Swift—as hacks and dunces. This work earned him so many enemies that he refused to leave his house without a pair of loaded pistols. The money Pope made from his translations had allowed him to retire to Twickenham, where he built a small villa and a famous garden and grotto. He died there at the age of fifty-six.

TIMES

Although he was the richest poet of his era, Pope frequently condemned writers who wrote for monetary gain. This might make him seem hypocritical, but in fact his whole culture was feeling a new and profound ambivalence about money, which underwent a major transformation during his lifetime. In the eighteenth century European economies for the first time began to produce paper currencies rather than relying on exchanges of gold and silver, and people started to write checks. Lottery tickets went on sale as a new thrill. Among the most important new financial instruments of the period was the joint stock company—where an individual investor could advance a small sum that would be lumped in with money from others. It became popular to buy shares in these companies, and this wave of enthusiasm enabled large-scale economic projects that would never have been possible before.

The most famous—and ill-fated—of the new joint stock ventures was the South Sea Company. In the early eighteenth century, the British government found itself deep in debt, and in 1711, they sold a substantial portion of the debt to the South Sea Company, promising a return of 6 percent interest. The company publicized the fact that they had bought the rights to all new trading opportunities in South America, since Spain had just opened up access to British ships. Having heard about gold and silver mines in Mexico and Peru, people rushed to buy shares in the company, and the price of stocks rose precipitously. The South Sea Company abruptly failed in 1720. It turned out that many of the glowing rumors about it had been false. The directors wanted to sell and get out quickly. "And thus," wrote a historian looking back in 1803, "were seen, in the space of eight months, the rise, progress, and fall of that mighty fabric, which, being wound up by mysterious springs to a wonderful height, had fixed the eyes and expectations of all Europe, but whose foundation, being fraud, illusion, credulity, and infatuation, fell to the ground as soon as the artful management of its directors was discovered."

Intangible and sometimes illusory, the new paper economy often seemed simply immoral. Pope saw the crash as "God punishing the avaritious." But it was also hugely tempting, since it was clearly now possible to amass a great fortune from very little. As Pope himself put it, "'Tis ignominious (in this Age of Hope and Golden Mountains) not to Venture." The poet had in fact invested in the South Sea Company, but on the advice of a wise broker, he got much of his money out before the crash, losing only a part of his growing fortune. Torn between excitement at a fast-growing economy where ordinary people could accumulate riches, and alarm at the greed, deception, and catastrophic failure that the new financial world made possible, the whole of Europe was caught up in wonder and uncertainty at the new, strange fact of wealth on paper.

Pope was particularly shrewd about putting the changing marketplace to use for his own writing career. Since he was a Catholic outsider, he could not depend on powerful patrons in the Anglican Church or the court, and he suffered particular hardships when new anti-Catholic laws diminished his family's property in 1714. But he figured out how to exploit a growing democratic and urban market for books and pamphlets. Pope retained his own copyright and acted as his own publisher. He also borrowed a trick out of the book of the new joint stock companies. That is, he sold subscriptions to his translation of Homer's *Iliad* before it appeared. Subscribers therefore "invested" in a promise rather than a concrete object, just as they bought stocks in new companies, and Pope could live on the cash that flowed in before the publication was complete. Unlike the South Sea Bubble, this turned out to be a good investment for his readers—and excellent for Pope's own finances. Where many contemporary writers might make a total £10 or £20 on a book they sold to a publisher, Pope made more than £800 on his *Iliad*, roughly equivalent to about $200,000 today. Thus he brought about his independence. As he put it proudly: "South-sea subscriptions take who please, / Leave me but Liberty and Ease!"

WORK

Pope's *Essay on Man* ambitiously sets out to consider humanity in relation to the universe, to itself, to society, and to happiness. He draws on a number of intellectual traditions—Catholic and Protestant theology, Platonic and Stoic philosophy, his own period's interest in a natural order—to reinforce the assumption of a timeless and universal human nature. Above all, the text is, like Milton's *Paradise Lost*, a theodicy—a genre that asks how, if God is good, there can be evil in the world. The first section of the poem, included here, begins by insisting on the necessary limitations of human judgment: we see only parts, not the whole. And yet, our ignorance of future events and our hope for eternal life give us the possibility of happiness. He explores the nature of human pride and the place of humans in the Great Chain of Being that stretches from God down to the minutest living things, suggesting that this order extends farther than we can know and that any attempt to interfere with it will destroy the whole.

Pope draws us into the poem by addressing us directly, reminding us of our own tendencies to presumption. "In Pride, in reas'ning Pride, our error lies": we all share bewilderment at our situation, we all need to interpret it, we all face, every day, our necessary limitations. The poet rapidly shifts tone and perspective, sometimes berating his readers, sometimes reminding us (and himself) of his own participation in the universal dilemma, some-times assuming a godlike perspective and suggesting his superior knowledge. And as he moves among voices and viewpoints, he comes to the conclusion that although we cannot see it, the universe works according to a design that is good, and thus demands "our absolute submission . . . to Providence."

Pope conceded that it was difficult to write a philosophical argument in poetic form, but he defended his choice. "This I might have done in prose," he wrote, "but I chose verse, and even rhyme, for two reasons. The one will appear obvious; that principles, maxims, or precepts, so written, both strike the reader more strongly at first, and are more easily retained by him afterwards: the other may seem odd, but it is true: I found I could express them more shortly this way than in prose itself; and nothing is more certain than that much of the force as well as grace of arguments or instructions depends on their conciseness." Forceful and concise, Pope's lines also offer concrete imagery—such as the Indian looking up at the clouds to find God or the eye of the fly, which sees more minutely than the human eye. And his perfectly turned couplets remind us of the complex dualities of humankind, at once godlike and animal, fallen and saved, capable of happy triviality and grim seriousness.

In the later eighteenth century, Pope's writing came under attack. Romantic poets such as **William Wordsworth** saw Pope's elegant verse couplets as artificial, mechanical, lacking "soul." But he remained a well-loved poet for his moral wisdom and his remarkable technical skill. Most famous today for lines we may not even recognize as his—such as "A little learning is a dangerous thing" and "Hope springs eternal in the human breast"—Pope embodies a whole literary era in England, which has come to be known as the "age of Pope."

An Essay on Man

To Henry St. John, Lord Bolingbroke

EPISTLE I

ARGUMENT OF THE NATURE AND STATE OF MAN, WITH RESPECT TO THE UNIVERSE. Of man in the abstract—I. That we can judge only with regard to our own system, being ignorant of the relations of systems and things, ver. 17, &c.—II. That man is not to be deemed imperfect, but a being suited to his place and rank in the creation, agreeable to the general order of things, and conformable to ends and relations to him unknown, ver. 35, &c.—III. That it is partly upon his ignorance of future events, and partly upon the hope of a future state, that all his happiness in the present depends, ver. 77, &c.—IV. The pride of aiming at more knowledge, and pretending to more perfection, the cause of man's error and misery. The impiety of putting himself in the place of God, and judging of the fitness or unfitness, perfection or imperfection, justice or injustice of his dispensations, ver. 113, &c.—V. The absurdity of conceiting himself the final cause of the creation, or expecting that perfection in the moral world which is not in the natural, ver. 131, &c.—VI. The unreasonableness of his complaints against Providence, while on the one hand he demands the perfections of the angels, and on the other the bodily qualifications of the brutes; though, to possess any of the sensitive faculties in a higher degree, would render him miserable, ver. 173, &c.—VII. That throughout the whole visible world, an universal order and gradation in the sensual and mental faculties is observed, which causes a subordination of creature to creature, and of all creatures to man. The gradations of sense, instinct, thought, reflection, reason: that reason alone countervails all the other faculties, ver. 207.—VIII. How much further this order and subordination of living creatures may extend, above and below us; were any part of which broken, not that part only, but the whole connected creation must be destroyed, ver. 233—IX. The extravagance, madness, and pride of such a desire, ver. 259.—X. The consequence of all, the absolute submission due to Providence, both as to our present and future state, ver. 281, &c., to the end.

> Awake, my St. John![1] leave all meaner things
> To low ambition, and the pride of Kings.
> Let us (since Life can little more supply
> Than just to look about us and to die)
> Expatiate free o'er all this scene of Man;   5
> A mighty maze! but not without a plan;
> A Wild, where weeds and flowers promiscuous shoot;
> Or Garden, tempting with forbidden fruit.
> Together let us beat this ample field,
> Try what the open, what the covert yield;   10
> The latent tracts, the giddy heights, explore

1. Henry St. John, Viscount Bolingbroke, Pope's friend, who had thus far neglected to keep his part of their friendly bargain: Pope was to write his philosophical speculations in verse; Bolingbroke was to write his in prose.

Of all who blindly creep, or sightless soar;
Eye Nature's walks, shoot Folly as it flies,
And catch the Manners living as they rise;
Laugh where we must, be candid where we can;   15
But vindicate the ways of God to man.[2]

    I. Say first, of God above, or Man below,
What can we reason, but from what we know?
Of Man, what see we but his station here,
From which to reason, or to which refer?   20
Through worlds unnumbered though the God be known,
'Tis ours to trace him only in our own.
He, who through vast immensity can pierce,
See worlds on worlds compose one universe,
Observe how system into system runs,   25
What other planets circle other suns,
What varied Being peoples every star,
May tell why Heaven has made us as we are.
But of this frame the bearings, and the ties,
The strong connections, nice dependencies,   30
Gradations just, has thy pervading soul
Looked through? or can a part contain the whole?
    Is the great chain,[3] that draws all to agree,
And drawn supports, upheld by God, or thee?

    II. Presumptuous Man! the reason wouldst thou find,   35
Why formed so weak, so little, and so blind?
First, if thou canst, the harder reason guess,
Why formed no weaker, blinder, and no less?
Ask of thy mother earth, why oaks are made
Taller or stronger than the weeds they shade?   40
Or ask of yonder argent fields above,
Why Jove's satellites are less than JOVE?
    Of Systems possible, if 'tis confest.
That Wisdom infinite must form the best,
Where all must full[4] or not coherent be,   45
And all that rises, rise in due degree;
Then, in the scale of reasoning life, 'tis plain,
There must be, somewhere, such a rank as Man:
And all the question (wrangle e'er so long)
Is only this, if God has placed him wrong?   50
    Respecting Man, whatever wrong we call,
May, must be right, as relative to all.
In human works, though laboured on with pain,

2. Cf. Milton's *Paradise Lost* 1.26. Pope's theme is essentially the same as Milton's, and even the opening image of the garden reminds one of the earlier poet's Paradise.
3. A reference to the popular 18th-century notion of the Great Chain of Being, in which elements of the universe took their places in a hierarchy ranging from the lowest matter to God.
4. Theorists of the Great Chain of Being believed that there must be no gaps in the chain.

A thousand movements scarce one purpose gain;
In God's, one single can its end produce;   55
Yet serves to second too some other use.
So Man, who here seems principal alone,
Perhaps acts second to some sphere unknown,
Touches some wheel, or verges to some goal;
'Tis but a part we see, and not a whole.   60
    When the proud steed shall know why Man restrains
His fiery course, or drives him o'er the plains;
When the dull Ox, why now he breaks the clod,
Is now a victim, and now Egypt's God:
Then shall Man's pride and dullness comprehend   65
His actions', passions', being's use and end;
Why doing, suffering, checked, impelled; and why
This hour a slave, the next a deity.
    Then say not Man's imperfect, Heaven in fault;
Say rather, Man's as perfect as he ought: 70
His knowledge measured to his state and place;
His time a moment, and a point his space.
If to be perfect in a certain sphere,
What matter, soon or late, or here or there?
The blest to-day is as completely so,   75
As who began a thousand years ago.

    III. Heaven from all creatures hides the book of Fate,
All but the page prescribed, their present state:
From brutes what men, from men what spirits know:
Or who could suffer Being here below?   80
The lamb thy riot dooms to bleed to-day,
Had he thy Reason, would he skip and play?
Pleased to the last, he crops the flowery food,
And licks the hand just raised to shed his blood.
Oh blindness to the future! kindly given,   85
That each may fill the circle marked by Heaven:
Who sees with equal eye, as God of all,
A hero perish, or a sparrow fall,
Atoms or systems into ruin hurled,
And now a bubble burst, and now a world.   90
    Hope humbly then; with trembling pinions soar;
Wait the great teacher Death; and God adore.
What future bliss, he gives not thee to know,
But gives that Hope to be thy blessing now.
Hope springs eternal in the human breast: 95
Man never Is, but always To be blest:
The soul, uneasy and confined from home,
Rests and expatiates in a life to come.
    Lo, the poor Indian! whose untutored mind
Sees God in clouds, or hears him in the wind;   100
His soul, proud Science never taught to stray
Far as the solar walk, or milky way;
Yet simple Nature to his hope has given,

Behind the cloud-topt hill, an humbler heaven;
Some safer world in depth of woods embraced,   105
Some happier island in the watery waste,
Where slaves once more their native land behold,
No fiends torment, no Christians thirst for gold.
To Be, contents his natural desire,
He asks no Angel's wing, no Seraph's fire;   110
But thinks, admitted to that equal sky,
His faithful dog shall bear him company.

    IV. Go, wiser thou! and, in thy scale of sense,
Weigh thy Opinion against Providence;
Call imperfection what thou fanciest such,   115
Say, here he gives too little, there too much:
Destroy all Creatures for thy sport or gust,
Yet cry, If Man's unhappy, God's unjust;
If Man alone engross not Heaven's high care,
Alone made perfect here, immortal there: 120
Snatch from his hand the balance and the rod,
Re-judge his justice, be the GOD of GOD.
In Pride, in reasoning Pride, our error lies;
All quit their sphere, and rush into the skies.
Pride still is aiming at the blest abodes,   125
Men would be Angels, Angels would be Gods.
Aspiring to be Gods, if Angels fell,
Aspiring to be Angels, Men rebel:
And who but wishes to invert the laws
Of ORDER, sins against the Eternal Cause.   130

    V. Ask for what end the heavenly bodies shine,
Earth for whose use? Pride answers, "'Tis for mine:
For me kind Nature wakes her genial Power,
Suckles each herb, and spreads out ev'ry flower;
Annual for me, the grape, the rose, renew,   135
The juice nectareous, and the balmy dew;
For me, the mine a thousand treasures brings;
For me, health gushes from a thousand springs;
Seas roll to waft me, suns to light me rise;
My footstool earth, my canopy the skies."   140
    But errs not Nature from this gracious end,
From burning suns when livid deaths descend,
When earthquakes swallow, or when tempests sweep
Towns to one grave, whole nations to the deep?
"No," 'tis replied, "the first Almighty Cause   145
Acts not by partial, but by general laws;
The exceptions few; some change since all began:
And what created perfect?"—Why then Man?
If the great end be human happiness,
Then Nature deviates; and can man do less?   150
As much that end a constant course requires
Of showers and sunshine, as of man's desires;

As much eternal springs and cloudless skies,
As Men forever temperate, calm, and wise.
If plagues or earthquakes break not Heaven's design, 155
Why then a Borgia, or a Catiline?[5]
Who knows but He whose hand the lightning forms,
Who heaves old Ocean, and who wings the storms;
Pours fierce Ambition in a Caesar's mind,
Or turns young Ammon[6] loose to scourge mankind? 160
From pride, from pride, our very reasoning springs;
Account for moral, as for natural things:
Why charge we Heaven in those, in these acquit?
In both, to reason right is to submit.
 Better for Us, perhaps, it might appear, 165
Where there all harmony, all virtue here;
That never air or ocean felt the wind;
That never passion discomposed the mind.
But ALL subsists by elemental strife;
And Passions are the elements of Life. 170
The general ORDER, since the whole began,
Is kept in Nature, and is kept in Man.

 VI. What would this Man? Now upward will he soar,
And little less than Angel, would be more;
Now looking downwards, just as grieved appears 175
To want the strength of bulls, the fur of bears.
Made for his use all creatures if he call,
Say what their use, had he the powers of all?
Nature to these, without profusion, kind,
The proper organs, proper powers assigned; 180
Each seeming want compénsated of course,
Here with degrees of swiftness, there of force;
All in exact proportion to the state;
Nothing to add, and nothing to abate.
Each beast, each insect, happy in its own: 185
Is Heaven unkind to Man, and Man alone?
Shall he alone, whom rational we call,
Be pleased with nothing, if not blessed with all?
 The bliss of Man (could Pride that blessing find)
Is not to act or think beyond mankind; 190
No powers of body or of soul to share,
But what his nature and his state can bear.
Why has not Man a microscopic eye?
For this plain reason, Man is not a Fly.
Say what the use, were finer optics[7] given, 195
T' inspect a mite, not comprehend the heaven?

5. Roman who conspired against the state in 63 B.C.E. Cesare Borgia (1476–1507), an Italian prince notorious for his crimes.
6. Alexander the Great, who when he visited the oracle of Zeus Ammon in Egypt was hailed by the priest there as son of the god.
7. Eyes.

Or touch, if tremblingly alive all o'er,
To smart and agonize at every pore?
Or quick effluvia[8] darting through the brain,
Die of a rose in aromatic pain?   200
If nature thundered in his opening ears,
And stunned him with the music of the spheres,[9]
How would he wish that Heaven had left him still
The whispering Zephyr, and the purling rill?
Who finds not Providence all good and wise,   205
Alike in what it gives, and what denies?

    VII. Far as Creation's ample range extends,
The scale of sensual, mental powers ascends:
Mark how it mounts, to Man's imperial race,
From the green myriads in the peopled grass: 210
What modes of sight betwixt each wide extreme,
The mole's dim curtain, and the lynx's[1] beam:
Of smell, the headlong lioness between,
And hound sagacious[2] on the tainted green:
Of hearing, from the life that fills the Flood,   215
To that which warbles through the vernal wood:
The spider's touch, how exquisitely fine!
Feels at each thread, and lives along the line:
In the nice bee, what sense so subtly true
From poisonous herbs extracts the healing dew?   220
How Instinct varies in the grovelling swine,
Compared, half-reasoning elephant, with thine!
'Twixt that, and Reason, what a nice barriér,
For ever separate, yet for ever near!
Remembrance and Reflection how allied;   225
What thin partitions Sense from Thought divide:
And Middle natures,[3] how they long to join,
Yet never pass the insuperable line!
Without this just gradation, could they be
Subjected, these to those, or all to thee?   230
The powers of all subdued by thee alone,
Is not thy Reason all these powers in one?

    VIII. See, through this air, this ocean, and this earth,
All matter quick, and bursting into birth.
Above, how high, progressive life may go!   235
Around, how wide! how deep extend below!
Vast chain of Being! which from God began,
Natures ethereal, human, angel, man,

8. Stream of minute particles.
9. The old notion that the movement of the planets created a "higher" music.
1. According to legend, one of the keenest sighted animals. "Dim curtain": the mole's poor vision.
2. Here, exceptionally quick of scent.
3. Animals that seem to share the characteristics of several different classes, e.g., the duck-billed platypus.

Beast, bird, fish, insect, what no eye can see,
No glass can reach; from Infinite to thee,   240
From thee to Nothing.—On superior powers
Were we to press, inferior might on ours:
Or in the full creation leave a void,
Where, one step broken, the great scale's destroyed:
From Nature's chain whatever link you strike,   245
Tenth or ten thousandth, breaks the chain alike.
     And, if each system in gradation roll
Alike essential to the amazing Whole,
The least confusion but in one, not all
That system only, but the Whole must fall.   250
Let Earth unbalanced from her orbit fly,
Planets and Suns run lawless through the sky;
Let ruling angels from their spheres be hurled,
Being on Being wrecked, and world on world;
Heaven's whole foundations to their center nod,   255
And Nature tremble to the throne of God.
All this dread ORDER break—for whom? for thee?
Vile worm!—oh Madness! Pride! Impiety!

     IX. What if the foot, ordained the dust to tread,
Or hand, to toil, aspired to be the head?   260
What if the head, the eye, or ear repined
To serve mere engines to the ruling Mind?
Just as absurd for any part to claim
To be another, in this general frame:
Just as absurd, to mourn the tasks or pains,   265
The great directing MIND of ALL ordains.
     All are but parts of one stupendous whole,
Whose body Nature is, and God the soul;
That, changed through all, and yet in all the same;
Great in the earth, as in the ethereal frame;   270
Warms in the sun, refreshes in the breeze,
Glows in the stars, and blossoms in the trees,
Lives through all life, extends through all extent,
Spreads undivided, operates unspent;
Breathes in our soul, informs our mortal part,   275
As full, as perfect, in a hair as heart;
As full, as perfect, in vile Man that mourns,
As the rapt Seraph that adores and burns:
To him no high, no low, no great, no small;
He fills, he bounds, connects, and equals all.   280

     X. Cease then, nor ORDER imperfection name:
Our proper bliss depends on what we blame.
Know thy own point: this kind, this due degree
Of blindness, weakness, Heaven bestows on thee.
Submit.—In this, or any other sphere,   285
Secure to be as blest as thou canst bear:
Safe in the hand of one disposing Power,

Or in the natal, or the mortal hour.
All Nature is but Art, unknown to thee;
All Chance, Direction, which thou canst not see;   290
All Discord, Harmony not understood;
All partial Evil, universal Good:
And, spite of Pride, in erring Reason's spite,
One truth is clear, WHATEVER IS, IS RIGHT.[4]

4. Epistle II deals with "the Nature and State of Man with respect to himself, as an Individual"; Epistle III examines "the Nature and State of Man with respect to Society"; and the last epistle concerns "the Nature and State of Man with Respect to Happiness."

VOLTAIRE
(FRANÇOIS-MARIE AROUET)
1694–1778

I magine a writer so outspoken and so fearless that although his work landed him in prison and in exile— more than once—he never stopped writing defiantly. If he could not publish his work openly, he would have it printed secretly and smuggled across borders. If he could not circulate it by the post, he would have it hand-carried in suitcases and distributed by trusted friends. He seized freedom of speech even when it was not granted to him, and he used it to mock corrupt priests and self-regarding kings. The sheer gutsiness of Voltaire is breathtaking. In an atmosphere of stern censorship and absolute power, he managed to live to the ripe age of eighty-three, writing lively denunciations of dominant orthodoxies and powerful authorities almost every day. And his darkly comic imagination propelled him to enormous fame. He was so successful that he grew richer than many kings in Europe.

His witty, light prose, and his clear and accessible style allowed him to popularize many of the revolutionary goals of the Enlightenment—human rights, the value of freedom and tolerance, the hope for progress through reasoned debate, and the urgent desire to end human suffering where we can. It is in no small part thanks to Voltaire that these ideals shape our own political landscape today.

LIFE AND TIMES

Bold, witty, and rebellious, François-Marie Arouet was a trouble to his parents as a child and became a trouble to the authorities for the rest of his life. He was born near Paris in 1694 to a middle-class family. At the age of ten he went to a boarding school run by Jesuits, where he developed an enthusiasm for literature and a passionate opposition to organized religion. His father wanted him to pursue a career in law, but he soon gave it up to write poetry and plays. So sparkling and brilliant was his conversation that he won powerful friends, but his propensity for satire also brought him enemies, and an attack on the acting head of state got him locked in the Bastille prison in Paris for almost a year. While there, he committed himself to writing, and his first play, *Oedipus*, turned into a huge success, bringing him considerable wealth and establishing his reputation.

The young writer, who was now known by his pen name, "Voltaire," spent three years in exile in England after a quarrel with a French nobleman. There he met the writers Jonathan Swift and **Alexander Pope**. He enjoyed the freedom from censorship and punishment allowed to writers in England, and returned to France with an even stronger sense of his right to dissent and oppose authority. His many subversive writings, called by the authorities "most dangerous to religion and civil order," earned him another spell of exile from Paris, which he spent with his longtime mistress and intellectual companion Madame du Châtelet. In 1750, Voltaire moved to Potsdam, in Prussia, where he joined the court of the young King Frederick, later to be known as Frederick the Great, who loved the arts and wanted philosophy and literature to flourish. Voltaire, like many other Enlightenment thinkers, did not see democracy as the best form of government. The masses seemed to him to impede reason, freedom, and progress (he said he would "rather obey one lion than 200 rats"). The regime he idealized was the enlightened despot—a sensitive, rational king who welcomed dissent and sought the counsel of philosophers like himself. Early on, Frederick promised to live up to that ideal, but Voltaire was soon to be disappointed. He and Frederick argued; Frederick

waged violent warfare and asserted power high-handedly. Voltaire was invited to leave.

He took up residence for the rest of his life at Ferney, a town on the border between France and Switzerland, so that he could escape from France easily if necessary. It was here that he wrote the best-selling *Candide*—and a great deal more. Travelers and visitors brought suitcases filled with Voltaire's "scandal-sheets" back with them to Paris where the public eagerly gobbled them up. He repeatedly attacked religious extremism and stultifying tradition and argued for universal human rights. And he refused the traditional literary goal of immortality, casting his writing as a response to current debates and events.

Voltaire was no atheist (he once said that "if God did not exist it would be necessary to invent him"). His own religion is usually known as Deism; that is, faith in a God who created the world and then stands back, allowing nature to follow its own laws and never intervening. The Deists' signature metaphor was God as a watchmaker: the world he made was a mechanism, which then ticked away on its own. As far as human beings were concerned, God gave them reason, and then left them free to use it. Deists disagreed about whether God had instilled human beings with a love of virtue, and whether there was an afterlife of rewards and punishments. Voltaire claimed that it was impossible for humans to know anything beyond their senses—so God's will must remain mysterious—and he believed that humans should use their senses and their reason to understand how the world works and, to the best of our ability, to make it better.

By the time of Voltaire's death, he had become a national hero. In all, he had produced enough work to fill 135 volumes, in a range of genres including tragedy, epic, philosophy, history, fiction, and journalism. In death as in life, he continued to generate scandal and division. Clergy in Paris refused to let him be buried in hallowed ground, so friends smuggled his body out of the city—propping it up on the journey like a sleeping passenger—and brought it to a monastery to be laid to rest. Later, leaders of the French Revolution, who had been inspired by Voltaire's attacks on authority and religion, had his body exhumed and reburied in Paris to huge national fanfare.

WORK

Voltaire wrote *Candide* in part as a response to a piece of news that shook him, and many of his contemporaries, badly. On November 1, 1755, a devastating earthquake hit Lisbon, in Portugal. Upwards of thirty thousand people died. Voltaire, writing almost obsessively about this tragedy in his letters, wondered how anyone could make a case for an optimistic philosophy in light of it. He worried over Alexander Pope's assertion in his *Essay on Man* that "Whatever is, is right." Could anyone really believe that this was God's will—that a just and rational God had created this world and that it was, in the words of the German philosopher Gottfried Wilhelm Leibniz, "the best of all possible worlds"? Voltaire's absurd philosopher Pangloss ("all-tongue") is a caricature of Leibniz.

Though philosophical, *Candide* is so brief and so easy to read that it was immediately popular with a wide range of readers. Voltaire deliberately opted for short, cheap, excitingly readable texts. Long works "will never make a revolution," he argued, and wrote that "if the New Testament had cost 4,200 sesterces, the Christian religion would never have taken root." Thus *Candide's* brevity may be seen as part of its power.

It is also deliberately entertaining. Voltaire combines a lively appetite for humor with a horrifying sense of the real existence of evil. The exuberance and extravagance of the sufferings characters undergo may even prompt us to laugh: the plight of the old woman whose buttock has been cut off to make rump steak for her starving companions, the weeping of two girls whose monkey-lovers have been killed, the glum circumstances of six exiled, poverty-stricken kings. But Voltaire also manages to keep his readers off balance. Raped, cut to pieces, hanged, stabbed in the belly, the central characters of *Candide* keep coming back to life at opportune moments, as though no disaster could have permanent effects. Such reassuring fantasy at first suggests that it is all a joke, designed to ridicule an outmoded philosophical system. And yet, reality keeps intruding. An admiral really did face a firing squad and die for failing to engage an enemy ferociously enough. Those six hungry kings were actual historical figures who were dispossessed. The Lisbon earthquake was so real that it haunted Voltaire for years. And his satirical pen attacks genuine social problems as various as military discipline, class hierarchy, greed, religious extremism, slavery, and even the publishing industry. The extravagances of the story are therefore uncomfortably matched by the extravagances of real life, and despite the comic lightness of the telling, Voltaire demands that the reader confront these horrors.

The fantastic and exaggerated nature of the events stands out against the simplicity of the narrative style. Candide is a naive traveler who does not grasp the ironies he witnesses. He travels widely, taking in Europe, South America, and the Ottoman Empire, where Catholics, Protestants, and Muslims all emerge as cruel and hypocritical. The only exception is the mythical Eldorado, which takes place almost exactly at the half-way point of the text, where corruption, crime, malice, and poverty do not exist. Candide nonetheless insists on leaving Eldorado to find his beloved Cunégonde. Readers have often wondered about the role of this paradise in an otherwise bleak picture of human experience: does Eldorado suggest that human beings are capable of virtue, and if so, then why does Voltaire compel his protagonist to leave? Is it too stagnant, too isolated, too dull? Is it like the Garden of Eden, a paradise no longer home to fallen humanity? The fact that Candide admires Milton's *Paradise Lost* and that the novella concludes with the protagonist cultivating a garden suggests that Voltaire may have been rethinking the story of Adam and Eve in his own imaginative way.

Candide encapsulated the many problems that stoked Voltaire's anger and fed his satire: absolutism and religious bigotry, unnecessary bloodshed, restrictions on freedom of speech and religion, and the intolerable reality of human suffering. This story has always been the most famous work of its author's incalculably influential career. Voltaire inspired leaders of the American Revolution—Thomas Jefferson, Thomas Paine, and Benjamin Franklin—and helped to shape the United States Constitution. The French Revolutionaries held Voltaire up as a hero, as did generations fighting against religious intolerance. He was hotly reviled by those who wanted to maintain the authority of established churches, and some went so far as to call him the Antichrist. But in the centuries that have followed, Voltaire's ideas have become part of the common fabric of our ideals.

Candide, or Optimism[1]

translated from the German of Doctor Ralph with the additions which were found in the Doctor's pocket when he died at Minden in the Year of Our Lord 1759

CHAPTER I

How Candide Was Brought up in a Fine Castle and How He Was Driven Therefrom

There lived in Westphalia,[2] in the castle of the Baron of Thunder-Ten-Tronckh, a young man on whom nature had bestowed the perfection of gentle manners. His features admirably expressed his soul; he combined an honest mind with great simplicity of heart; and I think it was for this reason that they called him Candide. The old servants of the house suspected that he was the son of the Baron's sister by a respectable, honest gentleman of the neighborhood, whom she had refused to marry because he could prove only seventy-one quarterings,[3] the rest of his family tree having been lost in the passage of time.

---

1. Translated and with notes by Robert M. Adams.
2. A province of western Germany, near Holland and the lower Rhineland. Flat, boggy, and drab, it is noted chiefly for its excellent ham. In a letter to his niece, written during his German expedition of 1750, Voltaire described the "vast, sad, sterile, detestable countryside of Westphalia."
3. Genealogical divisions of one's family tree. Seventy-one of them is a grotesque number to have, representing something over 2,000 years of uninterrupted nobility.

The Baron was one of the most mighty lords of Westphalia, for his castle had a door and windows. His great hall was even hung with a tapestry. The dogs of his courtyard made up a hunting pack on occasion, with the stable-boys as huntsmen; the village priest was his grand almoner. They all called him "My Lord," and laughed at his stories.

The Baroness, who weighed in the neighborhood of three hundred and fifty pounds, was greatly respected for that reason, and did the honors of the house with a dignity which rendered her even more imposing. Her daughter Cunégonde,[4] aged seventeen, was a ruddy-cheeked girl, fresh, plump, and desirable. The Baron's son seemed in every way worthy of his father. The tutor Pangloss was the oracle of the household, and little Candide listened to his lectures with all the good faith of his age and character.

Pangloss gave instruction in metaphysico-theologico-cosmoloonigology.[5] He proved admirably that there cannot possibly be an effect without a cause and that in this best of all possible worlds the Baron's castle was the best of all castles and his wife the best of all possible Baronesses.

—It is clear, said he, that things cannot be otherwise than they are, for since everything is made to serve an end, everything necessarily serves the best end. Observe: noses were made to support spectacles, hence we have spectacles. Legs, as anyone can plainly see, were made to be breeched, and so we have breeches. Stones were made to be shaped and to build castles with; thus My Lord has a fine castle, for the greatest Baron in the province should have the finest house; and since pigs were made to be eaten, we eat pork all year round.[6] Consequently, those who say everything is well are uttering mere stupidities; they should say everything is for the best.

Candide listened attentively and believed implicitly; for he found Miss Cunégonde exceedingly pretty, though he never had the courage to tell her so. He decided that after the happiness of being born Baron of Thunder-Ten-Tronckh, the second order of happiness was to be Miss Cunégonde; the third was seeing her every day, and the fourth was listening to Master Pangloss, the greatest philosopher in the province and consequently in the entire world.

One day, while Cunégonde was walking near the castle in the little woods that they called a park, she saw Dr. Pangloss in the underbrush; he was giving a lesson in experimental physics to her mother's maid, a very attractive and obedient brunette. As Miss Cunégonde had a natural bent for the sciences, she watched breathlessly the repeated experiments which were going on; she saw clearly the doctor's sufficient reason, observed both cause and effect, and returned to the house in a distracted and pensive frame of mind, yearning for knowledge and dreaming that she might be the sufficient reason of young Candide—who might also be hers.

As she was returning to the castle, she met Candide, and blushed; Candide blushed too. She greeted him in a faltering tone of voice; and Candide talked to

4. Cunégonde gets her odd name from Kunigunda (wife to Emperor Henry II) who walked barefoot and blindfolded on red-hot irons to prove her chastity; Pangloss gets his name from Greek words meaning "all-tongue."
5. The "looney" buried in this burlesque word corresponds to a buried *nigaud*—"booby" in the French. Christian Wolff, disciple of Leibniz, invented and popularized the word "cosmology." The catch phrases in the following sentence, echoed by popularizers of Leibniz, make reference to the determinism of his system, its linking of cause with effect, and its optimism.
6. The argument from design supposes that everything in this world exists for a specific reason; Voltaire objects not to the argument as a whole, but to the abuse of it.

her without knowing what he was saying. Next day, as everyone was rising from the dinner table, Cunégonde and Candide found themselves behind a screen; Cunégonde dropped her handkerchief, Candide picked it up; she held his hand quite innocently, he kissed her hand quite innocently with remarkable vivacity and emotion; their lips met, their eyes lit up, their knees trembled, their hands wandered. The Baron of Thunder-Ten-Tronckh passed by the screen and, taking note of this cause and this effect, drove Candide out of the castle by kicking him vigorously on the backside. Cunégonde fainted; as soon as she recovered, the Baroness slapped her face; and everything was confusion in the most beautiful and agreeable of all possible castles.

CHAPTER 2

What Happened to Candide Among the Bulgars[7]

Candide, ejected from the earthly paradise, wandered for a long time without knowing where he was going, weeping, raising his eyes to heaven, and gazing back frequently on the most beautiful of castles which contained the most beautiful of Baron's daughters. He slept without eating, in a furrow of a plowed field, while the snow drifted over him; next morning, numb with cold, he dragged himself into the neighboring village, which was called Waldberghoff-trarbk-dikdorff; he was penniless, famished, and exhausted. At the door of a tavern he paused forlornly. Two men dressed in blue[8] took note of him:

—Look, chum, said one of them, there's a likely young fellow of just about the right size.

They approached Candide and invited him very politely to dine with them.

—Gentlemen, Candide replied with charming modesty, I'm honored by your invitation, but I really don't have enough money to pay my share.

—My dear sir, said one of the blues, people of your appearance and your merit don't have to pay; aren't you five feet five inches tall?

—Yes, gentlemen, that is indeed my stature, said he, making a bow.

—Then, sir, you must be seated at once; not only will we pay your bill this time, we will never allow a man like you to be short of money; for men were made only to render one another mutual aid.

—You are quite right, said Candide; it is just as Dr. Pangloss always told me, and I see clearly that everything is for the best.

They beg him to accept a couple of crowns, he takes them, and offers an I.O.U.; they won't hear of it, and all sit down at table together.

—Don't you love dearly . . . ?

—I do indeed, says he, I dearly love Miss Cunégonde.

—No, no, says one of the gentlemen, we are asking if you don't love dearly the King of the Bulgars.

—Not in the least, says he, I never laid eyes on him.

—What's that you say? He's the most charming of kings, and we must drink his health.

---

7. Voltaire chose this name to represent the Prussian troops of Frederick the Great because he wanted to make an insinuation of pederasty against both the soldiers and their master. Cf. French *bougre*, English "bugger."

8. The recruiting officers of Frederick the Great, much feared in 18th-century Europe, wore blue uniforms. Frederick had a passion for sorting out his soldiers by size; several of his regiments would accept only six-footers.

—Oh, gladly, gentlemen; and he drinks.

—That will do, they tell him; you are now the bulwark, the support, the defender, the hero of the Bulgars; your fortune is made and your future assured.

Promptly they slip irons on his legs and lead him to the regiment. There they cause him to right face, left face, present arms, order arms, aim, fire, doubletime, and they give him thirty strokes of the rod. Next day he does the drill a little less awkwardly and gets only twenty strokes; the third day, they give him only ten, and he is regarded by his comrades as a prodigy.

Candide, quite thunderstruck, did not yet understand very clearly how he was a hero. One fine spring morning he took it into his head to go for a walk, stepping straight out as if it were a privilege of the human race, as of animals in general, to use his legs as he chose.[9] He had scarcely covered two leagues when four other heroes, each six feet tall, overtook him, bound him, and threw him into a dungeon. At the court-martial they asked which he preferred, to be flogged thirty-six times by the entire regiment or to receive summarily a dozen bullets in the brain. In vain did he argue that the human will is free and insist that he preferred neither alternative; he had to choose; by virtue of the divine gift called "liberty" he decided to run the gauntlet thirty-six times, and actually endured two floggings. The regiment was composed of two thousand men. That made four thousand strokes, which laid open every muscle and nerve from his nape to his butt. As they were preparing for the third beating, Candide, who could endure no more, begged as a special favor that they would have the goodness to smash his head. His plea was granted; they bandaged his eyes and made him kneel down. The King of the Bulgars, passing by at this moment, was told of the culprit's crime; and as this king had a rare genius, he understood, from everything they told him of Candide, that this was a young metaphysician, extremely ignorant of the ways of the world, so he granted his royal pardon, with a generosity which will be praised in every newspaper in every age. A worthy surgeon cured Candide in three weeks with the ointments described by Dioscorides.[1] He already had a bit of skin back and was able to walk when the King of the Bulgars went to war with the King of the Abares.[2]

CHAPTER 3

How Candide Escaped from the Bulgars, and What Became of Him

Nothing could have been so fine, so brisk, so brilliant, so well-drilled as the two armies. The trumpets, the fifes, the oboes, the drums, and the cannon produced such a harmony as was never heard in hell. First the cannons battered down about six thousand men on each side; then volleys of musket fire removed from

9. This episode was suggested by the experience of a Frenchman named Courtilz, who had deserted from the Prussian army and been bastinadoed for it. Voltaire intervened with Frederick to gain his release. But it also reflects the story that Wolff, Leibniz's disciple, got into trouble with Frederick's father when someone reported that his doctrine denying free will had encouraged several soldiers to desert. "The argument of the grenadier," who was said to have pleaded preestablished harmony to justify his desertion, so infuriated the king that he had Wolff expelled from the country.

1. Dioscorides' treatise on *materia medica*, dating from the 1st century C.E., was not the most up to date.

2. A tribe of semicivilized Scythians, who might be supposed at war with the Bulgars; allegorically, the Abares are the French, who opposed the Prussians in the Seven Years' War (1756–63). According to the title page of 1761, "Doctor Ralph," the dummy author of *Candide*, himself perished at the battle of Minden (Westphalia) in 1759.

the best of worlds about nine or ten thousand rascals who were cluttering up its surface. The bayonet was a sufficient reason for the demise of several thousand others. Total casualties might well amount to thirty thousand men or so. Candide, who was trembling like a philosopher, hid himself as best he could while this heroic butchery was going on.

Finally, while the two kings in their respective camps celebrated the victory by having *Te Deums* sung, Candide undertook to do his reasoning of cause and effect somewhere else. Passing by mounds of the dead and dying, he came to a nearby village which had been burnt to the ground. It was an Abare village, which the Bulgars had burned, in strict accordance with the laws of war. Here old men, stunned from beatings, watched the last agonies of their butchered wives, who still clutched their infants to their bleeding breasts; there, disemboweled girls, who had first satisfied the natural needs of various heroes, breathed their last; others, half-scorched in the flames, begged for their death stroke. Scattered brains and severed limbs littered the ground.

Candide fled as fast as he could to another village; this one belonged to the Bulgars, and the heroes of the Abare cause had given it the same treatment. Climbing over ruins and stumbling over corpses, Candide finally made his way out of the war area, carrying a little food in his knapsack and never ceasing to dream of Miss Cunégonde. His supplies gave out when he reached Holland; but having heard that everyone in that country was rich and a Christian, he felt confident of being treated as well as he had been in the castle of the Baron before he was kicked out for the love of Miss Cunégonde.

He asked alms of several grave personages, who all told him that if he continued to beg, he would be shut up in a house of correction and set to hard labor.

Finally he approached a man who had just been talking to a large crowd for an hour on end; the topic was charity. Looking doubtfully at him, the orator demanded:

—What are you doing here? Are you here to serve the good cause?

—There is no effect without a cause, said Candide modestly; all events are linked by the chain of necessity and arranged for the best. I had to be driven away from Miss Cunégonde, I had to run the gauntlet, I have to beg my bread until I can earn it; none of this could have happened otherwise.

—Look here, friend, said the orator, do you think the Pope is Antichrist?[3]

—I haven't considered the matter, said Candide; but whether he is or not, I'm in need of bread.

—You don't deserve any, said the other; away with you, you rascal, you rogue, never come near me as long as you live.

Meanwhile, the orator's wife had put her head out of the window, and, seeing a man who was not sure the Pope was Antichrist, emptied over his head a pot full of————Scandalous! The excesses into which women are led by religious zeal!

A man who had never been baptized, a good Anabaptist[4] named Jacques, saw this cruel and heartless treatment being inflicted on one of his fellow creatures, a

---

3. Voltaire is satirizing extreme Protestant sects that have sometimes seemed to make hatred of Rome the sum and substance of their creed.
4. Holland, as the home of religious liberty, had offered asylum to the Anabaptists, whose radical views on property and religious discipline had made them unpopular during the 16th century. Granted tolerance, they settled down into respectable burghers. Since this behavior confirmed some of Voltaire's major theses, he had a high opinion of contemporary Anabaptists.

featherless biped possessing a soul;[5] he took Candide home with him, washed him off, gave him bread and beer, presented him with two florins, and even undertook to give him a job in his Persian-rug factory—for these items are widely manufactured in Holland. Candide, in an ecstasy of gratitude, cried out:

—Master Pangloss was right indeed when he told me everything is for the best in this world; for I am touched by your kindness far more than by the harshness of that black-coated gentleman and his wife.

Next day, while taking a stroll about town, he met a beggar who was covered with pustules, his eyes were sunken, the end of his nose rotted off, his mouth twisted, his teeth black, he had a croaking voice and a hacking cough, and spat a tooth every time he tried to speak.

CHAPTER 4

How Candide Met His Old Philosophy Tutor, Doctor Pangloss, and What Came of It

Candide, more touched by compassion even than by horror, gave this ghastly beggar the two florins that he himself had received from his honest Anabaptist friend Jacques. The phantom stared at him, burst into tears, and fell on his neck. Candide drew back in terror.

—Alas, said one wretch to the other, don't you recognize your dear Pangloss any more?

—What are you saying? You, my dear master! you, in this horrible condition? What misfortune has befallen you? Why are you no longer in the most beautiful of castles? What has happened to Miss Cunégonde, that pearl among young ladies, that masterpiece of Nature?

—I am perishing, said Pangloss.

Candide promptly led him into the Anabaptist's stable, where he gave him a crust of bread, and when he had recovered:—Well, said he, Cunégonde?

—Dead, said the other.

Candide fainted. His friend brought him around with a bit of sour vinegar which happened to be in the stable. Candide opened his eyes.

—Cunégonde, dead! Ah, best of worlds, what's become of you now? But how did she die? It wasn't of grief at seeing me kicked out of her noble father's elegant castle?

—Not at all, said Pangloss; she was disemboweled by the Bulgar soldiers, after having been raped to the absolute limit of human endurance; they smashed the Baron's head when he tried to defend her, cut the Baroness to bits, and treated my poor pupil exactly like his sister. As for the castle, not one stone was left on another, not a shed, not a sheep, not a duck, not a tree; but we had the satisfaction of revenge, for the Abares did exactly the same thing to a nearby barony belonging to a Bulgar nobleman.

At this tale Candide fainted again; but having returned to his senses and said everything appropriate to the occasion, he asked about the cause and effect, the sufficient reason, which had reduced Pangloss to his present pitiful state.

—Alas, said he, it was love; love, the consolation of the human race, the preservative of the universe, the soul of all sensitive beings, love, gentle love.

5. Plato's famous minimal definition of man, which he corrected by the addition of a soul to distinguish man from a plucked chicken.

—Unhappy man, said Candide, I too have had some experience of this love, the sovereign of hearts, the soul of our souls; and it never got me anything but a single kiss and twenty kicks in the rear. How could this lovely cause produce in you such a disgusting effect?

Pangloss replied as follows:—My dear Candide! you knew Paquette, that pretty maidservant to our august Baroness. In her arms I tasted the delights of paradise, which directly caused these torments of hell, from which I am now suffering. She was infected with the disease, and has perhaps died of it. Paquette received this present from an erudite Franciscan, who took the pains to trace it back to its source; for he had it from an elderly countess, who picked it up from a captain of cavalry, who acquired it from a marquise, who caught it from a page, who had received it from a Jesuit, who during his novitiate got it directly from one of the companions of Christopher Columbus. As for me, I shall not give it to anyone, for I am a dying man.

—Oh, Pangloss, cried Candide, that's a very strange genealogy. Isn't the devil at the root of the whole thing?

—Not at all, replied that great man; it's an indispensable part of the best of worlds, a necessary ingredient; if Columbus had not caught, on an American island, this sickness which attacks the source of generation and sometimes prevents generation entirely—which thus strikes at and defeats the greatest end of Nature herself—we should have neither chocolate nor cochineal. It must also be noted that until the present time this malady, like religious controversy, has been wholly confined to the continent of Europe. Turks, Indians, Persians, Chinese, Siamese, and Japanese know nothing of it as yet; but there is a sufficient reason for which they in turn will make its acquaintance in a couple of centuries. Meanwhile, it has made splendid progress among us, especially among those big armies of honest, well-trained mercenaries who decide the destinies of nations. You can be sure that when thirty thousand men fight a pitched battle against the same number of the enemy, there will be about twenty thousand with the pox on either side.

—Remarkable indeed, said Candide, but we must see about curing you.

—And how can I do that, said Pangloss, seeing I don't have a cent to my name? There's not a doctor in the whole world who will let your blood or give you an enema without demanding a fee. If you can't pay yourself, you must find someone to pay for you.

These last words decided Candide; he hastened to implore the help of his charitable Anabaptist, Jacques, and painted such a moving picture of his friend's wretched state that the good man did not hesitate to take in Pangloss and have him cured at his own expense. In the course of the cure, Pangloss lost only an eye and an ear. Since he wrote a fine hand and knew arithmetic, the Anabaptist made him his bookkeeper. At the end of two months, being obliged to go to Lisbon on business, he took his two philosophers on the boat with him. Pangloss still maintained that everything was for the best, but Jacques didn't agree with him.

—It must be, said he, that men have corrupted Nature, for they are not born wolves, yet that is what they become. God gave them neither twenty-four-pound cannon nor bayonets, yet they have manufactured both in order to destroy themselves. Bankruptcies have the same effect, and so does the justice which seizes the goods of bankrupts in order to prevent the creditors from getting them.[6]

---

6. Voltaire had suffered losses from various bankruptcy proceedings.

—It was all indispensable, replied the one-eyed doctor, since private misfortunes make for public welfare, and therefore the more private misfortunes there are, the better everything is.

While he was reasoning, the air grew dark, the winds blew from all directions, and the vessel was attacked by a horrible tempest within sight of Lisbon harbor.

CHAPTER 5

Tempest, Shipwreck, Earthquake, and What Happened to Doctor Pangloss, Candide, and the Anabaptist, Jacques

Half of the passengers, weakened by the frightful anguish of seasickness and the distress of tossing about on stormy waters, were incapable of noticing their danger. The other half shrieked aloud and fell to their prayers, the sails were ripped to shreds, the masts snapped, the vessel opened at the seams. Everyone worked who could stir, nobody listened for orders or issued them. The Anabaptist was lending a hand in the after part of the ship when a frantic sailor struck him and knocked him to the deck; but just at that moment, the sailor lurched so violently that he fell head first over the side, where he hung, clutching a fragment of the broken mast. The good Jacques ran to his aid, and helped him to climb back on board, but in the process was himself thrown into the sea under the very eyes of the sailor, who allowed him to drown without even glancing at him. Candide rushed to the rail, and saw his benefactor rise for a moment to the surface, then sink forever. He wanted to dive to his rescue; but the philosopher Pangloss prevented him by proving that the bay of Lisbon had been formed expressly for this Anabaptist to drown in. While he was proving the point *a priori*, the vessel opened up and everyone perished except for Pangloss, Candide, and the brutal sailor who had caused the virtuous Anabaptist to drown; this rascal swam easily to shore, while Pangloss and Candide drifted there on a plank.

When they had recovered a bit of energy, they set out for Lisbon; they still had a little money with which they hoped to stave off hunger after escaping the storm.

Scarcely had they set foot in the town, still bewailing the loss of their benefactor, when they felt the earth quake underfoot; the sea was lashed to a froth, burst into the port, and smashed all the vessels lying at anchor there. Whirlwinds of fire and ash swirled through the streets and public squares; houses crumbled, roofs came crashing down on foundations, foundations split; thirty thousand inhabitants of every age and either sex were crushed in the ruins.[7] The sailor whistled through his teeth, and said with an oath:—There'll be something to pick up here.

—What can be the sufficient reason of this phenomenon? asked Pangloss.

—The Last Judgment is here, cried Candide.

But the sailor ran directly into the middle of the ruins, heedless of danger in his eagerness for gain; he found some money, laid violent hands on it, got drunk, and, having slept off his wine, bought the favors of the first streetwalker he could

---

7. The great Lisbon earthquake and fire occurred on November 1, 1755; between thirty and forty thousand deaths resulted.

find amid the ruins of smashed houses, amid corpses and suffering victims on every hand. Pangloss however tugged at his sleeve.

—My friend, said he, this is not good form at all; your behavior falls short of that required by the universal reason; it's untimely, to say the least.

—Bloody hell, said the other, I'm a sailor, born in Batavia; I've been four times to Japan and stamped four times on the crucifix;[8] get out of here with your universal reason.

Some falling stonework had struck Candide; he lay prostrate in the street, covered with rubble, and calling to Pangloss:—For pity's sake bring me a little wine and oil; I'm dying.

—This earthquake is nothing novel, Pangloss replied; the city of Lima, in South America, underwent much the same sort of tremor, last year; same causes, same effects; there is surely a vein of sulphur under the earth's surface reaching from Lima to Lisbon.

—Nothing is more probable, said Candide; but, for God's sake, a little oil and wine.

—What do you mean, probable? replied the philosopher; I regard the case as proved.

Candide fainted and Pangloss brought him some water from a nearby fountain.

Next day, as they wandered amid the ruins, they found a little food which restored some of their strength. Then they fell to work like the others, bringing relief to those of the inhabitants who had escaped death. Some of the citizens whom they rescued gave them a dinner as good as was possible under the circumstances; it is true that the meal was a melancholy one, and the guests watered their bread with tears; but Pangloss consoled them by proving that things could not possibly be otherwise.

—For, said he, all this is for the best, since if there is a volcano at Lisbon, it cannot be somewhere else, since it is unthinkable that things should not be where they are, since everything is well.

A little man in black, an officer of the Inquisition,[9] who was sitting beside him, politely took up the question, and said:—It would seem that the gentleman does not believe in original sin, since if everything is for the best, man has not fallen and is not liable to eternal punishment.

—I most humbly beg pardon of your excellency, Pangloss answered, even more politely, but the fall of man and the curse of original sin entered necessarily into the best of all possible worlds.

—Then you do not believe in free will? said the officer.

—Your excellency must excuse me, said Pangloss; free will agrees very well with absolute necessity, for it was necessary that we should be free, since a will which is determined . . .

Pangloss was in the middle of his sentence, when the officer nodded significantly to the attendant who was pouring him a glass of port, or Oporto, wine.

---

8. The Japanese, originally receptive to foreign visitors, grew fearful that priests and proselytizers were merely advance agents of empire and expelled both the Portuguese and Spanish early in the 17th century. Only the Dutch were allowed to retain a small foothold, under humiliating conditions, of which the notion of stamping on the crucifix is symbolic. It was never what Voltaire suggests here, an actual requirement for entering the country.

9. Specifically, a *familier* or *poursuivant*, an undercover agent with powers of arrest.

CHAPTER 6

How They Made a Fine Auto-da-Fé to Prevent Earthquakes, and How Candide Was Whipped

After the earthquake had wiped out three quarters of Lisbon, the learned men of the land could find no more effective way of averting total destruction than to give the people a fine auto-da-fé;[1] the University of Coimbra had established that the spectacle of several persons being roasted over a slow fire with full ceremonial rites is an infallible specific against earthquakes.

In consequence, the authorities had rounded up a Biscayan convicted of marrying a woman who had stood godmother to his child, and two Portuguese who while eating a chicken had set aside a bit of bacon used for seasoning.[2] After dinner, men came with ropes to tie up Doctor Pangloss and his disciple Candide, one for talking and the other for listening with an air of approval; both were taken separately to a set of remarkably cool apartments, where the glare of the sun is never bothersome; eight days later they were both dressed in *san-benitos* and crowned with paper mitres;[3] Candide's mitre and *san-benito* were decorated with inverted flames and with devils who had neither tails nor claws; but Pangloss's devils had both tails and claws, and his flames stood upright. Wearing these costumes, they marched in a procession, and listened to a very touching sermon, followed by a beautiful concert of plainsong. Candide was flogged in cadence to the music; the Biscayan and the two men who had avoided bacon were burned, and Pangloss was hanged, though hanging is not customary. On the same day there was another earthquake, causing frightful damage.[4]

Candide, stunned, stupefied, despairing, bleeding, trembling, said to himself:—If this is the best of all possible worlds, what are the others like? The flogging is not so bad, I was flogged by the Bulgars. But oh my dear Pangloss, greatest of philosophers, was it necessary for me to watch you being hanged, for no reason that I can see? Oh my dear Anabaptist, best of men, was it necessary that you should be drowned in the port? Oh Miss Cunégonde, pearl of young ladies, was it necessary that you should have your belly slit open?

He was being led away, barely able to stand, lectured, lashed, absolved, and blessed, when an old woman approached and said,—My son, be of good cheer and follow me.

CHAPTER 7

How an Old Woman Took Care of Candide, and How He Regained What He Loved

Candide was of very bad cheer, but he followed the old woman to a shanty; she gave him a jar of ointment to rub himself, left him food and drink; she showed him a tidy little bed; next to it was a suit of clothing.

1. Literally, "act of faith," a public ceremony of repentance and humiliation. Such an auto-da-fé was actually held in Lisbon, June 20, 1756.
2. The Biscayan's fault lay in marrying someone within the forbidden bounds of relationship, an act of spiritual incest. The men who declined pork or bacon were understood to be crypto-Jews.
3. The cone-shaped paper cap (intended to resemble a bishop's mitre) and flowing yellow cape were customary garb for those pleading before the Inquisition.
4. In fact, the second quake occurred December 21, 1755.

—Eat, drink, sleep, she said; and may Our Lady of Atocha, Our Lord St. Anthony of Padua, and Our Lord St. James of Compostela watch over you. I will be back tomorrow.

Candide, still completely astonished by everything he had seen and suffered, and even more by the old woman's kindness, offered to kiss her hand.

—It's not *my* hand you should be kissing, said she. I'll be back tomorrow; rub yourself with the ointment, eat and sleep.

In spite of his many sufferings, Candide ate and slept. Next day the old woman returned bringing breakfast; she looked at his back and rubbed it herself with another ointment; she came back with lunch; and then she returned in the evening, bringing supper. Next day she repeated the same routine.

—Who are you? Candide asked continually. Who told you to be so kind to me? How can I ever repay you?

The good woman answered not a word; she returned in the evening, and without food.

—Come with me, says she, and don't speak a word.

Taking him by the hand, she walks out into the countryside with him for about a quarter of a mile; they reach an isolated house, quite surrounded by gardens and ditches. The old woman knocks at a little gate, it opens. She takes Candide up a secret stairway to a gilded room furnished with a fine brocaded sofa; there she leaves him, closes the door, disappears. Candide stood as if entranced; his life, which had seemed like a nightmare so far, was now starting to look like a delightful dream.

Soon the old woman returned; on her feeble shoulder leaned a trembling woman, of a splendid figure, glittering in diamonds, and veiled.

—Remove the veil, said the old woman to Candide.

The young man stepped timidly forward, and lifted the veil. What an event! What a surprise! Could it be Miss Cunégonde? Yes, it really was! She herself! His knees give way, speech fails him, he falls at her feet, Cunégonde collapses on the sofa. The old woman plies them with brandy, they return to their senses, they exchange words. At first they could utter only broken phrases, questions and answers at cross purposes, sighs, tears, exclamations. The old woman warned them not to make too much noise, and left them alone.

—Then it's really you, said Candide, you're alive, I've found you again in Portugal. Then you never were raped? You never had your belly ripped open, as the philosopher Pangloss assured me?

—Oh yes, said the lovely Cunégonde, but one doesn't always die of these two accidents.

—But your father and mother were murdered then?

—All too true, said Cunégonde, in tears.

—And your brother?

—Killed too.

—And why are you in Portugal? and how did you know I was here? and by what device did you have me brought to this house?

—I shall tell you everything, the lady replied; but first you must tell me what has happened to you since that first innocent kiss we exchanged and the kicking you got because of it.

Candide obeyed her with profound respect; and though he was overcome, though his voice was weak and hesitant, though he still had twinges of pain from his beating, he described as simply as possible everything that had happened to him since the time of their separation. Cunégonde lifted her eyes to heaven; she wept at the death of the good Anabaptist and at that of Pangloss; after which she told the following story to Candide, who listened to every word while he gazed on her with hungry eyes.

CHAPTER 8

Cunégonde's Story

—I was in my bed and fast asleep when heaven chose to send the Bulgars into our castle of Thunder-Ten-Tronckh. They butchered my father and brother, and hacked my mother to bits. An enormous Bulgar, six feet tall, seeing that I had swooned from horror at the scene, set about raping me; at that I recovered my senses, I screamed and scratched, bit and fought, I tried to tear the eyes out of that big Bulgar—not realizing that everything which had happened in my father's castle was a mere matter of routine. The brute then stabbed me with a knife on my left thigh, where I still bear the scar.

—What a pity! I should very much like to see it, said the simple Candide.

—You shall, said Cunégonde; but shall I go on?

—Please do, said Candide.

So she took up the thread of her tale:—A Bulgar captain appeared, he saw me covered with blood and the soldier too intent to get up. Shocked by the monster's failure to come to attention, the captain killed him on my body. He then had my wound dressed, and took me off to his quarters, as a prisoner of war. I laundered his few shirts and did his cooking; he found me attractive, I confess it, and I won't deny that he was a handsome fellow, with a smooth, white skin; apart from that, however, little wit, little philosophical training; it was evident that he had not been brought up by Doctor Pangloss. After three months, he had lost all his money and grown sick of me; so he sold me to a Jew named Don Issachar, who traded in Holland and Portugal, and who was mad after women. This Jew developed a mighty passion for my person, but he got nowhere with it; I held him off better than I had done with the Bulgar soldier; for though a person of honor may be raped once, her virtue is only strengthened by the experience. In order to keep me hidden, the Jew brought me to his country house, which you see here. Till then I had thought there was nothing on earth so beautiful as the castle of Thunder-Ten-Tronckh; I was now undeceived.

—One day the Grand Inquisitor took notice of me at mass; he ogled me a good deal, and made known that he must talk to me on a matter of secret business. I was taken to his palace; I told him of my rank; he pointed out that it was beneath my dignity to belong to an Israelite. A suggestion was then conveyed to Don Issachar that he should turn me over to My Lord the Inquisitor. Don Issachar, who is court banker and a man of standing, refused out of hand. The inquisitor threatened him with an auto-da-fé. Finally my Jew, fearing for his life, struck a bargain by which the house and I would belong to both of them as joint tenants; the Jew would get Mondays, Wednesdays, and the Sabbath, the inquisitor would get the other days of the week. That has been the arrangement for six months now. There have been quarrels; sometimes it has not been clear whether the night from Saturday to Sunday belonged to the old or the new dispensation. For my part, I have so far been able to hold both of them off; and that, I think, is why they are both still in love with me.

—Finally, in order to avert further divine punishment by earthquake, and to terrify Don Issachar, My Lord the Inquisitor chose to celebrate an auto-da-fé. He did me the honor of inviting me to attend. I had an excellent seat; the ladies were served with refreshments between the mass and the execution. To tell you the truth, I was horrified to see them burn alive those two Jews and that decent Biscayan who had married his child's godmother; but what was my surprise, my terror, my grief, when I saw, huddled in a *san-benito* and wearing a mitre, someone who looked like Pangloss! I rubbed my eyes, I watched his every move, I saw him hanged; and I fell back in a swoon. Scarcely had I come to my senses again, when I saw you stripped for the lash; that was the peak of my horror, consternation, grief, and despair. I may tell you, by the way, that your skin is even whiter and more delicate than that of my Bulgar captain. Seeing you, then, redoubled the torments which were already overwhelming me. I shrieked aloud, I wanted to call out, 'Let him go, you brutes!' but my voice died within me, and my cries would have been useless. When you had been thoroughly thrashed: 'How can it be,' I asked myself, 'that agreeable Candide and wise Pangloss have come to Lisbon, one to receive a hundred whiplashes, the other to be hanged by order of My Lord the Inquisitor, whose mistress I am? Pangloss must have deceived me cruelly when he told me that all is for the best in this world.'

—Frantic, exhausted, half out of my senses, and ready to die of weakness, I felt as if my mind were choked with the massacre of my father, my mother, my brother, with the arrogance of that ugly Bulgar soldier, with the knife slash he inflicted on me, my slavery, my cookery, my Bulgar captain, my nasty Don Issachar, my abominable inquisitor, with the hanging of Doctor Pangloss, with that great plainsong *miserere* which they sang while they flogged you—and above all, my mind was full of the kiss which I gave you behind the screen, on the day I saw you for the last time. I praised God, who had brought you back to me after so many trials. I asked my old woman to look out for you, and to bring you here as soon as she could. She did just as I asked; I have had the indescribable joy of seeing you again, hearing you and talking with you once more. But you must be frightfully hungry; I am, myself; let us begin with a dinner.

So then and there they sat down to table; and after dinner, they adjourned to that fine brocaded sofa, which has already been mentioned; and there they were when the eminent Don Issachar, one of the masters of the house, appeared. It was the day of the Sabbath; he was arriving to assert his rights and express his tender passion.

CHAPTER 9

*What Happened to Cunégonde, Candide, the Grand Inquisitor,
and a Jew*

This Issachar was the most choleric Hebrew seen in Israel since the Babylonian captivity.

—What's this, says he, you bitch of a Christian, you're not satisfied with the Grand Inquisitor? Do I have to share you with this rascal, too?

So saying, he drew a long dagger, with which he always went armed, and, supposing his opponent defenceless, flung himself on Candide. But our good Westphalian had received from the old woman, along with his suit of clothes, a fine sword. Out it came, and though his manners were of the gentlest, in short order he laid the Israelite stiff and cold on the floor, at the feet of the lovely Cunégonde.

—Holy Virgin! she cried. What will become of me now? A man killed in my house! If the police find out, we're done for.

—If Pangloss had not been hanged, said Candide, he would give us good advice in this hour of need, for he was a great philosopher. Lacking him, let's ask the old woman.

She was a sensible body, and was just starting to give her opinion of the situation, when another little door opened. It was just one o'clock in the morning, Sunday morning. This day belonged to the inquisitor. In he came, and found the whipped Candide with a sword in his hand, a corpse at his feet, Cunégonde in terror, and an old woman giving them both good advice.

Here now is what passed through Candide's mind in this instant of time; this is how he reasoned:—If this holy man calls for help, he will certainly have me burned, and perhaps Cunégonde as well; he has already had me whipped without mercy; he is my rival; I have already killed once; why hesitate?

It was a quick, clear chain of reasoning; without giving the inquisitor time to recover from his surprise, he ran him through, and laid him beside the Jew.

—Here you've done it again, said Cunégonde; there's no hope for us now. We'll be excommunicated, our last hour has come. How is it that you, who were born so gentle, could kill in two minutes a Jew and a prelate?

—My dear girl, replied Candide, when a man is in love, jealous, and just whipped by the Inquisition, he is no longer himself.

The old woman now spoke up and said:—There are three Andalusian steeds in the stable, with their saddles and bridles; our brave Candide must get them ready: my lady has some gold coin and diamonds; let's take to horse at once, though I can only ride on one buttock; we will go to Cadiz. The weather is as fine as can be, and it is pleasant to travel in the cool of the evening.

Promptly, Candide saddled the three horses. Cunégonde, the old woman, and he covered thirty miles without a stop. While they were fleeing, the Holy Brotherhood[5] came to investigate the house; they buried the inquisitor in a fine church, and threw Issachar on the dunghill.

Candide, Cunégonde, and the old woman were already in the little town of Avacena, in the middle of the Sierra Morena; and there, as they sat in a country inn, they had this conversation.

CHAPTER 10

In Deep Distress, Candide, Cunégonde, and the Old Woman
Reach Cadiz; They Put to Sea

—Who then could have robbed me of my gold and diamonds? said Cunégonde, in tears. How shall we live? what shall we do? where shall I find other inquisitors and Jews to give me some more?

—Ah, said the old woman, I strongly suspect that reverend Franciscan friar who shared the inn with us yesterday at Badajoz. God save me from judging him unfairly! But he came into our room twice, and he left long before us.

—Alas, said Candide, the good Pangloss often proved to me that the fruits of the earth are a common heritage of all, to which each man has equal right. On

---

5. A semireligious order with police powers, very active in 18th-century Spain.

these principles, the Franciscan should at least have left us enough to finish our journey. You have nothing at all, my dear Cunégonde?

—Not a maravedi, said she.

—What to do? said Candide.

—We'll sell one of the horses, said the old woman; I'll ride on the croup behind my mistress, though only on one buttock, and so we will get to Cadiz.

There was in the same inn a Benedictine prior; he bought the horse cheap. Candide, Cunégonde, and the old woman passed through Lucena, Chillas, and Lebrixa, and finally reached Cadiz. There a fleet was being fitted out and an army assembled, to reason with the Jesuit fathers in Paraguay, who were accused of fomenting among their flock a revolt against the kings of Spain and Portugal near the town of St. Sacrement.[6] Candide, having served in the Bulgar army, performed the Bulgar manual of arms before the general of the little army with such grace, swiftness, dexterity, fire, and agility, that they gave him a company of infantry to command. So here he is, a captain; and off he sails with Miss Cunégonde, the old woman, two valets, and the two Andalusian steeds which had belonged to My Lord the Grand Inquisitor of Portugal.

Throughout the crossing, they spent a great deal of time reasoning about the philosophy of poor Pangloss.

—We are destined, in the end, for another universe, said Candide; no doubt that is the one where everything is well. For in this one, it must be admitted, there is some reason to grieve over our physical and moral state.

—I love you with all my heart, said Cunégonde; but my soul is still harrowed by thoughts of what I have seen and suffered.

—All will be well, replied Candide; the sea of this new world is already better than those of Europe, calmer and with steadier winds. Surely it is the New World which is the best of all possible worlds.

—God grant it, said Cunégonde; but I have been so horribly unhappy in the world so far, that my heart is almost dead to hope.

—You pity yourselves, the old woman told them; but you have had no such misfortunes as mine.

Cunégonde nearly broke out laughing; she found the old woman comic in pretending to be more unhappy than she.

—Ah, you poor old thing, said she, unless you've been raped by two Bulgars, been stabbed twice in the belly, seen two of your castles destroyed, witnessed the murder of two of your mothers and two of your fathers, and watched two of your lovers being whipped in an auto-da-fé, I do not see how you can have had it worse than me. Besides, I was born a baroness, with seventy-two quarterings, and I have worked in a scullery.

—My lady, replied the old woman, you do not know my birth and rank; and if I showed you my rear end, you would not talk as you do, you might even speak with less assurance.

These words inspired great curiosity in Candide and Cunégonde, which the old woman satisfied with this story.

6. Actually, Colonia del Sacramento. Voltaire took great interest in the Jesuit role in Paraguay, which he has much oversimplified and largely misrepresented here in the interests of his satire. In 1750 they did, however, offer armed resistance to an agreement made between Spain and Portugal. They were subdued and expelled in 1769.

CHAPTER 11

The Old Woman's Story

—My eyes were not always bloodshot and red-rimmed, my nose did not always touch my chin, and I was not born a servant. I am in fact the daughter of Pope Urban the Tenth and the Princess of Palestrina.[7] Till the age of fourteen, I lived in a palace so splendid that all the castles of all your German barons would not have served it as a stable; a single one of my dresses was worth more than all the assembled magnificence of Westphalia. I grew in beauty, in charm, in talent, surrounded by pleasures, dignities, and glowing visions of the future. Already I was inspiring the young men to love; my breast was formed—and what a breast! white, firm, with the shape of the Venus de Medici;[8] and what eyes! what lashes, what black brows! What fire flashed from my glances and outshone the glitter of the stars, as the local poets used to tell me! The women who helped me dress and undress fell into ecstasies, whether they looked at me from in front or behind; and all the men wanted to be in their place.

—I was engaged to the ruling prince of Massa-Carrara; and what a prince he was! as handsome as I, softness and charm compounded, brilliantly witty, and madly in love with me. I loved him in return as one loves for the first time, with a devotion approaching idolatry. The wedding preparations had been made, with a splendor and magnificence never heard of before; nothing but celebrations, masks, and comic operas, uninterruptedly; and all Italy composed in my honor sonnets of which not one was even passable. I had almost attained the very peak of bliss, when an old marquise who had been the mistress of my prince invited him to her house for a cup of chocolate. He died in less than two hours, amid horrifying convulsions. But that was only a trifle. My mother, in complete despair (though less afflicted than I), wished to escape for a while the oppressive atmosphere of grief. She owned a handsome property near Gaeta.[9] We embarked on a papal galley gilded like the altar of St. Peter's in Rome. Suddenly a pirate ship from Salé swept down and boarded us. Our soldiers defended themselves as papal troops usually do; falling on their knees and throwing down their arms, they begged of the corsair absolution *in articulo mortis*.[1]

—They were promptly stripped as naked as monkeys, and so was my mother, and so were our maids of honor, and so was I too. It's a very remarkable thing, the energy these gentlemen put into stripping people. But what surprised me even more was that they stuck their fingers in a place where we women usually admit only a syringe. This ceremony seemed a bit odd to me, as foreign usages always do when one hasn't traveled. They only wanted to see if we didn't have some diamonds hidden there; and I soon learned that it's a custom of long standing among the genteel folk who swarm the seas. I learned that my lords the very religious knights of Malta never overlook this ceremony when they capture

---

7. Voltaire left behind a comment on this passage, a note first published in 1829: "Note the extreme discretion of the author; hitherto there has never been a pope named Urban X; he avoided attributing a bastard to a known pope. What circumspection! what an exquisite conscience!"

8. A famous Roman sculpture of Venus in marble from the 1st century B.C.E. that belonged to the Medici family in Italy; 18th-century Europeans considered it to be one of the best surviving works of art from ancient times.

9. About halfway between Rome and Naples.

1. Literally, when at the point of death. Absolution from a corsair in the act of murdering one is of very dubious validity.

Turks, whether male or female; it's one of those international laws which have never been questioned.

—I won't try to explain how painful it is for a young princess to be carried off into slavery in Morocco with her mother. You can imagine everything we had to suffer on the pirate ship. My mother was still very beautiful; our maids of honor, our mere chambermaids, were more charming than anything one could find in all Africa. As for myself, I was ravishing, I was loveliness and grace supreme, and I was a virgin. I did not remain so for long; the flower which had been kept for the handsome prince of Massa-Carrara was plucked by the corsair captain; he was an abominable negro, who thought he was doing me a great favor. My Lady the Princess of Palestrina and I must have been strong indeed to bear what we did during our journey to Morocco. But on with my story; these are such common matters that they are not worth describing.

—Morocco was knee deep in blood when we arrived. Of the fifty sons of the emperor Muley-Ismael,[2] each had his faction, which produced in effect fifty civil wars, of blacks against blacks, of blacks against browns, halfbreeds against halfbreeds; throughout the length and breadth of the empire, nothing but one continual carnage.

—Scarcely had we stepped ashore, when some negroes of a faction hostile to my captor arrived to take charge of his plunder. After the diamonds and gold, we women were the most prized possessions. I was now witness of a struggle such as you never see in the temperate climate of Europe. Northern people don't have hot blood; they don't feel the absolute fury for women which is common in Africa. Europeans seem to have milk in their veins; it is vitriol or liquid fire which pulses through these people around Mount Atlas. The fight for possession of us raged with the fury of the lions, tigers, and poisonous vipers of that land. A Moor snatched my mother by the right arm, the first mate held her by the left; a Moorish soldier grabbed one leg, one of our pirates the other. In a moment's time almost all our girls were being dragged four different ways. My captain held me behind him while with his scimitar he killed everyone who braved his fury. At last I saw all our Italian women, including my mother, torn to pieces, cut to bits, murdered by the monsters who were fighting over them. My captive companions, their captors, soldiers, sailors, blacks, browns, whites, mulattoes, and at last my captain, all were killed, and I remained half dead on a mountain of corpses. Similar scenes were occurring, as is well known, for more than three hundred leagues around, without anyone skimping on the five prayers a day decreed by Mohammed.

—With great pain, I untangled myself from this vast heap of bleeding bodies, and dragged myself under a great orange tree by a neighboring brook, where I collapsed, from terror, exhaustion, horror, despair, and hunger. Shortly, my weary mind surrendered to a sleep which was more of a swoon than a rest. I was in this state of weakness and languor, between life and death, when I felt myself touched by something which moved over my body. Opening my eyes, I saw a white man, rather attractive, who was groaning and saying under his breath: 'O che sciagura d'essere senza coglioni!'[3]

---

2. Having reigned for more than fifty years, a potent and ruthless sultan of Morocco, he died in 1727 and left his kingdom in much the condition described.

3. "Oh what a misfortune to have no testicles!"

CHAPTER 12

The Old Woman's Story Continued

—Amazed and delighted to hear my native tongue, and no less surprised by what this man was saying, I told him that there were worse evils than those he was complaining of. In a few words, I described to him the horrors I had undergone, and then fainted again. He carried me to a nearby house, put me to bed, gave me something to eat, served me, flattered me, comforted me, told me he had never seen anyone so lovely, and added that he had never before regretted so much the loss of what nobody could give him back.

'I was born at Naples,' he told me, 'where they caponize two or three thousand children every year; some die of it, others acquire a voice more beautiful than any woman's, still others go on to become governors of kingdoms.[4] The operation was a great success with me, and I became court musician to the Princess of Palestrina . . .'

'Of my mother,' I exclaimed.

'Of your mother,' cried he, bursting into tears; 'then you must be the princess whom I raised till she was six, and who already gave promise of becoming as beautiful as you are now!'

'I am that very princess; my mother lies dead, not a hundred yards from here, buried under a pile of corpses.'

—I told him my adventures, he told me his: that he had been sent by a Christian power to the King of Morocco, to conclude a treaty granting him gunpowder, cannon, and ships with which to liquidate the traders of the other Christian powers.

'My mission is concluded,' said this honest eunuch; 'I shall take ship at Ceuta and bring you back to Italy. *Ma che sciagura d'essere senza coglioni!*'

—I thanked him with tears of gratitude, and instead of returning me to Italy, he took me to Algiers and sold me to the dey of that country. Hardly had the sale taken place, when that plague which has made the rounds of Africa, Asia, and Europe broke out in full fury at Algiers. You have seen earthquakes; but tell me, young lady, have you ever had the plague?

—Never, replied the baroness.

—If you had had it, said the old woman, you would agree that it is far worse than an earthquake. It is very frequent in Africa, and I had it. Imagine, if you will, the situation of a pope's daughter, fifteen years old, who in three months' time had experienced poverty, slavery, had been raped almost every day, had seen her mother quartered, had suffered from famine and war, and who now was dying of pestilence in Algiers. As a matter of fact, I did not die; but the eunuch and the dey and nearly the entire seraglio of Algiers perished.

—When the first horrors of this ghastly plague had passed, the slaves of the dey were sold. A merchant bought me and took me to Tunis; there he sold me to another merchant, who resold me at Tripoli; from Tripoli I was sold to Alexandria, from Alexandria resold to Smyrna, from Smyrna to Constantinople. I ended by belonging to an aga of janizaries, who was shortly ordered to defend Azov against the besieging Russians.[5]

---

4. The castrato Farinelli (1705–1782), originally a singer, came to exercise considerable political influence on the kings of Spain, Philip V and Ferdinand VI.

5. Azov, near the mouth of the Don, was besieged by the Russians under Peter the Great in 1695–96. "Janizaries": an elite corps of the Ottoman armies.

—The aga, who was a gallant soldier, took his whole seraglio with him, and established us in a little fort amid the Maeotian marshes,[6] guarded by two black eunuchs and twenty soldiers. Our side killed a prodigious number of Russians, but they paid us back nicely. Azov was put to fire and sword without respect for age or sex; only our little fort continued to resist, and the enemy determined to starve us out. The twenty janizaries had sworn never to surrender. Reduced to the last extremities of hunger, they were forced to eat our two eunuchs, lest they violate their oaths. After several more days, they decided to eat the women too.

—We had an imam,[7] very pious and sympathetic, who delivered an excellent sermon, persuading them not to kill us altogether.

'Just cut off a single rumpsteak from each of these ladies,' he said, 'and you'll have a fine meal. Then if you should need another, you can come back in a few days and have as much again; heaven will bless your charitable action, and you will be saved.'

—His eloquence was splendid, and he persuaded them. We underwent this horrible operation. The imam treated us all with the ointment that they use on newly circumcised children. We were at the point of death.

—Scarcely had the janizaries finished the meal for which we furnished the materials, when the Russians appeared in flat-bottomed boats; not a janizary escaped. The Russians paid no attention to the state we were in; but there are French physicians everywhere, and one of them, who knew his trade, took care of us. He cured us, and I shall remember all my life that when my wounds were healed, he made me a proposition. For the rest, he counselled us simply to have patience, assuring us that the same thing had happened in several other sieges, and that it was according to the laws of war.

—As soon as my companions could walk, we were herded off to Moscow. In the division of booty, I fell to a boyar who made me work in his garden, and gave me twenty whiplashes a day; but when he was broken on the wheel after about two years, with thirty other boyars, over some little court intrigue,[8] I seized the occasion; I ran away; I crossed all Russia; I was for a long time a chambermaid in Riga, then at Rostock, Vismara, Leipzig, Cassel, Utrecht, Leyden, The Hague, Rotterdam; I grew old in misery and shame, having only half a backside and remembering always that I was the daughter of a Pope; a hundred times I wanted to kill myself, but always I loved life more. This ridiculous weakness is perhaps one of our worst instincts; is anything more stupid than choosing to carry a burden that really one wants to cast on the ground? to hold existence in horror, and yet to cling to it? to fondle the serpent which devours us till it has eaten out our heart?

—In the countries through which I have been forced to wander, in the taverns where I have had to work, I have seen a vast number of people who hated their existence; but I never saw more than a dozen who deliberately put an end to their own misery: three negroes, four Englishmen, four Genevans, and a German professor named Robeck.[9] My last post was as servant to the Jew Don Issachar; he

---

6. The Roman name of the so-called Sea of Azov, a shallow swampy lake near the town.
7. In effect, a chaplain.
8. Voltaire had in mind an ineffectual conspiracy against Peter the Great known as the "revolt of the streltsy" or musketeers, which took place in 1698. Though easily put down, it

provoked from the emperor a massive and atrocious program of reprisals.
9. Johann Robeck (1672–1739) published a treatise advocating suicide and showed his conviction by drowning himself at the age of sixty-seven.

attached me to your service, my lovely one; and I attached myself to your destiny, till I have become more concerned with your fate than with my own. I would not even have mentioned my own misfortunes, if you had not irked me a bit, and if it weren't the custom, on shipboard, to pass the time with stories. In a word, my lady, I have had some experience of the world, I know it; why not try this diversion? Ask every passenger on this ship to tell you his story, and if you find a single one who has not often cursed the day of his birth, who has not often told himself that he is the most miserable of men, then you may throw me overboard head first.

CHAPTER 13

How Candide Was Forced to Leave the Lovely Cunégonde and the Old Woman

Having heard out the old woman's story, the lovely Cunégonde paid her the respects which were appropriate to a person of her rank and merit. She took up the wager as well, and got all the passengers, one after another, to tell her their adventures. She and Candide had to agree that the old woman had been right.

—It's certainly too bad, said Candide, that the wise Pangloss was hanged, contrary to the custom of auto-da-fé; he would have admirable things to say of the physical evil and moral evil which cover land and sea, and I might feel within me the impulse to dare to raise several polite objections.

As the passengers recited their stories, the boat made steady progress, and presently landed at Buenos Aires. Cunégonde, Captain Candide, and the old woman went to call on the governor, Don Fernando d'Ibaraa y Figueroa y Mascarenes y Lampourdos y Souza. This nobleman had the pride appropriate to a man with so many names. He addressed everyone with the most aristocratic disdain, pointing his nose so loftily, raising his voice so mercilessly, lording it so splendidly, and assuming so arrogant a pose, that everyone who met him wanted to kick him. He loved women to the point of fury; and Cunégonde seemed to him the most beautiful creature he had ever seen. The first thing he did was to ask directly if she were the captain's wife. His manner of asking this question disturbed Candide; he did not dare say she was his wife, because in fact she was not; he did not dare say she was his sister, because she wasn't that either; and though this polite lie was once common enough among the ancients,[1] and sometimes serves moderns very well, he was too pure of heart to tell a lie.

—Miss Cunégonde, said he, is betrothed to me, and we humbly beg your excellency to perform the ceremony for us.

Don Fernando d'Ibaraa y Figueroa y Mascarenes y Lampourdos y Souza twirled his moustache, smiled sardonically, and ordered Captain Candide to go drill his company. Candide obeyed. Left alone with My Lady Cunégonde, the governor declared his passion, and protested that he would marry her tomorrow, in church or in any other manner, as it pleased her charming self. Cunégonde asked for a quarter-hour to collect herself, consult the old woman, and make up her mind.

The old woman said to Cunégonde:—My lady, you have seventy-two quarterings and not one penny; if you wish, you may be the wife of the greatest lord in South America, who has a really handsome moustache; are you going to insist on

---

1. Voltaire has in mind Abraham's adventures with Sarah (Genesis 12) and Isaac's with Rebecca (Genesis 26).

your absolute fidelity? You have already been raped by the Bulgars; a Jew and an inquisitor have enjoyed your favors; miseries entitle one to privileges. I assure you that in your position I would make no scruple of marrying My Lord the Governor, and making the fortune of Captain Candide.

While the old woman was talking with all the prudence of age and experience, there came into the harbor a small ship bearing an alcalde and some alguazils.[2] This is what had happened.

As the old woman had very shrewdly guessed, it was a long-sleeved Franciscan who stole Cunégonde's gold and jewels in the town of Badajoz, when she and Candide were in flight. The monk tried to sell some of the gems to a jeweler, who recognized them as belonging to the Grand Inquisitor. Before he was hanged, the Franciscan confessed that he had stolen them, indicating who his victims were and where they were going. The flight of Cunégonde and Candide was already known. They were traced to Cadiz, and a vessel was hastily dispatched in pursuit of them. This vessel was now in the port of Buenos Aires. The rumor spread that an alcalde was aboard, in pursuit of the murderers of My Lord the Grand Inquisitor. The shrewd old woman saw at once what was to be done.

—You cannot escape, she told Cunégonde, and you have nothing to fear. You are not the one who killed my lord, and, besides, the governor, who is in love with you, won't let you be mistreated. Sit tight.

And then she ran straight to Candide:—Get out of town, she said, or you'll be burned within the hour.

There was not a moment to lose; but how to leave Cunégonde, and where to go?

CHAPTER 14

How Candide and Cacambo Were Received by the Jesuits of Paraguay

Candide had brought from Cadiz a valet of the type one often finds in the provinces of Spain and in the colonies. He was one quarter Spanish, son of a half-breed in the Tucuman;[3] he had been choirboy, sacristan, sailor, monk, merchant, soldier, and lackey. His name was Cacambo, and he was very fond of his master because his master was a very good man. In hot haste he saddled the two Andalusian steeds.

—Hurry, master, do as the old woman says; let's get going and leave this town without a backward look.

Candide wept:—O my beloved Cunégonde! must I leave you now, just when the governor is about to marry us! Cunégonde, brought from so far, what will ever become of you?

—She'll become what she can, said Cacambo; women can always find something to do with themselves; God sees to it; let's get going.

—Where are you taking me? where are we going? what will we do without Cunégonde? said Candide.

—By Saint James of Compostela, said Cacambo, you were going to make war against the Jesuits, now we'll go make war for them. I know the roads pretty well, I'll bring you to their country, they will be delighted to have a captain who knows

2. Police officers.
3. A province of Argentina, to the northwest of Buenos Aires.

the Bulgar drill; you'll make a prodigious fortune. If you don't get your rights in one world, you will find them in another. And isn't it pleasant to see new things and do new things?

—Then you've already been in Paraguay? said Candide.

—Indeed I have, replied Cacambo; I was cook in the College of the Assumption, and I know the government of Los Padres[4] as I know the streets of Cadiz. It's an admirable thing, this government. The kingdom is more than three hundred leagues across; it is divided into thirty provinces. Los Padres own everything in it, and the people nothing; it's a masterpiece of reason and justice. I myself know nothing so wonderful as Los Padres, who in this hemisphere make war on the kings of Spain and Portugal, but in Europe hear their confessions; who kill Spaniards here, and in Madrid send them to heaven; that really tickles me; let's get moving, you're going to be the happiest of men. Won't Los Padres be delighted when they learn they have a captain who knows the Bulgar drill!

As soon as they reached the first barricade, Cacambo told the frontier guard that a captain wished to speak with My Lord the Commander. A Paraguayan officer ran to inform headquarters by laying the news at the feet of the commander. Candide and Cacambo were first disarmed and deprived of their Andalusian horses. They were then placed between two files of soldiers; the commander was at the end, his three-cornered hat on his head, his cassock drawn up, a sword at his side, and a pike in his hand. He nods, and twenty-four soldiers surround the newcomers. A sergeant then informs them that they must wait, that the commander cannot talk to them, since the reverend father provincial has forbidden all Spaniards from speaking, except in his presence, and from remaining more than three hours in the country.

—And where is the reverend father provincial? says Cacambo.

—He is reviewing his troops after having said mass, the sergeant replies, and you'll only be able to kiss his spurs in three hours.

—But, says Cacambo, my master the captain, who, like me, is dying from hunger, is not Spanish at all, he is German; can't we have some breakfast while waiting for his reverence?

The sergeant promptly went off to report this speech to the commander.

—God be praised, said this worthy; since he is German, I can talk to him; bring him into my bower.

Candide was immediately led into a leafy nook surrounded by a handsome colonnade of green and gold marble and trellises amid which sported parrots, hummingbirds,[5] guinea fowl, and all the rarest species of birds. An excellent breakfast was prepared in golden vessels; and while the Paraguayans ate corn out of wooden bowls in the open fields under the glare of the sun, the reverend father commander entered into his bower.

He was a very handsome young man, with an open face, rather blonde in coloring, with ruddy complexion, arched eyebrows, liquid eyes, pink ears, bright red lips, and an air of pride, but a pride somehow different from that of a Spaniard or a Jesuit. Their confiscated weapons were restored to Candide and Cacambo, as

4. The Jesuit fathers.
5. In this passage and several later ones, Voltaire uses in conjunction two words, both of which mean hummingbird. The French system of classifying hummingbirds, based on the work of the celebrated Buffon, distinguishes oiseaux-mouches with straight bills from colibris with curved bills. This distinction is wholly fallacious. Hummingbirds have all manner of shaped bills, and the division of species must be made on other grounds entirely.

well as their Andalusian horses; Cacambo fed them oats alongside the bower, always keeping an eye on them for fear of an ambush.

First Candide kissed the hem of the commander's cassock, then they sat down at the table.

—So you are German? said the Jesuit, speaking in that language.

—Yes, your reverence, said Candide.

As they spoke these words, both men looked at one another with great surprise, and another emotion which they could not control.

—From what part of Germany do you come? said the Jesuit.

—From the nasty province of Westphalia, said Candide; I was born in the castle of Thunder-Ten-Tronckh.

—Merciful heavens! cries the commander. Is it possible?

—What a miracle! exclaims Candide.

—Can it be you? asks the commander.

—It's impossible, says Candide.

They both fall back in their chairs, they embrace, they shed streams of tears.

—What, can it be you, reverend father! you, the brother of the lovely Cunégonde! you, who were killed by the Bulgars! you, the son of My Lord the Baron! you, a Jesuit in Paraguay! It's a mad world, indeed it is. Oh, Pangloss! Pangloss! how happy you would be, if you hadn't been hanged.

The commander dismissed his negro slaves and the Paraguayans who served his drink in crystal goblets. He thanked God and Saint Ignatius a thousand times, he clasped Candide in his arms, their faces were bathed in tears.

—You would be even more astonished, even more delighted, even more beside yourself, said Candide, if I told you that My Lady Cunégonde, your sister, who you thought was disemboweled, is enjoying good health.

—Where?

—Not far from here, in the house of the governor of Buenos Aires; and to think that I came to make war on you!

Each word they spoke in this long conversation added another miracle. Their souls danced on their tongues, hung eagerly at their ears, glittered in their eyes. As they were Germans, they sat a long time at table, waiting for the reverend father provincial; and the commander spoke in these terms to his dear Candide.

CHAPTER 15

How Candide Killed the Brother of His Dear Cunégonde

—All my life long I shall remember the horrible day when I saw my father and mother murdered and my sister raped. When the Bulgars left, that adorable sister of mine was nowhere to be found; so they loaded a cart with my mother, my father, myself, two serving girls, and three little murdered boys, to carry us all off for burial in a Jesuit chapel some two leagues from our ancestral castle. A Jesuit sprinkled us with holy water; it was horribly salty, and a few drops got into my eyes; the father noticed that my lid made a little tremor; putting his hand on my heart, he felt it beat; I was rescued, and at the end of three weeks was as good as new. You know, my dear Candide, that I was a very pretty boy; I became even more so; the reverend father Croust,[6] superior of the abbey, conceived a most tender friendship for me; he accepted me as a novice, and shortly after, I was sent

6. A Jesuit rector at Colmar with whom Voltaire had quarreled in 1754.

to Rome. The Father General had need of a resupply of young German Jesuits. The rulers of Paraguay accept as few Spanish Jesuits as they can; they prefer foreigners, whom they think they can control better. I was judged fit, by the Father General, to labor in this vineyard. So we set off, a Pole, a Tyrolean, and myself. Upon our arrival, I was honored with the posts of subdeacon and lieutenant; today I am a colonel and a priest. We are giving a vigorous reception to the King of Spain's men; I assure you they will be excommunicated as well as trounced on the battlefield. Providence has sent you to help us. But is it really true that my dear sister, Cunégonde, is in the neighborhood, with the governor of Buenos Aires?

Candide reassured him with a solemn oath that nothing could be more true. Their tears began to flow again.

The baron could not weary of embracing Candide; he called him his brother, his savior.

—Ah, my dear Candide, said he, maybe together we will be able to enter the town as conquerors, and be united with my sister Cunégonde.

—That is all I desire, said Candide; I was expecting to marry her, and I still hope to.

—You insolent dog, replied the baron, you would have the effrontery to marry my sister, who has seventy-two quarterings! It's a piece of presumption for you even to mention such a crazy project in my presence.

Candide, terrified by this speech, answered:—Most reverend father, all the quarterings in the world don't affect this case; I have rescued your sister out of the arms of a Jew and an inquisitor; she has many obligations to me, she wants to marry me. Master Pangloss always taught me that men are equal; and I shall certainly marry her.

—We'll see about that, you scoundrel, said the Jesuit baron of Thunder-Ten-Tronckh; and so saying, he gave him a blow across the face with the flat of his sword. Candide immediately drew his own sword and thrust it up to the hilt in the baron's belly; but as he drew it forth all dripping, he began to weep.

—Alas, dear God! said he, I have killed my old master, my friend, my brother-in-law; I am the best man in the world, and here are three men I've killed already, and two of the three were priests.

Cacambo, who was standing guard at the entry of the bower, came running.

—We can do nothing but sell our lives dearly, said his master; someone will certainly come; we must die fighting.

Cacambo, who had been in similar scrapes before, did not lose his head; he took the Jesuit's cassock, which the commander had been wearing, and put it on Candide; he stuck the dead man's square hat on Candide's head, and forced him onto horseback. Everything was done in the wink of an eye.

—Let's ride, master; everyone will take you for a Jesuit on his way to deliver orders; and we will have passed the frontier before anyone can come after us.

Even as he was pronouncing these words, he charged off, crying in Spanish:—Way, make way for the reverend father colonel!

CHAPTER 16

What Happened to the Two Travelers with Two Girls, Two Monkeys, and the Savages Named Biglugs

Candide and his valet were over the frontier before anyone in the camp knew of the death of the German Jesuit. Foresighted Cacambo had taken care to fill his satchel with bread, chocolate, ham, fruit, and several bottles of wine.

They pushed their Andalusian horses forward into unknown country, where there were no roads. Finally a broad prairie divided by several streams opened before them. Our two travelers turned their horses loose to graze; Cacambo suggested that they eat too, and promptly set the example. But Candide said:—How can you expect me to eat ham when I have killed the son of My Lord the Baron, and am now condemned never to see the lovely Cunégonde for the rest of my life? Why should I drag out my miserable days, since I must exist far from her in the depths of despair and remorse? And what will the *Journal de Trévoux*[7] say of all this?

Though he talked this way, he did not neglect the food. Night fell. The two wanderers heard a few weak cries which seemed to be voiced by women. They could not tell whether the cries expressed grief or joy; but they leaped at once to their feet, with that uneasy suspicion which one always feels in an unknown country. The outcry arose from two girls, completely naked, who were running swiftly along the edge of the meadow, pursued by two monkeys who snapped at their buttocks. Candide was moved to pity; he had learned marksmanship with the Bulgars, and could have knocked a nut off a bush without touching the leaves. He raised his Spanish rifle, fired twice, and killed the two monkeys.

—God be praised, my dear Cacambo! I've saved these two poor creatures from great danger. Though I committed a sin in killing an inquisitor and a Jesuit, I've redeemed myself by saving the lives of two girls. Perhaps they are two ladies of rank, and this good deed may gain us special advantages in the country.

He had more to say, but his mouth shut suddenly when he saw the girls embracing the monkeys tenderly, weeping over their bodies, and filling the air with lamentations.

—I wasn't looking for quite so much generosity of spirit, said he to Cacambo; the latter replied:—You've really fixed things this time, master; you've killed the two lovers of these young ladies.

—Their lovers! Impossible! You must be joking, Cacambo; how can I believe you?

—My dear master, Cacambo replied, you're always astonished by everything. Why do you think it so strange that in some countries monkeys succeed in obtaining the good graces of women? They are one quarter human, just as I am one quarter Spanish.

—Alas, Candide replied, I do remember now hearing Master Pangloss say that such things used to happen, and that from these mixtures there arose pans, fauns, and satyrs, and that these creatures had appeared to various grand figures of antiquity; but I took all that for fables.

—You should be convinced now, said Cacambo; it's true, and you see how people make mistakes who haven't received a measure of education. But what I fear is that these girls may get us into real trouble.

These sensible reflections led Candide to leave the field and to hide in a wood. There he dined with Cacambo; and there both of them, having duly cursed the inquisitor of Portugal, the governor of Buenos Aires, and the baron, went to sleep on a bed of moss. When they woke up, they found themselves unable to move;

---

7. A newspaper published by the Jesuit order, founded in 1701 and consistently hostile to Voltaire.

the reason was that during the night the Biglugs,[8] natives of the country, to whom the girls had complained of them, had tied them down with cords of bark. They were surrounded by fifty naked Biglugs, armed with arrows, clubs, and stone axes. Some were boiling a caldron of water, others were preparing spits, and all cried out:—It's a Jesuit, a Jesuit! We'll be revenged and have a good meal; let's eat some Jesuit, eat some Jesuit!

—I told you, my dear master, said Cacambo sadly, I said those two girls would play us a dirty trick.

Candide, noting the caldron and spits, cried out:—We are surely going to be roasted or boiled. Ah, what would Master Pangloss say if he could see these men in a state of nature? All is for the best, I agree; but I must say it seems hard to have lost Miss Cunégonde and to be stuck on a spit by the Biglugs.

Cacambo did not lose his head.

—Don't give up hope, said he to the disconsolate Candide; I understand a little of the jargon these people speak, and I'm going to talk to them.

—Don't forget to remind them, said Candide, of the frightful inhumanity of eating their fellow men, and that Christian ethics forbid it.

—Gentlemen, said Cacambo, you have a mind to eat a Jesuit today? An excellent idea; nothing is more proper than to treat one's enemies so. Indeed, the law of nature teaches us to kill our neighbor, and that's how men behave the whole world over. Though we Europeans don't exercise our right to eat our neighbors, the reason is simply that we find it easy to get a good meal elsewhere; but you don't have our resources, and we certainly agree that it's better to eat your enemies than to let the crows and vultures have the fruit of your victory. But, gentlemen, you wouldn't want to eat your friends. You think you will be spitting a Jesuit, and it's your defender, the enemy of your enemies, whom you will be roasting. For my part, I was born in your country; the gentleman whom you see is my master, and far from being a Jesuit, he has just killed a Jesuit, the robe he is wearing was stripped from him; that's why you have taken a dislike to him. To prove that I am telling the truth, take his robe and bring it to the nearest frontier of the kingdom of Los Padres; find out for yourselves if my master didn't kill a Jesuit officer. It won't take long; if you find that I have lied, you can still eat us. But if I've told the truth, you know too well the principles of public justice, customs, and laws, not to spare our lives.

The Biglugs found this discourse perfectly reasonable; they appointed chiefs to go posthaste and find out the truth; the two messengers performed their task like men of sense, and quickly returned bringing good news. The Biglugs untied their two prisoners, treated them with great politeness, offered them girls, gave them refreshments, and led them back to the border of their state, crying joyously:—He isn't a Jesuit, he isn't a Jesuit!

Candide could not weary of exclaiming over his preservation.

—What a people! he said. What men! what customs! If I had not had the good luck to run a sword through the body of Miss Cunégonde's brother, I would have been eaten on the spot! But, after all, it seems that uncorrupted nature is good, since these folk, instead of eating me, showed me a thousand kindnesses as soon as they knew I was not a Jesuit.

8. Voltaire's name is "Oreillons" from Spanish "Orejones," a name mentioned in Garcilaso de Vega's *Historia General del Perú* (1609), on which Voltaire drew for many of the details in his picture of South America.

CHAPTER 17

Arrival of Candide and His Servant at the Country of Eldorado, and What They Saw There

When they were out of the land of the Biglugs, Cacambo said to Candide:—
You see that this hemisphere is no better than the other; take my advice, and let's get back to Europe as soon as possible.

—How to get back, asked Candide, and where to go? If I go to my own land, the Bulgars and Abares are murdering everyone in sight; if I go to Portugal, they'll burn me alive; if we stay here, we risk being skewered any day. But how can I ever leave that part of the world where Miss Cunégonde lives?

—Let's go toward Cayenne, said Cacambo, we shall find some Frenchmen there, for they go all over the world; they can help us; perhaps God will take pity on us.

To get to Cayenne was not easy; they knew more or less which way to go, but mountains, rivers, cliffs, robbers, and savages obstructed the way everywhere. Their horses died of weariness; their food was eaten; they subsisted for one whole month on wild fruits, and at last they found themselves by a little river fringed with coconut trees, which gave them both life and hope.

Cacambo, who was as full of good advice as the old woman, said to Candide:—
We can go no further, we've walked ourselves out; I see an abandoned canoe on the bank, let's fill it with coconuts, get into the boat, and float with the current; a river always leads to some inhabited spot or other. If we don't find anything pleasant, at least we may find something new.

—Let's go, said Candide, and let Providence be our guide.

They floated some leagues between banks sometimes flowery, sometimes sandy, now steep, now level. The river widened steadily; finally it disappeared into a chasm of frightful rocks that rose high into the heavens. The two travelers had the audacity to float with the current into this chasm. The river, narrowly confined, drove them onward with horrible speed and a fearful roar. After twenty-four hours, they saw daylight once more; but their canoe was smashed on the snags. They had to drag themselves from rock to rock for an entire league; at last they emerged to an immense horizon, ringed with remote mountains. The countryside was tended for pleasure as well as profit; everywhere the useful was joined to the agreeable. The roads were covered, or rather decorated, with elegantly shaped carriages made of a glittering material, carrying men and women of singular beauty, and drawn by great red sheep which were faster than the finest horses of Andalusia, Tetuan, and Mequinez.

—Here now, said Candide, is a country that's better than Westphalia.

Along with Cacambo, he climbed out of the river at the first village he could see. Some children of the town, dressed in rags of gold brocade, were playing quoits at the village gate; our two men from the other world paused to watch them; their quoits were rather large, yellow, red, and green, and they glittered with a singular luster. On a whim, the travelers picked up several; they were of gold, emeralds, and rubies, and the least of them would have been the greatest ornament of the Great Mogul's throne.

—Surely, said Cacambo, these quoit players are the children of the king of the country.

The village schoolmaster appeared at that moment, to call them back to school.

—And there, said Candide, is the tutor of the royal household.

The little rascals quickly gave up their game, leaving on the ground their quoits and playthings. Candide picked them up, ran to the schoolmaster, and presented them to him humbly, giving him to understand by sign language that their royal highnesses had forgotten their gold and jewels. With a smile, the schoolmaster tossed them to the ground, glanced quickly but with great surprise at Candide's face, and went his way.

The travelers did not fail to pick up the gold, rubies, and emeralds.

—Where in the world are we? cried Candide. The children of this land must be well trained, since they are taught contempt for gold and jewels.

Cacambo was as much surprised as Candide. At last they came to the finest house of the village; it was built like a European palace. A crowd of people surrounded the door, and even more were in the entry; delightful music was heard, and a delicious aroma of cooking filled the air. Cacambo went up to the door, listened, and reported that they were talking Peruvian; that was his native language, for every reader must know that Cacambo was born in Tucuman, in a village where they talk that language exclusively.

—I'll act as interpreter, he told Candide; it's an hotel, let's go in.

Promptly two boys and two girls of the staff, dressed in cloth of gold, and wearing ribbons in their hair, invited them to sit at the host's table. The meal consisted of four soups, each one garnished with a brace of parakeets, a boiled condor which weighed two hundred pounds, two roast monkeys of an excellent flavor, three hundred birds of paradise in one dish and six hundred hummingbirds in another, exquisite stews, delicious pastries, the whole thing served up in plates of what looked like rock crystal. The boys and girls of the staff poured them various beverages made from sugar cane.

The diners were for the most part merchants and travelers, all extremely polite, who questioned Cacambo with the most discreet circumspection, and answered his questions very directly.

When the meal was over, Cacambo as well as Candide supposed he could settle his bill handsomely by tossing onto the table two of those big pieces of gold which they had picked up; but the host and hostess burst out laughing, and for a long time nearly split their sides. Finally they subsided.

—Gentlemen, said the host, we see clearly that you're foreigners; we don't meet many of you here. Please excuse our laughing when you offered us in payment a couple of pebbles from the roadside. No doubt you don't have any of our local currency, but you don't need it to eat here. All the hotels established for the promotion of commerce are maintained by the state. You have had meager entertainment here, for we are only a poor town; but everywhere else you will be given the sort of welcome you deserve.

Cacambo translated for Candide all the host's explanations, and Candide listened to them with the same admiration and astonishment that his friend Cacambo showed in reporting them.

—What is this country, then, said they to one another, unknown to the rest of the world, and where nature itself is so different from our own? This probably is the country where everything is for the best; for it's absolutely necessary that such a country should exist somewhere. And whatever Master Pangloss said of the matter, I have often had occasion to notice that things went badly in Westphalia.

CHAPTER 18

What They Saw in the Land of Eldorado

Cacambo revealed his curiosity to the host, and the host told him:—I am an ignorant man and content to remain so; but we have here an old man, retired from the court, who is the most knowing person in the kingdom, and the most talkative.

Thereupon he brought Cacambo to the old man's house. Candide now played second fiddle, and acted as servant to his own valet. They entered an austere little house, for the door was merely of silver and the paneling of the rooms was only gold, though so tastefully wrought that the finest paneling would not surpass it. If the truth must be told, the lobby was only decorated with rubies and emeralds; but the patterns in which they were arranged atoned for the extreme simplicity.

The old man received the two strangers on a sofa stuffed with bird-of-paradise feathers, and offered them several drinks in diamond carafes; then he satisfied their curiosity in these terms.

—I am a hundred and seventy-two years old, and I heard from my late father, who was liveryman to the king, about the astonishing revolutions in Peru which he had seen. Our land here was formerly part of the kingdom of the Incas, who rashly left it in order to conquer another part of the world, and who were ultimately destroyed by the Spaniards. The wisest princes of their house were those who had never left their native valley; they decreed, with the consent of the nation, that henceforth no inhabitant of our little kingdom should ever leave it; and this rule is what has preserved our innocence and our happiness. The Spaniards heard vague rumors about this land, they called it Eldorado;[9] and an English knight named Raleigh even came somewhere close to it about a hundred years ago; but as we are surrounded by unscalable mountains and precipices, we have managed so far to remain hidden from the rapacity of the European nations, who have an inconceivable rage for the pebbles and mud of our land, and who, in order to get some, would butcher us all to the last man.

The conversation was a long one; it turned on the form of the government, the national customs, on women, public shows, the arts. At last Candide, whose taste always ran to metaphysics, told Cacambo to ask if the country had any religion.

The old man grew a bit red.

—How's that? he said. Can you have any doubt of it? Do you suppose we are altogether thankless scoundrels?

Cacambo asked meekly what was the religion of Eldorado. The old man flushed again.

—Can there be two religions? he asked. I suppose our religion is the same as everyone's, we worship God from morning to evening.

—Then you worship a single deity? said Cacambo, who acted throughout as interpreter of the questions of Candide.

—It's obvious, said the old man, that there aren't two or three or four of them. I must say the people of your world ask very remarkable questions.

Candide could not weary of putting questions to this good old man; he wanted to know how the people of Eldorado prayed to God.

9. The myth of this land of gold somewhere in Central or South America had been widespread since the 16th century. *The Discovery of Guiana*, published in 1595, described Sir Walter Ralegh's infatuation with the myth of Eldorado and served to spread the story still further.

—We don't pray to him at all, said the good and respectable sage; we have nothing to ask him for, since everything we need has already been granted; we thank God continually.

Candide was interested in seeing the priests; he had Cacambo ask where they were. The old gentleman smiled.

—My friends, said he, we are all priests; the king and all the heads of household sing formal psalms of thanksgiving every morning, and five or six thousand voices accompany them.

—What! you have no monks to teach, argue, govern, intrigue, and burn at the stake everyone who disagrees with them?

—We should have to be mad, said the old man; here we are all of the same mind, and we don't understand what you're up to with your monks.

Candide was overjoyed at all these speeches, and said to himself:—This is very different from Westphalia and the castle of My Lord the Baron; if our friend Pangloss had seen Eldorado, he wouldn't have called the castle of Thunder-Ten-Tronckh the finest thing on earth; to know the world one must travel.

After this long conversation, the old gentleman ordered a carriage with six sheep made ready, and gave the two travelers twelve of his servants for their journey to the court.

—Excuse me, said he, if old age deprives me of the honor of accompanying you. The king will receive you after a style which will not altogether displease you, and you will doubtless make allowance for the customs of the country if there are any you do not like.

Candide and Cacambo climbed into the coach; the six sheep flew like the wind, and in less than four hours they reached the king's palace at the edge of the capital. The entryway was two hundred and twenty feet high and a hundred wide; it is impossible to describe all the materials of which it was made. But you can imagine how much finer it was than those pebbles and sand which we call gold and jewels.

Twenty beautiful girls of the guard detail welcomed Candide and Cacambo as they stepped from the carriage, took them to the baths, and dressed them in robes woven of hummingbird feathers; then the high officials of the crown, both male and female, led them to the royal chamber between two long lines, each of a thousand musicians, as is customary. As they approached the throne room, Cacambo asked an officer what was the proper method of greeting his majesty: if one fell to one's knees or on one's belly; if one put one's hands on one's head or on one's rear; if one licked up the dust of the earth—in a word, what was the proper form?[1]

—The ceremony, said the officer, is to embrace the king and kiss him on both cheeks.

Candide and Cacambo fell on the neck of his majesty, who received them with all the dignity imaginable, and asked them politely to dine.

In the interim, they were taken about to see the city, the public buildings rising to the clouds, the public markets and arcades, the fountains of pure water and of rose water, those of sugar cane liquors which flowed perpetually in the great plazas paved with a sort of stone which gave off odors of gilly-flower and rose petals. Candide asked to see the supreme court and the hall of parliament; they told him

1. Candide's questions are probably derived from those of Gulliver on a similar occasion, in the third part of *Gulliver's Travels*.

there was no such thing, that lawsuits were unknown. He asked if there were prisons, and was told there were not. What surprised him more, and gave him most pleasure, was the palace of sciences, in which he saw a gallery two thousand paces long, entirely filled with mathematical and physical instruments.

Having passed the whole afternoon seeing only a thousandth part of the city, they returned to the king's palace. Candide sat down to dinner with his majesty, his own valet Cacambo, and several ladies. Never was better food served, and never did a host preside more jovially than his majesty. Cacambo explained the king's witty sayings to Candide, and even when translated they still seemed witty. Of all the things which astonished Candide, this was not, in his eyes, the least astonishing.

They passed a month in this refuge. Candide never tired of saying to Cacambo:— It's true, my friend, I'll say it again, the castle where I was born does not compare with the land where I now am; but Miss Cunégonde is not here, and you doubtless have a mistress somewhere in Europe. If we stay here, we shall be just like everybody else, whereas if we go back to our own world, taking with us just a dozen sheep loaded with Eldorado pebbles, we shall be richer than all the kings put together, we shall have no more inquisitors to fear, and we shall easily be able to retake Miss Cunégonde.

This harangue pleased Cacambo; wandering is such pleasure, it gives a man such prestige at home to be able to talk of what he has seen abroad, that the two happy men resolved to be so no longer, but to take their leave of his majesty.

—You are making a foolish mistake, the king told them; I know very well that my kingdom is nothing much; but when you are pretty comfortable somewhere, you had better stay there. Of course I have no right to keep strangers against their will, that sort of tyranny is not in keeping with our laws or our customs; all men are free; depart when you will, but the way out is very difficult. You cannot possibly go up the river by which you miraculously came; it runs too swiftly through its underground caves. The mountains which surround my land are ten thousand feet high, and steep as walls; each one is more than ten leagues across; the only way down is over precipices. But since you really must go, I shall order my engineers to make a machine which can carry you conveniently. When we take you over the mountains, nobody will be able to go with you, for my subjects have sworn never to leave their refuge, and they are too sensible to break their vows. Other than that, ask of me what you please.

—We only request of your majesty, Cacambo said, a few sheep loaded with provisions, some pebbles, and some of the mud of your country.

The king laughed.

—I simply can't understand, said he, the passion you Europeans have for our yellow mud; but take all you want, and much good may it do you.

He promptly gave orders to his technicians to make a machine for lifting these two extraordinary men out of his kingdom. Three thousand good physicists worked at the problem; the machine was ready in two weeks' time, and cost no more than twenty million pounds sterling, in the money of the country. Cacambo and Candide were placed in the machine; there were two great sheep, saddled and bridled to serve them as steeds when they had cleared the mountains, twenty pack sheep with provisions, thirty which carried presents consisting of the rarities of the country, and fifty loaded with gold, jewels, and diamonds. The king bade tender farewell to the two vagabonds.

It made a fine spectacle, their departure, and the ingenious way in which they were hoisted with their sheep up to the top of the mountains. The technicians bade them good-bye after bringing them to safety, and Candide had now no other desire and no other object than to go and present his sheep to Miss Cunégonde.

—We have, said he, enough to pay off the governor of Buenos Aires—if, indeed, a price can be placed on Miss Cunégonde. Let us go to Cayenne, take ship there, and then see what kingdom we can find to buy up.

CHAPTER 19

What Happened to Them at Surinam, and How Candide
Got to Know Martin

The first day was pleasant enough for our travelers. They were encouraged by the idea of possessing more treasures than Asia, Europe, and Africa could bring together. Candide, in transports, carved the name of Cunégonde on the trees. On the second day two of their sheep bogged down in a swamp and were lost with their loads; two other sheep died of fatigue a few days later; seven or eight others starved to death in a desert; still others fell, a little after, from precipices. Finally, after a hundred days' march, they had only two sheep left. Candide told Cacambo:—My friend, you see how the riches of this world are fleeting; the only solid things are virtue and the joy of seeing Miss Cunégonde again.

—I agree, said Cacambo, but we still have two sheep, laden with more treasure than the king of Spain will ever have; and I see in the distance a town which I suspect is Surinam; it belongs to the Dutch. We are at the end of our trials and on the threshold of our happiness.

As they drew near the town, they discovered a negro stretched on the ground with only half his clothes left, that is, a pair of blue drawers; the poor fellow was also missing his left leg and his right hand.

—Good Lord, said Candide in Dutch, what are you doing in that horrible condition, my friend?

—I am waiting for my master, Mr. Vanderdendur,[2] the famous merchant, answered the negro.

—Is Mr. Vanderdendur, Candide asked, the man who treated you this way?

—Yes, sir, said the negro, that's how things are around here. Twice a year we get a pair of linen drawers to wear. If we catch a finger in the sugar mill where we work, they cut off our hand; if we try to run away, they cut off our leg: I have undergone both these experiences. This is the price of the sugar you eat in Europe. And yet, when my mother sold me for ten Patagonian crowns on the coast of Guinea, she said to me: 'My dear child, bless our witch doctors, reverence them always, they will make your life happy; you have the honor of being a slave to our white masters, and in this way you are making the fortune of your father and mother.' Alas! I don't know if I made their fortunes, but they certainly did not make mine. The dogs, monkeys, and parrots are a thousand times less unhappy than we are. The Dutch witch doctors who converted me tell me every Sunday that we are all sons of Adam, black and white alike. I am no genealogist;

---

2. A name perhaps intended to suggest Van-Duren, a Dutch bookseller with whom Voltaire had quarreled. In particular, the incident of gradually raising one's price recalls Van-Duren, to whom Voltaire had successively offered 1,000, 1,500, 2,000, and 3,000 florins for the return of the manuscript of Frederick the Great's *Anti-Machiavel*.

but if these preachers are right, we must all be remote cousins; and you must admit no one could treat his own flesh and blood in a more horrible fashion.

—Oh Pangloss! cried Candide, you had no notion of these abominations! I'm through, I must give up your optimism after all.

—What's optimism? said Cacambo.

—Alas, said Candide, it is a mania for saying things are well when one is in hell.

And he shed bitter tears as he looked at this negro, and he was still weeping as he entered Surinam.

The first thing they asked was if there was not some vessel in port which could be sent to Buenos Aires. The man they asked was a Spanish merchant who undertook to make an honest bargain with them. They arranged to meet in a café; Candide and the faithful Cacambo, with their two sheep, went there to meet with him.

Candide, who always said exactly what was in his heart, told the Spaniard of his adventures, and confessed that he wanted to recapture Miss Cunégonde.

—I shall take good care *not* to send you to Buenos Aires, said the merchant; I should be hanged, and so would you. The lovely Cunégonde is his lordship's favorite mistress.

This was a thunderstroke for Candide; he wept for a long time; finally he drew Cacambo aside.

—Here, my friend, said he, is what you must do. Each one of us has in his pockets five or six millions' worth of diamonds; you are cleverer than I; go get Miss Cunégonde in Buenos Aires. If the governor makes a fuss, give him a million; if that doesn't convince him, give him two millions; you never killed an inquisitor, nobody will suspect you. I'll fit out another boat and go wait for you in Venice. That is a free country, where one need have no fear either of Bulgars or Abares or Jews or inquisitors.

Cacambo approved of this wise decision. He was in despair at leaving a good master who had become a bosom friend; but the pleasure of serving him overcame the grief of leaving him. They embraced, and shed a few tears; Candide urged him not to forget the good old woman. Cacambo departed that very same day; he was a very good fellow, that Cacambo.

Candide remained for some time in Surinam, waiting for another merchant to take him to Italy, along with the two sheep which were left him. He hired servants and bought everything necessary for the long voyage; finally Mr. Vanderdendur, master of a big ship, came calling.

—How much will you charge, Candide asked this man, to take me to Venice—myself, my servants, my luggage, and those two sheep over there?

The merchant set a price of ten thousand piastres; Candide did not blink an eye.

—Oh, ho, said the prudent Vanderdendur to himself, this stranger pays out ten thousand piastres at once, he must be pretty well fixed.

Then, returning a moment later, he made known that he could not set sail under twenty thousand.

—All right, you shall have them, said Candide.

—Whew, said the merchant softly to himself, this man gives twenty thousand piastres as easily as ten.

He came back again to say he could not go to Venice for less than thirty thousand piastres.

—All right, thirty then, said Candide.

—Ah ha, said the Dutch merchant, again speaking to himself; so thirty thousand piastres mean nothing to this man; no doubt the two sheep are loaded with immense treasures; let's say no more; we'll pick up the thirty thousand piastres first, and then we'll see.

Candide sold two little diamonds, the least of which was worth more than all the money demanded by the merchant. He paid him in advance. The two sheep were taken aboard. Candide followed in a little boat, to board the vessel at its anchorage. The merchant bides his time, sets sail, and makes his escape with a favoring wind. Candide, aghast and stupefied, soon loses him from view.

—Alas, he cries, now there is a trick worthy of the old world!

He returns to shore sunk in misery; for he had lost riches enough to make the fortunes of twenty monarchs.

Now he rushes to the house of the Dutch magistrate, and, being a bit disturbed, he knocks loudly at the door; goes in, tells the story of what happened, and shouts a bit louder than is customary. The judge begins by fining him ten thousand piastres for making such a racket; then he listens patiently to the story, promises to look into the matter as soon as the merchant comes back, and charges another ten thousand piastres as the costs of the hearing.

This legal proceeding completed the despair of Candide. In fact he had experienced miseries a thousand times more painful, but the coldness of the judge, and that of the merchant who had robbed him, roused his bile and plunged him into a black melancholy. The malice of men rose up before his spirit in all its ugliness, and his mind dwelt only on gloomy thoughts. Finally, when a French vessel was ready to leave for Bordeaux, since he had no more diamond-laden sheep to transport, he took a cabin at a fair price, and made it known in the town that he would pay passage and keep, plus two thousand piastres, to any honest man who wanted to make the journey with him, on condition that this man must be the most disgusted with his own condition and the most unhappy man in the province.

This drew such a crowd of applicants as a fleet could not have held. Candide wanted to choose among the leading candidates, so he picked out about twenty who seemed companionable enough, and of whom each pretended to be more miserable than all the others. He brought them together at his inn and gave them a dinner, on condition that each would swear to tell truthfully his entire history. He would select as his companion the most truly miserable and rightly discontented man, and among the others he would distribute various gifts.

The meeting lasted till four in the morning. Candide, as he listened to all the stories, remembered what the old woman had told him on the trip to Buenos Aires, and of the wager she had made, that there was nobody on the boat who had not undergone great misfortunes. At every story that was told him, he thought of Pangloss.

—That Pangloss, he said, would be hard put to prove his system. I wish he was here. Certainly if everything goes well, it is in Eldorado and not in the rest of the world.

At last he decided in favor of a poor scholar who had worked ten years for the booksellers of Amsterdam. He decided that there was no trade in the world with which one should be more disgusted.

This scholar, who was in fact a good man, had been robbed by his wife, beaten by his son, and deserted by his daughter, who had got herself abducted by a Portuguese. He had just been fired from the little job on which he existed; and the preachers of Surinam were persecuting him because they took him for a Socinian.[3] The others, it is true, were at least as unhappy as he, but Candide hoped the scholar would prove more amusing on the voyage. All his rivals declared that Candide was doing them a great injustice, but he pacified them with a hundred piastres apiece.

CHAPTER 20

What Happened to Candide and Martin at Sea

The old scholar, whose name was Martin, now set sail with Candide for Bordeaux. Both men had seen and suffered much; and even if the vessel had been sailing from Surinam to Japan via the Cape of Good Hope, they would have been able to keep themselves amused with instances of moral evil and physical evil during the entire trip.

However, Candide had one great advantage over Martin, that he still hoped to see Miss Cunégonde again, and Martin had nothing to hope for; besides, he had gold and diamonds, and though he had lost a hundred big red sheep loaded with the greatest treasures of the earth, though he had always at his heart a memory of the Dutch merchant's villainy, yet, when he thought of the wealth that remained in his hands, and when he talked of Cunégonde, especially just after a good dinner, he still inclined to the system of Pangloss.

—But what about you, Monsieur Martin, he asked the scholar, what do you think of all that? What is your idea of moral evil and physical evil?

—Sir, answered Martin, those priests accused me of being a Socinian, but the truth is that I am a Manichee.[4]

—You're joking, said Candide; there aren't any more Manichees in the world.

—There's me, said Martin; I don't know what to do about it, but I can't think otherwise.

—You must be possessed of the devil, said Candide.

—He's mixed up with so many things of this world, said Martin, that he may be in me as well as elsewhere; but I assure you, as I survey this globe, or globule, I think that God has abandoned it to some evil spirit—all of it except Eldorado. I have scarcely seen one town which did not wish to destroy its neighboring town, no family which did not wish to exterminate some other family. Everywhere the weak loathe the powerful, before whom they cringe, and the powerful treat them like brute cattle, to be sold for their meat and fleece. A million regimented assassins roam Europe from one end to the other, plying the trades of murder and robbery in an organized way for a living, because there is no more honest form of work for them; and in the cities which seem to enjoy peace and where the arts are flourishing, men are devoured by more envy, cares, and anxieties than a whole town experiences when it's under siege. Private griefs are

<hr>

3. A follower of Faustus and Laelius Socinus, 16th-century Polish theologians who proposed a form of "rational" Christianity that exalted the rational conscience and minimized such mysteries as the Trinity. The Socinians, by a special irony, were vigorous optimists.
4. Mani, a Persian sage and philosopher of the 3rd century, taught (probably under the influence of traditions stemming from Zoroaster and the worshipers of the sun god Mithra) that the earth is a field of dispute between two almost equal powers, one of light and one of darkness, both of which must be propitiated.

worse even than public trials. In a word, I have seen so much and suffered so much, that I am a Manichee.

—Still there is some good, said Candide.

—That may be, said Martin, but I don't know it.

In the middle of this discussion, the rumble of cannon was heard. From minute to minute the noise grew louder. Everyone reached for his spyglass. At a distance of some three miles they saw two vessels fighting; the wind brought both of them so close to the French vessel that they had a pleasantly comfortable seat to watch the fight. Presently one of the vessels caught the other with a broadside so low and so square as to send it to the bottom. Candide and Martin saw clearly a hundred men on the deck of the sinking ship; they all raised their hands to heaven, uttering fearful shrieks; and in a moment everything was swallowed up.

—Well, said Martin, that is how men treat one another.

—It is true, said Candide, there's something devilish in this business.

As they chatted, he noticed something of a striking red color floating near the sunken vessel. They sent out a boat to investigate; it was one of his sheep. Candide was more joyful to recover this one sheep than he had been afflicted to lose a hundred of them, all loaded with big Eldorado diamonds.

The French captain soon learned that the captain of the victorious vessel was Spanish and that of the sunken vessel was a Dutch pirate. It was the same man who had robbed Candide. The enormous riches which this rascal had stolen were sunk beside him in the sea, and nothing was saved but a single sheep.

—You see, said Candide to Martin, crime is punished sometimes; this scoundrel of a Dutch merchant has met the fate he deserved.

—Yes, said Martin; but did the passengers aboard his ship have to perish too? God punished the scoundrel, and the devil drowned the others.

Meanwhile the French and Spanish vessels continued on their journey, and Candide continued his talks with Martin. They disputed for fifteen days in a row, and at the end of that time were just as much in agreement as at the beginning. But at least they were talking, they exchanged their ideas, they consoled one another. Candide caressed his sheep.

—Since I have found you again, said he, I may well rediscover Miss Cunégonde.

CHAPTER 21

Candide and Martin Approach the Coast of France: They Reason Together

At last the coast of France came in view.

—Have you ever been in France, Monsieur Martin? asked Candide.

—Yes, said Martin, I have visited several provinces. There are some where half the inhabitants are crazy, others where they are too sly, still others where they are quite gentle and stupid, some where they venture on wit; in all of them the principal occupation is love-making, the second is slander, and the third stupid talk.

—But, Monsieur Martin, were you ever in Paris?

—Yes, I've been in Paris; it contains specimens of all these types; it is a chaos, a mob, in which everyone is seeking pleasure and where hardly anyone finds it, at least from what I have seen. I did not live there for long; as I arrived, I was robbed of everything I possessed by thieves at the fair of St. Germain; I myself was taken for a thief, and spent eight days in jail, after which I took a proofreader's job to earn enough money to return on foot to Holland. I knew the writing gang, the intriguing gang, the gang with fits and convulsions.[5] They say there are some very civilized people in that town; I'd like to think so.

—I myself have no desire to visit France, said Candide; you no doubt realize that when one has spent a month in Eldorado, there is nothing else on earth one wants to see, except Miss Cunégonde. I am going to wait for her at Venice; we will cross France simply to get to Italy; wouldn't you like to come with me?

—Gladly, said Martin; they say Venice is good only for the Venetian nobles, but that on the other hand they treat foreigners very well when they have plenty of money. I don't have any; you do, so I'll follow you anywhere.

—By the way, said Candide, do you believe the earth was originally all ocean, as they assure us in that big book belonging to the ship's captain?[6]

—I don't believe that stuff, said Martin, nor any of the dreams which people have been peddling for some time now.

—But why, then, was this world formed at all? asked Candide.

—To drive us mad, answered Martin.

—Aren't you astonished, Candide went on, at the love which those two girls showed for the monkeys in the land of the Biglugs that I told you about?

—Not at all, said Martin, I see nothing strange in these sentiments; I have seen so many extraordinary things that nothing seems extraordinary any more.

—Do you believe, asked Candide, that men have always massacred one another as they do today? That they have always been liars, traitors, ingrates, thieves, weaklings, sneaks, cowards, backbiters, gluttons, drunkards, misers, climbers, killers, calumniators, sensualists, fanatics, hypocrites, and fools?

—Do you believe, said Martin, that hawks have always eaten pigeons when they could get them?

—Of course, said Candide.

—Well, said Martin, if hawks have always had the same character, why do you suppose that men have changed?

—Oh, said Candide, there's a great deal of difference, because freedom of the will . . .

As they were disputing in this manner, they reached Bordeaux.

CHAPTER 22

What Happened in France to Candide and Martin

Candide paused in Bordeaux only long enough to sell a couple of Eldorado pebbles and to fit himself out with a fine two-seater carriage, for he could no longer do without his philosopher Martin; only he was very unhappy to part with his sheep, which he left to the academy of science in Bordeaux. They proposed, as the theme of that year's prize contest, the discovery of why the wool of the sheep was red; and the prize was awarded to a northern scholar[7] who demonstrated by A plus B minus C divided by Z that the sheep ought to be red and die of sheep rot.

---

5. The Jansenists, a sect of strict Catholics, became notorious for spiritual ecstasies. Their public displays reached a height during the 1720s, and Voltaire described them in *Le Siècle de Louis XIV* (chap. 37), as well as in the article "Convulsions" in the *Philosophical* *Dictionary*.

6. The Bible: Genesis I.

7. Maupertuis Le Lapon, philosopher and mathematician, whom Voltaire had accused of trying to adduce mathematical proofs of the existence of God.

But all the travelers with whom Candide talked in the roadside inns told him:—We are going to Paris.

This general consensus finally inspired in him too a desire to see the capital; it was not much out of his road to Venice.

He entered through the Faubourg Saint-Marceau,[8] and thought he was in the meanest village of Westphalia.

Scarcely was Candide in his hotel, when he came down with a mild illness caused by exhaustion. As he was wearing an enormous diamond ring, and people had noticed among his luggage a tremendously heavy safe, he soon found at his bedside two doctors whom he had not called, several intimate friends who never left him alone, and two pious ladies who helped to warm his broth. Martin said:—I remember that I too was ill on my first trip to Paris; I was very poor; and as I had neither friends, pious ladies, nor doctors, I got well.

However, as a result of medicines and bleedings, Candide's illness became serious. A resident of the neighborhood came to ask him politely to fill out a ticket, to be delivered to the porter of the other world.[9] Candide wanted nothing to do with it. The pious ladies assured him it was a new fashion; Candide replied that he wasn't a man of fashion. Martin wanted to throw the resident out the window. The cleric swore that without the ticket they wouldn't bury Candide. Martin swore that he would bury the cleric if he continued to be a nuisance. The quarrel grew heated; Martin took him by the shoulders and threw him bodily out the door; all of which caused a great scandal, from which developed a legal case.

Candide got better; and during his convalescence he had very good company in to dine. They played cards for money; and Candide was quite surprised that none of the aces were ever dealt to him, and Martin was not surprised at all.

Among those who did the honors of the town for Candide there was a little abbé from Perigord, one of those busy fellows, always bright, always useful, assured, obsequious, and obliging, who waylay passing strangers, tell them the scandal of the town, and offer them pleasures at any price they want to pay. This fellow first took Candide and Martin to the theatre. A new tragedy was being played. Candide found himself seated next to a group of wits. That did not keep him from shedding a few tears in the course of some perfectly played scenes. One of the commentators beside him remarked during the intermission:—You are quite mistaken to weep, this actress is very bad indeed; the actor who plays with her is even worse; and the play is even worse than the actors in it. The author knows not a word of Arabic, though the action takes place in Arabia; and besides, he is a man who doesn't believe in innate ideas. Tomorrow I will show you twenty pamphlets written against him.

—Tell me, sir, said Candide to the abbé, how many plays are there for performance in France?

—Five or six thousand, replied the other.

—That's a lot, said Candide; how many of them are any good?

8. A district on the left bank, notably grubby in the 18th century. "As I entered [Paris] through the Faubourg Saint-Marceau, I saw nothing but dirty stinking little streets, ugly black houses, a general air of squalor and poverty, beggars, carters, menders of clothes, sellers of herb-drinks and old hats." Jean-Jacques Rousseau, *Confessions*, Book IV.

9. In the middle of the 18th century in France, it became customary to require persons who were grievously ill to sign *billets de confession*, without which they could not be given absolution, admitted to the last sacraments, or buried in consecrated ground.

—Fifteen or sixteen, was the answer.

—That's a lot, said Martin.

Candide was very pleased with an actress who took the part of Queen Elizabeth in a rather dull tragedy[1] that still gets played from time to time.

—I like this actress very much, he said to Martin, she bears a slight resemblance to Miss Cunégonde; I should like to meet her.

The abbé from Perigord offered to introduce him. Candide, raised in Germany, asked what was the protocol, how one behaved in France with queens of England.

—You must distinguish, said the abbé; in the provinces, you take them to an inn; at Paris they are respected while still attractive, and thrown on the dunghill when they are dead.[2]

—Queens on the dunghill! said Candide.

—Yes indeed, said Martin, the abbé is right; I was in Paris when Miss Monime herself[3] passed, as they say, from this life to the other; she was refused what these folk call 'the honors of burial,' that is, the right to rot with all the beggars of the district in a dirty cemetery; she was buried all alone by her troupe at the corner of the Rue de Bourgogne; this must have been very disagreeable to her, for she had a noble character.

—That was extremely rude, said Candide.

—What do you expect? said Martin; that is how these folk are. Imagine all the contradictions, all the incompatibilities you can, and you will see them in the government, the courts, the churches, and the plays of this crazy nation.

—Is it true that they are always laughing in Paris? asked Candide.

—Yes, said the abbé, but with a kind of rage too; when people complain of things, they do so amid explosions of laughter; they even laugh as they perform the most detestable actions.

—Who was that fat swine, said Candide, who spoke so nastily about the play over which I was weeping, and the actors who gave me so much pleasure?

—He is a living illness, answered the abbé, who makes a business of slandering all the plays and books; he hates the successful ones, as eunuchs hate successful lovers; he's one of those literary snakes who live on filth and venom; he's a folliculator . . .

—What's this word *folliculator*? asked Candide.

—It's a folio filler, said the abbé, a Fréron.[4]

It was after this fashion that Candide, Martin, and the abbé from Perigord chatted on the stairway as they watched the crowd leaving the theatre.

—Although I'm in a great hurry to see Miss Cunégonde again, said Candide, I would very much like to dine with Miss Clairon,[5] for she seemed to me admirable.

The abbé was not the man to approach Miss Clairon, who saw only good company.

---

1. *Le Comte d'Essex* by Thomas Corneille.
2. Voltaire engaged in a long and vigorous campaign against the rule that actors and actresses could not be buried in consecrated ground. The superstition probably arose from a feeling that by assuming false identities they drained their own souls.
3. Adrienne Lecouvreur (1690–1730), so called because she made her debut as Monime in Racine's *Mithridate*. Voltaire had assisted at her secret midnight funeral and wrote an indignant poem about it.
4. A successful and popular journalist who had attacked several of Voltaire's plays, including *Tancrède*.
5. Actually Claire Leris (1723–1803). She had played the lead role in *Tancrède* and was for many years a leading figure on the Paris stage.

—She has an engagement tonight, he said; but I shall have the honor of introducing you to a lady of quality, and there you will get to know Paris as if you had lived here for years.

Candide, who was curious by nature, allowed himself to be brought to the lady's house, in the depths of the Faubourg St.-Honoré; they were playing faro;[6] twelve melancholy punters held in their hands a little sheaf of cards, blank summaries of their bad luck. Silence reigned supreme, the punters were pallid, the banker uneasy; and the lady of the house, seated beside the pitiless banker, watched with the eyes of a lynx for the various illegal redoublings and bets at long odds which the players tried to signal by folding the corners of their cards; she had them unfolded with a determination which was severe but polite, and concealed her anger lest she lose her customers. The lady caused herself to be known as the Marquise of Parolignac.[7] Her daughter, fifteen years old, sat among the punters and tipped off her mother with a wink to the sharp practices of these unhappy players when they tried to recoup their losses. The abbé from Perigord, Candide, and Martin came in; nobody arose or greeted them or looked at them; all were lost in the study of their cards.

—My Lady the Baroness of Thunder-Ten-Tronckh was more civil, thought Candide.

However, the abbé whispered in the ear of the marquise, who, half rising, honored Candide with a gracious smile and Martin with a truly noble nod; she gave a seat and dealt a hand of cards to Candide, who lost fifty thousand francs in two turns; after which they had a very merry supper. Everyone was amazed that Candide was not upset over his losses; the lackeys, talking together in their usual lackey language, said:—He must be some English milord.

The supper was like most Parisian suppers: first silence, then an indistinguishable rush of words; then jokes, mostly insipid, false news, bad logic, a little politics, a great deal of malice. They even talked of new books.

—Have you seen the new novel by Dr. Gauchat, the theologian?[8] asked the abbé from Perigord.

—Oh yes, answered one of the guests; but I couldn't finish it. We have a horde of impudent scribblers nowadays, but all of them put together don't match the impudence of this Gauchat, this doctor of theology. I have been so struck by the enormous number of detestable books which are swamping us that I have taken up punting at faro.

—And the *Collected Essays* of Archdeacon T————[9] asked the abbé, what do you think of them?

—Ah, said Madame de Parolignac, what a frightful bore he is! He takes such pains to tell you what everyone knows; he discourses so learnedly on matters which aren't worth a casual remark! He plunders, and not even wit-

6. A game of cards, about which it is necessary to know only that a number of punters play against a banker or dealer. The pack is dealt out two cards at a time, and each player may bet on any card as much as he pleases. The sharp practices of the punters consist essentially of tricks for increasing their winnings without corresponding risks.

7. A *paroli* is an illegal redoubling of one's bet; her name therefore implies a title grounded in cardsharping.

8. He had written against Voltaire, and Voltaire suspected him (wrongly) of having written the novel *L'Oracle des nouveaux philosophes*.

9. His name was Trublet, and he had said, among other disagreeable things, that Voltaire's epic poem, the *Henriade*, made him yawn and that Voltaire's genius was "the perfection of mediocrity."

tily, the wit of other people! He spoils what he plunders, he's disgusting! But he'll never disgust me again; a couple of pages of the archdeacon have been enough for me.

There was at table a man of learning and taste, who supported the marquise on this point. They talked next of tragedies; the lady asked why there were tragedies which played well enough but which were wholly unreadable. The man of taste explained very clearly how a play could have a certain interest and yet little merit otherwise; he showed succinctly that it was not enough to conduct a couple of intrigues, such as one can find in any novel, and which never fail to excite the spectator's interest; but that one must be new without being grotesque, frequently touch the sublime but never depart from the natural; that one must know the human heart and give it words; that one must be a great poet without allowing any character in the play to sound like a poet; and that one must know the language perfectly, speak it purely, and maintain a continual harmony without ever sacrificing sense to mere sound.

—Whoever, he added, does not observe all these rules may write one or two tragedies which succeed in the theatre, but he will never be ranked among the good writers; there are very few good tragedies; some are idylls in well-written, well-rhymed dialogue, others are political arguments which put the audience to sleep, or revolting pomposities; still others are the fantasies of enthusiasts, barbarous in style, incoherent in logic, full of long speeches to the gods because the author does not know how to address men, full of false maxims and emphatic commonplaces.

Candide listened attentively to this speech and conceived a high opinion of the speaker; and as the marquise had placed him by her side, he turned to ask her who was this man who spoke so well.

—He is a scholar, said the lady, who never plays cards and whom the abbé sometimes brings to my house for supper; he knows all about tragedies and books, and has himself written a tragedy that was hissed from the stage and a book, the only copy of which ever seen outside his publisher's office was dedicated to me.

—What a great man, said Candide, he's Pangloss all over.

Then, turning to him, he said:—Sir, you doubtless think everything is for the best in the physical as well as the moral universe, and that nothing could be otherwise than as it is?

—Not at all, sir, replied the scholar, I believe nothing of the sort. I find that everything goes wrong in our world; that nobody knows his place in society or his duty, what he's doing or what he ought to be doing, and that outside of mealtimes, which are cheerful and congenial enough, all the rest of the day is spent in useless quarrels, as of Jansenists against Molinists,[1] parliament-men against churchmen, literary men against literary men, courtiers against courtiers, financiers against the plebs, wives against husbands, relatives against relatives—it's one unending warfare.

---

1. The Jansenists (from Corneille Jansen, 1585–1638) were a relatively strict party of religious reform; the Molinists (from Luis Molina) were the party of the Jesuits. Their central issue of controversy was the relative importance of divine grace and human will to the salvation of man.

Candide answered:—I have seen worse; but a wise man, who has since had the misfortune to be hanged, taught me that everything was marvelously well arranged. Troubles are just the shadows in a beautiful picture.

—Your hanged philosopher was joking, said Martin; the shadows are horrible ugly blots.

—It is human beings who make the blots, said Candide, and they can't do otherwise.

—Then it isn't their fault, said Martin.

Most of the faro players, who understood this sort of talk not at all, kept on drinking; Martin disputed with the scholar, and Candide told part of his story to the lady of the house.

After supper, the marquise brought Candide into her room and sat him down on a divan.

—Well, she said to him, are you still madly in love with Miss Cunégonde of Thunder-Ten-Tronckh?

—Yes, ma'am, replied Candide. The marquise turned upon him a tender smile.

—You answer like a young man of Westphalia, said she; a Frenchman would have told me: 'It is true that I have been in love with Miss Cunégonde; but since seeing you, madame, I fear that I love her no longer.'

—Alas, ma'am, said Candide, I will answer any way you want.

—Your passion for her, said the marquise, began when you picked up her handkerchief; I prefer that you should pick up my garter.

—Gladly, said Candide, and picked it up.

—But I also want you to put it back on, said the lady; and Candide put it on again.

—Look you now, said the lady, you are a foreigner; my Paris lovers I sometimes cause to languish for two weeks or so, but to you I surrender the very first night, because we must render the honors of the country to a young man from Westphalia.

The beauty, who had seen two enormous diamonds on the two hands of her young friend, praised them so sincerely that from the fingers of Candide they passed over to the fingers of the marquise.

As he returned home with his Perigord abbé, Candide felt some remorse at having been unfaithful to Miss Cunégonde; the abbé sympathized with his grief; he had only a small share in the fifty thousand francs which Candide lost at cards, and in the proceeds of the two diamonds which had been half-given, half-extorted. His scheme was to profit, as much as he could, from the advantage of knowing Candide. He spoke at length of Cunégonde, and Candide told him that he would beg forgiveness for his beloved for his infidelity when he met her at Venice.

The Perigordian overflowed with politeness and unction, taking a tender interest in everything Candide said, everything he did, and everything he wanted to do.

—Well, sir, said he, so you have an assignation at Venice?

—Yes indeed, sir, I do, said Candide; it is absolutely imperative that I go there to find Miss Cunégonde.

And then, carried away by the pleasure of talking about his love, he recounted, as he often did, a part of his adventures with that illustrious lady of Westphalia.

—I suppose, said the abbé, that Miss Cunégonde has a fine wit and writes charming letters.

—I never received a single letter from her, said Candide; for, as you can imagine, after being driven out of the castle for love of her, I couldn't write; shortly I learned that she was dead; then I rediscovered her; then I lost her again, and I have now sent, to a place more than twenty-five hundred leagues from here, a special agent whose return I am expecting.

The abbé listened carefully, and looked a bit dreamy. He soon took his leave of the two strangers, after embracing them tenderly. Next day Candide, when he woke up, received a letter, to the following effect:

—Dear sir, my very dear lover, I have been lying sick in this town for a week, I have just learned that you are here. I would fly to your arms if I could move. I heard that you had passed through Bordeaux; that was where I left the faithful Cacambo and the old woman, who are soon to follow me here. The governor of Buenos Aires took everything, but left me your heart. Come; your presence will either return me to life or cause me to die of joy.

This charming letter, coming so unexpectedly, filled Candide with inexpressible delight, while the illness of his dear Cunégonde covered him with grief. Torn between these two feelings, he took gold and diamonds, and had himself brought, with Martin, to the hotel where Miss Cunégonde was lodging. Trembling with emotion, he enters the room; his heart thumps, his voice breaks. He tries to open the curtains of the bed, he asks to have some lights.

—Absolutely forbidden, says the serving girl; light will be the death of her.

And abruptly she pulls shut the curtain.

—My dear Cunégonde, says Candide in tears, how are you feeling? If you can't see me, won't you at least speak to me?

—She can't talk, says the servant.

But then she draws forth from the bed a plump hand, over which Candide weeps a long time, and which he fills with diamonds, meanwhile leaving a bag of gold on the chair.

Amid his transports, there arrives a bailiff followed by the abbé from Perigord and a strong-arm squad.

—These here are the suspicious foreigners? says the officer; and he has them seized and orders his bullies to drag them off to jail.

—They don't treat visitors like this in Eldorado, says Candide.

—I am more a Manichee than ever, says Martin.

—But, please sir, where are you taking us? says Candide.

—To the lowest hole in the dungeons, says the bailiff.

Martin, having regained his self-possession, decided that the lady who pretended to be Cunégonde was a cheat, the abbé from Perigord was another cheat who had imposed on Candide's innocence, and the bailiff still another cheat, of whom it would be easy to get rid.

Rather than submit to the forms of justice, Candide, enlightened by Martin's advice and eager for his own part to see the real Cunégonde again, offered the bailiff three little diamonds worth about three thousand pistoles apiece.

—Ah, my dear sir! cried the man with the ivory staff, even if you have committed every crime imaginable, you are the most honest man in the world. Three diamonds! each one worth three thousand pistoles! My dear sir! I would gladly die for you, rather than take you to jail. All foreigners get arrested here; but let me manage it; I have a brother at Dieppe in Normandy; I'll take you to him; and if you have a bit of a diamond to give him, he'll take care of you, just like me.

—And why do they arrest all foreigners? asked Candide.

The abbé from Perigord spoke up and said:—It's because a beggar from Atreba-tum[2] listened to some stupidities; that made him commit a parricide, not like the one of May, 1610, but like the one of December, 1594, much on the order of several other crimes committed in other years and other months by other beggars who had listened to stupidities.

The bailiff then explained what it was all about.[3]

—Foh! what beasts! cried Candide. What! monstrous behavior of this sort from a people who sing and dance? As soon as I can, let me get out of this country, where the monkeys provoke the tigers. In my own country I've lived with bears; only in Eldorado are there proper men. In the name of God, sir bailiff, get me to Venice where I can wait for Miss Cunégonde.

—I can only get you to Lower Normandy, said the guardsman.

He had the irons removed at once, said there had been a mistake, dismissed his gang, and took Candide and Martin to Dieppe, where he left them with his brother. There was a little Dutch ship at anchor. The Norman, changed by three more diamonds into the most helpful of men, put Candide and his people aboard the vessel, which was bound for Portsmouth in England. It wasn't on the way to Venice, but Candide felt like a man just let out of hell; and he hoped to get back on the road to Venice at the first possible occasion.

CHAPTER 23

Candide and Martin Pass the Shores of England; What They See There

—Ah, Pangloss! Pangloss! Ah, Martin! Martin! Ah, my darling Cunégonde! What is this world of ours? sighed Candide on the Dutch vessel.

—Something crazy, something abominable, Martin replied.

—You have been in England; are people as crazy there as in France?

—It's a different sort of crazy, said Martin. You know that these two nations have been at war over a few acres of snow near Canada, and that they are spend-ing on this fine struggle more than Canada itself is worth.[4] As for telling you if there are more people in one country or the other who need a strait jacket, that is a judgment too fine for my understanding; I know only that the people we are going to visit are eaten up with melancholy.

As they chatted thus, the vessel touched at Portsmouth. A multitude of people covered the shore, watching closely a rather bulky man who was kneeling, his eyes blindfolded, on the deck of a man-of-war. Four soldiers, stationed directly in

---

2. The Latin name for the district of Artois, from which came Robert-François Damiens, who tried to stab Louis XV in 1757. The assas-sination failed, like that of Châtel, who tried to kill Henri IV in 1594, but unlike that of Ravail-lac, who succeeded in killing him in 1610.
3. The point, in fact, is not too clear since arresting foreigners is an indirect way at best to guard against homegrown fanatics, and the position of the abbé from Perigord in the whole transaction remains confused. Has he called in the officer just to get rid of Candide? If so, why is he sardonic about the very suspicions he is trying to foster? Candide's reaction is to the notion that Frenchmen should be capable of political assassination at all; it seems excessive.
4. The wars of the French and English over Canada dragged intermittently through the 18th century till the peace of Paris sealed England's conquest (1763). Voltaire thought the French should concentrate on developing Louisiana, where the Jesuit influence was less marked.

front of this man, fired three bullets apiece into his brain, as peaceably as you would want; and the whole assemblage went home, in great satisfaction.[5]

—What's all this about? asked Candide. What devil is everywhere at work?

He asked who was that big man who had just been killed with so much ceremony.

—It was an admiral, they told him.

—And why kill this admiral?

—The reason, they told him, is that he didn't kill enough people; he gave battle to a French admiral, and it was found that he didn't get close enough to him.

—But, said Candide, the French admiral was just as far from the English admiral as the English admiral was from the French admiral.

—That's perfectly true, came the answer; but in this country it is useful from time to time to kill one admiral in order to encourage the others.

Candide was so stunned and shocked at what he saw and heard, that he would not even set foot ashore; he arranged with the Dutch merchant (without even caring if he was robbed, as at Surinam) to be taken forthwith to Venice.

The merchant was ready in two days; they coasted along France, they passed within sight of Lisbon, and Candide quivered. They entered the straits, crossed the Mediterranean, and finally landed at Venice.

—God be praised, said Candide, embracing Martin; here I shall recover the lovely Cunégonde. I trust Cacambo as I would myself. All is well, all goes well, all goes as well as possible.

CHAPTER 24

About Paquette and Brother Giroflée

As soon as he was in Venice, he had a search made for Cacambo in all the inns, all the cafés, all the stews—and found no trace of him. Every day he sent to investigate the vessels and coastal traders; no news of Cacambo.

—How's this? said he to Martin. I have had time to go from Surinam to Bordeaux, from Bordeaux to Paris, from Paris to Dieppe, from Dieppe to Portsmouth, to skirt Portugal and Spain, cross the Mediterranean, and spend several months at Venice—and the lovely Cunégonde has not come yet! In her place, I have met only that impersonator and that abbé from Perigord. Cunégonde is dead, without a doubt; and nothing remains for me too but death. Oh, it would have been better to stay in the earthly paradise of Eldorado than to return to this accursed Europe. How right you are, my dear Martin; all is but illusion and disaster.

He fell into a black melancholy, and refused to attend the fashionable operas or take part in the other diversions of the carnival season; not a single lady tempted him in the slightest. Martin told him:—You're a real simpleton if you think a half-breed valet with five or six millions in his pockets will go to the end of the world to get your mistress and bring her to Venice for you. If he finds her, he'll take her for himself; if he doesn't, he'll take another. I advise you to forget about your servant Cacambo and your mistress Cunégonde.

---

5. Candide has witnessed the execution of Admiral John Byng, defeated off Minorca by the French fleet under Galisonnière and executed by firing squad on March 14, 1757. Voltaire had intervened to avert the execution.

Martin was not very comforting. Candide's melancholy increased, and Martin never wearied of showing him that there is little virtue and little happiness on this earth, except perhaps in Eldorado, where nobody can go.

While they were discussing this important matter and still waiting for Cunégonde, Candide noticed in St. Mark's Square a young Theatine[6] monk who had given his arm to a girl. The Theatine seemed fresh, plump, and flourishing; his eyes were bright, his manner cocky, his glance brilliant, his step proud. The girl was very pretty, and singing aloud; she glanced lovingly at her Theatine, and from time to time pinched his plump cheeks.

—At least you must admit, said Candide to Martin, that these people are happy. Until now I have not found in the whole inhabited earth, except Eldorado, anything but miserable people. But this girl and this monk, I'd be willing to bet, are very happy creatures.

—I'll bet they aren't, said Martin.

—We have only to ask them to dinner, said Candide, and we'll find out if I'm wrong.

Promptly he approached them, made his compliments, and invited them to his inn for a meal of macaroni, Lombardy partridges, and caviar, washed down with wine from Montepulciano, Cyprus, and Samos, and some Lacrima Christi. The girl blushed but the Theatine accepted gladly, and the girl followed him, watching Candide with an expression of surprise and confusion, darkened by several tears. Scarcely had she entered the room when she said to Candide:—What, can it be that Master Candide no longer knows Paquette?

At these words Candide, who had not yet looked carefully at her because he was preoccupied with Cunégonde, said to her:—Ah, my poor child! so you are the one who put Doctor Pangloss in the fine fix where I last saw him.

—Alas, sir, I was the one, said Paquette; I see you know all about it. I heard of the horrible misfortunes which befell the whole household of My Lady the Baroness and the lovely Cunégonde. I swear to you that my own fate has been just as unhappy. I was perfectly innocent when you knew me. A Franciscan, who was my confessor, easily seduced me. The consequences were frightful; shortly after My Lord the Baron had driven you out with great kicks on the backside, I too was forced to leave the castle. If a famous doctor had not taken pity on me, I would have died. Out of gratitude, I became for some time the mistress of this doctor. His wife, who was jealous to the point of frenzy, beat me mercilessly every day; she was a gorgon. The doctor was the ugliest of men, and I the most miserable creature on earth, being continually beaten for a man I did not love. You will understand, sir, how dangerous it is for a nagging woman to be married to a doctor. This man, enraged by his wife's ways, one day gave her as a cold cure a medicine so potent that in two hours' time she died amid horrible convulsions. Her relatives brought suit against the bereaved husband; he fled the country, and I was put in prison. My innocence would never have saved me if I had not been rather pretty. The judge set me free on condition that he should become the doctor's successor. I was shortly replaced in this post by another girl, dismissed without any payment, and obliged to continue this abominable trade which you men find so pleasant and which for us is nothing but a bottomless pit of misery. I went to ply the trade in Venice. Ah, my dear sir, if you could imagine what it is like to

6. A Catholic order founded in 1524 by Cardinal Cajetan and G. P. Caraffa, later Pope Paul IV.

have to caress indiscriminately an old merchant, a lawyer, a monk, a gondolier, an abbé; to be subjected to every sort of insult and outrage; to be reduced, time and again, to borrowing a skirt in order to go have it lifted by some disgusting man; to be robbed by this fellow of what one has gained from that; to be shaken down by the police, and to have before one only the prospect of a hideous old age, a hospital, and a dunghill, you will conclude that I am one of the most miserable creatures in the world.

Thus Paquette poured forth her heart to the good Candide in a hotel room, while Martin sat listening nearby. At last he said to Candide:—You see, I've already won half my bet.

Brother Giroflée[7] had remained in the dining room, and was having a drink before dinner.

—But how's this? said Candide to Paquette. You looked so happy, so joyous, when I met you; you were singing, you caressed the Theatine with such a natural air of delight; you seemed to me just as happy as you now say you are miserable.

—Ah, sir, replied Paquette, that's another one of the miseries of this business; yesterday I was robbed and beaten by an officer, and today I have to seem in good humor in order to please a monk.

Candide wanted no more; he conceded that Martin was right. They sat down to table with Paquette and the Theatine; the meal was amusing enough, and when it was over, the company spoke out among themselves with some frankness.

—Father, said Candide to the monk, you seem to me a man whom all the world might envy; the flower of health glows in your cheek, your features radiate pleasure; you have a pretty girl for your diversion, and you seem very happy with your life as a Theatine.

—Upon my word, sir, said Brother Giroflée, I wish that all the Theatines were at the bottom of the sea. A hundred times I have been tempted to set fire to my convent, and go turn Turk. My parents forced me, when I was fifteen years old, to put on this detestable robe, so they could leave more money to a cursed older brother of mine, may God confound him! Jealousy, faction, and fury spring up, by natural law, within the walls of convents. It is true, I have preached a few bad sermons which earned me a little money, half of which the prior stole from me; the remainder serves to keep me in girls. But when I have to go back to the monastery at night, I'm ready to smash my head against the walls of my cell; and all my fellow monks are in the same fix.

Martin turned to Candide and said with his customary coolness:

—Well, haven't I won the whole bet?

Candide gave two thousand piastres to Paquette and a thousand to Brother Giroflée.

—I assure you, said he, that with that they will be happy.

—I don't believe so, said Martin; your piastres may make them even more unhappy than they were before.

—That may be, said Candide; but one thing comforts me, I note that people often turn up whom one never expected to see again; it may well be that, having rediscovered my red sheep and Paquette, I will also rediscover Cunégonde.

—I hope, said Martin, that she will some day make you happy; but I very much doubt it.

—You're a hard man, said Candide.

7. His name means "carnation" and Paquette means "daisy."

—I've lived, said Martin.

—But look at these gondoliers, said Candide; aren't they always singing?

—You don't see them at home, said Martin, with their wives and squalling children. The doge has his troubles, the gondoliers theirs. It's true that on the whole one is better off as a gondolier than as a doge; but the difference is so slight, I don't suppose it's worth the trouble of discussing.

—There's a lot of talk here, said Candide, of this Senator Pococurante,[8] who has a fine palace on the Brenta and is hospitable to foreigners. They say he is a man who has never known a moment's grief.

—I'd like to see such a rare specimen, said Martin.

Candide promptly sent to Lord Pococurante, asking permission to call on him tomorrow.

CHAPTER 25

Visit to Lord Pococurante, Venetian Nobleman

Candide and Martin took a gondola on the Brenta, and soon reached the palace of the noble Pococurante. The gardens were large and filled with beautiful marble statues; the palace was handsomely designed. The master of the house, sixty years old and very rich, received his two inquisitive visitors perfectly politely, but with very little warmth; Candide was disconcerted and Martin not at all displeased.

First two pretty and neatly dressed girls served chocolate, which they whipped to a froth. Candide could not forbear praising their beauty, their grace, their skill.

—They are pretty good creatures, said Pococurante; I sometimes have them into my bed, for I'm tired of the ladies of the town, with their stupid tricks, quarrels, jealousies, fits of ill humor and petty pride, and all the sonnets one has to make or order for them; but, after all, these two girls are starting to bore me too.

After lunch, Candide strolled through a long gallery, and was amazed at the beauty of the pictures. He asked who was the painter of the two finest.

—They are by Raphael, said the senator; I bought them for a lot of money, out of vanity, some years ago; people say they're the finest in Italy, but they don't please me at all; the colors have all turned brown, the figures aren't well modeled and don't stand out enough, the draperies bear no resemblance to real cloth. In a word, whatever people may say, I don't find in them a real imitation of nature. I like a picture only when I can see in it a touch of nature itself, and there are none of this sort. I have many paintings, but I no longer look at them.

As they waited for dinner, Pococurante ordered a concerto performed. Candide found the music delightful.

—That noise? said Pococurante. It may amuse you for half an hour, but if it goes on any longer, it tires everybody though no one dares to admit it. Music today is only the art of performing difficult pieces, and what is merely difficult cannot please for long. Perhaps I should prefer the opera, if they had not found ways to make it revolting and monstrous. Anyone who likes bad tragedies set to music is welcome to them; in these performances the scenes serve only to introduce, inappropriately, two or three ridiculous songs designed to show off the actress's sound box. Anyone who wants to, or who can, is welcome to swoon with pleasure at the sight of a castrate wriggling through the role of Caesar or Cato,

---

8. His name means "small care."

and strutting awkwardly about the stage. For my part, I have long since given up these paltry trifles which are called the glory of modern Italy, and for which monarchs pay such ruinous prices.

Candide argued a bit, but timidly; Martin was entirely of a mind with the senator.

They sat down to dinner, and after an excellent meal adjourned to the library. Candide, seeing a copy of Homer in a splendid binding, complimented the noble lord on his good taste.

—That is an author, said he, who was the special delight of great Pangloss, the best philosopher in all Germany.

—He's no special delight of mine, said Pococurante coldly. I was once made to believe that I took pleasure in reading him; but that constant recital of fights which are all alike, those gods who are always interfering but never decisively, that Helen who is the cause of the war and then scarcely takes any part in the story, that Troy which is always under siege and never taken—all that bores me to tears. I have sometimes asked scholars if reading it bored them as much as it bores me; everyone who answered frankly told me the book dropped from his hands like lead, but that they had to have it in their libraries as a monument of antiquity, like those old rusty coins which can't be used in real trade.

Your Excellence doesn't hold the same opinion of Virgil? said Candide.

—I concede, said Pococurante, that the second, fourth, and sixth books of his *Aeneid* are fine; but as for his pious Aeneas, and strong Cloanthes, and faithful Achates, and little Ascanius, and that imbecile King Latinus, and middle-class Amata, and insipid Lavinia, I don't suppose there was ever anything so cold and unpleasant. I prefer Tasso and those sleepwalkers' stories of Ariosto.

—Dare I ask, sir, said Candide, if you don't get great enjoyment from reading Horace?

—There are some maxims there, said Pococurante, from which a man of the world can profit, and which, because they are formed into vigorous couplets, are more easily remembered; but I care very little for his trip to Brindisi, his description of a bad dinner, or his account of a quibblers' squabble between some fellow Pupilus, whose words he says *were full of pus,* and another whose words *were full of vinegar.*[9] I feel nothing but extreme disgust at his verses against old women and witches; and I can't see what's so great in his telling his friend Maecenas that if he is raised by him to the ranks of lyric poets, he will strike the stars with his lofty forehead. Fools admire everything in a well-known author. I read only for my own pleasure; I like only what is in my style.

Candide, who had been trained never to judge for himself, was much astonished by what he heard; and Martin found Pococurante's way of thinking quite rational.

—Oh, here is a copy of Cicero, said Candide. Now this great man I suppose you're never tired of reading.

—I never read him at all, replied the Venetian. What do I care whether he pleaded for Rabirius or Cluentius? As a judge, I have my hands full of lawsuits. I might like his philosophical works better, but when I saw that he had doubts about everything, I concluded that I knew as much as he did, and that I needed no help to be ignorant.

---

9. *Satires* 1.7; Pococurante, with gentlemanly negligence, has corrupted Rupilius to Pupilus. Horace's poems against witches are *Epodes* 5.8, 12; the one about striking the stars with his lofty forehead is *Odes* 1.1.

—Ah, here are eighty volumes of collected papers from a scientific academy, cried Martin; maybe there is something good in them.

—There would be indeed, said Pococurante, if one of these silly authors had merely discovered a new way of making pins; but in all those volumes there is nothing but empty systems, not a single useful discovery.

—What a lot of stage plays I see over there, said Candide, some in Italian, some in Spanish and French.

—Yes, said the senator, three thousand of them, and not three dozen good ones. As for those collections of sermons, which all together are not worth a page of Seneca, and all these heavy volumes of theology, you may be sure I never open them, nor does anybody else.

Martin noticed some shelves full of English books.

—I suppose, said he, that a republican must delight in most of these books written in the land of liberty.

—Yes, replied Pococurante, it's a fine thing to write as you think; it is mankind's privilege. In all our Italy, people write only what they do not think; men who inhabit the land of the Caesars and Antonines dare not have an idea without the permission of a Dominican. I would rejoice in the freedom that breathes through English genius, if partisan passions did not corrupt all that is good in that precious freedom.

Candide, noting a Milton, asked if he did not consider this author a great man.

—Who? said Pococurante. That barbarian who made a long commentary on the first chapter of Genesis in ten books of crabbed verse?[1] That clumsy imitator of the Greeks, who disfigures creation itself, and while Moses represents the eternal being as creating the world with a word, has the messiah take a big compass out of a heavenly cupboard in order to design his work? You expect me to admire the man who spoiled Tasso's hell and devil? who disguises Lucifer now as a toad, now as a pigmy? who makes him rehash the same arguments a hundred times over? who makes him argue theology? and who, taking seriously Ariosto's comic story of the invention of firearms, has the devils shooting off cannon in heaven? Neither I nor anyone else in Italy has been able to enjoy these gloomy extravagances. The marriage of Sin and Death, and the monster that Sin gives birth to, will nauseate any man whose taste is at all refined; and his long description of a hospital is good only for a gravedigger. This obscure, extravagant, and disgusting poem was despised at its birth; I treat it today as it was treated in its own country by its contemporaries. Anyhow, I say what I think, and care very little whether other people agree with me.

Candide was a little cast down by this speech; he respected Homer, and had a little affection for Milton.

—Alas, he said under his breath to Martin, I'm afraid this man will have a supreme contempt for our German poets.

—No harm in that, said Martin.

—Oh what a superior man, said Candide, still speaking softly, what a great genius this Pococurante must be! Nothing can please him.

Having thus looked over all the books, they went down into the garden. Candide praised its many beauties.

---

1. The first edition of *Paradise Lost* had ten books, which Milton later expanded to twelve.

—I know nothing in such bad taste, said the master of the house; we have nothing but trifles here; tomorrow I am going to have one set out on a nobler design.

When the two visitors had taken leave of his excellency:—Well now, said Candide to Martin, you must agree that this was the happiest of all men, for he is superior to everything he possesses.

—Don't you see, said Martin, that he is disgusted with everything he possesses? Plato said, a long time ago, that the best stomachs are not those which refuse all food.

—But, said Candide, isn't there pleasure in criticizing everything, in seeing faults where other people think they see beauties?

—That is to say, Martin replied, that there's pleasure in having no pleasure?

—Oh well, said Candide, then I am the only happy man . . . or will be, when I see Miss Cunégonde again.

—It's always a good thing to have hope, said Martin.

But the days and the weeks slipped past; Cacambo did not come back, and Candide was so buried in his grief, that he did not even notice that Paquette and Brother Giroflée had neglected to come and thank him.

CHAPTER 26

About a Supper that Candide and Martin Had with Six Strangers, and Who They Were

One evening when Candide, accompanied by Martin, was about to sit down for dinner with the strangers staying in his hotel, a man with a soot-colored face came up behind him, took him by the arm, and said:—Be ready to leave with us, don't miss out.

He turned and saw Cacambo. Only the sight of Cunégonde could have astonished and pleased him more. He nearly went mad with joy. He embraced his dear friend.

—Cunégonde is here, no doubt? Where is she? Bring me to her, let me die of joy in her presence.

—Cunégonde is not here at all, said Cacambo, she is at Constantinople.

—Good Heavens, at Constantinople! but if she were in China, I must fly there, let's go.

—We will leave after supper, said Cacambo; I can tell you no more; I am a slave, my owner is looking for me, I must go wait on him at table; mum's the word; eat your supper and be prepared.

Candide, torn between joy and grief, delighted to have seen his faithful agent again, astonished to find him a slave, full of the idea of recovering his mistress, his heart in a turmoil, his mind in a whirl, sat down to eat with Martin, who was watching all these events coolly, and with six strangers who had come to pass the carnival season at Venice.

Cacambo, who was pouring wine for one of the strangers, leaned respectfully over his master at the end of the meal, and said to him:—Sire, Your Majesty may leave when he pleases, the vessel is ready.

Having said these words, he exited. The diners looked at one another in silent amazement, when another servant, approaching his master, said to him:—Sire, Your Majesty's litter is at Padua, and the bark awaits you.

The master nodded, and the servant vanished. All the diners looked at one another again, and the general amazement redoubled. A third servant, approaching a third stranger, said to him:—Sire, take my word for it, Your Majesty must stay here no longer; I shall get everything ready.

Then he too disappeared.

Candide and Martin had no doubt, now, that it was a carnival masquerade. A fourth servant spoke to a fourth master:—Your Majesty will leave when he pleases—and went out like the others. A fifth followed suit. But the sixth servant spoke differently to the sixth stranger, who sat next to Candide. He said:—My word, sire, they'll give no more credit to Your Majesty, nor to me either; we could very well spend the night in the lockup, you and I. I've got to look out for myself, so good-bye to you.

When all the servants had left, the six strangers, Candide, and Martin remained under a pall of silence. Finally Candide broke it.

—Gentlemen, said he, here's a funny kind of joke. Why are you all royalty? I assure you that Martin and I aren't.

Cacambo's master spoke up gravely then, and said in Italian:—This is no joke, my name is Achmet the Third.[2] I was grand sultan for several years; then, as I had dethroned my brother, my nephew dethroned me. My viziers had their throats cut; I was allowed to end my days in the old seraglio. My nephew, the Grand Sultan Mahmoud, sometimes lets me travel for my health; and I have come to spend the carnival season at Venice.

A young man who sat next to Achmet spoke after him, and said:—My name is Ivan; I was once emperor of all the Russias.[3] I was dethroned while still in my cradle; my father and mother were locked up, and I was raised in prison; I sometimes have permission to travel, though always under guard, and I have come to spend the carnival season at Venice.

The third said:—I am Charles Edward, king of England;[4] my father yielded me his rights to the kingdom, and I fought to uphold them; but they tore out the hearts of eight hundred of my partisans, and flung them in their faces. I have been in prison; now I am going to Rome, to visit the king, my father, dethroned like me and my grandfather; and I have come to pass the carnival season at Venice.

The fourth king then spoke up, and said:—I am a king of the Poles;[5] the luck of war has deprived me of my hereditary estates; my father suffered the same losses; I submit to Providence like Sultan Achmet, Emperor Ivan, and King Charles Edward, to whom I hope heaven grants long lives; and I have come to pass the carnival season at Venice.

The fifth said:—I too am a king of the Poles;[6] I lost my kingdom twice, but Providence gave me another state, in which I have been able to do more good than all the Sarmatian kings ever managed to do on the banks of the Vistula. I too have submitted to Providence, and I have come to pass the carnival season at Venice.

It remained for the sixth monarch to speak.

2. Ottoman ruler (1673–1736); he was deposed in 1730.

3. Ivan VI reigned from his birth in 1740 until 1756, then was confined in the Schlusselberg, and executed in 1764.

4. This is the Young Pretender (1720–1788), known to his supporters as Bonnie Prince Charlie. The defeat so theatrically described took place at Culloden, April 16, 1746.

5. Augustus III (1696–1763), Elector of Saxony and King of Poland, dethroned by Frederick the Great in 1756.

6. Stanislas Leczinski (1677–1766), father-in-law of Louis XV, who abdicated the throne of Poland in 1736, was made Duke of Lorraine and in that capacity befriended Voltaire.

—Gentlemen, said he, I am no such great lord as you, but I have in fact been a king like any other. I am Theodore; I was elected king of Corsica.[7] People used to call me *Your Majesty*, and now they barely call me *Sir*; I used to coin currency, and now I don't have a cent; I used to have two secretaries of state, and now I scarcely have a valet; I have sat on a throne, and for a long time in London I was in jail, on the straw; and I may well be treated the same way here, though I have come, like your majesties, to pass the carnival season at Venice.

The five other kings listened to his story with noble compassion. Each one of them gave twenty sequins to King Theodore, so that he might buy a suit and some shirts; Candide gave him a diamond worth two thousand sequins.

—Who in the world, said the five kings, is this private citizen who is in a position to give a hundred times as much as any of us, and who actually gives it?[8]

Just as they were rising from dinner, there arrived at the same establishment four most serene highnesses, who had also lost their kingdoms through the luck of war, and who came to spend the rest of the carnival season at Venice. But Candide never bothered even to look at these newcomers because he was only concerned to go find his dear Cunégonde at Constantinople.

CHAPTER 27

Candide's Trip to Constantinople

Faithful Cacambo had already arranged with the Turkish captain who was returning Sultan Achmet to Constantinople to make room for Candide and Martin on board. Both men boarded ship after prostrating themselves before his miserable highness. On the way, Candide said to Martin:—Six dethroned kings that we had dinner with! and yet among those six there was one on whom I had to bestow charity! Perhaps there are other princes even more unfortunate. I myself have only lost a hundred sheep, and now I am flying to the arms of Cunégonde. My dear Martin, once again Pangloss is proved right, all is for the best.

—I hope so, said Martin.

—But, said Candide, that was a most unlikely experience we had at Venice. Nobody ever saw, or heard tell of, six dethroned kings eating together at an inn.

—It is no more extraordinary, said Martin, than most of the things that have happened to us. Kings are frequently dethroned; and as for the honor we had from dining with them, that's a trifle which doesn't deserve our notice.[9]

Scarcely was Candide on board than he fell on the neck of his former servant, his friend Cacambo.

—Well! said he, what is Cunégonde doing? Is she still a marvel of beauty? Does she still love me? How is her health? No doubt you have bought her a palace at Constantinople.

---

7. Theodore von Neuhof (1690–1756), an authentic Westphalian, an adventurer and a soldier of fortune, who in 1736 was (for about eight months) the elected king of Corsica. He spent time in an Amsterdam as well as a London debtor's prison.
8. Voltaire was very conscious of his situation as a man richer than many princes; in 1758 he

had money on loan to no fewer than three highnesses, Charles Eugene, Duke of Wurtemburg; Charles Theodore, Elector Palatine; and the Duke of Saxe-Gotha.
9. Another late change adds the following question:—*What does it matter whom you dine with as long as you fare well at table?* I have omitted it, again on literary grounds.

—My dear master, answered Cacambo, Cunégonde is washing dishes on the shores of the Propontis, in the house of a prince who has very few dishes to wash; she is a slave in the house of a onetime king named Ragotski,[1] to whom the Great Turk allows three crowns a day in his exile; but, what is worse than all this, she has lost all her beauty and become horribly ugly.

—Ah, beautiful or ugly, said Candide, I am an honest man, and my duty is to love her forever. But how can she be reduced to this wretched state with the five or six millions that you had?

—All right, said Cacambo, didn't I have to give two millions to Señor don Fernando d'Ibaraa y Figueroa y Mascarenes y Lampourdos y Souza, governor of Buenos Aires, for his permission to carry off Miss Cunégonde? And didn't a pirate cleverly strip us of the rest? And didn't this pirate carry us off to Cape Matapan, to Melos, Nicaria, Samos, Petra, to the Dardanelles, Marmora, Scutari? Cunégonde and the old woman are working for the prince I told you about, and I am the slave of the dethroned sultan.

—What a lot of fearful calamities linked one to the other, said Candide. But after all, I still have a few diamonds, I shall easily deliver Cunégonde. What a pity that she's become so ugly!

Then, turning toward Martin, he asked:—Who in your opinion is more to bepitied, the Emperor Achmet, the Emperor Ivan, King Charles Edward, or myself?

—I have no idea, said Martin; I would have to enter your hearts in order to tell.

—Ah, said Candide, if Pangloss were here, he would know and he would tell us.

—I can't imagine, said Martin, what scales your Pangloss would use to weigh out the miseries of men and value their griefs. All I will venture is that the earth holds millions of men who deserve our pity a hundred times more than King Charles Edward, Emperor Ivan, or Sultan Achmet.

—You may well be right, said Candide.

In a few days they arrived at the Black Sea canal. Candide began by repurchasing Cacambo at an exorbitant price; then, without losing an instant, he flung himself and his companions into a galley to go search out Cunégonde on the shores of Propontis, however ugly she might be.

There were in the chain gang two convicts who bent clumsily to the oar, and on whose bare shoulders the Levantine[2] captain delivered from time to time a few lashes with a bullwhip. Candide naturally noticed them more than the other galley slaves, and out of pity came closer to them. Certain features of their disfigured faces seemed to him to bear a slight resemblance to Pangloss and to that wretched Jesuit, that baron, that brother of Miss Cunégonde. The notion stirred and saddened him. He looked at them more closely.

—To tell you the truth, he said to Cacambo, if I hadn't seen Master Pangloss hanged, and if I hadn't been so miserable as to murder the baron, I should think they were rowing in this very galley.

At the names of 'baron' and 'Pangloss' the two convicts gave a great cry, sat still on their bench, and dropped their oars. The Levantine captain came running, and the bullwhip lashes redoubled.

—Stop, stop, captain, cried Candide. I'll give you as much money as you want.

1. Francis Leopold Rakoczy (1676–1735), who was briefly king of Transylvania in the early 18th century. After 1720 he was interned in Turkey.
2. From the eastern Mediterranean.

—What, can it be Candide? cried one of the convicts.

—What, can it be Candide? cried the other.

—Is this a dream? said Candide. Am I awake or asleep? Am I in this galley? Is that My Lord the Baron, whom I killed? Is that Master Pangloss, whom I saw hanged?

—It is indeed, they replied.

—What, is that the great philosopher? said Martin.

—Now, sir, Mr. Levantine Captain, said Candide, how much money do you want for the ransom of My Lord Thunder-Ten-Tronckh, one of the first barons of the empire, and Master Pangloss, the deepest metaphysician in all Germany?

—Dog of a Christian, replied the Levantine captain, since these two dogs of Christian convicts are barons and metaphysicians, which is no doubt a great honor in their country, you will give me fifty thousand sequins for them.

—You shall have them, sir, take me back to Constantinople and you shall be paid on the spot. Or no, take me to Miss Cunégonde.

The Levantine captain, at Candide's first word, had turned his bow toward the town, and he had them rowed there as swiftly as a bird cleaves the air.

A hundred times Candide embraced the baron and Pangloss.

—And how does it happen I didn't kill you, my dear baron? and my dear Pangloss, how can you be alive after being hanged? and why are you both rowing in the galleys of Turkey?

—Is it really true that my dear sister is in this country? asked the baron.

—Yes, answered Cacambo.

—And do I really see again my dear Candide? cried Pangloss.

Candide introduced Martin and Cacambo. They all embraced; they all talked at once. The galley flew, already they were back in port. A Jew was called, and Candide sold him for fifty thousand sequins a diamond worth a hundred thousand, while he protested by Abraham that he could not possibly give more for it. Candide immediately ransomed the baron and Pangloss. The latter threw himself at the feet of his liberator, and bathed them with tears; the former thanked him with a nod, and promised to repay this bit of money at the first opportunity.

—But is it really possible that my sister is in Turkey? said he.

—Nothing is more possible, replied Cacambo, since she is a dishwasher in the house of a prince of Transylvania.

At once two more Jews were called; Candide sold some more diamonds; and they all departed in another galley to the rescue of Cunégonde.

CHAPTER 28

What Happened to Candide, Cunégonde, Pangloss, Martin, &c.

—Let me beg your pardon once more, said Candide to the baron, pardon me, reverend father, for having run you through the body with my sword.

—Don't mention it, replied the baron. I was a little too hasty myself, I confess it; but since you want to know the misfortune which brought me to the galleys, I'll tell you. After being cured of my wound by the brother who was apothecary to the college, I was attacked and abducted by a Spanish raiding party; they jailed me in Buenos Aires at the time when my sister had just left. I asked to be sent to Rome, to the father general. Instead, I was named to serve as almoner in Constantinople, under the French ambassador. I had not been a week on this job when I chanced one evening on a very handsome young ichoglan.[3] The evening was hot; the young man wanted to take a swim; I seized the occasion, and went with him. I did not know that it is a capital offense for a Christian to be found naked with a young Moslem. A cadi sentenced me to receive a hundred blows with a cane on the soles of my feet, and then to be sent to the galleys. I don't suppose there was ever such a horrible miscarriage of justice. But I would like to know why my sister is in the kitchen of a Transylvanian king exiled among Turks.

—But how about you, my dear Pangloss, said Candide; how is it possible that we have met again?

—It is true, said Pangloss, that you saw me hanged; in the normal course of things, I should have been burned, but you recall that a cloudburst occurred just as they were about to roast me. So much rain fell that they despaired of lighting the fire; thus I was hanged, for lack of anything better to do with me. A surgeon bought my body, carried me off to his house, and dissected me. First he made a cross-shaped incision in me, from the navel to the clavicle. No one could have been worse hanged than I was. In fact, the executioner of the high ceremonials of the Holy Inquisition, who was a subdeacon, burned people marvelously well, but he was not in the way of hanging them. The rope was wet, and tightened badly; it caught on a knot; in short, I was still breathing. The cross-shaped incision made me scream so loudly that the surgeon fell over backwards; he thought he was dissecting the devil, fled in an agony of fear, and fell downstairs in his flight. His wife ran in, at the noise, from a nearby room; she found me stretched out on the table with my cross-shaped incision, was even more frightened than her husband, fled, and fell over him. When they had recovered a little, I heard her say to him: 'My dear, what were you thinking of, trying to dissect a heretic? Don't you know those people are always possessed of the devil? I'm going to get the priest and have him exorcised.' At these words, I shuddered, and collected my last remaining energies to cry: 'Have mercy on me!' At last the Portuguese barber[4] took courage; he sewed me up again; his wife even nursed me; in two weeks I was up and about. The barber found me a job and made me lackey to a Knight of Malta who was going to Venice; and when this master could no longer pay me, I took service under a Venetian merchant, whom I followed to Constantinople.

—One day it occurred to me to enter a mosque; no one was there but an old imam and a very attractive young worshipper who was saying her prayers. Her bosom was completely bare; and between her two breasts she had a lovely bouquet of tulips, roses, anemones, buttercups, hyacinths, and primroses. She dropped her bouquet, I picked it up, and returned it to her with the most respectful attentions. I was so long getting it back in place that the imam grew angry, and, seeing that I was a Christian, he called the guard. They took me before the cadi, who sentenced me to receive a hundred blows with a cane on the soles of my feet, and then to be sent to the galleys. I was chained to the same galley and precisely the same bench as My Lord the Baron. There were in this galley four young fellows from Marseilles, five Neapolitan priests, and two Corfu monks, who assured us that these things happen every day. My Lord the Baron asserted that he had suffered a greater injustice than I; I, on the other hand, proposed that it was much more permissible to replace a bouquet in a bosom than to be found

---

3. A page to the sultan.
4. The two callings of barber and surgeon, since they both involved sharp instruments, were interchangeable in the early days of medicine.

naked with an ichoglan. We were arguing the point continually, and getting twenty lashes a day with the bullwhip, when the chain of events within this universe brought you to our galley, and you ransomed us.

—Well, my dear Pangloss, Candide said to him, now that you have been hanged, dissected, beaten to a pulp, and sentenced to the galleys, do you still think everything is for the best in this world?

—I am still of my first opinion, replied Pangloss; for after all I am a philosopher, and it would not be right for me to recant since Leibniz could not possibly be wrong, and besides pre-established harmony is the finest notion in the world, like the plenum and subtle matter.[5]

CHAPTER 29

How Candide Found Cunégonde and the Old Woman Again

While Candide, the baron, Pangloss, Martin, and Cacambo were telling one another their stories, while they were disputing over the contingent or non-contingent events of this universe, while they were arguing over effects and causes, over moral evil and physical evil, over liberty and necessity, and over the consolations available to one in a Turkish galley, they arrived at the shores of Propontis and the house of the prince of Transylvania. The first sight to meet their eyes was Cunégonde and the old woman, who were hanging out towels on lines to dry.

The baron paled at what he saw. The tender lover Candide, seeing his lovely Cunégonde with her skin weathered, her eyes bloodshot, her breasts fallen, her cheeks seamed, her arms red and scaly, recoiled three steps in horror, and then advanced only out of politeness. She embraced Candide and her brother; everyone embraced the old woman; Candide ransomed them both.

There was a little farm in the neighborhood; the old woman suggested that Candide occupy it until some better fate should befall the group. Cunégonde did not know she was ugly, no one had told her; she reminded Candide of his promises in so firm a tone that the good Candide did not dare to refuse her. So he went to tell the baron that he was going to marry his sister.

—Never will I endure, said the baron, such baseness on her part, such insolence on yours; this shame at least I will not put up with; why, my sister's children would not be able to enter the Chapters in Germany.[6] No, my sister will never marry anyone but a baron of the empire.

Cunégonde threw herself at his feet, and bathed them with her tears; he was inflexible.

—You absolute idiot, Candide told him, I rescued you from the galleys, I paid your ransom, I paid your sister's; she was washing dishes, she is ugly, I am good enough to make her my wife, and you still presume to oppose it! If I followed my impulses, I would kill you all over again.

—You may kill me again, said the baron, but you will not marry my sister while I am alive.

---

5. Rigorous determinism requires that there be no empty spaces in the universe, so wherever it seems empty, one posits the existence of the "plenum." "Subtle matter" describes the soul, the mind, and all spiritual agencies—which can, therefore, be supposed subject to the influence and control of the great world machine, which is, of course, visibly material. Both are concepts needed to round out the system of optimistic determinism.

6. Knightly assemblies.

CHAPTER 30

Conclusion

At heart, Candide had no real wish to marry Cunégonde; but the baron's extreme impertinence decided him in favor of the marriage, and Cunégonde was so eager for it that he could not back out. He consulted Pangloss, Martin, and the faithful Cacambo. Pangloss drew up a fine treatise, in which he proved that the baron had no right over his sister and that she could, according to all the laws of the empire, marry Candide morganatically.[7] Martin said they should throw the baron into the sea. Cacambo thought they should send him back to the Levantine captain to finish his time in the galleys, and then send him to the father general in Rome by the first vessel. This seemed the best idea; the old woman approved, and nothing was said to his sister; the plan was executed, at modest expense, and they had the double pleasure of snaring a Jesuit and punishing the pride of a German baron.

It is quite natural to suppose that after so many misfortunes, Candide, married to his mistress, and living with the philosopher Pangloss, the philosopher Martin, the prudent Cacambo, and the old woman—having, besides, brought back so many diamonds from the land of the ancient Incas—must have led the most agreeable life in the world. But he was so cheated by the Jews[8] that nothing was left but his little farm; his wife, growing every day more ugly, became sour-tempered and insupportable; the old woman was ailing and even more ill-humored than Cunégonde. Cacambo, who worked in the garden and went into Constantinople to sell vegetables, was worn out with toil, and cursed his fate. Pangloss was in despair at being unable to shine in some German university. As for Martin, he was firmly persuaded that things are just as bad wherever you are; he endured in patience. Candide, Martin, and Pangloss sometimes argued over metaphysics and morals. Before the windows of the farmhouse they often watched the passage of boats bearing effendis, pashas, and cadis into exile on Lemnos, Mytilene, and Erzeroum; they saw other cadis, other pashas, other effendis coming, to take the place of the exiles and to be exiled in their turn. They saw various heads, neatly impaled, to be set up at the Sublime Porte.[9] These sights gave fresh impetus to their discussions; and when they were not arguing, the boredom was so fierce that one day the old woman ventured to say:—I should like to know which is worse, being raped a hundred times by negro pirates, having a buttock cut off, running the gauntlet in the Bulgar army, being flogged and hanged in an auto-da-fé, being dissected and rowing in the galleys—experiencing, in a word, all the miseries through which we have passed—or else just sitting here and doing nothing?

—It's a hard question, said Candide.

These words gave rise to new reflections, and Martin in particular concluded that man was bound to live either in convulsions of misery or in the lethargy of boredom. Candide did not agree, but expressed no positive opinion. Pangloss asserted that he had always suffered horribly; but having once declared that everything was marvelously well, he continued to repeat the opinion and didn't believe a word of it.

7. A morganatic marriage confers no rights on the partner of lower rank or on the offspring.
8. Voltaire's anti-Semitism, derived from various unhappy experiences with Jewish financiers, is not the most attractive aspect of his personality.

9. The gate of the sultan's palace is often used by extension to describe his government as a whole. But it was in fact a real gate where the heads of traitors and public enemies were gruesomely exposed.

One thing served to confirm Martin in his detestable opinions, to make Candide hesitate more than ever, and to embarrass Pangloss. It was the arrival one day at their farm of Paquette and Brother Giroflée, who were in the last stages of misery. They had quickly run through their three thousand piastres, had split up, made up, quarreled, been jailed, escaped, and finally Brother Giroflée had turned Turk. Paquette continued to ply her trade everywhere, and no longer made any money at it.

—I told you, said Martin to Candide, that your gifts would soon be squandered and would only render them more unhappy. You have spent millions of piastres, you and Cacambo, and you are no more happy than Brother Giroflée and Paquette.

—Ah ha, said Pangloss to Paquette, so destiny has brought you back in our midst, my poor girl! Do you realize you cost me the end of my nose, one eye, and an ear? And look at you now! eh! what a world it is, after all!

This new adventure caused them to philosophize more than ever.

There was in the neighborhood a very famous dervish, who was said to be the best philosopher in Turkey; they went to ask his advice. Pangloss was spokesman, and he said:—Master, we have come to ask you to tell us why such a strange animal as man was created.

—What are you getting into? answered the dervish. Is it any of your business?

—But, reverend father, said Candide, there's a horrible lot of evil on the face of the earth.

—What does it matter, said the dervish, whether there's good or evil? When his highness sends a ship to Egypt, does he worry whether the mice on board are comfortable or not?

—What shall we do then? asked Pangloss.

—Hold your tongue, said the dervish.

—I had hoped, said Pangloss, to reason a while with you concerning effects and causes, the best of possible worlds, the origin of evil, the nature of the soul, and pre-established harmony.

At these words, the dervish slammed the door in their faces.

During this interview, word was spreading that at Constantinople they had just strangled two viziers of the divan,[1] as well as the mufti, and impaled several of their friends. This catastrophe made a great and general sensation for several hours. Pangloss, Candide, and Martin, as they returned to their little farm, passed a good old man who was enjoying the cool of the day at his doorstep under a grove of orange trees. Pangloss, who was as inquisitive as he was explanatory, asked the name of the mufti who had been strangled.

—I know nothing of it, said the good man, and I have never cared to know the name of a single mufti or vizier. I am completely ignorant of the episode you are discussing. I presume that in general those who meddle in public business sometimes perish miserably, and that they deserve their fate; but I never listen to the news from Constantinople; I am satisfied with sending the fruits of my garden to be sold there.

Having spoken these words, he asked the strangers into his house; his two daughters and two sons offered them various sherbets which they had made themselves, Turkish cream flavored with candied citron, orange, lemon, lime, pineapple, pistachio, and mocha coffee uncontaminated by the inferior coffee of Batavia and the East Indies. After which the two daughters of this good Moslem perfumed the beards of Candide, Pangloss, and Martin.

1. Intimate advisers of the sultan.

—You must possess, Candide said to the Turk, an enormous and splendid property?

I have only twenty acres, replied the Turk; I cultivate them with my children, and the work keeps us from three great evils, boredom, vice, and poverty.

Candide, as he walked back to his farm, meditated deeply over the words of the Turk. He said to Pangloss and Martin:—This good old man seems to have found himself a fate preferable to that of the six kings with whom we had the honor of dining.

—Great place, said Pangloss, is very perilous in the judgment of all the philosophers; for, after all, Eglon, king of the Moabites, was murdered by Ehud; Absalom was hung up by the hair and pierced with three darts; King Nadab, son of Jeroboam, was killed by Baasha; King Elah by Zimri; Ahaziah by Jehu; Athaliah by Jehoiada; and Kings Jehoiakim, Jeconiah, and Zedekiah were enslaved. You know how death came to Croesus, Astyages, Darius, Dionysius of Syracuse, Pyrrhus, Perseus, Hannibal, Jugurtha, Ariovistus, Caesar, Pompey, Nero, Otho, Vitellius, Domitian, Richard II of England, Edward II, Henry VI, Richard III, Mary Stuart, Charles I, the three Henrys of France, and the Emperor Henry IV? You know . . .

—I know also, said Candide, that we must cultivate our garden.

—You are perfectly right, said Pangloss; for when man was put into the garden of Eden, he was put there *ut operaretur eum*, so that he should work it; this proves that man was not born to take his ease.

—Let's work without speculation, said Martin; it's the only way of rendering life bearable.

The whole little group entered into this laudable scheme; each one began to exercise his talents. The little plot yielded fine crops. Cunégonde was, to tell the truth, remarkably ugly; but she became an excellent pastry cook. Paquette took up embroidery; the old woman did the laundry. Everyone, down even to Brother Giroflée, did something useful; he became a very adequate carpenter, and even an honest man; and Pangloss sometimes used to say to Candide:—All events are linked together in the best of possible worlds for, after all, if you had not been driven from a fine castle by being kicked in the backside for love of Miss Cunégonde, if you hadn't been sent before the Inquisition, if you hadn't traveled across America on foot, if you hadn't given a good sword thrust to the baron, if you hadn't lost all your sheep from the good land of Eldorado, you wouldn't be sitting here eating candied citron and pistachios.

—That is very well put, said Candide, but we must cultivate our garden.

MARY WOLLSTONECRAFT

1759–1797

Consorting with radicals in England who favored the French Revolution, with its overthrow of traditional authority and its embrace of universal principles of equality and reason, Mary Wollstonecraft launched a powerful argument for inalienable human rights in her essay *A Vindication of the Rights of Men* (1791). Here she relied on rational principles to attack justifications for traditional privilege and power. She followed this essay in 1792 with the even more radical *A Vindication of the Rights of Woman*, where she argued that marriage was no better than prostitution, and that education and unequal laws for women at the time subjected them to a condition similar to slavery. For these political views, Wollstonecraft was widely mocked in her own lifetime. And when it emerged after her death that she had had a child out of wedlock, her reputation sank so low that few readers were willing to open her "immoral" books for more than a century. It was only in the 1960s that she became known as the great founder of feminism. Wollstonecraft also left a legacy of a different kind: her second daughter, Mary, the only legitimate child of Wollstonecraft and fellow radical writer William Godwin, grew up to write *Frankenstein*, one of the most influential works of nineteenth-century literature.

From A Vindication of the Rights of Woman

* * *

Men and women must be educated, in a great degree, by the opinions and manners of the society they live in. In every age there has been a stream of popular opinion that has carried all before it, and given a family character, as it were, to the century. It may then fairly be inferred, that, till society be differently constituted, much cannot be expected from education. It is, however, sufficient for my present purpose to assert, that, whatever effect circumstances have on the abilities, every being may become virtuous by the exercise of its own reason; for if but one being was created with vicious inclinations, that is positively bad, what can save us from atheism? or if we worship a God, is not that God a devil?

Consequently, the most perfect education, in my opinion, is such an exercise of the understanding as is best calculated to strengthen the body and form the heart. Or, in other words, to enable the individual to attain such habits of virtue as will render it independent. In fact, it is a farce to call any being virtuous whose virtues do not result from the exercise of its own reason. This was Rousseau's opinion[1] respecting men: I extend it to women, and confidently assert that they have been drawn out of their sphere by false refinement, and not by an endeavour to acquire masculine qualities. Still the regal homage which they

---

1. Jean-Jacques Rousseau (1712–1778), philosopher from Geneva whose ideas about human equality and freedom inspired many revolutionaries; he also wrote about education.

receive is so intoxicating, that till the manners of the times are changed, and formed on more reasonable principles, it may be impossible to convince them that the illegitimate power, which they obtain, by degrading themselves, is a curse, and that they must return to nature and equality, if they wish to secure the placid satisfaction that unsophisticated affections impart. But for this epoch we must wait—wait, perhaps, till kings and nobles, enlightened by reason, and, preferring the real dignity of man to childish state, throw off their gaudy hereditary trappings: and if then women do not resign the arbitrary power of beauty—they will prove that they have *less* mind than man.

I may be accused of arrogance; still I must declare what I firmly believe, that all the writers who have written on the subject of female education and manners from Rousseau to Dr. Gregory,[2] have contributed to render women more artificial, weak characters, than they would otherwise have been; and, consequently, more useless members of society. I might have expressed this conviction in a lower key; but I am afraid it would have been the whine of affectation, and not the faithful expression of my feelings, of the clear result, which experience and reflection have led me to draw. When I come to that division of the subject, I shall advert to the passages that I more particularly disapprove of, in the works of the authors I have just alluded to; but it is first necessary to observe, that my objection extends to the whole purport of those books, which tend, in my opinion, to degrade one half of the human species, and render women pleasing at the expense of every solid virtue.

Though, to reason on Rousseau's ground, if man did attain a degree of perfection of mind when his body arrived at maturity, it might be proper, in order to make a man and his wife *one*, that she should rely entirely on his understanding; and the graceful ivy, clasping the oak that supported it, would form a whole in which strength and beauty would be equally conspicuous. But, alas! husbands, as well as their helpmates, are often only overgrown children; nay, thanks to early debauchery, scarcely men in their outward form—and if the blind lead the blind, one need not come from heaven to tell us the consequence.

Many are the causes that, in the present corrupt state of society, contribute to enslave women by cramping their understandings and sharpening their senses. One, perhaps, that silently does more mischief than all the rest, is their disregard of order.

To do every thing in an orderly manner, is a most important precept, which women, who, generally speaking, receive only a disorderly kind of education, seldom attend to with that degree of exactness that men, who from their infancy are broken into method, observe. This negligent kind of guess-work, for what other epithet can be used to point out the random exertions of a sort of instinctive common sense, never brought to the test of reason? prevents their generalizing matters of fact—so they do to-day, what they did yesterday, merely because they did it yesterday.

This contempt of the understanding in early life has more baneful consequences than is commonly supposed; for the little knowledge which women of strong minds attain, is, from various circumstances, of a more desultory kind than the knowledge of men, and it is acquired more by sheer observations on

---

2. John Gregory (1724–1773), Scottish physician who wrote an influential book on educating girls called *A Father's Legacy to his Daughters* (1774).

real life, than from comparing what has been individually observed with the results of experience generalized by speculation. Led by their dependent situation and domestic employments more into society, what they learn is rather by snatches; and as learning is with them, in general, only a secondary thing, they do not pursue any one branch with that persevering ardour necessary to give vigor to the faculties, and clearness to the judgment. In the present state of society, a little learning is required to support the character of a gentleman; and boys are obliged to submit to a few years of discipline. But in the education of women, the cultivation of the understanding is always subordinate to the acquirement of some corporeal accomplishment; even while enervated by confinement and false notions of modesty, the body is prevented from attaining that grace and beauty which relaxed half-formed limbs never exhibit. Besides, in youth their faculties are not brought forward by emulation; and having no serious scientific study, if they have natural sagacity it is turned too soon on life and manners. They dwell on effects, and modifications, without tracing them back to causes; and complicated rules to adjust behaviour are a weak substitute for simple principles.

As a proof that education gives this appearance of weakness to females, we may instance the example of military men, who are, like them, sent into the world before their minds have been stored with knowledge or fortified by principles. The consequences are similar; soldiers acquire a little superficial knowledge, snatched from the muddy current of conversation, and, from continually mixing with society, they gain, what is termed a knowledge of the world; and this acquaintance with manners and customs has frequently been confounded with a knowledge of the human heart. But can the crude fruit of casual observation, never brought to the test of judgment, formed by comparing speculation and experience, deserve such a distinction? Soldiers, as well as women, practice the minor virtues with punctilious politeness. Where is then the sexual difference, when the education has been the same? All the difference that I can discern, arises from the superior advantage of liberty, which enables the former to see more of life.

It is wandering from my present subject, perhaps, to make a political remark; but, as it was produced naturally by the train of my reflections, I shall not pass it silently over.

Standing armies can never consist of resolute, robust men; they may be well disciplined machines, but they will seldom contain men under the influence of strong passions, or with very vigorous faculties. And as for any depth of understanding, I will venture to affirm, that it is as rarely to be found in the army as amongst women; and the cause, I maintain, is the same. It may be further observed, that officers are also particularly attentive to their persons, fond of dancing, crowded rooms, adventures, and ridicule.[3] Like the *fair* sex, the business of their lives is gallantry.—They were taught to please, and they only live to please. Yet they do not lose their rank in the distinction of sexes, for they are still reckoned superior to women, though in what their superiority consists, beyond what I have just mentioned, it is difficult to discover.

3. Why should women be censured with petulant acrimony, because they seem to have a passion for a scarlet coat? Has not education placed them more on a level with soldiers than any other class of men? [Wollstonecraft's note].

The great misfortune is this, that they both acquire manners before morals, and a knowledge of life before they have, from reflection, any acquaintance with the grand ideal outline of human nature. The consequence is natural; satisfied with common nature, they become a prey to prejudices, and taking all their opinions on credit, they blindly submit to authority. So that, if they have any sense, it is a kind of instinctive glance, that catches proportions, and decides with respect to manners; but fails when arguments are to be pursued below the surface, or opinions analyzed.

May not the same remark be applied to women? Nay, the argument may be carried still further, for they are both thrown out of a useful station by the unnatural distinctions established in civilized life. Riches and hereditary honours have made cyphers of women to give consequence to the numerical figure;[4] and idleness has produced a mixture of gallantry and despotism into society, which leads the very men who are the slaves of their mistresses to tyrannize over their sisters, wives, and daughters. This is only keeping them in rank and file, it is true. Strengthen the female mind by enlarging it, and there will be an end to blind obedience; but, as blind obedience is ever sought for by power, tyrants and sensualists are in the right when they endeavour to keep women in the dark, because the former only want slaves, and the latter a plaything. The sensualist, indeed, has been the most dangerous of tyrants, and women have been duped by their lovers, as princes by their ministers, whilst dreaming that they reigned over them.

---

4. Wealth and hereditary privilege have made women into "cyphers"—zeroes—which are nothing in themselves but valuable when added to the end of numbers.

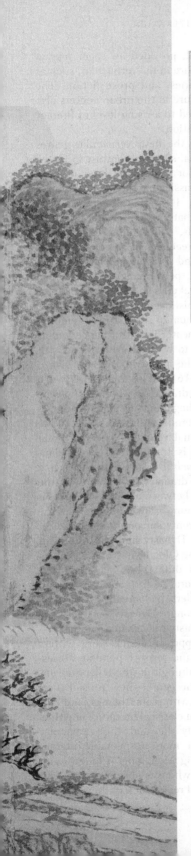

II

Early Modern Chinese Vernacular Literature

An early twentieth-century version of this anthology would probably not have featured a section on "Chinese Vernacular Literature." Although the vernacular stories and novels in this volume are now regarded as unquestionable masterpieces, the status of vernacular literature was until recently far below that of the ancient and authoritative genres of classical poetry, prose, and tales. The last two dynasties of imperial China, the Ming (1368–1644) and Qing (1644–1911), bristled with artistic and literary creativity, and the classical genres thrived in an intellectual climate of unprecedented variety and sophistication. At the same time, new literatures formed, written not in the scholastic classical language but in the living vernacular of everyday speech. This literature was much more adept at handling themes and topics that had been outside the purview of classical literature, such as sex, violence, corruption, social satire, and slapstick humor. Vernacular literatures in China could lay claim to a richer, or at least more wide-ranging, portrait of the lives of Chinese readers, and thus had a broad appeal across class lines.

From the series *Landscapes after Ancient Masters*, ca. 1675, by Wang Hui (ca. 1632–ca. 1717).

THE MONGOLS AND THE RISE OF VERNACULAR LITERATURE

The beginnings of written vernacular literature in China are intimately connected to the drastic political and social changes during the Yuan Dynasty (1279–1368). Several decades after completing the conquest of North China, Mongol armies crossed the Yangzi River and conquered the Southern Song Dynasty in 1279. Although they assumed a Chinese dynastic title and some of the trappings of Chinese imperial government, the Mongols did not base their state on Confucian principles, for which they often showed contempt. To the great shock of Chinese intellectuals, the Mongols suspended the examination system, by which members of the educated elite had been recruited for government service during previous dynasties. The long-established link among classical literature, an education in the Confucian Classics, and service in the government was temporarily broken. As a consequence, classical literature temporarily lost its place as the core around which public, social, and private life were organized. Instead, literature in the vernacular such as plays, verse romances, and prose fiction emerged, laying the groundwork for their subsequent triumph.

VERNACULAR LITERATURE OF THE MING DYNASTY: PLAYS, STORIES, NOVELS

With the Ming Dynasty the civil service examinations regained their importance as a venue for a political career and thus created again a national culture of shared elite education, leading to a renewal of classical literature. At the same time an emergent urban bourgeoisie, increasingly literate and

influential, provided an eager market for literature in the vernacular, such as plays, stories, and prose fiction. The print culture in the urban centers also contributed to a rising level of literacy and education.

One of the new, vernacular genres was drama, since in contrast to Greek culture, for example, China did not have a classical tradition of dramatic literature. It was during the Ming Dynasty that *chuanqi* drama ("records of marvels," also known as "Kunqu Opera") reached its high point. An opulent and sprawling form of romantic drama, performances often spread over several days and attracted increasingly sophisticated crowds of connoisseurs. Chuanqi drama was enjoyed both as theater in performance and as literature to be read. Most famous of all was the playwright Tang Xianzu (1550–1616) and his *Peony Pavilion,* a romantic drama in which the lovers meet in beguiling dream encounters and the heroine is brought back to life for the final reunion. The last great play in this tradition is Kong Shangren's *Peach Blossom Fan* (1699), a historical drama that intertwines the love story between a courtesan and an aspiring young exam candidate with the chaotic events surrounding the fall of the Ming Dynasty and the establishment of the Qing Dynasty.

As with drama, vernacular stories, rooted in oral performances presented by storytellers, had already existed during the Mongol Dynasty, but with the Ming Dynasty they gained in complexity and appeal. Master story writers collected and rewrote popular stories. While retaining the storyteller conventions of the genre, they infused their narratives with plots, themes, and language from classical literature and thus successfully elevated the vernacular story to a more respectable literary genre. Feng Menglong, a failed exam candidate who was obsessed both with the rarified realms of Confucian scholarship and the popular gossip of low life, was the most versatile writer of vernacular stories during the Ming.

The Ming and the Qing are the age of the great Chinese historical romances and novels, which were often lengthy elaborations of older stories. On some level Chinese popular literature can be described as a vast tapestry of interrelated stories. This was a literature whose strength lay not in inventing new plots but in filling in details and saying what had been omitted in older ones. A dramatist might take one incident from a story cycle and develop it into a play. A fiction writer might spin out a short story in a novel. A number of these historical romances survive, the most famous being *The Romance of the Three Kingdoms* (*Sanguo yanyi*)—attributed to Luo Guanzhong (earliest printed version 1522)—an elaboration of the official history of the struggle between the three kingdoms that succeeded the Han Dynasty (206 B.C.E.–220 C.E.). In *The Romance of the Three Kingdoms*, the somewhat dry historical account about remote events of the third century was transformed into a dazzling saga of battles, clever stratagems, and martial heroism. Stories of a famous group of twelfth-century bandits, like Robin Hood representing justice against corrupt authority, developed into the novel *Water Margin* (*Shuihuzhuan*) (early 1500s). One small incident in *Water Margin* was elaborated into the saga of a corrupt sensualist whose greed and sexual escapades give a vivid if skewed portrait of urban life in Ming China in the novel *Golden Lotus* (*Jin Pingmei*) (1617). And the rather prosaic story of the travel of the Tang Dynasty (618–907) monk Xuanzang to India in search for Buddhist scriptures became **Journey to the West** (1592) by **Wu Cheng'en**, a brilliant novel populated with fantastic creatures including a wily monkey, who masters larger-than-life challenges with supernatural powers.

An illustrated page from a 1581 edition of *The Romance of the Three Kingdoms*.

CHINA
FROM MING TO QING
1640–1760

SIBERIA
(to RUSSIA by 1689)

Lake Baikal

Nerchinsk•

MANCHURIA

Lake Balkash

ZUNGHARIA

OUTER MONGOLIA
Gobi Desert

Mukden
(Shenyang)

Kashgar
XINJIANG Hami

EAST TURKESTAN

INNER MONGOLIA

Beijing

KOREA

Sea of Japan

JAPAN

Great Wall
Lanzhou

SHANDONG

Grand Canal

Yellow R.

Xi'an• Kaifeng
SHAANXI   Yangzhou
Nanjing• •Suzhou

East China Sea

HIMALAYAS

TIBET

Lhasa•

NEPAL

SICHUAN

HUBEI Hangzhou• Ningbo
Chongqing•
Lake Dongting   Lake Poyang
Yangtze •Changsha

Ryukyu Islands

INDIA

BURMA

YUNNAN

Guangzhou
(Canton)

Fuzhou•

Taiwan

Pacific Ocean

LAOS

Aomen•
(Macao)

Hainan

SIAM

VIETNAM

South China Sea

PHILIPPINES

Manchu homeland

Manchu expansion
(before 1644)

Manchu expansion
1644–60

Manchu expansion
to 1760

The core territory
of the Ming Empire
(to 1644)

Areas paying tribute
to Manchu China

0   400   800   1200   1600   2000 kilometers
0   200   400   600   800   1000   600 miles

LITERATURE AND THE INTELLECTUAL CLIMATE DURING THE QING DYNASTY

In 1644 Manchu armies from the Northeast descended into China and established a new dynasty, the Qing, which would rule China until the Republican revolution in 1911. Once again under non-Chinese rule, and forced to wear the Manchu *queue* (a long ponytail) as a mark of submission, many Chinese harbored strong anti-Manchu sentiments. The Manchus, for their part, became very sensitive to native opposition. Censors whose job was to survey current writings for hostility to the regime continually discovered slights, both real and imagined, against the dynasty. The late seventeenth and eighteenth centuries, known as the "literary inquisition," had a chilling effect on writing.

Qing intellectual culture rejected the radical individualism of the later Ming, when personal freedom had been celebrated at the expense of social responsibility. Early Qing intellectuals held this late Ming ethos responsible for the decline of the dynasty. In particular, intellectuals turned away from a brand of Confucianism propagated by the Ming thinker Wang Yangming (1472–1529), who had claimed that humans possessed inborn knowledge that simply needed to be rediscovered, not learned. Accordingly, studies of canonical texts by even the greatest sages like Confucius became little more than aids in the process of subjective rediscovery.

The reaction against Ming subjectivism saw not only a conservative public morality but also a new historical and philological rigor in determining the origin, transformation, and meaning of early canonical texts. This empirical approach to the canon was called "evidential learning" and it was closely analogous to the development of Western historical philology, which treated sacred texts as historical documents. The new emphasis on historical scholarship had profound consequences for both China and the West, each of which had depended to some degree on the authority of received texts. In China, as in the West, empiricism in scholarship became linked to other forms of empiricism, such as natural philosophy and science.

The debates about the interpretation of the Confucian Classics were just one aspect of the complex presence of Confucianism in Qing society. Confucianism was a form of governance, a state cult, a tool of civil service recruitment, a tradition of textual study, and

a system of public morals and personal ethics that was to guide all aspects of life. Its rigid demands for sociopolitical success and stern moral self-cultivation failed in basic ways to address the complexities of human nature and the pressures of living in an increasingly complex world. Except among a very few committed thinkers, it was a philosophical position that invited gross hypocrisy. Vernacular literature, on the other hand, celebrated liberty, violent energy, and passion. Though such works often contained elements of neo-Confucian ethics and were later given pious neo-Confucian interpretations, by and large they either voiced qualities that neo-Confucianism sought to repress or savagely attacked society as a world of false appearances and secret evils. The hypocrisy of Confucian elite values had already been dramatically exposed in plays and stories since the Yuan Dynasty, but two Qing novels contain particularly trenchant representations of the ambiguities of Confucianism's grip on society. Wu Jingzi's (1701–1754) *The Scholars*

Portrait of a Confucian Scholar (late eighteenth century), attributed to the Korean painter Yi Che-gwan.

hovers between satire of petrified Confucian institutions—such as the civil service examination system—and the ideal vision of a true form of Confucianism. **Cao Xueqin's *The Story of the Stone*** (1791), an epic family saga of glamour and decline, conveys an even more ambiguous picture of the ideals and evils of Confucianism in the broader context of intellectual, artistic, and sexual aspirations in life.

Vernacular literature is an enthralling and varied body of literature that thrived alongside the classical tradition in early modern China and influenced many later writers. The intellectuals of the first half of the twentieth century, who called for a literary revolution that would abolish classical Chinese and the privileges that were associated with it, propelled this body of literature into the limelight and belligerently declared it to be the "true" tradition of Chinese literature: it spoke the language of the people; it decried hypocrisy, violence, and corruption through money and power; and it celebrated passion, truth, love, and heroic loyalty to oneself and one's principles. At the beginning of the twenty-first century, when China's revolutionary rhetoric has lost its earlier edge, we can recognize vernacular literature as a complementary, equal part to the classical tradition, from which it drew generously while also significantly expanding and enriching its literary themes and expressive power.

WU CHENG'EN
ca. 1500–1582

Nothing is impossible in *The Journey to the West*. People and fantastic creatures are whisked through the universe, a magic monkey can create thousands of companions by blowing on a wisp of his hair, and virgin monks can become pregnant. The novel has won over generations of readers with its unusual blend of a fast-paced, suspenseful martial-arts narrative and religious allegory, as well as its vivid satirical portrait of the workings and failings of human and heavenly bureaucracies.

The Journey to the West was not the work of a single person. First published in 1592, the novel is a product of the cumulative retelling of the story, which circulated orally and was adapted and transformed through the centuries. The final form of these stories in this vast, sprawling compendium of one hundred chapters transformed the traditional material into a great work of literature. Scholars are not entirely certain whether Wu Cheng'en did indeed give final shape to the story and was the author of the 1592 edition of *The Journey to the West*. But a local gazetteer of his home prefecture connects this title to his name. This piece of evidence is further supported by the fact that Wu had a reputation for being a versatile poet (there are over 1,700 poems in the novel), and for writing on mythical and supernatural subjects in a satirical style. Also, he was a native of a region in southeast China, whose dialect appears in the novel. We do not know much more about Wu than that he was a minor official serving under the Ming Dynasty (1368–1644).

The core of the story had a historical basis in the journey of the monk Xuanzang, or Tripitaka (596–664), who traveled from China to India in search of Buddhist scriptures during the reign of Emperor Taizong, one of the most splendid emperors of the Tang Dynasty (618–907). At the time, travel to the Western territories was forbidden and Tripitaka could have faced arrest and execution for his transgression. But when he returned seventeen years later with the coveted scriptures, he earned immediate imperial patronage and was allowed to settle down, translate the new scriptures, and propagate them. He spent the last twenty years of his life in the Tang capital of Chang'an (modern-day Xi'an), translating hundreds of sutras and other Buddhist texts from Sanskrit into Chinese, more than any other person before him had ever done. He did write a brief record of his experience during his travels. The account of the historical Xuanzang had virtually nothing to do with the much-later novel, but it may have served as the early basis from which the story began to be retold. Pilgrimages to India were by no means unique to Chinese monks of this era, but Tripitaka's journey somehow captured the popular imagination; it was retold in stories and plays, until it finally emerged as *The Journey to the West*.

As Xuanzang's journey was retold, the most important addition was his acquisition of a wondrous disciple named Sun Wukong, "Monkey Aware-of-Vacuity." Monkey had already made his appearance in a twelfth-century version of the story and came to so dominate the full novel version that the first major English translation of the novel, published in 1943, was named after this character: *Monkey*. An argument can be made, from a Buddhist point of view, that Tripitaka, however inept and timorous, is the novel's true hero. But for most readers the monkey's splendid vitality and boundless humor remain the center of interest. Tripitaka is also accompanied by the ever-hungry and lustful Bajie (alternately called "Pigsy"), a Daoist immortal who was banned to the human world for flirting with a goddess and who becomes increasingly unsympathetic as the journey progresses. Tripitaka's third disciple and protector is the gentle Sha monk (also called "Sandy"), a former marshal of the hosts of Heaven who was sent to the bottom of a river to expiate the sin of having broken the crystal cup of the Jade Emperor, a powerful Daoist deity.

Throughout their journey, the four travelers are watched over, and sometimes interact with, a number of otherworldly beings: an assortment of benign bodhisattvas (buddhas who linger in this world to help others) and a Daoist pantheon of unruly and sometimes dangerous deities. On the earthly plane the pilgrims move through a landscape of strange kingdoms and monsters, stopping sometimes to help those in need or to protect themselves from harm. Some of the earthly monsters belong to the places where the pilgrims find them, but many of the demons and temptresses that the travelers encounter are either exiles and escapees from the heavenly realm or are sent on purpose to test the pilgrims. Although the story of the Buddhist monk at times shows the traditional hostility of Buddhism against Daoism, Xuanzang's quest has a broader, conciliatory message that sees Confucianism, Buddhism, and Daoism as complementary truths. As the Buddha says about the scriptures before the monk and his companions set out to India, they "are for the cultivation of immortality and the gate to ultimate virtue." Thus Buddhist scriptures also serve the purpose of fulfilling the Daoist desire for self-preservation and immortality as well as the Confucian quest for moral virtue.

Surrounded by three guardian disciples who are endowed with a more general, allegorical meaning, Tripitaka is the only truly human character in *The Journey to the West*. He is easily frightened, sometimes petulant, and never knows what to do. He is not so much driven on the pilgrimage by determined resolve as merely carried along by it. Yet he alone is the character destined for full Buddhahood at the end, and his apparent lack of concern for the quest and for his disciples has been interpreted as the true manifestation of Buddhist detachment. Although "Pilgrim," the monkey king, grows increasingly devoted to his master through the course of the novel, Tripitaka never fully trusts him, however much he depends on him. If there is a difficult Buddhist lesson in the novel, it is to grasp how Tripitaka, the ordinary man as saint, can be the novel's true hero. He is the empty center of the group, kept alive and carried forward by his more powerful and active disciples, both willing and unwilling. Yet he remains the master, and without him the pilgrimage would not exist.

Both Pilgrim and Bajie are creatures of desire, though the nature of their desires differs greatly. Pilgrim, who had once lived an idyllic life with his monkey subjects in Water Curtain Cave at Flower-Fruit Mountain, is, in the novel's early chapters, driven by a hunger for knowledge and immortality which takes him around the earth and the heavens. In the first stage of his existence, Pilgrim's curiosity is never perfectly directed; it is a turbulence of spirit that always leads to mischief and an urge to create chaos. He acquires skills and magic tools that make him more powerful, but since he uses them unwisely, they only lead him to ever more outrageous escapades. After wreaking havoc in Heaven and being subdued by the god Erlang, he is imprisoned by the Buddha under a mountain for five hundred years. Finally Monkey is given a chance to redeem himself by guarding Tripitaka on his pilgrimage to India as "Pilgrim."

During the course of the pilgrimage, the monkey becomes increasingly bound both to his master and to the quest itself, without ever losing his energy and humor. Despite occasional outbursts of his former mischief making, the quest becomes for Pilgrim a structured series of challenges by which he can focus and discipline his rambunctious intellect. The journey is driven forward by Pilgrim alone, with Tripitaka ever willing to give up in despair and Bajie always ready to be seduced or return to his wife. Monkey understands the world with a comic detachment that is in some ways akin to Buddhist detachment, and this detachment makes him always more resourceful and often wiser than Tripitaka. Yet in his fierce energy and sheer joy in the use of his mind, Monkey falls short of the Buddhist ideal of true tranquility, while remaining the hero for unenlightened mortals.

Pilgrim is a complex character with many contradictions, as is perhaps fitting for a creature that may be seen in some sense as an allegory of the human mind. Bajie, on the other hand, is a straightforward and predictable emblem of human sensual appetites. In his initial domestic setting, as the unwelcome son-in-law on Mr. Gao's farm, Bajie was at least reliable and hardworking. But in the enforced celibacy of the pilgrimage, he grows increasingly slothful and undependable. Now and then on the journey he is permitted to gorge himself, but every time he finds a beautiful woman, something prevents him from satisfying his sexual appetite. Never having freely chosen the quest, Bajie is always distracted by his desire to go home to his wife—or to take another along the way. Yet his preoccupation with food and sex often makes him an endearing character.

The selections printed here treat the monkey's birth and early apprenticeship, and Tripitaka's dispatch to India, which is destined by the Buddha, overseen by the Bodhisattva Guanyin, and endorsed by Emperor Taizong. The next two sequences show the adventures and challenges Tripitaka and his companions encounter in two peculiar countries: one, a Daoist kingdom that suppresses Buddhists, where the Buddhist pilgrims straighten out the record with hilarious interventions for the sake of their brothers in faith; and the other, a kingdom of women in which the monk is erroneously impregnated by the water of a stream crossing its territory. While searching for a cure they have to resist the attack of female charms and a female scorpion monster. Finally, in the last sections of our selection they reach their goal in India and receive the scriptures. Whisked back to China by divine winds, they are rewarded in a solemn ceremony by the emperor back home in the capital of Chang'an, according to their merits.

Critics count *The Journey to the West* among the greatest novels of traditional China, along with **Cao Xueqin's The Story of the Stone**. In the modern period it has inspired films, musicals, television series, comic books, anime adaptations, and computer games. They all capture facets of *The Journey to the West*, whose sprawling imagination and playful esprit make it unlike any other book.

From The Journey to the West[1]

From *Chapter 1*

The divine root being conceived, the origin appears;
The moral nature cultivated, the Great Dao is born.

* * *

There was on top of that very mountain[2] an immortal stone, which measured thirty-six feet and five inches in height and twenty-four feet in circumference. The height of thirty-six feet and five inches corresponded to the three hundred and sixty-five cyclical degrees, while the circumference of twenty-four feet corresponded to the twenty-four solar terms of the calendar. On the stone were also nine perforations and eight holes, which corresponded to the Palaces of the Nine Constellations and the Eight Trigrams. Thought it lacked the shade of trees on all sides, it was set off by epidendrums on the left and right. Since the creation of the world, it had been nourished for a long period by the seeds of Heaven and Earth and by the essences of the sun and the moon, until, quickened by divine inspiration, it became pregnant with a divine embryo. One day, it split open, giving birth to a stone egg about the size of a playing ball. Exposed to the wind, it was transformed into a stone monkey endowed with fully developed features and limbs. Having learned at once to climb and run, this monkey also bowed to the four quarters, while two beams of golden light flashed from his eyes to reach even the Palace of the Polestar. The light disturbed the Great

1. Translated by Anthony Yu.   2. Flower-Fruit-Mountain.

Benevolent Sage of Heaven, the Celestial Jade Emperor[3] of the Most Venerable Deva, who, attended by his divine ministers, was sitting in the Cloud Palace of the Golden Arches, in the Treasure Hall of the Divine Mists. Upon seeing the glimmer of the golden beams, he ordered Thousand-Mile Eye and Fair-Wind Ear to open the South Heaven Gate and to look out. At this command the two captains went out to the gate, and, having looked intently and listened clearly, they returned presently to report. "Your subjects, obeying your command to locate the beams, discovered that they came from the Flower-Fruit Mountain at the border of the small Aolai Country, which lies to the east of the East Pūrvavideha Continent. On this mountain is an immortal stone which has given birth to an egg. Exposed to the wind, it has been transformed into a monkey, who, when bowing to the four quarters, has flashed from his eyes those golden beams that reached the Palace of the Polestar. Now that he is taking some food and drink, the light is about to grow dim." With compassionate mercy the Jade Emperor declared, "These creatures from the world below are born of the essences of Heaven and Earth, and they need not surprise us."

That monkey in the mountain was able to walk, run, and leap about; he fed on grass and shrubs, drank from the brooks and streams, gathered mountain flowers, and searched out fruits from trees. He made his companions the tiger and the lizard, the wolf and the leopard; he befriended the civet and the deer, and he called the gibbon and the baboon his kin. At night he slept beneath stony ridges, and in the morning he sauntered about the caves and the peaks, Truly,

> In the mountain there is no passing of time;
> The cold recedes, but one knows not the year.

One very hot morning, he was playing with a group of monkeys under the shade of some pine trees to escape the heat. Look at them, each amusing himself in his own way by

> Swinging from branches to branches,
> Searching for flowers and fruits;
> They played two games or three
> With pebbles and with pellets;
> They circled sandy pits;
> They built rare pagodas;
> They chased the dragonflies;
> They ran down small lizards:
> Bowing low to the sky,
> They worshiped Bodhisattvas;
> They pulled the creeping vines;
> They plaited mats with grass;
> They searched to catch the louse
> They bit or crushed with their nails;
> They dressed their furry coats;
> They scraped their fingernails;
> Some leaned and leaned;

3. The chief deity in the Daoist pantheon.

Some rubbed and rubbed;
Some pushed and pushed;
Some pressed and pressed;
Some pulled and pulled;
Some tugged and tugged.
Beneath the pine forest they played without a care,
Washing themselves in the green-water stream.

So, after the monkeys had frolicked for a while, they went to bathe in the mountain stream and saw that its currents bounced and splashed like rumbling melons. As the old saying goes,

Fowls have their fowl speech,
And beasts have their beast language.

The monkeys said to each other, "We don't know where this water comes from. Since we have nothing to do today, let us follow the stream up to its source to have some fun." With a shriek of joy, they dragged along males and females, calling out to brothers and sisters, and scrambled up the mountain alongside the stream. Reaching its source, they found a great waterfall. What they saw was

A column of rising white rainbows,
A thousand fathoms of dancing waves—
Which the sea wind buffets but cannot sever,
On which the river moon shines and reposes.
Its cold breath divides the green ranges;
Its tributaries moisten the blue-green hillsides.
This torrential body, its name a cascade,
Seems truly like a hanging curtain.

All the monkeys clapped their hands in acclaim: "Marvelous water! Marvelous water! So this waterfall is distantly connected with the stream at the base of the mountain, and flows directly out, even to the great ocean." They said also, "If any of us had the ability to penetrate the curtain and find out where the water comes from without hurting himself, we would honor him as king." They gave the call three times, when suddenly the stone monkey leaped out from the crowd. He answered the challenge with a loud voice. "I'll go in! I'll go in!" What a monkey! For

Today his fame will spread wide.
His fortune arrives with the time;
He's fated to live in this place,
Sent by a king to this godly palace.

Look at him! He closed his eyes, crouched low, and with one leap he jumped straight through the waterfall. Opening his eyes at once and raising his head to look around, he saw that there was neither water not waves inside, only a gleaming, shining bridge. He paused to collect himself and looked more carefully again: it was a bridge made of sheet iron. The water beneath it surged through a hole in the rock to reach the outside, filling in all the space under the arch. With bent body he climbed on the bridge, looking about as he walked, and discovered a beautiful place that seemed to be some kind of residence. Then he saw

> Fresh mosses piling up indigo,
> White clouds like jade afloat,
> And luminous sheens of mist and smoke;
> Empty windows, quiet rooms,
> And carved flowers growing smoothly on benches;
> Stalactites suspended in milky caves;
> Rare blossoms voluminous over the ground.
> Pans and stoves near the wall show traces of fire;
> Bottles and cups on the table contain leftovers.
> The stone seats and beds were truly lovable;
> The stone pots and bowls were more praiseworthy.
> There were, furthermore, a stalk or two of tall bamboos,
> And three or five sprigs of plum flowers.
> With a few green pines always draped in rain,
> This whole place indeed resembled a home.

After staring at the place for a long time, he jumped across the middle of the bridge and looked left and right. There in the middle was a stone tablet on which was inscribed in regular, large letters:

> The Blessed Land of Flower-Fruit Mountain,
> The Cave Heaven of Water-Curtain Cave.

Beside himself with delight, the stone monkey quickly turned around to go back out and, closing his eyes and crouching again, leaped out of the water. "A great stroke of luck," he exclaimed with two loud guffaws, "a great stroke of luck." The other monkeys surrounded him and asked, "How is it inside? How deep is the water?" The stone monkey replied, "There isn't any water at all. There's a sheet iron bridge, and beyond it is a piece of Heaven-sent property." "What do you mean that there's property in there?" asked the monkeys.

Laughing, the stone monkey said, "This water splashes through a hole in the rock and fills the space under the bridge. Beside the bridge there is a stone mansion with trees and flowers. Inside are stone ovens and stoves, stone pots and pans, stone beds and benches. A stone tablet in the middle has the inscription,

> "The Blessed Land of the Flower-Fruit Mountain,
> The Cave Heaven of the Water-Curtain Cave.

This is truly the place for us to settle in. It is, moreover, very spacious inside and can hold thousands of the young and old. Let's all go live in there, and spare ourselves from being subject to the whims of Heaven. For we have in there

> A retreat from the wind,
> A shelter from the rain.
> You fear no frost or snow;

You hear no thunderclap.
Mist and smoke are brightened,
Warmed by a holy light—
The pines are ever green:
Rare flowers, daily new."

When the monkeys heard that, they were delighted, saying. "You go in first and lead the way." The stone monkey closed his eyes again, crouched low, and jumped inside. "All of you," he cried. "Follow me in! Follow me in!" The braver of the monkeys leaped in at once, but the more timid ones stuck out their heads and then drew them back, scratched their ears, rubbed their jaws, and chattered noisily. After milling around for some time, they too bounded inside. Jumping across the bridge, they were all soon snatching dishes, clutching bowls, or fighting for stoves and beds—shoving and pushing things hither and thither. Befitting their stubbornly prankish nature, the monkeys could not keep still for a moment and stopped only when they were utterly exhausted. The stone monkey then solemnly took a seat above and spoke to them: "Gentlemen! 'If a man lacks trustworthiness, it is difficult to know what he can accomplish!'[4] You yourselves promised just now that whoever could get in here and leave again without hurting himself would be honored as king. Now that I have come in and gone out, gone out and come in, and have found for all of you this Heavenly grotto in which you may reside securely and enjoy the privilege of raising a family, why don't you honor me as your king?" When the monkeys heard this, they all folded their hands on their breasts and obediently prostrated themselves. Each one of them then lined up according to rank and age, and, bowing reverently, they intoned. "Long live our great king!" From that moment, the stone monkey ascended the throne of kingship. He did away with the word "stone" in his name and assumed the title, Handsome Monkey King. There is a testimonial poem which says:

When triple spring mated to produce all things,
A divine stone was quickened by the sun and moon.
The egg changed to a monkey, perfecting the Great Way.
He took a name, matching elixir's success.
Formless, his inward shape is thus concealed:
His outer frame by action is plainly known.
In every age all persons will yield to him;
Named a king, a sage, he is free to roam.

The Handsome Monkey King thus led a flock of gibbons and baboons, some of whom were appointed by him as his officers and ministers. They toured the Flower-Fruit Mountain in the morning, and they lived in the Water-Curtain Cave by night. Living in concord and sympathy, they did not mingle with bird or beast but enjoyed their independence in perfect happiness. For such were their activities:

In the spring they gathered flowers for food and drink.
In the summer they went in quest of fruits for sustenance.

4. From the Confucian *Analects*.

In the autumn they amassed taros and chestnuts to ward off time.
In the winter they searched for yellow-sperms[5] to live out the year.

The Handsome Monkey King had enjoyed this insouciant existence for three
or four hundred years when one day, while feasting with the rest of the monkeys, he suddenly grew sad and shed a few tears. Alarmed, the monkeys surrounded him, bowed down, and asked, "What is disturbing the Great King?" The
Monkey King replied, "Though I am very happy at the moment, I am a little
concerned about the future. Hence I'm distressed." The monkeys all laughed
and said, "The Great King indeed does not know contentment! Here we daily
have a banquet on an immortal mountain in a blessed land, in an ancient cave
on a divine continent. We are not subject to the unicorn or the phoenix, nor
are we governed by the rulers of mankind. Such independence and comfort are
immeasurable blessings. Why, then, does he worry about the future?" The
Monkey King said, "Though we are not subject to the laws of man today, nor
need we be threatened by the rule of any bird or beast, old age and physical
decay in the future will disclose the secret sovereignty of Yama, King of the
Underworld. If we die, shall we not have lived in vain, not being able to rank
forever among the Heavenly beings?"

When the monkeys heard this, they all covered their faces and wept mournfully, each one troubled by his own impermanence. But look! From among the
ranks a bareback monkey suddenly leaped forth and cried aloud, "If the Great
King is so farsighted, it may well indicate the sprouting of his religious inclination. There are, among the five major divisions of all living creatures, only
three species that are not subject to Yama, King of the Underworld." The Monkey King said, "Do you know who they are?" The monkey said, "They are the
Buddhas, the immortals, and the holy sages; these three alone can avoid the
Wheel of Transmigration as well as the process of birth and destruction, and
live as long as Heaven and Earth, the mountains and the streams." "Where do
they live?" asked the Monkey King. The monkey said, "They do not live beyond
the world of the Jambūdvīpa for they dwell within ancient caves on immortal
mountains." When the Monkey King heard this, he was filled with delight, saying, "Tomorrow I shall take leave of you all and go down the mountain. Even if
I have to wander with the clouds to the corners of the sea or journey to the
distant edges of Heaven, I intend to find these three kinds of people. I will
learn from them how to be young forever and escape the calamity inflicted by
King Yama." Lo, this utterance at once led him

To leap free of the Transmigration Net,
And be the Great Sage, Equal to Heaven.

All the monkeys clapped their hands in acclamation, saying, "Wonderful! Wonderful! Tomorrow we shall scour the mountain ranges to gather plenty of
fruits, so that we may send the Great King off with a great banquet."

Next day the monkeys duly went to gather immortal peaches, to pick rare
fruits, to dig out mountain herbs, and to chop yellow-sperms. They brought in
an orderly manner every variety of orchids and epidendrums, exotic plants and

---

5. Plant whose roots were used for medicinal purposes.

strange flowers. They set out the stone chairs and stone tables, covering the tables with immortal wines and food. Look at the

> Golden balls and pearly pellets,
> Red ripeness and yellow plumpness.
> Golden balls and pearly pellets are the cherries,
> Their colors truly luscious.
> Red ripeness and yellow plumpness are the plums,
> Their taste—a fragrant tartness.
> Fresh lungans
> Of sweet pulps and thin skins.
> Fiery lychees
> Of small pits and red sacks.
> Green fruits of the Pyrus are presented by the branches.
> The loquats yellow with buds are held with their leaves.
> Pears like rabbit heads and dates like chicken hearts
> Dispel your thirst, your sorrow, and the effects of wine.
> Fragrant peaches and soft almonds
> Are sweet as the elixir of life:
> Crisply fresh plums and strawberries
> Are sour like cheese and buttermilk.
> Red pulps and black seeds compose the ripe watermelons.
> Four cloves of yellow rind enfold the big persimmons.
> When the pomegranates are split wide,
> Cinnabar grains glisten like specks of ruby:
> When the chestnuts are cracked open,
> Their tough brawns are hard like cornelian.
> Walnut and silver almonds fare well with tea.
> Coconuts and grapes may be pressed into wine.
> Hazelnuts, yews, and crabapples overfill the dishes.
> Kumquats, sugarcanes, tangerines, and oranges crowd the tables.
> Sweet yams are baked,
> Yellow-sperms overboiled,
> The tubers minced with seeds of waterlily,
> And soup in stone pots simmers on a gentle fire.
> Mankind may boast its delicious dainties,
> But what can best the pleasure of mountain monkeys.

The monkeys honored the Monkey King with the seat at the head of the table, while they sat below according to their age and rank. They drank for a whole day, each of the monkeys taking a turn to go forward and present the Monkey King with wine, flowers, and fruits. Next day the Monkey King rose early and gave the instruction, "Little ones, cut me some pinewood and make me a raft. Then find me a bamboo for the pole, and gather some fruits and the like. I'm about to leave." When all was ready, he got onto the raft by himself. Pushing off with all his might, he drifted out toward the great ocean and, taking advantage of the wind, set sail for the border of South Jambūdvīpa Continent. Here is the consequence of this journey:

> The Heaven-born monkey, strong in magic might,
> He left the mount and rode the raft to catch fair wind:

> *He drifted across the sea to seek immortals' way,*
> *Determined in heart and mind to achieve great things.*
> *It's his lot, his portion, to quit earthly zeals:*
> *Calm and carefree, he'll face a lofty sage.*
> *He'd meet, I think, a true, discerning friend:*
> *The source disclosed, all dharma will be known.*

It was indeed his fortune that, after he had boarded the wooden raft, a strong southeast wind which lasted for days sent him to the northwestern coast, the border of the South Jambūdvīpa Continent. He took the pole to test the water, and, finding it shallow one day, he abandoned the raft and jumped ashore. On the beach there were people fishing, hunting wild geese, digging clams, and draining salt. He approached them and, making a weird face and some strange antics, he scared them into dropping their baskets and nets and scattering in all directions. One of them could not run and was caught by the Monkey King, who stripped him of his clothes and put them on himself, aping the way humans wore them. With a swagger he walked through counties and prefectures, imitating human speech and human manners in the marketplaces. He rested by night and dined in the morning, but he was bent on finding the way of the Buddhas, immortals, and holy sages, on discovering the formula for eternal youth. He saw, however, that the people of the world were all seekers after profit and fame: there was not one who showed concern for his appointed end. This is their condition:

> *When will end this quest for fortune and fame,*
> *This tyrant of early rising and retiring late?*
> *Riding on mules they long for noble steeds;*
> *By now prime ministers, they hope to be kings.*
> *For food and raiment they suffer stress and strain,*
> *Never fearing Yama's call to reckoning.*
> *Seeking wealth and power to give to sons of sons,*
> *There's not one ever willing to turn back.*

The Monkey King searched diligently for the way of immortality, but he had no chance of meeting it. Going through big cities and visiting small towns, he unwittingly spent eight or nine years on the South Jambūdvīpa Continent before he suddenly came upon the Great Western Ocean. He thought that there would certainly be immortals living beyond the ocean; so, having built himself a raft like the previous one, he once again drifted across the Western Ocean until he reached the West Aparagodānīya Continent. After landing, he searched for a long time, when all at once he came upon a tall and beautiful mountain with thick forests at its base. Since he was afraid neither of wolves and lizards nor of tigers and leopards, he went straight to the top to look around. It was indeed a magnificent mountain:

> *A thousand peaks stand like rows of spears,*
> *Like ten thousand cubits of screen widespread.*
> *The sun's beams lightly enclose the azure mist;*
> *In darkening rain, the mount's color turns cool and green.*
> *Dry creepers entwine old trees;*

Ancient fords edge secluded paths.
Rare flowers and luxuriant grass.
Tall bamboos and lofty pines.
Tall bamboos and lofty pines
For ten thousand years grow green in this blessed land.
Rare flowers and luxuriant grass
In all seasons bloom as in the Isles of the Blest.
The calls of birds hidden are near.
The sounds of streams rushing are clear.
Deep inside deep canyons the orchids interweave.
On every ridge and crag sprout lichens and mosses.
Rising and falling, the ranges show a fine dragon's pulse.[6]
Here in reclusion must an eminent man reside.

As he was looking about, he suddenly heard the sound of a man speaking deep within the woods. Hurriedly he dashed into the forest and cocked his ear to listen. It was someone singing, and the song went thus:

I watch chess games, my ax handle's rotted.
I crop at wood, zheng zheng the sound.
I walk slowly by the cloud's fringe at the valley's entrance.
Selling my firewood to buy some wine.
I am happy and laugh without restraint.
When the path is frosted in autumn's height,
I face the moon, my pillow the pine root.
Sleeping till dawn
I find my familiar woods.
I climb the plateaus and scale the peaks
To cut dry creepers with my ax.

When I gather enough to make a load,
I stroll singing through the marketplace
And trade it for three pints of rice,
With nary the slightest bickering
Over a price so modest.
Plots and schemes I do not know;
Without vainglory or attaint
My life's prolonged in simplicity.
Those I meet,
If not immortals, would be Daoists,
Seated quietly to expound the Yellow Court.

When the Handsome Monkey King heard this, he was filled with delight, saying, "So the immortals are hiding in this place." He leaped at once into the forest. Looking again carefully, he found a woodcutter chopping firewood with his ax. The man he saw was very strangely attired.

On his head he wore a wide splint hat
Of seed-leaves freshly cast from new bamboos.

6. One of the magnetic currents recognized by geomancers.

On his body he wore a cloth garment
Of gauze woven from the native cotton.
Around his waist he tied a winding sash
Of silk spun from an old silkworm.
On his feet he had a pair of straw sandals,
With laces rolled from withered sedge.
In his hands he held a fine steel ax;
A sturdy rope coiled round and round his load.
In breaking pines or chopping trees
Where's the man to equal him?

The Monkey King drew near and called out: "Reverend immortal! Your disciple raises his hands." The woodcutter was so flustered that he dropped his ax as he turned to return the salutation. "Blasphemy! Blasphemy!" he said, "I, a foolish fellow with hardly enough clothes or food! How can I beat the title of immortal?" The Monkey King said, "If you are not an immortal, how is it that you speak his language?" The woodcutter said, "What did I say that sounded like the language of an immortal?" The Monkey King said, "When I came just now to the forest's edge, I heard you singing, 'Those I meet, if not immortals, would be Daoists, seated quietly to expound the *Yellow Court*.' The *Yellow Court* contains the perfected words of the Way and Virtue.[7] What can you be but an immortal?"

Laughing, the woodcutter said, "I can tell you this much: the tune of that lyric is named 'A Court Full of Blossoms,' and it was taught to me by an immortal, a neighbor of mine. He saw that I had to struggle to make a living and that my days were full of worries: so he told me to recite the poem whenever I was troubled. This, he said, would both comfort me and rid me of my difficulties. It happened that I was anxious about something just now; so I sang the song. It didn't occur to me that I would be overheard."

The Monkey King said, "If you are a neighbor of the immortal, why don't you follow him in the cultivation of the Way? Wouldn't it be nice to learn from him the formula for eternal youth?" The woodcutter said, "My lot has been a hard one all my life. When I was young, I was indebted to my parents' nurture until I was eight or nine. As soon as I began to have some understanding of human affairs, my father unfortunately died, and my mother remained a widow. I had no brothers or sisters; so there was no alternative but for me alone to support and care for my mother. Now that my mother is growing old, all the more I dare not leave her. Moreover, my fields are rather barren and desolate, and we haven't enough food or clothing. I can't do more than chop two bundles of firewood to take to the market in exchange for a few pennies to buy a few pints of rice. I cook that myself, serving it to my mother with the tea that I make. That's why I can't practice austerities."

The Monkey King said, "According to what you have said, you are indeed a gentleman of filial piety, and you will certainly be rewarded in the future. I hope, however, that you will show me the way to the immortal's abode, so that I may reverently call upon him." "It's not far. It's not far," the woodcutter said.

---

7. Also the title of the ancient Chinese Daoist classic, the *Daodejing* (*The Classic of the Way and Virtue*).

"This mountain is called the Mountain of Mind and Heart, and in it is the Cave of Slanting Moon and Three Stars. Inside the cave is an immortal by the name of the Patriarch Subodhi, who has already sent out innumerable disciples. Even now there are thirty or forty persons who are practicing austerities with him. Follow this narrow path and travel south for about seven or eight miles, and you will come to his home." Grabbing at the woodcutter, the Monkey King said. "Honored brother, go with me. If I receive any benefit, I will not forget the favor of your guidance." "What a boneheaded fellow you are!" the woodcutter said, "I have just finished telling you these things, and you still don't understand. If I go with you, won't I be neglecting my livelihood? And who will take care of my mother? I must chop my firewood. You go on by yourself!"

When the Monkey King heard this, he had to take his leave. Emerging from the deep forest, he found the path and went past the slope of a hill. After he had traveled seven or eight miles, a cave dwelling indeed came into sight. He stood up straight to take a better look at this splendid place, and this was what he saw:

> Mist and smoke in diffusive brilliance,
> Flashing lights from the sun and moon,
> A thousand stalks of old cypress,
> Ten thousand stems of tall bamboo.
> A thousand stalks of old cypress
> Draped in rain half fill the air with tender green;
> Ten thousand stems of tall bamboo
> Held in smoke will paint the glen chartreuse.
> Strange flowers spread brocades before the door.
> Jadelike grass emits fragrance beside the bridge.
> On ridges protruding grow moist green lichens;
> On hanging cliffs cling the long blue mosses.
> The cries of immortal cranes are often heard.
> Once in a while a phoenix soars overhead.
> When the cranes cry,
> Their sounds reach through the marsh to the distant sky.
> When the phoenix soars up,
> Its plume with five bright colors embroiders the clouds.
> Black apes and white deer may come or hide:
> Gold lions and jade elephants may leave or hide.
> Look with care at this blessed, holy place:
> It has the true semblance of Paradise.

He noticed that the door of the cave was tightly shut; all was quiet, and there was no sign of any human inhabitant. He turned around and suddenly perceived, at the top of the clif, a stone slab approximately eight feet wide and over thirty feet tall. On it was written in large letters:

> The Mountain of Mind and Heart;
> The Cave of Slanting Moon and Three Stars.

Immensely pleased, the Handsome Monkey King said, "People here are truly honest. This mountain and this cave really do exist!" He stared at the place for a long time but dared not knock. Instead, he jumped onto the branch of a pine tree, picked a few pine seeds and ate them, and began to play.

After a moment he heard the door of the cave open with a squeak, and an immortal youth walked out. His bearing was exceedingly graceful; his features were highly refined. This was certainly no ordinary young mortal, for he had

> His hair bound with two cords of silk,
> A wide robe with two sleeves of wind.
> His body and face seemed most distinct,
> For visage and mind were both detached.
> Long a stranger to all worldly things
> He was the mountain's ageless boy.
> Untainted even with a speck of dust,
> He feared no havoc by the seasons wrought.

After coming through the door, the boy shouted, "Who is causing disturbance here?" With a bound the Monkey King leaped down from the tree, and went up to him bowing. "Immortal boy," he said, "I am a seeker of the way of immortality. I would never dare cause any disturbance." With a chuckle, the immortal youth asked, "Are you a seeker of the Way?" "I am indeed," answered the Monkey King. "My master at the house," the boy said, "has just left his couch to give a lecture on the platform. Before even announcing his theme, however, he told me to go out and open the door, saying, 'There is someone outside who wants to practice austerities. You may go and receive him.' It must be you, I suppose." The Monkey King said, smiling, "It is I, most assuredly!" "Follow me in then," said the boy. With solemnity the Monkey King set his clothes in order and followed the boy into the depths of the cave. They passed rows and rows of lofty towers and huge alcoves, of pearly chambers and carved arches. After walking through innumerable quiet chambers and empty studios, they finally reached the base of the green jade platform. Patriarch Subodhi was seen seated solemnly on the platform, with thirty lesser immortals standing below in rows. He was truly

> An immortal of great ken and purest mien,
> Master Subodhi, whose wondrous form of the West
> Had no end or birth for the work of Double Three.[8]
> His whole spirit and breath were with mercy filled.
> Empty, spontaneous, it could change at will,
> His Buddha-nature able to do all things.
> The same age as Heaven had his majestic frame.
> Fully tried and enlightened was this grand priest.

As soon as the Handsome Monkey King saw him, he prostrated himself and kowtowed times without number, saying, "Master! Master! I, your pupil, pay you my sincere homage." The Patriarch said, "Where do you come from? Let's hear you state clearly your name and country before you kowtow again." The Monkey King said, "Your pupil came from the Water-Curtain Cave of the Flower-Fruit Mountain, in the Aolai Country of the East Pūrvavideha Continent." "Chase him out of here!" the Patriarch shouted. "He is nothing but a liar

8. A higher form of meditation, reflecting a doubling of the three standard practices.

and a fabricator of falsehood. How can he possibly be interested in attaining enlightenment?" The Monkey King hastened to kowtow unceasingly and to say, "Your pupil's word is an honest one, without any deceit." The Patriarch said, "If you are telling the truth, how is it that you mention the East Pūrvavideha Continent? Separating that place and mine are two great oceans and the entire region of the South Jambūdvīpa Continent. How could you possibly get here?" Again kowtowing, the Monkey King said, "Your pupil drifted across the oceans and trudged through many regions for more than ten years before finding this place." The Patriarch said, "If you have come on a long journey in many stages, I'll let that pass. What is your *xing*?" The Monkey King again replied, "I have no *xing*.[9] If a man rebukes me, I am not offended; if he hits me, I am not angered. In fact, I simply repay him with a ceremonial greeting and that's all. My whole life's without ill temper." "I'm not speaking of your temper," the Patriarch said, "I'm asking after the name of your parents." "I have no parents either," said the Monkey King. The Patriarch said, "If you have no parents, you must have been born from a tree." "Not from a tree," said the Monkey King, "but from a rock. I recall that there used to be an immortal stone on the Flower-Fruit Mountain. I was born the year the stone split open."

When the Patriarch heard this, he was secretly pleased, and said, "Well, evidently you have been created by Heaven and Earth. Get up and show me how you walk." Snapping erect, the Monkey King scurried around a couple of times. The Patriarch laughed and said. "Though your features are not the most attractive, you do resemble a monkey (*husun*) that feeds on pine seeds. This gives me the idea of deriving your surname from your appearance. I intended to call you by the name *Hu*. Now, when the accompanying animal radical is dropped from this word, what's left is a compound made up of the two characters, *gu* and *yue*. *Gu* means aged and *yue* means female, but an aged female cannot reproduce. Therefore, it is better to give you the surname of *Sun*. When the accompanying animal radical is dropped from this word, we have the compound of *zi* and *xi*. *Zi* means a boy and *xi* means a baby, so that the name exactly accords with the Doctrine of the Baby. So your surname will be 'Sun.'"

When the Monkey King heard this, he was filled with delight. "Splendid! Splendid!" he cried, kowtowing, "At last I know my surname. May the master be even more gracious! Since I have received the surname, let me be given also a personal name, so that it may facilitate your calling and commanding me." The Patriarch said, "Within my tradition are twelve characters which have been used to name the pupils according to their divisions. You are one who belongs to the tenth generation." "Which twelve characters are they?" asked the Monkey King. The Patriarch said, "They are: wide (*guang*), great (*da*), wise (*zhi*), intelligence (*hui*), true (*zhen*), conforming (*ru*), nature (*xing*), sea (*hai*), sharp (*ying*), wake-to (*wu*), complete (*yuan*), and awakening (*jue*). Your rank falls precisely on the word 'wake-to' (*wu*). You will hence be given the religious name 'Wake-to-Vacuity' (*wukong*). All right?" "Splendid! Splendid!" said the Monkey King, laughing, "henceforth I shall be called Sun Wukong." So it was thus:

> At nebula's first clearing there was no name;
> Smashing stubborn vacuity requires wake-to-vacuity.

9. A pun on *xing* meaning both "surname" and "temper."

We do not know what fruit of Daoist cultivation he succeeded in attaining afterward; let's listen to the explanation in the next chapter.

* * *

From *Chapter 12*

The Tang emperor, firm in sincerity, convenes the Grand Mass;
Guanyin, revealing herself, converts Gold Cicada.[1]

* * *

The work was finished and reported; Taizong[2] was exceedingly pleased. He then gathered many officials together in order that a public notice be issued to invite monks for the celebration of the Grand Mass of Land and Water, so that those orphaned souls in the Region of Darkness might find salvation. The notice went throughout the empire, and officials of all regions were asked to recommend monks illustrious for their holiness to go to Chang'an for the Mass. In less than a month's time, the various monks from the empire had arrived. The Tang emperor ordered the court historian, Fu Yi, to select an illustrious priest to take charge of the ceremonies. When Fu Yi received the order, however, he presented a memorial to the Throne which attempted to dispute the worth of Buddha. The memorial said:

> The teachings of the Western Territory deny the relations of ruler and subject, of father and son.[3] With the doctrines of the Three Ways and the Sixfold Path, they beguile and seduce the foolish and the simpleminded. They emphasize the sins of the past in order to ensure the felicities of the future. By chanting in Sanskrit, they seek a way of escape. We submit, however, that birth, death, and the length of one's life are ordered by nature; but the conditions of public disgrace or honor are determined by human volition. These phenomena are not, as some philistines would now maintain, ordained by Buddha. The teachings of Buddha did not exist in the time of the Three Kings and the Five Emperors,[4] and yet those rulers were wise, their subjects loyal, and their reigns long-lasting. It was not until the period of Emperor Ming in the Han dynasty that the worship of foreign gods was established, but this meant only that priests of the Western Territory were permitted to propagate their faith. The event, in fact, represented a foreign intrusion in China, and the teachings are hardly worthy to be believed.

When Taizong saw the memorial, he had it distributed among the various officials for discussion. At that time the prime minister Xiao Yu came forward and prostrated himself to address the Throne, saying, "The teachings of Buddha, which have flourished in several previous dynasties, seek to exalt the good

---

1. Guanyin is the Bodhisattva of Mercy. "Gold Cicada" refers to the monk Xuanzang who was considered the reincarnation of the Buddha's second disciple, named Master Gold Cicada. Because he failed to follow the master's teachings, he was banished and reborn in China. His acquisition of the scriptures and adherence to Buddhism allow him in the end to reach Buddhahood.
2. Emperor Taizong of the Tang Dynasty, who ruled from 626 to 649 and dispatched Xuanzang to India.
3. "Buddhism denies the principles of our Confucianism." The "teachings of the Western Territory" refer to Buddhism and the "relations of ruler and subject, of father and son" stands for the Confucian emphasis on social hierarchies.
4. Sage rulers of High Antiquity, long before Buddhism reached China from India.

and to restrain what is evil. In this way they are covertly an aid to the nation, and there is no reason why they should be rejected. For Buddha after all is also a sage, and he who spurns a sage is himself lawless. I urge that the dissenter be severely punished."

Taking up the debate with Xiao Yu, Fu Yi contended that propriety had its foundation in service to one's parents and ruler. Yet Buddha forsook his parents and left his family; indeed, he defied the Son of Heaven[5] all by himself, just as he used an inherited body to rebel against his parents. Xiao Yu, Fu Yi went on to say, was not born in the wilds, but by his adherence to this doctrine of parental denial, he confirmed the saying that an unfilial son had in fact no parents. Xiao Yu, however, folded his hands in front of him and declared, "Hell was established precisely for people of this kind." Taizong thereupon called on the Lord High Chamberlain, Zhang Daoyuan, and the President of the Grand Secretariat, Zhang Shiheng, and asked how efficacious the Buddhist exercises were in the procurement of blessings. The two officials replied, "The emphasis of Buddha is on purity, benevolence, compassion, the proper fruits, and the unreality of things. It was Emperor Wu of the Northern Zhou dynasty who set the Three Religions in order. The Chan Master, Da Hui, also had extolled those concepts of the dark and the distant. Generations of people revered such saints as the Fifth Patriarch, who became man, or the Bodhidharma, who appeared in his sacred form; none of them proved to be inconspicuous in grace and power. Moreover, it has been held since antiquity that the Three Religions are most honorable, not to be destroyed or abolished. We beseech therefore, Your Majesty to exercise your clear and sagacious judgment." Highly pleased, Taizong said, "The words of our worthy subjects are not unreasonable. Anyone who disputes them further will be punished." He thereupon ordered Wei Zheng, Xiao Yu, and Zhang Daoyuan to invite the various Buddhist priests to prepare the site for the Grand Mass and to select from among them someone of great merit and virtue to preside over the ceremonies. All the officials then bowed their heads to the ground to thank the emperor before withdrawing. From that time also came the law that any person who denounces a monk or Buddhism will have his arms broken.

Next day the three court officials began the process of selection at the Mountain-River Platform, and from among the priests gathered there they chose an illustrious monk of great merit. "Who is this person?" you ask.

> Gold Cicada was his former divine name.
> As heedless he was of the Buddha's talk,
> He had to suffer in this world of dust,
> To fall in the net by being born a man.
> He met misfortune as he came to Earth,
> And evildoers even before his birth.
> His father: Chen, a zhuangyuan from Haizhou.
> His mother's sire: chief of this dynasty's court.
> Fated by his natal star to fall in the stream,
> He followed tide and current, chased by mighty waves.
> At Gold Mountain, the island, he had great fortune;

5. The Chinese emperor.

For the abbot, Qian'an, raised him up.
He met his true mother at age eighteen,
And called on her father at the capital.
A great army was sent by Chief Kaishan
To stamp out the vicious crew at Hongzhou.
The zhuangyuan Guangrui escaped his doom:
Son united with sire—how worthy of praise!
They saw the king to receive his favor;
Their names resounded in Lingyan Tower.
Declining office, he wished to be a monk,
To seek at Hongfu Temple the Way of Truth,
A former child of Buddha, nicknamed River Float,
Had a religious name of Chen Xuanzang.

So that very day the multitude selected the priest Xuanzang, a man who had been a monk since childhood, who maintained a vegetarian diet, and who had received the commandments the moment he left his mother's womb. His maternal grandfather was Yin Kaishan, one of the chief army commanders of the present dynasty. His father, Chen Guangrui, had taken the prize of zhuangyuan and was appointed Grand Secretary of the Wenyuan Chamber. Xuanzang, however, had no love for glory or wealth, being dedicated wholly to the pursuit of Nirvāna. Their investigations revealed that he had an excellent family background and the highest moral character. Not one of the thousands of classics and sūtras had he failed to master; none of the Buddhist chants and hymns was unknown to him. The three officials led Xuanzang before the Throne. After going through elaborate court ritual, they bowed to report, "Your subjects, in obedience to your holy decree, have selected an illustrious monk by the name of Chen Xuanzang." Hearing the name, Taizong thought silently for a long time and said, "Can Xuanzang be the son of Grand Secretary Chen Guangrui?" Child River Float kowtowed and replied, "That is indeed your subject." "This is a most appropriate choice," said Taizong, delighted. "You are truly a monk of great virtue and devotion. We therefore appoint you the Grand Expositor of the Faith, Supreme Vicar of Priests." Xuanzang touched his forehead to the ground to express his gratitude and to receive his appointment. He was given, furthermore, a cassock of knitted gold and five colors, a Vairocana hat, and the instruction diligently to seek out all worthy monks and to rank all these ācāryas[6] in order. They were to follow the imperial decree and proceed to the Temple of Transformation, where they would begin the ceremony after selecting a propitious day and hour.

Xuanzang bowed again to receive the decree and left. He went to the Temple of Transformation and gathered many monks together; they made ready the beds, built the platforms, and rehearsed the music. A total of one thousand two hundred worthy monks, young and old, were chosen, who were further separated into three divisions, occupying the rear, middle, and front portions of the hall. All the preparations were completed and everything was put in order before the Buddhas.

*   *   *

6. Spiritual masters, another word for Buddhist priests.

We shall now tell you about the Bodhisattva Guanyin of the Potalaka Mountain in the South Sea, who, since receiving the command of Tathāgata,[7] was searching in the city of Chang'an for a worthy person to be the seeker of scriptures. For a long time, however, she did not encounter anyone truly virtuous. Then she learned that Taizong was extolling merit and virtue and selecting illustrious monks to hold the Grand Mass. When she discovered, moreover, that the chief priest and celebrant was the monk Child River Float, who was a child of Buddha born from paradise and who happened also to be the very elder whom she had sent to this incarnation, the Bodhisattva was exceedingly pleased. She immediately took the treasures bestowed by Buddha and carried them out with Moksa to sell them on the main streets of the city. "What were these treasures?" you ask. There were the embroidered cassock with rare jewels and the nine-ring priestly staff. But she kept hidden the Golden, the Constrictive, and the Prohibitive Fillets for use in a later time, putting up for sale only the cassock and the priestly staff.

Now in the city of Chang'an there was one of those foolish monks who had not been selected to participate in the Grand Mass but who happened to possess a few strands of pelf. Seeing the Bodhisattva, who had changed herself into a monk covered with scabs and sores, bare-footed and bare-headed, dressed in rags, and holding up for sale the glowing cassock, he approached and asked, "You filthy monk, how much do you want for your cassock?" "The price of the cassock," said the Bodhisattva, "is five thousand taels of silver; for the staff, two thousand." The foolish monk laughed and said, "This filthy monk is mad! A lunatic! You want seven thousand taels of silver for two such common articles? They are not worth that much even if wearing them would make you immortal or turn you into a buddha. Take them away! You'll never be able to sell them!" The Bodhisattva did not bother to argue with him; she walked away and proceeded on her journey with Moksa.

After a long while, they came to the Eastern Flower Gate and ran right into the chief minister Xiao Yu, who was just returning from court. His outriders were shouting to clear the streets, but the Bodhisattva boldly refused to step aside. She stood on the street holding the cassock and met the chief minister head on. The chief minister pulled in his reins to look at this bright, luminous cassock, and asked his subordinates to inquire about the price of the garment. "I want five thousand taels for the cassock," said the Bodhisattva, "and two thousand for the staff." "What is so good about them," said Xiao Yu, "that they should be so expensive?" "This cassock," said the Bodhisattva, "has something good about it, and something bad, too. For some people it may be very expensive, but for others it may cost nothing at all."

"What's good about it," asked Xiao Yu, "and what's bad about it?"

"He who wears my cassock," said the Bodhisattva, "will not fall into perdition, will not suffer in Hell, will not encounter violence, and will not meet tigers and wolves. That's how good it is! But if the person happens to be a foolish monk who relishes pleasures and rejoices in iniquities, or a priest who obeys neither the dietary laws nor the commandments, or a worldly fellow who attacks the sūtras and slanders the Buddha, he will never even get to see my

7. The Buddha.

cassock. That's what's bad about it!" The chief minister asked again, "What do you mean, it will be expensive for some and not expensive for others?" "He who does not follow the Law of Buddha," said the Bodhisattva, "or revere the Three Jewels will be required to pay seven thousand taels if he insists on buying my cassock and my staff. That's how expensive it'll be! But if he honors the Three Jewels, rejoices in doing good deeds, and obeys our Buddha, he is a person worthy of these things. I shall willingly give him the cassock and the staff to establish an affinity of goodness with him. That's what I meant when I said that for some it would cost nothing."

When Xiao Yu heard these words, his face could not hide his pleasure, for he knew that this was a good person. He dismounted at once and greeted the Bodhisattva ceremoniously, saying, "Your Holy Eminence, please pardon whatever offense Xiao Yu might have caused. Our Great Tang Emperor is a most religious person, and all the officials of his court are like-minded. In fact, we have just begun a Grand Mass of Land and Water, and this cassock will be most appropriate for the use of Chen Xuanzang, the Grand Expositor of the Faith. Let me go with you to have an audience with the Throne."

The Bodhisattva was happy to comply with the suggestion. They turned around and went into the Eastern Flower Gate. The Custodian of the Yellow Door went inside to make the report, and they were summoned to the Treasure Hall, where Xiao Yu and the two monks covered with scabs and sores stood below the steps. "What does Xiao Yu want to report to us?" asked the Tang emperor. Prostrating himself before the steps, Xiao Yu said, "Your subject going out of the Eastern Flower Gate met by chance these two monks, selling a cassock and a priestly staff. I thought of the priest, Xuanzang, who might wear this garment. For this reason, we asked to have an audience with Your Majesty."

Highly pleased, Taizong asked for the price of the cassock. The Bodhisattva and Moksa stood at the foot of the steps but did not bow at all. When asked the price of the cassock, the Bodhisattva replied, "Five thousand taels for the cassock and two thousand for the priestly staff." "What's so good about the cassock," said Taizong, "that it should cost so much?" The Bodhisattva said:

> "Of this cassock,
> A dragon which wears but one shred
> Will miss the woe of being devoured by the great roc;
> Or a crane on which one thread is hung
> Will transcend this world and reach the place of the gods.
> Sit in it:
> Ten thousand gods will salute you!
> Move with it:
> Seven Buddhas will follow you!
> This cassock was made of silk drawn from ice silkworm
> And threads spun by skilled craftsmen.
> Immortal girls did the weaving;
> Divine maidens helped at the loom.
> Bit by bit, the parts were sewn and embroidered.
> Stitch by stitch, it arose—a brocade from the heddle,
> Its pellucid weave finer than ornate blooms.
> Its colors, brilliant, emit precious light.

Wear it, and crimson mist will surround your frame.
Doff it, and see the colored clouds take flight.
Outside the Three Heavens' door its primal light was seen;
Before the Five Mountains its magic aura grew.
Inlaid are layers of lotus from the West,
And hanging pearls shine like planets and stars.
On four corners are pearls which glow at night;
On top stays fastened an emerald.
Though lacking the all-seeing primal form.
It's held by Eight Treasures all aglow.
This cassock
You keep folded at leisure;
You wear it to meet sages.
When it's kept folded at leisure,
Its rainbowlike hues cut through a thousand wrappings.
When you wear it to meet sages,
All Heaven takes fright—both demons and gods!
On top are the rddhi pearl,
The māni pearl,
The dust-clearing pearl,
The wind-stopping pearl.
There are also the red cornelian,
The purple coral,
The luminescent pearl,
The Sāriputra.
They rob the moon of its whiteness;
They match the sun in its redness.
In waves its divine aura imbues the sky;
In flashes its brightness lifts up its perfection.
In waves its divine aura imbues the sky,
Flooding the Gate of Heaven.
In flashes its brightness lifts up its perfection,
Lighting up the whole world.
Shining upon the mountains and the streams.
It wakens tigers and leopards;
Lighting up the isles and the seas,
It moves dragons and fishes,
Along its edges hang two chains of melted gold,
And joins the collars a ring of snow-white jade.
The poem says:
The august Three Jewels, this venerable Truth—
It judges all Four Creatures on the Sixfold Path.
The mind enlightened knows and holds God's Law and man's;
The soul illumined can transmit the lamp of wisdom.
The solemn guard of one's body is Vajradhātu;[8]
Like ice in a jade pitcher is the purified mind.
Since Buddha caused this cassock to be made,
Which of ten thousand kalpas can harm a monk?"

---

8. Golden or diamond element in the universe, signifying the indestructible wisdom of a particular Buddha.

When the Tang emperor, who was up in the Treasure Hall, heard these words, he was highly pleased. "Tell me, priest," he asked again, "What's so good about the nine-ring priestly staff?" "My staff," said the Bodhisattva, "has on it

> Nine joined-rings made of iron and set in bronze,
> And nine joints of vine immortal ever young.
> When held, it scorns the sight of aging bones:
> It leaves the mount to return with fleecy clouds.
> It roamed through Heaven with the Fifth Patriarch:
> It broke Hell's gate where Lo Bo sought his Mom.
> Not soiled by the fifth of this red-dust world,
> It gladly trails the god-monk up Mount Jade.⁹"

When the Tang emperor heard these words, he gave the order to have the cassock spread open so that he might examine it carefully from top to bottom. It was indeed a marvelous thing! "Venerable Elder of the Great Law,"[1] he said, "we shall not deceive you. At this very moment we have exalted the Religion of Mercy and planted abundantly in the fields of blessing. You may see many priests assembled in the Temple of Transformation to perform the Law and the sūtras. In their midst is a man of great merit and virtue, whose religious name is Xuanzang. We wish, therefore, to purchase these two treasure objects from you to give them to him. How much do you really want for these things?" Hearing these words, the Bodhisattva and Moksa folded their hands and gave praise to the Buddha. "If he is a man of virtue and merit," she said to the Throne, bowing, "this humble cleric is willing to give them to him. I shall not accept any money." She finished speaking and turned at once to leave. The Tang emperor quickly asked Xiao Yu to hold her back. Standing up in the Hall, he bowed low before saying, "Previously you claimed that the cassock was worth five thousand taels of silver, and the staff two thousand. Now that you see we want to buy them, you refuse to accept payment. Are you implying that we would bank on our position and take your possession by force? That's absurd! We shall pay you according to the original sum you asked for: please do not refuse it."

Raising her hands for a salutation, the Bodhisattva said, "This humble cleric made a vow before, stating that anyone who reveres the Three Treasures, rejoices in virtue, and submits to our Buddha will be given these treasures free. Since it is clear that Your Majesty is eager to magnify virtues to rest in excellence, and to honor our Buddhist faith by having an illustrious monk proclaim the Great Law, it is my duty to present these gifts to you. I shall take no money for them. They will be left here and this humble cleric will take leave of you." When the Tang emperor saw that she was so insistent, he was very pleased. He ordered the Court of Banquets to prepare a huge vegetarian feast to thank the Bodhisattva, who firmly declined that also. She left amiably and went back to her hiding place at the Temple of the Local Spirit, which we shall mention no further.

* * *

9. Abode of the Queen Mother of the West, a Daoist deity. 1. The "Great Law" of Buddhism.

Time went by like the snapping of fingers, and the formal celebration of the Grand Mass on the seventh day was to take place. Xuanzang presented the Tang emperor with a memorial, inviting him to raise the incense. News of these good works was circulating throughout the empire. Upon receiving the notice, Taizong sent for his carriage and led many of his officials, both civil and military, as well as his relatives and the ladies of the court, to the temple. All the people of the city—young and old, nobles and commoners—went along also to hear the preaching. At the same time the Bodhisattva said to Moksa, "Today is the formal celebration of the Grand Mass, the first seventh of seven such occasions. It's about time for you and me to join the crowd. First, we want to see how the mass is going; second, we want to find out whether Gold Cicada is worthy of my treasures; and third, we can discover what division of Buddhism he is preaching about."

* * *

On the platform, that Master of the Law recited for a while the *Sūtra of Life and Deliverance for the Dead*; he then lectured for a while on the *Heavenly Treasure Chronicle for Peace in the Nation*, after which he preached for a while on the *Scroll on Merit and Self-Cultivation*. The Bodhisattva drew near and thumped her hands on the platform, calling out in a loud voice, "Hey, monk! You only know how to talk about the teachings of the Little Vehicle. Don't you know anything about the Great Vehicle?"[2] When Xuanzang heard this question, he was filled with delight. He turned and leaped down from the platform, raised his hands and saluted the Bodhisattva, saying, "Venerable Teacher, please pardon your pupil for much disrespect. I only know that the priests who came before me all talk about the teachings of the Little Vehicle. I have no idea what the Great Vehicle teaches." "The doctrines of your Little Vehicle," said the Bodhisattva, "cannot save the damned by leading them up to Heaven; they can only mislead and confuse mortals. I have in my possession Tripitaka, three collections of the Great Vehicle Laws of Buddha, which are able to send the lost to Heaven, to deliver the afflicted from their sufferings, to fashion ageless bodies, and to break the cycles of coming and going."

As they were speaking, the officer in charge of incense and the inspection of halls went to report to the emperor, saying, "The Master was just in the process of lecturing on the wondrous Law when he was pulled down by two scabby mendicants, babbling some kind of nonsense." The king ordered them to be arrested, and the two monks were taken by many people and pushed into the hall in the rear. When the monk saw Taizong, she neither raised her hands nor made a bow; instead, she lifted her face and said, "What do you want of me, Your Majesty?" Recognizing her, the Tang emperor said, "Aren't you the monk who brought us the cassock the other day?" "I am," said the Bodhisattva. "If you have come to listen to the lecture," said Taizong, "you may as well take some vegetarian food. Why indulge in this wanton discussion with our Master and disturb the lecture hall, delaying our religious service?"

2. "Little Vehicle" and "Great Vehicle" refer to two forms of Buddhism. Hīnayāna Buddhism, the "Little Vehicle," is focused more on ascetic practices and individual salvation, while Mahāyāna Buddhism, the "Great Vehicle," which became dominant in East Asia, emphasizes care for others.

"What that Master of yours was lecturing on," said the Bodhisattva, "happens to be the teachings of the Little Vehicle, which cannot lead the lost up to Heaven. In my possession is the Tripitaka, the Great Vehicle Law of Buddha, which is able to save the damned, deliver the afflicted, and fashion the indestructible body." Delighted, Taizong asked eagerly, "Where is your Great Vehicle Law of Buddha?" "At the place of our lord, Tathāgata," said the Bodhisattva, "in the Great Temple of Thunderclap, located in India of the Great Western Heaven.[3] It can untie the knot of a hundred enmities; it can dispel unexpected misfortunes." "Can you remember any of it?" said Taizong. "Certainly," said the Bodhisattva. Taizong was overjoyed and said, "Let the Master lead this monk to the platform to begin a lecture at once."

Our Bodhisattva led Moksa and flew up onto the high platform. She then trod on the hallowed clouds to rise up into the air and revealed her true salvific form, holding the pure vase with the willow branch. At her left stood the virile figure of Moksa carrying the rod. The Tang emperor was so overcome that he bowed to the sky and worshiped, as civil and military officials all knelt on the ground and burned incense. Throughout the temple, there was not one of the monks, nuns, Taoists, secular persons, scholars, craftsmen, and merchants, who did not bow down and exclaim, "Dear Bodhisattva! Dear Bodhisattva!" We have a song as a testimony. They saw only

Auspicious mist in diffusion
And dharmakāya[4] veiled by holy light.
In the bright air of ninefold Heaven
A lady immortal appeared.
That Bodhisattva
Wore on her head a cap
Fastened by leaves of gold
And set with flowers of jade,
With tassels of dangling pearls,
All aglow with golden light.
On her body she had
A robe of fine blue silk.
Lightly colored
And simply fretted
By circling dragons
And soaring phoenixes.
Down in front was hung
A pair of fragrant girdle-jade,
Which glowed with the moon
And danced with the wind,
Overlaid with precious pearls
And with imperial jade.
Around her waist was tied
An embroidered velvet skirt
Of ice-worm silk
And piped in gold,
In which she topped the colored clouds

3. Destination of Xuanzang's trip to India. 4. The spiritual form embodying Buddhahood.

And crossed the jasper sea.
Before her she led
A cockatoo with red beak and yellow plumes,
Which had roamed the Eastern Ocean
And throughout the world
To foster deeds of mercy and filial piety.
She held in her hands
A grace-dispensing and world-sustaining precious vase,
In which was planted
A twig of pliant willow,
That could moisten the blue sky,
And sweep aside all evil—
All clinging fog and smoke.
Her jade rings joined the embroidered loops,
And gold lotus grew thick beneath her feet.
In three days how often she came and went:
This very Guanshiyin⁵ who saves from pain and woe.

So pleased by the vision was Tang Taizong that he forgot about his empire; so enthralled were the civil and military officials that they completely ignored court etiquette. Everyone was chanting, "Namo Bodhisattva Guanshiyin!"

Taizong at once gave the order for a skilled painter to sketch the true form of the Bodhisattva. No sooner had he spoken than a certain Wu Daozi was selected, who could portray gods and sages and was a master of the noble perspective and lofty vision. (This man, in fact, was the one who would later paint the portraits of meritorious officials in the Lingyan Tower.) Immediately he opened up his magnificent brush to record the true form. The hallowed clouds of the Bodhisattva gradually drifted away, and in a little while the golden light disappeared. From midair came floating down a slip of paper on which were plainly written several lines in the style of the *gāthā*:⁶

We greet the great Ruler of Tang
With scripts most sublime of the West.
The way: a hundred and eight thousand miles.
Seek earnestly this Mahāyāna,⁷
These Books, when they reach your fair state,
Can redeem damned spirits from Hell.
If someone is willing to go,
He'll become a Buddha of gold.

When Taizong saw the *gāthā*, he said to the various monks: "Let's stop the Mass. Wait until I have sent someone to bring back the scriptures of the Great Vehicle. We shall then renew our sincere effort to cultivate the fruits of virtue." Not one of the officials disagreed with the emperor, who then asked in the temple, "Who is willing to accept our commission to seek scriptures from Buddha in the Western Heaven?" Hardly had he finished speaking when the

5. Full name of Guanyin, meaning "She who listens to the voices of the world."
6. A verse.

7. Again, this refers to Mahāyāna Buddhism common in East Asia.

Master of the Law stepped from the side and saluted him, saying, "Though your poor monk has no talents, he is ready to perform the service of a dog and a horse. I shall seek these true scriptures on behalf of Your Majesty, that the empire of our king may be firm and everlasting." Highly pleased, the Tang emperor went forward to raise up the monk with his royal hands, saying, "If the Master is willing to express his loyalty this way, undaunted by the great distance or by the journey over mountains and streams, we are willing to become bond brothers with you." Xuanzang touched his forehead to the ground to express his gratitude. Being indeed a righteous man, the Tang emperor went at once before Buddha's image in the temple and bowed to Xuanzang four times, addressing him as "our brother and holy monk."

Deeply moved, Xuanzang said, "Your Majesty, what ability and what virtue does your poor monk possess that he should merit such affection from your Heavenly Grace? I shall not spare myself in this journey, but I shall proceed with all diligence until I reach the Western Heaven. If I do not attain my goal, or the true scriptures, I shall not return to our land even if I have to die. I would rather fall into eternal perdition in Hell." He thereupon lifted the incense before Buddha and made that his vow. Highly pleased, the Tang emperor ordered his carriage back to the palace to wait for the auspicious day and hour, when official documents could be issued for the journey to begin. And so the Throne withdrew as everyone dispersed.

Xuanzang also went back to the Temple of Great Blessing. The many monks of that temple and his several disciples, who had heard about the quest for the scriptures, all came to see him. They asked, "Is it true that you have vowed to go to the Western Heaven?" "It is," said Xuanzang. "O Master," one of his disciples said, "I have heard people say that the way to the Western Heaven is long, filled with tigers, leopards, and all kinds of monsters. I fear that there will be departure but no return for you, as it will be difficult to safeguard your life."

"I have already made a great vow and a profound promise," said Xuanzang, "that if I do not acquire the true scriptures, I shall fall into eternal perdition in Hell. Since I have received such grace and favor from the king, I have no alternative but to serve my country to the utmost of my loyalty. It is true, of course, that I have no knowledge of how I shall fare on this journey or whether good or evil awaits me." He said to them again, "My disciples, after I leave, wait for two or three years, or six or seven years. If you see the branches of the pine trees within our gate pointing eastward, you will know that I am about to return. If not, I shall not be coming back." The disciples all committed his words firmly to memory.

The next morning Taizong held court and gathered all the officials together. They wrote up the formal rescript stating the intent to acquire scriptures and stamped it with the seal of free passage. The President of the Imperial Board of Astronomy then came with the report, "Today the positions of the planets are especially favorable for men to make a journey of great length." The Tang emperor was most delighted. Thereafter the custodian of the Yellow Gate also made a report, saying, "The Master of the Law awaits your pleasure outside the court." The emperor summoned him up to the treasure hall and said, "Royal Brother, today is an auspicious day for the journey, and your rescript for free passage is ready. We also present you with a bowl made of purple gold for you to collect alms on your way. Two attendants have been selected to accompany you, and a horse will be your means of travel. You may begin your journey at once."

Highly pleased, Xuanzang expressed his gratitude and received his gifts, not displaying the least desire to linger. The Tang emperor called for his carriage and led many officials outside the city gate to see him off. The monks in the Temple of Great Blessing and the disciples were already waiting there with Xuanzang's winter and summer clothing. When the emperor saw them, he ordered the bags to be packed on the horses first, and then asked an officer to bring a pitcher of wine. Taizong lifted his cup to toast the pilgrim saying, "What is the byname of our Royal Brother?" "Your poor monk," said Xuanzang, "is a person who has left the family. He dares not assume a byname." "The Bodhisattva said earlier," said Taizong, that there were three collections of scriptures in the Western Heaven. Our Brother can take that as a byname and call himself Tripitaka.[8] How about it?" Thanking him, Xuanzang accepted the wine and said, "Your Majesty, wine is the first prohibition of priesthood. Your poor monk has practiced abstinence since birth." "Today's journey," said Taizong, "is not to be compared with any ordinary event. Please drink one cup of this dietary wine, and accept our good wishes that go along with the toast." Xuanzang dared not refuse; he took the wine and was about to drink, when he saw Taizong stoop down to scoop up a handful of dirt with his fingers and sprinkle it in the wine. Tripitaka had no idea what this gesture meant.

"Dear Brother," said Taizong, laughing, "how long will it take you to come back from this trip to the Western Heaven?" "Probably in three years time," said Tripitaka, "I'll be returning to our noble nation." "The years are long and the journey is great," said Taizong. "Drink this, Royal Brother, and remember: Treasure a handful of dirt from your home, but love not ten thousand taels of foreign gold." Then Tripitaka understood the meaning of the handful of dirt sprinkled in his cup: he thanked the emperor once more and drained the cup. He went out of the gate and left, as the Tang emperor returned in his carriage. We do not know what will happen to him on this journey; let's listen to the explanation in the next chapter.

* * *

From *Chapter 44*

The dharma-body in primary cycle meets the force of the cart;
The mind, righting monstrous deviates, crosses the spine-ridge pass.

* * *

When the monks saw the two Daoists, they were terrified;[1] every one of them redoubled his effort to pull desperately at the cart. "So, that's it!" said Pilgrim, comprehending the situation all at once. "These monks must be awfully afraid of the Daoists, for if not, why should they be tugging so hard at the carts? I have heard someone say that there is a place on the road to the West where Daoism is revered and Buddhism is set for destruction. This must be the place. I would like to go back and report this to Master, but I still don't know the

---

8. The monk carries hereafter the name "Buddhist Canon."
1. In the intervening chapters Tripitaka, the monk Xuanzang, has gained his three disciples: Pilgrim (the monkey, Sun Wukong), Sha

Monk (or Sha Wujing), and Zhu Bajie. Having been subjected to numerous ordeals on the way to India in pursuit of the scriptures, they here enter a land where Buddhists are enslaved by Daoists.

whole truth and he might blame me for bringing him surmises, saying that even a smart person like me can't be counted on for a reliable report. Let me go down there and question them thoroughly before I give Master an answer."

"Whom would he question?" you ask. Dear Great Sage! He lowered his cloud and with a shake of his torso, he changed at the foot of the city into a wandering Daoist of the Completed Authenticity sect, with an exorcist hamper hung on his left arm. Striking a hollow wooden fish with his hands and chanting lyrics of Daoist themes, he walked up to the two Daoists near the city gate. "Masters," he said, bowing, "this humble Daoist raises his hand." Returning his salute, one of the Daoists said, "Sir, where did you come from?" "This disciple," said Pilgrim, "has wandered to the corners of the sea and to the edges of Heaven. I arrived here this morning with the sole purpose of collecting subscriptions for good works. May I ask the two masters which street in this city is favorable towards the Dao, and which alley is inclined towards piety? This humble Daoist would like to go there and beg for some vegetarian food." Smiling, the Daoist said, "O Sir! Why do you speak in such a disgraceful manner?" "What do you mean by disgraceful?" said Pilgrim. "If you want to *beg* for vegetarian food," said the Daoist, "isn't that disgraceful?" Pilgrim said, "Those who have left the family live by begging. If I didn't beg, where would I have money to buy food?"

Chuckling, the Daoist said, "You've come from afar, and you don't know anything about our city. In this city of ours, not only the civil and military officials are fond of the Dao, the rich merchants and men of prominence devoted to piety, but even the ordinary citizens, young and old, will bow to present us food once they see us. It is, in fact, a trivia matter, hardly worth mentioning. What's most important about our city is that His Majesty, the king, is also fond of the Dao and devoted to piety." "This humble cleric is first of all quite young," said Pilgrim, "and second, he is indeed from afar. In truth I'm ignorant of the situation here. May I trouble the two masters to tell me the name of this place and give me a thorough account of how the king has come to be so devoted to the cause of Dao—for the sake of fraternal feelings among us Daoists?" The Daoist said, "This city has the name of the Cart Slow Kingdom, and the ruler on the precious throne is a relative of ours."

When Pilgrim heard these words, he broke into loud guffaws, saying, "I suppose that a Daoist has become king." "No," said the Daoist. "What happened was that twenty years ago, this region had a drought, so severe that not a single drop of rain fell from the sky and all grains and plants perished. The king and his subjects, the rich as well as the poor—every person was burning incense and praying to Heaven for relief. Just when it seemed that nothing else could preserve their lives, three immortals suddenly descended from the sky and saved us all." "Who were these immortals?" asked Pilgrim. "Our masters," said the Daoist. "What are their names?" said Pilgrim. The Daoist replied, "The eldest master is called the Tiger-Strength Great Immortal; the second master, the Deer-Strength Great Immortal; and the third master, Goat-Strength Great Immortal." "What kinds of magic power do your esteemed teachers possess?" asked Pilgrim. The Daoist said, "Summoning the wind and the rain for my masters would be as easy as flipping over one's palms; they point at water and it will change into oil; they touch stones and change them into gold, as quickly as one turns over in bed. With this kind of magic power, they are thus able to rob the creative genius of Heaven and Earth, to alter the mysteries of the stars and constellations. The king and his subjects have such profound respect for them that all of us Daoists are claimed as royal kin." Pilgrim said, "This ruler is lucky, all right. After all, the proverb says, 'Magic moves ministers!' He certainly can't lose to claim kinship with your old masters, if they possess such powers. Alas! I wonder if I had even that tiniest spark of affinity, such that I could have an audience with the old masters?" Chuckling, the Daoist replied, "If you want to see our masters, it's not difficult at all. The two of us are their bosom disciples. Moreover, our masters are so devoted to the Way and so deferential to the pious that the mere mention of the word 'Dao' would bring them out of the door, fall of welcome. If we two were to introduce you, we would need to exert our themselves no more vigorously than to blow away some ashes."

Bowing deeply, Pilgrim said, "I am indebted to you for your introduction. Let us go into the city then." "Let's wait a moment," said one of the Daoists. "You sit here while we two finish our official business first. Then we'll go with you." Pilgrim said, "Those of us who have left the family are without cares or ties; we are completely free. What do you mean by official business?" The Daoist pointed with his finger at the monks on the beach and said, "Their work happens to be the means of livelihood for us. Lest they become indolent, we have come to check them off the roll before we go with you." Smiling, Pilgrim said, "You must be mistaken, Masters. Buddhists and Daoists are all people who have left the family. For what reason are they working for our support? Why are they willing to submit to our roll call?"

The Daoist said, "You have no idea that in the year when we were all praying for rain, the monks bowed to Buddha on one side while the Daoists petitioned the Pole Star on the other, all for the sake of finding some food for the country. The monks, however, were useless, their empty chants of sūtras wholly without efficacy. As soon as our masters arrived on the scene, they summoned the wind and the rain and the bitter affliction was removed from the multitudes. It was then that the Court became terribly vexed at the monks, saying that they were completely ineffective and that they deserved to have their monasteries wrecked and their Buddha images destroyed. Their travel rescripts were revoked and they were not permitted to return to their native regions. His Majesty gave them to us instead and they were to serve as bondsmen: they are the ones who tend the fires in our temple, who sweep the grounds, and who guard the gates. Since we have some buildings in the rear which are not completely finished, we have ordered these monks here to haul bricks, tiles, and timber for the construction. But for fear of their mischief, indolence, and unwillingness to pull the cart, we have come to investigate and make the roll call."

When Pilgrim heard that, he tugged at the Daoist as tears rolled from his eyes. "I said that I might not have the good affinity to see your old masters," he said, "and true enough I don't." "Why not?" asked the Daoist. "This humble Daoist is making a wide tour of the world," said Pilgrim, "both for the sake of eking out a living and for finding a relative." "What sort of relative do you have?" said the Daoist. Pilgrim said, "I have an uncle, who since his youth had left the family and shorn his hair to become a monk. Because of famine some years ago he had to go abroad to beg for alms and hadn't returned since. As I remembered our ancestral benevolence, I decided that I would make a special effort to find him along the way. It's very likely, I suppose, that he is detained here and cannot go home. I must find him somehow and get to see him before I can go inside the city with you." "That's easy," said the Daoist. "The two of us can sit here while you go down to the beach to make the roll call for us. There should be five hundred of them on the roll. Take a look and see if your uncle is among them. If he is, we'll let him go for the sake of the fact that you, too, are a fellow Daoist. Then we'll go inside the city with you. How about that?"

Pilgrim thanked them profusely, and with a deep bow he took leave of the Daoists. Striking up his wooden fish, he headed down to the beach, passing the double passes as he walked down the narrow path from the steep ridge. All those monks knelt down at once and kowtowed, saying in unison, "Father, we have not been indolent. Not even half a person from the five hundred is missing—we are all here pulling the cart." Snickering to himself, Pilgrim thought: "These monks must have been awfully abused by the Daoists. They are terrified even when they see a fake Daoist like me. If a real Daoist goes near them, they will probably die of fear." Waving his hand, Pilgrim said, "Get up, and don't be afraid! I'm not here to inspect your work, I'm here to find a relative." When those monks heard that he was looking for a relative, they surrounded him on all sides, every one of them sticking out his head and coughing, hoping that he would be claimed as kin. "Which of us is his relative?" they said. After he had looked at them for a while, Pilgrim burst into laughter. "Father," said the monks, "you don't seem to have found your relative. Why are you laughing instead?" Pilgrim said, "You want to know why I'm laughing? I'm laughing at how immature you monks are! It was because of your having been born under an unlucky star that your parents, for fear of your bringing misfortune upon them or for not bringing with you additional brothers and sisters, turned you out of the family and made you priests. How could you then not follow the Three Jewels and not revere the law of Buddha? Why aren't you reading the sūtras and chanting the litanies? Why do you serve the Daoists and allow them to exploit you as bondsmen and slaves?" "Venerable Father," said the monks, "are you here to ridicule us? You must have come from abroad, and you have no idea of our plight." "Indeed I'm from abroad," said Pilgrim, "and I truly have no idea of what sort of plight you have."

As they began to weep, the monks said, "The ruler of our country is wicked and partial. All he cares for are those persons like you, Venerable Father, and those whom he hates are us Buddhists." "Why is that?" asked Pilgrim. "Because the need for wind and rain," said one of the monks, "caused three immortal elders to come here. They deceived our ruler and persuaded him to tear down our monasteries and revoke our travel rescripts, forbidding us to return to our native regions. He would not, moreover, permit us to serve even in any secular capacity except as slaves in the household of those immortal elders. Our agony is unbearable! If any Daoist mendicant shows up in this region, they would immediately request the king to grant him an audience and a handsome reward; but if a monk appears, regardless of whether he is from nearby or afar, he will be seized and sent to be a servant in the house of the immortals." Pilgrim said, "Could it be that those Daoists are truly in possession of some mighty magic, potent enough to seduce the king? If it's only a matter of summoning the wind and the rain, then it is merely a trivial trick of heterodoxy. How could it sway a ruler's heart?" The monks said, "They know how to manipulate cinnabar and refine lead, to sit in meditation in order to nourish their spirits. They point to water and it changes into oil; they touch stones and transform them into pieces of gold. Now they are in the process of building a huge temple for the Three Pure Ones, in which they can perform rites to Heaven and Earth and read scriptures night and day, to the end that the king will remain youthful for ten thousand years. Such enterprise undoubtedly pleases the king."

"So that's how it is!" said Pilgrim. "Why don't you all run away and be done with it?" "Father, we can't!" said the monks. "Those immortal elders have obtained permission from the king to have our portraits painted and hung up in all four quarters of the kingdom. Although the territory of this Cart Slow Kingdom is quite large, there is a picture of monks displayed in the marketplace of every village, town, county, and province. It bears on top the royal inscription that any official who catches a monk will be elevated three grades, and any private citizen who does so will receive a reward of fifty taels of white silver. That's why we can never escape. Let's not say monks—but even those who have cut their hair short or are getting bald will find it difficult to get past the officials. They are everywhere, the detectives and the runners! No matter what you do, you simply can't flee. We have no alternative but to remain here and suffer."

* * *

There were three old Daoists resplendent in their ritual robes, and Pilgrim thought they had to be the Tiger-Strength, Deer-Strength, and Goat-Strength Immortals. Below them there was a motley crew of some seven or eight hundred Daoists; lined up on opposite sides, they were beating drums and gongs, offering incense, and saying prayers. Secretly pleased, Pilgrim said to himself, "I would like to go down there and fool with them a bit, but as the proverb says,

> A silk fiber is no thread;
> A single hand cannot clap.

Let me go back and alert Bajie and Sha Monk. Then we can return and have some fun."

He dropped down from the auspicious cloud and went straight back to the abbot's hall, where he found Bajie and Sha Monk asleep head to foot in one bed. Pilgrim tried to wake Wujing first, and as he stirred, Sha Monk said, "Elder Brother, you aren't asleep yet?" "Get up now," said Pilgrim, "for you and I are going to enjoy ourselves." "In the dead of night," said Sha Monk, "how could we enjoy ourselves when our mouths are dried and our eyes won't stay open?" Pilgrim said, "There is indeed in this city a Temple of the Three Pure Ones. Right now the Daoists in the temple are conducting a mass, and their main hall is filled with all kinds of offerings. The buns are big as barrels, and their cakes must weigh fifty or sixty pounds each. There are also countless rice condiments and fresh fruits. Come with me and we'll go enjoy ourselves!" When Zhu Bajie heard in his sleep that there were good things to eat, he immediately woke up, saying, "Elder Brother, aren't you going to take care of me too?" "Brother," said Pilgrim, "if you want to eat, don't make all these noises and wake up Master. Just follow me."

The two of them slipped on their clothes and walked quietly out the door. They trod on the cloud with Pilgrim and rose into the air. When Idiot saw the flare of lights, he wanted immediately to go down there had not Pilgrim pulled him back. "Don't be so impatient," said Pilgrim, "wait till they disperse. Then we can go down there." Bajie said, "But obviously they are having such a good time praying. Why would they want to disperse? "Let me use a little magic," said Pilgrim, "and they will."

Dear Great Sage! He made the magic sign with his fingers and recited a spell before he drew in his breath facing the ground toward the southwest. Then he blew it out and at once a violent whirlwind assailed the Three Pure Ones Hall, smashing flower vases and candle stands and tearing up all the ex-votos hanging on the four walls. As lights and torches were all blown out, the Daoists became terrified. Tiger-Strength Immortal said, "Disciples, let's disperse. Since this divine wind has extinguished all our lamps, torches, and incense, each of us should retire. We can rise earlier tomorrow morning to recite a few more scrolls of scriptures and make up for what we miss tonight." The various Daoists indeed retreated.

Our Pilgrim leading Bajie and Sha Monk lowered the clouds and dashed up to the Three Pure Ones Hall. Without bothering to find out whether it was raw or cooked, Idiot grabbed one of the cakes and gave it a fierce bite. Pilgrim whipped out the iron rod and tried to give his hand a whack. Hastily withdrawing his hand to dodge the blow, Bajie said, "I haven't even found out the taste yet, and you're trying to hit me already?" "Don't be so rude," said Pilgrim. "Let's sit down with proper manners and then we may treat ourselves." "Aren't you embarrassed?" said Bajie. "You are stealing food, you know, and you still want proper manners! If you were invited here, what would you do then?" Pilgrim said, "Who are these bodhisattvas sitting up there?" "What do you mean by who are these bodhisattvas?" chuckled Bajie. "Can't you recognize the Three Pure Ones?" "Which Three Pure Ones?" said Pilgrim. "The one in the middle," said Bajie, "is the Honorable Divine of the Origin; the one on the left is the Enlightened Lord of Spiritual Treasures; and the one on the right is Laozi.[2]" Pilgrim said, "We have to take on their appearances. Only then can we eat safely and comfortably." When he caught hold of the delicious fragrance coming from the offerings, Idiot could wait no longer. Climbing up onto the tall platform, he gave the figure of Laozi a shove with his snout and pushed it to the floor, saying, "Old fellow, you have sat here long enough! Now let old Hog take your place for a while!" So Bajie changed himself into Laozi, while Pilgrim took on the appearance of the Honorable Divine of the Origin and Sha Monk became the Enlightened Lord of Spiritual Treasures. All the original images were pushed down to the floor. The moment they sat down, Bajie began to gorge himself with the huge buns. "Could you wait one moment?" said Pilgrim. "Elder Brother," said Bajie, "we have changed into their forms. Why wait any longer?"

"Brother," said Pilgrim, "it's small thing to eat, but giving ourselves away is no small matter! These holy images we pushed on the floor could be found by those Daoists who had to rise early to strike the bell or sweep the grounds. If they stumbled over them, wouldn't our secret be revealed? Why don't you see if you can hide them somewhere?" Bajie said, "This is an unfamiliar place, and I don't even know where to begin to look for a hiding spot." "Just now when we entered the hall," Pilgrim said, "I chanced to notice a little door on our right.

---

2. Famous ancient philosophical master, to whom the book *Laozi* is ascribed, and central deity of the Daoist pantheon.

Judging from the foul stench coming through it, I think it must be a Bureau of Five-Grain Transmigration. Send them in there."

Idiot, in truth, was rather good at crude labor! He leaped down, threw the three images over his shoulder, and carried them out of the hall. When be kicked open the door, he found a huge privy inside. Chuckling to himself he said, "This Bimawen truly has a way with words! He even bestows on a privy a sacred title! The Bureau of Five-Grain Transmigration, what a name!" Still hauling the images on this shoulders, Idiot began to mumble this prayer to them:

> "O Pure Ones Three,
> I'll confide in thee:
> From afar we came,
> Staunch foes of bogies.
> We'd like a treat,
> But nowhere's cozy.
> We borrow your seats
> For a while only.
> You've sat too long,
> Now go to the privy.
> In times past you've enjoyed countless good things
> By being pure and clean Daoists.
> Today you can't avoid facing something dirty
> When you become Honorable Divines Most Smelly!"

After he had made his supplication, he threw them inside with a splash and half of his robe was soiled by the muck. As he walked back into the hall, Pilgrim said, "Did you hide them well?" "Well enough," said Bajie, "but some of the filth stained my robe. It still stinks. I hope it won't make you retch." "Never mind," said Pilgrim, laughing, "you just come and enjoy yourself. I wonder if we could all make a clean getaway!" After Idiot changed back into the form of Laozi, the three of them took their seats and abandoned themselves to enjoyment. They ate the huge buns first; then they gobbled down the side dishes, the rice condiments, the dumplings, the baked goods, the cakes, the deep-fried dishes, and the steamed pastries—regardless of whether these were hot or cold. Pilgrim Sun, however, was not too fond of anything cooked; all he had were a few pieces of fruit, just to keep the other two company. Meanwhile Bajie and Sha Monk went after the offerings like comets chasing the moon, like wind mopping up the clouds! In no time at all, they were completely devoured. When there was nothing left for them to eat, they, instead of leaving, remained seated there to chat and wait for the food to digest.

* * *

From Chapter 46

Heresy flaunts its strength to make orthodoxy;
Mind Monkey shows his saintliness to slay the deviates.

We were telling you that when the king saw Pilgrim Sun's ability to summon dragons and command sages, he immediately applied his treasure seal to the travel rescript. He was about to hand it back to the Tang monk and permit him to take up the journey once more, when the three Daoists went forward and prostrated themselves before the steps of the Hall of Golden Chimes. The king left his dragon throne hurriedly and tried to raise them with his hands. "National Preceptors," he said, "why do you three go through such a great ceremony with us today?" "Your Majesty," said the Daoists, "we have been upholding your reign and providing security for your people here for these twenty years. Today this priest has made use of some paltry tricks of magic and robbed us of all our credit and ruined our reputation. Just because of one rainstorm, Your Majesty has pardoned even their crime of murder. Are we not being treated lightly? Let Your Majesty withhold their rescript for the moment and allow us brothers to wage another contest with them. We shall see what happens then."

* * *

Just then, the Tiger-Strength Great Immortal walked out from the Pavilion of Cultural Florescence after he had been washed and combed. "Your Majesty," he said as he walked up the hall, "this monk knows the magic of object removal. Give me the chest, and I'll destroy his magic. Then we can have another contest with him." "What do you want to do?" said the king. Tiger-Strength said, "His magic can remove only lifeless objects but not a human body. Put this Daoist youth in the chest, and he'll never be able to remove him." The youth indeed was hidden in the chest, which was then brought down again from the hall to be placed before the steps. "You, monk," said the king, "guess again what sort of treasure we have inside." Tripitaka said, "Here it comes again!" "Let me go and have another look," said Pilgrim. With a buzz, he flew off and crawled inside, where he found a Daoist lad. Marvelous Great Sage! What readiness of mind! Truly

>   Such agility is rare in the world!
>   Such cleverness is uncommon indeed!

Shaking his body once, he changed himself into the form of one of those old Daoists, whispering as he entered the chest, "Disciple."

"Master," said the lad, "how did you come in here?" "With the magic of invisibility," said Pilgrim. The lad said, "Do you have some instructions for me?" "The priest saw you enter the chest," said Pilgrim, "and if he made his guess a Daoist lad, wouldn't we lose to him again? That's why I came here to discuss the matter with you. Let's shave your head, and we'll then make them guess that you are a monk." The Daoist lad said, "Do whatever you want, Master, just so that we win. For if we lose to them again, not only our reputation will be ruined, but the court also may no longer revere us." "Exactly," said Pilgrim. "Come over here, my child. When we defeat them, I'll reward you handsomely." He changed his golden-hooped rod into a sharp razor, and hugging the lad, he said, "Darling, try to endure the pain for a moment. Don't make any noise! I'll shave your head." In a little while, the lad's hair was completely shorn, rolled into a ball, and stuffed into one of the corners of the chest. He put away the razor, and rubbing the lad's bald head, he said, "My child, your head looks like a monk's all right, but your clothes don't fit. Take them off and let me change them for you." What the Daoist lad had on was a crane's-down robe of spring-onion white silk, embroidered with the cloud pattern and trimmed with brocade. When he took it off, Pilgrim blew on it his immortal breath, crying, "Change!" It changed instantly into a monk shirt of brown color, which Pilgrim helped him put on. He then pulled off two pieces of hair which he changed into a wooden fish and a tap. "Disciple," said Pilgrim, as he handed over the fish and the tap to the lad, "you must listen carefully. If you hear someone call for the Daoist youth, don't ever leave this chest. If someone calls 'Monk,' then you may push open the chest door, strike up the wooden fish, and walk out chanting a Buddhist sūtra. Then it'll be complete success for us." "I only know," said the lad, "how to recite the *Three Officials Scripture*, the *Northern Dipper Scripture*, or the *Woe-Dispelling Scripture*. I don't know how to recite any Buddhist sūtra." Pilgrim said, "Can you chant the name of Buddha?" "You mean Amitābha,"[1] said the lad. "Who doesn't know that?" "Good enough! Good enough!" said Pilgrim. "You may chant the name of Buddha. It'll spare me from having to teach you anything new. Remember what I've told you. I'm leaving." He changed back into a mole-cricket and crawled out, after which, he flew back to the ear of the Tang monk and said, "Master, just guess it's a monk." Tripitaka said, "This time I know I'll win." "How could you be so sure?" said Pilgrim, and Tripitaka replied, "The sūtras said, 'The Buddha, the Dharma, and the Sangha are the Three Jewels.' A monk therefore is a treasure."

As they were thus talking among themselves, the Tiger-Strength Great Immortal said, "Your Majesty, this third time it is a Daoist youth." He made the declaration several times, but nothing happened nor did anyone make an appearance. Pressing his palms together, Tripitaka said, "It's a monk." With all his might, Bajie screamed: "It's a monk in the chest!" All at once the youth kicked open the chest and walked out, striking the wooden fish and chanting the name of Buddha. So delighted were the two rows of civil and military officials that they shouted bravos repeatedly; so astonished were the three Daoists that they could not utter a sound. "These priests must have the assistance from spirits and gods," said the king. "How could a Daoist enter the chest and come out a monk? Even if he had an attendant with him, he might have been able to have his head shaved. How could he know how to take up the chanting of Buddha's name? O Preceptors! Please let them go!"

"Your Majesty," said the Tiger-Strength Great Immortal, "as the proverb says, 'The warrior has found his equal, the chess player his match.' We might as well make use of what we learned in our youth at Zhongnan Mountain and challenge them to a greater competition." "What did you learn?" said the king. Tiger-Strength said, "We three brothers all have acquired some magic abilities: cut off our heads, and we can put them back on our necks; open our chests and gouge out our hearts, and they will grow back again: inside a cauldron of boiling oil, we can take baths." Highly startled the king said, "These three things are all roads leading to certain death!" "Only because we have such magic power," said Tiger-Strength, "do we dare make so bold a claim. We won't quit until we have waged this contest with them." The king said in a loud voice, "You priests from the Land of the East, our National Preceptors are unwilling

---

1. "Buddha of Infinite Light," who presides over the Pure Land Paradise in the West, where believers who call his name can be reborn.

to let you go. They wish to wage one more contest with you in head cutting, stomach ripping, and going into a cauldron of boiling oil to take a bath."

Pilgrim was still assuming the form of the mole-cricket, flying back and forth to make his secret report. When he heard this, he retrieved his hair, which had been changed into his substitute, and he himself changed at once back into his true form. "Lucky! Lucky!" he cried with loud guffaws. "Business has come to my door!" "These three things," said Bajie, "will certainly make you lose your life. How could you say that business has come to your door?" "You still have no idea of my abilities!" said Pilgrim. "Elder Brother," said Bajie, "you are quite clever, quite capable in those transformations. Aren't those skills something already? What more abilities do you have?" Pilgrim said,

"*Cut off my head and I still can speak.*
Sever my arms, I still can beat you up!
My legs amputated, I still can walk.
My belly, ripped open, will heal again,
Smooth and snug as a wonton people make:
A tiny pinch and it's completely formed.
To bathe in boiling oil is easier still;
It's like warm liquid cleansing me of dirt."

When Bajie and Sha Monk heard these words, they roared with laughter. Pilgrim went forward and said, "Your Majesty, this young priest knows how to have his head cut off." "How did you acquire such an ability?" asked the king. "When I was practicing austerities in a monastery some years ago," said Pilgrim, "I met a mendicant Chan[2] master, who taught me the magic of head cutting. I don't know whether it works or not, and that's why I want to try it out right now." "This priest is so young and ignorant!" said the king, chuckling. "Is head cutting something to try out? The head is, after all, the very fountain of the six kinds of *yang* energies[3] in one's body. If you cut it off. you'll die." "That's what we want," said Tiger-Strength. "Only then can our feelings be relieved!" Besotted by the Daoist's words, the foolish ruler immediately gave the decree for an execution site to be prepared.

Once the command was given, three thousand imperial guards took up their positions outside the gate of the court. The king said, "Monk, go and cut off your head first." "I'll go first! I'll go first!" said Pilgrim merrily. He folded his hands before his chest and shouted, "National Preceptors, pardon my presumption for taking my turn first!" He turned swiftly and was about to dash out. The Tang monk grabbed him, saying, "O Disciple! Be careful! Where you are going isn't a playground!" "No fear!" said Pilgrim. "Take off your hands! Let me go!"

The Great Sage went straight to the execution site, where he was caught hold of by the executioner and bound with ropes. He was then led to a tall mound and pinned down on top of it. At the cry "Kill," his head came off with a swishing sound. Then the executioner gave the head a kick, and it rolled off like a watermelon to a distance of some forty paces away. No blood, however, spurted from the neck of Pilgrim. Instead, a voice came from inside his stom-

---

2. Also known as Zen (Japanese). A Buddhist sect.

3. According to traditional medicine the body consists of a mixture of *yin* and *yang* energies.

ach, crying, "Come, head!" So alarmed was the Deer-Strength Great Immortal by the sight of such ability that he at once recited a spell and gave this charge to the local spirit and patron deity: "Hold down that head. When I have defeated the monk, I'll persuade the king to turn your little shrines into huge temples, your idols of clay into true bodies of gold." The local spirit and the god, you see, had to serve him since he knew the magic of the five thunders. Secretly, they indeed held Pilgrim's head down. Once more Pilgrim cried, "Come, head!" But the head stayed on the ground as if it had taken root; it would not move at all. Somewhat anxious, Pilgrim rolled his hands into fists and wrenched his body violently. The ropes all snapped and fell off; at the cry "Grow," a head sprang up instantly from his neck. Every one of the executioners and every member of the imperial guards became terrified, while the officer in charge of the execution dashed inside the court to make this report: "Your Majesty, that young priest had his head cut off, but another head has grown up." "Sha Monk," said Bajie, giggling, "we truly had no idea that Elder Brother has this kind of talent!" "If he knows seventy-two ways of transformation," said Sha Monk, "he may have altogether seventy-two heads!"

Hardly had he finished speaking when Pilgrim came walking back, saying, "Master." Exceedingly pleased, Tripitaka said, "Disciple, did it hurt?" "Hardly," said Pilgrim, "it's sort of fun!" "Elder Brother," said Bajie, "do you need ointment for the scar?" "Touch me," said Pilgrim, "and see if there's any scar." Idiot touched him and he was dumbfounded. "Marvelous! Marvelous!" he giggled. "It healed perfectly. You can't feel even the slightest scar!"

As the brothers were chatting happily among themselves, they heard the king say, "Receive your rescript. We give you a complete pardon. Go away!" Pilgrim said, "We'll take the rescript all right, but we want the National Preceptor to go there and cut his head off too! He should try something new!" "Great National Preceptor," said the king, "the priest is not willing to pass you up. If you want to compete with him, please try not to frighten us." Tiger-Strength had no choice but to go up to the site, where he was bound and pinned to the ground by several executioners. One of them lifted the sword and cut off his head, which was then kicked some thirty paces away. Blood did not spurt from his trunk either, and he, too, gave a cry, "Come, head!" Hurriedly pulling off a piece of hair, Pilgrim blew on it his immortal breath, crying, "Change!" It changed into a yellow hound, which dashed into the execution site, picked up the Daoist's head with its mouth, and ran to drop it into the imperial moat. The Daoist, meanwhile, called for his head three times without success. He did not, you see, have the ability of Pilgrim, and there was no possibility that he could produce another head. All at once, bright crimson gushed out from his trunk. Alas!

> Though he could send for wind and call for rain,
> How could he match an immortal of the right fruit?

In a moment, he fell to the dust, and those gathered about him discovered that he was actually a headless tiger with yellow fur.

* * *

We tell you now instead about those monks who succeeded in escaping with their lives. When they heard of the decree that was promulgated, every one of them was delighted and began to return to the city to search for the Great Sage Sun,[4] to thank him, and to return his hairs. Meanwhile, the elder, after the banquet was over, obtained the rescript from the king, who led the queen, the concubines, and two rows of civil and military officials out the gate of the court to see the priests off, As they came out, they found many monks kneeling on both sides of the road, saying "Father Great Sage, Equal to Heaven, we are the monks who escaped with our lives on the beach. When we heard that Father had wiped out the demons and rescued us, and when we further heard that our king had issued a decree commanding our return, we came here to present to you the hairs and to thank you for your Heavenly grace." "How many of you came back?" asked Pilgrim, chuckling, and they replied, "All five hundred. None's missing." Pilgrim shook his body once and immediately retrieved his hairs. Then he said to the king and the laypeople, "These monks indeed were released by old Monkey. The cart was smashed after old Monkey tossed it through the double passes and up the steep ridge, and it was Monkey also who beat to death those two perverse Daoists. After such pestilence has been exterminated this day, you should realize that the true way is the gate of Chan. Hereafter you should never believe in false doctrines. I hope you will honor the unity of the Three Religions: revere the monks, revere also the Daoists, and take care to nurture the talented. Your kingdom, I assure you, will be secure forever." The king gave his assent and his thanks repeatedly before he escorted the Tang monk out of the city. And so, this was the purpose of their journey:

> A *diligent search for the three canons;*
> A *strenuous quest for the primal light.*

We do not know what will happen to master and disciples; let's listen to the explanation in the next chapter.

* * *

From *Chapter 53*

> The Chan[1] *Master, taking food, is demonically conceived;*
> *Yellow Hag brings water to dissolve the perverse pregnancy.*

* * *

Walking to the side of the boat, Pilgrim said, "You are the one ferrying the boat?" "Yes," said the woman. "Why is the ferryman not here?" asked Pilgrim. "Why is the ferrywoman punting the boat?" The woman smiled and did not reply; she pulled out the gangplank instead and set it up. Sha Monk then poled the luggage into the boat, followed by the master holding onto Pilgrim. Then they moved the boat sideways so that Bajie could lead the horse to step into it. After the gangplank was put away, the woman punted the boat away from shore and, in a moment, rowed it across the river.

After they reached the western shore, the elder asked Sha Monk to untie one of the wraps and take out a few pennies for the woman. Without disputing the price, the woman tied the boat to a wooden pillar by the water and walked into

---

4. Sun Wukong, the monkey.   1. Again, Zen (Japanese), a Buddhist sect.

one of the village huts nearby, giggling loudly all the time. When Tripitaka saw how clear the water was, he felt thirsty and told Bajie: "Get the almsbowl and fetch some water for me to drink." "I was just about to drink some myself," said Idiot, who took out the almsbowl and bailed out a full bowl of water to hand over to the master. The master drank less than half of the water, and when Idiot took the bowl back, he drank the rest of it in one gulp before he helped his master to mount the horse once more.

After master and disciples resumed their journey to the West, they had hardly traveled half an hour when the elder began to groan as he rode. "Stomachache!" he said, and Bajie behind him also said, "I have a stomachache, too." Sha Monk said, "It must be the cold water you drank." But before he even finished speaking, the elder cried out: "The pain's awful!" Bajie also screamed: "The pain's awful!" As the two of them struggled with this unbearable pain, their bellies began to swell in size steadily. Inside their abdomens, there seemed to be a clot of blood or a lump of flesh, which could be felt clearly by the hand, kicking and jumping wildly about. Tripitaka was in great discomfort when they came upon a small village by the road; two bundles of hay were tied to some branches on a tall tree nearby. "Master, that's good!" said Pilgrim. "The house over there must be an inn. Let me go over there to beg some hot liquid for you. I'll ask them also whether there is an apothecary around, so that I can get some ointment for your stomachache."

Delighted by what he heard, Tripitaka whipped his white horse and soon arrived at the village. As he dismounted, he saw an old woman sitting on a grass mound outside the village gate and knitting hemp. Pilgrim went forward and bowed to her with palms pressed together saying, "Popo,[2] this poor monk has come from the Great Tang in the Land of the East. My master is the royal brother of the Tang court. Because he drank some water from the river back there after we crossed it, he is having a stomachache." Breaking into loud guffaws, the woman said, "You people drank some water from the river?" "Yes," replied Pilgrim, "we drank some of the clean river water east of here." Giggling loudly, the old woman said, "What a joke! What a joke! Come in, all of you. I'll explain to you."

Pilgrim went to take hold of Tang monk while Sha Monk held up Bajie; moaning with every step the two sick men walked into the thatched hut to take a seat, their stomachs protruding and their faces turning yellow from the pain. "Popo," Pilgrim kept saying, "please make some hot liquid for my master. We'll thank you." Instead of boiling water, however, the old woman dashed inside, laughing and yelling, "Come and look, all of you!"

With loud clip-clops, several middle-aged women ran out from within to stare at the Tang monk, grinning stupidly all the time. Enraged, Pilgrim gave a yell and ground his teeth together, so frightening the whole crowd of them that they turned to flee, stumbling all over. Pilgrim darted forward and caught hold of the old woman, crying, "Boil some water quick and I'll spare you!" "O Father!" said the old woman, shaking violently, "boiling water is useless, because it won't cure their stomachaches. Let me go, and I'll tell you." Pilgrim released her, and she said, "This is the Nation of Women of Western Liang.[3] There are

2. Granny.
3. In the *Record of the Western Territories of the Great Tang*, a diary by the historical Xuanzang, he mentions a Western kingdom of women.

only women in our country, and not even a single male can be found here. That's why we were amused when we saw you. That water your master drank is not the best, for the river is called Child-and-Mother River. Outside our capital we also have a Male Reception Post-house, by the side of which there is also a Pregnancy Reflection Stream. Only after reaching her twentieth year would someone from this region dare go and drink that river's water, for she would feel the pain of conception soon after she took a drink. After three days, she would go to the Male Reception Post-house and look at her reflection in the stream. If a double reflection appears, it means that she will give birth to a child. Since your master drank some water from the Child-and-Mother River, he too has become pregnant and will give birth to a child. How could hot water cure him?"

When Tripitaka heard this, he paled with fright. "O disciple," he cried, "what shall we do?" "O father!" groaned Bajie as he twisted to spread his legs further apart, "we are men, and we have to give birth to babies? Where can we find a birth canal? How could the fetus come out?" With a chuckle Pilgrim said, "According to the ancients, 'A ripe melon will fall by itself.' When the time comes, you may have a gaping hole at your armpit and the baby will crawl out."

When Bajie heard this, he shook with fright, and that made the pain all the more unbearable. "Finished! Finished!" he cried. "I'm dead! I'm dead!" "Second Elder Brother," said Sha Monk, laughing, "stop writhing! Stop writhing! You may hurt the umbilical cord and end up with some sort of prenatal sickness." Our Idiot became more alarmed than ever. Tears welling up in his eyes, he tugged at Pilgrim and said, "Elder Brother, please ask the Popo to see if they have some midwives here who are not too heavy-handed. Let's find a few right away. The movement inside is becoming more frequent now. It must be labor pain. It's coming! It's coming!" Again Sha Monk said chuckling, "Second Elder Brother, if it's labor pain, you'd better sit still. I fear you may puncture the water bag."

"O Popo," said Tripitaka with a moan, "do you have a physician here? I'll ask my disciple to go there and ask for a prescription. We'll take the drug and have an abortion." "Even drugs are useless," said the old woman, "but due south of here there is a Male-Undoing Mountain. In it there is a Child Destruction Cave, and inside the cave there is an Abortion Stream. You must drink a mouthful of water from the stream before the pregnancy can be terminated. But nowadays, it's not easy to get that water. Last year, a Daoist by the name of True Immortal Compliant came on the scene and he changed the name of the Child Destruction Cave to the Shrine of Immortal Assembly. Claiming the water from the Abortion Stream as his possession, he refused to give it out freely. Anyone who wants the water must present monetary offerings together with meats, wines, and fruit baskets. After bowing to him in complete reverence, you will receive a tiny bowl of the water. But all of you are mendicants. Where could you find the kind of money you need to spend for something like this? You might as well suffer here and wait for the births." When Pilgrim heard this, he was filled with delight. "Popo," he said, "how far is it from here to the Male-Undoing Mountain?" "About three thousand miles," replied the old woman. "Excellent! Excellent!" said Pilgrim. "Relax, Master! Let old Monkey go and fetch some of that water for you to drink."

* * *

When Pilgrim saw him, he pressed his palms together before him and bowed, saying, "This poor monk is Sun Wukong." "Are you the real Sun Wukong," said the master with a laugh, "or are you merely assuming his name and surname?" "Look at the way the master speaks!" said Pilgrim. "As the proverb says, 'A gentleman changes neither his name when he stands, nor his surname when he sits.' What would be the reason for me to assume someone else's name?" The master asked, "Do you recognize me?" "Since I made repentance in the Buddhist gate and embraced with all sincerity the teaching of the monks," said Pilgrim, "I have only been climbing mountains and fording waters. I have lost contact with all the friends of my youth. Because I have never been able to visit you, I have never beheld your honorable countenance before. When we asked for our way in a village household west of the Child-and-Mother River, they told me that the master is called the True Immortal Compliant. That's how I know your name." The master said, "You are walking on your way, and I'm cultivating my realized immortality. Why did you come to visit me?" "Because my master drank by mistake the water of the Child-and-Mother River," replied Pilgrim, "and his stomachache turned into a pregnancy. I came especially to your immortal mansion to beg you for a bowl of water from the Abortion Stream, in order that my master might be freed from this ordeal."

"Is your master Tripitaka Tang?" asked the master, his eyes glowering. "Yes, indeed!" answered Pilgrim. Grinding his teeth together, the master said spitefully, "Have you run into a Great King Holy Child?" "That's the nickname of the fiend, Red Boy," said Pilgrim, "who lived in the Fiery Cloud Cave by the Dried Pine Stream, in the Roaring Mountain. Why does the True Immortal ask after him?" "He happens to be my nephew," replied the master, "and the Bull Demon King is my brother. Some time ago my elder brother told me in a letter that Sun Wukong, the eldest disciple of Tripitaka Tang, was such a rascal that he brought his son great harm. I didn't know where to find you for vengeance, but you came instead to seek me out. And you're asking me for water?" Trying to placate him with a smile, Pilgrim said, "You are wrong, Sir. Your elder brother used to be my friend, for both of us belonged to a league of seven bond brothers when we were young. I just didn't know about you, and so I did not come to pay my respect in your mansion. Your nephew is very well off, for he is now the attendant of the Bodhisattva Guanyin. He has become the Boy of Goodly Wealth, with whom even we cannot compare. Why do you blame me instead?"

"You brazen monkey!" shouted the master. "Still waxing your tongue! Is my nephew better off being a king by himself, or being a slave to someone? Stop this insolence and have a taste of my hook!" Using the iron rod to parry the blow, the Great Sage said, "Please don't use the language of war, Sir. Give me some water and I'll leave." "Brazen monkey!" scolded the master. "You don't know any better! If you can withstand me for three rounds, I'll give you the water. If not, I'll chop you up as meat sauce to avenge my nephew." "You damned fool!" scolded Pilgrim. "You don't know what's good for you! If you want to fight, get up here and watch my rod!" The master at once countered with his compliant hook, and the two of them had quite a fight before the Shrine of Immortal Assembly.

The sage monk drinks from this procreant stream,
And Pilgrim must th' Immortal Compliant seek.

Who knows the True Immortal is a fiend,
Who safeguards by force the Abortion Stream?
When these two meet, they speak as enemies
Feuding, and resolved not to give one whit.
The words thus traded engender distress;
Rancor and malice so bent on revenge.
This one, whose master's life is threatened, comes seeking water;
That one for losing his nephew refuses to yield.
Fierce as a scorpion's the compliant hook;
Wild like a dragon's the golden-hooped rod.
Madly it stabs the chest, what savagery!
Aslant, it hooks the legs, what subtlety!
The rod aiming down there[4] inflicts grave wounds;
The hook, passing shoulders, will whip the head.
The rod slaps the waist—"a hawk holds a bird."
The hook swipes the head—"a mantis hits its prey."
They move here and there, both striving to win;
They turn and close in again and again.
The hook hooks, the rod strikes, without letup—
On either side victory cannot be seen.

* * *

The two of them began their fighting outside the shrine, and as they struggled and danced together, they gradually moved to the mountain slope below. We shall leave this bitter contest for a moment.

We tell you instead about our Sha Monk, who crashed inside the door, holding the bucket. He was met by the Daoist, who barred the way at the well and said, "Who are you that you dare come to get our water?" Dropping the bucket, Sha Monk took out his fiend-routing treasure staff and, without a word, brought it down on the Daoist's head. The Daoist was unable to dodge fast enough, and his left arm and shoulder were broken by this one blow. Falling to the ground, he lay there struggling for his life. "I wanted to slaughter you, cursed beast," scolded Sha Monk, "but you are, after all, a human being. I still have some pity for you, and I'll spare you. Let me bail out the water." Crying for Heaven and Earth to help him, the Daoist crawled slowly to the rear, while Sha Monk lowered the bucket into the well and filled it to the brim. He then walked out of the shrine and mounted the cloud and fog before he shouted to Pilgrim, "Big Brother, I have gotten the water and I'm leaving. Spare him! Spare him!" When the Great Sage heard this, he stopped the hook with his iron rod and said, "I was about to exterminate you, but you have not committed a crime. Moreover, I still have regard for the feelings of your brother, the Bull Demon King. When I first came here, I was hooked by you twice and didn't get my water. When I returned, I came with the trick of enticing the tiger to leave the mountain and deceived you into fighting me, so that my brother could go inside to get the water. If old Monkey is willing to use his real abilities to fight with you, don't say there is only one of you so-called True Immortal Compliants; even if there were several of you, I would beat you all to death. But to kill is not as

4. I.e., the genitals.

good as to let live, and so I'm going to spare you and permit you to have a few more years. From now on if anyone wishes to obtain the water, you must not blackmail the person."

Not knowing anything better, that bogus immortal brandished his hook and once more attempted to catch Pilgrim's legs. The Great Sage evaded the blade of his hook and then rushed forward, crying, "Don't run!" The bogus immortal was caught unprepared and he was pushed head over heels to the ground, unable to get up. Grabbing the compliant hook the Great Sage snapped it in two; then he bundled the pieces together and, with another bend, broke them into four segments. Throwing them on the ground, he said, "Brazen, cursed beast! Still dare to be unruly?" Trembling all over, the bogus immortal took the insult and dared not utter a word. Our Great Sage, in peals of laughter, mounted the cloud to rise into the air, and we have a testimonial poem. The poem says:

> You need true water to smelt true lead;
> With dried mercury true water mixes well.
> True mercury and lead have no maternal breath;
> Elixir is divine drug and cinnabar.
> In vain the child conceived attains a form;
> Earth Mother has achieved merit with ease.
> Heresy pushed down, right faith's affirmed;
> The lord of the mind, all smiles, now goes back.

Mounting the auspicious luminosity, the Great Sage caught up with Sha Monk. Having acquired the true water, they were filled with delight as they returned to where they belonged. After they lowered the clouds and went up to the village hut, they found Zhu Bajie leaning on the door post and groaning, his belly huge and protruding. Walking quietly up to him, Pilgrim said, "Idiot, when did you enter the delivery room?" Horrified, Idiot said, "Elder Brother, don't make fun of me. Did you bring the water?" Pilgrim was about to tease him some more when Sha Monk followed him in, laughing as he said, "Water's coming! Water's coming!" Enduring the pain, Tripitaka rose slightly and said, "O disciples, I've caused you a lot of trouble." That old woman, too, was most delighted, and all of her relatives came out to kowtow, crying, "O bodhisattva! This is our luck! This is our luck!" She took a goblet of flowered porcelain, filled it half full, and handed it to Tripitaka, saying, "Old master, drink it slowly. All you need is a mouthful and the pregnancy will dissolve." "I don't need any goblet," said Bajie, "I'll just finish the bucket." "O Venerable Father, don't scare people to death!" said the old woman. "If you drink this bucket of water, your stomach and your intestines will all be dissolved."

Idiot was so taken aback that he dared not misbehave; he drank only half a goblet. In less than the time of a meal, the two of them experienced sharp pain and cramps in their bellies, and then their intestines growled four or five times. After that, Idiot could no longer contain himself: both waste and urine poured out of him. The Tang monk, too, felt the urge to relieve himself and wanted to go to a quiet place. "Master," said Pilgrim, "you mustn't go out to a place where there is a draft. If you are exposed to the wind, I fear that you may catch some postnatal illness." At once the old woman brought to them two night pots so that the two of them could find relief. After several bowel movements, the pain stopped and the swelling of their bellies gradually subsided as the lump of blood and flesh dissolved. The relatives of the old woman also boiled some white rice congee and presented it to them to strengthen their postnatal weakness.

"Popo," said Bajie, "I have a healthy constitution, and I have no need to strengthen any postnatal weakness. You go and boil me some water, so that I can take a bath before I eat the congee." "Second Elder Brother," said Sha Monk, "you can't take a bath. If water gets inside someone within a month after birth, the person will be sick." Bajie said, "But I have not given proper birth to anything; at most, I only have had a miscarriage. What's there to be afraid of? I must wash and clean up." Indeed, the old woman prepared some hot water for them to clean their hands and feet. The Tang monk then ate about two bowls of congee, but Bajie consumed over fifteen bowls and he still wanted more. "Coolie," chuckled Pilgrim, "don't eat so much. If you get a sandbag belly, you'll look quite awful." "Don't worry, don't worry," replied Bajie. "I'm no female hog. So, what's there to be afraid of?" The family members indeed went to prepare some more rice.

The old woman then said to the Tang monk, "Old master, please bestow this water on me." Pilgrim said, "Idiot, you are not drinking the water anymore?" "My stomachache is gone," said Bajie, "and the pregnancy, I suppose, must be dissolved. I'm quite fine now. Why should I drink any more water?" "Since the two of them have recovered," said Pilgrim, "we'll give this water to your family." After thanking Pilgrim, the old woman poured what was left of the water into a porcelain jar, which she buried in the rear garden. She said to the rest of the family, "This jar of water will take care of my funeral expenses." Everyone in that family, young and old, was delighted. A vegetarian meal was prepared and tables were set out to serve to the Tang monk. He and his disciples had a leisurely dinner and then rested.

*   *   *

From *Chapter 54*

Dharma-nature, going west, reaches the Women Nation;
Mind Monkey devises a plan to flee the fair sex.

We tell you now about Tripitaka and his disciples, who left the household at the village and followed the road westward. In less than forty miles, they came upon the boundary of Western Liang. Pointing ahead as he rode along, the Tang monk said, "Wukong, we are approaching a city, and from the noise and hubbub coming from the markets, I suppose it must be the Nation of Women. All of you must take care to behave properly. Keep your desires under control and don't let them violate the teachings of our gate of Law." When the three disciples heard this, they obeyed the strict admonition. Soon they reached the head of the street that opened to the eastern gate. The people there, with long skirts and short blouses, powdered faces and oily heads, were all women regardless of whether they were young or old. Many of them were doing business on the streets, and when they saw the four of them walking by, they all clapped their hands in acclaim and laughed aloud, crying happily, "Human seeds are coming! Human seeds are coming!" Tripitaka was so startled that he reined in his horse; all at once the street was blocked, completely filled with women, and all you could hear were laughter and chatter. Bajie began to holler wildly: "I'm a pig for sale! I'm a pig for sale!" "Idiot," said Pilgrim, "stop this nonsense. Bring out your old features, that's all!" Indeed, Bajie shook his head a couple of times and stuck up his two rush-leaf fan ears; then he wriggled his lips like two hanging lotus roots and gave a yell, so frightening those women that they all fell and stumbled. We have a testimonial poem, and the poem says:

> The sage monk, seeking Buddha, reached Western Liang,
> A land full of females but without one male.
> Farmers, scholars, workers, and those in trade,
> The fishers and plowers were women all.
> Maidens lined the streets, crying "Human seeds!"
> Young girls filled the roads to greet the comely men.
> If Wuneng did not show his ugly face,
> The siege by the fair sex would be pain indeed.

In this way, the people became frightened and none dared go forward; everyone was rubbing her hands and squatting down. They shook their heads, bit their fingers, and crowded both sides of the street, trembling all over but still eager to stare at the Tang monk. The Great Sage Sun had to display his hideous face in order to open up the road, while Sha Monk, too, played monster to keep order. Leading the horse, Bajie stuck out his snout and waved his ears. As the whole entourage proceeded, the pilgrims discovered that the houses in the city were built in orderly rows while the shops had lavish displays. There were merchants selling rice and salt; there were wine and tea houses.

> There were bell and drum towers with goods piled high;
> Bannered pavilions with screens hung low.

As master and disciples followed the street through its several turns, they came upon a woman official standing in the street and crying, "Visitors from afar should not enter the city gate without permission. Please go to the post-house and enter your names on the register. Allow this humble official to announce you to the Throne. After your rescript is certified, you will be permitted to pass through." Hearing this, Tripitaka dismounted; then he saw a horizontal plaque hung over the gate of an official mansion nearby, and on the plaque were the three words, Male Reception Post-house. "Wukong," said the elder; "what that family in the village said is true. There is indeed a Male Reception Post-house." "Second Elder Brother," said Sha Monk, laughing, "go and show yourself at the Pregnancy Reflection Stream and see if there's a double reflection." Bajie replied, "Don't play with me! Since I drank that cup of water from the Abortion Stream, the pregnancy has been dissolved. Why should I show myself?" Turning around, Tripitaka said to him, "Wuneng, be careful with your words." He then went forward to greet the woman official, who led them inside the post-house.

* * *

They had hardly finished speaking when the two women officials arrived and bowed deeply to the elder, who returned their salutations one by one, saying, "This humble cleric is someone who has left the family. What virtue or talent do I have that I dare let you bow to me?" When the Grand Preceptor saw how impressive the elder looked, she was delighted and thought to herself: "Our nation is truly quite lucky! Such a man is most worthy to be the husband of our ruler." After the officials made their greetings, they stood on either side of the Tang monk and said, "Father royal brother, we wish you ten thousand happinesses!" "I'm someone who has left the family," replied Tripitaka. "Where do those happinesses come from?" Again bending low, the Grand Preceptor said, "This is the Nation of Women in the Western Liang, and since time immemorial, there is not a single male in our country. We are lucky at this time to have the arrival of father royal brother. Your subject, by the decree of my ruler, has come especially to offer a proposal of marriage." "My goodness! My goodness!" said Tripitaka. "This poor monk has arrived at your esteemed region all by himself, without the attendance of either son or daughter. I have with me only three mischievous disciples, and I wonder to which of us is offered this marriage proposal." The post-house clerk said, "Your lowly official just now went into court to present my report, and my ruler, in great delight, told us of an auspicious dream she had last night. She dreamed that

> Luminous hues grew from the screens of gold,
> Refulgent rays spread from the mirrors of jade.

When she learned that the royal brother is a man from the noble nation of China, she was willing to use the wealth of her entire nation to ask you to be her live-in husband. You would take the royal seat facing south to be called the man set apart from others,[1] and our ruler would be the queen. That was why she gave the decree for the Grand Preceptor to serve as the marriage go-between and this lowly official to officiate at the wedding. We came especially to offer you this proposal." When Tripitaka heard these words, he bowed his head and fell into complete silence. "When a man finds the time propitious," said the Grand Preceptor, "he should not pass up such an opportunity. Though there is, to be sure, such a thing in the world as asking a husband to live in the wife's family, the dowry of a nation's wealth is rare indeed. May we ask the royal brother to give his quick consent, so that we may report to our ruler." The elder, however, became more dumb and deaf than ever.

Sticking out his pestlelike snout, Bajie shouted, "Grand Preceptor, go back and tell your ruler that my master happens to be an arhat who has attained the Way after a long process of cultivation. He will never fall in love with the dowry of a nation's wealth, nor will he be enamored with even beauty that can topple an empire. You may as well certify the travel rescript quickly and send them off to the West. Let me stay here to be the live-in husband. How's that?" When the Grand Preceptor heard this, her heart quivered and her gall shook, unable to answer at all. The clerk of the post-house said, "Though you may be a male, your looks are hideous. Our ruler will not find you attractive." "You are much too inflexible," said Bajie, laughing. "As the proverb says,

> The thick willow's a basket, the thin, a barrel—
> Who in the world will take a man as an ugly fellow?"

---

1. The "man set apart from others" is an elevated expression for the emperor.

Pilgrim said, "Idiot, stop this foolish talk. Let Master make up his mind: if he wants to leave, let him leave, and if he wants to stay, let him stay. Let's not waste the time of the marriage go-between."

"Wukong," said Tripitaka, "What do you think I ought to do?" "In old Monkey's opinion," replied Pilgrim, "perhaps it's good that you stay here. As the ancients said, 'One thread can tie up a distant marriage.' Where will you ever find such a marvelous opportunity?" Tripitaka said, "Disciple, if we remain here to dote on riches and glory, who will go to acquire scriptures in the Western Heaven? Won't the waiting kill my emperor of the Great Tang?" The Grand Preceptor said, "In the presence of the royal brother, your humble official dares not hide the truth. The wish of our ruler is only to offer you the proposal of marriage. After your disciples have attended the wedding banquet, provisions will be given them and the travel rescript will be certified, so that they may proceed to the Western Heaven to acquire the scriptures." "What the Grand Preceptor said is most reasonable," said Pilgrim, "and we need not be difficult about this. We are willing to let our master remain here to become the husband of your mistress. Certify our rescript quickly and send us off to the West. When we have acquired the scriptures, we will return here to visit father and mother and ask for travel expenses so that we may go back to the Great Tang." Both the Grand Preceptor and the clerk of the post-house bowed to Pilgrim as they said, "We thank this teacher for his kind assistance in concluding this marriage." Bajie said, "Grand Preceptor, don't use only your mouth to set the table! Since we have given our consent, tell your mistress to prepare us a banquet first. Let us have an engagement drink. How about it?" "Of course! Of course!" said the Grand Preceptor. "We'll send you a feast at once." In great delight, the Grand Preceptor left with the clerk of the post-house.

We tell you now about our elder Tang, who caught hold of Pilgrim immediately and berated him, crying, "Monkey head! Your tricks are killing me! How could you say such things and ask me to get married here while you people go to the Western Heaven to see Buddha? Even if I were to die, I would not dare do this." "Relax, Master," said Pilgrim, "old Monkey's not ignorant of how you feel. But since we have reached this place and met this kind of people, we have no alternative but to meet plot with plot." "What do you mean by that?" asked Tripitaka.

Pilgrim said, "If you persist in refusing them, they will not certify our travel rescript nor will they permit us to pass through. If they grow vicious and order many people to cut you up and use your flesh to make those so-called fragrant bags, do you think that we will treat them with kindness? We will, of course, bring out our abilities which are meant to subdue demons and dispel fiends. Our hands and feet are quite heavy, you know, and our weapons ferocious. Once we lift our hands, the people of this entire nation will be wiped out. But you must think of this, however. Although they are now blocking our path, they are no fiendish creatures or monster-spirits; all of them in this country are humans. And you have always been a man committed to kindness and compassion, refusing to hurt even one sentient being on our way. If we slaughter all these common folk here, can you bear it? That would be true wickedness."

When Tripitaka heard this, he said, "Wukong, what you have just said is most virtuous. But I fear that if the queen asks me to enter the palace, she will want me to perform the conjugal rite with her. How could I consent to lose my original *yang* and destroy the virtue of Buddhism, to leak my true sperm and fall from the humanity of our faith?" "Once we have agreed to the marriage," said Pilgrim, "she will no doubt follow royal etiquette and send her carriage out of the capital to receive you. Don't refuse her. Take a ride in her phoenix carriage and dragon chariot to go up to the treasure hall, and then sit down on the throne facing south. Ask the queen to take out her imperial seal and summon us brothers to go into court. After you have stamped the seal on the rescript, tell the queen to sign the document also and give it back to us. Meanwhile, you can also tell them to prepare a huge banquet; call it a wedding feast as well as a farewell party for us. After the banquet, ask for the chariot once more on the excuse that you want to see us off outside the capital before you return to consummate the marriage with the queen. In this way, both ruler and subjects will be duped into false happiness; they will no longer try to block our way, nor will they have any cause to become vicious. Once we reach the outskirts of the capital, you will come down from the dragon chariot and Sha Monk will help you to mount the white horse immediately. Old Monkey will then use his magic of immobility to make all of them, ruler and subjects, unable to move. We can then follow the main road to the West. After one day and one night, I will recite a spell to recall the magic and release all of them, so that they can wake up and return to the city. For one thing, their lives will be preserved, and for another, your primal soul will not be hurt. This is a plot called Fleeing the Net by a False Marriage. Isn't it a doubly advantageous act?" When Tripitaka heard these words, he seemed as if he were snapping out of a stupor or waking up from a dream. So delighted was he that he forgot all his worries and thanked Pilgrim profusely, saying, "I'm deeply grateful for my worthy disciple's lofty intelligence." And so, the four of them were united in their decision, and we shall leave them for the moment.

* * *

After putting everything in order, Pilgrim, Bajie, and Sha Monk faced the imperial carriage and cried out in unison, "The queen need not go any further. We shall take our leave now." Descending slowly from the dragon chariot, the elder raised his hands toward the queen and said, "Please go back, Your Majesty, and let this poor monk go to acquire scriptures." When the queen heard this, she paled with fright and tugged at the Tang monk. "Royal brother darling," she cried, "I'm willing to use the wealth of my entire nation to ask you to be my husband. Tomorrow you shall ascend the tall treasure throne to call yourself king, and I am to be your queen. You have even eaten the wedding feast. Why are you changing your mind now?" When Bajie heard what she said, he became slightly mad. Pouting his snout and flapping his ears wildly, he charged up to the carriage, shouting, "How could we monks marry a powdered skeleton like you? Let my master go on his journey!" When the queen saw that hideous face and ugly behavior, she was scared out of her wits and fell back into the carriage. Sha Monk pulled Tripitaka out of the crowd and was just helping him to mount the horse when another girl dashed out from somewhere and shouted, "Royal brother Tang, where are you going? Let's you and I make some love!" "You stupid hussy!" cried Sha Monk and, whipping out his treasure staff, brought it down hard on the head of the girl. Suddenly calling up a cyclone, the girl carried away the Tang monk with a loud whoosh and both of them vanished without a trace. Alas! Thus it was that

> Having just left the fair sex net,
> Then the demon of love he met.

We do not know whether that girl is a human or a fiend, or whether the old master will die or live; let's listen to the explanation in the next chapter.

From *Chapter 55*

Deviant form makes lustful play for Tripitaka Tang;
Upright nature safeguards the uncorrupted self.

* * *

We now tell you about Sha Monk, who was grazing the horse before the mountain slope when he heard some hog-grunting. As he raised his head, he saw Bajie dashing back, lips pouted and grunting as he ran. "What in the world . . . ?" said Sha Monk, and our Idiot blurted out: "It's awful! It's awful! This pain! This pain!" Hardly had he finished speaking when Pilgrim also arrived. "Dear Idiot!" he chuckled. "Yesterday you said I had a brain tumor, but now you are suffering from the plague of the swollen lip!" "I can't bear it!" cried Bajie. "The pain's acute! It's terrible! It's terrible!"

The three of them were thus in sad straits when they saw an old woman approaching from the south on the mountain road, her left hand carrying a little bamboo basket with vegetables in it. "Big Brother," said Sha Monk, "look at that old lady approaching. Let me find out from her what sort of a monster-spirit this is and what kind of weapon she has that can inflict a wound like this." "You stay where you are," said Pilgrim, "and let old Monkey question her." When Pilgrim stared at the old woman carefully, he saw that there were auspicious clouds covering her head and fragrant mists encircling her body. Recognizing all at once who she was, Pilgrim shouted. "Brothers, kowtow quickly! The lady is Bodhisattva!" Ignoring his pain, Bajie hurriedly went to his knees while Sha Monk bent low, still holding the reins of the horse. The Great Sage Sun, too, pressed his palms together and knelt down, all crying. "We submit to the great and compassionate, the efficacious savior, Bodhisattva Guanshiyin."

When the Bodhisattva saw that they recognized her primal light, she at once trod on the auspicious clouds and rose to midair to reveal her true form, the one which carried the fish basket. Pilgrim rushed up there also to say to her, bowing. "Bodhisattva, pardon us for not receiving you properly. We were desperately trying to rescue our master and we had no idea that the Bodhisattva was descending to earth. Our present demonic ordeal is hard to overcome indeed, and we beg the Bodhisattva to help us." "This monster-spirit," said the Bodhisattva. "is most formidable. Those tridents of hers happen to be two front claws, and what gave you such a painful stab is actually a stinger on her tail. It's called the Horse-Felling Poison, for she herself is a scorpion spirit. Once upon a time she happened to be listening to a lecture in the Thunderclap Monastery. When Tathāgata[1] saw her, he wanted to push her away with his hand, but she turned around and gave the left thumb of the Buddha a stab. Even Tathāgata found the pain unbearable! When he ordered the arhats to seize her, she fled here. If you want to rescue the Tang monk, you must find a special friend of mine for even I cannot go near her." Bowing again, Pilgrim said, "I beg the Bodhisattva to reveal to whom it is that your disciple should go to ask for assistance." "Go to the East Heaven Gate," replied the Bodhisattva, "and ask for help from the Star Lord Orionis in the Luminescent Palace. He is the

---

1. Again, the Buddha.

one to subdue this monster-spirit." When she finished speaking, she changed into a beam of golden light to return to South Sea.

Dropping down from the clouds, the Great Sage Sun said to Bajie and Sha Monk, "Relax, Brothers, we've found someone to rescue Master." "From where?" asked Sha Monk, and Pilgrim replied, "Just now the Bodhisattva told me to seek the assistance of the Star Lord Orionis. Old Monkey will go immediately." With swollen lips, Bajie grunted: "Elder Brother, please ask the god for some medicine for the pain." "No need for medicine," said Pilgrim with a laugh. "After one night, the pain will go away like mine." "Stop talking," said Sha Monk. "Go quickly!"

Dear Pilgrim! Mounting his cloud-somersault, he arrived instantly at the East Heaven Gate, where he was met by the Devarāja Virūdhaka. "Great Sage," said the devarāja, bowing, "where are you going?" "On our way to acquire scriptures in the West," replied Pilgrim, "the Tang monk ran into another demonic obstacle. I must go to the Luminescent Palace to find the Star God of the Rising Sun." As he spoke, Tao, Zhang, Xin, and Deng, the four Grand Marshals, also approached him to ask where he was going. "I have to find the Star Lord Orionis," said Pilgrim, "and ask him to rescue my master from a monster-spirit." One of the grand marshals said, "By the decree of the Jade Emperor this morning, the god went to patrol the Star-Gazing Terrace." "Is that true?" asked Pilgrim. "All of us humble warriors," replied Grand Marshal Xin, "left the Dipper Palace with him at the same time. Would we dare speak falsehood?" "It has been a long time," said Grand Marshal Tao, "and he might be back already. The Great Sage should go to the Luminescent Palace first, and if he's not there, then you can go to the Star-Gazing Terrace."

Delighted, the Great Sage took leave of them and arrived at the gate of the Luminescent Palace. Indeed, there was no one in sight, and as he turned to leave, he saw a troop of soldiers approaching, followed by the god, who still had on his court regalia made of golden threads. Look at

> His cap of five folds ablaze with gold;
> His court tablet of most lustrous jade.
> A seven-star sword, cloud patterned, hung from his robe;
> An eight-treasure belt, lucent, wrapped around his waist.
> His pendant jangled as if striking a tune;
> It rang like a bell in a strong gust of wind.
> Kingfisher fans parted and Orionis came
> As celestial fragrance the courtyard filled.

Those soldiers walking in front saw Pilgrim standing outside the Luminescent Palace, and they turned quickly to report: "My lord, the Great Sage Sun is here." Stopping his cloud and straightening his court attire, the god ordered the soldiers to stand on both sides in two rows while he went forward to salute his visitor, saying, "Why has the Great Sage come here?"

"I have come here," replied Pilgrim, "especially to ask you to save my master from an ordeal." "Which ordeal," asked the god, "and where?" "In the Cave of the Lute at the Toxic Foe Mountain," Pilgrim answered "which is located in the State of Western Liang." "What sort of monster is there in the cave," asked the god again, "that has made it necessary for you to call on this humble deity?"

Pilgrim said, "Just now the Bodhisattva Guanyin, in her epiphany, revealed to us that it was a scorpion spirit. She told us further that only you, sir, could overcome it. That is why I have come to call on you." "I should first go back and report to the Jade Emperor," said the god, "but the Great Sage is already here, and you have, moreover, the Bodhisattva's recommendation. Since I don't want to cause you delay, I dare not ask you for tea. I shall go with you to subdue the monster-spirit first before I report to the Throne."

When the Great Sage heard this, he at once went out of the East Heaven Gate with the god and sped to the State of Western Liang. Seeing the mountain ahead, Pilgrim pointed at it and said, "This is it." The god lowered his cloud and walked with Pilgrim up to the stone screen beneath the mountain slope. When Sha Monk saw them, he said, "Second Elder Brother, please rise. Big Brother has brought back the star god." His lips still pouting, Idiot said, "Pardon! Pardon! I'm ill, and I cannot salute you." "You are a man who practices self-cultivation," said the star god. "What kind of sickness do you have?" "Earlier in the morning," replied Bajie, "we fought with the monster-spirit, who gave me a stab on my lip. It still hurts."

The star god said, "Come up here, and I'll cure it for you." Taking his hand away from his snout, Idiot said, "I beg you to cure it, and I'll thank you most heartily." The star god used his hand to give Bajie's lip a stroke before blowing a mouthful of breath on it. At once, the pain ceased. In great delight, our Idiot went to his knees, crying, "Marvelous! Marvelous!" "May I trouble the star god to touch the top of my head also?" said Pilgrim with a grin. "You weren't poisoned," said the star god. "Why should I touch you?" Pilgrim replied, "Yesterday, I was poisoned, but after one night the pain is gone. The spot, however, still feels somewhat numb and itchy, and I fear that it may act up when the weather changes. Please cure it for me." The star god indeed touched the top of his head and blew a mouthful of breath on it. The remaining poison was thus eliminated, and Pilgrim no longer felt the numbness or the itch. "Elder Brother," said Bajie, growing ferocious, "let's go and beat up that bitch!" "Exactly!" said the star god. "You provoke her to come out, the two of you, and I'll subdue her."

Leaping up the mountain slope, Pilgrim and Bajie again went behind the stone screen. With his mouth spewing abuses and his hands working like a pair of fuel-gatherer hooks, our Idiot used his rake to remove the rocks piled up in front of the cave in no time at all. He then dashed up to the second-level door, and one blow of his rake reduced it to powder. The little fiends inside were so terrified that they fled inside to report: "Madam, those two ugly men have destroyed even our second-level door!" The fiend was just about to untie the Tang monk so that he could be fed some tea and rice. When she heard that the door had been broken down, she jumped out of the flower arbor and stabbed Bajie with the trident. Bajie met her with the rake, while Pilgrim assisted him with his iron rod. Rushing at her opponents, the fiend wanted to use her poisonous trick again, but Pilgrim and Bajie perceived her intentions and retreated immediately.

The fiend chased them beyond the stone screen, and Pilgrim shouted: "Orionis, where are you?" Standing erect on the mountain slope, the star god revealed his true form. He was, you see, actually a huge, double-combed rooster, about seven feet tall when he held up his head. He faced the fiend and crowed once: immediately the fiend revealed her true form, which was that of a scorpion about the size of a lute. The star god crowed again, and the fiend, whose whole body became paralyzed, died before the slope. We have a testimonial poem for you, and the poem says:

> Like tasseled balls his embroidered neck and comb,
> With long, hard claws and angry, bulging eyes,
> He perfects the Five Virtues forcefully;
> His three crows are done heroically.
> No common, clucking fowl about the hut,
> He's Heaven's star showing his holy name.
> In vain the scorpion seeks the human ways;
> She now her true, original form displays.

Bajie went forward and placed one foot on the back of the creature, saying, "Cursed beast! You can't use your Horse-Felling Poison this time!" Unable to make even a twitch, the fiend was pounded into a paste by the rake of the Idiot. Gathering up again his golden beams, the star god mounted the clouds and left, while Pilgrim led Bajie and Sha Monk to bow to the sky, saying, "Sorry for all your inconvenience! In another day, we shall go to your palace to thank you in person."

* * *

From *Chapter 98*

> *Only when ape and horse are tamed will shells be cast;*
> *With merit and work perfected, they see the Real.*

We shall now tell you about the Tang monk and his three disciples, who set out on the main road.

In truth the land of Buddha in the West[1] was quite different from other regions. What they saw everywhere were gemlike flowers and jasperlike grasses, aged cypresses and hoary pines. In the regions they passed through, every family was devoted to good works, and every household would feed the monks.

> They met people in cultivation beneath the hills
> And saw travellers reciting sūtras in the woods.

Resting at night and journeying at dawn, master and disciples proceeded for some six or seven days when they suddenly caught sight of a row of tall buildings and noble lofts. Truly

> They soar skyward a hundred feet,
> Tall and towering in the air.
> You look down to see the setting sun
> And reach out to pluck the shooting stars.
> Spacious windows engulf the universe;
> Lofty pillars join with the cloudy screens.

---

1. The pilgrims have now reached India, the destination of their trip.

Yellow cranes bring letters[2] as autumn trees age;
Phoenix-sheets come with the cool evening breeze.
These are the treasure arches of a spirit palace,
The pearly courts and jeweled edifices,
The immortal hall where the Way is preached,
The cosmos where sūtras are taught.
The flowers bloom in the spring;
Pines grow green after the rain.
Purple agaric and divine fruits, fresh every year.
Phoenixes gambol, potent in every manner.

Lifting his whip to point ahead, Tripitaka said, "Wukong, what a lovely place!"

"Master," said Pilgrim, "you insisted on bowing down even in a specious region, before false images of Buddha. Today you have arrived at a true region with real images of Buddha, and you still haven't dismounted. What's your excuse?"

So taken aback was Tripitaka when he heard these words that he leaped down from the horse. Soon they arrived at the entrance to the buildings. A Daoist lad, standing before the gate, called out, "Are you the scripture seeker from the Land of the East?" Hurriedly tidying his clothes, the elder raised his head and looked at his interrogator.

He wore a robe of silk
And held a jade duster.
He wore a robe of silk
Often to feast at treasure lofts and jasper pools;
He held a jade yak's-tail
To wave and dust in the purple mansions.
From his arm hangs a sacred register,
And his feet are shod in sandals.
He floats—a true feathered-one;[3]
He's winsome—indeed uncanny!
Long life attained, he lives in this fine place;
Immortal, he can leave the world of dust.
The sage monk knows not our Mount Spirit guest:
The Immortal Golden Head of former years.

The Great Sage, however, recognized the person. "Master," he cried, "this is the Great Immortal of the Golden Head, who resides in the Yuzhen Daoist Temple at the foot of the Spirit Mountain."

Only then did Tripitaka realize the truth, and he walked forward to make his bow. With laughter, the great immortal said, "So the sage monk has finally arrived this year. I have been deceived by the Bodhisattva Guanyin. When she received the gold decree from Buddha over ten years ago to find a scripture seeker in the Land of the East, she told me that he would be here after two or three years. I waited year after year for you, but no news came at all. Hardly have I anticipated that I would meet you this year!"

2. Immortals are thought to send their communications through magic birds like yellow cranes and blue phoenixes.
3. Immortal or transcendent being.

Pressing his palms together, Tripitaka said, "I'm greatly indebted to the great immortal's kindness. Thank you! Thank you!" The four pilgrims, leading the horse and toting the luggage, all went inside the temple before each of them greeted the great immortal once more. Tea and a vegetarian meal were ordered. The immortal also asked the lads to heat some scented liquid for the sage monk to bathe, so that he could ascend the land of Buddha. Truly,

> It's good to bathe when merit and work are done,
> When nature's tamed and the natural state is won.
> All toils and labors are now at rest;
> Law and obedience have renewed their zest.
> At māra's end they reach indeed Buddha-land;
> Their woes dispelled, before Śramana[4] they stand.
> Unstained, they are washed of all filth and dust.
> To a diamond body[5] return they must.

After master and disciples had bathed, it became late and they rested in the Yuzhen Temple.

Next morning the Tang monk changed his clothing and put on his brocade cassock and his Vairocana hat. Holding the priestly staff, he ascended the main hall to take leave of the great immortal. "Yesterday you seemed rather dowdy," said the great immortal, chuckling, "but today everything is fresh and bright. As I look at you now, you are a true of son of Buddha!" After a bow, Tripitaka wanted to set out at once.

"Wait a moment," said the great immortal. "Allow me to escort you." "There's no need for that," said Pilgrim. "Old Monkey knows the way."

"What you know happens to be the way in the clouds," said the great immortal, "a means of travel to which the sage monk has not yet been elevated. You must still stick to the main road."

"What you say is quite right," replied Pilgrim. "Though old Monkey has been to this place several times, he has always come and gone on the clouds and he has never stepped on the ground. If we must stick to the main road, we must trouble you to escort us a distance. My master's most eager to bow to Buddha. Let's not dally." Smiling broadly, the great immortal held the Tang monk's hand

> To lead Candana up the gate of Law.

The way that they had to go, you see, did not lead back to the front gate. Instead, they had to go through the central hall of the temple to go out the rear door. Immediately behind the temple, in fact, was the Spirit Mountain, to which the great immortal pointed and said, "Sage Monk, look at the spot half-way up the sky, shrouded by auspicious luminosity of five colors and a thousand folds of hallowed mists. That's the tall Spirit Vulture Peak, the holy region of the Buddhist Patriarch."

The moment the Tang monk saw it, he began to bend low. With a chuckle, Pilgrim said, "Master, you haven't reached that place where you should bow down. As the proverb says, 'Even within sight of a mountain you can ride a

---

4. Wandering ascetic.   5. The incorruptible body of Buddhahood.

horse to death!' You are still quite far from that principality. Why do you want to bow down now? How many times does your head need to touch the ground if you kowtow all the way to the summit?"

"Sage Monk," said the great immortal, "you, along with the Great Sage, Heavenly Reeds, and Curtain-Raising, have arrived at the blessed land when you can see Mount Spirit. I'm going back." Thereupon Tripitaka bowed to take leave of him.

* * *

Highly pleased, the elder said, "Disciples, stop your frivolity! There's a boat coming." The three of them leaped up and stood still to stare at the boat. When it drew near, they found that it was a bottomless one. With his fiery eyes and diamond pupils, Pilgrim at once recognized that the ferryman was in fact the Conductor Buddha, also named the Light of Ratnadhvaja. Without revealing the Buddha's identity, however, Pilgrim simply said, "Over here! Punt it this way!"

Immediately the boatman punted it up to the shore. "Ahoy! Ahoy!" he cried. Terrified by what he saw, Tripitaka said, "How could this bottomless boat of yours carry anybody?" The Buddhist Patriarch said, "This boat of mine

Since creation's dawn has achieved great fame;
Punted by me, it has e'er been the same.
Upon the wind and wave it's still secure:
With no end or beginning its joy is sure.
It can return to One, completely clean,
Through ten thousand kalpas a sail serene.
Though bottomless boats may ne'er cross the sea,
This ferries all souls through eternity."

Pressing his palms together to thank him, the Great Sage Sun said, "I thank you for your great kindness in coming to receive and lead my master. Master, get on the boat. Though it is bottomless, it is safe. Even if there are wind and waves, it will not capsize."

The elder still hesistated, but Pilgrim took him by the shoulder and gave him a shove. With nothing to stand on, that master tumbled straight into the water, but the boatman swiftly pulled him out. As he stood on the side of the boat, the master kept shaking out his clothes and stamping his feet as he grumbled at Pilgrim. Pilgrim, however, helped Sha Monk and Bajie to lead the horse and tote the luggage into the boat. As they all stood on the gunwale, the Buddhist Patriarch gently punted the vessel away from shore. All at once they saw a corpse floating down the upstream, the sight of which filled the elder with terror.

"Don't be afraid, Master," said Pilgrim, laughing. "It's actually you!"

"It's you! It's you!" said Bajie also.

Clapping his hands, Sha Monk also said, "It's you! It's you!"

Adding his voice to the chorus, the boatman also said, "That's you! Congratulations! Congratulations!" Then the three disciples repeated this chanting in unison as the boat was punted across the water. In no time at all, they crossed the Divine Cloud-Transcending Stream all safe and sound. Only then did

Tripitaka turn and skip lightly onto the other shore. We have here a testimonial poem, which says:

> Delivered from their mortal flesh and bone,
> A primal spirit of mutual love has grown.
> Their work done, they become Buddhas this day,
> Free of their former six-six senses[6] sway.

Truly this is what is meant by the profound wisdom and the boundless dharma which enable a person to reach the other shore.

The moment the four pilgrims went ashore and turned around, the boatman and even the bottomless boat had disappeared. Only then did Pilgrim point out that it was the Conductor Buddha, and immediately Tripitaka awoke to the truth. Turning quickly, he thanked his three disciples instead.

* * *

Highly pleased, Holy Father Buddha at once asked the Eight Bodhisattvas, the Four Vajra Guardians, the Five Hundred Arhats, the Three Thousand Guardians, the Eleven Great Orbs, and the Eighteen Guardians of Monasteries to form two rows for the reception. Then he issued the golden decree to summon in the Tang monk. Again the word was passed from section to section, from gate to gate: "Let the sage monk enter." Meticulously observing the rules of ritual propriety, our Tang monk walked through the monastery gate with Wukong, Wuneng, and Wujing, still leading the horse and toting the luggage. Thus it was that

> Commissioned that year, a resolve he made
> To leave with rescript the royal steps of jade.
> The hills he'd climb to face the morning dew
> Or rest on a boulder when the twilight fades.
> He totes his faith to ford three thousand streams,
> His staff trailing o'er endless palisades.
> His every thought's on seeking the right fruit.
> Homage to Buddha will this day be paid.

The four pilgrims, on reaching the Great Hero Treasure Hall, prostrated themselves before Tathāgata. Thereafter, they bowed to all the attendants of Buddha on the left and right. This they repeated three times before kneeling again before the Buddhist Patriarch to present their traveling rescript to him. After reading it carefully, Tathāgata handed it back to Tripitaka, who touched his head to the ground once more to say, "By the decree of the Great Tang Emperor in the Land of the East, your disciple Xuanzang has come to this treasure monastery to beg you for the true scriptures for the redemption of the multitude. I implore the Buddhist Patriarch to vouchsafe his grace and grant me my wish, so that I may soon return to my country."

To express the compassion of his heart, Tathāgata opened his mouth of mercy and said to Tripitaka, "Your Land of the East belongs to the South

---

6. Intensive form of the six impure qualities engendered by the objects and organs of sense: sight, sound, smell, taste, touch, and idea.

Jambūdvīpa Continent. Because of your size and your fertile land, your prosperity and population, there is a great deal of greed and killing, lust and lying, oppression and deceit. People neither honor the teachings of Buddha nor cultivate virtuous karma; they neither revere the three lights nor respect the five grains. They are disloyal and unfilial, unrighteous and unkind, unscrupulous and self-deceiving. Through all manners of injustice and taking of lives, they have committed boundless transgressions. The fullness of their iniquities therefore has brought on them the ordeal of hell and sent them into eternal darkness and perdition to suffer the pains of pounding and grinding and of being transformed into beasts. Many of them will assume the forms of creatures with fur and horns; in this manner they will repay their debts by having their flesh made for food for mankind. These are the reasons for their eternal perdition in Avīci without deliverance.

"Though Confucius had promoted his teachings of benevolence, righteousness, ritual, and wisdom, and though a succession of kings and emperors had established such penalties as transportation, banishment, hanging, and beheading, these institutions had little effect on the foolish and the blind, the reckless and the antinomian.

"Now, I have here three baskets of scriptures which can deliver humanity from its afflictions and dispel its calamities. There is one basket of vinaya, which speak of Heaven; a basket of śāstras, which tell of the Earth; and a basket of sūtras, which redeem the damned. Altogether these three baskets of scriptures contain thirty-five titles written in fifteen thousand one hundred and forty-four scrolls. They are truly the pathway to the realization of immortality and the gate to ultimate virtue. Every concern of astronomy, geography, biography, flora and fauna, utensils, and human affairs within the Four Great Continents of this world is recorded therein. Since all of you have traveled such a great distance to come here, I would have liked to give the entire set to you. Unfortunately, the people of your region are both stupid and headstrong. Mocking the true words, they refuse to recognize the profound significance of our teachings of Śramaṇa."

Then Buddha turned to call out: "Ānanda[7] and Kāśyapa, take the four of them to the space beneath the precious tower. Give them a vegetarian meal first. After the maigre, open our treasure loft for them and select a few scrolls from each of the thirty-five divisions of our three canons, so that they may take them back to the Land of the East as a perpetual token of grace."

The two Honored Ones obeyed and took the four pilgrims to the space beneath the tower, where countless rare dainties and exotic treasures were laid out in a seemingly endless spread. Those deities in charge of offerings and sacrifices began to serve a magnificent feast of divine food, tea, and fruit—viands of a hundred flavors completely different from those of the mortal world. After master and disciples had bowed to give thanks to Buddha, they abandoned themselves to enjoyment. In truth

> Treasure flames, gold beams on their eyes have shined;
> Strange fragrance and feed even more refined.
> Boundlessly fair the tow'r of gold appears;

7. Devout disciple of the Buddha.

> *There's immortal music that clears the ears.*
> *Such divine fare and flower humans rarely see;*
> *Long life's attained through strange food and fragrant tea.*
> *Long have they endured a thousand forms of pain.*
> *This day in glory the Way they're glad to gain.*

This time it was Bajie who was in luck and Sha Monk who had the advantage, for what the Buddhist Patriarch had provided for their complete enjoyment was nothing less than such viands as could grant them longevity and health and enable them to transform their mortal substance into immortal flesh and bones.

When the four pilgrims had finished their meal, the two Honored Ones who had kept them company led them up to the treasure loft. The moment the door was opened, they found the room enveloped in a thousand layers of auspicious air and magic beams, in ten thousand folds of colored fog and hallowed clouds. On the sūtra cases and jeweled chests red labels were attached, on which the titles of the books were written in clerkly script. After Ānanda and Kāśyapa had shown all the titles to the Tang monk, they said to him, "Sage Monk, having come all this distance from the Land of the East, what sort of small gifts have you brought for us? Take them out quickly! We'll be pleased to hand over the scriptures to you."

On hearing this, Tripitaka said, "Because of the great distance, your disciple, Xuanzang, has not been able to make such preparation."

"How nice! How nice!" said the two Honored Ones, snickering. "If we imparted the scriptures to you gratis, our posterity would starve to death!"

When Pilgrim saw them fidgeting and fussing, refusing to hand over the scriptures, he could not refrain from yelling, "Master, let's go tell Tathāgata about this! Let's make him come himself and hand over the scriptures to old Monkey!"

"Stop shouting!" said Ānanda. "Where do you think you are that you dare indulge in such mischief and waggery? Get over here and receive the scriptures!" Controlling their annoyance, Bajie and Sha Monk managed to restrain Pilgrim before they turned to receive the books. Scroll after scroll were wrapped and laid on the horse. Four additional luggage wraps were bundled up for Bajie and Sha Monk to tote, after which the pilgrims went before the jeweled throne again to kowtow and thank Tathāgata. As they walked out the gates of the monastery, they bowed twice whenever they came upon a Buddhist Patriarch or a Bodhisattva. When they reached the main gate, they also bowed to take leave of the priests and nuns, the upāsakas and upāsikās, before descending the mountain. We shall now leave them for the moment.

We tell you now that there was up in the treasure loft the aged Dīpamkara, also named the Buddha of the Past, who overheard everything and understood immediately that Ānanda and Kāśyapa had handed over to the pilgrims scrolls of scriptures that were actually wordless. Chuckling to himself, he said, "Most of the priests in the Land of the East are so stupid and blind that they will not recognize the value of these wordless scriptures. When that happens, won't it have made this long trek of our sage monk completely worthless?"

* * *

In a little while they reached the temple gates, where they were met by the multitude with hands folded in their sleeves. "Has the sage monk returned to ask for an exchange of scriptures?" they asked, laughing. Tripitaka nodded his affirmation, and the Vajra Guardians permitted them to go straight inside. When they arrived before the Great Hero Hall, Pilgrim shouted, "Tathāgata, we master and disciples had to experience ten thousand stings and a thousand demons in order to come bowing from the Land of the East. After you had specifically ordered the scriptures to be given to us, Ānanda and Kāśyapa sought a bribe from us; when they didn't succeed, they conspired in fraud and deliberately handed over wordless texts to us. Even if we took them, what good would they do? Pardon me, Tathāgata, but you must deal with this matter!"

"Stop shouting!" said the Buddhist Patriarch with a chuckle. "I knew already that the two of them would ask you for a little present. After all, the holy scriptures are not to be given lightly, nor are they to be received gratis. Some time ago, in fact, a few of our sage priests went down the mountain and recited these scriptures in the house of one Elder Zhao in the Kingdom of Śrāvastī, so that the living in his family would all be protected from harm and the deceased redeemed from perdition. For all that service they managed to charge him only three pecks and three pints of rice. I told them that they had made far too cheap a sale and that their posterity would have no money to spend. Since you people came with empty hands to acquire scriptures, blank texts were handed over to you. But these blank texts are actually true, wordless scriptures, and they are just as good as those with words. However, those creatures in your Land of the East are so foolish and unenlightened that I have no choice but to impart to you now the texts with words."

"Ānanda and Kāśyapa," he then called out, "quickly select for them a few scrolls from each of the titles of true scriptures with words, and then come back to me to report the total number."

The two Honored Ones again led the four pilgrims to the treasure loft, where they once more demanded a gift from the Tang monk. Since he had virtually nothing to offer, Tripitaka told Sha Monk to take out the alms bowl of purple gold. With both hands he presented it to the Honored Ones, saying, "Your disciple in truth has not brought with him any gift, owing to the great distance and my own poverty. This alms bowl, however, was bestowed by the Tang emperor in person, in order that I could use it to beg for my maigre, throughout the journey. As the humblest token of my gratitude, I am presenting it to you now, and I beg the Honored Ones to accept it. When I return to the court and make my report to the Tang emperor, a generous reward will certainly be forthcoming. Only grant us the true scriptures with words, so that His Majesty's goodwill will not be thwarted nor the labor of this lengthy journey be wasted." With a gentle smile, Ānanda took the alms bowl. All those vīra who guarded the precious towers, the kitchen helpers in charge of sacrifices and incense, and the Honored Ones who worked in the treasure loft began to clap one another on the back and tickle one another on the face. Snapping their fingers and curling their lips, every one of them said, "How shameless! How shameless! Asking the scripture seeker for a present!"

After a while, the two Honored Ones became rather embarrassed, though Ānanda continued to clutch firmly at the alms bowl. Kāśyapa, however, went into the loft to select the scrolls and handed them item by item to Tripitaka. "Disciples," said Tripitaka, "take a good look at these, and make sure that they are not like the earlier ones."

The three disciples examined each scroll as they received it, and this time all the scrolls had words written on them. Altogether they were given five thousand and forty-eight scrolls, making up the number of a single canon. After being properly packed, the scriptures were loaded onto the horse. An additional load was made for Bajie to tote, while their own luggage was toted by Sha Monk. As Pilgrim led the horse, the Tang monk took up his priestly staff and gave his Vairocana hat a press and his brocade cassock a shake.

* * *

From Chapter 99

Nine times nine ends the count and Māra's all destroyed;
The work of three times three[1] done, the Dao reverts to its root.

We shall not speak of the Eight Vajra Guardians escorting the Tang monk back to his nation. We turn instead to those Guardians of the Five Quarters, the Four Sentinels, the Six Gods of Darkness and the Six Gods of Light, and the Guardians of Monasteries, who appeared before the triple gates and said to the Bodhisattva Guanyin, "Your disciples had received the Bodhisattva's dharma decree to give secret protection to the sage monk. Now that the work of the sage monk is completed, and the Bodhisattva has returned the Buddhist Patriarch's golden decree to him, we too request permission from the Bodhisattva to return your dharma decree to you."

Highly pleased also, the Bodhisattva said, "Yes, yes! You have my permission." Then she asked, "What was the disposition of the four pilgrims during their journey?"

"They showed genuine devotion and determination," replied the various deities, "which could hardly have escaped the penetrating observation of the Bodhisattva. The Tang monk, after all, had endured unspeakable sufferings. Indeed, all the ordeals which he had to undergo throughout his journey have been recorded by your disciples. Here is the complete account." The Bodhisattva started to read the registry from its beginning, and this was the content:

> *The Guardians in obedience to your decree*
> *Record with care the Tang monk's calamities.*
> *Gold Cicada banished is the first ordeal;*
> *Being almost killed after birth is the second ordeal;*
> *Delivered of mortal stock at Cloud-Transcending Stream*
>   *is the eightieth ordeal;*
> *The journey: one hundred and eight thousand miles.*
> *The sage monk's ordeals are clearly on file.*

After the Bodhisattva had read through the entire registry of ordeals, she said hurriedly, "Within our order of Buddhism, nine times nine is the crucial means by which one returns to immortality. The sage monk has undergone eighty ordeals. Because one ordeal, therefore, is still lacking, the sacred number is not yet complete."

1. Work of advanced meditation. Double three, equaling nine, is an auspicious number. "*Māra's*": of the evil demon who tried to tempt the Buddha.

At once she gave this order to one of the Guardians: "Catch the Vajra Guardians and create one more ordeal." Having received this command, the Guardian soared toward the east astride the clouds. After a night and a day he caught the Vajra Guardians and whispered in their ears, "Do this and this . . . ! Don't fail to obey the dharma decree of the Bodhisattva." On hearing these words, the Eight Vajra Guardians immediately retrieved the wind that had borne aloft the four pilgrims, dropping them and the horse bearing the scriptures to the ground. Alas! Truly such is

> Nine times nine, hard task of immortality!
> Firmness of will yields the mysterious key.
> By bitter toil you must the demons spurn;
> Cultivation will the proper way return.
> Regard not the scriptures as easy things.
> So many are the sage monk's sufferings!
> Learn of the old, wondrous Kinship of the Three:[2]
> Elixir won't gel if there's slight errancy.

When his feet touched profane ground, Tripitaka became terribly frightened. Bajie, however, roared with laughter, saying, "Good! Good! Good! This is exactly a case of 'More haste, less speed'!"

"Good! Good! Good!" said Sha Monk. "Because we've speeded up too much, they want us to take a little rest here." "Have no worry," said the Great Sage. "As the proverb says,

> For ten days you sit on the shore;
> In one day you may pass nine beaches."

"Stop matching your wits, you three!" said Tripitaka. "Let's see if we can tell where we are." Looking all around, Sha Monk said, "I know the place! I know the place! Master, listen to the sound of water!"

Pilgrim said, "The sound of water, I suppose, reminds you of your ancestral home." "Which is the Flowing-Sand River," said Bajie. "No! No!" said Sha Monk. "This happens to be the Heaven-Reaching River." Tripitaka said, "O Disciples! Take a careful look and see which side of the river we're on."

Vaulting into the air, Pilgrim shielded his eyes with his hand and took a careful survey of the place before dropping down once more. "Master," he said, "this is the west bank of the Heaven-Reaching River."

"Now I remember," said Tripitaka. "There was a Chen Village on the east bank. When we arrived here that year, you rescued their son and daughter. In their gratitude to us, they wanted to make a boat to take us across. Eventually we were fortunate enough to get across on the back of a white turtle. I recall, too, that there was no human habitation whatever on the west bank. What shall we do this time?"

"I thought that only profane people would practice this sort of fraud," said Bajie. "Now I know that even the Vajra Guardians before the face of Buddha can practice fraud! Buddha commanded them to take us back east. How could they just abandon us in mid-journey? Now we're in quite a bind! How are we

---

2. Reputedly the earliest book on alchemy; from the 2nd century C.E.

going to get across?" "Stop grumbling, Second Elder Brother!" said Sha Monk. "Our master has already attained the Way, for he had already been delivered from his mortal frame previously at the Cloud-Transcending Stream. This time he can't possibly sink in water. Let's all of us exercise our magic of Displacement and take Master across."

"You can't take him over! You can't take him over!" said Pilgrim, chuckling to himself. Now, why did he say that? If he were willing to exercise his magic powers and reveal the mystery of flight, master and disciples could cross even a thousand rivers. He knew, however, that the Tang monk had not yet perfected the sacred number of nine times nine. That one remaining ordeal made it necessary for them to be detained at the spot.

As master and disciples conversed and walked slowly up to the edge of the water, they suddenly heard someone calling, "Tang Sage Monk! Tang Sage Monk! Come this way! Come this way!" Startled, the four of them looked all around but could not see any sign of a human being or a boat. Then they caught sight of a huge, white, scabby-headed turtle at the shoreline. "Old Master," he cried with outstretched neck, "I have waited for you for so many years! Have you returned only at this time?"

"Old Turtle," replied Pilgrim, smiling, "we troubled you in a year past, and today we meet again." Tripitaka, Bajie, and Sha Monk could not have been more pleased. "If indeed you want to serve us," said Pilgrim, "come up on the shore." The turtle crawled up the bank. Pilgrim told his companions to guide the horse onto the turtle's back. As before, Bajie squatted at the rear of the horse, while the Tang monk and Sha Monk took up positions to the left and to the right of the horse. With one foot on the turtle's head and another on his neck, Pilgrim said, "Old Turtle, go steadily."

His four legs outstretched, the old turtle moved through the water as if he were on dry level ground, carrying all five of them—master, disciples, and the horse—straight toward the eastern shore. Thus it is that

> In Advaya's[3] gate the dharma profound
> Reveals Heav'n and Earth and demons confounds.
> The original visage now they see;
> Causes find perfection in one body.
> Freely they move when Triyāna's won,
> And when the elixir's nine turns are done.
> The luggage and the staff there's no need to tote,
> Glad to return on old turtle afloat.

Carrying the pilgrims on his back, the old turtle trod on the waves and proceeded for more than half a day. Late in the afternoon they were near the eastern shore when he suddenly asked this question: "Old Master, in that year when I took you across, I begged you to question Tathāgata, once you got to see him, when I would find my sought-after refuge and how much longer would I live. Did you do that?"

Now, that elder, since his arrival at the Western Heaven, had been preoccupied with bathing in the Yuzhen Temple, being renewed at Cloud-Transcending

---

3. Gateway to Buddha-nature.

Stream, and bowing to the various sage monks, Bodhisattvas, and Buddhas. When he walked up the Spirit Mountain, he fixed his thought on the worship of Buddha and on the acquisition of scriptures, completely banishing from his mind all other concerns. He did not, of course, ask about the allotted age of the old turtle. Not daring to lie, however, he fell silent and did not answer the question for a long time. Perceiving that Tripitaka had not asked the Buddha for him, the old turtle shook his body once and dove with a splash into the depths. The four pilgrims, the horse, and the scriptures all fell into the water as well. Ah! It was fortunate that the Tang monk had cast off his mortal frame and attained the Way. If he were like the person he had been before, he would have sunk straight to the bottom. The white horse, moreover, was originally a dragon, while Bajie and Sha Monk both were quite at home in the water. Smiling broadly, Pilgrim made a great display of his magic powers by hauling the Tang monk right out of the water and onto the eastern shore. But the scriptures, the clothing, and the saddle were completely soaked.

* * *

From *Chapter 100*

They return to the Land of the East;
The five sages attain immortality.

* * *

We tell you now instead about the Eight Vajra Guardians, who employed the second gust of fragrant wind to carry the four pilgrims back to the Land of the East. In less than a day, the capital, Chang'an, gradually came into view. That Emperor Taizong, you see, had escorted the Tang monk out of the city three days before the full moon in the ninth month of the thirteenth year of the Zhenguan reign period. By the sixteenth year, he had already asked the Bureau of Labor to erect a Scripture-Watch Tower outside the Western-Peace Pass to receive the holy books. Each year Taizong would go personally to that place for a visit. It so happened that he had gone again to the tower that day when he caught sight of a skyful of auspicious mists drifting near from the West, and he noticed at the same time strong gusts of fragrant wind.

Halting in midair, the Vajra Guardians cried, "Sage Monk, this is the city Chang'an. It's not convenient for us to go down there, for the people of this region are quite intelligent, and our true identity may become known to them. Even the Great Sage Sun and his two companions needn't go; you yourself can go, hand over the scriptures, and return at once. We'll wait for you in the air so that we may all go back to report to Buddha."

"What the Honored Ones say may be most appropriate," said the Great Sage, "but how could my master tote all those scriptures? How could he lead the horse at the same time? We will have to escort him down there. May we trouble you to wait a while in the air? We dare not tarry."

"When the Bodhisattva Guanyin spoke to Tathāgata the other day," said the Vajra Guardians, "she assured him that the whole trip should take only eight days, so that the canonical number would be fulfilled. It's already more than four days now. We fear that Bajie might become so enamored of the riches down below that we will not be able to meet our appointed schedule."

"When Master attains Buddhahood," said Bajie, chuckling, "I, too, will attain Buddhahood. How could I become enamored of riches down below? Stupid old ruffians! Wait for me here, all of you! As soon as we have handed over the scriptures, I'll return with you and be canonized." Idiot took up the pole, Sha Monk led the horse, and Pilgrim supported the sage monk. Lowering their cloud, they dropped down beside the Scripture-Watch Tower.

When Taizong and his officials saw them, they all descended the tower to receive them. "Has the royal brother returned?" said the emperor. The Tang monk immediately prostrated himself, but he was raised by the emperor's own hands. "Who are these three persons?" asked the emperor once more.

"They are my disciples made during our journey," replied the Tang monk. Highly pleased, Taizong at once ordered his attendants, "Saddle one of our chariot horses for our royal brother to ride. We'll go back to the court together." The Tang monk thanked him and mounted the horse, closely followed by the Great Sage wielding his golden-hooped rod and by Bajie and Sha Monk toting the luggage and supporting the other horse. The entire entourage thus entered together the city of Chang'an. Truly

> A banquet of peace was held years ago.
> When lords, civil and martial, made a grand show.
> A priest preached the law in a great event;
> From Golden Chimes the king his subject sent.
> Tripitaka was given a royal rescript,
> For Five Phases matched the cause of holy script.
> Through bitter smelting all demons were purged.
> Merit done, they now on the court converged.

The Tang monk and his three disciples followed the Throne into the court, and soon there was not a single person in the city of Chang'an who had not learned of the scripture seekers' return.

We tell you now about those priests, young and old, of the Temple of Great Blessing, which was also the old residence of the Tang monk in Chang'an. That day they suddenly discovered that the branches of a few pine trees within the temple gate were pointing eastward. Astonished, they cried, "Strange! Strange! There was no strong wind to speak of last night. Why are all the tops of these trees twisted in this manner?"

One of the former disciples of Tripitaka said, "Quickly, let's get our proper clerical garb. The old master who went away to acquire scriptures must have returned."

"How do you know that?" asked the other priests.

"At the time of his departure," the old disciple said, "he made the remark that he might be away for two or three years, or for six or seven years. Whenever we noticed that these pine-tree tops were pointing to the east, it would mean that he has returned. Since my master spoke the holy words of a true Buddha, I know that the truth has been confirmed this day."

They put on their clothing hurriedly and left; by the time they reached the street to the west, people were already saying that the scripture seeker had just arrived and been received into the city by His Majesty. When they heard the news, the various monks dashed forward and ran right into the imperial chariot.

Not daring to approach the emperor, they followed the entourage instead to the gate of the court. The Tang monk dismounted and entered the court with the emperor. The dragon horse, the scripture packs, Pilgrim, Bajie, and Sha Monk were all placed beneath the steps of jade, while Taizong commanded the royal brother to ascend the hall and take a seat.

After thanking the emperor and taking his seat, the Tang monk asked that the scripture scrolls be brought up. Pilgrim and his companions handed them over to the imperial attendants, who presented them in turn to the emperor for inspection. "How many scrolls of scriptures are there," asked Taizong, "and how did you acquire them?"

"When your subject arrived at the Spirit Mountain and bowed to the Buddhist Patriarch," replied Tripitaka, "he was kind enough to ask Ānanda and Kāśyapa, the two Honored Ones, to lead us to the precious tower first for a meal. Then we were brought to the treasure loft, where the scriptures were bestowed on us. Those Honored Ones asked for a gift, but we were not prepared and did not give them any. They gave us some scriptures anyway, and after thanking the Buddhist Patriarch, we headed east, but a monstrous wind snatched away the scriptures. My humble disciple fortunately had a little magic power; he gave chase at once, and the scriptures were thrown and scattered all over. When we unrolled the scrolls, we saw that they were all wordless, blank texts. Your subjects in great fear went again to bow and plead before Buddha. The Buddhist Patriarch said, 'When these scriptures were created, some Bhikṣu sage monks left the monastery and recited some scrolls for one Elder Zhao in the Śrāvastī Kingdom. As a result, the living members of that family were granted safety and protection, while the deceased attained redemption. For such great service they only managed to ask the elder for three pecks and three pints of rice and a little gold. I told them that it was too cheap a sale, and that their descendants would have no money to spend.' Since we learned that even the Buddhist Patriarch anticipated that the two Honored Ones would demand a gift, we had little choice but to offer them that alms bowl of purple gold which Your Majesty had bestowed on me. Only then did they willingly turn over the true scriptures with writing to us. There are thirty-five titles of these scriptures, and several scrolls were selected from each title. Altogether, there are now five thousand and forty-eight scrolls, the number of which makes up one canonical sum."

More delighted than ever, Taizong gave this command: "Let the Court of Imperial Entertainments prepare a banquet in the East Hall so that we may thank our royal brother." Then he happened to notice Tripitaka's three disciples standing beneath the steps, all with extraordinary looks, and he therefore asked, "Are your noble disciples foreigners?"

Prostrating himself, the elder said, "My eldest disciple has the surname of Sun, and his religious name is Wukong. Your subject also addresses him as Pilgrim Sun. He comes from the Water Curtain Cave of the Flower-Fruit Mountain, located in the Aolai Country in the East Pūrvavideha Continent. Because he caused great disturbance in the Celestial Palace, he was imprisoned in a stone box by the Buddhist Patriarch and pressed beneath the Mountain of Two Frontiers in the region of the Western barbarians. Thanks to the admonitions of the Bodhisattva Guanyin, he was converted to Buddhism and became my disciple when I freed him. Throughout my journey I relied heavily on his protection.

"My second disciple has the surname of Zhu, and his religious name is Wu-neng. Your subject also addresses him as Zhu Bajie. He comes from the Cloudy Paths Cave of Fuling Mountain. He was playing the fiend at the Old Gao Village of Tibet when the admonitions of the Bodhisattva and the power of the Pilgrim caused him to become my disciple. He made his merit on our journey by toting the luggage and helping us to ford the waters.

"My third disciple has the surname of Sha, and his religious name is Wujing. Your subject also addresses him as Sha Monk. Originally he was a fiend at the Flowing-Sand River. Again the admonitions of the Bodhisattva persuaded him to take the vows of Buddhism. By the way, the horse is not the one my Lord bestowed on me."

Taizong said, "The color and the coat seem all the same. Why isn't it the same horse?"

"When your subject reached the Eagle Grief Stream in the Serpent Coil Mountain and tried to cross it," replied Tripitaka, "the original horse was devoured by this horse. Pilgrim managed to learn from the Bodhisattva that this horse was originally the prince of the Dragon King of the Western Ocean. Convicted of a crime, he would have been executed had it not been for the intervention of the Bodhisattva, who ordered him to be the steed of your subject. It was then that he changed into a horse with exactly the same coat as that of my original mount. I am greatly indebted to him for taking me over mountains and summits and through the most treacherous passages. Whether it be carrying me on my way there or bearing the scriptures upon our return, we are much beholden to his strength."

On hearing these words, Taizong complimented him profusely before asking again, "This long trek to the Western Region, exactly how far is it?"

Tripitaka said, "I recall that the Bodhisattva told us that the distance was a hundred and eight thousand miles. I did not make a careful record on the way. All I know is that we have experienced fourteen seasons of heat and cold. We encountered mountains and ridges daily; the forests we came upon were not small, and the waters we met were wide and swift. We also went through many kingdoms, whose rulers had affixed their seals and signatures on our document." Then he called out: "Disciples, bring up the travel rescript and present it to our Lord."

It was handed over immediately. Taizong took a look and realized that the document had been issued on the third day before the full moon, in the ninth month of the thirteenth year during the Zhenguan reign period. Smiling, Taizong said, "We have caused you the trouble of taking a long journey. This is now the twenty-seventh year of the Zhenguan period!" The travel rescript bore the seals of the Precious Image Kingdom, the Black Rooster Kingdom, the Cart Slow Kingdom, the Kingdom of Women in Western Liang, the Sacrifice Kingdom, the Scarlet-Purple Kingdom, the Bhikṣu Kingdom, the Dharma-Destroying Kingdom. There were also the seals of the Phoenix-Immortal Prefecture, the Jade-Flower County, and the Gold-Level Prefecture. After reading through the document, Taizong put it away.

Soon the officer in attendance to the Throne arrived to invite them to the banquet. As the emperor took the hand of Tripitaka and walked down the steps of the hall, he asked once more, "Are your noble disciples familiar with the etiquette of the court?"

"My humble disciples," replied Tripitaka, "all began their careers as monsters deep in the wilds or a mountain village, and they have never been instructed in the etiquette of China's sage court. I beg my Lord to pardon them."

Smiling, Taizong said, "We won't blame them! We won't blame them! Let's all go to the feast set up in the East Hall." Tripitaka thanked him once more before calling for his three disciples to join them. Upon their arrival at the hall, they saw that the opulence of the great nation of China was indeed different from all ordinary kingdoms. You see

> The doorway o'erhung with brocade,
> The floor adorned with red carpets,
> The whirls of exotic incense,
> And fresh victuals most rare.
> The amber cups
> And crystal goblets
> Are gold-trimmed and jade-set;
> The gold platters
> And white-jade bowls
> Are patterned and silver-rimmed.
> The tubers thoroughly cooked,
> The taros sugar-coated;
> Sweet, lovely button mushrooms,
> Unusual, pure seaweeds.
> Bamboo shoots, ginger-spiced, are served a few times;
> Malva leafs, honey-drenched, are mixed several ways.
> Wheat-glutens fried with xiangchun leaves:[1]
> Wood-ears cooked with bean-curd skins.
> Rock ferns and fairy plants;
> Fern flour and dried wei-leaves.
> Radishes cooked with Sichuan peppercorns;
> Melon strands stirred with mustard powder.
> These few vegetarian dishes are so-so,
> But the many rare fruits quite steal the show!
> Walnuts and persimmons,
> Lung-ans and lychees.
> The chestnuts of Yizhou and Shandong's dates;
> The South's ginko fruits and hare-head pears.
> Pine-seeds, lotus-seeds, and giant grapes;
> Fei-nuts, melon seeds, and water chestnuts.
> "Chinese olives"and wild apples;
> Crabapples and Pyrus-pears;
> Tender stalks and young lotus roots;
> Crisp plums and "Chinese strawberries."
> Not one species is missing;
> Not one kind is wanting.
> There are, moreover, the steamed mille-feuilles, honeyed pastries, and
>   fine viands;
> And there are also the lovely wines, fragrant teas, and strange dainties.

1. From a fragrant, slightly spicy plant.

> An endless spread of a hundred flavors, true noble fare.
> Western barbarians with great China can never compare!

Master and three disciples were grouped together with the officials, both civil and military, on both sides of the emperor Taizong, who took the seat in the middle. The dancing and the music proceeded in an orderly and solemn manner, and in this way they enjoyed themselves thoroughly for one whole day. Truly

> The royal banquet rivals the sage kings':
> True scriptures acquired excess blessings bring.
> Forever these will prosper and remain
> As Buddha's light shines on the king's domain.

When it became late, the officials thanked the emperor; while Taizong withdrew into his palace, the various officials returned to their residences. The Tang monk and his disciples, however, went to the Temple of Great Blessing, where they were met by the resident priests kowtowing. As they entered the temple gate, the priests said, "Master, the top of these trees were all suddenly pointing eastward this morning. We remembered your words and hurried out to the city to meet you. Indeed, you did arrive!" The elder could not have been more pleased as they were ushered into the abbot's quarters. By then, Bajie was not clamoring at all for food or tea, nor did he indulge in any mischief. Both Pilgrim and Sha Monk behaved most properly, for they had become naturally quiet and reserved since the Dao in them had come to fruition. They rested that night.

Taizong held court next morning and said to the officials, "We did not sleep the whole night when we reflected on how great and profound has been the merit of our brother, such that no compensation is quite adequate. We finally composed in our head several homely sentences as a mere token of our gratitude, but they have not yet been written down." Calling for one of the secretaries from the Central Drafting Office, he said, "Come, let us recite our composition for you, and you take it down sentence by sentence." The composition was as follows:

> We have heard how the Two Primary Forces[2] which manifest themselves in Heaven and Earth in the production of life are represented by images, whereas the invisible powers of the four seasons bring about transformation of things through the hidden action of heat and cold. By scanning Heaven and Earth, even the most ignorant may perceive their rudimentary laws. Even the thorough understanding of yin and yang, however, has seldom enabled the worthy and wise to comprehend fully their ultimate principle. It is easy to recognize that Heaven and Earth do contain yin and yang because there are images. It is difficult to comprehend fully how yin and yang pervade Heaven and Earth because the forces themselves are invisible. That images may manifest the minute is a fact that does not perplex even the foolish, whereas forms hidden in what is invisible are what confuse even the learned.
>
> How much more difficult it is, therefore, to understand the way of Buddhism, which exalts the void, uses the dark, and exploits the silent in order to succor the myriad grades of living things and exercise control over the entire world. Its spiritual

---

2. Probably forces of darkness and light, of yin and yang.

authority is the highest, and its divine potency has no equal. Its magnitude impregnates the entire cosmos; there is no space so tiny that it does not permeate it. Birthless and deathless, it does not age after a thousand kalpas; half-hidden and half-manifest, it brings a hundred blessings even now. A wondrous way most mysterious, those who follow it cannot know its limit. A law flowing silent and deep, those who draw on it cannot fathom its source. How, therefore, could those benighted ordinary mortals not be perplexed if they tried to plumb its depths?

Now, this great Religion arose in the Land of the West. It soared to the court of the Han period in the form of a radiant dream,[3] which flowed with its mercy to enlighten the Eastern territory. In antiquity, during the time when form and abstraction were clearly distinguished, the words of the Buddha, even before spreading, had already established their goodly influence. In a generation when he was both frequently active in and withdrawn from the world, the people beheld his virtue and honored it. But when he returned to Nirvāṇa and generations passed by, the golden images concealed his true form and did not reflect the light of the universe. The beautiful paintings, though unfolding lovely portraits, vainly held up the figure of thirty-two marks.[4] Nonetheless his subtle doctrines spread far and wide to save men and beasts from the three unhappy paths, and his traditions were widely proclaimed to lead all creatures through the ten stages toward Buddhahood. Moreover, the Buddha made scriptures, which could be divided into the Great and the Small Vehicles. He also possessed the Law, which could be transmitted either in the correct or in the deviant method.

Our priest Xuanzang, a Master of the Law, is a leader within the Gate of Law. Devoted and intelligent as a youth, he realized at an early age the merit of the three forms of immateriality. When grown he comprehended the principles of the spiritual, including first the practice of the four forms of patience.[5] Neither the pine in the wind nor the moon mirrored in water can compare with his purity and radiance. Even the dew of Heaven and luminous gems cannot surpass the clarity and refinement of his person. His intelligence encompassed even those elements which seemingly had no relations, and his spirit could perceive that which had yet to take visible forms. Having transcended the lure of the six senses, he was such an outstanding figure that in all the past he had no rival. He concentrated his mind on the internal verities, mourning all the time the mutilation of the correct doctrines. Worrying over the mysteries, he lamented that even the most profound treatises had errors.

He thought of revising the teachings and reviving certain arguments, so as to disseminate what he had received to a wider audience. He would, moreover, strike out the erroneous and preserve the true to enlighten the students. For this reason he longed for the Pure Land and a pilgrimage to the Western Territories. Risking dangers he set out on a long journey, with only his staff for his companion on this solitary expedition. Snow drifts in the morning would blanket his roadway; sand storms at dusk would blot out the horizon. Over ten thousand miles of mountains and streams he proceeded, pushing aside mist and smoke. Through a thousand alternations of heat and cold he advanced amidst frost and

---

3. Reference to a famous legend about China's first contact with Buddhism. Emperor Ming of the Han (r. 58–75 B.C.E.) dreamed that a golden deity was flying in front of his palace. The next morning one minister identified the deity in the dream as the flying Buddha from India.
4. Special physical marks on the body of the Buddha.
5. Four forms of patience: endurance under shame, hatred, physical hardship, and in pursuit of faith [translator's Note].

rain. As his zeal was great, he considered his task a light one, for he was determined to succeed.

He toured throughout the Western World for fourteen years,[6] going to all the foreign nations in quest of the proper doctrines. He led the life of an ascetic beneath twin śāla trees[7] and by the eight rivers of India. At the Deer Park and on the Vulture Peak he beheld the strange and searched out the different. He received ultimate truths from the senior sages and was taught the true doctrines by the highest worthies. Penetrating into the mysteries, he mastered the most profound lessons. The way of the Triyāna and Six Commandments he learned by heart; a hundred cases of scriptures forming the canon flowed like waves from his lips.

Though the countries he visited were innumerable, the scriptures he succeeded in acquiring had a definite number. Of those important texts of the Mahāyāna he received, there are thirty-five titles in altogether five thousand and forty-eight scrolls. When they are translated and spread through China, they will proclaim the surpassing merit of Buddhism, drawing the cloud of mercy from the Western extremity to shower the dharma-rain on the Eastern region. The Holy Religion, once incomplete, is now returned to perfection. The multitudes, once full of sins, are now brought back to blessing. Like that which quenches the fire in a burning house, Buddhism works to save humanity lost on its way to perdition. Like a golden beam shining on darkened waters, it leads the voyagers to climb the other shore safely.

Thus we know that the wicked will fall because of their iniquities, but the virtuous will rise because of their affinities. The causes of such rise and fall are all self-made by man. Consider the cinnamon flourishing high on the mountain, its flowers nourished by cloud and mist, or the lotus growing atop the green waves, its leaves unsoiled by dust. This is not because the lotus is by nature clean or because the cinnamon itself is chaste, but because what the cinnamon depends on for its existence is lofty, and thus it will not be weighed down by trivia; and because what the lotus relies on is pure, and thus impurity cannot stain it. Since even the vegetable kingdom, which is itself without intelligence, knows that excellence comes from an environment of excellence, how can humans who understand the great relations not search for well-being by following well-being?

May these scriptures abide forever as the sun and moon and may the blessings they confer spread throughout the universe!

After the secretary had finished writing this treatise, the sage monk was summoned. At the time, the elder was already waiting outside the gate of the court. When he heard the summons, he hurried inside and prostrated himself to pay homage to the emperor.

Taizong asked him to ascend the hall and handed him the document. When he had finished reading it, the priest went to his knees again to express his gratitude. "The style and rhetoric of my Lord," said the priest, "are lofty and classical, while the reasoning in the treatise is both profound and subtle. I would like to know, however, whether a title has been chosen for this composition."

"We composed it orally last night,"[8] replied Taizong, "as a token of thanks to our royal brother. Will it be acceptable if I title this 'Preface to the Holy

---

6. Perhaps a deliberate deviation from the nearly seventeen years of the pilgrimage indicated in the historical sources.

7. Trees under which the Buddha died and passed into nirvana.

8. The emperor's declaration here was actually a note written in reply to a formal memorial of thanks submitted to the historical Xuanzang [translator's note].

Religion'?" The elder kowtowed and thanked him profusely. Once more Taizong said,

> "Our talents pale before the imperial tablets,
> And our words cannot match the bronze and stone inscriptions.
> As for the esoteric texts,
> Our ignorance thereof is even greater.
> Our treatise orally composed
> Is actually quite unpolished—
> Like mere spilled ink on tablets of gold.
> Or broken tiles in a forest of pearls.
> Writing it in self-interest,
> We have quite ignored even embarrassment.
> It is not worth your notice,
> And you should not thank us."

All the officials present, however, congratulated the emperor and made arrangements immediately to promulgate the royal essay on Holy Religion inside and outside the capital.

Taizong said, "We would like to ask the royal brother to recite the true scriptures for us. How about it?"

"My Lord," said the elder, "if you want me to recite the true scriptures, we must find the proper religious site. The treasure palace is no place for recitation." Exceedingly pleased, Taizong asked his attendants, "Among the monasteries of Chang'an, which is the purest one?"

From among the ranks stepped forth the Grand Secretary, Xiao Yu, who said, "The Wild-Goose Pagoda Temple in the city is purest of all." At once Taizong gave this command to the various officials: "Each of you take several scrolls of these true scriptures and go reverently with us to the Wild-Goose Pagoda Temple. We want to ask our royal brother to expound the scriptures to us." Each of the officials indeed took up several scrolls and followed the emperor's carriage to the temple. A lofty platform with proper appointments was then erected. As before, the elder told Bajie and Sha Monk to hold the dragon horse and mind the luggage, while Pilgrim was to serve him by his side. Then he said to Taizong, "If my Lord would like to circulate the true scriptures throughout his empire, copies should be made before they are dispersed. We should treasure the originals and not handle them lightly."

Smiling, Taizong said, "The words of our royal brother are most appropriate! Most appropriate!" He thereupon ordered the officials in the Hanlin Academy and the Central Drafting Office to make copies of the true scriptures. For them he also erected another temple east of the capital and named it the Temple for Imperial Transcription.

* * *

We must tell you now about those Eight Great Vajra Guardians, who mounted the fragrant wind to lead the elder, his three disciples, and the white horse back to Spirit Mountain. The round trip was made precisely within a period of eight days. At that time the various divinities of Spirit Mountain were all assembled before Buddha to listen to his lecture. Ushering master and disciples before his presence, the Eight Vajra Guardians said, "Your disciples by your golden decree have escorted the sage monk and his companions back to the Tang nation. The scriptures have been handed over. We now return to surrender your decree." The Tang monk and his disciples were then told to approach the throne of Buddha to receive their appointments.

"Sage Monk," said Tathāgata, "in your previous incarnation you were originally my second disciple named Master Gold Cicada. Because you failed to listen to my exposition of the law and slighted my great teaching, your true spirit was banished to find another incarnation in the Land of the East. Happily you submitted and, by remaining faithful to our teaching, succeeded in acquiring the true scriptures. For such magnificent merit, you will receive a great promotion to become the Buddha of Candana Merit.

"Sun Wukong, when you caused great disturbance at the Celestial Palace, I had to exercise enormous dharma power to have you pressed beneath the Mountain of Five Phases. Fortunately your Heaven-sent calamity came to an end, and you embraced the Buddhist religion. I am pleased even more by the fact that you were devoted to the scourging of evil and the exaltation of good. Throughout your journey you made great merit by smelting the demons and defeating the fiends. For being faithful in the end as you were in the beginning, I hereby give you the grand promotion and appoint you the Buddha Victorious in Strife.

"Zhu Wuneng, you were originally an aquatic deity of the Heavenly River, the Marshal of Heavenly Reeds. For getting drunk during the Festival of Immortal Peaches and insulting the divine maiden, you were banished to an incarnation in the Region Below which would give you the body of a beast. Fortunately you still cherished and loved the human form, so that even when you sinned at the Cloudy Paths Cave in Fuling Mountain, you eventually submitted to our great religion and embraced our vows. Although you protected the sage monk on his way, you were still quite mischievous, for greed and lust were never wholly extinguished in you. For the merit of toting the luggage, however, I hereby grant you promotion and appoint you Janitor of the Altars."

"They have all become Buddhas!" shouted Bajie. "Why am I alone made Janitor of the Altars?"

"Because you are still talkative and lazy," replied Tathāgata, "and you retain an enormous appetite. Within the four great continents of the world, there are many people who observe our religion. Whenever there are Buddhist services, you will be asked to clear the altars. That's an appointment which offers you plenty of enjoyment. How could it be bad?

"Sha Wujing, you were originally the Great Curtain-Raising Captain. Because you broke a crystal chalice during the Festival of Immortal Peaches, you were banished to the Region Below, where at the River of Flowing-Sand you sinned by devouring humans. Fortunately you submitted to our religion and remained firm in your faith. As you escorted the sage monk, you made merit by leading his horse over all those mountains. I hereby grant you promotion and appoint you the Golden-Bodied Arhat."

Then he said to the white horse, "You were originally the prince of Dragon King Guangjin of the Western Ocean. Because you disobeyed your father's command and committed the crime of unfiliality, you were to be executed. Fortunately you made submission to the Law and accepted our vows. Because you carried the sage monk daily on your back during his journey to the West and because you also took the holy scriptures back to the East, you too have made merit. I hereby grant you promotion and appoint you one of the dragons belonging to the Eight Classes of Supernatural Beings."

The elder, his three disciples, and the horse all kowtowed to thank the Buddha, who ordered some of the guardians to take the horse to the Dragon-Transforming Pool at the back of the Spirit Mountain. After being pushed into the pool, the horse stretched himself, and in a little while he shed his coat, horns began to grow on his head, golden scales appeared all over his body, and silver whiskers emerged on his cheeks. His whole body shrouded in auspicious air and his four paws wrapped in hallowed clouds, he soared out of the pool and circled inside the monastery gate, on top of one of the Pillars that Support Heaven.

As the various Buddhas gave praise to the great dharma of Tathāgata, Pilgrim Sun said also to the Tang monk, "Master, I've become a Buddha now, just like you. It can't be that I still must wear a golden fillet! And you wouldn't want to clamp my head still by reciting that so-called Tight-Fillet Spell, would you? Recite the Loose-Fillet Spell quickly and get it off my head. I'm going to smash it to pieces, so that that so-called Bodhisattva can't use it anymore to play tricks on other people."

"Because you were difficult to control previously," said the Tang monk, "this method had to be used to keep you in hand. Now that you have become a Buddha, naturally it will be gone. How could it be still on your head? Try touching your head and see." Pilgrim raised his hand and felt along his head, and indeed the fillet had vanished. So at that time, Buddha Candana, Buddha Victorious in Strife, Janitor of the Altars, and Golden-Bodied Arhat all assumed the position of their own rightful fruition. The Heavenly dragon-horse too returned to immortality, and we have a testimonial poem for them. The poem says:

> One reality fallen to the dusty plain
> Fuses with Four Signs and cultivates self again.
> In Five Phases terms forms are but silent and void;
> The hundred fiends' false names one should all avoid.
> The great Bodhi's the right Candana fruition;
> Appointments complete their rise from perdition.
> When scriptures spread throughout the world the gracious light,
> Henceforth five sages live within Advaya's heights.

At the time when these five sages assumed their positions, the various Buddhist Patriarchs, Bodhisattvas, sage priests, arhats, guardians, bhikṣus, upāsakas and upāsikās, the immortals of various mountains and caves, the grand divinities, the Gods of Darkness and Light, the Sentinels, the Guardians of Monasteries, and all the immortals and preceptors who had attained the Way all came to listen to the proclamation before retiring to their proper stations. Look now at

> Colored mists crowding the Spirit Vulture Peak,
> And hallowed clouds gathered in the world of bliss.
> Gold dragons safely sleeping,
> Jade tigers resting in peace;
> Black hares scampering freely,

Snakes and turtles circling at will.
Phoenixes, red and blue, gambol pleasantly;
Black apes and white deer saunter happily.
Strange flowers of eight periods,
Divine fruits of four seasons,
Hoary pines and old junipers,
Jade cypresses and aged bamboos.
Five-colored plums often blossoming and bearing fruit;
Millennial peaches frequently ripening and fresh.
A thousand flowers and fruits vying for beauty;
A whole sky full of auspicious mists.

Pressing their palms together to indicate their devotion, the holy congregation all chanted:

I submit to Dipamkara, the Buddha of Antiquity.
I submit to Bhaiṣajya-vaidūrya-prabhāṣa, the Physician and Buddha
   of Crystal Lights.
I submit to the Buddha Śākyamuni.
I submit to the Buddha of the Past, Present, and Future.
I submit to the Buddha of Pure Joy.
I submit to the Buddha Vairocana.
I submit to the Buddha, King of the Precious Banner.
I submit to the Maitreya, the Honored Buddha.
I submit to the Buddha Amitābha.
I submit to Sukhāvativyūha, the Buddha of Infinite Life.
I submit to the Buddha who Receives and Leads to Immorality.
I submit to the Buddha of Diamond Indestructibility.
I submit to Sūrya, the Buddha of Precious Light.
I submit to Mañjuśrī, the Buddha of the Race of Honorable Dragon
   Kings.
I submit to the Buddha of Zealous Progress and Virtue.
I submit to Candraprabha, the Buddha of Precious Moonlight.
I submit to the Buddha of Presence without Ignorance.
I submit to Varuna, the Buddha of Sky and Water.
I submit to the Buddha Nārāyaṇa.
I submit to the Buddha of Radiant Meritorious Works.
I submit to the Buddha of Talented Meritorious Works.
I submit to Svāgata, the Buddha of the Well-Departed.
I submit to the Buddha of Candana Light.
I submit to the Buddha of Jeweled Banner.
I submit to the Buddha of the Light of Wisdom Torch.
I submit to the Buddha of the Light of Sea-Virtue.
I submit to the Buddha of Great Mercy Light.
I submit to the Buddha, King of Compassion-Power.
I submit to the Buddha, Leader of the Sages.
I submit to the Buddha of Vast Solemnity.
I submit to the Buddha of Golden Radiance.
I submit to the Buddha of Luminous Gifts.
I submit to the Buddha Victorious in Wisdom.

I submit to the Buddha, Quiescent Light of the World.
I submit to the Buddha, Light of the Sun and Moon.
I submit to the Buddha, Light of the Sun-and-Moon Pearl.
I submit to the Buddha, King of the Victorious Banner.
I submit to the Buddha of Wondrous Tone and Sound.
I submit to the Buddha, Banner of Permanent Light.
I submit to the Buddha, Lamp that Scans the World.
I submit to the Buddha, King of Surpassing Dharma.
I submit to the Buddha of Sumeru Light.
I submit to the Buddha, King of Great Wisdom.
I submit to the Buddha of Golden Sea Light.
I submit to the Buddha of Great Perfect Light.
I submit to the Buddha of the Gift of Light.
I submit to the Buddha of Candana Merit.
I submit to the Buddha Victorious in Strife.
I submit to the Bodhisattva Guanshiyin.
I submit to the Bodhisattva, Great Power-Coming.
I submit to the Bodhisattva Mañjuśrī.
I submit to the Bodhisattva Viśvabhadra and other Bodhisattvas.
I submit to the various Bodhisattvas of the Great Pure Ocean.
I submit to the Bodhisattva, the Buddha of Lotus Pool and Ocean
    Assembly.
I submit to the various Bodhisattvas in the Western Heaven of
    Ultimate Bliss.
I submit to the Great Bodhisattvas, the Three Thousand Guardians.
I submit to the Great Bodhisattvas, the Five Hundred Arhats.
I submit to the Bodhisattva, Bhikṣu-ikṣṇi.
I submit to the Bodhisattva of Boundless and Limitless Dharma.
I submit to the Bodhisattva, Diamond Great Scholar-Sage.
I submit to the Bodhisattva, Janitor of the Altars.
I submit to the Bodhisattva, Golden-Bodied Arhat of Eight Jewels.
I submit to the Bodhisattva of Vast Strength, the Heavenly Dragon
    of Eight Divisions of Supernatural Beings.

Such are these various Buddhas in all the worlds.

> *I wish to use these merits*
> *To adorn Buddha's pure land—*
> *To repay fourfold grace above*
> *And save those on three paths below.*
> *If there are those who see and hear,*
> *Their minds will find enlightenment.*
> *Their births with us in paradise*
> *Will be this body's recompense.*
> *All the Buddhas of past, present, future in all the world,*
> *The various Honored Bodhisattvas and Mahāsattvas,*
> Mahā-prajñā-pāramitā![9]

9. The Great Perfection of Wisdom.

CAO XUEQIN

ca. 1715–1763

Of the world's great novels perhaps only *Don Quixote* rivals *The Story of the Stone* as the embodiment of a modern nation's cultural identity, much as the epic once embodied cultural identity in the ancient world. For Chinese readers of the past two centuries, *The Story of the Stone* (also known as *The Dream of the Red Chamber*) has come to represent the best and worst of traditional China in its final phase. It is the story of an extended family, centered around its women, maids, and outside relations, that asks tantalizing questions about the nature of love and lust, the differences between male and female sensibilities, the corrupting effects of money and power, and the reality of truth and illusion. Even after the twentieth century, a century of war, revolution, and social experiment that saw the dissolution of the traditional extended family, *The Story of the Stone* has retained its power to move people's hearts and minds. It is generally considered the greatest Chinese novel of all time.

THE CAO CLAN AND CAO XUEQIN

Cao Xueqin came from a Han Chinese family, the dominant ethnic group in China, but his ancestors had been captured and forced into service by the Manchus, a people from the northeastern border of the Ming Empire (1368–1644), who had conquered China and set up their own Chinese-style Manchu empire, the Qing (1644–1911). Having fought on the victors' side certainly added to the family's fortunes with the first Qing emperors, and several generations of the Cao family served in a prominent and lucrative official position as Imperial Textile Commissioner in Nanjing, the old southern capital. Given the fame of the Cao family, it is surprising how little we know about Cao Xueqin's life. We do know of the sudden demise of the family when Cao was in his teens. A new emperor suddenly confiscated their opulent mansion and properties, probably due to political intrigues. The family was reduced to poverty and forced to relocate to Beijing. Cao Xueqin may have passed a low-level civil service examination and served in minor offices. Between 1740 and 1750 he was at work on *The Story of the Stone*, and toward the end of his life he lived in the suburbs of Beijing, struggling to support himself by selling his paintings—painting being a typical pastime of Chinese literati and writers.

THE ORIGIN OF *THE STORY OF THE STONE*

The novel itself has a peculiar genesis. The first eighty chapters are the work of Cao Xueqin, who probably wrote the novel, in at least five drafts, between 1740 and 1750. There is another figure in the process of the novel's composition, however, someone who used the pseudonym "Red Inkstone" (or more properly "He of the Red Inkstone Studio") and who added commentary and made corrections to the manuscript. He was obviously a close friend or relative of Cao Xueqin and his comments suggest that the characters in the main portion of the novel are based on real people. This remark and the lack of information about Cao's life has inspired scholars and lovers of *The Story of the Stone* to identify historical figures and events in the novel. Biographical readings of the novel are often far-fetched and clearly born from the desire to get an inch closer to the masterful mind behind this epic novel. Still, the demise of Cao's own family in young age certainly resonates with the novel's minute chronicling of a grand family's glory and doom.

The novel was unfinished when Cao died and he probably never intended it for publication. But it did circulate widely in Beijing in manuscript copies, whose many variations show a complex process of revision. One version of the manuscript came into the hands of the writer Gao E (ca. 1740–ca. 1815), who probably completed the story by adding another forty chapters, finally publishing a full 120–chapter version in 1791, about a half century after Cao Xueqin had begun to write it. Due to the supreme status of *The Story of the Stone* and its complicated textual history, the novel has given birth to a separate field in Chinese literary studies. The transformations of the novel in its manuscript versions, the role of the mysterious Red Inkstone (and of another early commentator who calls himself "Odd Tablet"), and the relation of the characters to Cao's life are questions that continue to engage professional and amateur scholars of "Redology" or "Red Studies" (named after the novel's alternative title).

THE WORLDS OF
THE STORY OF THE STONE

Chinese novels are, as a rule, very long, and *The Story of the Stone* is longer than most, taking up five substantial volumes in its complete English translation. The narrative is impossible to summarize and difficult to excerpt. It has a cast of about four hundred characters, both major and minor, who appear and disappear in intricately interwoven incidents and interspersed sequences of episodes. The novel's opulent cast of characters plays out its social dramas in equally opulent surroundings. The daily life in the Jia household is spent with birthday parties, poetry contests, opera performances, and artistic pastimes, and these aristocratic pursuits are captured in a vocabulary of luxurious abundance, detailing the charms of buildings, the exotic recipes of expensive medicines, the texture of exquisite clothes, makeup, and features of sophisticated landscape gardening.

This ornate world of splendor that is described in lovingly realist detail and fills a large part of the novel comes, literally, out of nowhere, out of the cosmic void. As the title tells us, the novel is the story of a magical and conscious stone, the one block left over when the goddess Nü-wa repaired the damaged vault of the sky in the mythic past. Transported into the mortal world by a pair of priests, a Buddhist and a Daoist, the stone is destined to find enlightenment by suffering the pains of love, loss, and disillusion as a human being. It does so when it is incarnated as the sole legitimate male heir of the powerful household of the Jias, which is about to pass from the height of prosperity into decline. The novel unfolds in an unnamed city, which blends features of Beijing and Nanjing. Miraculously, the baby is born with an inscribed piece of jade in his mouth, from which he is given his name Baoyu ("Precious Jade") and which he wears always. In a novel filled with ominous puns and double entendres, "yu" ("jade") puns on "desire." Baoyu has a delicate preference for girls, once claiming that "girls are made of water, boys are made of mud." He has a remarkable sensibility for the world of lyrical poetry, artistic reverie and rarified intellectual pleasures. And he is said to possess a "lust of the mind." His grandmother dotes on him and often protects him from the callous attacks of his stern father who considers him a n'er-do-well dreamer, pampered by the weak women around him. The father is disgusted with Baoyu's lack of interest in serious Confucian studies, which would prepare him for the civil service examinations and a successful career in the Qing bureaucracy. The strident conflict between father and heir unmasks the hypocrisy of Confucian scholasticism and its creatures, such as the sycophant "literary gentlemen" surrounding Baoyu's father. Beyond the father-son conflict, the darker sides of Qing Confucianism surface in briberies, corruption and outrageous cover-ups of murders perpetrated by Confucian magistrates at the expense of people of lower social status.

In addition to Baoyu, the human metamorphosis of the Stone, one other central character originates in the supernatural frame story and its fanciful landscape: the Crimson Pearl Flower, a semidivine plant. While Stone is serving at the court of the goddess Disenchantment before being born into the human world as Baoyu, he takes a fancy to this flower and waters it with sweet dew. This eventually brings the flower to life in the form of a fairy girl, who is obsessed with repaying the kindness of Stone, and for his gift of sweet dew she owes him the "debt of tears." The girl is born as Baoyu's cousin, the delicate and high-strung Lin Daiyu (Daiyu means "Black Jade"). The early chapters of the novel are devoted to the supernatural frame story and to bringing the characters together in the household of the all too human Jia family. In chapters seventeen and eighteen, Baoyu's elder sister, an imperial concubine, has been permitted to pay a visit to her home— an unusual break with court protocol that displays the emperor's favor to her and her family. In her honor a huge

garden ("Prospect Garden") is constructed on the grounds of the family compound. After the imperial concubine's departure, the adolescent girls of the extended family are allowed to take up residence in the various buildings in the garden, and Baoyu is also permitted to live there with his maids. The world of the garden is one of adolescent love in full flower, though we never forget the violent and ugly world outside, a world that can barely be held at bay.

The love between Baoyu and Daiyu forms the core of the novel. Each is intensely sensitive to the other, and neither can express what he or she feels. Communication between them often depends on subtle gestures with implicit meanings that are inevitably misunderstood. Both believe in a perfect understanding of hearts, but even in the charmed world of the garden, closeness eludes them. The novel often juxtaposes brutish characters (usually male) with those possessed of a finer sensibility; but in the case of Daiyu, sensibility is carried to the extreme. Daiyu's relation to Baoyu is balanced out by that of another distant relation, Xue Baochai, whose plump good looks and gentle common sense are the very opposite of Daiyu's frailty and histrionic morbidity. Baochai ("Precious Hairpin") has a golden locket with an inscription that matches Baoyu's jade, and the marriage of "jade and gold" is being seriously considered by older members of the family. Eventually, in Gao E's ending for the novel, as Daiyu is dying of consumption, Baoyu will be tricked into marrying Baochai, falling dangerously ill as he realizes the plot. In passing the grueling civil service examination Baoyu finally carries out his obligation toward the family line, but the novel ends on a twist.

Although the triangle of Baoyu, Daiyu, and Baochai stands at the center of the novel, scores of subplots involve characters of all types. The reader easily becomes absorbed in the intensity of the family's internal relationships, always to be reminded of how those relationships touch and are touched by the world outside. There is a vast establishment of close and distant family members, personal maids, and servants, each with his or her own status. Although personal maids have some responsibilities, the number of maids attached to each family member is primarily a mark of status, while for a girl from a poor family, the position of personal maid is very desirable, providing room, board, and income to send to her own family. Because the Jias have social power, the actions taken by family members to serve its interests and loyalties can also be seen as corruption. In some cases the corruption is obvious, but the reader is also induced to identify with the family and to take many acts of power and privilege for granted. At the same time, the outside world has the capacity to impinge on the protected space of the family, and the reader sees these forces from the point of view of the insider, as intrusions. It is a world of concentric circles of proximity, both of kinship and affinity. Petty details and private loves and hates grow larger and larger as they approach the center. And above all this hovers the Buddhist and Daoist lesson about the illusory nature of a world driven by emotions that cause only suffering, both to one's self and others.

The lesson of illusion is underscored by the family name Jia, a real Chinese surname that can mean "false" or "feigned." Puns ominously underlie many proper names in the novel. The names of Zhen Shiyin and Jia Yucun, who introduce the Jia household in the first chapters from the sidelines, can alternatively mean "true things are hidden" and "false words remain." The most emblematic statement of the novel's play with truth and illusion stands on a tablet over the entrance to the "Land of Illusion": "Truth becomes fiction when the fiction's true. Real becomes not-real when the unreal's real."

The selections printed here include the opening frame story, the first few chapters of the novel that gradually introduce the reader into the Jia household. We then move to the building of the Prospect Garden for the visit of the imperial concubine, which becomes a space of poetic passions and artistic pursuits, and an almost metaphysical realm of blissful love for Baoyu and the adolescent women around him. We pick up the story again much later, with chapters 96 through 98, when the family fortunes have declined and Daiyu enters a final bout of illness when she learns that Baoyu is to be married to Baochai. With the final selections, from chapters 119 and 120, we witness Baoyu's triumphant success in the civil service examinations, as well as the novel's sudden and surprising ending. At the end, Stone is whisked from the stage of his human incarnation by the Buddhist and Daoist monks.

Although nothing can replace the experience of reading the whole novel, the selective glimpses of Stone's world and story presented here make for a contagious experience with the greatest and last novel of traditional China. A few decades after the publication of the novel, Western powers forced China into wars, carved out colonial enclaves, and helped bring down the Qing Dynasty. Stone is a full-fledged creature of traditional China, but the metaphor of fateful decline that pervades his trials in the human world came to resonate differently for readers who witnessed the painful end of twenty-two centuries of imperial China in the twentieth century.

From The Story of the Stone[1]

CHARACTERS

AROMA, NIGHTINGALE, Snowgoose, Tealeaf, Crimson etc.: Maids in the Jia Household

AUNT XUE: widowed sister of Lady Wang and mother of Xue Pan and Xue Baochai

FENG YUAN: Caltrop's first purchaser, murdered by Xue Pan's servants

GRANDMOTHER JIA: née Shi; widow of Baoyu's paternal grandfather and head of the Rongguo branch of the Jia family

GRANNY LIU: old countrywoman patronized by Wang Xifeng and the Rongguo Jias

JIA BAOYU: incarnation of Stone; the eldest surviving son of Jia Zheng and Lady Wang of Rongguo House

JIA LAN: Baoyu's deceased elder brother

JIA RONG: son of Cousin Zhen and Youshi

JIA SHE: Jia Zheng's elder brother, Baoyu's uncle

JIA TANCHUN: daughter of Jia Zheng and "Aunt" Zhao; half-sister of Baoyu

JIA YINGCHUN: daughter of Jia She by a concubine

JIA YUANCHUN: daughter of Jia Zheng and Lady Wang and elder sister of Baoyu; the Imperial Concubine

JIA YUCUN: careerist claiming relationship with the Rongguo family

JIA ZHEN: also "Cousin Zhen"; son of Jia Jing; acting head of the senior (Ningguo) branch of the Jia family

JIAN ZHENG: Baoyu's father; the younger of Grandmother Jia's two sons

LADY XING: wife of Jia She and mother of Jia Lian

LENG ZIXING: an antique dealer; friend of Jia Yucun

LIN DAIYU: incarnation of the Crimson Pearl Flower; daughter of Lin Ruhai and Jia Zheng's sister, Jia Min

LIN RUHAI: Daiyu's father; the Salt Commissioner of Yangchow

QINSHI (OR KEQING): wife of Jia Rong

WANG XIFENG: wife of Jia Lan and niece of Lady Wang and Aunt Xue

XUE BAOCHAI: daughter of Aunt Xue

XUE PAN: son of Aunt Xue and reckless elder brother of Baochai

ZHEN SHIYIN: retired gentleman of Soochow; father of Caltrop

ZHEN YINGLIAN: daughter of Zhen Shiyin, later know as Caltrop

FROM CHAPTER I

Zhen Shiyin makes the Stone's acquaintance in a dream
And Jia Yu-cun finds that poverty is not incompatible with romantic feelings

GENTLE READER,

What, you may ask, was the origin of this book?

Though the answer to this question may at first seem to border on the absurd, reflection will show that there is a good deal more in it than meets the eye.

Long ago, when the goddess Nü-wa was repairing the sky, she melted down a great quantity of rock and, on the Incredible Crags of the Great Fable Mountains, moulded the amalgam into thirty-six thousand, five hundred and one large

---

1. Chapters 1–17 are translated by David Hawkes.

Genealogy of the Ningguo and Rongguo Houses of the Jia Clan

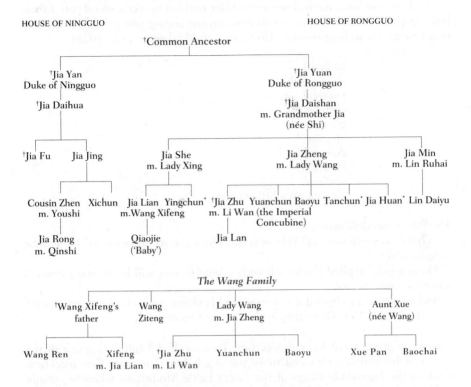

m. married   †dead before the beginning of the novel   *son or daughter by a concubine

building blocks, each measuring seventy-two feet by a hundred and forty-four feet square. She used thirty-six thousand five hundred of these blocks in the course of her building operations, leaving a single odd block unused, which lay, all on its own, at the foot of Greensickness Peak in the aforementioned mountains.

Now this block of stone, having undergone the melting and moulding of a goddess, possessed magic powers. It could move about at will and could grow or shrink to any size it wanted. Observing that all the other blocks had been used for celestial repairs and that it was the only one to have been rejected as unworthy, it became filled with shame and resentment and passed its days in sorrow and lamentation.

One day, in the midst of its lamentings, it saw a monk and a Taoist approaching from a great distance, each of them remarkable for certain eccentricities of manner and appearance. When they arrived at the foot of Greensickness Peak, they sat down on the ground and began to talk. The monk, catching sight of a lustrous, translucent stone—it was in fact the rejected building block which had now shrunk itself to the size of a fan-pendant[2] and looked very attractive in

2. Jade decoration strung from the bottom of a fan.

its new shape—took it up on the palm of his hand and addressed it with a smile:

'Ha, I see you have magical properties! But nothing to recommend you. I shall have to cut a few words on you so that anyone seeing you will know at once that you are something special. After that I shall take you to a certain

> brilliant
> successful
> poetical
> cultivated
> aristocratic
> elegant
> delectable
> luxurious
> opulent
> locality on a little trip'.

The stone was delighted.

'What words will you cut? Where is this place you will take me to? I beg to be enlightened.'

'Do not ask,' replied the monk with a laugh. 'You will know soon enough when the time comes.'

And with that he slipped the stone into his sleeve and set off at a great pace with the Taoist. But where they both went to I have no idea.

Countless aeons went by and a certain Taoist called Vanitas in quest of the secret of immortality chanced to be passing below that same Greensickness Peak in the Incredible Crags of the Great Fable Mountains when he caught sight of a large stone standing there, on which the characters of a long inscription were clearly discernible.

Vanitas read the inscription through from beginning to end and learned that this was a once lifeless stone block which had been found unworthy to repair the sky, but which had magically transformed its shape and been taken down by the Buddhist mahāsattva[3] Impervioso and the Taoist illuminate Mysterioso into the world of mortals, where it had lived out the life of a man before finally attaining nirvana and returning to the other shore.[4] The inscription named the country where it had been born, and went into considerable detail about its domestic life, youthful amours, and even the verses, mottoes and riddles it had written. All it lacked was the authentication of a dynasty and date. On the back of the stone was inscribed the following quatrain:

> Found unfit to repair the azure sky
> Long years a foolish mortal man was I.
> My life in both worlds on this stone is writ:
> Pray who will copy out and publish it?

3. Wise man.
4. That is, achieving enlightenment and passing beyond the cycles of rebirth.

From his reading of the inscription Vanitas realized that this was a stone of some consequence. Accordingly he addressed himself to it in the following manner:

'Brother Stone, according to what you yourself seem to imply in these verses, this story of yours contains matter of sufficient interest to merit publication and has been carved here with that end in view. But as far as I can see (a) it has no discoverable dynastic period, and (b) it contains no examples of moral grandeur among its characters—no statesmanship, no social message of any kind. All I can find in it, in fact, are a number of females, conspicuous, if at all, only for their passion or folly or for some trifling talent or insignificant virtue. Even if I were to copy all this out, I cannot see that it would make a very remarkable book.'

'Come, your reverence,' said the stone (for Vanitas had been correct in assuming that it could speak) 'must you be so obtuse? All the romances ever written have an artificial period setting—Han or Tang for the most part. In refusing to make use of that stale old convention and telling my *Story of the Stone* exactly as it occurred, it seems to me that, far from *depriving* it of anything, I have given it a freshness these other books do not have.

'Your so-called "historical romances", consisting, as they do, of scandalous anecdotes about statesmen and emperors of bygone days and scabrous attacks on the reputations of long-dead gentlewomen, contain more wickedness and immorality than I care to mention. Still worse is the "erotic novel", by whose filthy obscenities our young folk are all too easily corrupted. And the "boudoir romances", those dreary stereotypes with their volume after volume all pitched on the same note and their different characters undistinguishable except by name (all those ideally beautiful young ladies and ideally eligible young bachelors)—even they seem unable to avoid descending sooner or later into indecency.

'The trouble with this last kind of romance is that it only gets written in the first place because the author requires a framework in which to show off his love-poems. He goes about constructing this framework quite mechanically, beginning with the names of his pair of young lovers and invariably adding a third character, a servant or the like, to make mischief between them, like the *chou*[5] in a comedy.

'What makes these romances even more detestable is the stilted, bombastic language—inanities dressed in pompous rhetoric, remote alike from nature and common sense and teeming with the grossest absurdities.

'Surely my "number of females", whom I spent half a lifetime studying with my own eyes and ears, are preferable to this kind of stuff? I do not claim that they are better people than the ones who appear in books written before my time; I am only saying that the contemplation of their actions and motives may prove a more effective antidote to boredom and melancholy. And even the inelegant verses with which my story is interlarded could serve to entertain and amuse on those convivial occasions when rhymes and riddles are in demand.

5. The stock role of the clown in a play.

'All that my story narrates, the meetings and partings, the joys and sorrows, the ups and downs of fortune, are recorded exactly as they happened. I have not dared to add the tiniest bit of touching-up, for fear of losing the true picture.

'My only wish is that men in the world below may sometimes pick up this tale when they are recovering from sleep or drunkenness, or when they wish to escape from business worries or a fit of the dumps, and in doing so find not only mental refreshment but even perhaps, if they will heed its lesson and abandon their vain and frivolous pursuits, some small arrest in the deterioration of their vital forces. What does your reverence say to that?'

For a long time Vanitas stood lost in thought, pondering this speech. He then subjected the *Story of the Stone* to a careful second reading. He could see that its main theme was love; that it consisted quite simply of a true record of real events; and that it was entirely free from any tendency to deprave and corrupt. He therefore copied it all out from beginning to end and took it back with him to look for a publisher.

As a consequence of all this, Vanitas, starting off in the Void (which is Truth) came to the contemplation of Form (which is Illusion); and from Form engendered Passion; and by communicating Passion, entered again into Form; and from Form awoke to the Void (which is Truth). He therefore changed his name from Vanitas to Brother Amor, or the Passionate Monk, (because he had approached Truth by way of Passion), and changed the title of the book from *The Story of the Stone* to *The Tale of Brother Amor*.

Old Kong Meixi from the homeland of Confucius called the book *A Mirror for the Romantic*. Wu Yufeng called it *A Dream of Golden Days*. Cao Xueqin in his Nostalgia Studio worked on it for ten years, in the course of which he rewrote it no less than five times, dividing it into chapters, composing chapter headings, renaming it *The Twelve Beauties of Jinling*, and adding an introductory quatrain. Red Inkstone restored the original title when he recopied the book and added his second set of annotations to it.

This, then, is a true account of how *The Story of the Stone* came to be written.

> Pages full of idle words
> Penned with hot and bitter tears:
> All men call the author fool;
> None his secret message hears.

The origin of *The Story of the Stone* has now been made clear. The same cannot, however, be said of the characters and events which it recorded. Gentle reader, have patience! This is how the inscription began:

Long, long ago the world was tilted downwards towards the south-east; and in that lower-lying south-easterly part of the earth there is a city called Soochow; and in Soochow the district around the Chang-men Gate is reckoned one of the two or three wealthiest and most fashionable quarters in the world of men. Outside the Chang-men Gate is a wide thoroughfare called Worldly Way; and somewhere off Worldly Way is an area called Carnal Lane. There is an old temple in the Carnal Lane area which, because of the way it is bottled up inside a narrow *cul-de-sac*, is referred to locally as Bottle-gourd Temple. Next door to Bottle-gourd Temple lived a gentleman of private means called Zhen Shiyin and his wife Fengshi, a kind, good woman with a profound sense of decency and decorum. The household was not a particularly wealthy one, but they were nevertheless looked up to by all and sundry as the leading family in the neighbourhood.

Zhen Shiyin himself was by nature a quiet and totally unambitious person. He devoted his time to his garden and to the pleasures of wine and poetry. Except for a single flaw, his existence could, indeed, have been described as an idyllic one. The flaw was that, although already past fifty, he had no son, only a little girl, just two years old, whose name was Yinglian.

Once, during the tedium of a burning summer's day, Shiyin was sitting idly in his study. The book had slipped from his nerveless grasp and his head had nodded down onto the desk in a doze. While in this drowsy state he seemed to drift off to some place he could not identify, where he became aware of a monk and a Taoist walking along and talking as they went.

'Where do you intend to take that thing you are carrying?' the Taoist was asking.

'Don't you worry about him!' replied the monk with a laugh. 'There is a batch of lovesick souls awaiting incarnation in the world below whose fate is due to be decided this very day. I intend to take advantage of this opportunity to slip our little friend in amongst them and let him have a taste of human life along with the rest.'

'Well, well, so another lot of these amorous wretches is about to enter the vale of tears,' said the Taoist. 'How did all this begin? And where are the souls to be reborn?'

'You will laugh when I tell you,' said the monk. 'When this stone was left unused by the goddess, he found himself at a loose end and took to wandering about all over the place for want of better to do, until one day his wanderings took him to the place where the fairy Disenchantment lives.

'Now Disenchantment could tell that there was something unusual about this stone, so she kept him there in her Sunset Glow Palace and gave him the honorary title of Divine Luminescent Stone-in-Waiting in the Court of Sunset Glow.

'But most of his time he spent west of Sunset Glow exploring the banks of the Magic River. There, by the Rock of Rebirth, he found the beautiful Crimson Pearl Flower, for which he conceived such a fancy that he took to watering her every day with sweet dew, thereby conferring on her the gift of life.

'Crimson Pearl's substance was composed of the purest cosmic essences, so she was already half-divine; and now, thanks to the vitalizing effect of the sweet dew, she was able to shed her vegetable shape and assume the form of a girl.

'This fairy girl wandered about outside the Realm of Separation, eating the Secret Passion Fruit when she was hungry and drinking from the Pool of Sadness when she was thirsty. The consciousness that she owed the stone something for his kindness in watering her began to prey on her mind and ended by becoming an obsession.

'"I have no sweet dew here that I can repay him with," she would say to herself. "The only way in which I could perhaps repay him would be with the tears shed during the whole of a mortal lifetime if he and I were ever to be reborn as humans in the world below."

'Because of this strange affair, Disenchantment has got together a group of amorous young souls, of which Crimson Pearl is one, and intends to send them down into the world to take part in the great illusion of human life. And as today happens to be the day on which this stone is fated to go into the world too, I am taking him with me to Disenchantment's tribunal for the purpose of getting him registered and sent down to earth with the rest of these romantic creatures.'

'How very amusing!' said the Taoist. 'I have certainly never heard of a debt of tears before. Why shouldn't the two of us take advantage of this opportunity to go down into the world ourselves and save a few souls? It would be a work of merit.'

'That is exactly what I was thinking,' said the monk. 'Come with me to Disenchantment's palace to get this absurd creature cleared. Then, when this last batch of romantic idiots goes down, you and I can go down with them. At present about half have already been born. They await this last batch to make up the number.'

'Very good, I will go with you then,' said the Taoist. Shiyin heard all this conversation quite clearly, and curiosity impelled him to go forward and greet the two reverend gentlemen. They returned his greeting and asked him what he wanted.

'It is not often that one has the opportunity of listening to a discussion of the operations of *karma*[6] such as the one I have just been privileged to overhear,' said Shiyin. 'Unfortunately I am a man of very limited understanding and have not been able to derive the full benefit from your conversation. If you would have the very great kindness to enlighten my benighted understanding with a somewhat fuller account of what you were discussing, I can promise you the most devout attention. I feel sure that your teaching would have a salutary effect on me and—who knows—might save me from the pains of hell.'

The reverend gentlemen laughed. 'These are heavenly mysteries and may not be divulged. But if you wish to escape from the fiery pit, you have only to remember us when the time comes, and all will be well.'

Shi-yin saw that it would be useless to press them. 'Heavenly mysteries must not, of course, be revealed. But might one perhaps inquire what the "absurd creature" is that you were talking about? Is it possible that I might be allowed to see it?'

'Oh, as for that,' said the monk: 'I think it is on the cards for you to have a look at *him*,' and he took the object from his sleeve and handed it to Shiyin.

Shi-yin took the object from him and saw that it was a clear, beautiful jade on one side of which were carved the words 'Magic Jade'. There were several columns of smaller characters on the back, which Shiyin was just going to examine more closely when the monk, with a cry of 'Here we are, at the frontier of Illusion', snatched the stone from him and disappeared, with the Taoist, through a big stone archway above which

THE LAND OF ILLUSION

was written in large characters. A couplet in smaller characters was inscribed vertically on either side of the arch:

> Truth becomes fiction when the fiction's true;
> Real becomes not-real where the unreal's real.

6. The accumulation of good and bad deeds that determines a soul's future lives.

Shiyin was on the point of following them through the archway when suddenly a great clap of thunder seemed to shake the earth to its very foundations, making him cry out in alarm.

And there he was sitting in his study, the contents of his dream already half forgotten, with the sun still blazing on the ever-rustling plantains outside, and the wet-nurse at the door with his little daughter Yinglian in her arms. Her delicate little pink-and-white face seemed dearer to him than ever at that moment, and he stretched out his arms to take her and hugged her to him.

After playing with her for a while at his desk, he carried her out to the front of the house to watch the bustle in the street. He was about to go in again when he saw a monk and a Taoist approaching, the monk scabby-headed and barefoot, the Taoist tousle-haired and limping. They were behaving like madmen, shouting with laughter and gesticulating wildly as they walked along.

When this strange pair reached Shiyin's door and saw him standing there holding Yinglian, the monk burst into loud sobs. 'Patron,' he said, addressing Shiyin, 'what are you doing, holding in your arms that ill-fated creature who is destined to involve both her parents in her own misfortune?'

Shiyin realized that he was listening to the words of a madman and took no notice. But the monk persisted:

'Give her to me! Give her to me!'

Shiyin was beginning to lose patience and, clasping his little girl more tightly to him, turned on his heel and was about to re-enter the house when the monk pointed his finger at him, roared with laughter, and then proceeded to intone the following verses:

'Fond man, your pampered child to cherish so—
That caltrop-glass which shines on melting snow!
Beware the high feast of the fifteenth day,
When all in smoke and fire shall pass away!'

Shiyin heard all this quite plainly and was a little worried by it. He was thinking of asking the monk what lay behind these puzzling words when he heard the Taoist say, 'We don't need to stay together. Why don't we part company here and each go about his own business? Three *kalpas*[7] from now I shall wait for you on Beimang Hill. Having joined forces again there, we can go together to the Land of Illusion to sign off.'

'Excellent!' said the other. And the two of them went off and soon were both lost to sight.

'There must have been something behind all this,' thought Shiyin to himself. 'I really ought to have asked him what he meant, but now it is too late.'

He was still standing outside his door brooding when Jia Yucun, the poor student who lodged at the Bottle-gourd Temple next door, came up to him. Yucun was a native of Huzhou and came from a family of scholars and bureaucrats which had, however, fallen on bad times when Yucun was born. The family fortunes on both his father's and mother's side had all been spent, and the members of the family had themselves gradually died off until only Yucun was left. There were no prospects for him in his home town, so he had

7. An aeon, an extraordinarily long span of cosmic time.

set off for the capital, in search of fame and fortune. Unfortunately he had got no further than Soochow when his funds ran out, and he had now been living there in poverty for a year, lodging in this temple and keeping himself alive by working as a copyist. For this reason Shiyin saw a great deal of his company.

As soon as he caught sight of Shiyin, Yucun clasped his hands in greeting and smiled ingratiatingly. 'I could see you standing there gazing, sir. Has anything been happening in the street?'

'No, no,' said Shiyin. 'It just happened that my little girl was crying, so I brought her out here to amuse her. Your coming is most opportune, dear boy. I was beginning to feel most dreadfully bored. Won't you come into my little den, and we can help each other to while away this tedious hot day?'

So saying, he called for a servant to take the child indoors, while he himself took Yucun by the hand and led him into his study, where his boy served them both with tea. But they had not exchanged half-a-dozen words before one of the servants rushed in to say that 'Mr Yan had come to pay a call.' Shiyin hurriedly rose up and excused himself: 'I seem to have brought you here under false pretences. I do hope you will forgive me. If you don't mind sitting on your own here for a moment, I shall be with you directly.'

Yucun rose to his feet too. 'Please do not distress yourself on my account, sir. I am a regular visitor here and can easily wait a bit.' But by the time he had finished saying this, Shiyin was already out of the study and on his way to the guestroom.

Left to himself, Yucun was flicking through some of Shiyin's books of poetry in order to pass the time, when he heard a woman's cough outside the window. Immediately he jumped up and peered out to see who it was. The cough appeared to have come from a maid who was picking flowers in the garden. She was an unusually good-looking girl with a rather refined face: not a great beauty, by any means, but with something striking about her. Yucun gazed at her spellbound.

Having now finished picking her flowers, this anonymous member of the Zhen household was about to go in again when, on some sudden impulse, she raised her head and caught sight of a man standing in the window. His hat was frayed and his clothing threadbare; yet, though obviously poor, he had a fine, manly physique and handsome, well-proportioned features.

The maid hastened to remove herself from this male presence; but as she went she thought to herself, 'What a fine-looking man! But so shabby! The family hasn't got any friends or relations as poor as that. It must be that Jia Yucun the master is always on about. No wonder he says that he won't stay poor long. I remember hearing him say that he's often wanted to help him but hasn't yet found an opportunity.' And thinking these thoughts she could not forbear to turn back for another peep or two.

Yucun saw her turn back and, at once assuming that she had taken a fancy to him, was beside himself with delight. What a perceptive young woman she must be, he thought, to have seen the genius underneath the rags! A real friend in trouble!

After a while the boy came in again and Yucun elicited from him that the visitor in the front room was now staying to dinner. It was obviously out of the question to wait much longer, so he slipped down the passage-way at the side of the house and let himself out by the back gate. Nor did Shiyin invite him round again when, having at last seen off his visitor, he learned that Yucun had already left.

But then the Mid Autumn festival arrived and, after the family convivialities were over, Shiyin had a little dinner for two laid out in his study and went in person to invite Yucun, walking to his temple lodgings in the moonlight.

Ever since the day the Zhens' maid had, by looking back twice over her shoulder, convinced him that she was a friend, Yucun had had the girl very much on his mind, and now that it was festival time, the full moon of Mid Autumn lent an inspiration to his romantic impulses which finally resulted in the following octet:

> 'Ere on ambition's path my feet are set,
> Sorrow comes often this poor heart to fret.
> Yet, as my brow contracted with new care,
> Was there not one who, parting, turned to stare?
> Dare I, that grasp at shadows in the wind,
> Hope, underneath the moon, a friend to find?
> Bright orb, if with my plight you sympathize,
> Shine first upon the chamber where she lies.'

Having delivered himself of this masterpiece, Yucun's thoughts began to run on his unrealized ambitions and, after much head-scratching and many heavenward glances accompanied by heavy sighs, he produced the following couplet, reciting it in a loud, ringing voice which caught the ear of Shiyin, who chanced at that moment to be arriving:

> 'The jewel in the casket bides till one shall come to buy.
> The jade pin in the drawer hides, waiting its time to fly.'[8]

Shi-yin smiled. 'You are a man of no mean ambition, Yucun.'

'Oh no!' Yucun smiled back deprecatingly. 'You are too flattering. I was merely reciting at random from the lines of some old poet. But what brings you here, sir?'

'Tonight is Mid Autumn night,'[9] said Shiyin. 'People call it the Festival of Reunion. It occurred to me that you might be feeling rather lonely here in your monkery, so I have arranged for the two of us to take a little wine together in my study. I hope you will not refuse to join me.'

Yucun made no polite pretence of declining. 'Your kindness is more than I deserve,' he said. 'I accept gratefully.' And he accompanied Shiyin back to the study next door.

Soon they had finished their tea. Wine and various choice dishes were brought in and placed on the table, already laid out with cups, plates, and so forth, and

8. Yucun is thinking of the jade hairpin given by a visiting fairy to an early Chinese emperor; the hairpin later turned into a white swallow and flew away into the sky. Metaphors of flying were frequently used to hint at success in the civil service examinations.

9. The fifteenth day of the eighth month, when, according to the lunar calendar, the moon is at its brightest.

the two men took their places and began to drink. At first they were rather slow and ceremonious; but gradually, as the conversation grew more animated, their potations too became more reckless and uninhibited. The sounds of music and singing which could now be heard from every house in the neighbourhood and the full moon which shone with cold brilliance overhead seemed to increase their elation, so that the cups were emptied almost as soon as they touched their lips, and Yucun, who was already a sheet or so in the wind, was seized with an irrepressible excitement to which he presently gave expression in the form of a quatrain, ostensibly on the subject of the moon, but really about the ambition he had hitherto been at some pains to conceal:

'In thrice five nights her perfect O is made,
Whose cold light bathes each marble balustrade.
As her bright wheel starts on its starry ways,
On earth ten thousand heads look up and gaze.'

'Bravo!' said Shiyin loudly. 'I have always insisted that you were a young fellow who would go up in the world, and now, in these verses you have just recited, I see an augury of your ascent. In no time at all we shall see you up among the clouds! This calls for a drink!' And, saying this, he poured Yucun a large cup of wine.

Yucun drained the cup, then, surprisingly, sighed:

'Don't imagine the drink is making me boastful, but I really do believe that if it were just a question of having the sort of qualifications now in demand, I should stand as good a chance as any of getting myself on to the list of candidates. The trouble is that I simply have no means of laying my hands on the money that would be needed for lodgings and travel expenses. The journey to the capital is a long one, and the sort of money I can earn from my copying is not enough—'

'Why ever didn't you say this before?' said Shiyin interrupting him. 'I have long wanted to do something about this, but on all the occasions I have met you previously, the conversation has never got round to this subject, and I haven't liked to broach it for fear of offending you. Well, now we know where we are. I am not a very clever man, but at least I know the right thing to do when I see it. Luckily, the next Triennial is only a few months ahead. You must go to the capital without delay. A spring examination triumph will make you feel that all your studying has been worthwhile. I shall take care of all your expenses. It is the least return I can make for your friendship.' And there and then he instructed his boy to go with all speed and make up a parcel of fifty taels of the best refined silver and two suits of winter clothes.

'The almanac gives the nineteenth as a good day for travelling,' he went on, addressing Yucun again. 'You can set about hiring a boat for the journey straight away. How delightful it will be to meet again next winter when you have distinguished yourself by soaring to the top over all the other candidates!'

Yucun accepted the silver and the clothes with only the most perfunctory word of thanks and without, apparently, giving them a further moment's thought, for he continued to drink and laugh and talk as if nothing had happened. It was well after midnight before they broke up.

After seeing Yucun off, Shiyin went to bed and slept without a break until the sun was high in the sky next morning. When he awoke, his mind was still running on the conversation of the previous night. He thought he would write a couple of introductory letters for Yucun to take with him to the capital, and arrange for him to call on the family of an official he was acquainted with who might be able to put him up; but when he sent a servant to invite him over, the servant brought back word from the temple as follows:

'The monk says that Mr Jia set out for the capital at five o'clock this morning, sir. He says he left a message to pass on to you. He said to tell you, "A scholar should not concern himself with almanacs, but should act as the situation demands," and he said there wasn't time to say good-bye.'

So Shiyin was obliged to let the matter drop.

* * *

FROM **CHAPTER 2**

A daughter of the Jias ends her days in Yangchow City
And Leng Zixing discourses on the Jias of Rongguo House.

* * *

[Yucun] now thought that in order to give the full rural flavour to his outing he would treat himself to a few cups of wine in a little country inn and accordingly directed his steps towards the near-by village. He had scarcely set foot inside the door of the village inn when one of the men drinking at separate tables inside rose up and advanced to meet him with a broad smile.

'Fancy meeting you!'

It was an antique dealer called Leng Zixing whom Yucun had got to know some years previously when he was staying in the capital. Yucun had a great admiration for Zixing as a practical man of business, whilst Zixing for his part was tickled to claim acquaintanceship with a man of Yucun's great learning and culture. On the basis of this mutual admiration the two of them had got on wonderfully well, and Yucun now returned the other's greeting with a pleased smile.

'My dear fellow! How long have you been here? I really had no idea you were in these parts. It was quite an accident that I came here today at all. What an extraordinary coincidence!'

'I went home at the end of last year to spend New Year with the family,' said Zixing. 'On my way back to the capital I thought I would stop off and have a few words with a friend of mine who lives hereabouts, and he very kindly invited me to spend a few days with him. I hadn't got any urgent business waiting for me, so I thought I might as well stay on a bit and leave at the middle of the month. I came out here on my own because my friend has an engagement today. I certainly didn't expect to run into *you* here.'

Zixing conducted Yucun to his table as he spoke and ordered more wine and some fresh dishes to be brought. The two men then proceeded, between leisurely sips of wine, to relate what each had been doing in the years that had elapsed since their last meeting.

Presently Yucun asked Zixing if anything of interest had happened recently in the capital.

'I can't think of anything particularly deserving of mention,' said Zixing. 'Except, perhaps, for a very small but very unusual event that took place in your own clan there.'

'What makes you say that?' said Yucun, 'I have no family connections in the capital.'

'Well, it's the same name,' said Zixing. 'They must be the same clan.'

Yucun asked him what family he could be referring to.

'I fancy you wouldn't disown the Jias of the Rongguo mansion as unworthy of you.'

'Oh, you mean them,' said Yucun. 'There are so many members of my clan, it's hard to keep up with them all. Since the time of Jia Fu of the Eastern Han dynasty there have been branches of the Jia clan in every province of the empire. The Rongguo branch is, as a matter of fact, on the same clan register as my own; but since they are exalted so far above us socially, we don't normally claim the connection, and nowadays we are completely out of touch with them.'

Zixing sighed. 'You shouldn't speak about them in that way, you know. Nowadays both the Rong and Ning mansions are in a greatly reduced state compared with what they used to be.'

'When I was last that way the Rong and Ning mansions both seemed to be fairly humming with life. Surely nothing could have happened to reduce their prosperity in so short a time?'

'Ah, you may well ask. But it's a long story.'

'Last time I was in Jinling,' went on Yucun, 'I passed by their two houses one day on my way to Shitoucheng to visit the ruins. The Ningguo mansion along the eastern half of the road and the Rongguo mansion along the western half must between them have occupied the greater part of the north side frontage of that street. It's true that there wasn't much activity outside the main entrances, but looking up over the outer walls I had a glimpse of the most magnificent and imposing halls and pavilions, and even the rocks and trees of the gardens beyond seemed to have a sleekness and luxuriance that were certainly not suggestive of a family whose fortunes were in a state of decline.'

'Well! For a Palace Graduate Second Class, you ought to know better than that! Haven't you ever heard the old saying, "The beast with a hundred legs is a long time dying"? Although I say they are not as prosperous as they used to be in years past, of course I don't mean to say that there is not still a world of difference between *their* circumstances and those you would expect to find in the household of your average government official. At the moment the numbers of their establishment and the activities they engage in are, if anything, on the increase. Both masters and servants all lead lives of luxury and magnificence. And they still have plenty of plans and projects under way. But they can't bring themselves to economize or make any adjustment in their accustomed style of living. Consequently, though outwardly they still manage to keep up appearances, inwardly they are beginning to feel the pinch. But that's a small matter. There's something much more seriously wrong with them than that. They are not able to turn out good sons, those stately houses, for all their pomp and show. The males in the family get more degenerate from one generation to the next.'

'Surely,' said Yucun with surprise, 'it is inconceivable that such highly cultured households should not give their children the best education possible? I say nothing of other families, but the Jias of the Ning and Rong households used to be famous for the way in which they brought up their sons. How could they come to be as you describe?'

'I assure you, it is precisely those families I am speaking of. Let me tell you something of their history. The Duke of Ningguo and the Duke of Rongguo were two brothers by the same mother. Ningguo was the elder of the two. When he died, his eldest son, Jia Daihua, inherited his post. Daihua had two sons. The elder, Jia Fu, died at the age of eight or nine, leaving only the second son, Jia Jing, to inherit. Nowadays Jia Jing's only interest in life is Taoism. He spends all his time over retorts and crucibles concocting elixirs, and refuses to be bothered with anything else.

'Fortunately he had already provided himself with a son, Jia Zhen, long before he took up this hobby. So, having set his mind on turning himself into an immortal, he has given up his post in favour of this son. And what's more he refuses outright to live at home and spends his time fooling around with a pack of Taoists somewhere outside the city walls.

'This Jia Zhen has got a son of his own, a lad called Jia Rong, just turned sixteen. With old Jia Jing out of the way and refusing to exercise any authority, Jia Zhen has thrown his responsibilities to the winds and given himself up to a life of pleasure. He has turned that Ningguo mansion upside down, but there is no one around who dares gainsay him.

'Now I come to the Rong household—it was there that this strange event occurred that I was telling you about. When the old Duke of Rongguo died, his eldest son, Jia Daishan, inherited his emoluments. He married a girl from a very old Nanking family, the daughter of Marquis Shi, who bore him two sons, Jia She and Jia Zheng.

'Daishan has been dead this many a year, but the old lady is still alive. The elder son, Jia She, inherited; but he's only a very middling sort of person and doesn't play much part in running the family. The second son, though, Jia Zheng, has been mad keen on study ever since he was a lad. He is a very upright sort of person, straight as a die. He was his grandfather's favourite. He would have sat for the examinations, but when the emperor saw Daishan's testamentary memorial that he wrote on his death bed, he was so moved, thinking what a faithful servant the old man had been, that he not only ordered the elder son to inherit his father's position, but also gave instructions that any other sons of his were to be presented to him at once, and on seeing Jia Zheng he gave him the post of Supernumerary Executive Officer, brevet rank, with instructions to continue his studies while on the Ministry's payroll. From there he has now risen to the post of Under Secretary.

'Sir Zheng's lady was formerly a Miss Wang. Her first child was a boy called Jia Zhu. He was already a Licensed Scholar at the age of fourteen. Then he married and had a son. But he died of an illness before he was twenty. The second child she bore him was a little girl, rather remarkable because she was born on New Year's day. Then after an interval of twelve years or more she suddenly had another son. He was even more remarkable, because at the moment of his birth he had a piece of beautiful, clear, coloured jade in his mouth with a lot of writing on it. They gave him the name "Baoyu" as a consequence. Now tell me if you don't think that is an extraordinary thing.'

'It certainly is,' Yucun agreed. 'I should not be at all surprised to find that there was something very unusual in the heredity of that child.'

'Humph,' said Zixing. 'A great many people have said that. That is the reason why his old grandmother thinks him such a treasure. But when they celebrated the First Twelve-month and Sir Zheng tested his disposition by putting a lot of objects in front of him and seeing which he would take hold of, he stretched out his little hand and started playing with some women's things—combs, bracelets, pots of rouge and powder and the like—completely ignoring all the other objects. Sir Zheng was very displeased. He said he would grow up to be a rake, and ever since then he hasn't felt much affection for the child. But to the old lady he's the very apple of her eye.

'But there's more that's unusual about him than that. He's now rising ten and unusually mischievous, yet his mind is as sharp as a needle. You wouldn't find one in a hundred to match him. Some of the childish things he says are most extraordinary. He'll say, "Girls are made of water and boys are made of mud. When I am with girls I feel fresh and clean, but when I am with boys I feel stupid and nasty." Now isn't that priceless! He'll be a lady-killer when he grows up, no question of that.'

Yucun's face assumed an expression of unwonted severity. 'Not so. By no means. It is a pity that none of you seem to understand this child's heredity. Most likely even my esteemed kinsman Sir Jia Zheng is mistaken in treating the boy as a future libertine. This is something that no one but a widely read person, and one moreover well-versed in moral philosophy and in the subtle arcana of metaphysical science could possibly understand.'

Observing the weighty tone in which these words were uttered, Zixing hurriedly asked to be instructed, and Yucun proceeded as follows:

'The generative processes operating in the universe provide the great majority of mankind with natures in which good and evil are commingled in more or less equal proportions. Instances of exceptional goodness and exceptional badness are produced by the operation of beneficent or noxious ethereal influences, of which the former are symptomatized by the equilibrium of society and the latter by its disequilibrium.

'Thus,

> Yao,
> Shun,
> Yu,
> Tang,
> King Wen,
> King Wu,
> the Duke of Zhou,
> the Duke of Shao,
> Confucius,
> Mencius,
> Dong Zhongshu,
> Han Yu,
> Zhou Dunyi,
> the Cheng brothers,
> Zhu Xi and
> Zhang Zai[1]

---

1. List of most virtuous figures in Chinese history, ranging from sage kings and philosophical masters to scholar-officials.

—all instances of exceptional goodness—were born under the influence of benign forces, and all sought to promote the well-being of the societies in which they lived; whilst

> Chi You,
> Gong Gong,
> Jie,
> Zhou,
> the First Qin Emperor,
> Wang Mang,
> Cao Cao,
> Huan Wen,
> An Lushan and
> Qin Kuai[2]

—all instances of exceptional badness—were born under the influence of harmful forces, and all sought to disrupt the societies in which they lived.

'Now,[3] the good cosmic fluid with which the natures of the exceptionally good are compounded is a pure, quintessential humour; whilst the evil fluid which infuses the natures of the exceptionally bad is a cruel, perverse humour.

'Therefore, our age being one in which beneficent ethereal influences are in the ascendant, in which the reigning dynasty is well-established and society both peaceful and prosperous, innumerable instances are to be found, from the palace down to the humblest cottage, of individuals endowed with the pure, quintessential humour.

'Moreover, an unused surplus of this pure, quintessential humour, unable to find corporeal lodgement, circulates freely abroad until it manifests itself in the form of sweet dews and balmy winds, asperged and effused for the enrichment and refreshment of all terrestial life.

'Consequently, the cruel and perverse humours, unable to circulate freely in the air and sunlight, subside, by a process of incrassation and coagulation, into the bottoms of ditches and ravines.

'Now, should these incrassate humours chance to be stirred or provoked by wind or weather into a somewhat more volatile and active condition, it sometimes happens that a stray wisp or errant flocculus may escape from the fissure or concavity in which they are contained; and if some of the pure, quintessential humour should chance to be passing overhead at that same moment, the two will become locked in irreconcilable conflict, the good refusing to yield to the evil, the evil persisting in its hatred of the good. And just as wind, water, thunder and lightning meeting together over the earth can neither dissipate nor yield one to another but produce an explosive shock resulting in the downward emission of rain, so does this clash of humours result in the forcible downward expulsion of the evil humour, which, being thus forced downwards, will find its way into some human creature.

'Such human recipients, whether they be male or female, since they are already amply endowed with the benign humour before the evil humour is injected, are incapable of becoming either greatly good or greatly bad; but place them in the company of ten thousand others and you will find that they

---

2. List of archetypal villains in Chinese history, ranging from rulers, to ministers, to rebels.
3. The translator highlights the particularly dry, scholastic line of argument in these few paragraphs by italicizing the cumbersome connective words.

are superior to all the rest in sharpness and intelligence and inferior to all the rest in perversity, wrongheadedness and eccentricity. Born into a rich or noble household they are likely to become great lovers or the occasion of great love in others; in a poor but well-educated household they will become literary rebels or eccentric aesthetes; even if they are born in the lowest stratum of society they are likely to become great actors or famous *hetaerae*. Under no circumstances will you find them in servile or menial positions, content to be at the beck and call of mediocrities.

'For examples I might cite:

> Xu You,
> Tao Yuanming,
> Ruan Ji,
> Ji Kang,
> Liu Ling,
> the Wang and Xie clans of the Jin period,
> Gu Kaizhi,
> the last ruler of Chen,
> the emperor Minghuang of the Tang dynasty,
> the emperor Huizong of the Song dynasty,
> Liu Tingzhi,
> Wen Tingyun,
> Mi Fei,
> Shi Yannian,
> Liu Yong and
> Qin Guan;

or, from more recent centuries:

> Ni Zan,
> Tang Yin and
> Zhu Yunming;

or again, for examples of the last type:

> Li Guinian,
> Huang Fanchuo,
> Jing Xinmo,
> Zhuo Wenjun,
> Little Red Duster,
> Xue Tao,
> Cui Yingying and
> Morning Cloud.[4]

All of these, though their circumstances differed, were essentially the same.'
'You mean,' Zixing interposed,

> 'Zhang victorious is a hero,
> Zhang beaten is a lousy knave?'

---

4. Lists of eccentric and extraordinary individuals from the Chinese tradition, including figures such as recluses, poets, emperors, painters, and courtesans.

'Precisely so,' said Yucun. 'I should have told you that during the two years after I was cashiered I travelled extensively in every province of the empire and saw quite a few remarkable children in the course of my travels; so that just now when you mentioned this Baoyu I felt pretty certain what type of boy he must be. But one doesn't need to go very far afield for another example. There is one in the Zhen family in Nanking—I am referring to the family of the Zhen who is Imperial Deputy Director-General of the Nanking Secretariat. Perhaps you know who I mean?'

'Who doesn't?' said Zixing. 'There is an old family connection between the Zhen family and the Jias of whom we have just been speaking, and they are still on very close terms with each other. I've done business with them myself for longer than I'd care to mention.'

'Last year when I was in Nanking,' said Yucun, smiling at the recollection, 'I was recommended for the post of tutor in their household. I could tell at a glance, as soon as I got inside the place, that for all the ducal splendour this was a family "though rich yet given to courtesy", in the words of the Sage, and that it was a rare piece of luck to have got a place in it. But when I came to teach my pupil, though he was only at the first year primary stage, he gave me more trouble than an examination candidate.

'He was indeed a comedy. He once said, "I must have two girls to do my lessons with me if I am to remember the words and understand the sense. Otherwise my mind will simply not work." And he would often tell the little pages who waited on him, "The word 'girl' is very precious and very pure. It is much more rare and precious than all the rarest beasts and birds and plants in the world. So it is most extremely important that you should never, never violate it with your coarse mouths and stinking breath. Whenever you need to say it, you should first rinse your mouths out with clean water and scented tea. And if ever I catch you slipping up, I shall have holes drilled through your teeth and lace them up together."

'There was simply no end to his violence and unruliness. Yet as soon as his lessons were over and he went inside to visit the girls of the family, he became a completely different person—all gentleness and calm, and as intelligent and well-bred as you please.

'His father gave him several severe beatings but it made no difference. Whenever the pain became too much for him he would start yelling "Girls! girls!" Afterwards, when the girls in the family got to hear about it, they made fun of him. "Why do you always call to us when you are hurt? I suppose you think we shall come and plead for you to be let off. You ought to be ashamed of yourself!" But you should have heard his answer. He said, "Once when the pain was very bad, I thought that perhaps if I shouted the word 'girls' it might help to ease it. Well," he said, "I just called out once, and the pain really was quite a bit better. So now that I have found this secret remedy, I just keep on shouting 'Girls! girls! girls!' whenever the pain is at its worst." I could not help laughing.

'But because his grandmother doted on him so much, she was always taking the child's part against me and his father. In the end I had to hand in my notice. A boy like that will never be able to keep up the family traditions or listen to the advice of his teachers and friends. The pity of it is, though, that the girls in that family are all exceptionally good.'

'The three at present in the Jia household are also very fine girls,' said Zixing. 'Sir Jia Zheng's eldest girl, Yuanchun, was chosen for her exceptional virtue and cleverness to be a Lady Secretary in the Imperial Palace.[5] The next in age after her and eldest of the three still at home is called Yingchun. She is the daughter of Sir Jia She by one of his secondary wives. After her comes another daughter of Sir Zheng's, also a concubine's child, called Tanchun. The youngest, Xichun, is sister-german to Mr Jia Zhen of the Ningguo mansion. Old Lady Jia is very fond of her granddaughters and keeps them all in her own apartments on the Rongguo side. They all study together, and I have been told that they are doing very well.'

'One of the things I liked about the Zhen family,' said Yucun, 'was their custom of giving the girls the same sort of names as the boys, unlike the majority of families who invariably use fancy words like "*chun*", "*hong*", "*xiang*", "*yu*", and so forth. How comes it that the Jias should have followed the vulgar practice in this respect?'

'They didn't,' said Zixing. 'The eldest girl was called "Yuanchun" because she was in fact born on the first day of spring. The others were given names with "*chun*" in them to match hers. But if you go back a generation, you will find that among the Jias too the girls had names exactly like the boys'.

'I can give you proof. Your present employer's good lady is sister-german to Sir She and Sir Zheng of the Rong household. Her name, before she married, was Jia Min. If you don't believe me, you make a few inquiries when you get home and you'll find it is so.'

Yucun clapped his hands with a laugh. 'Of course! I have often wondered why it is that my pupil Daiyu always pronounces "*min*" as "*mi*" when she is reading and, if she has to write it, always makes the character with one or two strokes missing. Now I understand. No wonder her speech and behaviour are so unlike those of ordinary children! I always supposed that there must have been something remarkable about the mother for her to have produced so remarkable a daughter. Now I know that she was related to the Jias of the Rong household, I am not surprised.

'By the way, I am sorry to say that last month the mother passed away.'

Zixing sighed. 'Fancy her dying so soon! She was the youngest of the three. And the generation before them are all gone, every one. We shall have to see what sort of husbands they manage to find for the younger generation!'

'Yes, indeed,' said Yucun. 'Just now you mentioned that Sir Zheng had this boy with the jade in his mouth and you also mentioned a little grandson left behind by his elder son. What about old Sir She? Surely he must have a son?'

'Since Sir Zheng had the boy with the jade, he has had another son by a concubine,' said Zixing, 'but I couldn't tell you what he's like. So at present he has two sons and one grandson. Of course, we don't know what the future may bring.

'But you were asking about Sir She. Yes, he has a son too, called Jia Lian. He's already a young man in his early twenties. He married his own kin, the niece of his Uncle Zheng's wife, Lady Wang. He's been married now for four or five years. Holds the rank of a Sub-prefect by purchase. He's another member of the family who doesn't find responsibilities congenial. He knows his way around, though, and has a great gift of the gab, so at present he stays at home

---

5. Baoyu's sister became an imperial concubine.

with his Uncle Zheng and helps him manage the family's affairs. However, ever since he married this young lady I mentioned, everyone high and low has joined in praising *her*, and he has been put into the shade rather. She is not only a *very* handsome young woman, she also has a very ready tongue and a very good head—more than a match for most men, I can tell you.'

'You see, I was not mistaken,' said Yucun. 'All these people you and I have been talking about are probably examples of that mixture of good and evil humours I was describing to you.'

'Well, I don't know about that,' said Zixing. 'Instead of sitting here setting other people's accounts to rights, let's have another drink!'

* * *

FROM CHAPTER 3

Lin Ruhai recommends a private tutor to his brother-in-law
And old Lady Jia extends a compassionate welcome to the motherless child

* * *

On the day of her arrival in the capital, Daiyu stepped ashore to find covered chairs from the Rong mansion for her and her women and a cart for the luggage ready, waiting on the quay.

She had often heard her mother say that her Grandmother Jia's home was not like other people's houses. The servants she had been in contact with during the past few days were comparatively low-ranking ones in the domestic hierarchy, yet the food they ate, the clothes they wore, and everything about them was quite out of the ordinary. Daiyu tried to imagine what the people who employed these superior beings must be like. When she arrived at their house she would have to watch every step she took and weigh every word she said, for if she put a foot wrong they would surely laugh her to scorn.

Daiyu got into her chair and was soon carried through the city walls. Peeping through the gauze panel which served as a window, she could see streets and buildings more rich and elegant and throngs of people more lively and numerous than she had ever seen in her life before. After being carried for what seemed a very great length of time, she saw, on the north front of the east-west street through which they were passing, two great stone lions crouched one on each side of a triple gateway whose doors were embellished with animal-heads. In front of the gateway ten or so splendidly dressed flunkeys sat in a row. The centre of the three gates was closed, but people were going in and out of the two side ones. There was a board above the centre gate on which were written in large characters the words:

NINGGUO HOUSE

Founded and Constructed by
Imperial Command

Daiyu realized that this must be where the elder branch of her grandmother's family lived. The chair proceeded some distance more down the street and presently there was another triple gate, this time with the legend

RONGGUO HOUSE

above it.

Ignoring the central gate, her bearers went in by the western entrance and after traversing the distance of a bow-shot inside, half turned a corner and set the chair down. The chairs of her female attendants which were following behind were set down simultaneously and the old women got out. The places of Daiyu's bearers were taken by four handsome, fresh-faced pages of seventeen or eighteen. They shouldered her chair and, with the old women now following on foot, carried it as far as an ornamental inner gate. There they set it down again and then retired in respectful silence. The old women came forward to the front of the chair, held up the curtain, and helped Daiyu to get out.

Each hand resting on the outstretched hand of an elderly attendant, Daiyu passed through the ornamental gate into a courtyard which had balustraded loggias running along its sides and a covered passage-way through the centre. The foreground of the courtyard beyond was partially hidden by a screen of polished marble set in an elaborate red sandalwood frame. Passing round the screen and through a small reception hall beyond it, they entered the large courtyard of the mansion's principal apartments. These were housed in an imposing five-frame building resplendent with carved and painted beams and rafters which faced them across the courtyard. Running along either side of the courtyard were galleries hung with cages containing a variety of different-coloured parrots, cockatoos, white-eyes, and other birds. Some gaily-dressed maids were sitting on the steps of the main building opposite. At the appearance of the visitors they rose to their feet and came forward with smiling faces to welcome them.

'You've come just at the right time! Lady Jia[1] was only this moment asking about you.'

Three or four of them ran to lift up the door-curtain, while another of them announced in loud tones,

'Miss Lin is here!'

As Daiyu entered the room she saw a silver-haired old lady advancing to meet her, supported on either side by a servant. She knew that this must be her Grandmother Jia and would have fallen on her knees and made her kotow, but before she could do so her grandmother had caught her in her arms and pressing her to her bosom with cries of 'My pet!' and 'My poor lamb!' burst into loud sobs, while all those present wept in sympathy, and Daiyu felt herself crying as though she would never stop. It was some time before those present succeeded in calming them both down and Daiyu was at last able to make her kotow.

Grandmother Jia now introduced those present.

'This is your elder uncle's wife, Aunt Xing. This is your Uncle Zheng's wife, Aunt Wang. This is Li Wan, the wife of your Cousin Zhu, who died.'

Daiyu kotowed to each of them in turn.

'Call the girls!' said Grandmother Jia. 'Tell them that we have a very special visitor and that they need not do their lessons today.'

There was a cry of 'Yes ma'am' from the assembled maids, and two of them went off to do her bidding.

Presently three girls arrived, attended by three nurses and five or six maids.

1. Baoyu's grandmother.

The first girl was of medium height and slightly plumpish, with cheeks as white and firm as a fresh lychee and a nose as white and shiny as soap made from the whitest goose-fat. She had a gentle, sweet, reserved manner. To look at her was to love her.

The second girl was rather tall, with sloping shoulders and a slender waist. She had an oval face under whose well-formed brows large, expressive eyes shot out glances that sparkled with animation. To look at her was to forget all that was mean or vulgar.

The third girl was undersized and her looks were still somewhat babyish and unformed.

All three were dressed in identical skirts and dresses and wore identical sets of bracelets and hair ornaments.

Daiyu rose to meet them and exchanged curtseys and introductions. When she was seated once more, a maid served tea, and a conversation began on the subject of her mother: how her illness had started, what doctors had been called in, what medicines prescribed, what arrangements had been made for the funeral, and how the mourning had been observed. This conversation had the foreseeable effect of upsetting the old lady all over again.

'Of all my girls your mother was the one I loved the best,' she said, 'and now she's been the first to go, and without my even being able to see her again before the end. I can't help being upset!' And holding fast to Daiyu's hand, she once more burst into tears. The rest of the company did their best to comfort her, until at last she had more or less recovered.

Everyone's attention now centred on Daiyu. They observed that although she was still young, her speech and manner already showed unusual refinement. They also noticed the frail body which seemed scarcely strong enough to bear the weight of its clothes, but which yet had an inexpressible grace about it, and realizing that she must be suffering from some deficiency, asked her what medicine she took for it and why it was still not better.

'I have always been like this,' said Daiyu. 'I have been taking medicine ever since I could eat and been looked at by ever so many well-known doctors, but it has never done me any good. Once, when I was only three, I can remember a scabby-headed old monk came and said he wanted to take me away and have me brought up as a nun; but of course, Mother and Father wouldn't hear of it. So he said, "Since you are not prepared to give her up, I am afraid her illness will never get better as long as she lives. The only way it might get better would be if she were never to hear the sound of weeping from this day onwards and never to see any relations other than her own mother and father. Only in those conditions could she get through her life without trouble." Of course, he was quite crazy, and no one took any notice of the things he said. I'm still taking Ginseng Tonic Pills.'

'Well, that's handy,' said Grandmother Jia. 'I take the Pills myself. We can easily tell them to make up a few more each time.'

She had scarcely finished speaking when someone could be heard talking and laughing in a very loud voice in the inner courtyard behind them.

'Oh dear! I'm late,' said the voice. 'I've missed the arrival of our guest.'

'Everyone else around here seems to go about with bated breath,' thought Daiyu. 'Who can this new arrival be who is so brash and unmannerly?'

Even as she wondered, a beautiful young woman entered from the room behind the one they were sitting in, surrounded by a bevy of serving women and maids. She was dressed quite differently from the others present, gleaming like some fairy princess with sparkling jewels and gay embroideries.

Her chignon was enclosed in a circlet of gold filigree and clustered pearls. It was fastened with a pin embellished with flying phoenixes, from whose beaks pearls were suspended on tiny chains.

Her necklet was of red gold in the form of a coiling dragon.

Her dress had a fitted bodice and was made of dark red silk damask with a pattern of flowers and butterflies in raised gold thread.

Her jacket was lined with ermine. It was of a slate-blue stuff with woven insets in coloured silks.

Her under-skirt was of a turquoise-coloured imported silk crêpe embroidered with flowers.

She had, moreover,

> eyes like a painted phoenix,
> eyebrows like willow-leaves,
> a slender form,
> seductive grace;
> the ever-smiling summer face
> of hidden thunders showed no trace;
> the ever-bubbling laughter started
> almost before the lips were parted.

'You don't know her,' said Grandmother Jia merrily. 'She's a holy terror this one. What we used to call in Nanking a "peppercorn". You just call her "Peppercorn Feng".[2] She'll know who you mean!'

Daiyu was at a loss to know how she was to address this Peppercorn Feng until one of the cousins whispered that it was 'Cousin Lian's wife', and she remembered having heard her mother say that her elder uncle, Uncle She, had a son called Jia Lian who was married to the niece of her Uncle Zheng's wife, Lady Wang. She had been brought up from earliest childhood just like a boy, and had acquired in the schoolroom the somewhat boyish-sounding name of Wang Xifeng. Daiyu accordingly smiled and curtseyed, greeting her by her correct name as she did so.

Xifeng took Daiyu by the hand and for a few moments scrutinized her carefully from top to toe before conducting her back to her seat beside Grandmother Jia.

'She's a beauty, Grannie dear! If I hadn't set eyes on her today, I shouldn't have believed that such a beautiful creature could exist! And everything about her so *distingué*! She doesn't take after your side of the family, Grannie. She's more like a Jia. I don't blame you for having gone on so about her during the past few days—but poor little thing! What a cruel fate to have lost Auntie like that!' and she dabbed at her eyes with a handkerchief.

'I've only just recovered,' laughed Grandmother Jia. 'Don't you go trying to start me off again! Besides, your little cousin is not very strong, and we've only just managed to get *her* cheered up. So let's have no more of this!'

In obedience to the command Xifeng at once exchanged her grief for merriment.

2. Nickname for Wang Xifeng.

'Yes, of course. It was just that seeing my little cousin here put everything else out of my mind. It made me want to laugh and cry all at the same time. I'm afraid I quite forgot about you, Grannie dear. I deserve to be spanked, don't I?'

She grabbed Daiyu by the hand.

'How old are you dear? Have you begun school yet? You musn't feel home-sick here. If there's anything you want to eat or anything you want to play with, just come and tell me. And you must tell me if any of the maids or the old nan-nies are nasty to you.'

Daiyu made appropriate responses to all of these questions and injunctions.

Xifeng turned to the servants.

'Have Miss Lin's things been brought in yet? How many people did she bring with her? You'd better hurry up and get a couple of rooms swept out for them to rest in.'

While Xifeng was speaking, the servants brought in tea and various plates of food, the distribution of which she proceeded to supervise in person.

Daiyu noticed her Aunt Wang questioning Xifeng on the side:

'Have this month's allowances been paid out yet?'

'Yes. By the way, just now I went with some of the women to the upstairs store-room at the back to look for that satin. We looked and looked, but we couldn't find any like the one you described yesterday. Perhaps you misremembered.'

'Oh well, if you can't find it, it doesn't really matter,' said Lady Wang. Then, after a moment's reflection, 'You'd better pick out a couple of lengths presently to have made up into clothes for your little cousin here. If you think of it, send someone round in the evening to fetch them!'

'It's already been seen to. I knew she was going to arrive within a day or two, so I had some brought out in readiness. They are waiting back at your place for your approval. If you think they are all right, they can be sent over straight away.'

Lady Wang merely smiled and nodded her head without saying anything.

The tea things and dishes were now cleared away, and Grandmother Jia ordered two old nurses to take Daiyu round to see her uncles; but Uncle She's wife, Lady Xing, hurriedly rose to her feet and suggested that it would be more convenient if she were to take her niece round herself.

'Very well,' said Grandmother Jia. 'You go now, then. There is no need for you to come back afterwards.'

So having, together with Lady Wang, who was also returning to her quarters, taken leave of the old lady, Lady Xing went off with Daiyu, attended across the courtyard as far as the covered way by the rest of the company.

A carriage painted dark blue and hung with kingfisher-blue curtains had been drawn up in front of the ornamental gateway by some pages. Into this Aunt Xing ascended hand in hand with Daiyu. The old women pulled down the carriage blind and ordered the pages to take up the shafts, the pages drew the carriage into an open space and harnessed mules to it, and Daiyu and her aunt were driven out of the west gate, eastwards past the main gate of the Rong mansion, in again through a big black-lacquered gate, and up to an inner gate, where they were set down again.

Holding Daiyu by the hand, Aunt Xing led her into a courtyard in the middle of what she imagined must once have been part of the mansion's gardens. This impression was strengthened when they passed through a third gateway into the quarters occupied by her uncle and aunt; for here the smaller scale and quiet elegance of the halls, galleries and loggias were quite unlike the heavy magnificence and imposing grandeur they had just come from, and ornamental trees and artificial rock formations, all in exquisite taste, were to be seen on every hand.

As they entered the main reception hall, a number of heavily made-up and expensively dressed maids and concubines, who had been waiting in readiness, came forward to greet them.

Aunt Xing asked Daiyu to be seated while she sent a servant to call Uncle She. After a considerable wait the servant returned with the following message:

'The Master says he hasn't been well these last few days, and as it would only upset them both if he were to see Miss Lin now, he doesn't feel up to it for the time being. He says, tell Miss Lin not to grieve and not to feel homesick. She must think of her grandmother and her aunts as her own family now. He says that her cousins may not be very clever girls, but at least they should be company for her and help to take her mind off things. If she finds anything at all here to distress her, she is to speak up at once. She mustn't feel like an outsider. She is to make herself completely at home.'

Daiyu stood up throughout this recital and murmured polite assent whenever assent seemed indicated. She then sat for about another quarter of an hour before rising to take her leave. Her Aunt Xing was very pressing that she should have a meal with her before she went, but Daiyu smilingly replied that though it was very kind of her aunt to offer, and though she ought really not to refuse, nevertheless she still had to pay her respects to her Uncle Zheng, and feared that it would be disrespectful if she were to arrive late. She hoped that she might accept on another occasion and begged her aunt to excuse her.

'In that case, never mind,' said Lady Xing, and instructed the old nurses to see her to her Uncle Zheng's in the same carriage she had come by. Daiyu formally took her leave, and Lady Xing saw her as far as the inner gate, where she issued a few more instructions to the servants and watched her niece's carriage out of sight before returning to her rooms.

Presently they re-entered the Rong mansion proper and Daiyu got down from the carriage. There was a raised stone walk running all the way up to the main gate, along which the old nurses now conducted her. Turning right, they led her down a roofed passage-way along the back of a south-facing hall, then through an inner gate into a large courtyard.

The big building at the head of the courtyard was connected at each end to galleries running through the length of the side buildings by means of 'stag's head' roofing over the corners. The whole formed an architectural unit of greater sumptuousness and magnificence than anything Daiyu had yet seen that day, from which she concluded that this must be the main inner hall of the whole mansion.

High overhead on the wall facing her as she entered the hall was a great blue board framed in gilded dragons, on which was written in large gold characters

THE HALL OF EXALTED FELICITY

with a column of smaller characters at the side giving a date and the words '. . . written for Our beloved Subject, Jia Yuan, Duke of Rongguo', followed by the

Emperor's private seal, a device containing the words 'kingly cares' and 'royal brush' in archaic seal-script.

A long, high table of carved red sandalwood, ornamented with dragons, stood against the wall underneath. In the centre of this was a huge antique bronze *ding*, fully a yard high, covered with a green patina. On the wall above the *ding* hung a long vertical scroll with an ink-painting of a dragon emerging from clouds and waves, of the kind often presented to high court officials in token of their office. The *ding* was flanked on one side by a smaller antique bronze vessel with a pattern of gold inlay and on the other by a crystal bowl. At each side of the table stood a row of eight yellow cedar-wood armchairs with their backs to the wall; and above the chairs hung, one on each side, a pair of vertical ebony boards inlaid with a couplet in characters of gold:

(on the right-hand one)

May the jewel of learning shine in this house more effulgently than the sun and
    moon.

(on the left-hand one)

May the insignia of honour glitter in these halls more brilliantly than the
    starry sky.

This was followed by a colophon in smaller characters:

With the Respectful Compliments of your Fellow-
Student, Mu Shi, Hereditary Prince of Dongan.

Lady Wang did not, however, normally spend her leisure hours in this main reception hall, but in a smaller room on the east side of the same building. Accordingly the nurses conducted Daiyu through the door into this side apartment.

Here there was a large kang[3] underneath the window, covered with a scarlet Kashmir rug. In the middle of the kang was a dark-red bolster with a pattern of medallions in the form of tiny dragons, and a long russet-green seating strip in the same pattern. A low rose-shaped table of coloured lacquer-work stood at each side. On the left-hand one was a small, square, four-legged *ding*, together with a bronze ladle, metal chopsticks, and an incense container. On the right-hand one was a narrow-waisted Ru-ware imitation *gu*[4] with a spray of freshly cut flowers in it.

In the part of the room below the kang there was a row of four big chairs against the east wall. All had footstools in front of them and chair-backs and seat-covers in old rose brocade sprigged with flowers. There were also narrow side-tables on which tea things and vases of flowers were arranged, besides other furnishings which it would be superfluous to enumerate.

The old nurses invited Daiyu to get up on the kang; but guessing that the brocade cushions arranged one on each side near the edge of it must be her uncle's and aunt's places, she deemed it more proper to sit on one of the chairs against the wall below. The maids in charge of the apartment served tea, and as she sipped it Daiyu observed that their clothing, makeup, and deportment were

---

3. A heated bed-stove.   4. *Ding* and *gu* are vessel types.

quite different from those of the maids she had seen so far in other parts of the mansion.

Before she had time to finish her tea, a smiling maid came in wearing a dress of red damask and a black silk sleeveless jacket which had scalloped borders of some coloured material.

'The Mistress says will Miss Lin come over to the other side, please.'

The old nurses now led Daiyu down the east gallery to a reception room at the side of the courtyard. This too had a kang. It was bisected by a long, low table piled with books and tea things. A much-used black satin back-rest was pushed up against the east wall. Lady Wang was seated on a black satin cushion and leaning against another comfortable-looking back-rest of black satin somewhat farther forward on the opposite side.

Seeing her niece enter, she motioned her to sit opposite her on the kang, but Daiyu felt sure that this must be her Uncle Zheng's place. So, having observed a row of three chairs near the kang with covers of flower-sprigged brocade which looked as though they were in fairly constant use, she sat upon one of those instead. Only after much further pressing from her aunt would she get up on the kang, and even then she would only sit beside her and not in the position of honour opposite.

'Your uncle is in retreat today,' said Lady Wang. 'He will see you another time. There is, however, something I have got to talk to you about. The three girls are very well-behaved children, and in future, when you are studying or sewing together, even if once in a while they may grow a bit high-spirited, I can depend on them not to go too far. There is only one thing that worries me. I have a little monster of a son who tyrannizes over all the rest of this household. He has gone off to the temple today in fulfilment of a vow and is not yet back; but you will see what I mean this evening. The thing to do is never to take any notice of him. None of your cousins dare provoke him.'

Daiyu had long ago been told by her mother that she had a boy cousin who was born with a piece of jade in his mouth and who was exceptionally wild and naughty. He hated study and liked to spend all his time in the women's apartments with the girls; but because Grandmother Jia doted on him so much, no one ever dared to correct him. She realized that it must be this cousin her aunt was now referring to.

'Do you mean the boy born with the jade, Aunt?' she asked. 'Mother often told me about him at home. She told me that he was one year older than me and that his name was Baoyu. But she said that though he was very wilful, he always behaved very nicely to girls. Now that I am here, I suppose I shall be spending all my time with my girl cousins and not in the same part of the house as the boys. Surely there will be no danger of *my* provoking him?'

Lady Wang gave a rueful smile. 'You little know how things are here! Baoyu is a law unto himself. Because your grandmother is so fond of him she has thoroughly spoiled him. When he was little he lived with the girls, so with the girls he remains now. As long as they take no notice of him, things run quietly enough. But if they give him the least encouragement, he at once becomes excitable, and then there is no end to the mischief he may get up to. That is why I counsel you to ignore him. He can be all honey-sweet words one minute and ranting and raving like a lunatic the next. So don't believe anything he says.'

Daiyu promised to follow her aunt's advice.

Just then a maid came in with a message that 'Lady Jia said it was time for dinner', whereupon Lady Wang took Daiyu by the hand and hurried her out through a back door. Passing along a verandah which ran beneath the rear eaves of the hall they came to a corner gate through which they passed into an alley-way running north and south. At the south end it was traversed by a narrow little building with a short passage-way running through its middle. At the north end was a white-painted screen wall masking a medium-sized gateway leading to a small courtyard in which stood a very little house.

'That,' said Lady Wang, pointing to the little house, 'is where your Cousin Lian's wife, Wang Xifeng, lives, in case you want to see her later on. She is the person to talk to if there is anything you need.'

There were a few young pages at the gate of the courtyard who, when they saw Lady Wang coming, all stood to attention with their hands at their sides.

Lady Wang now led Daiyu along a gallery, running from east to west, which brought them out into the courtyard behind Grandmother Jia's apartments. Entering these by a back entrance, they found a number of servants waiting there who, as soon as they saw Lady Wang, began to arrange the table and chairs for dinner. The ladies of the house themselves took part in the service. Li Wan brought in the cups, Xifeng laid out the chopsticks, and Lady Wang brought in the soup.

The table at which Grandmother Jia presided, seated alone on a couch, had two empty chairs on either side. Xifeng tried to seat Daiyu in the one on the left nearer to her grandmother—an honour which she strenuously resisted until her grandmother explained that her aunt and her elder cousins' wives would not be eating with them, so that, since she was a guest, the place was properly hers. Only then did she ask permission to sit, as etiquette prescribed. Grandmother Jia then ordered Lady Wang to be seated. This was the cue for the three girls to ask permission to sit. Yingchun sat in the first place on the right opposite Daiyu, Tanchun sat second on the left, and Xichun sat second on the right.

While Li Wan and Xifeng stood by the table helping to distribute food from the dishes, maids holding fly-whisks, spittoons, and napkins ranged themselves on either side. In addition to these, there were numerous other maids and serving-women in attendance in the outer room, yet not so much as a cough was heard throughout the whole of the meal.

When they had finished eating, a maid served each diner with tea on a little tray. Daiyu's parents had brought their daughter up to believe that good health was founded on careful habits, and in pursuance of this principle, had always insisted that after a meal one should allow a certain interval to elapse before taking tea in order to avoid indigestion. However, she could see that many of the rules in this household were different from the ones she had been used to at home; so, being anxious to conform as much as possible, she accepted the tea. But as she did so, another maid proferred a spittoon, from which she inferred that the tea was for rinsing her mouth with. And it was not, in fact, until they had all rinsed out their mouths and washed their hands that another lot of tea was served, this time for drinking.

Grandmother Jia now dismissed her lady servers, observing that she wished to enjoy a little chat with her young grandchildren without the restraint of their grown-up presence.

Lady Wang obediently rose to her feet and, after exchanging a few pleasantries, went out, taking Li Wan and Wang Xifeng with her.

Grandmother Jia asked Daiyu what books she was studying.

'The Four Books,'[5] said Daiyu, and inquired in turn what books her cousins were currently engaged on.

'Gracious, child, they don't study books,' said her grandmother; 'they can barely read and write!'

While they were speaking, a flurry of footsteps could be heard outside and a maid came in to say that Baoyu was back.

'I wonder,' thought Daiyu, 'just what sort of graceless creature this Baoyu is going to be!'

The young gentleman who entered in answer to her unspoken question had a small jewel-encrusted gold coronet on the top of his head and a golden headband low down over his brow in the form of two dragons playing with a large pearl.

He was wearing a narrow-sleeved, full-skirted robe of dark red material with a pattern of flowers and butterflies in two shades of gold. It was confined at the waist with a court girdle of coloured silks braided at regular intervals into elaborate clusters of knotwork and terminating in long tassels.

Over the upper part of his robe he wore a jacket of slate-blue Japanese silk damask with a raised pattern of eight large medallions on the front and with tasselled borders.

On his feet he had half-length dress boots of black satin with thick white soles.

As to his person, he had:
a face like the moon of Mid-Autumn,
a complexion like flowers at dawn,
a hairline straight as a knife-cut,
eyebrows that might have been painted by an artist's brush,
a shapely nose, and
eyes clear as limpid pools,
   that even in anger seemed to smile,
   and, as they glared, beamed tenderness the while.

Around his neck he wore a golden torque in the likeness of a dragon and a woven cord of coloured silks to which the famous jade was attached.

Daiyu looked at him with astonishment. How strange! How very strange! It was as though she had seen him somewhere before, he was so extraordinarily familiar. Baoyu went straight past her and saluted his grandmother, who told him to come after he had seen his mother, whereupon he turned round and walked straight out again.

Quite soon he was back once more, this time dressed in a completely different outfit.

The crown and circlet had gone. She could now see that his side hair was dressed in a number of small braids plaited with red silk, which were drawn round to join the long hair at the back in a single large queue of glistening jet black, fastened at intervals from the nape downwards with four enormous pearls and ending in a jewelled gold clasp. He had changed his robe and jacket for a rather more worn-looking rose-coloured gown, sprigged with flowers. He

---

5. The Neoconfucian canon: *Analects, Mencius, Doctrine of the Mean,* and *The Great Learning.*

wore the gold torque and his jade as before, and she observed that the collection of objects round his neck had been further augmented by a padlock-shaped amulet and a lucky charm. A pair of ivy-coloured embroidered silk trousers were partially visible beneath his gown, thrust into black and white socks trimmed with brocade. In place of the formal boots he was wearing thick-soled crimson slippers.

She was even more struck than before by his fresh complexion. The cheeks might have been brushed with powder and the lips touched with rouge, so bright was their natural colour.

> His glance was soulful,
> yet from his lips the laughter often leaped;
>   a world of charm upon that brow was heaped;
>   a world of feeling from those dark eyes peeped.

In short, his outward appearance was very fine. But appearances can be misleading. A perceptive poet has supplied two sets of verses, to be sung to the tune of *Moon On West River*, which contain a more accurate appraisal of our hero than the foregoing descriptions.

I

> Oft-times he sought out what would make him sad;
> Sometimes an idiot seemed and sometimes mad.
> Though outwardly a handsome sausage-skin,
> He proved to have but sorry meat within.
> A harum-scarum, to all duty blind,
> A doltish mule, to study disinclined;
> His acts outlandish and his nature queer;
> Yet not a whit cared he how folk might jeer!

2

> Prosperous, he could not play his part with grace,
> Nor, poor, bear hardship with a smiling face.
> So shamefully the precious hours he'd waste
> That both indoors and out he was disgraced.
> For uselessness the world's prize he might bear;
> His gracelessness in history has no peer.
> Let gilded youths who every dainty sample
> Not imitate this rascal's dire example!

'Fancy changing your clothes before you have welcomed the visitor!' Grandmother Jia chided indulgently on seeing Baoyu back again. 'Aren't you going to pay your respects to your cousin?'

Baoyu had already caught sight of a slender, delicate girl whom he surmised to be his Aunt Lin's daughter and quickly went over to greet her. Then, returning to his place and taking a seat, he studied her attentively. How different she seemed from the other girls he knew!

> Her mist-wreathed brows at first seemed to frown, yet were
>   not frowning;

Her passionate eyes at first seemed to smile, yet were not
  merry.
Habit had given a melancholy cast to her tender face;
Nature had bestowed a sickly constitution on her delicate
  frame.
Often the eyes swam with glistening tears;
Often the breath came in gentle gasps.
In stillness she made one think of a graceful flower reflected
  in the water;
In motion she called to mind tender willow shoots caressed by
  the wind.
She had more chambers in her heart than the martyred Bi Gan;
And suffered a tithe more pain in it than the beautiful Xi Shi.[6]

Having completed his survey, Baoyu gave a laugh.

'I have seen this cousin before.'

'Nonsense!' said Grandmother Jia. 'How could you possibly have done?'

'Well, perhaps not,' said Baoyu, 'but her face seems so familiar that I have the impression of meeting her again after a long separation.'

'All the better,' said Grandmother Jia. 'That means that you should get on well together.'

Baoyu moved over again and, drawing a chair up beside Daiyu, recommenced his scrutiny.

Presently: 'Do you study books yet, cousin?'

'No,' said Daiyu. 'I have only been taking lessons for a year or so. I can barely read and write.'

'What's your name?'

Daiyu told him.

'What's your school-name?'

'I haven't got one.'

Baoyu laughed. 'I'll give you one, cousin. I think "Frowner" would suit you perfectly.'

'Where's your reference?' said Tanchun.

'In the *Encyclopedia of Men and Objects Ancient and Modern* it says that somewhere in the West there is a mineral called "dai" which can be used instead of eye-black for painting the eyebrows with. She has this "dai" in her name and she knits her brows together in a little frown. I think it's a splendid name for her!'

'I expect you made it up,' said Tanchun scornfully.

'What if I did?' said Baoyu. 'There are lots of made-up things in books—apart from the *Four Books*, of course.'

He returned to his interrogation of Daiyu.

'Have you got a jade?'

The rest of the company were puzzled, but Daiyu at once divined that he was asking her if she too had a jade like the one he was born with.

---

6. A famous beauty from early China known for a slight frown. "More chambers . . . Bi Gan": When Bi Gan tried to restrain the behavior of the last tyrannical ruler of the Shang Dynasty (ca. 1500–1045 B.C.E.), the ruler retorted that he had heard that a sage had a heart with seven openings and that he would have to tear his heart out to ascertain this truth.

'No,' said Daiyu. 'That jade of yours is a very rare object. You can't expect everybody to have one.'

This sent Baoyu off instantly into one of his mad fits. Snatching the jade from his neck he hurled it violently on the floor as if to smash it and began abusing it passionately.

'Rare object! Rare object! What's so lucky about a stone that can't even tell which people are better than others? Beastly thing! I don't want it!'

The maids all seemed terrified and rushed forward to pick it up, while Grandmother Jia clung to Baoyu in alarm.

'Naughty, naughty boy! Shout at someone or strike them if you like when you are in a nasty temper, but why go smashing that precious thing that your very life depends on?'

'None of the girls has got one,' said Baoyu, his face streaming with tears and sobbing hysterically. 'Only I have got one. It always upsets me. And now this new cousin comes here who is as beautiful as an angel and she hasn't got one either, so I *know* it can't be any good.'

'Your cousin did have a jade once,' said Grandmother Jia, coaxing him like a little child, 'but because when Auntie died she couldn't bear to leave her little girl behind, they had to let her take the jade with her instead. In that way your cousin could show her mamma how much she loved her by letting the jade be buried with her; and at the same time, whenever Auntie's spirit looked at the jade, it would be just like looking at her own little girl again.

'So when your cousin said she hadn't got one, it was only because she didn't want to boast about the good, kind thing she did when she gave it to her mamma. Now you put yours on again like a good boy, and mind your mother doesn't find out how naughty you have been.'

So saying, she took the jade from the hands of one of the maids and hung it round his neck for him. And Baoyu, after reflecting for a moment or two on what she had said, offered no further resistance.

* * *

FROM CHAPTER 17

The inspection of the new garden becomes a test of talent
And Rongguo House makes itself ready for an important visitor

* * *

One day Cousin Zhen came to Jia Zheng with his team of helpers to report that work on the new garden had been completed.

'Uncle She has already had a look,' said Cousin Zhen. 'Now we are only waiting for you to look round it to tell us if there is anything you think will need altering and also to decide what inscriptions ought to be used on the boards everywhere.'

Jia Zheng reflected a while in silence.

'These inscriptions are going to be difficult,' he said eventually. 'By rights, of course, Her Grace should have the privilege of doing them herself; but she can scarcely be expected to make them up out of her head without having seen any of the views which they are to describe. On the other hand, if we wait until she has already visited the garden before asking her, half the pleasure of the visit will be lost. All those prospects and pavilions—even the rocks and trees and flowers will seem somehow incomplete without that touch of poetry which only the written word can lend a scene.'

'My dear patron, you are so right,' said one of the literary gentlemen who sat with him. 'But we have had an idea. The inscriptions for the various parts of the garden obviously cannot be dispensed with; nor, equally obviously, can they be decided in advance. Our suggestion is that we should compose provisional names and couplets to suit the places where inscriptions are required, and have them painted on rectangular paper lanterns which can be hung up temporarily—either horizontally or vertically as the case may be—when Her Grace comes to visit. We can ask her to decide on the permanent names after she has inspected the garden. Is not this a solution of the dilemma?'

'It is indeed,' said Jia Zheng. 'When we look round the garden presently, we must all try to think of words that can be used. If they seem suitable, we can keep them for the lanterns. If not, we can call for Yucun to come and help us out.'

'Your own suggestions are sure to be admirable, Sir Zheng,' said the literary gentlemen ingratiatingly. 'There will be no need to call in Yucun.'

Jia Zheng smiled deprecatingly.

'I am afraid it is not as you imagine. In my youth I had at best only indifferent skill in the art of writing verses about natural objects—birds and flowers and scenery and the like; and now that I am older and have to devote all my energies to official documents and government papers, I am even more out of touch with this sort of thing than I was then; so that even if I were to try my hand at it, I fear that my efforts would be rather dull and pedantic ones. Instead of enhancing the interest and beauty of the garden, they would probably have a deadening effect upon both.'

'That doesn't matter,' the literary gentlemen replied. 'We can *all* try our hands at composing. If each of us contributes what he is best at, and if we then select the better attempts and reject the ones that are not so good, we should be able to manage all right.'

'That seems to me a very good suggestion,' said Jia Zheng. 'As the weather today is so warm and pleasant, let us all go and take a turn round the garden now!'

So saying he rose to his feet and conducted his little retinue of literary luminaries towards the garden. Cousin Zhen hurried on ahead to warn those in charge that they were coming.

As Baoyu was still in very low spirits these days because of his grief for Qin Zhong, Grandmother Jia had hit on the idea of sending him into the newly made garden to play. By unlucky chance she had selected this very day on which to try out her antidote. He had in fact only just entered the garden when Cousin Zhen came hurrying towards him.

'Better get out of here!' said Cousin Zhen with an amused smile. 'Your father will be here directly!'

Baoyu streaked back towards the gate, a string of nurses and pages hurrying at his heels. But he had only just turned the corner on coming out of it when he almost ran into the arms of Jia Zheng and his party coming from the opposite direction. Escape was impossible. He simply had to stand meekly to one side and await instructions.

Jia Zheng had recently received a favourable report on Baoyu from his teacher Jia Dairu in which mention had been made of his skill in composing couplets. Although the boy showed no aptitude for serious study, Dairu had said, he nevertheless possessed a certain meretricious talent for versification not undeserving of commendation. Because of this report, Jia Zheng ordered Baoyu to accompany him into the garden, intending to put his aptitude to the test. Baoyu, who knew nothing either of Dairu's report or of his father's intentions, followed with trepidation.

As soon as they reached the gate they found Cousin Zhen at the head of a group of overseers waiting to learn Jia Zheng's wishes.

'I want you to close the gate,' said Jia Zheng, 'so that we can see what it looks like from outside before we go in.'

Cousin Zhen ordered the gate to be closed, and Jia Zheng stood back and studied it gravely.

It was a five-frame gate-building with a hump-backed roof of half-cylinder tiles. The wooden lattice-work of the doors and windows was finely carved and ingeniously patterned. The whole gatehouse was quite unadorned by colour or gilding, yet all was of the most exquisite workmanship. Its walls stood on a terrace of white marble carved with a pattern of passion-flowers in relief, and the garden's whitewashed circumference wall to left and right of it had a footing made of black-and-white striped stone blocks arranged so that the stripes formed a simple pattern. Jia Zheng found the unostentatious simplicity of this entrance greatly to his liking, and after ordering the gates to be opened, passed on inside.

A cry of admiration escaped them as they entered, for there, immediately in front of them, screening everything else from their view, rose a steep, verdure-clad hill.

'Without this hill,' Jia Zheng somewhat otiosely observed, 'the whole garden would be visible as one entered, and all its mystery would be lost.'

The literary gentlemen concurred. 'Only a master of the art of landscape could have conceived so bold a stroke,' said one of them.

As they gazed at this miniature mountain, they observed a great number of large white rocks in all kinds of grotesque and monstrous shapes, rising course above course up one of its sides, some recumbent, some upright or leaning at angles, their surfaces streaked and spotted with moss and lichen or half concealed by creepers, and with a narrow, zig-zag path only barely discernible to the eye winding up between them.

'Let us begin our tour by following this path,' said Jia Zheng. 'If we work our way round towards the other side of the hill on our way back, we shall have made a complete circuit of the garden.'

He ordered Cousin Zhen to lead the way, and leaning on Baoyu's shoulder, began the winding ascent of the little mountain. Suddenly on the mountain-side above his head, he noticed a white rock whose surface had been polished to mirror smoothness and realized that this must be one of the places which had been prepared for an inscription.

'Aha, gentlemen!' said Jia Zheng, turning back to address the others who were climbing up behind him. 'What name are we going to choose for this mountain?'

'Emerald Heights,' said one.

'Embroidery Hill,' said another.

Another proposed that they should call it 'Little Censer' after the famous Censer Peak in Kiangsi. Another proposed 'Little Zhongnan'. Altogether some twenty or thirty names were suggested—none of them very seriously, since the literary gentlemen were aware that Jia Zheng intended to test Baoyu and were anxious not to make the boy's task too difficult. Baoyu understood and was duly grateful.

When no more names were forthcoming Jia Zheng turned to Baoyu and asked him to propose something himself.

'I remember reading in some old book,' said Baoyu, 'that "to recall old things is better than to invent new ones; and to recut an ancient text is better than to engrave a modern". We ought, then, to choose something old. But as this is not the garden's principal "mountain" or its chief vista, strictly speaking there is no justification for having an inscription here at all—unless it is to be something which implies that this is merely a first step towards more important things ahead. I suggest we should call it "Pathway to Mysteries" after the line in Chang Jian's poem about the mountain temple:

A path winds upwards to mysterious places.

A name like that would be more distinguished.'

There was a chorus of praise from the literary gentlemen:

'Exactly right! Wonderful! Our young friend with his natural talent and youthful imagination succeeds immediately where we old pedants fail!'

Jia Zheng gave a deprecatory laugh:

'You mustn't flatter the boy! People of his age are adept at making a little knowledge go a long way. I only asked him as a joke, to see what he would say. We shall have to think of a better name later on.'

As he spoke, they passed through a tunnel of rock in the mountain's shoulder into an artificial ravine ablaze with the vari-coloured flowers and foliage of many varieties of tree and shrub which grew there in great profusion. Down below, where the trees were thickest, a clear stream gushed between the rocks. After they had advanced a few paces in a somewhat northerly direction, the ravine broadened into a little flat-bottomed valley and the stream widened out to form a pool. Gaily painted and carved pavilions rose from the slopes on either side, their lower halves concealed amidst the trees, their tops reaching into the blue. In the midst of the prospect below them was a handsome bridge:

> In a green ravine
> A jade stream sped.
> A stair of stone
> Plunged to the brink.
> Where the water widened
> To a placid pool,
> A marble baluster
> Ran round about.
> A marble bridge crossed it
> With triple span,
> And a marble lion's maw
> Crowned each of the arches.

Over the centre of the bridge there was a little pavilion, which Jia Zheng and the others entered and sat down in.

'Well, gentlemen!' said Jia Zheng. 'What are we going to call it?'

'Ou-yang Xiu[1] in his *Pavilion of the Old Drunkard* speaks of "a pavilion poised above the water",' said one of them. 'What about "Poised Pavilion"?'

'"Poised Pavilion" is good,' said Jia Zheng, 'but *this* pavilion was put here in order to dominate the water it stands over, and I think there ought to be some reference to water in its name. I seem to recollect that in that same essay you mention Ou-yang Xiu speaks of the water "gushing between twin peaks". Could we not use the word "gushing" in some way?'

'Yes, yes!' said one of the literary gentlemen. '"Gushing Jade" would do splendidly.'

Jia Zheng fondled his beard meditatively, then turned to Baoyu and asked him for *his* suggestion.

'I agreed with what you said just now, Father,' said Baoyu, 'but on second thought it seems to me that though it may have been all right for Ou-yang Xiu to use the word "gushing" in describing the source of the river Rang, it doesn't really suit the water round this pavilion. Then again, as this is a Separate Residence specially designed for the reception of a royal personage, it seems to me that something rather formal is called for, and that an expression taken from the *Drunkard's Pavilion* might seem a bit improper. I think we should try to find a rather more imaginative, less obvious sort of name.'

'I hope you gentlemen are all taking this in!' said Jia Zheng sarcastically. 'You will observe that when we suggest something original we are recommended to prefer the old to the new, but that when we *do* make use of an old text we are "improper" and "unimaginative"!—Well, carry on then! Let's have your suggestion!'

'I think "Drenched Blossoms" would be more original and more tasteful than "Gushing Jade".'

Jia Zheng stroked his beard and nodded silently. The literary gentlemen could see that he was pleased and hastened to commend Baoyu's remarkable ability.

'That's the two words for the framed board on top,' said Jia Zheng. 'Not a very difficult task. But what about the seven-word lines for the sides?'

Baoyu glanced quickly round, seeking inspiration from the scene, and presently came up with the following couplet:

'Three pole-thrust lengths of bankside willows green,
    One fragrant breath of bankside flowers sweet.'

Jia Zheng nodded and a barely perceptible smile played over his features. The literary gentlemen redoubled their praises.

They now left the pavilion and crossed to the other side of the pool. For a while they walked on, stopping from time to time to admire the various rocks and flowers and trees which they passed on their way, until suddenly they found themselves at the foot of a range of whitewashed walls enclosing a small retreat almost hidden among the hundreds and hundreds of green bamboos which grew in a

1. A well-known scholar-official of the 11th century.

dense thicket behind them. With cries of admiration they went inside. A cloister-like covered walk ran round the walls from the entrance to the back of the fore-court and a cobbled pathway led up to the steps of the terrace. The house was a tiny three-frame one, two parts latticed, the third part windowless. The tables, chairs and couches which furnished it seemed to have been specially made to fit the interior. A door in the rear wall opened onto a garden of broad-leaved plan-tains dominated by a large flowering pear-tree and overlooked on either side by two diminutive lodges built at right angles to the back of the house. A stream gushed through an opening at the foot of the garden wall into a channel barely a foot wide which ran to the foot of the rear terrace and thence round the side of the house to the front, where it meandered through the bamboos of the forecourt before finally disappearing through another opening in the surrounding wall.

'This must be a pleasant enough place at any time,' said Jia Zheng with a smile. 'But just imagine what it would be like to sit studying beside the window here on a moonlight night! It is pleasures like that which make a man feel he has not lived in vain!'

As he spoke, his glance happened to fall on Baoyu, who instantly became so embarrassed that he hung his head in shame. He was rescued by the timely intervention of the literary gentlemen who changed the subject from that of study to a less dangerous topic. Two of them suggested that the name given to this retreat should be a four-word one. Jia Zheng asked them what four words they proposed.

'"Where Bends the Qi"' said one of them, no doubt having in mind the song in the *Poetry Classic*[2] which begins with the words

> See in that nook where bends the Qi,
> The green bamboos, how graceful grown!

'No,' said Jia Zheng. 'Too obvious!'

'"North of the Sui",' said the other, evidently thinking of the ancient Rabbit Garden of the Prince of Liang in Suiyang—also famous for its bamboos and running water.

'No,' said Jia Zheng. 'Still too obvious!'

'You'd better ask Cousin Bao again,' said Cousin Zhen, who stood by listening.

'He always insists on criticizing everyone else's suggestions before he will deign to make one of his own,' said Jia Zheng. 'He is a worthless creature.'

'That's all right,' said the others. 'His criticisms are very good ones. He is in no way to blame for making them.'

'You shouldn't let him get away with it!' said Jia Zheng. 'All right!' he went on, turning to Baoyu. 'Today we will indulge you up to the hilt. Let's have your criticisms, and after that we'll hear your own proposal. What about the two suggestions that have just been made? Do you think either of them could be used?'

'Neither of them seems quite right to me,' said Baoyu in answer to the question.

'In what way "not quite right"?' said Jia Zheng with a scornful smile.

2. The *Classic of Poetry*.

'Well,' said Baoyu, 'This is the first building our visitor will enter when she looks over the garden, so there ought to be some word of praise for the Emperor at this point. If we want a classical reference with imperial symbolism, I suggest "The Phoenix Dance", alluding to that passage in the *History Classic* about the male and female phoenixes alighting "with measured gambollings" in the Emperor's courtyard.'

'What about "Bend of the Qi" and "North of the Sui"?' said Jia Zheng. 'Aren't they classical allusions? If not, I should like to know what they are!'

'Yes,' said Baoyu, 'but they are too contrived. "The Phoenix Dance" is more fitting.'

There was a loud murmur of assent from the literary gentlemen. Jia Zhong nodded and tried not to look pleased.

'Young idiot!—A "small capacity but a great self-conceit", gentlemen—All right!' he ordered: 'now the couplet!'

So Baoyu recited the following couplet:

'From the empty cauldron the steam still rises after the brewing
    of tea.
By the darkening window the fingers are still cold after the game
    of Go.'

Jia Zheng shook his head:
'Nothing very remarkable about *that*!'

* * *

They had been moving on meanwhile, and he now led them into the largest of the little thatched buildings, from whose simple interior with its paper windows and plain deal furniture all hint of urban refinement had been banished. Jia Zheng was inwardly pleased. He stared hard at Baoyu:
'How do you like *this* place, then?'

With secret winks and nods the literary gentlemen urged Baoyu to make a favourable reply, but he wilfully ignored their promptings.

'Not nearly as much as "The Phoenix Dance".'

His father snorted disgustedly.

'Ignoramus! You have eyes only for painted halls and gaudy pavilions—the rubbishy trappings of wealth. What can *you* know of the beauty that lies in quietness and natural simplicity? This is a consequence of your refusal to study properly.'

'Your rebuke is, of course, justified, Father,' Baoyu replied promptly, 'but then I have never really understood what it was the ancients *meant* by "natural".'

The literary gentlemen, who had observed a vein of mulishness in Baoyu which boded trouble, were surprised by the seeming naïveté of this reply.

'Why, fancy not knowing what "natural" means—you who have such a good understanding of so much else! "Natural" is that which is *of nature*, that is to say, that which is produced by nature as opposed to that which is produced by human artifice.'

'There you are, you see!' said Baoyu. 'A farm set down in the middle of a place like this is obviously the product of human artifice. There are no neighbouring villages, no distant prospects of city walls; the mountain at the back doesn't belong to any system; there is no pagoda rising from some tree-hid monastery in the hills above; there is no bridge below leading to a near-by market town. It sticks up out of nowhere, in total isolation from everything else. It isn't even a particularly remarkable view—not nearly so "natural" in either form or spirit as those other places we have seen. The bamboos in those other places may have been planted by human hand and the streams diverted out of their natural courses, but there was no *appearance* of artifice. That's why, when the ancients use the term "natural" I have my doubts about what they really meant. For example, when they speak of a "natural painting", I can't help wondering if they are not referring to precisely that forcible interference with the landscape to which I object: putting hills where they are not meant to be, and that sort of thing. However great the skill with which this is done; the results are never quite . . .'

His discourse was cut short by an outburst of rage from Jia Zheng.

'Take that boy out of here!'

Baoyu fled.

'Come back!'

He returned.

'You still have to make a couplet on this place. If it isn't satisfactory, you will find yourself reciting it to the tune of a slapped face!'

Baoyu stood quivering with fright and for some moments was unable to say anything. At last he recited the following couplet:

> 'Emergent buds swell where the washerwoman soaks her cloth.
> A fresh tang rises where the cress-gatherer fills his pannier.'

Jia Zheng shook his head:

'Worse and worse.'

He led them out of the 'village' and round the foot of the hill:

> through flowers and foliage,
> by rock and rivulet,
> past rose-crowned pergolas
> and rose-twined trellises,
> through small pavillions
> embowered in peonies,
> where scent of sweet-briers stole,
> or pliant plantains waved—

until they came to a place where a musical murmur of water issued from a cave in the rock. The cave was half-veiled by a green curtain of creeper, and the water below was starred with bobbing blossoms.

'What a delightful spot!' the literary gentlemen exclaimed.

'Very well, gentlemen. What are you going to call it?' said Jia Zheng.

Inevitably the literary gentlemen thought of Tao Yuanming's fisherman of Wuling and his Peach-blossom Stream.[3]

3. Allusion to Tao Qian's (or Tao Yuanming's) vision of a utopian society, the *Peach Blossom Spring*.

'"The Wuling Stream",' said one of them. 'The name is ready-made for this place. No need to look further than that.'

Jia Zheng laughed:

'The same trouble again, I am afraid. It is the name of a real place. In any case, it is too hackneyed.'

'All right,' said the others good-humouredly. 'In that case simply call it "Refuge of the Qins".'[4] Their minds still ran on the Peach-blossom Stream and its hidden paradise.

'That's even more inappropriate!' said Baoyu. '"Refuge of the Qins" would imply that the people here were fugitives from tyranny. How can we possibly call it that? I suggest "Smartweed Bank and Flowery Harbour".'

'Rubbish!' said Jia Zheng.

* * *

Baoyu was now longing to get back to the girls, but as no dismissal was forthcoming from his father, he followed him along with the others into his study. Fortunately Jia Zheng suddenly recollected that Baoyu was still with him:

'Well, run along then! Your grandmother will be worrying about you. I take it you're not still waiting for more?'

At last Baoyu could withdraw. But as soon as he was in the courtyard outside, he was waylaid by a group of Jia Zheng's pages who laid hands on him and prevented him from going.

'You've done well today, haven't you, coming out top with all those poems? You have *us* to thank for that! Her Old Ladyship sent round several times asking about you, but because the Master was so pleased with you, we told her not to worry. If we hadn't done that, you wouldn't have had the chance to show off your poems! Everyone says they were better than all the others. What about sharing your good luck with us?'

Baoyu laughed good-naturedly.

'All right. A string of cash each.'

'Who wants a measly string of cash? Give us that little purse you're wearing!' And without a 'by your leave' they began to despoil him, beginning with the purse and his fan-case, of all his trinkets, until every one of the objects he carried about him had been taken from him.

'Now,' they said, 'we'll see you back in style!'

And closing round him, they marched him back to Grandmother Jia's apartment in triumphal procession.

Grandmother Jia had been waiting for him with some anxiety, and was naturally delighted to see him come in apparently none the worse for his experience.

Soon after, when he was back in his own room, Aroma came in to pour him some tea and noticed that all the little objects he usually carried about his waist had disappeared.

'Where have the things from your belt gone?' she said. 'I suppose those worthless pages have taken them again.'

Daiyu overheard her and came up to inspect. Sure enough, not one of the things was there.

---

4. In Tao Qian's *Peach Blossom Spring* the inhabitants were said to have fled political upheavals and the draconian rule of the Qin Dynasty (221–206 B.C.E.), China's first empire.

'So you've given away that little purse I gave you? Very well, then. You needn't expect me to give you anything in future, however much you want it!'

With these words she went off to her own room in a temper, and taking up a still unfinished perfume sachet which she was making for him at his own request, she began to cut it up with her embroidery scissors. Baoyu, observing that she was angry, had hurried after her—but it was too late. The sachet was already cut to pieces.

Although it had not been finished, Baoyu could see that the embroidery was very fine, and it made him angry to think of the hours and hours of work so wantonly destroyed. Tearing open his collar he took out the little embroidered purse which had all along been hanging round his neck and held it out for her to see.

'Look! What's that? When have I ever given anything of yours to someone else?'

Daiyu knew that he must have treasured her gift to have worn it inside his clothing where there was no risk of its being taken from him. She regretted her over-hasty destruction of the sachet and hung her head in silence.

'You needn't have cut it up,' said Baoyu. 'I know it's only because you hate giving things away. Here, you can have this back too since you're so stingy!'

He tossed the purse into her lap and turned to go. Daiyu burst into tears of rage, and picking up the little purse, attacked that too with her scissors. Baoyu hurried back and caught her by the wrist.

'Come, cuzzy dear!' he said with a laugh. 'Have mercy on it!'

Daiyu threw down the scissors and wiped her streaming eyes.

'You shouldn't blow hot and cold by turns. If you want to quarrel, let's quarrel properly and have nothing to do with each other!'

She got up on the kang in a great huff, and turning her back on him, sobbed into her handkerchief and affected to ignore his presence. But Bao-yu got up beside her, and with many soothing words and affectionate endearments humbly entreated her forgiveness.

* * *

FROM CHAPTER 96[1]

Xifeng conceives an ingenious plan of deception
And Frowner[2] is deranged by an inadvertent disclosure

* * *

The time had come round for the triennial review of civil servants stationed in the capital. Jia Zheng's Board gave him a high commendation, and in the second month the Board of Civil Office presented him for an audience with the Emperor. His Majesty, in view of Jia Zheng's record as a 'diligent, frugal, conscientious and prudent servant of the Throne', appointed him immediately to the post of Grain Intendant for the province of Kiangsi. The same day, Jia Zheng offered his humble acceptance and gratitude for the honour, and suggested a day for his departure. Friends and relatives were all eager to celebrate, but he was not in festive mood. He was loth to leave the capital at a time when

1. Chapters 96–120 are translated by John Minford.   2. Lin Daiyu's nickname.

things were so unsettled at home, although at the same time he knew that he could not delay his departure.

He was pondering this dilemma, when a message came to summon him to Grandmother Jia's presence. He made his way promptly to her apartment, where he found Lady Wang also present, despite her illness. He paid his respects to Grandmother Jia, who told him to be seated and then began:

'In a few days, you will be leaving us to take up your post. There is something I should like to discuss with you, if you are willing.'

The old lady's eyes were wet with tears. Jia Zheng rose swiftly to his feet, and said:

'Whatever you have to say, Mother, please speak: your word is my command.'

'I shall be eighty-one this year,' said Grandmother Jia, sobbing as she spoke. 'You are going away to a post in the provinces, and with your elder brother still at home, you will not be able to apply for early retirement to come and look after me. When you are gone, of the ones closest to my heart I shall only have Baoyu left to me. And he, poor darling, is in such a wretched state, I don't know what we can do for him! The other day I sent out Lai Sheng's wife to have the boy's fortune told. The man's reading was uncanny. What he said was: "This person must marry a lady with a destiny of gold, to help him and support him. He must be given a marriage as soon as possible to turn his luck. If not, he may not live." Now I know you don't believe in such things, which is why I sent for you, to talk it over with you. You and his mother must discuss it among yourselves. Are we to save him, or are we to do nothing and watch him fade away?'

Jia Zheng smiled anxiously.

'Could I, who as a child received such tender love and care from you, Mother, not have fatherly feelings myself? It is just that I have been exasperated by his repeated failure to make progress in his studies, and have perhaps been too ambitious for him. You are perfectly right in wanting to see him married. How could I possibly wish to oppose you? I am concerned for the boy, and his recent illness has caused me great anxiety. But as you have kept him from me, I have not ventured to say anything. I should like to see him now for myself, and form my own impression of his condition.'

Lady Wang saw that his eyes were moist, and knew that he was genuinely concerned. She told Aroma to fetch Baoyu and help him into the room. He walked in, and when Aroma told him to pay his respects to his father, did exactly as she said. Jia Zheng saw how emaciated his face had grown, how lifeless his eyes were. His son was like some pathetic simpleton. He told them to take him back to his room.

* * *

A day or two after these events, Daiyu, having eaten her breakfast, decided to take Nightingale with her to visit Grandmother Jia. She wanted to pay her respects, and also thought the visit might provide some sort of distraction for herself. She had hardly left the Naiad's House, when she remembered that she had left her handkerchief at home, and sent Nightingale back to fetch it, saying that she would walk ahead slowly and wait for her to catch up. She had just reached the corner behind the rockery at Drenched Blossoms Bridge—the very spot where she had once buried the flowers with Baoyu—when all of a sudden she heard the sound of sobbing. She stopped at once and listened. She could not tell whose voice it was, nor could she distinguish what it was that the voice was complaining of, so tearfully and at such length. It really was most puzzling. She moved forward again cautiously and as she turned the corner, saw before her the source of the sobbing, a maid with large eyes and thick-set eyebrows.

Before setting eyes on this girl, Daiyu had guessed that one of the many maids in the Jia household must have had an unhappy love-affair, and had come here to cry her heart out in secret. But now she laughed at the very idea. 'How could such an ungainly creature as this know the meaning of love?' she thought to herself. 'This must be one of the odd-job girls, who has probably been scolded by one of the senior maids.' She looked more closely, but still could not place the girl. Seeing Daiyu, the maid ceased her weeping, wiped her cheeks, and rose to her feet.

'Come now, what are you so upset about?' inquired Daiyu.

'Oh Miss Lin!' replied the maid, amid fresh tears. 'Tell me if you think it fair. *They* were talking about it, and how was I to know better? Just because I say one thing wrong, is that a reason for sister to start hitting me?'

Daiyu did not know what she was talking about. She smiled, and asked again:

'Who is your sister?'

'Pearl,' answered the maid.

From this, Daiyu concluded that she must work in Grandmother Jia's apartment.

'And what is your name?'

'Simple.'

Daiyu laughed. Then:

'Why did she hit you? What did you say that was so wrong?'

'That's what I'd like to know! It was only to do with Master Bao marrying Miss Chai!'

The words struck Daiyu's ears like a clap of thunder. Her heart started thumping fiercely. She tried to calm herself for a moment, and told the maid to come with her. The maid followed her to the secluded corner of the garden, where the Flower Burial Mound was situated. Here Daiyu asked her:

'Why should she hit you for mentioning Master Bao's marriage to Miss Chai?'

'Her Old Ladyship, Her Ladyship and Mrs Lian,' replied Simple, 'have decided that as the Master is leaving soon, they are going to arrange with Mrs Xue to marry Master Bao and Miss Chai as quickly as possible. They want the wedding to turn his luck, and then . . .'

Her voice tailed off. She stared at Daiyu, laughed and continued:

'Then, as soon as those two are married, they are going to find a husband for you, Miss Lin.'

Daiyu was speechless with horror. The maid went on regardless:

'But how was I to know that they'd decided to keep it quiet, for fear of embarrassing Miss Chai? All I did was say to Aroma, that serves in Master Bao's room: "Won't it be a fine to-do here soon, when Miss Chai comes over, or Mrs Bao . . . what *will* we have to call her?" That's all I said. What was there in that to hurt sister Pearl? Can *you* see, Miss Lin? She came across and hit me straight in the face and said I was talking rubbish and disobeying orders, and would be dismissed from service! How was I to know their Ladyships didn't want us to mention it? Nobody told me, and she just hit me!'

She started sobbing again. Daiyu's heart felt as though oil, soy-sauce, sugar and vinegar had all been poured into it at once. She could not tell which flavour predominated, the sweet, the sour, the bitter or the salty. After a few moments' silence, she said in a trembling voice:

'Don't talk such rubbish. Any more of that, and you'll be beaten again. Off you go!'

She herself turned back in the direction of the Naiad's House. Her body felt as though it weighed a hundred tons, her feet were as wobbly as if she were walking on cotton-floss. She could only manage one step at a time. After an age, she still had not reached the bank by Drenched Blossoms Bridge. She was going so slowly, with her feet about to collapse beneath her, and in her giddiness and confusion had wandered off course and increased the distance by about a hundred yards. She reached Drenched Blossoms Bridge only to start drifting back again along the bank in the direction she had just come from, quite unaware of what she was doing.

Nightingale had by now returned with the handkerchief, but could not find Daiyu anywhere. She finally saw her, pale as snow, tottering along, her eyes staring straight in front of her, meandering in circles. Nightingale also caught sight of a maid disappearing in the distance beyond Daiyu, but could not make out who it was. She was most bewildered, and quickened her step.

'Why are you turning back again, Miss?' she asked softly. 'Where are you heading for?'

Daiyu only heard the blurred outline of this question. She replied:

'I want to ask Baoyu something.'

Nightingale could not fathom what was going on, and could only try to guide her on her way to Grandmother Jia's apartment. When they came to the entrance, Daiyu seemed to feel clearer in mind. She turned, saw Nightingale supporting her, stopped for a moment, and asked:

'What are you doing here?'

'I went to fetch your handkerchief,' replied Nightingale, smiling anxiously. 'I saw you over by the bridge and hurried across. I asked you where you were going, but you took no notice.'

'Oh!' said Daiyu with a smile. 'I thought you had come to see Baoyu. What else did we come here for?'

Nightingale could see that her mind was utterly confused. She guessed that it was something that the maid had said in the garden, and only nodded with a faint smile in reply to Daiyu's question. But to herself she was trying to imagine what sort of an encounter this was going to be, between the young master who had already lost his wits, and her young mistress who was now herself a little touched. Despite her apprehensions, she dared not prevent the meeting, and helped Daiyu into the room. The funny thing was that Daiyu now seemed to have recovered her strength. She did not wait for Nightingale but raised the portière herself, and walked into the room. It was very quiet inside. Grandmother Jia had retired for her afternoon nap. Some of the maids had sneaked off to play, some were having forty winks themselves and others had gone to wait on Grandmother Jia in her bedroom. It was Aroma who came out to see who was there, when she heard the swish of the portière. Seeing that it was Dai-yu, she greeted her politely:

'Please come in and sit down, Miss.'

'Is Master Bao at home?' asked Daiyu with a smile.

Aroma did not know that anything was amiss, and was about to answer, when she saw Nightingale make an urgent movement with her lips from behind Daiyu's back, pointing to her mistress and making a warning gesture with her hand. Aroma had no idea what she meant and dared not ask. Undeterred, Daiyu walked on into Baoyu's room. He was sitting up in bed, and when she came in made no move to get up or welcome her, but remained where he was, staring at her and giving a series of silly laughs. Daiyu sat down uninvited, and she too began to smile and stare back at Baoyu. There were no greetings exchanged, no courtesies, in fact no words of any kind. They just sat there staring into each other's faces and smiling like a pair of half-wits. Aroma stood watching, completely at a loss.

Suddenly Daiyu said:

'Baoyu, why are you sick?'

Baoyu laughed.

'I'm sick because of Miss Lin.'

Aroma and Nightingale grew pale with fright. They tried to change the subject, but their efforts only met with silence and more senseless smiles. By now it was clear to Aroma that Daiyu's mind was as disturbed as Baoyu's.

'Miss Lin has only just recovered from her illness,' she whispered to Nightingale. 'I'll ask Ripple to help you take her back. She should go home and lie down.' Turning to Ripple, she said: 'Go with Nightingale and accompany Miss Lin home. And no stupid chattering on the way, mind.'

Ripple smiled, and without a word came over to help Nightingale. The two of them began to help Daiyu to her feet. Daiyu stood up at once, unassisted, still staring fixedly at Baoyu, smiling and nodding her head.

'Come on, Miss!' urged Nightingale. 'It's time to go home and rest.'

'Of course!' exclaimed Daiyu. 'It's time!'

She turned to go. Still smiling and refusing any assistance from the maids, she strode out at twice her normal speed. Ripple and Nightingale hurried after her. On leaving Grandmother Jia's apartment, Daiyu kept on walking, in quite the wrong direction. Nightingale hurried up to her and took her by the hand.

'This is the way, Miss.'

Still smiling, Daiyu allowed herself to be led, and followed Nightingale towards the Naiad's House. When they were nearly there, Nightingale exclaimed:

'Lord Buddha be praised! Home at last!'

She had no sooner uttered these words when she saw Daiyu stumble forwards onto the ground, and give a loud cry. A stream of blood came gushing from her mouth.

To learn if she survived this crisis, please read the next chapter.

FROM **CHAPTER** 97

Lin Daiyu burns her poems to signal the end of her heart's folly
And Xue Baochai leaves home to take part in a solemn rite

* * *

Next day, Xifeng came over after breakfast. Wishing to sound out Baoyu according to her plan, she advanced into his room and said:

'Congratulations, Cousin Bao! Uncle Zheng has already chosen a lucky day for your wedding! Isn't that good news?'

Baoyu stared at her with a blank smile, and nodded his head faintly.

'He is marrying you,' went on Xifeng, with a studied smile, 'to your cousin Lin. Are you happy?'

Baoyu burst out laughing. Xifeng watched him carely, but could not make out whether he had understood her, or was simply raving. She went on:

'Uncle Zheng says, you are to marry Miss Lin, *if* you get better. But not if you carry on behaving like a half-wit.'

Baoyu's expression suddenly changed to one of utter seriousness, as he said:

'I'm not a half-wit. You're the half-wit.'

He stood up.

'I am going to see Cousin Lin, to set her mind at rest.'

Xifeng quickly put out a hand to stop him.

'She knows already. And, as your bride-to-be, she would be much too embarrassed to receive you now.'

'What about when we're married? Will she see me then?'

Xifeng found this both comic and somewhat disturbing.

'Aroma was right,' she thought to herself. 'Mention Daiyu, and while he still talks like an idiot, he at least seems to understand what's going on. I can see we shall be in real trouble, if he sees through our scheme and finds out that his bride is not to be Daiyu after all.'

In reply to his question, she said, suppressing a smile:

'If you behave, she will see you. But not if you continue to act like an imbecile.'

To which Baoyu replied:

'I have given my heart to Cousin Lin. If she marries me, she will bring it with her and put it back in its proper place.'

Now this was madman's talk if ever, thought Xifeng, She left him, and walked back into the outer room, glancing with a smile in Grandmother Jia's direction. The old lady too found Baoyu's words both funny and distressing.

'I heard you both myself,' she said to Xifeng. 'For the present, we must ignore it. Tell Aroma to do her best to calm him down. Come, let us go.'

Lady Wang joined them, and the three ladies went across to Aunt Xue's. On arrival there, they pretended to be concerned about the course of Xue Pan's affair. Aunt Xue expressed her profound gratitude for this concern, and gave them the latest news. After they had all taken tea, Aunt Xue was about to send for Baochai, when Xifeng stopped her, saying:

'There is no need to tell Cousin Chai that we are here, Auntie.'

With a diplomatic smile, she continued:

'Grandmother's visit today is not purely a social one. She has something of importance to say, and would like you to come over later so that we can all discuss it together.'

Aunt Xue nodded.

'Of course.'

After a little more chat, the three ladies returned.

That evening Aunt Xue came over as arranged, and after paying her respects to Grandmother Jia, went to her sister's apartment. First there was the inevitable scene of sisterly commiseration over Wang Ziteng's death. Then Aunt Xue said:

'Just now when I was at Lady Jia's, young Bao came out to greet me and seemed quite well. A little thin perhaps, but certainly not as ill as I had been led to expect from your description and Xifeng's.'

'No, it is really not that serious,' said Xifeng. 'It's only Grandmother who will worry so. Her idea is that it would be reassuring for Sir Zheng to see Baoyu married before he leaves, as who knows when he will be able to come home from his new posting. And then from Baoyu's own point of view, it might be just the thing to turn his luck. With Cousin Chai's golden locket to counteract the evil influence, he should make a good recovery.'

Aunt Xue was willing enough to go along with the idea, but was concerned that Baochai might feel rather hard done by.

'I see nothing against it,' she said. 'But I think we should all take time to think it over properly.'

In accordance with Xifeng's plan, Lady Wang went on:

'As you have no head of family present, we should like you to dispense with the usual trousseau. Tomorrow you should send Ke to let Pan know that while we proceed with the wedding, we shall continue to do our utmost to settle his court-case.'

She made no mention of Baoyu's feelings for Daiyu, but continued:

'Since you have given your consent, the sooner they are married, the sooner things will look up for everyone.'

At this point, Faithful came in to take back a report to Grandmother Jia. Though Aunt Xue was still concerned about Baochai's feelings, she saw that in the circumstances she had no choice, and agreed to everything they had suggested. Faithful reported this to Grandmother Jia, who was delighted and sent her back again to ask Mrs Xue to explain to Baochai why it was that things were being done in this way, so that she would not feel unfairly treated. Aunt Xue agreed to do this, and it was settled that Xifeng and Jia Lian would act as official go-betweens. Xifeng retired to her apartment, while Aunt Xue and Lady Wang stayed up talking together well into the night.

Next day, Aunt Xue returned to her apartment and told Baochai the details of the proposal, adding:

'I have already given my consent.'

At first Baochai hung her head in silence. Then she began to cry. Aunt Xue said all that she could to comfort her, and went to great lengths to explain the reasoning behind the decision. Baochai retired to her room, and Baoqin went in to keep her company and cheer her up. Aunt Xue also spoke to Ke, instructing him as follows:

'You must leave tomorrow. Find out the latest news of Pan's judgement, and then convey this message to him. Return as soon as you possibly can.'

*   *   *

Daiyu meanwhile, for all the medicine she took, continued to grow iller with every day that passed. Nightingale did her utmost to raise her spirits. Our story finds her standing once more by Daiyu's bedside, earnestly beseeching her:

'Miss, now that things have come to this pass, I simply must speak my mind. We know what it is that's eating your heart out. But can't you see that your fears are groundless? Why, look at the state Baoyu is in! How can he possibly get married, when he's so ill? You must ignore these silly rumours, stop fretting and let yourself get better.'

Daiyu gave a wraithlike smile, but said nothing. She started coughing again and brought up a lot more blood. Nightingale and Snowgoose came closer and watched her feebly struggling for breath. They knew that any further attempt to rally her would be to no avail, and could do nothing but stand there watching and weeping. Each day Nightingale went over three or four times to tell Grandmother Jia, but Faithful, judging the old lady's attitude towards Daiyu to have hardened of late, intercepted her reports and hardly mentioned Daiyu to her mistress. Grandmother Jia was preoccupied with the wedding arrangements, and in the absence of any particular news of Daiyu, did not show a great deal of interest in the girl's fate, considering it sufficient that she should be receiving medical attention.

Previously, when she had been ill, Daiyu had always received frequent visits from everyone in the household, from Grandmother Jia down to the humblest maidservant. But now not a single person came to see her. The only face she saw looking down at her was that of Nightingale. She began to feel her end drawing near, and struggled to say a few words to her:

'Dear Nightingale! Dear sister! Closest friend! Though you were Grandmother's maid before you came to serve me, over the years you have become as a sister to me . . .'

She had to stop for breath. Nightingale felt a pang of pity, was reduced to tears and could say nothing. After a long silence, Daiyu began to speak again, searching for breath between words:

'Dear sister! I am so uncomfortable lying down like this. Please help me up and sit next to me.'

'I don't think you should sit up, Miss, in your condition. You might get cold in the draught.'

Daiyu closed her eyes in silence. A little later she asked to sit up again. Nightingale and Snowgoose felt they could no longer deny her request. They propped her up on both sides with soft pillows, while Nightingale sat by her on the bed to give further support. Daiyu was not equal to the effort. The bed where she sat on it seemed to dig into her, and she struggled with all her remaining strength to lift herself up and ease the pain. She told Snowgoose to come closer.

'My poems . . .'

Her voice failed, and she fought for breath again. Snowgoose guessed that she meant the manuscripts she had been revising a few days previously, went to fetch them and laid them on Daiyu's lap. Daiyu nodded, then raised her eyes and gazed in the direction of a chest that stood on a stand close by. Snowgoose did not know how to interpret this and stood there at a loss. Daiyu stared at her now with feverish impatience. She began to cough again and brought up another mouthful of blood. Snowgoose went to fetch some water, and Daiyu rinsed her mouth and spat into the spittoon. Nightingale wiped her lips with a handkerchief. Daiyu took the handkerchief from her and pointed to the chest. She tried to speak, but was again seized with an attack of breathlessness and closed her eyes.

'Lie down, Miss,' said Nightingale. Daiyu shook her head. Nightingale thought she must want one of her handkerchiefs, and told Snowgoose to open the chest and bring her a plain white silk one. Daiyu looked at it, and dropped it on the bed. Making a supreme effort, she gasped out:

'The ones with the writing on . . .'

Nightingale finally realized that she meant the handkerchiefs Baoyu had sent her, the ones she had inscribed with her own poems. She told Snowgoose to fetch them, and herself handed them to Daiyu, with these words of advice:

'You must lie down and rest, Miss. Don't start wearing yourself out. You can look at these another time, when you are feeling better.'

Daiyu took the handkerchiefs in one hand and without even looking at them, brought round her other hand (which cost her a great effort) and tried with all her might to tear them in two. But she was so weak that all she could achieve was a pathetic trembling motion. Nightingale knew that Baoyu was the object of all this bitterness but dared not mention his name, saying instead:

'Miss, there is no sense in working yourself up again.'

Daiyu nodded faintly, and slipped the handkerchiefs into her sleeve.

'Light the lamp,' she ordered.

Snowgoose promptly obeyed. Daiyu looked into the lamp, then closed her eyes and sat in silence. Another fit of breathlessness. Then:

'Make up the fire in the brazier.'

Thinking she wanted it for the extra warmth, Nightingale protested:

'You should lie down, Miss, and have another cover on. And the fumes from the brazier might be bad for you.'

Daiyu shook her head, and Snowgoose reluctantly made up the brazier, placing it on its stand on the floor. Daiyu made a motion with her hand, indicating that she wanted it moved up onto the kang. Snowgoose lifted it and placed it there, temporarily using the floor-stand, while she went out to fetch the special stand they used on the kang. Daiyu, far from resting back in the warmth, now inclined her body slightly forward—Nightingale had to support her with both hands as she did so. Daiyu took the handkerchiefs in one hand. Staring into the flames and nodding thoughtfully to herself, she dropped them into the brazier. Nightingale was horrified, but much as she would have liked to snatch them from the flames, she did not dare move her hands and leave Daiyu unsupported. Snowgoose was out of the room, fetching the brazier-stand, and by now the handkerchiefs were all ablaze.

'Miss!' cried Nightingale. 'What are you doing?'

As if she had not heard, Daiyu reached over for her manuscripts, glanced at them and let them fall again onto the kang. Nightingale, anxious lest she burn these too, leaned up against Daiyu and freeing one hand, reached out with it to take hold of them. But before she could do so, Daiyu had picked them up again and dropped them in the flames. The brazier was out of Nightingale's reach, and there was nothing she could do but look on helplessly.

Just at that moment Snowgoose came in with the stand. She saw Daiyu drop something into the fire, and without knowing what it was, rushed forward to try and save it. The manuscripts had caught at once and were already ablaze. Heedless of the danger to her hands, Snowgoose reached into the flames and pulled out what she could, throwing the paper on the floor and stamping frantically on it. But the fire had done its work, and only a few charred fragments remained.

Daiyu closed her eyes and slumped back, almost causing Nightingale to topple over with her. Nightingale, her heart thumping in great agitation, called Snowgoose over to help her settle Daiyu down again. It was too late now to send for anyone. And yet, what if Daiyu should die during the night, and the only people there were Snowgoose, herself and the one or two other junior maids in the Naiad's House? They passed a restless night. Morning came at last, and Daiyu seemed a little more comfortable. But after breakfast she suddenly began coughing and vomiting, and became tense and feverish again. Nightingale could see that she had reached a crisis.

* * *

FROM CHAPTER 98

Crimson Pearl's suffering spirit returns to the Realm of Separation
And the convalescent Stone-in-waiting weeps at the scene of past affection

On his return from seeing his father, Baoyu, as we have seen, regressed into a worse state of stupor and depression than ever. He was too lacking in energy to move, and could eat nothing, but fell straight into a heavy slumber. Once more the doctor was called, once more he took Baoyu's pulses and made out a prescription, which was administered to no effect. He could not even recognize the people around him. And yet, if helped into a sitting position, he could still pass for someone in normal health. Provided he was not called upon to do anything, there were no external symptoms to indicate how seriously ill he was. He continued like this for several days, to the increasing anxiety of the family, until the Ninth Day after the wedding, when according to tradition the newly-married couple should visit the bride's family. If they did not go, Aunt Xue would be most offended. But if they went with Baoyu in his present state, whatever were they to say? Knowing that his illness was caused by his attachment to Daiyu, Grandmother Jia would have liked to make a clean breast of it and tell Aunt Xue. But she feared that this too might cause offence and ill-feeling. It was also difficult for her to be of any comfort to Baochai, who was in a delicate position as a new member of the Jia family. Such comfort could only be rendered by a visit from the girl's mother, which would be difficult if they had already offended her by not celebrating the Ninth Day. It must be gone through with. Grandmother Jia imparted her views on the matter to Lady Wang and Xifeng:

'It is only Baoyu's mind that has been temporarily affected. I don't think a little excursion would do him any harm. We must prepare two small sedan-chairs, and send a maid to support him. They can go through the Garden. Once the Ninth Day has been properly celebrated, we can ask Mrs Xue to come over and comfort Baochai, while we do our utmost to restore Baoyu to health. They will both benefit.'

Lady Wang agreed and immediately began making the necessary preparations. Baochai acquiesced in the charade out of a sense of conjugal duty, while Baoyu in his moronic state was easily manipulated. Baochai now knew the full truth, and in her own mind blamed her mother for making a foolish decision. But now that things had gone this far she said nothing. Aunt Xue herself, when she witnessed Baoyu's pitiful condition, began to regret having ever given her consent, and could only bring herself to play a perfunctory part in the proceedings.

When they returned home, Baoyu's condition seemed to grow worse. By the next day he could not even sit up in bed. This deterioration continued daily, until he could no longer swallow medicine or water. Aunt Xue was there, and she and the other ladies in their frantic despair scoured the city for eminent physicians, without finding one that could diagnose the illness. Finally they discovered, lodging in a broken-down temple outside the city, a down-and-out practitioner by the name of Bi Zhian, who diagnosed it as a case of severe emotional shock, aggravated by a failure to dress in accordance with the seasons and by irregular eating habits, with consequent accumulation of choler and obstruction of the humours. In short, an internal disorder made worse by external factors. He made out a prescription in accordance with this diagnosis, which was administered that evening. At about ten o'clock it began to take effect. Baoyu began to show signs of consciousness and asked for water to drink. Grandmother Jia, Lady Wang and all the other ladies congragated round the sick-bed felt that they could at last have a brief respite from their vigil, and Aunt Xue was invited to bring Baochai with her to Grandmother Jia's apartment to rest for a while.

His brief access of clarity enabled Baoyu to understand the gravity of his illness. When the others had gone and he was left alone with Aroma, he called her over to his side and taking her by the hand said tearfully:

'Please tell me how Cousin Chai came to be here? I remember Father marrying me to Cousin Lin. Why has *she* been made to go? Why has Cousin Chai taken her place? She has no right to be here! I'd like to tell her so, but I don't want to offend her. How has Cousin Lin taken it? Is she very upset?'

Aroma did not dare tell him the truth, but merely said:

'Miss Lin is ill.'

'I must go and see her,' insisted Baoyu. He wanted to get up, but days of going without food and drink had so sapped his strength that he could no longer move, but could only weep bitterly and say:

'I know I am going to die! There's something on my mind, something very important, that I want you to tell Grannie for me, Cousin Lin and I are both ill. We are both dying. It will be too late to help us when we are dead: but if they prepare a room for us now and if we are taken there before it is too late, we can at least be cared for together while we are still alive, and be laid out together when we die. Do this for me, for friendship's sake!'

Aroma found this plea at once disturbing, comical and moving. Baochai, who happened to be passing with Oriole, heard every word and took him to task straight away.

'Instead of resting and trying to get well, you make yourself iller with all this gloomy talk! Grandmother has scarcely stopped worrying about you for a moment, and here you are causing more trouble for her. She is over eighty now and may not live to acquire a title because of your achievements; but at least, by leading a good life, you can repay her a little for all that she has suffered for your sake. And I hardly need mention the agonies Mother has endured in bringing you up. You are the only son she has left. If you were to die, think how she would suffer! As for me, I am wretched enough as it is; you don't need to make a widow of me. Three good reasons why even if you want to die, the powers above will not let you and you will not be able to. After four or five days of proper rest and care, your illness will pass, your strength will be restored and you will be yourself again.'

For a while Baoyu could think of no reply to this homily. Finally he gave a silly laugh and said:

'After not speaking to me for so long, here you are lecturing me. You are wasting your breath.'

Encouraged by this response to go a step further, Baochai said:

'Let me tell you the plain truth, then. Some days ago, while you were unconscious, Cousin Lin passed away.'

With a sudden movement, Baoyu sat up and cried out in horror:

'It can't be true!'

'It is. Would I lie about such a thing? Grandmother and Mother knew how fond you were of each other, and wouldn't tell you because they were afraid that if they did, you would die too.'

Baoyu began howling unrestrainedly and slumped back in his bed. Suddenly all was pitch black before his eyes. He could not tell where he was and was beginning to feel very lost, when he thought he saw a man walking towards him and asked in a bewildered tone of voice:

'Would you be so kind as to tell me where I am?'

'This,' replied the stranger, 'is the road to the Springs of the Nether World. Your time is not yet come. What brings you here?'

'I have just learned of the death of a friend and have come to find her. But I seem to have lost my way.'

'Who is this friend of yours?'

'Lin Daiyu of Soochow.'

The man gave a chilling smile:

'In life Lin Daiyu was no ordinary mortal, and in death she has become no ordinary shade. An ordinary mortal has two souls which coalesce at birth to vitalize the physical frame, and disperse at death to rejoin the cosmic flux. If you consider the impossibility of tracing even such ordinary human entities in the Nether World, you will realize what a futile task it is to look for Lin Daiyu. You had better return at once.'

After standing for a moment lost in thought, Baoyu asked again:

'But if as you say, death is a dispersion, how can there be such a place as the Nether World?'

'There is,' replied the man with a superior smile, 'and yet there is not, such a place. It is a teaching, devised to warn mankind in its blind attachment to the idea of life and death. The Supreme Wrath is aroused by human folly in all forms—whether it be excessive ambition, premature death self-sought, or futile self-destruction through debauchery and a life of overweening violence. Hell is the place where souls such as these are imprisoned and made to suffer countless torments in expiation of their sins. This search of yours for Lin Daiyu is a case of futile self-delusion. Daiyu has already returned to the Land of Illusion and if you really want to find her you must cultivate your mind and strengthen your spiritual nature. Then one day you will see her again. But if you throw your life away, you will be guilty of premature death self-sought and will be confined to Hell. And then, although you may be allowed to see your parents, you will certainly never see Daiyu again.'

When he had finished speaking, the man took a stone from within his sleeve and threw it at Baoyu's chest. The words he had spoken and the impact of the stone as it landed on his chest combined to give Baoyu such a fright that he would have returned home at once, if he had only known which way to turn. In his confusion he suddenly heard a voice, and turning, saw the figures of Grandmother Jia, Lady Wang, Baochai, Aroma and his other maids standing in a circle around him, weeping and calling his name. He was lying on his own bed. The red lamp was on the table. The moon was shining brilliantly through the window. He was back among the elegant comforts of his own home. A moment's reflection told him that what he had just experienced had been a dream. He was in a cold sweat. Though his mind felt strangely lucid, thinking only intensified his feeling of helpless desolation, and he uttered several profound sighs.

Baochai had known of Daiyu's death for several days. While Grandmother Jia had forbidden the maids to tell him for fear of further complicating his illness, she felt she knew better. Aware that it was Daiyu who lay at the root of his illness and that the loss of his jade was only a secondary factor, she took the opportunity of breaking the news of her death to him in this abrupt manner, hoping that by severing his attachment once and for all she would enable his sanity and health to be restored. Grandmother Jia, Lady Wang and company were not aware of her intentions and at first reproached her for her lack of caution. But when they saw Baoyu regain consciousness, they were all greatly relieved and went at once to the library to ask doctor Bi to come in and examine his patient again. The doctor carefully took his pulses.

'How odd!' he exclaimed. 'His pulses are deep and still, his spirit calm, the oppression quite dispersed. Tomorrow he must take a regulative draught, which I shall prescribe, and he should make a prompt and complete recovery.'

The doctor left and the ladies all returned to their apartments in much improved spirits.

Although at first Aroma greatly resented the way in which Baochai had broken the news, she did not dare say so. Oriole, on the other hand, reproved her mistress in private for having been, as she put it, too hasty.

'What do you know about such things?' retorted Baochai. 'Leave this to me. I take full responsibility.'

Baochai ignored the opinions and criticisms of those around her and continued to keep a close watch on Baoyu's progress, probing him judiciously, like an acupunturist with a needle.

A day or two later, he began to feel a slight improvement in himself, though his mental equilibrium was still easily disturbed by the least thought of Daiyu. Aroma was constantly at his side, with such words of consolation as:

'The Master chose Miss Chai as your bride for her more dependable nature. He thought Miss Lin too difficult and temperamental for you, and besides there was always the fear that she would not live long. Then later Her Old Ladyship thought you were not in a fit state to know what was best for you and would only be upset and make yourself iller if you knew the truth, so she made Snowgoose come over, to try and make things easier for you.'

This did nothing to lessen his grief, and he often wept inconsolably. But each time he thought of putting an end to his life, he remembered the words of the stranger in his dream; and then he thought of the distress his death would cause his mother and grandmother and knew that he could not tear himself away from them. He also reflected that Daiyu was dead, and that Baochai was a fine lady in her own right; there must after all have been some truth in the bond of gold and jade. This thought eased his mind a little. Baochai could see that things were improving, and herself felt calmer as a result. Every day she scrupulously performed her duties towards Grandmother Jia and Lady Wang, and when these were completed, did all she could to cure Baoyu of his grief. He was still not able to sit up for long periods, but often when he saw her sitting by his bedside he would succumb to his old weakness for the fairer sex. She tried to rally him in an earnest manner, saying:

'The important thing is to take care of your health. Now that we are married, we have a whole lifetime ahead of us.'

He was reluctant to listen to her advice. But since his grandmother, his mother, Aunt Xue and all the others took it in turns to watch over him during the day, and since Baochai slept on her own in an adjoining room, and he was waited on at night by one or two maids of Grandmother Jia's, he found himself left with little choice but to rest and get well again. And as time went by and Baochai proved herself a gentle and devoted companion, he found that a small part of his love for Daiyu began to transfer itself to her. But this belongs to a later part of our story.

* * *

FROM CHAPTER 119

Baoyu becomes a Provincial Graduate and severs worldly ties
The House of Jia receives Imperial favour and renews ancestral glory

* * *

The time drew near for the examination. All the family were full of eager anticipation, hoping that the two boys would write creditable compositions and bring the family honour. All except for Baochai; while it was true that Baoyu had prepared well, she had also on occasions noticed a strange indifference in his behaviour. Her first concern was that the two boys, for both of whom this was the first venture of its kind, might get hurt or have some accident in the crush of men and vehicles around the examination halls. She was more particularly worried for Baoyu, who had not been out at all since his encounter with the monk. His delight in studying seemed to her the result of a somewhat too hasty and not altogether convincing conversion, and she had a premonition that something untoward was going to happen. So, on the day before the big event, she dispatched Aroma and a few of the junior maids to go with Candida and her helpers and make sure that the candidates were both properly prepared. She herself inspected their things and put them out in readiness, and then went over with Li Wan to Lady Wang's apartment, where she selected a few of the more trusty family retainers to accompany them the next day, for fear they might be jolted or trampled on in the crowds.

The big day finally arrived, and Baoyu and Jia Lan changed into smart but unostentatious clothes. They came over in high spirits to bid farewell to Lady Wang, who gave them a few parting words of advice:

'This is the first examination for both of you, and although you are such big boys now, it will still be the first time either of you has been away from me for a whole day. You may have gone out in the past, but you were always surrounded by your maids and nurses. You have never spent the night away on your own like this. Today, when you both go into the examination, you are bound to feel rather lonely with none of the family by you. You must take special care. Finish your papers and come out as early as possible, and then be sure to find one of the family servants and come home as soon as you can. We shall be worrying about you.'

As she spoke, Lady Wang herself was greatly moved by the occasion. Jia Lan made all the appropriate responses, but Baoyu remained silent until his mother had quite finished speaking. Then he walked up to her, knelt at her feet and with tears streaming down his cheeks kowtowed to her three times and said:

'I could never repay you adequately for all you have done for me, Mother. But if I can do this one thing successfully, if I can do my very best and pass this examination, then perhaps I can bring you a little pleasure. Then my worldly duty will be accomplished and I will at least have made some small return for all the trouble I have caused you.'

Lady Wang was still more deeply moved by this:

'It is a very fine thing, what you are setting out to do. It is only a shame that your grandmother couldn't be here to witness it.'

She wept as she spoke and put her arms around him to draw him to her. Baoyu remained kneeling however and would not rise.

'Even though Grandmother is not here,' he said, 'I am sure she knows about it and is happy. So really it is just as if she were present. What separates us is only matter. We are together in spirit.'

*   *   *

At last came the day when the examinations were due to be concluded and the students released from their cells.[1] Lady Wang was eagerly awaiting the return of Baoyu and Jia Lan, and when midday came and there was still no sign of either of them, she, Li Wan and Baochai all began to worry and sent one servant after another to find out what had become of them. The servants could obtain no news, and not one of them dared to return empty handed. Later another batch was dispatched on the same mission, with the same result. The three ladies were beside themselves with anxiety.

When evening came, someone returned at last: it was Jia Lan. They were delighted to see him, and immediately asked:

'Where is Baoyu?'

He did not even greet them but burst into tears.

'Lost!' he sobbed.

For several minutes Lady Wang was struck dumb. Then she collapsed senseless onto her couch. Luckily Suncloud and one or two other maids were at

---

1. During the several days of the examinations, candidates were sequestered in individual exam cells.

hand to support her, and they brought her round, themselves sobbing hysterically the while. Baochai stared in front of her with a glazed expression in her eyes, while Aroma sobbed her heart out. The only thing they could find time to do between their fits of sobbing was to scold Jia Lan:

'Fool! You were with Baoyu—how could he get lost?'

'Before the examinations we stayed in the same room, we ate together and slept together. Even when we went in we were never far apart, we were always within sight of each other. This morning Uncle Bao finished his paper early and waited for me. We handed in our papers at the same time and left together. When we reached the Dragon Gate outside there was a big crowd and I lost sight of him. The servants who had come to fetch us asked me where he was and Li Gui told them: "One minute he was just over there clear as daylight, the next minute he was gone. How can he have disappeared so suddenly in the crowd?" I told Li Gui and the others to split up into search parties, while I took some men and looked in all the cubicles. But there was no sign of him. That's why I'm so late back.'

Lady Wang had been sobbing throughout this, without saying a word. Baochai had already more or less guessed the truth. Aroma continued to weep inconsolably. Jia Qiang and the other men needed no further orders but set off immediately in several directions to join in the search. It was a sad sight, with everyone in the lowest of spirits and the welcome-home party prepared in vain. Jia Lan forgot his own exhaustion and wanted to go out with the others. But Lady Wang kept him back:

'My child! Your uncle is lost; if we lost you as well, it would be more than we could bear! You have a rest now, there's a good boy!'

He was reluctant to stay behind, but acquiesced when Youshi added her entreaties to Lady Wang's.

The only person present who seemed unsurprised was Xichun. She did not feel free to express her thoughts, but instead inquired of Baochai:

'Did Baoyu have his jade with him when he left?'

'Of course he did,' she replied. 'He never goes anywhere without it.'

Xichun was silent. Aroma remembered how they had had to waylay Baoyu and snatch the jade from his hands, and she had an overwhelming suspicion that today's mishap was that monk's doing too. Her heart ached with grief, tears poured down her cheeks and she began wailing despondently. Memories flooded back of the affection Baoyu had shown her. 'I annoyed him sometimes, I know, and then he'd be cross. But he always had a way of making it up. He was so kind to me, and so thoughtful. In heated moments he often would vow to become a monk. I never believed him. And now he's gone!'

It was two o'clock in the morning by now, and still there was no sign of Baoyu. Li Wan, afraid that Lady Wang would injure herself through excess of grief, did her best to console her and advised her to retire to bed. The rest of the family accompanied her to her room, except for Lady Xing who returned to her own apartment, and Jia Huan, who was still lying low and had not dared to make an appearance at all. Lady Wang told Jia Lan to go back to his room, and herself spent a sleepless night. Next day at dawn some of the servants dispatched the previous day returned, to report that they had searched everywhere and failed to find the slightest trace of Baoyu. During the morning a stream of relations including Aunt Xue, Xue Ke, Shi Xiangyun, Baoqin and old Mrs Li came to enquire after Lady Wang's health and to ask for news of Baoyu.

After several days of this, Lady Wang was so consumed with grief that she could neither eat nor drink, and her very life seemed in danger. Then suddenly a servant announced a messenger from the Commandant of the Haimen Coastal Region, who brought news that Tanchun was due to arrive in the capital the following day. Although this could not totally dispel her grief at Baoyu's disappearance, Lady Wang felt some slight comfort at the thought of seeing Tanchun again. The next day, Tanchun arrived at Rongguo House and they all went out to the front to greet her, finding her lovelier than ever and most prettily dressed. When Tanchun saw how Lady Wang had aged, and how red-eyed everyone in the family was, tears sprang to her eyes, and it was a while before she could stop weeping and greet them all properly. She was also distressed to see Xichun in a nun's habit, and wept again to learn of Baoyu's strange disappearance and the many other family misfortunes. But she had always been gifted with a knack of finding the right thing to say, and her natural equanimity restored a degree of calm to the gathering and gave some real comfort to Lady Wang and the rest of the family. The next day her husband came to visit, and when he learned how things stood he begged her to stay at home and console her family. The maids and old serving-women who had accompanied her to her new home were thus granted a welcome reunion with their old friends.

The entire household, masters and servants alike, still waited anxiously day and night for news of Baoyu. Very late one night, during the fifth watch, some servants came as far as the inner gate, announcing that they had indeed wonderful news to report, and a couple of the junior maids hurried in to the inner apartments, without stopping to inform the senior maids.

'Ma'am, ladies!' they announced. 'Wonderful news!'

Lady Wang thought that Baoyu must at last have been found and rising from her bed she exclaimed with delight:

'Where did they find him? Send him in at once to see me!'

'He has been placed seventh on the roll of successful candidates!' the maid cried.

'But has he been *found?*'

The maid was silent. Lady Wang sat down again.

'*Who* came seventh?' asked Tanchun.

'Mr Bao.'

As they were talking they heard a voice outside shouting:

'Master Lan has passed too!'

A servant went hurrying out to receive the official notice, on which it was written that Jia Lan had been placed one hundred and thirtieth on the roll.

Since there was still no news of Baoyu's whereabouts, Li Wan did not feel free to express her feelings of pride and joy; and Lady Wang, delighted as she was that Jia Lan had passed, could not help thinking to herself:

'If only Baoyu were here too, what a happy celebration it would be!'

Baochai alone was still plunged in gloom, though she felt it inappropriate to weep. The others were busy offering their congratulations and trying to look on the cheerful side:

'Since it was Baoyu's fate to pass, he cannot remain lost for long. In a day or two he is sure to be found.'

This plausible suggestion brought a momentary smile to Lady Wang's cheeks, and the family seized on this opportunity to persuade her to eat and drink a little. A moment later Tealeaf's voice could be heard calling excitedly from the inner gate:

'Now that Mr Bao has passed, he is sure to be found soon!'

'What makes you so sure of that?' they asked him.

'There's a saying: "If a man once passes the examination, the whole world learns his name." Now everyone will know Mr Bao's name wherever he goes, and someone will be sure to bring him home.'

'That Tealeaf may be a cheeky little devil, but there's something in what he says,' agreed the maids.

Xichun differed:

'How could a grown man like Baoyu be lost? If you ask me, he has deliberately severed his ties with the world and chosen the life of a monk. And in that case he *will* be hard to find.'

This set the ladies weeping all over again.

'It is certainly true,' said Li Wan, 'that since ancient times many men have renounced worldly rank and riches to become Buddhas or Saints.'

'But if he rejects his own mother and father,' sobbed Lady Wang, 'then he's failing in his duty as a son. And in that case how can he ever hope to become a Saint or a Buddha?'

'It is best to be ordinary,' commented Tanchun. 'Baoyu was always different. He had that jade of his ever since he was born, and everyone always thought it lucky. But looking back, I can see that it's brought him nothing but bad luck. If a few more days go by and we still cannot find him I don't want to upset you, Mother—but I think in that case we must resign ourselves to the fact that this is something decreed by fate and beyond our understanding. It would be better not to think of him as having ever been born from your womb. His destiny is after all the fruit of karma, the result of your accumulated merit in several lifetimes.'

Baochai listened to this in silence. Aroma could bear it no longer; her heart ached, she felt dizzy and sank to the ground in a faint. Lady Wang seemed most concerned for her, and told one of the maids to help her up.

Jia Huan was feeling extremely out of sorts. On top of his disgrace in the Qiao-jie affair, there was now the added humiliation of having to watch both his brother and nephew pass their examinations. He cursed Qiang and Yun for having dragged him into this trouble. Tanchun was sure to take him to task now that she was back. And yet he dared not try to hide. He was altogether in a state of abject misery.

The next day Jia Lan had to attend court to give thanks for his successful graduation. There he met Zhen Baoyu[2] and discovered that he too had passed. So now all three of them belonged to the same 'class'. When Lan mentioned Baoyu's strange disappearance, Zhen Baoyu sighed and offered a few words of consolation.

---

2. Son of a friend of Baoyu's father. The Zhens, also a wealthy southern family, had close ties with the Jias.

The Chief Examiner presented the successful candidates' compositions to the throne, and His Majesty read them through one by one and found them all to be well balanced and cogent, displaying both breadth of learning and soundness of judgement. When he noticed two Nanking Jias in seventh and one hundred and thirtieth place, he asked if they were any relation of the late Jia Concubine. One of his ministers went to summon Jia Baoyu and Jia Lan for questioning on this matter. Jia Lan, on arrival, explained the circumstances of his uncle's disappearance and gave a full account of the three preceding generations of the family, all of which was transmitted to the throne by the minister. His Majesty, as a consequence of this information, being a monarch of exceptional enlightenment and compassion, instructed his minister, in consideration of the family's distinguished record of service, to submit a full report on their case. This the minister did and drafted a detailed memorial on the subject. His Majesty's concern was such that on reading this memorial he ordered the minister to re-examine the facts that had led to Jia She's conviction. Subsequently the Imperial eye lighted upon yet another memorial describing the success of the recent campaign to quell the coastal disturbances, 'causing the seas to be at peace and the rivers to be cleansed, and leaving the honest citizenry free to pursue their livelihood unmolested once more'. His Majesty was overjoyed at this good news and ordered his council of ministers to deliberate on suitable rewards and also to pronounce a general amnesty throughout the Empire.

When Jia Lan had left court and had gone to pay his respects to his examiner, he learned of the amnesty and hurried home to tell Lady Wang and the rest of the family. They all seemed delighted, though their pleasure was marred by Baoyu's continued absence. Aunt Xue was particularly happy at the news, and set about making preparations for the payment of Xue Pan's fine, since his death sentence would now be commuted as part of the amnesty.

A few days later it was announced that Zhen Baoyu and his father had called to offer their congratulations, and Lady Wang sent Jia Lan out to receive them. Shortly afterwards Jia Lan returned with a broad smile on his face:

'Good news, Grandmother! Uncle Zhen Baoyu's father has heard at court of an edict pardoning both Great-uncle She and Uncle Zhen from Ningguo House, and restoring the hereditary Ningguo rank to Uncle Zhen. Grandfather is to keep the hereditary Rongguo rank and after his period of mourning will be reinstated as a Permanent Secretary in the Board of Works. All the family's confiscated property is to be restored. His Majesty has read Uncle Bao's composition and was extremely struck by it. When he discovered that the candidate concerned was Her Late Grace's younger brother, and when the Prince of Beijing added a few words of commendation, His Majesty expressed a desire to summon him to court for an audience. The ministers then told him that Uncle Bao had disappeared after the examination (it was I who informed them of this in the first place), and that he was at present being looked for everywhere, without success, whereupon His Majesty issued another edict, ordering all the garrisons in the capital to make a thorough search for him. You can set your mind at rest now, Grandmother. With His Majesty taking a personal interest in the matter, Uncle Bao is sure to be found!'

Lady Wang and the rest of the family were delighted and congratulated each other on this new turn of events.

* * *

FROM **CHAPTER** 120

*Zhen Shiyin expounds the Nature of Passion and Illusion
And Jia Yucun concludes the Dream of Golden Days*

* * *

Jia Zheng had arrived in Nanking with Grandmother Jia's coffin, accompanied by Jia Rong and the coffins of Qinshi, Xifeng, Daiyu and Faithful. They made arrangements for the Jia family members to be interred, and then Jia Rong took Daiyu's coffin to her own family graveyard to be buried there, while Jia Zheng saw to the construction of the tombs. Then one day a letter arrived from home, in which he read of the success achieved by Baoyu and Jia Lan in their examinations—which gave him great pleasure—and of Baoyu's disappearance, which disturbed him greatly and made him decide to cut short his stay and hurry home. On his return journey he learned of the amnesty decreed by the Emperor, and received another letter from home telling him that Jia She and Cousin Zhen had been pardoned, and their titles restored. Much cheered by this news, he pressed on towards home, travelling by day and night.

On the day when his boat reached the post-station at Piling, there was a sudden cold turn in the weather and it began to snow. He moored in a quiet, lonely stretch of the canal and sent his servants ashore to deliver a few visiting-cards and to apologize to his friends in the locality, saying that since his boat was due to set off again at any moment he would not be able to call on them in person or entertain them aboard. Only one page-boy remained to wait on him while he sat in the cabin writing a letter home (to be sent on ahead by land). When he came to write about Baoyu, he paused for a moment and looked up. There, up on deck, standing in the very entrance to his cabin and silhouetted dimly against the snow, was the figure of a man with shaven head and bare feet, wrapped in a large cape made of crimson felt. The figure knelt down and bowed to Jia Zheng, who did not recognize the features and hurried out on deck, intending to raise him up and ask him his name. The man bowed four times, and now stood upright, pressing his palms together in monkish greeting. Jia Zheng was about to reciprocate with a respectful bow of the head when he looked into the man's eyes and with a sudden shock recognized him as Baoyu.

'Are you not my son?' he asked.

The man was silent and an expression that seemed to contain both joy and sorrow played on his face. Jia Zheng asked again:

'If you are Baoyu, why are you dressed like this? And what brings you to this place?'

Before Baoyu could reply two other men appeared on the deck, a Buddhist monk and a Taoist, and holding him between them they said:

'Come, your earthly karma is complete. Tarry no longer.'

The three of them mounted the bank and strode off into the snow. Jia Zheng went chasing after them along the slippery track, but although he could spy them ahead of him, somehow they always remained just out of reach. He could hear all three of them singing some sort of a song:

'On Greensickness Peak
I dwell;

In the Cosmic Void
I roam.
Who will pass over,
Who will go with me,
Who will explore
The supremely ineffable
Vastly mysterious
Wilderness
To which I return!'

Jia Zheng listened to the song and continued to follow them until they rounded the slope of a small hill and suddenly vanished from sight. He was weak and out of breath by now with the exertion of the chase, and greatly mystified by what he had seen. Looking back he saw his page-boy, hurrying up behind him.

'Did you see those three men just now?' he questioned him.

'Yes, sir, I did,' replied the page. 'I saw you following them, so I came too. Then they disappeared and I could see no one but you.'

Jia Zheng wanted to continue, but all he could see before him was a vast expanse of white, with not a soul anywhere. He knew there was more to this strange occurrence than he could understand, and reluctantly he turned back and began to retrace his steps.

The other servants had returned to their master's boat to find the cabin empty and were told by the boatman that Jia Zheng had gone on shore in pursuit of two monks and a Taoist. They followed his footsteps through the snow and when they saw him coming towards them in the distance hurried forward to meet him, and then all returned to the boat together. Jia Zheng sat down to regain his breath and told them what had happened. They sought his authority to mount a search for Baoyu in the area, but Jia Zheng dismissed the idea.

'You do not understand,' he said with a sigh. 'This was indeed no supernatural apparition; I saw these men with my own eyes. I heard them singing, and the words of their song held a most profound and mysterious meaning. Baoyu came into the world with his jade, and there was always something strange about it. I knew it for an ill omen. But because his grandmother doted on him so, we nurtured him and brought him up until now. That monk and that Taoist I have seen before, three times altogether. The first time was when they came to extol the virtues of the jade; the second was when Baoyu was seriously ill and the monk came and said a prayer over the jade, which seemed to cure Baoyu at once; the third time was when he restored the jade to us after it had been lost. He was sitting in the hall one minute, and the next he had vanished completely. I thought it strange at the time and could only conclude that perhaps Baoyu was in some way blessed and that these two holy men had come to protect him. But the truth of the matter must be that he himself is a being from a higher realm who has descended into the world to experience the trials of this human life. For these past nineteen years he has been doted on in vain by his poor grandmother! Now at last I understand!'

As he said these words, tears came to his eyes.

'But surely,' protested one of the servants, 'if Mr Bao was really a Buddhist Immortal, what need was there for him to bother with passing his exams before disappearing?'

'How can you ever hope to understand these things?' replied Jia Zheng with a sigh. 'The constellations in the heavens, the hermits in their hills, the spirits in their caves, each has a particular configuration, a unique temperament. When did you ever see Baoyu willingly work at his books? And yet if once he applied himself, nothing was beyond his reach. His temperament was certainly unique.'

In an effort to restore his spirits, the servants turned the conversation to Jia Lan's success in the exams and the revival of the family fortunes. Then Jia Zheng completed and sealed his letter, in which he related his encounter with Baoyu and instructed the family not to brood over their loss too much, and dispatched one of the servants to deliver it to Rongguo House while he himself continued his journey by boat. But of this no more.

* * *

III

Early Modern Japanese Popular Literature

Japan's transition from the late medieval age of civil wars to an early modern world of peace and order is one of the most dramatic turning points in Japanese history. The new military rulers of the Tokugawa shogunate (1603–1868) created peace and order, imposed strict social hierarchies and forceful policies, and laid the foundations for economic prosperity and a new cultural flourishing. As the traditional elites and great military clans lost their influence and power, they also witnessed the rise of social newcomers. Commoners, a crucial driving force in Japan's commercial revolution, made their fortune in the rapidly growing great cities. Even the lower social classes, for the first time in Japanese history, had broader access to education under the Tokugawa. The new social prominence of the commoners and the great leap in literacy gave birth to a new type of literature: popular fiction, haikai poetry, and popular theater such as kabuki and puppet theater. This literature captured the pleasures and challenges of the lives of the new commoner class and their vibrant urban milieu.

A portrait of the seventeenth-century Japanese poet Bashō, with the text of one of his most famous haikus: "An old pond— / A frog leaps in, / The sound of water." (See p. 614.)

313

RUSSIAN
EMPIRE

Hokkaidō

HOKKAIDŌ

Hokkaidō

TOKUGAWA JAPAN
1603–1867

```
0    50    100         200 kilometers

0  20  40  60 80 100 120 miles
```

K I N K I

Regional name
and boundary

Owari

Domain name
and boundary

Ōgaki

Bashō's 1689 journey
from Edo to Ōgaki as
recorded in *The Narrow
Road to the Deep North*

N
W E
S

TŌHOKU

Akita   Morioka

Kisakata   Hiraizumi
Dewagoe (Naruko)   Ishi-no-maki
Obanazawa   Matsushima
Sakata   Shiogama
Mount Hagaro   Ōishida   Sendai
Yamagata   Ryūshakoji
Yonezawa
Iizuka
Echigo (Niigata)   Asaka (Fukushima)

Sukagawa

Shirakawa Barrier
Nasu
Kurobane
Nikkō

Ichiburi Barrier   Muronoyashima

K A N T Ō
Honshū   Sōka

Kanazawa   Edo (Tokyo)
Komatsu   CHŪBU
Daishōji   Kamakura
Maruoka
Fukui   *Mount Fuji* ▲
Iro-no-hama
Tsuruga
Ōgaki

Sea of Japan

HOKURIKU

Owari

KOREA

Kyoto
Nara
Osaka   ★ Ise Shrine

Kii

Tsushima

CHŪGOKU

Chōsu

Sanyō

SHIKOKU
Tosa
Shikoku

Inland

Pacific Ocean

KYŪSHŪ

Kumamoto

Nagasaki
Dejima   Shimabara

Kyūshū

Satsuma

East China Sea

Tanegashima

THE TOKUGAWA CLAN

Since the late twelfth century, in the wake of the civil wars chronicled in *The Tales of the Heike*, Japan had been governed by a series of military clans who held de facto power on behalf of politically impotent emperors. The first military government, the Kamakura shogunate (1185–1333) ruled from Kamakura near modern-day Tokyo. The Ashikaga shogunate (1336–1573) ruled from Muromachi, a quarter in Kyoto. But after 1467 Japan descended into 150 years of chaos and bloodshed until the beginning of the seventeenth century, when one clan, the Tokugawa, managed to reunify Japan and to set up a new military government in Edo, modern-day Tokyo.

The Tokugawa shoguns created a rigid class society, consisting of samurai, farmers, artisans, and merchants. The old aristocracy and Buddhist and Shintō priests stood outside of this hierarchy, although priests ranked equal to the samurai class. The shoguns' vast bureaucracy was staffed by samurai retainers. With no more wars to fight, these former soldiers became bureau-crats, and with a government to run they clustered in the cities. Removed from the land and their previous military and agricultural pursuits, the urban samurai developed new needs, which were promptly met by enterprising urban commoners—such as merchants and artisans—whose numbers swelled in response to economic opportunity. Even the traditional ways of commerce evolved under the Tokugawa. Because rice, which had long been the traditional standard of exchange, was unwieldy and inconvenient in an urban setting, coined money took its place in business transactions. The growth of a money economy had a slow but irreversible effect on every aspect of Japanese life.

Cities grew into bustling centers of commercial activity and changed under the impact of new policies. To prevent power challenges from the provinces, the shogun required his most prestigious retainers, the so-called "domain lords," to keep estates in Edo in addition to their castles in the provinces. Their women and children were held as hostages of sorts in Edo, while the domain lords lived in alternating years

This late eighteenth-century woodblock print by Katsukawa Shunshō depicts a street scene in Edo's Yoshiwara pleasure quarter.

in the provinces and in Edo. This policy changed the face of Edo, as wealth from the provinces flooded into the city and commercial and cultural exchange between the provinces and the political center increased. The shoguns were also worried about public morals. To control prostitution, they consolidated brothels that were previously spread out into "officially licensed pleasure quarters." The pleasure quarters were surrounded by a moat and only accessible through a main gate, to monitor entering clients and to prevent courtesans from leaving at their own will. The largest pleasure quarters—Yoshiwara in Edo, Shimabara in Kyoto, and Shinmachi in Osaka—quickly became proverbial. They appear again and again in popular literature as sites where fortunes were spent on music, dance, songs, and sex; purses and families ruined; hearts broken, and double love suicides planned.

Connected to the pleasure quarters both geographically and in spirit, the theater districts embodied the heartbeat of the early modern era. Although medieval Noh theater continued to thrive as an elegant, courtly entertainment for the upper classes that was sponsored by the Tokugawa shoguns, commoners crowded into the urban theater districts to witness the new forms of theater—*kabuki* and puppet plays—that emerged in the seventeenth century. Both kabuki—an opulent form of dance-drama with live actors—and

A detail from an early seventeenth-century folding screen showing Portuguese merchants in Japan.

puppet theater—narrative chanting (*jōruri*) performed by one chanter accompanied by a banjō-like *shamisen* and the miming with large puppets—dramatized issues of contemporary Edo society. They often staged current events. Whether in the guise of "historical dramas" or of "contemporary-life dramas" such as **Chikamatsu Monzaemon's** *Love Suicides at Amijima,* popular theater touched upon hot issues of the day: the repressive class system which led to clashes between people's individual desires and societal expectations; grisly acts of desperation, in particular double suicides of lovers whose union was unacceptable to Tokugawa society; or the hypocrisy of authority figures who propagated the values of Confucian virtue and honor but were actually driven by vanity, greed, and pettiness. Although actors and courtesans were considered outcasts, together with entertainers and beggars, they were the heroes of their age, darlings of an early modern celebrity cult. The newly popular *ukiyo-e* woodblock prints ("pictures of the floating world") depicted the world of the pleasure quarters and the world of theater: Mass-produced portraits of courtesans and actors show the faces of the giddy and voluptuous creativity of early modern Japan. It is therefore not surprising that the pleasure quarters and the theater district were at times subject to censorship and repression by the authorities.

The Tokugawa shoguns were also worried about outside threats. Portuguese traders had first reached Japan in 1543 when blown ashore by a typhoon. European merchants brought a few products that would have a major impact on Japan: firearms and New World crops such as corn, sweet potatoes, and tobacco. Catholic missionaries who were seeking converts outside of Europe to combat the reformation movements

back home followed in the wake of these merchants and traders. Francis Xavier, a priest of the recently founded Jesuit order, reached Japan in 1549 and, like many missionaries who followed him, had a keen interest in Asian cultures and was sensitive to indigenous beliefs and practices. But ultimately quarrels between different Catholic orders over how to present Christianity in East Asia and how to accommodate radically different cultural values and religious traditions damaged the credibility of the missionaries in the eyes of East Asian rulers. Repressions against Christianity began in Japan in 1587, and the Tokugawa shoguns quickly decided that the foreigners must go. By 1639 the shoguns had forbidden the practice of Christianity, overseas travel, and the importation of foreign books. European traders and Christian missionaries were expelled under threat of execution. Japanese converts were sometimes tortured or killed if they refused to abjure their Christian beliefs.

Although the period when Christian missionaries worked in Japan was relatively brief, they helped inspire a development that altered the face of Japan within a century: mass printing. Japanese had imported printed texts from China as early as the eighth century and had subsequently used the technology of woodblock printing to print Buddhist sutras. But until the late sixteenth century all books except for Buddhist texts circulated in extremely small, restricted numbers in manuscript format. Manuscripts were expensive, because they had to be copied by an expert hand; therefore access to book knowledge was limited to those few who owned copies as members of elite families or who had the means to have them copied. After Christian missionaries set up a printing press with movable type and published among others a Japanese translation of Aesop's

Fables (*Isoho monogatari* or "Tales of Isoho") in 1594, the first shogun, Tokugawa Ieyasu, had prominent Confucian texts, along with administrative and military works, printed with movable type in the early 1600s. Classical works of vernacular literature, such as an abridged version of *The Tale of Genji* and *Essays in Idleness*, followed soon in luxury editions. In the 1630s movable type printing was replaced with woodblock printing, which was more suitable to print the cursive Japanese *kana* syllabary, and commercial publishing houses opened. Seventeenth-century Japan underwent a printing revolution. Classical Chinese and Japanese texts were printed quickly and sold to the urban population in the dozens of bookstores that sprung up in response.

As a result, literacy levels soared. Until 1600 only aristocrats and the Buddhist clergy received an extensive education, while peasants and many samurai could not read or write. By the mid-seventeenth century, most of the samurai, artisans, merchants, and even some farmers had gained basic literacy. A growing network of private schools for the merchant class and domain schools for the samurai class made this drastic change possible.

The advent of mass printing fuelled the speed of both reading and writing. At one point, for example, on a single day in 1680, Saikaku composed in a frenzied single sitting a four-thousand-verse sequence. But not everybody followed the acceleration of the printing revolution. The entire oeuvre of **Matsuo Bashō** (1644–1694), generally considered the most famous haiku writer of all time, contains only about a thousand verses and Bashō seems to have disdained Saikaku's prolific literary output as well as the commercialization of literature he saw happening around him.

Despite their different outlook, both Bashō and Saikaku belonged to the new world of early modern popular literature. There was a strong awareness of the polar dynamic between popular (*zoku*) literature and refined or elegant (*ga*) literature. Refined literature was rooted in the classical traditions. Chinese-style poetry and classical *waka* poetry continued to stress aristocratic topics and relied on a fixed vocabulary of acceptable themes and diction—romantic love (in the case of waka), the seasons, spring warblers, or cherry blossoms. Popular literature, in turn, became expert in depicting bad places such as the theater districts and the pleasure quarters in vulgar language or celebrating themes and earthy expressions of simple commoner life— courtesans, potatoes, or piss. Popular linked verse (*haikai no renga*), which gave birth to the genre of haiku, became a major ground for experimenting with novel combinations of high and low diction, classical and popular themes, and Chinese and Japanese styles. Bashō's **The Narrow Road to the Deep North**, a poetic diary of his travels through northeastern Japan, is a brilliant example of how the literary tradition could be recaptured and recast through a new poetic language that preserved all the rich resonances of that tradition.

Early modern popular literature was one part of the revolution in lifestyles and forms of entertainment of this era. Actors, courtesans, adventurers, shopkeepers, rice brokers, moneylenders, fashion-plate wives, and precocious sons and daughters all created their own new cosmopolitan customs. *Kabuki* playwrights, haiku poets, woodblock artists, and best-selling novelists all captured in their own genres an intimate glimpse of kinetic bourgeois life—blunt, expansive, iconoclastic, irrepressibly playful. For the first time ordinary people became standard literary characters, and the material and sexual aspects of life were deemed worthy subjects of literature. We should note that the rich and varied spectrum of literary production in the early modern period also included sophisticated debates about the philological and historical interpretation of the Chinese Confucian Classics and the canonical works of Japan such as *The Man'yōshū* (*Collection of Myriad Leaves*) and *The Tale of Genji,* and thus the classical genres never went completely out of style, but popular literary forms—popular theater, fiction, and haiku—were the truly novel genres that emerged from the great transformations of early modern Japan.

THE WORLD OF HAIKU

Haiku is the best-known form of Japanese poetry and a testament to the importance of poetry within Japanese culture even today. With its evocative power and ability to surprise with unexpected juxtapositions, haiku is also the only Japanese genre to have spread beyond the Japanese archipelago. Haiku written in English have become a part of Anglophone literature and are used for elementary education in poetry. And poets throughout Europe, India, and the world bring the genre to life in many different languages. Today haiku is without doubt the shortest poetic form of world literature with a truly global reach.

Haikai, which can mean "comic" or "unorthodox" poetry and is the origin of haiku, was both a literary genre and a distinctive attitude towards language, the literary tradition, and life. Haikai poets wrote not only new popular verse; they also pioneered a new style in writing prose essays (*haibun*) such as travelogues, and they produced striking ink paintings (*haiga*), which are as sparsely and poignantly sketched in ink as haikus are sketched in words. Although there were many different schools of haikai with competing claims about their craft, they shared a basic spirit: they all venerated novelty produced against the backdrop of the classical past. They enjoyed collages of high and low culture, relished the clashes resulting from inserting every-

Woman Admiring Plum Blossoms at Night (mid-eighteenth century), by Suzuki Harunobu.

day, vulgar expressions of the new popular culture into the nuanced vocabulary of previous elite traditions, or blending Chinese and Japanese elements, which had previously been carefully kept apart. Enamored of puns, wit, and parody, haikai poets thus rewrote the tradition in often playful and humorous ways. Haiku became more than simply another form of poetry: it became an expression of modern life.

The seventeenth century, when haikai became popular, was a period of drastic change. After a prolonged period of civil wars, the military clan of the Tokugawa brought back order and prosperity when they established themselves as shoguns in Edo, modern-day Tokyo, on behalf of the emperors, the symbolical heads of state residing in Kyoto. A new class of urban commoners, including merchants and samurai, became a driving economic and cultural force. Commercial printing took off and bookstores selling popular literature targeting the new commoner class dotted the alleys of the expanding urban centers of Osaka, Edo, and Kyoto. Thanks to domain and temple schools, the literacy rate among samurai, merchants, and even peasants increased dramatically within the short span of half a century. Copies of Chinese and Japanese classics were now affordable to almost all classes of society, and a vibrant popular culture of vernacular literature, which often parodied classical models, thrived alongside Neo-Confucian studies and classical scholarship. Haikai had a large share in this new commercial book culture: during the second half of the seventeenth century 650 separate haikai titles were published in Kyoto alone. They represented the second most popular category of printed books after Buddhist devotional texts.

Originally haiku was the "hokku," the "opening verse" in a longer sequence of linked poems, which typically included a greeting to the host of a poetry session. The "opening verse," with a 5-7-5 syllable pattern, was followed by a verse with a 7-7 pattern, and capped by a third verse, again in 5-7-5 patterns continuing in alternation until the completion of the sequence. Sequences of 36, 100, or even 1,000 poems, composed alone or in a group, were the most common forms of linked verse. Haiku stood at the end of a long process of gradual shrinking of traditional verse forms. After the capacious "long verse poems" (*chōka*) in the eighth-century *Man'yōshū* (*Collection of Myriad Leaves*), the much shorter waka form, in a 5-7-5-7-7 pattern (also called *tanka* or "short poem") became the classical verse form since the tenth-century *Kokinshū* (*Collection of Ancient and Modern Poems*). Beginning with the fourteenth century, classical linked verse, the forerunner of popular linked verse, cut the waka pattern further down into alternating units of 5-7-5 and 7-7. Hokku appeared independently in prose texts and paintings in the seventeenth century. These short poems were not called haiku until the 1890s when the poet and critic Masaoka Shiki (1867–1902) coined the term "haiku" for poems in the 5-7-5 pattern.

Haiku typically contains a "seasonal word" (*kigo*), which evokes a host of associations relating landscape to mood (for example autumn wind to desolation), and a "cutting word" (*kireji*), which usually stands at the end of the first or second line and divides the haiku into two parts. A good example is a haiku by the haiku master **Matsuo Bashō** (1644–1694). On one of his travels, ghosts of fallen warriors appeared to Bashō along the shore of Akashi, where troops of the aristocratic Heike clan were massacred in the civil wars at the end of the twelfth century (described in *The Tales of the Heike*). Bashō captured the tragic spirit of the site in this humorous haiku:

> Octopus traps—
> fleeting dreams under
> a summer moon

Bashō must have seen local fishermen at Akashi lowering their octopus traps in the afternoon and hoping for a good catch the next morning. Tragic memory, traditional imagery, and the vignette of the simple fisherman life experienced by the poet-traveler clash in these few syllables. The classical image of the "summer moon," suggesting brevity of life and impermanence of all things, is juxtaposed with the all-too-real octopus traps. But the vulgar traps of the poet's actual experience are also the traps which once captured the Heike warriors, putting an end to their short-lived glory, short like a summer night.

Haikai exponentially expanded the topics on which one could write. If a poem introduced a word on which previous poets could never seriously compose, this "haikai word" was elevated to the status of the poetic, infusing literary language with the earthy, unrefined presence of contemporary commoner life.

The excitement over novelty was not only directed against the classical tradition, but also against the haikai tradition itself. Bashō's famous haiku of 1686 shook up the firm convictions of what "frogs" were expected to do in a classical poem:

> An old pond—
> A frog leaps in,
> The sound of water

Frogs appeared in spring, calling out to their mates with their beautiful voices, next to the bright yellow blossoms of the globeflower that typically grew next to a crystal-clear murmuring mountain stream. Bashō's haikai creature could hardly be more different from the "poetic essence" of the classical frog: not singing in spring, not in love, not enjoying its sparkling mountain stream, but stuck in a stagnant pond associated with the dead season of winter. As Bashō shook up classical frog poems, later haiku poets kept shaking up Bashō's poem:

> Jumping in,
> Washing off an old poem—
> A frog
>
> (Yosa Buson, 1716–1783)

> A new pond—
> Without the sound of
> A frog jumping in
>
> (Ryōkan, 1758–1831)

Both in today's Japan and in the West, haiku has become a different genre. It is no longer devoted to the rewriting of classical Chinese and Japanese poetry, as knowledge of these traditions has declined. But newer forms of haiku are thriving. As it is one of the few poetic genres of truly global reach, its fate lies in the hands of poets who write in many different languages and live in diverse locales. But haiku is still a poetry of small things and of everyday experience that preserves the sparkles of the particular in its universal appeal.

KITAMURA KIGIN

Kitamura Kigin (1624–1705) was a prominent member of the Teimon school of haikai. He emphasized the importance of classical waka poetry and Heian vernacular literature such as *The Tale of Genji* and *The Pillow Book*, on which he wrote commentaries. In his youth the future haikai master **Bashō** studied with him for a while.

"Fireflies" comes from a haikai manual Kigin wrote in 1648. This how-to manual is an early example of the poetic almanacs sold in Japanese bookstores today. In the entry on the topic of "fireflies," the reader can experience the quick-witted jumps between traditional poetic associations and funny new meanings.

From The Mountain Well

Fireflies[1]

In composing haikai about fireflies, those that mingle among the wild pinks are said to share the feelings of Prince Hyōbukyō and the ones that jump at the lilies are said to be like the amorous Minamoto Itaru.[2] The ones that fly on Mount

1. Translated by and with notes adapted from Haruo Shirane.
2. Situations in which fireflies helped lovers glimpse their object of desire: In the "Fireflies" chapter of *The Tale of Genji*, Prince Hyōbukyō, Genji's brother, sees the young Tamakazura in the light of fireflies, which Genji

cleverly releases behind the screen where she is sitting, and the prince falls instantly in love. The "wild pinks" refer to Tamakazura. In another romantic tale from the Heian Period, Minamoto Itaru peers into a woman's carriage aided by the light from fireflies.

Hiyoshi are compared to the red buttocks of monkeys, and the ones that glitter on Mount Inari are thought to be fox fires.[3] Fireflies are also said to be the soul of China's Baosi or the fire that shone in our country's Tamamo no mae.[4] Furthermore, poetry reveals the way in which the fireflies remain still on a moonlit night while wagging their rear ends in the darkness, or the way they light up the water's edge as if camphor or moxa were in the river, or the way they look like stars—like the Pleiades or shooting stars.

At Mount Kōya
Even the fireflies in the valley
are holy men[5]

3. The messenger to the god of the Hiyoshi Shrine on Mount Hiei, northeast of Kyoto, was said to be a monkey. Inari Shrine, also near Kyoto, was associated with both foxes and "fox fires," strange lights appearing in the hills and fields at night.
4. A nine-tailed golden fox that bewitched Emperor Toba by disguising itself as a beautiful woman. The emperor loved Tamamo no mae, but the light she radiated was so painful

to him that he had to have her exorcised. Tamamo no mae was believed to be a reincarnation of the Chinese beauty Baosi.
5. The headquarters of the Buddhist esoteric sect and an area with numerous monasteries and temples. The poem puns on *hijiri*, which means both "holy men" and "fire buttock" (lower part of a hearth), and implies homosexuality, not uncommon for Buddhist priests in the medieval period.

MATSUO BASHŌ

During his lifetime Matsuo Bashō (1644–1694) was only one of many haikai masters. He was not even part of the prominent haikai circles in the major cities of Kyoto, Osaka, or Edo, but spent much time on the road and eventually settled on the outskirts of Edo, supported by patrons and friends. Although Bashō was a socially marginal figure, like the travelers, outcasts, beggars, and old people who feature in his poetry, he and his school of haikai came to embody the art of haiku.

Bashō was born into a former samurai family that had fallen low in a small castle town thirty miles southeast of Kyoto. After serving the lord of the local castle, where he also developed his tastes for haikai poetry, he moved to Edo at the age of twenty-nine and installed himself as a haikai master, making his

living from teaching poetry. A few years later, in 1680, Bashō retreated to a "Banana plant hut" (Bashō-an), from which he took his pen-name, on the Sumida River in the outskirts of Edo. For the next four years he would write in a style heavily tinged by Chinese recluse poetry, before setting out on travels in 1684, during which he wrote poetic travel diaries.

In 1689 he set out with his travel companion Sora on a five-month journey to explore the Northeast, a trip which resulted in *The Narrow Road to the Deep North*, included in the selections here. The journey depicted in *Narrow Road* is a pilgrimage through nature, but it is also a very conscious emulation of the conventions of the past as Bashō seeks inspiration from famous poetic sites. In another sense it is a travel through language. Some places evoke the frail aesthetics of Heian waka, while others are tinged with reminiscences of Chinese poets, such as Du Fu and Li Bo. Both Bashō and his travel companion Sora kept a travel diary of sorts. Sora's diary, not published until 1943, shows that the majority of the fifty haiku in Bashō's travelogue were actually written after the journey or were revisions of earlier poems, and that Bashō made himself look far more ascetic and contemplative in the process of revision. *The Narrow Road to the Deep North* is thus not a diary but an idealized version of his travels.

Bashō was always on the move in search for new poetic themes, new language, and new objects. In his travel diaries he accomplished nothing less than influencing how people saw some of the most defining sites of Japanese identity. He gave the haikai movement a distinctive prose style. Previous classical linked verse had always stayed in the aristocratic realm of waka, never developing a prose language of its own. But with the innovations of haikai prose, haikai poetry reached a new degree of freedom, where poetry, prose, painting, and lifestyle flowed seamlessly into one another.

From The Narrow Road to the Deep North[1]

* * *

The months and days, the travelers of a hundred ages;
the years that come and go, voyagers too.
floating away their lives on boats,
growing old as they lead horses by the bit,
for them, each day a journey, travel their home.
Many, too, are the ancients who perished on the road.
Some years ago, seized by wanderlust, I wandered along the shores
    of the sea.

Then, last autumn, I swept away the old cobwebs in my dilapidated dwelling on the river's edge. As the year gradually came to an end and spring arrived, filling the sky with mist, I longed to cross the Shirakawa Barrier, the most revered of poetic places. Somehow or other, I became possessed by a spirit, which crazed my soul. Unable to sit still, I accepted the summons of the Deity of the Road. No sooner had I repaired the holes in my trousers, attached a new cord to my rain hat, and cauterized my legs with moxa than my thoughts were on the famous moon at Matsushima. I turned my dwelling over to others and moved to Sanpū's villa.

Time even for the grass hut
to change owners—
house of dolls[2]

I left a sheet of eight linked verses on the pillar of the hermitage.

I started out on the twenty-seventh day of the Third Month.

1. Translated by Haruo Shirane. For the route of Bashō's travels, see the map on p. 314.
2. It is the time of the Doll Festival, in the

Third Month, when dolls representing the emperor, the empress, and their attendants are displayed in every household.

The dawn sky was misting over; the moon lingered, giving off a pale light; the peak of Mount Fuji appeared faintly in the distance. I felt uncertain, wondering whether I would see again the cherry blossoms on the boughs at Ueno and Yanaka. My friends had gathered the night before to see me off and joined me on the boat. When I disembarked at a place called Senju, my breast was overwhelmed by thoughts of the "three thousand leagues ahead," and standing at the crossroads of the illusory world, I wept at the parting.

> Spring going—
> birds crying and tears
> in the eyes of the fish

Making this my first journal entry, we set off but made little progress. People lined the sides of the street, seeing us off, it seemed, as long as they could see our backs.

Was it the second year of Genroku?[3] On a mere whim, I had resolved that I would make a long journey to the Deep North. Although I knew I would probably suffer, my hair growing white under the distant skies of Wu, I wanted to view those places that I had heard of but never seen and placed my faith in an uncertain future, not knowing if I would return alive. We barely managed to reach the Sōka post station that night. The luggage that I carried over my bony shoulders began to cause me pain. I had departed on the journey thinking that I need bring only myself, but I ended up carrying a coat to keep me warm at night, a night robe, rain gear, inkstone, brush, and the like, as well as the farewell presents that I could not refuse. All these became a burden on the road.

We paid our respects to the shrine at Muro-no-yashima, Eight Islands of the Sealed Room. Sora, my travel companion, noted: "This deity is called the Goddess of the Blooming Cherry Tree and is the same as that worshiped at Mount Fuji. Since the goddess entered a sealed hut and burned herself giving birth to Hohodemi, the God of Emitting Fire, and proving her vow, they call the place Eight Islands of the Sealed Room. The custom of including smoke in poems on this place also derives from this story. It is forbidden to consume a fish called *konoshiro*, or shad, which is thought to smell like flesh when burned. The essence of this shrine history is already known to the world."

On the thirtieth, we stopped at the foot of Nikkō Mountain. The owner said, "My name is Buddha Gozaemon. People have given me this name because I make honesty my first concern in all matters. As a consequence, you can relax for one night on the road. Please stay here." I wondered what kind of buddha had manifested itself in this soiled world to help someone like me, traveling like a beggar priest on a pilgrimage. I observed the actions of the innkeeper carefully and saw that he was neither clever nor calculating. He was nothing but honesty—the type of person that Confucius referred to when he said, "Those who are strong in will and without pretension are close to humanity." I had nothing but respect for the purity of his character.

On the first of the Fourth Month, we paid our respects to the holy mountain. In the distant past, the name of this sacred mountain was written with the characters Nikkōzan, Two Rough Mountain, but when Priest Kūkai[4] established a

---

3. 1689.
4. Famous 9th-century priest and calligrapher who studied in China and introduced esoteric Buddhism into Japan.

temple here, he changed the name to Nikkō, Light of the Sun. Perhaps he was able to see a thousand years into the future. Now this venerable light shines throughout the land, and its benevolence flows to the eight corners of the earth, and the four classes—warrior, samurai, artisan, and merchant—all live in peace. Out of a sense of reverence and awe, I put my brush down here.

> Awe inspiring!
> on the green leaves, budding leaves
> light of the sun

Black Hair Mountain, enshrouded in mist, the snow still white.

> Shaving my head
> at Black Hair Mountain—
> time for summer clothes
>
> Sora

Sora's family name is Kawai; his personal name is Sōgoro. He lived near me, helping me gather wood and heat water, and was delighted at the thought of sharing with me the sights of Matsushima and Kisagata. At the same time, he wanted to help me overcome the hardships of travel. On the morning of the departure, he shaved his hair, changed to dark black robes, and took on the Buddhist name of Sōgō. That is why he wrote the Black Hair Mountain poem. I thought that the words "time for summer clothes"[5] were particularly effective.

Climbing more than a mile up a mountain, we came to a waterfall. From the top of the cavern, the water flew down a hundred feet, falling into a blue pool of a thousand rocks. I squeezed into a hole in the rocks and entered the cavern: they say that this is called Back-View Falls because you can see the waterfall from the back, from inside the cavern.

> Secluded for a while
> in a waterfall—
> beginning of summer austerities[6]

. . .

There is a mountain-priest temple called Kōmyōji. We were invited there and prayed at the Hall of Gyōja.

> Summer mountains—
> praying to the tall clogs
> at journey's start[7]

. . .

5. The first day of the Fourth Month was the date for changing from winter to summer clothing.
6. Period in which Buddhist practitioners remained indoors, fasting, reciting scripture, and practicing austerities.

7. At the beginning of the journey, the traveler bows before the high clogs, a prayer for the foot strength of En no Gyōja, the founder of a mountain priest sect believed to have gained superhuman powers from rigorous mountain training.

The willow that was the subject of Saigyō's[8] poem, "Where a Crystal Stream Flows," still stood in the village of Ashino, on a footpath in a rice field. The lord of the manor of this village had repeatedly said, "I would like to show you this willow," and I had wondered where it was. Today I was able to stand in its very shade.

> Whole field of
> rice seedlings planted—I part
> from the willow

The days of uncertainty piled one on the other, and when we came upon the Shirakawa Barrier, I finally felt as if I had settled into the journey. I can understand why that poet had written, "Had I a messenger, I would send a missive to the capital!" One of three noted barriers, the Shirakawa Barrier captured the hearts of poets. With the sound of the autumn wind in my ears and the image of the autumn leaves in my mind, I was moved all the more by the tops of the green-leafed trees. The flowering of the wild rose amid the white deutzia clusters made me feel as if I were crossing over snow. . . .

At the Sukagawa post station, we visited a man named Tōkyū. He insisted that we stay for four or five days and asked me how I had found the Shirakawa Barrier. I replied, "My body and spirit were tired from the pain of the long journey; my heart overwhelmed by the landscape. The thoughts of the distant past tore through me, and I couldn't think straight." But feeling it would be a pity to cross the barrier without producing a single verse, I wrote:

> Beginnings of poetry—
> rice-planting songs
> of the Deep North

This opening verse was followed by a second verse and then a third; before we knew it, three sequences. . . .

The next day we went to Shinobu[9] Village and visited Shinobu Mottling Rock. The rock was in a small village, half buried, deep in the shade of the mountain. A child from the village came and told us, "In the distant past, the rock was on top of this mountain, but the villagers, angered by the visitors who had been tearing up the barley grass to test the rock, pushed it down into the valley, where it lies face down." Perhaps that was the way it had to be.

> Planting rice seedlings
> the hands—in the distant past pressing
> the grass of longing

> . . .

---

8. Celebrated 12th-century poet. Bashō thinks here of the following poem: "I thought to pause on the roadside where a crystal stream flows beneath a willow and stood rooted to the spot."
9. One of the place names with the longest poetic history in the Deep North. The "Mottling Rock" was thought to have been used to imprint cloth with patterns of *Shinobugusa*, literally "longing grass," a typical local product. The plant was associated with wild and uncontrollable longing.

The Courtyard Inscribed-Stone was in Taga Castle in the village of Ichikawa. More than six feet high and about three feet wide; the moss had eaten away the rock, and the letters were faint. On the memorial, which listed the number of miles to the four borders of the province: "This castle was built in 724 by Lord Ono no Azumabito, the Provincial Governor and General of the Barbarian-Subduing Headquarters. In 762, on the first of the Twelfth Month, it was rebuilt by the Councillor and Military Commander of the Eastern Seaboard, Lord Emi Asakari." The memorial belonged to the era of the sovereign Shōmu. Famous places in poetry have been collected and preserved; but mountains crumble, rivers shift, roads change, rock are buried in dirt; trees age, saplings replace them; times change, generations come and go. But here, without a doubt, was a memorial of a thousand years: I was peering into the heart of the ancients. The virtues of travel, the joys of life, forgetting the weariness of travel, I shed only tears. . . .

It was already close to noon when we borrowed a boat and crossed over to Matsushima. The distance was more than two leagues, and we landed on the shore of Ojima. It has been said many times, but Matsushima is the most beautiful place in all of Japan. First of all, it can hold its head up to Dongting Lake or West Lake. Letting in the sea from the southeast, it fills the bay, three leagues wide, with the tide of Zhejiang.[1] Matsushima has gathered countless islands: the high ones point their fingers to heaven; those lying down crawl over the waves. Some are piled two deep; some, three deep. To the left, the islands are separated from one another; to the right, they are linked. Some seem to be carrying islands on their backs; others, to be embracing them like a person caressing a child. The green of the pine is dark and dense, the branches and leaves bent by the salty sea breeze—as if they were deliberately twisted. A soft, tranquil landscape, like a beautiful lady powdering her face. Did the god of the mountain create this long ago, in the age of the gods? Is this the work of the Creator? What words to describe this?

The rocky shore of Ojima extended out from the coast and became an island protruding into the sea. Here were the remains of Priest Ungo's dwelling and the rock on which he meditated. Again, one could see, scattered widely in the shadow of the pines, people who had turned their backs on the world. They lived quietly in grass huts, the smoke from burning rice ears and pinecones rising from the huts. I didn't know what kind of people they were, but I was drawn to them, and when I approached, the moon was reflected on the sea, and the scenery changed again, different from the afternoon landscape. When we returned to the shore and took lodgings, I opened the window. It was a two-story building, and I felt like a traveler sleeping amid the wind and the clouds: to a strange degree it was a good feeling.

> Matsushima—
> borrow the body of a crane
> cuckoo!![2]

> > > Sora

1. Flattering comparisons to well-known scenic sites in China. The tidal bore in Hangzhou, Zhejiang Province, was already famous in ancient China.
2. Typical summer bird. The gist of the poem is:

"Your song is appealing, cuckoo, but the stately white crane is the bird we expect to see at Matsushima [Pine Isles]." Pines and cranes were a conventional pair, both symbols of longevity.

I closed my mouth and tried to sleep but couldn't. When I left my old hermitage, Sodō had given me a Chinese poem on Matsushima, and Hara Anteki had sent me a waka on Matsugaurashima. Opening my knapsack, I made those poems my friends for the night. There also were hokku by Sanpū and Jokushi.[3]

* * *

On the twelfth we headed for Hiraizumi. We had heard of such places as the Pine at Anewa and the Thread-Broken Bridge, but there were few human traces, and finding it difficult to recognize the path normally used by the rabbit hunters and woodcutters, we ended up losing our way and came out at a harbor called Ishi no maki. Across the water we could see Kinkazan the Golden Flower Mountain, where the "Blooming of the Golden Flower"[4] poem had been composed as an offering to the emperor. Several hundred ferry boats gathered in the inlet; human dwellings fought for space on the shore; and the smoke from the ovens rose high. It never occurred to me that I would come across such a prosperous place. We attempted to find a lodging, but no one gave us a place for the night. Finally, we spent the night in an impoverished hovel and, at dawn, wandered off again onto an unknown road. Looking afar at Sode no watari, Obuchi no maki, Mano no kayahara, and other famous places, we made our way over a dike that extended into the distance. We followed the edge of a lonely and narrow marsh, lodged for the night at a place called Toima, and then arrived at Hiraizumi: a distance, I think, of more than twenty leagues.

The glory of three generations of Fujiwara[5] vanished in the space of a dream; the remains of the Great Gate stood two miles in the distance. Hidehira's headquarters had turned into rice paddies and wild fields. Only Kinkeizan, Golden Fowl Hill, remained as it was. First, we climbed Takadachi, Castle-on-the-Heights, from where we could see the Kitakami, a broad river that flowed from the south. The Koromo River rounded Izumi Castle, and at a point beneath Castle-on-the-Heights, it dropped into the broad river. The ancient ruins of Yasuhira[6] and others, lying behind Koromo Barrier, appear to close off the southern entrance and guard against the Ainu barbarians. Selecting his loyal retainers, Yoshitsune fortified himself in the castle, but his glory quickly turned to grass. "The state is destroyed; rivers and hills remain. The city walls turn to spring; grasses and trees are green." With these lines from Du Fu[7] in my head, I lay down my bamboo hat, letting the time and tears flow.

3. Bashō's disciples. "Hokku": the first three lines of a linked-verse sequence, from which haiku evolved.
4. Ōtomo no Yakamochi, an important poet in the *Man'yōshū*, composed a poem for the emperor when gold was discovered in the area: "For our sovereign's reign, / an auspicious augury: / among the mountains of the Deep North / in the east, / golden flowers have blossomed."
5. In the 12th century, members of a local branch of the powerful Fujiwara family—Kiyohira, Motohira, and Hidehira—had built up a flourishing power base in the north. Hiraizumi was the tragic site of the forced suicide of Minamoto no Yoshitsune, a heroic warrior of the Genpei Wars (1180–85) fought between the Taira/Heike and the Minamoto/Genji.

6. Son of Fujiwara Hidehira, whose fight with his brother destroyed the clan's prosperity in the region. After killing his brother, Yasuhira was in turn killed by the Minamoto/Genji chieftain Yoritomo, the founder of the Kamakura shogunate in 1185.
7. Minamoto no Yoshitsune won the crucial battles in the Genpei Wars, chronicled in *The Tales of the Heike*, and gave the Heike/Taira their death blow in 1185. Since his half-brother Yoritomo had become ever more suspicious of him, he sought refuge with the Fujiwara in Hiraizumi. Fujiwara no Yasuhira eventually betrayed him to Yoritomo and Yoshitsune was forced into suicide in 1189. Bashō compares Yoshitsune's tragedy to Du Fu's poem "View in Spring," written in a tragic moment when the Chinese capital was taken by rebels.

> Summer grasses—
> the traces of dreams
> of ancient warriors
>
> In the deutzia
> Kanefusa[8] appears
> white haired

Sora

The two halls about which we had heard such wonderful things were open. The Sutra Hall held the statues of the three chieftains, and the Hall of Light contained the coffins of three generations, preserving three sacred images.[9] The seven precious substances were scattered and lost; the doors of jewels, torn by the wind; the pillars of gold, rotted in the snow. The hall should have turned into a mound of empty, abandoned grass, but the four sides were enclosed, covering the roof with shingles, surviving the snow and rain. For a while, it became a memorial to a thousand years.

> Have the summer rains
> come and gone, sparing
> the Hall of Light?

Gazing afar at the road that extended to the south, we stopped at the village of Iwade. We passed Ogurazaki and Mizu no ojima, and from Narugo Hot Springs we proceeded to Passing-Water Barrier and attempted to cross into Dewa Province. Since there were few travelers on this road, we were regarded with suspicion by the barrier guards, and it was only after considerable effort that we were able to cross the barrier. We climbed a large mountain, and since it had already grown dark, we caught sight of a house of a border guard and asked for lodging. For three days, the wind and rain were severe, forcing us to stay in the middle of a boring mountain.

> Fleas, lice—
> a horse passes water
> by my pillow

. . .

I visited a person named Seifū at Obanazawa. Though wealthy, he had the spirit of a recluse. Having traveled repeatedly to the capital, he understood the tribulations of travel and gave me shelter for a number of days. He eased the pain of the long journey.

> Taking coolness
> for my lodging
> I relax

. . .

8. A loyal retainer of Yoshitsune. Some legends claim that he helped Yoshitsune's wife and children commit suicide and also saw his master to his end, before himself dying. "Deutzia": a white summer flower.

9. Of Amida Buddha, the Buddha presiding over the Pure Land Paradise in the West, and his attendants Kannon and Seishi. The coffins contained the mummified remains of Hidehira, his father, and his grandfather.

In Yamagata there was a mountain temple, the Ryūshaku-ji, founded by the high priest Jikaku,[1] an especially pure and tranquil place. People had urged us to see this place at least once, so we backtracked from Obanazawa, a distance of about seven leagues. It was still light when we arrived. We borrowed a room at a temple at the mountain foot and climbed to the Buddha hall at the top. Boulders were piled on boulders; the pines and cypress had grown old; the soil and rocks were aged, covered with smooth moss. The doors to the temple buildings at the top were closed, not a sound to be heard. I followed the edge of the cliff, crawling over the boulders, and then prayed at the Buddhist hall. It was a stunning scene wrapped in quiet—I felt my spirit being purified.

> Stillness—
> sinking deep into the rocks
> cries of the cicada

The Mogami River originates in the Deep North; its upper reaches are in Yamagata. As we descended, we encountered frightening rapids with names like Scattered Go Stones and Flying Eagle. The river skirts the north side of Mount Itajiki and then finally pours into the sea at Sakata. As I descended, passing through the dense foliage, I felt as if the mountains were covering the river on both sides. When filled with rice, these boats are apparently called "rice boats." Through the green leaves, I could see the falling waters of White-Thread Cascade. Sennindō, Hall of the Wizard, stood on the banks, directly facing the water. The river was swollen with rain, making the boat journey perilous.

> Gathering the rains
> of the wet season—swift
> the Mogami River
>
> . . .

Haguroyama, Gassan, and Yudono are called the Three Mountains of Dewa. At Haguroyama, Feather Black Mountain—which belongs to the Tōeizan Temple in Edo, in Musashi Province—the moon of Tendai[2] concentration and contemplation shines, and the lamp of the Buddhist Law of instant enlightenment glows. The temple quarters stand side by side, and the ascetics devote themselves to their calling. The efficacy of the divine mountain, whose prosperity will last forever, fills people with awe and fear.

On the eighth, we climbed Gassan, Moon Mountain. With purification cords around our necks and white cloth wrapped around our heads, we were led up the mountain by a person called a strongman. Surrounded by clouds and mist, we walked over ice and snow and climbed for twenty miles. Wondering if we had passed Cloud Barrier, beyond which the sun and moon move back and forth, I ran out of breath, my body frozen. By the time we reached the top, the sun had set and the moon had come out. We spread bamboo grass on the ground and lay down, waiting for the dawn. When the sun emerged and the clouds cleared away, we descended to Yudono, Bathhouse Mountain.

---

1. Better known as Ennin (794–864), a famous Japanese priest who studied in China and helped establish Tendai Buddhism in Japan.

2. A Buddhist sect that originated from Tiantai (Japanese Tendai) Mountain in southern China and was established in Japan in the 9th century.

On the side of the valley were the so-called Blacksmith Huts. Here blacksmiths collect divine water, purify their bodies and minds, forge swords admired by the world, and engrave them with "Moon Mountain." I hear that in China they harden swords in the sacred water at Dragon Spring, and I was reminded of the ancient story of Gan Jiang and Mo Ye, the two Chinese who crafted famous swords.[3] The devotion of these masters to the art was extraordinary. Sitting down on a large rock for a short rest, I saw a cherry tree about three feet high, its buds half open. The tough spirit of the late-blooming cherry tree, buried beneath the accumulated snow, remembering the spring, moved me. It was as if I could smell the "plum blossom in the summer heat," and I remembered the pathos of the poem by Priest Gyōson.[4] Forbidden to speak of the details of this sacred mountain, I put down my brush.

When we returned to the temple quarters, at Priest Egaku's behest, we wrote down verses about our pilgrimage to the Three Mountains.

> Coolness—
> faintly a crescent moon over
> Feather Black Mountain

> Cloud peaks
> crumbling one after another—
> Moon Mountain

> Forbidden to speak—
> wetting my sleeves
> at Bathhouse Mountain!

Left Haguro and at the castle town of Tsurugaoka were welcomed by the samurai Nagayama Shigeyuki. Composed a round of haikai. Sakichi accompanied us this far. Boarded a boat and went down to the port of Sakata. Stayed at the house of a doctor named En'an Fugyoku.

> From Hot Springs Mountain
> to the Bay of Breezes,
> the evening cool

> Pouring the hot day
> into the sea—
> Mogami River

Having seen all the beautiful landscapes—rivers, mountains, seas, and coasts— I now prepared my heart for Kisagata. From the port at Sakata moving northeast, we crossed over a mountain, followed the rocky shore, and walked across the sand—all for a distance of ten miles. The sun was on the verge of setting when we arrived. The sea wind blew sand into the air; the rain turned everything to mist,

3. Gan Jiang was a Chinese swordsmith who forged two famous swords with his wife, Moye. 4. "Plum blossoms in summer heat" is a Zen phrase for the unusual ability to achieve enlightenment. The plum tree blossoms open in early spring and never last until the summer. The poem by Gyōson (1055–1135), composed when he discovered cherries blooming out of season, reads: "Let us sympathize / with one another, / cherry tree on the mountain: / were it not for your blossoms, / I would have no friend at all."

hiding Chōkai Mountain. I groped in the darkness. Having heard that the landscape was exceptional in the rain,[5] I decided that it must also be worth seeing after the rain, too, and squeezed into a fisherman's thatched hut to wait for the rain to pass.

By the next morning the skies had cleared, and with the morning sun shining brightly, we took a boat to Kisagata. Our first stop was Nōin Island, where we visited the place where Nōin had secluded himself for three years. We docked our boat on the far shore and visited the old cherry tree on which Saigyō had written the poem about "a fisherman's boat rowing over the flowers."[6] On the shore of the river was an imperial mausoleum, the gravestone of Empress Jingū.[7] The temple was called Kanmanju Temple. I wondered why I had yet to hear of an imperial procession to this place.

We sat down in the front room of the temple and raised the blinds, taking in the entire landscape at one glance. To the south, Chōkai Mountain held up the heavens, its shadow reflected on the bay of Kisagata; to the west, the road came to an end at Muyamuya Barrier; and to the east, there was a dike. The road to Akita stretched into the distance. To the north was the sea, the waves pounding into the bay at Shiogoshi, Tide-Crossing. The face of the bay, about two and a half miles in width and length, resembled Matsushima but with a different mood. If Matsushima was like someone laughing, Kisagata resembled a resentful person filled with sorrow and loneliness. The land was as if in a state of anguish.

> Kisagata—
> Xi Shi[8] asleep in the rain
> flowers of the silk tree

> In the shallows—
> cranes wetting their legs
> coolness of the sea

> . . .

Reluctant to leave Sakata, the days piled up; now I turn my gaze to the far-off clouds of the northern provinces. Thoughts of the distant road ahead fill me with anxiety; I hear it is more than 325 miles to the castle town in Kaga. After we crossed Nezu-no-seki, Mouse Barrier, we hurried toward Echigo and came to Ichiburi, in Etchū Province. Over these nine days, I suffered from the extreme heat, fell ill, and did not record anything.

> The Seventh Month—
> the sixth day, too, is different
> from the usual night[9]

5. Bashō compares Kisakata to the famous West Lake in China, of which the Chinese poet Su Shi (or Su Dongpo, 1037–1101) wrote: "The sparkling, brimming waters are beautiful in sunshine; / The view when a misty rain veils the mountains is exceptional too."
6. From a poem attributed to Saigyō: "The cherry trees at Kisakata are buried in waves—a fisherman's boat rowing over the flowers."
7. Legendary empress said to have ruled in the second half of the 4th century.
8. A legendary beauty of early China, whose charms were used to bring down an enemy state. Xi Shi was known for a constant frown, which enhanced her beauty.
9. Because people were preparing for the Tanabata Festival, which was held on the seventh day of the Seventh Month in honor of the stars Altair (the herd boy) and Vega (the weaver maiden). Legend held that the two lovers were separated by the Milky Way, except for this one night, when they would meet for their annual rendezvous.

> A wild sea—
> stretching to Sado Isle
> the River of Heaven

Today, exhausted from crossing the most dangerous places in the north country—places with names like Children Forget Parents, Parents Forget Children, Dogs Turn Back, Horses Sent Back—I drew up my pillow and lay down to sleep, only to hear in the adjoining room the voices of two young women. An elderly man joined in the conversation, and I gathered that they were women of pleasure from a place called Niigata in Echigo Province. They were on a pilgrimage to Ise Shrine, and the man was seeing them off as far as the barrier here at Ichiburi. They seemed to be writing letters and giving him other trivial messages to take back to Niigata tomorrow. Like "the daughters of the fishermen, passing their lives on the shore where the white waves roll in,"[1] they had fallen low in this world, exchanging vows with every passerby. What terrible lives they must have had in their previous existence for this to occur. I fell asleep as I listened to them talk. The next morning, they came up to us as we departed. "The difficulties of road, not knowing our destination, the uncertainty and sorrow—it makes us want to follow your tracks. We'll be inconspicuous. Please bless us with your robes of compassion, link us to the Buddha," they said tearfully.

"We sympathize with you, but we have many stops on the way. Just follow the others. The gods will make sure that no harm occurs to you." Shaking them off with these remarks, we left, but the pathos of their situation lingered with us.

> Under the same roof
> women of pleasure also sleep—
> bush clover and moon[2]

I dictated this to Sora, who wrote it down. . . .

We visited Tada Shrine where Sanemori's helmet and a piece of his brocade robe were stored. They say that long ago when Sanemori belonged to the Genji clan, Lord Yoshitomo offered him the helmet. Indeed, it was not the armor of a common soldier. A chrysanthemum and vine carved design inlaid with gold extended from the visor to the ear flaps, and a two-horn frontpiece was attached to the dragon head. After Sanemori died in battle, Kiso Yoshinaka attached a prayer sheet to the helmet and offered it to the shrine. Higuchi Jirō acted as Kiso's messenger. It was as if the past were appearing before my very eyes.

> "How pitiful!"
> beneath the warrior helmet
> cries of a cricket[3]

> . . .

1. From an anonymous poem: "Since I am the daughter of a fisherman, passing my life on the shore where the white waves roll in, I have no home."

2. Bashō shows surprise that two very different parties—the young prostitutes and the male priest-travelers—have something in common. The bush clover, the object of love in classical poetry, suggests the prostitutes, while the moon, associated with enlightenment and clarity, implies Bashō and his priest friend.

3. An allusion to a scene from *The Tales of the Heike*, in which the warrior Sanemori, who did not want other soldiers to realize his advanced age, dyed his white hair black and fought valiantly to death, slain by retainers of Yoshinaka. A Noh play connects the washing and identification of Sanemori's head, which occurred at the place Bashō is visiting here, to the cry of a cricket, a poetic image of autumn, decline, and loneliness.

The sixteenth. The skies had cleared, and we decided to gather little red shells at Iro-no-hama, Color Beach, seven leagues across the water. A man named Ten'ya made elaborate preparations—lunch boxes, wine flasks, and the like—and ordered a number of servants to go with us on the boat. Enjoying a tailwind, we arrived quickly. The beach was dotted with a few fisherman's huts and a dilapidated Lotus Flower temple. We drank tea, warmed up saké, and were overwhelmed by the loneliness of the evening.

> Loneliness—
> an autumn beach judged
> superior to Suma's[4]

> Between the waves—
> mixed with small shells
> petals of bush clover

I had Tōsai write down the main events of that day and left it at the temple.

Rotsū came as far as the Tsuruga harbor to greet me, and together we went to Mino Province. With the aid of horses, we traveled to Ōgaki. Sora joined us from Ise. Etsujin galloped in on horseback, and we gathered at the house of Jokō. Zensenshi, Keiko, Keiko's sons, and other intimate acquaintances visited day and night. For them, it was like meeting someone who had returned from the dead. They were both overjoyed and sympathetic. Although I had not yet recovered from the weariness of the journey, we set off again on the sixth of the Ninth Month. Thinking to pay our respects to the great shrine at Ise, we boarded a boat.

> Autumn going—
> parting for Futami
> a clam pried from its shell

4. A coastal town well-known for people who spent their time in exile, such as the poet Ariwara no Yukihira (ca. 893) and Genji, the protagonist of *The Tale of Genji*.

MORIKAWA KYORIKU

Morikawa Kyoriku (1656–1715) was one of the most important disciples of **Bashō**. In his treatise *Haikai Dialogue* (1697), he argues that the "combination poem," which combines two unexpected elements in a single haiku, is the central technique of Bashō's school. In this short extract from his treatise, we have the privilege of glancing into the poet's mind at work, as he tries to find the perfect words to link an unlikely couple of things: "scent of plum blossoms" and "blue lacquer bowl."

From Haikai Dialogue[1]

Recently, I thought that "scent of plum blossoms" would make a good combination with "blue lacquer bowl" and tried various middle phrases, but none of them felt right.

> Scent of plum blossoms—
> pickled vegetables and
> a blue lacquer bowl

> Scent of plum blossoms—
> arranged in a row
> blue lacquer bowls

> Scent of plum blossoms
> from somewhere or other
> a blue lacquer bowl

I tried these various possibilities, but none of them was successful. When the subject matter and the combination are excellent but a good hokku[2] does not materialize, it means that the necessary intermediary has yet to be found. After more searching, I came up with the following:

> Scent of plum blossoms—
> beneath the guest's nose
> a blue lacquer bowl

1. Translated by Haruo Shirane.
2. Again, the first three lines of a linked-verse sequence, now usually called "haiku."

YOSA BUSON

Unlike many other haikai poets, Yosa Buson (1716–1783) came from a peasant family living outside of Osaka. Around the age of twenty he studied haikai poetry in Edo with a student of one of Bashō's students. He moved to Kyoto in his mid-thirties and devoted himself to Chinese-style literati painting. He ultimately became the head of his own school, succeeding his previous teacher. While Bashō sought novelty mostly in the everyday, Buson favored a "departure from the common," the pursuit of another, imaginary world inspired mostly by classical Chinese literature. In "Preface to Shōha's Haiku Collection," which he wrote in 1777 for Shōha, a wealthy merchant who studied Chinese-style poetry with well-known poets in Edo, Buson explains the attraction of mixing popular haikai with highbrow Chinese poetry. *New Flower Gathering* (1784, published 1797), his own collection, is a series of haiku and prose anecdotes that captures his infatuation with the strange and curious. One of the anecdotes, "The Badger," shows the serious, spiritual purposes that haiku could be put to by the eighteenth century.

Preface to Shōha's Haiku Collection[1]

I once met with Shōha at his villa in western Kyoto. When Shōha asked me about haikai, I said, "Although haikai greatly values the use of common language, it nonetheless departs from the common. That is, haikai departs from the common while using the common. The doctrine of departure from the common [*rizoku*] is most difficult to understand. It is like the famous Zen master who said, 'Listen to the sound of one hand clapping.'[2] The principle of departure from the common is the zen of haikai." Shōha was immediately enlightened.

He asked again, "Your explanation of departure from the common is, in its essence, profound and mysterious. Doesn't it mean finding a way to accomplish the deed by oneself? Isn't there another way? Isn't there a quicker way to change naturally, to depart from the common without others knowing it, without knowing it oneself?" I answered, "There is: Chinese poetry. From the beginning you've been very skilled at Chinese poetry. You needn't look elsewhere."

Shōha had doubts and asked again, "Now Chinese poetry and haikai differ in character. And yet you tell me to disregard haikai and discuss Chinese poetry—isn't this a roundabout approach?" I answered, "Painters assume that there is only one method for departing from the common, that if one reads many books, one's literary inclinations will increase and one's common or vulgar inclinations will decrease. Students must pay attention to this. To depart from the common in painting, they must throw away their brushes and read books. In this case, how can there be a distance between Chinese poetry and haikai?" Shōha immediately understood.

From New Flower Gathering

The Badger[1]

Jōū of Yūki acquired a second house and had an old man stay there as a caretaker. Even though it was in the middle of town, it was surrounded by trees and luxuriant with plants, and because it was a place where one could escape the hustle and bustle of the world, I myself stayed there for quite some time.

The old man had nothing to do there other than keep the place clean. One time he spent the long autumn night praying over his beads in the light of a single lamp while I stayed in the back room, working on my haikai and my Chinese poetry. Eventually I grew tired, and I spread out the blankets and pulled them over my head. But just as I was drifting off to sleep, there was a tapping sound on the shutters by the veranda. There must have been some twenty or thirty taps. My heart beat faster, and I thought, "How strange!" But when I got out of bed and quietly slid open the shutter to take a look, there was nothing. When I went back to bed and pretended to be asleep, there was the same tapping sound. Once again I got out of bed and looked outside, but found nothing. "How very strange," I thought, and consulted the old caretaker: "What should we do?" The caretaker responded, "It's that badger again. The next time it starts tapping like that, quickly open the shutter and chase after it. I'll come around from the back door, and it will probably be hiding under the fence." I saw that he was holding a switch.

---

1. Translated by Jack Stoneman.
2. A well-known Zen paradox.
1. Translated by Cheryl Crowley. There is a rich popular lore associated with the Japanese *tanuki*, here translated as "badger" (sometimes also called "raccoon dog").

I went back to bed and once more pretended to be asleep. Again there was the sound of tapping. When I shouted, "Aha!" opened the shutter, and ran out, the old man came out too, yelling, "Gotcha!" But there was nothing there, so we both got very angry. Even though we looked in every corner of the property, we couldn't find a thing.

This went on for some five nights running. Wearied by it all, I finally came to the conclusion that I could no longer stay there. But then a servant of Jōū's house came and said, "You will not be disturbed tonight, sir. This morning one of the villagers shot an old badger in a place called Yabushita. I know for sure that all that fuss and trouble was the work of this badger. Rest well tonight."

And indeed, from that night on, all the noises ceased. I began to think sadly that the animal that I had thought of as a nuisance had really offered me some comfort from the loneliness of my lodging. I felt pity for the badger's soul and wondered whether we had formed a karmic bond. For that reason I called on a cleric named Priest Zenku, made a donation, and for one night chanted the *nen-butsu*[2] in order that the badger might eventually achieve buddhahood.

> Late in autumn
> transformed into a buddha
> —the badger

A badger had come to the door to visit, and people said he made tapping sounds with his tail, but that was not the case. In fact, he had pressed his back against the door.

2. "Calling the name of Amida Buddha," who presided over the Pure Land Paradise in the West, helped people attain Buddhahood.

CHIKAMATSU MONZAEMON
1653–1725

The early eighteenth century in Japan was perhaps the only period in the history of theater when puppets performing for adult audiences were more popular than real-life actors. Although puppetry exists in many cultures and often has a long history as a folk art, in Japan it became a major literary form with acclaimed playwrights and sophisticated puppeteers. No playwright in this tradition was more popular or influential than Chikamatsu Monzaemon,

and his play *The Love Suicides at Amijima* (1721) is considered one of his greatest masterpieces.

THE RISE OF PUPPET
THEATER IN JAPAN

Beginning with the Heian Period (794–1185) puppeteer troupes roamed the capital and the provinces in search for audiences, competing with other low-class entertainers who thrived on the fringes of the aristocratic culture at the court in Kyoto. But puppet theater entered a new stage as a literary art form in 1684, when Takemoto Gidayū, a famous chanter, founded his own puppet theater in Osaka. Gidayū was an acclaimed performer of *jōruri*, popular narrative chanting that took its name from the heroine of a well-known tale and that was accompanied by a banjolike instrument called a *shamisen* ("three flavor strings"). The shamisen had recently been imported from Okinawa, then a kingdom south of Japan, and had become a popular instrument in the demimonde of the pleasure quarters. Gidayū convinced Chikamatsu to collaborate with him. Gidayū's invitation was fortunate: Chikamatsu would become the most brilliant playwright in the history of Japanese puppet theater.

Puppet theater thrived in the early modern milieu of the Tokugawa Shogunate (1600–1868), the military regime of the Tokugawa family that ruled from Edo, modern-day Tokyo. Also called the "Edo Period," this era saw an unprecedented growth of commercial culture. Urbanization accelerated, book printing caught on and fostered various genres of popular literature, while also enabling the spread of education and the flourishing of Confucianism and scholarship. Licensed pleasure quarters thrived, attracting customers of all social classes. Yet Tokugawa society was based on strict status order. Under the symbolic authority of the emperor, who resided in Kyoto, and the Tokugawa shoguns, the de facto power holders in Edo, there were four social classes: samurai (warriors), peasants, artisans, and merchants. Actors and entertainers were considered outcasts, together with prostitutes and beggars. Marriage outside one's class was forbidden, although in practice the boundaries were more fluid. Medieval Noh theater often borrowed themes and language from classical literature and addressed the higher rungs of Edo society, mostly samurai and rich merchants; it was sponsored by the shoguns as official state theater. In contrast to the high-class Noh theater, the new popular theater of the Edo Period—Kabuki and puppet theater—attracted commoners by staging current events and addressing concerns of contemporary society.

THE ELEMENTS OF PUPPET THEATER

Puppet theater performances include three elements: puppets; shamisen music; and jōruri chanting. The puppets are up to three-quarters of life-size. At first they were handled by one person, but they quickly became more complex creatures requiring the manipulation of three men, a head puppeteer in charge of the head and right hand, and two assistants responsible in turn for the left hand and the feet. Unlike puppetry that uses strings or other devices to make the puppeteers invisible to the audience, Japanese puppeteers are in full view on stage, dressed in black. The assistants' heads are covered with black hoods, while the calm face of the main puppeteer is visible above the head of the puppet. During the eighteenth century the puppets became ever more sophisticated, as the genre competed with other forms of popular theater such as Kabuki, an opulent popular genre of dance-drama with live actors. Crucial technical inventions that enhanced the puppets' appeal were the introduction of movable eyelids and mouths, and prehensile hands that could now wield swords, tissue paper, and other props.

During performance, the shamisen player and the chanter sit on an auxiliary stage protruding into the theater at stage left. Although the puppeteers, the shamisen player, and the chanter usually do not make eye contact, their performance is carefully synchronized and the percussive strumming of the shamisen helps pace the narrative and timing of the action. The central star

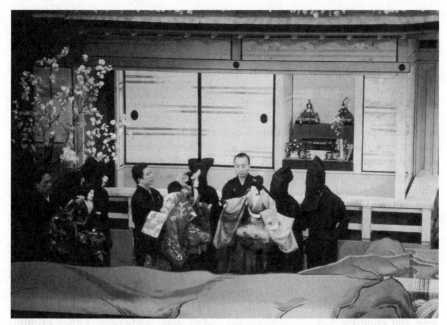

A contemporary puppet-theater performance in Osaka.

of puppet theater is the chanter. He intones the entire text of the play, taking in turn the roles of all puppet protagonists and of the narrator. At times he must switch among the voices of a timid child, a swashbuckling warrior, and an enamored lady within a few sentences. A master chanter uttering the last dramatic words of a famed young beauty in utmost despair before taking her life can make an audience forget that he is an old man who is turning the script's pages with his coarse and wrinkled hands.

Although in its heyday, puppet theater had raging success and reached a broad spectrum of early modern Japanese society, it has long since been eclipsed by other forms of mass entertainment. Today the Japanese government sponsors puppet theater as a traditional art form that is struggling in the modern world. But its reputation has spread beyond Japan and it dazzles even those first-time spectators outside Japan who consider themselves immune to the perplexing power of puppets to evoke the deepest human feelings.

THE LOVE SUICIDES AT AMIJIMA

Chikamatsu was born into a provincial samurai family. He served in the households of the imperial aristocracy in Kyoto before moving to Osaka, a bustling commercial hub at the time. He produced his first plays in the 1680s. Although after 1693 he devoted most of his energies to kabuki, in 1703 he reconnected with Gidayū and wrote exclusively for Gidayū's puppet theater during the last two decades of his life.

Chikamatsu wrote about one hundred puppet plays. His earlier plays were mostly historical dramas common at the time, but this subject changed in 1703, when he pioneered a new subgenre: the "contemporary-life play." In that year a shopkeeper from Osaka had committed double suicide with a prostitute from the Sonezaki pleasure quarters, because at the time people believed that they could be reborn with their lover "on the same lotus" in the Buddhist Pure Land if they committed suicide together. Three weeks after the event Chikamatsu's *The Love Suicides at Sonezaki* premiered with roaring success. It was the first time that such a scandalous contemporary event was depicted on the puppet theater stage. Chikamatsu would write twenty-four contemporary-life plays inspired by actual events during his lifetime.

The Love Suicides at Amijima, Chikamatsu's masterwork, was first performed in Osaka in 1721, and quickly adapted for the kabuki stage, as happened often with successful plays. In the play the Osaka paper merchant Jihei, with a wife and children, falls desperately in love with Koharu, a prostitute under contract at a Sonezaki establishment. This situation upsets a complicated network of social relationships and obligations between husband and wife, parent and child, and even among prostitute, madam, and customer. Koharu, a prostitute far below Jihei's social status, refuses other customers, Jihei squanders the sparse resources of his shop, his father-in-law demands a divorce, his brother tries to save him, while his wife develops an admirable bond of loyalty with Koharu. The clashes between social obligations and the desire for personal happiness are irreconcilable. Unlike in other "love

suicide" plays, where suicide is the unforeseen final outcome, in *The Love Suicides at Amijima* suicide is on the horizon from the beginning and nobody can in the end avert the tragic end of the lovers, however hard they try. Despite the dark subject matter, the play glistens with moments of social comedy.

The play became so successful that the authorities intervened. While Noh theater was patronized by the shoguns and the warrior elite, popular theater was seen by the elite classes as potentially subversive and incendiary and was often subject to censorship. Some of the prohibitions concerned the actors; for example, women and young boys were banned from the stage in 1629 and 1652, respectively, because of the seductive appeal they had for adult male audiences. Other prohibitions concerned the plays' subject matter: a year after *The Love Suicides at Amijima* premiered, the government prohibited plays on "love suicide" since they seemed to inspire waves of real-live suicides of lovers whose social class and life circumstances forbade their union. Prohibitions fostered inventiveness and playwrights started to disguise their staging of current events by setting the action in the distant past. Yet, since everybody in the audience knew what lay behind the historical veil, these plays remained contemporary-life plays of sorts and thus sustained the immense popularity of puppet theater.

From The Love Suicides at Amijima[1]

CHARACTERS

JIHEI, *a paper merchant, age twenty-eight*

MAGOEMON, *a flour merchant, Jihei's brother*

GOZAEMON, *Jihei's father-in-law*

TAHEI, *Jihei's rival for Koharu*

DEMBEI, *Proprietor of the Yamato House*

SANGORŌ, *Jihei's servant*

KANTARŌ, *Jihei's son, age six*

OSUE, *Jihei's daughter, age four*

KOHARU, *a courtesan belonging to the Kinokuni House in Sonezaki, a pleasure quarter in the northern part of Ōsaka*

OSAN, *Jihei's wife*

OSAN'S MOTHER (*also Jihei's aunt*), *age fifty-six*

ACT I

* * *

SCENE: *The Kawachi House, a Sonezaki teahouse.*

NARRATOR Koharu slips away, under cover of the crowd, and hurries into the Kawachi House.

PROPRIETRESS Well, well, I hadn't expected you so soon.—It's been ages even since I've heard your name mentioned. What a rare visitor you are, Koharu! And what a long time it's been!

NARRATOR The proprietress greets Koharu cheerfully.

KOHARU Oh—you can be heard as far as the gate. Please don't call me Koharu in such a loud voice. That horrible Ri Tōten[2] is out there. I beg you, keep your voice down.

NARRATOR Were her words overheard? In bursts a party of three men.

TAHEI I must thank you first of all, dear Koharu, for bestowing a new name on me, Ri Tōten. I never was called *that* before. Well, friends, this is the Koharu I've confided to you about—the good-hearted, good-natured, good-in-bed Koharu. Step up and meet the whore who's started all the rivalry! Will I soon be the lucky man and get Koharu for my wife? Or will Kamiya Jihei ransom her?

NARRATOR He swaggers up.

KOHARU I don't want to hear another word. If you think it's such an achievement to start unfounded rumors about someone you don't even know, throw yourself into it, say what you please. But I don't want to hear.

NARRATOR She steps away suddenly, but he sidles up again.

TAHEI You may not want to hear me, but the clink of my gold coins will make you listen! What a lucky girl you are! Just think—of all the many men in Temma and the rest of Osaka, you chose Jihei the paper dealer, the father

1. Translated by Donald Keene. A rarely performed opening scene, omitted here, shows Koharu making her way to the teahouse in Sonezaki to meet a samurai customer (the disguised Magoemon, Jihei's brother). The audience learns that Koharu is in love with Jihei, while Tahei, a man she dislikes, is trying to buy out her contract. When Koharu sees Tahei in the street, she escapes.
2. Villain in another puppet play.

of two children, with his cousin for his wife and his uncle for his father-in-law! A man whose business is so tight he's at his wits' ends every sixty days merely to pay the wholesalers' bills! Do you think he'll be able to fork over nearly ten *kamme* to ransom you? That reminds me of the mantis who picked a fight with an oncoming vehicle![3] But look at me—I haven't a wife, a father-in-law, a father, or even an uncle, for that matter. Tahei the Lone Wolf—that's the name I'm known by. I admit that I'm no match for Jihei when it comes to bragging about myself in the Quarter, but when it comes to money, I'm an easy winner. If I pushed with all the strength of my money, who knows what I might conquer?—How about it, men?—Your customer tonight, I'm sure, is none other than Jihei, but I'm taking over. The Lone Wolf's taking over. Hostess! Bring on the saké! On with the saké!

PROPRIETRESS What are you saying? Her customer tonight is a samurai, and he'll be here any moment. Please amuse yourself elsewhere.

NARRATOR But Tahei's look is playful.

TAHEI A customer's a customer, whether he's a samurai or a townsman. The only difference is that one wears swords and the other doesn't. But even if this samurai wears his swords he won't have five or six—there'll only be two, the broadsword and dirk. I'll take care of the samurai and borrow Koharu afterwards. (*To* KOHARU.) You may try to avoid me all you please, but some special connection from a former life must have brought us together. I owe everything to that ballad-singing priest—what a wonderful thing the power of prayer is! I think I'll recite a prayer of my own. Here, this ashtray will be my bell, and my pipe the hammer. This is fun.

> *Chan Chan Cha Chan Chan.*
> *Ei Ei Ei Ei Ei.*
> Jihei the paper dealer—
> Too much love for Koharu
> Has made him a foolscap,
> He wastepapers sheets of gold
> Till his fortune's shredded to confetti
> And Jihei himself is like scrap paper
> You can't even blow your nose on!
> Hail, Hail Amida Buddha!
> *Namaida Namaida Namaida.*

NARRATOR As he prances wildly, roaring his song, a man appears at the gate, so anxious not to be recognized that he wears, even at night, a wicker hat.[4]

TAHEI Well, Toilet paper's showed up! That's quite a disguise! Why don't you come in, Toilet paper? If my prayer's frightened you, say a Hail Amida![5] Here, I'll take off your hat!

NARRATOR He drags the man in and examines him: it is the genuine article, a two-sworded samurai, somber in dress and expression, who glares at Tahei

3. Allusion to an ancient Chinese text, where it is an image for someone who does not know his own limitations. "*Kamme*": one *kamme* corresponded to 3.75 kilograms (or 8.3 pounds) of silver. The price is extremely high.
4. Customers visiting the pleasure quarter by day usually wore deep wicker hats, concealing their faces, in order to preserve the secrecy of their visits; this customer wears the hat even at night.
5. A word play on *ami*, part of the name of Amida Buddha (the "Buddha of Infinite Light" promising rebirth in the Western Paradise of the Pure Land) and *ami*gasa, meaning "woven hat."

through his woven hat, his eyeballs round as gongs. Tahei, unable to utter either a Hail or an Amida, gasps "Haaa!" in dismay, but his face is unflinching.

TAHEI Koharu, I'm a townsman. I've never worn a sword, but I've lots of New Silver[6] at my place, and I think that the glint could twist a mere couple of swords out of joint. Imagine that wretch from the toilet paper shop, with a capital as thin as tissue, trying to compete with the Lone Wolf! That's the height of impertinence! I'll wander down now from Sakura Bridge to Middle Street, and if I meet that Wastepaper along the way, I'll trample him under foot. Come on, men.

NARRATOR Their gestures, at least, have a cavalier assurance as they swagger off, taking up the whole street.

The samurai customer patiently endures the fool, indifferent to his remarks because of the surroundings, but every word of gossip about Jihei, whether for good or ill, affects Koharu. She is so depressed that she stands there blankly, unable even to greet her guest. Sugi, the maid from the Kinokuni House, runs up from home, looking annoyed.

SUGI When I left you here a while ago, Miss Koharu, your guest hadn't appeared yet, and they gave me a terrible scolding when I got back for not having checked on him. I'm very sorry, sir, but please excuse me a minute.

NARRATOR She lifts the woven hat and examines the face.

SUGI Oh—it's not him! There's nothing to worry about, Koharu. Ask your guest to keep you for the whole night, and show him how sweet you can be. Give him a barrelful of nectar![7] Good-by, madam, I'll see you later, honey.

NARRATOR She takes her leave with a cloying stream of puns. The extremely hard-baked[8] samurai is furious.

SAMURAI What's the meaning of this? You'd think from the way she appraised my face that I was a tea canister or a porcelain cup! I didn't come here to be trifled with. It's difficult enough for me to leave the Residence even by day, and in order to spend the night away I had to ask the senior officer's permission and sign the register. You can see how complicated the regulations make things. But I'm in love, miss, just from hearing about you, and I wanted very badly to spend a night with you. I came here a while ago without an escort and made the arrangements with the teahouse. I had been looking forward to your kind reception, a memory to last me a lifetime, but you haven't so much as smiled at me or said a word of greeting. You keep your head down, as if you were counting money in your lap. Aren't you afraid of getting a stiff neck? Madam—I've never heard the like. Here I come to a teahouse, and I must play the part of night nurse in a maternity room!

PROPRIETRESS You're quite right, sir. Your surprise is entirely justified, considering that you don't know the reasons. This girl is deeply in love with a customer named Kamiji. It's been Kamiji today and Kamiji tomorrow, with nobody else allowed a chance at her. Her other customers have scattered in every direction, like leaves in a storm. When two people get so carried away with each other, it often leads to trouble, for both the customer and the girl. In the first place, it inteferes with business, and the owner, whoever

6. Good-quality coinage common around 1720.
7. The translator has changed the imagery from puns on saltiness in the original (soy sauce, green vegetables, etc.) to puns on sweetness.
8. Technical term from pottery making, meaning "hard-fired."

he may be, is bound to prevent it. That's why all her guests are examined. Koharu is naturally depressed—it's only to be expected. You are annoyed, which is equally to be expected. But, speaking as the proprietress here, it seems to me that the essential thing is for you to meet each other halfway and cheer up. Come, have a drink.—Act a little more lively, Koharu.

NARRATOR   Koharu, without answering, lifts her tear-stained face.

KOHARU   Tell me, samurai, they say that, if you're going to kill yourself any-way, people who die during the Ten Nights[9] are sure to become Buddhas. Is that really true?

SAMURAI   How should I know? Ask the priest at your family temple.

KOHARU   Yes, that's right. But there's something I'd like to ask a samurai. If you're committing suicide, it'd be a lot more painful, wouldn't it, to cut your throat rather than hang yourself?

SAMURAI   I've never tried cutting my throat to see whether or not it hurt. Please ask more sensible questions.—What an unpleasant girl!

NARRATOR   Samurai though he is, he looks nonplussed.

PROPRIETRESS   Koharu, that's a shocking way to treat a guest the first time you meet him. I'll go and get my husband. We'll have some saké together. That ought to liven things a bit.

NARRATOR   The gate she leaves is illumined by the evening moon low in the sky; the clouds and the passers in the street have thinned.

For long years there has lived in Temma, the seat of the mighty god, though not a god himself, Kamiji, a name often bruited by the gongs of worldly gossip, so deeply, hopelessly, is he tied to Koharu by the ropes[1] of an ill-starred love. Now is the tenth moon, the month when no gods will unite them;[2] they are thwarted in their love, unable to meet. They swore in the last letters they exchanged that if only they could meet, that day would be their last. Night after night Jihei, ready for death, trudges to the Quarter, distract-edly, as though his soul had left a body consumed by the fires of love.

At a roadside eating stand he hears people gossiping about Koharu. "She's at Kawashō with a samurai customer," someone says, and immediately Jihei decides, "It will be tonight!"

He peers through the latticework window and sees a guest in the inside room, his face obscured by a hood. Only the moving chin is visible, and Jihei cannot hear what is said.

JIHEI   Poor Koharu! How thin her face is! She keeps it averted from the lamp. In her heart she's thinking only of me. I'll signal her that I'm here, and we'll run off together. Then which will it be—Umeda or Kitano?[3] Oh—I want to tell her I'm here. I want to call her.

---

9. A period in the Tenth Month when special Buddhist services were conducted in temples of the Pure Land sect. It was believed that people who died during this period immedi-ately became Buddhas.
1. The sacred ropes at a Shintō shrine. "Temma . . . god": one of the main districts of Ōsaka, Temma was the site of the Tenjin Shrine, dedicated to the deified poet-official

Sugawara no Michizane (845–903). "Kamiji": the word kami, for "paper," sounds like kami, "god."
2. The Tenth Month was when the gods were believed to gather at Izumo, an ancient province on Japan's southwestern shore; they thus were absent from the rest of Japan.
3. Both places had well-known cemeteries.

NARRATOR   He beckons with his heart, his spirit flies to her, but his body, like a cicada's cast-off shell, clings to the latticework. He weeps with impatience.

The guest in the inside room gives a great yawn.

SAMURAI   What a bore, playing nursemaid to a prostitute with worries on her mind!—The street seems quiet now. Let's go to the end room. We can at least distract ourselves by looking at the lanterns. Come with me.

NARRATOR   They go together to the outer room. Jihei, alarmed, squeezes into the patch of shadow under the lattice window. Inside they do not realize that anyone cavesdrops.

SAMURAI   I've been noticing your behavior and the little things you've said this evening. It's plain to me that you intend a love suicide with Kamiji, or whatever his name is—the man the hostess mentioned. I'm sure I'm right. I realize that no amount of advice or reasoning is likely to penetrate the ears of somebody bewitched by the god of death, but I must say that you're exceedingly foolish. The boy's family won't blame him for his recklessness, but they will blame and hate you. You'll be shamed by the public exposure of your body. Your parents may be dead, for all I know, but if they're alive, you'll be punished in hell as a wicked daughter. Do you suppose that you'll become a Buddha? You and your lover won't even be able to fall smoothly into hell together! What a pity—and what a tragedy! This is only our first meeting but, as a samurai, I can't let you die without trying to save you. No doubt money's the problem. I'd like to help, if five or ten *ryō* would be of service. I swear by the god Hachiman and by my good fortune as a samurai that I will never reveal to anyone what you tell me. Open your heart without fear.

NARRATOR   He whispers these words. She joins her hands and bows.

KOHARU   I'm extremely grateful. Thank you for your kind words and for swearing an oath to me, someone you've never had for a lover or even a friend. I'm so grateful that I'm crying.—Yes, it's as they say, when you've something on your mind it shows on your face. You were right. I have promised Kamiji to die with him. But we've been completely prevented from meeting by my master, and Jihei, for various reasons, can't ransom me at once. My contracts with my former master[4] and my present one still have five years to run. If somebody else claimed me during that time, it would be a blow to me, of course, but a worse disgrace to Jihei's honor. He suggested that it would be better if we killed ourselves, and I agreed. I was caught by obligations from which I could not withdraw, and I promised him before I knew what I was doing. I said, "We'll watch for a chance, and I'll slip out when you give the signal." "Yes," he said, "slip out somehow." Ever since then I've been leading a life of uncertainty, never knowing from one day to the next when my last hour will come.

I have a mother living in a back alley south of here. She has no one but me to depend on, and she does piecework to eke out a living. I keep thinking that after I'm dead she'll become a beggar or an outcast, and maybe she'll die of starvation. That's the only sad part about dying. I have just this one life. I'm ashamed that you may think me a coldhearted woman, but I must endure the shame. The most important thing is that I don't want to die. I beg you, please help me to stay alive.

---

4. The master at the bathhouse where Koharu worked before.

NARRATOR   As she speaks the samurai nods thoughtfully. Jihei, crouching outside, hears her words with astonishment; they are so unexpected to his manly heart that he feels like a monkey who has tumbled from a tree. He is frantic with agitation.

JIHEI (*to himself*)   Then was everything a lie? Ahhh—I'm furious! For two whole years I've been bewitched by that rotten she-fox! Shall I break in and kill her with one blow of my sword? Or shall I satisfy my anger by shaming her to her face?

NARRATOR   He gnashes his teeth and weeps in chagrin. Inside the house Koharu speaks through her tears.

KOHARU   It's a curious thing to ask, but would you please show the kindness of a samurai and become my customer for the rest of this year and into next spring? Whenever Jihei comes, intent on death, please interfere and force him to postpone and postpone his plan. In this way our relations can be broken quite naturally. He won't have to kill himself, and my life will also be saved.—What evil connection from a former existence made us promise to die? How I regret it now!

NARRATOR   She weeps, leaning on the samurai's knee.

SAMURAI   Very well, I'll do as you ask. I think I can help you.—But there's a draft blowing. Somebody may be watching.

NARRATOR   He slams shut the latticework *shōji*. Jihei, listening outside, is in a frenzy.

JIHEI   Exactly what you'd expect from a whore, a cheap whore! I misjudged her foul nature. She robbed the soul from my body, the thieving harlot! Shall I slash her down or run her through? What am I to do?

NARRATOR   The shadows of two profiles fall on the *shōji*.

JIHEI   I'd like to give her a taste of my fist and trample her.—What are they chattering about? See how they nod to each other! Now she's bowing to him, whispering and sniveling. I've tried to control myself—I've pressed my chest, I've stroked it—but I can't stand any more. This is too much to endure!

NARRATOR   His heart pounds wildly as he unsheathes his dirk, a Magoroku of Seki. "Koharu's side must be here," he judges, and stabs through an opening in the latticework. But Koharu is too far away for his thrust, and though she cries out in terror, she remains unharmed. Her guest instantly leaps at Jihei, grabs his hands, and jerks them through the latticework. With his sword knot he quickly and securely fastens Jihei's hands to the window upright.

SAMURAI   Don't make any outcry, Koharu. You are not to look at him.

NARRATOR   At this moment the proprietor and his wife return. They exclaim in alarm.

SAMURAI   This needn't concern you. Some ruffian ran his sword through the *shōji*, and I've tied his arms to the latticework. I have my own way of dealing with him. Don't untie the cord. If you attract a crowd, the place is sure to be thrown in an uproar. Let's all go inside. Come with me, Koharu. We'll go to bed.

NARRATOR   Koharu answers, "Yes," but she recognizes the handle of the dirk, and the memory—if not the blade—transfixes her breast.

KOHARU   There're always people doing crazy things in the Quarter when they've had too much to drink. Why don't you let him go without making any trouble? I think that's best, don't you, Kawashō?

SAMURAI Out of the question. Do as I say—inside, all of you. Koharu, come along.

NARRATOR Jihei can still see their shadows even after they enter the inner room, but he is bound to the spot, his hands held in fetters which grip him the tighter as he struggles, his body beset by suffering as he tastes a living shame worse than a dog's.[5] More determined than ever to die, he sheds tears of blood, a pitiful sight.

Tahei the Lone Wolf returns from his carousing.

TAHEI That's Jihei standing by Kawashō's window. I'll give him a tossing.

NARRATOR He catches Jihei by the collar and starts to lift him over his back.

JIHEI Owww!

TAHEI Owww? What kind of weakling are you? Oh, I see—you're tied here. You must've been pulling off a robbery. You dirty pickpocket! You rotten pickpocket!

NARRATOR He drubs Jihei mercilessly.

TAHEI You burglar! You convict!

NARRATOR He kicks him wildly.

TAHEI Kamiya Jihei's been caught burgling, and they've tied him up!

NARRATOR Passersby and people of the neighborhood, attracted by his shouts, quickly gather. The samurai rushes from the house.

SAMURAI Who's calling him a burglar? You? Tell what Jihei's stolen! Out with it!

NARRATOR He seizes Tahei and forces him into the dirt. Tahei rises to his feet only for the samurai to kick him down again and again. He grips Tahei.

SAMURAI Jihei! Trample him to your heart's content!

NARRATOR He pushes Tahei under Jihei's feet. Bound though he is, Jihei stamps furiously over Tahei's face. Tahei, thoroughly trampled and covered with mire, gets to his feet and glares around him.

TAHEI (to bystander) How could you fools stand there calmly and let him step on me? I've memorized every one of your faces, and I intend to pay you back. Remember that!

NARRATOR He makes his escape, still determined to have the last word. The spectators burst out laughing.

VOICES Listen to him brag, even after he's been trampled on! Let's throw him from the bridge and give him a drink of water! Don't let him get away!

NARRATOR They chase after him. When the crowd has dispersed, the samurai approaches Jihei and unfastens the knots. He shows his face with his hood removed.

JIHEI Magoemon! My brother! How shaming!

NARRATOR He sinks to the ground and weeps, prostrating himself in the dirt.

KOHARU Are you his brother, sir?

NARRATOR Koharu runs to them. Jihei, catching her by the front of the kimono, forces her to the ground.

JIHEI Beast! She-fox! I'd sooner trample on you than on Tahei!

NARRATOR He raises his foot, but Magoemon calls out.

MAGOEMON That's the kind of foolishness responsible for all your trouble. A prostitute's business is to deceive men. Have you just now waked up to that?

---

5. Allusion to a proverb of Buddhist origin: "Suffering follows one like a dog."

I've seen to the bottom of her heart the very first time I met her, but you're so scatter-brained that in over two years of intimacy with the woman you never discovered what she was thinking. Instead of stamping on Koharu, why don't you use your feet on your own misguided disposition?—It's deplorable. You're my younger brother, but you're almost thirty, and you've got a six-year-old boy and a four-year-old girl, Kantarō and Osue. You run a shop with a thirty-six-foot frontage,[6] but you don't seem to realize that your whole fortune's collapsing. You shouldn't have to be lectured to by your brother. Your father-in-law is your aunt's husband, and your mother-in-law is your aunt. They've always been like real parents to you. Your wife Osan is my cousin too. The ties of marriage are multiplied by those of blood. But when the family has a reunion the only subject of discussion is our mortification over your incessant visits to Sonezaki. I feel sorry for our poor aunt. You know what a stiff-necked gentleman of the old school her husband Gozaemon is. He's forever flying into a rage and saying, "We've been tricked by your nephew. He's deserted our daughter. I'll take Osan back and ruin Jihei's reputation throughout Temma." Our aunt, with all the heartache to bear herself, sometimes sides with him and sometimes with you. She's worried herself sick. What an ingrate, not to appreciate how she's defended you in your shame! This one offense is enough to make you the target for Heaven's future punishment!

I realized that your marriage couldn't last much longer at this rate. I decided, in the hopes of relieving our aunt's worries, that I'd see with my own eyes what kind of woman Koharu was, and work out some sort of solution afterwards. I consulted the proprietor here, then came myself to investigate the cause of your sickness. I see now how natural it was that you should desert your wife and children. What a faithful prostitute you discovered! I congratulate you!

And here I am, Magoemon the Miller,[7] known far and wide for my paragon of a brother, dressed up like a masquerader at a festival or maybe a lunatic! I put on swords for the first time in my life, and announced myself, like a bit player in a costume piece, as an officer at a residence. I feel like an absolute idiot with these swords, but there's nowhere I can dispose of them now.—It's so infuriating—and ridiculous—that it's given me a pain in the chest.

NARRATOR   He gnashes his teeth and grimaces, attempting to hide his tears. Koharu, choking the while with emotion, can only say:

KOHARU   Yes, you're entirely right.

NARRATOR   The rest is lost in tears. Jihei pounds the earth with his fist.

JIHEI   I was wrong. Forgive me, Magoemon. For three years I've been possessed by that witch. I've neglected my parents, relatives—even my wife and children—and wrecked my fortune, all because I was deceived by Koharu, that sneak thief! I'm utterly mortified. But I'm through with her now, and I'll never set foot here again. Weasel! Vixen! Sneak thief! Here's proof that I've broken with her!

NARRATOR   He pulls out the amulet bag which has rested next to his skin.

6. A large shop.
7. A dealer in flour (for noodles). His shop

name Konaya—"the flour merchant"—is used almost as a surname.

JIHEI Here are the written oaths we've exchanged, one at the beginning of each month, twenty-nine in all. I return them. This means our love and affection are over. Take them.

NARRATOR He flings the notes at her.

JIHEI Magoemon, collect from her my pledges. Please make sure you get them all. Then burn them with your own hands. (*To* KOHARU.) Hand them to my brother.

KOHARU As you wish.

NARRATOR In tears, she surrenders the amulet bag. Magoemon opens it.

MAGOEMON One, two, three, four . . . ten . . . twenty-nine. They're all here. There's also a letter from a woman. What's this?

NARRATOR He starts to unfold it.

KOHARU That's an important letter. I can't let you see it.

NARRATOR She clings to Magoemon's arm, but he pushes her away. He holds the letter to the lamplight and examines the address, "To Miss Koharu from Kamiya Osan." As soon as he reads the words, he casually thrusts the letter into his kimono.

MAGOEMON Koharu. A while ago I swore by my good fortune as a samurai, but now Magoemon the Miller swears by his good fortune as a businessman that he will show this letter to no one, not even his wife. I alone will read it, then burn it with the oaths. You can trust me. I will not break this oath.

KOHARU Thank you. You save my honor.

NARRATOR She bursts into tears again.

JIHEI (*laughs contemptuously*) Save your honor! You talk like a human being! (*To* MAGOEMON.) I don't want to see her cursed face another minute. Let's go. No—I can't hold so much resentment and bitterness! I'll kick her one in the face, a memory to treasure for the rest of my life. Excuse me, please.

NARRATOR He strides up to Koharu and stamps on the ground.

JIHEI For three years I've loved you, delighted in you, longed for you, adored you, but today my foot will say my only farewells.

NARRATOR He kicks her sharply on the forehead and bursts into tears. The brothers leave, forlorn figures. Koharu, unhappy woman, raises her voice in lament as she watches them go. Is she faithful or unfaithful? Her true feelings are hidden in the words penned by Jihei's wife, a letter no one has seen. Jihei goes his separate way without learning the truth.

ACT 2

SCENE: *The house and shop of Kamiya* JIHEI.

TIME: *Ten days later.*

NARRATOR The busy street that runs straight to Tenjin Bridge named for the god of Temma, bringer of good fortune, is known as the Street Before the Kami,[8] and here a paper shop does business under the name Kamiya Jihei. The paper is honestly sold, the shop well situated; it is a long established firm, and customers come thick as raindrops.

---

8. Again, wordplay on *kami* (god) and *kami* (paper).

Outside crowds pass in the street, on their way to the Ten Nights service, while inside the husband dozes in the *kotatsu*,[9] shielded from draughts by a screen at his pillow. His wife Osan keeps solitary, anxious watch over shop and house.

OSAN The days are so short—it's dinnertime already, but Tama still hasn't returned from her errand to Ichinokawa.[1] I wonder what can be keeping her. That scamp Sangorō isn't back either. The wind is freezing. I'm sure the children will both be cold. He doesn't even realize that it's time for Osue to be nursed. Heaven preserve me from ever becoming such a fool! What an infuriating creature!

NARRATOR She speaks to herself.

KANTARŌ Mama, I've come back all by myself.

NARRATOR Her son, the older child, runs up to the house.

OSAN Kantarō—is that you? What's happened to Osue and Sangorō?

KANTARŌ They're playing by the shrine. Osue wanted her milk and she was bawling her head off.

OSAN I was sure she would. Oh—your hands and feet are frozen stiff as nails! Go and warm yourself at the *kotatsu*. Your father's sleeping there.—What am I to do with that idiot?

NARRATOR She runs out impatiently to the shop just as Sangorō shuffles back, alone.

OSAN Come here, you fool! Where have you left Osue?

SANGORŌ You know, I must've lost her somewhere. Maybe somebody's picked her up. Should I go back for her?

OSAN How could you? If any harm has come to my precious child, I'll beat you to death!

NARRATOR But even as she screams at him, the maid Tama returns with Osue on her back.

TAMA The poor child—I found her in tears at the corner. Sangorō, when you're supposed to look after the child, do it properly.

OSAN You poor dear. You must want your milk.

NARRATOR She joins the others by the *kotatsu* and suckles the child.

OSAN Tama—give that fool a taste of something that he'll remember![2]

NARRATOR Sangorō shakes his head.

SANGORŌ No, thanks. I gave each of the children two tangerines just a while ago at the shrine, and I tasted five myself.

NARRATOR Fool though he is, bad puns come from him nimbly enough, and the others can only smile despite themselves.

TAMA Oh—I've become so involved with this half-wit that I almost forgot to tell you, ma'am, that Mr. Magoemon and his aunt[3] are on their way here from the west.

OSAN Oh dear! I'll have to wake Jihei in that case. (*To* JIHEI.) Please get up. Mother and Magoemon are coming. They'll be upset again if you let them see you, a businessman, sleeping in the afternoon, with the day so short as it is.

9. A low, quilt-covered table under which a charcoal burner is placed as a source of heat.
1. Site of a large vegetable market near the north end of Tenjin Bridge, named, again, after the god "Tenjin," the deified Michizane.
2. A pun on two meanings of *kurawasu*: "to make eat" and "to beat."
3. Magoemon's and Jihei's aunt, who is also Osan's mother.

JIHEI   All right.

NARRATOR   He struggles to a sitting position and, with his abacus in one hand, pulls his account book to him with the other.

JIHEI   Two into ten goes five, three into nine goes three, three into six goes two, seven times eight is fifty-six.

NARRATOR   His fifty-six-year old aunt enters with Magoemon.

JIHEI   Magoemon, aunt. How good of you. Please come in. I was in the midst of some urgent calculations. Four nines makes thirty-six *momme*. Three sixes make eighteen *fun*. That's two *momme* less two *fun*.[4] Kantarō! Osue! Granny and Uncle have come! Bring the tobacco tray! One times three makes three. Osan,[5] serve the tea!

NARRATOR   He jabbers away.

AUNT   We haven't come for tea or tobacco. Osan, you're young I know, but you're the mother of two children, and your excessive forbearance does you no credit. A man's dissipation can always be traced to his wife's carelessness. Remember, it's not only the man who's disgraced when he goes bankrupt and his marriage breaks up. You'd do well to take notice of what's going on and assert yourself a bit more.

MAGOEMON   It's foolish to hope for any results, aunt. The scoundrel even deceives me, his elder brother. Why should he take to heart criticism from his wife? Jihei—you played me for a fool. After showing me how you returned Koharu's pledges, here you are, not ten days later, redeeming her! What does this mean? I suppose your urgent calulations are of Koharu's debts! I've had enough!

NARRATOR   He snatches away the abacus and flings it clattering into the hallway.

JIHEI   You're making an enormous fuss without any cause. I haven't crossed the threshold since the last time I saw you except to go twice to the wholesalers in Imabashi and once to the Tenjin Shrine. I haven't even thought of Koharu, much less redeemed her.

AUNT   None of your evasions! Last evening at the Ten Nights service I heard the people in the congregation gossiping. Everybody was talking about the great patron from Temma who'd fallen in love with a prostitute named Koharu from the Kinokuni House in Sonezaki. They said he'd driven away her other guests and was going to ransom her in the next couple of days. There was all kinds of gossip about the abundance of money and fools even in these days of high prices.

My husband Gozaemon has been hearing about Koharu constantly, and he's sure that her great patron from Temma must be you, Jihei. He told me, "He's your nepbew, but for me he's a stranger, and my daughter's happiness is my chief concern. Once he ransoms the prostitute he'll no doubt sell his wife to a brothel. I intend to take her back before he starts selling her clothes."

He was halfway out of the house before I could restrain him. "Don't get so excited. We can settle this calmly. First we must make sure whether or not the rumors are true."

---

4. Meaningless calculations. Twenty *fun* made two *momme* (and one *kamme* made one thousand *momme*).
5. The name Osan echoes the word "three" (*san*).

That's why Magoemon and I are here now. He was telling me a while ago that the Jihei of today was not the Jihei of yesterday—that you'd broken all connections with Sonezaki and completely reformed. But now I hear that you've had a relapse. What disease can this be?

Your father was my brother. When the poor man was on his deathbed, he lifted his head from the pillow and begged me to look after you, as my son-in-law and nephew. I've never forgotten those last words, but your perversity has made a mockery of his request!

NARRATOR   She collapses in tears of resentment. Jihei claps his hands in sudden recognition.

JIHEI   I have it! The Koharu everybody's gossiping about is the same Koharu, but the great patron who's to redeem her is a different man. The other day, as my brother can tell you, Tahei—they call him the Lone Wolf because he hasn't any family or relations—started a fight and was trampled on. He gets all the money he needs from his home town, and he's been trying for a long time to redeem Koharu. I've always prevented him, but I'm sure he's decided that now is his chance. I have nothing to do with it.

NARRATOR   Osan brightens at his words.

OSAN   No matter how forbearing I might be—even if I were an angel—you don't suppose I'd encourage my husband to redeem a prostitute! In this instance at any rate there's not a word of untruth in what my husband has said. I'll be a witness to that, Mother.

NARRATOR   Husband's and wife's words tally perfectly.

AUNT   Then it's true?

NARRATOR   The aunt and nephew clap their hands with relief.

MAGOEMON   Well, I'm happy it's over, anyway. To make us feel doubly reassured, will you write an affidavit which will dispel any doubts your stubborn uncle may have?

JIHEI   Certainly. I'll write a thousand if you like.

MAGOEMON   Splendid! I happen to have bought this on the way here.

NARRATOR   Magoemon takes from the fold of his kimono a sheet of oath-paper from Kumano, the sacred characters formed by flocks of crows.[6] Instead of vows of eternal love, Jihei now signs under penalty of Heaven's wrath an oath that he will sever all ties and affections with Koharu. "If I should lie, may Bonten and Taishaku above, and the Four Great Kings below afflict me!"[7] So the text runs, and to it is appended the names of many Buddhas and gods. He signs his name, Kamiya Jihei, in bold characters, imprints the oath with a seal of blood, and proffers it.

OSAN   It's a great relief to me too. Mother, I have you and Magoemon to thank. Jihei and I have had two children, but this is his firmest pledge of affection. I hope you share my joy.

AUNT   Indeed we do. I'm sure that Jihei will settle down and his business will improve, now that he's in this frame of mind. It's been entirely for his sake and for love of the grandchildren that we've intervened. Come, Magoemon,

---

6. The charms issued by the Shintō shrine at Kumano were printed on the face with six Chinese characters, the strokes of which were in the shape of crows. The reverse side of the charms was used for writing oaths.

7. A formal oath. Bonten (Brahma) and Taishaku (Indra), though Hindu gods, were considered protective deities of the Buddhist law. The four Deva kings served under Indra and were also protectors of Buddhism.

let's be on our way. I'm anxious to set my husband's mind at ease.—It's become chilly here. See that the children don't catch cold.—This too we owe to the Buddha of the Ten Nights. I'll say a prayer of thanks before I go. Hail, Amida Buddha!

NARRATOR   She leaves, her heart innocent as Buddha's. Jihei is perfunctory even about seeing them to the door. Hardly have they crossed the threshold than he slumps down again at the *kotatsu*. He pulls the checked quilting over his head.

OSAN   You still haven't forgotton Sonezaki, have you?

NARRATOR   She goes up to him in disgust and tears away the quilting. He is weeping; a waterfall of tears streams along the pillow, deep enough to bear him afloat. She tugs him upright and props his body against the *kotatsu* frame. She stares into his face.

OSAN   You're acting outrageously, Jihei. You shouldn't have signed that oath if you felt so reluctant to leave her. The year before last, on the middle day of the Boar of the tenth moon,[8] we lit the first fire in the *kotatsu* and celebrated by sleeping here together, pillow to pillow. Ever since then—did some demon or snake creep into my bosom that night?—for two whole years I've been condemned to keep watch over an empty nest. I thought that tonight at least, thanks to Mother and Magoemon, we'd share sweet words in bed as husbands and wives do, but my pleasure didn't last long. How cruel of you, how utterly heartless! Go ahead, cry your eyes out, if you're so attached to her. Your tears will flow into Shijimi River and Koharu, no doubt, will ladle them out and drink them! You're ignoble, inhuman.

NARRATOR   She embraces his knees and throws herself over him, moaning in supplication. Jihei wipes his eyes.

JIHEI   If tears of grief flowed from the eyes and tears of anger from the ears, I could show my heart without saying a word. But my tears all pour in the same way from my eyes, and there's no difference in their color. It's not surprising that you can't tell what's in my heart. I have not a shred of attachment left for that vampire in human skin, but I bear a grudge against Tahei. He has all the money he wants, no wife or children. He's schemed again and again to redeem her, but Koharu refused to give in, at least until I broke with her. She told me time and again, "You have nothing to worry about. I'll never let myself be redeemed by Tahei, not even if my ties with you are ended and I can no longer stay by your side. If my master is induced by Tahei's money to deliver me to him, I'll kill myself in a way that'll do you credit!" But think—not ten days have passed since I broke with her, and she's to be redeemed by Tahei! That rotten whore! That animal! No, I haven't a trace of affection left for her, but I can just hear how Tahei will be boasting. He'll spread the word around Osaka that my business has come to a standstill and I'm hard pressed for money. I'll meet with contemptuous stares from the wholesalers. I'll be dishonored. My heart is broken and my body burns with shame. What a disgrace! How maddening! I've passed the stage of shedding hot tears, tears of blood, sticky tears—my tears now are of molten iron!

NARRATOR   He collapses with weeping. Osan pales with alarm.

---

8. It was customary to light the first fire of the winter on this day.

OSAN If that's the situation, poor Koharu will surely kill herself.

JIHEI You're too well bred, despite your intelligence, to understand her likes! What makes you suppose that faithless creature would kill herself? Far from it—she's probably taking moxa treatments and medicine to prolong her life!

OSAN No, that's not true. I was determined never to tell you so long as I lived, but I'm afraid of the crime I'd be committing if I concealed the facts and let her die with my knowledge. I will reveal my great secret. There is not a grain of deceit in Koharu. It was I who schemed to end the relations between you. I could see signs that you were drifting towards suicide. I felt so unhappy that I wrote a letter, begging her as one woman to another to break with you, though I knew how painful it would be. I asked her to save your life. The letter must have moved her. She answered that she would give you up, though you were more precious than life itself, because she could not shirk her duty to me. I've kept her letter with me ever since—it's been like a protective charm. Could such a noble-hearted woman violate her promise and brazenly marry Tahei? When a woman—I no less than another—has given herself completely to a man, she does not change. I'm sure she'll kill herself. I'm sure of it. Ahhh—what a dreadful thing to have happened! Save her, please.

NARRATOR Her voice rises in agitation. Her husband is thrown into a turmoil.

JIHEI There was a letter in an unknown woman's hand among the written oaths she surrendered to my brother. It must have been from you. If that's the case, Koharu will surely commit suicide.

OSAN Alas! I'd be failing in the obligations I owe her as another woman if I allowed her to die. Please go to her at once. Don't let her kill herself.

NARRATOR Clinging to her husband, she melts in tears.

JIHEI But what can I possibly do? It'd take half the amount of her ransom in earnest money merely to keep her out of Tahei's clutches. I can't save Koharu's life without administering a dose of 750 momme in New Silver.[9] How could I raise that much money in my present financial straits? Even if I crush my body to powder, where will the money come from?

OSAN Don't exaggerate the difficulties. If that's all you need, it's simple enough.

NARRATOR She goes to the wardrobe, and opening a small drawer takes out a bag fastened with cords of twisted silk. She unhesitantly tears it open and throws down a packet which Jihei retrieves.

JIHEI What's this? Money? Four hundred momme in New Silver? How in the world—

NARRATOR He stares astonished at this money he never put there.

OSAN I'll tell you later where this money came from. I've scraped it together to pay the bill for Iwakuni paper that falls due the day after tomorrow. We'll have to ask Magoemon to help us keep the business from betraying its insolvency. But Koharu comes first. The packet contains 400 momme. That leaves 350 momme to raise.

---

9. Koharu's situation is described in terms of the money needed to cure a sickness. If 750 me is half the sum needed to redeem Koharu, the total of 1,500 me (or 6,000 me in Old Silver) is considerably less than the 10 kamme, or 10,000 me in Old Silver.

NARRATOR   She unlocks a large drawer. From the wardrobe lightly fly kite-colored Hachijō silks;[1] a Kyoto crepe kimono lined in pale brown, insubstantial as her husband's life which flickers today and may vanish tomorrow; a padded kimono of Osue's, a flaming scarlet inside and out—Osan flushes with pain to part with it; Kantarō's sleeveless, unlined jacket—if she pawns this, he'll be cold this winter. Next comes a garment of striped Gunnai silk lined in pale blue and never worn, and then her best formal costume—heavy black silk dyed with her family crest, an ivy leaf in a ring. They say that those joined by marriage ties can even go naked at home, though outside the house clothes make the man she snatches up even her husband's finery, a silken cloak, making fifteen articles in all.

OSAN   The very least the pawnshop can offer is 350 *momme* in New Silver.

NARRATOR   Her face glows as though she already held the money she needs; she hides in the one bundle her husband's shame and her own obligation, and puts her love in besides.

OSAN   It doesn't matter if the children and I have nothing to wear. My husband's reputation concerns me more. Ransom Koharu. Save her. Assert your honor before Tahei.

NARRATOR   But Jihei's eyes remain downcast all the while, and he is silently weeping.

JIHEI   Yes, I can pay the earnest money and keep her out of Tahei's hands. But once I've redeemed her, I'll either have to maintain her in a separate establishment or bring her here. Then what will become of you?

NARRATOR   Osan is at a loss to answer.

OSAN   Yes, what shall I do? Shall I become your children's nurse or the cook? Or perhaps the retired mistress of the house?

NARRATOR   She falls to the floor with a cry of woe.

JIHEI   That would be too selfish. I'd be afraid to accept such generosity. Even if the punishment for my crimes against my parents, against Heaven, against the gods and the Buddhas fails to strike me, the punishment for my crimes against my wife alone will be sufficient to destroy all hope for the future life. Forgive me, I beg you.

NARRATOR   He joins his hands in tearful entreaty.

OSAN   Why should you bow before me? I don't deserve it. I'd be glad to rip the nails from my fingers and toes, to do anything which might serve my husband. I've been pawning my clothes for some time in order to scrape together the money for the paper wholesalers' bills. My wardrobe is empty, but I don't regret it in the least. But it's too late now to talk of such things. Hurry, change your cloak and go to her with a smile.

NARRATOR   He puts on an under kimono of Gunnai silk, a robe of heavy black silk, and a striped cloak. His sash of figured damask holds a dirk of middle length worked in gold: Buddha surely knows that tonight it will be stained with Koharu's blood.

JIHEI   Sangorō! Come here!

---

1. Woven with a warp of brown and a woof of yellow thread to give a color like that of a kite. "Kite" also suggests that the material "flies" out of the cupboard.

NARRATOR   Jihei loads the bundle on the servant's back, intending to take him along. Then he firmly thrusts the wallet next to his skin and starts towards the gate.

VOICE   Is Jihei at home?

NARRATOR   A man enters, removing his fur cap. They see—good heavens!—that it is Gozaemon.

OSAN *and* JIHEI   Ahhh—how fortunate that you should come at this moment!

NARRATOR   Husband and wife are upset and confused. Gozaemon snatches away Sangorō's bundle and sits heavily. His voice is sharp.

GOZAEMON   Stay where you are, harlot!—My esteemed son-in-law, what a rare pleasure to see you dressed in your finest attire, with a dirk and a silken cloak! Ahhh—that's how a gentleman of means spends his money! No one would take you for a paper dealer. Are you perchance on your way to the New Quarter? What commendable perseverance! You have no need for your wife, I take it—Give her a divorce. I've come to take her home with me.

NARRATOR   He speaks needles and his voice is bitter. Jihei has not a word to reply.

OSAN   How kind of you, Father, to walk here on such a cold day. Do have a cup of tea.

NARRATOR   Offering the teacup serves as an excuse for edging closer.

OSAN   Mother and Magoemon came here a while ago, and they told my husband how much they disapproved of his visits to the New Quarter. Jihei was in tears and he wrote out an oath swearing he had reformed. He gave it to Mother. Haven't you seen it yet?

GOZAEMON   His written oath? Do you mean this?

NARRATOR   He takes the paper from his kimono.

GOZAEMON   Libertines scatter vows and oaths wherever they go, as if they were monthly statements of accounts. I thought there was something peculiar about this oath, and now that I am here I can see I was right. Do you still swear to Bonten and Taishaku? Instead of such nonsense, write out a bill of divorcement!

NARRATOR   He rips the oath to shreds and throws down the pieces. Husband and wife exchange looks of alarm, stunned into silence. Jihei touches his hands to the floor and bows his head.

JIHEI   Your anger is justified. If I were still my former self, I would try to offer explanations, but today I appeal entirely to your generosity. Please let me stay with Osan. I promise that even if I become a beggar or an outcast and must sustain life with the scraps that fall from other people's chopsticks, I will hold Osan in high honor and protect her from every harsh and bitter experience. I feel so deeply indebted to Osan that I cannot divorce her. You will understand that this is true as time passes and I show you how I apply myself to my work and restore my fortune. Until then please shut your eyes and allow us to remain together.

NARRATOR   Tears of blood stream from his eyes and his face is pressed to the matting in contrition.

GOZAEMON   The wife of an outcast! That's all the worse. Write the bill of divorcement at once! I will verify and seal the furniture and clothes Osan brought in her dowry.

NARRATOR   He goes to the wardrobe. Osan is alarmed.

OSAN   My clothes are all here. There's no need to examine them.

NARRATOR   She runs up to forestall him, but Gozaemon pushes her aside and jerks open a drawer.

GOZAEMON   What does this mean?

NARRATOR   He opens another drawer: it too is empty. He pulls out every last drawer, but not so much as a foot of patchwork cloth is to be seen. He tears open the wicker hampers, long boxes, and clothes chests.

GOZAEMON   Stripped bare, are they?

NARRATOR   His eyes set in fury. Jihei and Osan huddle under the striped *kotatsu* quilts, ready to sink into the fire with humiliation.

GOZAEMON   This bundle looks suspicious.

NARRATOR   He unties the knots and dumps out the contents.

GOZAEMON   As I thought! You were sending these to the pawnshop, I take it. Jihei—you'd strip the skin from your wife's and your children's bodies to squander the money on your whore! Dirty thief! You're my wife's nephew, but an utter stranger to me, and I'm under no obligation to suffer for your sake. I'll explain to Magoemon what has happened and ask him to make good whatever inroads you've already made on Osan's belongings. But first, the bill of divorcement!

NARRATOR   Even if Jihei could escape through seven padlocked doors, eight thicknesses of chains, and a hundred girdling walls, he could not evade so stringent a demand.

JIHEI   I won't use a brush to write the bill of divorcement. Here's what I'll do instead! Good-by, Osan.

NARRATOR   He lays his hand on his dirk, but Osan clings to him.

OSAN   Father—Jihei admits that he's done wrong and he's apologized in every way. You press your advantage too hard. Jihei may be a stranger, but his children are your grandchildren. Have you no affection for them? I will not accept a bill of divorcement.

NARRATOR   She embraces her husband and raises her voice in tears.

GOZAEMON   Very well. I won't insist on it. Come with me, woman.

NARRATOR   He pulls her to her feet.

OSAN   No, I won't go. What bitterness makes you expose to such shame a man and wife who still love each other? I will not suffer it.

NARRATOR   She pleads with him, weeping, but he pays her no heed.

GOZAEMON   Is there some greater shame? I'll shout it through the town!

NARRATOR   He pulls her up, but she shakes free. Caught by the wrist she totters forward when—alas!—her toes brush against her sleeping children. They open their eyes.

CHILDREN   Mother dear, why is Grandfather, the bad man, taking you away? Whom will we sleep beside now?

NARRATOR   They call out after her.

OSAN   My poor dears! You've never spent a night away from Mother's side since you were born. Sleep tonight beside your father. (*To* JIHEI.) Please don't forget to give the children their tonic before breakfast.—Oh, my heart is broken!

NARRATOR   These are her parting words. She leaves her children behind, abandoned as in the woods; the twin-trunked bamboo of conjugal love is sundered forever.

ACT 3

SCENE 1: *Sonezaki New Quarter, in front of the Yamato House.*

TIME: *That night.*

NARRATOR   This is Shijimi River, the haunt of love and affection. Its flowing water and the feet of passersby are stilled now at two in the morning, and the full moon shines clear in the sky. Here in the street a dim doorway lantern is marked "Yamatoya Dembei" in a single scrawl. The night watchman's clappers take on a sleepy cadence as he totters by on uncertain legs. The very thickness of his voice crying, "Beware of fire! Beware of fire!" tells how far advanced the night is. A serving woman from the upper town comes along, followed by a palanquin. "It's terribly late," she remarks to the bearers as she clatters open the side door of the Yamato House and steps inside.

SERVANT   I've come to take back Koharu of the Kinokuni House.

NARRATOR   Her voice is faintly heard outside. A few moments later, after hardly time enough to exchange three or four words of greeting, she emerges.

SERVANT   Koharu is spending the night. Bearers, you may leave now and get some rest. (*To proprietress, inside the doorway.*) Oh, I forgot to tell you, madam. Please keep an eye on Koharu. Now that the ransom to Tahei has been arranged and the money's been accepted, we're merely her custodians. Please don't let her drink too much saké.

NARRATOR   She leaves, having scattered at the doorway the seeds that before morning will turn Jihei and Koharu to dust.

At night between two and four even the teahouse kettle rests; the flame flickering in the low candle stand narrows; and the frost spreads in the cold river-wind of the deepening night. The master's voice breaks the stillness.

DEMBEI (*to* JIHEI)   It's still the middle of the night. I'll send somebody with you. (*To servants.*) Mr. Jihei is leaving. Wake Koharu. Call her here.

NARRATOR   Jihei slides open the side door.

JIHEI   No, Dembei, not a word to Koharu. I'll be trapped here till dawn if she hears I'm leaving. That's why I'm letting her sleep and slipping off this way. Wake her up after sunrise and send her back then. I'm returning home now and will leave for Kyoto immediately on business. I have so many engagements that I may not be able to return in time for the interim payment.[2] Please use the money I gave you earlier this evening to clear my account. I'd like you also to send 150 *me* of Old Silver to Kawashō for the moon-viewing party last month. Please get a receipt. Give Saietsubō[3] from Fukushima one piece of silver as a contribution to the Buddhist altar he's bought, and tell him to use it for a memorial service. Wasn't there something else? Oh yes—give Isoichi a tip of four silver coins. That's the lot. Now you can close up and get to bed. Good-by. I'll see you when I return from Kyoto.

NARRATOR   Hardly has he taken two or three steps than he turns back.

2. On the last day of the Tenth Month, one of the times during the year for making payments.

3. Name of a male entertainer in the Fukushima quarter, west of Sonezaki.

JIHEI I forgot my dirk. Fetch it for me, won't you?—Yes, Dembei, this is one respect in which it's easier being a townsman. If I were a samurai and forgot my sword, I'd probably commit suicide on the spot!

DEMBEI I completely forgot that I was keeping it for you. Yes, here's the knife with it.

NARRATOR He gives the dirk to Jihei, who fastens it firmly into his sash.

JIHEI I feel secure as long as I have this. Good night!

NARRATOR He goes off.

DEMBEI Please come back to Osaka soon! Thank you for your patronage!

NARRATOR With this hasty farewell Dembei rattles the door bolt shut; then not another sound is heard as the silence deepens. Jihei pretends to leave, only to creep back again with stealthy steps. He clings to the door of the Yamato House. As he peeps within he is startled by shadows moving towards him. He takes cover at the house across the way until the figures pass.

Magoemon the Miller, his heart pulverized with anxiety over his younger brother, comes first, followed by the apprentice Sangorō with Jihei's son Kantarō on his back. They hurry along until they spy the lantern of the Yamato House. Magoemon pounds on the door.

MAGOEMON Excuse me. Kamiya Jihei's here, isn't he? I'd like to see him a moment.

NARRATOR Jihei thinks, "It's my brother!" but dares not stir from his place of concealment. From inside a man's sleep-laden voice is heard.

DEMBEI Jihei left a while ago saying he was going up to Kyoto. He's not here.

NARRATOR Not another sound is heard. Magoemon's tears fall unchecked.

MAGOEMON (to himself) I ought to have met him on the way if he'd been going home. I can't understand what takes him to Kyoto. Ahhh—I'm trembling all over with worry. I wonder if he didn't take Koharu with him.

NARRATOR The thought pierces his heart; unable to bear the pain, he pounds again on the door.

DEMBEI Who is it, so late at night? We've gone to bed.

MAGOEMON I'm sorry to disturb you, but I'd like to ask one more thing. Has Koharu of the Kinokuni House left? I was wondering if she mightn't have gone with Jihei.

DEMBEI What's that? Koharu's upstairs, fast asleep.

MAGOEMON That's a relief, anyway. There's no fear of a lovers' suicide. But where is he hiding himself causing me all this anxiety? He can't imagine the agony of suspense that the whole family is going through on his account. I'm afraid that bitterness towards his father-in-law may make him forget himself and do something rash. I brought Kantarō along, hoping he would help to dissuade Jihei, but the gesture was in vain. I wonder why I failed to meet him?

NARRATOR He murmurs to himself, his eyes moist with tears. Jihei's hiding place is close enough for him to hear every word. He chokes with emotion, but can only swallow his tears.

MAGOEMON Sangorō! Where does the fool go night after night? Don't you know anywhere else?

NARRATOR Sangorō imagines that he himself is the fool referred to.

SANGORŌ I know a couple of places, but I'm too embarrassed to mention them.

MAGOEMON You know them? Where are they? Tell me.

SANGORŌ Please don't scold me when you've heard. Every night I wander down below the warehouses by the market.

MAGOEMON Imbecile! Who's asking about that? Come on, let's search the back streets. Don't let Kantarō catch a chill. The poor kid's having a cold time of it, thanks to that useless father of his. Still, if the worst the boy experiences is the cold I won't complain. I'm afraid that Jihei may cause him much greater pain. The scoundrel!

NARRATOR But beneath the rancor in his heart of hearts is profound pity.

MAGOEMON Let's look at the back street!

NARRATOR They pass on. As soon as their figures have gone off a distance Jihei runs from his hiding place. Standing on tiptoes he gazes with yearning after them and cries out in his heart.

JIHEI He cannot leave me to my death, though I am the worst of sinners! I remain to the last a burden to him! I'm unworthy of such kindness!

NARRATOR He joins his hands and kneels in prayer.

JIHEI If I may make one further request of your mercy, look after my children!

NARRATOR These are his only words; for a while he chokes with tears.

JIHEI At any rate, our decision's been made. Koharu must be waiting.

NARRATOR He peers through a crack in the side door of the Yamato House and glimpses a figure.

JIHEI That's Koharu, isn't it? I'll let her know I'm here.

NARRATOR He clears his throat, their signal. "Ahem, ahem"—the sound blends with the clack of wooden clappers as the watchman comes from the upper street, coughing in the night wind. He hurries on his round of fire warning, "Take care! Beware!" Even this cry has a dismal sound to one in hiding. Jihei, concealing himself like the god of Katsuragi,[4] lets the watchman pass. He sees his chance and rushes to the side door, which softly opens from within.

JIHEI Koharu?

KOHARU Were you waiting? Jihei—I want to leave quickly.

NARRATOR She is all impatience, but the more hastily they open the door, the more likely people will be to hear the casters turning. They lift the door; it gives a moaning that thunders in their ears and in their hearts. Jihei lends a hand from the outside, but his fingertips tremble with the trembling of his heart. The door opens a quarter of an inch, a half, an inch—an inch ahead are the tortures of hell, but more than hell itself they fear the guardian-demon's eyes. At last the door opens, and with the joy of New Year's morn[5] Koharu slips out. They catch each other's hands. Shall they go north or south, west or east? Their pounding hearts urge them on, though they know not to what destination: turning their backs on the moon reflected in Shijimi River, they hurry eastward as fast as their legs will carry them.

---

4. The god was so ashamed of his ugliness that he ventured forth only at night.

5. Mention of the New Year is connected with Koharu's name, with *haru* meaning "spring."

SCENE 2: *The farewell journey of many bridges.*

NARRATOR

The running hand in texts of Nō is always Konoe style;
An actor in a woman's part is sure to wear a purple hat.[6]
Does some teaching of the Buddha as rigidly decree
That men who spend their days in evil haunts must end like this?
Poor creatures, though they would discover today their destiny in the Sutra of Cause and Effect, tomorrow the gossip of the world will scatter like blossoms the scandal of Kamiya Jihei's love suicide, and, carved in cherry wood, his story to the last detail will be printed in illustrated sheets.[7]

Jihei, led on by the spirit of death—if such there be among the gods—is resigned to this punishment for neglect of his trade. But at times—who could blame him?—his heart is drawn to those he has left behind, and it is hard to keep walking on. Even in the full moon's light, this fifteenth night of the tenth moon,[8] he cannot see his way ahead—a sign perhaps of the darkness in his heart? The frost now falling will melt by dawn but, even more quickly than this symbol of human frailty, the lovers themselves will melt away. What will become of the fragrance that lingered when he held her tenderly at night in their bedchamber?

This bridge, Tenjin Bridge, he has crossed every day, morning and night, gazing at Shijimi River to the west. Long ago, when Tenjin, then called Michizane,[9] was exiled to Tsukushi, his plum tree, following its master, flew in one bound to Dazaifu, and here is Plum-field Bridge. Green Bridge recalls the aged pine that followed later, and Cherry Bridge the tree that withered away in grief over parting. Such are the tales still told, bespeaking the power of a single poem.

JIHEI   Though born the parishioner of so holy and mighty a god, I shall kill you and then myself. If you ask the cause, it was that I lacked even the wisdom that might fill a tiny Shell Bridge.[1] Our stay in this world has been short as an autumn day. This evening will be the last of your nineteen, of my twenty-eight years. The time has come to cast away our lives. We

---

6. The Konoe style of calligraphy was used in books with Noh texts. Custom also decreed that young male actors playing the parts of women cover their foreheads with a square of purple cloth to disguise the fact that they were shaven.
7. These sheets mentioned here featured current scandals, such as lovers' suicides. "Cause and Effect": a sacred scripture of Buddhism, which says: "If you wish to know the past cause, look at the present effect; if you wish to know the future effect, look at the present cause." "Cherry wood": the blocks from which illustrated books were printed were often of cherry wood.
8. November 14, 1720. In the lunar calendar the full moon occurs on the fifteenth of the month.
9. Sugawara no Michizane, unfairly slandered at court, was exiled to Dazaifu on Japan's southernmost main island of Kyushu. When he was about to depart, he composed a poem of

farewell to his favorite plum tree. Legend has it that the tree, moved by his master's poem, flew after him to Kyushu, while the cherry tree in Michizane's garden withered away in grief. Only the pine seemed indifferent, but after Michizane complained in a poem, the pine tree also flew to Kyushu to join his master.
1. The lovers' journey takes them over twelve bridges altogether. They proceed first along the north bank of Shijimi River ("Shell River") to Shijimi Bridge, where they cross to Dōjima. At Little Naniwa Bridge they cross back again to Sonezaki. Continuing eastward, they cross Horikawa, then cross the Temma Bridge over the Ōkawa. At "Eight Houses" (Hakkenya) they journey eastward along the south bank of the river as far as Kyō Bridge (Sutra Bridge). They cross this bridge to the tip of land at Katamachi and then take the Onari Bridge to the final destination, Amijima.

promised we'd remain together faithfully, till you were an old woman and I an old man, but before we knew each other three full years, we have met this disaster. Look, here is Ōe Bridge. We follow the river from Little Naniwa Bridge to Funairi Bridge. The farther we journey, the closer we approach the road to death.

NARRATOR   He laments. She clings to him.

KOHARU   Is this already the road to death?

NARRATOR   Falling tears obscure from each the other's face and threaten to immerse even the Horikawa bridges.

JIHEI   A few steps north and I could glimpse my house, but I will not turn back. I will bury in my breast all thoughts of my children's future, all pity for my wife. We cross southward over the river. Why did they call a place with as many buildings as a bridge has piers "Eight Houses"? Hurry, we want to arrive before the down-river boat from Fushimi comes—with what happy couples sleeping aboard!

Next is Temma Bridge, a frightening name[2] for us about to depart this world. Here the two streams Yodo and Yamato join in one great river, as fish with water, and as Koharu and I, dying on one blade will cross together the River of Three Fords.[3] I would like this water for our tomb offering!

KOHARU   What have we to grieve about? Though in this world we could not stay together, in the next and through each successive world to come until the end of time we shall be husband and wife. Every summer for my devotions[4] I have copied the All Compassionate and All Merciful Chapter of the Lotus Sutra, in the hope that we may be reborn on one lotus.

NARRATOR   They cross over Kyō Bridge and reach the opposite shore.[5]

KOHARU   If I can save living creatures at will when once I mount a lotus calyx in Paradise and become a Buddha, I want to protect women of my profession, so that never again will there be love suicides.

NARRATOR   This unattainable prayer stems from worldly attachment, but it touchingly reveals her heart.

They cross Onari Bridge.[6] The waters of Noda Creek are shrouded with morning haze; the mountain tips show faintly white.

JIHEI   Listen—the voices of the temple bells begin to boom. How much farther can we go on this way? We are not fated to live any longer—let us make an end quickly. Come this way.

NARRATOR   Tears are strung with the 108 beads of the rosaries in their hands. They have come now to Amijima, to the Daichō Temple; the overflowing sluice gate of a little stream beside a bamboo thicket will be their place of death.

---

2. The characters used for Temma mean literally "demon."
3. A river in the Buddhist underworld that had to be crossed to reach the world of the dead. One blade plus two people equal "Three Fords."
4. It was customary for Buddhist monks and some of the laity in Japan to observe a summer retreat to practice austerities.
5. This location implies Nirvana. "Kyō Bridge": called "Sutra Bridge."
6. The word "Onari" implies "to become a Buddha."

SCENE 3: *Amijima.*

JIHEI   No matter how far we walk, there'll never be a spot marked "For Suicides." Let us kill ourselves here.

NARRATOR   He takes her hand and sits on the ground.

KOHARU   Yes, that's true. One place is as good as another to die. But I've been
thinking on the way that if they find our dead bodies together people will
say that Koharu and Jihei committed a lovers' suicide. Osan will think then
that I treated as mere scrap paper the letter I sent promising her, when she
asked me not to kill you, that I would not, and vowing to break all relations.
She will be sure that I lured her precious husband into a lovers' suicide. She
will despise me as a one-night prostitute, a false woman with no sense of
decency. I fear her contempt more than the slander of a thousand or ten
thousand strangers. I can imagine how she will resent and envy me. That is
the greatest obstacle to my salvation. Kill me here, then choose another
spot, far away, for yourself.

NARRATOR   She leans against him. Jihei joins in her tears of pleading.

JIHEI   What foolish worries! Osan has been taken back by my father-in-law.
I've divorced her. She and I are strangers now. Why should you feel obliged
to a divorced woman? You were saying on the way that you and I will be
husband and wife through each successive world until the end of time.
Who can criticize us, who can be jealous if we die side by side?

KOHARU   But who is responsible for your divorce? You're even less reasonable
than I. Do you suppose that our bodies will accompany us to the afterworld?
We may die in different places, our bodies may be pecked by kites and
crows, but what does it matter as long as our souls are twined together?
Take me with you to heaven or to hell!

NARRATOR   She sinks again in tears.

JIHEI   You're right. Our bodies are made of earth, water, fire, and wind, and
when we die they revert to emptiness. But our souls will not decay, no matter how often reborn. And here's a guarantee that our souls will be married
and never part!

NARRATOR   He whips out his dirk and slashes off his black locks at the base
of the top knot.

JIHEI   Look, Koharu. As long as I had this hair I was Kamiya Jihei, Osan's
husband, but cutting it has made me a monk. I have fled the burning house
of the three worlds of delusion; I am a priest, unencumbered by wife, children, or worldly possessions. Now that I no longer have a wife named Osan,
you owe her no obligations either.

NARRATOR   In tears he flings away the hair.

KOHARU   I am happy.

NARRATOR   Koharu takes up the dirk and ruthlessly, unhesitantly, slices
through her flowing Shimada coiffure. She casts aside the tresses she has
so often washed and combed and stroked. How heartbreaking to see their
locks tangled with the weeds and midnight frost of this desolate field!

JIHEI   We have escaped the inconstant world, a nun and a priest. Our duties
as husband and wife belong to our profane past. It would be best to choose
quite separate places for our deaths, a mountain for one, the river for the
other. We will pretend that the ground above this sluice gate is a mountain.

You will die there. I shall hang myself by this stream. The time of our deaths will be the same, but the method and place will differ. In this way we can honor to the end our duty to Osan. Give me your under sash.

NARRATOR   Its fresh violet color and fragrance will be lost in the winds of impermanence; the crinkled silk long enough to wind twice round her body will bind two worlds, this and the next. He firmly fastens one end to the crosspiece of the sluice, then twists the other into a noose for his neck. He will hang for love of his wife like the "pheasant in the hunting grounds."[7]

Koharu watches Jihei prepare for his death. Her eyes swim with tears, her mind is distraught.

KOHARU   Is that how you're going to kill yourself?—If we are to die apart, I have only a little while longer by your side. Come near me.

NARRATOR   They take each other's hands.

KOHARU   It's over in a moment with a sword, but I'm sure you'll suffer. My poor darling!

NARRATOR   She cannot stop the silent tears.

JIHEI   Can suicide ever be pleasant, whether by hanging or cutting the throat? You mustn't let worries over trifles disturb the prayers of your last moments. Keep your eyes on the westward-moving moon, and worship it as Amida himself.[8] Concentrate your thoughts on the Western Paradise. If you have any regrets about leaving the world, tell me now, then die.

KOHARU   I have none at all, none at all. But I'm sure you must be worried about your children.

JIHEI   You make me cry all over again by mentioning them. I can almost see their faces, sleeping peacefully, unaware, poor dears, that their father is about to kill himself. They're the one thing I can't forget.

NARRATOR   He droops to the ground with weeping. The voices of the crows leaving their nests at dawn rival his sobs. Are the crows mourning his fate? The thought brings more tears.

JIHEI   Listen to them. The crows have come to guide us to the world of the dead. There's an old saying that every time somebody writes an oath on the back of a Kumano charm, three crows of Kumano die on the holy mountain. The first words we've written each New Year have been vows of love, and how often we've inscribed oaths at the beginning of the month! If each oath has killed three crows, what a multitude must have perished! Their cries have always sounded like "beloved, beloved," but hatred for our crime of taking life makes their voices ring tonight "revenge, revenge!"[9] Whose fault is it they demand revenge? Because of me you will die a painful death. Forgive me!

NARRATOR   He takes her in his arms.

KOHARU   No, it's my fault!

---

7. A reference to a poem from the 8th-century anthology *Collection of Myriad Leaves* (*Man'yōshū*): "The pheasant foraging in the fields of spring reveals his whereabouts to man as he cries for his mate."
8. Amida's Western Paradise of the Pure Land lies in the west. The moon is frequently used as a symbol of Buddhist enlightenment.
9. The cries have always sounded like *kawai, kawai* ("beloved"), but now they sound like *mukui, mukui* ("revenge").

NARRATOR They cling to each other, face pressed to face; their sidelocks, drenched with tears, freeze in the winds blowing over the fields. Behind them echoes the voice of the Daichō Temple.

JIHEI Even the long winter night seems short as our lives.

NARRATOR Dawn is already breaking, and matins can be heard. He draws her to him.

JIHEI The moment has come for our glorious end. Let there be no tears on your face when they find you later.

KOHARU There won't be any.

NARRATOR She smiles. His hands, numbed by the frost, tremble before the pale vision of her face, and his eyes are first to cloud. He is weeping so profusely that he cannot control the blade.

KOHARU Compose yourself—but be quick!

NARRATOR Her encouragement lends him strength; the invocations to Amida carried by the wind urge a final prayer. *Namu Amida Butsu.* He thrusts in the saving sword.[1] Stabbed, she falls backwards, despite his staying hand, and struggles in terrible pain. The point of the blade has missed her windpipe, and these are the final tortures before she can die. He writhes with her in agony, then painfully summons his strength again. He draws her to him, and plunges his dirk to the hilt. He twists the blade in the wound, and her life fades away like an unfinished dream at dawning.

He arranges her corpse head to the north, face to the west, lying on her right side,[2] and throws his cloak over her. He turns away at last, unable to exhaust with tears his grief over parting. He pulls the sash to him and fastens the noose around his neck. The service in the temple has reached the closing section, the prayers for the dead. "Believers and unbelievers will equally share in the divine grace," the voices proclaim, and at the final words Jihei jumps from the sluice gate.

JIHEI May we be reborn on one lotus! Hail Amida Buddha!

NARRATOR For a few moments he writhes like a gourd swinging in the wind, but gradually the passage of his breath is blocked as the stream is dammed by the sluice gate, where his ties with this life are snapped.

Fishermen out for the morning catch find the body in their net.[3]

FISHERMEN A dead man! Look, a dead man! Come here, everybody!

NARRATOR The tale is spread from mouth to mouth. People say that they who were caught in the net of Buddha's vow immediately gained salvation and deliverance, and all who hear the tale of the Love Suicides at Amijima are moved to tears.

---

1. The invocations of Amida's name freed one from spiritual obstacles, just as a sword freed one from physical obstacles.
2. The dead were arranged in this manner because the historical Buddha, Shakyamuni Buddha, chose this position when he died and passed into Nirvana.
3. The vow of the Buddha to save all sentient beings is likened to a net that catches people in its meshes. "Net" (*ami*) is echoed a few lines later in the name "Amijima."

IV

An Age of Revolutions in Europe and the Americas

If you were born in 1765, and you happened to live to a ripe old age, you would witness two dramatic revolutions. Together these revolutions would create a period of staggering upheaval unparalleled in prior human history. Whether you happened to find yourself in Texas or London or Buenos Aires, you would see daily life change for almost everyone—rich and poor, rural and urban—and the workings of governments and markets forever transformed. You would have to learn a whole new vocabulary to describe your social world: the terms "factory," "middle class," "capitalism," "industry," "journalism," "liberal," and "conservative" would come into use during your lifetime. You would learn of workers moving to cities in vast numbers. They would live in dismal conditions of filth, disease, and hunger, and at times would erupt in violent protest. You would listen to orators denouncing tyranny and demanding new rights and freedoms. You would hear about an ordinary soldier who rose to conquer most of Europe, and his name, Napoleon, would provoke either a chill of fear or a shiver of exhilaration. You would watch new constitutions take effect and new nations assert themselves. You would see the very map of the world redrawn.

Liberty Leading the People, 1830, Eugène Delacroix.

THE INDUSTRIAL REVOLUTION

The first of the two great upheavals was the industrial revolution, which began in England and then radiated outward, as other nations copied English innovations and as England's increasing commercial and military power conquered large portions of the globe. Before the 1780s economies everywhere changed only at a glacially slow pace. Most of Europe's inhabitants were peasants who worked the land which their forefathers had worked for generations before them, typically growing their own food and making their own clothes, and paying rent to their landowners in exchange for military protection. Many, including Russian serfs, were under the legal control of their landowners and thus forbidden to move from the places where they were born. But agriculture in England was different. There, large landowners rented tracts of land to tenant farmers, who then hired laborers to work for them. The farmers could get rich by finding new markets for their products, and the workers could move if they saw opportunities elsewhere. Here were the seeds of an entirely new, fast-growing capitalist economy. In the eighteenth century, English farmers started to turn into entrepreneurs, looking for faster and better ways to make profits from their lands. In order to attract investors, the nation needed to keep the economy growing, and in order to keep the economy growing, it needed to increase production and find new markets. Colonial expansion seemed like a perfect solution: England fought to acquire and control vast territories abroad, especially in North America, which would provide new land to till and new natural resources to use. Entrepreneurs also found new markets in the colonies to buy the goods which England produced.

The great spur for this new global economy was cotton. Grown and har-

An engraving depicting the interior of the Swainson & Birley Mill in Lancashire, England, ca. 1830.

vested by slaves in the colonies, the raw material was shipped to English entrepreneurs, whose textile factories spun and wove the slave-picked cotton into finished cloth. They eagerly developed new technologies to keep production growing, and that meant that iron and steel industries grew too, allowing for the ever faster production of machines for manufacture and transportation. Railways expanded swiftly. Historians often date the great acceleration of the economy to the 1780s, which was the moment when English exports surpassed imports for the first time. The growth was breathtaking and unprecedented. In 1785 England imported 11 million pounds of raw cotton; by 1850 the English were importing 588 million pounds. They established trade monopolies with India and Latin America, compelling overseas consumers to buy English goods, which meant that exports grew at an astonishing rate: English mill owners had sold more than two billion yards of cotton cloth by the middle of the nineteenth century. England had become the hub of a new world economy, and other nations rushed to imitate English techniques of production. Factories sprang up everywhere.

Wentworth Street, Whitechapel, 1872, Gustave Doré. A late 19th-century depiction of the squalor in London's slums.

Not everyone benefited from this extraordinary growth. The workers who moved off ancestral lands to crowd into new industrial centers labored in unregulated factories, often inhaling dust or having their limbs broken in machines. Employers looked for the cheapest labor, typically hiring women and children, and forced them to work 14- and even 16-hour days. Barely paid a subsistence wage, the new urban working class made do with living conditions that were even more appalling than conditions in the factories where they worked. Cities grew at such a fast rate that urban populations quickly outpaced the availability of necessities such as adequate housing and the supply of clean water. The result was a sequence of major epidemics, including cholera and typhoid fever, which overwhelmed congested slums but hardly touched the middle and upper classes. To add to the general hardships for the poor, the economy had already begun the international cycles of boom and bust that would characterize the next two centuries. In periods of poor growth, unemployed workers literally starved. Feelings of angry discontent grew rapidly alongside the new economy.

Overseas, too, large populations began to suffer from industrialization. The huge acceleration in the English economy had absolutely depended on slavery. Six million slaves had been captured and sent from Africa to the Americas in the eighteenth century alone, many to serve the booming cotton trade. Meanwhile, India's economy plunged. Until the eighteenth century, India had had a thriving manufacturing sector that produced gorgeous textiles for export, but the new factory-made cloth from England came in at low prices and depressed the market. Many workers in India were forced back into agriculture, which deindustrialized India's economy, setting it on a slower track. Latin America, too, increasingly organized its economies around exports to England—including sugar, coffee, and silver—which made the new Latin American nations worryingly dependent on agriculture and on economic decisions made in England.

DEMOCRATIC REVOLUTIONS

As the industrial revolution was producing vast wealth, changing labor practices, molding a class of angry urban workers, rapidly expanding cities, and creating new and uneven global trade relations, a second revolution was also taking place. This revolution was political. Intent on throwing off old hierarchies that gave power to kings and compelled everyone else to act as obedient subjects, revolutionaries in North America and France argued that ordinary people should take political decision making into their own hands. This was a democratic revolution that, like the industrial revolution, had global effects, transforming expectations about basic rights and freedoms worldwide.

In North America, colonial subjects became increasingly resentful of the power of the English king, who made both political and economic decisions that favored England. In 1776 they declared independence not only from English rule but from the whole structure of the old regime, rejecting its hereditary monarchy in favor of a new elected president. They vested power in "the people," insisting that governments should derive their power only from the consent of the governed. This was a radical new foundation for politics, and it inspired many later constitutions.

In Europe, another, even more dramatic political revolution was brewing. The French monarchy had become ever more absolutist, and peasants were growing resentful of the traditional taxes and tithes they had to pay. Bad harvests in 1788 and 1789 doubled the cost of bread, but the king seemed entirely indifferent to the fate of a starving people. (When told that the peasants were calling for bread, Queen Marie Antoinette is famous for responding, "Let them eat cake.") On July 14, 1789, a loosely organized armed mob stormed the Bastille prison—a symbol of royal power—and called for the liberation of the French people. The news spread quickly. Within a month, uprisings all across France had wrecked the traditional feudal social hierarchy and ushered in a new era. The Declaration of the Rights of Man and of the Citizen, issued by the French National Assembly in August, asserted the equality and freedom of all men and abolished all privileges based on birth. The revolutionary government insisted on ruling by reason, not by tradition. They adopted the innovative new metric system, separated church and state, abolished slavery in the French colonies, and granted equal rights to everyone, including, for the first time, Jews. The French Revolution also helped to unleash a new force in world affairs: nationalism. France was no longer a land possessed by a powerful ruling family, but stood for a self-governing and autonomous "people." In a powerful symbolic gesture, the revolutionaries renamed 1789 as "Year Zero," suggesting that nothing that had happened before the revolution mattered. They then stunned Europe by sending the king to his death in 1793, executing him with a sleek new machine intended to make killing more humane: the guillotine.

The French Revolution sent shock waves around the world. Throughout Europe and the Americas, suddenly it seemed possible that people might rise

The siege of the Bastille, July 1789.

up against their oppressors, violently opposing traditional authority in the name of individual human rights. Huge divisions emerged between those who saw the revolutionaries as vicious and reckless, and those who heralded them as the opening of a whole new chapter in human history.

Other European powers, fearful that revolution might spread into their territories, went to war with France in 1792, and the whole country threatened to collapse in disarray. A small group of radicals, called the Jacobins, seized control and united the nation under a strong centralized dictatorship, mobilizing the nation for war and sending all traitors—and potential traitors—to the guillotine. Their short period of leadership in 1793–94 has come to be known as the "Reign of Terror." The blood they shed sickened many observers who had once sympathized with the aims of the revolution,

and the "Reign of Terror" has, ever since, been seen as a symbol of revolutionary violence taken too far.

As the new French government faltered and changed leadership, a talented young soldier who had helped the French to defeat the British at Toulon in 1793 was rising up through the ranks. Born on the remote island of Corsica, Napoleon Bonaparte had few advantages of birth or connections, but his genius for military strategy, his extraordinary ambition, and his own huge popularity allowed him to take advantage of government weakness during a wave of foreign invasions and to position himself as the new leader of France. In 1799 he installed a new dictatorship and through a vast military campaign redrew the map of Europe, bringing large parts of Spain, Germany, Austria, Italy, and Poland under French control. He crowned himself emperor in 1804. Ravenous

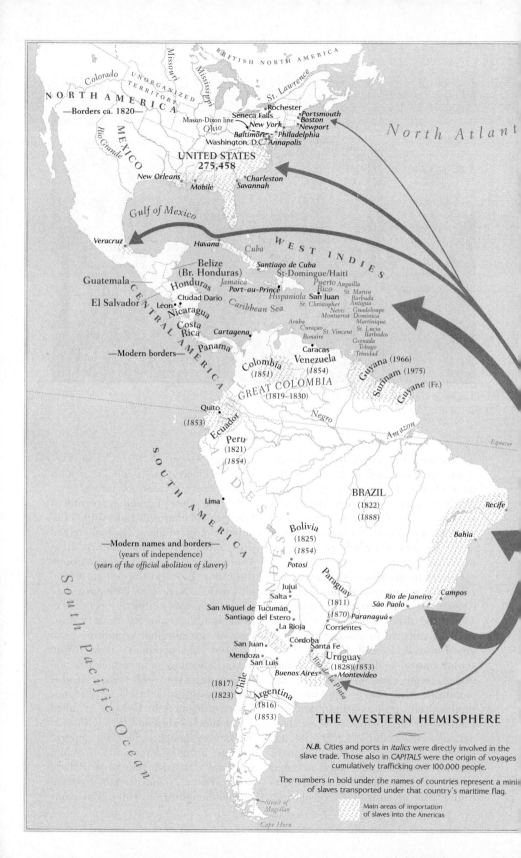

NORTH AMERICA
—Borders ca. 1820—

BRITISH NORTH AMERICA

Colorado

Missouri

Mississippi

UNORGANIZED TERRITORY

St. Lawrence

Rochester
Portsmouth
Boston
Newport

Rio Grande

MEXICO

Ohio

Seneca Falls
New York

Mason-Dixon line

Baltimore
Philadelphia
Washington, D.C. Annapolis

UNITED STATES
275,458

New Orleans

Charleston
Savannah

Mobile

Gulf of Mexico

North Atlant

Veracruz

Havana
Cuba

WEST INDIES

Belize
(Br. Honduras)

Santiago de Cuba

St-Domingue/Haiti

Guatemala

Honduras

Jamaica
Port-au-Prince

Puerto
Rico

Anguilla
St. Martin
Barbuda

Ciudad Dario

San Juan

Antigua

El Salvador

León

Nicaragua

Hispaniola

St. Christopher

Nevis
Montserrat

Guadeloupe
Dominica

Caribbean Sea

Aruba

Curaçao

St. Vincent

Martinique

CENTRAL AMERICA

Costa
Rica

Bonaire

St. Lucia
Barbados

Cartagena

Grenada
Tobago
Trinidad

Panama

Caracas

—Modern borders—

Colombia
(1851)

Venezuela
(1854)

Guyana (1966)

Surinam (1975)

GREAT COLOMBIA
(1819–1830)

Guyane (Fr.)

Quito

Negro

Amazon

Equator

(1853)

Ecuador

Peru
(1821)

(1854)

SOUTH AMERICA

ANDES

BRAZIL
(1822)

Recife

(1888)

Lima

Bahia

Bolivia
(1825)

—Modern names and borders—
(years of independence)
(years of the official abolition of slavery)

(1854)

Potosí

Paraguay

Jujui

Rio de Janeiro

Campos

Salta

São Paolo

San Miguel de Tucumán

(1811)

Paranaguá

Santiago del Estero

(1870)

La Rioja

Corrientes

San Juan

Córdoba

Santa Fe

Mendoza

Uruguay
(1828)(1853)

San Luis

Buenos Aires

Montevideo

South Pacific Ocean

(1817)

(1823)

Chile

Rio de la Plata

Argentina
(1816)

THE WESTERN HEMISPHERE

(1853)

N.B. Cities and ports in *italics* were directly involved in the
slave trade. Those also in *CAPITALS* were the origin of voyages
cumulatively trafficking over 100,000 people.

The numbers in bold under the names of countries represent a mini
of slaves transported under that country's maritime flag.

Strait of
Magellan

Cape Horn

Main areas of importation
of slaves into the Americas

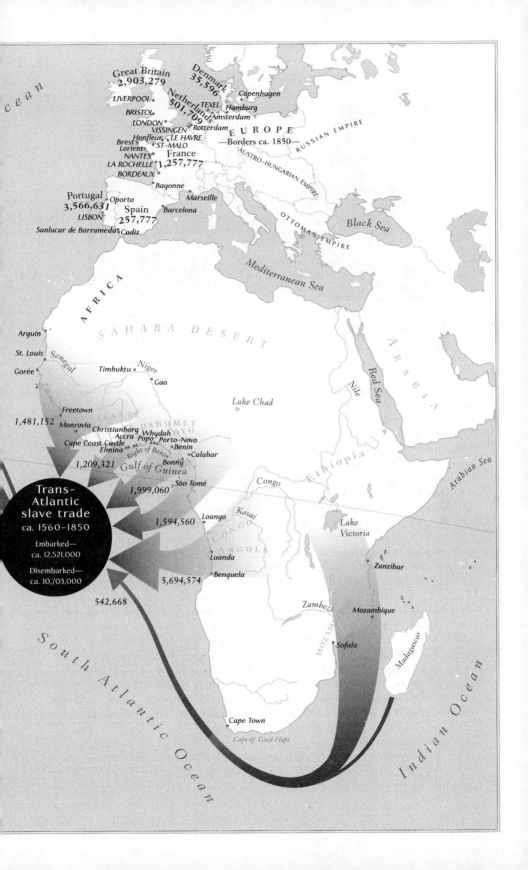

Great Britain
2,903,279
LIVERPOOL
BRISTOL
LONDON
VISSINGEN
Honfleur LE HAVRE
Brest ST-MALO
Lorient
NANTES France
LA ROCHELLE 1,257,777
BORDEAUX
Bayonne

Denmark
35,596
Copenhagen
TEXEL Hamburg
Netherlands Amsterdam
501,709 Rotterdam

EUROPE
—Borders ca. 1850—

RUSSIAN EMPIRE

AUSTRO-HUNGARIAN EMPIRE

Portugal Oporto
3,566,631 Spain Marseille
LISBON 257,777 Barcelona
Sanlucar de Barrameda Cadiz

OTTOMAN EMPIRE

Black Sea

Mediterranean Sea

ocean

AFRICA

SAHARA DESERT

Arguin

St. Louis
Gorée Senegal
Timbuktu Niger
Gao

ARABIA

Red Sea

Nile

Lake Chad

1,481,152
Freetown
Monrovia
Christianborg Whydah
Accra Popo Porto-Novo
Cape Coast Castle Benin
Elmina Bight of Benin Calabar
1,209,321 Gulf of Guinea Bonny

DAHOMEY

Ethiopia

Arabian Sea

**Trans-
Atlantic
slave trade**
ca. 1560–1850

Embarked—
ca. 12,521,000

Disembarked—
ca. 10,703,000

542,668

1,999,060 São Tomé
Congo
1,594,560 Loango Kasai
Luanda
5,694,574 Benguela

Lake
Victoria
Zanzibar

Zambezi Mozambique

Sofala

Madagascar

South Atlantic Ocean

Cape Town
Cape of Good Hope

Indian Ocean

The execution of Louis XVI on January 21, 1793, intensified the political divisions in France that followed the revolution. Later in the year, and into 1794, the "Reign of Terror" was responsible for the execution of thousands of "enemies of the revolution."

for power, he tried and failed to conquer the vast territories of Russia, and he did not succeed in controlling Egypt for long, but his meteoric career was unlike any the world had ever seen. When he was finally defeated by the British at the Battle of Waterloo in 1815, he left a powerful myth behind: the brilliant individual who, by sheer talent, could conquer whole nations.

Napoleon left a number of crucial political legacies too. Though he ruled by dictatorship and reinstated slavery in the French colonies, he also consolidated many of the principles of the French Revolution. Known as the Napoleonic Code, his new legal system was modeled after the civil code of ancient Rome: it abolished hereditary privileges, opened government careers to individuals on the basis of ability rather than birth, and established freedom of religion. In conquering much of Europe, Napoleon managed to wipe away many vestiges of old feudal institutions across the continent. And when he occupied Spain in 1808, he destabilized its power over its colonies, opening the way for a wave of

independence movements across South and Central America. Inspired by the ideals of the American and French Revolutions, groups mostly composed of *criollos*—South Americans of European ancestry—led new nations to freedom from Spanish imperial rule. By 1825 Mexico, Peru, Brazil, Bolivia, Colombia, Venezuela, Chile, Uruguay, Ecuador, and Paraguay had all taken their places on the map as independent states.

Both the industrial revolution and the political revolution continued to haunt the generations that followed. Absolute monarchies kept crumbling, as outraged people rose up to demand new rights. Exploited workers also mobilized, organizing strikes and protests against economic and political inequalities. They began to call themselves the "proletariat" or "working class" for the first time. Each insurgency inspired other outbreaks, producing a kind of revolutionary contagion across Europe and the Americas that reached its peak in the extraordinary year of 1848, called the "Springtime of the Peoples," when revolutions broke out in France, Austria, Hungary, Switzer-

Napoleon at the Battle of Waterloo, 1815, Charles Auguste Steuben. Most artists' portrayals of Napoleon, even in defeat (as here, where he is shown during the Battle of Waterloo), reinforced a romanticized, heroic ideal.

land, Spain, Germany, Italy, Denmark, and Romania. This was the year that Karl Marx and Friedrich Engels published the *Communist Manifesto*, which ended with the battle cry: "Workers of the world, unite!" It was in this year that the French abolished slavery for good. And it was in the same year that women's rights activists in the United States organized their first convention at Seneca Falls, New York, where, in a deliberate echo of the Declaration of Independence, they made the case "that all men and women are created equal."

LITERATURE IN THE AGE OF REVOLUTIONS

Utopian dreams have always driven political revolutionaries. In fact, there can be no revolution without acts of imagination. If the old world must be banished and a new world put in its place, what should that new world look like? The first wave of American and

French revolutionaries were inspired by the work of eighteenth-century Enlightenment thinkers who envisioned a society governed by reason rather than by custom or superstition. In particular, the philosopher and novelist **Jean-Jacques Rousseau** powerfully stirred the French revolutionaries by imagining a universal emancipation from tyranny: "Man is born free," he wrote, "but everywhere is in chains." The industrial revolution, too, depended on the workings of the imagination: it was spurred by new schemes for increasing the speed of production, for the invention of huge new machines and the creation of fast modes of communication and transportation. It was fueled, too, by dreams of unprecedented wealth.

Since imagination seemed so crucial to the making of these modern revolutions, writers and artists began to see themselves as playing an important role in the tumult of the times. Art, it seemed, could have the power to transform the world. Many writers eagerly

REVOLUTIONARY EUROPE
1848

Centers of major revolutionary uprisings, 1819–1848

ST. PETERSBURG

ckholm

Baltic Sea

Riga

Moscow

RUSSIAN EMPIRE

Volga

a

Vistula

Warsaw

Łodz

Dneiper

Kiev

aków

Dneister

NGARIAN EMPIRE

Prut

CARPATHIAN MOUNTAINS

Pest

da

Danube

Belgrade

Bucharest

Danube

Black Sea

OTTOMAN EMPIRE

ISTANBUL

ASIA MINOR

Aegean Sea

GREECE

Euphrates

Rhodes

Cyprus

Crete

The artist Francisco Goya, whose life spanned the years covered in this section of the anthology, spent most of his career as a portraitist for the wealthy. But late in his career, he also privately devoted his art to chronicling the horrors of war during and after Napoleon's siege of Spain in the early 1800s. The series of prints that resulted—called *The Disasters of War* (*Los Desastres de la Guerra*)—hinted at the stylistic upheavals that would follow later in the century. In this image, called simply *Why?* (*Por qué?*), French soldiers garrotte a Spanish prisoner.

threw themselves into the fray. In the 1790s, for example, the English poet **William Blake** boldly wore the red cap symbolizing the liberty and equality of the French Revolution, and he used his poetry to decry the corruption of church and government, as well as the poverty and enslavement of the people. Still strongly inspired by the French Revolution, in the 1840s the German poet **Heinrich Heine** supported a workers' uprising in a poem called "**The Silesian Weavers,**" which cursed unbearable economic and political inequalities. Similarly, English poet **Elizabeth Barrett Browning** helped to persuade her contemporaries to put limits on child labor in factories with her poem, "**The Cry of the Children.**" Meanwhile, the Venezuelan-born poet **Andrés Bello** came to be known as the "artistic liberator" of Latin America for throwing off the dominance of European themes

and ideas, and later the Cuban **José Martí** combined the roles of revolutionary fighter, political prisoner, and heroic national poet. All of these writers are included in this volume.

For a hundred years, the French Revolution continued to haunt literary writers. Had it ushered in a great new world based on equality and freedom, or had its violence and bloodshed produced meaningless destruction? The Anglo-Irish writer Edmund Burke called the French revolutionaries a "swinish multitude"; British poets **William Wordsworth** and Samuel Taylor Coleridge were at first caught up in the enthusiasm for the democratic ideals of the French Revolution, but the Reign of Terror horrified them and turned them into conservative voices. Charles Dickens, in his *Tale of Two Cities* (1859), exposed the terrible impoverishment of both the London poor and the French peasantry, and yet did not support the French Revolution: the sinister revolutionary Madame Defarge represents vengeful bloodshed. On the other hand, the revolutionaries continued to inspire passionate adherents. "Whatever else may be said of it," asserts a character in Victor Hugo's novel *Les Misérables* (1862), "the French Revolution was the greatest step forward by mankind since the coming of Christ." And whichever side one took, according to the English poet Percy Shelley, the French Revolution was simply "the master theme of the epoch in which we live."

The upheavals of this revolutionary moment did not only provide compelling subject matter for writers. This was a period that dramatically altered the very forms of art. Until the nineteenth century, artists in Europe had mostly worked for the old wealthy elites: powerful aristocrats or the Catholic Church. Now they began to create works of art for "the people." In this context, tradi-tional modes of writing often seemed ill-suited to new democratic ideals. What was needed was a revolution in style and form. Thus when Wordsworth and Coleridge collaborated on a volume of poetry in 1798, they outright rejected "the gaudiness and inane phraseology" of earlier poetry in favor of "language really used by men." For generations to follow, writers would struggle to capture the revolutionary tumult of the times in startling and sometimes uncomfortable new forms, insisting on experimenting, on innovating, on seeing the world afresh—and never getting buried in old routines. This impulse to revolutionize the way people saw the world was to become part of the definition of art itself. The late nineteenth-century painter Paul Gauguin maintained that every artist was "either a plagiarist or a revolutionary." And if those were the only choices, then what self-respecting artist wouldn't choose revolution?

JEAN-JACQUES ROUSSEAU
1712–1778

Jean-Jacques Rousseau played a significant role in three different revolutions: in politics, his work inspired and shaped revolutionary sentiment in the American colonies and France; in philosophy, he proposed radically unsettling ideas about human nature, justice, and progress that disrupted the dominant Enlightenment thinking of the moment and helped to spark the Romantic movement; and in literature, he invented a major new genre: the modern autobiography. The kind of life story he tells in the *Confessions* is now so familiar as to feel ordinary, recounting in detail the author's emotional life, including formative childhood experiences of desire, pain, and guilt. But in its moment this narrative broke with established conventions, erupting onto the literary scene as a shock so great that it was banned altogether. The text did not appear in full until more than a hundred years after it was written.

LIFE

As a young man, Rousseau did not seem bound for intellectual greatness. Born in the Protestant city of Geneva in 1712, the second son of a watch-maker, he spent very little time in school. Rousseau's mother died a few days after he was born, and his father, after having gotten himself involved in a violent quarrel, fled Geneva when Jean-Jacques was ten, sending his son to live with relatives. The boy did not seem adept enough to learn watchmaking, so at the age of thirteen he was apprenticed to an engraver, who turned out to be cruel and violent. Three years later, Rousseau ran away from Geneva and, craving the protection of a beautiful Catholic woman named Françoise-Louise de Warens, converted to Catholicism. Then began a period of aimless wandering, as Rousseau lived on and off with Madame de Warens, working for short periods as a domestic servant, a music teacher, a surveyor's clerk, and a tutor. Even in his thirties, he was given to idle drifting and was unable to hold down a job for long.

Despite his lack of formal schooling, the young Rousseau always read voraciously. In early childhood he developed a passionate enthusiasm for ancient Greek and Roman writers. A particular favorite was Plutarch, who wrote morally instructive biographies of ancient emperors and military leaders, including Julius Caesar and Alexander the Great. Rousseau was such an avid reader that while he was an apprentice he went so far as to sell his clothes in order to get his hands on books.

Madame de Warens helped the young man to pursue his intellectual interests and encouraged him to learn music. Their emotional relationship has become well known thanks to Rousseau's account of it in the *Confessions*. Rousseau called her "Mamma," while she called him "Little One." They became lovers in the period from 1733 to 1738, although, Rousseau writes, he felt considerable discomfort joining sexual longings with his love for this maternal figure. To make matters more complicated still, their household often included other men, with Rousseau at times the less favored figure in the *ménage à trois*. And yet, long after their relationship was over, he continued to speak of his lasting love for Madame de Warens and her pivotal importance in his life.

At the age of thirty, Rousseau went to Paris, where he became a personal assistant to a powerful and aristocratic family. In this period he met many important Enlightenment philosophers, and he contributed a few entries to the grand *Encyclopédie* they were compiling. At the same time that he was attracting patronage in the most refined Parisian circles, he started living with a barely literate chambermaid named Thérèse Levasseur, a relationship that lasted for three decades and finally resulted in marriage. He had five children with her—all of whom, shockingly, he insisted on leaving in a Paris orphanage.

Late in 1749 Rousseau was considering competing for an essay prize: the challenge was to write about whether advances in the arts and sciences had brought about a purification of human morals. As he was thinking about this question, he experienced a sudden flash of inspiration that would change his life. In one moment of "illumination," he said, he realized that intellectual advances had brought not moral purification but corruption, not improvement but decline. Human beings in a state of nature were compassionate and good; it was society itself that was to blame for creating inequality, greed, and aggression. He abruptly rejected the achievements that the Enlightenment philosophers were calling "progress."

The essay won first prize, and it made Rousseau famous. "I dared to strip man's nature naked," he wrote, "and showed that his supposed improvement was the true fount of all his miseries."

In the years that followed, Rousseau developed these innovative ideas. In 1754 he ascribed all of the evils of human experience to property and inequality: "You are undone if you once forget that the fruits of the earth belong to us all, and the earth itself to nobody." Deciding to live the simple life that he extolled in his works, he returned to Geneva, where he converted back to Protestantism. This second conversion prompted some detractors to accuse him of insincerity and opportunism. Soon after, he made a new enemy when he published a condemnation of the French philosopher **Voltaire**. Two years later he denounced the theater as a cause of moral corruption, and launched personal attacks. He soon found himself isolated and labeled a traitor. From this point onward, he constantly suspected that others were conspiring against him.

Julie, or the New Heloise, Rousseau's only novel, was published in 1761. The best-selling novel of the entire eighteenth century, *Julie* extolled passionate, authentic feeling, sincere faith, and rustic nature, and it struck audiences as dramatically different from most contemporary fiction, which prized artful wit and sophistication. Readers were enthralled, and Rousseau became one of the first literary celebrities. "Women were intoxicated by both the book and its author," he boasted, "and there were hardly any, even in the highest ranks, whose conquest I might not have made if I had undertaken it."

The year after *Julie* appeared, Rousseau developed his thinking in two major philosophical works. The first, *The Social Contract*, made the radical case that legitimate government rests on the will of the people. When rulers fail to protect the populace, Rousseau argued, they break the social contract, and the people are then free to choose new rulers. Thomas Jefferson would rely on this argument when he came to write the Declaration of Independence. The second major work, *Émile*, another major best seller, was a treatise on education which argued that children should be allowed to develop according to their senses and lived experience, and should be kept from books until the age of 12. This idea inspired numerous educational programs, including Montessori schools. In *Émile*, Rousseau also made a case for "natural religion," arguing that a knowledge of God comes not from orthodox doctrine or from revelation, but from one's own observations of nature. Parliaments in both Paris and Geneva saw the book as subversive and called for it to be banned and burned, while the French government ordered Rousseau's arrest. He escaped to a Prussian town, where he asked a priest if he could take communion. His detractors were shocked: was this the man who had just condemned all established religion? Then, in 1764, an anonymous pamphlet—which turned out to have been written by Voltaire—revealed that Rousseau had abandoned all five of his children. Since the moral purpose of *Émile* was to teach readers how to raise and educate children, this latest scandal seemed to many to expose Rousseau as a thoroughgoing hypocrite. In response, he began to write a defense of himself that would shield him from public blame—a story of his own life. This was to become the *Confessions*.

Looking for refuge from scandal and capture, Rousseau fled to England to stay with the philosopher David Hume in 1766. He had become so suspicious of those around him that after a few months he became convinced that Hume was part of a large conspiracy against him, and he wrote a public letter accusing his host of persecuting him. After wandering in exile, he finally settled down in Paris in 1770. A warrant was still out for his arrest, but no one seemed eager to enforce it, and he quietly took up copying music for a living. He also finished the *Confessions*. Since he knew that he would not be permitted to publish it, he confined himself to reading portions aloud to intimate aristocratic audiences. Even these readings alarmed many of his listeners, however, who feared that their own secrets would become public in Rousseau's narrative. Former friends convinced the police to ban these events. After an intense period of despair and hopelessness, Rousseau grew comparatively serene until his death in 1778.

CENSORSHIP AND SUBVERSION IN ROUSSEAU'S FRANCE

Rousseau was not the only writer of his time to endure censorship. At the beginning of the eighteenth century, France had been ruled for decades by an absolute monarch, Louis XIV, who consolidated power so effectively that he is remembered for his stark declaration, "I am the state." Under his rule, Catholic France became the most powerful nation in Europe. It was also highly repressive, silencing criticism of the state and persecuting Protestants who lived within French borders. The king's great-grandson, Louis XV, came to the throne in 1715, a less able and decisive ruler than his predecessor. After several serious military losses, sex scandals, and spending sprees, his popularity sank, and although the government controlled all publications and ordered the death penalty for any writer who attacked religious or state authority, a lively underground book and

pamphlet trade flourished. The literate population of France almost doubled between 1680 and 1780, and it included an ever greater variety of readers, including women and artisans. Printed works became cheaper and more available, and audiences began to change their habits, shifting from the conventional practice of reading a small number of works many times over to a new pattern of reading numerous works quickly, thereby gaining access to an unprecedented array of genres and points of view.

From the 1720s onward, a large network of underground printers published philosophical works outside of France in Protestant cities such as Geneva or Amsterdam and had them smuggled across the borders in oxcarts, or sewn into women's petticoats. A few publishers hid inflammatory pages inside respectable books such as Bibles. The king's advisors realized that they were losing the battle and in the 1750s became more permissive, but such an outpouring of radical publications followed that the state imposed new bans. Paradoxically, outlawing a work helped it to sell more copies, which meant that Louis XV's censorship helped to set off a vigorous public debate. For the first time, a democratic public sphere was emerging. Literary success began to depend on a wide reading public, rather than on specific patrons. And as those beyond the elite enjoyed a growing access to such innovative works, their willingness to tolerate the conventions of the old regime would start to falter.

Among the most influential critics of authority in Rousseau's time were the Enlightenment philosophers, such as Voltaire, who forcefully attacked the Catholic Church, and the Baron de Montesquieu, who denounced despotism and the slave trade. These thinkers called for individual reason to take the place of traditional authority, and they argued that human history was progressing toward perfection by casting off old habits and fetters. This was no marginal academic argument: it threatened to rock the very foundations of the state. Rousseau's friend Denis Diderot remained under police surveillance for years and was for a time imprisoned in a dungeon for writing subversively about religion. Later, his great Enlightenment project, the *Encyclopédie*, worried those in power by promising to diffuse knowledge widely, allowing ordinary people access to unsettling new ideas about natural rights, science, and religious tolerance. In the late 1750s Enlightenment thinkers felt intensely vulnerable, and it was in these same years that Rousseau—subversive and inflammatory in his own right—began to attack them from a new angle. Exalting feeling over reason, rejecting scientific advances, and imagining a return to uncorrupted nature as the key to human happiness, Rousseau became the lightning rod for critiques of Enlightenment reason and the personification of a whole new movement that would come to be known as Romanticism. Indeed, it was Rousseau's writing that first introduced a wide audience to the values that Romantic writers and artists would enthusiastically take up in the generations to follow: an admiration for simplicity and naturalness, a pleasure in the imagination, an assertion of the importance of unique, sincere, individual experience, and, in place of reason, a celebration of the whole range of emotions, from passionate love and intense horror to patriotic loyalty and harrowing grief.

WORK

Before Rousseau's *Confessions*, European readers had sometimes encoun-tered life stories written by aristocrats and military heroes, which recounted their heroic exploits, and they had read confessional religious works, where authors had told stories about faith and conversion. But they had never seen anything quite like a modern autobiography. For the first time, an author's intimate emotional life became the subject of his work. The *Confessions* therefore helped to revolutionize notions of what a life was and what it meant. This was a text that took the uniqueness of individual feeling more seriously than any text had done before, prizing honest self-knowledge as a new moral value. In the process, it also offered a new kind of hero: the isolated but extraordinary individual, unhappy in his solitude but brave in his resistance to social mores. Rousseau departed from convention, too, in his insistence on the importance of childhood memories as essential to the formation of adult personality. Since previous writers had generally considered children's experience inconsequential, the *Confessions* challenged the most basic expectations about what was relevant to an understanding of the self. And then, even more strangely, the narrative focused specifically on sexual pleasures—including the pleasure of being spanked as a child—which struck many of Rousseau's first readers as embarrassingly petty. But these episodes would turn out to have a lasting impact. More than a century later, Sigmund Freud looked back on the *Confessions* as the forerunner of psychoanalysis, and into our own time, biographers, memoir writers, novelists, therapists, and talk-show hosts continue to understand childhood sexuality as a crucial shaping factor in an adult's life.

The book opens with Rousseau's own sense of his radical originality: "I am resolved on an undertaking that has no model and will have no imitator."

Given this claim to being without precedent, Rousseau's title intriguingly suggests the opposite: by calling his autobiography the *Confessions*, he suggests that he is in fact modeling his own work on a famous fourth-century Christian story of spiritual conversion, St. Augustine's *Confessions*. And so he invites us to consider whether or not Augustine's autobiography acts as a "model" for his own work.

This is just one of many paradoxes and contradictions that readers have noticed in Rousseau. On the one hand, for example, he casts himself as a solitary outcast. On the other hand, the *Confessions* repeatedly mentions that its author is an international celebrity, hounded by adoring fans across Europe. In another seeming paradox, Rousseau borrows from the conventionally masculine genre of the public figure's memoir, while he draws equally from the much more feminine, private, domestic style of the novel to describe his childhood and love affairs. Rousseau himself said, "I would rather be a man of paradoxes than a man of prejudices," and it is possible to see these paradoxes forming the very backbone of the work. After all, while the *Confessions* presents the private, emotional life of a unique person, it also uses this personal experience to explore larger ideas about the relationship between the individual and society—the very ideas that are also at the heart of Rousseau's philosophical works.

The *Confessions* can therefore be seen to interrogate and break down conventional distinctions between private and public, unique and representative, masculine and feminine.

Many readers have been troubled by yet another tension in the text. Rousseau insists throughout that he is telling the unvarnished truth about himself, however shameful, including acts of theft and masturbation. And yet, he also says that he intends the text to vindicate him to a wide public—to show that he is, by nature, essentially good. The struggle for truth and the attempt at self-justification can seem starkly at odds. In his own time, however, Rousseau's innovative style strengthened his claims to truth telling. Most contemporary writers reveled in elaborate wit and wordplay, but Rousseau spoke frankly and powerfully in the first person, giving his readers a startling new sense of direct contact with the author. Inventing a style of prose that felt unusually plain and honest, Rousseau helped to provoke a new appetite for authenticity in life-writing. Meanwhile, his insistence on direct democracy, natural rights, the value of authentic emotion, and the perils of property ownership would win numerous followers, political, philosophical, and literary. Napoleon himself is reputed to have said that Rousseau caused the French Revolution, and added, "without the Revolution, you would not have had me."

Confessions[1]

This is the only portrait of a man, painted exactly according to nature and in all its truth, that exists and will probably ever exist. Whoever you may be, whom destiny or my trust has made the arbiter of the fate of these notebooks, I entreat you, in the name of my misfortunes, of your compassion, and of all human kind, not to destroy a unique and useful work, which may serve as a first point of comparison in the study of man that certainly is yet to be begun, and not to take away from the honour of my memory the only sure monument to my character that has not been disfigured by my enemies. Finally, were you yourself to be one of those implacable enemies, cease to be so towards my ashes, and do not pursue your cruel injustice beyond the term both of my life and yours; so that you might do yourself the credit of having been, once at least, generous and good, when you might have been wicked and vindictive; if, that is, the evil directed at a man who has never himself done nor wanted to do any could properly bear the name of vengeance.

Part One

BOOK ONE

Intus, et in cute.[2]

I am resolved on an undertaking that has no model and will have no imitator. I want to show my fellow-men a man in all the truth of nature; and this man is to be myself.

Myself alone. I feel my heart and I know men. I am not made like any that I have seen; I venture to believe that I was not made like any that exist. If I am not more deserving, at least I am different. As to whether nature did well or ill to break the mould in which I was cast, that is something no one can judge until after they have read me.

Let the trumpet of judgement sound when it will, I will present myself with this book in my hand before the Supreme Judge. I will say boldly: 'Here is what I have done, what I have thought, what I was. I have told the good and the bad with equal frankness. I have concealed nothing that was ill, added nothing that was good, and if I have sometimes used some indifferent ornamentation, this has only ever been to fill a void occasioned by my lack of memory; I may have supposed to be true what I knew could have been so, never what I knew to be false. I have shown myself as I was, contemptible and vile when that is how I was, good, generous, sublime, when that is how I was; I have disclosed my innermost self as you alone know it to be. Assemble about me, Eternal Being, the numberless host of my fellow-men; let them hear my confessions, let them groan at my unworthiness, let them blush at my wretchedness. Let each of them, here on the steps of your throne, in turn reveal his heart with the same sincerity; and then let one of them say to you, if he dares: *I was better than that man.*'

1. Translated by Angela Scholar.
2. "Inside and under the skin" (Latin), from Roman satirist Aulus Persius Flaccus (34– 62 C.E.), referring to a man who looks back sadly on his loss of virtue.

I was born in 1712 in Geneva, the son of Isaac Rousseau and Suzanne Bernard, citizens.[3] Since an already modest family fortune to be divided between fifteen children had reduced to almost nothing my father's share of it, he was obliged to depend for his livelihood on his craft as a watchmaker, at which, indeed, he excelled. My mother, who was the daughter of M. Bernard, the minister, was wealthier; she was beautiful and she was good; and my father had not won her easily. They had loved one another almost from the day they were born; at the age of eight or nine years they were already taking walks together every evening along the Treille; by ten years they were inseparable. The sympathy, the harmony between their souls, reinforced the feelings that habit had formed. Tender and sensitive by nature, they were both of them waiting only for the moment when they would find another person of like disposition, or rather this moment was waiting for them, and each of them gave his heart to the first that opened to receive it. The destiny that had seemed to oppose their passion served only to kindle it. Unable to win his lady, the young man was consumed with grief; she counselled him to travel and to forget her. He travelled, to no avail, and returned more in love than ever. He found the woman he loved still tender and true. After such a test all that remained was for them to love one another till the end of their days; they swore to do so, and Heaven blessed the vow.

Gabriel Bernard, my mother's brother, fell in love with one of my father's sisters; but she consented to marry the brother only on condition that her brother marry the sister. Love prevailed, and the two weddings took place on the same day. And so my uncle was the husband of my aunt, and their children were my first cousins twice over. By the end of the first year a child had been born on each side; but there was to be a further separation.

My uncle Bernard was an engineer; he went away to serve in the Empire and in Hungary under Prince Eugène. He distinguished himself during the siege and the battle of Belgrade.[4] After the birth of my only brother, my father departed for Constantinople to take up a post as watchmaker to the seraglio. While he was away my mother's beauty, intelligence, and accomplishments[5] won her many admirers. M. de La Closure, the French resident in Geneva, was one of the most assiduous in his attentions. His passion must have been keenly felt; since thirty years later he still softened visibly when he spoke of her to me. My mother had more than her virtue with which to defend herself, she loved her husband tenderly; she pressed him to return; he abandoned everything and came. I was the sad fruit of this homecoming. Ten months later, I was born, weak and sickly; I cost my mother her life, and my birth was the first of my misfortunes.

---

3. Geneva, unlike its larger neighbors Savoy and France, was a republic with an elected legislature, though only a small number of adult men counted as citizens.

4. François-Eugène, Prince of Savoy (1663–1736), led the Hungarian army to victory in the Battle of Belgrade, a famous and surprising triumph over the Turkish army in 1717.

5. These were too brilliant for her condition in life, for her father, the minister, adored her, and had taken great care over her education. She could draw and sing, she accompanied herself on the theorbo [a stringed instrument], she was well read and could write tolerable verse. Here is a little rhyme she wrote impromptu, while out walking with her sister-in-law and their children during the absence of her brother and her husband, in response to a remark that someone made to her about these latter:

These two young men, though far from here,
In many ways to us are dear;
They are our friends, our lovers;
Our husbands and our brothers,
And the fathers of these children here.
[Rousseau's note]

I never knew how my father bore his loss; but I do know that he never got over it. He thought he could see my mother in me, without being able to forget that I had deprived him of her; he never caressed me without my sensing, from his sighs, from his urgent embraces, that a bitter regret was mingled with them, for which, however, they were the more tender. He had only to say to me: 'Let's talk about your mother, Jean-Jacques,' and I would reply: 'Very well, Father, and then we'll weep together,' and these words alone were enough to move him to tears. 'Ah!' he would sigh, 'bring her back to me, comfort me for losing her; fill the emptiness she has left in my soul. Would I love you as much if you were only my son?' Forty years after losing her he died in the arms of a second wife, but with the name of the first on his lips, and her image deep in his heart.

Such were the authors of my days. Of all the gifts bestowed on them by heaven, the only one they bequeathed to me was a tender heart; but to this they owed their happiness, just as I owe it all my misfortune.

I was born almost dying; they despaired of saving me. I already carried within me the germ of an indisposition which has worsened with the years, and which now allows me some occasional respite only in order that I might endure another, more cruel, form of suffering. One of my father's sisters, an amiable and virtuous young woman, took such good care of me that she saved me. She is still alive as I write this, and at eighty years old cares for a husband who is younger than she, but ravaged by drink. I forgive you, dear Aunt, for having preserved my life, and it grieves me that I cannot, at the end of your days, repay you for the tender care you lavished on me at the beginning of mine. My nurse Jacqueline, too, is still alive and in sound health. The hands that opened my eyes at my birth may yet close them at my death.

I had feelings before I had thoughts: that is the common lot of humanity. But I was more affected by it than others are. I have no idea what I did before the age of five or six: I do not know how I learned to read; all I remember is what I first read and its effect on me; this is the moment from which I date my first uninterrupted consciousness of myself. My mother had left some romances.[6] We began to read them after supper, my father and I. Our first intention was simply that I should practise my reading with the help of some entertaining books; but we soon became so engrossed in them that we spent whole nights taking it in turns to read to one another without interruption, unable to break off until we had finished the whole volume. Sometimes my father, hearing the swallows at dawn, would say shamefacedly: 'We'd better go to bed now; I'm more of a child than you are.'

By this dangerous method I acquired in a short time not only a marked facility for reading and comprehension, but also an understanding, unique in one of my years, of the passions. I had as yet no ideas about things, but already I knew every feeling. I had conceived nothing; I had felt everything. This rapid succession of confused emotions did not damage my reason, since as yet I had none; but it provided me with one of a different temper; and left me with some bizarre and romantic notions about human life, of which experience and reflection have never quite managed to cure me.

6. Novels, often fanciful tales of adventure and heroism.

The romances lasted us until the summer of 1719. The following winter we found something else. Since my mother's books were exhausted, we resorted to what we had inherited of her father's library. Fortunately it contained some good books; and this could scarcely have been otherwise, since this library had been collected by a man who was not only an ordained minister and even, for such was the fashion of the day, a scholar, but also a man of taste and intelligence. Le Sueur's *History of Church and Empire*, Bossuet's discourses on universal history, Plutarch's on famous men, Nani's *History of Venice*, Ovid's *Metamorphoses*, La Bruyère, Fontenelle's *Plurality of Worlds* and his *Dialogues of the Dead*, and some volumes of Molière,[7] all these were moved into my father's studio, and there, every day, I read to him while he worked. I acquired a taste for these works that was rare, perhaps unique, in one of my age. Plutarch, in particular, became my favourite author. The pleasure I took in reading and rereading him cured me in part of my passion for romances, and I soon preferred Agesilaus, Brutus, and Aristides to Orondate, Artamène, and Juba.[8] These interesting books, and the conversations they occasioned between my father and me, shaped that free, republican spirit, that proud and indomitable character, that impatience with servitude and constraint, which it has been my torment to possess all my life in circumstances not at all favourable to its development. My mind was full of Athens and Rome; I lived, as it were, in the midst of their great men; I was, besides, by birth a citizen of a republic and the son of a father whose love for his country was his greatest passion, and I was fired by his example; I thought of myself as a Greek or a Roman; I became the person whose life I was reading: when I recounted acts of constancy and fortitude that had particularly struck me, my eyes would flash and my voice grow louder. One day at table, while I was relating the story of Scaevola,[9] my family were alarmed to see me stretch out my hand and, in imitation of his great deed, place it on a hot chafing-dish.

I had a brother seven years older than I, who was learning my father's trade. The extreme affection that was lavished upon me meant that he was a little neglected, which is not something of which I can approve. His upbringing suffered in consequence. He fell into dissolute ways even before the age at which one can, properly speaking, be considered dissolute. He was placed with a new master, from whom he ran away just as he had done at home. I hardly ever saw him; I can hardly claim to have known him; but I nevertheless loved him dearly, and he loved me too, in as far as such a rascal is capable of love. I remember once when my father, in a rage, was chastising him severely, throwing myself impetuously between the two of them and flinging my arms around him. I thus protected him by taking on my own body all the blows destined for

7. The pseudonym of Jean Baptiste de Poquelin (1622–1673), French comic playwright. Jean Le Sueur (c. 1602–1681), French historian and Protestant minister. Jacques-Bénigne Bossuet (1627–1704), French bishop, writer, and orator. Plutarch (46–119), Roman historian and biographer. Giovanni Battista Nani (1616–1678), Venetian writer, historian, and ambassador. Ovid (43 B.C.E.–16 C.E.), Roman poet. Jean de la Bruyère (1645–1696), French satirist. Bernard le Bovier de Fontenelle (1657–1757), French writer, scientist, and philosopher.

8. Agesilaus, Brutus, and Aristides are historical figures; Orondate and Juba are characters from novels by Gauthier de Costes, called la Calprenède (1610–1663); Artamène is the hero of a long novel by Madeleine de Scudéry (1607–1701).

9. Gaius Mucius Scaevola, a mythical Roman hero who held his right hand in a fire without showing any signs of pain.

him, and I kept this up so determinedly that my father was obliged in the end to spare him, either because he was moved by my cries and my tears, or because he was afraid of hurting me more than him. My brother went from bad to worse and in the end ran off and disappeared forever. A little while later we heard that he was in Germany. He never once wrote. No more was ever heard of him; and so it was that I became an only son.

If this poor boy's upbringing was neglected, the same could not be said of his brother, for royal princes could not have been cared for more zealously than I was during my early years, idolized by everyone around me, and, which is rarer, treated always as a much-loved child and never as a spoiled one. Never once while I remained in my father's house was I allowed to roam the streets alone with the other children; never was it necessary either to discourage in me or to indulge any of those fanciful whims which are generally attributed to nature, and which are entirely the product of upbringing. I had my childish faults: I prattled, I was greedy, I sometimes told lies. No doubt I stole fruit, sweets, things to eat; but I never, just for the fun of it, did any harm or damage, got others into trouble, or teased dumb animals. I remember on one occasion, however, peeing into the kettle belonging to one of our neighbours, Mme Clot, while she was at church. I must confess, too, that this memory still makes me laugh, for Mme Clot, although otherwise a thoroughly good person, was the grumpiest old woman I ever knew in my life. Such is the true but brief history of my childhood misdemeanours.

How could I have learnt bad ways, when I was offered nothing but examples of mildness and surrounded by the best people in the world? It was not that the people around me—my father, my aunt, my nurse, our relatives, our friends, our neighbours—obeyed me, but rather that they loved me; and I loved them in return. My whims were so little encouraged and so little opposed that it never occurred to me to have any. I am ready to swear that, until I was myself subjected to the rule of a master, I never even knew what a caprice was. When I was not reading or writing with my father, or going for walks with my nurse, I was always with my aunt, watching her at her embroidery, hearing her sing, sitting or standing at her side; and I was happy. Her good-humour, her gentleness, her agreeable features, all these have so imprinted themselves on my memory, that I can still see in my mind's eye her manner, her glance, her whole air; I still remember the affectionate little things she used to say; I could describe how she was dressed, and how she wore her hair, even to the two black curls which, after the fashion of the day, framed her temples.

I am convinced that it is to her that I owe the taste, or rather passion, for music that developed in me fully only much later. She knew a prodigious number of songs and airs, which she sang in a small, sweet voice. This excellent young woman possessed a serenity of soul that banished far from her and from everyone around her any reverie or sadness. I was so enchanted by her singing that, not only have many of her songs lingered in my memory, but, now that I have lost her, others too, totally forgotten since childhood, return to haunt me as I grow older, with a charm I cannot convey. Who would have thought that, old driveller that I am, worn out with worry and care, I should suddenly catch myself humming these little tunes in a voice already cracked and quavering, and weeping like a child? One air in particular has come back to me in full, although the words of the second verse have repeatedly resisted all my efforts to remember them, even though I dimly recall the rhymes. Here is the beginning followed by what I have been able to remember of the rest.

> Tircis,[1] I dare not stay
> Beneath the sturdy oak
> To hear your pipe's sweet play;
> Already I'm the talk
> Of all our village folk
>
> . . . .
> . . . a shepherd's vows
> . . . his repose
> . . . allows
> For always the thorn lies under the rose.

What is it about this song, I wonder, that so beguiles and moves my heart? It has a capricious charm I do not understand at all; nevertheless, I am quite incapable of singing it through to the end without dissolving into tears. I have often been on the point of writing to Paris to enquire about the rest of the words, in case there should be anyone there who still knows them. But I suspect that some of the pleasure I take in recalling this little tune would fade if I knew for certain that others apart from my poor aunt Suzanne had sung it.

Such were the affections that marked my entry into life; thus there began to take shape or to manifest themselves within me this heart, at once so proud and so tender, and this character, effeminate and yet indomitable, which, continually fluctuating between weakness and courage, between laxity and virtue, has to the end divided me against myself and ensured that abstinence and enjoyment, pleasure and wisdom have all eluded me equally.

This upbringing was interrupted by an accident whose consequences have affected my life ever since. My father had a quarrel with a M. Gautier, a French captain, who had relatives in the council.[2] This Gautier, an insolent and cowardly fellow, suffered a nose-bleed and, out of revenge, accused my father of having drawn his sword on him inside the city limits. My father, threatened with imprisonment, insisted that, in accordance with the law, his accuser be taken into custody with him. Unable to obtain this, he chose to leave Geneva and to exile himself for the rest of his life rather than give way on a point where it seemed to him that both his honour and his liberty were compromised.

I remained behind under the guardianship of my uncle Bernard, who at the time was employed on the fortifications of Geneva. His eldest daughter had died, but he had a son the same age as myself. We were sent off together to Bossey to board with the minister, M. Lambercier, so that, along with some Latin, we might acquire that hotchpotch of knowledge which usually accompanies it under the name of education.

Two years spent in this village softened, somewhat, my Roman harshness and restored my childhood to me. At Geneva, where nothing was imposed on me, I had loved reading and study; it was almost my only amusement. At Bossey I was made to work, and thus grew to love the games that served as relaxation. The countryside was so new to me that I never tired of enjoying it. I came to love it

---

1. A shepherd from pastoral poetry. 2. The legislature of Geneva.

with a passion that has never faded. The memory of the happy days I spent there has filled me with regret for rural life and its pleasures at every stage of my existence until the one that took me back there. M. Lambercier was a sensible man who, while not neglecting our education, did not overburden us with schoolwork. The proof that he went about this in the right way is that, in spite of my dislike of any form of compulsion, I have never remembered my hours of study with any distaste, and that, while I did not learn much from him, what I did learn, I learned without difficulty and have never forgotten.

This simple country life bestowed on me a gift beyond price in opening up my heart to friendship. Up until then I had only known feelings that, although exalted, were imaginary. Living peaceably day after day with my cousin Bernard, I became warmly attached to him, and soon felt a more tender affection for him than I had for my brother, and one that has not been erased by time. He was a tall boy, lanky and very thin, as mild-tempered as he was feeble-bodied, and who did not take unfair advantage of the preference that, as the son of my guardian, he was shown by the whole household. We shared the same tasks, the same amusements, the same tastes; we were on our own together; we were of the same age; each of us needed a friend; so that to be separated was for both of us, so to speak, to be annihilated. Although we rarely had occasion to demonstrate our mutual attachment, it was strong, and not only could we not bear to be separated for a moment, but we could not imagine ever being able to bear it. Since we both of us responded readily to affection and were good-humoured when not crossed, we always agreed about everything. If, as the favourite of our guardians, he took precedence over me when we were with them, when we were alone the advantage was mine, and this redressed the balance between us. When he was at a loss during lessons, I whispered the answer to him; when my exercise was finished, I helped him with his, and in games, where I was the more inventive, he always followed my lead. In other words, our characters were so compatible and the friendship that united us so real, that, during the more than five years that we were virtually inseparable, whether at Bossey or in Geneva, we often, it is true, fell out, but we never needed to be separated, none of our quarrels lasted for more than a quarter of an hour, and neither of us ever once informed against the other. These remarks may seem puerile, but they nevertheless draw attention to an example that is perhaps unique among children.

The kind of life I led at Bossey suited me so well that it would have fixed my character for ever, if only it had lasted longer. It was founded on feelings that were at once tender, affectionate, and tranquil. Never, I believe, has any individual of our species possessed less natural vanity than I do. I would soar to heights of sublime feeling, but as promptly fall back into my habitual indolence. To be loved by all who came near me was my most urgent wish. I was by nature gentle, so too was my cousin; so indeed were our guardians. During two whole years I neither witnessed nor was the victim of any kind of violence. Everything fostered the tendencies that nature herself had planted in my heart. I knew no greater happiness than to see everyone content with me and with the world in general. I will never forget how, when it was my turn in chapel to recite my catechism, nothing distressed me more, if I happened to hesitate in my replies, than to see on Mlle Lambercier's face signs of anxiety and distress. I was more upset by this than by the shame of failing in public, although that, too, affected me greatly: for, not much moved by praise, I was always susceptible to shame, and I can safely say that the expectation of a reprimand from Mlle Lambercier alarmed me less than did the fear of causing her pain.

And indeed, she was not afraid, any more than was her brother, to show severity when this was necessary; but since her severity was almost always justified and never excessive, it provoked in me feelings of distress rather than of rebellion. I was more concerned about occasioning displeasure than about being chastised, for marks of disapprobation seemed more cruel to me than physical punishment. I find it embarrassing to go into greater detail, but I must. How promptly we would change our methods of dealing with the young if only the long-term effects of the one that is presently employed, always indiscriminately and often indiscreetly, could be foreseen! The lesson that may be learned from just one example of this, as common as it is pernicious, is so important that I have decided to give it.

Just as Mlle Lambercier felt for us the affection of a mother, so too she had a mother's authority, which she sometimes exerted to the point of inflicting common childhood punishments on us, when we had deserved this. For a while she restricted herself to threats of punishment which were quite new to me and which I found very frightening; but after the threat had been carried out, I discovered that it was less terrible in the event than it had been in anticipation, and, what is even more bizarre, that this punishment made me even fonder of the woman who had administered it. Indeed, it took all the sincerity of my affection for her and all my natural meekness to prevent me from seeking to merit a repetition of the same treatment; for I had found in the pain inflicted, and even in the shame that accompanied it, an element of sensuality which left me with more desire than fear at the prospect of experiencing it again from the same hand. It is true that, since without doubt some precocious sexual instinct entered into all this, the same punishment received from her brother would not have seemed to me at all pleasant. But given his temperament, this arrangement was not something that needed to be feared, so that, if I resisted the temptation to earn punishment, this was solely because I was afraid of vexing Mlle de Lambercier; for so great is the power that human kindness exercises over me, even if it has its origin in the senses, that in my heart the former will always prevail over the latter.

This second offence, which I had avoided without fearing it, duly occurred, but without involving any misdeed or at least any conscious act of will on my part, so that it was with a clear conscience that I as it were profited from it. But this second was also the last: for Mlle de Lambercier, who no doubt inferred from some sign I gave that the punishment was not achieving its aim, declared that she could not continue with it, that it exhausted her too much. Up until then we had slept in her room and sometimes, in winter, even in her bed. Two days later we were moved to another room, and I had henceforward the honour, which I would gladly have foregone, of being treated by her as a big boy.

Who would have believed that this ordinary form of childhood punishment, meted out to a boy of eight years[3] by a young woman of thirty, should have decided my tastes, my desires, my passions, my whole self, for the rest of my

3. Rousseau was in fact eleven years old at the time, not eight.

life, and in a direction that was precisely the opposite of what might naturally have been expected? My senses were inflamed, but at the same time my desires, confused and indeed limited by what I had already experienced, never thought of looking for anything else. My blood had burned within my veins almost from the moment of my birth, but I kept myself pure of any taint until an age when even the coldest and slowest of temperaments begins to develop. Long tormented, but without knowing why, I devoured with ardent gaze all the beautiful women I encountered. My imagination returned to them again and again, but only to deploy them in its own way, and to make of each of them another Mlle de Lambercier.

This bizarre taste, which persisted beyond adolescence and indeed drove me to the verge of depravity and madness, nevertheless preserved in me those very standards of upright behaviour which it might have been expected to undermine. If ever an upbringing was proper and chaste, it was certainly the one that I had received. My three aunts were not only persons of exemplary respectability, they also practised a reticence that women have long since abandoned. My father, who liked his pleasures but was gallant in the old style, never uttered, even in the presence of the women he most admired, a single word that would make a virgin blush, and the consideration that is due to children has never been more scrupulously observed than it was in my family and in front of me. M. Lambercier's household was no less strict in this regard, and indeed a very good servant was dismissed for having said something a little too free and easy in front of us. Not only had I reached adolescence before I had any clear idea about sexual union, but such confused ideas as I did have always took some odious and disgusting form. I had a horror of common prostitutes that I have never lost; I could not look at a debauchee without disdain, without dread even, so extreme was the aversion that I had felt for debauchery ever since, going to Saconnex one day along a hollow lane, I saw holes in the earth along both sides of the path and was told that this was where these people did their coupling. What I had seen dogs doing always came into my mind too when I thought of how it might be for people, and the very memory was enough to sicken me.

These prejudices, which I owed to my upbringing and which were sufficient in themselves to delay the first eruptions of a combustible temperament, were further reinforced, as I have said, by the false direction in which I had been led by the first stirrings of sensuality. I imagined only what I had experienced; in spite of a troublesome agitation in the blood, I concentrated all my desires on the kind of pleasure I already knew, without ever getting as far as that which I had been made to think of as odious, and which so closely resembled the other, although I had not the least suspicion of this. When, in the midst of my foolish fantasies, of my wild erotic flights, and of the extravagant actions to which they sometimes drove me, I resorted in imagination to the assistance of the other sex, I never dreamt that it could be put to any other use than that which I burned to make of it.

In this way, then, in spite of an ardent, lascivious, and very precocious temperament, not only did I pass beyond the age of puberty without desiring, without knowing, any sensual pleasures beyond those to which Mlle de Lambercier had quite innocently introduced me; but also, when at last the passing years had made me a man, it was again the case that what should have ruined me preserved me. The taste I had acquired as a child, instead of disappearing, became so identified with that other pleasure that I was never able to dissociate it from the desires aroused through the senses; and this vagary, in conjunction with my natural timidity, has always inhibited me in my approaches to women, because I dare not tell them everything, but nor am I able to perform everything; since my kind of pleasure, of which the other sort is only the end point, cannot be extracted by the man who desires it, nor guessed at by the woman who alone can bestow it. And so I have spent my life coveting but never declaring myself to the women I loved most. Never daring to reveal my proclivities, I have at least kept them amused with relationships that allowed my mind to dwell on them. To lie at the feet of an imperious mistress, to obey her commands, to be obliged to beg for her forgiveness, these were sweet pleasures, and the more my inflamed imagination roused my blood, the more I played the bashful lover. This way of making love does not, needless to say, result in very rapid progress, nor does it pose much threat to the virtue of the women who are its object. I have thus possessed very few, but have nevertheless achieved much pleasure in my own way, that is, through my imagination. Thus it is that my senses, conspiring with my timid nature and my romantic spirit, have kept my heart pure and my behaviour honourable, thanks to those very inclinations which, if I had been a little bolder perhaps, would have plunged me into the most brutish pleasure-seeking.

I have taken the first step, and the most painful, into the dark and miry labyrinth of my confessions. It is not what is criminal that it is the hardest to reveal, but what is laughable or shameful. But from now on I can feel certain of myself: after what I have just dared to say, nothing can stop me.

* * *

BOOK TWO

My landlady who, as I have said, had taken a liking to me, told me that she might have found a situation for me, and that a lady of quality wanted to see me. This was enough to convince me that I was at last embarked upon adventures in high places, for this was the idea I always came back to. It turned out, however, not to be as brilliant as I had imagined. I was taken to see the lady by the servant who had told her about me. She questioned me, cross-examined me, and was, apparently, satisfied, for all of a sudden I found myself in her service, not exactly as a favourite, but as a footman. I was dressed in the same colour as the other servants, except that they had a shoulder-knot which I was not given; since there was no braid on her livery, it looked very little different from any ordinary suit of clothes. Such was the unexpected fulfilment of all my high hopes!

The Comtesse de Vercellis, whose household I had entered, was a widow with no children. Her husband had been from Piedmont; as for her, I have always assumed that she came from Savoy, since I could not imagine a Piedmontese speaking French so well and with such a pure accent. She was in her middle years, distinguished in appearance, cultivated in mind, with a great love and knowledge of French literature. She wrote a great deal and always in

French. Her letters had the turn of phrase and the grace, almost, of Mme de Sévigné's:[4] some of them might even have been taken for hers. My main task, not at all an unpleasant one, was to take dictation of these letters, since she was prevented by a breast cancer, which caused her much suffering, from writing them herself.

Mme de Vercellis possessed not only great intelligence but a steadfast and noble soul. I watched her during her last illness, I saw her suffer and die without betraying a moment's weakness, without making the least apparent effort to contain herself, without abandoning her woman's dignity, and without suspecting that there was any philosophy in all of this; indeed, the word 'philosophy' was not yet in vogue, and she would not have known it in the sense in which it is used today. This strength of character was so marked as to be indistinguishable, sometimes, from coldness. She always seemed to me to be as indifferent to the feelings of others as she was to her own, so that, if she performed good works among the poor and needy, she did so because this was good in itself rather than out of any true compassion. I experienced something of this indifference during the three months I was with her. It would have been natural for her to conceive a liking for a young man of some promise, who was continually in her presence, and for it to occur to her, as she felt death approach, that afterwards he would still need help and support; however, either because she did not think me worthy of any special attention, or because the people who watched over her saw to it that she thought only of them, she did nothing for me.

I well remember, however, the curiosity she showed while getting to know me. She would sometimes ask me about myself; she liked me to show her the letters I was writing to Mme de Warens, and to describe my feelings to her. But she went about discovering them in quite the wrong way, since she never revealed hers to me. My heart was eager to pour itself out, provided it felt that another was open to receive it. Cold and curt interrogation, however, with no hint either of approbation or of blame at my replies, did not inspire me with confidence. Unable to judge whether my chatter was pleasing or displeasing, I became fearful and would try, not so much to say what I felt, as to avoid saying anything that might harm me. I have since observed that this habit of coldly interrogating people whom you are trying to get to know is fairly common among women who pride themselves on their intelligence. They imagine that, by revealing nothing of their own feelings, they will the better succeed in discovering yours; what they do not realize is that they thereby deprive you of the courage to reveal them. Anyone subjected to close questioning will, for that very reason, be put on his guard, and if he suspects that, far from inspiring any real interest, he is merely being made to talk, he will either lie, say nothing, or watch his tongue even more carefully than before, preferring to be thought a fool than to be the dupe of someone's mere curiosity. It is, in short, pointless to attempt to see into the heart of another while affecting to conceal one's own.

Mme de Vercellis never said a word to me that expressed affection, pity, or benevolence. She questioned me coldly, I replied with reserve. My replies were so timid that she must have found them beneath her notice, and become

---

4. French writer Marie de Rabutin-Chantal, marquise de Sévigné (1626–1696), famous for her letters.

bored. Towards the end she asked me no more questions and spoke to me only if she wanted me to do something for her. She judged me on the basis not so much of what I was but of what she had made me, and because she regarded me as nothing more than a footman, she prevented me from appearing to be anything else.

I think that this was my first experience of that malign play of hidden self-interest which has so often impeded me in life and which has left me with a very natural aversion towards the apparent order that produces it. Mme de Vercellis's heir, since she had no children, was a nephew, the Comte de la Roque, who was assiduous in his attentions towards her. In addition, her principal servants, seeing that her end was near, were determined not to be forgotten, and all in all she was surrounded by so many over-zealous people that it was unlikely that she would find time to think of me. The head of her household was a certain M. Lorenzini, an artful man, whose wife, even more artfully, had so insinuated herself into the good graces of her mistress that she was treated by her as a friend rather than a paid servant. She had persuaded her to take on as chambermaid a niece of hers, called Mlle Pontal, a crafty little creature who gave herself the airs of a lady's maid; together, she and her aunt were so successful in ingratiating themselves with their mistress that she saw only through their eyes and acted only through their agency. I had not the good fortune to find favour with these three people; I obeyed them, but I did not serve them; I did not see why, as well as attending our common mistress, I should be a servant to her servants. I presented, moreover, something of a threat to them. They could see very well that I was not in my rightful place; they feared that Madame would see it too, and that what she might do to rectify this would diminish their own inheritance; for people of that sort are too greedy to be fair, and look upon any legacy made to others as depriving them of what is properly theirs. And so they made a concerted effort to keep me out of her sight. She liked writing letters. It was a welcome distraction for someone in her condition; they discouraged it and persuaded her doctor to oppose it on the grounds that it was too tiring for her. On the pretext that I did not understand my duties, they hired in my place two great oafs to carry her about in her chair; and in short, they were so successful in all this that, when she came to make her will, I had not even entered her room during the whole of the previous week. It is true that thereafter I entered as before, and was more assiduous in my attentions than anyone else; for the poor woman's sufferings distressed me greatly, while the constancy with which she bore them inspired admiration and affection in me; indeed I shed genuine tears in that room, unnoticed by her or by anyone else.

At last we lost her. I saw her die. In life she had been a woman of wit and good sense; in death she was a sage. I can safely say that she endeared the Catholic religion to me by the serenity of spirit with which she fulfilled its duties, without omission and without affectation. She was by nature serious, but towards the end of her illness she assumed an air of gaiety, which was too constant to be simulated, and which was as though lent her by reason itself to compensate for the gravity of her situation. It was only during her last two days that she stayed in bed, and even then she kept up a tranquil conversation with the people round about her. At last, unable to speak and already in the throes of death, she gave a great fart. 'Good,' she said, as she turned over: 'A woman who farts cannot be dead.' These were the last words she uttered.

She had bequeathed a year's wages to each of her menial servants; but, since my name did not appear on her household list, I received nothing; in spite of this, the Comte de la Roque gave me thirty francs and let me keep the new suit of clothes which, although I was wearing it, M. Lorenzini had wanted to take away from me. He even promised to try to find me a new position and gave me permission to go and see him. I went two or three times, but without managing to speak to him. Easily deterred, I did not go again. As we will soon see, this was a mistake.

If only this were all that I have to relate about my time with Mme de Vercellis! But although my situation appeared unchanged, I was not the same on leaving her house as I had been when I entered it. I took away with me the enduring memory of a crime and the intolerable burden of a remorse, with which even now, after forty years, my conscience is still weighed down, and whose bitter knowledge, far from fading, becomes more painful with the years. Who would have thought that a child's misdeed could have such cruel consequences? But it is because of these all too probable consequences that my heart is denied any consolation. I may have caused to perish, in shameful and miserable circumstances, a young woman who, amiable, honest, and deserving, was, without a doubt, worth a great deal more than I.

It is almost inevitable that the dispersal of a household should generate a certain confusion and that items should go astray. And yet, such was the loyalty of the servants and the vigilance of M. and Mme Lorenzini that nothing was missing from the inventory. All that was lost was a little ribbon, silver and rose-coloured and already quite old, which belonged to Mlle Pontal. Many other, better things had been within my reach; but I was tempted only by this ribbon, I stole it, and since I made little attempt to conceal it, I was soon found with it. They asked me where I had got it. I hesitated, stammered, and finally said, blushing, that Marion had given it to me. Marion was a young girl from the Maurienne,[5] whom Mme de Vercellis had engaged as a cook when, because she no longer entertained and had more need of nourishing soups than of delicate ragouts, she decided to dismiss her own. Not only was Marion pretty, with a freshness of complexion that is found only in the mountains, and, above all, an air of modesty and sweetness that won the heart of everyone who saw her, she was also a good girl, virtuous and totally loyal. There was thus great surprise when I named her. I was regarded as scarcely less trustworthy, and so an enquiry was thought to be necessary to establish which of us was the thief. She was summoned; a large crowd of people was present, among them the Comte de la Roque. She arrived, was shown the ribbon, and, shamelessly, I made my accusation; taken aback, she said nothing, then threw me a glance which would have disarmed the devil himself, but which my barbarous heart resisted. At length she denied the charge, firmly but calmly, remonstrated with me, urged me to recollect myself and not to bring disgrace upon an innocent girl who had never done me any harm; I persisted in my infernal wickedness, however, repeated my accusation, and asserted to her face that it was she who had given me the ribbon. The poor girl began to cry, but said no more than, 'Ah Rousseau, and I always thought you had a good character! How wretched you are making me, and yet I would not for anything be in your

5. A province in the kingdom of Savoy.

place.' And that was all. She continued to defend herself with steadfast simplicity but without permitting herself any attack on me. The contrast between her moderation and my decided tone worked against her. It did not seem natural to suppose that there could be such diabolical effrontery on the one hand and such angelic sweetness on the other. No formal conclusion was reached, but the presumption was in my favour. Because of the general upheaval, the matter was left there, and the Comte de la Roque, dismissing us both, contented himself with saying that the conscience of the guilty party would be certain to avenge the innocent. This was no vain prophecy, but is every day fulfilled anew.

I do not know what became of the victim of my false witness; it seems unlikely that, after this, she would easily have found another good situation. She had suffered an imputation to her honour that was cruel in every way. The theft was trifling; nevertheless, it was a theft and, what was worse, had been used to seduce a young boy; finally, the lie and the obstinacy with which she clung to it left nothing to be hoped for from someone who combined so many vices. I fear, too, that wretchedness and destitution were not the worst of the dangers I exposed her to. Who knows to what extremes despair and injured innocence might not, at her age, have driven her? Ah, if my remorse at having made her unhappy is intolerable, only judge how it feels to have perhaps reduced her to being worse off than myself!

At times I am so troubled by this cruel memory, and so distressed, that I lie sleepless in my bed, imagining the poor girl advancing towards me to reproach me for my crime as though I had committed it only yesterday. While I still enjoyed some tranquillity in life it tormented me less, but in these tempestuous times it deprives me of the sweetest consolation known to persecuted innocence; it brings home to me the truth of an observation I think I have made in another work, that remorse is lulled during times of good fortune and aggravated in adversity. And yet I have never been able to bring myself to unburden my heart of this confession by entrusting it to a friend. I have never, in moments of the greatest intimacy, divulged it to anyone, even to Mme de Warens. The most that I have been able to do has been to confess my responsibility for an atrocious deed, without ever saying of what exactly it consisted. This burden, then, has lain unalleviated on my conscience until this very day; and I can safely say that the desire to be in some measure relieved of it has greatly contributed to the decision I have taken to write my confessions.

I have been outspoken in the confession I have just made, and surely no one could think that I have in any way sought to mitigate the infamy of my crime. But I would not be fulfilling the purpose of this book if I did not at the same time reveal my own innermost feelings, and if I were afraid to excuse myself, even where the truth of the matter calls for it. I have never been less motivated by malice than at this cruel moment, and when I accused this unfortunate girl, it is bizarre, but it is true, that it was my fondness for her that was the cause of it. She was on my mind, and I had simply used as an excuse the first object that presented itself to me. I accused her of having done what I wanted to do, and of having given me the ribbon, because my intention had been to give it to her. When she appeared shortly afterwards I was stricken with remorse, but the presence of so many people was stronger than my repentance. It was not that

I was afraid of being punished but that I was afraid of being put to shame; and I feared shame more than death, more than crime, more than anything in the world. I would have wanted the earth to swallow me up and bury me in its depths. It was shame alone, unconquerable shame, that prevailed over everything and was the cause of all my impudence; and the more criminal I became, the more my terror at having to admit it made me bold. All I could think of was the horror of being found out and of being denounced, publicly and to my face, as a thief, a liar, a slanderer. The confusion that seized my whole being robbed me of any other feeling. If I had been given time to collect myself, I would unquestionably have admitted everything. If M. de la Roque had taken me aside and had said to me: 'Don't ruin this poor girl. If you are guilty, own up to it now,' I would have thrown myself at his feet forthwith; of that I am perfectly certain. But, when what I needed was encouragement, all I received was intimidation. My age, too, was a consideration that it is only fair to take into account. I was scarcely more than a child, or rather I still was one. Real wickedness is even more criminal in a young person than in an adult, but what is merely weakness is much less so, and my offence, when it comes down to it, was little more. Thus its memory distresses me less because of any evil in the act itself than because of that which it must have caused. It has even had the good effect of preserving me for the rest of my life from any inclination towards crime, because of the terrible impression that has remained with me of the only one I ever committed, and I suspect that my aversion towards lying comes in large part from remorse at having been capable of one that was so wicked. If, as I venture to believe, such a crime can be expiated, it must surely have been so by the many misfortunes that burden my old age; by forty years of rectitude and honour in difficult circumstances; indeed, poor Marion has found so many avengers in this world that, however grave my offence against her, I am not too afraid that I will carry the guilt for it into the next. That is all that I had to say on this subject. May I be spared from ever having to speak of it again.

JOHANN WOLFGANG VON GOETHE

1749–1832

Few writers have ever surpassed Goethe in global fame and influence. He was perhaps the last European to live up to the ideal of the Renaissance man: skilled in the arts, in science, and in politics. He made groundbreaking contributions not only in all the major literary genres, but also in art criticism and the study of classical culture. He did extensive work in the fields of botany, mineralogy, comparative anatomy, and optics. And he occupied many administrative and political positions at the court of Weimar, where he was responsible for finance, the military, and mining, as well as for the Weimar Court Theatre, which he turned from an amateur theater to a professional troupe that premiered many of his own plays. Distrusting both the French Revolution, whose effects he witnessed at close hand, and growing nationalist movements in Germany and elsewhere, Goethe did not consider himself a German, but a European, and he coined the visionary notion of "world literature," eager to open Europe to the intellectual and artistic production of the non-European world.

Goethe was born into a middle-class family in Frankfurt. Despite an early interest in the arts and the theater, he followed his father's wishes and studied law. But Goethe's artistic ambitions could not be held back for long and he soon started to publish literary works. His first significant play, *Götz of Berlechingen* (1773), was shaped by his discovery of Shakespeare, whom he especially admired for being willing to violate the strict rules of drama that prevailed at the time. Yet the most important work of Goethe's early period was a novel, *The Sorrows of Young Werther* (1774), which turned Goethe into the representative of a literary movement called *Sturm und Drang* ("storm and stress") that emphasized the expression of feelings over the strictures of literary form. Centered on subjective impressions, extreme emotions, and literary outbursts, the novel leads its tragic protagonist, who is caught in a love triangle, to his eventual suicide. *The Sorrows of Young Werther* prompted mass hysteria, also called "Werther fever," allegedly leading to several copycat suicides as well as to the marketing of Werther paraphernalia. Goethe became a European celebrity virtually overnight.

A year later, Duke Karl August of Weimar called the young writer to his elegant but provincial court, where Goethe first served as educator, but soon fulfilled more important functions and was ultimately elevated to the aristocracy. It was here, amid his extensive duties, that Goethe began his mature, more classical works: his influential novel, *Wilhelm Meister's Apprenticeship*, as well as the plays *Egmont, Iphigenia on Tauris, Torquato Tasso,* and *Faust.* He began all of these works shortly after he had arrived at Weimar, but they went through innumerable revisions, during which he slowly forged a new, less unruly and more measured style, leaving the earlier "storm and stress" behind.

Goethe was inspired by an extended voyage to Italy (1786–88), and he became the chief representative of a revival of classical forms and ideas in Germany and Europe more generally. This journey led him to revise *Faust* and other works in accordance with the classical ideal. He collected classical sculpture (he contented himself with replicas) and adapted classical stories, poetry, and drama. But the theater stood at the center of the classical revival. He worried about the training of actors, developing guidelines later published as *Rules for Actors* (1803, 1832), and intervened in all other aspects of theater production. He also insisted on introducing international playwrights, including Shakespeare, Calderón, and Goldoni, to his provincial audience. Thus, although Goethe had started the Weimar Court Theatre as a vehicle for his revival of classical drama, he opened it to a variety of dramatic styles.

In the first decades of the nineteenth century, Goethe finally completed the long-awaited first part of *Faust* (1806). While he left his mark on numerous fields and genres, *Faust* stands out as his masterpiece. He began writing it in his early twenties and continued to work on it until his death. Even more than many of his other texts, it underwent significant changes, from the first drafts in the 1770s, through the publication of the first part in 1808, to the

Goethe in the Roman Campagna, 1786–1787, Johann Heinrich Wilhelm Tischbein.

final version of the second part, completed just before his last birthday in 1832.

For *Faust* Goethe relied on an old folk legend, a quintessentially medieval morality tale, in which an arrogant scholar gives in to the temptations of the devil, makes a famous pact to trade his soul for the use of black magic, and finally suffers in hell for his sins. In the course of his many revisions, Goethe transformed this simple material into a text that captured the spirit and desires of modernity. Although he preserved important set pieces such as the pact with the devil, what mattered to Goethe was the relation between abstract learning and sensuous experience, as well as the nature of human striving. He used the character of Faust to explore the transformative energies unleashed by modern science, philosophy, and industry.

In revising the old legend, Goethe changed its moral structure. While earlier Fausts were always lost to the devil, Goethe has Faust escape Mephistopheles' clutches at the end of *Faust II*. This decision thoroughly alters the morality play, which had punished a blaspheming protagonist as a warning to Christian audiences. Goethe still depicts Faust as a sinner, as the earlier versions had done. But now Faust's sinning has to be balanced against his irreverent and limitless thirst for knowledge, which for Goethe has great esteem. Paradoxically, the very quality that drives Faust to his pact with the devil is the one that will lead him to salvation.

The "Prologue in Heaven" shows this shift. It is one of several scenes that frame the play before its proper action begins. Borrowed from the beginning of the biblical book of Job, the "Prologue" depicts a debate between God and Mephistopheles that ends in a wager. Mephistopheles has permission to lead Faust into temptation because God is certain that Faust's restless striving, his search for true knowledge, will eventually lead him back on the right path. Besides the "Prologue," Goethe also introduces the text with a "Dedication," in which he evokes the youthful world in which he began this work some thirty years ago. And he presents a kind of curtain riser, a "Prelude in the Theater," in which a Manager, a Poet, and a Clown debate their respective visions of a theater, poised between popular entertainment and high art, a debate undoubtedly grounded in Goethe's experience as a dramatist and theater director.

The main drama of *Faust I* can be divided into two parts. The first part introduces us to the medieval Doctor, who has mastered all the higher disciplines of the university—philosophy, law, medicine, and theology—but who still has not learned the inner essence of the world. Dissatisfied with this insufficient knowledge, he turns to the dangerous domains of magic and alchemy, and it is this daring that is, for Goethe, Faust's most modern attribute. Shunning inherited pieties and religious prejudices, Faust is ready to sacrifice everything to knowledge. He also longs to experience life to the fullest, and this makes him especially susceptible to the enticements of Mephistopheles, who offers him wide experience and the satisfaction of his sensual desires.

In the second part of *Faust I*, Mephistopheles tries to satisfy Faust's demands and yearnings. Although he often dismisses Mephistopheles' efforts at satisfaction as "mere spectacle," Faust nevertheless tries them all, culminating in the famous, orgiastic "Walpurgisnight" scene, a delirious meeting of all creatures of the night. None of these sensuous pleasures, however, can give Faust the kind of satisfaction he derives from the culminating event of the play:

the seduction of Gretchen. It is with Gretchen that *Faust* earns its title to tragedy. Gretchen represents different pleasures from the other experiences provided by Mephistopheles. Faust genuinely falls in love with her, praising her innocence and simple religious faith. And yet he alternately neglects her and showers her with presents as he pursues, and finally achieves, his physical satisfaction, leading to a tragic end. Here the first part of *Faust* ends. These tragic events will be blissfully forgotten in the second part, which takes Faust and Mephistopheles on a wild tour through politics, science, and learning.

Not only did Goethe revise the Faust legend to rescue Faust from damnation at the end of part two, but in the first part, he shaped another, and possibly more radical, revision of the historical tale. For the real protagonist of this part is not Faust, who is alternatively pompous, idealistic, and fatuous, who does not know himself, and who manages to bring everything, including poor Gretchen, to ruin. Instead, the real protagonist is the witty, realistic, and caustic Mephistopheles. It is Mephistopheles who criticizes the medieval world of Faust, and who deflates his grandiose speeches, including his self-serving declarations of love for Gretchen. Mephistopheles is the spirit of negation, as he says of himself, but it is a negation that serves to criticize authority. Mephistopheles thus embodies the principle of critique, of questioning all kinds of inherited religious belief and orthodoxies. Since this critical spirit is central to modernity, Mephistopheles becomes the truly modern character in the play. And Goethe clandestinely turns Mephistopheles into the main protagonist. He has all the best and wittiest lines. In the theater, he simply steals the show.

Outdoing a modernized Faust with an even more modern Mephistopheles, Goethe was also daring in his use of structure and form. The play rejects the narrow rules of Aristotelian drama, constraining time and space, and instead presents a play of epic length that is composed of loosely connected scenes. *Faust* contains passages in different meters and rhyme schemes as well as in prose. It includes interludes, an allegorical dream, a satire of the university, erotic songs, and scenes of outright bacchanalia. It seeks to encompass the entirety of the modern world, aspiring to a rare totality in its hybrid form. Thus *Faust* has been considered a total work of art, a modern epic, and a strikingly new type of drama.

Faust is so startling in its dramatic innovations that Goethe himself never sought to mount even the more manageable first part in his own Weimar Court Theatre, and in fact he did not even consider it fit for the stage. When it was performed at another theater a few years before his death, he did not show much interest in the production.

The much more difficult, allegorical second part has been performed even less often. Given the length of both parts taken together, few theaters have ever tried to produce the entirety of Goethe's *Faust*. In the course of the twentieth century, however, the first part attracted the most renowned theater directors, composers, and actors. French composers Hector Berlioz and Charles Gounod based operas on it, and in the twentieth century, Gertrude Stein's *Doctor Faustus Lights the Lights* is among the most modernist responses to Goethe's text. Filmmakers have turned to it again and again for inspiration, including F. W. Murnau in 1926 and Czech director Jan Švankmajer in 1994. Goethe's *Faust* has thus remained an important touchstone for two centuries of art, a testament to Goethe's ability to turn a simple medieval morality tale into a complex investigation of modernity.

Faust[1]

Prologue in Heaven[2]

THE LORD. THE HEAVENLY HOST. *Then* MEPHISTOPHELES.[3] *The three* ARCHANGELS *advance to front.*

RAPHAEL   The sun sounds out his ancient measure
 In contest with each brother sphere,
 Marching round and around, with steps of thunder,
 His appointed circle year after year.
 To see him lends us angels strength,   5
 But what he *is*, oh who can say?
 The inconceivably great works are great
 As on the first creating day.
GABRIEL   And swift, past all conception swift,
 The jeweled globe spins on its axletree,   10
 Celestial brightness alternating

1. Translated by Martin Greenberg.
2. The scene is patterned on Job 1.6–12 and 2.1–6.
3. The origin of the name remains debatable. It may come from Hebrew, Persian, or Greek, with such meanings as "destroyer-liar," "no friend of Faust," and "no friend of light."

With shuddering night's obscurity.
Against the rock-bound littoral
The sea is backwards seething hurled
And rock and sea together hurtle   15
With the eternally turning world.
MICHAEL   And tempests, vying, howling riot
From sea to land, from land to sea,
Linking in tremendous circuit
A chain of blazing energy.   20
The lightning bolt makes ready for
The thunderclap a ruinous way—
Yet Lord, your servants most prefer
The stiller motions of your day.
ALL THREE   From seeing this we draw our strength,   25
But what You *are*, oh who can say?
And all your great works are as great
As on the first creating day.
MEPHISTOPHELES   Lord, since you've stopped by here again,
    liking to know
How all of us are doing, for which we're grateful,   30
And since you've never made me feel *de trop*,
Well, here I am too with your other people.
Excuse, I hope, my lack of eloquence,
Though this whole host, I'm sure, will think I'm stupid.
Coming from me, high-sounding sentiments   35
Would only make you laugh—that is, provided
Laughing was a thing Your Worship still did.
About suns and worlds I don't know beans, I only see
How mortals find their lives pure misery.
Earth's little god's shaped out of the same old clay,   40
He's the same queer fish he was on the first day.
He'd be much better off, in my opinion, without
The bit of heavenly light you dealt him out.
He calls it Reason and the use he puts it to?
To act more beastly than beasts ever do.   45
To me he seems, if you'll pardon my saying so,
Like a long-legged grasshopper all of whose leaping
Only lands him back in the grass again chirping
The tune he's always chirped. And if only he'd
Stay put in the grass! But no! It's an absolute need   50
With him to creep and crawl and strain and sweat
And stick his nose in every pile of dirt.
THE LORD   Is that all you have got to say to me?
Is that all you can do, accuse eternally?
Is nothing ever right for you down there, sir?   55
MEPHISTOPHELES   No, nothing, Lord—all's just as bad as ever.
I really pity humanity's myriad miseries,
I swear I hate tormenting the poor ninnies.

THE LORD   Do you know Faust?
MEPHISTOPHELES   The Doctor?[4]
THE LORD   My good servant.
MEPHISTOPHELES   You[5] don't say! Well, he serves you, I think, very queerly, 60
   Finds meat and drink, the fool, in nothing earthly,
   Drives madly on, there's in him such a torment,
   He himself is half aware he's crazy;
   Heaven's brightest stars he imperiously requires,
   And from the earth its most exciting pleasures,   65
   And all that's near at hand or far and wide
   Leaves your good servant quite unsatisfied.
THE LORD   If today his service shows confused, disordered,
   With my help he'll see his way clearly forward.
   When the sapling greens, the gardener can feel certain   70
   Flower and fruit shall follow in due season.
MEPHISTOPHELES   Would you care to bet on that? You'll lose, I tell you,
   If you'll give me leave to lead the fellow
   Gently down my broad, my primrose path.
THE LORD   As long as Faustus walks the earth   75
   I shan't, I promise, interfere.
   While still man strives, still he must err.
MEPHISTOPHELES   Well thanks, Lord, for it's not the dead and gone
   I like dealing with. By far what I prefer
   Are round and rosy cheeks. When corpses come   80
   A-knocking, sorry, Master's left the house;
   My way of working's the cat's way with a mouse.
THE LORD   So it's agreed, you have my full consent.
   Divert the soul of Faust from its true source
   And if you're able, lead him along, Hell bent   85
   With you, upon the downward course—
   Then blush for shame when you find you must admit:
   Impelled in this direction, then in that one,
   A good man still knows which way is the right one.
MEPHISTOPHELES   Of course, of course! Yet I'll seduce him from it   90
   Soon enough. I'm not afraid I'll lose my bet.
   And after I have won it,
   You won't, I trust, begrudge me
   My whoops of triumph, shouts of victory.
   Dust he'll eat   95
   And find that he enjoys it, exactly like
   That old aunt of mine, the famous snake.
THE LORD   There too feel free, you have carte blanche.
   I've never hated your likes much;
   I find, of all the spirits of denial,   100

---

4. Of philosophy.
5. In the German text, Mephistopheles shifts
back and forth between the informal word for
"you" (*du*) and the more formal, respectful
mode of address (*ihr*).

You jeerers not my severest trial.
Man's very quick to slacken in his effort,
What he likes best is Sunday peace and quiet;
So I'm glad to give him a devil—for his own good,
To prod and poke and incite him as a devil should.   105
[*To the* ANGELS] But you who are God's true and faithful progeny—
Delight in the world's wealth of living beauty!
May the force that makes all life-forms to evolve
Enfold you in the dear confines of love,
And the fitfulness, the flux of all appearance—   110
By enduring thoughts give enduring forms to its transience.
    [*The Heavens close, the* ARCHANGELS *withdraw.*]
MEPHISTOPHELES   I like to see the Old Man now and then,
And take good care I don't fall out with him.
How very decent of a Lord Celestial
To talk man to man with the Devil of all people.   115

Part I

NIGHT

In a narrow, high-vaulted Gothic room, FAUST, *seated restlessly in an armchair at his desk.*

FAUST   I've studied, alas, philosophy,
Law and medicine, recto and verso,
And how I regret it, theology also,
Oh God, how hard I've slaved away,
With what result? Poor foolish old man,   120
I'm no whit wiser than when I began!
I've got a Master of Arts degree,
On top of that a Ph.D.,
For ten long years, around and about,
Upstairs, downstairs, in and out,   125
I've led my students by the nose
With what result?—that nobody knows,
Or ever shall know, the tiniest crumb!
Which is why I feel completely undone.
    Of course I'm cleverer than these stuffed shirts,   130
These Doctors, M.A.s, Scribes and Priests,
I'm not bothered by a doubt or a scruple,
I'm not afraid of Hell or the Devil—
But the consequence is, my mirth's all gone.
No longer can I fool myself   135
I'm able to teach anyone
How to be better, love true worth;
I've got no money or property,
Worldly honors or celebrity—
A dog wouldn't put up with this life!   140
Which is why I've turned to magic,

Seeking to know, by ways occult,
From ghostly mouths, spells difficult;
So I no longer need to sweat
Painfully explaining what
I don't know anything about; 145
So I may penetrate the power
That holds the universe together,
Behold the source whence all proceeds
And no more torture words, words, words. 150

O full moon, melancholy-bright,
Friend I've watched for, many a night,
Till your quiet-shining circle
Appeared above my high-piled table,
If only you might never again 155
Look down from above on my pain,
If only I might stray at will
In your mild light, high on the hill,
Haunt with spirits upland hollows,
Fade with you in dim-lit meadows, 160
And soul no longer gasping in
The stink of learning's midnight oil,
Bathe in your dews till well again!

Oh misery! Oh am I still
Stuck here in this dismal prison? 165
A musty goddamned hole in the wall
Where even the golden light of heaven
Can only weakly make its way through
The painted panes of the gothic window;
Where all about me shelves of books 170
Rise up to the vault in stacks,
Books gray with dust, worm-eaten, rotten,
With soot-stained paper for a curtain;
Where instruments, retorts and glasses
Are crammed in everywhere a space is; 175
And squeezed in somehow with these things
My family's ancient furnishings
Make complete the sad confusion—
Call this a world, this world you live in?

Can you still wonder why your heart 180
Should clench in your breast so anxiously?
Why your every impulse is stopped short
By an inexplicable misery?
Instead of Nature's flourishing garden
God created and man to dwell there, 185
Rubbish, dirt are everywhere
Your gaze turns, old bones, a skeleton.

Off, off, to the open countryside!
And this mysterious book, inscribed
By Nostradamus'[6] own hand—   190
What better help to master the secrets
Of how the stars turn in their orbits,
From Nature learn to understand
The spirits' power to speak to spirits;
Sitting here and racking your brains   195
To puzzle out the sacred signs—
What a sterile, futile business!
Spirits, I feel your presence around me:
Announce yourselves if you hear me!
    [*He opens the book and his eye encounters the sign of
    the Macrocosm.*[7]]
The pure bliss flooding all my senses   200
Seeing this! Through every nerve and vein
I feel youth's fiery, fresh spirit race again.
Was it a god marked out these signs
By which my agitated bosom's stilled,
By which my bleak heart's filled with joy,   205
By whose mysterious agency
The powers of Nature all around me stand revealed?
Am *I* a god? All's bright as day!
By these pure tracings I can see,
At my soul's feet, great Nature unconcealed.   210
And the sage's words—I understand them, finally:
"The spirit world is not barred shut,
It's your closed mind, your dead heart!
Stand up unappalled, my scholar,
And bathe your breast in the rose of Aurora!"   215
    [*He contemplates the sign.*]
How all is woven one, uniting,
Each in the other living, working!
How Heavenly Powers rise, descend,
Passing gold vessels from hand to hand!
On wings that scatter sweet-smelling blessings   220
Everywhere they post in earth
And make a universal harmony sound forth!
Oh, what a show! But a show, nothing more!
How, infinite Nature, lay hold of you, where?
Where find your all-life-giving fountains?—breasts that sustain   225
The earth and the heavens, which my shrunken breast
Yearns for with a feverish thirst—
You flow, overflow, must I keep on thirsting in vain?

---

6. The Latin name of the French astrologer and physician Michel de Notredame (1503–1566). His collection of rhymed prophecies, *The Centuries*, appeared in 1555.

7. The great world (literal trans.); the universe as a whole. It represents the ordered, harmonious universe in its totality.

[*Morosely, he turns the pages of the book and comes on the sign of the Spirit of Earth.*[8]]

What a different effect this sign has on me!
Spirit of Earth, how nearer you are to me!   230
Already fresh lifeblood pours through every vein,
Already I'm aglow as if with new wine—
Now I have the courage to dare
To venture into the world and bear
The ill and well of life, to battle   235
Storms, when the ship splits, not to tremble.

The air grows dark overhead—
The moon's put out her light,
The oil lamp looks like dying.
Vapors rise, red flashes dart   240
Around my head—fright,
Shuddering down from the vault,
Seizes me by the throat!
Spirit I have invoked, hovering near:
Reveal yourself!   245
Ha! How my heart beats! All of my being's
Fumbling and groping amid never felt feelings!
Spirit, I feel I am yours, body and breath!
Appear! Oh, you must! Though it costs me my life!

    [*He seizes the book and pronounces the* SPIRIT's *mystic spell.*
    A red flame flashes, in the midst of which the SPIRIT *appears.*]

SPIRIT   Who's calling?   250
FAUST [*Averting his face.*]   Overpowering! Dreadful!
SPIRIT   Potently you've drawn me here,
  A parched mouth sucking at my sphere.
  And now—?
FAUST   Oh, you're unbearable!
SPIRIT   You're breathless from your implorations   255
  To see my face, to hear me speak,
  I've yielded to your supplications
  And here I am.—Well, worried sick
  I find the superman! I come at your bidding
  And you're struck dumb! Is this the mind   260
  That builds a whole interior world, doting
  On its own creation, puffed to find
  Itself quite on a par, the equal,
  Of us spirits? Wherever is that Faust
  Who urged himself just now with boastful   265
  Claims on me, made such a fuss?
  You're Faust? The one who at my breath's

---

8. This figure seems to be a symbol for the energy of terrestrial nature—neither good nor bad, merely powerful.

Least touch, shudders to his depths,
A thing that wriggles off scared, a worm!
FAUST   *I* shrink back from you, an airy flame?   270
I'm him, yes Faust, your equal, the same.
SPIRIT   In flood tides of life, in tempests of action,
I surge upwards, sink low,
Going here, going there,
Birth and the grave,   275
Unstopping exertion,
An eternal sea heaving,
A weaving, unweaving,
A life all aglow—
So seated before time's whirring loom   280
I weave divinity's living costume.
FAUST   We're equals, I know! I feel so close to you, near,
You busy spirit ranging everywhere!
SPIRIT   It's your idea of me you're equal to,
Not me! [*Vanishes.*]   285
FAUST [*Deflated.*]   Not you?
Then who?
Me, made in God's own image,
Not even equal to you?
        [*A knocking.*]
Death! My famulus[9]—I know that knock.   290
Finis my supremest moment—worse luck!
That visions richer than I could have guessed
Should be scattered by a shuffling dryasdust!
        [WAGNER *in dressing gown and nightcap, carrying a lamp.*
        FAUST *turns around impatiently.*]
WAGNER   Excuse me, sir, but wasn't that
Your voice I heard declaiming? A Greek tragedy,   295
I'm sure. Well, that's an art that comes in handy
Nowadays. I'd love to master it.
People say, how often I have heard it,
Actors could really give lessons to the clergy.
FAUST   Yes, so parsons can make a stage out of the pulpit—   300
Something I've seen done in more than one case.
WAGNER   Oh dear, to be so cooped up in one's study all day,
Seeing the world only now and then, on holiday,
Seeing people from far off, as if through a spyglass—
How persuade them to any effect in that way?   305
FAUST   Unless you really feel it, no, you cannot—
Unless the words your lips declare are heartfelt
And by their soul-born spontaneous power,
Seize with delight the soul of your hearer.
But no! Stick in your seats, you scholars!   310
Paste bits and pieces together, cook up

9. Assistant to a medieval scholar.

A beggar's stew from others' leftovers,
Over a flame you've sweated to coax up
From your own little heap of smoldering ashes,
Filling with wonder all the jackasses,   315
If that's the kind of stuff your taste favors—
But you'll never get heart to cleave to heart
Unless you spear from your own heart.
WAGNER   Still and all, a good delivery is what
Makes the orator. I'm far behind in that art.   320
FAUST   Advance yourself in an honest way!
Don't play the fool in cap and bells!
Good sense, good understanding, they
Are art enough, speak for themselves.
When you have something serious to say   325
What need is there for hunting up
Fancy words, high-sounding phrases?
Your brilliant speeches, smartened up
With bits and pieces collected out
Of a miscellany of commonplaces   330
From all the languages spoken by all the races,
Are about as bracing as the foggy autumnal breeze
Swaying the last leaves on the trees.
WAGNER   Dear God, but art is long
And our life—lots shorter.   335
Often in the middle of my labor
My confidence and courage falter.
How hard it is to master all the stuff
For dealing with each and every source,
And before you've traveled half the course,   340
Poor devil, you have gone and left this life.
FAUST   Parchment, tell me—that's the sacred fount
You drink out of, to slake your eternal thirst?
The only true refreshment that exists
You get from where? Yourself—where all things start.   345
WAGNER   But sir, it's such a pleasure, isn't it,
To enter into another age's spirit,
To see what the sages before us thought
And measure how far since we've got.
FAUST   As far as to the stars, no doubt!   350
Your history, why, it's a joke;
Bygone times are a seven-sealed book.[1]
What you call an age's spirit
Is nothing more than your own spirit
With the age reflected as you see it.   355
And it's pathetic, what's to be seen in your mirror!
One look and off I head for the exit:
A trash can, strewn attic, junk-filled cellar,

1. Revelation 5.1.

At best a blood-and-thunder thriller
Improved with the most high-minded sentiments   360
Exactly suited for mouthing by marionettes.
WAGNER   But this great world, the human mind and heart,
They are things everyone wants to know about.
FAUST   Yes, know as the world, knows knowing!
Who wants to know the real truth, tell me?   365
Those few with vision, feeling, understanding
Who failed to stand guard, most unwisely,
Over their tongues, speaking their minds and hearts
For the mob to hear—you know what's been their fate:
They were crucified, burnt, torn to bits.   370
But we must break off, friend, it's getting late.
WAGNER   I love such serious conversation, I do!
I'd stay up all night gladly talking to you.
But, sir, it's Easter Sunday in the morning
And perhaps I may ask you a question or two then, if you're willing? 375
I've studied hard, with unrelaxing zeal,
I know a lot, but I want, sir, to know all. [*Exit.*]
FAUST [*Alone.*]   Such fellows keep their hopes up by forever
Busying themselves with trivialities,
Dig greedily in the ground for treasure,   380
And when they turn a worm up—what ecstacies!
That banal, commonplace human accents
Should fill air just now filled with spirits' voices!
Still, this one time you've earned my thanks,
Oh sorriest, oh shallowest of wretches!   385
You snatched me from the grip of a dejection
So profound I was nearly driven off
My head. So gigantic was the apparition
It made me feel no bigger than a dwarf—

Me, the image of God, certain in my belief   390
Soon, soon I'd behold the mirror of eternal truth
Whose near presence I felt; already savoring
The celestial glory, stripped of all mortal clothing—
Me, higher placed than the angels, dreaming brashly
With the strength I possess I could flow freely,   395
Godlike creative, through Nature's live body—
Well, it had to be paid for: a single word
Thundered out knocked me flat, all vain conceit curbed.
No, I can't claim we are equals, presumptuously!
Though strong enough to draw you down to me,   400
Holding on to you was another matter entirely.
In that exalted-humbling moment of pure delight
I felt myself at once both small and great.
And then you thrust me remorselessly back
Into uncertainty, which is all of humanity's fate.   405

Who'll tell me what to do? Not to do?
Still seek out the spirits to learn what they know?
Oh what we do, as much as what's done to us,
Obstructs the way stretching clearly before us.

The noblest conceptions our minds ever attained   410
Are watered down more and more, corrupted, profaned;
When we've gained a bit of the good of the world as our prize,
Then the better's dismissed as delusion and lies;
Those radiant sentiments, once our breath of life,
Grow dim and expire in the madding crowd's strife.   415
Time was that hope and brave imagination
Boldly reached as far as to infinity,
But now misfortune piling on misfortune,
A little, confined space will satisfy.
It's then, heart-deep, Care builds her nest,   420
Dithering nervously, killing joy, ruining rest,
Masking herself as this, as that concern
For house and home, for wife and children,
Fearing fire and flood, daggers and poison;
You shrink back in terror from imagined blows   425
And cry over losing what you never in fact lose.

Oh no, I'm no god, only too well do I know it!
A worm's what I am, wriggling through the soot
And finding his nourishment in it,
Whom the passerby treads underfoot.   430

These high walls, every shelf crammed, every niche,
Dust is what shrinks them to a stifling cell,
This moth-eaten world with its oddments and trash,
It's the reason I feel shut up in jail.
And here I'll discover what it is that I lack?   435
Devour thousands of books so as to learn, shall I,
Mankind has always been stretched on the rack,
With now and then somebody, somewhere, who's been happy?
You, empty skull there, smirking so, I know why—
What does it tell me if not that your brain,   440
Whirling like mine, sought the bright sun of truth,
Only to wander, night-bewildered, in vain.
And all that apparatus, you mock me, you laugh
With your every wheel, cylinder, cog and ratchet;
I stood at the door, sure you provided the key,   445
Yet for all the bit's cunning design I couldn't unlatch it.
Mysterious even in broad daylight,
Nature lets no one part her veil,
And what she keeps hidden, out of sight,
All your levers and wrenches can't make her reveal.   450

You, ancient stuff I've left lying about,
You're here, and why?—my father[2] found you useful.
And you, old scrolls, have gathered soot
For as long as the lamp's smoked on this table.
Much better to have squandered the little I got   455
Than find myself sweating under the lot.
It's from our fathers, what we inherit,
To possess it really we have to earn it.
What you don't use is a dead weight,
What's worthwhile is what you spontaneously create.   460

But why do I find I must stare in that corner,
Is that bottle a magnet enchanting my sight?
Why is everything all at once brighter, clearer,
Like woods when the moon's up and floods them with light?

Vial, I salute you, exceptional, rare thing,   465
And reverently bring you down from the shelf,
Honoring in you man's craft and cunning;
Quintessence of easeful sleeping potions,
Pure distillation of subtle poisons,
Do your master the kindness that lies in your power!   470
One look at you and my agony lessens,
One touch and my feverish straining grows calmer
And my tight-stretched spirit bit by bit slackens.
The spirit's flood tide runs more and more out,
My way is clear, into death's immense sea;   475
The bright waters glitter before my feet,
A new day is dawning, new shores calling to me.

A fiery chariot, bird-winged, swoops down on me,
I am ready to follow new paths and higher,
Aloft into new spheres of purest activity.   480
An existence so exalted, so godlike a rapture,
Does the worm of a minute ago deserve it?
No matter. Never falter! Turn your back bravely
On the sunlight, sweet sunlight, of our earth forever!
Tear wide open those dark gates boldly   485
Which the whole world skulks past with averted heads.
The time has come to disprove by deeds,
Because the gods are great, man's a derision,
To cringe back no more from that black pit
Whose unspeakable tortures are your own invention,   490
To struggle toward that narrow gate
Around which all Hell flames in constant eruption,
To do it calmly, without regret,
Even at the risk of utter extinction.

2. Later we find that Faust's father was a doctor of medicine.

And now let me lift this long forgotten   495
Crystal wine cup out of its chest.
You used to shine bright at the family feast,
Making the solemn guests' faces lighten
When you went round with each lively toast.
The figures artfully cut in the crystal,   500
Which it was the duty of all at the table
In turn to make up rhymes about,
Then drain the cup at a single draught—
How they recall the nights of my youth!
But now there's no passing you on to my neighbor,   505
Or thinking up rhymes to parade my quick wit;³
Here is a juice that is quick too—to intoxicate,
A brownish liquid, see, filling the beaker,
Chosen by me, by me mixed together,
My last drink! Which now I lift up in festal greeting   510
To the bright new day I see dawning!
    [He raises the cup to his lips. Bells peal, a choir bursts into song.]
CHORUS OF ANGELS
    Christ is arisen!
    Joy to poor mortals
    By their own baleful,
    Inherited, subtle   515
    Failings imprisoned.
FAUST   What deep-sounding burden, what tremelo strain
  Arrest the glass before I can drink?
  Does that solemn ringing already proclaim
  The glorious advent of Holy Week?   520
  Already, choirs, are you intoning
  What angels' lips sang once, a comforting chant,
  Above the sepulcher's darkness sounding,
  Certain assurance of a new covenant?
CHORUS OF WOMEN
    With spices and balm, we   525
    Prepared the body,
    Faithful ones all, we
    Laid him out in the tomb;
    Clean in linen we wound him
    And bound up his hair—   530
    Oh, what do we find now?
    Christ is not here.
CHORUS OF ANGELS
    Christ is arisen!
    Blest is the man of love,
    He who the anguishing,   535

---

3. Faust here alludes to the drinking of toasts. The maker of a toast often produced impromptu
rhymes.

Bitter, exacting test,
Salvation bringing, passed.

FAUST   But why do you seek me out in the dust,
You music of Heaven, mild and magnificent?
Sound out where men and women are simple,   540
Your message is clear but it leaves me indifferent,
And where no belief is, no miracle's possible.
The spheres whence those glad tidings ring
Are not for me to try and enter—
Yet all's familiar from when I was young   545
And back to life I feel myself sent for.
Years ago loving Heaven's kiss
Flew down to me in the Sabbath stillness,
Oh, how the bells rang with such promise,
And fervently praying to Jesus, what bliss!   550
A yearning so sweet, not to be comprehended,
Drove me out into green wood and field,
In me an inner world expanded
As my cheeks ran wet from eyes tear-filled.
Your song gave the signal for the games we rejoiced in   555
When the springtime arrived with its gay festival,
Innocent childhood's remembered emotion
Holds me back from the last step of all—
O sound away, sound away, sweet songs of Heaven,
Earth claims me again, my tears well up, fall.   560

CHORUS OF DISCIPLES
Only just buried,
Ascended already,
Living sublimely,
Up rising in glory!
Joy of becoming, his,   565
Near to creating's bliss.
He on the earth's hard crust
Left us, his own, his best,
To languish and wait—
Oh! how we pity,   570
Master, your fate!

CHORUS OF ANGELS
Christ is arisen
From the bowels of decay,
Strike off your fetters
And shout for joy!   575
By good works praising him,
By loving raising him,
Feeding the least of all,
Preaching him east and west to all,
Promising bliss to all.   580
You have the Master near,
You have him here.

OUTSIDE THE CITY GATE

All sorts of people out walking.

SOME APPRENTICES   Where are you fellows off to?
OTHERS   To the hunters' lodge—over that way.
FIRST BUNCH   Well, we're on our way to the old mill.   585
ONE APPRENTICE   The river inn—that's what I say.
SECOND APPRENTICE   The way there's not pleasant, I feel.
SECOND BUNCH   And what about you?
THIRD APPRENTICE   I'll stick with the rest of us here.
FOURTH APPRENTICE   Let's go up to the village. There, I can promise you   590
   The best-looking girls, the best-tasting beer,
   And some very good roughhousing too.
FIFTH APPRENTICE   My, but aren't you greedy!
   A third bloody nose—don't you care?
   I'll never go there, it's too scary.   595
SERVANT GIRL   No, no, I'm turning back, no, I won't stay.
ANOTHER   We're sure to find him at those poplar trees.
FIRST GIRL   Is that supposed to make me jump for joy?
   It's you he wants to walk with, wants to please,
   And you're the one he'll dance with. Fine   600
   For you. And for me what? The spring sunshine!
THE OTHER   He's not alone, I know, today. He said
   He'd bring his friend—you know, that curlyhead.
A STUDENT   Those fast-stepping girls there, look at the heft of them!
   Into action, old fellow, we're taking out after them.   605
   Beer with body, tobacco with a good sharp taste
   And red-cheeked housemaids in their Sunday best
   Are just the things to make your Hermann happiest.
A BURGHER'S DAUGHTER   Oh look over there, such fine-looking boys!
   Really, I think they are simply outrageous,   610
   They have their pick of the nicest girls,
   Instead they run after overweight wenches.
SECOND STUDENT [*To the first*]   Hold up, go slow! I see two more,
   And the pair of them dressed so pretty, so proper.
   But I know that one! She lives next door,   615
   And she, I can tell you, I think I could go for.
   They loiter along, eyes lowered decorously,
   But after saying no twice, they'll jump at our company.
FIRST STUDENT   No, no—all that bowing and scraping, it makes me
     feel ill at ease,
   If we don't get a move on we'll lose our two birds in the bushes.   620
   The work-reddened hand that swings the broom Saturdays
   On Sundays knows how to give the softest caresses.
A BURGHER   No, you can have him, our new Mayor,
   Since he took office he's been a dictator,
   All he's done is make the town poorer,   625
   Every day I get madder and madder,

When he says a thing's so, not a peep, not a murmur,
Dare we express—and the taxes climb higher.

A BEGGAR [*Singing.*]
    Good sirs and all you lovely ladies,
    Healthy in body and handsome in dress,   630
    Turn, oh turn your eyes on me, please,
    And pity the beggarman's distress!
    Must I grind the organ fruitlessly,
    Only the charitable know true joy.
    This day when all the world dance merrily,   635
    Make it for me a harvest day.

ANOTHER BURGHER   On a Sunday or holiday nothing in all my experience
  Beats talking about war and rumors of war,
  When leagues away, in Turkey, for instance,
  Armies are wading knee deep in gore.   640
  You stand at the window, take long pulls at your schooner,
  And watch the gaily colored boats glide past,
  And then at sunset go home in the best of humor
  And praise God for the peace by which we're blest.

THIRD BURGHER   Yes, neighbor, yes, exactly my opinion.   645
  Let them go and beat each other's brains in,
  Let them turn the whole world upside down,
  As long as things are just as always in our town.

OLD CRONE [*To the* BURGHERS' DAUGHTERS.]
  Well, how smart we are! *And* so pretty and young.
  I'd like to see the man who could resist you.   650
  But not so proud, my dears! Just come along,
  Oh, I know how to get what you want for you.

BURGHER'S DAUGHTER   Agatha, come! The awful fright!
  I'm afraid of being seen with that witchwoman.
  It's true that last St. Andrew's Eve[4]   655
  She showed me in a glass my very own one.

HER FRIEND   And mine she showed me in a crystal sphere
  Looking a soldier, with swaggering friends around him,
  And though I watch out everywhere,
  I have no luck, I never seem to find him.   660

SOLDIERS
    Castles have ramparts,
    Great walls and towers,
    Girls turn their noses up
    At soldier-boy lovers—
    We'll make both ours!   665
    Boldly adventure
    And rake in the pay!

---

4. November 29, the traditional time for young girls to consult fortune-tellers about their future lovers or husbands.

Hear the shrill bugle
Summon to battle,
Forward to rapture 670
Or forward to ruin!
Oh what a struggle!
Our life—oh how stirring!
Haughty girls, high-walled castles,
We'll make them surrender! 675
Boldly adventure
And rake in the pay!
—And after, the soldiers
Go marching away.

[FAUST *and* WAGNER]

FAUST   The streams put off their icy mantle 680
Under the springtime's quickening smile.
Hope's green banner flies in the valley;
White-bearded winter, old and frail,
Retreats back up into the mountains,
And still retreating, down he sends 685
Feeble volleys of sleet showers,
Whitening in patches new-green plains.
But the sun can bear with white no longer,
When life stirs, shaping all anew,
He wants a scene that has some color, 690
And since there's nowhere yet one flower,
Holiday crowds have got to do.
Now face about, and looking down
From the hilltop back to town,
See the brightly colored crowd 695
Pouring like a spring flood
Through the gaping, gloomy arch
To bask in the sun all love so much.
They celebrate the Savior's Rising,
For they themselves today are risen: 700
From airless rooms in huddled houses,
From drudgery at counters and benches,
From under cumbrous roofs and gables,
From crowded, suffocating alleys,
From the mouldering dimness of the churches, 705
They hurry to where all is brightness.
And look there, how the eager crowd
Scatters through the fields and gardens.
How over the river's length and breadth
Skiffs and sculls are busily darting, 710
And that last boat, packed near to sinking,
Already's pulled a good ways off.
Even from distant mountain slopes
Bright colored clothes wink back at us.

Now I can hear it, the village commotion,   715
Out here, you can tell, is the people's true heaven,
Young and old crying exultingly:
Here I am human, here I can be free.
WAGNER   To go for a walk with you, dear Doctor,
Is a treat for my mind as well as honoring me;   720
But by myself I'd never come near here,
For I can't abide the least vulgarity.
The fiddling, shrieking, clashing bowls
For me are all an unbearable uproar,
All scream and shout like possessed souls   725
And call it music, call it pleasure.
PEASANTS [*Singing and dancing under the linden tree.*]
        The shepherd dressed up in his best,
        Pantaloons and flowered vest,
            Oh my, how brave and handsome!
        Within the broad-leaved linden's shade   730
        Madly spun both man and maid,
            Tra-la! Tra-la!
            Tra-la-la-la! Tra-lay!
        The fiddle bow flew, and then some.
        He flung himself into their midst   735
        And seized a young thing round the waist,
            While saying, "Care to dance, ma'am?"
        The snippy miss she tossed her head,
        "You boorish shepherd boy!" she said,
            Tra-la! Tra-la!   740
            Tra-la-la-la! Tra-lay!
        "Observe, do, some decorum!"
        But round the circle swiftly wheeled,
        To right and left the dancers whirled,
            Till all the breath flew from them.   745
        They got so red, they got so warm,
        They rested, panting, arm in arm,
            Tra-la! Tra-la!
            Tra-la-la-la! Tra-lay!
        And breast to breast—a twosome.   750

        "I'll thank you not to make so free!
        We girls know well how men betray,
            What snakes lurk in your bosom!"
        But still he wheedled her away—
        Far off they heard the fiddles play,   755
            Tra-la! Tra-la!
            Tra-la-la-la! Tra-lay!
        The shouting, uproar, bedlam.
OLD PEASANT   Professor, welcome! Oh how kind
To join us common folk today,   760
Though such a fine man, learned mind,

Not to scorn our holiday.
So please accept out best cup, sir,
Brimful with the freshest beer;
We hope that it will quench your thirst,   765
But more than that, we pray and hope
Your sum of days may be increased
By as many drops as fill the cup!
FAUST   Friends, thanks for this refreshment, I
In turn wish you all health and joy.   770
    [*The people make a circle around him.*]
OLD PEASANT   Indeed it's only right that you
Should be with us this happy day,
Who when our times were hard, a true
Friend he proved in every way.
Many a one stands in his boots here   775
Whom your good father, the last minute,
Snatched from the hot grip of the fever,
That time he quelled the epidemic.[5]
And you yourself, a youngster then,
Never shrank back; every house   780
The pest went in, you did too.
Out they carried many a corpse,
But never yours. Much you went through;
Us you saved, and God saved you.
ALL   Health to our tried and trusty friend,   785
And may his kindness have no end.
FAUST   Bow down to him who dwells above,
Whose love shows us how we should love.
    [*He continues on with* WAGNER.]
WAGNER   The gratification you must get from all of this,
From knowing the reverence these people hold you in!   790
The man whose gifts can gain him such advantages,
Oh, he's a lucky one in my opinion.
Who is it, each one asks as he runs to see,
Fathers point you out to their boys,
The fiddle stops, the dancers pause,   795
And as you pass between the rows
Of people, caps fly in the air, why,
Next you know they'll all be on their knees
As if the Host itself[6] were passing by.
FAUST   A few steps more to that rock where we'll rest   800
A bit, shall we, from our walk. How often
I would sit alone here thinking, sighing,
And torture myself with praying, fasting, crying.
So much hope I had then, such great trust—
I'd wring my hands, I'd weep, fall on my knees,   805

5. Pestilence or plague.
6. The Eucharist, the consecrated bread of the Sacrament.

Believing God, in this way forced
To look below, would cry halt to the disease.
But now these people's generous praise of me
I find a mockery. If only you could see
Into my heart, you'd realize 810
How little worthy father and son were really.
    My father was an upright man, a lonely,
Brooding soul who searched great Nature's processes
With a head crammed full of the most bizarre hypotheses.
Shutting himself with fellow masters up in 815
The vaulted confines of their vaporous Black Kitchen,
He mixed together opposites according
To innumerable recipes. A bold Red Lion,
Handsome suitor he, took for wedding
Partner a pure White Lily, the two uniting 820
In a tepid bath; then being tested by fire,
The pair precipitately fled
From one bridal chamber to another,
Till there appeared within the glass
The young Queen, dazzlingly dressed 825
In every color of the spectrum:
The Sovereign Remedy—a futile nostrum.
The patients died; none stopped to inquire
How many there were who'd got better.[7]
    So with our infernal electuary 830
We killed our way across the country.
I poisoned, myself, by prescription, thousands,
They sickened and faded; yet I must live to see
On every side the murderers' fame emblazoned.
WAGNER   But why be so distressed, there is no reason. 835
If an honest man with conscientious devotion
Practises the arts his forebears practised,
It's understandable, it's what's to be expected.
A youth who is respectful of his father
Listens and soaks up all he has to teach; 840
If the grown man lengthens science's reach,
His son in turn can reach goals even farther.
FAUST   Oh, he's a happy man who hopes
To keep from drowning in these seas of error!
What we know least, we need the most, 845
And what we do know is no use whatever.
    But such cheerlessness blasphemes
The quiet sweetness of this shining hour.
Look how the sunset's level beams
Gild those cottages in their green bower, 850
The brightness fades, the sun makes his adieu,
Hurrying off to kindle new life elsewhere—

7. This confusing sequence evokes a kind of medicine closely allied to magic.

If only I had wings to rise into
The air and follow ever after!
Then I would see the whole world at my feet,   855
Quietly shining in the eternal sunset,
The peaks ablaze, the valleys gone to sleep,
And babbling into golden stream the silver runlet.
The savage mountain with its plunging cliffs
Should never balk my godlike soaring,   860
And there's the ocean, see, already swelling
Before my wondering gaze, with its sun-warmed gulfs.
But finally the bright god looks like sinking,
Whereupon a renewed urgency
Drives me on to drink his eternal light,   865
The day always before, behind the night,
The heavens overhead, below the heaving sea . . .

    A lovely dream!—and meanwhile it grows dark.
Oh dear, oh dear, that our frames should lack
Wings with which to match the spirit's soaring.   870
Still our nature's such that all of us
Know feelings that strive upwards, always straining,
When high above, lost in the azure emptiness,
The skylark pours out his shrill rhapsody,
When over fir-clad mountain peaks   875
The eagle on his broad wings gyres silently,
And passing over prairies, over lakes,
The homeward-bound crane labors steadily.
WAGNER   Well, I've had more than one odd moment, I have,
But I have never felt those impulses you have.   880
Soon enough you get your fill of woods and things,
I don't really envy birds their wings.
How different are the pleasures of the intellect,
Sustaining one from page to page, from book to book,
And warming winter nights with dear employment   885
And with the consciousness your life's so lucky.
And goodness, when you spread out an old parchment,
Heaven's fetched straight down into your study.
FAUST   You know the one great driving force,
May you never know the other!   890
Two souls live in me, alas,
Irreconcilable with one another.
One, lusting for the world with all its might,
Grapples it close, greedy of all its pleasures,
The other rises up, up from the dirt,   895
Up to the blest fields where dwell our great forebears.

    O beings of the air, if you exist,
Holding sway between the heavens and earth,
Come down to me out of the golden mist

And translate me to a new, a vivid life!   900
Oh, if I only had a magic mantle
To bear me off to unknown lands,
I'd never trade it for the costliest gowns,
Or for a cloak however rich and royal.

WAGNER   Never call them down, the dreadful swarm   905
That swoop and hover through the atmosphere,
Bringing mankind every kind of harm
From every corner of the terrestrial sphere.
From the North they bare their razor teeth
And prick you with their arrow-pointed tongues,   910
From the East, sighing with parched breath,
They eat away your dessicated lungs;
And when from Southern wastes they gust and sough,
Fire on fire on your sunk head heaping,
From the West they send for your relief   915
Cooling winds—then drown fields just prepared for reaping.
Their ears are cocked, on trickery intent,
Seem dutiful while scheming to defeat us,
Their pretense is that they are heaven-sent
And lisp like angels even as they cheat us.   920
    However, come, let's go, the world's turned gray
And chilly, evening mists are rising!
At nightfall it's indoors you want to be.
But why should you stand still, astonished, staring?
What can you see in the dusk to find upsetting?   925

FAUST   Don't you see that black dog in the stubble,
Coursing back and forth?

WAGNER   I do. I noticed him.
A while back. What about him?

FAUST   Look again.
What kind of creature is it?

WAGNER   Kind? A poodle—
Worried where his master is, and always   930
Sniffing about to find his scent.

FAUST   Look, he's
Circling around us, coming near and nearer.
Unless I'm much mistaken, a wake of fire
Is streaming after him.

WAGNER   I see nothing
But a black-haired poodle. Your eyes are playing   940
Tricks on you, perhaps.

FAUST   I think I see
Him winding a magic snare, quietly,
Around our feet, a noose which he'll pull tight
In the future, when the time is right.

WAGNER   He's circling us because he's timid and uncertain;   945
He's missed his master, come on men unknown to him.

FAUST   The circle's getting tighter, he's much closer!

WAGNER   You see!—a dog, it's no ghost, sir.
   He growls suspiciously, he hesitates,
   He wags his tail, lies down and waits.   950
   Never fear, it's all just dog behavior.
FAUST   Come here, doggie, come here, do.
WAGNER   A silly poodle, a poor creature,
   When you stop, he stops too.
   Speak to him, he'll leap and bark,   955
   Throw something, he will fetch it back,
   Go after your stick right into the river.
FAUST   I guess you're right, it's just what he's been taught;
   I see no sign of anything occult.
WAGNER   A dog so good, so well-behaved by nature—   960
   Why, even a philosopher would stoop to pet him.
   Some students trained him, found him an apt scholar—
   Sir, he deserves you should adopt him.
      [*They enter at the City Gate.*]

FAUST'S STUDY [I]

FAUST [*Entering with the poodle.*]
   Behind me lie the fields and meadows
   Shrouded in the lowering dark,   965
   In dread of what waits in the shadows
   Our better soul now starts awake.
   Our worser one, unruly, reckless,
   Quietens and starts to nod;
   In me the love of my own fellows   970
   Begins to stir, and the love of God.

   Poodle, stop! How you race around! A dozen
   Dogs you seem. Why all that sniffing at the door?
   Here's my best cushion, it's yours to doze on,
   Behind the stove, there on the floor.   975
   Just now when we came down the hillside
   You gambolled like the friendliest beast.
   I'm glad to take you in, provide
   Your keep—provided you're a silent guest.

   When once again the lamp light brightens   980
   With its soft glow your narrow cell,
   Oh in your breast how then it lightens,
   And deeper in your heart as well.
   Again you hear the voice of reason,
   And hope revives, it breathes afresh,   985
   You long to drink the living waters,
   Mount upwards to our being's source.

   You're growling, poodle! Animal squealings
   Hardly suit the exalted feelings

Filling my soul to overflowing. 990
We're used to people ridiculing
What they hardly understand,
Grumbling at the good and beautiful—
It makes them so uncomfortable!
Do dogs now emulate mankind? 995
   Yet even with the best of will
I feel my new contentment fail.
Why must the waters cease so soon
And leave us thirsting once again?
Oh, this has happened much too often! 1000
But there's an answer to it all:
I mean the supernatural,
I mean our hope of revelation,
Which nowhere shines so radiant
As here in the New Testament. 1005
I'll look right now at the original[8]
And see if it is possible
For me to make a true translation
Into my beloved German.
   [He opens the volume and begins.]
"In the beginning was the Word"[9]—so goes 1010
The text. And right off I am given pause!
A little help, please, someone, I'm unable
To see the *word* as first, most fundamental.
If I am filled with the true spirit
I'll find a better way to say it. 1015
So: "In the beginning *mind* was"—right?
Give plenty of thought to what you write,
Lest your pen prove too impetuous:
Is it mind that makes and moves the universe?
Shouldn't it be: "In the beginning
Power was, before it nothing"? 1020
Yet even as I write this down on paper
Something tells me don't stop there, go further.
The Spirit's prompt in aid; now, now, indeed
I know for sure: "In the beginning was the *deed*!" 1025

If this cell's one that we'll be sharing,
Poodle, stop that barking, yelping!
You're giving me a splitting headache,
I can't put up with such a roommate.
I'm sorry to say that one of us 1030
Has got to quit the premises.
It goes against the grain with me
To renege on hospitality,
But there's the door, dog, leave, goodbye.

8. That is, the Greek.   9. John 1.1.

But what's that I'm seeing,   1035
A shadow or real thing?
It beggars belief—
My poodle swells up huger than life!
He heaves up his hulk—
No dog has such bulk!   1040
What a spook I have brought
Into my house without thought.
He looks, with his fierce eyes and jaws,
Just like a hippopotamus—
But I've got you, you're caught!   1045
For a half-hellhound like you are,
Solomon's Key[1] is what is called for.

SPIRITS [*Outside the door.*]

Someone is locked in there!
No one's allowed in there!
Like a fox hunters snared,   1050
Old Scratch shivers, he's scared.
Be careful, watch out!
Hover this way, now that,
About and again about,
You'll soon find he's got out.   1055
If you can help him,
Don't let him sit there,
All of us owe him
For many a favor.

FAUST   Against such a creature, my first defense: 1060
The Spell of the Four Elements.

Salamander glow hot,
Undine, wind about,
Sylph, melt quick,
Kobold,[2] to work.   1065

Ignorance
Of the elements,
Their powers and properties,
Denies you all mastery
Over the demonry.   1070

Vanish in flames,
Salamander!
Undine, make babbling streams
All flow together!

1. The *Clavicula Salomonis*, a standard work used
by magicians for conjuring. In many medieval legends, Solomon was noted as a great magician.

2. A spirit of the earth. "Salamander": spirit
of fire. "Undine": spirit of water. "Sylph": spirit
of air.

Glitter meteor-beauteous,   1075
Aërial Sylph!
Give household help to us,
Incubus! Incubus!
Come out, come out, enough's enough.

None of the four   1080
Is in the cur.
Calmly he lies there, grinning at me,
My spells glance off him harmlessly.
   Now hear me conjure
With something stronger.   1085

   Are you, grim fellow,
   Escaped here from Hell below?
   Then look at this symbol
   Before which the legions
   Of devils and demons   1090
   Fearfully bow.

How his hair bristles, how he swells up now!

   Creature cast into darkness,
   Can you make out its meaning?
   The never-begotten One.   1095
   Wholly ineffable One,
   Carelessly pierced in the side One,
   Whose blood in the heavens
   Is everywhere streaming?

Behind the stove by me sent,   1100
Bulging big as an elephant,
The entire cell filling,
Into mist himself willing—
—No, no, not through the ceiling!
At my feet fall, Master's bidding!   1105
My threats as you see are scarcely idle—
With fire I'll rout you out, yes, I will!
Wait if you wish,
For my triune[3] light's hot flash,
Wait till you force me   1110
To employ my most potent sorcery.
      [*The smoke clears, and* MEPHISTOPHELES, *dressed as an
      itinerant student, emerges from behind the stove.*]
MEPHISTO   Why all the racket? What's your wish, sir?
FAUST   So it's you who was the poodle!
   I have to laugh—a wandering scholar!

3. Perhaps the Trinity or a triangle with divergent rays.

MEPHISTO   My greetings to you, learned doctor,   1115
   You really had me sweating hard there.
FAUST   And what's your name?
MEPHISTO   Your question's trivial
   From one who finds words superficial,
   Who strives to pass beyond mere seeming
   And penetrate the heart of being.[4]   1120
FAUST   With gentry like yourself, it's common
   To find the name declares what you are
   Very plainly. I'll just mention
   Lord of the Flies,[5] Destroyer, Liar.
   So say who you are, if you would.   1125
MEPHISTO   A humble part of that great power
   Which always means evil, always does good.
FAUST   Those riddling words mean what, I'd like to know.
MEPHISTO   I am the spirit that says no,
   No always! And how right I am! For certainly   1130
   It's only fitting everything that comes to be
   Should cease to be. And so they do.
   Still better nothing ever was. Hence sin,
   And havoc and ruin—all you call evil, in sum—
   For me's the element that I swim in.   1135
FAUST   A part, you say? You look like the whole works to me.
MEPHISTO   I say what's so, it isn't modesty—
   Man in his world of self's a fool,
   He likes to think he's all in all.
   I'm part of the part which was all at first,   1140
   A part of the dark out of which light burst,
   Arrogant light which now usurps the air
   And seeks to thrust Night from her ancient chair,
   To no avail. Since light is one with all
   Things bodily, making them beautiful,   1145
   Streams from them, from them is reflected,
   Since light by matter's manifested—
   When by degrees all matter's burnt up and no more,
   Why, then light shall not matter any more.
FAUST   Oh, now I understand your office: 1150
   Since you can't wreck Creation wholesale,
   You're going at it bit by bit, retail.
MEPHISTO   And making, I fear, little progress.
   The opposite of nothing-at-all,
   The *something*, this great shambling world,   1155
   In spite of how I exert myself against it,
   Phlegmatically endures my every onset
   By earthquake, fire, tidal wave and storm:

---

4. Mephistopheles refers to Faust's substitution of *Deed* for *Word* in the passage from John (see line 1025).

5. An almost literal translation of the name of the Philistine deity Beelzebub.

Next day the land and sea again are calm.
And all that *stuff*, those animal and human species— 1160
I can hardly make a dent in them.
The numbers I've already buried, armies!
Yet fresh troops keep on marching up again.
That's how it is, it's enough to drive you crazy!
From air, from water, from the earth 1165
Seeds innumerable sprout forth
In dry and wet and cold and warm!
If I hadn't kept back fire for myself,
What the devil could I call my own?

FAUST   So against the good, the never-resting, 1170
Beneficent creative force
In impotent spite you ball your fist and
Try to arrest life's onward course?
Look around for work that's more rewarding,
You singular son of old Chaos! 1175

MEPHISTO   Well, it's a subject for discussion—
At our next meeting. Now I wish
To go. That is, with your permission.

FAUST   But why should *you* ask *me* for leave?
We've struck up an acquaintance, we two, 1180
Drop in on me whenever you please.
There's the door and there's the window,
And ever reliable, there's the chimney.

MEPHISTO   Well . . . you see . . . an obstacle
Keeps me from dropping *out*—so sorry! 1185
That witch's foot chalked on your doorsill.

FAUST   The pentagram's[6] the difficulty?
But if it's that that has you stopped,
How did you ever manage an entry?
And how should a devil like you get trapped? 1190

MEPHISTO   Well, look close and you'll see that
A corner's open: the outward pointing
Angle's lines don't quite meet.

FAUST   What a stroke of luck! I'm thinking
Now you are my prisoner. 1195
Pure chance has put you in my power!

MEPHISTO   The poodle dashed right in, saw nothing;
But now the case is the reverse:
The Devil can't get out of the house!

FAUST   There's the window, why don't you use it? 1200

MEPHISTO   It's an iron law we devils can't flout,
The way we come in, we've got to go out,
We're free as to entrée, but not as to exit.

FAUST   So even in Hell there's law and order!
I'm glad, for then a man might sign 1205
A contract with you gentlemen.

6. A magic five-pointed star designed to keep away evil spirits.

MEPHISTO   Whatever we promise, you get, full measure,
    There's no cutting corners, no skulduggery—
    But it's not a thing to be done in a hurry;
    Let's save the subject for our next get-together.   1210
    And as for now, I beg you earnestly,
    Release me from the spell that binds me!
FAUST   Why rush off, stay a while, do.
    I'd love to hear some more from you.
MEPHISTO   Let me go now. I swear I'll come back,   1215
    Then you can ask me whatever you like.
FAUST   Trapping you was never my thought,
    You trapped yourself, it's your own fault.
    Who's nabbed the Devil must keep a tight grip,
    You don't grab him again once he gives you the slip.   1220
MEPHISTO   Oh, all right! To please you I
    Will stay and keep you company;
    Provided with my arts you let me
    Entertain you in my own way.
FAUST   Delighted, go ahead. But please   1225
    Make sure those arts of yours amuse!
MEPHISTO   You'll find, my friend, your senses, in one hour,
    More teased and roused than all the long dull year.
    The songs the fluttering spirits murmur in your ear,
    The visions they unfold of sweet desire,   1230
    Oh they are more than just tricks meant to fool.
    By Arabian scents you'll be delighted,
    Your palate tickled, never sated,
    The ravishing sensations you will feel!
    No preparation's needed, none.   1235
    Here we are. Let the show begin!
SPIRITS   Open, you gloomy
        Vaulted ceiling above him,
        Let the blue ether
        Look benignly in on him,   1240
        And dark cloudbanks scatter
        So that all is fair for him!
        Starlets are glittering,
        Milder suns glowing,
        Angelic troops shining   1245
        In celestial beauty
        Hover past smiling,
        Bending and bowing.
        Ardent desire
        Follows them yearning;   1250
        And their robes streaming ribbons
        Veil the fields, veil the meadows,
        Veil the arbors where lovers
        In pensive surrender
        Give themselves to each other   1255
        For ever and ever.

Arbor on arbor!
Vines clambering and twining!
Their heavy clusters,
Poured into presses, 1260
Pour out purple wines
Which descend in dark streams
Over beds of bright stones
Down the vineyards' steep slopes
To broaden to lakes 1265
At the foot of green hills.
Birds blissfully drink there,
With beating wings sunwards soar,
Soar towards the golden isles
Shimmering hazily 1270
On the horizon;
Where we hear voices
Chorusing jubilantly,
Where we see dancers
Whirling exuberantly 1275
Over the meadows,
Here, there and everywhere.
Some climb the heights,
Some swim in the lakes,
Others float in the air— 1280
Joying in life, all,
Beneath the paradisal
Stars glowing with love
Afar in the distance.
MEPHISTO   Asleep! Oh bravely done, my every airy youngling! 1285
Into a drowse you've sung him, never stumbling.
I am in your debt for this performance.
—As for you, sir, you were never born
To keep the Prince of Darkness down!
Let sweet dream-shapes crowd round him in confusion, 1290
Drown him in a deep sea of delusion.
But from this doorsill-magic to be freed
A rat's tooth is the thing I need.
No point to conjuring long-windedly—
There's one rustling nearby, he'll soon hear me. 1295

The lord of flies and rats and mice,
Of frogs and bedbugs, worms and lice,
Commands you forth from your dark hole
To gnaw, beast, for me that doorsill
Whereon I dab this drop of oil! 1300
—And there you are! Begin, begin!
The corner that is pointing in,
That's the one that shuts me in;

One last crunch to clear my way:
Now Faustus, till we meet next—dream away! 1305
FAUST [*Awakening.*] Deceived again, am I, by tricks,
　Those vanished spirits just a hoax,
　A dream the Devil, nothing more,
　The dog I took home just a cur?

FAUST'S STUDY [II]

FAUST, MEPHISTOPHELES.

FAUST　A knock, was that? Come in! Who is it this time? 1310
MEPHISTO　Me.
FAUST　　　　　Come in!
MEPHISTO　　　　　　　　You have to say it still a third time.
FAUST　All right, all right—come in!
MEPHISTO　　　　　　　　　Good, very good!
　We two will get along, I see, just as we should.
　I've come here dressed up as a grandee.[7] Why?
　To help you drive your blues away! 1315
　In a scarlet suit, all over gold braid,
　Across my shoulders a stiff silk cape,
　A gay cock's feather in my cap,
　At my side a gallant's long blade—
　And bringing you advice that's short and sweet: 1320
　Put fine clothes on like me, cut loose a bit,
　Be free and easy, man, throw off your yoke
　And find out what real life is like.
FAUST　In any clothes, I'd feel the misery
　Of this cramped, suffocating life on earth. 1325
　I'm too old for a life of gaity,
　Too young to live for nothing, wait for death.
　The world—what has it got to say to me?
　Renounce all that you long for, all—renounce!
　That's the truth that all pronounce 1330
　So sagely, so interminably,
　The non-stop croak, the universal chant:
　You can't have what you want, you can't!
　I awake each morning, how? Horrified,
　On the verge of tears, to confront a day 1335
　Which at its close will not have satisfied
　One smallest wish of mine, not one. Why,
　Even a hint of pleasure, some pleasantness,
　Withers in the air of mean-spirited fault-finding;

7. In the popular plays based on the Faust legend, the Devil often appeared as a monk when the play catered to a Protestant audience and as a noble squire when the audience was mainly Catholic.

My lively nature's quick inventiveness 1340
Is thwarted by cares that seem to have no ending.
And when the night draws on and all is hushed,
I go to bed not soothed at last but apprehensively,
Well knowing what awaits me is not rest,
But wild and whirling dreams that terrify me. 1345
The god who dwells inside my breast,
Able to stir me to my depths,
The master strength of all my strengths
Is impotent to effect a single thing outside me;
And so I find existence burdensome, wretched, 1350
Death eagerly desired, my life hated.

MEPHISTO   Yet the welcome men give death is never wholehearted.

FAUST   Oh that man's blest who, conquering gloriously,
Death winds the blood-stained laurel round his brows,
Who after dancing the night through furiously 1355
Death finds him in a girl's arms in a drowse.
If only, overwhelmed by the Spirit's power,
In raptures I had died right then and there!

MEPHISTO   And yet that very night, I seem to remember,
A fellow didn't down a drink I saw him prepare. 1360

FAUST   Spying around, I see, is what you like to do.

MEPHISTO   I don't know everything, but I know a thing or two.

FAUST   If a sweet, familiar harmony
When I was staggering, steadied me,
Beguiled what's left of childhood feeling 1365
From a time when all was smiling, gay,
Well, never again! I pronounce a curse on
All false and flattering persuasion,
All tales that cheat the soul, constrain
It to endure this vale of pain. 1370
First I curse man's mind for thinking
Much too well of itself; I curse
The show of things, so dazzling, glittering,
That assails us through our every sense;
Our dreams of fame, of our name's enduring, 1375
Oh what a sham, I curse them too;
I curse as hollow all our having,
Curse wife and child, peasant and plow;
I curse Mammon[8] when he incites us
With dreams of treasure to reckless deeds, 1380
Or plumps the cushions for our pleasure
As we lie lazily at ease;
Curse comfort sucked out of the grape,
Curse love on its pinnacle of bliss,

---

8. The Aramaic word for "riches," used in the New Testament of the Bible. Medieval writers interpreted the word as a proper noun, the name of the Devil, as representing greed.

Curse faith, so false, curse all vain hope, 1385
And patience most of all I curse!
SPIRIT CHORUS [*Invisible.*]
    Oh, what a pity,
    Now you've destroyed it!
    The world once so lovely,
    How you have wrecked it! 1390
    Down it goes, smashed
    By a demigod's fist!
    Out of existence
    We sweep its poor remnants,
    Sorrowing over 1395
    Beauty now lost forever.
    —Then build again, better,
    Potent son of the earth,
    Build a new world, a fairer,
    Inside your own self, 1400
    Within your own heart!
    With a mind clear and strong,
    On your lips a new song,
    Come, make a fresh start!
MEPHISTO   Lesser ones, these are, 1405
  Of my order.
  Active be, cheerful,
  Is their sage counsel.
  Out of your loneliness,
  Spiritless lustlessness, 1410
  Their voices draw you
  Into the wide world before you.

  Stop making love to your misery,
  It gnaws away at you like a vulture;
  Even in the meanest company 1415
  You'd feel yourself a man like any other.
  Not that I'm proposing to
  Thrust you down among the rabble.
  I'm not your grandest devil, no,
  But still, throw in with me—that way, united, 1420
  Together life's long road we'll travel,
  And my, how I would be delighted!
  I'll do your will as if my will,
  Every wish of yours fulfill,
  By your leave 1425
  Be your bond servant, be your slave.
FAUST   And in return what must I do?
MEPHISTO   There's plenty of time for that, forget it.
FAUST   No, no, the Devil must have his due,
  He doesn't do things for the hell of it, 1430
  Just to see another fellow through.

So let's hear the terms, what the fine print is;
Having you for a servant's a tricky business.
MEPHISTO   I promise I will serve your wishes—here,
  A slave who'll do your bidding faithfully;   1435
  But if we meet each other—there,
  Why, you must do the same for me.
FAUST   That "there" of yours—it doesn't scare me off;
  If you pull this world down about my ears,
  Let the other one come on, who cares?   1440
  My joys are part and parcel of this earth,
  It's under this sun that I suffer,
  And once it's goodbye, last leave taken,
  Then let whatever happens happen,
  And that is that. About the hereafter   1445
  We have had enough palaver,
  More than I want to hear, by far:
  If still we love and hate each other,
  If some stand high and some stand lower,
  Et cetera, et cetera.   1450
MEPHISTO   In that case an agreement's easy.
  Come, dare it! Come, your signature!
  Oh, how my tricks will tickle your fancy!
  I'll show you things no man has seen before.
FAUST   You poor devil, really, what have you got to offer?   1455
  The mind of man in its sublime endeavor,
  Tell me, have you ever understood it?
  Oh yes indeed, you've bread, and when I eat it
  I'm hungry still; you've yellow gold, it's flighty,
  Quicksilver-like it's gone, my purse is empty.   1460
  Games of chance no man can win at ever;
  Girls who wind me in their arms, their lover,
  While eyeing up a fresh one over my shoulder.
  There's fame, last failing of a noble nature,
  It shoots across the sky a second, then it's over—   1465
  Oh yes, do show me fruit that rots as you try
  To pick it, trees whose leaves bud daily, daily die!
MEPHISTO   Marvels like that? For a devil, not so daunting.
  I'm good for whatever you have in mind.
  —But friend, the day comes when you find   1470
  A share of your own in life's good things,
  And peace and quiet, are what you're wanting.
FAUST   If ever you see me loll at ease,
  Then it's all yours, you can have it, my life!
  If ever you fool me with flatteries   1475
  Into feeling satisfied with myself,
  Or tempt me with visions of luxuries,
  That's my last day on earth breathed,
  I'll bet you!
MEPHISTO   Done! A bet!

FAUST   A bet—agreed!
  If ever I plead with the passing moment,   1480
  "Linger awhile, you are so fair!"
  Then chain me up in close confinement,
  Then serving me's no more your care,
  Then let the death bell toll my finish,
  Then unreluctantly I'll perish,   1485
  The clock may stop, hands break, fall off,
  And time for me be over with.
MEPHISTO   Think twice. Forgetting's not a thing we do.
FAUST   Of course, quite right—a bet's a bet.
  This isn't anything I'm rushing into.   1490
  But if I fall into a rut,
  I'm a slave, no matter who to,
  To this or that one or to you.
MEPHISTO   My service starts now—no procrastinating!—
  At the dinner tonight for the just-made Ph.D.s.   1495
  But there's one thing: you know, for emergencies,
  I'd like to have our arrangement down in writing.
FAUST   In black and white you want it, pedant!
  You've never learnt a *man's* word's your best warrant?
  It's not enough for you that I'm committed   1500
  By what I promise till the end of days?
  —Yet the world's a flood sweeps all along before it,
  And why should I feel my word holds always?
  A strange idea, but that's the way we are,
  And who would want it otherwise?   1505
  That man's blessed who keeps his conscience clear,
  He'll regret no sacrifice.
  But parchment signed and stamped and sealed,
  Is a bogey all recoil from, scared.
  The pen does in the living word,   1510
  Only sealing wax and vellum count, honor must yield.
  Base spirit, say what you require!
  Brass or marble, parchment or paper?
  Shall I write with quill, with stylus, chisel,
  I leave it up to you, you devil!   1515
MEPHISTO   Why get so hot, make extravagant speeches?
  Ranting away does no good.
  A scrap of paper takes care of the business.
  And sign it with a drop of blood.
FAUST   Oh, all right. If that's what makes you happy,   1520
  I'll go along with the childish comedy.
MEPHISTO   Blood's a very special ink, you know.
FAUST   Are you afraid that I won't keep our bargain?
  With every sinew I'll strive, never slacken!
  So I've promised, that's what I will do.   1525
  I had ideas too big for me,
  Your level's mine, that's all I'm good for.

The Spirit laughed derisively,
Nature won't allow me near her.
Thinking is done with for me, I'm through,   1530
Learning I've loathed since long ago.
—Then fling ourselves into the dance
Of sensual extravagance!
Bring on your miracles, each one,
Veiled in impenetrable sorcery!   1535
We'll plunge into time's racing current,
The vortex of activity,
Where pleasure and distress,
Setbacks and success,
May come as they come, by turn-about, however;   1540
To be always up and doing is man's nature!
MEPHISTO   No limits restrain you, do just as you like.
A little taste here, a nibble, a lick,
You see something there, snatch it up on the run,
Let all that you do with gusto be done,   1545
Only don't be bashful, wade right in.
FAUST   I told you, I'm not out to enjoy myself, have fun,
I want frenzied excitements, gratifications that are painful,
Love and hatred violently mixed,
Anguish that enlivens, inspiriting trouble.   1550
Cured of my thirst to know at last,
I'll never again shun anything distressful;
From now on my wish is to undergo
What people everywhere undergo, their whole portion,
Make mine their heights and depths, their weal and woe,   1555
Everything human encompass in my one person,
And so enlarge my own self to embrace theirs, all,
And shipwreck with them when at last we shipwreck, all.
MEPHISTO   Believe me, I have chewed and chewed
At that tough meat, mankind, since long ago,   1560
From birth to death work at it, still that food
Is indigestible as sourdough.
Only a God can take in all of them,
The whole lot. For He dwells in eternal light,
While we poor devils are stuck down below   1565
In darkness and gloom, lacking even candlelight,
And all *you* qualify for is, half day, half night.
FAUST   Nevertheless I will!
MEPHISTO   Fine! Right!
Still, there's one thing worries me.
The time allotted you is very short,   1570
But art has always been around and shall be,
So listen, hear what is my thought:
Hire a poet, learn by his instruction.
Let the good gentleman search his mind
By careful, persevering reflection,   1575

And every noble attribute he can find
Heap on the head of his honored creation:
    The lion's fierceness,
    Mild hart's swiftness,
    Italian fieriness,   1580
    Northern steadiness.
Let him master for you the difficult feat
Of combining magnanimity with deceit,
How, driven by youthful impulsiveness, unrestrained,
To fall in love as beforehand planned.   1585
Such a creature—my, I'd love to know him!
I'd call him Mr. Microcosm.
FAUST   What am I, then, if it can never be:
The realization of all human possibility,
That crown my soul so avidly reaches for?   1590
MEPHISTO   In the end you are—just what you are.
Wear wigs high-piled with curls, oh millions,
Stick your legs in yard-high hessians,
You're still you, the one you always were.
FAUST   I feel it now, how pointless my long grind   1595
To make mine all the treasures of man's mind;
When I sit back and interrogate my soul,
No new powers answer to my call,
I'm not a hair's breadth more in height,
A step nearer to the infinite.   1600
MEPHISTO   The way you see things, my dear Faust,
Is superficial—I speak frankly.
If you go on repining weakly,
We'll lose our seat at life's rich feast.
Hell, man, you have hands and feet,   1605
A headpiece and a pair of balls,
And savors from fruit fresh and sweet,
That pleasure's yours, entirely yours.
If I've six studs, a sturdy span,
That horsepower's mine, my property,   1610
My coach bowls on, ain't I the man,
Two dozen legs I've got for me!
    Sir, come on, quit all that thinking,
Into the world, the pair of us!
The man who lives in his head only's   1615
Like a donkey in the rough
Led round and round by the bad fairies,
While green grass grows a stone's throw off.
FAUST   And how do we begin?
MEPHISTO   By clearing out—just leaving.
A torture chamber this place is, and that's the truth.   1620
You call it living, to be boring
Yourself and your young men to death?
Leave that to Dr. Bacon Fat next door!

Why toil and moil at threshing heaps of straw?
Anyhow, the deepest knowledge you possess   1625
You daren't let on to before your class.
—Oh now I hear one in the passageway!
FAUST   I can't see him—tell him to go away.
MEPHISTO   The poor boy's been so patient, don't be cross;
    We mustn't let him leave here *désolé*.   1630
    Let's have your cap and gown, Herr Doctor.
    Won't I look the fine professor!
        [*Changes clothes.*]
    Count on me to know just what to say,
    Fifteen minutes's all I need for it—
    Meanwhile get ready for our little junket!   1635

                                          [*Exit* FAUST.]

MEPHISTO [*Wearing* FAUST's *gown.*]   Despise learning, heap contempt
        on reason,
    The human race's best possession,
    Only let the lying spirit draw you
    Over into mumbo-jumbo,
    Make-believe and pure illusion—   1640
    And then you're mine, for sure I have you,
    No matter what we just agreed to.
    Fate's given him a spirit knows no measure,
    On and on it strives relentlessly,
    It soars away disdaining every pleasure,   1645
    Yet I will lead him deep into debauchery
    Where all is shallow, meaningless,
    I'll have him writhing, ravening, berserk;
    Before his lips' insatiable greediness
    I'll dangle food and drink, he'll shriek   1650
    In vain for relief from his torturing dryness.
    And even if he weren't the Devil's already,
    He'd still be sure to perish horribly.
        [*Enter a* STUDENT.]
STUDENT   Allow me, sir, but I am a beginner
    And come in quest of an adviser,   1655
    One whom all the people here
    Greatly esteem, indeed revere.
MEPHISTO   I thank you for your courtesy.
    But I'm a man, as you can see,
    Like any other. Perhaps you should look further.   1660
STUDENT   It's you, sir, you, I want for adviser!
    I came here full of youthful zeal,
    Eager to learn everything worthwhile.
    Mother cried to see me go;
    I've got an allowance, not much, but it'll do.   1665
MEPHISTO   You've come to the right place, my son.
STUDENT   But I'm ready to turn right around and run!
    It seems so sad inside these walls,

My heart misgives me; I find all's
Confined, shut in; there's nothing green,   1670
Not even a single tree to be seen.
I can't, on the beach in the lecture hall,
Hear or see or think at all!
MEPHISTO   It's a matter of getting used to things first.
An infant starts out fighting the breast,   1675
But soon it's feeding lustily.
Just so your appetite will sharpen day by day
The more you nurse at Wisdom's bosom.
STUDENT   I'll cling tight to her bosom, happily,
But where do I find her, by what way?   1680
MEPHISTO   First of all, then—have you chosen
A faculty?
STUDENT   Well, you see,
I'd like to be a learned man.
The earth below, the heavens on high—
All those things I long to understand,   1685
All the sciences; all nature.
MEPHISTO   You've got the right idea; however,
It demands close application.
STUDENT   Oh never fear, I'm in this heart and soul;
But still, a fellow gets so dull   1690
Without time off for recreation,
In the long and lovely days of summer.
MEPHISTO   Time slips away so fast you need to use it
Rationally, and not abuse it.
And for that reason I advise you: 1695
The Principles of Logic *primo*!
We will drill your mind by rote,
Strap it in the Spanish boot
So it never shall forget
The road that's been marked out for it   1700
And stray about incautiously,
A will-o'-the-wisp, this way, that way.
Day after day you'll be taught
All you once did just like that,
Like eating and drinking, thoughtlessly,   1705
Now needs a methodology—
Order and system: *A, B, C!*
   Our thinking instrument behaves
Like a loom: every thread
At a step on the treadle's set in motion,   1710
Back and forth the shuttle's sped,
The strands flow too fast for the eye,
A blow of the batten and there's cloth, woven!
Now enter your philosopher, he
Proves all is just as it should be: 1715
A being thus and B also,

Then C and D inevitably follow;
And if there were no A and B,
There'd never be a C and D.
They're struck all of a heap, his admiring hearers,   1720
But still, it doesn't make them weavers.
How do you study something living?
Drive out the spirit, deny it being,
So there're just parts with which to deal,
Gone is what binds it all, the soul.   1725
With lifeless pieces as the only things real,
The wonder's where's the life of the whole—
Encheiresis naturae,[9] the chemists then call it,
Make fools of themselves and never know it.
STUDENT   I have trouble following what you say.   1730
MEPHISTO   You'll get the hang of it by and by,
When you learn to distinguish and classify.
STUDENT   How stupid all this makes me feel;
It spins around in my head like a wheel.
MEPHISTO   Next metaphysics—a vital part   1735
Of scholarship, its very heart.
Exert your faculties to venture
Beyond the boundaries of our nature,
Gain intelligence the brain
Has difficulty taking in,   1740
And whether it goes in or not,
There's always a big word for it.
Be very sure, your first semester,
To do things right, attend each lecture.
Five of them you'll have daily;   1745
Be in your seat when the bell peals shrilly.
Come to class with your homework done,
The sections memorized, each one,
So you are sure nothing's mistook
And no word's said not in the book.   1750
Still, all you hear set down in your notes
As if it came from the Holy Ghost.
STUDENT   No need to say that to me twice,
I realize notes help a lot;
What you've got down in black and white   1755
Goes home with you to a safe place.
MEPHISTO   But your faculty—you've still not told me.
STUDENT   Well, I don't think the law would hold me.
MEPHISTO   I can't blame you, law is no delight.
What's jurisprudence?—a stupid rite   1760
That's handed down, a kind of contagion,
Passed from generation to generation,

---

9. The natural process by which substances are united into a living organism—a name for an
action no one understands.

From people to people, region to region;
What once made sense becomes nonsensical,
And benefaction a bothersome burden.   1765
O grandsons to come, how I do wince for you all!
As for the rights we have from Nature as her heir—
Never a word about *them* will you hear!

STUDENT   I hate the stuff now more than ever!
How lucky I am to have you for adviser.   1770
Perhaps I'll take theology.

MEPHISTO   I shouldn't want to lead you astray,
But it's a science, if you'll allow me to say it,
Where it's easy to lose your way.
There's so much poison hidden in it,   1775
It's very nearly impossible
To tell what's toxic from what's medicinal.
Here again it's safer to choose
One single master and echo his words dutifully—
As a general rule, put your trust in *words*,   1780
They'll guide you safely past doubt and dubiety
Into the Temple of Absolute Certainty.

STUDENT   But shouldn't words convey ideas, a meaning?

MEPHISTO   Of course they should! But why overdo it?
It's exactly when ideas are lacking   1785
Words come in so handy as a substitute.
With words we argue pro and con,
With words invent a whole system.
Believe in words! Have faith in them!
No jot or tittle shall pass from them.   1790

STUDENT   Forgive me, I've another query,
My last one and then I'll go.
Medicine, sir—what might you care to tell me
About that study I should know?
Three years, my God, are terribly short   1795
For so vast a field for the mind to survey;
A pointer or two would provide a start
And advance one quicker on one's way.

MEPHISTO [*Aside*]   Enough of all this academic chatter.
Back again to deviltry!   1800
[*Aloud*]   Medicine's an easy art to master.
Up and down you study the whole world
Only so as to discover
In the end it's all up to the Lord.
Plough your way through all the sciences you please,   1805
Each learns only what he can;
But the man who understands his opportunities,
Him I call a man.
You seem a pretty strapping fellow,
Not one to hang back bashfully.   1810
If you don't doubt yourself, I know,

Nobody else will doubt you, nobody.
Above all learn your way with women
If you mean to practise medicine;
The aches and pains that torture them   1815
From one place only, one, all stem.
Cure there, cure all. Act halfway decent
And you'll find the whole sex acquiescent.
With an M.D. you enjoy great credit,
Your art, they're sure, beats others' arts.   1820
The doctor, when he pays a visit,
For greeting reaches for those parts
It takes a layman years to get at;
You feel her pulse with extra emphasis,
And your arm slipping with an ardent glance   1825
Around her slender waist,
See if it's because she's so tight-laced.

STUDENT   Oh, that's much better—practical, down to earth!
MEPHISTO   All theory, my dear boy, is gray,
And green the golden tree of life.   1830
STUDENT   I swear it seems a dream to me!
Would you permit me, sir, to impose on
Your generous kindness another day
And drink still more draughts of your wisdom?
MEPHISTO   I'm glad to help you in any way.   1835
STUDENT   I mustn't leave without presenting
You my album. Do write something
In it for me, would you?
MEPHISTO   Happily.
   [Writes and hands back the album.]
STUDENT [Reading.]   Eritis sicut Deus, scientes bonum et malum.[1]
   [Closes the book reverently and exits.]
MEPHISTO   Faithfully follow that good old verse,   1840
That favorite line of my aunt's, the snake,
And for all your precious godlikeness,
You'll end up how? A nervous wreck.
   [Enter FAUST.]
FAUST   And now where to?
MEPHISTO   Wherever you like.
First we'll mix with little people, then with great.   1845
The pleasure and the profit you will get
From our course—and never pay tuition for it!
FAUST   But me and my long beard—we're hardly suited
For the fast life. I feel myself defeated
Even before we start. I've never been   1850
A fellow to fit in. Among other men

---

1. A slight alteration of the serpent's words to Eve in Genesis: "Ye shall be as God, knowing good
and evil" (Latin).

I feel so small, so mortified—I freeze.
Oh, in the world I'm always ill at ease!
MEPHISTO   My friend, that's all soon changed, it doesn't matter;
With confidence comes *savoir-vivre*.   1855
FAUST   But how do we get out of here?
Where are your horses, groom and carriage?
MEPHISTO   By air's how we make our departure,
On my cloak—you'll enjoy the voyage.
But take care, on so bold a venture,   1860
You're sparing in the matter of luggage.
I'll heat some gas, that way we'll lift up
Quickly off the face of earth;
If we're light enough we'll rise right up—
I offer my congratulations, sir, on your new life!   1865

AUERBACH'S CELLAR IN LEIPZIG

Drinkers carousing.

FROSCH   Faces glum and glasses empty?
I don't call this much of a party.
You fellows seem wet straw tonight,
Who always used to blaze so bright.
BRANDER   It's your fault—he just sits there, hardly speaks!   1870
Where's the horseplay, where's the dirty jokes?
FROSCH   [*Emptying a glass of wine on his head.*]
There! Both at once!
BRANDER   O horse and swine!
FROSCH   You asked for it, so don't complain.
SIEBEL   Out in the street if you want to punch noses!
—Now take a deep breath and roar out a chorus   1875
In praise of the grape and the jolly god Bacchus.
Come, all together with a rollicking round-o!
ALTMAYER   Stop, stop, man, I'm wounded, cotton, quick, someone
       fetch some,
The terrible fellow has burst me an eardrum!
SIEBEL   Hear the sound rumble above in the vault?   1880
That tells you you're hearing the true bass note.
FROSCH   That's right! Out the door, whoever don't like it!
With a do-re-mi,
ALTMAYER   And a la-ti-do,
FROSCH   We will have us a concert!   1885
       [*Sings.*]
       Our dear Holy Roman Empire,
       How does the damn thing hold together?
BRANDER   Oh, but that's dreadful, and dreadfully sung,
A dreary, disgusting *political* song!
Thank the Lord when you wake each morning   1890
You're not the one must keep the Empire running.

It's a blessing I'm grateful for
To be neither Kaiser nor Chancellor.
But we, too, need a chief for our group,
So let's elect ourselves a pope.   1895
To all of us here I'm sure it's well known
What a man must do to sit on that throne.
FROSCH [*Singing.*]
    Nightingale, fly away, o'er lawn, o'er bower,
    Tell her I love her ten thousand times over.
SIEBEL   Enough of that love stuff, it turns my stomach.   1900
FROSCH   Ten thousand times, though it drives you frantic!
    [*Sings.*]
    Unbar the door, the night is dark!
    Unbar the door, my love, awake!
    Bar up the door now it's daybreak.
SIEBEL   Go on, then, boast about her charms, her favor,   1905
But I will have the latest laugh of all.
She played me false—just wait, she'll play you falser.
A horned imp's what I wish her, straight from Hell,
To dawdle with her in the dust of crossroads,
And may an old goat stinking from the Brocken   1910
Bleat "Goodnight, dearie," to her, galloping homewards.
A fellow made of honest flesh and blood
For a slut like that is much too good.
What kind of love note would I send that scarecrow?—
A beribboned rock tossed through her kitchen window.   1915
BRANDER [*Banging on the table.*]
Good fellows, your attention! None here will deny
I know what should be done and shouldn't at all.
Now we have lovers in our company
Whom we must treat in manner suitable
To their condition, our jollity,   1920
With a song just lately written. So mind the air
And come in on the chorus loud and clear!
    [*He sings.*]
    A rat lived downstairs in the cellar,
    Dined every day on lard and butter,
    His paunch grew round as any burgher's,   1925
    As round as Dr. Martin Luther's.[2]
    The cook put poison down for it,
    Oh, how it groaned, the pangs it felt,
       As if by Cupid smitten.
CHORUS [*Loud and clear.*]
       As if by Cupid smitten!   1930
BRANDER
    It rushed upstairs, it raced outdoors
    And drank from every gutter,

---

2. Martin Luther (1483–1546), German leader of the Protestant Reformation, hence an object
of distaste for Catholics.

It gnawed the woodwork, scratched the floors,
Its fever burned still hotter,
In agony it hopped and squealed   1935
Oh, piteously the the beast appealed,
    As if by Cupid smitten.
CHORUS
    As if by Cupid smitten!
BRANDER
Its torment drove it, in broad day,
Out into the kitchen,   1940
Collapsing on the hearth, it lay
Panting hard and twitching.
But that cruel Borgia smiled with pleasure,
That's it, that's that rat's final seizure,
    As if by Cupid smitten.   1945
CHORUS
    As if by Cupid smitten!
SIEBEL   You find it funny, you coarse louts,
  Oh, quite a stunt, so very cunning,
  To put down poison for poor rats!
BRANDER   You like rats, do you, find them charming?   1950
ALTMAYER   O big of gut and bald of pate!
  Losing out's subdued the oaf;
  What he sees in the bloated rat
  'S the spitting image of himself.
    [FAUST *and* MEPHISTOPHELES *enter.*]
MEPHISTO   What your case calls for, Doctor, first,   1955
  Is some diverting company,
  To teach you life affords some gaiety.
  For these men every night's a feast
  And every day a holiday;
  With little wit but lots of zest   1960
  All spin inside their little orbit
  Like young cats chasing their own tails.
  As long as the landlord grants them credit
  And they are spared a splitting headache,
  They find life good, unburdened by travails. 1965
BRANDER   They're travelers is what your Brander says,
  You can tell it by their foreign ways,
  They've not been here, I'll bet, an hour.
FROSCH   Right, right! My Leipzig's an attraction, how I love her,
  A little Paris spreading light and culture!   1970
SIEBEL   Who might they be? What's your guess?
FROSCH   Leave it to me. I'll fill their glass,
  Gently extract, as you do a baby's tooth,
  All there 's to know about them, the whole truth.
  I'd say we're dealing with nobility,   1975
  They look so proud, so dissatisfied, to me.
BRANDER   They're pitchmen at the Fair, is what I think.
ALTMAYER   Maybe so.

FROSCH   Now watch me go to work.

MEPHISTO [*To* FAUST.]

   These dolts can't ever recognize Old Nick

   Even when he's got them by the neck.   1980

FAUST   Gentlemen, good day.

SIEBEL   Thank you, the same.

    [*Aside, obliquely studying* MEPHISTOPHELES.]

   What the hell, the fellow limps, he's lame![3]

MEPHISTO   We'd like to join you, sirs, if you'll allow it.

   But our landlord's wine looks so-so, I am thinking,

   So the company shall make up for it.   1985

ALTMAYER   Particular, you are, about your drinking?

FROSCH   Fresh from Dogpatch, right? From supper

   On cabbage soup with Goodman Clodhopper?

MEPHISTO   We couldn't stop on this trip, more's the pity!

   But last time he went on so tenderly   1990

   About his Leipzig kith and kin,

   And sent his very best to you, each one.

    [*Bowing to* FROSCH.]

ALTMAYER [*Aside to* FROSCH.]

   Score one for him. He's got some wit.

SIEBEL   A sly one, he is.

FROSCH   Wait, I'll fix him yet!

MEPHISTO   Unless I err, weren't we just now hearing   1995

   Some well-schooled voices joined in choral singing?

   Voices, I am sure, must resonate

   Inside this vault to very fine effect.

FROSCH   You know music professionally, I think.

MEPHISTO   Oh no—the spirit's eager, but the voice is weak.   2000

ALTMAYER   Give us a song!

MEPHISTO   Whatever you'd like to hear.

SIEBEL   The latest, nothing we've heard before.

MEPHISTO   Easily done. We've just come back from Spain,

   Land where the air breathes song, the rivers run wine.

    [*Sings.*]

     Once upon a time a King   2005

       Had a flea, a big one—

FROSCH   Did you hear that? A flea, goddamn!

   I'm all for fleas, myself, I am.

MEPHISTO [*Sings.*]

     Once upon a time a King

       Had a flea, a big one,   2010

     Doted fondly on the thing

       With fatherly affection.

     Calling his tailor in, he said,

       Fetch needles, thread and scissors,

---

3. By tradition, the Devil had a cloven foot, split like a sheep's hoof.

Measure the Baron up for shirts,   2015
    Measure him, too, for trousers.
BRANDER   And make it perfectly clear to the tailor
He must measure exactly, sew perfect stitches,
If he's fond of his head, not the least little error,
Not a wrinkle, you hear, not one, in those breeches!   2020
MEPHISTO
    Glowing satins, gleaming silks
       Now were the flea's attire,
    Upon his chest red ribbons crossed
       And a great star shone like fire,
    In sign of his exalted post   2025
       As the King's First Minister.
    His sisters, cousins, uncles, aunts
       Enjoyed great influence too—
    The bitter torments that that Court's
       Nobility went through!   2030
    And the Queen as well, and her lady's maid,
       Though bitten till delirious,
    Forbore to squash the fleas, afraid
       To incur the royal animus.
    But we free souls, we squash all fleas   2035
       The instant they light on us!
CHORUS [*Loud and clear.*]
    But we free souls, we squash all fleas
       The instant they light on us!
FROSCH   Bravo, bravo! That was fine!
SIEBEL   May every flea's fate be the same!   2040
BRANDER   Between finger and nail, then crack! and they're done for.
ALTMAYER   Long live freedom, long live wine!
MEPHISTO   I'd gladly drink a glass in freedom's honor,
If only your wine was a little better.[4]
SIEBEL   Again! You try, sir, our good humor!   2045
MEPHISTO   I'm sure our landlord wouldn't take it kindly,
For otherwise I'd treat this company
To wine that's wine—straight out of our own cellar.
SIEBEL   Go on, go on, let the landlord be my worry.
FROSCH   You're princes, you are, if you're able   2050
To put good wine upon the table;
But a drop or two, well, that's no trial at all,
To judge right what I need's a real mouthful.
ALTMAYER [*In an undertone.*]   They're from the Rhineland,
I would swear.
MEPHISTO   Let's have an auger, please.   2055
BRANDER   What for?
Don't tell me you've barrels piled outside the door!
ALTMAYER   There's a basket of tools—look, over there.

---

4. That is, not cursed.

MEPHISTO [*Picking out an auger, to* FROSCH.]
  Now gentlemen—name what you'll have, please?
FROSCH   What do you mean? We have a choice?
MEPHISTO   Whatever you wish, I'll produce. 2060
ALTMAYER [*To* FROSCH.]   Licking his lips already, he is!
FROSCH   Fine, fine! For me—a Rhine wine any day,
  The best stuff's from the Fatherland, I say.
MEPHISTO [*Boring a hole in the table edge at* FROSCH'S *place.*]
  Some wax to stop the holes with, quick!
ALTMAYER   Hell, it's just a sideshow trick. 2065
MEPHISTO [*To* BRANDER.]
  And you?
BRANDER   The best champagne you have, friend, please,
  With lots of sparkle, lots of fizz.

     [MEPHISTOPHELES *goes round the table boring holes at all the places,*
     which one of the drinkers stops with bungs made of wax.]

  You can't always avoid what's foreign;
  About pleasure I'm nonpartisan. 2070
  A man who's a true German can't stand Frenchmen,
  But he can stand their wine, oh how he can!
SIEBEL [*As* MEPHISTOPHELES *reaches his place.*]
  I confess your dry wines don't
  Please my palate, I'll take sweet.
MEPHISTO   Tokay[5] for you! Coming up shortly! 2075
ALTMAYER   No, gentlemen! Look at me honestly,
  The whole thing's meant to make fools of us.
MEPHISTO   Come on, my friend, I'm not so obtuse!
  Trying something like that on you would be risky.
  So what's your pleasure, I'm waiting—speak! 2080
ALTMAYER   Whatever you like, just don't take all week.
MEPHISTO [*All the holes are now bored and stopped; gesturing grotesquely*]
  Grapes grow on the vine,
  Horns on the head of the goat,
  O vinestock of hard wood,
  O juice of the tender grape! 2085
  And a wooden table shall,
  When summoned, yield wine as well!
  O depths of Nature, mysterious, secret,
  Here is a miracle—if you believe it!
  Now pull the plugs, all, drink and be merry! 2090
ALL [*Drawing the bungs and the wine each drinker asked for gushing*
  into his glass.]
  Sweet fountain, flowing for us only!
MEPHISTO   But take good care you don't spill any.
  [*They drink glass after glass.*]

5. A sweet Hungarian wine.

ALL [*Singing.*]
   How lovely everything is, I'm dreaming!
   Like cannibals having a feast,
   Like pigs in a pen full of slops!   2095
MEPHISTO The people feel free, what a time they're having!
FAUST I'd like to go now—nincompoops!
MEPHISTO Before we do, you must admire
  Their swinishness in its full splendor.
SIEBEL [*Spilling wine on the floor, where it bursts into flame.*]
  All Hell's afire, I burn, I burn!   2100
MEPHISTO [*Conjuring the flame.*]
  Peace, my own element, down, down!
   [*To the drinkers.*]
  Only a pinch, for the present, of the purgatorial fire.
SIEBEL What's going on here? For this you'll pay dear!
  You don't seem to know the kind of men you have here.
FROSCH Once is enough for that kind of business!   2105
ALTMAYER Throw him out on his ear, but quietly, no fuss!
SIEBEL You've got your nerve, trying out upon us
  Stuff like that—damned hocus-pocus!
MEPHISTO Quiet, you tub of guts!
SIEBEL   Bean pole, you!
  Now he insults us. I know what to do.   2110
BRANDER A taste of our fists is what: one-two, one-two.
ALTMAYER [*Drawing a bung and flames shooting out at him.*]
  I'm on fire, I'm on fire!
SIEBEL   It's witchcraft, no mistaking!
  Stick him, the rogue, he's free for the taking!
   [*They draw their knives and fall on* MEPHISTOPHELES.]
MEPHISTO [*Gesturing solemnly.*]
  False words, false shapes
  Addle wits, muddle senses!   2115
  Let here and otherwheres
  Exchange places!
   [*All stand astonished and gape at each other.*]
ALTMAYER Where am I? What a lovely country!
FROSCH Such vineyards! Do my eyes deceive me?
SIEBEL And grapes you only need to reach for!   2120
BRANDER Just look inside this green arbor!
  What vines, what grapes! Cluster on cluster!
   [*He seizes* SIEBEL *by the nose. The others do the same to each
   other and raise their knives.*]
MEPHISTO Unspell, illusion, eyes and ears!
  —Take note the Devil's a jester, my dears!
   [*He vanishes with* FAUST; *the drinkers recoil from each other.*]
SIEBEL What's happened?   2125
ALTMAYER   What?
FROSCH   Was that your nose?
BRANDER [*To* SIEBEL.] And I'm still holding on to yours!

ALTMAYER   The shock I felt—in every limb!
  Get me a chair, I'm caving in.
FROSCH   But what the devil was it, tell me.
SIEBEL   Only let me catch that scoundrel,   2130
  He won't go home alive, believe me!
ALTMAYER   I saw him, horsed upon a barrel,
  Vault straight out through the cellar door—
  My feet feel leaden, so unnatural.
      [*Turning toward the table.*]
  Well—maybe some wine's still trickling here.   2135
SIEBEL   Lies, all, lies! Deluded! Dupes!
FROSCH   I was drinking wine, I'd swear.
BRANDER   But what was it with all those grapes?
ALTMAYER   Now try and tell me, you know-it-alls,
  There's no such thing as miracles!   2140

WITCH'S KITCHEN

A low hearth, and on the fire a large cauldron. In the steam rising up from it, various figures can be glimpsed. A SHE-APE *is seated by the cauldron, skimming it to keep it from boiling over. The* MALE *with their young crouches close by, warming himself. Hanging on the walls and from the ceiling are all sorts of strange objects, the household gear of a witch.*

FAUST, MEPHISTOPHELES.

FAUST   Why, it's revolting, all this crazy witchery!
  Are you telling me I'll be born a new man
  Here amid this lunatic confusion?
  Is an ancient hag the doctor who will cure me?
  And the mess that that beast's boiling, that's the remedy   2145
  To cancel thirty years, unbow my back?
  If you can do no better, the outlook's black
  For me, the hopes I nursed are dead already.
  Hasn't man's venturesome mind, instructed by Nature,
  Discovered some sort of potent elixer?   2150
MEPHISTO   Now you're speaking sensibly!
  There *is* a natural way to recover your youth;
  But that's another business entirely
  And not your sort of thing, is my belief.
FAUST   No, no, come on, I want to hear it.   2155
MEPHISTO   All right. It's simple: you don't need to worry
  About money, doctors, necromancy.
  Go out into the fields right now, this minute,
  Start digging and hoeing with never a stop or a respite.
  Confine yourself and your thoughts to the narrowest sphere, 2160
  Eat nothing but the plainest kind of fare,
  Live with the cattle as cattle, don't think it too low
  To spread your own dung on the fields that you plow.
  So there you have it, the sane way, the healthy,
  To keep yourself young till the age of eighty!   2165

FAUST   Yes, not my sort of thing, I'm afraid,
   Humbling myself to work with a spade;
   So straitened a life would never suit me.

MEPHISTO   So it's back to the witch, my friend, are we?

FAUST   That horrible hag—no one else will do?   2170
   Why can't *you* concoct the brew?

MEPHISTO   A nice thing that, to waste the time of the Devil
   When his every moment is claimed by the business of evil!
   Please understand. Not only skill and science
   Are called for here, but also patience: 2175
   A mind must keep at it for years, very quietly,
   Only time can supply the mixture its potency.
   Such a deal of stuff goes into the process,
   All very strange, all so secret.
   The Devil, it's true, taught her how to do it,   2180
   But it's no business of his to brew it.
      [*Seeing the* APES.]
   See here, those creatures, aren't they pretty!
   That one's the housemaid, that one's the flunkey.
      [*To the* APES.]
   Madam is not at home, it seems?

APES   Flew up the chimney   2185
   To dine out with friends.

MEPHISTO   And her feasting, how long does it usually take her?

APES   As long as we warm our paws by the fire.

MEPHISTO [*To* FAUST.]   What do you think of this elegant folk?

FAUST   Noisome enough to make me puke.   2190

MEPHISTO   Well, just this sort of causerie
   Is what I find most pleases me.
      [*To the* APES.]
   Tell me, you ugly things, oh do,
   What's that you're stirring there, that brew?

APES   Beggars' soup, it's thin stuff, goes down easy.   2195

MEPHISTO   Your public's assured—they like what's wishy-washy.

HE-APE [*Sidling up to* MEPHISTOPHELES *fawningly*.]
   Oh roll the dice quick,
   How I long to be rich!
   I need some good luck,
   It's wrong, so few have so much.   2200
   With a purse full of thaler,
   An ape passes for clever.

MEPHISTO   How very happy that monkey would be
   If he could buy chances in the lottery.
      [*Meanwhile the young* APES *have been rolling around a big ball
      to which they now give a push forward.*]

HE-APE   The world, sirs, behold it!   2205
   Down goes the upside,
   Up goes the downside,
   And never a respite.
   Touch it, it'll ring,

It's like glass, fractures easily.   2210
When all's said and done,
A hollow, void thing.
Here it shines brightly,
Here, even brighter.
—Oops, ain't I nimble!   2215
But you, son, be careful
And keep a safe distance,
Or it's your last day.
The thing's made of clay,
A knock, and it's fragments.   2220
MEPHISTO   What is that sieve for?
HE-APE [*Taking it down.*]
If you came here to thieve,
It would be my informer.
[*He scampers across to the* SHE-APE *and has her look through it.*]
Look through the sieve!
Now say, do you know him?   2225
Or you don't dare name him?
MEPHISTO [*Approaching the fire.*]   And this pot over here?
APES
Oh, you're a blockhead, sir—
Don't know what a pot's for!
Nor a kettle neither.
MEPHISTO   What a rude creature!   2230
HE-APE
Here, take this duster,
Sit down in the armchair.
[*Presses* MEPHISTOPHELES *down in the chair.*]
FAUST [*Who meanwhile has been standing in front of a mirror,*
going forward to peer into it from close up and then stepping back.]
What do I see? What a marvellous vision
Shows itself in this magic glass!
Love, lend me your wings, your swiftest, to pass   2235
Through the air to the heaven she must dwell in!
Oh dear, unless I stay fixed to this spot,
If I dare to move nearer even a bit,
Mist blurs the vision and obscures her quite.
Woman unrivaled, beauty absolute!   2240
Can such things be, a creature so lovely?
The body so indolently stretched out there
Surely epitomizes all that is heavenly.
Can such a marvel inhabit down here?
MEPHISTO   Of course when a god's sweated six whole days,   2245
And himself cries bravo in his works praise,
You can be certain the results are first class;
Look all you want now in the glass,
But I can find you just such a prize,
And lucky the man, his bliss is assured,   2250
Who can bring home such a beauty to his bed and board.

[FAUST *continues to stare into the mirror, while*
MEPHISTOPHELES, *leaning back comfortably in the armchair and toying
with the feather duster, talks on.*]
Here I sit like a king on a throne,
Scepter in hand, all I'm lacking's my crown.
APES [*Who have been performing all sorts of queer, involved movements,
with loud cries bring* MEPHISTOPHELES *a crown.*]
    Here, your majesty,
    If you would,   2255
    Glue up the crown
    With sweat and blood!
    [*Their clumsy handling of the crown causes it to break in two,
    and they cavort around with the pieces.*]
    Oh, oh, now it's broken!
    We look and we listen,
    We chatter, scream curses,   2260
    And make up our verses—
FAUST [*Still gazing raptly into the mirror.*]
  Good God, how my mind reels, it's going to snap!
MEPHISTO [*Nodding toward the* APES.]
  My own head's starting to spin like a top.
APES
    And if by some fluke
    The words happen to suit   2265
    Then the rhyme makes a thought!
FAUST [*As above.*]   I feel like my insides are on fire!
  Let's go, we've got to get out of here.
MEPHISTO [*Keeping his seat.*]   They tell the truth, these poets do,
  You've got to give the creatures their due.   2270
    [*The cauldron, neglected by the* SHE-APE, *starts to boil over, causing
    a great tongue of flame to shoot up in the chimney.* THE WITCH *comes
    in riding down the flame, shrieking hideously.*]
THE WITCH   It hurts, it hurts!
  Monkeys, apes, incompetent brutes!
  Forgetting the pot and singeing your mistress—
  The servants I have! Utterly useless!
    [*Catching sight of* FAUST *and* MEPHISTOPHELES.]
  What's this? What's this?   2275
  Who are you? Explain!
  What's your business?
  Got in by chicane!
  Hellfires parch and make
  Your bones crack, your bones break!   2280
  [*She plunges the spoon into the cauldron and scatters fire
  over* FAUST, MEPHISTOPHELES *and the* APES. *The apes whine.*]
MEPHISTOPHELES [*Turning the duster upside down and hitting out
violently among the glasses and jars with the butt end.*]
    In pieces, in pieces,
    Spilt soup and smashed dishes!
    It's all in fun, really—

Beating time, you old carcass,
To your melody.   2285
        [THE WITCH *starts back in rage and fear.*]
Can't recognize me, rattlebones, old donkey, you?
Can't recognize your lord and master?
Why I don't chop up you and your monkey crew
Into the littlest bits and pieces is a wonder!
No respect at all for my red doublet?   2290
And my cock's feather means nothing to you, beldam?
Is my face masked, or can you plainly see it?
Must I tell *you* of all people who I am?
THE WITCH   Oh sir, forgive my discourteous salute!
But I look in vain for your cloven foot,   2295
And your two ravens, where are they?
MEPHISTO   All right, this time you're let off—I remember,
It's been so long since we've seen each other.
Also, the world's grown so cultured today,
Even the Devil's been swept up in it.   2300
The northern bogey has made his departure,
No horns now, no tail, to make people shiver,
And as for my hoof, though I can't do without it,
Socially it would raise too many eyebrows,
So like a lot of other young fellows   2305
I've padded my calves to try and conceal it.
THE WITCH [*Dancing with glee.*]
I'm out of my mind with delight, I swear!
My lord Satan's dropped out of the air.
MEPHISTO   Woman, that name—I forbid you to use it.
THE WITCH   Why not? Whyever now refuse it?   2310
MEPHISTO   Since God knows when, it belongs to mythology,
But that's hardly improved the morals of humanity.
The Evil One's no more, evil ones more than ever.
Address me as Baron, that will do,
A gentleman of rank like any other.   2315
And if you doubt my blood is blue,
See, here's my house's arms, the noblest ever!
        [*He makes an indecent gesture.*]
THE WITCH [*Laughing excessively.*]
Ha, ha! It's you, I see now, it's clear—
The same old rascal you always were!
MEPHISTO [*To* FAUST.]   Observe, friend, my diplomacy   2320
And learn the art of witch-mastery.
THE WITCH   Gentlemen, now what's your pleasure?
MEPHISTO   A generous glass of your famous liquor.
But please, let it be from your oldest supply;
It doubles in strength as the years multiply.   2325
THE WITCH   At once! Here I've got, as it happens, a bottle
From which I myself every now and then tipple,
And what is more, it's lost all its stink.

I'll gladly pour you out a cup.
  [*Under her breath.*]
But if the fellow's unprepared, the drink   2330
Might kill him, you know, before an hour's up.
MEPHISTO I know the man well, he'll thrive upon it.
I wish him the best your kitchen affords.
Now draw your circle, say the words,
And pour him out a brimming goblet.   2335
  [*Making bizarre gestures,* THE WITCH *draws a circle and sets*
  down an assortment of strange objects inside it. All the glasses
  start to ring and the pots to resound, providing a kind of musical
  accompaniment. Last of all, she brings out a great tome and
  stands the APES *in the circle to serve as a lectern and to hold up*
  the torches. Then she signals FAUST *to approach.*]
FAUST [*To* MEPHISTOPHELES.]
What's to be hoped for from this, would you tell me?
That junk of hers, her waving her arms crazily,
All the vulgar tricks she is performing,
Well do I know them, don't find them amusing.
MEPHISTO Jokes, just jokes! It's not all that serious;   2340
Really, you're being much too difficult.
Of course hocus-pocus, she's a sorceress—
How else can her potion produce a result?
  [*He presses* FAUST *inside the circle.*]
THE WITCH [*Declaiming from the book, with great emphasis.*]
  Listen and learn!
  From one make ten,   2345
  And let two go,
  And add three in,
  And you are rich.
  Now cancel four!
  From five and six,   2350
  So says the witch,
  Make seven and eight—
  Thus all's complete.
  And nine is one,
  And ten is none,   2355
  And that's the witch's one-times-one.
FAUST I think the old woman's throwing a fit.
MEPHISTO We're nowhere near the end of it.
I know the book, it's all like that.
The time I've wasted over it!   2360
For a thoroughgoing paradox is what
Bemuses fools and wise men equally.
The trick's old as the hills yet it's still going strong:
With Three-in-One and One-in-Three[6]
Lies are sown broadcast, truth may go hang.   2365

---

6. The Christian doctrine of the Trinity.

Who questions professors about the claptrap they teach—
Who wants to debate and dispute with a fool?
People dutifully think, hearing floods of fine speech,
It can't be such big words mean nothing at all.

THE WITCH [*Continuing.*]
    The power of science   2370
    From the whole world kept hidden!
    Who don't have a thought,
    To them it is given
    Unbidden, unsought,
    It's theirs without sweat.   2375

FAUST   Did you hear that, my God, what nonsense,
It's giving me a headache, phew!
It makes me think I'm listening to
A hundred thousand fools in chorus.

MEPHISTO   Enough, enough, O excellent Sibyl!   2380
Bring on the potion, fill the stoup,
Your drink won't give my friend here trouble,
He's earned his Ph.D. in many a bout.
    [THE WITCH *very ceremoniously pours the potion into a bowl;*
    when FAUST *raises it to his lips, a low flame plays over it.*]
Drink, now drink, no need to diddle,
It'll put you into a fine glow.   2385
When you've got a sidekick in the Devil,
Why should some fire frighten you so?
    [THE WITCH *breaks the circle and* FAUST *steps out.*]
Now let's be off, you mustn't dally.

THE WITCH   I hope that little nip, sir, hits the spot!

MEPHISTO [*To* THE WITCH.]   Madam, thanks. If I can help *you* out,   2390
Don't fail, upon Walpurgis Night,[7] to ask me.

THE WITCH [*To* FAUST.]   Here is a song, sir, carol it now and then,
You'll find it assists the medicine.

MEPHISTO   Come away quick! You must do as I say.
To soak up the potion body and soul,   2395
A man's got to sweat a bucketful.
And after, I'll teach you the gentleman's way
Of wasting your time expensively.
Soon yours the delight outdelights all things—
Boy Cupid astir in you, stretching his wings.   2400

FAUST   One more look in the mirror, let me—
That woman was inexpressibly lovely!

MEPHISTO   No, no, soon enough, before you, vis-à-vis,
    Yours the fairest of fair women, I guarantee.
    [*Aside.*] With that stuff in him, old Jack will   2405
    Soon see a Helen in every Jill.

---

7. May Day Eve (April 30), when witches are supposed to assemble on the Brocken, the highest peak in the Harz Mountains, which are in central Germany.

A STREET

FAUST. MARGARETE *passing by.*

FAUST   Pretty lady, here is my arm—
  Would you allow me to see you home?
MARGARETE   I'm neither pretty nor a lady,
  And I can find my way unaided.   2410
        [*She escapes his arm and passes by.*]
FAUST   By God, what a lovely girl,
  I've never seen her like, a pearl!
  A good girl, too, and quick-witted,
  Her behavior modest and yet spirited,
  Those red, ripe lips and cheeks abloom   2415
  Will haunt me till the crack of doom!
  The way she looked down, so demure,
  Had for me such allure!
  And bringing me up short, quite speechless—
  Oh that was charming, that was priceless!   2420
        [*Enter* MEPHISTOPHELES.]
FAUST   Get me that girl, do you hear, you must!
MEPHISTO   What girl?
FAUST   The one who just went past.
MEPHISTO   Oh, her. She's just been to confession
  To be absolved of all her sins.
  I sidled near the box to listen: 2425
  She could have spared herself her pains,
  She is the soul of innocence
  And has no reason, none at all,
  To visit the confessional.
  Her kind is too much for me.   2430
FAUST   She's over fourteen, isn't she?
MEPHISTO   Well, listen to him, an instant Don Juan,[8]
  Demands every favor, his shyness all gone,
  Conceitedly thinks it offends his honor
  To leave unplucked every pretty flower.   2435
  But it doesn't go so easy always.
FAUST   Dear Doctor of What's Right and Proper,
  Spare me your lectures, I can do without.
  Let me tell you it straight out:
  If I don't hold that darling creature   2440
  Tight in my arms this very night,
  We're through, we two, come twelve midnight.
MEPHISTO   Impossible! That's out of the question!
  I must have two weeks at least
  To spy out a propitious occasion.   2445

---

8. The German reads *Hans Liederlich*, meaning a profligate because *liederlich* means "careless"
or "dissolute."

FAUST   With several hours or so, at the most,
   I could seduce her handily—
   Don't need the Devil to pimp for me.
MEPHISTO   You're talking like a Frenchman now.
   Calm down, there's no cause for vexation.   2450
   You'll find that instant gratification
   Disappoints; if you allow
   For compliments and billets doux,
   Whisperings and rendezvous,
   The pleasure's felt so much more keenly.   2455
   Italian novels teach you exactly.
FAUST   I've no use for your slow-paced courting;
   My appetite needs no supporting.
MEPHISTO   Please, I'm being serious.
   With such a pretty little miss   2460
   You mustn't be impetuous
   And assault the fortress frontally.
   What's called for here is strategy.
FAUST   Something of hers, do you hear, I require!
   Come, show me the way to the room she sleeps in,   2465
   Get me a scarf, a glove, a ribbon,
   A garter with which to feed my desire!
MEPHISTO   To prove to you my earnest intention
   By every means to further your passion,
   Not losing a minute, without delay,   2470
   I'll take you to her room today.
FAUST   I'll see her, yes? And have her?
MEPHISTO   No!
   She'll be at a neighbor's—you *must* go slow!
   Meanwhile alone there, in her room,
   You can breathe in her own person's perfume   2475
   And dream of the delights to come.
FAUST   Can we start now?
MEPHISTO   Too soon! Be patient!
FAUST   Then find me a pretty thing for a present.

                                    [*Exit.*]

MEPHISTO   Presents already? The man's proving a lover!
   Now for his gift. I know there's treasure   2480
   Buried in many an out-of-the-way corner.
   Off I go to reconnoiter!

EVENING

A small room, very neat and clean.

MARGARETE [*As she braids her hair and puts it up.*]
   I'd give a lot to know, I would.
   Who the gentleman was today.
   He seemed a fine man, decent, good,   2485
   And from a noble house, I'm sure;

It shows on him as plain as day.
And so bold! Who else would dare?

                                    [*Exit.*]
      [MEPHISTOPHELES, FAUST.]
MEPHISTO   Come in now, in!—but take care, softly.
FAUST [*After a silent interval.*]   Leave, please leave, I'd like
   to be alone.   2490
MEPHISTO [*Sniffing around.*]   Not every girl keeps things so clean.
                                    [*Exit.*]
FAUST   Welcome, evening's twilight gloom,
   Stealing through this holy room.
   Possess my heart, O love's sweet anguish,
   That lives in hope, in hope must languish   2495
   Stillness reigns here, breathing quietly
   Peace, good order and contentment—
   What riches in this poverty,
   What bliss there is in this confinement!
      [*He flings himself into a leather armchair by the bed.*]
   Receive me as in generations past   2500
   You received the happy and distressed;
   How often, I know, children crowded around
   This chair where their grandfather sat enthroned.
   Perhaps my darling too, a round-cheeked child,
   Grateful for her Christmas present, held   2505
   Reverentially his shrunken hand.
   I feel, dear girl, where you are all is comfort,
   Where you are order, goodness all abound;
   Maternally instructed by your spirit,
   Daily you spread the clean cloth on the table,   2510
   Sprinkle the sand on the floor so evenly[9]—
   O lovely hand! Hand of a lovely angel
   That's made of this cottage something heavenly.
   And here—!
      [*He lifts a bed curtain.*]
          Why am I seized with awe-struck bliss?
   Here I could linger hour after hour.   2515
   Nature! Shaping here in dreaming peace
   The indwelling angel out of the budding creature.
   Here warm life in her tender bosom swelled,
   Here by a pure and holy weaving
   Of the strands, was revealed   2520
   The celestial being.

   But me? What is it brought me here?
   See how shaken I am, how nervous!
   What do I want? Why is my heart so anxious?
   Poor Faust, I hardly know you any more.   2525

---

9. Floors were sprinkled with sand after cleaning.

Has this room put a spell on me?
I came here burning up with lust,
And melt with love now, helplessly.
Are we blown about by every gust?

And if she came in now, this minute,   2530
How I would pay dear, I would, for it.
The big talker, Herr Professor,
Would dwindle to nothing, grovel before her.

MEPHISTO [*Entering.*]   Hurry! I saw her, she's coming up.

FAUST   Hurry indeed, I'll never come here again!   2535

MEPHISTO   Here's a jewel box I snatched up
When I—but who cares how or when.
Put it in the closet there,
She'll jump for joy when she comes on it.
It's got a number of choice things in it,   2540
Meant for another—but I declare,
Girls are girls, they're all the same,
The only thing that matters is the game.

FAUST   Should I, I wonder?

MEPHISTO   *Should* you, you say!
Do you mean to keep it for yourself?   2545
If what you're after's treasure, pelf,
Then I have wasted my whole day,
Been put to a lot of needless bother.
I hope you aren't some awful miser—
After all my head-scratching, scheming, labor!   2550
        [*He puts the box in the closet and shuts it.*]
Come on, let's go!
Our aim? Your darling's favor,
So you may do with her as you'd like to do.
And you do what?—only gape,
As if going into your lecture hall,   2555
There before you in human shape
Stood physics and metaphysics, old and stale.
                                              [*Exit.*]

MARGARETE [*With a lamp.*]   How close, oppressive it's in here.
        [*She opens the window.*]
And yet outside it isn't warm.
I feel, I don't know why, so queer—   2560
I wish Mother would come home.
I shivering so in every limb.
What a foolish, frightened girl I am!
        [*She sings as she undresses.*]
        There was a king in Thule,[1]

---

1. The fabled *ultima Thule* of Latin literature—those distant lands just beyond the reach of every explorer. Goethe wrote the bal-lad in 1774; it was published in 1782 and set to music by several composers.

No truer man drank up, 2565
To whom his mistress, dying,
Gave a golden cup.

Nothing he held dearer.
Amid the feasting's noise
Each time he drained the beaker 2570
Tears started in his eyes.

And when death knocked, he tallied
His towns and treasure up,
Yielded his heirs all gladly,
All except the cup. 2575

In the great hall of his fathers,
In the castle by the sea,
He and his knights sat down to
Their last revelry.

Up stood the old carouser, 2580
A last time knew wine's warmth,
Then pitched his beloved beaker
Down into the gulf.

He saw it fall and founder,
Deep in the sea it sank, 2585
His eyes grew dim and never
Another drop he drank.
[*She opens the closet to put her clothes away and sees the jewel box.*]
How did this pretty box get here?
I locked the closet, I'm quite sure.
Whatever's in the box? Maybe 2590
Mother took it in pledge today.
And there's the little key on a ribbon.
I think I'd like to open it.
—Look at all this, God in Heaven!
I've never seen the like of it! 2595
Jewels! And *such* jewels, that a fine lady
Might wear on a great holiday.
How would the necklace look on me?
Who is it owns these wonderful things?
[*She puts the jewelry on and stands in front of the mirror.*]
I wish they were mine, these lovely earrings! 2600
When you put them on, you're changed completely.
What good's your pretty face, your youth?
Nice to have but little worth.
Men praise you, do it half in pity,
The thing on their mind is money, money. 2605
Gold is their god, all,
Oh us poor people!

OUT WALKING

FAUST *strolling up and down, thinking. To him* MEPHISTOPHELES.

MEPHISTO   By true love cruelly scorned! By Hellfire fierce and fiery!
  If only I could think of worse to swear by!
FAUST   What's eating you, now what's the trouble? 2610
  Such a face I've not seen till today.
MEPHISTO   The Devil take me, that's what I would say,
  If it didn't so happen I'm the Devil.
FAUST   Are you in your right mind—behaving
  Like a madman, wildly raving? 2615
MEPHISTO   The jewels I got for Gretchen,[2] just imagine—
  Every piece a damned priest's stolen!
  The minute her mother saw them, she
  Began to tremble fearfully.
  The woman has a nose! It's stuck 2620
  Forever in her prayerbook;
  She knows right off, by the smell alone,
  If something's sacred or profane;
  One whiff of the jewelry was enough
  To tell her something's wrong with the stuff. 2625
  My child—she cried—and listen well to me,
  All property obtained unlawfully
  Does body and soul a mortal injury.
  These jewels we'll consecrate to the Blessed Virgin,
  And for reward have showers of manna from Heaven. 2630
  Our little Margaret pouted, loath—
  Why look a gift horse[3] in the mouth?
  And surely the one who gave her it
  So generously, was hardly wicked.
  Her mother sent for the priest, and he, 2635
  Seeing how the land lay,
  Was mightily pleased. You've done, he said,
  Just as you should, mother and maid.
  Who overcometh, is repaid.
  The Church's stomach's very capacious, 2640
  Gobbles up whole realms, everything precious,
  Nor once suffers qualms, not even belches.
  The Church alone, dear sister, God has named
  Receiver of goods unlawfully obtained.
FAUST   That's the way the whole world over, 2645
  From a king to a Jew, so all do, ever.
MEPHISTO   So then he pockets brooches, chains and rings
  As if they were quite ordinary things,
  And gives the women as much of a thank-you

2. Diminutive of the German *Margarete*. She is given this name through much of the play.
3. Like the wooden horse in which Greek sol- diers entered Troy to capture it; an emblem of potential treachery.

As a body gets for a mouldy potato,   2650
  In Heaven, he says, you'll be compensated—
  And makes off leaving them feeling elevated.
FAUST   And Gretchen?
MEPHISTO   Sits there restlessly,
  Her mind confused, her will uncertain,
  Thinks about jewels night and day,   2655
  Even more about her unknown patron.
FAUST   I can't bear that she should suffer.
  Find her new ones immediately!
  Poor stuff, those others, hardly suit her.
MEPHISTO   Oh yes indeed! With a snap of the fingers!   2660
FAUST   Do what I say, march, man—how he lingers!
  Insinuate yourself with her neighbor!
  Damn it, devil, you move so sluggishly!
  Fetch Gretchen new and better jewelry!
MEPHISTO   Yes, yes, just as you wish, Your Majesty.   2665

                           [*Exit* FAUST.]

A lovesick fool! To amuse his girl he'd blow up
  Sun, moon, stars, the whole damn shop.

THE NEIGHBOR'S HOUSE

MARTHE [*Alone.*]   May God forgive that man of mine,
  He's done me wrong—disappeared
  Into the night without a word   2670
  And left me here to sleep alone.
  I never gave him cause for grief
  But loved him as a faithful wife.
    [*She weeps.*]
  Suppose he's dead—oh I feel hopeless!
  If only I had an official notice.   2675
    [*Enter* MARGARETE.]
MARGARETE   Frau Marthe!
MARTHE   Gretel, what's wrong, tell me!
MARGARETE   I feel so weak I'm near collapse!
  Just now I found another box
  Inside my closet. Ebony,
  And such things in it, much more splendid   2680
  Than the first ones, I'm dumbfounded!
MARTHE   Never a word to your mother about it,
  Or the priest will have all the next minute.
MARGARETE   Just look at this, and this, and this here!
MARTHE [*Decking her out in the jewels.*]
  Oh, what a lucky girl you are!   2685
MARGARETE   But I mustn't be seen in the streets with such jewelry,
  And never in church. Oh, it's too cruel!
MARTHE   Come over to me whenever you're able,
  Here you can wear them without worry,

March back and forth in front of the mirror—   2690
Won't we enjoy ourselves together!
And when it's a holiday, some such occasion,
You can start wearing them, with discretion.
First a necklace, then a pearl earring,
Your mother'll never notice a thing.   2695
And if she does we'll think of something.

MARGARETE   Who put the jewelry in my closet?
There's something that's not right about it.
        [*A knock.*]
Dear God above, can that be Mother?

MARTHE [*Peeping through the curtain.*]
Please come in!—No, it's a stranger.   2700
        [*Enter* MEPHISTOPHELES.]

MEPHISTO   With your permission, my good women!
I beg you to excuse the intrusion.
        [*Steps back deferentially from* MARGARETE.]
I'm looking for Frau Marthe Schwerdtlein.

MARTHE   I'm her. And what have you to say, sir?

MEPHISTO [*Under his breath to her.*]
Now I know who you are, that's enough.   2705
You have a lady under your roof,
I'll go away and come back later.

MARTHE [*Aloud.*]   Goodness, child, you won't believe me,
What the gentleman thinks is, you're a lady!

MARGARETE   A poor girl's what I am, no more.   2710
The gentleman's kind—I thank you, sir.
These jewels don't belong to me.

MEPHISTO   Ah, it's not just the jewelry,
It's the Fräulein herself, so clear-eyed, serene.
—So delighted I'm allowed to remain.   2715

MARTHE   Why are you here, if you'll pardon the question?

MEPHISTO   I wish my news were pleasanter.
Don't blame me, the messenger:
Your husband's dead. He sent his affection.

MARTHE   The good man's dead, gone, departed?   2720
Then I'll die too. Oh, I'm broken-hearted!

MARGARETE   Marthe dear, it's too violent, your sorrow!

MEPHISTO   Hear the sad story I've come to tell you.

MARGARETE   As long as I live I'll never love, no,
It would kill me with grief to lose my man so.   2725

MEPHISTO   Joy's latter end is sorrow—and sorrow's joy.

MARTHE   Tell me how the dear man died.

MEPHISTO   He's buried in Padua, beside
The blessed saint, sweet Anthony,
In hallowed ground where he can lie   2730
In rest eternal, quietly.

MARTHE   And nothing else, sir, that is all?

MEPHISTO   A last request. He enjoins you solemnly:

Let three hundred masses be sung for his soul!
As for anything else, my pocket's empty. 2735
MARTHE What! No gold coin, jewel, souvenir,
Such as every journeyman keeps in his wallet,
And would sooner go hungry and beg than sell it?
MEPHISTO Nothing, I'm sorry to say, Madam dear.
However—he never squandered his money, 2740
And he sincerely regretted his sins,
Regretted even more he was so unlucky.
MARGARETE Why must so many be so unhappy!
I'll pray for him often, sing requiems.
MEPHISTO What a lovable creature, there's none dearer! 2745
What you should have now, right away,
Is a good husband. It's true what I say.
MARGARETE Oh no, it's not time yet, that must come later.
MEPHISTO If not now a husband, meanwhile a lover.
What blessing from Heaven, which one of life's charms 2750
Rivals holding a dear thing like you in one's arms.
MARGARETE With us people here it isn't the custom.
MEPHISTO Custom or not, it's what's done and by more than some.
MARTHE Go on with your story, sir, go on!
MEPHISTO He lay on a bed of half-rotten straw, 2755
Better at least than a dunghill, and there
He died as a Christian, knowing well
Much remained outstanding on his bill.
"Oh how," he cried, "I hate myself!
To abandon my trade, desert my wife! 2760
It kills me even to think of it.
If only she would forgive and forget!"
MARTHE [*Weeping.*] I did, long ago! He's forgiven, dear man.
MEPHISTO "But she's more to blame, God knows, than I am."
MARTHE Liar! How shameless! At death's very door! 2765
MEPHISTO His mind wandered as the end drew near,
If I'm anything of a connoisseur here.
"No pleasure," he said, "no good times, nor anything nice;
First getting children, then getting them fed,
By fed meaning lots more things than bread. 2770
With never a moment for having my bite in peace."
MARTHE How could he forget my love and loyalty,
My hard work day and night, the drudgery!
MEPHISTO He didn't forget, he remembered all tenderly.
"When we set sail from Malta's port," he said, 2775
"For wife and children fervently I prayed.
And Heaven, hearing, smiled down kindly,
For we captured a Turkish vessel, stuffed
With the Sultan's treasure. How we rejoiced!
Our courage being recompensed, 2780
I left the ship with a fatter purse
Than ever I'd owned before in my life."

MARTHE   Treasure! Do you think he buried it?
MEPHISTO   Who knows what's become of it?
  In Naples, where he wandered about,   2785
  A pretty miss with a kind heart
  Showed the stranger such good will
  Till the day he died he felt it still.
MARTHE   The villain! Robbing his children, his wife!
  And for all his misery, dire need,   2790
  He would never give up his scandalous life.
MEPHISTO   Well, he's been paid, the man is dead.
  If I were in your shoes, my dear,
  I'd mourn him decently a year
  And meanwhile keep an eye out for another.   2795
MARTHE   Dear God, I'm sure it won't be easy
  To find, on this earth, his successor;
  So full of jokes he was, so jolly!
  But he was restless, always straying,
  Loved foreign women, foreign wine,   2800
  And how he loved, drat him, dice-playing!
MEPHISTO   Oh well, I'm sure things worked out fine
  If he was equally forgiving.
  With such an arrangement, why, I swear
  I'd marry you myself, my dear!   2805
MARTHE   Oh sir, you would? You're joking, I'm sure!
MEPHISTO [*Aside.*]   Time to leave! This one's an ogress,
  She'd sue the Devil for breach of promise!
        [*To* GRETCHEN.]
  And what's your love life like, my charmer?
MARGARETE   What do you mean?   2810
MEPHISTO [*Aside.*]   Oh you good girl,
  All innocence! [*Aloud.*] And now farewell.
MARGARETE   Farewell.
MARTHE   Quick, one last matter,
  If you would. I want to know
  If I might have some proof to show
  How and when my husband died   2815
  And where the poor man now is laid?
  I like to have things right and proper,
  With a notice published in the paper.
MEPHISTO   Madam, yes. To attest the truth,
  Two witnesses must swear an oath.   2820
  I know someone, a good man; we
  Will go before the notary.
  I'll introduce you to him.
MARTHE   Do.
MEPHISTO   And she'll be here, your young friend, too?—
  A very fine fellow who's been all over,   2825
  So polite to ladies, so urbane his behavior.
MARGARETE   I'd blush for shame before the gentleman.

MEPHISTO   No, not before a king or any man!
MARTHE   We'll wait for you tonight, the two of us,
   Inside my garden, just behind the house.   2830

A STREET

FAUST, MEPHISTOPHELES.

FAUST   Well? What's doing? When am I going to have her?
MEPHISTO   Bravo, bravo, I can see you're all on fire.
   Very shortly Gretchen will be all yours.
   This evening you will meet her at her neighbor's.
   The worthy Mistress Marthe, I confess,   2835
   Needs no instruction as a procuress.
FAUST   Good work.
MEPHISTO   There's something we must do for her, however.
FAUST   One good turn deserves another.
MEPHISTO   All it is is swear an oath
   Her husband's buried in the earth,   2840
   At Padua in consecrated ground.
FAUST   So we must make a trip there—very smart!
MEPHISTO   *Sancta simplicitas!*[4] Whoever said that?
   Just swear an oath. What's wrong? You frowned.
FAUST   If that's the best you're able, count me out.   2845
MEPHISTO   The saintly fellow! Turned devout!
   Declaring falsely—Heaven forbid!—
   Is something Faustus never did.
   Haven't you pontificated
   About God and the world, undisconcerted,   2850
   About man, man's mind and heart and being,
   As bold as brass, without blushing?
   Look at it closely and what's the truth?
   You know as much about those things
   As you know about Herr Schwerdtlein's death.   2855
FAUST   You always were a sophist and a liar.
MEPHISTO   Indeed, indeed. If we look ahead a little further,
   To tomorrow, what do we see?
   You swearing, oh so honorably,
   Your soul is Gretchen's—cajoling and deceiving her.   2860
FAUST   My soul, and all my heart as well.
MEPHISTO   Oh wonderful!
   You'll swear undying faith and love eternal,
   Go on about desire unique and irresistible,
   About longing, boundless, infinite:
   That, too, with all your heart—I'll bet!   2865
FAUST   With all my heart! And now enough.
   What I feel, an emotion of such depth,

---

4. Holy simplicity (Latin).

Such turbulence—when I try to find
A name for it and nothing comes to mind,
And cast about, search heaven and earth   2870
For words to express its transcendent worth,
And call the fire in which I burn
Eternal, yes, eternal, yes, undying!
Do you really mean to tell me
That's just devil's doing, deception, lying?   2875
MEPHISTO   Say what you please, I'm right.
FAUST   One word more, one only,
And then I'll save my breath. A man who is unyielding,
Sure, absolutely, he's right, and has a tongue in his mouth—
Is right. So come, I'm sick of arguing.
You're right, and the reason's simple enough: 2880
I must do what I must, can't help myself.

                                    A GARDEN

MARGARETE *with* FAUST, *her arm linked with his;* MARTHE *with*
MEPHISTOPHELES. *The two couples stroll up and down.*

MARGARETE   You are too kind, sir, I am sure it's meant
    To spare a simple girl embarrassment.
    A traveler finds whatever amusement he can,
    You've been all over, you're a gentleman—   2885
    How can anything I say
    Interest you in any way?
FAUST   To me one word of yours, a loving look
    'S worth all the wisdom in the great world's book.
        [*He kisses her hand.*]
MARGARETE   No, no, sir, please, you mustn't! How could you kiss   2890
    A hand so ugly—red and coarse?
    You can't imagine all the work I do;
    My mother must have things just so.
        [*They walk on.*]
MARTHE   And you, sir, I believe, you constantly travel?
MEPHISTO   Business, business! It is so demanding!   2895
    Leaving a place you like can be so painful,
    Duty's duty, its voice strict, commanding.
MARTHE   How fine when young and full of ginger,
    To travel the world, see all that's doing.
    But with the years worse times arrive and worser,   2900
    And find me, just do, someone somewhere choosing
    To crawl to his grave a lonely bachelor.
MEPHISTO   When I look at what's ahead, I tremble.
MARTHE   Then, sir, bethink yourself while you're still able.
        [*They walk on.*]
MARGARETE   Yes, out of sight is out of mind.   2905
    It's second nature with you, gallantry;

But you have heaps of friends of every kind
    Cleverer by far, oh much, than me.
FAUST   Dear girl, believe me, what's called cleverness
    Is mostly shallowness and vanity.   2910
MARGARETE   What do you mean?
FAUST   God, isn't it a pity
    That unspoiled innocence and simpleness
    Should never know itself and its own worth,
    That meekness, lowliness, those highest gifts
    Kindly Nature endows us with—   2915
MARGARETE   You'll think of me for a moment or two,
    I'll have hours enough to think of you.
FAUST   You're alone a good deal, are you?
MARGARETE   Our family's very small, it's true,
    But still it has to be looked to.   2920
    We have no maid, I sweep the floors, I cook and knit
    And sew, do all the errands, morning and night.
    Mother's very careful about money,
    All's accounted for to the last penny.
    Not that she really needs to pinch and save;   2925
    We could afford much more than others have.
    My father left us a good bit,
    With a small dwelling added to it,
    And a garden just outside the city.
    But lately I've lived quietly.   2930
    My brother is a soldier. My little sister died.
    The trouble that she cost me, the poor child!
    But I loved her very much, I'd gladly do
    It all again.
FAUST   An angel, if at all like you.
MARGARETE   All the care of her was mine,   2935
    And she was very fond of her sister.
    My father died before she was born,
    And Mother, well, we nearly lost her;
    It took so long, oh many months, till she got better.
    It was out of the question she should nurse   2940
    The poor little crying thing herself,
    So I nursed her, on milk and water,
    I felt she was my own daughter.
    In my arms, upon my lap,
    She smiled and kicked, grew round and plump.   2945
FAUST   The happiness it must have given you!
MARGARETE   But it was hard on me so often, too.
    Her crib stood at my bedside, near my head,
    A slightest movement, cradle's creak,
    And instantly I was awake;   2950
    I'd give her a bottle, or take her into my bed.
    If still she fretted, up I'd raise,
    Walk up and down with her, swaying and crooning,

And be at the washtub early the next morning;
To market after that, and getting the hearth to blaze,   2955
And so it went, day after day, always.
Home's not always cheerful, be it said;
But still—how good your supper, good your bed.
[*They walk on.*]

MARTHE   It's very hard on us poor women,
You bachelors don't listen, you're so stubborn!   2960

MEPHISTO   What's needed are more charmers like yourself
To bring us bachelors down from off the shelf.

MARTHE   There's never, sir, been anyone? Confess!
You've never lost your heart to one of us?

MEPHISTO   How does the proverb go? A loving wife,   2965
And one's own hearthside, are more worth
Than all the gold that's hidden in the earth.

MARTHE   I mean, you've had no wish, yourself?

MEPHISTO   Oh, everywhere I've been received politely.

MARTHE   No, what I mean is, hasn't there been somebody   2970
Who ever made your heart beat? Seriously?

MEPHISTO   It's never a joking matter with women, believe me.

MARTHE   Oh, you don't understand!

MEPHISTO   So sorry! Still,
I can see that you are—amiable.
[*They walk on.*]

FAUST   You recognized me, angel, instantly   2975
When I came through the gate into the garden?

MARGARETE   I dropped my eyes. Didn't you see?

FAUST   And you'll forgive the liberty, you'll pardon
My swaggering up in that insulting fashion
When you came out of the church door?   2980

MARGARETE   I was shocked. Never before
Had I been spoken to like that.
I'm a good girl. Who would dare
To be so free with me, so smart?
It seemed to me at once you thought   2985
There's a girl who can be bought
On the spot. Did I look a flirt?
Is that so, tell! Well, I'll admit
A voice spoke "Isn't he nice?" in my breast,
And oh how vexed with myself I felt   2990
That I wasn't vexed with you in the least.

FAUST   Dear girl!

MARGARETE   Just wait.
[*Picking a daisy and plucking the petals one by one.*]

FAUST   What is it for, a bouquet?

MARGARETE   Only a little game of ours.

FAUST   A game, is it?

MARGARETE   Never mind. I'm afraid you'll laugh at me.
[*Murmuring to herself as she plucks the petals.*]

FAUST What are you saying?   2995
MARGARETE [*Under her breath.*]
                        Loves me—loves me not—
FAUST Oh, what a creature, heavenly!
MARGARETE [*Continuing.*] He loves me—not—he loves me—not—
        [*Plucking the last petal and crying out delightedly.*]
    He loves me!
FAUST   Dearest, yes! Yes, let the flower be
    The oracle by which the truth is said.
    He loves you! Do you understand?   3000
    He loves you! Let me take your hand.
        [*He takes her hands in his.*]
MARGARETE I'm afraid!
FAUST No, no, never! Read the look
    On my face, feel my hands gripping yours—
    They tell you what's impossible   3005
    Ever to put in words:
    Utter surrender, and such rapture
    As must never end, must last forever!
    Yes, forever! An end—it would betoken
    Utter despair, a heart forever broken!   3010
    No—no end! No end!
        [MARGARETE *squeezes his hands, frees herself and runs away.*
        He doesn't move for a moment, thinking, then follows her.]
MARTHE It's getting dark.
MEPHISTO   That's right. We have to go.
MARTHE Please forgive me if I don't invite
    You in. But ours is such a nasty-minded street,
    You'd think people had no more to do   3015
    Than watch their neighbors' every coming and going.
    The gossip that goes on here, about nothing!
    But where are they, our little couple?
MEPHISTO   Flew
    Up that path like butterflies.
MARTHE   He seems to like her.
MEPHISTO And she him. Which is the way the world wags ever.   3020

                    A SUMMERHOUSE

GRETCHEN *runs in and hides behind the door, putting her fingertips*
to her lips and peeping through a crack.
MARGARETE Here he comes!
FAUST   You're teasing me, are you?
    I've got you now. [*Kisses her.*]
MARGARETE [*Holding him around and returning the kiss.*]
                        I love you, yes, I do!
        [MEPHISTOPHELES *knocks.*]
FAUST [*Stamping his foot.*]
    Who's there?

MEPHISTO   A friend.

FAUST   A fiend!

MEPHISTO   We must be on our way.

MARTHE [*Coming up.*]   Yes, sir, it's late.   3025

FAUST   I'd like to walk you home.

MARGARETE   My mother, I'm afraid. . . . Goodbye!

FAUST   So we must say

  Goodbye? Goodbye!

MARGARETE   I hope I'll see you soon.

                              [*Exit* FAUST *and* MEPHISTOPHELES.]

  Good God, the thoughts that fill the head
  Of such a man, oh it's astounding!
  I stand there dumbly, my face red,   3030
  And stammer yes to everything.
  I don't understand. What in the world
  Does he see in me, an ignorant child?

                    A CAVERN IN THE FOREST

FAUST [*Alone.*]   Sublime Spirit, all that I asked for, all,
  You gave me. Not for nothing was it,   3035
  The face you showed me, all ablaze with fire.
  You gave me glorious Nature for my kingdom.
  With the power to feel, to delight in her—nor as
  A spectator only, coolly admiring her wonders,
  But letting me see deep into her bosom   3040
  As a man sees deep into a dear friend's heart.
  Before me you make pass all living things,
  From high to low, and teach me how to know
  My brother creatures in the silent woods, the streams, the air.
  And when the shrieking storm winds make the forest   3045
  Groan, toppling the giant fir whose fall
  Bears nearby branches down with it and crushes
  Neighboring trees so that the hill returns
  A hollow thunder—oh, then you lead me to
  The shelter of this cave, lay bare my being to myself,   3050
  And all the mysteries hidden in my depths
  Unfold themselves and open to the day.
  And when I see the moon ascend the sky,
  Shedding a pure, assuaging light, out
  Of the walls of rock, the dripping bushes, float   3055
  The silver figures of antiquity
  And temper meditation's austere joy.

  That nothing perfect's ever ours, oh but
  I know it now. Together with the rapture
  That I owe you, by which I am exalted   3060
  Nearer and still nearer to the gods, you gave me
  A familiar, a creature whom already
  I can't do without, though he's a cold

And shameless devil who drags me down
In my own eyes and with a whispered word   3065
Makes all you granted me to be as nothing.
The longing that I feel for that enchanting
Figure of a girl, he busily blows up
Into a leaping flame. And so desire
Whips me, stumbling on, to seize enjoyment,   3070
And once enjoyed, I languish for desire.
    [*Enter* MEPHISTOPHELES.]
MEPHISTO   Aren't you fed up with it by now,
This mooning about? How can it still
Amuse you? You do it for a while,
All right; but enough's enough, on to the new!   3075
FAUST   Why, when I'm feeling a bit better,
Do you badger me with your insidious chatter?
MEPHISTO   A breather you want? Very well, I grant it.
But don't speak so, as if you really meant it—
I wouldn't shed tears, losing a companion   3080
Who is so mad, so rude, so sullen.
I have my hands full every minute—
Impossible to tell what pleases you or doesn't.
FAUST   Why, that's just perfect, isn't it?
He bores me stiff and wants praise for it.   3085
MEPHISTO   You poor earthly creature, would
You ever have managed at all without me?
Whom do you have to thank for being cured
Of your mad ideas, your feverish frenzy?
If not for me you would have disappeared   3090
From off the face of earth already.
What kind of life do you call it, dully fretting
Owl-like in caves, or toad-like feeding
On oozing moss and dripping stone?
That's a way to spend your time? Go on!   3095
You're still living in your head—I have to say so;
Only the old Dr. Faust would carry on so.
FAUST   Try to understand: my life's renewed
When I wander, musing, in wild Nature.
But even if you could, I know you would   3100
Begrudge me, Devil that you are, my rapture.
MEPHISTO   Your superterrestrial joys! So spiritual!
To sprawl on a hillside at night in the damp dewfall,
Clasping heaven and earth blissfully to your bosom,
Swelling up godlike in your enthusiasm,   3105
Driven by vague intimations, delving
Down to the bottommost depths of the earth;
Feeling each day of Creation unfolding,
All six at once, inside yourself,
Arrogantly elated, by what I can't imagine.   3110
And having ceased to be a mortal being,
Ecstatically immerged with everything existing.

And your conclusion from such exalted insight?—
    [*Making a gesture.*]
I forbid myself to say, it's not polite.

FAUST   For shame!   3115

MEPHISTO   So that's not to your taste at all, sir?
You're right, "shame"'s right, the moral comment called for.
Never a word, when chaste ears are about,
Of what chaste hearts can't do without.
Oh well, go on, amuse yourself
By duping now and then yourself.   3120
Yet you can't keep on in this way much longer.
You look done in again, almost a goner.
And if you persist in this fashion,
You'll go mad with baffled passion.
Enough, I say! Your sweetheart sits down there   3125
And all's a dismal prison for her.
You haunt her mind continually,
She's mad about you, oh completely.
At first your passion, like a freshet,
Swollen with melted snow, overflowing   3130
Its peaceful banks, engulfed a soul unknowing.
But now the flood's thinned to a streamlet.
Instead of playing monarch of the wood,
My opinion is the Herr Professor
Should make the silly little creature   3135
Some return, in gratitude.
For her the hours creep along,
She stands at the window, watching the clouds
Pass slowly over the old town walls,
"Lend me, sweet bird, your wings," is the song   3140
She sings all day and half the night.
Sometimes she's cheerful, mostly she's downhearted,
Sometimes she cries as if brokenhearted,
Then she's calm again and seems all right,
And heart-sick always.   3145

FAUST   Serpent! Snake!

MEPHISTO [*Aside.*]   I'll have you yet!

FAUST   Away, you monster from some stinking fen!
Don't mention her, the soul itself of beauty,
Don't make my half-crazed senses crave again   3150
The sweetness of that lovely body!

MEPHISTO   Then what? She thinks you've taken flight,
And I must say, the girl's half right.

FAUST   Far off as I may wander, she's still near me,
She fills my thoughts both day and night,   3155
I even envy the Lord's body her warm kiss
Bestowed upon it at the Mass.[5]

5. When the bread of Communion miraculously turns to the body of Christ.

MEPHISTO   I understand. I've often envied *you*
    Her pair of roes that feed among the lilies.[6]
FAUST   Pimp, you! I won't hear your blasphemies!   3160
MEPHISTO   Fine! Insult me! And I laugh at you.
    The God that made you girls and boys
    Himself was first to recognize,
    And practice, what's the noblest calling,
    The furnishing of opportunities.   3165
    Away! A crying shame this, never linger!
    You act as if hard fate were dragging
    You to death, not to your true love's chamber.
FAUST   Heaven's out-heavened when she holds me tight,
    And though I'm warmed to life upon her breast,   3170
    Do I ever once forget her plight?
    A fugitive is what I am, a beast
    That's houseless, restless, purposeless,
    A furious, impatient cataract
    That plunges down from rock to rock to the abyss.   3175
    And she, her senses unawakened, a child still,
    Dwelt in her cottage on the Alpine meadow,
    Her life the same domestic ritual
    Within a little world where fell no shadow.
    And I, abhorred by God,   3180
    Was not content to batter
    Rocks to bits, I had
    To undermine her peace and overwhelm her!
    This sacrifice you claimed, Hell, as your due!
    Help me, Devil, please, to shorten   3185
    The anxious time I must go through!
    Let happen quick what has to happen!
    Let her fate fall on me, too, crushingly,
    And both together perish, her and me!
MEPHISTO   All worked up again, all in a sweat!   3190
    On your way, you fool, and comfort her.
    When blockheads think there's no way out,
    They give up instantly, they're done for.
    Long live the man who keeps on undeterred!
    I'd rate your progress as a devil pretty fair;   3195
    But tell me, what is there that's more absurd
    Than a moping devil, mewling in despair?

GRETCHEN'S ROOM

GRETCHEN [*Alone at her spinning wheel.*]
      My heart is heavy,
      My peace is gone,

---

6. Compare Song of Solomon 4.5: "Thy two breasts are like two young roes that are twins, which feed among the lilies."

I'll never know any
Peace again.   3200

For me it's death
Where he is not,
The whole green earth
All waste, all rot.   3205

My poor poor head
Is in a whirl,
I'm mad, for sure
A poor mad girl.

My heart is heavy,   3210
My peace is gone,
I'll never know any
Peace again.

I look out the window,
Walk out the door,   3215
Him, only him,
I look for.

His bold walk,
His princely person,
His look,
His eyes' persuasion,   3220

And his sweet speech—
Magicalness!
His fingers' touch,
And oh, his kiss!

My heart is heavy,   3225
My peace is gone,
I'll never know any
Peace again.

With aching breast   3230
I strain so toward him,
Oh if I just
Could catch and hold him,

And kiss and kiss him,
Never ceasing,   3235
Though I should die in
His arms kissing.

MARTHE'S GARDEN

MARGARETE, FAUST

MARGARETE   Heinrich,[7] the truth—I have to insist!
FAUST   As far as I'm able.
MARGARETE   Well, tell me, you must,
  About your religion—how do you feel?   3240
  You're such a good man, kind and intelligent,
  But I suspect you are indifferent.
FAUST   Enough of that, my child. You know quite well
  I cherish you so very dearly,
  For those I love I'd give my life up gladly,   3245
  And I never interfere with people's faith.
MARGARETE   That isn't right, you've got to have belief!
FAUST   You do?
MARGARETE   I know you think I am a dunce!
  You don't respect the sacraments.   3250
FAUST   I do respect them.
MARGARETE   Not enough to go to Mass.
  And tell me when you last went to confess?
  Do you believe in God?
FAUST   Who, my dear,
  Can say, I believe in God?
  Ask any priest or learned scholar   3255
  And what you get by way of answer
  Sounds like a joke, like words run wild.
MARGARETE   So you don't believe in him?
FAUST   Don't misunderstand me, lovely child.
  Who dares name him,   3260
  Dares affirm him,
  Declares I believe?
  And who, feeling doubt,
  Ventures to say right out,
  I don't believe?   3265
  The All-embracing,
  All-sustaining
  Sustains and embraces
  Himself and you and me.
  Overhead the great sky arches,   3270
  Firm lies the earth beneath our feet,
  And the friendly shining stars, don't they
  Mount aloft eternally?
  Don't my eyes, seeking your eyes, meet?
  And all that is, doesn't it weigh   3275
  On your mind and heart,
  In eternal secrecy working,

7. That is, Faust. In the legend, Faust's name was generally Johann (John). Goethe changed it
to Heinrich (Henry).

Visibly, invisibly about you?
Fill heart with it to overflowing
In an ecstasy of blissful feeling,   3280
Which then call what you would:
Happiness! Heart! Love! Call it God!—
I know no name for it, seek
For none. Feeling is all,
Names noise and smoke   3285
Dimming the heavenly fire.

MARGARETE   I guess what you say is all right,
  The priest speaks so, or pretty near,
  Except his language isn't yours, not quite.

FAUST   I speak as all speak here below,   3290
  All souls beneath bright heaven's day,
  They use the language that they know,
  And I use mine. Why shouldn't I?

MARGARETE   It sounds fine when it's put your way,
  But something's wrong, there's still a question: 3295
  The truth is, you are not a Christian.

FAUST   Now darling!

MARGARETE   I have suffered so much, I can't sleep
  To see the company you keep.

FAUST   Company?

MARGARETE   That man you always have with you,   3300
  I loathe him, oh how much I do;
  In all my life I can't remember
  Anything that's made me shiver
  More than his face has, so horrid, hateful!

FAUST   Silly thing, don't be so fearful.   3305

MARGARETE   His presence puts my blood into a turmoil.
  I like people, most of them indeed;
  But even as I long for you,
  I think of him with secret dread—
  And he's a scoundrel, he is too!   3310
  If I'm unjust, forgive me, Lord.

FAUST   It takes all kinds to make a world.

MARGARETE   I wouldn't want to have his kind around me!
  His lips curl so sarcastically,
  Half angrily,   3315
  When he pokes his head inside the door.
  You can see there's nothing he cares for,
  It's written on his face as plain as day
  He loves no one, we're all his enemy.
  I'm so happy with your arms around me,   3320
  I'm yours, and feel so warm, so free, so easy,
  But when he's here it knots up so inside me.

FAUST   You angel, you, atremble with foreboding!

MARGARETE   What I feel's so strong, so overwhelming,
  That let him join us anywhere   3325

And right away I almost fear
I don't love you anymore.
And when he's near, my lips refuse to pray,
Which causes me such agony.
Don't you feel the same way too?   3330
FAUST   It's just that you dislike him so.
MARGARETE   I must go now.
FAUST   Shall we never
Pass a quiet time alone together,
Breast pressed to breast, our two souls one?
MARGARETE   Oh, if I only slept alone   3335
I'd draw the bolt for you tonight, yes, gladly.
But my mother sleeps so lightly,
And if we were surprised by her
I know I'd die right then and there.
FAUST   Angel, there's no need to worry.   3340
Here's a vial—three drops only
In her cup will subdue nature
And lull her into pleasant slumber.
MARGARETE   What is there that I'd say no to
When you ask?   3345
It won't harm her, though,
There is no risk?
FAUST   If there were,
Would I suggest you give it her?
MARGARETE   Let me only look at you   3350
And I don't know, I have to do
Your least wish.
I have gone so far already,
How much farther's left for me to go?
                                                       [Exit.]

     [Enter MEPHISTOPHELES.]
MEPHISTO   The girl's a goose! I hope she's gone.   3355
FAUST   Spying around, are you, again?
MEPHISTO   I heard it all, yes, every bit of it,
How she put the Doctor through his catechism,
From which he'll have, I trust, much benefit.
Does a fellow stick to the old, the true religion?—   3360
That's what all the girls are keen to know.
If he minds there, they think, he'll mind us too.
FAUST   Monster, lacking the least comprehension
How such a soul, so loving, pure,
Whose faith is all in all to her,   3365
The sole means to obtain salvation,
Should be tormented by the fear
The one she loves is damned forever!
MEPHISTO   You transcendental, hot and sensual Romeo,
See how a little skirt's got you in tow.   3370
FAUST   You misbegotten thing of filth and fire!

MEPHISTO   And she's an expert, too, in physiognomy.
  When I come in, she feels—what, she's not sure;
  This face I wear hides a dark mystery;
  I am genius of some kind, a bad one,   3375
  About that she is absolutely certain,
  Even the Devil, very possibly.
  Now about tonight—?
FAUST   What's it to you?
MEPHISTO   I get my fun out of it too.

AT THE WELL

GRETCHEN *and* LIESCHEN *carrying pitchers.*

LIESCHEN   You've heard about our Barbara, have you?   3380
GRETCHEN   No, not a word. I hardly see a soul.
LIESCHEN   Sybil told me; yes, the whole thing's true.
  She's gone and done it now, the little fool.
  You see what comes of being so stuck up!
GRETCHEN   What comes?   3385
LIESCHEN   Oh, it smells bad, I tell you, phew!—
  When she eats now, she's feeding two.
GRETCHEN   Oh dear!
LIESCHEN   Serves her right, if you ask me.
  How she kept after him, without a letup
  Gadding about, the pair, and gallivanting
  Off to the village for the music, dancing,   3390
  She had to be first always, everywhere,
  While he with wine and sweet cakes courted her.
  She thought her beauty echoed famously,
  Accepted his gifts shamelessly.
  They kissed and fondled by the hour,   3395
  Till it was goodbye to her little flower.
GRETCHEN   The poor thing!
LIESCHEN   Poor thing, you say!
  While we two sat home spinning the whole day
  And our mothers wouldn't let us out at night,
  She was where?—out hugging her sweetheart   3400
  On a bench or up a dark alley,
  And never found an hour passed too slowly.
  Well, now she's got to pay for it—
  Shiver in church, in her sinner's shift.
GRETCHEN   He'll marry her. How can he not?   3405
LIESCHEN   He won't—he can't.
  That one's too smart.
  He'll find a girlfriend elsewhere in a trice,
  In fact he's gone.
GRETCHEN   But that's not nice!   3410
LIESCHEN   And if he does, she'll rue the day,

The boys will snatch her bridal wreath away
And we'll throw dirty straw down in her doorway.[8]

[*Exit.*]

GRETCHEN [*Turning to go home.*]
How full of blame I used to be, how scornful
Of any girl who got herself in trouble!   3415
I couldn't find words enough to express
My disgust for others' sinfulness.
Black as all their misdeeds seemed to be,
I blackened them still more, so cruelly,
And still they weren't black enough for me.   3420
I blessed myself, was smug and proud
To think I was so very good,
And who's the sinner now? Me, me, oh God!
Yet everything that brought me to it,
God, was so good, oh, was so sweet!   3425

THE CITY WALL

*In a niche in the wall, an image of the Mater Dolorosa[9] at the foot of the cross,
with pots of flowers before it.*

GRETCHEN [*Putting fresh flowers in the pots.*]
Look down, O
Thou sorrow-rich Lady,
On my need—in thy infinite mercy, aid me!

With the sword in your heart,
With your eternal hurt,   3430
Upwards you look to your son's death.

To the Father you gaze up,
Send sighs upon sighs up
For His grief and your own sore grief.

Who's there knows   3435
How it gnaws
Deep inside me, the pain?
The heart-anguish I suffer,
Fright, tremblings, desire?
You only know, you alone!   3440

I go no matter where,
The pain goes with me there,

---

8. In Germany, this treatment was reserved
for young women who had sexual relations
before marriage.

9. "Sorrowful mother" (Latin; literal trans.);
that is, the Virgin Mary in mourning.

Inside my bosom aching!
No sooner I'm alone
I moan, I moan, I moan—   3445
Mary, my heart is breaking!

From the box outside my window,
Dropping tears like dew,
Leaning into the dawning,
I picked these flowers for you.   3450

Into my bedroom early
The bright sun put his head,
Found me bolt upright sitting
Miserably on my bed.

Help! Save me from shame and death!   3455
Look down, O
Thou sorrow-rich Lady,
On my need—in thy infinite mercy, aid me!

NIGHT

The street outside GRETCHEN's *door.*

VALENTINE [*A soldier,* GRETCHEN's *brother.*]
    Whenever at a bout the boys
    Would fill the tavern with the noise   3460
    Of their loud bragging, swearing Mattie,
    Handsome Kate or blushing Mary
    The finest girl in all the country,
    Confirming what they said by drinking
    Many a bumper, I'd say nothing,   3465
    My elbows on the table propped
    Till all their boasting at last stopped.
    And then I'd stroke my beard and smiling,
    Say there was no point to quarreling
    About taste; but tell me where   3470
    There was one who could compare,
    A virgin who could hold a candle
    To my beloved sister, Gretel?
    Clink, clank, you heard the tankards rattle
    All around and voices shout   3475
    He's right, he is, she gets our vote,
    Among all her sex she has no equal!
    Which stopped those others cold. But now!—
    I could tear my hair out, all,
    Run right up the side of the wall!   3480
    All the drunks are free to crow
    Over me, to needle, sneer,
    And I'm condemned to sitting there

Like a man with debts unpaid
Who sweats in fear lest something's said. 3485
I itch to smash them all, those beggars,
But still that wouldn't make them liars.

Who's sneaking up here? Who is that?
There's two! And one I bet's that rat.
When I lay my hands on him 3490
He won't be going home again!
    [FAUST, MEPHISTOPHELES.]
FAUST   How through the window of the vestry, look,
  The flickering altar lamp that's always lit,
  Upward throws its light, while dim and weak,
  By darkness choked, a gleam dies at our feet. 3495
  Just so all's night and gloom within my soul.
MEPHISTO   And me, I'm itching like a tomcat on his prowls,
  That slinks past fire ladders, hugs building walls.
  An honest devil I am, after all;
  It's nothing serious, the little thievery 3500
  I have in mind, the little lechery—
  It merely shows Walpurgis Night's already
  Spooking up and down inside me.
  Still another night of waiting, then
  The glorious season's here again 3505
  When a fellow finds out waking beats
  Sleeping life away between the sheets.
FAUST   That flickering light I see, is that
  Buried treasure rising, what?
MEPHISTO   Very soon you'll have the pleasure 3510
  Of lifting out a pot of treasure.
  The other day I stole a look—
  Such lovely coins, oh you're in luck!
FAUST   No necklace, bracelet, some such thing
  My darling can put on, a ring? 3515
MEPHISTO   I think I glimpsed a string of pearls—
  Just the thing to please the girls.
FAUST   Good, good. It makes me feel unhappy
  When I turn up with my hands empty.
MEPHISTO   Why should you mind it if you can 3520
  Enjoy a free visit now and then?
  Look up, how the heavens sparkle, starfull,
  Time for a song, a cunning one, artful:
  I'll sing her a ballad that's moral, proper,
  So as to delude the baggage the better. 3525
    [Sings to the guitar.]
      What brings you out before[1]
      Your sweet William's door,

1. Lines 3526–41 are adapted by Goethe from Shakespeare's Hamlet 4.5.

O Katherine, my dear,
  In dawning's chill?
You pretty child, beware,   3530
The maid that enters there,
Out she shall come ne'er
  A maiden still.

Girls, listen, trust no one,
Or when all's said and done,   3535
You'll find yourselves *undone*
  And, poor things, damned.
Of your good selves take care,
Yield nothing though he swear,
Until your finger wear   3540
  A silver band.

VALENTINE [*Advancing.*]
  Luring who here with that braying,
Abominable ratcatcher!
The devil take that thing you're playing,
And then take you, you guitar scratcher!   3545
MEPHISTO   Smashed my guitar! Now it's no good at all.
VALENTINE   What I'll smash next's your skull!
MEPHISTO [*To* FAUST.]   Hold your ground, Professor! At the ready!
  Stick close to me, I'll show you how.
Out with your pigsticker now!   3550
You do the thrusting, I will parry.
VALENTINE   Parry that!
MEPHISTO   Why not?
VALENTINE   And this one too!
MEPHISTO   So delighted, I am, to oblige you.
VALENTINE   It's the Devil I think I'm fighting!
  What's this? My hand is feeling feeble.   3555
MEPHISTO [*To* FAUST.]   Stick him!
VALENTINE [*Falling.*]   Oh!
MEPHISTO   See how the lout's turned civil.
  What's called for now is legwork. Off and running!
In no time they will raise a hue and cry.
I can manage sheriffs without trouble,
But not the High Judiciary.   3560
                        [*Exeunt.*]

MARTHE [*Leaning out of the window.*]
  Neighbors, help!
GRETCHEN   [*Leaning out of her window.*]
          A light, a light!
MARTHE   They curse and brawl, they scream and fight.
CROWD   Here's one on the ground. He's dead.
MARTHE [*Coming out.*]   Where are the murderers? All fled?
GRETCHEN [*Coming out.*]
  Who's lying here?   3565
CROWD   Your mother's son.

GRETCHEN   My God, the misery! On and on!
VALENTINE   I'm dying! Well, it's soon said, that,
 And sooner done. You women, don't
 Stand there blubbering away.
 Come here, I've something I must say.   3570
  [*All gather around him.*]
 Gretchen, look here, you're young yet,
 A green girl, not so smart about
 Managing her business.
 We know it, don't we, you and me,
 You're a whore, quietly—   3575
 Go public, don't be shy, miss.
GRETCHEN   My brother! God! What wretchedness!
VALENTINE   You can leave God out of this.
 What's done can't ever be undone,
 And as things went, so they'll go on.   3580
 You let in one at the back door,
 Soon there'll be others, more and more—
 A whole dozen, hot for pleasure,
 And then the whole town for good measure.

 Shame is born in hugger-mugger,   3585
 The lying-in veiled in black night,
 And she is swaddled up so tight
 In hopes the ugly thing will smother.
 But as she thrives, grows bigger, bolder,
 The hussy's eager to step out,   3590
 Though she has grown no prettier.
 The more she's hateful to the sight,
 The more the creature seeks the light.

 I look ahead and I see what?
 The honest people of this place   3595
 Standing back from you, you slut,
 As from a plague-infected corpse.
 When they look you in the face
 You'll cringe with shame, pierced to the heart.
 In church they'll drive you from the altar,   3600
 No wearing gold chains any more,
 No putting on a fine lace collar
 For skipping round on the dance floor.
 You'll hide in dark and dirty corners
 With limping cripples, lousy beggars.   3605
 God may pardon you at last,
 But here on earth you stand accurst!
MARTHE   Look up to God and ask his mercy!
 Don't add to all your other sins
 Sacrilege and blasphemy.   3610
VALENTINE   If I could only lay my hands
 On your scrawny, dried-up body,

Vile panderer, repulsive bawd,
Then I might hope to find forgiveness
Ten times over from the Lord! 3615
GRETCHEN My brother! Oh, what hellish anguish!
VALENTINE Stop your bawling, all your to-do.
When you said goodbye to honor,
That is what gave me the worst blow.
And now I go down in the earth, 3620
Passing through the sleep of death
To God—who in his life was a brave soldier.

[*Dies.*]

THE CATHEDRAL

Requiem mass, organ music, singing. GRETCHEN *among a crowd of worshippers. Behind her an* EVIL SPIRIT.

EVIL SPIRIT Oh, it was different,
Wasn't it, Gretchen,
When you then, an innocent, 3625
Used to come here
To the altar and kneeling,
Prattle out prayers
From the worn little prayer book,
Half childish playing, 3630
Half God adoring,
Gretchen!
In your heart's hidden
What horrid sin?

Do you pray for the soul of your mother, 3635
Who by your contriving slept on,
On into pain and more pain?
That blood on your doorstep, whose is it?
And under your heart, that faint stirring,
A quickening in you, what is it?— 3640
Affrighting both you and itself
With its foreboding presence.
GRETCHEN Misery! Misery!
To be rid of these thoughts
That go round and around in me, 3645
Accusing, accusing!
CHOIR *Dies irae, dies illa*
Solvet saeclum in favilla.[2]
[*Organ music.*]
EVIL SPIRIT The wrath of God grips you!
The trumpet is sounding, 3650

2. "Day of wrath, that day that dissolves the world into ashes" (Latin). The choir sings a famous mid-13th-century hymn by Thomas Celano (ca. 1200–ca. 1255).

The sepulchers quaking,
And your heart,
From its ashen peace waking,
Trembles upwards in flames
Of burning qualms!   3655

GRETCHEN   To be out of here, gone!
I feel as if drowning
In the organ's sound,
Dissolving into nothing
In the singing's profound.   3660

CHOIR   *Judex ergo cum sedebit,*
Quidquid latet apparebit,
Nil inultum remanebit.[3]

GRETCHEN   I feel so oppressed here!
The pillars imprison me!   3665
The vaulting presses
Down on me! Air!

EVIL SPIRIT   Hide yourself, try! Sin and shame
Never stay hidden.
Air! Light!   3670
Poor thing that you are!

CHOIR   *Quid sum miser tunc dicturus?*
Quem patronum rogaturus,
Cum vix justus sit securus?[4]

EVIL SPIRIT   The blessed avert   3675
Their faces from you.
Pure souls snatch back
Hands once offered you.
Poor thing!

CHOIR   *Quid sum miser tunc dicturus?*   3680

GRETCHEN   Neighbor, your smelling salts!
     [*She swoons.*]

WALPURGIS NIGHT

The Harz Mountains, near Schierke and Elend. FAUST, MEPHISTOPHELES.

MEPHISTO   What you would like now is a broomstick, right?
Myself, give me a tough old billy goat.
We've got a ways to go, still, on this route.

FAUST   While legs hold up and breath comes freely,   3685
This knotty blackthorn's all I want.
Hastening our journey, what's the point?
To loiter through each winding valley,
Then clamber up this rocky slope
Down which that stream there tumbles ceaselessly—   3690

---

3. "When the judge shall be seated, what is hidden shall appear, nothing shall remain unavenged" (Latin).

4. "What shall I say in my wretchedness? To whom shall I appeal when scarcely the righteous man is safe?" (Latin.)

That's what gives the pleasure to our tramp.
The spring has laid her finger on the birch,
Even the fir tree feels her touch,
Then mustn't our limbs feel new energy?

MEPHISTO   Must they? I don't feel that way, not me.   3695
My season's strictly wintertime,
I'd much prefer we went through ice and snow.
The waning moon, making its tardy climb
Up the sky, gives off a reddish glow
So sad and dim, at every step you run   3700
Into a tree or stumble on a stone.
You won't mind my begging assistance
Of some will-o'-the-wisp?[5] And there's one no great distance,
Shining for all his worth, so merrily.
—Hello there, friend, we'd like your company!   3705
Why blaze away so uselessly, for nothing?
Do us a favor, light up this path we're climbing.

WILL-O'-THE-WISP   I hope the deep respect I hold you in, sir,
Will keep in check my all-too-skittish temper;
The way we go is zigzag, that's our nature.   3710

MEPHISTO   Trying to ape mankind, poor silly flame.
Now listen to me: fly straight, in the Devil's name,
Or out I'll blow your feeble, flickering light!

WILL-O'-THE-WISP   Yes, yes, you give the orders here, quite right;
I'll do what you require, eagerly.   3715
But don't forget, the mountain on this night
Is mad with magic, witchcraft, sorcery,
And if Jack-o'-Lantern is your guide,
Don't expect more than he can provide.

FAUST, MEPHISTOPHELES, WILL-O'-THE-WISP [*Singing in turn*]
We have entered, as it seems,   3720
Realm of magic, realm of dreams.
Lead us well and win the honor
His to have, bright-shining creature,
By whose flicker we may hasten
Forward through this wide, waste region!   3725

See the trees, one then another,
Spinning past us fast and faster,
And the cliffs impending over,
And the jutting crags, like noses
Winds blow through with snoring noises!   3730

Over stones and through the heather
Rills and runnels downwards hasten.
Is that water splashing, listen,
Is it singing, that soft murmur,
Is it love's sweet voice, lamenting   3735

5. A wavering light formed by marsh gas. In German folklore, it was thought to lead travelers to
their destruction.

For the days when all was heaven?
How our hearts hoped, loving, yearning!
And like a tale, an old, familiar,
Echo once more tells it over.

Whoo-oo! owl's hoot's heard nearer,   3740
Cry of cuckoo and of plover—
Still not nested, still awake?
Are those lizards in the brake,
Straggle-legged, big of belly?
And roots, winding every which way   3745
In the rock and sand, send far out
Shoots to snare and make us cry out;
Tree warts, swollen, gross excrescents,
Send their tentacles like serpents
Out to catch us. And mice scamper   3750
In great packs of every color
Through the moss and through the heather.
And the glowworms swarm around us
In dense clouds and only lead us
Hither, thither, to confuse us.   3755

Tell me, are we standing still, or
Still advancing, climbing higher?
Everything spins round us wildly,
Rocks and trees grin at us madly,
And the errant lights, their number   3760
Ever greater, puffed up, swagger,
MEPHISTO   Seize hold of my coattails, quick,
   We're coming to a middling peak
   Where you'll marvel at the sight
   Of Mammon's mountain, burning bright.[6]   3765
FAUST   How strange that glow is, there, far down,
   Dim and reddish, like the dawn.
   Its faint luminescence reaches
   Deep into the yawning gorges.
   Mist rises here and streams away there,   3770
   Penetrated by pale fire.
   Here, like a thin thread, the glimmer
   Creeps along, then like a fountain
   Overflowing, spills down the mountain,
   And vein-like, spreading all about   3775
   Winds along the entire valley,
   And here, squeezed through a narrow gully,
   Collects into a pool apart.
   Sparks fly about as if a hand
   Were scattering golden grains of sand.   3780

6. Mammon is imagined as leading a group of fallen angels in digging out gold and gems from the
ground of hell, presumably for Satan's palace, as described in Milton's *Paradise Lost* 1.678 ff.

And look there, how from base to top
The whole cliffside is lit up.
MEPHISTO   Holiday time Lord Mammon's castle
  Puts on a show that has no equal.
  Don't you agree? You saw it, luckily.   3785
  I hear our guests arriving—not so quietly!
FAUST   What a gale of wind is blowing,
  Buffeting my back and shoulders!
MEPHISTO   Clutch with your fingers that outcropping
  Or you'll fall to your death among the boulders.   3790
  The mist is making it darker than ever.
  Hear how the trees are pitching and tossing!
  Frightened, the owls fly up in a flutter.
  The evergreen palace's pillars are creaking
  And cracking, boughs snapping and breaking,   3795
  As down the trunks thunder
  With a shriek of roots tearing,
  Piling up on each other
  In a fearful disorder!
  And through the wreckage-strewn ravines   3800
  The hurtling storm blast howls and keens.
  And hear those voices in the air,
  Some faroff and others near?
  That's the witches' wizard singing,
  Along the mountain shrilly ringing.   3805
CHORUS OF WITCHES
      The witches ride up to the Brocken,
      Stubble's yellow, new grain green.
      The great host meets upon the peak and
      There Urian[7] mounts his throne.
      So over stock and stone go stumping,   3810
      Witches farting, billy goats stinking!
VOICE   Here comes Mother Baubo[8] now,
  Riding on an old brood sow.
CHORUS
      Honor to whom honor is due!
      Old Baubo to the head of the queue!   3815
      A fat pig and a fat frau on her,
      And all the witches following after!
VOICE   How did you come?
VOICE   Ilsenstein way.
  I peeked in an owl's nest, passing by,
  Oh how it stared!   3820
VOICE   Oh go to hell, all!
  Why such a rush, such a mad scramble?

7. A name for the devil.
8. In Greek mythology, the nurse of Demeter, noted for her obscenity and bestiality.

VOICE   Too fast, too fast, my bottom's skinned sore!
  Oh my wounds! Look here and here!
CHORUS OF WITCHES
    Broad the way and long the road,
    What a bumbling, stumbling crowd!   3825
    Broomstraw scratches, pitchfork's pushed,
    Mother's ripped and baby's crushed.
HALF-CHORUS OF WARLOCKS
    We crawl like snails lugging their whorled shell,
    The women have got a good mile's lead.
    When where you're going's to the Devil,   3830
    It's woman knows how to get up speed.
OTHER HALF-CHORUS
    A mile or so, why should we care?
    Women may get the start of us,
    But for all of their forehandedness,
    One jump carries a man right there.   3835
VOICE [*Above.*]   Come along with us, you down at the lake.
VOICE [*From below.*]   Is there anything better we would like?
  We scrub ourselves clean as a whistle,
  But it's no use, still we're infertile.
BOTH CHORUSES
    The wind is still, the stars are fled,   3840
    The veiled moon's glad to hide her head.
    Rushing and roaring, the magic chorus
    Scatters sparks by the thousands around us.
VOICE [*From below.*]   Wait, please wait, only a minute!
VOICE [*Above.*]   A voice from that crevice, did you hear it?   3845
VOICE [*From below.*]   Take me along, don't forget me!
  For three hundred years I've tried to climb
  Up to the summit—all in vain.
  I long for creatures who are like me.
BOTH CHORUSES
    Straddle a broomstick, a pitchfork's fine too,   3850
    Get up on a goat, a plain stick will do.
    Who can't make it up today
    Forever is done for, and so bye-bye.
HALF-WITCH [*From below.*]   I trot breathlessly, and yet
  How far ahead the rest have got.   3855
  No peace at all at home, and here
  It's no better. Dear, oh dear!
CHORUS OF WITCHES
    The unction gives us hags a lift,
    A bit of rag will do for a sail,
    Any tub's a fine sky boat—   3860
    Don't fly now and you never will.
BOTH CHORUSES
    And when we've gained the very top,

Light down, swooping, to a stop.
We'll darken the heath entirely
With all our swarming witchery.   3865
    [*They alight.*]
MEPHISTO   What a crowding and shoving, rushing and clattering,
    Hissing and shrieking, pushing and chattering,
    Burning and sparking, stinking and kicking!
    We're among witches, no mistaking!
    Stick close to me or we'll lose each other.   3870
    But where are you?
FAUST   Here, over here!
MEPHISTO   Already swept away so far!
    I must show this mob who's master.
    Out of the way of Voland the Devil,
    Out of the way, you charming rabble!   3875
    Doctor, hang on, we'll make a quick dash
    And get ourselves out of this terrible crush—
    Even for me it's too much to endure.
    Yonder's a light has a strange lure,
    Those bushes, I don't know why, attract me,   3880
    Quick now, dive in that shrubbery!
FAUST   Spirit of Contradiction! However,
    Lead the way!—He's clever, my devil:
    Walpurgis Night up the Brocken we scramble
    So as to do what? Hide ourselves in a corner!   3885
MEPHISTO   Just look at that fire there, shining brightly,
    Clubmen are meeting, how nice all looks, sprightly.
    You don't feel alone when the company's fewer.
FAUST   But I would feel much happier
    To be on the summit. I can make out   3890
    A red glow and black smoke swirling,
    Satanwards a great crowd's toiling,
    And there, I don't have any doubt,
    Many a riddle's at last resolved.
MEPHISTO   And many another riddle revealed.   3895
    Let the great world rush on crazily,
    We'll pass the time here cozily;
    And doing what has been for a long time the thing done,
    Inside that great world contrive us a little one.
    Look there, young witches, all stark naked,   3900
    And old ones wisely petticoated.
    Don't sulk, be nice, if only to please me;
    Much fun at small cost, really it's easy.
    I hear music, a damned racket!
    You must learn not to mind it.   3905
    No backing out now, in with me!
    You'll meet a distinguished company
    And again be much obliged to me.
    —Now what do you think of this place, my friend?

Our eyes can hardly see to its end.   3910
A hundred fires, all in a row,
People dance, people chatter, make love, drink and cook,
Did you ever in your life see such a show?
Find me the like, hard as ever you look!
FAUST   And when we enter into the revel,   3915
  What part will you play, magician or devil?
MEPHISTO   I travel incognito normally,
  But when it comes to celebrations
  A man must show his decorations.
  The Garter's never been awarded me,[9]   3920
  But in these parts the split hoof's much respected.
  That snail there, do you see it, creeping forwards,
  Its face pushing this way, that way, towards us?
  Already I've been smelt out, I'm detected.
  Even if deception was my aim,   3925
  Here there's no denying who I am.
  Come on, we'll go along from fire to fire,
  The go-between me, you the lover.
    [*Addressing several figures huddled around a fading fire.*]
  Old sirs, you keep apart, you're hardly merry,
  You'd please me better if you joined the party.   3930
  You ought to be carousing with the youngsters,
  At home we're all alone enough, we oldsters.
GENERAL   Put no trust in nations, for the people,
  In spite of all you've done, are never grateful.
  It's with them always as it is with women,   3935
  The young come first, and we—ignored, forgotten.
MINISTER OF STATE   The world has got completely off the track.
  Oh, they were men, the older generation!
  When it was us held every high position,
  That was the golden age, and no mistake.   3940
PARVENU   We were no simpletons ourselves, we weren't,
  And often did the things we shouldn't.
  But everything's turned topsy-turvy, now
  That we are foursquare with the status quo.
AUTHOR   Who wants, today, to read a book   3945
  With a modicum of sense or wit?
  And as for our younger folk,
  I've never seen such rude conceit.
MEPHISTO [*Suddenly transformed into an old man.*]
  For Judgment Day all now are ripe and ready
  Since I shan't ever again climb Brocken's top;   3950
  And considering, too, my wine of life is running cloudy,
  The world also is coming to a stop.
JUNK-DEALER WITCH   Good sirs, don't pass me unawares,
  Don't miss this opportunity!

9. That is, he has no decoration of nobility, such as the Order of the Garter.

Look here, will you, at my wares, 3955
What richness, what variety!
Yet there is not a single item
Hasn't served to claim a victim,
Nowhere on earth will you find such a stall!
No dagger here but it has drunk hot blood, 3960
No cup but from it deadly poison's flowed
To waste a body once robust and hale,
No gem but has seduced a loving girl,
No sword but has betrayed an ally or a friend,
Or struck an adversary from behind. 3965

MEPHISTO   Auntie, think about the times you live in—
What's past is done! Done and gone!
The new, the latest, that's what you should deal in;
The nouveau only, turns us on.

FAUST   Oh let me not forget I'm me, me only! 3970
This is a fair to beat all fairs, believe me!

MEPHISTO   The scrambling mob climbs upwards, jostling, rushed,
You think you're pushing and you're being pushed.

FAUST   Who's that there?

MEPHISTO   Look at her close.
Lilith.¹ 3975

FAUST   Lilith? What's she to us?

MEPHISTO   Adam's wife, his first. Beware of her.
Her beauty's one boast is her dangerous hair.
When Lilith winds it tight around young men
She doesn't soon let go of them again. 3980

FAUST   Look, one old witch, one young one, there they sit—
They've waltzed around a lot already, I will bet!

MEPHISTO   Tonight's no night for resting, but for fun,
Let's join the dance, a new one's just begun.

FAUST [*Dancing with the* YOUNG WITCH.]
A lovely dream I dreamt one day: 3985
I saw a green-leaved apple tree,
Two apples swayed upon a stem,
So tempting! I climbed up for them.

THE PRETTY WITCH   Ever since the days of Eden
Apples have been man's desire. 3990
How overjoyed I am to think, sir,
Apples grow, too, in my garden.

MEPHISTO [*Dancing with the* OLD WITCH.]
A naughty dream I dreamt one day:
I saw a tree split up the middle—
A huge cleft, phenomenal! 3995
And yet it pleased me every way.

1. According to rabbinical legend, Adam's first wife; the *female* mentioned in Genesis 1.27: "So God created man in his own image, in the image of God created he him; male and female created he them." After Eve was created, Lilith became a ghost who seduced men and inflicted evil on children.

THE OLD WITCH   Welcome, welcome, to you, sire,
   Cloven-footed cavalier!
   Stand to with a proper stopper,
   Unless you fear to come a cropper.   4000
PROCTOPHANTASMIST[2]   Accurst tribe, so bold, presumptuous!
   Hasn't it been proven past disputing
   Spirits all are footless, they lack standing?
   And here you're footing like the rest of us!
THE PRETTY WITCH [Dancing.]
   What's he doing here, at our party?   4005
FAUST [Dancing.]
   Him? You find him everywhere, that killjoy;
   We others dance, he does the criticizing.
   Every step one takes requires analyzing;
   Until it's jawed about, it hasn't yet occurred.
   He can't stand how we go forward undeterred;   4010
   If you keep going around in the same old circle,
   As he plods year in, year out on his treadmill,
   You might be favored with his good opinion,
   Provided you most humbly beg it of him.
PROCTOPHANTASMIST   Still here, are you? It's an outrage!   4015
   Vanish, ours is the Enlightened Age—
   You devils, no respect for rule and regulation.
   We've grown so wise, yet ghosts still walk in Tegel.[3]
   How long I've toiled to banish superstition,
   Yet it lives on. The whole thing is a scandal!   4020
THE PRETTY WITCH   Stop, stop, how boring, all your gabble!
PROCTOPHANTASMIST   I tell you to your face you ghostly freaks,
   I'll not endure this tyranny of spooks—
   My spirit finds you spirits much too spiritual!
      [They go on dancing.]
   I see I'm getting nowhere with these devils,   4025
   Still, it will add a chapter to my travels,
   And I hope, before my sands of life run out,
   To put foul fiends and poets all to rout.
MEPHISTO   He'll go and plump himself down in a puddle—
   It solaces him for all his ghostly trouble—   4030
   And purge away his spirit and these other spirits
   By having leeches feed on where the M'sieur sits.[4]
      [To FAUST, who has broken off dancing and withdrawn.]
   What's this? You've left your partner in the lurch
   As she was sweetly singing, pretty witch.

2. A German coinage meaning "one who exorcises evil spirits by sitting in a pond and applying leeches to his behind" (see lines 4029–32). The figure caricatures Friedrich Nicolai (1733–1811), who opposed modern movements in German thought and literature and had parodied Goethe's *The Sorrows of Young Werther* (1774).

3. A town near Berlin where ghosts had been reported.
4. Nicolai claimed that he had been bothered by ghosts but had repelled them by applying leeches to his rump.

FAUST   Ugh! From her mouth a red mouse sprung   4035
  In the middle of her song.
MEPHISTO   Is that anything to fuss about?
  And anyway it wasn't gray, was it?
  To take on so, to me, seems simply rudeness
  When you are sporting with your Phyllis.   4040
FAUST   And then I saw—
MEPHISTO   Saw what?
FAUST   Look there, Mephisto,
  At that lovely child, so pale with sorrow,
  Standing by herself. How lifelessly
  She makes her way along, with piteous pains,
  As if her feet were bound in cruel chains.   4045
  I must confess, it looks like Gretchen.
MEPHISTO   Let it be!
  It's bad, that thing, a lifeless shape, a wraith
  No man ever wants to meet up with.
  Your blood freezes under her dead stare,
  Almost turned to stone, you are.   4050
  Medusa,[5] did you ever hear of her?
FAUST   Yes, yes, those are a corpse's eyes
  No loving hand was by to close.
  That's Gretchen's breast, which she so often
  Gave to me to rest my head on,   4055
  That shape her dear, her lovely body
  She gave to me to enjoy freely.
MEPHISTO   It's all magic, idiot!
  Each thinks her his sweetheart.
FAUST   What rapture! And what suffering!   4060
  I stand here spellbound by her look.
  How strange, that bit of scarlet string
  That ornaments her lovely neck,
  No thicker than a knife blade's back.
MEPHISTO   Right you are. I see it, too.   4065
  She's also perfectly able to
  Tuck her head beneath her arm
  And stroll about. Perseus—remember him?—
  He was the one who hacked it off her.
  —Man, I'd think you'd have enough of   4070
  The mad ideas your head is stuffed with!
  Come, we'll climb this little hill where
  All's as lively as inside the Prater.[6]
  And unless somebody has bewitched me,
  The thing I see there is a theater.   4075
  What's happening?

5. The Gorgon with hair of serpents whose glance turned people to stone.
6. A famous park in Vienna.

SERVIBILIS   A play, a new one, starting shortly,
   Last of seven. With us here it's customary
   To offer a full repertory.
   The playwright's a rank amateur,
   Amateurs, too, the whole company.   4080
   Well, I must hurry off now, please excuse me,
   I need to raise the curtain—amateurishly!
MEPHISTO   How right it is that I should find you here, sirs;
   The Blocksberg's just the place for amateurs.

WALPURGIS NIGHT'S DREAM;

OR

OBERON AND TITANIA'S GOLDEN WEDDING

INTERMEZZO[7]

STAGE MANAGER [*To crew.*]   Today we'll put by paint and canvas,   4085
   Mieding's[8] brave sons, all.
   Nature paints the scene for us:
   Gray steep and mist-filled vale.
HERALD   For the wedding to be golden,
   Years must pass, full fifty;   4090
   But if the quarrel is made up, then
   It is golden truly.
OBERON   Spirits hovering all around,
   Appear, dear imps, to me here!
   King and Queen are once more bound   4095
   Lovingly together.
PUCK[9]   Here's Puck, my lord, who spins and whirls
   And cuts a merry caper,
   A hundred follow at his heels,
   Skipping to the measure.   4100
ARIEL[1]   Ariel strikes up his song,
   The notes as pure as silver;
   Philistines all around him throng,
   But those, too, with true culture.
OBERON   Wives and husbands, learn from us   4105
   How two hearts unite:
   To find connubial happiness,
   Only separate.
TITANIA   If Master sulks and Mistress pouts,
   Here's the remedy: 4110
   Send her on a trip down south,
   Him the other way.

---

7. Brief interlude. Oberon and Titania are king and queen of the fairies.
8. Johann Martin Mieding (died 1782), a master carpenter and scene builder in the Weimar theater.
9. A mischievous spirit.
1. A helpful sprite.

FULL ORCHESTRA [*Fortissimo.*]   Buzzing fly and humming gnat
    And all their consanguinity,
    Frog's hoarse croak, cicada's chat   4115
    Compose our symphony.
SOLO   Here I come, the bagpipes, who's
    Only a soap bubble.
    Hear me through my stumpy nose
    Tootle-doodle-doodle.   4120
A BUDDING IMAGINATION   A spider's foot, a green toad's gut,
    Two winglets—though a travesty
    Devoid of life and nature, yet
    It does as nonsense poetry.
A YOUNG COUPLE   Short steps, smart leaps, all done neatly   4125
    On the scented lawn—
    I grant you foot it very featly,
    Yet we remain un-airborne.
AN INQUIRING TRAVELER   Can it be a fairground fraud,
    The shape at which I'm looking?   4130
    Oberon the handsome god
    Still alive and kicking?
A PIOUS BELIEVER   I don't see claws, nor any tail,
    And yet it's indisputable:
    Like Greece's gods, his dishabille   4135
    Betrays the pagan devil.
AN ARTIST OF THE NORTH   Here everything I undertake
    Is weak, is thin, is sketchy;
    But I'm preparing soon to make
    My Italian journey.   4140
A STICKLER FOR DECORUM   I'm here, and most unhappily,
    Where all's impure, improper;
    Among this riotous witchery
    Only two wear powder.
A YOUNG WITCH   Powder, like a petticoat,   4145
    Is right for wives with gray hair;
    But I'll sit naked on my goat,
    Show off my strapping figure.
A MATRON   We are too well bred by far
    To bandy words about: 4150
    But may you, young thing that you are,
    Drop dead, and soon, cheap tart!
THE CONDUCTOR   Don't crowd so round the naked charmer,
    On with the concerto!
    Frog and blowfly, gnat, cicada—   4155
    Mind you keep the tempo.
A WEATHERCOCK [*Pointing one way.*]
    No better company than maids
    Like these, kind and complaisant,
    And bachelors to match, old boys
    Agog all, all impatient!   4160

WEATHERCOCK [*Pointing the other way.*]
    And if the earth don't open up
    And swallow this lewd rabble,
    Off I'll race at a great clip,
    Myself go to the Devil.
SATIRICAL EPIGRAMS [XENIEN[2]]   We are gadflies, plant our sting   4165
    In hides highborn and bourgeois,
    By so doing honoring
    Satan, our dear dada.
HENNINGS[3]   Look there at the pack of them,
    Like schoolboys jeering meanly.   4170
    Next, I'm sure, they all will claim
    It's all in fun, friends, really.
MUSAGET[4] ["LEADER OF THE MUSES"]
    If I joined these witches here,
    I'm sure I'd not repine;
    I know I'd find it easier   4175
    To lead them than the Nine.
[A JOURNAL] FORMERLY [ENTITLED] "THE SPIRIT OF THE AGE"[5]
    What counts is knowing the right people,
    With me, sir, you'll go places;
    The Blocksberg's got a place for all,
    Like Germany's Parnassus.[6]   4180
THE INQUIRING TRAVELER   Who's that fellow who's so stiff
    And marches so majestical?
    He sniffs away for all he's worth
    "Pursuing things Jesuitical."
A CRANE   An earnest fisherman I am   4185
    In clear and muddy waters,
    And thus you see a pious man
    Hobnobbing with devils.
A CHILD OF THIS WORLD   All occasions serve the godly
    In their work. Atop   4190
    The Blocksberg, even there, they
    Set up religious shop.
A DANCER   What's that drumming, a new team
    Of musicians coming?
    No, no, they're bitterns in the stream   4195
    All together booming.
THE DANCING MASTER   How cautiously each lifts a foot,
    Draws back in fear of tripping,

2. Literally, polemical verses written by Goethe and Friedrich von Schiller (1759–1805). The characters here are versions of Goethe himself.
3. August Adolf von Hennings (1746–1826), publisher of a journal called *Genius of the Age* that had attacked Schiller.
4. The title of a collection of Hennings's poetry.
5. That is, former "Genius of the Age"; probably alludes to the journal's change of title in 1800 to *Genius of the Nineteenth Century*.
6. A mountain sacred to Apollo and the Muses; hence, figuratively, the locale of poetic excellence.

The knock-kneed hop, they jump the stout,
Heedless how they're looking.   4200
THE FIDDLER   This riffraff's so hate-filled, each lusts
To slit the other's throat;
Orpheus with his lute tamed beasts,[7]
These march to the bagpipes' note.
A DOGMATIST   You can't rattle me by all   4205
Your questionings and quibbles;
The Devil is perfectly evil, hence real—
For the perfect entails existence: so devils.
AN IDEALIST   The mind's creative faculty
This time has gone too far.   4210
If everything I see is me,
I'm crazy, that's for sure.
A REALIST   It's pandemonium, it's mad,
I'm floored, I am, dumbfounded.
This is the first time I have stood   4215
On ground on nothing founded.
A SUPERNATURALIST   The presence of these devils here
For me's reassuring evidence;
From the demonical I infer
The angelical's existence.   4220
A SKEPTIC   They see a flickering light and gloat,
There's treasure there, oh surely;
Devil's a word that pairs with doubt,
This is a place that suits me.
CONDUCTOR   Frogs in leaves, grasshoppers grass,   4225
What damned amateurs!
Cicadas chirr, mosquitos buzz—
Call yourselves performers!
THE SMART ONES   Sans all souci[8] we are, shift
About with lightning speed;   4230
When walking on the feet is out,
We walk on the head.
THE NOT-SO-SMART ONES   At court we sat down to free dinners,
And now all doors are shut.
We've worn out our dancing slippers   4235
And must limp barefoot.
WILL-O'-THE-WISPS   We're from the muddy flats, marais,
Such is our lowly origin.
Today we shine as chevaliers
And dance in the cotillion.   4240
A SHOOTING STAR   I shot across the sky's expanse,
A meteor, blazing bright.
Now fallen, I sprawl in the grass—
Who'll help me to my feet?

7. In Greek mythology, Orpheus's music was   8. "Without any care or unhappiness"
said to have the power to quiet wild animals.   (French).

THE BRUISERS Look out, look out, we're coming through,   4245
    Trampling your lawn.
    We're spirits too, but spirits who
    Have lots of beef and brawn.
PUCK How you tramp, so heavily,
    Like infant elephants.   4250
    Elfin Puck's tread be today
    Heaviest of stamps.
ARIEL Or gave you wings, our kindly Nature,
    Or gave you them the Spirit?
    As I fly, fly close after,   4255
    Up to the rose hill's summit.
ORCHESTRA [*Pianissimo.*]
    Shrouding mists and trailing clouds
    Lighten in the dawning,
    Breeze stirs leaves, wind rattles reeds,
    And all, all, gone in the morning.   4260

AN OVERCAST DAY. A FIELD

FAUST *and* MEPHISTOPHELES.

FAUST In misery! In despair! Stumbling about pitifully over the earth
for so long, and now a prisoner! A condemned criminal, shut up in a
dungeon and suffering horrible torments, the poor unfortunate child!
It's come to this, to this! And not a word about it breathed to me, you
treacherous, odious spirit! Stand there rolling your Devil's eyes   4265
around in rage, oh do! Brazen it out with your intolerable presence!
A prisoner! In misery, irremediable misery! Delivered up to evil spirits
and the stony-hearted justice of mankind! And meanwhile you distract me with your insipid entertainments, keep her situation, more
desperate every day, from me, and leave her to perish helplessly!   4270
MEPHISTO She's not the first.
FAUST You dog, you monster! Change him, O you infinite Spirit,
change the worm back into a dog, give it back the shape it wore those
evenings when it liked to trot ahead of me and roll under the feet of
some innocent wayfarer, tripping him up and leaping on him as he   4275
fell. Give it back its favorite shape so it can crawl on its belly in the
sand before me, and I can kick it as it deserves, the abomination!—
Not the first!—Such misery, such misery! It's inconceivable, humanly
inconceivable, that more than one creature should ever have plumbed
such depths of misery, that the first who did, writhing in her last   4280
agony under the eyes of the Eternal Forgiveness, shouldn't have expiated the guilt of all the others who came after! I am cut to the quick,
pierced to the marrow, by the suffering of this one being—you grin
indifferently at the fate of thousands!
MEPHISTO So once again we're at our wits' end, are we—reached the   4285
point where you fellows start feeling your brain is about to explode?
Why did you ever throw in with us if you can't see the thing through?

You'd like to fly, but don't like heights. Did we force ourselves on you
or you on us?

FAUST   Don't snarl at me that way with those wolfish fangs of yours, it   4290
sickens me!—Great and glorious Spirit, Spirit who vouchsafed to
appear to me, who knows me in my heart and soul, why did you tie
me to this scoundrel who diets on destruction, delights to hurt?

MEPHISTO   Finished yet?

FAUST   Save her or you'll pay for it! With a curse on you, the dreadful-   4295
est there is, for thousands of years to come!

MEPHISTO   I'm powerless to strike off the Great Avenger's chains or
draw his bolts.—Save her indeed!—Who's the one who ruined her, I
would like to know—you or me?

　　　　　[FAUST *looks around wildly.*]

Looking for a thunderbolt, are you? A good thing you wretched mor-   4300
tals weren't given them. That's the tyrant's way of getting out of
difficulties—strike down any innocent person who makes an objection, gets in his way.

FAUST   Take me to where she is, you hear? She's got to be set free.

MEPHISTO   In spite of the risk you would run? There's blood guilt on   4305
the town because of what you did. Where murder was, there the
avenging spirits hover, waiting for the murderer to return.

FAUST   That from you, that too? Death and destruction, a world's
worth, on your head, you monster! Take me there, I say, and set her
free!   4310

MEPHISTO   All right, all right, I'll carry you there. But hear what I can
do—do you think all the powers of heaven and earth are mine? I'll
muddle the turnkey's senses, then you seize his keys and lead her out.
Only a human hand can do it. I'll keep watch. The spirit horses are
ready. Off I'll carry both of you. That's what I can do.   4315

FAUST   Away then!

NIGHT. OPEN COUNTRY

FAUST *and* MEPHISTOPHELES *going by on black horses at a furious gallop.*

FAUST   What's that they're doing at the ravenstone?

MEPHISTO   Cooking up, getting up, something, who cares?

FAUST   Soaring up, swooping down, bowing and stooping.

MEPHISTO   A pack of witches.   4320

FAUST   Strewing stuff, consecrating.

MEPHISTO   Keep going, keep going!

A PRISON

FAUST [*With a bunch of keys and carrying a lamp, at a narrow iron door.*]
I shudder as I haven't for so long—
She's shut up inside these dank walls, poor thing,
And all her crime was love, the brave, the illusory.   4325
You're hanging back from going in!

You're afraid of meeting her eyes again!
In, in, your hesitation's her death, hurry!
   [*He puts the key in the lock.*]
SINGING [*From withins.*]
   My mother, the whore,
   She's the one slew me!   4330
   My father, the knave,
   He's the one ate me!
   My sister, wee thing,
   Heaped up my bones
   Under cool stones.   4335
   Then I became a pretty woodbird—
   Fly away, fly away!
FAUST [*Unlocking the door.*]   She doesn't dream her lover's listening.
   Hears her chains rattle, the straw rustling.
      [*He enters.*]
MARGARETE [*Cowering on her paillasse.*]
   They're coming, they're coming! How bitter, death, bitter!   4340
FAUST [*Whispering.*]   Hush, dear girl, hush! You'll soon be free.
MARGARETE [*Groveling before him.*]
   If your heart's human, think how I suffer.
FAUST   You'll wake the guards. Speak quietly.
      [*Taking hold of the chains to unlock them.*]
MARGARETE [*On her knees.*]   Headsman, so early, it isn't right.
   Have mercy on me! Too soon, too soon!   4345
   You come for me in the dead of night—
   Isn't it time enough at dawn?
      [*Stands up.*]
   I'm still so young, too young surely—
   Still I must die.
   How pretty I was, that's what undid me.   4350
   He held me so close, now he's far away,
   My wreath pulled apart, the flowers scattered.
   Don't grip me so hard. Please, won't you spare me?
   What did I ever do to you?
   Don't let me beg in vain for mercy.   4355
   I never before laid eyes on you.
FAUST   It's unendurable, her misery.
MARGARETE   What can I do, I'm in your power.
   Only let me nurse my baby first,
   All night long I hugged the dear creature;   4360
   How mean they were, snatched it from my breast,
   And now they say I murdered it.
   I'll never be happy, no, never again.
   They sing songs about me in the street;
   It's wicked of them.   4365
   There's an old fairy tale ends that way—
   What has it got to do with me?

FAUST [*Falling at her feet.*]   It's me here who loves you, me,
 at your feet,
 To rescue you from this miserable fate.
MARGARETE [*kneeling beside him.*]
 We'll kneel down, that's right, and pray to the saints.   4370
 Look, under those steps,
 Below the doorsill,
 All Hell's a-boil!
 The Evil One
 In his horrible rage   4375
 Makes such a noise.
FAUST [*Crying out.*]   Gretchen! Gretchen!
MARGARETE [*Listening.*]   That was my darling's own dear voice!
  [*She jumps up, the chains fall away.*]
 I heard him call. Where can he be?
 No one may stop me now, I'm free!   4380
 Into his arms I'll run so fast,
 Lie on his breast at last, at last.
 Gretchen, he called, from there on the sill.
 Through all the howlings and gnashings of Hell,
 Through the furious, devilish sneering and scorn,   4385
 I heard a dear voice, its sound so well known.
FAUST It's me!
MARGARETE It's you! Oh, say it again.
  [*Catching hold of him.*]
 It's him! Where is the torture now, it's him!
 Where's my fear of the prison, the chains they hung on me,
 It's you, it's you, you've come here to save me!   4390
 I'm saved!
 —I see it before me, so very plainly,
 The street I saw you the first time on,
 I see Marthe and me where we waited for you
 In the sunlit garden.   4395
FAUST [*Pulling her toward the door.*]
 Come along, come!
MARGARETE   Don't go, stay here!
 I love it so being wherever you are.
  [*Caressing him.*]
FAUST Hurry!
 If you don't hurry,
 The price we will pay!   4400
MARGARETE What? Don't know how to kiss anymore?
 Parted from me a short time only
 And quite forgotten what lips are for?
 Why am I frightened with your arms around me?
 Time was, at a word or a look from you,   4405
 Heaven herself threw her arms around me
 And you kissed me as if you'd devour me.
 Kiss me, kiss me!

Or I'll kiss you!
    [*She embraces him.*]
What cold lips you have,   4410
You don't speak, look dumbly.
What's become of your love?
Who took it from me?
    [*She turns away from him.*]
FAUST   Come, follow me! Darling, be brave!
  Oh, the kisses I'll give you, my love—   4415
  Only come now, we'll slip through that door.
MARGARETE [*Turning back to him.*]
  Is it really you? Can I be sure?
FAUST   Yes, it's me—you must come!
MARGARETE   You strike off my chains,
  Take me into your arms.
  How is it you don't shrink away from me?   4420
  Have you any idea who you're letting go free?
FAUST   Hurry, hurry! The night's almost over.
MARGARETE   I murdered my mother,
  Drowned my infant,
  Weren't both of us given it—you too its parent—   4425
  Equally? It's you, I can hardly believe it.
  Give me your hand. No, I haven't dreamt it.
  Your dear hand.—But your hand is wet!
  Wipe it off, there's blood on it!
  My God, my God, what did you do?   4430
  Put away your sword,
  I beg you to!
FAUST   What's past is done, forget it all.
  You're killing me.
MARGARETE   No, live on still.   4435
  I'll tell you how the graves should be;
  Tomorrow you must see to it.
  Give my mother the best spot,
  My brother put alongside her,
  Me, put me some distance off,   4440
  Yet not too far,
  And at my right breast put my baby.
  Nobody else shall lie beside me.
  When I used to press up close to you,
  How sweet it was, pure happiness,   4445
  But now I can't, it's over, all such bliss—
  I feel it as an effort I must make,
  That I must force myself on you,
  And you, I feel, resist me, push me back.
  And yet it's you, with your good, kind look.   4450
FAUST   If it's me, then come, we can't delay.
MARGARETE   Out there?
FAUST   Out there, away!

MARGARETE   If the grave's out there, death waiting for me,
   Come, yes, come! The two of us together!
   But only to the last place, there, no other.   4455
      —You're going now?
   I'd go too if I could, Heinrich, believe me!
FAUST   You can! All you need is the will. Come on!
   The way is clear.
MARGARETE   No, I mayn't, for me all hope is gone.   4460
   It's useless, flight. They'd keep, I'm sure,
   A sharp watch out. I'd find it dreadful
   To have to beg my bread of people,
   Beg with a bad conscience, too;
   Dreadful to have to wander about   4465
   Where all is strange and new,
   Only to end up getting caught.
FAUST   But I'll stick to you!
MARGARETE   Quick, be quick!
   Save your poor child—   4470
   Run! Keep to the track
   That follows the brook;
   Over the bridge,
   Into the wood,
   Left where the plank is,   4475
   There, in the pool—
   Reach down, quick, catch it!
   It's fighting for breath!
   It's struggling still!
   Save it, save it!   4480
FAUST   Get hold of yourself!
   One step and you're free, dear girl!
MARGARETE   If only we were well past the hill!
   On the rock over there Mother sits, all atremble—
   Not a sign does she makes, doesn't speak.   4485
   On the rock over there Mother sits, head awobble,
   To look at her gives me a chill,
   She slept so long she will never wake.
   She slept so we might have our pleasure—
   The happy hours we passed together!   4490
FAUST   If all my persuading is no use,
   I'll have to carry you off by force.
MARGARETE   Let go, let go, how dare you compel me!
   You're gripping my arm so brutally!
   I always did what you wanted, once.   4495
FAUST   Soon day will be breaking! Darling, darling!
MARGARETE   Day? Yes, day, my last one, dawning,
   My wedding day it should have been.
   Not a word to a soul you've already been with your Gretchen.
   My poor wreath!   4500
   All's over and done.

We'll see one another again,
But not to go dancing.
The crowd presses in—not a sound, nothing,
Not the cry of a child. 4505
They are too many
For square and alley
To hold.
The bell calls, the staff's shattered,
I'm seized and I'm fettered 4510
And borne away, bound, to the block.
Every neck shivers with shock
As the axe-blade's brought down on my own.
Dumb lies the world as the grave.

FAUST I wish I had never been born! 4515

MEPHISTOPHELES [*Appearing outside*]
Come, come, or all's up with you, friend—
Debating, vacillating, useless jabbering!
My horses are trembling.
A minute or two and it's day.

MARGARETE Who's that rising up out of the ground? 4520
It's him, him, oh drive him away!
It's holy here, what is he after?
It's me he is after, it's me!

FAUST   Live, hear me, live!

MARGARETE It's the judgment of God! I surrender!

MEPHISTO Die both of you, I have to leave. 4525

MARGARETE In your hands, our Father! Oh, save me!
You angelical hosts, stand about me,
Draw up in your ranks to protect me!
I'm afraid of you, Heinrich, afraid!

MEPHISTO She's condemned! 4530

VOICE [*From above.*]
                    She is saved!

MEPHISTO [*To* FAUST, *peremptorily.*]
Come with me!
        [*He disappears with* FAUST.]

VOICE [*From within, dying away.*]
Heinrich! Heinrich!

FREDERICK DOUGLASS
1818?–1895

There was no more important African American public figure in the nineteenth century than Frederick Douglass. Born into slavery, he could easily have remained illiterate his whole life. But with extraordinary ingenuity and perseverance, he taught himself to read, and soon turned himself into such an electrifying antislavery speaker and writer that some audiences simply could not believe that he had grown up a slave. Even skeptics found themselves won over by his charismatic personality, acerbic wit, and skillful arguments. Douglass's eloquence became a powerful weapon in the war against slavery, as he edited an influential abolitionist newspaper, stirred crowded lecture halls in the United States, Great Britain, and Ireland, and published his best-selling *Narrative of the Life of Frederick Douglass, an American Slave, Written by Himself* (1845).

LIFE

Frederick Augustus Washington Bailey was born in Talbot County in the slave state of Maryland sometime around 1818. He barely knew his mother, a slave, and never knew the identity of his father, probably a white man and perhaps his owner. At first he lived in his grandmother's cabin, and then at the age of six he went to live in the house of his owner, the chief overseer of a vast plantation belonging to one of the wealthiest men in Maryland. It was during this period, as Douglass recounts in horrifying detail in his autobiography, that he first witnessed the daily cruelty suffered by plantation slaves.

An important turning point came in 1826 when Frederick was sent to live with Hugh and Sophia Auld, relatives of his owner in Baltimore. One of the most famous episodes in the autobiography tells of the moment when Hugh Auld discovered that his wife was teaching the slave to read. He burst out angrily that literacy would make Frederick "discontented" and "unmanageable" and so "would forever unfit him to be a slave." This reprimand transformed the slave's life: "From that moment," Douglass writes, "I understood the pathway from slavery to freedom." In the seven years that he remained with the Aulds, Douglass used his best resources to learn how to read and write, discovering two texts that would significantly shape his later career: Caleb Bingham's *The Columbian Orator* (1807), and the speeches of Thomas Sheridan, an eighteenth-century Irish actor and educator. Both were guides to public speaking.

In 1833 Hugh Auld's brother, Thomas, who had become Frederick Bailey's official owner, called him back to work on his plantation. Thomas Auld was a cruel master, but he found the slave so unruly that he sent him to a harsh "slave breaker" for a year to tame him. Douglass was not tamed, however; he defied and bested this notoriously brutal master in a long physical struggle, which, he says, resolved him to break free from slavery altogether: "however long I might remain a slave in form, the day passed forever when I could be a slave in fact."

After a first abortive attempt at escape, Douglass returned to Hugh Auld in Baltimore, where he learned caulking skills in the shipyard and began to turn his weekly wages over to his master. During this period of relative independence he met and fell in love with a free black woman named Anna Murray. Then, in 1838, he managed a successful escape. In the *Narrative* he was reluctant to divulge his strategies in case publicizing them would endanger other slaves trying to escape, but much later, after slavery had ended, he told the full story. First he disguised himself as a sailor and borrowed the identification papers of a free black seaman; then he traveled by train and ferry to New York, and with the help of abolitionists, moved to New Bedford, Massachusetts. There he married Murray, changed his name, and worked odd jobs to make a living. He also began to read an abolitionist newspaper, *The Liberator*. In 1841 he met its celebrated and controversial editor, William Lloyd Garrison, who invited Douglass to work for him as a traveling lecturer, telling the story of his life and selling subscriptions to the newspaper.

This marked the beginning of Douglass's extraordinarily successful public career. From the outset, his lectures moved his audiences to laughter, tears, and rapt attention. "As a speaker, he has few equals," claimed a contemporary editor. "I would give twenty thousand dollars if I could deliver an address in that manner," said another. In a context where apologists for slavery argued that Southern slaves were contented—living comfortable lives with kindly owners—Douglass's story offered a compelling counternarrative. And yet, from the beginning, he was also accused of fabricating the facts. His oratorical elegance and skill were so striking that a few abolitionists pleaded with him to put a little more "plantation" into his speech, so that he would seem more authentic. Douglass refused.

The public lectures paved the way for the *Narrative of the Life of Frederick Douglass* in two ways. First, although Douglass's speeches regularly told of the cruelties of slaveholding, mocked hypocritical proslavery ministers, and asked Northern audiences to confront inequality and prejudice in the free states, the centerpiece of his lectures was his own life story. He had tested it out on audience after audience; he knew it had power, and he was eager to disseminate it widely. Second, given the many accusations of fraud against Douglass, he wanted to publish details about the people and places he had known as a slave, so that others could confirm the truthfulness of his account. But publishing the details also put Douglass in danger. There was always the threat that a fugitive slave would be recaptured and sent back to the South, and now his owners could recognize him from his narrative and come to claim him. Douglass left the United States for England in 1845, just a few months after the autobiography appeared.

For two years Douglass traveled through Great Britain and Ireland, lecturing to enthusiastic crowds. By 1848 the *Narrative* had gone through nine editions in England alone, and it was translated into French and German. Douglass was surprised at the relative lack of racial prejudice he encountered in Britain. Among the warmest receptions he had was from Daniel O'Connell, the leader of the struggle against British colonial rule in Ireland. In England two Quakers gave Douglass the money to buy his own freedom, and in December of 1846 he became officially a free man.

Back in the United States, Douglass broke from Garrison's organization. Garrison was a powerful voice in the antislavery cause, but he paid Douglass less than the white lecturers on his circuit and patronized him, urging him to focus only on telling the story of his own life because, Garrison suggested, a black man was not capable of analyzing slavery as a large-scale social problem. Garrison also refused to fight for the vote for African Americans. Setting up on his own, Douglass launched an antislavery newspaper called the *North Star* in Rochester, New York. This city was an important stop on the underground railroad—the secret route organized around safe houses which fugitive slaves followed to Canada. The Douglass household harbored so many runaway slaves that there were sometimes as many as eleven fugitives staying in the house at a time. But the city was less committed to full racial equality than the Douglasses had hoped: their oldest daughter, Rosetta, was not allowed to attend public school, and the private school she attended forbade her to learn with the white students. Douglass began a campaign to end segregation in the schools. In 1848 he attended the women's rights convention in Seneca Falls, and he emerged as a stalwart champion of women's suffrage. The motto of the *North Star* marked his commitment to gender as well as racial equality: "Right is of no sex," it read. "Truth is of no color."

When the Civil War broke out in 1861, Douglass led efforts to persuade Congress and President Lincoln to allow African American men to enlist in the Union Army. This struggle succeeded, and in 1863, Douglass actively recruited soldiers to fight, including his own two sons, Lewis and Charles. After the war was over, he led the campaign for black suffrage, and prevailed in 1870 with the passage of the Fifteenth Amendment to the U.S. Constitution, which states that citizens cannot be denied the vote "on account of race, color, or previous condition of servitude."

The following years saw Douglass working tirelessly to expose and denounce discrimination and violence. He moved to Washington, D.C., where he held several government offices. In 1889

he accepted the position of consul-general to Haiti and moved there, but later resigned when he was told that he was too sympathetic to Haitian interests. His wife died in 1882, and Douglass later married Helen Pitts, a white woman. After speaking at the National Council of Women, he died of a heart attack in 1895. On hearing the news of Douglass's death, the women's rights activist Elizabeth Cady Stanton remembered hearing him speak for the first time: "He stood there like an African prince, majestic in his wrath, as with wit, satire, and indignation he graphically described the bitterness of slavery. . . . Thus it was that I first saw Frederick Douglass, and wondered that any mortal man should have ever tried to subjugate a being with such talents, intensified with the love of liberty."

SLAVERY AND ABOLITION

In the southern United States in the nineteenth century, slaves worked in fields, in homes, and in mines; they built railroads and canals; they processed sugar and iron. But by far the most significant use of slave labor involved cotton production. Eli Whitney's 1793 invention of the cotton gin had accelerated the cleaning of cotton, and worldwide demand for cotton textiles—a source of cheap and lightweight clothing—had skyrocketed. But this was a crop that still needed to be handpicked in the fields. The booming cotton trade therefore demanded lots of arable land and a huge supply of labor—conditions met easily by the slave economy of the United States South. Nearly three quarters of all U.S. slaves labored on cotton plantations, and by 1840 the southern United States produced more than half of the world's cotton. Cotton helped to drive the whole nation's economy, contributing substantially to the growth of Northern industry, shipping, and banking. It powered the global economy too. African traders used the term *americani* to refer to inexpensive cottons from the United States. And even after Britain had officially abolished slavery in its own territories, British traders imported vast quantities of cotton picked by U.S. slaves, and British mills turned this raw material into textiles for sale around the world. About 10 percent of Britain's wealth came from the cotton trade. In 1858 U.S. Senator James Hammond of South Carolina declared, "You dare not make war upon cotton. No power on earth dare make war upon it. Cotton is king!"

Intent on reaping as much profit as possible from their crops, plantation holders increasingly turned to the "gang system" to organize slave labor. Groups of slaves, under the command of an overseer, were forced—typically with whips, clubs, and threats—to perform a single repetitive task from the break of dawn until night. To increase efficiency, slaveholders would often rotate corn and cotton—ready at different times of the year—and use the corn to feed both slaves and animals on the plantation.

The state of Maryland, where Douglass was a slave, differed from most of the South. Maryland farms mostly grew tobacco rather than cotton, and the demand for tobacco was on the decline. Also, by the time that Frederick Douglass was born, Maryland had the highest number of free black men and women in the United States, more than half of its African American population. (By contrast, more than 99 percent of black people in Alabama, Texas, and Mississippi were slaves.) Working in the bustling city of Baltimore, surrounded by free blacks, Douglass had significantly more opportunities for escape than the plantation would have afforded.

Maryland was reputed to have a less harsh and dehumanizing slaveholder population than the "deep" South. In this respect as in many others, Douglass's *Narrative* challenged his readers' assumptions. In general the abolition-

ists felt that the best weapon against slavery was a campaign to reveal its horrors as fully and as accurately as possible. They went to significant trouble to demonstrate the evils of slavery and to confirm the truth of their claims. Some former slaves on the lecture circuit corroborated their accounts of violence by baring scars on their backs to horrified audiences.

Apart from organizing lecture tours and publishing books, abolitionists also sent volleys of pamphlets by mail to Southern states. But Southerners were not the only targets. As the abolitionist movement grew in the 1830s, activists increasingly focused their attention on the indifference of white Northerners, who mostly kept quiet on the subject of slavery. Neither major political party would mention it. And even in the North, angry mobs would descend on antislavery meetings and smash their printing presses. Douglass himself had his hand broken in Indiana. Dedicating themselves to exposing slavery to a wide public, abolitionists showed just how risky—and how powerful—words could be.

WORK

While the truthfulness of Douglass's story was a central question for his contemporaries, recent readers have been more inclined to admire the literary artfulness of the *Narrative*, its metaphorical richness, rhetorical complexity, and careful construction. Douglass casts his life as a long process of self-transformation—from an object, or an animal, to a free human being with a name. The contrast between the openings of the *Narrative* and of **Rousseau's Confessions** is instructive. Rousseau begins by proclaiming that he differs from everyone else in his unique personality and character. Douglass, on the other hand, starts by reporting what he does *not* know of himself. He must guess his own age, he doesn't know his birthday, he has only rumor to tell him of his father's identity. Although he knows his mother, he spends virtually no time with her; she comes to him and leaves him in the dark. Most children develop their sense of who they are by precisely the clues missing in Douglass's experience: age, parentage, and such ritual occasions as birthdays. Douglass has only a generic identity: slave. Everything in Douglass's early experience denies his individuality and declares his lack of particularized identity. By the end, however, he claims a right to affirm himself: "I subscribe myself, FREDERICK DOUGLASS." The name itself is a triumph, not his father's or his mother's but the freshly bestowed name of his freedom. Each step of the way to this point— learning to read, learning to write, acquiring a name—has involved a painful self-testing, but the *word* proves for Douglass quite literally a means to salvation.

If Douglass wins himself a name and an identity by the end of the *Narrative*, the triumphant individual is not the sole focus of the story. Along the way, Douglass uses his own experience to throw light on slavery in general. The first pages in fact tell us little about the uniqueness of the author, and Douglass is careful to explain how his own circumstances are common to many slaves. He also repeatedly argues that individuals emerge out of their circumstances. He goes to some trouble to show how masters systematically *create* the slaves' mindset, deliberately starving them of intellectual or spiritual nourishment. But he makes it clear that the masters, too, are created by their conditions. Sophia Auld begins as a compassionate and generous person, but the experience of owning another human being makes her suspicious and mean-spirited. Many readers have seen the *Narrative* as fundamentally a story of self-transformation in which the illiterate and unthinking slave is prompted to recognize the injustice of his experience and to insist on his full person-

hood, but Douglass reminds us many times along the way that self-transformation always involves a set of opportunities, and that under slightly different conditions, this slave might never have sought out his freedom.

There is one way that Douglass's story has disappointed recent readers. He affirms his own manhood—rejecting the bestial and objectified status of the slave—but does so at the expense of women's experience. He entirely omits descriptions of important women in his life, such as his grandmother, who raised him, and his wife-to-be. He does give graphic depictions of women slaves enduring physical violence, and he refers to the rape of slaves by masters more than once. But since his central image for slavery is a physical struggle for dominance between men, and since he depicts women mostly as lacerated bodies, Douglass's *Narrative* cannot be said to speak for all slaves.

In recounting the internal and external shifts that take him from slave to free man, Douglass's story draws on a number of other genres. As in spiritual autobiographies, the *Narrative* calls attention to moments of revelation, when the central figure undergoes a kind of conversion experience, and sees himself and his world in a fresh light. As in rags-to-riches stories, Douglass tells us how he makes a dramatic rise in social status and wealth through virtues such as perseverance, bravery, self-reliance, and determination. He draws on the sentimental novel, too, in offering us images of innocent victims whose abuses tug at our heartstrings. And the *Narrative* draws on the language of politics, economics, and religious sermons, woven together throughout the text. But perhaps most important, this autobiography belongs in the tradition of the slave narrative, which, by Douglass's time, had become a well-established genre. There had been literally thousands of first-person accounts of slavery published since the late eighteenth century, and slave narratives had become a major American genre. They were so popular that most American readers might never have encountered an autobiography written by anyone other than a slave. Among these many narratives, Douglass's has been widely recognized as the richest, most subtle, and most beautifully conceived, remaining worthwhile reading not only for its searing indictment of slavery, but also for its complex literary artistry.

Narrative of the Life of Frederick Douglass, An American Slave[1]

CHAPTER I

I was born in Tuckahoe, near Hillsborough, and about twelve miles from Easton, in Talbot county, Maryland. I have no accurate knowledge of my age, never having seen any authentic record containing it. By far the larger part of the slaves know as little of their ages as horses know of theirs, and it is the wish of most masters within my knowledge to keep their slaves thus ignorant. I do not remember to have ever met a slave who could tell of his birthday. They seldom come nearer to it than planting-time, harvest-time, cherry-time, spring-time, or fall-time. A want of information concerning my own was a source of unhappiness to me even during childhood. The white children could tell their ages. I could not tell why I ought to be deprived of the same privilege. I was not allowed to make any inquiries of my master concerning it. He deemed all such inquiries on the part of a slave improper and impertinent, and evidence of a restless spirit. The nearest estimate I can give makes me now between twenty-seven and twenty-eight years of age. I come to this, from hearing my master say, some time during 1835, I was about seventeen years old.

My mother was named Harriet Bailey. She was the daughter of Isaac and Betsey Bailey, both colored, and quite dark. My mother was of a darker complexion than either my grandmother or grandfather.

My father was a white man. He was admitted to be such by all I ever heard speak of my parentage. The opinion was also whispered that my master was my father; but of the correctness of this opinion, I know nothing; the means of knowing was withheld from me. My mother and I were separated when I was but an infant—before I knew her as my mother. It is a common custom, in the part of Maryland from which I ran away, to part children from their mothers at a very early age. Frequently, before the child has reached its twelfth month, its mother is taken from it, and hired out on some farm a considerable distance off, and the child is placed under the care of an old woman, too old for field labor. For what this separation is done, I do not know, unless it be to hinder the development of the child's affection toward its mother, and to blunt and destroy the natural affection of the mother for the child. This is the inevitable result.

I never saw my mother, to know her as such, more than four or five times in my life; and each of those times was very short in duration, and at night.

1. The text, printed in its entirety, is that of the first American edition, published by the Massachusetts Anti-Slavery Society in Boston in 1845.

She was hired by a Mr. Stewart, who lived about twelve miles from my home. She made her journeys to see me in the night, travelling the whole distance on foot, after the performance of her day's work. She was a field hand, and a whipping is the penalty of not being in the field at sunrise, unless a slave has special permission from his or her master to the contrary—a permission which they seldom get, and one that gives to him that gives it the proud name of being a kind master. I do not recollect of ever seeing my mother by the light of day. She was with me in the night. She would lie down with me, and get me to sleep, but long before I waked she was gone. Very little communication ever took place between us. Death soon ended what little we could have while she lived, and with it her hardships and suffering. She died when I was about seven years old, on one of my master's farms, near Lee's Mill. I was not allowed to be present during her illness, at her death, or burial. She was gone long before I knew anything about it. Never having enjoyed, to any considerable extent, her soothing presence, her tender and watchful care, I received the tidings of her death with much the same emotions I should have probably felt at the death of a stranger.

Called thus suddenly away, she left me without the slightest intimation of who my father was. The whisper that my master was my father, may or may not be true; and, true or false, it is of but little consequence to my purpose whilst the fact remains, in all its glaring odiousness, that slaveholders have ordained, and by law established, that the children of slave women shall in all cases follow the condition of their mothers; and this is done too obviously to administer to their own lusts, and make a gratification of their wicked desires profitable as well as pleasurable; for by this cunning arrangement, the slaveholder, in cases not a few, sustains to his slaves the double relation of master and father.

I know of such cases; and it is worthy of remark that such slaves invariably suffer greater hardships, and have more to contend with, than others. They are, in the first place, a constant offence to their mistress. She is ever disposed to find fault with them; they can seldom do any thing to please her; she is never better pleased than when she sees them under the lash, especially when she suspects her husband of showing to his mulatto children favors which he withholds from his black slaves. The master is frequently compelled to sell this class of his slaves, out of deference to the feelings of his white wife; and, cruel as the deed may strike any one to be, for a man to sell his own children to human flesh-mongers, it is often the dictate of humanity for him to do so; for, unless he does this, he must not only whip them himself, but must stand by and see one white son tie up his brother, of but few shades darker complexion than himself, and ply the gory lash to his naked back; and if he lisp one word of disapproval, it is set down to his parental partiality, and only makes a bad matter worse, both for himself and the slave whom he would protect and defend.

Every year brings with it multitudes of this class of slaves. It was doubtless in consequence of a knowledge of this fact, that one great statesman of the south predicted the downfall of slavery by the inevitable laws of population. Whether this prophecy is ever fulfilled or not, it is nevertheless plain that a very different-looking class of people are springing up at the south, and are now held in slavery, from those originally brought to this country from Africa; and if their increase will do no other good, it will do away the force of the argument, that God cursed Ham,[2] and therefore American slavery is right. If the lineal descendants of Ham are alone to be scripturally enslaved, it is certain that slavery at the south must soon become unscriptural; for thousands are ushered into the world, annually, who, like myself, owe their existence to white fathers, and those fathers most frequently their own masters.

I have had two masters. My first master's name was Anthony. I do not remember his first name. He was generally called Captain Anthony—a title which, I presume, he acquired by sailing a craft on the Chesapeake Bay. He was not considered a rich slaveholder. He owned two or three farms, and about thirty slaves. His farms and slaves were under the care of an overseer. The overseer's name was Plummer. Mr. Plummer was a miserable drunkard, a profane swearer, and a savage monster. He always went armed with a cowskin and a heavy cudgel. I have known him to cut and slash the women's heads so horribly, that even master would be enraged at his cruelty, and would threaten to whip him if he did not mind himself. Master, however, was not a humane slaveholder. It required extraordinary barbarity on the part of an overseer to affect him. He was a cruel man, hardened by a long life of slaveholding. He would at times seem to take great pleasure in whipping a slave. I have often been awakened at the dawn of day by the most heartrending shrieks of an own aunt of mine, whom he used to tie up to a joist, and whip upon her naked back till she was literally covered with blood. No words, no tears, no prayers, from his gory victim, seemed to move his iron heart from its bloody purpose. The louder she screamed, the harder he whipped; and where the blood ran fastest, there he whipped longest. He would whip her to make her scream, and whip her to make her hush; and not until overcome by fatigue, would he cease to swing the blood-clotted cowskin. I remember the first time I ever witnessed this horrible exhibition. I was quite a child, but I well remember it. I never shall forget it whilst I remember any thing. It was the first of a long series of such outrages, of which I was doomed to be a witness and a participant. It struck me with awful force. It was the blood-stained gate, the entrance to the hell of slavery, through which I was about to pass. It was a most terrible spectacle. I wish I could commit to paper the feelings with which I beheld it.

This occurrence took place very soon after I went to live with my old master, and under the following circumstances. Aunt Hester went out one night,— where or for what I do not know,—and happened to be absent when my master desired her presence. He had ordered her not to go out evenings, and warned her that she must never let him catch her in company with a young man, who was paying attention to her, belonging to Colonel Lloyd. The young man's name was Ned Roberts, generally called Lloyd's Ned. Why master was so careful of her, may be safely left to conjecture. She was a woman of noble form, and of graceful proportions, having very few equals, and fewer superiors, in personal appearance, among the colored or white women of our neighborhood.

2. It was widely thought that Noah cursed his second son, Ham, for mocking him; that black skin resulted from the curse; and that all black people descended from Ham. In fact, according to Genesis 9.20–27 and 10.6–14, Noah cursed not Ham but Ham's son Canaan, while Ham's son Cush was black.

Aunt Hester had not only disobeyed his orders in going out, but had been found in company with Lloyd's Ned; which circumstance, I found, from what he said while whipping her, was the chief offence. Had he been a man of pure morals himself, he might have been thought interested in protecting the innocence of my aunt; but those who knew him will not suspect him of any such virtue. Before he commenced whipping Aunt Hester, he took her into the kitchen, and stripped her from neck to waist, leaving her neck, shoulders, and back, entirely naked. He then told her to cross her hands, calling her at the same time a d—d b—h. After crossing her hands, he tied them with a strong rope, and led her to a stool under a large hook in the joist, put in for the purpose. He made her get upon the stool, and tied her hands to the hook. She now stood fair for his infernal purpose. Her arms were stretched up at their full length, so that she stood upon the ends of her toes. He then said to her, "Now, you d—d b—h, I'll learn you how to disobey my orders!" and after rolling up his sleeves, he commenced to lay on the heavy cowskin, and soon the warm, red blood (amid heart-rending shrieks from her, and horrid oaths from him) came dripping to the floor. I was so terrified and horror-stricken at the sight, that I hid myself in a closet, and dared not venture out till long after the bloody transaction was over. I expected it would be my turn next. It was all new to me. I had never seen any thing like it before. I had always lived with my grandmother on the outskirts of the plantation, where she was put to raise the children of the younger women. I had therefore been, until now, out of the way of the bloody scenes that often occurred on the plantation.

CHAPTER II

My master's family consisted of two sons, Andrew and Richard; one daughter, Lucretia, and her husband, Captain Thomas Auld. They lived in one house, upon the home plantation of Colonel Edward Lloyd. My master was Colonel Lloyd's clerk and superintendent. He was what might be called the overseer of the overseers. I spent two years of childhood on this plantation in my old master's family. It was here that I witnessed the bloody transaction recorded in the first chapter; and as I received my first impressions of slavery on this plantation, I will give some description of it, and of slavery as it there existed. The plantation is about twelve miles north of Easton, in Talbot county, and is situated on the border of Miles River. The principal products raised upon it were tobacco, corn, and wheat. These were raised in great abundance; so that, with the products of this and the other farms belonging to him, he was able to keep in almost constant employment a large sloop, in carrying them to market at Baltimore. This sloop was named *Sally Lloyd*, in honor of one of the colonel's daughters. My master's son-in-law, Captain Auld, was master of the vessel; she was otherwise manned by the colonel's own slaves. Their names were Peter, Isaac, Rich, and Jake. These were esteemed very highly by the other slaves, and looked upon as the privileged ones of the plantation; for it was no small affair, in the eyes of the slaves, to be allowed to see Baltimore.

Colonel Lloyd kept from three to four hundred slaves on his home plantation, and owned a large number more on the neighboring farms belonging to him. The names of the farms nearest to the home plantation were Wye Town and New Design. "Wye Town" was under the overseership of a man named

Noah Willis. New Design was under the overseership of a Mr. Townsend. The overseers of these, and all the rest of the farms, numbering over twenty, received advice and direction from the managers of the home plantation. This was the great business place. It was the seat of government for the whole twenty farms. All disputes among the overseers were settled here. If a slave was convicted of any high misdemeanor, became unmanageable, or evinced a determination to run away, he was brought immediately here, severely whipped, put on board the sloop, carried to Baltimore, and sold to Austin Woolfolk, or some other slave-trader, as a warning to the slaves remaining.

Here, too, the slaves of all the other farms received their monthly allowance of food, and their yearly clothing. The men and women slaves received, as their monthly allowance of food, eight pounds of pork, or its equivalent in fish, and one bushel of corn meal. Their yearly clothing consisted of two coarse linen shirts, one pair of linen trousers, like the shirts, one jacket, one pair of trousers for winter, made of coarse negro cloth, one pair of stockings, and one pair of shoes; the whole of which could not have cost more than seven dollars. The allowance of the slave children was given to their mothers, or the old women having the care of them. The children unable to work in the field had neither shoes, stockings, jackets, nor trousers, given to them; their clothing consisted of two coarse linen shirts per year. When these failed them, they went naked until the next allowance-day. Children from seven to ten years old, of both sexes, almost naked, might be seen at all seasons of the year.

There were no beds given the slaves, unless one coarse blanket be considered such, and none but the men and women had these. This, however, is not considered a very great privation. They find less difficulty from the want of beds, than from the want of time to sleep; for when their day's work in the field is done, the most of them having their washing, mending, and cooking to do, and having few or none of the ordinary facilities for doing either of these, very many of their sleeping hours are consumed in preparing for the field the coming day; and when this is done, old and young, male and female, married and single, drop down side by side, on one common bed,—the cold, damp floor,—each covering himself or herself with their miserable blankets; and here they sleep till they are summoned to the field by the driver's horn. At the sound of this, all must rise, and be off to the field. There must be no halting; every one must be at his or her post; and woe betides them who hear not this morning summons to the field; for if they are not awakened by the sense of hearing, they are by the sense of feeling: no age nor sex finds any favor. Mr. Severe, the overseer, used to stand by the door of the quarter, armed with a large hickory stick and heavy cowskin, ready to whip any one who was so unfortunate as not to hear, or, from any other cause, was prevented from being ready to start for the field at the sound of the horn.

Mr. Severe was rightly named: he was a cruel man. I have seen him whip a woman, causing the blood to run half an hour at the time; and this, too, in the midst of her crying children, pleading for their mother's release. He seemed to take pleasure in manifesting his fiendish barbarity. Added to his cruelty, he was a profane swearer. It was enough to chill the blood and stiffen the hair of an ordinary man to hear him talk. Scarce a sentence escaped him but that was commenced or concluded by some horrid oath. The field was the place to witness his cruelty and profanity. His presence made it both the field of blood and of blasphemy. From the rising till the going down of the sun, he was cursing, raving, cutting, and slashing among the slaves of the field, in the most frightful manner. His career was short. He died very soon after I went to Colonel Lloyd's; and he died as he lived, uttering, with his dying groans, bitter curses and horrid oaths. His death was regarded by the slaves as the result of a merciful providence.

Mr. Severe's place was filled by a Mr. Hopkins. He was a very different man. He was less cruel, less profane, and made less noise, than Mr. Severe. His course was characterized by no extraordinary demonstrations of cruelty. He whipped, but seemed to take no pleasure in it. He was called by the slaves a good overseer.

The home plantation of Colonel Lloyd wore the appearance of a country village. All the mechanical operations for all the farms were performed here. The shoemaking and mending, the blacksmithing, cartwrighting, coopering, weaving, and grain-grinding, were all performed by the slaves on the home plantation. The whole place wore a business-like aspect very unlike the neighboring farms. The number of houses, too, conspired to give it advantage over the neighboring farms. It was called by the slaves the *Great House Farm.* Few privileges were esteemed higher, by the slaves of the out-farms, than that of being selected to do errands at the Great House Farm. It was associated in their minds with greatness. A representative could not be prouder of his election to a seat in the American Congress, than a slave on one of the out-farms would be of his election to do errands at the Great House Farm. They regarded it as evidence of great confidence reposed in them by their overseers; and it was on this account, as well as a constant desire to be out of the field from under the driver's lash, that they esteemed it a high privilege, one worth careful living for. He was called the smartest and most trusty fellow, who had this honor conferred upon him the most frequently. The competitors for this office sought as diligently to please their overseers, as the office-seekers in the political parties seek to please and deceive the people. The same traits of character might be seen in Colonel Lloyd's slaves, as are seen in the slaves of the political parties.

The slaves selected to go to the Great House Farm, for the monthly allowance for themselves and their fellow-slaves, were peculiarly enthusiastic. While on their way, they would make the dense old woods, for miles around, reverberate with their wild songs, revealing at once the highest joy and the deepest sadness. They would compose and sing as they went along, consulting neither time nor tune. The thought that came up, came out—if not in the word, in the sound;—and as frequently in the one as in the other. They would sometimes sing the most pathetic sentiment in the most rapturous tone, and the most rapturous sentiment in the most pathetic tone. Into all of their songs they would manage to weave something of the Great House Farm. Especially would they do this, when leaving home. They would then sing most exultingly the following words:—

> "I am going away to the Great House Farm!
> O, yea! O, yea! O!"

This they would sing, as a chorus, to words which to many would seem unmeaning jargon, but which, nevertheless, were full of meaning to themselves. I have sometimes thought that the mere hearing of those songs would do more to impress some minds with the horrible character of slavery, than the reading of whole volumes of philosophy on the subject could do.

I did not, when a slave, understand the deep meaning of those rude and apparently incoherent songs. I was myself within the circle; so that I neither saw nor heard as those without might see and hear. They told a tale of woe which was then altogether beyond my feeble comprehension; they were tones loud, long, and deep; they breathed the prayer and complaint of souls boiling over with the bitterest anguish. Every tone was a testimony against slavery, and a prayer to god for deliverance from chains. The hearing of those wild notes always depressed my spirit, and filled me with ineffable sadness. I have frequently found myself in tears while hearing them. The mere recurrence to those songs, even now, afflicts me; and while I am writing these lines, an expression of feeling has already found its way down my cheek. To those songs I trace my first glimmering conception of the dehumanizing character of slavery. I can never get rid of that conception. Those songs still follow me, to deepen my hatred of slavery, and quicken my sympathies for my brethren in bonds. If any one wishes to be impressed with the soul-killing effects of slavery, let him go to Colonel Lloyd's plantation, and, on allowance-day, place himself in the deep pine woods, and there let him, in silence, analyze the sounds that shall pass through the chambers of his soul,—and if he is not thus impressed, it will only be because "there is no flesh in his obdurate heart."

I have often been utterly astonished, since I came to the north, to find persons who could speak of the singing, among slaves, as evidence of their contentment and happiness. It is impossible to conceive of a greater mistake. Slaves sing most when they are most unhappy. The songs of the slave represent the sorrows of his heart; and he is relieved by them, only as an aching heart is relieved by its tears. At least, such is my experience. I have often sung to drown my sorrow, but seldom to express my happiness. Crying for joy, and singing for joy, were alike uncommon to me while in the jaws of slavery. The singing of a man cast away upon a desolate island might be as appropriately considered as evidence of contentment and happiness, as the singing of a slave; the songs of the one and of the other are prompted by the same emotion.

CHAPTER III

Colonel Lloyd kept a large and finely cultivated garden, which afforded almost constant employment for four men, besides the chief gardener (Mr. M'Durmond). This garden was probably the greatest attraction of the place. During the summer months, people came from far and near—from Baltimore, Easton, and Annapolis—to see it. It abounded in fruits of almost every description, from the hardy apple of the north to the delicate orange of the south. This garden was not the least source of trouble on the plantation. Its excellent fruit was quite a temptation to the hungry swarms of boys, as well as the older slaves, belonging to the colonel, few of whom had the virtue or the vice to resist it. Scarcely a day passed, during the summer, but that some slave had to take the lash for stealing fruit. The colonel had to resort to all kinds of stratagems to keep his slaves out of the garden. The last and most successful one was that of tarring his fence all around; after which, if a slave was caught with tar upon his person, it was deemed sufficient proof that he had either been into the garden, or had tried to get in. In either case, he was severely whipped by the chief gardener. This plan worked well; the slaves became as fearful of tar as of the lash. They seemed to realize the impossibility of touching *tar* without being defiled.[3]

The colonel also kept a splendid riding equipage. His stable and carriage-house presented the appearance of some of our large city livery establishments. His horses were of the finest form and noblest blood. His carriage-house contained three splendid coaches, three or four gigs, besides dearborns and barouches[4] of the most fashionable style.

This establishment was under the care of two slaves—old Barney and young Barney—father and son. To attend to this establishment was their sole work. But it was by no means an easy employment; for in nothing was Colonel Lloyd more particular than in the management of his horses. The slightest inattention to these was unpardonable, and was visited upon those, under whose care they were placed, with the severest punishment; no excuse could shield them, if the colonel only suspected any want of attention to his horses—a supposition which he frequently indulged, and one which, of course, made the office of old and young Barney a very trying one. They never knew when they were safe from punishment. They were frequently whipped when least deserving, and escaped whipping when most deserving it. Every thing depended upon the looks of the horses, and the state of Colonel Lloyd's own mind when his horses were brought to him for use. If a horse did not move fast enough, or hold his head high enough, it was owing to some fault of his keepers. It was painful to stand near the stable-door, and hear the various complaints against the keepers when a horse was taken out for use. "This horse has not had proper attention. He has not been sufficiently rubbed and curried, or he has not been properly fed; his food was too wet or too dry; he got it too soon or too late; he was too hot or too cold; he had too much hay, and not enough of grain; or he had too much grain, and not enough of hay; instead of old Barney's attending to the horse, he had very improperly left it to his son." To all these complaints, no matter how unjust, the slave must answer never a word. Colonel Lloyd could not brook any contradiction from a slave. When he spoke, a slave must stand, listen, and tremble; and such was literally the case. I have seen Colonel Lloyd make old Barney, a man between fifty and sixty years of age, uncover his bald head, kneel down upon the cold, damp ground, and receive upon his naked and toil-worn shoulders more than thirty lashes at the time. Colonel Lloyd had three sons—Edward, Murray, and Daniel,—and three sons-in-law, Mr. Winder, Mr. Nicholson, and Mr. Lowndes. All of these lived at the Great House Farm, and enjoyed the luxury of whipping the servants when they pleased, from old Barney down to William Wilkes, the coach-driver. I have seen Winder make one of the house-servants stand off from him a suitable distance to be touched with the end of his whip, and at every stroke raise great ridges upon his back.

To describe the wealth of Colonel Lloyd would be almost equal to describing the riches of Job.[5] He kept from ten to fifteen house-servants. He was said to

---

3. Cf. the proverb "He who touches pitch shall be defiled."
4. Light four-wheeled carriages (*dearborns*) and carriages with a front seat for the driver and two facing back seats for couples (*barouches*).
5. Job 1.3: "His substance also was seven thousand sheep, and three thousand camels, and five hundred yoke of oxen, and five hundred she asses, and a very great household; so that this man was the greatest of all the men of the East."

own a thousand slaves, and I think this estimate quite within the truth. Colonel Lloyd owned so many that he did not know them when he saw them; nor did all the slaves of the out-farms know him. It is reported of him, that, while riding along the road one day, he met a colored man, and addressed him in the usual manner of speaking to colored people on the public highways of the south: "Well, boy, whom do you belong to?" "To Colonel Lloyd," replied the slave. "Well, does the colonel treat you well?" "No, sir," was the ready reply. "What, does he work you too hard?" "Yes, sir." "Well, don't he give you enough to eat?" "Yes, sir, he gives me enough, such as it is."

The colonel, after ascertaining where the slave belonged, rode on; the man also went on about his business, not dreaming that he had been conversing with his master. He thought, said, and heard nothing more of the matter, until two or three weeks afterwards. The poor man was then informed by his overseer that, for having found fault with his master, he was now to be sold to a Georgia trader. He was immediately chained and handcuffed; and thus, without a moment's warning, he was snatched away, and forever sundered, from his family and friends, by a hand more unrelenting than death. This is the penalty of telling the truth, of telling the simple truth, in answer to a series of plain questions.

It is partly in consequence of such facts, that slaves, when inquired of as to their condition and the character of their masters, almost universally say they are contented, and that their masters are kind. The slaveholders have been known to send in spies among their slaves, to ascertain their views and feelings in regard to their condition. The frequency of this has had the effect to establish among the slaves the maxim, that a still tongue makes a wise head. They suppress the truth rather than take the consequences of telling it, and in so doing prove themselves a part of the human family. If they have any thing to say of their masters, it is generally in their masters' favor, especially when speaking to an untried man. I have been frequently asked, when a slave, if I had a kind master, and do not remember ever to have given a negative answer; nor did I, in pursuing this course, consider myself as uttering what was absolutely false; for I always measured the kindness of my master by the standard of kindness set up among slaveholders around us. Moreover, slaves are like other people, and imbibe prejudices quite common to others. They think their own better than that of others. Many, under the influence of this prejudice, think their own masters are better than the masters of other slaves; and this, too, in some cases, when the very reverse is true. Indeed, it is not uncommon for slaves even to fall out and quarrel among themselves about the relative goodness of their masters, each contending for the superior goodness of his own over that of the others. At the very same time, they mutually execrate their masters when viewed separately. It was so on our plantation. When Colonel Lloyd's slaves met the slaves of Jacob Jepson, they seldom parted without a quarrel about their masters; Colonel Lloyd's slaves contending that he was the richest, and Mr. Jepson's slaves that he was the smartest, and most of a man. Colonel Lloyd's slaves would boast his ability to buy and sell Jacob Jepson. Mr. Jepson's slaves would boast his ability to whip Colonel Lloyd. These quarrels would almost always end in a fight between the parties, and those that whipped were supposed to have gained the point at issue. They seemed to think that the greatness of their masters was transferable to themselves. It was considered as being bad enough to be a slave; but to be a poor man's slave was deemed a disgrace indeed!

CHAPTER IV

Mr. Hopkins remained but a short time in the office of overseer. Why his career was so short, I do not know, but suppose he lacked the necessary severity to suit Colonel Lloyd. Mr. Hopkins was succeeded by Mr. Austin Gore, a man possessing, in an eminent degree, all those traits of character indispensable to what is called a first-rate overseer. Mr. Gore had served Colonel Lloyd, in the capacity of overseer, upon one of the out-farms, and had shown himself worthy of the high station of overseer upon the home or Great House Farm.

Mr. Gore was proud, ambitious, and persevering. He was artful, cruel, and obdurate. He was just the man for such a place, and it was just the place for such a man. It afforded scope for the full exercise of all his powers, and he seemed to be perfectly at home in it. He was one of those who could torture the slightest look, word, or gesture, on the part of the slave, into impudence, and would treat it accordingly. There must be no answering back to him; no explanation was allowed a slave, showing himself to have been wrongfully accused. Mr. Gore acted fully up to the maxim laid down by slaveholders,—"It is better that a dozen slaves suffer under the lash, than that the overseer should be convicted, in the presence of the slaves, of having been at fault." No matter how innocent a slave might be—it availed him nothing, when accused by Mr. Gore of any misdemeanor. To be accused was to be convicted, and to be convicted was to be punished; the one always following the other with immutable certainty. To escape punishment was to escape accusation; and few slaves had the fortune to do either, under the overseership of Mr. Gore. He was just proud enough to demand the most debasing homage of the slave, and quite servile enough to crouch, himself, at the feet of the master. He was ambitious enough to be contented with nothing short of the highest rank of overseers, and persevering enough to reach the height of his ambition. He was cruel enough to inflict the severest punishment, artful enough to descend to the lowest trickery, and obdurate enough to be insensible to the voice of a reproving conscience. He was, of all the overseers, the most dreaded by the slaves. His presence was painful; his eye flashed confusion; and seldom was his sharp, shrill voice heard, without producing horror and trembling in their ranks.

Mr. Gore was a grave man, and, though a young man, he indulged in no jokes, said no funny words, seldom smiled. His words were in perfect keeping with his looks, and his looks were in perfect keeping with his words. Overseers will sometimes indulge in a witty word, even with the slaves; not so with Mr. Gore. He spoke but to command, and commanded but to be obeyed; he dealt sparingly with his words, and bountifully with his whip, never using the former where the latter would answer as well. When he whipped, he seemed to do so from a sense of duty, and feared no consequences. He did nothing reluctantly, no matter how disagreeable; always at his post, never inconsistent. He never promised but to fulfil. He was, in a word, a man of the most inflexible firmness and stone-like coolness.

His savage barbarity was equalled only by the consummate coolness with which he committed the grossest and most savage deeds upon the slaves under his charge. Mr. Gore once undertook to whip one of Colonel Lloyd's slaves, by the name of Demby. He had given Demby but few stripes, when, to get rid of the scourging, he ran and plunged himself into a creek, and stood there at the depth of his shoulders, refusing to come out. Mr. Gore told him that he would give him three calls, and that, if he did not come out at the third call, he would shoot him. The first call was given. Demby made no response, but stood his ground. The second and third calls were given with the same result. Mr. Gore then, without consultation or deliberation with any one, not even giving Demby an additional call, raised his musket to his face, taking deadly aim at his standing victim, and in an instant poor Demby was no more. His mangled body sank out of sight, and blood and brains marked the water where he had stood.

A thrill of horror flashed through every soul upon the plantation, excepting Mr. Gore. He alone seemed cool and collected. He was asked by Colonel Lloyd and my old master, why he resorted to this extraordinary expedient. His reply was, (as well as I can remember,) that Demby had become unmanageable. He was setting a dangerous example to the other slaves,—one which, if suffered to pass without some such demonstration on his part, would finally lead to the total subversion of all rule and order upon the plantation. He argued that if one slave refused to be corrected, and escaped with his life, the other slaves would soon copy the example; the result of which would be, the freedom of the slaves, and the enslavement of the whites. Mr. Gore's defence was satisfactory. He was continued in his station as overseer upon the home plantation. His fame as an overseer went abroad. His horrid crime was not even submitted to judicial investigation. It was committed in the presence of slaves, and they of course could neither institute a suit, nor testify against him; and thus the guilty perpetrator of one of the bloodiest and most foul murders goes unwhipped of justice, and uncensured by the community in which he lives. Mr. Gore lived in St. Michael's, Talbot county, Maryland, when I left there; and if he is still alive, he very probably lives there now; and if so, he is now, as he was then, as highly esteemed and as much respected as though his guilty soul had not been stained with his brother's blood.

I speak advisedly when I say this,—that killing a slave, or any colored person, in Talbot county, Maryland, is not treated as a crime, either by the courts or the community. Mr. Thomas Lanman, of St. Michael's, killed two slaves, one of whom he killed with a hatchet, by knocking his brains out. He used to boast of the commission of the awful and bloody deed. I have heard him do so laughingly, saying, among other things, that he was the only benefactor of his country in the company, and that when others would do as much as he had done, we should be relieved of "the d——d niggers."

The wife of Mr. Giles Hicks, living but a short distance from where I used to live, murdered my wife's cousin, a young girl between fifteen and sixteen years of age, mangling her person in the most horrible manner, breaking her nose and breastbone with a stick, so that the poor girl expired in a few hours afterward. She was immediately buried, but had not been in her untimely grave but a few hours before she was taken up and examined by the coroner, who decided that she had come to her death by severe beating. The offence for which this girl was thus murdered was this:—She had been set that night to mind Mrs. Hicks's baby, and during the night she fell asleep, and the baby cried. She, having lost her rest for several nights previous, did not hear the crying. They were both in the room with Mrs. Hicks. Mrs. Hicks, finding the girl slow to move, jumped from her bed, seized an oak stick of wood by the fireplace, and with it broke the girl's nose and breastbone, and thus ended her life.

I will not say that this most horrid murder produced no sensation in the community. It did produce sensation, but not enough to bring the murderess to punishment. There was a warrant issued for her arrest, but it was never served. Thus she escaped not only punishment, but even the pain of being arraigned before a court for her horrid crime.

Whilst I am detailing bloody deeds which took place during my stay on Colonel Lloyd's plantation, I will briefly narrate another, which occurred about the same time as the murder of Demby by Mr. Gore.

Colonel Lloyd's slaves were in the habit of spending a part of their nights and Sundays in fishing for oysters, and in this way made up the deficiency of their scanty allowance. An old man belonging to Colonel Lloyd, while thus engaged, happened to get beyond the limits of Colonel Lloyd's, and on the premises of Mr. Beal Bondly. At this trespass, Mr. Bondly took offence, and with his musket came down to the shore, and blew its deadly contents into the poor old man.

Mr. Bondly came over to see Colonel Lloyd the next day, whether to pay him for his property, or to justify himself in what he had done, I know not. At any rate, this whole fiendish transaction was soon hushed up. There was very little said about it at all, and nothing done. It was a common saying, even among little white boys, that it was worth a half-cent to kill a "nigger," and a half-cent to bury one.

CHAPTER V

As to my own treatment while I lived on Colonel Lloyd's plantation, it was very similar to that of the other slave children. I was not old enough to work in the field, and there being little else than field work to do, I had a great deal of leisure time. The most I had to do was to drive up the cows at evening, keep the fowls out of the garden, keep the front yard clean, and run off errands for my old master's daughter, Mrs. Lucretia Auld. The most of my leisure time I spent in helping Master Daniel Lloyd in finding his birds, after he had shot them. My connection with Master Daniel was of some advantage to me. He became quite attached to me, and was a sort of protector of me. He would not allow the older boys to impose upon me, and would divide his cakes with me.

I was seldom whipped by my old master, and suffered little from any thing else than hunger and cold. I suffered much from hunger, but much more from cold. In hottest summer and coldest winter, I was kept almost naked—no shoes, no stockings, no jacket, no trousers, nothing on but a coarse tow linen shirt, reaching only to my knees. I had no bed. I must have perished with cold, but that, the coldest nights, I used to steal a bag which was used for carrying corn to the mill. I would crawl into this bag, and there sleep on the cold, damp, clay floor, with my head in and feet out. My feet had been so cracked with the frost, that the pen with which I am writing might be laid in the gashes.

We were not regularly allowanced. Our food was coarse corn meal boiled. This was called *mush*. It was put into a large wooden tray or trough, and set down upon the ground. The children were then called, like so many pigs, and like so many pigs they would come and devour the mush; some with oyster-shells, others with pieces of shingle, some with naked hands, and none with spoons. He that ate fastest got most; he that was strongest secured the best place; and few left the trough satisfied.

I was probably between seven and eight years old when I left Colonel Lloyd's plantation. I left it with joy. I shall never forget the ecstasy with which I received the intelligence that my old master (Anthony) had determined to let me go to Baltimore, to live with Mr. Hugh Auld, brother to my old master's son-in-law, Captain Thomas Auld. I received this information about three days before my departure. They were three of the happiest days I ever enjoyed. I spent the most part of all these three days in the creek, washing off the plantation scurf, and preparing myself for my departure.

The pride of appearance which this would indicate was not my own. I spent the time in washing, not so much because I wished to, but because Mrs. Lucretia had told me I must get all the dead skin off my feet and knees before I could go to Baltimore; for the people in Baltimore were very cleanly, and would laugh at me if I looked dirty. Besides, she was going to give me a pair of trousers, which I should not put on unless I got all the dirt off me. The thought of owning a pair of trousers was great indeed! It was almost a sufficient motive, not only to make me take off what would be called by pig-drovers the mange, but the skin itself. I went at it in good earnest, working for the first time with the hope of reward.

The ties that ordinarily bind children to their homes were all suspended in my case. I found no severe trial in my departure. My home was charmless; it was not home to me; on parting from it, I could not feel that I was leaving any thing which I could have enjoyed by staying. My mother was dead, my grand-mother lived far off, so that I seldom saw her. I had two sisters and one brother, that lived in the same house with me; but the early separation of us from our mother had well nigh blotted the fact of our relationship from our memories. I looked for home elsewhere, and was confident of finding none which I should relish less than the one which I was leaving. If, however, I found in my new home hardship, hunger, whipping, and nakedness, I had the consolation that I should not have escaped any one of them by staying. Having already had more than a taste of them in the house of my old master, and having endured them there, I very naturally inferred my ability to endure them elsewhere, and especially at Baltimore; for I had something of the feeling about Baltimore that is expressed in the proverb, that "being hanged in England is preferable to dying a natural death in Ireland." I had the strongest desire to see Baltimore. Cousin Tom, though not fluent in speech, had inspired me with that desire by his eloquent description of the place. I could never point out any thing at the Great House, no matter how beautiful or powerful, but that he had seen some-thing at Baltimore far exceeding, both in beauty and strength, the object which I pointed out to him. Even the Great House itself, with all its pictures, was far inferior to many buildings in Baltimore. So strong was my desire, that I thought a gratification of it would fully compensate for whatever loss of comforts I should sustain by the exchange. I left without a regret, and with the highest hopes of future happiness.

We sailed out of Miles River for Baltimore on a Saturday morning. I remem-ber only the day of the week, for at that time I had no knowledge of the days of the month, nor the months of the year. On setting sail, I walked aft, and gave to Colonel Lloyd's plantation what I hoped would be the last look. I then placed myself in the bows of the sloop, and there spent the remainder of the day in looking ahead, interesting myself in what was in the distance rather than in things near by or behind.

In the afternoon of that day, we reached Annapolis, the capital of the State. We stopped but a few moments, so that I had no time to go on shore. It was the first large town that I had ever seen, and though it would look small compared with some of our New England factory villages, I thought it a wonderful place for its size—more imposing even than the Great House Farm!

We arrived at Baltimore early on Sunday morning, landing at Smith's Wharf, not far from Bowley's Wharf. We had on board the sloop a large flock of sheep; and after aiding in driving them to the slaughterhouse of Mr. Curtis on Louden Slater's Hill, I was conducted by Rich, one of the hands belonging on board of the sloop, to my new home in Alliciana Street, near Mr. Gardner's ship-yard, on Fells Point.

Mr. and Mrs. Auld were both at home, and met me at the door with their little son Thomas, to take care of whom I had been given. And here I saw what I had never seen before; it was a white face beaming with the most kindly emotions; it was the face of my new mistress, Sophia Auld. I wish I could describe the rapture that flashed through my soul as I beheld it. It was a new and strange sight to me, brightening up my pathway with the light of happiness. Little Thomas was told, there was his Freddy,—and I was told to take care of little Thomas; and thus I entered upon the duties of my new home with the most cheering prospect ahead.

I look upon my departure from Colonel Lloyd's plantation as one of the most interesting events of my life. It is possible, and even quite probable, that but for the mere circumstance of being removed from that plantation to Baltimore, I should have to-day, instead of being here seated by my own table, in the enjoyment of freedom and the happiness of home, writing this Narrative, been confined in the galling chains of slavery. Going to live at Baltimore laid the foundation, and opened the gateway, to all my subsequent prosperity. I have ever regarded it as the first plain manifestation of that kind providence which has ever since attended me, and marked my life with so many favors. I regarded the selection of myself as being somewhat remarkable. There were a number of slave children that might have been sent from the plantation to Baltimore. There were those younger, those older, and those of the same age. I was chosen from among them all, and was the first, last, and only choice.

I may be deemed superstitious, and even egotistical, in regarding this event as a special interposition of divine Providence in my favor. But I should be false to the earliest sentiments of my soul, if I suppressed the opinion. I prefer to be true to myself, even at the hazard of incurring the ridicule of others, rather than to be false, and incur my own abhorrence. From my earliest recollection, I date the entertainment of a deep conviction that slavery would not always be able to hold me within its foul embrace; and in the darkest hours of my career in slavery, this living word of faith and spirit of hope departed not from me, but remained like ministering angels to cheer me through the gloom. This good spirit was from God, and to him I offer thanksgiving and praise.

CHAPTER VI

My new mistress proved to be all she appeared when I first met her at the door,—a woman of the kindest heart and finest feelings. She had never had a slave under her control previously to myself, and prior to her marriage she had been dependent upon her own industry for a living. She was by trade a weaver; and by constant application to her business, she had been in a good degree preserved from the blighting and dehumanizing effects of slavery. I was utterly astonished at her goodness. I scarcely knew how to behave towards her. She was entirely unlike any other white woman I had ever seen. I could not approach her as I was accustomed to approach other white ladies. My early instruction was all out of place. The crouching servility, usually so acceptable a quality in a slave, did not answer when manifested toward her. Her favor was not gained by it; she seemed to be disturbed by it. She did not deem it impudent or unmannerly for a slave to look her in the face. The meanest slave was put fully at ease in her presence, and none left without feeling better for having seen her. Her face was made of heavenly smiles, and her voice of tranquil music.

But, alas! this kind heart had but a short time to remain such. The fatal poison of irresponsible power was already in her hands, and soon commenced its infernal work. That cheerful eye, under the influence of slavery, soon became red with rage; that voice, made all of sweet accord, changed to one of harsh and horrid discord; and that angelic face gave place to that of a demon.

Very soon after I went to live with Mr. and Mrs. Auld, she very kindly commenced to teach me the A, B, C. After I had learned this, she assisted me in learning to spell words of three or four letters. Just at this point of my progress, Mr. Auld found out what was going on, and at once forbade Mrs. Auld to instruct me further, telling her, among other things, that it was unlawful, as well as unsafe, to teach a slave to read. To use his own words, further, he said, "If you give a nigger an inch, he will take an ell. A nigger should know nothing but to obey his master—to do as he is told to do. Learning would *spoil* the best nigger in the world. Now," said he, "if you teach that nigger (speaking of myself) how to read, there would be no keeping him. It would forever unfit him to be a slave. He would at once become unmanageable, and of no value to his master. As to himself, it could do him no good, but a great deal of harm. It would make him discontented and unhappy." These words sank deep into my heart, stirred up sentiments within that lay slumbering, and called into existence an entirely new train of thought. It was a new and special revelation, explaining dark and mysterious things, with which my youthful understanding had struggled, but struggled in vain. I now understood what had been to me a most perplexing difficulty—to wit, the white man's power to enslave the black man. It was a grand achievement, and I prized it highly. From that moment, I understood the pathway from slavery to freedom. It was just what I wanted, and I got it at a time when I the least expected it. Whilst I was saddened by the thought of losing the aid of my kind mistress, I was gladdened by the invaluable instruction which, by the merest accident, I had gained from my master. Though conscious of the difficulty of learning without a teacher, I set out with high hope, and a fixed purpose, at whatever cost of trouble, to learn how to read. The very decided manner with which he spoke, and strove to impress his wife with the evil consequences of giving me instruction, served to convince me that he was deeply sensible of the truths he was uttering. It gave me the best assurance that I might rely with the utmost confidence on the results which, he said, would flow from teaching me to read. What he most dreaded, that I most desired. What he most loved, that I most hated. That which to him

was a great evil, to be carefully shunned, was to me a great good, to be diligently sought; and the argument which he so warmly urged, against my learning to read, only served to inspire me with a desire and determination to learn.
In learning to read, I owe almost as much to the bitter opposition of my master,
as to the kindly aid of my mistress. I acknowledge the benefit of both.

I had resided but a short time in Baltimore before I observed a marked difference, in the treatment of slaves, from that which I had witnessed in the country. A city slave is almost a freeman, compared with a slave on the plantation.
He is much better fed and clothed, and enjoys privileges altogether unknown
to the slave on the plantation. There is a vestige of decency, a sense of shame,
that does much to curb and check those outbreaks of atrocious cruelty so commonly enacted upon the plantation. He is a desperate slaveholder, who will
shock the humanity of his nonslaveholding neighbors with the cries of his lacerated slave. Few are willing to incur the odium attaching to the reputation
of being a cruel master; and above all things, they would not be known as
not giving a slave enough to eat. Every city slaveholder is anxious to have it
known of him, that he feeds his slaves well; and it is due to them to say, that
most of them do give their slaves enough to eat. There are, however, some
painful exceptions to this rule. Directly opposite to us, on Philpot Street, lived
Mr. Thomas Hamilton. He owned two slaves. Their names were Henrietta
and Mary. Henrietta was about twenty-two years of age, Mary was about fourteen; and of all the mangled and emaciated creatures I ever looked upon, these
two were the most so. His heart must be harder than stone, that could look
upon these unmoved. The head, neck, and shoulders of Mary were literally cut
to pieces. I have frequently felt her head, and found it nearly covered with
festering sores, caused by the lash of her cruel mistress. I do not know that
her master ever whipped her, but I have been an eye-witness to the cruelty of
Mrs. Hamilton. I used to be in Mr. Hamilton's house nearly every day.
Mrs. Hamilton used to sit in a large chair in the middle of the room, with a
heavy cowskin always by her side, and scarce an hour passed during the day
but was marked by the blood of one of these slaves. The girls seldom passed
her without her saying, "Move faster, you *black gip!*"[6] at the same time giving
them a blow with the cowskin over the head or shoulders, often drawing the
blood. She would then say, "Take that, you *black gip!*"—continuing, "If you
don't move faster, I'll move you!" Added to the cruel lashings to which these
slaves were subjected, they were kept nearly half-starved. They seldom knew
what it was to eat a full meal. I have seen Mary contending with the pigs for
the offal thrown into the street. So much was Mary kicked and cut to pieces,
that she was oftener called "*pecked*" than by her name.

CHAPTER VII

I lived in Master Hugh's family about seven years. During this time, I succeeded in learning to read and write. In accomplishing this, I was compelled to
resort to various stratagems. I had no regular teacher. My mistress, who had
kindly commenced to instruct me, had, in compliance with the advice and
direction of her husband, not only ceased to instruct, but had set her face

6. Cheat, swindler.

against my being instructed by any one else. It is due, however, to my mistress to say of her, that she did not adopt this course of treatment immediately. She at first lacked the depravity indispensable to shutting me up in mental darkness. It was at least necessary for her to have some training in the exercise of irresponsible power, to make her equal to the task of treating me as though I were a brute.

My mistress was, as I have said, a kind and tender-hearted woman; and in the simplicity of her soul she commenced, when I first went to live with her, to treat me as she supposed one human being ought to treat another. In entering upon the duties of a slaveholder, she did not seem to perceive that I sustained to her the relation of a mere chattel, and that for her to treat me as a human being was not only wrong, but dangerously so. Slavery proved as injurious to her as it did to me. When I went there, she was a pious, warm, and tender-hearted woman. There was no sorrow or suffering for which she had not a tear. She had bread for the hungry, clothes for the naked, and comfort for every mourner that came within her reach. Slavery soon proved its ability to divest her of these heavenly qualities. Under its influence, the tender heart became stone, and the lamblike disposition gave way to one of tiger-like fierceness. The first step in her downward course was in her ceasing to instruct me. She now commenced to practise her husband's precepts. She finally became even more violent in her opposition than her husband himself. She was not satisfied with simply doing as well as he had commanded; she seemed anxious to do better. Nothing seemed to make her more angry than to see me with a newspaper. She seemed to think that here lay the danger. I have had her rush at me with a face made all up of fury, and snatch from me a newspaper, in a manner that fully revealed her apprehension. She was an apt woman; and a little experience soon demonstrated, to her satisfaction, that education and slavery were incompatible with each other.

From this time I was most narrowly watched. If I was in a separate room any considerable length of time, I was sure to be suspected of having a book, and was at once called to give an account of myself. All this, however, was too late. The first step had been taken. Mistress, in teaching me the alphabet, had given me the *inch*, and no precaution could prevent me from taking the *ell*.

The plan which I adopted, and the one by which I was most successful, was that of making friends of all the little white boys whom I met in the street. As many of these as I could, I converted into teachers. With their kindly aid, obtained at different times and in different places, I finally succeeded in learning to read. When I was sent of errands, I always took my book with me, and by going one part of my errand quickly, I found time to get a lesson before my return. I used also to carry bread with me, enough of which was always in the house, and to which I was always welcome; for I was much better off in this regard than many of the poor white children in our neighborhood. This bread I used to bestow upon the hungry little urchins, who, in return, would give me that more valuable bread of knowledge. I am strongly tempted to give the names of two or three of those little boys, as a testimonial of the gratitude and affection I bear them; but prudence forbids;—not that it would injure me, but it might embarrass them; for it is almost an unpardonable offence to teach slaves to read in this Christian country. It is enough to say of the dear little fellows, that they lived on Philpot Street, very near Durgin and Bailey's ship-yard. I used to talk this matter of slavery over with them. I would sometimes say to them, I wished I could be as free as they would be when they got to be men. "You will be free as soon as you are twenty-one, *but I am a slave for life!* Have not I as good a right to be free as you have?" These words used to trouble them; they would express for me the liveliest sympathy, and console me with the hope that something would occur by which I might be free.

I was now about twelve years old, and the thought of being *a slave for life* began to bear heavily upon my heart. Just about this time, I got hold of a book entitled "The Columbian Orator."[7] Every opportunity I got, I used to read this book. Among much of other interesting matter, I found in it a dialogue between a master and his slave. The slave was represented as having run away from his master three times. The dialogue represented the conversation which took place between them, when the slave was retaken the third time. In this dialogue, the whole argument in behalf of slavery was brought forward by the master, all of which was disposed of by the slave. The slave was made to say some very smart as well as impressive things in reply to his master—things which had the desired though unexpected effect; for the conversation resulted in the voluntary emancipation of the slave on the part of the master.

In the same book, I met with one of Sheridan's[8] mighty speeches on and in behalf of Catholic emancipation. These were choice documents to me. I read them over and over again with unabated interest. They gave tongue to interesting thoughts of my own soul, which had frequently flashed through my mind, and died away for want of utterance. The moral which I gained from the dialogue was the power of truth over the conscience of even a slaveholder. What I got from Sheridan was a bold denunciation of slavery, and a powerful vindication of human rights. The reading of these documents enabled me to utter my thoughts, and to meet the arguments brought forward to sustain slavery; but while they relieved me of one difficulty, they brought on another even more painful than the one of which I was relieved. The more I read, the more I was led to abhor and detest my enslavers. I could regard them in no other light than a band of successful robbers, who had left their homes, and gone to Africa, and stolen us from our homes, and in a strange land reduced us to slavery. I loathed them as being the meanest as well as the most wicked of men. As I read and contemplated the subject, behold! that very discontentment which Master Hugh had predicted would follow my learning to read had already come, to torment and sting my soul to unutterable anguish. As I writhed under it, I would at times feel that learning to read had been a curse rather than a blessing. It had given me a view of my wretched condition, without the remedy. It opened my eyes to the horrible pit, but to no ladder upon which to get out. In moments of agony, I envied my fellow-slaves for their stupidity. I have often wished myself a beast. I preferred the condition of the meanest reptile to my own. Any thing, no matter what, to get rid of thinking! It was this everlasting thinking of my condition that tormented me. There was no getting rid of it. It was pressed upon me by every object within sight or hearing, animate or inanimate. The silver trump of freedom had roused my soul to eternal wakefulness.

---

7. Caleb Bingham, *The Columbian Orator: Containing a Variety of Original and Selected Pieces: Together with Rules, Calculated to Improve Youth and Others in the Ornamental and Useful Art of Eloquence* (1807).
8. Thomas Sheridan (1719–1788), Irish actor, lecturer, and writer on elocution.

Freedom now appeared, to disappear no more forever. It was heard in every sound, and seen in every thing. It was ever present to torment me with a sense of my wretched condition. I saw nothing without seeing it, I heard nothing without hearing it, and felt nothing without feeling it. It looked from every star, it smiled in every calm, breathed in every wind, and moved in every storm.

I often found myself regretting my own existence, and wishing myself dead; and but for the hope of being free, I have no doubt but that I should have killed myself, or done something for which I should have been killed. While in this state of mind, I was eager to hear any one speak of slavery. I was a ready listener. Every little while, I could hear something about the abolitionists. It was some time before I found what the word meant. It was always used in such connections as to make it an interesting word to me. If a slave ran away and succeeded in getting clear, or if a slave killed his master, set fire to a barn, or did any thing very wrong in the mind of a slaveholder, it was spoken of as the fruit of *abolition*. Hearing the word in this connection very often, I set about learning what it meant. The dictionary afforded me little or no help. I found it was "the act of abolishing"; but then I did not know what was to be abolished. Here I was perplexed. I did not dare to ask any one about its meaning, for I was satisfied that it was something they wanted me to know very little about. After a patient waiting, I got one of our city papers, containing an account of the number of petitions from the north, praying for the abolition of slavery in the District of Columbia, and of the slave trade between the States. From this time I understood the words *abolition* and *abolitionist*, and always drew near when that word was spoken, expecting to hear something of importance to myself and fellow-slaves. The light broke in upon me by degrees. I went one day down on the wharf of Mr. Waters; and seeing two Irishmen unloading a scow of stone, I went, unasked, and helped them. When we had finished, one of them came to me and asked me if I were a slave. I told him I was. He asked, "Are ye a slave for life?" I told him that I was. The good Irishman seemed to be deeply affected by the statement. He said to the other that it was a pity so fine a little fellow as myself should be a slave for life. He said it was a shame to hold me. They both advised me to run away to the north; that I should find friends there, and that I should be free. I pretended not to be interested in what they said, and treated them as if I did not understand them; for I feared they might be treacherous. White men have been known to encourage slaves to escape, and then, to get the reward, catch them and return them to their masters. I was afraid that these seemingly good men might use me so; but I nevertheless remembered their advice, and from that time I resolved to run away. I looked forward to a time at which it would be safe for me to escape. I was too young to think of doing so immediately; besides, I wished to learn how to write, as I might have occasion to write my own pass. I consoled myself with the hope that I should one day find a good chance. Meanwhile, I would learn to write.

The idea as to how I might learn to write was suggested to me by being in Durgin and Bailey's ship-yard, and frequently seeing the ship carpenters, after hewing, and getting a piece of timber ready for use, write on the timber the name of that part of the ship for which it was intended. When a piece of timber was intended for the larboard side, it would be marked thus—"L." When a piece was for the starboard side, it would be marked thus—"S." A piece for the larboard forward, would be marked thus—"L.F." When a piece was for starboard side forward, it would be marked thus—"S.F." For larboard aft, it would be marked thus—"L.A." For starboard aft, it would be marked thus—"S.A." I soon learned the names of these letters, and for what they were intended when placed upon a piece of timber in the ship-yard. I immediately commenced copying them, and in a short time was able to make the four letters named. After that, when I met with any boy who I knew could write, I would tell him I could write as well as he. The next word would be, "I don't believe you. Let me see you try it." I would then make the letters which I had been so fortunate as to learn, and ask him to beat that. In this way I got a good many lessons in writing, which it is quite possible I should never have gotten in any other way. During this time, my copy-book was the board fence, brick wall, and pavement; my pen and ink was a lump of chalk. With these, I learned mainly how to write. I then commenced and continued copying the Italics in Webster's Spelling Book, until I could make them all without looking on the book. By this time, my little Master Thomas had gone to school, and learned how to write, and had written over a number of copy-books. These had been brought home, and shown to some of our near neighbors, and then laid aside. My mistress used to go to class meeting at the Wilk Street meetinghouse every Monday afternoon, and leave me to take care of the house. When left thus, I used to spend the time in writing in the spaces left in Master Thomas's copy-book, copying what he had written. I continued to do this until I could write a hand very similar to that of Master Thomas. Thus, after a long, tedious effort for years, I finally succeeded in learning how to write.

CHAPTER VIII

In a very short time after I went to live at Baltimore, my old master's youngest son Richard died; and in about three years and six months after his death, my old master, Captain Anthony, died, leaving only his son, Andrew, and daughter, Lucretia, to share his estate. He died while on a visit to see his daughter at Hillsborough. Cut off thus unexpectedly, he left no will as to the disposal of his property. It was therefore necessary to have a valuation of the property, that it might be equally divided between Mrs. Lucretia and Master Andrew. I was immediately sent for, to be valued with the other property. Here again my feelings rose up in detestation of slavery. I had now a new conception of my degraded condition. Prior to this, I had become, if not insensible to my lot, at least partly so. I left Baltimore with a young heart overborne with sadness, and a soul full of apprehension. I took passage with Captain Rowe, in the schooner *Wild Cat*, and, after a sail of about twenty-four hours, I found myself near the place of my birth. I had now been absent from it almost, if not quite, five years. I, however, remembered the place very well. I was only about five years old when I left it, to go and live with my old master on Colonel Lloyd's plantation; so that I was now between ten and eleven years old.

We were all ranked together at the valuation. Men and women, old and young, married and single, were ranked with horses, sheep, and swine. There were horses and men, cattle and women, pigs and children, all holding the same rank in the scale of being, and all were subjected to the same narrow examination. Silvery-headed age and sprightly youth, maids and matrons, had to undergo the same indelicate inspection. At this moment, I saw more clearly than ever the brutalizing effects of slavery upon both slave and slaveholder.

After the valuation, then came the division. I have no language to express the high excitement and deep anxiety which were felt among us poor slaves during this time. Our fate for life was now to be decided. We had no more voice in that decision than the brutes among whom we were ranked. A single word from the white men was enough—against all our wishes, prayers, and entreaties—to sunder forever the dearest friends, dearest kindred, and strongest ties known to human beings. In addition to the pain of separation, there was the horrid dread of falling into the hands of Master Andrew. He was known to us all as being a most cruel wretch,—a common drunkard, who had, by his reckless mismanagement and profligate dissipation, already wasted a large portion of his father's property. We all felt that we might as well be sold at once to the Georgia traders, as to pass into his hands; for we knew that that would be our inevitable condition,—a condition held by us all in the utmost horror and dread.

I suffered more anxiety than most of my fellow-slaves. I had known what it was to be kindly treated; they had known nothing of the kind. They had seen little or nothing of the world. They were in very deed men and women of sorrow, and acquainted with grief.[9] Their backs had been made familiar with the bloody lash, so that they had become callous; mine was yet tender; for while at Baltimore I got few whippings, and few slaves could boast of a kinder master and mistress than myself; and the thought of passing out of their hands into those of Master Andrew—a man who, but a few days before, to give me a sample of his bloody disposition, took my little brother by the throat, threw him on the ground, and with the heel of his boot stamped upon his head till the blood gushed from his nose and ears—was well calculated to make me anxious as to my fate. After he had committed this savage outrage upon my brother, he turned to me, and said that was the way he meant to serve me one of these days,—meaning, I suppose, when I came into his possession.

Thanks to a kind Providence, I fell to the portion of Mrs. Lucretia, and was sent immediately back to Baltimore, to live again in the family of Master Hugh. Their joy at my return equalled their sorrow at my departure. It was a glad day to me. I had escaped a [fate] worse than lion's jaws. I was absent from Baltimore, for the purpose of valuation and division, just about one month, and it seemed to have been six.

Very soon after my return to Baltimore, my mistress, Lucretia, died, leaving her husband and one child, Amanda; and in a very short time after her death, Master Andrew died. Now all the property of my old master, slaves included, was in the hands of strangers,—strangers who had had nothing to do with accumulating it. Not a slave was left free. All remained slaves, from the youngest to the oldest. If any one thing in my experience, more than another, served to deepen my conviction of the infernal character of slavery, and to fill me with unutterable loathing of slaveholders, it was their base ingratitude to my poor old grandmother. She had served my old master faithfully from youth to old age. She had been the source of all his wealth; she had peopled his plantation

---

9. In Isaiah 53.3, the Lord's servant is described as "a man of sorrows, and acquainted with grief."

with slaves; she had become a great grandmother in his service. She had rocked him in infancy, attended him in childhood, served him through life, and at his death wiped from his icy brow the cold death-sweat, and closed his eyes forever. She was nevertheless left a slave—a slave for life—a slave in the hands of strangers; and in their hands she saw her children, her grandchildren, and her great-grandchildren, divided, like so many sheep, without being gratified with the small privilege of a single word, as to their or her own destiny. And, to cap the climax of their base ingratitude and fiendish barbarity, my grandmother, who was now very old, having outlived my old master and all his children, having seen the beginning and end of all of them, and her present owners finding she was of but little value, her frame already racked with the pains of old age, and complete helplessness fast stealing over her once active limbs, they took her to the woods, built her a little hut, put up a little mud-chimney, and then made her welcome to the privilege of supporting herself there in perfect loneliness; thus virtually turning her out to die! If my poor old grandmother now lives, she lives to suffer in utter loneliness; she lives to remember and mourn over the loss of children, the loss of grandchildren, and the loss of great-grandchildren. They are, in the language of the slave's poet, Whittier,—

"Gone, gone, sold and gone
To the rice swamp dank and lone,
Where the slave-whip ceaseless swings,
Where the noisome insect stings,
Where the fever-demon strews
Poison with the falling dews,
Where the sickly sunbeams glare
Through the hot and misty air:—
Gone, gone, sold and gone
To the rice swamp dank and lone,
From Virginia hills and waters—
Woe is me, my stolen daughters!"[1]

The hearth is desolate. The children, the unconscious children, who once sang and danced in her presence, are gone. She gropes her way, in the darkness of age, for a drink of water. Instead of the voices of her children, she hears by day the moans of the dove, and by night the screams of the hideous owl. All is gloom. The grave is at the door. And now, when weighed down by the pains and aches of old age, when the head inclines to the feet, when the beginning and ending of human existence meet, and helpless infancy and painful old age combine together—at this time, this most needful time, the time for the exercise of that tenderness and affection which children only can exercise towards a declining parent—my poor old grandmother, the devoted mother of twelve children, is left all alone, in yonder little hut, before a few dim embers. She stands—she sits—she staggers—she falls—she groans—she dies—and there are none of her children or grandchildren present, to wipe from her wrinkled

1. John Greenleaf Whittier, American poet (1807–1892), wrote a large group of antislavery poems. This one is *The Farewell of a Vir-* *ginia Slave Mother to her Daughters Sold into Southern Bondage.*

brow the cold sweat of death, or to place beneath the sod her fallen remains. Will not a righteous God visit[2] for these things?

In about two years after the death of Mrs. Lucretia, Master Thomas married his second wife. Her name was Rowena Hamilton. She was the eldest daughter of Mr. William Hamilton. Master now lived in St. Michael's. Not long after his marriage, a misunderstanding took place between himself and Master Hugh; and as a means of punishing his brother, he took me from him to live with himself at St. Michael's. Here I underwent another most painful separation. It, however, was not so severe as the one I dreaded at the division of property; for, during this interval, a great change had taken place in Master Hugh and his once kind and affectionate wife. The influence of brandy upon him, and of slavery upon her, had effected a disastrous change in the characters of both; so that, as far as they were concerned, I thought I had little to lose by the change. But it was not to them that I was attached. It was to those little Baltimore boys that I felt the strongest attachment. I had received many good lessons from them, and was still receiving them, and the thought of leaving them was painful indeed. I was leaving, too, without the hope of ever being allowed to return. Master Thomas had said he would never let me return again. The barrier betwixt himself and brother he considered impassable.

I then had to regret that I did not at least make the attempt to carry out my resolution to run away; for the chances of success are tenfold greater from the city than from the country.

I sailed from Baltimore for St. Michael's in the sloop *Amanda*, Captain Edward Dodson. On my passage, I paid particular attention to the direction which the steamboats took to go to Philadelphia. I found, instead of going down, on reaching North Point they went up the bay, in a north-easterly direction. I deemed this knowledge of the utmost importance. My determination to run away was again revived. I resolved to wait only so long as the offering of a favorable opportunity. When that came, I was determined to be off.

CHAPTER IX

I have now reached a period of my life when I can give dates. I left Baltimore, and went to live with Master Thomas Auld, at St. Michael's, in March, 1832. It was now more than seven years since I lived with him in the family of my old master, on Colonel Lloyd's plantation. We of course were now almost entire strangers to each other. He was to me a new master, and I to him a new slave. I was ignorant of his temper and disposition; he was equally so of mine. A very short time, however, brought us into full acquaintance with each other. I was made acquainted with his wife not less than with himself. They were well matched, being equally mean and cruel. I was now, for the first time during a space of more than seven years, made to feel the painful gnawings of hunger—a something which I had not experienced before since I left Colonel Lloyd's plantation. It went hard enough with me then, when I could look back to no period at which I had enjoyed a sufficiency. It was tenfold harder after living in Master Hugh's family, where I had always had enough to eat, and of that

2. I.e., visit vengeance. Cf. Exodus 32.34: "Nevertheless, in the day when I visit I will visit their sin upon them."

which was good. I have said Master Thomas was a mean man. He was so. Not to give a slave enough to eat, is regarded as the most aggravated development of meanness even among slaveholders. The rule is, no matter how coarse the food, only let there be enough of it. This is the theory; and in the part of Maryland from which I came, it is the general practice,—though there are many exceptions. Master Thomas gave us enough of neither coarse nor fine food. There were four of us slaves in the kitchen—my sister Eliza, my aunt Priscilla, Henny, and myself; and we were allowed less than a half of a bushel of corn-meal per week, and very little else, either in the shape of meat or vegetables. It was not enough for us to subsist upon. We were therefore reduced to the wretched necessity of living at the expense of our neighbors. This we did by begging and stealing, whichever came handy in the time of need, the one being considered as legitimate as the other. A great many times have we poor creatures been nearly perishing with hunger, when food in abundance lay mouldering in the safe and smoke-house, and our pious mistress was aware of the fact; and yet that mistress and her husband would kneel every morning, and pray that God would bless them in basket and store!

Bad as all slaveholders are, we seldom meet one destitute of every element of character commanding respect. My master was one of this rare sort. I do not know of one single noble act ever performed by him. The leading trait in his character was meanness; and if there were any other element in his nature, it was made subject to this. He was mean; and, like most other mean men, he lacked the ability to conceal his meanness. Captain Auld was not born a slave-holder. He had been a poor man, master only of a Bay craft. He came into pos-session of all his slaves by marriage; and of all men, adopted slaveholders are the worst. He was cruel, but cowardly. He commanded without firmness. In the enforcement of his rules, he was at times rigid, and at times lax. At times, he spoke to his slaves with the firmness of Napoleon and the fury of a demon; at other times, he might well be mistaken for an inquirer who had lost his way. He did nothing of himself. He might have passed for a lion, but for his ears.[3] In all things noble which he attempted, his own meanness shone most conspicu-ous. His airs, words, and actions, were the airs, words, and actions of born slaveholders, and, being assumed, were awkward enough. He was not even a good imitator. He possessed all the disposition to deceive, but wanted the power. Having no resources within himself, he was compelled to be the copyist of many, and being such, he was forever the victim of inconsistency; and of consequence he was an object of contempt, and was held as such even by his slaves. The luxury of having slaves of his own to wait upon him was something new and unprepared for. He was a slaveholder without the ability to hold slaves. He found himself incapable of managing his slaves either by force, fear, or fraud. We seldom called him "master"; we generally called him "Captain Auld," and were hardly disposed to title him at all. I doubt not that our conduct had much to do with making him appear awkward, and of consequence fretful. Our want of reverence for him must have perplexed him greatly. He wished to have us call him master, but lacked the firmness necessary to command us to do so. His wife used to insist upon our calling him so, but to no purpose. In

---

3. A variation on Aesop's fable of the ass in a lion's skin who frightened all of the animals. The fox says: "I would have been frightened too if I had not heard you bray."

August, 1832, my master attended a Methodist camp-meeting held in the Bay-side, Talbot county, and there experienced religion. I indulged a faint hope that his conversion would lead him to emancipate his slaves, and that, if he did not do this, it would, at any rate, make him more kind and humane. I was disap-pointed in both these respects. It neither made him to be humane to his slaves, nor to emancipate them. If it had any effect on his character, it made him more cruel and hateful in all his ways; for I believe him to have been a much worse man after his conversion than before. Prior to his conversion, he relied upon his own depravity to shield and sustain him in his savage barbarity; but after his conversion, he found religious sanction and support for his slaveholding cru-elty. He made the greatest pretensions to piety. His house was the house of prayer. He prayed morning, noon, and night. He very soon distinguished him-self among his brethren, and was soon made a class-leader and exhorter. His activity in revivals was great, and he proved himself an instrument in the hands of the church in converting many souls. His house was the preachers' home. They used to take great pleasure in coming there to put up; for while he starved us, he stuffed them. We have had three or four preachers there at a time. The names of those who used to come most frequently while I lived there, were Mr. Storks, Mr. Ewery, Mr. Humphry, and Mr. Hickey. I have also seen Mr. George Cookman at our house. We slaves loved Mr. Cookman. We believed him to be a good man. We thought him instrumental in getting Mr. Samuel Harrison, a very rich slaveholder, to emancipate his slaves; and by some means got the impression that he was laboring to effect the emancipation of all the slaves. When he was at our house, we were sure to be called in to prayers. When the others were there, we were sometimes called in and sometimes not. Mr. Cookman took more notice of us than either of the other ministers. He could not come among us without betraying his sympathy for us, and, stupid as we were, we had the sagacity to see it.

While I lived with my master in St. Michael's, there was a white young man, a Mr. Wilson, who proposed to keep a Sabbath school for the instruction of such slaves as might be disposed to learn to read the New Testament. We met but three times, when Mr. West and Mr. Fairbanks, both class-leaders, with many others, came upon us with sticks and other missiles, drove us off, and forbade us to meet again. Thus ended our little Sabbath school in the pious town of St. Michael's.

I have said my master found religious sanction for his cruelty. As an example, I will state one of many facts going to prove the charge. I have seen him tie up a lame young woman, and whip her with a heavy cowskin upon her naked shoulders, causing the warm red blood to drip; and, in justification of the bloody deed, he would quote this passage of Scripture—"He that knoweth his master's will, and doeth it not, shall be beaten with many stripes."[4]

Master would keep this lacerated young woman tied up in this horrid situa-tion four or five hours at a time. I have known him to tie her up early in the morning, and whip her before breakfast; leave her, go to his store, return to dinner, and whip her again, cutting her in the places already made raw with his cruel lash. The secret of master's cruelty toward "Henny" is found in the fact of her being almost helpless. When quite a child, she fell into the fire, and burned

4. Luke 12.47.

herself horribly. Her hands were so burnt that she never got the use of them. She could do very little but bear heavy burdens. She was to master a bill of expense; and as he was a mean man, she was a constant offence to him. He seemed desirous of getting the poor girl out of existence. He gave her away once to his sister; but, being a poor gift, she was not disposed to keep her. Finally, my benevolent master, to use his own words, "set her adrift to take care of herself." Here was a recently-converted man, holding on upon the mother, and at the same time turning out her helpless child, to starve and die! Master Thomas was one of the many pious slaveholders who hold slaves for the very charitable purpose of taking care of them.

My master and myself had quite a number of differences. He found me unsuitable to his purpose. My city life, he said, had had a very pernicious effect upon me. It had almost ruined me for every good purpose, and fitted me for every thing which was bad. One of my greatest faults was that of letting his horse run away, and go down to his father-in-law's farm, which was about five miles from St. Michael's. I would then have to go after it. My reason for this kind of carelessness, or carefulness, was, that I could always get something to eat when I went there. Master William Hamilton, my master's father-in-law, always gave his slaves enough to eat. I never left there hungry, no matter how great the need of my speedy return. Master Thomas at length said he would stand it no longer. I had lived with him nine months, during which time he had given me a number of severe whippings, all to no good purpose. He resolved to put me out, as he said, to be broken; and, for this purpose, he let me for one year to a man named Edward Covey. Mr. Covey was a poor man, a farm-renter. He rented the place upon which he lived, as also the hands with which he tilled it. Mr. Covey had acquired a very high reputation for breaking young slaves, and this reputation was of immense value to him. It enabled him to get his farm tilled with much less expense to himself than he could have had it done without such a reputation. Some slaveholders thought it not much loss to allow Mr. Covey to have their slaves one year, for the sake of the training to which they were subjected, without any other compensation. He could hire young help with great ease, in consequence of this reputation. Added to the natural good qualities of Mr. Covey, he was a professor of religion—a pious soul—a member and a class-leader in the Methodist church. All of this added weight to his reputation as a "nigger-breaker." I was aware of all the facts, having been made acquainted with them by a young man who had lived there. I nevertheless made the change gladly; for I was sure of getting enough to eat, which is not the smallest consideration to a hungry man.

CHAPTER X

I left Master Thomas's house, and went to live with Mr. Covey, on the 1st of January, 1833. I was now, for the first time in my life, a field hand. In my new employment, I found myself even more awkward than a country boy appeared to be in a large city. I had been at my new home but one week before Mr. Covey gave me a very severe whipping, cutting my back, causing the blood to run, and raising ridges on my flesh as large as my little finger. The details of this affair are as follows: Mr. Covey sent me, very early in the morning of one of our coldest days in the month of January, to the woods, to get a load of wood. He gave me a team of unbroken oxen. He told me which was the in-hand ox, and which the off-hand ox. He then tied the end of a large rope around the horns of the in-hand ox, and gave me the other end of it, and told me, if the oxen started to run, that I must hold on upon the rope. I had never driven oxen before, and of course I was very awkward. I, however, succeeded in getting to the edge of the woods with little difficulty; but I had got a very few rods into the woods, when the oxen took fright, and started full tilt, carrying the cart against trees, and over stumps, in the most frightful manner. I expected every moment that my brains would be dashed out against the trees. After run-ning thus for a considerable distance, they finally upset the cart, dashing it with great force against a tree, and threw themselves into a dense thicket. How I escaped death, I do not know. There I was, entirely alone, in a thick wood, in a place new to me. My cart was upset and shattered, my oxen were entangled among the young trees, and there was none to help me. After a long spell of effort, I succeeded in getting my cart righted, my oxen disentangled, and again yoked to the cart. I now proceeded with my team to the place where I had, the day before, been chopping wood, and loaded my cart pretty heavily, thinking in this way to tame my oxen. I then proceeded on my way home. I had now con-sumed one half of the day. I got out of the woods safely, and now felt out of danger. I stopped my oxen to open the woods gate; and just as I did so, before I could get hold of my ox-rope, the oxen again started, rushed through the gate, catching it between the wheel and the body of the cart, tearing it to pieces, and coming within a few inches of crushing me against the gate-post. Thus twice, in one short day, I escaped death by the merest chance. On my return, I told Mr. Covey what had happened, and how it happened. He ordered me to return to the woods again immediately. I did so, and he followed on after me. Just as I got into the woods, he came up and told me to stop my cart, and that he would teach me how to trifle away my time, and break gates. He then went to a large gum-tree, and with his axe cut three large switches, and, after trimming them up neatly with his pocket-knife, he ordered me to take off my clothes. I made him no answer, but stood with my clothes on. He repeated his order. I still made him no answer, nor did I move to strip myself. Upon this he rushed at me with the fierceness of a tiger, tore off my clothes, and lashed me till he had worn out his switches, cutting me so savagely as to leave the marks visible for a long time after. This whipping was the first of a number just like it, and for similar offences.

I lived with Mr. Covey one year. During the first six months, of that year, scarce a week passed without his whipping me. I was seldom free from a sore back. My awkwardness was almost always his excuse for whipping me. We were worked fully up to the point of endurance. Long before day we were up, our horses fed, and by the first approach of day we were off to the field with our hoes and ploughing teams. Mr. Covey gave us enough to eat, but scarce time to eat it. We were often less than five minutes taking our meals. We were often in the field from the first approach of day till its last lingering ray had left us; and at saving-fodder time, midnight often caught us in the field binding blades.[5]

5. Gathering cut grain into bundles or sheaves.

Covey would be out with us. The way he used to stand it was this. He would spend the most of his afternoons in bed. He would then come out fresh in the evening, ready to urge us on with his words, example, and frequently with the whip. Mr. Covey was one of the few slaveholders who could and did work with his hands. He was a hard-working man. He knew by himself just what a man or a boy could do. There was no deceiving him. His work went on in his absence almost as well as in his presence; and he had the faculty of making us feel that he was ever present with us. This he did by surprising us. He seldom approached the spot where we were at work openly, if he could do it secretly. He always aimed at taking us by surprise. Such was his cunning, that we used to call him, among ourselves, "the snake." When we were at work in the cornfield, he would sometimes crawl on his hands and knees to avoid detection, and all at once he would rise nearly in our midst, and scream out, "Ha, ha! Come, come! Dash on, dash on!" This being his mode of attack, it was never safe to stop a single minute. His comings were like a thief in the night. He appeared to us as being ever at hand. He was under every tree, behind every stump, in every bush, and at every window, on the plantation. He would sometimes mount his horse, as if bound to St. Michael's, a distance of seven miles, and in half an hour after- wards you would see him coiled up in the corner of the wood-fence, watching every motion of the slaves. He would, for this purpose, leave his horse tied up in the woods. Again, he would sometimes walk up to us, and give us orders as though he was upon the point of starting on a long journey, turn his back upon us, and make as though he was going to the house to get ready; and, before he would get half way thither, he would turn short and crawl into a fence-corner, or behind some tree, and there watch us till the going down of the sun.

Mr. Covey's *forte* consisted in his power to deceive. His life was devoted to planning and perpetrating the grossest deceptions. Every thing he possessed in the shape of learning or religion, he made conform to his disposition to deceive. He seemed to think himself equal to deceiving the Almighty. He would make a short prayer in the morning, and a long prayer at night; and, strange as it may seem, few men would at times appear more devotional than he. The exercises of his family devotions were always commenced with singing; and, as he was a very poor singer himself, the duty of raising the hymn generally came upon me. He would read his hymn, and nod at me to commence. I would at times do so; at others, I would not. My noncompliance would almost always produce much confusion. To show himself independent of me, he would start and stagger through with his hymn in the most discordant manner. In this state of mind, he prayed with more than ordinary spirit. Poor man! such was his disposition, and success at deceiving, I do verily believe that he sometimes deceived him- self into the solemn belief, that he was a sincere worshipper of the most high God; and this, too, at a time when he may be said to have been guilty of com- pelling his woman slave to commit the sin of adultery. The facts in the case are these: Mr. Covey was a poor man; he was just commencing in life; he was only able to buy one slave; and, shocking as is the fact, he bought her, as he said, for a *breeder*. This woman was named Caroline. Mr. Covey bought her from Mr. Thomas Lowe, about six miles from St. Michael's. She was a large, able- bodied woman, about twenty years old. She had already given birth to one child, which proved her to be just what he wanted. After buying her, he hired a married man of Mr. Samuel Harrison, to live with him one year; and him he used to fasten up with her every night! The result was, that, at the end of the year, the miserable woman gave birth to twins. At this result Mr. Covey seemed to be highly pleased, both with the man and the wretched woman. Such was his joy, and that of his wife, that nothing they could do for Caroline during her confinement was too good, or too hard, to be done. The children were regarded as being quite an addition to his wealth.

If at any one time of my life more than another, I was made to drink the bitterest dregs of slavery, that time was during the first six months of my stay with Mr. Covey. We were worked in all weathers. It was never too hot or too cold; it could never rain, blow, hail, or snow, too hard for us to work in the field. Work, work, work, was scarcely more the order of the day than of the night. The longest days were too short for him, and the shortest nights too long for him. I was somewhat unmanageable when I first went there, but a few months of this discipline tamed me. Mr. Covey succeeded in breaking me. I was broken in body, soul, and spirit. My natural elasticity was crushed, my intellect languished, the disposition to read departed, the cheerful spark that lingered about my eye died; the dark night of slavery closed in upon me; and behold a man transformed into a brute!

Sunday was my only leisure time. I spent this in a sort of beast-like stupor, between sleep and wake, under some large tree. At times I would rise up, a flash of energetic freedom would dart through my soul, accompanied with a faint beam of hope, that flickered for a moment, and then vanished. I sank down again, mourning over my wretched condition. I was sometimes prompted to take my life, and that of Covey, but was prevented by a combination of hope and fear. My sufferings on this plantation seem now like a dream rather than a stern reality.

Our house stood within a few rods of the Chesapeake Bay, whose broad bosom was ever white with sails from every quarter of the habitable globe. Those beautiful vessels, robed in purest white, so delightful to the eye of freemen, were to me so many shrouded ghosts, to terrify and torment me with thoughts of my wretched condition. I have often, in the deep stillness of a summer's Sabbath, stood all alone upon the lofty banks of that noble bay, and traced, with saddened heart and tearful eye, the countless number of sails moving off to the mighty ocean. The sight of these always affected me powerfully. My thoughts would compel utterance; and there, with no audience but the Almighty, I would pour out my soul's complaint, in my rude way, with an apostrophe[6] to the moving multitude of ships:—

"You are loosed from your moorings, and are free; I am fast in my chains, and am a slave! You move merrily before the gentle gale, and I sadly before the bloody whip! You are freedom's swift-winged angels, that fly round the world; I am confined in bands of iron! O that I were free! O, that I were on one of your gallant decks, and under your protecting wing! Alas! betwixt me and you, the turbid waters roll. Go on, go on. O that I could also go! Could I but swim! If I could fly! O, why was I born a man, of whom to make a brute! The glad ship is gone; she hides in the dim distance. I am left in the hottest hell of unending slavery. O God, save me! God, deliver me! Let me be free! Is there any God?

6. An exclamatory form of address.

Why am I a slave? I will run away. I will not stand it. Get caught, or get clear, I'll try it. I had as well die with ague as the fever. I have only one life to lose. I had as well be killed running as die standing. Only think of it; one hundred miles straight north, and I am free! Try it? Yes! God helping me, I will. It cannot be that I shall live and die a slave. I will take to the water. This very bay shall bear me into freedom. The steam boats steered in a north-east course from North Point. I will do the same; and when I get to the head of the bay, I will turn my canoe adrift, and walk straight through Delaware into Pennsylvania. When I get there, I shall not be required to have a pass; I can travel without being disturbed. Let but the first opportunity offer, and, come what will, I am off. Meanwhile, I will try to bear up under the yoke. I am not the only slave in the world. Why should I fret? I can bear as much as any of them. Besides, I am but a boy, and all boys are bound to some one. It may be that my misery in slavery will only increase my happiness when I get free. There is a better day coming."

Thus I used to think, and thus I used to speak to myself; goaded almost to madness at one moment, and at the next reconciling myself to my wretched lot.

I have already intimated that my condition was much worse, during the first six months of my stay at Mr. Covey's, than in the last six. The circumstances leading to the change in Mr. Covey's course toward me form an epoch in my humble history. You have seen how a man was made a slave; you shall see how a slave was made a man. On one of the hottest days of the month of August, 1833, Bill Smith, William Hughes, a slave named Eli, and myself, were engaged in fanning wheat.[7] Hughes was clearing the fanned wheat from before the fan, Eli was turning, Smith was feeding, and I was carrying wheat to the fan. The work was simple, requiring strength rather than intellect; yet, to one entirely unused to such work, it came very hard. About three o'clock of that day, I broke down; my strength failed me; I was seized with a violent aching of the head, attended with extreme dizziness; I trembled in every limb. Finding what was coming, I nerved myself up, feeling it would never do to stop work. I stood as long as I could stagger to the hopper with grain. When I could stand no longer, I fell, and felt as if held down by an immense weight. The fan of course stopped; every one had his own work to do; and no one could do the work of the other, and have his own go on at the same time.

Mr. Covey was at the house, about one hundred yards from the treading-yard where we were fanning. On hearing the fan stop, he left immediately, and came to the spot where we were. He hastily inquired what the matter was. Bill answered that I was sick, and there was no one to bring wheat to the fan. I had by this time crawled away under the side of the post and rail-fence by which the yard was enclosed, hoping to find relief by getting out of the sun. He then asked where I was. He was told by one of the hands. He came to the spot, and, after looking at me awhile, asked me what was the matter. I told him as well as I could, for I scarce had strength to speak. He then gave me a savage kick in the side, and told me to get up. I tried to do so, but fell back in the attempt. He gave me another kick, and again told me to rise. I again tried, and succeeded in gaining my feet; but, stooping to get the tub with which I was feeding the fan,

7. Separating the grain from the chaff.

I again staggered and fell. While down in this situation, Mr. Covey took up the hickory slat with which Hughes had been striking off the half-bushel measure, and with it gave me a heavy blow upon the head, making a large wound, and the blood ran freely; and with this again told me to get up. I made no effort to comply, having now made up my mind to let him do his worst. In a short time after receiving this blow, my head grew better. Mr. Covey had now left me to my fate. At this moment I resolved, for the first time, to go to my master, enter a complaint, and ask his protection. In order to [do] this, I must that afternoon walk seven miles; and this, under the circumstances, was truly a severe undertaking. I was exceedingly feeble; made so as much by the kicks and blows which I received, as by the severe fit of sickness to which I had been subjected. I, however, watched my chance, while Covey was looking in an opposite direction, and started for St. Michael's. I succeeded in getting a considerable distance on my way to the woods, when Covey discovered me, and called after me to come back, threatening what he would do if I did not come. I disregarded both his calls and his threats, and made my way to the woods as fast as my feeble state would allow; and thinking I might be overhauled by him if I kept the road, I walked through the woods, keeping far enough from the road to avoid detection, and near enough to prevent losing my way. I had not gone far before my little strength again failed me. I could go no farther. I fell down, and lay for a considerable time. The blood was yet oozing from the wound on my head. For a time I thought I should bleed to death; and think now that I should have done so, but that the blood so matted my hair as to stop the wound. After lying there about three quarters of an hour, I nerved myself up again, and started on my way, through bogs and briers, barefooted and bareheaded, tearing my feet sometimes at nearly every step; and after a journey of about seven miles, occupying some five hours to perform it, I arrived at master's store. I then presented an appearance enough to affect any but a heart of iron. From the crown of my head to my feet, I was covered with blood. My hair was all clotted with dust and blood; my shirt was stiff with blood. My legs and feet were torn in sundry places with briers and thorns, and were also covered with blood. I suppose I looked like a man who had escaped a den of wild beasts, and barely escaped them. In this state I appeared before my master, humbly entreating him to interpose his authority for my protection. I told him all the circumstances as well as I could, and it seemed, as I spoke, at times to affect him. He would then walk the floor, and seek to justify Covey by saying he expected I deserved it. He asked me what I wanted. I told him, to let me get a new home; that as sure as I lived with Mr. Covey again, I should live with but to die with him; that Covey would surely kill me; he was in a fair way for it. Master Thomas ridiculed the idea that there was any danger of Mr. Covey's killing me, and said that he knew Mr. Covey; that he was a good man, and that he could not think of taking me from him; that, should he do so, he would lose the whole year's wages; that I belonged to Mr. Covey for one year, and that I must go back to him, come what might; and that I must not trouble him with any more stories, or that he would himself *get hold of me*. After threatening me thus, he gave me a very large dose of salts, telling me that I might remain in St. Michael's that night, (it being quite late) but that I must be off back to Mr. Covey's early in the morning; and that if I did not, he would *get hold of me*, which meant that he would whip me. I remained all night, and, according to his orders, I started off to Covey's in the morning, (Saturday morning), wearied in body and broken in spirit. I got no supper that night, or breakfast that morning. I reached Covey's about nine o'clock; and just as I was getting over the fence that divided Mrs. Kemp's fields from ours, out ran Covey with his cowskin, to give me another whipping. Before he could reach me, I succeeded in getting to the cornfield; and as the corn was very high, it afforded me the means of hiding. He seemed very angry, and searched for me a long time. My behavior was altogether unaccountable. He finally gave up the chase, thinking, I suppose, that I must come home for something to eat; he would give himself no further trouble in looking for me. I spent that day mostly in the woods, having the alternative before me,—to go home and be whipped to death, or stay in the woods and be starved to death. That night, I fell in with Sandy Jenkins, a slave with whom I was somewhat acquainted. Sandy had a free wife who lived about four miles from Mr. Covey's; and it being Saturday, he was on his way to see her. I told him my circumstances, and he very kindly invited me to go home with him. I went home with him, and talked this whole matter over, and got his advice as to what course it was best for me to pursue. I found Sandy an old adviser. He told me, with great solemnity, I must go back to Covey; but that before I went, I must go with him into another part of the woods, where there was a certain *root*, which, if I would take some of it with me, carrying it *always on my right side*, would render it impossible for Mr. Covey, or any other white man, to whip me. He said he had carried it for years; and since he had done so, he had never received a blow, and never expected to while he carried it. I at first rejected the idea, that the simple carrying of a root in my pocket would have any such effect as he had said, and was not disposed to take it; but Sandy impressed the necessity with much earnestness, telling me it could do no harm, if it did no good. To please him, I at length took the root, and, according to his direction, carried it upon my right side. This was Sunday morning. I immediately started for home; and upon entering the yard gate, out came Mr. Covey on his way to meeting. He spoke to me very kindly, bade me drive the pigs from a lot near by, and passed on towards the church. Now, this singular conduct of Mr. Covey really made me begin to think that there was something in the *root* which Sandy had given me; and had it been on any other day than Sunday, I could have attributed the conduct to no other cause than the influence of that root; and as it was, I was half inclined to think the *root* to be something more than I at first had taken it to be. All went well till Monday morning. On this morning, the virtue of the *root* was fully tested. Long before daylight, I was called to go and rub, curry, and feed, the horses. I obeyed, and was glad to obey. But whilst thus engaged, whilst in the act of throwing down some blades from the loft, Mr. Covey entered the stable with a long rope; and just as I was half out of the loft, he caught hold of my legs, and was about tying me. As soon as I found what he was up to, I gave a sudden spring, and as I did so, he holding to my legs, I was brought sprawling on the stable floor. Mr. Covey seemed now to think he had me, and could do what he pleased; but at this moment—from whence came the spirit I don't know—I resolved to fight; and, suiting my action to the resolution, I seized Covey hard by the throat; and as I did so, I rose. He held on to me, and I to him. My resistance was so entirely unexpected, that Covey seemed taken all aback. He trembled like a leaf. This gave me assurance, and I held him uneasy, causing the blood to run where

I touched him with the ends of my fingers. Mr. Covey soon called out to Hughes for help. Hughes came, and, while Covey held me, attempted to tie my right hand. While he was in the act of doing so, I watched my chance, and gave him a heavy kick close under the ribs. This kick fairly sickened Hughes, so that he left me in the hands of Mr. Covey. This kick had the effect of not only weakening Hughes, but Covey also. When he saw Hughes bending over with pain, his courage quailed. He asked me if I meant to persist in my resistance. I told him I did, come what might; that he had used me like a brute for six months, and that I was determined to be used so no longer. With that, he strove to drag me to a stick that was lying just out of the stable door. He meant to knock me down. But just as he was leaning over to get the stick, I seized him with both hands by his collar, and brought him by a sudden snatch to the ground. By this time, Bill came. Covey called upon him for assistance. Bill wanted to know what he could do. Covey said, "Take hold of him, take hold of him!" Bill said his master hired him out to work, and not to help to whip me; so he left Covey and myself to fight our own battle out. We were at it for nearly two hours. Covey at length let me go, puffing and blowing at a great rate, saying that if I had not resisted, he would not have whipped me half so much. The truth was, that he had not whipped me at all. I considered him as getting entirely the worst end of the bargain; for he had drawn no blood from me, but I had from him. The whole six months afterwards, that I spent with Mr. Covey, he never laid the weight of his finger upon me in anger. He would occasionally say, he didn't want to get hold of me again. "No," thought I, "you need not; for you will come off worse than you did before."

This battle with Mr. Covey was the turning-point in my career as a slave. It rekindled the few expiring embers of freedom, and revived within me a sense of my own manhood. It recalled the departed self-confidence, and inspired me again with a determination to be free. The gratification afforded by the triumph was a full compensation for whatever else might follow, even death itself. He only can understand the deep satisfaction which I experienced, who has himself repelled by force the bloody arm of slavery. I felt as I never felt before. It was a glorious resurrection, from the tomb of slavery, to the heaven of freedom. My long-crushed spirit rose, cowardice departed, bold defiance took its place; and I now resolved that, however long I might remain a slave in form, the day had passed forever when I could be a slave in fact. I did not hesitate to let it be known of me, that the white man who expected to succeed in whipping, must also succeed in killing me.

From this time I was never again what might be called fairly whipped, though I remained a slave four years afterwards. I had several fights, but was never whipped.

It was for a long time a matter of surprise to me why Mr. Covey did not immediately have me taken by the constable to the whipping-post, and there regularly whipped for the crime of raising my hand against a white man in defence of myself. And the only explanation I can now think of does not entirely satisfy me; but such as it is, I will give it. Mr. Covey enjoyed the most unbounded reputation for being a first-rate overseer and negro-breaker. It was of considerable importance to him. That reputation was at stake; and had he sent me—a boy about sixteen years old—to the public whipping-post, his reputation would have been lost; so, to save his reputation, he suffered me to go unpunished.

My term of actual service to Mr. Edward Covey ended on Christmas day, 1833. The days between Christmas and New Year's day are allowed as holidays; and, accordingly, we were not required to perform any labor, more than to feed and take care of the stock. This time we regarded as our own, by the grace of our masters; and we therefore used or abused it nearly as we pleased. Those of us who had families at a distance, were generally allowed to spend the whole six days in their society. This time, however, was spent in various ways. The staid, sober, thinking and industrious ones of our number would employ themselves in making corn-brooms, mats, horse-collars, and baskets; and another class of us would spend the time in hunting opossums, hares, and coons. But by far the larger part engaged in such sports and merriments as playing ball, wrestling, running foot-races, fiddling, dancing, and drinking whisky; and this latter mode of spending the time was by far the most agreeable to the feelings of our masters. A slave who would work during the holidays was considered by our masters as scarcely deserving them. He was regarded as one who rejected the favor of his master. It was deemed a disgrace not to get drunk at Christmas; and he was regarded as lazy indeed, who had not provided himself with the necessary means, during the year, to get whisky enough to last him through Christmas.

From what I know of the effect of these holidays upon the slave, I believe them to be among the most effective means in the hands of the slaveholder in keeping down the spirit of insurrection. Were the slaveholders at once to abandon this practice, I have not the slightest doubt it would lead to an immediate insurrection among the slaves. These holidays serve as conductors, or safety-valves, to carry off the rebellious spirit of enslaved humanity. But for these, the slave would be forced up to the wildest desperation; and woe betide the slaveholder, the day he ventures to remove or hinder the operation of those conductors! I warn him that, in such an event, a spirit will go forth in their midst, more to be dreaded than the most appalling earthquake.

The holidays are part and parcel of the gross fraud, wrong, and inhumanity of slavery. They are professedly a custom established by the benevolence of the slaveholders; but I undertake to say, it is the result of selfishness, and one of the grossest frauds committed upon the down-trodden slave. They do not give the slaves this time because they would not like to have their work during its continuance, but because they know it would be unsafe to deprive them of it. This will be seen by the fact, that the slaveholders like to have their slaves spend those days just in such a manner as to make them as glad of their ending as of their beginning. Their object seems to be, to disgust their slaves with freedom, by plunging them into the lowest depths of dissipation. For instance, the slaveholders not only like to see the slave drink of his own accord, but will adopt various plans to make him drunk. One plan is, to make bets on their slaves, as to who can drink the most whisky without getting drunk; and in this way they succeed in getting whole multitudes to drink to excess. Thus, when the slave asks for virtuous freedom, the cunning slaveholder, knowing his ignorance, cheats him with a dose of vicious dissipation, artfully labelled with the name of liberty. The most of us used to drink it down, and the result was just what might be supposed: many of us were led to think that there was little to choose between liberty and slavery. We felt, and very properly too, that we had almost as well be slaves to man as to rum. So, when the holidays ended, we staggered up from the filth of our wallowing, took a long breath, and marched to the field,—feeling, upon the whole, rather glad to go, from what our master had deceived us into a belief was freedom, back to the arms of slavery.

I have said that this mode of treatment is a part of the whole system of fraud and inhumanity of slavery. It is so. The mode here adopted to disgust the slave with freedom, by allowing him to see only the abuse of it, is carried out in other things. For instance, a slave loves molasses; he steals some. His master, in many cases, goes off to town, and buys a large quantity; he returns, takes his whip, and commands the slave to eat the molasses, until the poor fellow is made sick at the very mention of it. The same mode is sometimes adopted to make the slaves refrain from asking for more food than their regular allowance. A slave runs through his allowance, and applies for more. His master is enraged at him; but, not willing to send him off without food, gives him more than is necessary, and compels him to eat it within a given time. Then, if he complains that he cannot eat it, he is said to be satisfied neither full nor fasting, and is whipped for being hard to please! I have an abundance of such illustrations of the same principle, drawn from my own observation, but think the cases I have cited sufficient. The practice is a very common one.

On the first of January, 1834, I left Mr. Covey, and went to live with Mr. William Freeland, who lived about three miles from St. Michael's. I soon found Mr. Freeland a very different man from Mr. Covey. Though not rich, he was what would be called an educated southern gentleman. Mr. Covey, as I have shown, was a well-trained negro-breaker and slave-driver. The former (slaveholder though he was) seemed to possess some regard for honor, some reverence for justice, and some respect for humanity. The latter seemed totally insensible to all such sentiments. Mr. Freeland had many of the faults peculiar to slaveholders, such as being very passionate and fretful; but I must do him the justice to say, that he was exceedingly free from those degrading vices to which Mr. Covey was constantly addicted. The one was open and frank, and we always knew where to find him. The other was a most artful deceiver, and could be understood only by such as were skilful enough to detect his cunningly-devised frauds. Another advantage I gained in my new master was, he made no pretensions to, or profession of, religion; and this, in my opinion, was truly a great advantage. I assert most unhesitatingly, that the religion of the south is a mere covering for the most horrid crimes,—a justifier of the most appalling barbarity,—a sanctifier of the most hateful frauds,—and a dark shelter under which the darkest, foulest, grossest, and most infernal deeds of slaveholders find the strongest protection. Were I to be again reduced to the chains of slavery, next to that enslavement, I should regard being the slave of a religious master the greatest calamity that could befall me. For of all slaveholders with whom I have ever met, religious slaveholders are the worst. I have ever found them the meanest and basest, the most cruel and cowardly, of all others. It was my unhappy lot not only to belong to a religious slaveholder, but to live in a community of such religionists. Very near Mr. Freeland lived the Rev. Daniel Weeden, and in the same neighborhood lived the Rev. Rigby Hopkins. These were members and ministers in the Reformed Methodist Church. Mr. Weeden owned, among others, a woman slave, whose name I have forgotten. This woman's back, for weeks, was kept literally raw, made so by the lash of this merciless, *religious* wretch. He used to hire hands. His maxim was, Behave well or behave ill, it is the duty of a master occasionally to whip a slave, to remind him of his master's authority. Such was his theory, and such his practice.

Mr. Hopkins was even worse than Mr. Weeden. His chief boast was his ability to manage slaves. The peculiar feature of his government was that of whipping slaves in advance of deserving it. He always managed to have one or more of his slaves to whip every Monday morning. He did this to alarm their fears, and strike terror into those who escaped. His plan was to whip for the smallest offences, to prevent the commission of large ones. Mr. Hopkins could always find some excuse for whipping a slave. It would astonish one, unaccustomed to a slaveholding life, to see with what wonderful ease a slaveholder can find things, of which to make occasion to whip a slave. A mere look, word, or motion,—a mistake, accident, or want of power,—are all matters for which a slave may be whipped at any time. Does a slave look dissatisfied? It is said, he has the devil in him, and it must be whipped out. Does he speak loudly when spoken to by his master? Then he is getting high-minded, and should be taken down a button-hole lower. Does he forget to pull off his hat at the approach of a white person? Then he is wanting in reverence, and should be whipped for it. Does he ever venture to vindicate his conduct, when censured for it? Then he is guilty of impudence,—one of the greatest crimes of which a slave can be guilty. Does he ever venture to suggest a different mode of doing things from that pointed out by his master? He is indeed presumptuous, and getting above himself; and nothing less than a flogging will do for him. Does he, while ploughing, break a plough,—or, while hoeing, break a hoe? It is owing to his carelessness, and for it a slave must always be whipped. Mr. Hopkins could always find something of this sort to justify the use of the lash, and he seldom failed to embrace such opportunities. There was not a man in the whole county, with whom the slaves who had the getting their own home, would not prefer to live, rather than with this Rev. Mr. Hopkins. And yet there was not a man any where round, who made higher professions of religion, or was more active in revivals,—more attentive to the class, love-feast, prayer and preaching meetings, or more devotional in his family,—that prayed earlier, later, louder, and longer,—than this same reverend slave-driver, Rigby Hopkins.

But to return to Mr. Freeland, and to my experience while in his employment. He, like Mr. Covey, gave us enough to eat; but, unlike Mr. Covey, he also gave us sufficient time to take our meals. He worked us hard, but always between sunrise and sunset. He required a good deal of work to be done, but gave us good tools with which to work. His farm was large, but he employed hands enough to work it, and with ease, compared with many of his neighbors. My treatment, while in his employment, was heavenly, compared with what I experienced at the hands of Mr. Edward Covey.

Mr. Freeland was himself the owner of but two slaves. Their names were Henry Harris and John Harris. The rest of his hands he hired. These consisted of myself, Sandy Jenkins,[8] and Handy Caldwell. Henry and John were quite

8. This is the same man who gave me the roots to prevent my being whipped by Mr. Covey. He was "a clever soul." We used frequently to talk about the fight with Covey, and as often as we did so, he would claim my success as the result of the roots which he gave me. This superstition is very common among the more ignorant slaves. A slave seldom dies but that his death is attributed to trickery [Douglass's note].

intelligent, and in a very little while after I went there, I succeeded in creating in them a strong desire to learn how to read. This desire soon sprang up in the others also. They very soon mustered up some old spelling-books, and nothing would do but that I must keep a Sabbath school. I agreed to do so, and accordingly devoted my Sundays to teaching these my loved fellow-slaves how to read. Neither of them knew his letters when I went there. Some of the slaves of the neighboring farms found what was going on, and also availed themselves of this little opportunity to learn to read. It was understood, among all who came, that there must be as little display about it as possible. It was necessary to keep our religious masters at St. Michael's unacquainted with the fact, that, instead of spending the Sabbath in wrestling, boxing, and drinking whisky, we were trying to learn how to read the will of God; for they had much rather see us engaged in those degrading sports, than to see us behaving like intellectual, moral, and accountable beings. My blood boils as I think of the bloody manner in which Messrs. Wright Fairbanks and Garrison West, both class-leaders, in connection with many others, rushed in upon us with sticks and stones, and broke up our virtuous little Sabbath school, at St. Michael's—all calling themselves Christians! humble followers of the Lord Jesus Christ! But I am again digressing.

I held my Sabbath school at the house of a free colored man, whose name I deem it imprudent to mention; for should it be known, it might embarrass him greatly, though the crime of holding the school was committed ten years ago. I had at one time over forty scholars, and those of the right sort, ardently desiring to learn. They were of all ages, though mostly men and women. I look back to those Sundays with an amount of pleasure not to be expressed. They were great days to my soul. The work of instructing my dear fellow-slaves was the sweetest engagement with which I was ever blessed. We loved each other, and to leave them at the close of the Sabbath was a severe cross indeed. When I think that those precious souls are to-day shut up in the prison-house of slavery, my feelings overcome me, and I am almost ready to ask, "Does a righteous God govern the universe? and for what does he hold the thunders in his right hand, if not to smite the oppressor, and deliver the spoiled out of the hand of the spoiler?" These dear souls came not to Sabbath school because it was popular to do so, nor did I teach them because it was reputable to be thus engaged. Every moment they spent in that school, they were liable to be taken up, and given thirty-nine lashes. They came because they wished to learn. Their minds had been starved by their cruel masters. They had been shut up in mental darkness. I taught them, because it was the delight of my soul to be doing something that looked like bettering the condition of my race. I kept up my school nearly the whole year I lived with Mr. Freeland; and, beside my Sabbath school, I devoted three evenings in the week, during the winter, to teaching the slaves at home. And I have the happiness to know, that several of those who came to Sabbath school learned how to read; and that one, at least, is now free through my agency.

The year passed off smoothly. It seemed only about half as long as the year which preceded it. I went through it without receiving a single blow. I will give Mr. Freeland the credit of being the best master I ever had, *till I became my own master*. For the ease with which I passed the year, I was, however, somewhat indebted to the society of my fellow-slaves. They were noble souls; they not only possessed loving hearts, but brave ones. We were linked and interlinked with each other. I loved them with a love stronger than any thing I have experienced since. It is sometimes said that we slaves do not love and confide in each other. In answer to this assertion, I can say, I never loved any or confided in any people more than my fellow-slaves, and especially those with whom I lived at Mr. Freeland's. I believe we would have died for each other. We never undertook to do any thing, of any importance, without a mutual consultation. We never moved separately. We were one; and as much so by our tempers and dispositions, as by the mutual hardships to which we were necessarily subjected by our condition as slaves.

At the close of the year 1834, Mr. Freeland again hired me of my master, for the year 1835. But, by this time, I began to want to live *upon free land* as well as *with Freeland*; and I was no longer content, therefore, to live with him or any other slaveholder. I began, with the commencement of the year, to prepare myself for a final struggle, which should decide my fate one way or the other. My tendency was upward. I was fast approaching manhood, and year after year had passed, and I was still a slave. These thoughts roused me—I must do something. I therefore resolved that 1835 should not pass without witnessing an attempt, on my part, to secure my liberty. But I was not willing to cherish this determination alone. My fellow-slaves were dear to me. I was anxious to have them participate with me in this, my life-giving determination. I therefore, though with great prudence, commenced early to ascertain their views and feelings in regard to their condition, and to imbue their minds with thoughts of freedom. I bent myself to devising ways and means for our escape, and meanwhile strove, on all fitting occasions, to impress them with the gross fraud and inhumanity of slavery. I went first to Henry, next to John, then to the others. I found, in them all, warm hearts and noble spirits. They were ready to hear, and ready to act when a feasible plan should be proposed. This was what I wanted. I talked to them of our want of manhood, if we submitted to our enslavement without at least one noble effort to be free. We met often, and consulted frequently, and told our hopes and fears, recounted the difficulties, real and imagined, which we should be called on to meet. At times we were almost disposed to give up, and try to content ourselves with our wretched lot; at others, we were firm and unbending in our determination to go. Whenever we suggested any plan, there was shrinking—the odds were fearful. Our path was beset with the greatest obstacles; and if we succeeded in gaining the end of it, our right to be free was yet questionable—we were yet liable to be returned to bondage. We could see no spot, this side of the ocean, where we could be free. We knew nothing about Canada. Our knowledge of the north did not extend farther than New York; and to go there, and be forever harassed with the frightful liability of being returned to slavery—with the certainty of being treated tenfold worse than before—the thought was truly a horrible one, and one which it was not easy to overcome. The case sometimes stood thus: At every gate through which we were to pass, we saw a watchman—at every ferry a guard—on every bridge a sentinel—and in every wood a patrol. We were hemmed in upon every side. Here were the difficulties, real or imagined—the good to be sought, and the evil to be shunned. On the one hand, there stood slavery, a stern reality, glaring frightfully upon us,—its robes already crimsoned with the blood of millions, and even now feasting itself greedily upon our own flesh. On the other hand, away back in the dim distance, under the flickering light of the north star, behind some craggy hill or snow-covered mountain, stood a doubtful freedom—half frozen—beckoning us to come and share its hospitality. This in itself was sometimes enough to stagger us; but when we permitted ourselves to survey the road, we were frequently appalled. Upon either side we saw grim death, assuming the most horrid shapes. Now it was starvation, causing us to eat our own flesh;—now we were contending with the waves, and were drowned;—now we were overtaken, and torn to pieces by the fangs of the terrible blood-hound. We were stung by scorpions, chased by wild beasts, bitten by snakes, and finally, after having nearly reached the desired spot,—after swimming rivers, encountering wild beasts, sleeping in the woods, suffering hunger and nakedness,—we were overtaken by our pursuers, and, in our resistance, we were shot dead upon the spot! I say, this picture sometimes appalled us, and made us

> "rather bear those ills we had,
> Than fly to others, that we knew not of."[9]

In coming to a fixed determination to run away, we did more than Patrick Henry,[1] when he resolved upon liberty or death. With us it was a doubtful liberty at most, and almost certain death if we failed. For my part, I should prefer death to hopeless bondage.

Sandy, one of our number, gave up the notion, but still encouraged us. Our company then consisted of Henry Harris, John Harris, Henry Bailey, Charles Roberts, and myself. Henry Bailey was my uncle, and belonged to my master. Charles married my aunt: he belonged to my master's father-in-law, Mr. William Hamilton.

The plan we finally concluded upon was, to get a large canoe belonging to Mr. Hamilton, and upon the Saturday night previous to Easter holidays, paddle directly up the Chesapeake Bay. On our arrival at the head of the bay, a distance of seventy or eighty miles from where we lived, it was our purpose to turn our canoe adrift, and follow the guidance of the north star till we got beyond the limits of Maryland. Our reason for taking the water route was, that we were less liable to be suspected as runaways; we hoped to be regarded as fishermen; whereas, if we should take the land route, we should be subjected to interruptions of almost every kind. Any one having a white face, and being so disposed, could stop us, and subject us to examination.

The week before our intended start, I wrote several protections, one for each of us. As well as I can remember, they were in the following words, to wit:—

"This is to certify that I, the undersigned, have given the bearer, my servant, full liberty to go to Baltimore, and spend the Easter holidays. Written with mine own hand, &c., 1835.

"WILLIAM HAMILTON,
"Near St. Michael's, in Talbot county, Maryland."

9. Shakespeare's *Hamlet* 3.1.81–82: "rather bear those ills we have, / Than fly to others, that we know not of."

1. American statesman and orator (1736–1799) whose most famous utterance was "Give me liberty or give me death."

We were not going to Baltimore; but, in going up the bay, we went toward Baltimore, and these protections were only intended to protect us while on the bay.

As the time drew near for our departure, our anxiety became more and more intense. It was truly a matter of life and death with us. The strength of our determination was about to be fully tested. At this time, I was very active in explaining every difficulty, removing every doubt, dispelling every fear, and inspiring all with the firmness indispensable to success in our undertaking; assuring them that half was gained the instant we made the move; we had talked long enough; we were now ready to move; if not now, we never should be; and if we did not intend to move now, we had as well fold our arms, sit down, and acknowledge ourselves fit only to be slaves. This, none of us were prepared to acknowledge. Every man stood firm; and at our last meeting, we pledged ourselves afresh, in the most solemn manner, that, at the time appointed, we would certainly start in pursuit of freedom. This was in the middle of the week, at the end of which we were to be off. We went, as usual, to our several fields of labor, but with bosoms highly agitated with thoughts of our truly hazardous undertaking. We tried to conceal our feelings as much as possible; and I think we succeeded very well.

After a painful waiting, the Saturday morning, whose night was to witness our departure, came. I hailed it with joy, bring what of sadness it might. Friday night was a sleepless one for me. I was, by common consent, at the head of the whole affair. The responsibility of success or failure lay heavily upon me. The glory of the one, and the confusion of the other, were alike mine. The first two hours of that morning were such as I never experienced before, and hope never to again. Early in the morning, we went, as usual, to the field. We were spreading manure; and all at once, while thus engaged, I was overwhelmed with an indescribable feeling, in the fulness of which I turned to Sandy, who was near by, and said, "We are betrayed!" "Well," said he, "that thought has this moment struck me." We said no more. I was never more certain of any thing.

The horn was blown as usual, and we went up from the field to the house for breakfast. I went for the form, more than for want of any thing to eat that morning. Just as I got to the house, in looking out at the lane gate, I saw four white men, with two colored men. The white men were on horseback, and the colored ones were walking behind, as if tied. I watched them a few moments till they got up to our lane gate. Here they halted, and tied the colored men to the gate-post. I was not yet certain as to what the matter was. In a few moments, in rode Mr. Hamilton, with a speed betokening great excitement. He came to the door, and inquired if Master William was in. He was told he was at the barn. Mr. Hamilton, without dismounting, rode up to the barn with extraordinary speed. In a few moments, he and Mr. Freeland returned to the house. By this time, the three constables rode up, and in great haste dismounted, tied their horses, and met Master William and Mr. Hamilton returning from the barn; and after talking awhile, they all walked up to the kitchen door. There was no one in the kitchen but myself and John. Henry and Sandy were up at the barn. Mr. Freeland put his head in at the door, and called me by name, saying, there were some gentlemen at the door who wished to see me. I stepped to the door, and inquired what they wanted. They at once seized me, and, without giving me any satisfaction, tied me—lashing my hands closely together. I insisted upon knowing what the matter was. They at length said, that they had learned I had been in a "scrape," and that I was to be examined before my master; and if their information proved false, I should not be hurt.

In a few moments, they succeeded in tying John. They then turned to Henry, who had by this time returned, and commanded him to cross his hands. "I won't!" said Henry, in a firm tone, indicating his readiness to meet the consequences of his refusal. "Won't you?" said Tom Graham, the constable. "No, I won't!" said Henry, in a still stronger tone. With this, two of the constables pulled out their shining pistols, and swore, by their Creator, that they would make him cross his hands or kill him. Each cocked his pistol, and, with fingers on the trigger, walked up to Henry, saying, at the same time, if he did not cross his hands, they would blow his damned heart out. "Shoot me, shoot me!" said Henry; "you can't kill me but once. Shoot, shoot,—and be damned! *I won't be tied!*" This he said in a tone of loud defiance; and at the same time, with a motion as quick as lightning, he with one single stroke dashed the pistols from the hand of each constable. As he did this, all hands fell upon him, and, after beating him some time, they finally overpowered him, and got him tied.

During the scuffle, I managed, I know not how, to get my pass out, and, without being discovered, put it into the fire. We were all now tied; and just as we were to leave for Easton jail, Betsy Freeland, mother of William Freeland, came to the door with her hands full of biscuits, and divided them between Henry and John. She then delivered herself of a speech, to the following effect:—addressing herself to me, she said, *"You devil! You yellow devil!* it was you that put it into the heads of Henry and John to run away. But for you, you long-legged mulatto devil! Henry nor John would never have thought of such a thing." I made no reply, and was immediately hurried off towards St. Michael's. Just a moment previous to the scuffle with Henry, Mr. Hamilton suggested the propriety of making a search for the protections which he had understood Frederick had written for himself and the rest. But, just at the moment he was about carrying his proposal into effect, his aid was needed in helping to tie Henry; and the excitement attending the scuffle caused them either to forget, or to deem it unsafe, under the circumstances, to search. So we were not yet convicted of the intention to run away.

When we got about half way to St. Michael's, while the constables having us in charge were looking ahead, Henry inquired of me what he should do with his pass. I told him to eat it with his biscuit, and own nothing; and we passed the word around, *"Own nothing"*; and *"Own nothing!"* said we all. Our confidence in each other was unshaken. We were resolved to succeed or fail together, after the calamity had befallen us as much as before. We were now prepared for any thing. We were to be dragged that morning fifteen miles behind horses, and then to be placed in the Easton jail. When we reached St. Michael's, we underwent a sort of examination. We all denied that we ever intended to run away. We did this more to bring out the evidence against us, than from any hope of getting clear of being sold; for, as I have said, we were ready for that. The fact was, we cared but little where we went, so we went together. Our greatest concern was about separation. We dreaded that more than any thing this side of death. We found the evidence against us to be the testimony of one person; our master would not tell who it was; but we came to a unanimous decision among ourselves as to who their informant was. We were sent off to the jail at Easton. When we got there, we were delivered up to the sheriff, Mr. Joseph Graham, and by him placed in jail. Henry, John, and myself, were placed in one room together—Charles, and Henry Bailey, in another. Their object in separating us was to hinder concert.

We had been in jail scarcely twenty minutes, when a swarm of slave traders, and agents for slave traders, flocked into jail to look at us, and to aseertain if we were for sale. Such a set of beings I never saw before! I felt myself surrounded by so many fiends from perdition. A band of pirates never looked more like their father, the devil. They laughed and grinned over us, saying, "Ah, my boys! we have got you, haven't we?" And after taunting us in various ways, they one by one went into an examination of us, with intent to ascertain our value. They would impudently ask us if we would not like to have them for our masters. We would make them no answer, and leave them to find out as best they could. Then they would curse and swear at us, telling us that they could take the devil out of us in a very little while, if we were only in their hands.

While in jail, we found ourselves in much more comfortable quarters than we expected when we went there. We did not get much to eat, nor that which was very good; but we had a good clean room, from the windows of which we could see what was going on in the street, which was very much better than though we had been placed in one of the dark, damp cells. Upon the whole, we got along very well, so far as the jail and its keeper were concerned. Immediately after the holidays were over, contrary to all our expectations, Mr. Hamilton and Mr. Freeland came up to Easton, and took Charles, the two Henrys, and John, out of jail, and carried them home, leaving me alone. I regarded this separation as a final one. It caused me more pain than any thing else in the whole transaction. I was ready for any thing rather than separation. I supposed that they had consulted together, and had decided that, as I was the whole cause of the intention of the others to run away, it was hard to make the innocent suffer with the guilty; and that they had, therefore, concluded to take the others home, and sell me, as a warning to the others that remained. It is due to the noble Henry to say, he seemed almost as reluctant at leaving the prison as at leaving home to come to the prison. But we knew we should, in all probability, be separated, if we were sold; and since he was in their hands, he concluded to go peaceably home.

I was now left to my fate. I was all alone, and within the walls of a stone prison. But a few days before, and I was full of hope. I expected to have been safe in a land of freedom; but now I was covered with gloom, sunk down to the utmost despair. I thought the possibility of freedom was gone. I was kept in this way about one week, at the end of which, Captain Auld, my master, to my surprise and utter astonishment, came up, and took me out, with the intention of sending me, with a gentleman of his acquaintance, into Alabama. But, from some cause or other, he did not send me to Alabama, but concluded to send me back to Baltimore, to live again with his brother Hugh, and to learn a trade.

Thus, after an absence of three years and one month, I was once more permitted to return to my old home at Baltimore. My master sent me away, because there existed against me a very great prejudice in the community, and he feared I might be killed.

In a few weeks after I went to Baltimore, Master Hugh hired me to Mr. William Gardner, an extensive ship-builder, on Fell's Point. I was put there to learn how to calk. It, however, proved a very unfavorable place for the accomplishment of this object. Mr. Gardner was engaged that spring in building two large man-of-war brigs, professedly for the Mexican government. The vessels were to be launched in the July of that year, and in failure thereof, Mr. Gardner was to lose a considerable sum; so that when I entered, all was hurry. There was no time to learn any thing. Every man had to do that which he knew how to do. In entering the shipyard, my orders from Mr. Gardner were, to do whatever the carpenters commanded me to do. This was placing me at the beck and call of about seventy-five men. I was to regard all these as masters. Their word was to be my law. My situation was a most trying one. At times I needed a dozen pair of hands. I was called a dozen ways in the space of a single minute. Three or four voices would strike my ear at the same moment. It was—"Fred., come help me to cant this timber here."—"Fred., come carry this timber yonder."—"Fred., bring that roller here."—"Fred., go get a fresh can of water."—"Fred., come help saw off the end of this timber."—"Fred., go quick, and get the crowbar."—"Fred., hold on the end of this fall."—"Fred., go to the blacksmith's shop, and get a new punch."—"Hurra,[2] Fred.! run and bring me a cold chisel."—"I say, Fred., bear a hand, and get up a fire as quick as lightning under that steam-box."—"Halloo, nigger! come, turn this grindstone."—"Come, come! move, move! and *bowse*[3] this timber forward."—"I say, darky, blast your eyes, why don't you heat up some pitch?"—"Halloo! halloo! halloo!" (Three voices at the same time.) "Come here!—Go there!—Hold on where you are! Damn you, if you move, I'll knock your brains out!"

This was my school for eight months, and I might have remained there longer, but for a most horrid fight I had with four of the white apprentices, in which my left eye was nearly knocked out, and I was horribly mangled in other respects. The facts in the case were these: Until a very little while after I went there, white and black ship-carpenters worked side by side, and no one seemed to see any impropriety in it. All hands seemed to be very well satisfied. Many of the black carpenters were freemen. Things seemed to be going on very well. All at once, the white carpenters knocked off, and said they would not work with free colored workmen. Their reason for this, as alleged, was, that if free colored carpenters were encouraged, they would soon take the trade into their own hands, and poor white men would be thrown out of employment. They therefore felt called upon at once to put a stop to it. And, taking advantage of Mr. Gardner's necessities, they broke off, swearing they would work no longer, unless he would discharge his black carpenters. Now, though this did not extend to me in form, it did reach me in fact. My fellow-apprentices very soon began to feel it degrading to them to work with me. They began to put on airs, and talk about the "niggers" taking the country, saying we all ought to be killed; and, being encouraged by the journeymen, they commenced making my condition as hard as they could, by hectoring me around, and sometimes striking me. I, of course, kept the vow I made after the fight with Mr. Covey, and struck back again, regardless of consequences; and while I kept them from combining,

2. Hurry.

3. Lift or haul (usually with the help of block and tackle).

I succeeded very well; for I could whip the whole of them, taking them separately. They, however, at length combined, and came upon me, armed with sticks, stones, and heavy handspikes. One came in front with a half brick. There was one at each side of me, and one behind me. While I was attending to those in front, and on either side, the one behind ran up with the handspike, and struck me a heavy blow upon the head. It stunned me. I fell, and with this they all ran upon me, and fell to beating me with their fists. I let them lay on for a while, gathering strength. In an instant, I gave a sudden surge, and rose to my hands and knees. Just as I did that, one of their number gave me, with his heavy boot, a powerful kick in the left eye. My eyeball seemed to have burst. When they saw my eye closed, and badly swollen, they left me. With this I seized the handspike, and for a time pursued them. But here the carpenters interfered, and I thought I might as well give it up. It was impossible to stand my hand against so many. All this took place in sight of not less than fifty white ship-carpenters, and not one interposed a friendly word; but some cried, "Kill the damned nigger! Kill him! kill him! He struck a white person." I found my only chance for life was in flight. I succeeded in getting away without an additional blow, and barely so; for to strike a white man is death by Lynch law,— and that was the law in Mr. Gardner's ship-yard; nor is there much of any other out of Mr. Gardner's ship-yard.

I went directly home, and told the story of my wrongs to Master Hugh; and I am happy to say of him, irreligious as he was, his conduct was heavenly, compared with that of his brother Thomas under similar circumstances. He listened attentively to my narration of the circumstances leading to the savage outrage, and gave many proofs of his strong indignation of it. The heart of my once overkind mistress was again melted into pity. My puffed-out eye and blood-covered face moved her to tears. She took a chair by me, washed the blood from my face, and, with a mother's tenderness, bound up my head, covering the wounded eye with a lean piece of fresh beef. It was almost compensation for my suffering to witness, once more, a manifestation of kindness from this, my once affectionate old mistress. Master Hugh was very much enraged. He gave expression to his feelings by pouring out curses upon the heads of those who did the deed. As soon as I got a little the better of my bruises, he took me with him to Esquire Watson's, on Bond Street, to see what could be done about the matter. Mr. Watson inquired who saw the assault committed. Master Hugh told him it was done in Mr. Gardner's ship-yard, at midday, where there were a large company of men at work. "As to that," he said, "the deed was done, and there was no question as to who did it." His answer was, he could do nothing in the case, unless some white man would come forward and testify. He could issue no warrant on my word. If I had been killed in the presence of a thousand colored people, their testimony combined would have been insufficient to have arrested one of the murderers. Master Hugh, for once, was compelled to say this state of things was too bad. Of course, it was impossible to get any white man to volunteer his testimony in my behalf, and against the white young men. Even those who may have sympathized with me were not prepared to do this. It required a degree of courage unknown to them to do so; for just at that time, the slightest manifestation of humanity toward a colored person was denounced as abolitionism, and that name subjected its bearer to frightful liabilities. The watchwords of the bloody-minded in that region, and in those days, were, "Damn the abolitionists!" and "Damn the niggers!" There was nothing done, and probably nothing would have been done if I had been killed. Such was, and such remains, the state of things in the Christian city of Baltimore.

Master Hugh, finding he could get no redress, refused to let me go back again to Mr. Gardner. He kept me himself, and his wife dressed my wound till I was again restored to health. He then took me into the ship-yard of which he was foreman, in the employment of Mr. Walter Price. There I was immediately set to calking, and very soon learned the art of using my mallet and irons. In the course of one year from the time I left Mr. Gardner's, I was able to command the highest wages given to the most experienced calkers. I was now of some importance to my master. I was bringing him from six to seven dollars per week. I sometimes brought him nine dollars per week: my wages were a dollar and a half a day. After learning how to calk, I sought my own employment, made my own contracts, and collected the money which I earned. My pathway became much more smooth than before; my condition was now much more comfortable. When I could get no calking to do, I did nothing. During these leisure times, those old notions about freedom would steal over me again. When in Mr. Gardner's employment, I was kept in such a perpetual whirl of excitement, I could think of nothing, scarcely, but my life; and in thinking of my life, I almost forgot my liberty. I have observed this in my experience of slavery,—that whenever my condition was improved, instead of its increasing my contentment, it only increased my desire to be free, and set me to thinking of plans to gain my freedom. I have found that, to make a contented slave, it is necessary to make a thoughtless one. It is necessary to darken his moral and mental vision, and, as far as possible, to annihilate the power of reason. He must be made to feel that slavery is right; and he can be brought to that only when he ceases to be a man.

I was now getting, as I have said, one dollar and fifty cents per day. I contracted for it; I earned it; it was paid to me; it was rightfully my own; yet, upon each returning Saturday night, I was compelled to deliver every cent of that money to Master Hugh. And why? Not because he earned it,—not because he had any hand in earning it,—not because I owed it to him,—nor because he possessed the slightest shadow of a right to it; but solely because he had the power to compel me to give it up. The right of the grim-visaged pirate upon the high seas is exactly the same.

CHAPTER XI

I now come to that part of my life during which I planned, and finally succeeded in making, my escape from slavery. But before narrating any of the peculiar circumstances, I deem it proper to make known my intention not to state all the facts connected with the transaction. My reasons for pursuing this course may be understood from the following: First, were I to give a minute statement of all the facts, it is not only possible, but quite probable, that others would thereby be involved in the most embarrassing difficulties. Secondly, such a statement would most undoubtedly induce greater vigilance on the part of slaveholders than has existed heretofore among them; which would, of course, be the means of guarding a door whereby some dear brother bondman might escape his galling chains. I deeply regret the necessity that impels me to suppress any thing of importance connected with my experience in slavery. It would afford me great pleasure indeed, as well as materially add to the interest of my narrative, were I at liberty to gratify a curiosity, which I know exists in the minds of many, by an accurate statement of all the facts pertaining to my most fortunate escape. But I must deprive myself of this pleasure, and the curious of the gratification which such a statement would afford. I would allow myself to suffer under the greatest imputations which evil-minded men might suggest, rather than exculpate myself, and thereby run the hazard of closing the slightest avenue by which a brother slave might clear himself of the chains and fetters of slavery.

I have never approved of the very public manner in which some of our western friends have conducted what they call the *underground railroad*,[4] but which, I think, by their open declarations, has been made most emphatically the *upperground railroad*. I honor those good men and women for their noble daring, and applaud them for willingly subjecting themselves to bloody persecution, by openly avowing their participation in the escape of slaves. I, however, can see very little good resulting from such a course, either to themselves or the slaves escaping; while, upon the other hand, I see and feel assured that those open declarations are a positive evil to the slaves remaining, who are seeking to escape. They do nothing towards enlightening the slave, whilst they do much towards enlightening the master. They stimulate him to greater watchfulness, and enhance his power to capture his slave. We owe something to the slaves south of the line[5] as well as to those north of it; and in aiding the latter on their way to freedom, we should be careful to do nothing which would be likely to hinder the former from escaping from slavery. I would keep the merciless slaveholder profoundly ignorant of the means of flight adopted by the slave. I would leave him to imagine himself surrounded by myriads of invisible tormentors, ever ready to snatch from his infernal grasp his trembling prey. Let him be left to feel his way in the dark; let darkness commensurate with his crime hover over him; and let him feel that at every step he takes, in pursuit of the flying bondman, he is running the frightful risk of having his hot brains dashed out by an invisible agency. Let us render the tyrant no aid; let us not hold the light by which he can trace the footprints of our flying brother. But enough of this. I will now proceed to the statement of those facts, connected with my escape, for which I am alone responsible, and for which no one can be made to suffer but myself.

In the early part of the year 1838, I became quite restless. I could see no reason why I should, at the end of each week, pour the reward of my toil into the purse of my master. When I carried to him my weekly wages, he would, after counting the money, look me in the face with a robber-like fierceness, and ask, "Is this all?" He was satisfied with nothing less than the last cent. He would, however, when I made him six dollars, sometimes give me six cents, to encourage me. It had the opposite effect. I regarded it as a sort of admission of my right to the whole. The fact that he gave me any part of my wages was

4. A system set up by opponents of slavery to help fugitive slaves from the South escape to free states and to Canada.

5. The Mason-Dixon line, the boundary between Pennsylvania and Maryland and between slave and free states.

proof, to my mind, that he believed me entitled to the whole of them. I always felt worse for having received any thing; for I feared that the giving me a few cents would ease his conscience, and make him feel himself to be a pretty honorable sort of robber. My discontent grew upon me. I was ever on the look-out for means of escape; and, finding no direct means, I determined to try to hire my time, with a view of getting money with which to make my escape. In the spring of 1838, when Master Thomas came to Baltimore to purchase his spring goods, I got an opportunity, and applied to him to allow me to hire my time. He unhesitatingly refused my request, and told me this was another stratagem by which to escape. He told me I could go nowhere but that he could get me; and that, in the event of my running away, he should spare no pains in his efforts to catch me. He exhorted me to content myself, and be obedient. He told me, if I would be happy, I must lay out no plans for the future. He said, if I behaved myself properly, he would take care of me. Indeed, he advised me to complete thoughtlessness of the future, and taught me to depend solely upon him for happiness. He seemed to see fully the pressing necessity of setting aside my intellectual nature, in order to [insure] contentment in slavery. But in spite of him, and even in spite of myself, I continued to think, and to think about the injustice of my enslavement, and the means of escape.

About two months after this, I applied to Master Hugh for the privilege of hiring my time. He was not acquainted with the fact that I had applied to Master Thomas, and had been refused. He too, at first, seemed disposed to refuse; but, after some reflection, he granted me the privilege, and proposed the following terms: I was to be allowed all my time, make all contracts with those for whom I worked, and find my own employment; and, in return for this liberty, I was to pay him three dollars at the end of each week; find myself in calking tools, and in board and clothing. My board was two dollars and a half per week. This, with the wear and tear of clothing and calking tools, made my regular expenses about six dollars per week. This amount I was compelled to make up, or relinquish the privilege of hiring my time. Rain or shine, work or no work, at the end of each week the money must be forthcoming, or I must give up my privilege. This arrangement, it will be perceived, was decidedly in my master's favor. It relieved him of all need of looking after me. His money was sure. He received all the benefits of slave-holding without its evils; while I endured all the evils of a slave, and suffered all the care and anxiety of a freeman. I found it a hard bargain. But, hard as it was, I thought it better than the old mode of getting along. It was a step towards freedom to be allowed to bear the responsibilities of a freeman, and I was determined to hold on upon it. I bent myself to the work of making money. I was ready to work at night as well as day, and by the most untiring perseverance and industry, I made enough to meet my expenses, and lay up a little money every week. I went on thus from May till August. Master Hugh then refused to allow me to hire my time longer. The ground for his refusal was a failure on my part, one Saturday night, to pay him for my week's time. This failure was occasioned by my attending a camp meeting about ten miles from Baltimore. During the week, I had entered into an engagement with a number of young friends to start from Baltimore to the camp ground early Saturday evening; and being detained by my employer, I was unable to get down to Master Hugh's without disappointing the company. I knew that Master Hugh was in no special need of the money that night. I therefore decided to go to camp meeting, and upon my return pay him the three dollars. I staid at the camp meeting one day longer than I intended when I left. But as soon as I returned, I called upon him to pay him what he considered his due. I found him very angry; he could scarce restrain his wrath. He said he had a great mind to give me a severe whipping. He wished to know how I dared go out of the city without asking his permission. I told him I hired my time, and while I paid him the price which he asked for it, I did not know that I was bound to ask him when and where I should go. This reply troubled him, and, after reflecting a few moments, he turned to me, and said I should hire my time no longer; that the next thing he should know of, I would be running away. Upon the same plea, he told me to bring my tools and clothing home forthwith. I did so; but instead of seeking work, as I had been accustomed to do previously to hiring my time, I spent the whole week without the performance of a single stroke of work. I did this in retaliation. Saturday night, he called upon me as usual for my week's wages. I told him I had no wages; I had done no work that week. Here we were upon the point of coming to blows. He raved, and swore his determination to get hold of me. I did not allow myself a single word; but was resolved, if he laid the weight of his hand upon me, it should be blow for blow. He did not strike me, but told me that he would find me in constant employment in future. I thought the matter over during the next day, Sunday, and finally resolved upon the third day of September, as the day upon which I would make a second attempt to secure my freedom. I now had three weeks during which to prepare for my journey. Early on Monday morning, before Master Hugh had time to make any engagement for me, I went out and got employment of Mr. Butler, at his ship-yard near the draw-bridge, upon what is called the City Block, thus making it unnecessary for him to seek employment for me. At the end of the week, I brought him between eight and nine dollars. He seemed very well pleased, and asked me why I did not do the same the week before. He little knew what my plans were. My object in working steadily was to remove any suspicion he might entertain of my intent to run away; and in this I succeeded admirably. I suppose he thought I was never better satisfied with my condition than at the very time during which I was planning my escape. The second week passed, and again I carried him my full wages; and so well pleased was he, that he gave me twenty-five cents, (quite a large sum for a slaveholder to give a slave,) and bade me to make a good use of it. I told him I would.

Things went on without very smoothly indeed, but within there was trouble. It is impossible for me to describe my feelings as the time of my contemplated start drew near. I had a number of warm-hearted friends in Baltimore,— friends that I loved almost as I did my life,—and the thought of being separated from them forever was painful beyond expression. It is my opinion that thousands would escape from slavery, who now remain, but for the strong cords of affection that bind them to their friends. The thought of leaving my friends was decidedly the most painful thought with which I had to contend. The love of them was my tender point, and shook my decision more than all things else. Besides the pain of separation, the dread and apprehension of a failure exceeded what I had experienced at my first attempt. The appalling defeat I then sustained returned to torment me. I felt assured that, if I failed in this attempt, my case would be a hopeless one—it would seal my fate as a slave forever. I could not hope to get off with any thing less than the severest punishment, and being placed beyond the means of escape. It required no very vivid imagination to depict the most frightful scenes through which I should have to pass, in case I failed. The wretchedness of slavery, and the blessedness of freedom, were perpetually before me. It was life and death with me. But I remained firm, and, according to my resolution, on the third day of September, 1838, I left my chains, and succeeded in reaching New York without the slightest interruption of any kind. How I did so,— what means I adopted,— what direction I travelled, and by what mode of conveyance,—I must leave unexplained, for the reasons before mentioned.

I have been frequently asked how I felt when I found myself in a free State. I have never been able to answer the question with any satisfaction to myself. It was a moment of the highest excitement I ever experienced. I suppose I felt as one may imagine the unarmed mariner to feel when he is rescued by a friendly man-of-war from the pursuit of a pirate. In writing to a dear friend, immediately after my arrival at New York, I said I felt like one who had escaped a den of hungry lions. This state of mind, however, very soon subsided; and I was again seized with a feeling of great insecurity and loneliness. I was yet liable to be taken back, and subjected to all the tortures of slavery. This in itself was enough to damp the ardor of my enthusiasm. But the loneliness overcame me. There I was in the midst of thousands, and yet a perfect stranger; without home and without friends, in the midst of thousands of my own brethren— children of a common Father, and yet I dared not to unfold to any one of them my sad condition. I was afraid to speak to any one for fear of speaking to the wrong one, and thereby falling into the hands of money-loving kidnappers, whose business it was to lie in wait for the panting fugitive, as the ferocious beasts of the forest lie in wait for their prey. The motto which I adopted when I started from slavery was this—"Trust no man!" I saw in every white man an enemy, and in almost every colored man cause for distrust. It was a most painful situation; and, to understand it, one must needs experience it, or imagine himself in similar circumstances. Let him be a fugitive slave in a strange land—a land given up to be the hunting-ground for slaveholders—whose inhabitants are legalized kidnappers—where he is every moment subjected to the terrible liability of being seized upon by his fellow-men, as the hideous crocodile seizes upon his prey!—I say, let him place himself in my situation— without home or friends—without money or credit—wanting shelter, and no one to give it—wanting bread, and no money to buy it,—and at the same time let him feel that he is pursued by merciless men-hunters, and in total darkness as to what to do, where to go, or where to stay,—perfectly helpless both as to the means of defence and means of escape,—in the midst of plenty, yet suffering the terrible gnawings of hunger,—in the midst of houses, yet having no home,—among fellow-men, yet feeling as if in the midst of wild beasts, whose greediness to swallow up the trembling and half-famished fugitive is only equalled by that with which the monsters of the deep swallow up the helpless fish upon which they subsist,—I say, let him be placed in this most trying situation,—the situation in which I was placed,—then, and not till then, will he fully appreciate the hardships of, and know how to sympathize with, the toil-worn and whip-scarred fugitive slave.

Thank Heaven, I remained but a short time in this distressed situation. I was relieved from it by the humane hand of Mr. DAVID RUGGLES,[6] whose vigilance, kindness, and perseverance, I shall never forget. I am glad of an opportunity to express, as far as words can, the love and gratitude I bear him. Mr. Ruggles is now afflicted with blindness, and is himself in need of the same kind offices which he was once so forward in the performance of toward others. I had been in New York but a few days, when Mr. Ruggles sought me out, and very kindly took me to his boarding-house at the corner of Church and Lespenard Streets. Mr. Ruggles was then very deeply engaged in the memorable *Darg* case, as well as attending to a number of other fugitive slaves, devising ways and means for their successful escape; and, though watched and hemmed in on almost every side, he seemed to be more than a match for his enemies. Very soon after I went to Mr. Ruggles, he wished to know of me where I wanted to go; as he deemed it unsafe for me to remain in New York. I told him I was a calker, and should like to go where I could get work. I thought of going to Canada; but he decided against it, and in favor of my going to New Bedford, thinking I should be able to get work there at my trade. At this time, Anna,[7] my intended wife, came on; for I wrote to her immediately after my arrival at New York, (notwithstanding my homeless, houseless, and helpless condition,) informing her of my successful flight, and wishing her to come on forthwith. In a few days after her arrival, Mr. Ruggles called in the Rev. J. W. C. Pennington, who, in the presence of Mr. Ruggles, Mrs. Michaels, and two or three others, performed the marriage ceremony, and gave us a certificate, of which the following is an exact copy:—

"THIS may certify, that I joined together in holy matrimony Frederick Johnson[8] and Anna Murray, as man and wife, in the presence of Mr. David Ruggles and Mrs. Michaels.

"JAMES W. C. PENNINGTON.
"*New York, Sept. 15, 1838.*"

Upon receiving this certificate, and a five-dollar bill from Mr. Ruggles, I shouldered one part of our baggage, and Anna took up the other, and we set out forthwith to take passage on board of the steamboat John W. Richmond for Newport, on our way to New Bedford. Mr. Ruggles gave me a letter to a Mr. Shaw in Newport, and told me, in case my money did not serve me to New Bedford, to stop in Newport and obtain further assistance; but upon our arrival at Newport, we were so anxious to get to a place of safety, that, notwithstanding we lacked the necessary money to pay our fare, we decided to take seats in the stage, and promise to pay when we got to New Bedford. We were encouraged to do this by two excellent gentlemen, residents of New Bedford, whose names I afterward ascertained to be Joseph Ricketson and William C. Taber. They seemed at once to understand our circumstances, and gave us such assurance of their friendliness as put us fully at ease in their presence. It was good indeed to meet with such friends, at such a time. Upon reaching New Bedford, we were directed to the house of Mr. Nathan Johnson, by whom we

6. A black abolitionist (1810–1849), at this time living in New York, who helped many slaves to escape.

7. She was free [Douglass's note].

8. I had changed my name from Frederick *Bailey* to that of *Johnson* [Douglass's note].

were kindly received, and hospitably provided for. Both Mr. and Mrs. Johnson took a deep and lively interest in our welfare. They proved themselves quite worthy of the name of abolitionists. When the stage-driver found us unable to pay our fare, he held on upon our baggage as security for the debt. I had but to mention the fact to Mr. Johnson, and he forthwith advanced the money.

We now began to feel a degree of safety, and to prepare ourselves for the duties and responsibilities of a life of freedom. On the morning after our arrival at New Bedford, while at the breakfast-table, the question arose as to what name I should be called by. The name given me by my mother was, "Frederick Augustus Washington Bailey." I, however, had dispensed with the two middle names long before I left Maryland so that I was generally known by the name of "Frederick Bailey." I started from Baltimore bearing the name of "Stanley." When I got to New York, I again changed my name to "Frederick Johnson," and thought that would be the last change. But when I got to New Bedford, I found it necessary again to change my name. The reason of this necessity was, that there were so many Johnsons in New Bedford, it was already quite difficult to distinguish between them. I gave Mr. Johnson the privilege of choosing me a name, but told him he must not take from me the name of "Frederick." I must hold on to that, to preserve a sense of my identity. Mr. Johnson had just been reading the "Lady of the Lake,"[9] and at once suggested that my name be "Douglass." From that time until now I have been called "Frederick Douglass"; and as I am more widely known by that name than by either of the others, I shall continue to use it as my own.

I was quite disappointed at the general appearance of things in New Bedford. The impression which I had received respecting the character and condition of the people of the north, I found to be singularly erroneous. I had very strangely supposed, while in slavery, that few of the comforts, and scarcely any of the luxuries, of life were enjoyed at the north, compared with what were enjoyed by the slaveholders of the south. I probably came to this conclusion from the fact that northern people owned no slaves. I supposed that they were about upon a level with the non-slaveholding population of the south. I knew *they* were exceedingly poor, and I had been accustomed to regard their poverty as the necessary consequence of their being non-slaveholders. I had somehow imbibed the opinion that, in the absence of slaves, there could be no wealth, and very little refinement. And upon coming to the north, I expected to meet with a rough, hard-handed, and uncultivated population, living in the most Spartan-like simplicity, knowing nothing of the ease, luxury, pomp, and grandeur of southern slaveholders. Such being my conjectures, any one acquainted with the appearance of New Bedford may very readily infer how palpably I must have seen my mistake.

In the afternoon of the day when I reached New Bedford, I visited the wharves, to take a view of the shipping. Here I found myself surrounded with the strongest proofs of wealth. Lying at the wharves, and riding in the stream, I saw many ships of the finest model, in the best order, and of the largest size. Upon the right and left, I was walled in by granite warehouses of the widest dimensions, stowed to their utmost capacity with the necessaries and comforts of life. Added to this, almost every body seemed to be at work, but noiselessly

9. A narrative poem by Sir Walter Scott (1810) about the fortunes of the Douglas clan in Scotland.

so, compared with what I had been accustomed to in Baltimore. There were no loud songs heard from those engaged in loading and unloading ships. I heard no deep oaths or horrid curses on the laborer. I saw no whipping of men; but all seemed to go smoothly on. Every man appeared to understand his work, and went at it with a sober, yet cheerful earnestness, which betokened the deep interest which he felt in what he was doing, as well as a sense of his own dignity as a man. To me this looked exceedingly strange. From the wharves I strolled around and over the town, gazing with wonder and admiration at the splendid churches, beautiful dwellings, and finely-cultivated gardens; evincing an amount of wealth, comfort, taste, and refinement, such as I had never seen in any part of slaveholding Maryland.

Every thing looked clean, new, and beautiful. I saw few or no dilapidated houses, with poverty-stricken inmates; no half-naked children and barefooted women, such as I had been accustomed to see in Hillsborough, Easton, St. Michael's, and Baltimore. The people looked more able, stronger, healthier, and happier, than those of Maryland. I was for once made glad by a view of extreme wealth, without being saddened by seeing extreme poverty. But the most astonishing as well as the most interesting thing to me was the condition of the colored people, a great many of whom, like myself, had escaped thither as a refuge from the hunters of men. I found many, who had not been seven years out of their chains, living in finer houses, and evidently enjoying more of the comforts of life, than the average of slave-holders in Maryland. I will venture to assert that my friend Mr. Nathan Johnson (of whom I can say with a grateful heart, "I was hungry, and he gave me meat; I was thirsty, and he gave me drink; I was a stranger, and he took me in")[1] lived in a neater house; dined at a better table; took, paid for, and read, more newspapers; better understood the moral, religious, and political character of the nation,—than nine tenths of the slave-holders in Talbot county Maryland. Yet Mr. Johnson was a working man. His hands were hardened by toil, and not his alone, but those also of Mrs. Johnson. I found the colored people much more spirited than I had supposed they would be. I found among them a determination to protect each other from the blood-thirsty kidnapper, at all hazards. Soon after my arrival, I was told of a circumstance which illustrated their spirit. A colored man and a fugitive slave were on unfriendly terms. The former was heard to threaten the latter with informing his master of his whereabouts. Straightway a meeting was called among the colored people, under the stereotyped notice, "Business of importance!" The betrayer was invited to attend. The people came at the appointed hour, and organized the meeting by appointing a very religious old gentleman as president, who, I believe, made a prayer, after which he addressed the meeting as follows: *Friends, we have got him here, and I would recommend that you young men just take him outside the door, and kill him!*" With this, a number of them bolted at him; but they were intercepted by some more timid than themselves, and the betrayer escaped their vengeance, and has not been seen in New Bedford since. I believe there have been no more such threats, and should there be hereafter, I doubt not that death would be the consequence.

1. Matthew 25.35: "For I was an hungered, and ye gave me meat: I was thirsty, and ye gave me drink: I was a stranger, and ye took me in."

I found employment, the third day after my arrival, in stowing a sloop with a load of oil. It was new, dirty, and hard work for me; but I went at it with a glad heart and a willing hand. I was now my own master. It was a happy moment, the rapture of which can be understood only by those who have been slaves. It was the first work, the reward of which was to be entirely my own. There was no Master Hugh standing ready, the moment I earned the money, to rob me of it. I worked that day with a pleasure I had never before experienced. I was at work for myself and newly-married wife. It was to me the starting-point of a new existence. When I got through with that job, I went in pursuit of a job of calking; but such was the strength of prejudice against color, among the white calkers, that they refused to work with me, and of course I could get no employment.[2] Finding my trade of no immediate benefit, I threw off my calking habiliments, and prepared myself to do any kind of work I could get to do. Mr. Johnson kindly let me have his woodhorse and saw, and I very soon found myself a plenty of work. There was no work too hard—none too dirty. I was ready to saw wood, shovel coal, carry the hod, sweep the chimney, or roll oil casks,—all of which I did for nearly three years in New Bedford, before I became known to the anti-slavery world.

In about four months after I went to New Bedford there came a young man to me, and inquired if I did not wish to take the "Liberator."[3] I told him I did; but, just having made my escape from slavery, I remarked that I was unable to pay for it then. I, however, finally became a subscriber to it. The paper came, and I read it from week to week with such feelings as it would be quite idle for me to attempt to describe. The paper became my meat and my drink. My soul was set all on fire. Its sympathy for my brethren in bonds—its scathing denunciations of slaveholders—its faithful exposures of slavery—and its powerful attacks upon the upholders of the institution—sent a thrill of joy through my soul, such as I had never felt before!

I had not long been a reader of the "Liberator," before I got a pretty correct idea of the principles, measures and spirit of the anti-slavery reform. I took right hold of the cause. I could do but little; but what I could, I did with a joyful heart, and never felt happier than when in an anti-slavery meeting. I seldom had much to say at the meetings, because what I wanted to say was said so much better by others. But, while attending an anti-slavery convention at Nantucket, on the 11th of August, 1841, I felt strongly moved to speak, and was at the same time much urged to do so by Mr. William C. Coffin, a gentleman who had heard me speak in the colored people's meeting at New Bedford. It was a severe cross, and I took it up reluctantly. The truth was, I felt myself a slave, and the idea of speaking to white people weighed me down. I spoke but a few moments, when I felt a degree of freedom, and said what I desired with considerable ease. From that time until now, I have been engaged in pleading the cause of my brethren—with what success, and with what devotion, I leave those acquainted with my labors to decide.

2. I am told that colored persons can now get employment at calking in New Bedford—a result of antislavery effort [Douglass's note].

3. William Lloyd Garrison's antislavery newspaper, which began publication in 1831.

APPENDIX

I find, since reading over the foregoing Narrative, that I have, in several instances, spoken in such a tone and manner, respecting religion, as may possibly lead those unacquainted with my religious views to suppose me an opponent of all religion. To remove the liability of such misapprehension, I deem it proper to append the following brief explanation. What I have said respecting and against religion, I mean strictly to apply to the *slaveholding religion* of this land, and with no possible reference to Christianity proper; for, between the Christianity of this land, and the Christianity of Christ, I recognize the widest possible difference—so wide, that to receive the one as good, pure, and holy, is of necessity to reject the other as bad, corrupt, and wicked. To be the friend of the one, is of necessity to be the enemy of the other. I love the pure, peaceable, and impartial Christianity of Christ: I therefore hate the corrupt, slaveholding, women-whipping, cradle-plundering, partial and hypocritical Christianity of this land. Indeed, I can see no reason, but the most deceitful one, for calling the religion of this land Christianity. I look upon it as the climax of all misnomers, the boldest of all frauds, and the grossest of all libels. Never was there a clearer case of "stealing the livery of the court of heaven to serve the devil in." I am filled with unutterable loathing when I contemplate the religious pomp and show, together with the horrible inconsistencies, which every where surround me. We have men-stealers for ministers, women-whippers for missionaries, and cradle-plunderers for church members. The man who wields the blood-clotted cowskin during the week fills the pulpit on Sunday, and claims to be a minister of the meek and lowly Jesus. The man who robs me of my earnings at the end of each week meets me as a class-leader on Sunday morning, to show me the way of life, and the path of salvation. He who sells my sister, for purposes of prostitution, stands forth as the pious advocate of purity. He who proclaims it a religious duty to read the Bible denies me the right of learning to read the name of the God who made me. He who is the religious advocate of marriage robs whole millions of its sacred influence, and leaves them to the ravages of wholesale pollution. The warm defender of the sacredness of the family relation is the same that scatters whole families,—sundering husbands and wives, parents and children, sisters and brothers,—leaving the hut vacant, and the hearth desolate. We see the thief preaching against theft, and the adulterer against adultery. We have men sold to build churches, women sold to support the gospel, and babes sold to purchase Bibles for the *poor heathen! all for the glory of God and the good of souls!* The slave auctioneer's bell and the church-going bell chime in with each other, and the bitter cries of the heart-broken slave are drowned in the religious shouts of his pious master. Revivals of religion and revivals in the slave-trade go hand in hand together. The slave prison and the church stand near each other. The clanking of fetters and the rattling of chains in the prison, and the pious psalm and solemn prayer in the church, may be heard at the same time. The dealers in the bodies and souls of men erect their stand in the presence of the pulpit, and they mutually help each other. The dealer gives his blood-stained gold to support the pulpit, and the pulpit, in return, covers his infernal business with the garb of Christianity. Here we have religion and robbery the allies of each other—devils dressed in angels' robes, and hell presenting the semblance of paradise.

"Just God! and these are they,
   Who minister at thine altar, God of right!
Men who their hands, with prayer and blessing, lay
   On Israel's ark of light.

"What! preach, and kidnap men?
   Give thanks, and rob thy own afflicted poor?
Talk of thy glorious liberty, and then
   Bolt hard the captive's door?

"What! servants of thy own
   Merciful Son, who came to seek and save
The homeless and the outcast, fettering down
   The tasked and plundered slave!

"Pilate and Herod friends!
   Chief priests and rulers, as of old, combine!
Just God and holy! is that church which lends
   Strength to the spoiler thine?"

The Christianity of America is a Christianity, of whose votaries it may be as truly said, as it was of the ancient scribes and Pharisees, "They bind heavy burdens, and grievous to be borne, and lay them on men's shoulders, but they themselves will not move them with one of their fingers. All their works they do for to be seen of men.—— They love the uppermost rooms at feasts, and the chief seats in the synagogues, ... and to be called of men, Rabbi, Rabbi.——But woe unto you, scribes and Pharisees, hypocrites! for ye neither go in yourselves, neither suffer ye them that are entering to go in. Ye devour widows' houses, and for a pretence make long prayers; therefore ye shall receive the greater damnation. Ye compass sea and land to make one proselyte, and when he is made, ye make him twofold more the child of hell than yourselves.——Woe unto you, scribes and Pharisees, hypocrites! for ye pay tithe of mint, and anise, and cumin, and have omitted the weightier matters of the law, judgment, mercy, and faith; these ought ye to have done, and not to leave the other undone. Ye blind guides! which strain at a gnat, and swallow a camel. Woe unto you, scribes and Pharisees, hypocrites! for ye make clean the outside of the cup and of the platter; but within, they are full of extortion and excess.——Woe unto you, scribes and Pharisees, hypocrites! for ye are like unto whited sepulchres, which indeed appear beautiful outward, but are within full of dead men's bones, and of all uncleanness. Even so ye also outwardly appear righteous unto men, but within ye are full of hypocrisy and iniquity."[4]

Dark and terrible as is this picture, I hold it to be strictly true of the overwhelming mass of professed Christians in America. They strain at a gnat, and swallow a camel. Could anything be more true of our churches? They would be shocked at the proposition of fellowshipping a *sheep*-stealer; and at the same time they hug to their communion a *man*-stealer, and brand me with being an infidel, if I find fault with them for it. They attend with Pharisaical strictness to the outward forms of religion, and at the same time neglect the weightier matters of the law, judgment, mercy, and faith. They are always ready to sacrifice, but seldom to show mercy. They are they who are represented as professing to love

4. Matthew 23.

God whom they have not seen, whilst they hate their brother whom they have seen. They love the heathen on the other side of the globe. They can pray for him, pay money to have the Bible put into his hand, and missionaries to instruct him; while they despise and totally neglect the heathen at their own doors.

Such is, very briefly, my view of the religion of this land; and to avoid any misunderstanding, growing out of the use of general terms, I mean, by the religion of this land, that which is revealed in the words, deeds, and actions, of those bodies, north and south, calling themselves Christian churches, and yet in union with slaveholders. It is against religion, as presented by these bodies, that I have felt it my duty to testify.

I conclude these remarks by copying the following portrait of the religion of the south, (which is, by communion and fellowship, the religion of the north) which I soberly affirm is "true to the life," and without caricature or the slightest exaggeration. It is said to have been drawn, several years before the present anti-slavery agitation began, by a northern Methodist preacher, who, while residing at the south, had an opportunity to see slaveholding morals, manners, and piety, with his own eyes. "Shall I not visit for these things? saith the Lord. Shall not my soul be avenged on such a nation as this?"[5]

"A Parody.

"Come, saints and sinners, hear me tell
How pious priests whip Jack and Nell,
And women buy and children sell,
And preach all sinners down to hell,
   And sing of heavenly union.

"They'll bleat and baa, dona[6] like goats,
Gorge down black sheep, and strain at motes,
Array their backs in fine black coats,
Then seize their negroes by their throats,
   And choke, for heavenly union.

"They'll church you if you sip a dram,
And damn you if you steal a lamb;
Yet rob old Tony, Doll, and Sam,
Of human rights, and bread and ham;
   Kidnapper's heavenly union.

"They'll loudly talk of Christ's reward,
And bind his image with a cord,
And scold, and swing the lash abhorred,
And sell their brother in the Lord
   To handcuffed heavenly union.

"They'll read and sing a sacred song,
And make a prayer both loud and long,
And teach the right and do the wrong,
Hailing the brother, sister throng,
   With words of heavenly union.

---

5. Jeremiah 5.9.

6. Believed to be a printer's error in the original edition for "go on" or "go n-a-a-ah."

"We wonder how such saints can sing,
Or praise the Lord upon the wing,
Who roar, and scold, and whip, and sting,
And to their slaves and mammon cling,
   In guilty conscience union.

"They'll raise tobacco, corn, and rye,
And drive, and thieve, and cheat, and lie,
And lay up treasures in the sky,
By making switch and cowskin fly,
   In hope of heavenly union.

"They'll crack old Tony on the skull,
And preach and roar like Bashan bull,
Or braying ass, of mischief full,
Then seize old Jacob by the wool,
   And pull for heavenly union.

"A roaring, ranting, sleek man-thief,
Who lived on mutton, veal, and beef,
Yet never would afford relief
To needy, sable sons of grief,
   Was big with heavenly union.

"'Love not the world,' the preacher said,
And winked his eye, and shook his head;
He seized on Tom, and Dick, and Ned,
Cut short their meat, and clothes, and bread,
   Yet still loved heavenly union.

"Another preacher whining spoke
Of One whose heart for sinners broke:
He tied old Nanny to an oak,
And drew the blood at every stroke,
   And prayed for heavenly union.

"Two others oped their iron jaws,
And waved their children-stealing paws;
There sat their children in gewgaws;
By stinting negroes' backs and maws,
   They kept up heavenly union.

"All good from Jack another takes,
And entertains their flirts and rakes,
Who dress as sleek as glossy snakes,
And cram their mouths with sweetened cakes;
   And this goes down for union."

Sincerely and earnestly hoping that this little book may do something toward throwing light on the American slave system, and hastening the glad day of deliverance to the millions of my brethren in bonds—faithfully relying upon the power of truth, love, and justice, for success in my humble efforts—and solemnly pledging my self anew to the sacred cause,—I subscribe myself,

                        FREDERICK DOUGLASS.

Lynn, Mass., April 28, 1845.

LYRIC POETRY IN THE
LONG NINETEENTH CENTURY

The twentieth century is often considered the era of radical experimentation in poetry, but in fact throughout the nineteenth century poets around the world were inventing startling new poetic forms and resisting traditional expectations. Among the most important movements was what we now know as Romanticism, which shaped all of the arts—literature, visual art, and music—and lasted roughly from the 1780s to the 1830s in Europe and the Americas. *Romanticism* often feels like a frustratingly loose term, encompassing so many styles and practices that it ceases to mean anything at all. It is associated with nature, and especially wild and untamed natural settings. It is often defined as a rejection of neoclassical styles—the revival of Greek and Roman traditions that had grown dominant in the eighteenth century—as well as a rejection of reason as the organizing principle for art and society. Romanticism tended to valorize the ordinary individual, the solitary soul, the visionary, even the outcast. The term evokes imagination, excess, spontaneity, freedom, and revolution. Romantic art often dwells in wild, ghostly, and exotic settings, and embraces a turn inward to the emotions, dreams, and fantasies. Romanticism is also associated with nationalism and folk traditions. Its dominant literary form is the lyric poem, though there were Romantic novels, dramas, plays, and autobiographies.

One way to grasp Romanticism as a concept is to investigate the crucial role that nature plays in the period. Before the 1780s in Europe, there was very little art that depicted natural scenes apart from the highly artful tradition of pastoral—which tended to portray flute-playing, classical-style shepherds in distinctly sheepless environments. Romantic artists were really the first group in the West to take nature as an important subject matter in and of itself: turning away from the manners and artifices of social life, writers and artists celebrated the beauties of vast skies and towering mountains, a world free from court intrigues and urban poverty. But why did this new focus on nature emerge at this particular moment? Two different historical explanations help to make sense of the shift. First, as the industrial revolution forced huge masses of people out of agricultural life and into crowded cities, nature became exotic—and therefore interesting and valuable—in a whole new way. That is, when the majority of people lived in the countryside, it had seemed ordinary, mundane. But as more and more people began to lead urban lives, while railways cut ugly gashes through the fields and black smoke billowed into the sky, nature's beauty began to seem rare and precious—and increasingly under threat. From this perspective, the sudden upsurge in artistic treatments of nature makes sense as a way to capture and honor an increasingly vulnerable natural environment.

There is also a second explanation for the new embrace of nature.

In the eighteenth century, both absolute monarchies and new kinds of human knowledge—including science and statistics—valued control over nature. The gardens built by King Louis XIV of France at his grand palace of Versailles followed a rigid geometrical design, marking the power to subdue and order the natural world in accordance with the demands of human reason. Resisting old regimes of power, some radical late-eighteenth-century thinkers rejected this entwining of order and authority, and saw a return to the wildness of nature as a new model of expressive freedom, liberated from the constraints of reason and authority. Nature could be not only a source of beauty and inspiration, but a very foundation for a new kind of society that would replace the rule of absolute monarchs and rigid regulations. This new society would be based on the fulfillment of what was natural within human beings. Thus thinkers started to explore and celebrate nature as a kind of foundation for human experience, putting forward "natural laws" as the basis for social organizations, and crafting new state constitutions based on them. Here we see the emergence of new ideas about human rights—the notion that certain freedoms are given by nature alone and cannot justly be taken away by any government. Also emergent was a notion of a human community based not on kings or laws but on natural ties that united a group—an organic set of folk traditions that bound a people together indissolubly. Called "romantic nationalists," these thinkers celebrated local folklore, language, and customs—and often ethnic and racial differences—as the basis for national identity.

This revolutionary set of political ideals went hand in hand with a thoroughgoing revolution in poetry. Throwing off classical models, poets now looked to children and to "primitive" peoples who seemed closer to nature as models for social experience. They sought out new poetic forms that would capture natural rhythms and patterns of human speech. They turned to traditional folk and fairy tales for inspiration, and wrote in local dialects that had seemed low and coarse in the era of neoclassicism. And they valued not rigid conventions but what seemed most natural in the self: impulsiveness, excess, imaginative freedom. **William Wordsworth** cast the best new poetry as "the spontaneous overflow of powerful feelings," and **John Keats** wrote that "if poetry comes not as naturally as the leaves to a tree it had better not come at all." Instead of insisting on reason, art, and order as their sources of inspiration, poets looked to the unconscious mind, to spiritual awakening, and to dreams. They also valued ruins and relics of past times and exotic settings—anything that would jolt readers out of their entrenched sense of order and habit. Some of these Romantic themes contradicted each other—exotic settings and local traditions, individualism and racial foundations for communities—but they coexisted as a constellation of reactions against the dominant eighteenth-century values of order, reason, and authority.

For many writers—especially in England—the ideal poetic form for these new principles seemed to be the lyric. A lyric poem expresses a process of perception, thought, or emotion, often in the first person. Traditionally a marginal European form compared to epic, elegy, pastoral, and the satires popular in the eighteenth century, lyric grew so powerfully central to the definition of poetry in the nineteenth century that today it seems to have little in the way of competition. And it is thanks to the Romantics, with their insistence on turning away from the imitation of classical forms and toward the truth of inner experience—toward the individual's sincere, spontaneous feeling—that lyric came to prominence. Lyric has few set rules—one can choose any meter, stanza length, or structuring arc—and so it embodies the freedom from set conventions that Romantic poets valued. And its focus on processes of thought and feeling allowed poets to celebrate the great range of human emotion that seemed to have been suddenly released from rigid authority—imagination and desire, memory and mourning, speculation and idealism, and above all, a passionate interest in the truth of nature as a guide to beauty, freedom, community, and humanity itself. This volume collects Romantic poems from Britain, Germany, Russia, Italy, and Venezuela.

EXPERIMENTAL POETS AT MID-CENTURY

Romanticism has no clear end point, and in fact, writers can still be called "Romantic" today if their values seem to fit the mood and spirit of the period. But it is true that some poets in the middle of the nineteenth century began to turn a critical eye on some of the most crucial Romantic presumptions. These transitional figures, such as **Elizabeth Barrett Browning**, **Heinrich Heine**, and **Walt Whitman**, continued some of the impulses of Romantic poetry but experimented with transforming its voice and subject matter. Both Barrett Browning and Heine rejected the solitary first-person perspective of the individual poet in order to write in the collective voice of oppressed workers, attempting an unusual poetry in which whole groups would speak as one. Both also expressed bitterness at the betrayal of Romantic ideals by industrial exploitation and thus maintained the values of the Romantics even as they turned away from the natural landscapes that had so inspired

their predecessors. Walt Whitman took Romanticism to a new extreme: he used the first-person voice of lyric in the interests of speaking for a nation emancipated from oppression, and yet his experimental voice pushed past the style and focus of his European forebears toward a wholly new poetic form that paved the way for the free verse that would become popular in the twentieth century. **Emily Dickinson** can also be seen to be in dialogue— and sometimes in tension—with her Romantic precursors. All of these transitional poets pushed at the boundaries of convention, inventing new and sometimes profoundly unsettling poetic forms, but they formed no single school or movement. In India, the poet **Ghalib** was creating a transitional poetry too. While most Indian poets at the time were rejecting the influence of Britain, which was the new imperial power in the region, and positioning themselves as either purely Hindu or purely Muslim in reaction to European power, Ghalib deliberately brought together Muslim and Hindu traditions and remained intrigued by European culture. While working in traditional forms, he refused to be contained by any single school or nation.

EMERGENT MODERNISM

Just after the midpoint of the nineteenth century, a handful of French poets launched innovations that would have a profound influence on world literature. **Charles Baudelaire** is sometimes called "the first modern poet." His successors—Stéphane Mallarmé, **Paul Verlaine**, and **Arthur Rimbaud**— built on his resistance to poetic convention and together came to be known as the Symbolists. Preserving the Romantic notion of the poet as a seer or visionary, they brought together intensely evocative images that were not necessarily related by any external logic. In fact, they rejected the notion that poetic language should communicate or resolve itself into clear meanings. The goal was not to make sense; rather, they developed a deliberately allusive, sometimes brutally coarse poetry that played with multiple and shifting perspectives and frequently led to a blurring of boundaries between real and imaginary. They even abandoned the notion of the lyric speaker as a stable self, assuming that language precedes and makes up the self, rather than the other way around. For the Symbolists, poetry should be purified of everything but language itself.

The Symbolists were the first of a series of movements that would soon come to be known as *avant-garde*. Originally a military term, it means "advance guard" and evokes the image of artists doing battle. In this case, the war was being waged in the name of the future. Artists of the avant-garde saw themselves not as representing the world as it was but as bringing in a new world through startling breaks in perception. They shattered old views in favor of disconcerting new modes of seeing, which they hoped would then usher in radically new ways of living. Impressionism in painting, a famous avant-garde move-ment like Symbolism in poetry, literally broke color apart to lay bare its components of light and human perception.

In their struggle to make a radical break from the past, the Symbolists marked the beginnings of Modernism, an international movement that would flourish in the first half of the twentieth century. Already in the 1890s, the influence of the Symbolists could be felt far from Paris. Nicaraguan-born poet **Rubén Darío** was in fact the first person to use the term *modernismo* to describe what was happening in the arts. He drew on the inspiration of the French Symbolists but also brought indigenous American traditions into his work to create a new poetic movement in Latin America.

But perhaps the spirit of these avant-garde movements was not so new as it sometimes claimed to be. It was the Romantics of a century before, after all, who had insisted on freeing art from the past and experimenting with new forms and styles. The Modernists therefore drew upon a tradition of innovation launched by their Romantic precursors. And thus, while they inaugurated revolutionary new art forms for the new century, the Modernists remained in many ways Romanticism's rightful heirs.

WILLIAM BLAKE
1757–1827

William Blake condemned authority of all kinds. He cast priests and kings as responsible for exploiting the poor, repressing sexuality, and stifling art, and he admired the devil himself for his disobedience. "I must Create a System or be enslaved by another Man's," claims one of his characters. But the rebellious Blake also harbored profound religious beliefs, developing his own unorthodox visions of divine love, justice, and creativity. When asked if he believed in the divinity of Jesus Christ, he is reported to have said, "*He is the only God,*" and then added: "And so am I and so are you." Some of his contemporaries hailed him as a saint: one legend has it that on his deathbed he burst out in songs of joy. To many others, he seemed a pitiable madman. Only a few admirers in his own time acclaimed him as the creative visionary he would appear to later generations.

LIFE

Born in 1757 in London, Blake was the third of six children. His father kept a hosiery shop, and both parents were lower-middle-class Londoners, radical in their politics and unorthodox in their religion. He grew up among small tradesmen and artisans, who typically took pride in their skilled labor and had a tradition of political radicalism that pitted them against the aristocratic elite. At the age of ten, Blake started drawing school, and at fourteen he was apprenticed to an engraver who taught him complex techniques of engraving and printmaking. He had no formal education beyond drawing school, but he read widely, including history, philosophy, classical literature, the Bible, Shakespeare, Milton, and other English poets, and he began writing poetry himself at around the age of thirteen. From childhood onward he repeatedly saw visions. "I write when commanded by the spirits," he once said, "and the moment I have written I see the words fly about the room in all directions." After exhibiting engravings and watercolors at the prestigious Royal Academy of Arts in 1779, Blake went to work as an engraver for Joseph Johnson, a bookseller and publisher who associated with the most influential radical thinkers of the Enlightenment period.

At the age of 25 Blake married Catherine Boucher, an illiterate daughter of a small farmer, whom he taught to read and write. By all accounts, their married life was a happy one, if occasionally tempestuous, and Catherine actively helped William in his work. The couple had no children.

In the late 1780s Blake developed a revolutionary new technique which he called "illuminated printing." Conventional print shops at the time separated the printing of images and words, integrating them only in the final stage of book production. Blake's method, by contrast, involved combining visual and written materials. He drew and wrote directly on the same copper plate, which then formed the basis for print reproductions. This process allowed Blake to adopt a much more spontaneous multimedia artistic practice than was usual, and ensured that the end product was entirely his own: he was at once the writer, the illustrator, and the printer. In characteristically visionary fashion, Blake explained that the spirit of his dead brother Robert had come to teach him this new technique.

Excited by the radical energies unleashed by the French Revolution in 1789, Blake threw himself into his creative endeavors and produced many of his greatest works in the following few years. *Songs of Innocence* in 1789 marked the beginnings of Blake's innovations. Frustrated with the poetry of his contemporaries, he looked backward to ancient ballads and sixteenth- and seventeenth-century English poetry for models. But he also took his work into some startlingly new poetic directions, including experimental rhythms, prophecies, themes of madness and jealousy, and the beginnings of a grand cosmological history. He wrote directly about politics while also pursuing his growing interest in myths and symbols.

All of his books combined words and images, but Blake grew gradually more absorbed with freestanding visual images, and in 1795 he abandoned poetry altogether for a period and produced some of the greatest works in the history of British printmaking: twelve large color prints that showed a range of subjects, from the creation of Adam and Blake's own mythological figures to Isaac Newton. Blake experimented with adding glue to paint to produce a deeper color and a more complex texture than his earlier watercolor images.

Printing his own images and books involved such costly and painstaking labor that Blake struggled to make ends meet. Eventually he went to work for private patrons, but even then his path was not smooth: he repeatedly broke with benefactors, including the domineering William Hayley, who moved Blake from London to the seaside village of Felpham and employed him mostly as a drawing teacher and illustrator. Hayley tried to pull Blake away from his visionary art, and Blake, frustrated and angry, called him "the Enemy of my Spiritual Life."

A soldier came into the Blakes' garden in Felpham one day in 1803, uttering threats and curses; Blake physically pushed him out. The artist went on trial for sedition, then punishable by hanging. In the end, he was acquitted, but the experience drove him further into isolation than ever. He spent the rest of his life back in London, poor and obscure. In his final years, a group of young painters recognized Blake's innovations in visual art, hailing him as a genius and an inspiration. He began to feel less angry and isolated, and his last few years were probably his happiest. But although he had finally won admiration as a visual artist, it was only long after his death that Blake's extraordinary inventiveness as a poet would be understood and acclaimed.

TIMES

Blake was not alone in wanting to see tyrannical and corrupt authorities toppled, but he was often seen as eccentric even among revolutionaries. For example, the Enlightenment thinkers who frequented Joseph Johnson's shop—including Thomas Paine and **Mary Wollstonecraft**—wanted to see the monarchy overthrown and replaced with a new and more democratic society; Blake shared these ideals, but he rejected their insistence on cold rationality, mechanical science, and individual rights, envisioning a more spiritual, imaginative, and collective future. He wrote, "God is not a mathematical diagram." In a striking visual image, he depicted Isaac Newton—who was one of the heroes of the Enlightenment—as unable to appreciate the wonders of the natural world, obsessed only with tracing abstract geometrical patterns on the ground.

Blake put a much greater emphasis on economic inequality than most English supporters of the French Revolution. While many of his Enlightenment contemporaries argued for legal rights and political representation, Blake fiercely condemned the vast economic gulf between rich and poor. This was a moment when working conditions were changing dramatically: factories were springing up in urban centers, drawing vast numbers of laborers from the rural countryside, and machines were beginning to replace traditional craftsmanship. Blake angrily denounced a society willing to thrust workers into "dark Satanic Mills." Britain was at this time becoming the first and wealthiest industrialized nation, but in the process it was also putting small children to work for long hours, allowing laborers to be injured and disfigured by machines, and offering little help to those who were too old or too ill to work. Chimney sweeps, notorious as emblems of child labor, endured particularly severe hardships. Typically, these boys started working around the age of five, and by the time they had grown too large to climb chimneys, at twelve or thirteen, their bodies had been deformed and broken, rendered incapable of further work. In "The Chimney Sweeper," Blake expressed horror at the life of the laboring child who worked in darkness, inhaled soot and smoke, and had to endure burns, bruises, and debilitating illnesses.

It was not an easy time to speak out against injustice. The 1790s saw a wave of repressive laws that clamped down on dissenting expression in Britain. Public speakers, inflamed by the French Revolution, were trying to whip up antimonarchical sentiment and crowds were actively protesting—even at one point attacking the king's carriage. The British government responded harshly, suspending habeas corpus (the right not to be detained indefinitely without trial), banning most meetings larger than fifty people, and prosecuting "wicked and seditious writing." In 1793 France declared war on England, and the two nations were at war almost continuously until 1815. The wars intensified popular unrest, and revolutionary sympathizers were forced underground. Blake's former employer, Joseph Johnson, landed in jail for nine months for publishing an antiwar pamphlet. Blake himself published some of his work anonymously, and stopped work on his epic poem, *The French Revolution*, as fellow writers and publishers around him began to go to jail. Blake's explicit engagements with poverty, slavery, and revolution gave way to more cryptic, biblical, and mythological themes.

But it would also be a mistake to imagine too strict a separation between Blake's politics and his religion. British law had long denied civil liberties to those who did not belong to the Church of England, and many Protestants, such as Methodists, Baptists, and Presbyterians—called Dissenters—had a robust tradition of resistance to official power. They wove together their religious beliefs with their political opposition. Blake was no exception. His parents, like many other urban artisans and small shopkeepers, moved among Protestant denominations, and spent some time with the Moravian Church. Blake himself was drawn to the mystical, charitable Swedenborg Church of the New Jerusalem, though he later criticized and rejected its doctrines. The 1780s and '90s saw a rise in evangelical and millenarian enthusiasm, and many Dissenters took the French Revolution to be the sign of a coming apocalypse. Blake repeatedly treated politics in terms of biblical models, and he, like many of his dissenting contemporaries, understood political revolutions as a violent purifying process that would bring about prophecies foretold in the Bible. In Blake's *Jerusalem*, one character asks, "Are not Religion & Politics the same thing? Brotherhood is Religion." Although Blake can seem eccentric among his rationalist Enlightenment contemporaries, then, his fusion of radical political beliefs and unorthodox, mystical spirituality was not entirely unusual among Dissenters in London.

WORK

Blake called for an open, accessible, democratic poetry and claimed that children were often the best readers of his work. His poems typically reject regular rhythms and conventional images in favor of unorthodox forms and unusually plain, forceful language. But he also opted for complicated systems of allegorical images and symbols, and in his stories characters often meld into others, change names, and appear and disappear in new guises. Not surprisingly, then, Blake's meanings remain a subject of fierce debate after two centuries. Many readers protest that much of his work is impenetrable and obscure—precisely the opposite of what Blake himself seems to have intended. And yet this debate might not have surprised or bothered Blake, since deliberate oppositions are often at the very heart of his work. He moves back and forth between innocence and experience, mystical vision and wry irony, joyful optimism and bleak prophecy, visual art and poetry. In *The Marriage of Heaven and Hell*—a union of opposites—Blake invites us to see conflict as a vital force: "Without Contraries is no progression. Attraction and Repulsion, Reason and Energy, Love and Hate, are necessary to Human existence. From these contraries spring what the religious call Good & Evil. Good is the passive that obeys Reason. Evil is the active springing from Energy."

In *Songs of Innocence*, Blake explores in simple language what it would be like to perceive the world through the eyes of a child. This means rendering familiar ideas radically unfamiliar. For instance, if we are accustomed to living in a culture that associates darkness with evil, then what does it feel like to be a dark-skinned child? His later *Songs of Experience* (1794) offers a set of companion pieces that return to the same subject matter from a more knowing perspective. Blake juxtaposes the two sets of poems, inviting us to think about the different ways that an innocent child and an experienced adult might understand God, love, and justice. There are echoes and recurrences within as well as across these two groups of poems, and perhaps this is not surprising: after all, Blake's major occupation throughout his life involved making copies—as an engraver, printmaker, and printer—and he seems to have been at least as interested in ideas of doubling and repetition as he was in uniqueness and originality. But he also complicates many of these echoes. In the famous "Tyger," for example, he rhymes "symmetry" and "eye"—a sight rhyme or pairing that might look like a rhyme but does not sound like one. He also unsettles conventional distinctions: the usual lines dividing human and divine states dissolve, for example, and the child leads the poet, rather than the other way around. These apparently simple but highly complex poems have remained Blake's most famous and beloved works.

SONGS OF INNOCENCE AND OF EXPERIENCE

SHEWING THE TWO CONTRARY STATES OF THE HUMAN SOUL

From Songs of Innocence[1]

Introduction

Piping down the valleys wild
Piping songs of pleasant glee
On a cloud I saw a child,
And he laughing said to me,

"Pipe a song about a Lamb";   5
So I piped with merry chear;
"Piper pipe that song again"—
So I piped, he wept to hear.

"Drop thy pipe thy happy pipe
Sing thy songs of happy chear";   10
So I sung the same again
While he wept with joy to hear.

"Piper sit thee down and write
In a book that all may read"—
So he vanished from my sight.   15
And I plucked a hollow reed,

And I made a rural pen,
And I stained the water clear,
And I wrote my happy songs
Every child may joy to hear.   20

The Lamb

Little Lamb, who made thee?
Dost thou know who made thee?
Gave thee life & bid thee feed,
By the stream & o'er the mead;
Gave thee clothing of delight,   5
Softest clothing wooly bright;
Gave thee such a tender voice,
Making all the vales rejoice!
Little Lamb who made thee?
Dost thou know who made thee?   10

---

1. The text for all of Blake's works is edited by David V. Erdman and Harold Bloom. *Songs of Innocence* (1789) was later combined with *Songs of Experience* (1794), and the poems were etched and accompanied by Blake's illustrations, the process accomplished by copper engravings stamped on paper, then colored by hand.

Little Lamb I'll tell thee,
Little Lamb I'll tell thee!
He is callèd by thy name,
For he calls himself a Lamb:
He is meek & he is mild, 15
He became a little child:
I a child & thou a lamb,
We are callèd by his name.[1]
  Little Lamb God bless thee.
  Little Lamb God bless thee. 20

The Little Black Boy

My mother bore me in the southern wild,
And I am black, but O! my soul is white;
White as an angel is the English child:
But I am black as if bereaved of light.

My mother taught me underneath a tree, 5
And sitting down before the heat of day,
She took me on her lap and kissèd me,
And pointing to the east, began to say:

"Look on the rising sun: there God does live,
And gives his light, and gives his heat away; 10
And flowers and trees and beasts and men receive
Comfort in morning, joy in the noon day.

"And we are put on earth a little space,
That we may learn to bear the beams of love,
And these black bodies and this sun-burnt face 15
Is but a cloud, and like a shady grove.

"For when our souls have learned the heat to bear,
The cloud will vanish; we shall hear his voice,
Saying: 'Come out from the grove, my love & care,
And round my golden tent like lambs rejoice.'" 20

Thus did my mother say, and kissèd me;
And thus I say to little English boy:
When I from black and he from white cloud free,
And round the tent of God like lambs we joy,

I'll shade him from the heat till he can bear 25
To lean in joy upon our father's knee;
And then I'll stand and stroke his silver hair,
And be like him, and he will then love me.

1. I.e., Christians use the name of Christ to designate themselves.

Holy Thursday[1]

'Twas on a Holy Thursday, their innocent faces clean,
The children walking two & two, in red & blue & green,[2]
Grey headed beadles[3] walked before with wands as white as snow,
Till into the high dome of Paul's they like Thames' waters flow.

O what a multitude they seemed, these flowers of London town! 5
Seated in companies they sit with radiance all their own.
The hum of multitudes was there, but multitudes of lambs,
Thousands of little boys & girls raising their innocent hands.

Now like a mighty wind they raise to heaven the voice of song,
Or like harmonious thunderings the seats of heaven among. 10
Beneath them sit the agèd men, wise guardians[4] of the poor;
Then cherish pity, lest you drive an angel from your door.[5]

The Chimney Sweeper

When my mother died I was very young,
And my father sold me[1] while yet my tongue
Could scarcely cry " 'weep![2] 'weep! 'weep! 'weep!"
So your chimneys I sweep & in soot I sleep.

There's little Tom Dacre, who cried when his head 5
That curled like a lamb's back, was shaved, so I said,
"Hush, Tom! never mind it, for when your head's bare,
You know that the soot cannot spoil your white hair."

And so he was quiet, & that very night,
As Tom was a-sleeping he had such a sight! 10
That thousands of sweepers, Dick, Joe, Ned, & Jack,
Were all of them locked up in coffins of black;

And by came an Angel who had a bright key,
And he opened the coffins & set them all free;
Then down a green plain, leaping, laughing they run, 15
And wash in a river and shine in the Sun;

---

1. Ascension Day, forty days after Easter, when children from charity schools were marched to St. Paul's Cathedral.
2. Each school had its own distinctive uniform.
3. Ushers and minor functionaries, whose job was to maintain order.
4. The governors of the charity schools.
5. See Hebrews 13.2: "Be not forgetful to entertain strangers: for thereby some have entertained angels unawares."

1. It was common practice in Blake's day for fathers to sell, or indenture, their children to become chimney sweeps. The average age at which such children began working was six or seven; they were generally employed for seven years, until they were too big to ascend the chimneys.
2. The child's lisping effort to say "sweep," as he walks the streets looking for work.

Then naked[3] & white, all their bags left behind,
They rise upon clouds, and sport in the wind.
And the Angel told Tom, if he'd be a good boy,
He'd have God for his father & never want joy.   20

And so Tom awoke; and we rose in the dark
And got with our bags & our brushes to work.
Tho' the morning was cold, Tom was happy & warm;
So if all do their duty, they need not fear harm.

From Songs of Experience

Introduction

Hear the voice of the Bard!
Who Present, Past, & Future sees;
   Whose ears have heard
   The Holy Word
That walked among the ancient trees;[1]   5

Calling the lapsèd Soul
And weeping in the evening dew;[2]
   That might control
   The starry pole,
And fallen, fallen light renew!   10

"O Earth, O Earth, return!
Arise from out the dewy grass;
   Night is worn,
   And the morn
Rises from the slumberous mass.   15

"Turn away no more;
Why wilt thou turn away?
   The starry floor
   The watery shore
Is given thee till the break of day."   20

Earth's Answer

Earth raised up her head,
From the darkness dread & drear.
   Her light fled:

3. They climbed up the chimneys naked.
1. Genesis 3.8: "And [Adam and Eve] heard the voice of the Lord God walking in the garden in the cool of the day."
2. Blake's ambiguous use of pronouns makes for interpretive difficulties. It would seem that *The Holy Word* (Jehovah, a name for God in the Old Testament of the Bible) calls *the lapsèd Soul*, and weeps—not the Bard.

Stony dread!
And her locks covered with grey despair.   5

"Prisoned on watery shore
Starry Jealousy does keep my den,
Cold and hoar
Weeping o'er
I hear the Father[1] of the ancient men.   10

"Selfish father of men,
Cruel, jealous, selfish fear!
Can delight
Chained in night
The virgins of youth and morning bear?   15

"Does spring hide its joy
When buds and blossoms grow?
Does the sower
Sow by night,
Or the plowman in darkness plow?   20

"Break this heavy chain
That does freeze my bones around;
Selfish! vain!
Eternal bane!
That free Love with bondage bound."   25

The Tyger

Tyger! Tyger! burning bright
In the forests of the night,
What immortal hand or eye
Could frame thy fearful symmetry?

In what distant deeps or skies   5
Burnt the fire of thine eyes?
On what wings dare he aspire?
What the hand dare seize the fire?

And what shoulder, & what art,
Could twist the sinews of thy heart?   10
And when thy heart began to beat,
What dread hand? & what dread feet?

---

1. In Blake's later prophetic works, one of the four Zoas, representing the four chief faculties of humankind, is Urizen. In general, he stands for the orthodox conception of the Divine Creator, sometimes Jehovah in the Old Testament, often the God conceived by Newton and Locke—in all instances a tyrant associated with excessive rationalism and sexual repression, and the opponent of the imagination and creativity. This may be "the Holy Word" in line 4 of "Introduction" (p. 585).

What the hammer? what the chain?
In what furnace was thy brain?
What the anvil? what dread grasp   15
Dare its deadly terrors clasp?

When the stars threw down their spears,
And watered heaven with their tears,
Did he smile his work to see?
Did he who made the Lamb make thee?   20

Tyger! Tyger! burning bright
In the forests of the night,
What immortal hand or eye
Dare frame thy fearful symmetry?

The Sick Rose

O Rose, thou art sick.
The invisible worm
That flies in the night
In the howling storm

Has found out thy bed   5
Of crimson joy,
And his dark secret love
Does thy life destroy.

London

I wander thro' each chartered[1] street,
Near where the chartered Thames does flow,
And mark in every face I meet
Marks of weakness, marks of woe.

In every cry of every Man,   5
In every Infant's cry of fear,
In every voice, in every ban,
The mind-forged manacles I hear:

How the Chimney-sweeper's cry
Every blackening Church appalls;[2]   10
And the hapless Soldier's sigh
Runs in blood down Palace walls.

---

1. Hired (literally). Blake implies that the streets and the river are controlled by commercial interests.

2. Makes white (literally), punning also on *appall* (to dismay) and *pall* (the cloth covering a corpse or bier).

But most thro' midnight streets I hear
How the youthful Harlot's curse
Blasts the new-born Infant's tear,[3]   15
And blights with plagues the Marriage hearse.

The Chimney Sweeper

A little black thing among the snow
Crying "'weep, 'weep," in notes of woe!
"Where are thy father & mother? say?"
"They are both gone up to the church to pray.

"Because I was happy upon the heath,   5
And smiled among the winter's snow;
They clothèd me in the clothes of death,
And taught me to sing the notes of woe.

"And because I am happy, & dance & sing,
They think they have done me no injury,   10
And are gone to praise God & his Priest & King,
Who make up a heaven of our misery."

3. The harlot infects the parents with venereal disease, and thus the infant is inflicted with neonatal blindness.

WILLIAM WORDSWORTH
1770–1850

After Wordsworth, English poetry would never be the same again. The sense that poets should convey intensely personal, individual expression—which now feels like the ordinary stuff of poetry—can be traced to Wordsworth's deliberate rejection of his eighteenth-century precursors. He turned readers' attention away from classical models and Gothic supernatural stories to everyday emotion and imagination, championing the sponta- neity of authentic feeling. Like **Jean-Jacques Rousseau**, he approached children's experience as crucial and determinative, in defiance of many of his contemporaries, who considered childhood trivial. And he chose to focus on common people—often poor and marginal figures such as elderly farmers and vagrant beggars. Just as important, Wordsworth also launched a new set of stylistic values for poetry, jettisoning "the gaudiness and inane phraseology" of contemporary poets in favor of a language that would feel direct, authentic, and plain. And finally, Wordsworth committed himself in surprising new ways to honoring the natural world as a benevolent nurturer and guide, and many have credited him with launching an ecological consciousness that continues to inspire environmentalists today.

LIFE

William Wordsworth was born in the small town of Cockermouth, in England's wild and rugged Lake District, in 1770. He was the second of four sons. His only sister, Dorothy, was a year younger. Separated for long periods as children, William and Dorothy were extremely close as adults. Their father worked as a lawyer and was often forced to travel, and their mother died when Wordsworth was eight years old. The boy was sent to a grammar school in the countryside, where he learned Greek and Latin and committed large portions of Shakespeare and Milton to memory. After his father's death in 1783, he began to feel restless and unsettled. While at Cambridge University, he failed to apply himself to his studies. "I am doomed to be an idler thro' my whole life," he wrote.

Wordsworth's perspective on the world took a turn in the summer of 1790, when he and a friend set off for a walking tour of France and the Alps. It was a critical moment in French history: the country was "mad with joy in consequence of the revolution," as Wordsworth put it. He also had a love affair with a Frenchwoman named Annette Vallon and had a child with her. He returned to England in 1793, meaning to make some money so that he could marry Vallon, but Britain went to war with France, and Wordsworth was not permitted to cross back for a decade.

The following few years were the most difficult of Wordsworth's life. He had no source of income, and his revolutionary sympathies made him an outsider in England. He moved to London and for a time became a disciple of the anarchist William Godwin, who favored the abolition of marriage and all forms of government. In 1795 Wordsworth began a formative friendship with another young radical poet, Samuel Taylor Coleridge. So close did Wordsworth and Coleridge become that they deliberately moved to within walking distance of one another in rural Somerset. There they entertained revolutionary thinkers and were suspected of being spies: "a mischievous gang of disaffected Englishmen," reported a government agent, "a Sett of violent Democrats." In fact, however, both Wordsworth and Coleridge were horrified by the bloody turn the revolution in France had taken, and they soon began to lose faith in radical politics. Loving the beauty of the countryside and each other's company, the two poets started to work together on a different kind of revolutionary ideal: the production of a new kind of poetry. Together, in 1798, they published a collection of poems called *Lyrical Ballads*. It contained works that would count among their best loved, including Wordsworth's "Tintern Abbey" and "We Are Seven," and Coleridge's "Rime of the Ancient Mariner." They published the first edition anonymously. ("Wordsworth's name is nothing," Coleridge explained, and "to a large number of persons mine *stinks*.")

This book succeeded in accomplishing a revolution in English poetry. Radically democratic, it focused on subject matter conventionally ignored by poets—the lives of lowly people, such as the very poor, the insane, children, shepherds, and tinkers. This new subject matter, Wordsworth wrote, demanded a simple and unaffected language, like the prose spoken by ordinary people. Thus *Lyrical Ballads* prized not only humble and simple subjects but also the poet's own internal state of mind, a focus that would become ever more important to Wordsworth's work. In 1801 he included a new preface, which has become as well known as his poetry. Here he put forward his revolutionary new ideas: "I have proposed to myself to imitate, and, as far as is possible, to adopt the very language of men," he wrote. Famously, he defined poetry as "the spontaneous overflow of powerful feelings," explaining that it comes from "emotion recollected in tranquility."

Critics were not prepared for this innovative volume, and Wordsworth's poetry garnered almost entirely hostile reviews. One critic wrote, "Than the volumes now before us we never saw any thing better calculated to excite disgust and anger in a lover of poetry. The drivelling nonsense of some of Mr. Wordsworth's poems is insufferable, and it is equally insufferable that such nonsense should have been written by a man capable, as he is, of writing well." Even Wordsworth's fellow poet, Lord Byron, wrote contemptuously of this "dull" poetry, which, he said, "shows / That prose is verse, and verse is merely prose."

In 1799 William and his sister Dorothy moved to Grasmere in the Lake District, near where they had grown up. Coleridge took a house nearby, and Wordsworth married a friend named Mary Hutchinson. At the time, Dorothy was reportedly so upset by the wedding that she could not attend the ceremony, but she and Mary settled into a happy domestic life in Grasmere. The Wordsworths went on to have five children.

Wordsworth was appalled by Napoleon's rise to power across Europe, and his political views turned increasingly conservative. Meanwhile, his life entered a period of stability, punctuated with several tragic events. He lost two young children to illness, and his friendship with Coleridge faltered. The Wordsworths had hosted Coleridge for lengthy periods, but he remained moody and depressed, and in 1810 the two poets quarreled. Although they patched up their friendship, they never regained their former closeness. In the following years, Wordsworth became very much part of the conservative establishment. He was appointed distributor of stamps, collecting taxes on government documents, a civil service job that seemed to many contemporary radicals to represent a betrayal of his earlier commitment to the artist's independence. In 1818 he campaigned for the Tories—the conservative party—in local elections.

It was in the last phase of Wordsworth's life that he became popular and widely respected, both in Britain and the United States, though the poetry he wrote in his final years is now usually considered much weaker than his earlier work. In 1843 Queen Victoria bestowed the title of Poet Laureate on him, and he received visiting fans from around the world, including the American writer Ralph Waldo Emerson. He died on April 23, traditionally thought to be Shakespeare's birth- and death-day, in 1850.

WORDSWORTH'S READERS

Expanding cities and industrialization brought with them a new kind of reading public. Before Wordsworth's time, writers had mostly published on a small scale for that tiny proportion of the public who were literate, many of whom would have known the writer personally. But around the turn of the nineteenth century, cheaper means of publication, rapidly increasing literacy, and growing leisure time for reading meant that printed matter suddenly started to reach a newly large and anonymous mass market. A few writers, including the poet Byron, became literary celebrities, selling every copy of a new work on its first day of publication and earning thousands of pounds from their writing. Other writers could not make ends meet unless they turned to private patrons. Wordsworth, for most of his life, knew that he was reaching the traditionally small literate audience but aspired to the new mass market, often uncertain of his readers. He was trying out a new kind of democratic style and subject matter in his poetry, but was he actually reaching the working classes? Women? Radicals?

The uncertainty about audience gave way to a new sense of the literary marketplace over the next couple of decades, as the reading public in Britain increased markedly, reaching more widely into the reaches of the upper working classes—skilled artisans, shopkeepers, clerks, and servants. Churches played a major role in a dramatic expansion of literacy: Evangelicals insisted on reading as essential to spiritual development, and they set up charity schools and distributed Bibles and didactic tracts to the poor. Between 1804 and 1819 the British and Foreign Bible Society printed two and a half million Bibles for domestic use alone. Since print remained relatively costly, working people often banded together to buy newspapers, which they read aloud in pubs.

British opinion was split over the political consequences of this expanding readership. The government often feared the energetic radical press and worried that reading would incite revolutionary sentiment. They imposed a severe censorship, especially during the French Revolution and the Napoleonic wars. Others, however, held that education would quell agitation and increase worker productivity. "An instructed and intelligent people," wrote Scottish philosopher Adam Smith, "are always more decent and orderly than an ignorant and stupid one."

WORK

Since Wordsworth's style is often purposefully simple, his poetry can seem deceptively uncomplicated. For many readers, its pleasures lie in the philosophical questions it poses. "Tintern Abbey" asks what makes a self a self: how do we become what we are? "We Are Seven" interrogates the abstraction of death and asks whether the dead may be considered part of the human community. And the "Ode on Intimations of Immortality" considers the immortality of the soul, using Plato's ideas as a touchstone.

But the poems also reward a close attention to their language. On first reading, Wordsworth's invocations of nature might seem simple acts of homage, but in fact the relationship between the poet and the natural world varies from poem to poem, and sometimes within the same poem. Even the most seemingly straightforward Wordsworthian lines often yield more questions than answers. Consider, for example, the title of the poem "Lines Composed a Few Miles above Tintern Abbey, on Revisiting the Banks of the Wye during a Tour, July 13, 1798." Why such a curiously long and descriptive title, going to such trouble to mark the place and date of composition? The poem itself, surprisingly, says nothing at all about the ruined abbey. Some readers have noted that Wordsworth is careful to use the title to note his position "above" the landscape; others have remarked on the date, which commemorates the anniversary of the day *before* the French Revolution started, hinting that Wordsworth's explorations of memory and selfhood in this poem are bound up with his ambivalence about the revolution. How is it, Wordsworth's poetry insistently asks, that complex conceptions of faith, nature, selfhood, community, and knowledge are revealed in the most commonplace language that we use?

Wordsworth is famous for his plain style and his philosophical explorations, but he is also notable for his ease in moving among poetic forms and genres. "Tintern Abbey" is composed in the regular and highly traditional English form of iambic pentameter. The other genre represented here is the sonnet, a form that had languished for a couple of centuries but became popular again in the late eighteenth century. Wordsworth was among many Romantic poets—among them, numerous women—who

brought the sonnet back to prominence. He wrote a poem called "Scorn not the Sonnet," which reminds the reader of the sonnet's illustrious history, begun by the Italian poet Petrarch and later taken up by Shakespeare and Milton. Wordsworth was clearly self-conscious about his place in this poetic tradition. The two examples included here, "Composed upon Westminster Bridge" and "The World Is Too Much with Us," steer clear of the sonnet's traditional focus on romantic love, meditating instead on the specific conditions of modern, industrial, and urban society, thus pointedly bringing this traditional poetic form into the present. In re-imagining the sonnet, then, as in his innovative ideas about democracy, poetic style, nature, childhood, and the importance of individual experience, Wordsworth is a quintessentially modern poet.

Lines Composed a Few Miles above Tintern Abbey

On Revisiting the Banks of the Wye During a Tour, July 13, 1798

Five years have past; five summers, with the length
Of five long winters! and again I hear
These waters, rolling from their mountain-springs
With a soft inland murmur.—Once again
Do I behold these steep and lofty cliffs, 5
That on a wild secluded scene impress
Thoughts of more deep seclusion; and connect
The landscape with the quiet of the sky.
The day is come when I again repose
Here, under this dark sycamore, and view 10
These plots of cottage-ground, these orchard-tufts,
Which at this season, with their unripe fruits,
Are clad in one green hue, and lose themselves
'Mid groves and copses. Once again I see
These hedge-rows, hardly hedge-rows, little lines 15
Of sportive wood run wild: these pastoral farms,
Green to the very door; and wreaths of smoke
Sent up, in silence, from among the trees!
With some uncertain notice, as might seem

Of vagrant dwellers in the houseless woods,   20
Or of some Hermit's cave, where by his fire
The Hermit sits alone.

              These beauteous forms,
Through a long absence, have not been to me
As is a landscape to a blind man's eye:
But oft, in lonely rooms, and 'mid the din   25
Of towns and cities, I have owed to them,
In hours of weariness, sensations sweet,
Felt in the blood, and felt along the heart;
And passing even into my purer mind,
With tranquil restoration:—feelings too   30
Of unremembered pleasure: such, perhaps,
As have no slight or trivial influence
On that best portion of a good man's life,
His little, nameless, unremembered, acts
Of kindness and of love. Nor less, I trust,   35
To them I may have owed another gift,
Of aspect more sublime; that blessèd mood,
In which the burthen of the mystery,
In which the heavy and the weary weight
Of all this unintelligible world,   40
Is lightened:—that serene and blessèd mood,
In which the affections gently lead us on,—
Until, the breath of this corporeal frame
And even the motion of our human blood
Almost suspended, we are laid asleep   45
In body, and become a living soul:
While with an eye made quiet by the power
Of harmony, and the deep power of joy,
We see into the life of things.

                If this
Be but a vain belief, yet, oh! how oft—   50
In darkness and amid the many shapes
Of joyless daylight; when the fretful stir
Unprofitable, and the fever of the world,
Have hung upon the beatings of my heart—
How oft, in spirit, have I turned to thee,   55
O sylvan Wye! thou wanderer thro' the woods,
How often has my spirit turned to thee!

   And now, with gleams of half-extinguished thought,
With many recognitions dim and faint,
And somewhat of a sad perplexity,   60
The picture of the mind revives again:
While here I stand, not only with the sense
Of present pleasure, but with pleasing thoughts
That in this moment there is life and food

For future years. And so I dare to hope, 65
Though changed, no doubt, from what I was when first
I came among these hills; when like a roe
I bounded o'er the mountains, by the sides
Of the deep rivers, and the lonely streams,
Wherever nature led: more like a man 70
Flying from something that he dreads, than one
Who sought the thing he loved. For nature then
(The coarser pleasures of my boyish days,
And their glad animal movements all gone by)
To me was all in all.—I cannot paint 75
What then I was. The sounding cataract
Haunted me like a passion: the tall rock,
The mountain, and the deep and gloomy wood,
Their colours and their forms, were then to me
An appetite; a feeling and a love, 80
That had no need of a remoter charm,
By thought supplied, nor any interest
Unborrowed from the eye.—That time is past,
And all its aching joys are now no more,
And all its dizzy raptures. Not for this 85
Faint I, nor mourn nor murmur; other gifts
Have followed; for such loss, I would believe,
Abundant recompense. For I have learned
To look on nature, not as in the hour
Of thoughtless youth; but hearing oftentimes 90
The still, sad music of humanity,
Nor harsh nor grating, though of ample power
To chasten and subdue. And I have felt
A presence that disturbs me with the joy
Of elevated thoughts; a sense sublime 95
Of something far more deeply interfused,
Whose dwelling is the light of setting suns,
And the round ocean and the living air,
And the blue sky, and in the mind of man:
A motion and a spirit, that impels 100
All thinking things, all objects of all thought,
And rolls through all things. Therefore am I still
A lover of the meadows and the woods,
And mountains; and of all that we behold
From this green earth; of all the mighty world 105
Of eye, and ear,—both what they half create,
And what perceive; well pleased to recognise
In nature and the language of the sense,
The anchor of my purest thoughts, the nurse,
The guide, the guardian of my heart, and soul 110
Of all my moral being.

                  Nor perchance,
If I were not thus taught, should I the more

Suffer my genial[1] spirits to decay:
For thou art with me here upon the banks
Of this fair river; thou my dearest Friend,   115
My dear, dear Friend; and in thy voice I catch
The language of my former heart, and read
My former pleasures in the shooting lights
Of thy wild eyes. Oh! yet a little while
May I behold in thee what I was once,   120
My dear, dear Sister! and this prayer I make,
Knowing that Nature never did betray
The heart that loved her; 'tis her privilege,
Through all the years of this our life, to lead
From joy to joy: for she can so inform   125
The mind that is within us, so impress
With quietness and beauty, and so feed
With lofty thoughts, that neither evil tongues,
Rash judgments, nor the sneers of selfish men,
Nor greetings where no kindness is, nor all   130
The dreary intercourse of daily life,
Shall e'er prevail against us, or disturb
Our cheerful faith, that all which we behold
Is full of blessings. Therefore let the moon
Shine on thee in thy solitary walk;   135
And let the misty mountain-winds be free
To blow against thee: and, in after years,
When these wild ecstasies shall be matured
Into a sober pleasure; when thy mind
Shall be a mansion for all lovely forms,   140
Thy memory be as a dwelling-place
For all sweet sounds and harmonies; oh! then,
If solitude, or fear, or pain, or grief
Should be thy portion, with what healing thoughts
Of tender joy wilt thou remember me,   145
And these my exhortations! Nor, perchance—
If I should be where I no more can hear
Thy voice, nor catch from thy wild eyes these gleams
Of past existence—wilt thou then forget
That on the banks of this delightful stream   150
We stood together; and that I, so long
A worshipper of Nature, hither came
Unwearied in that service; rather say
With warmer love—oh! with far deeper zeal
Of holier love. Nor wilt thou then forget   155
That after many wanderings, many years
Of absence, these steep woods and lofty cliffs,
And this green pastoral landscape, were to me
More dear, both for themselves and for thy sake!

1. Generative, creative.

Composed upon Westminster Bridge, September 3, 1802

Earth has not anything to show more fair:
Dull would he be of soul who could pass by
A sight so touching in its majesty;
This City now doth, like a garment, wear
The beauty of the morning; silent, bare,   5
Ships, towers, domes, theatres, and temples lie
Open unto the fields, and to the sky;
All bright and glittering in the smokeless air.
Never did sun more beautifully steep
In his first splendour, valley, rock, or hill;   10
Ne'er saw I, never felt, a calm so deep!
The river glideth at his own sweet will:
Dear God! the very houses seem asleep;
And all that mighty heart is lying still!

The World Is Too Much with Us

The world is too much with us; late and soon,
Getting and spending, we lay waste our powers:
Little we see in Nature that is ours;
We have given our hearts away, a sordid boon![1]
This Sea that bares her bosom to the moon,   5
The winds that will be howling at all hours,
And are up-gathered now like sleeping flowers;
For this, for everything, we are out of tune;
It moves us not.—Great God! I'd rather be
A Pagan suckled in a creed outworn;   10
So might I, standing on this pleasant lea,
Have glimpses that would make me less forlorn;
Have sight of Proteus[2] rising from the sea;
Or hear old Triton[3] blow his wreathèd horn.

1. Gift. "Sordid": refers to the act of giving the heart away.
2. An old man of the sea who, in the *Odyssey*, could assume a variety of shapes.
3. A sea deity, usually represented as blowing on a conch shell.

ANNA BUNINA

1774–1829

It was not easy to work as a woman writer in early nineteenth-century Russia, even for those who came from the highest ranks of the aristocracy. Women were largely dependent on husbands or fathers for their keep, and they received meager educations compared to their male counterparts. The small handful of women who did publish their writing typically won disparaging and sometimes hostile comments from critics and male writers, who insisted that women could act as readers and inspirations, but could not compose anything of value. It was in this context that the remarkable Anna Petrovna Bunina published a startling range of poems, in multiple styles and on themes that ranged from nationalistic military songs to conversational, intimate lyrics on love and mortality.

Born into an aristocratic family in 1774, Bunina struggled to maintain her independence. Her inheritance was so small that she soon exhausted it on attempts to improve her education, learning to read Latin and Greek and to speak a number of foreign languages. She started publishing her work in her late twenties, and soon attracted mentors and patrons. Remaining unmarried, she barely made ends meet as a poverty-stricken writer until her death in 1829 from breast cancer. And yet, although she was poor, her independence was an extraordinary accomplishment: she was the first Russian woman to earn her living as a writer. At the time it was rare for even male Russian writers to live by the pen. Only about 250 titles were published in Russia each year between 1800 and 1820, compared to 4,500 in France. As few as 6 percent of Russian men could read in 1800, and 4 percent of women. A financial turning point for Bunina came in 1808, when she published a manual for women poets called *The Rules of Poetry*. Here she explained principles of genre and meter in order to educate women who might not have taken up writing otherwise. The Administration of Schools adopted it as a textbook, and the ensuing profits allowed Bunina to become self-sufficient.

Some critics hailed Bunina as a "Russian Sappho," comparable to the great ancient Greek woman poet. Others, including the legendary writer Alexander Pushkin, scorned her as "the goddess of the lady-chatterboxes." Writers in the generation that followed hers saw her as painfully old-fashioned, and felt particular contempt for women poets who were only able to produce "a poetic knitting of stockings." Bunina's reputation never recovered, though readers have begun to show a renewed interest in recent years.

Bunina's poems frequently took gender as an explicit theme. Her "Conversation Between Me and the Women" sets up a dialogue between the poet and a chorus of modern, cosmopolitan women who reject Russian poetry and want the poetess to sing them flattering verses. She refuses, claiming that male readers will be the judges of her fame. But this seems like a puzzling conclusion. Is Bunina also writing for men in *this* poem, which is so clearly focused on women readers and writers? Is she trivializing women, or taking them seriously? And is she indicating her own preference for Russian styles and subjects, or is she undermining them by claiming that she writes about tsars and heroes merely for the approbation of a masculine readership? Bunina's ironic meditation on the role of the woman poet raises more questions than it answers.

Conversation Between Me and the Women[1]

THE WOMEN

Our sister dear, what joy for us!
You are a poetess! your palette's able,
Holding all shades, to paint an ode, a fable;
Your heart must brim with praise for us!
A man's tongue, though . . . Ah, God preserve us, dear!   5
Sharp as a knife is sharp!
In Paris, London—as in Russia here—
   They're all the same! On just one string they harp:
Naught but abuse—and ladies always suffer!
We wait for madrigals—it's epigrams they offer.   10
Don't expect brothers, husbands, fathers, sons
   To praise you even once.
How long we've lacked a songstress of our own!
So, do you sing? Pray answer, yes or no?

ME

Yes, yes, dear sisters! Thanks be to Providence   15
I have been singing now for five years since.

THE WOMEN

And in those years, what have you sung and how?
Though few of us, in truth, have Russian educations,
And Russian verses make such complications!
Besides, you know, they aren't in fashion now.   20

ME

I sing all Nature's beauteous hues,
Above the flood the hornèd sickle moon;
I count the little drops of dew,
I hymn the sun's ascension in the morn.
Flocks gambolling in the fields enjoy my care: 25
I give reed pipes unto the shepherdesses,
Flowers I entwine in their companions' tresses,
   That are so flaxen-fair;
I order them to take each other's hands,
   To caper to a dance,   30

1. Translated by Sibelan Forrester.

And as their fleet feet pass,
To trample not a single blade of grass.
Up to the heavens rocky crags I raise,
   I plant out branchy trees
To rest an old man in their shady breeze   35
   On summer's sultry days;
I search the roses for bright insects' wings,
    And, having summoned feathered birds to sing,
   I languish pale
To the sweet warble of the nightingale.   40
Or, all at once, freeing the horse's manes.
   I order them to race the wind;
And with their hooves dust to the clouds they fling.
I draw a corn-field crowned with ears of grain,
    Which, from the sun's bright rays   45
     Takes on the look of seas
Of molten gold,
   Sways, ripples, dazzles, shines—
    Blinding the eye,
As humble ploughmen their reward behold.   50
In fortifying my own timid voice
Through Nature's loveliness,
   I'm braver in a flash!

THE WOMEN

Fie! what balderdash!
There's not one word in this for us!   55
Tell us what good such singing does?
What use are all your livestock, polled and horned
   To us, who weren't as herdsmen born?
So, with the beasts you feel at home?
Well! . . . if that's your topic, then,   60
    Hide in a den,
   Among the fields, pray, roam,
And never haunt the capitals in vain!

ME

O no, dear sisters, come!
People are also in my ken.   65

THE WOMEN

Commendable! but whom *have* you sung, then?

ME

At times I've hymned the deeds of mighty men,
   Who, when the bloody fight drew near,
Declared for faith and Tsar; they knew no fear.

Shaking with my lament the field of quarrels   70
   I bore them thence away with laurels,
      Dropping a tear.
At times I've left this grievous task,
And passed to those who keep the laws,
I've filled my soul with cheer,   75
And rested 'neath their aegis, free from cares.
   At times to poets I've inclined my ear
And bent the knee before their thunderous lyres.
   At times
   Moved by esteem,   80
I've made the chemist or astronomer my theme.

THE WOMEN

And here again we're missing from your rhymes!
   You do us quite a service!
So what good *are* you? Don't you make things worse?
   Why did you bother learning to sing verse?   85
You ought to take your themes from your own circle.
'Tis only men you honour with your lays,
As if their sex alone deserved your praise.
You traitress! Give our case some thought!
   For is this what you ought?   90
Are their own founts of flattery too few,
Or can they boast of more than our virtue?

ME

It's true, my dears, you are no less,
   But understand:
With men, not you, the courts of taste are manned   95
   Where authors all must stand,
And all an author's fame is in their hands,
And none can help loving himself the best.[2]

---

2. May I be forgiven for this jest in deference to the merry Muses, who love to mix business with idleness, lies with truth, and to enliven conversation with innocent playfulness [Bunina's note].

ANDRÉS BELLO

1781–1865

Sometimes known as "the artistic liberator" of Spanish America, Andrés Bello wrote at a moment when Latin American nations were throwing off the yoke of colonial rule. He insisted that it was time for poetry "to leave effete Europe . . . and fly to where Columbus's world / opens its great scene." And yet, while his work replaces the familiar natural landscape of European romantic poetry—mountains and daffodils—with a distinctively Latin American landscape, with cocoa beans and palm trees, yucca and sugar cane, Bello was not a thoroughgoing revolutionary. He began his life as a monarchist, an advocate of Spanish colonial rule, and only gradually became a supporter of democratic elections. Steadfastly, he favored long-term goals of stability and order, even in nature. In the "Ode to Tropical Agriculture," what he praises is not wilderness but human cultivation—plants in "proud rows and orderly design."

Born in Caracas, Venezuela, in 1781, Bello began working for the colonial government in 1802 and oversaw projects of national scope—including the first smallpox vaccination, which he made the subject of a poetic ode and a play. In response to the conquest of Spain by Napoleon in 1810, Venezuela claimed independence and established a series of military governments. One regime sent Bello on a diplomatic mission to London. He stayed there for nineteen years, working in temporary positions that left him too poor to return to Venezuela. It was in London, racked by homesickness, that he composed his most famous poetry, including the "Ode to Tropical Agriculture" in 1826. Three years later, the Chilean government invited him to work for their Foreign Ministry, and he went to live in Santiago, where he founded the University of Chile and became its rector until his death in 1865. Among the famous works he completed there were *Castilian Grammar Intended for Use by Americans* (1847), the first specifically Latin American grammar, and the Civil Code of Chile, which is still in force today. Over the course of his life, he exerted an astonishing breadth of influence—as a poet, essayist, editor, civil servant, diplomat, philosopher, grammarian, educator, and legal thinker.

Bello's poetry combines classical and romantic impulses. In "Ode to Tropical Agriculture" we find resonances of the Roman georgics of Virgil and Horace, who celebrate civic virtue, the simple life of farmers, and the beauties of nature. Bello also invokes the Roman republic as a model for the rising Latin American nations. But it would be a mistake to read Bello as simply nostalgic for an ancient past: he urges poets to draw inspiration from their native landscapes, suggesting that the unique characteristics of current politics, history, and geography will shape a dramatic and powerful art for the future.

Ode to Tropical Agriculture[1]

Hail, fertile zone, that circumscribes
the errant course of your enamored sun,
and, caressed by its light,

1. Translated by Frances M. Lopez-Morillas.

brings forth all living things
in each of your many climes!   5
You weave the summer's wreath of golden grain,
and offer grapes to the bubbling pail.
Your glorious groves lack no tone
of purple fruit, or red, or gold. In them the wind
imbibes a thousand odors, and innumerable flocks   10
crop your green meadow, from the plain
bordered by the horizon, to the mountain heights,
ever hoary with inaccessible snow.

       You give sweet sugarcane, whose pure sap
makes the world disdain the honeycomb.   15
In coral urns you prepare the beans
that overflow the foaming chocolate cup.
Living red teems on your cactus plants,
outdoing the purple of Tyre.[2]
And the splendid dye of your indigo   20
imitates the sapphire's glow.
Wine is yours, which the piercèd agave
pours out for Anahuac's happy brood.[3]
Yours too is the leaf that solaces
the tedium of idle hours, when its soft smoke   25
rises in wandering spirals.
You clothe with jasmine the bush of Sheba,[4]
and give it the perfume that cools
the wild fever of riotous excess.
For your children the lofty palm brings forth   30
its varied products, and the pineapple ripens
its ambrosia. The yucca grows its snowy bread,
and the potato yields its fair fruit,
and cotton opens to the gentle breeze
its golden roses and its milk-white fleece.   35
For you the passion plant displays
its fresh green branches, and sweet globes
and dangling flowers hang from climbing branches.
For you maize, proud chief of the tribe of grains
swells its ears; and for you the banana plant   40
sags under dulcet weight. Banana, first
of all the plants that Providence has offered
to happy tropic's folk with generous hand;
it asks no care by human arts, but freely yields
its fruit. It needs no pruning hook or plow.   45
No care does it require, only such heed
as a slave's hand can steal from daily toil.
It grows with swiftness, and when it is outworn
its full-grown children take its place.

2. Precious purple dye produced in the ancient Phoenician city of Tyre and used only for members of the emperor's family.
3. Anahuac is the Aztec region in the Valley of Mexico.
4. Ancient kingdom mentioned in the Hebrew Bible and the Qur'an.

But, fertile zone, though rich,   50
why did not Nature work with equal zeal
to make its indolent dwellers follow her?
Oh, would that they could recognize the joy
that beckons from the simple farmer's home,
and spurn vain luxury, false brilliance,   55
and the city's evil idleness!
What vain illusion has a grip on those
whom Fortune has made masters of this land,
so happy, rich and varied as it is,
to make them leave hereditary soil,   60
forsaking it to mercenary hands?
Shut in blind clamor of the wretched cities,
where sick ambition fans the flames
of civil strife, or indolence exhausts
the love of country. There it is   65
that luxury saps customs, and vices trap
unwary youth in ever stronger bonds.
There, youth does not tire from manly exercise,
but sickens in the arms of treacherous beauty
that sells its favors to the highest bidder;   70
whose pastime is to light the flame of outlaw love
in the chaste bosom of a youth.
Or dawn will find him drunk, perhaps,
at the base, sordid gaming table.

Meanwhile the wife lends an eager ear   75
to the ardent lover's seductive flattery.
The tender virgin grows in her mother's school
of dissipation and flirtation, and that example
spurs her to sin before she wishes to.
Is this the way to form the heroic spirits   80
that bravely found and undergird the state?
How will strong and modest youth emerge,
our country's hope and pride,
from the hubbub of foolish revels
or the choruses of lewd dances?   85
Can the man who even in the cradle
slept to the murmur of lascivious songs,
a man who curls his hair and scents himself,
and dresses with almost feminine care
and spends the day in idleness,   90
or worse, in criminal lust: can such a man
hold firmly to the reins of law,
or be serene in doubtful combat, or confront
the haughty spirit of a tyrannous leader?
Triumphant Rome did not thus view   95
the arts of peace and war; rather, she gave
the reins of state to the strong hand,
tanned by the sun and hardened by the plow,
who raised his sons under a smoky peasant roof,
and made the world submit to Latin valor.   100

Oh, you who are the fortunate possessors,
born in this beautiful land,
where bountiful Nature parades her gifts
as if to win you and attract you!
Break the harsh enchantment   105
that holds you prisoner within walls.
The common man, working at crafts,
the merchant who loves luxury and must have it,
those who pant after high place and noisy honour,
the troop of parasitic flatterers,   110
live happily in that filthy chaos.
The land is your heritage; enjoy it.
Do you love freedom? Go then to the country,
Not where the rich man lives
amid armed satellites, and where   115
Fashion, that universal dame,
drags reason tied to her triumphal car.
Go not where foolish common folk adore
Fortune, and nobles the adulation of the mob.
Or do you love virtue? then the best teacher   120
is the solitary calm where man's soul,
judge only of itself, displays its actions.
Do you seek lasting joys, and happiness,
as much as is given to man on earth?
Where laughter is close to tears, and always,   125
ah, always, among the flowers pricks the thorn?
Go and enjoy the farmer's life, his lovely peace,
untroubled by bitterness and envy.
His soft bed is prepared for him
by labor, purest air, and great content,   130
and the flavor of food easily won.
He is untouched by wasteful gluttony,
and in the safe haven of his loyal home
is host to health and happiness.
Go breathe the mountain air, that gives   135
lost vigor to the tired body, and retards
fretful old age, and tinges pink
the face of beauty. Is the flame of love,
tempered by modesty, less sweet, perchance?
Or is beauty less attractive   140
without false ornament and lying paint?
Does the heart hear unmoved
the innocent language that expresses love
openly, the intent equal to the promise?
No need to rehearse before the mirror   145
a laugh, a step, a gesture;
no lack there of an honest face
flushed with modesty and health, nor does
the sidelong glance cast by a timid lover
lose its way to the soul.   150
Could you expect a marriage bond to form,
arranged by an alien hand, tyrant of love,

swayed by base interests, for repute or fortune,
happier than one where taste and age agree,
and free choice reigns, and mutual ardor?　　　　　　　　155

　　　　There too are duties to perform: heal, oh heal
the bitter wounds of war; place the fertile soil,
now harsh and wild, under the unaccustomed yoke
of human skill, and conquer it.
Let pent-up pond and water mill　　　　　　　　　　　160
remember where their waters flowed,
let the axe break the matted trees
and fire burn the forest; in its barren splendor
let a long gash be cut.
Give shelter in the valleys　　　　　　　　　　　　　165
to thirsty sugarcane; in the cool mountains make
pear trees and apples forget their mother, Spain.
Make coffee trees adorn the slopes;
on river banks, let the maternal shade
of the *bucare* tree[5] guard the tender cacao plants.　　　170
Let gardens flourish, orchards laugh with joy.
Is this blind error, foolish fantasy?
Oh agriculture, wetnurse of mankind,
heeding your voice, now comes the servile crowd
with curving sickles armed.　　　　　　　　　　　　175
It bursts into the dark wood's tangled growth.
I hear voices and distant sounds, the axe's noise.
Far off, echo repeats its blows; the ancient tree
for long the challenge of the laboring crowd,
groans, and trembles from a hundred axes,　　　　　　180
topples at last, and its tall summit falls.
The wild beast flees; the doleful bird
leaves its sweet nest, its fledgling brood,
seeking a wood unknown to humankind.
What do I see? a tall and crackling flame　　　　　　　185
spills over the dry ruins of the conquered forest.
The roaring fire is heard afar,
black smoke eddies upward, piling cloud on cloud.
And only dead trunks, only ashes remain
of what before was lovely green and freshness,　　　　190
the tomb of mortal joy, plaything of the wind.
But the wild growth of savage, tangled plants
gives way to fruitful plantings, that display
their proud rows and orderly design.
Branch touches branch, and steals　　　　　　　　　195
the light of day from sturdy shoots.
Now the first flower displays its buds,
lovely to see and breathing joyful hope.
Hope, that laughing mops the tired farmer's brow,
Hope, that from afar　　　　　　　　　　　　　　　200
paints the rich fruit, the harvest's bounty

5. Coral tree that provides the shade needed for growing cocoa beans.

that carries off the tribute of the fields
in heaping baskets and in billowing skirts,
and under the weight of plenty, the farmer's due,
makes vast storehouses creak and groan.   205

       Dear God! let not the Equator's farming folk
sweat vainly; be moved to pity and compassion.
Let them return now from their sad despair
with renewed spirit, and after such alarms,
anxiety and turmoil, and so many years   210
of fierce destruction and of military crimes,
may beg your mercy more than in the past.
May rustic piety, but no less sincere
find favor in your eyes. Let them not weep
for a vanished golden dream, a lying vision,   215
a future without tears, a smiling future
that lightens all the troubles of today.
Let not unseasonable rains
ruin the tender crops; let not the pitiless tooth
of gnawing insects devour them.   220
Let not the savage storm destroy,
or the tree's maternal sap
dry up in summer's long and heated thirst.
For you, supreme arbiter of fate,
were pleased at long last to remove the yoke   225
of foreign rule, and with your blessing
to raise American man toward heaven,
to make his freedom root and thrive.
Bury accursed war in deep abyss,
and, for fear of vengeful sword,   230
let the distrustful farmer not desist
from noble toil, that nourishes
families and whole countries too.
May anxious worry leave their souls,
and plows no longer sadly rust.   235
We have atoned enough for the savage conquest
of our unhappy fathers.
No matter where we look, do we not see
a stubbled wilderness where once were fields,
and cities too? Who can sum up the dreadful count   240
of deaths, proscriptions, tortures,
and orphans left abandoned?
The ghosts of Montezuma, Atahualpa,[6]
sleep now, glutted with Spanish blood.
Ah! from your lofty seat,   245
where choirs of winged angels veil their faces
in awe before the splendor of your face
(if luckless humankind deserves, perchance,

---

6. Montezuma II (ca. 1466–1529), Aztec emperor taken prisoner and killed during the Spanish conquest. "Atahualpa": last Inca emperor (1497–1533), captured and executed by the Spanish.

a single glance from you),
send down an angel, angel of peace, to make   250
the rude Spaniard forget his ancient tyranny,
and, reverent, hear the sacred vow,
the essential law you gave to men;
may he stretch out his unarmed hand,
(alas, too stained with blood!)   255
to his wronged brother.
And if innate gentleness should sleep
make it awake in the American breast.
The brave heart that scorns obscure content,
that beats more strongly in the bloody hap   260
of battle, and greedy for power or fame,
loves noble perils,
deems an insult, worthy of contempt,
and spurns the prize not given by his country.
May he find freedom sweeter far than power,   265
and olive branch more fair than laurel crown.
Let the soldier-citizen put off
the panoply of war; let the victory wreath
hang on his country's altar,
and glory be the only prize of merit.   270
Then may my country see the longed-for day
when peace will triumph:
peace, that fills the world
with joy, serenity, and happiness.
Man will return rejoicing to his task;   275
the ship lifts anchor, and entrusts herself
to friendly winds. Workshops swarm, farms teem,
the scythes do not suffice to cut the grain.

      Oh, youthful nations, with early laurels crowned,
who rise before the West's astonished gaze!   280
Honor the fields, honor the simple life,
and the farmer's frugal simplicity.
Thus freedom will dwell in you forever,
ambition be restrained, law have its temple.
Your people will set out bravely   285
on the hard, steep path of immortality,
always citing your example.
Those who come after you will imitate you eagerly,
adding new names to those whose fame
they now acclaim. For they will say, "Sons, sons   290
are these of men who won the Andes' heights;
those who in Boyacá, and on Maipo's sands,
and in Junín, and Apurima's glorious field,[7]
humbled in victory the lion of Spain."

7. Sites of military victories by revolutionary forces against Spanish colonial rule. "Andes": mountain range that runs along the west coast of South America. "Boyacá": a state in Colombia. "Maipo": river in Chile. "Junín": large lake in Peru. "Apurima": the Apurimac River in Peru, the source of the Amazon.

JOHN KEATS

1795–1821

John Keats established himself as one of the greatest of all English poets in a career that lasted less than five years. His first published work appeared in 1816, and his life ended—"blighted in the bud," as the poet Percy Shelley put it—in 1821, just as he had reached the height of his powers. Readers have long speculated about what would have happened to his writing, and to the history of English poetry, if he had lived just a few years longer. Keats himself knew well that his life could be cut short; he had watched his mother and brother die of tuberculosis, and he diagnosed his own mortal illness. Written in the full awareness of a terrifying mortality, Keats's poetry exults in the intensity of bodily, sensual experience. And even in this briefest of writing careers, Keats produced a varied, original, and formally dazzling body of work. His linguistic richness, taut craftsmanship, and skill in harmonizing sounds and rhythms have influenced many poets to follow, while he grapples with themes that have moved generations of readers: aching desire, the dreadful coming of death, and the seductive power of beauty.

LIFE

John Keats began his life in comparatively lowly surroundings. He was the eldest son of an ostler, a laborer who looked after horses at a London inn, and the inn-owner's daughter. His father died when he was eight years old, and Keats's mother remarried within a few months. At the time Keats was a student at the progressive Enfield Academy, where the schoolmasters embraced political reform, skepticism, and religious dissent. The young Keats often started fights with other boys, earning a reputation for a hot temper. Called "little Keats" into adulthood, he never grew taller than five feet in height. After his father's death he began to work extraordinarily hard at his studies, hungrily reading poetry in particular, including the work of Edmund Spenser—his favorite poet—as well as Virgil, Chaucer, Dante, Shakespeare, Milton, **Wordsworth**, and Byron.

Miserable in her second marriage, Keats's mother disappeared altogether for some time. Eventually she returned to her children, but only after she had begun to suffer from a deadly case of tuberculosis. John nursed her in her final illness, caring for her passionately and possessively. She died when he was fourteen years old. Soon afterward, Keats's guardian decided to apprentice him to a surgeon. These were the days before anesthesia, which meant patients writhed in pain under the surgeon's knife. Keats found this horrifying, and he stayed with his medical training only long enough to become an apothecary—the lowest rung on the medical ladder—before dedicating himself to writing poetry. His first volume garnered many harshly critical reviews, including one that called him "an uneducated and flimsy stripling."

At the end of 1818 Keats's younger brother Tom died of tuberculosis, and the poet threw himself into writing, producing all of his greatest work in just one remarkable year: "The Eve of Saint Agnes," "La Belle Dame sans Merci," "Lamia," the completion of his long poem *Hyperion*, all of his great odes. This was the same year as the Peterloo Massacre, the government's violent killing of peaceful civilians. It was also the year that Keats fell in love with a London neighbor named Fanny Brawne. He was possessive, she flirtatious, and his letters reveal him as an impassioned and jealous lover.

Their love was doomed, however, by Keats's poverty and growing ill-health. A history of debts, unwise loans, and ongoing struggles to earn money prevented Keats from proposing marriage. Then, early in 1820, he suffered a lung hemorrhage. His medical training led him to recognize this as his "death warrant." He was told that he would not survive another British winter, and so he set out for Italy. It was in this final stretch of his life that his work finally earned favorable reviews, and Keats felt hopeful that he would eventually be ranked with the great English poets. He died in Rome at the age of twenty-five.

KEATS AND THE "COCKNEY SCHOOL" OF POETRY

In 1817 the radical poet and editor Leigh Hunt published Keats's first poem and hailed him as one of the most exciting of a new generation of poets who were casting off the orderly, decorous, neoclassical poetic styles associated with the eighteenth century—in particular the work of **Alexander Pope**. Detractors lumped Keats and Hunt together as the "Cockney School" of poets. Cockneys are working-class Londoners from the heart of the city, and this name conveyed contempt for what critics saw as the poets' low social class, lack of education, and vulgarity. "Back to the shop, Mr John," urged one snobbish reviewer assessing Keats's work.

There was no question that the Cockney poets were up to something quite new. They flagrantly broke with

poetic convention in a number of obvious ways: their work sparkled with clever, innovative turns of phrase—often making adverbs out of participles, such as "crushingly," or turning verbs into adjectives, as in "scattery light." They also refused Pope's favorite form of "closed couplets," which contained a completed sentence in two rhyming lines, in favor of "open couplets," where the thought spilled out beyond the end of the rhyme. Even more shockingly, they delighted in erotic imagery and sensuous language, which invited readers to linger on bodily pleasures: "delicious" was a particular favorite.

The Cockney poets also led a return to the roughness and sensuous vitality of the pagan ancient Greeks, which they saw as fundamentally different from the eighteenth-century English version of the Greeks as delicate "toys." Keats's poem "On First Looking into Chapman's Homer" would have seemed polemical at the time: the poet is pointedly celebrating Chapman's "loud and bold" seventeenth-century translation of the ancient Greek poet over the neatly rhymed, standard translation of his own time—that of Alexander Pope. (When one of Keats's readers expressed surprise that he evoked the Greeks so well, despite his meager education, Percy Shelley answered curtly, "He *was* a Greek.")

Contemporaries contrasted the Cockney School with the poets they called the "Lake School"—most prominently **William Wordsworth** and Samuel Taylor Coleridge. Keats mulled a great deal on Wordsworth, who provided both inspiration and irritation for the younger poet. In place of the "egotistical sublime"—Keats's term for Wordsworth's focus on the self—he embraced the model of the "chameleon poet" who has "no identity" but takes delight in things other than himself. Keats also criticized Coleridge, who lacked what he famously called "negative capability": "when a man is capable of being in uncertainties, Mysteries, doubts, without any irritable reaching after fact & reason."

WORKS

Keats's work richly rewards the reader in a broad range of ways. His luxurious language and sumptuous imagery invite us to take pleasure in the sensuous beauty of poetry; his meticulous crafting of poetic forms—the architecture of lines, stanzas, and figures—is flawless; his numerous allusions to other writers are thoughtful and suggestive; and his uses of poetic forms to dwell on death, love, pain, art, and nature are philosophically penetrating. For many readers, Keats is among the very few poets in English who have combined these elements with such skill.

Keats's poetry insistently dwells on antitheses and contradictions. "Ode to a Nightingale," for example, opens with the oxymoronic claim that "numbness" can give "pain." This poem also foregrounds a fundamental Keatsian opposition: the distance between the fully sensuous experience of human bodies, which are doomed to die, and that which lasts beyond the human lifespan but has no experience of its pleasures—in this case, the transcendent song of the nightingale. But far from offering a simple contrast between these two states, Keats often pushes one of these so far that it turns into its opposite: in "Ode to a Nightingale," the poet longs for a lived experience of wine and sunshine so intense that he will "fade away" and become like the immortal nightingale, remote from lived experience. Leigh

Hunt spoke of Keats's "poetical *concentrations*," and it is typical of his poetry to find conflicting experiences fused together. In "Ode to a Nightingale," for example, the poet speaks of "tasting . . . the country green," an example of synaesthesia—the mixing up of the senses—that violates conventional distinctions. And yet it would be misleading to see Keats as consumed only with oppositions and contradictions. His poems are thick with linguistic activity—meticulously wrought metaphors, puns, allusions, echoes within and across poems, and multiple kinds of poetic diction—all working together in a single text.

Keats's odes, perhaps his greatest works of all, participate in a tradition of English odes that are addressed to a serious and dignified object—such as an artwork, a mood, or a mythological figure. Keats, like other writers of odes, uses these objects to reflect on the nature and power of poetry. Each of his odes responds to and builds on the one before, and they echo and oppose one another in provocative ways. For example, "Ode to a Nightingale" and "Ode on a Grecian Urn" are like mirror images: the first compares poetry to music, suppressing visual experience in favor of aural; the second contrasts poetry to visual art while suppressing sound.

Keats is an architect of poetic structure: he cares deeply about the ways that stanzas, rhymes, rhythms, and line lengths punctuate, organize, and work together in complex composite wholes. But he is more than a mere craftsman: Keats's intricate structures are there to serve his exquisite meditations on poetry, love, and the looming fact of death.

On First Looking into Chapman's Homer[1]

Much have I traveled in the realms of gold,
   And many goodly states and kingdoms seen;
   Round many western islands have I been
Which bards in fealty to Apollo[2] hold.
Oft of one wide expanse had I been told   5
   That deep-browed Homer ruled as his demesne;[3]
   Yet did I never breathe its pure serene
Till I heard Chapman speak out loud and bold:
Then felt I like some watcher of the skies
   When a new planet swims into his ken;   10
Or like stout Cortez[4] when with eagle eyes
   He stared at the Pacific—and all his men
Looked at each other with a wild surmise—
   Silent, upon a peak in Darien.

Ode on a Grecian Urn

I

Thou still unravished bride of quietness,
   Thou foster-child of silence and slow time,
Sylvan historian, who canst thus express
   A flowery tale more sweetly than our rhyme:
What leaf-fringed legend haunts about thy shape   5
   Of deities or mortals, or of both,
      In Tempe or the dales of Arcady?[1]
   What men or gods are these? What maidens loth?
What mad pursuit? What struggle to escape?
      What pipes and timbrels? What wild ecstasy?   10

II

Heard melodies are sweet, but those unheard
   Are sweeter; therefore, ye soft pipes, play on;
Not to the sensual ear, but, more endeared,
   Pipe to the spirit ditties of no tone:

1. Keats's friend and former teacher Charles Cowden Clarke had introduced Keats to George Chapman's (1559?–1634) translations of the *Iliad* (1611) and the *Odyssey* (1616) the night before this poem was written.
2. The Greek god of poetic inspiration.
3. Realm, kingdom.
4. In fact, Vasco Núñez de Balboa (ca. 1475–1519), Spanish conquistador, not Hernán Cortés (1485–1547), another Spaniard, was the European explorer who first saw the Pacific from Darién, Panama.
1. A mountainous region in the Peloponnese, traditionally regarded as the place of ideal rustic, bucolic contentment. "Tempe": a valley in Thessaly between Mount Olympus and Mount Ossa.

Fair youth, beneath the trees, thou canst not leave   15
   Thy song, nor ever can those trees be bare;
     Bold lover, never, never canst thou kiss,
Though winning near the goal—yet, do not grieve;
     She cannot fade, though thou hast not thy bliss,
     For ever wilt thou love, and she be fair!   20

III

Ah, happy, happy boughs! that cannot shed
   Your leaves, nor ever bid the Spring adieu;
And, happy melodist, unwearièd,
   For ever piping songs for ever new;
More happy love! more happy, happy love!   25
   For ever warm and still to be enjoyed,
     For ever panting, and for ever young;
All breathing human passion far above,
     That leaves a heart high-sorrowful and cloyed,
     A burning forehead, and a parching tongue.   30

IV

Who are these coming to the sacrifice?
   To what green altar, O mysterious priest,
Lead'st thou that heifer lowing at the skies,
   And all her silken flanks with garlands drest?
What little town by river or sea shore,   35
   Or mountain-built with peaceful citadel,
     Is emptied of this folk, this pious morn?
And, little town, thy streets for evermore
Will silent be; and not a soul to tell
     Why thou art desolate, can e'er return.   40

V

O Attic shape! Fair attitude! with brede[2]
   Of marble men and maidens overwrought,
With forest branches and the trodden weed;
   Thou, silent form, dost tease us out of thought
As doth eternity: Cold Pastoral!   45
   When old age shall this generation waste,
     Thou shalt remain, in midst of other woe
Than ours, a friend to man, to whom thou say'st,
   "Beauty is truth, truth beauty,"—that is all
     Ye know on earth, and all ye need to know.   50

---

2. Pattern. "Attic": classical (literally, Athenian).

Ode to a Nightingale

I

My heart aches, and a drowsy numbness pains
  My sense, as though of hemlock I had drunk,
Or emptied some dull opiate to the drains
  One minute past, and Lethe-wards[1] had sunk:
'Tis not through envy of thy happy lot,   5
  But being too happy in thy happiness,
    That thou, light-winged Dryad[2] of the trees,
      In some melodious plot
  Of beechen green, and shadows numberless,
    Singest of summer in full-throated ease.   10

II

O for a draught of vintage! that hath been
  Cooled a long age in the deep-delvèd earth,
Tasting of Flora[3] and the country green,
  Dance, and Provençal[4] song, and sunburnt mirth!
O for a beaker full of the warm South!   15
  Full of the true, the blushful Hippocrene,[5]
    With beaded bubbles winking at the brim,
      And purple-stainèd mouth;
That I might drink, and leave the world unseen,
  And with thee fade away into the forest dim: 20

III

Fade far away, dissolve, and quite forget
  What thou among the leaves hast never known,
The weariness, the fever, and the fret
  Here, where men sit and hear each other groan;
Where palsy shakes a few, sad, last gray hairs,   25
  Where youth grows pale, and spectre-thin, and dies;
    Where but to think is to be full of sorrow
      And leaden-eyed despairs;
Where beauty cannot keep her lustrous eyes,
  Or new love pine at them beyond tomorrow.   30

1. I.e., toward Lethe, the river of forgetfulness in Greek mythology.
2. Wood nymph.
3. The goddess of flowers and spring; here, flowers.
4. From Provence, the region in France associated with the troubadours.
5. The fountain on Mount Helicon, in Greece, sacred to the muse of poetry.

IV

Away! away! for I will fly to thee,
  Not charioted by Bacchus and his pards,[6]
But on the viewless wings of Poesy,
  Though the dull brain perplexes and retards:
Already with thee! tender is the night,   35
  And haply[7] the Queen-Moon is on her throne,
    Clustered around by all her starry Fays;[8]
      But here there is no light,
  Save what from heaven is with the breezes blown
    Through verdurous glooms and winding mossy ways.   40

V

I cannot see what flowers are at my feet,
  Nor what soft incense hangs upon the boughs,
But, in embalmèd darkness, guess each sweet
  Wherewith the seasonable month endows
The grass, the thicket, and the fruit-tree wild;   45
  White hawthorn, and the pastoral eglantine;
    Fast-fading violets covered up in leaves;
      And mid-May's eldest child,
  The coming musk-rose, full of dewy wine,
    The murmurous haunt of flies on summer eves.   50

VI

Darkling[9] I listen; and for many a time
  I have been half in love with easeful Death,
Called him soft names in many a musèd rhyme,
  To take into the air my quiet breath;
Now more than ever seems it rich to die,   55
  To cease upon the midnight with no pain,
    While thou art pouring forth thy soul abroad
      In such an ecstasy!
Still wouldst thou sing, and I have ears in vain—
  To thy high requiem become a sod.[1]   60

VII

Thou wast not born for death, immortal Bird!
  No hungry generations tread thee down;
The voice I hear this passing night was heard
  In ancient days by emperor and clown:

6. Leopards. Bacchus (Dionysus) was traditionally supposed to be accompanied by leopards, lions, goats, and so on.
7. By chance.
8. Fairies.
9. In the dark.
1. I.e., like dirt, unable to hear.

Perhaps the self-same song that found a path   65
   Through the sad heart of Ruth, when, sick for home,
      She stood in tears amid the alien corn;[2]
         The same that ofttimes hath
Charmed magic casements, opening on the foam
      Of perilous seas, in faery lands forlorn.   70

                              VIII

Forlorn! the very word is like a bell
   To toll me back from thee to my sole self!
Adieu! the fancy cannot cheat so well
   As she is famed to do, deceiving elf.
Adieu! adieu! thy plaintive anthem fades   75
   Past the near meadows, over the still stream,
      Up the hill-side; and now 'tis buried deep
         In the next valley-glades:
Was it a vision, or a waking dream?
   Fled is that music:—do I wake or sleep?   80

2. See the Book of Ruth. After her Ephrathite husband died, she returned to his native land with her mother-in-law.

HEINRICH HEINE

1797–1856

Born to Jewish parents in the German city of Düsseldorf, Heinrich Heine became one of the most famous of all German poets. He wrote at a historical moment dominated by Romantic literature, but experienced a growing disillusionment with the ideals of his contemporaries. "The Romantic School" was "where I spent the most agreeable days of my youth," he wrote, but he "ended up by beating the schoolmaster." He turned his sardonic pen on the very themes that had first animated him: instead of dreams, he focused on harsh awakenings; in place of beautiful love, he concentrated on falling out of love; and he treated nature itself with ironic detachment. He continued to rely on traditional rhyming forms, evocative of simple folk songs, but he deliberately modernized their content, and put them to complex, ironic, and often humorous ends.

Politically, Heine was a radical. He was a friend of Karl Marx, though he remained wary of communism. Early in his life he refused to use his poetic voice as a vehicle for political opinions, arguing that poetry belonged to a higher, more transcendent realm. (He once compared political poets to dancing bears.) But in the 1840s he would write a number of rousing poems on current political events: "The Silesian Weavers" commemorates a protest by Prussian laborers whose wages had fallen below starvation levels.

Throughout his life, the poet maintained an ambivalent relationship to both his Jewishness and his Germanness. Napoleon's conquest of Germany brought with it a guarantee of full civil rights to Jews, but after his defeat, many German cities and states reverted to repressive laws. In Frankfurt, for example, only twelve Jewish couples were permitted to marry in any given year. Heine was allowed to study law but not to practice, and he converted to Christianity in order to find work. He rejected Jewish communities and beliefs until late in life, but remained fiercely critical of Christian Germany. "Wherever they burn books," he wrote, "they will also, in the end, burn human beings."

[A pine is standing lonely][1]

A pine is standing lonely
In the North on a bare plateau.
He sleeps; a bright white blanket
Enshrouds him in ice and snow.

He's dreaming of a palm tree   5
Far away in the Eastern land
Lonely and silently mourning
On a sunburnt rocky strand.

To Tell the Truth[1]

When springtime comes, the sun and showers
Bring out a host of dancing flowers;
And when at night the moon peeps through,
The stars begin to twinkle too;
And when the bard sees two blue eyes,   5
Soulful songs materialise;—
But songs and stars and dancing flowers
And azure eyes and April showers,
However popular such stuff,
It's never *really* quite enough.   10

[A young man loves a maiden]

A young man loves a maiden
Who chooses another instead;

1. Translated by Hal Draper, as are the other Heine selections except "To tell the Truth."

1. Translated by T. J. Reed and David Cram.

This other loves still another
And these two haply[1] wed.

The maiden out of anger   5
Marries, with no regard,
The first good man she runs into—
The young lad takes it hard.

It is so old a story,
Yet somehow always new;   10
And he that has just lived it,
It breaks his heart in two.

The Silesian Weavers[1]

In somber eyes no tears of grieving;
Grinding their teeth, they sit at their weaving;
"O Germany, at your shroud we sit,
We're weaving a threefold curse in it—
    We're weaving, we're weaving!   5

"A curse on the god we prayed to, kneeling
With cold in our bones, with hunger reeling;
We waited and hoped, in vain persevered,
He scorned us and duped us, mocked and jeered—
    We're weaving, we're weaving!   10

"A curse on the king[2] of the rich man's nation
Who hardens his heart at our supplication,
Who wrings the last penny out of our hides
And lets us be shot like dogs besides—
    We're weaving, we're weaving!   15

"A curse on this false fatherland, teeming
With nothing but shame and dirty scheming,
Where every flower is crushed in a day,
Where worms are regaled on rot and decay—
    We're weaving, we're weaving!   20

"The shuttle[3] flies, the loom creaks loud,
Night and day we weave your shroud—
Old Germany, at your shroud we sit,
We're weaving a threefold curse in it,
    We're weaving, we're weaving!"   25

---

1. By chance.
1. Silesia was a province of the kingdom of
Prussia in northeast Germany. This poem was
occasioned by violent uprisings of weavers
protesting intolerable working conditions during June 1844.

2. Friedrich Wilhelm IV (1795–1861).
Heine's poem is prophetic: in 1848 the king,
though not deposed, was forced by revolution
to grant a constitution to Prussia.
3. Device used for weaving cloth on a loom.

GHALIB

1797–1869

Ghalib is probably the most frequently quoted poet of the nineteenth and twentieth centuries in India and Pakistan, where tens of millions of people know some of his Urdu poems by heart. His popularity, which has only grown since his death nearly one and a half centuries ago, is especially remarkable given the complexity of his work. Despite the fact that he is a difficult poet, his phrases, images, and ideas have become part of the common speech of Urdu and Hindi, which are closely interrelated languages. He wrote haunting love poems in a style that still seems contemporary, and his words and emotions are on the lips of young and old lovers everywhere on the subcontinent.

LIFE AND TIMES

Indians in the nineteenth century passed from one vast imperial power to another. The Muslim Mughal Empire, which at its height commanded 100 million people, had once boasted great wealth and military might. But some Hindu kingdoms put up resistance to Mughal control, and by the middle of the eighteenth century they had helped to weaken the empire. In 1804, the British East India Company officially took control. This had been a trading company, bringing Indian tea, cotton, silk, spices, and opium into Britain, but it gradually took power as the official government of the Indian subcontinent. British administrators, feeling superior to the Indians, began a campaign to impose their own moral, linguistic, and cultural traditions on India. Christian missionaries arrived in ever larger numbers, and increasingly, the British back home were whipped into an enthusi-asm for advancing the "backward" peoples of India. Ironically, it was partly thanks to British imperialism that the Indians could be seen as backward in the first place. India had once had a lively economy based on handcrafts—in 1700 it had been the world's leading exporter of woven cloth—but Britain's cheap factory-made textiles and its demand for raw materials from India had forced many workers back into a more peasant-based and rural economy. Meanwhile, the imposition of European ideas produced reactions in the form of increased sectarian Hindu and Muslim feeling, fostering more intolerance between these two groups. A major blow to British imperialism came in 1857, when Hindu soldiers rebelled against the British army, triggering a larger insurrection by both Hindu and Muslim leaders. The British violently suppressed the rebellion, a brutality that left lasting scars. By the middle of the nineteenth century, English had replaced Persian as the official language of law, diplomacy, and administration.

Born in Agra in December 1797, Asadullah Khan—later known by his literary pseudonym, Ghalib ("Conqueror" in Persian and Urdu)—was a descendant of Turkish military settlers in north India. His grandfather as well as his father and an uncle, who ranked as minor nobles in the Muslim ruling class of the nineteenth century, served in the Mughal emperor's army. After his father died, when he was five, and his uncle, who then supported the extended family, died only three years later, Ghalib was raised mostly among his mother's relatives. When he was thirteen, his family (then in financial decline) arranged his marriage to an eleven-year-old girl from a wealthier segment of the nobility. In 1810 he moved to Delhi, where the young couple lived in comfortable circumstances with support from her family, a dependence that was to continue for the rest of his life. The young poet, who had begun to write Urdu verse and prose at seven and in Persian by the age of nine, matured rapidly in the next few years, completing a significant portion of his oeuvre of Urdu poetry by 1816, when he was nineteen.

However, in 1822, partly in response to widespread incomprehension and criticism of his early poetry, Ghalib stopped writing verse in Urdu and switched to Persian as his only poetic medium—a practice he adhered to until 1850. Persian had been the premier literary language of Muslim society across Asia for much of the preceding seven or eight hundred years; and, since the end of the sixteenth century, it had also been the official imperial language of the subcontinent under the Mughals. By the 1840s Ghalib had produced a large body of poetry and prose in Persian, and he had become a prominent Indian authority on the language and its literature.

Despite his renown, much of Ghalib's adult life was marked by bitter disappointments. He spent most of the 1820s unsuccessfully seeking an aristocratic patron near Delhi; in 1827–30, he tried in vain to secure a British pension in Calcutta; and in 1842 he failed to get a position as Persian instructor at Delhi College, a new British-Indian institution. Ghalib's public humiliations reached a peak in 1847, when he was arrested for gambling in his home and imprisoned for three months. His personal and family life also proved to be deeply unhappy during this period. He and his wife had seven children, but none survived beyond the age of fifteen months, a cycle of tragedies that contributed to their emotional alienation from each other. In the 1840s

Ghalib adopted his wife's adult nephew 'Arif as his son, but the untimely deaths of both 'Arif and his wife from tuberculosis in 1852 only added to the poet's sorrows. Ghalib's elegy for 'Arif—included here as "It Was Essential"—remains one of his most famous poems today, a memorable mourning of human mortality and a celebration of family life and familial love. And yet his deepest emotional relationship—one that haunted him for more than forty years after its tragic end—may have been with a low-caste Hindu courtesan, who died very young and whose loss he mourned publicly at her funeral and in his letters and poetry.

The year 1850 brought significant changes to the poet's literary and professional life, and alleviated his financial circumstances to some extent. Emperor Bahadur Shah Zafar—who proved to be the last in the long line of Mughal rulers on Delhi's throne—commissioned Ghalib to write a history of the dynasty in Persian; and, four years later, the emperor finally appointed him as royal tutor and court poet. At Zafar's urging, Ghalib also resumed writing poetry and prose in Urdu, the "mixed" language (combining Hindi syntax and Persian vocabulary) that was the first language of north-Indian Muslims. In the 1850s and 1860s Ghalib became the most sought-after master of Urdu and Persian poetry among Muslim as well as Hindu writers, developing a rich and voluminous correspondence in Urdu with more than four hundred friends and admirers of various faiths across the subcontinent.

The events of 1857, however, transformed Ghalib's life and his beloved city of Delhi irreversibly. The "Mutiny" (now often called the First Indian War of Independence from British rule) started that summer and quickly overtook the Mughal capital, where large-scale violence ravaged all segments of Muslim and Hindu society over several months, first with the arrival of large contingents of Indian soldiers rebelling against the British colonial army, and subsequently with British retaliation. After crushing the uprising and arresting and deporting the emperor, the British administration and British militias summarily executed some 3,000 citizens of Delhi and razed the most densely populated part of the city (now known as Old Delhi), exiling its inhabitants to the surrounding countryside. Several hundreds of Ghalib's fellow-courtiers, friends, acquaintances, and neighbors—Hindu, Muslim, and Sikh—lost their lives, families, homes, or property; and for many months he lived in fear of his own life and the safety of his family. In 1858 he published *Dastanbuy*, his personal account of these events, which testified to his political innocence in the Mughal court's complicity with the rebels.

Ghalib survived the catastrophe of 1857 by a dozen years, but as a broken and lonely man. He wrote some of his best late poems in Urdu in the 1850s and early 1860s, but old age, deteriorating eyesight and hearing, and long illness increasingly confined him to his dilapidated home in Delhi; much of this is foreshadowed in his first poem in our selection, "Now Go and Live in a Place." Despite his personal difficulties, however, he kept up a vivid and generous correspondence with younger poets and admirers, including the close Hindu friends who preserved his works. These letters became a celebrated part of his oeuvre in his own lifetime, when, in 1868, they were collected and published as *Urdu-i-mu'alla*.

Looking back from our own times, Ghalib's life and poetry seem to represent the Indian subcontinent's transition from tradition to modernity in all its many-sided complexity. He was the last major poet to be trained in the traditional disciplines (language, poetics, philosophy, and theology), and to work only in inherited forms, even as Indian

society engaged fully with Western-style modernity. He was the first—and last—traditional writer to publish his work in the print medium in his own lifetime (which he did around its midpoint), and to experience at first hand the extraordinary transformation that print culture brings to long-standing cultures of manuscript circulation, by fundamentally changing the nature of authorship, the author-audience connection, and literary reputation itself. He also underwent this experience by positioning himself quite uniquely in the shadowy space between tradition and modernity. While most of his contemporaries confronted the British presence in India from the perspective of a traditional "Hindu" or "Muslim" identity, Ghalib explicitly located himself in a prior synthesis of Muslim and Hindu cultures (or a hybrid Indo-Islamic civilization) that was open to a productive interaction with European culture. His life and career thus give us a glimpse into the unusual "triangle" of Muslim, Hindu, and European cultures intersecting in unprecedented proximity in the turmoil of nineteenth-century India.

WORK

Ghalib composed his poetry entirely in the inherited verse forms and genres of Persian and Urdu, both influenced heavily by Arabic traditions and the literary conventions of Islam. His favorite form in both Persian and Urdu was the *ghazal*, but he also wrote the equivalents of odes, panegyrics, satires, epigrams, epithalamiums, verse-epistles, prayers, and chronograms. The *ghazal*, invented in classical Arabic but widely practiced in Persian and Urdu, among other languages, over the past millennium, is technically one of the most demanding metrical forms in world poetry. A *ghazal* consists of a sequence of couplets—most often between five and twelve in number—in a single meter; and each couplet is end-stopped, hence representing one complete poetic thought. All the couplets in a *ghazal* have to be connected to each other by end-rhyme; the rhyme, however, has to occur at the end of each couplet, not in an isolated word but in an entire phrase. This "rhyming phrase" has two required parts: a final word or set of words that is repeated in each couplet, and hence serves as a refrain; and a word preceding the refrain that rhymes with the corresponding word in each of the other couplets. The rhyming phrase in a *ghazal* thus consists of a "mono-rhyme" followed by a refrain. The following metrical translation of two separate couplets from an Urdu *ghazal* by Ghalib captures this pattern in English, with the repeated word "good" at the end of each couplet defining the refrain, and "more" and "restore" representing the mono-rhyme that precedes it.

> The beauty of the moon, its sheer
>   beauty when it's full, is good—
> And yet, compared to it, her beauty
>   dazzles like the sun, is more than
>   good.

> When my face lights up merely
>   because she has looked at me,
> She thinks, mistakenly, the patient's
>   on the mend, restored for good.

The stringent rules of the *ghazal* also require that the opening couplet contain this rhyme-and-repetition pattern in both its lines (rather than only in the second one), thus defining the paradigm strongly; and that the closing couplet contain the poet's literary pseudonym, thus embedding the author's signature in the *ghazal* itself. This complicated structure leaves the poet free to make each couplet an entire miniature poem that is thematically and rhetorically independent of the other couplets. At the same time, it challenges him to create a thematic continuity against impossible prosodic odds. In the history of the *ghazal* across Arabic, Persian, and Urdu, Ghalib stands out as an astonishing craftsman who could construct continuous poetic arguments within the strictest constraints of meter, repetition, and rhyme, without sacrificing wit, emotional integrity, intellectual rigor, and range of experience. Among the examples included in our selection, his versatility with the *ghazal* is especially evident in "I've Made My Home Next Door to You," "It Was Essential," and "My Tongue Begs for the Power of Speech."

The poems below display Ghalib's imaginative range and depth in several genres in Urdu. The three poems just mentioned, together with "Now Go and Live in a Place," are translations of complete *ghazals*, and they capture the recursive structure of the form as closely as possible in metrical English, while retaining the semantic richness of the originals. Of these, "I've Made My Home Next Door to You" is represented in two parallel translations, one rendering the *ghazal* as a "secular" piece (a lover's plea and complaint), and the other highlighting the same text as a "sacred" poem (about love between God and human beings); the original conveys both meanings simultaneously, which is impossible to achieve in a single English version. In contrast, "Where's the Foothold" is a translation of a complete poem that is composed as a single unrhymed couplet, but is nevertheless classified among Ghalib's *ghazals* in Urdu. The separate "Selection of Couplets" offers self-contained verses taken from a dozen different *ghazals*, each presenting a complete and independent poetic thought with epigrammatic force. The final piece, "My Salary," is an excerpt from one of Ghalib's miscellaneous poems, addressed to Emperor Bahadur Shah Zafar, who was formally his literary student as well as his royal employer;

in this unusual verse epistle, he sought to improve his working conditions and salary as court poet. Most of the poems here contain "Ghalib" as the poet's signature, and hence they may belong to the latter half of his career; the exception is the prayer, "My Tongue Begs for the Power of Speech," which refers to him as "Asad," the pseudonym he used often as a young man.

Ghalib's value as a poet also rests on his larger cultural position. In the predominantly Sunni Muslim community of nineteenth-century Delhi, he professed to be a Shi'a; in the midst of organized Sunni Islam, with its mosques, public prayers and rituals, and powerful clerics, he adopted a radical and subversive Sufism in private, as evident from "I've Made My Home Next Door to You." He did not practice the five daily prayers or the weekly Friday prayer, did not fast during the month of Ramadan, and did not undertake the pilgrimage to Mecca; at the same time, he conspicuously violated the taboo against alcohol—among the "sins committed" that he mentions in the third piece in our "Selection of Couplets." Moreover, as the fifth couplet in that selection shows, he openly advocated a complete reconciliation between Islam and Hinduism, arguing for a secular merger in shared ways of everyday life. Ghalib was also a universal humanist before his time, as the sixth couplet indicates: in his view, being fully human was more essential than, and prior to, being either Muslim or Hindu, believer or infidel. He actively sympathized with, acted for, and spoke out on behalf of the poor and the dispossessed, and he was doggedly committed to the freedom of thought and speech, always speaking his mind tactfully yet forcefully, regardless of his interlocutor's status or power. At the same time, his contemporaries valued him immensely for his personal kindness and generos-

ity: he had a remarkable gift for friendship, and he conducted himself with wit, humor, and dignity even with his enemies. We see all these qualities vividly at work in his extraordinary prayer, "My Tongue Begs for the Power of Speech," which remained unpublished in his lifetime, perhaps because of its subversively modern message.

Ghalib was one of the last figures in a seven-century tradition of Persian writing in India; while his Persian prose was a model for a few later writers, his Persian poetry (about 11,000 verses) has had little effect on later poets in India or Pakistan, and none on poets in Iran. In contrast, his Urdu prose (in his letters) and especially his Urdu poetry have deeply influenced writers and readers in every generation after him. His *ghazals* have perpetuated this traditional form among Indian, Pakistani, and diasporic Urdu writers down to the present; and, just as importantly, they have spread the *ghazal* tradition among other contemporary Indian languages, such as Punjabi, Hindi, and Marathi. Since the international commemoration of the centenary of Ghalib's death in 1969, dozens of American, British, and Irish poets—from Adrienne Rich to Paul Muldoon—have cultivated the Ghalib-style *ghazal* in English, building on its earlier history as an international form that **Goethe** had adapted in German from his Persian favorite, Hafiz, and that **Lorca** had used in his avant-garde Spanish *gacelas*. Since the mid-twentieth century, in India as well as Pakistan, Ghalib's *ghazals* have been set to music and performed, live and in recordings, by many popular singers, and his life and work have been the subjects of several films and a television serial. One and a half centuries after his death, Ghalib remains a living presence in the two countries that have inherited his poetic legacy.

[Now go and live in a place]¹

Now go and live in a place where no one lives—
no one who fathoms your verse, no one who shares your speech.

Build yourself a house, as if without a wall or gate—
no neighbour to keep you company, no watchman to keep you safe.

If you fall ill, no one to nurse you there—   5
and if you die, no one to mourn you there.

[Be merciful and send for me]

Be merciful and send for me,
anytime you please—
   I'm not some moment
that has passed
   and can't come back again.   5

Why do I complain
about my rival's power²
   as though I were a weakling?
My cause isn't so lost
   it can't be taken up again.   10

I just can't lay my hands
on poison, darling,
   and even if I could,
I couldn't swallow it—
   because I've made a vow   15

that we two shall be one again.

[Where's the foothold]

Where's the foothold, Lord,
for desire's second step?

I found this barren world—
this wilderness of possibilities—

to be an imprint   5
of just the first step.

---

1. All the poems in this selection are translated by Vinay Dharwadker.
2. The woman addressed in this poem may be
a courtesan, and one of her other suitors
would then be the speaker's rival. Like other
Muslim aristocrats in 19th-century India,
Ghalib frequently visited courtesans, especially
in his youth and early adulthood.

[I've made my home next door to you]

1. The secular version

I've made my home next door to you, without being asked,
    without a word being said—
you still can't find my whereabouts without my help,
    without a word being said.

She says to me: "Since you don't have   5
    the power of words, how can you tell
what's in someone else's heart—
    without a word being said?"

I've work to do with her—I have to make it work—
    though no one in the world   10
can even speak her name without the word
    "tormentor" having to be said.

There's nothing in my heart, or else,
    even if my life were on the line,
I wouldn't hold my tongue,   15
    I wouldn't leave a thing unsaid.

I won't stop worshipping the one I love—
    that idol of an infidel—
even though the world won't let me go
    without the phrase "You infidel!" being said.[3]   20

Ghalib, don't press your case on her
    again and again and again.
Your state's completely evident to her—
    without a word being said.

2. The sacred version

I've made my home next door to You, without being asked,
    without a word being said—
You still can't find my whereabouts without my help,
    without a word being said.

He says to me: "Since you don't have   5
    the power of words, how can you tell
what's in someone else's heart—
    without a word being said?"

I've work to do with Him—I have to make it work—
    though no one in the world   10

3. Following Sufi mystical tradition, Ghalib often represents the beloved woman in his *ghazals* as an "infidel," someone who has not submitted to the true faith (Islam), and who is also sexually unfaithful or incapable of fidelity. The image is provocative because it suggests that she may not be a Muslim, which is why the speaker himself is accused of being disloyal to his religion. Ghalib may be referring here to the low-caste Hindu courtesan with whom he fell in love as a young man, and whose early tragic death he mourned much of his adult life.

can even speak His Name without the word
   "Tormentor" having to be said.[4]

There's nothing in my heart, or else,
   even if my life were on the line,
I wouldn't hold my tongue,
   I wouldn't leave a thing unsaid.

15

I won't stop worshipping the One I love—
   that Idol of an Infidel—
even though the world won't let me go
   without the phrase "You infidel!" being said.[5]

20

Ghalib, don't press your case on Him
   again and again and again.
Your state's completely evident to Him—
   without a word being said.

Couplets

1

Ghalib, it's no use
forcing your way with love:
   it's a form of fire
that doesn't catch when lit
and doesn't die when doused.

2

I have hopes,
I have hopes of faithfulness
from her—
     she
who doesn't have a clue
what faithfulness might be.

3

Dear God:
if there are punishments
for sins committed,

there also ought to be
rewards
for sins craved

but not committed.

---

4. In Sufi poetry in Persian and Urdu, God is often portrayed as a Beloved who torments worshipers, much as a beloved woman may torment a suitor in order to deepen his emotional dependence on her.

5. From the perspective of orthodox Islam, this characterization is theologically provocative; it suggests that God himself is not "faithful" to the faith that focuses on him.

4

What I have
isn't a case of love
but madness—

I grant you that.

But then it's true—
your reputation rests
upon the fact that it was you

who drove me mad.

5

We're monotheists,
we believe in the unity of God.[6]
For them, our message is:
Abandon your rituals![7]

But when communities
have cancelled their differences
and mingled and merged,
they've already converged

upon a common faith.[8]

6

Just this
that it's so hard
to make each task
look easy.

So too
it isn't simple
for humans
to be human.[9]

7

There are other poets
in the world
who're also very good:

6. The "we" in this verse refers to the fraternity of Muslims; Ghalib here repeats Islam's central claim that it believes in one God and in his absolute unity.

7. "They" and "them" refer to Hindus; Ghalib here alludes to the standard Muslim position that Hinduism valorizes many gods, the worship of idols, and numerous rituals.

8. This is Ghalib's famous argument for a "secularization" of both Islam and Hinduism, in which the two communities, after living with each other for centuries, have already created a shared way of life in practice, and hence ought not to be ideologically pitted against each other anymore.

9. The last word in this verse translates *insan* in the Urdu original, which points explicitly to Ghalib's emphasis on *insaniyat*, literally "humanism" as well as "the set of qualities that render a creature fully human." Like his much younger contemporary Rabindranath Tagore, Ghalib was a proponent of a "universal humanism."

but Ghalib's style
of saying things, they say,
is something else.

8

Tonight, somewhere,
    you're sleeping by the side
of another lover, a stranger:
    otherwise, what reason would you have
for visiting my dreams
    and smiling your half-smile?

9

I've been
set free
from the prison of love
a hundred times—

but what can I do
if the heart itself
proves to be
an enemy of freedom?

10

Pulling
that image
from my memory—

of your finger
imprinted with designs
in henna[1]—

was exactly like
pulling a fingernail
from my flesh.

11

If no one but You
    is manifest,
if nothing but You
    exists, O Lord,

1. Among Muslims as well as Hindus in India, henna is used as a cosmetic, both routinely and for brides at weddings. Dry henna leaves are crushed and mixed into a paste, which is applied in designs or patterns on the skin, especially the forearms, palms and hands, and soles and feet.

then what's this great commotion
all about?

12

The news was hot—
that Ghalib would self-destruct,
and all his parts
would go flying!
I, too, went to see the show—
but the promised mayhem
never materialized.

[It was essential]

Elegy for his wife's nephew and adopted son, 'Arif[2]

It was essential
that you wait for me
    for a few more days.
Why did you leave alone—
now wait alone
    for a few more days.   5

If your gravestone hasn't
worn it down for me,
    my head will soon be dust—
for I'll be rubbing my brow   10
upon your threshold
    for a few more days.

You arrived yesterday—
and, now, today you say,
    "I'm leaving."
I agree that staying forever   15
isn't good—but stay with us
    for a few more days.

As you depart you say,
"We'll meet once more   20
    on Doomsday."[3]
How great—
that doom will have its day
    on one more day.

2. 'Arif was a young adult when Ghalib and his wife formally adopted him, but both the young man and his wife died prematurely due to ill health. This *ghazal*, Ghalib's famous elegy for 'Arif, also celebrates family life and domesticity.

3. The day specified in the Qur'an on which the world will end, and on which Allah will call the living and the dead to Judgment.

Yes, oh yes,   25
O wise and ancient sky,
   'Arif was young—
what would have gone so wrong
if he hadn't died
   for a few more days?   30

You were the moon
of the fourteenth night,
   the full moon of my home[4]—
why didn't that remain
the picture of my household   35
   for a few more days?

You weren't so uptight
about the give-and-take of life—
   couldn't Death have been
bribed and dissuaded   40
from pressing His case
   for a few more days?

Fine, you hated me,
and fought with Nayyir[5]—
   but you didn't even stay   45
to watch, with pleasure,
your children's boisterous games
   for a few more days.

Our time together didn't pass
through every sort of circumstance,   50
   to seal enduring bonds—
dead before your time,
you should have passed the time with us
   for a few more days.

Those of you around me   55
are fools to ask,
   "Ghalib, why are you still living?"
It's my destiny
to continue to wish for death
   for a few more days.   60

---

4. Each month on the Muslim lunar calendar in India begins with the new moon; the full moon thus appears on the fourteenth night of the month. In Urdu *ghazals*, the full moon is a multifaceted image of beauty, happiness, and blessedness.

5. A relative of Ghalib's who lived in his neighborhood in Ballimaran, Old Delhi; for 'Arif, Nayyir was one of the "elders" in the extended family to be treated with respect and affection.

[My tongue begs for the power of speech]⁶

My tongue begs
for the power of speech
    that is Your gift to us;
for silence gets
its style of representation
    from Your gift to us.   5

The melancholic weeping
of those who live with disappointment
    is Your gift to us;
daybreak's smothered lamp   10
and autumn's wilted bloom
    are Your gifts to us.

The blossoming of wonder
at the sights we see
    is tough Love's gift: 15
the henna on the feet of death,⁷
the blood of slaughter's victims
    are Your gifts to us.

The predawn hour's concupiscence,
the contrivance of effects   20
    that follow later—
the flood of tears,
the colours of grief—
    are all Your gifts to us.

Garden after garden   25
multiplies the mirrors
    that fill desire's lap;
the hope that flowers there,
immersed in spring's displays,
    is Your gift to us.   30

Devotion is the veil⁸
that keeps our hubris hidden,
    held in check;

6. One of Ghalib's most technically skilled, thematically complex, and powerful *ghazals*, which he did not publish in his lifetime and which was discovered in the 1970s among his papers. Written with an almost entirely Persian vocabulary and syntax, linguistically and poetically it lies on the thin line separating Ghalib's Urdu and Persian verse. An intensely personal prayer, it is the poet's most direct and sustained conversation with, and tribute to, God.

7. Henna is a traditional cosmetic in India; this image suggests the death of a young woman, perhaps a bride, in the prime of her life.
8. Islam enjoins women always to remain behind a veil outside the *zenana*, the "women's quarters" in a home; theologically, God is "veiled" from human eyes, as is any form of true piety or "devotion" to God.

the brow that scrapes the ground,
the square prayer mat,[9]   35
    are Your gifts to us.

Our farce-like search for mercy,
our secretive retreat
    behind a festival's facade—
the firmness of our courage,   40
our sorrow at the tests we fail—
    are all Your gifts to us.

Asad, in the season of roses,
in an arbour that enchants us
    with its overarching latticework,   45
the winding walk, the bracing easterly,
the flowerbed in bloom
    are all Your gifts to us.

Petition: My Salary

*The conclusion of a petition in verse,
addressed to Bahadur Shah Zafar, the last Mughal emperor,
with its famous final lines*[1]

My master and my pupil! . . .
My salary, agreed upon,
is paid to me
in the strangest way.
The custom is   5
to consecrate the dead
once in six months—
that's the basis
on which the world runs.
But if you look at me,   10
you'll see that I am
a prisoner of life, not death—
and six-monthly paydays[2]
fall only twice a year.

9. One of the "pillars" of Islam is the set of five prayers that a Muslim must offer at prescribed times every day, facing in the direction of the Ka'aba in Mecca; since the prayers must be performed, in part, while kneeling on the ground, most Muslims use a personal mat for the purpose.
1. Emperor Bahadur Shah, who wrote verse under the pen name "Zafar," appointed Ghalib as his court poet and poetry teacher in 1854. This poem is a formal petition in verse addressed to the emperor.
2. Ghalib was paid his salary twice a year, rather than once a month; he compares this biannual schedule to the customary practice, among Muslims in India, of remembering the dead twice a year.

All I do each month
is take out a debt,
with wrangles over interest
repeated endlessly—
my money-lender has become
a partner
in one-third of my earnings.
Today, the world
has no one like me—
a poet of worth
who speaks beautifully.
If you wish to hear
an epic of war,
my tongue's a sharp sword;
if you convene an assembly,
my pen's a cloud
that rains down pearls.
It's a violation of etiquette
not to praise poetry,
it's an act of violence
not to love me.
I'm your slave
and I wander naked,
I'm your servant
and all I eat is debt.
Let my salary be paid
month by month,
let my life
cease to be a burden.
And now I conclude
my discourse
of prayer and supplication—
my business isn't poetry.
May you live
safe and sound
for a thousand years,
may the days
in every year
be fifty thousand.[3]

15

20

25

30

35

40

45

50

3. The final sentence of this poem, its concluding verse, has become the most widespread benediction or blessing in Urdu and Hindi in northern Indian society and is used especially on birthdays, at partings or departures, and at life-cycle ceremonies.

GIACOMO LEOPARDI
1798–1837

Giacomo Leopardi is one of Italy's greatest lyric poets. Born into an aristocratic family in a dreary provincial town, he was extraordinarily precocious, learning faster than any tutor could teach him. As an adolescent, he read several hundred pages a day, translated and commented on ancient texts, and wrote volumes of his own plays, essays, and poems. Yet it was far from a happy childhood. In his well-known diary, Leopardi explained that his mother purposefully reproached her children in order to "make them well aware of their defects . . . and to convince them with a fierce, pitiless veracity of their inevitable misery." In late adolescence, Leopardi's health began to break down—he became almost blind, his spine curved over—and his family encouraged him to become a priest. But he had begun to lose faith in God, and what followed was thoroughgoing, even paralyzing skepticism, as he began to see human life as little more than agonizing suffering. Even as he grew to be a famous poet, he remained almost completely trapped in his parents' house, with no income of his own. He had three painful experiences of unrequited love, and died at the age of thirty-nine.

It is not surprising, then, that Leopardi is, above all, a poet of despair, one who casts life as doomed, sorrowful, and purposeless. And yet both natural and artistic beauty seem to provide a brief respite from this anguish. His own art has often felt to readers strangely uplifting, filled with pleasure and solace, despite the sadness of his themes. In his most famous lyric, "The Infinite" (1819), the poet has the sublime feeling—both pleasurable and frightening—of imagining infinity, which extends beyond his own restricted vision, and he willingly celebrates the feeling of drowning in this endlessness. Readers have long appreciated the musical beauty of "To Silvia" (1828). The despairing late poem "To Himself" (1833) was written after Leopardi had been rejected by a woman he loved. While most other Italian Romantic writers looked outward—toward national political struggles—Leopardi resolutely turned inward, to explore the painful intensity of an individual human life.

The Infinite[1]

This lonely hill has always been so dear
To me, and dear the hedge which hides away
The reaches of the sky. But sitting here
And wondering, I fashion in my mind
The endless spaces far beyond, the more 5
Than human silences, and deepest peace;
So that the heart is on the edge of fear.

---

1. All three poems are translated by Ottavio M. Casale.

And when I hear the wind come blowing through
The trees, I pit its voice against that boundless
Silence and summon up eternity,   10
And the dead seasons, and the present one,
Alive with all its sound. And thus it is
In this immensity my thought is drowned:
And sweet to me the foundering in this sea.

To Himself

Now you may rest forever,
My tired heart. The last illusion is dead
That I believed eternal. Dead. I can
So clearly see—not only hope is gone
But the desire to be deceived as well.   5
Rest, rest forever.
You have beaten long enough. Nothing is worth
Your smallest motion, nor the earth your sighs.
This life is bitterness
And vacuum, nothing else. The world is mud.   10
From now on calm yourself.
Despair for the last time. The only gift
Fate gave our kind was death. Henceforth, heap scorn
Upon yourself, Nature, the ugly force
That, hidden, orders universal ruin,   15
And the boundless emptiness of everything.

To Sylvia

Sylvia. Do you remember still
The moments of your mortal lifetime here,
When such a loveliness
Shone in the elusive laughter of your eyes,
And you, contemplative and gay, climbed toward   5
The summit of your youth?

The tranquil chambers held,
The paths re-echoed, your perpetual song,
When at your woman's tasks
You sat, content to concentrate upon   10
The future beckoning within your mind.
It was the fragrant May,
And thus you passed your time.

I often used to leave
The dear, belabored pages which consumed   15
So much of me and of my youth, and from

Ancestral balconies
Would lean to hear the music of your voice,
Your fingers humming through
The intricacies of the weaving work.   20
And I would gaze upon
The blue surrounding sky,
The paths and gardens golden in the sun,
And there the far-off sea, and here the mountain.
No human tongue can tell   25
What I felt then within my brimming heart.

    What tendernesses then,
What hopes, what hearts were ours, O Sylvia mine!
How large a thing seemed life, and destiny!
When I recall those bright anticipations,   30
Bitterness invades,
And I turn once again to mourn my lot.
O Nature, Nature, why
Do you not keep the promises you gave?
Why trick the children so?   35

    Before the winter struck the summer grass,
You died, my gentle girl,
Besieged by hidden illness and possessed.
You never saw the flowering of your years.
Your heart was never melted by the praise   40
Of your dark hair, your shy,
Enamoured eyes. Nor did you with your friends
Conspire on holidays to talk of love.

    The expectation failed
As soon for me, and fate denied my youth.   45
Ah how gone by, gone by,
You dear companion of my dawning time,
The hope that I lament!
Is this the world we knew? And these the joys
The love, the labors, happenings we shared?   50
And this the destiny
Of human beings? My poor one, when
The truth rose up, you fell,
And from afar you pointed me the way
To coldest death and the stark sepulchre.   55

ELIZABETH BARRETT BROWNING
1806–1861

Elizabeth Barrett Browning was by far the most famous woman poet writing in English in the nineteenth century. She was adored to the point of hero-worship both in England and in the United States. In her view, poetry was capable of acting as a powerful vehicle for social protest, and in fact, when she wrote about slavery, women's rights, prostitution, and child labor, her audiences were often inspired to vocal debate and political action. Though widely acclaimed as both a poetic genius and a moral authority, after her death her fame was eclipsed by that of her husband, Robert Browning, and later writers dismissed her as a sentimental feminine soul rather than an accomplished poet in her own right. But this was a mistake. Few poets have been more technically skilled than Barrett Browning. She uses a vast range of existing poetic forms with staggering dexterity and subtlety, and when these forms are not enough, she boldly invents strange and innovative new rhythms, stanza structures, and rhyme schemes.

The eldest of twelve children, Elizabeth Barrett Moulton-Barrett was born to a prosperous English family that had made its money from slave plantations in Jamaica. Her education was highly unusual for an Englishwoman of her time: sitting in on her brother's private lessons, she learned Latin and Greek, and later taught herself Hebrew. She began writing poetry at the age of six and published her first volume at thirteen. Exceptionally learned, she translated the ancient Greek dramatist Aeschylus and experimented with writing epic poetry—something women were strongly discouraged from doing. As she came to understand the source of her family's wealth, she deliberately tried to distance herself from slavery, both renouncing money earned from plantation labor and writing antislavery poetry for abolitionist periodicals in the United States. A mysterious lung disease and a fall from a horse made her an invalid, and she spent much of her early adulthood confined to her bedroom, addicted to morphine. Her tyrannical father wanted none of his children to marry and leave his house, and he kept her secluded even as she became an increasingly prominent poet. This was to change, however, when the young poet Robert Browning launched a passionate correspondence with her. In 1846, when she was 39 and he 33, they eloped to Italy, where she recovered her strength and bore a son. The following years were exceptionally happy and productive. Elizabeth Barrett Browning died, in her husband's arms, unforgiven by her father, in 1861.

"The Cry of the Children" appeared in response to a government report about child laborers in mines and factories, who were expected to work as many as sixteen hours a day unprotected by any safety regulations. Rejecting the intensely personal voice of lyric poetry, Barrett Browning here makes confrontational direct addresses to her readers and adopts a collective first-person-plural "we" for the voice of the child workers. She also invents an uncomfortable, confrontational new rhythm rather than relying on existing poetic conventions. One reviewer wrote that "the cadence, lingering, broken, and full of wail, is one of the most perfect adaptations of sound to sense in literature." This poem was so powerful that Barrett Browning was credited with inspiring the British parliament to pass new laws regulating child labor.

Very different in tone and form are the *Sonnets from the Portuguese*—a series of love poems which Barrett Browning presented as if they were translations from a fictional Portuguese original. Typically, in these poems, she will use a single dominant image—the musician, the colorful gift, the sacrifice—and follow the logic of this image to a surprising conclusion. For example, in Sonnet III, she pictures her beloved as the chief musician at a royal court, while she is stuck outside, the wandering minstrel. But while casting herself as a marginal figure humbles her, it also masculinizes her in a context where women are closely associated with the home, deliberately shut in rather than out. Always noteworthy is the poet's use of the *volta*, or "turn" in the sonnet form—a break between the first two quatrains (sets of four lines) and the closing six lines. Barrett Browning will often turn here from question to answer, or from beloved to lover. But in the case of her most famous sonnet, "How Do I Love Thee? Let Me Count the Ways," it is intriguing to note that she makes no obvious turn at all.

In her own time, Barrett Browning's fierce frankness on politics, women's desire, and the power of poetry consistently drew attention to the ways that she defied conventional feminine constraints. One of her contemporaries wrote that she was the first woman writer to mix "masculine vigour, breadth, and culture" with "feminine subtlety of perception, feminine quickness of sensibility, and feminine tenderness."

The Cry of the Children

"Φευ, φευ, τιπροσδερκεσθέ μ' ὄμμασιν, τέκνα;"
—*Medea*[1]

Do ye hear the children weeping, O my brothers,
    Ere the sorrow comes with years?
They are leaning their young heads against their mothers,
    And *that* cannot stop their tears.
The young lambs are bleating in the meadows,   5
    The young birds are chirping in the nest,
The young fawns are playing with the shadows,
    The young flowers are blowing toward the west—
But the young, young children, O my brothers,
    They are weeping bitterly!   10
They are weeping in the playtime of the others,
    In the country of the free.

Do you question the young children in the sorrow
    Why their tears are falling so?

---

1. Greek tragedy by Euripides (ca. 480–406 B.C.E.) about the mythological figure of Medea, a mother who kills her own children; Medea speaks the line in Greek: "Alas, my children, why do you look at me?"

The old man may weep for his to-morrow   15
    Which is lost in Long Ago;
The old tree is leafless in the forest,
    The old year is ending in the frost,
The old wound, if stricken, is the sorest,
    The old hope is hardest to be lost: 20
But the young, young children, O my brothers,
    Do you ask them why they stand
Weeping sore before the bosoms of their mothers,
    In our happy Fatherland?

They look up with their pale and sunken faces,   25
    And their looks are sad to see,
For the man's hoary anguish draws and presses
    Down the cheeks of infancy;
"Your old earth," they say, "is very dreary,"
    "Our young feet," they say, "are very weak;   30
Few paces have we taken, yet are weary—
    Our grave-rest is very far to seek:
Ask the aged why they weep, and not the children,
    For the outside earth is cold,
And we young ones stand without, in our bewildering,   35
    And the graves are for the old."

"True," say the children, "it may happen
    That we die before our time:
Little Alice died last year, her grave is shapen
    Like a snowball, in the rime.   40
We looked into the pit prepared to take her:
    Was no room for any work in the close clay!
From the sleep wherein she lieth none will wake her,
    Crying, 'Get up, little Alice! it is day.'
If you listen by that grave, in sun and shower,   45
    With your ear down, little Alice never cries;
Could we see her face, be sure we should not know her,
    For the smile has time for growing in her eyes:
And merry go her moments, lulled and stilled in
    The shroud by the kirk[2] chime.   50
It is good when it happens," say the children,
    "That we die before our time."

Alas, alas, the children! they are seeking
    Death in life, as best to have:
They are binding up their hearts away from breaking,   55
    With a ceremen[3] from the grave.
Go out, children, from the mine and from the city,
    Sing out, children, as the little thrushes do;
Pluck your handfuls of the meadow-cowslips pretty,
    Laugh aloud, to feel your fingers let them through! 60

2. Church.   3. Shroud.

But they answer, "Are your cowslips of the meadows
    Like our weeds anear the mine?
Leave us quiet in the dark of the coal-shadows,
    From your pleasures fair and fine!

"For oh," say the children, "we are weary,   65
    And we cannot run or leap;
If we cared for any meadows, it were merely
    To drop down in them and sleep.
Our knees tremble sorely in the stooping,
  We fall upon our faces, trying to go;   70
And, underneath our heavy eyelids drooping,
  The reddest flower would look as pale as snow.
For, all day, we drag our burden tiring
    Through the coal-dark, underground;
Or, all day, we drive the wheels of iron   75
    In the factories, round and round.

"For, all day, the wheels are droning, turning;
    Their wind comes in our faces,
Till our hearts turn, our heads with pulses burning,
    And the walls turn in their places: 80
Turns the sky in the high window blank and reeling,
  Turns the long light that drops adown the wall,
Turn the black flies that crawl along the ceiling,
  All are turning, all the day, and we with all.
And all day, the iron wheels are droning,   85
    And sometimes we could pray,
'O ye wheels,' (breaking out in a mad moaning)
    'Stop! be silent for to-day!'"

Ay, be silent! Let them hear each other breathing
    For a moment, mouth to mouth!   90
Let them touch each other's hands, in a fresh wreathing
    Of their tender human youth!
Let them feel that this cold metallic motion
  Is not all the life God fashions or reveals:
Let them prove their living souls against the notion   95
  That they live in you, or under you, O wheels!
Still, all day, the iron wheels go onward,
    Grinding life down from its mark;
And the children's souls, which God is calling sunward,
    Spin on blindly in the dark.   100

Now tell the poor young children; O my brothers,
    To look up to Him and pray;
So the blessed One who blesseth all the others,
    Will bless them another day.
They answer, "Who is God that He should hear us,   105
  While the rushing of the iron wheels is stirred?
When we sob aloud, the human creatures near us

Pass by, hearing not, or answer not a word.
And *we* hear not (for the wheels in their resounding)
    Strangers speaking at the door: 110
Is it likely God, with angels singing round Him,
    Hears our weeping any more?

Two words, indeed, of praying we remember,
    And at midnight's hour of harm,
'Our Father,' looking upward in the chamber, 115
    We say softly for a charm.
We know no other words except 'Our Father.'
    And we think that, in some pause of angels' song,
God may pluck them with the silence sweet to gather,
    And hold both within His right hand which is strong. 120
'Our Father!' If He heard us, He would surely
    (For they call Him good and mild)
Answer, smiling down the steep world very purely,
    'Come and rest with me, my child.'

"But, no!" say the children, weeping faster, 125
    "He is speechless as a stone:
And they tell us, of His image is the master
    Who commands us to work on.
Go to!" say the children,—"up in Heaven,
    Dark, wheel-like, turning clouds are all we find. 130
Do not mock us; grief has made us unbelieving:
    We look up for God, but tears have made us blind."
Do you hear the children weeping and disproving,
    O my brothers, what ye preach?
For God's possible is taught by His world's loving, 135
    And the children doubt of each.

And well may the children weep before you!
    They are weary ere they run;
They have never seen the sunshine, nor the glory
    Which is brighter than the sun. 140
They know the grief of man, without its wisdom;
    They sink in man's despair, without its calm;
Are slaves, without the liberty in Christdom,
    Are martyrs, by the pang without the palm:
Are worn as if with age, yet unretrievingly 145
    The harvest of its memories cannot reap,—
Are orphans of the earthly love and heavenly.
    Let them weep! let them weep!

They look up with their pale and sunken faces,
    And their look is dread to see, 150
For they mind you of their angels in high places,
    With eyes turned on Deity.
"How long," they say, "how long, O cruel nation,
    Will you stand, to move the world, on a child's heart,—

Stifle down with a mailed[4] heel its palpitation,   155
    And tread onward to your throne amid the mart?
Our blood splashes upward, O gold-heaper,
    And your purple shows your path!
But the child's sob in the silence curses deeper
    Than the strong man in his wrath."   160

From Sonnets from the Portuguese

III

Unlike are we, unlike, O princely Heart!
Unlike our uses and our destinies.
Our ministering two angels look surprise
On one another, as they strike athwart
Their wings in passing. Thou, bethink thee, art   5
A guest for queens to social pageantries,
With gages from a hundred brighter eyes
Than tears even can make mine, to play thy part
Of chief musician. What hast *thou* to do
With looking from the lattice-lights at me,   10
A poor, tired, wandering singer, singing through
The dark, and leaning up a cypress tree?[1]
The chrism is on thine head,—on mine, the dew,—
And Death must dig the level where these agree.

VIII

What can I give thee back, O liberal
And princely giver, who hast brought the gold
And purple[2] of thine heart, unstained, untold,
And laid them on the outside of the wall
For such as I to take or leave withal,   5
In unexpected largesse? am I cold,
Ungrateful, that for these most manifold
High gifts, I render nothing back at all?
Not so; not cold,—but very poor instead.
Ask God who knows. For frequent tears have run   10
The colours from my life, and left so dead
And pale a stuff, it were not fitly done
To give the same as pillow to thy head.
Go farther! let it serve to trample on.

---

4. Armored, as with chainmail.
1. The cypress was connected to death in both
Greek and Roman mythology.

2. Traditionally, purple comes from a dye so
expensive that it was reserved for royalty.

XXXV

If I leave all for thee, wilt thou exchange
And be all to me? Shall I never miss
Home-talk and blessing and the common kiss
That comes to each in turn, nor count it strange,
When I look up, to drop on a new range   5
Of walls and floors, another home than this?
Nay, wilt thou fill that place by me which is
Filled by dead eyes too tender to know change?
That's hardest. If to conquer love, has tried,
To conquer grief, tries more, as all things prove;   10
For grief indeed is love and grief beside.
Alas, I have grieved so I am hard to love.
Yet love me—wilt thou? Open thine heart wide,
And fold within the wet wings of thy dove.

XLIII

How do I love thee? Let me count the ways.
I love thee to the depth and breadth and height
My soul can reach, when feeling out of sight
For the ends of Being and ideal Grace.
I love thee to the level of everyday's   5
Most quiet need, by sun and candlelight.
I love thee freely, as men strive for Right;
I love thee purely, as they turn from Praise.
I love thee with the passion put to use
In my old griefs, and with my childhood's faith.   10
I love thee with a love I seemed to lose
With my lost saints,—I love thee with the breath,
Smiles, tears, of all my life!—and, if God choose,
I shall but love thee better after death.

ALFRED, LORD TENNYSON
1809–1892

Alfred Tennyson exerted such a powerful influence on English poetry in the nineteenth century that the rebellious American poet **Walt Whitman** called him "the Boss." By the last decades of the century, British audiences looked to this post-Romantic poet as a voice of the whole nation, and readers of all classes could recite at least a few of his poems from memory.

Many of his poems were set to music, and his works became a standard part of school curricula in Britain, the United States, Ireland, and India well into the twentieth century. The Modernist writers who followed found Tennyson's influence so stifling that they struggled to reject his legacy. (The Irish novelist **James Joyce** mockingly renamed him "Lawn Tennyson" to suggest that the poetry was tame and trivial.) And yet, Tennyson's appeal has long outlasted his fiercest critics. Using gorgeously melodious language to investigate the intensities of love, loss, longing, doubt, and despair, Tennyson remains one of the most moving of English poets.

Growing up in a family troubled by drunkenness, violence, and madness, Alfred Tennyson was the fourth of twelve children born in the space of fourteen years. The family was descended from the highest ranks of the aristocracy, but Tennyson's own father had been disinherited: he struggled to make ends meet while his younger brother enjoyed the immense riches of the ancestral estate. Given to paranoia and raging, abusive violence, Tennyson's father sunk into alcoholism in the 1820s. As soon as he could, Tennyson escaped the family home for Cambridge University. There he joined an undergraduate society called the Apostles, many of whom would become the leading intellectual lights of the nineteenth century in England. In particular he befriended a talented and brilliant young man named Arthur Henry Hallam, who encouraged Tennyson to write poetry, predicting that he would be recognized as the most important poetic genius of his time. Hallam died suddenly in 1833 at age twenty-two, plunging Tennyson into grief. He would later memorialize his friend in his great and wide-ranging elegy, *In Memoriam* (1850).

Tennyson's first two volumes of poetry, published in the 1830s, broke in surprising ways with Romantic themes and conventions. In luxuriantly musical cadences that evoked moods, personalities, and sensations, these poems seemed to their first audiences technically and thematically adventurous. Many of them explored an inexplicable melancholy and immobility. Reviewers at the time offered mostly harsh words, considering the work mystifying and pretentious. With his later volumes, Tennyson's fame and popularity grew; he became the favorite poet of Queen Victoria, who named him Poet Laureate in 1850. And yet, as Tennyson gained recognition, he lost some of his daringly experimental edge.

In his greatest early works, Tennyson explores feelings, thoughts, and experiences not through the poet's own voice, as the Romantics so often did, but instead through figures other than himself—for instance, Ulysses, the hero of Homer's *Odyssey*. Tennyson wrote many poems in a genre called the dramatic monologue: a poem, such as *Ulysses*, in which the writer adopts a persona and speaks in the first person from that perspective.

Tennyson not only rejects himself as the source of poetic emotion, he also explores odd, neglected moments from the lives of the characters he chooses: in this case, Ulysses as an old man, when his celebrated days of heroic action are over. Tennyson draws on great literary forebears—Shakespeare, Homer, the Arthurian tradition—and yet concentrates on marginal experiences which his precursors ignored. Homer, after all, did not bother to think about what it might be like to be an epic hero past his prime. Tennyson's poems therefore rethink what literary tradition has left out.

Notably, too, Tennyson departs from many of the Romantic poets in his evocations of nature. Ulysses broods on that which lies beyond the natural and social environments that confine him. With

Tennyson, nature ceases to provide a model, an outlet, or a source of solace, while social relations remain broken and discouraging. His is a bleaker, less prom- ising world than that of the Romantics— but it is also one that has resonated with readers from that day to this.

Ulysses[1]

It little profits that an idle king,
By this still hearth, among these barren crags,
Matched with an aged wife, I mete and dole
Unequal laws unto a savage race,
That hoard, and sleep, and feed, and know not me.   5
   I cannot rest from travel; I will drink
Life to the lees.[2] All times I have enjoyed
Greatly, have suffered greatly, both with those
That loved me, and alone; on shore, and when
Through scudding drifts the rainy Hyades[3]   10
Vexed the dim sea. I am become a name;
For always roaming with a hungry heart
Much have I seen and known—cities of men
And manners, climates, councils, governments,
Myself not least, but honored of them all—   15
And drunk delight of battle with my peers,
Far on the ringing plains of windy Troy,
I am a part of all that I have met;
Yet all experience is an arch wherethrough
Gleams that untraveled world whose margin fades   20
Forever and forever when I move.
How dull it is to pause, to make an end,
To rust unburnished, not to shine in use!
As though to breathe were life! Life piled on life
Were all too little, and of one to me   25
Little remains; but every hour is saved
From that eternal silence, something more,
A bringer of new things; and vile it were
For some three suns to store and hoard myself,
And this gray spirit yearning in desire   30

1. In Dante's *Inferno*, Ulysses—the Roman name for the Greek hero Odysseus—persuades his crew to go on a new adventure rather than return home to his wife in Ithaca; Tennyson merges Dante's Ulysses with Homer's Odysseus, giving us a character who has spent time in Ithaca and then, in old age, sets out on a new journey.
2. That is, to the very end. (Lees are the dregs that settle at the bottom of a bottle of wine.)
3. Cluster of stars supposed to portend rain.

To follow knowledge like a sinking star,
Beyond the utmost bound of human thought.

This is my son, mine own Telemachus,
To whom I leave the scepter and the isle—
Well-loved of me, discerning to fulfill   35
This labor, by slow prudence to make mild
A rugged people, and through soft degrees
Subdue them to the useful and the good.
Most blameless is he, centered in the sphere
Of common duties, decent not to fail   40
In offices of tenderness, and pay
Meet[4] adoration to my household gods,
When I am gone. He works his work, I mine.

There lies the port; the vessel puffs her sail;
There gloom the dark, broad seas. My mariners,   45
Souls that have toiled, and wrought, and thought with me—
That ever with a frolic welcome took
The thunder and the sunshine, and opposed
Free hearts, free foreheads—you and I are old;
Old age hath yet his honor and his toil.   50
Death closes all; but something ere the end,
Some work of noble note, may yet be done,
Not unbecoming men that strove with Gods.
The lights begin to twinkle from the rocks;
The long day wanes; the slow moon climbs; the deep   55
Moans round with many voices. Come, my friends,
'Tis not too late to seek a newer world.
Push off, and sitting well in order smite
The sounding furrows; for my purpose holds
To sail beyond the sunset, and the baths   60
Of all the western stars, until I die.
It may be that the gulfs will wash us down;
It may be we shall touch the Happy Isles,[5]
And see the great Achilles, whom we knew.
Though much is taken, much abides; and though   65
We are not now that strength which in old days
Moved earth and heaven, that which we are, we are—
One equal temper of heroic hearts,
Made weak by time and fate, but strong in will
To strive, to seek, to find, and not to yield.

4. Proper, appropriate.

5. Summery paradise in the western ocean for heroes.

WALT WHITMAN
1819–1892

Walt Whitman left an astonishing legacy. In rejecting conventional rhyme and meter he managed, almost single-handedly, to make free verse seem like the most appropriate form for a truly modern poetry. He insisted on a homegrown American art that would supplant European influence. He cast the poet as a fighter and a leader. He prized free and full sexual pleasure, celebrating "the body electric." And he gave voice to a vast range of ordinary people who had gone largely unnoticed by poets before him. "I am big—I contain multitudes," he wrote. Affirmative, inclusive, energetic, defiant, and radically experimental, Whitman ushered in a whole new era in American poetry.

LIFE

Born on Long Island, Whitman moved with his family to Brooklyn as a child. His father deeply admired American democracy, naming three of his sons George Washington, Thomas Jefferson, and Andrew Jackson. The young Whitman grew up among Deists and Quakers, creeds that favored an internal spirituality over formal religious doctrines. He left school at the age of eleven and worked odd jobs, first as a printer, later as a schoolteacher, builder, bookstore owner, journalist, and poet. He spent a few months in New Orleans and came to love the South, though he vehemently opposed slavery and petitioned to prevent its westward expansion. During the Civil War, Whitman felt a passionate admiration for Abraham Lincoln and was devoted to the Union cause. He was also deeply moved by the soldiers at the front, so much so that he went to Washington as a volunteer nurse, helping to care for the Civil War wounded and witnessing firsthand the devastating spectacle of corpses and amputated limbs. While in Washington he worked as a clerk in several government departments, including the Bureau of Indian Affairs. In 1865 Whitman met Peter Doyle, a young horsecar conductor who became his companion and almost certainly his lover. A few years later he settled in Camden, New Jersey, where he remained for the rest of his life.

WORK

Whitman began writing in his youth, producing a good deal of bad poetry and a novel about temperance, the movement advocating abstinence from alcohol. But something altogether different emerged in 1855 with his innovative collection of poems, *Leaves of Grass*. This volume departed from convention in startling ways. First of all, it did not look like the poetry of his contemporaries: there were no rhymes; the lines varied widely in length; and the words followed no particular rhythm. Second, the collection's themes were shocking: many readers were appalled by the unusually vivid sexual imagery and the intense evocations of bodily pleasure. Whitman also overturned convention by insisting on a vehemently democratic kind of verse, appealing to the common reader and celebrating the most overlooked people, from slaves and prostitutes to immigrants and prisoners. Finally, his poetic language was eccentrically various, moving between beauty and slang, between spirituality and obscenity. This was a poetry that aimed to include all of modern life. A poet fails, Whitman wrote, "if he does not flood himself with the immediate age as with vast oceanic tides . . . if he be not himself the age transfigured."

Whitman always loved the theater, and he deliberately adopted many voices and personae in his poetry. The *I* of his poems represents many selves. Perhaps most famously, the poet ventriloquizes a new urban type called the "b'hoy," a rebellious young working-class New Yorker known for his idle loafing and his willingness to fight, as well as his insolent, loud, slangy way of speaking. Whitman saw ordinary speech as the best source for poetry. "Language," he wrote, "is not an abstract construction of the learn'd, or of the dictionary-makers, but is something arising out of the work, needs, ties, joys, affections, tastes, of long generations of humanity, and has its bases broad and low, close to the ground. Its final decisions are made by the masses." Whitman's long lines also follow the patterns of ordinary language: rather than forming sentences broken up in accordance with conventions of rhyme or meter, each line is a statement complete in itself.

The innovations of *Leaves of Grass* did not sit well with the volume's first readers. "Walt Whitman," wrote one reviewer, "is as unacquainted with art as a hog is with mathematics." Another dismissed the book as "a mass of stupid filth." Even Henry David Thoreau said, "It is as if beasts spoke." Whitman was unperturbed by these attacks: he had intended to unsettle his readers, and he even publicized his most venomous reviews as a way of promoting his work.

But Whitman would soon come to be seen as one of the great poets of the United States, perhaps the greatest. In part this was because the nation was such a crucial focus for his work. He was deliberately writing a new, quin-

tessentially American poetry, an art form that would leave European values and traditions behind to celebrate a modern, pluralistic democracy. At a moment when Europe was widely assumed to represent the standard for art and culture, Whitman wrote: "The Americans of all nations at any time upon the earth, have probably the fullest poetical nature. The United States themselves are essentially the greatest poem." And if the nation was a poem, the poet was its best leader. With the exception of Lincoln, Whitman despised politicians ("swarms of cringers, suckers, doughfaces, planners of the sly involutions for their own preferment to city offices or state legislatures or the judiciary or congress or the presidency"), and, as the United States fractured on the eve of Civil War, he imagined the poet alone as capable of healing and uniting the nation.

His way of healing, of course, involved confrontation and defiance. "I think agitation is the most important factor of all," he wrote. "To stir, to question, to suspect, to examine, to denounce!" What upset his contemporaries most was his willingness to defy conventions of silence around sex and sexuality. In 1882 he was threatened with an obscenity prosecution. Intriguingly, Whitman's contemporaries objected more to his eroticized representations of women than to the explicit expressions of male-male desire that appear often in his works. This was a cultural and historical context in which the "manly love" Whitman celebrated could be understood in idealized, nonsexual terms.

Whitman reworked *Leaves of Grass* many times, revising old poems and including new ones. Over time, he included explicitly patriotic work and toned down the most sexually offensive passages. By the end of his life he had come to seem not the rebellious purveyor of scandalous experiments, but simply "the good gray poet."

From Song of Myself[1]

I

I celebrate myself, and sing myself,
And what I assume you shall assume,
For every atom belonging to me as good belongs to you.

I loafe and invite my soul,
I lean and loafe at my ease observing a spear of summer grass.   5

My tongue, every atom of my blood, formed from this soil, this air,
Born here of parents born here from parents the same, and their parents
     the same,
I, now thirty-seven years old in perfect health begin,
Hoping to cease not till death.

Creeds and schools in abeyance,   10
Retiring back a while sufficed at what they are, but never forgotten,
I harbor for good or bad, I permit to speak at every hazard,
Nature without check with original energy.

* * *

4

Trippers and askers surround me,
People I meet, the effect upon me of my early life or the ward and city
     I live in, or the nation,
The latest dates, discoveries, inventions, societies, authors old and new,
My dinner, dress, associates, looks, compliments, dues,
The real or fancied indifference of some man or woman I love,   5
The sickness of one of my folks or of myself, or ill-doing or loss or lack of
     money, or depressions or exaltations,
Battles, the horrors of fratricidal war, the fever of doubtful news, the fitful
     events;
These come to me days and nights and go from me again,
But they are not the Me myself.

Apart from the pulling and hauling stands what I am,   10
Stands amused, complacent, compassionating, idle, unitary,
Looks down, is erect, or bends an arm on an impalpable certain rest,
Looking with side-curved head curious what will come next,
Both in and out of the game and watching and wondering at it.

Backward I see in my own days where I sweated through fog with linguists and
     contenders,
I have no mockings or arguments, I witness and wait.   15

* * *

1. First published in 1855. This text is from the 1891–92 edition of *Leaves of Grass*, the so-
called Deathbed Edition.

7

Has any one supposed it lucky to be born?
I hasten to inform him or her it is just as lucky to die, and I know it.

I pass death with the dying and birth with the new-washed babe, and
    am not contained between my hat and boots,
And peruse manifold objects, no two alike and every one good,
The earth good and the stars good, and their adjuncts all good.   5

I am not an earth nor an adjunct of an earth,
I am the mate and companion of people, all just as immortal and fathomless as
    myself,
(They do not know how immortal, but I know.)

Every kind for itself and its own, for me mine male and female,
For me those that have been boys and that love women,   10
For me the man that is proud and feels how it stings to be slighted,
For me the sweet-heart and the old maid, for me mothers and the mothers
    of mothers,
For me lips that have smiled, eyes that have shed tears,
For me children and the begetters of children.

Undrape! you are not guilty to me, nor stale nor discarded,   15
I see through the broadcloth and gingham whether or no,
And am around, tenacious, acquisitive, tireless, and cannot be shaken away.

* * *

16

I am of old and young, of the foolish as much as the wise,
Regardless of others, ever regardful of others,
Maternal as well as paternal, a child as well as a man,
Stuffed with the stuff that is coarse and stuffed with the stuff that is fine,
One of the Nation of many nations, the smallest the same and the largest
    the same,   5
A Southerner soon as a Northerner, a planter nonchalant and hospitable down
    by the Oconee[2] I live,
A Yankee bound my own was ready for trade, my joints the limberest joints
    on earth and the sternest joints on earth,
A Kentuckian walking the vale of the Elkhorn in my deer-skin leggings, a
    Louisianian or Georgian,
A boatman over lakes or bays or along coasts, a Hoosier, Badger, Buckeye;
At home on Kanadian snow-shoes or up in the bush, or with fishermen off
    Newfoundland,   10
At home in the fleet of ice-boats, sailing with the rest and tacking,
At home on the hills of Vermont or in the woods of Maine, or the Texan
    ranch,

2. River in Georgia.

Comrade of Californians, comrade of free North-Westerners, (loving their
    big proportions,)
Comrade of raftsmen and coalmen, comrade of all who shake hands and
    welcome to drink and meat,
A learner with the simplest, a teacher of the thoughtfullest,   15
A novice beginning yet experient of myriads of seasons,
Of every hue and caste am I, of every rank and religion,
A farmer, mechanic, artist, gentleman, sailor, quaker,
Prisoner, fancy-man, rowdy, lawyer, physician, priest.

I resist any thing better than my own diversity,   20
Breathe the air but leave plenty after me,
And am not stuck up, and am in my place.

(The moth and the fish-eggs are in their place,
The bright suns I see and the dark suns I cannot see are in their place,
The palpable is in its place and the impalpable is in its place.)   25

*   *   *

21

I am the poet of the Body and I am the poet of the Soul,
The pleasures of heaven are with me and the pains of hell are with me,
The first I graft and increase upon myself, the latter I translate into a new
    tongue.

I am the poet of the woman the same as the man,
And I say it is as great to be a woman as to be a man,   5
And I say there is nothing greater than the mother of men.

I chant the chant of dilation or pride,
We have had ducking and deprecating about enough,
I show that size is only development.

Have you outstript the rest? are you the President?   10
It is a trifle, they will more than arrive there every one, and still pass on.

I am he that walks with the tender and growing night,
I call to the earth and sea half-held by the night.

Press close bare-bosomed night—press close magnetic nourishing night!
Night of south winds—night of the large few stars!   15
Still nodding night—mad naked summer night.

Smile O voluptuous cool-breathed earth!
Earth of the slumbering and liquid trees!
Earth of departed sunset—earth of the mountains misty-topt!
Earth of the vitreous pour of the full moon just tinged with blue!   20
Earth of shine and dark mottling the tide of the river!
Earth of the limpid gray of clouds brighter and clearer for my sake!

Far-swooping elbowed earth—rich apple-blossomed earth!
Smile, for your lover comes.

Prodigal, you have given me love—therefore I to you give love!   25
O unspeakable passionate love.

* * *

24

Walt Whitman, a kosmos, of Manhattan the son,
Turbulent, fleshy, sensual, eating, drinking and breeding,
No sentimentalist, no stander above men and women or apart from them,
No more modest than immodest.

Unscrew the locks from the doors!   5
Unscrew the doors themselves from their jambs!

Whoever degrades another degrades me,
And whatever is done or said returns at last to me.

Through me the afflatus surging and surging, through me the current and
     index.

I speak the pass-word primeval, I give the sign of democracy,   10
By God! I will accept nothing which all cannot have their counterpart of
     on the same terms.

* * *

32

I think I could turn and live with animals, they are so placid and self-
     contained,
I stand and look at them long and long.

They do not sweat and whine about their condition,
They do not lie awake in the dark and weep for their sins,
They do not make me sick discussing their duty to God,   5
Not one is dissatisfied, not one is demented with the mania of owning things,
Not one kneels to another, nor to his kind that lived thousands of years ago,
Not one is respectable or unhappy over the whole earth.

So they show their relations to me and I accept them,
They bring me tokens of myself, they evince them plainly in their
     possession.   10

I wonder where they get those tokens,
Did I pass that way huge times ago and negligently drop them?

Myself moving forward then and now and forever,
Gathering and showing more always and with velocity,

Infinite and omnigenous,[3] and the like of these among them,   15
Not too exclusive toward the reachers of my remembrancers,
Picking out here one that I love, and now go with him on brotherly terms.

A gigantic beauty of a stallion, fresh and responsive to my caresses,
Head high in the forehead, wide between the ears,
Limbs glossy and supple, tail dusting the ground,   20
Eyes full of sparkling wickedness, ears finely cut, flexibly moving.

His nostrils dilate as my heels embrace him,
His well-built limbs tremble with pleasure as we race around and return.

I but use you a minute, then I resign you, stallion,
Why do I need your paces when I myself out-gallop them?   25
Even as I stand or sit passing faster than you.

* * *

46

I know I have the best of time and space, and was never measured and
    never will be measured.

I tramp a perpetual journey, (come listen all!)
My signs are a rain-proof coat, good shoes, and a staff cut from the woods,
No friend of mine takes his ease in my chair,
I have no chair, no church, no philosophy,   5
I lead no man to a dinner-table, library, exchange,
But each man and each woman of you I lead upon a knoll,
My left hand hooking you round the waist,
My right hand pointing to landscapes of continents and the public road.
Not I, not any one else can travel that road for you,   10
You must travel it for yourself.

It is not far, it is within reach,
Perhaps you have been on it since you were born and did not know,
Perhaps it is everywhere on water and on land.

Shoulder your duds dear son, and I will mine, and let us hasten forth,   15
Wonderful cities and free nations we shall fetch as we go.

* * *

51

The past and present wilt—I have filled them, emptied them,
And proceed to fill my next fold of the future.

Listener up there! what have you to confide to me?
Look in my face while I snuff the sidle of evening[4]

---

3. Belonging to all races.   4. I.e., smell the fragrance of the slowly
                                                 descending evening.

(Talk honestly, no one else hears you, and I stay only a minute longer.)   5
Do I contradict myself?
Very well then I contradict myself,
(I am large, I contain multitudes.)

I concentrate toward them that are nigh, I wait on the door-slab.

Who has done his day's work? who will soonest be through with his
   supper?   10
Who wishes to walk with me?

Will you speak before I am gone? will you prove already too late?

52

The spotted hawk swoops by and accuses me, he complains of my gab
  and my loitering.

I too am not a bit tamed, I too am untranslatable,
I sound my barbaric yawp over the roofs of the world.

The last scud of day holds back for me,
It flings my likeness after the rest and true as any on the shadowed wilds,   5
It coaxes me to the vapor and the dusk.

I depart as air, I shake my white locks at the runaway sun,
I effuse my flesh in eddies, and drift it in lacy jags.

I bequeath myself to the dirt to grow from the grass I love,
If you want me again look for me under your boot-soles.   10

You will hardly know who I am or what I mean,
But I shall be good health to you nevertheless,
And filter and fibre your blood.

Failing to fetch me at first keep encouraged,
Missing me one place search another,   15
I stop somewhere waiting for you.

CHARLES BAUDELAIRE
1821–1867

Crowds and prostitutes, boredom and hypocrisy, garbage and cheap perfume: from these ugly materials, Charles Baudelaire crafted such shocking, painful, and exquisite poetry that he became the most widely read French poet around the globe. Haunted by a vision of human nature as fallen and corrupt, he was drawn to explore his own weaknesses and transgressions, as well as the sins of society. Lust, hatred, laziness, a disabling self-awareness, a horror of death and decay, and above all an all-encompassing *ennui*—a kind of disgusted, existential boredom—consumed the poet. But it is not only this anguished worldview that makes Baudelaire so significant: for many thinkers who followed, he opened the way to understanding what it means to be modern, to live in the exciting, disorienting, technologically changing, often hideous world of the industrialized city. And for writers, what is so extraordinary about Baudelaire is that he examined the unsettling shocks of modernity through perfectly controlled and beautiful art forms.

LIFE

Born in Paris in 1821, Baudelaire quickly became a rebellious youth. His elderly father died when he was six, and his mother married a stern military man whom the young Baudelaire came to detest. In his late teens, he was expelled from boarding school and sent away on a boat to India to remove him from bad influences. He jumped ship on the African island of Mauritius, then slowly wended his way home without ever reaching India. Back in Paris, he began to consort with artists, bohemians, and prostitutes in the famous Latin Quarter. By his early twenties, he had contracted syphilis and had started to spend his father's inheritance with alarming speed, buying up gorgeous furniture, dandyish clothing, and costly paintings. In 1842 he fell passionately in love with a woman named Jeanne Duval, an actress of African descent, who lived with him on and off for most of his adult life. To his family, he seemed to be going nowhere. His mother was disturbed at his spending habits and obtained a court order to control his finances. Humiliated, Baudelaire remained for the rest of his life dependent on an allowance dispensed by the family lawyer.

In 1845 he published a work of art criticism that established his reputation as a writer, and he would go on to write important reviews of painting and photography, championing the most daring contemporary art. In the 1850s he reviewed and translated the works of American writer Edgar Allan Poe, who shared his dedication to beauty, his fascination with death, and his passion for perfectly crafted writing. Only in 1857, at the age of thirty-six, did his first slim volume of poetry appear. With its horrifyingly evocative images of lust, duplicity, and decay, *The Flowers of Evil* was fully intended to scandalize its readers. It succeeded. French authorities seized the book and fined the writer, making Baudelaire famous—but more reviled than admired. Ever more ill and in debt, Baudelaire spent his last years in distress. He added new poems to *The Flowers of Evil* and began to write some experimental works that would come to be known as *Paris Spleen*. He died in 1867, leaving behind few admirers. At the graveside, in the pouring rain, accompanied by a few stragglers, only one close friend predicted that Baudelaire would someday be recognized as a "poet of genius."

BAUDELAIRE'S PARIS

Most French poets of the first half of the nineteenth century were drawn to the beauties of the natural world: to mountains, lakes, and flowers. Baudelaire was different. "I find myself incapable of feeling moved by vegetation," he wrote. Instead, he observed the social life of the city.

At the time, Paris was an exciting and disorienting place. It grew rapidly over the first few decades of the nineteenth century, as new industries drew peasants from the impoverished countryside in search of work. Competing for badly paid jobs, the urban poor were visible everywhere, many of them sick from factory smoke, or reduced to beggary and prostitution. Also visible in the city, however, were the glossy carriages and flamboyant dresses of the rich. Commentators often remarked that on a single stroll through the city one might find ragpickers searching through street refuse for scraps to sell, as well as glittering new shopping arcades offering seductive, mass-produced commodities for wealthy consumers. Everything in this modern world, it seemed, could be bought and sold.

During the 1850s the streets of Paris underwent a huge transformation, as the government razed winding old alleyways and installed clean, wide boulevards in their place. These smooth streets radiated outward to allow easy access to the city center from many directions. The poor were evicted and moved in large numbers to the suburbs, while gleaming new apartment houses, street cafes, shops, and theaters rose up quickly. In this new urban milieu, one encountered vast numbers of strangers. Dramatically unlike village life, the city typically felt both crowded and lonely, both stimulating and alienating. Baudelaire used the term *flâneur*—meaning "saunterer"—to refer to those who wandered alone and detached through urban streets to experience the city's fleeting spectacles. Many of the first *flâneurs* were writers who found a new kind of inspiration in this fragmented experience. And so the bustling commercial city became an important literary theme, supplanting rural beauty for self-consciously "modern" writers in the decades to follow.

WORK

It is difficult to grasp just how shocking Baudelaire's work must have seemed to his contemporaries. French poets before him typically worked in what was called the "noble style," which was formal and elevated, deliberately remote from everyday speech. Poets were not supposed to refer to ordinary objects (even the word "nose" was forbidden as prosaic). We can only imagine, then, how outrageous Baudelaire's deliberately brutal wording— "pissing hogwash" or "lecherous whore"— must have seemed. And not only did he offer up explicit, often coarse, images of the body, but his contemporaries were horrified to find him willing to connect sexual desire to the horrors of sadism and putrefaction, as we see in his poem "A Carcass."

And yet it would be misleading to see Baudelaire as rejecting beauty: he luxuriated in gorgeous, lavish, and exotic images, and crafted passages of lyrical magnificence. Unlike some of his other rebellious-poet contemporaries—such as **Walt Whitman**, born just two years before him—Baudelaire loved strictly traditional metrical forms and rhyme schemes. And so it is worth exploring the ways that the poet associates the shockingly foul with the traditionally lovely. Even the very title of his volume, *The Flowers of Evil*, signals the juxtaposition of beauty with corruption.

Always attracted by dissonance and contrast, Baudelaire is famous for his irony—his willingness to undermine one perspective with another more-knowing, cynical point of view. Many of his works explore both lived experience and the desire to stand skeptically apart from that experience. In the process, Baudelaire's poetic speakers often emerge as self-divided, torn between beautiful ideals and what he called "spleen," a thoroughgoing disgust with life. (The ancient Greeks had believed that sadness originated with fluids of the spleen.)

Late in his life, Baudelaire experimented with "prose poems"—then highly innovative and, according to many of his contemporaries, confusingly paradoxical. Dissolving the distinction between poetry and prose, these brief pieces lack the line breaks associated with poetry, but they feel like lyric, capturing brief moments of experience in compressed and meditative passages. For Baudelaire, this kind of writing was momentous: he claimed to dream of "the miracle of a poetic prose, musical, without rhythm and without rhyme, supple enough and rugged enough to adapt itself to the lyrical impulses of the soul."

THE FLOWERS OF EVIL

To the Reader[1]

Infatuation, sadism, lust, avarice
possess our souls and drain the body's force;
we spoonfeed our adorable remorse,
like whores or beggars nourishing their lice.

Our sins are mulish, our confessions lies;   5
we play to the grandstand with our promises,
we pray for tears to wash our filthiness,
importantly pissing hogwash through our styes.

The devil, watching by our sickbeds, hissed
old smut and folk-songs to our soul, until   10
the soft and precious metal of our will
boiled off in vapor for this scientist.

Each day his flattery[2] makes us eat a toad,
and each step forward is a step to hell,
unmoved, though previous corpses and their smell   15
asphyxiate our progress on this road.

Like the poor lush who cannot satisfy,
we try to force our sex with counterfeits,

---

1. Translated by Robert Lowell. The translation pays primary attention to the insistent rhythm of the original poetic language and

keeps the *abba* rhyme scheme.
2. The devil is literally described as a puppet master controlling our strings.

die drooling on the deliquescent tits,
mouthing the rotten orange we suck dry.   20

Gangs of demons are boozing in our brain—
ranked, swarming, like a million warrior-ants,[3]
they drown and choke the cistern of our wants;
each time we breathe, we tear our lungs with pain.

If poison, arson, sex, narcotics, knives   25
have not yet ruined us and stitched their quick,
loud patterns on the canvas of our lives,
it is because our souls are still too sick.[4]

Among the vermin, jackals, panthers, lice,
gorillas and tarantulas that suck   30
and snatch and scratch and defecate and fuck
in the disorderly circus of our vice,

there's one more ugly and abortive birth.
It makes no gestures, never beats its breast,
yet it would murder for a moment's rest,[5]   35
and willingly annihilate the earth.

It's BOREDOM. Tears have glued its eyes together.
You know it well, my Reader. This obscene
beast chain-smokes yawning for the guillotine—
you—hypocrite Reader—my double—my brother!   40

Correspondences[1]

Nature is a temple whose living colonnades
Breathe forth a mystic speech in fitful sighs;
Man wanders among symbols in those glades
Where all things watch him with familiar eyes.

Like dwindling echoes gathered far away   5
Into a deep and thronging unison
Huge as the night or as the light of day,
All scents and sounds and colors meet as one.

Perfumes there are as sweet as the oboe's sound,
Green as the prairies, fresh as a child's caress,[2]   10
—And there are others, rich, corrupt, profound[3]

---

3. Literally, intestinal worms.
4. Literally, not bold enough.
5. Literally, swallow the world in a yawn.
1. Translated by Richard Wilbur. The transla-

tion keeps the intricate melody of the sonnet's
original rhyme scheme.
2. Literally, flesh.
3. Literally, triumphant.

And of an infinite pervasiveness,
Like myrrh, or musk, or amber,[4] that excite
The ecstasies of sense, the soul's delight.

Her Hair[1]

O fleece, that down the neck waves to the nape!
O curls! O perfume nonchalant and rare!
O ecstacy! To fill this alcove[2] shape
With memories that in these tresses sleep,
I would shake them like pennons in the air!   5

Languorous Asia, burning Africa,
And a far world, defunct almost, absent,
Within your aromatic forest stay!
As other souls on music drift away,
Mine, o my love! still floats upon your scent.   10

I shall go there where, full of sap, both tree
And man swoon in the heat of southern climes;
Strong tresses, be the swell that carries me!
I dream upon your sea of ebony
Of dazzling sails, of oarsmen, masts and flames: 15

A sun-drenched and reverberating port,
Where I imbibe color and sound and scent;
Where vessels, gliding through the gold and moire,
Open their vast arms as they leave the shore
To clasp the pure and shimmering firmament.   20

I'll plunge my head, enamored of its pleasure,
In this black ocean where the other hides;
My subtle spirit then will know a measure
Of fertile idleness and fragrant leisure,
Lulled by the infinite rhythm of its tides!   25

Pavilion, of blue-shadowed tresses spun,
You give me back the azure from afar;
And where the twisted locks are fringed with down
Lurk mingled odors I grow drunk upon
Of oil of coconut, of musk and tar.   30

A long time! always! my hand in your hair
Will sow the stars of sapphire, pearl, ruby,
That you be never deaf to my desire,
My oasis and gourd whence I aspire
To drink deep of the wine of memory![3]   35

4. Or ambergris, a substance secreted by whales. Ambergris and musk (a secretion of the male musk deer) are used in making perfume.
1. Translated by Doreen Bell. The translation emulates the French original's challenging *abaab* rhyme pattern.
2. Bedroom.
3. The last two lines are a question: "Are you not . . . ?"

A Carcass[1]

Remember, my love, the item you saw
    That beautiful morning in June:
By a bend in the path a carcass reclined
    On a bed sown with pebbles and stones;

Her legs were spread out like a lecherous whore,   5
    Sweating out poisonous fumes,
Who opened in slick invitational style
    Her stinking and festering womb.

The sun on this rottenness focused its rays
    To cook the cadaver till done,   10
And render to Nature a hundredfold gift
    Of all she'd united in one.

And the sky cast an eye on this marvelous meat
    As over the flowers in bloom.
The stench was so wretched that there on the grass   15
    You nearly collapsed in a swoon.

The flies buzzed and droned on these bowels of filth
    Where an army of maggots arose,
Which flowed like a liquid and thickening stream
    On the animate rags of her clothes.[2]   20

And it rose and it fell, and pulsed like a wave,
    Rushing and bubbling with health.
One could say that this carcass, blown with vague breath,
    Lived in increasing itself.

And this whole teeming world made a musical sound   25
    Like babbling brooks and the breeze,
Or the grain that a man with a winnowing-fan
    Turns with a rhythmical ease.

The shapes wore away as if only a dream
    Like a sketch that is left on the page   30
Which the artist forgot and can only complete
    On the canvas, with memory's aid.

From back in the rocks, a pitiful bitch
    Eyed us with angry distaste,
Awaiting the moment to snatch from the bones   35
    The morsel she'd dropped in her haste.

1. Translated by James McGowan with special attention to imagery. The alternation of long and short lines in English emulates the French meter's rhythmic swing between twelve- and eight-syllable lines in an *abab* rhyme scheme.
2. By extension. The torn flesh is described as "living rags."

—And you, in your turn, will be rotten as this:
    Horrible, filthy, undone,
Oh sun of my nature and star of my eyes,
    My passion, my angel[3] in one!   40

Yes, such will you be, oh regent of grace,
    After the rites have been read,
Under the weeds, under blossoming grass
    As you molder with bones of the dead.

Ah then, oh my beauty, explain to the worms   45
    Who cherish your body so fine,
That I am the keeper for corpses of love
    Of the form, and the essence divine![4]

Invitation to the Voyage[1]

    My child, my sister, dream
    How sweet all things would seem
Were we in that kind land to live together,
    And there love slow and long,
    There love and die among   5
Those scenes that image you, that sumptuous weather.
    Drowned suns that glimmer there
    Through cloud-disheveled air
Move me with such a mystery as appears
    Within those other skies   10
    Of your treacherous eyes
When I behold them shining through their tears.

There, there is nothing else but grace and measure,
Richness, quietness, and pleasure.

    Furniture that wears   15
    The lustre of the years
Softly would glow within our glowing chamber,
    Flowers of rarest bloom
    Proffering their perfume
Mixed with the vague fragrances of amber;   20
    Gold ceilings would there be,
    Mirrors deep as the sea,
The walls all in an Eastern splendor hung—
    Nothing but should address

3. Series of conventional Petrarchan images that idealize the beloved.
4. "Any form created by man is immortal. For form is independent of matter . . ." (from Baudelaire's journal *My Heart Laid Bare* 80).
1. Translated by Richard Wilbur. The translation maintains both the rhyme scheme and the rocking motion of the original meter, which follows an unusual pattern of two five-syllable lines followed by one seven-syllable line, and a seven-syllable couplet as refrain.

The soul's loneliness,   25
Speaking her sweet and secret native tongue.

There, there is nothing else but grace and measure,
Richness, quietness, and pleasure.

    See, sheltered from the swells
    There in the still canals   30
Those drowsy ships that dream of sailing forth;
    It is to satisfy
    Your least desire, they ply
Hither through all the waters of the earth.
    The sun at close of day   35
    Clothes the fields of hay,
Then the canals, at last the town entire
    In hyacinth and gold:
    Slowly the land is rolled
Sleepward under a sea of gentle fire.   40

There, there is nothing else but grace and measure,
Richness, quietness, and pleasure.

Spleen LXXXI[1]

When the low heavy sky weighs like a lid
Upon the spirit aching for the light
And all the wide horizon's line is hid
By a black day sadder than any night;

When the changed earth is but a dungeon dank   5
Where batlike Hope goes blindly fluttering
And, striking wall and roof and mouldered plank,
Bruises his tender head and timid wing;

When like grim prison bars stretch down the thin,
Straight, rigid pillars of the endless rain,   10
And the dumb throngs of infamous spiders spin
Their meshes in the caverns of the brain,

Suddenly, bells leap forth into the air,
Hurling a hideous uproar to the sky
As 'twere a band of homeless spirits who fare   15
Through the strange heavens, wailing stubbornly.

And hearses, without drum or instrument,
File slowly through my soul; crushed, sorrowful,
Weeps Hope, and Grief, fierce and omnipotent,
Plants his black banner on my drooping skull.   20

1. Translated by Sir John Squire in accord with the original rhyme scheme.

The Voyage[1]

To Maxime du Camp[2]

I

The child, in love with prints and maps,
Holds the whole world in his vast appetite.
How large the earth is under the lamplight!
But in the eyes of memory, how the world is cramped!

We set out one morning, brain afire,   5
Hearts fat with rancor and bitter desires,
Moving along to the rhythm of wind and waves,
Lull the inner infinite on the finite of seas:

Some are glad, glad to leave a degraded home;
Others, happy to shake off the horror of their hearts,   10
Still others, astrologers drowned in the eyes of woman—
Oh the perfumes of Circe,[3] the power and the pig!—

To escape conversion to the Beast, get drunk
On space and light and the flames of skies;
The tongue of the sun and the ice that bites   15
Slowly erase the mark of the Kiss.

But the true voyagers are those who leave
Only to be going; hearts nimble as balloons,
They never diverge from luck's black sun,
And with or without reason, cry, Let's be gone!   20

Desire to them is nothing but clouds,
They dream, as a draftee dreams of the cannon,
Of vast sensualities, changing, unknown,
Whose name the spirit has never pronounced!

II

We imitate—horrible!—the top and ball   25
In their waltz and bounce; even in sleep
We're turned and tormented by Curiosity,
Who, like a mad Angel, lashes the stars.

Peculiar fortune that changes its goal,
And being nowhere, is anywhere at all!   30

---

1. Translated by Charles Henri Ford. The French poem is written in the traditional twelve-syllable (alexandrine) line with an *abab* rhyme scheme.
2. A wry dedication to the progress-oriented author of *Modern Songs* (1855), which began "I was born a traveler."
3. In Homer's *Odyssey*, an island sorceress who changed visitors into beasts. Odysseus's men were transformed into pigs.

And Man, who is never untwisted from hope,
Scrambling like a madman to get some rest!

The soul's a three-master seeking Icaria;[4]
A voice on deck calls: "Wake up there!"
A voice from the mast-head, vehement, wild: 35
"Love . . . fame . . . happiness!" We're on the rocks!

Every island that the lookout hails
Becomes the Eldorado[5] foretold by Fortune;
Then Imagination embarks on its orgy
But runs aground in the brightness of morning.   40

Poor little lover of visionary fields!
Should he be put in irons, dumped in the sea,
This drunken sailor, discoverer of Americas,
Mirage that makes the gulf more bitter?

So the old vagabond, shuffling in mud,   45
Dreams, nose hoisted, of a shining paradise,
His charmed eye lighting on Capua's[6] coast
At every candle aglow in a hovel.

III

Astounding voyagers! what noble stories
We read in your eyes, deeper than seas;   50
Show us those caskets, filled with rich memories,
Marvelous jewels, hewn from stars and aether.

Yes, we would travel, without sail or steam!
Gladden a little our jail's desolation,
Sail over our minds, stretched like a canvas,   55
All your memories, framed with gold horizons.

Tell us, what have you seen?

IV

              "We have seen stars
And tides; we have seen sands, too,
And, despite shocks and unforeseen disasters,
We were often bored, just as we are here.   60

4. Greek island in the Aegean Sea named after the mythological Icarus, who, escaping from prison using wings made by his father, Daedalus, plunged into nearby waters and drowned when the wings gave way. His name was associated with utopian flights, as in Étienne Cabet's novel about a utopian community, *Voyage to Icaria* (1840). "Three-master": a ship.
5. Fabled country of gold and abundance.
6. City on the Volturno River in southern Italy, famous for its luxury and sensuality.

The glory of sun on a violet sea,
The glory of cities in the setting sun,
Kindled our hearts with torment and longing
To plunge into the sky's magnetic reflections.

Neither the rich cities nor sublime landscapes,   65
Ever possessed that mysterious attraction
Of Change and Chance having fun with the clouds.
And always Desire kept us anxious!

—Enjoyment adds force to Appetite!
Desire, old tree nurtured by pleasure,   70
Although your dear bark thicken and harden,
Your branches throb to hold the sun closer!

Great tree, will you outgrow the cypress?
Still we have gathered carefully
Some sketches for your hungry album,   75
Brothers, for whom all things from far away

Are precious! We've bowed down to idols;
To thrones encrusted with luminous rocks;
To figured palaces whose magic pomp
Would ruin your bankers with a ruinous dream;   80

To costumes that intoxicate the eye,
To women whose teeth and nails are dyed,
To clever jugglers, fondled by the snake."[7]

V

And then, and what more?

VI

"O childish minds!

Not to forget the principal thing,   85
We saw everywhere, without looking for it,
From top to toe of the deadly scale,
The tedious drama of undying sin:

Woman, low slave, vain and stupid,
Without laughter self-loving, and without disgust,   90
Man, greedy despot, lewd, hard and covetous,
Slave of the slave, rivulet in the sewer;

---

7. Snake charmers. The images in this stanza evoke India.

The hangman exulting, the martyr sobbing;
Festivals that season and perfume the blood;[8]
The poison of power unnerving the tyrant,   95
The masses in love with the brutalizing whip;

Many religions, very like our own,
All climbing to heaven; and Holiness,
Like a delicate wallower in a feather bed,
Seeking sensation from hair shirts and nails.   100

Jabbering humanity, drunk with its genius,
As crazy now as it was in the past,
Crying to God in its raging agony:
'O master, fellow creature, I curse thee forever!'

And then the least stupid, brave lovers of Lunacy,   105
Fleeing the gross herd that Destiny pens in,
Finding release in the vast dreams of opium!
—Such is the story, the whole world over."

VII

Bitter knowledge that traveling brings!
The globe, monotonous and small, today,   110
Yesterday, tomorrow, always, throws us our image:
An oasis of horror in a desert of boredom!

Should we go? Or stay? If you can stay, stay;
But go if you must. Some run, some hide
To outwit Time, the enemy so vigilant and   115
Baleful. And many, alas, must run forever

Like the wandering Jew[9] and the twelve apostles,
Who could not escape his relentless net[1]
By ship or by wheel; while others knew how
To destroy him without leaving home.   120

When finally he places his foot on our spine,
May we be able to hope and cry, Forward!
As in days gone by when we left for China,
Eyes fixed on the distance, hair in the wind,

With heart as light as a young libertine's   125
We'll embark on the sea of deepening shadows.

8. Literally, "Festivals seasoned and perfumed
by blood."
9. According to medieval legend, a Jew who
mocked Christ on his way to the cross and was
condemned to wander unceasingly until Judgment Day.
1. These three stanzas describe Time (ultimately Death) as a Roman gladiator, the
retiarius, who used a net to trap his opponent.

Do you hear those mournful, enchanting voices[2]
That sing: "Come this way, if you would taste

The perfumed Lotus. Here you may pick
Miraculous fruits for which the heart hungers.   130
Come and drink deep of this strange,
Soft afternoon that never ends?"

Knowing his voice, we visualize the phantom—
It is our Pylades there, his arms outstretched.
While she whose knees we used to kiss cries out,   135
"For strength of heart, swim back to your Electra!"[3]

VIII

O Death, old captain, it is time! weigh anchor!
This country confounds us; hoist sail and away!
If the sky and sea are black as ink,
Our hearts, as you know them, burst with blinding rays.   140

Pour us your poison, that last consoling draft!
For we long, so the fire burns in the brain,
To sound the abyss, Hell or Heaven, what matter?
In the depths of the Unknown, we'll discover the New!

---

2. The voices of the dead, luring the sailor to the Lotus-land of ease and forgetfulness.
3. In Greek mythology, Orestes and Pylades were close friends ready to sacrifice their lives for each other. Electra was Orestes' faithful sister, who saved him from the Furies.

EMILY DICKINSON
1830–1886

In the 1880s, visitors to Amherst, Massachusetts, gossiped about the strange woman, dressed only in white gowns, who never left her father's house—except once, it was rumored, "to see a new church, when she crept out by night, and viewed it by moonlight." Neighbors and friends knew that this woman wrote, but she published only ten poems during her lifetime, and even those appeared anonymously. She begged those closest to her to burn her papers after her death. They refused, instead startling audiences by publishing Emily Dickinson's unusual lyrics, with their passionate intensity, broken meter, slant rhymes, and unconventional dashes and capitalizations. From the moment that they first appeared, these poems have been beloved by both readers and critics. Dickinson's works can seem, on the one hand, like child-like and accessible meditations on such universal themes as death, faith, and nature, and on the other hand, like highly artful, philosophically demanding, and radically innovative experiments in lyric form. It is with this unlikely combination of innocence and sophistication that the mysterious Dickinson has become one of the best-known of American poets.

LIFE

Born to a prominent Amherst family—her father was elected to Congress—Dickinson attended Amherst Academy and later, for a year, the Mount Holyoke Female Seminary. Conflicted and ambivalent about Christian orthodoxy even as a child, she resisted the Puritan attitudes that surrounded her, especially at school. "Christ is calling everyone here," she wrote, "and I am standing alone in rebellion." This sense of isolation would only deepen. From early in her twenties, she confined herself almost entirely to her family home, leading the life of a recluse with her tyrannical father and absent-minded mother. She did have close attachments to her brother and sister, and she developed a few close friendships, though she pursued these mainly through correspondence. Some of her works reflect on the pain of unrequited love and erotic desire, and biographers have speculated about Dickinson's passions, but no scholar has been able to determine indisputably the name of the one—or ones—she loved.

Dickinson began writing verse seriously in the 1850s, putting groups of her poems together in fascicles—booklets of pages bound together by hand. In these works she seldom remarked on the burning issues of the day, from slavery and women's rights to the violence of the

Civil War. Concerned with domestic matters and the torments of the soul, she can seem excruciatingly inward-looking. But her literary life was expansive. She wrote more than a thousand letters, linking herself to the outside world more readily by mail than by face-to-face contact. Dickinson also read widely. Shakespeare was a major touchstone (she once asked: "why is any other book needed?"), and she named **John Keats**, **Elizabeth Barrett Browning**, Robert Browning, and Charlotte Brontë as among her foremost inspirations.

In 1862, after seeing an article with advice for aspiring writers by Thomas Wentworth Higginson, Dickinson wrote to solicit his opinion of her poems. He was both enthusiastic and shocked, warning her away from publishing such unconventional work. Their friendship continued to the end of Dickinson's life. After her death, Dickinson's sister Lavinia was surprised to discover almost two thousand poems stashed away in a box, and she began the difficult task of trying to figure out how to edit and organize these works for publication, a process that has puzzled and divided editors ever since. Higginson was one of the first to publish volumes of Dickinson's poetry, editing the work to make it seem as conventional as he could.

WORK

With singular conviction and independence, Dickinson produced poetry unlike anyone else of her time. Her works are noteworthy, first of all, for their brevity and compression, throwing readers immediately into the thick of the poem, eschewing any preparation. And while she draws on familiar poetic themes—nature, death, love, and faith—she pushes her explorations of feeling to their most extreme intensity, and her images persistently unsettle expectation. Nature can turn out to be revolting, as when a bird devours a worm; the grandest subjects can turn ordinary, as when death appears as an everyday conveyance; and the human body can be estranged from itself, turned into a corpse, a gun, or a tomb.

Dickinson's use of meter is as striking as her imagery. She relies most heavily on popular metrical patterns associated with Protestant hymns, such as common meter (quatrains that begin with one line of eight syllables followed by a line of six syllables, repeated to form an 8/6/8/6 pattern). But while she depends on the hymnal, she also breaks with it. Sometimes she speeds up or slows down its familiar rhythms; and sometimes she even interrupts them altogether. For example, she introduces dashes that cluster syllables together in a way that interrupts the feeling of a smooth rhythm (as in the first line of one of her most famous poems, "I heard a Fly buzz—when I died"); or she changes meter suddenly (as in "I like to see it lap the Miles," a poem that opens and closes with common-meter quatrains but swerves into a different pattern altogether in the third stanza). Dickinson's rhymes also play with traditional patterns. In "A Bird came down the Walk," for example, she offers us a couple of perfect rhymes (saw/raw, Grass/pass). But in the same poem she gives us two slant rhymes (Crumb/home, seam/swim), and in the middle, where one expects a rhyme, she presents sounds that share a rough resemblance but do not rhyme at all (around/Head).

Perhaps most strikingly experimental of all is Dickinson's use of punctuation. Her dramatic dashes are famous, and the manuscripts suggest that they are even more innovative than they look on the printed page. In her own handwriting, Dickinson's dashes are of varying lengths, and sometimes turn up or down (a few are completely vertical). These marks do not always work the same way: sometimes her dashes draw thoughts together; at other times they separate them. And finally, while Dickinson capitalizes many important proper nouns, such as Soul and Beauty, she also opts to capitalize some unexpected words: Onset, for example, or Buckets.

That Dickinson never published these outrageously unconventional and demanding poems might not surprise us. Higginson had led her to believe that the world would not appreciate them, and the few of her poems that did appear in print in her lifetime were heavily edited to conform to unadventurous tastes. "Publication—is the Auction / Of the Mind of Man," she wrote, disgusted by the idea of selling what she cared for most. And so she withdrew to what she called the "freedom" of her narrow room to create great poetry for herself alone.

216

Safe in their Alabaster Chambers—
Untouched by Morning
And untouched by Noon—
Sleep the meek members of the Resurrection—
Rafter of satin,   5
And Roof of stone.

Light laughs the breeze
In her Castle above them—
Babbles the Bee in a stolid Ear,
Pipe the Sweet Birds in ignorant cadence—   10
Ah, what sagacity perished here!

258

There's a certain Slant of light,
Winter Afternoons—
That oppresses, like the Heft
Of Cathedral Tunes—

Heavenly Hurt, it gives us—   5
We can find no scar,
But internal difference,
Where the Meanings, are—

None may teach it—Any—
'Tis the Seal Despair—   10
An imperial affliction
Sent us of the Air—

When it comes, the Landscape listens—
Shadows—hold their breath—
When it goes, 'tis like the Distance   15
On the look of Death—

303

The Soul selects her own Society—
Then—shuts the Door—
To her divine Majority—
Present no more—

Unmoved—she notes the Chariots—pausing   5
At her low Gate—
Unmoved—an Emperor be kneeling
Upon her Mat—

I've known her—from an ample nation—
Choose One—   10
Then—close the Valves of her attention—
Like Stone—

328

A Bird came down the Walk—
He did not know I saw—
He bit an Angleworm in halves
And ate the fellow, raw,

And then he drank a Dew   5
From a convenient Grass—

And then hopped sidewise to the Wall
To let a Beetle pass—

He glanced with rapid eyes
That hurried all around—
They looked like frightened Beads, I thought—   10
He stirred his Velvet Head

Like one in danger, Cautious,
I offered him a Crumb
And he unrolled his feathers   15
And rowed him softer home—

Than Oars divide the Ocean,
Too silver for a seam—
Or Butterflies, off Banks of Noon
Leap, plashless as they swim.   20

341

After great pain, a formal feeling comes—
The Nerves sit ceremonious, like Tombs—
The stiff Heart questions was it He, that bore,
And Yesterday, or Centuries before?

The Feet, mechanical, go round—   5
Of Ground, or Air, or Ought[1]—
A Wooden way
Regardless grown,
A Quartz contentment, like a stone—

This is the Hour of Lead—   10
Remembered, if outlived,
As Freezing persons, recollect the Snow—
First—Chill—then Stupor—then the letting go—

435

Much Madness is divinest Sense—
To a discerning Eye—
Much Sense—the starkest Madness—
'Tis the Majority
In this, as All, prevail—   5
Assent—and you are sane—
Demur—you're straightway dangerous—
And handled with a Chain—

1. Zero.

449

I died for Beauty—but was scarce
Adjusted in the Tomb
When One who died for Truth, was lain
In an adjoining Room—

He questioned softly "Why I failed"?   5
"For Beauty", I replied—
"And I—for Truth—Themself are One—
We Brethren, are", He said—

And so, as Kinsmen, met a Night—
We talked between the Rooms—   10
Until the Moss had reached our lips—
And covered up—our names—

465

I heard a Fly buzz—when I died—
The Stillness in the Room
Was like the Stillness in the Air—
Between the Heaves of Storm—

The Eyes around—had wrung them dry—   5
And Breaths were gathering firm
For that last Onset—when the King
Be witnessed—in the Room—

I willed my Keepsakes—Signed away
What portion of me be   10
Assignable—and then it was
There interposed a Fly—

With Blue—uncertain stumbling Buzz—
Between the light—and me—
And then the Windows failed—and then   15
I could not see to see—

519

'Twas warm—at first—like Us—
Until there crept upon
A Chill—like frost upon a Glass—
Till all the scene—be gone.

The Forehead copied Stone—   5
The Fingers grew too cold
To ache—and like a Skater's Brook—
The busy eyes—congealed—

It straightened—that was all—
It crowded Cold to Cold
It multiplied indifference—   10
As[1] Pride were all it could—

And even when with Cords—
'Twas lowered, like a Weight—
It made no Signal, nor demurred,   15
But dropped like Adamant.

585

I like to see it lap the Miles—
And lick the Valleys up—
And stop to feed itself at Tanks—
And then—prodigious step

Around a Pile of Mountains—   5
And supercilious peer
In Shanties—by the sides of Roads—
And then a Quarry pare

To fit its Ribs
And crawl between
Complaining all the while   10
In horrid—hooting stanza—
Then chase itself down Hill—

And neigh like Boanerges[1]—
Then—punctual as a Star   15
Stop—docile and omnipotent
At its own stable door—

632

The Brain—is wider than the Sky—
For—put them side by side—
The one the other will contain
With ease—and You—beside—

The Brain is deeper than the sea—   5
For—hold them—Blue to Blue—
The one the other will absorb—
As Sponges—Buckets—do—

---

1. As if.
1. "Sons of thunder," name given by Jesus to the brothers and disciples James and John, presumably because they were thunderous preachers.

The Brain is just the weight of God—
For—Heft them—Pound for Pound—   10
And they will differ—if they do—
As Syllable from Sound—

657

I dwell in Possibility—
A fairer House than Prose—
More numerous of Windows—
Superior—for Doors—

Of Chambers as the Cedars—   5
Impregnable of Eye—
And for an Everlasting Roof
The Gambrels¹ of the Sky—

Of Visitors—the fairest—
For Occupation—This—   10
The spreading wide my narrow Hands
To gather Paradise—

712

Because I could not stop for Death—
He kindly stopped for me—
The Carriage held but just Ourselves—
And Immortality.

We slowly drove—He knew no haste   5
And I had put away
My labor and my leisure too,
For His Civility—

We passed the School, where Children strove
At Recess—in the Ring—   10
We passed the Fields of Gazing Grain—
We passed the Setting Sun—

Or rather—He passed Us—
The Dews drew quivering and chill—
For only Gossamer, my Gown—   15
My Tippet—only Tulle¹—

We paused before a House that seemed
A Swelling of the Ground—

---

1. Slopes, as in the large, arched roofs often   1. Fine, silken netting. "Tippet": a scarf.
seen on barns.

The Roof was scarcely visible—
The Cornice—in the Ground—   20

Since then—'tis Centuries—and yet
Feels shorter than the Day
I first surmised the Horses' Heads
Were toward Eternity—

754

My Life had stood—a Loaded Gun—
In Corners—till a Day
The Owner passed—identified—
And carried Me away—

And now We roam in Sovereign Woods—   5
And now We hunt the Doe—
And every time I speak for Him—
The Mountains straight reply—

And do I smile, such cordial light
Upon the Valley glow—   10
It is as a Vesuvian face[1]
Had let its pleasure through—

And when at Night—Our good Day done—
I guard My Master's Head—
'Tis better than the Eider-Duck's   15
Deep Pillow—to have shared—

To foe of His—I'm deadly foe—
None stir the second time—
On whom I lay a Yellow Eye—
Or an emphatic Thumb—   20

Though I than He—may longer live
He longer must—than I—
For I have but the power to kill,
Without—the power to die—

1084

At Half past Three, a single Bird
Unto a silent Sky
Propounded but a single term
Of cautious melody.

---

1. A face glowing with light like that from an erupting volcano.

At Half past Four, Experiment   5
Had subjugated test
And lo, Her silver Principle
Supplanted all the rest.

At Half past Seven, Element
Nor Implement, be seen—   10
And Place was where the Presence was
Circumference between.

1129

Tell all the Truth but tell it slant—
Success in Circuit lies
Too bright for our infirm Delight
The Truth's superb surprise

As Lightning to the Children eased   5
With explanation kind
The Truth must dazzle gradually
Or every man be blind—

1207

He preached upon "Breadth" till it argued him narrow—
The Broad are too broad to define
And of "Truth" until it proclaimed him a Liar—
The Truth never flaunted a Sign—

Simplicity fled from his counterfeit presence   5
As Gold the Pyrites[1] would shun—
What confusion would cover the innocent Jesus
To meet so enabled[2] a Man!

1564

Pass to thy Rendezvous of Light,
Pangless except for us—
Who slowly ford the Mystery
Which thou hast leaped across!

---

1. Iron bisulfide, sometimes called fool's gold.   2. Competent.

1593

There came a Wind like a Bugle—
It quivered through the Grass
And a Green Chill upon the Heat
So ominous did pass
We barred the Windows and the Doors   5
As from an Emerald Ghost—
The Doom's electric Moccasin[1]
That very instant passed—
On a strange Mob of panting Trees
And Fences fled away   10
And Rivers where the Houses ran
Those looked that lived—that Day—
The Bell within the steeple wild
The flying tidings told—
How much can come   15
And much can go,
And yet abide the World!

1. I.e., water moccasin, a poisonous snake.

PAUL VERLAINE
1844–1896

Most famous today for his decadent and bohemian life, Paul Verlaine spent time in prison for shooting his lover, and he passed his final years frequenting bars in Paris, hopelessly addicted to the notoriously dangerous green liquor, absinthe. But he was also, at the time, thought to be France's best poet. "You must have music first of all," he wrote, and indeed his poetry has often been praised above all for its rhythms and sounds. It is no accident, then, that he became a figurehead for the Symbolist movement—hailed as a "Prince of Poets" by those artists who felt that writing should capture suggestive, atmospheric hints and feelings rather than reporting on the world. And if the flamboyant **Rimbaud** is better known to modern readers, it is Verlaine whose asymmetrical lines and fleeting images most influenced twentieth-century poets in their rejection of traditional poetic forms and their exploration of free verse.

Born in Metz, Verlaine was the only son of indulgent parents. He began publishing poetry in his early twenties, and he would go on to write no fewer than twenty-four volumes, making him one of the most prolific poets of the nineteenth century. By his mid-twenties Verlaine was having problems with alcoholism and showing signs of sudden, violent rage, attacking his mother more than once. In an attempt to reform himself and settle down, he married Mathilde Mauté, a devout Catholic and sister of a friend. The next year, however, he met the seventeen-year old poet, Arthur Rimbaud, and they began a tempestuous relationship that ended his marriage. This new love affair, however, was also to be short-lived. In 1873 Verlaine shot Rimbaud in the arm and went to jail for two years. It was during this time that he published his most admired work, *Songs Without Words*, and critics have often remarked that Verlaine's best poetry was composed during the most tumultuous periods in his life. While in prison, Verlaine also turned to the religion of his childhood, Catholicism. When he was released from jail he took up with a new lover and together they tried farming, but this venture failed and Verlaine moved back in with his mother. Thrown into jail a second time for violence, he emerged to face a terrible end. His last years were spent in poverty and alcohol addiction. During his last decade, however, his literary reputation was on the rise. The next generation of poets in France and England looked on him as a master, admiring both his poetry and his non-conformist ways.

In Verlaine's writing, his imagery is often elusive and fragmentary, even vague, and he evokes moods rather than describing detailed realities. He lavishes attention on sound, not only pursuing a variety of rhymes, but also exploring the many rich possibilities of assonance—the echoing of vowel sounds—and the repetition of consonants. He was especially fascinated by rhythms throughout his career, sometimes opting for long, slow lines, sometimes for broken and fragmentary ones. One of the most interesting examples of Verlaine's experiments in rhythm is the poem "Wooden Horses," which follows an insistent, harsh tempo to evoke a busy merry-go-round in an amusement park. The final poem included here, called "The Art of Poetry," outlines Verlaine's program for breaking from poetic tradition. No more even rhythms; no more fixed images with clear outlines and colors; no more witty epigrams or attempts at persuasion. These all belong to an outdated category Verlaine calls "literature"; they are not authentic poetry. Poetry, for Verlaine, must involve the joys of shade and nuance, and must pursue the *vers impair*, a poetic line with an odd number of syllables that often creates a floating effect. In French, "The Art of Poetry" follows a nine-syllable line, but otherwise it does not always practice what it preaches. For example, if all poetry should involve suggestion, dream, and nuance rather than definition, persuasion, and exactitude, then "The Art of Poetry," with its prescriptive formulas ("You must have music first of all," and "Never the Color, always the Shade"), does not meet its own requirements. Perhaps Verlaine decided to write one last work of ordinary "literature" in order to send conventional poetry to its grave. If so, he succeeded. This poem became Verlaine's most famous and was taken up as the unofficial manifesto of the Symbolist movement, which helped to revolutionize European poetry.

Autumn Song[1]

With long sobs
the violin-throbs
  of autumn wound
my heart with languorous
and monotonous   5
  sound.

Choking and pale
when I mind the tale
  the hours keep,
my memory strays   10
down other days
  and I weep;

and I let me go
where ill winds blow,
  now here, now there,   15
harried and sped,
even as a dead
  leaf, anywhere.

Wooden Horses[1]

By Saint-Gille
let's away,
my light-footed bay. —V. Hugo[2]

Turn, good wooden horses, round
a hundred turns, a thousand turns.
Forever turn till the axles burn,
turn, turn, to the oboes' sound.

The big soldier and the fattest maid   5
ride your backs as if in their chamber,
because their masters have also made
an outing today in the Bois de la Cambre.[3]

Turn, turn, horses of their hearts,
while all around your whirling there   10
are the clever sharpers[4] at their art;
turn to the cornet's bragging blare.

---

1. All poems translated by C. F. MacIntyre. The poem is one of the "Mournful Land-scapes" in *Saturnian Poems* (1866).
1. From *Songs Without Words* (1874).
2. French poet (1802–1885). Saint-Gilles is a suburb of Brussels, Belgium, with a public fairground.
3. An elegant park south of Brussels.
4. Literally, pickpockets.

It's as much fun as getting dead
drunk, to ride in this silly ring!
Good for the belly, bad for the head,   15
a plenty good and a plenty bad thing.

Turn, turn, no need today
of any spurs to make you bound,
galloping around and round,
turn, turn, without hope of hay.   20

And hurry, horses of their love,
already night is falling here
and the pigeon flies to join the dove,
far from madame, far from the fair.

Turn! Turn! Slow evening comes,   25
in velvet, buttoned up with stars.
Away the lovers go, in pairs.
Turn to the beat of the joyous drums.

The Art of Poetry[1]

You must have music first of all,
and for that a rhythm uneven[2] is best,
vague in the air and soluble,
with nothing heavy and nothing at rest.

You must not scorn to do some wrong   5
in choosing the words to fill your lines:
nothing more dear than the tipsy song
where the Undefined and Exact combine.

It is the veiled and lovely eye,
the full noon quivering with light;   10
it is, in the cool of an autumn sky,
the blue confusion of stars at night!

Never the Color, always the Shade,
always the nuance is supreme!
Only by shade is the trothal made   15
between flute and horn, of dream with dream!

Epigram's an assassin! Keep
away from him, fierce Wit, and vicious

1. From *Yesteryear and Yesterday* (1884), written in 1874.
2. The *vers impair* (line with an uneven number of syllables), which gives traditional
French readers a sense of "nothing at rest."
This poem uses a nine-syllable line and—as
here—often illustrates its points.

laughter that makes the Azure[3] weep,
and from all that garlic of vulgar dishes!   20

Take Eloquence and wring his neck!
You would do well, by force and care,
wisely to hold Rhyme in check,
or she's off—if you don't watch—God knows where!

Oh, who will tell the wrongs of Rhyme?   25
What crazy negro or deaf child
made this trinket for a dime,
sounding hollow and false when filed?

Let there be music, again and forever!
Let your verse be a quick-wing'd thing and light—   30
such as one feels when a new love's fervor
to other skies wings the soul in flight.

Happy-go-lucky, let your lines
disheveled run where the dawn winds lure,
smelling of wild mint, smelling of thyme . . .   35
and all the rest is literature.

---

3. The sky's unbroken azure was, for many Symbolists, an image of absolute poetry as opposed to vulgarity.

JOSÉ MARTÍ

1853–1895

The Cuban writer José Martí always entwined his revolutionary political activities with his art. Arrested at the age of sixteen for writing subversive literature, he was killed twenty-six years later by a Spanish bullet in a war for Cuban independence. In the intervening years, he became known as an orator, a teacher, a diplomat, a widely respected journalist, a political and literary essayist, a groundbreaking poet, and a committed organizer of the struggle to free Cuba from Spanish colonial rule. His most important works, *Our America* (1891) and *Versos Sencillos* (*Simple Songs*, 1891), helped to formulate the concept of America for Latin Americans. Martí's dedication to freedom and human rights and his committed antiracism made him a political hero (today his face appears on Cuban coins, and the Havana airport is named after him), while his deliberately simplified poetic diction and his rejection of conventional Spanish verse forms paved the way for Latin American *modernismo*, the exciting experimental poetry that emerged at the end of the nineteenth century.

Martí's best-known poem, "I Am an Honest Man," with its values of sincerity, simplicity, and intense emotion, astonished readers when it first appeared, dramatically overturning dominant traditions of Spanish poetry that had valued complex, artful structures and Romantic sentimentality. This poem has long been beloved by Cubans, but it became world famous when it was set to the tune of *Guantanamera* ("the woman from Guantánamo"), a popular Cuban melody. Julián Orbón, a musician and composer, wanted to dignify this popular song and did so by borrowing celebrated words for it from the martyred poet-hero Martí. It is now the unofficial anthem of both island and exiled Cubans, and musicians around the world have translated and recorded it. The U.S. folk singer Pete Seeger helped to propel the song to international fame in the 1960s.

I Am an Honest Man[1]

(Guantanamera)

I am an honest man
From where the palm grows
And before I die I wish
To fling my verses from my soul.
I come from everywhere   5
And I am going toward everywhere:
Among the arts, I am art
In the mountains, I am a mountain.
I know the strange names
Of the herbs and flowers   10
And of mortal deceits
And of sublime pains.
I have seen in the dark night
Rain over my head
The pure rays of lightning   15
Of divine beauty.
I saw wings born in men
Of beautiful women:
And coming out of rubbish
Butterflies flying.   20
I have seen a man live
With his dagger at his side,
Without ever saying the name
Of she who had killed him.
Rapid, like a reflection,   25
I saw my soul, twice
When the poor old man died,
When she said good-bye to me.
I trembled once—at the fence,
At the entrance to the vineyard—   30
When a barbarous bee
Stung my daughter in the forehead.

1. Translated by Aviva Chomsky.

I felt joy once, such that
Nobody ever felt joy: when
The mayor read the sentence   35
Of my death, crying.
I hear a sigh, across
The lands and the sea
And it is not a sigh, it is
That my son is going to wake up.   40
They say that from the jeweler
I took the best jewel,
I took a sincere friend
And left love aside.

ARTHUR RIMBAUD
1854–1891

In a brief, dazzling literary career, which lasted from the age of fifteen to the age of twenty, Arthur Rimbaud expanded the visionary and experimental possibilities of modern poetry. Taking literally the ancient notion of the poet as a prophet, he determined to push poetic vision beyond all familiar bounds, violently and dramatically, "by the systematic derangement *of all the senses.*" Rimbaud dedicated himself to a transformation of existence that exceeded even the written word: in ordinary life, he actively rebelled against rules of etiquette and conventional morality to produce a revolutionary reimagining of experience intended to explode entrenched patterns of thought and usher in a radically different future. Idealistic, defiant, deliberately rude, bitter, profoundly anti-conventional and astonishingly talented, Rimbaud, as one admirer explained, passed like a lightning bolt through French literature.

Jean-Nicholas-Arthur Rimbaud was born on October 20, 1854, in Charleville, a town in northeastern France. His military father abandoned the family when Arthur was seven, and his embittered mother raised her four children in a repressive, disciplinary atmosphere. Rimbaud was a highly gifted student who read widely, but he was also unruly, running away from home more than once to live as a vagrant. In 1871 the seventeen-year-old writer sent some of his work to an established Parisian poet, **Paul Verlaine**, who was so impressed that he invited Rimbaud to stay with him in Paris. Expecting to meet a man in his twenties, Verlaine was shocked to behold the "real head of a child, chubby and fresh, on a big, bony rather clumsy body of a still-growing adolescent." Far from innocent, however, Rimbaud sneered and swore, stole books and broke objects, and deliberately used literary magazines as toilet paper. He also wrote staggeringly innovative works of poetry. Verlaine was drawn to this gifted and uncompromising outsider, and the two began a tumultuous love affair, which ended two years later when Verlaine went to prison for shooting his young lover in a fight. At the age of nineteen Rimbaud decided to renounce poetry, and he traveled as a commercial trader to Cyprus, Java, and Aden, eventually becoming a gunrunner in Abyssinia (now Ethiopia). Falling ill with a cancerous tumor in one knee, he returned to France to die in 1891, one month after his thirty-seventh birthday.

Rimbaud's work resists Romantic traditions of lyric poetry that cherish the self as the site and source of meaningful experience. He suggests instead that multiple, disjointed, and borrowed experiences precede the self, making it what it is. One should not say "I think," he wrote, but rather "I am being thought," as if our thoughts come before us, rather than the other way around. In one of his most famous lines, he claimed "je est un autre" ("I is an other"), his deliberate grammatical error signaling a whole new way of regarding the self as if it were an external object.

We can see one radical revision of the lyric "I" in Rimbaud's most famous poem, "The Drunken Boat," which speaks from the perspective of the boat itself, one that leaves the rivers of Europe for the sea, where it experiences a thoroughgoing freedom and encounters a kind of total reality, both beautiful and terrifying, both creative and destructive, and ends in failure and the desire for self-annihilation, longing to be only a poor child's paper boat sailing in a black puddle. Rimbaud had at this point in his life never seen the sea, but the images he has borrowed from adventure novels, newspapers, and epic poetry allow him to bring together bits and pieces of imaginative intensity to see the world from the strange and unknowable vantage point of a boat.

The bitter prose poem, A Season in Hell, also unsettles the conventional first-person narrative. On the one hand it seems to be autobiographical, offering insight into the poet's life, but on the other hand it gives us as much hallucination as fact, and it turns into disjointed images in place of a coherent story: "I saw very plainly a mosque in place of a factory, a school of drummers composed of angels. . . . I became a fabulous opera." Similarly, the *Illuminations* offer a series of transformations that leave only traces of their points of departure, immersing the reader in free associations, cutting short all logical organization to develop an almost musical organization of themes and images. And "Barbarian," set outside recognizable parameters of time and space, gives us a vision— without logic or story—that operates according to a pattern of oppositions: red and white, heat and cold, subterranean volcanoes and starry sky. All of these works swing between an ideal world and the pain of repugnant and sordid realities, and all of them explode— often violently—dreams of a coherent and stable self.

The Drunken Boat[1]

As I descended black, impassive Rivers,
I sensed that haulers[2] were no longer guiding me:
Screaming Redskins took them for their targets,
Nailed nude to colored stakes: barbaric trees.

---

1. Translated by Stephen Stepanchev.
2. The image is of a commercial barge being towed along a canal.

I was indifferent to all my crews;   5
I carried English cottons, Flemish wheat.
When the disturbing din of haulers ceased,
The Rivers let me ramble where I willed.

Through the furious ripping of the sea's mad tides,
Last winter, deafer than an infant's mind,   10
I ran! And drifting, green Peninsulas
Did not know roar more gleefully unkind.

A tempest blessed my vigils on the sea.
Lighter than a cork I danced on the waves,
Those endless rollers, as they say, of graves: 15
Ten nights beyond a lantern's[3] silly eye!

Sweeter than sourest apple-flesh to children,
Green water seeped into my pine-wood hull
And washed away blue wine[4] stains, vomitings,
Scattering rudder, anchor, man's lost rule.   20

And then I, trembling, plunged into the Poem
Of the Sea,[5] infused with stars, milk-white,
Devouring azure greens; where remnants, pale
And gnawed, of pensive corpses fell from light;

Where, staining suddenly the blueness, delirium.   25
The slow rhythms of the pulsing glow of day,
Stronger than alcohol and vaster than our lyres,
The bitter reds of love ferment the way!

I know skies splitting into light, whirled spouts
Of water, surfs, and currents: I know the night,   30
The dawn exalted like a flock of doves, pure wing,
And I have seen what men imagine they have seen.

I saw the low sun stained with mystic horrors,
Lighting long, curdled clouds of violet,
Like actors in a very ancient play,   35
Waves rolling distant thrills like lattice[6] light!

I dreamed of green night, stirred by dazzling snows,
Of kisses rising to the sea's eyes, slowly,
The sap-like coursing of surprising currents,
And singing phosphors,[7] flaring blue and gold!   40

I followed, for whole months, a surge like herds
Of insane cattle in assault on the reefs,

3. Port beacons.
4. A cheap, ordinary, bitter wine.
5. A play on words, "Poem" suggests "creation" (Greek *poiein*, "making"); "Sea," the source or

"mother" of life, sounds the same as "mother" in French (*mer / mère*).
6. Like the ripple of venetian blinds.
7. *Noctiluca*, tiny marine animals.

Unhopeful that three Marys,[8] come on luminous feet,
Could force a muzzle on the panting seas!

Yes, I struck incredible Floridas[9]   45
That mingled flowers and the eyes of panthers
In skins of men! And rainbows bridled green
Herds beneath the horizon of the seas.

I saw the ferment of enormous marshes, weirs
Where a whole Leviathan[1] lies rotting in the weeds!   50
Collapse of waters within calms at sea,
And distances in cataract toward chasms!

Glaciers, silver suns, pearl waves, and skies like coals,
Hideous wrecks at the bottom of brown gulfs
Where giant serpents eaten by red bugs   55
Drop from twisted trees and shed a black perfume!

I should have liked to show the young those dolphins
In blue waves, those golden fish, those fish that sing.
—Foam like flowers rocked my sleepy drifting,
And, now and then, fine winds supplied me wings.   60

When, feeling like a martyr, I tired of poles and zones,
The sea, whose sobbing made my tossing sweet,
Raised me its dark flowers, deep and yellow whirled,
And, like a woman, I fell on my knees . . .[2]

Peninsula, I tossed upon my shores   65
The quarrels and droppings of clamorous, blond-eyed birds.
I sailed until, across my rotting cords,
Drowned men, spinning backwards, fell asleep! . . .

Now I, a lost boat in the hair of coves,[3]
Hurled by tempest into a birdless air,   70
I, whose drunken carcass neither Monitors
Nor Hansa ships[4] would fish back for men's care;

Free, smoking, rigged with violet fogs,
I, who pierced the red sky like a wall
That carries exquisite mixtures for good poets,   75
Lichens of sun and azure mucus veils;

Who, spotted with electric crescents, ran
Like a mad plank, escorted by seashores,

8. A legend that the three biblical Marys crossed the sea during a storm to land in Camargue, a region in southern France famous for its horses and bulls.
9. A name (plural) given to any exotic country.
1. Vast biblical sea monster (Job 41.1–10).
2. The poet's ellipses; nothing has been omitted.
3. Seaweed.
4. Vessels belonging to the German Hanseatic League of commercial maritime cities. "Monitors": armored coast guard ships, after the iron-clad Union warship *Monitor* of the American Civil War.

When cudgel blows of hot Julys struck down
The sea-blue skies upon wild water spouts;   80

I, who trembled, feeling the moan at fifty leagues
Of rutting Behemoths[5] and thick Maelstroms, I,
Eternal weaver of blue immobilities,
I long for Europe with its ancient quays!

I saw sidereal archipelagoes! and isles   85
Whose delirious skies are open to the voyager:
—Is it in depthless nights you sleep your exile,
A million golden birds, O future Vigor?—

But, truly, I have wept too much! The dawns disturb.
All moons are painful, and all suns break bitterly: 90
Love has swollen me with drunken torpors.
Oh, that my keel might break and spend me in the sea!

Of European waters I desire
Only the black, cold puddle in a scented twilight
Where a child of sorrows squats and sets the sails   95
Of a boat as frail as a butterfly in May.

I can no longer, bathed in languors, O waves,
Cross the wake of cotton-bearers on long trips,
Nor ramble in a pride of flags and flares,
Nor swim beneath the horrible eyes of prison ships.[6]   100

From A Season in Hell[1]

Night of Hell

I have swallowed a first-rate draught of poison.—Thrice blessed be the counsel that came to me!—My entrails are on fire. The violence of the venom
wrings my limbs, deforms me, fells me. I am dying of thirst, I am suffocating, I
cannot cry out. This is hell, the everlasting punishment! Mark how the fire
surges up again! I am burning properly. There you are, demon!

I had caught a glimpse of conversion to righteousness and happiness, salvation. May I describe the vision; the atmosphere of hell does not permit hymns!
It consisted of millions of charming creatures, a sweet sacred concert, power
and peace, noble ambitions, and goodness knows what else.

Noble ambitions![2]

---

5. Biblical animal resembling a hippopotamus
(Job 40.15–24).
6. Portholes of ships tied at anchor and used
as prisons.
1. Translated by Enid Rhodes Peschel. *Night
of Hell* is the second section (after the preface) of the autobiographical *A Season in Hell.*
The first section, *Bad Blood,* describes his soli-

tary childhood and sense of being a member of
an "inferior race." It also contrasts an authoritarian and hypocritical European society with
African paganism, which is seen as a freer and
more natural existence.
2. Mockery of his childhood idealism and
attraction to traditional Catholicism.

And yet this is life!—What if damnation is eternal! A man who chooses to mutilate himself is rightly damned, isn't he? I believe that I am in hell, consequently I am there.[3] This is the effect of the catechism. I am the slave of my baptism.[4] Parents, you have caused my affliction and you have caused your own. Poor innocent!—Hell cannot assail pagans.—This is life, nevertheless! Later, the delights of damnation will be deeper. A crime, quickly, that I may sink to nothingness, in accordance with human law.

Be silent, do be silent! . . . There is shame, reproof, in this place: Satan who says that the fire is disgraceful, that my wrath is frightfully foolish.—Enough! . . . The errors that are whispered to me, enchantments, false perfumes, childish melodies.[5]—And to say that I possess truth, that I understand justice: I have a sound and steady judgment, I am prepared for perfection . . . Pride.—The skin of my head is drying up. Pity! Lord, I am terrified. I am thirsty, so thirsty! Ah! childhood, the grass, the rain, the lake upon the stones, *the moonlight when the bell tower was striking twelve*[6] . . . the devil is in the bell tower, at that hour. Mary! Blessed Virgin! . . . —The horror of my stupidity.

Over there, are they not honest-souls, who wish me well? . . . Come . . . I have a pillow over my mouth, they don't hear me, they are phantoms. Besides, no one ever thinks of others. Let no one approach. I reek of burning, that's certain.

The hallucinations are countless. It's exactly what I've always had: no more faith in history, neglect of principles. I shall be silent about this: poets and visionaries would be jealous. I am a thousand times the richest, let us be avaricious like the sea.

Now then! the clock of life has just stopped. I am no longer in the world.— Theology is serious, hell is certainly *below*—and heaven above.—Ecstasy, nightmare, sleep in a nest of flames.

What pranks during my vigilance in the country . . . Satan, Ferdinand,[7] races with wild seeds . . . Jesus walks on the purplish briers, without bending them . . . Jesus used to walk on the troubled waters.[8] The lantern revealed him to us, a figure standing, pale and with brown tresses, beside a wave of emerald. . . .

I am going to unveil all the mysteries: mysteries religious or natural, death, birth, futurity, antiquity, cosmogony, nothingness, I am a master of phantasmagories.

Listen! . . .

I have all the talents!—There is nobody here and there is somebody: I would not wish to scatter my treasure.—Do you wish for Negro chants, dances of houris?[9] Do you wish me to vanish, to dive in search of the *ring*?[1] Do you? I shall produce gold, cures.

Rely, then, upon me: faith comforts, guides, heals. All of you, come,—even the little children,[2]—that I may console you, that one may pour out his heart

3. A parody of French philosopher René Descartes's (1596–1650) phrase "I think, therefore I am," which had become a symbol of well-ordered thought.
4. Because baptism creates the possibility of both heaven and hell.
5. The poetic visions and harmonies that Rimbaud explored with Paul Verlaine.
6. A collection of romanticized childhood memories.
7. Peasant name for the devil.
8. Jesus' disciples saw him walking on the sea at night (John 6.16–21).
9. Beautiful virgins in the Koranic paradise.
1. At the end of Wagner's opera *Götterdämmerung*, Hagen plunges into the river Rhine to recapture the golden ring of world power.
2. Parody of Jesus' words "Suffer little children, and forbid them not, to come unto me" (Matthew 19.14).

for you,—the marvelous heart!—Poor men, laborers! I do not ask for prayers; with your confidence alone, I shall be happy.

—And let's think of me. This makes me miss the world very little. I have the good fortune not to suffer any longer. My life was nothing but sweet follies, regrettably.

Bah! let's make all the grimaces imaginable.

Decidedly, we are out of the world. No more sound. My sense of touch has disappeared. Ah! my castle, my Saxony,[3] my forest of willows. The evenings, the mornings, the nights, the days . . . Am I weary!

I ought to have my hell for wrath, my hell for pride,—and the hell of the caress; a concert of hells.

I am dying of weariness. This is the tomb, I am going to the worms, horror of horrors! Satan, jester, you wish to undo me, with your spells. I protest. I protest! one jab of the pitchfork, one lick of fire.

Ah! to rise again to life! To cast eyes upon our deformities. And that poison, that kiss a thousand times accursed! My weakness, the cruelty of the world! Dear God, your mercy, hide me, I regard myself too poorly!—I am hidden and I am not.

It is the fire that rises again with the soul condemned to it.

From THE ILLUMINATIONS[1]

The Bridges[2]

Crystal-gray skies. A bizarre pattern of bridges, some of them straight, others convex, still others descending or veering off at angles to the first ones, and these shapes multiplying in the other illuminated circuits of the canal,[3] but all of them so long and delicate that the riverbanks burdened with domes fall away and diminish. Some of these bridges are still lined with hovels.[4] Others support masts, signals, frail parapets. Minor chords meet and leave each other, ropes climb up from the banks. One can make out a red jacket, perhaps other costumes and musical instruments. Are these popular tunes, fragments of concerts offered by the aristocracy, snatches of public hymns? The water is gray and blue, wide as an arm of the sea.—A white ray, falling from the top of the sky, wipes out this bit of theatricality.

Barbarian

Long after the days and the seasons, and the beings and the countries,

The pennant of bloody meat[1] against the silk of arctic seas and flowers; (they don't exist.)

---

3. Germanic duchy, part of Rimbaud's visionary memories.
1. This and the following selection are translated by John Ashbery.
2. An impressionistic memory of London.
3. The river Thames as it winds through the city.
4. Houses were once built on London Bridge.
1. Perhaps a reference to the Danish flag (a white cross on a red field), which Rimbaud would have seen on a visit to Iceland, then a Danish possession.

Recovered from old fanfares of heroism—which still attack our hearts and heads—far from the ancient assassins—

Oh! The pennant of bloody meat against the silk of arctic seas and flowers; (they don't exist)

Sweetness!

Live coals raining down gusts of frost,—Sweetness!—those flashes in the rain of the wind of diamonds thrown down by the terrestrial heart eternally charred for us.—O world!—

(Far from the old refuges and the old fires that we can hear, can smell,)

The live coals and the foam. Music, wheeling of abysses and shock of ice floes against the stars.

O Sweetness, O world, O music! And there, shapes, sweat, tresses and eyes, floating. And the white, boiling tears.—O sweetness!—and the voice of woman reaching to the depths of the aretic volcanoes and caverns.

The pennant. . . .

RUBÉN DARÍO

1867–1916

Rubén Darío was the first poet of *Modernismo*—a movement that revolutionized Spanish American poetry. He was inspired by the French Symbolists, and he fused their poetic innovations with a range of traditions, including his own indigenous ancestry, occult science, and ancient Greek mythology, to create a startling new sensibility. Darío's life, like his poetry, spanned continents and historical moments. He was born in Nicaragua, lived in Chile and Argentina, worked for the Colombian government, and spent many years in Europe as a reporter and diplomat, managing to serve as a bridge between countries and generations. When two later writers, **Pablo Neruda** and **García Lorca**, paid homage to Darío in 1933, they called him "that great Nicaraguan, Argentinian, Chilean, and Spanish poet" whose poetry, "crisscrossed with sounds and dreams . . . stands solidly outside of norms, forms, and schools."

LIFE

Rubén Darío was born Félix Rubén García y Sarmiento in a small village in Nicaragua now called Ciudad Darío (Darío City). His parents separated when he was only eight months old, and he was sent to live with an aunt and uncle in the old city of Léon. His autobiography describes the impression made on him by the antiquated house and the ghostly horror stories told after dinner, which gave him nightmares. Before he was eight, he had made a name for himself as a child-poet and soon became well known in the region. At fourteen he began submitting articles to newspapers, and in 1886 he moved to Chile, where he worked as a journalist and wrote poetry. It was here, two years later, that he published *Azul (Blue)*, a collection of his writing that would come to be recognized as a turning point in Spanish American literary history.

In 1891 Nicaragua arranged to send a delegation to Spain for the fourth centennial of the European discovery of America, and Darío went as secretary to the delegation. Exhilarated by the warm reception he experienced as a representative of Spanish American letters, he moved to Argentina with new confidence in his role as a spokesperson for Latin American literature and culture.

Darío married twice and had two children who survived to adulthood. In the early years of the twentieth century, he lived in Madrid and then in Paris. Eventually, suffering from cirrhosis of the liver and barely making a living in Europe, he returned to Nicaragua, where he died in 1916. After his death, the government ordered national mourning and granted him the burial honors of a high-level minister, while the Church performed funeral services usually reserved for royalty.

BETWEEN TWO EMPIRES

To have grown up in Nicaragua in the late nineteenth century was to find oneself caught between two empires. Though the Spanish government had lost most of its colonies in the fierce battles for independence that had been waged in the early decades of the nineteenth century, Spain still exerted its powerful influence over Latin America through language and institutions—including the Catholic Church—as well as continued political control of Cuba and Puerto Rico. Meanwhile, the United States had become the major power in the region and was threatening to use its military strength against European states that might try to exert authority in the hemisphere. The 1823 Monroe Doctrine had proclaimed that the United States would interpret any European attempt to interfere with territory in the Americas as an act of aggression and would retaliate. Thus, when Cuba began to struggle for independence in 1868, tensions between Spain and the United States began to mount until 1898 when war erupted, and with Spain's defeat the United States took over almost all of Spain's remaining colonies, including the Philippines, Guam, and Puerto Rico. The Spanish-American War, as it came to be called, established the United States as an imperial power far more frightening to many in Latin America than Spain.

It was in this context that Darío turned toward Spain, and away from the United States. At the very end of the nineteenth century he traveled to Spain as a journalist to report on that country's defeat in the Spanish-American War. He quickly became a figure in Spanish intellectual and literary circles, and saw European culture as a rich resource for poets and intellectuals, while the United States seemed to him aggressive, greedy, and culturally barbaric. He started to envision a new literary geography that would include modern Spanish and Latin American writers, but would remain proudly separate from the looming influence of the United States. And yet his opposition to the U.S. was not absolute. At times Darío offered homage to the American poet **Walt Whitman**, and he remained fully conscious of Spain's long history of torturing and exploiting Indian peoples. Thus, like many of his contemporaries, he remained suspicious of both empires, and he longed for a Latin American cultural and political renewal that would entail a new kind of self-determination.

WORK

Although Darío is known for modernizing Latin American poetry, he was not one to discard traditional literary forms and conventions. His works deliberately recall forms with a long history—such as the *blasón* (blazon), a love poem that lists the beauties of the beloved. He also drew on age-old images, such as the swan, Darío's favorite symbol of artistic inspiration—ideally beautiful, and yet haunted by doubt, with its neck swerving into the shape of a question mark. All of this suggests a deep debt to tradition. But what felt strikingly new to his contemporaries was Darío's style. The poems, short stories, and sketches in the early collection *Blue* seemed far more similar to the evocative, jewel-like recent work of French Symbolist writers—such as **Verlaine**, one of Darío's great heroes—than to contemporary Spanish-language writers, who tended to favor long rhetorical passages. His sentences were surprisingly short, with rhythmic and stylistic variations; he preferred foreign, even exotic subjects, and rare and musical words. "Words should paint the color of a sound, the aroma of a star; they should capture the very soul of things," he wrote. Like many of the French Symbolists, then, he evoked ideal beauties in rich images rather than describing gritty realities, and he concentrated his attention on the musical qualities of his verse. He also purified his language of anything coarse or vulgar and produced a rigorously flawless technical brilliance that was entirely different from any poetry that had been written in Spanish before. At the same time, there was always a sense of melancholy, of longing and doubt, as if the pursuit of the ideal was always doomed to failure.

Darío's final collection, *Songs of Life and Hope*, continued the emphasis on musicality and technical perfection but also displayed a new poetic awakening to contemporary political and cultural concerns, as well as a somber interrogation of the poet's own mortality, as we see in the poem "Fatality." These final poems, including "Leda" and "To Roosevelt," invite a new sense of violence that breaks from the perfectly crafted, ideal gems that are the early work.

Darío's influence was already so overpowering by 1910 that a young Mexican poet named Enrique González Martínez urged his fellow poets to "wring the swan's neck." And yet poets have continued to return to Darío for inspiration. Indeed, his work has had such a profound impact that some literary historians have broken the story of Spanish-language poetry into two periods—before and after Darío.

Blazon[1]

For the Countess of Peralta

The snow-white Olympic[2] swan,
with beak of rose-red agate,
preens his eucharistic[3] wing,
which he opens to the sun like a fan.

His shining neck is curved   5
like the arm of a lyre,
like the handle of a Greek amphora,[4]
like the prow of a ship.

He is the swan of divine origin
whose kiss mounted through fields   10
of silk to the rosy peaks
of Leda's[5] sweet hills.

White king of Castalia's fount,
his triumph illumines the Danube;[6]
Da Vinci was his baron in Italy;   15
Lohengrin[7] is his blond prince.

His whiteness is akin to linen,
to the buds of white roses,
to the diamantine white
of the fleece of an Easter lamb.   20

He is the poet of perfect verses,
and his lyric cloak is of ermine;
he is the magic, the regal bird
who, dying, rhymes the soul in his song.

This wingèd aristocrat displays   25
white lilies on a blue field;
and Pompadour,[8] gracious and lovely,
has stroked his feathers.

---

1. This and the following poems are translated by Lysander Kemp. "Blazon": both a heraldic coat of arms and a poem that enumerates various qualities of the beloved.
2. Associated with Mount Olympus, home of the gods in Greek mythology.
3. Like the white wafer used in the Eucharist, the Christian ritual of communion.
4. Large two-handled jar used in ancient Greece for storing wine or oil.
5. In Greek mythology, a nymph raped by Zeus, who had taken the form of a swan; she gave birth to Helen of Troy.

6. A major river in central Europe. "Castalia's fount": the spring of Castalia on Mount Parnassus, home of the Greek Muses.
7. The "Swan Knight" of Wagner's opera Lohengrin (1850). "Da Vinci": Leonardo da Vinci (1452–1519), the Renaissance artist and inventor.
8. The Marquise de Pompadour (1721–1764) was the mistress of King Louis XV of France. "White lilies on a blue field": the fleur-de-lis. The coat of arms of the French kings displayed white lilies on a blue background.

He rows and rows on the lake
where dreams wait for the unhappy, 30
where a golden gondola waits
for the sweetheart of Louis of Bavaria.[9]

Countess, give the swans your love,
for they are gods of an alluring land
and are made of perfume and ermine, 35
of white light, of silk, and of dreams.

To Roosevelt[1]

The voice that would reach you, Hunter, must speak
in Biblical tones, or in the poetry of Walt Whitman.[2]
You are primitive and modern, simple and complex;
you are one part George Washington and one part Nimrod.[3]
    You are the United States 5
future invader of our naive America[4]
with its Indian blood, an America
that still prays to Christ and still speaks Spanish.

You are a strong, proud model of your race;
you are cultured and able; you oppose Tolstoy.[5] 10
You are an Alexander-Nebuchadnezzar,[6]
breaking horses and murdering tigers.
(You are a Professor of Energy,
as the current lunatics say).

You think that life is a fire, 15
that progress is an irruption,
that the future is wherever
your bullet strikes.

No.

The United States is grand and powerful.
Whenever it trembles, a profound shudder 20
runs down the enormous backbone of the Andes.[7]
If it shouts, the sound is like the roar of a lion.

9. The mad king of Bavaria (1864–86) who built a fairytale castle and retired from the world; he was Wagner's patron for many years.
1. President of the United States from 1901 to 1909, Theodore Roosevelt was well known as a hunter and as a political expansionist.
2. American poet (1819–1892) and author of *Leaves of Grass* (1855) whose poetry Darío liked and to whom he addressed a poem.
3. Mighty hunter and king of ancient Assyria (see Genesis 10.8–12).

4. I.e., Spanish-speaking South America.
5. The Russian count and novelist Leo Tolstoy (1828–1910) in his later works preached piety, morality, and a simple peasant life.
6. A combination of the Macedonian conqueror Alexander the Great (356–323 B.C.E.) and Nebuchadnezzar (630–562 B.C.E.), king of Babylon, who destroyed Jerusalem and made its inhabitants slaves.
7. A mountain chain running the length of South America.

And Hugo said to Grant:[8] "The stars are yours."
(The dawning sun of the Argentine barely shines;
the star of Chile is rising . . .)[9] A wealthy country, 25
joining the cult of Mammon to the cult of Hercules;[1]
while Liberty, lighting the path
to easy conquest, raises her torch in New York.
But our own America, which has had poets
since the ancient times of Nezahualcóyotl;[2] 30
which preserved the footprints of great Bacchus,
and learned the Panic[3] alphabet once,
and consulted the stars; which also knew Atlantis[4]
(whose name comes ringing down to us in Plato)
and has lived, since the earliest moments of its life, 35
in light, in fire, in fragrance, and in love—
the America of Moctezuma and Atahualpa,[5]
the aromatic America of Columbus,
Catholic America, Spanish America,
the America where noble Cuauhtémoc said: 40
"I am not on a bed of roses"[6]—our America,
trembling with hurricanes, trembling with Love:
O men with Saxon[7] eyes and barbarous souls,
our America lives. And dreams: And loves.
And it is the daughter of the Sun. Be careful. 45
Long live Spanish America!
A thousand cubs of the Spanish lion are roaming free.
Roosevelt, you must become, by God's own will,
the deadly Rifleman and the dreadful Hunter
before you can clutch us in your iron claws. 50

And though you have everything, you are lacking one thing:
God!

Leda

The swan in shadow seems to be of snow;
his beak is translucent amber in the daybreak;
gently that first and fleeting glow of crimson
tinges his gleaming wings with rosy light.

8. Ulysses S. Grant (1822–1885), Union general in the Civil War and president from 1869 to 1877. "Hugo": Darío admired the 19th-century French writer Victor Hugo (1802–1885).
9. The flags of Argentina and Chile display a sun and a star, respectively.
1. The Greek demigod known for his strength. "Mammon": in the New Testament, a false god who personified riches and greed.
2. An Aztec ruler and early poet.
3. Belonging to the woodland god Pan, a follower of Bacchus. "Bacchus": the Greek god of wine and fertility.
4. The lost civilization of Atlantis, described in Plato's dialogues *Timaeus* and *Critias*.
5. Last Inca emperor (r. 1532–33), captured and held for ransom before being strangled by Pizarro's soldiers. "Moctezuma": Montezuma II (1466–1520), Aztec emperor in Mexico, slain for his wealth by Spanish invaders.
6. Words spoken to a fellow prisoner by the last Aztec emperor (d. 1525) while he was being tortured by Spanish invaders.
7. Of Germanic or British ancestry; here, North Americans.

And then, on the azure waters of the lake,   5
when dawn has lost its colors, then the swan,
his wings outspread, his neck a noble arc,
is turned to burnished silver by the sun.

The bird from Olympus, wounded by love, swells out
his silken plumage, and clasping her in his wings   10
he ravages Leda there in the singing water,
his beak seeking the flower of her lips.

She struggles, naked and lovely, and is vanquished,
and while her cries turn sighs and die away,
the screen of teeming foliage parts and the wild   15
green eyes of Pan[1] stare out, wide with surprise.

Fatality

The tree is happy because it is scarcely sentient;
the hard rock is happier still, it feels nothing:
there is no pain as great as being alive,
no burden heavier than that of conscious life.

To be, and to know nothing, and to lack a way,   5
and the dread of having been, and future terrors . . .
And the sure terror of being dead tomorrow,
and to suffer all through life and through the darkness,

and through what we do not know and hardly suspect . . .
And the flesh that tempts us with bunches of cool grapes,   10
and the tomb that awaits us with its funeral sprays,
and not to know where we go,
nor whence we came! . . .

---

1. The horned shepherd god of woods and field.

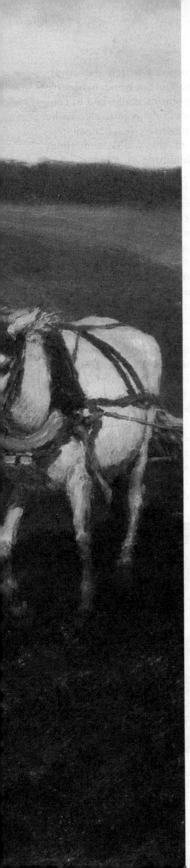

V

Realism Across the Globe

As the world grew closer together in the nineteenth century, thanks to rapidly expanding empires and new methods of transportation and communication, including the steamship and the telegraph, literary movements were able to spread fast, too. Writers could find inspiration in texts composed across the world; they could nurture new ideas at home that then spread quickly outward; and they could readily mix and fuse traditions that came from different continents. "World literature" as a globally interconnected phenomenon became a reality in this period. Symbolism, for example—the poetic movement launched by **Charles Baudelaire** in Paris—had an impact as far away as Nicaragua and Japan, and the *ghazal*, an Arabic poetic form used for many centuries in India and Persia, inspired imitators in nineteenth-century Europe, including **Johann Wolfgang von Goethe**, who made it a popular poetic form in Germany, and Thomas Hardy in Britain.

One of the most powerfully influential global artistic movements in the nineteenth century was realism. It began in Britain and France, hotbeds of industrial and political revolution, but it soon spread worldwide. And yet realism in literature did not always arise in response to European influences.

Leo Tolstoi Ploughing a Field, 1882, by Ilya Yefimovich Repin.

697

For example, **Higuchi Ichiyō**, a Japanese woman writer, published fiction at the end of the nineteenth century that departed from Japanese literary conventions, startling and enchanting her readers with a new style and subject matter that felt fresh and lifelike. She focused on poor and marginal characters in the city as they struggle to make choices in a forbidding economic environment. She also purposefully incorporated colloquial speech and lively dialogue that sounded more natural than the speech of traditional literary characters. And she did all this without ever having read a European novel. Similarly, it would be a mistake to see **Joaquim Maria Machado de Assis** in Brazil, **Rabindranath Tagore** in India, and Rebecca Harding Davis in the United States as mere imitators of the European model: they invented techniques, subjects, and plots, they altered conventions, and they experimented with styles to generate realisms all their own.

Despite its rich variety, realist writing around the world tended to share some crucial aims and characteristics. In the nineteenth century many artists felt a new urgency to tell the unvarnished truth about the world, to observe social life unsentimentally, and to convey it as objectively as possible. To be sure, the struggle to give a realistic representation of the world—sometimes called verisimilitude or mimesis—was nothing new. But while artists for many generations had been aiming at truth in their representations of the world, the nineteenth century ushered in a new realist philosophy, shocking new subject matter, and a specific new constellation of literary techniques.

The revolutionary overturning of old regimes and hierarchies, the rise of democracy and the middle class, and the industrial revolution—which created smoky, grimy cities teeming with an impoverished working class—had already inspired writers to throw off old literary forms and conventions. In Europe and the Americas, the Romantic poets (described in detail in this volume) had sought to liberate literature from the grip of traditional courtly manners and traditions to focus instead on nature as a model of freedom and beauty. For them, the natural environment offered an antidote to the arti-

The Stonebreakers, 1848, by Gustave Courbet. A realist masterpiece that was destroyed in the Allied bombing of Dresden during World War II, this painting now exists only in reproductions and photographs.

fices and injustices of human societies. Realist writers, by and large, lost faith in this ideal: nature no longer seemed to provide a plausible alternative. Now all that was left of reality was what you could see with your naked eyes: gritty, ugly industries; the power of money; starving, broken workers; social hierarchies; dirt, decay, and disease. The realists thus shocked their audiences by representing characters who for centuries had been considered too low and coarse for art: ragged orphans and exhausted workers, washerwomen and prostitutes, drunks and thieves. They routinely chose the city over the countryside for their settings. And they were willing to lavish their descriptive attention on squalid surroundings—sickening slums, smoggy factories, dusty barrooms. Gone was the equation of art with beauty: visual art and literature could now be deliberately, powerfully hideous.

The realists were not only concerned with the unfortunate, however. In throwing off the ideals associated with earlier art forms, realist artists often threw their energies into representing the commonplace—the mundane experience of ordinary people. They wanted to capture the world as it was, and that meant describing plausible individuals in recognizable circumstances. Realism is as closely associated with middle-class characters, then, as it is with the poor, and many of the most famous realist writers of the nineteenth century—including Honoré de Balzac, Charles Dickens, and **Fyodor Dostoyevsky**—wrote fiction that deliberately cut across different classes, showing encounters between rich and poor in an attempt to give a realistic picture of a whole society.

While some realist writers tried to capture entire nations and social classes, others focused intensively on a few individuals. Some put their emphasis on internal, psychological reality, others on the shaping force of external circumstances. Usually those who stuck to the small scale implied larger social relationships, and they used individual characters to represent whole groups, but their fictions do feel more local and intimate than the vast and sprawling novels of the period—*Bleak House* or *War and Peace*—that contain many characters and strive to represent a whole nation. These differences were in part philosophical, revolving around the question of what it is possible to know. What *is* reality?

Place de la Concorde, 1875, by Edgar Degas. A portrait of a moment in the lives of the well-to-do.

Reading by Lamplight, 1858, by James Abbott McNeill Whistler.

Can we rely on our senses, or do we need to turn to facts and statistics, theories about hidden causes and social structures? Can we see reality from a single, individual perspective, or do we need to take a bird's-eye view?

The realists did not always agree about what constituted reality or how best to capture it in words or paint, but in general they resisted symbols and allegories, sentimentality and sensationalism, otherworldly ideals and timeless values in favor of the literal, the specific, and observable—the social world as it appeared in the here and the now. They tended to focus on the immediate, material causes of social misery and looked to scientists and social thinkers for solutions, rather than aspiring to transcendent or beautiful ideals. Though frequently the writers themselves were religious, realism was typically a secular project that put its emphasis on empirical experience— what we can know through our senses— rather than on providential explanations. Many realist writers were influenced by currents in science, and a later offshoot of realism, called naturalism, turned to the evolutionary science of Charles

Darwin for a brutal explanatory model: human beings would only survive to the extent that they could adapt to their social environments; those who proved unfit would die.

Realist writers introduced a whole new range of formal techniques that transformed the literary landscape. Most wrote novels or short stories, though realist drama changed the history of theater in the late nineteenth century. The novel had the advantage of being relatively formless: it could be long or short; it could include many central characters or a single protagonist; it could be told in the first person or the third person; it could focus on domestic settings or foreign travel; and it could entwine many stories or follow a single main path. Unlike more traditional and compact forms, such as the sonnet or *ghazal*, it could swallow up other kinds of writing—letters, dialogue, description, history, biography, satire, even poetry—without being bound by the rules of any of those particular forms itself. In Europe, the novel was a new genre in the eighteenth century—hence its name "novel"—and its flexibility as a form allowed it to adapt to many different kinds of philosophies and social circumstances. Often written and read by more women than men, novels were a popular form that did not acquire a serious, highbrow status until the beginning of the twentieth century.

The novel and drama suited the aims of realism in some very specific ways. Prose is of course prosaic—suited to capturing ordinariness and even ugliness. Realist writers often opted for plain, unstylized diction and usually tried to convey the many ways of speaking that characterized the social groups they represented, including dialect speech. Prose and drama lend themselves much better to this linguistic variety than does poetry, with its strict forms and connotations of artful beauty. Fiction also lends itself well to movement between action and description: it can pause the plot to include highly detailed depictions of the characters and their environments. For writers wanting to capture the whole social world in a style that seemed objective, the omniscient third-person narrator provided the perfect, impersonal perspective. Other writers opted for first-person narrators, guided only by their own senses and experience as they try to make sense of the world. Fiction can accommodate both of these perspectives easily, and some realist novels even move back and forth between the narrator's bird's-eye view and the characters' more restricted knowledge.

The elements of both character and plot raised particular challenges and opportunities for realist writers. Some realists tried to present uniquely individual characters, conveying some of the complexity of real people in the world; others felt that the truth lay instead in types, and they used individual characters to represent whole social groups—the outraged worker, the subjugated wife, the social climber. As for plot, realist writers often tried to

Rue Transnonain, 1834, by Honoré Daumier. This lithograph was Daumier's attempt to document the massacre of nineteen people, including women and children, by the French National Guard on April 14, 1834, in response to a strike of silk weavers in Lyon, France.

steer clear of sensational events and neat endings, which jeopardized the goal of unvarnished truth telling, but they also wanted to keep their readers absorbed. One solution was to put characters in believable social situations where they faced ethical dilemmas. The dramatic interest of the plot then lay in having the character make a difficult choice. Should the heroine choose respectable poverty or agree to a luxurious but disreputable life as a kept woman? Should the hero climb the social ladder at the expense of an innocent victim?

One of the advantages of dramatizing ethical predicaments is that these allowed fiction to engage the question of moral action in the new social environments of the nineteenth century. Can individuals have an impact on unjust social relationships? What responsibility does each of us have toward others in a city, a nation, or a densely inter-connected world? For many realists, the purpose of describing the social world in great detail—with a particular emphasis on poverty and injustice—was to prompt readers to try to change that world.

With its emphasis on ordinary language, new social circumstances, and plausible human predicaments, realism transformed the literary landscape across the globe, inviting writers everywhere to try to capture the troubled, painful, struggling worlds of their own experience. And the mark these writers left remains palpable everywhere today, as realism continues to exert a powerful cultural force, still part of the daily fare of television, fiction, drama, and film around the world. Realism is nothing if not a capacious, roomy genre—able to move across borders and oceans, and as it moves, to take up new social relationships, new styles, new perspectives, and new resolutions.

FYODOR DOSTOYEVSKY

1821–1881

At seven o'clock on a bitter winter morning in 1849, a young man, meagerly dressed and shivering, went to meet his death. He had been convicted of circulating subversive writings that attacked both the Russian Orthodox Church and the tsar. Led to a platform surrounded by a crowd, he looked out over a cart filled with coffins. He heard his name and faced a firing squad. A priest administered his last rites and pressed him to confess. His cap was pulled over his face. Then, just as the firing squad took aim, a carriage screeched to a halt, and a messenger leapt out, shouting, "Long live the tsar! The good tsar!" Fyodor Dostoyevsky had been allowed to live. Astonished and thankful, he pledged his lifelong loyalty to the tsar. Drawing on this and other experiences from his eventful life, he would go on to write some of the most gripping fiction of the nineteenth century, works characterized by dramatic extremes of authority and subjection. Intense and unforgettable, Dostoyevsky's characters are often, like their author, wracked by violence, guilt, obsession, and addiction.

LIFE

Fyodor Dostoyevsky was born in 1821, the son of a doctor in Moscow. He was the second of six children. The family lived next to a hospital for poor people, which also housed a morgue. Their father was stern and efficient, their mother compassionate, and both were devout members of the Russian Orthodox Church. The children were encouraged to read widely, and Fyodor became an admirer of such writers as William Shakespeare, Pierre Corneille, **Johann Wolfgang von Goethe**, and Charles Dickens.

In 1837 Dostoyevsky's beloved mother died, and his father sent him to be educated at the military Academy for Engineers in St. Petersburg. On the way there, he witnessed an act of violence that later became a famous scene in *Crime and Punishment*, one of his best-known novels. A government courier, after throwing back a few shots of vodka, jumped into a carriage and started beating the peasant driver mercilessly. The driver, in turn, began to thrash his horses. Dostoyevsky retained a lifelong fascination with what he considered the basic human desire to subdue those weaker than oneself. After his mother's death, his father withdrew and became violent, drinking excessively, talking aloud to his dead wife, and beating his servants. In 1839 he was mysteriously murdered on his own estate, probably by his serfs.

Once Dostoyevsky had finished his engineering courses, he worked at a government job, which he found as "tiresome as potatoes." He lived beyond his means, gambling and eating in expensive restaurants. Soon he quit his job to write *Poor Folk*, his first novel, which turned out to be a great success, especially with political radicals. In the revolutionary year 1848, he took up with a group of subversive St. Petersburg socialists and atheists. A spy who had infiltrated the group informed on them, leading to Dostoyevsky's arrest and death sentence.

After being pardoned at the last moment by the tsar, the writer was exiled to hard labor in remote Siberia.

For four years he marched with shackles on his legs, moving snow and firing bricks. "Every minute," he wrote later, "weighed upon my soul like a stone." The only book he was allowed was the New Testament, and he was not permitted to write letters or receive them. Dostoyevsky's thinking and writing would be transformed by the experience: in Siberia, he found renewed faith in the Orthodox Christianity of his childhood and artistic inspiration in the religious and folk traditions of the poorest Russian people.

Dostoyevsky served out the next four years of his sentence as a soldier in the small town of Semipalatinsk, where he fell in love for the first time with a married woman. In 1857, after her husband died, they were married. Then began a period of restlessness. The marriage was not a success. The couple traveled to Western Europe, where they were poor and unhappy. Ill with epilepsy and subject to increasingly serious episodes of the disease, Dostoyevsky gambled compulsively, squandering all of the money he had begged relatives to give him. As Dostoyevsky and his wife grew ever more estranged and her health declined from tuberculosis, he fell in love with another woman who disappointed him and then left him.

It was in 1864, during the lowest point of his bitter wandering, that he composed *Notes from Underground*. Soon after this his wife died, and he began work on the manuscript that would become *Crime and Punishment*, a novel about a young man named Raskolnikov who believes that he is superior to the ordinary run of humanity and therefore not subject to the usual moral laws. He kills two women with an axe and is consumed both with guilt and with the terror of being caught. Dostoyevsky burned the first draft of this novel and then rewrote it from scratch. All the while, he was miserably poor, forced to plead with acquaintances for money and to sell everything he owned, including most of his clothes.

The next phase of the writer's life proved slightly more stable. He married a much younger woman with good business sense who managed his publications and their finances better than he had done on his own, though he remained in debt until the last year of his life. They had four children. The last, Alyosha, died from epilepsy at the age of three, and Dostoyevsky, heartbroken, blamed himself for having passed on the disease. His final novel, *The Brothers Karamazov*, features not only the murder of a father but also a saintly son named Alyosha. This novel proved extremely popular, hailed by fellow writer **Leo Tolstoy** as the best of the century. A life packed with dramatic incidents and great suffering came to an end soon after. At the time of his death in 1881, Dostoyevsky was acclaimed as one of the greatest Russian writers of all time. Thirty thousand people attended his funeral.

TIMES

By the middle of the nineteenth century, Russians had a long tradition of ambivalence toward Western Europe. On the one hand, Russia had been instituting Western-inspired reforms since the late seventeenth century, borrowing ideas about military organization, industry, law, and culture from France, Britain, and Germany. Most highborn Russians spoke French almost as a native language. On the other hand, the Russians had proudly fought off the invasion of Napoleon's French troops in 1812, and some saw European influences as weakening and corrupting Russian traditions. Tsar Nicholas I, who ruled the Russian empire from 1825 to 1855, instituted a policy he called Official Nationalism. He believed in exerting absolute power himself, and he imposed a regime of strict suppression, punishing dissenters, censoring subversive publications, and demanding allegiance to the Russian nation. He also insisted that everyone at court speak Russian. Nicholas I was followed by a very different kind of leader, Tsar Alexander II, who looked to the West for reformist ideas. His most sweeping reform was the abolition of serfdom—the possession of peasants by landowners, a system very much like slavery. He also introduced trial by jury and modest forms of representative government. His relatively liberal administration came to an end when he was assassinated in 1881.

Russian thinkers in this period tended to divide themselves into two broad camps. The first, called the Westernizers, favored European-style modernizations. Many of these were moderate liberals who defended gradual progress toward rights and freedoms, welcoming Alexander II's reforms, but others were more radical and utopian, imagining that only a thoroughgoing revolution would bring about the change Russia needed. Both liberals and radicals believed that the Western European Enlightenment, with its emphasis on reason and on universal rights, offered the best model for Russia's future.

Other Russians resisted this wholehearted embrace of Western Enlightenment values. Most of these, known as Slavophiles, envisioned all of the Slavic peoples uniting around a unique set of spiritual and cultural traditions, including a shared loyalty to the Orthodox Church. Dostoyevsky, after his brief flirtation with European radicalism, helped to bring into being a movement called "Native Soil" conservatism. He imagined all of Russia, rich and poor, joined in a new national union that would be spiritually superior to all of Western Europe. Somewhat ambivalent about the Orthodox Church, he was always drawn to the image of Christ

as a loving figure of universal reconciliation and self-sacrifice who could regenerate the nation. He saw the Russian peasantry as a repository of great spiritual wealth, and he felt that intellectuals must now return to their native soil to create a new bond with the vast mass of the people through *sobornost*, or spiritual oneness.

These "native soil" views sometimes come as a surprise to readers of Dostoyevsky's fiction, since he delves so compellingly into the minds of dogmatic atheists and violent killers that it seems he must in some way have shared their perspective. But part of what makes Dostoyevsky remarkable is his capacity to see from multiple, often conflicting viewpoints, and perhaps this is not surprising, given the extraordinary range of his experiences: his pious childhood, his fraternizing with socialists and atheists, his incarceration in a Siberian prison with murderous convicts and devout peasants, his humiliating poverty, his addiction to gambling, and his misery in love.

WORK

From the outset, *Notes from Underground* poses questions about what kind of human one should be. The narrator begins, "I am a sick man. . . . I am a spiteful man. I am a most unpleasant man." But if this character is sick, then what does it mean to be healthy? If he is spiteful and unpleasant, are others good and generous? Or, as the underground man suggests at times, are we all actually versions of him, and is humanity therefore sick, spiteful, and unpleasant? In the first few pages, the narrator compares himself to an insect, a mouse, a monkey, a slave, a peasant, and a civilized European. Later he mocks those who see humans as musical instruments—mechanical devices. But if we are not bugs, animals, machines, slaves, or civilized people, then what is the proper model for thinking about what it means to be human?

Dostoyevsky does not give us a character who can answer any of these questions to our satisfaction. Constantly contradicting himself, he calls himself a "paradoxicalist," taking pleasure in spitefulness and pride in pain. One of the most tortuous aspects of the narrator's experience is his acute self-awareness. He is horrified at being seen by others and then more troubled still by the idea that he may not be seen. And he cannot escape his obsessive self-consciousness even when alone, since he is always watching and judging himself and imagining himself through the eyes of others. Indeed, although he is painfully lonely, he is never truly free of the social world. We see him always in dialogue, constantly responding to another's views, anticipating someone else's response, even when that someone else is himself.

The "underground man" moves back and forth between casting his intense self-awareness as unique and seeing it as representative of all humanity. But Dostoyevsky also hints at a third possibility: that his antihero is a particular social type, a representative of a specifically *modern* condition. The "underground man" is a new kind of rootless urban intellectual, bombarded with fashionably progressive ideas about science, who cannot reason his way to any kind of satisfying conclusion. *Notes from Underground* is packed with references to contemporary ideas. For example, the socialist utopian novel *What Is to Be Done?*, published in 1863 (just a year prior to *Notes from Underground*), with its vision of an intrinsically good human nature governed by scientific laws, is one of the central targets of Dostoyevsky's biting critique, as is Charles Darwin's theory of evolution, first translated into Russian in 1864. The narrator also mocks an 1863 controversy over N. N. Ge's painting *The Last Supper*, which offered a star-

tling realism, showing Jesus recumbent and thoughtful instead of upright and authoritative, and presenting his disciples as scared and puzzled. This attention to up-to-date ideas was no accident: Dostoyevsky saw his own time as a "thunderous epoch permeated with so many colossal, astounding, and rapidly shifting actual events" that he could not imagine writing historical fiction, such as Leo Tolstoy's hugely popular *War and Peace*, which was set in 1812. *Notes from Underground*, then, may be less about the human condition in general than about the specific dilemma of being an educated man in modern, urban Russia.

Dostoyevsky captures this troubled mindset through a carefully crafted and complex work of literature. It is split into two quite distinct parts: in the first section we hear about the narrator from his own perspective in the present, and in the second we move backwards in time to see him through his encounters with others. The genre of *Notes from Underground* has long puzzled readers. It certainly draws on the tradition of the confession, as the narrator makes a declaration of guilt to an implied audience. And yet religious confessions require feelings of repentance, whereas Dostoyevsky's narrator defends himself and resists expressions of contrition. Is this novel, as some readers have believed, a parody of a confession? In many ways, the narrator is most like **Jean-Jacques Rousseau**, whose secular *Confessions* was the first text to explore the intimate psychological life of the author, including petty experiences of guilt and shame. And yet *Notes from Underground* is hardly a straightforward autobiography. The text's split structure does not follow a chronological arc. Instead, it gives us a picture of the narrator in two different pieces, first present and then past.

On first reading, this text may seem to meander with the narrator's tortured perceptions, but in fact it is tightly organized. After the long first section, in which he is entirely alone, we see him engaging with a sequence of other people, each of whom is lower on the social ladder than the one before. First, he becomes obsessed with a stranger—a military officer who is socially superior to him and snubs him by failing to recognize his existence. Next he meets with a group of his peers, schoolmates who refuse to take him seriously as an equal. In the final section we see him try to assert his superiority over two others: his dignified servant Apollon and the compassionate, self-sacrificing prostitute Liza.

However extreme and contradictory his characters, Dostoyevsky laid claim to a specific version of realism in his fiction. "They call me a psychologist," he said, but "it's not true. I'm merely a realist in a higher sense, that is to say I describe all the depths of the human soul." Reaching low, into the depths of the soul, as a way of achieving a "higher realism," his literature is nothing if not paradoxical. But Dostoyevsky's brilliance lies precisely in its capacity to fold together extremes—it is in the poorest prostitute that one finds the greatest spiritual wealth, and in the cruelest spite that a man can experience pleasure. Not surprisingly, then, Dostoyevsky's realism did not involve attention to the humdrum, as did the work of other realists, but offered up extremes of emotion and violence. "What most people regard as fantastic and exceptional is sometimes for me the very essence of reality," he wrote. "Everyday trivialities and a conventional view of them, in my opinion, not only fall short of realism but are even contrary to it."

Dostoyevsky influenced an astonishing array of writers and thinkers. From **Franz Kafka** and William Faulkner to **Gabriel García Márquez** and Ralph Ellison, some of the most imaginative minds of the following century acknowledged him as an inspiration. Perhaps the most unexpected of these was Albert Einstein. "Dostoyevsky," he wrote, "gives me more than any scientist."

Notes from Underground[1]

I

Underground[2]

I

I am a sick man. . . .[3] I am a spiteful man. I am a most unpleasant man. I think my liver is diseased. Then again, I don't know a thing about my illness; I'm not even sure what hurts. I'm not being treated and never have been, though I

---

1. Translated by Michael Katz.
2. Both the author of these notes and the *Notes* themselves are fictitious, of course. Nevertheless, people like the author of these notes not only may, but actually must exist in our society, considering the general circumstances under which our society was formed. I wanted to bring before the public with more prominence than usual one of the characters of the recent past. He's a representative of the current generation. In the excerpt entitled "Underground" this person introduces himself and his views, and, as it were, wants to explain the reasons why he appeared and why he had to appear in our midst. The following excerpt [*Apropos of Wet Snow*] contains the actual "notes" of this person about several events in his life [Dostoyevsky's note].
3. The ellipses are Dostoyevsky's and do not indicate omissions from the text.

respect both medicine and doctors. Besides, I'm extremely superstitious—well at least enough to respect medicine. (I'm sufficiently educated not to be superstitious; but I am, anyway.) No, gentlemen, it's out of spite that I don't wish to be treated. Now then, that's something you probably won't understand. Well, I do. Of course, I won't really be able to explain to you precisely who will be hurt by my spite in this case; I know perfectly well that I can't possibly "get even" with doctors by refusing their treatment; I know better than anyone that all this is going to hurt me alone, and no one else. Even so, if I refuse to be treated, it's out of spite. My liver hurts? Good, let it hurt even more!

I've been living this way for some time—about twenty years. I'm forty now. I used to be in the civil service. But no more. I was a nasty official. I was rude and took pleasure in it. After all, since I didn't accept bribes, at least I had to reward myself in some way. (That's a poor joke, but I won't cross it out. I wrote it thinking that it would be very witty; but now, having realized that I merely wanted to show off disgracefully, I'll make a point of not crossing it out!) When petitioners used to approach my desk for information, I'd gnash my teeth and feel unending pleasure if I succeeded in causing someone distress. I almost always succeeded. For the most part they were all timid people: naturally, since they were petitioners. But among the dandies there was a certain officer whom I particularly couldn't bear. He simply refused to be humble, and he clanged his saber in a loathsome manner. I waged war with him over that saber for about a year and a half. At last I prevailed. He stopped clanging. All this, however, happened a long time ago, during my youth. But do you know, gentlemen, what the main component of my spite really was? Why, the whole point, the most disgusting thing, was the fact that I was shamefully aware at every moment, even at the moment of my greatest bitterness, that not only was I not a spiteful man, I was not even an embittered one, and that I was merely scaring sparrows to no effect and consoling myself by doing so. I was foaming at the mouth—but just bring me some trinket to play with, just serve me a nice cup of tea with sugar, and I'd probably have calmed down. My heart might even have been touched, although I'd probably have gnashed my teeth out of shame and then suffered from insomnia for several months afterward. That's just my usual way.

I was lying about myself just now when I said that I was a nasty official. I lied out of spite. I was merely having some fun at the expense of both the petitioners and that officer, but I could never really become spiteful. At all times I was aware of a great many elements in me that were just the opposite of that. I felt how they swarmed inside me, these contradictory elements. I knew that they had been swarming inside me my whole life and were begging to be let out; but I wouldn't let them out, I wouldn't, I deliberately wouldn't let them out. They tormented me to the point of shame; they drove me to convulsions and—and finally I got fed up with them, oh how fed up! Perhaps it seems to you, gentlemen, that I'm repenting about something, that I'm asking your forgiveness for something? I'm sure that's how it seems to you. . . . But really, I can assure you, I don't care if that's how it seems. . . .

Not only couldn't I become spiteful, I couldn't become anything at all: neither spiteful nor good, neither a scoundrel nor an honest man, neither a hero nor an insect. Now I live out my days in my corner, taunting myself with the spiteful and entirely useless consolation that an intelligent man cannot seriously become anything and that only a fool can become something. Yes, sir, an intelligent man in the nineteenth century must be, is morally obliged to be, principally a characterless creature; a man possessing character, a man of action, is fundamentally a limited creature. That's my conviction at the age of forty. I'm forty now; and, after all, forty is an entire lifetime; why it's extreme old age. It's rude to live past forty, it's indecent, immoral! Who lives more than forty years? Answer sincerely, honestly. I'll tell you who: only fools and rascals. I'll tell those old men that right to their faces, all those venerable old men, all those silver-haired and sweet-smelling old men! I'll say it to the whole world right to its face! I have a right to say it because I myself will live to sixty. I'll make it to seventy! Even to eighty! . . . Wait! Let me catch my breath. . . .

You probably think, gentlemen, that I want to amuse you. You're wrong about that, too. I'm not at all the cheerful fellow I seem to be, or that I may seem to be; however, if you're irritated by all this talk (and I can already sense that you are irritated), and if you decide to ask me just who I really am, then I'll tell you: I'm a collegiate assessor. I worked in order to have something to eat (but only for that reason); and last year, when a distant relative of mine left me six thousand rubles in his will, I retired immediately and settled down in this corner. I used to live in this corner before, but now I've settled down in it. My room is nasty, squalid, on the outskirts of town. My servant is an old peasant woman, spiteful out of stupidity; besides, she has a foul smell. I'm told that the Petersburg climate is becoming bad for my health, and that it's very expensive to live in Petersburg with my meager resources. I know all that; I know it better than all those wise and experienced advisers and admonishers. But I shall remain in Petersburg; I shall not leave Petersburg! I shall not leave here because . . . Oh, what difference does it really make whether I leave Petersburg or not?

Now, then, what can a decent man talk about with the greatest pleasure? Answer: about himself.

Well, then, I too will talk about myself.

II

Now I would like to tell you, gentlemen, whether or not you want to hear it, why it is that I couldn't even become an insect. I'll tell you solemnly that I wished to become an insect many times. But not even that wish was granted. I swear to you, gentlemen, that being overly conscious is a disease, a genuine, full-fledged disease. Ordinary human consciousness would be more than sufficient for everyday human needs—that is, even half or a quarter of the amount of consciousness that's available to a cultured man in our unfortunate nineteenth century, especially to one who has the particular misfortune of living in St. Petersburg, the most abstract and premeditated city in the whole world.[4] (Cities can be either premeditated or unpremeditated.) It would have been entirely sufficient, for example, to have the consciousness with which all so-called spontaneous people and men of action are endowed. I'll bet that you think I'm writing all this to show off, to make fun of these men of action, that I'm clanging my saber just like that officer did to show off in bad taste. But,

4. St. Petersburg was conceived of as an imposing city; plans called for regular streets, broad avenues, and spacious squares.

gentlemen, who could possibly be proud of his illnesses and want to show them off?

But what am I saying? Everyone does that; people do take pride in their illnesses, and I, perhaps, more than anyone else. Let's not argue; my objection is absurd. Nevertheless, I remain firmly convinced that not only is being overly conscious a disease, but so is being conscious at all. I insist on it. But let's leave that alone for a moment. Tell me this: why was it, as if on purpose, at the very moment, indeed, at the precise moment that I was most capable of becoming conscious of the subtleties of everything that was "beautiful and sublime,"[5] as we used to say at one time, that I didn't become conscious, and instead did such unseemly things, things that . . . well, in short, probably everyone does, but it seemed as if they occurred to me deliberately at the precise moment when I was most conscious that they shouldn't be done at all? The more conscious I was of what was good, of everything "beautiful and sublime," the more deeply I sank into the morass and the more capable I was of becoming entirely bogged down in it. But the main thing is that all this didn't seem to be occurring accidentally; rather, it was as if it all had to be so. It was as if this were my most normal condition, not an illness or an affliction at all, so that finally I even lost the desire to struggle against it. It ended when I almost came to believe (perhaps I really did believe) that this might really have been my normal condition. But at first, in the beginning, what agonies I suffered during that struggle! I didn't believe that others were experiencing the same thing; therefore, I kept it a secret about myself all my life. I was ashamed (perhaps I still am even now); I reached the point where I felt some secret, abnormal, despicable little pleasure in returning home to my little corner on some disgusting Petersburg night, acutely aware that once again I'd committed some revolting act that day, that what had been done could not be undone, and I used to gnaw and gnaw at myself inwardly, secretly, nagging away, consuming myself until finally the bitterness turned into some kind of shameful, accursed sweetness and at last into genuine, earnest pleasure! Yes, into pleasure, real pleasure! I absolutely mean that. . . . That's why I first began to speak out, because I want to know for certain whether other people share this same pleasure. Let me explain: the pleasure resulted precisely from the overly acute consciousness of one's own humiliation; from the feeling that one had reached the limit; that it was disgusting, but couldn't be otherwise; you had no other choice—you could never become a different person; and that even if there were still time and faith enough for you to change into something else, most likely you wouldn't even want to change, and if you did, you wouldn't have done anything, perhaps because there really was nothing for you to change into. But the main thing and the final point is that all of this was taking place according to normal and fundamental laws of overly acute consciousness and of the inertia which results directly from these laws; consequently, not only couldn't one change, one simply couldn't do anything at all. Hence it follows, for example, as a result of this overly acute consciousness, that one is absolutely right in being a

---

5. This phrase originated in Edmund Burke's *Philosophical Inquiry into the Origin of Our Ideas of the Sublime and Beautiful* (1756) and was repeated in Immanuel Kant's *Observations on the Feeling of the Beautiful and the Sublime* (1756). It became a cliché in the writings of Russian critics during the 1830s.

scoundrel, as if this were some consolation to the scoundrel. But enough of this. . . . Oh, my, I've gone on rather a long time, but have I really explained anything? How can I explain this pleasure? But I will explain it! I shall see it through to the end! That's why I've taken up my pen. . . .

For example, I'm terribly proud. I'm as mistrustful and as sensitive as a hunchback or a dwarf; but, in truth, I've experienced some moments when, if someone had slapped my face, I might even have been grateful for it. I'm being serious. I probably would have been able to derive a peculiar sort of pleasure from it—the pleasure of despair, naturally, but the most intense pleasures occur in despair, especially when you're very acutely aware of the hopelessness of your own predicament. As for a slap in the face—why, here the conscious-ness of being beaten to a pulp would overwhelm you. The main thing is, no matter how I try, it still turns out that I'm always the first to be blamed for everything and, what's even worse, I'm always the innocent victim, so to speak, according to the laws of nature. Therefore, in the first place, I'm guilty inas-much as I'm smarter than everyone around me. (I've always considered myself smarter than everyone around me, and sometimes, believe me, I've been ashamed of it. At the least, all my life I've looked away and never could look people straight in the eye.) Finally, I'm to blame because even if there were any magnanimity in me, it would only have caused more suffering as a result of my being aware of its utter uselessness. After all, I probably wouldn't have been able to make use of that magnanimity: neither to forgive, as the offender, per-haps, had slapped me in accordance with the laws of nature, and there's no way to forgive the laws of nature; nor to forget, because even if there were any laws of nature, it's offensive nonetheless. Finally, even if I wanted to be entirely unmagnanimous, and had wanted to take revenge on the offender, I couldn't be revenged on anyone for anything because, most likely, I would never have decided to do anything, even if I could have. Why not? I'd like to say a few words about that separately.

III

Let's consider people who know how to take revenge and how to stand up for themselves in general. How, for example, do they do it? Let's suppose that they're seized by an impulse to take revenge—then for a while nothing else remains in their entire being except for that impulse. Such an individual sim-ply rushes toward his goal like an enraged bull with lowered horns; only a wall can stop him. (By the way, when actually faced with a wall such individuals, that is, spontaneous people and men of action, genuinely give up. For them a wall doesn't constitute the evasion that it does for those of us who think and consequently do nothing; it's not an excuse to turn aside from the path, a pre-text in which a person like me usually doesn't believe, but one for which he's always extremely grateful. No, they give up in all sincerity. For them the wall possesses some kind of soothing, morally decisive and definitive meaning, per-haps even something mystical . . . But more about the wall later.) Well, then, I consider such a spontaneous individual to be a genuine, normal person, just as tender mother nature wished to see him when she lovingly gave birth to him on earth. I'm green with envy at such a man. He's stupid, I won't argue with you about that; but perhaps a normal man is supposed to be stupid—how do we know? Perhaps it's even very beautiful. And I'm all the more convinced of the suspicion, so to speak, that if, for example, one were to take the antithesis of a normal man—that is, a man of overly acute consciousness, who emerged, of course, not from the bosom of nature, but from a laboratory test tube (this is almost mysticism, gentlemen, but I suspect that it's the case), then this test tube man sometimes gives up so completely in the face of his antithesis that he himself, with his overly acute consciousness, honestly considers himself not as a person, but a mouse. It may be an acutely conscious mouse, but a mouse nonetheless, while the other one is a person and consequently, . . . and so on and so forth. But the main thing is that he, he himself, considers himself to be a mouse; nobody asks him to do so, and that's the important point. Now let's take a look at this mouse in action. Let's assume, for instance, that it feels offended (it almost always feels offended), and that it also wishes to be revenged. It may even contain more accumulated malice than *l'homme de la nature et de la vérité*.[6] The mean, nasty, little desire to pay the offender back with evil may indeed rankle in it even more despicably than in *l'homme de la nature et de la vérité*, because *l'homme de la nature et de la vérité*, with his innate stupidity, considers his revenge nothing more than justice, pure and simple; but the mouse, as a result of its overly acute consciousness, rejects the idea of justice. Finally, we come to the act itself, to the very act of revenge. In addition to its original nastiness, the mouse has already managed to pile up all sorts of other nastiness around itself in the form of hesitations and doubts; so many unresolved questions have emerged from that one single question, that some kind of fatal blow is concocted unwillingly, some kind of stinking mess consisting of doubts, anxieties and, finally, spittle showered upon it by the spontaneous men of action who stand by solemnly as judges and arbiters, roaring with laughter until their sides split. Of course, the only thing left to do is dismiss it with a wave of its paw and a smile of assumed contempt which it doesn't even believe in, and creep ignominiously back into its mousehole. There, in its disgusting, stinking underground, our offended, crushed, and ridiculed mouse immediately plunges into cold, malicious, and, above all, everlasting spitefulness. For forty years on end it will recall its insult down to the last, most shameful detail; and each time it will add more shameful details of its own, spitefully teasing and irritating itself with its own fantasy. It will become ashamed of that fantasy, but it will still remember it, rehearse it again and again, fabricating all sorts of incredible stories about itself under the pretext that they too could have happened; it won't forgive a thing. Perhaps it will even begin to take revenge, but only in little bits and pieces, in trivial ways, from behind the stove, incognito, not believing in its right to be revenged, nor in the success of its own revenge, and knowing in advance that from all its attempts to take revenge, it will suffer a hundred times more than the object of its vengeance, who might not even feel a thing. On its deathbed it will recall everything all over again, with interest compounded over all those years and. . . . But it's precisely in that cold, abominable state of half-despair and

---

6. "The man of nature and truth" (French). The basic idea is borrowed from Jean-Jacques Rousseau's *Confessions* (1782–89), namely, that human beings in a state of nature are honest and direct and that they are corrupted only by civilization.

half-belief, in that conscious burial of itself alive in the underground for forty years because of its pain, in that powerfully created, yet partly dubious hopelessness of its own predicament, in all that venom of unfulfilled desire turned inward, in all that fever of vacillation, of resolutions adopted once and for all and followed a moment later by repentance—herein precisely lies the essence of that strange enjoyment I was talking about earlier. It's so subtle, sometimes so difficult to analyze, that even slightly limited people, or those who simply have strong nerves, won't understand anything about it. "Perhaps," you'll add with a smirk, "even those who've never received a slap in the face won't understand," and by so doing you'll be hinting to me ever so politely that perhaps during my life I too have received such a slap in the face and that therefore I'm speaking as an expert. I'll bet that's what you're thinking. Well, rest assured, gentlemen, I've never received such a slap, although it's really all the same to me what you think about it. Perhaps I may even regret the fact that I've given so few slaps during my lifetime. But that's enough, not another word about this subject which you find so extremely interesting.

I'll proceed calmly about people with strong nerves who don't understand certain refinements of pleasure. For example, although under particular circumstances these gentlemen may bellow like bulls as loudly as possible, and although, let's suppose, this behavior bestows on them the greatest honor, yet, as I've already said, when confronted with impossibility, they submit immediately. Impossibility—does that mean a stone wall? What kind of stone wall? Why, of course, the laws of nature, the conclusions of natural science and mathematics. As soon as they prove to you, for example, that it's from a monkey you're descended,[7] there's no reason to make faces; just accept it as it is. As soon as they prove to you that in truth one drop of your own fat is dearer to you than the lives of one hundred thousand of your fellow creatures and that this will finally put an end to all the so-called virtues, obligations, and other such similar ravings and prejudices, just accept that too; there's nothing more to do, since two times two is a fact of mathematics. Just you try to object.

"For goodness sake," they'll shout at you, "it's impossible to protest: it's two times two makes four! Nature doesn't ask for your opinion; it doesn't care about your desires or whether you like or dislike its laws. You're obliged to accept it as it is, and consequently, all its conclusions. A wall, you see, is a wall . . . etc. etc." Good Lord, what do I care about the laws of nature and arithmetic when for some reason I dislike all these laws and I dislike the fact that two times two makes four? Of course, I won't break through that wall with my head if I really don't have the strength to do so, nor will I reconcile myself to it just because I'm faced with such a stone wall and lack the strength.

As though such a stone wall actually offered some consolation and contained some real word of conciliation, for the sole reason that it means two times two makes four. Oh, absurdity of absurdities! How much better it is to understand it all, to be aware of everything, all the impossibilities and stone walls; not to be reconciled with any of those impossibilities or stone walls if it so disgusts you; to reach, by using the most inevitable logical combinations, the most revolting

7. A reference to the theory of evolution by natural selection developed by Charles Darwin (1809–1882). A book on the subject was translated into Russian in 1864.

conclusions on the eternal theme that you are somehow or other to blame even for that stone wall, even though it's absolutely clear once again that you're in no way to blame, and, as a result of all this, while silently and impotently gnashing your teeth, you sink voluptuously into inertia, musing on the fact that, as it turns out, there's no one to be angry with; that an object cannot be found, and perhaps never will be; that there's been a substitution, some sleight of hand, a bit of cheating, and that it's all a mess—you can't tell who's who or what's what; but in spite of all these uncertainties and sleights-of-hand, it hurts you just the same, and the more you don't know, the more it hurts!

<h2 style="text-align:center">IV</h2>

"Ha, ha, ha! Why, you'll be finding enjoyment in a toothache next!" you cry out with a laugh.

"Well, what of it? There is some enjoyment even in a toothache," I reply. I've had a toothache for a whole month; I know what's what. In this instance, of course, people don't rage in silence; they moan. But these moans are insincere; they're malicious, and malice is the whole point. These moans express the sufferer's enjoyment; if he didn't enjoy it, he would never have begun to moan. This is a good example, gentlemen, and I'll develop it. In the first place, these moans express all the aimlessness of the pain which consciousness finds so humiliating, the whole system of natural laws about which you really don't give a damn, but as a result of which you're suffering nonetheless, while nature isn't. They express the consciousness that while there's no real enemy to be identified, the pain exists nonetheless; the awareness that, in spite of all possible Wagenheims,[8] you're still a complete slave to your teeth; that if someone so wishes, your teeth will stop aching, but that if he doesn't so wish, they'll go on aching for three more months; and finally, that if you still disagree and protest, all there's left to do for consolation is flagellate yourself or beat your fist against the wall as hard as you can, and absolutely nothing else. Well, then, it's these bloody insults, these jeers coming from nowhere, that finally generate enjoyment that can sometimes reach the highest degree of voluptuousness. I beseech you, gentlemen, to listen to the moans of an educated man of the nineteenth century who's suffering from a toothache, especially on the second or third day of his distress, when he begins to moan in a very different way than he did on the first day, that is, not simply because his tooth aches; not the way some coarse peasant moans, but as a man affected by progress and European civilization, a man "who's renounced both the soil and the common people," as they say nowadays. His moans become somehow nasty, despicably spiteful, and they go on for days and nights. Yet he himself knows that his moans do him no good; he knows better than anyone else that he's merely irritating himself and others in vain; he knows that the audience for whom he's trying so hard, and his whole family, have now begun to listen to him with loathing; they don't believe him for a second, and they realize full well that he could moan in a different, much simpler way, without all the flourishes and affectation, and

---

8. The *General Address Book of St. Petersburg* listed eight dentists named Wagenheim; contemporary readers would have recognized the name from signs throughout the city.

that he's only indulging himself out of spite and malice. Well, it's precisely in this awareness and shame that the voluptuousness resides. "It seems I'm disturbing you, tearing at your heart, preventing anyone in the house from getting any sleep. Well, then, you won't sleep; you too must be aware at all times that I have a toothache. I'm no longer the hero I wanted to pass for earlier, but simply a nasty little man, a rogue. So be it! I'm delighted that you've seen through me. Does it make you feel bad to hear my wretched little moans? Well, then, feel bad. Now let me add an even nastier flourish. . . ." You still don't understand, gentlemen? No, it's clear that one has to develop further and become even more conscious in order to understand all the nuances of this voluptuousness! Are you laughing? I'm delighted. Of course my jokes are in bad taste, gentlemen; they're uneven, contradictory, and lacking in self-assurance. But that's because I have no respect for myself. Can a man possessing consciousness ever really respect himself?

V

Well, and is it possible, is it really possible for a man to respect himself if he even presumes to find enjoyment in the feeling of his own humiliation? I'm not saying this out of any feigned repentance. In general I could never bear to say: "I'm sorry, Daddy, and I won't do it again," not because I was incapable of saying it, but, on the contrary, perhaps precisely because I was all too capable, and how! As if on purpose it would happen that I'd get myself into some sort of mess for which I was not to blame in any way whatsoever. That was the most repulsive part of it. What's more, I'd feel touched deep in my soul; I'd repent and shed tears, deceiving even myself of course, though not feigning in the least. It seemed that my heart was somehow playing dirty tricks on me. . . . Here one couldn't even blame the laws of nature, although it was these very laws that continually hurt me during my entire life. It's disgusting to recall all this, and it was disgusting even then. Of course, a moment or so later I would realize in anger that it was all lies, lies, revolting, made-up lies, that is, all that repentance, all that tenderness, all those vows to mend my ways. But you'll ask why I mauled and tortured myself in that way? The answer is because it was so very boring to sit idly by with my arms folded; so I'd get into trouble. That's the way it was. Observe yourselves better, gentlemen; then you'll understand that it's true. I used to think up adventures for myself, inventing a life so that at least I could live. How many times did it happen, well, let's say, for example, that I took offense, deliberately, for no reason at all? All the while I knew there was no reason for it; I put on airs nonetheless, and would take it so far that finally I really did feel offended. I've been drawn into such silly tricks all my life, so that finally I lost control over myself. Another time, even twice, I tried hard to fall in love. I even suffered, gentlemen, I can assure you. In the depths of my soul I really didn't believe that I was suffering; there was a stir of mockery, but suffer I did, and in a genuine, normal way at that; I was jealous, I was beside myself with anger. . . . And all as a result of boredom, gentlemen, sheer boredom; I was overcome by inertia. You see, the direct, legitimate, immediate result of consciousness is inertia, that is, the conscious sitting idly by with one's arms folded. I've referred to this before. I repeat, I repeat emphatically: all spontaneous men and men of action are so active precisely because they're stupid and limited. How can one explain this? Here's how: as a result of their limitations they mistake immediate and secondary causes for primary ones, and thus they're convinced more quickly and easily than other people that they've located an indisputable basis for action, and this puts them at ease; that's the main point. For, in order to begin to act, one must first be absolutely at ease, with no lingering doubts whatsoever. Well, how can I, for example, ever feel at ease? Where are the primary causes I can rely upon, where's the foundation? Where shall I find it? I exercise myself in thinking, and consequently, with me every primary cause drags in another, an even more primary one, and so on to infinity. This is precisely the essence of all consciousness and thought. And here again, it must be the laws of nature. What's the final result? Why, the very same thing. Remember: I was talking about revenge before. (You probably didn't follow.) I said: a man takes revenge because he finds justice in it. That means, he's found a primary cause, a foundation: namely, justice. Therefore, he's completely at ease, and, as a result, he takes revenge peacefully and successfully, convinced that he's performing an honest and just deed. But I don't see any justice here at all, nor do I find any virtue in it whatever; consequently, if I begin to take revenge, it's only out of spite. Of course, spite could overcome everything, all my doubts, and therefore could successfully serve instead of a primary cause precisely because it's not a cause at all. But what do I do if I don't even feel spite (that's where I began before)? After all, as a result of those damned laws of consciousness, my spite is subject to chemical disintegration. You look—and the object vanishes, the arguments evaporate, a guilty party can't be identified, the offense ceases to be one and becomes a matter of fate, something like a toothache for which no one's to blame, and, as a consequence, there remains only the same recourse: that is, to bash the wall even harder. So you throw up your hands because you haven't found a primary cause. Just try to let yourself be carried away blindly by your feelings, without reflection, without a primary cause, suppressing consciousness even for a moment; hate or love, anything, just in order not to sit idly by with your arms folded. The day after tomorrow at the very latest, you'll begin to despise yourself for having deceived yourself knowingly. The result: a soap bubble and inertia. Oh, gentlemen, perhaps I consider myself to be an intelligent man simply because for my whole life I haven't been able to begin or finish anything. All right, suppose I am a babbler, a harmless, annoying babbler, like the rest of us. But then what is to be done[9] if the direct and single vocation of every intelligent man consists in babbling, that is, in deliberately talking in endless circles?

VI

Oh, if only I did nothing simply as a result of laziness. Lord, how I'd respect myself then. I'd respect myself precisely because at least I'd be capable of being lazy; at least I'd possess one more or less positive trait of which I could be cer-

---

9. Reference to a then-new novel by Nikolai Chernyshevsky (1828–1889) called *What Is to Be Done?* (1863). Dostoyevsky disliked the main idea of the novel, which was that Russians could be freed from the delusions of tra- dition and faith by scientific knowledge and could build a rational new nation; *Notes from Underground* is in part a response to Cherny- shevsky.

tain. Question: who am I? Answer: a sluggard. Why, it would have been very pleasant to hear that said about oneself. It would mean that I'd been positively identified; it would mean that there was something to be said about me. "A sluggard!" Why, that's a calling and a vocation, a whole career! Don't joke, it's true. Then, by rights I'd be a member of the very best club and would occupy myself exclusively by being able to respect myself continually. I knew a gentleman who prided himself all his life on being a connoisseur of Lafite.[1] He considered it his positive virtue and never doubted himself. He died not merely with a clean conscience, but with a triumphant one, and he was absolutely correct. I should have chosen a career for myself too: I would have been a sluggard and a glutton, not an ordinary one, but one who, for example, sympathized with everything beautiful and sublime. How do you like that? I've dreamt about it for a long time. The "beautiful and sublime" have been a real pain in the neck during my forty years, but then it's been *my* forty years, whereas then—oh, then it would have been otherwise! I would've found myself a suitable activity at once—namely, drinking to everything beautiful and sublime. I would have seized upon every opportunity first to shed a tear into my glass and then drink to everything beautiful and sublime. Then I would have turned everything into the beautiful and sublime; I would have sought out the beautiful and sublime in the nastiest, most indisputable trash. I would have become as tearful as a wet sponge. An artist, for example, has painted a portrait of Ge.[2] At once I drink to the artist who painted that portrait of Ge because I love everything beautiful and sublime. An author has written the words, "Just as you please,"[3] at once I drink to "Just as you please," because I love everything "beautiful and sublime." I'd demand respect for myself in doing this, I'd persecute anyone who didn't pay me any respect. I'd live peacefully and die triumphantly—why, it's charming, perfectly charming! And what a belly I'd have grown by then, what a triple chin I'd have acquired, what a red nose I'd have developed—so that just looking at me any passerby would have said, "Now that's a real plus! That's something really positive!" Say what you like, gentlemen, it's extremely pleasant to hear such comments in our negative age.

VII

But these are all golden dreams. Oh, tell me who was first to announce, first to proclaim that man does nasty things simply because he doesn't know his own true interest; and that if he were to be enlightened, if his eyes were to be opened to his true, normal interests, he would stop doing nasty things at once and would immediately become good and noble, because, being so enlightened and understanding his real advantage, he would realize that his own advantage really did lie in the good; and that it's well known that there's not a single man capable of acting knowingly against his own interest; consequently, he would,

1. A variety of red wine from Médoc in France.
2. N. N. Ge (1831–1894), Russian artist who rebelled against official styles in favor of a new realism in art; just before *Notes from Underground* appeared, Ge's *Last Supper* (1863) provoked considerable controversy in St. Petersburg because the painter had refused the conventional imagery of Jesus seated at a long table and instead showed him reclined and meditative, with his disciples confused and frightened.
3. An attack on the writer M. E. Saltykov-Shchedrin, who published a sympathetic review of Ge's painting titled *Just As You Please*.

so to speak, begin to do good out of necessity. Oh, the child! Oh, the pure, innocent babe! Well, in the first place, when was it during all these millennia, that man has ever acted only in his own self interest? What does one do with the millions of facts bearing witness to the one fact that people knowingly, that is, possessing full knowledge of their own true interests, have relegated them to the background and have rushed down a different path, that of risk and chance, compelled by no one and nothing, but merely as if they didn't want to follow the beaten track, and so they stubbornly, willfully forged another way, a difficult and absurd one, searching for it almost in the darkness? Why, then, this means that stubbornness and willfulness were really more pleasing to them than any kind of advantage. . . . Advantage! What is advantage? Will you take it upon yourself to define with absolute precision what constitutes man's advantage? And what if it turns out that man's advantage sometimes not only may, but even must in certain circumstances, consist precisely in his desiring something harmful to himself instead of something advantageous? And if this is so, if this can ever occur, then the whole theory falls to pieces. What do you think, can such a thing happen? You're laughing; laugh, gentlemen, but answer me: have man's advantages ever been calculated with absolute certainty? Aren't there some which don't fit, can't be made to fit into any classification? Why, as far as I know, you gentlemen have derived your list of human advantages from averages of statistical data and from scientific-economic formulas. But your advantages are prosperity, wealth, freedom, peace, and so on and so forth; so that a man who, for example, expressly and knowingly acts in opposition to this whole list, would be, in your opinion, and in mine, too, of course, either an obscurantist or a complete madman, wouldn't he? But now here's what's aston-ishing: why is it that when all these statisticians, sages, and lovers of humanity enumerate man's advantages, they invariably leave one out? They don't even take it into consideration in the form in which it should be considered, although the entire calculation depends upon it. There would be no great harm in considering it, this advantage, and adding it to the list. But the whole point is that this particular advantage doesn't fit into any classification and can't be found on any list. I have a friend, for instance. . . . But gentlemen! Why, he's your friend, too! In fact, he's everyone's friend! When he's preparing to do something, this gentleman straight away explains to you eloquently and clearly just how he must act according to the laws of nature and truth. And that's not all: with excitement and passion he'll tell you all about genuine, normal human interests; with scorn he'll reproach the shortsighted fools who understand neither their own advantage nor the real meaning of virtue; and then—exactly a quarter of an hour later, without any sudden outside cause, but precisely because of something internal that's stronger than all his interests—he does a complete about-face; that is, he does something which clearly contradicts what he's been saying: it goes against the laws of reason and his own advantage, in a word, against everything. . . . I warn you that my friend is a collective person-age; therefore it's rather difficult to blame only him. That's just it, gentlemen; in fact, isn't there something dearer to every man than his own best advantage, or (so as not to violate the rules of logic) isn't there one more advantageous advantage (exactly the one omitted, the one we mentioned before), which is more important and more advantageous than all others and, on behalf of which, a man will, if necessary, go against all laws, that is, against reason, honor, peace, and prosperity—in a word, against all those splendid and useful things, merely in order to attain this fundamental, most advantageous advantage which is dearer to him than everything else?

"Well, it's advantage all the same," you say, interrupting me. Be so kind as to allow me to explain further; besides, the point is not my pun, but the fact that this advantage is remarkable precisely because it destroys all our classifications and constantly demolishes all systems devised by lovers of humanity for the happiness of mankind. In a word, it interferes with everything. But, before I name this advantage, I want to compromise myself personally; therefore I boldly declare that all these splendid systems, all these theories to explain to mankind its real, normal interests so that, by necessarily striving to achieve them, it would immediately become good and noble—are, for the time being, in my opinion, nothing more than logical exercises! Yes, sir, logical exercises! Why, even to maintain a theory of mankind's regeneration through a system of its own advantages, why, in my opinion, that's almost the same as . . . well, claiming, for instance, following Buckle,[4] that man has become kinder as a result of civilization; consequently, he's becoming less bloodthirsty and less inclined to war. Why, logically it all even seems to follow. But man is so partial to systems and abstract conclusions that he's ready to distort the truth intentionally, ready to deny everything that he himself has ever seen and heard, merely in order to justify his own logic. That's why I take this example, because it's such a glaring one. Just look around: rivers of blood are being spilt, and in the most cheerful way, as if it were champagne. Take this entire nineteenth century of ours during which even Buckle lived. Take Napoleon—both the great and the present one.[5] Take North America—that eternal union.[6] Take, finally, that ridiculous Schleswig-Holstein[7]. . . . What is it that civilization makes kinder in us? Civilization merely promotes a wider variety of sensations in man and . . . absolutely nothing else. And through the development of this variety man may even reach the point where he takes pleasure in spilling blood. Why, that's even happened to him already. Haven't you noticed that the most refined bloodshedders are almost always the most civilized gentlemen to whom all these Attila the Huns and Stenka Razins[8] are scarcely fit to hold a candle; and if they're not as conspicuous as Attila and Stenka Razin, it's precisely because they're too common and have become too familiar to us. At least if man hasn't become more bloodthirsty as a result of civilization, surely he's become bloodthirsty in a nastier, more repulsive way than before. Previously man saw justice in bloodshed and exterminated whomever he wished with a

4. In his *History of Civilization in England* (1857–61), Henry Thomas Buckle (1821–1862) argued that the development of civilization necessarily leads to the cessation of war. Russia had recently been involved in fierce fighting in the Crimea (1853–56).

5. The French emperors Napoleon I (1769–1821) and his nephew Napoleon III (1808–1873), both of whom engaged in numerous wars, though on vastly different scales.

6. The United States was in the middle of its Civil War (1861–65).

7. The German duchies of Schleswig and Holstein, held by Denmark since 1773, were reunited with Prussia after a brief war in 1864.

8. Cossack leader (d. 1671) who organized a peasant rebellion in Russia. Attila (406?–453 C.E.), king of the Huns, who conducted devastating wars against the Roman emperors.

clear conscience; whereas now, though we consider bloodshed to be abominable, we nevertheless engage in this abomination even more than before. Which is worse? Decide for yourselves. They say that Cleopatra (forgive an example from Roman history) loved to stick gold pins into the breasts of her slave girls and take pleasure in their screams and writhing. You'll say that this took place, relatively speaking, in barbaric times; that these are barbaric times too, because (also comparatively speaking), gold pins are used even now; that even now, although man has learned on occasion to see more clearly than in barbaric times, *he's still far from having learned* how to act in accordance with the dictates of reason and science. Nevertheless, you're still absolutely convinced that he will learn how to do so, as soon as he gets rid of some bad, old habits and as soon as common sense and science have completely re-educated human nature and have turned it in the proper direction. You're convinced that then man will voluntarily stop committing blunders, and that he will, so to speak, never willingly set his own will in opposition to his own normal interests. More than that: then, you say, science itself will teach man (though, in my opinion, that's already a luxury) that in fact he possesses neither a will nor any whim of his own, that he never did, and that he himself is nothing more than a kind of piano key or an organ stop;[9] that, moreover, there still exist laws of nature, so that everything he's done has been not in accordance with his own desire, but in and of itself, according to the laws of nature. Consequently, we need only discover these laws of nature, and man will no longer have to answer for his own actions and will find it extremely easy to live. All human actions, it goes without saying, will then be tabulated according to these laws, mathematically, like tables of logarithms up to 108,000, and will be entered on a schedule; or even better, certain edifying works will be published, like our contemporary encyclopedic dictionaries, in which everything will be accurately calculated and specified so that there'll be no more actions or adventures left on earth.

At that time, it's still you speaking, new economic relations will be established, all ready-made, also calculated with mathematical precision, so that all possible questions will disappear in a single instant, simply because all possible answers will have been provided. Then the crystal palace[1] will be built. And then . . . Well, in a word, those will be our halcyon days. Of course, there's no way to guarantee (now this is me talking) that it won't be, for instance, terribly boring then (because there won't be anything left to do, once everything has been calculated according to tables); on the other hand, everything will be extremely rational. Of course, what don't people think up out of boredom! Why, even gold pins get stuck into other people out of boredom, but that wouldn't matter. What's really bad (this is me talking again) is that for all I know, people might even be grateful for those gold pins. For man is stupid, phenomenally stupid. That is, although he's not really stupid at all, he's really so ungrateful that it's hard to find another being quite like him. Why, I, for

9. A reference to the last discourse of the French philosopher Denis Diderot (1713–1784) in the *Conversation of D'Alembert and Diderot* (1769).
1. An allusion to the crystal palace described in Vera Pavlovna's fourth dream in Cherny-

shevsky's *What Is to Be Done?* and to the actual building designed by Sir Joseph Paxton, erected for the Great Exhibition in London in 1851 and at that time admired as the newest wonder of architecture; Dostoyevsky described it in *Winter Notes on Summer Impressions* (1863).

example, wouldn't be surprised in the least, if, suddenly, for no reason at all, in the midst of this future, universal rationalism, some gentleman with an offensive, rather, a retrograde and derisive expression on his face were to stand up, put his hands on his hips, and declare to us all: "How about it, gentlemen, what if we knock over all this rationalism with one swift kick for the sole purpose of sending all these logarithms to hell, so that once again we can live according to our own stupid will!" But that wouldn't matter either; what's so annoying is that he would undoubtedly find some followers; such is the way man is made. And all because of the most foolish reason, which, it seems, is hardly worth mentioning: namely, that man, always and everywhere, whoever he is, has preferred to act as he wished, and not at all as reason and advantage have dictated; one might even desire something opposed to one's own advantage, and sometimes (this is now my idea) one *positively must do so*. One's very own free, unfettered desire, one's own whim, no matter how wild, one's own fantasy, even though sometimes roused to the point of madness—all this constitutes precisely that previously omitted, most advantageous advantage which isn't included under any classification and because of which all systems and theories are constantly smashed to smithereens. Where did these sages ever get the idea that man needs any normal, virtuous desire? How did they ever imagine that man needs any kind of rational, advantageous desire? Man needs only one thing—his own *independent* desire, whatever that independence might cost and wherever it might lead. And as far as desire goes, the devil only knows. . . .

VIII

"Ha, ha, ha! But in reality even this desire, if I may say so, doesn't exist!" you interrupt me with a laugh. "Why science has already managed to dissect man so now we know that desire and so-called free choice are nothing more than . . ."

Wait, gentlemen, I myself wanted to begin like that. I must confess that even I got frightened. I was just about to declare that the devil only knows what desire depends on and perhaps we should be grateful for that, but then I remembered about science and I . . . stopped short. But now you've gone and brought it up. Well, after all, what if someday they really do discover the formula for all our desires and whims, that is, the thing that governs them, precise laws that produce them, how exactly they're applied, where they lead in each and every case, and so on and so forth, that is, the genuine mathematical formula—why, then all at once man might stop desiring, yes, indeed, he probably would. Who would want to desire according to some table? And that's not all: he would immediately be transformed from a person into an organ stop or something of that sort; because what is man without desire, without will, and without wishes if not a stop in an organ pipe? What do you think? Let's consider the probabilities—can this really happen or not?

"Hmmm . . . ," you decide, "our desires are mistaken for the most part because of an erroneous view of our own advantage. Consequently, we sometimes desire pure rubbish because, in our own stupidity, we consider it the easiest way to achieve some previously assumed advantage. Well, and when all this has been analyzed, calculated on paper (that's entirely possible, since it's repugnant and senseless to assume in advance that man will never come to understand the laws of nature) then, of course, all so-called desires will no longer exist. For if someday desires are completely reconciled with reason, we'll follow reason instead of desire simply because it would be impossible, for example, while retaining one's reason, to *desire* rubbish, and thus knowingly oppose one's reason, and desire something harmful to oneself. . . . And, since all desires and reasons can really be tabulated, since someday the laws of our so-called free choice are sure to be discovered, then, all joking aside, it may be possible to establish something like a table, so that we could actually desire according to it. If, for example, someday they calculate and demonstrate to me that I made a rude gesture because I couldn't possibly refrain from it, that I had to make precisely that gesture, well, in that case, what sort of *free choice* would there be, especially if I'm a learned man and have completed a course of study somewhere? Why, then I'd be able to calculate in advance my entire life for the next thirty years; in a word, if such a table were to be drawn up, there'd be nothing left for us to do; we'd simply have to accept it. In general, we should be repeating endlessly to ourselves that at such a time and in such circumstances nature certainly won't ask our opinion; that we must accept it as is, and not as we fantasize it, and that if we really aspire to prepare a table, a schedule, and, well . . . well, even a laboratory test tube, there's nothing to be done—one must even accept the test tube! If not, it'll be accepted even without you. . . ."

Yes, but that's just where I hit a snag! Gentlemen, you'll excuse me for all this philosophizing; it's a result of my forty years in the underground! Allow me to fantasize. Don't you see: reason is a fine thing, gentlemen, there's no doubt about it, but it's only reason, and it satisfies only man's rational faculty, whereas desire is a manifestation of all life, that is, of all human life, which includes both reason, as well as all of life's itches and scratches. And although in this manifestation life often turns out to be fairly worthless, it's life all the same, and not merely the extraction of square roots. Why, take me, for instance; I quite naturally want to live in order to satisfy all my faculties of life, not merely my rational faculty, that is, some one-twentieth of all my faculties. What does reason know? Reason knows only what it's managed to learn. (Some things it may never learn; while this offers no comfort, why not admit it openly?) But human nature acts as a whole, with all that it contains, consciously and unconsciously; and although it may tell lies, it's still alive. I suspect, gentlemen, that you're looking at me with compassion; you repeat that an enlightened and cultured man, in a word, man as he will be in the future, cannot knowingly desire something disadvantageous to himself, and that this is pure mathematics. I agree with you: it really is mathematics. But I repeat for the one-hundredth time, there is one case, only one, when a man may intentionally, consciously desire even something harmful to himself, something stupid, even very stupid, namely: in order *to have the right* to desire something even very stupid and not be bound by an obligation to desire only what's smart. After all, this very stupid thing, one's own whim, gentlemen, may in fact be the most advantageous thing on earth for people like me, especially in certain cases. In particular, it may be more advantageous than any other advantage, even in a case where it causes obvious harm and contradicts the most sensible conclusions of reason about advantage—because in any case it preserves for us what's most important and precious, that is, our personality and our individuality. There are some people who maintain that in fact this is more precious to man than anything else; of course, desire can, if it so chooses, coincide with reason, especially if it doesn't abuse this option, and chooses to coincide in moderation; this is useful and sometimes even commendable. But very often, even most of the time, desire absolutely and stubbornly disagrees with reason and . . . and . . . and, do you know, sometimes this is also useful and even very commendable? Let's assume, gentlemen, that man isn't stupid. (And really, this can't possibly be said about him at all, if only because if he's stupid, then who on earth is smart?) But even if he's not stupid, he is, nevertheless, monstrously ungrateful. Phenomenally ungrateful. I even believe that the best definition of man is this: a creature who walks on two legs and is ungrateful. But that's still not all; that's still not his main defect. His main defect is his perpetual misbehavior, perpetual from the time of the Great Flood to the Schleswig-Holstein period of human destiny. Misbehavior, and consequently, imprudence; for it's long been known that imprudence results from nothing else but misbehavior. Just cast a glance at the history of mankind; well, what do you see? Is it majestic? Well, perhaps it's majestic; why, the Colossus of Rhodes,[2] for example—that alone is worth something! Not without reason did Mr Anaevsky[3] report that some people consider it to be the product of human hands, while others maintain that it was created by nature itself. Is it colorful? Well, perhaps it's also colorful; just consider the dress uniforms, both military and civilian, of all nations at all times— why, that alone is worth something, and if you include everyday uniforms, it'll make your eyes bulge; not one historian will be able to sort it all out. Is it monotonous? Well, perhaps it's monotonous, too: men fight and fight; now they're fighting; they fought first and they fought last—you'll agree that it's really much too monotonous. In short, anything can be said about world history, anything that might occur to the most disordered imagination. There's only one thing that can't possibly be said about it—that it's rational. You'll choke on the word. Yet here's just the sort of thing you'll encounter all the time: why, in life you're constantly running up against people who are so well-behaved and so rational, such wise men and lovers of humanity who set themselves the lifelong goal of behaving as morally and rationally as possible, so to speak, to be a beacon for their nearest and dearest, simply in order to prove that it's really possible to live one's life in a moral and rational way. And so what? It's a well-known fact that many of these lovers of humanity, sooner or later, by the end of their lives, have betrayed themselves: they've pulled off some caper, sometimes even quite an indecent one. Now I ask you: what can one expect from man as a creature endowed with such strange qualities? Why, shower him with all sorts of earthly blessings, submerge him in happiness over his head so that only little bubbles appear on the surface of this happiness, as if on water, give him such economic prosperity that he'll have absolutely nothing left to do except sleep, eat gingerbread, and worry about the continuation of world history—even then, out of pure ingratitude, sheer perversity, he'll commit some repulsive act. He'll even risk losing his gingerbread, and will intentionally desire the most wicked rubbish, the most uneconomical absurdity, simply in order to inject his own pernicious fantastic element into all this positive rationality. He wants to hold onto those most fantastic dreams, his own indecent stupidity solely for the purpose of assuring himself (as if it were necessary) that men are still men and not piano keys, and that even if the laws

2. A large bronze statue of the Greek sun god, Helios, built between 292 and 280 B.C.E. in the harbor of Rhodes (an island in the Aegean Sea) and considered one of the Seven Wonders of the Ancient World.
3. A. E. Anaevsky was a critic whose articles were frequently ridiculed in literary polemics of the period.

of nature play upon them with their own hands, they're still threatened by being overplayed until they won't possibly desire anything more than a schedule. But that's not all: even if man really turned out to be a piano key, even if this could be demonstrated to him by natural science and pure mathematics, even then he still won't become reasonable; he'll intentionally do something to the contrary, simply out of ingratitude, merely to have his own way. If he lacks the means, he'll cause destruction and chaos, he'll devise all kinds of suffering and have his own way! He'll leash a curse upon the world; and, since man alone can do so (it's his privilege and the thing that most distinguishes him from other animals), perhaps only through this curse will he achieve his goal, that is, become really convinced that he's a man and not a piano key! If you say that one can also calculate all this according to a table, this chaos and darkness, these curses, so that the mere possibility of calculating it all in advance would stop everything and that reason alone would prevail—in that case man would go insane deliberately in order not to have reason, but to have his own way! I believe this, I vouch for it, because, after all, the whole of man's work seems to consist only in proving to himself constantly that he's a man and not an organ stop! Even if he has to lose his own skin, he'll prove it; even if he has to become a troglodyte, he'll prove it. And after that, how can one not sin, how can one not praise the fact that all this hasn't yet come to pass and that desire still depends on the devil knows what . . . ?

You'll shout at me (if you still choose to favor me with your shouts) that no one's really depriving me of my will; that they're merely attempting to arrange things so that my will, by its own free choice, will coincide with my normal interests, with the laws of nature, and with arithmetic.

But gentlemen, what sort of free choice will there be when it comes down to tables and arithmetic, when all that's left is two times two makes four? Two times two makes four even without my will. Is that what you call free choice?

IX

Gentlemen, I'm joking of course, and I myself know that it's not a very good joke; but, after all, you can't take everything as a joke. Perhaps I'm gnashing my teeth while I joke. I'm tormented by questions, gentlemen; answer them for me. Now, for example, you want to cure man of his old habits and improve his will according to the demands of science and common sense. But how do you know not only whether it's possible, but even if it's *necessary* to remake him in this way? Why do you conclude that human desire *must* undoubtedly be improved? In short, how do you know that such improvement will really be to man's advantage? And, to be perfectly frank, why are you so *absolutely* convinced that not to oppose man's real, normal advantage guaranteed by the conclusions of reason and arithmetic is really always to man's advantage and constitutes a law for all humanity? After all, this is still only an assumption of yours. Let's suppose that it's a law of logic, but perhaps not a law of humanity. Perhaps, gentlemen, you're wondering if I'm insane? Allow me to explain. I agree that man is primarily a creative animal, destined to strive consciously toward a goal and to engage in the art of engineering, that, is, externally and incessantly building new roads for himself *wherever they lead*. But sometimes he may want to swerve aside precisely because he's *compelled* to build these roads, and perhaps also because, no matter how stupid the spontaneous man of action may generally be, nevertheless it sometimes occurs to him that the road, as it turns out, almost always leads *somewhere or other*, and that the main thing isn't so much where it goes, but the fact that it does, and that the well-behaved child, disregarding the art of engineering, shouldn't yield to pernicious idleness which, as is well known, constitutes the mother of all vices. Man loves to create and build roads; that's indisputable. But why is he also so passionately fond of destruction and chaos? Now, then, tell me. But I myself want to say a few words about this separately. Perhaps the reason that he's so fond of destruction and chaos (after all, it's indisputable that he sometimes really loves it, and that's a fact) is that he himself has an instinctive fear of achieving his goal and completing the project under construction? How do you know if perhaps he loves his building only from afar, but not from close up; perhaps he only likes building it, but not living in it, leaving it afterward *aux animaux domestiques*,[4] such as ants or sheep, or so on and so forth. Now ants have altogether different tastes. They have one astonishing structure of a similar type, forever indestructible—the anthill.

The worthy ants began with the anthill, and most likely, they will end with the anthill, which does great credit to their perseverance and steadfastness. But man is a frivolous and unseemly creature and perhaps, like a chess player, he loves only the process of achieving his goal, and not the goal itself. And, who knows (one can't vouch for it), perhaps the only goal on earth toward which mankind is striving consists merely in this incessant process of achieving or to put it another way, in life itself, and not particularly in the goal which, of course, must always be none other than two times two makes four, that is, a formula; after all, two times two makes four is no longer life, gentlemen, but the beginning of death. At least man has always been somewhat afraid of this two times two makes four, and I'm afraid of it now, too. Let's suppose that the only thing man does is search for this two times two makes four; he sails across oceans, sacrifices his own life in the quest; but to seek it out and find it—really and truly, he's very frightened. After all, he feels that as soon as he finds it, there'll be nothing left to search for. Workers, after finishing work, at least receive their wages, go off to a tavern, and then wind up at a police station—now that's a full week's occupation. But where will man go? At any rate a certain awkwardness can be observed each time he approaches the achievement of similar goals. He loves the process, but he's not so fond of the achievement, and that, of course is terribly amusing. In short, man is made in a comical way; obviously there's some sort of catch in all this. But two times two makes four is an insufferable thing, nevertheless. Two times two makes four—why, in my opinion, it's mere insolence. Two times two makes four stands there brazenly with its hands on its hips, blocking your path and spitting at you. I agree that two times two makes four is a splendid thing; but if we're going to lavish praise, then two times two makes five is sometimes also a very charming little thing.

4. "To domestic animals" (French).

And why are you so firmly, so triumphantly convinced that only the normal and positive—in short, only well-being is advantageous to man? Doesn't reason ever make mistakes about advantage? After all, perhaps man likes something other than well-being? Perhaps he loves suffering just as much? Perhaps suffering is just as advantageous to him as well-being? Man sometimes loves suffering terribly, to the point of passion, and that's a fact. There's no reason to study world history on this point; if indeed you're a man and have lived at all, just ask yourself. As far as my own personal opinion is concerned, to love only well-being is somehow even indecent. Whether good or bad, it's sometimes also very pleasant to demolish something. After all, I'm not standing up for suffering here, nor for well-being, either. I'm standing up for . . . my own whim and for its being guaranteed to me whenever necessary. For instance, suffering is not permitted in vaudevilles,[5] that I know. It's also inconceivable in the crystal palace; suffering is doubt and negation. What sort of crystal palace would it be if any doubt were allowed? Yet, I'm convinced that man will never renounce real suffering, that is, destruction and chaos. After all, suffering is the sole cause of consciousness. Although I stated earlier that in my opinion consciousness is man's greatest misfortune, still I know that man loves it and would not exchange it for any other sort of satisfaction. Consciousness, for example, is infinitely higher than two times two. Of course, after two times two, there's nothing left, not merely nothing to do, but nothing to learn. Then the only thing possible will be to plug up your five senses and plunge into contemplation. Well, even if you reach the same result with consciousness, that is, having nothing left to do, at least you'll be able to flog yourself from time to time, and that will liven things up a bit. Although it may be reactionary, it's still better than nothing.

X[6]

You believe in the crystal palace, eternally indestructible, that is, one at which you can never stick out your tongue furtively nor make a rude gesture, even with your fist hidden away. Well, perhaps I'm so afraid of this building precisely because it's made of crystal and it's eternally indestructible, and because it won't be possible to stick one's tongue out even furtively.

Don't you see: if it were a chicken coop instead of a palace, and if it should rain, then perhaps I could crawl into it so as not to get drenched; but I would still not mistake a chicken coop for a palace out of gratitude, just because it sheltered me from the rain. You're laughing, you're even saying that in this case there's no difference between a chicken coop and a mansion. Yes, I reply, if the only reason for living is to keep from getting drenched.

But what if I've taken it into my head that this is not the only reason for living, and, that if one is to live at all, one might as well live in a mansion? Such is my wish, my desire. You'll expunge it from me only when you've changed my desires. Well, then, change them, tempt me with something else, give me some other ideal. In the meantime, I still won't mistake a chicken coop for a palace.

---

5. A dramatic genre, popular on the Russian stage, consisting of scenes from contemporary life acted with a satirical twist, often in racy dialogue.

6. This chapter was badly mutilated by the censor, as Dostoyevsky makes clear in the letter to his brother Mikhail, dated March 26, 1864.

But let's say that the crystal palace is a hoax, that according to the laws of nature it shouldn't exist, and that I've invented it only out of my own stupidity, as a result of certain antiquated, irrational habits of my generation. But what do I care if it doesn't exist? What difference does it make if it exists only in my own desires, or, to be more precise, if it exists as long as my desires exist? Perhaps you're laughing again? Laugh, if you wish; I'll resist all your laughter and I still won't say I'm satiated if I'm really hungry; I know all the same that I won't accept a compromise, an infinitely recurring zero, just because it exists according to the laws of nature and it *really* does exist. I won't accept as the crown of my desires a large building with tenements for poor tenants to be rented for a thousand years and, just in case, with the name of the dentist Wagenheim on the sign. Destroy my desires, eradicate my ideals, show me something better and I'll follow you. You may say, perhaps, that it's not worth getting involved; but, in that case, I'll say the same thing in reply. We're having a serious discussion; if you don't grant me your attention, I won't grovel for it. I still have my underground.

And, as long as I'm still alive and feel desire—may my arm wither away before it contributes even one little brick to that building! Never mind that I myself have just rejected the crystal palace for the sole reason that it won't be possible to tease it by sticking out one's tongue at it. I didn't say that because I'm so fond of sticking out my tongue. Perhaps the only reason I got angry is that among all your buildings there's still not a single one where you don't feel compelled to stick out your tongue. On the contrary, I'd let my tongue be cut off out of sheer gratitude, if only things could be so arranged that I'd no longer want to stick it out. What do I care if things can't be so arranged and if I must settle for some tenements? Why was I made with such desires? Can it be that I was made this way only in order to reach the conclusion that my entire way of being is merely a fraud? Can this be the whole purpose? I don't believe it.

By the way, do you know what? I'm convinced that we underground men should be kept in check. Although capable of sitting around quietly in the underground for some forty years, once he emerges into the light of day and bursts into speech, he talks on and on and on. . . .

XI

The final result, gentlemen, is that it's better to do nothing! Conscious inertia is better! And so, long live the underground! Even though I said that I envy the normal man to the point of exasperation, I still wouldn't want to be him under the circumstances in which I see him (although I still won't keep from envying him. No, no, in any case the underground is more advantageous!) At least there one can . . . Hey, but I'm lying once again! I'm lying because I know myself as surely as two times two, that it isn't really the underground that's better, but something different, altogether different, something that I long for, but I'll never be able to find! To hell with the underground! Why, here's what would be better: if I myself were to believe even a fraction of everything I've written. I swear to you, gentlemen, that I don't believe one word, not one little word of all that I've scribbled. That is, I do believe it, perhaps, but at the very same time, I don't know why, I feel and suspect that I'm lying like a trooper.

"Then why did you write all this?" you ask me.

"What if I'd shut you up in the underground for forty years with nothing to do and then came back forty years later to see what had become of you? Can a man really be left alone for forty years with nothing to do?"

"Isn't it disgraceful, isn't it humiliating!" you might say, shaking your head in contempt. "You long for life, but you try to solve life's problems by means of a logical tangle. How importunate, how insolent your outbursts, and how frightened you are at the same time! You talk rubbish, but you're constantly afraid of them and make apologies. You maintain that you fear nothing, but at the same time you try to ingratiate yourself with us. You assure us that you're gnashing your teeth, yet at the same time you try to be witty and amuse us. You know that your witticisms are not very clever, but apparently you're pleased by their literary merit. Perhaps you really have suffered, but you don't even respect your own suffering. There's some truth in you, too, but no chastity; out of the pettiest vanity you bring your truth out into the open, into the marketplace, and you shame it. . . . You really want to say something, but you conceal your final word out of fear because you lack the resolve to utter it; you have only cowardly impudence. You boast about your consciousness, but you merely vacillate, because even though your mind is working, your heart has been blackened by depravity, and without a pure heart, there can be no full, genuine consciousness. And how importunate you are; how you force yourself upon others; you behave in such an affected manner. Lies, lies, lies!"

Of course, it was I who just invented all these words for you. That, too, comes from the underground. For forty years in a row I've been listening to all your words through a crack. I've invented them myself, since that's all that's occurred to me. It's no wonder that I've learned it all by heart and that it's taken on such a literary form. . . .

But can you really be so gullible as to imagine that I'll print all this and give it to you to read? And here's another problem I have: why do I keep calling you "gentlemen"? Why do I address you as if you really were my readers? Confessions such as the one I plan to set forth here aren't published and given to other people to read. Anyway, I don't possess sufficient fortitude, nor do I consider it necessary to do so. But don't you see, a certain notion has come into my mind, and I wish to realize it at any cost. Here's the point.

Every man has within his own reminiscences certain things he doesn't reveal to anyone, except, perhaps, to his friends. There are also some that he won't reveal even to his friends, only to himself perhaps, and even then, in secret. Finally, there are some which a man is afraid to reveal even to himself; every decent man has accumulated a fair number of such things. In fact, it can even be said that the more decent the man, the more of these things he's accumulated. Anyway, only recently I myself decided to recall some of my earlier adventures; up to now I've always avoided them, even with a certain anxiety. But having decided not only to recall them, but even to write them down, now is when I wish to try an experiment: is it possible to be absolutely honest even with one's own self and not to fear the whole truth? Incidentally, I'll mention that Heine maintains that faithful autobiographies are almost impossible, and that a man is sure to lie about himself.[7] In Heine's opinion, Rousseau, for

7. A reference to the work *On Germany* (1853–54) by the German poet Heinrich Heine (1797–1856), in which on the very first page Heine speaks of Rousseau as lying and inventing disgraceful incidents about himself for his *Confessions.*

example, undoubtedly told untruths about himself in his confession and even lied intentionally, out of vanity. I'm convinced that Heine is correct; I understand perfectly well that sometimes it's possible out of vanity alone to impute all sorts of crimes to oneself, and I can even understand what sort of vanity that might be. But Heine was making judgments about a person who confessed to the public. I, however, am writing for myself alone and declare once and for all that if I write as if I were addressing readers, that's only for show, because it's easier for me to write that way. It's a form, simply a form; I shall never have any readers. I've already stated that. . . . I don't want to be restricted in any way by editing my notes. I won't attempt to introduce any order or system. I'll write down whatever comes to mind.

Well, now, for example, someone might seize upon my words and ask me, if you really aren't counting on any readers, why do you make such compacts with yourself, and on paper no less; that is, if you're not going to introduce any order or system, if you're going to write down whatever comes to mind, etc., etc.? Why do you go on explaining? Why do you keep apologizing?

"Well, imagine that," I reply.

This, by the way, contains an entire psychology. Perhaps it's just that I'm a coward. Or perhaps it's that I imagine an audience before me on purpose, so that I behave more decently when I'm writing things down. There may be a thousand reasons.

But here's something else: why is it that I want to write? If it's not for the public, then why can't I simply recall it all in my own mind and not commit it to paper?

Quite so; but somehow it appears more dignified on paper. There's something more impressive about it; I'll be a better judge of myself; the style will be improved. Besides, perhaps I'll actually experience some relief from the process of writing it all down. Today, for example, I'm particularly oppressed by one very old memory from my distant past. It came to me vividly several days ago and since then it's stayed with me, like an annoying musical motif that doesn't want to leave you alone. And yet you must get rid of it. I have hundreds of such memories; but at times a single one emerges from those hundreds and oppresses me. For some reason I believe that if I write it down I can get rid of it. Why not try?

Lastly, I'm bored, and I never do anything. Writing things down actually seems like work. They say that work makes a man become good and honest. Well, at least there's chance.

It's snowing today, an almost wet, yellow, dull snow. It was snowing yesterday too, a few days ago as well. I think it was apropos of the wet snow that I recalled this episode and now it doesn't want to leave me alone. And so, let it be a tale apropos of wet snow.

II

Apropos of Wet Snow

> When from the darkness of delusion
> I saved your fallen soul
> With ardent words of conviction,
> And, full of profound torment,
> Wringing your hands, you cursed

The vice that had ensnared you;
When, punishing by recollection
Your forgetful conscience,
You told me the tale
Of all that had happened before,
And, suddenly, covering your face,
Full of shame and horror,
You tearfully resolved,
Indignant, shaken . . .
Etc., etc., etc.
    From the poetry of N. A. Nekrasov[8]

I

At that time I was only twenty-four years old. Even then my life was gloomy, disordered, and solitary to the point of savagery. I didn't associate with anyone; I even avoided talking, and I retreated further and further into my corner. At work in the office I even tried not to look at anyone; I was aware not only that my colleagues considered me eccentric, but that they always seemed to regard me with a kind of loathing. Sometimes I wondered why it was that no one else thinks that others regard him with loathing. One of our office-workers had a repulsive pock-marked face which even appeared somewhat villainous. It seemed to me that with such a disreputable face I'd never have dared look at anyone. Another man had a uniform so worn that there was a foul smell emanating from him. Yet, neither of these two gentlemen was embarrassed— neither because of his clothes, nor his face, nor in any moral way. Neither one imagined that other people regarded him with loathing; and if either had so imagined, it wouldn't have mattered at all, as long as their supervisor chose not to view him that way. It's perfectly clear to me now, because of my unlimited vanity and the great demands I accordingly made on myself, that I frequently regarded myself with a furious dissatisfaction verging on loathing; as a result, I intentionally ascribed my own view to everyone else. For example, I despised my own face; I considered it hideous, and I even suspected that there was something repulsive in its expression. Therefore, every time I arrived at work, I took pains to behave as independently as possible, so that I couldn't be suspected of any malice, and I tried to assume as noble an expression as possible. "It may not be a handsome face," I thought, "but let it be noble, expressive, and above all, extremely *intelligent*." But I was agonizingly certain that my face couldn't possibly express all these virtues. Worst of all, I considered it positively stupid. I'd have been reconciled if it had looked intelligent. In fact, I'd even have agreed to have it appear repulsive, on the condition that at the same time people would find my face terribly intelligent.

Of course, I hated all my fellow office-workers from the first to the last and despised every one of them; yet, at the same time it was as if I were afraid of them. Sometimes it happened that I would even regard them as superior to me. At this time these changes would suddenly occur: first I would despise them,

8. A Russian poet and editor of radical sympathies (1821–1878). The poem quoted dates from 1845 and is untitled. It ends with the lines "And enter my house bold and free / To become its full mistress!"

then I would regard them as superior to me. A cultured and decent man cannot be vain without making unlimited demands on himself and without hating himself, at times to the point of contempt. But, whether hating them or regarding them as superior, I almost always lowered my eyes when meeting anyone. I even conducted experiments: could I endure someone's gaze? I'd always be the first to lower my eyes. This infuriated me to the point of madness. I slavishly worshipped the conventional in everything external. I embraced the common practice and feared any eccentricity with all my soul. But how could I sustain it? I was morbidly refined, as befits any cultured man of our time. All others resembled one another as sheep in a flock. Perhaps I was the only one in the whole office who constantly thought of himself as a coward and a slave; and I thought so precisely because I was so cultured. But not only did I think so, it actually was so: I was a coward and a slave. I say this without any embarrassment. Every decent man of our time is and must be a coward and a slave. This is his normal condition. I'm deeply convinced of it. This is how he's made and what he's meant to be. And not only at the present time, as the result of some accidental circumstance, but in general at all times, a decent man must be a coward and a slave. This is a law of nature for all decent men on earth. If one of them should happen to be brave about something or other, we shouldn't be comforted or distracted: he'll still lose his nerve about something else. That's the single and eternal way out. Only asses and their mongrels are brave, and even then, only until they come up against a wall. It's not worthwhile paying them any attention because they really don't mean anything at all.

There was one more circumstance tormenting me at that time: no one was like me, and I wasn't like anyone else. "I'm alone," I mused, "and they are *everyone*"; and I sank deep into thought.

From all this it's clear that I was still just a boy.

The exact opposite would also occur. Sometimes I would find it repulsive to go to the office: it reached the point where I would often return home from work ill. Then suddenly, for no good reason at all, a flash of skepticism and indifference would set in (everything came to me in flashes); I would laugh at my own intolerance and fastidiousness, and reproach myself for my *romanticism*. Sometimes I didn't even want to talk to anyone; at other times it reached a point where I not only started talking, but I even thought about striking up a friendship with others. All my fastidiousness would suddenly disappear for no good reason at all. Who knows? Perhaps I never really had any, and it was all affected, borrowed from books. I still haven't answered this question, even up to now. And once I really did become friends with others; I began to visit their houses, play préférence,[9] drink vodka, talk about promotions. . . . But allow me to digress.

We Russians, generally speaking, have never had any of those stupid, transcendent German romantics, or even worse, French romantics, on whom nothing produces any effect whatever: the earth might tremble beneath them, all of France might perish on the barricades, but they remain the same, not even changing for decency's sake; they go on singing their transcendent songs, so to speak, to their dying day, because they're such fools. We here on Russian soil have no fools. It's a well-known fact; that's precisely what distinguishes us

9. A card game for three players.

from foreigners. Consequently, transcendent natures cannot be found among us in their pure form. That's the result of our "positive" publicists and critics of that period, who hunted for the Kostanzhouglo and the Uncle Pyotr Ivanoviches,[1] foolishly mistaking them for our ideal and slandering our own romantics, considering them to be the same kind of transcendents as one finds in Germany or France. On the contrary, the characteristics of our romantics are absolutely and directly opposed to the transcendent Europeans; not one of those European standards can apply here. (Allow me to use the word "romantic"—it's an old-fashioned little word, well-respected and deserving, familiar to everyone.) The characteristics of our romantics are to understand everything, *to see everything, often to see it much more clearly than our most positive minds*; not to be reconciled with anyone or anything, but, at the same time, not to balk at anything; to circumvent everything, to yield on every point, to treat everyone diplomatically; never to lose sight of some useful, practical goal (an apartment at government expense, a nice pension, a decoration)—to keep an eye on that goal through all his excesses and his volumes of lyrical verse, and, at the same time, to preserve intact the "beautiful and sublime" to the end of their lives; and, incidentally, to preserve themselves as well, wrapped up in cotton like precious jewelry, if only, for example, for the sake of that same "beautiful and sublime." Our romantic has a very broad nature and is the biggest rogue of all, I can assure you of that . . . even by my own experience. Of course, all this is true if the romantic is smart. But what am I saying? A romantic is always smart; I merely wanted to observe that although we've had some romantic fools, they really don't count at all, simply because while still in their prime they would degenerate completely into Germans, and, in order to preserve their precious jewels more comfortably, they'd settle over there, either in Weimar or in the Black Forest. For instance, I genuinely despised my official position and refrained from throwing it over merely out of necessity, because I myself sat there working and received good money for doing it. And, as a result, please note, I still refrained from throwing it over. Our romantic would sooner lose his mind (which, by the way, very rarely occurs) than give it up, if he didn't have another job in mind; nor is he ever kicked out, unless he's hauled off to the insane asylum as the "King of Spain,"[2] and only if he's gone completely mad. Then again, it's really only the weaklings and towheads who go mad in our country. An enormous number of romantics later rise to significant rank. What extraordinary versatility! And what a capacity for the most contradictory sensations! I used to be consoled by these thoughts back then, and still am even nowadays. That's why there are so many "broad natures" among us, people who never lose their ideals, no matter how low they fall; even though they never lift a finger for the sake of their ideals, even though they're outrageous villains and thieves, nevertheless they respect their original ideals to the point of tears and are extremely honest men at heart. Yes, only among us Russians

1. A character in Ivan Goncharov's novel *A Common Story* (1847); a high bureaucrat, a factory owner who teaches lessons of sobriety and good sense to the romantic hero, Alexander Aduyev. Konstanzhouglo is the ideal efficient landowner in the second part of Nikolai Gogol's novel *Dead Souls* (1852).

2. An allusion to the hero of Gogol's short story "Diary of a Madman" (1835). Poprishchin, a low-ranking civil servant, sees his aspirations crushed by the enormous bureaucracy. He ends by going insane and imagining himself to be king of Spain.

can the most outrageous scoundrel be absolutely, even sublimely honest at heart, while at the same time never ceasing to be a scoundrel. I repeat, nearly always do our romantics turn out to be very efficient rascals (I use the word "rascal" affectionately); they suddenly manifest such a sense of reality and positive knowledge that their astonished superiors and the general public can only click their tongues at them in amazement.

Their versatility is really astounding; God only knows what it will turn into, how it will develop under subsequent conditions, and what it holds for us in the future. The material is not all that bad! I'm not saying this out of some ridiculous patriotism or jingoism. However, I'm sure that once again you think I'm joking. But who knows? Perhaps it's quite the contrary, that is, you're convinced that this is what I really think. In any case, gentlemen, I'll consider that both of these opinions constitute an honor and a particular pleasure. And do forgive me for this digression.

Naturally, I didn't sustain any friendships with my colleagues, and soon I severed all relations after quarreling with them; and, because of my youthful inexperience at the same time, I even stopped greeting them, as if I'd cut them off entirely. That, however, happened to me only once. On the whole, I was always alone.

At home I spent most of my time reading. I tried to stifle all that was constantly seething within me with external sensations. And of all external sensations available, only reading was possible for me. Of course, reading helped a great deal—it agitated, delighted, and tormented me. But at times it was terribly boring. I still longed to be active; and suddenly I sank into dark, subterranean, loathsome depravity—more precisely, petty vice. My nasty little passions were sharp and painful as a result of my constant, morbid irritability. I experienced hysterical fits accompanied by tears and convulsions. Besides reading, I had nowhere else to go—that is, there was nothing to respect in my surroundings, nothing to attract me. In addition, I was overwhelmed by depression; I possessed a hysterical craving for contradictions and contrasts; and, as a result, I plunged into depravity. I haven't said all this to justify myself. . . . But, no, I'm lying. I did want to justify myself. It's for myself, gentlemen, that I include this little observation. I don't want to lie. I've given my word.

I indulged in depravity all alone, at night, furtively, timidly, sordidly, with a feeling of shame that never left me even in my most loathsome moments and drove me at such times to the point of profanity. Even then I was carrying around the underground in my soul. I was terribly afraid of being seen, met, recognized. I visited all sorts of dismal places.

Once, passing by some wretched little tavern late at night, I saw through a lighted window some gentlemen fighting with billiard cues; one of them was thrown out the window. At some other time I would have been disgusted; but just then I was overcome by such a mood that I envied the gentleman who'd been tossed out; I envied him so much that I even walked into the tavern and entered the billiard room. "Perhaps," I thought, "I'll get into a fight, and they'll throw me out the window, too."

I wasn't drunk, but what could I do—after all, depression can drive a man to this kind of hysteria. But nothing came of it. It turned out that I was incapable of being tossed out the window; I left without getting into a fight.

As soon as I set foot inside, some officer put me in my place.

I was standing next to the billiard table inadvertently blocking his way as he wanted to get by; he took hold of me by the shoulders and without a word of warning or explanation, moved me from where I was standing to another place, and he went past as if he hadn't even noticed me. I could have forgiven even a beating, but I could never forgive his moving me out of the way and entirely failing to notice me.

The devil knows what I would have given for a genuine, ordinary quarrel, a decent one, a more *literary* one, so to speak. But I'd been treated as if I were a fly. The officer was about six feet tall, while I'm small and scrawny. The quarrel, however, was in my hands; all I had to do was protest, and of course they would've thrown me out the window. But I reconsidered and preferred . . . to withdraw resentfully.

I left the tavern confused and upset and went straight home; the next night I continued my petty vice more timidly, more furtively, more gloomily than before, as if I had tears in my eyes—but I continued nonetheless. Don't conclude, however, that I retreated from that officer as a result of any cowardice; I've never been a coward at heart, although I've constantly acted like one in deed, but—wait before you laugh—I can explain this. I can explain anything, you may rest assured.

Oh, if only this officer had been the kind who'd have agreed to fight a duel! But no, he was precisely one of those types (alas, long gone) who preferred to act with their billiard cues or, like Gogol's Lieutenant Pirogov,[3] by appealing to the authorities. They didn't fight duels; in any case, they'd have considered fighting a duel with someone like me, a lowly civilian, to be indecent. In general, they considered duels to be somehow inconceivable, free-thinking, French, while they themselves, especially if they happened to be six feet tall, offended other people rather frequently.

In this case I retreated not out of any cowardice, but because of my unlimited vanity. I wasn't afraid of his height, nor did I think I'd receive a painful beating and get thrown out the window. In fact, I'd have had sufficient physical courage; it was moral fortitude I lacked. I was afraid that everyone present— from the insolent billiard marker to the foul-smelling, pimply little clerks with greasy collars who used to hang about—wouldn't understand and would laugh when I started to protest and speak to them in literary Russian. Because, to this very day, it's still impossible for us to speak about a point of honor, that is, not about honor itself, but a point of honor (*point d'honneur*), except in literary language. One can't even refer to a "point of honor" in everyday language. I was fully convinced (a sense of reality, in spite of all my romanticism!) that they would all simply split their sides laughing, and that the officer, instead of giving me a simple beating, that is, an inoffensive one, would certainly apply his knee to my back and drive me around the billiard table; only then perhaps would he have the mercy to throw me out the window. Naturally, this wretched story of mine couldn't possibly end with this alone. Afterward I used to meet this officer frequently on the street and I observed him very carefully. I don't know whether he ever recognized me. Probably not; I reached that conclusion

3. One of two main characters in Gogol's short story "Nevsky Prospect" (1835). A shallow and self-satisfied officer, he mistakes the wife of a German artisan for a woman of easy virtue and receives a sound thrashing. He decides to lodge an official complaint but, after consuming a cream-filled pastry, thinks better of it.

from various observations. As for me, I stared at him with malice and hatred, and continued to do so for several years! My malice increased and became stronger over time. At first I began to make discreet inquiries about him. This was difficult for me to do, since I had so few acquaintances. But once, as I was following him at a distance as though tied to him, someone called to him on the street: that's how I learned his name. Another time I followed him back to his own apartment and for a ten-kopeck piece learned from the doorman where and how he lived, on what floor, with whom, etc.—in a word, all that could be learned from a doorman. One morning, although I never engaged in literary activities, it suddenly occurred to me to draft a description of this officer as a kind of exposé, a caricature, in the form of a tale. I wrote it with great pleasure. I exposed him; I even slandered him. At first I altered his name only slightly, so that it could be easily recognized; but then, upon careful reflection, I changed it. Then I sent the tale off to *Notes of the Fatherland*.[4] But such exposés were no longer in fashion, and they didn't publish my tale. I was very annoyed by that. At times I simply choked on my spite. Finally, I resolved to challenge my opponent to a duel. I composed a beautiful, charming letter to him, imploring him to apologize to me; in case he refused, I hinted rather strongly at a duel. The letter was composed in such a way that if that officer had possessed even the smallest understanding of the "beautiful and sublime," he would have come running, thrown his arms around me, and offered his friendship. That would have been splendid! We would have led such a wonderful life! Such a life! He would have shielded me with his rank; I would have ennobled him with my culture, and, well, with my ideas. Who knows what might have come of it! Imagine it, two years had already passed since he'd insulted me; my challenge was the most ridiculous anachronism, in spite of all the cleverness of my letter in explaining and disguising that fact. But, thank God (to this day I thank the Almighty with tears in my eyes), I didn't send that letter. A shiver runs up and down my spine when I think what might have happened if I had. Then suddenly . . . suddenly, I got my revenge in the simplest manner, a stroke of genius! A brilliant idea suddenly occurred to me. Sometimes on holidays I used to stroll along Nevsky Prospect at about four o'clock in the afternoon, usually on the sunny side. That is, I didn't really stroll; rather, I experienced innumerable torments, humiliations, and bilious attacks. But that's undoubtedly just what I needed. I darted in and out like a fish among the strollers, constantly stepping aside before generals, cavalry officers, hussars, and young ladies. At those moments I used to experience painful spasms in my heart and a burning sensation in my back merely at the thought of my dismal apparel as well as the wretchedness and vulgarity of my darting little figure. This was sheer torture, uninterrupted and unbearable humiliation at the thought, which soon became an incessant and immediate sensation, that I was a fly in the eyes of society, a disgusting, obscene fly—smarter than the rest, more cultured, even nobler—all that goes without saying, but a fly, nonetheless, who incessantly steps aside, insulted and injured by everyone. For what reason did I inflict this torment on myself? Why did I stroll along Nevsky Prospect? I don't know. But something simply *drew* me there at every opportunity.

Then I began to experience surges of that pleasure about which I've already spoken in the first chapter. After the incident with the officer I was drawn

---

4. A radical literary and political journal published in St. Petersburg from 1839 to 1867.

there even more strongly; I used to encounter him along Nevsky most often, and it was there that I could admire him. He would also go there, mostly on holidays. He, too, would give way before generals and individuals of superior rank; he, too, would spin like a top among them. But he would simply trample people like me, or even those slightly superior; he would walk directly toward them, as if there were empty space ahead of him; and under no circumstance would he ever step aside. I revelled in my malice as I observed him, and . . . bitterly stepped aside before him every time. I was tortured by the fact that even on the street I found it impossible to stand on an equal footing with him. "Why is it you're always first to step aside?" I badgered myself in insane hysteria, at times waking up at three in the morning. "Why always you and not he? After all, there's no law about it; it isn't written down anywhere. Let it be equal, as it usually is when people of breeding meet: he steps aside halfway and you halfway, and you pass by showing each other mutual respect." But that was never the case, and I continued to step aside, while he didn't even notice that I was yielding to him. Then a most astounding idea suddenly dawned on me. "What if," I thought, "what if I were to meet him and . . . not step aside? Deliberately not step aside, even if it meant bumping into him: how would that be?" This bold idea gradually took such a hold that it afforded me no peace. I dreamt about it incessantly, horribly, and even went to Nevsky more frequently so that I could imagine more clearly how I would do it. I was in ecstasy. The scheme was becoming more and more possible and even probable to me. "Of course, I wouldn't really collide with him," I thought, already feeling more generous toward him in my joy, "but I simply won't turn aside. I'll bump into him, not very painfully, but just so, shoulder to shoulder, as much as decency allows. I'll bump into him the same amount as he bumps into me." At last I made up my mind completely. But the preparations took a very long time. First, in order to look as presentable as possible during the execution of my scheme, I had to worry about my clothes. "In any case, what if, for example, it should occasion a public scandal? (And the public there was *superflu*:[5] a countess, Princess D., and the entire literary world.) It was essential to be well-dressed; that inspires respect and in a certain sense will place us immediately on an equal footing in the eyes of high society." With that goal in mind I requested my salary in advance, and I purchased a pair of black gloves and a decent hat at Churkin's store. Black gloves seemed to me more dignified, more *bon ton*[6] than the lemon-colored ones I'd considered at first. "That would be too glaring, as if the person wanted to be noticed"; so I didn't buy the lemon-colored ones. I'd already procured a fine shirt with white bone cufflinks; but my overcoat constituted a major obstacle. In and of itself it was not too bad at all; it kept me warm; but it was quilted and had a raccoon collar, the epitome of bad taste. At all costs I had to replace the collar with a beaver one, just like on an officer's coat. For this purpose I began to frequent the Shopping Arcade; and, after several attempts, I turned up some cheap German beaver. Although these German beavers wear out very quickly and soon begin to look shabby, at first, when they're brand new, they look very fine indeed; after all, I only needed it for a single occasion. I asked the price: it was still expensive. After considerable reflection I resolved to sell my raccoon collar. I decided to request a loan for

---

5. "Excessively refined" (French).   6. "In good taste" (French).

the remaining amount—a rather significant sum for me—from Anton Antonych Setochkin, my office chief, a modest man, but a serious and solid one, who never lent money to anyone, but to whom, upon entering the civil service, I'd once been specially recommended by an important person who'd secured the position for me. I suffered terribly. It seemed monstrous and shameful to ask Anton Antonych for money. I didn't sleep for two or three nights in a row; in general I wasn't getting much sleep those days, and I always had a fever. I would have either a vague sinking feeling in my heart, or else my heart would suddenly begin to thump, thump, thump! . . . At first Anton Antonych was surprised, then he frowned, thought it over, and finally gave me the loan, after securing from me a note authorizing him to deduct the sum from my salary two weeks later. In this way everything was finally ready; the splendid beaver reigned in place of the mangy raccoon, and I gradually began to get down to business. It was impossible to set about it all at once, in a foolhardy way; one had to proceed in this matter very carefully, step by step. But I confess that after many attempts I was ready to despair: we didn't bump into each other, no matter what! No matter how I prepared, no matter how determined I was—it seems that we're just about to bump, when I look up—and once again I've stepped aside while he's gone by without even noticing me. I even used to pray as I approached him that God would grant me determination. One time I'd fully resolved to do it, but the result was that I merely stumbled and fell at his feet because, at the very last moment, only a few inches away from him, I lost my nerve. He stepped over me very calmly, and I bounced to one side like a rubber ball. That night I lay ill with a fever once again and was delirious. Then, everything suddenly ended in the best possible way. The night before I decided once and for all not to go through with my pernicious scheme and to give it all up without success; with that in mind I went to Nevsky Prospect for one last time simply in order to see how I'd abandon the whole thing. Suddenly, three paces away from my enemy, I made up my mind unexpectedly; I closed my eyes and—we bumped into each other forcefully, shoulder to shoulder! I didn't yield an inch and walked by him on a completely equal footing! He didn't even turn around to look at me and pretended that he hadn't even noticed; but he was merely pretending, I'm convinced of that. To this very day I'm convinced of that! Naturally, I got the worst of it; he was stronger, but that wasn't the point. The point was that I'd achieved my goal, I'd maintained my dignity, I hadn't yielded one step, and I'd publicly placed myself on an equal social footing with him. I returned home feeling completely avenged for everything. I was ecstatic. I rejoiced and sang Italian arias. Of course, I won't describe what happened to me three days later; if you've read the first part entitled "Underground," you can guess for yourself. The officer was later transferred somewhere else; I haven't seen him for some fourteen years. I wonder what he's doing nowadays, that dear friend of mine! Whom is he trampling underfoot?

II

But when this phase of my nice, little dissipation ended I felt terribly nauseated. Remorse set in; I tried to drive it away because it was too disgusting. Little by little, however, I got used to that, too. I got used to it all; that is, it wasn't that I got used to it, rather, I somehow voluntarily consented to endure it. But I had a way out that reconciled everything—to escape into "all that was beautiful and sublime," in my dreams, of course. I was a terrible dreamer; I dreamt for three months in a row, tucked away in my little corner. And well you may believe that in those moments I was not at all like the gentleman who, in his faint-hearted anxiety, had sewn a German beaver onto the collar of his old overcoat. I suddenly became a hero. If my six-foot-tall lieutenant had come to see me then, I'd never have admitted him. I couldn't even conceive of him at that time. It's hard to describe now what my dreams consisted of then, and how I could've been so satisfied with them, but I was. Besides, even now I can take pride in them at certain times. My dreams were particularly sweet and vivid after my little debauchery; they were filled with remorse and tears, curses and ecstasy. There were moments of such positive intoxication, such happiness, that I felt not even the slightest trace of mockery within me, really and truly. It was all faith, hope and love. That's just it: at the time I believed blindly that by some kind of miracle, some external circumstance, everything would suddenly open up and expand; a vista of appropriate activity would suddenly appear—beneficent, beautiful, and most of all, *ready-made* (what precisely, I never knew, but, most of all, it had to be ready-made), and that I would suddenly step forth into God's world, almost riding on a white horse and wearing a laurel wreath. I couldn't conceive of a secondary role; and that's precisely why in reality I very quietly took on the lowest one. Either a hero or dirt—there was no middle ground. That was my ruin because in the dirt I consoled myself knowing that at other times I was a hero, and that the hero covered himself with dirt; that is to say, an ordinary man would be ashamed to wallow in filth, but a hero is too noble to become defiled; consequently, he can wallow. It's remarkable that these surges of everything "beautiful and sublime" occurred even during my petty depravity, and precisely when I'd sunk to the lowest depths. They occurred in separate spurts, as if to remind me of themselves; however, they failed to banish my depravity by their appearance. On the contrary, they seemed to add spice to it by means of contrast; they came in just the right amount to serve as a tasty sauce. This sauce consisted of contradictions, suffering, and agonizing internal analysis; all of these torments and trifles lent a certain piquancy, even some meaning to my depravity—in a word, they completely fulfilled the function of a tasty sauce. Nor was all this even lacking in a measure of profundity. Besides, I would never have consented to the simple, tasteless, spontaneous little debauchery of an ordinary clerk and have endured all that filth! How could it have attracted me then and lured me into the street late at night? No, sir, I had a noble loophole for everything. . . .

But how much love, oh Lord, how much love I experienced at times in those dreams of mine, in those "escapes into everything beautiful and sublime." Even though it was fantastic love, even though it was never directed at anything human, there was still so much love that afterward, in reality, I no longer felt any impulse to direct it: that would have been an unnecessary luxury. However, everything always ended in a most satisfactory way by a lazy and intoxicating transition into art, that is, into beautiful forms of being, ready-made, largely borrowed from poets and novelists, and adapted to serve every possible need. For instance, I would triumph over everyone; naturally, everyone else grovelled in the dust and was voluntarily impelled to acknowledge my superiority, while I would forgive them all for everything. Or else, being a famous poet and chamberlain, I would fall in love; I'd receive an enormous fortune and would immediately sacrifice it all for the benefit of humanity, at the same time confessing before all peoples my own infamies, which, needless to say, were not simple infamies, but contained a great amount of "the beautiful and sublime," something in the style of Manfred.[7] Everyone would weep and kiss me (otherwise what idiots they would have been), while I went about barefoot and hungry preaching new ideas and defeating all the reactionaries of Austerlitz.[8] Then a march would be played, a general amnesty declared, and the Pope would agree to leave Rome and go to Brazil;[9] a ball would be hosted for all of Italy at the Villa Borghese on the shores of Lake Como,[1] since Lake Como would have been moved to Rome for this very occasion; then there would be a scene in the bushes, etc., etc.—as if you didn't know. You'll say that it's tasteless and repugnant to drag all this out into the open after all the raptures and tears to which I've confessed. But why is it so repugnant? Do you really think I'm ashamed of all this or that it's any more stupid than anything in your own lives, gentlemen? Besides, you can rest assured that some of it was not at all badly composed. . . . Not everything occurred on the shores of Lake Como. But you're right; in fact, it is tasteless and repugnant. And the most repugnant thing of all is that now I've begun to justify myself before you. And even more repugnant is that now I've made that observation. But enough, otherwise there'll be no end to it: each thing will be more repugnant than the last. . . .

I was never able to dream for more than three months in a row, and I began to feel an irresistible urge to plunge into society. To me plunging into society meant paying a visit to my office chief, Anton Antonych Setochkin. He's the only lasting acquaintance I've made during my lifetime; I too now marvel at this circumstance. But even then I would visit him only when my dreams had reached such a degree of happiness that it was absolutely essential for me to embrace people and all humanity at once; for that reason I needed to have at least one person on hand who actually existed. However, one could only call upon Anton Antonych on Tuesdays (his receiving day); consequently, I always had to adjust the urge to embrace all humanity so that it occurred on Tuesday. This Anton Antonych lived near Five Corners,[2] on the fourth floor, in four small, low-ceilinged rooms, each smaller than the last, all very frugal and yellowish in appearance. He lived with his two daughters and an aunt who used to serve tea. The daughters, one thirteen, the other fourteen, had little snub noses. I was very embarrassed by them because they used to whisper all the time and giggle to each other. The host usually sat in his study on a leather couch in front of a table together with some gray-haired guest, a civil servant either from our office or another one. I never saw more than two or three guests there, and they were always the same ones. They talked about excise

---

7. The romantic hero of Byron's poetic tragedy *Manfred* (1817), a lonely, defiant figure whose past conceals some mysterious crime.
8. The site of Napoleon's great victory in December 1805 over the combined armies of the Russian tsar Alexander I and the Austrian emperor Francis II.
9. Napoleon announced his annexation of the Papal States to France in 1809 and was promptly excommunicated by Pope Pius VII.

The pope was imprisoned and forced to sign a new concordat, but in 1814 he returned to Rome in triumph.
1. Located in the foothills of the Italian Alps in Lombardy. Villa Borghese was the elegant summer palace built by Scipione Cardinal Borghese outside the Porta del Popolo in Rome.
2. A well-known landmark in St. Petersburg.

taxes, debates in the Senate, salaries, promotions, His Excellency and how to please him, and so on and so forth. I had the patience to sit there like a fool next to these people for four hours or so; I listened without daring to say a word to them or even knowing what to talk about. I sat there in a stupor; several times I broke into a sweat; I felt numbed by paralysis; but it was good and useful. Upon returning home I would postpone for some time my desire to embrace all humanity.

I had one other sort of acquaintance, however, named Simonov, a former schoolmate of mine. In fact, I had a number of schoolmates in Petersburg, but I didn't associate with them, and I'd even stopped greeting them along the street. I might even have transferred into a different department at the office so as not to be with them and to cut myself off from my hated childhood once and for all. Curses on that school and those horrible years of penal servitude. In short, I broke with my schoolmates as soon as I was released. There remained only two or three people whom I would greet upon encountering them. One was Simonov, who hadn't distinguished himself in school in any way; he was even-tempered and quiet, but I detected in him a certain independence of character, even honesty. I don't even think that he was all that limited. At one time he and I experienced some rather bright moments, but they didn't last very long and somehow were suddenly clouded over. Evidently he was burdened by these recollections, and seemed in constant fear that I would lapse into that former mode. I suspect that he found me repulsive, but not being absolutely sure, I used to visit him nonetheless.

So once, on a Thursday, unable to endure my solitude, and knowing that on that day Anton Antonych's door was locked, I remembered Simonov. As I climbed the stairs to his apartment on the fourth floor, I was thinking how burdensome this man found my presence and that my going to see him was rather useless. But since it always turned out, as if on purpose, that such reflections would impel me to put myself even further into an ambiguous situation, I went right in. It had been almost a year since I'd last seen Simonov.

III

I found two more of my former schoolmates there with him. Apparently they were discussing some important matter. None of them paid any attention to me when I entered, which was strange since I hadn't seen them for several years. Evidently they considered me some sort of ordinary house fly. They hadn't even treated me like that when we were in school together, although they'd all hated me. Of course, I understood that they must despise me now for my failure in the service and for the fact that I'd sunk so low, was badly dressed, and so on, which, in their eyes, constituted proof of my ineptitude and insignificance. But I still hadn't expected such a degree of contempt. Simonov was even surprised by my visits. All this disconcerted me; I sat down in some distress and began to listen to what they were saying.

The discussion was serious, even heated, and concerned a farewell dinner which these gentlemen wanted to organize jointly as early as the following day for their friend Zverkov, an army officer who was heading for a distant province. Monsieur Zverkov had also been my schoolmate all along. I'd begun to hate him especially in the upper grades. In the lower grades he was merely an attractive, lively lad whom everyone liked. However, I'd hated him in the lower grades, too, precisely because he was such an attractive, lively lad. He was perpetually a poor student and had gotten worse as time went on; he managed to graduate, however, because he had influential connections. During his last year at school he'd come into an inheritance of some two hundred serfs, and, since almost all the rest of us were poor, he'd even begun to brag. He was an extremely uncouth fellow, but a nice lad nonetheless, even when he was bragging. In spite of our superficial, fantastic, and high-flown notions of honor and pride, all of us, except for a very few, would fawn upon Zverkov, the more so the more he bragged. They didn't fawn for any advantage; they fawned simply because he was a man endowed by nature with gifts. Moreover, we'd somehow come to regard Zverkov as a cunning fellow and an expert on good manners. This latter point particularly infuriated me. I hated the shrill, self-confident tone of his voice, his adoration for his own witticisms, which were terribly stupid in spite of his bold tongue; I hated his handsome, stupid face (for which, however, I'd gladly have exchanged my own intelligent one), and the impudent bearing typical of officers during the 1840s. I hated the way he talked about his future successes with women. (He'd decided not to get involved with them yet, since he still hadn't received his officer's epaulettes; he awaited those epaulettes impatiently.) And he talked about all the duels he'd have to fight. I remember how once, although I was usually very taciturn, I suddenly clashed with Zverkov when, during our free time, he was discussing future exploits with his friends; getting a bit carried away with the game like a little puppy playing in the sun, he suddenly declared that not a single girl in his village would escape his attention—that it was his *droit de seigneur*,[3] and that if the peasants even dared protest, he'd have them all flogged, those bearded rascals; and he'd double their quit-rent.[4] Our louts applauded, but I attacked him—not out of any pity for the poor girls or their fathers, but simply because everyone else was applauding such a little insect. I got the better of him that time, but Zverkov, although stupid, was also cheerful and impudent. Therefore he laughed it off to such an extent that, in fact, I really didn't get the better of him. The laugh remained on his side. Later he got the better of me several times, but without malice, just so, in jest, in passing, in fun. I was filled with spite and hatred, but I didn't respond. After graduation he took a few steps toward me; I didn't object strongly because I found it flattering; but soon we came to a natural parting of the ways. Afterward I heard about his barrack-room successes as a lieutenant and about his *binges*. Then there were other rumors—about his *successes* in the service. He no longer bowed to me on the street; I suspected that he was afraid to compromise himself by acknowledging such an insignificant person as myself. I also saw him in the theater once, in the third tier, already sporting an officer's gold braids. He was fawning and grovelling before the daughters of some aged general. In those three years he'd let himself go, although he was still as handsome and agile as before; he sagged somehow and had begun to put on weight; it was clear that by the age of thirty

3. "Lord's privilege" (French); the feudal lord's right to spend the first night with the bride of a newly married serf.

4. The annual sum paid in cash or produce by serfs to landowners for the right to farm their land in feudal Russia, as opposed to the *corvée*, a certain amount of labor owed.

he'd be totally flabby. So it was for this Zverkov, who was finally ready to depart, that our schoolmates were organizing a farewell dinner. They'd kept up during these three years, although I'm sure that inwardly they didn't consider themselves on an equal footing with him.

One of Simonov's two guests was Ferfichkin, a Russified German, a short man with a face like a monkey, a fool who made fun of everybody, my bitterest enemy from the lower grades—a despicable, impudent show-off who affected the most ticklish sense of ambition, although, of course, he was a coward at heart. He was one of Zverkov's admirers and played up to him for his own reasons, frequently borrowing money from him. Simonov's other guest, Trudolyubov, was insignificant, a military man, tall, with a cold demeanor, rather honest, who worshipped success of any kind and was capable of talking only about promotions. He was a distant relative of Zverkov's, and that, silly to say, lent him some importance among us. He'd always regarded me as a nonentity; he treated me not altogether politely, but tolerably.

"Well, if each of us contributes seven rubles," said Trudolyubov, "with three of us that makes twenty-one altogether—we can have a good dinner. Of course, Zverkov won't have to pay."

"Naturally," Simonov agreed, "since we're inviting him."

"Do you really think," Ferfichkin broke in arrogantly and excitedly, just like an insolent lackey bragging about his master-the-general's medals, "do you really think Zverkov will let us pay for everything? He'll accept out of decency, but then he'll order *half a dozen bottles* on his own."

"What will the four of us do with half a dozen bottles?" asked Trudolyubov, only taking note of the number.

"So then, three of us plus Zverkov makes four, twenty-one rubles, in the Hôtel de Paris, tomorrow at five o'clock," concluded Simonov definitively, since he'd been chosen to make the arrangements.

"Why only twenty-one?" I asked in trepidation, even, apparently, somewhat offended. "If you count me in, you'll have twenty-eight rubles instead of twenty-one."

It seemed to me that to include myself so suddenly and unexpectedly would appear as quite a splendid gesture and that they'd all be smitten at once and regard me with respect.

"Do you really want to come, too?" Simonov inquired with displeasure, managing somehow to avoid looking at me. He knew me inside out.

It was infuriating that he knew me inside out.

"And why not? After all, I was his schoolmate, too, and I must admit that I even feel a bit offended that you've left me out," I continued, just about to boil over again.

"And how were we supposed to find you?" Ferfichkin interjected rudely.

"You never got along very well with Zverkov," added Trudolyubov frowning. But I'd already latched on and wouldn't let go.

"I think no one has a right to judge that," I objected in a trembling voice, as if God knows what had happened. "Perhaps that's precisely why I want to take part now, since we didn't get along so well before."

"Well, who can figure you out . . . such lofty sentiments . . . ," Trudolyubov said with an ironic smile.

"We'll put your name down," Simonov decided, turning to me. "Tomorrow at five o'clock at the Hôtel de Paris. Don't make any mistakes."

"What about the money?" Ferfichkin started to say in an undertone to Simonov while nodding at me, but he broke off because Simonov looked embarrassed.

"That'll do," Trudolyubov said getting up. "If he really wants to come so much, let him."

"But this is our own circle of friends," Ferfichkin grumbled, also picking up his hat. "It's not an official gathering. Perhaps we really don't want you at all. . . ."

They left. Ferfichkin didn't even say goodbye to me as he went out; Trudolyubov barely nodded without looking at me. Simonov, with whom I was left alone, was irritated and perplexed, and he regarded me in a strange way. He neither sat down nor invited me to.

"Hmmm . . . yes . . . , so, tomorrow. Will you contribute your share of the money now? I'm asking just to know for sure," he muttered in embarrassment.

I flared up; but in doing so, I remembered that I'd owed Simonov fifteen rubles for a very long time, which debt, moreover, I'd forgotten, but had also never repaid.

"You must agree, Simonov, that I couldn't have known when I came here . . . oh, what a nuisance, but I've forgotten. . . ."

He broke off and began to pace around the room in even greater irritation. As he paced, he began to walk on his heels and stomp more loudly.

"I'm not detaining you, am I?" I asked after a few moments of silence.

"Oh, no!" he replied with a start. "That is, in fact, yes. You see, I still have to stop by at . . . It's not very far from here . . . ," he added in an apologetic way with some embarrassment.

"Oh, good heavens! Why didn't you say so?" I exclaimed, seizing my cap; moreover I did so with a surprisingly familiar air, coming from God knows where.

"But it's really not far . . . only a few steps away . . . ," Simonov repeated, accompanying me into the hallway with a bustling air which didn't suit him well at all. "So, then, tomorrow at five o'clock sharp!" he shouted to me on the stairs. He was very pleased that I was leaving. However, I was furious.

"What possessed me, what on earth possessed me to interfere?" I gnashed my teeth as I walked along the street. "And for such a scoundrel, a pig like Zverkov! Naturally, I shouldn't go. Of course, to hell with them. Am I bound to go, or what? Tomorrow I'll inform Simonov by post. . . ."

But the real reason I was so furious was that I was sure I'd go. I'd go on purpose. The more tactless, the more indecent it was for me to go, the more certain I'd be to do it.

There was even a definite impediment to my going: I didn't have any money. All I had was nine rubles. But of those, I had to hand over seven the next day to my servant Apollon for his monthly wages; he lived in and received seven rubles for his meals.

Considering Apollon's character it was impossible not to pay him. But more about that rascal, that plague of mine, later.

In any case, I knew that I wouldn't pay him his wages and that I'd definitely go.

That night I had the most hideous dreams. No wonder: all evening I was burdened with recollections of my years of penal servitude at school and I couldn't get rid of them. I'd been sent off to that school by distant relatives on whom I was dependent and about whom I've heard nothing since. They dispatched me, a lonely boy, crushed by their reproaches, already introspective, taciturn, and regarding everything around him savagely. My schoolmates received me with spiteful and pitiless jibes because I wasn't like any of them. But I couldn't tolerate their jibes; I couldn't possibly get along with them as easily as they got along with each other. I hated them all at once and took refuge from everyone in fearful, wounded and excessive pride. Their crudeness irritated me. Cynically they mocked my face and my awkward build; yet, what stupid faces they all had! Facial expressions at our school somehow degenerated and became particularly stupid. Many attractive lads had come to us, but in a few years they too were repulsive to look at. When I was only sixteen I wondered about them gloomily; even then I was astounded by the pettiness of their thoughts and the stupidity of their studies, games and conversations. They failed to understand essential things and took no interest in important, weighty subjects, so that I couldn't help considering them beneath me. It wasn't my wounded vanity that drove me to it; and, for God's sake, don't repeat any of those nauseating and hackneyed clichés, such as, "I was merely a dreamer, whereas they already understood life." They didn't understand a thing, not one thing about life, and I swear, that's what annoyed me most about them. On the contrary, they accepted the most obvious, glaring reality in a fantastically stupid way, and even then they'd begun to worship nothing but success. Everything that was just, but oppressed and humiliated, they ridiculed hard-heartedly and shamelessly. They mistook rank for intelligence; at the age of sixteen they were already talking about occupying comfortable little niches. Of course, much of this was due to their stupidity and the poor examples that had constantly surrounded them in their childhood and youth. They were monstrously depraved. Naturally, even this was more superficial, more affected cynicism; of course, their youth and a certain freshness shone through their depravity; but even this freshness was unattractive and manifested itself in a kind of rakishness. I hated them terribly, although, perhaps, I was even worse than they were. They returned the feeling and didn't conceal their loathing for me. But I no longer wanted their affection; on the contrary, I constantly longed for their humiliation. In order to avoid their jibes, I began to study as hard as I could on purpose and made my way to the top of the class. That impressed them. In addition, they all began to realize that I'd read certain books which they could never read and that I understood certain things (not included in our special course) about which they'd never even heard. They regarded this with savagery and sarcasm, but they submitted morally, all the more since even the teachers paid me some attention on this account. Their jibes ceased, but their hostility remained, and relations between us became cold and strained. In the end I myself couldn't stand it: as the years went by, my need for people, for friends, increased. I made several attempts to get closer to some of them; but these attempts always turned out to be unnatural and ended of their own accord. Once I even had a friend of sorts. But I was already a despot at heart; I wanted to exercise unlimited power over his soul; I wanted to instill in him contempt for his surroundings; and I demanded from him a disdainful and definitive break with those surroundings. I frightened him with my passionate friendship, and I reduced him to tears and convulsions. He was a naive and giving soul, but as soon as he'd surrendered himself to me totally, I began to despise him and reject him immediately—as if I only needed to achieve a victory over him, merely to subjugate him. But I was unable to conquer them all; my one friend was not at all like them, but rather a rare exception. The first thing I did upon leaving school was abandon the special job in the civil service for which I'd been trained, in order to sever all ties, break with my past, cover it over with dust. . . . The devil only knows why, after all that, I'd dragged myself over to see this Simonov! . . .

Early the next morning I roused myself from bed, jumped up in anxiety, just as if everything was about to start happening all at once. But I believed that some radical change in my life was imminent and was sure to occur that very day. Perhaps because I wasn't used to it, but all my life, at any external event, albeit a trivial one, it always seemed that some sort of radical change would occur. I went off to work as usual, but returned home two hours earlier in order to prepare. The most important thing, I thought, was not to arrive there first, or else they'd all think I was too eager. But there were thousands of most important things, and they all reduced me to the point of impotence. I polished my boots once again with my own hands. Apollon wouldn't polish them twice in one day for anything in the world; he considered it indecent. So I polished them myself, after stealing the brushes from the hallway so that he wouldn't notice and then despise me for it afterward. Next I carefully examined my clothes and found that everything was old, shabby, and worn out. I'd become too slovenly. My uniform was in better shape, but I couldn't go to dinner in a uniform. Worst of all, there was an enormous yellow stain on the knee of my trousers. I had an inkling that the spot alone would rob me of nine-tenths of my dignity. I also knew that it was unseemly for me to think that. "But this isn't the time for thinking. Reality is now looming," I thought, and my heart sank. I also knew perfectly well at that time, that I was monstrously exaggerating all these facts. But what could be done? I was no longer able to control myself, and was shaking with fever. In despair I imagined how haughtily and coldly that "scoundrel" Zverkov would greet me; with what dull and totally relentless contempt that dullard Trudolyubov would regard me; how nastily and impudently that insect Ferfichkin would giggle at me in order to win Zverkov's approval; how well Simonov would understand all this and how he'd despise me for my wretched vanity and cowardice; and worst of all, how petty all this would be, not *literary*, but commonplace. Of course, it would have been better not to go at all. But that was no longer possible; once I began to feel drawn to something, I plunged right in, head first. I'd have reproached myself for the rest of my life: "So, you retreated, you retreated before reality, you retreated!" On the contrary, I desperately wanted to prove to all this "rabble" that I really wasn't the coward I imagined myself to be. But that's not all: in the strongest paroxysm of cowardly fever I dreamt of gaining the upper hand, of conquering them, of carrying them away, compelling them to love me—if only "for the nobility of my thought and my indisputable wit." They would abandon Zverkov; he'd sit by in silence and embarassment, and I'd crush him. Afterward, perhaps, I'd be reconciled with Zverkov and drink to our *friendship*, but what was most spiteful and insulting for me was that I knew even then, I knew completely and for sure, that I didn't need any of this at all; that in fact I really didn't want to crush them, conquer them, or attract them, and that if I could have ever achieved all that, I'd be the first to say that it wasn't worth a damn. Oh, how I prayed to God that this day would pass quickly! With inexpressible anxiety I approached the window, opened the transom,[5] and peered out into the murky mist of the thickly falling wet snow. . . .

At last my worthless old wall clock sputtered out five o'clock. I grabbed my hat, and, trying not to look at Apollon—who'd been waiting since early morning to receive his wages, but didn't want to be the first one to mention it out of pride—I slipped out the door past him and intentionally hired a smart cab with my last half-ruble in order to arrive at the Hôtel de Paris in style.

IV

I knew since the day before that I'd be the first one to arrive. But it was no longer a question of who was first.

Not only was no one else there, but I even had difficulty finding our room. The table hadn't even been set. What did it all mean? After many inquiries I finally learned from the waiters that dinner had been ordered for closer to six o'clock, instead of five. This was also confirmed in the buffet. It was too embarrassing to ask any more questions. It was still only twenty-five minutes past five. If they'd changed the time, they should have let me know; that's what the city mail was for. They shouldn't have subjected me to such "shame" in my own eyes and . . . and, at least not in front of the waiters. I sat down. A waiter began to set the table. I felt even more ashamed in his presence. Toward six o'clock candles were brought into the room in addition to the lighted lamps already there, yet it hadn't occurred to the waiters to bring them in as soon as I'd arrived. In the next room two gloomy customers, angry-looking and silent, were dining at separate tables. In one of the distant rooms there was a great deal of noise, even shouting. One could hear the laughter of a whole crowd of people, including nasty little squeals in French—there were ladies present at that dinner. In short, it was disgusting. Rarely had I passed a more unpleasant hour, so that when they all arrived together precisely at six o'clock, I was initially overjoyed to see them, as if they were my liberators, and I almost forgot that I was supposed to appear offended.

Zverkov, obviously the leader, entered ahead of the rest. Both he and they were laughing; but, upon seeing me, Zverkov drew himself up, approached me unhurriedly, bowed slightly from the waist almost coquettishly, and extended his hand politely, but not too, with a kind of careful civility, almost as if he were a general both offering his hand, but also guarding against something. I'd imagined, on the contrary, that as soon as he entered he'd burst into his former, shrill laughter with occasional squeals, and that he'd immediately launch into his stale jokes and witticisms. I'd been preparing for them since the previous evening; but in no way did I expect such condescension, such courtesy characteristic of a general. Could it be that he now considered himself so immeasurably superior to me in all respects? If he'd merely wanted to offend me by this superior attitude, it wouldn't have been so bad, I thought; I'd manage to pay him back somehow. But what if, without any desire to offend, the notion had crept into his dumb sheep's brain that he really was immeasurably

---

5. A small hinged pane in the window of a Russian house, used for ventilation especially during the winter when the main part of the window is sealed.

superior to me and that he could only treat me in a patronizing way? From this possibility alone I began to gasp for air.

"Have you been waiting long?" Trudolyubov asked.

"I arrived at five o'clock sharp, just as I was told yesterday," I answered loudly and with irritation presaging an imminent explosion.

"Didn't you let him know that we changed the time?" Trudolyubov asked, turning to Simonov.

"No, I didn't. I forgot," he replied, but without any regret; then, not even apologizing to me, he went off to order the hors d'oeuvres.

"So you've been here for a whole hour, you poor fellow!" Zverkov cried sarcastically, because according to his notions, this must really have been terribly amusing. That scoundrel Ferfichkin chimed in after him with nasty, ringing laughter that sounded like a dog's yapping. My situation seemed very amusing and awkward to him, too.

"It's not the least bit funny!" I shouted at Ferfichkin, getting more and more irritated. "The others are to blame, not me. They neglected to inform me. It's, it's, it's . . . simply preposterous."

"It's not only preposterous, it's more than that," muttered Trudolyubov, naively interceding on my behalf. "You're being too kind. It's pure rudeness. Of course, it wasn't intentional. And how could Simonov have . . . hmm!"

"If a trick like that had been played on me," said Ferfichkin, "I'd . . ."

"Oh, you'd have ordered yourself something to eat," interrupted Zverkov, "or simply asked to have dinner served without waiting for the rest of us."

"You'll agree that I could've done that without asking anyone's permission," I snapped. "If I did wait, it was only because . . ."

"Let's be seated, gentlemen," cried Simonov upon entering. "Everything's ready. I can vouch for the champagne; it's excellently chilled. . . . Moreover, I didn't know where your apartment was, so how could I find you?" he said turning to me suddenly, but once again not looking directly at me. Obviously he was holding something against me. I suspect he got to thinking after what had happened yesterday.

Everyone sat down; I did, too. The table was round. Trudolyubov sat on my left, Simonov, on my right. Zverkov sat across; Ferfichkin, next to him, between Trudolyubov and him.

"Tell-l-l me now, are you . . . in a government department?" Zverkov continued to attend to me. Seeing that I was embarrassed, he imagined in earnest that he had to be nice to me, encouraging me to speak. "Does he want me to throw a bottle at his head, or what?" I thought in a rage. Unaccustomed as I was to all this, I was unnaturally quick to take offense.

"In such and such an office," I replied abruptly, looking at my plate.

"And . . . is it p-p-profitable? Tell-l-l me, what ma-a-de you decide to leave your previous position?"

"What ma-a-a-de me leave my previous position was simply that I wanted to," I dragged my words out three times longer than he did, hardly able to control myself. Ferfichkin snorted. Simonov looked at me ironically; Trudolyubov stopped eating and began to stare at me with curiosity.

Zverkov was jarred, but didn't want to show it.

"Well-l, and how is the support?"

"What support?"

"I mean, the s-salary?"

"Why are you cross-examining me?"

However, I told him right away what my salary was. I blushed terribly.

"That's not very much," Zverkov observed pompously.

"No, sir, it's not enough to dine in café-restaurants!" added Ferfichkin insolently.

"In my opinion, it's really very little," Trudolyubov observed in earnest.

"And how thin you've grown, how you've changed . . . since . . . ," Zverkov added, with a touch of venom now, and with a kind of impudent sympathy, examining me and my apparel.

"Stop embarrassing him," Ferfichkin cried with a giggle.

"My dear sir, I'll have you know that I'm not embarrassed," I broke in at last. "Listen! I'm dining in this 'café-restaurant' at my own expense, my own, not anyone else's; note that, Monsieur Ferfichkin."

"Wha-at? And who isn't dining at his own expense? You seem to be . . ." Ferfichkin seized hold of my words, turned as red as a lobster, and looked me straight in the eye with fury.

"Just so-o," I replied, feeling that I'd gone a bit too far, "and I suggest that it would be much better if we engaged in more intelligent conversation."

"It seems that you're determined to display your intelligence."

"Don't worry, that would be quite unnecessary here."

"What's all this cackling, my dear sir? Huh? Have you taken leave of your senses in that *duh*-partment of yours?"

"Enough, gentlemen, enough," cried Zverkov authoritatively.

"How stupid this is!" muttered Simonov.

"Really, it is stupid. We're gathered here in a congenial group to have a farewell dinner for our good friend, while you're still settling old scores," Trudolyubov said, rudely addressing only me. "You forced yourself upon us yesterday; don't disturb the general harmony now. . . ."

"Enough, enough," cried Zverkov. "Stop it, gentlemen, this'll never do. Let me tell you instead how I very nearly got married a few days ago . . ."

There followed some scandalous, libelous anecdote about how this gentleman very nearly got married a few days ago. There wasn't one word about marriage, however; instead, generals, colonels, and even gentlemen of the bed chamber figured prominently in the story, while Zverkov played the leading role among them all. Approving laughter followed; Ferfichkin even squealed.

Everyone had abandoned me by now, and I sat there completely crushed and humiliated.

"Good Lord, what kind of company is this for me?" I wondered. "And what a fool I've made of myself in front of them all! But I let Ferfichkin go too far. These numbskulls think they're doing me an honor by allowing me to sit with them at their table, when they don't understand that it's I who's done them the honor, and not the reverse. 'How thin I've grown! What clothes!' Oh, these damned trousers! Zverkov's already noticed the yellow spot on my knee. . . . What's the use? Right now, this very moment, I should stand up, take my hat, and simply leave without saying a single word. . . . Out of contempt! And tomorrow—I'll even be ready for a duel. Scoundrels! It's not the seven rubles I care about. But they may think that . . . To hell with it! I don't care about the seven rubles. I'm leaving at once! . . ."

Of course, I stayed.

In my misery I drank Lafite and sherry by the glassful. Being unaccustomed to it, I got drunk very quickly; the more intoxicated I became, the greater my annoyance. Suddenly I felt like offending them all in the most impudent manner—and then I'd leave. To seize the moment and show them all who I really was—let them say: even though he's ridiculous, he's clever . . . and . . . and . . . in short, to hell with them!

I surveyed them all arrogantly with my dazed eyes. But they seemed to have forgotten all about me. *They* were noisy, boisterous and merry. Zverkov kept on talking. I began to listen. He was talking about some magnificent lady whom he'd finally driven to make a declaration of love. (Of course, he was lying like a trooper.) He said that he'd been assisted in this matter particularly by a certain princeling, the hussar Kolya, who possessed some three thousand serfs.

"And yet, this same Kolya who has three thousand serfs hasn't even come to see you off," I said, breaking into the conversation suddenly. For a moment silence fell.

"You're drunk already," Trudolyubov said, finally deigning to notice me, and glancing contemptuously in my direction. Zverkov examined me in silence as if I were an insect. I lowered my eyes. Simonov quickly began to pour champagne.

Trudolyubov raised his glass, followed by everyone but me.

"To your health and to a good journey!" he cried to Zverkov. "To old times, gentlemen, and to our future, hurrah!"

Everyone drank up and pressed around to exchange kisses with Zverkov. I didn't budge; my full glass stood before me untouched.

"Aren't you going to drink?" Trudolyubov roared at me, having lost his patience and turning to me menacingly.

"I wish to make my own speech, all by myself . . . and then I'll drink, Mr. Trudolyubov."

"Nasty shrew!" Simonov muttered.

I sat up in my chair, feverishly seized hold of my glass, and prepared for something extraordinary, although I didn't know quite what I'd say.

"*Silence!*" cried Ferfichkin. "And now for some real intelligence!" Zverkov waited very gravely, aware of what was coming.

"Mr. Lieutenant Zverkov," I began, "you must know that I detest phrases, phrasemongers, and corsetted waists. . . . That's the first point; the second will follow."

Everyone stirred uncomfortably.

"The second point: I hate obscene stories and the men who tell them.[6] I especially hate the men who tell them!"

"The third point: I love truth, sincerity and honesty," I continued almost automatically, because I was beginning to become numb with horror, not knowing how I could be speaking this way. . . . "I love thought, Monsieur Zverkov. I love genuine comradery, on an equal footing, but not . . . hmmm . . . I

6. A phrase borrowed from the inveterate liar Nozdryov, one of the provincial landowners in the first volume of Gogol's *Dead Souls* (1842).

love . . . But, after all, why not? I too will drink to your health, Monsieur Zverkov. Seduce those Circassian[7] maidens, shoot the enemies of the fatherland, and . . . and . . . To your health, Monsieur Zverkov!"

Zverkov rose from his chair, bowed, and said: "I'm most grateful."

He was terribly offended and had even turned pale.

"To hell with him," Trudolyubov roared, banging his fist down on the table.

"No, sir, people should be whacked in the face for saying such things!" squealed Ferfichkin.

"We ought to throw him out!" muttered Simonov.

"Not a word, gentlemen, not a move!" Zverkov cried triumphantly, putting a stop to this universal indignation. "I'm grateful to you all, but I can show him myself how much I value his words."

"Mr. Ferfichkin, tomorrow you'll give me satisfaction for the words you've just uttered!" I said loudly, turning to Ferfichkin with dignity.

"Do you mean a duel? Very well," he replied, but I must have looked so ridiculous as I issued my challenge, it must have seemed so out of keeping with my entire appearance, that everyone, including Ferfichkin, collapsed into laughter.

"Yes, of course, throw him out! Why, he's quite drunk already," Trudolyubov declared in disgust.

"I shall never forgive myself for letting him join us," Simonov muttered again.

"Now's the time to throw a bottle at the lot of them," I thought. So I grabbed a bottle and . . . poured myself another full glass.

". . . No, it's better to sit it out to the very end!" I went on thinking. "You'd be glad, gentlemen, if I left. But nothing doing! I'll stay here deliberately and keep on drinking to the very end, as a sign that I accord you no importance whatsoever. I'll sit here and drink because this is a tavern, and I've paid good money to get in. I'll sit here and drink because I consider you to be so many pawns, nonexistent pawns. I'll sit here and drink . . . and sing too, if I want to, yes, sir, I'll sing because I have the right to . . . sing . . . hmm."

But I didn't sing. I just tried not to look at any of them; I assumed the most carefree poses and waited impatiently until they would be the first to speak to me. But, alas, they did not. How much, how very much I longed to be reconciled with them at that moment! The clock struck eight, then nine. They moved from the table to the sofa. Zverkov sprawled on the couch, placing one foot on the round table. They brought the wine over, too. He really had ordered three bottles at his own expense. Naturally, he didn't invite me to join them. Everyone surrounded him on the sofa. They listened to him almost with reverence. It was obvious they liked him. "What for? What for?" I wondered to myself. From time to time they were moved to drunken ecstasy and exchanged kisses. They talked about the Caucasus,[8] the nature of true passion, card games, profitable positions in the service; they talked about the income of a certain hussar Podkharzhevsky, whom none of them knew personally, and they

7. Women from the region between the Black Sea and the Caspian Sea, famous for their beauty and much in demand as concubines in the Ottoman Empire.

8. Region in which various peoples opposed Russian rule, and thus a constant source of trouble for the Russian Empire.

rejoiced that his income was so large; they talked about the unusual beauty and charm of Princess D., whom none of them had ever seen; finally, they arrived at the question of Shakespeare's immortality.

I smiled contemptuously and paced up and down the other side of the room, directly behind the sofa, along the wall from the table to the stove and back again. I wanted to show them with all my might that I could get along without them; meanwhile, I deliberately stomped my boots, thumping my heels. But all this was in vain. *They* paid me no attention. I had the forbearance to pace like that, right in front of them, from eight o'clock until eleven, in the very same place, from the table to the stove and from the stove back to the table. "I'm pacing just as I please, and no one can stop me." A waiter who came into the room paused several times to look at me; my head was spinning from all those turns; there were moments when it seemed that I was delirious. During those three hours I broke out in a sweat three times and then dried out. At times I was pierced to the heart with a most profound, venomous thought: ten years would pass, twenty, forty; and still, even after forty years, I'd remember with loathing and humiliation these filthiest, most absurd, and horrendous moments of my entire life. It was impossible to humiliate myself more shamelessly or more willingly, and I fully understood that, fully; nevertheless, I continued to pace from the table to the stove and back again. "Oh, if you only knew what thoughts and feelings I'm capable of, and how cultured I really am!" I thought at moments, mentally addressing the sofa where my enemies were seated. But my enemies behaved as if I weren't even in the room. Once, and only once, they turned to me, precisely when Zverkov started in about Shakespeare, and I suddenly burst into contemptuous laughter. I snorted so affectedly and repulsively that they broke off their conversation immediately and stared at me in silence for about two minutes, in earnest, without laughing, as I paced up and down, from the table to the stove, while *I paid not the slightest bit of attention to them.* But nothing came of it; they didn't speak to me. A few moments later they abandoned me again. The clock struck eleven.

"Gentlemen," exclaimed Zverkov, getting up from the sofa, "Now let's all go *to that place.*"[9]

"Of course, of course!" the others replied.

I turned abruptly to Zverkov. I was so exhausted, so broken, that I'd have slit my own throat to be done with all this! I was feverish; my hair, which had been soaked through with sweat, had dried and now stuck to my forehead and temples.

"Zverkov, I ask your forgiveness," I said harshly and decisively. "Ferfichkin, yours too, and everyone's, everyone's. I've insulted you all!"

"Aha! So a duel isn't really your sort of thing!" hissed Ferfichkin venomously.

His remark was like a painful stab to my heart.

"No, I'm not afraid of a duel, Ferfichkin! I'm ready to fight with you tomorrow, even after we're reconciled. I even insist upon it, and you can't refuse me. I want to prove that I'm not afraid of a duel. You'll shoot first, and I'll fire into the air."

"He's amusing himself," Simonov observed.

"He's simply taken leave of his senses!" Trudolyubov added.

9. I.e., a brothel.

"Allow us to pass; why are you blocking our way? . . . Well, what is it you want?" Zverkov asked contemptuously. They were all flushed, their eyes glazed. They'd drunk a great deal.

"I ask for your friendship, Zverkov, I've insulted you, but . . ."

"Insulted me? You? In-sul-ted me? My dear sir, I want you to know that never, under any circumstances, could you possibly insult *me*!"

"And that's enough from you. Out of the way!" Trudolyubov added. "Let's go."

"Olympia is mine, gentlemen, that's agreed!" cried Zverkov.

"We won't argue, we won't," they replied, laughing.

I stood there as if spat on. The party left the room noisily, and Trudolyubov struck up a stupid song. Simonov remained behind for a brief moment to tip the waiters. All of a sudden I went up to him.

"Simonov! Give me six rubles," I said decisively and desperately.

He looked at me in extreme amazement with his dulled eyes. He was drunk, too.

"Are you really going *to that place* with us?"

"Yes!"

"I have no money!" he snapped; then he laughed contemptuously and headed out of the room.

I grabbed hold of his overcoat. It was a nightmare.

"Simonov! I know that you have some money. Why do you refuse me? Am I really such a scoundrel? Beware of refusing me: if you only knew, if you only knew why I'm asking. Everything depends on it, my entire future, all my plans. . . ."

Simonov took out the money and almost threw it at me.

"Take it, if you have no shame!" he said mercilessly, then ran out to catch up with the others.

I remained behind for a minute. The disorder, the leftovers, a broken glass on the floor, spilled wine, cigarette butts, drunkenness and delirium in my head, agonizing torment in my heart; and finally, a waiter who'd seen and heard everything and who was now looking at me with curiosity.

"*To that place!*" I cried. "Either they'll all fall on their knees, embracing me, begging for my friendship, or . . . or else, I'll give Zverkov a slap in the face."

V

"So here it is, here it is at last, a confrontation with reality," I muttered, rushing headlong down the stairs. "This is no longer the Pope leaving Rome and going to Brazil; this is no ball on the shores of Lake Como!"

"You're a scoundrel," the thought flashed through my mind, "if you laugh at that now."

"So what!" I cried in reply. "Everything is lost now, anyway!"

There was no sign of them, but it didn't matter. I knew where they were going.

At the entrance stood a solitary, late-night cabby in a coarse peasant coat powdered with wet, seemingly warm snow that was still falling. It was steamy and stuffy outside. The little shaggy piebald nag was also dusted with snow and was coughing; I remember that very well. I headed for the rough-hewn sledge; but as soon as I raised one foot to get in, the recollection of how Simonov had just given me six rubles hit me with such force that I tumbled into the sledge like a sack.

"No! There's a lot I have to do to make up for that!" I cried. "But make up for it I will or else I'll perish on the spot this very night. Let's go!" We set off. There was an entire whirlwind spinning around inside my head.

"They won't fall on their knees to beg for my friendship. That's a mirage, an indecent mirage, disgusting, romantic, and fantastic; it's just like the ball on the shores of Lake Como. Consequently, I *must* give Zverkov a slap in the face! I am obligated to do it. And so, it's all decided; I'm rushing there to give him a slap in the face."

"Hurry up!"

The cabby tugged at the reins.

"As soon as I go in, I'll slap him. Should I say a few words first before I slap him in the face? No! I'll simply go in and slap him. They'll all be sitting there in the drawing room; he'll be on the sofa with Olympia. That damned Olympia! She once ridiculed my face and refused me. I'll drag Olympia around by the hair and Zverkov by the ears. No, better grab one ear and lead him around the room like that. Perhaps they'll begin to beat me, and then they'll throw me out. That's even likely. So what? I'll still have slapped him first; the initiative will be mine. According to the laws of honor, that's all that matters. He'll be branded, and nothing can wipe away that slap except a duel.[1] He'll have to fight. So just let them beat me now! Let them, the ingrates! Trudolyubov will hit me hardest, he's so strong. Ferfichkin will sneak up alongside and will undoubtedly grab my hair, I'm sure he will. But let them, let them. That's why I've come. At last these blockheads will be forced to grasp the tragedy in all this! As they drag me to the door, I'll tell them that they really aren't even worth the tip of my little finger!"

"Hurry up, driver, hurry up!" I shouted to the cabby.

He was rather startled and cracked his whip. I'd shouted very savagely.

"We'll fight at daybreak, and that's settled. I'm through with the department. Ferfichkin recently said duh-partment, instead of department. But where will I get pistols? What nonsense! I'll take my salary in advance and buy them. And powder? Bullets? That's what the second will attend to. And how will I manage to do all this by daybreak? And where will I find a second? I have no acquaintances. . . ."

"Nonsense!" I shouted, whipping myself up into even more of a frenzy, "Nonsense!"

"The first person I meet on the street will have to act as my second, just as he would pull a drowning man from the water. The most extraordinary possibilities have to be allowed for. Even if tomorrow I were to ask the director himself to act as my second, he too would have to agree merely out of a sense of chivalry, and he would keep it a secret! Anton Antonych . . ."

The fact of the matter was that at that very moment I was more clearly and vividly aware than anyone else on earth of the disgusting absurdity of my intentions and the whole opposite side of the coin, but . . .

"Hurry up, driver, hurry, you rascal, hurry up!"

---

1. Duels as a means of resolving points of honor were officially discouraged but still fairly common.

"Hey, sir!" that son of the earth replied.

A sudden chill came over me.

"Wouldn't it be better . . . wouldn't it be better . . . to go straight home right now? Oh, my God! Why, why did I invite myself to that dinner yesterday? But no, it's impossible. And my pacing for three hours from the table to the stove? No, they, and no one else will have to pay me back for that pacing! They must wipe out that disgrace!"

"Hurry up!"

"What if they turn me over to the police? They wouldn't dare! They'd be afraid of a scandal. And what if Zverkov refuses the duel out of contempt? That's even likely; but I'll show them. . . . I'll rush to the posting station when he's supposed to leave tomorrow; I'll grab hold of his leg, tear off his overcoat just as he's about to climb into the carriage. I'll fasten my teeth on his arm and bite him. 'Look, everyone, see what a desperate man can be driven to!' Let him hit me on the head while others hit me from behind. I'll shout to the whole crowd, 'Behold, here's a young puppy who's going off to charm Circassian maidens with my spit on his face!'"

"Naturally, it'll all be over after that. The department will banish me from the face of the earth. They'll arrest me, try me, drive me out of the service, send me to prison; ship me off to Siberia for resettlement. Never mind! Fifteen years later when they let me out of jail, a beggar in rags, I'll drag myself off to see him. I'll find him in some provincial town. He'll be married and happy. He'll have a grown daughter. . . . I'll say, 'Look, you monster, look at my sunken cheeks and my rags. I've lost everything—career, happiness, art, science, a *beloved woman*—all because of you. Here are the pistols. I came here to load my pistol, and . . . and I forgive you.' Then I'll fire into the air, and he'll never hear another word from me again. . . ."

I was actually about to cry, even though I knew for a fact at that very moment that all this was straight out of Silvio and Lermontov's *Masquerade*.[2] Suddenly I felt terribly ashamed, so ashamed that I stopped the horse, climbed out of the sledge, and stood there amidst the snow in the middle of the street. The driver looked at me in amazement and sighed.

What was I to do? I couldn't go there—that was absurd; and I couldn't drop the whole thing, because then it would seem like . . . Oh, Lord! How could I drop it? After such insults!

"No!" I cried, throwing myself back into the sledge. "It's predestined; it's fate! Drive on, hurry up, *to that place!*"

In my impatience, I struck the driver on the neck with my fist.

"What's the matter with you? Why are you hitting me?" cried the poor little peasant, whipping his nag so that she began to kick up her hind legs.

Wet snow was falling in big flakes; I unbuttoned my coat, not caring about the snow. I forgot about everything else because now, having finally resolved on the slap, *I felt with horror that it was imminent* and that *nothing on earth could possibly stop it.* Lonely street lamps shone gloomily in the snowy mist like torches at a funeral. Snow got in under my overcoat, my jacket, and my necktie, and melted there. I didn't button up; after all, everything was lost, anyway.

---

2. A drama by Mikhail Lermontov (1835) about romantic conventions of love and honor. Silvio is the protagonist of Alexander Push- kin's short story "The Shot" (1830), about a man dedicated to revenge. Both works conclude with bizarre twists.

At last we arrived. I jumped out, almost beside myself, ran up the stairs, and began to pound at the door with my hands and feet. My legs, especially my knees, felt terribly weak. The door opened rather quickly; it was as if they knew I was coming. (In fact, Simonov had warned them that there might be someone else, since at this place one had to give notice and in general take precautions. It was one of those "fashionable shops" of the period that have now been eliminated by the police. During the day it really was a shop; but in the evening men with recommendations were able to visit as guests.) I walked rapidly through the darkened shop into a familiar drawing-room where there was only one small lit candle, and I stopped in dismay: there was no one there.

"Where are they?" I asked.

Naturally, by now they'd all dispersed. . . .

Before me stood a person with a stupid smile, the madam herself, who knew me slightly. In a moment a door opened, and another person came in.

Without paying much attention to anything, I walked around the room, and, apparently, was talking to myself. It was as if I'd been delivered from death, and I felt it joyously in my whole being. I'd have given him the slap, certainly, I'd certainly have given him the slap. But now they weren't here and . . . everything had vanished, everything had changed! . . . I looked around. I still couldn't take it all in. I glanced up mechanically at the girl who'd come in: before me there flashed a fresh, young, slightly pale face with straight dark brows and a serious, seemingly astonished look. I liked that immediately; I would have hated her if she'd been smiling. I began to look at her more carefully, as though with some effort: I'd still not managed to collect my thoughts. There was something simple and kind in her face, but somehow it was strangely serious. I was sure that she was at a disadvantage as a result, and that none of those fools had even noticed her. She couldn't be called a beauty, however, even though she was tall, strong, and well built. She was dressed very simply. Something despicable took hold of me; I went up to her. . . .

I happened to glance into a mirror. My overwrought face appeared extremely repulsive: it was pale, spiteful and mean; and my hair was dishevelled. "It doesn't matter. I'm glad," I thought. "In fact, I'm even delighted that I'll seem so repulsive to her; that pleases me. . . ."

VI

Somewhere behind a partition a clock was wheezing as if under some strong pressure, as though someone were strangling it. After this unnaturally prolonged wheezing there followed a thin, nasty, somehow unexpectedly hurried chime, as if someone had suddenly leapt forward. It struck two. I recovered, although I really hadn't been asleep, only lying there half-conscious.

It was almost totally dark in the narrow, cramped, low-ceilinged room, which was crammed with an enormous wardrobe and cluttered with cartons, rags, and all sorts of old clothes. The candle burning on the table at one end of the room flickered faintly from time to time, and almost went out completely. In a few moments total darkness would set in.

It didn't take long for me to come to my senses; all at once, without any effort, everything returned to me, as though it had been lying in ambush ready to pounce on me again. Even in my unconscious state some point had constantly remained in my memory, never to be forgotten, around which my sleepy visions had gloomily revolved. But it was a strange thing: everything that had happened to me that day now seemed, upon awakening, to have occurred in the distant past, as if I'd long since left it all behind.

My mind was in a daze. It was as though something were hanging over me, provoking, agitating, and disturbing me. Misery and bile were welling inside me, seeking an outlet. Suddenly I noticed beside me two wide-open eyes, examining me curiously and persistently. The gaze was coldly detached, sullen, as if belonging to a total stranger. I found it oppressive.

A dismal thought was conceived in my brain and spread throughout my whole body like a nasty sensation, such as one feels upon entering a damp, mouldy underground cellar. It was somehow unnatural that only now these two eyes had decided to examine me. I also recalled that during the course of the last two hours I hadn't said one word to this creature, and that I had considered it quite unnecessary; that had even given me pleasure for some reason. Now I'd suddenly realized starkly how absurd, how revolting as a spider, was the idea of debauchery, which, without love, crudely and shamelessly begins precisely at the point where genuine love is consummated. We looked at each other in this way for some time, but she didn't lower her gaze before mine, nor did she alter her stare, so that finally, for some reason, I felt very uneasy.

"What's your name?" I asked abruptly, to put an end to it quickly.

"Liza," she replied, almost in a whisper, but somehow in a very unfriendly way; and she turned her eyes away.

I remained silent.

"The weather today . . . snow . . . foul!" I observed, almost to myself, drearily placing one arm behind my head and staring at the ceiling.

She didn't answer. The whole thing was obscene.

"Are you from around here?" I asked her a moment later, almost angrily, turning my head slightly toward her.

"No."

"Where are you from?"

"Riga," she answered unwillingly.

"German?"

"No, Russian."

"Have you been here long?"

"Where?"

"In this house."

"Two weeks." She spoke more and more curtly. The candle had gone out completely; I could no longer see her face.

"Are your mother and father still living?"

"Yes . . . no . . . they are."

"Where are they?"

"There . . . in Riga."

"Who are they?"

"Just . . ."

"Just what? What do they do?"

"Tradespeople."

"Have you always lived with them?"

"Yes."

"How old are you?"

"Twenty."

"Why did you leave them?"

"Just because . . ."

That "just because" meant: leave me alone, it makes me sick. We fell silent.

Only God knows why, but I didn't leave. I too started to feel sick and more depressed. Images of the previous day began to come to mind all on their own, without my willing it, in a disordered way. I suddenly recalled a scene that I'd witnessed on the street that morning as I was anxiously hurrying to work. "Today some people were carrying a coffin and nearly dropped it," I suddenly said aloud, having no desire whatever to begin a conversation, but just so, almost accidentally.

"A coffin?"

"Yes, in the Haymarket; they were carrying it up from an underground cellar."

"From a cellar?"

"Not a cellar, but from a basement . . . well, you know . . . from down-stairs . . . from a house of ill repute . . . There was such filth all around. . . . Egg-shells, garbage . . . it smelled foul . . . it was disgusting."

Silence.

"A nasty day to be buried!" I began again to break the silence.

"Why nasty?"

"Snow, slush . . ." (I yawned.)

"It doesn't matter," she said suddenly after a brief silence.

"No, it's foul. . . ." (I yawned again.) "The grave diggers must have been curs-ing because they were getting wet out there in the snow. And there must have been water in the grave."

"Why water in the grave?" she asked with some curiosity, but she spoke even more rudely and curtly than before. Something suddenly began to goad me on.

"Naturally, water on the bottom, six inches or so. You can't ever dig a dry grave at Volkovo cemetery."

"Why not?"

"What do you mean, why not? The place is waterlogged. It's all swamp. So they bury them right in the water. I've seen it myself . . . many times. . . ."

(I'd never seen it, and I'd never been to Volkovo cemetery, but I'd heard about it from other people.)

"Doesn't it matter to you if you die?"

"Why should I die?" she replied, as though defending herself.

"Well, someday you'll die; you'll die just like that woman did this morning. She was a . . . she was also a young girl . . . she died of consumption."

"The wench should have died in the hospital. . . ." (She knows all about it, I thought, and she even said "wench" instead of "girl.")

"She owed money to her madam," I retorted, more and more goaded on by the argument. "She worked right up to the end, even though she had consump-tion. The cabbies standing around were chatting with the soldiers, telling them all about it. Her former acquaintances, most likely. They were all laughing. They were planning to drink to her memory at the tavern." (I invented a great deal of this.)

Silence, deep silence. She didn't even stir.

"Do you think it would be better to die in a hospital?"

"Isn't it just the same? . . . Besides, why should I die?" she added irritably.

"If not now, then later?"

"Well, then later . . ."

"That's what you think! Now you're young and pretty and fresh—that's your value. But after a year of this life, you won't be like that any more; you'll fade."

"In a year?"

"In any case, after a year your price will be lower," I continued, gloating. "You'll move out of here into a worse place, into some other house. And a year later, into a third, each worse and worse, and seven years from now you'll end up in a cellar on the Haymarket. Even that won't be so bad. The real trouble will come when you get some disease, let's say a weakness in the chest . . . or you catch cold or something. In this kind of life it's no laughing matter to get sick. It takes hold of you and may never let go. And so, you die."

"Well, then, I'll die," she answered now quite angrily and stirred quickly.

"That'll be a pity."

"For what?"

"A pity to lose a life."

Silence.

"Did you have a sweetheart? Huh?"

"What's it to you?"

"Oh, I'm not interrogating you. What do I care? Why are you angry? Of course, you may have had your own troubles. What's it to me? Just the same, I'm sorry."

"For whom?"

"I'm sorry for you."

"No need . . . ," she whispered barely audibly and stirred once again.

That provoked me at once. What! I was being so gentle with her, while she . . .

"Well, and what do you think? Are you on the right path then?"

"I don't think anything."

"That's just the trouble—you don't think. Wake up, while there's still time. And there is time. You're still young and pretty; you could fall in love, get married, be happy.[3] . . ."

"Not all married women are happy," she snapped in her former, rude manner.

"Not all, of course, but it's still better than this. A lot better. You can even live without happiness as long as there's love. Even in sorrow life can be good; it's good to be alive, no matter how you live. But what's there besides . . . stench? Phew!"

I turned away in disgust; I was no longer coldly philosophizing. I began to feel what I was saying and grew excited. I'd been longing to expound these cherished *little ideas* that I'd been nurturing in my corner. Something had suddenly caught fire in me, some kind of goal had "manifested itself" before me.

"Pay no attention to the fact that I'm here. I'm no model for you. I may be even worse than you are. Moreover, I was drunk when I came here." I hastened nonetheless to justify myself. "Besides, a man is no example to a woman. It's a different thing altogether; even though I degrade and defile myself, I'm still no one's slave; if I want to leave, I just get up and go. I shake it all off and I'm a

---

3. A popular theme treated by Gogol, Chernyshevsky, and Nekrasov, among others. Typically, an innocent and idealistic young man attempts to rehabilitate a prostitute or "fallen" woman.

different man. But you must realize right from the start that you're a slave. Yes, a slave! You give away everything, all your freedom. Later, if you want to break this chain, you won't be able to; it'll bind you ever more tightly. That's the kind of evil chain it is. I know. I won't say anything else; you might not even understand me. But tell me this, aren't you already in debt to your madam? There, you see!" I added, even though she hadn't answered, but had merely remained silent; but she was listening with all her might. "There's your chain! You'll never buy yourself out. That's the way it's done. It's just like selling your soul to the devil. . . .

"And besides . . . I may be just as unfortunate, how do you know, and I may be wallowing in mud on purpose, also out of misery. After all, people drink out of misery. Well, I came here out of misery. Now, tell me, what's so good about this place? Here you and I were . . . intimate . . . just a little while ago, and all that time we didn't say one word to each other; afterward you began to examine me like a wild creature, and I did the same. Is that the way people love? Is that how one person is supposed to encounter another? It's a disgrace, that's what it is!"

"Yes!" she agreed with me sharply and hastily. The haste of her answer surprised even me. It meant that perhaps the very same idea was flitting through her head while she'd been examining me earlier. It meant that she too was capable of some thought. . . . "Devil take it; this is odd, this *kinship*," I thought, almost rubbing my hands together. "Surely I can handle such a young soul."

It was the sport that attracted me most of all.

She turned her face closer to mine, and in the darkness it seemed that she propped her head up on her arm. Perhaps she was examining me. I felt sorry that I couldn't see her eyes. I heard her breathing deeply.

"Why did you come here?" I began with some authority.

"Just so . . ."

"But think how nice it would be living in your father's house! There you'd be warm and free; you'd have a nest of your own."

"And what if it's worse than that?"

"I must establish the right tone," flashed through my mind. "I won't get far with sentimentality."

However, that merely flashed through my mind. I swear that she really did interest me. Besides, I was somewhat exhausted and provoked. After all, artifice goes along so easily with feeling.

"Who can say?" I hastened to reply. "All sorts of things can happen. Why, I was sure that someone had wronged you and was more to blame than you are. After all, I know nothing of your life story, but a girl like you doesn't wind up in this sort of place on her own accord. . . ."

"What kind of a girl am I?" she whispered hardly audibly; but I heard it.

"What the hell! Now I'm flattering her. That's disgusting! But, perhaps it's a good thing. . . ." She remained silent.

"You see, Liza, I'll tell you about myself. If I'd had a family when I was growing up, I wouldn't be the person I am now. I think about this often. After all, no matter how bad it is in your own family—it's still your own father and mother, and not enemies or strangers. Even if they show you their love only once a year, you still know that you're at home. I grew up without a family; that must be why I turned out the way I did—so unfeeling."

I waited again.

"She might not understand," I thought. "Besides, it's absurd—all this moralizing."

"If I were a father and had a daughter, I think that I'd have loved her more than my sons, really," I began indirectly, talking about something else in order to distract her. I confess that I was blushing.

"Why's that?"

Ah, so she's listening!

"Just because. I don't know why, Liza. You see, I knew a father who was a stern, strict man, but he would kneel before his daughter and kiss her hands and feet; he couldn't get enough of her, really. She'd go dancing at a party, and he'd stand in one spot for five hours, never taking his eyes off her. He was crazy about her; I can understand that. At night she'd be tired and fall asleep, but he'd wake up, go in to kiss her, and make the sign of the cross over her while she slept. He used to wear a dirty old jacket and was stingy with everyone else, but would spend his last kopeck on her, buying her expensive presents; it afforded him great joy if she liked his presents. A father always loves his daughters more than their mother does. Some girls have a very nice time living at home. I think that I wouldn't even have let my daughter get married."

"Why not?" she asked with a barely perceptible smile.

"I'd be jealous, so help me God. Why, how could she kiss someone else? How could she love a stranger more than her own father? It's even painful to think about it. Of course, it's all nonsense; naturally, everyone finally comes to his senses. But I think that before I'd let her marry, I'd have tortured myself with worry. I'd have found fault with all her suitors. Nevertheless, I'd have ended up by allowing her to marry whomever she loved. After all, the one she loves always seems the worst of all to the father. That's how it is. That causes a lot of trouble in many families."

"Some are glad to sell their daughters, rather than let them marry honorably," she said suddenly.

Aha, so that's it!

"That happens, Liza, in those wretched families where there's neither God nor love," I retorted heatedly. "And where there's no love, there's also no good sense. There are such families, it's true, but I'm not talking about them. Obviously, from the way you talk, you didn't see much kindness in your own family. You must be very unfortunate. Hmm . . . But all this results primarily from poverty."

"And is it any better among the gentry? Honest folk live decently even in poverty."

"Hmmm . . . Yes. Perhaps. There's something else, Liza. Man only likes to count his troubles; he doesn't calculate his happiness. If he figured as he should, he'd see that everyone gets his share. So, let's say that all goes well in a particular family; it enjoys God's blessing, the husband turns out to be a good man, he loves you, cherishes you, and never leaves you. Life is good in that family. Sometimes, even though there's a measure of sorrow, life's still good. Where isn't there sorrow? If you choose to get married, *you'll find out for yourself.* Consider even the first years of a marriage to the one you love: what happiness, what pure bliss there can be sometimes! Almost without exception. At first even quarrels with your husband turn out well. For some women, the more they love their husbands, the more they pick fights with them. It's true; I once knew a woman like that. 'That's how it is,' she'd say. 'I love you very much and I'm tormenting you out of love, so that you'll feel it.' Did you know that one can torment a person intentionally out of love? It's mostly women who do that. Then she thinks to herself, 'I'll love him so much afterward, I'll be so affectionate, it's no sin to torment him a little now.' At home everyone would rejoice over you, and it would be so pleasant, cheerful, serene, and honorable. . . . Some other women are very jealous. If her husband goes away, I knew one like that, she can't stand it; she jumps up at night and goes off on the sly to see. Is he there? Is he in that house? Is he with that one? Now that's bad. Even she herself knows that it's bad; her heart sinks and she suffers because she really loves him. It's all out of love. And how nice it is to make up after a quarrel, to admit one's guilt or forgive him! How nice it is for both of them, how good they both feel at once, just as if they'd met again, married again, and begun their love all over again. No one, no one at all has to know what goes on between a husband and wife, if they love each other. However their quarrel ends, they should never call in either one of their mothers to act as judge or to hear complaints about the other one. They must act as their own judges. Love is God's mystery and should be hidden from other people's eyes, no matter what happens. This makes it holier, much better. They respect each other more, and a great deal is based on this respect. And, if there's been love, if they got married out of love, why should love disappear? Can't it be sustained? It rarely happens that it can't be sustained. If the husband turns out to be a kind and honest man, how can the love disappear? The first phase of married love will pass, that's true, but it's followed by an even better kind of love. Souls are joined together and all their concerns are managed in common; there'll be no secrets from one another. When children arrive, each and every stage, even a very difficult one, will seem happy, as long as there's both love and courage. Even work is cheerful; even when you deny yourself bread for your children's sake, you're still happy. After all, they'll love you for it afterward; you're really saving for your own future. Your children will grow up, and you'll feel that you're a model for them, a support. Even after you die, they'll carry your thoughts and feelings all during their life. They'll take on your image and likeness, since they received it from you. Consequently, it's a great obligation. How can a mother and father keep from growing closer? They say it's difficult to raise children. Who says that? It's heavenly joy! Do you love little children, Liza? I love them dearly. You know—a rosy little boy, suckling at your breast; what husband's heart could turn against his wife seeing her sitting there holding his child? The chubby, rosy little baby sprawls and snuggles; his little hands and feet are plump; his little nails are clean and tiny, so tiny it's even funny to see them; his little eyes look as if he already understood everything. As he suckles, he tugs at your breast playfully with his little hand. When the father approaches, the child lets go of the breast, bends way back, looks at his father, and laughs—as if God only knows how funny it is—and then takes to suckling again. Afterward, when he starts cutting teeth, he'll sometimes bite his mother's breast; looking at her sideways his little eyes seem to say, 'See, I bit you!' Isn't this pure bliss—the three of them, husband, wife, and child, all together? You can forgive a great deal for such moments. No, Liza, I think you must first learn how to live by yourself, and only afterward blame others."

"It's by means of images," I thought to myself, "just such images that I can get to you," although I was speaking with considerable feeling, I swear it; and all at once I blushed. "And what if she suddenly bursts out laughing—where will I hide then?" That thought drove me into a rage. By the end of my speech I'd really become excited, and now my pride was suffering somehow. The silence lasted for a while. I even considered shaking her.

"Somehow you . . ." she began suddenly and then stopped.

But I understood everything already: something was trembling in her voice now, not shrill, rude or unyielding as before, but something soft and timid, so timid that I suddenly was rather ashamed to watch her and felt guilty.

"What?" I asked with tender curiosity.

"Well, you . . ."

"What?"

"You somehow . . . it sounds just like a book," she said, and once again something which was noticeably sarcastic was suddenly heard in her voice.

Her remark wounded me dreadfully. That's not what I'd expected.

Yet, I didn't understand that she was intentionally disguising her feelings with sarcasm; that was usually the last resort of people who are timid and chaste of heart, whose souls have been coarsely and impudently invaded; and who, until the last moment, refuse to yield out of pride and are afraid to express their own feelings to you. I should've guessed it from the timidity with which on several occasions she tried to be sarcastic, until she finally managed to express it. But I hadn't guessed, and a malicious impulse took hold of me.

"Just you wait," I thought.

VII

"That's enough, Liza. What do books have to do with it, when this disgusts me as an outsider? And not only as an outsider. All this has awakened in my heart . . . Can it be, can it really be that you don't find it repulsive here? No, clearly habit means a great deal. The devil only knows what habit can do to a person. But do you seriously think that you'll never grow old, that you'll always be pretty, and that they'll keep you on here forever and ever? I'm not even talking about the filth. . . . Besides, I want to say this about your present life: even though you're still young, good-looking, nice, with soul and feelings, do you know, that when I came to a little while ago, I was immediately disgusted to be here with you! Why, a man has to be drunk to wind up here. But if you were in a different place, living as nice people do, I might not only chase after you, I might actually fall in love with you. I'd rejoice at a look from you, let alone a word; I'd wait for you at the gate and kneel down before you; I'd think of you as my betrothed and even consider that an honor. I wouldn't dare have any impure thoughts about you. But here, I know that I need only whistle, and you, whether you want to or not, will come to me, and that I don't have to do your bidding, whereas you have to do mine. The lowliest peasant may hire himself out as a laborer, but he doesn't make a complete slave of himself; he knows that it's only for a limited term. But what's your term? Just think about it. What are you giving up here? What are you enslaving? Why, you're enslaving your soul, something you don't really own, together with your body! You're giving away your love to be defiled by any drunkard! Love! After all, that's all there is!

It's a precious jewel, a maiden's treasure, that's what it is! Why, to earn that love a man might be ready to offer up his own soul, to face death. But what's your love worth now? You've been bought, all of you; and why should anyone strive for your love, when you offer everything even without it? Why, there's no greater insult for a girl, don't you understand? Now, I've heard that they console you foolish girls, they allow you to see your own lovers here. But that's merely child's play, deception, making fun of you, while you believe it. And do you really think he loves you, that lover of yours? I don't believe it. How can he, if he knows that you can be called away from him at any moment? He'd have to be depraved after all that. Does he possess even one drop of respect for you? What do you have in common with him? He's laughing at you and stealing from you at the same time—so much for his love. It's not too bad, as long as he doesn't beat you. But perhaps he does. Go on, ask him, if you have such a lover, whether he'll ever marry you. Why, he'll burst out laughing right in your face, if he doesn't spit at you or smack you. He himself may be worth no more than a few lousy kopecks. And for what, do you think, did you ruin your whole life here? For the coffee they give you to drink, or for the plentiful supply of food? Why do you think they feed you so well? Another girl, an honest one, would choke on every bite, because she'd know why she was being fed so well. You're in debt here, you'll be in debt, and will remain so until the end, until such time comes as the customers begin to spurn you. And that time will come very soon; don't count on your youth. Why, here youth flies by like a stage-coach. They'll kick you out. And they'll not merely kick you out, but for a long time before that they'll pester you, reproach you, and abuse you—as if you hadn't ruined your health for the madam, hadn't given up your youth and your soul for her in vain, but rather, as if you'd ruined her, ravaged her, and robbed her. And don't expect any support. Your friends will also attack you to curry her favor, because they're all in bondage here and have long since lost both conscience and pity. They've become despicable, and there's nothing on earth more despicable, more repulsive, or more insulting than their abuse. You'll lose everything here, everything, without exception—your health, youth, beauty, and hope—and at the age of twenty-two you'll look as if you were thirty-five, and even that won't be too awful if you're not ill. Thank God for that. Why, you probably think that you're not even working, that it's all play! But there's no harder work or more onerous task than this one in the whole world and there never has been. I'd think that one's heart alone would be worn out by crying. Yet you dare not utter one word, not one syllable; when they drive you out, you leave as if you were the guilty one. You'll move to another place, then to a third, then somewhere else, and finally you'll wind up in the Haymarket. And there they'll start beating you for no good reason at all; it's a local custom; the clients there don't know how to be nice without beating you. You don't think it's so disgusting there? Maybe you should go and have a look sometime, and see it with your own eyes. Once, at New Year's, I saw a woman in a doorway. Her own kind had pushed her outside as a joke, to freeze her for a little while because she was wailing too much; they shut the door behind her. At nine o'clock in the morning she was already dead drunk, dishevelled, half-naked, and all beaten up. Her face was powdered, but her eyes were bruised; blood was streaming from her nose and mouth; a certain cabby had just fixed her up. She was sitting on a stone step, holding a piece of salted fish in her hand; she was howling, wailing something about her 'fate,' and slapping the fish against the stone step. Cabbies and drunken soldiers had gathered around the steps and were taunting her. Don't you think you'll wind up the same way? I wouldn't want to believe it myself, but how do you know, perhaps eight or ten years ago this same girl, the one with the salted fish, arrived here from somewhere or other, all fresh like a little cherub, innocent, and pure; she knew no evil and blushed at every word. Perhaps she was just like you—proud, easily offended, unlike all the rest; she looked like a queen and knew that total happiness awaited the man who would love her and whom she would also love. Do you see how it all ended? What if at the very moment she was slapping the fish against that filthy step, dead drunk and dishevelled, what if, even at that very moment she'd recalled her earlier, chaste years in her father's house when she was still going to school, and when her neighbor's son used to wait for her along the path and assure her that he'd love her all his life and devote himself entirely to her, and when they vowed to love one another forever and get married as soon as they grew up! No, Liza, you'd be lucky, very lucky, if you died quickly from consumption somewhere in a corner, in a cellar, like that other girl. In a hospital, you say? All right—they'll take you off, but what if the madam still requires your services? Consumption is quite a disease—it's not like dying from a fever. A person continues to hope right up until the last minute and declares that he's in good health. He consoles himself. Now that's useful for your madam. Don't worry, that's the way it is. You've sold your soul; besides, you owe her money—that means you don't dare say a thing. And while you're dying, they'll all abandon you, turn away from you—because there's nothing left to get from you. They'll even reproach you for taking up space for no good reason and for taking so long to die. You won't even be able to ask for something to drink, without their hurling abuse at you: 'When will you croak, you old bitch? You keep on moaning and don't let us get any sleep—and you drive our customers away.' That's for sure; I've overheard such words myself. And as you're breathing your last, they'll shove you into the filthiest corner of the cellar—into darkness and dampness; lying there alone, what will you think about then? After you die, some stranger will lay you out hurriedly, grumbling all the while, impatiently—no one will bless you, no one will sigh over you; they'll merely want to get rid of you as quickly as possible. They'll buy you a wooden trough and carry you out as they did that poor woman I saw today; then they'll go off to a tavern and drink to your memory. There'll be slush, filth, and wet snow in your grave—why bother for the likes of you? 'Let her down, Vanyukha; after all, it's her fate to go down with her legs up, that's the sort of girl she was. Pull up on that rope, you rascal!' 'It's okay like that.' 'How's it okay? See, it's lying on its side. Was she a human being or not? Oh, never mind, cover it up.' They won't want to spend much time arguing over you. They'll cover your coffin quickly with wet, blue clay and then go off to the tavern. . . . That'll be the end of your memory on earth; for other women, children will visit their graves, fathers, husbands—but for you—no tears, no sighs; no remembrances. No one, absolutely no one in the whole world, will ever come to visit you; your name will disappear from the face of the earth, just as if you'd never been born and had never existed. Mud and filth, no matter how you pound on the lid of your coffin at night when other corpses arise: 'Let me out, kind people, let me live on earth for a little while! I lived, but I didn't really see life; my life went down the drain; they drank it away in a tavern at the Haymarket; let me out, kind people, let me live in the world once again!'"

I was so carried away by my own pathos that I began to feel a lump forming in my throat, and . . . I suddenly stopped, rose up in fright, and, leaning over apprehensively, I began to listen carefully as my own heart pounded. There was cause for dismay.

For a while I felt that I'd turned her soul inside out and had broken her heart; the more I became convinced of this, the more I strived to reach my goal as quickly and forcefully as possible. It was the sport, the sport that attracted me; but it wasn't only the sport. . . .

I knew that I was speaking clumsily, artificially, even bookishly; in short, I didn't know how to speak except "like a book." But that didn't bother me, for I knew, I had a premonition, that I would be understood and that this bookishness itself might even help things along. But now, having achieved this effect, I suddenly lost all my nerve. No, never, never before had I witnessed such despair! She was lying there, her face pressed deep into a pillow she was clutching with her hands. Her heart was bursting. Her young body was shuddering as if she were having convulsions. Suppressed sobs shook her breast, tore her apart, and suddenly burst forth in cries and moans. Then she pressed her face even deeper into the pillow: she didn't want anyone, not one living soul, to hear her anguish and her tears. She bit the pillow; she bit her hand until it bled (I noticed that afterward); or else, thrusting her fingers into her dishevelled hair, she became rigid with the strain, holding her breath and clenching her teeth. I was about to say something, to ask her to calm down; but I felt that I didn't dare. Suddenly, all in a kind of chill, almost in a panic, I groped hurriedly to get out of there as quickly as possible. It was dark: no matter how I tried, I couldn't end it quickly. Suddenly I felt a box of matches and a candlestick with a whole unused candle. As soon as the room was lit up, Liza started suddenly, sat up, and looked at me almost senselessly, with a distorted face and a half-crazy smile. I sat down next to her and took her hands; she came to and threw herself at me, wanting to embrace me, yet not daring to. Then she quietly lowered her head before me.

"Liza, my friend, I shouldn't have . . . you must forgive me," I began, but she squeezed my hands so tightly in her fingers that I realized I was saying the wrong thing and stopped.

"Here's my address, Liza. Come to see me."

"I will," she whispered resolutely, still not lifting her head.

"I'm going now, good-bye . . . until we meet again."

I stood up; she did, too, and suddenly blushed all over, shuddered, seized a shawl lying on a chair, threw it over her shoulders, and wrapped herself up to her chin. After doing this, she smiled again somewhat painfully, blushed, and looked at me strangely. I felt awful. I hastened to leave, to get away.

"Wait," she said suddenly as we were standing in the hallway near the door, and she stopped me by putting her hand on my overcoat. She quickly put the candle down and ran off; obviously she'd remembered something or wanted to show me something. As she left she was blushing all over, her eyes were gleaming, and a smile had appeared on her lips—what on earth did it all mean? I waited against my own will; she returned a moment later with a glance that seemed to beg forgiveness for something. All in all it was no longer the same face or the same glance as before—sullen, distrustful, obstinate. Now her glance was imploring, soft, and, at the same time, trusting, affectionate, and timid. That's how children look at people whom they love very much, or when they're asking for something. Her eyes were light hazel, lovely, full of life, as capable of expressing love as brooding hatred.

Without any explanation, as if I were some kind of higher being who was supposed to know everything, she held a piece of paper out toward me. At that moment her whole face was shining with a most naive, almost childlike triumph. I unfolded the paper. It was a letter to her from some medical student containing a high-flown, flowery, but very respectful declaration of love. I don't remember the exact words now, but I can well recall the genuine emotion that can't be feigned shining through that high style. When I'd finished reading the letter, I met her ardent, curious, and childishly impatient gaze. She'd fixed her eyes on my face and was waiting eagerly to see what I'd say. In a few words, hurriedly, but with some joy and pride, she explained that she'd once been at a dance somewhere, in a private house, at the home of some "very, very good people, *family people*, where they *knew nothing*, nothing at all," because she'd arrived at this place only recently and was just . . . well, she hadn't quite decided whether she'd stay here and she'd certainly leave as soon as she'd paid off her debt. . . . Well, and this student was there; he danced with her all evening and talked to her. It turned out he was from Riga; he'd known her as a child, they'd played together, but that had been a long time ago; he was acquainted with her parents—but he knew nothing, absolutely nothing *about this place* and he didn't even suspect it! And so, the very next day, after the dance, (only some three days ago), he'd sent her this letter through the friend with whom she'd gone to the party . . . and . . . well, that's the whole story."

She lowered her sparkling eyes somewhat bashfully after she finished speaking.

The poor little thing, she'd saved this student's letter as a treasure and had run to fetch this one treasure of hers, not wanting me to leave without knowing that she too was the object of sincere, honest love, and that someone exists who had spoken to her respectfully. Probably that letter was fated to lie in her box without results. But that didn't matter; I'm sure that she'll guard it as a treasure her whole life, as her pride and vindication; and now, at a moment like this, she remembered it and brought it out to exult naively before me, to raise herself in my eyes, so that I could see it for myself and could also think well of her. I didn't say a thing; I shook her hand and left. I really wanted to get away. . . . I walked all the way home in spite of the fact that wet snow was still falling in large flakes. I was exhausted, oppressed, and perplexed. But the truth was already glimmering behind that perplexity. The ugly truth!

VIII

It was some time, however, before I agreed to acknowledge that truth. I awoke the next morning after a few hours of deep, leaden sleep. Instantly recalling the events of the previous day, even I was astonished at my *sentimentality* with Liza last night, at all of yesterday's "horror and pity." "Why, it's an attack of old woman's nervous hysteria, phew!" I decided. "And why on earth did I force my address on her? What if she comes? Then again, let her come, it doesn't make any difference. . . ." But *obviously* that was not the main, most important matter: I had to make haste and rescue at all costs my reputation in the eyes of Zverkov and Simonov. That was my main task. I even forgot all about Liza in the concerns of that morning.

First of all I had to repay last night's debt to Simonov immediately. I resolved on desperate means: I would borrow the sum of fifteen rubles from Anton Antonych. As luck would have it, he was in a splendid mood that morning and gave me the money at once, at my first request. I was so delighted that I signed a promissory note with a somewhat dashing air, and told him *casually* that on the previous evening "I'd been living it up with some friends at the Hôtel de Paris. We were holding a farewell dinner for a comrade, one might even say, a childhood friend, and, you know—he's a great carouser, very spoiled—well, naturally; he comes from a good family, has considerable wealth and a brilliant career; he's witty and charming, and has affairs with certain ladies, you understand. We drank up an extra 'half-dozen bottles' and . . ." There was nothing to it; I said all this very easily, casually, and complacently.

Upon arriving home I wrote to Simonov at once.

To this very day I recall with admiration the truly gentlemanly, good-natured, candid tone of my letter. Cleverly and nobly, and, above all, without unnecessary words, I blamed myself for everything. I justified myself, "if only I could be allowed to justify myself," by saying that, being so totally unaccustomed to wine, I'd gotten drunk with the first glass, which (supposedly) I'd consumed even before their arrival, as I waited for them in the Hôtel de Paris between the hours of five and six o'clock. In particular, I begged for Simonov's pardon; I asked him to convey my apology to all the others, especially to Zverkov, whom, "I recall, as if in a dream," it seems, I'd insulted. I added that I'd have called upon each of them, but was suffering from a bad headache, and, worst of all, I was ashamed. I was particularly satisfied by the "certain lightness," almost casualness (though, still very proper), unexpectedly reflected in my style; better than all possible arguments, it conveyed to them at once that I regarded "all of last night's unpleasantness" in a rather detached way, and that I was not at all, not in the least struck down on the spot as you, gentlemen, probably suspect. On the contrary, I regard this all serenely, as any self-respecting gentleman would. The true story, as they say, is no reproach to an honest young man.

"Why, there's even a hint of aristocratic playfulness in it," I thought admiringly as I reread my note. "And it's all because I'm such a cultured and educated man! Others in my place wouldn't know how to extricate themselves, but I've gotten out of it, and I'm having a good time once again, all because I'm an 'educated and cultured man of our time.' It may even be true that the whole thing occurred as a result of that wine yesterday. Hmmm . . . well, no, it wasn't really the wine. And I didn't have anything to drink between five and six o'clock when I was waiting for them. I lied to Simonov; it was a bold-faced lie—yet I'm not ashamed of it even now. . . ."

But, to hell with it, anyway! The main thing is, I got out of it.

I put six rubles in the letter, sealed it up, and asked Apollon to take it to Simonov. When he heard that there was money in it, Apollon became more respectful and agreed to deliver it. Toward evening I went out for a stroll. My head was still aching and spinning from the events of the day before. But as evening approached and twilight deepened, my impressions changed and became more confused, as did my thoughts. Something hadn't yet died within me, deep within my heart and conscience; it didn't want to die, and it expressed itself as burning anguish. I jostled my way along the more populous, commercial streets, along Meshchanskaya, Sadovaya, near the Yusupov Garden. I particularly liked to stroll along these streets at twilight, just as they became most crowded with all sorts of pedestrians, merchants, and tradesmen, with faces preoccupied to the point of hostility, on their way home from a hard day's work. It was precisely the cheap bustle that I liked, the crass prosaic quality. But this time all that street bustle irritated me even more. I couldn't get a hold of myself or puzzle out what was wrong. Something was rising, rising up in my soul continually, painfully, and didn't want to settle down. I returned home completely distraught. It was just as if some crime were weighing on my soul.

I was constantly tormented by the thought that Liza might come to see me. It was strange, but from all of yesterday's recollections, the one of her tormented me most, somehow separately from all the others. I'd managed to forget the rest by evening, to shrug everything off, and I still remained completely satisfied with my letter to Simonov. But in regard to Liza, I was not at all satisfied. It was as though I were tormented by her alone. "What if she comes?" I thought continually. "Well, so what? It doesn't matter. Let her come. Hmm. The only unpleasant thing is that she'll see, for instance, how I live. Yesterday I appeared before her such a . . . hero . . . but now, hmm! Besides, it's revolting that I've sunk so low. The squalor of my apartment. And I dared go to dinner last night wearing such clothes! And that oilcloth sofa of mine with its stuffing hanging out! And my dressing gown that doesn't quite cover me! What rags! . . . She'll see it all—and she'll see Apollon. That swine will surely insult her. He'll pick on her, just to be rude to me. Of course, I'll be frightened, as usual. I'll begin to fawn before her, wrap myself up in my dressing gown. I'll start to smile and tell lies. Ugh, the indecency! And that's not even the worst part! There's something even more important, nastier, meaner! Yes, meaner! Once again, I'll put on that dishonest, deceitful mask! . . ."

When I reached this thought, I simply flared up.

"Why deceitful? How deceitful? Yesterday I spoke sincerely. I recall that there was genuine feeling in me, too. I was trying no less than to arouse noble feelings in her . . . and if she wept, that's a good thing; it will have a beneficial effect. . . ."

But I still couldn't calm down.

All that evening, even after I returned home, even after nine o'clock, when by my calculations Liza could no longer have come, her image continued to haunt me, and, what's most important, she always appeared in one and the same form. Of all that had occurred yesterday, it was one moment in particular which stood out most vividly: that was when I lit up the room with a match and saw her pale, distorted face with its tormented gaze. What a pitiful, unnatural, distorted smile she'd had at that moment! But little did I know then that even fifteen years later I'd still picture Liza to myself with that same pitiful, distorted, and unnecessary smile which she'd had at that moment.

The next day I was once again prepared to dismiss all this business as nonsense, as the result of overstimulated nerves; but most of all, as exaggeration. I was well aware of this weakness of mine and sometimes was even afraid of it; "I exaggerate everything, that's my problem," I kept repeating to myself hour after hour. And yet, "yet, Liza may still come, all the same"; that was the refrain which concluded my reflections. I was so distressed that I sometimes became furious. "She'll come! She'll definitely come!" If not today, then tomorrow, she'll seek me out! That's just like the damned romanticism of all these *pure hearts*! Oh, the squalor, the stupidity, the narrowness of these "filthy, sentimental souls!' How could all this not be understood, how on earth could it not be understood? . . ." But at this point I would stop myself, even in the midst of great confusion.

"And how few, how very few words were needed," I thought in passing, "how little idyllic sentiment (what's more, the sentiment was artificial, bookish, composed) was necessary to turn a whole human soul according to my wishes at once. That's innocence for you! That's virgin soil!"

At times the thought occurred that I might go to her myself "to tell her everything," and to beg her not to come to me. But at this thought such venom arose in me that it seemed I'd have crushed that "damned" Liza if she'd suddenly turned up next to me. I'd have insulted her, spat at her, struck her, and chased her away!

One day passed, however, then a second, and a third; she still hadn't come, and I began to calm down. I felt particularly reassured and relaxed after nine o'clock in the evening, and even began to daydream sweetly at times. For instance, I'd save Liza, precisely because she'd come to me, and I'd talk to her. . . . I'd develop her mind, educate her. At last I'd notice that she loved me, loved me passionately. I'd pretend I didn't understand. (For that matter, I didn't know why I'd pretend; most likely just for the effect.) At last, all embarrassed, beautiful, trembling, and sobbing, she'd throw herself at my feet and declare that I was her saviour and she loved me more than anything in the world. I'd be surprised, but . . . "Liza," I'd say, "Do you really think that I haven't noticed your love? I've seen everything. I guessed, but dared not be first to make a claim on your heart because I had such influence over you, and because I was afraid you might deliberately force yourself to respond to my love out of gratitude, that you might forcibly evoke within yourself a feeling that didn't really exist. No, I didn't want that because it would be . . . despotism. . . . It would be indelicate (well, in short, here I launched on some European, George Sandian,[4] inexplicably lofty subtleties . . .). But now, now—you're mine, you're my creation, you're pure and lovely, you're my beautiful wife."

> And enter my house bold and free
> To become its full mistress![5]

---

4. George Sand was the pseudonym of the French woman novelist Aurore Dudevant (1804–1876), famous also as a promoter of feminism.

5. The last lines of the poem by Nekrasov used as the epigraph of Part II of this story (see pp. 729–30).

"Then we'd begin to live happily together, travel abroad, etc., etc." In short, it began to seem crude even to me, and I ended it all by sticking my tongue out at myself.

"Besides, they won't let her out of there, the 'bitch,'" I thought. "After all, it seems unlikely that they'd release them for strolls, especially in the evening (for some reason I was convinced that she had to report there every evening, precisely at seven o'clock). Moreover, she said that she'd yet to become completely enslaved there, and that she still had certain rights; that means, hmm. Devil take it, she'll come, she's bound to come!"

It was a good thing I was distracted at the time by Apollon's rudeness. He made me lose all patience. He was the bane of my existence, a punishment inflicted on me by Providence. We'd been squabbling constantly for several years now and I hated him. My God, how I hated him! I think that I never hated anyone in my whole life as much as I hated him, especially at those times. He was an elderly, dignified man who worked part-time as a tailor. But for some unknown reason he despised me, even beyond all measure, and looked down upon me intolerably. However, he looked down on everyone. You need only glance at that flaxen, slicked-down hair, at that single lock brushed over his forehead and greased with vegetable oil, at his strong mouth, always drawn up in the shape of the letter V,[6] and you felt that you were standing before a creature who never doubted himself. He was a pedant of the highest order, the greatest one I'd ever met on earth; in addition he possessed a sense of self-esteem appropriate perhaps only to Alexander the Great, King of Macedonia. He was in love with every one of his buttons, every one of his fingernails—absolutely in love, and he looked it! He treated me quite despotically, spoke to me exceedingly little, and, if he happened to look at me, cast a steady, majestically self-assured, and constantly mocking glance that sometimes infuriated me. He carried out his tasks as if he were doing me the greatest of favors. Moreover, he did almost nothing at all for me; nor did he assume that he was obliged to do anything. There could be no doubt that he considered me the greatest fool on earth, and, that if he "kept me on," it was only because he could receive his wages from me every month. He agreed to "do nothing" for seven rubles a month. I'll be forgiven many of my sins because of him. Sometimes my hatred reached such a point that his gait alone would throw me into convulsions. But the most repulsive thing about him was his lisping. His tongue was a bit larger than normal or something of the sort; as a result, he constantly lisped and hissed. Apparently, he was terribly proud of it, imagining that it endowed him with enormous dignity. He spoke slowly, in measured tones, with his hands behind his back and his eyes fixed on the ground. It particularly infuriated me when he used to read the Psalter to himself behind his partition. I endured many battles on account of it. He was terribly fond of reading during the evening in a slow, even singsong voice, as if chanting over the dead. It's curious, but that's how he ended up: now he hires himself out to recite the Psalter over the dead; in addition, he exterminates rats and makes shoe polish. But at that time I couldn't get rid of him; it was as if he were chemically linked to my own existence. Besides, he'd never have agreed to leave for anything. It was impossible for me to live in a furnished room: my

6. The last letter of the old Russian alphabet, triangular in shape.

own apartment was my private residence, my shell, my case, where I hid from all humanity. Apollon, the devil only knows why, seemed to belong to this apartment, and for seven long years I couldn't get rid of him.

It was impossible, for example, to delay paying him his wages for even two or three days. He'd make such a fuss that I wouldn't know where to hide. But in those days I was so embittered by everyone that I decided, heaven knows why or for what reason, to *punish* Apollon by not paying him his wages for two whole weeks. I'd been planning to do this for some time now, about two years, simply in order to teach him that he had no right to put on such airs around me, and that if I chose to, I could always withhold his wages. I resolved to say nothing to him about it and even remain silent on purpose, to conquer his pride and force him to be the first one to mention it. Then I would pull all seven rubles out of a drawer and show him that I actually had the money and had intentionally set it aside, but that "I didn't want to, didn't want to, simply didn't want to pay him his wages, and that I didn't want to simply because *that's what I wanted*," because such was "my will as his master," because he was disrespectful and because he was rude. But, if he were to ask respectfully, then I might relent and pay him; if not, he might have to wait another two weeks, or three, or even a whole month. . . .

But, no matter how angry I was, he still won. I couldn't even hold out for four days. He began as he always did, because there had already been several such cases (and, let me add, I knew all this beforehand; I knew his vile tactics by heart), to wit: he would begin by fixing an extremely severe gaze on me. He would keep it up for several minutes in a row, especially when meeting me or accompanying me outside of the house. If, for example, I held out and pretended not to notice these stares, then he, maintaining his silence as before, would proceed to further tortures. Suddenly, for no reason at all, he'd enter my room quietly and slowly, while I was pacing or reading; he'd stop at the door, place one hand behind his back, thrust one foot forward, and fix his gaze on me, no longer merely severe, but now utterly contemptuous. If I were suddenly to ask him what he wanted, he wouldn't answer at all. He'd continue to stare at me reproachfully for several more seconds; then, compressing his lips in a particular way and assuming a very meaningful air, he'd turn slowly on the spot and slowly withdraw to his own room. Two hours later he'd emerge again and suddenly appear before me in the same way. It's happened sometimes that in my fury I hadn't even asked what he wanted, but simply raised my head sharply and imperiously, and begun to stare reproachfully back at him. We would stare at each other thus for some two minutes or more; at last he'd turn slowly and self-importantly, and withdraw for another few hours.

If all this failed to bring me back to my senses and I continued to rebel, he'd suddenly begin to sigh while staring at me. He'd sigh heavily and deeply, as if trying to measure with each sigh the depth of my moral decline. Naturally, it would end with his complete victory: I'd rage and shout, but I was always forced to do just as he wished on the main point of dispute.

This time his usual maneuvers of "severe stares" had scarcely begun when I lost my temper at once and lashed out at him in a rage. I was irritated enough even without that.

"Wait!" I shouted in a frenzy, as he was slowly and silently turning with one hand behind his back, about to withdraw to his own room. "Wait! Come back, come back, I tell you!" I must have bellowed so unnaturally that he turned around and even began to scrutinize me with a certain amazement. He continued, however, not to utter one word, and that was what infuriated me most of all.

"How dare you come in here without asking permission and stare at me? Answer me!"

But after regarding me serenely for half a minute, he started to turn around again.

"Wait!" I roared, rushing up to him. "Don't move! There! Now answer me: why do you come in here to stare?"

"If you've got any orders for me now, it's my job to do 'em," he replied after another pause, lisping softly and deliberately, raising his eyebrows, and calmly shifting his head from one side to the other—what's more, he did all this with horrifying composure.

"That's not it! That's not what I'm asking you about, you executioner!" I shouted, shaking with rage. "I'll tell you myself, you executioner, why you came in here. You know that I haven't paid you your wages, but you're so proud that you don't want to bow down and ask me for them. That's why you came in here to punish me and torment me with your stupid stares, and you don't even sus-s-pect, you torturer, how stupid it all is, how stupid, stupid, stupid, stupid!"

He would have turned around silently once again, but I grabbed hold of him.

"Listen," I shouted to him. "Here's the money, you see! Here it is! (I pulled it out of a drawer.) All seven rubles. But you won't get it, you won't until you come to me respectfully, with your head bowed, to ask my forgiveness. Do you hear?"

"That can't be!" he replied with some kind of unnatural self-confidence.

"It will be!" I shrieked. "I give you my word of honor, it will be!"

"I have nothing to ask your forgiveness for," he said as if he hadn't even noticed my shrieks, "because it was you who called me an 'executioner,' and I can always go lodge a complaint against you at the police station."

"Go! Lodge a complaint!" I roared. "Go at once, this minute, this very second! You're still an executioner! Executioner! Executioner!" But he only looked at me, then turned and, no longer heeding my shouts, calmly withdrew to his own room without looking back.

"If it hadn't been for Liza, none of this would have happened!" I thought to myself. Then, after waiting a minute, pompously and solemnly, but with my heart pounding heavily and forcefully, I went in to see him behind the screen.

"Apollon!" I said softly and deliberately, though gasping for breath, "go at once, without delay to fetch the police supervisor!"

He'd already seated himself at his table, put on his eyeglasses, and picked up something to sew. But, upon hearing my order, he suddenly snorted with laughter.

"At once! Go this very moment! Go, go, or you can't imagine what will happen to you!"

"You're really not in your right mind," he replied, not even lifting his head, lisping just as slowly, and continuing to thread his needle. "Who's ever heard of a man being sent to fetch a policeman against himself? And as for trying to frighten me, you're only wasting your time, because nothing will happen to me."

"Go," I screeched, seizing him by the shoulder. I felt that I might strike him at any moment.

I never even heard the door from the hallway suddenly open at that very moment, quietly and slowly, and that someone walked in, stopped, and began to examine us in bewilderment. I glanced up, almost died from shame, and ran back into my own room. There, clutching my hair with both hands, I leaned my head against the wall and froze in that position.

Two minutes later I heard Apollon's deliberate footsteps.

"There's *some woman* asking for you," he said, staring at me with particular severity; then he stood aside and let her in—it was Liza. He didn't want to leave, and he scrutinized us mockingly.

"Get out, get out!" I commanded him all flustered. At that moment my clock strained, wheezed, and struck seven.

IX

And enter my house bold and free,
To become its full mistress!
From the same poem.[7]

I stood before her, crushed, humiliated, abominably ashamed; I think I was smiling as I tried with all my might to wrap myself up in my tattered, quilted dressing gown—exactly as I'd imagined this scene the other day during a fit of depression. Apollon, after standing over us for a few minutes, left, but that didn't make things any easier for me. Worst of all was that she suddenly became embarrassed too, more than I'd ever expected. At the sight of me, of course.

"Sit down," I said mechanically and moved a chair up to the table for her, while I sat on the sofa. She immediately and obediently sat down, staring at me wide-eyed, and, obviously, expecting something from me at once. This naive expectation infuriated me, but I restrained myself.

She should have tried not to notice anything, as if everything were just as it should be, but she . . . And I vaguely felt that she'd have to pay dearly *for everything*.

"You've found me in an awkward situation, Liza," I began, stammering and realizing that this was precisely the wrong way to begin.

"No, no, don't imagine anything!" I cried, seeing that she'd suddenly blushed. "I'm not ashamed of my poverty. . . . On the contrary, I regard it with pride. I'm poor, but noble. . . . One can be poor and noble," I muttered. "But . . . would you like some tea?"

"No . . . ," she started to say.

"Wait!"

I jumped up and ran to Apollon. I had to get away somehow.

"Apollon," I whispered in feverish haste, tossing down the seven rubles which had been in my fist the whole time, "here are your wages. There, you see, I've given them to you. But now you must rescue me: bring us some tea and a dozen rusks from the tavern at once. If you don't go, you'll make me a very miserable

7. I.e., from the poem quoted on pp. 729–30 and 769.

man. You have no idea who this woman is. . . . This means—everything! You may think she's . . . But you've no idea at all who this woman really is!"

Apollon, who'd already sat down to work and had put his glasses on again, at first glanced sideways in silence at the money without abandoning his needle; then, paying no attention to me and making no reply, he continued to fuss with the needle he was still trying to thread. I waited there for about three minutes standing before him with my arms folded à la Napoleon.[8] My temples were soaked in sweat. I was pale, I felt that myself. But, thank God, he must have taken pity just looking at me. After finishing with the thread, he stood up slowly from his place, slowly pushed back his chair, slowly took off his glasses, slowly counted the money and finally, after inquiring over his shoulder whether he should get a whole pot, slowly walked out of the room. As I was returning to Liza, it occurred to me: shouldn't I run away just as I was, in my shabby dressing gown, no matter where, and let come what may.

I sat down again. She looked at me uneasily. We sat in silence for several minutes.

"I'll kill him." I shouted suddenly, striking the table so hard with my fist that ink splashed out of the inkwell.

"Oh, what are you saying?" she exclaimed, startled.

"I'll kill him, I'll kill him!" I shrieked, striking the table in an absolute frenzy, but understanding full well at the same time how stupid it was to be in such a frenzy.

"You don't understand, Liza, what this executioner is doing to me. He's my executioner. . . . He's just gone out for some rusks; he . . ."

And suddenly I burst into tears. It was a nervous attack. I felt so ashamed amidst my sobs, but I couldn't help it. She got frightened.

"What's the matter? What's wrong with you?" she cried, fussing around me.

"Water, give me some water, over there!" I muttered in a faint voice, realizing full well, however, that I could've done both without the water and without the faint voice. But I was *putting on an act*, as it's called, in order to maintain decorum, although my nervous attack was genuine.

She gave me some water while looking at me like a lost soul. At that very moment Apollon brought in the tea. It suddenly seemed that this ordinary and prosaic tea was horribly inappropriate and trivial after everything that had happened, and I blushed. Liza stared at Apollon with considerable alarm. He left without looking at us.

"Liza, do you despise me?" I asked, looking her straight in the eye, trembling with impatience to find out what she thought.

She was embarrassed and didn't know what to say.

"Have some tea," I said angrily. I was angry at myself, but she was the one who'd have to pay, naturally. A terrible anger against her suddenly welled up in my heart; I think I could've killed her. To take revenge I swore inwardly not to say one more word to her during the rest of her visit. "She's the cause of it all," I thought.

Our silence continued for about five minutes. The tea stood on the table; we didn't touch it. It reached the point of my not wanting to drink on purpose, to make it even more difficult for her; it would be awkward for her to begin alone.

8. In the style of Napoleon.

Several times she glanced at me in sad perplexity. I stubbornly remained silent. I was the main sufferer, of course, because I was fully aware of the despicable meanness of my own spiteful stupidity; yet, at the same time, I couldn't restrain myself.

"I want to . . . get away from . . . that place . . . once and for all," she began just to break the silence somehow; but, poor girl, that was just the thing she shouldn't have said at that moment, stupid enough as it was to such a person as me, stupid as I was. My own heart even ached with pity for her tactlessness and unnecessary straightforwardness. But something hideous immediately suppressed all my pity; it provoked me even further. Let the whole world go to hell. Another five minutes passed.

"Have I disturbed you?" she began timidly, barely audibly, and started to get up.

But as soon as I saw this first glimpse of injured dignity, I began to shake with rage and immediately exploded.

"Why did you come here? Tell me why, please," I began, gasping and neglecting the logical order of my words. I wanted to say it all at once, without pausing for breath; I didn't even worry about how to begin.

"Why did you come here? Answer me! Answer!" I cried, hardly aware of what I was saying. "I'll tell you, my dear woman, why you came here. You came here because I spoke some *words of pity* to you that time. Now you've softened, and want to hear more 'words of pity.' Well, you should know that I was laughing at you then. And I'm laughing at you now. Why are you trembling? Yes, I was laughing at you! I'd been insulted, just prior to that, at dinner, by those men who arrived just before me that evening. I came intending to thrash one of them, the officer; but I didn't succeed; I couldn't find him; I had to avenge my insult on someone, to get my own back; you turned up and I took my anger out at you, and I laughed at you. I'd been humiliated, and I wanted to humiliate someone else; I'd been treated like a rag, and I wanted to exert some power. . . . That's what it was; you thought that I'd come there on purpose to save you, right? Is that what you thought? Is that it?"

I knew that she might get confused and might not grasp all the details, but I also knew that she'd understand the essence of it very well. That's just what happened. She turned white as a sheet; she wanted to say something. Her lips were painfully twisted, but she collapsed onto a chair just as if she'd been struck down with an ax. Subsequently she listened to me with her mouth gaping, her eyes wide open, shaking with awful fear. It was the cynicism, the cynicism of my words that crushed her. . . .

"To save you!" I continued, jumping up from my chair and rushing up and down the room in front of her, "to save you from what? Why, I may be even worse than you are. When I recited that sermon to you, why didn't you throw it back in my face? You should have said to me, 'Why did you come here? To preach morality or what?' Power, it was the power I needed then, I craved the sport, I wanted to reduce you to tears, humiliation, hysteria—that's what I needed then! But I couldn't have endured it myself, because I'm such a wretch. I got scared. The devil only knows why I foolishly gave you my address. Afterward, even before I got home, I cursed you like nothing on earth on account of that address. I hated you already because I'd lied to you then, because it was all playing with words, dreaming in my own mind. But, do you know what I really want now? For you to get lost, that's what! I need some peace. Why, I'd sell the whole world for a kopeck if people would only stop bothering me. Should the world go to hell, or should I go without my tea? I say, let the world go to hell as long as I can always have my tea. Did you know that or not? And I know perfectly well that I'm a scoundrel, a bastard, an egotist, and a sluggard. I've been shaking from fear for the last three days wondering whether you'd ever come. Do you know what disturbed me most of all these last three days? The fact that I'd appeared to you then as such a hero, and that now you'd suddenly see me in this torn dressing gown, dilapidated and revolting. I said before that I wasn't ashamed of my poverty; well, you should know that I am ashamed, I'm ashamed of it more than anything, more afraid of it than anything, more than if I were a thief, because I'm so vain; it's as if the skin's been stripped away from my body so that even wafts of air cause pain. By now surely even you've guessed that I'll never forgive you for having come upon me in this dressing gown as I was attacking Apollon like a vicious dog. Your saviour, your former hero, behaving like a mangy, shaggy mongrel, attacking his own lackey, while that lackey stood there laughing at me! Nor will I ever forgive you for those tears which, like an embarrassed old woman, I couldn't hold back before you. And I'll never forgive *you* for all that I'm confessing now. Yes—you, you alone must pay for everything because you turned up like this, because I'm a scoundrel, because I'm the nastiest, most ridiculous, pettiest, stupidest, most envious worm of all those living on earth who're no better than me in any way, but who, the devil knows why, never get embarrassed, while all my life I have to endure insults from every louse—that's my fate. What do I care that you don't understand any of this? What do I care, what do I care about you and whether or not you perish there? Why, don't you realize how much I'll hate you now after having said all this with your being here listening to me? After all, a man can only talk like this once in his whole life, and then only in hysteria! . . . What more do you want? Why, after all this, are you still hanging around here tormenting me? Why don't you leave?"

But at this point a very strange thing suddenly occurred.

I'd become so accustomed to inventing and imagining everything according to books, and picturing everything on earth to myself just as I'd conceived of it in my dreams, that at first I couldn't even comprehend the meaning of this strange occurrence. But here's what happened: Liza, insulted and crushed by me, understood much more than I'd imagined. She understood out of all this what a woman always understands first of all, if she sincerely loves—namely, that I myself was unhappy.

The frightened and insulted expression on her face was replaced at first by grieved amazement. When I began to call myself a scoundrel and a bastard, and my tears had begun to flow (I'd pronounced this whole tirade in tears), her whole face was convulsed by a spasm. She wanted to get up and stop me; when I'd finished, she paid no attention to my shouting, "Why are you here? Why don't you leave?" She only noticed that it must have been very painful for me to utter all this. Besides, she was so defenseless, the poor girl. She considered herself immeasurably beneath me. How could she get angry or take offense? Suddenly she jumped up from the chair with a kind of uncontrollable impulse, and yearning toward me, but being too timid and not daring to stir from her place, she extended her arms in my direction. . . . At this moment my heart leapt inside me, too. Then suddenly she threw herself at me, put her arms around my neck, and burst into tears. I, too, couldn't restrain myself and sobbed as I'd never done before.

"They won't let me . . . I can't be . . . good!" I barely managed to say; then I went over to the sofa, fell upon it face down, and sobbed in genuine hysterics for a quarter of an hour. She knelt down, embraced me, and remained motionless in that position.

But the trouble was that my hysterics had to end sometime. And so (after all, I'm writing the whole loathsome truth), lying there on the sofa and pressing my face firmly into that nasty leather cushion of mine, I began to sense gradually, distantly, involuntarily, but irresistibly, that it would be awkward for me to raise my head and look Liza straight in the eye. What was I ashamed of? I don't know, but I was ashamed. It also occurred to my overwrought brain that now our roles were completely reversed; now she was the heroine, and I was the same sort of humiliated and oppressed creature she'd been in front of me that evening—only four days ago. . . . And all this came to me during those few minutes as I lay face down on the sofa!

My God! Was it possible that I envied her?

I don't know; to this very day I still can't decide. But then, of course, I was even less able to understand it. After all, I couldn't live without exercising power and tyrannizing over another person. . . . But . . . but, then, you really can't explain a thing by reason; consequently, it's useless to try.

However, I regained control of myself and raised my head; I had to sooner or later. . . . And so, I'm convinced to this day that it was precisely because I felt too ashamed to look at her, that another feeling was suddenly kindled and burst into flame in my heart—the feeling of domination and possession. My eyes gleamed with passion; I pressed her hands tightly. How I hated her and felt drawn to her simultaneously! One feeling intensified the other. It was almost like revenge! . . . At first there was a look of something resembling bewilderment, or even fear, on her face, but only for a brief moment. She embraced me warmly and rapturously.

X

A quarter of an hour later I was rushing back and forth across the room in furious impatience, constantly approaching the screen to peer at Liza through the crack. She was sitting on the floor, her head leaning against the bed, and she must have been crying. But she didn't leave, and that's what irritated me. By this time she knew absolutely everything. I'd insulted her once and for all, but . . . there's nothing more to be said. She guessed that my outburst of passion was merely revenge, a new humiliation for her, and that to my former, almost aimless, hatred there was added now a *personal, envious* hatred of her. . . . However, I don't think that she understood all this explicitly; on the other hand, she fully understood that I was a despicable man, and, most important, that I was incapable of loving her.

I know that I'll be told this is incredible—that it's impossible to be as spiteful and stupid as I am; you may even add that it was impossible not to return, or at least to appreciate, this love. But why is this so incredible? In the first place, I could no longer love because, I repeat, for me love meant tyrannizing and demonstrating my moral superiority. All my life I could never even conceive of any other kind of love, and I've now reached the point that I sometimes think that love consists precisely in a voluntary gift by the beloved person of the right to tyrannize over him. Even in my underground dreams I couldn't conceive of love in any way other than a struggle. It always began with hatred and ended with moral subjugation; afterward, I could never imagine what to do with the subjugated object. And what's so incredible about that, since I'd previously managed to corrupt myself morally; I'd already become unaccustomed to "real life," and only a short while ago had taken it into my head to reproach her and shame her for having come to hear "words of pity" from me. But I never could've guessed that she'd come not to hear words of pity at all, but to love me, because it's in that kind of love that a woman finds her resurrection, all her salvation from whatever kind of ruin, and her rebirth, as it can't appear in any other form. However, I didn't hate her so much as I rushed around the room and peered through the crack behind the screen. I merely found it unbearably painful that she was still there. I wanted her to disappear. I longed for "peace and quiet"; I wanted to remain alone in my underground. "Real life" oppressed me—so unfamiliar was it—that I even found it hard to breathe.

But several minutes passed, and she still didn't stir, as if she were oblivious. I was shameless enough to tap gently on the screen to remind her. . . . She started suddenly, jumped up, and hurried to find her shawl, hat, and coat, as if she wanted to escape from me. . . . Two minutes later she slowly emerged from behind the screen and looked at me sadly. I smiled spitefully; it was forced, however, for *appearance's sake only*; and I turned away from her look.

"Good-bye," she said, going toward the door.

Suddenly I ran up to her, grabbed her hand, opened it, put something in . . . and closed it again. Then I turned away at once and bolted to the other corner, so that at least I wouldn't be able to see. . . .

I was just about to lie—to write that I'd done all this accidentally, without knowing what I was doing, in complete confusion, out of foolishness. But I don't want to lie; therefore I'll say straight out, that I opened her hand and placed something in it . . . out of spite. It occurred to me to do this while I was rushing back and forth across the room and she was sitting there behind the screen. But here's what I can say for sure: although I did this cruel thing deliberately, it was not from my heart, but from my stupid head. This cruelty of mine was so artificial, cerebral, intentionally invented, *bookish*, that I couldn't stand it myself even for one minute—at first I bolted to the corner so as not to see, and then, out of shame and in despair, I rushed out after Liza. I opened the door into the hallway and listened. "Liza! Liza!" I called down the stairs, but timidly, in a soft voice.

There was no answer; I thought I could hear her footsteps at the bottom of the stairs.

"Liza!" I cried more loudly.

No answer. But at that moment I heard down below the sound of the tight outer glass door opening heavily with a creak and then closing again tightly. The sound rose up the stairs.

She'd gone. I returned to my room deep in thought. I felt horribly oppressed.

I stood by the table near the chair where she'd been sitting and stared senselessly into space. A minute or so passed, then I suddenly started: right before me on the chair I saw . . . in a word, I saw the crumpled blue five-ruble note, the very one I'd thrust into her hand a few moments before. It was the same one; it couldn't be any other; I had none other in my apartment. So she'd managed to toss it down on the table when I'd bolted to the other corner.

So what? I might have expected her to do that. Might have expected it? No. I was such an egotist, in fact, I so lacked respect for other people, that I couldn't even conceive that she'd ever do that. I couldn't stand it. A moment later, like a madman, I hurried to get dressed. I threw on whatever I happened to find, and rushed headlong after her. She couldn't have gone more than two hundred paces when I ran out on the street.

It was quiet; it was snowing heavily, and the snow was falling almost perpendicularly, blanketing the sidewalk and the deserted street. There were no passers-by; no sound could be heard. The street lights were flickering dismally and vainly. I ran about two hundred paces to the crossroads and stopped.

"Where did she go? And why am I running after her? Why? To fall down before her, sob with remorse, kiss her feet, and beg her forgiveness! That's just what I wanted. My heart was being torn apart; never, never will I recall that moment with indifference. But—why?" I wondered. "Won't I grow to hate her, perhaps as soon as tomorrow, precisely because I'm kissing her feet today? Will I ever be able to make her happy? Haven't I found out once again today, for the hundredth time, what I'm really worth? Won't I torment her?"

I stood in the snow, peering into the murky mist, and thought about all this.

"And wouldn't it be better, wouldn't it," I fantasized once I was home again, stifling the stabbing pain in my heart with such fantasies, "wouldn't it be better if she were to carry away the insult with her forever? Such an insult—after all, is purification; it's the most caustic and painful form of consciousness. Tomorrow I would have defiled her soul and wearied her heart. But now that insult will never die within her; no matter how abominable the filth that awaits her, that insult will elevate and purify her . . . by hatred . . . hmm . . . perhaps by forgiveness as well. But will that make it any easier for her?"

And now, in fact, I'll pose an idle question of my own. Which is better: cheap happiness or sublime suffering? Well, come on, which is better?

These were my thoughts as I sat home that evening, barely alive with the anguish in my soul. I'd never before endured so much suffering and remorse; but could there exist even the slightest doubt that when I went rushing out of my apartment, I'd turn back again after going only halfway? I never met Liza afterward, and I never heard anything more about her. I'll also add that for a long time I remained satisfied with my theory about the use of insults and hatred, in spite of the fact that I myself almost fell ill from anguish at the time.

Even now, after so many years, all this comes back to me as *very unpleasant*. A great deal that comes back to me now is very unpleasant, but . . . perhaps I should end these *Notes* here? I think that I made a mistake in beginning to write them. At least, I was ashamed all the time I was writing this *tale*: consequently, it's not really literature, but corrective punishment. After all, to tell you long stories about how, for example, I ruined my life through moral decay in my corner, by the lack of appropriate surroundings, by isolation from any living beings, and by futile malice in the underground—so help me God, that's not very interesting. A novel needs a hero, whereas here all the traits of an anti-hero have been assembled *deliberately*; but the most important thing is that all this produces an extremely unpleasant impression because we've all become estranged from life, we're all cripples, every one of us, more or less. We've become so estranged that at times we feel some kind of revulsion for genuine "real life," and therefore we can't bear to be reminded of it. Why, we've reached a point where we almost regard "real life" as hard work, as a job, and we've all agreed in private that it's really better in books. And why do we sometimes fuss, indulge in whims, and make demands? We don't know ourselves. It'd be even worse if all our whimsical desires were fulfilled. Go on, try it. Give us, for example, a little more independence; untie the hands of any one of us, broaden our sphere of activity, relax the controls, and . . . I can assure you, we'll immediately ask to have the controls reinstated. I know that you may get angry at me for saying this, you may shout and stamp your feet: "Speak for yourself," you'll say, "and for your own miseries in the underground, but don't you dare say 'all of us.'" If you'll allow me, gentlemen; after all, I'm not trying to justify myself by saying all of us. What concerns me in particular, is that in my life I've only taken to an extreme that which you haven't even dared to take halfway; what's more, you've mistaken your cowardice for good sense; and, in so deceiving yourself, you've consoled yourself. So, in fact, I may even be "more alive" than you are. Just take a closer look! Why, we don't even know where this "real life" lives nowadays, what it really is, and what it's called. Leave us alone without books and we'll get confused and lose our way at once—we won't know what to join, what to hold on to, what to love or what to hate, what to respect or what to despise. We're even oppressed by being men—men with real bodies and blood of *our very own*. We're ashamed of it; we consider it a disgrace and we strive to become some kind of impossible "general-human-beings." We're stillborn; for some time now we haven't been conceived by living fathers; we like it more and more. We're developing a taste for it. Soon we'll conceive of a way to be born from ideas. But enough; I don't want to write any more "from Underground. . . ."

However, the "notes" of this paradoxalist don't end here. He couldn't resist and kept on writing. But it also seems to us that we might as well stop here.

GUSTAVE FLAUBERT
1821–1880

Living mostly as a hermit in a small country town, Gustave Flaubert threw himself into the making of art. He saw literature as a realm superior to the "stupidity" and "mediocrity" of lived experience. He labored over every sentence he wrote, sometimes taking as much as a week to complete a paragraph, determined to perfect the style of each phrase. He did travel, spending months at a time in Paris and taking journeys to North Africa, Syria, Turkey, and Italy. He was even in Paris to witness the revolution of 1848, as workers rose up against the monarchy and demanded the vote. But Flaubert's greatest excitement lay in the tormented process of writing: "I get drunk on ink as others do on wine," he wrote. "I love my work with a frenetic and perverted love, as the ascetic loves the hair shirt that scratches his belly."

LIFE

Gustave Flaubert was the son of a chief surgeon in the provincial French town of Rouen. When he was fourteen, he developed an unrequited passion for an older married woman. A few years later he went to Paris to study law, which he hated. Anxious and unhappy, he failed his exams and suffered a sudden nervous breakdown, which sent him back to his family home in the small town of Croisset near Rouen, where he would stay for most of his life with his mother. It was there that he began to write seriously.

In 1846, on a visit to Paris, he met the beautiful Louise Colet, a professional writer who lived and worked among bohemian artists. This was Flaubert's only serious love affair, though it would take place mostly by correspondence—for him reality never lived up to the imagination—and he treated her coldly. Otherwise, he frequented prostitutes and had some fleeting sexual relationships with men. His mother declared that his "passion for sentences" had "dried up" his heart.

Flaubert's works did not make it easily into the world. In 1849 he asked his two closest friends to read a draft of his first novel, *The Temptation of Saint Anthony*. "We think you should throw it in the fire and never speak of it again," they advised. He put it aside and labored for five years on his masterpiece, *Madame Bovary* (1857). He said he wanted to write "a book about nothing," one held together by the "internal force of its style" alone. The

protagonist he developed for this was a doctor's wife who longs to lead a romantic life like that of the heroines she encounters in books. She seeks out grand love affairs but is doomed to a narrow middle-class life among mediocrities in the provinces. Though sales of *Madame Bovary* were strong, critics denounced it as repugnant, consumed with the ugly banality of everyday life and offering nothing uplifting or consoling. One critic famously charged that Flaubert wielded his pen as a surgeon wields a scalpel. The novel was so shocking in its distanced and ironic treatment of adultery that Flaubert was tried for "offending public morals and religion." Although he was acquitted, *Madame Bovary* maintained its reputation as an immoral book for decades. Now it is viewed as one of the great works of nineteenth-century realism—perhaps the greatest. In 1869 Flaubert published *Sentimental Education*, a novel about the generation that lived through the revolutions of 1848. It flopped with the public, and the reviewers at the time sneered, although it has been enormously influential and highly regarded since.

Flaubert returned to *The Temptation of Saint Anthony* late in life, burying his manuscript in the ground temporarily when the Prussians invaded Normandy in 1870. In a period of despondency, when he was struggling financially and grieving over the loss of his mother and several close friends, he wrote *Three Tales* (1877), which included *A Simple Heart*. As Flaubert's body succumbed to syphilis, he told his niece, "Sometimes I think I'm liquefying like an old Camembert cheese." He died from a brain hemorrhage in 1880.

WORK

"It's no easy business to be simple," Flaubert said, pointing us to the great paradox at the center of *A Simple*

Heart. On the one hand, this is a straightforward tale of a relatively uneventful life: there is nothing complex or convoluted about the prose, about the chronology of events, or about the protagonist's experience. On the other hand, the sophisticated Flaubert invites us to see the world from the perspective of a naïve, exploited, illiterate servant woman whose last great love is a stuffed parrot, and allows us to understand her viewpoint as serious and sad rather than absurd or contemptible. The contemporary British novelist Julian Barnes, in a novel called *Flaubert's Parrot*, puts it this way: "Imagine the technical difficulty of writing a story in which a badly stuffed bird with a ridiculous name ends up standing for one third of the Trinity, and in which the intention is neither satirical, sentimental nor blasphemous. Imagine further telling the story from the point of view of an ignorant old woman without making it sound derogatory or coy." If we remember that Flaubert labored over every single sentence, suffering the "torments of style," we can read the simplicity he represents here as the result of a complex and careful artistic process.

Three elements of the story's highly refined technique are worth noticing. First of all, its economy: Flaubert distills his protagonist's experience into brief, clipped sentences. No word is wasted, and often it is tiny details that carry rich significance. For example, when the narrator tells us that Félicité's nephew keeps her "amused by telling her stories full of nautical jargon," he suggests that she cherishes precisely what she cannot understand—a language of her nephew's that is foreign to her. Second, Flaubert is famous for the impersonality or objectivity of his narrative style: he never intrudes his own feelings or opinions, maintaining a deliberate detachment. He wrote that "the author in his work should be like God in the universe—present everywhere and visible nowhere." Finally, it is worth paying attention to the story's structure: Félicité's experience follows the same pattern again and again—she falls in love and experiences a short period of happiness; this is followed by some kind of parting or death and a long spell of grief. But each time she falls in love with a new object, and the sequence of beloved objects is itself intriguing: first it is a lover, then the little girl in her care, then her nephew, then an elderly neighbor, then a live parrot, and finally the same parrot, stuffed. If on the one hand Flaubert seems to suggest a decline from human to animal to dead thing, on the other hand he suggests an ascent, as Félicité moves from erotic love to a wider, more charitable love and finally to a kind of mystical and heavenly adoration.

The parrot's role in the text goes beyond Félicité's love for it. As an animal from overseas brought to the town by an outsider-bureaucrat, it is above all a strange and foreign thing. Yet parrots learn to repeat human phrases, and so it becomes a strange echo of the social world it inhabits. First it learns Félicité's own expressions of respect and humility: "Your servant, sir!" and "Hail Mary!" Later it imitates Madame Aubain, and when the doorbell rings, it screams out "Félicité! The door, the door!" And yet it refuses to obey the rules of class and decorum itself, mocking the corrupt Boulais with screeches of laughter and leaving its droppings everywhere. At once symbolizing the stupidity and rote clichés of human life and acting as a focus for sincere love and spiritual veneration, the parrot remains one of Flaubert's most startling and fascinating figures.

Félicité too emerges as more complex than she may at first appear. On the one hand, Flaubert uses her to explore the psychology of servitude: what makes a person willingly accept the monotony and humiliation of spending a lifetime serving the needs of callous and thoughtless others? Intellectually, she is certainly simple: she has so little power of abstract thought that she cannot understand how a map works, and her understanding of religious doctrine is limited indeed. Compared to an animal herself, she bears numerous interesting relations to animals in the text. On the other hand, Flaubert allows her simplicity to feel powerful and moving and even sometimes surprising. For example, Félicité experiences an intense identification with Virginie at the moment of her first communion, and then disappointment with her own experience of taking communion the following day. She herself cannot interpret this difference, but Flaubert implies that sincere feeling may take place by way of concrete realities—people and objects—rather than abstractions. Indeed, Félicité endows not only animals but her cherished collection of things with meaning and value. And along the way, although she is cheated, exploited, discounted, and misguided, she reaches moments of heroism and even sublimity.

Flaubert wrote the story at a moment when he himself was thinking back over his life with sadness. Félicité's life is set in the very places that had been his own haunts in childhood: all of the place names are real, and many of the farms and beach scenes evoke specific spots the writer remembered with fondness. Flaubert's early readers assumed that the detached writer must feel scorn for his simple heroine, but he declared otherwise: *A Simple Heart* is "not at all ironic, as you suppose, but on the contrary very serious and very sad. I want to arouse people's pity, to make sensitive souls weep, since I am one myself."

A Simple Heart[1]

I

For half a century the women of Pont-l'Évêque[2] envied Mme Aubain her maidservant Félicité.

In return for a hundred francs a year she did all the cooking and the housework, the sewing, the washing, and the ironing. She could bridle a horse, fatten poultry, and churn butter, and she remained faithful to her mistress, who was by no means an easy person to get on with.

Mme Aubain had married a young fellow who was good-looking but badly-off, and who died at the beginning of 1809, leaving her with two small children and a pile of debts. She then sold all her property except for the farms of Toucques and Geffosses, which together brought in five thousand francs a year at the most, and left her house at Saint-Melaine for one behind the covered market which was cheaper to run and had belonged to her family.

This house had a slate roof and stood between an alley-way and a lane leading down to the river. Inside there were differences in level which were the cause of many a stumble. A narrow entrance-hall separated the kitchen from

1. Translated by Robert Baldick. 2. Town in the rural French province of Normandy.

the parlour, where Mme Aubain sat all day long in a wicker easy-chair by the window. Eight mahogany chairs were lined up against the white-painted wainscoting, and under the barometer stood an old piano loaded with a pyramid of boxes and cartons. On either side of the chimney-piece, which was carved out of yellow marble in the Louis Quinze style, there was a tapestry-covered armchair, and in the middle was a clock designed to look like a temple of Vesta.[3] The whole room smelt a little musty, as the floor was on a lower level than the garden.

On the first floor was 'Madame's' bedroom—very spacious, with a patterned wallpaper of pale flowers and a portrait of 'Monsieur' dressed in what had once been the height of fashion. It opened into a smaller room in which there were two cots, without mattresses. Then came the drawing-room, which was always shut up and full of furniture covered with dustsheets. Next there was a passage leading to the study, where books and papers filled the shelves of a book-case in three sections built round a big writing-table of dark wood. The two end panels were hidden under pen-and-ink drawings, landscapes in gouache, and etchings by Audran,[4] souvenirs of better days and bygone luxury. On the second floor a dormer window gave light to Félicité's room, which looked out over the fields.

Every day Félicité got up at dawn, so as not to miss Mass, and worked until evening without stopping. Then, once dinner was over, the plates and dishes put away, and the door bolted, she piled ashes on the log fire and went to sleep in front of the hearth, with her rosary in her hands. Nobody could be more stubborn when it came to haggling over prices, and as for cleanliness, the shine on her saucepans was the despair of all the other servants. Being of a thrifty nature, she ate slowly, picking up from the table the crumbs from her loaf of bread—a twelve-pound loaf which was baked specially for her and lasted her twenty days.

All the year round she wore a kerchief of printed calico fastened behind with a pin, a bonnet which covered her hair, grey stockings, a red skirt, and over her jacket a bibbed apron such as hospital nurses wear.

Her face was thin and her voice was sharp. At twenty-five she was often taken for forty; once she reached fifty, she stopped looking any age in particular. Always silent and upright and deliberate in her movements, she looked like a wooden doll driven by clock-work.

2

Like everyone else, she had had her love-story.

Her father, a mason, had been killed when he fell off some scaffolding. Then her mother died, and when her sisters went their separate ways, a farmer took her in, sending her, small as she was, to look after the cows out in the fields. She went about in rags, shivering with cold, used to lie flat on the ground to

3. The ancient temple of Vesta, Roman goddess of the hearth, is a round building with a conical roof supported by columns. "Louis Quinze style": ornate furniture style dating from the 18th century.
4. Claude Audran III (1658–1734), French painter, sculptor, engraver, and decorator.

drink water out of the ponds, would be beaten for no reason at all, and was finally turned out of the house for stealing thirty sous,[5] a theft of which she was innocent. She found work at another farm, looking after the poultry, and as she was liked by her employers the other servants were jealous of her.

One August evening—she was eighteen at the time—they took her off to the fête[6] at Colleville. From the start she was dazed and bewildered by the noise of the fiddles, the lamps in the trees, the medley of gaily coloured dresses, the gold crosses and lace, and the throng of people jigging up and down. She was standing shyly on one side when a smart young fellow, who had been leaning on the shaft of a cart, smoking his pipe, came up and asked her to dance. He treated her to cider, coffee, girdle-cake, and a silk neckerchief, and imagining that she knew what he was after, offered to see her home. At the edge of a field of oats, he pushed her roughly to the ground. Thoroughly frightened, she started screaming for help. He took to his heels.

Another night, on the road to Beaumont, she tried to get past a big, slow-moving waggon loaded with hay, and as she was squeezing by she recognized Théodore.

He greeted her quite calmly, saying that she must forgive him for the way he had behaved to her, as 'it was the drink that did it.'

She did not know what to say in reply and felt like running off.

Straight away he began talking about the crops and the notabilities of the commune, saying that his father had left Colleville for the farm at Les Écots, so that they were now neighbours.

'Ah!' she said.

He added that his family wanted to see him settled but that he was in no hurry and was waiting to find a wife to suit his fancy. She lowered her head. Then he asked her if she was thinking of getting married. She answered with a smile that it was mean of him to make fun of her.

'But I'm not making fun of you!' he said. 'I swear I'm not!'

He put his left arm round her waist, and she walked on supported by his embrace. Soon they slowed down. There was a gentle breeze blowing, the stars were shining, the huge load of hay was swaying about in front of them, and the four horses were raising clouds of dust as they shambled along. Then, without being told, they turned off to the right. He kissed her once more and she disappeared into the darkness.

The following week Théodore got her to grant him several rendezvous.

They would meet at the bottom of a farm-yard, behind a wall, under a solitary tree. She was not ignorant of life as young ladies are, for the animals had taught her a great deal; but her reason and an instinctive sense of honour prevented her from giving way. The resistance she put up inflamed Théodore's passion to such an extent that in order to satisfy it (or perhaps out of sheer naivety) he proposed to her. At first she refused to believe him, but he swore that he was serious.

Soon afterwards he had a disturbing piece of news to tell her: the year before, his parents had paid a man to do his military service for him, but now

---

5. About the price of a good dinner.   6. "Festival" (French).

he might be called up again any day, and the idea of going into the army frightened him. In Félicité's eyes this cowardice of his appeared to be a proof of his affection, and she loved him all the more for it. Every night she would steal out to meet him, and every night Théodore would plague her with his worries and entreaties.

In the end he said that he was going to the Prefecture himself to make inquiries, and that he would come and tell her how matters stood the following Sunday, between eleven and midnight.

At the appointed hour she hurried to meet her sweetheart, but found one of his friends waiting for her instead.

He told her that she would not see Théodore again. To make sure of avoiding conscription, he had married a very rich old woman, Mme Lehoussais of Toucques.

Her reaction was an outburst of frenzied grief. She threw herself on the ground, screaming and calling on God, and lay moaning all alone in the open until sunrise. Then she went back to the farm and announced her intention of leaving. At the end of the month, when she had received her wages, she wrapped her small belongings up in a kerchief and made her way to Pont-l'Évêque.

In front of the inn there, she sought information from a woman in a widow's bonnet, who, as it happened, was looking for a cook. The girl did not know much about cooking, but she seemed so willing and expected so little that finally Mme Aubain ended up by saying: 'Very well, I will take you on.'

A quarter of an hour later Félicité was installed in her house.

At first she lived there in a kind of fearful awe caused by 'the style of the house' and by the memory of 'Monsieur' brooding over everything. Paul and Virginie, the boy aged seven and the girl barely four, seemed to her to be made of some precious substance. She used to carry them about pick-a-back,[7] and when Mme Aubain told her not to keep on kissing them she was cut to the quick. All the same, she was happy now, for her pleasant surroundings had dispelled her grief.

On Thursdays, a few regular visitors came in to play Boston,[8] and Félicité got the cards and the footwarmers ready beforehand. They always arrived punctually at eight, and left before the clock struck eleven.

Every Monday morning the second-hand dealer who lived down the alley put all his junk out on the pavement. Then the hum of voices began to fill the town, mingled with the neighing of horses, the bleating of lambs, the grunting of pigs, and the rattle of carts in the streets.

About midday, when the market was in full swing, a tall old peasant with a hooked nose and his cap on the back of his head would appear at the door. This was Robelin, the farmer from Geffosses. A little later, and Liébard, the farmer from Toucques, would arrive—a short, fat, red-faced fellow in a grey jacket and leather gaiters fitted with spurs.

Both men had hens or cheeses they wanted to sell to 'Madame.' But Félicité was up to all their tricks and invariably outwitted them, so that they went away full of respect for her.

7. Piggy-back.   8. A card game.

From time to time Mme Aubain had a visit from an uncle of hers, the Marquis de Grémanville, who had been ruined by loose living and was now living at Falaise on his last remaining scrap of property. He always turned up at lunchtime, accompanied by a hideous poodle which dirtied all the furniture with its paws. However hard he tried to behave like a gentleman, even going so far as to raise his hat every time he mentioned 'my late father,' the force of habit was usually too much for him, for he would start pouring himself one glass after another and telling bawdy stories. Félicité used to push him gently out of the house, saying politely: 'You've had quite enough, Monsieur de Grémanville. See you another time!' and shutting the door on him.

She used to open it with pleasure to M. Bourais, who was a retired solicitor. His white tie and his bald head, his frilled shirt-front and his ample brown frock-coat, the way he had of rounding his arm to take a pinch of snuff, and indeed everything about him made an overwhelming impression on her such as we feel when we meet some outstanding personality.

As he looked after 'Madame's' property, he used to shut himself up with her for hours in 'Monsieur's' study. He lived in dread of compromising his reputation, had a tremendous respect for the Bench, and laid claim to some knowledge of Latin.

To give the children a little painless instruction, he made them a present of a geography book with illustrations. These represented scenes in different parts of the world, such as cannibals wearing feather head-dresses, a monkey carrying off a young lady, Bedouins in the desert, a whale being harpooned, and so on.

Paul explained these pictures to Félicité, and that indeed was all the education she ever had. As for the children, they were taught by Guyot, a poor devil employed at the Town Hall, who was famous for his beautiful handwriting, and who had a habit of sharpening his penknife on his boots.

When the weather was fine the whole household used to set off early for a day at the Geffosses farm.

The farm-yard there was on a slope, with the house in the middle; and the sea, in the distance, looked like a streak of grey. Félicité would take some slices of cold meat out of her basket, and they would have their lunch in a room adjoining the dairy. It was all that remained of a country house which had fallen into ruin, and the wallpaper hung in shreds, fluttering in the draught. Mme Aubain used to sit with bowed head, absorbed in her memories, so that the children were afraid to talk. 'Why don't you run along and play?' she would say, and away they went.

Paul climbed up into the barn, caught birds, played ducks and drakes on the pond, or banged with a stick on the great casks, which sounded just like drums.

Virginie fed the rabbits, or scampered off to pick cornflowers, showing her little embroidered knickers as she ran.

One autumn evening they came home through the fields. The moon, which was in its first quarter, lit up part of the sky, and there was some mist floating like a scarf over the winding Toucques. The cattle, lying out in the middle of the pasture, looked peacefully at the four people walking by. In the third field a few got up and made a half circle in front of them.

'Don't be frightened!' said Félicité, and crooning softly, she stroked the back of the nearest animal. It turned about and the others did the same. But while they were crossing the next field they suddenly heard a dreadful bellowing. It came from a bull which had been hidden by the mist, and which now came towards the two women.

Mme Aubain started to run.

'No! No!' said Félicité. 'Not so fast!'

All the same they quickened their pace, hearing behind them a sound of heavy breathing which came nearer and nearer. The bull's hooves thudded like hammers on the turf, and they realized that it had broken into a gallop. Turning round, Félicité tore up some clods of earth and flung them at its eyes. It lowered its muzzle and thrust its horns forward, trembling with rage and bellowing horribly.

By now Mme Aubain had got to the end of the field with her two children and was frantically looking for a way over the high bank. Félicité was still backing away from the bull, hurling clods of turf which blinded it, and shouting: 'Hurry! Hurry!'

Mme Aubain got down into the ditch, pushed first Virginie and then Paul up the other side, fell once or twice trying to climb the bank, and finally managed it with a valiant effort.

The bull had driven Félicité back against a gate, and its slaver was spurting into her face. In another second it would have gored her, but she just had time to slip between two of the bars, and the great beast halted in amazement.

This adventure was talked about at Pont-l'Évêque for a good many years, but Félicité never prided herself in the least on what she had done, as it never occurred to her that she had done anything heroic.

Virginie claimed all her attention, for the fright had affected the little girl's nerves, and M. Poupart, the doctor, recommended sea-bathing at Trouville.

In those days the resort had few visitors. Mme Aubain made inquiries, consulted Bourais, and got everything ready as though for a long journey.

Her luggage went off in Liébard's cart the day before she left. The next morning he brought along two horses, one of which had a woman's saddle with a velvet back, while the other carried a cloak rolled up to make a kind of seat on its crupper. Mme Aubain sat on this, with Liébard in front. Félicité looked after Virginie on the other horse, and Paul mounted M. Lechaptois's donkey, which he had lent them on condition they took great care of it.

The road was so bad that it took two hours to travel the five miles to Toucques. The horses sank into the mud up to their pasterns and had to jerk their hind-quarters to get out; often they stumbled in the ruts, or else they had to jump. In some places, Liébard's mare came to a sudden stop, and while he waited patiently for her to move off again, he talked about the people whose properties bordered the road, adding moral reflexions to each story. For instance, in the middle of Toucques, as they were passing underneath some windows set in a mass of nasturtiums, he shrugged his shoulders and said: 'There's a Madame Lehoussais lives here. Now instead of taking a young man, she . . .'

Félicité did not hear the rest, for the horses had broken into a trot and the donkey was galloping along. All three turned down a bridle-path, a gate swung open, a couple of boys appeared, and everyone dismounted in front of a manure-heap right outside the farm-house door.

Old Mother Liébard welcomed her mistress with every appearance of pleasure. She served up a sirloin of beef for lunch, with tripe and black pudding, a fricassee of chicken, sparkling cider, a fruit tart and brandy-plums, garnishing the whole meal with compliments to Madame, who seemed to be enjoying better health, to Mademoiselle, who had turned into a 'proper little beauty,' and to Monsieur Paul, who had 'filled out a lot.' Nor did she forget their deceased grandparents, whom the Liébards had known personally, having been in the family's service for several generations.

Like its occupants, the farm had an air of antiquity. The ceiling-beams were worm-eaten, the walls black with smoke, and the window-panes grey with dust. There was an oak dresser laden with all sorts of odds and ends—jugs, plates, pewter bowls, wolf-traps, sheep-shears, and an enormous syringe which amused the children. In the three yards outside there was not a single tree without either mushrooms at its base or mistletoe in its branches. Several had been blown down and had taken root again at the middle; all of them were bent under the weight of their apples. The thatched roofs, which looked like brown velvet and varied in thickness, weathered the fiercest winds, but the cart-shed was tumbling down. Mme Aubain said that she would have it seen to, and ordered the animals to be reharnessed.

It took them another half-hour to reach Trouville. The little caravan dismounted to make their way along the Écores, a cliff jutting right out over the boats moored below; and three minutes later they got to the end of the quay and entered the courtyard of the Golden Lamb, the inn kept by Mère David.

After the first few days Virginie felt stronger, as a result of the change of air and the sea-bathing. Not having a costume, she went into the water in her chemise and her maid dressed her afterwards in a customs officer's hut which was used by the bathers.

In the afternoons they took the donkey and went off beyond the Roches-Noires,[9] in the direction of Hennequeville. To begin with, the path went uphill between gentle slopes like the lawns in a park, and then came out on a plateau where pastureland and ploughed fields alternated. On either side there were holly-bushes standing out from the tangle of brambles, and here and there a big dead tree spread its zigzag branches against the blue sky.

They almost always rested in the same field, with Deauville on their left, Le Havre on their right, and the open sea in front. The water glittered in the sunshine, smooth as a mirror, and so still that the murmur it made was scarcely audible; unseen sparrows could be heard twittering, and the sky covered the whole scene with its huge canopy. Mme Aubain sat doing her needlework, Virginie plaited rushes beside her, Félicité gathered lavender, and Paul, feeling profoundly bored, longed to get up and go.

Sometimes they crossed the Toucques in a boat and hunted for shells. When the tide went out, sea-urchins, ormers, and jelly-fish were left behind; and the children scampered around, snatching at the foam-flakes carried on the wind.

9. "Black rocks," visible on the Normandy coast at low tide.

The sleepy waves, breaking on the sand, spread themselves out along the shore. The beach stretched as far as the eye could see, bounded on the land side by the dunes which separated it from the Marais, a broad meadow in the shape of an arena. When they came back that way, Trouville, on the distant hillside, grew bigger at every step, and with its medley of oddly assorted houses seemed to blossom out in gay disorder.

On exceptionally hot days they stayed in their room. The sun shone in dazzling bars of light between the slats of the blind. There was not a sound to be heard in the village, and not a soul to be seen down in the street. Everything seemed more peaceful in the prevailing silence. In the distance caulkers were hammering away at the boats, and the smell of tar was wafted along by a sluggish breeze.

The principal amusement consisted in watching the fishing-boats come in. As soon as they had passed the buoys, they started tacking. With their canvas partly lowered and their foresails blown out like balloons they glided through the splashing waves as far as the middle of the harbour, where they suddenly dropped anchor. Then each boat came alongside the quay, and the crew threw ashore their catch of quivering fish. A line of carts stood waiting, and women in cotton bonnets rushed forward to take the baskets and kiss their men.

One day one of these women spoke to Félicité, who came back to the inn soon after in a state of great excitement. She explained that she had found one of her sisters—and Nastasie Barette, now Leroux, made her appearance, with a baby at her breast, another child holding her right hand, and on her left a little sailor-boy, his arms akimbo and his cap over one ear.

Mme Aubain sent her off after a quarter of an hour. From then on they were forever hanging round the kitchen or loitering about when the family went for a walk, though the husband kept out of sight.

Félicité became quite attached to them. She bought them a blanket, several shirts, and a stove; and it was clear that they were bent on getting all they could out of her.

This weakness of hers annoyed Mme Aubain, who in any event disliked the familiar way in which the nephew spoke to Paul. And so, as Virginie had started coughing and the good weather was over, she decided to go back to Pont-l'Évêque.

M. Bourais advised her on the choice of a school; Caen[1] was considered the best, so it was there that Paul was sent. He said good-bye bravely, feeling really rather pleased to be going to a place where he would have friends of his own.

Mme Aubain resigned herself to the loss of her son, knowing that it was unavoidable. Virginie soon got used to it. Félicité missed the din he used to make, but she was given something new to do which served as a distraction: from Christmas onwards she had to take the little girl to catechism every day.

3

After genuflecting at the door, she walked up the centre aisle under the nave, opened the door of Mme Aubain's pew, sat down, and started looking about her.

1. A cathedral school.

The choir stalls were all occupied, with the boys on the right and the girls on the left, while the curé[2] stood by the lectern. In one of the stained-glass windows in the apse the Holy Ghost looked down on the Virgin; another window showed her kneeling before the Infant Jesus; and behind the tabernacle there was a wood-carving of St. Michael slaying the dragon.[3]

The priest began with a brief outline of sacred history. Listening to him, Félicité saw in imagination the Garden of Eden, the Flood, the Tower of Babel, cities burning, peoples dying, and idols being overthrown; and this dazzling vision left her with a great respect for the Almighty and profound fear of His wrath.

Then she wept as she listened to the story of the Passion.[4] Why had they crucified Him, when He loved children, fed the multitudes, healed the blind, and had chosen out of humility to be born among the poor, on the litter of a stable? The sowing of the seed, the reaping of the harvest, the pressing of the grapes— all those familiar things of which the Gospels speak had their place in her life. God had sanctified them in passing, so that she loved the lambs more tenderly for love of the Lamb of God, and the doves for the sake of the Holy Ghost.

She found it difficult, however, to imagine what the Holy Ghost looked like, for it was not just a bird but a fire as well, and sometimes a breath.[5] She wondered whether that was its light she had seen flitting about the edge of the marshes at night, whether that was its breath she had felt driving the clouds across the sky, whether that was its voice she had heard in the sweet music of the bells. And she sat in silent adoration, delighting in the coolness of the walls and the quiet of the church.

Of dogma she neither understood nor even tried to understand anything. The curé discoursed, the children repeated their lesson, and she finally dropped off to sleep, waking up suddenly at the sound of their sabots[6] clattering across the flagstones as they left the church.

It was in this manner, simply by hearing it expounded, that she learnt her catechism, for her religious education had been neglected in her youth. From then on she copied all Virginie's observances, fasting when she did and going to confession with her. On the feast of Corpus Christi the two of them made an altar of repose together.[7]

The preparations for Virginie's first communion caused her great anxiety. She worried over her shoes, her rosary, her missal, and her gloves. And how she trembled as she helped Mme Aubain to dress the child!

All through the Mass her heart was in her mouth. One side of the choir was hidden from her by M. Bourais, but directly opposite her she could see the flock of maidens, looking like a field of snow with their white crowns perched on top of their veils; and she recognized her little darling from a distance by her

2. "Priest" (French).
3. Satan, depicted as a dragon in the Book of Revelation, is cast out of heaven by St. Michael.
4. The crucifixion and death of Christ.
5. The Holy Spirit appears as both fire and breath (or wind) in the Bible.

6. Heavy wooden shoes.
7. The resting-place for the Eucharist during the Tridduum, the holiest three days of the Christian year. "Corpus Christi": "Body of Christ" (Latin), a liturgical celebration of Christ's gift of himself, in the form of bread and wine, during the mass.

dainty neck and her rapt attitude. The bell tinkled.[8] Every head bowed low, and there was a silence. Then, to the thunderous accompaniment of the organ, choir and congregation joined in singing the *Agnus Dei*.[9] Next the boys' procession began, and after that the girls got up from their seats. Slowly, their hands joined in prayer, they went towards the brightly lit altar, knelt on the first step, received the Host one by one, and went back to their places in the same order. When it was Virginie's turn, Félicité leant forward to see her, and in one of those imaginative flights born of real affection, it seemed to her that she herself was in the child's place. Virginie's face became her own, Virginie's dress clothed her, Virginie's heart was beating in her breast; and as she closed her eyes and opened her mouth, she almost fainted away.

Early next morning she went to the sacristy and asked M. le Curé to give her communion. She received the sacrament with all due reverence, but did not feel the same rapture as she had the day before.

Mme Aubain wanted her daughter to possess every accomplishment, and since Guyot could not teach her English or music, she decided to send her as a boarder to the Ursuline[1] Convent at Honfleur.

Virginie raised no objection, but Félicité went about sighing at Madame's lack of feeling. Then she thought that perhaps her mistress was right: such matters, after all, lay outside her province.

Finally the day arrived when an old waggonette stopped at their door, and a nun got down from it who had come to fetch Mademoiselle. Félicité hoisted the luggage up on top, gave the driver some parting instructions, and put six pots of jam, a dozen pears, and a bunch of violets in the boot.

At the last moment Virginie burst into a fit of sobbing. She threw her arms round her mother, who kissed her on the forehead, saying: 'Come now, be brave, be brave.' The step was pulled up and the carriage drove away.

Then Mme Aubain broke down, and that evening all her friends, M. and Mme Lormeau, Mme Lechaptois, the Rochefeuille sisters, M. de Houppeville, and Bourais, came in to console her.

To begin with she missed her daughter badly. But she had a letter from her three times a week, wrote back on the other days, walked round her garden, did a little reading, and thus contrived to fill the empty hours.

As for Félicité, she went into Virginie's room every morning from sheer force of habit and looked round it. It upset her not having to brush the child's hair any more, tie her bootlaces, or tuck her up in bed; and she missed seeing her sweet face all the time and holding her hand when they went out together. For want of something to do, she tried making lace, but her fingers were too clumsy and broke the threads. She could not settle to anything, lost her sleep, and, to use her own words, was 'eaten up inside.'

To 'occupy her mind,' she asked if her nephew Victor might come and see her, and permission was granted.

He used to arrive after Mass on Sunday, his cheeks flushed, his chest bare, and smelling of the countryside through which he had come. She laid a place

---

8. The bell marks the moment of transubstantiation during the mass.
9. "Lamb of God" (Latin); a plea for God's mercy.

1. Catholic religious order concerned with the education of girls.

for him straight away, opposite hers, and they had lunch together. Eating as little as possible herself, in order to save the expense, she stuffed him so full of food that he fell asleep after the meal. When the first bell for vespers rang, she woke him up, brushed his trousers, tied his tie, and set off for church, leaning on his arm with all a mother's pride.

His parents always told him to get something out of her—a packet of brown sugar perhaps, some soap, or a little brandy, sometimes even money. He brought her his clothes to be mended, and she did the work gladly, thankful for anything that would force him to come again.

In August his father took him on a coasting trip. The children's holidays were just beginning, and it cheered her up to have them home again. But Paul was turning capricious and Virginie was getting too old to be addressed familiarly— a state of affairs which put a barrier of constraint between them.

Victor went to Morlaix, Dunkirk, and Brighton in turn, and brought her a present after each trip. The first time it was a box covered with shells, the second a coffee cup, the third a big gingerbread man. He was growing quite handsome, with his trim figure, his little moustache, his frank open eyes, and the little leather cap that he wore on the back of his head like a pilot. He kept her amused by telling her stories full of nautical jargon.

One Monday—it was the fourteenth of July 1819,[2] a date she never forgot— Victor told her that he had signed on for an ocean voyage, and that on the Wednesday night he would be taking the Honfleur packet to join his schooner, which was due to sail shortly from Le Havre. He might be away, he said, for two years.

The prospect of such a long absence made Félicité extremely unhappy, and she felt she must bid him godspeed once more. So on the Wednesday evening, when Madame's dinner was over, she put on her clogs and swiftly covered the ten miles between Pont-l'Évêque and Honfleur.

When she arrived at the Calvary[3] she turned right instead of left, got lost in the shipyards, and had to retrace her steps. Some people she spoke to advised her to hurry. She went right round the harbour, which was full of boats, constantly tripping over moorings. Then the ground fell away, rays of light crisscrossed in front of her, and for a moment she thought she was going mad, for she could see horses up in the sky.

On the quayside more horses were neighing, frightened by the sea. A derrick was hoisting them into the air and dropping them into one of the boats, which was already crowded with passengers elbowing their way between barrels of cider, baskets of cheese, and sacks of grain. Hens were cackling and the captain swearing, while a cabin-boy stood leaning on the cats-head, completely indifferent to it all. Félicité, who had not recognized him, shouted: 'Victor!' and he raised his head. She rushed forward, but at that very moment the gangway was pulled ashore.

2. The national holiday called Bastille Day, which commemorates the start of the French Revolution.
3. Public crucifix.

The packet moved out of the harbour with women singing as they hauled it along, its ribs creaking and heavy waves lashing its bows. The sail swung round, hiding everyone on board from view, and against the silvery, moonlit sea the boat appeared as a dark shape that grew ever fainter, until at last it vanished in the distance.

As Félicité was passing the Calvary, she felt a longing to commend to God's mercy all that she held most dear; and she stood there praying for a long time, her face bathed in tears, her eyes fixed upon the clouds. The town was asleep, except for the customs officers walking up and down. Water was pouring ceaselessly through the holes in the sluice-gate, making as much noise as a torrent. The clocks struck two.

The convent parlour would not be open before daybreak, and Madame would be annoyed if she were late; so, although she would have liked to give a kiss to the other child, she set off for home. The maids at the inn were just waking up as she got to Pont-l'Évêque.

So the poor lad was going to be tossed by the waves for months on end! His previous voyages had caused her no alarm. People came back from England and Brittany; but America, the Colonies, the Islands, were all so far away, somewhere at the other end of the world.

From then on Félicité thought of nothing but her nephew. On sunny days she hoped he was not too thirsty, and when there was a storm she was afraid he would be struck by lightning. Listening to the wind howling in the chimney or blowing slates off the roof, she saw him being buffeted by the very same storm, perched on the top of a broken mast, with his whole body bent backwards under a sheet of foam; or again—and these were reminiscences of the illustrated geography-book—he was being eaten by savages, captured by monkeys in a forest, or dying on a desert shore. But she never spoke of her worries.

Mme Aubain had worries of her own about her daughter. The good nuns said that she was an affectionate child, but very delicate. The slightest emotion upset her, and she had to give up playing the piano.

Her mother insisted on regular letters from the convent. One morning when the postman had not called, she lost patience and walked up and down the room, between her chair and the window. It was really extraordinary! Four days without any news!

Thinking her own example would comfort her, Félicité said:

'I've been six months, Madame, without news.'

'News of whom?'

The servant answered gently:

'Why—of my nephew.'

'Oh, your nephew!' And Mme Aubain started pacing up and down again, with a shrug of her shoulders that seemed to say: 'I wasn't thinking of him—and indeed, why should I? Who cares about a young, good-for-nothing cabinboy? Whereas my daughter—why, just think!'

Although she had been brought up the hard way, Félicité was indignant with Madame, but she soon forgot. It struck her as perfectly natural to lose one's head where the little girl was concerned. For her, the two children were of equal importance; they were linked together in her heart by a single bond, and their destinies should be the same.

The chemist[4] told her that Victor's ship had arrived at Havana: he had seen this piece of information in a newspaper.

Because of its association with cigars, she imagined Havana as a place where nobody did anything but smoke, and pictured Victor walking about among crowds of Negroes in a cloud of tobacco-smoke. Was it possible, she wondered, 'in case of need' to come back by land? And how far was it from Pont-l'Évêque? To find out she asked M. Bourais.

He reached for his atlas, and launched forth into an explanation of latitudes and longitudes, smiling like the pedant he was at Félicité's bewilderment. Finally he pointed with his pencil at a minute black dot inside a ragged oval patch, saying:

'There it is.'

She bent over the map, but the network of coloured lines meant nothing to her and only tired her eyes. So when Bourais asked her to tell him what was puzzling her, she begged him to show her the house where Victor was living. He threw up his hands, sneezed, and roared with laughter, delighted to come across such simplicity. And Félicité—whose intelligence was so limited that she probably expected to see an actual portrait of her nephew—could not make out why he was laughing.

It was a fortnight later that Liébard came into the kitchen at market-time, as he usually did, and handed her a letter from her brother-in-law. As neither of them could read, she turned to her mistress for help.

Mme Aubain, who was counting the stitches in her knitting, put it down and unsealed the letter. She gave a start, and, looking hard at Félicité, said quietly:

'They have some bad news for you . . . Your nephew . . .'

He was dead. That was all the letter had to say.

Félicité dropped on to a chair, leaning her head against the wall and closing her eyelids, which suddenly turned pink. Then, with her head bowed, her hands dangling, and her eyes set, she kept repeating:

'Poor little lad! Poor little lad!'

Liébard looked at her and sighed. Mme Aubain was trembling slightly. She suggested that she should go and see her sister at Trouville, but Félicité shook her head to indicate that there was no need for that.

There was a silence. Old Liébard thought it advisable to go.

Then Félicité said:

'It doesn't matter a bit, not to them it doesn't.'

Her head fell forward again, and from time to time she unconsciously picked up the knitting needles lying on the worktable.

Some women went past carrying a tray full of dripping linen.

Catching sight of them through the window, she remembered her own washing; she had passed the lye through it the day before and today it needed rinsing. So she left the room.

Her board and tub were on the bank of the Toucques. She threw a pile of chemises down by the water's edge, rolled up her sleeves, and picked up her battledore. The lusty blows she gave with it could be heard in all the neighbouring gardens.

4. Pharmacist.

The fields were empty, the river rippling in the wind; at the bottom long weeds were waving to and fro, like the hair of corpses floating in the water. She held back her grief, and was very brave until the evening; but in her room she gave way to it completely, lying on her mattress with her face buried in the pillow and her fists pressed against her temples.

Long afterwards she learnt the circumstances of Victor's death from the captain of his ship. He had gone down with yellow fever, and they had bled him too much at the hospital. Four doctors had held him at once. He had died straight away, and the chief doctor had said:

'Good! There goes another!'

His parents had always treated him cruelly. She preferred not to see them again, and they made no advances, either because they had forgotten about her or out of the callousness of the poor.

Meanwhile Virginie was growing weaker. Difficulty in breathing, fits of coughing, protracted bouts of fever, and mottled patches on the cheekbones all indicated some deep-seated complaint. M. Poupart had advised a stay in Provence. Mme Aubain decided to follow this suggestion, and, if it had not been for the weather at Pont-l'Évêque, she would have brought her daughter home at once.

She arranged with a jobmaster[5] to drive her out to the convent every Tuesday. There was a terrace in the garden, overlooking the Seine, and there Virginie, leaning on her mother's arm, walked up and down over the fallen vine-leaves. Sometimes, while she was looking at the sails in the distance, or at the long stretch of horizon from the Château de Tancarville to the lighthouses of Le Havre, the sun would break through the clouds and make her blink. Afterwards they would rest in the arbour. Her mother had secured a little cask of excellent Malaga,[6] and, laughing at the idea of getting tipsy, Virginie used to drink a thimbleful, but no more.

Her strength revived. Autumn slipped by, and Félicité assured Mme Aubain that there was nothing to fear. But one evening, coming back from some errand in the neighbourhood, she found M. Poupart's gig standing at the door. He was in the hall, and Mme Aubain was tying on her bonnet.

'Give me my foot warmer, purse, gloves. Quickly now!'

Virginie had pneumonia and was perhaps past recovery.

'Not yet!' said the doctor; and the two of them got into the carriage with snow-flakes swirling around them. Night was falling and it was very cold.

Félicité rushed into the church to light a candle, and then ran after the gig. She caught up with it an hour later, jumped lightly up behind, and hung on to the fringe. But then a thought struck her: the courtyard had not been locked up, and burglars might get in. So she jumped down again.

At dawn the next day she went to the doctor's. He had come home and gone out again on his rounds. Then she waited at the inn, thinking that somebody who was a stranger to the district might call there with a letter. Finally, when it was twilight, she got into the coach for Lisieux.

---

5. One who loans horses and carriages.   6. A Spanish dessert wine.

The convent was at the bottom of a steep lane. When she was half-way down the hill, she heard a strange sound which she recognized as a death-bell tolling.

'It's for somebody else,' she thought, as she banged the door-knocker hard.

After a few minutes she heard the sound of shuffling feet, the door opened a little way, and a nun appeared.

The good sister said with an air of compunction that 'she had just passed away.' At that moment the bell of Saint-Léonard was tolled more vigorously than ever.

Félicité went up to the second floor. From the doorway of the room she could see Virginie lying on her back, her hands clasped together, her mouth open, her head tilted back under a black crucifix that leant over her, her face whiter than the curtains that hung motionless on either side. Mme Aubain was clinging to the foot of the bed and sobbing desperately. The Mother Superior stood on the right. Three candlesticks on the chest of drawers added touches of red to the scene, and fog was whitening the windows. Some nuns led Mme Aubain away.

For two nights Félicité never left the dead girl. She said the same prayers over and over again, sprinkled holy water on the sheets, then sat down again to watch. At the end of her first vigil, she noticed that the child's face had gone yellow, the lips were turning blue, the nose looked sharper, and the eyes were sunken. She kissed them several times, and would not have been particularly surprised if Virginie had opened them again: to minds like hers the supernatural is a simple matter. She laid her out, wrapped her in a shroud, put her in her coffin, placed a wreath on her, and spread out her hair. It was fair and amazingly long for her age. Félicité cut off a big lock, half of which she slipped into her bosom, resolving never to part with it.

The body was brought back to Pont-l'Évêque at the request of Mme Aubain, who followed the hearse in a closed carriage.

After the Requiem Mass, it took another three-quarters of an hour to reach the cemetery. Paul walked in front, sobbing. Then came M. Bourais, and after him the principal inhabitants of the town, the women all wearing long black veils, and Félicité. She was thinking about her nephew; and since she had been unable to pay him these last honours, she felt an added grief, just as if they were burying him with Virginie.

Mme Aubain's despair passed all bounds. First of all she rebelled against God, considering it unfair of Him to have taken her daughter from her—for she had never done any harm, and her conscience was quite clear. But was it? She ought to have taken Virginie to the south; other doctors would have saved her life. She blamed herself, wished she could have joined her daughter, and cried out in anguish in her dreams. One dream in particular obsessed her. Her husband, dressed like a sailor, came back from a long voyage, and told her amid tears that he had been ordered to take Virginie away—whereupon they put their heads together to discover somewhere to hide her.

One day she came in from the garden utterly distraught. A few minutes earlier—and she pointed to the spot—father and daughter had appeared to her, doing nothing, but simply looking at her.

For several months she stayed in her room in a kind of stupor. Félicité scolded her gently telling her that she must take care of herself for her son's sake, and also in remembrance of 'her.'

'Her?' repeated Mme Aubain, as if she were waking from a sleep. 'Oh, yes, of course! You don't forget her, do you!' This was an allusion to the cemetery, where she herself was strictly forbidden to go.

Félicité went there every day. She would set out on the stroke of four, going past the houses, up the hill, and through the gate, until she came to Virginie's grave. There was a little column of pink marble with a tablet at its base, and a tiny garden enclosed by chains. The beds were hidden under a carpet of flowers. She watered their leaves and changed the sand, going down on her knees to fork the ground thoroughly. The result was that when Mme Aubain was able to come here, she experienced a feeling of relief, a kind of consolation.

Then the years slipped by, each one like the last, with nothing to vary the rhythm of the great festivals: Easter, the Assumption, All Saints' Day.[7] Domestic events marked dates that later served as points of reference. Thus in 1825 a couple of glaziers whitewashed the hall; in 1827 a piece of the roof fell into the courtyard and nearly killed a man; and in the summer of 1828 it was Madame's turn to provide the bread for consecration. About this time Bourais went away in a mysterious fashion; and one by one the old acquaintances disappeared: Guyot, Liébard, Mme Lechaptois, Robelin, and Uncle Grémanville, who had been paralysed for a long time.

One night the driver of the mail-coach brought Pont-l'Évêque news of the July Revolution.[8] A few days later a new sub-prefect[9] was appointed. This was the Baron de Larsonnière, who had been a consul in America, and who brought with him, besides his wife, his sister-in-law and three young ladies who were almost grown-up. They were to be seen on their lawn, dressed in loose-fitting smocks; and they had a Negro servant and a parrot. They paid a call on Mme Aubain, who made a point of returning it. As soon as Félicité saw them coming, she would run and tell her mistress. But only one thing could really awaken her interest, and that was her son's letters.

He seemed to be incapable of following any career and spent all his time in taverns. She paid his debts, but he contracted new ones, and the sighs Mme Aubain heaved as she knitted by the window reached Félicité at her spinning-wheel in the kitchen.

The two women used to walk up and down together beside the espalier, forever talking of Virginie and debating whether such and such a thing would have appealed to her, or what she would have said on such and such an occasion.

All her little belongings were in a cupboard in the children's bedroom. Mme Aubain went through them as seldom as possible. One summer day she resigned herself to doing so, and the moths were sent fluttering out of the cupboard.

Virginie's frocks hung in a row underneath a shelf containing three dolls, a few hoops, a set of toy furniture, and the wash-basin she had used. Besides the frocks, they took out her petticoats, her stockings and her handkerchiefs, and spread them out on the two beds before folding them up again. The sunlight

7. Catholic holy days that mark the arrival of souls into heaven.
8. The July Revolution of 1830 toppled the French king Charles X and established a new constitutional monarchy.
9. Government official responsible for a region.

streamed in on these pathetic objects, bringing out the stains and showing up the creases made by the child's movements. The air was warm, the sky was blue, a blackbird was singing, and everything seemed to be utterly at peace.

They found a little chestnut-coloured hat, made of plush with a long nap; but the moths had ruined it. Félicité asked if she might have it. The two women looked at each other and their eyes filled with tears. Then the mistress opened her arms, the maid threw herself into them, and they clasped each other in a warm embrace, satisfying their grief in a kiss which made them equal.

It was the first time that such a thing had happened, for Mme Aubain was not of a demonstrative nature. Félicité was as grateful as if she had received a great favour, and henceforth loved her mistress with dog-like devotion and religious veneration.

Her heart grew softer as time went by.

When she heard the drums of a regiment coming down the street she stood at the door with a jug of cider and offered the soldiers a drink. She looked after the people who went down with cholera. She watched over the Polish refugees,[1] and one of them actually expressed a desire to marry her. But they fell out, for when she came back from the Angelus[2] one morning, she found that he had got into her kitchen and was calmly eating an oil-and-vinegar salad.

After the Poles it was Père Colmiche, an old man who was said to have committed fearful atrocities in '93.[3] He lived by the river in a ruined pig-sty. The boys of the town used to peer at him through the cracks in the walls, and threw pebbles at him which landed on the litter where he lay, constantly shaken by fits of coughing. His hair was extremely long, his eyelids inflamed, and on one arm there was a swelling bigger than his head. Félicité brought him some linen, tried to clean out his filthy hovel, and even wondered if she could install him in the wash-house without annoying Madame. When the tumour had burst, she changed his dressings every day, brought him some cake now and then, and put him out in the sun on a truss of hay. The poor old fellow would thank her in a faint whisper, slavering and trembling all the while, fearful of losing her and stretching his hands out as soon as he saw her moving away.

He died, and she had a Mass said for the repose of his soul.

That same day a great piece of good fortune came her way. Just as she was serving dinner, Mme de Larsonnière's Negro appeared carrying the parrot in its cage, complete with perch, chain, and padlock. The Baroness had written a note informing Mme Aubain that her husband had been promoted to a Prefecture and they were leaving that evening; she begged her to accept the parrot as a keepsake and a token of her regard.

This bird had engrossed Félicité's thoughts for a long time, for it came from America, and that word reminded her of Victor. So she had asked the Negro all about it, and once she had even gone so far as to say:

'How pleased Madame would be if it were hers!'

---

1. After the July Revolution, a spirit of revolt spread throughout Europe, prompting Poles and other Europeans to seek refuge in France.
2. A daily prayer to the Virgin Mary.

3. I.e., 1793, the height of the Reign of Terror during the French Revolution when thousands of people were guillotined.

The Negro had repeated this remark to his mistress, who, unable to take the parrot with her, was glad to get rid of it in this way.

4

His name was Loulou. His body was green, the tips of his wings were pink, his poll blue, and his breast golden.

Unfortunately he had a tiresome mania for biting his perch, and also used to pull his feathers out, scatter his droppings everywhere, and upset his bath water. He annoyed Mme Aubain, and so she gave him to Félicité for good.

Félicité started training him, and soon he could say: 'Nice boy! Your servant, sir! Hail, Mary!' He was put near the door, and several people who spoke to him said how strange it was that he did not answer to the name of Jacquot, as all parrots were called Jacquot.[4] They likened him to a turkey or a block of wood, and every sneer cut Félicité to the quick. How odd, she thought, that Loulou should be so stubborn, refusing to talk whenever anyone looked at him!

For all that, he liked having people around him, because on Sundays, while the Rochefeuille sisters, M. Houppeville and some new friends—the apothecary Onfroy, M. Varin, and Captain Mathieu—were having their game of cards, he would beat on the window-panes with his wings and make such a din that it was impossible to hear oneself speak.

Bourais's face obviously struck him as terribly funny, for as soon as he saw it he was seized with uncontrollable laughter. His shrieks rang round the courtyard, the echo repeated them, and the neighbours came to their windows and started laughing too. To avoid being seen by the bird, M. Bourais used to creep along by the wall, hiding his face behind his hat, until he got to the river, and then come into the house from the garden. The looks he gave the parrot were far from tender.

Loulou had once been cuffed by the butcher's boy for poking his head into his basket; and since then he was always trying to give him a nip through his shirt. Fabu threatened to wring his neck, although he was not a cruel fellow, in spite of his tattooed arms and bushy whiskers. On the contrary, he rather liked the parrot, so much so indeed that in a spirit of jovial camaraderie he tried to teach him a few swear-words. Félicité, alarmed at this development, put the bird in the kitchen. His little chain was removed and he was allowed to wander all over the house.

Coming downstairs, he used to rest the curved part of his beak on each step and then raise first his right foot, then his left; and Félicité was afraid that this sort of gymnastic performance would make him giddy. He fell ill and could neither talk nor eat for there was a swelling under his tongue such as hens sometimes have. She cured him by pulling this pellicule out with her fingernails. One day M. Paul was silly enough to blow the smoke of his cigar at him; another time Mme Lormeau started teasing him with the end of her parasol, and he caught hold of the ferrule with his beak. Finally he got lost.

Félicité had put him down on the grass in the fresh air, and left him there for a minute. When she came back, the parrot had gone. First of all she looked for

4. A species of parrot native to the island of St. Lucia in the West Indies.

him in the bushes, by the river and on the rooftops, paying no attention to her mistress's shouts of: 'Be careful, now! You must be mad!' Next she went over all the gardens in Pont-l'Évêque, stopping passersby and asking them: 'You don't happen to have seen my parrot by any chance?' Those who did not know him already were given a description of the bird. Suddenly she thought she could make out something green flying about behind the mills at the foot of the hill. But up on the hill there was nothing to be seen. A pedlar told her that he had come upon the parrot a short time before in Mère Simon's shop at Saint-Melaine. She ran all the way there, but no one knew what she was talking about. Finally she came back home, worn out, her shoes falling to pieces, and death in her heart. She was sitting beside Madame on the garden-seat and telling her what she had been doing, when she felt something light drop on her shoulder. It was Loulou! What he had been up to, no one could discover: perhaps he had just gone for a little walk round the town.

Félicité was slow to recover from this fright, and indeed never really got over it.

As the result of a chill she had an attack of quinsy,[5] and soon after that her ears were affected. Three years later she was deaf, and she spoke at the top of her voice, even in church. Although her sins could have been proclaimed over the length and breadth of the diocese without dishonour to her or offence to others, M. le Curé thought it advisable to hear her confession in the sacristy.

Imaginary buzzings in the head added to her troubles. Often her mistress would say: 'Heavens, how stupid you are!' and she would reply: 'Yes, Madame,' at the same time looking all around her for something.

The little circle of her ideas grew narrower and narrower, and the pealing of bells and the lowing of cattle went out of her life. Every living thing moved about in a ghostly silence. Only one sound reached her ears now, and that was the voice of the parrot.

As if to amuse her, he would reproduce the click-clack of the turn-spit, the shrill call of a man selling fish, and the noise of the saw at the joiner's across the way; and when the bell rang he would imitate Mme Aubain's 'Félicité ! The door, the door !'

They held conversations with each other, he repeating *ad nauseam* the three phrases in his repertory, she replying with words which were just as disconnected but which came from the heart. In her isolation, Loulou was almost a son or a lover to her. He used to climb up her fingers, peck at her lips, and hang on to her shawl; and as she bent over him, wagging her head from side to side as nurses do, the great wings of her bonnet and the wings of the bird quivered in unison.

When clouds banked up in the sky and there was a rumbling of thunder, he would utter piercing cries, no doubt remembering the sudden downpours in his native forests. The sound of the rain falling roused him to frenzy. He would flap excitedly around, shoot up to the ceiling, knocking everything over, and fly out of the window to splash about in the garden. But he would soon come back to perch on one of the firedogs, hopping about to dry his feathers and showing tail and beak in turn.

5. Tonsillitis.

One morning in the terrible winter of 1837, when she had put him in front of the fire because of the cold she found him dead in the middle of his cage, hanging head down with his claws caught in the bars. He had probably died of a stroke, but she thought he had been poisoned with parsley,[6] and despite the absence of any proof, her suspicions fell on Fabu.

She wept so much that her mistress said to her: 'Why don't you have him stuffed?'

Félicité asked the chemist's advice, remembering that he had always been kind to the parrot. He wrote to Le Havre, and a man called Fellacher agreed to do the job. As parcels sometimes went astray on the mail-coach, she decided to take the parrot as far as Honfleur herself.

On either side of the road stretched an endless succession of apple-trees, all stripped of their leaves, and there was ice in the ditches. Dogs were barking around the farms; and Félicité, with her hands tucked under her mantlet, her little black sabots and her basket, walked briskly along the middle of the road.

She crossed the forest, passed Le Haut-Chêne, and got as far as Saint-Gatien.

Behind her, in a cloud of dust, and gathering speed as the horses galloped downhill, a mail-coach swept along like a whirlwind. When he saw this woman making no attempt to get out of the way, the driver poked his head out above the hood, and he and the postilion shouted at her. His four horses could not be held in and galloped faster, the two leaders touching her as they went by. With a jerk of the reins the driver threw them to one side, and then, in a fury, he raised his long whip and gave her such a lash, from head to waist, that she fell flat on her back.

The first thing she did on regaining consciousness was to open her basket. Fortunately nothing had happened to Loulou. She felt her right cheek burning, and when she touched it her hand turned red; it was bleeding.

She sat down on a heap of stones and dabbed her face with her handkerchief. Then she ate a crust of bread which she had taken the precaution of putting in her basket, and tried to forget her wound by looking at the bird.

As she reached the top of the hill at Ecquemauville, she saw the lights of Honfleur twinkling in the darkness like a host of stars, and the shadowy expanse of the sea beyond. Then a sudden feeling of faintness made her stop; and the misery of her childhood, the disappointment of her first love, the departure of her nephew, and the death of Virginie all came back to her at once like the waves of a rising tide, and, welling up in her throat, choked her.

When she got to the boat she insisted on speaking to the captain, and without telling him what was in her parcel, asked him to take good care of it.

Fellacher kept the parrot a long time. Every week he promised it for the next; after six months he announced that a box had been sent off, and nothing more was heard of it. It looked as though Loulou would never come back, and Félicité told herself: 'They've stolen him for sure!'

At last he arrived—looking quite magnificent, perched on a branch screwed into a mahogany base, one foot in the air, his head cocked to one side, and biting a nut which the taxidermist, out of a love of the grandiose, had gilded.

Félicité shut him up in her room.

6. Fool's Parsley, a poisonous plant resembling parsley in appearance.

This place, to which few people were ever admitted, contained such a quantity of religious bric-à-brac and miscellaneous oddments that it looked like a cross between a chapel and a bazaar.

A big wardrobe prevented the door from opening properly. Opposite the window that overlooked the garden was a little round one looking on to the courtyard. There was a table beside the bed, with a water-jug, a couple of combs, and a block of blue soap in a chipped plate. On the walls there were rosaries, medals, several pictures of the Virgin, and a holy-water stoup made out of a coconut. On the chest of drawers, which was draped with a cloth just like an altar, was the shell box Victor had given her, and also a watering-can and a ball, some copy-books, the illustrated geography book, and a pair of ankle-boots. And on the nail supporting the looking-glass, fastened by its ribbons, hung the little plush hat.

Félicité carried this form of veneration to such lengths that she even kept one of Monsieur's frock-coats. All the old rubbish Mme Aubain had no more use for, she carried off to her room. That was how there came to be artificial flowers along the edge of the chest of drawers, and a portrait of the Comte d'Artois[7] in the window-recess.

With the aid of a wall-bracket, Loulou was installed on a chimney-breast that jutted out into the room. Every morning when she awoke, she saw him in the light of the dawn, and then she remembered the old days, and the smallest details of insignificant actions, not in sorrow but in absolute tranquillity.

Having no intercourse with anyone, she lived in the torpid state of a sleep-walker. The Corpus Christi processions roused her from this condition, for she would go round the neighbours collecting candlesticks and mats to decorate the altar of repose which they used to set up in the street.

In church she was forever gazing at the Holy Ghost, and one day she noticed that it had something of the parrot about it. This resemblance struck her as even more obvious in a colour-print depicting the baptism of Our Lord. With its red wings and its emerald-green body, it was the very image of Loulou.

She bought the print and hung it in the place of the Comte d'Artois, so that she could include them both in a single glance. They were linked together in her mind, the parrot being sanctified by this connexion with the Holy Ghost, which itself acquired new life and meaning in her eyes. God the Father could not have chosen a dove as a means of expressing Himself, since doves cannot talk, but rather one of Loulou's ancestors. And although Félicité used to say her prayers with her eyes on the picture, from time to time she would turn slightly towards the bird.

She wanted to join the Children of Mary,[8] but Mme Aubain dissuaded her from doing so.

An important event now loomed up—Paul's wedding.

After starting as a lawyer's clerk, he had been in business, in the Customs, and in Inland Revenue, and had even begun trying to get into the Department

---

7. Charles Philippe, Comte d' Artois (1757–1836), reigned as King Charles X from 1824 until 1830, when he was overthrown in the July Revolution.

8. Society of laywomen who pledge to imitate the Virgin Mary.

of Woods and Forests, when, at the age of thirty-six, by some heaven-sent inspiration, he suddenly discovered his real vocation—in the Wills and Probate Department. There he proved so capable that one of the auditors had offered him his daughter in marriage and promised to use his influence on his behalf.

Paul, grown serious-minded, brought her to see his mother. She criticized the way things were done at Pont-l'Évêque, put on airs, and hurt Félicité's feelings. Mme Aubain was relieved to see her go.

The following week came news of M. Bourais's death in an inn in Lower Brittany. Rumours that he had committed suicide were confirmed, and doubts arose as to his honesty. Mme Aubain went over her accounts and was soon conversant with the full catalogue of his misdeeds—embezzlement of interest, secret sales of timber, forged receipts, etc. Besides all this, he was the father of an illegitimate child, and had had 'relations with a person at Dozulé.'

These infamies upset Mme Aubain greatly. In March 1853 she was afflicted with a pain in the chest; her tongue seemed to be covered with a film; leeches failed to make her breathing any easier; and on the ninth evening of her illness she died. She had just reached the age of seventy-two.

She was thought to be younger because of her brown hair, worn in bandeaux round her pale, pock-marked face. There were few friends to mourn her, for she had a haughty manner which put people off. Yet Félicité wept for her as servants rarely weep for their masters. That Madame should die before her upset her ideas, seemed to be contrary to the order of things, monstrous and unthinkable.

Ten days later—the time it took to travel hot-foot from Besançon—the heirs arrived. The daughter-in-law ransacked every drawer, picked out some pieces of furniture and sold the rest; and then back they went to the Wills and Probate Department.

Madame's arm-chair, her pedestal table, her foot warmer, and the eight chairs had all gone. Yellow squares in the centre of the wall-panels showed where the pictures had hung. They had carried off the two cots with their mattresses, and no trace remained in the cupboard of all Virginie's things. Félicité climbed the stairs to her room, numbed with sadness.

The next day there was a notice on the door, and the apothecary shouted in her ear that the house was up for sale.

She swayed on her feet, and was obliged to sit down.

What distressed her most of all was the idea of leaving her room, which was so suitable for poor Loulou. Fixing an anguished look on him as she appealed to the Holy Ghost, she contracted the idolatrous habit of kneeling in front of the parrot to say her prayers. Sometimes the sun, as it came through the little window, caught his glass eye, so that it shot out a great luminous ray which sent her into ecstasies.

She had a pension of three hundred and eighty francs a year which her mistress had left her. The garden kept her in vegetables. As for clothes, she had enough to last her till the end of her days, and she saved on lighting by going to bed as soon as darkness fell.

She went out as little as possible, to avoid the second-hand dealer's shop, where some of the old furniture was on display. Ever since her fit of giddiness, she had been dragging one leg; and as her strength was failing, Mère Simon, whose grocery business had come to grief, came in every morning to chop wood and pump water for her.

Her eyes grew weaker. The shutters were not opened any more. Years went by, and nobody rented the house and nobody bought it.

For fear of being evicted, Félicité never asked for any repairs to be done. The laths in the roof rotted, and all through one winter her bolster was wet. After Easter she began spitting blood.

When this happened Mère Simon called in a doctor. Félicité wanted to know what was the matter with her, but she was so deaf that only one word reached her: 'Pneumonia.' It was a word she knew, and she answered gently: 'Ah! like Madame,' thinking it natural that she should follow in her mistress's footsteps.

The time to set up the altars of repose was drawing near.

The first altar was always at the foot of the hill, the second in front of the post office, the third about half-way up the street. There was some argument as to the siting of this one, and finally the women of the parish picked on Mme Aubain's courtyard.

The fever and the tightness of the chest grew worse. Félicité fretted over not doing anything for the altar. If only she could have put something on it! Then she thought of the parrot. The neighbours protested that it would not be seemly, but the curé gave his permission, and this made her so happy that she begged him to accept Loulou, the only thing of value she possessed, when she died.

From Tuesday to Saturday, the eve of Corpus Christi, she coughed more and more frequently. In the evening her face looked pinched and drawn, her lips stuck to her gums, and she started vomiting. At dawn the next day, feeling very low, she sent for a priest.

Three good women stood by her while she was given extreme unction. Then she said that she had to speak to Fabu.

He arrived in his Sunday best, very ill at ease in this funereal atmosphere.

'Forgive me,' she said, making an effort to stretch out her arm. 'I thought it was you who had killed him.'

What could she mean by such nonsense? To think that she had suspected a man like him of murder! He got very indignant and was obviously going to make a scene.

'Can't you see,' they said, 'that she isn't in her right mind any more?'

From time to time Félicité would start talking to shadows. The women went away. Mère Simon had her lunch.

A little later she picked Loulou up and held him out to Félicité, saying:

'Come now, say good-bye to him.'

Although the parrot was not a corpse, the worms were eating him up. One of his wings was broken, and the stuffing was coming out of his stomach. But she was blind by now, and she kissed him on the forehead and pressed him against her cheek. Mère Simon took him away from her to put him on the altar.

5

The scents of summer came up from the meadows; there was a buzzing of flies; the sun was glittering in the river and warming the slates of the roof. Mère Simon had come back into the room and was gently nodding off to sleep.

The noise of church bells woke her up; the congregation was coming out from vespers. Félicité's delirium abated. Thinking of the procession, she could see it as clearly as if she had been following it.

All the school-children, the choristers, and the firemen were walking along the pavements, while advancing up the middle of the street came the church officer armed with his halberd, the beadle carrying a great cross, the school-master keeping an eye on the boys, and the nun fussing over her little girls— three of the prettiest, looking like curly-headed angels, were throwing rose-petals into the air. Then came the deacon, with both arms outstretched, conducting the band, and a couple of censer-bearers who turned round at every step to face the Holy Sacrament, which the curé, wearing his splendid chasuble, was carrying under a canopy of poppy-red velvet held aloft by four churchwardens. A crowd of people surged along behind, between the white cloths covering the walls of the houses, and eventually they got to the bottom of the hill.

A cold sweat moistened Félicité's temples. Mère Simon sponged it up with a cloth, telling herself that one day she would have to go the same way.

The hum of the crowd increased in volume, was very loud for a moment, then faded away.

A fusillade shook the window-panes. It was the postilions saluting the monstrance. Félicité rolled her eyes and said as loud as she could: 'Is he all right?'— worrying about the parrot.

She entered into her death-agony. Her breath, coming ever faster, with a rattling sound, made her sides heave. Bubbles of froth appeared at the corners of her mouth, and her whole body trembled.

Soon the booming of the ophicleides,[9] the clear voices of the children, and the deep voices of the men could be heard near at hand. Now and then everything was quiet, and the tramping of feet, deadened by a carpet of flowers, sounded like a flock moving across pasture-land.

The clergy appeared in the courtyard. Mère Simon climbed on to a chair to reach the little round window, from which she had a full view of the altar below.

It was hung with green garlands and adorned with a flounce in English needle-point lace. In the middle was a little frame containing some relics, there were two orange-trees at the corners, and all the way along stood silver candlesticks and china vases holding sunflowers, lilies, peonies, foxgloves, and bunches of hydrangea. This pyramid of bright colours stretched from the first floor right down to the carpet which was spread out over the pavement. Some rare objects caught the eye: a silver-gilt sugar-basin wreathed in violets, some pendants of Alençon gems gleaming on a bed of moss, and two Chinese screens with landscape decorations. Loulou, hidden under roses, showed nothing but his blue poll, which looked like a plaque of lapis lazuli.

The churchwardens, the choristers, and the children lined up along the three sides of the courtyard. The priest went slowly up the steps and placed his great

9. Bugles.

shining gold sun[1] on the lace altar cloth. Everyone knelt down. There was a deep silence. And the censers, swinging at full tilt, slid up and down their chains.

A blue cloud of incense was wafted up into Félicité's room. She opened her nostrils wide and breathed it in with a mystical, sensuous fervour. Then she closed her eyes. Her lips smiled. Her heart-beats grew slower and slower, each a little fainter and gentler, like a fountain running dry, an echo fading away. And as she breathed her last, she thought she could see, in the opening heavens, a gigantic parrot hovering above her head.

1. Used in Catholic services, the vessel called a "monstrance" resembles a sun.

LEO TOLSTOY

1828–1910

A gambler, womanizer, and aristocrat of the highest rank, Count Leo Tolstoy was also a vegetarian, pacifist, and anarchist, and a passionate advocate for the Russian peasantry. He was world-famous for his wisdom on the subject of marriage, but suffered through a remarkably stormy marriage himself. He became widely known as a moral and religious sage, but was excommunicated from the Russian Orthodox Church. He produced some of the century's best fiction but came to believe that novels were immoral. And yet this heap of contradictions should not be seen as the mark of a hypocrite. Tolstoy was always fully conscious of the disparity between his ideals and his life. "Blame *me*," he wrote, "and not the path I tread." This painful self-division reflects his intense, lifelong struggle to find the best way to live in the world—how to respond to the pressures of guilt and pleasure, authority and money, sex and war. And it suggests the source of one of his great talents as a writer: the capacity to represent a vast, various, and conflicting array of desires and ideals.

LIFE

Born in 1828, Tolstoy was the fourth of five children. Both of his parents belonged to the highest class of Russian society—aristocrats who had access to the tsar and the tsar's court. And yet Tolstoy never took advantage of his high birth to pursue a grand career as a diplomat or courtier. Having lost his mother at the age of two and his father at nine, he spent a relatively isolated youth. Much of his long life was passed on the family estate, Yasnaya Polyana, about 130 miles from Moscow, in the company of his close family members and his serfs—Russian peasants who were the property of aristocratic landowners, much like slaves.

Despite the fact that he was an orphan and moved from one guardian to another, Tolstoy looked back on his childhood as idyllic. He was close to his siblings, and together they imagined a perfect society based on the ideal of universal love. At the age of fourteen Tolstoy started to visit brothels, which prompted terrible bouts of remorse and self-revulsion. After his first experience, he claimed to have stood next to the bed and wept. A few years later he started to write in a diary, which he then kept compulsively for the rest of his life. This daily writing often furnished material for his fiction, as well as developing his skills and habits as a writer. Here, he would explore questions about how to act and what to believe, wondering about the purpose and meaning of life. He would also repeatedly make vows to give up his dalliances with women, and just as often break his promise. Thus began a chronicle of sex and shame, played out in countless affairs with women, almost all of them members of the peasant class.

Intending to take up a diplomatic career, Tolstoy went to the provincial university at Kazan to study Arabic, Turko-Tartar, French, and German. He later switched to law, a course of study open only to the highest-ranking aristocrats. But this too he dropped in 1847 when he inherited the family estate, a large sum of money, and the ownership of over three hundred serfs. This sudden inheritance allowed him to drift aimlessly for a while, moving in aristocratic circles in the cities of St. Petersburg and Moscow, where he spent night after night at gambling tables.

Tolstoy's life changed radically in 1851 when he followed his older brother Nikolay, a soldier, to the mountains of the Caucasus, where the Russian army was protecting the hotly contested boundary between Russia and the Ottoman and Persian empires. It was here, observing military life and conflict, that Tolstoy began publishing his work. He decided to join the army and to serve in the war between Russia and Britain in Crimea. There he witnessed appalling devastation, incompetence, and confusion. He also gambled away his fortune, observed the heat of battle and the pettiness of military life, and became a literary sensation with his detailed descriptions of the war in *Sebastopol Sketches* (1854). He began to be known in literary circles as an emerging genius, and in government circles as a potentially dangerous critic.

Although he had been an indifferent student, Tolstoy was a great reader, and from adolescence he passionately admired the French Romantic **Jean-Jacques Rousseau**, who argued against the artificiality of social manners and institutions in favor of the simplicity of life in and through nature. Tolstoy read widely in European and American literature, from **Johann Wolfgang von Goethe** to Harriet Beecher Stowe. One of his greatest influences was the English novelist Charles Dickens, who was highly popular in Russia. Tolstoy would often read a Dickens novel when he needed a catalyst to begin writing himself.

At the age of thirty-four, Tolstoy, now a famous writer, married Sofya Andreyevna Bers, an eighteen-year-old, upper-class St. Petersburg girl. A day after he proposed, he offered his fiancée the chance to read his diaries, which recorded, among other things, twenty years of sexual activity with prostitutes, gypsies, and serfs. "I forgive you," she said to him after reading it, "but it's dreadful." From the beginning, both Tolstoys wrote constantly about one another in their diaries, and read each other's accounts, leading to many jealous battles—and perhaps the most documented marriage in history. Over their long and tumultuous life together, Sofya bore thirteen children, made four handwritten copies of the 1,500-page *War and Peace*, and did her best to protect her husband's literary property.

By his mid-thirties, Tolstoy had run afoul of the Russian government. As a local justice of the peace, he had made eccentric and radical decisions, taking the side of serfs against his fellow landowners, and he had founded an experimental school for peasant children at Yasnaya Polyana based on new theories of education emerging out of France, Belgium, Germany, and England. Instead of cramming children with information, Tolstoy argued, it made sense for education to draw on their own experience. This seemed dangerously foreign, and his writing seemed unsettling, too. The tsar, concerned about threats to his life and his regime, had a team of censors who excised paragraphs from a number of Tolstoy's early short stories. In 1862 the police made a raid on his house. They found little evidence of subversive writings or activity, but the search infuriated Tolstoy, whose antigovernment sentiment increased as he grew older. Arguing that governments always relied on violence, he became a vocal anarchist and pacifist, advocating civil disobedience rather than submission to the state.

Tolstoy's two greatest works, *War and Peace* (1865–69) and *Anna Karenina* (1875–77), were hugely popular and established him as the greatest novelist of the Russian experience. *War and Peace* was an epic that recounted Napoleon's invasion of Russia in 1812, a huge swarming story of a nation's resistance to a foreign power. Tolstoy unsettles the myth of Napoleon as one of the world's greatest heroes, interpreting history instead as a struggle of anonymous collective forces; events are the consequences of waves of irrational communal feeling. *Anna Karenina* is a moving story of marriage and adultery that juxtaposes characters who are searching for meaning and fulfillment. Its hero, Levin, ends a painful struggle with the promise of salvation,

adopting the ideal of a simple life in which we should "remember God." So bound up with national pride were these two works that they survived successive waves of censorship. In fact, the repressive Russian government was so fearful of making a martyr out of the much-beloved novelist that they left Tolstoy almost entirely alone, even while they imprisoned and executed a vast number of his fellow writers for subversive antitsarist sentiment. As Tolstoy became an increasingly outspoken critic of the state, his own fiction protected him.

After he published *Anna Karenina* Tolstoy underwent an acute personal and spiritual crisis, thrown into such despair by the pointlessness of existence that he considered suicide (a despair shared by some of the characters in the novel). Then he had a conversion experience that set him on a new path. After exploring and rejecting the Russian Orthodox Church, he began to pursue his own search for God. It was the peasants who seemed to Tolstoy to know how to live best, and in the late 1870s he started to try to live a peasant life, dressing like them, eating peasant food, and even making his own shoes. Rereading the Gospels closely, he founded his own religion. This involved rejecting any idea of an afterlife and following the model of Jesus' life as closely as possible, giving away wealth and rejecting all forms of violence. Tolstoy's first work of fiction after his conversion was *The Death of Ivan Ilyich* in 1886.

The last decades of his life saw Tolstoy writing mostly religious and philosophical treatises. By the 1880s the writer was arguing in favor of complete sexual abstinence. He condemned literature and singled out Shakespeare as particularly bad. He became an outspoken vegetarian. At one point, an elderly relative visiting Yasnaya Polyana asked that meat be served to her; when she came to the table, she discovered a meat cleaver at her place and a live chicken tied to her chair. In his later years, many followers saw Tolstoy as a wise prophet and made long journeys to Yasnaya Polyana from distant places to meet the great man. They often reported that he seemed larger than life—saintly and heroic.

At Tolstoy's death in 1910 students rioted, anarchists were rounded up by the police, and thousands of people followed his coffin. Seven years later, when Russia erupted in political turmoil, some saw the first tide of communism as a "Tolstoyan revolution." But Tolstoy left another kind of political legacy as well. So influential was his notion of nonviolent resistance for a young Indian man named Mohandas Gandhi that he called his first political base "Tolstoy farm."

TIMES

In the century leading up to Tolstoy's birth, Russian society was divided into three major groups: the aristocracy, which was small in number but exerted all of the nation's political power; town merchants, who had fixed duties and privileges; and serfs, who made up the vast majority of the population but had no power at all. The aristocrats were the only Russians who could attend universities, hold civil service positions, and remain exempt from taxation. Meanwhile, serfs had neither freedom nor authority: one tsar after another reduced serfs' rights, and by the middle of the eighteenth century, serfs were forbidden to travel and had the legal status of personal property, exactly like slaves. When Tolstoy was young, 23 million Russians were privately owned serfs.

This drastically lopsided political and social system was clearly unstable, and anxious tsars struggled to stave off outright revolution. Alexander II emancipated the serfs in 1861 for purely pragmatic reasons: "It is better to abolish serfdom from above," he explained, "than to wait for the time when it will begin to abolish itself from below." The emancipation did not put an end to social unrest, however. By 1880 there had been six attempts to kill the tsar by anarchists and nihilists. Alexander increased his secret police force, imposed severe censorship, and promised political reforms. In 1881 an assassin succeeded in killing him, and he was succeeded by his son, Alexander III, who rejected his father's reform efforts in favor of harsh and repressive measures, including even tighter censorship and persecution of non-Orthodox minorities, especially Jews. Most writers were persecuted—thrown in jail or kept under house arrest. In this context, it is astonishing that Tolstoy managed to remain free, especially given his sharp and vocal criticism of both church and state.

In Russian intellectual circles, one urgent question constantly reemerged in the nineteenth century: should Russia follow the lead of a modernizing Western Europe in terms of culture, politics, and industry, or should the nation instead reach for models drawn from its own religious and national history, developing its own distinctive heritage? On the one side, the so-called Westernizers, based largely in St. Petersburg, argued for liberal democracy, religious freedom, and the emancipation of the serfs. They spoke French, and often felt ashamed of Russian backwardness. On the other side, the Moscow-based Slavophiles resisted rationalism and technological innovation, embraced the Russian Orthodox Church, and typically favored bringing together all Slavic peoples under the Russian tsar. Tolstoy belonged to neither camp—or to both. While he favored European models of education and rejected the Orthodox Church, he also prized the Russian peasantry as a source of national renewal and meaning.

Tolstoy's great novels, *War and Peace* and *Anna Karenina*, told vast and sweeping realist stories of nineteenth-century Russian life, filled with vivid depictions of aristocratic pursuits, military battles, and the complexities of love and marriage. Later he turned to a different kind of writing, producing impassioned and often didactic stories and nonfiction essays in favor of spiritual principles. *The Death of Ivan Ilyich*, the story included here, falls midway between these two phases of his career. As the first piece of fiction written after the writer's conversion, it has seemed to many readers to combine Tolstoy's earlier, richly realistic representations of contemporary life with his later turn to religious ideals.

There may be a biographical source for this novella. In 1856—thirty years before he began writing it—Tolstoy's brother Dmitry had died of tuberculosis in the arms of a prostitute. Revolted by his brother's emaciated body and the smell of illness, Tolstoy felt remarkably little concern for Dmitry and selfishly rushed back to St. Petersburg to enjoy his growing literary fame. This experience—Dmitry's death, his own indifference, and his resulting guilt—seems to have provided the writer with the contrasting perspectives he explores in *The Death of Ivan Ilyich*.

This is the story of an average man of the prosperous middle class who faces the unbearable fact that he is soon going to die. Tolstoy is famous for peppering his prose with startlingly opinionated, intrusive judgments, and among the most famous of these is the narrator's assessment of his protagonist's life at the opening of chapter II: "Ivan Ilyich's life had been the most simple and most ordinary and therefore most terrible."

The relationship between terror and ordinariness here appears straightforward and categorical, but the story then asks us to think about how we respond to such blunt claims of truth. Ivan Ilyich himself knows that everyone must die—"Caius is a man, men are mortal, therefore Caius is mortal"—but he rebels against applying this to himself: "he was not Caius, not an abstract man, but a creature quite, quite separate from all others." What, Tolstoy asks us, is the relationship between abstract, universal truths and our intensely felt personal experience?

Ordinary social life, it seems, allows us to avoid this question, as characters immerse themselves in card games, interior decorating, career advancement, financial dealings, and the desire to "live pleasantly." Ivan Ilyich, whose first symptoms of illness appear when he tries to hang his curtains properly, comes to see his family, friends, and doctors as false and deceitful. Gerasim, the peasant, represents the only appealing alternative described in the narrative.

Tolstoy experiments with perspective, choosing to begin the story at its chronological endpoint, as the news of Ivan Ilyich's death comes to his acquaintances. For them it appears as an interruption of ordinary life, and we see the event through their uncomfortable eyes. It is only after this introduction that the narrator switches to Ivan Ilyich's perspective. In the first draft, two characters, Peter Ivanovich and Ivan Ilyich, told the story in the first person. Later Tolstoy shifted to a third-person omniscient narrator, who filters our experience through these two characters.

Tolstoy not only multiplies perspectives, he also multiplies metaphors: dying is like being "thrust into a narrow, deep black sack"; it is also like a "stone falling downwards," like flying, and "like the sensation one sometimes experiences in a railway carriage when one thinks one is going backwards while one is really going forwards." Death emerges variously as nothingness, a black hole, a judge (like the character himself), and perhaps most memorably, as *"It."* In Russian this pronoun is feminine and thus closer to the English *"She."* As death slowly comes to the protagonist, language itself begins to break down. In the final chapter, he starts screaming, "I won't," but this becomes simply "Oh! Oh! Oh!"—a sound that lasts for three solid days. In his final moments of illumination, the protagonist tries to ask his son to "forgive" him but says only "forgo." As Ivan Ilyich's viewpoint develops and changes, the story narrows in time and space; the focus tightens, his range of movements contracts, the chapters get shorter, and the time of the events shrinks.

Guy de Maupassant, a French writer whom Tolstoy admired, read *The Death of Ivan Ilyich* late in his own life, and said, sadly: "I realize that everything I have done now was to no purpose, and that my ten volumes are worthless."

The Death of Ivan Ilyich[1]

I

During an interval in the Melvinski trial in the large building of the Law Courts the members and public prosecutor met in Ivan Egorovich Shebek's private room, where the conversation turned on the celebrated Krasovski case. Fëdor Vasilievich warmly maintained that it was not subject to their jurisdiction, Ivan Egorovich maintained the contrary, while Peter Ivanovich, not having entered into the discussion at the start, took no part in it but looked through the *Gazette* which had just been handed in.

"Gentlemen," he said, "Ivan Ilyich has died!"

"You don't say!"

"Here read it yourself," replied Peter Ivanovich, handing Fëdor Vasilievich the paper still damp from the press. Surrounded by a black border were the words: "Praskovya Fëdorovna Golovina, with profound sorrow, informs relatives and friends of the demise of her beloved husband Ivan Ilyich Golovin, Member of the Court of Justice, which occurred on February the 4th of this year 1882. The funeral will take place on Friday at one o'clock in the afternoon."

Ivan Ilyich had been a colleague of the gentlemen present and was liked by them all. He had been ill for some weeks with an illness said to be incurable. His post had been kept open for him, but there had been conjectures that in case of his death Alexeev might receive his appointment, and that either Vinnikov or Shtabel would succeed Alexeev. So on receiving the news of Ivan Ilyich's death the first thought of each of the gentlemen in that private room was of the changes and promotions it might occasion among themselves or their acquaintances.

"I shall be sure to get Shtabel's place or Vinnikov's," thought Fëdor Vasilievich. "I was promised that long ago, and the promotion means an extra eight hundred rubles a year for me besides the allowance."

1. Translated by Louise Maude and Aylmer Maude.

"Now I must apply for my brother-in-law's transfer from Kaluga," thought Peter Ivanovich. "My wife will be very glad, and then she won't be able to say that I never do anything for her relations."

"I thought he would never leave his bed again," said Peter Ivanovich aloud. "It's very sad."

"But what really was the matter with him?"

"The doctors couldn't say—at least they could, but each of them said something different. When last I saw him I thought he was getting better."

"And I haven't been to see him since the holidays. I always meant to go."

"Had he any property?"

"I think his wife had a little—but something quite trifling."

"We shall have to go to see her, but they live so terribly far away."

"Far away from you, you mean. Everything's far away from your place."

"You see, he never can forgive my living on the other side of the river," said Peter Ivanovich, smiling at Shebek. Then, still talking of the distances between different parts of the city, they returned to the Court.

Besides considerations as to the possible transfers and promotions likely to result from Ivan Ilyich's death, the mere fact of the death of a near acquaintance aroused, as usual, in all who heard of it the complacent feeling that, "it is he who is dead and not I."

Each one thought or felt, "Well, he's dead but I'm alive!" But the more intimate of Ivan Ilyich's acquaintances, his so-called friends, could not help thinking also that they would now have to fulfil the very tiresome demands of propriety by attending the funeral service and paying a visit of condolence to the widow.

Fëdor Vasilievich and Peter Ivanovich had been his nearest acquaintances. Peter Ivanovich had studied law with Ivan Ilyich and had considered himself to be under obligations to him.

Having told his wife at dinner-time of Ivan Ilyich's death, and of his conjecture that it might be possible to get her brother transferred to their circuit, Peter Ivanovich sacrificed his usual nap, put on his evening clothes, and drove to Ivan Ilyich's house.

At the entrance stood a carriage and two cabs. Leaning against the wall in the hall downstairs near the cloak-stand was a coffin-lid covered with cloth of gold, ornamented with gold cord and tassels, that had been polished up with metal powder. Two ladies in black were taking off their fur cloaks. Peter Ivanovich recognized one of them as Ivan Ilyich's sister, but the other was a stranger to him. His colleague Schwartz was just coming downstairs, but on seeing Peter Ivanovich enter he stopped and winked at him, as if to say: "Ivan Ilyich has made a mess of things—not like you and me."

Schwartz's face with his Piccadilly whiskers, and his slim figure in evening dress, had as usual an air of elegant solemnity which contrasted with the playfulness of his character and had a special piquancy here, or so it seemed to Peter Ivanovich.

Peter Ivanovich allowed the ladies to precede him and slowly followed them upstairs. Schwartz did not come down but remained where he was, and Peter Ivanovich understood that he wanted to arrange where they should play bridge that evening. The ladies went upstairs to the widow's room, and Schwartz with seriously compressed lips but a playful look in his eyes, indicated by a twist of his eyebrows the room to the right where the body lay.

Peter Ivanovich, like everyone else on such occasions, entered feeling uncertain what he would have to do. All he knew was that at such times it is always safe to cross oneself. But he was not quite sure whether one should make obeisances while doing so. He therefore adopted a middle course. On entering the room he began crossing himself and made a slight movement resembling a bow. At the same time, as far as the motion of his head and arm allowed, he surveyed the room. Two young men—apparently nephews, one of whom was a high-school pupil—were leaving the room, crossing themselves as they did so. An old woman was standing motionless, and a lady with strangely arched eyebrows was saying something to her in a whisper. A vigorous, resolute Church Reader,[2] in a frock-coat, was reading something in a loud voice with an expression that precluded any contradiction. The butler's assistant, Gerasim, stepping lightly in front of Peter Ivanovich, was strewing something on the floor. Noticing this, Peter Ivanovich was immediately aware of a faint odour of a decomposing body.

The last time he had called on Ivan Ilyich, Peter Ivanovich had seen Gerasim in the study. Ivan Ilyich had been particularly fond of him and he was performing the duty of a sick nurse.

Peter Ivanovich continued to make the sign of the cross slightly inclining his head in an intermediate direction between the coffin, the Reader, and the icons on the table in a corner of the room. Afterwards, when it seemed to him that this movement of his arm in crossing himself had gone on too long, he stopped and began to look at the corpse.

The dead man lay, as dead men always lie, in a specially heavy way, his rigid limbs sunk in the soft cushions of the coffin, with the head forever bowed on the pillow. His yellow waxen brow with bald patches over his sunken temples was thrust up in the way peculiar to the dead, the protruding nose seeming to press on the upper lip. He was much changed and had grown even thinner since Peter Ivanovich had last seen him, but, as is always the case with the dead, his face was handsomer and above all more dignified than when he was alive. The expression on the face said that what was necessary had been accomplished, and accomplished rightly. Besides this there was in that expression a reproach and a warning to the living. This warning seemed to Peter Ivanovich out of place, or at least not applicable to him. He felt a certain discomfort and so he hurriedly crossed himself once more and turned and went out of the door—too hurriedly and too regardless of propriety, as he himself was aware.

Schwartz was waiting for him in the adjoining room with legs spread wide apart and both hands toying with his top-hat behind his back. The mere sight of that playful, well-groomed, and elegant figure refreshed Peter Ivanovich. He felt that Schwartz was above all these happenings and could not surrender to any depressing influences. His very look said that this incident of a church service for Ivan Ilyich could not be a sufficient reason for infringing the order of the session—in other words, that it would certainly not prevent his unwrapping a new pack of cards and shuffling them that evening while a footman placed four fresh candles on the table: in fact, that there was no reason for

---

2. High position in the minor orders of the Eastern Orthodox Church, responsible for reading from scripture during services.

supposing that this incident would hinder their spending the evening agreeably. Indeed he said this in a whisper as Peter Ivanovich passed him, proposing that they should meet for a game at Fëdor Vasilievich's. But apparently Peter Ivanovich was not destined to play bridge that evening. Praskovya Fëdorovna (a short, fat woman who despite all efforts to the contrary had continued to broaden steadily from her shoulders downwards and who had the same extraordinary arched eyebrows as the lady who had been standing by the coffin), dressed all in black, her head covered with lace, came out of her own room with some other ladies, conducted them to the room where the dead body lay, and said: "The service will begin immediately. Please go in."

Schwartz, making an indefinite bow, stood still, evidently neither accepting nor declining this invitation. Praskovya Fëdorovna recognizing Peter Ivanovich, sighed, went close up to him, took his hand, and said: "I know you were a true friend to Ivan Ilyich . . ." and looked at him awaiting some suitable response. And Peter Ivanovich knew that, just as it had been the right thing to cross himself in that room, so what he had to do here was to press her hand, sigh, and say, "Believe me . . ." So he did all this and as he did it felt that the desired result had been achieved: that both he and she were touched.

"Come with me. I want to speak to you before it begins," said the widow. "Give me your arm."

Peter Ivanovich gave her his arm and they went to the inner rooms, passing Schwartz who winked at Peter Ivanovich compassionately.

"That does for our bridge! Don't object if we find another player. Perhaps you can cut in when you do escape," said his playful look.

Peter Ivanovich sighed still more deeply and despondently, and Praskovya Fëdorovna pressed his arm gratefully. When they reached the drawing-room, upholstered in pink cretonne[3] and lighted by a dim lamp, they sat down at the table—she on a sofa and Peter Ivanovich on a low hassock, the springs of which yielded spasmodically under his weight. Praskovya Fëdorovna had been on the point of warning him to take another seat, but felt that such a warning was out of keeping with her present condition and so changed her mind. As he sat down on the hassock Peter Ivanovich recalled how Ivan Ilyich had arranged this room and had consulted him regarding this pink cretonne with green leaves. The whole room was full of furniture and knick-knacks, and on her way to the sofa the lace of the widow's black shawl caught on the carved edge of the table. Peter Ivanovich rose to detach it, and the springs of the hassock, relieved of his weight, rose also and gave him a push. The widow began detaching her shawl herself, and Peter Ivanovich again sat down, suppressing the rebellious springs of the hassock under him. But the widow had not quite freed herself and Peter Ivanovich got up again, and again the hassock rebelled and even creaked. When this was all over she took out a clean cambric handkerchief and began to weep. The episode with the shawl and the struggle with the hassock had cooled Peter Ivanovich's emotions and he sat there with a sullen look on his face. This awkward situation was interrupted by Sokolov, Ivan Ilyich's butler, who came to report that the plot in the cemetery that Praskovya Fëdorovna had chosen would cost two hundred rubles. She stopped weeping and, looking

3. Heavy upholstery fabric, often printed with a fancy or gaudy pattern.

at Peter Ivanovich with the air of a victim, remarked in French[4] that it was very hard for her. Peter Ivanovich made a silent gesture signifying his full conviction that it must indeed be so.

"Please smoke," she said in a magnanimous yet crushed voice, and turned to discuss with Sokolov the price of the plot for the grave.

Peter Ivanovich while lighting his cigarette heard her inquiring very circumstantially into the prices of different plots in the cemetery and finally decide which she would take. When that was done she gave instructions about engaging the choir. Sokolov then left the room.

"I look after everything myself," she told Peter Ivanovich, shifting the albums that lay on the table; and noticing that the table was endangered by his cigarette-ash, she immediately passed him an ashtray, saying as she did so: "I consider it an affectation to say that my grief prevents my attending to practical affairs. On the contrary, if anything can—I won't say console me, but—distract me, it is seeing to everything concerning him." She again took out her handkerchief as if preparing to cry, but suddenly, as if mastering her feeling, she shook herself and began to speak calmly. "But there is something I want to talk to you about."

Peter Ivanovich bowed, keeping control of the springs of the hassock, which immediately began quivering under him.

"He suffered terribly the last few days."

"Did he?" said Peter Ivanovich.

"Oh, terribly! He screamed unceasingly, not for minutes but for hours. For the last three days he screamed incessantly. It was unendurable. I cannot understand how I bore it; you could hear him three rooms off. Oh, what I have suffered!"

"Is it possible that he was conscious all that time?" asked Peter Ivanovich.

"Yes," she whispered. "To the last moment. He took leave of us a quarter of an hour before he died, and asked us to take Vasya away."

The thought of the sufferings of this man he had known so intimately, first as a merry little boy, then as a school-mate, and later as a grown-up colleague, suddenly struck Peter Ivanovich with horror, despite an unpleasant consciousness of his own and this woman's dissimulation. He again saw that brow, and that nose pressing down on the lip, and felt afraid for himself.

"Three days of frightful suffering and then death! Why, that might suddenly, at any time, happen to me," he thought, and for a moment felt terrified. But— he did not himself know how—the customary reflection at once occurred to him that this had happened to Ivan Ilyich and not to him, and that it should not and could not happen to him, and that to think that it could would be yielding to depression which he ought not to do, as Schwartz's expression plainly showed. After which reflection Peter Ivanovich felt reasured, and began to ask with interest about the details of Ivan Ilyich's death, as though death was an accident natural to Ivan Ilyich but certainly not to himself.

After many details of the really dreadful physical sufferings Ivan Ilyich had endured (which details he learnt only from the effect those sufferings had produced on Praskovya Fëdorovna's nerves) the widow apparently found it necessary to get to business.

---

4. It was common for members of the upper classes in Russia in the 19th century to speak French to one another.

"Oh, Peter Ivanovich, how hard it is! How terribly, terribly hard!" and she again began to weep.

Peter Ivanovich sighed and waited for her to finish blowing her nose. When she had done so he said, "Believe me . . ." and she again began talking and brought out what was evidently her chief concern with him—namely, to question him as to how she could obtain a grant of money from the government on the occasion of her husband's death. She made it appear that she was asking Peter Ivanovich's advice about her pension, but he soon saw that she already knew about that to the minutest detail, more even than he did himself. She knew how much could be got out of the government in consequence of her husband's death, but wanted to find out whether she could possibly extract something more. Peter Ivanovich tried to think of some means of doing so, but after reflecting for a while and, out of propriety, condemning the government for its niggardliness, he said he thought that nothing more could be got. Then she sighed and evidently began to devise means of getting rid of her visitor. Noticing this, he put out his cigarette, rose, pressed her hand, and went out into the anteroom.

In the dining-room where the clock stood that Ivan Ilyich had liked so much and had bought at an antique shop, Peter Ivanovich met a priest and a few acquaintances who had come to attend the service, and he recognized Ivan Ilyich's daughter, a handsome young woman. She was in black and her slim figure appeared slimmer than ever. She had a gloomy, determined, almost angry expression, and bowed to Peter Ivanovich as though he were in some way to blame. Behind her, with the same offended look, stood a wealthy young man, an examining magistrate, whom Peter Ivanovich also knew and who was her fiancé, as he had heard. He bowed mournfully to them and was about to pass into the death-chamber, when from under the stairs appeared the figure of Ivan Ilyich's schoolboy son, who was extremely like this father. He seemed a little Ivan Ilyich, such as Peter Ivanovich remembered when they studied law together. His tear-stained eyes had in them the look that is seen in the eyes of boys of thirteen or fourteen who are not pure-minded.

When he saw Peter Ivanovich he scowled morosely and shamefacedly. Peter Ivanovich nodded to him and entered the death-chamber. The service began: candles, groans, incense, tears, and sobs. Peter Ivanovich stood looking gloomily down at his feet. He did not look once at the dead man, did not yield to any depressing influence, and was one of the first to leave the room. There was no one in the anteroom, but Gerasim darted out of the dead man's room, rummaged with his strong hands among the fur coats to find Peter Ivanovich's and helped him on with it.

"Well, friend Gerasim," said Peter Ivanovich, so as to say something. "It's a sad affair, isn't it?"

"It's God's will. We shall all come to it some day," said Gerasim, displaying his teeth—the even, white teeth of a healthy peasant—and, like a man in the thick of urgent work, he briskly opened the front door, called the coachman, helped Peter Ivanovich into the sledge, and sprang back to the porch as if in readiness for what he had to do next.

Peter Ivanovich found the fresh air particularly pleasant after the smell of incense, the dead body, and carbolic acid.

"Where to, sir?" asked the coachman.

"It's not too late even now. . . . I'll call round on Fëdor Vasilievich."

He accordingly drove there and found them just finishing the first rubber,[5] so that it was quite convenient for him to cut in.

II

Ivan Ilyich's life had been most simple and most ordinary and therefore most terrible.

He had been a member of the Court of Justice, and died at the age of forty-five. His father had been an official who after serving in various ministries and departments in Petersburg had made the sort of career which brings men to positions from which by reason of their long service they cannot be dismissed, though they are obviously unfit to hold any responsible position, and for whom therefore posts are specially created, which though fictitious, carry salaries of from six to ten thousand rubles that are not fictitious, and in receipt of which they live on to a great age.

Such was the Privy Councillor and superfluous member of various superflous institutions, Ilya Efimovich Golovin.

He had three sons, of whom Ivan Ilyich was the second. The eldest son was following in his father's footsteps only in another department, and was already approaching that stage in the service at which a similar sinecure would be reached. The third son was a failure. He had ruined his prospects in a number of positions and was now serving in the railway department. His father and brothers, and still more their wives, not merely disliked meeting him, but avoided remembering his existence unless compelled to do so. His sister had married Baron Greff, a Petersburg official of her father's type. Ivan Ilyich was *le phénix de la famille*[6] as people said. He was neither as cold and formal as his elder brother nor as wild as the younger, but was a happy mean between them—an intelligent, polished, lively and agreeable man. He had studied with his younger brother at the School of Law, but the latter had failed to complete the course and was expelled when he was in the fifth class. Ivan Ilyich finished the course well. Even when he was at the School of Law he was just what he remained for the rest of his life: a capable, cheerful, good-natured, and sociable man, though strict in the fulfilment of what he considered to be his duty: and he considered his duty to be what was so considered by those in authority. Neither as a boy nor as a man was he a toady, but from early youth was by nature attracted to people of high station as a fly is drawn to the light, assimilating their ways and views of life and establishing friendly relations with them. All the enthusiasms of childhood and youth passed without leaving much trace on him; he succumbed to sensuality, to vanity, and latterly among the highest classes to liberalism, but always within limits which his instinct unfailingly indicated to him as correct.

At school he had done things which had formerly seemed to him very horrid and made him feel disgusted with himself when he did them; but when later on he saw that such actions were done by people of good position and that they

5. A round of a card game.
6. "The phoenix of the family" (French). The word *phoenix* is used here to mean "rare bird," "prodigy."

did not regard them as wrong, he was able not exactly to regard them as right, but to forget about them entirely or not be at all troubled at remembering them.

Having graduated from the School of Law and qualified for the tenth rank of the civil service, and having received money from his father for his equipment, Ivan Ilyich ordered himself clothes at Scharmer's, the fashionable tailor, hung a medallion inscribed *respice finem*[7] on his watch-chain, took leave of his professor and the prince who was patron of the school, had a farewell dinner with his comrades at Donon's first-class restaurant, and with his new and fashionable portmanteau, linen, clothes, shaving and other toilet appliances, and a travelling rug, all purchased at the best shops, he set off for one of the provinces where, through his father's influence, he had been attached to the governor as an official for special service.

In the province Ivan Ilyich soon arranged as easy and agreeable a position for himself as he had at the School of Law. He performed his official tasks, made his career, and at the same time amused himself pleasantly and decorously. Occasionally he paid official visits to country districts, where he behaved with dignity both to his superiors and inferiors, and performed the duties entrusted to him, which related chiefly to the sectarians,[8] with an exactness and incorruptible honesty of which he could not but feel proud.

In official matters, despite his youth and taste for frivolous gaiety, he was exceedingly reserved, punctilious, and even severe; but in society he was often amusing and witty, and always good-natured, correct in his manner, and *bon enfant*, as the governor and his wife—with whom he was like one of the family—used to say of him.

In the province he had an affair with a lady who made advances to the elegant young lawyer, and there was also a milliner; and there were carousals with aides-de-camp who visited the district, and after-supper visits to a certain outlying street of doubtful reputation; and there was too some obsequiousness to his chief and even to his chief's wife, but all this was done with such a tone of good breeding that no hard names could be applied to it. It all came under the heading of the French saying: *"Il faut que jeunesse se passe."*[9] It was all done with clean hands, in clean linen, with French phrases, and above all among people of the best society and consequently with the approval of people of rank.

So Ivan Ilyich served for five years and then came a change in his official life. The new and reformed judicial institutions were introduced, and new men were needed. Ivan Ilyich became such a new man. He was offered the post of Examining Magistrate, and he accepted it though the post was in another province and obliged him to give up the connexions he had formed and to make new ones. His friends met to give him a send-off; they had a group-photograph taken and presented him with a silver cigarette-case, and he set off to his new post.

7. "Regard the end" (a Latin motto).
8. The Old Believers, a large group of Russians (about 25 million in 1900), members of a sect that originated in a break with the Orthodox Church in the 17th century; they were subject to many legal restrictions.
9. "Youth must have its fling" [translators' note].

As examining magistrate Ivan Ilyich was just as *comme il faut*[1] and decorous a man, inspiring general respect and capable of separating his official duties from his private life, as he had been when acting as an official on special service. His duties now as examining magistrate were far more interesting and attractive than before. In his former position it had been pleasant to wear an undress uniform made by Scharmer, and to pass through the crowd of petitioners and officials who were timorously awaiting an audience with the governor, and who envied him as with free and easy gait he went straight into his chief's private room to have a cup of tea and a cigarette with him. But not many people had then been directly dependent on him—only police officials and the sectarians when he went on special missions—and he liked to treat them politely, almost as comrades, as if he were letting them feel that he who had the power to crush them was treating them in this simple, friendly way. There were then but few such people. But now, as an examining magistrate, Ivan Ilyich felt that everyone without exception, even the most important and self-satisfied, was in his power, and that he need only write a few words on a sheet of paper with a certain heading, and this or that important, self-satisfied person would be brought before him in the role of an accused person or a witness, and if he did not choose to allow him to sit down, would have to stand before him and answer his questions. Ivan Ilyich never abused his power; he tried on the contrary to soften its expression, but the consciousness of it and of the possibility of softening its effect, supplied the chief interest and attraction of his office. In his work itself, especially in his examinations, he very soon acquired a method of eliminating all considerations irrelevant to the legal aspect of the case, and reducing even the most complicated case to a form in which it would be presented on paper only in its externals, completely excluding his personal opinion of the matter, while above all observing every prescribed formality. The work was new and Ivan Ilyich was one of the first men to apply the new Code of 1864.[2]

On taking up the post of examining magistrate in a new town, he made new acquaintances and connexions, placed himself on a new footing, and assumed a somewhat different tone. He took up an attitude of rather dignified aloofness towards the provincial authorities, but picked out the best circle of legal gentlemen and wealthy gentry living in the town and assumed a tone of slight dissatisfaction with the government, of moderate liberalism, and of enlightened citizenship. At the same time, without at all altering the elegance of his toilet, he ceased shaving his chin and allowed his beard to grow as it pleased.

Ivan Ilyich settled down very pleasantly in this new town. The society there, which inclined towards opposition to the governor, was friendly, his salary was larger, and he began to play *vint* [a form of bridge], which he found added not a little to the pleasure of life, for he had a capacity for cards, played good-humouredly, and calculated rapidly and astutely, so that he usually won.

After living there for two years he met his future wife, Praskovya Fëdorovna Mikhel, who was the most attractive, clever, and brilliant girl of the set in which he moved, and among other amusements and relaxations from his

---

1. Literally, "as one must" (French); proper.
2. The emancipation of the serfs in 1861 was followed by a thorough all-round reform of judicial proceedings [translators' note].

labours as examining magistrate, Ivan Ilyich established light and playful relations with her.

While he had been an official on special service he had been accustomed to dance, but now as an examining magistrate it was exceptional for him to do so. If he danced now, he did it as if to show that though he served under the reformed order of things, and had reached the fifth official rank, yet when it came to dancing he could do it better than most people. So at the end of an evening he sometimes danced with Praskovya Fëdorovna, and it was chiefly during these dances that he captivated her. She fell in love with him. Ivan Ilyich had at first no definite intention of marrying, but when the girl fell in love with him he said to himself: "Really, why shouldn't I marry?"

Praskovya Fëdorovna came of a good family, was not bad looking, and had some little property. Ivan Ilyich might have aspired to a more brilliant match, but even this was good. He had his salary, and she, he hoped, would have an equal income. She was well connected, and was a sweet, pretty, and thoroughly correct young woman. To say that Ivan Ilyich married because he fell in love with Praskovya Fëdorovna and found that she sympathized with his views of life would be as incorrect as to say that he married because his social circle approved of the match. He was swayed by both these considerations: the marriage gave him personal satisfaction, and at the same time it was considered the right thing by the most highly placed of his associates.

So Ivan Ilyich got married.

The preparations for marriage and the beginning of married life, with its conjugal caresses, the new furniture, new crockery, and new linen, were very pleasant until his wife became pregnant—so that Ivan Ilyich had begun to think that marriage would not impair the easy, agreeable, gay, and always decorous character of his life, approved of by society and regarded by himself as natural, but would even improve it. But from the first months of his wife's pregnancy, something new, unpleasant, depressing, and unseemly, and from which there was no way of escape, unexpectedly showed itself.

His wife, without any reason—*de gaieté de coeur*[3] as Ivan Ilyich expressed it to himself—began to disturb the pleasure and propriety of their life. She began to be jealous without any cause, expected him to devote his whole attention to her, found fault with everything, and made coarse and ill-mannered scenes.

At first Ivan Ilyich hoped to escape from the unpleasantness of this state of affairs by the same easy and decorous relation to life that had served him heretofore: he tried to ignore his wife's disagreeable moods, continued to live in his usual easy and pleasant way, invited friends to his house for a game of cards, and also tried going out to his club or spending his evenings with friends. But one day his wife began upbraiding him so vigorously, using such coarse words, and continued to abuse him every time he did not fulfil her demands, so resolutely and with such evident determination not to give way till he submitted—that is, till he stayed at home and was bored just as she was—that he became alarmed. He now realized that matrimony—at any rate with Praskovya Fëdorovna—was not always conducive to the pleasures and amenities of life, but on the contrary often infringed both comfort and propriety, and that he must therefore entrench himself against such infringement. And Ivan Ilyich

3. Literally, "from gaiety of heart" (French); from sheer impulsiveness.

began to seek for means of doing so. His official duties were the one thing that imposed upon Praskovya Fëdorovna, and by means of his official work and the duties attached to it he began struggling with his wife to secure his own independence.

With the birth of their child, the attempts to feed it and the various failures in doing so, and with the real and imaginary illnesses of mother and child, in which Ivan Ilyich's sympathy was demanded but about which he understood nothing, the need of securing for himself an existence outside his family life became still more imperative.

As his wife grew more irritable and exacting and Ivan Ilyich transferred the centre of gravity of his life more and more to his official work, so did he grow to like his work better and became more ambitious than before.

Very soon, within a year of his wedding, Ivan Ilyich had realized that marriage, though it may add some comforts to life, is in fact a very intricate and difficult affair towards which in order to perform one's duty, that is, to lead a decorous life approved of by society, one must adopt a definite attitude just as towards one's official duties.

And Ivan Ilyich evolved such an attitude towards married life. He only required of it those conveniences—dinner at home, housewife, and bed— which it could give him, and above all that propriety of external forms required by public opinion. For the rest he looked for light-hearted pleasure and propriety, and was very thankful when he found them, but if he met with antagonism and querulousness he at once retired into his separate fenced-off world of official duties, where he found satisfaction.

Ivan Ilyich was esteemed a good official, and after three years was made Assistant Public Prosecutor. His new duties, their importance, the possibility of indicting and imprisoning anyone he chose, the publicity his speeches received, and the success he had in all these things, made his work still more attractive.

More children came. His wife became more and more querulous and ill-tempered, but the attitude Ivan Ilyich had adopted towards his home life rendered him almost impervious to her grumbling.

After seven years' service in that town he was transferred to another province as Public Prosecutor. They moved, but were short of money and his wife did not like the place they moved to. Though the salary was higher the cost of living was greater, besides which two of their children died and family life became still more unpleasant for him.

Praskovya Fëdorovna blamed her husband for every inconvenience they encountered in their new home. Most of the conversations between husband and wife, especially as to the children's education, led to topics which recalled former disputes, and those disputes were apt to flare up again at any moment. There remained only those rare periods of amorousness which still came to them at times but did not last long. These were islets at which they anchored for a while and then again set out upon that ocean of veiled hostility which showed itself in their aloofness from one another. This aloofness might have grieved Ivan Ilyich had he considered that it ought not to exist, but he now regarded the position as normal, and even made it the goal at which he aimed in family life. His aim was to free himself more and more from those unpleasantnesses and to give them a semblance of harmlessness and propriety. He attained this by spending less and less time with his family, and when obliged to be at home he tried to safeguard his position by the presence of outsiders. The chief thing however was that he had his official duties. The whole interest of his life now centered in the official world and that interest absorbed him. The consciousness of his power, being able to ruin anybody he wished to ruin, the importance, even the external dignity of his entry into court, or meetings with his subordinates, his success with superiors and inferiors, and above all his masterly handling of cases, of which he was conscious—all this gave him pleasure and filled his life, together with chats with his colleagues, dinners, and bridge. So that on the whole Ivan Ilyich's life continued to flow as he considered it should do—pleasantly and properly.

So things continued for another seven years. His eldest daughter was already sixteen, another child had died, and only one son was left, a school-boy and a subject of dissensions. Ivan Ilyich wanted to put him in the School of Law, but to spite him Praskovya Fëdorovna entered him at the High School. The daughter had been educated at home and had turned out well: the boy did not learn badly either.

III

So Ivan Ilyich lived for seventeen years after his marriage. He was already a Public Prosecutor of long standing, and had declined several proposed transfers while awaiting a more desirable post, when an unanticipated and unpleasant occurrence quite upset the peaceful course of his life. He was expecting to be offered the post of presiding judge in a University town, but Hoppe somehow came to the front and obtained the appointment instead. Ivan Ilyich became irritable, reproached Hoppe, and quarrelled both with him and with his immediate superiors—who became colder to him and again passed him over when other appointments were made.

This was in 1880, the hardest year of Ivan Ilyich's life. It was then that it became evident on the one hand that his salary was insufficient for them to live on, and on the other that he had been forgotten, and not only this, but that what was for him the greatest and most cruel injustice appeared to others a quite ordinary occurrence. Even his father did not consider it his duty to help him. Ivan Ilyich felt himself abandoned by everyone, and that they regarded his position with a salary of 3,500 rubles as quite normal and even fortunate. He alone knew that with the consciousness of the injustices done him, with his wife's incessant nagging, and with the debts he had contracted by living beyond his means his position was far from normal.

In order to save money that summer he obtained leave of absence and went with his wife to live in the country at her brother's place.

In the country, without his work, he experienced *ennui* for the first time in his life, and not only *ennui* but intolerable depression, and he decided that it was impossible to go on living like that, and that it was necessary to take energetic measures.

Having passed a sleepless night pacing up and down the veranda, he decided to go to Petersburg and bestir himself, in order to punish those who had failed to appreciate him and to get transferred to another ministry.

Next day, despite many protests from his wife and her brother, he started for Petersburg with the sole object of obtaining a post with a salary of five thousand rubles a year. He was no longer bent on any particular department, or tendency, or kind of activity. All he now wanted was an appointment to another post with a salary of five thousand rubles, either in the administration, in the banks, with the railways, in one of the Empress Marya's Institutions,[4] or even in the customs—but it had to carry with it a salary of five thousand rubles and be in a ministry other than that in which they had failed to appreciate him.

And this quest of Ivan Ilyich's was crowned with remarkable and unexpected success. At Kursk an acquaintance of his, F. I. Ilyin, got into the first-class carriage, sat down beside Ivan Ilyich, and told him of a telegram just received by the governor of Kursk announcing that a change was about to take place in the ministry: Peter Ivanovich was to be superseded by Ivan Semënovich.

The proposed change, apart from its significance for Russia, had a special significance for Ivan Ilyich, because by bringing forward a new man, Peter Petrovich, and consequently his friend Zachar Ivanovich, it was highly favourable for Ivan Ilyich, since Zachar Ivanovich was a friend and colleague of his.

In Moscow his news was confirmed, and on reaching Petersburg Ivan Ilyich found Zachar Ivanovich and received a definite promise of an appointment in his former department of Justice.

A week later he telegraphed to his wife: "Zachar in Miller's place. I shall receive appointment on presentation of report."

Thanks to this change of personnel, Ivan Ilyich had unexpectedly obtained an appointment in his former ministry which placed him two stages above his former colleagues besides giving him five thousand rubles salary and three thousand five hundred rubles for expenses connected with his removal. All his ill humour towards his former enemies and the whole department vanished, and Ivan Ilyich was completely happy.

He returned to the country more cheerful and contented than he had been for a long time. Praskovya Fëdorovna also cheered up and a truce was arranged between them. Ivan Ilyich told of how he had been fêted by everybody in Petersburg, how all those who had been his enemies were put to shame and now fawned on him, how envious they were of his appointment, and how much everybody in Petersburg had liked him.

Praskovya Fëdorovna listened to all this and appeared to believe it. She did not contradict anything, but only made plans for their life in the town to which they were going. Ivan Ilyich saw with delight that these plans were his plans, that he and his wife agreed, and that, after a stumble, his life was regaining its due and natural character of pleasant lightheartedness and decorum.

Ivan Ilyich had come back for a short time only, for he had to take up his new duties on the 10th of September. Moreover, he needed time to settle into the new place, to move all his belongings from the province, and to buy and order many additional things: in a word, to make such arrangements as he had resolved on, which were almost exactly what Praskovya Fëdorovna too had decided on.

Now that everything had happened so fortunately, and that he and his wife were at one in their aims and moreover saw so little of one another they got on together better than they had done since the first years of marriage. Ivan Ilyich had thought of taking his family away with him at once, but the insistence of

---

4. Reference to the charitable organization founded by the Empress Marya, wife of Paul I, late in the 18th century.

his wife's brother and her sister-in-law, who had suddenly become particularly amiable and friendly to him and his family, induced him to depart alone.

So he departed, and the cheerful state of mind induced by his success and by the harmony between his wife and himself, the one intensifying the other, did not leave him. He found a delightful house, just the thing both he and his wife had dreamt of. Spacious, lofty reception rooms in the old style, a convenient and dignified study, rooms for his wife and daughter, a study for his son—it might have been specially built for them. Ivan Ilyich himself superintended the arrangements, chose the wallpapers, supplemented the furniture (preferably with antiques which he considered particularly *comme il faut*), and supervised the upholstering. Everything progressed and progressed and approached the ideal he had set himself: even when things were only half completed they exceeded his expectations. He saw what a refined and elegant character, free from vulgarity, it would all have when it was ready. On falling asleep he pictured to himself how the reception-room would look. Looking at the yet unfinished drawing-room he could see the fireplace, the screen, the what-not, the little chairs dotted here and there, the dishes and plates on the walls, and the bronzes, as they would be when everything was in place. He was pleased by the thought of how his wife and daughter, who shared his taste in this matter, would be impressed by it. They were certainly not expecting as much. He had been particularly successful in finding, and buying cheaply, antiques which gave a particularly aristocratic character to the whole place. But in his letters he intentionally understated everything in order to be able to surprise them. All this so absorbed him that his new duties—though he liked his official work— interested him less than he had expected. Sometimes he even had moments of absent-mindedness during the Court Sessions, and would consider whether he should have straight or curved cornices for his curtains. He was so interested in it all that he often did things himself, rearranging the furniture, or rehanging the curtains. Once when mounting a step-ladder to show the upholsterer, who did not understand, how he wanted the hangings draped, he made a false step and slipped, but being a strong and agile man he clung on and only knocked his side against the knob of the window frame. The bruised place was painful but the pain soon passed, and he felt particularly bright and well just then. He wrote: "I feel fifteen years younger." He thought he would have everything ready by September, but it dragged on till mid-October. But the result was charming not only in his eyes but to everyone who saw it.

In reality it was just what is usually seen in the houses of people of moderate means who want to appear rich, and therefore succeed only in resembling others like themselves: there were damasks, dark wood, plants, rugs, and dull and polished bronzes—all the things people of a certain class have in order to resemble other people of that class. His house was so like the others that it would never have been noticed, but to him it all seemed to be quite exceptional. He was very happy when he met his family at the station and brought them to the newly furnished house all lit up, where a footman in a white tie opened the door into the hall decorated with plants, and when they went on into the drawing room and the study uttering exclamations of delight. He conducted them everywhere, drank in their praises eagerly, and beamed with pleasure. At tea that evening, when Praskovya Fëdorovna among other things asked him about his fall, he laughed, and showed them how he had gone flying and had frightened the upholsterer.

"It's a good thing I'm a bit of an athlete. Another man might have been killed, but I merely knocked myself, just here; it hurts when it's touched, but it's passing off already—it's only a bruise."

So they began living in their new home—in which, as always happens, when they got thoroughly settled in they found they were just one room short—and with the increased income, which as always was just a little (some five hundred rubles) too little, but it was all very nice.

Things went particularly well at first, before everything was finally arranged and while something had still to be done: this thing bought, that thing ordered, another thing moved, and something else adjusted. Though there were some disputes between husband and wife, they were both so well satisfied and had so much to do that it all passed off without any serious quarrels. When nothing was left to arrange it became rather dull and something seemed to be lacking, but they were then making acquaintances, forming habits, and life was growing fuller.

Ivan Ilyich spent his mornings at the law court and came home to dinner, and at first he was generally in a good humour, though he occasionally became irritable just on account of his house. (Every spot on the tablecloth or the upholstery, and every broken window-blind string, irritated him. He had devoted so much trouble to arranging it all that every disturbance of it distressed him.) But on the whole his life ran its course as he believed life should do: easily, pleasantly, and decorously.

He got up at nine, drank his coffee, read the paper, and then put on his undress uniform and went to the law courts. There the harness in which he worked had already been stretched to fit him and he donned it without a hitch: petitioners, inquiries at the chancery, the chancery itself, and the sittings public and administrative. In all this the thing was to exclude everything fresh and vital, which always disturbs the regular course of official business, and to admit only official relations with people, and then only on official grounds. A man would come, for instance, wanting some information. Ivan Ilyich, as one in whose sphere the matter did not lie, would have nothing to do with him: but if the man had some business with him in his official capacity, something that could be expressed on officially stamped paper, he would do everything, positively everything he could within the limits of such relations, and in doing so would maintain the semblance of friendly human relations, that is, would observe the courtesies of life. As soon as the official relations ended, so did everything else. Ivan Ilyich possessed this capacity to separate his real life from the official side of affairs and not mix the two, in the highest degree, and by long practice and natural aptitude had brought it to such a pitch that sometimes, in the manner of a virtuoso, he would even allow himself to let the human and official relations mingle. He let himself do this just because he felt that he could at any time he chose resume the strictly official attitude again and drop the human relation. And he did it all easily, pleasantly, correctly, and even artistically. In the intervals between the sessions he smoked, drank tea, chatted a little about politics, a little about general topics, a little about cards, but most of all about official appointments. Tired, but with the feelings of a virtuoso—one of the first violins who has played his part in an orchestra with precision—he would return home to find that his wife and daughter had been out paying calls, or had a visitor, and that his son had been to school, had done his homework with his tutor, and was duly learning what is taught at High Schools. Everything was as it should be. After dinner, if they had no visitors,

Ivan Ilyich sometimes read a book that was being much discussed at the time, and in the evening settled down to work, that is, read official papers, compared the depositions of witnesses, and noted paragraphs of the Code applying to them. This was neither dull nor amusing. It was dull when he might have been playing bridge, but if no bridge was available it was at any rate better than doing nothing or sitting with his wife. Ivan Ilyich's chief pleasure was giving little dinners to which he invited men and women of good social position, and just as his drawing-room resembled all other drawing-rooms so did his enjoyable little parties resemble all other such parties.

Once they even gave a dance. Ivan Ilyich enjoyed it and everything went off well, except that it led to a violent quarrel with his wife about the cakes and sweets. Praskovya Fëdorovna had made her own plans, but Ivan Ilyich insisted on getting everything from an expensive confectioner and ordered too many cakes, and the quarrel occurred because some of those cakes were left over and the confectioner's bill came to forty-five rubles. It was a great and disagreeable quarrel. Praskovya Fëdorovna called him "a fool and an imbecile," and he clutched at his head and made angry allusions to divorce.

But the dance itself had been enjoyable. The best people were there, and Ivan Ilyich had danced with Princess Trufonova, a sister of the distinguished founder of the Society "Bear my Burden."

The pleasures connected with his work were pleasures of ambition; his social pleasures were those of vanity; but Ivan Ilyich's greatest pleasure was playing bridge. He acknowledged that whatever disagreeable incident happened in his life, the pleasure that beamed like a ray of light above everything else was to sit down to bridge with good players, not noisy partners, and of course to four-handed bridge (with five players it was annoying to have to stand out, though one pretended not to mind), to play a clever and serious game (when the cards allowed it) and then to have supper and drink a glass of wine. After a game of bridge, especially if he had won a little (to win a large sum was unpleasant), Ivan Ilyich went to bed in specially good humour.

So they lived. They formed a circle of acquaintances among the best people and were visited by people of importance and by young folk. In their views as to their acquaintances, husband, wife, and daughter were entirely agreed, and tacitly and unanimously kept at arm's length and shook off the various shabby friends and relations who, with much show of affection, gushed into the drawing-room with its Japanese plates on the walls. Soon these shabby friends ceased to obtrude themselves and only the best people remained in the Golovins' set.

Young men made up to Lisa, and Petrishchev, an examining magistrate and Dmitri Ivanovich Petrishchev's son and sole heir, began to be so attentive to her that Ivan Ilyich had already spoken to Praskovya Fëdorovna about it, and considered whether they should not arrange a party for them, or get up some private theatricals.

So they lived, and all went well, without change, and life flowed pleasantly.

IV

They were all in good health. It could not be called ill health if Ivan Ilyich sometimes said that he had a queer taste in his mouth and felt some discomfort in his left side.

But this discomfort increased and, though not exactly painful, grew into a sense of pressure in his side accompanied by ill humour. And his irritability became worse and worse and began to mar the agreeable, easy, and correct life that had established itself in the Golovin family. Quarrels between husband and wife became more and more frequent, and soon the ease and amenity disappeared and even the decorum was barely maintained. Scenes again became frequent, and very few of those islets remained on which husband and wife could meet without an explosion. Praskovya Fëdorovna now had good reason to say that her husband's temper was trying. With characteristic exaggeration she said he had always had a dreadful temper, and that it had needed all her good nature to put up with it for twenty years. It was true that now the quarrels were started by him. His bursts of temper always came just before dinner, often just as he began to eat his soup. Sometimes he noticed that a plate or dish was chipped, or the food was not right, or his son put his elbow on the table, or his daughter's hair was not done as he liked it, and for all this he blamed Praskovya Fëdorovna. At first she retorted and said disagreeable things to him, but once or twice he fell into such a rage at the beginning of dinner that she realized it was due to some physical derangement brought on by taking food, and so she restrained herself and did not answer, but only hurried to get the dinner over. She regarded this self-restraint as highly praiseworthy. Having come to the conclusion that her husband had a dreadful temper and made her life miserable, she began to feel sorry for herself, and the more she pitied herself the more she hated her husband. She began to wish he would die; yet she did not want him to die because then his salary would cease. And this irritated her against him still more. She considered herself dreadfully unhappy just because not even his death could save her, and though she concealed her exasperation, that hidden exasperation of hers increased his irritation also.

After one scene in which Ivan Ilyich had been particularly unfair and after which he had said in explanation that he certainly was irritable but that it was due to his not being well, she said that if he was ill it should be attended to, and insisted on his going to see a celebrated doctor.

He went. Everything took place as he had expected and as it always does. There was the usual waiting and the important air assumed by the doctor, with which he was so familiar (resembling that which he himself assumed in court), and the sounding and listening, and the questions which called for answers that were foregone conclusions and were evidently unnecessary, and the look of importance which implied that "if only you put yourself in our hands we will arrange everything—we know indubitably how it has to be done, always in the same way for everybody alike." It was all just as it was in the law courts. The doctor put on just the same air towards him as he himself put on towards an accused person.

The doctor said that so-and-so indicated that there was so-and-so inside the patient, but if the investigation of so-and-so did not confirm this, then he must assume that and that. If he assumed that and that, then . . . and so on. To Ivan Ilyich only one question was important: was his case serious or not? But the doctor ignored that inappropriate question. From his point of view it was not the one under consideration, the real question was to decide between a floating kidney, chronic catarrh, or appendicitis. It was not a question of Ivan

Ilyich's life or death, but one between a floating kidney and appendicitis. And that question the doctor solved brilliantly, as it seemed to Ivan Ilyich, in favour of the appendix, with the reservation that should an examination of the urine give fresh indications the matter would be reconsidered. All this was just what Ivan Ilyich had himself brilliantly accomplished a thousand times in dealing with men on trial. The doctor summed up just as brilliantly, looking over his spectacles triumphantly and even gaily at the accused. From the doctor's summing up Ivan Ilyich concluded that things were bad, but that for the doctor, and perhaps for everybody else, it was a matter of indifference, though for him it was bad. And this conclusion struck him painfully, arousing in him a great feeling of pity for himself and of bitterness towards the doctor's indifference to a matter of such importance.

He said nothing of this, but rose, placed the doctor's fee on the table, and remarked with a sigh: "We sick people probably often put inappropriate questions. But tell me, in general, is this complaint dangerous or not? . . ."

The doctor looked at him sternly over his spectacles with one eye, as if to say: "Prisoner, if you will not keep to the questions put to you, I shall be obliged to have you removed from the court."

"I have already told you what I consider necessary and proper. The analysis may show something more." And the doctor bowed.

Ivan Ilyich went out slowly, seated himself disconsolately in his sledge, and drove home. All the way home he was going over what the doctor had said, trying to translate those complicated, obscure, scientific phrases into plain language and find in them an answer to the question: "Is my condition bad? Is it very bad? Or is there as yet nothing much wrong?" And it seemed to him that the meaning of what the doctor had said was it was very bad. Everything in the streets seemed depressing. The cabmen, the houses, the passers-by, and the shops, were dismal. His ache, this dull gnawing ache that never ceased for a moment, seemed to have acquired a new and more serious significance from the doctor's dubious remarks. Ivan Ilyich now watched it with a new and oppressive feeling.

He reached home and began to tell his wife about it. She listened, but in the middle of his account his daughter came in with her hat on, ready to go out with her mother. She sat down reluctantly to listen to this tedious story, but could not stand it long, and her mother too did not hear him to the end.

"Well, I am very glad," she said. "Mind now to take your medicine regularly. Give me the prescription and I'll send Gerasim to the chemist's." And she went to get ready to go out.

While she was in the room Ivan Ilyich had hardly taken time to breathe, but he sighed deeply when she left it.

"Well," he thought, "perhaps it isn't so bad after all."

He began taking his medicine and following the doctor's directions, which had been altered after the examination of the urine. But then it happened that there was a contradiction between the indications drawn from the examination of the urine and the symptoms that showed themselves. It turned out that what was happening differed from what the doctor had told him, and that he had either forgotten, or blundered, or hidden something from him. He could not, however, be blamed for that, and Ivan Ilyich still obeyed his orders implicitly and at first derived some comfort from doing so.

From the time of his visit to the doctor, Ivan Ilyich's chief occupation was the exact fulfilment of the doctor's instructions regarding hygiene and the taking of medicine, and the observation of his pain and his excretions. His chief interests came to be people's ailments and people's health. When sickness, deaths, or recoveries were mentioned in his presence, especially when the illness resembled his own, he listened with agitation which he tried to hide, asked questions, and applied what he heard to his own case.

The pain did not grow less, but Ivan Ilyich made efforts to force himself to think that he was better. And he could do this so long as nothing agitated him. But as soon as he had any unpleasantness with his wife, any lack of success in his official work, or held bad cards at bridge, he was at once acutely sensible of his disease. He had formerly borne such mischances, hoping soon to adjust what was wrong, to master it and attain success, or make a grand slam. But now every mischance upset him and plunged him into despair. He would say to himself. "There now, just as I was beginning to get better and the medicine had begun to take effect, comes this accursed misfortune, or unpleasantness . . ." And he was furious with the mishap, or with the people who were causing the unpleasantness and killing him, for he felt that this fury was killing him but could not restrain it. One would have thought that it should have been clear to him that this exasperation with circumstances and people aggravated his illness, and that he ought therefore to ignore unpleasant occurrences. But he drew the very opposite conclusion: he said that he needed peace, and he watched for everything that might disturb it and became irritable at the slightest infringement of it. His condition was rendered worse by the fact that he read medical books and consulted doctors. The progress of his disease was so gradual that he could deceive himself when comparing one day with another— the difference was so slight. But when he consulted the doctors it seemed to him that he was getting worse, and even very rapidly. Yet despite this he was continually consulting them.

That month he went to see another celebrity, who told him almost the same as the first had done but put his questions rather differently, and the interview with this celebrity only increased Ivan Ilyich's doubts and fears. A friend of a friend of his, a very good doctor, diagnosed his illness again quite differently from the others, and though he predicted recovery, his questions and suppositions bewildered Ivan Ilyich still more and increased his doubts. A homeopathist diagnosed the disease in yet another way, and prescribed medicine which Ivan Ilyich took secretly for a week. But after a week, not feeling any improvement and having lost confidence both in the former doctor's treatment and in this one's, he became still more despondent. One day a lady acquaintance mentioned a cure effected by a wonder-working icon. Ivan Ilyich caught himself listening attentively and beginning to believe that it had occurred. This incident alarmed him. "Has my mind really weakened to such an extent?" he asked himself. "Nonsense! It's all rubbish. I mustn't give way to nervous fears but having chosen a doctor must keep strictly to his treatment. That is what I will do. Now it's all settled. I won't think about it, but will follow the treatment seriously till summer, and then we shall see. From now there must be no more of this wavering!" This was easy to say but impossible to carry out. The pain in his side oppressed him and seemed to grow worse and more incessant, while the taste in his mouth grew stranger and stranger. It seemed to him that his breath had a disgusting smell, and he was conscious of a loss of appetite and strength. There was no deceiving himself: something terrible, new, and more important than anything before in his life, was taking place within him of which he alone was aware. Those about him did not understand or would not understand it, but thought everything in the world was going on as usual. That tormented Ivan Ilyich more than anything. He saw that his household, especially his wife and daughter who were in a perfect whirl of visiting, did not understand anything of it and were annoyed that he was so depressed and so exacting, as if he were to blame for it. Though they tried to disguise it he saw that he was an obstacle in their path, and that his wife had adopted a definite line in regard to his illness and kept to it regardless of anything he said or did. Her attitude was this: "You know," she would say to her friends, "Ivan Ilyich can't do as other people do, and keep to the treatment prescribed for him. One day he'll take his drops and keep strictly to his diet and go to bed in good time, but the next day unless I watch him he'll suddenly forget his medicine, eat sturgeon—which is forbidden—and sit up playing cards till one o'clock in the morning."

"Oh, come, when was that?" Ivan Ilyich would ask in vexation. "Only once at Peter Ivanovich's."

"And yesterday with Shebek."

"Well, even if I hadn't stayed up, this pain would have kept me awake."

"Be that as it may you'll never get well like that, but will always make us wretched."

Praskovya Fëdorovna's attitude to Ivan Ilyich's illness, as she expressed it both to others and to him, was that it was his own fault and was another of the annoyances he caused her. Ivan Ilyich felt that this opinion escaped her involuntarily—but that did not make it easier for him.

At the law courts too, Ivan Ilyich noticed, or thought he noticed, a strange attitude towards himself. It sometimes seemed to him that people were watching him inquisitively as a man whose place might soon be vacant. Then again, his friends would suddenly begin to chaff him in a friendly way about his low spirits, as if the awful, horrible, and unheard-of thing that was going on within him, incessantly gnawing at him and irresistibly drawing him away, was a very agreeable subject for jests. Schwartz in particular irritated him by his jocularity, vivacity, and savoir-faire, which reminded him of what he himself had been ten years ago.

Friends came to make up a set and they sat down to cards. They dealt, bending the new cards to soften them, and he sorted the diamonds in his hand and found he had seven. His partner said "No trumps" and supported him with two diamonds. What more could be wished for? It ought to be jolly and lively. They would make a grand slam. But suddenly Ivan Ilyich was conscious of that gnawing pain, that taste in his mouth, and it seemed ridiculous that in such circumstances he should be pleased to make a grand slam.

He looked at his partner Mikhail Mikhaylovich, who rapped the table with his strong hand and instead of snatching up the tricks pushed the cards courteously and indulgently towards Ivan Ilyich that he might have the pleasure of gathering them up without the trouble of stretching out his hand for them. "Does he think I am too weak to stretch out my arm?" thought Ivan Ilyich, and forgetting what he was doing he over-trumped his partner, missing the grand slam by three tricks. And what was most awful of all was that he saw how upset Mikhail Mikhaylovich was about it but did not himself care. And it was dreadful to realize why he did not care.

They all saw that he was suffering, and said: "We can stop if you are tired. Take a rest." Lie down? No, he was not at all tired, and he finished the rubber. All were gloomy and silent. Ivan Ilyich felt that he had diffused this gloom over them and could not dispel it. They had supper and went away, and Ivan Ilyich was left alone with the consciousness that his life was poisoned and was poisoning the lives of others, and that this poison did not weaken but penetrated more and more deeply into his whole being.

With this consciousness, and with physical pain besides the terror, he must go to bed, often to lie awake the greater part of the night. Next morning he had to get up again, dress, go to the law courts, speak, and write; or if he did not go out, spend at home those twenty-four hours a day each of which was a torture. And he had to live thus all alone on the brink of an abyss, with no one who understood or pitied him.

V

So one month passed and then another. Just before the New Year his brother-in-law came to town and stayed at their house. Ivan Ilyich was at the law courts and Praskovya Fëdorovna had gone shopping. When Ivan Ilyich came home and entered his study he found his brother-in-law there—a healthy, florid man—unpacking his portmanteau himself. He raised his head on hearing Ivan Ilyich's footsteps and looked up at him for a moment without a word. That stare told Ivan everything. His brother-in-law opened his mouth to utter an exclamation of surprise but checked himself, and that action confirmed it all.

"I have changed, eh?"

"Yes, there is a change."

And after that, try as he would to get his brother-in-law to return to the subject of his looks, the latter would say nothing about it. Praskovya Fëdorovna came home and her brother went out to her. Ivan Ilyich locked the door and began to examine himself in the glass, first full face, then in profile. He took up a portrait of himself taken with his wife, and compared it with what he saw in the glass. The change in him was immense. Then he bared his arms to the elbow, looked at them, drew the sleeves down again, sat down on an ottoman, and grew blacker than night.

"No, no, this won't do!" he said to himself, and jumped up, went to the table, took up some law papers and began to read them, but could not continue. He unlocked the door and went into the reception-room. The door leading to the drawing-room was shut. He approached it on tiptoe and listened.

"No, you are exaggerating!" Praskovya Fëdorovna was saying.

"Exaggerating! Don't you see it? Why, he's a dead man! Look at his eyes—there's no light in them. But what is it that is wrong with him?"

"No one knows. Nikolaevich [that was another doctor] said something, but I don't know what. And Leshchetitsky [this was the celebrated specialist] said quite the contrary . . ."

Ivan Ilyich walked away, went to his own room, lay down and began musing: "The kidney, a floating kidney." He recalled all the doctors had told him of how it detached itself and swayed about. And by an effort of imagination he tried to catch that kidney and arrest it and support it. So little was needed for this, it seemed to him. "No, I'll go to see Peter Ivanovich again." [That was the friend whose friend was a doctor.] He rang, ordered the carriage, and got ready to go.

"Where are you going, *Jean*?"[5] asked his wife, with a specially sad and exceptionally kind look.

This exceptionally kind look irritated him. He looked morosely at her.

"I must go to see Peter Ivanovich."

He went to see Peter Ivanovich, and together they went to see his friend, the doctor. He was in, and Ivan Ilyich had a long talk with him.

Reviewing the anatomical and physiological details of what in the doctor's opinion was going on inside him, he understood it all.

There was something, a small thing, in the vermiform appendix. It might all come right. Only stimulate the energy of one organ and check the activity of another, then absorption would take place and everything would come right. He got home rather late for dinner, ate his dinner, and conversed cheerfully, but could not for a long time bring himself to go back to work in his room. At last, however, he went to his study and did what was necessary, but the consciousness that he had put something aside—an important, intimate matter which he would revert to when his work was done—never left him. When he had finished his work he remembered that this intimate matter was the thought of his vermiform appendix. But he did not give himself up to it, and went to the drawing-room for tea. There were callers there, including the examining magistrate who was a desirable match for his daughter, and they were conversing, playing the piano, and singing. Ivan Ilyich, as Praskovya Fëdorovna remarked, spent that evening more cheerfully than usual, but he never for a moment forgot that he had postponed the important matter of the appendix. At eleven o'clock he said good-night and went to his bedroom. Since his illness he had slept alone in a small room next to his study. He undressed and took up a novel by Zola,[6] but instead of reading it he fell into thought, and in his imagination that desired improvement in the vermiform appendix occurred. There was the absorption and evacuation and the reestablishment of normal activity. "Yes, that's it!" he said to himself. "One need only assist nature, that's all." He remembered his medicine, rose, took it, and lay down on his back watching for the beneficent action of the medicine and for it to lessen the pain. "I need only take it regularly and avoid all injurious influences. I am already feeling better, much better." He began touching his side: it was not painful to the touch. "There, I really don't feel it. It's much better already." He put out the light and turned on his side. . . . "The appendix is getting better, absorption is occurring." Suddenly he felt the old, familiar, dull, gnawing pain, stubborn and serious. There was the same familiar loathsome taste in his mouth. His heart sank and he felt dazed. "My God! My God!" he muttered. "Again, again! And it will never cease." And suddenly the matter presented itself in a quite different aspect. "Vermiform appendix! Kidney!" he said to himself. "It's not a question of appendix or kidney, but of life and . . . death. Yes, life was there and now it

---

5. French for Ivan (in English, John).
6. Émile Zola (1840–1902), French novelist, author of the *Rougon-Macquart* novels (*Nana*, *Germinal*, etc.). Tolstoy condemned Zola for his naturalistic theories and considered his novels crude.

is going, going and I cannot stop it. Yes. Why deceive myself? Isn't it obvious to everyone but me that I'm dying, and that it's only a question of weeks, days . . . it may happen this moment. There was light and now there is darkness. I was here and now I'm going there! Where?" A chill came over him, his breathing ceased, and he felt only the throbbing of his heart.

"When I am not, what will there be? There will be nothing. Then where shall I be when I am no more? Can this be dying? No, I don't want to!" He jumped up and tried to light the candle, felt for it with trembling hands, dropped candle and candlestick on the floor, and fell back on his pillow.

"What's the use? It makes no difference," he said to himself, staring with wide-open eyes into the darkness. "Death. Yes, death. And none of them know or wish to know it, and they have no pity for me. Now they are playing." (He heard through the door the distant sound of a song and its accompaniment.) "It's all the same to them, but they will die too! Fools! I first, and they later, but it will be the same for them. And now they are merry . . . the beasts!"

Anger choked him and he was agonizingly, unbearably miserable. "It is impossible that all men have been doomed to suffer this awful horror!" He raised himself.

"Something must be wrong. I must calm myself—must think it all over from the beginning." And he again began thinking. "Yes, the beginning of my illness: I knocked my side, but I was still quite well that day and the next. It hurt a little, then rather more. I saw the doctors, then followed despondency and anguish, more doctors, and I drew nearer to the abyss. My strength grew less and I kept coming nearer and nearer, and now I have wasted away and there is no light in my eyes. I think of the appendix—but this is death! I think of mending the appendix, and all the while here is death! Can it really be death!" Again terror seized him and he gasped for breath. He leant down and began feeling for the matches, pressing with his elbow on the stand beside the bed. It was in his way and hurt him, he grew furious with it, pressed on it still harder, and upset it. Breathless and in despair he fell on his back, expecting death to come immediately.

Meanwhile the visitors were leaving. Praskovya Fëdorovna was seeing them off. She heard something fall and came in.

"What has happened?"

"Nothing. I knocked it over accidentally."

She went out and returned with a candle. He lay there panting heavily, like a man who has run a thousand yards, and stared upwards at her with a fixed look.

"What is it, *Jean*?"

"No . . . o . . . thing. I upset it." ("Why speak of it? She won't understand," he thought.)

And in truth she did not understand. She picked up the stand, lit his candle, and hurried away to see another visitor off. When she came back he still lay on his back, looking upwards.

"What is it? Do you feel worse?"

"Yes."

She shook her head and sat down.

"Do you know, *Jean*, I think we must ask Leshchetitsky to come and see you here."

This meant calling in the famous specialist, regardless of expense. He smiled malignantly and said "No." She remained a little longer and then went up to him and kissed his forehead.

While she was kissing him he hated her from the bottom of his soul and with difficulty refrained from pushing her away.

"Good-night. Please God you'll sleep."

"Yes."

VI

Ivan Ilyich saw that he was dying, and he was in continual despair.

In the depth of his heart he knew he was dying, but not only was he not accustomed to the thought, he simply did not and could not grasp it.

The syllogism he had learned from Kiesewetter's *Logic*:[7] "Caius is a man, men are mortal, therefore Caius is mortal," had always seemed to him correct as applied to Caius, but certainly not as applied to himself. That Caius—man in the abstract—was mortal, was perfectly correct, but he was not Caius, not an abstract man, but a creature quite, quite separate from all others. He had been little Vanya, with a mamma and a papa, with Mitya and Volodya, with the toys, a coachman and a nurse, afterwards with Katenka and with all the joys, griefs, and delights of childhood, boyhood, and youth. What did Caius know of the smell of that striped leather ball Vanya had been so fond of? Had Caius kissed his mother's hand like that, and did the silk of her dress rustle so for Caius? Had he rioted like that at school when the pastry was bad? Had Caius been in love like that? Could Caius preside at a session as he did? "Caius really was mortal, and it was right for him to die; but for me, little Vanya, Ivan Ilyich, with all my thoughts and emotions, it's altogether a different matter. It cannot be that I ought to die. That would be too terrible."

Such was his feeling.

"If I had to die like Caius I should have known it was so. An inner voice would have told me so, but there was nothing of the sort in me and I and all my friends felt that our case was quite different from that of Caius. And now here it is!" he said to himself. "It can't be. It's impossible! But here it is. How is this? How is one to understand it?"

He could not understand it, and tried to drive this false, incorrect, morbid thought away and to replace it by other proper and healthy thoughts. But that thought, and not the thought only but the reality itself, seemed to come and confront him.

And to replace that thought he called up a succession of others, hoping to find in them some support. He tried to get back into the former current of thoughts that had once screened the thought of death from him. But strange to say, all that had formerly shut off, hidden, and destroyed, his consciousness of death, no longer had that effect. Ivan Ilyich now spent most of his time in attempting to re-establish that old current. He would say to himself: "I will take up my duties again—after all I used to live by them." And banishing all doubts

7. Karl Kiesewetter (1766–1819) was a German popularizer of Kant's philosophy. His *Outline of Logic According to Kantian Princi-* *ples* (1796) was widely used in Russian adaptations as a schoolbook.

he would go to the law courts, enter into conversation with his colleagues, and sit carelessly as was his wont, scanning the crowd with a thoughtful look and leaning both his emaciated arms on the arms of his oak chair; bending over as usual to a colleague and drawing his papers nearer he would interchange whispers with him, and then suddenly raising his eyes and sitting erect would pronounce certain words and open the proceedings. But suddenly in the midst of those proceedings the pain in his side, regardless of the stage the proceedings had reached, would begin its own gnawing work. Ivan Ilyich would turn his attention to it and try to drive the thought of it away, but without success. It would come and stand before him and look at him, and he would be petrified and the light would die out of his eyes, and he would again begin asking himself whether It alone was true. And his colleagues and subordinates would see with surprise and distress that he, the brilliant and subtle judge, was becoming confused and making mistakes. He would shake himself, try to pull himself together, manage somehow to bring the sitting to a close, and return home with the sorrowful consciousness that his judicial labours could not as formerly hide from him what he wanted them to hide, and could not deliver him from It. And what was worst of all was that It drew his attention to itself not in order to make him take some action but only that he should look at It, look it straight in the face: look at it without doing anything, suffer inexpressibly.

And to save himself from this condition Ivan Ilyich looked for consolations— new screens—and new screens were found and for a while seemed to save him, but then they immediately fell to pieces or rather became transparent, as It penetrated them and nothing could veil It.

In these latter days he would go into the drawing-room he had arranged— that drawing-room where he had fallen and for the sake of which (how bitterly ridiculous it seemed) he had sacrificed his life—for he knew that his illness originated with that knock. He would enter and see that something had scratched the polished table. He would look for the cause of this and find that it was the bronze ornamentation of an album, that had got bent. He would take up the expensive album which he had lovingly arranged, and feel vexed with his daughter and her friends for their untidiness—for the album was torn here and there and some of the photographs turned upside down. He would put it carefully in order and bend the ornamentation back into position. Then it would occur to him to place all those things in another corner of the room, near the plants. He would call the footman, but his daughter or wife would contradict him, and he would dispute and grow angry. But that was all right, for then he did not think about It. It was invisible.

But then, when he was moving something himself, his wife would say: "Let the servants do it. You will hurt yourself again." And suddenly It would flash through the screen and he would see it. It was just a flash, and he hoped it would disappear, but he would involuntarily pay attention to his side. "It sits there as before, gnawing just the same!" And he could no longer forget It, but could distinctly see it looking at him from behind the flowers. "What is it all for?"

"It really is so! I lost my life over that curtain as I might have done when storming a fort. Is that possible? How terrible and how stupid. It can't be true! It can't, but it is."

He would go to his study, lie down, and again be alone with It: face to face with It. And nothing could be done with It except to look at it and shudder.

VII

How it happened it is impossible to say because it came about step by step, unnoticed, but in the third month of Ivan Ilyich's illness, his wife, his daughter, his son, his acquaintances, the doctors, the servants, and above all he himself, were aware that the whole interest he had for other people was whether he would soon vacate his place, and at last release the living from the discomfort caused by his presence and be himself released from his sufferings.

He slept less and less. He was given opium and hypodermic injections of morphine, but this did not relieve him. The dull depression he experienced in a somnolent condition at first gave him a little relief, but only as something new; afterwards it became as distressing as the pain itself or even more so.

Special foods were prepared for him by the doctors' orders, but all those foods became increasingly distasteful and disgusting to him.

For his excretions also special arrangements had to be made, and this was a torment to him every time—a torment from the uncleanliness, the unseemliness, and the smell, and from knowing that another person had to take part in it.

But just through this most unpleasant matter, Ivan Ilyich obtained comfort. Gerasim, the butler's young assistant, always came in to carry the things out. Gerasim was a clean, fresh peasant lad, grown stout on town food and always cheerful and bright. At first the sight of him, in his clean Russian peasant costume, engaged on that disgusting task embarrassed Ivan Ilyich.

Once when he got up from the commode too weak to draw up his trousers, he dropped into a soft armchair and looked with horror at his bare, enfeebled thighs with the muscles so sharply marked on them.

Gerasim with a firm light tread, his heavy boots emitting a pleasant smell of tar and fresh winter air, came in wearing a clean Hessian apron, the sleeves of his print shirt tucked up over his strong bare young arms; and refraining from looking at his sick master out of consideration for his feelings, and restraining the joy of life that beamed from his face, he went up to the commode.

"Gerasim!" said Ivan Ilyich in a weak voice.

Gerasim started, evidently afraid he might have committed some blunder, and with a rapid movement turned his fresh, kind, simple young face which just showed the first downy sign of a beard.

"Yes, sir?"

"That must be very unpleasant for you. You must forgive me. I am helpless."

"Oh, why, sir," and Gerasim's eyes beamed and he showed his glistening white teeth, "what's a little trouble? It's a case of illness with you, sir."

And his deft strong hands did their accustomed task, and he went out of the room stepping lightly. Five minutes later he as lightly returned.

Ivan Ilyich was still sitting in the same position in the armchair.

"Gerasim," he said when the latter had replaced the freshly-washed utensil. "Please come here and help me." Gerasim went up to him. "Lift me up. It is hard for me to get up, and I have sent Dmitri away."

Gerasim went up to him, grasped his master with his strong arms deftly but gently, in the same way that he stepped—lifted him, supported him with one hand, and with the other drew up his trousers and would have set him down again, but Ivan Ilyich asked to be led to the sofa. Gerasim, without an effort and without apparent pressure, led him, almost lifting him, to the sofa and placed him on it.

"Thank you. How easily and well you do it all!"

Gerasim smiled again and turned to leave the room. But Ivan Ilyich felt his presence such a comfort that he did not want to let him go.

"One thing more, please move up that chair. No, the other one—under my feet. It is easier for me when my feet are raised."

Gerasim brought the chair, set it down gently in place, and raised Ivan Ilyich's legs on to it. It seemed to Ivan Ilyich that he felt better while Gerasim was holding up his legs.

"It's better when my legs are higher," he said. "Place that cushion under them."

Gerasim did so. He again lifted the legs and placed them, and again Ivan Ilyich felt better while Gerasim held his legs. When he set them down Ivan Ilyich fancied he felt worse.

"Gerasim," he said. "Are you busy now?"

"Not at all, sir," said Gerasim, who had learnt from the townsfolk how to speak to gentlefolk.

"What have you still to do?"

"What have I to do? I've done everything except chopping the logs for tomorrow."

"Then hold my legs up a bit higher, can you?"

"Of course I can. Why not?" And Gerasim raised his master's legs higher and Ivan Ilyich thought that in that position he did not feel any pain at all.

"And how about the logs?"

"Don't trouble about that, sir. There's plenty of time."

Ivan Ilyich told Gerasim to sit down and hold his legs, and began to talk to him. And strange to say it seemed to him that he felt better while Gerasim held his legs up.

After that Ivan Ilyich would sometimes call Gerasim and get him to hold his legs on his shoulders, and he liked talking to him. Gerasim did it all easily, willingly, simply, and with a good nature that touched Ivan Ilyich. Health, strength, and vitality in other people were offensive to him, but Gerasim's strength and vitality did not mortify but soothed him.

What tormented Ivan Ilyich most was the deception, the lie, which for some reason they all accepted, that he was not dying but was simply ill, and that he only need keep quiet and undergo a treatment and then something very good would result. He however knew that do what they would nothing would come of it, only still more agonizing suffering and death. This deception tortured him—their not wishing to admit what they all knew and what he knew, but wanting to lie to him concerning his terrible condition, and wishing and forcing him to participate in that lie. Those lies—lies enacted over him on the eve of his death and destined to degrade this awful, solemn act to the level of their visitings, their curtains, their sturgeon for dinner—were a terrible agony for Ivan Ilyich. And strangely enough, many times when they were going through their antics over him he had been within a hairbreadth of calling out to them: "Stop lying! You know and I know that I am dying. Then at least stop lying about it!" But he had never had the spirit to do it. The awful, terrible act of his dying was, he could see, reduced by those about him to the level of a casual, unpleasant, and almost indecorous incident (as if someone entered a drawing-room diffusing an unpleasant odour) and this was done by that very decorum which he had served all his life long. He saw that no one felt for him, because no one even wished to grasp his position. Only Gerasim recognized and pitied him. And so Ivan Ilyich felt at ease only with him. He felt comforted when Gerasim supported his legs (sometimes all night long) and refused to go to bed, saying: "Don't you worry, Ivan Ilyich. I'll get sleep enough later on," or when he suddenly became familiar and exclaimed: "If you weren't sick it would be another matter, but as it is, why should I grudge a little trouble?" Gerasim alone did not lie; everything showed that he alone understood the facts of the case and did not consider it necessary to disguise them, but simply felt sorry for his emaciated and enfeebled master. Once when Ivan Ilyich was sending him away he even said straight out: "We shall all of us die, so why should I grudge a little trouble?"—expressing the fact that he did not think his work burdensome, because he was doing it for a dying man and hoped someone would do the same for him when his time came.

Apart from this lying, or because of it, what most tormented Ivan Ilyich was that no one pitied him as he wished to be pitied. At certain moments after prolonged suffering he wished most of all (though he would have been ashamed to confess it) for someone to pity him as a sick child is pitied. He longed to be petted and comforted. He knew he was an important functionary, that he had a beard turning grey, and that therefore what he longed for was impossible, but still he longed for it. And in Gerasim's attitude towards him there was something akin to what he wished for, and so that attitude comforted him. Ivan Ilyich wanted to weep, wanted to be petted and cried over, and then his colleague Shebek would come, and instead of weeping and being petted, Ivan Ilyich would assume a serious, severe, and profound air, and by force of habit would express his opinion on a decision of the Court of Appeal and would stubbornly insist on that view. This falsity around him and within him did more than anything else to poison his last days.

VIII

It was morning. He knew it was morning because Gerasim had gone, and Peter the footman had come and put out the candles, drawn back one of the curtains, and begun quietly to tidy up. Whether it was morning or evening, Friday or Sunday, made no difference, it was all just the same: the gnawing, unmitigated, agonizing pain, never ceasing for an instant, the consciousness of life inexorably waning but not yet extinguished, the approach of that ever dreaded and hateful Death which was the only reality, and always the same falsity. What were days, weeks, hours, in such a case?

"Will you have some tea, sir?"

"He wants things to be regular, and wishes the gentlefolk to drink tea in the morning," thought Ivan Ilyich, and only said "No."

"Wouldn't you like to move onto the sofa, sir?"

"He wants to tidy up the room, and I'm in the way. I am uncleanliness and disorder," he thought, and said only:

"No, leave me alone."

The man went on bustling about. Ivan Ilyich stretched out his hand. Peter came up, ready to help.

"What is it, sir?"

"My watch."

Peter took the watch which was close at hand and gave it to his master.

"Half-past eight. Are they up?"

"No sir, except Vladimir Ivanich" (the son) "who has gone to school. Praskovya Fëdorovna ordered me to wake her if you asked for her. Shall I do so?"

"No, there's no need to." "Perhaps I'd better have some tea," he thought, and added aloud: "Yes, bring me some tea."

Peter went to the door, but Ivan Ilyich dreaded being left alone. "How can I keep him here? Oh yes, my medicine." "Peter, give me my medicine." "Why not? Perhaps it may still do me some good." He took a spoonful and swallowed it. "No, it won't help. It's all tomfoolery, all deception," he decided as soon as he became aware of the familiar, sickly, hopeless taste. "No, I can't believe in it any longer. But the pain, why this pain? If it would only cease just for a moment!" And he moaned. Peter turned towards him. "It's all right. Go and fetch me some tea."

Peter went out. Left alone Ivan Ilyich groaned not so much with pain, terrible though that was, as from mental anguish. Always and forever the same, always these endless days and nights. If only it would come quicker! If only *what* would come quicker? Death, darkness? . . . No, no! Anything rather than death!

When Peter returned with the tea on a tray, Ivan Ilyich stared at him for a time in perplexity, not realizing who and what he was. Peter was disconcerted by that look and his embarrassment brought Ivan Ilyich to himself.

"Oh, tea! All right, put it down. Only help me to wash and put on a clean shirt."

And Ivan Ilyich began to wash. With pauses for rest, he washed his hands and then his face, cleaned his teeth, brushed his hair, and looked in the glass. He was terrified by what he saw, especially by the limp way in which his hair clung to his pallid forehead.

While his shirt was being changed he knew that he would be still more frightened at the sight of his body, so he avoided looking at it. Finally he was ready. He drew on a dressing-gown, wrapped himself in a plaid, and sat down in the armchair to take his tea. For a moment he felt refreshed, but as soon as he began to drink the tea he was again aware of the same taste, and the pain also returned. He finished it with an effort, and then lay down stretching out his legs, and dismissed Peter.

Always the same. Now a spark of hope flashes up, then a sea of despair rages, and always pain; always pain, always despair, and always the same. When alone he had a dreadful and distressing desire to call someone, but he knew beforehand that with others present it would be still worse. "Another dose of morphine—to lose consciousness. I will tell him, the doctor, that he must think of something else. It's impossible, impossible, to go on like this."

An hour and another pass like that. But now there is a ring at the door bell. Perhaps it's the doctor? It is. He comes in fresh, hearty, plump, and cheerful, with that look on his face that seems to say: "There now, you're in a panic about something, but we'll arrange it all for you directly!" The doctor knows this expression is out of place here, but he has put it on once for all and can't take it off—like a man who has put on a frock-coat in the morning to pay a round of calls.

The doctor rubs his hands vigorously and reassuringly.

"Brr! How cold it is! There's such a sharp frost; just let me warm myself!" he says, as if it were only a matter of waiting till he was warm, and then he would put everything right.

"Well now, how are you?"

Ivan Ilyich feels that the doctor would like to say: "Well, how are our affairs?" but that even he feels that this would not do, and says instead: "What sort of a night have you had?"

Ivan Ilyich looks at him as much as to say: "Are you really never ashamed of lying?" But the doctor does not wish to understand this question, and Ivan Ilyich says: "Just as terrible as ever. The pain never leaves me and never subsides. If only something . . ."

"Yes, you sick people are always like that. . . . There, now I think I'm warm enough. Even Praskovya Fëdorovna, who is so particular, could find no fault with my temperature. Well, now I can say good-morning," and the doctor presses his patient's hand.

Then, dropping his former playfulness, he begins with a most serious face to examine the patient, feeling his pulse and taking his temperature, and then begins the sounding and auscultation.

Ivan Ilyich knows quite well and definitely that all this is nonsense and pure deception, but when the doctor, getting down on his knee, leans over him, putting his ear first higher then lower, and performs various gymnastic movements over him with a significant expression on his face, Ivan Ilyich submits to it all as he used to submit to the speeches of the lawyers, though he knew very well that they were all lying and why they were lying.

The doctor, kneeling on the sofa, is still sounding him when Praskovya Fëdorovna's silk dress rustles at the door and she is heard scolding Peter for not having let her know of the doctor's arrival.

She comes in, kisses her husband, and at once proceeds to prove that she has been up a long time already, and only owing to a misunderstanding failed to be there when the doctor arrived.

Ivan Ilyich looks at her, scans her all over, sets against her the whiteness and plumpness and cleanness of her hands and neck, the gloss of her hair, and the sparkle of her vivacious eyes. He hates her with his whole soul. And the thrill of hatred he feels for her makes him suffer from her touch.

Her attitude towards him and his disease is still the same. Just as the doctor had adopted a certain relation to his patient which he could not abandon, so had she formed one towards him—that he was not doing something he ought to do and was himself to blame, and that she reproached him lovingly for this—and she could not now change that attitude.

"You see he doesn't listen to me and doesn't take his medicine at the proper time. And above all he lies in a position that is no doubt bad for him—with his legs up."

She described how he made Gerasim hold his legs up.

The doctor smiled with a contemptuous affability that said: "What's to be done? These sick people do have foolish fancies of that kind, but we must forgive them."

When the examination was over the doctor looked at his watch, and then Praskovya Fëdorovna announced to Ivan Ilyich that it was of course as he pleased, but she had sent to-day for a celebrated specialist who would examine him and have a consultation with Michael Danilovich (their regular doctor).

"Please don't raise any objections. I am doing this for my own sake," she said ironically, letting it be felt that she was doing it all for his sake and only said this to leave him no right to refuse. He remained silent, knitting his brows. He felt that he was so surrounded and involved in a mesh of falsity that it was hard to unravel anything.

Everything she did for him was entirely for her own sake, and she told him she was doing for herself what she actually was doing for herself, as if that was so incredible that he must understand the opposite.

At half-past eleven the celebrated specialist arrived. Again the sounding began and the significant conversations in his presence and in other rooms, about the kidneys and the appendix, and the questions and answers, with such an air of importance that again, instead of the real question of life and death which now alone confronted him, the question arose of the kidney and the appendix which were not behaving as they ought to and would now be attacked by Michael Danilovich and the specialist and forced to amend their ways.

The celebrated specialist took leave of him with a serious though not hopeless look, and in reply to the timid question in Ivan Ilyich, with eyes glistening with fear and hope, put to him as to whether there was a chance of recovery, said that he could not vouch for it but there was a possibility. The look of hope with which Ivan Ilyich watched the doctor out was so pathetic that Praskovya Fëdorovna, seeing it, even wept as she left the room to hand the doctor his fee.

The gleam of hope kindled by the doctor's encouragement did not last long. The same room, the same pictures, curtains, wallpaper, medicine bottles, were all there, and the same aching suffering body, and Ivan Ilyich began to moan. They gave him a subcutaneous injection and he sank into oblivion.

It was twilight when he came to. They brought him his dinner and he swallowed some beef tea with difficulty, and then everything was the same again and night was coming on.

After dinner, at seven o'clock, Praskovya Fëdorovna came into the room in evening dress, her full bosom pushed up by her corset, and with traces of powder on her face. She had reminded him in the morning that they were going to the theatre. Sarah Bernhardt[8] was visiting the town and they had a box, which he had insisted on their taking. Now he had forgotten about it and her toilet offended him, but he concealed his vexation when he remembered that he had himself insisted on their securing a box and going because it would be an instructive and aesthetic pleasure for the children.

Praskovya Fëdorovna came in, self-satisfied but yet with a rather guilty air. She sat down and asked how he was, but, as he saw, only for the sake of asking and not in order to learn about it, knowing that there was nothing to learn— and then went on to what she really wanted to say: that she would not on any account have gone but that the box had been taken and Helen and their daughter were going, as well as Petrishchev (the examining magistrate, their daughter's fiancé) and that it was out of the question to let them go alone; but

---

8. Stage name of French actress Rosine Bernard (1844–1923), famed for romantic and tragic roles.

that she would have much preferred to sit with him for a while; and he must be sure to follow the doctor's orders while she was away.

"Oh, and Fëdor Petrovich" (the fiancé) "would like to come in. May he? And Lisa?"

"All right."

Their daughter came in in full evening dress, her fresh young flesh exposed (making a show of that very flesh which in his own case caused so much suffering), strong, healthy, evidently in love, and impatient with illness, suffering, and death, because they interfered with her happiness.

Fëdor Petrovich came in too, in evening dress, his hair curled à la Capoul, a tight stiff collar round his long sinewy neck, an enormous white shirt-front and narrow black trousers tightly stretched over his strong thighs. He had one white glove tightly drawn on, and was holding his opera hat in his hand.

Following him the schoolboy crept in unnoticed, in a new uniform, poor little fellow, and wearing gloves. Terribly dark shadows showed under his eyes, the meaning of which Ivan Ilyich knew well.

His son had always seemed pathetic to him, and now it was dreadful to see the boy's frightened look of pity. It seemed to Ivan Ilyich that Vasya was the only one besides Gerasim who understood and pitied him.

They all sat down and again asked how he was. A silence followed. Lisa asked her mother about the opera-glasses, and there was an altercation between mother and daughter as to who had taken them and where they had been put. This occasioned some unpleasantness.

Fëdor Petrovich inquired of Ivan Ilyich whether he had ever seen Sarah Bernhardt. Ivan Ilyich did not at first catch the question, but then replied: "No, have you seen her before?"

"Yes, in *Adrienne Lecouvreur*."[9]

Praskovya Fëdorovna mentioned some rôles in which Sarah Bernhardt was particularly good. Her daughter disagreed. Conversation sprang up as to the elegance and realism of her acting—the sort of conversation that is always repeated and is always the same.

In the midst of the conversation Fëdor Petrovich glanced at Ivan Ilyich and became silent. The others also looked at him and grew silent. Ivan Ilyich was staring with glittering eyes straight before him, evidently indignant with them. This had to be rectified, but it was impossible to do so. The silence had to be broken, but for a time no one dared to break it and they all became afraid that the conventional deception would suddenly become obvious and the truth become plain to all. Lisa was the first to pluck up courage and break that silence, but by trying to hide what everybody was feeling, she betrayed it.

"Well, if we are going it's time to start," she said, looking at her watch, a present from her father, and with a faint and significant smile at Fëdor Petrovich relating to something known only to them. She got up with a rustle of her dress.

They all rose, said good-night, and went away.

When they had gone it seemed to Ivan Ilyich that he felt better; the falsity had gone with them. But the pain remained—that same pain and that same

9. A play (1849) by the French dramatist Eugène Scribe (1791–1861), in which the heroine was a famous actress of the 18th century. Tolstoy considered Scribe, who wrote over four hundred plays, a shoddy, commercial playwright.

fear that made everything monotonously alike, nothing harder and nothing easier. Everything was worse.

Again minute followed minute and hour followed hour. Everything remained the same and there was no cessation. And the inevitable end of it all became more and more terrible.

"Yes, send Gerasim here," he replied to a question Peter asked.

IX

His wife returned late at night. She came in on tiptoe, but he heard her, opened his eyes, and made haste to close them again. She wished to send Gerasim away and to sit with him herself, but he opened his eyes and said: "No, go away."

"Are you in great pain?"

"Always the same."

"Take some opium."

He agreed and took some. She went away.

Till about three in the morning he was in a state of stupefied misery. It seemed to him that he and his pain were being thrust into a narrow, deep black sack, but though they were pushed further and further in they could not be pushed to the bottom. And this, terrible enough in itself, was accompanied by suffering. He was frightened yet wanted to fall through the sack, he struggled but yet co-operated. And suddenly he broke through, fell, and regained consciousness. Gerasim was sitting at the foot of the bed dozing quietly and patiently, while he himself lay with his emaciated stockinged legs resting on Gerasim's shoulders; the same shaded candle was there and the same unceasing pain.

"Go away, Gerasim," he whispered.

"It's all right, sir. I'll stay a while."

"No. Go away."

He removed his legs from Gerasim's shoulders, turned sideways onto his arm, and felt sorry for himself. He only waited till Gerasim had gone into the next room and then restrained himself no longer but wept like a child. He wept on account of his helplessness, his terrible loneliness, the cruelty of man, the cruelty of God, and the absence of God.

"Why hast Thou done all this? Why hast Thou brought me here? Why, dost Thou torment me so terribly?"

He did not expect an answer and yet wept because there was no answer and could be none. The pain again grew more acute, but he did not stir and did not call. He said to himself: "Go on! Strike me! But what is it for? What have I done to Thee? What is it for?"

Then he grew quiet and not only ceased weeping but even held his breath and became all attention. It was as though he were listening not to an audible voice but to a voice of his soul, to the current of thoughts arising within him.

"What is it you want?" was the first clear conception capable of expression in words, that he heard.

"What do you want? What do you want?" he repeated to himself.

"What do I want? To live and not to suffer," he answered.

And again he listened with such concentrated attention that even his pain did not distract him.

"To live? How?" asked his inner voice.

"Why, to live as I used to—well and pleasantly."

"As you lived before, well and pleasantly?" the voice repeated.

And in imagination he began to recall the moments of his pleasant life. But strange to say none of those best moments of his pleasant life now seemed at all what they had then seemed—none of them except the first recollections of childhood. There, in childhood, there had been something really pleasant with which it would be possible to live if it could return. But the child who had experienced that happiness existed no longer, it was like a reminiscence of somebody else.

As soon as the period began which had produced the present Ivan Ilyich, all that had then seemed joys now melted before his sight and turned into something trivial and often nasty.

And the further he departed from childhood and the nearer he came to the present the more worthless and doubtful were the joys. This began with the School of Law. A little that was really good was still found there—there was light-heartedness, friendship, and hope. But in the upper classes there had already been fewer of such good moments. Then during the first years of his official career, when he was in the service of the Governor, some pleasant moments again occurred: they were the memories of love for a woman. Then all became confused and there was still less of what was good; later on again there was still less that was good, and the further he went the less there was. His marriage, a mere accident, then the disenchantment that followed it, his wife's bad breath and the sensuality and hypocrisy: then that deadly official life and those preoccupations about money, a year of it, and two, and ten, and twenty, and always the same thing. And the longer it lasted the more deadly it became. "It is as if I had been going downhill while I imagined I was going up. And that is really what it was. I was going up in public opinion, but to the same extent life was ebbing away from me. And now it is all done and there is only death."

"Then what does it mean? Why? It can't be that life is so senseless and horrible. But if it really has been so horrible and senseless, why must I die and die in agony? There is something wrong!"

"Maybe I did not live as I ought to have done," it suddenly occurred to him. "But how could that be, when I did everything properly?" he replied, and immediately dismissed from his mind this, the sole solution of all the riddles of life and death, as something quite impossible.

"Then what do you want now? To live? Live how? Live as you lived in the law courts when the usher proclaimed 'The judge is coming!' The judge is coming, the judge!" he repeated to himself. "Here he is, the judge. But I am not guilty!" he exclaimed angrily. "What is it for?" And he ceased crying, but turning his face to the wall continued to ponder on the same question: Why, and for what purpose, is there all this horror? But however much he pondered he found no answer. And whenever the thought occurred to him, as it often did, that it all resulted from his not having lived as he ought to have done, he at once recalled the correctness of his whole life, and dismissed so strange an idea.

X

Another fortnight passed. Ivan Ilyich now no longer left his sofa. He would not lie in bed but lay on the sofa, facing the wall nearly all the time. He suffered ever the same unceasing agonies and in his loneliness pondered always on the same insoluble question: "What is this? Can it be that it is Death?" And the inner voice answered: "Yes, it is Death."

"Why these sufferings?" And the voice answered, "For no reason—they just are so." Beyond and besides this there was nothing.

From the very beginning of his illness, ever since he had first been to see the doctor, Ivan Ilyich's life had been divided between two contrary and alternating moods: now it was despair and the expectation of this uncomprehended and terrible death, and now hope and an intently interested observation of the functioning of his organs. Now before his eyes there was only a kidney or an intestine that temporarily evaded its duty, and now only that incomprehensible and dreadful death from which it was impossible to escape.

These two states of mind had alternated from the very beginning of his illness, but the further it progressed the more doubtful and fantastic became the conception of the kidney, and the more real the sense of impending death.

He had but to call to mind what he had been three months before and what he was now, to call to mind with what regularity he had been going downhill, for every possibility of hope to be shattered.

Latterly during that loneliness in which he found himself as he lay facing the back of the sofa, a loneliness in the midst of a populous town and surrounded by numerous acquaintances and relations but that yet could not have been more complete anywhere—either at the bottom of the sea or under the earth—during that terrible loneliness Ivan Ilyich had lived only in memories of the past. Pictures of his past rose before him one after another. They always began with what was nearest in time and then went back to what was most remote—to his childhood—and rested there. If he thought of the stewed prunes that had been offered him that day, his mind went back to the raw shrivelled French plums of his childhood, their peculiar flavour and the flow of saliva when he sucked their stones, and along with the memory of that taste came a whole series of memories of those days: his nurse, his brother, and their toys. "No, I mustn't think of that. . . . It is too painful," Ivan Ilyich said to himself, and brought himself back to the present—to the button on the back of the sofa and the creases in its morocco. "Morocco is expensive, but it does not wear well: there had been a quarrel about it. It was a different kind of quarrel and a different kind of morocco that time when we tore father's portfolio and were punished, and mamma brought us some tarts. . . ." And again his thoughts dwelt on his childhood, and again it was painful and he tried to banish them and fix his mind on something else.

Then again together with that chain of memories another series passed through his mind—of how his illness had progressed and grown worse. There also the further back he looked the more life there had been. There had been more of what was good in life and more of life itself. The two merged together. "Just as the pain went on getting worse and worse, so my life grew worse and worse," he thought. "There is one bright spot there at the back, at the beginning of life, and afterwards all becomes blacker and blacker and proceeds more and more rapidly—in inverse ratio to the square of the distance from death," thought Ivan Ilyich. And the example of a stone falling downwards with increasing velocity entered his mind. Life, a series of increasing sufferings, flies further and further towards its end—the most terrible suffering. "I am flying. . . ." He shuddered, shifted himself, and tried to resist, but was already aware that resistance was impossible, and again with eyes weary of gazing but unable to cease seeing what was before them, he stared at the back of the sofa and waited—awaiting that dreadful fall and shock and destruction.

"Resistance is impossible!" he said to himself. "If I could only understand what it is all for! But that too is impossible. An explanation would be possible if it could be said that I have not lived as I ought to. But it is impossible to say that," and he remembered all the legality, correctitude, and propriety of his life. "That at any rate can certainly not be admitted," he thought, and his lips smiled ironically as if someone could see that smile and be taken in by it. "There is no explanation! Agony, death. . . . What for?"

XI

Another two weeks went by in this way and during that fortnight an event occurred that Ivan Ilyich and his wife had desired. Petrishchev formally proposed. It happened in the evening. The next day Praskovya Fëdorovna came into her husband's room considering how best to inform him of it, but that very night there had been a fresh change for the worse in his condition. She found him still lying on the sofa but in a different position. He lay on his back, groaning and staring fixedly straight in front of him.

She began to remind him of his medicines, but he turned his eyes towards her with such a look that she did not finish what she was saying; so great an animosity, to her in particular, did that look express.

"For Christ's sake let me die in peace!" he said.

She would have gone away, but just then their daughter came in and went up to say good morning. He looked at her as he had done at his wife, and in reply to her inquiry about his health said dryly that he would soon free them all of himself. They were both silent and after sitting with him for a while went away.

"Is it our fault?" Lisa said to her mother. "It's as if we were to blame! I am sorry for papa, but why should we be tortured?"

The doctor came at his usual time. Ivan Ilyich answered "Yes" and "No," never taking his angry eyes from him, and at last said: "You know you can do nothing for me, so leave me alone."

"We can ease your sufferings."

"You can't even do that. Let me be."

The doctor went into the drawing-room and told Praskovya Fëdorovna that the case was very serious and that the only resource left was opium to allay her husband's sufferings, which must be terrible.

It was true, as the doctor said, that Ivan Ilyich's physical sufferings were terrible, but worse than the physical sufferings were his mental sufferings which were his chief torture.

His mental sufferings were due to the fact that that night, as he looked at Gerasim's sleepy, good-natured face with its prominent cheek-bones, the question suddenly occurred to him: "What if my whole life has really been wrong?"

It occurred to him that what had appeared perfectly impossible before, namely that he had not spent his life as he should have done, might after all be true. It occurred to him that his scarcely perceptible attempts to struggle against what was considered good by the most highly placed people, those scarcely noticeable impulses which he had immediately suppressed, might have been the real thing, and all the rest false. And his professional duties and the whole arrangement of his life and of his family, and all his social and official interests, might all have been false. He tried to defend all those things to himself and suddenly felt the weakness of what he was defending. There was nothing to defend.

"But if that is so," he said to himself, "and I am leaving this life with the consciousness that I have lost all that was given me and it is impossible to rectify it—what then?"

He lay on his back and began to pass his life in review in quite a new way. In the morning when he saw first his footman, then his wife, then his daughter, and then the doctor, their every word and movement confirmed to him the awful truth that had been revealed to him during the night. In them he saw himself—all that for which he had lived—and saw clearly that it was not real at all, but a terrible and huge deception which had hidden both life and death. This consciousness intensified his physical suffering tenfold. He groaned and tossed about, and pulled at his clothing which choked and stifled him. And he hated them on that account.

He was given a large dose of opium and became unconscious, but at noon his sufferings began again. He drove everybody away and tossed from side to side.

His wife came to him and said:

"*Jean*, my dear, do this for me. It can't do any harm and often helps. Healthy people often do it."

He opened his eyes wide.

"What? Take communion? Why? It's unnecessary! However . . ."

She began to cry.

"Yes, do, my dear. I'll send for our priest. He is such a nice man."

"All right. Very well," he muttered.

When the priest came and heard his confession, Ivan Ilyich was softened and seemed to feel a relief from his doubts and consequently from his sufferings, and for a moment there came a ray of hope. He again began to think of the vermiform appendix and the possibility of correcting it. He received the sacrament with tears in his eyes.

When they laid him down again afterwards he felt a moment's ease, and the hope that he might live awoke in him again. He began to think of the operation that had been suggested to him. "To live! I want to live!" he said to himself.

His wife came in to congratulate him after his communion, and when uttering the usual conventional words she added:

"You feel better, don't you?"

Without looking at her he said "Yes."

Her dress, her figure, the expression of her face, the tone of her voice, all revealed the same thing. "This is wrong, it is not as it should be. All you have lived for and still live for is falsehood and deception, hiding life and death from you." And as soon as he admitted that thought, his hatred and his agonizing physical suffering again sprang up, and with that suffering a consciousness of the unavoidable, approaching end. And to this was added a new sensation of grinding shooting pain and a feeling of suffocation.

The expression of his face when he uttered that "yes" was dreadful. Having uttered it, he looked her straight in the eyes, turned on his face with a rapidity extraordinary in his weak state and shouted:

"Go away! Go away and leave me alone!"

XII

From that moment the screaming began that continued for three days, and was so terrible that one could not hear it through two closed doors without horror. At the moment he answered his wife he realized that he was lost, that there was no return, that the end had come, the very end, and his doubts were still unsolved and remained doubts.

"Oh! Oh! Oh!" he cried in various intonations. He had begun by screaming "I won't!" and continued screaming on the letter "o."

For three whole days, during which time did not exist for him, he struggled in that black sack into which he was being thrust by an invisible, resistless force. He struggled as a man condemned to death struggles in the hands of the executioner, knowing that he cannot save himself. And every moment he felt that despite all his efforts he was drawing nearer and nearer to what terrified him. He felt that his agony was due to his being thrust into that black hole and still more to his not being able to get right into it. He was hindered from getting into it by his conviction that his life had been a good one. That very justification of his life held him fast and prevented his moving forward, and it caused him most torment of all.

Suddenly some force struck him in the chest and side, making it still harder to breathe, and he fell through the hole and there at the bottom was a light. What had happened to him was like the sensation one sometimes experiences in a railway carriage when one thinks one is going backwards while one is really going forwards and suddenly becomes aware of the real direction.

"Yes, it was all not the right thing," he said to himself, "but that's no matter. It can be done. But what *is* the right thing?" he asked himself, and suddenly grew quiet.

This occurred at the end of the third day, two hours before his death. Just then his schoolboy son had crept softly in and gone up to the bedside. The dying man was still screaming desperately and waving his arms. His hand fell on the boy's head, and the boy caught it, pressed it to his lips, and began to cry.

At that very moment Ivan Ilyich fell through and caught sight of the light, and it was revealed to him that though his life had not been what it should have been, this could still be rectified. He asked himself, "What *is* the right thing?" and grew still, listening. Then he felt that someone was kissing his hand. He opened his eyes, looked at his son, and felt sorry for him. His wife came up to him and he glanced at her. She was gazing at him open-mouthed, with undried tears on her nose and cheek and a despairing look on her face. He felt sorry for her too.

"Yes, I am making them wretched," he thought. "They are sorry, but it will be better for them when I die." He wished to say this but had not the strength to utter it. "Besides, why speak? I must act," he thought. With a look at his wife he indicated his son and said: "Take him away . . . sorry for him . . . sorry for you too. . . ." He tried to add, "forgive me," but said "forgo" and waved his hand, knowing that He whose understanding mattered would understand.

And suddenly it grew clear to him that what had been oppressing him and would not leave him was all dropping away at once from two sides, from ten sides, and from all sides. He was sorry for them, he must act so as not to hurt them: release them and free himself from these sufferings. "How good and how simple!" he thought. "And the pain?" he asked himself. "What has become of it? Where are you, pain?"

He turned his attention to it.

"Yes, here it is. Well, what of it? Let the pain be."

"And death . . . where is it?"

He sought his former accustomed fear of death and did not find it. "Where is it? What death?" There was no fear because there was no death.

In place of death there was light.

"So that's what it is!" he suddenly exclaimed aloud. "What joy!"

To him all this happened in a single instant, and the meaning of that instant did not change. For those present his agony continued for another two hours. Something rattled in his throat, his emaciated body twitched, then the gasping and rattle became less and less frequent.

"It is finished!" said someone near him.

He heard these words and repeated them in his soul.

"Death is finished," he said to himself. "It is no more!"

He drew in a breath, stopped in the midst of a sigh, stretched out, and died.

HENRIK IBSEN

1828–1906

Writing in an era when drama had become a second-rate occupation, with most gifted writers turning instead to novels or poetry, Henrik Ibsen restored prestige and relevance to the theater. Over the course of the nineteenth century, the invention of new theatrical machinery and techniques had turned theater into spectacle. Theater producers spent their time and money on special effects, dazzling audiences with lighting, horses, or even nautical battles in addition to, of course, trying to sign the latest acting stars. One might compare nineteenth-century theater with present-day Hollywood and its focus on blockbuster action movies packed with special effects and star actors. Ibsen showed Europe that theater could be more than just spectacle, that it could be an art form addressing the most serious moral and social questions of the time. The theatergoing public was first shocked, and later thrilled, to have controversial themes presented on the stage, and to have them presented not through special effects but through carefully drawn characters and well-constructed dramatic situations. Honing his dramatic technique over half a century, Ibsen almost single-handedly brought a new seriousness to the theater, and he has been regarded as the originator of modern drama ever since.

Ibsen achieved his unparalleled success against all odds. He was born in Skien, a small town in Norway, far removed from the cultural centers of Europe, and he spoke Norwegian, a marginal language unlikely to launch a European career in literature. When Ibsen left his provincial home at the age of fifteen, he was apprenticed to a chemist. Only at the age of twenty-two was he able to free himself from his apprenticeship—and from a liaison with a maid that had resulted in an illegitimate child—and move to the capital, Christiania (now Oslo), to study for the university entrance exam. During this time his first play was performed. After a few years spent learning the craft, he assumed positions of greater responsibility—as artistic director and dramaturge—at theaters in Bergen and Christiania.

Ibsen at first learned from the standard dramatic form of the time, the so-called well-made play. Popularized by the French playwrights Victorien Sardou and Augustine-Eugène Scribe, the well-made play revolved around complicated plots and well-timed confrontations. Immensely popular with audiences, well-made plays excelled at fast-moving action, intrigues, alliances, and sudden revelations.

But Ibsen would soon turn against these sensational formulas. In two plays, *Brand* (1866) and *Peer Gynt* (1867), Ibsen startlingly rejected not only the well-made play, but the theater as such. He wrote these works as "dramatic poems," plays that were not supposed to be performed but were written exclusively to be read. All the rules that governed conventional stage action could thus be circumvented entirely. Drawing on literary models such as **Goethe's** *Faust* and Byron's *Don Juan*, *Peer Gynt* freely mixes fantasy and reality, conjuring mountain trolls, mad German philosophers, and the devil himself. The play established Ibsen as a writer of European significance.

And so Europe, rather than Norway, became Ibsen's home: he would spend the next twenty-seven years on the continent, mostly in Italy and Germany, before moving back to Norway at the age of sixty-three. After *Brand* and *Peer Gynt* had secured his Europe-wide reputation, he changed course and started writing for the stage once more, but in an entirely different style. He gave up on Norway's past and chose to write, once and for all, about the world he knew best: the contemporary Norwegian middle class. His singular purpose was to lay bare the ugly reality behind the façade of middle-class respectability, to expose the lies of bourgeois characters and indeed of bourgeois society as a whole. The five plays of this period, *The Pillars of Society* (1877), *A Doll's House* (1879), *Ghosts* (1881), *Enemy of the People* (1882), and *The Wild Duck* (1884), made Ibsen notorious throughout Europe and established him as an author of shock, confrontation, and revolt.

The main reason why these plays caused such consternation and excitement is that they introduced realism to the theater. Realism had already been established in the novel, but not in drama. In these realist plays, Ibsen wrote in ordinary language and devoted his drama to undoing deceit and pretense, to unveiling hidden motives and past misdeeds so that the truth would shine forth on the stage. Realism, for Ibsen, meant creating a theater of emotional and moral truth, where audiences could understand both the subjective experience and the objective conditions of modern life.

After becoming notorious with his realist plays, Ibsen changed course once more. He had been trying to write modern versions of Greek tragedy for a long while, but it was only in the last phase of his career that he managed to give definite shape to the tragedy of modern middle-class life. Of these plays *Hedda Gabler* (1890) is the most compelling and famous. It is set in the same bourgeois milieu as his realist plays, but is no longer directed towards social deceptions and pretense. Instead it is interested in the bourgeois characters themselves, presenting them in all their complexity, with the hidden yearnings and fantasies that take them outside of the constricted worlds in which they live.

Hedda Gabler is a play about the daughter of a general who marries Tesman, an aspiring scholar waiting for his university post. As the play begins, we see almost immediately that the marriage is unequal and unsettled. Tesman is eager to start his new life and he is clearly proud of his trophy wife. Hedda, by contrast, is dismissive of his affectionate tone and also his values. She snubs him, is impatient, abruptly changes the topic of conversation, and sulks. There is a clear class difference between them. As the daughter of a general, Hedda is used to an upper-middle-class life. Tesman, by contrast, is lower middle class, with all the difference in habit and taste that entails. The collision between Hedda's and Tesman's respective classes, expectations, and attitudes centers on the bourgeois home. Gradually we learn that Hedda only married Tesman and convinced him to get the house out of boredom, feeling that no other options were available to her. But now she finds herself trapped: trapped in her marriage and trapped in the house.

Far from merely a setting for the characters, the house and its furnishings emerge as the main object of Hedda's scorn. The play revolves around furniture and what it represents: class and taste. Hedda despises those objects associated with Tesman and his class, and she admires the remnants of her former life. Tesman's scholarly study is also a set of objects: the handicrafts of the Middle Ages. For Ibsen tangible things become pawns in larger struggles between classes and wills.

Hedda Gabler, bored and without a function except to bear children—a thought she rejects with horror—manipulates every single character in the play, from Tesman and his aunt to Løvborg and his companion, her old school friend, Mrs. Elvsted. She gets them to do her bidding through force, lies, flattery, and utter ruthlessness. As the play progresses, we find her destroying careers and lives without blinking an eye. Hedda sees plotting as an end in itself and for this reason she is often seen as a modern version of Medea or Lady Macbeth.

The main victim of Hedda's plotting is Tesman's rival, Løvborg, who has written nothing less than a book about the future (after completing one about the history of civilization). Ibsen again here focuses on an object, Løvberg's sole manuscript, which becomes a central plot device, a stage prop that drives the action forward. Ibsen had learned from the well-made play how to weave objects and characters into suspenseful plots. But these props are rich in meaning too, throwing light on characters and themes, multifaceted devices that develop a life of their own.

Hedda Gabler may be a manipulator, but she is a manipulator with a vision. She is driven by her hunger for a more fulfilling, ideal, and beautiful life. She fantasizes about acts of heroism and beauty, and she tries to bring about such acts by directing the people around her the way a director assigns roles to actors. She shares her desire for a better life with many tragic characters of Ibsen's later plays, characters who cannot get rid of the chains that bind them to their houses, their objects, their habits, their class, and their past. Ibsen's attitude towards his characters' desire for beauty tends to be ambivalent. On the one hand, he sympathizes with them, even with the cold-hearted Hedda Gabler. On the other hand, his plays show that the single-minded desire to achieve an ideal life leads to destruction. Hedda Gabler's vision is an escape fantasy, the stuff of historical and idealist plays of the kind Ibsen had written in his youth. Ibsen saw both: the intense longing to live a life of ideals as well as the destructive effects of that idealism.

Since his own time, Ibsen's work has inspired important actors and directors worldwide. In England, George Bernard Shaw and the writer William Archer led what some have called the Ibsen campaign, turning the Norwegian playwright into the central figure in modern British drama, and the influential Russian director Konstantin Stanislavsky, whose Moscow Art Theater promoted an acting style based on authentic emotional responses, drew on Ibsen's drama. His later plays, including *Hedda Gabler*, have attracted a different set of directors, less interested in naturalism and truth telling than in symbolism and poetry. Film directors drawn to surrealism and suggestive stage craft, such as Ingmar Bergman, continue to be attracted first and foremost to Ibsen's late plays.

Ibsen's influential career is full of enigmas and contradictions. He began with historical dramas, looking to the past, and yet he would become the herald of modern drama. He rejected the dramatic techniques of standard nineteenth-century drama, but he also managed to transform them into something that seemed new, shocking, and modern to his audience. He received the most attention for his realist plays but later turned realism itself in a more poetic and symbolist direction. In the end, he created a dramatic oeuvre of unparalleled variety and complexity, and this versatility has allowed him to become one of the most popular dramatists of all time. Today, he ranks second only to Shakespeare as the world's most-performed playwright. Shocking and novel when it was first presented to audiences, Ibsen's work has also stood the test of time.

Hedda Gabler[1]

CHARACTERS

GEORGE TESMAN, *research fellow in cultural history*
HEDDA TESMAN, *his wife*
MISS JULIANE TESMAN, *his aunt*

MRS. ELEVSTED
JUDGE BRACK
EILERT LØVBORG
BERTA, *the maid to the Tesmans*

The action takes place in the fashionable west side of Christiania, Norway's capital.

---

1. Translated by Rick Davis and Brian Johnston.

Act 1

A large, pleasantly and tastefully furnished drawing room, decorated in somber tones. In the rear wall is a wide doorway with the curtains pulled back. This doorway leads into a smaller room decorated in the same style. In the right wall of the drawing room is a folding door leading into the hall. In the opposite wall, a glass door, also with its curtains pulled back. Outside, through the windows, part of a covered veranda can be seen, along with trees in their autumn colors. In the foreground, an oval table surrounded by chairs. Downstage, near the right wall, is a broad, dark porcelain stove, a high-backed armchair, a footstool with cushions and two stools. Up in the right-hand corner, a corner-sofa and a small round table. Downstage, on the left side, a little distance from the wall, a sofa. Beyond the glass door, a piano. On both sides of the upstage doorway stand shelves displaying terra cotta and majolica objects. By the back wall of the inner room, a sofa, a table and a couple of chairs can be seen. Above the sofa hangs the portrait of a handsome elderly man in a general's uniform. Above the table, a hanging lamp with an opalescent glass shade. There are many flowers arranged in vases and glasses all around the drawing room. More flowers lie on the tables. The floors of both rooms are covered with thick rugs.

Morning light. The sun shines in through the glass door.

[MISS JULIE TESMAN, *with hat and parasol, comes in from the hall, followed by* BERTA, *who carries a bouquet wrapped in paper.* MISS TESMAN *is a kindly, seemingly good-natured lady of about sixty-five, neatly but simply dressed in a grey visiting outfit.* BERTA *is a housemaid, getting on in years, with a homely and somewhat rustic appearance.*]

MISS TESMAN [*Stops just inside the doorway, listens, and speaks softly.*]   Well—
I believe they're just now getting up!
BERTA [*Also softly.*]   That's what I said, Miss. Just think—the steamer got in so
late last night, and then—Lord, the young mistress wanted so much unpacked
before she could settle down.
MISS TESMAN   Well, well. Let them have a good night's sleep at least. But—
they'll have some fresh morning air when they come down. [*She crosses to
the glass door and throws it wide open.*]
BERTA [*By the table, perplexed, holding the bouquet.*]   Hmm. Bless me if I
can find a spot for these. I think I'd better put them down here, Miss. [*Puts
the bouquet down on the front of the piano.*]
MISS TESMAN   So, Berta dear, now you have a new mistress. As God's my
witness, giving you up was a heavy blow.
BERTA   And me, Miss—what can I say? I've been in yours and Miss Rina's
service for so many blessed years—
MISS TESMAN   We must bear it patiently, Berta. Truly, there's no other way.
You know George has to have you in the house with him—he simply has to.
You've looked after him since he was a little boy.
BERTA   Yes, but Miss—I keep worrying about her, lying there at home—so
completely helpless, poor thing. And that new girl! She'll never learn how to
take care of sick people.

MISS TESMAN   Oh, I'll teach her how soon enough. And I'll be doing most of the work myself, you know. Don't you worry about my sister, Berta dear.

BERTA   Yes, but there's something else, Miss. I'm so afraid I won't satisfy the new mistress—

MISS TESMAN   Ffft—Good Lord—there might be a thing or two at first—

BERTA   Because she's so particular about things—

MISS TESMAN   Well, what do you expect? General Gabler's daughter—the way she lived in the general's day! Do you remember how she would go out riding with her father? In that long black outfit, with the feather in her hat?

BERTA   Oh, yes—I remember that all right. But I never thought she'd make a match with our Mr. Tesman.

MISS TESMAN   Neither did I. But—while I'm thinking about it, don't call George "Mister Tesman" any more. Now it's "Doctor Tesman."

BERTA   Yes—that's what the young mistress said as soon as they came in last night. So it's true?

MISS TESMAN   Yes, it's really true. Think of it, Berta—they've made him a doctor. While he was away, you understand. I didn't know a thing about it, until he told me himself, down at the pier.

BERTA   Well, he's so smart he could be anything he wanted to be. But I never thought he'd take up curing people too!

MISS TESMAN   No, no, no. He's not that kind of doctor. [*Nods significantly.*] As far as that goes, you might have to start calling him something even grander soon.

BERTA   Oh no! What could that be?

MISS TESMAN   [*Smiling.*] Hmm—wouldn't you like to know? [*Emotionally.*] Oh, dear God . . . if our sainted Joseph could look up from his grave and see what's become of his little boy. [*She looks around.*] But, Berta—what's this now? Why have you taken all the slipcovers off the furniture?

BERTA   The mistress told me to. She said she can't stand covers on chairs.

MISS TESMAN   But are they going to use this for their everyday living room?

BERTA   Yes, they will. At least she will. He—the doctor—he didn't say anything.

> [GEORGE TESMAN *enters, humming, from the right of the inner room, carrying an open, empty suitcase. He is a youthful-looking man of thirty-three, of medium height, with an open, round, and cheerful face, blond hair and beard. He wears glasses and is dressed in comfortable, somewhat disheveled clothes.*]

MISS TESMAN   Good morning, good morning, George!

TESMAN   Aunt Julie! Dear Aunt Julie! [*Goes over and shakes her hand.*] All the way here—so early in the day! Hm!

MISS TESMAN   Yes, you know me—I just had to peek in on you a little.

TESMAN   And after a short night's sleep at that!

MISS TESMAN   Oh, that's nothing at all to me.

TESMAN   So—you got home all right from the pier, hm?

MISS TESMAN   Yes, as it turned out, thanks be to God. The Judge was kind enough to see me right to the door.

TESMAN   We felt so bad that we couldn't take you in the carriage—but you saw how many trunks and boxes Hedda had to bring.

MISS TESMAN   Yes, it was amazing.

BERTA [*To* TESMAN.]   Perhaps I should go in and ask the mistress if there's anything I can help her with.

TESMAN   No, thank you, Berta. You don't have to do that. If she needs you, she'll ring—that's what she said.

BERTA [*Going out to right.*]   Very well.

TESMAN   Ah—but—Berta—take this suitcase with you.

BERTA [*Takes the case.*]   I'll put it in the attic.

TESMAN   Just imagine, Auntie. I'd stuffed that whole suitcase with notes— just notes! The things I managed to collect in those archives—really incredible! Ancient, remarkable things that no one had any inkling of.

MISS TESMAN   Ah yes—you certainly haven't wasted any time on your honeymoon.

TESMAN   Yes—I can really say that's true. But, Auntie, take off your hat— Here, let's see. Let me undo that ribbon, hm?

MISS TESMAN [*While he does so.*]   Ah, dear God—this is just what it was like when you were home with us.

TESMAN [*Examining the hat as he holds it.*]   My, my—isn't this a fine, elegant hat you've got for yourself.

MISS TESMAN   I bought it for Hedda's sake.

TESMAN   For Hedda's—hm?

MISS TESMAN   Yes, so Hedda won't feel ashamed of me if we go out for a walk together.

TESMAN [*Patting her cheek.*]   You think of everything, Auntie Julie, don't you? [*Putting her hat on a chair by the table.*] And now—let's just settle down here on the sofa until Hedda comes. [*They sit. She puts her parasol down near the sofa.*]

MISS TESMAN [*Takes both his hands and gazes at him.*]   What a blessing to have you here, bright as day, right before my eyes again, George. Sainted Joseph's own boy!

TESMAN   For me too. To see you again, Aunt Julie—who've been both father and mother to me.

MISS TESMAN   Yes, I know you'll always have a soft spot for your old aunts.

TESMAN   But no improvement at all with Rina, hm?

MISS TESMAN   Oh dear no—and none to be expected poor thing. She lies there just as she has all these years. But I pray that Our Lord lets me keep her just a little longer. Otherwise I don't know what I'd do with my life, George. Especially now, you know—when I don't have you to take care of any more.

TESMAN [*Patting her on the back.*]   There. There. There.

MISS TESMAN   Oh—just to think that you've become a married man, George. And that you're the one who carried off Hedda Gabler! Beautiful Hedda Gabler. Imagine—with all her suitors.

TESMAN [*Hums a little and smiles complacently.*]   Yes, I believe I have quite a few friends in town who envy me, hm?

MISS TESMAN   And then—you got to take such a long honeymoon—more than five—almost six months . . .

TESMAN   Yes, but it was also part of my research, you know. All those archives I had to wade through—and all the books I had to read!

MISS TESMAN   I suppose you're right. [*Confidentially and more quietly.*] But listen, George—isn't there something—something extra you want to tell me?

TESMAN   About the trip?

MISS TESMAN   Yes.

TESMAN   No—I can't think of anything I didn't mention in my letters. I was given my doctorate—but I told you that yesterday.

MISS TESMAN   So you did. But I mean—whether you might have any—any kind of—prospects—?

TESMAN   Prospects?

MISS TESMAN   Good Lord, George—I'm your old aunt.

TESMAN   Well of course I have prospects.

MISS TESMAN   Aha!

TESMAN   I have excellent prospects of becoming a professor one of these days. But Aunt Julie dear, you already know that.

MISS TESMAN   [*With a little laugh.*]   You're right, I do. [*Changing the subject.*] But about your trip. It must cost a lot.

TESMAN   Well, thank God, that huge fellowship paid for a good part of it.

MISS TESMAN   But how did you make it last for the both of you?

TESMAN   That's the tricky part, isn't it?

MISS TESMAN   And on top of that, when you're travelling with a lady! That's always going to cost you more, or so I've heard.

TESMAN   You're right—it was a bit more costly. But Hedda just had to have that trip, Auntie. She really had to. There was no choice.

MISS TESMAN   Well, I suppose not. These days a honeymoon trip is essential, it seems. But now tell me—have you had a good look around the house?

TESMAN   Absolutely! I've been up since dawn.

MISS TESMAN   And what do you think about all of it?

TESMAN   It's splendid! Only I can't think of what we'll do with those two empty rooms between the back parlor and Hedda's bedroom.

MISS TESMAN   [*Lightly laughing.*]   My dear George—when the time comes, you'll think of what to do with them.

TESMAN   Oh, of course—as I add to my library, hm?

MISS TESMAN   That's right, my boy—of course I was thinking about your library.

TESMAN   Most of all I'm just so happy for Hedda. Before we got engaged she'd always say how she couldn't imagine living anywhere but here—in Prime Minister Falk's house.

MISS TESMAN   Yes—imagine. And then it came up for sale just after you left for your trip.

TESMAN   Aunt Julie, we really had luck on our side, hm?

MISS TESMAN   But the expense, George. This will all be costly for you.

TESMAN   [*Looks at her disconcertedly.*]   Yes. It might be. It might be, Auntie.

MISS TESMAN   Ah, God only knows.

TESMAN   How much, do you think? Approximately. Hm?

MISS TESMAN   I can't possibly tell before all the bills are in.

TESMAN   Luckily Judge Brack lined up favorable terms for me—he wrote as much to Hedda.

MISS TESMAN   That's right—don't you ever worry about that, my boy. All this furniture, and the carpets? I put up the security for it.

TESMAN   Security? You? Dear Auntie Julie, what kind of security could you give?

MISS TESMAN   I took out a mortgage on our annuity.

TESMAN   What? On your—and Aunt Rina's annuity!

MISS TESMAN   I couldn't think of any other way.

TESMAN [*Standing in front of her.*]   Have you gone completely out of your mind, Auntie? That annuity is all you and Aunt Rina have to live on.

MISS TESMAN   Now, now, take it easy. It's just a formality, you understand. Judge Brack said so. He was good enough to arrange it all for me. Just a formality, he said.

TESMAN   That could very well be, but all the same . . .

MISS TESMAN   You'll be earning your own living now, after all. And, good Lord, so what if we do have to open the purse a little, spend a little bit at first? That would only make us happy.

TESMAN   Auntie . . . you never get tired of sacrificing yourself for me.

MISS TESMAN [*Rises and lays her hands on his shoulders.*]   What joy do I have in the world, my dearest boy, other than smoothing out the path for you? You, without a father or mother to take care of you . . . but we've reached our destination, my dear. Maybe things looked black from time to time. But, praise God, George, you've come out on top!

TESMAN   Yes, it's really amazing how everything has gone according to plan.

MISS TESMAN   And those who were against you—those who would have blocked your way—they're at the bottom of the pit. They've fallen, George. And the most dangerous one, he fell the farthest. Now he just lies there where he fell, the poor sinner.

TESMAN   Have you heard anything about Eilert—since I went away, I mean?

MISS TESMAN   Nothing, except they say he published a new book.

TESMAN   What? Eilert Løvborg? Just recently, hm?

MISS TESMAN   That's what they say. God only knows how there could be anything to it. But when *your* book comes out—now that will be something else again, won't it, George? What's it going to be about?

TESMAN   It will deal with the Domestic Craftsmanship Practices of Medieval Brabant.[2]

MISS TESMAN   Just think—you can write about that kind of thing too.

TESMAN   However, it might be quite a while before that book is ready. I've got all these incredible collections that have to be put in order first.

MISS TESMAN   Ordering and collecting—you're certainly good at that. You're not the son of sainted Joseph for nothing.

TESMAN   And I'm so eager to get going. Especially now that I've got my own snug house and home to work in.

MISS TESMAN   And most of all, now that you've got her—your heart's desire, dear, dear George!

2. In the Middle Ages, Brabant was a duchy located in parts of what are now Belgium and the Netherlands.

TESMAN [*Embracing her.*]   Yes, Auntie Julie! Hedda . . . that's the most beautiful thing of all! [*Looking toward the doorway.*] I think that's her, hm?

> [HEDDA *comes in from the left side of the inner room. She is a lady of twenty-nine. Her face and figure are aristocratic and elegant. Her complexion is pale. Her eyes are steel-grey, cold and clear. Her hair is an attractive medium brown but not particularly full. She is wearing a tasteful, somewhat loose-fitting morning gown.*]

MISS TESMAN [*Going to meet* HEDDA.]   Good morning, Hedda, my dear. Good morning.

HEDDA [*Extending her hand.*]   Good morning, Miss Tesman, my dear. You're here so early. How nice of you.

MISS TESMAN [*Looking somewhat embarrassed.*]   Well now, how did the young mistress sleep in her new home?

HEDDA   Fine thanks. Well enough.

TESMAN [*Laughing.*]   Well enough! That's a good one, Hedda. You were sleeping like a log when I got up.

HEDDA   Yes, lucky for me. But of course you have to get used to anything new, Miss Tesman. A little at a time. [*Looks toward the window.*] Uch! Look at that. The maid opened the door. I'm drowning in all this sunlight.

MISS TESMAN [*Going to the door.*]   Well then, let's close it.

HEDDA   No, no, don't do that. Tesman my dear, just close the curtains. That gives a gentler light.

TESMAN [*By the door.*]   All right, all right. Now then, Hedda. You've got both fresh air and sunlight.

HEDDA   Yes, fresh air. That's what I need with all these flowers all over the place. But Miss Tesman, won't you sit down?

MISS TESMAN   No, but thank you. Now that I know everything's all right here, I've got to see about getting home again. Home to that poor dear who's lying there in pain.

TESMAN   Be sure to give her my respects, won't you? And tell her I'll stop by and look in on her later today.

MISS TESMAN   Yes, yes I'll certainly do that. But would you believe it, George? [*She rustles around in the pocket of her skirt.*] I almost forgot. Here, I brought something for you.

TESMAN   And what might that be, Auntie, hm?

MISS TESMAN [*Brings out a flat package wrapped in newspaper and hands it to him.*]   Here you are, my dear boy.

TESMAN [*Opening it.*]   Oh my Lord. You kept them for me, Aunt Julie. Hedda, isn't this touching, hm?

HEDDA   Well, what is it?

TESMAN   My old house slippers. My slippers.

HEDDA   Oh yes, I remember how often you talked about them on our trip.

TESMAN   Yes, well, I really missed them. [*Goes over to her.*] Now you can see them for yourself, Hedda.

HEDDA [*Moves over to the stove.*]   Oh, no thanks. I don't really care to.

TESMAN [*Following after her.*]   Just think, Aunt Rina lying there embroidering for me, sick as she was. Oh, you couldn't possibly believe how many memories are tangled up in these slippers.

HEDDA [*By the table.*]   Not for me.

MISS TESMAN   Hedda's quite right about that, George.

TESMAN   Yes, but now that she's in the family I thought—

HEDDA   That maid won't last, Tesman.

MISS TESMAN   Berta—?

TESMAN   What makes you say that, hm?

HEDDA [*Pointing.*]   Look, she's left her old hat lying there on that chair.

TESMAN [*Terrified, dropping the slippers on the floor.*]   Hedda—!

HEDDA   What if someone came in and saw that.

TESMAN   But Hedda—that's Aunt Julie's hat.

HEDDA   Really?

MISS TESMAN [*Taking the hat.*]   Yes, it really is. And for that matter it's not so old either, my dear little Hedda.

HEDDA   Oh, I really didn't get a good look at it, Miss Tesman.

MISS TESMAN [*Tying the hat on her head.*]   Actually I've never worn it before today—and the good Lord knows that's true.

TESMAN   And an elegant hat it is too. Really magnificent.

MISS TESMAN [*She looks around.*]   Oh that's as may be, George. My parasol? Ah, here it is. [*She takes it.*] That's mine too. [*She mutters.*] Not Berta's.

TESMAN   A new hat and a new parasol. Just think, Hedda.

HEDDA   Very charming, very attractive.

TESMAN   That's true, hm? But Auntie, take a good look at Hedda before you go. Look at how charming and attractive she is.

MISS TESMAN   Oh my dear, that's nothing new. Hedda's been lovely all her life. [*She nods and goes across to the right.*]

TESMAN [*Following her.*]   Yes, but have you noticed how she's blossomed, how well she's filled out on our trip?

HEDDA   Oh, leave it alone!

MISS TESMAN [*Stops and turns.*]   Filled out?

TESMAN   Yes, Aunt Julie. You can't see it so well right now in that gown—but I, who have a little better opportunity to—

HEDDA [*By the glass door impatiently.*]   Oh you don't have the opportunity for anything.

TESMAN   It was that mountain air down in the Tyrol.

HEDDA [*Curtly interrupting.*]   I'm the same as when I left.

TESMAN   You keep saying that. But it's true, isn't it Auntie?

MISS TESMAN [*Folding her hands and gazing at* HEDDA.]   Lovely . . . lovely . . . lovely. That's Hedda. [*She goes over to her and with both her hands takes her head, bends it down, kisses her hair.*]   God bless and keep Hedda Tesman for George's sake.

HEDDA [*Gently freeing herself.*]   Ah—! Let me out!

MISS TESMAN [*With quiet emotion.*]   I'll come look in on you two every single day.

TESMAN   Yes, Auntie, do that, won't you, hm?

MISS TESMAN   Good-bye, good-bye.

[*She goes out through the hall door.* TESMAN *follows her out. The door remains half open.* TESMAN *is heard repeating his greetings to Aunt Rina and his thanks for the slippers. While this is happening,* HEDDA

*walks around the room raising her arms and clenching her fists as if in
a rage. Then she draws the curtains back from the door, stands there
and looks out. After a short time,* TESMAN *comes in and closes the door
behind him.*]

TESMAN [*Picking up the slippers from the floor.*] What are you looking at,
Hedda?

HEDDA [*Calm and controlled again.*] Just the leaves. So yellow and so
withered.

TESMAN [*Wrapping up the slippers and placing them on the table.*] Yes,
well—we're into September now.

HEDDA [*Once more uneasy.*] Yes—It's already—already September.

TESMAN Didn't you think Aunt Julie was acting strange just now, almost
formal? What do you suppose got into her?

HEDDA I really don't know her. Isn't that the way she usually is?

TESMAN No, not like today.

HEDDA [*Leaving the glass door.*] Do you think she was upset by the hat
business?

TESMAN Not really. Maybe a little, for just a moment—

HEDDA But where did she get her manners, flinging her hat around any
way she likes here in the drawing room. People just don't act that way.

TESMAN Well, I'm sure she won't do it again.

HEDDA Anyway, I'll smooth everything over with her soon enough.

TESMAN Yes, Hedda, if you would do that.

HEDDA When you visit them later today, invite her here for the evening.

TESMAN Yes, that's just what I'll do. And there's one more thing you can
do that would really make her happy.

HEDDA Well?

TESMAN If you just bring yourself to call her Aunt Julie, for my sake,
Hedda, hm?

HEDDA Tesman, for God's sake, don't ask me to do that. I've told you
that before. I'll try to call her Aunt once in a while and that's enough.

TESMAN Oh well, I just thought that now that you're part of the family . . .

HEDDA Hmm. I don't know—[*She crosses upstage to the doorway.*]

TESMAN [*After a pause.*] Is something the matter, Hedda?

HEDDA I was just looking at my old piano. It really doesn't go with these
other things.

TESMAN As soon as my salary starts coming in, we'll see about trading it
in for a new one.

HEDDA Oh, no, don't trade it in. I could never let it go. We'll leave it in
the back room instead. And then we'll get a new one to put in here. I
mean, as soon as we get the chance.

TESMAN [*A little dejectedly.*] Yes, I suppose we could do that.

HEDDA [*Taking the bouquet from the piano.*] These flowers weren't here
when we got in last night.

TESMAN I suppose Aunt Julie brought them.

HEDDA [*Looks into the bouquet.*] Here's a card. [*Takes it out and reads.*]
"Will call again later today." Guess who it's from.

TESMAN Who is it, hm?

HEDDA It says Mrs. Elvsted.

TESMAN   Really. Mrs. Elvsted. She used to be Miss Rysing.

HEDDA   Yes, that's the one. She had all that irritating hair she'd always be fussing with. An old flame of yours, I've heard.

TESMAN [*Laughs.*]   Oh, not for long and before I knew you, Hedda. And she's here in town. How about that.

HEDDA   Strange that she should come visiting us. I hardly know her except from school.

TESMAN   Yes, and of course I haven't seen her since—well God knows how long. How could she stand it holed up out there so far from everything, hm?

HEDDA [*Reflects a moment and then suddenly speaks.*]   Just a minute, Tesman. Doesn't he live out that way, Eilert Løvborg, I mean?

TESMAN   Yes, right up in that area.

[BERTA *comes in from the hallway.*]

BERTA   Ma'am, she's back again. The lady who came by with the flowers an hour ago. [*Pointing.*] Those you've got in your hand, Ma'am.

HEDDA   Is she then? Please ask her to come in.

[BERTA *opens the door for* MRS. ELVSTED *and then leaves.* MRS. ELVSTED *is slender with soft, pretty features. Her eyes are light blue, large, round and slightly protruding. Her expression is one of alarm and question. Her hair is remarkably light, almost a white gold and exceptionally rich and full. She is a couple of years younger than Hedda. Her costume is a dark visiting dress, tasteful but not of the latest fashion.*]

HEDDA [*Goes to meet her in a friendly manner.*]   Hello my dear Mrs. Elvsted. So delightful to see you again.

MRS. ELVSTED [*Nervous, trying to control herself.*]   Yes, it's been so long since we've seen each other.

TESMAN [*Shakes her hand.*]   And we could say the same, hm?

HEDDA   Thank you for the lovely flowers.

MRS. ELVSTED   I would have come yesterday right away but I heard you were on a trip—

TESMAN   So you've just come into town, hm?

MRS. ELVSTED   Yesterday around noon. I was absolutely desperate when I heard you weren't home.

HEDDA   Desperate, why?

TESMAN   My dear Miss Rysing—I mean Mrs. Elvsted.

HEDDA   There isn't some sort of trouble—?

MRS. ELVSTED   Yes there is—and I don't know another living soul to turn to here in town.

HEDDA [*Sets the flowers down on the table.*]   All right then, let's sit down here on the sofa.

MRS. ELVSTED   Oh no, I'm too upset to sit down.

HEDDA   No you're not. Come over here. [*She draws* MRS. ELVSTED *to the sofa and sits beside her.*]

TESMAN   Well, and now Mrs.—

HEDDA   Did something happen up at your place?

MRS. ELVSTED   Yes—That's it—well, not exactly—Oh, I don't want you to misunderstand me—

HEDDA   Well then the best thing is just to tell it straight out, Mrs. Elvsted—why?

TESMAN   That's why you came here, hm?

MRS. ELVSTED   Yes, of course. So I'd better tell you, if you don't already know, that Eilert Løvborg is in town.

HEDDA   Løvborg?

TESMAN   Eilert Løvborg's back again? Just think, Hedda.

HEDDA   Good Lord, Tesman, I can hear.

MRS. ELVSTED   He's been back now for about a week. The whole week alone here where he can fall in with all kinds of bad company. This town's a dangerous place for him.

HEDDA   But my dear Mrs. Elvsted, how does this involve you?

MRS. ELVSTED   [*With a scared expression, speaking quickly.*]   He was the children's tutor.

HEDDA   Your children?

MRS. ELVSTED   My husband's. I don't have any.

HEDDA   The stepchildren then?

MRS. ELVSTED   Yes.

TESMAN   [*Somewhat awkwardly.*]   But was he sufficiently—I don't know how to say this—sufficiently regular in his habits to be trusted with that kind of job, hm?

MRS. ELVSTED   For the past two years no one could say anything against him.

TESMAN   Really, nothing. Just think, Hedda.

HEDDA   I hear.

MRS. ELVSTED   Nothing at all, I assure you. Not in any way. But even so, now that I know he's here in the city alone and with money in his pocket I'm deathly afraid for him.

TESMAN   But why isn't he up there with you and your husband, hm?

MRS. ELVSTED   When the book came out he was too excited to stay up there with us.

TESMAN   Yes, that's right. Aunt Julie said he'd come out with a new book.

MRS. ELVSTED   Yes, a major new book on the progress of civilization—in its entirety I mean. That was two weeks ago. And it's been selling wonderfully. Everyone's reading it. It's created a huge sensation—why?

TESMAN   All that really? Must be something he had lying around from his better days.

MRS. ELVSTED   From before, you mean?

TESMAN   Yes.

MRS. ELVSTED   No, he wrote the whole thing while he was up there living with us. Just in the last year.

TESMAN   That's wonderful to hear, Hedda. Just think!

MRS. ELVSTED   Yes, if only it continues.

HEDDA   Have you met him here in town?

MRS. ELVSTED   No, not yet. I had a terrible time hunting down his address but this morning I finally found it.

HEDDA   [*Looks searchingly.*]   I can't help thinking this is a little odd on your husband's part.

MRS. ELVSTED [*Starts nervously.*]   My husband—What?

HEDDA   That he'd send you to town on this errand. That he didn't come himself to look for his friend.

MRS. ELVSTED   Oh no, no, no. My husband doesn't have time for that. And anyway I had to do some shopping too.

HEDDA [*Smiling slightly.*]   Oh well, that's different then.

MRS. ELVSTED [*Gets up quickly, ill at ease.*]   And now I beg you, Mr. Tesman, please be kind to Eilert Løvborg if he comes here—and I'm sure he will. You were such good friends in the old days. You have interests in common. The same area of research, as far as I can tell.

TESMAN   Yes, that used to be the case anyway.

MRS. ELVSTED   Yes, that's why I'm asking you—from the bottom of my heart to be sure to—that you'll—that you'll keep a watchful eye on him. Oh, Mr. Tesman, will you do that—will you promise me that?

TESMAN   Yes, with all my heart, Mrs. Rysing.

HEDDA   Elvsted.

TESMAN   I'll do anything in my power for Eilert. You can be sure of it.

MRS. ELVSTED   Oh, that is so kind of you. [*She presses his hands.*] Many, many thanks. [*Frightened.*] Because my husband thinks so highly of him.

HEDDA [*Rising.*]   You should write to him, Tesman. He might not come to you on his own.

TESMAN   Yes, that's the way to do it, Hedda, hm?

HEDDA   And the sooner the better. Right now, I think.

MRS. ELVSTED [*Beseechingly.*]   Yes, if you only could.

TESMAN   I'll write to him this moment. Do you have his address, Mrs. Elvsted?

MRS. ELVSTED   Yes. [*She takes a small slip of paper from her pocket and hands it to him.*] Here it is.

TESMAN   Good, good. I'll go write him—[*Looks around just a minute.*]—Where are my slippers? Ah, here they are. [*Takes the packet and is about to leave.*]

HEDDA   Make sure your note is very friendly—nice and long too.

TESMAN   Yes, you can count on me.

MRS. ELVSTED   But please don't say a word about my asking you to do it.

TESMAN   Oh, that goes without saying.

[*TESMAN leaves to the right through the rear room.*]

HEDDA [*Goes over to* MRS. ELVSTED, *smiles and speaks softly.*]   There, now we've killed two birds with one stone.

MRS. ELVSTED   What do you mean?

HEDDA   Didn't you see that I wanted him out of the way?

MRS. ELVSTED   Yes, to write the letter—

HEDDA   So I could talk to you alone.

MRS. ELVSTED [*Confused.*]   About this thing?

HEDDA   Yes, exactly, about this thing.

MRS. ELVSTED [*Apprehensively.*]   But there's nothing more to it, Mrs. Tesman, really there isn't.

HEDDA   Ah, but there is indeed. There's a great deal more. I can see that much. Come here, let's sit down together. Have a real heart-to-heart talk.

[*She forces* MRS. ELVSTED *into the armchair by the stove and sits down herself on one of the small stools.*]

MRS. ELVSTED [*Nervously looking at her watch.*] Mrs. Tesman, I was just thinking of leaving.

HEDDA Now you can't be in such a hurry, can you? Talk to me a little bit about how things are at home.

MRS. ELVSTED Oh, that's the last thing I want to talk about.

HEDDA But to me? Good Lord, we went to the same school.

MRS. ELVSTED Yes, but you were one class ahead of me. Oh, I was so afraid of you then.

HEDDA Afraid of me?

MRS. ELVSTED Horribly afraid. Whenever we'd meet on the stairs you always used to pull my hair.

HEDDA No, did I do that?

MRS. ELVSTED Yes, you did—and once you said you'd burn it off.

HEDDA Oh, just silly talk, you know.

MRS. ELVSTED Yes, but I was so stupid in those days and anyway since then we've gotten to be so distant from each other. Our circles have just been totally different.

HEDDA Well let's see if we can get closer again. Listen now, I know we were good friends in school. We used to call each other by our first names.

MRS. ELVSTED No, no, I think you're mistaken.

HEDDA I certainly am not. I remember it perfectly and so we have to be perfectly open with each other just like in the old days. [*Moves the stool closer.*] There now. [*Kisses her cheek.*] Now you must call me Hedda.

MRS. ELVSTED [*Pressing and patting her hands.*] Oh, you're being so friendly to me. I'm just not used to that.

HEDDA There, there, there. I'll stop being so formal with you and I'll call you my dear Thora.

MRS. ELVSTED My name is Thea.

HEDDA That's right, of course, I meant Thea. [*Looks at her compassionately.*] So you're not used to friendship, Thea, in your own home?

MRS. ELVSTED If I only had a home, but I don't. I've never had one.

HEDDA [*Glances at her.*] I suspected it might be something like that.

MRS. ELVSTED [*Staring helplessly before her.*] Yes, yes, yes.

HEDDA I can't exactly remember now, but didn't you go up to Sheriff Elvsted's as a housekeeper?

MRS. ELVSTED Actually I was supposed to be a governess but his wife—at that time—she was an invalid, mostly bedridden, so I had to take care of the house too.

HEDDA So in the end you became mistress of your own house.

MRS. ELVSTED [*Heavily.*] Yes, that's what I became.

HEDDA Let me see. How long has that been?

MRS. ELVSTED Since I was married?

HEDDA Yes.

MRS. ELVSTED Five years now.

HEDDA That's right, it must be about that.

MRS. ELVSTED Oh these five years—! Or the last two or three anyway—! Ah, Mrs. Tesman, if you could just imagine.

HEDDA [*Slaps her lightly on the hand.*] Mrs. Tesman; really, Thea.

MRS. ELVSTED No, no, of course, I'll try to remember. Anyway, Hedda, if you could only imagine.

HEDDA [*Casually.*] It seems to me that Eilert Løvborg's been living up there for about three years, hasn't he?

MRS. ELVSTED [*Looks uncertainly at her.*] Eilert Løvborg? Yes, that's about right.

HEDDA Did you know him from before—from here in town?

MRS. ELVSTED Hardly at all. I mean his name of course.

HEDDA But up there he'd come to visit you at the house?

MRS. ELVSTED Yes, every day. He'd read to the children. I couldn't manage everything myself, you see.

HEDDA No, of course not. And what about your husband? His work must take him out of the house quite a bit.

MRS. ELVSTED Yes, as you might imagine. He's the sheriff so he has to go traveling around the whole district.

HEDDA [*Leaning against the arm of the chair.*] Thea, my poor sweet Thea— You've got to tell me everything just the way it is.

MRS. ELVSTED All right, but you've got to ask the questions.

HEDDA So, Thea, what's your husband really like? I mean, you know, to be with? Is he good to you?

MRS. ELVSTED [*Evasively.*] He thinks he does everything for the best.

HEDDA I just think he's a little too old for you. He's twenty years older, isn't he?

MRS. ELVSTED [*Irritatedly.*] There's that too. There's a lot of things. I just can't stand being with him. We don't have a single thought in common, not a single thing in the world, he and I.

HEDDA But doesn't he care for you at all in his own way?

MRS. ELVSTED I can't tell what he feels. I think I'm just useful to him, and it doesn't cost very much to keep me. I'm very inexpensive.

HEDDA That's a mistake.

MRS. ELVSTED [*Shaking her head.*] Can't be any other way, not with him. He only cares about himself and maybe about the children a little.

HEDDA And also for Eilert Løvborg, Thea.

MRS. ELVSTED [*Stares at her.*] For Eilert Løvborg? Why do you think that?

HEDDA Well, my dear, he sent you all the way into town to look for him. [*Smiling almost imperceptibly.*] And besides, you said so yourself, to Tesman.

MRS. ELVSTED [*With a nervous shudder.*] Oh yes, I suppose I did. No, I'd better just tell you the whole thing. It's bound to come to light sooner or later anyway.

HEDDA But my dear Thea.

MRS. ELVSTED All right, short and sweet. My husband doesn't know that I'm gone.

HEDDA What, your husband doesn't know?

MRS. ELVSTED Of course not. Anyway he's not at home. He was out traveling. I just couldn't stand it any longer, Hedda, it was impossible. I would have been so completely alone up there.

HEDDA Well, then what?

MRS. ELVSTED Then I packed some of my things, just the necessities, all in secret, and I left the house.

HEDDA Just like that?

MRS. ELVSTED Yes, and I took the train to town.

HEDDA Oh, my good, dear Thea. You dared to do that!

MRS. ELVSTED [*Gets up and walks across the floor.*] Well, what else could I do?

HEDDA What do you think your husband will say when you go home again?

MRS. ELVSTED [*By the table looking at her.*] Up there to him?

HEDDA Of course, of course.

MRS. ELVSTED I'm never going back up there.

HEDDA [*Gets up and goes closer to her.*] So you've really done it? You've really run away from everything?

MRS. ELVSTED Yes, I couldn't think of anything else to do.

HEDDA But you did it—so openly.

MRS. ELVSTED Oh, you can't keep something like that a secret anyway.

HEDDA Well, what do you think people will say about you, Thea?

MRS. ELVSTED They'll say whatever they want, God knows. [*She sits tired and depressed on the sofa.*] But I only did what I had to do.

HEDDA [*After a brief pause.*] So what will you do with yourself now?

MRS. ELVSTED I don't know yet. All I know is that I've got to live here where Eilert Løvborg lives if I'm going to live at all.

HEDDA [*Moves a chair closer from the table, sits beside her and strokes her hands.*] Thea, my dear, how did it come about, this—bond between you and Eilert Løvborg?

MRS. ELVSTED Oh, it just happened, little by little. I started to have a kind of power over him.

HEDDA Really?

MRS. ELVSTED He gave up his old ways—and not because I begged him to. I never dared do that. But he started to notice that those kinds of things upset me, so he gave them up.

HEDDA [*Concealing an involuntary, derisive smile.*] So you rehabilitated him, as they say. You, little Thea.

MRS. ELVSTED That's what he said, anyway. And for his part he's made a real human being out of me. Taught me to think, to understand all sorts of things.

HEDDA So he read to you too, did he?

MRS. ELVSTED No, not exactly, but he talked to me. Talked without stopping about all sorts of great things. And then there was that wonderful time when I shared in his work, when I helped him.

HEDDA You got to do that?

MRS. ELVSTED Yes. Whenever he wrote anything, we had to agree on it first.

HEDDA Like two good comrades.

MRS. ELVSTED [*Eagerly.*] Yes, comrades. Imagine, Hedda, that's what he called it too. I should feel so happy, but I can't yet because I don't know how long it will last.

HEDDA Are you that unsure of him?

MRS. ELVSTED [*Dejectedly.*] There's the shadow of a woman between Eilert Løvborg and me.

HEDDA [*Stares intently at her.*] Who could that be?

MRS. ELVSTED I don't know. Someone from his past. Someone he's never really been able to forget.

HEDDA What has he told you about all this?

MRS. ELVSTED He's only talked about it once and very vaguely.

HEDDA Yes, what did he say?

MRS. ELVSTED He said that when they broke up she was going to shoot him with a pistol.

HEDDA [*Calm and controlled.*] That's nonsense, people just don't act that way here.

MRS. ELVSTED No they don't—so I think it's got to be that red-haired singer that he once—

HEDDA Yes, that could well be.

MRS. ELVSTED Because I remember they used to say about her that she went around with loaded pistols.

HEDDA Well, then it's her, of course.

MRS. ELVSTED [*Wringing her hands.*] Yes, but Hedda, just think, I hear this singer is in town again. Oh, I'm so afraid.

HEDDA [*Glancing toward the back room.*] Shh, here comes Tesman. [*She gets up and whispers.*] Now, Thea, all of this is strictly between you and me.

MRS. ELVSTED [*Jumping up.*] Oh yes, yes, for God's sake!

[GEORGE TESMAN, *a letter in his hand, comes in from the right side of the inner room.*]

TESMAN There now, the epistle is prepared.

HEDDA Well done—but Mrs. Elvsted's got to leave now, I think. Just a minute, I'll follow you as far as the garden gate.

TESMAN Hedda dear, do you think Berta could see to this?

HEDDA [*Takes the letter.*] I'll instruct her.

[BERTA *comes in from the hall.*]

BERTA Judge Brack is here. Says he'd like to pay his respects.

HEDDA Yes, ask the Judge to be so good as to come in, and then—listen here now—Put this letter in the mailbox.

BERTA [*Takes the letter.*] Yes, ma'am.

[*She opens the door for* JUDGE BRACK *and then goes out.* JUDGE BRACK *is forty-five years old, short, well built and moves easily. He has a round face and an aristocratic profile. His short hair is still almost black. His eyes are lively and ironic. He has thick eyebrows and a thick moustache, trimmed square at the ends. He is wearing outdoor clothing, elegant, but a little too young in style. He has a monocle in one eye. Now and then he lets it drop.*]

BRACK [*Bows with his hat in his hand.*] Does one dare to call so early?

HEDDA One does dare.

TESMAN [*Shakes his hand.*] You're welcome any time. Judge Brack, Mrs. Rysing. [HEDDA *sighs.*]

BRACK [*Bows.*] Aha, delighted.

HEDDA [*Looks at him laughing.*] Nice to see you by daylight for a change, Judge.

BRACK Do I look different?

HEDDA Yes, younger.

BRACK   You're too kind.

TESMAN   Well, how about Hedda, hm? Doesn't she look fine? Hasn't she filled out?

HEDDA   Stop it now. You should be thanking Judge Brack for all of his hard work—

BRACK   Nonsense. It was my pleasure.

HEDDA   There's a loyal soul. But here's my friend burning to get away. Excuse me, Judge, I'll be right back.

[*Mutual good-byes.* MRS. ELVSTED *and* HEDDA *leave by the hall door.*]

BRACK   Well, now, your wife's satisfied, more or less?

TESMAN   Oh yes, we can't thank you enough. I gather there might be a little more rearrangement here and there and one or two things still missing. A couple of small things yet to be procured.

BRACK   Is that so?

TESMAN   But nothing for you to worry about. Hedda said that she'd look for everything herself. Let's sit down.

BRACK   Thanks. Just for a minute. [*Sits by the table.*] Now, my dear Tesman, there's something we need to talk about.

TESMAN   Oh yes, ah, I understand. [*Sits down.*] Time for a new topic. Time for the serious part of the celebration, hm?

BRACK   Oh, I wouldn't worry too much about the finances just yet— although I must tell you that it would have been better if we'd managed things a little more frugally.

TESMAN   But there was no way to do that. You know Hedda, Judge, you know her well. I couldn't possibly ask her to live in a middle-class house.

BRACK   No, that's precisely the problem.

TESMAN   And luckily it can't be too long before I get my appointment.[3]

BRACK   Well, you know, these things often drag on and on.

TESMAN   Have you heard anything further, hm?

BRACK   Nothing certain. [*Changing the subject.*] But there is one thing. I've got a piece of news for you.

TESMAN   Well?

BRACK   Your old friend Eilert Løvborg's back in town.

TESMAN   I already know.

BRACK   Oh, how did you find out?

TESMAN   She told me, that lady who just left with Hedda.

BRACK   Oh, I see. I didn't quite get her name.

TESMAN   Mrs. Elvsted.

BRACK   Ah yes, the sheriff's wife. Yes, he's been staying up there with them.

TESMAN   And I'm so glad to hear that he's become a responsible person again.

BRACK   Yes, one is given to understand that.

TESMAN   And he's come out with a new book, hm?

BRACK   He has indeed.

TESMAN   And it's caused quite a sensation.

BRACK   It's caused an extraordinary sensation.

---

3. Tesman expects to be appointed to a professorship. These positions were much less numerous and more socially prominent than their contemporary American counterparts.

TESMAN   Just think, isn't that wonderful to hear. With all his remarkable talents, I was absolutely certain he was down for good.

BRACK   That was certainly the general opinion.

TESMAN   But I can't imagine what he'll do with himself now. What will he live on, hm?

[During these last words, HEDDA has entered from the hallway.]

HEDDA [To BRACK, laughing a little scornfully.]   Tesman is constantly going around worrying about what to live on.

TESMAN   My Lord, we're talking about Eilert Løvborg, dear.

HEDDA [Looking quickly at him.]   Oh yes? [Sits down in the armchair by the stove and asks casually.] What's the matter with him?

TESMAN   Well, he must have spent his inheritance a long time ago, and he can't really write a new book every year, hm? So I was just asking what was going to become of him.

BRACK   Perhaps I can enlighten you on that score.

TESMAN   Oh?

BRACK   You might remember that he has some relatives with more than a little influence.

TESMAN   Unfortunately they've pretty much washed their hands of him.

BRACK   In the old days they thought of him as the family's great shining hope.

TESMAN   Yes, in the old days, possibly, but he took care of that himself.

HEDDA   Who knows? [Smiles slightly.] Up at the Elvsteds' he's been the target of a reclamation project.

BRACK   And there's this new book.

TESMAN   Well, God willing, they'll help him out some way or another. I've just written to him, Hedda, asking him to come over this evening.

BRACK   But my dear Tesman, you're coming to my stag party[4] this evening. You promised me on the pier last night.

HEDDA   Had you forgotten, Tesman?

TESMAN   Yes, to be perfectly honest, I had.

BRACK   For that matter, you can be sure he won't come.

TESMAN   Why do you say that, hm?

BRACK [Somewhat hesitantly getting up and leaning his hands on the back of his chair.]   My dear Tesman, you too, Mrs. Tesman, in good conscience I can't let you go on living in ignorance of something like this.

TESMAN   Something about Eilert, hm?

BRACK   About both of you.

TESMAN   My dear Judge, tell me what it is.

BRACK   You ought to prepare yourself for the fact that your appointment might not come through as quickly as you expect.

TESMAN [Jumps up in alarm.]   Has something held it up?

BRACK   The appointment might just possibly be subject to a competition.

TESMAN   A competition! Just think of that, Hedda!

HEDDA [Leans further back in her chair.]   Ah yes—yes.

TESMAN   But who on earth would it—surely not with—?

BRACK   Yes, precisely, with Eilert Løvborg.

4. A party for men only, whether single or married.

TESMAN [*Clasping his hands together.*]   No, no, this is absolutely unthinkable, absolutely unthinkable, hm?

BRACK   Hmm—well, we might just have to learn to get used to it.

TESMAN   No, but Judge Brack, that would be incredibly inconsiderate. [*Waving his arms.*] Because—well—just look, I'm a married man. We went and got married on this very prospect, Hedda and I. Went and got ourselves heavily into debt. Borrowed money from Aunt Julie too. I mean, good Lord, I was as much as promised the position, hm?

BRACK   Now, now, you'll almost certainly get it but first there'll have to be a contest.

HEDDA [*Motionless in the armchair.*]   Just think, Tesman, it will be a sort of match.

TESMAN   But Hedda, my dear, how can you be so calm about this?

HEDDA   Oh I'm not, not at all. I can't wait for the final score.

BRACK   In any case, Mrs. Tesman, it's a good thing that you know how matters stand. I mean, before you embark on any more of these little purchases I hear you're threatening to make.

HEDDA   What's that got to do with this?

BRACK   Well, well, that's another matter. Good-bye. [*To* TESMAN.] I'll come by for you when I take my afternoon walk.

TESMAN   Oh yes, yes, forgive me—I don't know if I'm coming or going.

HEDDA [*Reclining, stretching out her hand.*]   Good-bye, Judge, and do come again.

BRACK   Many thanks. Good-bye, good-bye.

TESMAN [*Following him to the door.*]   Good-bye, Judge. You'll have to excuse me.

[JUDGE BRACK *goes out through the hallway door.*]

TESMAN [*Pacing about the floor.*]   We should never let ourselves get lost in a wonderland, Hedda, hm?

HEDDA [*Looking at him and smiling.*]   Do you do that?

TESMAN   Yes, well, it can't be denied. It was like living in wonderland to go and get married and set up housekeeping on nothing more than prospects.

HEDDA   You may be right about that.

TESMAN   Well, at least we have our home, Hedda, our wonderful home. The home both of us dreamt about, that both of us craved, I could almost say, hm?

HEDDA [*Rises slowly and wearily.*]   The agreement was that we would live in society, that we would entertain.

TESMAN   Yes, good Lord, I was so looking forward to that. Just think, to see you as a hostess in our own circle. Hm. Well, well, well, for the time being at least we'll just have to make do with each other, Hedda. We'll have Aunt Julie here now and then. Oh you, you should have such a completely different—

HEDDA   To begin with, I suppose I can't have the liveried footmen.[5]

TESMAN   Ah no, unfortunately not. No footmen. We can't even think about that right now.

---

5. Uniformed servants.

HEDDA   And the horse!

TESMAN [*Horrified.*]   The horse.

HEDDA   I suppose I mustn't think about that any more.

TESMAN   No, God help us, you can see that for yourself.

HEDDA [*Walking across the floor.*]   Well, at least I've got one thing to amuse myself with.

TESMAN [*Beaming with pleasure.*]   Ah, thank God for that, and what is that, Hedda?

HEDDA [*In the center doorway looking at him with veiled scorn.*]   My pistols, George.

TESMAN [*Alarmed.*]   Pistols?

HEDDA [*With cold eyes.*]   General Gabler's pistols.

   [*She goes through the inner room and out to the left.*]

TESMAN [*Running to the center doorway and shouting after her.*]   No, for the love of God, Hedda, dearest, don't touch those dangerous things. For my sake, Hedda, hm?

Act 2

The TESMANS' *rooms as in the first act except that the piano has been moved out and an elegant little writing table with a bookshelf has been put in its place. Next to the sofa a smaller table has been placed. Most of the bouquets have been removed.* MRS. ELVSTED's *bouquet stands on the larger table in the foreground. It is afternoon.*

[HEDDA, *dressed to receive visitors, is alone in the room. She stands by the open glass door loading a pistol. The matching pistol lies in an open pistol case on the writing table.*]

HEDDA [*Looking down into the garden and calling.*]   Hello again, Judge.

BRACK [*Is heard some distance below.*]   Likewise, Mrs. Tesman.

HEDDA [*Raises the pistol and aims.*]   Now, Judge Brack, I am going to shoot you.

BRACK [*Shouting from below.*]   No, no, no. Don't stand there aiming at me like that.

HEDDA   That's what you get for coming up the back way. [*She shoots.*]

BRACK   Are you out of your mind?

HEDDA   Oh, good Lord, did I hit you?

BRACK [*Still outside.*]   Stop this nonsense.

HEDDA   Then come on in, Judge.

   [JUDGE BRACK, *dressed for a bachelor party, comes in through the glass doors. He carries a light overcoat over his arm.*]

BRACK   In the devil's name, are you still playing this game? What were you shooting at?

HEDDA   Oh, I just stand here and shoot at the sky.

BRACK [*Gently taking the pistol out of her hands.*]   With your permission, ma'am? [*Looks at it.*] Ah, this one. I know it well. [*Looks around.*] And where do we keep the case? I see, here it is. [*Puts the pistol inside and shuts the case.*] All right, we're through with these little games for today.

HEDDA   Then what in God's name am I to do with myself?

BRACK   No visitors?

HEDDA   [*Closes the glass door.*]   Not a single one. Our circle is still in the country.

BRACK   Tesman's not home either, I suppose.

HEDDA   [*At the writing table, locks the pistol case in the drawer.*]   No, as soon as he finished eating he was off to the aunts. He wasn't expecting you so early.

BRACK   Hmm, I never thought of that. Stupid of me.

HEDDA   [*Turns her head, looks at him.*]   Why stupid?

BRACK   Then I would have come a little earlier.

HEDDA   [*Going across the floor.*]   Then you wouldn't have found anyone here at all. I've been in my dressing room since lunch.

BRACK   Isn't there even one little crack in the door wide enough for a negotiation?

HEDDA   Now that's something you forgot to provide for.

BRACK   That was also stupid of me.

HEDDA   So we'll just have to flop down here and wait. Tesman won't be home any time soon.

BRACK   Well, well, Lord knows I can be patient.

[HEDDA *sits in the corner of the sofa.* BRACK *lays his overcoat over the back of the nearest chair and sits down, keeps his hat in his hand. Short silence. They look at each other.*]

HEDDA   So?

BRACK   [*In the same tone.*]   So?

HEDDA   I asked first.

BRACK   [*Leaning a little forward.*]   Yes, why don't we allow ourselves a cozy little chat, Mrs. Hedda.

HEDDA   [*Leaning further back in the sofa.*]   Doesn't it feel like an eternity since we last talked together? A few words last night and this morning, but I don't count them.

BRACK   Like this, between ourselves, just the two of us?

HEDDA   Well, yes, more or less.

BRACK   I wished you were back home every single day.

HEDDA   The whole time I was wishing the same thing.

BRACK   You, really, Mrs. Hedda? Here I thought you were having a wonderful time on your trip.

HEDDA   Oh yes, you can just imagine.

BRACK   But that's what Tesman always wrote.

HEDDA   Yes, him! He thinks it's the greatest thing in the world to go scratching around in libraries. He loves sitting and copying out old parchments or whatever they are.

BRACK   [*Somewhat maliciously.*]   Well, that's his calling in the world, at least in part.

HEDDA   Yes, so it is, and no doubt it's—but for me, oh dear Judge, I've been so desperately bored.

BRACK   [*Sympathetically.*]   Do you really mean that? You're serious?

HEDDA   Yes, you can imagine it for yourself. Six whole months never meeting with a soul who knew the slightest thing about our circle. No one we could talk with about our kinds of things.

BRACK Ah no, I'd agree with you there. That would be a loss.

HEDDA Then what was most unbearable of all.

BRACK Yes?

HEDDA To be together forever and always—with one and the same person.

BRACK [*Nodding agreement.*] Early and late, yes, night and day, every waking and sleeping hour.

HEDDA That's it, forever and always.

BRACK Yes, all right, but with our excellent Tesman I would have imagined that you might—

HEDDA Tesman is—a specialist, dear Judge.

BRACK Undeniably.

HEDDA And specialists aren't so much fun to travel with. Not for the long run anyway.

BRACK Not even the specialist that one loves?

HEDDA Uch, don't use that syrupy word.

BRACK [*Startled.*] Mrs. Hedda.

HEDDA [*Half laughing, half bitterly.*] Well, give it a try for yourself. Hearing about the history of civilization every hour of the day.

BRACK Forever and always.

HEDDA Yes, yes, yes. And then his particular interest, domestic crafts in the Middle Ages. Uch, the most revolting thing of all.

BRACK [*Looks at her curiously.*] But, tell me now, I don't quite understand how—hmmm.

HEDDA That we're together? George Tesman and I, you mean?

BRACK Well, yes. That's a good way of putting it.

HEDDA Good Lord, do you think it's so remarkable?

BRACK I think—yes and no, Mrs. Hedda.

HEDDA I'd danced myself out, dear Judge. My time was up. [*Shudders slightly.*] Uch, no, I'm not going to say that or even think it.

BRACK You certainly have no reason to think it.

HEDDA Ah, reasons—[*Looks watchfully at him.*] And George Tesman? Well, he'd certainly be called a most acceptable man in every way.

BRACK Acceptable and solid, God knows.

HEDDA And I can't find anything about him that's actually ridiculous, can you?

BRACK Ridiculous? No—I wouldn't quite say that.

HEDDA Hmm. Well, he's a very diligent archivist anyway. Some day he might do something interesting with all of it. Who knows.

BRACK [*Looking at her uncertainly.*] I thought you believed, like everyone else, that he'd turn out to be a great man.

HEDDA [*With a weary expression.*] Yes, I did. And then when he went around constantly begging with all his strength, begging for permission to let him take care of me, well, I didn't see why I shouldn't take him up on it.

BRACK Ah well, from that point of view . . .

HEDDA It was a great deal more than any of my other admirers were offering.

BRACK [*Laughing.*] Well, of course I can't answer for all the others, but as far as I'm concerned you know very well that I've always maintained a certain respect for the marriage bond, that is, in an abstract kind of way, Mrs. Hedda.

HEDDA [*Playfully.*] Oh, I never had any hopes for you.

BRACK All I ask is an intimate circle of good friends, friends I can be of service to in any way necessary. Places where I am allowed to come and go as a trusted friend.

HEDDA Of the man of the house, you mean.

BRACK [*Bowing.*] No, to be honest, of the lady. Of the man as well, you understand, because you know that kind of—how should I put this— that kind of triangular arrangement is really a magnificent convenience for everyone concerned.

HEDDA Yes, you can't imagine how many times I longed for a third person on that trip. Ach, huddled together alone in a railway compartment.

BRACK Fortunately, the wedding trip is over now.

HEDDA [*Shaking her head.*] Oh no, it's a very long trip. It's nowhere near over. I've only come to a little stopover on the line.

BRACK Then you should jump out, stretch your legs a little, Mrs. Hedda.

HEDDA I'd never jump out.

BRACK Really?

HEDDA No, because there's always someone at the stop who—

BRACK [*Laughing.*] Who's looking at your legs, you mean?

HEDDA Yes, exactly.

BRACK Yes, but for heaven's sake.

HEDDA [*With a disdainful gesture.*] I don't hold with that sort of thing. I'd rather remain sitting, just like I am now, a couple alone. On a train.

BRACK But what if a third man climbed into the compartment with the couple?

HEDDA Ah yes. Now that's quite different.

BRACK An understanding friend, a proven friend—

HEDDA Who can be entertaining on all kinds of topics—

BRACK And not a specialist in any way!

HEDDA [*With an audible sigh.*] Yes, that would be a relief.

BRACK [*Hears the front door open and glances toward it.*] The triangle is complete.

HEDDA [*Half audibly.*] And there goes the train.

[GEORGE TESMAN *in a gray walking suit and with a soft felt hat comes in from the hallway. He is carrying a large stack of unbound books under his arm and in his pockets.*]

TESMAN [*Goes to the table by the corner, sofa.*] Phew—hot work lugging all these here. [*Puts the books down.*] Would you believe I'm actually sweating, Hedda? And you're already here, Judge, hm. Berta didn't mention anything about that.

BRACK [*Getting up.*] I came up through the garden.

HEDDA What are all those books you've got there?

TESMAN [*Stands leafing through them.*] All the new works by my fellow specialists. I've absolutely got to have them.

HEDDA By your fellow specialists.

BRACK Ah, the specialists, Mrs. Tesman. [BRACK *and* HEDDA *exchange a knowing smile.*]

HEDDA   You need even more of these specialized works?

TESMAN   Oh, yes, my dear Hedda, you can never have too many of these. You have to keep up with what's being written and published.

HEDDA   Yes, you certainly must do that.

TESMAN   [*Searches among the books.*] And look here, I've got Eilert Løvborg's new book too. (*Holds it out.*) Maybe you'd like to look at it, Hedda, hm?

HEDDA   No thanks—or maybe later.

TESMAN   I skimmed it a little on the way.

HEDDA   And what's your opinion as a specialist?

TESMAN   I think the argument's remarkably thorough. He never wrote like this before. [*Collects the books together.*] Now I've got to get all these inside. Oh, it's going to be such fun to cut the pages.[6] Then I'll go and change. [*To* BRACK.] We don't have to leave right away, hm?

BRACK   No, not at all. No hurry at all.

TESMAN   Good, I'll take my time then. [*Leaves with the books but stands in the doorway and turns.*] Oh, Hedda, by the way, Aunt Julie won't be coming over this evening.

HEDDA   Really? Because of that hat business?

TESMAN   Not at all. How could you think that of Aunt Julie? No, it's just that Aunt Rina is very ill.

HEDDA   She always is.

TESMAN   Yes, but today she's gotten quite a bit worse.

HEDDA   Well, then it's only right that the other one should stay at home with her. I'll just have to make the best of it.

TESMAN   My dear, you just can't believe how glad Aunt Julie was, in spite of everything, at how healthy and rounded out you looked after the trip.

HEDDA   [*Half audibly getting up.*]   Oh, these eternal aunts.

TESMAN   Hm?

HEDDA   [*Goes over to the glass door.*]   Nothing.

TESMAN   Oh, all right. [*He goes out through the rear room and to the right.*]

BRACK   What were you saying about a hat?

HEDDA   Oh, just a little run-in with Miss Tesman this morning. She'd put her hat down there on that chair [*Looks at him smiling.*] and I pretended I thought it was the maid's.

BRACK   [*Shaking his head.*]   My dear Mrs. Hedda, how could you do such a thing to that harmless old lady.

HEDDA   [*Nervously walking across the floor.*]   Oh, you know—these things just come over me like that and I can't resist them. [*Flings herself into the armchair by the stove.*] I can't explain it, even to myself.

BRACK   [*Behind the armchair.*]   You're not really happy—that's the heart of it.

HEDDA   [*Staring in front of her.*]   And why should I be happy? Maybe you can tell me.

BRACK   Yes. Among other things, be happy you've got the home that you've always longed for.

---

6. Books used to be sold with the pages folded but uncut; one had to cut the pages to read the book.

HEDDA [*Looks up at him and laughs.*] You also believe that myth?

BRACK There's nothing to it?

HEDDA Yes, heavens, there's something to it.

BRACK So?

HEDDA And here's what it is. I used George Tesman to walk me home from parties last summer.

BRACK Yes, regrettably I had to go another way.

HEDDA Oh yes, you certainly were going a different way last summer.

BRACK [*Laughs.*] Shame on you, Mrs. Hedda. So you and Tesman . . .

HEDDA So we walked past here one evening and Tesman, the poor thing, was twisting and turning in his agony because he didn't have the slightest idea what to talk about and I felt sorry that such a learned man—

BRACK [*Smiling skeptically.*] You did . . .

HEDDA Yes, if you will, I did, and so just to help him out of his torment I said, without really thinking about it, that this was the house I would love to live in.

BRACK That was all?

HEDDA For that evening.

BRACK But afterward?

HEDDA Yes, dear Judge, my thoughtlessness has had its consequences.

BRACK Unfortunately, our thoughtlessness often does, Mrs. Hedda.

HEDDA Thanks, I'm sure. But it so happens that George Tesman and I found our common ground in this passion for Prime Minister Falk's villa. And after that it all followed. The engagement, the marriage, the honeymoon and everything else. Yes, yes, Judge, I almost said: you make your bed, you have to lie in it.

BRACK That's priceless. Essentially what you're telling me is you didn't care about any of this here.

HEDDA God knows I didn't.

BRACK What about now, now that we've made it into a lovely home for you?

HEDDA Ach, I feel an air of lavender and dried roses in every room—or maybe Aunt Julie brought that in with her.

BRACK [*Laughing.*] No, I think that's probably a relic of the eminent prime minister's late wife.

HEDDA Yes, that's it, there's something deathly about it. It reminds me of a corsage the day after the ball. [*Folds her hands at the back of her neck, leans back in her chair and gazes at him.*] Oh, my dear Judge, you can't imagine how I'm going to bore myself out here.

BRACK What if life suddenly should offer you some purpose or other, something to live for? What about that, Mrs. Hedda?

HEDDA A purpose? Something really tempting for me?

BRACK Preferably something like that, of course.

HEDDA God knows what sort of purpose that would be. I often wonder if— [*Breaks off.*] No, that wouldn't work out either.

BRACK Who knows. Let me hear.

HEDDA If I could get Tesman to go into politics, I mean.

BRACK [*Laughing.*] Tesman? No, you have to see that politics, anything like that, is not for him. Not in his line at all.

HEDDA No, I can see that. But what if I could get him to try just the same?

BRACK   Yes, but why should he do that if he's not up to it? Why would you want him to?

HEDDA   Because I'm bored, do you hear me? [*After a pause.*] So you don't think there's any way that Tesman could become a cabinet minister?

BRACK   Hmm, you see my dear Mrs. Hedda, that requires a certain amount of wealth in the first place.

HEDDA   [*Rises impatiently.*]   Yes, that's it, this shabby little world I've ended up in. [*Crosses the floor.*] That's what makes life so contemptible, so completely ridiculous. That's just what it is.

BRACK   I think the problem's somewhere else.

HEDDA   Where's that?

BRACK   You've never had to live through anything that really shakes you up.

HEDDA   Anything serious, you mean.

BRACK   Yes, you could call it that. Perhaps now, though, it's on its way.

HEDDA   [*Tosses her head.*]   You mean that competition for that stupid professorship? That's Tesman's business. I'm not going to waste a single thought on it.

BRACK   No, forget about that. But when you find yourself facing what one calls in elegant language a profound and solemn calling—[*Smiling.*] a new calling, my dear little Mrs. Hedda.

HEDDA   [*Angry.*]   Quiet. You'll never see anything like that.

BRACK   [*Gently.*]   We'll talk about it again in a year's time, at the very latest.

HEDDA   [*Curtly.*]   I don't have any talent for that, Judge. I don't want anything to do with that kind of calling.

BRACK   Why shouldn't you, like most other women, have an innate talent for a vocation that—

HEDDA   [*Over by the glass door.*]   Oh, please be quiet. I often think I only have one talent, one talent in the world.

BRACK   [*Approaching.*]   And what is that may I ask?

HEDDA   [*Standing, staring out.*]   Boring the life right out of me. Now you know. [*Turns, glances toward the inner room and laughs.*] Perfect timing; here comes the professor.

BRACK   [*Warning softly.*]   Now, now, now, Mrs. Hedda.

  [GEORGE TESMAN, *in evening dress, carrying his gloves and hat, comes in from the right of the rear room.*]

TESMAN   Hedda, no message from Eilert Løvborg?

HEDDA   No.

BRACK   Do you really think he'll come?

TESMAN   Yes, I'm almost certain he will. What you told us this morning was just idle gossip.

BRACK   Oh?

TESMAN   Yes, at least Aunt Julie said she couldn't possibly believe that he would stand in my way anymore. Just think.

BRACK   So, then everything's all right.

TESMAN   [*Puts his hat with his gloves inside on a chair to the right.*]   Yes, but I'd like to wait for him as long as I can.

BRACK   We have plenty of time. No one's coming to my place until seven or even half past.

TESMAN   Meanwhile, we can keep Hedda company and see what happens, hm?

HEDDA [*Sets* BRACK's *overcoat and hat on the corner sofa.*]   At the very worst, Mr. Løvborg can stay here with me.

BRACK [*Offering to take his things.*]   At the worst, Mrs. Tesman, what do you mean?

HEDDA   If he won't go out with you and Tesman.

TESMAN [*Looking at her uncertainly.*]   But, Hedda dear, do you think that would be quite right, him staying here with you? Remember, Aunt Julie can't come.

HEDDA   No, but Mrs. Elvsted will be coming and the three of us can have a cup of tea together.

TESMAN   Yes, that's all right then.

BRACK [*Smiling.*]   And I might add, that would be the best plan for him.

HEDDA   Why so?

BRACK   Good Lord, Mrs. Tesman, you've had enough to say about my little bachelor parties in the past. Don't you agree they should be open only to men of the highest principle?

HEDDA   That's just what Mr. Løvborg is now, a reclaimed sinner.

[BERTA *comes in from the hall doorway.*]

BERTA   Madam, there's a gentleman who wishes to—

HEDDA   Yes, please, show him in.

TESMAN [*Softly.*]   It's got to be him. Just think.

[EILERT LØVBORG *enters from the hallway. He is slim and lean, the same age as* TESMAN, *but he looks older and somewhat haggard. His hair and beard are dark brown. His face is longish, pale, with patches of red over the cheekbones. He is dressed in an elegant suit, black, quite new dark gloves and top hat. He stops just inside the doorway and bows hastily. He seems somewhat embarrassed.*]

TESMAN [*Goes to him and shakes his hands.*]   Oh my dear Eilert, we meet again at long last.

LØVBORG [*Speaks in a low voice.*]   Thanks for the letter, George. [*Approaches* HEDDA.] May I shake your hand also, Mrs. Tesman?

HEDDA [*Takes his hand.*]   Welcome, Mr. Løvborg. [*With a gesture.*] I don't know if you two gentlemen—

LØVBORG [*Bowing.*]   Judge Brack, I believe.

BRACK [*Similarly.*]   Indeed. It's been quite a few years—

TESMAN [*To* LØVBORG, *his hands on his shoulders.*]   And now Eilert, make yourself completely at home. Right, Hedda? I hear you're going to settle down here in town, hm?

LØVBORG   Yes, I will.

TESMAN   Well, that's only sensible. Listen, I got your new book. I haven't really had time to read it yet.

LØVBORG   You can save yourself the trouble.

TESMAN   What do you mean?

LØVBORG   There's not much to it.

TESMAN   How can you say that?

BRACK   But everyone's been praising it so highly.

LØVBORG   Exactly as I intended—so I wrote the sort of book that everyone can agree with.

BRACK   Very clever.

TESMAN   Yes, but my dear Eilert.

LØVBORG   Because I want to reestablish my position, begin again.

TESMAN [*A little downcast.*] Yes, I suppose you'd want to, hm.

LØVBORG [*Smiling, putting down his hat and pulling a package wrapped in paper from his coat pocket.*]   But when this comes out, George Tesman—this is what you should read. It's the real thing. I've put my whole self into it.

TESMAN   Oh yes? What's it about?

LØVBORG   It's the sequel.

TESMAN   Sequel to what?

LØVBORG   To my book.

TESMAN   The new one?

LØVBORG   Of course.

TESMAN   But my dear Eilert, that one takes us right to the present day.

LØVBORG   So it does—and this one takes us into the future.

TESMAN   The future. Good Lord! We don't know anything about that.

LØVBORG   No, we don't—but there are still one or two things to say about it, just the same. [*Opens the packages.*] Here, you'll see.

TESMAN   That's not your handwriting, is it?

LØVBORG   I dictated it. [*Turns the pages.*] It's written in two sections. The first is about the cultural forces which will shape the future, and this other section [*Turning the pages.*] is about the future course of civilization.

TESMAN   Extraordinary. It would never occur to me to write about something like that.

HEDDA [*By the glass door, drumming on the pane.*] Hmm, no, no.

LØVBORG [*Puts the papers back in the packet and sets it on the table.*]   I brought it along because I thought I might read some of it to you tonight.

TESMAN   Ah, that was very kind of you, Eilert, but this evening [*Looks at* BRACK.] I'm not sure it can be arranged—

LØVBORG   Some other time then, there's no hurry.

BRACK   I should tell you, Mr. Løvborg, we're having a little party at my place this evening, mostly for Tesman, you understand—

LØVBORG [*Looking for his hat.*] Aha, well then I'll—

BRACK   No, listen, why don't you join us?

LØVBORG [*Briefly but firmly.*] No, that I can't do, but many thanks just the same.

BRACK   Oh come now, you certainly can do that. We'll be a small, select circle and I guarantee we'll be "lively," as Mrs. Hed—Mrs. Tesman would say.

LØVBORG   No doubt, but even so—

BRACK   And then you could bring your manuscript along and read it to Tesman at my place. I've got plenty of rooms.

TESMAN   Think about that, Eilert. You could do that, hm?

HEDDA [*Intervening.*] Now, my dear, Mr. Løvborg simply doesn't want to. I'm quite sure Mr. Løvborg would rather settle down here and have supper with me.

LØVBORG [*Staring at her.*] With you, Mrs. Tesman?

HEDDA   And with Mrs. Elvsted.

LØVBORG   Ah—[*Casually.*] I saw her this morning very briefly.

HEDDA Oh did you? Well, she's coming here; so you might almost say it's essential that you stay here, Mr. Løvborg. Otherwise she'll have no one to see her home.

LØVBORG That's true. Yes, Mrs. Tesman, many thanks. I'll stay.

HEDDA I'll go and have a word with the maid.

[*She goes over to the hall door and rings.* BERTA *enters.* HEDDA *speaks quietly to her and points toward the rear room.* BERTA *nods and goes out again.*]

TESMAN [*At the same time to* LØVBORG.] Listen, Eilert, your lecture—Is it about this new subject? About the future?

LØVBORG Yes.

TESMAN Because I heard down at the bookstore that you'd be giving a lecture series here this fall.

LØVBORG I plan to. Please don't hold it against me.

TESMAN No, God forbid, but—?

LØVBORG I can easily see how this might make things awkward.

TESMAN [*Dejectedly.*] Oh, for my part, I can't expect you to—

LØVBORG But I'll wait until you get your appointment.

TESMAN You will? Yes but—yes but—you won't be competing then?

LØVBORG No. I only want to conquer you in the marketplace of ideas.

TESMAN But, good Lord, Aunt Julie was right after all. Oh yes, yes, I was quite sure of it. Hedda, imagine, my dear—Eilert Løvborg won't stand in our way.

HEDDA [*Curtly.*] Our way? Leave me out of it.

[*She goes up toward the rear room where* BERTA *is placing a tray with decanters and glasses on the table.* HEDDA *nods approvingly, comes forward again.* BERTA *goes out.*]

TESMAN [*Meanwhile.*] So, Judge Brack, what do you say about all this?

BRACK Well now, I say that honor and victory, hmm—they have a powerful appeal—

TESMAN Yes, yes, I suppose they do but all the same—

HEDDA [*Looking at* TESMAN *with a cold smile.*] You look like you've been struck by lightning.

TESMAN Yes, that's about it—or something like that, I think—

BRACK That was quite a thunderstorm that passed over us, Mrs. Tesman.

HEDDA [*Pointing toward the rear room.*] Won't you gentlemen go in there and have a glass of punch?

BRACK [*Looking at his watch.*] For the road? Yes, not a bad idea.

TESMAN Wonderful, Hedda, wonderful! And I'm in such a fantastic mood now.

HEDDA You too, Mr. Løvborg, if you please.

LØVBORG [*Dismissively.*] No, thank you, not for me.

BRACK Good Lord, cold punch isn't exactly poison, you know.

LØVBORG Maybe not for everybody.

HEDDA Then I'll keep Mr. Løvborg company in the meantime.

TESMAN Yes, yes, Hedda dear, you do that.

[TESMAN *and* BRACK *go into the rear room, sit down and drink punch, smoking cigarettes and talking animatedly during the following.* EILERT LØVBORG *remains standing by the stove and* HEDDA *goes to the writing table.*]

HEDDA [*In a slightly raised voice.*]   Now, if you like, I'll show you some photographs. Tesman and I—we took a trip to the Tyrol on the way home.
[*She comes over with an album and lays it on the table by the sofa, seating herself in the farthest corner.* EILERT LØVBORG *comes closer, stooping and looking at her. Then he takes a chair and sits on her left side with his back to the rear room.*]

HEDDA [*Opening the album.*]   Do you see these mountains, Mr. Løvborg? That's the Ortler group. Tesman's written a little caption. Here. "The Ortler group near Meran."[7]

LØVBORG [*Who has not taken his eyes off her from the beginning, says softly and slowly.*]   Hedda Gabler.

HEDDA [*Glances quickly at him.*]   Shh, now.

LØVBORG [*Repeating softly.*]   Hedda Gabler.

HEDDA [*Staring at the album.*]   Yes, so I was once, when we knew each other.

LØVBORG   And from now—for the rest of my life—do I have to teach myself never to say Hedda Gabler?

HEDDA [*Turning the pages.*]   Yes, you have to. And I think you'd better start practicing now. The sooner the better, I'd say.

LØVBORG [*In a resentful voice.*]   Hedda Gabler married—and then—with George Tesman.

HEDDA   That's how it goes.

LØVBORG   Ah, Hedda, Hedda—how could you have thrown yourself away like that?

HEDDA [*Looks sharply at him.*]   What? Now stop that.

LØVBORG   Stop what, what do you mean?

HEDDA   Calling me Hedda and[8]—
[TESMAN *comes in and goes toward the sofa.*]

HEDDA [*Hears him approaching and says casually.*]   And this one here, Mr. Løvborg, this was taken from the Ampezzo Valley. Would you just look at these mountain peaks. [*Looks warmly up at* TESMAN.] George, dear, what were these extraordinary mountains called?

TESMAN   Let me see. Ah, yes, those are the Dolomites.

HEDDA   Of course. Those, Mr. Løvborg, are the Dolomites.

TESMAN   Hedda, dear, I just wanted to ask you if we should bring some punch in here, for you at least.

HEDDA   Yes, thank you my dear. And a few pastries perhaps.

TESMAN   Any cigarettes?

HEDDA   No.

TESMAN   Good.
[*He goes into the rear room and off to the right.* BRACK *remains sitting, from time to time keeping his eye on* HEDDA *and* LØVBORG.]

7. I.e., Merano, a city in the Austrian Tyrol, since 1918 in Italy. The scenic features mentioned here and later are tourist attractions. The Ortler group and the Dolomites are Alpine mountain ranges. The Ampezzo Valley lies beyond the Dolomites to the east. The Brenner Pass is a major route through the Alps to Austria.

8. This line is interpolated in an attempt to suggest the difference between the informal *du* (thee or thou) and the formal *de* (you) in the Norwegian text. Løvborg has just addressed Hedda in the informal manner and she is warning him not to [translators' note].

LØVBORG [*Quietly, as before.*] Then answer me, Hedda—how could you go and do such a thing?

HEDDA [*Apparently absorbed in the album.*] If you keep talking to me that way, I just won't speak to you.

LØVBORG Not even when we're alone together?

HEDDA No. You can think whatever you want but you can't talk about it.

LØVBORG Ah, I see. It offends your love for George Tesman.

HEDDA [*Glances at him and smiles.*] Love? Don't be absurd.

LØVBORG Not love then either?

HEDDA But even so—nothing unfaithful. I will not allow it.

LØVBORG Answer me just one thing—

HEDDA Shh.

[TESMAN, *with a tray, enters from the rear room.*]

TESMAN Here we are, here come the treats. [*He places the tray on the table.*]

HEDDA Why are you serving us yourself?

TESMAN [*Filling the glasses.*] I have such a good time waiting on you, Hedda.

HEDDA But now you've gone and poured two drinks and Mr. Løvborg definitely does not want—

TESMAN No, but Mrs. Elvsted's coming soon.

HEDDA Yes, that's right, Mrs. Elvsted.

TESMAN Did you forget about her?

HEDDA We were just sitting here so completely wrapped up in these. [*Shows him a picture.*] Do you remember this little village?

TESMAN Yes, that's the one below the Brenner Pass. We spent the night there—

HEDDA —and ran into all those lively summer visitors.

TESMAN Ah yes, that was it. Imagine—if you could have been with us, Eilert, just think. [*He goes in again and sits with* BRACK.]

LØVBORG Just answer me one thing—

HEDDA Yes?

LØVBORG In our relationship—wasn't there any love there either? No trace? Not a glimmer of love in any of it?

HEDDA I wonder if there really was. For me it was like we were two good comrades, two really good, faithful friends. [*Smiling.*] I remember you were particularly frank and open.

LØVBORG That's how you wanted it.

HEDDA When I look back on it, there was something really beautiful—something fascinating, something brave about this secret comradeship, this secret intimacy that no living soul had any idea about.

LØVBORG Yes, Hedda, that's true isn't it? That was it. When I'd come to your father's in the afternoon—and the General would sit in the window reading his newspaper with his back toward the room—

HEDDA And us on the corner sofa.

LØVBORG Always with the same illustrated magazine in front of us.

HEDDA Instead of an album, yes.

LØVBORG Yes, Hedda—and when I made all those confessions to you—telling you things about myself that no one else knew in those days. Sat there and told you how I'd lost whole days and nights in drunken frenzy, frenzy that would last for days on end. Ah, Hedda—what kind of power was in you that drew these confessions out of me?

HEDDA You think it was a power in me?

LØVBORG Yes. I can't account for it in any other way. And you'd ask me all those ambiguous leading questions—

HEDDA Which you understood implicitly—

LØVBORG How did you sit there and question me so fearlessly?

HEDDA Ambiguously?

LØVBORG Yes, but fearlessly all the same. Questioning me about—About things like that.

HEDDA And how could you answer them, Mr. Løvborg?

LØVBORG Yes, yes. That's just what I don't understand anymore. But now tell me, Hedda, wasn't it love underneath it all? Wasn't that part of it? You wanted to purify me, to cleanse me—when I'd seek you out to make my confessions. Wasn't that it?

HEDDA No, no, not exactly.

LØVBORG Then what drove you?

HEDDA Do you find it so hard to explain that a young girl—when it becomes possible—in secret—

LØVBORG Yes?

HEDDA That she wants a glimpse of a world that—

LØVBORG That—

HEDDA That is not permitted to her.

LØVBORG So that was it.

HEDDA That too, that too—I almost believe it.

LØVBORG Comrades in a quest for life. So why couldn't it go on?

HEDDA That was your own fault.

LØVBORG You broke it off.

HEDDA Yes, when it looked like reality threatened to spoil the situation. Shame on you, Eilert Løvborg, how could you do violence to your comrade in arms?

LØVBORG [Clenching his hands together.] Well, why didn't you do it for real? Why didn't you shoot me dead right then and there like you threatened to?

HEDDA Oh, I'm much too afraid of scandal.

LØVBORG Yes, Hedda, underneath it all, you're a coward.

HEDDA A terrible coward. [Changes her tone.] Lucky for you. And now you've got plenty of consolation up there at the Elvsteds'.

LØVBORG I know what Thea's confided to you.

HEDDA And no doubt you've confided to her about us.

LØVBORG Not one word. She's too stupid to understand things like this.

HEDDA Stupid?

LØVBORG In things like this she's stupid.

HEDDA And I'm a coward. [Leans closer to him without looking him in the eyes and says softly.] Now I'll confide something to you.

LØVBORG [In suspense.] What?

HEDDA My not daring to shoot you—

LØVBORG Yes?!

HEDDA —that wasn't my worst cowardice that evening.

LØVBORG [*Stares at her a moment, understands and whispers passionately.*] Ah, Hedda Gabler, now I see the hidden reason why we're such comrades. This craving for life in you—

HEDDA [*Quietly, with a sharp glance at him.*] Watch out, don't believe anything of the sort.

[*It starts to get dark. The hall door is opened by* BERTA.]

HEDDA [*Clapping the album shut and crying out with a smile.*] Ah, finally. Thea, darling, do come in.

[MRS. ELVSTED *enters from the hall. She is in evening dress. The door is closed after her.*]

HEDDA [*On the sofa, stretching out her arms.*] Thea, my sweet, you can't imagine how I've been expecting you.

[MRS. ELVSTED, *in passing, exchanges a greeting with the gentlemen in the inner room, crosses to the table, shakes* HEDDA'*s hand.* EILERT LØVBORG *has risen. He and* MRS. ELVSTED *greet each other with a single nod.*]

MRS. ELVSTED Perhaps I should go in and have a word with your husband.

HEDDA Not at all. Let them sit there. They'll be on their way soon.

MRS. ELVSTED They're leaving?

HEDDA Yes, they're going out on a little binge.

MRS. ELVSTED [*Quickly to* LØVBORG.] You're not?

LØVBORG No.

HEDDA Mr. Løvborg . . . he'll stay here with us.

MRS. ELVSTED [*Takes a chair and sits down beside him.*] It's so nice to be here.

HEDDA No, you don't, little Thea, not there. Come right over here next to me. I want to be in the middle between you.

MRS. ELVSTED All right, whatever you like. [*She goes around the table and sits on the sofa to the right of* HEDDA. LØVBORG *takes his chair again.*]

LØVBORG [*After a brief pause, to* HEDDA.] Isn't she lovely to look at?

HEDDA [*Gently stroking her hair.*] Only to look at?

LØVBORG Yes. We're true comrades, the two of us. We trust each other completely and that's why we can sit here and talk so openly and boldly together.

HEDDA With no ambiguity, Mr. Løvborg.

LØVBORG Well—

MRS. ELVSTED [*Softly, clinging to* HEDDA.] Oh, Hedda, I'm so lucky. Just think, he says I've inspired him too.

HEDDA [*Regards her with a smile.*] No, dear, does he say that?

LØVBORG And she has the courage to take action, Mrs. Tesman.

MRS. ELVSTED Oh God, me, courage?

LØVBORG Tremendous courage when it comes to comradeship.

HEDDA Yes, courage—yes! That's the crucial thing.

LØVBORG Why is that, do you suppose?

HEDDA Because then—maybe—life has a chance to be lived. [*Suddenly changing her tone.*] But now, my dearest Thea. Why don't you treat yourself to a nice cold glass of punch?

MRS. ELVSTED No thank you, I never drink anything like that.

HEDDA Then for you, Mr. Løvborg.

LØVBORG   No thank you, not for me either.

MRS. ELVSTED   No, not for him either.

HEDDA [*Looking steadily at him.*]   But if I insisted.

LØVBORG   Doesn't matter.

HEDDA [*Laughing.*]   Then I have absolutely no power over you? Ah, poor me.

LØVBORG   Not in that area.

HEDDA   But seriously now, I really think you should, for your own sake.

MRS. ELVSTED   No, Hedda—

LØVBORG   Why is that?

HEDDA   Or to be more precise, for others' sakes.

LØVBORG   Oh?

HEDDA   Because otherwise people might get the idea that you don't, deep down inside, feel really bold, really sure of yourself.

LØVBORG   Oh, from now on people can think whatever they like.

MRS. ELVSTED   Yes, that's right, isn't it.

HEDDA   I saw it so clearly with Judge Brack a few minutes ago.

LØVBORG   What did you see?

HEDDA   That condescending little smile when you didn't dare join them at the table.

LØVBORG   Didn't dare? I'd just rather stay here and talk with you, of course.

MRS. ELVSTED   That's only reasonable, Hedda.

HEDDA   How was the Judge supposed to know that? I saw how he smiled and shot a glance at Tesman when you didn't dare join them in their silly little party.

LØVBORG   Didn't dare. You're saying I don't dare.

HEDDA   Oh, I'm not. But that's how Judge Brack sees it.

LØVBORG   Well let him.

HEDDA   So you won't join them?

LØVBORG   I'm staying here with you and Thea.

MRS. ELVSTED   Yes, Hedda, you can be sure he is.

HEDDA [*Smiling and nodding approvingly to* LØVBORG.]   What a strong foundation you've got. Principles to last a lifetime. That's what a man ought to have. [*Turns to* MRS. ELVSTED.] See now, wasn't that what I told you when you came here this morning in such a panic—

LØVBORG [*Startled.*]   Panic?

MRS. ELVSTED [*Terrified.*]   Hedda, Hedda, no.

HEDDA   Just see for yourself. No reason at all to come running here in mortal terror. [*Changing her tone.*] There, now all three of us can be quite jolly.

LØVBORG [*Shocked.*]   What does this mean, Mrs. Tesman?

MRS. ELVSTED   Oh God, oh God, Hedda. What are you doing? What are you saying?

HEDDA   Keep calm now. That disgusting Judge is sitting there watching you.

LØVBORG   In mortal terror on my account?

MRS. ELVSTED [*Quietly wailing.*]   Oh, Hedda—

LØVBORG [*Looks at her steadily for a moment; his face is drawn.*]   So that, then, was how my brave, bold comrade trusted me.

MRS. ELVSTED [*Pleading.*]   Oh, my dearest friend, listen to me—

LØVBORG [*Takes one of the glasses of punch, raises it and says in a low, hoarse voice.*]   Your health, Thea. [*Empties the glass, takes another.*]

MRS. ELVSTED [*Softly.*]   Oh Hedda, Hedda—how could you want this to happen?

HEDDA   Want it? I want this? Are you mad?

LØVBORG   And your health too, Mrs. Tesman. Thanks for the truth. Long may it live. [*He drinks and goes to refill the glass.*]

HEDDA [*Placing her hand on his arm.*]   That's enough for now. Remember, you're going to the party.

MRS. ELVSTED   No, no, no.

HEDDA   Shh. They're watching us.

LØVBORG [*Putting down the glass.*]   Thea, be honest with me now.

MRS. ELVSTED   Yes.

LØVBORG   Was your husband told that you came here to look for me?

MRS. ELVSTED [*Wringing her hands.*]   Oh, Hedda, listen to what he's asking me!

LØVBORG   Did he arrange for you to come to town to spy on me? Maybe he put you up to it himself. Aha, that's it. He needed me back in the office again. Or did he just miss me at the card table?

MRS. ELVSTED [*Softly moaning.*]   Oh, Løvborg, Løvborg—

LØVBORG [*Grabs a glass intending to fill it.*]   Skøal to the old Sheriff too.

HEDDA [*Preventing him.*]   No more now. Remember, you're going out to read to Tesman.

LØVBORG [*Calmly putting down his glass.*]   Thea, that was stupid of me. What I did just now. Taking it like that I mean. Don't be angry with me, my dear, dear comrade. You'll see. Both of you and everyone else will see that even though I once was fallen—now I've raised myself up again, with your help, Thea.

MRS. ELVSTED [*Radiant with joy.*]   Oh God be praised.

[*Meanwhile* BRACK *has been looking at his watch. He and* TESMAN *get up and come into the drawing room.*]

BRACK [*Taking his hat and overcoat.*]   Well, Mrs. Tesman, our time is up.

HEDDA   Yes, it must be.

LØVBORG [*Rising.*]   Mine too.

MRS. ELVSTED [*Quietly pleading.*]   Løvborg, don't do it.

HEDDA [*Pinching her arm.*]   They can hear you.

MRS. ELVSTED [*Crying out faintly.*]   Ow.

LØVBORG [*To* BRACK.]   You were kind enough to ask me along.

BRACK   So you're coming after all.

LØVBORG   Yes, thanks.

BRACK   I'm delighted.

LØVBORG [*Putting the manuscript packet in his pocket and saying to* TESMAN.]   I'd really like you to look at one or two things before I send it off.

TESMAN   Just think, that will be splendid. But, Hedda dear, how will you get Mrs. Elvsted home?

HEDDA   Oh, there's always a way out.

LØVBORG [*Looking at the ladies.*]   Mrs. Elvsted? Well, of course, I'll come back for her. [*Coming closer.*]   Around ten o'clock, Mrs. Tesman, will that do?

HEDDA   Yes, that will be fine.

TESMAN   Well, everything's all right then; but don't expect me that early, Hedda.

HEDDA   No dear, you stay just as long—as long as you like.

MRS. ELVSTED   [*With suppressed anxiety.*]   Mr. Løvborg—I'll stay here until you come.

LØVBORG   [*His hat in his hand.*]   That's understood.

BRACK   All aboard then, the party train's pulling out. Gentlemen, I trust it will be a lively trip, as a certain lovely lady suggested.

HEDDA   Ah yes, if only that lovely lady could be there—invisible, of course.

BRACK   Why invisible?

HEDDA   To hear a little of your liveliness, Judge, uncensored.

BRACK   [*Laughing.*]   Not recommended for the lovely lady.

TESMAN   [*Also laughing.*]   You really are the limit, Hedda. Think of it.

BRACK   Well, well, my ladies. Good night. Good night.

LØVBORG   [*Bowing as he leaves.*]   Until ten o'clock, then.

> [BRACK, LØVBORG *and* TESMAN *leave through the hall door. At the same time* BERTA *comes in from the rear room with a lighted lamp which she places on the drawing room table, going out the way she came in.*]

MRS. ELVSTED   [*Has gotten up and wanders uneasily about the room.*]   Oh, Hedda, where is all this going?

HEDDA   Ten o'clock—then he'll appear. I see him before me with vine leaves in his hair,[9] burning bright and bold.

MRS. ELVSTED   Yes, if only it could be like that.

HEDDA   And then you'll see—then he'll have power over himself again. Then he'll be a free man for the rest of his days.

MRS. ELVSTED   Oh God yes—if only he'd come back just the way you see him.

HEDDA   He'll come back just that way and no other. [*Gets up and comes closer.*] You can doubt him as much as you like. I believe in him. And so we'll see—

MRS. ELVSTED   There's something behind this, something else you're trying to do.

HEDDA   Yes, there is. Just once in my life I want to help shape someone's destiny.

MRS. ELVSTED   Don't you do that already?

HEDDA   I don't and I never have.

MRS. ELVSTED   Not even your husband?

HEDDA   Oh yes, that was a real bargain. Oh, if you could only understand how destitute I am while you get to be so rich. [*She passionately throws her arms around her.*] I think I'll burn your hair off after all.

MRS. ELVSTED   Let me go, let me go. I'm afraid of you.

BERTA   [*In the doorway.*]   Tea is ready in the dining room, Madam.

HEDDA   Good. We're on our way.

MRS. ELVSTED   No, no, no! I'd rather go home alone! Right now!

---

9. Like Bacchus, the Greek god of wine, and his followers.

HEDDA   Nonsense! First you're going to have some tea, you little bubble-head, and then—at ten o'clock—Eilert Løvborg—with vine leaves in his hair! [*She pulls* MRS. ELVSTED *toward the doorway almost by force.*]

Act 3

The room at the TESMANS'. *The curtains are drawn across the center door-way and also across the glass door. The lamp covered with a shade burns low on the table. In the stove, with its door standing open, there has been a fire that is almost burned out.*

[MRS. ELVSTED, *wrapped in a large shawl and with her feet on a footstool, sits sunk back in an armchair.* HEDDA, *fully dressed, lies sleeping on the sofa with a rug over her.*]

MRS. ELVSTED   [*After a pause suddenly straightens herself in the chair and listens intently. Then she sinks back wearily and moans softly.*]   Still not back . . . Oh God, oh God . . . Still not back.

[BERTA *enters tiptoeing carefully through the hall doorway; she has a letter in her hand.*]

MRS. ELVSTED   Ah—did someone come?

BERTA   Yes, a girl came by just now with this letter.

MRS. ELVSTED   [*Quickly stretching out her hand.*]   A letter? Let me have it.

BERTA   No ma'am, it's for the doctor.

MRS. ELVSTED   Oh.

BERTA   It was Miss Tesman's maid who brought it. I'll put it on the table here.

MRS. ELVSTED   Yes, do that.

BERTA   [*Puts down the letter.*]   I'd better put out the lamp; it's starting to smoke.

MRS. ELVSTED   Yes, put it out. It'll be light soon anyway.

BERTA   [*Putting out the light.*]   Oh, ma'am, it's already light.

MRS. ELVSTED   So, morning and still not back—!

BERTA   Oh, dear Lord—I knew all along it would go like this.

MRS. ELVSTED   You knew?

BERTA   Yes, when I saw a certain person was back in town. And then when he went off with them—oh we'd heard plenty about that gentleman.

MRS. ELVSTED   Don't speak so loud, you'll wake your mistress.

BERTA   [*Looks over to the sofa and sighs.*]   No, dear Lord—let her sleep, poor thing. Shouldn't I build the stove up a little more?

MRS. ELVSTED   Not for me, thanks.

BERTA   Well, well then. [*She goes out quietly through the hall doorway.*]

HEDDA   [*Awakened by the closing door, looks up.*]   What's that?

MRS. ELVSTED   Only the maid.

HEDDA   [*Looking around.*]   In here—! Oh, now I remember. [*Straightens up, stretches sitting on the sofa and rubs her eyes.*] What time is it, Thea?

MRS. ELVSTED   [*Looks at her watch.*]   It's after seven.

HEDDA   What time did Tesman get in?

MRS. ELVSTED   He hasn't.

HEDDA   Still?

MRS. ELVSTED [*Getting up.*]   No one's come back.

HEDDA   And we sat here waiting and watching until almost four.

MRS. ELVSTED [*Wringing her hands.*]   Waiting for him!

HEDDA [*Yawning and speaking with her hand over her mouth.*]   Oh yes—we could have saved ourselves the trouble.

MRS. ELVSTED   Did you finally manage to sleep?

HEDDA   Yes, I think I slept quite well. Did you?

MRS. ELVSTED   Not a wink. I couldn't, Hedda. It was just impossible for me.

HEDDA [*Gets up and goes over to her.*]   Now, now, now. There's nothing to worry about. I know perfectly well how it all turned out.

MRS. ELVSTED   Yes, what do you think? Can you tell me?

HEDDA   Well, of course they dragged it out dreadfully up at Judge Brack's.

MRS. ELVSTED   Oh God yes—that must be true. But all the same—

HEDDA   And then you see, Tesman didn't want to come home and create a fuss by ringing the bell in the middle of the night. [*Laughing.*] He probably didn't want to show himself either right after a wild party like that.

MRS. ELVSTED   For goodness sake—where would he have gone?

HEDDA   Well, naturally, he went over to his aunt's and laid himself down to sleep there. They still have his old room standing ready for him.

MRS. ELVSTED   No, he's not with them. A letter just came for him from Miss Tesman. It's over there.

HEDDA   Oh? [*Looks at the inscription.*] Yes, that's Aunt Julie's hand all right. So then, he's still over at Judge Brack's and Eilert Løvborg—he's sitting—reading aloud with vine leaves in his hair.

MRS. ELVSTED   Oh, Hedda, you don't even believe what you're saying.

HEDDA   You are such a little noodlehead, Thea.

MRS. ELVSTED   Yes, unfortunately I probably am.

HEDDA   And you look like you're dead on your feet.

MRS. ELVSTED   Yes, I am. Dead on my feet.

HEDDA   And so now you're going to do what I tell you. You'll go into my room and lie down on my bed.

MRS. ELVSTED   Oh no, no—I couldn't get to sleep anyway.

HEDDA   Yes, you certainly will.

MRS. ELVSTED   But your husband's bound to be home any time now and I've got to find out right away—

HEDDA   I'll tell you as soon as he comes.

MRS. ELVSTED   Promise me that, Hedda?

HEDDA   Yes, that you can count on. Now just go in and sleep for a while.

MRS. ELVSTED   Thanks. At least I'll give it a try. [*She goes in through the back room.*]

> [HEDDA *goes over to the glass door and draws back the curtains. Full daylight floods the room. She then takes a small hand mirror from the writing table, looks in it and arranges her hair. Then she goes to the hall door and presses the bell. Soon after* BERTA *enters the doorway.*]

BERTA   Did Madam want something?

HEDDA   Yes, build up the stove a little bit. I'm freezing in here.

BERTA Lord, in no time at all it'll be warm in here. [*She rakes the embers and puts a log inside. She stands and listens.*] There's the front doorbell, Madam.

HEDDA So, go answer it. I'll take care of the stove myself.

BERTA It'll be burning soon enough. [*She goes out through the hall door.*] [HEDDA *kneels on the footstool and puts more logs into the stove. After a brief moment,* GEORGE TESMAN *comes in from the hall. He looks weary and rather serious. He creeps on tiptoes toward the doorway and is about to slip through the curtains.*]

HEDDA [*By the stove, without looking up.*] Good morning.

TESMAN [*Turning around.*] Hedda. [*Comes nearer.*] What in the world— Up so early, hm?

HEDDA Yes, up quite early today.

TESMAN And here I was so sure you'd still be in bed. Just think, Hedda.

HEDDA Not so loud. Mrs. Elvsted's lying down in my room.

TESMAN Has Mrs. Elvsted been here all night?

HEDDA Yes. No one came to pick her up.

TESMAN No, no, they couldn't have.

HEDDA [*Shuts the door of the stove and gets up.*] So, did you have a jolly time at the Judge's?

TESMAN Were you worried about me?

HEDDA No, that would never occur to me. I asked if you had a good time.

TESMAN Yes, I really did, for once, in a manner of speaking—Mostly in the beginning, I'd say. We'd arrived an hour early. How about that? And Brack had so much to get ready. But then Eilert read to me.

HEDDA [*Sits at the right of the table.*] So, tell me.

TESMAN Hedda, you can't imagine what this new work will be like. It's one of the most brilliant things ever written, no doubt about it. Think of that.

HEDDA Yes, yes, but that's not what I'm interested in.

TESMAN But I have to confess something, Hedda. After he read—something horrible came over me.

HEDDA Something horrible?

TESMAN I sat there envying Eilert for being able to write like that. Think of it, Hedda.

HEDDA Yes, yes, I'm thinking.

TESMAN And then, that whole time, knowing that he—even with all the incredible powers at his command—is still beyond redemption.

HEDDA You mean he's got more of life's courage in him than the others?

TESMAN No, for heaven sakes—he just has no control over his pleasures.

HEDDA And what happened then—at the end?

TESMAN Well, Hedda, I guess you'd have to say it was a bacchanal.

HEDDA Did he have vine leaves in his hair?

TESMAN Vine leaves? No, I didn't see anything like that. But he did make a long wild speech for the woman who had inspired him in his work. Yes—that's how he put it.

HEDDA Did he name her?

TESMAN No, he didn't, but I can only guess that it must be Mrs. Elvsted. Wouldn't you say?

HEDDA Hmm—where did you leave him?

TESMAN   On the way back. Most of our group broke up at the same time and Brack came along with us to get a little fresh air. And you see, we agreed to follow Eilert home because—well—he was so far gone.

HEDDA   He must have been.

TESMAN   But here's the strangest part, Hedda! Or maybe I should say the saddest. I'm almost ashamed for Eilert's sake—to tell you—

HEDDA   So?

TESMAN   There we were walking along, you see, and I happened to drop back a bit, just for a couple of minutes, you understand.

HEDDA   Yes, yes, good Lord but—

TESMAN   And then when I was hurrying to catch up—can you guess what I found in the gutter, hm?

HEDDA   How can I possibly guess?

TESMAN   Don't ever tell a soul, Hedda. Do you hear? Promise me that for Eilert's sake. [*Pulls a package out of his coat pocket.*] Just think—this is what I found.

HEDDA   That's the package he had with him here yesterday, isn't it?

TESMAN   That's it. His precious, irreplaceable manuscript—all of it. And he's lost it—without even noticing it. Oh just think, Hedda—the pity of it—

HEDDA   Well, why didn't you give it back to him right away?

TESMAN   Oh, I didn't dare do that—The condition he was in—

HEDDA   You didn't tell any of the others that you found it either?

TESMAN   Absolutely not. I couldn't, you see, for Eilert's sake.

HEDDA   So nobody knows you have Eilert's manuscript? Nobody at all?

TESMAN   No. And they mustn't find out either.

HEDDA   What did you talk to him about later?

TESMAN   I didn't get a chance to talk to him any more. We got to the city limits, and he and a couple of the others went a different direction. Just think—

HEDDA   Aha, they must have followed him home then.

TESMAN   Yes, I suppose so. Brack also went his way.

HEDDA   And, in the meantime, what became of the bacchanal?

TESMAN   Well, I and some of the others followed one of the revelers up to his place and had morning coffee with him—or maybe we should call it morning-after coffee, hm? Now, I'll rest a bit—and as soon as I think Eilert has managed to sleep it off, poor man, then I've got to go over to him with this.

HEDDA   [*Reaching out for the envelope.*]   No, don't give it back. Not yet, I mean. Let me read it first.

TESMAN   Oh no.

HEDDA   Oh, for God's sake.

TESMAN   I don't dare do that.

HEDDA   You don't dare?

TESMAN   No, you can imagine how completely desperate he'll be when he wakes up and realizes he can't find the manuscript. He's got no copy of it. He said so himself.

HEDDA   [*Looks searchingly at him.*]   Couldn't it be written again?

TESMAN No, I don't believe that could ever be done because the inspiration—you see—

HEDDA Yes, yes—That's the thing, isn't it? [*Casually.*] But, oh yes—there's a letter here for you.

TESMAN No, think of that.

HEDDA [*Hands it to him.*] It came early this morning.

TESMAN From Aunt Julie, Hedda. What can it be? [*Puts the manuscript on the other stool, opens the letter and jumps up.*] Oh Hedda—poor Aunt Rina's almost breathing her last.

HEDDA It's only what's expected.

TESMAN And if I want to see her one more time, I've got to hurry. I'll charge over there right away.

HEDDA [*Suppressing a smile.*] You'll charge?

TESMAN Oh, Hedda dearest—if you could just bring yourself to follow me. Just think.

HEDDA [*Rises and says wearily and dismissively.*] No, no. Don't ask me to do anything like that. I won't look at sickness and death. Let me stay free from everything ugly.

TESMAN Oh, good Lord, then—[*Darting around.*] My hat—? My overcoat—? Ah, in the hall—Oh, I hope I'm not too late, Hedda, hm?

HEDDA Then charge right over—

[BERTA *appears in the hallway.*]

BERTA Judge Brack is outside.

HEDDA Ask him to come in.

TESMAN At a time like this! No, I can't possibly deal with him now.

HEDDA But I can. [*To* BERTA.] Ask the Judge in.

[BERTA *goes out.*]

HEDDA [*In a whisper.*] The package, Tesman. [*She snatches it off the stool.*]

TESMAN Yes, give it to me.

HEDDA No, I'll hide it until you get back.

[*She goes over to the writing table and sticks the package in the bookcase.* TESMAN *stands flustered, and can't get his gloves on.* BRACK *enters through the hall doorway.*]

HEDDA [*Nodding to him.*] Well, you're an early bird.

BRACK Yes, wouldn't you say. [*To* TESMAN.] You're going out?

TESMAN Yes, I've got to go over to my aunt's. Just think, the poor dear is dying.

BRACK Good Lord, is she really? Then don't let me hold you up for even a moment, at a time like this—

TESMAN Yes, I really must run—Good-bye. Good-bye. [*He hurries through the hall doorway.*]

HEDDA [*Approaches.*] So, things were livelier than usual at your place last night, Judge.

BRACK Oh yes, so much so that I haven't even been able to change clothes, Mrs. Hedda.

HEDDA You too.

BRACK As you see. But, what has Tesman been telling you about last night's adventures?

HEDDA Oh, just some boring things. He went someplace to drink coffee.

BRACK I've already looked into the coffee party. Eilert Løvborg wasn't part of that group, I presume.

HEDDA No, they followed him home before that.

BRACK Tesman too?

HEDDA No, but a couple of others, he said.

BRACK [*Smiles.*] George Tesman is a very naïve soul, Mrs. Hedda.

HEDDA God knows, he is. But is there something more behind this?

BRACK I'd have to say so.

HEDDA Well then, Judge, let's be seated. Then you can speak freely. [*She sits to the left side of the table,* BRACK *at the long side near her.*] Well, then—

BRACK I had certain reasons for keeping track of my guests—or, more precisely, some of my guests' movements last night.

HEDDA For example, Eilert Løvborg?

BRACK Yes, indeed.

HEDDA Now I'm hungry for more.

BRACK Do you know where he and a couple of the others spent the rest of the night, Mrs. Hedda?

HEDDA Why don't you tell me, if it can be told.

BRACK Oh, it's certainly worth the telling. It appears that they found their way into a particularly animated soirée.[1]

HEDDA A lively one?

BRACK The liveliest.

HEDDA Tell me more, Judge.

BRACK Løvborg had received an invitation earlier—I knew all about that. But he declined because, as you know, he's made himself into a new man.

HEDDA Up at the Elvsteds', yes. But he went just the same?

BRACK Well, you see, Mrs. Hedda—unfortunately, the spirit really seized him at my place last evening.

HEDDA Yes, I hear he was quite inspired.

BRACK Inspired to a rather powerful degree. And so, he started to reconsider, I assume, because we men, alas, are not always so true to our principles as we ought to be.

HEDDA Present company excepted, Judge Brack. So, Løvborg—?

BRACK Short and sweet—He ended up at the salon of a certain Miss Diana.

HEDDA Miss Diana?

BRACK Yes, it was Miss Diana's soirée for a select circle of ladies and their admirers.

HEDDA Is she a redhead?

BRACK Exactly.

HEDDA A sort of a—singer?

BRACK Oh, yes—She's also that. And a mighty huntress—of men, Mrs. Hedda. You must have heard of her. Eilert Løvborg was one of her most strenuous admirers—in his better days.

HEDDA And how did all this end?

---

1. "Evening party" (French).

BRACK   Apparently less amicably than it began. Miss Diana, after giving him the warmest of welcomes, soon turned to assault and battery.

HEDDA   Against Løvborg?

BRACK   Oh, yes. He accused her, or one of her ladies, of robbing him. He insisted that his pocketbook was missing, along with some other things. In short, he seems to have created a dreadful spectacle.

HEDDA   And what did that lead to?

BRACK   A regular brawl between both the men and the women. Luckily the police finally got there.

HEDDA   The police too?

BRACK   Yes. It's going to be quite a costly little romp for Eilert Løvborg. What a madman.

HEDDA   Well!

BRACK   Apparently, he resisted arrest. It seems he struck one of the officers on the ear, and ripped his uniform to shreds, so he had to go to the police station.

HEDDA   How do you know all this?

BRACK   From the police themselves.

HEDDA   [Gazing before her.]   So, that's how it ended? He had no vine leaves in his hair.

BRACK   Vine leaves, Mrs. Hedda?

HEDDA   [Changing her tone.]   Tell me now, Judge, why do you go around snooping and spying on Eilert Løvborg?

BRACK   For starters, I'm not a completely disinterested party—especially if the hearing uncovers the fact that he came straight from my place.

HEDDA   There's going to be a hearing?

BRACK   You can count on it. Be that as it may, however—My real concern was my duty as a friend of the house to inform you and Tesman of Løvborg's nocturnal adventures.

HEDDA   Why, Judge Brack?

BRACK   Well, I have an active suspicion that he'll try to use you as a kind of screen.

HEDDA   Oh! What makes you think that?

BRACK   Good God—we're not that blind, Mrs. Hedda. Wait and see. This Mrs. Elvsted—she won't be in such a hurry to leave town again.

HEDDA   If there's anything going on between those two, there's plenty of places they can meet.

BRACK   Not one single home. Every respectable house will be closed to Eilert Løvborg from now on.

HEDDA   And mine should be too—Is that what you're saying?

BRACK   Yes. I have to admit it would be more than painful for me if this man secured a foothold here. If this—utterly superfluous—and intrusive individual—were to force himself into—

HEDDA   Into the triangle?

BRACK   Precisely! It would leave me without a home.

HEDDA   [Looks smilingly at him.]   I see—The one cock of the walk—That's your goal.

BRACK   [Slowly nodding and dropping his voice.]   Yes, that's my goal. And it's a goal that I'll fight for—with every means at my disposal.

HEDDA [*Her smile fading.*] You're really a dangerous man, aren't you—when push comes to shove.

BRACK You think so?

HEDDA Yes, I'm starting to. And that's all right—just as long as you don't have any kind of hold on me.

BRACK [*Laughing ambiguously.*] Yes, Mrs. Hedda—you might be right about that. Of course, then, who knows whether I might not find some way or other—

HEDDA Now listen, Judge Brack! That sounds like you're threatening me.

BRACK [*Gets up.*] Oh, far from it. A triangle, you see—is best fortified by free defenders.

HEDDA I think so too.

BRACK Well, I've had my say so I should be getting back. Good-bye, Mrs. Hedda. [*He goes toward the glass doors.*]

HEDDA Out through the garden?

BRACK Yes, it's shorter for me.

HEDDA And then, it's also the back way.

BRACK That's true. I have nothing against back ways. Sometimes they can be very piquant.

HEDDA When there's sharpshooting.

BRACK [*In the doorway, laughing at her.*] Oh, no—you never shoot your tame cocks.

HEDDA [*Also laughing.*] Oh, no, especially when there's only one—
    [*Laughing and nodding they take their farewells. He leaves. She closes the door after him.* HEDDA *stands for a while, serious, looking out. Then she goes and peers through the curtains in the back wall. She goes to the writing table, takes Løvborg's package from the bookcase, and is about to leaf through it.* BERTA's *voice, raised in indignation, is heard out in the hall.* HEDDA *turns and listens. She quickly locks the package in the drawer and sets the key on the writing table.* EILERT LØVBORG, *wearing his overcoat and carrying his hat, bursts through the hall doorway. He looks somewhat confused and excited.*]

LØVBORG [*Turned toward the hallway.*] And I'm telling you, I've got to go in! And that's that! [*He closes the door, sees* HEDDA, *controls himself immediately, and bows.*]

HEDDA [*By the writing table.*] Well, Mr. Løvborg, it's pretty late to be calling for Thea.

LØVBORG Or a little early to be calling on you. I apologize.

HEDDA How do you know that she's still here?

LØVBORG I went to where she was staying. They told me she'd been out all night.

HEDDA [*Goes to the table.*] Did you notice anything special when they told you that?

LØVBORG [*Looks inquiringly at her.*] Notice anything?

HEDDA I mean—did they seem to have any thought on the subject—one way or the other?

LØVBORG [*Suddenly understanding.*] Oh, of course, it's true. I'm dragging her down with me. Still, I didn't notice anything. Tesman isn't up yet, I suppose?

HEDDA   No, I don't think so.

LØVBORG   When did he get home?

HEDDA   Very late.

LØVBORG   Did he tell you anything?

HEDDA   Yes. I heard Judge Brack's was very lively.

LØVBORG   Nothing else?

HEDDA   No, I don't think so. I was terribly tired, though—

[MRS. ELVSTED *comes in through the curtains at the back.*]

MRS. ELVSTED   [*Runs toward him.*]   Oh, Løvborg—at last!

LØVBORG   Yes, at last, and too late.

MRS. ELVSTED   [*Looking anxiously at him.*]   What's too late?

LØVBORG   Everything's too late. I'm finished.

MRS. ELVSTED   Oh no, no—Don't say that!

LØVBORG   You'll say it too, when you've heard—

MRS. ELVSTED   I won't listen—

HEDDA   Shall I leave you two alone?

LØVBORG   No, stay—You too, I beg you.

MRS. ELVSTED   But I won't listen to anything you tell me.

LØVBORG   I don't want to talk about last night.

MRS. ELVSTED   What is it, then?

LØVBORG   We've got to go our separate ways.

MRS. ELVSTED   Separate!

HEDDA   [*Involuntarily.*]   I knew it!

LØVBORG   Because I have no more use for you, Thea.

MRS. ELVSTED   You can stand there and say that! No more use for me! Can't I help you now, like I did before? Won't we go on working together?

LØVBORG   I don't plan to work any more.

MRS. ELVSTED   [*Desperately.*]   Then what do I have to live for?

LØVBORG   Just try to live your life as if you'd never known me.

MRS. ELVSTED   I can't do that.

LØVBORG   Try, Thea. Try, if you can. Go back home.

MRS. ELVSTED   [*Defiantly.*]   Where you are, that's where I want to be. I won't let myself be just driven off like this. I want to stay at your side—be with you when the book comes out.

HEDDA   [*Half aloud, tensely.*]   Ah, the book—Yes.

LØVBORG   [*Looking at her.*]   Mine and Thea's, because that's what it is.

MRS. ELVSTED   Yes, that's what I feel it is. That's why I have a right to be with you when it comes out. I want to see you covered in honor and glory again, and the joy. I want to share that with you too.

LØVBORG   Thea—our book's never coming out.

HEDDA   Ah!

MRS. ELVSTED   Never coming out?

LØVBORG   It can't ever come out.

MRS. ELVSTED   [*In anxious foreboding.*]   Løvborg, what have you done with the manuscript?

HEDDA   [*Looking intently at him.*]   Yes, the manuscript—?

MRS. ELVSTED   What have you—?

LØVBORG   Oh, Thea, don't ask me that.

MRS. ELVSTED   Yes, yes, I've got to know. I have the right to know.

LØVBORG   The manuscript—all right then, the manuscript—I've ripped it up into a thousand pieces.

MRS. ELVSTED [*Screams.*]   Oh no, no!

HEDDA [*Involuntarily.*]   But that's just not—!

LØVBORG [*Looking at her.*]   Not true, you think?

HEDDA [*Controls herself.*]   All right then. Of course it is, if you say so. It sounds so ridiculous.

LØVBORG   But it's true, just the same.

MRS. ELVSTED [*Wringing her hands.*]   Oh God—oh God, Hedda. Torn his own work to pieces.

LØVBORG   I've torn my own life to pieces. I might as well tear up my life's work too—

MRS. ELVSTED   And you did that last night!

LØVBORG   Yes. Do you hear me? A thousand pieces. Scattered them all over the fjord.[2] Way out where there's pure salt water. Let them drift in it. Drift with the current in the wind. Then, after a while, they'll sink. Deeper and deeper. Like me, Thea.

MRS. ELVSTED   You know, Løvborg, all this with the book—? For the rest of my life, it will be just like you'd killed a little child.

LØVBORG   You're right. Like murdering a child.

MRS. ELVSTED   But then, how could you—! That child was partly mine, too.

HEDDA [*Almost inaudibly.*]   Ah, the child—

MRS. ELVSTED [*Sighs heavily.*]   So it's finished? All right, Hedda, now I'm going.

HEDDA   You're not going back?

MRS. ELVSTED   Oh, I don't know what I'm going to do. I can't see anything out in front of me. [*She goes out through the hall doorway.*]

HEDDA [*Standing a while, waiting.*]   Don't you want to see her home, Mr. Løvborg?

LØVBORG   Through the streets? So that people can get a good look at us together?

HEDDA   I don't know what else happened to you last night but if it's so completely beyond redemption—

LØVBORG   It won't stop there. I know that much. And I can't bring myself to live that kind of life again either. Not again. Once I had the courage to live life to the fullest, to break every rule. But she's taken that out of me.

HEDDA [*Staring straight ahead.*]   That sweet little fool has gotten hold of a human destiny. [*Looks at him.*] And you're so heartless to her.

LØVBORG   Don't call it heartless.

HEDDA   To go and destroy the thing that has filled her soul for this whole long, long time. You don't call that heartless?

LØVBORG   I can tell you the truth, Hedda.

HEDDA   The truth?

LØVBORG   First, promise me—Give me your word that Thea will never find out what I'm about to confide to you.

---

2. "Inlet of the sea" (Norwegian).

HEDDA   You have my word.

LØVBORG   Good. Then I'll tell you—What I stood here and described—It wasn't true.

HEDDA   About the manuscript?

LØVBORG   Yes. I haven't ripped it up. I didn't throw it in the fjord, either.

HEDDA   No, well—so—Where is it?

LØVBORG   I've destroyed it just the same. Utterly and completely, Hedda!

HEDDA   I don't understand any of this.

LØVBORG   Thea said that what I'd done seemed to her like murdering a child.

HEDDA   Yes, she did.

LØVBORG   But killing his child—that's not the worst thing a father can do to it.

HEDDA   Not the worst?

LØVBORG   No. And the worst—that is what I wanted to spare Thea from hearing.

HEDDA   And what is the worst?

LØVBORG   Imagine, Hedda, a man—in the very early hours of the morning—after a wild night of debauchery, came home to the mother of his child and said, "Listen—I've been here and there to this place and that place, and I had our child with me in this place and that place. And the child got away from me. Just got away. The devil knows whose hands it's fallen into, who's got a hold of it."

HEDDA   Well—when you get right down to it—it's only a book—

LØVBORG   All of Thea's soul was in that book.

HEDDA   Yes, I can see that.

LØVBORG   And so, you must also see that there's no future for her and me.

HEDDA   So, what will your road be now?

LØVBORG   None. Only to see to it that I put an end to it all. The sooner the better.

HEDDA   [Comes a step closer.]   Eilert Løvborg—Listen to me now—Can you see to it that—that when you do it, you bathe it in beauty?

LØVBORG   In beauty? [Smiles.] With vine leaves in my hair, as you used to imagine?

HEDDA   Ah, no. No vine leaves—I don't believe in them any longer. But in beauty, yes! For once! Good-bye. You've got to go now. And don't come here any more.

LØVBORG   Good-bye, Mrs. Tesman. And give my regards to George Tesman. [He is about to leave.]

HEDDA   No, wait! Take a souvenir to remember me by.
[She goes over to the writing table, opens the drawer and the pistol case. She returns to LØVBORG with one of the pistols.]

LØVBORG   [Looks at her.]   That's the souvenir?

HEDDA   [Nodding slowly.]   Do you recognize it? It was aimed at you once.

LØVBORG   You should have used it then.

HEDDA   Here, you use it now.

LØVBORG   [Puts the pistol in his breast pocket.]   Thanks.

HEDDA   In beauty, Eilert Løvborg. Promise me that.

LØVBORG   Good-bye, Hedda Gabler. [He goes out the hall doorway.]

[HEDDA *listens a moment at the door. Afterward, she goes to the writing table and takes out the package with the manuscript, looks inside the wrapper, pulls some of the pages half out and looks at them. She then takes it all over to the armchair by the stove and sits down. She has the package in her lap. Soon after she opens the stove door and then opens the package.*]

HEDDA [*Throws one of the sheets into the fire and whispers to herself.*] Now, I'm burning your child, Thea—You with your curly hair. [*Throws a few more sheets into the fire.*] Your child and Eilert Løvborg's. [*Throws in the rest.*] Now I'm burning—burning the child.

Act 4

The same room at the TESMANS'. *It is evening. The drawing room is in darkness. The rear room is lit with a hanging lamp over the table. The curtains are drawn across the glass door.*

[HEDDA, *dressed in black, wanders up and down in the darkened room. Then she goes into the rear room, and over to the left side. Some chords are heard from the piano. Then she emerges again, and goes into the drawing room.* BERTA *comes in from the right of the rear room, with a lighted lamp, which she places on the table in front of the sofa, in the salon. Her eyes show signs of crying, and she has black ribbons on her cap. She goes quietly and carefully to the right.* HEDDA *goes over to the glass door, draws the curtains aside a little, and stares out into the darkness. Soon after,* MISS TESMAN *enters from the hallway dressed in black with a hat and a veil.* HEDDA *goes over to her and shakes her hand.*]

MISS TESMAN Yes, here I am, Hedda—in mourning black. My poor sister's struggle is over at last.

HEDDA As you can see, I've already heard. Tesman sent me a note.

MISS TESMAN Yes, he promised he would but I thought I should bring the news myself. This news of death into this house of life.

HEDDA That was very kind of you.

MISS TESMAN Ah, Rina shouldn't have left us right now. Hedda's house is no place for sorrow at a time like this.

HEDDA [*Changing the subject.*] She died peacefully, Miss Tesman?

MISS TESMAN Yes, so gently—Such a peaceful release. And she was happy beyond words that she got to see George once more and could say a proper good-bye to him. Is it possible he's not home yet?

HEDDA No. He wrote saying I shouldn't expect him too early. But, please sit down.

MISS TESMAN No, thank you, my dear—blessed Hedda. I'd like to, but I have so little time. She'll be dressed and arranged the best that I can. She'll look really splendid when she goes to her grave.

HEDDA Can I help you with anything?

MISS TESMAN Oh, don't even think about it. These kinds of things aren't for Hedda Tesman's hands or her thoughts either. Not at this time. No, no.

HEDDA   Ah—thoughts—Now they're not so easy to master—

MISS TESMAN   [*Continuing.*]   Yes, dear God, that's how this world goes. Over at my house we'll be sewing a linen shroud for Aunt Rina, and here there will be sewing too, but of a whole different kind, praise God.

[GEORGE TESMAN *enters through a hall door.*]

HEDDA   Well, it's good you're finally here.

TESMAN   You here, Aunt Julie, with Hedda. Just think.

MISS TESMAN   I was just about to go, my dear boy. Well. Did you manage to finish everything you promised to?

TESMAN   No, I'm afraid I've forgotten half of it. I have to run over there tomorrow again. Today my brain is just so confused. I can't keep hold of two thoughts in a row.

MISS TESMAN   George, my dear, you mustn't take it like that.

TESMAN   Oh? How should I take it, do you think?

MISS TESMAN   You must be joyful in your sorrow. You must be glad for what has happened, just as I am.

TESMAN   Ah, yes. You're thinking of Aunt Rina.

HEDDA   You'll be lonely now, Miss Tesman.

MISS TESMAN   For the first few days, yes. But that won't last long, I hope. Our sainted Rina's little room won't stand empty. That much I know.

TESMAN   Really? Who'll be moving in there, hm?

MISS TESMAN   Oh, there's always some poor invalid or other who needs care and attention, unfortunately.

HEDDA   You'd really take on a cross like that again?

MISS TESMAN   Cross? God forgive you child. It's not a cross for me.

HEDDA   But a complete stranger—

MISS TESMAN   It's easy to make friends with sick people. And I so badly need someone to live for. Well, God be praised and thanked—there'll be a thing or two to keep an old aunt busy here in this house soon enough.

HEDDA   Oh, please don't think about us.

TESMAN   Yes. The three of us could be quite cozy here if only—

HEDDA   If only—?

TESMAN   [*Uneasily.*]   Oh, it's nothing. Everything'll be fine. Let's hope, hm?

MISS TESMAN   Well, well, you two have plenty to talk about, I'm sure. [*Smiling.*] And Hedda may have something to tell you, George. Now it's home to Rina. [*Turning in the doorway.*] Dear Lord, isn't it strange to think about. Now Rina's both with me and our sainted Joseph.

TESMAN   Yes, just think, Aunt Julie, hm?

[MISS TESMAN *leaves through the hall door.*]

HEDDA   [*Follows* TESMAN *with cold, searching eyes.*]   I think all this has hit you harder than your aunt.

TESMAN   Oh, it's not just this death. It's Eilert I'm worried about.

HEDDA   [*Quickly.*]   Any news?

TESMAN   I wanted to run to him this afternoon and tell him that his manuscript was safe—in good hands.

HEDDA   Oh? Did you find him?

TESMAN   No, he wasn't home. But later I met Mrs. Elvsted, and she told me he'd been here early this morning.

HEDDA Yes, just after you left.

TESMAN And apparently he said that he'd ripped the manuscript up into a thousand pieces, hm?

HEDDA That's what he said.

TESMAN But, good God, he must have been absolutely crazy. So you didn't dare give it back to him, Hedda?

HEDDA No, he didn't get it back.

TESMAN But, you told him we had it?

HEDDA No. [*Quickly.*] Did you tell Mrs. Elvsted?

TESMAN No, I didn't want to. But you should have told him. What would happen if in his desperation he went and did something to himself? Let me have the manuscript, Hedda. I'll run it over to him right away. Where did you put it?

HEDDA [*Cold and impassively leaning on the armchair.*] I don't have it any more.

TESMAN Don't have it! What in the world do you mean?

HEDDA I burned it up—every page.

TESMAN [*Leaps up in terror.*] Burned? Burned? Eilert's manuscript!

HEDDA Don't shout like that. The maid will hear you.

TESMAN Burned! But good God—! No, no, no—That's absolutely impossible.

HEDDA Yes, but all the same it's true.

TESMAN Do you have any idea what you've done, Hedda? That's—that's criminal appropriation of lost property. Think about that. Yes, just ask Judge Brack, then you'll see.

HEDDA Then it's probably wise for you not to talk about it, isn't it? To the Judge or anyone else.

TESMAN How could you have gone and done something so appalling? What came over you? Answer me that, Hedda, hm?

HEDDA [*Suppressing an almost imperceptible smile.*] I did it for your sake, George.

TESMAN My sake?

HEDDA Remember you came home this morning and talked about how he had read to you?

TESMAN Yes, yes.

HEDDA You confessed that you envied him.

TESMAN Good God, I didn't mean it literally.

HEDDA Nevertheless, I couldn't stand the idea that someone would over shadow you.

TESMAN [*Exclaiming between doubt and joy.*] Hedda—Oh, is this true?— What you're saying?—Yes, but. Yes, but. I never noticed that you loved me this way before. Think of that!

HEDDA Well, you need to know—that at a time like this—[*Violently breaking off.*] No, no—go and ask your Aunt Julie. She'll provide all the details.

TESMAN Oh, I almost think I understand you, Hedda. [*Clasps his hands together.*] No, good God—Can it be, hm?

HEDDA Don't shout like that. The maid can hear you.

TESMAN [*Laughing in extraordinary joy.*] The maid! Oh, Hedda, you are priceless. The maid—why it's—why it's Berta. I'll go tell Berta myself.

HEDDA [*Clenching her hands as if frantic.*]   Oh, I'm dying—Dying of all this.

TESMAN   All what, Hedda, what?

HEDDA [*Coldly controlled again.*]   All this—absurdity—George.

TESMAN   Absurdity? I'm so incredibly happy. Even so, maybe I shouldn't say anything to Berta.

HEDDA   Oh yes, go ahead. Why not?

TESMAN   No, no. Not right now. But Aunt Julie, yes, absolutely. And then, you're calling me George. Just think. Oh, Aunt Julie will be so happy—so happy.

HEDDA   When she hears I've burned Eilert Løvborg's manuscript for your sake?

TESMAN   No, no, you're right. All this with the manuscript. No. Of course, nobody can find out about that. But, Hedda—you're burning for me—Aunt Julie really must share in that. But I wonder—all this—I wonder if it's typical with young wives, hm?

HEDDA   You'd better ask Aunt Julie about that too.

TESMAN   Oh yes, I certainly will when I get the chance. [*Looking uneasy and thoughtful again.*] No, but, oh no, the manuscript. Good Lord, it's awful to think about poor Eilert, just the same.

[MRS. ELVSTED, *dressed as for her first visit with hat and coat, enters through the hall door.*]

MRS. ELVSTED [*Greets them hurriedly and speaks in agitation.*]   Oh, Hedda, don't be offended that I've come back again.

HEDDA   What happened to you, Thea?

TESMAN   Something about Eilert Løvborg?

MRS. ELVSTED   Oh yes, I'm terrified that he's had an accident.

HEDDA [*Grips her arm.*]   Ah, do you think so?

TESMAN   Good Lord, where did you get that idea, Mrs. Elvsted?

MRS. ELVSTED   I heard them talking at the boarding house—just as I came in. There are the most incredible rumors about him going around town today.

TESMAN   Oh yes, imagine, I heard them too. And still I can swear he went straight home to sleep. Just think.

HEDDA   So—What were they saying at the boarding house?

MRS. ELVSTED   Oh, I couldn't get any details, either because they didn't know or—or they saw me and stopped talking. And I didn't dare ask.

TESMAN [*Uneasily pacing the floor.*]   Let's just hope—you misunderstood.

MRS. ELVSTED   No, I'm sure they were talking about him. Then I heard them say something about the hospital—

TESMAN   Hospital?

HEDDA   No—That's impossible.

MRS. ELVSTED   I'm deathly afraid for him, so I went up to his lodgings and asked about him there.

HEDDA   You dared to do that?

MRS. ELVSTED   What else should I have done? I couldn't stand the uncertainty any longer.

TESMAN   You didn't find him there either, hm?

MRS. ELVSTED No. And the people there didn't know anything at all. They said he hadn't been home since yesterday afternoon.

TESMAN Yesterday? How could they say that?

MRS. ELVSTED It could only mean one thing—Something terrible's happened to him.

TESMAN You know, Hedda—What if I were to go into town and ask around at different places—?

HEDDA No! You stay out of this.

[JUDGE BRACK, *carrying his hat, enters through the hall door, which* BERTA *opens and closes after him. He looks serious and bows in silence.*]

TESMAN Oh, here you are, Judge, hm?

BRACK Yes, it was essential for me to see you this evening.

TESMAN I see you got the message from Aunt Julie.

BRACK Yes, that too.

TESMAN Isn't it sad, hm?

BRACK Well, my dear Tesman, that depends on how you look at it.

TESMAN [*Looks at him uneasily.*] Has anything else happened?

BRACK Yes, it has.

HEDDA [*Tensely.*] Something sad, Judge Brack?

BRACK Once again, it depends on how you look at it, Mrs. Tesman.

MRS. ELVSTED [*In an uncontrollable outburst.*] It's Eilert Løvborg.

BRACK [*Looks briefly at her.*] How did you guess, Mrs. Elvsted? Do you already know something—?

MRS. ELVSTED [*Confused.*] No, no, I don't know anything but—

TESMAN Well, for God's sake, tell us what it is.

BRACK [*Shrugging his shoulders.*] Well then—I'm sorry to tell you—that Eilert Løvborg has been taken to the hospital. He is dying.

MRS. ELVSTED [*Crying out.*] Oh God, oh God.

TESMAN Dying?

HEDDA [*Involuntarily.*] So quickly—?

MRS. ELVSTED [*Wailing.*] And we were quarrelling when we parted, Hedda.

HEDDA [*Whispers.*] Now, Thea—Thea.

MRS. ELVSTED [*Not noticing her.*] I'm going to him. I've got to see him alive.

BRACK It would do you no good, Mrs. Elvsted. No visitors are allowed.

MRS. ELVSTED At least tell me what happened. What—?

TESMAN Yes, because he certainly wouldn't have tried to—hm?

HEDDA Yes, I'm sure that's what he did.

TESMAN Hedda. How can you—

BRACK [*Who is watching her all the time.*] Unfortunately, Mrs. Tesman, you've guessed right.

MRS. ELVSTED Oh, how awful.

TESMAN To himself, too. Think of it.

HEDDA Shot himself!

BRACK Right again, Mrs. Tesman.

MRS. ELVSTED [*Tries to compose herself.*] When did this happen, Mr. Brack?

BRACK Just this afternoon, between three and four.

TESMAN Oh, my God—Where did he do it, hm?

BRACK [*Slightly uncertain.*]   Where? Oh, I suppose at his lodgings.

MRS. ELVSTED   No, that can't be. I was there between six and seven.

BRACK   Well then, some other place. I don't know precisely. All I know is that he was found—he'd shot himself—in the chest.

MRS. ELVSTED   Oh, how awful to think that he should die like that.

HEDDA [*To* BRACK.]   In the chest?

BRACK   Yes, like I said.

HEDDA   Not through the temple?

BRACK   The chest, Mrs. Tesman.

HEDDA   Well, well. The chest is also good.

BRACK   What was that, Mrs. Tesman?

HEDDA [*Evasively.*]   Oh, nothing—nothing.

TESMAN   And the wound is fatal, hm?

BRACK   The wound is absolutely fatal. In fact, it's probably already over.

MRS. ELVSTED   Yes, yes, I can feel it. It's over. It's all over. Oh, Hedda—!

TESMAN   Tell me, how did you find out about all this?

BRACK [*Curtly.*]   From a police officer. One I spoke with.

HEDDA [*Raising her voice.*]   Finally—an action.

TESMAN   God help us, Hedda, what are you saying?

HEDDA   I'm saying that here, in this—there is beauty.

BRACK   Uhm, Mrs. Tesman.

TESMAN   Beauty! No, don't even think it.

MRS. ELVSTED   Oh, Hedda. How can you talk about beauty?

HEDDA   Eilert Løvborg has come to terms with himself. He's had the courage to do what had to be done.

MRS. ELVSTED   No, don't ever believe it was anything like that. What he did, he did in a moment of madness.

TESMAN   It was desperation.

MRS. ELVSTED   Yes, madness. Just like when he tore his book in pieces.

BRACK [*Startled.*]   The book. You mean his manuscript? Did he tear it up?

MRS. ELVSTED   Yes, last night.

TESMAN [*Whispering softly.*]   Oh, Hedda, we'll never get out from under all this.

BRACK   Hmm, that's very odd.

TESMAN [*Pacing the floor.*]   To think that Eilert Løvborg should leave the world this way. And then not to leave behind the work that would have made his name immortal.

MRS. ELVSTED   Oh, what if it could be put together again.

TESMAN   Yes—just think—what if it could? I don't know what I wouldn't give—

MRS. ELVSTED   Maybe it can, Mr. Tesman.

TESMAN   What do you mean?

MRS. ELVSTED [*Searching in the pocket of her skirt.*]   See this? I saved all the notes he dictated from.

HEDDA [*A step closer.*]   Ah.

TESMAN   You saved them, Mrs. Elvsted, hm?

MRS. ELVSTED   Yes, they're all here. I brought them with me when I came to town, and here they've been. Tucked away in my pocket—

TESMAN   Oh, let me see them.

MRS. ELVSTED [*Gives him a bundle of small papers.*] But they're all mixed up, completely out of order.

TESMAN Just think. What if we could sort them out. Perhaps if the two of us helped each other.

MRS. ELVSTED Oh yes. Let's at least give it a try—

TESMAN It will happen. It must happen. I'll give my whole life to this.

HEDDA You, George, your life?

TESMAN Yes, or, anyway, all the time I have. Every spare minute. My own research will just have to be put aside. Hedda—you understand, don't you, hm? I owe this to Eilert's memory.

HEDDA Maybe so.

TESMAN Now, my dear Mrs. Elvsted, let's pull ourselves together. God knows there's no point brooding about what's happened. We've got to try to find some peace of mind so that—

MRS. ELVSTED Yes, yes, Mr. Tesman. I'll do my best.

TESMAN Well. So, come along then. We've got to get started on these notes right away. Where should we sit? Here? No. In the back room. Excuse us, Judge. Come with me, Mrs. Elvsted.

MRS. ELVSTED Oh God—if only it can be done.

> [TESMAN *and* MRS. ELVSTED *go into the rear room. She takes her hat and coat off. Both sit at the table under the hanging lamp and immerse themselves in eager examination of the papers. Hedda goes across to the stove and sits in the armchair. Soon after,* BRACK *goes over to her.*]

HEDDA [*Softly.*] Ah, Judge—This act of Eilert Løvborg's—there's a sense of liberation in it.

BRACK Liberation, Mrs. Hedda? Yes, I guess it's a liberation for him, all right.

HEDDA I mean, for me. It's a liberation for me to know that in this world an act of such courage, done in full, free will, is possible. Something bathed in a bright shaft of sudden beauty.

BRACK [*Smiles.*] Hmm—Dear Mrs. Hedda—

HEDDA Oh, I know what you're going to say, because you're a kind of specialist too, after all, just like—Ah well.

BRACK [*Looking steadily at her.*] Eilert Løvborg meant more to you than you might admit—even to yourself. Or am I wrong?

HEDDA I don't answer questions like that. All I know is that Eilert Løvborg had the courage to live life his own way, and now—his last great act— bathed in beauty. He—had the will to break away from the banquet of life—so soon.

BRACK It pains me, Mrs. Hedda—but I'm forced to shatter this pretty illusion of yours.

HEDDA Illusion?

BRACK Which would have been taken away from you soon enough.

HEDDA And what's that?

BRACK He didn't shoot himself—so freely.

HEDDA Not freely?

BRACK No. This whole Eilert Løvborg business didn't come off exactly the way I described it.

HEDDA [*In suspense.*] Are you hiding something? What is it?

BRACK   I employed a few euphemisms for poor Mrs. Elvsted's sake.

HEDDA   Such as—?

BRACK   First, of course, he's already dead.

HEDDA   At the hospital?

BRACK   Yes. And without regaining consciousness.

HEDDA   What else?

BRACK   The incident took place somewhere other than his room.

HEDDA   That's insignificant.

BRACK   Not completely. I have to tell you—Eilert Løvborg was found shot in—Miss Diana's boudoir.

HEDDA   [*About to jump up but sinks back again.*]   That's impossible, Judge. He can't have gone there again today.

BRACK   He was there this afternoon. He came to demand the return of something that he said they'd taken from him. He talked crazily about a lost child.

HEDDA   Ah, so that's why—

BRACK   I thought maybe he was referring to his manuscript but I hear he'd already destroyed that himself so I guess it was his pocketbook.

HEDDA   Possibly. So—that's where he was found.

BRACK   Right there, with a discharged pistol in his coat pocket, and a fatal bullet wound.

HEDDA   In the chest, yes?

BRACK   No—lower down.

HEDDA   [*Looks up at him with an expression of revulsion.*]   That too! Oh absurdity—! It hangs like a curse over everything I so much as touch.

BRACK   There's still one more thing, Mrs. Hedda. Also in the ugly category.

HEDDA   And what is that?

BRACK   The pistol he had with him—

HEDDA   [*Breathless.*]   Well, what about it?

BRACK   He must have stolen it.

HEDDA   [*Jumping up.*]   Stolen? That's not true. He didn't.

BRACK   There's no other explanation possible. He must have stolen it—Shh.

[TESMAN *and* MRS. ELVSTED *have gotten up from the table in the rear room and come into the living room.*]

TESMAN   [*With papers in both hands.*]   Hedda, my dear—I can hardly see anything in there under that lamp. Just think—

HEDDA   I'm thinking.

TESMAN   Do you think you might let us sit a while at your desk, hm?

HEDDA   Oh, gladly. [*Quickly.*] No, wait. Let me just clean it up a bit first.

TESMAN   Oh, not necessary, Hedda. There's plenty of room.

HEDDA   No, no, I'll just straighten it up, I'm telling you. I'll just move these things here under the piano for a while.

[*She has pulled an object covered with sheet music out of the bookcase. She adds a few more sheets and carries the whole pile out to the left of the rear room.* TESMAN *puts the papers on the desk and brings over the lamp from the corner table. He and* MRS. ELVSTED *sit and continue their work.*]

HEDDA   Well, Thea, my sweet. Are things moving along with the memorial?

MRS. ELVSTED   [*Looks up at her dejectedly.*]   Oh, God—It's going to be so difficult to find the order in all of this.

TESMAN   But it must be done. There's simply no other choice. And finding
the order in other people's papers—that's precisely what I'm meant for.
[HEDDA *goes over to the stove and sits on one of the stools.* BRACK *stands over
her, leaning over the armchair.*]

HEDDA [*Whispers.*]   What were you saying about the pistol?

BRACK [*Softly.*]   That he must have stolen it.

HEDDA   Why stolen exactly?

BRACK   Because there shouldn't be any other way to explain it, Mrs. Hedda.

HEDDA   I see.

BRACK [*Looks briefly at her.*]   Eilert Løvborg was here this morning, am I
correct?

HEDDA   Yes.

BRACK   Were you alone with him?

HEDDA   Yes, for a while.

BRACK   You didn't leave the room at all while he was here?

HEDDA   No.

BRACK   Think again. Weren't you out of the room, even for one moment?

HEDDA   Yes. Perhaps. Just for a moment—out in the hallway.

BRACK   And where was your pistol case at that time?

HEDDA   I put it under the—

BRACK   Well, Mrs. Hedda—

HEDDA   It was over there on the writing table.

BRACK   Have you looked since then to see if both pistols are there?

HEDDA   No.

BRACK   It's not necessary. I saw the pistol Løvborg had, and I recognized
it immediately from yesterday, and from before as well.

HEDDA   Have you got it?

BRACK   No, the police have it.

HEDDA   What will the police do with that pistol?

BRACK   Try to track down its owner.

HEDDA   Do you think they can do that?

BRACK [*Bends over her and whispers.*]   No, Hedda Gabler, not as long as I
keep quiet.

HEDDA [*Looking fearfully at him.*]   And what if you don't keep quiet—then
what?

BRACK   Then the way out is to claim that the pistol was stolen.

HEDDA   I'd rather die.

BRACK [*Smiling.*]   People make those threats but they don't act on them.

HEDDA [*Without answering.*]   So—let's say the pistol is not stolen and the
owner is found out? What happens then?

BRACK   Well, Hedda—then there'll be a scandal.

HEDDA   A scandal?

BRACK   Oh, yes, a scandal. Just what you're so desperately afraid of. You'd
have to appear in court, naturally. You and Miss Diana. She'd have to
detail how it all occurred. Whether it was an accident or a homicide.
Was he trying to draw the pistol to threaten her? Is that when the gun
went off? Did she snatch it out of his hands to shoot him, and then put
the pistol back in his pocket? That would be thoroughly in character for
her. She's a feisty little thing, that Miss Diana.

HEDDA   But all this ugliness has got nothing to do with me.

BRACK   No. But you would have to answer one question. Why did you give the pistol to Eilert Løvborg? And what conclusions would people draw from the fact that you gave it to him?

HEDDA [*Lowers her head.*]   That's true. I didn't think of that.

BRACK   Well. Fortunately you have nothing to worry about as long as I keep quiet.

HEDDA [*Looking up at him.*]   So I'm in your power now, Judge. You have a hold over me from now on.

BRACK [*Whispering more softly.*]   Dearest Hedda—Believe me—I won't abuse my position.

HEDDA   But in your power. Totally subject to your demands—And your will. Not free. Not free at all. [*She gets up silently.*] No, that's one thought I just can't stand. Never!

BRACK [*Looks mockingly at her.*]   One can usually learn to live with the inevitable.

HEDDA [*Returning his look.*]   Maybe so. [*She goes over to the writing table, suppressing an involuntary smile and imitating* TESMAN's *intonation.*] Well, George, this is going to work out, hm?

TESMAN   Oh, Lord knows, dear. Anyway, at this rate, it's going to be months of work.

HEDDA [*As before.*]   No, just think. [*Runs her fingers lightly through* MRS. ELVSTED's *hair.*] Doesn't it seem strange, Thea. Here you are, sitting together with Tesman—just like you used to sit with Eilert Løvborg.

MRS. ELVSTED   Oh, God, if only I could inspire your husband too.

HEDDA   Oh, that will come—in time.

TESMAN   Yes, you know what, Hedda—I really think I'm beginning to feel something like that. But why don't you go over and sit with Judge Brack some more.

HEDDA   Can't you two find any use for me here?

TESMAN   No, nothing in the world. [*Turning his head.*] From now on, my dear Judge, you'll have to be kind enough to keep Hedda company.

BRACK [*With a glance at* HEDDA.]   That will be an infinite pleasure for me.

HEDDA   Thanks, but I'm tired tonight. I'll go in there and lie down on the sofa for a while.

TESMAN   Yes, do that, Hedda, hm?

[HEDDA *goes into the rear room and draws the curtains after her. Short pause. Suddenly she is heard to play a wild dance melody on the piano.*]

MRS. ELVSTED [*Jumping up from her chair.*]   Oh—what's that?

TESMAN [*Running to the doorway.*]   Oh, Hedda, my dear—Don't play dance music tonight. Just think of poor Aunt Rina and of Eilert Løvborg too.

HEDDA [*Putting her head out from between the curtains.*]   And Aunt Julie and all the rest of them too. From now on I shall be quiet. [*She closes the curtains again.*]

TESMAN [*At the writing table.*]   This can't be making her very happy—Seeing us at this melancholy work. You know what, Mrs. Elvsted—You're going to move in with Aunt Julie. Then I can come over in the evening, and we can sit and work there, hm?

MRS. ELVSTED   Yes, maybe that would be the best—

HEDDA [*From the rear room.*]   I can hear you perfectly well, Tesman. So, how am I supposed to get through the evenings out here?

TESMAN [*Leafing through the papers.*]   Oh, I'm sure Judge Brack will be good enough to call on you.

BRACK [*In the armchair, shouts merrily.*]   I'd be delighted, Mrs. Tesman. Every evening. Oh, we're going to have some good times together, the two of us.

HEDDA [*Loudly and clearly.*]   Yes, that's what you're hoping for, isn't it, Judge? You, the one and only cock of the walk—

[*A shot is heard within.* TESMAN, MRS. ELVSTED *and* BRACK *all jump to their feet.*]

TESMAN   Oh, she's playing around with those pistols again.

[*He pulls the curtains aside and runs in.* MRS. ELVSTED *follows.* HEDDA *is stretched out lifeless on the sofa. Confusion and cries.* BERTA *comes running in from the right.*]

[*Shrieking to* BRACK.] Shot herself! Shot herself in the temple! Just think!

BRACK [*Half prostrate in the armchair.*]   But God have mercy—People just don't act that way!

END OF PLAY

JOAQUIM MARIA MACHADO DE ASSIS
1839–1908

No one could have predicted that Joaquim Maria Machado de Assis would became Brazil's greatest writer. Born the grandson of freed slaves in a dilapidated corner of Rio de Janeiro, subject to fits of epilepsy, afflicted with a pronounced stutter, and having no more than an elementary school education, this man of color became the first president of Brazil's Academy of Letters and one of the most innovative, playful, and technically adventurous writers of the whole nineteenth century. Particularly skilled at revealing gaps between high-flown rhetoric and bleak reality, Machado—as he is called—used his fiction to expose hypocrisy and pretension at the heart of Brazilian society.

Machado's father was a housepainter of mixed race, his mother a white Portuguese woman who died when he was a small child. He taught himself largely by listening in on lessons at a girls' school where his stepmother worked in the kitchen. In his early teens he took a job as an apprentice printer and began to write for publication. By the age of twenty-five he was a literary star, having established himself as an editor, translator, poet, and writer of criticism and drama. Elegant, reserved, and courteous, he was happily married to the sister of a close poet friend. Despite his literary success, he took bureaucratic posts in the Brazilian government to ensure a steady income.

Machado eventually became best known for his novels and short stories, which in the 1880s broke with all established schools and styles. Drawing on a huge range of influences that included Shakespeare and Jonathan Swift, Machado often anticipated twentieth-century Modernist fiction by experimenting with unreliable narrators and mischievous addresses to the reader. But he also expanded the possibilities of realism, exploring the complex psychology and social structures of modern urban life.

The city of Rio de Janeiro was an especially strange and frustrating place to live in the late nineteenth century. Brazil abolished slavery only in 1888, when Machado was forty-nine years old—the last country in the Americas to do so. Over the previous three centuries Brazil had brought in four and a half million Africans, more slaves than any other nation in the New World. Even very poor people—some of them free blacks—often owned a slave or two. The social life of Rio de Janeiro looked quite peculiar to nineteenth-century observers: its elite class turned to Europe for fashion and ideas, imitating especially the upper classes in France and Britain; its "middle class" was typically quite poor, composed of white immigrants from Europe and free black workers; and the whole city was propped up by slave labor.

Machado, more than any of his contemporaries, set out to expose the attitudes and the lies that sustained this lopsided society. Slavery often remains on the margins of Machado's work, but he had a longstanding fascination with questions of authority and control. How do people wield power? Why do others submit? "The Rod of Justice" (1891), our selection below, follows a subtle chain of influence, as a young seminary student tries to figure out how to escape a career in the priesthood. He locates his best chance of help in his godfather's mistress, who herself is eager to show her power over both her lover and her slaves. As the main character is torn between ideals of justice and compassion on the one hand and a desire to realize his own freedom on the other, Machado reveals the subtle and conflicting sources of power organizing Brazilian society.

The Rod of Justice[1]

Damião ran away from the seminary at eleven o'clock in the morning, on a Friday in August. I am not sure of the year, but it was before 1850.[2] After a few minutes he stopped in embarrassment. He had not counted on the effect his appearance would have on other people—a seminarist in his cassock, hurrying along with a dazed, fearful look. He did not recognize the streets, he kept missing his way and retracing his steps. Finally he stopped altogether. Where would he go? Home? No, that was where his father was, and his father would send him back to the seminary, after a good trouncing. He had not settled upon a place of refuge, because his departure had been planned for a later date: an unforeseen circumstance hastened it. Where would he go? He thought of his

---

1. Translated by Helen Caldwell.

2. The end of the international slave trade in Brazil.

godfather, João Carneiro, a soft muttonhead with no will of his own. He'd be of no help. It was he who took him to the seminary in the first place and presented him to the rector.

"I bring you the great-man-to-be," he had said to the rector.

"Let him enter, let the great man enter, provided he be also meek and good. True greatness is humble. Young man . . ."

Such was his introduction. Not long after, he ran away. And now we see him in the street, dazed, uncertain, with no idea of where to take refuge, or even ask for advice. He mentally ran over the houses of relatives and friends without regarding any one of them with much favor. Suddenly he cried out, "I'll go beg Sinhá[3] Rita to protect me! She will send for my godfather, tell him that she wants me to leave the seminary . . . Maybe . . ."

Sinhá Rita was a widow, the sweetheart of João Carneiro. Damião had certain vague ideas about this situation and decided to turn it to his advantage. Where did she live? He was so confused that it was several minutes before he could remember where her house was. It was in the Largo do Capim.[4]

"Holy name of Jesus! What's this?" screamed Sinhá Rita sitting upright on the settee where she had been reclining. Damião entered terror-stricken. At the very moment of reaching the house, he had seen a priest walking along, had given the door a shove, and by great good luck it was neither locked nor bolted. Once inside, he peeked through the lattice to watch the padre. The latter had not noticed him, and kept on his way.

"But what's this, Senhor Damião?" the mistress of the house again screamed, for it was only now that she recognized him. "What are you doing here?"

Damião, trembling, scarcely able to speak, told her not to be afraid, it was nothing, he would explain everything.

"There, there, go ahead and explain."

"First of all, I have not perpetrated any crime, that I swear! Wait."

Sinhá Rita looked at him with a startled air, and all the little slave girls—those of the household and those from outside—who were seated around the room before their work cushions, all stopped moving their bobbins and their hands. Sinhá Rita made her living, for the most part, by teaching lacemaking, drawn work, and embroidery. While the boy caught his breath, she ordered the little girls back to work, and waited. At last Damião poured out everything: the misery the seminary caused him, he was sure he could never be a good padre. He spoke with passion and begged her to save him.

"How? I can't do anything."

"Yes, you can, if you really want to."

"No," she answered, shaking her head, "I'm not butting into your family's affairs. I scarcely know them. And your father—they say he has a terrible temper!"

Damião saw his hopes fading. He knelt at her feet, kissed her hands in desperation.

"You can do a great deal, Sinhá Rita. I beg you for the love of God—by whatever you hold most sacred, by the soul of your late husband—save me from death, because I'll kill myself if I have to go back to that place."

3. Variant of *senhora*, or "mistress"; used by slaves as a form of address.

4. Street in Rio de Janeiro where there was a hangman's scaffold and a slave cemetery.

Sinhá Rita, flattered by the young man's entreaties, tried to recall him to a more cheerful frame of mind. A priest's life was holy and fine, she told him, time would teach him it was better to overcome one's dislikes, and one day . . .

"No, nohow, never!" he retorted shaking his head and kissing her hands, and he kept repeating that it would be his death.

Even then, Sinhá Rita hesitated, for a long time. Finally she asked him why he did not go talk to his godfather.

"My godfather? He's even worse than papa, he doesn't pay any attention to what I say, I don't believe he'd pay attention to anyone . . ."

"No?" interrupted Sinhá Rita, her pride pricked. "Well, I'll show him whether he'll pay attention or not . . ."

She called a slave and ordered him in a loud voice to go to João Carneiro's house and tell him to come at once, and if he was not at home to ask where he could be found, and to run and tell him that she had to speak to him immediately.

"Get along, darky!"

Damião sighed heavily.

To cover up the authority with which she had given these orders, she explained to the youth that Senhor João Carneiro had been a friend of her dead husband and had got her some of these slaves as pupils. Then, as Damião continued to lean gloomily against the door jamb, she smiled and tweaked his nose, "Come, come, your reverence! Don't worry, everything will be all right."

Sinhá Rita was forty years old by her baptismal certificate, but her eyes were seven and twenty. She was a fine figure of a woman, lively, merry, and fond of a joke, but, if need be, fierce as the devil. She set out to cheer the boy up, and it was not hard for her. In a little while they were both laughing: she told him funny stories and asked him to tell her some, which he did with singular wit and charm. One of them, thanks to his crazy capering and grimacing, was so absurd that it made one of Sinhá Rita's pupils laugh: she had forgotten her work to stare at the young man and listen to him. Sinhá Rita grabbed a birch rod that was lying beside the settee and called out in a threatening voice, "Lucretia, mind the rod!"

The little girl lowered her head to parry the blow, but the blow did not fall. It was a warning. If her task was not finished at nightfall, Lucretia would receive the usual punishment. Damião looked at the child: she was a little Negress, a frail wisp of a thing with a scar on her forehead and a burn on her left hand. She was eleven years old. Damião noticed that she kept coughing, but inwardly, and muffled, so as not to interrupt the conversation. He was sorry for the little black girl, and resolved to protect her if she did not finish her task. Sinhá Rita would not refuse to forgive her . . . Besides, she had laughed because she found him amusing; the fault was his, if it is a fault to be witty.

At this point, João Carneiro arrived. He turned pale when he saw his godson there, and looked at Sinhá Rita, who wasted no time in preliminaries. She told him it was necessary to remove the boy from the seminary, that he had no talent for an ecclesiastical life, and better one priest the less than a bad priest. One could love and serve Our Lord out in the world just as well.

João Carneiro was thunderstruck. For several minutes he could find nothing to say. Finally he opened his mouth and began to reprimand his godson for coming and bothering "strangers," and then he asserted he would punish him.

"Punish, nothing!" interrupted Sinhá Rita. "Punish for what? Go on, go talk to the boy's father."

"I don't guarantee anything. I don't believe it will be possible to . . ."

"And I guarantee it will be possible, it has to be. If you have a will to do it, senhor," she continued in an insinuating tone, "everything is bound to be arranged. Keep after him; he'll give in. Get along, João Carneiro, your godson is not going back to the seminary. I tell you, he is not going back . . ."

"But, my dear senhora . . ."

"Go, go on."

João Carneiro was in no hurry to leave, and he could not remain. He was caught between two opposing forces. It really made no difference to him whether his godson ended up a priest, a doctor, a lawyer, or what—even if he turned out to be a good-for-nothing bum and loafer. But, the worst of it was, he was being pushed into a terrible struggle against the most intimate feelings of his friend the boy's father, with no certainty as to the result. If the result proved negative, he would have another fight on his hands with Sinhá Rita, whose final words were, "I tell you he is not going back." There was bound to be a row. João Carneiro's gaze became unsteady, his eyelids twitched, his chest heaved, and the eyes he turned upon Sinhá Rita were full of supplication, mixed with a mild gleam of censure. Why couldn't she ask something else of him? Why couldn't she command him to walk up Tijuca in a pouring rain, or up Jacarèpaguá?[5] But to persuade his godson's father, like that, to change his son's whole career . . . He knew the man, he was quite capable of breaking a water pitcher over his head. Oh, if his godson would only drop dead, then and there, of a fit of apoplexy! It would be a solution, cruel, it is true, but conclusive.

"Well?" insisted Sinhá Rita.

He held up his hand for her to wait. He scratched his beard, hunting for an expedient. God in heaven! a decree of the pope dissolving the Church, or at the least abolishing seminaries, would fix up everything. João Carneiro would go back home and play *três-setes*.[6] Imagine Napoleon's barber entrusted with the command of the battle of Austerlitz[7] . . . But the Church lived on, seminaries lived on, his godson lived on, shrunk against the wall, his eyes downcast, hoping, and giving no promise of an apoplectic solution.

"Be off, be off," said Sinhá Rita, handing him his hat and cane.

There was no help for it. The barber put the razor in its case, girded on his sword, and sallied forth to battle. Damião began to breathe again. Outwardly, however, he was the same, eyes fixed on the ground, dispirited. This time, Sinhá Rita chucked him under the chin. "Come on to dinner, and stop brooding."

"Do you really think, senhora, that he'll do anything?"

"He'll do everything," she asserted with a self-confident air. "Come along or the soup'll get cold."

In spite of Sinhá Rita's boisterous good humor and his own lighthearted nature, Damião was less cheerful at dinner than he had been earlier in the day. He distrusted his godfather's flabby character. Still, he ate a good dinner, and

5. Neighborhoods in Rio de Janeiro.
6. Card game.
7. Defining victory in Napoleon's military

career, often considered the height of his tactical genius; Austerlitz is the present-day Slavkov, a town in the Czech Republic.

toward the end returned to his jesting mood of that morning. During dessert he heard the sound of voices in the sitting room and asked if they had come to arrest him.

"It must be the girls."

They got up from the table and went into the other room. The "girls" were five young women of the neighborhood who came every afternoon to take coffee with Sinhá Rita, and stayed until nightfall.

The pupils finished their dinner and returned to their work cushions. Sinhá Rita was mistress of all this womenfolk—slaves of her own household and from outside. The whisper of the bobbins and the chattering of the "girls" were such worldly echoes, so far from theology and Latin, that the young man gave himself up to them and forgot those other things.

During the first few minutes there was a certain constraint on the part of the neighbor women, but it soon wore off. One of them sang a popular song, to a guitar accompaniment played by Sinhá Rita. And so the afternoon passed quickly. Sinhá Rita asked Damião to tell a certain funny story that had particularly delighted her. It was the one that had made Lucretia laugh.

"Come on, Senhor Damião, don't be coy, the girls have to leave. You'll be crazy about it."

There was nothing for Damião to do but obey. Although the announcement and the expectation served to lessen the drollery and the effect, the story ended amid the loud laughter of the girls. Damião, pleased with himself, did not forget Lucretia, and glanced in her direction to see if she had laughed too. He saw her with her head bent over the work cushion, trying to complete her task. She was not laughing, or she may have been laughing inwardly, just as she coughed.

The neighbor women left, and the day was gone in earnest. Damião's soul grew dark before the night. What was happening? Every other second he went and peered through the lattice and returned each time more downhearted. Not a sign of his godfather. It was certain his father had made him shut up, called a couple of slaves, gone to the police station for an officer, and was on his way thither to seize him by force and drag him back to the seminary. He asked Sinhá Rita if the house happened to have a back door, he ran into the yard and figured he could jump over the wall. He tried to find out if there was a way of escape down the Rua da Valla, or if it was better to speak to one of the neighbors, and see if they would take him in. The worst thing was the cassock: if Sinhá Rita could only get him a man's jacket, an old coat . . . Sinhá Rita just happened to have a man's jacket in the house, a remembrance—or a forgetfulness—of João Carneiro.

"I do have a jacket . . . that belonged to my late husband," she said with a laugh, "but why are you so scared? Everything will be all right. Don't worry."

Finally, at nightfall, there appeared one of his godfather's slaves with a letter for Sinhá Rita. The business was not yet settled; the father was furious and wanted to smash things. He had shouted "no sir," the young dandy would go to the seminary, or he would have him locked up in the Aljube[8] or on a prison ship. João Carneiro fought hard to get him not to make a decision right away, to sleep on it, and think over carefully whether it was *right* to offer the Church

---

8. Archbishop's prison, famous for its abominable conditions.

such an unruly and vicious character. He explained in the letter that he had spoken in this manner the better to win his case. He did not consider it yet won, but he would go to see him the next day and have another try. He concluded by saying that the young man should go to his house.

Damião finished reading the letter and glanced toward Sinhá Rita. She is my only hope, he thought. Sinhá Rita sent for her inkstand of carved horn, and on the same sheet of paper, below the letter itself, she wrote this reply: "Joãozinho,[9] either you rescue the boy, or we never see each other again." She folded the paper and sealed it with wax, handed it to the slave, and told him to take it back with all speed. She returned to the job of cheering up the seminarist, for he was once more very low and shrouded in despair. She told him to rest easy and leave the matter to her.

"They'll find out what I'm made of! No, I won't stand for any foolishness!"

It was now time to gather up the pieces of needle-work. Sinhá Rita inspected them. All the others had finished their tasks. Only Lucretia still sat before her cushion, moving the bobbins in and out, for some time now without seeing. Sinhá Rita came to where she sat, saw that the allotted task was not finished, became furious, and grabbed her by the ear.

"Ah! low-down good-for-nothing!"

"Nhanhã, Nhanhã,[1] for the love of God! by Our Lady that is in heaven!"

"Trashy good-for-nothing! Our Lady does not protect lazy-bones."

With a tremendous effort, Lucretia wrenched herself free from the hands of her mistress, and ran out of the room. The mistress went after her and grabbed her.

"Come back here!"

"Mistress, forgive me!" coughed the little black girl.

"No, I won't forgive you! Where is the rod?"

They both came back into the sitting room: one held by the ear, struggling, crying, begging; the other saying "no," that she was going to punish her.

"Where is the rod?"

The rod lay on the floor by the settee, on the other side of the room. Sinhá Rita was unwilling to loose her hold on the little girl and yelled to the seminarist, "Senhor Damião, give me that rod, if you please!"

Damião froze . . . Cruel moment! A cloud passed before his eyes. Yes, he had sworn to protect the little girl; it was because of him that she was behind with her work . . .

"Give me the rod, Senhor Damião!"

Damião finally started to walk toward the settee. The little Negress begged him then by all he held most sacred, in the name of his mother, his father, of Our Lord . . .

"Help me, sweet young master!"

Sinhá Rita, her face on fire, her eyes starting from her head, kept calling for the rod, without letting go of the little black girl, who was now held in a fit of coughing.

Damião was pricked by an uneasy sense of guilt, but he wanted so much to get out of the seminary! He reached the settee, picked up the rod, and handed it to Sinhá Rita.

9. Diminutive nickname for João, a term of endearment.   1. Variant of *senhora*, mistress.

ANTON CHEKHOV
1860–1904

Anton Chekhov visited **Leo Tolstoy** late in the great novelist's life. Tolstoy embraced him warmly, and said: "I can't stand your plays. Shakespeare's are terrible, but yours are worse!" Tolstoy particularly objected that the dramas lacked purpose. "Where does one get to with your heroes?" he asked the young dramatist. "From the sofa to the privy and from the privy back to the sofa?" The ever-modest Chekhov was apparently amused, finding it hard to take offense at a judgment that likened him to Shakespeare. And perhaps he was pleased, too, that Tolstoy's perplexity got at the very heart of Chekhov's innovative drama, which both puzzled and startled his early audiences by refusing grand actions and melodramatic plots: no deaths, no great love affairs, no shocking revelations. Tolstoy was looking for heroes, and Chekhov refuses to give us any, avoiding the conventional focus on a single protagonist in favor of a constellation of characters, each of whom—even the most minor—can lay claim to a separate life and perspective. Aged servants and bumbling tutors have as much to say as aristocrats and beauties. His plays are like life, Chekhov said, "just as complex and just as simple."

Anton Chekhov was born in the thriving Russian seaport town of Taganrog in 1860. His grandfather had been a serf who eventually saved enough money to purchase his freedom. Chekhov himself never forgot how narrowly he had escaped being born into serfdom, and he struggled his whole life against feelings of subservience and inferiority.

Chekhov's father owned a grimy and decrepit grocery store, and he forced his children to work there. A tyrannical man, he had outbursts of temper, beat his children, insulted his wife, and held fervent religious beliefs. When Chekhov was sixteen, his father went bankrupt and to escape his debtors slunk off to Moscow, where his family soon joined him. They left only Anton to fend for himself in Taganrog. Survival was difficult. His parents insisted that he send them money, so he sold the family furniture and lived with relatives, begging them for small sums.

In 1879 Chekhov won a scholarship to study medicine at Moscow University. In Moscow he found his family poverty stricken and gloomy, his two older brothers spending what money they earned on drinking and women. Anton took financial responsibility for all of them, writing humorous stories for magazines to make money while studying medicine. He was so prolific that by the age of twenty-six, he had published over four hundred short pieces in popular magazines, as well as two books of stories.

During this period Chekhov developed two techniques as a writer that would serve him for the rest of his life. First, his medical training taught him a close attention to details, and readers have long praised his skill as an objective observer of subtle signs and gestures. Second, his work as a humor writer demanded brevity: he frequently wrote for a magazine called *Splinters*, which had a strict limit of one hundred words, forcing the young writer to express his ideas within tight constraints. A friend once found him condensing a story by Tolstoy; he frequently did this kind of exercise, he explained, to practice conciseness.

In his third year of medical school, Chekhov began writing for more serious literary magazines. He was now launched on two careers, and he managed to work as both a physician and a writer until he died. "Medicine is my lawful wife," he once said. "Writing is my mistress." His medical practice was draining, since he often treated poor patients for nothing and was called out to visit the sick in the middle of the night. Alarmingly, he started showing symptoms of tuberculosis in 1884.

Chekhov's first full-length play, *Ivanov*, was staged in 1887. The production was a disaster: none of the actors had learned their lines, and one was clearly drunk onstage. Chekhov later dismissed his early plays as conventional and frivolous. It would be another decade before his drama would be treated as seriously as his short fiction, which was making him famous. He won the prestigious Pushkin Prize for his short stories in 1888.

Surprising everyone who knew him, Chekhov decided to write a report about Sakhalin, a penal colony off the coast of Siberia that was notorious for its appalling conditions. What he found was worse even than he had imagined: a "perfect hell." Chained to wheelbarrows, flogged, starved, and sometimes raped and murdered, the prisoners endured a life of daily horror. The women survived mostly by prostitution. Since the Russian government had never collected much information about the prisoners and their families, Chekhov decide to perform a full census of the island himself. This was a massive task, and the writer took notes on the brutal conditions as he traveled around, offering his medical services to sick prisoners. When he returned, he lobbied for reform of Sakhalin, especially for the island's children, and in 1894 he published a long and detailed

book on the colony, filled with statistics and shocking truths. The press praised the book; the public was scandalized by the conditions in Sakhalin, and the government began to undertake reforms.

On his return to Moscow, Chekhov bought an estate. It was symbolic indeed for the grandson of a serf to become a landlord, and Chekhov acted in characteristically generous fashion, building schools, roads, and bridges, and providing free health education and medical care to the poor in his district. He also wrote a troubling and controversial short story called "Peasants," which exposed the harsh realities of life for the poorest Russians.

In the 1890s Chekhov finally turned his hand to writing drama again, and this time the plays he wrote were radically experimental, casting off the conventions of sensational melodrama that had dominated Russian theater and ushering in a new style that stressed ensembles rather than heroes and moods rather than actions. The first of these dramas, *The Seagull*, had such a disastrous opening that Chekhov vowed never to write another play. But even this failure marked the beginning of a new era in Russian drama. In 1897 a new theater opened in Moscow, dedicated to naturalistic, modern styles, and its great director, Konstantin Stanislavsky, saw *The Seagull* as the ideal play to mark this innovation. His new production astonished its first audiences. When the curtain fell on the first act, there was total silence. The hush went on for so long that one actress tried to keep from sobbing aloud. But then the audience burst into such wild applause that the actors were too stunned to take their bow. What followed were rave reviews and packed houses. Stanislavky's production of *The Seagull* was hailed as "one of the greatest events in the history of Russian theater and one of the greatest new developments in the history of world drama." The Moscow Art Theater took the seagull as its emblem, and it staged all of Chekhov's late dramatic works, including his very last, *The Cherry Orchard*, our selection here.

The Moscow Art Theater launched a new phase in Chekhov's personal life as well. He fell in love with one of the actresses in *The Seagull*, Olga Knipper, and married her in 1901, at the age of forty-one. They moved to Yalta, where they hoped that his health would improve. It did not. Chekhov died of tuberculosis in 1904.

TIMES

Huge social inequalities, fast-paced economic change, and rising political instability produced the pervasive anxiety that characterized Russia at the end of the nineteenth century. The country had begun a phase of rapid industrialization—about a century later than most of Western Europe—and saw a dramatic rise in the production of coal, steel, iron, oil, textiles, and beet sugar after 1850. Its population exploded from 50 million in 1860 to about 100 million in 1900. Russian cities grew quickly, and the railroad system expanded dramatically. Tsar Alexander II officially abolished serfdom in 1861, diminishing the traditional influence of landowners, while business and bureaucratic sectors grew and employed ever larger numbers of recently urbanized workers. Newly rich merchants and professionals began to buy property from the old aristocracy.

This profound shift in wealth and power brought a sense of impending crisis. Social groups that had new access to wealth and education frequently expressed anger at the autocratic tsarist regime, and voices across the class spectrum criticized the government for allowing the poor to suffer miserable hardships. Numerous high-ranking officials, including Tsar Alexander II himself in 1881, were assassinated by anarchists and other revolutionary groups. The government tried to crack down on social turmoil with widespread arrests. Writers and intellectuals lived in constant fear that they would be thrown into prison, and their work was often censored. Chekhov was among the writers who signed a petition for freedom of the press, which brought him under the surveillance of the tsar's secret police. The end of the century witnessed massive demonstrations against tsarist authority, with students often acting as the leading agitators. In 1901 the Russian Minister of Education tried to draft two hundred student leaders into the army. In *The Cherry Orchard*, the perpetual student Trofimov would have evoked these dissidents for contemporary audiences, and in fact the censors forced Chekhov to revise his character's most inflammatory speeches.

In the final years of Chekhov's life, Russian society was turning ever more volatile. Tsar Nicholas II was a weak-willed leader, inclined to bow to the dictates of reactionary ministers. Russian liberals clamored for constitutional reforms, while increasingly visible socialists responded to widespread crop failures, cholera epidemics, and grinding rural poverty by demanding outright revolution. In 1904 mounting tensions between Japan and Russia exploded into war. The very day that Chekhov died, July 15, 1904, a homemade bomb thrown by a socialist revolutionary killed the Minister of the Interior in his carriage. A year later the Imperial Guard killed a thousand peaceful demonstrators who had been singing patriotic songs and hymns. "Bloody Sunday," as this event came to be called, inflamed anti-monarchical sentiment, launched the Russian Revolution of 1905, and heralded the ultimate end of tsarism. In 1917 the Bolshevik-led revolution would bring about a wholly new kind of social organization—the communist state.

Writers and artists working in this atmosphere of violence and instability hotly debated the proper role of the arts. Should art act as provocative political opposition, offering criticism of the status quo and images of a better future? Should it instead glorify the nation, prompting patriotism and loyalty? Or should art retain a fierce independence from politics and dedicate itself to purely aesthetic aims and aspirations? Chekhov had friends who propounded all of these positions. Throughout his career Chekhov stood up for oppressed and marginalized groups, and yet his plays often steer clear of strong political and moral messages. But from the 1930s onward, Chekhov was also destined to become a favorite among Soviet leaders, who insisted that his plays be produced across the USSR. Meanwhile, in the West his work was taken to stand for individualism and human dignity. Throughout the twentieth century, Chekhov remained widely popular around the world—and exceptionally difficult to categorize.

WORK

Since The Cherry Orchard's first production, people have debated whether the play is a comedy or a tragedy. The original director, Stanislavsky, saw the play as a tear-jerker: he wept when he read the text for the first time, and many directors since have foregrounded the pain and loss at the center of the play. Chekhov himself, however, insisted that it was a comic farce, to be played at an almost breakneck speed. (He imagined the fourth act taking just a quick twelve minutes, while Stanislavsky stretched it to last forty.) Conventional comedies end in marriage, tragedies in death, and this play does end with the death of the ancient servant Firs, whom the family has forgotten to send to a nursing home. On the other hand, slapstick moments occur throughout the play, as when Várya smacks her beloved Lopákhin over the head by mistake.

Carlotta's magic tricks and Yepikhódov's comically grandiose language compete for attention with passages of poetic beauty. Chekhov wrote that directors like Stanislavsky were misreading him: "First they turn me into a weeper and then into a boring writer." In the century since its premiere, directors and actors have had to wrestle with the question of the proper mood and pace for The Cherry Orchard, which can change significantly from production to production.

Productions of The Cherry Orchard also have to grapple with the political implications of the play. Since the Russian Revolution of 1917, it has been difficult to avoid reading the play as a warning of the coming Russian Revolution. The single event in the drama—the sale of a beautiful but unprofitable aristocratic estate—suggests the passing of the old regime and the coming of a new order. Like the vast expanse of Russia, the orchard is huge—bigger than any real orchard—and like prerevolutionary Russian land it is owned by the few rather than the many. Toward the end of the second act, Trofímov says explicitly, "This whole country is our orchard." But Chekhov does not agitate for revolution here: instead he captures a feeling of stagnation, the quiet before the storm.

Soviet directors tended to cast the workers as heroic characters—serious and grand—while the aristocrats appeared decadent and foolish. But it is equally plausible to represent the socialist student as a naïve idealist with his head so much in the clouds that he cannot even make it down a flight of stairs. Many Western productions have played The Cherry Orchard in this way. A third perspective—probably closest to Chekhov's own—is to see the cast as an ensemble, with no one character claiming the heroic center. In such productions, Chekhov offers us representatives from many social groups, all comically misguided but all sympathetic as well.

Chekhov's characters are caught at a moment when each faces an uncertain future, and their fates are shaped by their particular relationship to the sale of the orchard. The event of the auction invites us to witness not a clear standoff between old and new, but rather a set of mixed and ambivalent social perspectives: that of Lopákhin, the son of a serf turned rich businessman, who buys the estate that had enslaved his forefathers, but only after having tried to save it for the aristocracy; or that of Firs, the loyal servant, who sees his own emancipation as the tragic loss of a better, more stable order. And Chekhov uses the orchard to display the experiences not only of multiple classes but also of multiple generations: the oldest look nostalgically backward to the past; the youngest yearn for the future; and those in the middle handle the practical necessities of the present. Through just a handful of actors, Chekhov thus captures the experience of large-scale historical change and gives us a surprisingly wide cross-section of Russian society.

At the same time, this playwright diminishes the usual scale of the dramatic action. As the only major event in the play, the sale of the orchard takes place offstage, and what happens onstage is largely banter, offhand remarks, distracted conversation, foundering intentions, and other markers of sheer ordinariness. Notably, Chekhov paid considerable attention to writing meticulous stage directions, which some readers have found poetic in themselves, and which suggest that he cared a great deal about the smallest details of clothing, setting, and blocking.

If Chekhov overturns conventional distinctions between comedy and tragedy, and frustrates a traditional reliance on grand heroes and exciting plots, he is perhaps at his most innovative when it comes to the play's extraordinarily complex structure. *The Cherry Orchard* is more like a musical composition than a traditional dramatic plot: certain words, themes, and images appear, then reappear later, somewhat changed, like leitmotifs. The play organizes itself around multiple, overlapping patterns: it follows the cycle of the cherry trees, from their first blossoming in an unseasonably cold early spring to the axe that chops them down at the end, but it also follows the fates of three young women, Ánya, Várya, and Dunyásha, each of whom considers the possibility of marriage, just as it tracks the intensity of loss, from the mother's loss of her child to the aristocrats' loss of their land. Echoes and resonances among the characters reverberate in visible groupings onstage: clusters of characters converge and then disperse; and their collective moods shift, like a network of emotions with its own life. Chekhov's play also follows the model of music in quite a literal way: it organizes itself around specific, nonverbal *sounds*: the mysterious, sad noise like a harp string breaking or an echo in a mine shaft, the racket of the axes chopping down the cherry trees, and more comically, Yepikhódov's squeaking boots (which resonate with Pishchik's name, meaning "squeaker"). Throughout, too, music plays a prominent role: among Chekhov's many specific stage directions are details about the music played by the Jewish orchestra, Yepikhódov's guitar, and Ranévskaya's humming. As one director wrote to Chekhov: "Your play is abstract, like a Tchaikovsky symphony."

Although Chekhov's admirers have disagreed about the nature of *The Cherry Orchard*, from those who compared it to a musical abstraction to those who praised it as a politically charged historical chronicle, there has been no disputing its radical originality and its contribution to the history of drama. As Chekhov himself said, in characteristically self-effacing fashion: "I think that, however boring it may be, there's something new about my play."

The Cherry Orchard

A Comedy in Four Acts[1]

CHARACTERS

LIUBÓV RANYÉVSKAYA [Lyúba, Liúba Andréyevna], *who owns the estate*
ÁNYA, *her daughter, seventeen years old*
VÁRYA, *her adopted daughter, twenty-four years old*
LEONÍD GÁYEV [Lonya, Lyónya Andréyich], *Liubóv's brother*
YERMOLÁI LOPÁKHIN [Yermolái Alexéyich], *a businessman*
PÉTYA TROFÍMOV, *a graduate student*
BORÍS SEMYÓNOV-PÍSHCHIK, *who owns land in the neighborhood*

CARLOTTA, *the governess*
SEMYÓN YEPIKHÓDOV, *an accountant*
DUNYÁSHA [Avdótya Fyódorovna, Dunyáhsa Kozoyédov], *the maid*
FIRS, *the butler, eighty-seven years old*
YÁSHA, *the valet*
A HOMELESS MAN
THE STATIONMASTER
THE POSTMASTER
GUESTS, SERVANTS

The action takes place on Ranyévskaya's estate.

Act 1

[*A room they still call the nursery. A side door leads to* ÁNYA's *room. Almost dawn; the sun is about to rise. It's May; the cherry orchard is already in bloom, but there's a chill in the air. The windows are shut. Enter* DUNYÁSHA *with a lamp, and* LOPÁKHIN *with a book in his hand.*]

LOPÁKHIN   The train's finally in, thank God. What time is it?

DUNYÁSHA   Almost two. [*She blows out the lamp.*] It's getting light.

LOPÁKHIN   How late is the train this time? Must be at least two hours. [*He yawns and stretches.*] That was dumb. I came over on purpose just to meet them at the station, and then I fell asleep. Sat right here and fell asleep. Too bad. You should have woke me up.

DUNYÁSHA   I thought you already left. [*She listens.*] Listen, that must be them.

LOPÁKHIN [*he listens*]   No, they still have the luggage to get, and all that. [*Pause*] She's been away five years now; no telling how she's changed. She was always a good person. Very gentle, never caused a fuss. I remember one time when I was a kid, fifteen or so, they had my old man working in the store down by the village, and he hit me, hard, right in the face; my nose started to bleed. And we had to come up here to make a delivery or something; he was still drunk. And Liubóv Andréyevna—she wasn't much older than I was, kind of thin—she brought me inside the house, right into the nursery here, and washed the blood off my face for me. "Don't cry," she told me. "Don't cry, poor boy; you'll live long enough to get married." [*Pause*] Poor boy . . . Well, my father was poor, but take a look at me now, all dressed up, brand-new suit and tan shoes. Silk purse out of a sow's ear, I guess . . . I'm rich now, got lots of money, but when you think about it, I

1. Translated by Paul Schmidt.

guess I'm still a poor boy from the country. [*He flips the pages of the book.*] I tried reading this book, couldn't figure out a word it said. Put me to sleep.

    [*Pause.*]

DUNYÁSHA The dogs were barking all night long; they know their mistress is coming home.

LOPÁKHIN Don't be silly.

DUNYÁSHA I'm so excited I'm shaking. I may faint.

LOPÁKHIN You're getting too full of yourself, Dunyásha. Look at you, all dressed up like that, and that hairdo. You watch out for that. You got to remember who you are.

    [*Enter* YEPIKHÓDOV *with a bunch of flowers; he wears a jacket and tie and brightly polished boots, which squeak loudly. As he comes in, he drops the flowers.*]

YEPIKHÓDOV [*picking up the flowers*] Here. The gardener sent these over; he said put them on the dining room table. [*He gives the flowers to* DUNYÁSHA.]

LOPÁKHIN And bring me a beer.

DUNYÁSHA Right away.

    [*She goes out.*]

YEPIKHÓDOV It's freezing this morning—it must be in the thirties—and the cherry blossoms are out already. I cannot abide the climate here. [*He sighs.*] I never have abided it, ever. [*Beat*][2] Yermolái Alexéyich, would you examinate something for me, please? Day before yesterday I bought myself a new pair of boots, and listen to them squeak, will you? I just cannot endear it. Do you know anything I can put on them?

LOPÁKHIN Will you shut up? You drive me crazy.

YEPIKHÓDOV Every day something awful happens to me. It's like a habit. But I don't complain. I just try to keep smiling.

[*Enter* DUNYÁSHA; *she brings* LOPÁKHIN *a beer.*]

YEPIKHÓDOV I'm going. [*He bumps into a chair, which falls over.*] You see? [*He seems proud of it.*] You see what I was referring about? Excuse my expressivity, but what a concurrence. It's almost uncanny, isn't it?

    [*He leaves.*]

DUNYÁSHA You know what? That Yepikhódov proposed to me!

LOPÁKHIN Oh?

DUNYÁSHA I just don't know what to think. He's kind of nice. . . . He's a real quiet boy, but then he opens his mouth, and you can't ever understand what he's talking about. I mean, it sounds nice, but it just doesn't make any sense. I do like him, though. Kind of. And he's crazy about me. It's funny, you know, every day something awful happens to him. People around here call him Double Trouble.

LOPÁKHIN [*he listens*] That must be them.

DUNYÁSHA It's them! Oh, I don't know what's the matter with me! I feel so funny; I'm cold all over.

LOPÁKHIN It really is them this time. Let's go; we should be there at the door. You think she'll recognize me? It's been five years.

2. Pause.

DUNYÁSHA [*excited*]   Oh, my God! I'm going to faint! I think I'm going to faint!

[*The sound of two carriages outside the house.* LOPÁKHIN *and* DUNYÁSHA *hurry out. The stage is empty. The sound outside gets louder.* FIRS, *leaning heavily on his cane, crosses the room, heading for the door; he wears an old-fashioned butler's livery and a top hat; he says something to himself, but you can't make out the words. The offstage noise and bustle increases. A voice: "Here we are . . . this way." Enter* LIUBÓV ANDRÉYEVNA, ÁNYA, *and* CARLOTTA, *dressed in traveling clothes.* VÁRYA *wears an overcoat, and a kerchief on her head.* GÁYEV, SEMYÓNOV-PÍSHCHIK, LOPÁKHIN, DUNYÁSHA *with a bundle and an umbrella, Servants with the luggage—all pass across the stage.*]

ÁNYA   Here we are. Oh, Mama, do you remember this room?

LIUBÓV ANDRÉYEVNA   The nursery!

VÁRYA   It's freezing; my hands are like ice. We kept your room exactly as you left it, Mama. The white and lavender one.

LIUBÓV ANDRÉYEVNA   The nursery! Oh, this house, this beautiful house! I slept in this room when I was a child. . . . [*She weeps.*] And I feel like a child again! [*She hugs* GÁYEV, VÁRYA, *then* GÁYEV *again.*] And Várya hasn't changed at all—still looks like a nun! And Dunyásha dear! Of course I remember you! [*She hugs* DUNYÁSHA.]

GÁYEV   The train was two hours late. What kind of efficiency is that? Eh?

CARLOTTA   And my dog loves nuts.

SEMYÓNOV-PÍSHCHIK   Really! I don't believe it!

[*Everyone leaves, except* ÁNYA *and* DUNYÁSHA.]

DUNYÁSHA   We've been up all night, waiting. . . . [*She takes* ÁNYA's *coat and hat.*]

ÁNYA   I've been up for four nights now. . . . I didn't sleep the whole trip. And now I'm freezing.

DUNYÁSHA   When you went away it was still winter, it was snowing, and now look! Oh, sweetie, you're back! [*She laughs and hugs* Ánya.] I've been up all night, waiting to see you. Sweetheart, I just can't wait—I've got to tell you what happened. I can't wait another minute!

ÁNYA [*wearily*]   Now what?

DUNYÁSHA   Yepikhódov proposed the day after Easter! He wants to marry me!

ÁNYA   That's all you ever think about. . . . [*She fixes her hair.*] I lost all my hairpins. . . .

DUNYÁSHA   I just don't know what to do about him. He really, really loves me!

ÁNYA [*looking through the door to her room*]   My own room, just as if I'd never left. I'm back home! Tomorrow I'll get up and go for a walk in the orchard. I just wish I could get some sleep. I didn't sleep the whole trip, I was so worried.

DUNYÁSHA   Pétya's here. He got here day before yesterday.

ÁNYA [*joyfully*]   Pétya!

DUNYÁSHA   He's staying out in the barn. Said he didn't want to bother anybody. [*She looks at her watch.*] He told me to get him up, but Várya said not to. You let him sleep, she said.

[*Enter* VÁRYA. *She has a big bunch of keys attached to her belt.*]

VÁRYA   Dunyásha, go get the coffee. Mama wants her coffee.

DUNYÁSHA   Oh, I forgot!

  [*She goes out.*]

VÁRYA   You're back. Thank God! You're home again! [*She embraces Ánya.*] My angel is home again! My beautiful darling!

ÁNYA   You won't believe what I've been through!

VÁRYA   I can imagine.

ÁNYA   I left just before Easter; it was cold. Carlotta never shut up the whole trip; she kept doing those silly tricks of hers. I don't know why you had to stick me with her.

VÁRYA   Darling, you couldn't go all that way by yourself! You're only seventeen!

ÁNYA   We got to Paris, it was cold and snowy, and my French is just awful! Mama was living in this fifth-floor apartment, we had to walk up, we get there and there's all these French people, some old priest reading some book, and it was crowded, and everybody was smoking these awful cigarettes—and I felt so sorry for Mama, I just threw my arms around her and couldn't let go. And she was so glad to see me, she cried—

VÁRYA [*almost crying*]   I know, I know . . .

ÁNYA   And she sold the villa in Mentón,[3] and the money was already gone, all of it! And I spent everything you gave me for the trip; I haven't got a thing left. And Mama still doesn't understand! We have dinner at the train station, and she orders the most expensive things on the menu, and then she tips the waiters a ruble[4] each! And Carlotta does the same! And Yásha expects the same treatment—he's just awful. You know, Yásha, that flunky of Mama's—he came back with us.

VÁRYA   I saw him, the lazy good-for-nothing.

ÁNYA   So what happened? Did you get the interest paid?

VÁRYA   With what?

ÁNYA   Oh, my God, my God . . .

VÁRYA   The place goes up for sale in August.

ÁNYA   Oh, my God.

  [LOPÁKHIN *sticks his head in the doorway and makes a mooing sound, then goes away.*]

VÁRYA   Oh, that man! I'd like to— [*She shakes her fist.*]

ÁNYA [*she hugs her*]   Várya, did he propose yet? [VÁRYA *shakes her head no.*] But you know he loves you! Why don't the two of you just sit down and be honest with each other? What are you waiting for?

VÁRYA   I don't think anything will ever come of it. He's always so busy, he never has time for me. He just isn't interested! It's hard for me when I see him, but I don't care anymore. Everybody talks about us getting married, people even congratulate me, but there's nothing. . . . I mean, it's all just a dream. [*A change of tone*] Oh, you've got a new pin, a little bee. . . .

ÁNYA [*with a sigh*]   I know. Mama bought it for me. [*She goes into her room and starts to giggle, like a little girl.*] You know what? In Paris I went for a ride in a balloon!

VÁRYA   Oh, darling, you're back! My angel is home again!

---

3. Resort town on the French Riviera.
4. Basic unit of Russian currency, worth about $20; one ruble is equal to one hundred kopecks.

[DUNYÁSHA *comes in, carrying a tray with coffee things, and begins setting them out on the table.* VÁRYA *stands at the doorway and talks to* ÁNYA *in the other room.*]

You know, dear, I spend the livelong day trying to keep this house going, and all I do is dream. I want to see you married off to somebody rich, then I can rest easy. And I think then I'll go away by myself, maybe live in a convent, or just go traveling: Kiev, Moscow . . . spend all my time making visits to churches. I'd start walking and just go and go and go. That would be heaven!

ÁNYA Listen to the birds in the orchard! What time is it?

VÁRYA It must be almost three. You should get some sleep, darling. [*She goes into* ÁNYA'S *room.*] Yes, that would be heaven!

[*Enter* YÁSHA *with a suitcase and a lap robe. He walks with an affected manner.*]

YÁSHA I beg pardon! May I intrude?

DUNYÁSHA I didn't even recognize you, Yásha. You got so different there in France.

YÁSHA *I'm* sorry—who are you exactly?

DUNYÁSHA When you left, I wasn't any higher than this. [*She holds her hand a distance from the floor.*] I'm Dunyásha. You know, Dunyásha Kozoyédov. Don't you remember me?

YÁSHA Well! You sure turned out cute, didn't you? [*He looks around carefully, then grabs and kisses her; she screams and drops a saucer;* YÁSHA *leaves in a hurry.*]

VÁRYA [*at the door, annoyed*] Now what happened?

DUNYÁSHA [*almost in tears*] I broke a saucer.

VÁRYA [*ironically*] Well, isn't that lucky!

ÁNYA [*entering*] Somebody should let Mama know Pétya's here.

VÁRYA I told them to let him sleep.

ÁNYA [*lost in thought*] Father died six years ago, and a month later our little brother, Grísha, drowned. Sweet boy, he was only seven. And Mama couldn't face it, that's why she went away, just went away and never looked back. [*Shivers.*] And I understand exactly how she felt. I wish she knew that.

[*Pause.*]

And Pétya Trofímov was Grísha's tutor. He might remind her . . .

[*Enter* FIRS *in his old-fashioned butler's livery. He crosses to the table and begins looking over the coffee things.*]

FIRS The missus will have her breakfast here. [*He puts on a pair of white gloves.*] Is the coffee ready? [*To* DUNYÁSHA, *crossly*] Where's the cream? Go get the cream!

DUNYÁSHA Oh, my God, I'm sorry. . . .

[*Hurries off.*]

FIRS [*he starts fussing with the coffee things*] Young flibbertigibbet . . . [*He mumbles to himself.*] They're all back from Paris. . . . In the old days they went to Paris too . . . had to go the whole way in a horse and buggy. [*He laughs.*]

VÁRYA Firs, what are you talking about?

FIRS Beg pardon? [*Joyfully*] The missus is home! Going to see her at last! Now I can die happy. . . . [*He starts to cry with joy.*]

[*Enter* LIUBÓV, GÁYEV, LOPÁKHIN, *and* SEMYÓNOV-PÍSHCHIK, *who wears a crumpled linen suit. As* GÁYEV *enters, he gestures as if he were making a billiard shot.*]

LIUBÓV ANDRÉYEVNA   How did it go? I'm trying to remember. . . . Yellow ball in the side pocket! Bank shot off the corner!

GÁYEV   And right down the middle! Oh, sister, sister, just think . . . when you and I were little we used to sleep in this room, and now I'm almost fifty-one! Strange, isn't it?

LOPÁKHIN   Time sure passes. . . .

GÁYEV [*beat*]   Say again?

LOPÁKHIN   I said, time sure passes.

GÁYEV [*looking at* LOPÁKHIN]   Who's wearing that cheap cologne?

ÁNYA   I'm going to bed. Good night, Mama. [*She kisses her mother.*]

LIUBÓV ANDRÉYEVNA   Oh, my darling little girl, my baby! Are you glad you're home? I still can't quite believe I'm here.

ÁNYA   Good night, Uncle.

GÁYEV [*he kisses her*]   God bless you, dear. You're getting to look so much like your mother! Liúba, she looks just like you when you were her age. She really does.

> [ÁNYA *says good night to* LOPÁKHIN *and* PÍSHCHIK, *goes into her room, and closes the door behind her.*]

LIUBÓV ANDRÉYEVNA   She's tired to death.

PÍSHCHIK   Well, that's such a long trip!

VÁRYA   Gentlemen, please. It's almost three; time you were going.

LIUBÓV ANDRÉYEVNA [*laughs*]   You're the same as ever, Várya. [*Hugs and kisses her.*] Just let me have my coffee, then we'll all be going.

> [FIRS *puts a pillow beneath her feet.*]

Thank you, dear. I've really gotten addicted to coffee; I drink it day and night. You old darling, you! Thank you.

VÁRYA   I'll just go make sure they've got everything unloaded.

> [*Goes out.*]

LIUBÓV ANDRÉYEVNA   I can't believe I'm really here! [*Laughs.*] I feel like jumping up and waving my arms in the air! [*Covers her face with her hands.*] It's still like a dream. I love this country, really I do, I adore it. I started to cry every time I looked out the train windows. [*Almost in tears*] But I do need my coffee! Thank you, Firs, thank you, darling. I'm so glad you're still alive.

FIRS   Day before yesterday.

GÁYEV   He doesn't hear too well anymore.

LOPÁKHIN   Time for me to go. I have to leave for Hárkow[5] at five. I'm really disappointed; I was looking forward to seeing you, have a chance to talk. . . . You look wonderful, just the way you always did.

PÍSHCHIK [*breathes hard*]   Better than she always did. That Paris outfit. . . . She makes me feel young again!

LOPÁKHIN   Your brother here thinks I'm crude, calls me a money grubber. That doesn't bother me; he can call me whatever he wants. I just hope you'll trust me the way you used to, look at me the way you used to. . . . My God, my father slaved for your father and grandfather, my whole family worked for yours; but you, you treated me different. You did so much for me I forgot about all that. Fact is, I . . . I love you like you were family . . . more, even.

---

5. Kharkov, city in present-day Ukraine.

LIUBÓV ANDRÉYEVNA   I can't sit still; I'm just not in the mood! [*Gets up excitedly, moves about the room.*] I'm so happy I could die! I know I sound stupid—go ahead, laugh. . . . Dear old bookcase. . . . [*Kisses the bookcase.*] My little desk . . .

GÁYEV   Did I tell you Nanny died while you were away?

LIUBÓV ANDRÉYEVNA [*sits back down and drinks her coffee*]   Yes, you wrote me. God rest her.

GÁYEV   Stásy died too. And Petrúsha Kosói quit and moved into town; he works at the police station. [*Takes out a little box of hard candies and puts one in his mouth.*]

PÍSHCHIK   Dáshenka—you remember Dáshenka? My daughter? Anyway, she sends her regards. . . .

LOPÁKHIN   Well, I'd like to give you some very good news. [*Looks at his watch.*] Afraid there's no time to talk now, though; I've got to go. Well, just to make it short, you know you haven't kept up the mortgage payments on your place here. So now they foreclosed and your estate is up for sale. At auction. They set a date already, August twenty-second, but don't you worry, you can rest easy. We can take care of this—I've got a great idea. Now listen, here's how it works: your place here is fifteen miles from town, and it's only a short drive from the train station. All you've got to do is clear out the old cherry orchard, plus that land down by the river, and subdivide! You lease the plots, build vacation homes, and I swear that'll bring you in twenty-five thousand[6] a year, maybe more.

GÁYEV   What an outrageous thing to say!

LIUBÓV ANDRÉYEVNA   Excuse me . . . Excuse me, I don't think I quite understand. . . .

LOPÁKHIN   You'll get at least twenty-five hundred an acre! And if you start advertising right away, I swear to God come this fall you won't have a single plot left. You see what I'm saying? Your troubles are over! Congratulations! The location is terrific; the river's a real selling point. Only thing is, you've got to start clearing right away. Get rid of all the old buildings. This house, for instance, will have to go. You can't get people to live in a barn like this anymore. And you'll have to cut down that old cherry orchard.

LIUBÓV ANDRÉYEVNA   Cut down the cherry orchard? My dear man, you don't understand! Our cherry orchard is a landmark! It's famous for miles around!

LOPÁKHIN   The only thing famous about it is how big it is. You only get cherries every two years, and even then you can't get rid of them. Nobody buys them. It's just not a commercial crop.

GÁYEV   Our cherry orchard is mentioned in the encyclopedia![7]

LOPÁKHIN [*looks at his watch*]   We have to think of something to do and then do it. Otherwise the cherry orchard will be sold at auction on August twenty-second, this house and all the land with it. Make up your minds! Believe me, I've thought this through; there isn't any other way to do it. There just isn't.

FIRS   Back in the old days, forty, fifty years ago, they used to make dried cherries, pickled cherries, preserved cherries, cherry jam, and sometimes—

6. Roughly equivalent to $500,000 today (all references to money are in rubles).
7. Probably a reference to the *Great Russian Encyclopedic Dictionary* (1890–1906), an authoritative 86-volume reference work published by F. A. Brockhaus and I. A. Efron.

GÁYEV   Oh, Firs, just shut up.

FIRS   —sometimes they sent them off to Moscow by the wagonload. People paid a lot for them! Back then the dried cherries were soft and juicy and sweet, and they smelled just lovely; back then they knew how to fix them. . . .

LIUBÓV ANDRÉYEVNA   Does anybody know how to fix them nowadays?

FIRS   Nope. They all forgot.

PÍSHCHIK   Tell us about Paris. What was it like? Did you eat frogs?

LIUBÓV ANDRÉYEVNA   I ate crocodiles.

PÍSHCHIK   Crocodiles? Really! I don't believe it!

LOPÁKHIN   You see, it used to be out here in the country there were only landlords and poor farmers, but now all of a sudden there are summer people moving in; they want vacation homes. Every town you can name is surrounded by them—it's the coming thing. In twenty years they'll expand and multiply! Right now maybe they're only places to relax on the weekend, but I bet you eventually people will put down roots out here, they'll create neighborhoods, and then your cherry orchard will blossom and bear fruit once again—and even bring in a profit!

GÁYEV [indignantly]   That's outrageous!

　　　　[Enter VÁRYA and YÁSHA.]

VÁRYA   Mama, a couple of telegrams came for you. [Takes a key and opens the old bookcase; the lock creaks.] Here they are.

LIUBÓV ANDRÉYEVNA   They're from Paris. [She tears them up without opening them.] I'm through with Paris.

GÁYEV   Liúba, have you any idea how old this bookcase is? Last week I pulled out the bottom drawer, and there was the date on the back, burned right into the wood. A hundred years! This bookcase is exactly a hundred years old! What do you say to that, eh? We should have a birthday celebration. Of course, it's an inanimate object, any way you look at it, but still, it's a . . . well, it's a . . . a bookcase.

PÍSHCHIK   A hundred years old! Really! I don't believe it!

GÁYEV   Yes, yes, it is. [He caresses the bookcase.] Dear old bookcase! Wonderful old bookcase! I rejoice in your existence. For a hundred years now you have borne the shining ideals of goodness and justice, a hundred years have not dimmed your silent summons to useful labor. To generations of our family [Almost in tears] you have offered courage, a belief in a better future, you have instructed us in ideals of goodness and social awareness. . . .

　　　　[Pause.]

LOPÁKHIN   Right. Well . . .

LIUBÓV ANDRÉYEVNA   Oh, Lonya, you're still the same as ever!

GÁYEV [somewhat embarrassed]   Yellow ball in the side pocket! Bank shot off the center!

LOPÁKHIN   Well, I've got to be off.

YÁSHA [gives LIUBÓV a pillbox]   Isn't it perhaps time for your pills?

PÍSHCHIK   No, no, no, dear lady! Never take medicine! Won't do any good! Won't do any harm either, though. Watch! [Takes the pillbox, dumps the contents into his hand, puts them in his mouth, and swallows them with a swig of beer.] There! All gone!

LIUBÓV ANDRÉYEVNA [alarmed]   Are you out of your mind?

PÍSHCHIK   I have just taken all your pills for you.

LOPÁKHIN   What a glutton.

[*Everybody laughs.*]

FIRS   He was here over the holidays, ate half a crock of pickles. . . . [*Mumbles.*]

LIUBÓV ANDRÉYEVNA   What's he mumbling about?

VÁRYA   He's been going on like that for the last three years. We're used to it by now.

YÁSHA   He's getting senile.

[*Enter* CARLOTTA, *in a white dress with a lorgnette on a chain. She starts to cross the room.*]

LOPÁKHIN   Oh, excuse me, Carlotta, I didn't get a chance to say hello yet. [*Tries to kiss her hand.*]

CARLOTTA [*takes her hand away*]   I let you kiss my hand, first thing I know, you'll want to kiss my elbow, then my shoulder . . .

LOPÁKHIN   This isn't my lucky day.

[*Everybody laughs.*]

Carlotta, show us a trick!

LIUBÓV ANDRÉYEVNA   Yes, do, Carlotta—show us a trick!

CARLOTTA   Not now. I'm off to bed.

[*Leaves.*]

LOPÁKHIN   Well, I'll see you in three weeks. [*Kisses* LIUBÓV's *hand.*] Goodbye now. I've got to be off. [*To* GÁYEV] Goodbye. [*Hugs* PÍSHCHIK.] So long. [*Shakes hands with* VÁRYA, *then with* FIRS *and* YÁSHA.] I sort of hate to leave. [*To* LIUBÓV] Think over what I said about subdividing the place. You decide to do it, let me know, and I'll take care of everything. I'll get you a loan of fifty thousand. Think it over now, seriously.

VÁRYA [*angry*]   Will you please just go?

LOPÁKHIN   I'm going, I'm going.

[*Leaves.*]

GÁYEV   What a bore. Oh, excuse me, *pardon*,[8] I forgot—that's Várya's boy-friend. He's going to marry our Várya.

VÁRYA   Uncle, will you please not talk nonsense?

LIUBÓV ANDRÉYEVNA   Oh, but Várya, that's wonderful! He's a fine man!

PÍSHCHIK   One of the finest, in fact . . . the very, very finest . . . My Dáshenka always says . . . she says . . . she says a lot of things. [*Snores, but immediately wakes up.*] Dear lady, yes, always respected you, hmm. . . . You think you could lend me, say, two hundred and forty rubles? Mortgage payment, you know, due tomorrow . . .

VÁRYA [*terrified*]   We can't; we don't have any!

LIUBÓV ANDRÉYEVNA   I'm afraid that's the truth. We haven't any money.

PÍSHCHIK   I'll get it somewhere. [*Laughs.*] I never give up hope. There was that time I thought I was finished, it was all over, and all of a sudden— boom! The railroad cut across some of my land and paid me for it. You'll see, something will turn up tomorrow or the next day. Dáshenka will win two hundred thousand in the lottery; she just bought a ticket.

LIUBÓV ANDRÉYEVNA   Well, the coffee's gone. We might as well go to bed.

---

8. Gáyev uses the French word *pardon* (excuse me); it was typical for upper-class Russians in the 19th century to speak French to one another.

FIRS [*takes out a clothes brush and brushes* GÁYEV's *clothes; scolds him*]   You've got on the wrong trousers again. What am I supposed to do with you?

VÁRYA [*softly*]   Ánya's asleep. [*Quietly opens the window.*] The sun's coming up; it's not as cold as it was. Look, Mama, what wonderful trees! Smell the perfume! Oh, Lord! And the orioles are singing!

GÁYEV [*opens another window*]   The whole orchard is white. You remember, Liúba? That long path, stretched out like a ribbon, on and on, the way it used to shine in the moonlight? You remember? You haven't forgotten?

LIUBÓV ANDRÉYEVNA   Oh, my childhood! My innocence! I slept in this room, I could look out over the orchard, when I woke up in the morning I was happy, and it all looked exactly the same as this! Nothing has changed! [*Laughs delightedly.*] White, white, all white! My whole orchard is white! Autumn was dark and drizzly, and winter was cold, but now you're young again, flowering with happiness—the angels of heaven have never abandoned you. If only I could shake off this weight I've been carrying so long. If only I could forget my past!

GÁYEV   Yes, and now they're selling the orchard to pay our debts. Strange, isn't it?

LIUBÓV ANDRÉYEVNA   Look! There . . . in the orchard . . . it's Mother! In her white dress! [*Laughs delightedly.*] It's Mother!

GÁYEV   Where?

VÁRYA   Oh, Mama, for God's sake . . .

LIUBÓV ANDRÉYEVNA   It's all right; I was just imagining things. There to the right, by the path to the summerhouse, that little white tree all bent over . . . it looked just like a woman.

[*Enter* TROFÍMOV. *He is dressed like a student and wears wire-rimmed glasses.*]
What a glorious orchard! All those white blossoms, and the blue sky—

TROFÍMOV   Liubóv Andréyevna!

[*She turns to look at him.*]
I don't mean to disturb you; I just wanted to say hello. [*Shakes her hand warmly.*] They told me to wait until later, but I couldn't. . . .

[LIUBÓV *stares at him, bewildered.*]

VÁRYA   It's Pétya Trofímov. . . .

TROFÍMOV   Pétya Trofímov—I was your little boy Grísha's tutor. . . . Have I really changed all that much?

[LIUBÓV *embraces him and begins to weep softly.*]

GÁYEV [*embarrassed*]   Liúba, that'll do, that'll do. . . .

VÁRYA [*weeps*]   Oh, Pétya, I told you to wait till tomorrow.

LIUBÓV ANDRÉYEVNA   Grísha . . . my little boy. Grísha . . . my son . . .

VÁRYA   Oh, Mama, don't; it was God's will.

TROFÍMOV [*gently, almost in tears*]   There, there . . .

LIUBÓV ANDRÉYEVNA [*weeps softly*]   My little boy drowned, lost forever . . . Why? What for? My dear boy, why? [*Quiets down.*] Ánya's asleep, and here I am carrying on like this. . . . Pétya, what's happened to you? You used to be such a nice-looking boy. What happened? You look dreadful. You've gotten so old!

TROFÍMOV   Some lady on the train called me a high-class tramp.

LIUBÓV ANDRÉYEVNA   You were only a boy then, just out of high school, you were adorable, and now you've got glasses and you're losing your hair. And haven't you graduated yet? [*Goes to the door.*]

TROFÍMOV   I suppose I'm what you'd call a permanent graduate student.

LIUBÓV ANDRÉYEVNA [*kisses* GÁYEV, *then* VÁRYA]   Time for bed. You've gotten old too, Leoníd.

PÍSHCHIK [*follows* LIUBÓV]   Time for bed, time to go . . . Ooh, my gout! I'd better stay the night. Now, dear, look, look . . . Liubóv Andréyevna, tomorrow morning I need . . . two hundred and forty rubles. . . .

GÁYEV   He never gives up, does he?

PÍSHCHIK   Two hundred and forty rubles; my mortgage payment due. . . .

LIUBÓV ANDRÉYEVNA   Darling, I simply have no money.

PÍSHCHIK   But, dear, I'll give it right back. . . . It's such a *trivial* amount. . . .

LIUBÓV ANDRÉYEVNA   Oh, all right. Leoníd will get it for you. Leoníd, you give him the money.

GÁYEV   I should give him money? That'll be the day.

LIUBÓV ANDRÉYEVNA   We have to give it to him; he needs it. He'll give it back.

[*Exit* LIUBÓV, TROFÍMOV, PÍSHCHIK, *and* FIRS. GÁYEV, VÁRYA, *and* YÁSHA *remain.*]

GÁYEV   She still thinks money grows on trees. [*To* YÁSHA] My good man, will you leave us, please? Go back to the barn, where you belong.

YÁSHA [*smiles*]   Leoníd Andréyich, you're the same as you always were.

GÁYEV   What say? [*To* VÁRYA] What did he just say?

VÁRYA [*to* YÁSHA]   Your mother came in from the country to see you. She's been sitting in the kitchen for two days now, waiting.

YÁSHA   Oh, for God's sake, can't she leave me alone?

VÁRYA   You are really disgraceful!

YÁSHA   That's all I need right now. Why couldn't she wait till tomorrow? [*Goes out.*]

VÁRYA   Mama hasn't changed; she's the same as she always was. If it were up to her, she'd give away everything.

GÁYEV   Yes. . . . [*Pause*] Someone gets sick, you know, and the doctor tries one thing after another, that means there's no cure. I've been thinking and thinking, racking my brains, I come up with one thing, then another, but the truth is, none of them will work. It would be wonderful if somebody left us a lot of money, it would be wonderful if we could marry off Ánya to somebody with a lot of money, it would be wonderful if we could go see Ánya's godmother in Yároslavl,[9] try to borrow the money from her. She's very, very rich.

VÁRYA [*weeps*]   If only God would help us!

GÁYEV   Oh, stop crying. She's very, very rich, but she doesn't like us. Because in the first place, my sister married a mere lawyer instead of a man with a title. . . .

[ÁNYA *appears in the doorway.*]

She married a lawyer, and then her behavior has not been—how shall I put it?—particularly exemplary. She's a lovely woman, goodhearted, charming, and of course she's my sister and I love her very much, and there are extenuating circumstances and such, but the fact is, she's what you'd have to call a . . . a loose woman. And she doesn't care who knows it; you can feel it in every move she makes.

9. Russian city northeast of Moscow.

VÁRYA [whispers] Ánya's here.

GÁYEV What say? [Pause] Funny, I must have gotten something in my eye: I can't see too well. . . . Did I tell you what happened Thursday, when I was at the county courthouse?

[ÁNYA comes into the room.]

VÁRYA Why aren't you asleep?

ÁNYA I tried. I couldn't sleep.

GÁYEV Kitten . . . [Kisses ÁNYA's cheek, then her hands.] My dear child . . . [Almost in tears] You're more than just my niece, you're my angel, you know that? You're my whole world, believe me, believe me. . . .

ÁNYA I believe you, Uncle. And I love you; we all love you. . . . But, Uncle dear, you should learn not to talk so much. The things you were saying just now about Mama, about your own sister . . . What were you saying all that for?

GÁYEV I know, I know. . . . [Covers his face with her hand.] It's awful, I know. My God, a few minutes ago I made a speech to a piece of furniture. . . . It was so stupid! The thing is, I never realize how stupid I sound until I'm done.

VÁRYA She's right, Uncle. You just have to learn to keep still, that's all.

ÁNYA If you do, you'll feel much better about yourself, you know you will. . . .

GÁYEV I will, I will, I promise. [Kisses ÁNYA's and VÁRYA's hands.] I'll keep still. Only right now I have to talk a little more. Business! On Thursday I was at the county courthouse; there was a group of us talking—just this and that—and it turns out I might be able to arrange a promissory note for enough money to pay off the mortgage.

VÁRYA If only God would help us!

GÁYEV I'm going in on Tuesday, I'll talk to them again. [To VÁRYA] Don't whine! [To ÁNYA] Your mother will talk to Lopákhin; he can't refuse to help her. And you, as soon as you're rested, you go to Yároslavl, go talk to your godmother. There. We'll be operating on three fronts at once; we're sure to succeed. We will pay off this mortgage, I know we will. . . . [He pops a hard candy into his mouth.] I swear by my honor, I swear by anything you want, the estate will not be sold! [Excitedly] I swear by my own happiness! Here, you have my hand on it. You may call me . . . dishonorable, call me anything you will, if I ever let this estate go on the auction block! I swear by my entire existence!

ÁNYA [her calm mood has returned; she is happy] You're so smart, Uncle! You're such a wonderful man! [Hugs GÁYEV.] Now I feel better! So much better! I'm happy again!

[Enter FIRS.]

FIRS [reproachfully] Leoníd Andréyich, why aren't you in bed, like decent God-fearing people?

GÁYEV I'm coming, I'm coming. You go to bed, Firs. I can get undressed by myself. All right, children, nighty-night. We can talk about the details tomorrow, now it's time for bed. [Kisses ÁNYA and VÁRYA.] I am a man of the eighties, you know. People don't think much of that era now, but I can tell you frankly that I have had the courage of my convictions and often had to pay the price.[1]

---

1. When Alexander III (1845–1894) became tsar in 1881, he initiated repressive measures to combat liberal and revolutionary elements in Russian society.

But these local peasants all love me. You have to get to know them, that's all. You have to get to know them, and—

ÁNYA   Uncle. You're at it again.

VÁRYA   Just be quiet, Uncle.

FIRS [angrily]   Leoníd Andréyich!

GÁYEV   I'm coming, I'm coming. . . . Go to bed now. Yellow ball in the side pocket! Clean shot!

[Goes out; FIRS follows him, limping.]

ÁNYA   I feel much better. I don't much want to go to Yároslavl, I don't like my godmother, but I feel better now. Thanks to Uncle [Sits down.]

VÁRYA   We've got to get some sleep. I'm going to bed. Oh, there's something came up since you left. You know we've got all those old retired servants living out back—Paulina, old Karp, and the rest of them. And what happened, they started inviting people in to spend the night. Well, it's annoying, but I never said a thing. Then what happened was, they started telling everybody all they were getting to eat was beans. Because I was so cheap, you see. It was that old Karp was doing it. So I said to myself, All right, that's the way you want it, all right, just wait, and I sent for him [Yawns], and in he comes, so I say, Karp, you're such an idiot—[Looks at ÁNYA.] Ánya!

[Pause.]

She's asleep. [Lifts ÁNYA by the arms.] Come on, time for bed. . . . Come on, let's go. . . . [Leads her off.] My angel fell asleep! Come on. . . . [They start out.]

[In the distance, beyond the orchard, a shepherd plays a pipe. TROFÍMOV enters, sees ÁNYA and VÁRYA, stops.]

VÁRYA   Shh! She's asleep. . . . Come on, darling, let's go. . . .

ÁNYA [softly, half asleep]   I was so tired. . . . All those bells . . . Uncle dear . . . and Mama. Uncle and Mama.

VÁRYA   Come on, darling, come on. . . .

[They go off into ÁNYA's room.]

TROFÍMOV [deeply moved]   My sunshine! My springtime!

Curtain.

Act 2

[An open space. The overgrown rain of an abandoned chapel. There is a well beside it and some large stones that must once have been grave markers. An old bench. Beyond, the road to the Gáyev estate. On one side a shadowy row of poplar trees; they mark the limits of the cherry orchard. A row of telegraph poles, and on the far distant horizon, on a clear day, you can just make out the city. It's late afternoon, almost sunset. CARLOTTA, YÁSHA, and DUNYÁSHA are sitting on the bench; YEPIKHÓDOV stands nearby, strumming his guitar; each seems lost in his own thoughts. CARLOTTA wears an old military cap and is adjusting the strap on a hunting rifle.]

CARLOTTA [meditatively]   I haven't got a birth certificate, so I don't know how old I really am. I just think of myself as young. When I was a little girl, Mama and my father used to travel around to fairs and put on shows, good ones. I did back flips, things like that. And after they died this German woman brought me up, taught me a few things. And that was it. Then I grew up and had to go to work. As a governess. Where I'm from . . . who I am . . . no idea. Who my parents were—maybe they weren't even married—no idea. [*Takes a large cucumber pickle out of her pocket and takes a bite.*] No idea at all.

[*Pause.*]

And I feel like talking all the time, but there's no one to talk to. No one.

YEPIKHÓDOV [*plays the guitar and sings*]

"What do I care for the rest of the world,
or care what it cares for me . . . "[2]

Very agreeable, playing a mandolin.

DUNYÁSHA   That's not a mandolin, it's a guitar. [*Takes out a compact with a mirror and powders herself.*]

YEPIKHÓDOV   When a man is madly in love, a guitar is a mandolin. [*Sings.*]

"As long as my heart is on fire with love,
and the one I love loves me."

[YÁSHA *sings harmony.*]

CARLOTTA   Oof! You people sound like hyenas.

DUNYÁSHA   But it must have been just lovely, being in Europe.

YÁSHA   Oh, it was. Quite, quite lovely. I have to agree with you there. [*Yawns, then lights a cigar.*]

YEPIKHÓDOV   That's understandable. In Europe, things have already come to a complex.

YÁSHA [*beat*]   I suppose you could say that.

YEPIKHÓDOV   I'm a true product of the educational system; I read all the time. All the right books too, but I have no chosen directive in life. For me, strictly speaking, it's live or shoot myself. That's why I always carry a loaded pistol. See? [*Takes out a revolver.*]

CARLOTTA   All done. Time to go. [*Slings the rifle over her shoulder.*] You're a very smart man, Yepikhódov, and a very scary one. Ooh! The women must adore you. [*Starts off.*] They're all so dumb, these smart boys. Never anyone to talk to . . . Always alone, all by myself, no one to talk to . . . and I still don't know who I am. Or why. No idea.

[*Walks slowly off.*]

YEPIKHÓDOV   I should explain, by the way, for the sake of expressivity, that fate has been, ah, *rigorous* to me. I am, strictly speaking, tempest-tossed. Always have been. Now, you may say to me, Oh, you're imagining things, but then why, when I wake up this morning—here's an example—and I look down, why is there this spider on my stomach? Detrimentally large too. [*Makes a circle with his two hands.*] Big as that. Or take a beer, let's say. I go to drink it, what do I see floating around in it? Something highly unappreciative, like a cockroach.

[*Pause.*]

Have you ever read Henry Thomas Buckle?[3]

[*Pause.*]

---

2. Words from a popular turn-of-the-century ballad.
3. English historian (1821–1862) who wrote

A History of Civilization in England (1857–61), considered daringly freethinking and materialistic.

May I design to disturb you, Avdótya Fyódorovna, with something I have to say?

DUNYÁSHA So say it.

YEPIKHÓDOV Preferentially alone. [*Sighs.*]

DUNYÁSHA [*embarrassed*] All right. . . . Only first get me my wrap; it's by the kitchen door. It's getting kind of damp.

YEPIKHÓDOV Ah, I see. Yes, get the wrap, of course. Now I know what to do with my gun.

[*Takes his guitar and goes off, strumming.*]

YÁSHA Double Trouble. He's an idiot, if you ask me. [*Yawns.*]

DUNYÁSHA I hope to God he doesn't shoot himself.

[*Pause.*]

I get upset over every little thing anymore. Ever since I started working for them here, I've gotten used to their *lifestyle*. Just look at my hands. Look at how white they are, just like I was rich. I'm different now from like I was. I'm more delicate, I'm more sensitive; everything upsets me. . . . It's just awful how things upset me. So if you cheat on me, Yásha, I may just have a nervous breakdown.

YÁSHA [*kisses her*] Oh, you little cutie! Just remember, though: a girl has to watch her step. What I'm after is a *nice* girl.

DUNYÁSHA I really love you, Yásha, I really do. You're so smart, you know so many things. . . .

[*Pause.*]

YÁSHA [*yawns*] Yeah. . . . But my theory is, a girl says she loves you, she's not a nice girl.

[*Pause.*]

Nothing like smoking a cigar out here in the fresh air. . . . [*Listens.*] Somebody's coming. . . . It's them. . . .

[DUNYÁSHA *hugs him impulsively.*]

YÁSHA Go on back to the house. Go back the other way, make believe you've been swimming down by the river, so they don't think we've been . . . we've been getting together out here like this. I don't want them to think that.

DUNYÁSHA [*a little cough*] That cigar smoke is giving me a headache. . . .

[*Goes out.*]

[YÁSHA *sits beside the chapel wall. Enter* LIUBÓV, GÁYEV, *and* LOPÁKHIN.]

LOPÁKHIN You have to make up your mind one way or the other; time's running out. There's no argument left. You want to subdivide or don't you? Just give me an answer, one word, yes or no.

LIUBÓV ANDRÉYEVNA Who's been smoking those cheap cigars? [*Sits down.*]

GÁYEV Everything's so convenient, now that there's the railroad. We went into town just to have lunch. Yellow ball in the side pocket! What do you say—why don't we go back to the house, eh? Have ourselves a little game . . .

LIUBÓV ANDRÉYEVNA Let's wait till later.

LOPÁKHIN Just one word! [*Imploringly*] Why don't you give me an answer?

GÁYEV [*yawns*] To what?

LIUBÓV ANDRÉYEVNA [*rummages in her purse*] Yesterday I had a lot of money, today it's all gone. My poor Várya feeds us all on soup to economize, the poor old people get nothing but beans, and I just spend and spend. . . . [*Drops her purse; gold coins spill out.*] Oh, I've spilled everything. . . .

YÁSHA   Here, allow me. [*Picks up the money.*]

LIUBÓV ANDRÉYEVNA   Oh, please do, Yásha: thank you. And why I had to go into that town for lunch—that stupid restaurant of yours, those stupid musicians, those stupid tablecloths; they smelled of soap. . . . Why do we drink so much, Lyónya? And eat so much? Why do we talk so much? The whole time we were in the restaurant, you kept talking, and none of it made any sense. Talking about the seventies, about Symbolism.[4] And to who? The waiters! Talking about Symbolism to waiters!

LOPÁKHIN   Yes.

GÁYEV [*makes a deprecating gesture*]   I'm incorrigible, I suppose. . . . [*To* YÁSHA, *irritably*] What are *you* doing here? Why are you always underfoot every time I turn around?

YÁSHA [*laughs*]   Because every time I hear your voice it makes me laugh.

GÁYEV   Either he goes or I do!

LIUBÓV ANDRÉYEVNA   Yásha, please . . . just go 'way, will you?

YÁSHA [*gives* LIUBÓV *her purse*]   I'm going. Right now. [*Barely containing his laughter*] Right this very minute . . .
        [*Goes out.*]

LOPÁKHIN   You know who DeriGánov is? You know how much money he has? You know he's planning to buy your property? They say he's coming to the auction himself.

LIUBÓV ANDRÉYEVNA   Who told you that?

LOPÁKHIN   Everybody in town knows about it.

GÁYEV   The old lady in Yároslavl promised to send money. . . . But when, and how much, she didn't say.

LOPÁKHIN   How much will she send? A hundred thousand? Two hundred?

LIUBÓV ANDRÉYEVNA   Ten or fifteen thousand. And we're lucky to get that much.

LOPÁKHIN   Excuse me, but you people . . . I have never met anyone so unbusinesslike, so impractical, so . . . so *crazy* as the pair of you! Somebody tells you flat out your land is about to be sold, you don't even seem to understand!

LIUBÓV ANDRÉYEVNA   But what should we do? Just tell us what we should do!

LOPÁKHIN   I tell you every day what you should do! Every day I come out here and say the same thing. The cherry orchard and the rest of the land has to be subdivided and developed for leisure homes, and it has to be done right away. The auction date is getting closer! Can't you understand? All you have to do is make up your mind to subdivide, you'll have more money than even you can spend! Your troubles will be over!

LIUBÓV ANDRÉYEVNA   Subdivide, leisure homes . . . excuse me, but it's all so hopelessly vulgar.

GÁYEV   I couldn't agree more.

---

4. Symbolism was an unsettling artistic movement, launched by French poets Stéphane Mallarmé and Paul Verlaine in the late 19th century; they emphasized evocative images and sounds rather than logic or facts. "The seventies": a time of peasant unrest in Russia.

LOPÁKHIN You people drive me crazy! Another minute, I'll be shouting my head off! Oh, I give up, I give up! Why do I even bother? [*To* GÁYEV] You're worse than an old lady!

GÁYEV What say?

LOPÁKHIN I said you're an old lady! [*Starts to leave.*]

LIUBÓV ANDRÉYEVNA [*fearfully*] No, no, no, please, my dear, don't go. Please. I'm sure we'll think of something.

LOPÁKHIN What's there to think of?

LIUBÓV ANDRÉYEVNA Please. Don't go. Things are easier when you're around. . . .

> [*Pause.*]

> I keep waiting for something to happen. It's as if the house were about to fall down around our ears or something. . . .

GÁYEV [*meditatively*] Yellow ball in the side pocket . . . Clean shot down the middle . . .

LIUBÓV ANDRÉYEVNA We're guilty of so many sins, I know—

LOPÁKHIN Sins? What are you talking about?

GÁYEV [*pops a hard candy into his mouth*] People say I've eaten up my entire inheritance in candy. [*Laughs.*]

LIUBÓV ANDRÉYEVNA All my sins . . . I've always wasted money, just thrown it away like a madwoman, and I married a man who never paid a bill in his life. He was an alcoholic; he drank himself to death—on champagne. And I was so unhappy I fell in love with another man, *unfortunately*, and had an affair with him, and that was when—that was the first thing, my first punishment, right down there, in the river, my little boy drowned, and I left, I went to France, I left and never wanted to come back, I never wanted to see that river again, I just closed my eyes and *ran*, forgot about everything, and that man followed me. He just wouldn't let up. And he was so mean to me, so cruel! I bought a villa in Mentón because he got sick while we were there, and for the next three years I never had a moment's peace, day or night. He tormented me from his sickbed. I could feel my soul dry up. And last year I couldn't afford the villa anymore, so I sold it and we moved to Paris, and once we were in Paris he took everything I had left and ran off with another woman, and I tried to kill myself. It was so stupid, and so shameful! Finally all I wanted was to come back home, to where I was born, to my daughter. [*Wipes away her tears.*] Oh, dear God, dear God, forgive me! Forgive me my sins! Don't punish me again! [*Takes a telegram from her purse.*] This came today, from Paris. . . . He says he's sorry, he wants me back. . . . [*Tears up the telegram.*] Where's [*Listens.*] . . . where's that music coming from?

GÁYEV That's our famous local orchestra. Those Jewish musicians, you remember? Four fiddles, a clarinet, and a double bass.

LIUBÓV ANDRÉYEVNA Are they still around? We should have them over some evening and throw a party.

LOPÁKHIN [*listens*] I don't hear anything. [*Sings to himself.*]

> "Ooh-la-la . . .
> Just a little bit of money
> makes a lady very French . . ."[5]

---

5. Satirical reference to Russian efforts to imitate Parisian culture since the time of Tsar Peter the Great (1672–1725).

[*Laughs.*] I went to the theater last night, saw this musical. Very funny.

LIUBÓV ANDRÉYEVNA   I doubt there was anything funny about it. You ought to stop going to see playacting and take a good look at your own reality. What a boring life you lead! And what uninteresting things you talk about.

LOPÁKHIN   Well . . . yeah, there's some truth to that. It is a pretty dumb life we lead. . . .

[*Pause.*]

My father was a . . . he was a dirt farmer, an idiot, never understood me, never taught me anything, just got drunk and beat me up. With a stick. Fact is, I'm not much better myself. Never did well in school, my writing's terrible, I'm ashamed if anybody sees it. I write like a pig.

LIUBÓV ANDRÉYEVNA   My dear man, you should get married.

LOPÁKHIN   Yes. . . . Yes, I should.

LIUBÓV ANDRÉYEVNA   And you should marry our Várya. She's a wonderful girl.

LOPÁKHIN   She is.

LIUBÓV ANDRÉYEVNA   Her people were quite ordinary, but she works like a dog, and the main thing is, she loves you. And you like her, I know you do. You always have.

LOPÁKHIN   Look, I've got nothing against it. I . . . She's wonderful girl.

[*Pause.*]

GÁYEV   They offered me a position at the bank. Six thousand a year. Did I tell you?

LIUBÓV ANDRÉYEVNA   Don't be silly! You stay right here where you belong.

[*Enter* FIRS, *carrying an overcoat.*]

FIRS   Sir, sir, please put this on. It's getting damp.

GÁYEV [*puts it on*]   Firs, you're getting to be a bore.

FIRS   That so? Went out this morning, didn't even tell me. [*Tries to adjust* GÁYEV's *clothes.*]

LIUBÓV ANDRÉYEVNA   Poor Firs! You've gotten so old!

FIRS   Beg pardon?

LOPÁKHIN   She said you got very old!

FIRS   I've lived a long time. They were trying to marry me off way back before your daddy was born. [*Laughs.*] By the time we got our freedom back,[6] I was already head butler. I had all the freedom I needed, so I stayed right here with the masters.

[*Pause.*]

I remember everybody got all excited about it, but they never even knew what they were getting excited about.

LOPÁKHIN   Oh, sure, things were wonderful back in the good old days! They had the right to beat you if they wanted, remember?

FIRS [*doesn't hear*]   That's right. Masters stood by the servants, servants stood by the masters. Nowadays it's all mixed up; you can't tell who's who.

GÁYEV   Shut up, Firs. . . . I have to go into town tomorrow. A friend promised to introduce me to someone who might be able to arrange a loan. Some general.

---

6. Tsar Alexander II emancipated the serfs in 1861.

LOPÁKHIN   That's never going to work. Trust me, you won't get enough even for the interest payments.

LIUBÓV ANDRÉYEVNA   He's imagining things. There's no general.

[*Enter* ÁNYA, VÁRYA, *and* TROFÍMOV.]

GÁYEV   Here come our young people.

ÁNYA   Mama's resting.

LIUBÓV ANDRÉYEVNA [*tenderly*]   Here we are, dears, over here. [*Kisses* ÁNYA *and* VÁRYA.] If you only knew how much I love you both. Come sit here by me . . . that's right.

[*They all sit down.*]

LOPÁKHIN   Our permanent graduate student seems to spend all his time studying the ladies.

TROFÍMOV   Mind your own business.

LOPÁKHIN   Almost in his fifties, he's still in school.

TROFÍMOV   Just stop the silly jokes, will you?

LOPÁKHIN   Oh, the *scholar* is losing his temper!

TROFÍMOV   Will you please just leave me alone?

LOPÁKHIN [*laughs*]   Let me ask you a question: You look at me, what do you see?

TROFÍMOV   When I look at you, Yermolái Alexéyich, what I see is a rich man. One who will soon be a millionaire. You are as necessary a part of the evolution of the species as the wild animal that eats up anything in its path.

[*Everybody laughs.*]

VÁRYA   Forget biology, Pétya. You should stick to counting stars.

LIUBÓV ANDRÉYEVNA   I want to hear more about what we were talking about last night.

TROFÍMOV   What were we talking about?

GÁYEV   About human dignity.

TROFÍMOV   We talked about a lot last night, but we never got anywhere. You people talk about human dignity as if it were something mystical. I suppose it is, in a way, for you anyway, but when you really get down to it, what have humans got to be proud of? Biologically we're pretty minor specimens— besides which, the great majority of human beings are vulgar and unhappy and totally *un*dignified. We should stop patting ourselves on the back and get to work.

GÁYEV   You still have to die.

TROFÍMOV   Who says? Anyway, what does that mean, to die? Maybe we have a hundred senses, and all we lose when we die are the five we're familiar with, and the other ninety-five go on living.

LIUBÓV ANDRÉYEVNA   Oh, Pétya, you're so smart!

LOPÍKHIN [*with irony*]   Oh, yes, very.

TROFÍMOV   Remember, human beings are constantly progressing, and their power keeps growing. Things that seem impossible to us nowadays, the day will come when they're not a problem at all, only we have to work toward that day. We have to seek out the truth. We don't do that, you know. Most of the people in this country aren't working toward anything. People I come in contact with—at the university, for instance—they're supposed to be educated, but they're not interested in the truth. They're not interested in much of anything, actually. They certainly don't *do* much. They call themselves intellectuals and think that gives them the right to look down on the rest of the world. They never read anything worthwhile, they're completely ignorant where science is concerned, they talk about art and they don't even know what it is they're talking about. They take themselves so seriously, they're full of theories and ideas, but just go look at the cities they live in. Miles and miles of slums, where people go hungry and where they live packed into unheated tenements full of cockroaches and garbage, and their lives are full of violence and immorality. So what are all the theories for? To keep people like us from seeing all that. Where are the day-care centers they talk so much about, and the literacy programs? It's all just talk. You go out to the parts of town where the poor people live, you can't find them. All you find is dirt and ignorance and crime. That's why I don't like all this talk, all these theories. Bothers me, makes me afraid. If that's all our talk is good for, we'd better just shut up.

LOPÁKHIN   I get up at five and work from morning to night, and you know, my business involves a lot of money, my own and other people's, so I see lots of people, see what they're like. And you just try to get anything accomplished: you'll see how few decent, honest people there really are. Sometimes at night I can't sleep, and I think: Dear God, you gave us this beautiful earth to live on, these great forests, these wide fields, the broad horizons . . . by rights we should be giants.

LIUBÓV ANDRÉYEVNA   What do you want giants for? The only good giants are in fairy tales. Real ones would scare you to death.

　　[*Upstage,* YEPIKHÓDOV *strolls by, playing his guitar.*]

　　[*Dreamily*] There goes Yepikhódov. . . .

ÁNYA [*dreamily*]   There goes Yepikhódov. . . .

GÁYEV   The sun, ladies and gentlemen, has just set.

TROFÍMOV   Yes.

GÁYEV [*as if reciting a poem, but not too loud*]   O wondrous nature, cast upon us your eternal rays, forever beautiful, forever indifferent. . . . Mother, we call you; life and death reside within you; you bring forth and lay waste—

VÁRYA [*pleading*]   Uncle, please!

ÁNYA   Uncle, you're doing it again.

TROFÍMOV   We'd rather have the yellow ball in the side pocket.

GÁYEV   Sorry, sorry. I'll keep still.

　　[*They all sit in silence. The only sound we hear is old* FIRS *mumbling. Suddenly a distant sound seems to fall from the sky, a sad sound, like a harp string breaking. It dies away.*]

LIUBÓV ANDRÉYEVNA   What was that?

LOPÁKHIN   Can't tell. Sounds like it could be an echo from a mine shaft. But it must be far away.

GÁYEV   Or some kind of bird . . . like a heron.

TROFÍMOV   Or an owl.

LIUBÓV ANDRÉYEVNA [*shivers*]   Makes me nervous.

　　[*Pause.*]

FIRS   It's like just before the trouble started. They heard an owl screech, and the kettle wouldn't stop whistling. . . .

GÁYEV   Before what trouble?

FIRS   The day we got our freedom back.

　　[*Pause.*]

LIUBÓV ANDRÉYEVNA   My dears, it's getting dark; we should be going in. [*To* ÁNYA] You've got tears in your eyes, darling. What's the matter? [*Hugs* ÁNYA.]

ÁNYA   Nothing, Mama. It's all right.

TROFÍMOV   Someone's coming.

> [*Enter a* HOMELESS MAN *in a white cap and an overcoat; he's slightly drunk.*]

HOMELESS MAN   Can anyone please tell me, can I get to the train station this way?

GÁYEV   Of course you can. Just follow this road.

HOMELESS MAN   Much obliged. [*Bows.*] Wonderful weather we're having . . . [*Recites.*] "Behold one of the poor in spirit, just trying to inherit a little of the earth. . . ."[7] [*To* VÁRYA] Listen, you think you could spare some money for a hungry man?

> [VÁRYA *is terrified; she screams.*]

LOPÁKHIN [*angrily*]   Now hold on just a minute!

LIUBÓV ANDRÉYEVNA [*panicked*]   Here . . . here . . . take this. [*Fumbles in her purse.*] Oh, I don't seem to have anything smaller. Here, take this. [*Gives him a gold piece.*]

HOMELESS MAN   Very much obliged!

> [*Goes out.*]
>
> [*Everybody laughs.*]

VÁRYA   Get me out of here! Oh, please get me out! Mama, how could you! We can't even feed the servants, and you go and give him a gold piece!

LIUBÓV ANDRÉYEVNA   I know, darling, I'm just stupid about money. When we get home I'll give you whatever I've got left; you can take care of it. Yermolái Alexéyich, can you lend me some money?

LOPÁKHIN   Of course.

LIUBÓV ANDRÉYEVNA   My darlings, it really is time to go in. Várya dear, we've just gotten you engaged. Congratulations.

VÁRYA [*almost in tears*]   Mama, that's nothing to joke about!

LOPÁKHIN   Amelia, get thee to a nunnery![8]

GÁYEV   Look how my hands shake. I don't know if I could play billiards anymore. . . .

LOPÁKHIN   Nymph, in thy horizons be all my sins remembered![9]

LIUBÓV ANDRÉYEVNA   Please, let's go. It's almost suppertime.

VÁRYA   He scared me half to death. I can feel my heart pounding.

LOPÁKHIN   But keep in mind, the cherry orchard is going to be sold. On August twenty-second! You hear what I'm saying? You've got to think about this! You've got to!

> [*They all go off except* ÁNYA *and* TROFÍMOV.]

ÁNYA [*laughs*]   I'm so glad that tramp scared Várya off. Now we can be alone.

TROFÍMOV   Várya's afraid we're going to fall in love; that's why she never leaves us alone. She's so narrow-minded; she simply can't understand that we are

---

7. Reference to Jesus' Sermon on the Mount: "Blessed are the poor in spirit, for theirs is the kingdom of heaven. . . . Blessed are the meek, for they shall inherit the earth" (Matthew 5.3, 5).

8. Hamlet, in Shakespeare's play, suspects Ophelia of spying for her father and sends her off with "Get thee to a nunnery!" (3.1.22).

9. Lopákhin transforms a line from *Hamlet*: "Nymph, in thy orisons, / Be all my sins remembered" (3.1.91–92).

above love. Our goal is to get rid of the silly illusions that keep us from being free and happy. We are moving forward, toward the future! Toward one bright star that burns ahead of us! Forward, friends! Come join us in our journey!

ÁNYA [*claps her hands*]   Oh, you talk so beautifully!

[*Pause.*]

It's just heavenly out here today!

TROFÍMOV   Yes, the weather's been really good lately.

ÁNYA   I don't know what it is you've done to me, Pétya, but I don't love the cherry orchard anymore, not the way I used to. I used to think there was no place on earth like our orchard.

TROFÍMOV   This whole country is our orchard. It's a big country and a beautiful one; it has lots of wonderful places in it.

[*Pause.*]

Just think, Ánya: your grandfather, and his father, and his father's fathers, they *owned* the people who slaved away for them all over this estate, and now the voices and faces of human beings hide behind every cherry in the orchard, every leaf, every tree trunk. Can't you see them? And hear them? And owning human beings has left its mark on all of you. Look at your mother and your uncle! They live off the labor of others, they always have, and they've never even noticed! They owe their entire lives to those other people, people they wouldn't even let walk through the front gate of their beloved cherry orchard! This whole country has fallen behind; it'll take us at least two hundred years to catch up. The thing is, we don't have any real sense of our own history; all we do is sit around and talk, talk, talk, then we feel depressed, so we go out and get drunk. If there's one thing that's clear to me, it's this: if we want to have any real life in the present, we have to do something to make up for our past, we have to get over it, and the only way to do that is to make sacrifices, get down to work, and work harder than we've ever worked before. Do you understand what I mean, Ánya?

ÁNYA   The house we live in isn't our house anymore. It hasn't ever been, really. And I'll leave it all behind, I promise you I will.

TROFÍMOV   Yes, you will! Throw away your house keys and go as far away as you can! You'll be free as the wind.

ÁNYA [*radiant*]   I love the way you say things!

TROFÍMOV   You have to understand me, Ánya. I'm not thirty yet, I'm still young; I may still be in school, but I've learned a lot. Winter comes, sometimes I get cold and hungry, or sick and upset, I don't have a cent to my name; things work out or they don't. . . . But no matter what, my heart and soul are always full of feelings, all kinds . . . I can't even explain them. And I feel happiness coming, Ánya, I can feel it. I can almost see it—

ÁNYA [*dreamily*]   Look, the moon's rising.

[*The sound of* YEPIKHÓDOV's *guitar, still playing the same mournful song. The moon rises. Somewhere beyond the poplar trees,* VÁRYA *can be heard calling.*]

VÁRYA [*off*]   Ánya! Ánya, where are you?

TROFÍMOV   Yes, the moon is rising.

[*Pause.*]

It's happiness, that's what it is: it's rising, it's coming closer and closer, I can hear it. And even if we miss it, if we never find it, that's all right! Someone will!

VÁRYA [off]   Ánya! Ánya, where are you?

TROFÍMOV [angrily]   That Várya! Why won't she let us alone!

ÁNYA   Don't let her bother you. Let's take a walk by the river. It's so nice there.

TROFÍMOV   All right, let's go.

[They leave. The stage is empty.]

VÁRYA [off]   Ánya! Ánya!

Curtain.

Act 3

[*A sitting room, separated from the ballroom in back by an archway. The chandeliers are lit. From the entrance hall comes the sounds of an orchestra, the Jewish musicians* GÁYEV *mentioned in Act 2. Evening. In the ballroom, everyone is dancing a grande ronde.* SEMYÓNOV-PÍSHCHIK's *voice is heard calling the figures of the dance: "Promenade à une paire!"*[1] *The dancers dance through the sitting room in pairs in the following order:* PÍSHCHIK *and* CARLOTTA, TROFÍMOV *and* LIUBÓV ANDREYÉVNA, ÁNYA *and the* POSTMASTER, VÁRYA *and the* STATIONMASTER, *etc.* VÁRYA *is in tears, which she tries to wipe away as she dances. The final pair includes* DUNYÁSHA. *As the dancers return to the ballroom,* PÍSHCHIK *calls out: "Grande roude, balancez!" and "Les cavaliers à genoux et remercier vos dames."*[2] FIRS *in his butler's uniform crosses the stage, carrying a seltzer bottle on a tray.* PÍSHCHIK *and* TROFÍMOV *come into the sitting room.*]

PÍSHCHIK   I'm prone to strokes, already had two of 'em, I really shouldn't be dancing, but you know what they say: When in Rome. Besides, I'm really strong as a horse. Speaking of Romans, my father—what a joker he was—he used to claim our family was descended from the emperor Caligula's horse—you know, the one he made a senator?[3] [*Sits down.*] The only problem is we have no money. [*His head nods, he snores, then immediately wakes up.*] So the only thing I ever think about is money.

TROFÍMOV   Your father was right. You do look a little like a horse.

PÍSHCHIK   Nothing wrong with horses. Wonderful animals. If I had one, I could sell it. . . .

[*From the adjacent billiard room come the sounds of a game.* VÁRYA *appears in the archway.*]

TROFÍMOV [*teases her*]   Mrs. Lopákhin! Mrs. Lopákhin!

VÁRYA [*angrily*]   High-class tramp!

TROFÍMOV   Yes, I'm a high-class tramp, and I'm proud of it!

VÁRYA [*bitterly*]   We've hired an orchestra! And what are we supposed to pay them with?

[*Goes out.*]

---

1. "Promenade with your partner!" (French).
2. "Make a large circle, swing with your arms! Gentlemen, kneel and thank your ladies!" (French).
3. The mad emperor Caligula (12–41 C.E.) brought his favorite horse into the Roman senate to make it a senator.

TROFÍMOV [*to* PÍSHCHIK]   All the energy you've used trying to find money to pay your mortgage, if you'd spent that energy on something else, you could have moved the world.

PÍSHCHIK   Nietzsche,[4] you know, the philosopher—a great thinker, Nietzsche, a man of genius, one of the great minds of the century—now Nietzsche, you know, says, in his memoirs, that counterfeit money's just as good as real. . . .

TROFÍMOV   I didn't know you'd read Nietzsche.

PÍSHCHIK   Well . . . actually, Dáshenka told me. And I'm desperate enough. I'm ready to start counterfeiting. I need three hundred and ten rubles, day after tomorrow. All I've got so far is a hundred and thirty. . . . [*He feels in his pockets anxiously.*] It's gone! My money's gone! [*Almost in tears*] I've lost my money! [*Joyfully*] Oh, here it is! It slipped down into the lining of my coat! God, I'm all in a sweat!

   [*Enter* LIUBÓV *and* CARLOTTA.]

LIUBÓV ANDREYÉVNA [*she hums a dance tune*]   Why is it taking so long? What's Leoníd doing all this time in town? He should be back by now. [*Calls to* DUNYÁSHA *in the ballroom.*] Dunyásha, tell the musicians they can take a break.

TROFÍMOV   They probably postponed the auction.

LIUBÓV ANDREYÉVNA   I suppose it was a mistake to hire an orchestra. Or to have a party in the first place. Oh, well . . . what difference does it make? [*Sits down and hums quietly.*]

CARLOTTA [*hands* PÍSHCHIK *a deck of cards*]   Here's the deck. Pick a card, any card. . . . No, no, just think of one.

PÍSHCHIK   All right, I'm thinking of one.

CARLOTTA   Good. Now shuffle the deck. Very good. Now give it to me. Observe, my dear Píshchik! *Eins, zwei, drei!*[5] Now look in your jacket pocket, and you will find your card.

PÍSHCHIK [*takes a card from his jacket pocket*]   That's it, the eight of spades! [*Amazed*] Really! I don't believe it!

CARLOTTA [*holds out the deck to* TROFÍMOV]   Quick, what's the top card?

TROFÍMOV   The top card? Oh . . . uh . . . the queen of spades.

CARLOTTA   Correct! [*To* PÍSHCHIK] Now which card's on top?

PÍSHCHIK   Ace of hearts!

CARLOTTA   Correct! [*Claps her hands, and the deck disappears.*] Well, isn't this a lovely day we're having?

   [*A mysterious woman's voice answers; it seems to come from the floor-boards: "A lovely day indeed. I couldn't agree more."*]

Whoever you are, I adore you!

   [*The voice: "I adore you too!"*]

MASTER [*applauds*]   Bravo! A lady ventriloquist!

PÍSHCHIK [*amazed*]   Really! I don't believe it! Carlotta, you are amazing! I'm completely in love with you!

---

4. Friedrich Nietzsche (1844–1900), influen-   5. "One, two, three!" (German).
tial German philosopher.

CARLOTTA   In love? [*Shrugs her shoulders.*] What do you know about love? *Guter Mensch aber schlechter Musikant.*[6]

TROFÍMOV [*slaps* PÍSHCHIK *on the shoulder*]   You're just an old horse!

CARLOTTA   All right, everybody, watch closely! One more trick! [*Takes a lap robe from a chair.*] See, what a lovely blanket! I'm thinking of selling it. [*Shakes out the lap robe and holds it up.*] Who wants to buy?

PÍSHCHIK [*amazed*]   Really! I don't believe it!

CARLOTTA   *Eins, zwei, drei!* [*Quickly raises the lap robe.*]

　　[ÁNYA *appears behind the lap robe; she curtsies, runs to her mother and kisses her, then runs back into the ballroom. General applause and cries of delight.*]

LIUBÓV ANDREYÉVNA [*applauding*]   Bravo! Bravo!

CARLOTTA   Now one more! *Eins, zwei, drei!*

　　[*She raises the lap robe;* VÁRYA *appears; she takes a bow.*]

PÍSHCHIK   Really! I don't believe it!

CARLOTTA   That's all. The show is over.

　　[*Throws the lap robe to* PÍSHCHIK, *takes a bow, goes through the ballroom and out.*]

PÍSHCHIK [*goes after her*]   Enchanting! What a woman! What a woman! [*Goes out.*]

LIUBÓV ANDRÉYEVNA   Leoníd still isn't back from town yet. I don't understand what could be taking him so long! It's got to be all over by now: either the estate has been sold or they've postponed the auction. Why does he have to keep us in suspense like this?

VÁRYA [*tries to comfort her*]   Uncle bought the estate, I'm sure he has.

TROFÍMOV [*ironically*]   Oh, I'm sure.

VÁRYA   Ánya's godmother sent him a power of attorney to buy the estate in her name; she agreed to take over the mortgage. She did it for Ánya. So God *has* helped us. Uncle has saved the estate.

LIUBÓV ANDREYÉVNA   The old lady in Yároslavl sent us fifteen thousand to buy the place in her name—she doesn't trust us—but that's not even enough to pay the interest. [*Covers her face with her hands.*] My fate . . . my entire life . . . It's all being decided today.

TROFÍMOV [*teases* VÁRYA]   Mrs. Lopákhin! Mrs. Lopákhin!

VÁRYA [*angrily*]   And you're a permanent graduate student! Who's been suspended twice!

LIUBÓV ANDRÉYEVNA   Don't get so angry, Várya; he's only teasing you. What's wrong with that? And what's wrong with Lopákhin? If you want to marry him, do; he's a nice man. Interesting, even. If you don't want to marry him, don't; nobody's forcing you.

VÁRYA   It's not a joking matter, Mama, believe me. I'm serious about him. He is a nice man, and I like him.

LIUBÓV ANDRÉYEVNA   Then go ahead and marry him! I don't understand what you're waiting for!

VÁRYA   Mama, I can't propose to him myself! For two years now everybody's been telling me to marry him, everybody, but he never mentions it. Or he

6. "A good man but a bad musician" (German); that is, an incompetent (from the poet Heinrich Heine).

jokes about it! Look, I understand, he's busy getting rich, he doesn't have time for me. Oh, if I had just a little money—I don't care how much, even a couple of hundred—I'd get out of here and go someplace far away. I'd go join a convent.

TROFÍMOV Now, there's an exalted idea!

VÁRYA [to TROFÍMOV] I thought students were supposed to be smart! [Her tone softens; almost crying.] Oh, Pétya, you used to be so nice-looking, and now you're getting old! [To LIUBÓV, in a normal tone] It's just that I need something to do all the time, Mama; it's the way I am. I can't sit around and do nothing.

[Enter YÁSHA.]

YÁSHA [barely controlling his laughter] Yepikhódov broke a billiard cue! [Goes out.]

VÁRYA What is Yepikhódov doing here? Who asked him to come? And what's he doing playing billiards? I just don't understand these people. . . .

[Goes out.]

LIUBÓV ANDRÉYEVNA Pétya, don't tease her like that; you can see she's upset already.

TROFÍMOV Oh, she's such a busybody, always poking her nose into other people's business. She hasn't left Ánya and me alone the whole summer; she's afraid we're having a . . . an affair. What business is it of hers? Besides, it's not true. I'd never do anything so sordid. We're above love!

LIUBÓV ANDRÉYEVNA And I, I suppose, am beneath love. [Upset] Why isn't Leoníd back yet? I just want to know: has the estate been sold or not? The whole disaster seems so impossible to me, I don't know what to think, or do. . . . Oh, God, I'm losing my mind! I want to scream, or do something completely stupid . . . Help me, Pétya! Save me! Say something, say something!

TROFÍMOV Whether they sell it or not, does it make any difference really? You can't go back to the past. Everything here came to an end a long time ago. Try to calm down. You can't go on deceiving yourself; at least once in your life you have to look the truth straight in the eye.

LIUBÓV ANDRÉYEVNA What truth? You seem so sure what's truth and what isn't, but I'm not. I've lost any sense of it. I've lost sight of the truth. You're so sure of yourself, aren't you, so sure you have all the answers to everything, but darling, have you ever really had to live with one of your answers? You're too young. Of course you look into the future and see a brave new world, you don't expect any difficulties, but that's because you know nothing about life! Yes, you have more courage than my generation has, and better morals, and you're better educated, but for God's sake have a little sense of what it's like for me, and be easier on me. Pétya, I was born here! My parents lived here all their lives; so did my grandfather. I love this house! Without the cherry orchard my life makes no sense, and if you have to sell it, you might as well sell me with it. [She embraces TROFÍMOV and kisses his forehead.] And it was here my son drowned, you know that. . . . [Weeps.] Have some feeling for me, Pétya, you're such a good, sweet boy.

TROFÍMOV I pity you. [Beat] I do, from the bottom of my heart.

LIUBÓV ANDRÉYEVNA You should have said that differently, just a little differently. . . . [Takes out her handkerchief; a telegram falls to the floor.] You can't imagine how miserable I am today. All this noise, and every new sound makes me shake. I can't get away from it, but then when I'm alone in my room I can't stand the silence. Don't judge me, Pétya! I love you like one of my own family; I'd be very happy to see you and Ánya married, you know I would, only, darling, you must finish school first! You have *got* to graduate! You don't do anything except drift around from place to place—what kind of life is that? It's true, isn't it? Isn't that the truth? And we have to do something about that beard of yours; it's so scraggly. . . . [*Laughs.*] You've gotten so funny-looking!

TROFÍMOV [*picks up the telegram*]   I have no desire to be good-looking.

LIUBÓV ANDRÉYEVNA   The telegram's from Paris. I get a new one every day. One yesterday, now again today. That madman is sick again and in trouble. . . . He wants me to forgive him, he wants me back . . . and I suppose I should go back to Paris to be with him. Now see, Pétya, you're giving me that superior look, but darling, what am I supposed to do? He's sick, he's alone, he's unhappy, and who has he got to look after him? To give him his medicine and keep him out of trouble? And I love him—why do I have to pretend I don't, or not talk about it? I love him. That's just the way it is: I love him. I love him! He's a millstone around my neck, and he'll drown me with him, but he's *my* millstone! I love him and I can't live without him! [*Grabs* TROFÍMOV's *hand.*] Don't judge me, Pétya, don't think badly of me, just don't say anything, please just don't say anything. . . .

TROFÍMOV [*almost in tears*]   But for God's sake, you have to face the facts! He robbed you blind!

LIUBÓV ANDRÉYEVNA   No, no, please, you mustn't say that, you mustn't—

TROFÍMOV   He doesn't care a thing for you—you're the only person who doesn't seem to understand that! He's rotten!

LIUBÓV ANDRÉYEVNA [*gets angry but tries to control it*]   And you, you're what? Twenty-six, twenty-seven? Listen to you: you sound like you'd never even graduated to long pants!

TROFÍMOV   That's fine with me!

LIUBÓV ANDRÉYEVNA   You're supposed to be a man; at your age you ought to know something about love. You ought to be in love yourself! [*Angrily*] Really! You think you're so smart, you're just a kid who doesn't know the first thing about it, you're probably a virgin, you're ridiculous, you're grotesque—

TROFÍMOV [*horrified*]   What are you saying!

LIUBÓV ANDREYÉVNA   "I'm above love!" You're not above love; you've just never gotten down to it! You're all wet, like Firs says. At your age, you ought to be sleeping with someone!

TROFÍMOV [*horrified*]   What a terrible thing to say! That's terrible! [*He runs toward the ballroom, covering his ears.*] That's just horrible. . . . I can't listen to that; I'm leaving. [*Goes out, but reappears immediately.*] All is over between us!

[*Goes out into the entrance hall.*]

LIUBÓV ANDRÉYEVNA [*calls after him*]   Pétya, wait a minute! Come back! I was just joking, Pétya, don't be so silly! Pétya!

[*A great clatter from the entrance hall; someone has fallen downstairs.* ÁNYA *and* VÁRYA *scream.*]

What happened?

[ÁNYA *and* VÁRYA *suddenly howl with laughter.*]

ÁNYA [*runs in, laughing*]   Pétya just fell headfirst down the stairs!

[*Runs out.*]

LIUBÓV ANDRÉYEVNA   Oh, what a silly boy!

[*The* STATIONMASTER *in the ballroom gets on a chair and begins declaiming the opening lines of "The Magdalen" by Alexei Tolstoy.*[7]]

STATIONMASTER   "The splendid ballroom gleams with gold and candles,
a crowd of dancers whirls around the room;
and there apart, an empty glass beside her,
behold the fallen beauty, the lost, the doomed.

Her lavish gown and jewels make all eyes wonder,
her shameless glance bespeaks a life of sin;
young men and old cast longing glances at her—
see, how her fatal beauty draws them in!"

[*Everyone gathers to listen, but soon the orchestra returns and the strains of a waltz are heard from the entrance hall. The reading breaks off, and everybody begins to dance.* TROFÍMOV, ÁNYA, *and* VÁRYA *come in from the entrance hall.*]

LIUBÓV ANDRÉYEVNA   Pétya . . . oh, darling, I'm *so* sorry. . . . You sweet thing, please forgive me. . . . Come on, let's dance. [*Dances with* TROFÍMOV.]

[ÁNYA *and* VÁRYA *dance together.* FIRS *enters, leans his walking stick against the side door.* YÁSHA *appears and stands watching the dancers.*]

YÁSHA   What's the matter, pops?

FIRS   I don't feel so good. The old days, we had a dance, we had generals and barons and admirals; nowadays we have to send out for the postmaster and the stationmaster. And they're none too eager to come, either. Oh, I'm getting old and feeble. The old master, their grandfather, anybody got sick, he used to dose 'em all with sealing wax. Didn't matter what they had, they all got sealing wax. I've been taking sealing wax myself now for nigh onto twenty years. Take some every day. That's probably why I'm still alive.

YÁSHA   You're getting boring, pops. [*Yawns.*] Time for you to crawl off and die.

FIRS   Oh, you . . . you young flibbertigibbet. [*Mumbles.*]

[TROFÍMOV *and* LIUBÓV *dance through the ballroom, into the sitting room.*]

LIUBÓV ANDRÉYEVNA   Merci.[8] I need to sit down and rest a bit. . . . [*Sits.*] I'm so tired.

[*Enter* ÁNYA.]

ÁNYA [*upset*]   There was a man in the kitchen just now, he said the cherry orchard's already been sold!

LIUBÓV ANDRÉYEVNA   Who bought it?

ÁNYA   He didn't say. And he's gone now. [*Dances with* TROFÍMOV; *they dance off across the ballroom.*]

YÁSHA   That was just some old guy talking crazy. It wasn't anybody from around here.

FIRS   And Leoníd Andréyich still isn't back. All he had on was his topcoat; you watch, he'll catch cold. He's all wet, that one.

LIUBÓV ANDRÉYEVNA   I'll never live through this. Yásha, go out and see if anybody knows who bought it.

---

7. Russian writer (1817–1875), a distant relative of Leo Tolstoy, and author of *The Magdalen*, a play about a prostitute.
8. "Thank you" (French).

YÁSHA   It was just some old guy. He left long ago. [*Laughs.*]

LIUBÓV ANDRÉYEVNA [*somewhat annoyed*]   What are you laughing at? What's so funny?

YÁSHA   That Yepikhódov. What a dope. Old Double Trouble.

LIUBÓV ANDRÉYEVNA   Firs, suppose the estate is sold—where are you going to go?

FIRS   I'll go wherever you tell me to.

LIUBÓV ANDRÉYEVNA   What's the matter? Your face looks so funny. . . . Are you sick? You should go to bed.

FIRS   Yes . . . [*Smirks.*] Yes, sure, go to bed, and then who'll take care of things? I'm the only one you've got.

YÁSHA   Liubóv Andréyevna, there's a favor I have *got* to ask you; it's very important. If you go back to Paris, please take me with you. Please! You've got to! I positively cannot stay around here. [*Looks around, lowers his voice.*] You can see for yourself this place is hopeless. The whole country's a mess, nobody has any culture, it's boring, the food is lousy, and there's that old Firs drooling all over the place and talking like an idiot. Please, take me with you—you've just got to!
    [*Enter* PÍSHCHIK.]

PÍSHCHIK   Beautiful lady, what about a waltz? Just one little waltz! [LIUBÓV *crosses to him.*] You dazzler, you! And what about a loan, just one little loan, just a hundred and eighty, that's all I need. [*They begin to dance.*] Just a hundred and eighty . . .
    [*They dance off into the ballroom.*]

YÁSHA [*sings to himself*]   "Can't you see my heart is breaking . . ."
    [*In the ballroom, a figure appears dressed in checkered trousers and a gray top hat, jumping and waving its arms. We hear shouts of "Bravo, Carlotta!"*]

DUNYÁSHA [*stops to powder her nose*]   The missus told me to dance—there's too many gentlemen and not enough ladies—so I did, I've been dancing all night and my heart won't stop beating, and you know what, Firs? Just now, the postmaster, you know? He said something almost made me faint.
    [*The orchestra stops playing.*]

FIRS   What did he say?

DUNYÁSHA   That I was like a flower. That's what he said.

YÁSHA [*yawns*]   What does he know about it?
    [*Goes out.*]

DUNYÁSHA   Just like a flower. I'm a very romantic girl, really. I just adore that kind of talk.

FIRS   You're out of your mind.
    [*Enter* YEPIKHÓDOV.]

YEPIKHÓDOV [*to* DUNYÁSHA]   Why are you deliberating not to notice me? You act as if I wasn't here, like I was a bug or something. [*Sighs.*] Ah, life!

DUNYÁSHA   Excuse me?

YEPIKHÓDOV   Of course, you may be right. [*Sighs.*] But if you look at it, let's say, from a . . . a point of view, then you're the faulty one—excuse my expressivity—because you led me on. Into this predictament. Look at me! Every day something awful happens to me. It's like a habit. But I can look disaster in the face and keep smiling. You gave me your word, you know, and you even—

DUNYÁSHA   Do you mind? Let's talk about it later. Right now I'd rather be left alone. With my dreams. [*Plays with a fan.*]

YEPIKHÓDOV Every day. Something awful. But all I do—excuse my expressivity—is try to keep smiling. Sometimes I even laugh.
[*Enter* VÁRYA *from the ballroom.*]

VÁRYA [*to* YEPIKHÓDOV] Are you still here? I thought I told you to go home. Really, you have no consideration. [*To* DUNYÁSHA] Dunyásha, go back to the kitchen! [*To* YEPIKHÓDOV] You come in here and start playing billiards, you break one of our cues, now you hang around in here as if we'd invited you.

YEPIKHÓDOV Excuse my expressivity, but you have no right to penalize me.

VÁRYA I'm not penalizing you, I'm telling you! All you do here is wander around and bump into the furniture. You're supposed to be working for us, and you don't do a thing. I don't know why we hired you in the first place.

YEPIKHÓDOV [*offended*] Whether I work or not or wander around or not or play billiards or not is none of your business! You do not have the know-it-all to make my estimation!

VÁRYA How dare you talk to me like that! [*In a rage*] How dare you! What do you mean, I don't have the know-it-all? You get yourself out of here right this minute! Right this minute!

YEPIKHÓDOV [*apprehensively*] I wish you wouldn't use language like that—

VÁRYA [*beside herself*] Get out of here right this minute! Out! [*He goes to the door; she follows him.*] Double Trouble! I don't want to see hide or hair of you, I don't want to lay eyes on you ever again! [YEPIKHÓDOV *goes out; from behind the door we hear him screech: "I'll call the police on you!"*] Oh, you coming back for more? [*Grabs the stick that* FIRS *has left by the door.*] Come on . . . Come on . . . Come on, I'll show you! All right, all right, you asked for it—[*Swings the stick; the door opens, and she hits* LOPÁKHIN *over the head as he enters.*]

LOPÁKHIN Thanks a lot.

VÁRYA [*still angry, sarcastic*] Oh, I'm so sorry!

LOPÁKHIN S'all right. Always appreciate a warm welcome.

VÁRYA I don't need appreciation. [*Walks off, then turns and asks gently.*] I didn't hurt you, did I?

LOPÁKHIN No, I'm fine. Just a whopping big lump, that's all.
[*Voices from the ballroom: "Lopákhin! Lopákhin's here! He's back! Lopákhin's back!" People crowd into the sitting room.*]

PÍSHCHIK The great man in person! [*Hugs* LOPÁKHIN.] Is that cognac I smell? It is! You've been celebrating! Well, so have we. Join the party!

LIUBÓV ANDRÉYEVNA It's you, Yermolái Alexéyich. Where have you been all this time? Where's Leoníd?

LOPÁKHIN He's coming; we took the same train.

LIUBÓV ANDRÉYEVNA What happened? Did they have the auction? Tell me!

LOPÁKHIN [*embarrassed, afraid to show his joy*] The auction was all over by four this afternoon, but we missed the train. We had to wait for the nine-thirty. [*Exhales heavily.*] Oof! My head is really spinning. . . .
[*Enter* GÁYEV; *he holds a wrapped package in one hand, wipes his eyes with the other.*]

LIUBÓV ANDRÉYEVNA Lyónya, what's the matter? Lyónya! [*Impatiently, beginning to cry*] For God's sake, what happened!

GÁYEV [*weeps and can't answer her; makes a despairing gesture with his free hand and turns to* FIRS] Here, take these . . . some anchovies . . . imported. I haven't eaten a thing all day. You have no idea what I've been through! [*The door to the billiard room is open; we hear the click of billiard balls and*

YÁSHA's *voice: "Seven ball in the left pocket!"* GÁYEV's *expression changes; he stops crying.*] I'm all worn out. Firs, come help me get ready for bed.

[*Goes through the ballroom and out;* FIRS *follows him.*]

PÍSHCHIK   What about the auction? Tell us what happened!

LIUBÓV ANDRÉYEVNA   Is the cherry orchard sold?

LOPÁKHIN   It's sold.

LIUBÓV ANDRÉYEVNA   Who bought it?

LOPÁKHIN   I did.

[*Pause.* LIUBÓV *is overcome; she would fall, if she weren't standing beside a table and the armchair.* VÁRYA *takes the keys from her belt, throws them on the floor, crosses the room, and goes out.*]

I did! I bought it! No, wait, don't go, please. I'm still a little mixed up about it, I can't talk yet. . . . [*Laughs.*] We get to the auction, and there's Derigánov, all ready and waiting. Leoníd Andréyich only had fifteen thousand, so right away Derigánov raises the bid to thirty, that's on top of the balance on the mortgage. So I see what he's up to, and I bid against him. Raise it to forty. He bids forty-five. I bid fifty-five. See, he was raising by five, and I double him, I raise him ten each time. Anyway, finally it's all over, and I got it! Ninety thousand plus the balance on the mortgage.[9] And now the cherry orchard is mine! Mine! [*A loud laugh*] My God, the cherry orchard belongs to me! Tell me I'm drunk, tell me it's all a dream, I'm making this up—[*Stomps on the floor.*] And don't anybody laugh! My God, if my father and my grandfather could be here now and see this, see *me*, their Yermolái, the boy they beat, who went barefoot in winter and never went to school, see how that poor boy just bought the most beautiful estate in the whole world! I bought the estate where my father and my grandfather slaved away their lives, where they wouldn't even let them in the kitchen! My God, I must be dreaming—I can't believe all this is happening! [*Picks up* VÁRYA's *keys; smiles gently.*] See, she threw away her keys; she knows she isn't running the place anymore. . . . [*Jingles the keys.*] Well, that's all right.

[*The orchestra starts tuning up again.*]

That's it, let's have some music—come on, I want to hear it! Everybody come watch! Come on and watch what I do! I'm going to chop down every tree in that cherry orchard, every goddamn one of them, and then I'm going to develop that land! Watch me! I'm going to do something our children and grandchildren can be proud of! Come on, you musicians, play!

[*The orchestra begins to play,* LIUBÓV *curls up in the armchair and weeps bitterly.*]

LOPÁKHIN [*reproachfully*]   Oh, why didn't you listen to me? You dear woman, you dear good woman, you can't ever go back to the past. [*With tears in his eyes*] Oh, if only we could change things, if only life were different, this unhappy, messy life . . .

PÍSHCHIK [*takes his arm; quietly*]   She's crying. Come on, we'll go in the other room, leave her alone for a while. Come on. . . . [*Leads him into the ballroom.*]

LOPÁKHIN   What's the matter? Tell the band to keep playing! Louder! [*Ironic*] It's my house now! The cherry orchard belongs to me! I can do what I want

---

9. The winning bid for the estate was equivalent to nearly $2 million today—about twice what Lopákhin had offered to lend Liubóv and her family to save the estate (act 1).

to! [*Bumps into a small table, almost knocking over a candlestick.*] Don't worry about that: I can pay for it! I can pay for everything!

[*Goes out with* PÍSHCHIK.]

[*The sitting room is empty except for* LIUBÓV, *who sits lightly clenched and weeping bitterly. The orchestra plays softly. Suddenly* ÁNYA *and* TROFÍMOV *enter.* ÁNYA *goes and kneels before her mother.* TROFÍMOV *remains by the archway.*]

ÁNYA Mama! Mama, you're crying. Mama dear, I love you, I'll take care of you. The cherry orchard is sold, it's gone now, that's the truth, Mama, that's the truth, but don't cry. You still have your life to lead, you're still a good person. . . . Come with me, Mama, we'll go away, someplace far away from here. We'll plant a new orchard, even better than this one, you'll see, Mama, you'll understand, and you'll feel a new kind of joy, like a light in your soul. . . . Let's go, Mama. Let's go!

Curtain.

Act 4

[*The same room as Act 1. The curtains have been taken down, the pictures are gone from the walls, and there are only a few pieces of furniture shoved into a corner, as if for sale. The place feels empty. By the doorway, a pile of trunks, suitcases, etc. The door on the right is open; we hear* ÁNYA *and* VÁRYA *talking in the room beyond.* LOPÁKHIN *stands waiting. Beside him,* YÁSHA *holds a tray of glasses filled with champagne. Through the door we see* YEPIKHÓDOV *in the front hall, fastening the straps on a trunk. The sound of murmured voices offstage; some of the local people have come to say goodbye.* GÁYEV's *voice: "Thank you all, good people, thanks, thanks very much for coming."*]

YÁSHA It's some of these poor yokels, come to say goodbye. I'm of the opinion, you know, these people around here . . . ? They're okay, but they're . . . they're just a bunch of know-nothings.

[*The murmur of voices dies away.* LIUBÓV *and* GÁYEV *come in from the entrance hall; she has stopped crying, but she is shaking slightly, and her face is pale. She cannot speak.*]

GÁYEV You gave them all the money you had, Liúba. You can't do that! You can't do that anymore!

LIUBÓV ANDREYÉVNA I couldn't help it! I just couldn't help it!

[*They both go out.* LOPÁKHIN *follows them to the door.*]

LOPÁKHIN Wait, please. How about a little glass of champagne, just to celebrate? I forgot to bring some from town, but I got this one bottle at the station. It was all they had.

[*Pause.*]

No? What's the matter, don't you want any? [*Comes back from the door.*] If I'd known that, I wouldn't have bought it. I don't feel like any myself.

[YÁSHA *carefully puts the tray down on a chair.*]

Go on, Yásha, you might as well have one.

YASHA *Bon voyage!* And here's to the girls we leave behind! [*Drinks.*] This is not your real French champagne, I can tell.

LOPÁKHIN Cost me enough.

[*Pause.*]

It's cold as hell in here.

YÁSHA They figured they were going away today anyway—they decided not to heat the place. [*Laughs.*]

LOPÁKHIN What's with you?

YÁSHA I'm laughing because everything worked out just the way I wanted.

LOPÁKHIN It's October already, but the sun's out; it feels like summer. Good weather for home builders. [*Looks at his watch, then at the door.*] Listen, everybody, you got forty-six minutes till train time! And it's twenty minutes from here to the station, so you better get a move on.

[*Enter* TROFÍMOV *from outside; he's wearing an overcoat.*]

TROFÍMOV It must be time to go. The carts are here. Where the hell are my galoshes? I've lost them somewhere. [*At the door*] Ánya, where are my galoshes? I can't find them anyplace!

LOPÁKHIN I'm off to Hárkov. I'll be taking the same train as you. Off to Hárkov, spend the winter there. I've been hanging around here too long, doing nothing; I can't stand that. I got to keep working, otherwise I don't know what to do with my hands; if they're not doing something, they feel like they don't belong to me.

TROFÍMOV So. We're leaving, and you're going back to your useful labors in the real world.

LOPÁKHIN Have a glass of champagne.

TROFÍMOV No, thanks.

LOPÁKHIN So you're off to Moscow?

TROFÍMOV Yes. I'll go into town with them today, and then leave tomorrow for Moscow.

LOPAKHIN Sure. I'll bet all those professors are waiting for you to show up, wouldn't want to start their lectures without you!

TROFÍMOV Mind your own business.

LOPÁKHIN How long you say you've been at that university?

TROFÍMOV Come on! Think up something new, will you? You're getting boring. [*Pokes around, looking for his galoshes.*] You know, we probably won't ever see each other again, so you mind my giving you a little advice? As a farewell present? Don't wave your arms around so much. Bad habit. And this development you're putting in out here—you think that's going to improve the world? You think your leisure home buyers are going to turn into yeoman farmers? That's a lot of arm waving too. Well, what the hell. I like you anyway. You've got nice hands. Gentle and sensitive. You could have been an artist. And you're like that inside too—gentle and sensitive.

LOPÁKHIN [*hugs him*] Goodbye, boy. Thanks for everything. Here, let me give you a little money. You may need it for the trip.

TROFÍMOV What for? I don't need money!

LOPÁKHIN What *for*? You don't have any!

TROFÍMOV I do too. Thanks all the same. I got paid for a translation I did. I have money right here in my pocket. [*Worried*] I just wish I could find my galoshes!

VÁRYA [*from the next room*] Here they are! The smelly things . . . [*Throws a pair of galoshes into the room.*]

TROFÍMOV What are you always getting mad for? Hmm . . . These aren't my galoshes.

LOPÁKHIN   This past spring I planted a big crop of poppies. Three hundred acres. Sold the poppy seed, made forty thousand clear. And when those poppies were all in flower, what a picture that was! So look, I just made forty thousand, I can afford to loan you some money. Why turn up your nose at it? Because you think I'm just a dirt farmer?

TROFÍMOV   So your father was a dirt farmer. Mine worked in a drugstore. What does that prove?

[LOPÁKHIN *takes out his wallet.*]

Forget it, forget it. Look, you could give me a couple of hundred thousand, I still wouldn't take it. I'm a free man. And you people, everything you think is so valuable, it doesn't mean a thing to me. I don't care whether you're rich or poor; you've got no power over me. I can do without you, I can go right on past you, because I am proud and I am strong. Humanity is moving onward, toward a higher truth and a higher happiness, higher than anyone can imagine. And I'm ahead of the rest!

LOPÁKHIN   You think you'll ever get there?

TROFÍMOV   I'll get there.

[*Pause.*]

I'll get there. Or I'll make sure the rest of them get there.

[*From the orchard comes the sound of axes; they've started chopping down the cherry trees.*]

LOPÁKHIN   Well, boy, goodbye. Time to go. You and I don't see eye to eye, but life goes on anyway. Whenever I work real hard, round the clock practically, that clears my mind somehow, and for a minute I think maybe I know what we're all here for. But God, boy, think of the thousands of people in this country who don't know what they're doing or why they're doing it. But . . . I guess that doesn't have much to do with the price of eggs. They told me Leoníd Andréyich got a job at the bank, six thousand a year. He won't last; he's too lazy.

ÁNYA [*at the door*]   Mama asks you to please wait until she's gone before you start cutting down the orchard.

TROFÍMOV   I agree. That isn't very tactful, you know.

[*Goes out into the front hall.*]

LOPÁKHIN   All right, all right, I'll take care of it. God, these people . . .

[*Goes out after him.*]

ÁNYA   Have they taken Firs to the nursing home?

YÁSHA   I told them about it this morning. So I imagine they have.

ÁNYA [*to* YEPIKHÓDOV, *who crosses the room*]   Yepikhódov, could you please go and make sure they've taken Firs to the nursing home?

YÁSHA [*offended*]   I already told them this morning! Why keep asking?

YEPIKHÓDOV   The aged Firs, in my ultimate opinion, is beyond nursing. They ought to take him to the cemetery. And I can only envy him. [*Sets a suitcase down on a cardboard hatbox and crushes it.*] There. Finally. Wouldn't you know.

[*Goes out.*]

YÁSHA [*snickers*]   Old Double Trouble.

VÁRYA [*from the next room*]   Have they taken Firs to the nursing home?

ÁNYA   They took him this morning.

VÁRYA   Then why didn't they take the letter for the doctor?

ÁNYA   They must have forgotten. We'll have to send someone after them with it.

VÁRYA Where's Yásha? Tell him his mother is here; she wants to say goodbye.

YÁSHA [*with a dismissive gesture*] What a bore! Why can't she just leave me alone?

[DUNYÁSHA *has been drifting in and out, fussing with the baggage; now that she sees* YÁSHA *alone, she goes to him.*]

DUNYÁSHA Oh . . . oh, Yásha, why won't you even look at me? You're going away . . . you're leaving me behind. . . . [*Starts to cry and throws her arms around his neck.*]

YÁSHA What are you crying about? [*Drinks some champagne.*] Six days from now, I'll be back in Paris. Tomorrow we get on the express train, and we're off! And that's the last you'll ever see of me! I can't hardly believe it myself. *Vive la France!*[1] I can't live around here anymore; it's just not my kind of place. They're all so ignorant, and I can't stand that. [*Drinks more champagne.*] What are you crying about? If you'd been a nice girl, you wouldn't have anything to cry about.

DUNYÁSHA [*powders her nose in a mirror*] Don't forget to send me a letter from Paris. Because I loved you, Yásha, I really did. I'm a very sensitive person, Yásha, I really am—

YÁSHA Watch it, someone's coming. [*He starts fussing with the luggage, whistling quietly.*]

[*Enter* LIUBÓV, GÁYEV, ÁNYA, *and* CARLOTTA.]

GÁYEV We should be going. We're already a little late. [*Looks at* YÁSHA.] Who smells like herring?

LIUBÓV ANDRÉYEVNA We've only got ten minutes; then we absolutely must start out. [*Glances around the room.*] Goodbye, house! Wonderful old house! Winter's almost here, and come spring you'll be gone. They'll tear you down. Think of everything these walls have seen! [*Kisses* ÁNYA *with great feeling.*] My treasure, look at you! You're radiant today! Your eyes are shining like diamonds! Are you happy? Really happy?

ÁNYA Oh, yes, Mama, really! We're starting a new life!

GÁYEV She's right—everything worked out extremely well. Before the cherry orchard was sold we were at our wit's end—remember how painful it was?— and now everything's finally settled, once and for all, no turning back, and see? We've all calmed down. We're even rather happy. I'm going to work at the bank, I'm about to become a financier! Yellow ball in the side pocket . . . And you look better than you have in a long time, Lyúba; you do, you know.

LIUBÓV ANDRÉYEVNA I know. My nerves have quieted down. You're quite right.
[*Someone holds out her hat and coat.*]
And I sleep much better now. Take my things, Yásha, will you? It's time to go. [*To* ÁNYA] Darling, we'll see each other soon enough. I'm off to Paris—I kept the money your godmother in Yároslavl sent to buy the estate. [*A hard laugh*] Thank God for the old lady! That ought to get me through the winter at least. . . .

ÁNYA And you'll come back soon, won't you? You promise? I'll study hard and get my diploma, and then I'll get a job and help you out. We can read together the way we used to, can't we? [*Kisses her mother's hands.*] We'll spend long autumn evenings together; we'll read lots of books and learn all

---

1. "Long live France!" (French).

about the wonderful new world of the future. . . . [*Dreamily*] Don't forget, Mama, you promised. . . .

LIUBÓV ANDRÉYEVNA   I will, my angel, I promise. [*Embraces her.*]

[*Enter* LOPÁKHIN. CARLOTTA *hums a tune under her breath.*]

GÁYEV   Carlotta must be happy; she's singing!

CARLOTTA   [*picks up a bundle that looks like a baby in swaddling clothes*] Here's my little baby. Bye, bye, baby . . .

[*We hear a baby's voice: "Wah! Wah!"*]

Shh, baby, shh, shh . . . good little children don't cry. . . .

[*Again: "Wah! Wah!"*]

I feel so sorry for the poor thing. [*Hurls the bundle to the floor.*] You will find me a job, won't you? I can't go on like this anymore.

LOPÁKHIN   Don't worry, Carlotta; we'll take care of you.

GÁYEV   Everybody's just thrown us away. Várya's leaving. . . . All of a sudden we're useless.

CARLOTTA   How can I live in that town of yours? There must be someplace I can go. . . . [*Hums.*] What difference does it make . . . ?

[*Enter* PÍSHCHIK.]

LOPÁKHIN   Here comes the wonder boy.

PÍSHCHIK [*panting*]   Ooh, give me a minute . . . I'm all worn out. Good morning, good morning, good morning. Could I get a drink of water?

GÁYEV [*sarcastic*]   You're sure it isn't money you want? You'll all have to excuse me if I remove myself from the approaching negotiations.

[*Goes out.*]

PÍSHCHIK   I'm so glad to see you all. . . . Dear lady . . . I've been a stranger, I know. [*To* LOPÁKHIN] And you're here too. Delighted, delighted, a man I admire, always have. . . . Here. Here. This is for you. [*Gives* LOPÁKHIN *money.*] Four hundred. And I still owe you eight hundred and forty.

LOPÁKHIN [*a bewildered shrug*]   I must be dreaming. Where did you get money?

PÍSHCHIK   Wait a minute; let me cool off. Well, it was an absolutely extraordinary thing. These Englishmen showed up, they poked around on my land, found some kind of white clay. . . . [*To* LIUBÓV] Here . . . Here's the four hundred. You've been so kind . . . so sweet . . . [*Gives her money.*] And you'll have the rest before you know it. [*Takes a drink of water.*] You know, there was a young man on the train just now, he was saying . . . there was this philosopher, he said, who wanted us all to jump off the roof. "Jump!" he said. "Jump!" That was his whole philosophy. [*Amazed*] Really! I don't believe it! Give me some more water. . . .

LOPÁKHIN   What Englishmen are you talking about?

PÍSHCHIK   I gave them a lease on the land, the place where the clay is, a twenty-four-year lease. And now excuse me, but I'm off. Lots of people to see, pay back what I owe. I owe money all over the place. [*Takes a drink of water.*] Well, I just wanted to say hello. I'll come by again on Thursday.

LIUBÓV ANDRÉYEVNA   But we're leaving for town today. And tomorrow I'm going back to Paris.

PÍSHCHIK   What? [*Astonished*] Leaving for town? Oh, my . . . Oh, of course; the furniture's gone. And all these trunks. I didn't realize. [*Almost in tears*] I didn't realize. Great thinkers, these English . . . God bless you all. And be happy. I didn't realize. Well, all things must come to an end. [*Kisses* LIUBÓV's *hand.*]

I'll come to an end myself one of these days. And when I do, I want you all to say: "Semyónov-Píshchik . . . he was a good old horse. God bless him." Wonderful weather we're having. Yes. . . . [*Starts out, overcome with emotion, stops in the doorway and turns.*] Oh, by the way, Dáshenka says hello.
[*Goes out.*]

LIUBÓV ANDRÉYEVNA   Now we can go. There are just two things still on my mind. The first is old Firs. [*Looks at her watch.*] We've still got five minutes. . . .

ÁNYA   Mama, they took Firs to the nursing home this morning. Yásha took care of it.

LIUBÓV ANDRÉYEVNA   . . . And then there's our Várya. She's used to getting up early and working around here all day long, and now she's . . . out of a job. Like a fish out of water. Poor thing—she's so nervous, she cries, she's losing weight . . .
[*Pause.*]
You know, Yermolái Alexéyich—well, of course you know—I'd always dreamed . . . always dreamed she'd marry you; you know we all think it's a wonderful idea. . . . [*Whispers to* ÁNYA, *who nods to* CARLOTTA; *they both leave.*] She loves you, you like her. . . . I don't know why, I just don't know why the two of you keep avoiding the issue. Really!

LOPÁKHIN   I don't know why either. It's all a little funny. Well, I don't mind. If there's still time, I'll do it. . . . All right, *basta*,[2] let's just get it over with. But I don't know, I don't think I can propose without you—

LIUBÓV ANDRÉYEVNA   Of course you can. All it takes is a minute. I'll send her right in. . . .

LOPÁKHIN   We've even got some champagne all ready. [*Looks at the tray of empty glasses.*] Or at least we did. Somebody must have drunk it all up.
[YÁSHA *coughs.*]
Guzzled it down, I should say.

LIUBÓV ANDRÉYEVNA   Wonderful! We'll leave you alone. Yásha, *allez!*[3] I'll go call her. [*At the door*] Várya, leave that alone; come here a minute, will you? Come on, dear!
[*Goes out with* YÁSHA.]

LOPÁKHIN [*looks at his watch*]   Well . . .
[*Pause. A few stifled laughs and whispers behind the door. Finally* VÁRYA *enters.*]

VÁRYA [*examines the luggage; takes her time*]   That's funny, I can't find them. . . .

LOPÁKHIN   What are you looking for?

VÁRYA   I packed them myself, and now I don't remember where.
[*Pause.*]

LOPÁKHIN   What . . . ah . . . where are you off to, Várya?

VÁRYA   Me? I'm going to work for the Ragúlins. I talked to them about it already; they need a housekeeper. And look after things, you know. . . .

LOPÁKHIN   All the way over there? That's fifty miles away.
[*Pause.*]
Well, looks like this is the end of things around here. . . .

VÁRYA [*still examining the luggage*]   Where are they . . . ? Or maybe I put them in the trunk. You're right: this is the end of things here. The end of one life—

2. "That's enough" (Italian).   3. "Go on!" (French).

LOPÁKHIN   I'm going too. To Hárkov. Taking the same train, actually. I've got a million things waiting for me. I'm leaving Yepikhódov, though. Hired him to take charge here.

VÁRYA   You hired *who*?

LOPÁKHIN   Last year this time it was snowing already, remember? Today it's still sunny. Nice day. A little chilly, though . . . It was freezing this morning; must have been in the thirties.

VÁRYA   I didn't notice.

[*Pause.*]

Anyway, the thermometer's broken.

[*Pause. A voice from outside calls: "Lopákhin!"*]

LOPÁKHIN [*as if he'd been waiting for the call*]   I'm coming!

[*Goes out.*]

[VÁRYA *sits down on the floor, leans her head on a bundle of dresses, and cries. The door opens;* LIUBÓV *enters carefully.*]

LIUBÓV ANDRÉYEVNA   Well?

[*Pause.*]

We have to go.

VÁRYA [*already stopped crying, wipes her eyes*]   Right, Mama, we have to go. I can get to the Ragúlins' today, if I don't miss the train.

LIUBÓV ANDRÉYEVNA   Ánya, get your coat on.

[*Enter* ÁNYA, GÁYEV, CARLOTTA. GÁYEV *wears a winter overcoat. Servants and drivers come in to pick up the luggage.* YEPIKHÓDOV *directs the operation.*]

Well, we're ready to start.

ÁNYA [*joyfully*]   Ready to start!

GÁYEV   My dear friends, my very dear friends! On this occasion, this farewell to our beloved house, I cannot keep still. I feel I must say a few words to express the emotion that overwhelms me, overwhelms us all—

ÁNYA [*pleads*]   Uncle, please!

VÁRYA   That's enough, Uncle.

GÁYEV [*crushed*]   All right . . . Yellow ball in the side pocket . . . I'll keep still.

[*Enter* TROFÍMOV, *then* LOPÁKHIN.]

TROFÍMOV   Ladies and gentlemen, time to go! You'll be late!

LOPÁKHIN   Yepikhódov, get my coat.

LIUBÓV ANDRÉYEVNA   Let me stay a little minute longer. I never really noticed these walls before, or the ceilings. I want a last look, one last long look. . . .

GÁYEV   I remember when I was six, I was watching out that window, right over there. It was a holy day, Trinity Sunday,[4] I think, and I saw Father on his way to church. . . .

LIUBÓV ANDRÉYEVNA   Have we got everything?

LOPÁKHIN   I guess so. [*To* YEPIKHÓDOV, *who helps him on with his coat*] You keep an eye on things, Yepikhódov.

YEPIKHÓDOV [*loud, businesslike tone*]   You can count on me, Yermolái Alexéyich!

LOPÁKHIN   Why are you talking like that all of a sudden?

YEPIKHÓDOV   I just had a drink—water. . . . It went down the wrong way.

YÁSHA [*with contempt*]   Dumb hick!

LIUBÓV ANDRÉYEVNA   We're all going away. There won't be a soul left on the place. . . .

---

4. Also known as Pentecost, a Christian holy day occurring on the seventh Sunday after Easter.

LOPÁKHIN   But wait till you see what happens here come spring!

[VÁRYA *grabs an umbrella from the luggage, as if she were going to hit him.* LOPÁKHIN *pretends to be terrified.*]

VÁRYA   Don't get excited. It was just a joke.

TROFÍMOV   You've all got to get moving! It's time to go! You'll miss your train!

VÁRYA   Here's your galoshes, Pétya, behind this suitcase. [*With tears in her eyes*] Smelly old things . . .

TROFÍMOV [*puts them on*]   It's time to go!

GÁYEV [*deeply moved, afraid he'll start crying*]   Yes, the train . . . mustn't miss the train . . . Yellow ball in the side pocket, white in the corner . . .

LIUBÓV ANDRÉYEVNA   Let's go!

LOPÁKHIN   Everybody here? Nobody left? [*Closes and locks the door, left.*] Got to lock up; I've got a few things stored here. All right, let's go!

ÁNYA   Goodbye, house! Goodbye, old life!

TROFÍMOV   No, hello, new life!

[*Goes out with* ÁNYA.]

[VÁRYA *looks around the room again; she's not eager to go.* YÁSHA *goes out with* CARLOTTA *and her little dog.*]

LOPÁKHIN   So. Until next spring. Come on, let's go, everybody. Goodbye!

[LIUBÓV *and* GÁYEV *are left alone. It's as if they'd been waiting for this moment. They throw their arms around each other and burst out crying, but try to keep the others outside from hearing.*]

GÁYEV [*in despair*]   Oh, sister, sister . . .

LIUBÓV ANDRÉYEVNA   Oh, my orchard, my beautiful orchard! My life, my youth, my happiness, goodbye! Goodbye! Goodbye!

[ÁNYA's *voice, joyful:* "Mama!" TROFÍMOV's *voice, joyful, excited:* "Yoo-hoo!"] These walls, these windows, for the last time . . . And Mama loved this room . . .

GÁYEV   Oh, sister, sister . . .

[ÁNYA: "Mama!" TROFÍMOV: "Yoo-hoo!"]

LIUBÓV ANDRÉYEVNA   We're coming!

[*They leave.*]

[*The stage is empty. We hear the sound of the door being locked, then the carriages as they drive away. It grows very quiet. In the silence, we hear the occasional sound of an ax chopping down the cherry trees, a mournful, lonely sound. Then we hear steps. Enter* FIRS *from the door, right. He wears his usual butler's livery, but with bedroom slippers. He's very ill.*]

FIRS [*goes to the door, tries the handle*]   Locked. They're gone. [*Sits on the sofa.*] They forgot about me. That's all right; I'll just sit here for a bit. . . . And Leoníd Andréyich probably forgot his winter coat. [*A worried sigh*] I should have looked. . . . He's still all wet, that one. . . . [*Mumbles something we can't make out.*] Well, it's all over now, and I never even had a life to live. . . . [*Lies back.*] I'll just lie here for a bit. . . . No strength left, nothing left, not a thing . . . Oh, you. You young flibbertigibbet. [*Lies there, no longer moving.*]

[*In the distance we hear a sound that seems to come from the sky, a sad sound, like a string snapping. It dies away. Everything grows quiet. We can hear the occasional sound of an ax on a tree.*]

Curtain.

RABINDRANATH TAGORE

1861–1941

Rabindranath Tagore, the first Asian to receive the Nobel Prize (in 1913), won the award for literature—specifically for his contribution to poetry. But, by the end of his career in 1941, Tagore had become an international influence not only with his poetry but also with his novels, novellas, short stories, plays, and essays; and his continuing, broader impact on the modern world has been as much due to his other artistic work as a musician, painter, and performer, as to his activism as an educator, political thinker, and cosmopolitan intellectual. The challenge he poses for readers today is to understand how he interwove these roles into a remarkably productive career, and how he combined his diverse talents into coherent individual works.

LIFE AND TIMES

Tagore was born in Calcutta in 1861, into one of India's most famous families. His grandfather, Dwarkanath Tagore, amassed a great fortune in agriculture, mining, banking, and trade in British India, and helped establish such major institutions in the city as Hindu College (known as Presidency College today), Calcutta Medical College, the National Library, and the Agricultural and Horticultural Society of India. Dwarkanath also cofounded the Brahmo Sabha, an influential association dedicated to far-reaching reforms of Hindu religious and social life, which Rabindranath's father, Debendranath, expanded and renamed as the Brahmo Samaj. Growing up in an exceptionally talented family and a stimulating cultural environment, almost all of Debendranath's fourteen surviving children—of whom Rabindranath was the youngest—became notable writers, artists, intellectuals, and civil servants in a late-colonial India that was shaped by this legacy of reformist activism.

Tagore was educated in several schools in Calcutta but rebelled against formal education so strongly that, after the age of fourteen, he was trained by tutors at home in history, science, mathematics, literature, and art, as well as in Bengali, Sanskrit, and English. He spent 1878–80 in England, first in Brighton and then in London, but returned to India after failing to complete a law degree at University College. Back in Calcutta, he published his first book of poems in Bengali in 1880; two years later, his family arranged his marriage to Mrinalini Devi, with whom he had three daughters and two sons. What followed proved to be one of the most fertile periods in his artistic career: between 1891 and 1895 he wrote forty-two short stories, single-handedly establishing this modern genre in India, besides inventing what we now recognize as Indian realism and aesthetic modernism.

A reformist and activist in education, Tagore founded a school at Shantiniketan, about a hundred miles northwest of Calcutta, in 1901; twenty years later, he launched a college called Vishwa Bharati at the same site, which became Vishwa Bharati University in 1951 (a decade after his death), an unconventional "open-air" teaching and research institution that continues to serve as an international model for alternative education in the arts and humanities today. Tagore's two elder daughters were married in 1901, but the next few years brought several tragedies to the family: his wife died in 1902, his middle daughter the following year, his father in 1905, and his younger son two years later. Despite this emotional devastation, Tagore remained productive and innovative during the first decade of the twentieth century, publishing several important works, including the novel *Chokher Bali* (*A Speck of Sand in the Eye*, 1903), and a book of poems, *Gitanjali* (*An Offering of Songs*, 1910), which was the primary citation by the Noble Prize Committee in 1913.

After the award, Tagore's range of activities and influence became truly global, as he visited some thirty countries, including Russia, China, Japan, Vietnam, Argentina, the United States, Iran, Iraq, Bulgaria, Germany, and Sweden. He lectured on the most pressing issues of the time, speaking out in *Nationalism* (1917), a pioneering early-twentieth-century critique of this phenomenon, and he became a moral and political authority in the international arena. In 1919 he rejected the British knighthood bestowed on him a few years earlier, in protest against the British massacre of Indians at a peaceful rally in Jallianwalla Bagh, Amritsar. Even though his health deteriorated in the late 1930s, he continued to write poems and stories until the final months of his life.

Although Tagore's career as a writer was full, it was only one part of his creative life. Over several decades he also wrote more than 2,200 songs and set them to music; unique in style, they constitute an entire genre of modern South Asian music, known as *Rabindra-sangit*. India and Bangladesh would both use songs written and set to music by Tagore for their national anthems. In 1928 he also took up drawing and painting, and produced a large number of artworks in the last dozen years of his life, mostly in graphite, pen and ink, wash, and watercolor; his visual art has been exhibited in several major cities around the world. Moreover, he wrote or composed more than sixty-five works for the stage, including short and long plays as well as operatic works and dance-dramas, and Tagore himself performed in them in India as well as during his visits to Europe.

Tagore's influence on modern life and literature has been as multifarious and far-reaching as his output in many media. In his own time, he became a notable representative of universal humanism, especially of a "spiritual" version of it; seventy years after his death, he continues to be celebrated as a model of cosmopolitanism. Tagore has left a lasting impression in many unexpected places around the world. Modern education in the Czech Republic, for example, still carries the impact of his pedagogic experiments in the arts and humanities. The main waterfront in the beautiful resort town of Balatonfured, Hungary, is called the Tagore Promenade; dozens of artists gather there regularly to paint in the open air. The Abbey Theater in Dublin staged Tagore's play *The Post Office* (1912); **James Joyce** watched a performance during one of his rare visits to his native city, and he modeled the twin characters Shem and Shaun in *Finneganns Wake* (1939) on the central character in the play.

WORK

Tagore was fluent in Bengali and English, but he wrote almost all his literary works originally in Bengali. In the second half of his six-decade-long career he translated and supervised the translation of most of his work into English; he also wrote numerous book reviews, articles, and public lectures directly in English, and carried on an extensive English correspondence with many associates around the world. He described himself as first and foremost a poet; his language in his verse as well as his prose was always lyrical. The hallmark of his prose style was its poetic and musical quality: it was infused with the rhythms and melodic sounds of spoken Bengali, as well as with the figures of speech and thought that we normally associate with poetry.

Tagore was not a systematic thinker, and he was rarely successful in explaining his ideas and philosophical positions at length in expository prose; but his insights and intuitions ran deep, and he was able to express them in imaginative structures of startling originality. He was equally at home in song, narrative, and drama; many of his poems, tales, and plays display an effortless organic unity, as though they "came to him" fully formed, without needing any conscious artistry or intervention on his part. One of the unusual aspects of Tagore's work is that each of the genres in which he wrote serves a different artistic function, and all the genres together complement each other imaginatively.

Our selection here consists of a short story that, like many of Tagore's shorter pieces of fiction, is realistic in style, organization, and effect. "Punishment" (1892) is set in the Bengal countryside (probably in what is now west-central Bangladesh) in the late nineteenth century. It is told crisply from the perspective of a narrator whose omniscience and veracity play crucial roles in the story; and its theme is the administration of justice, in this case in the British colonial justice system. "Punishment," in fact, is the first modern short story in world literature about the legal phenomenon that lawyers and judges call "the Rashomon effect." Named after the famous Japanese art film *Rashomon* (1950), directed by Akira Kurosawa, this is a universal phenomenon: whenever there are two or more eyewitnesses to an event or a crime, even their most truthful accounts of what happened differ fundamentally from each other. When a judge or a jury has to decide a case solely on the basis of eyewitness

accounts, without material evidence to clinch the matter, there is no purely rational way to choose between equally reliable but conflicting eyewitness testimonies given under oath. In Tagore's story, written nearly seventy years before the movie, the problem of conflicting testimony goes much deeper: for different reasons, the various eyewitnesses produce dishonest as well as truthful accounts of a spontaneous murder. When the colonial judge (an Englishman) assesses the witnesses' stories, he has no means of separating the truth from the fabrications, even though the murderer confesses fully in court. The judge then arrives at a decision that is blatantly biased (by class and gender), bringing the story to its famous surprise ending. The narrative combines social realism with psychological realism to confront the troubling questions of what constitutes justice under such circumstances and how we might solve this most intractable of problems.

This story is drawn from Tagore's early work, and it represents his writing in the realistic mode. His poetry, novelistic fiction, and plays take us in other directions, but his short stories remain among his most memorable pieces. Tagore is not a writer who fits into the usual model of linear development in which the later writing supersedes the earlier on the grounds of maturity. Since he attempts rather different kinds of effects in different genres, his output in any one genre frequently brings together his best qualities, regardless of chronology. "Punishment" already displays the skills for which Tagore is most celebrated: vivid and diverse characters who come alive in a few brushstrokes and invite our deeper sympathies; evolving human situations that refuse to stand still; problems and dilemmas that turn up in many different times, places, and guises; and insights into the larger rhythms and patterns of life that fully engage our emotions and reveal a great deal about ourselves.

Punishment[1]

I

When the brothers Dukhiram Rui and Chidam Rui went out in the morning with their heavy farm-knives, to work in the fields, their wives would quarrel and shout. But the people nearby were as used to the uproar as they were to other customary, natural sounds. When they heard the shrill screams of the women, they would say, "They're at it again"—that is, what was happening was only to be expected: it was not a violation of Nature's rules. When the sun rises at dawn, no one asks why; and whenever the two wives in this *kuri*-caste[2] household let fly at each other, no one was at all curious to investigate the cause.

Of course this wrangling and disturbance affected the husbands more than the neighbours, but they did not count it a major nuisance. It was as if they were riding together along life's road in a cart whose rattling, clattering, unsprung wheels were inseparable from the journey. Indeed, days when there was no noise, when everything was uncannily silent, carried a greater threat of unpredictable doom.

The day on which our story begins was like this. When the brothers returned home at dusk, exhausted by their work, they found the house eerily quiet. Outside, too, it was extremely sultry. There had been a sharp shower in the afternoon, and clouds were still massing. There was not a breath of wind. Weeds and scrub round the house had shot up after the rain: the heavy scent of damp vegetation, from these and from the waterlogged jute-fields, formed a solid wall all around. Frogs croaked from the milkman's pond behind the house, and the buzz of crickets filled the leaden sky.

Not far off the swollen Padma[3] looked flat and sinister under the mounting clouds. It had flooded most of the grain-fields, and had come close to the houses. Here and there, roots of mango and jackfruit trees on the slipping bank stuck up out of the water, like helpless hands clawing at the air for a last fingerhold.

That day, Dukhiram and Chidam had been working near the zamindar's office. On a sandbank opposite, paddy[4] had ripened. The paddy needed to be cut before the sandbank was washed away, but the village people were busy either in their own fields or in cutting jute: so a messenger came from the office and forcibly engaged the two brothers. As the office roof was leaking in places, they also had to mend that and make some new wickerwork panels: it had taken them all day. They couldn't come home for lunch; they just had a snack from the office. At times they were soaked by the rain; they were not paid normal labourers' wages; indeed, they were paid mainly in insults and sneers.

When the two brothers returned at dusk, wading through mud and water, they found the younger wife, Chandara, stretched on the ground with her sari[5] spread out. Like the sky, she had wept buckets in the afternoon, but had now given way to sultry exhaustion. The elder wife, Radha, sat on the verandah sullenly: her eighteen-month son had been crying, but when the brothers came in they saw him lying naked in a corner of the yard, asleep.

1. Translated by William Radice.
2. In Bengal, a low caste originally of bird catchers, but by the 19th century, general laborers.
3. A major river in what is now Bangladesh.
4. The rice crop. "Zamindar": landlord.
5. A long strip of cloth draped around the body; Indian women's traditional clothing.

Dukhiram, famished, said gruffly, "Give me my food."

Like a spark on a sack of gunpowder, the elder wife exploded, shrieking out, "Where is there food? Did you give me anything to cook? Must I earn money myself to buy it?"

After a whole day of toil and humiliation, to return—raging with hunger—to a dark, joyless, foodless house, to be met by Radha's sarcasm, especially her final jibe, was suddenly unendurable. "What?" he roared, like a furious tiger, and then, without thinking, plunged his knife into her head. Radha collapsed into her sister-in-law's lap, and in minutes she was dead.

"What have you done?" screamed Chandara, her clothes soaked with blood. Chidam pressed his hand over her mouth. Dukhiram, throwing aside the knife, fell to his knees with his head in his hands, stunned. The little boy woke up and started to wail in terror.

Outside there was complete quiet. The herd-boys were returning with the cattle. Those who had been cutting paddy on the far sandbanks were crossing back in groups in a small boat—with a couple of bundles of paddy on their heads as payment. Everyone was heading for home.

Ramlochan Chakravarti, pillar of the village, had been to the post office with a letter, and was now back in his house, placidly smoking. Suddenly he remembered that his sub-tenant Dukhiram was very behind with his rent: he had promised to pay some today. Deciding that the brothers must be home by now, he threw his chadar[6] over his shoulders, took his umbrella, and stepped out.

As he entered the Ruis' house, he felt uneasy. There was no lamp alight. On the dark verandah, the dim shapes of three or four people could be seen. In a corner of the verandah there were fitful, muffled sobs: the little boy was trying to cry for his mother, but was stopped each time by Chidam.

"Dukhi," said Ramlochan nervously, "are you there?"

Dukhiram had been sitting like a statue for a long time; now, on hearing his name, he burst into tears like a helpless child.

Chidam quickly came down from the verandah into the yard, to meet Ramlochan. "Have the women been quarelling again?" Ramlochan asked. "I heard them yelling all day."

Chidam, all this time, had been unable to think what to do. Various impossible stories occurred to him. All he had decided was that later that night he would move the body somewhere. He had never expected Ramlochan to come. He could think of no swift reply. "Yes," he stumbled, "today they were quarrelling terribly."

"But why is Dukhi crying so?" asked Ramlochan, stepping towards the verandah.

Seeing no way out now, Chidam blurted, "In their quarrel, *Chotobau* struck at *Barobau's*[7] head with a farm-knife."

When immediate danger threatens, it is hard to think of other dangers. Chidam's only thought was to escape from the terrible truth—he forgot that a lie can be even more terrible. A reply to Ramlochan's question had come instantly to mind, and he had blurted it out.

"Good grief," said Ramlochan in horror. "What are you saying? Is she dead?"

"She's dead," said Chidam, clasping Ramlochan's feet.

---

6. In Bengal, a sheet of cloth draped around the shoulders, usually worn by men but sometimes by women.

7. "Elder Daughter-in-Law"; members of a family address each other by kinship terms. *Chotobau*: "Younger Daughter-in-Law."

Ramlochan was trapped. *"Rām, Rām,"*[8] he thought, "what a mess I've got into this evening. What if I have to be a witness in court?" Chidam was still clinging to his feet, saying, *"Thākur,*[9] how can I save my wife?"

Ramlochan was the village's chief source of advice on legal matters. Reflecting further he said, "I think I know a way. Run to the police station: say that your brother Dukhi returned in the evening wanting his food, and because it wasn't ready he struck his wife on the head with his knife. I'm sure that if you say that, she'll get off."

Chidam felt a sickening dryness in his throat. He stood up and said, *"Thākur,* if I lose my wife I can get another, but if my brother is hanged, how can I replace him?" In laying the blame on his wife, he had not seen it that way. He had spoken without thought; now, imperceptibly, logic and awareness were returning to his mind.

Ramlochan appreciated his logic. "Then say what actually happened," he said. "You can't protect yourself on all sides."

He had soon, after leaving, spread it round the village that Chandara Rui had, in a quarrel with her sister-in-law, split her head open with a farm-knife. Police charged into the village like a river in flood. Both the guilty and the innocent were equally afraid.

II

Chidam decided he would have to stick to the path he had chalked out for himself. The story he had given to Ramlochan Chakravarti had gone all round the village; who knew what would happen if another story was circulated? But he realized that if he kept to the story he would have to wrap it in five more stories if his wife was to be saved.

Chidam asked Chandara to take the blame on to herself. She was dumbfounded. He reassured her: "Don't worry—if you do what I tell you, you'll be quite safe." But whatever his words, his throat was dry and his face was pale.

Chandara was not more than seventeen or eighteen. She was buxom, well-rounded, compact and sturdy—so trim in her movements that in walking, turning, bending or climbing there was no awkwardness at all. She was like a brand-new boat: neat and shapely, gliding with ease, not a loose joint anywhere. Everything amused and intrigued her; she loved to gossip; her bright, restless, deep black eyes missed nothing as she walked to the *ghāt,*[1] pitcher on her hip, parting her veil slightly with her finger.

The elder wife had been her exact opposite: unkempt, sloppy and slovenly. She was utterly disorganized in her dress, housework, and the care of her child. She never had any proper work in hand, yet never seemed to have time for anything. The younger wife usually refrained from comment, for at the mildest barb Radha would rage and stamp and left fly at her, disturbing everyone around.

Each wife was matched by her husband to an extraordinary degree. Dukhiram was a huge man—his bones were immense, his nose was squat, in his eyes and expression he seemed not to understand the world very well, yet he never questioned it either. He was innocent yet fearsome: a rare combination of power and helplessness. Chidam, however, seemed to have been carefully

8. God's name, repeated to express great emotion.
9. "Master" or "lord," term of address for gods and upper-class (*brāhmaṇa*) men. *Tagore* is an anglicized form of *Thākur*.
1. Steps leading down to a pond or river; meeting place, especially for women, who go there to get water or to wash clothes.

carved from shiny black rock. There was not an inch of excess fat on him, not a wrinkle or dimple anywhere. Each limb was a perfect blend of strength and finesse. Whether jumping from a riverbank, or punting[2] a boat, or climbing up bamboo-shoots for sticks, he showed complete dexterity, effortless grace. His long black hair was combed with oil back from his brow and down to his shoulders—he took great care over his dress and appearance. Although he was not unresponsive to the beauty of other women in the village, and was keen to make himself charming in their eyes, his real love was for his young wife. They quarrelled sometimes, but there was mutual respect too: neither could defeat the other. There was a further reason why the bond between them was firm: Chidam felt that a wife as nimble and sharp as Chandara could not be wholly trusted, and Chandara felt that all eyes were on her husband—that if she didn't bind him tightly to her she might one day lose him.

A little before the events in this story, however, they had a major row. Chandara had noticed that when her husband's work took him away for two days or more, he brought no extra earnings. Finding this ominous, she also began to overstep the mark. She would hang around by the *ghāt*, or wander about talking rather too much about Kashi Majumdar's middle son.

Something now seemed to poison Chidam's life. He could not settle his attention on his work. One day his sister-in-law rounded on him: she shook her finger and said in the name of her dead father, "That girl runs before the storm. How can I restrain her? Who knows what ruin she will bring?"

Chandara came out of the next room and said sweetly, "What's the matter, *Didi?*"[3] and a fierce quarrel broke out between them.

Chidam glared at his wife and said, "If I ever hear that you've been to the *ghāt* on your own, I'll break every bone in your body."

"The bones will mend again," said Chandara, starting to leave. Chidam sprang at her, grabbed her by the hair, dragged her back to the room and locked her in.

When he returned from work that evening he found that the room was empty. Chandara had fled three villages away, to her maternal uncle's house. With great difficulty Chidam persuaded her to return, but he had to surrender to her. It was as hard to restrain his wife as to hold a handful of mercury; she always slipped through his fingers. He did not have to use force any more, but there was no peace in the house. Ever-fearful love for his elusive young wife wracked him with intense pain. He even once or twice wondered if it would be better if she were dead: at least he would get some peace then. Human beings can hate each other more than death.

It was at this time that the crisis hit the house.

When her husband asked her to admit to the murder, Chandara stared at him, stunned; her black eyes burnt him like fire. Then she shrank back, as if to escape his devilish clutches. She turned her heart and soul away from him. "You've nothing to fear," said Chidam. He taught her repeatedly what she should say to the police and the magistrate. Chandara paid no attention—sat like a wooden statue whenever he spoke.

2. Propelling a boat with a long pole.
3. "Elder Sister," respectful form of address for Bengali women.

Dukhiram relied on Chidam for everything. When he told him to lay the blame on Chandara, Dukhiram said, "But what will happen to her?" "I'll save her," said Chidam. His burly brother was content with that.

III

This was what he instructed his wife to say: "The elder wife was about to attack me with the vegetable-slicer. I picked up a farm-knife to stop her, and it somehow cut into her." This was all Ramlochan's invention. He had generously supplied Chidam with the proofs and embroidery that the story would require.

The police came to investigate. The villagers were sure now that Chandara had murdered her sister-in-law, and all the witnesses confirmed this. When the police questioned Chandara, she said, "Yes, I killed her."

"Why did you kill her?"

"I couldn't stand her anymore."

"Was there a brawl between you?"

"No."

"Did she attack you first?"

"No."

"Did she ill-treat you?"

"No."

Everyone was amazed at these replies, and Chidam was completely thrown off balance. "She's not telling the truth," he said. "The elder wife first—"

The inspector silenced him sharply. He continued according to the rules of cross-examination and repeatedly received the same reply: Chandara would not accept that she had been attacked in any way by her sister-in-law. Such an obstinate girl was never seen! She seemed absolutely bent on going to the gallows; nothing would stop her. Such fierce, passionate pride! In her thoughts, Chandara was saying to her husband, "I shall give my youth to the gallows instead of to you. My final ties in this life will be with them."

Chandara was arrested, and left her home for ever, by the paths she knew so well, past the festival carriage, the market-place, the _ghāt_, the Majumdars' house, the post office, the school—an ordinary, harmless, flirtatious, fun-loving village wife; leaving a shameful impression on all the people she knew. A bevy of boys followed her, and the women of the village, her friends and companions— some of them peering through their veils, some from their doorsteps, some from behind trees—watched the police leading her away and shuddered with embarrassment, fear and contempt.

To the Deputy Magistrate, Chandara again confessed her guilt, claiming no ill-treatment from her sister-in-law at the time of the murder. But when Chidam was called to the witness-box he broke down completely, weeping, clasping his hands and saying, "I swear to you, sir, my wife is innocent." The magistrate sternly told him to control himself, and began to question him. Bit by bit the true story came out.

The magistrate did not believe him, because the chief, most trustworthy, most educated witness—Ramlochan Chakravarti—said: "I appeared on the scene a little after the murder. Chidam confessed everything to me and clung to my feet saying, 'Tell me how I can save my wife.' I did not say anything one way or the other. Then Chidam said, 'If I say that my elder brother killed his wife in a fit of fury because his food wasn't ready, then she'll get off.' I said, 'Be careful, you rogue: don't say a single false word in court—there's no worse offence than that.'" Ramlochan had previously prepared lots of stories that would save Chandara, but when he found that she herself was bending her neck to receive the noose, he decided, "Why take the risk of giving false evidence now? I'd better say what little I know." So Ramlochan said what he knew—or rather said a little more than he knew.

The Deputy Magistrate committed the case to a sessions trial.[4] Meanwhile in fields, houses, markets and bazaars, the sad or happy affairs of the world carried on; and just as in previous years, torrential monsoon rains fell on to the new rice-crop.

Police, defendant and witnesses were all in court. In the civil court opposite hordes of people were waiting for their cases. A Calcutta lawyer had come on a suit about the sharing of a pond behind a kitchen; the plaintiff had thirty-nine witnesses. Hundreds of people were anxiously waiting for hair-splitting judgements, certain that nothing, at present, was more important. Chidam stared out of the window at the constant throng, and it seemed like a dream. A koel-bird[5] was hooting from a huge banyan tree in the compound: no courts or cases in his world!

Chandara said to the judge, "Sir, how many times must I go on saying the same thing?"

The judge explained, "Do you know the penalty for the crime you have confessed?"

"No," said Chandara.

"It is death by the hanging."

"Then please give it to me, sir," said Chandara. "Do what you like—I can't take any more."

When her husband was called to the court, she turned away. "Look at the witness," said the judge, "and say who he is."

"He is my husband," said Chandara, covering her face with her hands.

"Does he not love you?"

"He loves me greatly."

"Do you not love him?"

"I love him greatly."

When Chidam was questioned, he said, "I killed her."

"Why?"

"I wanted my food and my sister-in-law didn't give it to me."

When Dukhiram came to give evidence, he fainted. When he had come round again, he answered, "Sir, I killed her."

"Why?"

"I wanted a meal and she didn't give it to me."

After extensive cross-examination of various other witnesses, the judge concluded that the brothers had confessed to the crime in order to save the younger wife from the shame of the noose. But Chandara had, from the police investigation right through to the sessions trial, said the same thing repeatedly—she had not budged an inch from her story. Two barristers did their utmost to save her from the death-sentence, but in the end were defeated by her.

---

4. A trial that is settled through a special *ses-*
sions court in one continuous sitting.

5. Common Indian songbird.

Who, on that auspicious night when, at a very young age, a dusky, diminutive, round-faced girl had left her childhood dolls in her father's house and come to her in-laws' house, could have imagined these events? Her father, on his deathbed, had happily reflected that at least he had made proper arrangements for his daughter's future.

In gaol,[6] just before the hanging, a kindly Civil Surgeon asked Chandara, "Do you want to see anyone?"

"I'd like to see my mother," she replied.

"Your husband wants to see you," said the doctor. "Shall I call him?"

"To hell with him,"[7] said Chandara.

6. Jail.
7. "Death to him" (literal trans.); an expression usually uttered in jest.

HIGUCHI ICHIYŌ
1872–1896

The first major Japanese woman writer in six centuries, the poverty-stricken, barely educated Higuchi Ichiyō seemed to emerge out of nowhere. She crafted brief, sensitive stories that borrowed from the luxuriant language of classical Japanese literature while representing a stark and sordid modern world: bedraggled orphans in the streets, mistreated prostitutes, and the urban working class—potters, rickshaw drivers, seamstresses. Knowing nothing about European literary movements, she developed a realism all her own, focusing on the lives of poor and insignificant city dwellers. She was quickly hailed as one of the great writers of her time—praised as inventive, highly skillful, and deeply moving. She died suddenly at the age of twenty-four, leaving a mark on Japanese literature in a writing career that lasted just four years.

LIFE

Higuchi Natsu was born at a time when Japanese women were not expected to receive much in the way of education, but she read as widely as she could, immersing herself in classical literature. She especially loved *The Tale of Genji* and from an early age wrote poetry in a classical style. Her father was determined to leave his peasant roots behind, and he managed to become a bureaucrat in Tokyo. Intrigued by the fast money he saw entrepreneurs earning around him, he then sunk all of his money into a business that failed miserably. He died, destitute, when Ichiyō was seventeen. She packed up her mother and sister and moved to the fringes of Tokyo's red-light district, where she took in sewing and laundry while struggling to make literary connections. The family had barely enough money to put food on the table.

The young woman met her literary mentor, Nakarai Tōsui, while working as his washerwoman. He was a journalist and hack novelist, writing in an increasingly outmoded style that was deliberately playful, even frivolous. He appeared handsome, elegant, and sophisticated. She fell in love with him immediately, as she records in her lively diary, but he did not reciprocate her feeling; eventually she had to break with him when gossip about them began to compromise her reputation. In the meanwhile, however, he did launch her career as a writer, helping her to get her first stories published under the pen name Higuchi Ichiyō (the second name meaning "single leaf").

Ichiyō's novella *Child's Play*, which appeared in 1895 and 1896, made her suddenly famous. It follows a number of children living on the margins of Tokyo's red-light district as they come of age. Leaders of Japan's literary establishment were astonished by the fresh talent of a writer unschooled in Western fiction, and the general public was equally enthusiastic. She began to publish one brilliant story after another for a miraculous fourteen months. Fan clubs arose; students begged her to teach them about *The Tale of Genji*; and one besotted enthusiast stole the handwritten nameplate from her door so that he could have a piece of her writing. But by this time, having lived on a meager diet in grim poverty for years, Ichiyō was suffering from an advanced case of tuberculosis. No doctor could save her.

TIMES

In 1868 a new Japanese emperor took the name Meiji ("enlightened rule"). At the time, the Japanese economy was mostly agricultural, and the nation did not have a strong military. Europe and the United States had been putting pressure on Japan to sign unbalanced trade treaties, and the Japanese realized that they had little power to resist. But this situation was about to change dramatically. By 1912, the end of the Meiji period, the government of the military dictator, or *shogun*, and his *samurai*, in power since the seventeenth century, had fallen in favor of a constitutional monarchy, with a representative system of local government and a bicameral legislature. The new regime had established a new legal system and a ministry of education to oversee the training of future generations, while newspapers sprang up to circulate information and debate about the modern state. The country had built up its military, winning wars against China and Russia, and established itself as an international power. Perhaps most important, Japan had invested in industry—importing new technologies from the West, installing telegraph and telephone lines, and laying railways. Suddenly whole new industries opened up, and with the collapse of old feudal structures, people found themselves free to move around in search of work. "Advances" could be seen everywhere, from new brick buildings several stories high to streetlights and telegraph poles, and fashionable people wore bowler hats and petticoats, following the styles from London and Paris. As Tokyo grew into a modern metropolis, the number of rats was alleged to have topped eight million.

Writers, too, got caught up in the enthusiasm for modernization and looked in the direction of Europe for ideas. Japanese audiences eagerly read new translations: Defoe's *Robinson Crusoe*, Aesop's *Fables*, *Hamlet*, **Dostoyevsky's** *Crime and Punishment*. Many male writers were now educated at the new Japanese universities, fully exposed to the latest intellectual currents from around the world. Encouraged to think of themselves as potential leaders of the new Japan, they became purposefully worldly. The new novelists found European realism especially intriguing, and they began to write fiction that examined the subtlest feelings of ordinary, middle-class people and explored the contemporary social world.

WORK

Isolated from the male writers who were at the time inspired by European literature to reinvent the Japanese novel as serious social and psychological fiction, Ichiyō belonged to no established or emerging school of writing. Her mentor, Nakarai, with his frivolous, unfashionable style, was clearly not the right guide to bring her into the modern age. And so she accomplished this feat almost entirely alone. Drawing on the materials of her lived experience—her own marginal social status, her struggles with money, and her squalid surroundings—she began to paint a rich picture of the alleyways and brothels in Tokyo's poorest neighborhoods, where threadbare merchants and day-laborers, fortune-tellers and hangers-on, jugglers and minstrels catered to the rough and colorful "pleasure quarter." She had a particular predilection for adolescent characters, and some of her readers saw these figures as metaphors for the new Japan, on the brink of full maturity and feeling all of the excitement, the pain—and the disappointment—of growing up. Indeed, unlike many writers in the West, Ichiyō tended to cast the experience of coming of age as a loss and a threat rather than a fulfilling promise.

"Separate Ways," Ichiyō's final short story, captures the world of Tokyo's struggling poor almost entirely in a compact dialogue between its two main characters. Here she shows a woman at a crossroads, able to choose between two kinds of life—one of respectable independence and poverty, the other of sexual dependence and luxury—but she gives us the woman's choice mostly through the eyes of a feisty street urchin who is her friend. Throughout, in fact, the narrator remains very much in the background, offering very little explicit description and no judgment of her characters or their feelings; we learn almost everything we know about them through what they say and what is said about them. Although it is an unsentimental, restrained narrator who takes us into Tokyo's urban underclass, the dialogue itself is full of feeling—colloquial, spirited, disapproving, even aggressive. Thus we are immersed in a contentious social world, and like the story's characters, must find our way to our own judgments about how best to live in that world.

While focusing on the modern urban poor, Ichiyō throughout her career preserved an attachment to the style of classical Japanese literature, filling her elegantly brief stories with skillful plays on words, literary allusions, and passages of lyrical beauty that were quite different from the new literary realism of male writers borrowing from Western models. Poised perfectly between old and new, Higuchi Ichiyō has been called both the last woman writer of old Japan and the first woman writer of Japanese modernity.

Separate Ways[1]

There was someone outside, tapping at her window.

"Okyō? Are you home?"

"Who is it? I'm already in bed," she lied. "Come back in the morning."

"I don't care if you are in bed. Open up! It's me—Kichizō, from the umbrella shop."

"What a bothersome boy you are. Why do you come so late at night? I suppose you want some rice cakes again," she chuckled. "Just a minute. I'm coming."

Okyō, a stylish woman in her early twenties, put her sewing down and hurried into the front hall. Her abundant hair was tied back simply—she was too busy to fuss with it—and over her kimono she wore a long apron and a jacket. She opened the lattice, then the storm door.

"Sorry," Kichizō said as he barged in.

Dwarf, they called him. He was a pugnacious little one. He was sixteen, and he worked as an apprentice at the umbrella shop, but to look at him one would think he was eleven or twelve. He had spindly shoulders and a small face. He was a bright-looking boy, but so short that people teased him and dubbed him "Dwarf."

"Pardon me." He went right for the brazier.

"You won't find enough fire in there to toast any of your rice cakes. Go get some charcoal from the cinder box in the kitchen. You can heat the cakes yourself. I've got to get this done tonight." She took up her sewing again. "The owner of the pawnshop on the corner ordered it to wear on New Year's."[2]

"Hmm. What a waste, on that old baldie. Why don't I wear it first?"

"Don't be ridiculous. Don't you know what they say? 'He who wears another's clothes will never get anywhere in life.' You're a hopeless one, you are. You shouldn't say such things."

"I never did expect to be successful. I'll wear anybody's clothes—it's all the same to me. Remember what you promised once? When your luck changes, you said you'd make me a good kimono. Will you really?" He wasn't joking now.

"If only I could sew you a nice kimono, it would be a happy day. I'd gladly do it. But look at me. I don't have enough money to dress myself properly. I'm sewing to support myself. These aren't gifts I'm making." She smiled at him. "It's a dream, that promise."

"That's all right. I'm not asking for it now. Wait until some good luck comes. At least say you will. Don't you want to make me happy? That would be a sight, though, wouldn't it?" The boy had a wistful smile on his face. "Me dressed up in a fancy kimono!"

"And if you succeed first, Kichizō, promise me you'll do the same. That's a pledge I'd like to see come true."

"Don't count on it. I'm not going to succeed."

"How do you know?"

---

1. Translated by Robert Lyons Danly.

2. New Year's Day is the most significant holiday of the year in Japan.

"I know, that's all. Even if someone came along and insisted on helping me, I'd still rather stay where I am. Oiling umbrellas suits me fine. I was born to wear a plain kimono with workman's sleeves[3] and a short band around my waist. To me, all 'good luck' means is squeezing a little money from the change when I'm sent to buy persimmon juice.[4] If I hit the target someday, shooting arrows through a bamboo pole,[5] that's about all the good luck I can hope for. But someone like you, from a good family—why, fortune will come to greet you in a carriage. I don't mean a man's going to come and take you for his mistress, or something. Don't get the wrong idea." He toyed with the fire in the brazier and sighed over his fate.

"It won't be a fine carriage that comes for me. I'll be going to hell in a hand-cart." Okyō leaned against her yardstick and turned to Kichizō. "I've had so many troubles on my mind, sometimes it feels as if my heart's on fire."

Kichizō went to fetch the charcoal from the kitchen, as he always did.

"Aren't you going to have any rice cakes?"

Okyō shook her head. "No thank you."

"Then I'll go ahead. That old tightwad at the umbrella shop is always complaining. He doesn't know how to treat people properly. I was sorry when the old woman died. *She* was never like that. These new people! I don't talk to any of them. Okyō, what do you think of Hanji at the shop? He's a mean one, isn't he? He's so stuck-up. He's the owner's son, but, you know, I still can't think of him as a future boss. Whenever I have the chance, I like to pick a fight and cut him down to size." Kichizō set the rice cakes on the wire net above the brazier. "Oh, it's hot!" he shouted, blowing on his fingers. "I wonder why it is—you seem almost like a sister to me, Okyō. Are you sure you never had a younger brother?"

"I was an only child. I never had any brothers or sisters."

"So there really is no connection between us. Boy, I'd sure be glad if someone like you would come and tell me she was my sister. I'd hug her so tight . . . After that, I wouldn't care if I died. What was I, born from a piece of wood? I've never run into anyone who was a relative of mine. You don't know how many times I've thought about it: if I'm never, ever going to meet anyone from my own family, I'd be better off dying right now. Wouldn't I? But it's odd. I still want to go on living. I have this funny dream. The few people who've been the least bit kind to me all of a sudden turn out to be my mother and father and my brother and sister. And then I think, I want to live a little longer. Maybe if I wait another year, someone will tell me the truth. So I go on oiling umbrellas, even if it doesn't interest me a bit. Do you suppose there's anyone in the world as strange as I am? I don't have a mother or a father, Okyō. How could a child be born without either parent? It makes me pretty odd." He tapped at the rice cakes and decided they were done.

"Don't you have some kind of proof of your identity? A charm with your name on it, for instance?[6] There must be something you have, some clue to your family's whereabouts."

3. The kimono is a traditional Japanese robe; workman's sleeves are short.
4. Persimmons are a common fruit in Japan, sometimes used for fermented drinks.
5. A game played at carnivals that involved trying to hit a target.
6. Children were given paper charms with their names on them to carry for safety and good luck.

"Nothing. My friends used to tease me. They said I was left underneath a bridge when I was born, so I'd be taken for a beggar's baby. It may be true. Who knows? I may be the child of a tramp. One of those men who pass by in rags every day could be a kinsman. That old crippled lady with one eye who comes begging every morning—for all I know, she could be my mother. I used to wear a lion's mask and do acrobatics in the street," he said dejectedly, "before I worked at the umbrella shop. Okyō, if I were a beggar's boy, you wouldn't have been so nice to me, would you? You wouldn't have given me a second look."

"You shouldn't joke like that, Kichizō. I don't know what kind of people your parents were, but it makes no difference to me. These silly things you're saying— you're not yourself tonight. If I were you, I wouldn't let it bother me. Even if I were the child of an outcast, I'd make something of myself, whether I had any parents or not, no matter who my brothers were. Why are you whining around so?"

"I don't know," he said, staring at the floor. "There's something wrong with me. I don't seem to have any get-up-and-go."

* * *

She was dead now, but in the last generation the old woman Omatsu, fat as a *sumō* wrestler, had made a tidy fortune at the umbrella shop. It was a winter's night six years before that she had picked up Kichizō, performing his tumbler's act along the road, as she was returning from a pilgrimage.

"It's all right," she had assured him. "If the master gives us any trouble, we'll worry about it when the time comes. I'll tell him what a poor boy you are, how your companions abandoned you when your feet were too sore to go on walking. Don't worry about it. No one will raise an eyebrow. There's always room for a child or two. Who's going to care if we spread out a few boards for you to sleep on in the kitchen, and give you a little bit to eat? There's no risk in that. Why, even with a formal apprenticeship boys have been known to disappear. It doesn't prevent them from running off with things that don't belong to them. There are all kinds of people in this world. You know what they say: 'You don't know a horse till you ride it.' How can we tell whether we can use you in the shop if we don't give you a try? But listen, if you don't want to go back to that slum of yours, you're going to have to work hard. And learn how things are done. You'll have to make up your mind: this is where your home is. You're going to have to work, you know."

And work he did. Today, by himself, Kichizō could treat as many umbrellas as three adults, humming a tune as he went about his business. Seeing this, people would praise the dead lady's foresight: "Granny knew what she was doing."

The old woman, to whom he owed so much, had been dead two years now, and the present owners of the shop and their son Hanji were hard for Kichizō to take. But what was he to do? Even if he didn't like them, he had nowhere else to go. Had not his anger and resentment at them caused his very bones and muscles to contract? "Dwarf! Dwarf!" everybody taunted him. "Eating fish on the anniversary of your parents' death! It serves you right that you're so short. Round and round we go—look at him! The tiny monk who'll never grow!"[7]

---

7. Song from a children's game.

In his work, he could take revenge on the sniveling bullies, and he was perfectly ready to answer them with a clenched fist. But his valor sometimes left him. He didn't even know the date of his parents' death, he had no way to observe the yearly abstinences. It made him miserable, and he would throw himself down underneath the umbrellas drying in the yard and push his face against the ground to stifle his tears.

The boy was a little fireball. He had a violence about him that frightened the entire neighborhood. The sleeves of his plain kimono would swing as he flailed his arms, and the smell of oil from the umbrellas followed him through every season. There was no one to calm his temper, and he suffered all the more. If anyone were to show Kichizō a moment's kindness, he knew that he would cling to him and find it hard ever to let go.

In the spring Okyō the seamstress had moved into the neighborhood. With her quick wit, she was soon friendly with everyone. Her landlord was the owner of the umbrella shop, and so she was especially cordial to the members of the shop. "Bring over your mending anytime, boys. I don't care what condition it's in. There are so many people at your house, the mistress won't have time to tend to it. I'm always sewing anyway, one more stitch is nothing. Come and visit when you have time. I get lonely living by myself. I like people who speak their minds, and that rambunctious Kichizō—he's one of my favorites. Listen, the next time you lose your temper," she would tell him, "instead of hitting the little white dog at the rice shop, come over to my place. I'll give you my mallet, and you can take out your anger on the fulling block. That way, people won't be so upset with you. And you'll be helping me—it'll do us both good."

In no time Kichizō began to make himself at home. It was "Okyō, this" and "Okyō, that" until he had given the other workmen at the shop something new to tease him about. "Why, he's the mirror image of the great Chōemon!" they would laugh. "At the River Katsura, Ohan will have to carry *him*! Can't you see the little runt perched on top of her sash for the ride across the river? What a farce!"[8]

Kichizō was not without retort. "If you're so manly, why don't you ever visit Okyō? Which one of you can tell me each day what sweets she's put in the cookie jar? Take the pawnbroker with the bald spot. He's head over heels in love with her, always ordering sewing from her and coming round on one pretext or another, sending her aprons and neckpieces and sashes—trying to win her over. But she's never given him the time of day. Let alone treat him the way she does me! Kichizō from the umbrella shop—*I'm* the one who can go there any hour of the night, and when she hears it's me, she'll open the door in her nightgown. 'You haven't come to see me all day. Did something happen? I've been worried about you.' That's how she greets me. Who else gets treated that way? 'Hulking men are like big trees: not always good supports.' Size has nothing to do with it. Look at how the tiny peppercorn is prized."

8. Reference to a puppet play by the late-18th-century playwright Suga Sensuke, *The River Katsura and the Floodgate of Eternal Love* (1776), a story of two lovers, a middle-aged man named Chōemon and a teenaged girl named Ohan. In one scene Chōemon carries Ohan across the Katsura River.

"Listen to him!" they would yell, pelting Kichizō across the back.

But all he did was smile nonchalantly. "Thank you very much." If only he had a little height, no one would dare to tease him. As it was, the disdain he showed them was dismissed as nothing more than the impertinence of a little fool. He was the butt of all their jokes and the gossip they exchanged over tobacco.

On the night of the thirtieth of December, Kichizō was returning home. He had been up the hill to call on a customer with apologies for the late filling of an order. On his way back now he kept his arms folded across his chest and walked briskly, kicking a stone with the tip of his sandal. It rolled to the left and then to the right, and finally Kichizō kicked it into a ditch, chuckling aloud to himself. There was no one around to hear him. The moon above shone brightly on the white winter roads, but the boy was oblivious to the cold. He felt invigorated. He thought he would stop by Okyō's on the way home. As he crossed over to the back street, he was suddenly startled: someone appeared from behind him and covered his eyes. Whoever it was, the person could not keep from laughing.

"Who is it? Come on, who is it?" When he touched the hands held over his eyes, he knew who it was. "Ah, Okyō! I can tell by your snaky fingers. You shouldn't scare people."

Kichizō freed himself and Okyō laughed. "Oh, too bad! I've been discovered."

Over her usual jacket she was wearing a hood that came down almost to her eyes. She looked smart tonight, Kichizō thought as he surveyed her appearance. "Where've you been? I thought you told me you were too busy even to eat the next few days." The boy did not hide his suspicion. "Were you taking something to a customer?"

"I went to make some of my New Year's calls early," she said innocently.

"You're lying. No one receives greetings on the thirtieth. Where did you go? To your relatives?"

"As a matter of fact, I *am* going to a relative's—to live with a relative I hardly know. Tomorrow I'll be moving. It's so sudden, it probably surprises you. It *is* unexpected, even I feel a little startled. Anyway, you should be happy for me. It's not a bad thing that's happened."

"Really? You're not teasing, are you? You shouldn't scare me like this. If you went away, what would I do for fun? Don't ever joke about such things. You and your nonsense!" He shook his head at her.

"I'm not joking. It's just as you said once—good luck has come riding in a fancy carriage. So I can't very well stay on in a back tenement, can I? Now I'll be able to sew you that kimono, Kichizō."

"I don't want it. When you say 'Good luck has come,' you mean you're going off someplace worthless. That's what Hanji said the other day. 'You know Okyō the seamstress?' he said. 'Her uncle—the one who gives rub-downs over by the vegetable market—he's helped her find a new position. She's going into service with some rich family. Or so they say. But it sounds fishy to me—she's too old to learn sewing from some housewife. Somebody's going to set her up. I'm sure of it. She'll be wearing tasseled coats the next time we see her, la-de-da, and her hair all done up in ringlets, like a kept woman. You wait. With a face like hers, you don't think she's about to spend her whole life sewing, do you?' That's what he said. I told him he was full of it, and we had a big fight. But you *are* going to do it, aren't you? You're going off to be someone's mistress!"

"It's not that I want to. I don't have much choice. I suppose I won't be able to see you anymore, Kichizō, will I?"

With these few words, Kichizō withered. "I don't know, maybe it's a step up for you, but don't do it. It's not as if you can't make a living with your sewing. The only one you have to feed is yourself. When you're good at your work, why give it up for something so stupid? It's disgusting of you. Don't go through with it. It's not too late to change your mind." The boy was unyielding in his notion of integrity.

"Oh, dear," Okyō sighed. She stopped walking. "Kichizō, I'm sick of all the washing and sewing. Anything would be better. I'm tired of these drab clothes. I'd like to wear a crepe kimono, too, for a change—even if it is tainted."

They were bold words, and yet it didn't sound as if she herself fully comprehended them. "Anyway," she laughed, "come home with me. Hurry up now."

"What! I'm too disgusted. You go ahead," he said, but his long, sad shadow followed after her.

Soon they came to their street. Okyō stopped beneath the window where Kichizō always tapped for her. "Every night you come and knock at this window. After tomorrow night," she sighed, "I won't be able to hear your voice calling anymore. How terrible the world is."

"It's not the world. It's you."

Okyō went in first and lit a lamp. "Kichizō, come get warm," she called when she had the fire in the brazier going.

He stood by the pillar. "No, thanks."

"Aren't you chilly? It won't do to catch a cold."

"I don't care." He looked down at the floor as he spoke. "Leave me alone."

"What's the matter with you? You're acting funny. Is it something I said? If it is, please tell me. When you stand around with a long face like that and won't talk to me, it makes me worry."

"You don't have to worry about anything. This is Kichizō from the umbrella shop you're talking to. I don't need any woman to take care of me." He rubbed his back against the pillar. "How pointless everything turns out. What a life! People are friendly, and then they disappear. It's always the ones I like. Granny at the umbrella shop, and Kinu, the one with short hair, at the dyer's shop. First Granny dies of palsy. Then Kinu goes and throws herself into the well behind the dyer's—she didn't want to marry. Now you're going off. I'm always disappointed in the end. Why should I be surprised, I suppose? What am I but a boy who oils umbrellas? So what if I do the work of a hundred men? I'm not going to win any prizes for it. Morning and night, the only title I ever hear is 'Dwarf' . . . 'Dwarf'! I wonder if I'll ever get any taller. 'All things come to him who waits,' they say, but I wait and wait, and all I get is more unhappiness. Just the day before yesterday I had a fight with Hanji over you. Ha! I was so sure he was wrong. I told him you were the last person rotten enough to go off and do that kind of thing. Not five days have passed, and I have to eat crow. How could I have thought of you as a sister? You, with all your lies and tricks, and your selfishness. This is the last you'll ever see of me. Ever. Thanks for your kindness. Go on and do what you want. From now on, I won't have anything to do with anyone. It's not worth it. Good-by, Okyō."

He went to the front door and began to put his sandals on.

"Kichizō! You're wrong. I'm leaving here, but I'm not abandoning *you*. You're like my little brother. How can you turn on me?" From behind, she hugged him with all her might. "You're too impatient. You jump to conclusions."

"You mean you're not going to be someone's mistress?" Kichizō turned around.

"It's not the sort of thing anybody wants to do. But it's been decided. You can't change things."

He stared at her with tears in his eyes.

"Take your hands off me, Okyō."

ORATURE

The written word reached only a tiny sliver of the world's population before the twentieth century. The United Nations estimates that around 10 percent of the world was literate in 1850. By the 1920s the number was up to 28 percent. But low levels of literacy worldwide did not mean that people lacked stories and poetry, philosophy and religious wisdom. For most of human history, people used the spoken word to pass on laws, skills, common values, founding legends, and thrilling tales. In fact, world literature as we know it today would not exist without the nourishment of oral traditions. Homer's great ancient Greek epics, the *Iliad* and the *Odyssey*, began as oral tales, becoming "literature" only after generations had passed them down from memory. From Walt Disney's *Snow White* to Toni Morrison's Nobel Prize–winning fiction, from experimental poetry to African jazz, long and complex histories of oral performance continue to circulate as a living part of world culture, whether we recognize them or not.

The Ugandan linguist Pio Zirimu coined the term *orature* to convey the serious artistic value of oral expression. In most predominantly oral cultures, performance is a highly refined skill. Those who recite stories and poems aloud adopt individual performance styles and alter details for dramatic effect. A talented few come to be renowned as great artists. Unlike the fixed written word, an oral tradition is not a single, knowable object: live performances involve vocal modulations and cadences, dramatic silences and bodily movements that change with each telling; and performers often introduce creative transformations, adapting old stories to suit new circumstances. Live audiences respond to the teller in ways that can shape the telling, and they sometimes participate in the performance.

The relationship between oral literature and the written word took on a new importance in the nineteenth century. When it comes to reading and writing, this was a time of great unevenness and rapid change. In traditional agrarian societies such as Russia, where most people worked the land, only 5 percent of the population could read. But in the United States and Protestant Europe, where churches formed schools to teach people how to read the Bible, and industrialization and urbanization demanded new skills and new mobility, literacy rates reached almost universal levels. Around mid-century, about 60 percent of French and British people could read, 30 percent of Japanese people, and 5 percent across the Ottoman Empire. In some regions literacy rates varied by gender: in Brazil 12 percent of women were literate compared to 20 percent of men, and India's female literacy was at 8 percent across the country, while in the Kerala region almost a third of adult women could read. In the United States, the most important differentiating factor was race: while the United States boasted an 80 percent overall literacy rate in 1870, four-fifths of African Americans were illiterate because under slavery they had been denied education.

Zovave storyteller (North Africa, 1857). Photograph by Gustave le Gray.

Literacy rates rose dramatically in many places over the course of the century: in Argentina, adult literacy stood at less than one-third in 1869, but thanks to education reforms launched by Domingo Faustino Sarmiento, it rose to two-thirds by 1914. Toward the end of the nineteenth century, British colonial administrators in South Africa actually worried that too many black people were literate and so were beginning to rebel against the expectation that they would perform only the most menial kinds of work. Literacy, as the American slave **Frederick Douglass** had discovered, could be a powerful tool of resistance and political freedom. But so too could orature, which often eluded official scrutiny and could bring a sense of cohesion and solidarity to social groups under threat.

Interest in oral traditions rose sharply in the nineteenth century, as many nations made the shift to widespread literacy. When people learn how to read, they usually stop developing the skills and methods of memorization, and this means that oral traditions fade as literacy rates rise. Thanks to the huge upsurge in literacy, the nineteenth century saw the end of many vibrant oral traditions around the world. This threat of disappearing cultural riches prompted some, like **Jacob and Wilhelm Grimm**, to try to preserve spoken stories in print before they vanished. The Grimms' fairy tales, first published in 1812, included "Snow White" and "Hansel and Gretel," stories that had been passed down orally for generations. For the Grimms, fairy tales were important because they were thought to reveal a deep, longstanding cultural life that bound the German people together. And the Grimms were not the only ones to turn to folktales and fairy tales to build nationalist sentiment: around the world, traditional oral stories were often thought to be the authentic expressions of a unified people.

The nineteenth century was also a time when European powers were conquering peoples around the world, and some Europeans became fascinated by similarities between their own oral traditions and those they found thriving elsewhere. Did folktales provide a key to understanding a universal human nature? Did all cultures tell the same basic stories? The examples collected below suggest intriguing similarities between African stories and those told by slaves in the Americas and peasants in Europe: all of these groups return again and again to tales of oppressive labor. Many Europeans assumed that cultures in Africa and Asia represented "immature" stages in a single story of human development, and that one could see Europe as it had once been by studying Iroquois or Zulu culture in the present. In the 1870s, for example, a Dutch scholar by the name of Willem Bleek took advantage of the imprisonment of a number of nomadic Kung people by the British in southern Africa. These prisoners were the perfect subjects to teach him about oral traditions, he realized, since they could not wander off, as nomadic people were inclined to do. Acknowledging that the Kung were in danger of extinction because their traditional hunting and gathering lands had been seized by European settlers, Bleek said that he had made an urgent journey to collect their stories so that Europeans could come to know a disappearing race "that had made little, if any, advance since the far-distant days when members of it shot their flint-headed arrows at reindeer in France." Bleek assumed that oral stories from Africa needed to be transcribed as a way for Europeans to understand their own past—the prehistory of civilization—before they themselves eradicated that prehistory through colonization.

Although orature might have seemed fragile in the context of rapid industrialization and modernization, sometimes it survived, forceful and vigorous. The twelve million African slaves who crossed the ocean between the seventeenth and the nineteenth centuries carried stories, styles, and cadences to the United States, Latin America, and the Caribbean, which pervaded their new home cultures. The roots of jazz and hip-hop rhythms, for example, can be traced to African musical traditions. Collected below are three stories of **Anansi** the spider-trickster, a character who originates with the Ashanti people in West Africa and then travels on the slave ships, appearing in lots of different retellings in the Americas.

As vibrant oral cultures continued to coexist with rising literacy in the nineteenth century, many people tried their hands at translating oral stories and poems into written form. Among these were colonial administrators, missionaries, curious travelers, and scholars of language, folklore, and anthropology, as well as representatives of cultures under threat. The examples here reveal a range of motives: the British in West Africa, for example, wanted to study local lore so that they could control the Ashanti people, while the brothers Grimm feared that their own traditions were disappearing. Whether intending to oppress or to conserve, all of these writers had to make difficult choices in the translation from oral to written forms: should they try to express the particular style of one performer, or should they listen to multiple versions of the same story to try to distill the common features of a tradition? Should the written version convey the idiosyncratic features of spoken language— conversational interjections, cadences, repetitions, and colloquialisms—or should it follow a tidier, more conventionally literary style?

However they were preserved and transcribed, a vast range of oral traditions have survived into our time, nourishing the richness of modern world cultures, sometimes unseen or overlooked but nonetheless still vital. Many of the most prominent twentieth- and twenty-first-century writers around the world have drawn inspiration from orature. **William Butler Yeats**, the Irish poet, collected and published traditional tales from his own country and drew from them for his groundbreaking Modernist poetry, while the Nigerian novelist **Chinua Achebe** has made complex use of Igbo orature. American Indian writers, such as **Leslie Marmon Silko**, frequently ground their fiction in folktales passed down orally through the generations, while Indian-born **Salman Rushdie** deliberately stylizes traditional oral storytelling in his novels. Surprisingly, perhaps, even the most modern, technologically driven cultures have been built on oral foundations.

GERMAN FOLKTALE: THE THREE SPINNERS

The folktales and fairy tales collected by the brothers Grimm—Jacob (1785–1863) and Wilhelm (1786–1859)—have become some of the most famous stories in the world: "Little Red Riding Hood," "Rapunzel," "Hansel and Gretel," "Rumpelstiltskin," "Snow White," "Cinderella," and "Sleeping Beauty." The Grimm versions can be surprising or even shocking today. They include scenes of sexual and physical violence that seem like strange material for children. But in fact these stories were originally entertainment for a whole village.

The Grimms were the editors of these stories rather than their authors. They were serious German scholars who came of age just as Napoleon's French armies invaded and imposed new laws and customs, threatening to wipe out generations of traditional German lore. Eager to preserve a national heritage, the brothers set about collecting the stories told by peasants. Ironically, however, they did not hear actual peasants tell the tales. Instead, most of their sources were educated women who had absorbed traditional stories from household servants and nursemaids in their childhoods. The Grimms then heavily edited the stories. They were keen to preserve a rustic feel, sometimes inserting old proverbs for effect. But they also added new material that explored the psychological motives of the characters. In this way, they joined traditional folk elements with rounded characters who appealed to a growing middle-class audience. This combination would prove enormously popular, influencing many other collectors of folktales around the world and making these tales classics well beyond Germany within a generation.

"The Three Spinners" is not one of the most famous Grimm fairy tales, but it reveals the ways that traditional folktales could appeal to poor peasants. It is primarily about the burden of physical work, which is so oppressive that it deforms the very body of the worker. The story shows how the different social classes have strikingly different relationships to work, and it is interesting to speculate what its happy ending would have meant to those facing a life of hard and unrelenting labor.

The Three Spinners[1]

There was once a girl who was idle and would not spin, and her mother, say what she would, could not bring her to it. At last the mother lost her temper and beat her, at which the girl began to weep loudly. Now at this very moment the Queen drove by, and when she heard the weeping she stopped her carriage, went into the house, and asked the mother why she was beating her daughter so that the cries could be heard out in the road?

The woman was ashamed to tell how lazy her daughter was, and said,—

"I cannot get her to leave off spinning. She insists on spinning for ever and ever, and I am poor, and cannot get the flax for her." Then the Queen answered,—

---

1. Translated by Jack Zipes.

"There is nothing I like better to hear than spinning, and I am never happier than when the wheels are humming. Let me have your daughter with me in the palace; I have flax enough, and there she shall spin as much as she likes."

The mother was well pleased with this, and the Queen took the girl with her. When they had arrived at the palace, the Queen led the girl up into three rooms which were filled from the bottom to the top with the finest flax.

"Now spin me this flax," said she, "and when you have done it, you shall have my eldest son for a husband, even if you are poor. I care not for that; you are a hard-working girl, and that is enough."

The girl was scared out of her wits, for she could not have spun the flax, no, not if she had lived till she was three hundred years old, and had sat at it every day from morning till night. So when she was alone, she began to weep, and sat thus for three days without moving a finger. On the third day the Queen came, and wondered when she saw nothing had been spun yet; but the girl said she had not been able to begin because she felt so badly at leaving her mother's house. The Queen was sorry for her, but said when she was going away,—

"To-morrow you must begin to work."

When the girl was alone again, she did not know what to do, and in her distress went to the window. There she saw three women coming toward her; the first had a broad flat foot, the second had such a great under lip that it hung down over her chin, and the third had a broad thumb. They stood before the window, and looked up, and asked the girl what was the matter with her? She told her trouble, and they said they would help her, but added,—

"If you will invite us to the wedding, not be ashamed of us, and will call us your aunts; and if you will place us at your table, we will spin the flax for you, and that in a very short time."

"With all my heart," she replied; "do but come in and begin the work at once." Then she let in the three strange women, and cleared a place in the first room, where they sat down and began their spinning. One drew the thread and trod the wheel, the second wetted the thread, the third twisted it, and struck the table with her finger; and as often as she struck it, a skein of thread, that was spun in the finest manner possible, fell to the ground. The girl hid the three spinners from the Queen, and showed her, whenever she came, the great heap of spun thread, until the Queen could not praise her enough. When the first room was empty she went to the second, and at last to the third, and that too was quickly cleared. Then the three women took leave, and said to the girl,—

"Do not forget what you have promised us,—it will make your fortune."

When the maiden showed the Queen the empty rooms, and the great heap of yarn, she gave orders for the wedding. Her son was glad that he was to have such a clever and hard-working wife, and praised her well.

"I have three aunts," said the girl, "and as they have been very kind to me, I should not like to forget them in my good fortune; let me ask them to the wedding, and let them sit with us at table." The Queen and the bridegroom said,—

"Why not?" So when the feast began, the three women entered in strange dress, and the bride said,—

"Welcome, dear aunts."

"Ah," said the bridegroom, "how do you come by these odious friends?" He went to the one with the broad flat foot, and said,—

"How do you come by such a broad foot?"

"By treading," she answered, "by treading." Then the bridegroom went to the second and said,—

"How do you come by your falling lip?"

"By licking," she answered, "by licking." Then he asked the third,—

"How do you come by your broad thumb?"

"By twisting the thread," she answered, "by twisting the thread." On this the King's son took fright and said,—

"Neither now nor ever shall my beautiful bride touch a spinning-wheel." And thus she got rid of the hateful flax-spinning.

THREE ANANSI STORIES: GHANA, JAMAICA, UNITED STATES

Tricky, mischievous, mostly clever but sometimes very foolish, the spider Anansi manages to outsmart most other animals and sometimes even the gods. He is a trickster—a character who compensates for his physical weakness by using his cunning to play tricks on powerful characters. He can be a shape-shifter, and sometimes takes the form of a human, or a human-spider hybrid. Spiders spin webs that connect spaces: they are therefore border-crossers, and belong to no one place. They also hide in corners, and disappear easily. Anansi usually breaks taboos and upsets expectations. And he is almost always selfish, aiming to survive in hard conditions, stealing food and money or bamboozling other creatures into working to get food for him. Anansi's maneuvers do not always succeed: sometimes they backfire and he is temporarily set back, but he is nothing if not resilient, and he simply returns to his old tricks again in the next story.

For the Ashanti people of West Africa, where he originates, Anansi is almost always the underdog, though he sometimes takes on qualities of the gods. Ashanti village elders typically tell Anansi stories after dark, with an audience sitting in a circle to listen. Sometimes in the middle of a telling, an actor will enter the circle and start impersonating one of the characters, to the great amusement of those watching. The stories typically reinforce a shared sense of moral norms and appropriate behavior precisely by having Anansi break taboos in a humorous way. One characteristic of the African versions of the Anansi stories is that they often explain how the world has come to be the way it is. In Ghana, stories of all kinds are called *Anansesem*, and the first tale included here explains why all stories belong to Anansi.

The first English-language transcriber of the Anansi stories was R. S. Rattray, an anthropologist for the British government, which had established a colony called the Gold Coast (now Ghana). The more the British knew, they thought, the more successfully they would be able to assert and maintain power over the Ashanti. The collection of oral traditions was thus considered "of incalculable importance from an administrative point of view." The version included here comes out of a later collaboration between American anthropologist Harold Courlander and a student from Ghana, Albert Kofi Prempeh.

Trickster figures are found in many cultures, but what is most remarkable about the Anansi stories is their global reach. They can be found not only in West Africa but also in the Bahamas, Jamaica, Haiti, Trinidad, Barbados, Curaçao, Grenada, Costa Rica, Belize, Colombia, Nicaragua, Suriname, and the United States. The stories vary, and the character's name changes from place to place—Ananse, Annancy, Nansi, Aunt Nancy, Bre Nancy, Anansi Tori, and Ti Malice—but this oral tradition has remained remarkably resilient despite its transmission through centuries and across oceans.

The geographical scope of the Anansi tradition has everything to do with the slave trade. Enforced illiteracy meant that slaves who were taken from West Africa to the New World had severely restricted educations, but it also meant that they kept alive oral traditions that might have faded under different conditions. Oppressed by a system that was based on a hypocritical morality, and surrounded by an abundance that was denied to them, slaves might well find Anansi appealing: his egocentrism, his willingness to use cunning to survive, his undermining of authority, and his resistance to moral constraints all suggested ways of coping with cruel and hypocritical slaveholders.

As Anansi traveled to the Caribbean, Latin America, and the United States, he tended to lose the divine qualities which he sometimes had in West Africa. In the American versions, he also faces harsher realities; moreover, he is more inclined to trick characters who are weaker than he is, and more frequently his tricks go wrong and he loses. Sometimes his arrogance or his greed brings about a downfall. He also adapts to new social conditions, sometimes getting involved in gambling and bootlegging. The stories are frequently entangled with tales and characters from other traditions, including European and American Indian orature.

Walter Jekyll, a British folklorist, collected the Jamaican version of the Anansi story included here, published in 1906. The "men and boys" who told the stories he collected were his own paid workers. (The British government had abolished slavery in Jamaica in 1834.) Around the same time that he was transcribing these stories, Jekyll met and encouraged a young Jamaican poet, Claude McKay, urging him to write in his native dialect. With money and advice, Jekyll helped McKay to move to the United States, where he became a leading writer in New York's Harlem Renaissance.

Some slaves in the United States transformed Anansi into a mischievous female. The story included here features Brer Rabbit, a famous trickster figure of Cherokee origin, who meets a frightening spider named "Aunt Nancy." This melding of American Indian and African traditions was not uncommon. Before 1776 many Indians had been enslaved and made to work alongside African slaves, with English as their common language. With Julius Lester's retelling of "Brer Rabbit and Aunt Nancy," we see how far-flung oral traditions can cross the world, meet, enrich, and transform one another, all without the need of writing.

All Stories Are Anansi's

In the beginning, all tales and stories belonged to Nyame, the Sky God. But Kwaku Anansi, the spider, yearned to be the owner of all the stories known in the world, and he went to Nyame and offered to buy them.

The Sky God said: "I am willing to sell the stories, but the price is high. Many people have come to me offering to buy, but the price was too high for them. Rich and powerful families have not been able to pay. Do you think you can do it?"

Anansi replied to the Sky God: "I can do it. What is the price?"

"My price is three things," the Sky God said. "I must first have Mmoboro, the hornets. I must then have Onini, the great python. I must then have Osebo, the leopard. For these things I will sell you the right to tell all stories."

Anansi said: "I will bring them."

He went home and made his plans. He first cut a gourd from a vine and made a small hole in it. He took a large calabash and filled it with water. He went to the tree where the hornets lived. He poured some of the water over himself, so that he was dripping. He threw some water over the hornets, so that they too were dripping. Then he put the calabash on his head, as though to protect himself from a storm, and called out to the hornets: "Are you foolish people? Why do you stay in the rain that is falling?"

The hornets answered: "Where shall we go?"

"Go here, in this dry gourd," Anansi told them.

The hornets thanked him and flew into the gourd through the small hole. When the last of them had entered, Anansi plugged the hole with a ball of grass, saying: "Oh, yes, but you are really foolish people!"

He took his gourd full of hornets to Nyame, the Sky God. The Sky God accepted them. He said: "There are two more things."

Anansi returned to the forest and cut a long bamboo pole and some strong vines. Then he walked toward the house of Onini, the python, talking to himself. He said: "My wife is stupid. I say he is longer and stronger. My wife says he is shorter and weaker. I give him more respect. She gives him less respect. Is she right or am I right? I am right, he is longer. I am right, he is stronger."

When Onini, the python, heard Anansi talking to himself, he said: "Why are you arguing this way with yourself?"

The spider replied: "Ah, I have had a dispute with my wife. She says you are shorter and weaker than this bamboo pole. I say you are longer and stronger."

Onini said: "It's useless and silly to argue when you can find out the truth. Bring the pole and we will measure."

So Anansi laid the pole on the ground, and the python came and stretched himself out beside it.

"You seem a little short," Anansi said.

The python stretched further.

"A little more," Anansi said.

"I can stretch no more," Onini said.

"When you stretch at one end, you get shorter at the other end," Anansi said. "Let me tie you at the front so you don't slip."

He tied Onini's head to the pole. Then he went to the other end and tied the tail to the pole. He wrapped the vine all around Onini, until the python couldn't move.

"Onini," Anansi said, "it turns out that my wife was right and I was wrong. You are shorter than the pole and weaker. My opinion wasn't as good as my wife's. But you were even more foolish than I, and you are now my prisoner."

Anansi carried the python to Nyame, the Sky God, who said: "There is one thing more."

Osebo, the leopard, was next. Anansi went into the forest and dug a deep pit where the leopard was accustomed to walk. He covered it with small branches and leaves and put dust on it, so that it was impossible to tell where the pit was. Anansi went away and hid. When Osebo came prowling in the black of night, he stepped into the trap Anansi had prepared and fell to the bottom. Anansi heard the sound of the leopard falling, and he said: "Ah, Osebo, you are half-foolish!"

When morning came, Anansi went to the pit and saw the leopard there.

"Osebo," he asked, "what are you doing in this hole?"

"I have fallen into a trap," Osebo said. "Help me out."

"I would gladly help you," Anansi said. "But I'm sure that if I bring you out, I will have no thanks for it. You will get hungry, and later on you will be wanting to eat me and my children."

"I swear it won't happen!" Osebo said.

"Very well. Since you swear it, I will take you out," Anansi said.

He bent a tall green tree toward the ground, so that its top was over the pit, and he tied it that way. Then he tied a rope to the top of the tree and dropped the other end of it into the pit.

"Tie this to your tail," he said.

Osebo tied the rope to his tail.

"Is it well tied?" Anansi asked.

"Yes, it is well tied," the leopard said.

"In that case," Anansi said, "you are not merely half-foolish, you are all-foolish."

And he took his knife and cut the other rope, the one that held the tree bowed to the ground. The tree straightened up with a snap, pulling Osebo out of the hole. He hung in the air head downward, twisting and turning. And while he hung this way, Anansi killed him with his weapons.

Then he took the body of the leopard and carried it to Nyame, the Sky God, saying: "Here is the third thing. Now I have paid the price."

Nyame said to him: "Kwaku Anansi, great warriors and chiefs have tried, but they have been unable to do it. You have done it. Therefore, I will give you the stories. From this day onward, all stories belong to you. Whenever a man tells a story, he must acknowledge that it is Anansi's tale."

In this way Anansi, the spider, became the owner of all stories that are told. To Anansi all these tales belong.

Annancy, Monkey and Tiger

One day Annancy an' Tiger get in a rum-shop, drink an' drink, an' then Monkey commence to boast. Monkey was a great boaster.

Annancy say:—"You boast well; I wonder if you have sense as how you boast."

Monkey say:—"Get 'way you foolish fellah you, can come an' ask me if me have sense. You go t'rough de whole world you never see a man again have the sense I have."

Annancy say:—"Bro'er Monkey, how many sense you have, tell me?"

Monkey say:—"I have dem so till I can't count dem to you, for dem dé[1] all over me body."

Annancy say:—"Me no have much, only two, one fe[2] me an' one fe me friend."

One day Monkey was travelling an' was going to pass where Tiger live. Annancy was working on that same road.

As Monkey passing, Tiger was into a stone-hole an' jump out on the fellah an' catch him. All his sense was gone, no sense to let him get 'way. Tiger was so glad, have him before him well ready to kill.

Here come the clever man Mr. Annancy.

When he saw his friend Monkey in the hand of such a wicked man he was frighten, but he is going to use his sense.

He said:—"Marnin', Bro'er Tiger, I see you catch dat fellah; I was so glad to see you hold him so close in hand. You must eat him now. But before you eat him take you two hand an' cover you face an' kneel down with you face up to Massa God an' say, 'T'ank God fe what I goin' to receive.'"

An' so Tiger do.

An' by the time Tiger open his eyes Monkey an' Annancy was gone.

When they get to a distant Annancy said to Monkey:—"T'ink you say you have sense all over you 'kin, why you no been get 'way when Bro'er Tiger catch you?"

Monkey don't have nothing to say.

Annancy say:—"Me no tell you say me have two sense, one fe me an' one fe me friend? Well! a him me use to-day."

From that day Tiger hate Annancy up to now.

Jack Mantora me no choose any.[3]

Brer Rabbit and Aunt Nancy

Once a year all the creatures—winged and claw, big and little, long-tail, bobtail, and no-tail—had to go see Aunt Nancy. Aunt Nancy was the great-grandmother of the Witch-Rabbit, Mammy-Bammy-Big-Money. She ruled all the animals, even King Lion. When she wanted them to know that she was watching their every move, all she had to do was suck in her breath and the creatures would get a chill.

One year it came time for the creatures to go pay their respects.

"I ain't going!" Brer Rabbit announced.

"You got to go," the other animals argued with him.

"Says who? I don't feel like going way up in the country and into that thick swamp just to see Aunt Nancy."

"You better go," they told him.

"I done already been and seen. But, when you get where you going, ask Aunt Nancy to shake hands with you. Then you'll see what I saw."

1. There.
2. For.
3. Jamaican storytellers typically end Annancy stories with these words, indicating that the moral is not intended for any particular listener.

A late Ming Dynasty (ca. seventeenth century) ink-on-paper illustration of Dushi Huang, one of the "Yama" kings of the ten courts of the underworld. The concept of layers and courts of hell appears to have arisen from a blending of ideas from Daoism, Buddhism, and Chinese folk religion. In this image, Dushi Huang appears as a divine record-keeper, with a scroll and writing implements laid out before him.

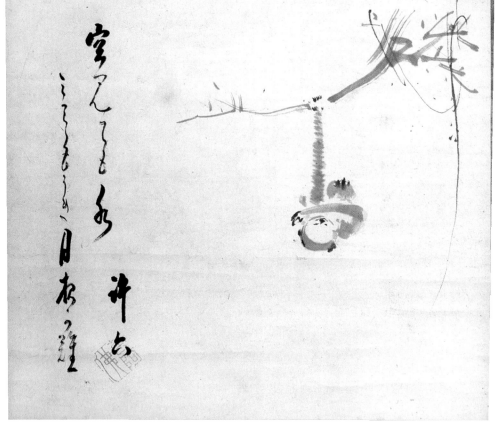

As literacy spread and flourished in Europe, more people kept "commonplace books"—journals in which one could record quotations from books one had read or compose one's own work. These pages from a mid-seventeenth-century commonplace book contain texts by two different hands; one text is a poem about tobacco.

Captain Lemuel Gulliver; of
Redriff Ætat. suæ 58.

TRAVELS

INTO SEVERAL

Remote Nations

OF THE

WORLD.

In ·Four PARTS.

By *LEMUEL GULLIVER,*
First a SURGEON, and then a CAP-
TAIN of several SHIPS.

VOL. I.

LONDON:
Printed for BENJ. MOTTE, *at the*
Middle Temple-Gate *in* Fleet-street.
MDCCXXVI.

Frontispiece and title page of *Travels Into Several Remote Nations of the World. In Four Parts. By Lemuel Gulliver, First a Surgeon, and then a Captain of Several Ships,* later known as *Gulliver's Travels,* by Jonathan Swift. Especially in its early history in English, much prose fiction was presented in a nonfiction guise, as a memoir or, as here, a travel journal of a real person.

Daytime in the Gay Quarters (ca. 1739), a woodblock color print by Okumura Masanobu
(1686–1764), a prolific Japanese print designer, painter, and publisher. The geisha in the

A posthumous portrait, by Miguel Cabrera (1695–1768), of Sor Juana Inés de la Cruz (1648–1695), a pioneering writer and thinker in New Spain. Sor Juana is revered as a major figure in Mexican literature, and as a brave and eloquent advocate of formal education for women.

This medallion, designed in 1787 by the English potter and ceramicist Josiah Wedgwood (1730–1795), features an inscription, "Am I not a man and a brother?" that became one of the most recognizable mottoes of the abolitionist movement. The medallion became a wildly popular fashion accessory among people sympathetic to the abolitionist cause, and thus raised public awareness of the issue.

LIBERTÉ DE LA PRESSE

This 1820 oil painting by Dutch artist Johannes Jelgerhuis (1770–1836) of the bookshop of Pieter Meijer Warnars in Amsterdam provides a wonderfully detailed portrait of early nineteenth-century middle-class book selling.

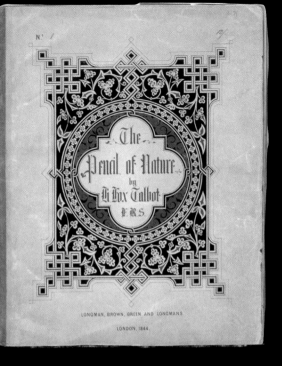

The Pencil of Nature, assembled and published in 1844 by William Henry Fox Talbot (1800–1877), was the first commercially available book illustrated with photographs. Shown here are the cover of the first issue (it was published in six installments) and one of the "plates" inside that issue: Fox's 1841 photograph "Bust of Patroclus."

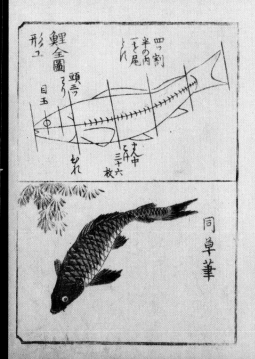

Sketches of swimming carp from *A Picture Book Miscellany* (1849), a book by the Japanese ukiyo-e artist Utagawa Hiroshige (1797–1858) that displays his commitment to realistic renderings of subjects from nature.

SKETCHES IN JAPAN BY OUR SPECIAL ARTIST: THE STORYTELLER (A DAILY SCENE) IN YOKOHAMA.

A street scene from 1861 in Yokohoma, Japan, shows a storyteller (center, seated on small stage) accompanying himself with a stringed instrument.

The world's first commercially produced typewriter: the Hansen Writing Ball designed by Rasmus Malling-Hansen (1835–1890), minister and principal at the Danish Royal Institute for the Deaf. First designed in 1865 and improved over the next fifteen years, Hansen's machine would eventually be overshadowed by late nineteenth-century typewriters that allowed one to see the result on paper as one typed (rather than operating 'blind,' as with the writing ball).

A photograph of Queen Victoria (1819–1901) in July 1893 accompanied by her Indian "Munshi" (personal secretary and attendant), Abdul Karim, who was one of her closest confidants during the final fifteen years of her reign. The queen was an early adopter of the typewriter, which she used for her official correspondence.

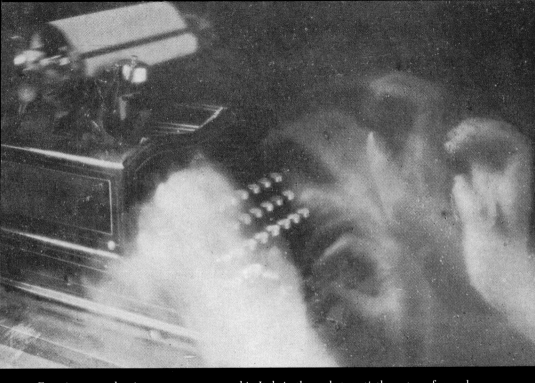

Futurism, a modernist movement centered in Italy in the early twentieth century, focused on the technologies and dynamism of modern life. This photograph (*Dattilografa*, 1913) by Anton Giulio Bragaglia (1890–1960) captures the spirit of the futurist movement perfectly, portraying writing as an energetic and technology-enhanced activity.

The Reader (Woman in Grey), 1920, an oil painting by the twentieth-century's most famous artist, Pablo Picasso (1881–1973).

Soviet propaganda poster, 1921. The text reads, "From the gloom to the light; from battle to books; from grief to happiness."

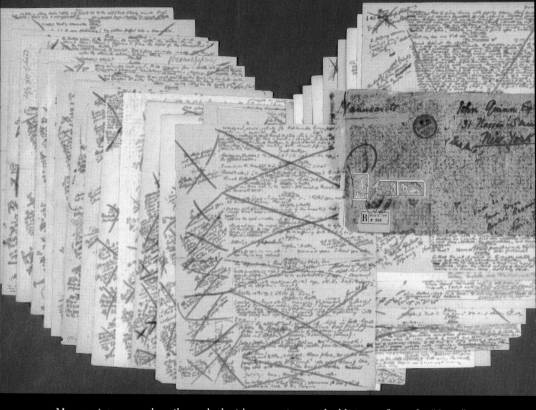

Manuscript pages—heavily marked with corrections and additions—from the "Circe" chapter of James Joyce's novel *Ulysses* (1922).

Portrait of Virginia Woolf (1882–1941) taken in 1902, and a page from Woolf's draft notebook for her novel *Mrs. Dalloway* (1925). Surveying the history of literature and finding so few women, Woolf had this to say in *A Room of One's Own* (1929): "I would venture to guess that Anon, who wrote so many poems without signing them, was often a woman."

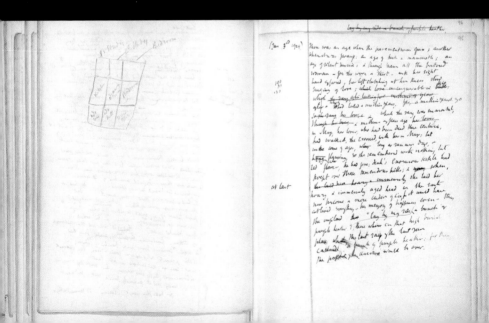

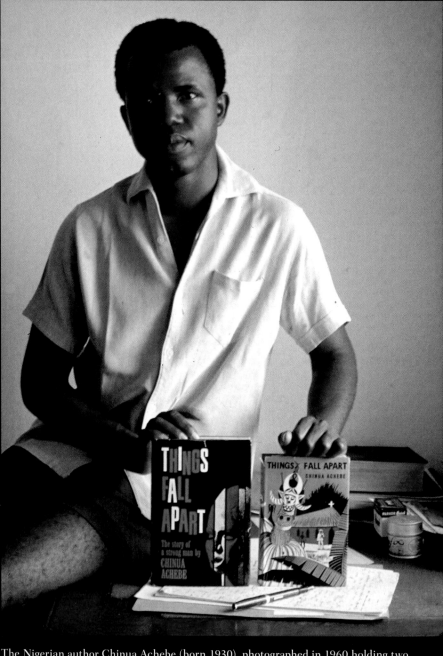

The Nigerian author Chinua Achebe (born 1930), photographed in 1960 holding two editions of his book *Things Fall Apart* (1958), which would become the most widely read and respected African novel in English.

Participants in a 2010 calligraphy contest in the city of Xian, Shanxi Province, China.

The cover of the first American edition of T. S. Eliot's modernist masterpiece, *The Waste Land*, published in 1922, and the opening menu of an ebook/app version of the poem, released in 2011. Clearly, the new media and technologies of the twenty-first century will change the way we read and experience poetry, drama, fiction, and other writing. But in what ways? How quickly?

The creatures went off. After a while they came to Aunt Nancy's house. If you had seen her house, you would've said it looked like a big chunk of fog.

Brer Bear hollered, "Hallooooo!"

Aunt Nancy came out wearing a big black cloak and sat down on a pine stump. Her eyeballs sparkled red like they were on fire.

"Let me call the roll to be sure everybody is here," she said in a voice like chalk on a blackboard.

"Brer Wolf!"

"Here!"

"Brer Possum!"

"Here!"

Finally she got to the last one. "Brer Rabbit!"

Silence.

"Brer Rabbit!"

More silence.

"BRER RABBIT!!!!!"

Silence and more silence.

"Did Brer Rabbit send an excuse as to why he ain't here?" Aunt Nancy asked the creatures.

Brer Wolf said, "No, he didn't."

Brer Bear added, "He said to tell you howdy and he told us to tell you to shake hands with us and remember him in your dreams."

Aunt Nancy rolled her eyes and chomped her lips together. "Is that what he told you? Well, you tell him that if he'll come, I'll shake hands with him. Tell him that if he don't come, then I'll come and shake hands with him where he lives."

Brer Bear persisted. "Why won't you shake hands with us? You're hurting my feelings."

Aunt Nancy rolled her eyes again. She got up. But her cloak got caught on the tree stump and slipped off. The creatures looked. She was half woman and half spider, with seven arms and no hands. That's why her house looked like fog. It was a web.

The creatures got away from there as fast as their legs could take them.

When they got back and told Brer Rabbit what they had seen, he chuckled but didn't say a word.

That was the last time the animals went to see Aunt Nancy.

U.S. SLAVE STORY:
ALL GOD'S CHILLEN HAD WINGS

Geographically and culturally isolated from the mainland, the islands off the coast of Georgia and South Carolina are home to a group of African Americans called "Gullah," who retained African stories, rituals, intonations, common words, and even grammatical constructions well into the twentieth century. Many of their linguistic practices can be traced to Bantu, a family of languages found across central and southern Africa. In the early part of the twentieth century, Caesar Grant, a Gullah worker on John's Island off the coast of South Carolina, told a story of slaves making plans in a language not understood by their masters and escaping from a cruel slave driver by intoning an African word that allows them to fly away. A white novelist named John Bennett wrote Grant's story down, though he felt free to translate many of the teller's Gullah phrases into standard English. Bennett published the story in 1943, concerned that the grim and ghostly Gullah stories common in Charleston would vanish with the older generations who had lived under slavery.

Across the American South there were many versions of this legend of slaves who could fly. The great African American poet Langston Hughes (1902–1967) claimed that this story was important because it showed that there was more to slave folklore than humorous trickster tales. Later, the U.S. novelist Toni Morrison (b. 1931) shaped her novel *Song of Solomon* around this oral tradition. The image of flying slaves, she has said, "is everywhere—people used to talk about it, it's in the spirituals and gospels. Perhaps it was wishful thinking: escape, death, and all that. But suppose it wasn't. What might that mean?"

All God's Chillen Had Wings

Once all Africans could fly like birds; but owing to their many transgressions, their wings were taken away. There remained, here and there, in the sea islands and out-of-the-way places in the low country, some who had been overlooked, and had retained the power of flight, though they looked like other men.

There was a cruel master on one of the sea islands who worked his people till they died. When they died he bought others to take their places. These also he killed with overwork in the burning summer sun, through the middle hours of the day, although this was against the law.

One day, when all the worn-out Negroes were dead of overwork, he bought, of a broker in the town, a company of native Africans just brought into the country, and put them at once to work in the cottonfield.

He drove them hard. They went to work at sunrise and did not stop until dark. They were driven with unsparing harshness all day long, men, women and children. There was no pause for rest during the unendurable heat of the midsummer noon, though trees were plenty and near. But through the hardest hours, when fair plantations gave their Negroes rest, this man's driver pushed the work along without a moment's stop for breath, until all grew weak with heat and thirst.

There was among them one young woman who had lately borne a child. It was her first; she had not fully recovered from bearing, and should not have been sent to the field until her strength had come back. She had her child with her, as the other women had, astraddle on her hip, or piggyback.

The baby cried. She spoke to quiet it. The driver could not understand her words. She took her breast with her hand and threw it over her shoulder that the child might suck and be content. Then she went back to chopping knot-grass; but being very weak, and sick with the great heat, she stumbled, slipped and fell.

The driver struck her with his lash until she rose and staggered on.

She spoke to an old man near her, the oldest man of them all, tall and strong, with a forked beard. He replied; but the driver could not understand what they said; their talk was strange to him.

She returned to work; but in a little while she fell again. Again the driver lashed her until she got to her feet. Again she spoke to the old man. But he said: "Not yet, daughter; not yet." So she went on working, though she was very ill.

Soon she stumbled and fell again. But when the driver came running with his lash to drive her on with her work, she turned to the old man and asked: "Is it time yet, daddy?" He answered: "Yes, daughter; the time has come. Go; and peace be with you!". . . and stretched out his arms toward her . . . so.

With that she leaped straight up into the air and was gone like a bird, flying over field and wood.

The driver and overseer ran after her as far as the edge of the field; but she was gone, high over their heads, over the fence, and over the top of the woods, gone, with her baby astraddle of her hip, sucking at her breast.

Then the driver hurried the rest to make up for her loss; and the sun was very hot indeed. So hot that soon a man fell down. The overseer himself lashed him to his feet. As he got up from where he had fallen the old man called to him in an unknown tongue. My grandfather told me the words that he said; but it was a long time ago, and I have forgotten them. But when he had spoken, the man turned and laughed at the overseer, and leaped up into the air, and was gone, like a gull, flying over field and wood.

Soon another man fell. The driver lashed him. He turned to the old man. The old man cried out to him, and stretched out his arms as he had done for the other two; and he, like them, leaped up, and was gone through the air, flying like a bird over field and wood.

Then the overseer cried to the driver, and the master cried to them both: "Beat the old devil! He is the doer!"

The overseer and the driver ran at the old man with lashes ready; and the master ran too, with a picket pulled from the fence, to beat the life out of the old man who had made those Negroes fly.

But the old man laughed in their faces, and said something loudly to all the Negroes in the field, the new Negroes and the old Negroes.

And as he spoke to them they all remembered what they had forgotten, and recalled the power which once had been theirs. Then all the Negroes, old and new, stood up together; the old man raised his hands; and they all leaped up into the air with a great shout; and in a moment were gone, flying, like a flock of crows, over the field, over the fence, and over the top of the wood; and behind them flew the old man.

The men went clapping their hands; and the women went singing; and those who had children gave them their breasts; and the children laughed and sucked as their mothers flew, and were not afraid.

The master, the overseer, and the driver looked after them as they flew, beyond the wood, beyond the river, miles on miles, until they passed beyond the last rim of the world and disappeared in the sky like a handful of leaves. They were never seen again.

Where they went I do not know; I never was told. Nor what it was that the old man said . . . that I have forgotten. But as he went over the last fence he made a sign in the master's face, and cried "Kuli-ba! Kuli-ba!" I don't know what that means.

But if I could only find the old wood sawyer, he could tell you more; for he was there at the time, and saw the Africans fly away with their women and children. He is an old, old man, over ninety years of age, and remembers a great many strange things.

MALAGASY WISDOM POETRY

While many songs and stories that flourished in the nineteenth century focused on the realities of back-breaking labor, scarce resources, and the desire for freedom, not all oral traditions offered such grim fare. On the island of Madagascar, off the east coast of Africa, oral poetry conveyed traditional knowledge and explored the delights and torments of love. *Ohabolana*, the Malagasy word for wise proverbs, expresses cultural values and guides for living. There are *ohabolana* for a huge range of different emotions and circumstances. Widely respected as ancient and authoritative, these are typically brief and rhythmic, which means that they can be easily remembered and transmitted. *Hainteny*, or Malagasy wisdom poetry, deals mostly with love, including initial attraction, the joy of union, jealousy, feelings of abandonment, and bitter blame. Despite the patriarchal social structure, Malagasy women are comparatively free, and love poetry can be spoken by a man or a woman. Some are dialogues, spoken by two sparring parties as in a contest. Much of the complexity of *hainteny* does not translate: poems about thunder may include words that sound thunderous, for example, and double meanings are common in the original. But the selection included here gives a sense of the wit, profundity, and compact poetic structure characteristic of the Malagasy oral tradition.

Both *ohabolana* and *hainteny* are traditions that belonged originally to the Merina people, a group who arrived on Madagascar from the Malay-Indonesian archipelago in the fifteenth century. Despite many waves of migration from East Africa, Indonesia, and India, this large island shares the Malagasy language and many Malagasy cultural institutions and traditions. The culture remained predominantly oral until 1850. Much of the traditional poetry and prose has been recorded, but some is irretrievably lost, in part thanks to Protestant missionaries in the nineteenth century who excised and distorted a great deal as they transcribed. "I have . . . thought it necessary to cut out anything that might be considered 'dirty,'" wrote a Norwegian missionary in 1877, "which has thus reduced the collection very considerably." (Since Malagasy people accept sex before marriage, their own cultural expectations and those of Christian missionaries often came into conflict.) The selections included here were transcribed by the French writer Jean Paulhan (1884–1968), who worked as a teacher in Madagascar between 1908 and 1910. His translations of Malagasy oral poetry inspired the surrealist French poets Guillaume Apollinaire (1880–1918) and Paul Éluard (1895–1952).

Ohabolana

Life is like the aroma of a cooking-pot:
when it is uncovered, it escapes [i.e., departs].

God is not the property of one person alone.

Death is not a condemnation,
but part of a tax.

I hate the passage of time,
for it causes beauty to pass.

Man falls no lower than his knees.

Sometimes she is like spilled coral
and sometimes like a startled swarm of beetles.

Justice is like a fire:
if it is covered, it burns [you].

Justice resembles a dream:
it cannot be acquired except in bed;
and it is like a straight tree:
it cannot be found except in the forest.

Hainteny

I love you.
- And how do you love me?
- I love you as I love money.
- Then you do not love me,

for if you are hungry, you will exchange me for food.
- I love you as I love the door.
- Then you do not love me:
it is surely loved, but it is pushed continually.
- I love you as I love the *lambamena*.[1]
- Then you do not love me,
for we will be united only in death.
- I love you as I love the *voatavo*:[2]
fresh, I eat you;
dry, I make you into a cup;
broken, I fashion you into a *valiha*[3] bridge:
I will play there along the edge of the road.

————————

How, then, do you love me?
- I love you as I love rice.
- Then you do not love me,
for you will make a meal of me when you are hungry.
How, then, do you love me?
- I love you as I love water.
- Then you do not love me,
for you will make your love follow your sweat.
How, then, do you love me?
- I love you as I love my *lamba*.[4]
- Then you do not love me,
for if you are in debt, you will exchange me
and no longer remember me.
How, then, do you love me?
- I love you as I love honey.
- Then you do not love me,
for there are still dregs that you remove.
How, then, do you love me?
- I love you as I love the ruling prince.
- Then you truly love me.
- His passage inspires awe,
his glance causes me shame.
- You truly love me, then;
my desires are fulfilled,
my searching is complete.
- I love you as I love my father and mother:
alive in the same house,
dead in the same wood.

————————

1. Shroud.
2. Gourd or pumpkin.
3. A zither made of bamboo.
4. Traditional shawl.

I am a friendless child
who plays alone with the dust,
a chick that has fallen into a ditch:
if it calls out, its voice is small;
if it flies, its wings are weak;
if it waits, it fears the savage cat.
Do not make our love a love of stones:
broken, they cannot be joined.
But make it a love of lips:
although angry, they approach each other.

What does blame resemble?
It resembles the wind:
I have heard its name, but I have not seen its face.
But what does blame resemble?
It is not heaped up like the clouds;
it does not lie on its back like the hills;
it is not the passing man, to whom is said, "Enter the house;"
it is not the visitor, to whom is said, "Return;"
it is not the seated man, to whom is said, "May I pass?"
But it resembles the slippery path:
he who is not careful falls.
A rock at the side of the road:
he who does not see it trips.
A deep abyss:
he who looks at it becomes dizzy
and it kills him when he falls.
Like the freezing cold:
unseen, it numbs.
May it be removed!
Removed in the morning, may it have no meal!
Removed in the evening, may it have no bed!
Removed in the summer, may the floods take it!
Removed in the winter, may it be burned with the grass!
Above, let it not press down;
below, let it not be revived;
on two sides, let it not crush;
in front, let it not be able to stop;
behind, let it not be able to pursue!

NAVAJO CEREMONY: THE NIGHT CHANT

Navajo ceremonialism ranks among the glories of native American achievement. Directed primarily toward restoring a harmony between individuals and the environment, the ceremonies called Nightway, Mountainway, Beautyway, Enemyway, and Blessingway—to name only a few of the best known—create a spiritual universe of song, prayer, drama, and graphic art. These are healing ceremonies that have proven their therapeutic power and earned the respect of Western medicine. In fact, they cross the boundaries of art, religion, and science. Their shared quest for *beauty*—a broad term that includes perfection, normality, success, and well-being—reflects a central value of Navajo culture, located mostly in the southwestern United States, in Arizona and New Mexico.

With its induction of new initiates, its unique all-night sing, and its lofty portrayal of deities, the famous Nightway chant occupies a place of honor among these "ways." Its nineteenth-century translator, Washington Matthews, a U.S. army surgeon posted to New Mexico, called it by the name "Night Chant." Although a large audience of relatives, friends, and visitors usually attend the Nightway ceremony, a single person is its focus. Each of the Navajo ceremonials is said to be effective against a particular group of illnesses, and the Night Chant heals strokes and other disorders of the brain. It remains in huge demand every year. But the value of the ceremony also goes beyond the task of healing one person: the host who sponsors it gains prestige, and it provides opportunities for broader cultural reaffirmation, socializing, and spiritual renewal.

Performed in only fall or winter, the Night Chant falls into two four-day parts, followed by a climactic ninth-night reprise, the night of nights, in which the ceremonial leader, or chanter, summons the long-awaited spirit of thunder. At this point the ceremony breaks free in a torrent of song that continues unabated until dawn. In the first part the emphasis is on rites that exorcise evil influences and invoke the distant gods. The second part is distinguished by spacious and intricate sand paintings made of dry pigments sprinkled on the earth. The paintings depict the gods and allow the sick to take on some divine invulnerability. Through it all, the ceremonial leader directs the song recitals and intones the prescribed prayers. The two selections included here are the prayer to thunder that begins the final night and the last of the Finishing Songs that bring it to a close.

From The Night Chant[1]

Prayer to Thunder[2]

* * *

In Tsegíhi,[3]
In the house made of the dawn,
In the house made of the evening twilight,

1. Translated by Washington Matthews.
2. In performance each line is first recited by the chanter, then repeated by the patient.

3. Pronounced *tsay-gee'-hee*, a distant canyon and site of the *house made of the dawn* (line 2), a prehistoric ruin, regarded as the home of deities.

In the house made of the dark cloud,
In the house made of the he-rain,
In the house made of the dark mist,
In the house made of the she-rain,[4]
In the house made of pollen,[5]
In the house made of grasshoppers,
Where the dark mist curtains the doorway,
The path to which is on the rainbow,
Where the zigzag lightning stands high on top,
Where the he-rain stands high on top,
Oh, male divinity![6]
With your moccasins of dark cloud, come to us.
With your leggings of dark cloud, come to us.
With your shirt of dark cloud, come to us.
With your headdress of dark cloud, come to us.
With your mind enveloped in dark cloud, come to us.
With the dark thunder above you, come to us soaring.
With the shapen cloud at your feet, come to us soaring.
With the far darkness made of the dark cloud
   over your head, come to us soaring.
With the far darkness made of the he-rain
   over your head, come to us soaring.
With the far darkness made of the dark mist
   over your head, come to us soaring.
With the far darkness made of the she-rain
   over your head, come to us soaring.
With the zigzag lightning flung out on high
   over your head, come to us soaring.
With the rainbow hanging high over your head,
   come to us soaring.
With the far darkness made of the dark cloud on
   the ends of your wings, come to us soaring.
With the far darkness made of the he-rain on
   the ends of your wings, come to us soaring.
With the far darkness made of the dark mist
   on the ends of your wings, come to us soaring.
With the far darkness made of the she-rain
   on the ends of your wings, come to us soaring.
With the zigzag lightning flung out on high
   on the ends of your wings, come to us soaring.
With the rainbow hanging high on the ends of
   your wings, come to us soaring.
With the near darkness made of the dark cloud, of
   the he-rain, of the dark mist, and of the
   she-rain, come to us.
With the darkness on the earth, come to us.

5

10

15

20

25

30

35

---

4. Rain without thunder. "He-rain": rain with thunder.

5. Emblem of peace, of happiness, of prosperity [translator's note].

6. Thunder, regarded as a bird.

With these I wish the foam floating on the flowing
    water over the roots of the great corn.
I have made your sacrifice.
I have prepared a smoke[7] for you.
My feet restore for me.
My limbs restore for me.   40
My body restore for me.
My mind restore for me.
My voice restore for me.
Today, take out your spell for me.
Today, take away your spell for me.   45
Away from me you have taken it.
Far off from me it is taken.
Far off you have done it.
Happily I recover.
Happily my interior becomes cool.   50
Happily my eyes regain their power.
Happily my head becomes cool.
Happily my limbs regain their power.
Happily I hear again.
Happily for me *the spell*[8] is taken off.   55
Happily may I walk.
Impervious to pain, may I walk.
Feeling light within, may I walk.
With lively feelings, may I walk.
Happily abundant dark clouds I desire.   60
Happily abundant dark mists I desire.
Happily abundant passing showers I desire.
Happily an abundance of vegetation I desire.
Happily an abundance of pollen I desire.
Happily abundant dew I desire.   65
Happily may fair white corn, to the ends of the
    earth, come with you.
Happily may fair yellow corn, to the ends of the
    earth, come with you.
Happily may fair blue corn, to the ends of the
    earth, come with you.
Happily may fair corn of all kinds, to the ends
    of the earth, come with you.
Happily may fair plants of all kinds, to the ends
    of the earth, come with you.   70
Happily may fair goods of all kinds, to the ends
    of the earth, come with you.
Happily may fair jewels of all kinds, to the ends
    of the earth, come with you.
With these before you, happily may they come with you.
With these behind you, happily may they come with you.
With these below you, happily may they come with you.   75

7. Painted reed filled with native tobacco,   8. Words added by the translator.
offered as a sacrifice.

With these above you, happily may they come with you.
With these all around you, happily may they come with you.
Thus happily you accomplish your tasks.
Happily the old men will regard you.
Happily the old women will regard you.   80
Happily the young men will regard you.
Happily the young women will regard you.
Happily the boys will regard you.
Happily the girls will regard you.
Happily the children will regard you.   85
Happily the chiefs will regard you.
Happily, as they scatter in different directions,
    they will regard you.
Happily, as they approach their homes, they will
    regard you.
Happily may their roads home be on the trail of pollen.
Happily may they all get back.   90
In beauty I walk.
With beauty before me, I walk.
With beauty behind me, I walk.
With beauty below me, I walk.
With beauty above me, I walk.   95
With beauty all around me, I walk.
It is finished in beauty,
It is finished in beauty,
It is finished in beauty,
It is finished in beauty.   100

Finishing Song

From the pond in the white valley—
The young man doubts it—
He takes up his sacrifice,
With that he now heals.
With that your kindred thank you now.   5

From the pools in the green meadow[9]—
The young woman doubts it—
He takes up his sacrifice,[1]
With that he now heals.
With that your kindred thank you now.   10

9. A contrast of landscapes, of the beginning and end of a stream. It rises in a green valley in the mountains and flows down to the lower plains, where it spreads into a single sheet of water. As the dry season approaches, it shrinks, leaving a white saline efflorescence called alkali. The male is associated with the sterile, unattractive alkali flat in the first stanza, while the female is named with the pleasant moun-tain meadow in the second stanza [adapted from translator's note].
1. The deity accepts the sacrificial offering (see p. 1000, n. 7) and effects the healing that benefits the patient and his kindred—though young men and young women, with the irrev-erence of youth, may doubt the truth of the ceremony.

VI

Modernity
and Modernism,
1900–1945

A t the beginning of the twentieth century, the
world was interconnected as never before. New means of transportation, such as
the steamship, the railroad, the automobile, and the
airplane, allowed people in the industrialized West
to cover vast distances quickly. Other technologies,
such as the telegraph and the telephone, allowed
them to communicate instantaneously. In the decades to come, such inventions, powered either by
electricity or by the internal combustion engine,
along with improvements in agriculture, nutrition,
public health, and medical care, would foster remarkable growth in human health and material
prosperity. Infant mortality declined and world population more than tripled, from under two billion to
around six billion. In unprecedented numbers, people were living in large cities; correspondingly, the
experience of urban life is one of the major themes
of twentieth-century literature. Together, these vast
transformations in human experience can be characterized as *modernization*.

Yet the technological advances that undeniably
improved human life led, as well, to the production
of weapons that were increasingly effective, and
therefore increasingly destructive. As distant parts of
the globe grew closer through trade, immigration,

"Books!" (1925), a promotional poster by the Russian artist
Alexander Rodchenko (1891–1956).

and communications, they often came into deadly conflict. Indeed, the twentieth century was the bloodiest in human history: as many as 200 million died in wars, revolutions, genocides, and related famines. In response to the century's horrors, the old dream of a unified, peaceful world became ever more appealing; and to many, in the splendid light of new technologies and optimistic ideas of progress, it even seemed achievable as never before. Frequently, those who sought to end war looked to supranational bodies, such as the League of Nations, the United Nations, the European Community (later the European Union), the Organization of American States, and the Organization for African Unity, as the future guarantors of "peaceful coexistence," a term that gained currency during the Cold War to refer to the arms race between the United States and the Soviet Union.

A caricature of Cecil John Rhodes, perhaps the most famous supporter of British colonialism and imperialism in the late nineteenth century, here straddling the continent of Africa. The wires in his hands are telegraph cables. The cartoon was drawn soon after Rhodes announced his intention to connect Cape Town, South Africa, with Cairo, Egypt, by telegraph and rail.

MODERNITY AND CONFLICT IN WORLD HISTORY, 1900–1945

As Europe and North America became industrialized over the course of the nineteenth century, they extended their political power to cover most of the globe. By 1900, after centuries of European expansion, there were no longer, in the words of **Joseph Conrad's Heart of Darkness**, any "blank spaces" on the map. Within a few years, explorers would even reach the North and South Poles. At the 1884 Berlin Conference, the European powers had carved up Africa among themselves; they also controlled most of southern Asia. The remaining independent nations in the Americas and the antipodes maintained close ties with their former colonial masters—Britain, Spain, France, Portugal, and the Netherlands. The small kingdom of Belgium and the recently unified nations of Germany and Italy sought to acquire overseas empires of their own. The British Empire was still at its zenith, and since Britain retained colonial possessions in all parts of the world, it was known as "the empire on which the sun never sets."

Yet as the twentieth century advanced, the sun did set on the British Empire— and on every other European empire as well. During the first half of the century, the world system that the European powers dominated experienced massive crises in the forms of two world wars, the Russian Revolution, the Great Depression, and the Holocaust. These upheavals became central concerns for the literature of the period and contributed to a rethinking of traditional literary forms and techniques.

The First World War (1914–18) took place mainly in Europe; it was the most mechanized war to date and killed some 15 million people. Much of the war on the Western Front (in Belgium and France) was characterized by stale-

Emmeline Pankhurst, a leading British suffragette, is shown here speaking in the early 1920s, several years after passage of the 1918 Representation of the People Act, which acknowledged the right of women over thirty to vote. In the 1920s, Pankhurst devoted herself to speaking out against Bolshevism and in favor of British imperialism.

mate, as each side ferociously defended entrenched positions with machine guns, resulting in massive battles over tiny slices of territory, as at Ypres, Vimy Ridge, and Verdun. It was only after the United States joined the war, in 1917, that the Allies (France, Britain and its colonies, Italy, and the United States) gained the initiative and were able to repel Germany.

In the East, Germany and Austria-Hungary drove deep into Russian territory. Russia's near-defeat contributed to the revolution of 1917, in which the Bolsheviks under V. I. Lenin sought to establish a Communist "dictatorship of the proletariat," with a tiny vanguard of party members taking power in the name of the working classes. During the succeeding decades, forced collectivization of agriculture and enterprise (which led to widespread famine), as well as purges of people considered enemies of the Communist Party (especially under Lenin's successor, Joseph Stalin), caused tens of millions of deaths, both in Russia and in other former territories of the Russian Empire,

such as the Ukraine. (They were united under the Communist regime of the Soviet Union.) The Communist movement, initially supportive of some literary experiments, increasingly restricted the scope of acceptable artistic expression in the countries where it gained control. In response, a dissident literature developed, published abroad or in informal, private editions that could circulate without being censored. Writers such as **Anna Akhmatova** and **Alexander Solzhenitsyn** had to work within these constraints.

The Treaty of Versailles (1919) formalized the end of the war, and of four great empires—the German, Austro-Hungarian, Russian, and Ottoman—dividing most of Central and Eastern Europe into a multitude of smaller nations (some of which would later be reabsorbed by the resurgent Soviet Union and Nazi Germany). The treaty also founded the first of the great international organizations, the League of Nations—which, despite its idealistic beginnings, proved incapable of enforcing the demilitarization of Germany.

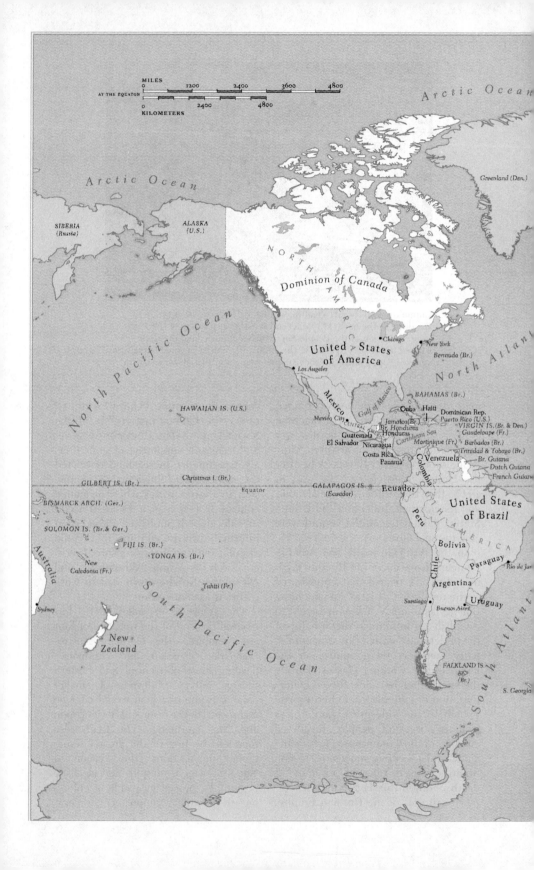

THE WORLD
1913

The British Empire

Spitsbergen (Nor.)

Arctic Ocean

Iceland (Den.)

SIBERIA

Russian Empire

Sweden
Norway
St. Petersburg
Moscow

MONGOLIA   MANCHURIA

Great
Britain
Dublin
London
Netherlands
Denmark
Germany
Berlin Warsaw
Belgium Lux.
Paris
Switz. Vienna Austro-
France Venice Hungary
Portugal
Madrid Rome Italy
Spain
AZORES (Port.)
Gibraltar (Br.)
Madeira (Port.)
Morocco
Algeria Tunisia
Malta (Br.)
Mediterranean
Libya
(It.)

Chinese Republic

Peking
(Beijing)
Wethaiwei (Br.)
Korea
(Jap.)
Seoul
Tokyo
Japan

Shanghai

Serbia Romania
Alb. Greece
Bulgaria Black Sea
Mont.
Istanbul
Ottoman Empire
Cyprus (Br.) Beirut
Alexandria Jerusalem
Persia
Afghanistan
TIBET
New
Delhi Nepal Bhutan
British India
Bombay
(Mumbai)
Burma
Hanoi
Okinawa (Japan)
Formosa (Jap.)
Hong Kong (Br.)
Macao (Port.)
Hainan
PHILIPPINES (U.S.)

CANARIES (Sp.)
Rio de Oro (Sp.)
Cape Verde (Port.)
French West Africa
Gambia
Portuguese Guinea
Sierra
Leone
Liberia
Togoland
(Ger.)
Gold
Coast
Nigeria
Ibadan
Cameroon
(Ger.)
Sp. Guinea
Fr. Congo

Cairo
Egypt
Red Sea
Bahrein (Br.)
Arabia
Aden
Oman
Arabian Sea
Bay of Bengal
Siam
French Indochina
Br. N. Borneo
Sarawak
Brunei
Malay
States

C
A
Anglo-
Egyptian
Sudan
Eritrea
(It.)
Fr. Somaliland
Socotra I. (Br.)
British Somaliland
Abyssinia
Italian Somaliland
Uganda
B. E. Africa
Kenya
Nairobi
ANDAMAN IS.
(Br.)
LACCADIVES (Br.)
Ceylon
MALDIVES (Br.) Equator
Dutch East Indies
NEW
GUINEA
Papua

Ascension I. (Br.)
Kabinda
(Port.)
Belgian
Congo
German E. Africa
Nyasaland
Zanzibar (Br.)
SEYCHELLES (Br.)
CHAGOS ARCH. (Br.)
COCOS IS. (Br.)
Christmas I. (Br.)

St. Helena I. (Br.)
Angola
(Port.)
Rhodesia
Mozambique (Port.)
Ger. S.W. Africa
Walvis Bay (Br.)
Bechuanaland
Johannesburg
Swaziland
Union of
South Africa
Basutoland
Mauritius (Br.)
Réunion (Fr.)
Madagascar (Fr.)

Ocean

Tristan da Cunha I. (Br.)

Indian Ocean

Commonwealth
of
Australia

TASMANIA

Kerguélen I. (Fr.)

ANTARCTICA

Making matters worse, the Allies' demand for huge reparations contributed to the economic chaos in Germany that, in turn, furthered the cause of the National Socialists (Nazis). The party came to power under Adolf Hitler in 1933 with a program of national rearmament and authoritarian politics held together by the glue of anti-Semitism. The Nazis were unremittingly hostile to modern literature, and writers such as **Thomas Mann** and Bertolt Brecht went into exile.

Beginning on October 24, 1929, the liberal capitalist world also experienced financial disaster, with the stock market crash that heralded the Great Depression. Within a few years, a third of American workers were unemployed; hunger and joblessness spread throughout the industrialized world. Despite fears that radical parties like the Communists or the Nazis would emerge from the economic devastation in the United States, Franklin D. Roosevelt (president from 1933 to 1945) was able to reverse the worst effects of the Depression with the New Deal, which included public works spending and the introduction of Social Security and other forms of protection for the elderly and the unemployed. "The only thing we have to fear," the president told an anxious public, "is fear itself."

Germany annexed Austria and invaded Czechoslovakia in 1938. After Hitler's military forces invaded Poland in 1939, the Second World War began, with Germany rapidly conquering most of continental Europe. France fell in 1940, and the following year Germany invaded the Soviet Union. Germany allied itself with both Fascist Italy and authoritarian Japan, which had earlier conquered Korea and occupied China. The United States entered the war after the surprise Japanese attack on Pearl Harbor, Hawaii, on December 7, 1941. It took almost three years for the Allies to find a foothold in Western Europe;

In November 1940, the Nazis closed off a portion of Warsaw, Poland, and designated it a Jewish ghetto—essentially condemning 400,000 people to an urban prison. Predictably, nearly 100,000 of the people in the ghetto died of disease and starvation over the next year and a half. Among those trapped behind the wall were these two children, begging for food.

during that time, the most intense battles took place in the Soviet Union.

Once Germany controlled much of Eastern Europe, Hitler, who had enforced anti-Semitic policies and encouraged persecution of the Jews on such occasions as *Kristallnacht,* or the Night of Broken Glass (on November 9, 1938), took even more extreme measures. His troops massacred large numbers of Jews (and also Poles) between 1939 and 1941, while others were either forced into ghettos or transported to concentration camps. Starting in 1941, Hitler authorized the so-called Final Solution, aimed at destroying the Jewish people. In the end, his death squads and camps would exterminate six million Jews (more than half the Jewish population of Europe), as well as several million Poles, Gypsies, homosexuals, and political enemies of the Nazis.

The war in Europe ended when the Soviets entered Berlin in May 1945; Hitler had committed suicide the previous month. Fighting still raged in the

Pacific, and the United States dropped atomic bombs on Hiroshima and on Nagasaki, obliterating those Japanese cities and starting the nuclear age. The cessation of the global hostilities, which had resulted in some sixty million deaths, took place on August 14, 1945. The return to peacetime brought much relief, but also the sense that a new era of conflict was at hand. The wartime British prime minister Winston Churchill spoke of an "iron curtain" that had "descended across the Continent." The aftermath of the Second World War led quickly to the Cold War, in which most nations aligned themselves with either the capitalist West or the Communist East.

MODERNISM IN WORLD LITERATURE

Writers around the world responded to these cataclysmic events with an unprecedented wave of literary experimentation, known collectively as *modernism*, which linked the political crises with a crisis of representation—a sense that the old ways of portraying the human experience were no longer adequate. The modernists therefore broke away from such conventions as standard plots, verse forms, narrative techniques, and the boundaries of genre. They often grouped themselves in avant-garde movements with names like futurism, Dadaism, and surrealism, seeing their literary experiments in the context of a broader search for a type of society to replace the broken prewar consensus.

The modernist crisis of representation also reflected a broader "crisis of reason" that had begun in Europe in the late nineteenth century, as radical thinkers challenged the ability of human reason to understand the world. In the wake of Charles Darwin's discovery of the process of natural selection, human beings could no longer be so easily distinguished from the other animals; the animal nature of human existence was a crucial concept to three thinkers from the nineteenth century who wielded significant influence in the twentieth. Karl Marx saw the struggle between social classes for control of the means of economic production as the motor force of history; his thought inspired the Communist revolutions in Russia and China during the twentieth century and also the more moderate Socialist and Communist Parties of Western Europe. Friedrich Nietzsche attacked both a belief in God and the conviction that humans are fundamentally rational. His emphasis on the variety of perspectives from which we shape our notions of truth would have a substantial affect on both modernists and post-modernists. Sigmund Freud published the first major work of psychoanalysis, *The Interpretation of Dreams*, in 1900. His exploration of the unconscious, the power of sexual and destructive instincts, the shaping force of early childhood, and the Oedipal conflict between fathers and sons led many writers to reimagine the wellsprings of family interactions. More specifically, Freud's stress on the hidden, or "latent," meanings contained in dreams, jokes, and slips of the tongue lent itself to creative wordplay.

The title of this work by the Belgian painter René Magritte (1898–1967), *La Trahison des Images* (1929), translates as *The Treason of Images*. "Ceci n'est pas une pipe" means "This is not a pipe."

Although Pablo Picasso's *Guernica* (1937) memorializes a historical event—the bombing of Guernica, in the Basque region of Spain, in April 1937, during the Spanish Civil War—the painting stresses the psychological horror, rather than the physical appearance, of the event.

While philosophers and psychologists were examining the dynamics of the human mind, scientists found that the natural world does not necessarily function in the way it appears to. The most famous of the scientific discoveries of the early twentieth century was Albert Einstein's theory of relativity (Special Theory, 1905; General Theory, 1915). Other discoveries around the turn of the century, such as radioactivity, X-rays, and quantum theory, presented counterintuitive understandings of the physical universe that conflicted with classical Newtonian physics and even with common sense.

Modernism began in Europe and can be traced both to these new currents of thought and to the experimental literature of the late nineteenth century, including the symbolist poets and the realist novelists. Like such symbolists as **Charles Baudelaire** and Stéphane Mallarmé, the modernist poets held a high conception of the power and significance of poetry. In their works, they often drew on symbolist techniques, such as ambiguous and esoteric meanings. **T. S. Eliot's** *The Waste Land* (1922) responded to the prevalent sense of devastation after the First World War and was seen at the

time as the high-water mark of modernism in the English language.

Modernist fiction followed the realists, especially **Gustave Flaubert**, in attempting to portray life "as it is" by using precise language. Modernists found, however, that in depicting characters, settings, and events with directness and without sentiment, they discovered mysteries that lay beyond language. The great modern novelists, including Conrad, **Marcel Proust**, Thomas Mann, **James Joyce**, and **Virginia Woolf**, all started out by writing realistic works in the manner of Flaubert or **Leo Tolstoy**. The great difference, which became more apparent as the modernists reached maturity, was that the realists tended to balance their attention between the objective, outside world and the inner world of their characters, whereas the modernists shifted the balance toward interiority. Thus, rather than offer objective descriptions of the outside world, they increasingly focused on the more limited perspective of an individual, often idiosyncratic, character. In this approach they were following the lead of another great nineteenth-century precursor, **Fyodor Dostoyevsky**.

Bertolt Brecht and Kurt Weill's *The Threepenny Opera*, staged at the Kammer (Chamber) Theater, Moscow, in 1930.

It would be too simple to say that the modernists did away with the omniscient narrator. They might retain a narrator who seemed to be observing the characters and events with an objective, all-knowing eye, but the authors counterbalanced such narrators with storytellers like Conrad's Marlow or Proust's Marcel, who were themselves characters in the stories they related and whose reliability might therefore be in doubt. Joyce's story **"The Dead,"** with its narrator who sees into the mind of the protagonist Gabriel Conroy, could easily belong to the nineteenth century, but Joyce later pioneered the move toward a deeper interiority in two novels, *A Portrait of the Artist as a Young Man* (1916) and *Ulysses* (1922)—the latter is, in fact, the most famous and influential of all modernist novels. The new method, called "the stream of consciousness," was well described by another of its great practitioners, Woolf, when she wrote: "Let us record the atoms as they fall upon the mind in the order in which they fall, let us trace the pattern, however disconnected and incoherent in

appearance, which each sight or incident scores upon the consciousness."

A similar, possibly even farther-reaching transformation took place in the theater. Just as novelists questioned the role of an omniscient narrator, dramatists challenged the separation of the audience from the action of the play—specifically, the tradition of the "fourth wall." According to this concept, developed in realist and naturalist theater of the nineteenth century, the actors on stage went about their business as if they did not know that an audience was watching them. In different ways, the major modernist playwrights, represented in this section by **Luigi Pirandello**, broke down the fourth wall. Pirandello introduced a playful "metatheater," calling attention to the fictionality of his works by having his characters debate the nature of drama. In Bertolt Brecht's Epic Theater, audience members were encouraged not to identify with the characters and be carried away by the drama but to think critically about the actions they were witnessing. The German writer's notion of an "estrangement effect" that would shock audiences out of their complacency was linked closely to broader modernist theories in which the task of art was to break through our habitual assumptions to make the world appear strange and new.

Many of these modernist experiments took place on the level of form; but modernism also entailed a change in the content of literature, specifically in the inclusion of previously taboo subject matter (especially sexuality), as well as greater attention to shifting social roles (often relating to the impact of feminism). Woolf was famous both as a novelist and as an essayist on feminist issues. Her work *A Room of One's Own* makes the case for women's writing and, more broadly, for women's admission into traditionally male professions and institutions of learning, which were gradually becoming more open to women during the first decades of the century. Feminism had won a major victory with the achievement of women's suffrage in 1918 in Britain; the United States would guarantee all women the vote in 1920. Conrad's novel *Heart of Darkness* criticizes the actions of European imperialists in Africa, although he seems to make an exception for the British Empire. Joyce addresses the political situation of Ireland in the midst of its quest for independence from Britain. **Franz Kafka's** work has been seen as a commentary on the status of the Jews in a hostile world. Mann addresses homosexuality, which was becoming socially acceptable even though it remained illegal in many countries. Even the seemingly most intimate of works, Proust's **Swann's Way**, documents the social changes that France was undergoing in the late nineteenth century. (In subsequent volumes of his masterpiece, *Remembrance of Things Past*, Proust also treats both anti-Semitism and homosexuality at length.) In their later works, Mann and Proust were conscious of reconstructing the bygone Europe of the years before the First World War.

Modernist experimentation persisted in various forms throughout the century. Somewhat younger than the European novelists represented here, **Jorge Luis Borges** wrote short pieces that present alternative universes; in "**The Garden of Forking Paths**," the fictional universe he creates starts out as a commentary on a work of history. Whereas Pirandello's play with theatricality came to be known as "metatheater," Borges's games with the border between fact and fiction have been called "metafiction" or even "metahistory." Borges is also representative of the mobility of writers in the twentieth century: educated mostly in Europe, he returned home to Argentina and formed a bridge between European modernism and the significant expansion of Latin American fiction in the second half of the century.

Asian writers followed European and American developments with interest and typically responded in one of three ways. Some embraced modern Western themes and styles; others, while drawing on nineteenth-century European realist forms, tended to blend them with more traditional Asian subject matter or linguistic styles. Finally, a substantial number of Asian writers embraced Communist or Socialist politics and a related style of politically engaged fiction. Often, a single writer would combine more than one of these responses. For example, in Japan, **Akutagawa Ryūnosuke** draws on techniques of European modernism but also mines old Japanese tales for material. In China, **Lu Xun** combines modernist techniques with a more satirical attitude to contemporary Chinese society.

In other parts of the world, nationalist movements against colonization were gathering force and would result in a wave of independence after the Second

A self-portrait, circa 1939, of Tsuguharu Foujita (1886–1968), a Tokyo-born artist who applied traditional Japanese printing, painting, and coloring techniques to works that were otherwise modernist in style.

World War. The African American writer and activist W. E. B. Du Bois had said early in the century that "the problem of the Twentieth Century is the problem of the color line." Literature played a major role both in the articulation of this challenge and in the attempts to solve it. During the 1920s, when, in the words of Langston Hughes, "Harlem was in vogue," a group of African American intellectuals and writers enjoyed unprecedented success in what came to be known as the Harlem Renaissance. During the 1930s, a group

of African and Caribbean intellectuals, led by **Léopold Sédar Senghor** and Aimé Césaire, met in Paris, where they had come to pursue higher education, and formed the Négritude movement. It would celebrate the culture of Africa and the African diaspora and provide intellectual support and political leadership for decolonization movements after the war.

These developments pointed the way to a postwar and postcolonial literature that often rejected the formal experiments of the modernist generation and sought a more direct engagement with the pressing political issues of the day, such as decolonization, civil rights, and economic empowerment. The Holocaust also presented a distinct challenge to writers who sought to record the unspeakable: some took a straightforward, documentary style, while others turned to a minimalist, almost mystical language. While Europe, after 1945, set about rebuilding the cities destroyed in the war, much of the rest of the world entered a period of decolonization, establishing nation-states on the basis of the principles (democracy, equality) that the Allies had defended during the war and that they now had to acknowledge as the basis for their colonies' self-determination. The postwar world would inspire both avant-garde literary movements and a return to more traditional forms, but the literature of the twentieth century had been decisively marked by the experiments of the modernists, who created a diverse, remarkable range of masterpieces during a period of continual social crisis.

JOSEPH CONRAD
1857–1924

Born in Polish Ukraine, learning English at twenty-one, and then serving as a sailor for sixteen years, Joseph Conrad nonetheless became a prolific, innovative writer of English fiction. Works like *Heart of Darkness* and *Lord Jim* have influenced novelists throughout the twentieth century, because of Conrad's ability to evoke the feel and color of distant places as well as the complexity of human responses to moral crisis. Conrad's sense of separation and exile, his yearning for the kinship and solidarity of humanity, permeates these works, along with the despairing vision of a universe in which even the most ardent idealist finds no ultimate meaning or moral value.

He was born Jozef Teodor Konrad Korzeniowski on December 3, 1857, the only child of Polish patriots who were involved in resistance to Russian rule. (He changed his name to the more English-sounding Conrad for the publication of his first novel, in 1895.) Their country had been partitioned through most of the nineteenth century among Russia, Prussia, and Austria. The town where Conrad was born, now part of Ukraine, had traditionally been ruled by the Polish aristocracy, and Conrad's family bore a coat of arms. When his father was condemned for conspiracy in 1862, the family went into exile in northern Russia, where Conrad's mother died three years later from tuberculosis. Conrad's father, a poet and a translator, supported the small family by translating Shakespeare and Victor Hugo; Conrad himself read English novels by William Makepeace Thackeray, Walter Scott, and Charles Dickens in Polish and in French translation. When his father,

too, succumbed to tuberculosis in 1869, the eleven-year-old orphan went to live with his maternal uncle, Tadeusz Bobrowski, who sent him to school in Cracow (in Austrian-ruled Poland) and Switzerland. Bobrowski supported his orphaned nephew both financially and emotionally, and, when Conrad asked to fulfill a long-standing dream of going to sea, he gave him an annual allowance (which Conrad consistently overspent) and helped him find a berth in the merchant marine. The decision to go to sea reflected the gallant and romantic aspirations of a child who had often been frail and sickly; it also marked a permanent departure from the nation that his parents had fought and, as Conrad saw it, died for.

During the next few years, he worked on French ships, traveling to the West Indies and participating in various activities—some of which, such as smuggling, were probably illegal—that would play a role in his novels of the sea. He also lost money at the casino in Monte Carlo, may have had an unhappy romance, and attempted suicide. Many events of these years are known only through the fictionalized versions Conrad used in short stories written years later. After signing onto a British ship in 1878 to avoid conscription by the French or the Russians (he had just turned twenty-one), Conrad visited England for the first time, speaking the language only haltingly. He served for sixteen years on British merchant ships, earning his Master's Certificate in 1886 (the same year that he became a British subject) and learning English fast and well. During this period, he made trips to the Far East and India that would provide material for his fiction throughout his writing career, including major works like The Nigger of the "Narcissus" (1897) and Typhoon (1903). When he married in 1896, he turned his back on the sea as a profession and, buoyed by the publication of his first novel, Almayer's Folly (1895), chose writing as his new career. His early novels, including An Outcast of the Islands (1896), established his initial literary reputation as an exotic storyteller and novelist of adventure at sea.

Among the many voyages that furnished material for his fiction, one stands out as the most emotional and intense: the trip up the Congo River that Conrad made in 1890, straight into the heart of King Leopold II's privately owned Congo Free State. Like many nineteenth-century explorers, Conrad was fascinated by the mystery of this "dark" (because uncharted by Europeans) continent, and he persuaded a relative to find him a job as pilot on a Belgian merchant steamer. The steamer that Conrad was supposed to pilot had been damaged, and while he waited for a replacement, his supervisors shifted him to another where he could help out and learn about the river. The boat traveled upstream to collect a seriously ill trader, Georges Antoine Klein (who died on the return trip), and Conrad, after speaking with Klein and observing the inhuman conditions imposed by slave labor and the ruthless search for ivory, returned seriously ill and traumatized by his journey. The experience marked Conrad both physically and mentally. After a few years, he began to write about it with a moral rage that emerged openly at first and subsequently in more complex, ironic form. An Outpost of Progress, a harshly satirical story of two murderous incompetents in a jungle trading post, was published in 1897, and Conrad wrote Heart of Darkness two years later; it appeared in Blackwood's Magazine in 1899 and in the volume "Youth" and Other Stories in 1902.

Along with Lord Jim (1900) and Nostromo (1904), this volume established him as one of the leading novelists of the day. He became friendly with other writers such as Henry James, Stephen Crane, H. G. Wells, John Galsworthy, and Ford Madox Ford. Yet he preferred a quiet life in the country to the attractions of literary London. From 1898 he lived on Pent Farm in Kent, near James, Wells, and Crane. He found writing difficult, often suffering from insomnia and physical ailments while trying to complete a novel (one biographer remarks that each of his later novels "cost him a tooth"). His novels from this period, The Secret Agent (1907) and Under Western Eyes (1911), revolve around political conflicts, but Conrad usually refrained from taking sides in politics—his interest lay in the effect that espionage and intrigue have on individual character. He hated autocratic rule but opposed revolution and was skeptical of social reform movements. His two abiding political commitments were to his adoptive homeland, England, and to the cause of Polish independence; he traveled to Poland on the eve of the First World War, returning with difficulty to England once war broke out. Although he had struggled financially throughout his writing life, Conrad had his first popular success with Chance (1913), which is now less highly regarded than his other works. His later works returned, typically with a more optimistic tone, to the Eastern settings with which he began. They have not received much appreciation from critics, although The Shadow Line (1917) recaptures some of the earlier works' appreciation of the moment of crisis in a youthful life.

HEART OF DARKNESS

Although the subject matter of Heart of Darkness is clearly one of the reasons for its continued influence, equally important is Conrad's introduction of many literary techniques that would be central to modern fiction. In the preface to *The Nigger of the "Narcissus,"* Conrad describes the task of the writer as "before all, to make you *see*," and his works stress the visual perception of reality. His technique of registering the way that a scene appears to an individual before explaining the scene's contents has been described as "delayed decoding"; it is an element of his literary impressionism, his emphasis on how the mind processes the information that the senses provide. In *Heart of Darkness*, Conrad records first the impressions that an event makes on Marlow and only later Marlow's arrival at an explanation of the event. The reader must continually decide when to accept Marlow's account as accurate and when to treat it as ironic and unreliable. Marlow describes his experiences in Africa from a position of experience, having contemplated the episode for many years, but the reader, like the narrator, may question some aspects of Marlow's story as self-justification. Conrad also uses symbolism in a distinctly modern way. As he later wrote, "a work of art is very seldom limited to one exclusive meaning and not necessarily tending to a definite conclusion. And this for the reason that the nearer it approaches art, the more it acquires a symbolic character." Frequently, Marlow's story seems to carry symbolic overtones that are not easily extracted from the story as a simple kernel of wisdom. This symbolic character has its exemplar in the primary narrator's comment that "the yarns of seamen have a direct simplicity, the whole meaning of which lies within the shell of a cracked nut. . . . [But to Marlow,] the meaning of an episode was not inside like a kernel but outside, enveloping the tale which brought it out only as a glow brings out a haze." *Heart of Darkness* does not reveal its meaning in digestible morsels, like the kernel of a nut. Rather, its meanings evade the interpreter; they are larger than the story itself. The story's hazy atmosphere, rich symbolic suggestiveness, and complex narrative structure have all appealed to later readers and writers. Although it was published at the end of the nineteenth century, *Heart of Darkness* became one of the most influential works of the twentieth century. It greatly influenced Nobel Prize winners **T. S. Eliot,** William Faulkner, **Gabriel García Márquez,** V. S. Naipaul, and **J. M. Coetzee.** In the second half of the century, the novella was seen as so relevant to the aftermath of imperialism that the filmmaker Francis Ford Coppola used it as the basis of his film about the Vietnam War, *Apocalypse Now.*

The "darkness" of the title exemplifies this symbolism. Although it is both a conventional metaphor for obscurity and evil and a cliché referring to Africa and the "unenlightened" state of its indigenous population, the story leaves it unclear where the heart of darkness is located: in the "uncivilized" jungle or in the hearts of the European imperialists. Leopold II of Belgium, who owned the trading company that effectively was the Congo Free State, gained a free hand in the area after calling an international conference in 1876 "to open to civilization the only part of our globe where Christianity has not penetrated and to pierce the darkness which envelops the entire population." Leopold had pledged to end the slave trade in central Africa, but his rule continued slavery under another guise, extracting forced labor for infrastructure projects, such as road building, that were poorly managed. Throughout the novella, Conrad plays on images of darkness and savagery and complicates any simple opposition by associating moral darkness—the evil that lurks within humans and underlies their predatory idealism—with a white exterior, beginning with the town (Brussels) that serves as the Belgian firm's headquarters and that Marlow describes as a "whited sepulchre."

Still, it is not surprising that later critics and writers, most notably the Nigerian novelist and essayist **Chinua Achebe**, would criticize *Heart of Darkness* for its racist portrayal of Africans. Marlow's words and behavior—indeed, the selectivity of his narrative—can be as distant and cruelly patronizing as those of any European colonialist. Yet he also recognizes his "kinship" with the Africans and often sees them as morally superior to the Europeans; Marlow's quiet critique of imperialism has inspired many postcolonial writers. For the most part, however, the Africans in his story constitute the back-ground for the strange figure of Kurtz, the charismatic, once idealistic, now totally corrupt trader who becomes the destination of Marlow's journey. Marlow's strange bond with this maddened soul stems initially from a desire to see a man whom others have described to him as a universal genius—an "emissary of pity, and science, and progress" and part of the "gang of virtue." In time, though, it becomes a horrified fascination with someone who has explored moral extremes to their furthest end. Kurtz's famous judgment on what he has lived and seen—"The horror! The horror!"—speaks at once to personal despair, to the political realities of imperialism, and to a broader sense of the human condition.

Heart of Darkness

1

The *Nellie*, a cruising yawl,[1] swung to her anchor without a flutter of the sails, and was at rest. The flood had made, the wind was nearly calm, and being bound down the river, the only thing for it was to come to[2] and wait for the turn of the tide.

The sea-reach of the Thames stretched before us like the beginning of an interminable waterway. In the offing[3] the sea and the sky were welded together without a joint, and in the luminous space the tanned sails of the barges drifting up with the tide seemed to stand still in red clusters of canvas sharply peaked, with gleams of varnished sprits. A haze rested on the low shores that ran out to sea in vanishing flatness. The air was dark above Gravesend,[4] and farther back still seemed condensed into a mournful gloom, brooding motionless over the biggest, and the greatest, town on earth.

The Director of Companies was our captain and our host. We four affectionately watched his back as he stood in the bows looking to seaward. On the whole river there was nothing that looked half so nautical. He resembled a pilot, which to a seaman is trustworthiness personified. It was difficult to realise his work was not out there in the luminous estuary, but behind him, within the brooding gloom.

1. A two-masted boat.
2. To come to a standstill in a fixed position.
3. The part of the sea distant but visible from the shore.
4. A port on the Thames River, and the last major town in the estuary.

Between us there was, as I have already said somewhere, the bond of the sea.[5] Besides holding our hearts together through long periods of separation, it had the effect of making us tolerant of each other's yarns—and even convictions. The Lawyer—the best of old fellows—had, because of his many years and many virtues, the only cushion on deck, and was lying on the only rug. The Accountant had brought out already a box of dominoes, and was toying architecturally with the bones. Marlow sat cross-legged right aft, leaning against the mizzenmast.[6] He had sunken cheeks, a yellow complexion, a straight back, an ascetic aspect, and, with his arms dropped, the palms of hands outwards, resembled an idol. The Director, satisfied the anchor had good hold, made his way aft and sat down amongst us. We exchanged a few words lazily. Afterwards there was silence on board the yacht. For some reason or other we did not begin that game of dominoes. We felt meditative, and fit for nothing but placid staring. The day was ending in a serenity of still and exquisite brilliance. The water shone pacifically; the sky, without a speck, was a benign immensity of unstained light; the very mist on the Essex marshes was like a gauzy and radiant fabric, hung from the wooded rises inland, and draping the low shores in diaphanous folds. Only the gloom to the west, brooding over the upper reaches, became more sombre every minute, as if angered by the approach of the sun.

And at last, in its curved and imperceptible fall, the sun sank low, and from glowing white changed to a dull red without rays and without heat, as if about to go out suddenly, stricken to death by the touch of that gloom brooding over a crowd of men.

Forthwith a change came over the waters, and the serenity became less brilliant but more profound. The old river in its broad reach rested unruffled at the decline of day, after ages of good service done to the race that peopled its banks, spread out in the tranquil dignity of a waterway leading to the uttermost ends of the earth. We looked at the venerable stream not in the vivid flush of a short day that comes and departs for ever, but in the august light of abiding memories. And indeed nothing is easier for a man who has, as the phrase goes, "followed the sea" with reverence and affection, than to evoke the great spirit of the past upon the lower reaches of the Thames. The tidal current runs to and fro in its unceasing service, crowded with memories of men and ships it has borne to the rest of home or to the battles of the sea. It had known and served all the men of whom the nation is proud, from Sir Francis Drake to Sir John Franklin, knights all, titled and untitled—the great knights-errant of the sea. It had borne all the ships whose names are like jewels flashing in the night of time, from the *Golden Hind* returning with her round flanks full of treasure, to be visited by the Queen's Highness and thus pass out of the gigantic tale, to the *Erebus* and *Terror*,[7] bound on other conquests—and that never returned. It had known the ships and the men. They had sailed from Deptford, from

5. "The bond of the sea" appears in "Youth," Conrad's first story to feature Marlow. "Youth" and *Heart of Darkness* were first published in book form as part of the same volume, with "Youth" immediately preceding *Heart of Darkness*.

6. The mast aft (to the rear) of the mainmast on any ship with two or more masts.

7. The *Erebus* and the *Terror* were ships commanded by Arctic explorer Sir John Franklin (1786–1847) and lost in an attempt to find a passage from the Atlantic Ocean to the Pacific. *Golden Hind*: the ship in which Elizabethan explorer Sir Francis Drake (1540–1596) sailed around the world.

Greenwich, from Erith—the adventurers and the settlers; kings' ships and the ships of men on 'Change; captains, admirals, the dark "interlopers"[8] of the Eastern trade, and the commissioned "generals" of East India fleets. Hunters for gold or pursuers of fame, they all had gone out on that stream, bearing the sword, and often the torch, messengers of the might within the land, bearers of a spark from the sacred fire.[9] What greatness had not floated on the ebb of that river into the mystery of an unknown earth! . . . The dreams of men, the seed of commonwealths, the germs of empires.

The sun set; the dusk fell on the stream, and lights began to appear along the shore. The Chapman lighthouse, a three-legged thing erect on a mudflat, shone strongly. Lights of ships moved in the fairway[1]—a great stir of lights going up and going down. And farther west on the upper reaches the place of the monstrous town[2] was still marked ominously on the sky, a brooding gloom in sunshine, a lurid glare under the stars.

"And this also," said Marlow suddenly, "has been one of the dark places of the earth."

He was the only man of us who still "followed the sea." The worst that could be said of him was that he did not represent his class. He was a seaman, but he was a wanderer too, while most seamen lead, if one may so express it, a sedentary life. Their minds are of the stay-at-home order, and their home is always with them—the ship; and so is their country—the sea. One ship is very much like another, and the sea is always the same. In the immutability of their surroundings the foreign shores, the foreign faces, the changing immensity of life, glide past, veiled not by a sense of mystery but by a slightly disdainful ignorance; for there is nothing mysterious to a seaman unless it be the sea itself, which is the mistress of his existence and as inscrutable as Destiny. For the rest, after his hours of work, a casual stroll or a casual spree on shore suffices to unfold for him the secret of a whole continent, and generally he finds the secret not worth knowing. The yarns of seamen have a direct simplicity, the whole meaning of which lies within the shell of a cracked nut. But Marlow was not typical (if his propensity to spin yarns be excepted), and to him the meaning of an episode was not inside like a kernel but outside, enveloping the tale which brought it out only as a glow brings out a haze, in the likeness of one of these misty halos that sometimes are made visible by the spectral illumination of moonshine.

His remark did not seem at all surprising. It was just like Marlow. It was accepted in silence. No one took the trouble to grunt even; and presently he said, very slow:

"I was thinking of very old times, when the Romans first came here, nineteen hundred years ago[3]—the other day. . . . Light came out of this river since—you

8. Private ships intruding on the East India Company's legal trade monopoly. "Deptford, Greenwich, Erith": ports on the Thames between London and Gravesend. "'Change": the stock exchange.

9. An allusion to the myth of Prometheus, who stole fire from the gods to give to humankind; by extension, refers to civilization, human ingenuity, and adventurousness.

1. A navigable passage in a river between rocks or sandbanks; the usual route into or out of a port.

2. I.e., London.

3. Romans first invaded England under Julius Caesar, in 55 and 54 B.C.E. These attempts were unsuccessful; in 43 C.E. a lengthy and effective conquest began.

say Knights? Yes; but it is like a running blaze on a plain, like a flash of light-ning in the clouds. We live in the flicker—may it last as long as the old earth keeps rolling! But darkness was here yesterday. Imagine the feelings of a com-mander of a fine—what d'ye call 'em?—trireme[4] in the Mediterranean, ordered suddenly to the north; run overland across the Gauls[5] in a hurry; put in charge of one of these craft the legionaries[6]—a wonderful lot of handy men they must have been too—used to build, apparently by the hundred, in a month or two, if we may believe what we read. Imagine him here—the very end of the world, a sea the colour of lead, a sky the colour of smoke, a kind of ship about as rigid as a concertina[7]—and going up this river with stores, or orders, or what you like. Sandbanks, marshes, forests, savages—precious little to eat fit for a civi-lised man, nothing but Thames water to drink. No Falernian wine[8] here, no going ashore. Here and there a military camp lost in a wilderness, like a needle in a bundle of hay—cold, fog, tempests, disease, exile, and death—death skulk-ing in the air, in the water, in the bush. They must have been dying like flies here. Oh yes—he did it. Did it very well, too, no doubt, and without thinking much about it either, except afterwards to brag of what he had gone through in his time, perhaps. They were men enough to face the darkness. And perhaps he was cheered by keeping his eye on a chance of promotion to the fleet at Ravenna[9] by and by, if he had good friends in Rome and survived the awful climate. Or think of a decent young citizen in a toga—perhaps too much dice, you know—coming out here in the train of some prefect, or tax-gatherer, or trader, even, to mend his fortunes. Land in a swamp, march through the woods, and in some inland post feel the savagery, the utter savagery, had closed round him—all that mysterious life of the wilderness that stirs in the forest, in the jungles, in the hearts of wild men. There's no initiation either into such mysteries. He has to live in the midst of the incomprehensible, which is also detestable. And it has a fascination, too, that goes to work upon him. The fascination of the abomination—you know. Imagine the growing regrets, the longing to escape, the powerless disgust, the surrender, the hate."

He paused.

"Mind," he began again, lifting one arm from the elbow, the palm of the hand outwards, so that, with his legs folded before him, he had the pose of a Buddha preaching in European clothes and without a lotus-flower[1]—"Mind, none of us would feel exactly like this. What saves us is efficiency—the devo-tion to efficiency. But these chaps were not much account, really. They were no colonists; their administration was merely a squeeze, and nothing more, I suspect. They were conquerors, and for that you want only brute force—nothing to boast of, when you have it, since your strength is just an accident arising from the weakness of others. They grabbed what they could get for the sake of what was to be got. It was just robbery with violence, aggravated murder

---

4. A Roman galley with three banks of oars.
5. Name used by the Romans to refer to the three regions of what is now France.
6. The members of a legion, a unit of Roman infantrymen.
7. An instrument resembling an accordion, with a bellows and buttons on either end: hence, not rigid at all.

8. Wine from a famous wine-making district in southern Italy.
9. Once a major Roman port on the Adriatic Sea.
1. Siddhartha Gautama, founder of Bud-dhism, is traditionally portrayed seated cross-legged on a lotus flower.

on a great scale, and men going at it blind—as is very proper for those who tackle a darkness. The conquest of the earth, which mostly means the taking it away from those who have a different complexion or slightly flatter noses than ourselves, is not a pretty thing when you look into it too much. What redeems it is the idea only. An idea at the back of it; not a sentimental pretence but an idea; and an unselfish belief in the idea—something you can set up, and bow down before, and offer a sacrifice to. . . ."

He broke off. Flames glided in the river, small green flames, red flames, white flames, pursuing, overtaking, joining, crossing each other—then separating slowly or hastily. The traffic of the great city went on in the deepening night upon the sleepless river. We looked on, waiting patiently—there was nothing else to do till the end of the flood; but it was only after a long silence, when he said, in a hesitating voice, "I suppose you fellows remember I did once turn fresh-water sailor for a bit," that we knew we were fated, before the ebb began to run,[2] to hear about one of Marlow's inconclusive experiences.

"I don't want to bother you much with what happened to me personally," he began, showing in this remark the weakness of many tellers of tales who seem so often unaware of what their audience would best like to hear; "yet to understand the effect of it on me you ought to know how I got out there, what I saw, how I went up that river to the place where I first met the poor chap. It was the farthest point of navigation and the culminating point of my experience. It seemed somehow to throw a kind of light on everything about me—and into my thoughts. It was sombre enough too—and pitiful—not extraordinary in any way—not very clear either. No, not very clear. And yet it seemed to throw a kind of light.

"I had then, as you remember, just returned to London after a lot of Indian Ocean, Pacific, China Seas—a regular dose of the East—six years or so, and I was loafing about, hindering you fellows in your work and invading your homes, just as though I had got a heavenly mission to civilise you. It was very fine for a time, but after a bit I did get tired of resting. Then I began to look for a ship—I should think the hardest work on earth. But the ships wouldn't even look at me. And I got tired of that game too.

"Now when I was a little chap I had a passion for maps. I would look for hours at South America, or Africa, or Australia, and lose myself in all the glories of exploration. At that time there were many blank spaces[3] on the earth, and when I saw one that looked particularly inviting on a map (but they all look that) I would put my finger on it and say, When I grow up I will go there. The North Pole was one of these places, I remember. Well, I haven't been there yet, and shall not try now. The glamour's off. Other places were scattered about the Equator, and in every sort of latitude all over the two hemispheres. I have been in some of them, and . . . well, we won't talk about that. But there was one yet—the biggest, the most blank, so to speak—that I had a hankering after.

"True, by this time it was not a blank space any more. It had got filled since my boyhood with rivers and lakes and names. It had ceased to be a blank space of delightful mystery—a white patch for a boy to dream gloriously over. It had become a place of darkness. But there was in it one river especially, a mighty

2. "Flood" and "ebb": the rise and fall of the tide in the river.

3. I.e., regions unexplored by Europeans at the time and hence left blank on European maps.

big river,[4] that you could see on the map, resembling an immense snake uncoiled, with its head in the sea, its body at rest curving afar over a vast country, and its tail lost in the depths of the land. And as I looked at the map of it in a shop-window, it fascinated me as a snake would a bird—a silly little bird. Then I remembered there was a big concern, a Company for trade on that river. Dash it all! I thought to myself, they can't trade without using some kind of craft on that lot of fresh water—steamboats![5] Why shouldn't I try to get charge of one? I went on along Fleet Street,[6] but could not shake off the idea. The snake had charmed me.

"You understand it was a Continental concern, that Trading Society;[7] but I have a lot of relations living on the Continent, because it's cheap and not so nasty as it looks, they say.

"I am sorry to own I began to worry them. This was already a fresh departure for me. I was not used to get things that way, you know. I always went my own road and on my own legs where I had a mind to go. I wouldn't have believed it of myself; but, then—you see—I felt somehow I must get there by hook or by crook. So I worried them. The men said, 'My dear fellow,' and did nothing. Then—would you believe it?—I tried the women. I, Charlie Marlow, set the women to work—to get a job. Heavens! Well, you see, the notion drove me. I had an aunt, a dear enthusiastic soul. She wrote: 'It will be delightful. I am ready to do anything, anything for you. It is a glorious idea. I know the wife of a very high personage in the Administration, and also a man who has lots of influence with,' etc. etc. She was determined to make no end of fuss to get me appointed skipper of a river steamboat, if such was my fancy.

"I got my appointment—of course; and I got it very quick. It appears the Company had received news that one of their captains had been killed in a scuffle with the natives. This was my chance, and it made me the more anxious to go. It was only months and months afterwards, when I made the attempt to recover what was left of the body, that I heard the original quarrel arose from a misunderstanding about some hens. Yes, two black hens. Fresleven—that was the fellow's name, a Dane—thought himself wronged somehow in the bargain, so he went ashore and started to hammer the chief of the village with a stick. Oh, it didn't surprise me in the least to hear this, and at the same time to be told that Fresleven was the gentlest, quietest creature that ever walked on two legs. No doubt he was; but he had been a couple of years already out there engaged in the noble cause, you know, and he probably felt the need at last of asserting his self-respect in some way. Therefore he whacked the old nigger mercilessly, while a big crowd of his people watched him, thunderstruck, till some man—I was told the chief's son—in desperation at hearing the old chap yell, made a tentative jab with a spear at the white man—and of course it went quite easy between the shoulder-blades. Then the whole population cleared into the forest, expecting all kinds of calamities to happen, while, on the other hand, the steamer Fresleven commanded left also in a bad panic, in charge of

4. The Congo River.
5. Flat-bottomed steamboats were essential for navigating the shallow waters of the Congo.
6. A major street in central London, famous as a publishing center.
7. The trading company—specifically, a Belgian company that operated ships on the Congo River in the protectorate of King Leopold II of Belgium.

the engineer, I believe. Afterwards nobody seemed to trouble much about Fresleven's remains, till I got out and stepped into his shoes. I couldn't let it rest, though; but when an opportunity offered at last to meet my predecessor, the grass growing through his ribs was tall enough to hide his bones. They were all there. The supernatural being had not been touched after he fell. And the village was deserted, the huts gaped black, rotting, all askew within the fallen enclosures. A calamity had come to it, sure enough. The people had vanished. Mad terror had scattered them, men, women, and children, through the bush, and they had never returned. What became of the hens I don't know either. I should think the cause of progress got them, anyhow. However, through this glorious affair I got my appontment, before I had fairly begun to hope for it.

"I flew around like mad to get ready, and before forty-eight hours I was crossing the Channel to show myself to my employers, and sign the contract. In a very few hours I arrived in a city that always makes me think of a whited sepulchre.[8] Prejudice no doubt. I had no difficulty in finding the Company's offices. It was the biggest thing in the town, and everybody I met was full of it. They were going to run an overseas empire, and make no end of coin by trade.

"A narrow and deserted street in deep shadow, high houses, innumerable windows with venetian blinds, a dead silence, grass sprouting between the stones, imposing carriage archways right and left, immense double doors standing ponderously ajar. I slipped through one of these cracks, went up a swept and ungarnished staircase, as arid as a desert, and opened the first door I came to. Two women, one fat and the other slim, sat on straw-bottomed chairs, knitting black wool.[9] The slim one got up and walked straight at me—still knitting with downcast eyes—and only just as I began to think of getting out of her way, as you would for a somnambulist, stood still, and looked up. Her dress was as plain as an umbrella-cover, and she turned round without a word and preceded me into a waiting-room. I gave my name, and looked about. Deal table in the middle, plain chairs all round the walls, on one end a large shining map, marked with all the colours of a rainbow. There was a vast amount of red— good to see at any time, because one knows that some real work is done in there, a deuce of a lot of blue, a little green, smears of orange, and, on the East Coast, a purple patch, to show where the jolly pioneers of progress drink the jolly lager-beer.[1] However, I wasn't going into any of these. I was going into the yellow. Dead in the centre. And the river was there—fascinating—deadly—like a snake. Ough! A door opened, a white-haired secretarial head, but wearing a compassionate expression, appeared, and a skinny forefinger beckoned me into

---

8. The city is based on Brussels. "Whited sepulchre": a biblical allusion, Matthew 23.27: "Woe unto you, scribes and Pharisees, hypocrites! for ye are like unto whited sepulchres, which indeed appear beautiful outward, but are within full of dead men's bones, and of all uncleanness."
9. The knitters allude to at least two sources: in Charles Dickens's *Tale of Two Cities*, the villainous Madame Defarge knits the names of those she condemns to die. In Greek mythology, the Fates were usually three women spin-

ning, measuring, and cutting the thread of life.
1. The map shows territories claimed by European nations in the aftermath of the Berlin Conference of 1884–85: red is England, Conrad's adopted nation; blue territories belonged to France; and purple, Germany. Although color schemes varied, in the map Marlow is looking at, orange presumably refers to Portugal and green to Italy, which also had holdings in Africa. Yellow stands for the Congo Free State, controlled by King Leopold II.

the sanctuary. Its light was dim, and a heavy writing desk squatted in the middle. From behind that structure came out an impression of pale plumpness in a frockcoat. The great man himself. He was five feet six, I should judge, and had his grip on the handle-end of ever so many millions. He shook hands, I fancy, murmured vaguely, was satisfied with my French. *Bon voyage.*[2]

"In about forty-five seconds I found myself again in the waiting-room with the compassionate secretary, who, full of desolation and sympathy, made me sign some document. I believe I undertook amongst other things not to disclose any trade secrets. Well, I am not going to.

"I began to feel slightly uneasy. You know I am not used to such ceremonies, and there was something ominous in the atmosphere. It was just as though I had been let into some conspiracy—I don't know—something not quite right; and I was glad to get out. In the outer room the two women knitted black wool feverishly. People were arriving, and the younger one was walking back and forth introducing them. The old one sat on her chair. Her flat cloth slippers were propped up on a foot-warmer, and a cat reposed on her lap. She wore a starched white affair on her head, had a wart on one cheek, and silver-rimmed spectacles hung on the tip of her nose. She glanced at me above the glasses. The swift and indifferent placidity of that look troubled me. Two youths with foolish and cheery countenances were being piloted over, and she threw at them the same quick glance of unconcerned wisdom. She seemed to know all about them and about me too. An eerie feeling came over me. She seemed uncanny and fateful. Often far away there I thought of these two, guarding the door of Darkness, knitting black wool as for a warm pall, one introducing, introducing continuously to the unknown, the other scrutinising the cheery and foolish faces with unconcerned old eyes. *Ave!* Old knitter of black wool. *Morituri te salutant.*[3] Not many of those she looked at ever saw her again—not half, by a long way.

"There was yet a visit to the doctor. 'A simple formality,' assured me the secretary, with an air of taking an immense part in all my sorrows. Accordingly a young chap wearing his hat over the left eyebrow, some clerk I suppose—there must have been clerks in the business, though the house was as still as a house in a city of the dead—came from somewhere upstairs, and led me forth. He was shabby and careless, with ink-stains on the sleeves of his jacket, and his cravat was large and billowy, under a chin shaped like the toe of an old boot. It was a little too early for the doctor, so I proposed a drink, and thereupon he developed a vein of joviality. As we sat over our vermuths[4] he glorified the Company's business, and by and by I expressed casually my surprise at him not going out there. He became very cool and collected all at once. 'I am not such a fool as I look, quoth Plato to his disciples,' he said sententiously, emptied his glass with great resolution, and we rose.

"The old doctor felt my pulse, evidently thinking of something else the while. 'Good, good for there,' he mumbled, and then with a certain eagerness asked me whether I would let him measure my head. Rather surprised, I said Yes, when he produced a thing like callipers and got the dimensions back and front

---

2. "Have a good trip" (French).
3. "Those who are about to die salute you" (Latin): the greeting of gladiators to the Roman emperor before beginning combat in the arena.

4. Vermuth, now known as vermouth, is wine fortified with alcohol and, usually, additional flavors.

and every way, taking notes carefully. He was an unshaven little man in a threadbare coat like a gaberdine, with his feet in slippers, and I thought him a harmless fool. 'I always ask leave, in the interests of science, to measure the crania of those going out there,'⁵ he said. 'And when they come back too?' I asked. 'Oh, I never see them,' he remarked; 'and, moreover, the changes take place inside, you know.' He smiled, as if at some quiet joke. 'So you are going out there. Famous. Interesting too.' He gave me a searching glance, and made another note. 'Ever any madness in your family?' he asked, in a matter-of-fact tone. I felt very annoyed. 'Is that question in the interests of science too?' 'It would be,' he said, without taking notice of my irritation, 'interesting for science to watch the mental changes of individuals, on the spot, but . . .' 'Are you an alienist?' I interrupted. 'Every doctor should be—a little,' answered that original⁶ imperturbably. 'I have a little theory which you Messieurs who go out there must help me to prove. This is my share in the advantages my country shall reap from the possession of such a magnificent dependency. The mere wealth I leave to others. Pardon my questions, but you are the first Englishman coming under my observation . . .' I hastened to assure him I was not in the least typical. 'If I were,' said I, 'I wouldn't be talking like this with you.' 'What you say is rather profound, and probably erroneous,' he said, with a laugh. 'Avoid irritation more than exposure to the sun. Adieu. How do you English say, eh? Good-bye. Ah! Good-bye. Adieu. In the tropics one must before everything keep calm.' . . . He lifted a warning forefinger. . . . 'Du calme, du calme. Adieu.'⁷

"One thing more remained to do—say good-bye to my excellent aunt. I found her triumphant. I had a cup of tea—the last decent cup of tea for many days— and in a room that most soothingly looked just as you would expect a lady's drawing-room to look, we had a long quiet chat by the fireside. In the course of these confidences it became quite plain to me I had been represented to the wife of the high dignitary, and goodness knows to how many more people besides, as an exceptional and gifted creature—a piece of good fortune for the Company—a man you don't get hold of every day. Good heavens! and I was going to take charge of a two-penny-halfpenny river-steamboat with a penny whistle attached! It appeared, however, I was also one of the Workers, with a capital—you know. Something like an emissary of light, something like a lower sort of apostle. There had been a lot of such rot let loose in print and talk just about that time,⁸ and the excellent woman, living right in the rush of all that humbug, got carried off her feet. She talked about 'weaning those ignorant millions from their horrid ways,' till, upon my word, she made me quite uncomfortable. I ventured to hint that the Company was run for profit.

"'You forget, dear Charlie, that the labourer is worthy of his hire,'⁹ she said brightly. It's queer how out of touch with truth women are. They live in a world of their own, and there had never been anything like it, and never can be. It is

5. The doctor may practice some form of phrenology, a pseudoscience holding that personality traits could be determined by the shape and size of the skull.
6. Unusual or eccentric person. "Alienist": early term for a psychiatrist.
7. "Calm, calm. Goodbye" (French).
8. Initially, Leopold II was viewed as a philanthropist—bringing missionaries to pagans and, it was thought, using Belgian military forces to rescue the native people from homegrown slave traders.
9. The aunt quotes Luke 10.7, one of Christ's instructions to his disciples as they depart to proselytize: to make themselves welcome in the homes they visit.

too beautiful altogether, and if they were to set it up it would go to pieces before the first sunset. Some confounded fact we men have been living contentedly with ever since the day of creation would start up and knock the whole thing over.

"After this I got embraced, told to wear flannel, be sure to write often, and so on—and I left. In the street—I don't know why—a queer feeling came to me that I was an impostor. Odd thing that I, who used to clear out for any part of the world at twenty-four hours' notice, with less thought than most men give to the crossing of a street, had a moment—I won't say of hesitation, but of startled pause, before this commonplace affair. The best way I can explain it to you is by saying that, for a second or two, I felt as though, instead of going to the centre of a continent, I were about to set off for the centre of the earth.[1]

"I left in a French steamer, and she called in every blamed port they have out there, for, as far as I could see, the sole purpose of landing soldiers and custom-house officers.[2] I watched the coast. Watching a coast as it slips by the ship is like thinking about an enigma. There it is before you—smiling, frowning, inviting, grand, mean, insipid, or savage, and always mute with an air of whispering, Come and find out. This one was almost featureless, as if still in the making, with an aspect of monotonous grimness. The edge of a colossal jungle, so dark green as to be almost black, fringed with white surf, ran straight, like a ruled line, far, far away along a blue sea whose glitter was blurred by a creeping mist. The sun was fierce, the land seemed to glisten and drip with steam. Here and there greyish-whitish specks showed up clustered inside the white surf, with a flag flying above them perhaps—settlements some centuries old, and still no bigger than pin-heads on the untouched expanse of their background. We pounded along, stopped, landed soldiers; went on, landed custom-house clerks to levy toll in what looked like a God-forsaken wilderness, with a tin shed and a flag-pole lost in it; landed more soldiers—to take care of the custom-house clerks presumably. Some, I heard, got drowned in the surf; but whether they did or not, nobody seemed particularly to care. They were just flung out there, and on we went. Every day the coast looked the same, as though we had not moved; but we passed various places—trading places—with names like Gran' Bassam, Little Popo;[3] names that seemed to belong to some sordid farce acted in front of a sinister back-cloth. The idleness of a passenger, my isolation amongst all these men with whom I had no point of contact, the oily and languid sea, the uniform sombreness of the coast, seemed to keep me away from the truth of things, within the toil of a mournful and senseless delusion. The voice of the surf heard now and then was a positive pleasure, like the speech of a brother. It was something natural, that had its reason, that had a meaning. Now and then a boat from the shore gave one a momentary contact with reality. It was paddled by black fellows. You could see from afar the white of their eyeballs glistening. They shouted, sang; their bodies streamed with perspiration; they had faces like grotesque masks—these chaps; but they had bone, muscle, a wild vitality, an intense energy of movement, that was as

---

1. Jules Verne's science fiction novel *Journey to the Center of the Earth* (1864) featured characters encountering prehistoric animals of greater age in successive layers of the earth.
2. Colonial officials.

3. The former name of Aného, a coastal city in Togo, then under German control. "Gran' Bassam": Grand-Bassam, a city in Côte d'Ivoire, was then a French colony and a major seaport.

natural and true as the surf along their coast. They wanted no excuse for being there. They were a great comfort to look at. For a time I would feel I belonged still to a world of straightforward facts; but the feeling would not last long. Something would turn up to scare it away. Once, I remember, we came upon a man-of-war anchored off the coast. There wasn't even a shed there, and she was shelling the bush. It appears the French had one of their wars going on thereabouts. Her ensign dropped limp like a rag; the muzzles of the long six-inch guns stuck out all over the low hull; the greasy, slimy swell swung her up lazily and let her down, swaying her thin masts. In the empty immensity of earth, sky, and water, there she was, incomprehensible, firing into a continent. Pop, would go one of the six-inch guns; a small flame would dart and vanish, a little white smoke would disappear, a tiny projectile would give a feeble screech—and nothing happened. Nothing could happen. There was a touch of insanity in the proceeding, a sense of lugubrious drollery in the sight; and it was not dissipated by somebody on board assuring me earnestly there was a camp of natives—he called them enemies!—hidden out of sight somewhere.

"We gave her her letters (I heard the men in that lonely ship were dying of fever at the rate of three a day) and went on. We called at some more places with farcical names, where the merry dance of death and trade goes on in a still and earthy atmosphere as of an overheated catacomb; all along the formless coast bordered by dangerous surf, as if Nature herself had tried to ward off intruders; in and out of rivers, streams of death in life, whose banks were rotting into mud, whose waters, thickened into slime, invaded the contorted mangroves, that seemed to writhe at us in the extremity of an impotent despair. Nowhere did we stop long enough to get a particularised impression, but the general sense of vague and oppressive wonder grew upon me. It was like a weary pilgrimage amongst hints for nightmares.

"It was upward of thirty days before I saw the mouth of the big river. We anchored off the seat of the government.[4] But my work would not begin till some two hundred miles farther on. So as soon as I could I made a start for a place thirty miles higher up.

"I had my passage on a little sea-going steamer. Her captain was a Swede, and knowing me for a seaman, invited me on the bridge. He was a young man, lean, fair, and morose, with lanky hair and a shuffling gait. As we left the miserable little wharf, he tossed his head contemptuously at the shore. 'Been living there?' he asked. I said, 'Yes.' 'Fine lot these government chaps—are they not?' he went on, speaking English with great precision and considerable bitterness. 'It is funny what some people will do for a few francs a month. I wonder what becomes of that kind when it goes up country?' I said to him I expected to see that soon. 'So-o-o!' he exclaimed. He shuffled athwart, keeping one eye ahead vigilantly. 'Don't be too sure,' he continued. 'The other day I took up a man who hanged himself on the road. He was a Swede, too.' 'Hanged himself! Why, in God's name?' I cried. He kept on looking out watchfully. 'Who knows? The sun too much for him, or the country perhaps.'

"At last we opened a reach.[5] A rocky cliff appeared, mounds of turned-up earth by the shore, houses on a hill, others with iron roofs, amongst a waste of

4. The capital of the Congo Free State was Boma, a port at the mouth of the Congo.   5. Found an open, visible stretch of river.

excavations, or hanging to the declivity. A continuous noise of the rapids above hovered over this scene of inhabited devastation. A lot of people, mostly black and naked, moved about like ants. A jetty projected into the river. A blinding sunlight drowned all this at times in a sudden recrudescence of glare. 'There's your Company's station,' said the Swede, pointing to three wooden barrack-like structures on the rocky slope. 'I will send your things up. Four boxes did you say? So. Farewell.'

"I came upon a boiler[6] wallowing in the grass, then found a path leading up the hill. It turned aside for the boulders, and also for an undersized railway truck lying there on its back with its wheels in the air. One was off. The thing looked as dead as the carcass of some animal. I came upon more pieces of decaying machinery, a stack of rusty nails. To the left a clump of trees made a shady spot, where dark things seemed to stir feebly. I blinked, the path was steep. A horn tooted to the right, and I saw the black people run. A heavy and dull detonation shook the ground, a puff of smoke came out of the cliff, and that was all. No change appeared on the face of the rock. They were building a railway. The cliff was not in the way or anything; but this objectless blasting was all the work going on.

"A slight clinking behind me made me turn my head. Six black men advanced in a file, toiling up the path. They walked erect and slow, balancing small baskets full of earth on their heads, and the clink kept time with their footsteps. Black rags were wound round their loins, and the short ends behind waggled to and fro like tails. I could see every rib, the joints of their limbs were like knots in a rope; each had an iron collar on his neck, and all were connected together with a chain whose bights[7] swung between them, rhythmically clinking. Another report from the cliff made me think suddenly of that ship of war I had seen firing into a continent. It was the same kind of ominous voice; but these men could by no stretch of imagination be called enemies. They were called criminals, and the outraged law, like the bursting shells, had come to them, an insoluble mystery from the sea. All their meagre breasts panted together, the violently dilated nostrils quivered, the eyes stared stonily uphill. They passed me within six inches, without a glance, with that complete, deathlike indifference of unhappy savages. Behind this raw matter one of the reclaimed, the product of the new forces at work, strolled despondently, carrying a rifle by its middle. He had a uniform jacket with one button off, and seeing a white man on the path, hoisted his weapon to his shoulder with alacrity. This was simple prudence, white men being so much alike at a distance that he could not tell who I might be. He was speedily reassured, and with a large, white, rascally grin, and a glance at his charge, seemed to take me into partnership in his exalted trust. After all, I also was a part of the great cause of these high and just proceedings.

"Instead of going up, I turned and descended to the left. My idea was to let that chain-gang get out of sight before I climbed the hill. You know I am not particularly tender; I've had to strike and to fend off. I've had to resist and to attack sometimes—that's only one way of resisting—without counting the exact cost, according to the demands of such sort of life as I had blundered into. I've seen the devil of violence, and the devil of greed, and the devil of hot desire; but, by all the stars! these were strong, lusty, red-eyed devils, that

6. A machine for converting water into steam.   7. The dangling excess of chain.

swayed and drove men—men, I tell you. But as I stood on this hillside, I fore-saw that in the blinding sunshine of that land I would become acquainted with a flabby, pretending, weak-eyed devil of a rapacious and pitiless folly. How insidious he could be, too, I was only to find out several months later and a thousand miles farther. For a moment I stood appalled, as though by a warn-ing. Finally I descended the hill, obliquely, towards the trees I had seen.

"I avoided a vast artificial hole somebody had been digging on the slope, the purpose of which I found it impossible to divine. It wasn't a quarry or a sandpit, anyhow. It was just a hole. It might have been connected with the philanthropic desire of giving the criminals something to do. I don't know. Then I nearly fell into a very narrow ravine, almost no more than a scar in the hillside. I discov-ered that a lot of imported drainage-pipes for the settlement had been tumbled in there. There wasn't one that was not broken. It was a wanton smash-up. At last I got under the trees. My purpose was to stroll into the shade for a moment; but no sooner within than it seemed to me I had stepped into the gloomy circle of some Inferno.[8] The rapids were near, and an uninterrupted, uniform, head-long, rushing noise filled the mournful stillness of the grove, where not a breath stirred, not a leaf moved, with a mysterious sound—as though the tearing pace of the launched earth had suddenly become audible.

"Black shapes crouched, lay, sat between the trees, leaning against the trunks, clinging to the earth, half coming out, half effaced within the dim light, in all the attitudes of pain, abandonment, and despair. Another mine[9] on the cliff went off, followed by a slight shudder of the soil under my feet. The work was going on. The work! And this was the place where some of the helpers had withdrawn to die.

"They were dying slowly—it was very clear. They were not enemies, they were not criminals, they were nothing earthly now—nothing but black shadows of disease and starvation, lying confusedly in the greenish gloom. Brought from all the recesses of the coast in all the legality of time contracts, lost in uncongenial surroundings, fed on unfamiliar food, they sickened, became inefficient, and were then allowed to crawl away and rest.[1] These moribund shapes were free as air—and nearly as thin. I began to distinguish the gleam of eyes under the trees. Then, glancing down, I saw a face near my hand. The black bones reclined at full length with one shoulder against the tree, and slowly the eyelids rose and the sunken eyes looked up at me, enormous and vacant, a kind of blind, white flicker in the depths of the orbs, which died out slowly. The man seemed young—almost a boy—but you know with them it's hard to tell. I found nothing else to do but to offer him one of my good Swede's ship's biscuits I had in my pocket. The fingers closed slowly on it and held—there was no other movement and no other glance. He had tied a bit of white worsted[2] round his neck—Why? Where did he get it? Was it a badge—an ornament—a charm—a propitiatory act? Was there any idea at all connected with it? It looked startling round his black neck, this bit of white thread from beyond the seas.

8. Hell, often of fire. The term is associated with the portrayal of hell in the *Inferno*, the first section of the *Divine Comedy*, by Dante Alighieri (ca. 1265–1321).
9. Explosive charge.

1. The workers and porters who provided the infrastructure of the Congo Free State were often conscripts: overworked, underfed, and beaten, they died in enormous numbers.
2. Wool fabric.

"Near the same tree two more bundles of acute angles sat with their legs drawn up. One, with his chin propped on his knees, stared at nothing, in an intolerable and appalling manner: his brother phantom rested its forehead, as if overcome with a great weariness; and all about others were scattered in every pose of contorted collapse, as in some picture of a massacre or a pestilence. While I stood horror-struck, one of these creatures rose to his hands and knees, and went off on all-fours towards the river to drink. He lapped out of his hand, then sat up in the sunlight, crossing his shins in front of him, and after a time let his woolly head fall on his breastbone.

"I didn't want any more loitering in the shade, and I made haste towards the station. When near the buildings I met a white man, in such an unexpected elegance of get-up that in the first moment I took him for a sort of vision. I saw a high starched collar, white cuffs, a light alpaca[3] jacket, snowy trousers, a clear necktie, and varnished boots. No hat. Hair parted, brushed, oiled, under a green-lined parasol held in a big white hand. He was amazing, and had a penholder behind his ear.

"I shook hands with this miracle, and I learned he was the Company's chief accountant, and that all the book-keeping was done at this station. He had come out for a moment, he said, 'to get a breath of fresh air.' The expression sounded wonderfully odd, with its suggestion of sedentary desk-life. I wouldn't have mentioned the fellow to you at all, only it was from his lips that I first heard the name of the man who is so indissolubly connected with the memories of that time. Moreover, I respected the fellow. Yes; I respected his collars, his vast cuffs, his brushed hair. His appearance was certainly that of a hairdresser's dummy; but in the great demoralisation of the land he kept up his appearance. That's backbone. His starched collars and got-up shirt-fronts were achievements of character. He had been out nearly three years; and, later, I could not help asking him how he managed to sport such linen. He had just the faintest blush, and said modestly, 'I've been teaching one of the native women about the station. It was difficult. She had a distaste for the work.' Thus this man had verily accomplished something. And he was devoted to his books, which were in apple-pie order.

"Everything else in the station was in a muddle,—heads, things, buildings. Strings of dusty niggers with splay feet arrived and departed; a stream of manufactured goods, rubbishy cottons, beads, and brass-wire sent into the depths of darkness, and in return came a precious trickle of ivory.[4]

"I had to wait in the station for ten days—an eternity. I lived in a hut in the yard, but to be out of the chaos I would sometimes get into the accountant's office. It was built of horizontal planks, and so badly put together that, as he bent over his high desk, he was barred from neck to heels with narrow strips of sunlight. There was no need to open the big shutter to see. It was hot there too; big flies buzzed fiendishly, and did not sting, but stabbed. I sat generally on the floor, while, of faultless appearance (and even slightly scented), perching on a high stool, he wrote, he wrote. Sometimes he stood up for exercise.

3. An expensive fine wool that comes from a South American animal of the same name.
4. Congolese were not allowed currency, and the enormous disparity between the value of goods returning from the Congo and the value of goods being sent there eventually gave activists the first hint of the forced labor conditions that would turn public opinion against Leopold.

When a truckle-bed[5] with a sick man (some invalided agent from up country) was put in there, he exhibited a gentle annoyance. 'The groans of this sick person' he said, 'distract my attention. And without that it is extremely difficult to guard against clerical errors in this climate.'

"One day he remarked, without lifting his head, 'In the interior you will no doubt meet Mr Kurtz.' On my asking who Mr Kurtz was, he said he was a first-class agent; and seeing my disappointment at this information, he added slowly, laying down his pen, 'He is a very remarkable person.' Further questions elicited from him that Mr Kurtz was at present in charge of a trading-post, a very important one, in the true ivory-country, at 'the very bottom of there. Sends in as much ivory as all the others put together . . .' He began to write again. The sick man was too ill to groan. The flies buzzed in a great peace.

"Suddenly there was a growing murmur of voices and a great tramping of feet. A caravan had come in. A violent babble of uncouth sounds burst out on the other side of the planks. All the carriers were speaking together, and in the midst of the uproar the lamentable voice of the chief agent was heard 'giving it up' tearfully for the twentieth time that day. . . . He rose slowly. 'What a frightful row,' he said. He crossed the room gently to look at the sick man, and returning, said to me, 'He does not hear.' 'What! Dead?' I asked, startled. 'No, not yet,' he answered, with great composure. Then, alluding with a toss of the head to the tumult in the station-yard, 'When one has got to make correct entries, one comes to hate those savages—hate them to the death.' He remained thoughtful for a moment. 'When you see Mr Kurtz,' he went on, 'tell him from me that everything here'—he glanced at the desk—'is very satisfactory. I don't like to write to him—with those messengers of ours you never know who may get hold of your letter—at that Central Station.' He stared at me for a moment with his mild, bulging eyes. 'Oh, he will go far, very far,' he began again. 'He will be a somebody in the Administration before long. They, above—the Council in Europe, you know—mean him to be.'

"He turned to his work. The noise outside had ceased, and presently in going out I stopped at the door. In the steady buzz of flies the homeward-bound agent was lying flushed and insensible; the other, bent over his books, was making correct entries of perfectly correct transactions; and fifty feet below the doorstep I could see the still tree-tops of the grove of death.

"Next day I left that station at last, with a caravan of sixty men, for a two-hundred-mile tramp.

"No use telling you much about that. Paths, paths, everywhere; a stamped-in network of paths spreading over the empty land, through long grass, through burnt grass, through thickets, down and up chilly ravines, up and down stony hills ablaze with heat; and a solitude, a solitude, nobody, not a hut. The population had cleared out a long time ago. Well, if a lot of mysterious niggers armed with all kinds of fearful weapons suddenly took to travelling on the road between Deal and Gravesend,[6] catching the yokels right and left to carry heavy loads for them, I fancy every farm and cottage thereabouts would get empty very soon. Only here the dwellings were gone too. Still, I passed through several abandoned

5. I.e., trundle bed, a low portable bed that is on castors and that may be slid under a higher bed when not being used.

6. Deal, like Gravesend, is a coastal town in southeastern England.

villages. There's something pathetically childish in the ruins of grass walls. Day after day, with the stamp and shuffle of sixty pair of bare feet behind me, each pair under a 60-lb. load. Camp, cook, sleep, strike camp, march. Now and then a carrier dead in harness, at rest in the long grass near the path, with an empty water-gourd and his long staff lying by his side. A great silence around and above. Perhaps on some quiet night the tremor of far-off drums, sinking, swelling, a tremor vast, faint; a sound weird, appealing, suggestive, and wild—and perhaps with as profound a meaning as the sound of bells in a Christian country. Once a white man in an unbuttoned uniform, camping on the path with an armed escort of lank Zanzibaris,[7] very hospitable and festive—not to say drunk. Was looking after the upkeep of the road, he declared. Can't say I saw any road or any upkeep, unless the body of a middle-aged negro, with a bullet-hole in the forehead, upon which I absolutely stumbled three miles farther on, may be considered as a permanent improvement. I had a white companion too, not a bad chap, but rather too fleshy and with the exasperating habit of fainting on the hot hillsides, miles away from the least bit of shade and water. Annoying, you know, to hold your own coat like a parasol over a man's head while he is coming-to. I couldn't help asking him once what he meant by coming there at all. 'To make money, of course. What do you think?' he said scornfully. Then he got fever, and had to be carried in a hammock slung under a pole. As he weighed sixteen stone[8] I had no end of rows with the carriers. They jibbed, ran away, sneaked off with their loads in the night—quite a mutiny. So, one evening, I made a speech in English with gestures, not one of which was lost to the sixty pairs of eyes before me, and the next morning I started the hammock off in front all right. An hour afterwards I came upon the whole concern wrecked in a bush—man, hammock, groans, blankets, horrors. The heavy pole had skinned his poor nose. He was very anxious for me to kill somebody, but there wasn't the shadow of a carrier near. I remembered the old doctor—'It would be interesting for science to watch the mental changes of individuals, on the spot.' I felt I was becoming scientifically interesting. However, all that is to no purpose. On the fifteenth day I came in sight of the big river again, and hobbled into the Central Station. It was on a back water surrounded by scrub and forest, with a pretty border of smelly mud on one side, and on the three others enclosed by a crazy fence of rushes. A neglected gap was all the gate it had, and the first glance at the place was enough to let you see the flabby devil was running that show. White men with long staves in their hands appeared languidly from amongst the buildings, strolling up to take a look at me, and then retired out of sight somewhere. One of them, a stout, excitable chap with black moustaches, informed me with great volubility and many digressions, as soon as I told him who I was, that my steamer was at the bottom of the river. I was thunderstruck. What, how, why? Oh, it was 'all right.' The 'manager himself' was there. All quite correct. 'Everybody had behaved splendidly! splendidly!'—'You must,' he said in agitation, 'go and see the general manager at once. He is waiting!'

"I did not see the real significance of that wreck at once. I fancy I see it now, but I am not sure—not at all. Certainly the affair was too stupid—when I think

7. Mercenary soldiers from the island of Zanzibar, off the east African coast.

8. I.e., 224 pounds (1 stone equals 14 pounds).

of it—to be altogether natural. Still . . . But at the moment it presented itself simply as a confounded nuisance. The steamer was sunk. They had started two days before in a sudden hurry up the river with the manager on board, in charge of some volunteer skipper, and before they had been out three hours they tore the bottom out of her on stones, and she sank near the south bank. I asked myself what I was to do there, now my boat was lost. As a matter of fact, I had plenty to do in fishing my command out of the river. I had to set about it the very next day. That, and the repairs when I brought the pieces to the station, took some months.

"My first interview with the manager was curious. He did not ask me to sit down after my twenty-mile walk that morning. He was commonplace in complexion, in feature, in manners, and in voice. He was of middle size and of ordinary build. His eyes, of the usual blue, were perhaps remarkably cold, and he certainly could make his glance fall on one as trenchant and heavy as an axe. But even at these times the rest of his person seemed to disclaim the intention. Otherwise there was only an indefinable, faint expression of his lips, something stealthy—a smile—not a smile—I remember it, but I can't explain. It was unconscious, this smile was, though just after he had said something it got intensified for an instant. It came at the end of his speeches like a seal applied on the words to make the meaning of the commonest phrase appear absolutely inscrutable. He was a common trader, from his youth up employed in these parts—nothing more. He was obeyed, yet he inspired neither love nor fear, nor even respect. He inspired uneasiness. That was it! Uneasiness. Not a definite mistrust—just uneasiness—nothing more. You have no idea how effective such a . . . a . . . faculty can be. He had no genius for organising, for initiative, or for order even. That was evident in such things as the deplorable state of the station. He had no learning, and no intelligence. His position had come to him—why? Perhaps because he was never ill . . . He had served three terms of three years out there . . . Because triumphant health in the general rout of constitutions is a kind of power in itself. When he went home on leave he rioted on a large scale—pompously. Jack ashore[9]—with a difference—in externals only. This one could gather from his casual talk. He originated nothing, he could keep the routine going—that's all. But he was great. He was great by this little thing that it was impossible to tell what could control such a man. He never gave that secret away. Perhaps there was nothing within him. Such a suspicion made one pause—for out there there were no external checks. Once when various tropical diseases had laid low almost every 'agent' in the station, he was heard to say, 'Men who come out here should have no entrails.' He sealed the utterance with that smile of his, as though it had been a door opening into a darkness he had in his keeping. You fancied you had seen things—but the seal was on. When annoyed at meal-times by the constant quarrels of the white men about precedence, he ordered an immense round table[1] to be made, for which a special house had to be built. This was the station's messroom. Where he sat was the first place—the rest were nowhere. One felt this to be his unalterable conviction. He was neither civil nor uncivil. He was quiet.

9. The carousing of seamen ("Jack Tar") on shore leave was proverbial.
1. King Arthur, legendary ruler of England, seated his knights at a round table so that none would take precedence over any of the others.

He allowed his 'boy'—an overfed young negro from the coast—to treat the white men, under his very eyes, with provoking insolence.

"He began to speak as soon as he saw me. I had been very long on the road. He could not wait. Had to start without me. The up-river stations had to be relieved. There had been so many delays already that he did not know who was dead and who was alive, and how they got on—and so on, and so on. He paid no attention to my explanations, and, playing with a stick of sealing-wax, repeated several times that the situation was 'very grave, very grave.' There were rumours that a very important station was in jeopardy, and its chief, Mr Kurtz, was ill. Hoped it was not true. Mr Kurtz was . . . I felt weary and irritable. Hang Kurtz, I thought. I interrupted him by saying I had heard of Mr Kurtz on the coast. 'Ah! So they talk of him down there,' he murmured to himself. Then he began again, assuring me Mr Kurtz was the best agent he had, an exceptional man, of the greatest importance to the Company; therefore I could understand his anxiety. He was, he said, 'very, very uneasy.' Certainly he fidgeted on his chair a good deal, exclaimed, 'Ah, Mr Kurtz!' broke the stick of sealing-wax and seemed dumbfounded by the accident. Next thing he wanted to know 'how long it would take to' . . . I interrupted him again. Being hungry, you know, and kept on my feet too, I was getting savage. 'How can I tell?' I said, 'I haven't even seen the wreck yet—some months, no doubt.' All this talk seemed to me so futile. 'Some months,' he said. 'Well, let us say three months before we can make a start. Yes. That ought to do the affair.' I flung out of his hut (he lived all alone in a clay hut with a sort of verandah) muttering to myself my opinion of him. He was a chattering idiot. Afterwards I took it back when it was borne in upon me startlingly with what extreme nicety he had estimated the time requisite for the 'affair.'

"I went to work the next day, turning, so to speak, my back on that station. In that way only it seemed to me I could keep my hold on the redeeming facts of life. Still, one must look about sometimes; and then I saw this station, these men strolling aimlessly about in the sunshine of the yard. I asked myself sometimes what it all meant. They wandered here and there with their absurd long staves in their hands, like a lot of faithless pilgrims bewitched inside a rotten fence. The word 'ivory' rang in the air, was whispered, was sighed. You would think they were praying to it. A taint of imbecile rapacity blew through it all, like a whiff from some corpse. By Jove! I've never seen anything so unreal in my life. And outside, the silent wilderness surrounding this cleared speck on the earth struck me as something great and invincible, like evil or truth, waiting patiently for the passing away of this fantastic invasion.

"Oh, these months! Well, never mind. Various things happened. One evening a grass shed full of calico, cotton prints, beads, and I don't know what else, burst into a blaze so suddenly that you would have thought the earth had opened to let an avenging fire consume all that trash. I was smoking my pipe quietly by my dismantled steamer, and saw them all cutting capers in the light, with their arms lifted high, when the stout man with moustaches came tearing down to the river, a tin pail in his hand, assured me that everybody was 'behaving splendidly, splendidly,' dipped about a quart of water and tore back again. I noticed there was a hole in the bottom of his pail.

"I strolled up. There was no hurry. You see the thing had gone off like a box of matches. It had been hopeless from the very first. The flame had leaped high, driven everybody back, lighted up everything—and collapsed. The shed was already a heap of embers glowing fiercely. A nigger was being beaten near by. They said he had caused the fire in some way; be that as it may, he was screeching most horribly. I saw him, later, for several days, sitting in a bit of shade looking very sick and trying to recover himself: afterwards he arose and went out—and the wilderness without a sound took him into its bosom again. As I approached the glow from the dark I found myself at the back of two men, talking. I heard the name of Kurtz pronounced, then the words, 'take advantage of this unfortunate accident.' One of the men was the manager. I wished him a good evening. 'Did you ever see anything like it—eh? it is incredible,' he said, and walked off. The other man remained. He was a first-class agent, young, gentlemanly, a bit reserved, with a forked little beard and a hooked nose. He was standoffish with the other agents, and they on their side said he was the manager's spy upon them. As to me, I had hardly ever spoken to him before. We got into talk, and by and by we strolled away from the hissing ruins. Then he asked me to his room, which was in the main building of the station. He struck a match, and I perceived that this young aristocrat had not only a silver-mounted dressing-case but also a whole candle all to himself. Just at that time the manager was the only man supposed to have any right to candles. Native mats covered the clay walls; a collection of spears, assegais,[2] shields, knives, was hung up in trophies. The business entrusted to this fellow was the making of bricks—so I had been informed; but there wasn't a fragment of a brick anywhere in the station, and he had been there more than a year—waiting. It seems he could not make bricks without something, I don't know what—straw maybe. Anyway, it could not be found there, and as it was not likely to be sent from Europe, it did not appear clear to me what he was waiting for. An act of special creation[3] perhaps. However, they were all waiting—all the sixteen or twenty pilgrims of them—for something; and upon my word it did not seem an uncongenial occupation, from the way they took it, though the only thing that ever came to them was disease—as far as I could see. They beguiled the time by backbiting and intriguing against each other in a foolish kind of way. There was an air of plotting about that station, but nothing came of it, of course. It was as unreal as everything else—as the philanthropic pretence of the whole concern, as their talk, as their government, as their show of work. The only real feeling was a desire to get appointed to a trading-post where ivory was to be had, so that they could earn percentages. They intrigued and slandered and hated each other only on that account—but as to effectually lifting a little finger—oh no. By heavens! there is something after all in the world allowing one man to steal a horse while another must not look at a halter. Steal a horse straight out. Very well. He has done it. Perhaps he can ride. But there is a way of looking at a halter that would provoke the most charitable of saints into a kick.

"I had no idea why he wanted to be sociable, but as we chatted in there it suddenly occurred to me the fellow was trying to get at something—in fact, pumping me. He alluded constantly to Europe, to the people I was supposed to know there—putting leading questions as to my acquaintances in the sepulchral city,

2. Slender hardwood javelins used as weapons.
3. The religious doctrine of "special creation" referred to a literal interpretation of Genesis in which the universe came into being by instant divine decree.

and so on. His little eyes glittered like mica[4] discs—with curiosity—though he tried to keep up a bit of superciliousness. At first I was astonished, but very soon I became awfully curious to see what he would find out from me. I couldn't possibly imagine what I had in me to make it worth his while. It was very pretty to see how he baffled himself, for in truth my body was full only of chills, and my head had nothing in it but that wretched steamboat business. It was evident he took me for a perfectly shameless prevaricator. At last he got angry, and, to conceal a movement of furious annoyance, he yawned. I rose. Then I noticed a small sketch in oils, on a panel, representing a woman, draped and blindfolded, carrying a lighted torch.[5] The background was sombre—almost black. The movement of the woman was stately, and the effect of the torchlight on the face was sinister.

"It arrested me, and he stood by civilly, holding an empty half-pint champagne bottle (medical comforts) with the candle stuck in it. To my question he said Mr Kurtz had painted this—in this very station more than a year ago—while waiting for means to go to his trading-post. 'Tell me, pray,' said I, 'who is this Mr Kurtz?'

"'The chief of the Inner Station,' he answered in a short tone, looking away. 'Much obliged,' I said, laughing. 'And you are the brickmaker of the Central Station. Every one knows that.' He was silent for a while. 'He is a prodigy,' he said at last. 'He is an emissary of pity, and science, and progress, and devil knows what else. We want,' he began to declaim suddenly, 'for the guidance of the cause entrusted to us by Europe, so to speak, higher intelligence, wide sympathies, a singleness of purpose.' 'Who says that?' I asked. 'Lots of them,' he replied. 'Some even write that; and so *he* comes here, a special being, as you ought to know.' 'Why ought I to know?' I interrupted, really surprised. He paid no attention. 'Yes. To-day he is chief of the best station, next year he will be assistant-manager, two years more and . . . but I daresay you know what he will be in two years' time. You are of the new gang—the gang of virtue. The same people who sent him specially also recommended you. Oh, don't say no. I've my own eyes to trust.' Light dawned upon me. My dear aunt's influential acquaintances were producing an unexpected effect upon that young man. I nearly burst into a laugh. 'Do you read the Company's confidential correspondence?' I asked. He hadn't a word to say. It was great fun. 'When Mr Kurtz,' I continued severely, 'is General Manager, you won't have the opportunity.'

"He blew the candle out suddenly, and we went outside. The moon had risen. Black figures strolled about listlessly, pouring water on the glow, whence proceeded a sound of hissing; steam ascended in the moonlight; the beaten nigger groaned somewhere. 'What a row the brute makes!' said the indefatigable man with the moustaches, appearing near us. 'Serve him right. Transgression—punishment—bang! Pitiless, pitiless. That's the only way. This will prevent all conflagrations for the future. I was just telling the manager . . .' He noticed my companion, and became crestfallen all at once. 'Not in bed yet,' he said, with a kind of servile heartiness; 'it's so natural. Ha! Danger—agitation.' He vanished. I went on to the river-side, and the other followed me. I heard a scathing murmur

---

4. A mineral silicate that separates into glittering layers.
5. Justice was traditionally portrayed as a

blindfolded woman, although usually bearing scales and a sword rather than a torch.

at my ear, 'Heap of muffs[6]—go to.' The pilgrims could be seen in knots gesticulating, discussing. Several had still their staves in their hands. I verily believe
they took these sticks to bed with them. Beyond the fence the forest stood up
spectrally in the moonlight, and through the dim stir, through the faint sounds of
that lamentable courtyard, the silence of the land went home to one's very
heart—its mystery, its greatness, the amazing reality of its concealed life. The
hurt nigger moaned feebly somewhere near by, and then fetched a deep sigh that
made me mend my pace away from there. I felt a hand introducing itself under
my arm. 'My dear sir,' said the fellow, 'I don't want to be misunderstood, and
especially by you, who will see Mr Kurtz long before I can have that pleasure. I
wouldn't like him to get a false idea of my disposition. . . .'

"I let him run on, this papier-mâché Mephistopheles,[7] and it seemed to me
that if I tried I could poke my forefinger through him, and would find nothing
inside but a little loose dirt, maybe. He, don't you see, had been planning to be
assistant-manager by and by under the present man, and I could see that the
coming of that Kurtz had upset them both not a little. He talked precipitately,
and I did not try to stop him. I had my shoulders against the wreck of my
steamer, hauled up on the slope like a carcass of some big river animal. The
smell of mud, of primeval mud, by Jove! was in my nostrils, the high stillness of
primeval forest was before my eyes; there were shiny patches on the black
creek. The moon had spread over everything a thin layer of silver—over the
rank grass, over the mud, upon the wall of matted vegetation standing higher
than the wall of a temple, over the great river I could see through a sombre gap
glittering, glittering, as it flowed broadly by without a murmur. All this was
great, expectant, mute, while the man jabbered about himself. I wondered
whether the stillness on the face of the immensity looking at us two were
meant as an appeal or as a menace. What were we who had strayed in here?
Could we handle that dumb thing, or would it handle us? I felt how big, how
confoundedly big, was that thing that couldn't talk and perhaps was deaf as
well. What was in there? I could see a little ivory coming out from there, and I
had heard Mr Kurtz was in there. I had heard enough about it too—God
knows! Yet somehow it didn't bring any image with it—no more than if I had
been told an angel or a fiend was in there. I believed it in the same way one of
you might believe there are inhabitants in the planet Mars. I knew once a
Scotch sailmaker who was certain, dead sure, there were people in Mars.[8] If
you asked him for some idea how they looked and behaved, he would get shy
and mutter something about 'walking on all-fours.' If you as much as smiled,
he would—though a man of sixty—offer to fight you. I would not have gone so
far as to fight for Kurtz, but I went for him near enough to a lie. You know I
hate, detest, and can't bear a lie, not because I am straighter than the rest of
us, but simply because it appals me. There is a taint of death, a flavour of mortality in lies—which is exactly what I hate and detest in the world—what I want
to forget. It makes me miserable and sick, like biting something rotten would

6. A "muff" is a foolish, stupid, feeble, or
incompetent person, especially in matters of
physical skill.
7. A devil, associated with the legend of Faust,
who sells his soul to Mephistopheles; in
exchange, the devil is to do his bidding on earth.

"Papier-mâché": method of constructing (e.g.,
masks, props, ornaments) using paper and glue;
suggestive of fragility, pretension, illusoriness.
8. H. G. Wells's *The War of the Worlds*, about
an invasion of Earth by aliens from Mars, was
first serialized in 1897.

do. Temperament, I suppose. Well, I went near enough to it by letting the young fool there believe anything he liked to imagine as to my influence in Europe. I became in an instant as much of a pretence as the rest of the bewitched pilgrims. This simply because I had a notion it somehow would be of help to that Kurtz whom at the time I did not see—you understand. He was just a word for me. I did not see the man in the name any more than you do. Do you see him? Do you see the story? Do you see anything? It seems to me I am trying to tell you a dream—making a vain attempt, because no relation of a dream can convey the dream-sensation, that commingling of absurdity, surprise, and bewilderment in a tremor of struggling revolt, that notion of being captured by the incredible which is of the very essence of dreams. . . ."

He was silent for a while.

". . . No, it is impossible; it is impossible to convey the life-sensation of any given epoch of one's existence—that which makes its truth, its meaning—its subtle and penetrating essence. It is impossible. We live, as we dream— alone. . . ."

He paused again as if reflecting, then added:

"Of course in this you fellows see more than I could then. You see me, whom you know. . . ."

It had become so pitch dark that we listeners could hardly see one another. For a long time already he, sitting apart, had been no more to us than a voice. There was not a word from anybody. The others might have been asleep, but I was awake. I listened, I listened on the watch for the sentence, for the word, that would give me the clue to the faint uneasiness inspired by this narrative that seemed to shape itself without human lips in the heavy night-air of the river.

". . . Yes—I let him run on," Marlow began again, "and think what he pleased about the powers that were behind me. I did! And there was nothing behind me! There was nothing but that wretched, old, mangled steamboat I was leaning against, while he talked fluently about 'the necessity for every man to get on.' 'And when one comes out here, you conceive, it is not to gaze at the moon.' Mr Kurtz was a 'universal genius,' but even a genius would find it easier to work with 'adequate tools—intelligent men.' He did not make bricks—why, there was a physical impossibility in the way—as I was well aware; and if he did secretarial work for the manager, it was because 'no sensible man rejects wantonly the confidence of his superiors.' Did I see it? I saw it. What more did I want? What I really wanted was rivets, by heaven! Rivets. To get on with the work—to stop the hole. Rivets I wanted. There were cases of them down at the coast—cases—piled up—burst—split! You kicked a loose rivet at every second step in that station yard on the hillside. Rivets had rolled into the grove of death. You could fill your pockets with rivets for the trouble of stooping down—and there wasn't one rivet to be found where it was wanted. We had plates that would do, but nothing to fasten them with. And every week the messenger, a lone negro, letter-bag on shoulder and staff in hand, left our station for the coast. And several times a week a coast caravan came in with trade goods—ghastly glazed calico that made you shudder only to look at it, glass beads value about a penny a quart, confounded spotted cotton handkerchiefs. And no rivets. Three carriers could have brought all that was wanted to set that steamboat afloat.

"He was becoming confidential now, but I fancy my unresponsive attitude must have exasperated him at last, for he judged it necessary to inform me he feared neither God nor devil, let alone any mere man. I said I could see that very well, but what I wanted was a certain quantity of rivets—and rivets were what really Mr Kurtz wanted, if he had only known it. Now letters went to the coast every week. . . . 'My dear sir,' he cried, 'I write from dictation.' I demanded rivets. There was a way—for an intelligent man. He changed his manner; became very cold, and suddenly began to talk about a hippopotamus; wondered whether sleeping on board the steamer (I stuck to my salvage night and day) I wasn't disturbed. There was an old hippo that had the bad habit of getting out on the bank and roaming at night over the station grounds. The pilgrims used to turn out in a body and empty every rifle they could lay hands on at him. Some even had sat up o' nights for him. All this energy was wasted, though. 'That animal has a charmed life,' he said; 'but you can say this only of brutes in this country. No man—you apprehend me?—no man here bears a charmed life.' He stood there for a moment in the moonlight with his delicate hooked nose set a little askew, and his mica eyes glittering without a wink, then, with a curt Good-night, he strode off. I could see he was disturbed and considerably puzzled, which made me feel more hopeful than I had been for days. It was a great comfort to turn from that chap to my influential friend, the battered, twisted, ruined, tinpot steamboat. I clambered on board. She rang under my feet like an empty Huntley & Palmer biscuit-tin[9] kicked along a gutter; she was nothing so solid in make, and rather less pretty in shape, but I had expended enough hard work on her to make me love her. No influential friend would have served me better. She had given me a chance to come out a bit—to find out what I could do. No, I don't like work. I had rather laze about and think of all the fine things that can be done. I don't like work—no man does—but I like what is in the work—the chance to find yourself. Your own reality—for yourself, not for others—what no other man can ever know. They can only see the mere show, and never can tell what it really means.

"I was not surprised to see somebody sitting aft, on the deck, with his legs dangling over the mud. You see I rather chummed with the few mechanics there were in that station, whom the other pilgrims naturally despised—on account of their imperfect manners, I suppose. This was the foreman—a boiler-maker by trade—a good worker. He was a lank, bony, yellow-faced man, with big intense eyes. His aspect was worried, and his head was as bald as the palm of my hand; but his hair in falling seemed to have stuck to his chin, and had prospered in the new locality, for his beard hung down to his waist. He was a widower with six young children (he had left them in charge of a sister of his to come out there), and the passion of his life was pigeon-flying. He was an enthusiast and a connoisseur. He would rave about pigeons. After work hours he used to sometimes come over from his hut for a talk about his children and his pigeons; at work, when he had to crawl in the mud under the bottom of the steamboat, he would tie up that beard of his in a kind of white serviette[1] he brought for the purpose. It had loops to go over his ears. In the evening he

9. Huntley & Palmer biscuits were made in Reading, England, and exported throughout the British Empire; they came in a variety of collectible tins.
1. Table napkin (French).

could be seen squatted on the bank rinsing that wrapper in the creek with great care, then spreading it solemnly on a bush to dry.

"I slapped him on the back and shouted 'We shall have rivets!' He scrambled to his feet exclaiming 'No! Rivets!' as though he couldn't believe his ears. Then in a low voice, 'You . . . eh?' I don't know why we behaved like lunatics. I put my finger to the side of my nose and nodded mysteriously. 'Good for you!' he cried, snapped his fingers above his head, lifting one foot. I tried a jig. We capered on the iron deck. A frightful clatter came out of that hulk, and the virgin forest on the other bank of the creek sent it back in a thundering roll upon the sleeping station. It must have made some of the pilgrims sit up in their hovels. A dark figure obscured the lighted doorway of the manager's hut, vanished, then, a second or so after, the doorway itself vanished too. We stopped, and the silence driven away by the stamping of our feet flowed back again from the recesses of the land. The great wall of vegetation, an exuberant and entangled mass of trunks, branches, leaves, boughs, festoons, motionless in the moonlight, was like a rioting invasion of soundless life, a rolling wave of plants, piled up, crested, ready to topple over the creek, to sweep every little man of us out of his little existence. And it moved not. A deadened burst of mighty splashes and snorts reached us from afar, as though an ichthyosaurus[2] had been taking a bath of glitter in the great river. 'After all,' said the boiler-maker in a reasonable tone, 'why shouldn't we get the rivets?' Why not, indeed! I did not know of any reason why we shouldn't. 'They'll come in three weeks,' I said confidently.

"But they didn't. Instead of rivets there came an invasion, an infliction, a visitation. It came in sections during the next three weeks, each section headed by a donkey carrying a white man in new clothes and tan shoes, bowing from that elevation right and left to the impressed pilgrims. A quarrelsome band of footsore sulky niggers trod on the heels of the donkey; a lot of tents, camp-stools, tin boxes, white cases, brown bales would be shot down in the court-yard, and the air of mystery would deepen a little over the muddle of the station. Five such instalments came, with their absurd air of disorderly flight with the loot of innumerable outfit shops and provision stores, that, one would think, they were lugging, after a raid, into the wilderness for equitable division. It was an inextricable mess of things decent in themselves but that human folly made look like the spoils of thieving.

"This devoted band called itself the Eldorado[3] Exploring Expedition, and I believe they were sworn to secrecy. Their talk, however, was the talk of sordid buccaneers: it was reckless without hardihood, greedy without audacity, and cruel without courage; there was not an atom of foresight or of serious intention in the whole batch of them, and they did not seem aware these things are wanted for the work of the world. To tear treasure out of the bowels of the land was their desire, with no more moral purpose at the back of it than there is in burglars breaking into a safe. Who paid the expenses of the noble enterprise I don't know; but the uncle of our manager was leader of that lot.

"In exterior he resembled a butcher in a poor neighbourhood, and his eyes had a look of sleepy cunning. He carried his fat paunch with ostentation on his

2. An extinct prehistoric marine reptile resembling a fish or a dolphin.
3. *El Dorado* (literally, "the gilded one," Span-ish); the mythical land of gold sought by the Spanish conquistadors in South America.

short legs, and during the time his gang infested the station spoke to no one but his nephew. You could see these two roaming about all day long with their heads close together in an everlasting confab.[4]

"I had given up worrying myself about the rivets. One's capacity for that kind of folly is more limited than you would suppose. I said Hang!—and let things slide. I had plenty of time for meditation, and now and then I would give some thought to Kurtz. I wasn't very interested in him. No. Still, I was curious to see whether this man, who had come out equipped with moral ideas of some sort, would climb to the top after all, and how he would set about his work when there."

2

"One evening as I was lying flat on the deck of my steamboat, I heard voices approaching—and there were the nephew and the uncle strolling along the bank. I laid my head on my arm again, and had nearly lost myself in a doze, when somebody said in my ear, as it were: 'I am as harmless as a little child, but I don't like to be dictated to. Am I the manager—or am I not? I was ordered to send him there. It's incredible.' . . . I became aware that the two were standing on the shore alongside the forepart of the steamboat, just below my head. I did not move; it did not occur to me to move: I was sleepy. 'It *is* unpleasant,' grunted the uncle. 'He has asked the Administration to be sent there,' said the other, 'with the idea of showing what he could do; and I was instructed accordingly. Look at the influence that man must have. Is it not frightful?' They both agreed it was frightful, then made several bizarre remarks: 'Make rain and fine weather—one man—the Council—by the nose'—bits of absurd sentences that got the better of my drowsiness, so that I had pretty near the whole of my wits about me when the uncle said, 'The climate may do away with this difficulty for you. Is he alone there?' 'Yes,' answered the manager; 'he sent his assistant down the river with a note to me in these terms: "Clear this poor devil out of the country, and don't bother sending more of that sort. I had rather be alone than have the kind of men you can dispose of with me." It was more than a year ago. Can you imagine such impudence?' 'Anything since then?' asked the other hoarsely. 'Ivory,' jerked the nephew; 'lots of it—prime sort—lots—most annoying, from him.' 'And with that?' questioned the heavy rumble. 'Invoice,' was the reply fired out, so to speak. Then silence. They had been talking about Kurtz.

"I was broad awake by this time, but, lying perfectly at ease, remained still, having no inducement to change my position. 'How did that ivory come all this way?' growled the elder man, who seemed very vexed. The other explained that it had come with a fleet of canoes in charge of an English half-caste[5] clerk Kurtz had with him; that Kurtz had apparently intended to return himself, the station being by that time bare of goods and stores, but after coming three hundred miles, had suddenly decided to go back, which he started to do alone in a small dugout with four paddlers, leaving the half-caste to continue down the river with the ivory. The two fellows there seemed astounded at anybody attempting such a thing. They were at a loss for an adequate motive. As for me, I seemed to see Kurtz for the first time. It was a distinct glimpse: the dugout, four paddling

4. Conversation.   5. Of mixed race.

savages, and the lone white man turning his back suddenly on the headquarters, on relief, on thoughts of home—perhaps; setting his face towards the depths of the wilderness, towards his empty and desolate station. I did not know the motive. Perhaps he was just simply a fine fellow who stuck to his work for its own sake. His name, you understand, had not been pronounced once. He was 'that man.' The half-caste, who, as far as I could see, had conducted a difficult trip with great prudence and pluck, was invariably alluded to as 'that scoundrel.' The 'scoundrel' had reported that the 'man' had been very ill—had recovered imperfectly. . . . The two below me moved away then a few paces, and strolled back and forth at some little distance. I heard: 'Military post—doctor—two hundred miles—quite alone now—unavoidable delays—nine months—no news—strange rumours.' They approached again, just as the manager was saying, 'No one, as far as I know, unless a species of wandering trader—a pestilential fellow, snapping ivory from the natives.' Who was it they were talking about now? I gathered in snatches that this was some man supposed to be in Kurtz's district, and of whom the manager did not approve. 'We will not be free from unfair competition till one of these fellows is hanged for an example,' he said. 'Certainly,' grunted the other; 'get him hanged! Why not? Anything—anything can be done in this country. That's what I say; nobody here, you understand, *here*, can endanger your position. And why? You stand the climate—you outlast them all. The danger is in Europe; but there before I left I took care to—' They moved off and whispered, then their voices rose again. 'The extraordinary series of delays is not my fault. I did my possible.' The fat man sighed, 'Very sad.' 'And the pestiferous absurdity of his talk,' continued the other; 'he bothered me enough when he was here. "Each station should be like a beacon on the road towards better things, a centre for trade of course, but also for humanising, improving, instructing." Conceive you[6]—that ass! And he wants to be manager! No, it's—' Here he got choked by excessive indignation, and I lifted my head the least bit. I was surprised to see how near they were—right under me. I could have spat upon their hats. They were looking on the ground, absorbed in thought. The manager was switching his leg with a slender twig: his sagacious relative lifted his head. 'You have been well since you came out this time?' he asked. The other gave a start. 'Who? I? Oh! Like a charm—like a charm. But the rest—oh, my goodness! All sick. They die so quick, too, that I haven't the time to send them out of the country—it's incredible!' 'H'm. Just so,' grunted the uncle. 'Ah! my boy, trust to this—I say, trust to this.' I saw him extend his short flipper of an arm for a gesture that took in the forest, the creek, the mud, the river—seemed to beckon with a dishonouring flourish before the sunlit face of the land a treacherous appeal to the lurking death, to the hidden evil, to the profound darkness of its heart. It was so startling that I leaped to my feet and looked back at the edge of the forest, as though I had expected an answer of some sort to that black display of confidence. You know the foolish notions that come to one sometimes. The high stillness confronted these two figures with its ominous patience, waiting for the passing away of a fantastic invasion.

"They swore aloud together—out of sheer fright, I believe—then, pretending not to know anything of my existence, turned back to the station. The sun was

6. "Just imagine." This phrase, like "I did my possible" (I did the best I could), above, and others throughout the novel, is a literal translation of the French spoken by Belgian traders.

low; and leaning forward side by side, they seemed to be tugging painfully uphill their two ridiculous shadows of unequal length, that trailed behind them slowly over the tall grass without bending a single blade.

"In a few days the Eldorado Expedition went into the patient wilderness, that closed upon it as the sea closes over a diver. Long afterwards the news came that all the donkeys were dead. I know nothing as to the fate of the less valuable animals.[7] They, no doubt, like the rest of us, found what they deserved. I did not inquire. I was then rather excited at the prospect of meeting Kurtz very soon. When I say very soon I mean it comparatively. It was just two months from the day we left the creek when we came to the bank below Kurtz's station.

"Going up that river was like travelling back to the earliest beginnings of the world, when vegetation rioted on the earth and the big trees were kings. An empty stream, a great silence, an impenetrable forest. The air was warm, thick, heavy, sluggish. There was no joy in the brilliance of sunshine. The long stretches of the waterway ran on, deserted, into the gloom of overshadowed distances. On silvery sandbanks hippos and alligators sunned themselves side by side. The broadening waters flowed through a mob of wooded islands; you lost your way on that river as you would in a desert, and butted all day long against shoals, trying to find the channel, till you thought yourself bewitched and cut off for ever from everything you had known once—somewhere—far away—in another existence perhaps. There were moments when one's past came back to one, as it will sometimes when you have not a moment to spare to yourself; but it came in the shape of an unrestful and noisy dream, remembered with wonder amongst the overwhelming realities of this strange world of plants, and water, and silence. And this stillness of life did not in the least resemble a peace. It was the stillness of an implacable force brooding over an inscrutable intention. It looked at you with a vengeful aspect. I got used to it afterwards; I did not see it any more; I had no time. I had to keep guessing at the channel; I had to discern, mostly by inspiration, the signs of hidden banks; I watched for sunken stones; I was learning to clap my teeth smartly before my heart flew out, when I shaved by a fluke some infernal sly old snag[8] that would have ripped the life out of the tin-pot steamboat and drowned all the pilgrims; I had to keep a look-out for the signs of dead wood we could cut up in the night for next day's steaming. When you have to attend to things of that sort, to the mere incidents of the surface, the reality—the reality, I tell you—fades. The inner truth is hidden—luckily, luckily. But I felt it all the same; I felt often its mysterious still-ness watching me at my monkey tricks, just as it watches you fellows perform-ing on your respective tight-ropes for—what is it? half a crown[9] a tumble—"

"Try to be civil, Marlow," growled a voice, and I knew there was at least one listener awake besides myself.

"I beg your pardon. I forgot the heartache which makes up the rest of the price. And indeed what does the price matter, if the trick be well done? You do your tricks very well. And I didn't do badly either, since I managed not to sink that steamboat on my first trip. It's a wonder to me yet. Imagine a blindfolded

---

7. I.e., humans.
8. A large branch or tree trunk embedded in the river bottom with one end pointing up.
9. British denomination of coin, equal to 2

shillings and 6 pence, or an eighth of a pound. Not much money: at the time, the value of a London cab fare or a generous tip.

man set to drive a van over a bad road. I sweated and shivered over that business considerably, I can tell you. After all, for a seaman, to scrape the bottom of the thing that's supposed to float all the time under his care is the unpardonable sin. No one may know of it, but you never forget the thump—eh? A blow on the very heart. You remember it, you dream of it, you wake up at night and think of it—years after—and go hot and cold all over. I don't pretend to say that steamboat floated all the time. More than once she had to wade for a bit, with twenty cannibals splashing around and pushing. We had enlisted some of these chaps on the way for a crew. Fine fellows—cannibals—in their place. They were men one could work with, and I am grateful to them. And, after all, they did not eat each other before my face: they had brought along a provision of hippo-meat which went rotten, and made the mystery of the wilderness stink in my nostrils. Phoo! I can sniff it now. I had the manager on board and three or four pilgrims with their staves—all complete. Sometimes we came upon a station close by the bank, clinging to the skirts of the unknown, and the white men rushing out of a tumble-down hovel, with great gestures of joy and surprise and welcome, seemed very strange—had the appearance of being held there captive by a spell. The word 'ivory' would ring in the air for a while—and on we went again into the silence, along empty reaches, round the still bends, between the high walls of our winding way, reverberating in hollow claps the ponderous beat of the stern-wheel.[1] Trees, trees, millions of trees, massive, immense, running up high; and at their foot, hugging the bank against the stream, crept the little begrimed steamboat, like a sluggish beetle crawling on the floor of a lofty portico. It made you feel very small, very lost, and yet it was not altogether depressing, that feeling. After all, if you were small, the grimy beetle crawled on—which was just what you wanted it to do. Where the pilgrims imagined it crawled to I don't know. To some place where they expected to get something, I bet! For me it crawled towards Kurtz—exclusively; but when the steam-pipes started leaking we crawled very slow. The reaches opened before us and closed behind, as if the forest had stepped leisurely across the water to bar the way for our return. We penetrated deeper and deeper into the heart of darkness. It was very quiet there. At night sometimes the roll of drums behind the curtain of trees would run up the river and remain sustained faintly, as if hovering in the air high over our heads, till the first break of day. Whether it meant war, peace, or prayer we could not tell. The dawns were heralded by the descent of a chill stillness; the woodcutters slept, their fires burned low; the snapping of a twig would make you start. We were wanderers on a prehistoric earth, on an earth that wore the aspect of an unknown planet. We could have fancied ourselves the first of men taking possession of an accursed inheritance, to be subdued at the cost of profound anguish and of excessive toil. But suddenly, as we struggled round a bend, there would be a glimpse of rush walls, of peaked grass-roofs, a burst of yells, a whirl of black limbs, a mass of hands clapping, of feet stamping, of bodies swaying, of eyes rolling, under the droop of heavy and motionless foliage. The steamer toiled along slowly on the edge of a black and incomprehensible frenzy. The prehistoric man was cursing us, praying to us, welcoming us—who could tell? We were cut off from the

---

1. The paddle wheel at the rear of the boat; the main source of propulsion on a steamboat.

comprehension of our surroundings; we glided past like phantoms, wondering and secretly appalled, as sane men would be before an enthusiastic outbreak in a madhouse. We could not understand because we were too far and could not remember, because we were travelling in the night of first ages, of those ages that are gone, leaving hardly a sign—and no memories.

"The earth seemed unearthly. We are accustomed to look upon the shackled form of a conquered monster, but there—there you could look at a thing monstrous and free. It was unearthly, and the men were—No, they were not inhuman. Well, you know, that was the worst of it—this suspicion of their not being inhuman. It would come slowly to one. They howled and leaped, and spun, and made horrid faces; but what thrilled you was just the thought of their humanity—like yours—the thought of your remote kinship with this wild and passionate uproar. Ugly. Yes, it was ugly enough; but if you were man enough you would admit to yourself that there was in you just the faintest trace of a response to the terrible frankness of that noise, a dim suspicion of there being a meaning in it which you—you so remote from the night of first ages—could comprehend. And why not? The mind of man is capable of anything—because everything is in it, all the past as well as all the future. What was there after all? Joy, fear, sorrow, devotion, valour, rage—who can tell?—but truth—truth stripped of its cloak of time. Let the fool gape and shudder—the man knows, and can look on without a wink. But he must at least be as much of a man as these on the shore. He must meet that truth with his own true stuff—with his own inborn strength. Principles? Principles won't do. Acquisitions, clothes, pretty rags—rags that would fly off at the first good shake. No; you want a deliberate belief. An appeal to me in this fiendish row—is there? Very well; I hear; I admit, but I have a voice too, and for good or evil mine is the speech that cannot be silenced. Of course, a fool, what with sheer fright and fine sentiments, is always safe. Who's that grunting? You wonder I didn't go ashore for a howl and a dance? Well, no—I didn't. Fine sentiments, you say? Fine sentiments be hanged! I had no time. I had to mess about with white-lead[2] and strips of woollen blanket helping to put bandages on those leaky steam-pipes—I tell you. I had to watch the steering, and circumvent those snags, and get the tin-pot along by hook or by crook. There was surface-truth enough in these things to save a wiser man. And between whiles I had to look after the savage who was fireman. He was an improved specimen; he could fire up a vertical boiler.[3] He was there below me, and, upon my word, to look at him was as edifying as seeing a dog in a parody of breeches and a feather hat, walking on his hind legs. A few months of training had done for that really fine chap. He squinted at the steam-gauge and at the water-gauge with an evident effort of intrepidity—and he had filed teeth too, the poor devil, and the wool of his pate shaved into queer patterns, and three ornamental scars on each of his cheeks. He ought to have been clapping his hands and stamping his feet on the bank, instead of which he was hard at work, a thrall to strange witchcraft, full of improving knowledge. He was useful because he had been instructed; and what he knew was this—that should the water in that transparent thing disappear, the evil spirit inside the boiler would get angry through the greatness of

2. Lead compound often used in white paint   3. A simple and easily fired narrow boiler.
for caulking seams and waterproofing timber.

his thirst, and take a terrible vengeance. So he sweated and fired up and watched the glass fearfully (with an impromptu charm, made of rags, tied to his arm, and a piece of polished bone, as big as a watch, stuck flatways through his lower lip), while the wooded banks slipped past us slowly, the short noise was left behind, the interminable miles of silence—and we crept on, towards Kurtz. But the snags were thick, the water was treacherous and shallow, the boiler seemed indeed to have a sulky devil in it, and thus neither that fireman nor I had any time to peer into our creepy thoughts.

"Some fifty miles below the Inner Station we came upon a hut of reeds, an inclined and melancholy pole, with the unrecognisable tatters of what had been a flag of some sort flying from it, and a neatly stacked wood-pile. This was unexpected. We came to the bank, and on the stack of firewood found a flat piece of board with some faded pencil-writing on it. When deciphered it said: 'Wood for you. Hurry up. Approach cautiously.' There was a signature, but it was illegible—not Kurtz—a much longer word. Hurry up. Where? Up the river? 'Approach cautiously.' We had not done so. But the warning could not have been meant for the place where it could be only found after approach. Something was wrong above. But what—and how much? That was the question. We commented adversely upon the imbecility of that telegraphic style.[4] The bush around said nothing, and would not let us look very far, either. A torn curtain of red twill hung in the doorway of the hut, and flapped sadly in our faces. The dwelling was dismantled; but we could see a white man had lived there not very long ago. There remained a rude table—a plank on two posts; a heap of rubbish reposed in a dark corner, and by the door I picked up a book. It had lost its covers, and the pages had been thumbed into a state of extremely dirty softness; but the back had been lovingly stitched afresh with white cotton thread, which looked clean yet. It was an extraordinary find. Its title was, *An Inquiry into some Points of Seamanship*, by a man Towser, Towson—some such name—Master in His Majesty's Navy.[5] The matter looked dreary reading enough, with illustrative diagrams and repulsive tables of figures, and the copy was sixty years old. I handled this amazing antiquity with the greatest possible tenderness, lest it should dissolve in my hands. Within, Towson or Towser was inquiring earnestly into the breaking strain of ships' chains and tackle, and other such matters. Not a very enthralling book; but at the first glance you could see there a singleness of intention, an honest concern for the right way of going to work, which made these humble pages, thought out so many years ago, luminous with another than a professional light. The simple old sailor, with his talk of chains and purchases,[6] made me forget the jungle and the pilgrims in a delicious sensation of having come upon something unmistakably real. Such a book being there was wonderful enough; but still more astounding were the notes pencilled in the margin, and plainly referring to the text. I couldn't believe my eyes! They were in cipher! Yes, it looked like cipher. Fancy a man lugging with him a book of that description into this nowhere and studying it—and making notes—in cipher at that! It was an extravagant mystery.

---

4. Using as few words as possible, as in a telegram.
5. I.e., the British Navy.
6. Nautical terms. "Chains": contrivances for fastening ropes supporting the mast to the deck and the sides of a ship. "Purchases": devices for applying or increasing force: pulleys, windlasses, etc.

"I had been dimly aware for some time of a worrying noise, and when I lifted my eyes I saw the wood-pile was gone, and the manager, aided by all the pilgrims, was shouting at me from the river-side. I slipped the book into my pocket. I assure you to leave off reading was like tearing myself away from the shelter of an old an solid friendship.

"I started the lame engine ahead. 'It must be this miserable trader—this intruder,' exclaimed the manager, looking back malevolently at the place we had left. 'He must be English,' I said. 'It will not save him from getting into trouble if he is not careful,' muttered the manager darkly. I observed with assumed innocence that no man was safe from trouble in this world.

"The current was more rapid now, the steamer seemed at her last gasp, the stern-wheel flopped languidly, and I caught myself listening on tiptoe for the next beat of the float,[7] for in sober truth I expected the wretched thing to give up every moment. It was like watching the last flickers of a life. But still we crawled. Sometimes I would pick out a tree a little way head to measure our progress towards Kurtz by, but I lost it invariably before we got abreast. To keep the eyes so long on one thing was too much for human patience. The manager displayed a beautiful resignation. I fretted and fumed and took to arguing with myself whether or no I would talk openly with Kurtz; but before I could come to any conclusion it occurred to me that my speech or my silence, indeed any action of mine, would be a mere futility. What did it matter what any one knew or ignored? What did it matter who was manager? One gets sometimes such a flash of insight. The essentials of this affair lay deep under the surface, beyond my reach, and beyond my power of meddling.

"Towards the evening of the second day we judged ourselves about eight miles from Kurtz's station. I wanted to push on; but the manager looked grave, and told me the navigation up there was so dangerous that it would be advisable, the sun being very low already, to wait where we were till next morning. Moreover, he pointed out that if the warning to approach cautiously were to be followed, we must approach in daylight—not at dusk, or in the dark. This was sensible enough. Eight miles meant nearly three hours' steaming for us, and I could also see suspicious ripples at the upper end of the reach. Nevertheless, I was annoyed beyond expression at the delay, and most unreasonably too, since one night more could not matter much after so many months. As we had plenty of wood, and caution was the word, I brought up in the middle of the stream. The reach was narrow, straight, with high sides like a railway cutting. The dusk came gliding into it long before the sun had set. The current ran smooth and swift, but a dumb immobility sat on the banks. The living trees, lashed together by the creepers and every living bush of the undergrowth, might have been changed into stone, even to the slenderest twig, to the lightest leaf. It was not sleep—it seemed unnatural, like a state of trance. Not the faintest sound of any kind could be heard. You looked on amazed, and began to suspect yourself of being deaf—then the night came suddenly, and struck you blind as well. About three in the morning some large fish leaped, and the loud splash made me jump as though a gun had been fired. When the sun rose there was a white fog, very warm and clammy, and more blinding than the night. It did not shift or drive; it was just there, standing all round you like something

7. The sound of the paddle ("paddle float") as it hits the water.

solid. At eight or nine, perhaps, it lifted as a shutter lifts. We had a glimpse of the towering multitude of trees, of the immense matted jungle, with the blazing little ball of the sun hanging over it—all perfectly still—and then the white shutter came down again, smoothly, as if sliding in greased grooves. I ordered the chain, which we had begun to heave in, to be paid out again. Before it stopped running with a muffled rattle, a cry, a very loud cry, as of infinite desolation, soared slowly in the opaque air. It ceased. A complaining clamour, modulated in savage discords, filled our ears. The sheer unexpectedness of it made my hair stir under my cap. I don't know how it struck the others: to me it seemed as though the mist itself had screamed, so suddenly, and apparently from all sides at once, did this tumultuous and mournful uproar arise. It culminated in a hurried outbreak of almost intolerably excessive shrieking, which stopped short, leaving us stiffened in a variety of silly attitudes, and obstinately listening to the nearly as appalling and excessive silence. 'Good God! What is the meaning—?' stammered at my elbow one of the pilgrims—a little fat man, with sandy hair and red whiskers, who wore side-spring boots, and pink pyjamas tucked into his socks. Two others remained open-mouthed a whole minute, then dashed into the little cabin, to rush out incontinently and stand darting scared glances, with Winchesters[8] at 'ready' in their hands. What we could see was just the steamer we were on, her outlines blurred as though she had been on the point of dissolving, and a misty strip of water, perhaps two feet broad, around her—and that was all. The rest of the world was nowhere, as far as our eyes and ears were concerned. Just nowhere. Gone, disappeared; swept off without leaving a whisper or a shadow behind.

"I went forward, and ordered the chain to be hauled in short, so as to be ready to trip the anchor and move the steamboat at once if necessary. 'Will they attack?' whispered an awed voice. 'We will all be butchered in this fog,' murmured another. The faces twitched with the strain, the hands trembled slightly, the eyes forgot to wink. It was very curious to see the contrast of expressions of the white men and of the black fellows of our crew, who were as much strangers to that part of the river as we, though their homes were only eight hundred miles away. The whites, of course greatly discomposed, had besides a curious look of being painfully shocked by such an outrageous row. The others had an alert, naturally interested expression; but their faces were essentially quiet, even those of the one or two who grinned as they hauled at the chain. Several exchanged short, grunting phrases, which seemed to settle the matter to their satisfaction. Their headman, a young, broad-chested black, severely draped in dark-blue fringed cloths, with fierce nostrils and his hair all done up artfully in oily ringlets, stood near me. 'Aha!' I said, just for good fellowship's sake. 'Catch 'im,' he snapped, with a bloodshot widening of his eyes and a flash of sharp teeth—'catch 'im. Give 'im to us.' 'To you, eh?' I asked; 'what would you do with them?' 'Eat 'im!' he said curtly, and, leaning his elbow on the rail, looked out into the fog in a dignified and profoundly pensive attitude. I would no doubt have been properly horrified, had it not occurred to me that he and his chaps must be very hungry: that they must have been growing increasingly hungry for at least this month past. They had been engaged for six months (I don't think a single one of them had any clear idea of time, as we at the end of countless ages have. They still belonged to the beginnings of time—had no inherited experience to teach them, as it were), and of course, as long as there was a piece of paper written over in accordance with some farcical law or other made down the river, it didn't enter anybody's head to trouble how they would live. Certainly they had brought with them some rotten hippo-meat, which couldn't have lasted very long, anyway, even if the pilgrims hadn't, in the midst of a shocking hullabaloo, thrown a considerable quantity of it overboard. It looked like a high-handed proceeding; but it was really a case of legitimate self-defence. You can't breathe dead hippo waking, sleeping, and eating, and at the same time keep your precarious grip on existence. Besides that, they had given them every week three pieces of brass wire, each about nine inches long; and the theory was they were to buy their provisions with that currency in river-side villages. You can see how *that* worked. There were either no villages, or the people were hostile, or the director, who like the rest of us fed out of tins, with an occasional old he-goat thrown in, didn't want to stop the steamer for some more or less recondite reasons. So, unless they swallowed the wire itself, or made loops of it to snare the fishes with, I don't see what good their extravagant salary could be to them. I must say it was paid with a regularity worthy of a large and honourable trading company. For the rest, the only thing to eat—though it didn't look eatable in the least—I saw in their possession was a few lumps of some stuff like half-cooked dough, of a dirty lavender colour, they kept wrapped in leaves, and now and then swallowed a piece of, but so small that it seemed done more for the look of the thing than for any serious purpose of sustenance. Why in the name of all the gnawing devils of hunger they didn't go for us—they were thirty to five—and have a good tuck-in for once, amazes me now when I think of it. They were big powerful men, with not much capacity to weigh the consequences, with courage, with strength, even yet, though their skins were no longer glossy and their muscles no longer hard. And I saw that something restraining, one of those human secrets that baffle probability, had come into play there. I looked at them with a swift quickening of interest—not because it occurred to me I might be eaten by them before very long, though I own to you that just then I perceived—in a new light, as it were—how unwholesome the pilgrims looked, and I hoped, yes, I positively hoped, that my aspect was not so—what shall I say?—so—unappetising: a touch of fantastic vanity which fitted well with the dream-sensation that pervaded all my days at that time. Perhaps I had a little fever too. One can't live with one's finger everlastingly on one's pulse. I had often 'a little fever,' or a little touch of other things—the playful paw-strokes of the wilderness, the preliminary trifling before the more serious onslaught which came in due course. Yes; I looked at them as you would on any human being, with a curiosity of their impulses, motives, capacities, weaknesses, when brought to the test of an inexorable physical necessity. Restraint! What possible restraint? Was it superstition, disgust, patience, fear—or some kind of primitive honour? No fear can stand up to hunger, no patience can wear it out, disgust simply does not exist where hunger is; and as to superstition, beliefs, and what you may call principles, they are less than chaff in a breeze. Don't you know the devilry of lingering starvation, its exasperating torment, its black thoughts, its sombre and brooding ferocity? Well, I do. It takes a man all his inborn strength to fight hunger properly. It's really easier to face bereavement, dishonour, and the perdition of one's soul—than this kind of prolonged hunger. Sad, but true. And these chaps too had no earthly reason for any kind of scruple. Restraint! I would just as soon have expected restraint from a hyena prowling amongst the corpses of a battlefield. But there was the fact facing me—the fact dazzling, to be seen, like the foam on the depths of the sea, like a ripple on an unfathomable enigma, a mystery greater—when I thought of it—than the curious, inexplicable note of desperate grief in this savage clamour that had swept by us on the river-bank, behind the blind whiteness of the fog.

"Two pilgrims were quarrelling in hurried whispers as to which bank. 'Left.' 'No, no; how can you? Right, right, of course.' 'It is very serious,' said the manager's voice behind me; 'I would be desolated if anything should happen to Mr. Kurtz before we came up.' I looked at him, and had not the slightest doubt he was sincere. He was just the kind of man who would wish to preserve appearances. That was his restraint. But when he muttered something about going on at once, I did not even take the trouble to answer him. I knew, and he knew, that it was impossible. Were we to let go our hold of the bottom, we would be absolutely in the air—in space. We wouldn't be able to tell where we were going to—whether up or down stream, or across—till we fetched against one bank or the other—and then we wouldn't know at first which it was. Of course I made no move. I had no mind for a smashup. You couldn't imagine a more deadly place for a shipwreck. Whether drowned at once or not, we were sure to perish speedily in one way or another. 'I authorise you to take all the risks,' he said, after a short silence. 'I refuse to take any,' I said shortly; which was just the answer he expected, though its tone might have surprised him. 'Well, I must defer to your judgment. You are captain,' he said, with marked civility. I turned my shoulder to him in sign of my appreciation, and looked into the fog. How long would it last? It was the most hopeless look-out. The approach to this Kurtz grubbing for ivory in the wretched bush was beset by as many dangers as though he had been an enchanted princess sleeping in a fabulous castle. 'Will they attack, do you think?' asked the manager, in a confidential tone.

"I did not think they would attack, for several obvious reasons. The thick fog was one. If they left the bank in their canoes they would get lost in it, as we would be if we attempted to move. Still, I had also judged the jungle of both banks quite impenetrable—and yet eyes were in it, eyes that had seen us. The river-side bushes were certainly very thick; but the undergrowth behind was evidently penetrable. However, during the short lift I had seen no canoes anywhere in the reach—certainly not abreast of the steamer. But what made the idea of attack inconceivable to me was the nature of the noise—of the cries we had heard. They had not the fierce character boding of immediate hostile intention. Unexpected, wild, and violent as they had been, they had given me an irresistible impression of sorrow. The glimpse of the steamboat had for some reason filled those savages with unrestrained grief. The danger, if any, I expounded, was from our proximity to a great human passion let loose. Even extreme grief may ultimately vent itself in violence—but more generally takes the form of apathy. . . .

"You should have seen the pilgrims stare! They had no heart to grin, or even to revile me; but I believe they thought me gone mad—with fright, maybe. I delivered a regular lecture. My dear boys, it was no good bothering. Keep a look-out? Well, you may guess I watched the fog for the signs of lifting as a cat watches a mouse; but for anything else our eyes were of no more use to us than if we had been buried miles deep in a heap of cottonwool. It felt like it too—choking, warm, stifling. Besides, all I said, though it sounded extravagant, was absolutely true to fact. What we afterwards alluded to as an attack was really an attempt at repulse. The action was very far from being aggressive—it was not even defensive, in the usual sense: it was undertaken under the stress of desperation, and in its essence was purely protective.

"It developed itself, I should say, two hours after the fog lifted, and its commencement was at a spot, roughly speaking, about a mile and a half below Kurtz's station. We had just floundered and flopped round a bend, when I saw an islet, a mere grassy hummock of bright green, in the middle of the stream. It was the only thing of the kind; but as we opened the reach more, I perceived it was the head of a long sandbank, or rather of a chain of shallow patches stretching down the middle of the river. They were discoloured, just awash, and the whole lot was seen just under the water, exactly as a man's backbone is seen running down the middle of his back under the skin. Now, as far as I did see, I could go to the right or to the left of this. I didn't know either channel, of course. The banks looked pretty well alike, the depth appeared the same; but as I had been informed the station was on the west side, I naturally headed for the western passage.

"No sooner had we fairly entered it than I became aware it was much narrower than I had supposed. To the left of us there was the long uninterrupted shoal, and to the right a high steep bank heavily overgrown with bushes. Above the bush the trees stood in serried ranks. The twigs overhung the current thickly, and from distance to distance a large limb of some tree projected rigidly over the stream. It was then well on in the afternoon, the face of the forest was gloomy, and a broad strip of shadow had already fallen on the water. In this shadow we steamed up—very slowly, as you may imagine. I sheered her well inshore—the water being deepest near the bank, as the sounding-pole[9] informed me.

"One of my hungry and forbearing friends was sounding in the bows just below me. This steamboat was exactly like a decked scow.[1] On the deck there were two little teak-wood houses, with doors and windows. The boiler was in the fore-end, and the machinery right astern. Over the whole there was a light roof, supported on stanchions. The funnel projected through that roof, and in front of the funnel a small cabin built of light planks served for a pilot-house. It contained a couch, two camp-stools, a loaded Martini-Henry[2] leaning in one corner, a tiny table, and the steering-wheel. It had a wide door in front and a broad shutter at each side. All these were always thrown open, of course. I spent my days perched up there on the extreme fore-end of that roof, before the door. At night I slept, or tried to, on the couch. An athletic black belonging to some coast tribe, and educated by my poor predecessor, was the helmsman. He sported a pair of brass earrings, wore a blue cloth wrapper from the waist to the

9. A pole with measurements, stuck in the water until it hits bottom, to determine the depth of a shallow body of water. "Sheered her well inshore": i.e., steered so as to be going upriver while close to the bank.

1. A large, flat-bottomed boat for cargo; in this case, with the addition of a deck.
2. A lever-action rifle taking an especially powerful charge; standard British service weapon of the time.

ankles, and thought all the world of himself. He was the most unstable kind of fool I had ever seen. He steered with no end of a swagger while you were by; but if he lost sight of you, he became instantly the prey of an abject funk, and would let that cripple of a steamboat get the upper hand of him in a minute.

"I was looking down at the sounding-pole, and feeling much annoyed to see at each try a little more of it stick out of that river, when I saw my poleman give up the business suddenly, and stretch himself flat on the deck, without even taking the trouble to haul his pole in. He kept hold on it though, and it trailed in the water. At the same time the fireman, whom I could also see below me, sat down abruptly before his furnace and ducked his head. I was amazed. Then I had to look at the river mighty quick, because there was a snag in the fairway. Sticks, little sticks, were flying about—thick; they were whizzing before my nose, dropping below me, striking behind me against my pilot-house. All this time the river, the shore, the woods, were very quiet—perfectly quiet. I could only hear the heavy splashing thump of the stern-wheel and the patter of these things. We cleared the snag clumsily. Arrows, by Jove! We were being shot at! I stepped in quickly to close the shutter on the land-side. That fool-helmsman, his hands on the spokes, was lifting his knees high, stamping his feet, champing his mouth, like a reined-in horse. Confound him! And we were staggering within ten feet of the bank. I had to lean right out to swing the heavy shutter, and I saw a face amongst the leaves on the level with my own, looking at me very fierce and steady; and then suddenly, as though a veil had been removed from my eyes, I made out, deep in the tangled gloom, naked breasts, arms, legs, glaring eyes— the bush was swarming with human limbs in movement, glistening, of bronze colour. The twigs shook, swayed, and rustled, the arrows flew out of them, and then the shutter came to. 'Steer her straight,' I said to the helmsman. He held his head rigid, face forward; but his eyes rolled, he kept on lifting and setting down his feet gently, his mouth foamed a little. 'Keep quiet!' I said in a fury. I might just as well have ordered a tree not to sway in the wind. I darted out. Below me there was a great scuffle of feet on the iron deck; confused exclamations; a voice screamed, 'Can you turn back?' I caught sight of a V-shaped ripple on the water ahead. What? Another snag! A fusillade[3] burst out under my feet. The pilgrims had opened with their Winchesters, and were simply squirting lead into that bush. A deuce of a lot of smoke came up and drove slowly forward. I swore at it. Now I couldn't see the ripple or the snag either. I stood in the doorway, peering, and the arrows came in swarms. They might have been poisoned, but they looked as though they wouldn't kill a cat. The bush began to howl. Our wood-cutters raised a warlike whoop; the report of a rifle just at my back deafened me. I glanced over my shoulder, and the pilot-house was yet full of noise and smoke when I made a dash at the wheel. The fool-nigger had dropped everything, to throw the shutter open and let off that Martini-Henry. He stood before the wide opening, glaring, and I yelled at him to come back, while I straightened the sudden twist out of that steamboat. There was no room to turn even if I had wanted to, the snag was somewhere very near ahead in that confounded smoke, there was no time to lose, so I just crowded her into the bank— right into the bank, where I knew the water was deep.

3. The simultaneous discharge of many firearms.

"We tore slowly along the overhanging bushes in a whirl of broken twigs and flying leaves. The fusillade below stopped short, as I had foreseen it would when the squirts got empty. I threw my head back to a glinting whizz that traversed the pilot-house, in at one shutter-hole and out at the other. Looking past that mad helmsman, who was shaking the empty rifle and yelling at the shore, I saw vague forms of men running bent double, leaping, gliding, distinct, incomplete, evanescent. Something big appeared in the air before the shutter, the rifle went overboard, and the man stepped back swiftly, looked at me over his shoulder in an extraordinary, profound, familiar manner, and fell upon my feet. The side of his head hit the wheel twice, and the end of what appeared a long cane clattered round and knocked over a little camp-stool. It looked as though after wrenching that thing from somebody ashore he had lost his balance in the effort. The thin smoke had blown away, we were clear of the snag, and looking ahead I could see that in another hundred yards or so I would be free to sheer off, away from the bank; but my feet felt so very warm and wet that I had to look down. The man had rolled on his back and stared straight up at me; both his hands clutched that cane. It was the shaft of a spear that, either thrown or lunged through the opening, had caught him in the side just below the ribs; the blade had gone in out of sight, after making a frightful gash; my shoes were full; a pool of blood lay very still, gleaming dark-red under the wheel; his eyes shone with an amazing lustre. The fusillade burst out again. He looked at me anxiously, gripping the spear like something precious, with an air of being afraid I would try to take it away from him. I had to make an effort to free my eyes from his gaze and attend to the steering. With one hand I felt above my head for the line of the steam whistle, and jerked out screech after screech hurriedly. The tumult of angry and warlike yells was checked instantly, and then from the depths of the woods went out such a tremulous and prolonged wail of mournful fear and utter despair as may be imagined to follow the flight of the last hope from the earth. There was a great commotion in the bush; the shower of arrows stopped, a few dropping shots rang out sharply—then silence, in which the languid beat of the stern-wheel came plainly to my ears. I put the helm hard a-starboard at the moment when the pilgrim in pink pyjamas, very hot and agitated, appeared in the doorway. 'The manager sends me—' he began in an official tone, and stopped short. 'Good God!' he said, glaring at the wounded man.

"We two whites stood over him, and his lustrous and inquiring glance enveloped us both. I declare it looked as though he would presently put to us some question in an understandable language; but he died without uttering a sound, without moving a limb, without twitching a muscle. Only in the very last moment, as though in response to some sign we could not see, to some whisper we could not hear, he frowned heavily, and that frown gave to his black death-mask an inconceivably sombre, brooding, and menacing expression. The lustre of inquiring glance faded swiftly into vacant glassiness. 'Can you steer?' I asked the agent eagerly. He looked very dubious; but I made a grab at his arm, and he understood at once I meant him to steer whether or no. To tell you the truth, I was morbidly anxious to change my shoes and socks. 'He is dead,' murmured the fellow, immensely impressed. 'No doubt about it,' said I, tugging like mad at the shoe-laces. 'And by the way, I suppose Mr Kurtz is dead as well by this time.'

"For the moment that was the dominant thought. There was a sense of extreme disappointment, as though I had found out I had been striving after something altogether without a substance. I couldn't have been more disgusted if I had travelled all this way for the sole purpose of talking with Mr Kurtz. Talking with . . . I flung one shoe overboard, and became aware that that was exactly what I had been looking forward to—a talk with Kurtz. I made the strange discovery that I had never imagined him as doing, you know, but as discoursing. I didn't say to myself, 'Now I will never see him,' or 'Now I will never shake him by the hand,' but, 'Now I will never hear him.' The man presented himself as a voice. Not of course that I did not connect him with some sort of action. Hadn't I been told in all the tones of jealousy and admiration that he had collected, bartered, swindled, or stolen more ivory than all the other agents together? That was not the point. The point was in his being a gifted creature, and that of all his gifts the one that stood out pre-eminently, that carried with it a sense of real presence, was his ability to talk, his words— the gift of expression, the bewildering, the illuminating, the most exalted and the most contemptible, the pulsating stream of light, or the deceitful flow from the heart of an impenetrable darkness.

"The other shoe went flying unto the devil-god of that river. I thought, By Jove! it's all over. We are too late; he has vanished—the gift has vanished, by means of some spear, arrow, or club. I will never hear that chap speak after all—and my sorrow had a startling extravagance of emotion, even such as I had noticed in the howling sorrow of these savages in the bush. I couldn't have felt more of lonely desolation somehow, had I been robbed of a belief or had missed my destiny in life. . . . Why do you sigh in this beastly way, somebody? Absurd? Well, absurd. Good Lord! mustn't a man ever—Here, give me some tobacco." . . .

There was a pause of profound stillness, then a match flared, and Marlow's lean face appeared, worn, hollow, with downward folds and dropped eyelids, with an aspect of concentrated attention; and as he took vigorous draws at his pipe, it seemed to retreat and advance out of the night in the regular flicker of the tiny flame. The match went out.

"Absurd!" he cried. "This is the worst of trying to tell . . . Here you all are, each moored with two good addresses, like a hulk with two anchors, a butcher round one corner, a policeman round another, excellent appetites, and temperature normal—you hear—normal from year's end to year's end. And you say, Absurd! Absurd be—exploded! Absurd! My dear boys, what can you expect from a man who out of sheer nervousness had just flung overboard a pair of new shoes? Now I think of it, it is amazing I did not shed tears. I am, upon the whole, proud of my fortitude. I was cut to the quick at the idea of having lost the inestimable privilege of listening to the gifted Kurtz. Of course I was wrong. The privilege was waiting for me. Oh yes, I heard more than enough. And I was right, too. A voice. He was very little more than a voice. And I heard—him— it—this voice—other voices—all of them were so little more than voices—and the memory of that time itself lingers around me, impalpable, like a dying vibration of one immense jabber, silly, atrocious, sordid, savage, or simply mean, without any kind of sense. Voices, voices—even the girl herself—now—"

He was silent for a long time.

"I laid the ghost of his gifts at last with a lie," he began suddenly. "Girl! What? Did I mention a girl? Oh, she is out of it—completely. They—the women I mean—are out of it—should be out of it. We must help them to stay in that beautiful world of their own, lest ours gets worse. Oh, she had to be out of it. You should have heard the disinterred body of Mr Kurtz saying, 'My Intended.' You would have perceived directly then how completely she was out of it. And the lofty frontal bone of Mr Kurtz! They say the hair goes on growing sometimes, but this—ah—specimen was impressively bald. The wilderness had patted him on the head, and, behold, it was like a ball—an ivory ball; it had caressed him, and—lo!—he had withered; it had taken him, loved him, embraced him, got into his veins, consumed his flesh, and sealed his soul to its own by the inconceivable ceremonies of some devilish initiation. He was its spoiled and pampered favourite. Ivory? I should think so. Heaps of it, stacks of it. The old mud shanty was bursting with it. You would think there was not a single tusk left either above or below the ground in the whole country. 'Mostly fossil,' the manager had remarked disparagingly. It was no more fossil than I am; but they call it fossil when it is dug up. It appears these niggers do bury the tusks sometimes—but evidently they couldn't bury this parcel deep enough to save the gifted Mr Kurtz from his fate. We filled the steamboat with it, and had to pile a lot on the deck. Thus he could see and enjoy as long as he could see, because the appreciation of this favour had remained with him to the last. You should have heard him say, 'My ivory.' Oh yes, I heard him. 'My Intended, my ivory, my station, my river, my—' everything belonged to him. It made me hold my breath in expectation of hearing the wilderness burst into a prodigious peal of laughter that would shake the fixed stars in their places. Everything belonged to him—but that was a trifle. The thing was to know what he belonged to, how many powers of darkness claimed him for their own. That was the reflection that made you creepy all over. It was impossible—it was not good for one either—trying to imagine. He had taken a high seat amongst the devils of the land—I mean literally. You can't understand. How could you?—with solid pavement under your feet, surrounded by kind neighbours ready to cheer you or to fall on you, stepping delicately between the butcher and the policeman, in the holy terror of scandal and gallows and lunatic asylums—how can you imagine what particular region of the first ages a man's untrammelled feet may take him into by the way of solitude—utter solitude without a policeman—by the way of silence—utter silence, where no warning voice of a kind neighbour can be heard whispering of public opinion? These little things make all the great difference. When they are gone you must fall back upon your own innate strength, upon your own capacity for faithfulness. Of course you may be too much of a fool to go wrong—too dull even to know you are being assaulted by the powers of darkness. I take it, no fool ever made a bargain for his soul with the devil: the fool is too much of a fool, or the devil too much of a devil—I don't know which. Or you may be such a thunderingly exalted creature as to be altogether deaf and blind to anything but heavenly sights and sounds. Then the earth for you is only a standing place—and whether to be like this is your loss or your gain I won't pretend to say. But most of us are neither one nor the other. The earth for us is a place to live in, where we must put up with sights, with sounds, with smells, too, by Jove!—breathe dead hippo, so to speak, and not be contaminated. And there, don't you see? your strength comes in, the faith in your ability for the digging of unostentatious holes to bury the stuff in—your power of devotion, not to yourself, but to an obscure, back-breaking business. And that's difficult enough. Mind, I am not trying to excuse or even explain—I am trying to account to myself for—for—Mr Kurtz—for the shade of Mr Kurtz. This initiated wraith[4] from the back of Nowhere honoured me with its amazing confidence before it vanished altogether. This was because it could speak English to me. The original Kurtz had been educated partly in England, and—as he was good enough to say himself—his sympathies were in the right place. His mother was half-English, his father was half-French. All Europe contributed to the making of Kurtz; and by and by I learned that, most appropriately, the International Society for the Suppression of Savage Customs[5] had entrusted him with the making of a report, for its future guidance. And he had written it too. I've seen it. I've read it. It was eloquent, vibrating with eloquence, but too high-strung, I think. Seventeen pages of close writing he had found time for! But this must have been before his—let us say—nerves went wrong, and caused him to preside at certain midnight dances ending with unspeakable rites, which—as far as I reluctantly gathered from what I heard at various times—were offered up to him—do you understand?—to Mr Kurtz himself. But it was a beautiful piece of writing. The opening paragraph, however, in the light of later information, strikes me now as ominous. He began with the argument that we whites, from the point of development we had arrived at, 'must necessarily appear to them [savages] in the nature of supernatural beings—we approach them with the might as of a deity,' and so on, and so on. 'By the simple exercise of our will we can exert a power for good practically unbounded,' etc. etc. From that point he soared and took me with him. The peroration was magnificent, though difficult to remember, you know. It gave me the notion of an exotic Immensity ruled by an august Benevolence. It made me tingle with enthusiasm. This was the unbounded power of eloquence—of words—of burning noble words. There were no practical hints to interrupt the magic current of phrases, unless a kind of note at the foot of the last page, scrawled evidently much later, in an unsteady hand, may be regarded as the exposition of a method. It was very simple, and at the end of that moving appeal to every altruistic sentiment it blazed at you, luminous and terrifying, like a flash of lightning in a serene sky: 'Exterminate all the brutes!' The curious part was that he had apparently forgotten all about that valuable postscriptum, because, later on, when he in a sense came to himself, he repeatedly entreated me to take good care of 'my pamphlet' (he called it), as it was sure to have in the future a good influence upon his career. I had full information about all these things, and, besides, as it turned out, I was to have the care of his memory. I've done enough for it to give me the indisputable right to lay it, if I choose, for an everlasting rest in the dust-bin of progress, amongst all the sweepings and, figuratively speaking, all the dead cats of civilisation. But then, you see, I can't choose. He won't be forgotten. Whatever he was, he was not common. He had the power to charm or frighten rudimentary souls into an aggravated witchdance in his honour; he could also fill the small souls of the pilgrims with bitter misgivings: he had one devoted friend at least, and he had conquered one soul in the world that was neither rudimentary nor tainted with

4. Either the spectral or immaterial appearance of a living being, often viewed as a portent of that person's death, or simply a ghost.
5. This society is fictional, but in 1889–90 the international Anti-Slavery Conference at Brussels in effect granted Leopold control of the Congo trade, ostensibly in return for his help in eliminating African slavers.

self-seeking. No; I can't forget him, though I am not prepared to affirm the fellow was exactly worth the life we lost in getting to him. I missed my late helmsman awfully—I missed him even while his body was still lying in the pilot-house. Perhaps you will think it passing strange this regret for a savage who was no more account than a grain of sand in a black Sahara. Well, don't you see, he had done something, he had steered; for months I had him at my back—a help—an instrument. It was a kind of partnership. He steered for me—I had to look after him, I worried about his deficiencies, and thus a subtle bond had been created, of which I only became aware when it was suddenly broken. And the intimate profundity of that look he gave me when he received his hurt remains to this day in my memory—like a claim of distant kinship affirmed in a supreme moment.

"Poor fool! If he had only left that shutter alone. He had no restraint, no restraint—just like Kurtz—a tree swayed by the wind. As soon as I had put on a dry pair of slippers, I dragged him out, after first jerking the spear out of his side, which operation I confess I performed with my eyes shut tight. His heels leaped together over the little doorstep; his shoulders were pressed to my breast; I hugged him from behind desperately. Oh! he was heavy, heavy; heavier than any man on earth, I should imagine. Then without more ado I tipped him overboard. The current snatched him as though he had been a wisp of grass, and I saw the body roll over twice before I lost sight of it for ever. All the pilgrims and the manager were then congregated on the awning-deck about the pilot-house, chattering at each other like a flock of excited magpies, and there was a scandalised murmur at my heartless promptitude. What they wanted to keep that body hanging about for I can't guess. Embalm it, maybe. But I had also heard another, and a very ominous, murmur on the deck below. My friends the wood-cutters were likewise scandalised, and with a better show of reason—though I admit that the reason itself was quite inadmissible. Oh, quite! I had made up my mind that if my late helmsman was to be eaten, the fishes alone should have him. He had been a very second-rate helmsman while alive, but now he was dead he might have become a first-class temptation, and possibly cause some startling trouble. Besides, I was anxious to take the wheel, the man in pink pyjamas showing himself a hopeless duffer at the business.

"This I did directly the simple funeral was over. We were going half-speed, keeping right in the middle of the stream, and I listened to the talk about me. They had given up Kurtz, they had given up the station; Kurtz was dead, and the station had been burnt—and so on—and so on. The red-haired pilgrim was beside himself with the thought that at least this poor Kurtz had been properly revenged. 'Say! We must have made a glorious slaughter of them in the bush. Eh? What do you think? Say?' He positively danced, the bloodthirsty little gingery beggar.[6] And he had nearly fainted when he saw the wounded man! I could not help saying, 'You made a glorious lot of smoke, anyhow.' I had seen, from the way the tops of the bushes rustled and flew, that almost all the shots had gone too high. You can't hit anything unless you take aim and fire from the shoulder; but these chaps fired from the hip with their eyes shut. The retreat, I maintained—and I was right—was caused by the screeching of the steam-whistle. Upon this they forgot Kurtz, and began to howl at me with indignant protests.

6. Red-haired rascal (British slang).

"The manager stood by the wheel murmuring confidentially about the necessity of getting well away down the river before dark at all events, when I saw in the distance a clearing on the river-side and the outlines of some sort of building. 'What's this?' I asked. He clapped his hands in wonder. 'The station!' he cried. I edged in at once, still going half-speed.

"Through my glasses I saw the slope of a hill interspersed with rare trees and perfectly free from undergrowth. A long decaying building on the summit was half buried in the high grass; the large holes in the peaked roof gaped black from afar; the jungle and the woods made a background. There was no enclosure or fence of any kind; but there had been one apparently, for near the house half a dozen slim posts remained in a row, roughly trimmed, and with their upper ends ornamented with round carved balls. The rails, or whatever there had been between, had disappeared. Of course the forest surrounded all that. The river-bank was clear, and on the water side I saw a white man under a hat like a cart-wheel beckoning persistently with his whole arm. Examining the edge of the forest above and below, I was almost certain I could see movements—human forms gliding here and there. I steamed past prudently, then stopped the engines and let her drift down. The man on the shore began to shout, urging us to land. 'We have been attacked,' screamed the manager. 'I know—I know. It's all right,' yelled back the other, as cheerful as you please. 'Come along. It's all right. I am glad.'

"His aspect reminded me of something I had seen—something funny I had seen somewhere. As I manœuvred to get alongside, I was asking myself, 'What does this fellow look like?' Suddenly I got it. He looked like a harlequin. His clothes had been made of some stuff that was brown holland[7] probably, but it was covered with patches all over, with bright patches, blue, red, and yellow—patches on the back, patches on the front, patches on elbows, on knees; coloured binding round his jacket, scarlet edging at the bottom of his trousers; and the sunshine made him look extremely gay and wonderfully neat withal, because you could see how beautifully all this patching had been done. A beardless, boyish face, very fair, no features to speak of, nose peeling, little blue eyes, smiles and frowns chasing each other over that open countenance like sunshine and shadow on a wind-swept plain. 'Look out, captain!' he cried; 'there's a snag lodged in here last night.' What! Another snag? I confess I swore shamefully. I had nearly holed my cripple, to finish off that charming trip. The harlequin on the bank turned his little pug nose up to me. 'You English?' he asked, all smiles. 'Are you?' I shouted from the wheel. The smiles vanished, and he shook his head as if sorry for my disappointment. Then he brightened up. 'Never mind!' he cried encouragingly. 'Are we in time?' I asked. 'He is up there,' he replied, with a toss of the head up the hill, and becoming gloomy all of a sudden. His face was like the autumn sky, overcast one moment and bright the next.

"When the manager, escorted by the pilgrims, all of them armed to the teeth, had gone to the house, this chap came on board. 'I say, I don't like this. These natives are in the bush,' I said. He assured me earnestly it was all right. 'They are simple people,' he added; 'well, I am glad you came. It took me all my time to keep them off.' 'But you said it was all right,' I cried. 'Oh, they meant no

7. Unbleached linen fabric. "Harlequin": a traditional clown figure known by his multicolored costume.

harm,' he said; and as I stared he corrected himself, 'Not exactly.' Then vivaciously, 'My faith, your pilot-house wants a clean up!' In the next breath he advised me to keep enough steam on the boiler to blow the whistle in case of any trouble. 'One good screech will do more for you than all your rifles. They are simple people,' he repeated. He rattled away at such a rate he quite overwhelmed me. He seemed to be trying to make up for lots of silence, and actually hinted, laughing, that such was the case. 'Don't you talk with Mr Kurtz?' I said. 'You don't talk with that man—you listen to him,' he exclaimed with severe exaltation. 'But now—' He waved his arm, and in the twinkling of an eye was in the uttermost depths of despondency. In a moment he came up again with a jump, possessed himself of both my hands, shook them continuously, while he gabbled: 'Brother sailor . . . honour . . . pleasure . . . delight . . . introduce myself . . . Russian . . . son of an arch-priest . . . Government of Tambov[8] . . . What? Tobacco! English tobacco; the excellent English tobacco! Now, that's brotherly. Smoke? Where's a sailor that does not smoke?'

"The pipe soothed him, and gradually I made out he had run away from school, had gone to sea in a Russian ship; ran away again; served some time in English ships; was now reconciled with the arch-priest. He made a point of that. 'But when one is young one must see things, gather experience, ideas; enlarge the mind.' 'Here!' I interrupted. 'You can never tell! Here I met Mr Kurtz,' he said, youthfully solemn and reproachful. I held my tongue after that. It appears he had persuaded a Dutch trading-house on the coast to fit him out with stores and goods, and had started for the interior with a light heart, and no more idea of what would happen to him than a baby. He had been wandering about that river for nearly two years alone, cut off from everybody and everything. 'I am not so young as I look. I am twenty-five,' he said. 'At first old Van Shuyten would tell me to go to the devil,' he narrated with keen enjoyment; 'but I stuck to him, and talked and talked, till at last he got afraid I would talk the hind-leg off his favourite dog, so he gave me some cheap things and a few guns, and told me he hoped he would never see my face again. Good old Dutchman, Van Shuyten. I sent him one small lot of ivory a year ago, so that he can't call me a little thief when I get back. I hope he got it. And for the rest I don't care. I had some wood stacked for you. That was my old house. Did you see?'

"I gave him Towson's book. He made as though he would kiss me, but restrained himself. 'The only book I had left, and I thought I had lost it,' he said, looking at it ecstatically. 'So many accidents happen to a man going about alone, you know. Canoes get upset sometimes—and sometimes you've got to clear out so quick when the people get angry.' He thumbed the pages. 'You made notes in Russian?' I asked. He nodded. 'I thought they were written in cipher,' I said. He laughed, then became serious. 'I had lots of trouble to keep these people off,' he said. 'Did they want to kill you?' I asked. 'Oh no!' he cried, and checked himself. 'Why did they attack us?' I pursued. He hesitated, then said shamefacedly, 'They don't want him to go.' 'Don't they?' I said curiously. He nodded a nod full of mystery and wisdom. 'I tell you,' he cried, 'this man has enlarged my mind.' He opened his arms wide, staring at me with his little blue eyes that were perfectly round."

<hr />

8. A province in Russia, south of Moscow, a cultural center.

3

"I looked at him, lost in astonishment. There he was before me, in motley,[9] as though he had absconded from a troupe of mimes, enthusiastic, fabulous. His very existence was improbable, inexplicable, and altogether bewildering. He was an insoluble problem. It was inconceivable how he had existed, how he had succeeded in getting so far, how he had managed to remain—why he did not instantly disappear. 'I went a little farther,' he said, 'then still a little farther—till I had gone so far that I don't know how I'll ever get back. Never mind. Plenty time. I can manage. You take Kurtz away quick—quick—I tell you.' The glamour of youth enveloped his particoloured rags, his destitution, his loneliness, the essential desolation of his futile wanderings. For months— for years—his life hadn't been worth a day's purchase; and there he was gallantly, thoughtlessly alive, to all appearance indestructible solely by the virtue of his few years and of his unreflecting audacity. I was seduced into something like admiration—like envy. Glamour urged him on, glamour kept him unscathed. He surely wanted nothing from the wilderness but space to breathe in and to push on through. His need was to exist, and to move onwards at the greatest possible risk, and with a maximum of privation. If the absolutely pure, uncalculating, unpractical spirit of adventure had ever ruled a human being, it ruled this be-patched youth. I almost envied him the possession of this modest and clear flame. It seemed to have consumed all thought of self so completely, that, even while he was talking to you, you forgot that it was he—the man before your eyes—who had gone through these things. I did not envy him his devotion to Kurtz, though. He had not meditated over it. It came to him, and he accepted it with a sort of eager fatalism. I must say that to me it appeared about the most dangerous thing in every way he had come upon so far.

"They had come together unavoidably, like two ships becalmed near each other, and lay rubbing sides at last. I suppose Kurtz wanted an audience, because on a certain occasion, when encamped in the forest, they had talked all night, or more probably Kurtz had talked. 'We talked of everything,' he said, quite transported at the recollection. 'I forgot there was such a thing as sleep. The night did not seem to last an hour. Everything! Everything! . . . Of love too.' 'Ah, he talked to you of love!' I said, much amused. 'It isn't what you think,' he cried, almost passionately. 'It was in general. He made me see things—things.'

"He threw his arms up. We were on deck at the time, and the head-man of my wood-cutters, lounging near by, turned upon him his heavy and glittering eyes. I looked around, and I don't know why, but I assure you that never, never before, did this land, this river, this jungle, the very arch of this blazing sky, appear to me so hopeless and so dark, so impenetrable to human thought, so pitiless to human weakness. 'And, ever since, you have been with him, of course?' I said.

"On the contrary. It appears their intercourse had been very much broken by various causes. He had, as he informed me proudly, managed to nurse Kurtz through two illnesses (he alluded to it as you would to some risky feat), but as a rule Kurtz wandered alone, far in the depths of the forest. 'Very often coming to this station, I had to wait days and days before he would turn up,' he said. 'Ah, it was worth waiting for!—sometimes.' 'What was he doing? exploring or what?'

9. Like a jester, who wore a distinctive multicolored costume.

I asked. 'Oh yes, of course'; he had discovered lots of villages, a lake too—he did not know exactly in what direction; it was dangerous to inquire too much—but mostly his expeditions had been for ivory. 'But he had no goods to trade with by that time,' I objected. 'There's a good lot of cartridges left even yet,' he answered, looking away. 'To speak plainly, he raided the country,'[1] I said. He nodded. 'Not alone, surely!' He muttered something about the villages round that lake. 'Kurtz got the tribe to follow him, did he?' I suggested. He fidgeted a little. 'They adored[2] him,' he said. The tone of these words was so extraordinary that I looked at him searchingly. It was curious to see his mingled eagerness and reluctance to speak of Kurtz. The man filled his life, occupied his thoughts, swayed his emotions. 'What can you expect?' he burst out; 'he came to them with thunder and lightning, you know—and they had never seen anything like it—and very terrible. He could be very terrible. You can't judge Mr Kurtz as you would an ordinary man. No, no, no! Now—just to give you an idea—I don't mind telling you, he wanted to shoot me too one day—but I don't judge him.' 'Shoot you!' I cried. 'What for?' 'Well, I had a small lot of ivory the chief of that village near my house gave me. You see I used to shoot game for them. Well, he wanted it, and wouldn't hear reason. He declared he would shoot me unless I gave him the ivory and then cleared out of the country, because he could do so, and had a fancy for it, and there was nothing on earth to prevent him killing whom he jolly well pleased. And it was true too. I gave him the ivory. What did I care! But I didn't clear out. No, no. I couldn't leave him. I had to be careful, of course, till we got friendly again for a time. He had his second illness then. Afterwards I had to keep out of the way; but I didn't mind. He was living for the most part in those villages on the lake. When he came down to the river, some-times he would take to me, and sometimes it was better for me to be careful. This man suffered too much. He hated all this, and somehow he couldn't get away. When I had a chance I begged him to try and leave while there was time; I offered to go back with him. And he would say yes, and then he would remain; go off on another ivory hunt; disappear for weeks; forget himself amongst these people—forget himself—you know.' 'Why! he's mad,' I said. He protested indig-nantly. Mr Kurtz couldn't be mad. If I had heard him talk, only two days ago, I wouldn't dare hint at such a thing. . . . I had taken up my binoculars while we talked, and was looking at the shore, sweeping the limit of the forest at each side and at the back of the house. The consciousness of there being people in that bush, so silent, so quiet—as silent and quiet as the ruined house on the hill—made me uneasy. There was no sign on the face of nature of this amazing tale that was not so much told as suggested to me in desolate exclamations, completed by shrugs, in interrupted phrases, in hints ending in deep sighs. The woods were unmoved, like a mask—heavy, like the closed door of a prison—they looked with their air of hidden knowledge, of patient expectation, of unap-proachable silence. The Russian was explaining to me that it was only lately that Mr Kurtz had come down to the river, bringing along with him all the fighting men of that lake tribe. He had been absent for several months—getting himself adored, I suppose—and had come down unexpectedly, with the intention to all appearance of making a raid either across the river or down stream. Evidently

1. Raids for ivory were a common practice, with little or no attempt to compensate natives for the stolen goods.
2. Literally, worshipped as a deity.

the appetite for more ivory had got the better of the—what shall I say?—less material aspirations. However, he had got much worse suddenly. 'I heard he was lying helpless, and so I came up—took my chance,' said the Russian. 'Oh, he is bad, very bad.' I directed my glass to the house. There were no signs of life, but there was the ruined roof, the long mud wall peeping above the grass, with three little square window-holes, no two of the same size; all this brought within reach of my hand, as it were. And then I made a brusque movement, and one of the remaining posts of that vanished fence leaped up in the field of my glass. You remember I told you I had been struck at the distance by certain attempts at ornamentation, rather remarkable in the ruinous aspect of the place. Now I had suddenly a nearer view, and its first result was to make me throw my head back as if before a blow. Then I went carefully from post to post with my glass, and I saw my mistake. These round knobs were not ornamental but symbolic; they were expressive and puzzling, striking and disturbing—food for thought and also for the vultures if there had been any looking down from the sky; but at all events for such ants as were industrious enough to ascend the pole. They would have been even more impressive, those heads on the stakes, if their faces had not been turned to the house. Only one, the first I had made out, was facing my way. I was not so shocked as you may think. The start back I had given was really nothing but a movement of surprise. I had expected to see a knob of wood there, you know. I returned deliberately to the first I had seen—and there it was, black, dried, sunken, with closed eyelids—a head that seemed to sleep at the top of that pole, and, with the shrunken dry lips showing a narrow white line of the teeth, was smiling too, smiling continuously at some endless and jocose dream of that eternal slumber.

"I am not disclosing any trade secrets. In fact the manager said afterwards that Mr Kurtz's methods[3] had ruined the district. I have no opinion on that point, but I want you clearly to understand that there was nothing exactly profitable in these heads being there. They only show that Mr Kurtz lacked restraint in the gratification of his various lusts, that there was something wanting in him—some small matter which, when the pressing need arose, could not be found under his magnificent eloquence. Whether he knew of this deficiency himself I can't say. I think the knowledge came to him at last—only at the very last. But the wilderness had found him out early, and had taken on him a terrible vengeance for the fantastic invasion. I think it had whispered to him things about himself which he did not know, things of which he had no conception till he took counsel with this great solitude—and the whisper had proved irresistibly fascinating. It echoed loudly within him because he was hollow at the core. . . . I put down the glass, and the head that had appeared near enough to be spoken to seemed at once to have leaped away from me into inaccessible distance.

"The admirer of Mr Kurtz was a bit crestfallen. In a hurried, indistinct voice he began to assure me he had not dared to take these—say, symbols—down. He was not afraid of the natives; they would not stir till Mr Kurtz gave the word. His ascendancy was extraordinary. The camps of these people surrounded the place, and the chiefs came every day to see him. They would

---

3. Perhaps an allusion to *Hamlet*, where Polonius comments on Hamlet's apparent insanity, "Though this be madness, yet there is method in 't."

crawl . . . 'I don't want to know anything of the ceremonies used when approaching Mr Kurtz,' I shouted. Curious, this feeling that came over me that such details would be more intolerable than those heads drying on the stakes under Mr Kurtz's windows. After all, that was only a savage sight, while I seemed at one bound to have been transported into some lightless region of subtle horrors, where pure, uncomplicated savagery was a positive relief, being something that had a right to exist—obviously—in the sunshine. The young man looked at me with surprise. I suppose it did not occur to him that Mr Kurtz was no idol of mine. He forgot I hadn't heard any of these splendid monologues on, what was it? on love, justice, conduct of life—or what not. If it had come to crawling before Mr Kurtz, he crawled as much as the veriest savage of them all. I had no idea of the conditions, he said: these heads were the heads of rebels. I shocked him excessively by laughing. Rebels! What would be the next definition I was to hear? There had been enemies, criminals, workers—and these were rebels. Those rebellious heads looked very subdued to me on their sticks. 'You don't know how such a life tries a man like Kurtz,' cried Kurtz's last disciple. 'Well, and you?' I said. 'I! I! I am a simple man. I have no great thoughts. I want nothing from anybody. How can you compare me to . . .?' His feelings were too much for speech, and suddenly he broke down. 'I don't understand,' he groaned. 'I've been doing my best to keep him alive, and that's enough. I had no hand in all this. I have no abilities. There hasn't been a drop of medicine or a mouthful of invalid food for months here. He was shamefully abandoned. A man like this, with such ideas. Shamefully! Shamefully! I—I—haven't slept for the last ten nights. . . .'

"His voice lost itself in the calm of the evening. The long shadows of the forest had slipped down hill while we talked, had gone far beyond the ruined hovel, beyond the symbolic row of stakes. All this was in the gloom, while we down there were yet in the sunshine, and the stretch of the river abreast of the clearing glittered in a still and dazzling splendour, with a murky and overshadowed bend above and below. Not a living soul was seen on the shore. The bushes did not rustle.

"Suddenly round the corner of the house a group of men appeared, as though they had come up from the ground. They waded waist-deep in the grass, in a compact body, bearing an improvised stretcher in their midst. Instantly, in the emptiness of the landscape, a cry arose whose shrillness pierced the still air like a sharp arrow flying straight to the very heart of the land; and, as if by enchantment, streams of human beings—of naked human beings—with spears in their hands, with bows, with shields, with wild glances and savage movements, were poured into the clearing by the darkfaced and pensive forest. The bushes shook, the grass swayed for a time, and then everything stood still in attentive immobility.

"'Now, if he does not say the right thing to them we are all done for,' said the Russian at my elbow. The knot of men with the stretcher had stopped too, halfway to the steamer, as if petrified. I saw the man on the stretcher sit up, lank and with an uplifted arm, above the shoulders of the bearers. 'Let us hope that the man who can talk so well of love in general will find some particular reason to spare us this time,' I said. I resented bitterly the absurd danger of our situation, as if to be at the mercy of that atrocious phantom had been a dishonouring necessity. I could not hear a sound, but through my glasses I saw the thin arm extended commandingly, the lower jaw moving, the eyes of that apparition shining darkly far in its bony head that nodded with grotesque jerks. Kurtz— Kurtz—that means 'short' in German—don't it? Well, the name was as true as everything else in his life—and death. He looked at least seven feet long. His covering had fallen off, and his body emerged from it pitiful and appalling as from a winding-sheet. I could see the cage of his ribs all astir, the bones of his arm waving. It was as though an animated image of death carved out of old ivory had been shaking its hand with menaces at a motionless crowd of men made of dark and glittering bronze. I saw him open his mouth wide—it gave him a weirdly voracious aspect, as though he had wanted to swallow all the air, all the earth, all the men before him. A deep voice reached me faintly. He must have been shouting. He fell back suddenly. The stretcher shook as the bearers staggered forward again, and almost at the same time I noticed that the crowd of savages was vanishing without any perceptible movement of retreat, as if the forest that had ejected these beings so suddenly had drawn them in again as the breath is drawn in a long aspiration.

"Some of the pilgrims behind the stretcher carried his arms—two shotguns, a heavy rifle, and a light revolver-carbine[4]—the thunderbolts of that pitiful Jupiter.[5] The manager bent over him murmuring as he walked beside his head. They laid him down in one of the little cabins—just a room for a bedplace and a camp-stool or two, you know. We had brought his belated correspondence, and a lot of torn envelopes and open letters littered his bed. His hand roamed feebly amongst these papers. I was struck by the fire of his eyes and the composed languor of his expression. It was not so much the exhaustion of disease. He did not seem in pain. This shadow looked satiated and calm, as though for the moment it had had its fill of all the emotions.

"He rustled one of the letters, and looking straight in my face said, 'I am glad.' Somebody had been writing to him about me. These special recommendations were turning up again. The volume of tone he emitted without effort, almost without the trouble of moving his lips, amazed me. A voice! a voice! It was grave, profound, vibrating, while the man did not seem capable of a whisper. However, he had enough strength in him—factitious[6] no doubt—to very nearly make an end of us, as you shall hear directly.

"The manager appeared silently in the doorway; I stepped out at once and he drew the curtain after me. The Russian, eyed curiously by the pilgrims, was staring at the shore. I followed the direction of his glance.

"Dark human shapes could be made out in the distance, flitting indistinctly against the gloomy border of the forest, and near the river two bronze figures, leaning on tall spears, stood in the sunlight under fantastic head-dresses of spotted skins, warlike and still in statuesque repose. And from right to left along the lighted shore moved a wild and gorgeous apparition of a woman.

"She walked with measured steps, draped in striped and fringed cloths, treading the earth proudly, with a slight jingle and flash of barbarous ornaments. She carried her head high; her hair was done in the shape of a helmet; she had brass leggings to the knee,[7] brass wire gauntlets to the elbow, a crimson spot on her

---

4. A rifle with a revolving clip.
5. The Roman god of the sky, ruler over the other gods.

6. Not natural; got up for a particular purpose; artificial.
7. From the ankle to the knee.

tawny cheek, innumerable necklaces of glass beads on her neck; bizarre things, charms, gifts of witch-men, that hung about her, glittered and trembled at every step. She must have had the value of several elephant tusks upon her. She was savage and superb, wild-eyed and magnificent; there was something ominous and stately in her deliberate progress. And in the hush that had fallen suddenly upon the whole sorrowful land, the immense wilderness, the colossal body of the fecund and mysterious life seemed to look at her, pensive, as though it had been looking at the image of its own tenebrous[8] and passionate soul.

"She came abreast of the steamer, stood still, and faced us. Her long shadow fell to the water's edge. Her face had a tragic and fierce aspect of wild sorrow and of dumb pain mingled with the fear of some struggling, half-shaped resolve. She stood looking at us without a stir, and like the wilderness itself, with an air of brooding over an inscrutable purpose. A whole minute passed, and then she made a step forward. There was a low jingle, a glint of yellow metal, a sway of fringed draperies, and she stopped as if her heart had failed her. The young fellow by my side growled. The pilgrims murmured at my back. She looked at us all as if her life had depended upon the unswerving steadiness of her glance. Suddenly she opened her bared arms and threw them up rigid above her head, as though in an uncontrollable desire to touch the sky, and at the same time the swift shadows darted out on the earth, swept around on the river, gathering the steamer into a shadowy embrace. A formidable silence hung over the scene.

"She turned away slowly, walked on, following the bank, and passed into the bushes to the left. Once only her eyes gleamed back at us in the dusk of the thickets before she disappeared.

"'If she had offered to come aboard I really think I would have tried to shoot her,' said the man of patches nervously. 'I had been risking my life every day for the last fortnight to keep her out of the house. She got in one day and kicked up a row about those miserable rags I picked up in the storeroom to mend my clothes with. I wasn't decent. At least it must have been that, for she talked like a fury to Kurtz for an hour, pointing at me now and then. I don't understand the dialect of this tribe. Luckily for me, I fancy Kurtz felt too ill that day to care, or there would have been mischief. I don't understand. . . . No—it's too much for me. Ah, well, it's all over now.'

"At this moment I heard Kurtz's deep voice behind the curtain: 'Save me!— save the ivory, you mean. Don't tell me. Save *me*! Why, I've had to save you. You are interrupting my plans now. Sick! Sick! Not so sick as you would like to believe. Never mind. I'll carry my ideas out yet—I will return. I'll show you what can be done. You with your little peddling notions—you are interfering with me. I will return. I . . .'

"The manager came out. He did me the honour to take me under the arm and lead me aside. 'He is very low, very low,' he said. He considered it necessary to sigh, but neglected to be consistently sorrowful. 'We have done all we could for him—haven't we? But there is no disguising the fact, Mr Kurtz has done more harm than good to the Company. He did not see the time was not ripe for vigorous action. Cautiously, cautiously—that's my principle. We must be cautious yet. The district is closed to us for a time. Deplorable! Upon the whole, the trade will suffer. I don't deny there is a remarkable quantity of ivory—mostly

8. Full of darkness or shadows; obscure; gloomy.

fossil. We must save it, at all events—but look how precarious the position is—and why? Because the method is unsound.' 'Do you,' said I, looking at the shore, 'call it "unsound method"?' 'Without doubt,' he exclaimed hotly, 'Don't you?' . . . 'No method at all,' I murmured after a while. 'Exactly,' he exulted. 'I anticipated this. Shows a complete want of judgment. It is my duty to point it out in the proper quarter.' 'Oh,' said I, 'that fellow—what's his name?—the brickmaker, will make a readable report for you.' He appeared confounded for a moment. It seemed to me I had never breathed an atmosphere so vile, and I turned mentally to Kurtz for relief—positively for relief. 'Nevertheless, I think Mr Kurtz is a remarkable man,' I said with emphasis. He started, dropped on me a cold heavy glance, said very quietly, 'He *was*,' and turned his back on me. My hour of favour was over; I found myself lumped along with Kurtz as a partisan of methods for which the time was not ripe: I was unsound! Ah! but it was something to have at least a choice of nightmares.

"I had turned to the wilderness really, not to Mr Kurtz, who, I was ready to admit, was as good as buried. And for a moment it seemed to me as if I also were buried in a vast grave full of unspeakable secrets. I felt an intolerable weight oppressing my breast, the smell of the damp earth, the unseen presence of victorious corruption, the darkness of an impenetrable night. . . . The Russian tapped me on the shoulder. I heard him mumbling and stammering something about 'brother seaman—couldn't conceal—knowledge of matters that would affect Mr Kurtz's reputation.' I waited. For him evidently Mr Kurtz was not in his grave; I suspect that for him Mr Kurtz was one of the immortals. 'Well!' said I at last, 'speak out. As it happens, I am Mr Kurtz's friend—in a way.'

"He stated with a good deal of formality that had we not been 'of the same profession,' he would have kept the matter to himself without regard to consequences. He suspected 'there was an active ill-will towards him on the part of these white men that—' 'You are right,' I said, remembering a certain conversation I had overheard. 'The manager thinks you ought to be hanged.' He showed a concern at this intelligence which amused me at first. 'I had better get out of the way quietly,' he said earnestly. 'I can do no more for Kurtz now, and they would soon find some excuse. What's to stop them? There's a military post three hundred miles from here.' 'Well, upon my word,' said I, 'perhaps you had better go if you have any friends amongst the savages near by.' 'Plenty,' he said. 'They are simple people—and I want nothing, you know.' He stood biting his lip, then: 'I don't want any harm to happen to these whites here, but of course I was thinking of Mr Kurtz's reputation—but you are a brother seaman and—' 'All right,' said I, after a time. 'Mr Kurtz's reputation is safe with me.' I did not know how truly I spoke.

"He informed me, lowering his voice, that it was Kurtz who had ordered the attack to be made on the steamer. 'He hated sometimes the idea of being taken away—and then again . . . But I don't understand these matters. I am a simple man. He thought it would scare you away—that you would give it up, thinking him dead. I could not stop him. Oh, I had an awful time of it this last month.' 'Very well,' I said. 'He is all right now.' 'Ye-e-es,' he muttered, not very convinced apparently. 'Thanks,' said I; 'I shall keep my eyes open.' 'But quiet—eh?' he urged anxiously. 'It would be awful for his reputation if anybody here—' I promised a complete discretion with great gravity. 'I have a canoe and three black fellows waiting not very far. I am off. Could you give me a few Martini-Henry cartridges?' I could, and did, with proper secrecy. He helped himself, with a wink at me, to a handful of my tobacco. 'Between sailors—you know—good English tobacco.' At the door of the pilot-house he turned round—'I say, haven't you a pair of shoes you could spare?' He raised one leg. 'Look.' The soles were tied with knotted strings sandal-wise under his bare feet. I rooted out an old pair, at which he looked with admiration before tucking it under his left arm. One of his pockets (bright red) was bulging with cartridges, from the other (dark blue) peeped 'Towson's Inquiry,' etc. etc. He seemed to think himself excellently well equipped for a renewed encounter with the wilderness. 'Ah! I'll never, never meet such a man again. You ought to have heard him recite poetry—his own too it was, he told me. Poetry!' He rolled his eyes at the recollection of these delights. 'Oh, he enlarged my mind!' 'Good-bye,' said I. He shook hands and vanished in the night. Sometimes I ask myself whether I had ever really seen him—whether it was possible to meet such a phenomenon! . . .

"When I woke up shortly after midnight his warning came to my mind with its hint of danger that seemed, in the starred darkness, real enough to make me get up for the purpose of having a look round. On the hill a big fire burned, illuminating fitfully a crooked corner of the station-house. One of the agents with a picket of a few of our blacks, armed for the purpose, was keeping guard over the ivory; but deep within the forest, red gleams that wavered, that seemed to sink and rise from the ground amongst confused columnar shapes of intense blackness, showed the exact position of the camp where Mr Kurtz's adorers were keeping their uneasy vigil. The monotonous beating of a big drum filled the air with muffled shocks and a lingering vibration. A steady droning sound of many men chanting each to himself some weird incantation came out from the black, flat wall of the woods as the humming of bees comes out of a hive, and had a strange narcotic effect upon my half-awake senses. I believe I dozed off leaning over the rail, till an abrupt burst of yells, an overwhelming outbreak of a pent-up and mysterious frenzy, woke me up in a bewildered wonder. It was cut short all at once, and the low droning went on with an effect of audible and soothing silence. I glanced casually into the little cabin. A light was burning within, but Mr Kurtz was not there.

"I think I would have raised an outcry if I had believed my eyes. But I didn't believe them at first—the thing seemed so impossible. The fact is I was completely unnerved by a sheer blank fright, pure abstract terror, unconnected with any distinct shape of physical danger. What made this emotion so overpowering was—how shall I define it?—the moral shock I received, as if something altogether monstrous, intolerable to thought and odious to the soul, had been thrust upon me unexpectedly. This lasted of course the merest fraction of a second, and then the usual sense of commonplace, deadly danger, the possibility of a sudden onslaught and massacre, or something of the kind, which I saw impending, was positively welcome and composing. It pacified me, in fact, so much, that I did not raise an alarm.

"There was an agent buttoned up inside an ulster[9] and sleeping on a chair on deck within three feet of me. The yells had not awakened him; he snored very slightly; I left him to his slumbers and leaped ashore. I did not betray Mr Kurtz—it was ordered I should never betray him—it was written I should be loyal to the

---

9. A long, loose overcoat, often with a belt.

nightmare of my choice. I was anxious to deal with this shadow by myself alone—and to this day I don't know why I was so jealous of sharing with any one the peculiar blackness of that experience.

"As soon as I got on the bank I saw a trail—a broad trail through the grass. I remember the exultation with which I said to myself, 'He can't walk—he is crawling on all-fours—I've got him.' The grass was wet with dew. I strode rapidly with clenched fists. I fancy I had some vague notion of falling upon him and giving him a drubbing. I don't know. I had some imbecile thoughts. The knitting old woman with the cat obtruded herself upon my memory as a most improper person to be sitting at the other end of such an affair. I saw a row of pilgrims squirting lead in the air out of Winchesters held to the hip. I thought I would never get back to the steamer, and imagined myself living alone and unarmed in the woods to an advanced age. Such silly things—you know. And I remember I confounded the beat of the drum with the beating of my heart, and was pleased at its calm regularity.

"I kept to the track though—then stopped to listen. The night was very clear; a dark blue space, sparkling with dew and starlight, in which black things stood very still. I thought I could see a kind of motion ahead of me. I was strangely cocksure of everything that night. I actually left the track and ran in a wide semicircle (I verily believe chuckling to myself) so as to get in front of that stir, of that motion I had seen—if indeed I had seen anything. I was circumventing Kurtz as though it had been a boyish game.

"I came upon him, and, if he had not heard me coming, I would have fallen over him too, but he got up in time. He rose, unsteady, long, pale, indistinct, like a vapour exhaled by the earth, and swayed slightly, misty and silent before me; while at my back the fires loomed between the trees, and the murmur of many voices issued from the forest. I had cut him off cleverly; but when actually confronting him I seemed to come to my senses, I saw the danger in its right proportion. It was by no means over yet. Suppose he began to shout? Though he could hardly stand, there was still plenty of vigour in his voice. 'Go away—hide yourself,' he said, in that profound tone. It was very awful. I glanced back. We were within thirty yards of the nearest fire. A black figure stood up, strode on long black legs, waving long black arms, across the glow. It had horns—antelope horns, I think—on its head. Some sorcerer, some witch-man no doubt: it looked fiend-like enough. 'Do you know what you are doing?' I whispered. 'Perfectly,' he answered, raising his voice for that single word: it sounded to me far off and yet loud, like a hail through a speaking-trumpet. If he makes a row we are lost, I thought to myself. This clearly was not a case for fisticuffs, even apart from the very natural aversion I had to beat that Shadow—this wandering and tormented thing. 'You will be lost,' I said—'utterly lost.' One gets sometimes such a flash of inspiration, you know. I did say the right thing, though indeed he could not have been more irretrievably lost than he was at this very moment, when the foundations of our intimacy were being laid—to endure—to endure—even to the end—even beyond.

"'I had immense plans,' he muttered irresolutely. 'Yes,' said I; 'but if you try to shout I'll smash your head with—' There was not a stick or a stone near. 'I will throttle you for good,' I corrected myself. 'I was on the threshold of great things,' he pleaded, in a voice of longing, with a wistfulness of tone that made my blood run cold. 'And now for this stupid scoundrel—' 'Your success in

Europe is assured in any case,' I affirmed steadily. I did not want to have the throttling of him, you understand—and indeed it would have been very little use for any practical purpose. I tried to break the spell—the heavy, mute spell of the wilderness—that seemed to draw him to its pitiless breast by the awakening of forgotten and brutal instincts, by the memory of gratified and monstrous passions. This alone, I was convinced, had driven him out to the edge of the forest, to the bush, towards the gleam of fires, the throb of drums, the drone of weird incantations; this alone had beguiled his unlawful soul beyond the bounds of permitted aspirations. And, don't you see, the terror of the position was not in being knocked on the head—though I had a very lively sense of that danger too—but in this, that I had to deal with a being to whom I could not appeal in the name of anything high or low. I had, even like the niggers, to invoke him—himself—his own exalted and incredible degradation. There was nothing either above or below him, and I knew it. He had kicked himself loose of the earth. Confound the man! he had kicked the very earth to pieces. He was alone, and I before him did not know whether I stood on the ground or floated in the air. I've been telling you what we said—repeating the phrases we pronounced—but what's the good? They were common everyday words—the familiar, vague sounds exchanged on every waking day of life. But what of that? They had behind them, to my mind, the terrific suggestiveness of words heard in dreams, of phrases spoken in nightmares. Soul! If anybody had ever struggled with a soul, I am the man. And I wasn't arguing with a lunatic either. Believe me or not, his intelligence was perfectly clear—concentrated, it is true, upon himself with horrible intensity, yet clear; and therein was my only chance—barring, of course, the killing him there and then, which wasn't so good, on account of unavoidable noise. But his soul was mad. Being alone in the wilderness, it had looked within itself, and, by heavens! I tell you, it had gone mad. I had—for my sins, I suppose, to go through the ordeal of looking into it myself. No eloquence could have been so withering to one's belief in mankind as his final burst of sincerity. He struggled with himself too. I saw it—I heard it. I saw the inconceivable mystery of a soul that knew no restraint, no faith, and no fear, yet struggling blindly with itself. I kept my head pretty well; but when I had him at last stretched on the couch, I wiped my forehead, while my legs shook under me as though I had carried half a ton on my back down that hill. And yet I had only supported him, his bony arm clasped round my neck—and he was not much heavier than a child.

"When next day we left at noon, the crowd, of whose presence behind the curtain of trees I had been acutely conscious all the time, flowed out of the woods again, filled the clearing, covered the slope with a mass of naked, breathing, quivering, bronze bodies. I steamed up a bit, then swung downstream, and two thousand eyes followed the evolutions of the splashing, thumping, fierce river-demon beating the water with its terrible tail and breathing black smoke into the air. In front of the first rank, along the river, three men, plastered with bright red earth from head to foot, strutted to and fro restlessly. When we came abreast again, they faced the river, stamped their feet, nodded their horned heads, swayed their scarlet bodies; they shook towards the fierce river-demon a bunch of black feathers, a mangy skin with a pendent tail—something that looked like a dried gourd; they shouted periodically together strings of amazing words that resembled no sounds of human language; and the deep murmurs of the crowd, interrupted suddenly, were like the responses of some satanic litany.

"We had carried Kurtz into the pilot-house: there was more air there. Lying on the couch, he stared through the open shutter. There was an eddy in the mass of human bodies, and the woman with helmeted head and tawny cheeks rushed out to the very brink of the stream. She put out her hands, shouted something, and all that wild mob took up the shout in a roaring chorus of articulated, rapid, breathless utterance.

"'Do you understand this?' I asked.

"He kept on looking out past me with fiery, longing eyes, with a mingled expression of wistfulness and hate. He made no answer, but I saw a smile, a smile of indefinable meaning, appear on his colourless lips that a moment after twitched convulsively. 'Do I not?' he said slowly, gasping, as if the words had been torn out of him by a supernatural power.

"I pulled the string of the whistle, and I did this because I saw the pilgrims on deck getting out their rifles with an air of anticipating a jolly lark. At the sudden screech there was a movement of abject terror through that wedged mass of bodies. 'Don't! don't you frighten them away,' cried someone on deck disconsolately. I pulled the string time after time. They broke and ran, they leaped, they crouched, they swerved, they dodged the flying terror of the sound. The three red chaps had fallen flat, face down on the shore, as though they had been shot dead. Only the barbarous and superb woman did not so much as flinch, and stretched tragically her bare arms after us over the sombre and glittering river.

"And then that imbecile crowd down on the deck started their little fun, and I could see nothing more for smoke.

"The brown current ran swiftly out of the heart of darkness, bearing us down towards the sea with twice the speed of our upward progress; and Kurtz's life was running swiftly too, ebbing, ebbing out of his heart into the sea of inexorable time. The manager was very placid, he had no vital anxieties now, he took us both in with a comprehensive and satisfied glance: the 'affair' had come off as well as could be wished. I saw the time approaching when I would be left alone of the party of 'unsound method.' The pilgrims looked upon me with disfavour. I was, so to speak, numbered with the dead. It is strange how I accepted this unforeseen partnership, this choice of nightmares forced upon me in the tenebrous land invaded by these mean and greedy phantoms.

"Kurtz discoursed. A voice! a voice! It rang deep to the very last. It survived his strength to hide in the magnificent folds of eloquence the barren darkness of his heart. Oh, he struggled! he struggled! The wastes of his weary brain were haunted by shadowy images now—images of wealth and fame revolving obsequiously round his unextinguishable gift of noble and lofty expression. My Intended, my station, my career, my ideas—these were the subjects for the occasional utterances of elevated sentiments. The shade of the original Kurtz frequented the bedside of the hollow sham, whose fate it was to be buried presently in the mould of primeval earth. But both the diabolic love and the unearthly hate of the mysteries it had penetrated fought for the possession of that soul satiated with primitive emotions, avid of lying fame, of sham distinction, of all the appearances of success and power.

"Sometimes he was contemptibly childish. He desired to have kings meet him at railway stations on his return from some ghastly Nowhere, where he intended to accomplish great things. 'You show them you have in you something that is really profitable, and then there will be no limits to the recognition of your ability,' he would say. 'Of course you must take care of the motives— right motives—always.' The long reaches that were like one and the same reach, monotonous bends that were exactly alike, slipped past the steamer with their multitude of secular[1] trees looking patiently after this grimy fragment of another world, the forerunner of change, of conquest, of trade, of massacres, of blessings. I looked ahead—piloting. 'Close the shutter,' said Kurtz suddenly one day; 'I can't bear to look at this.' I did so. There was a silence. 'Oh, but I will wring your heart yet!' he cried at the invisible wilderness.

"We broke down—as I had expected—and had to lie up for repairs at the head of an island. This delay was the first thing that shook Kurtz's confidence. One morning he gave me a packet of papers and a photograph—the lot tied together with a shoe-string. 'Keep this for me,' he said. 'This noxious fool' (meaning the manager) 'is capable of prying into my boxes when I am not looking.' In the afternoon I saw him. He was lying on his back with closed eyes, and I withdrew quietly, but I heard him mutter, 'Live rightly, die, die . . .' I listened. There was nothing more. Was he rehearsing some speech in his sleep, or was it a fragment of a phrase from some newspaper article? He had been writing for the papers and meant to do so again, 'for the furthering of my ideas. It's a duty.'

"His was an impenetrable darkness. I looked at him as you peer down at a man who is lying at the bottom of a precipice where the sun never shines. But I had not much time to give him, because I was helping the engine-driver to take to pieces the leaky cylinders, to straighten a bent connecting-rod, and in other such matters. I lived in an infernal mess of rust, filings, nuts, bolts, spanners, hammers, ratchet-drills—things I abominate, because I don't get on with them. I tended the little forge we fortunately had aboard; I toiled wearily in a wretched scrap-heap—unless I had the shakes too bad to stand.

"One evening coming in with a candle I was startled to hear him say a little tremulously, 'I am lying here in the dark waiting for death.' The light was within a foot of his eyes. I forced myself to murmur, 'Oh, nonsense!' and stood over him as if transfixed.

"Anything approaching the change that came over his features I have never seen before, and hope never to see again. Oh, I wasn't touched. I was fascinated. It was as though a veil had been rent. I saw on that ivory face the expression of sombre pride, of ruthless power, of craven terror—of an intense and hopeless despair. Did he live his life again in every detail of desire, temptation, and surrender during that supreme moment of complete knowledge? He cried in a whisper at some image, at some vision—he cried out twice, a cry that was no more than a breath:

"'The horror! The horror!'

"I blew the candle out and left the cabin. The pilgrims were dining in the mess-room, and I took my place opposite the manager, who lifted his eyes to give me a questioning glance, which I successfully ignored. He leaned back,

---

1. Centuries old (from *séculaire*, French).

serene, with that peculiar smile of his sealing the unexpressed depths of his meanness. A continuous shower of small flies streamed upon the lamp, upon the cloth, upon our hands and faces. Suddenly the manager's boy put his insolent black head in the doorway, and said in a tone of scathing contempt:

"'Mistah Kurtz—he dead.'

"All the pilgrims rushed out to see. I remained, and went on with my dinner. I believe I was considered brutally callous. However, I did not eat much. There was a lamp in there—light, don't you know—and outside it was so beastly, beastly dark. I went no more near the remarkable man who had pronounced a judgement upon the adventures of his soul on this earth. The voice was gone. What else had been there? But I am of course aware that next day the pilgrims buried something in a muddy hole.

"And then they very nearly buried me.

"However, as you see, I did not go to join Kurtz there and then. I did not. I remained to dream the nightmare out to the end, and to show my loyalty to Kurtz once more. Destiny. My destiny! Droll thing life is—that mysterious arrangement of merciless logic for a futile purpose. The most you can hope from it is some knowledge of yourself—that comes too late—a crop of unextinguishable regrets. I have wrestled with death. It is the most unexciting contest you can imagine. It takes place in an impalpable greyness, with nothing underfoot, with nothing around, without spectators, without clamour, without glory, without the great desire of victory, without the great fear of defeat, in a sickly atmosphere of tepid scepticism, without much belief in your own right, and still less in that of your adversary. If such is the form of ultimate wisdom, then life is a greater riddle than some of us think it to be. I was within a hair's-breadth of the last opportunity for pronouncement, and I found with humiliation that probably I would have nothing to say. This is the reason why I affirm that Kurtz was a remarkable man. He had something to say. He said it. Since I had peeped over the edge myself, I understand better the meaning of his stare, that could not see the flame of the candle, but was wide enough to embrace the whole universe, piercing enough to penetrate all the hearts that beat in the darkness. He had summed up—he had judged. 'The horror!' He was a remarkable man. After all, this was the expression of some sort of belief; it had candour, it had conviction, it had a vibrating note of revolt in its whisper, it had the appalling face of a glimpsed truth—the strange commingling of desire and hate. And it is not my own extremity I remember best—a vision of greyness without form filled with physical pain, and a careless contempt for the evanescence of all things— even of this pain itself. No! It is his extremity that I seem to have lived through. True, he had made that last stride, he had stepped over the edge, while I had been permitted to draw back my hesitating foot. And perhaps in this is the whole difference; perhaps all the wisdom, and all truth, and all sincerity, are just compressed into that inappreciable moment of time in which we step over the threshold of the invisible. Perhaps! I like to think my summing-up would not have been a word of careless contempt. Better his cry—much better. It was an affirmation, a moral victory paid for by innumerable defeats, by abominable terrors, by abominable satisfactions. But it was a victory! That is why I have remained loyal to Kurtz to the last, and even beyond, when a long time after I heard once more, not his own voice, but the echo of his magnificent eloquence thrown to me from a soul as translucently pure as a cliff of crystal.

"No, they did not bury me, though there is a period of time which I remember mistily, with a shuddering wonder, like a passage through some inconceivable world that had no hope in it and no desire. I found myself back in the sepulchral city resenting the sight of people hurrying through the streets to filch a little money from each other, to devour their infamous cookery, to gulp their unwholesome beer, to dream their insignificant and silly dreams. They trespassed upon my thoughts. They were intruders whose knowledge of life was to me an irritating pretence, because I felt so sure they could not possibly know the things I knew. Their bearing, which was simply the bearing of commonplace individuals going about their business in the assurance of perfect safety, was offensive to me like the outrageous flauntings of folly in the face of a danger it is unable to comprehend. I had no particular desire to enlighten them, but I had some difficulty in restraining myself from laughing in their faces, so full of stupid importance. I daresay I was not very well at that time. I tottered about the streets—there were various affairs to settle—grinning bitterly at perfectly respectable persons. I admit my behaviour was inexcusable, but then my temperature was seldom normal in these days. My dear aunt's endeavours to 'nurse up my strength' seemed altogether beside the mark. It was not my strength that wanted nursing, it was my imagination that wanted soothing. I kept the bundle of papers given me by Kurtz, not knowing exactly what to do with it. His mother had died lately, watched over, as I was told, by his Intended. A clean-shaven man, with an official manner and wearing gold-rimmed spectacles, called on me one day and made inquiries, at first circuitous, afterwards suavely pressing, about what he was pleased to denominate certain 'documents.' I was not surprised, because I had had two rows with the manager on the subject out there. I had refused to give up the smallest scrap out of that package, and I took the same attitude with the spectacled man. He became darkly menacing at last, and with much heat argued that the Company had the right to every bit of information about its 'territories.' And, said he, 'Mr Kurtz's knowledge of unexplored regions must have been necessarily extensive and peculiar—owing to his great abilities and to the deplorable circumstances in which he had been placed: therefore—' I assured him Mr Kurtz's knowledge, however extensive, did not bear upon the problems of commerce or administration. He invoked then the name of science. 'It would be an incalculable loss if,' etc. etc. I offered him the report on the 'Suppression of Savage Customs,' with the postscriptum torn off. He took it up eagerly, but ended by sniffing at it with an air of contempt. 'This is not what we had a right to expect,' he remarked. 'Expect nothing else,' I said. 'There are only private letters.' He withdrew upon some threat of legal proceedings, and I saw him no more; but another fellow, calling himself Kurtz's cousin, appeared two days later, and was anxious to hear all the details about his dear relative's last moments. Incidentally he gave me to understand that Kurtz had been essentially a great musician. 'There was the making of an immense success,' said the man, who was an organist, I believe, with lank grey hair flowing over a greasy coat-collar. I had no reason to doubt his statement; and to this day I am unable to say what was Kurtz's profession, whether he ever had any—which was the greatest of his talents. I had taken him for a painter who wrote for the papers, or else for a journalist who could paint—but even the cousin (who took snuff during the interview) could not tell me what he had been—exactly. He was a universal genius—on that point I agreed with the old chap, who thereupon blew his nose noisily into a large cotton handkerchief and withdrew in senile agitation, bearing off some family letters and memoranda without importance. Ultimately a journalist anxious to know something of the fate of his 'dear colleague' turned up. This visitor informed me Kurtz's proper sphere ought to have been politics 'on the popular side.' He had furry straight eyebrows, bristly hair cropped short, an eyeglass on a broad ribbon, and, becoming expansive, confessed his opinion that Kurtz really couldn't write a bit—'but heavens! how that man could talk! He electrified large meetings. He had faith—don't you see?—he had the faith. He could get himself to believe anything—anything. He would have been a splendid leader of an extreme party.' 'What party?' I asked. 'Any party,' answered the other. 'He was an—an—extremist.' Did I not think so? I assented. Did I know, he asked, with a sudden flash of curiosity, 'what it was that had induced him to go out there?' 'Yes,' said I, and forthwith handed him the famous Report for publication, if he thought fit. He glanced through it hurriedly, mumbling all the time, judged 'it would do,' and took himself off with this plunder.

"Thus I was left at last with a slim packet of letters and the girl's portrait. She struck me as beautiful—I mean she had a beautiful expression. I know that the sunlight can be made to lie too, yet one felt that no manipulation of light and pose could have conveyed the delicate shade of truthfulness upon those features. She seemed ready to listen without mental reservation, without suspicion, without a thought for herself. I concluded I would go and give her back her portrait and those letters myself. Curiosity? Yes; and also some other feeling perhaps. All that had been Kurtz's had passed out of my hands: his soul, his body, his station, his plans, his ivory, his career. There remained only his memory and his Intended—and I wanted to give that up too to the past, in a way—to surrender personally all that remained of him with me to that oblivion which is the last word of our common fate. I don't defend myself. I had no clear perception of what it was I really wanted. Perhaps it was an impulse of unconscious loyalty, or the fulfilment of one of those ironic necessities that lurk in the facts of human existence. I don't know. I can't tell. But I went.

"I thought his memory was like the other memories of the dead that accumulate in every man's life—a vague impress on the brain of shadows that had fallen on it in their swift and final passage; but before the high and ponderous door, between the tall houses of a street as still and decorous as a well-kept alley in a cemetery, I had a vision of him on the stretcher, opening his mouth voraciously, as if to devour all the earth with all its mankind. He lived then before me; he lived as much as he had ever lived—a shadow insatiable of splendid appearances, of frightful realities; a shadow darker than the shadow of the night, and draped nobly in the folds of a gorgeous eloquence. The vision seemed to enter the house with me—the stretcher, the phantom-bearers, the wild crowd of obedient worshippers, the gloom of the forests, the glitter of the reach between the murky bends, the beat of the drum, regular and muffled like the beating of a heart—the heart of a conquering darkness. It was a moment of triumph for the wilderness, an invading and vengeful rush which, it seemed to me, I would have to keep back alone for the salvation of another soul. And the memory of what I had heard him say afar there, with the horned shapes stirring at my back, in the glow of fires, within the patient woods, those broken phrases came back to me, were heard again in their ominous and terrifying simplicity. I remembered his abject pleading, his abject threats, the colossal scale of his vile desires, the meanness, the torment, the tempestuous anguish of his soul. And later on I seemed to see his collected languid manner, when he said one day, 'This lot of ivory now is really mine. The Company did not pay for it. I collected it myself at a very great personal risk. I am afraid they will try to claim it as theirs though. H'm. It is a difficult case. What do you think I ought to do—resist? Eh? I want no more than justice.' . . . He wanted no more than justice—no more than justice. I rang the bell before a mahogany door on the first floor, and while I waited he seemed to stare at me out of the glossy panel—stare with that wide and immense stare embracing, condemning, loathing all the universe. I seemed to hear the whispered cry, 'The horror! The horror!'

"The dusk was falling. I had to wait in a lofty drawing room with three long windows from floor to ceiling that were like three luminous and bedraped columns. The bent gilt legs and backs of the furniture shone in indistinct curves. The tall marble fireplace had a cold and monumental whiteness. A grand piano stood massively in a corner; with dark gleams on the flat surfaces like a sombre and polished sarcophagus. A high door opened—closed. I rose.

"She came forward, all in black, with a pale head, floating towards me in the dusk. She was in mourning. It was more than a year since his death, more than a year since the news came; she seemed as though she would remember and mourn for ever. She took both my hands in hers and murmured, 'I had heard you were coming.' I noticed she was not very young—I mean not girlish. She had a mature capacity for fidelity, for belief, for suffering. The room seemed to have grown darker, as if all the sad light of the cloudy evening had taken refuge on her forehead. This fair hair, this pale visage, this pure brow, seemed surrounded by an ashy halo from which the dark eyes looked out at me. Their glance was guileless, profound, confident, and trustful. She carried her sorrowful head as though she were proud of that sorrow, as though she would say, I—I alone know how to mourn for him as he deserves. But while we were still shaking hands, such a look of awful desolation came upon her face that I perceived she was one of those creatures that are not the playthings of Time. For her he had died only yesterday. And, by Jove! the impression was so powerful that for me too he seemed to have died only yesterday—nay, this very minute. I saw her and him in the same instant of time—his death and her sorrow—I saw her sorrow in the very moment of his death. Do you understand? I saw them together—I heard them together. She had said, with a deep catch of the breath, 'I have survived'; while my strained ears seemed to hear distinctly, mingled with her tone of despairing regret, the summing-up whisper of his eternal condemnation. I asked myself what I was doing there, with a sensation of panic in my heart as though I had blundered into a place of cruel and absurd mysteries not fit for a human being to behold. She motioned me to a chair. We sat down. I laid the packet gently on the little table, and she put her hand over it. . . . 'You knew him well,' she murmured, after a moment of mourning silence.

"'Intimacy grows quickly out there,' I said. 'I knew him as well as it is possible for one man to know another.'

"'And you admired him,' she said. 'It was impossible to know him and not to admire him. Was it?'

"'He was a remarkable man,' I said unsteadily. Then before the appealing fixity of her gaze, that seemed to watch for more words on my lips, I went on, 'It was impossible not to—'

"'Love him,' she finished eagerly, silencing me into an appalled dumbness. 'How true! how true! But when you think that no one knew him so well as I! I had all his noble confidence. I knew him best.'

"'You knew him best,' I repeated. And perhaps she did. But with every word spoken the room was growing darker, and only her forehead, smooth and white, remained illumined by the unextinguishable light of belief and love.

"'You were his friend,' she went on. 'His friend,' she repeated, a little louder. 'You must have been, if he had given you this, and sent you to me. I feel I can speak to you—and oh! I must speak. I want you—you who have heard his last words—to know I have been worthy of him. . . . It is not pride. . . . Yes! I am proud to know I understood him better than any one on earth—he told me so himself. And since his mother died I have had no one—no one—to—to—'

"I listened. The darkness deepened. I was not even sure whether he had given me the right bundle. I rather suspect he wanted me to take care of another batch of his papers which, after his death, I saw the manager examining under the lamp. And the girl talked, easing her pain in the certitude of my sympathy; she talked as thirsty men drink. I had heard that her engagement with Kurtz had been disapproved by her people. He wasn't rich enough or something. And indeed I don't know whether he had not been a pauper all his life. He had given me some reason to infer that it was his impatience of comparative poverty that drove him out there.

"'. . . Who was not his friend who had heard him speak once?' she was saying. 'He drew men towards him by what was best in them.' She looked at me with intensity. 'It is the gift of the great,' she went on, and the sound of her low voice seemed to have the accompaniment of all the other sounds, full of mystery, desolation, and sorrow, I had ever heard—the ripple of the river, the soughing[2] of the trees swayed by the wind, the murmurs of the crowds, the faint ring of incomprehensible words cried from afar, the whisper of a voice speaking from beyond the threshold of an eternal darkness. 'But you have heard him! You know!' she cried.

"'Yes, I know,' I said with something like despair in my heart, but bowing my head before the faith that was in her, before that great and saving illusion that shone with an unearthly glow in the darkness, in the triumphant darkness from which I could not have defended her—from which I could not even defend myself.

"'What a loss to me—to us!'—she corrected herself with beautiful generosity; then added in a murmur, 'To the world.' By the last gleams of twilight I could see the glitter of her eyes, full of tears—of tears that would not fall.

"'I have been very happy—very fortunate—very proud,' she went on. 'Too fortunate. Too happy for a little while. And now I am unhappy for—for life.'

"She stood up; her fair hair seemed to catch all the remaining light in a glimmer of gold. I rose too.

"'And of all this,' she went on mournfully, 'of all his promise, and of all his greatness, of his generous mind, of his noble heart, nothing remains—nothing but a memory. You and I—'

2. A rushing or murmuring sound.

"'We shall always remember him,' I said hastily.

"'No!' she cried. 'It is impossible that all this should be lost—that such a life should be sacrificed to leave nothing—but sorrow. You know what vast plans he had. I knew of them too—I could not perhaps understand—but others knew of them. Something must remain. His words, at least, have not died.'

"'His words will remain,' I said.

"'And his example,' she whispered to herself. 'Men looked up to him—his goodness shone in every act. His example—'

"'True,' I said; 'his example too. Yes, his example. I forgot that.'

"'But I do not. I cannot—I cannot believe—not yet. I cannot believe that I shall never see him again, that nobody will see him again, never, never, never.'

"She put out her arms as if after a retreating figure, stretching them back and with clasped pale hands across the fading and narrow sheen of the window. Never see him! I saw him clearly enough then. I shall see this eloquent phantom as long as I live, and I shall see her too, a tragic and familiar Shade, resembling in this gesture another one, tragic also, and bedecked with powerless charms, stretching bare brown arms over the glitter of the infernal stream, the stream of darkness. She said suddenly very low, 'He died as he lived.'

"'His end,' said I, with dull anger stirring in me, 'was in every way worthy of his life.'

"'And I was not with him,' she murmured. My anger subsided before a feeling of infinite pity.

"'Everything that could be done—' I mumbled.

"'Ah, but I believed in him more than any one on earth—more than his own mother, more than—himself. He needed me! Me! I would have treasured every sigh, every word, every sign, every glance.'

"I felt like a chill grip on my chest. 'Don't,' I said, in a muffled voice.

"'Forgive me. I—I—have mourned so long in silence—in silence. . . . You were with him—to the last? I think of his loneliness. Nobody near to understand him as I would have understood. Perhaps no one to hear. . . .'

"'To the very end,' I said shakily. 'I heard his very last words. . . .' I stopped in a fright.

"'Repeat them,' she murmured in a heart-broken tone. 'I want—I want—something—something—to—to live with.'

"I was on the point of crying at her, 'Don't you hear them?' The dusk was repeating them in a persistent whisper all around us, in a whisper that seemed to swell menacingly like the first whisper of a rising wind. 'The horror! The horror!'

"'His last word—to live with,' she insisted. 'Don't you understand I loved him—I loved him—I loved him!'

"I pulled myself together and spoke slowly.

"'The last word he pronounced was—your name.'

"I heard a light sigh and then my heart stood still, stopped dead short by an exulting and terrible cry, by the cry of inconceivable triumph and of unspeakable pain. 'I knew it—I was sure!' . . . She knew. She was sure. I heard her weeping; she had hidden her face in her hands. It seemed to me that the house would collapse before I could escape, that the heavens would fall upon my head. But nothing happened. The heavens do not fall for such a trifle. Would they have fallen, I wonder, if I had rendered Kurtz that justice which was his due? Hadn't he said he wanted only justice? But I couldn't. I could not tell her. It would have been too dark—too dark altogether. . . .'"

Marlow ceased, and sat apart, indistinct and silent, in the pose of a meditating Buddha. Nobody moved for a time. "We have lost the first of the ebb," said the Director suddenly. I raised my head. The offing was barred by a black bank of clouds, and the tranquil waterway leading to the uttermost ends of the earth flowed sombre under an overcast sky—seemed to lead into the heart of an immense darkness.

1899

THOMAS MANN
1875–1955

The greatest German novelist of the twentieth century, Thomas Mann also became an international figure to whom people looked for statements on art, modern society, and the human condition. Carrying on the nineteenth-century tradition of psychological realism, Mann took as his subject the cultural and spiritual crises of Europe at the turn of the century. His career spanned a time of great change, including the upheaval of two world wars and the disintegration of an entire society. Whereas other modern novelists such as **James Joyce**, William Faulkner, and **Virginia Woolf** stressed innovative language and style, Mann wrote in a more traditional, realistic style about the universal human conflicts between art and life, sensuality and intellect, individual and social will. Yet in his struggle with themes like time, subjectivity, and homosexuality, he too participated in the modernist movement that transformed the literature of the twentieth century.

Mann was born on June 6, 1875, in Lübeck, a historic seaport and commercial city in northern Germany. His father was a grain merchant and head of the family firm; his mother, who came from a German-Brazilian family, was known for her beauty and musical talent. The contrast between Nordic and Latin that plays such a large part in Mann's work began in his consciousness of his own heritage. Mann became acquainted with mortality early on: his father died when he was sixteen, and later both his sister and his son committed suicide. Although Thomas failed two years in school, he viewed the failure as liberating, since it relieved him of his parents' high expectations. He graduated from high school in 1894. Joining his family in Munich, where they had moved after his father's death, he worked as an unpaid apprentice in a fire insurance business, but was more interested in university lectures in history, political economy, and art. He decided against a business career after his first published story, *Fallen* (1896), received praise from the noted poet Richard Dehmel. He lived and wrote for two years in Italy before returning to Munich for a stint as manuscript reader for the satiric weekly *Simplicissimus*. In 1905 he married Katia Pringsheim, with whom he had six children. Yet as a young man he had experienced homosexual attractions, which continued throughout his life and became a recurring theme in his fiction. He recorded these attractions privately in his diary but never acted on them; he commented that "I would never have wanted to go to bed even with the Belvedere Apollo."

His first major work, *Buddenbrooks* (1901), describes the decline of a prosperous German family through four generations and is to some extent based on the history of the Mann family business. Nonetheless, the elements of autobiography are quickly absorbed into the universal themes of the inner decay of the German burgher ("bourgeois," or middle-class) tradition and its growing isolation from other segments of society—a decline paralleled in the portrait of a developing artistic sensitivity and its relation to death. Throughout his writings before and during the First World War, Mann established himself as an important spokesman for modern Germany. He argued with his brother Heinrich about politics; Heinrich was a passionate liberal, but Thomas defined freedom as "a moral, spiritual idea" and said that "for political freedom I've absolutely no interest." The political crises after the First World War shook Mann, however, and the subsequent rise of the Nazis changed his views. He rejected his early conservatism and defense of an authoritarian nationalist government (*Reflections of a Non-Political Man*, 1918) in favor of ardent support for democracy and liberal humanism.

One of the first signs of this new attitude was Mann's most famous novel, *The Magic Mountain* (1924), a bildungsroman (a novel of the protagonist's education and development) that uses the isolation of a mountaintop tuberculosis sanatorium to gain perspective on the philosophic issues of twentieth-century Europe. *The Magic Mountain* was immensely popular, and in 1929 its author received the Nobel Prize. As his international stature grew, Mann spoke out against the Nazis; his

wife, Katia, came from a Jewish family, and when Hitler rose to power in 1933, the Manns went into voluntary exile in neutral Switzerland. Stung by Mann's criticism, the Nazis revoked his citizenship. Moving to the United States in 1938, he wrote and lectured against Nazism, and in 1944 he became an American citizen. After the Second World War, Mann refused to live in Germany, arguing that the country had not expiated its crimes. He became an active advocate for the cause of peace; criticized by the House Un-American Activities Committee for his support of allegedly Communist peace organizations, Mann left the United States for Switzerland in 1952.

Mann's later works deal with the conflicts and interrelations between society and inspired individuals whose spiritual, intellectual, or artistic gifts set them apart. *Joseph and His Brothers* (1933–45) is a tetralogy that reimagines the biblical tale of Joseph, who, abandoned for dead by his brothers, survives and comes to power in Egypt. *Doctor Faustus* (1947), which Mann called "the novel of my epoch, dressed up in the story of a highly precarious and sinful artistic life," portrays the composer Adrian Leverkühn as a modern Faust who personifies the temptation and corruption of contemporary Germany. Well after the war, when Mann had moved to Zurich, he published a final, comic picture of the artist figure as a confidence man who uses his skill and ironic insight to manipulate society (*The Confessions of Felix Krull*, 1954). Mann's last work before his death, on August 12, 1955, the *Confessions* recapitulates his familiar themes, but in a lighthearted parody of the traditional bildungsroman that is a far cry from the moral seriousness of earlier tales.

Many of Mann's themes derive from the nineteenth-century German aesthetic tradition in which he grew up. The philosophers Schopenhauer and

Nietzsche and the composer Wagner had the most influence on his work: Arthur Schopenhauer (1788–1860) for his vision of the artist's suffering and development; Friedrich Nietzsche (1844–1900) for his portrait of the diseased artist overcoming chaos and decay to produce, through discipline and will, works that justify existence; and Richard Wagner (1813–1883) for embodying the complete artist who controlled all aspects of his work: music, lyrics, the very staging of his operas. Mann's well-known use of the verbal leitmotif is also borrowed from Wagner, whose operas are notable for the recurrent musical theme (the leitmotif) associated with a particular person, thing, action, or state of being. In Mann's literary adaptation, evocative phrases, repeated almost without change, link memories throughout the text and establish a cumulative emotional resonance. Inside the tradition of realistic narration, Mann creates a highly organized literary structure with subtly interrelated themes and images that build up rich associations of ideas: in his own words, an "epic prose composition . . . understood by me as spiritual thematic pattern, as a musical complex of associations." At the same time, Mann's works cultivate objectivity, distance, and irony, and no character—including the narrator—is immune from the author's critical eye. Indeed, it is in his tendency to treat realist techniques with irony that Mann most reveals himself as a modern, unable to accept narrative convention at face value.

DEATH IN VENICE

The work presented here, *Death in Venice*, is Mann's most famous novella, published in 1912, shortly after the author's vacation in Venice and two years before the First World War. Its sense of impending doom involves the cultural disintegration of the "European soul" (soon to be expressed in the war), which has its symbol in the corruption and death of the writer Gustav von Aschenbach during an epidemic. The story portrays a loss of psychological balance, a sickness of the artistic soul to match that of plague-ridden Venice masking its true condition before unsuspecting tourists. Erotic and artistic themes mingle as the respected Aschenbach, escaping a lifetime of laborious creation and self-discipline, allows himself to be swept away by the classical beauty of a young boy until he becomes a grotesque figure, dyeing his hair and rouging his cheeks in a vain attempt to appear young. Aschenbach's fatal obsession with Tadzio casts light on the artist's whole career.

Aschenbach has laboriously repressed emotions and spontaneity to achieve the disciplined, classical style of a master—and also to earn fame. Plagued by nervous exhaustion at the beginning of the story, he reacts to the sight of a foreign traveler with a "sudden, strange expansion of his inner space" and starts dreaming of exotic, dangerous landscapes. From the tropical swampland and tigers of the Ganges delta to the mountains of a later dream's Dionysiac revels, these visionary landscapes become a metaphor for all the subterranean impulses he has rejected in himself and for his art. Enigmatic figures guide Aschenbach's adventure of the emotions: the traveler, the grotesque old man on the boat, the gondolier, the street singer, and Tadzio himself, interpreted as a godlike figure out of Greek myth. Indeed, allusions to ancient myth and literature multiply rapidly as Aschenbach falls under Tadzio's spell and begins to rationalize his fascination as the artist's pursuit of divine beauty. Turning to Plato's *Phaedrus*, a dialogue that combines themes of love with the search for absolute beauty and truth, Aschenbach sketches his own "Platonic" argument as a meditation on the dual nature of the artist. "Who can untangle the riddle of the artist's essence and character?" asks the narrator. *Death in Venice* is a crystallization of Mann's work at its best, displaying the penetrating detail of his social and psychological realism, the power of his tightly interwoven symbolic structure, and the tragic force of his artist-hero's crisis.

Death in Venice[1]

CHAPTER I

On a spring afternoon in 19—,[2] a year that for months glowered threateningly over our continent, Gustav Aschenbach—or von[3] Aschenbach, as he had been known officially since his fiftieth birthday—set off alone from his dwelling in Prinzregentenstrasse[4] in Munich on a rather long walk. He had been overstrained by the difficult and dangerous morning's work, which just now required particular discretion, caution, penetration, and precision of will: even after his midday meal the writer had not been able to halt the running on of the productive machinery within him, that "motus animi continuus" which Cicero[5] claims is the essence of eloquence, nor had he been able to obtain the relaxing slumber so necessary to him once a day to relieve the increasing demands on his resources. Thus, he sought the open air right after tea, hoping that fresh air and exercise would restore him and help him to have a profitable evening.

It was early May, and after weeks of cold, wet weather a premature summer had set in. The Englischer Garten,[6] although only beginning to come into leaf, was as muggy as in August and at the end near the city was full of vehicles and people out for a stroll. Increasingly quiet paths led Aschenbach toward Aumeister,[7] where he spent a moment surveying the lively crowd in the beer garden, next to which several hackneys and carriages were lingering; but then as the sun went down he took a route homeward outside the park over the open fields and, since he felt tired and thunder clouds now threatened over Föhring,[8] he waited at the North Cemetery stop for the tram that would take him directly back into the city.

As it happened he found the tram stop and the surrounding area deserted. Neither on the paved Ungererstrasse, whose streetcar-tracks stretched in glistening solitude toward Schwabing, nor on the Föhringer Chaussee[9] was there

1. Translated by and some notes adapted from Clayton Koelb.
2. In 1911, when the story was written, the "Moroccan crisis" was precipitated when a German gunboat appeared off the coast of Agadir, prompting negotiations between France and Germany over their respective national interests. A series of similar diplomatic crises led to the outbreak of World War 1 in 1914.
3. From or of. "Von" appears only in the names of nobility. Aschenbach was made an honorary nobleman on his fiftieth birthday.
4. A street in Munich that forms the southern boundary of the Englischer Garten (English Garden). Mann lived in various apartments in this neighborhood.

5. Marcus Tullius Cicero (106–43 B.C.E.), Roman orator. "Motus animi continuus": the continuous motion of the spirit (Latin, attributed to Cicero).
6. The English Garden, a 900-acre public park with diverse attractions that extended from the city to the water meadows of the Isar River.
7. A beer garden in the northern section.
8. A district in Munich.
9. A street. Ungererstrasse is a street that borders the North Cemetery. Schwabing is another district in Munich.

a vehicle to be seen, nothing stirred behind the fences of the stonemasons' shops, where the crosses, headstones, and monuments for sale formed a second, untenanted graveyard, and the Byzantine architecture of the mortuary chapel across the way lay silent in the glow of the departing day. Its facade was decorated with Greek crosses and hieratic paintings in soft colors; in addition it displayed symmetrically arranged scriptural quotations in gold letters, such as, "They are entering the house of God," or, "May the eternal light shine upon them." Waiting, he found a few moments' solemn diversion in reading these formulations and letting his mind's eye bask in their radiant mysticism, when, returning from his reveries, he noticed a man in the portico, above the two apocalyptic beasts guarding the front steps. The man's not altogether ordinary appearance took his thoughts in a completely different direction.

It was not clear whether the man had emerged from the chapel through the bronze door or had climbed the steps up to the entry from the outside without being noticed. Aschenbach, without entering too deeply into the question, inclined to the first assumption. Moderately tall, thin, clean-shaven, and strikingly snub-nosed, the man belonged to the red-haired type and possessed a redhead's milky and freckled complexion. He was clearly not of Bavarian stock, and in any case the wide and straight-brimmed straw hat that covered his head lent him the appearance of a foreigner, of a traveler from afar. To be sure, he also wore the familiar native rucksack strapped to his shoulders and a yellowish Norfolk suit[1] apparently of loden cloth. He had a gray mackintosh over his left forearm, which he held supported against his side, and in his right hand he held a stick with an iron tip, which he propped obliquely against the ground, leaning his hip against its handle and crossing his ankles. With his head held up, so that his Adam's apple protruded nakedly from the thin neck that emerged from his loose sport shirt, he gazed intently into the distance with colorless, red-lashed eyes, between which stood two stark vertical furrows that went rather oddly with his short, turned-up nose. It may be that his elevated and elevating location had something to do with it, but his posture conveyed an impression of imperious surveillance, fortitude, even wildness. His lips seemed insufficient, perhaps because he was squinting, blinded, toward the setting sun or maybe because he was afflicted by a facial deformity—in any case they were retracted to such an extent that his teeth, revealed as far as the gums, menacingly displayed their entire white length.

It is entirely possible that Aschenbach had been somewhat indiscreet in his half-distracted, half-inquisitive survey of the stranger, for he suddenly realized that his gaze was being returned, and indeed returned so belligerently, so directly eye to eye, with such a clear intent to bring matters to a head and force the other to avert his eyes, that Aschenbach, with an awkward sense of embarrassment, turned away and began to walk along the fence, intending for the time being to pay no more attention to the fellow. In a moment he had forgotten about him. But perhaps the man had the look of the traveler about him, or perhaps because he exercised some physical or spiritual influence, Aschenbach's imagination was set working. He felt a sudden, strange expansion of his inner space, a rambling unrest, a youthful thirst for faraway places, a feeling so

1. A belted suit.

intense, so new—or rather so long unused and forgotten—that he stood rooted to the spot, his hands behind his back and his gaze to the ground, pondering the essence and direction of his emotion.

It was wanderlust and nothing more, but it was an overwhelming wanderlust that rose to a passion and even to a delusion. His desire acquired vision, and his imagination, not yet calmed down from the morning's work, created its own version of the manifold marvels and terrors of the earth, all of them at once now seeking to take shape within him. He saw, saw a landscape, a tropical swamp under a vaporous sky, moist, luxuriant, and monstrous, a sort of primitive wilderness of islands, morasses, and alluvial estuaries; saw hairy palm trunks rise up near and far out of rank fern brakes, out of thick, swollen, wildly blooming vegetation; saw wondrously formless trees sink their aerial roots into the earth through stagnant, green-shadowed pools, where exotic birds, their shoulders high and their bills shaped weirdly, stood motionless in the shallows looking askance amidst floating flowers that were white as milk and big as platters; saw the eyes of a lurking tiger sparkle between the gnarled stems of a bamboo thicket; and felt his heart pound with horror and mysterious desire. Then the vision faded, and with a shake of his head Aschenbach resumed his promenade along the fences bordering the headstone-makers' yard.

He had regarded travel, at least since he had commanded the financial resources to enjoy the advantages of global transportation at will, as nothing more than a measure he had to take for his health, no matter how much it went against his inclination. Too much taken up with the tasks that his problematic self and the European soul posed for him, too burdened with the obligation of productivity, too averse to distraction to be a success as a lover of the world's motley show, he had quite contented himself with the view of the earth's surface anyone could get without stirring very far from home. He had never even been tempted to leave Europe. Especially now that his life was slowly waning, now that his artist's fear of never getting finished—his concern that the sands might run out of the glass before he had done his utmost and given his all— could no longer be dismissed as pure fancy, his external existence had confined itself almost exclusively to the lovely city that had become his home and to the rustic country house he had built in the mountains where he spent the rainy summers.

Besides, even this impulse that had come over him so suddenly and so late in life was quickly moderated and set right by reason and a self-discipline practiced since early youth. He had intended to keep at the work to which he now devoted his life until he reached a certain point and then move out to the country. The thought of sauntering about the world, of thereby being seduced away from months of work, seemed all too frivolous, too contrary to plan, and ultimately impermissible. And yet he knew all too well why this temptation had assailed him so unexpectedly. He had to admit it to himself: it was the urge to escape that was behind this yearning for the far away and the new, this desire for release, freedom, and forgetfulness. It was the urge to get away from his work, from the daily scene of an inflexible, cold, and passionate service. Of course he loved this service and almost loved the enervating struggle, renewed each day, between his stubborn, proud, so-often-tested will and his growing lassitude, about which no one could be allowed to know and which the product of his toil could not be permitted to reveal in any way, by any sign of failure or of negligence. Yet it seemed reasonable not to overbend the bow and not to stifle obstinately the outbreak of such a vital need. He thought about his work, thought about the place where once again, today as yesterday, he had been forced to abandon it, a passage that would submit, it seemed, neither to patient care nor to surprise attack. He considered it again, sought once more to break through or untangle the logjam, then broke off the effort with a shudder of repugnance. The passage presented no extraordinary difficulty; what disabled him was the malaise of scrupulousness confronting him in the guise of an insatiable perfectionism. Even as a young man, to be sure, he had considered perfectionism the basis and most intimate essence of his talent, and for its sake he had curbed and cooled his emotions, because he knew that emotion inclines one to satisfaction with a comfortable approximation, a half of perfection. Was his enslaved sensitivity now avenging itself by leaving him, refusing to advance his project and give wings to his art, taking with it all his joy, all his delight in form and expression? It was not that he was producing bad work—that at least was the advantage of his advanced years; he felt every moment comfortably secure in his mastery. But, though the nation honored it, he himself was not pleased with his mastery, and indeed it seemed to him that his work lacked those earmarks of a fiery, playful fancy that, stemming from joy, gave more joy to his appreciative audience than did any inner content or weighty excellence. He was fearful of the summer in the country, all alone in the little house with the maid who prepared his meals and the servant who waited on him at table, fearful too of the familiar mountaintops and mountainsides that once more would surround him in his discontented, slow progress. And so what he needed was a respite, a kind of spur-of-the-moment existence, a way to waste some time, foreign air and an infusion of new blood, to make the summer bearable and productive. Travel it would be then—it was all right with him. Not too far, though, not quite all the way to the tigers. One night in a sleeping car and a siesta for three or maybe four weeks in some fashionable vacation spot in the charming south . . .

Such were his thoughts as the noise of the electric tram approached along the Ungererstrasse, and he decided as he got on to devote this evening to studying maps and time tables. Once aboard it occurred to him to look around for the man in the straw hat, his comrade in this excursion that had been, in spite of all, so consequential. But he could get no clear idea of the man's whereabouts; neither his previous location, nor the next stop, nor the tram car itself revealed any signs of his presence.

CHAPTER 2

Gustav Aschenbach, the author of the clear and vigorous prose epic on the life of Frederick the Great;[2] the patient artist who wove together with enduring diligence the novelistic tapestry *Maia*,[3] a work rich in characters and eminently successful in gathering together many human destinies under the shadow of a

2. King Frederick II (1712–1786) started Prussia on its rise to domination of Germany and made his court a prominent European cultural center.

3. In Hinduism, the illusory appearance of the world concealing a higher spiritual reality.

single idea; the creator of that powerful story bearing the title "A Man of Misery," which had earned the gratitude of an entire young generation by showing it the possibility for a moral resolution that passed through and beyond the deepest knowledge; the author, finally (and this completes the short list of his mature works), of the passionate treatment of the topic "Art and Intellect,"[4] an essay whose power of organization and antithetical eloquence had prompted serious observers to rank it alongside Schiller's "On Naïve and Sentimental Poetry";[5] Gustav Aschenbach, then, was born the son of a career civil servant in the justice ministry in L., a district capital in the province of Silesia. His ancestors had been officers, judges, and government functionaries, men who had led upright lives of austere decency devoted to the service of king and country. A more ardent spirituality had expressed itself once among them in the person of a preacher; more impetuous and sensuous blood had entered the family line in the previous generation through the writer's mother, the daughter of a Bohemian music director. It was from her that he had in his features the traits of a foreign race. The marriage of sober conscientiousness devoted to service with darker, more fiery impulses engendered an artist and indeed this very special artist.

Since his entire being was bent on fame, he emerged early on as, perhaps not exactly precocious, but nonetheless, thanks to the decisiveness and peculiar terseness of his style, surprisingly mature and ready to go before the public. He was practically still in high school when he made a name for himself. Ten years later he learned how to keep up appearances, to manage his fame from his writing desk, to produce gracious and significant sentences for his necessarily brief letters (for many demands are made on such a successful and reliable man). By the age of forty, exhausted by the tortures and vicissitudes of his real work, he had to deal with a daily flood of mail bearing stamps from countries in every corner of the globe.

Tending neither to the banal nor to the eccentric, his talent was such as to win for his stories both the acceptance of the general public and an admiring, challenging interest from a more discerning audience. Thus he found himself even as a young man obliged in every way to achieve and indeed to achieve extraordinary things. He had therefore never known sloth, never known the carefree, laissez-faire attitude of youth. When he got sick in Vienna around the age of thirty-five, a canny observer remarked about him to friends, "You see, Aschenbach has always lived like this"—and the speaker closed the fingers of his left hand into a fist—"never like this"—and he let his open hand dangle comfortably from the arm of the chair. How right he was! And the morally courageous aspect of it was that, possessing anything but a naturally robust constitution, he was not so much born for constant exertion as he was called to it.

Medical concerns had prevented him from attending school as a child and compelled the employment of private instruction at home. He had grown up alone and without companions, and yet he must have realized early on that he

---

4. *Frederick, Maia, A Man of Misery,* and *Art and Intellect* are titles of projects Mann had worked on and abandoned.

5. An influential essay by the German Romantic writer Friedrich Schiller (1759–1805).

belonged to a tribe in which talent was not so much a rarity as was the bodily frame talent needs to find its fulfillment, a tribe known for giving their best early in life but not for longevity. His watchword, however, was "Endure," and he saw in his novel about Frederick the Great precisely the apotheosis of this commandment, which seemed to him the essence of a selflessly active virtue. He harbored, moreover, a keen desire to live to a ripe old age, for he had long believed that an artistic career could be called truly great, encompassing, indeed truly worthy of honor only if the artist were allotted sufficient years to be fruitful in his own way at all stages of human life.

Since he thus bore the burdens of his talent on slender shoulders and wished to carry those burdens far, he was in great need of discipline. Fortunately for him discipline was his heritage at birth from his paternal side. At forty, at fifty, even at an age when others squander and stray, content to put their great plans aside for the time being, he started his day at an early hour by dousing his chest and back with cold water. Then, placing two tall wax candles in silver candlesticks at the head of his manuscript, he would spend two or three fervently conscientious morning hours sacrificing on the altar of art the powers he had assembled during his sleep. It was forgivable—indeed it even indicated the victory of his moral force—that uninformed readers mistook the Maia-world or the epic scroll on which unrolled Frederick's heroic life for the products of single sustained bursts of energy, whereas they actually grew into grandeur layer by layer, out of small daily doses of work and countless individual flashes of inspiration. These works were thoroughly excellent in every detail solely because their creator had endured for years under the pressure of a single project, bringing to bear a tenacity and perseverance similar to that which had conquered his home province,[6] and because he had devoted only his freshest and worthiest hours to actual composition.

If a work of the intellect is to have an immediate, broad, and deep effect, there must be a mysterious affinity, a correspondence between the personal fate of its originator and the more general fate of his contemporaries. People do not know why they accord fame to a particular work. Far from being experts, they suppose they see in it a hundred virtues that would justify their interest; but the real reason for their approval is something imponderable—it is sympathy. Aschenbach had actually stated forthrightly, though in a relatively inconspicuous passage, that nearly everyone achieving greatness did so under the banner of "Despite"—despite grief and suffering, despite poverty, destitution, infirmity, affliction, passion, and a thousand obstacles. But this was more than an observation, it was the fruit of experience; no, it was the very formula for his life and his fame, the key to his work. Was it any wonder, then, that it was also the basis for the moral disposition and outward demeanor of his most original fictional characters?

Early on an observant critic had described the new type of hero that this writer preferred, a figure returning over and over again in manifold variation: it was based on the concept of "an intellectual and youthful manliness which grits its teeth in proud modesty and calmly endures the swords and spears as

6. As a result of the Seven Years' War (1759–63), Frederick the Great wrested Silesia from Austria. Today, most of Silesia has become a region in southwestern Poland.

they pass through its body." It was a nice description, ingenious and precise, despite its seemingly excessive emphasis on passivity. For meeting one's fate with dignity, grace under pressure of pain, is not simply a matter of sufferance; it is an active achievement, a positive triumph, and the figure of St. Sebastian[7] is thus the most beautiful image, if not of art in general, then surely of the art under discussion here. Having looked at the characters in Aschenbach's narrated world, having seen the elegant self-discipline that managed right up to the last moment to hide from the eyes of the world the undermining process, the biological decline, taking place within; having seen the yellow, physically handicapped ugliness that nonetheless managed to kindle its smoldering ardor into a pure flame, managed even to catapult itself to mastery in the realm of beauty; or having seen the pale impotence that pulls out of the glowing depths of the spirit enough power to force a whole frivolous people to fall at the feet of the cross, at the feet of that very impotence; or the lovable charm that survives even the empty and rigorous service of pure form; or the false, dangerous life of the born deceiver, with the quick enervation of its longing and with its artfulness—having seen all these human destinies and many more besides, it was easy enough to doubt that there could be any other sort of heroism than that of weakness. In any case, what kind of heroism was more appropriate to the times than this? Gustav Aschenbach was the poet of all those who work on the edge of exhaustion, of the overburdened, worn down moralists of achievement who nonetheless still stand tall, those who, stunted in growth and short of means, use ecstatic feats of will and clever management to extract from themselves at least for a period of time the effects of greatness. Their names are legion, and they are the heroes of the age. And all of them recognized themselves in his work; they saw themselves justified, exalted, their praises sung. And they were grateful; they heralded his name.

He had been once as young and rough as the times and, seduced by them, had made public blunders and mistakes, had made himself vulnerable, had committed errors against tact and good sense in word and deed. But he had won the dignity toward which, in his opinion, every great talent feels an inborn urge and spur. One could say in fact that his entire development had been a conscious and defiant rise to dignity, beyond any twinge of doubt and of irony that might have stood in his way.

Pleasing the great mass of middle-class readers depends mainly on offering vividly depicted, intellectually undemanding characterizations, but passionately uncompromising youth is smitten only with what is problematic; and Aschenbach had been as problematic and uncompromising as any young man can be. He had pandered to the intellect, exhausted the soil of knowledge, milled flour from his seed corn, revealed secrets, put talent under suspicion, betrayed art. Indeed, while his portrayals entertained, elevated, invigorated the blissfully credulous among his readers, as a youthful artist it was his cynical observations on the questionable nature of art and of the artist's calling that had kept the twenty-year-old element fascinated.

---

7. A 3rd-century Roman martyr whose arrow-pierced body was a popular subject for Renaissance painters.

But it seems that nothing so quickly or so thoroughly blunts a high-minded and capable spirit as the sharp and bitter charm of knowledge; and it is certain that the melancholy, scrupulous thoroughness characteristic of the young seems shallow in comparison with the solemn decision of masterful maturity to disavow knowledge, to reject it, to move beyond it with head held high, to forestall the least possibility that it could cripple, dishearten, or dishonor his will, his capacity for action and feeling, or even his passion. How else could one interpret the famous story "A Man of Misery" save as an outbreak of disgust at the indecent psychologism then current? This disgust was embodied in the figure of that soft and foolish semi-villain who, out of weakness, viciousness, and moral impotence, buys a black-market destiny for himself by driving his wife into the arms of a beardless boy, who imagines profundity can justify committing the basest acts. The weight of the words with which the writer of that work reviled the vile announced a decisive turn away from all moral skepticism, from all sympathy with the abyss, a rejection of the laxity inherent in the supposedly compassionate maxim that to understand everything is to forgive everything. What was coming into play here—or rather, what was already in full swing—was that "miracle of ingenuousness reborn" about which there was explicit discussion, not without a certain mysterious emphasis, in one of the author's dialogues published only slightly later. Strange relationships! Was it an intellectual consequence of this "rebirth," of this new dignity and rigor, that just then readers began to notice an almost excessive increase in his sense of beauty, a noble purity, simplicity, and sense of proportion that henceforth gave his works such a palpable, one might say deliberately classical and masterful quality? But moral determination that goes beyond knowledge, beyond analytic and inhibiting perception—would that not also be a reduction, a moral simplification of the world and of the human soul and therefore also a growing potential for what is evil, forbidden, and morally unacceptable? And does form not have two faces? Is it not moral and amoral at the same time—moral insofar as form is the product and expression of discipline, but amoral and indeed immoral insofar as it harbors within itself by nature a certain moral indifference and indeed is essentially bent on forcing the moral realm to stoop under its proud and absolute scepter?

That is as may be. Since human development is human destiny, how could a life led in public, accompanied by the accolades and confidence of thousands, develop as does one led without the glory and the obligations of fame? Only those committed to eternal bohemianism would be bored and inclined to ridicule when a great talent emerges from its libertine chrysalis, accustoms itself to recognizing emphatically the dignity of the spirit, takes on the courtly airs of solitude, a solitude full of unassisted, defiantly independent suffering and struggle, and ultimately achieves power and honor in the public sphere. And how much playfulness, defiance, and indulgence there is in the way talent develops! A kind of official, educative element began in time to appear in Aschenbach's productions. His style in later years dispensed with the sheer audacity, the subtle and innovative shadings of his younger days, and moved toward the paradigmatic, the polished and traditional, the conservative and formal, even formulaic. Like Louis XIV[8]—as report would have it—the aging

---

8. King of France (1638–1715), the "great monarch" of the French classical period.

writer banished from his vocabulary every base expression. About this time it came to pass that the educational authorities began using selected passages from his works in their prescribed textbooks.[9] He seemed to sense the inner appropriateness of it, and he did not refuse when a German prince, newly ascended to the throne, bestowed on the author of *Frederick*, on his fiftieth birthday, a nonhereditary title.

Relatively early on, after a few years of moving about, a few tries at living here and there, he chose Munich as his permanent residence and lived there in bourgeois respectability such as comes to intellectuals sometimes, in exceptional cases. His marriage to a girl from a learned family, entered upon when still a young man, was terminated after only a short term of happiness by her death. A daughter, already married, remained to him. He never had a son.

Gustav Aschenbach was a man of slightly less than middle height, dark-haired and clean shaven. His head seemed a little too big for a body that was almost dainty. His hair, combed back, receding at the top, still very full at the temples, though quite gray, framed a high, furrowed, and almost embossed-looking brow. The gold frame of his rimless glasses cut into the bridge of his full, nobly curved nose. His mouth was large, sometimes relaxed and full, sometimes thin and tense; his cheeks were lean and hollow, and his well-proportioned chin was marked by a slight cleft. Important destinies seemed to have played themselves out on this long-suffering face, which he often held tilted somewhat to one side. And yet it was art alone, not a difficult and troubled life, that had taken over the task of chiseling these features. Behind this brow was born the scintillating repartee between Voltaire and King Frederick on the subject of war; these eyes, looking tiredly but piercingly through the glasses, had seen the bloody inferno of the field hospitals during the Seven Years' War.[1] Indeed, even on the personal level art provides an intensified version of life. Art offers a deeper happiness, but it consumes one more quickly. It engraves upon the faces of its servants the traces of imaginary, mental adventures and over the long term, even given an external existence of cloistered quietude, engenders in them a nervous sensitivity, an over-refinement, a weariness and an inquisitiveness such as are scarcely ever produced by a life full of extravagant passions and pleasures.

CHAPTER 3

Several obligations of both a practical and a literary nature forced the eager traveler to remain in Munich for about two weeks after his walk in the park. Finally he gave instructions for his country house to be prepared for his moving in within a month's time and, on a day sometime between the middle and end of May, he took the night train to Trieste, where he remained only twenty-four hours and where he boarded the boat to Pola[2] on the morning of the next day.

9. I.e., he received national recognition in the highly centralized German educational system.
1. A global war (1756–63) fought in Europe, North America, and India between European powers. François-Marie Arouet de Voltaire (1694–1778), French writer and philosopher,

was a guest at the court of Frederick the Great from 1750 until 1753, when he found it wise to leave after a disagreement.
2. Trieste (in Italy) and Pola (or Pula, in Croatia) are major ports at the head of the Adriatic Sea. Until 1919 they were Austrian possessions.

What he sought was someplace foreign, someplace isolated, but someplace nonetheless easy to get to. He thus took up residence on an Adriatic island, a destination that had been highly spoken of in recent years and lay not far from the Istrian coast. It was populated by locals dressed in colorful rags who spoke in wildly exotic accents, and the landscape was graced by rugged cliffs on the coast facing the open sea. But the rain and oppressive air, the provincial, exclusively Austrian clientele at the hotel, and the lack of the peaceful, intimate relation with the sea that only a soft sandy beach can offer—these things irritated him, denied him a sense of having found the place he was looking for; he was troubled by a pressure within him pushing in a direction he could not quite grasp; he studied ship schedules, he sought about for something; and suddenly the surprising but obvious destination came to him. If you wanted to reach in a single night someplace incomparable, someplace as out of the ordinary as a fairy tale, where did you go? The answer was clear. What was he doing here? He had gone astray. It was over there that he had wanted to go all along. He did not hesitate a moment in remedying his error and gave notice of his departure. A week and a half after his arrival on the island a swift motorboat carried him and his baggage through the early morning mist across the water to the military port, where he landed only long enough to find the gangway leading him onto the damp deck of a ship that was already getting up steam for a trip to Venice.[3]

It was an aged vessel, long past its prime, sooty, and gloomy, sailing under the Italian flag. In a cavernous, artificially lit cabin in the ship's interior—to which Aschenbach had been conducted with smirking politeness by a hunchbacked, scruffy sailor the moment he embarked—sat a goateed man behind a desk. With his hat cocked over his brow and a cigarette butt hanging from the corner of his mouth, his facial features were reminiscent of an old time ringmaster. He took down the passengers' personal information and doled out tickets with the grimacing, easy demeanor of the professional. "To Venice!" He repeated Aschenbach's request, stretching his arm to dip his pen in the congealed remains at the bottom of his slightly tilted inkwell. "To Venice, first class! There, sir, you're all taken care of." He inscribed great letters like crane's feet on a piece of paper, poured blue sand out of a box onto them, poured it back into an earthenware bowl, folded the paper with his yellow, bony fingers, and resumed writing. "What a fine choice for your destination!" he babbled in the meantime. "Ah, Venice, a wonderful city! A city that is irresistible to cultured people both for its history and for its modern charm!" The smooth swiftness of his movements and the empty chatter with which he accompanied them had an anesthetic and diversionary effect, as if he were concerned that the traveler should change his mind about his decision to go to Venice. He hastily took the money and dropped the change on the stained cloth covering the table with the practiced swiftness of a croupier.[4] "Enjoy yourself, sir!" he said with a theatrical bow. "It is an honor to be of service to you. . . . Next,

---

3. An ancient city whose network of bridges and canals links 118 islands in the Gulf of Venice. The Republic of Venice was headed by a doge (duke) and was a cultural, commercial, and political center in Europe from the 14th century.

4. Attendant at a gambling table who handles bets and money.

please!" he cried with his arm raised, acting as if he were still doing a brisk business, though in fact there was no one else there to do business with. Aschenbach returned above deck.

With one arm resting on the rail, he observed the passengers on board and the idle crowd loitering on the pier to watch the ship depart. The second-class passengers, both men and women, crouched on the forward deck using boxes and bundles as seats. A group of young people, apparently employees of businesses in Pola, who had banded together in great excitement for an excursion to Italy, formed the social set of the first upper deck. They made no little fuss over themselves and their plans, chattered, laughed, and took complacent enjoyment in their own continual gesturing. Leaning over the railing they called out in fluent and mocking phrases to various friends going about their business, briefcases under their arms, along the dockside street below, while the latter in turn made mock-threatening gestures with their walking sticks at the celebrants above. One of the merrymakers, wearing a bright yellow, overly fashionable summer suit, red tie, and a panama hat with a cockily turned-up brim, outdid all the others in his screeching gaiety. But scarcely had Aschenbach gotten a closer look at him when he realized with something like horror that this youth was not genuine. He was old, no doubt about it. There were wrinkles around his eyes and mouth. The faint carmine of his cheeks was rouge; the brown hair beneath the colorfully banded hat was a wig; his neck was shrunken and sinewy; his clipped mustache and goatee were dyed; the full, yellowish set of teeth he exposed when he laughed was a cheap set of dentures; and his hands, bedecked with signet rings on both forefingers, were those of an old man. With a shudder Aschenbach watched him and his interaction with his friends. Did they not know, had they not noticed that he was old, that he had no right to wear their foppish and colorful clothes, had no right to pretend to be one of their own? They apparently tolerated him in their midst as a matter of course, out of habit, and treated him as an equal, answering in kind without reluctance when he teasingly poked one of them in the ribs. But how could this be? Aschenbach covered his brow with his hand and closed his eyes, which were feeling inflamed from not getting enough sleep. It seemed to him that things were starting to take a turn away from the ordinary, as if a dreamy estrangement, a bizarre distortion of the world were setting in and would spread if he did not put a stop to it by shading his eyes a bit and taking another look around him. Just at this moment he experienced a sensation of motion and, looking up with an unreasoning terror, realized that the heavy and gloomy hulk of the ship was slowly parting company with the stone pier. The engines ran alternately forward and reverse, and inch by inch the band of oily, iridescent water between the pier and the hull of the ship widened. After a set of cumbersome maneuvers the steamer managed to point its bowsprit toward the open sea. Aschenbach went over to the starboard side, where the hunchback had set up a deck chair for him and a steward dressed in a stained tailcoat offered him service.

The sky was gray and the wind was moist. The harbor and the island were left behind, and soon all sight of land vanished beyond the misty horizon. Flakes of coal soot saturated with moisture fell on the scrubbed, never drying deck. No more than an hour later a canvas canopy was put up, since it had started to rain.

Wrapped in his cloak, a book on his lap, the traveler rested, and the hours passed by unnoticed. It stopped raining; the linen canopy was removed. The horizon was unobstructed. Beneath the overcast dome of the sky the immense disk of the desolate sea stretched into the distance all around. But in empty, undivided space our sense of time fails us, and we lose ourselves in the immeasurable. Strange and shadowy figures—the old fop, the goat-beard from below deck—invaded Aschenbach's mind as he rested. They gestured obscurely and spoke the confused speech of dreams. He fell asleep.

At noon they called him to lunch down in the corridorlike dining hall onto which opened the doors of all the sleeping quarters and in which stood a long table. He dined at one end, while at the other the business employees from Pola, including the old fop, had been carousing since ten o'clock with the jolly captain. The meal was wretched and he soon got up. He felt an urgent need to get out, to look at the sky, to see if it might not be brightening over Venice.

It had never occurred to him that anything else could happen, for the city had always received him in shining glory. But the sky and the sea remained overcast and leaden. From time to time a misty rain fell, and he came to the realization that he would approach a very different Venice by sea than the one he had previously reached by land. He stood by the foremast, gazing into the distance, awaiting the sight of land. He remembered the melancholy, enthusiastic poet of long ago who had furnished his dreams with the domes and bell towers rising from these waters. He softly repeated to himself some of those verses in which the awe, joy, and sadness of a former time had taken stately shape[5] and, easily moved by sensations thus already formed, looked into his earnest and weary heart to see if some new enthusiasm or entanglement, some late adventure of feeling might be in store for him, the idle traveler.

Then the flat coastline emerged on the right; the sea became populated with fishing boats; the barrier island with its beach appeared. The steamer soon left the island behind to the left, slipping at reduced speed through the narrow harbor named after it.[6] They came to a full stop in the lagoon in view of rows of colorfully wretched dwellings and awaited the arrival of the launch belonging to the health service.

An hour passed before it appeared. One had arrived and yet had not arrived; there was no great hurry and yet one felt driven by impatience. The young people from Pola had come up on deck, apparently yielding to a patriotic attraction to the military trumpet calls resounding across the water from the public garden. Full of excitement and Asti, they shouted cheers at the *bersaglieri*[7] conducting drills over there. It was disgusting, however, to see the state into which the made-up old coot's false fellowship with the young people had brought him. His aged brain had not been able to put up the same resistance to the wine as the younger and more vigorous heads, and he was wretchedly drunk. His vision blurred; a cigarette dangled from his shaking fingers; he stood swaying tipsily in place, pulled to and fro by intoxication, barely able to

---

5. The lines are probably from *Sonnets on Venice* (1825) by the German classical poet August Graf Platen (1796–1835): "My eye left the high seas behind / as the temples of [the architect Andrea] Palladio rose from the waters."

6. Both the barrier island and the harbor are called Lido. The island is the site of a famous resort.

7. Elite Italian troops. "Asti": or asti spumante, a sweet, sparkling Italian wine.

maintain his balance. Since he would have fallen over at the first step, he dared not move from the spot. Yet he maintained a woeful bravado, buttonholing everyone who came near; he stammered, blinked, giggled, raised his beringed, wrinkled forefinger in fatuous banter, and ran the tip of his tongue around the corners of his mouth in an obscenely suggestive manner. Aschenbach watched him from under a darkened brow and was once again seized by a feeling of giddiness, as if the world were displaying a slight but uncontrollable tendency to distort, to take on a bizarre and sneering aspect. It was a feeling, to be sure, that conditions prevented him from indulging, for just then the engine began anew its pounding, and the ship, interrupted so close to its destination, resumed its course through the canal of San Marco.[8]

Once more, then, it lay before him, that most astounding of landing places, that dazzling grouping of fantastic buildings that the republic presented to the awed gaze of approaching mariners: the airy splendor of the palace and the Bridge of Sighs; the pillars on the water's edge bearing the lion and the saint; the showy projecting flank of the fairy tale cathedral; the view toward the gate and the great clock.[9] It occurred to him as he raised his eyes that to arrive in Venice by land, at the railway station, was like entering a palace by a back door; that one ought not to approach this most improbable of cities save as he now did, by ship, over the high seas.

The engine stopped, gondolas swarmed about, the gangway was lowered, customs officials boarded and haughtily went about their duties; disembarkation could begin. Aschenbach let it be known that he desired a gondola to take him and his luggage over to the landing where he could get one of the little steamboats that ran between the city and the Lido; for it was his intention to take up residence by the sea. His wishes met with acquiescence; a call went down with his request to the water's surface where the gondoliers were quarreling with each other in dialect. He was still prevented from disembarking; his trunk presented problems; only with considerable difficulty could it be pulled and tugged down the ladderlike gangway. He therefore found himself unable for several moments to escape from the importunities of the ghastly old impostor, who, driven by some dark drunken impulse, was determined to bid elaborate farewell to the foreign traveler. "We wish you the happiest of stays," he bleated, bowing and scraping. "Keeping a fond memory of us! Au revoir, excusez, and bonjour,[1] your excellency!" He drooled, he batted his eyes, he licked the corners of his mouth, and the dyed goatee on his elderly chin bristled. "Our compliments," he babbled, two fingertips at his mouth, "our compliments to your beloved, your dearly beloved, your lovely beloved . . ." And suddenly his uppers fell out of his jaw onto his lower lip. Aschenbach took his chance to escape. "Your beloved, your sweet beloved . . ." He heard the cooing, hollow, obstructed sounds behind his back as he descended the gangway, clutching at the rope handrail as he went.

---

8. Saint Mark's Canal, named for the patron saint of Venice.
9. A large clock tower built in the late 15th century. "Bridge of Sighs": condemned prisoners walked over this bridge when proceeding to prison from the ducal palace. "Pillars": one is surmounted by a statue of St. Theodore stepping on a crocodile; the second, by a winged lion, emblem of St. Mark. "Cathedral": the Church of St. Mark.
1. "Goodbye, excuse me, and good-day" (French).

Who would not need to fight off a fleeting shiver, a secret aversion and anxiety, at the prospect of boarding a Venetian gondola for the first time or after a long absence? This strange conveyance, surviving unchanged since legendary times and painted the particular sort of black[2] ordinarily reserved for coffins, makes one think of silent, criminal adventures in a darkness full of splashing sounds; makes one think even more of death itself, of biers and gloomy funerals, and of that final, silent journey. And has anyone noticed that the seat of one of these boats, this armchair painted coffin-black and upholstered in dull black cloth, is one of the softest, most luxurious, most sleep-inducing seats in the world? Aschenbach certainly realized this as he sat down at the gondolier's feet, opposite his luggage lying in a copious pile in the bow. The oarsmen were still quarreling in a rough, incomprehensible language punctuated by threatening gestures. The peculiar quiet of this city of water, however, seemed to soften their voices, to disembody them, to disperse them over the sea. It was warm here in the harbor. Stroked by the mild breath of the sirocco,[3] leaning back into the cushions as the yielding element carried him, the traveler closed his eyes in the pleasure of indulging in an indolence both unaccustomed and sweet. The trip will be short, he thought; if only it could last forever! The gondola rocked softly, and he felt himself slip away from the crowded ship and the clamoring voices.

How quiet, ever more quiet it grew around him! Nothing could be heard but the splashing of the oar, the hollow slap of the waves against the gondola's prow, rising rigid and black above the water with its halberdlike beak—and then a third thing, a voice, a whisper. It was the murmur of the gondolier, who was talking to himself through his clenched teeth in fits and starts, emitting sounds that were squeezed out of him by the labor of his arms. Aschenbach looked up and realized with some astonishment that the lagoon was widening about him and that he was traveling in the direction of the open sea. It seemed, then, that he ought not to rest quite so peacefully but instead make sure his wishes were carried out.

"I told you to take me to the steamer landing," he said with a half turn toward the stern. The murmur ceased. He received no answer.

"I told you to take me to the steamer landing!" he repeated, turning around completely and looking up into the face of the gondolier, whose figure, perched on the high deck and silhouetted against the dun sky, towered behind him. The man had a disagreeable, indeed brutal-looking appearance; he wore a blue sailor suit belted with a yellow sash, and a shapeless straw hat that was beginning to come unraveled and was tilted rakishly on his head. His facial features and the blond, curly mustache under his short, turned-up nose marked him as clearly not of Italian stock. Although rather slender of build, so that one would not have thought him particularly well suited to his profession, he plied his oar with great energy, putting his whole body into every stroke. Several times he pulled his lips back with the strain, baring his white teeth. His reddish eyebrows puckered, he looked out over his passenger's head and replied in a decisive, almost curt tone of voice: "You are going to the Lido."

2. Legend explains the gondolas' traditional black through an ancient law forbidding ostentation.

3. A hot wind originating in the Sahara, which becomes humid as it picks up moisture over the Mediterranean.

Aschenbach responded, "Indeed. But I took the gondola only to get over to San Marco. I want to use the vaporetto."[4]

"You cannot use the vaporetto, sir."

"And why not?"

"Because the vaporetto does not accept luggage."

He was right about that; Aschenbach remembered. He said nothing. But the gruff, presumptuous manner of the man, so unlike the normal way of treating foreigners in this country, was not to be endured. He said, "That is my business. Perhaps I intend to put my luggage in storage. You will kindly turn back."

There was silence. The oar splashed, the waves slapped dully against the bow. And the murmuring and whispering began anew: the gondolier was talking to himself through his clenched teeth.

What to do? Alone at sea with this strangely insubordinate, uncannily resolute person, the traveler saw no way to enforce his wishes. And anyway, if he could just avoid getting angry, what a lovely rest he could have! Had he not wished the trip could last longer, could last forever? The smartest thing to do was to let matters take their course; more important, it was also the most pleasant thing to do. A magic circle of indolence seemed to surround the place where he sat, this low armchair upholstered in black, so gently rocked by the rowing of the autocratic gondolier behind him. The idea that he might have fallen into the hands of a criminal rambled about dreamily in Aschenbach's mind, but it was incapable of rousing his thoughts to active resistance. More annoying was the possibility that all this was simply a device by which to extort money from him. A sense of duty or of pride, the memory, as it were, that one must prevent such things, induced him once more to pull himself together. He asked, "What do you want for the trip?"

And the gondolier, looking out over him, answered, "You will pay."

It was clear what reply was necessary here. Aschenbach said mechanically, "I will pay nothing, absolutely nothing, if you take me where I do not want to go."

"You want to go to the Lido."

"But not with you."

"I row you well."

True enough, thought Aschenbach, and relaxed. True enough, you row me well. Even if you are just after my money, even if you send me to the house of Aides[5] with a stroke of your oar from behind, you will have rowed me well.

But no such thing occurred. In fact, some company even happened by in the form of a boat filled with musicians, both men and women, who waylaid the gondola, sailing obtrusively right alongside. They sang to the accompaniment of guitars and mandolins and filled the quiet air over the lagoon with the strains of their mercenary tourist lyrics. Aschenbach threw some money in the hat they held out to him, whereupon they fell silent and sailed off. The murmur of the gondolier became perceptible once again as he talked to himself in fits and starts.

4. Little steamboat (Italian); used for public transport.

5. A Greek spelling of "Hades," the ruler of the world of the dead in Greek and Roman mythol-ogy. The newly dead entered the underworld by paying a coin to the boatman, Charon, who then ferried them across the river Styx.

And so they arrived, bobbing in the wake of a steamer sailing back to the city. Two municipal officials walked up and down along the landing, their hands behind their backs and their faces turned to the lagoon. Aschenbach stepped from the gondola onto the dock assisted by one of those old men who seemed on hand, armed with a boathook, at every pier in Venice. Since he had no small coins with him, he crossed over to the hotel next to the steamer wharf to get change with which to pay the boatman an appropriate fee. His needs met in the lobby, he returned to find his baggage stowed on a cart on the dock. Gondola and gondolier had disappeared.

"He took off," said the old man with the boathook. "A bad man he was, sir, a man without a license. He's the only gondolier who doesn't have a license. The others telephoned over. He saw that we were on the lookout for him, so he took off."

Aschenbach shrugged his shoulders.

"You had a free ride, sir," the old man said, holding out his hat. Aschenbach threw some coins in it. He gave instructions that his luggage be taken to the Hotel des Bains[6] and then followed the cart along the boulevard of white blossoms, lined on both sides by taverns, shops, and boarding houses, that runs straight across the island to the beach.

He entered the spacious hotel from behind, from the garden terrace, and crossed the great lobby to reach the vestibule where the office was. Since he had a reservation, he was received with officious courtesy. A manager, a quiet, flatteringly polite little man with a black mustache and a French-style frock coat, accompanied him in the elevator to the third floor and showed him to his room. It was a pleasant place, furnished in cherry wood, decorated with highly fragrant flowers, and offering a view of the open sea through a set of tall windows. After the manager had withdrawn and while his luggage was being brought up and put in place in his room, he went up to one of the windows and looked out on the beach. It was nearly deserted in the afternoon lull, and the ocean, at high tide and bereft of sunshine, was sending long, low waves against the shore in a peaceful rhythm.

A lonely, quiet person has observations and experiences that are at once both more indistinct and more penetrating than those of one more gregarious; his thoughts are weightier, stranger, and never without a tinge of sadness. Images and perceptions that others might shrug off with a glance, a laugh, or a brief conversation occupy him unduly, become profound in his silence, become significant, become experience, adventure, emotion. Loneliness fosters that which is original, daringly and bewilderingly beautiful, poetic. But loneliness also fosters that which is perverse, incongruous, absurd, forbidden. Thus the events of the journey that brought him here—the ghastly old fop with his drivel about a beloved, the outlaw gondolier who was cheated of his reward—continued to trouble the traveler's mind. Though they did not appear contrary to reason, did not really give cause for second thoughts, the paradox was that they were nonetheless fundamentally and essentially odd, or so it seemed to him, and therefore troubling precisely because of this paradox. In the meantime his eyes greeted the sea, and he felt joy in knowing Venice to be in such comfortable

6. Hotel of the Baths (French, literal trans.); a famous seaside hotel.

proximity. He turned away at last, went to wash his face, gave some instructions to the maid with regard to completing arrangements to insure his comfort, and then put himself in the hands of the green-uniformed elevator operator, who took him down to the ground floor.

He took his tea on the terrace facing the sea, then went down to the shore and walked along the boardwalk for a good distance toward the Hotel Excelsior. When he got back it seemed about time to change for dinner. He did so slowly and precisely, the way he did everything, because he was used to working as he got dressed. Still, he found himself in the lobby a bit on the early side for dinner. There he found many of the hotel's guests gathered, unfamiliar with and affecting indifference to each other, sharing only the wait for the dinner bell. He picked up a newspaper from a table, sat down in a leather chair, and looked over the assembled company. It differed from that of his previous sojourn in a way that pleased him.

A broad horizon, tolerant and comprehensive, opened up before him. All the great languages of Europe melded together in subdued tones. Evening dress, the universal uniform of cultured society, provided a decorous external unity to the variety of humanity assembled here. There was the dry, long face of an American, a Russian extended family, English ladies, German children with French nannies. The Slavic component seemed to predominate. Polish was being spoken nearby.

It came from a group of adolescents and young adults gathered around a little wicker table under the supervision of a governess or companion. There were three young girls who looked to be fifteen to seventeen years old and a long-haired boy of maybe fourteen. Aschenbach noted with astonishment that the boy was perfectly beautiful. His face, pale and gracefully reserved, was framed by honey-colored curls. He had a straight nose and a lovely mouth and wore an expression of exquisite, divine solemnity. It was a face reminiscent of Greek statues from the noblest period of antiquity; it combined perfection of form with a unique personal charm that caused the onlooker to doubt ever having met with anything in nature or in art that could match its perfection. One could not help noticing, furthermore, that widely differing views on child-rearing had evidently directed the dress and general treatment of the siblings. The three girls, the eldest of whom was for all intents an adult, were got up in a way that was almost disfiguringly chaste and austere. Every grace of figure was suppressed and obscured by their uniformly habitlike half-length dresses, sober and slate-gray in color, tailored as if to be deliberately unflattering, relieved by no decoration save white, turned-down collars. Their smooth hair, combed tightly against their heads, made their faces appear nunnishly vacant and expressionless. It could only be a mother who was in charge here, one who never once considered applying to the boy the severity of upbringing that seemed required of her when it came to the girls. Softness and tenderness were the obvious conditions of the boy's existence. No one had yet been so bold as to take the scissors to his lovely hair, which curled about his brows, over his ears, and even further down the back of his neck—as it does on the statue of the "Boy Pulling a Thorn from his Foot."[7] His English sailor suit had puffy

7. A bronze Greco-Roman statue admired for the graceful pose and handsome appearance of the boy it depicts.

sleeves that narrowed at the cuff to embrace snugly the delicate wrists of his still childlike yet delicate hands. The suit made his slim figure seem somehow opulent and pampered with all its decoration, its bow, braidwork, and embroidery. He sat so that the observer saw him in profile. His feet were clad in black patent leather and arranged one in front of the other; one elbow was propped on the arm of his wicker chair with his cheek resting on his closed hand; his demeanor was one of careless refinement, quite without the almost submissive stiffness that seemed to be the norm for his sisters. Was he in poor health? Perhaps, for the skin of his face was white as ivory and stood out in sharp contrast to the darker gold of the surrounding curls. Or was he simply a coddled favorite, the object of a biased and capricious affection? Aschenbach was inclined to suppose the latter. There is inborn in every artistic disposition an indulgent and treacherous tendency to accept injustice when it produces beauty and to respond with complicity and even admiration when the aristocrats of this world get preferential treatment.

A waiter went about and announced in English that dinner was ready. Most of the company gradually disappeared through the glass door into the dining room. Latecomers passed by, arriving from the vestibule or from the elevators. Dinner was beginning to be served inside, but the young Poles still lingered by their wicker table. Aschenbach, comfortably seated in his deep armchair, his eyes captivated by the beautiful vision before him, waited with them.

The governess, a short, corpulent, rather unladylike woman with a red face, finally gave the sign to get up. With her brows raised she pushed back her chair and bowed as a tall lady, dressed in gray and white and richly bejeweled with pearls, entered the lobby. The demeanor of this woman was cool and measured; the arrangement of her lightly powdered hair and the cut of her clothes displayed the taste for simplicity favored by those who regard piety as an essential component of good breeding. She could have been the wife of a highly placed German official. Her jewelry was the only thing about her appearance that suggested fabulous luxury; it was priceless, consisting of earrings and a very long, triple strand of softly shimmering pearls, each as big as a cherry.

The boy and the girls had risen quickly. They bent to kiss their mother's hand while she, with a restrained smile on her well-preserved but slightly tired and rather pointy-nosed face, looked across the tops of their heads at the governess, to whom she directed a few words in French. Then she walked to the glass door. The young ones followed her, the girls in the order of their ages, behind them the governess, the boy last of all. For some reason he turned around before crossing the threshold. Since there was no one else left in the lobby, his strangely misty gray eyes met those of Aschenbach, who was sunk deep in contemplation of the departing group, his newspaper on his knees.

What he had seen was, to be sure, in none of its particulars remarkable. They did not go in to dinner before their mother; they had waited for her, greeted her respectfully when she came, and then observed perfectly normal manners going into the dining room. It was just that it had all happened so deliberately, with such a sense of discipline, responsibility, and self-respect, that Aschenbach felt strangely moved. He lingered a few moments more, then went along into the dining room himself. He was shown to his table, which, he noted with a brief twinge of regret, was very far away from that of the Polish family.

Tired but nonetheless mentally stimulated, he entertained himself during the tedious meal with abstract, even transcendent matters. He pondered the mysterious combination of regularity and individuality that is necessary to produce human beauty; proceeded then to the general problem of form and of art; and ultimately concluded that his thoughts and discoveries resembled those inspirations that come in dreams: they seem wonderful at the time, but in the sober light of day they show up as utterly shallow and useless. After dinner he spent some time smoking, sitting, and wandering about in the park, which was fragrant in the evening air. He went to bed early and passed the night in a sleep uninterruptedly deep but frequently enlivened by all sorts of dreams.

The next day the weather had gotten no better. There was a steady wind off the land. Under a pale overcast sky the sea lay in a dull calm, almost as if it had shriveled up, with a soberingly contracted horizon; it had receded so far from the beach that it uncovered several rows of long sandbars. When Aschenbach opened his window, he thought he could detect the stagnant smell of the lagoon.

He was beset by ill humor. He was already having thoughts of leaving. Once years ago, after several lovely weeks here in springtime, just such weather had been visited upon him and had made him feel so poorly that he had had to take flight from Venice like a fugitive. Was he not feeling once again the onset of the feverish listlessness he had felt then, the throbbing of his temples, the heaviness in his eyelids? To change his vacation spot yet again would be a nuisance; but if the wind did not shift soon, he simply could not remain here. He did not unpack everything, just in case. He ate at nine in the special breakfast room between the lobby and the dining room.

In this room prevailed the solemn stillness that great hotels aspire to. The waiters went about on tip-toe. The clink of the tea service and a half-whispered word were all one could hear. Aschenbach noticed the Polish girls and their governess at a table in the corner diagonally across from the door, two tables away. They sat very straight, their ash-blond hair newly smoothed down flat, their eyes red. They wore starched blue linen dresses with little white turned-down collars and cuffs, and they passed a jar of preserves to each other. They had almost finished their breakfast. The boy was not there.

Aschenbach smiled. Well, little Phaeacian, he thought. It seems you, and not they, have the privilege of sleeping to your heart's content. Suddenly cheered, he recited to himself the line:

"Changes of dress, warm baths, and downy beds."[8]

He ate his breakfast at a leisurely pace, received some mail that had been forwarded—delivered personally by the doorman, who entered the room with his braided hat in hand—and opened a few letters while he smoked a cigarette. Thus it happened that he was present for the entrance of the late sleeper they were waiting for over there in the corner.

He came through the glass door and traversed the silent room diagonally over to the table where his sisters sat. His carriage was extraordinarily graceful, not only in the way he held his torso but also in the way he moved his knees and set

---

8. A reference to Homer's *Odyssey* 8.249. The Phaeacians were a peaceful, happy people who showed hospitality to the shipwrecked Odysseus.

one white-shod foot in front of the other. He moved lightly, in a manner both gentle and proud, made more lovely still by the childlike bashfulness with which he twice lifted and lowered his eyelids as he went by, turning his face out toward the room. Smiling, he murmured a word in his soft, indistinct speech and took his place, showing his full profile to the observer. The latter was once more, and now especially, struck with amazement, indeed even alarm, at the truly godlike beauty possessed by this mortal child. Today the boy wore a lightweight sailor suit of blue and white striped cotton with a red silk bow on the chest, finished at the neck with a simple white upright collar. And above this collar, which did not even fit in very elegantly with the character of the costume, rose up that blossom, his face, a sight unforgettably charming. It was the face of Eros, with the yellowish glaze of Parian marble,[9] with delicate and serious brows, the temples and ears richly and rectangularly framed by soft, dusky curls.

Fine, very fine, thought Aschenbach with that professional, cool air of appraisal artists sometimes use to cover their delight, their enthusiasm when they encounter a masterpiece. He thought further: Really, if the sea and the sand were not waiting for me, I would stay here as long as you stay. With that, however, he departed, walking past the attentive employees through the lobby, down the terrace steps, and straight across the wooden walkway to the hotel's private beach. There he let a barefoot old man in linen pants, sailor shirt, and straw hat who managed affairs on the beach show him to his rented beach cabana and arrange a table and chair on its sandy, wooden platform. Then he made himself comfortable in his beach chair, which he had pulled through the pale yellow sand closer to the sea.

The beach scene, this view of a carefree society engaged in purely sensual enjoyment on the edge of the watery element, entertained and cheered him as it always did. The gray, smooth ocean was already full of wading children, swimmers, and colorful figures lying on the sandbars with their arms crossed behind their heads. Others were rowing about in little flat-bottomed boats painted red and blue, capsizing to gales of laughter. People sat on the platforms of the cabanas, arranged in a long neat row along the beach, as if they were little verandas. In front of them people played games, lounged lazily, visited and chatted, some dressed in elegant morning clothes and others enjoying the nakedness sanctioned by the bold and easy freedom of the place. Down on the moist, hard sand there were a few individuals strolling about in white beach robes or in loose, brightly colored bathing dresses. To the right some children had built an elaborate sand castle and bedecked it with little flags in the colors of every country. Vendors of mussels, cakes, and fruit knelt and spread their wares before them. On the left, a Russian family was encamped in front of one of the cabanas that were set at a right angle between the others and the sea, thus closing that end of the beach. The family included men with beards and huge teeth; languid women past their prime; a young lady from a Baltic country, sitting at an easel and painting the ocean to the accompaniment of cries of frustration; two affable, ugly children; and an old maid in a

---

9. White marble from the island of Paros was especially prized by sculptors in antiquity. Eros was the Greek god of love.

babushka, displaying the affectionately servile demeanor of a slave. They resided there in grateful enjoyment, called out endlessly the names of their unruly, giddy children, exchanged pleasantries at surprising length in their few words of Italian with the jocular old man from whom they bought candy, kissed each other on the cheeks, and cared not a whit for anyone who might witness their scene of shared humanity.

Well, then, I will stay, thought Aschenbach. Where could things be better? His hands folded in his lap, he let his eyes roam the ocean's distances, let his gaze slip out of focus, grow hazy, blur in the uniform distances, mistiness of empty space. He loved the sea from the depth of his being: first of all because a hardworking artist needs his rest from the demanding variety of phenomena he works with and longs to take refuge in the bosom of simplicity and enormity; and, second, because he harbors an affinity for the undivided, the immeasurable, the eternal, the void. It was a forbidden affinity, directly contrary to his calling, and seductive precisely for that reason. To rest in the arms of perfection is what all those who struggle for excellence long to do; and is the void not a form of perfection? But while he was thus dreaming away toward the depths of emptiness, the horizontal line of the sea's edge was crossed by a human figure. When he had retrieved his gaze from the boundless realms and refocused his eyes, he saw it was the lovely boy who, coming from the left, was passing before him across the sand. He went barefoot, ready to go in wading, his slim legs bare from the knees down. He walked slowly but with a light, proud step, as if he were used to going about without shoes, and looked around at the row of cabanas that closed the end of the beach. The Russian family was still there, gratefully leading its harmonious existence, but no sooner had he laid eyes on them than a storm cloud of angry contempt crossed his face. His brow darkened, his lips began to curl, and from one side of his mouth emerged a bitter grimace that gouged a furrow in his cheek. He frowned so deeply that his eyes seemed pressed inward and sunken, seemed to speak dark and evil volumes of hatred from their depths. He looked down at the ground, cast one more threatening glance backward, and then, shrugging his shoulders as if to discard something and get away from it, he left his enemies behind.

A sort of delicacy or fright, something like a mixture of respect and shame, caused Aschenbach to turn away as if he had not seen anything; for it is repugnant to a chance witness, if he is a serious person, to make use of his observations, even to himself. But Aschenbach felt cheered and shaken at the same time—that is, happiness overwhelmed him. This childish fanaticism directed against the most harmless, good-natured target imaginable put into a human perspective something that otherwise seemed divinely indeterminate. It transformed a precious creation of nature that had before been no more than a feast for the eyes into a worthy object of deeper sympathy. It endowed the figure of the youngster, who had already shone with significance because of his beauty, with an aura that allowed him to be taken seriously beyond his years.

Still turned away, Aschenbach listened to the boy's voice, his clear, somewhat weak voice, by means of which he was trying to hail from afar his playmates at work on the sand castle. They answered him, calling again and again his name or an affectionate variation on his name. Aschenbach listened with a certain curiosity, unable to distinguish anything more than two melodious syllables—something like Adgio or more frequently Adgiu, with a drawn-out *u* at the end of the cry. The sound made him glad, it seemed to him that its harmony suited its object, and he repeated it softly to himself as he turned back with satisfaction to his letters and papers.

With his small traveling briefcase on his knees, he took his fountain pen and began to attend to various matters of correspondence. But after a mere quarter of an hour he was feeling regret that he should thus take leave in spirit and miss out on this, the most charming set of circumstances he knew of, for the sake of an activity he carried on with indifference. He cast his writing materials aside and turned his attention back to the sea; and not long after, distracted by the voices of the youngsters at the sand castle, he turned his head to the right and let it rest comfortably on the back of his chair, where he could once more observe the comings and goings of the exquisite Adgio.

His first glance found him; the red bow on his breast could not be missed. He was engaged with some others in setting up an old board as a bridge over the moat around the sand castle, calling out advice on proper procedure and nodding his head. There were about ten companions with him, boys and girls, most of an age with him but a few younger, chattering in a confusion of tongues— Polish, French, and even some Balkan languages. But it was his name that most often resounded through it all. He was evidently popular, sought after, admired. One companion, likewise a Pole, a sturdy boy called something like Yashu, who wore a belted linen suit and had black hair slicked down with pomade, seemed to be his closest friend and vassal. With the work on the sand castle finished for the time being, they went off together along the beach, arms about each other, and the one called Yashu gave his beautiful partner a kiss.

Aschenbach was tempted to shake his finger at him. "Let me give you a piece of advice, Kritobulos," he thought and smiled to himself. "Take a year's journey. You will need at least that much time for your recovery."[1] And then he breakfasted on large, fully ripe strawberries that he obtained from a peddler. It had gotten very warm, although the sun had not managed to pierce the layer of mist that covered the sky. Lassitude seized his spirit, while his senses enjoyed the enormous, lulling entertainment afforded by the quiet sea. The task of puzzling out what name it was that sounded like Adgio struck the serious man as a fitting, entirely satisfying occupation. With the help of a few Polish memories he determined that it was probably Tadzio he had heard, the nickname for Tadeusz. It was pronounced Tadziu in the form used for direct address.

Tadzio was taking a swim. Aschenbach, who had lost sight of him for a moment, spotted his head and then his arm, which rose as it stroked. He was very far out; the water apparently stayed shallow for a long way. But already his family seemed to be getting concerned about him, already women's voices were calling to him from the cabanas, shouting out once more this name that ruled over the beach almost like a watchword and that possessed something both sweet and wild in its soft consonants and drawnout cry of *uuu* at the end. "Tadziu! Tadziu!" He turned back; he ran through the sea with his head thrown back, beating the resisting water into a foam with his legs. The sight of this

---

1. Recalling Socrates' advice to Kritoboulos when the latter kissed Alcibiades' handsome son (Xenophon's *Memorabilia* 1.3).

lively adolescent figure, seductive and chaste, lovely as a tender young god, emerging from the depths of the sky and the sea with dripping locks and escaping the clutches of the elements—it all gave rise to mythic images. It was a sight belonging to poetic legends from the beginning of time that tell of the origins of form and of the birth of the gods. Aschenbach listened with his eyes closed to this mythic song reverberating within him, and once again he thought about how good it was here and how he wanted to stay.

Later on Tadzio lay on the sand, resting from his swim, wrapped in a white beach towel that was drawn up under his right shoulder, his head resting on his bare arm. Even when Aschenbach refrained from looking at him, instead reading a few pages in his book, he almost never forgot who was lying nearby or forgot that it would cost him only a slight turn of his head to the right to bring the adorable sight back into view. It almost seemed to him that he was sitting here with the express purpose of keeping watch over the resting boy. Busy as he might be with his own affairs, he maintained his vigilant care for the noble human figure not far away on his right. A paternal kindness, an emotional attachment filled and moved his heart, the attachment that someone who produces beauty at the cost of intellectual self-sacrifice feels toward someone who naturally possesses beauty.

After midday he left the beach, returned to the hotel, and took the elevator up to his room. There he spent a considerable length of time in front of the mirror looking at his gray hair and his severe, tired face. At the same time he thought about his fame and about the fact that many people recognized him on the street and looked at him with respect, all on account of those graceful, unerringly accurate words of his. He called the roll of the long list of successes his talent had brought him, as many as he could think of, and even recalled his elevation to the nobility. He then retired to the dining room for lunch and ate at his little table. As he was entering the elevator when the meal was over, a throng of young people likewise coming from lunch crowded him to the back of the swaying little chamber. Tadzio was among them. He stood very close by, so close in fact that for the first time Aschenbach had the opportunity to view him not from a distance like a picture but minutely, scrutinizing every detail of his human form. Someone was talking to the boy, and while he was answering with his indescribably sweet smile they reached the second floor, where he got off, backing out, his eyes cast down. Beauty breeds modesty, Aschenbach thought and gave urgent consideration as to why. He had had occasion to notice, however, that Tadzio's teeth were not a very pleasing sight. They were rather jagged and pale and had no luster of health but rather a peculiar brittle transparency such as one sometimes sees in anemics. He is very sensitive, he is sickly, thought Aschenbach. He will probably not live long. And he refrained from trying to account for the feeling of satisfaction and reassurance that accompanied this thought.

He passed a couple of hours in his room and in the afternoon took the vaporetto across the stagnant-smelling lagoon to Venice. He got off at San Marco, took tea in the piazza,[2] and then, following his habitual routine in Venice, set off on a walk through the streets. It was this walk, however, that initiated a complete reversal of his mood and his plans.

---

2. A famous public square in front of the church, lined by restaurants and cafés.

The air in the little streets was odiously oppressive, so thick that the smells surging out of the dwellings, shops, and restaurants, a suffocating vapor of oil, perfume, and more, all hung about and failed to disperse. Cigarette smoke hovered in place and only slowly disappeared. The press of people in the small spaces annoyed rather than entertained him as he walked. The longer he went on, the more it became a torture. He was overwhelmed by that horrible condition produced by the sea air in combination with the sirocco, a state of both nervousness and debility at once. He began to sweat uncomfortably. His eyes ceased to function, his breathing was labored, he felt feverish, the blood pounded in his head. He fled from the crowded shop-lined streets across bridges into the poor quarter. There beggars molested him, and the evil emanations from the canals hindered his breathing. In a quiet piazza, one of those forgotten, seemingly enchanted little places in the interior of the city, he rested on the edge of a well, dried his forehead, and reached the conclusion that he would have to leave Venice.

For the second time, and this time definitively, it became clear that this city in this weather was particularly harmful to his health. To remain stubbornly in place obviously went against all reason, and the prospect of a change in the direction of the wind was highly uncertain. A quick decision had to be made. To return home this soon was out of the question. Neither his summer nor his winter quarters were prepared for his arrival. But this was not the only place with beaches on the ocean, and those other places did not have the noxious extra of the lagoon and its fever-inducing vapors. He recalled a little beach resort not far from Trieste that had been enthusiastically recommended to him. Why not go there and, indeed, without delay, so that yet another change of location would still be worthwhile? He declared himself resolved and stood up. At the next gondola stop he boarded a boat to take him to San Marco through the dim labyrinth of canals, under graceful marble balconies flanked by stone lions, around corners of slippery masonry, past mournful palace facades affixed with business insignia[3] reflected in the garbage-strewn water. He had trouble getting to his destination, since the gondolier was in league with lace and glass factories and made constant efforts to induce him to stop at them to sightsee and buy; and so whenever the bizarre journey through Venice began to weave its magic, the mercenary lust for booty afflicting this sunken queen of cities[4] did what it could to bring the enchanted spirit back to unpleasant reality.

Upon returning to the hotel he did not even wait for dinner but went right to the office and declared that unforeseen circumstances compelled him to depart the next morning. With many expressions of regret the staff acknowledged the payment of his bill. He dined and then passed the mild evening reading magazines in a rocking chair on the rear terrace. Before going to bed he did all his packing for the morning's departure.

He did not sleep especially well, as the impending move made him restless. When he opened the windows the next morning the sky was still overcast, but the air seemed fresher and . . . he already started to have second thoughts. Had he been hasty or wrong to give notice thus? Was it a result of his sick and unreliable condition? If he had just put it off a bit, if he had just made an

3. Once-stately Renaissance homes that now house businesses. 4. A major sea power by the 15th century, Venice was called Queen of the Seas.

attempt to get used to the Venetian air or to hold out for an improvement in the weather instead of losing heart so quickly! Then, instead of this hustle and bustle, he would have a morning on the beach like the one yesterday to look forward to. Too late. Now he would have to go ahead with it, to wish today what he wished for yesterday. He got dressed and at eight o'clock took the elevator down to breakfast on the ground floor.

The breakfast room was still empty when he entered. A number of individual guests arrived while he sat waiting for his order. With his teacup at his lips he watched the Polish girls and their attendant come in. Severe and morning-fresh, eyes still red, they proceeded to their table in the corner by the window. Immediately thereafter the doorman approached him with hat in hand to tell him it was time to leave. The car was ready, he said, to take him and some other travelers to the Hotel Excelsior, and from there a motor boat would convey them through the company's private canal to the railroad station. Time was pressing, he said. Aschenbach found it not at all pressing. There was more than an hour until the departure of his train. He was annoyed at the habitual hotel practice of packing departing guests off earlier than necessary and informed the doorman that he wanted to finish his breakfast in peace. The man withdrew hesitatingly only to show up again five minutes later. The car simply could not wait longer, he said. Very well, let it go and take his trunks with it, Aschenbach replied with annoyance. As for himself, he preferred to take the public steamer at the proper time and asked that they let him take care of his own arrangements. The employee bowed. Aschenbach, happy to have fended off this nuisance, finished his meal without haste and even had the waiter bring him a newspaper. Time had become short indeed when at last he got up to leave. And it just so happened that at that very moment Tadzio came in through the glass door.

He crossed the path of the departing traveler on his way to his family's table. He lowered his eyes modestly before the gray-haired, high-browed gentleman, only to raise them again immediately in his own charming way, displaying their soft fullness to him. Then he was past. Adieu, Tadzio, thought Aschenbach. I saw you for such a short time. And enunciating his thought as it occurred to him, contrary to his every habit, he added under his breath the words: "Bless-ings on you." He then made his departure, dispensed tips, received a parting greeting from the quiet little manager in the French frock coat, and left the hotel on foot, as he had arrived. Followed by a servant with his hand luggage, he traversed the island along the boulevard, white with flowers, that led to the steamer landing. He arrived, he took his seat—and what followed was a jour-ney of pain and sorrow through the uttermost depths of regret.

It was the familiar trip across the lagoon, past San Marco, up the Grand Canal. Aschenbach sat on the curved bench in the bow, his arm resting on the railing, his hand shading his eyes. They left the public gardens behind them; the Piazzetta once more revealed its princely splendor, and soon it too was left behind. Then came the great line of palaces, and as the waterway turned there appeared the magnificent marble arch of the Rialto.[5] The traveler looked, and his heart was torn. He breathed the atmosphere of the city, this slightly stag-nant smell of sea and of swamp from which he had felt so strongly compelled to

---

5. A famous, highly arched bridge over the Grand Canal.

flee, breathed it now deeply, in tenderly painful draughts. Was it possible that he had not known, had not considered how desperately he was attached to all this? What this morning had been a partial regret, a slight doubt as to the rightness of his decision, now became affliction, genuine pain, a suffering in his soul so bitter that it brought tears to his eyes more than once. He told himself he could not possibly have foreseen such a reaction. What was so hard to take, actually sometimes down-right impossible to endure, was the thought that he would never see Venice again, that this was a parting forever. Since it had become evident for the second time that the city made him sick, since for the second time he had been forced to run head over heels away, he would have to regard it henceforth as an impossible destination, forbidden to him, something he simply was not up to, something it would be pointless for him to try for again. Yes, he felt that, should he go away now, shame and spite would certainly prevent him from ever seeing the beloved city again, now that it had twice forced him to admit physical defeat. This conflict between the inclination of his soul and the capacity of his body seemed to the aging traveler suddenly so weighty and so important, his physical defeat so ignominious, so much to be resisted at all cost, that he could no longer grasp the ease with which he had reached the decision yesterday, without serious struggle, to acquiesce.

Meanwhile, the steamer was approaching the railway station, and his pain and helplessness were rising to the level of total disorientation. His tortured mind found the thought of departure impossible, the thought of return no less so. In such a state of acute inner strife he entered the station. It was already very late, he had not a moment to lose if he was to catch his train. He wanted to, and he did not want to. But time was pressing, it goaded him onward; he made haste to obtain his ticket and looked about in the bustle of the station for the hotel employee stationed here. This person appeared and announced that the large trunk was already checked and on its way. Already on its way? Yes indeed—to Como.[6] To Como? After a frantic exchange, after angry questions and embarrassed answers, the fact emerged that the trunk had been put together with the baggage of other, unknown travelers in the luggage office at the Hotel Excelsior and sent off in precisely the wrong direction.

Aschenbach had difficulty maintaining the facial expression expected under such circumstances. An adventurous joy, an unbelievable cheerfulness seized his breast from within like a spasm. The hotel employee sped off to see if he could retrieve the trunk and returned, as one might have expected, with no success whatever. Only then did Aschenbach declare that he did not wish to travel without his luggage and that he had decided to return and await the recovery of the trunk at the Hotel des Bains. Was the company boat still here at the station? The man assured him it was waiting right at the door. With an impressive display of Italian cajolery he persuaded the agent to take back Aschenbach's ticket. He swore he would telegraph ahead, that no effort would be spared to get the trunk back with all due speed, and . . . thus came to pass something very odd indeed. The traveler, not twenty minutes after his arrival at the station, found himself once again on the Grand Canal on his way back to the Lido.

6. A large lake and resort area in northwest Italy.

What a wondrous, incredible, embarrassing, odd and dreamlike adventure! Thanks to a sudden reversal of destiny, he was to see once again, within the very hour, places that he had thought in deepest melancholy he was leaving forever. The speedy little vessel shot toward its destination, foam flying before its bow, maneuvering with droll agility between gondolas and steamers, while its single passenger hid beneath a mask of annoyed resignation the anxious excitement of a boy playing hooky. Still from time to time his frame was shaken with laughter over this mischance, which he told himself could not have worked out better for the luckiest person in the world. Explanations would have to be made, amazed faces confronted, but then—so he told himself—all would be well again, a great disaster averted, a terrible error made right, and everything he thought he had left behind would be open to him once more, would be his to enjoy at his leisure. . . . And by the way, was it just the rapid movement of the boat, or could it really be that he felt a strong breeze off the ocean to complete his bliss?

The waves slapped against the concrete walls of the narrow canal that cut through the island to the Hotel Excelsior. A motor bus was waiting there for the returning traveler and conveyed him alongside the curling waves down the straight road to the Hotel des Bains. The little manager with the mustache and the cutaway frock coat came down the broad flight of steps to meet him.

With quiet cajolery the manager expressed his regret over the incident, declared it extremely embarrassing for himself personally and for the establishment, but expressed his emphatic approval of Aschenbach's decision to wait here for the return of his luggage. To be sure, his room was already taken, but another, by no means worse, stood ready. "Pas de chance, monsieur,"[7] said the elevator man with a smile as they glided upwards. And so the fugitive was billeted once again, and in a room that matched almost exactly his previous one in orientation and furnishings.

Tired, numb from the whirl of this strange morning, he distributed the contents of his small suitcase in his room and then sank down in an armchair by the open window. The sea had taken on a light green coloration, the air seemed thinner and purer, the beach with its cabanas and boats seemed more colorful, although the sky was still gray. Aschenbach looked out, his hands folded in his lap, content to be here once more, but shaking his head in reproach at his own fickle mood, his lack of knowledge of his own desires. He sat thus for perhaps an hour, resting and thoughtlessly dreaming. At noon he spied Tadzio, dressed in his striped linen suit with red bow, returning from the shore through the beach barrier and along the wooden walkway to the hotel. Aschenbach recognized him at once from his high vantage point even before he got a good look at him, and he was just about to form a thought something like: Look, Tadzio, you too have returned! But at that very moment he felt the casual greeting collapse and fall silent before the truth of his heart. He felt the excitement in his blood, the joy and pain in his soul, and recognized that it was because of Tadzio that his departure had been so difficult.

He sat quite still, quite unseen in his elevated location and looked into himself. His features were active; his brows rose; an alert, curious, witty smile

7. "No luck, sir" (French).

crossed his lips. Then he raised his head and with both his arms, which were hanging limp over the arms of his chair, he made a slow circling and lifting movement that turned his palms forward, as if to signify an opening and extending of his embrace. It was a gesture of readiness, of welcome, and of relaxed acceptance.

CHAPTER 4

The god with fiery cheeks[8] now, naked, directed his horses, four-abreast, fire-breathing, day by day through the chambers of heaven, and his yellow curls fluttered along with the blast of the east wind. A silky-white sheen lay on the Pontos,[9] its broad stretches undulating languidly. The sands burned. Under the silvery shimmering blue of the ether there were rustcolored canvas awnings spread out in front of the beach cabanas, and one passed the morning hours in the sharply framed patch of shade they offered. But the evening was also delightful, when the plants in the park wafted balsamic perfumes, the stars above paced out their circuits, and the murmur of the nightshrouded sea, softly penetrating, cast a spell on the soul. Such an evening bore the joyful promise of another festive day of loosely ordered leisure, bejeweled with count-less, thickly strewn possibilities of happy accidents.

The guest, whom accommodating mischance kept here, was far from dis-posed to see in the return of his belongings a reason to depart once more. He had been obliged to get along without a few things for a couple of days and to appear at meals in the great dining room wearing his traveling clothes. Then, when the errant baggage was finally set down once more in his room, he unpacked thoroughly and filled closets and drawers with his things, deter-mined for the time being to stay indefinitely, happy to be able to pass the morning's hours on the beach in his silk suit and to present himself once more at his little table at dinner time wearing proper evening attire.

The benevolent regularity of this existence had at once drawn him into its power; the soft and splendid calm of this lifestyle had him quickly ensnared. What a fine place to stay, indeed, combining the charms of a refined southern beach resort with the cozy proximity of the wondrous, wonder-filled city! Aschenbach was no lover of pleasure. Whenever and wherever it seemed proper to celebrate, to take a rest, to take a few days off, he soon had to get back—it was especially so in his younger days—anxiously and reluctantly back to the affliction of his high calling, the sacred, sober service of his day-to-day life. This place alone enchanted him, relaxed his will, made him happy. Some-times in the morning, under the canopy of his beach cabana, dreaming away across the blue of the southern sea, or sometimes as well on a balmy night, leaning back under the great starry sky on the cushions of a gondola taking him back home to the Lido from the Piazza San Marco, where he had tarried long—and the bright lights and the melting sounds of the serenade were left behind—he remembered his country home in the mountains, the site of his summertime struggles, where the clouds drifted through the garden, where in the evening fearful thunderstorms extinguished the lights in the house and the

8. Helios, Greek god of the sun (later equated with Apollo).

9. The sea (Greek, literal trans.); a figurative reference to the Adriatic Sea.

revens he fed soared to the tops of the spruce trees. Then it might seem to him that he had been transported to the land of Elysium[1] at the far ends of the earth, where a life of ease is bestowed upon mortals, where there is no snow, no winter, no storms or streaming rain, but rather always the cooling breath rising from Okeanos,[2] where the days run out in blissful leisure, trouble-free, struggle-free, dedicated only to the sun and its revels.

Aschenbach saw the boy Tadzio often, indeed almost continually; limited space and a regular schedule common to all the guests made it inevitable that the lovely boy was in his vicinity nearly all day, with brief interruptions. He saw, he met him everywhere: in the hotel's public places, on the cooling boat trips to the city and back, in the ostentation of the piazza itself; and often too in the streets and byways a chance encounter would take place. Chiefly, however, it was the mornings on the beach that offered him with delightful regularity an extended opportunity to study and worship the charming apparition. Yes, it was this narrow and constrained happiness, this regularly recurring good fortune that filled him with contentment and joy in life, that made his stay all the more dear to him and caused one sunny day after another to fall so agreeably in line.

He got up early, as he otherwise did under the relentless pressure of work, and was one of the first on the beach when the sun was still mild and the sea lay white in the glare of morning dreams. He gave a friendly greeting to the guard at the beach barrier, said a familiar hello to the barefoot old man who got his place ready, spreading the brown awning and arranging the cabana furniture on the platform, and settled in. Three hours or four were then his in which, as the sun rose to its zenith and grew fearsome in strength and the sea turned a deeper and deeper blue, he could watch Tadzio.

He would see him coming from the left along the edge of the sea, would see him from the back as he appeared from between the cabanas, or sometimes would suddenly discover, not without a happy shudder, that he had missed his arrival and that he was already there, already in the blue and white bathing suit that was now his only article of attire on the beach, that he was already up to his usual doings in sand and sun—his charmingly trivial, lazily irregular life that was both recreation and rest, filled with lounging, wading, digging, catching, resting, and swimming, watched over by the women on the platform who called to him, making his name resound with their high voices: "Tadziu! Tadziu!" He would come running to them gesturing excitedly and telling them what he had done, showing them what he had found or caught: mussels and sea horses, jelly fish, crabs that ran off going sideways. Aschenbach understood not a single word he said, and though it may have been the most ordinary thing in the world it was all a vague harmony to his ear. Thus, foreignness raised the boy's speech to the level of music, a wanton sun poured unstinting splendor over him, and the sublime perspectives of the sea always formed the background and aura that set off his appearance.

Soon the observer knew every line and pose of this noble body that displayed itself so freely; he exulted in greeting anew every beauty, familiar though it had

1. Located at the western edge of the Earth, a pleasant otherworld for those heroes favored by the gods.

2. According to Greek mythology, a river encircling the world.

become, and his admiration, the discreet arousal of his senses, knew no end. They called the boy to pay his compliments to a guest who was attending the ladies at the cabana; he came running, still wet from the sea; he tossed his curls, and as he held out his hand he stood on one foot while holding the other up on tiptoe. His body was gracefully poised in the midst of a charming turning motion, while his face showed an embarrassed amiability, a desire to please that came from an aristocratic sense of duty. Sometimes he would lie stretched out with his beach towel wrapped about his chest, his delicately chiseled arm propped in the sand, his chin in the hollow of his hand. The one called Yashu sat crouching by him, playing up to him, and nothing could have been more enchanting than the smiling eyes and lips with which the object of this flattery looked upon his inferior, his vassal. Or he would stand at the edge of the sea, alone, separated from his friends, very near Aschenbach, erect, his hands clasped behind his neck, slowly rocking on the balls of his feet and dreaming off into the blue yonder, while little waves that rolled in bathed his toes. His honey-colored hair clung in circles to his temples and his neck; the sun made the down shine on his upper back; the subtle definition of the ribs and the symmetry of his chest stood out through the tight-fitting material covering his torso; his armpits were still as smooth as those of a statue, the hollows behind his knees shone likewise, and the blue veins showing through made his body seem to be made of translucent material. What discipline, what precision of thought was expressed in the stretch of this youthfully perfect body! But was not the rigorous and pure will that had been darkly active in bringing this divine form into the clear light of day entirely familiar to the artist in him? Was this same will not active in him, too, when he, full of sober passion, freed a slender form from the marble mass of language,[3] a form he had seen with his spiritual eye and that he presented to mortal men as image and mirror of spiritual beauty?

Image and mirror! His eyes embraced the noble figure there on the edge of the blue, and in a transport of delight he thought his gaze was grasping beauty itself, the pure form of divine thought, the universal and pure perfection that lives in the spirit and which here, graceful and lovely, presented itself for worship in the form of a human likeness and exemplar. Such was his intoxication; the aging artist welcomed the experience without reluctance, even greedily. His intellect was in labor, his educated mind set in motion. His memory dredged up ancient images passed on to him in the days of his youth, thoughts not until now touched by the spark of his personal involvement. Was it not written that the sun turns our attention from intellectual to sensuous matters?[4] It was said that the sun numbs and enchants our reason and memory to such an extent that the soul in its pleasure forgets its ordinary condition; its amazed admiration remains fixed on the loveliest of sun-drenched objects. Indeed, only with the help of a body can the soul rise to the contemplation of still higher things. Amor[5] truly did as mathematicians have always done by assisting slow-learning children with concrete pictures of pure forms: so, too, did the god like

3. The Italian artist Michelangelo Buonarroti (1475–1564) explained that he created his statues by carving away the marble block until the figure within was set free.

4. In section 764E of the *Erotikos* (Dialogue on love) by the Greek essayist Plutarch (46–120).
5. The god of love (Latin).

to make use of the figure and coloration of human youth in order to make the spiritual visible to us, furnishing it with the reflected glory of beauty and thus making of it a tool of memory, so that seeing it we might then be set aflame with pain and hope.

Those, at any rate, were the thoughts of the impassioned onlooker. He was capable of sustaining just such a high pitch of emotion. He spun himself a charming tapestry out of the roar of the sea and the glare of the sun. He saw the ancient plane tree not far from the walls of Athens,[6] that sacred, shadowy place filled with the scent of willow blossoms, decorated with holy images and votive offerings in honor of the nymphs and of Achelous.[7] The stream flowed in crystal clarity over smooth pebbles past the foot of the wide-branched tree. The crickets sang. Two figures reclined on the grass that gently sloped so that you could lie with your head held up; they were sheltered here from the heat of the day—an older man and a younger, one ugly and one handsome, wisdom at the side of charm. Amidst polite banter and wooing wit Socrates taught Phaedrus about longing and virtue. He spoke to him of the searing terror that the sensitive man experiences when his eye lights on an image of eternal beauty; spoke to him of the appetites of the impious, bad man who cannot conceive of beauty when he sees beauty's image and is incapable of reverence; spoke of the holy fear that overcomes a noble heart when a godlike face or a perfect body appears before him—how he then trembles and is beside himself and scarcely dares turn his eyes upon the sight and honors him who has beauty, indeed would even sacrifice to him as to a holy image, if he did not fear looking foolish in the eyes of others. For beauty, my dear Phaedrus, beauty alone is both worthy of love and visible at the same time; beauty, mark me well, is the only form of spirit that our senses can both grasp and endure. For what should become of us if divinity itself, or reason and virtue and truth were to appear directly to our senses? Would we not be overcome and consumed in the flames of love, as Semele[8] was at the sight of Zeus? Thus beauty is the sensitive man's way to the spirit—just the way, just the means, little Phaedrus. . . . And then he said the subtlest thing of all, crafty wooer that he was: he said that the lover was more divine than the beloved, because the god was in the former and not in the latter—perhaps the tenderest, most mocking thought that ever was thought, a thought alive with all the guile and the most secret bliss of love's longing.

A writer's chief joy is that thought can become all feeling, that feeling can become all thought. The lonely author possessed and commanded at this moment just such a vibrant thought, such a precise feeling: namely, that nature herself would shiver with delight were intellect to bow in homage before beauty. He suddenly wanted to write. They say, to be sure, that Eros loves idleness; the god was made to engage in no other activity. But at this moment of crisis the excitement of the love-struck traveler drove him to productivity, and the occasion was almost a matter of indifference. The intellectual world had

6. A reference to the scene and some of the arguments in Plato's dialogue *Phaedrus*. Plato's school, or Academy, was located in a grove of plane trees outside Athens; in the dialogue, the young student Phaedrus tells Socrates of Lysias's speech on love, and Socrates responds with two speeches of his own.

7. A brook or small river in ancient Athens, here personified as a god.
8. The mortal mother of Zeus's son Dionysus. She perished in flames when the king of the gods appeared (at her request) in his divine glory.

been challenged to profess its views on a certain great and burning problem of culture and of taste, and the challenge had reached him. The problem was well known to him, was part of his experience; the desire to illuminate it with the splendor of his eloquence was suddenly irresistible. And what is more, he wanted to work here in the presence of Tadzio, to use the boy's physical frame as the model for his writing, to let his style follow the lines of that body that seemed to him divine, to carry his beauty into the realm of intellect as once the eagle carried the Trojan shepherd into the ethereal heavens.[9] Never had his pleasure in the word seemed sweeter to him, never had he known so surely that Eros dwelt in the word as now in the dangerous and delightful hours he spent at his rough table under the awning. There with his idol's image in full view, the music of his voice resounding in his ear, he formed his little essay after the image of Tadzio's beauty—composed that page-and-a-half of choice prose that soon would amaze many a reader with its purity, nobility, and surging depth of feeling. It is surely for the best that the world knows only the lovely work and not also its origins, not the conditions under which it came into being; for knowledge of the origins from which flowed the artist's inspiration would surely often confuse the world, repel it, and thus vitiate the effects of excellence. Strange hours! Strangely enervating effort! Strangely fertile intercourse between a mind and a body! When Aschenbach folded up his work and left the beach, he felt exhausted, even unhinged, as if his conscience were indicting him after a debauch.

The next morning as he was about to leave the hotel he chanced to notice from the steps that Tadzio was already on his way to the shore, alone; he was just approaching the beach barrier. He felt first a suggestion, then a compulsion: the wish, the simple thought that he might make use of the opportunity to strike up a casual, cheerful acquaintanceship with this boy who unwittingly had caused such a stir in his mind and heart, speak with him and enjoy his answer and his gaze. The lovely lad sauntered along; he could be easily caught up with; Aschenbach quickened his steps. He reached him on the walkway behind the cabanas, was about to put his hand on his head or on his shoulder, was about to let some word pass his lips, some friendly French phrase. But then he felt his heart beating like a hammer, perhaps only because of his rapid walk, so that he was short of breath and could only have spoken in a trembling gasp. He hesitated, tried to master himself, then suddenly feared he had been walking too long right behind the handsome boy, feared he might notice, might turn around with an inquiring look. He took one more run at him, but then he gave up, renounced his goal, and hung his head as he went by.

Too late! he thought at that moment. Too late! But was it really too late? This step he had failed to take might very possibly have led to something good, to something easy and happy, to a salutary return to reality. But it may have been that the aging traveler did not wish to return to reality, that he was too much in love with his own intoxication. Who can untangle the riddle of the artist's essence and character? Who can understand the deep instinctive fusion of discipline and a desire for licentiousness upon which that character is

9. The young Trojan prince Ganymede was tending flocks when Zeus, in the form of an eagle, carried him off to Olympus where he became Zeus's lover and the cupbearer to the gods.

based? For it is licentiousness to be unable to wish for a salutary return to reality. Aschenbach was no longer inclined to self-criticism. The taste, the intellectual constitution that came with his years, his self-esteem, maturity, and the simplicity of age made him disinclined to analyze the grounds for his behavior or to decide whether it was conscience or debauchery and weakness that caused him not to carry out his plan. He was confused; he feared that someone, if only the custodian on the beach, might have observed his accelerated gait and his defeat; he feared very much looking foolish. And all the while he made fun of himself, of his comically solemn anxiety. "We've been quite confounded," he thought, "and now we're as crestfallen as a gamecock that lets its wings droop during a fight.[1] It must surely be the god himself who thus destroys our courage at the very sight of loveliness, who crushes our proud spirit so deeply in the dust. . . ." His thoughts roamed playfully: he was far too arrogant to be fearful of a mere emotion.

He had already ceased to pay much attention to the extent of time he was allowing himself for his holiday; the thought of returning home did not even cross his mind. He had an ample amount of money sent to him by mail. His sole source of concern was the possible departure of the Polish family, but he had privately obtained information, thanks to casual inquiries at the hotel barber shop, that the Polish party had arrived only very shortly before he did. The sun tanned his face and hands, the bracing salt air stimulated his emotions. Just as he ordinarily used up all the resources he gathered from sleep, nourishment, or nature on literary work, so now he expended each contribution that sun, leisure, and sea air made to his daily increase in strength in a generous, extravagant burst of enthusiasm and sentiment.

He slept fitfully; the exquisitely uniform days were separated by short nights full of happy restlessness. To be sure he retired early, for at nine o'clock, when Tadzio had left the scene, the day was over as far as he was concerned. At the first glimmer of dawn, however, a softly penetrating pang of alarm awakened him, as his heart remembered its great adventure. No longer able to endure the pillow, he arose, wrapped himself in a light robe against the morning chill, and positioned himself at the open window to await the sunrise. This wonderful occurrence filled his sleep-blessed soul with reverence. Heaven, earth, and sea still lay in the ghostly, glassy pallor of dawn; a fading star still floated in the insubstantial distance. Then a breath of wind arose, a winged message from unapproachable abodes announcing that Eos was arising from the side of her spouse. There became visible on the furthest boundary between sea and sky that first sweet blush of red that reveals creation assuming perceptible form. The goddess was approaching, she who seduced young men, she who had stolen Kleitos and Kephalos and enjoyed the love of handsome Orion in defiance of all the envious Olympians.[2] A strewing of roses began there on the edge of the world, where all shone and blossomed in unspeakable purity. Childlike clouds, transfigured and luminous, hovered like attending Cupids in the rosy bluish fragrance. Purple light fell on the sea, then washed forward in waves.

---

1. From the Greek tragedian Phrynichus (512–476 B.C.E.), quoted in Plutarch's *Erotikos* (762E).
2. Eos, the Greek goddess of dawn, was known for seducing handsome young men, including Kleitos and Kephalos. When she took the hunter Orion for her lover, Artemis, the jealous goddess of the hunt, killed him with her arrows.

Golden spears shot up from below to the heights of the heavens, and the brilliance began to burn. Silently, with divine ascendancy, glow and heat and blazing flames spun upwards, as the brother-god's sacred chargers, hooves beating, mounted the heavens. The lonely, wakeful watcher sat bathed in the splendor of the god's rays; he closed his eyes and let the glory kiss his eyelids. With a confused, wondering smile on his lips he recognized feelings from long ago, early, exquisite afflictions of the heart that had withered in the severe service that his life had become and now returned so strangely transformed. He meditated, he dreamed. Slowly his lips formed a name, and still smiling, his face turned upward, his hands folded in his lap, he fell asleep once more in his armchair.

The whole day that had thus began in fiery celebration was strangely heightened and mythically transformed. Where did that breath of air come from, the one that suddenly played about his temples and ears so softly and significantly like a whisper from a higher realm? White feathery clouds stood in scattered flocks in the heavens like grazing herds that the gods tend. A stronger wind blew up; Poseidon's[3] steeds reared and ran, and the bulls obedient to the god with the blue-green locks lowered their horns and bellowed as they charged. But amid the boulders on the distant beach the waves hopped up like leaping goats. A magical world, sacred and animated by the spirit of Pan,[4] surrounded the beguiled traveler, and his heart dreamed tender fables. Often, as the sun set behind Venice, he would sit on a bench in the park to watch Tadzio, dressed in white with a colorful sash, delight in playing ball on the smooth, rolled gravel; and it was as if he were watching Hyacinthos, who had to die because two gods loved him.[5] Indeed he felt the painful envy Zephyros felt toward his rival in love, the god who abandoned his oracle, his bow, and his cithara to spend all his time playing with the beautiful boy. He saw the discus, directed by cruel jealousy, strike the lovely head; he too, turned pale as he received the stricken body; and the flower that sprang from that sweet blood bore the inscription of his unending lament. . . .

There is nothing stranger or more precarious than the relationship between people who know each other only by sight, who meet and watch each other every day, even every hour, yet are compelled by convention or their own whim to maintain the appearance of indifference and unfamiliarity, to avoid any word or greeting. There arises between them a certain restlessness and frustrated curiosity, the hysteria of an unsatisfied, unnaturally suppressed urge for acquaintanceship and mutual exchange, and in point of fact also a kind of tense respect. For people tend to love and honor other people so long as they are not in a position to pass judgment on them; and longing is the result of insufficient knowledge.

Some sort of relationship or acquaintance necessarily had to develop between Aschenbach and the young Tadzio, and with a pang of joy the older man was

---

3. God of the sea and brother of Zeus in Greek mythology, associated with the horse and the bull.
4. A Greek demigod, half man and half goat, associated with fertility and sexuality.
5. Apollo and Zephyr, god of the west wind, both loved the youth Hyacinthos. When Apollo accidentally killed him in a discus game— Zephyr blew the discus off course—a flower marked with the Greek syllables "ai ai" ("alas!") sprang from the boy's blood. Apollo is an archer and musician as well as the god of the Delphic oracle.

able to ascertain that his involvement and attentions were not altogether unre-quited. For example, what impelled the lovely boy no longer to use the board-walk behind the cabanas when he appeared on the beach in the morning but instead to saunter by toward his family's cabana on the front path, through the sand, past Aschenbach's customary spot, sometimes unnecessarily close by him, almost touching his table, his chair? Did Aschenbach's superior emo-tional energy exercise such an attraction, such a fascination on the tender, unreflecting object of those emotions? The writer waited daily for Tadzio's appearance; sometimes he would act as if he were busy when this event took place and let the lovely one pass by without seeming to notice. Sometimes, though, he would look up, and their eyes would meet. Both of them were gravely serious when it happened. In the refined and respectable bearing of the older man nothing betrayed his inner tumult; but in Tadzio's eyes there was the hint of an inquiry, of a thoughtful question. A hesitation became visible in his gait, he looked at the ground, he looked up again in his charming way, and when he was past there seemed to be something in his demeanor saying that only his good breeding prevented him from turning around.

One evening, however, something quite different happened. The Polish chil-dren and their governess were missing at the main meal in the large dining room. Aschenbach had taken note of it with alarm. Concerned about their absence, he was strolling in front of the hotel at the bottom of the terrace after dinner, dressed in his evening clothes and a straw hat, when he suddenly saw appear in the light of the arc lamps the nunlike sisters and their attendant, with Tadzio four steps behind. They were apparently returning from the steamer landing after having taken their meal for some reason in the city. It must have been cool on the water: Tadzio wore a dark blue sailor's coat with gold buttons and a sailor's hat to go with it. The sun and sea air had not browned him. His skin was the same marble-like yellow color it had been from the beginning. But today he seemed paler than usual, whether because of the cool temperature or because of the pallid moonglow cast by the lamps. His even brows showed in starker contrast, his eyes darkened to an even deeper tone. He was more beautiful than words could ever tell, and Aschenbach felt as he often had before the painful truth that words are capable only of praising physical beauty, not of rendering it visible.

He had not been expecting the exquisite apparition: it had come on unhoped for. He had not had time to fortify himself in a peaceful, respectable demeanor. Joy, surprise, and admiration might have been clearly displayed in the gaze that met that of the one he had so missed—and in that very second, it came to pass that Tadzio smiled. He smiled at Aschenbach, smiled eloquently, intimately, charmingly, and without disguise, with lips that began to open only as he smiled. It was the smile of Narcissus[6] leaning over the mirroring water, that deep, beguiled, unresisting smile that comes as he extends his arm toward the reflection of his own beauty—a very slightly distorted smile, distorted by the

6. A beautiful Greek youth who fell in love with his own image in a pool and drowned try-ing to reach it. "Tadzio's smile is Narcissus', who sees his own reflection—he sees it in the face of another / he sees his beauty in its effects. Coquettishness and tenderness are also in this smile" [Mann's note].

hopelessness of his desire to kiss the lovely lips of his shadow—a coquettish smile, curious and faintly pained, infatuated and infatuating.

He who had been the recipient of this smile rushed away with it as if it were a gift heavy with destiny. He was so thoroughly shaken that he was forced to flee the light of the terrace and the front garden and to seek with a hasty tread the darkness of the park in the rear. Strangely indignant and tender exhortations broke forth from him: "You must not smile so! Listen, no one is allowed to smile that way at anyone!" He threw himself on a bench; he breathed in the nocturnal fragrance of the plants, beside himself. Leaning back with his arms hanging at his sides, overpowered and shivering uncontrollably, he whispered the eternal formula of longing—impossible under these conditions, absurd, reviled, ridiculous, and yet holy and venerable even under these conditions—"I love you!"

CHAPTER 5

In the fourth week of his stay on the Lido Gustav Aschenbach made a number of disturbing discoveries regarding events in the outside world. In the first place it seemed to him that as the season progressed toward its height the number of guests at the hotel declined rather than increased. In particular it seemed that the German language ceased to be heard around him: lately his ear could detect only foreign sounds in the dining room and on the beach. He had taken to visiting the barbershop frequently, and in a conversation there one day he heard something that startled him. The barber had mentioned a German family that had just left after staying only a short time; then he added by way of flattering small talk, "But you're staying, sir, aren't you. You're not afraid of the disease." Aschenbach looked at him. "The disease?" he repeated. The man broke off his chatter, acted busy, ignored the question. When Aschenbach pressed the issue, he explained that he knew nothing and tried to change the subject with a stream of embarrassed eloquence.

That was at noon. In the afternoon Aschenbach sailed across to Venice in a dead calm and under a burning sun. He was driven by his mania to pursue the Polish children, whom he had seen making for the steamer landing along with their attendant. He did not find his idol at San Marco. But at tea, sitting at his round wrought-iron table on the shady side of the piazza, he suddenly smelled a peculiar aroma in the air, one that he now felt had been lurking at the edge of his consciousness for several days without his becoming fully aware of it. It was a medicinally sweet smell that put in mind thoughts of misery and wounds and ominous cleanliness. After a few moments' reflection he recognized it; then he finished his snack and left the piazza on the side opposite the cathedral. The odor became stronger in the narrow streets. At the street corners there were affixed printed posters in which the city fathers warned the population about certain illnesses of the gastric system that could be expected under these atmospheric conditions, advising that they should not eat oysters and mussels or use the water in the canals. The euphemistic nature of the announcement was obvious. Groups of local people stood together silently on the bridges and in the piazzas, and the foreign traveler stood among them, sniffing and musing.

There was a shopkeeper leaning in the doorway of his little vaulted quarters among coral necklaces and imitation amethyst trinkets, and Aschenbach asked him for some information about the ominous odor. The man took his measure with a heavy-lidded stare and then hastily put on a cheerful expression. "A precautionary measure, sir," he answered with many a gesture. "A police regulation that we must accept. The weather is oppressive, the sirocco is not conductive to good health. In short, you understand—perhaps they're being too careful. . . ." Aschenbach thanked him and went on. Even on the steamer that took him back to the Lido he could now detect the odor of disinfectant.

Once back at the hotel he went directly to the lobby to have a look at the newspapers. In the ones in foreign languages he found nothing. The German papers mentioned rumors, cited highly varying figures, quoted official denials, and offered doubts about their veracity. This explained the departure of the German and Austrian element. The citizens of other nations apparently knew nothing, suspected nothing, and were not yet concerned. "Best to keep quiet," thought Aschenbach anxiously, as he threw the papers back on the table. "Best to keep it under wraps." But at the same time his heart filled with a feeling of satisfaction over this adventure in which the outside world was becoming involved. For passion, like crime, does not sit well with the sure order and even course of everyday life; it welcomes every loosening of the social fabric, every confusion and affliction visited upon the world, for passion sees in such disorder a vague hope of finding an advantage for itself. Thus Aschenbach felt a dark satisfaction over the official cover-up of events in the dirty alleys of Venice. This heinous secret belonging to the city fused and became one with his own innermost secret, which he was likewise intent upon keeping. For the lovesick traveler had no concern other than that Tadzio might depart, and he recognized, not without a certain horror, that he would not know how to go on living were that to happen.

Recently he had not contented himself with allowing chance and the daily routine to determine his opportunities to see and be near the lovely lad; he pursued him, he lay in wait for him. On Sundays, for example, the Polish family never went to the beach. He guessed that they went to mass at San Marco. He followed speedily, entered the golden twilight of the sanctuary from the heat of the piazza, and found him, the one he had missed so, bent over a prie-dieu[7] taking part in the holy service. He stood in the background on the fissured mosaic floor, in the midst of a kneeling, murmuring crowd of people who kept crossing themselves, and felt the condensed grandeur of the oriental temple weigh voluptuously on his senses. Up in front the priest moved about, conducted his ritual, and chanted away, while incense billowed up and enshrouded the feeble flames of the altar candles. Mixed in with the sweet, heavy, ceremonial fragrance seemed to be another: the smell of the diseased city. But through all the haze and glitter Aschenbach saw how the lovely one up in front turned his head, looked for him, and found him.

When at last the crowd streamed out of the open portals into the shining piazza with its flocks of pigeons, the infatuated lover hid in the vestibule where

7. Pray God (French, literal trans.); a low bench on which to kneel during prayers, with a raised shelf for elbows or book.

he lay in wait, staking out his quarry. He saw the Polish family leave the church, saw the children take leave of their mother with great ceremony, saw her make for the Piazzetta on her way home. He ascertained that the lovely one, his cloisterly sisters, and the governess were on their way off to the right, through the clock tower gate, and into the Merceria,[8] and after giving them a reasonable head start he followed. He followed like a thief as they strolled through Venice. He had to stop when they lingered somewhere, had to flee into restaurants or courtyards to avoid them when they turned back. He lost them, got hot and tired as he searched for them over bridges and in dirty cul-de-sacs, and suffered long moments of mortal pain when he saw them coming toward him in a narrow passage where no escape was possible. And yet one cannot really say he suffered. He was intoxicated in head and heart, and his steps followed the instructions of the demon whose pleasure it is to crush under foot human reason and dignity.[9]

At some point or other Tadzio and his party would take a gondola, and Aschenbach, remaining hidden behind a portico or a fountain while they got in, did likewise shortly after they pulled away from the bank. He spoke quickly and in subdued tones to the gondolier, instructing him that a generous tip was in store for him if he would follow that gondola just now rounding the corner— but not too close, as unobtrusively as possible. Sweat trickled over his body as the gondolier, with the roguish willingness of a procurer, assured him in the same lowered tones that he would get service, that he would get conscientious service.

He leaned back in the soft black cushions and glided and rocked in pursuit of the other black, beak-prowed bark, to which his passion held him fastened as if by a chain. Sometimes he lost sight of it, and at those times he would feel worried and restless. But his boatman seemed entirely familiar with such assignments and always knew just how to bring the object of his desire back into view by means of clever maneuvers and quick passages and shortcuts. The air was still, and it smelled. The sun burned heavily through a haze that gave the sky the color of slate. Water gurgled against wood and stone. The cry of the gondolier, half warning and half greeting, received distant answer from out of the silent labyrinth as if by mysterious arrangement. Umbels of flowers hung down over crumbling walls from small gardens on higher ground. They were white and purple and smelled like almonds. Moorish window casings showed their forms in the haze. The marble steps of a church descended into the waters; a beggar crouching there and asserting his misery held out his hat and showed the whites of his eyes as if he were blind; a dealer in antiques stood before his cavelike shop and with fawning gestures invited the passerby to stop, hoping for a chance to swindle him. That was Venice, that coquettish, dubious beauty of a city, half fairy tale and half tourist trap, in whose noisome air the fine arts once thrived luxuriantly and where musicians were inspired to create sounds that cradle the listener and seductively rock him to sleep. To the traveler in the midst of his adventure it seemed as if his eyes were drinking in just this luxury, as if his ears were wooed by just such melodies. He remembered, too, that the city was sick and was keeping its secret out of pure greed, and he

---

8. Commercial district north of the Piazza San Marco.

9. Dionysus, originally an Eastern fertility god, worshipped with wild dances in ecstatic rites.

cast an even more licentious leer toward the gondola floating in the distance before him.

Entangled and besotted as he was, he no longer wished for anything else than to pursue the beloved object that inflamed him, to dream about him when he was absent and to speak amorous phrases, after the manner of lovers, to his mere shadow. His solitary life, the foreign locale, and his late but deep transport of ecstasy encouraged and persuaded him to allow himself the most bewildering transgressions without timidity or embarrassment. That is how it happened that on his return from Venice late in the evening he had stopped on the second floor of the hotel in front of the lovely one's door, leaned his brow against the hinge in complete intoxication, unable for a protracted period to drag himself away, heedless of the danger of being caught in such an outrageous position.

Still, there were moments when he paused and half came to his senses. How has this come to pass? he wondered in alarm. How did I come to this? Like everyone who has achieved something thanks to his natural talents, he had an aristocratic interest in his family background. At times when his life brought him recognition and success he would think about his ancestors and try to reassure himself that they would approve, that they would be pleased, that they would have had to admire him. Even here and now he thought about them, entangled as he was in such an illicit experience, seized by such exotic emotional aberrations. He thought about their rigorous self-possession, their manly respectability, and he smiled a melancholy smile. What would they say? But then what would they have said about his whole life, a life that had so diverged, one might say degenerated, from theirs, a life under the spell of art that he himself had mocked in the precocity of his youth, this life that yet so fundamentally resembled theirs? He too had done his service, he too had practiced a strict discipline; he too had been a soldier and a man of war, like many of them. For art was a war, a grinding battle that one was just no longer up to fighting for very long these days. It was a life of self-control and a life lived in despite, a harsh, steadfast, abstemious existence that he had made the symbol of a tender and timely heroism. He had every right to call it manly, call it courageous, and he wondered if the love-god who had taken possession of him might be particularly inclined and partial somehow to those who lived such a life. Had not that very god enjoyed the highest respect among the bravest nations of the earth? Did they not say that it was because of their courage that he had flourished in their cities? Numerous war heroes of ages past had willingly borne the yoke imposed by the god, for a humiliation imposed by the god did not count. Acts that would have been denounced as signs of cowardice when done in other circumstances and for other ends—prostrations, oaths, urgent pleas, and fawning behavior—none redounded to the shame of the lover, but rather he more likely reaped praise for them.[1]

Such was the infatuated thinker's train of thought; thus he sought to offer himself support; thus he attempted to preserve his dignity. But at the same time he stubbornly kept on the track of the dirty doings in the city's interior, that adventure of the outside world that darkly joined together with his heart's

---

1. A reference to the Athenian code of love as described by Pausanias in Plato's *Symposium*, sections 182d–e and 183b.

adventure and nourished his passion with vague, lawless hopes. Obsessed with finding out the latest and most reliable news about the status and progress of the disease, he went to the city's coffee houses and leafed through the German newspapers, which had long since disappeared from the table in the hotel lobby. He read alternating assertions and denials. The number of illnesses and deaths might be as high as twenty, forty, even a hundred or more; but then in the next article or next issue any outbreak of the epidemic, if not categorically denied, would be reported as limited to a few isolated cases brought in by foreigners. There were periodic doubts, warnings, and protests against the dangerous game being played by the Italian authorities. Reliable information was simply not available.

The solitary guest was nonetheless conscious of having a special claim on his share in the secret. Though he was excluded, he took a bizarre pleasure in pressing knowledgeable people with insidious questions and forcing those who were part of the conspiracy of silence to utter explicit lies. At breakfast one day in the main dining room, for example, he engaged the manager in conversation. This unobtrusive little person in his French frock coat was going about between the tables greeting everyone and supervising the help. He made a brief stop at Aschenbach's table, too, for a casual chat. Now then why, the guest just happened to ask very casually, why in the world had they been disinfecting Venice for all this time? "It's a police matter," the toady answered, "a measure intended to stop in due and timely fashion any and all unwholesome conditions, any disturbance of the public health that might come about owing to the brooding heat of this exceptionally warm weather." "The police are to be commended," replied Aschenbach. After the exchange of a few more meteorological observations the manager took his leave.

On that very same day, in the evening after dinner, it happened that a little band of street singers from the city performed in the hotel's front garden. They stood, two men and two women, next to the iron lamppost of an arc light and raised their faces, shining in the white illumination, toward the great terrace, where the guests were enjoying this traditional popular entertainment while drinking coffee and cooling beverages. Hotel employees—elevator boys, waiters, and office personnel—stood by listening at the entrances to the lobby. The Russian family, zealous and precise in taking their pleasure, had wicker chairs moved down into the garden so as to be nearer the performers. There they sat in a semi-circle, in their characteristically grateful attitude. Behind the ladies and gentlemen stood the old slave woman in her turbanlike headdress.

The low-life virtuosos were extracting sounds from a mandolin, a guitar, a harmonica, and a squeaky violin. Interspersed among the instrumental numbers were vocals in which the younger of the women blended her sharp, quavering voice with the sweet falsetto of the tenor in a love duet full of yearning. But the chief talent and real leader of the group was clearly the other man, the guitar player, who sang a kind of buffo[2] baritone while he played. Though his voice was weak, he was a gifted mime and projected remarkable comic energy. Often he would move away from the group, his great instrument under his arm, and advance toward the terrace with many a flourish. The audience rewarded his

2. Comic.

antics with rousing laughter. The Russians in particular, ensconced in their orchestra seats, displayed particular delight over all this southern vivacity and encouraged him with applause and cheers to ever bolder and more brazen behavior.

Aschenbach sat at the balustrade, cooling his lips from time to time with a mixture of pomegranate[3] juice and soda that sparkled ruby-red in his glass. His nerves greedily consumed the piping sounds, the vulgar, pining melodies; for passion numbs good taste and succumbs in all seriousness to enticements that a sober spirit would receive with humor or even reject scornfully. His features, reacting to the antics of the buffoon, had become fixed in a rigid and almost painful smile. He sat in an apparently relaxed attitude, and all the while he was internally tense and sharply attentive, for Tadzio stood no more than six paces away, leaning against the stone railing.

He stood there in the white belted suit that he sometimes wore to dinner, a figure of inevitable and innate grace, his left forearm on the railing, his ankles crossed, his right hand supported on his hip. He wore an expression that was not quite a smile but more an air of distant curiosity or polite receptivity as he looked down toward the street musicians. Sometimes he straightened up and, with a lovely movement of both arms that lifted his chest, he would pull his white blouse down through his leather belt. Occasionally, though—as the aging observer noted with triumph and even with horror, his reason staggering— Tadzio would turn his head to look across his left shoulder in the direction of the one who loved him, sometimes with deliberate hesitation, sometimes with sudden swiftness as if to catch him unawares. Their eyes never met, for an ignominious caution forced the errant lover to keep his gaze fearfully in check. The women guarding Tadzio were sitting in the back of the terrace, and things had reached the point that the smitten traveler had to take care lest his behavior should become noticeable and he fall under suspicion. Indeed his blood had nearly frozen on a number of occasions when he had been compelled to notice on the beach, in the hotel lobby, or in the Piazza San Marco that Tadzio was called away from his vicinity, that they were intent on keeping the boy away from him. He felt horribly insulted, and his pride flinched from unfamiliar tortures that his conscience prevented him from dismissing.

In the meantime the guitar player had begun singing a solo to his own accompaniment, a popular ditty in many verses that was quite the hit just then all over Italy. He was adept at performing it in a highly histrionic manner, and his band joined in the refrain each time, both with their voices and all their instruments. He was of a lean build, and even his face was thin to the point of emaciation. He stood there on the gravel in an attitude of impertinent bravura, apart from his fellow performers, his shabby felt hat so far back on his head that a roll of red hair surged forth from beneath the brim, and as he thumped the guitar strings, he hurled his buffooneries toward the terrace above in an insistent recitative. The veins on his brow swelled in response to his exertions. He seemed not to be of Venetian stock, more likely a member of the race of Neapolitan comics, half pimp, half actor, brutal and daring, dangerous and entertaining. The lyrics of his song were as banal as could be, but in his mouth

---

3. A tropical fruit with many seeds, associated in Greek mythology both with Persephone, the queen of Hades, and with the world of the dead.

they acquired an ambiguous, vaguely offensive quality because of his facial expressions and his gestures, his suggestive winks and his manner of letting his tongue play lasciviously at the corner of his mouth. His strikingly large Adam's apple protruded nakedly from his scrawny neck, which emerged from the soft collar of a sport shirt worn in incongruous combination with more formal city clothes. His pale, snubnosed face was beardless and did not permit an easy reckoning of his age; it seemed ravaged by grimaces and by vice. The two defi- ant, imperious, even wild-looking furrows that stood between his reddish eye- brows went rather oddly with the grin on his mobile lips. What particularly drew the attention of the lonely spectator, however, was his observation that this questionable figure seemed to carry with it its own questionable atmo- sphere. For every time the refrain began again the singer would commence a grotesque circular march, clowning and shaking the hands of his audience; every time his path would bring him directly underneath Aschenbach's spot, and every time that happened there wafted up to the terrace from his clothes and from his body a choking stench of carbolic acid.[4]

His song finished, he began collecting money. He started with the Russians, who produced a generous offering, and then ascended the steps. As bold as he had been during the performance, just so obsequious was he now. Bowing and scraping, he slithered about between the tables, a smile of crafty submissive- ness laying bare his large teeth, and all the while the two furrows between his red eyebrows stood forth menacingly. The guests surveyed with curiosity and some revulsion this strange being who was gathering in his livelihood. They threw coins in his hat from a distance and were careful not to touch him. The elimination of the physical separation between the performer and his respect- able audience always tends to produce a certain embarrassment, no matter how pleasurable the performance. The singer felt it and sought to excuse him- self by acting servile. He came up to Aschenbach, and with him came the smell, though no one else in the vicinity seemed concerned about it.

"Listen," the lonely traveler said in lowered tones, almost mechanically. "They are disinfecting Venice. Why?" The jester answered hoarsely: "Because of the police. That, sir, is the procedure when it gets hot like this and when the sirocco comes. The sirocco is oppressive. It's not conducive to good health. . . ." He spoke as if he were amazed that anyone could ask such questions, and he dem- onstrated by pushing with his open palm just how oppressive the sirocco was. "So there is no disease in Venice?" Aschenbach asked very quietly through his closed teeth. The tense muscles in the comedian's face produced a grimace of comic perplexity. "A disease? What sort of disease? Is the sirocco a disease? Do you suppose our police force is a disease? You like to make fun, don't you? A disease! Why on earth? Some preventive measures, you understand. A police regulation to minimize the effects of the oppressive weather . . . ," he gesticu- lated. "Very well," Aschenbach said once again, briefly and quietly, and he dropped an indecently large coin into the hat. Then he indicated with a look that the man should go. He obeyed with a grin and a bow. But even before he reached the steps two hotel employees intercepted him and, putting their faces very close to his, cross-examined him in whispers. He shrugged, he protested, he swore that he had been circumspect. You could tell. Dismissed, he returned

4. A chemical used as a disinfectant.

to the garden and, after making a few arrangements with his group by the light of the arc lamp, he stepped forward to offer one parting song.

It was a song the solitary traveler could not remember ever having heard before, an impudent Italian hit in an incomprehensible dialect embellished with a laughing refrain in which the whole group regularly joined, fortissimo. The refrain had neither words nor instrumental accompaniment; nothing was left but a certain rhythmically structured but still very natural-sounding laughter, which the soloist in particular was capable of producing with great talent and deceptive realism. Having reestablished a proper artistic distance between himself and his audience, he had regained all his former impudence. His artfully artificial laughter, directed impertinently up to the terrace, was the laughter of scorn. Even before the part of the song with actual lyrics had come to a close, one could see him begin to battle an irresistible itch. He would hiccup, his voice would catch, he would put his hand up to his mouth, he would twist his shoulders, and at the proper moment the unruly laughter would break forth, exploding in a hoot, but with such realism that it was infectious. It spread among the listeners so that even on the terrace an unfounded mirth set in, feeding on nothing but itself. This appeared only to double the singer's exuberance. He bent his knees, slapped his thighs, held his sides, fairly split with laughter; but he was no longer laughing, he was howling. He pointed his finger upwards, as if to say that there could be nothing funnier than the laughing audience up there, and soon everyone in the garden and on the veranda was laughing, including the waiters, elevator boys, and servants lingering in the doorways.

Aschenbach no longer reclined in his chair; he sat upright as if trying to defend himself or to flee. But the laughter, the rising smell of hospital sanitation, and the nearness of the lovely boy—all blended to cast a dreamy spell about him that held his mind and his senses in an unbreakable, inescapable embrace. In the general confusion of the moment he made so bold as to cast a glance at Tadzio, and when he did so he was granted the opportunity to see that the lovely lad answered his gaze with a seriousness equal to his own. It was as if the boy were regulating his behavior and attitude according to that of the man, as if the general mood of gaiety had no power over the boy so long as the man kept apart from it. This childlike and meaningful docility was so disarming, so overwhelming, that the gray-haired traveler could only with difficulty refrain from hiding his face in his hands. It had also seemed to him that Tadzio's habit of straightening up and taking a deep sighing breath suggested an obstruction in his breathing. "He is sickly; he will probably not live long," he thought once again with that sobriety that sometimes frees itself in some strange manner from intoxication and longing. Ingenuous solicitude mixed with a dissolute satisfaction filled his heart.

The Venetian singers had meanwhile finished their number and left, accompanied by applause. Their leader did not fail to adorn even his departure with jests. He bowed and scraped and blew kisses so that everyone laughed, which made him redouble his efforts. When his fellow performers were already gone, he pretended to back hard into a lamppost at full speed, then crept toward the gate bent over in mock pain. There at last he cast off the mask of the comic loser, unbent or rather snapped up straight, stuck his tongue out impudently at the guests on the terrace, and slipped into the darkness. The audience dispersed; Tadzio was already long gone from his place at the balustrade. But the lonely traveler remained sitting for a long time at his little table, nursing his pomegranate drink much to the annoyance of the waiters. The night progressed; time crumbled away. Many years ago in his parents' house there had been an hourglass. He suddenly could see the fragile and portentous little device once more, as though it were standing right in front of him. The rust-colored fine sand ran silently through the glass neck, and as it began to run out of the upper vessel a rapid little vortex formed.

In the afternoon of the very next day the obstinate visitor took a further step in his probing of the outside world, and this time he met with all possible success. What he did was to enter the English travel agency in the Piazza San Marco and, having changed some money at the cash register and having assumed the demeanor of a diffident foreigner, he directed his fateful question to the clerk who was taking care of him. The clerk was a wool-clad Briton, still young, his hair parted in the middle and eyes set close together, possessed of that steady, trustworthy bearing that stands out as so foreign and so remarkable among the roguishly nimble southerners. He began: "No cause for concern, sir. A measure of no serious importance. Such regulations are frequently imposed to ward off the ill effects of the heat and the sirocco. . . . " But when he raised his blue eyes he met the foreigner's gaze. It was a tired and rather sad gaze, and it was directed with an air of mild contempt toward his lips. The Englishman blushed. "That is," he continued in a low voice, somewhat discomfited, "the official explanation, which they see fit to stick to hereabouts. I can tell you, though, that there's a good deal more to it." And then, in his candid and comfortable language, he told the truth.

For some years now Asiatic cholera had shown an increasing tendency to spread and roam. The pestilence originated in the warm swamps of the Ganges delta,[5] rising on the foul-smelling air of that lushly uninhabitable primeval world, that wilderness of islands avoided by humankind where tigers lurk in bamboo thickets. It had raged persistently and with unusual ferocity throughout Hindustan; then it had spread eastwards to China and westwards to Afghanistan and Persia; and, following the great caravan routes, it had brought its horrors as far as Astrakhan and even Moscow. But while Europe was shaking in fear lest the specter should progress by land from Russia westward, it had emerged simultaneously in several Mediterranean port cities, having been carried in on Syrian merchant ships. It had raised its grisly head in Toulon and Malaga, shown its grim mask several times in Palermo and Naples, and seemed now firmly ensconced throughout Calabria and Apulia.[6] The northern half of the peninsula had so far been spared. On a single day in mid-May of this year, however, the terrible vibrioid[7] bacteria had been found on two emaciated, blackening corpses, that of a ship's hand and that of a woman who sold vegetables. These cases were hushed up. A week later, though, there were ten more, twenty more, thirty more, not localized but spread through various parts of the city. A man from the Austrian hinterlands who had come for a pleasant holiday of a few days in Venice died upon returning to his home town, exhibiting

---

5. In India.
6. Regions in southern Italy. Astrakhan, Toulon, Málaga, Palermo, and Naples are seaports in Russia, France, Spain, Sicily, and southern

Italy, respectively.
7. Belonging to a class of comma-shaped bacteria.

unmistakable symptoms. Thus it was that the first rumors of the affliction visited upon the city on the lagoon appeared in German newspapers. In response the Venetian authorities promulgated the assertion that matters of health had never been better in the city. They also immediately instituted the most urgent measures to counter the disease. But apparently the food supply—vegetables, meat, and milk—had been infected, for death, though denied and hushed up, devoured its way through the narrow streets. The early arrival of summer's heat made a lukewarm broth of the water in the canals and thus made conditions for the disease's spread particularly favorable. It almost seemed as though the pestilence had been reinvigorated, as if the tenacity and fecundity of its microscopic agitators had been redoubled. Cures were rare; out of a hundred infected eighty died, and in a particularly gruesome fashion, for the evil raged here with extreme ferocity. Often it took on its most dangerous form, commonly known as the "dry type." In such cases the body is unable to rid itself of the massive amounts of water secreted by the blood-vessels. In a few hours' time the patient dries up and suffocates, his blood as viscous as pitch, crying out hoarsely in his convulsions. It sometimes happened that a few lucky ones suffered only a mild discomfort followed by a loss of consciousness from which they would never again, or only rarely, awaken. At the beginning of June the quarantine wards of the Ospedale Civico quietly filled up, space became scarce in both of the orphanages, and a horrifyingly brisk traffic clogged the routes between the docks at the Fondamenta Nuove[8] and San Michele, the cemetery island. But the fear of adverse consequences to the city, concern for the newly opened exhibit of paintings in the public gardens, for the losses that the hotels, businesses, and the whole tourist industry would suffer in case of a panic or a boycott—these matters proved weightier in the city than the love of truth or respect for international agreements. They prompted the authorities stubbornly to maintain their policy of concealment and denial. The highest medical official in Venice, a man of considerable attainments, had angrily resigned his post and was surreptitiously replaced by a more pliable individual. The citizenry knew all about it, and the combination of corruption in high places with the prevailing uncertainty, the state of emergency in which the city was placed when death was striking all about, caused a certain demoralization of the lower levels of society. It encouraged those antisocial forces that shun the light, and they manifested themselves as immoderate, shameless, and increasingly criminal behavior. Contrary to the norm, one saw many drunks at evening time; people said that gangs of rogues made the streets unsafe at night; muggings and even murders multiplied. Already on two occasions it had come to light that alleged victims of the plague had in fact been robbed of their lives by their own relatives who administered poison. Prostitution and lasciviousness took on brazen and extravagant forms never before seen here and thought to be at home only in the southern parts of the country and in the seraglios of the orient.

The Englishman explained the salient points of these developments. "You would do well," he concluded, "to depart today rather than tomorrow. The imposition of a quarantine cannot be more than a few days off." "Thank you," said Aschenbach and left the agency.

---

8. New footings (Italian, literal trans.); the new piers. "Ospedale Civico": city hospital.

The piazza was sunless and sultry. Unsuspecting foreigners sat in the sidewalk cafes or stood in front of the cathedral completely covered with pigeons. They watched as the swarming birds beat their wings and jostled each other for their chance to pick at the kernels of corn offered to them in an open palm. In feverish excitement, triumphant in his possession of the truth, but with a taste of gall in his mouth and a fantastic horror in his heart, the lonely traveler paced back and forth over the flagstones of the magnificent plaza. He considered doing the decent thing, the thing that would cleanse him. Tonight after dinner he could go up to the lady with the pearls and speak to her. He planned exactly what he would say: "Permit me, Madame, stranger though I may be, to be of service to you with a piece of advice, a word of warning concerning a matter that has been withheld from you by self-serving people. Depart at once, taking Tadzio and your daughters with you. There is an epidemic in Venice." He could then lay his hand in farewell on the head of that instrument of a scornful deity, turn away, and flee this swamp. But at the same time he sensed that he was infinitely far from seriously wanting to take such a step. It would bring him back to his senses, would make him himself again; but when one is beside oneself there is nothing more abhorrent than returning to one's senses. He remembered a white building decorated with inscriptions that gleamed in the evening light, inscriptions in whose radiant mysticism his mind's eye had become lost. He remembered too that strange figure of the wanderer who had awakened in the aging man a young man's longing to roam in faraway and exotic places. The thought of returning home, of returning to prudence and sobriety, toil and mastery, was so repugnant to him that his face broke out in an expression of physical disgust. "Let them keep quiet," he whispered vehemently. And: "I will keep quiet!" The consciousness of his guilty complicity intoxicated him, just as small amounts of wine will intoxicate a weary brain. The image of the afflicted and ravaged city hovered chaotically in his imagination, incited in him inconceivable hopes, beyond all reason, monstrously sweet. How could that tender happiness he had dreamed of a moment earlier compare with these expectations? What value did art and virtue hold for him when he could have chaos? He held his peace and stayed.

That night he had a terrifying dream—if indeed one can call "dream" an experience that was both physical and mental, one that visited him in the depths of his sleep, in complete isolation as well as sensuous immediacy, but yet such that he did not see himself as physically and spatially present apart from its action. Instead, its setting was in his soul itself, and its events burst in upon him from outside, violently crushing his resistance, his deep, intellectual resistance, passing through easily and leaving his whole being, the culmination of a lifetime of effort, ravaged and annihilated.

It began with fear, fear and desire and a horrified curiosity about what was to come. Night ruled, and his senses were attentive; for from afar there approached a tumult, a turmoil, a mixture of noises: rattling, clarion calls and muffled thunder, shrill cheering on top of it all, and a certain howl with a drawn-out *uuu* sound at the end. All this was accompanied and drowned out by the gruesomely sweet tones of a flute playing a cooing, recklessly persistent tune that penetrated to the very bowels, where it cast a shameless enchantment. But there was a phrase, darkly familiar, that named what was coming: "*The stranger god!*"[9] A smoky glow welled up, and he recognized a mountain landscape like the one around his summer house. And in the fragmented light he could see people, animals, a swarm, a roaring mob, all rolling and plunging and whirling down from the forested heights, past tree-trunks and great moss-covered fragments of rock, overflowing the slope with their bodies, flames, tumult, and reeling circular dance. Women, stumbling over the fur skirts that hung too long from their belts, moaned, threw their heads back, shook their tambourines on high, brandished naked daggers and torches that threw off sparks, held serpents with flickering tongues by the middle of their bodies, or cried out, lifting their breasts in both hands. Men with horns on their brows, girdled with hides, their own skins shaggy, bent their necks and raised their arms and thighs, clashed brazen cymbals and beat furiously on drums, while smooth-skinned boys used garlanded staves to prod their goats, clinging to the horns so they could be dragged along, shouting with joy, when the goats sprang. And the ecstatic band howled the cry with soft consonants in the middle and a drawn-out *uuu* sound on the end, a cry that was sweet and wild at the same time, like none ever heard before: here it rang in the air like the bellowing of stags in rut; and there many voices echoed it back in anarchic triumph, using it to goad each other to dance and shake their limbs, never letting it fall silent. But it was all suffused and dominated by the deep, beckoning melody of the flute. Was it not also beckoning him, the resisting dreamer, with shameless persistence to the festival, to its excesses, and to its ultimate sacrifice? Great was his loathing, great his fear, sincere his resolve to defend his own against the foreign invader, the enemy of self-controlled and dignified intellect. But the noise and the howling, multiplied by the echoing mountainsides, grew, gained the upper hand, swelled to a madness that swept everything along with it. Fumes oppressed the senses: the acrid scent of the goats, the emanation of panting human bodies, a whiff as of stagnant water—and another smell perceptible through it all, a familiar reek of wounds and raging sickness. His heart pounded with the rhythm of the drum beats, his mind whirled, rage took hold of him and blinded him, he was overcome by a numbing lust, and his soul longed to join in the reeling dance of the god. Their obscene symbol,[1] gigantic, wooden, was uncovered and raised on high, and they howled out their watchword all the more licentiously. With foam on their lips they raved; they stimulated each other with lewd gestures and fondling hands; laughing and wheezing, they pierced each other's flesh with their pointed staves and then licked the bleeding limbs. Now among them, now a part of them, the dreamer belonged to the stranger god. Yes, they were he, and he was they, when they threw themselves on the animals, tearing and killing, devouring steaming gobbets of flesh, when on the trampled moss-covered ground there began an unfettered rite of copulation in sacrifice to the god. His soul tasted the lewdness and frenzy of surrender.

The afflicted dreamer awoke unnerved, shattered, a powerless victim of the demon. He no longer shunned the observant glances of people about him; he no longer cared if he was making himself a target of their suspicions. And in any case they were all departing, fleeing the sickness. Many cabanas now stood

---

9. Dionysus (also Bacchus), whose cult was brought to Greece from Thrace and Phrygia. The dream describes the orgiastic rites of his worship.
1. The phallus.

empty, the population of the dining room was seriously depleted, and in the city one only rarely saw a foreigner. The truth seemed to have leaked out, and in spite of the stubborn conniving of those with vested interests at stake, panic could no longer be averted. The lady with the pearls nonetheless remained with her family, perhaps because the rumors did not reach her or perhaps because she was too proud and fearless to succumb to them. Tadzio remained, and to Aschenbach, blind to all but his own concerns, it seemed at times that death and departure might very well remove all the distracting human life around them and leave him alone with the lovely one on this island. Indeed, in the mornings on the beach when his gaze would rest heavily, irresponsibly, fixedly on the object of his desire; or at the close of day when he would take up his shameful pursuit of the boy through narrow streets where loathsome death did its hushed-up business; then everything monstrous seemed to him to have a prosperous future, the moral law to have none.

He wished, like any other lover, to please his beloved and felt a bitter concern that it would not be possible. He added youthfully cheerful touches to his dress, took to using jewelry and perfume. Several times a day he took lengthy care getting dressed and then came down to the dining room all bedecked, excited and expectant. His aging body disgusted him when he looked at the sweet youth with whom he was smitten; the sight of his gray hair and his sharp facial features overwhelmed him with shame and hopelessness. He felt a need to restore and revive his body. He visited the barbershop more and more frequently.

Leaning back in the chair under the protective cloth, letting the manicured hands of the chattering barber care for him, he confronted the tortured gaze of his image in the mirror.

"Gray," he said with his mouth twisted.

"A bit," the man replied. "It's all because of a slight neglect, an indifference to externals—quite understandable in the case of important people, but still not altogether praiseworthy, all the less so since just such people ought not to harbor prejudices in matters of the natural and the artificial. If certain people were to extend the moral qualms they have about the cosmetic arts to their teeth, as logic compels, they would give no little offense. And anyway, we're only as old we feel in our hearts and minds. Gray hair can in certain circumstances give more of a false impression than the dye that some would scorn. In your case, sir, you have a right to your natural hair color. Will you allow me to give you back what is rightfully yours?"

"How?" Aschenbach inquired.

So the glib barber washed his customer's hair with two liquids, one clear and one dark, and it turned as black as it had been in youth. Then he rolled it with the curling iron into soft waves, stepped back and admired his handiwork.

"All that's left," he said, "is to freshen up the complexion a bit."

He went about, with ever renewed solicitude, moving from one task to another the way a person does who can never finish anything and is never satisfied. Aschenbach, resting comfortably, was in any case quite incapable of fending him off. Actually he was rather excited about what was happening, watching in the mirror as his brows took on a more decisive and symmetrical arch and his eyes grew in width and brilliance with the addition of a little shadow on the lids. A little further down he could see his skin, previously brown and leathery, perk up with a light application of delicate carmine rouge, his lips, pale and bloodless only a moment a ago, swell like raspberries, the furrows in his cheeks and mouth, the wrinkles around his eyes give way to a dab of cream and the glow of youth. His heart pounded as he saw in the mirror a young man in full bloom. The cosmetic artist finally pronounced himself satisfied and thanked the object of his ministrations with fawning politeness, the way such people do. "A minor repair job," he said as he put a final touch to Aschenbach's appearance. "Now, sir, you can go and fall in love without second thoughts." The beguiled lover went out, happy as in a dream, yet confused and timid. His tie was red, and his broad-brimmed straw hat was encircled by a band of many colors.

A tepid breeze had come up; it rained only seldom and then not hard, but the air was humid, thick, and full of the stench of decay. Rustling, rushing, and flapping sounds filled his ears. He burned with fever beneath his makeup, and it seemed to him that the air was filled with vile, evil windspirits, impure winged sea creatures who raked over, gnawed over, and defiled with garbage the meals of their victim.[2] For the sultry weather ruined one's appetite, and one could not suppress the idea that all the food was poisoned with infection.

Trailing the lovely boy one afternoon, Aschenbach had penetrated deep into the maze in the heart of the diseased city. He had lost his sense of direction, for the little streets, canals, bridges, and piazzas in the labyrinth all looked alike. He could no longer even tell east from west, since his only concern had been not to lose sight of the figure he pursued so ardently. He was compelled to a disgraceful sort of discretion that involved clinging to walls and seeking protection behind the backs of passersby, and so he did not for some time become conscious of the fatigue, the exhaustion which a high pitch of emotion and continual tension had inflicted on his body and spirit. Tadzio walked behind the rest of his family. In these narrow streets he would generally let the governess and the nunlike sisters go first, while he sauntered along by himself, occasionally turning his head to assure himself with a quick glance of his extraordinary dawn-gray eyes over his shoulder that his lover was still following. He saw him, and he did not betray him. Intoxicated by this discovery, lured onward by those eyes, tied to the apron string of his own passion, the lovesick traveler stole forth in pursuit of his unseemly hope—but ultimately found himself disappointed. The Polish family had gone across a tightly arched bridge, and the height of the arch had hidden them from their pursuer. When he was at last able to cross, he could no longer find them. He searched for them in three directions—straight ahead and to both sides along the narrow, dirty landing—but in vain. He finally had to give up, too debilitated and unnerved to go on.

His head was burning hot, his body was sticky with sweat, the scruff of his neck was tingling, an unbearable thirst assaulted him, and he looked about for immediate refreshment of any sort. In front of a small greengrocer's shop he bought some fruit, strawberries that were overripe and soft, and he ate them while he walked. A little piazza that was quite deserted and seemed enchanted

---

2. "Harpies: hideously thin, they flew swiftly in, fell with insatiable greed on whatever food was there, ate without being satisfied, and *befouled* whatever they left with their filth" [Mann's note]. See Virgil's *Aeneid* 3.210–62.

opened out before him. He recognized it, for it was here that weeks ago he had made his thwarted plan to flee the city. He collapsed on the steps of the well in the very middle of the plaza and rested his head on the stone rim. It was quiet, grass grew between the paving stones, refuse lay strewn about. Among the weathered buildings of varying heights around the periphery was one that looked rather palatial. It had Gothic-arched windows, now gaping emptily, and little balconies decorated with lions. On the ground floor of another there was a pharmacy. Warm gusts of wind from time to time carried the smell of carbolic acid.

He sat there, the master, the artist who had attained to dignity, the author of the "Man of Misery," that exemplary work which had with clarity of form renounced bohemianism and the gloomy murky depths, had condemned sympathy for the abyss, reviled the vile. There he sat, the great success who had overcome knowledge and outgrown every sort of irony, who had accustomed himself to the obligations imposed by the confidence of his large audience. There he sat, the author whose greatness had been officially recognized and whose name bore the title of nobility, the author whose style children were encouraged to emulate—sat there with his eyes shut, though from time to time a mocking and embarrassed look would slip sidelong out from underneath his lids, only to conceal itself again swiftly; and his slack, cosmetically enhanced lips formed occasional words that emerged out of the strange dream-logic engendered in his half-dozing brain.[3]

"For beauty, Phaedrus—mark me well—only beauty is both divine and visible at the same time, and thus it is the way of the senses, the way of the artist, little Phaedrus, to the spirit. But do you suppose, my dear boy, that anyone could ever attain to wisdom and genuine manly honor by taking a path to the spirit that leads through the senses? Or do you rather suppose (I leave the decision entirely up to you) that this is a dangerously delightful path, really a path of error and sin that necessarily leads astray? For you must know that we poets cannot walk the path of beauty without Eros joining our company and even making himself our leader; indeed, heroes though we may be after our own fashion, disciplined warriors though we may be, still we are as women, for passion is our exaltation, and our longing must ever be for love. That is our bliss and our shame. Do you see, then, that we poets can be neither wise nor honorable, that we necessarily go astray, that we necessarily remain dissolute adventurers of emotion? The masterly demeanor of our style is a lie and a folly, our fame and our honor a sham, the confidence accorded us by our public utterly ridiculous, the education of the populace and of the young by means of art a risky enterprise that ought not to be allowed. For how can a person succeed in educating others who has an inborn, irremediable, and natural affinity for the abyss? We may well deny it and achieve a certain dignity, but wherever we may turn that affinity abides. Let us say we renounce analytical knowledge; for knowledge, Phaedrus, has neither dignity nor discipline; it is knowing, understanding, forgiving, formless and unrestrained; it has sympathy for the abyss; it *is* the abyss. Let us therefore resolutely reject it, and henceforth our efforts will

---

3. Aschenbach adopts the role of Socrates in Plato's *Phaedrus* to examine the role of the artist. Although the Platonic dialogue briefly contrasts inspired art with mere technical perfection, it is chiefly concerned with moral choices and absolute beauty.

be directed only toward beauty, that is to say toward simplicity, grandeur, and a new discipline, toward reborn ingenuousness and toward form. But form and ingenuousness, Phaedrus, lead to intoxication and to desire, might lead the noble soul to horrible emotional outrages that his own lovely discipline would reject as infamous, lead him to the abyss. Yes, they too lead to the abyss. They lead us poets there, I say, because we are capable not of resolution but only of dissolution. And now I shall depart, Phaedrus; but you stay here until you can no longer see me, and then you depart as well."

A few days afterwards Gustav von Aschenbach left the hotel at a later hour than usual, since he was feeling unwell. He was struggling with certain attacks of dizziness that were only partly physical and were accompanied by a powerfully escalating sense of anxiety and indecision, a feeling of having no prospects and no way out. He was not at all sure whether these feelings concerned the outside world or his own existence. He noticed in the lobby a great pile of luggage prepared for departure, and when he asked the doorman who was leaving, he received for an answer the aristocratic Polish name he had in his heart been expecting to hear all along. He took it in with no change in the expression on his ravaged face, briefly raising his head as people do to acknowledge casually the receipt of a piece of information they do not need, and asked, "When?" The answer came: "After lunch." He nodded and went to the beach.

It was dreary there. Rippling tremors crossed from near to far on the wide, flat stretch of water between the beach and the first extended sandbar. Where so recently there had been color, life, and joy, it was now almost deserted, and an autumnal mood prevailed, a feeling that the season was past its prime. The sand was no longer kept clean. A camera with no photographer to operate it stood on its tripod at the edge of the sea, a black cloth that covered it fluttering with a snapping noise in a wind that now blew colder.

Tadzio and three or four playmates that still remained were active in front of his family's cabana to Aschenbach's right; and, resting in his beach chair approximately halfway between the ocean and the row of cabanas, with a blanket over his legs, Aschenbach watched him once more. Their play was unsupervised, since the women must have been busy with preparations for their departure. The game seemed to have no rules and quickly degenerated. The sturdy boy with the belted suit and the black, slicked-down hair who was called Yashu, angered and blinded by sand thrown in his face, forced Tadzio into a wrestling match, which ended swiftly with the defeat of the weaker, lovely boy. It seemed as if in the last moments before leave-taking the subservient feelings of the underling turned to vindictive cruelty as he sought to take revenge for a long period of slavery. The winner would not release his defeated opponent but instead kneeled on his back and pushed his face in the sand, persisting for so long that Tadzio, already out of breath from the fight, seemed in danger of suffocating. He made spasmodic attempts to shake off his oppressor, lay still for whole moments, then tried again with no more than a twitch. Horrified, Aschenbach wanted to spring to the rescue, but then the bully finally released his victim. Tadzio was very pale; he got up halfway and sat motionless for several minutes supported on one arm, his hair disheveled and his eyes darkening. Then he rose to his feet and slowly walked away. They called to him, cheerfully at first but then with pleading timidity. He paid no attention. The black-haired boy, apparently instantly regretting his transgression, caught up with him and tried to make up. A jerk of a lovely shoulder put him off. Tadzio crossed diagonally down to the water. He was barefoot and wore his striped linen suit with the red bow.

He lingered at the edge of the sea with his head hung down, drawing figures in the wet sand with his toe. Then he went into the shallows, which at their deepest point did not wet his knees, strode through them, and progressed idly to the sandbar. Upon reaching it he stood for a moment, his face turned to the open sea, then began to walk slowly to the left along the narrow stretch of uncovered ground. Separated from the mainland by the broad expanse of water, separated from his mates by a proud mood, he strode forth, a highly remote and isolated apparition with wind-blown hair, wandering about out there in the sea, in the wind, on the edge of the misty boundlessness. Once more he stopped to gaze outward. Suddenly, as if prompted by a memory or an impulse, he rotated his upper body in a lovely turn out of its basic posture, his hand resting on his hip, and looked over his shoulder toward the shore. The observer sat there as he had sat once before, when for the first time he had met the gaze of those dawn-gray eyes cast back at him from that threshold. His head, resting on the back of the chair, had slowly followed the movements of the one who was striding about out there; now his head rose as if returning the gaze, then sank on his chest so that his eyes looked out from beneath. His face took on the slack, intimately absorbed expression of deep sleep. It seemed to him, though, as if the pale and charming psychagogue[4] out there were smiling at him, beckoning to him; as if, lifting his hand from his hip, he were pointing outwards, hovering before him in an immensity full of promise. And, as so often before, he arose to follow him.

Minutes passed before anyone rushed to the aid of the man who had collapsed to one side in his chair. They carried him to his room. And later that same day a respectfully shaken world received the news of his death.

1912

4. Leader of souls to the underworld (Greek); a title of the god Hermes.

MARCEL PROUST
1871–1922

Marcel Proust's influence on twentieth-century literature is unequaled by that of any other writer, except **James Joyce**. Known primarily as a minor essayist until the age of forty, Proust devoted the last decade of his life to a massive sequence—*In Search of Lost Time* (À la recherche du temps perdu, 1913–27), also known in English as *Remembrance of Things Past*— that transformed the way writers and readers think about the novel as a form. It is a monumental construction coordinated down to its smallest part not by the progress of a traditional plot but by the narrator's intuition and "involuntary memory," and all external events are presented through the prism of the narrator's experience.

Proust was born on July 10, 1871, the older of two sons in a wealthy middle-class Parisian family. His father was a well-known doctor and professor of medicine, a Catholic from a small town outside Paris. His mother, a sensitive, scrupulous, and highly educated woman to whom Marcel was devoted, came from an urban Jewish family. When he was nine, Proust fell ill with severe asthma; thereafter, he spent his childhood holidays at a seaside resort in Normandy that became the model for the fictional Balbec, the setting for a portion of *In Search of Lost Time*. His asthma interfered with his favorite pastimes: walking in the country and smelling the flowering hawthorns near his aunt's home in Illiers (the fictional Combray, where the novel's protagonist grows up). In spite of his illness, which limited what he could do, Marcel graduated with honors from the Lycée Condorcet in Paris in 1889. He then did a year's military service at Orléans, which provided more material for his later novel. He went on to attend law school briefly and graduated with a degree in philosophy from the Sorbonne. As a student, Proust met many young writers and composers, and he frequented the salons of the wealthy bourgeoisie and the aristocracy of the Faubourg Saint-Germain (an elegant area of Paris), from which he drew much of the material for his portraits of society. He wrote for symbolist magazines, such as *Le Banquet* and *La Revue blanche*, and published a collection of essays, poems, and stories in an elegant book, *Pleasures and Days* (1896), but his work received relatively little attention from readers or critics. In 1899 (with his mother's help, since he knew little English), he began to translate the English social and art critic John Ruskin. He did not need to work, since his parents supported him, but he did briefly have a volunteer position at one of France's national libraries; after a few days' work, he went on permanent sick leave.

Proust is known as the author of one novel: the enormous, seven-volume exploration of time and consciousness called *In Search of Lost Time*. As early as 1895, he embarked on a shorter novel that traced the same themes and autobiographical awareness as his masterwork would, but *Jean Santeuil* (published posthumously in 1952) never found a coherent structure for its numerous episodes, and Proust abandoned it in 1899. Themes, ideas, and some episodes from the earlier novel were absorbed into *In Search of Lost Time*; the major difference (aside from length) between the two works is simply the highly sophisticated and subtle structure that Proust devised for the later one.

Proust's parents both died in 1905. The following year, his asthma worsening, he moved into a cork-lined, fumigated room in Paris, where he stayed until forced to move in 1919. From 1907 to 1914, he spent summers in the seacoast town of Cabourg (another source of material for the fictional Balbec), but when in Paris he emerged rarely from his apartment and then only late at night for dinners with friends. Proust was, he later said, "from the medical point of view, many different things, though in fact no one has ever known exactly what. But I am above all, and indisputably, an asthmatic." In an effort to control his symptoms, which he believed were exacerbated by drafts, sunlight, smells, noises, and digestive discomfort, he developed a number of rituals. For example, he ate only once a day, ordering in from high-end restaurants. He slept during the daylight hours, rising around eight in the evening and working through the night. He insisted that everything that touched his skin— bathwater, changes of clothes—had to be just his temperature, so his housekeeper kept extra shirts and long underwear in the oven.

While considering what to write next, Proust improved his style by creating a series of pastiches of great French writers. In 1909 he conceived the structure of his novel as a whole and wrote its first and last chapters together. A first draft was finished by September 1912, but Proust had difficulty finding a publisher and finally published the first volume, Swann's Way (Du côte de chez Swann), at his own expense, in 1913. Though this volume was a success, the First World War delayed publication of subsequent volumes, and Proust began the painstaking revision and enlargement of the whole manuscript (from fifteen hundred to four thousand pages, and three to seven parts) that was to occupy him until his death. He continually added material, even as his health deteriorated, often pasting strips onto earlier pages of the manuscript so that he could present a more detailed account of a particular incident or memory. Within a Budding Grove (À l'ombre des jeunes filles en fleurs, or "In the shadow of young girls in flower") won the prestigious Goncourt Prize in 1919, and The Guermantes Way (Le Côté de Guermantes) followed, in 1920–21. The last volume published in Proust's lifetime was Sodom and Gomorrah (Sodome et Gomorrhe II, 1922), and the remaining volumes—The Captive (La Prisonnière, 1923), The Fugitive (Albertine disparue, or "Albertine disappeared," 1925), and Time Regained (Le Temps retrouvé, 1927)—were released posthumously from manuscripts on which he had been working.

Throughout 1922, Proust's symptoms, particularly nausea, vomiting, and occasional delirium, grew more and more perilous. On November 18, after an especially bad week, his housekeeper, already alarmed by his deterioration, noticed the normally untidy Proust

"pulling up the sheet and picking up the papers strewn over the bed." "I'd never been at a deathbed before," she later wrote, "but in our village I'd heard people say that dying men gather things." By that afternoon three doctors, including the patient's brother, Robert Proust, had determined that he had only a few hours to live. Proust died before nightfall. A man who had always looked eerily young, he preserved enough of a glow in death to allow friends and colleagues to visit the bedroom over the weekend to pay their respects. When the writer Jean Cocteau visited, he remarked on the tall stacks of notebooks near the bed: "That pile of paper on his left was still alive, like watches ticking on the wrists of dead soldiers." Proust had achieved fame and was buried with military honors as a knight of the French Legion of Honor.

SWANN'S WAY

The selection presented here, from "Combray," is the first section of the first volume of In Search of Lost Time. Written almost completely in the first person and based on events in the author's life (although by no means purely autobiographical), the novel is famous both for its evocation of the closed world of Parisian society at the turn of the century and as a meditation on time. Proust was homosexual, and homosexuality eventually became a major theme in his writing. He once told another gay French writer, André Gide, that in a novel or short story one could say whatever one wanted about sexuality as long as the words were those of a fictional character: "never say I." Although the first-person pronoun appears on most pages of his novel, homosexuality is attributed to many characters but never to the narrator; likewise, in a novel with a number of Jewish characters, the narrator does not share Proust's religious heritage. Indeed, Proust took the events of his life and the traits of people he knew and rearranged them, combining them into fictional composites.

When *Swann's Way* appeared, in 1913, it was immediately seen as a new kind of fiction. Unlike nineteenth-century novels such as **Flaubert's** *Madame Bovary*, *In Search of Lost Time* has no clear and continuous plotline building to a denouement, nor (until the final volume, published in 1927) could the reader detect a consistent development of the central character, Marcel. Proust's plot acquires purpose only gradually, through the interconnection of several themes. Likewise, the characters, Marcel included, are not sketched in fully from the beginning, but rather are revealed piece by piece, evolving within the distinctive perspectives of individual chapters. Only at the end does the narrator recognize the meaning and value of what has preceded, and when he retells his story, he does so not from an omniscient, explanatory point of view but as the reliving and gradual assessment of Marcel's lifelong experience. Most of the novel sets forth a roughly chronological sequence of events, yet its opening pages swing through recollections of times and places before settling on the narrator's childhood in Combray. The second section, *Swann in Love (Un Amour de Swann)*, recounts the story of the title character in the third person. Thus the novel proceeds by apparently discontinuous blocks of recollection, bound together by the central consciousness of the narrator. This was always Proust's plan: he insisted that, from the beginning, he had in mind a fixed structure and a goal for the novel in its entirety that would reach down to the "solidity of the smallest parts." Still, his substantial revisions and expansion of the first draft enriched the existing structure; and as he was writing, history intruded: he moved the location of the fictional Combary to the front lines in order to include the war.

The overall theme of the novel is suggested by the translation of its title: "In Search of Lost Time." The narrator, "Marcel," who suggests but is not identical to the author, is an old man, weakened by a long illness, who puzzles over the events of his past, trying to find in them a significant pattern. He begins with his childhood, orderly and comfortable in the security of accepted manners and ideals in the family home at Combray. In succeeding volumes Marcel goes out into the world, experiences love and disappointment, discovers the disparity between idealized images of places and their crude, sometimes banal reality, and is increasingly overcome by disillusionment with himself and with society.

In the short ending chapter, things suddenly come into focus as Marcel reaches an understanding of the role of time. Abruptly reliving a childhood experience when he sees a familiar book and recognizing the ravages of time in the aged and enfeebled figures of his old friends, Marcel faces the approach of death with a sense of existential continuity and realizes that his vocation as an artist lies in giving form to this buried existence. Apparently lost, the past is still alive within us, a part of our being, and memory can recapture it to give coherence and depth to present identity. By the end of the last volume, *Time Regained*, Marcel has not yet begun to write, but paradoxically the book that he plans to write is already there: Proust's *In Search of Lost Time*.

"Swann's Way" is one of the two directions in which Marcel's family took walks from their home in Combray, toward Tansonville, home of Charles Swann, and is associated with various scenes and anecdotes of love and private life. The longer walk toward the estate of the Guermantes (*The Guermantes Way*), a fictional family of the highest aristocracy appearing frequently in the novel, evokes an aura of high society and French history, a more public sphere.

Fictional people and places mingle throughout with the real; here, names that are not annotated are Proust's inventions. The narrator of "Combray" is Marcel as an old man, and the French verb tense used in his recollections (here and throughout all but the final volume) is appropriately the imperfect, a tense of uncompleted action ("I used to . . . I would ask myself"). The famous first sentence points to a period in the narrator's life that is both private and somehow universal: "For a long time, I went to bed early." He would often wake up unsure where he was, what year it was, and even who he was. Proust then presents a kaleidoscopic vision of the many bedrooms where his narrator will sleep during the course of the novel, thus plunging the reader into the fictional world and demonstrating the instability of time and space.

The first chapter of "Combray" introduces the work's themes and methods, rather like the overture of an opera. All but one of the main characters appear or are mentioned, and the patterns of future encounters are set. Marcel, waiting anxiously for his beloved mother's response to a note sent down to her during dinner, suffers the same agony of separation as does Swann in his love for the promiscuous Odette, or the older Marcel himself for Albertine. The strange world of half-sleep, half-waking with which the novel begins prefigures later awakenings of memory. Long passages of intricate introspection, and sudden shifts of time and space, introduce us to the style and point of view of the rest of the book.

The selection ends with Proust's most famous image, summing up for many readers the world, the style, and the process of discovery of the author's vision. Nibbling at a madeleine (a small, rich cookielike pastry) that he has dipped in lime-blossom tea, Marcel suddenly has an overwhelming feeling of happiness. He soon associates this tantalizing, puzzling phenomenon with the memory of earlier times when he sipped tea with his aunt Leonie. He realizes that there is something valuable about such passive, spontaneous, and sensuous memory, quite different from the abstract operations of reason. Although the Marcel of "Combray" does not yet know it, he will pursue the elusive significance of this moment of happiness until, in *Time Regained*, he can, as a complete artist, bring it to the surface and link past and present in a fuller and richer vision.

Proust's novel has a unique architectural design that integrates large blocks of material: themes, situations, places, and events recur and are transformed across time. His long sentences and mammoth paragraphs reflect the slow, careful progression of thought among the changing objects of its perception. The ending paragraph of the "overture" is composed of two long sentences that encompass a wide range of meditative detail as the narrator not only recalls his childhood world—the old gray house, garden, public square and country roads, Swann's park, the river, the villagers, and indeed the whole town of Combray—but simultaneously compares the sudden recollection of the house to a stage set, and the unfolding village itself to the twists and turns of a Japanese paper flower expanding inside a bowl of water: here, inside the narrator's cup of lime-blossom tea. Characters are remembered in shifting settings and perspectives, creating a "multiple self" that is free to change and still remain the same.

Swann's Way[1]

Part 1. Combray

I

For a long time, I went to bed early. Sometimes, my candle scarcely out, my eyes would close so quickly that I did not have time to say to myself: "I'm falling asleep." And, half an hour later, the thought that it was time to try to sleep would wake me; I wanted to put down the book I thought I still had in my hands and blow out my light; I had not ceased while sleeping to form reflections on what I had just read, but these reflections had taken a rather peculiar turn; it seemed to me that I myself was what the book was talking about: a church, a quartet, the rivalry between François I and Charles V.[2] This belief lived on for a few seconds after my waking; it did not shock my reason but lay heavy like scales on my eyes and kept them from realizing that the candlestick was no longer lit. Then it began to grow unintelligible to me, as after metempsychosis do the thoughts of an earlier existence; the subject of the book detached itself from me, I was free to apply myself to it or not; immediately I recovered my sight and I was amazed to find a darkness around me soft and restful for my eyes, but perhaps even more so for my mind, to which it appeared a thing without cause, incomprehensible, a thing truly dark. I would ask myself what time it might be; I could hear the whistling of the trains which, remote or nearby, like the singing of a bird in a forest, plotting the distances, described to me the extent of the deserted countryside where the traveler hastens toward the nearest station; and the little road he is following will be engraved on his memory by the excitement he owes to new places, to unaccustomed activities, to the recent conversation and the farewells under the unfamiliar lamp that follow him still through the silence of the night, to the imminent sweetness of his return.

I would rest my cheeks tenderly against the lovely cheeks of the pillow, which, full and fresh, are like the cheeks of our childhood. I would strike a match to look at my watch. Nearly midnight. This is the hour when the invalid who has been obliged to go off on a journey and has had to sleep in an unfamiliar hotel, wakened by an attack, is cheered to see a ray of light under the door. How fortunate, it's already morning! In a moment the servants will be up, he will be able to ring, someone will come help him. The hope of being relieved gives him the courage to suffer. In fact he thought he heard footsteps; the steps approach, then recede. And the ray of light that was under his door has disappeared. It is midnight; they have just turned off the gas; the last servant has gone and he will have to suffer the whole night through without remedy.

I would go back to sleep, and would sometimes afterward wake again for brief moments only, long enough to hear the organic creak of the woodwork, open my eyes and stare at the kaleidoscope of the darkness, savor in a momentary glimmer of consciousness the sleep into which were plunged the furniture, the room, that whole of which I was only a small part and whose insensibility I

1. Translated by Lydia Davis.
2. Francis I (1496–1567), king of France, and Charles V (1500–1558), Holy Roman emperor and king of Spain, fought four wars over the empire's expansion in Europe.

would soon return to share. Or else while sleeping I had effortlessly returned to a period of my early life that had ended forever, rediscovered one of my childish terrors such as my great-uncle pulling me by my curls, a terror dispelled on the day—the dawn for me of a new era—when they were cut off. I had forgotten that event during my sleep, I recovered its memory as soon as I managed to wake myself up to escape the hands of my great-uncle, but as a precautionary measure I would completely surround my head with my pillow before returning to the world of dreams.

Sometimes, as Eve was born from one of Adam's ribs, a woman was born during my sleep from a cramped position of my thigh. Formed from the pleasure I was on the point of enjoying, she, I imagined, was the one offering it to me. My body, which felt in hers my own warmth, would try to find itself inside her, I would wake up. The rest of humanity seemed very remote compared with this woman I had left scarcely a few moments before; my cheek was still warm from her kiss, my body aching from the weight of hers. If, as sometimes happened, she had the features of a woman I had known in life, I would devote myself entirely to this end: to finding her again, like those who go off on a journey to see a longed-for city with their own eyes and imagine that one can enjoy in reality the charm of a dream. Little by little the memory of her would fade, I had forgotten the girl of my dream.

A sleeping man holds in a circle around him the sequence of the hours, the order of the years and worlds. He consults them instinctively as he wakes and reads in a second the point on the earth he occupies, the time that has elapsed before his waking; but their ranks can be mixed up, broken. If toward morning, after a bout of insomnia, sleep overcomes him as he is reading, in a position quite different from the one in which he usually sleeps, his raised arm alone is enough to stop the sun and make it retreat,[3] and, in the first minute of his waking, he will no longer know what time it is, he will think he has only just gone to bed. If he dozes off in a position still more displaced and divergent, after dinner sitting in an armchair for instance, then the confusion among the disordered worlds will be complete, the magic armchair will send him traveling at top speed through time and space, and, at the moment of opening his eyelids, he will believe he went to bed several months earlier in another country. But it was enough if, in my own bed, my sleep was deep and allowed my mind to relax entirely; then it would let go of the map of the place where I had fallen asleep and, when I woke in the middle of the night, since I did not know where I was, I did not even understand in the first moment who I was; I had only, in its original simplicity, the sense of existence as it may quiver in the depths of an animal; I was more destitute than a cave dweller; but then the memory—not yet of the place where I was, but of several of those where I had lived and where I might have been—would come to me like help from on high to pull me out of the void from which I could not have got out on my own; I crossed centuries of civilization in one second, and the image confusedly glimpsed of oil lamps, then of wingcollar shirts, gradually recomposed my self's original features.

Perhaps the immobility of the things around us is imposed on them by our certainty that they are themselves and not anything else, by the immobility of

---

3. If his uplifted arm prevents him from seeing the sunlight, he will think it is still night.

our mind confronting them. However that may be, when I woke thus, my mind restlessly attempting, without success, to discover where I was, everything revolved around me in the darkness, things, countries, years. My body, too benumbed to move, would try to locate, according to the form of its fatigue, the position of its limbs so as to deduce from this the direction of the wall, the placement of the furniture, so as to reconstruct and name the dwelling in which it found itself. Its memory, the memory of its ribs, its knees, its shoulders, offered in succession several of the rooms where it had slept, while around it the invisible walls, changing place according to the shape of the imagined room, spun through the shadows. And even before my mind, hesitating on the thresholds of times and shapes, had identified the house by reassembling the circumstances, it—my body—would recall the kind of bed in each one, the location of the doors, the angle at which the light came in through the windows, the existence of a hallway, along with the thought I had had as I fell asleep and that I had recovered upon waking. My stiffened side, trying to guess its orientation, would imagine, for instance, that it lay facing the wall in a big canopied bed and immediately I would say to myself: "Why, I went to sleep in the end even though Mama didn't come to say goodnight to me," I was in the country in the home of my grandfather, dead for many years; and my body, the side on which I was resting, faithful guardians of a past my mind ought never to have forgotten, recalled to me the flame of the night-light of Bohemian glass, in the shape of an urn, which hung from the ceiling by little chains, the mantelpiece of Siena marble,[4] in my bedroom at Combray, at my grandparents' house, in faraway days which at this moment I imagined were present without picturing them to myself exactly and which I would see more clearly in a little while when I was fully awake.

Then the memory of a new position would reappear; the wall would slip away in another direction: I was in my room at Mme. de Saint-Loup's,[5] in the country; good Lord! It's ten o'clock or even later, they will have finished dinner! I must have overslept during the nap I take every evening when I come back from my walk with Mme. de Saint-Loup, before putting on my evening clothes. For many years have passed since Combray, where, however late we returned, it was the sunset's red reflections I saw in the panes of my window. It is another sort of life one leads at Tansonville, at Mme. de Saint-Loup's, another sort of pleasure I take in going out only at night, in following by moonlight those lanes where I used to play in the sun; and the room where I fell asleep instead of dressing for dinner—from far off I can see it, as we come back, pierced by the flares of the lamp, a lone beacon in the night.

These revolving, confused evocations never lasted for more than a few seconds; often, in my brief uncertainty about where I was, I did not distinguish the various suppositions of which it was composed any better than we isolate, when we see a horse run, the successive positions shown to us by a kinetoscope.[6] But

4. Marble from central Italy, mottled and reddish in color. "Bohemian glass": likely to have been ornately engraved. Bohemia (now part of the Czech Republic) was a major center of the glass industry.
5. Charles Swann's daughter, Gilberte, who has married Robert de Saint-Loup, a nephew of the Guermantes.
6. An early moving-picture machine that showed photographs in rapid succession, giving the illusion of motion.

I had seen sometimes one, sometimes another, of the bedrooms I had inhabited in my life, and in the end I would recall them all in the long reveries that followed my waking: winter bedrooms in which, as soon as you are in bed, you bury your head in a nest braided of the most disparate things: a corner of the pillow, the top of the covers, a bit of shawl, the side of the bed and an issue of the *Débats roses*,[7] which you end by cementing together using the birds' technique of pressing down on it indefinitely; where in icy weather the pleasure you enjoy is the feeling that you are separated from the outdoors (like the sea swallow which makes its nest deep in an underground passage in the warmth of the earth) and where, since the fire is kept burning all night in the fireplace, you sleep in a great cloak of warm, smoky air, shot with the glimmers from the logs breaking into flame again, a sort of immaterial alcove, a warm cave dug out of the heart of the room itself, a zone of heat with shifting thermal contours, aerated by drafts which cool your face and come from the corners, from the parts close to the window or far from the hearth, and which have grown cold again: summer bedrooms where you delight in becoming one with the soft night, where the moonlight leaning against the half-open shutters casts its enchanted ladder to the foot of the bed, where you sleep almost in the open air, like a titmouse rocked by the breeze on the tip of a ray of light; sometimes the Louis XVI[8] bedroom, so cheerful that even on the first night I had not been too unhappy there and where the slender columns that lightly supported the ceiling stood aside with such grace to show and reserve the place where the bed was; at other times, the small bedroom with the very high ceiling, hollowed out in the form of a pyramid two stories high and partly paneled in mahogany, where from the first second I had been mentally poisoned by the unfamiliar odor of the vetiver,[9] convinced of the hostility of the violet curtains and the insolent indifference of the clock chattering loudly as though I were not there; where a strange and pitiless quadrangular cheval glass, barring obliquely one of the corners of the room, carved from deep inside the soft fullness of my usual field of vision a site for itself which I had not expected; where my mind, struggling for hours to dislodge itself, to stretch upward so as to assume the exact shape of the room and succeed in filling its gigantic funnel to the very top, had suffered many hard nights, while I lay stretched out in my bed, my eyes lifted, my ear anxious, my nostril restive, my heart pounding, until habit had changed the color of the curtains, silenced the clock, taught pity to the cruel oblique mirror, concealed, if not driven out completely, the smell of the vetiver and appreciably diminished the apparent height of the ceiling. Habit! That skillful but very slow housekeeper who begins by letting our mind suffer for weeks in a temporary arrangement; but whom we are nevertheless truly happy to discover, for without habit our mind, reduced to no more than its own resources, would be powerless to make a lodging habitable.

Certainly I was now wide-awake, my body had veered around one last time and the good angel of certainty had brought everything around me to a standstill, laid me down under my covers, in my bedroom, and put approximately

7. The evening edition of the daily newspaper *Le Journal des Débats*.
8. Furnished in late 18th-century style, named for the French king of the time and marked by great elegance.
9. The aromatic root of a tropical grass packaged as a moth repellent.

where they belonged in the darkness my chest of drawers, my desk, my fireplace, the window onto the street and the two doors. But even though I knew I was not in any of the houses of which my ignorance upon waking had instantly, if not presented me with the distinct picture, at least made me believe the presence possible, my memory had been stirred; generally I would not try to go back to sleep right away; I would spend the greater part of the night remembering our life in the old days, in Combray at my great-aunt's house, in Balbec,[1] in Paris, in Doncières, in Venice, elsewhere still, remembering the places, the people I had known there, what I had seen of them, what I had been told about them.

At Combray, every day, in the late afternoon, long before the moment when I would have to go to bed and stay there, without sleeping, far away from my mother and grandmother, my bedroom again became the fixed and painful focus of my preoccupations. They had indeed hit upon the idea, to distract me on the evenings when they found me looking too unhappy, of giving me a magic lantern,[2] which, while awaiting the dinner hour, they would set on top of my lamp; and, after the fashion of the first architects and master glaziers of the Gothic age, it replaced the opacity of the walls with impalpable iridescences, supernatural multicolored apparitions, where legends were depicted as in a wavering, momentary stained-glass window. But my sadness was only increased by this since the mere change in lighting destroyed the familiarity which my bedroom had acquired for me and which, except for the torment of going to bed, had made it tolerable to me. Now I no longer recognized it and I was uneasy there, as in a room in some hotel or "chalet" to which I had come for the first time straight from the railway train.

Moving at the jerky pace of his horse, and filled with a hideous design, Golo[3] would come out of the small triangular forest that velveted the hillside with dark green and advance jolting toward the castle of poor Geneviève de Brabant. This castle was cut off along a curved line that was actually the edge of one of the glass ovals arranged in the frame which you slipped between the grooves of the lantern. It was only a section of castle and it had a moor in front of it where Geneviève stood dreaming, wearing a blue belt. The castle and the moor were yellow, and I had not had to wait to see them to find out their color since, before the glasses of the frame did so, the bronze sonority of the name Brabant had shown it to me clearly. Golo would stop for a moment to listen sadly to the patter read out loud by my great-aunt,[4] which he seemed to understand perfectly, modifying his posture, with a meekness that did not exclude a certain majesty, to conform to the directions of the text; then he moved off at the same jerky pace. And nothing could stop his slow ride. If the lantern was moved, I could make out Golo's horse continuing to advance over the window curtains, swelling out with their folds, descending into their fissures. The body of Golo himself, in its essence as supernatural as that of his steed, accommodated every material obstacle, every hindersome object that he encountered by

1. The narrator's room at the fictional seaside resort of Balbec, a setting in the later novel *Within a Budding Grove.*
2. A kind of slide projector.
3. Villain of a 5th-century legend. He falsely accuses Geneviève de Brabant of adultery. Brabant was a principality in what is now Belgium.
4. Marcel's great-aunt is reading the story to him as they wait for dinner.

taking it as his skeleton and absorbing it into himself, even the doorknob he immediately adapted to and floated invincibly over with his red robe or his pale face as noble and as melancholy as ever, but revealing no disturbance at this transvertebration.

Certainly I found some charm in these brilliant projections, which seemed to emanate from a Merovingian[5] past and send out around me such ancient reflections of history. But I cannot express the uneasiness caused in me by this intrusion of mystery and beauty into a room I had at last filled with myself to the point of paying no more attention to the room than to that self. The anesthetizing influence of habit having ceased, I would begin to have thoughts, and feelings, and they are such sad things. That doorknob of my room, which differed for me from all other doorknobs in the world in that it seemed to open of its own accord, without my having to turn it, so unconscious had its handling become for me, was now serving as an astral body[6] for Golo. And as soon as they rang for dinner, I hastened to run to the dining room where the big hanging lamp, ignorant of Golo and Bluebeard,[7] and well acquainted with my family and beef casserole, shed the same light as on every other evening; and to fall into the arms of Mama, whom Geneviève de Brabant's misfortunes made all the dearer to me, while Golo's crimes drove me to examine my own conscience more scrupulously.

After dinner, alas, I soon had to leave Mama, who stayed there talking with the others, in the garden if the weather was fine, in the little drawing room to which everyone withdrew if the weather was bad. Everyone, except my grandmother, who felt that "it's a pity to shut oneself indoors in the country" and who had endless arguments with my father on days when it rained too heavily, because he sent me to read in my room instead of having me stay outdoors. "That's no way to make him strong and active," she would say sadly, "especially that boy, who so needs to build up his endurance and willpower." My father would shrug his shoulders and study the barometer, for he liked meteorology, while my mother, making no noise so as not to disturb him, watched him with a tender respect, but not so intently as to try to penetrate the mystery of his superior qualities. But as for my grandmother, in all weathers, even in a downpour when Françoise had rushed the precious wicker armchairs indoors so that they would not get wet, we would see her in the empty, rain-lashed garden, pushing back her disordered gray locks so that her forehead could more freely drink in the salubriousness of the wind and rain. She would say: "At last, one can breathe!" and would roam the soaked paths—too symmetrically aligned for her liking by the new gardener, who lacked all feeling for nature and whom my father had been asking since morning if the weather would clear—with her jerky, enthusiastic little step, regulated by the various emotions excited in her soul by the intoxication of the storm, the power of good health, the stupidity of my upbringing, and the symmetry of the gardens, rather than by the desire, quite unknown to her, to spare her plum-colored skirt the spots of mud under

---

5. The first dynasty of French kings (ca. 500–751).

6. Spiritual counterpart of the physical body. According to the doctrine of Theosophy (a spiritualist movement originating in 1875),

the astral body survives the death of the physical body.

7. The legendary wife murderer, presumably shown on another set of slides.

which it would disappear up to a height that was always, for her maid, a source of despair and a problem.

When these garden walks of my grandmother's took place after dinner, one thing had the power to make her come inside again: this was—at one of the periodic intervals when her circular itinerary brought her back, like an insect, in front of the lights of the little drawing room where the liqueurs were set out on the card table—if my great-aunt called out to her: "Bathilde! Come and stop your husband from drinking cognac!" To tease her, in fact (she had brought into my father's family so different a mentality that everyone poked fun at her and tormented her), since liqueurs were forbidden to my grandfather, my great-aunt would make him drink a few drops. My poor grandmother would come in, fervently beg her husband not to taste the cognac; he would become angry, drink his mouthful despite her, and my grandmother would go off again, sad, discouraged, yet smiling, for she was so humble at heart and so gentle that her tenderness for others, and the lack of fuss she made over her own person and her sufferings, came together in her gaze in a smile in which, unlike what one sees in the faces of so many people, there was irony only for herself, and for all of us a sort of kiss from her eyes, which could not see those she cherished without caressing them passionately with her gaze. This torture which my great-aunt inflicted on her, the spectacle of my grandmother's vain entreaties and of her weakness, defeated in advance, trying uselessly to take the liqueur glass away from my grandfather, were the kinds of things which you later become so accustomed to seeing that you smile as you contemplate them and take the part of the persecutor resolutely and gaily enough to persuade yourself privately that no persecution is involved; at that time they filled me with such horror that I would have liked to hit my great-aunt. But as soon as I heard: "Bathilde, come and stop your husband from drinking cognac!," already a man in my cowardice, I did what we all do, once we are grown up, when confronted with sufferings and injustices: I did not want to see them; I went up to sob at the very top of the house next to the schoolroom,[8] under the roofs, in a little room that smelled of orris root[9] and was also perfumed by a wild black-currant bush which had sprouted outside between the stones of the wall and extended a branch of flowers through the half-open window. Intended for a more specialized and more vulgar use, this room, from which during the day you could see all the way to the keep[1] of Roussainville-le-Pin, for a long time served me as a refuge, no doubt because it was the only one I was permitted to lock, for all those occupations of mine that demanded an inviolable solitude: reading, reverie, tears, and sensuous pleasure. Alas! I did not know that, much more than her husband's little deviations from his regimen, it was my weak will, my delicate health, the uncertainty they cast on my future that so sadly preoccupied my grandmother in the course of those incessant perambulations, afternoon and evening, when we would see, as it passed and then passed again, lifted slantwise toward the sky, her beautiful face with its brown furrowed cheeks, which with age had become almost mauve like the plowed fields in autumn, crossed, if she was

8. A room in the house dedicated to the children's schoolwork.

9. A powder then used as a room deodorizer.

1. The best-fortified tower of a medieval castle. "Vulgar use": it was used as a toilet.

going out, by a veil half raised, while upon them, brought there by the cold or some sad thought, an involuntary tear was always drying.

My sole consolation, when I went upstairs for the night, was that Mama would come and kiss me once I was in bed. But this goodnight lasted so short a time, she went down again so soon, that the moment when I heard her coming up, then the soft sound of her garden dress of blue muslin, hung with little cords of plaited straw, passing along the hallway with its double doors, was for me a painful one. It heralded the moment that was to follow it, when she had left me, when she had gone down again. So that I came to wish that this goodnight I loved so much would take place as late as possible, so as to prolong the time of respite in which Mama had not yet come. Sometimes when, after kissing me, she opened the door to go, I wanted to call her back, to say "kiss me one more time," but I knew that immediately her face would look vexed, because the concession she was making to my sadness and agitation by coming up to kiss me, by bringing me this kiss of peace, irritated my father, who found these rituals absurd, and she would have liked to try to induce me to lose the need for it, the habit of it, far indeed from allowing me to acquire that of asking her, when she was already on the doorstep, for one kiss more. And to see her vexed destroyed all the calm she had brought me a moment before, when she had bent her loving face down over my bed and held it out to me like a host[2] for a communion of peace from which my lips would draw her real presence and the power to fall asleep. But those evenings, when Mama stayed so short a time in my room, were still sweet compared to the ones when there was company for dinner and when, because of that, she did not come up to say goodnight to me. That company was usually limited to M. Swann, who, apart from a few acquaintances passing through, was almost the only person who came to our house at Combray, sometimes for a neighborly dinner (more rarely after that unfortunate marriage of his, because my parents did not want to receive his wife), sometimes after dinner, unexpectedly. On those evenings when, as we sat in front of the house under the large chestnut tree, around the iron table, we heard at the far end of the garden, not the copious high-pitched bell that drenched, that deafened in passing with its ferruginous,[3] icy, inexhaustible noise any person in the household who set it off by coming in "without ringing," but the shy, oval, golden double tinkling of the little visitors' bell, everyone would immediately wonder: "A visitor—now who can that be?" but we knew very well it could only be M. Swann; my great-aunt speaking loudly, to set an example, in a tone of voice that she strained to make natural, said not to whisper that way; that nothing is more disagreeable for a visitor just coming in who is led to think that people are saying things he should not hear; and they would send as a scout my grandmother, who was always glad to have a pretext for taking one more walk around the garden and who would profit from it by surreptitiously pulling up a few rose stakes on the way so as to make the roses look a little more natural, like a mother who runs her hand through her son's hair to fluff it up after the barber has flattened it too much.

We would all remain hanging on the news my grandmother was going to bring us of the enemy, as though there had been a great number of possible

---

2. Communion wafer.   3. Ironlike.

assailants to choose among, and soon afterward my grandfather would say: "I recognize Swann's voice." In fact one could recognize him only by his voice, it was difficult to make out his face, his aquiline nose, his green eyes under a high forehead framed by blond, almost red hair, cut Bressant-style,[4] because we kept as little light as possible in the garden so as not to attract mosquitoes, and I would go off, as though not going for that reason, to say that the syrups should be brought out; my grandmother placed a great deal of importance, considering it more amiable, on the idea that they should not seem anything exceptional, and for visitors only. M. Swann, though much younger, was very attached to my grandfather, who had been one of the closest friends of his father, an excellent man but peculiar, in whom, apparently, a trifle was sometimes enough to interrupt the ardor of his feelings, to change the course of his thinking. Several times a year I would hear my grandfather at the table telling anecdotes, always the same ones, about the behavior of old M. Swann upon the death of his wife, over whom he had watched day and night. My grandfather, who had not seen him for a long time, had rushed to his side at the estate the Swanns owned in the vicinity of Combray and, so that he would not be present at the coffining, managed to entice him for a while, all in tears, out of the death chamber. They walked a short way in the park, where there was a little sunshine. Suddenly M. Swann, taking my grandfather by the arm, cried out: "Oh, my old friend, what a joy it is to be walking here together in such fine weather! Don't you think it's pretty, all these trees, these hawthorns! And my pond—which you've never congratulated me on! You look as sad as an old nightcap. Feel that little breeze? Oh, say what you like, life has something to offer despite everything, my dear Amédée!" Suddenly the memory of his dead wife came back to him and, no doubt feeling it would be too complicated to try to understand how he could have yielded to an impulse of happiness at such a time, he confined himself, in a habitual gesture of his whenever a difficult question came into his mind, to passing his hand over his forehead, wiping his eyes and the lenses of his lorgnon. Yet he could not be consoled for the death of his wife, but, during the two years he survived her, would say to my grandfather: "It's odd, I think of my poor wife often, but I can't think of her for long at a time." "Often, but only a little at a time, like poor old Swann," had become one of my grandfather's favorite phrases, which he uttered apropos of the most different sorts of things. I would have thought Swann's father was a monster, if my grandfather, whom I considered a better judge and whose pronouncement, forming a legal precedent for me, often allowed me later to dismiss offenses I might have been inclined to condemn, had not exclaimed: "What! He had a heart of gold!"

For many years, even though, especially before his marriage, the younger M. Swann often came to see them at Combray, my great-aunt and my grandparents did not suspect that he had entirely ceased to live in the kind of society his family had frequented and that, under the sort of incognito which this name Swann gave him among us, they were harboring—with the perfect innocence of honest innkeepers who have under their roof, without knowing it, some celebrated highwayman—one of the most elegant members of the Jockey

4. Crew cut in front and longer in back: a hair style popularized by the actor Jean-Baptiste Bressant (1815–1886).

Club, a favorite friend of the Comte de Paris and the Prince of Wales, one of the men most sought after by the high society of the Faubourg Saint-Germain.[5]

Our ignorance of this brilliant social life that Swann led was obviously due in part to the reserve and discretion of his character, but also to the fact that bourgeois people in those days formed for themselves a rather Hindu notion of society and considered it to be made up of closed castes, in which each person, from birth, found himself placed in the station which his family occupied and from which nothing, except the accidents of an exceptional career or an unhoped-for marriage, could withdraw him in order to move him into a higher caste. M. Swann, the father, was a stockbroker; "Swann the son" would find he belonged for his entire life to a caste in which fortunes varied, as in a tax bracket, between such and such fixed incomes. One knew which had been his father's associations, one therefore knew which were his own, with which people he was "in a position" to consort. If he knew others, these were bachelor acquaintances on whom old friends of the family, such as my relatives, would close their eyes all the more benignly because he continued, after losing his parents, to come faithfully to see us; but we would have been ready to wager that these people he saw, who were unknown to us, were the sort he would not have dared greet had he encountered them when he was with us. If you were determined to assign Swann a social coefficient that was his alone, among the other sons of stockbrokers in a position equal to that of his parents, this coefficient would have been a little lower for him because, very simple in his manner and with a long-standing "craze" for antiques and painting, he now lived and amassed his collections in an old town house which my grandmother dreamed of visiting, but which was situated on the quai d'Orléans,[6] a part of town where my great-aunt felt it was ignominious to live. "But are you a connoisseur? I ask for your own sake, because you're likely to let the dealers unload some awful daubs on you," my great-aunt would say to him; in fact she did not assume he had any competence and even from an intellectual point of view had no great opinion of a man who in conversation avoided serious subjects and showed a most prosaic preciseness not only when he gave us cooking recipes, entering into the smallest details, but even when my grandmother's sisters talked about artistic subjects. Challenged by them to give his opinion, to express his admiration for a painting, he would maintain an almost ungracious silence and then, on the other hand, redeem himself if he could provide, about the museum in which it was to be found, about the date at which it had been painted, a pertinent piece of information. But usually he would content himself with trying to entertain us by telling a new story each time about something that had just happened to him involving people selected from among those we knew, the Combray pharmacist, our cook, our coachman. Certainly these tales made my great-aunt laugh, but she could not distinguish clearly if this was because of the absurd role Swann always assigned himself or because of the

---

5. A fashionable area of Paris on the left bank of the Seine; many of the French aristocracy lived there. "Jockey Club": an exclusive men's club devoted to horse racing, opera, and other diversions. Louis-Philippe-Albert d'Orléans, comte de Paris (1838–1894), was the heir apparent to the French throne, should the monarchy ever be restored; the Prince of Wales became, in 1901, King Edward VII of England.
6. A beautiful though less fashionable section in the heart of Paris, along the Seine.

wit he showed in telling them: "You are quite a character, Monsieur Swann!" Being the only rather vulgar person in our family, she took care to point out to strangers, when they were talking about Swann, that, had he wanted to, he could have lived on the boulevard Haussmann or the avenue de l'Opéra, that he was the son of M. Swann, who must have left four or five million,[7] but that this was his whim. One that she felt moreover must be so amusing to others that in Paris, when M. Swann came on New Year's Day to bring her her bag of marrons glacés,[8] she never failed, if there was company, to say to him: "Well, Monsieur Swann! Do you still live next door to the wine warehouse, so as to be sure of not missing the train when you go to Lyon?"[9] And she would look out of the corner of her eye, over her lorgnon, at the other visitors.

But if anyone had told my great-aunt that this same Swann, who, as the son of old M. Swann, was perfectly "qualified" to be received by all the "best of the bourgeoisie," by the most respected notaries or lawyers of Paris (a hereditary privilege he seemed to make little use of), had, as though in secret, quite a different life; that on leaving our house, in Paris, after telling us he was going home to bed, he retraced his steps as soon as he had turned the corner and went to a certain drawing room that no eye of any broker or broker's associate would ever contemplate, this would have seemed to my aunt as extraordinary as might to a better-educated lady the thought of being personally on close terms with Aristaeus[1] and learning that, after having a chat with her, he would go deep into the heart of the realms of Thetis, into an empire hidden from mortal eyes, where Virgil shows him being received with open arms; or—to be content with an image that had more chance of occurring to her, for she had seen it painted on our petits-fours plates at Combray—of having had as a dinner guest Ali Baba,[2] who, as soon as he knows he is alone, will enter the cave dazzling with unsuspected treasure.

One day when he had come to see us in Paris after dinner apologizing for being in evening clothes, Françoise having said, after he left, that she had learned from the coachman that he had dined "at the home of a princess," "Yes, a princess of the demimonde!"[3] my aunt had responded, shrugging her shoulders without raising her eyes from her knitting, with serene irony.

Thus, my great-aunt was cavalier in her treatment of him. Since she believed he must be flattered by our invitations, she found it quite natural that he never came to see us in the summertime without having in his hand a basket of peaches or raspberries from his garden and that from each of his trips to Italy he would bring me back photographs of masterpieces.

---

7. I.e., francs—nearly $1 million in the currency of the day, about $19 million in 2011. (The franc has since been replaced by the euro.) "Boulevard Haussmann" and "avenue de l'Opéra": large modern avenues where the wealthy bourgeoisie liked to live.
8. Candied chestnuts, a traditional Parisian New Year's gift.
9. The wine warehouse was close to the Gare de Lyon, the terminal from which trains left for the industrial city of Lyon and other destinations in southeastern France.
1. Son of the Greek god Apollo. In Virgil's *Fourth Georgic*, Aristacus seeks help from the sea nymph Thetis.
2. Hero of an *Arabian Nights* tale, a poor youth who discovers a robbers' cave filled with treasure.
3. Literally, "half-world" (French): women of questionable reputation, not quite members of society.

They did not hesitate to send him off in search of it when they needed a recipe for gribiche sauce[4] or pineapple salad for large dinners to which they had not invited him, believing he did not have sufficient prestige for one to be able to serve him up to acquaintances who were coming for the first time. If the conversation turned to the princes of the House of France:[5] "people you and I will never know, will we, and we can manage quite well without that, can't we," my great-aunt would say to Swann, who had, perhaps, a letter from Twickenham[6] in his pocket; she had him push the piano around and turn the pages on the evenings when my grandmother's sister sang, handling this creature, who was elsewhere so sought after, with the naive roughness of a child who plays with a collector's curio no more carefully than with some object of little value. No doubt the Swann who was known at the same time to so many clubmen was quite different from the one created by my great-aunt, when in the evening, in the little garden at Combray, after the two hesitant rings of the bell had sounded, she injected and invigorated with all that she knew about the Swann family the dark and uncertain figure who emerged, followed by my grandmother, from a background of shadows, and whom we recognized by his voice. But even with respect to the most insignificant things in life, none of us constitutes a material whole, identical for everyone, which a person has only to go look up as though we were a book of specifications or a last testament; our social personality is a creation of the minds of others. Even the very simple act that we call "seeing a person we know" is in part an intellectual one. We fill the physical appearance of the individual we see with all the notions we have about him, and of the total picture that we form for ourselves, these notions certainly occupy the greater part. In the end they swell his cheeks so perfectly, follow the line of his nose in an adherence so exact, they do so well at nuancing the sonority of his voice as though the latter were only a transparent envelope that each time we see this face and hear this voice, it is these notions that we encounter again, that we hear. No doubt, in the Swann they had formed for themselves, my family had failed out of ignorance to include a host of details from his life in the fashionable world that caused other people, when they were in his presence, to see refinements rule his face and stop at his aquiline nose as though at their natural frontier; but they had also been able to garner in this face disaffected of its prestige, vacant and spacious, in the depths of these depreciated eyes, the vague, sweet residue—half memory, half forgetfulness—of the idle hours spent together after our weekly dinners, around the card table or in the garden, during our life of good country neighborliness. The corporeal envelope of our friend had been so well stuffed with all this, as well as with a few memories relating to his parents, that this particular Swann had become a complete and living being, and I have the impression of leaving one person to go to another distinct from him, when, in my memory, I pass from the Swann I knew later with accuracy to that first Swann—to that first Swann in whom I rediscover the charming mistakes of my youth and who in fact resembles less

---

4. A seasoned mayonnaise that includes chopped hard-boiled eggs.
5. The French royal family, headed by the comte de Paris. The political climate was anti-royalist, and all claimants to the French throne and their heirs were banished from France by law in 1886.

6. Fashionable London suburb. The French royal family had a house there, which was, for some time, the residence of the exiled comte de Paris.

the other Swann than he resembles the other people I knew at the time, as though one's life were like a museum in which all the portraits from one period have a family look about them, a single tonality—to that first Swann abounding in leisure, fragrant with the smell of the tall chestnut tree, the baskets of raspberries, and a sprig of tarragon.

Yet one day when my grandmother had gone to ask a favor from a lady she had known at the Sacré-Coeur[7] (and with whom, because of our notion of the castes, she had not wished to remain in close contact despite a reciprocal congeniality), this lady, the Marquise de Villeparisis of the famous de Bouillon family, had said to her: "I believe you know M. Swann very well; he is a great friend of my nephew and niece, the des Laumes."[8] My grandmother had returned from her visit full of enthusiasm for the house, which overlooked some gardens and in which Mme. de Villeparisis had advised her to rent a flat, and also for a waistcoat maker and his daughter, who kept a shop in the courtyard where she had gone to ask them to put a stitch in her skirt, which she had torn in the stairwell. My grandmother had found these people wonderful, she declared that the girl was a gem and the waistcoat maker was most distinguished, the finest man she had ever seen. Because for her, distinction was something absolutely independent of social position. She went into ecstasies over an answer the waistcoat maker had given her, saying to Mama: "Sévigné[9] couldn't have said it any better!" and, in contrast, of a nephew of Mme. de Villeparisis whom she had met at the house: "Oh, my dear daughter, how common he is!"

Now the remark about Swann had had the effect, not of raising him in my great-aunt's estimation, but of lowering Mme. de Villeparisis. It seemed that the respect which, on my grandmother's faith, we accorded Mme. de Villeparisis created a duty on her part to do nothing that would make her less worthy, a duty in which she had failed by learning of Swann's existence, by permitting relatives of hers to associate with him. "What! She knows Swann? A person you claim is a relation of the Maréchal de MacMahon?"[1] My family's opinion regarding Swann's associations seemed confirmed later by his marriage to a woman of the worst social station, practically a cocotte, whom, what was more, he never attempted to introduce, continuing to come to our house alone, though less and less, but from whom they believed they could judge—assuming it was there that he had found her—the social circle, unknown to them, that he habitually frequented.

But one time, my grandfather read in a newspaper that M. Swann was one of the most faithful guests at the Sunday lunches given by the Duc de X . . ., whose father and uncle had been the most prominent statesmen in the reign of Louis-Philippe.[2] Now, my grandfather was interested in all the little facts that

7. A convent school in Paris, attended by daughters of the aristocracy and the wealthy bourgeoisie.

8. A fictional family, like the Guermantes. Proust strengthens the apparent reality of the Guermantes family, including the marquise de Villeparis, by relating them to the historical house of Bouillon, a famous aristocratic family that could trace its descent from the Middle Ages.

9. The marquise de Sévigné (1626–1696), known for her lively style in letters that described contemporary events and the life of the aristocracy.

1. Marshal of France (1808–1893), elected president of the French Republic in 1873.

2. King of France from 1830 to 1848, father of the comte de Paris.

could help him enter imaginatively into the private lives of men like Molé, the Duc Pasquier, the Duc de Broglie.[3] He was delighted to learn that Swann associated with people who had known them. My great-aunt, however, interpreted this news in a sense unfavorable to Swann: anyone who chose his associations outside the caste into which he had been born, outside his social "class," suffered in her eyes a regrettable lowering of his social position. It seemed to her that he gave up forthwith the fruit of all the good relations with well-placed people so honorably preserved and stored away for their children by foresightful families (my great-aunt had even stopped seeing the son of a lawyer we knew because he had married royalty and was therefore in her opinion demoted from the respected rank of lawyer's son to that of one of those adventurers, former valets or stableboys, on whom they say that queens sometimes bestowed their favors). She disapproved of my grandfather's plan to question Swann, the next evening he was to come to dinner, about these friends of his we had discovered. At the same time my grandmother's two sisters, old maids who shared her nobility of character, but not her sort of mind, declared that they could not understand what pleasure their brother-in-law could find in talking about such foolishness. They were women of lofty aspirations, who for that very reason were incapable of taking an interest in what is known as tittle-tattle, even if it had some historic interest, and more generally in anything that was not directly connected to an aesthetic or moral subject. The disinterestedness of their minds was such, with respect to all that, closely or distantly, seemed connected with worldly matters, that their sense of hearing—having finally understood its temporary uselessness when the conversation at dinner assumed a tone that was frivolous or merely pedestrian without these two old spinsters being able to lead it back to the subjects dear to them—would suspend the functioning of its receptive organs and allow them to begin to atrophy. If my grandfather needed to attract the two sisters' attention at such times, he had to resort to those bodily signals used by alienists with certain lunatics suffering from distraction: striking a glass repeatedly with the blade of a knife while speaking to them sharply and looking them suddenly in the eye, violent methods which these psychiatrists often bring with them into their ordinary relations with healthy people, either from professional habit or because they believe everyone is a little crazy.

They were more interested when, the day before Swann was to come to dinner, and had personally sent them a case of Asti wine, my aunt, holding a copy of the *Figaro*[4] in which next to the title of a painting in an exhibition of Corot,[5] these words appeared: "From the collection of M. Charles Swann," said: "Did you see this? Swann is 'front page news' in the *Figaro*." "But I've always told you he had a great deal of taste," said my grandmother. "Of course you would! Anything so long as your opinion is not the same as *ours*," answered my great-

3. Achille-Charles-Léon-Victor, duc de Broglie (1785–1870) had a busy public career that ended in 1851. Louis-Mathieu, comte Molé (1781–1855) held various cabinet positions before becoming premier of France in 1836. Duc Etienne-Denis Pasquier (1767–1862) also held important public positions up to 1837. All three were active during the reign of Louis-Philippe.

4. A leading Parisian newspaper. "Asti": an Italian white wine.

5. Jean-Baptiste-Camille Corot (1796–1875), a popular French landscape painter.

aunt, who, knowing that my grandmother was never of the same opinion as she, and not being quite sure that she herself was the one we always declared was right, wanted to extract from us a general condemnation of my grandmother's convictions against which she was trying to force us into solidarity with her own. But we remained silent. When my grandmother's sisters expressed their intention of speaking to Swann about this mention in the *Figaro,* my great-aunt advised them against it. Whenever she saw in others an advantage, however small, that she did not have, she persuaded herself that it was not an advantage but a detriment and she pitied them so as not to have to envy them. "I believe you would not be pleasing him at all; I am quite sure I would find it very unpleasant to see my name printed boldly like that in the newspaper, and I would not be at all gratified if someone spoke to me about it." But she did not persist in trying to convince my grandmother's sisters; for they in their horror of vulgarity had made such a fine art of concealing a personal allusion beneath ingenious circumlocutions that it often went unnoticed even by the person to whom it was addressed. As for my mother, she thought only of trying to persuade my father to agree to talk to Swann not about his wife but about his daughter, whom he adored and because of whom it was said he had finally entered into this marriage. "You might just say a word to him; just ask how she is: It must be so hard for him." But my father would become annoyed: "No, no; you have the most absurd ideas. It would be ridiculous."

But the only one of us for whom Swann's arrival became the object of a painful preoccupation was I. This was because on the evenings when strangers, or merely M. Swann, were present, Mama did not come up to my room. I had dinner before everyone else and afterward I came and sat at the table, until eight o'clock when it was understood that I had to go upstairs; the precious and fragile kiss that Mama usually entrusted to me in my bed when I was going to sleep I would have to convey from the dining room to my bedroom and protect during the whole time I undressed, so that its sweetness would not shatter, so that its volatile essence would not disperse and evaporate, and on precisely those evenings when I needed to receive it with more care, I had to take it, I had to snatch it brusquely, publicly, without even having the time and the freedom of mind necessary to bring to what I was doing the attention of those individuals controlled by some mania, who do their utmost not to think of anything else while they are shutting a door, so as to be able, when the morbid uncertainty returns to them, to confront it victoriously with the memory of the moment when they did shut the door. We were all in the garden when the two hesitant rings of the little bell sounded. We knew it was Swann; even so we all looked at one another questioningly and my grandmother was sent on reconnaissance. "Remember to thank him intelligibly for the wine, you know how delicious it is and the case is enormous," my grandfather exhorted his two sisters-in-law. "Don't start whispering," said my great-aunt. "How comfortable would you feel arriving at a house where everyone is speaking so quietly!" "Ah! Here's M. Swann. Let's ask him if he thinks the weather will be good tomorrow," said my father. My mother thought that one word from her would wipe out all the pain that we in our family might have caused Swann since his marriage. She found an opportunity to take him aside. But I followed her; I could not bring myself to part from her by even one step while thinking that very soon I would have to leave her in the dining room and that I would have to go up to my room without having the consolation I had on the other evenings, that she would come kiss me. "Now, M. Swann," she said to him, "do tell me about your daughter; I'm sure she already has a taste for beautiful things like her papa." "Here, come and sit with the rest of us on the veranda," said my grandfather, coming up to them. My mother was obliged to stop, but she derived from this very constraint one more delicate thought, like good poets forced by the tyranny of rhyme to find their most beautiful lines: "We can talk about her again when we're by ourselves," she said softly to Swann. "Only a mother is capable of understanding you. I'm sure her own mother would agree with me." We all sat down around the iron table. I would have preferred not to think about the hours of anguish I was going to endure that evening alone in my room without being able to go to sleep; I tried to persuade myself they were not at all important, since I would have forgotten them by tomorrow morning, and to fix my mind on ideas of the future that should have led me as though across a bridge beyond the imminent abyss that frightened me so. But my mind, strained by my preoccupation, convex like the glance which I shot at my mother, would not allow itself to be penetrated by any foreign impressions. Thoughts certainly entered it, but only on condition that they left outside every element of beauty or simply of playfulness that could have moved or distracted me. Just as a patient, by means of an anesthetic, can watch with complete lucidity the operation being performed on him, but without feeling anything, I could recite to myself some lines that I loved or observe the efforts my grandfather made to talk to Swann about the Duc d'Audiffret-Pasquier,[6] without the former making me feel any emotion, the latter any hilarity. Those efforts were fruitless. Scarcely had my grandfather asked Swann a question relating to that orator than one of my grandmother's sisters, in whose ears the question was resonating like a profound but untimely silence that should be broken for the sake of politeness, would address the other: "Just imagine, Céline,[7] I've met a young Swedish governess who has been telling me about cooperatives in the Scandinavian countries; the details are most interesting. We really must have her here for dinner one evening." "Certainly!" answered her sister Flora, "but I haven't been wasting my time either. At M. Vinteuil's I met a learned old man who knows Maubant[8] very well, and Maubant has explained to him in the greatest detail how he creates his parts. It's most interesting. He's a neighbor of M. Vinteuil's, I had no idea; and he's very nice." "M. Vinteuil isn't the only one who has nice neighbors," exclaimed my aunt Céline in a voice amplified by her shyness and given an artificial tone by her premeditation, while casting at Swann what she called a meaningful look. At the same time my aunt Flora, who had understood that this phrase was Céline's way of thanking Swann for the Asti, was also looking at Swann with an expression that combined congratulation and irony, either simply to emphasize her sister's witticism, or because she envied Swann for having inspired it, or because she could not help making fun of him since she thought he was being put on the spot. "I think we can manage to persuade the old gentleman to come for dinner," continued

6. The duc d'Audiffret-Pasquier (1823–1905) was president of the Chamber of Peers during the reign of Louis-Philippe.
7. A misprint—as the context makes clear, it is Céline who speaks and Flora who responds.
8. Henri-Polydore Maubant (1823–1902), an actor at the Comédie Française. "Vinteuil": a fictitious composer.

Flora; "when you get him started on Maubant or Mme. Materna,[9] he talks for hours without stopping." "That must be delightful," sighed my grandfather, in whose mind, unfortunately, nature had as completely failed to include the possibility of taking a passionate interest in Swedish cooperatives or the creation of Maubant's parts as it had forgotten to furnish those of my grandmother's sisters with the little grain of salt one must add oneself, in order to find some savor in it, to a story about the private life of Molé or the Comte de Paris. "Now, then," said Swann to my grandfather, "what I'm going to say has more to do than it might appear with what you were asking me, because in certain respects things haven't changed enormously. This morning I was rereading something in Saint-Simon[1] that would have amused you. It's in the volume about his mission to Spain; it's not one of the best, hardly more than a journal, but at least it's a marvelously well written one, which already makes it rather fundamentally different from the deadly boring journals we think we have to read every morning and evening." "I don't agree, there are days when reading the papers seems to me very pleasant indeed . . ." my aunt Flora interrupted, to show that she had read the sentence about Swann's Corot in Le Figaro. "When they talk about things or people that interest us!" said my aunt Céline, going one better. "I don't deny it," answered Swann with surprise. "What I fault the newspapers for is that day after day they draw our attention to insignificant things whereas only three or four times in our lives do we read a book in which there is something really essential. Since we tear the band off the newspaper so feverishly every morning, they ought to change things and put into the newspaper, oh, I don't know, perhaps . . . Pascal's Pensées![2] (He isolated this word with an ironic emphasis so as not to seem pedantic.) "And then, in the gilt-edged volume that we open only once in ten years," he added, showing the disdain for worldly matters affected by certain worldly men, "we would read that the Queen of Greece has gone to Cannes or that the Princesse de Léon has given a costume ball. This way, the proper proportions would be reestablished." But, feeling sorry he had gone so far as to speak even lightly of serious things: "What a lofty conversation we're having," he said ironically; "I don't know why we're climbing to such 'heights' "—and turning to my grandfather: "Well, Saint-Simon describes how Maulévrier[3] had the audacity to offer to shake hands with Saint-Simon's sons. You know, this is the same Maulévrier of whom he says: 'Never did I see in that thick bottle anything but ill-humor, vulgarity, and foolishness.'" "Thick or not, I know some bottles in which there is something quite different," said Flora vivaciously, determined that she too should thank Swann, because the gift of Asti was addressed to both of them. Céline laughed. Swann, disconcerted, went on: "'I cannot say whether it was

9. Amalie Materna (1845–1918), Austrian soprano who took part in the premiere of Wagner's Ring cycle at Bayreuth in 1876.
1. The memoirs of the duc de Saint-Simon (1675–1755) describe court life and intrigue during the reigns of Louis XIV and Louis XV. He was sent to Spain in 1721 to arrange the marriage of Louis XV to the daughter of the king of Spain.
2. The Thoughts of the religious philosopher

Blaise Pascal (1623–1662) are comments on the human condition and one of the major works of French classicism.
3. Jean-Baptiste-Louis Andrault, marquis de Maulévrier-Langeron (1677–1754), the French ambassador to Spain. Saint-Simon considered him of inferior birth and would not let his own children shake Maulévrier's hand (Memoirs, vol. 39).

ignorance or a trap,' wrote Saint-Simon. 'He tried to shake hands with my children. I noticed it in time to prevent him.'" My grandfather was already in ecstasies over "ignorance or a trap," but Mlle. Céline, in whom the name of Saint-Simon—a literary man—had prevented the complete anesthesia of her auditory faculties, was already growing indignant: "What? You admire that? Well, that's a fine thing! But what can it mean; isn't one man as good as the next? What difference does it make whether he's a duke or a coachman, if he's intelligent and good-hearted? Your Saint-Simon had a fine way of raising his children, if he didn't teach them to offer their hands to all decent people. Why, it's quite abominable. And you dare to quote that?" And my grandfather, terribly upset and sensing how impossible it would be, in the face of this obstruction, to try to get Swann to tell the stories that would have amused him, said quietly to Mama: "Now remind me of the line you taught me that comforts me so much at times like this. Oh, yes! 'What virtues, Lord, Thou makest us abhor!'[4] Oh, how good that is!"

I did not take my eyes off my mother, I knew that when we were at the table, they would not let me stay during the entire dinner and that, in order not to annoy my father, Mama would not let me kiss her several times in front of the guests as though we were in my room. And so I promised myself that in the dining room, as they were beginning dinner and I felt the hour approaching, I would do everything I could do alone in advance of this kiss which would be so brief and furtive, choose with my eyes the place on her cheek that I would kiss, prepare my thoughts so as to be able, by means of this mental beginning of the kiss, to devote the whole of the minute Mama would grant me to feeling her cheek against my lips, as a painter who can obtain only short sittings prepares his palette and, guided by his notes, does in advance from memory everything for which he could if necessary manage without the presence of the model. But now before the dinner bell rang my grandfather had the unwitting brutality to say: "The boy looks tired, he ought to go up to bed. We're dining late tonight anyway." And my father, who was not as scrupulous as my grandmother and my mother about honoring treaties, said: "Yes, go on now, up to bed with you." I tried to kiss Mama, at that moment we heard the dinner bell. "No, really, leave your mother alone, you've already said goodnight to each other as it is, these demonstrations are ridiculous. Go on now, upstairs!" And I had to leave without my viaticum;[5] I had to climb each step of the staircase, as the popular expression has it, "against my heart,"[6] climbing against my heart which wanted to go back to my mother because she had not, by kissing me, given it license to go with me. That detested staircase which I always entered with such gloom exhaled an odor of varnish that had in some sense absorbed, fixated, the particular sort of sorrow I felt every evening and made it perhaps even crueler to my sensibility because, when it took that olfactory form, my intelligence could no longer share in it. When we are asleep and a raging toothache is as yet perceived by us only in the form of a girl whom we attempt two hundred times to pull out of the water or a line by Molière[7] that we

4. Adaptation of a line from *Pompey's Death* (III.4), a tragedy by the French classical dramatist Pierre Corneille (1606–1684).
5. The communion wafer and wine given to the dying in Catholic rites.

6. The literal translation of a common phrase meaning "reluctantly" (French).
7. Jean-Baptiste Poquelin Molière (1622–1673), French classical dramatist.

repeat to ourselves incessantly, it is a great relief to wake up so that our intelligence can divest the idea of raging toothache of its disguise of heroism or cadence. It was the opposite of this relief that I experienced when my sorrow at going up to my room entered me in a manner infinitely swifter, almost instantaneous, at once insidious and abrupt, through the inhalation—far more toxic than the intellectual penetration—of the smell of varnish peculiar to that staircase. Once in my room, I had to stop up all the exits, close the shutters, dig my own grave by undoing my covers, put on the shroud of my nightshirt. But before burying myself in the iron bed which they had added to the room because I was too hot in the summer under the rep curtains of the big bed, I had a fit of rebelliousness, I wanted to attempt the ruse of a condemned man. I wrote to my mother begging her to come upstairs for something serious that I could not tell her in my letter. My fear was that Françoise, my aunt's cook who was charged with looking after me when I was at Combray, would refuse to convey my note. I suspected that, for her, delivering a message to my mother when there was company would seem as impossible as for a porter to hand a letter to an actor while he was onstage. With respect to things that could or could not be done she possessed a code at once imperious, extensive, subtle, and intransigent about distinctions that were impalpable or otiose (which made it resemble those ancient laws which, alongside such fierce prescriptions as the massacre of children at the breast, forbid one with an exaggerated delicacy to boil a kid in its mother's milk, or to eat the sinew from an animal's thigh).[8] This code, to judge from her sudden obstinacy when she did not wish to do certain errands that we gave her, seemed to have anticipated social complexities and worldly refinements that nothing in Françoise's associations or her life as a village domestic could have suggested to her; and we had to say to ourselves that in her there was a very old French past, noble and ill understood, as in those manufacturing towns where elegant old houses testify that there was once a court life, and where the employees of a factory for chemical products work surrounded by delicate sculptures representing the miracle of Saint Théophile or the four sons of Aymon.[9] In this particular case, the article of the code which made it unlikely that except in case of fire Françoise would go bother Mama in the presence of M. Swann for so small a personage as myself simply betokened the respect she professed not only for the family—as for the dead, for priests, and for kings—but also for the visitor to whom one was offering one's hospitality, a respect that would perhaps have touched me in a book but that always irritated me on her lips, because of the solemn and tender tones she adopted in speaking of it, and especially so this evening when the sacred character she conferred on the dinner might have the effect of making her refuse to disturb its ceremonial. But to give myself a better chance, I did not hesitate to lie and tell her that it was not in the least I who had wanted to write to Mama, but that it was Mama who, as she said goodnight to me, had exhorted me not to forget to send her an answer concerning something she had asked me to look for; and she would certainly be very annoyed if this note was not delivered to her. I think Françoise did not believe me, for, like those

8. References to the strict dietary laws of Deuteronomy 14.21 and Genesis 31.32, respectively.
9. The four sons of Aymon, heroic knights who together rode the magic horse Bayard. "Théophile": a cleric who was saved from damnation by the Virgin Mary after he repented for having signed a pact with the devil.

primitive men whose senses were so much more powerful than ours, she could immediately discern, from signs imperceptible to us, any truth that we wanted to hide from her; she looked at the envelope for five minutes as if the examination of the paper and the appearance of the writing would inform her about the nature of the contents or tell her which article of her code she ought to apply. Then she went out with an air of resignation that seemed to signify: "If it isn't a misfortune for parents to have a child like that!" She came back after a moment to tell me that they were still only at the ice stage, that it was impossible for the butler to deliver the letter right away in front of everyone, but that, when the mouth-rinsing bowls[1] were put round, they would find a way to hand it to Mama. Instantly my anxiety subsided; it was now no longer, as it had been only a moment ago, until tomorrow that I had left my mother, since my little note, no doubt annoying her (and doubly because this stratagem would make me ridiculous in Swann's eyes), would at least allow me, invisible and enraptured, to enter the same room as she, would whisper about me in her ear; since that forbidden, hostile dining room, where, just a moment before, the ice itself—the "granité"[2]—and the rinsing bowls seemed to me to contain pleasures noxious and mortally sad because Mama was enjoying them far away from me, was opening itself to me and, like a fruit that has turned sweet and bursts its skin, was about to propel, to project, all the way to my intoxicated heart, Mama's attention as she read my lines. Now I was no longer separated from her; the barriers were down, an exquisite thread joined us. And that was not all: Mama would probably come!

I thought Swann would surely have laughed at the anguish I had just suffered if he had read my letter and guessed its purpose; yet, on the contrary, as I learned later, a similar anguish[3] was the torment of long years of his life and no one, perhaps, could have understood me as well as he; in his case, the anguish that comes from feeling that the person you love is in a place of amusement where you are not, where you cannot join her, came to him through love, to which it is in some sense predestined, by which it will be hoarded, appropriated; but when, as in my case, this anguish enters us before love has made its appearance in our life, it drifts as it waits for it, vague and free, without a particular assignment, at the service of one feeling one day, of another the next, sometimes of filial tenderness or affection for a friend. And the joy with which I served my first apprenticeship when Françoise came back to tell me my letter would be delivered Swann too had known well, that deceptive joy given to us by some friend, some relative of the woman we love when, arriving at the house or theater where she is, for some dance, gala evening, or premiere at which he is going to see her, this friend notices us wandering outside, desperately awaiting some opportunity to communicate with her. He recognizes us, speaks to us familiarly, asks us what we are doing there. And when we invent the story that we have something urgent to say to his relative or friend, he assures us that nothing could be simpler, leads us into the hall, and promises to send her to us in five minutes. How we love him, as at that moment I loved Françoise—the well-intentioned intermediary who with a single word has just made tolerable, human, and almost propitious the unimaginable, infernal festivity into the thick

---

1. Bowls with warm water for rinsing were passed around at the end of the meal.
2. A sherbetlike ice served as a separate course or after dinner.
3. I.e., his unhappy love for Odette de Crécy, described later in *Swann in Love*.

of which we had been imagining that hostile, perverse, and exquisite vortices of pleasure were carrying away from us and inspiring with derisive laughter the woman we love! If we are to judge by him, the relative who has come up to us and is himself also one of the initiates in the cruel mysteries, the other guests at the party cannot have anything very demoniacal about them. Those inaccessible and excruciating hours during which she was about to enjoy unknown pleasures—now, through an unexpected breach, we are entering them; now, one of the moments which, in succession, would have composed those hours, a moment as real as the others, perhaps even more important to us, because our mistress is more involved in it, we can picture to ourselves, we possess it, we are taking part in it, we have created it, almost: the moment in which he will tell her we are here, downstairs. And no doubt the other moments of the party would not have been essentially very different from this one, would not have had anything more delectable about them that should make us suffer so, since the kind friend has said to us: "Why, she'll be delighted to come down! It'll be much nicer for her to chat with you than to be bored up there." Alas! Swann had learned by experience that the good intentions of a third person have no power over a woman who is annoyed to find herself pursued even into a party by someone she does not love. Often, the friend comes back down alone.

My mother did not come, and with no consideration for my pride (which was invested in her not denying the story that she was supposed to have asked me to let her know the results of some search) asked Françoise to say these words to me: "There is no answer," words I have so often since then heard the doormen in grand hotels or the footmen in bawdy houses bring back to some poor girl who exclaims in surprise: "What, he said nothing? Why, that's impossible! Did you really give him my note? All right, I'll go on waiting." And—just as she invariably assures him she does not need the extra gas jet which the doorman wants to light for her, and remains there, hearing nothing further but the few remarks about the weather exchanged by the doorman and a lackey whom he sends off suddenly, when he notices the time, to put a customer's drink on ice—having declined Françoise's offer to make me some tea or to stay with me, I let her return to the servant's hall, I went to bed and closed my eyes, trying not to hear the voices of my family, who were having their coffee in the garden. But after a few seconds, I became aware that, by writing that note to Mama, by approaching, at the risk of angering her, so close to her that I thought I could touch the moment when I would see her again, I had shut off from myself the possibility of falling asleep without seeing her again, and the beating of my heart grew more painful each minute because I was increasing my agitation by telling myself to be calm, to accept my misfortune. Suddenly my anxiety subsided, a happiness invaded me as when a powerful medicine begins to take effect and our pain vanishes: I had just formed the resolution not to continue trying to fall asleep without seeing Mama again, to kiss her at all costs even though it was with the certainty of being on bad terms with her for a long time after, when she came up to bed. The calm that came with the end of my distress filled me with an extraordinary joy, quite as much as did my expectation, my thirst for and my fear of danger. I opened the window noiselessly and sat down on the foot of my bed; I hardly moved so that I would not be heard from below. Outdoors, too, things seemed frozen in silent attention so as not to disturb the moonlight which, duplicating and distancing each thing by extending its shadow before it, denser and more concrete than itself, had at once thinned and enlarged the landscape like a map that had been folded and was now opened out. What needed to move, some foliage of the chestnut tree, moved. But its quivering, minute, complete, executed even in its slightest nuances and ultimate refinements, did not spill over onto the rest, did not merge with it, remained circumscribed. Exposed against this silence, which absorbed nothing of them, the most distant noises, those that must have come from gardens that lay at the other end of town, could be perceived detailed with such "finish" that they seemed to owe this effect of remoteness only to their pianissimo, like those muted motifs so well executed by the orchestra of the Conservatoire[4] that, although you do not lose a single note, you nonetheless think you are hearing them far away from the concert hall and all the old subscribers—my grandmother's sisters too, when Swann had given them his seats—strained their ears as if they were listening to the distant advances of an army on the march that had not yet turned the corner of the rue de Trévise.[5]

I knew that the situation I was now placing myself in was the one that could provoke the gravest consequences of all for me, coming from my parents, much graver in truth than a stranger would have supposed, the sort he would have believed could be produced only by truly shameful misdeeds. But in my upbringing, the order of misdeeds was not the same as in that of other children, and I had become accustomed to placing before all the rest (because there were probably no others from which I needed to be more carefully protected) those whose common characteristic I now understand was that you lapse into them by yielding to a nervous impulse. But at the time no one uttered these words, no one revealed this cause, which might have made me believe I was excusable for succumbing to them or even perhaps incapable of resisting them. But I recognized them clearly from the anguish that preceded them as well as from the rigor of the punishment that followed them; and I knew that the one I had just committed was in the same family as others for which I had been severely punished, though infinitely graver. When I went and placed myself in my mother's path at the moment she was going up to bed, and when she saw that I had stayed up to say goodnight to her again in the hallway, they would not let me continue to live at home, they would send me away to school the next day, that much was certain. Well! Even if I had had to throw myself out of the window five minutes later, I still preferred this. What I wanted now was Mama, to say goodnight to her, I had gone too far along the road that led to the fulfillment of that desire to be able to turn back now.

I heard the footsteps of my family, who were seeing Swann out; and when the bell on the gate told me he had left, I went to the window. Mama was asking my father if he had thought the lobster was good and if M. Swann had had more coffee-and-pistachio ice. "I found it quite ordinary," said my mother; "I think next time we'll have to try another flavor." "I can't tell you how changed I find Swann," said my great-aunt, "he has aged so!" My great-aunt was so used to seeing Swann always as the same adolescent that she was surprised to find him suddenly not as young as the age she continued to attribute to him. And my family was also beginning to feel that in him this aging was abnormal, exces-

4. The national music conservatory (academy) in Paris.
5. A street in Combray.

sive, shameful, and more deserved by the unmarried, by all those for whom it seems that the great day that has no tomorrow is longer than for others, because for them it is empty and the moments in it add up from morning on without then being divided among children. "I think he has no end of worries with that wretched wife of his who is living with a certain Monsieur de Charlus,[6] as all of Combray knows. It's the talk of the town." My mother pointed out that in spite of this he had been looking much less sad for some time now. "He also doesn't make that gesture of his as often, so like his father, of wiping his eyes and running his hand across his forehead. I myself think that in his heart of hearts he no longer loves that woman." "Why, naturally he doesn't love her anymore," answered my grandfather. "I received a letter from him about it a long time ago, by now, a letter with which I hastened not to comply and which leaves no doubt about his feelings, at least his feelings of love, for his wife. Well now! You see, you didn't thank him for the Asti," added my grandfather, turning to his two sisters-in-law. "What? We didn't thank him? I think, just between you and me, that I put it quite delicately," answered my aunt Flora. "Yes, you managed it very well: quite admirable," said my aunt Céline. "But you were very good too." "Yes, I was rather proud of my remark about kind neighbors." "What? Is that what you call thanking him?" exclaimed my grandfather. "I certainly heard that, but devil take me if I thought it was directed at Swann. You can be sure he never noticed." "But see here, Swann isn't stupid, I'm sure he appreciated it. After all, I couldn't tell him how many bottles there were and what the wine cost!" My father and mother were left alone there, and sat down for a moment; then my father said: "Well, shall we go up to bed?" "If you like, my dear, even though I'm not the least bit sleepy; yet it couldn't be that perfectly harmless coffee ice that's keeping me so wide-awake; but I can see a light in the servants' hall, and since poor Françoise has waited up for me, I'll go and ask her to unhook my bodice while you're getting undressed." And my mother opened the latticed door that led from the vestibule to the staircase. Soon, I heard her coming upstairs to close her window. I went without a sound into the hallway; my heart was beating so hard I had trouble walking, but at least it was no longer pounding from anxiety, but from terror and joy. I saw the light cast in the stairwell by Mama's candle. Then I saw Mama herself; I threw myself forward. In the first second, she looked at me with astonishment, not understanding what could have happened. Then an expression of anger came over her face, she did not say a single word to me, and indeed for much less than this they would go several days without speaking to me. If Mama had said one word to me, it would have been an admission that they could talk to me again and in any case it would perhaps have seemed to me even more terrible, as a sign that, given the gravity of the punishment that was going to be prepared for me, silence, and estrangement, would have been childish. A word would have been like the calm with which you answer a servant when you have just decided to dismiss him; the kiss you give a son you are sending off to enlist, whereas you would have refused it if you were simply going to be annoyed with him for a few days. But she heard my father coming up from the dressing room where he had gone to undress and, to avoid the scene he would make over me, she said to me in a

6. The brother of the duc de Guermantes.

voice choked with anger: "Run, run, so at least your father won't see you waiting like this as if you were out of your mind!" But I repeated to her: "Come say goodnight to me," terrified as I saw the gleam from my father's candle already rising up the wall, but also using his approach as a means of blackmail and hoping that Mama, to avoid my father's finding me there still if she continued to refuse, would say: "Go back to your room, I'll come." It was too late, my father was there in front of us. Involuntarily, though no one heard, I murmured these words: "I'm done for!"

It was not so. My father was constantly refusing me permission for things that had been authorized in the more generous covenants granted by my mother and grandmother because he did not bother about "principles" and for him there was no "rule of law."[7] For a completely contingent reason, or even for no reason at all, he would at the last minute deny me a certain walk that was so customary, so consecrated that to deprive me of it was a violation, or, as he had done once again this evening, long before the ritual hour he would say to me: "Go on now, up to bed, no arguments!" But also, because he had no principles (in my grandmother's sense), he was not strictly speaking intransigent. He looked at me for a moment with an expression of surprise and annoyance, then as soon as Mama had explained to him with a few embarrassed words what had happened, he said to her: "Go along with him, then. You were just saying you didn't feel very sleepy, stay in his room for a little while, I don't need anything." "But my dear," answered my mother timidly, "whether I'm sleepy or not doesn't change anything, we can't let the child get into the habit . . ." "But it isn't a question of habit," said my father, shrugging his shoulders, "you can see the boy is upset, he seems very sad; look, we're not executioners! You'll end by making him ill, and that won't do us much good! There are two beds in his room; go tell Françoise to prepare the big one for you and sleep there with him tonight. Now then, goodnight, I'm not as high-strung as the two of you, I'm going to bed."

It was impossible to thank my father; he would have been irritated by what he called mawkishness. I stood there not daring to move; he was still there in front of us, tall in his white nightshirt, under the pink and violet Indian cashmere shawl that he tied around his head now that he had attacks of neuralgia, with the gesture of Abraham in the engraving after Benozzo Gozzoli[8] that M. Swann had given me, as he told Sarah she must leave Issac's side. This was many years ago. The staircase wall on which I saw the rising glimmer of his candle has long since ceased to exist. In me, too, many things have been destroyed that I thought were bound to last forever and new ones have formed that have given birth to new sorrows and joys which I could not have foreseen then, just as the old ones have become difficult for me to understand. It was a very long time ago, too, that my father ceased to be able to say to Mama: "Go with the boy." The possibility of such hours will never be reborn for me. But for a little while now, I have begun to hear again very clearly, if I take care to listen, the sobs that I was strong enough to contain in front of my father and that broke out only when I found myself alone again with Mama. They have never

7. Natural law, supposed to govern international and public relations. Marcel sees his relationship with his mother and grandmother as a social contract; his father, who does not respect the rules, becomes the unpredictable tyrant.
8. Florentine painter (1420–1497) whose frescoes at Pisa contain scenes from the life of the biblical patriarch Abraham.

really stopped; and it is only because life is now becoming quieter around me that I can hear them again, like those convent bells covered so well by the clamor of the town during the day that one would think they had ceased altogether but which begin sounding again in the silence of the evening.

Mama spent that night in my room; when I had just committed such a misdeed that I expected to have to leave the house, my parents granted me more than I could ever have won from them as a reward for any good deed. Even at the moment when it manifested itself through this pardon, my father's conduct toward me retained that arbitrary and undeserved quality that characterized it and was due to the fact that it generally resulted from fortuitous convenience rather than a premeditated plan. It may even be that what I called his severity, when he sent me to bed, deserved that name less than my mother's or my grandmother's, for his nature, in certain respects more different from mine than theirs was, had probably kept him from discovering until now how very unhappy I was every evening, something my mother and my grandmother knew well; but they loved me enough not to consent to spare me my suffering, they wanted to teach me to master it in order to reduce my nervous sensitivity and strengthen my will. As for my father, whose affection for me was of another sort, I do not know if he would have been courageous enough for that: the one time he realized that I was upset, he had said to my mother: "Go and comfort him." Mama stayed in my room that night and, as though not to allow any remorse to spoil those hours which were so different from what I had had any right to expect, when Françoise, realizing that something extraordinary was happening when she saw Mama sitting next to me, holding my hand and letting me cry without scolding me, asked her: "Why, madame, now what's wrong with Monsieur that he's crying so?" Mama answered her: "Why, even he doesn't know, Françoise, he's in a state; prepare the big bed for me quickly and then go on up to bed yourself." And so, for the first time, my sadness was regarded no longer as a punishable offense but as an involuntary ailment that had just been officially recognized, a nervous condition for which I was not responsible; I had the relief of no longer having to mingle qualms of conscience with the bitterness of my tears, I could cry without sin. I was also not a little proud, with respect to Françoise, of this turnabout in human affairs which, an hour after Mama had refused to come up to my room and had sent the disdainful answer that I should go to sleep, raised me to the dignity of a grown-up and brought me suddenly to a sort of puberty of grief, of emancipation from tears. I ought to have been happy: I was not. It seemed to me that my mother had just made me a first concession which must have been painful to her, that this was a first abdication on her part from the ideal she had conceived for me, and that for the first time she, who was so courageous, had to confess herself beaten. It seemed to me that, if I had just gained a victory, it was over her, that I had succeeded, as illness, affliction, or age might have done, in relaxing her will, in weakening her judgment, and that this evening was the beginning of a new era, would remain as a sad date. If I had dared, now, I would have said to Mama: "No, I don't want you to do this, don't sleep here." But I was aware of the practical wisdom, the realism as it would be called now, which in her tempered my grandmother's ardently idealistic nature, and I knew that, now that the harm was done, she would prefer to let me at least enjoy the soothing pleasure of it and not disturb my father. To be sure, my mother's lovely face still shone with youth that evening when she so gently held my hands and tried to stop my tears; but it seemed to me that this was precisely what should not have been, her anger would have saddened me less than this new gentleness which my childhood had not known before; it seemed to me that with an impious and secret hand I had just traced in her soul a first wrinkle and caused a first white hair to appear. At the thought of this my sobs redoubled, and then I saw that Mama, who never let herself give way to any emotion with me, was suddenly overcome by my own and was trying to suppress a desire to cry. When she saw that I had noticed, she said to me with a smile: "There now, my little chick, my little canary, he's going to make his mama as silly as himself if this continues. Look, since you're not sleepy and your mama isn't either, let's not go on upsetting each other, let's do something, let's get one of your books." But I had none there. "Would you enjoy it less if I took out the books your grandmother will be giving you on your saint's day? Think about it carefully: you mustn't be disappointed not to have anything the day after tomorrow." On the contrary, I was delighted, and Mama went to get a packet of books, of which I could not distinguish, through the paper in which they were wrapped, more than their shape, short and thick, but which, in this first guise, though summary and veiled, already eclipsed the box of colors from New Year's Day and the silkworms from last year. They were *La Mare au Diable, François le Champi, La Petite Fadette,* and *Les Maîtres Sonneurs.*[9] My grandmother, as I learned afterward, had first chosen the poems of Musset, a volume of Rousseau, and *Indiana*;[1] for though she judged frivolous reading to be as unhealthy as sweets and pastries, it did not occur to her that a great breath of genius might have a more dangerous and less invigorating influence on the mind even of a child than would the open air and the sea breeze on his body. But as my father had nearly called her mad when he learned which books she wanted to give me, she had returned to the bookstore, in Jouy-le-Vicomte herself, so that I would not risk not having my present (it was a burning-hot day and she had come home so indisposed that the doctor had warned my mother not to let her tire herself out that way again) and she had resorted to the four pastoral novels of George Sand. "My dear daughter," she said to Mama, "I could not bring myself to give the boy something badly written."

In fact, she could never resign herself to buying anything from which one could not derive an intellectual profit, and especially that which beautiful things afford us by teaching us to seek our pleasure elsewhere than in the satisfactions of material comfort and vanity. Even when she had to make someone a present of the kind called "useful," when she had to give an armchair, silverware, a walking stick, she looked for "old" ones, as though, now that long desuetude had effaced their character of usefulness, they would appear more disposed to tell us about the life of people of other times than to serve the needs of our own life. She would have liked me to have in my room photographs of the most

---

9. *The Devil's Pool, François the Foundling Discovered in the Fields, Little Fadette,* and *The Master Bellringers,* all novels of idealized country life by the French woman writer George Sand (1806–1876).
1. The works of Alfred de Musset (1810–1857)

and Jean-Jacques Rousseau (1712–1778), often romantic and sometimes confessional, and George Sand's *Indiana* (1832), a novel of free love, would be thought unsuitable reading for a young child.

beautiful monuments or landscapes. But at the moment of buying them, and even though the thing represented had an aesthetic value, she would find that vulgarity and utility too quickly resumed their places in that mechanical mode of representation, the photograph. She would try to use cunning and, if not to eliminate commercial banality entirely, at least to reduce it, to substitute for the greater part of it more art, to introduce into it in a sense several "layers" of art: instead of photographs of Chartres Cathedral, the Fountains of Saint-Cloud, or Mount Vesuvius, she would make inquiries of Swann as to whether some great painter had not depicted them, and preferred to give me photographs of Chartres Cathedral by Corot, of the Fountains of Saint-Cloud by Hubert Robert, of Mount Vesuvius by Turner,[2] which made one further degree of art. But if the photographer had been removed from the representation of the masterpiece or of nature and replaced by a great artist, he still reclaimed his rights to reproduce that very interpretation. Having deferred vulgarity as far as possible, my grandmother would try to move it back still further. She would ask Swann if the work had not been engraved, preferring, whenever possible, old engravings that also had an interest beyond themselves, such as those that represent a masterpiece in a state in which we can no longer see it today (like the engraving by Morghen of Leonardo's *Last Supper* before its deterioration).[3] It must be said that the results of this interpretation of the art of gift giving were not always brilliant. The idea I formed of Venice from a drawing by Titian[4] that is supposed to have the lagoon in the background was certainly far less accurate than the one I would have derived from simple photographs. We could no longer keep count, at home, when my great-aunt wanted to draw up an indictment against my grandmother, of the armchairs she had presented to young couples engaged to be married or old married couples which, at the first attempt to make use of them, had immediately collapsed under the weight of one of the recipients. But my grandmother would have believed it petty to be overly concerned about the solidity of a piece of wood in which one could still distinguish a small flower, a smile, sometimes a lovely invention from the past. Even what might, in these pieces of furniture, answer a need, since it did so in a manner to which we are no longer accustomed, charmed her like the old ways of speaking in which we see a metaphor that is obliterated, in our modern language, by the abrasion of habit. Now, in fact, the pastoral novels of George Sand that she was giving me for my saint's day were, like an old piece of furniture, full of expressions that had fallen into disuse and turned figurative again, the sort you no longer find anywhere but in the country. And my grandmother had bought them in preference to others just as she would sooner have rented an estate on which there was a Gothic dovecote or another of those old things that exercise such a happy influence on the mind by filling it with longing for impossible voyages through time.

2. All photographs of paintings: the cathedral at Chartres, painted in 1830 by Corot; the fountains in the old park at Saint-Cloud, outside Paris, painted by Hubert Robert (1733–1809); and Vesuvius, a famous volcano near Naples, painted by J. M. W. Turner (1775–1851).
3. Leonardo da Vinci's *Last Supper* was the subject of a famous engraving by Raphael Morghen (1758–1833). The paints in the original fresco had deteriorated rapidly, and a major restoration took place only in the 19th century.
4. Tiziano Vecellio (1488?–1576), Renaissance painter of the Venetian school.

Mama sat down by my bed; she had picked up *François le Champi*, whose reddish cover and incomprehensible title[5] gave it, in my eyes, a distinct personality and a mysterious attraction. I had not yet read a real novel. I had heard people say that George Sand was an exemplary novelist. This already predisposed me to imagine something indefinable and delicious in *François le Champi*. Narrative devices intended to arouse curiosity or emotion, certain modes of expression that make one uneasy or melancholy, and that a reader with some education will recognize as common to many novels, appeared to me—who considered a new book not as a thing having many counterparts, but as a unique person, having no reason for existing but in itself—simply as a disturbing emanation of *François le Champi*'s peculiar essence. Behind those events so ordinary, those things so common, those words so current, I sensed a strange sort of intonation, accentuation. The action began; it seemed to me all the more obscure because in those days, when I read, I often daydreamed, for entire pages, of something quite different. And in addition to the lacunae that this distraction left in the story, there was the fact, when Mama was the one reading aloud to me, that she skipped all the love scenes. Thus, all the bizarre changes that take place in the respective attitudes of the miller's wife and the child and that can be explained only by the progress of a nascent love seemed to me marked by a profound mystery whose source I readily imagined must be in that strange and sweet name "Champi," which gave the child, who bore it without my knowing why, its vivid, charming purplish color. If my mother was an unfaithful reader she was also, in the case of books in which she found the inflection of true feeling, a wonderful reader for the respect and simplicity of her interpretation, the beauty and gentleness of the sound of her voice. Even in real life, when it was people and not works of art which moved her to compassion or admiration, it was touching to see with what deference she removed from her voice, from her motions, from her words, any spark of gaiety that might hurt some mother who had once lost a child, any recollection of a saint's day or birthday that might remind some old man of his advanced age, any remark about housekeeping that might seem tedious to some young scholar. In the same way, when she was reading George Sand's prose, which always breathes that goodness, that moral distinction which Mama had learned from my grandmother to consider superior to all else in life, and which I was to teach her only much later not to consider superior to all else in books too, taking care to banish from her voice any pettiness, any affectation which might have prevented it from receiving that powerful torrent, she imparted all the natural tenderness, all the ample sweetness they demanded to those sentences which seemed written for her voice and which remained, so to speak, entirely within the register of her sensibility. She found, to attack them in the necessary tone, the warm inflection that preexists them and that dictated them, but that the words do not indicate; with this inflection she softened as she went along any crudeness in the tenses of the verbs, gave the imperfect and the past historic the sweetness that lies in goodness, the melancholy that lies in tenderness, directed the sentence that was ending toward the one that was about to begin, sometimes hurrying, sometimes slowing down the pace of the syllables so as to bring them, though their quantities were different, into one uniform rhythm, she breathed into this very common prose a sort of continuous emotional life.

---

5. *Champi* ("foundling") is an old French word that the child Marcel would not have known.

My remorse was quieted, I gave in to the sweetness of that night in which I had my mother close to me. I knew that such a night could not be repeated; that the greatest desire I had in the world, to keep my mother in my room during those sad hours of darkness, was too contrary to the necessities of life and the wishes of others for its fulfillment, granted this night, to be anything other than artificial and exceptional. Tomorrow my anxieties would reawaken and Mama would not stay here. But when my anxieties were soothed, I no longer understood them; and then tomorrow night was still far away; I told myself I would have time to think of what to do, even though that time could not bring me any access of power, since these things did not depend on my will and seemed more avoidable to me only because of the interval that still separated them from me.

So it was that, for a long time, when, awakened at night, I remembered Combray again, I saw nothing of it but this sort of luminous panel, cut out among indistinct shadows, like those panels which the glow of a Bengal light[6] or some electric projection will cut out and illuminate in a building whose other parts remain plunged in darkness: at the rather broad base, the small parlor, the dining room, the opening of the dark path by which M. Swann, the unconscious author of my sufferings, would arrive, the front hall where I would head toward the first step of the staircase, so painful to climb, that formed, by itself, the very narrow trunk of this irregular pyramid; and, at the top, my bedroom with the little hallway and its glass-paned door for Mama's entrance; in a word, always seen at the same hour, isolated from everything that might surround it, standing out alone against the darkness, the bare minimum of scenery (such as one sees prescribed at the beginnings of the old plays for performances in the provinces) needed for the drama of my undressing; as though Combray had consisted only of two floors connected by a slender staircase and as though it had always been seven o'clock in the evening there. The fact is, I could have answered anyone who asked me that Combray also included other things and existed at other times of day. But since what I recalled would have been supplied to me only by my voluntary memory, the memory of the intelligence, and since the information it gives about the past preserves nothing of the past itself, I would never have had any desire to think about the rest of Combray. It was all really quite dead for me.

Dead forever? Possibly.

There is a great deal of chance in all this, and a second sort of chance event, that of our own death, often does not allow us to wait long for the favors of the first.

I find the Celtic belief very reasonable, that the souls of those we have lost are held captive in some inferior creature, in an animal, in a plant, in some inanimate object, effectively lost to us until the day, which for many never comes, when we happen to pass close to the tree, come into possession of the object that is their prison.[7] Then they quiver, they call out to us, and as soon as we have recognized them, the spell is broken. Delivered by us, they have overcome death and they return to live with us.

6. A steady, blue-colored firework often used   7. A belief attributed to Druids, the priests of
for signals.   the ancient Celtic peoples.

It is the same with our past. It is a waste of effort for us to try to summon it, all the exertions of our intelligence are useless. The past is hidden outside the realm of our intelligence and beyond its reach, in some material object (in the sensation that this material object would give us) which we do not suspect. It depends on chance whether we encounter this object before we die, or do not encounter it.

For many years, already, everything about Combray that was not the theater and drama of my bedtime had ceased to exist for me, when one day in winter, as I returned home, my mother, seeing that I was cold, suggested that, contrary to my habit, I have a little tea. I refused at first and then, I do not know why, changed my mind. She sent for one of those squat, plump cakes called *petites madeleines* that look as though they have been molded in the grooved valve of a scallop shell. And soon, mechanically, oppressed by the gloomy day and the prospect of another sad day to follow, I carried to my lips a spoonful of the tea in which I had let soften a bit of madeleine. But at the very instant when the mouthful of tea mixed with cake crumbs touched my palate, I quivered, attentive to the extraordinary thing that was happening inside me. A delicious pleasure had invaded me, isolated me, without my having any notion as to its cause. It had immediately rendered the vicissitudes of life unimportant to me, its disasters innocuous, its brevity illusory, acting in the same way that love acts, by filling me with a precious essence: or rather this essence was not merely inside me, it was me. I had ceased to feel mediocre, contingent, mortal. Where could it have come to me from—this powerful joy? I sensed that it was connected to the taste of the tea and the cake, but that it went infinitely far beyond it, could not be of the same nature. Where did it come from? What did it mean? How could I grasp it? I drink a second mouthful, in which I find nothing more than in the first, a third that gives me a little less than the second. It is time for me to stop, the virtue of the drink seems to be diminishing. Clearly, the truth I am seeking is not in the drink, but in me. The drink has awoken it in me, but does not know this truth, and can do no more than repeat indefinitely, with less and less force, this same testimony which I do not know how to interpret and which I want at least to be able to ask of it again and find again, intact, available to me, soon, for a decisive clarification. I put down the cup and turn to my mind. It is up to my mind to find the truth. But how? Such grave uncertainty, whenever the mind feels overtaken by itself; when it, the seeker, is also the obscure country where it must seek and where all its baggage will be nothing to it. Seek? Not only that: create. It is face-to-face with something that does not yet exist and that only it can accomplish, then bring into its light.

And I begin asking myself again what it could be, this unknown state which brought with it no logical proof, but only the evidence of its felicity, its reality, and in whose presence the other states of consciousness faded away. I want to try to make it reappear. I return in my thoughts to the moment when I took the first spoonful of tea. I find the same state again, without any new clarity. I ask my mind to make another effort, to bring back once more the sensation that is slipping away. And, so that nothing may interrupt the thrust with which it will try to grasp it again, I clear away every obstacle, every foreign idea, I protect my ears and my attention from the noises in the next room. But feeling my mind grow tired without succeeding, I now compel it to accept the very distraction I was denying it, to think of something else, to recover its strength before a supreme attempt. Then for a second time I create an empty space before it, I confront it again with the still recent taste of that first mouthful, and I feel something quiver in me, shift, try to rise, something that seems to have been unanchored at a great depth; I do not know what it is, but it comes up slowly; I feel the resistance and I hear the murmur of the distances traversed.

Undoubtedly what is palpitating thus, deep inside me, must be the image, the visual memory which is attached to this taste and is trying to follow it to me. But it is struggling too far away, too confusedly; I can just barely perceive the neutral glimmer in which the elusive eddying of stirred-up colors is blended; but I cannot distinguish the form, cannot ask it, as the one possible interpreter, to translate for me the evidence of its contemporary, its inseparable companion, the taste, ask it to tell me what particular circumstance is involved, what period of the past.

Will it reach the clear surface of my consciousness—this memory, this old moment which the attraction of an identical moment has come from so far to invite, to move, to raise up from the deepest part of me? I don't know. Now I no longer feel anything, it has stopped, gone back down perhaps; who knows if it will ever rise up from its darkness again? Ten times I must begin again, lean down toward it. And each time, the laziness that deters us from every difficult task, every work of importance, has counseled me to leave it, to drink my tea and think only about my worries of today, my desires for tomorrow, upon which I may ruminate effortlessly.

And suddenly the memory appeared. That taste was the taste of the little piece of madeleine which on Sunday mornings at Combray (because that day I did not go out before it was time for Mass), when I went to say good morning to her in her bedroom, my aunt Léonie would give me after dipping it in her infusion of tea or lime blossom. The sight of the little madeleine had not reminded me of anything before I tasted it; perhaps because I had often seen them since, without eating them, on the shelves of the pastry shops, and their image had therefore left those days of Combray and attached itself to others more recent; perhaps because of these recollections abandoned so long outside my memory, nothing survived, everything had come apart; the forms and the form, too, of the little shell made of cake, so fatly sensual within its severe and pious pleating—had been destroyed, or, still half asleep, had lost the force of expansion that would have allowed them to rejoin my consciousness. But, when nothing subsists of an old past, after the death of people, after the destruction of things, alone, frailer but more enduring, more immaterial, more persistent, more faithful, smell and taste still remain for a long time, like souls, remembering, waiting, hoping, upon the ruins of all the rest, bearing without giving way, on their almost impalpable droplet, the immense edifice of memory.

And as soon as I had recognized the taste of the piece of madeleine dipped in lime-blossom tea that my aunt used to give me (though I did not yet know and had to put off to much later discovering why this memory made me so happy), immediately the old gray house on the street, where her bedroom was, came like a stage set to attach itself to the little wing opening onto the garden that had been built for my parents behind it (that truncated section which was all I had seen before then); and with the house the town, from morning to night and in all weathers, the Square, where they sent me before lunch, the streets where I went on errands, the paths we took if the weather was fine. And as in that game in which the Japanese amuse themselves by filling a porcelain bowl with water and steeping in it little pieces of paper until then undifferentiated which, the moment they are immersed in it, stretch and bend, take color and distinctive shape, turn into flowers, houses, human figures, firm and recognizable, so now all the flowers in our garden and in M. Swann's park, and the water lilies on the Vivonne,[8] and the good people of the village and their little dwellings and the church and all of Combray and its surroundings, all of this, acquiring form and solidity, emerged, town and gardens alike, from my cup of tea.

1913

8. The local river.

JAMES JOYCE
1882–1941

More than any other writer of the twentieth century, James Joyce shaped modern literature. His experiments with narrative form helped to define the major literary movements of the century, from modernism to postmodernism. By developing methods of tracing individual consciousness, Joyce, along with **Marcel Proust** and **Virginia Woolf**, helped us to understand the functioning of the human mind. Equally capable of realistic portrayal of urban life in Dublin and playful deformations of the English language, Joyce expanded the possibilities of the novel— as a record of intimate human experiences, as a massive encyclopedia of human culture, and as a funhouse mirror that shows the world a transformed image of itself.

Joyce left Ireland as a young man but made his native country the subject of all his works. Born in Dublin on February 2, 1882, to May Murray and John Stanislaus Joyce, he was given the impressive name James Augustine Aloy-

sius Joyce; he was the eldest surviving child of what would soon be a large family (ten children plus three who died in infancy). His father held a well-paid and undemanding post in the civil service, and the family was comfortable until 1891, when his job was eliminated. John received a small pension and declined to take up more demanding work elsewhere. The Joyce family moved steadily down the social and economic scale, and life became difficult under the improvident guidance of a man whom Joyce later portrayed as "a drinker, a good fellow, a storyteller, somebody's secretary, something in a distillery, a tax-gatherer, a bankrupt, and at present a praiser of his own past."

Joyce attended the well-known Catholic preparatory school of Clongowes Wood College from the ages of six to nine, leaving when his family could no longer afford the tuition. Two years later, he was admitted as a scholarship student to Belvedere College in Dublin. Both were Jesuit schools and provided a rigorous Catholic training against which Joyce violently rebelled but which he never forgot. In Belvedere College, shaken by a dramatic hell-fire sermon shortly after his first experience with sex, he even seriously considered becoming a priest; in the end, the life of the senses and his sense of vocation as an artist won out. After graduating from Belvedere in 1898, Joyce entered another Catholic institution—University College, Dublin—where he rejected Irish tradition and looked abroad for new values. Teaching himself Norwegian in order to read **Henrik Ibsen** in the original, he criticized the writers of the Irish Literary Renaissance as provincial and showed no interest in joining their ranks. His first published piece was an essay on Ibsen, to which the great playwright responded in a brief note of thanks. Like the hero of his autobiographical novel, *A Portrait of the Artist as a Young Man* (1916), Stephen Dedalus, Joyce decided (in 1902) to escape the stifling conventions of his native country and leave for the Continent.

This trip did not last long. He studied medicine briefly, then for six months supported himself in Paris by giving English lessons, but when his mother became seriously ill, he was called home. After her death, he taught school for a time in Dublin and then returned to the Continent with Nora Barnacle, a country woman from western Ireland with whom he had two children and whom he married (after twenty-seven years of cohabitation) in 1931. The young couple moved to Trieste, where Joyce taught English in a Berlitz school and started writing both the short stories collected as *Dubliners* (1914) and an early version, partially published as *Stephen Hero* in 1944, of *A Portrait of the Artist as a Young Man*. He also wrote some mostly forgettable poetry and a play, *Exiles* (1918), that he had trouble getting produced. The couple remained poor for much of Joyce's life and relied on grants from the British government and gifts from wealthy patrons to allow Joyce to complete his literary projects. Joyce made a few brief business trips to Dublin, but, after 1912, never returned to the city.

When the First World War broke out, the Joyces moved to neutral Zurich, then after the war to Paris, where Joyce completed his most famous work, *Ulysses* (1922). In Paris he briefly met the other great novelist of the day, Marcel Proust, but claimed never to have read his work. He did, however, attend Proust's funeral. By now, Joyce was a celebrity and developed a circle of literary friends who supported and publicized his work. Throughout his life Joyce was a heavy drinker, and his conversation was legendary. His eyesight deteriorated as he devoted himself to the project he called *Work in Progress* (completed as *Finnegans Wake* in 1939). He sometimes relied on others, including the young Irish writer **Samuel Beckett**, to take dictation. These years were blighted by the mental illness of Joyce's daughter, Lucia, who ended up institutionalized for most of her life. The Joyces remained in Paris until the German occupation during the Second World War, when Joyce and his wife returned to Zurich, where Joyce died in 1941 after an operation for a perforated ulcer.

From *Dubliners* to *Ulysses* and *Finnegans Wake*, Joyce developed ways of exploring the lives and dreams of characters, including his youthful self, from the parochial Dublin society he had fled. Each of the major works presents innovative literary approaches that were to have a substantial impact on later writers. *A Portrait of the Artist as a Young Man* introduced into English the technique of stream of consciousness, as a means of capturing thoughts and emotions. Because it suggests the seemingly arbitrary manner in which thoughts and feelings often arise and then dissipate, stream-of-conscious writing may sound illogical or confusing; nevertheless it can indeed be convincing, since it gives the reader apparent access to the workings of a character's mind. The author's aim in employing the technique is to achieve a deeper understanding of human experience by displaying subconscious associations along with conscious thoughts. *Portrait* is based on Joyce's life until 1902, but the novel is clearly not a conventional autobiography and the reader recognizes in the first pages a radical experiment in fictional language. The novel's sophisticated symbolism and stress on dramatic dialogue hint at the radical break with narrative tradition that Joyce was preparing in *Ulysses*.

While introducing a host of stylistic devices to English, including an expanded form of stream of consciousness, a complex set of mythic parallels, and a series of literary parodies, *Ulysses* also provided one of the most celebrated instances of modern literary censorship. Its serial publication in the New York *Little Review* (from 1918 to 1920) was halted by the U.S. Post Office after a complaint, from the New York Society for the Prevention of Vice, that the work was obscene. The novel was outlawed and all available copies were actually burned in England and in America, until a 1933 decision by Judge Woolsey in federal district court lifted the ban in the United States. Although Joyce's descriptions have lost none of their pungency, it is hard to imagine a reader who would not be struck by another element—the density and mythic scope of this complex, symbolic, and linguistically innovative novel. Openly referring to an ancient predecessor, the *Odyssey* of Homer ("Ulysses" is the Latin name for the hero Odysseus), *Ulysses* structures numerous episodes to suggest parallels with the Greek epic, and transforms the twenty-year Homeric journey home into the daylong wanderings through Dublin of an unheroic advertising man, Leopold Bloom, and a rebellious young teacher and writer from *Portrait*, Stephen Dedalus. **T. S. Eliot** saw Joyce's use of ancient myth to explore modern life as "a way of controlling, of ordering, of giving a shape and significance to the immense panorama of futility and anarchy which is contemporary history." The first half of *Ulysses* uses stream-of-consciousness technique to explore Bloom's and Stephen's thoughts through the course of the day. By the second half of the novel, however, a number of intrusive and parodic narrators intervene in the action; Joyce's games with language and representation in this section were prime influences on postmodernism.

After the publication of *Ulysses*, Joyce spent the next seventeen years writing an even more complex work: *Finnegans Wake* (1939). Despite the title, a reference to a ballad in which the bricklayer Tim Finnegan is brought back to life at his wake when somebody spills whiskey on him, the novel is the multivoiced, multidimensional dream of Humphrey Chimpden Earwicker. *Finnegans Wake* expands on the encyclopedic series of literary and cultural references underlying *Ulysses*, in language that has been even more radically broken apart and reassembled than that of *Ulysses*. Digressing exuberantly in all directions at once, with complex puns and hybrid words that mix languages, *Finnegans Wake* is—in spite of its cosmic symbolism—a game of language and reference by an artist "hoppy on akkant of his joyicity."

"THE DEAD"

These influential literary experiments had their roots in Joyce's command of more traditional narrative technique. "The Dead," presented here, was the last and greatest story in Joyce's first published volume, *Dubliners*. The collection as a whole sketches aspects of life in the Irish capital as Joyce knew it, in which the parochialism, piety, and repressive conventions of life are shown stifling artistic and psychological development. Whether it is the young boy who arrives too late at the fair in "Araby," the poor-aunt laundress of "Clay," or the frustrated writer Gabriel Conroy of "The Dead," the characters in *Dubliners* dream of a better life against a dismal, impoverishing background whose cumulative effect is of despair. The style of *Dubliners* is more realistic than in Joyce's later fiction, but he already employs a structure of symbolic meanings and revelatory moments he called "epiphanies." Joyce wrote to his publisher that the collection would be "a chapter of the moral history of my country," and he further explained that he had chosen Dublin because it was the "centre of paralysis" in Ireland—a city of blunted hopes and lost dreams: desperately poor, with large slums and more people than jobs, it stagnated in political, religious, and cultural divisions that color the lives of the characters in the stories. The book is arranged, Joyce noted, in an order that represents four aspects of life in the city: "childhood, adolescence, maturity and public life." Individual stories focus on one or a few characters, who may dream of a better life but are eventually frustrated by, or sink voluntarily back into, their shabby reality. Stories often end with a moment of special insight (epiphany), evident to the reader but not always to the protagonist, that puts events into sharp and illuminating perspective.

Several aspects of "The Dead" recall—and transmute—elements in Joyce's life. As in other stories, the neighborhood setting is familiar from his youth. The real-life models for Miss Kate and Miss Julia were indeed music teachers. Mr. Bartell D'Arcy evokes a contemporary tenor who performed under a similar name. The figure of Gabriel Conroy—who writes reviews for local journals, dislikes Irish nationalism, and prefers European culture—physically resembles

Joyce—a lesser Joyce who might never have had the courage to leave home for Europe. The tale that Gretta tells Gabriel at the end of the story echoes Nora's experience.

"The Dead" is divided into three parts, chronicling the stages of the Misses Morkan's party and also the stages by which Gabriel Conroy moves from the rather pompous, insecure, and externally oriented figure of the beginning to a man who has been forced to reassess himself and human relationships at the end. The party is an annual dinner dance that takes place after the New Year, probably on January 6, the Catholic Feast of the Epiphany (which many have connected with Gabriel's personal epiphany at the end of the story). A jovial occasion, it brings together friends and acquaintances for an evening of music, dancing, sumptuous food, and a formal after-dinner speech that Gabriel delivers. The undercurrents are not always harmonious, however, for small anxieties and personal frictions crop up that both create a realistic picture and suggest tensions in contemporary Irish society: nationalism, religion, poverty, and class differences. Gabriel has a position to maintain, and he is determined to live up to his responsibilities: he is at once cultured speaker and intellectual, carver and master of ceremonies, and the man whom the Misses Morkan expect to take care of occasional problems like alcoholic guests. He is a complex character, both a writer of real imagination and a narcissistic figure who is so used to focusing on himself that he has drawn apart from other people.

Joyce's method in "The Dead" relies heavily on free indirect discourse, the presentation of a character's thoughts (without quotation marks) by the narrator. Joyce drew this style partly from **Flaubert**—in *Portrait*, Stephen Dedalus quotes Flaubert's idea of the artist who "like the God of the creation, remains within or behind or beyond or above his handiwork, invisible, refined out of existence, indifferent, paring his fingernails." Joyce's later development of stream of consciousness would allow the character's thoughts to be presented directly to the reader, sometimes without the intervention of a narrator, but in "The Dead" the narrator unobtrusively filters Gabriel's thoughts for us, allowing us to sympathize with Gabriel in his insecurity but also inviting us to judge him in his complacency.

The Dead

Lily, the caretaker's daughter, was literally run off her feet. Hardly had she brought one gentleman into the little pantry behind the office on the ground floor and helped him off with his overcoat than the wheezy hall-door bell clanged again and she had to scamper along the bare hallway to let in another guest. It was well for her she had not to attend to the ladies also. But Miss Kate and Miss Julia had thought of that and had converted the bathroom upstairs into a ladies' dressing-room. Miss Kate and Miss Julia were there, gossiping and laughing and fussing, walking after each other to the head of the stairs, peering down over the banisters and calling down to Lily to ask her who had come.

It was always a great affair, the Misses Morkan's annual dance. Everybody who knew them came to it, members of the family, old friends of the family, the members of Julia's choir, any of Kate's pupils that were grown up enough and even some of Mary Jane's pupils too. Never once had it fallen flat. For years and years it had gone off in splendid style as long as anyone could remember; ever since Kate and Julia, after the death of their brother Pat, had left the house in Stoney Batter and taken Mary Jane, their only niece, to live with them in the dark gaunt house on Usher's Island,[1] the upper part of which they had rented from Mr. Fulham, the cornfactor[2] on the ground floor. That was a good thirty years ago if it was a day. Mary Jane, who was then a little girl in short clothes, was now the main prop of the household for she had the organ[3] in Haddington Road. She had been through the Academy[4] and gave a pupils' concert every year in the upper room of the Antient Concert Rooms. Many of her pupils belonged to better-class families on the Kingstown and Dalkey line.[5] Old as they were, her aunts also did their share. Julia, though she was quite grey, was still the leading soprano in Adam and Eve's, and Kate, being too feeble to go about much, gave music lessons to beginners on the old square[6] piano in the back room. Lily, the caretaker's daughter, did housemaid's work for them. Though their life was modest they believed in eating well; the best of everything: diamond-bone sirloins, three-shilling tea and the best bottled stout.[7] But Lily seldom made a mistake in the orders so that she got on well with her three mistresses. They were fussy, that was all. But the only thing they would not stand was back answers.

---

1. Not an island, but an area in western Dublin on the south bank of the River Liffey. Stoney Batter is a street of small shops and a few houses in Dublin.
2. Dealer in grain.
3. I.e., earned money by playing the organ at church.

4. The Royal Academy of Music.
5. Railway to a fashionable section of Dublin.
6. I.e., upright. "Adam and Eve's": popular name (taken from a nearby inn) for a Dublin Catholic church.
7. Strong beer.

Of course they had good reason to be fussy on such a night. And then it was long after ten o'clock and yet there was no sign of Gabriel and his wife. Besides they were dreadfully afraid that Freddy Malins might turn up screwed.[8] They would not wish for worlds that any of Mary Jane's pupils should see him under the influence; and when he was like that it was sometimes very hard to manage him. Freddy Malins always came late but they wondered what could be keeping Gabriel: and that was what brought them every two minutes to the banisters to ask Lily had Gabriel or Freddy come.

—O, Mr. Conroy, said Lily to Gabriel when she opened the door for him, Miss Kate and Miss Julia thought you were never coming. Good-night, Mrs. Conroy.

—I'll engage they did, said Gabriel, but they forgot that my wife here takes three mortal hours to dress herself.

He stood on the mat, scraping the snow from his goloshes, while Lily led his wife to the foot of the stairs and called out:

—Miss Kate, here's Mrs. Conroy.

Kate and Julia came toddling down the dark stairs at once. Both of them kissed Gabriel's wife, said she must be perished alive and asked was Gabriel with her.

—Here I am as right as the mail,[9] Aunt Kate! Go on up. I'll follow, called out Gabriel from the dark.

He continued scraping his feet vigorously while the three women went upstairs, laughing, to the ladies' dressing-room. A light fringe of snow lay like a cape on the shoulders of his overcoat and like toecaps on the toes of his goloshes: and, as the buttons of his overcoat slipped with a squeaking noise through the snow-stiffened frieze, a cold fragrant air from out-of-doors escaped from crevices and folds.

—Is it snowing again, Mr. Conroy? asked Lily.

She had preceded him into the pantry to help him off with his overcoat. Gabriel smiled at the three syllables she had given his surname and glanced at her. She was a slim, growing girl, pale in complexion and with hay-coloured hair. The gas in the pantry made her look still paler. Gabriel had known her when she was a child and used to sit on the lowest step nursing a rag doll.

—Yes, Lily, he answered, and I think we're in for a night of it.

He looked up at the pantry ceiling, which was shaking with the stamping and shuffling of feet on the floor above, listened for a moment to the piano and then glanced at the girl, who was folding his overcoat carefully at the end of a shelf.

—Tell me, Lily, he said in a friendly tone, do you still go to school?

—O no, sir, she answered. I'm done schooling this year and more.

—O, then, said Gabriel gaily, I suppose we'll be going to your wedding one of these fine days with your young man, eh?

The girl glanced back at him over her shoulder and said with great bitterness:

—The men that is now is only all palaver[1] and what they can get out of you.

Gabriel coloured as if he felt he had made a mistake and, without looking at her, kicked off his goloshes and flicked actively with his muffler at his patent-leather shoes.

8. Drunk.   1. Fancy talk.
9. Reliable as mail delivery.

He was a stout tallish young man. The high colour of his cheeks pushed upwards even to his forehead where it scattered itself in a few formless patches of pale red; and on his hairless face there scintillated restlessly the polished lenses and the bright gilt rims of the glasses which screened his delicate and restless eyes. His glossy black hair was parted in the middle and brushed in a long curve behind his ears where it curled slightly beneath the groove left by his hat.

When he had flicked lustre into his shoes he stood up and pulled his waistcoat down more tightly on his plump body. Then he took a coin rapidly from his pocket.

—O Lily, he said, thrusting it into her hands, it's Christmastime, isn't it? Just . . . here's a little. . . .

He walked rapidly towards the door.

—O no, sir! cried the girl, following him. Really, sir, I wouldn't take it.

—Christmas-time! Christmas-time! said Gabriel, almost trotting to the stairs and waving his hand to her in deprecation.

The girl, seeing that he had gained the stairs, called out after him:

—Well, thank you, sir.

He waited outside the drawing-room door until the waltz should finish, listening to the skirts that swept against it and to the shuffling of feet. He was still discomposed by the girl's bitter and sudden retort. It had cast a gloom over him which he tried to dispel by arranging his cuffs and the bows of his tie. Then he took from his waistcoat pocket a little paper and glanced at the headings he had made for his speech. He was undecided about the lines from Robert Browning[2] for he feared they would be above the heads of his hearers. Some quotation that they could recognise from Shakespeare or from the Melodies[3] would be better. The indelicate clacking of the men's heels and the shuffling of their soles reminded him that their grade of culture differed from his. He would only make himself ridiculous by quoting poetry to them which they could not understand. They would think that he was airing his superior education. He would fail with them just as he had failed with the girl in the pantry. He had taken up a wrong tone. His whole speech was a mistake from first to last, an utter failure.

Just then his aunts and his wife came out of the ladies' dressing-room. His aunts were two small plainly dressed old women. Aunt Julia was an inch or so the taller. Her hair, drawn low over the tops of her ears, was grey; and grey also, with darker shadows, was her large flaccid face. Though she was stout in build and stood erect her slow eyes and parted lips gave her the appearance of a woman who did not know where she was or where she was going. Aunt Kate was more vivacious. Her face, healthier than her sister's, was all puckers and creases, like a shrivelled red apple, and her hair, braided in the same old-fashioned way, had not lost its ripe nut colour.

They both kissed Gabriel frankly. He was their favourite nephew, the son of their dead elder sister, Ellen, who had married T. J. Conroy of the Port and Docks.[4]

---

2. English poet (1812–1889) who had a contemporary reputation for obscurity.
3. Thomas Moore's (1779–1852) immensely popular *Irish Melodies*, a collection of poems with many set to old Irish melodies.
4. The Dublin Port and Docks Board, which regulated customs and shipping.

—Gretta tells me you're not going to take a cab back to Monkstown[5] tonight, Gabriel, said Aunt Kate.

—No, said Gabriel, turning to his wife, we had quite enough of that last year, hadn't we? Don't you remember, Aunt Kate, what a cold Gretta got out of it? Cab windows rattling all the way, and the east wind blowing in after we passed Merrion.[6] Very jolly it was. Gretta caught a dreadful cold.

Aunt Kate frowned severely and nodded her head at every word.

—Quite right, Gabriel, quite right, she said. You can't be too careful.

—But as for Gretta there, said Gabriel, she'd walk home in the snow if she were let.

Mrs. Conroy laughed.

—Don't mind him, Aunt Kate, she said. He's really an awful bother, what with green shades for Tom's eyes at night and making him do the dumb-bells, and forcing Eva to eat the stirabout.[7] The poor child! And she simply hates the sight of it! . . . O, but you'll never guess what he makes me wear now!

She broke out into a peal of laughter and glanced at her husband, whose admiring and happy eyes had been wandering from her dress to her face and hair. The two aunts laughed heartily too, for Gabriel's solicitude was a standing joke with them.

—Goloshes! said Mrs. Conroy. That's the latest. Whenever it's wet underfoot I must put on my goloshes. To-night even he wanted me to put them on, but I wouldn't. The next thing he'll buy me will be a diving suit.

Gabriel laughed nervously and patted his tie reassuringly while Aunt Kate nearly doubled herself, so heartily did she enjoy the joke. The smile soon faded from Aunt Julia's face and her mirthless eyes were directed towards her nephew's face. After a pause she asked:

—And what are goloshes, Gabriel?

—Goloshes, Julia! exclaimed her sister. Goodness me, don't you know what goloshes are? You wear them over your . . . over your boots, Gretta, isn't it?

—Yes, said Mrs. Conroy. Guttapercha[8] things. We both have a pair now. Gabriel says everyone wears them on the continent.

—O, on the continent, murmured Aunt Julia, nodding her head slowly.

Gabriel knitted his brows and said, as if he were slightly angered:

—It's nothing very wonderful but Gretta thinks it very funny because she says the word reminds her of Christy Minstrels.[9]

—But tell me, Gabriel, said Aunt Kate, with brisk tact. Of course, you've seen about the room. Gretta was saying . . .

—O, the room is all right, replied Gabriel. I've taken one in the Gresham.[1]

—To be sure, said Aunt Kate, by far the best thing to do. And the children, Gretta, you're not anxious about them?

—O, for one night, said Mrs. Conroy. Besides, Bessie will look after them.

—To be sure, said Aunt Kate again. What a comfort it is to have a girl like that, one you can depend on! There's that Lily, I'm sure I don't know what has come over her lately. She's not the girl she was at all.

5. Well-to-do suburb of Dublin.
6. Village on Dublin Bay.
7. Porridge.
8. A rubberlike substance.

9. "Goloshes" sounds like "golly shoes," which reminds Gretta of the Christy Minstrels, a popular blackface minstrel show.
1. Fashionable hotel in central Dublin.

Gabriel was about to ask his aunt some questions on this point but she broke off suddenly to gaze after her sister who had wandered down the stairs and was craning her neck over the banisters.

—Now, I ask you, she said, almost testily, where is Julia going? Julia! Julia! Where are you going?

Julia, who had gone halfway down one flight, came back and announced blandly:

—Here's Freddy.

At the same moment a clapping of hands and a final flourish of the pianist told that the waltz had ended. The drawing-room door was opened from within and some couples came out. Aunt Kate drew Gabriel aside hurriedly and whispered into his ear:

—Slip down, Gabriel, like a good fellow and see if he's all right, and don't let him up if he's screwed. I'm sure he's screwed. I'm sure he is.

Gabriel went to the stairs and listened over the banisters. He could hear two persons talking in the pantry. Then he recognised Freddy Malins' laugh. He went down the stairs noisily.

—It's such a relief, said Aunt Kate to Mrs. Conroy, that Gabriel is here. I always feel easier in my mind when he's here. . . . Julia, there's Miss Daly and Miss Power will take some refreshment. Thanks for your beautiful waltz, Miss Daly. It made lovely time.

A tall wizen-faced man, with a stiff grizzled moustache and swarthy skin, who was passing out with his partner said:

—And may we have some refreshment, too, Miss Morkan?

—Julia, said Aunt Kate summarily, and here's Mr. Browne and Miss Furlong. Take them in, Julia, with Miss Daly and Miss Power.

—I'm the man for the ladies, said Mr. Browne, pursing his lips until his moustache bristled and smiling in all his wrinkles. You know, Miss Morkan, the reason they are so fond of me is—

He did not finish his sentence, but, seeing that Aunt Kate was out of earshot, at once led the three young ladies into the back room. The middle of the room was occupied by two square tables placed end to end, and on these Aunt Julia and the caretaker were straightening and smoothing a large cloth. On the sideboard were arrayed dishes and plates, and glasses and bundles of knives and forks and spoons. The top of the closed square piano served also as a sideboard for viands and sweets. At a smaller sideboard in one corner two young men were standing, drinking hop-bitters.[2]

Mr. Browne led his charges thither and invited them all, in jest, to some ladies' punch, hot, strong and sweet. As they said they never took anything strong he opened three bottles of lemonade for them. Then he asked one of the young men to move aside, and, taking hold of the decanter, filled out for himself a goodly measure of whiskey. The young men eyed him respectfully while he took a trial sip.

—God help me, he said, smiling, it's the doctor's orders.

His wizened face broke into a broader smile, and the three young ladies laughed in musical echo to his pleasantry, swaying their bodies to and fro, with nervous jerks of their shoulders. The boldest said:

2. Unfermented beer.

—O, now, Mr. Browne, I'm sure the doctor never ordered anything of the kind.

Mr. Browne took another sip of his whiskey and said, with sidling mimicry:

—Well, you see, I'm like the famous Mrs. Cassidy, who is reported to have said: *Now, Mary Grimes, if I don't take it, make me take it, for I feel I want it.*

His hot face had leaned forward a little too confidentially and he had assumed a very low Dublin accent so that the young ladies, with one instinct, received his speech in silence. Miss Furlong, who was one of Mary Jane's pupils, asked Miss Daly what was the name of the pretty waltz she had played; and Mr. Browne, seeing that he was ignored, turned promptly to the two young men who were more appreciative.

A red-faced young woman, dressed in pansy,[3] came into the room, excitedly clapping her hands and crying:

—Quadrilles![4] Quadrilles!

Close on her heels came Aunt Kate, crying:

—Two gentlemen and three ladies, Mary Jane!

—O, here's Mr. Bergin and Mr. Kerrigan, said Mary Jane. Mr. Kerrigan, will you take Miss Power? Miss Furlong, may I get you a partner, Mr. Bergin. O, that'll just do now.

—Three ladies, Mary Jane, said Aunt Kate.

The two young gentlemen asked the ladies if they might have the pleasure, and Mary Jane turned to Miss Daly.

—O, Miss Daly, you're really awfully good, after playing for the last two dances, but really we're so short of ladies to-night.

—I don't mind in the least, Miss Morkan.

—But I've a nice partner for you, Mr. Bartell D'Arcy, the tenor. I'll get him to sing later on. All Dublin is raving about him.

—Lovely voice, lovely voice! said Aunt Kate.

As the piano had twice begun the prelude to the first figure Mary Jane led her recruits quickly from the room. They had hardly gone when Aunt Julia wandered slowly into the room, looking behind her at something.

—What is the matter, Julia? asked Aunt Kate anxiously. Who is it?

Julia, who was carrying in a column of table-napkins turned to her sister and said, simply, as if the question had surprised her:

—It's only Freddy, Kate, and Gabriel with him.

In fact right behind her Gabriel could be seen piloting Freddy Malins across the landing. The latter, a young man of forty, was of Gabriel's size and build, with very round shoulders. His face was fleshy and pallid, touched with colour only at the thick hanging lobes of his ears and at the wide wings of his nose. He had coarse features, a blunt nose, a convex and receding brow, tumid and pro-truded lips. His heavy-lidded eyes and the disorder of his scanty hair made him look sleepy. He was laughing heartily in a high key at a story which he had been telling Gabriel on the stairs and at the same time rubbing the knuckles of his left fist backwards and forwards into his left eye.

—Good-evening, Freddy, said Aunt Julia.

3. Violet.   4. An intricate square dance for four couples.

Freddy Malins bade the Misses Morkan good-evening in what seemed an offhand fashion by reason of the habitual catch in his voice and then, seeing that Mr. Browne was grinning at him from the sideboard, crossed the room on rather shaky legs and began to repeat in an undertone the story he had just told to Gabriel.

—He's not so bad, is he? said Aunt Kate to Gabriel.

Gabriel's brows were dark but he raised them quickly and answered:

—O no, hardly noticeable.

—Now, isn't he a terrible fellow! she said. And his poor mother made him take the pledge on New Year's Eve. But come on, Gabriel, into the drawing-room.

Before leaving the room with Gabriel she signalled to Mr. Browne by frowning and shaking her forefinger in warning to and fro. Mr. Browne nodded in answer and, when she had gone, said to Freddy Malins:

—Now, then, Teddy, I'm going to fill you out a good glass of lemonade just to buck you up.

Freddy Malins, who was nearing the climax of his story, waved the offer aside impatiently but Mr. Browne, having first called Freddy Malins' attention to a disarray in his dress,[5] filled out and handed him a full glass of lemonade. Freddy Malins' left hand accepted the glass mechanically, his right hand being engaged in the mechanical readjustment of his dress. Mr. Browne, whose face was once more wrinkling with mirth, poured out for himself a glass of whisky while Freddy Malins exploded, before he had well reached the climax of his story, in a kink of high-pitched bronchitic laughter and, setting down his untasted and overflowing glass, began to rub the knuckles of his left fist backwards and forwards into his left eye, repeating words of his last phrase as well as his fit of laughter would allow him.

Gabriel could not listen while Mary Jane was playing her Academy piece, full of runs and difficult passages, to the hushed drawing-room. He liked music but the piece she was playing had no melody for him and he doubted whether it had any melody for the other listeners, though they had begged Mary Jane to play something. Four young men, who had come from the refreshment-room to stand in the doorway at the sound of the piano, had gone away quietly in couples after a few minutes. The only persons who seemed to follow the music were Mary Jane herself, her hands racing along the key-board or lifted from it at the pauses like those of a priestess in momentary imprecation, and Aunt Kate standing at her elbow to turn the page.

Gabriel's eyes, irritated by the floor, which glittered with beeswax under the heavy chandelier, wandered to the wall above the piano. A picture of the balcony scene in *Romeo and Juliet* hung there and beside it was a picture of the two murdered princes[6] in the Tower which Aunt Julia had worked in red, blue and brown wools when she was a girl. Probably in the school they had gone to as girls that kind of work had been taught, for one year his mother had worked for him as a birthday present a waistcoat of purple tabinet,[7] with little foxes'

---

5. That his fly was open.
6. According to Shakespeare's *Richard III*, the young heirs to the British throne were murdered in the Tower of London by order of

their uncle, King Richard III. *Balcony scene*: Shakespeare's *Romeo and Juliet* 2.2.
7. A damasklike fabric.

heads upon it, lined with brown satin and having round mulberry buttons. It was strange that his mother had had no musical talent though Aunt Kate used to call her the brains carrier of the Morkan family. Both she and Julia had always seemed a little proud of their serious and matronly sister. Her photograph stood before the pierglass.[8] She held an open book on her knees and was pointing out something in it to Constantine who, dressed in a man-o'-war suit,[9] lay at her feet. It was she who had chosen the names for her sons for she was very sensible of the dignity of family life. Thanks to her, Constantine was now senior curate in Balbriggan and, thanks to her, Gabriel himself had taken his degree in the Royal University. A shadow passed over his face as he remembered her sullen opposition to his marriage. Some slighting phrases she had used still rankled in his memory; she had once spoken of Gretta as being country cute[1] and that was not true of Gretta at all. It was Gretta who had nursed her during all her last long illness in their house at Monkstown.

He knew that Mary Jane must be near the end of her piece for she was playing again the opening melody with runs of scales after every bar and while he waited for the end the resentment died down in his heart. The piece ended with a trill of octaves in the treble and a final deep octave in the bass. Great applause greeted Mary Jane as, blushing and rolling up her music nervously, she escaped from the room. The most vigorous clapping came from the four young men in the doorway who had gone away to the refreshment-room at the beginning of the piece but had come back when the piano had stopped.

Lancers were arranged. Gabriel found himself partnered with Miss Ivors. She was a frank-mannered talkative young lady, with a freckled face and prominent brown eyes. She did not wear a low-cut bodice and the large brooch which was fixed in the front of her collar bore on it an Irish device.

When they had taken their places she said abruptly:

—I have a crow to pluck[2] with you.

—With me? said Gabriel.

She nodded her head gravely.

—What is it? asked Gabriel, smiling at her solemn manner.

—Who is G. C.? answered Miss Ivors, turning her eyes upon him.

Gabriel coloured and was about to knit his brows, as if he did not understand, when she said bluntly:

—O, innocent Amy! I have found out that you write for *The Daily Express.*[3] Now, aren't you ashamed of yourself?

—Why should I be ashamed of myself? asked Gabriel, blinking his eyes and trying to smile.

—Well, I'm ashamed of you, said Miss Ivors frankly. To say you'd write for a rag like that. I didn't think you were a West Briton.[4]

A look of perplexity appeared on Gabriel's face. It was true that he wrote a literary column every Wednesday in *The Daily Express*, for which he was paid fifteen shillings. But that did not make him a West Briton surely. The books he received for review were almost more welcome than the paltry cheque. He

---

8. A large mirror.
9. A sailor suit.
1. Unintelligent (not acute).
2. A bone to pick; an argument.

3. Conservative Dublin newspaper opposed to Irish independence.
4. An Irishman who supports union with Britain (an insult).

loved to feel the covers and turn over the pages of newly printed books. Nearly every day when his teaching in the college was ended he used to wander down the quays to the second-hand booksellers, to Hickey's on Bachelor's Walk, to Webb's or Massey's on Aston's Quay, or to O'Clohissey's in the by-street. He did not know how to meet her charge. He wanted to say that literature was above politics. But they were friends of many years' standing and their careers had been parallel, first at the University and then as teachers: he could not risk a grandiose phrase with her. He continued blinking his eyes and trying to smile and murmured lamely that he saw nothing political in writing reviews of books.

When their turn to cross[5] had come he was still perplexed and inattentive. Miss Ivors promptly took his hand in a warm grasp and said in a soft friendly tone:

—Of course, I was only joking. Come, we cross now.

When they were together again she spoke of the University question,[6] and Gabriel felt more at ease. A friend of hers had shown her his review of Browning's poems. That was how she had found out the secret: but she liked the review immensely. Then she said suddenly:

—O, Mr. Conroy, will you come for an excursion to the Aran Isles[7] this summer? We're going to stay there a whole month. It will be splendid out in the Atlantic. You ought to come. Mr. Clancy is coming, and Mr. Kilkelly and Kathleen Kearney. It would be splendid for Gretta too if she'd come. She's from Connacht,[8] isn't she?

—Her people are, said Gabriel shortly.

—But you will come, won't you? said Miss Ivors, laying her warm hand eagerly on his arm.

—The fact is, said Gabriel, I have already arranged to go—

—Go where? asked Miss Ivors.

—Well, you know, every year I go for a cycling tour with some fellows and so—

—But where? asked Miss Ivors.

—Well, we usually go to France or Belgium or perhaps Germany, said Gabriel awkwardly.

—And why do you go to France and Belgium, said Miss Ivors, instead of visiting your own land?

—Well, said Gabriel, it's partly to keep in touch with the languages and partly for a change.

—And haven't you your own language to keep in touch with—Irish? asked Miss Ivors.

—Well, said Gabriel, if it comes to that, you know, Irish is not my language.

Their neighbours had turned to listen to the cross-examination. Gabriel glanced right and left nervously and tried to keep his good humour under the ordeal which was making a blush invade his forehead.

5. A step in the square dance.
6. Controversy over the establishment of Irish Catholic universities to rival the dominant Protestant tradition of Oxford and Cambridge in England, and Trinity College in Dublin.
7. Off the west coast of Ireland, idealized by the nationalists as an example of unspoiled Irish culture and language.
8. The westernmost province of Ireland.

—And haven't you your own land to visit, continued Miss Ivors, that you know nothing of, your own people, and your own country?

—O, to tell you the truth, retorted Gabriel suddenly, I'm sick of my own country, sick of it!

—Why? asked Miss Ivors.

Gabriel did not answer for his retort had heated him.

—Why? repeated Miss Ivors.

They had to go visiting together[9] and, as he had not answered her, Miss Ivors said warmly:

—Of course, you've no answer.

Gabriel tried to cover his agitation by taking part in the dance with great energy. He avoided her eyes for he had seen a sour expression on her face. But when they met in the long chain[1] he was surprised to feel his hand firmly pressed. She looked at him from under her brows for a moment quizzically until he smiled. Then, just as the chain was about to start again, she stood on tiptoe and whispered into his ear:

—West Briton!

When the lancers were over Gabriel went away to a remote corner of the room where Freddy Malins' mother was sitting. She was a stout feeble old woman with white hair. Her voice had a catch in it like her son's and she stuttered slightly. She had been told that Freddy had come and that he was nearly all right. Gabriel asked her whether she had had a good crossing. She lived with her married daughter in Glasgow and came to Dublin on a visit once a year. She answered placidly that she had had a beautiful crossing and that the captain had been most attentive to her. She spoke also of the beautiful house her daughter kept in Glasgow, and of all the nice friends they had there. While her tongue rambled on Gabriel tried to banish from his mind all memory of the unpleasant incident with Miss Ivors. Of course the girl or woman, or whatever she was, was an enthusiast but there was a time for all things. Perhaps he ought not to have answered her like that. But she had no right to call him a West Briton before people, even in joke. She had tried to make him ridiculous before people, heckling him and staring at him with her rabbit's eyes.

He saw his wife making her way towards him through the waltzing couples. When she reached him she said into his ear:

—Gabriel, Aunt Kate wants to know won't you carve the goose as usual. Miss Daly will carve the ham and I'll do the pudding.

—All right, said Gabriel.

—She's sending in the younger ones first as soon as this waltz is over so that we'll have the table to ourselves.

—Were you dancing? asked Gabriel.

—Of course I was. Didn't you see me? What words had you with Molly Ivors?

—No words. Why? Did she say so?

—Something like that. I'm trying to get that Mr. D'Arcy to sing. He's full of conceit, I think.

—There were no words, said Gabriel moodily, only she wanted me to go for a trip to the west of Ireland and I said I wouldn't.

His wife clasped her hands excitedly and gave a little jump.

—O, do go, Gabriel, she cried. I'd love to see Galway again.

—You can go if you like, said Gabriel coldly.

She looked at him for a moment, then turned to Mrs. Malins and said:

—There's a nice husband for you, Mrs. Malins.

While she was threading her way back across the room Mrs. Malins, without adverting to the interruption, went on to tell Gabriel what beautiful places there were in Scotland and beautiful scenery. Her son-in-law brought them every year to the lakes and they used to go fishing. Her son-in-law was a splendid fisher. One day he caught a fish, a beautiful big big fish, and the man in the hotel boiled it for their dinner.

Gabriel hardly heard what she said. Now that supper was coming near he began to think again about his speech and about the quotation. When he saw Freddy Malins coming across the room to visit his mother Gabriel left the chair free for him and retired into the embrasure of the window. The room had already cleared and from the back room came the clatter of plates and knives. Those who still remained in the drawing-room seemed tired of dancing and were conversing quietly in little groups. Gabriel's warm trembling fingers tapped the cold pane of the window. How cool it must be outside! How pleasant it would be to walk out alone, first along by the river and then through the park! The snow would be lying on the branches of the trees and forming a bright cap on the top of the Wellington Monument.[2] How much more pleasant it would be there than at the supper-table!

He ran over the headings of his speech: Irish hospitality, sad memories, the Three Graces, Paris,[3] the quotation from Browning. He repeated to himself a phrase he had written in his review: *One feels that one is listening to a thought-tormented music.* Miss Ivors had praised the review. Was she sincere? Had she really any life of her own behind all her propagandism? There had never been any ill-feeling between them until that night. It unnerved him to think that she would be at the supper-table, looking up at him while he spoke with her critical quizzing eyes. Perhaps she would not be sorry to see him fail in his speech. An idea came into his mind and gave him courage. He would say, alluding to Aunt Kate and Aunt Julia: *Ladies and Gentlemen, the generation which is now on the wane among us may have had its faults but for my part I think it had certain qualities of hospitality, of humour, of humanity, which the new and very serious and hypereducated generation that is growing up around us seems to me to lack.* Very good: that was one for Miss Ivors. What did he care that his aunts were only two ignorant old women?

A murmur in the room attracted his attention. Mr. Browne was advancing from the door, gallantly escorting Aunt Julia, who leaned upon his arm, smiling and hanging her head. An irregular musketry of applause escorted her also as

2. A tall obelisk in Phoenix Park, celebrating the duke of Wellington (1769–1852), an Anglo-Irish statesman and general, who served as British prime minister and commander-in-chief of the army.

3. The Trojan prince of Homer's *Iliad.* "Three Graces": daughters of Zeus and Eurynome in Greek mythology; they embodied (and bestowed) charm.

far as the piano and then, as Mary Jane seated herself on the stool, and Aunt Julia, no longer smiling, half turned so as to pitch her voice fairly into the room, gradually ceased. Gabriel recognized the prelude. It was that of an old song of Aunt Julia's—*Arrayed for the Bridal.*[4] Her voice, strong and clear in tone, attacked with great spirit the runs which embellish the air and though she sang very rapidly she did not miss even the smallest of the grace notes. To follow the voice, without looking at the singer's face, was to feel and share the excitement of swift and secure flight. Gabriel applauded loudly with all the others at the close of the song and loud applause was borne in from the invisible supper-table. It sounded so genuine that a little colour struggled into Aunt Julia's face as she bent to replace in the music-stand the old leather-bound song-book that had her initials on the cover. Freddy Malins, who had listened with his head perched sideways to hear her better, was still applauding when everyone else had ceased and talking animatedly to his mother who nodded her head gravely and slowly in acquiescence. At last, when he could clap no more, he stood up suddenly and hurried across the room to Aunt Julia whose hand he seized and held in both his hands, shaking it when words failed him or the catch in his voice proved too much for him.

—I was just telling my mother, he said, I never heard you sing so well, never. No, I never heard your voice so good as it is to-night. Now! Would you believe that now? That's the truth. Upon my word and honour that's the truth. I never heard your voice sound so fresh and so . . . so clear and fresh, never.

Aunt Julia smiled broadly and murmured something about compliments as she released her hand from his grasp. Mr. Browne extended his open hand towards her and said to those who were near him in the manner of a showman introducing a prodigy to an audience:

—Miss Julia Morkan, my latest discovery!

—He was laughing very heartily at this himself when Freddy Malins turned to him and said:

—Well, Browne, if you're serious you might make a worse discovery. All I can say is I never heard her sing half so well as long as I am coming here. And that's the honest truth.

—Neither did I, said Mr. Browne. I think her voice has greatly improved.

Aunt Julia shrugged her shoulders and said with meek pride:

—Thirty years ago I hadn't a bad voice as voices go.

—I often told Julia, said Aunt Kate emphatically, that she was simply thrown away in that choir. But she never would be said by me.

She turned as if to appeal to the good sense of the others against a refractory child while Aunt Julia gazed in front of her, a vague smile of reminiscence playing on her face.

—No, continued Aunt Kate, she wouldn't be said or led by anyone, slaving there in that choir night and day, night and day. Six o'clock on Christmas morning! And all for what?

—Well, isn't it for the honour of God, Aunt Kate? asked Mary Jane, twisting round on the piano-stool and smiling.

Aunt Kate turned fiercely on her niece and said:

---

4. An English lyric by George Linley; from the first act of Vincenzo Bellini's 1835 opera *I Puritani* (The Puritans).

—I know all about the honour of God, Mary Jane, but I think it's not at all honourable for the pope to turn out the women out of the choirs that have slaved there all their lives and put little whipper-snappers of boys over their heads.[5] I suppose it is for the good of the Church if the pope does it. But it's not just, Mary Jane, and it's not right.

She had worked herself into a passion and would have continued in defence of her sister for it was a sore subject with her but Mary Jane, seeing that all the dancers had come back, intervened pacifically:

—Now, Aunt Kate, you're giving scandal to Mr. Browne who is of the other persuasion.

Aunt Kate turned to Mr. Browne, who was grinning at this allusion to his religion, and said hastily:

—O, I don't question the pope's being right. I'm only a stupid old woman and I wouldn't presume to do such a thing. But there's such a thing as common everyday politeness and gratitude. And if I were in Julia's place I'd tell that Father Healy straight up to his face . . .

—And besides, Aunt Kate, said Mary Jane, we really are all hungry and when we are hungry we are all very quarrelsome.

—And when we are thirsty we are also quarrelsome, added Mr. Browne.

—So that we had better go to supper, said Mary Jane, and finish the discussion afterwards.

On the landing outside the drawing-room Gabriel found his wife and Mary Jane trying to persuade Miss Ivors to stay for supper. But Miss Ivors, who had put on her hat and was buttoning her cloak, would not stay. She did not feel in the least hungry and she had already overstayed her time.

—But only for ten minutes, Molly, said Mrs. Conroy. That won't delay you.

—To take a pick itself, said Mary Jane, after all your dancing.

—I really couldn't, said Miss Ivors.

—I am afraid you didn't enjoy yourself at all, said Mary Jane hopelessly.

—Ever so much, I assure you, said Miss Ivors, but you really must let me run off now.

—But how can you get home? asked Mrs. Conroy.

—O, it's only two steps up the quay.

Gabriel hesitated a moment and said:

—If you will allow me, Miss Ivors, I'll see you home if you really are obliged to go.

But Miss Ivors broke away from them.

—I won't hear of it, she cried. For goodness sake go in to your suppers and don't mind me. I'm quite well able to take care of myself.

—Well, you're the comical girl, Molly, said Mrs. Conroy frankly.

—Beannacht libh,[6] cried Miss Ivors, with a laugh, as she ran down the staircase.

Mary Jane gazed after her, a moody puzzled expression on her face, while Mrs. Conroy leaned over the banisters to listen for the hall-door. Gabriel asked himself was he the cause of her abrupt departure. But she did not seem to be in ill humour: she had gone away laughing. He stared blankly down the staircase.

5. In 1903, Pope Pius X decreed that all church singers be male.   6. Farewell: blessings on you (Irish).

At that moment Aunt Kate came toddling out of the supper-room, almost wringing her hands in despair.

—Where is Gabriel? she cried. Where on earth is Gabriel? There's everyone waiting in there, stage to let, and nobody to carve the goose!

—Here I am, Aunt Kate! cried Gabriel, with sudden animation, ready to carve a flock of geese, if necessary.

A fat brown goose lay at one end of the table and at the other end, on a bed of creased paper strewn with sprigs of parsley, lay a great ham, stripped of its outer skin and peppered over with crust crumbs, a neat paper frill round its shin and beside this was a round of spiced beef. Between these rival ends ran parallel lines of side-dishes: two little minsters[7] of jelly, red and yellow; a shallow dish full of blocks of blancmange and red jam, a large green leaf-shaped dish with a stalk-shaped handle, on which lay bunches of purple raisins and peeled almonds, a companion dish on which lay a solid rectangle of Smyrna figs, a dish of custard topped with grated nutmeg, a small bowl full of chocolates and sweets wrapped in gold and silver papers and a glass vase in which stood some tall celery stalks. In the center of the table there stood, as sentries to a fruit-stand which upheld a pyramid of oranges and American apples, two squat old-fashioned decanters of cut glass, one containing port and the other dark sherry. On the closed square piano a pudding in a huge yellow dish lay in waiting and behind it were three squads of bottles of stout and ale and minerals,[8] drawn up according to the colours of their uniforms, the first two black, with brown and red labels, the third and smallest squad white, with transverse green sashes.

Gabriel took his seat boldly at the head of the table and, having looked to the edge of the carver, plunged his fork firmly into the goose. He felt quite at ease now for he was an expert carver and liked nothing better than to find himself at the head of a well-laden table.

—Miss Furlong, what shall I send you? he asked. A wing or a slice of the breast?

—Just a small slice of the breast.

—Miss Higgins, what for you?

—O, anything at all, Mr. Conroy.

While Gabriel and Miss Daly exchanged plates of goose and plates of ham and spiced beef Lily went from guest to guest with a dish of hot floury potatoes wrapped in a white napkin. This was Mary Jane's idea and she had also suggested apple sauce for the goose but Aunt Kate had said that plain roast goose without apple sauce had always been good enough for her and she hoped she might never eat worse. Mary Jane waited on her pupils and saw that they got the best slices and Aunt Kate and Aunt Julia opened and carried across from the piano bottles of stout and ale for the gentlemen and bottles of minerals for the ladies. There was a great deal of confusion and laughter and noise, the noise of orders and counter-orders, of knives and forks, of corks and glass-stoppers. Gabriel began to carve second helpings as soon as he had finished the first round without serving himself. Everyone protested loudly so that he compromised by taking a long draught of stout for he had found the carving hot

7. Confectioneries shaped to look like cathedrals.

8. Carbonated drinks.

work. Mary Jane settled down quietly to her supper but Aunt Kate and Aunt Julia were still toddling round the table, walking on each other's heels, getting in each other's way and giving each other unheeded orders. Mr. Browne begged of them to sit down and eat their suppers and so did Gabriel but they said there was time enough so that, at last, Freddy Malins stood up and, capturing Aunt Kate, plumped her down on her chair amid general laughter.

When everyone had been well served Gabriel said, smiling:

—Now, if anyone wants a little more of what vulgar people call stuffing let him or her speak.

A chorus of voices invited him to begin his own supper and Lily came forward with three potatoes which she had reserved for him.

—Very well, said Gabriel amiably, as he took another preparatory draught, kindly forget my existence, ladies and gentlemen, for a few minutes.

He sat to his supper and took no part in the conversation with which the table covered Lily's removal of the plates. The subject of talk was the opera company which was then at the Theatre Royal. Mr. Bartell D'Arcy, the tenor, a dark-complexioned young man with a smart moustache, praised very highly the leading contralto of the company but Miss Furlong thought she had a rather vulgar style of production. Freddy Malins said there was a negro chieftain[9] singing in the second part of the Gaiety pantomime who had one of the finest tenor voices he had ever heard.

—Have you heard him? he asked Mr. Bartell D'Arcy across the table.

—No, answered Mr. Bartell D'Arcy carelessly.

—Because, Freddy Malins explained, now I'd be curious to hear your opinion of him. I think he has a grand voice.

—It takes Teddy to find out the really good things, said Mr. Browne familiarly to the table.

—And why couldn't he have a voice too? asked Freddy Malins sharply. Is it because he's only a black?

Nobody answered this question and Mary Jane led the table back to the legitimate opera. One of her pupils had given her a pass for *Mignon*.[1] Of course it was very fine, she said, but it made her think of poor Georgina Burns. Mr. Browne could go back farther still, to the old Italian companies that used to come to Dublin—Tietjens, Ilma de Murzka, Campanini, the great Trebelli, Giuglini, Ravelli, Aramburo.[2] Those were the days, he said, when there was something like singing to be heard in Dublin. He told too of how the top gallery of the old Royal used to be packed night after night, of how one night an Italian tenor had sung five encores to *Let Me Like a Soldier Fall*,[3] introducing a high C every time, and of how the gallery boys would sometimes in their enthusiasm unyoke the horses from the carriage of some great *prima donna* and pull her themselves through the streets to her hotel. Why did they never play the grand old operas now, he asked, *Dinorah, Lucrezia Borgia?*[4] Because they could not get the voices to sing them: that was why.

9. Actually, a blackface performer.
1. Popular French opera (1866) by Ambroise Thomas.
2. Famous opera singers.

3. From William V. Wallace's romantic light opera *Maritana* (1845).
4. Operas by Giacomo Meyerbeer (1859) and Gaetano Donizetti (1833), respectively.

—O, well, said Mr. Bartell D'Arcy, I presume there are as good singers today as there were then.

—Where are they? asked Mr. Browne defiantly.

—In London, Paris, Milan, said Mr. Bartell D'Arcy warmly. I suppose Caruso,[5] for example, is quite as good, if not better than any of the men you have mentioned.

—Maybe so, said Mr. Browne. But I may tell you I doubt it strongly.

—O, I'd give anything to hear Caruso sing, said Mary Jane.

—For me, said Aunt Kate, who had been picking a bone, there was only one tenor. To please me, I mean. But I suppose none of you ever heard of him.

—Who was he, Miss Morkan? asked Mr. Bartell D'Arcy politely.

—His name, said Aunt Kate, was Parkinson. I heard him when he was in his prime and I think he had then the purest tenor voice that was ever put into a man's throat.

—Strange, said Mr. Bartell D'Arcy. I never even heard of him.

—Yes, yes, Miss Morkan is right, said Mr. Browne. I remember hearing of old Parkinson but he's too far back for me.

—A beautiful pure sweet mellow English tenor, said Aunt Kate with enthusiasm.

Gabriel having finished, the huge pudding was transferred to the table. The clatter of forks and spoons began again. Gabriel's wife served out spoonfuls of the pudding and passed the plates down the table. Midway down they were held up by Mary Jane, who replenished them with raspberry or orange jelly or with blancmange and jam. The pudding was of Aunt Julia's making and she received praises for it from all quarters. She herself said that it was not quite brown enough.

—Well, I hope, Miss Morkan, said Mr. Browne, that I'm brown enough for you because, you know, I'm all brown.

All the gentlemen, except Gabriel, ate some of the pudding out of compliment to Aunt Julia. As Gabriel never ate sweets the celery had been left for him. Freddy Malins also took a stalk of celery and ate it with his pudding. He had been told that celery was a capital thing for the blood and he was just then under doctor's care. Mrs. Malins, who had been silent all through the supper, said that her son was going down to Mount Melleray[6] in a week or so. The table then spoke of Mount Melleray, how bracing the air was down there, how hospitable the monks were and how they never asked for a penny-piece from their guests.

—And do you mean to say, asked Mr. Browne incredulously, that a chap can go down there and put up there as if it were a hotel and live on the fat of the land and then come away without paying a farthing?

—O, most people give some donation to the monastery when they leave, said Mary Jane.

—I wish we had an institution like that in our Church, said Mr. Browne candidly.

He was astonished to hear that the monks never spoke, got up at two in the morning and slept in their coffins.[7] He asked what they did it for.

5. Enrico Caruso (1873–1921).
6. A Trappist abbey whose hospitality included the treatment of wealthy alcoholics.
7. The coffin story is a popular fiction.

—That's the rule of the order, said Aunt Kate firmly.

—Yes, but why? asked Mr. Browne.

Aunt Kate repeated that it was the rule, that was all. Mr. Browne still seemed not to understand. Freddy Malins explained to him, as best he could, that the monks were trying to make up for the sins committed by all the sinners in the outside world. The explanation was not very clear for Mr. Browne grinned and said:

—I like that idea very much but wouldn't a comfortable spring bed do them as well as a coffin?

—The coffin, said Mary Jane, is to remind them of their last end.

As the subject had grown lugubrious it was buried in a silence of the table during which Mrs. Malins could be heard saying to her neighbour in an indistinct undertone:

—They are very good men, the monks, very pious men.

The raisins and almonds and figs and apples and oranges and chocolates and sweets were now passed about the table and Aunt Julia invited all the guests to have either port or sherry. At first Mr. Bartell D'Arcy refused to take either but one of his neighbours nudged him and whispered something to him upon which he allowed his glass to be filled. Gradually as the last glasses were being filled the conversation ceased. A pause followed, broken only by the noise of the wine and by unsettlings of chairs. The Misses Morkan, all three, looked down at the tablecloth. Someone coughed once or twice and then a few gentlemen patted the table gently as a signal for silence. The silence came and Gabriel pushed back his chair and stood up.

The patting at once grew louder in encouragement and then ceased altogether. Gabriel leaned his ten trembling fingers on the tablecloth and smiled nervously at the company. Meeting a row of upturned faces he raised his eyes to the chandelier. The piano was playing a waltz tune and he could hear the skirts sweeping against the drawing-room door. People, perhaps, were standing in the snow on the quay outside, gazing up at the lighted windows and listening to the waltz music. The air was pure there. In the distance lay the park where the trees were weighted with snow. The Wellington Monument wore a gleaming cap of snow that flashed westward over the white field of Fifteen Acres.[8]

He began:

—Ladies and Gentlemen.

—It has fallen to my lot this evening, as in years past, to perform a very pleasing task but a task for which I am afraid my poor powers as a speaker are all too inadequate.

—No, no! said Mr. Browne.

—But, however that may be, I can only ask you to-night to take the will for the deed and to lend me your attention for a few moments while I endeavour to express to you in words what my feelings are on this occasion.

—Ladies and Gentlemen. It is not the first time that we have gathered together under this hospitable roof, around this hospitable board. It is not the first time that we have been the recipients—or perhaps, I had better say, the victims—of the hospitality of certain good ladies.

8. A section of Phoenix Park used for British military reviews.

He made a circle in the air with his arm and paused. Everyone laughed or smiled at Aunt Kate and Aunt Julia and Mary Jane who all turned crimson with pleasure. Gabriel went on more boldly:

—I feel more strongly with every recurring year that our country has no tradition which does it so much honour and which it should guard so jealously as that of its hospitality. It is a tradition that is unique as far as my experience goes (and I have visited not a few places abroad) among the modern nations. Some would say, perhaps, that with us it is rather a failing than anything to be boasted of. But granted even that, it is, to my mind, a princely failing, and one that I trust will long be cultivated among us. Of one thing, at least, I am sure. As long as this one roof shelters the good ladies aforesaid—and I wish from my heart it may do so for many and many a long year to come—the tradition of genuine warm-hearted courteous Irish hospitality, which our forefathers have handed down to us and which we in turn must hand down to our descendants, is still alive among us.

A hearty murmur of assent ran around the table. It shot through Gabriel's mind that Miss Ivors was not there and that she had gone away discourteously: and he said with confidence in himself:

—Ladies and Gentlemen.

—A new generation is growing up in our midst, a generation actuated by new ideas and new principles. It is serious and enthusiastic for these new ideas and its enthusiasm, even when it is misdirected, is, I believe, in the main sincere. But we are living in a skeptical and, if I may use the phrase, a thought-tormented age: and sometimes I fear that this new generation, educated or hypereducated as it is, will lack those qualities of humanity, of hospitality, of kindly humour which belonged to an older day. Listening tonight to the names of all those great singers of the past it seemed to me, I must confess, that we were living in a less spacious age. Those days might, without exaggeration, be called spacious days: and if they are gone beyond recall let us hope, at least, that in gatherings such as this we shall still speak of them with pride and affection, still cherish in our hearts the memory of those dead and gone great ones whose fame the world will not willingly let die.

—Hear, hear! said Mr. Browne loudly.

—But yet, continued Gabriel, his voice falling into a softer inflection, there are always in gatherings such as this sadder thoughts that will recur to our minds: thoughts of the past, of youth, of changes, of absent faces that we miss here tonight. Our path through life is strewn with many such sad memories: and were we to brood upon them always we could not find the heart to go on bravely with our work among the living. We have all of us living duties and living affections which claim, and rightly claim, our strenuous endeavours.

—Therefore, I will not linger on the past. I will not let any gloomy moralising intrude upon us here to-night. Here we are gathered together for a brief moment from the bustle and rush of our everyday routine. We are met here as friends, in the spirit of good-fellowship, as colleagues, also to a certain extent, in the true spirit of *camaraderie*, and as the guests of—what shall I call them?—the Three Graces of the Dublin musical world.

The table burst into applause and laughter at this sally. Aunt Julia vainly asked each of her neighbours in turn to tell her what Gabriel had said.

—He says we are the Three Graces, Aunt Julia, said Mary Jane.

Aunt Julia did not understand but she looked up, smiling, at Gabriel, who continued in the same vein:

—Ladies and Gentlemen.

—I will not attempt to play to-night the part that Paris played on another occasion.[9] I will not attempt to choose between them. The task would be an invidious one and one beyond my poor powers. For when I view them in turn, whether it be our chief hostess herself, whose good heart, whose too good heart, has become a byword with all who know her, or her sister, who seems to be gifted with perennial youth and whose singing must have been a surprise and a revelation to us all to-night, or, last but not least, when I consider our youngest hostess, talented, cheerful, hard-working and the best of nieces, I confess, Ladies and Gentlemen, that I do not know to which of them I should award the prize.

Gabriel glanced down at his aunts and, seeing the large smile on Aunt Julia's face and the tears which had risen to Aunt Kate's eyes, hastened to his close. He raised his glass of port gallantly, while every member of the company fingered a glass expectantly, and said loudly:

—Let us toast them all three together. Let us drink to their health, wealth, long life, happiness and prosperity and may they long continue to hold the proud and self-won position which they hold in their profession and the position of honour and affection which they hold in our hearts.

All the guests stood up, glass in hand, and, turning towards the three seated ladies, sang in unison, with Mr. Browne as leader:

> *For they are jolly gay fellows,*
> *For they are jolly gay fellows,*
> *For they are jolly gay fellows,*
> *Which nobody can deny.*

Aunt Kate was making frank use of her handkerchief and even Aunt Julia seemed moved. Freddy Malins beat time with his pudding-fork and the singers turned towards one another, as if in melodious conference, while they sang, with emphasis:

> *Unless he tells a lie,*
> *Unless he tells a lie,*

Then, turning once more towards their hostesses, they sang:

> *For they are jolly gay fellows,*
> *For they are jolly gay fellows,*
> *For they are jolly gay fellows,*
> *Which nobody can deny.*

The acclamation which followed was taken up beyond the door of the supper-room by many of the other guests and renewed time after time, Freddy Malins acting as officer with his fork on high.

---

9. Paris was required to judge a beauty contest between the Greek goddesses Hera, Athena, and Aphrodite; see p. 1182, n. 3.

The piercing morning air came into the hall where they were standing so that Aunt Kate said:

—Close the door, somebody. Mrs. Malins will get her death of cold.

—Browne is out there, Aunt Kate, said Mary Jane.

—Browne is everywhere, said Aunt Kate, lowering her voice.

Mary Jane laughed at her tone.

—Really, she said archly, he is very attentive.

—He has been laid on here like the gas, said Aunt Kate in the same tone, all during the Christmas.

She laughed herself this time good-humouredly and then added quickly:

—But tell him to come in, Mary Jane, and close the door. I hope to goodness he didn't hear me.

At that moment the hall-door was opened and Mr. Browne came in from the doorstep, laughing as if his heart would break. He was dressed in a long green overcoat with mock astrakhan cuffs and collar and wore on his head an oval fur cap. He pointed down the snow-covered quay from where the sound of shrill prolonged whistling was borne in.

—Teddy will have all the cabs in Dublin out, he said.

Gabriel advanced from the little pantry behind the office, struggling into his overcoat and, looking round the hall, said:

—Gretta not down yet?

—She's getting on her things, Gabriel, said Aunt Kate.

—Who's playing up there? asked Gabriel.

—Nobody. They're all gone.

—O no, Aunt Kate, said Mary Jane. Bartell D'Arcy and Miss O'Callaghan aren't gone yet.

—Someone is strumming at the piano, anyhow, said Gabriel.

Mary Jane glanced at Gabriel and Mr. Browne and said with a shiver:

—It makes me feel cold to look at you two gentlemen muffled up like that. I wouldn't like to face your journey home at this hour.

—I'd like nothing better this minute, said Mr. Browne stoutly, than a rattling fine walk in the country or a fast drive with a good spanking goer between the shafts.

—We used to have a very good horse and trap at home, said Aunt Julia sadly.

—The never-to-be-forgotten Johnny, said Mary Jane, laughing.

Aunt Kate and Gabriel laughed too.

—Why, what was wonderful about Johnny? asked Mr. Browne.

—The late lamented Patrick Morkan, our grandfather, that is, explained Gabriel, commonly known in his later years as the old gentleman, was a glue-boiler.

—O, now, Gabriel, said Aunt Kate, laughing, he had a starch mill.

—Well, glue or starch, said Gabriel, the old gentleman had a horse by the name of Johnny. And Johnny used to work in the old gentleman's mill, walking round and round in order to drive the mill. That was all very well; but now comes the tragic part about Johnny. One fine day the old gentleman thought he'd like to drive out with the quality to a military review in the park.

—The Lord have mercy on his soul, said Aunt Kate compassionately.

—Amen, said Gabriel. So the old gentleman, as I said, harnessed Johnny and put on his very best tall hat and his very best stock collar and drove out in grand style from his ancestral mansion somewhere near Back Lane,[1] I think.

Everyone laughed, even Mrs. Malins, at Gabriel's manner and Aunt Kate said:

—O now, Gabriel, he didn't live in Back Lane, really. Only the mill was there.

—Out from the mansion of his forefathers, continued Gabriel, he drove with Johnny. And everything went on beautifully until Johnny came in sight of King Billy's[2] statue: and whether he fell in love with the horse King Billy sits on or whether he thought he was back again in the mill, anyhow he began to walk round the statue.

Gabriel paced in a circle round the hall in his goloshes amid the laughter of the others.

—Round and round he went, said Gabriel, and the old gentleman, who was a very pompous old gentleman, was highly indignant. *Go on, sir! What do you mean, sir? Johnny! Johnny! Most extraordinary conduct! Can't understand the horse!*

The peals of laughter which followed Gabriel's imitation of the incident were interrupted by a resounding knock at the hall-door. Mary Jane ran to open it and let in Freddy Malins. Freddy Malins, with his hat well back on his head and his shoulders humped with cold, was puffing and steaming after his exertions.

—I could only get one cab, he said.

—O, we'll find another along the quay, said Gabriel.

—Yes, said Aunt Kate. Better not keep Mrs. Malins standing in the draught.

Mrs. Malins was helped down the front steps by her son and Mr. Browne and, after many manœuvres, hoisted into the cab. Freddy Malins clambered in after her and spent a long time settling her on the seat, Mr. Browne helping him with advice. At last she was settled comfortably and Freddy Malins invited Mr. Browne into the cab. There was a good deal of confused talk, and then Mr. Browne got into the cab. The cabman settled his rug over his knees, and bent down for the address. The confusion grew greater and the cabman was directed differently by Freddy Malins and Mr. Browne, each of whom had his head out through a window of the cab. The difficulty was to know where to drop Mr. Browne along the route and Aunt Kate, Aunt Julia and Mary Jane helped the discussion from the doorstep with cross-directions and contradictions and abundance of laughter. As for Freddy Malins he was speechless with laughter. He popped his head in and out of the window every moment, to the great danger of his hat, and told his mother how the discussion was progressing till at last Mr. Browne shouted to the bewildered cabman above the din of everybody's laughter:

—Do you know Trinity College?

—Yes, sir, said the cabman.

—Well, drive bang up against Trinity College gates, said Mr. Browne, and then we'll tell you where to go. You understand now?

---

1. A shabby street in a run-down area of Dublin.
2. William III, king of England from 1689 to 1702, defeated the Irish nationalists at the Battle of the Boyne.

—Yes, sir, said the cabman.

—Make like a bird for Trinity College.

—Right, sir, cried the cabman.

The horse was whipped up and the cab rattled off along the quay amid a chorus of laughter and adieus.

Gabriel had not gone to the door with the others. He was in a dark part of the hall gazing up the staircase. A woman was standing near the top of the first flight, in the shadow also. He could not see her face but he could see the terra-cotta and salmonpink panels of her skirt which the shadow made appear black and white. It was his wife. She was leaning on the banisters, listening to something. Gabriel was surprised at her stillness and strained his ear to listen also. But he could hear little save the noise of laughter and dispute on the front steps, a few chords struck on the piano and a few notes of a man's voice singing.

He stood still in the gloom of the hall, trying to catch the air that the voice was singing and gazing up at his wife. There was grace and mystery in her attitude as if she were a symbol of something. He asked himself what is a woman standing on the stairs in the shadow, listening to distant music, a symbol of. If he were a painter he would paint her in that attitude. Her blue felt hat would show off the bronze of her hair against the darkness and the dark panels of her skirt would show off the light ones. *Distant Music* he would call the picture if he were a painter.

The hall-door was closed; and Aunt Kate, Aunt Julia and Mary Jane came down the hall, still laughing.

—Well, isn't Freddy terrible? said Mary Jane. He's really terrible.

Gabriel said nothing but pointed up the stairs towards where his wife was standing. Now that the hall-door was closed the voice and the piano could be heard more clearly. Gabriel held up his hand for them to be silent. The song seemed to be in the old Irish tonality[3] and the singer seemed uncertain both of his words and of his voice. The voice, made plaintive by distance and by the singer's hoarseness, faintly illuminated the cadence of the air with words expressing grief:

> *O, the rain falls on my heavy locks*
> *And the dew wets my skin,*
> *My babe lies cold*[4] . . .

—O, exclaimed Mary Jane. It's Bartell D'Arcy singing and he wouldn't sing all the night. O, I'll get him to sing a song before he goes.

—O do, Mary Jane, said Aunt Kate.

Mary Jane brushed past the others and ran to the staircase but before she reached it the singing stopped and the piano was closed abruptly.

—O, what a pity! she cried. Is he coming down, Gretta?

Gabriel heard his wife answer yes and saw her come down towards them. A few steps behind her were Mr. Bartell D'Arcy and Miss O'Callaghan.

---

3. Based on five (and later seven) tones rather than the modern eight-tone scale.
4. From "The Lass of Aughrim," a ballad about a peasant girl seduced by a lord; when she brings her baby to the castle door, the lord's mother imitates his voice and sends her away. Mother and child are drowned at sea, and the repentant lord curses his mother.

—O, Mr. D'Arcy, cried Mary Jane, it's downright mean of you to break off like that when we were all in raptures listening to you.

—I have been at him all the evening, said Miss O'Callaghan, and Mrs. Conroy too and he told us he had a dreadful cold and couldn't sing.

—O, Mr. D'Arcy, said Aunt Kate, now that was a great fib to tell.

—Can't you see that I'm as hoarse as a crow? said Mr. D'Arcy roughly.

He went into the pantry hastily and put on his overcoat. The others, taken aback by his rude speech, could find nothing to say. Aunt Kate wrinkled her brows and made signs to the others to drop the subject. Mr. D'Arcy stood swathing his neck carefully and frowning.

—It's the weather, said Aunt Julia, after a pause.

—Yes, everybody has colds, said Aunt Kate readily, everybody.

—They say, said Mary Jane, we haven't had snow like it for thirty years; and I read this morning in the newspapers that the snow is general all over Ireland.

—I love the look of snow, said Aunt Julia sadly.

—So do I, said Miss O'Callaghan. I think Christmas is never really Christmas unless we have the snow on the ground.

—But poor Mr. D'Arcy doesn't like the snow, said Aunt Kate, smiling.

Mr. D'Arcy came from the pantry, fully swathed and buttoned, and in a repentant tone told them the history of his cold. Everyone gave him advice and said it was a great pity and urged him to be very careful of his throat in the night air. Gabriel watched his wife who did not join in the conversation. She was standing right under the dusty fanlight and the flame of the gas lit up the rich bronze of her hair which he had seen her drying at the fire a few days before. She was in the same attitude and seemed unaware of the talk about her. At last she turned towards them and Gabriel saw that there was colour on her cheeks and that her eyes were shining. A sudden tide of joy went leaping out of his heart.

—Mr. D'Arcy, she said, what is the name of that song you were singing?

—It's called *The Lass of Aughrim*, said Mr. D'Arcy, but I couldn't remember it properly. Why? Do you know it?

—*The Lass of Aughrim*, she repeated. I couldn't think of the name.

—It's a very nice air, said Mary Jane. I'm sorry you were not in voice to-night.

—Now, Mary Jane, said Aunt Kate, don't annoy Mr. D'Arcy. I won't have him annoyed.

Seeing that all were ready to start she shepherded them to the door where good-night was said:

—Well, good-night, Aunt Kate, and thanks for the pleasant evening.

—Good-night, Gabriel. Good-night, Gretta!

—Good-night, Aunt Kate, and thanks ever so much. Good-night, Aunt Julia.

—O, good-night, Gretta, I didn't see you.

—Good-night, Mr. D'Arcy. Good-night, Miss O'Callaghan.

—Good-night, Miss Morkan.

—Good-night, again.

—Good-night, all. Safe home.

—Good-night. Good-night.

The morning was still dark. A dull yellow light brooded over the houses and the river; and the sky seemed to be descending. It was slushy underfoot; and only streaks and patches of snow lay on the roofs, on the parapets of the quay and on the area railings. The lamps were still burning redly in the murky air and, across the river, the palace of the Four Courts[5] stood out menacingly against the heavy sky.

She was walking on before him with Mr. Bartell D'Arcy, her shoes in a brown parcel tucked under one arm and her hands holding her skirt up from the slush. She had no longer any grace of attitude but Gabriel's eyes were still bright with happiness. The blood went bounding along his veins; and the thoughts went rioting through his brain, proud, joyful, tender, valorous.

She was walking on before him so lightly and so erect that he longed to run after her noiselessly, catch her by the shoulders and say something foolish and affectionate into her ear. She seemed to him so frail that he longed to defend her against something and then to be alone with her. Moments of their secret life together burst like stars upon his memory. A heliotrope envelope was lying beside his breakfast-cup and he was caressing it with his hand. Birds were twittering in the ivy and the sunny web of the curtain was shimmering along the floor: he could not eat for happiness. They were standing on the crowded platform and he was placing a ticket inside the warm palm of her glove. He was standing with her in the cold, looking in through a grated window at a man making bottles in a roaring furnace. It was very cold. Her face, fragrant in the cold air, was quite close to his; and suddenly she called out to the man at the furnace:

—Is the fire hot, sir?

But the man could not hear her with the noise of the furnace. It was just as well. He might have answered rudely.

A wave of yet more tender joy escaped from his heart and went coursing in warm flood along his arteries. Like the tender fires of stars moments of their life together, that no one knew of or would ever know of, broke upon and illumined his memory. He longed to recall to her those moments, to make her forget the years of their dull existence together and remember only their moments of ecstasy. For the years, he felt, had not quenched his soul or hers. Their children, his writing, her household cares had not quenched all their souls' tender fire. In one letter that he had written to her then he had said: *Why is it that words like these seem to me so dull and cold? Is it because there is no word tender enough to be your name?*

Like distant music these words that he had written years before were borne towards him from the past. He longed to be alone with her. When the others had gone away, when he and she were in their room in the hotel, then they would be alone together. He would call her softly:

—Gretta!

Perhaps she would not hear at once: she would be undressing. Then something in his voice would strike her. She would turn and look at him.

At the corner of Winetavern Street they met a cab. He was glad of its rattling noise as it saved him from conversation. She was looking out of the window and seemed tired. The others spoke only a few words, pointing out some building or street. The horse galloped along wearily under the murky morning sky, dragging his old rattling box after his heels, and Gabriel was again in a cab with her, galloping to catch the boat, galloping to their honeymoon.

5. The Irish law courts building.

As the cab drove across O'Connell Bridge Miss O'Callaghan said:

—They say you never cross O'Connell Bridge without seeing a white horse.

—I see a white man this time, said Gabriel.

—Where? asked Mr. Bartell D'Arcy.

Gabriel pointed to the statue,[6] on which lay patches of snow. Then he nodded familiarly to it and waved his hand.

—Good-night, Dan, he said gaily.

When the cab drew up before the hotel Gabriel jumped out and, in spite of Mr. Bartell D'Arcy's protest, paid the driver. He gave the man a shilling over his fare. The man saluted and said:

—A prosperous New Year to you, sir.

—The same to you, said Gabriel cordially.

She leaned for a moment on his arm in getting out of the cab and while standing at the curbstone, bidding the others good-night. She leaned lightly on his arm, as lightly as when she had danced with him a few hours before. He had felt proud and happy then, happy that she was his, proud of her grace and wifely carriage. But now, after the kindling again of so many memories, the first touch of her body, musical and strange and perfumed, sent through him a keen pang of lust. Under cover of her silence he pressed her arm closely to his side; and, as they stood at the hotel door, he felt that they had escaped from their lives and duties, escaped from home and friends and run away together with wild and radiant hearts to a new adventure.

An old man was dozing in a great hooded chair in the hall. He lit a candle in the office and went before them to the stairs. They followed him in silence, their feet falling in soft thuds on the thickly carpeted stairs. She mounted the stairs behind the porter, her head bowed in the ascent, her frail shoulders curved as with a burden, her skirt girt tightly about her. He could have flung his arms about her hips and held her still for his arms were trembling with desire to seize her and only the stress of his nails against the palms of his hands held the wild impulse of his body in check. The porter halted on the stairs to settle his guttering candle. They halted too on the steps below him. In the silence Gabriel could hear the falling of the molten wax into the tray and the thumping of his own heart against his ribs.

The porter led them along a corridor and opened a door. Then he set his unstable candle down on a toilet-table and asked at what hour they were to be called in the morning.

—Eight, said Gabriel.

The porter pointed to the tap of the electric-light and began a muttered apology but Gabriel cut him short.

—We don't want any light. We have light enough from the street. And I say, he added, pointing to the candle, you might remove that handsome article, like a good man.

The porter took up his candle again, but slowly for he was surprised by such a novel idea. Then he mumbled good-night and went out. Gabriel shot the lock to.

6. Of Daniel O'Connell (1775–1847), called "The Liberator" by the Irish independence movement.

A ghostly light from the street lamp lay in a long shaft from one window to the door. Gabriel threw his overcoat and hat on a couch and crossed the room towards the window. He looked down into the street in order that his emotion might calm a little. Then he turned and leaned against a chest of drawers with his back to the light. She had taken off her hat and cloak and was standing before a large swinging mirror, unhooking her waist.[7] Gabriel paused for a few moments, watching her, and then said:

—Gretta!

She turned away from the mirror slowly and walked along the shaft of light towards him. Her face looked so serious and weary that the words would not pass Gabriel's lips. No, it was not the moment yet.

—You looked tired, he said.

—I am a little, she answered.

—You don't feel ill or weak?

—No, tired: that's all.

She went on to the window and stood there, looking out. Gabriel waited again and then, fearing that diffidence was about to conquer him, he said abruptly:

—By the way, Gretta!

—What is it?

—You know that poor fellow Malins? he said quickly.

—Yes. What about him?

—Well, poor fellow, he's a decent sort of chap after all, continued Gabriel in a false voice. He gave me back that sovereign I lent him and I didn't expect it really. It's a pity he wouldn't keep away from that Browne, because he's not a bad fellow at heart.

He was trembling now with annoyance. Why did she seem so abstracted? He did not know how he could begin. Was she annoyed, too, about something? If she would only turn to him or come to him of her own accord! To take her as she was would be brutal. No, he must see some ardour in her eyes first. He longed to be master of her strange mood.

—When did you lend him the pound? she asked, after a pause.

Gabriel strove to restrain himself from breaking out into brutal language about the sottish Malins and his pound. He longed to cry to her from his soul, to crush her body against his, to overmaster her. But he said:

—O, at Christmas, when he opened that little Christmas-card shop in Henry Street.

He was in such a fever of rage and desire that he did not hear her come from the window. She stood before him for an instant, looking at him strangely. Then, suddenly raising herself on tiptoe and resting her hands lightly on his shoulders, she kissed him.

—You are a very generous person, Gabriel, she said.

Gabriel, trembling with delight at her sudden kiss and at the quaintness of her phrase, put his hands on her hair and began smoothing it back, scarcely touching it with his fingers. The washing had made it fine and brilliant. His heart was brimming over with happiness. Just when he was wishing for it she had come to him of her own accord. Perhaps her thoughts had been running

---

7. I.e., loosening her waistband.

with his. Perhaps she had felt the impetuous desire that was in him and then the yielding mood had come upon her. Now that she had fallen to him so easily he wondered why he had been so diffident.

He stood, holding her head between his hands. Then, slipping one arm swiftly about her body and drawing her towards him, he said softly:

—Gretta dear, what are you thinking about?

She did not answer nor yield wholly to his arm. He said again, softly:

—Tell me what it is, Gretta. I think I know what is the matter. Do I know?

She did not answer at once. Then she said in an outburst of tears:

—O, I am thinking about that song, *The Lass of Aughrim.*

She broke loose from him and ran to the bed and, throwing her arms across the bed-rail, hid her face. Gabriel stood stock-still for a moment in astonishment and then followed her. As he passed in the way of the cheval-glass he caught sight of himself in full length, his broad, well-filled shirt-front, the face whose expression always puzzled him when he saw it in a mirror and his glimmering gilt-rimmed eyeglasses. He halted a few paces from her and said:

—What about the song? Why does that make you cry?

She raised her head from her arms and dried her eyes with the back of her hand like a child. A kinder note than he had intended went into his voice.

—Why, Gretta? he asked.

—I am thinking about a person long ago who used to sing that song.

—And who was the person long ago? asked Gabriel, smiling.

—It was a person I used to know in Galway when I was living with my grandmother, she said.

The smile passed away from Gabriel's face. A dull anger began to gather again at the back of his mind and the dull fires of his lust began to glow angrily in his veins.

—Someone you were in love with? he asked ironically.

—It was a young boy I used to know, she answered, named Michael Furey. He used to sing that song, *The Lass of Aughrim.* He was very delicate.

Gabriel was silent. He did not wish her to think that he was interested in this delicate boy.

—I can see him so plainly, she said after a moment. Such eyes as he had: big dark eyes! And such an expression in them—an expression!

—O then, you were in love with him? said Gabriel.

—I used to go out walking with him,[8] she said, when I was in Galway. A thought flew across Gabriel's mind.

—Perhaps that was why you wanted to go to Galway with that Ivors girl? he said coldly.

She looked at him and asked in surprise:

—What for?

Her eyes made Gabriel feel awkward. He shrugged his shoulders and said:

—How do I know? To see him perhaps.

She looked away from him along the shaft of light towards the window in silence.

—He is dead, she said at length. He died when he was only seventeen. Isn't it a terrible thing to die so young as that?

---

8. I.e., she dated him.

—What was he? asked Gabriel, still ironically.

—He was in the gasworks,[9] she said.

Gabriel felt humiliated by the failure of his irony and by the evocation of this figure from the dead, a boy in the gasworks. While he had been full of memories of their secret life together, full of tenderness and joy and desire, she had been comparing him in her mind with another. A shameful consciousness of his own person assailed him. He saw himself as a ludicrous figure, acting as a pennyboy[1] for his aunts, a nervous well-meaning sentimentalist, orating to vulgarians and idealising his own clownish lusts, the pitiable fatuous fellow he had caught a glimpse of in the mirror. Instinctively he turned his back more to the light lest she might see the shame that burned upon his forehead.

He tried to keep up his tone of cold interrogation but his voice when he spoke was humble and indifferent.

—I suppose you were in love with this Michael Furey, Gretta, he said.

—I was great[2] with him at that time, she said.

Her voice was veiled and sad. Gabriel, feeling now how vain it would be to try to lead her whither he had purposed, caressed one of her hands and said, also sadly:

—And what did he die of so young, Gretta? Consumption, was it?

—I think he died for me, she answered.

A vague terror seized Gabriel at this answer as if, at that hour when he had hoped to triumph, some impalpable and vindictive being was coming against him, gathering forces against him in its vague world. But he shook himself free of it with an effort of reason and continued to caress her hand. He did not question her again for he felt that she would tell him of herself. Her hand was warm and moist: it did not respond to his touch but he continued to caress it just as he had caressed her first letter to him that spring morning.

—It was in the winter, she said, about the beginning of the winter when I was going to leave my grandmother's and come up here to the convent. And he was ill at the time in his lodgings in Galway and wouldn't be let out and his people in Oughterard[3] were written to. He was in decline, they said, or something like that. I never knew rightly.

She paused for a moment and sighed.

—Poor fellow, she said. He was very fond of me and he was such a gentle boy. We used to go out together, walking, you know, Gabriel, like the way they do in the country. He was going to study singing only for his health. He had a very good voice, poor Michael Furey.

—Well; and then? asked Gabriel.

—And then when it came to the time for me to leave Galway and come up to the convent he was much worse and I wouldn't be let see him so I wrote a letter saying I was going up to Dublin and would be back in the summer and hoping he would be better then.

She paused for a moment to get her voice under control and then went on:

—Then the night before I left I was in my grandmother's house in Nun's Island,[4] packing up, and I heard gravel thrown up against the window. The

---

9. A utilities plant that manufactured coal gas. Working there was an unhealthy occupation.

1. Errand boy.

2. Close friends.

3. A small village in western Ireland.

4. An island in the western city of Galway, on which is located the Convent of Poor Clares.

window was so wet I couldn't see so I ran downstairs as I was and slipped out the back into the garden and there was the poor fellow at the end of the garden, shivering.

—And did you not tell him to go back? asked Gabriel.

—I implored of him to go home at once and told him he would get his death in the rain. But he said he did not want to live. I can see his eyes as well as well! He was standing at the end of the wall where there was a tree.

—And did he go home? asked Gabriel.

—Yes, he went home. And when I was only a week in the convent he died and he was buried in Oughterard where his people came from. O, the day I heard that, that he was dead!

She stopped, choking with sobs, and, overcome by emotion, flung herself face downward on the bed, sobbing in the quilt. Gabriel held her hand for a moment longer, irresolutely, and then, shy of intruding on her grief, let it fall gently and walked quietly to the window.

She was fast asleep.

Gabriel, leaning on his elbow, looked for a few moments unresentfully on her tangled hair and half-open mouth, listening to her deep-drawn breath. So she had that romance in her life: a man had died for her sake. It hardly pained him now to think how poor a part he, her husband, had played in her life. He watched her while she slept as though he and she had never lived together as man and wife. His curious eyes rested long upon her face and on her hair: and, as he thought of what she must have been then, in that time of her first girlish beauty, a strange friendly pity for her entered his soul. He did not like to say even to himself that her face was no longer beautiful but he knew that it was no longer the face for which Michael Furey had braved death.

Perhaps she had not told him all the story. His eyes moved to the chair over which she had thrown some of her clothes. A petticoat string dangled to the floor. One boot stood upright, its limp upper fallen down: the fellow of it lay upon its side. He wondered at his riot of emotions of an hour before. From what had it proceeded? From his aunt's supper, from his own foolish speech, from the wine and dancing, the merrymaking when saying goodnight in the hall, the pleasure of the walk along the river in the snow. Poor Aunt Julia! She, too, would soon be a shade with the shade of Patrick Morkan and his horse. He had caught that haggard look upon her face for a moment when she was singing *Arrayed for the Bridal*. Soon, perhaps, he would be sitting in that same drawing-room, dressed in black, his silk hat on his knees. The blinds would be drawn down and Aunt Kate would be sitting beside him, crying and blowing her nose and telling him how Julia had died. He would cast about in his mind for some words that might console her, and would find only lame and useless ones. Yes, yes: that would happen very soon.

The air of the room chilled his shoulders. He stretched himself cautiously along under the sheets and lay down beside his wife. One by one they were all becoming shades. Better pass boldly into that other world, in the full glory of some passion, than fade and wither dismally with age. He thought of how she who lay beside him had locked in her heart for so many years that image of her lover's eyes when he had told her that he did not wish to live.

Generous tears filled Gabriel's eyes. He had never felt like that himself towards any woman but he knew that such a feeling must be love. The tears gathered more thickly in his eyes and in the partial darkness he imagined he saw the form of a young man standing under a dripping tree. Other forms were near. His soul had approached that region where dwell the vast hosts of the dead. He was conscious of, but could not apprehend, their wayward and flickering existence. His own identity was fading out into a grey impalpable world: the solid world itself which these dead had one time reared and lived in was dissolving and dwindling.

A few light taps upon the pane made him turn to the window. It had begun to snow again. He watched sleepily the flakes, silver and dark, falling obliquely against the lamplight. The time had come for him to set out on his journey westward. Yes, the newspapers were right: snow was general all over Ireland. It was falling on every part of the dark central plain, on the treeless hills, falling softly upon the Bog of Allen and, farther westward, softly falling into the dark mutinous Shannon[5] waves. It was falling, too, upon every part of the lonely churchyard on the hill where Michael Furey lay buried. It lay thickly drifted on the crooked crosses and headstones, on the spears of the little gate, on the barren thorns. His soul swooned slowly as he heard the snow falling faintly through the universe and faintly falling, like the descent of their last end, upon all the living and the dead.

1914

5. An estuary of the Shannon River, west-southwest of Dublin. The Bog of Allen is southwest of Dublin.

FRANZ KAFKA
1883–1924

Franz Kafka's stories and novels contain such nightmarish scenarios that the word *Kafkaesque* has been coined to describe the most unpleasant and bizarre aspects of modern life, especially when it comes to bureaucracy. Despite the bleakness of the world he depicted, Kafka was in fact a highly amusing writer who, when reading his work to friends, would sometimes leave them laughing out loud. A master of dark humor and an artist of unique vision, Kafka captures perfectly the anxiety and absurdity of contemporary urban society.

Born in Prague, a majority Catholic, Czech-speaking city in the Austro-Hungarian Empire, to a nonobservant Jewish, German-speaking family, Kafka trained as a lawyer and went to work for an insurance company, while living at home with his parents. He began writing in his twenties and published his first short prose works in 1908. Around the same time, he developed a renewed interest in Judaism, which he had mostly ignored as a child. Although he was an attractive and popular person—in this respect not much like his character Gregor Samsa—he was never quite satisfied with his relationships with women or with his family. He was engaged three times, twice to the same woman, and broke off all three engagements. Kafka had a difficult relationship with his father, a self-made man who could not take his son's writing seriously. Having learned from friends about the psychoanalytic theories of Sigmund Freud, Kafka recognized the oedipal tension in aspects of his family life and expressed uneasiness with authority, especially parental authority, in his fiction. He also kept extensive diaries about his dissatisfaction with his personal and work life and, in his late thirties, wrote a long letter to his father harshly criticizing his upbringing.

Most of Kafka's writing published during his life consisted of short stories, parables, and two novellas, including *The Metamorphosis*, the selection here, which were released in six slim volumes. Kafka did not believe himself to be a successful author, although he had won a prestigious literary award, the Fontane Prize of the City of Berlin, for one of his early stories, "The Stoker." He wrote three long novels, *The Trial*, *The Castle*, and *Amerika*, but completed none of them. In despair, he asked his friend and executor, Max Brod, to have them all burned at his death. Brod disobeyed Kafka's instructions and, instead, had the three novels published posthumously. Apparently reflecting the guilt their author experienced over his relations with women, and his failure to get married, the three novels are haunted by regret and a sense of culpability, although the source of the characters' disquiet can never be identified with certainty.

Unlike some of his characters—resentful employees of large bureaucracies—Kafka was a successful senior executive who handled an array of business matters. Nonetheless, he was unhappy with his day job and blamed the hours he spent at work for his inability to complete the novels: in his mind, he was a failure both in life and in art. After developing tuberculosis in his mid-

thirties, Kafka quit his job, at age thirty-nine, in 1922. He published a number of stories, collected in *The Hunger Artist*, and traveled extensively, spending a year in Berlin; but as his health deteriorated, he eventually moved to a sanatorium outside Vienna, where he died. Once Brod released the novels and unfinished stories, the author's fame quickly grew. During the Great Depression and the political crises of the 1930s, Kafka became popular in the English-speaking world. Readers viewed his work as demonstrating the anxiety and isolation of modern life, particularly the problem of living in alienation from God, a major theme of existentialist philosophers after World War II. More recently, however, critics have emphasized Kafka's humor and the social contexts of his work, including his experiences in his native Prague.

Until the middle of the nineteenth century, Jews had been excluded from most aspects of Austro-Hungarian society. Kafka and his family felt a strong affinity for the emperor, who represented for them German high culture and whose family had emancipated the Jews. The old city of Prague, with its narrow streets, crowded apartment houses, Gothic cathedral, and huge medieval castle, was cosmopolitan for a small town. After 1918, Czechoslovakia became an independent republic, and Czech replaced German as the official language. Kafka was able to adapt—he knew Czech well—and in fact was one of the few "German" business executives who were retained after Czech independence. And yet he felt himself to be an outsider—a German-speaking Jew among Czech-speaking Christians. This feeling was no doubt reinforced by a resurgent anti-Semitism that coincided with the rise of Czech nationalism and that threatened the Jews' relatively recent emancipation. (Kafka didn't live to see the final confirmation of his sense of alienation and isolation, but his three sisters would later die in Nazi concentration camps.) In his thirties, Kafka studied Hebrew and Yiddish and became interested in the Yiddish theater; the Jewish Enlightenment of his friend Martin Buber (Austrian philosopher, 1878–1965); Jewish folklore; and the philosophical writings of Søren Kierkegaard (1813–1855). Kafka's work seldom discusses Judaism directly, but the sense of exclusion and persecution that underlies much of his writing may spring in part from his experience of anti-Semitism; certainly his interest in interpretation and the nature of language owes much to his understanding of Jewish thought.

THE METAMORPHOSIS

Written in 1912 and published in 1915, *The Metamorphosis*, Kafka's longest work published in his lifetime, was, as well, his most famous work released before his death. It is a consummate narrative: from the moment Gregor Samsa wakes up to find himself transformed into a "monstrous cockroach," the reader asks, "What happens next?" Although the events seem dreamlike, the narrator assures us "it was no dream," no nightmarish fantasy in which Gregor temporarily identified himself with other downtrodden vermin of society. Instead, this grotesque transformation is permanent, a single, unshakable fact that renders almost comic his family's calculations and attempts to adjust. Indeed, the events of the story are described in great detail, often with an emphasis on the kind of concrete, vivid imagery that plays a prominent role in dreams and in Freud's interpretations of them: the father's fist, the bug's blood, the sister's violin playing.

When the novella begins, Gregor seems to be simply a man in a bug suit, but as the tale progresses, his thinking becomes increasingly buglike, and he loses touch with the people around him. A major theme of the work is the meaning of humanity, and Gregor experiences a sense of exclusion from what Kafka calls the "human circle." As the author relays the protagonist's thoughts, the reader gets the impression that Gregor considers himself to be put upon: he has taken a job he dislikes in order to pay off his parents' debt. Yet even before his transformation, he felt that his family misunderstood him. Once he becomes a bug, he loses the power of speech: although he continues to think, he cannot express his thoughts. Thus, when he turns into a despised species, the lack of communication Gregor perceived as a man becomes an actuality.

"The terror of art," said Kafka in a conversation about *The Metamorphosis*, is that "the dream reveals the reality." This dream, which in the novella becomes Gregor's reality, sheds light on the intolerable nature of his former existence. Another aspect of his professional life is its mechanical rigidity, personal rivalries, and threatening suspicion of any deviation from the norm. Gregor himself is part of this world, as he shows when he fawns on the chief clerk and tries to manipulate him by criticizing their boss.

More disturbing is the transformation that takes place in Gregor's family, where the expected love and support turns into shamed acceptance and animal resentment now that Gregor has let the family down. Mother and sister are ineffectual, and their sympathy is slowly replaced by disgust. Gregor's father quickly reassumes his position of authority and beats the vermin back into his room: first with the newspaper and chief clerk's cane, and later with a barrage of apples from the family table. Gregor eventually becomes an "it" for whom the family feels no affection. Even before his transformation, Gregor seems to have lost all purpose in life except earning money to repay his parents' debts.

These frustrated desires contribute to the central conflict: whether Gregor can ever emerge from his bedroom and become part of the family again. The slapstick-like comedy of Gregor's attempts to use his insect body underlines the sense of exclusion and broadens the novella's appeal. Perhaps everyone has, occasionally, felt like an outsider, but Gregor's metamorphosis makes him an alien of a literal sort. His attitude at times reflects the sullenness of an unhappy teenager; at other times, he seems more like a terminal patient who fears placing an undue burden on his family. The theme of transformation goes back to Ovid's *Metamorphoses*, in which frustrated sexual desire often plays a role in turning people into plants or animals. The dark humor and uncanniness of Kafka's work links it to fantastic works by authors such as

Edgar Allan Poe (American, 1809–1849) and Heinrich Wilhelm Kleist (German, 1771–1811) and to the analysis of the psyche conducted, during Kafka's lifetime, by Sigmund Freud. Without directly blaming Gregor, Kafka sometimes seems to hint that his transformation results in part from the protagonist's desire to escape from human interaction.

Kafka exposes both the pathos and the humor of the situation, and for this reason the story retains its attraction today. He has been recognized as an important influence by a range of modern writers, including **Samuel Beckett**, Harold Pinter (English playwright, 1930–2008), and many Latin Americans—among them, **Jorge Luis Borges** and **Gabriel García Márquez**. Kafka was one of the great storytellers of modern life, capable of showing the emptiness that can lie at the heart even of a busy life in a crowded city apartment.

The Metamorphosis[1]

I

When Gregor Samsa awoke one morning from troubled dreams, he found himself changed into a monstrous cockroach in his bed. He lay on his tough, armoured back, and, raising his head a little, managed to see—sectioned off by little crescent-shaped ridges into segments—the expanse of his arched, brown belly, atop which the coverlet perched, forever on the point of slipping off entirely. His numerous legs, pathetically frail by contrast to the rest of him, waved feebly before his eyes.

'What's the matter with me?' he thought. It was no dream. There, quietly between the four familiar walls, was his room, a normal human room, if always a little on the small side. Over the table, on which an array of cloth samples was spread out—Samsa was a travelling salesman—hung the picture he had only recently clipped from a magazine, and set in an attractive gilt frame. It was a picture of a lady in a fur hat and stole, sitting bolt upright, holding in the direction of the onlooker a heavy fur muff into which she had thrust the whole of her forearm.

From there, Gregor's gaze directed itself towards the window, and the drab weather outside—raindrops could be heard plinking against the tin window-

1. Translated by Michael Hofmann.

ledges—made him quite melancholy. 'What if I went back to sleep for a while, and forgot about all this nonsense?' he thought, but that proved quite impossible, because he was accustomed to sleeping on his right side, and in his present state he was unable to find that position. However vigorously he flung himself to his right, he kept rocking on to his back. He must have tried it a hundred times, closing his eyes so as not to have to watch his wriggling legs, and only stopped when he felt a slight ache in his side which he didn't recall having felt before.

'Oh, my Lord!' he thought. 'If only I didn't have to follow such an exhausting profession! On the road, day in, day out. The work is so much more strenuous than it would be in head office, and then there's the additional ordeal of travelling, worries about train connections, the irregular, bad meals, new people all the time, no continuity, no affection. Devil take it! He felt a light itch at the top of his belly: slid a little closer to the bedpost, so as to be able to raise his head a little more effectively; found the itchy place, which was covered with a sprinkling of white dots the significance of which he was unable to interpret: assayed the place with one of his legs, but hurriedly withdrew it, because the touch caused him to shudder involuntarily.

He slid back to his previous position. 'All this getting up early,' he thought, 'is bound to take its effect. A man needs proper bed rest. There are some other travelling salesmen I could mention who live like harem women. Sometimes, for instance, when I return to the *pension* in the course of the morning, to make a note of that morning's orders, some of those gents are just sitting down to breakfast. I'd like to see what happened if I tried that out with my director some time; it would be the order of the boot just like that. That said, it might be just the thing for me. If I didn't have to exercise restraint for the sake of my parents, then I would have quit a long time ago; I would have gone up to the director and told him exactly what I thought of him. He would have fallen off his desk in surprise! That's a peculiar way he has of sitting anyway, up on his desk, and talking down to his staff from on high, making them step up to him very close because he's so hard of hearing. Well, I haven't quite given up hope: once I've got the money together to pay back what my parents owe him—it may take me another five or six years—then I'll do it, no question. Then we'll have the parting of the ways. But for the time being, I'd better look sharp, because my train leaves at five.'

And he looked across at the alarm clock, ticking away on the bedside table. 'Great heavenly Father!' he thought. It was half past six, and the clock hands were moving smoothly forward—in fact it was after half past, it was more like a quarter to seven. Had the alarm not gone off? He could see from the bed that it had been quite correctly set for four o'clock; it must have gone off. But how was it possible to sleep calmly through its ringing, which caused even the furniture to shake? Well, his sleep hadn't exactly been calm, but maybe it had been all the more profound. What to do now? The next train left at seven; to catch it meant hurrying like a madman, and his samples weren't yet packed, and he himself didn't feel exactly agile or vigorous. And even if he caught that train, he would still get a carpeting from the director, because the office boy would be on the platform at five o'clock, and would certainly have reported long since that Gregor hadn't been on the train. That boy was a real piece of work, so utterly beholden to the director, without any backbone or nous. Then what if he called in sick? That would be rather embarrassing and a little suspicious too, because in the course of the past five years, Gregor hadn't once been ill. The director was bound to retaliate by calling in the company doctor, would upbraid the parents for their idle son, and refute all objections by referring to the doctor, for whom there were only perfectly healthy but workshy patients. And who could say he was wrong, in this instance anyway? Aside from a continuing feeling of sleepiness that was quite unreasonable after such a long sleep, Gregor felt perfectly well, and even felt the stirrings of a healthy appetite.

As he was hurriedly thinking this, still no nearer to getting out of bed—the alarm clock was just striking a quarter to seven—there was a cautious knock on the door behind him. 'Gregor,' came the call—it was his mother—'it's a quarter to seven. Shouldn't you ought to be gone by now?' The mild voice. Gregor was dismayed when he heard his own in response. It was still without doubt his own voice from before, but with a little admixture of an irrepressible squeaking that left the words only briefly recognizable at the first instant of their sounding, only to set about them afterwards so destructively that one couldn't be at all sure what one had heard. Gregor had wanted to offer a full explanation of everything but, in these circumstances, kept himself to: 'All right, thank you, Mother, I'm getting up!' The wooden door must have muted the change in Gregor's voice, because his mother seemed content with his reply, and shuffled away. But the brief exchange had alerted other members of the family to the surprising fact that Gregor was still at home, and already there was his father, knocking on the door at the side of the room, feebly, but with his fist. 'Gregor, Gregor?' he shouted, 'what's the matter?' And after a little while, he came again, in a lower octave: 'Gregor! Gregor!' On the door on the other side of the room, meanwhile, he heard his sister lamenting softly: 'Oh, Gregor? Are you not well? Can I bring you anything?' To both sides equally Gregor replied. 'Just coming', and tried by careful enunciation and long pauses between the words to take any unusual quality from his voice. His father soon returned to his breakfast, but his sister whispered: 'Gregor, please, will you open the door.' Gregor entertained no thought of doing so; instead he gave silent thanks for the precaution, picked up on his travels, of locking every door at night, even at home.

His immediate intention was to get up calmly and leisurely, to get dressed and, above all, to have breakfast before deciding what to do next, because he was quite convinced he wouldn't arrive at any sensible conclusions as long as he remained in bed. There were many times, he remembered, when he had lain in bed with a sense of some dim pain somewhere in his body, perhaps from lying awkwardly, which then turned out, as he got up, to be mere imagining, and he looked forward to his present fanciful state gradually falling from him. He had not the least doubt that the alteration in his voice was just the first sign of a head-cold, always an occupational malady with travelling salesmen.

Casting off the blanket proved to be straightforward indeed; all he needed to do was to inflate himself a little, and it fell off by itself. But further tasks were more problematical, not least because of his great breadth. He would have needed arms and hands with which to get up: instead of which all he had were those numerous little legs, forever in varied movement, and evidently not under his control. If he wanted to bend one of them, then it was certain that that was the one that was next fully extended; and once he finally succeeded in performing whatever task he had set himself with that leg, then all its neglected fellows would be in a turmoil of painful agitation. 'Whatever I do, I mustn't loaf around in bed,' Gregor said to himself.

At first he thought he would get out of bed bottom half first, but this bottom half of himself, which he had yet to see, and as to whose specifications he was perfectly ignorant, turned out to be not very manoeuvrable; progress was slow; and when at last, almost in fury, he pushed down with all his strength, he misjudged the direction, and collided with the lower bedpost, the burning pain he felt teaching him that this lower end of himself might well be, for the moment, the most sensitive to pain.

He therefore tried to lever his top half out of bed first, and cautiously turned his head towards the edge of the bed. This was easily done, and, in spite of its breadth and bulk, the rest of his body slowly followed the direction of the head. But, now craning his neck in empty space well away from the bed, he was afraid to move any further, because if he were to fall in that position, it would take a miracle if he didn't injure his head. And he mustn't lose consciousness at any price; it were better then to stay in bed.

But as he sighed and lay there at the end of his endeavours, and once again beheld his legs struggling, if anything, harder than before, and saw no possibility of bringing any order or calm to their randomness, he told himself once more that he couldn't possibly stay in bed and that the most sensible solution was to try anything that offered even the smallest chance of getting free of his bed. At the same time, he didn't forget to remind himself periodically that clarity and calm were better than counsels of despair. At such moments, he levelled his gaze as sharply as possible at the window, but unfortunately there was little solace or encouragement to be drawn from the sight of the morning fog, which was thick enough to obscure even the opposite side of the street. 'Seven o'clock already,' he said to himself as his alarm clock struck another quarter, 'seven o'clock already, and still such dense fog.' And he lay there for a while longer, panting gently, as though perhaps expecting that silence would restore the natural order of things.

But then he said to himself: 'By quarter past seven, I must certainly have got out of bed completely. In any case, somebody will have come from work by then to ask after me, because the business opens before seven o'clock.' And he set about rhythmically rocking his body clear of the bed. If he dropped out of bed in that way, then he would try to raise his head sharply at the last moment, so that it remained uninjured. His back seemed to be tough; a fall on to the carpet would surely not do it any harm. What most concerned him was the prospect of the loud crash he would surely cause, which would presumably provoke anxiety, if not consternation, behind all the doors. But that was a risk he had to take.

As Gregor was already half-clear of the bed—this latest method felt more like play than serious exertion, requiring him only to rock himself from side to side— he thought how simple everything would be if he had some help. Two strong people—he thought of his father and the servant-girl—would easily suffice: they needed only to push their arms under his curved back, peel him out of bed, bend down under his weight, and then just pay attention while they flipped him over on to the floor, where his legs would hopefully come into their own. But then, even if the doors hadn't been locked, could he have really contemplated calling for help? Even in his extremity, he couldn't repress a smile at the thought.

He had already reached the point where his rocking was almost enough to send him off balance, and he would soon have to make up his mind once and for all what he was going to do, because it was ten past seven—when the door-bell rang. 'It must be someone from work.' he said to himself and went almost rigid, while his little legs, if anything, increased their agitation. For a moment there was silence. 'They won't open the door,' Gregor said to himself, from within some mad hope. But then of course, as always, the servant-girl walked with firm stride to the door and opened it. Gregor needed only to hear the first word from the visitor to know that it was the chief clerk in person. Why only was Gregor condemned to work for a company where the smallest lapse was greeted with the gravest suspicion? Were all the employees without exception scoundrels, were there really no loyal and dependable individuals among them, who, if once a couple of morning hours were not exploited for work, were driven so demented by pangs of conscience that they were unable to get out of bed? Was it really not enough to send a trainee to inquire—if inquiries were necessary at all—and did the chief clerk need to come in person, thereby demonstrating to the whole blameless family that the investigation of Gregor's delinquency could only be entrusted to the seniority and trained intelligence of a chief clerk? And more on account of the excitement that came over Gregor with these reflections, than as the result of any proper decision on his part, he powerfully swung himself right out of bed. There was a loud impact, though not a crash as such. The fall was somewhat muffled by the carpet: moreover, his back was suppler than Gregor had expected, and therefore the result was a dull thump that did not draw such immediate attention to itself. Only he had been a little careless of his head, and had bumped it: frantic with rage and pain, he turned and rubbed it against the carpet.

'Something's fallen down in there,' said the chief clerk in the hallway on the left. Gregor tried to imagine whether the chief clerk had ever experienced something similar to what had happened to himself today; surely it was within the bounds of possibility. But as if in blunt reply to this question, the chief clerk now took a few decisive steps next door, his patent-leather boots creaking. From the room on the right, his sister now whispered to Gregor: 'Gregor, the chief clerk's here.' 'I know,' Gregor replied to himself: but he didn't dare say it sufficiently loudly for his sister to hear him.

'Gregor,' his father now said from the left-hand room, 'the chief clerk has come, and wants to know why you weren't on the early train. We don't know what to tell him. He wants a word with you too. So kindly open the door. I'm sure he'll turn a blind eye to the untidiness in your room.' 'Good morning, Mr Samsa,' called the cheery voice of the chief clerk. 'He's not feeling well,' Gregor's mother interjected to the chief clerk, while his father was still talking by the door, he's not feeling well, believe me, Chief Clerk. How otherwise could Gregor miss his train! You know that boy has nothing but work in his head! It almost worries me that he never goes out on his evenings off; he's been in the city now for the past week, but he's spent every evening at home. He sits at the table quietly reading the newspaper, or studying the railway timetable. His only hobby is a little occasional woodwork. In the past two or three evenings, he's carved a little picture-frame: I think you'll be surprised by the workmanship: he's got it up on the wall in his room; you'll see it the instant Gregor opens the door. You've no idea how happy I am to see you, Chief Clerk; by ourselves we would never have been able to induce Gregor to open the door, he's so obstinate; and I'm sure he's not feeling well, even though he told us he was fine.' 'I'm just coming,' Gregor said slowly and deliberately, not stirring, so as not to miss a single word of the conversation outside. 'I'm sure you're right, madam,' said the chief clerk. 'I only hope it's nothing serious. Though again I have to say that—unhappily or otherwise—we businesspeople often find ourselves in the position of having to set aside some minor ailment, in the greater interest of our work.' 'So can we admit the chief clerk now?' asked his impatient father, knocking on the door again. 'No,' said Gregor. In the left-hand room there was now an awkward silence, while on the right his sister began to sob.

Why didn't his sister go and join the others? She had presumably only just got up, and hadn't started getting dressed yet. And then why was she crying? Because he wouldn't get up and admit the chief clerk, because he was in danger of losing his job, and because the director would then pursue his parents with the old claims? Surely those anxieties were still premature at this stage. Gregor was still here, and wasn't thinking at all about leaving the family. For now he was sprawled on the carpet, and no one who was aware of his condition could have seriously expected that he would allow the chief clerk into his room. But this minor breach of courtesy, for which he could easily find an explanation later, hardly constituted reason enough for Gregor to be sent packing. Gregor thought it was much more sensible for them to leave him alone now, rather than bother him with tears and appeals. It was just the uncertainty that afflicted the others and accounted for their behaviour.

'Mr Samsa,' the chief clerk now called out loudly, 'what's the matter? You've barricaded yourself into your room, you give us one-word answers, you cause your parents grave and needless anxiety and—this just by the by—you're neglecting your official duties in a quite unconscionable way. I am talking to you on behalf of your parents and the director, and I now ask you in all seriousness for a prompt and full explanation. I must say, I'm astonished. I'm astonished. I had taken you for a quiet and sensible individual, but you seem set on indulging a bizarre array of moods. This morning the director suggested a possible reason for your missing your train—it was to do with the authority to collect payments recently entrusted to you—but I practically gave him my word of honour that that couldn't be the explanation. Now, though, in view of your baffling obstinacy, I'm losing all inclination to speak up on your behalf. And your position is hardly the most secure. I had originally come with the intention of telling you as much in confidence, but as you seem to see fit to waste my time, I really don't know why your parents shouldn't get to hear about it as well. Your performances of late have been extremely unsatisfactory; it's admittedly not the time of year for the best results, we freely concede that; but a time of year for no sales, that doesn't exist in our calendars, Mr Samsa, and it mustn't exist.'

'But Chief Clerk,' Gregor exclaimed, in his excitement forgetting everything else, 'I'll let you in right away. A light indisposition, a fit of giddiness, have prevented me from getting up. I'm still lying in bed. But I feel almost restored. I'm even now getting out of bed. Just one moment's patience! It seems I'm not as much improved as I'd hoped. But I feel better just the same. How is it something like this can befall a person! Only last night I felt fine, my parents will confirm it to you, or rather, last night I had a little inkling already of what lay ahead. It probably showed in my appearance somewhere. Why did I not think to inform work! It's just that one always imagines that one will get over an illness without having to take time off. Chief Clerk, sir! Spare my parents! All those complaints you bring against me, they're all of them groundless: it's the first I've heard of any of them. Perhaps you haven't yet perused the last batch of orders I sent in. By the way, I mean to set out on the eight o'clock train—the couple of hours rest have done me the world of good. Chief Clerk, don't detain yourself any longer; I'll be at work myself presently. Kindly be so good as to let them know, and pass on my regards to the director!'

While Gregor blurted all this out, almost unaware of what he was saving, he had moved fairly effortlessly—no doubt aided by the practice he had had in bed—up to the bedside table, and now attempted to haul himself into an upright position against it. He truly had it in mind to open the door, to show himself and to speak to the chief clerk; he was eager to learn what the others, who were all clamouring for him, would say when they got to see him. If they were shocked, then Gregor would have no more responsibility, and could relax. Whereas if they took it all calmly, then he wouldn't have any cause for agitation either, and if he hurried, he might still get to the station by eight o'clock. To begin with he could get no purchase on the smooth bedside table, but at last he gave himself one more swing, and stood there upright; he barely noticed the pain in his lower belly, though it did burn badly. Then he let himself drop against the back of a nearby chair, whose edges he clasped with some of his legs. With that he had attained mastery over himself, and was silent, because now he could listen to the chief clerk.

'Did you understand a single word of that?' the chief clerk asked Gregor's parents, 'you don't suppose he's pulling our legs, do you?' 'In the name of God,' his mother cried, her voice already choked with tears, 'perhaps he's gravely ill, and we're tormenting him. Grete! Grete!' she called out. 'Mother?' his sister called back from the opposite side. They were communicating with one another through Gregor's room. 'Go to the doctor right away. Gregor's ill. Hurry and fetch the doctor. Were you able to hear him just now?' 'That was the voice of an animal,' said the chief clerk, strikingly much more quietly than his mother and her screaming. 'Anna! Anna!' his father shouted through the hallway, in the direction of the kitchen, and clapped his hands, 'get the locksmith right away!' And already two girls in rustling skirts were hurrying through the hallway—however had his sister managed to dress so quickly?—and out through the front door. There wasn't the bang of it closing either; probably they had left it open, as happens at times when a great misfortune has taken place.

Meanwhile, Gregor had become much calmer. It appeared his words were no longer comprehensible, though to his own hearing they seemed clear enough, clearer than before, perhaps because his ear had become attuned to the sound. But the family already had the sense of all not being well with him, and were ready to come to his assistance. The clarity and resolve with which the first instructions had been issued did him good. He felt himself back within the human ambit, and from both parties, doctor and locksmith, without treating them really in any way as distinct one from the other, he hoped for magnificent and surprising feats. In order to strengthen his voice for the decisive conversations that surely lay ahead, he cleared his throat a few times, as quietly as possible, as it appeared that even this sound was something other than a human cough, and he no longer trusted himself to tell the difference. Next door, things had become very quiet. Perhaps his parents were sitting at the table holding whispered consultations with the chief clerk, or perhaps they were all pressing their ears to the door, and listening.

Gregor slowly pushed himself across to the door with the chair, there let go of it and dropped against the door, holding himself in an upright position against it—the pads on his little legs secreted some sort of sticky substance—and there rested a moment from his exertions. And then he set himself with his mouth to turn the key in the lock. Unfortunately, it appeared that he had no teeth as such—what was he going to grip the key with?—but luckily his jaws were very powerful; with their help, he got the key to move, and he didn't stop to consider that he was certainly damaging himself in some way, because a brown liquid came out of his mouth, ran over the key, and dribbled on to the floor. 'Listen,' the chief clerk was saying next door, 'he's turning the key.' This was a great encouragement for Gregor; but they all of them should have called out to him, his father and mother too: 'Go, Gregor,' they should have shouted, 'keep at it, work at the lock!' And with the idea that they were all following his efforts with tense concentration, he bit fast on to the key with all the strength he possessed, to the point when he was ready to black out. The more the key moved in the door, the more he danced around the lock; now he was holding himself upright with just his mouth, and, depending on the position, he either hung from the key, or was pressing against it with the full weight of his body. The light click of the snapping lock brought Gregor round, as from a spell of unconsciousness. Sighing with relief, he said to himself: 'Well, I didn't need the locksmith after all,' and he rested his head on the door handle to open the door fully.

As he had had to open the door in this way, it was already fairly ajar while he himself was still out of sight. He first had to twist round one half of the door, and very cautiously at that, if he wasn't to fall flat on his back just at the point of making his entry into the room. He was still taken up with the difficult manoeuvre, and didn't have time to think about anything else, when he heard the chief clerk emit a sharp 'Oh!'—it actually sounded like the rushing wind—and then he saw him as well, standing nearest to the door, his hand pressed against his open mouth, and slowly retreating, as if being pushed back by an invisible but irresistible force. Gregor's mother—in spite of the chief clerk's arrival, she was standing there with her hair loose, though now it was standing up stiffly in the air—first looked at his father with folded hands, then took two steps towards Gregor and collapsed in the midst of her skirts spreading out around her, her face irretrievably sunk against her bosom. His father clenched his fist with a pugnacious expression, as if ready to push Gregor back into his room, then looked uncertainly round the living room, covered his eyes with his hands and cried, his mighty chest shaking with sobs.

Now Gregor didn't even set foot in the room, but leaned against the inside of the fixed half of the door, so that only half his body could be seen, and the head with which he was peering across at the others cocked on its side a little. It was much brighter now; a little section of the endless grey-black frontage of the building opposite—it was a hospital—could clearly be seen, with its rhythmically recurring windows; it was still raining, but now only in single large drops, individually fashioned and flung to the ground. The breakfast things were out on the table in profusion, because for his father breakfast was the most important meal of the day, which he liked to draw out for hours over the perusal of several newspapers. Just opposite, on the facing wall, was a photograph of Gregor from his period in the army, as a lieutenant, his hand on his sabre, smiling confidently, the posture and uniform demanding respect. The door to the hallway was open, and as the front door was open too one could see out to the landing, and the top of the flight of stairs down.

'Now,' said Gregor, in the knowledge that he was the only one present to have maintained his equanimity. 'I'm just going to get dressed, pack up my samples, and then I'll set off. Do you want to let me set out, do you? You see. Chief Clerk, you see, I'm not stubborn. I like my work; the travel is arduous, but I couldn't live without it. Where are you off to, Chief Clerk? To work? Is that right? Will you accurately report everything you've seen here? It is possible to be momentarily unfit for work, but that is precisely the time to remind oneself of one's former achievements, and to reflect that, once the present obstacle has been surmounted, one's future work will be all the more diligent and focused. As you know all too well. I am under a very great obligation to the director. In addition, I have responsibilities for my parents and my sister. I am in a jam, but I will work my way out of it. Only don't make it any harder for me than it is already! Give me your backing at head office! I know the travelling salesman is not held in the highest regard there. People imagine he earns a packet, and has a nice life on top of it. These and similar assumptions remain unexamined. But you, Chief Clerk, you have a greater understanding of the circumstances than the rest of the staff, you even, if I may say this to you in confidence, have an understanding superior to that of the director himself, who, as an entrepreneur, is perhaps too easily swayed against an employee. You are also very well aware that the travelling salesman, spending, as he does, the best part of the year away from head office, may all too easily fall victim to tittle-tattle, to mischance, and to baseless allegations, against which he has no way of defending himself— mostly even does not get to hear of—and when he returns exhausted from his travels, it is to find himself confronted directly by practical consequences of whose causes he is ignorant. Chief Clerk, don't leave without showing me by a word or two of your own that you at least partly agree with me!'

But the chief clerk had turned his back on Gregor the moment he had begun speaking, and only stared back at him with mouth agape, over his trembling shoulder. All the while Gregor was speaking, he wasn't still for a moment, but, without taking his eyes off Gregor, moved towards the door, but terribly gradually, as though in breach of some secret injunction not to leave the room. Already he was in the hallway, and to judge by the sudden movement with which he snatched his foot back out of the living room for the last time, one might have supposed he had burned his sole. Once in the hallway, he extended his right hand fervently in the direction of the stairs, as though some supernatural salvation there awaited him.

Gregor understood that he must on no account allow the chief clerk to leave in his present frame of mind, not if he wasn't to risk damage to his place in the company. His parents didn't seem to grasp this issue with the same clarity; over the course of many years, they had acquired the conviction that in this business Gregor had a job for life and, besides, they were so consumed by their anxieties of the present moment, that they had lost any premonitory sense they might have had. Gregor, though, had his. The chief clerk had to be stopped, calmed, convinced, and finally won over; the future of Gregor and his family depended on that! If only his sister were back already! There was a shrewd person: she had begun to cry even as Gregor was still lying calmly on his back. And no doubt the chief clerk, notorious skirt-chaser that he was, would have allowed himself to be influenced by her; she would have closed the front door, and in the hallway talked him out of his panic. But his sister wasn't there. Gregor would have to act on his own behalf. Without stopping to think that he didn't understand his given locomotive powers, without even thinking that this latest speech of his had possibly—no, probably—not been understood either, he left the shelter of the half-door and pushed through the opening, making for the chief clerk, who was laughably holding on to the balustrade on the landing with both hands. But straightaway, looking for a grip, Gregor dropped with a short cry on to his many little legs. No sooner had this happened, than for the first time that morning he felt a sense of physical well-being: the little legs had solid ground under them; they obeyed perfectly, as he noticed to his satisfaction, even seeking to carry him where he wanted to go; and he was on the point of believing a final improvement in his condition was imminent. But at that very moment, while he was still swaying from his initial impetus, not far from his mother and just in front of her on the ground, she, who had seemed so utterly immersed in herself, suddenly leaped into the air, arms wide, fingers spread, and screamed: 'Help, oh please God, help me!', inclined her head as though for a better view of Gregor, but then, quite at variance with that, ran senselessly away from him; she forgot the breakfast table was behind her; on reaching it, she hurriedly, in her distractedness, sat down on it, seeming oblivious to the fact that coffee was gushing all over the carpet from the large upset coffee pot.

'Mother, mother,' Gregor said softly, looking up at her. For the moment, he forgot all about the chief clerk; on the other hand, he couldn't help but move his jaws several times at the sight of the flowing coffee. At that his mother screamed again and fled from the table into the arms of Gregor's father who was rushing towards her. But now Gregor had no time for his parents: the chief clerk was already on the stairs; his chin on the balustrade, he stared behind him one last time. Gregor moved sharply to be sure of catching him up; the chief clerk must have sensed something, because he took the last few steps at a single bound and disappeared. 'Oof!' he managed to cry, the sound echoing through the stairwell. Regrettably, the consequence of the chief clerk's flight was finally to turn the senses of his father, who to that point had remained relatively calm, because, instead of himself taking off after the man, or at least not getting in the way of Gregor as he attempted to do just that, he seized in his right hand the chief clerk's cane, which he had left behind on a chair along with his hat and coat, with his left grabbed a large newspaper from the table, and, by stamping his feet, and brandishing stick and newspaper, attempted to drive Gregor back into his room. No pleas on Gregor's part were any use, no pleas were even understood. However imploringly he might turn his head, his father only stamped harder with his feet. Meanwhile, in spite of the cool temperature, his mother had thrown open a window on the other side of the room and, leaning out of it, plunged her face in her hands. A powerful draught was created between the stairwell and the street outside, the window curtains flew up, the newspapers rustled on the table, some individual pages fluttered across the floor. His father was moving forward implacably, emitting hissing sounds like a savage. Gregor had no practice in moving backwards, and he was moving, it had to be said, extremely slowly. If he had been able to turn round, he would have been back in his room in little or no time, but he was afraid lest the delay incurred in turning around would make his father impatient, and at any moment the stick in his father's hand threatened to strike him a fatal blow to the back of the head. Finally, Gregor had no alternative, because he noticed to his consternation that in his reversing he was unable to keep to a given course; and so, with continual fearful sidelong looks to his father, he started as quickly as possible, but in effect only very slowly, to turn round. It was possible that his father was aware of his good intentions, because he didn't obstruct him, but even directed the turning manoeuvre from a distance with gestures from his cane. If only there hadn't been those unbearable hissing sounds issuing from his father! They caused Gregor to lose all orientation. He had turned almost completely round, when, distracted by the hissing, he lost his way, and moved a little in the wrong direction. Then, when he found himself with his head successfully in the doorway, it became apparent that his body was too wide to slip through it. To his father, in his present frame of mind, it didn't remotely occur to open the other wing of the door, and so make enough space for Gregor. He was, rather, obsessed with the notion of getting Gregor back in his room posthaste. He could not possibly have countenanced the cumbersome preparations Gregor would have required to get up and perhaps so get around the door. Rather, as though there were no hindrance at all, he drove Gregor forward with even greater din: the sound to Gregor's ears was not that of one father alone: now it was really no laughing matter, and Gregor drove himself—happen what might—against the door. One side of his body was canted up, he found himself lifted at an angle in the doorway, his flank was rubbed raw, and some ugly stains appeared on the white door. Before long he was caught fast and could not have moved any more unaided, his little legs on one side were trembling in mid-air while those on the other found themselves painfully pressed against the ground—when from behind his father now gave him a truly liberating kick, and he was thrown, bleeding profusely, far into his room. The door was battered shut with the cane, and then at last there was quiet.

II

Not until dusk did Gregor awake from his heavy, almost comatose sleep. Probably he would have awoken around that time anyway, even if he hadn't been roused, because he felt sufficiently rested and restored. Still, it seemed to him as though a hurried footfall and a cautious shutting of the door to the hallway had awoken him. The pale gleam of the electric street-lighting outside showed on the ceiling and on the upper parts of the furniture, but down on the floor, where Gregor lay, it was dark. Slowly he rose and, groping clumsily with his feelers, whose function he only now began to understand, he made for the door, to see what had happened there. His whole left side was one long, unpleasantly stretched scab, and he was positively limping on his two rows of legs. One of his little legs had been badly hurt in the course of the morning's incidents—it was a wonder that it was only one—and it dragged after the rest inertly.

Not until he reached the door did he realize what had tempted him there; it was the smell of food. There stood a dish full of sweetened milk, with little slices of white bread floating in it. He felt like laughing for joy, because he was even hungrier now than he had been that morning, and straightaway he dunked his head into the milk past his eyes. But before long he withdrew it again in disappointment: it wasn't just that he found eating difficult on account of his damaged left flank—it seemed he could only eat if the whole of his body, panting, participated—more that he disliked the taste of milk, which otherwise was a favourite drink, and which his sister had certainly put out for him for that reason. In fact, he pulled his head away from the dish almost with revulsion, and crawled back into the middle of the room.

In the living room the gas-jet had been lit, as Gregor saw by looking through the crack in the door, but whereas usually at this time his father would be reading aloud to Gregor's mother or sometimes to his sister from the afternoon edition of the newspaper, there was now silence. Well, it was possible that this reading aloud, of which his sister had written and spoken to him many times, had been discontinued of late. But it was equally quiet to either side, even though it was hardly possible that there was no one home. 'What a quiet life the family used to lead,' Gregor said to himself, and, staring into the blackness, he felt considerable pride that he had made such a life possible for his parents and his sister, and in such a lovely flat. But what if all peace, all prosperity, all contentment, were to come to a sudden and terrible end? So as not to fall into such thoughts, Gregor thought he would take some exercise instead, and he crawled back and forth in the room.

Once in the course of the long evening one of the side-doors was opened a crack, and once the other, and then hurriedly closed again: someone seemed to feel a desire to step inside, but then again had too many cavils about so doing. Gregor took up position right against the living-room door, resolved to bring in the reluctant visitor in some way if he could, or, if nothing more, at least discover his identity; but then the door wasn't opened again, and Gregor waited in vain. Previously, when the doors were locked, everyone had tried to come in and see him, but now that he had opened one door himself, and the others had apparently been opened in the course of the day, no visitors came, and the keys were all on the outside too.

The light in the living room was left on far into the night, and that made it easy to verify that his parents and his sister had stayed up till then, because, as he could very well hear, that was when the three of them left on tiptoed feet. Now it was certain that no one would come in to Gregor's room until morning; so he had a long time ahead of him to reflect undisturbed on how he could reorder his life. But the empty high-ceilinged room where he was forced to lie flat on the floor disquieted him, without him being able to find a reason for his disquiet, because after all this was the room he had lived in these past five years—and with a half unconscious turn, and not without a little shame, he hurried under the sofa, where, even though his back was pressed down a little, and he was unable to raise his head, he straightaway felt very much at home, and only lamented the fact that his body was too broad to be entirely concealed under the sofa.

He stayed there all night, either half asleep, albeit woken by hunger at regular intervals, or kept half awake by anxieties and unclear hopes, which all seemed to lead to the point that he would comport himself quietly for the moment, and by patience and the utmost consideration for the family make the inconveniences he was putting them through in his present state a little bearable for them.

Early the next morning, while it was almost still night, Gregor had an opportunity to put his resolutions to the test, because the door from the hallway opened, and his sister, almost completely dressed, looked in on him with some agitation. It took her a while to find him, but when she spotted him under the sofa—my God, he had to be somewhere, he couldn't have flown off into space—she was so terrified that in an uncontrollable revulsion she slammed the door shut. But then, as if sorry for her behaviour, she straightaway opened the door again, and tiptoed in, as if calling on a grave invalid, or even a stranger. Gregor had pushed his head forward to the edge of the sofa, and observed her. Would she notice that he had left his milk, and then not by any means because he wasn't hungry, and would she bring in some different food that would suit him better? If she failed to do so of her own accord, then he preferred to die rather than tell her, even though he did feel an incredible urge to shoot out from under the sofa, hurl himself at his sister's feet, and ask her for some nice titbit to eat. But his sister was promptly startled by the sight of the full dish, from which only a little milk had been spilled round the edges. She picked it up right away, not with her bare hands but with a rag, and carried it out. Gregor was dying to see what she would bring him instead, and he entertained all sorts of conjectures on the subject. But never would he have been able to guess what in the goodness of her heart his sister did. She brought him, evidently to get a sense of his likes and dislikes, a whole array of things, all spread out on an old newspaper. There were some half-rotten vegetables; bones left over from dinner with a little congealed white sauce; a handful of raisins and almonds; a cheese that a couple of days ago Gregor had declared to be unfit for human consumption; a piece of dry bread, a piece of bread and butter, and a piece of bread and butter sprinkled with salt. In addition she set down a dish that was probably to be given over to Gregor's personal use, into which she had poured some water. Then, out of sheer delicacy, knowing that Gregor wouldn't be able to eat in from of her, she hurriedly left the room, even turning the key, just as a sign to Gregor that he could settle down and take his time over everything. Gregor's legs trembled as he addressed his meal. His wounds too must have completely healed over, for he didn't feel any hindrance, he was astonished to realize, and remembered how a little more than a month ago he had cut his finger with a knife, and only the day before yesterday the place still had hurt. 'I wonder if I have less sensitivity now?' he thought, as he sucked avidly on the cheese, which of all the proffered foodstuffs had most spontaneously and powerfully attracted him. Then, in rapid succession, and with eyes watering with satisfaction, he ate up the cheese, the vegetables and the sauce; the fresh foods, on the other hand, were not to his liking—he couldn't even bear the smell of them, and dragged such things as he wanted to eat a little way away from them. He was long done with everything, and was just lounging lazily where he had eaten, when his sister, to signal that he was to withdraw, slowly turned the key in the lock. That immediately stung him out of his drowsiness, and he dashed back under the sofa. But it cost him a great effort to remain there, even for the short time his sister was in the room, because his big meal had filled out his belly, and he was scarcely able to breathe in his little space. Amidst little fits of panic suffocation, he watched with slightly bulging eyes, as his sister, all unawares, swept everything together with a broom—not only the leftovers, but also those elements of food that Gregor hadn't touched, as though they too were now not good for anything, and as she hastily tipped everything into a bucket, on which she set a wooden lid, whereupon she carried everything back out. No sooner had she turned her back than Gregor came out from under the sofa, stretched and pulled himself up.

This was how Gregor was now fed every day, once in the morning, while his parents and the maid were still asleep, and a second time after lunch, when his parents had their little lie down, and his sister sent the maid out on some errand or other. For sure, none of them wanted Gregor to starve, but maybe they didn't want to confront in so much material detail the idea of him eating anything. Perhaps also his sister wanted to spare them a little grief, because certainly they were suffering enough as it was.

With what excuses the doctor and locksmith were got rid of on that first morning was something Gregor never learned, because as he was not able to make himself understood, it didn't occur to anyone, not even his sister, that he could understand others, and so, when his sister was in his room, he had to content himself with hearing her occasional sighs and appeals to various saints. Only later, once she had got adjusted to everything a little—of course there could be no question of becoming fully used to it—Gregor sometimes caught a well-intentioned remark, or one that was capable of being interpreted as such. He had a good appetite today, she said, when Gregor had dealt with his food in determined fashion, whereas, in the opposite case, which came to be the rule, she would sometimes say, almost sorrowfully: 'Oh, it's hardly been touched today.'

While Gregor was not given any news directly he was sometimes able to glean developments from the adjoining rooms, and whenever he heard anyone speaking, he would rush to the door in question, and press his whole body against it. Especially in the early days, there was no conversation that did not somehow, in some oblique way, deal with him. For two days, at each meal, there were debates as to how one ought to behave: and in between meals, the same subject was also discussed, because there were always at least two members of the household at home, probably as no one wanted to be alone at home, and couldn't in any case wholly leave it. On the very first day the cook had begged on her knees—it was unclear what and how much she knew about what had happened—to be let go right away, and when she took her leave a quarter of an hour later, she said thank-you for her dismissal, as if it was the greatest kindness she had experienced here, and, without anyone demanding it of her, gave the most solemn oath never to betray the least thing to anyone.

Now his sister had to do the cooking in harness with his mother; admittedly, it didn't create much extra work for her, because no one ate anything. Gregor kept hearing them vainly exhorting one another to eat, and receiving no reply, other than: 'Thank you, I've enough,' or words to that effect. Perhaps they didn't drink anything either. Often, his sister asked his father whether he would like a beer, and offered to fetch it herself, and when her father made no reply, she said, to get over his hesitation, that she could equally well send the janitor woman out for it, but in the end his father said a loud 'No', and there was an end of the matter.

Already in the course of that first day his father set out the fortunes and prospects of the family to his mother and sister. From time to time, he got up from the table and produced some certificate or savings book from his little home safe, which he had managed to rescue from the collapse of his business five years ago. One could hear him opening the complicated lock, and shutting it again after taking out the desired item. These explanations from his father constituted the first good news that had reached Gregor's ears since his incarceration. He had been of the view that the winding-up of the business had left his father with nothing—at any rate his father had never said anything to the contrary, and Gregor hadn't questioned him either. At the time Gregor had bent all his endeavours to helping the family to get over the commercial catastrophe, which had plunged them all into complete despair, as quickly as

possible. And so he had begun working with an especial zeal and almost overnight had moved from being a little junior clerk to a travelling salesman, who
of course had earning power of an entirely different order, and whose successes in the form of percentages were instantly turned into money, which
could be laid out on the table of the surprised and delighted family. They had
been good times, and they had never returned, at least not in that magnificence, even though Gregor went on to earn so much money that he was able to
bear, and indeed bore, the expenses of the whole family. They had just become
used to it, both the family and Gregor; they gratefully took receipt of his
money, which he willingly handed over, but there was no longer any particular
warmth about it. Only his sister had remained close to Gregor, and it was his
secret project to send her, who unlike himself loved music and played the
violin with great feeling, to the conservatory next year, without regard to the
great expense that was surely involved, and that needed to be earned, most
probably in some other fashion. In the course of Gregor's brief stays in the city,
the conservatory often came up in conversations with his sister, but always as
a beautiful dream, not conceivably to be realized, and their parents disliked
even such innocent references: but Gregor thought about it quite purposefully,
and meant to make a formal announcement about it at Christmas.

Such—in his present predicament—perfectly useless thoughts crowded his
head, while he stuck to the door in an upright position, listening. Sometimes,
from a general fatigue, he was unable to listen, and carelessly let his head drop
against the door, before holding it upright again, because even the little noise
he had made had been heard next door, and had caused them all to fall silent.
'Wonder what he's doing now,' said his father after a while, evidently turning
towards the door, and only then was the interrupted conversation gradually
resumed.

Because his father tended to repeat himself in his statements—partly because
he had long disregarded these matters, and partly because Gregor's mother
often didn't understand when they were first put to her—Gregor now had
plenty of occasion to hear that, in spite of the calamity, an admittedly small
nest egg had survived from the old days, and had grown a little over the intervening years through the compounding of interest. In addition to this, the
money that Gregor had brought home every month—he kept back no more
than a couple of guilder for himself—had not been used up completely, and
had accrued to another small lump sum. Behind his door, Gregor nodded
enthusiastically, delighted by this unexpected caution and prudence. The surplus funds might have been used to pay down his father's debt to the director,
thereby bringing closer the day when he might quit this job, but now it seemed
to him better done the way his father had done it.

Of course, the money was nowhere near enough for the family to live off the
interest, say; it might be enough to feed them all for a year or two, at most, but
no more. Really it was a sum that mustn't be touched, that ought to be set
aside for an emergency; money for day-to-day living expenses needed to be
earned. His father was a healthy, but now elderly man, who hadn't worked for
five years now, and who surely shouldn't expect too much of himself; in those
five years, which were the first holidays of a strenuous and broadly unsuccessful life, he had put on a lot of fat, and had slowed down considerably. And was
his old mother to go out and earn money, who suffered from asthma, to whom

merely going from one end of the flat to the other was a strain, and who spent every other day on the sofa struggling for breath in front of the open window? Or was his sister to make money, still a child with her seventeen years, and who so deserved to be left in the manner of her life heretofore, which had consisted of wearing pretty frocks, sleeping in late, helping out at the pub, taking part in a few modest celebrations and, above all, playing the violin. Whenever the conversation turned to the necessity of earning money, Gregor would let go of the door, and throw himself on to the cool leather sofa beside it, because he was burning with sorrow and shame.

Often he would lie there all night, not sleeping a wink, and just scraping against the leather for hours. Nor did he shun the great effort of pushing a chair over to the window, creeping up to the window-sill, and, propped against the armchair, leaning in the window, clearly in some vague recollection of the liberation he had once used to feel, gazing out of the window. For it was true to say that with each passing day his view of distant things grew fuzzier; the hospital across the road, whose ubiquitous aspect he had once cursed, he now no longer even saw, and if he hadn't known for a fact that he lived in the leafy, but perfectly urban Charlottenstrasse, he might have thought that his window gave on to a wasteland where grey sky merged indistinguishably with grey earth. His alert sister needed only to spot that the armchair had been moved across to the window once or twice, before she took to pushing the chair over there herself after tidying Gregor's room, and even leaving the inner window ajar.

Had Gregor been able to speak to his sister and to thank her for everything she had to do for him, he would have found it a little easier to submit to her ministrations; but, as it was, he suffered from them. His sister, for her part, clearly sought to blur the embarrassment of the whole thing, and the more time passed, the better able she was to do so, but Gregor was also able to see through everything more acutely. Even her entry was terrible for him. No sooner had she stepped into his room, than without even troubling to shut the door behind her—however much care she usually took to save anyone passing the sight of Gregor's room—she darted over to the window and flung it open with febrile hands, almost as if she were suffocating, and then, quite regardless of how cold it might be outside, she stood by the window for a while, taking deep breaths. She subjected Gregor to her scurrying and her din twice daily; for the duration of her presence, he trembled under the sofa, even though he knew full well that she would have been only too glad to spare him the awkwardness, had it been possible for her to remain in the same room as her brother with the window closed.

On one occasion—it must have been a month or so after Gregor's metamorphosis, and there was surely no more cause for his sister to get agitated about Gregor's appearance—she came in a little earlier than usual and saw Gregor staring out of the window, immobile, almost as though set up on purpose to give her a fright. Gregor would not have been surprised if she had stopped in her tracks, seeing as he impeded her from going over and opening the window, but not only did she not come in, she leaped back and locked the door; a stranger might have supposed that Gregor had been lying in wait for her, to bite her. Naturally, Gregor straightaway went and hid under the sofa, but he had to wait till noon for his sister to reappear, and then she seemed more agitated than usual. From that he understood that the sight of him was still unbearable to her and would continue to be unbearable to her, and that she probably had to control herself so as not to run away at the sight of that little portion of his body that peeped out from under the sofa. One day, in a bid to save her from that as well, he moved the tablecloth on to the sofa—the labour took him four hours—and arranged it in such a way that he was completely covered, and that his sister, even if she bent down, would be unable to see him. If this covering hadn't been required in her eyes, she could easily have removed it, because it was surely clear enough that it was no fun for Gregor to screen himself from sight so completely, but she left the cloth *in situ*, and once Gregor even thought he caught a grateful look from her, as he moved the cloth ever so slightly with his head to see how his sister was reacting to the new arrangement.

During the first fortnight, his parents would not be induced to come in and visit him, and he often heard their professions of respect for what his sister was now doing, whereas previously they had frequently been annoyed with her for being a somewhat useless girl. Now, though, both of them, father and mother, often stood outside Gregor's room while his sister was cleaning up inside, and no sooner had she come out than she had to tell them in precise detail how things looked in the room, what Gregor had eaten, how he had behaved this time, and whether there wasn't some sign of an improvement in his condition. His mother, by the way, quite soon wanted to visit Gregor herself, but his father and sister kept her from doing so with their common-sense arguments, to which Gregor listened attentively, and which met with his wholehearted approval. Later on, it took force to hold her back, and when she cried, 'Let me see Gregor, after all he is my unhappy son! Won't you understand that I have to see him?' then Gregor thought it might after all be a good thing if his mother saw him, not every day of course, but perhaps as often as once a week; she did have a much better grasp of everything than his sister, who, for all her pluck, was still a child, and ultimately had perhaps taken on such a difficult task purely out of childish high spirits.

Before very long, Gregor's desire to see his mother was granted. Gregor didn't care to sit in the window in the daytime out of regard for his parents, nor was he able to crawl around very much on the few square yards of floor; even at night he was scarcely able to lie quietly, his food soon stopped affording him the least pleasure, and so, to divert himself, he got into the habit of crawling all over the walls and ceiling. He was particularly given to hanging off the ceiling: it felt very different from lying on the floor; he could breathe more easily; a gentle thrumming vibration went through his body; and in the almost blissful distraction Gregor felt up there, it could even happen that to his own surprise he let himself go, and smacked down on the floor. Of course his physical mastery of his body was of a different order from what it had been previously, and so now he didn't hurt himself, even after a fall from a considerable height. His sister observed the new amusement Gregor had found for himself—as he crept here and there he couldn't avoid leaving some traces of his adhesive secretion—and she got it into her head to maximize the amount of crawling Gregor could do, by removing those pieces of furniture that got in his way, in particular the wardrobe and the desk. But it was not possible for her to do so unaided; she didn't dare ask her father for help; the maid would certainly not have helped, because while this girl of about sixteen had bravely stayed on after the cook's departure, she had also asked in return that she might keep the kitchen locked, and only have to open it when particularly required to do so; so Gregor's sister had no alternative but to ask her mother on an occasion when her father was away. Gregor's mother duly came along with cries of joy and excitement, only to lapse into silence outside Gregor's door. First, his sister checked to see that everything in the room was tidy; only then did she allow her mother to step inside. In a very great rush, Gregor had pulled the tablecloth down lower, with more pleats, and the whole thing really had the appearance of a cloth draped casually over the sofa. He also refrained from peeping out from underneath it; he declined to try to see his mother on this first visit, he was just happy she had come. 'It's all right, you won't see him,' said his sister, who was evidently taking her mother by the hand. Now Gregor heard the two weak women shifting the heavy old wardrobe from its place, and how his sister always did the bulk of the work, ignoring the warnings of his mother, who kept fearing she might over-strain herself. It took a very long time. It was probably after fifteen minutes of toil that his mother said it would be better to leave the wardrobe where it was, because firstly it was too heavy, they would never manage to get it moved before father's return, and by leaving it in the middle of the room they would only succeed in leaving an irritating obstruction for Gregor, and secondly it was by no means certain that they were doing Gregor a favour by removing that piece of furniture anyway. She rather thought the opposite; the sight of the empty stretch of wall clutched at her heart; and why shouldn't Gregor have a similar sensation too, seeing as he was long accustomed to his bedroom furni-ture, and was therefore bound to feel abandoned in the empty room. 'And isn't it the case as well,' his mother concluded very quietly—indeed she was barely talking above a whisper throughout, as though to prevent Gregor, whose where-abouts she didn't know, from even hearing the sound of her voice, seeing as she felt certain that he wasn't capable of understanding her words anyway—'isn't it the case as well, that by taking away his furniture, we would be showing him we were abandoning all hope of an improvement in his condition, and leaving him utterly to his own devices? I think it would be best if we try to leave the room in exactly the condition it was before, so that, if Gregor is returned to us, he will find everything unaltered, and will thereby be able to forget the intervening period almost as if it hadn't happened.'

As he listened to these words of his mother, Gregor understood that the want of any direct human address, in combination with his monotonous life at the heart of the family over the past couple of months, must have confused his understanding, because otherwise he would not have been able to account for the fact that he seriously wanted to have his room emptied out. Was it really his wish to have his cosy room, comfortably furnished with old heirlooms, trans-formed into a sort of cave, merely so that he would be able to crawl around in it freely, without hindrance in any direction—even at the expense of rapidly and utterly forgetting his human past? He was near enough to forgetting it now, and only the voice of his mother, which he hadn't heard for a long time, had reawak-ened the memory in him. Nothing was to be taken out; everything was to stay as it was: the positive influence of the furniture on his condition was indispens-able; and if the furniture prevented him from crawling around without rhyme or reason, then that was no drawback either, but a great advantage.

But his sister was unfortunately of a different mind; she had become accus-tomed, not without some justification either, to cast herself in the role of a sort of expert when Gregor's affairs were discussed with her parents, and so her mother's urgings now had the effect on his sister of causing her to insist on the removal not merely of the wardrobe and the desk, which was all she had originally proposed, but of all the furniture, with the sole exception of the indispensable sofa. It wasn't merely childish stubbornness and a surge of unexpected and hard-won self-confidence that prompted her to take this view; she had observed that Gregor needed a lot of space for his crawling, and in the course of it, so far as she had seen, made no use whatever of the furniture. Perhaps the natural enthusiasm of a girl of her age played a certain role too, a quality that seeks its own satisfaction in any matter, and this now caused Grete to present Gregor's situation in even starker terms, so that she might do even more for him than she had thus far. For it was unthinkable that anyone else would dare to set foot in a room where Gregor all alone made free with the bare walls.

And so she refused to abandon her resolution in the face of the arguments of her mother, who seemed to have been overwhelmed by uncertainty in this room, and who, falling silent, to the best of her ability helped his sister to remove the wardrobe from the room. Well, Gregor could do without the wardrobe if need be, but the writing-desk had to stay. And no sooner had the two women left with the wardrobe, against which they pressed themselves groaning with effort, than Gregor thrust his head out from under the sofa, to see how best, with due care and respect, he might intervene on his own behalf. It was unfortunate that it was his mother who came back in first, while Grete was still clasping the wardrobe in the next-door room, hefting it this way and that, without of course being able to budge it from the spot. His mother was not accustomed to the sight of Gregor, it could have made her ill, and so Gregor reversed hurriedly to the far end of the sofa, but was unable to prevent the cloth from swaying slightly. That was enough to catch his mother's attention. She paused, stood still for a moment, and then went back to Grete.

Even though Gregor kept telling himself there was nothing particular going on, just a few sticks of furniture being moved around, he soon had to admit to himself that the to-ing and fro-ing of the two women, their little exhortations to one another, the scraping of the furniture on the floor, did have the effect on him of a great turmoil nourished on all sides, and he was compelled to admit that, however he drew in his head and his legs and pressed his belly to the floor, he would be unable to tolerate much more of it. They were clearing his room out: taking away everything that was dear to him: they had already taken the wardrobe that contained his jigsaw and his other tools, now they were prising away the desk that seemed to have taken root in the floor, where he had done his homework at trade school, at secondary, even at elementary school—he really had no more time to consider the good intentions of the two women, whose existence he had practically forgotten, because they were now so exhausted they were doing their work in near silence, all that could be heard of them being their heavy footfalls.

And so he erupted forth—the women were just resting on the desk next door, to catch their breath—and four times changed his direction for he really didn't know what he should rescue first, when he saw the picture of the fur-clad woman all the more prominent now, because the wall on which it hung had now been cleared, crawled hurriedly up to it and pressed himself against the glass, which stuck to him and imparted a pleasant coolness to his hot belly. At least no one would now take away this picture, which Gregor now completely covered. He turned his head in the direction of the living room door, to see the women as they returned.

They hadn't taken much of a break, and here they came again; Grete had laid her arm around her mother, and was practically carrying her. 'Well, what shall we take next? Grete said, looking around. Then her eyes encountered those of Gregor, up on the wall. She kept her calm, probably only on account of the presence of her mother, inclined her face towards her, to keep her from looking around, and said, with a voice admittedly trembling and uncontrolled: 'Oh, let's just go back to the living room for a moment, shall we?' Grete's purpose was clear enough to Gregor; she wanted to get her mother to safety, and then chase him off the wall. Well, just let her try! He would perch on his picture, and never surrender it. He would rather fly in Grete's face.

But Grete's words served only to disquiet her mother, who stepped to one side, spotted the giant brown stain on the flowered wallpaper, and, before she had time to understand what she saw, she cried in a hoarse, screaming voice, 'Oh my God, oh my God!' and with arms outspread, as though abandoning everything she had, fell across the sofa, and didn't stir. 'Ooh, Gregor!' cried his sister, brandishing her fist and glowering at him. Since his metamorphosis, they were the first words she had directly addressed to him. She ran next door to find some smelling-salts to rouse her mother from her faint; Gregor wanted to help too—he could always go back and rescue the picture later on—but he was stuck fast to the glass, and had to break free of it by force; then he trotted next door as though he could give his sister some advice, as in earlier times; was forced to stand around idly behind her while she examined various different flasks; and gave her such a shock, finally, when she spun round, that a bottle crashed to the ground and broke. One splinter cut Gregor in the face, the fumes of some harshly corrosive medicine causing him to choke; Grete ended up by grabbing as many little flasks as she could hold, and ran with them to her mother; she slammed the door shut with her foot. Gregor was now shut off from his mother, who, through his fault, was possibly close to death; there was nothing he could do but wait; and assailed by reproach and dread, he began to crawl. He crawled over everything, the walls, the furniture, the ceiling, and finally in his despair, with the whole room already spinning round him, he dropped on to the middle of the dining table.

Some time passed. Gregor lay there dully, there was silence all round, perhaps it was a good sign. Then the bell rang. The maid, of course, was locked away in her kitchen, and so Grete had to go to the door. His father was back. 'What happened?' were his first words; Grete's appearance must have given everything away. She answered in muffled tones; clearly she must be pressing her face to her father's chest: 'Mother had a faint, but she's feeling better now. Gregor's got loose.' 'I knew it,' said his father. 'Wasn't I always telling you, but you women never listen.' Gregor understood that his father must have put the worst possible construction on Grete's all too brief account, and supposed that Gregor had perpetrated some act of violence. Therefore Gregor must try to mollify his father, because for an explanation there was neither time nor means. And so he fled to the door of his room, and pressed himself against it, so that his father, on stepping in from the hallway, might see right away that Gregor had every intention of going back promptly into his room, and there was no necessity to use force, he had only to open the door for him, and he would disappear through it right away.

But his father wasn't in the mood to observe such details: 'Ah!' he roared, the moment he entered, in a tone equally enraged and delighted. Gregor withdrew his head from the door, and turned to look at his father. He really hadn't imagined him the way he was; admittedly, he had been distracted of late by the novel sensation of crawling, and had neglected to pay attention to goings-on in the rest of the flat, as he had previously, and so really he should have been prepared to come upon some alterations. But really, really, was that still his father? The same man who had lain feebly buried in bed, when Gregor had set out formerly on a business trip; who had welcomed him back at night, in his nightshirt and rocking-chair; not even properly able to get to his feet any more, but merely raising both arms in token of his pleasure; and who on his infrequent walks on one or two Sundays per year, and on the most solemn holidays, walked between Gregor and his wife slowly enough anyway, but still slower than them, bundled into his old overcoat, feeling his way forward with his carefully jabbing stick, and each time he wanted to speak, stopping to gather his listeners about him? And now here he was fairly erect; wearing a smart blue uniform with gold buttons, like the doorman of a bank; over the stiff collar of his coat, the bulge of a powerful double-chin; under the bushy eyebrows an alert and vigorous expression in his black eyes; his habitually unkempt white hair now briskly parted and combed into a shining tidy arrangement. He threw his cap, which had on it a gold monogram, presumably that of the bank, across the whole room in an arc on to the sofa, and, hands in his pockets, with the skirts of his long coat trailing behind him, he walked up to Gregor with an expression of grim resolve. He probably didn't know himself what he would do next; but even so, he raised his feet to an uncommon height, and Gregor was startled by the enormous size of his bootsoles. But he didn't allow himself the leisure to stop and remark on it; he had understood from the first day of his new life that his father thought the only policy to adopt was one of the utmost severity towards him. And so he scurried along in front of his father, pausing when he stopped, and hurrying on the moment he made another movement. In this way, they circled the room several times, without anything decisive taking place, yes, even without the whole process having the appearance of a chase, because of its slow tempo. It was for that reason too that Gregor remained on the floor for the time being, because he was afraid that if he took to the walls or ceiling, his father night interpret that as a sign of particular wickedness on his part. Admittedly, Gregor had to tell himself he couldn't keep up even this slow pace for very long, because in the time his father took a single step, he needed to perform a whole multiplicity of movements. He was already beginning to get out of breath—even in earlier times his lungs hadn't been altogether reliable. As he teetered along, barely keeping his eyes open, in order to concentrate all his resources on his movement—in his dull-wittedness not even thinking of any other form of salvation beyond merely keeping going: and had almost forgotten that the walls were available to him, albeit obstructed by carefully carved items of furniture, full of spikes and obstructions—something whizzed past him, something had been hurled at him, something now rolling around on the floor in front of him. It was an apple; straightaway it was followed by another; Gregor in terror was rooted to the spot; there was no sense in keeping moving, not if his father had decided to have recourse to artillery. He had filled his pockets from the fruit bowl on the sideboard, and was hurling one apple after another, barely pausing to take aim.

These little red apples rolled around on the floor as though electrified, often caroming into one another. A feebly tossed apple brushed against Gregor's back, only to bounce off it harmlessly. One thrown a moment later, however, secured to pierce it. Gregor tried to drag himself away, as though the bewildering and scarcely credible pain might pass if he changed position; but he felt as though nailed to the spot, and in complete disorientation, he stretched out. With one last look he saw how the door to his room was flung open, and his mother ran out in front of his howling sister, in her chemise—his sister must have undressed her to make it easier for her to breathe after her fainting fit— how his mother ran towards his father, and as she ran her loosened skirts successively slipped to the floor, and how, stumbling over them she threw herself at his father, and embracing him, in complete union with him—but now Gregor's eyesight was failing him—with her hands clasping the back of his head, begged him to spare Gregor's life.

III

The grave wound to Gregor, from whose effects he suffered for over a month—as no one dared to remove the apple, it remained embedded in his flesh, as a visible memento—seemed to have reminded even his father that in spite of his current sorry and loathsome form, Gregor remained a member of the family, and must not be treated like an enemy, but as someone whom—all revulsion to the contrary—family duty compelled one to choke down, and who must be tolerated, simply tolerated.

Even if Gregor had lost his mobility, and presumably for good, so that now like an old invalid he took an age to cross his room—there could be no more question of crawling up out of the horizontal—this deterioration of his condition acquired a compensation, perfectly adequate in his view, in the fact that each evening now, the door to the living room, which he kept under sharp observation for an hour or two before it happened, was opened, so that, lying in his darkened room, invisible from the living room, he was permitted to see the family at their lit-up table, and, with universal sanction, as it were, though now in a completely different way than before, to listen to them talk together.

Admittedly, these were not now the lively conversations of earlier times, which Gregor had once called to mind with some avidity as he lay down exhausted in the damp sheets of some poky hotel room. Generally, things were very quiet. His father fell asleep in his armchair not long after supper was over; his mother and sister enjoined one another to be quiet; his mother, sitting well forward under the lamp, sewed fine linen for some haberdashery; his sister, who had taken a job as salesgirl, studied stenography and French in the evenings, in the hope of perhaps one day getting a better job. Sometimes his father would wake up, and as though unaware that he had been asleep, would say to his mother: 'Oh, you've been sewing all this time!' and promptly fall asleep again, while mother and sister exchanged tired smiles.

With an odd stubbornness, his father now refused to take off his uniform coat when he was at home; and while his dressing-gown hung uselessly on its hook, his fully dressed father dozed in his chair, as though ready at all times to be of service, waiting, even here, for the voice of his superior. As a result, the uniform, which even to begin with had not been new, in spite of all the precautions of mother and sister, rapidly lost its cleanliness, and Gregor often spent whole evenings staring at this comprehensively stained suit, with its invariably gleaming gold buttons, in which the old man slept so calmly and uncomfortably.

As soon as the clock struck ten, his mother would softly wake his father, and talk him into going to bed, because he couldn't sleep properly where he was, and proper sleep was precisely what he needed, given that he had to be back on duty at six in the morning. But with the obstinacy that characterized him ever since he had become a commissionaire, he would always insist on staying at table longer, even though he quite regularly fell asleep there, and it was only with the greatest difficulty that he was then persuaded to exchange his chair for bed. However Gregor's mother and sister pleaded and remonstrated with him, he would slowly shake his head for a whole quarter of an hour at a time, keep his eyes shut, and refuse to get up. Gregor's mother would tug at his sleeve, whisper blandishments in his ear, his sister would leave her work to support her mother, but all in vain. His father would only slump deeper into his chair. Only when the women took him under the arms did he open his eyes, look alternately at them both, and then usually say: 'What sort of life is this? What sort of peace and dignity in my old days?' And propped up by the women, he would cumbersomely get to his feet, as though he was a great weight on himself, let them conduct him as far as the door, then gesture to them, and go on himself, while Gregor's mother hurriedly threw down her sewing, and his sister her pen, to run behind him and continue to be of assistance.

Who in this exhausted and overworked family had the time to pay any more attention to Gregor than was absolutely necessary? The household seemed to shrink: the maid was now allowed to leave after all; a vast bony charwoman with a great mane of white hair came in the morning and evening to do the brunt of the work; everything else had to be done by mother, in addition to her copious needlework. Things even came to such a pass that various family jewels, in which mother and sister had once on special occasions decked themselves, were sold off, as Gregor learned one evening, from a general discussion of the prices that had been achieved. The bitterest complaint, however, concerned the impossibility of leaving this now far too large apartment, as there was no conceivable way of moving Gregor. Gregor understood perfectly well that it wasn't any regard for him that stood in the way of a move, because all it would have taken was a suitably sized shipping crate, with a few holes drilled in it for him to breathe through; no, what principally kept the family from moving to another flat was their complete and utter despair—the thought that they in all the circle of relatives and acquaintances had been singled out for such a calamity. The things the world requires of poor people, they performed to the utmost, his father running out to get breakfast for the little bank officials, his mother hurling herself at the personal linen of strangers, his sister trotting back and forth behind the desk, doing the bidding of the customers, but that was as far as the strength of the family reached. The wound in Gregor's back would start to play up again, when mother and sister came back, having taken his father to bed, and neglected their work to sit pressed together, almost cheek to cheek; when his mother pointed to Gregor's room and said, 'Will you shut the door now, Grete'; and when Gregor found himself once more in the dark, while next door the women were mingling their tears, or perhaps sitting staring dry-eyed at the table.

Gregor spent his days and nights almost without sleeping. Sometimes he thought that the next time they opened the door he would take the business of the family in hand, just exactly as he had done before; after a long time the director figured in his thoughts again, and the chief clerk, the junior clerk and the trainees, the dim-witted factotum, a couple of friends he had in other companies, a chambermaid in a hotel out in the provinces somewhere, a sweet, fleeting memory, a cashier in a hat shop whom he had courted assiduously, but far too slowly—all these appeared to him, together with others he never knew or had already forgotten, but instead of helping him and his family, they were all inaccessible to him, and he was glad when they went away again. And then he wasn't in the mood to worry about the family, but instead was filled with rage at how they neglected him, and even though he couldn't imagine anything for which he had an appetite, he made schemes as to how to inveigle himself into the pantry, to take there what was rightfully his, even if he didn't feel the least bit hungry now. No longer bothering to think what might please Gregor, his sister before going to work in the morning and afternoon now hurriedly shoved some food or other into Gregor's room with her foot, and in the evening reached in with the broom to hook it back out again, indifferent as to whether it had been only tasted or even—as most regularly happened—had remained quite untouched. The tidying of the room, which she now did always in the evening, really could not have been done more cursorily. The walls were streaked with grime, and here and there lay little tangled balls of dust and filth. At first, Gregor liked to take up position, for her coming, in the worst affected corners, as if to reproach her for their condition. But he could probably have stayed there for weeks without his sister doing anything better; after all, she could see the dirt as clearly as he could, she had simply taken it into her head to ignore it. And at the same time, with a completely new pernicketiness that seemed to have come over her, as it had indeed the whole family, she jealously guarded her monopoly on the tidying of Gregor's room. On one occasion, his mother had subjected Gregor's room to a great cleaning, involving several buckets full of water—the humidity was upsetting to Gregor, who lay miserably and motionlessly stretched out on the sofa—but his mother didn't get away with it either. Because no sooner had his sister noticed the change in Gregor's room that evening than, mortally offended, she ran into the sitting room, and ignoring her mother's imploringly raised hands, burst into a crying fit that her parents—her father had of course been shaken from his slumbers in his armchair—witnessed first with helpless surprise, and then they too were touched by it: his father on the one side blaming Gregor's mother for not leaving the cleaning of the room to his sister; while on the other yelling at the sister that she would never be allowed to clean Gregor's room again; while the mother tried to drag the father, who was quite beside himself with excitement, into the bedroom; his sister, shaken with sobs, pummelled at the table with her little fists, and Gregor hissed loudly in impotent fury that no one thought to shut the door, and save him from such a noise and spectacle.

But even if his sister, exhausted by office work, no longer had it in her to care for Gregor as she had done earlier, that still didn't mean that his mother had to take a hand to save Gregor from being utterly neglected. Because now there was the old charwoman. This old widow, who with her strong frame had survived everything that life had had to throw at her, was evidently quite undismayed by

Gregor. It wasn't that she was nosy, but she had by chance once opened the door to Gregor's room, and at the sight of Gregor, who, caught out, started to scurry hither and thither, even though no one was chasing him, merely stood there with her hands folded and watched in astonishment. Since then, she let no morning or evening slip without opening the door a crack and looking in on Gregor. To begin with, she called to him as well, in terms she probably thought were friendly, such things as: 'Come here, you old dung-beetle!' or 'Will you take a look at that old dung-beetle!' Gregor of course didn't reply, but ignored the fact that the door had been opened, and stayed just exactly where he was. If only this old charwoman, instead of being allowed to stand and gawp at him whenever she felt like it, had been instructed to clean his room every day! Early one morning—a heavy rain battered against the windowpanes, a sign already, perhaps, of the approaching spring—Gregor felt such irritation when the charwoman came along with her words that, albeit slowly and ponderously, he made as if to attack her. The charwoman, far from being frightened, seized a chair that was standing near the door, and as she stood there with mouth agape it was clear that she would only close it when she had brought the chair crashing down on Gregor's back. 'So is that as far as it goes then?' she asked, as Gregor turned away, and she calmly put the chair back in a corner.

Gregor was now eating almost nothing at all. Only sometimes, happening to pass the food that had been put out for him, he would desultorily take a morsel in his mouth, and keep it there for hours, before usually spitting it out again. At first he thought it was grief about the condition of his room that was keeping him from eating, but in fact the alterations to his room were the things he came to terms with most easily. They had started pushing things into his room that would otherwise have been in the way, and there were now a good many such items, since one room in the flat had been let out to a trio of bachelors. These serious-looking gentlemen—all three wore full beards, as Gregor happened to see once, peering through a crack in the door—were insistent on hygiene, not just where their own room was concerned, but throughout the flat where they were now tenants, and therefore most especially in the kitchen. Useless or dirty junk was something for which they had no tolerance. Besides, they had largely brought their own furnishings with them. For that reason, many things had now become superfluous that couldn't be sold, and that one didn't want to simply throw away either. All these things came into Gregor's room. And also the ash-can and the rubbish-bin from the kitchen. Anything that seemed even temporarily surplus to requirements was simply slung into Gregor's room by the charwoman, who was always in a tearing rush; it was fortunate that Gregor rarely saw more than the hand and the object in question, whatever it was. It might be that the charwoman had it in mind to reclaim the things at some future time, or to go in and get them all out one day, but what happened was that they simply lay where they had been thrown, unless Gregor, crawling about among the junk, happened to displace some of it, at first perforce, because there was simply no more room in which to move, but later on with increasing pleasure, even though, after such peregrinations he would find himself heart-sore and weary to death, and wouldn't move for many hours.

Since the tenants sometimes took their supper at home in the shared living room, the door to it remained closed on some evenings, but Gregor hardly missed the opening of the door. After all, there were enough evenings when it had been open, and he had not profited from it, but, instead, without the family noticing at all, had merely lain still in the darkest corner of his room. On one occasion, however, the charwoman had left the door to the living room slightly ajar, and it remained ajar, even when the tenants walked in that evening, and the lights were turned on. They took their places at the table, where previously father, mother and Gregor had sat, unfurled their napkins and took up their eating irons. Straightaway his mother appeared in the doorway carrying a dish of meat, and hard behind her came his sister with a bowl heaped with potatoes. The food steamed mightily. The tenants inclined themselves to the dishes in front of them, as though to examine them before eating, and the one who was sitting at the head of the table, and who seemed to have some authority over the other two flanking him, cut into a piece of meat in the dish, as though to check whether it was sufficiently done, and didn't have to be sent back to the kitchen. He seemed content with what he found, and mother and sister, who had been watching in some trepidation, broke into relieved smiles.

The family were taking their meal in the kitchen. Even so, before going in there, the father came in and with a single reverence, cap in hand, walked once round the table. All the tenants got up and muttered something into their beards. Once they were on their own again, they ate in near silence. It struck Gregor that out of all the various sounds one could hear, it was that of their grinding teeth that stood out, as though to demonstrate to Gregor that teeth were needed to eat with, and the best toothless gums were no use. 'But I do have an appetite,' Gregor said to himself earnestly, 'only not for those things. The way those tenants fill their boots, while I'm left to starve!'

On that same evening—Gregor couldn't recall having heard the violin once in all this time—it sounded from the kitchen. The tenants had finished their supper, the one in the middle had produced a newspaper, and given the other two a page apiece, and now they were leaning back, reading and smoking. When the violin sounded, they pricked up their ears, got up and tiptoed to the door of the hallway where they stayed pressed together. They must have been heard from the kitchen, because father called: 'Do the gentlemen have any objection to the music? It can be stopped right away.' 'On the contrary,' said the middle gentleman, 'mightn't the young lady like to come in to us and play here, where it's more cosy and convenient?' 'Only too happy to oblige,' called the father, as if he were the violin player. The gentlemen withdrew to their dining room and waited. Before long up stepped the father with the music stand, the mother with the score, and the sister with the violin. Calmly the sister set everything up in readiness; the parents, who had never let rooms before, and therefore overdid politeness towards the tenants, didn't even dare to sit in their own chairs; Gregor's father leaned in the doorway, his right hand pushed between two buttons of his closed coat; Gregor's mother was offered a seat by one of the gentleman, and, not presuming to move, remained sitting just where the gentleman had put her, off in a corner.

The sister began to play; father and mother, each on their respective side, attentively followed the movements of her hands. Gregor, drawn by the music, had slowly inched forward, and his head was already in the living room. He was no longer particularly surprised at his lack of discretion, where previously this discretion had been his entire pride. Even though now he would have had additional cause to remain hidden, because as a result of the dust that lay everywhere in his room, and flew up at the merest movement, he himself was covered with dust; on his back and along his sides he dragged around an assortment of threads, hairs and bits of food; his indifference to everything was far too great for him to lie down on his back, as he had done several times a day before, and rub himself clean on the carpet. And, in spite of his condition, he felt no shame at moving out on to the pristine floor of the living room.

Admittedly, no one paid him any regard. The family was completely absorbed by the violin playing; the tenants, on the other hand, hands in pockets, had initially taken up position far too close behind the music stand, so that they all could see the music, which must surely be annoying to his sister, but before long, heads lowered in half-loud conversation, they retreated to the window, where they remained, nervously observed by the father. It really did look all too evident that they were disappointed in their expectation of hearing some fine or entertaining playing, were fed up with the whole performance, and only suffered themselves to be disturbed out of politeness. The way they all blew their cigar smoke upwards from their noses and mouths indicated in particular a great nervousness on their part. And yet his sister was playing so beautifully. Her face was inclined to the side, and sadly and searchingly her eyes followed the columns of notes. Gregor crept a little closer and held his head close to the ground, so as to be prepared to meet her gaze. Could he be an animal, to be so moved by music? It was as though he sensed a way to the unknown sustenance he longed for. He was determined to go right up to his sister, to pluck at her skirt, and so let her know she was to come into his room with her violin, because no one rewarded music here as much as he wanted to reward it. He would not let her out of his room, at least not as long as he lived; for the first time his frightening form would come in useful for him; he would appear at all doors to his room at once, and hiss in the faces of attackers: but his sister wasn't to be forced, she was to remain with him of her own free will; she was to sit by his side on the sofa, and he would tell her he was resolved to send her to the conservatory, and that, if the calamity hadn't struck, he would have told everyone so last Christmas—was Christmas past? surely it was—without brooking any objections. After this declaration, his sister would burst into tears of emotion, and Gregor would draw himself up to her oxter and kiss her on the throat, which, since she'd started going to the office, she wore exposed, without a ribbon or collar.

'Mr Samsa!' cried the middle of the gentlemen, and not bothering to say another word, pointed with his index finger at the slowly advancing Gregor. The violin stopped, the middle gentleman first smiled, shaking his head, at his two friends, and then looked at Gregor once more. His father seemed to think it his first priority, even before driving Gregor away, to calm the tenants, though they were not at all agitated, and in fact seemed to find Gregor more entertaining than they had the violin playing. He hurried over to them, and with outspread arms tried simultaneously to push them back into their room, and with his body to block their sight of Gregor. At this point, they seemed to lose their temper. It wasn't easy to tell whether it was the father's behaviour or the understanding now dawning on them that they had been living next door to someone like Gregor. They called on the father for explanations, they too started waving their arms around, plucked nervously at their beards, and were slow to retreat into their room. In the meantime, Gregor's sister had overcome the confusion that had befallen her after the sudden interruption in her play-ing, had, after holding her violin and bow in her slackly hanging hands a while and continuing to read the score as if still playing, suddenly got a grip on her-self, deposited the instrument in the lap of her mother who was still sitting on her chair struggling for breath, and ran into the next room, which the tenants, yielding now to pressure from her father, were finally more rapidly nearing. Gregor could see how, under the practised hands of his sister, the blankets and pillows on the beds flew up in the air and were plumped and pulled straight. Even before the gentlemen had reached their room, she was finished with making the beds, and had slipped out. Father seemed once more so much in the grip of his stubbornness that he quite forgot himself towards the tenants. He merely pushed and pushed, till the middle gentleman stamped thunder-ously on the floor, and so brought him to a stop. 'I hereby declare,' he said, raising his hand and with his glare taking in also mother and sister, 'that as a result of the vile conditions prevailing in this flat and in this family'—here, he spat emphatically on the floor—'I am giving notice with immediate effect. I of course will not pay one cent for the days I have lived here, in fact I will think very carefully whether or not to proceed with—believe me—very easily sub-stantiated claims against you.' He stopped and looked straight ahead of him, as though waiting for something else. And in fact his two friends chimed in with the words: 'We too are giving in our notice, with immediate effect.' Thereupon he seized the doorknob, and slammed the door with a mighty crash.

Gregor's father, with shaking hands, tottered to his chair, and slumped down into it: it looked as though he were settling to his regular evening snooze, but the powerful nodding of his somehow disconnected head showed that he was very far from sleeping. All this time, Gregor lay just exactly where he had been when the tenants espied him. Disappointment at the failure of his plan, per-haps also a slight faintness from his long fasting kept him from being able to move. With a certain fixed dread he awaited the calamity about to fall upon his head. Even the violin failed to startle him, when it slipped through the trem-bling fingers of his mother, and with a jangling echo fell to the floor.

'Dear parents,' said his sister, and brought her hand down on the table top to obtain silence, 'things cannot go on like this. You might not be able to see it, but I do. I don't want to speak the name of my brother within the hearing of that monster, and so I will merely say: we have to try to get rid of it. We did as much as humanly possible to try and look after it and tolerate it. I don't think anyone can reproach us for any measure we have taken or failed to take.'

'She's right, a thousand times right,' his father muttered to himself. His mother, who—with an expression of derangement in her eyes—was still expe-riencing difficulty breathing, started coughing softly into her cupped hand.

His sister ran over to her mother, and held her by the head. The sister's words seemed to have prompted some more precise form of thought in the father's mind, and he sat up and was toying with his doorman's cap among the plates, which still hadn't been cleared after the tenants' meal, from time to time shooting a look at the silent Gregor.

'We must try and get rid of it,' the sister now said, to her father alone, as her mother was caught up in her coughing and could hear nothing else, 'otherwise it'll be the death of you. I can see it coming. If we have to work as hard as we are all at present doing, it's not possible to stand this permanent torture at home as well. I can't do it any more either.' And she burst into such a flood of tears that they flowed down on to her mother's face, from which she wiped them away, with mechanical movements of her hand.

'My child,' said her father compassionately and with striking comprehension, 'but what shall we do?'

Grete merely shrugged her shoulders as a sign of the uncertainty into which—in striking contrast to her previous conviction—she had now fallen in her weeping.

'If only he understood us,' said the father, with rising intonation; the sister, still weeping, waved her hand violently to indicate that such a thing was out of the question.

'If only he understood us,' the father repeated, by closing his eyes accepting the sister's conviction of the impossibility of it, 'then we might come to some sort of settlement with him. But as it is . . .'

'We must get rid of it,' cried the sister again, 'that's the only thing for it, Father. You just have to put from your mind any thought that it's Gregor. Our continuing to think that it was, for such a long time, therein lies the source of our misfortune. But how can it be Gregor? If it was Gregor, he would long ago have seen that it's impossible for human beings to live together with an animal like that, and he would have left of his own free will. That would have meant I didn't have a brother, but we at least could go on with our lives, and honour his memory. But as it is, this animal hounds us, drives away the tenants, evidently wants to take over the whole flat, and throw us out on to the street. Look, Father,' she suddenly broke into a scream, 'he's coming again!' And in an access of terror wholly incomprehensible to Gregor, his sister even quit her mother, actually pushing herself away from her chair, as though she would rather sacrifice her mother than remain anywhere near Gregor, and dashed behind her father, who, purely on the basis of her agitation, got to his feet and half-raised his arms to shield the sister.

Meanwhile, Gregor of course didn't have the least intention of frightening anyone, and certainly not his sister. He had merely begun to turn around, to make his way back to his room, which was a somewhat laborious, and eye-catching process, as, in consequence of his debility he needed his head to help with such difficult manoeuvres, raising it many times and bashing it against the floor. He stopped and looked around. His good intentions seemed to have been acknowledged; it had just been a momentary fright he had given them. Now they all looked at him sadly and silently. There lay his mother in her armchair, with her legs stretched out and pressed together, her eyes falling shut with fatigue; his father and sister were sitting side by side, his sister having placed her hand on her father's neck.

Well, maybe they'll let me turn around now, thought Gregor, and recommenced the manoeuvre. He was unable to suppress the odd grunt of effort, and needed to take periodic rests as well. But nobody interfered with him, and he was allowed to get on with it by himself. Once he had finished his turn, he straightaway set off wandering back. He was struck by the great distance that seemed to separate him from his room, and was unable to understand how, in his enfeebled condition, he had just a little while ago covered the same distance, almost without noticing. Intent on making the most rapid progress he could, he barely noticed that no word, no exclamation from his family distracted him. Only when he was in the doorway did he turn his head, not all the way, as his neck felt a little stiff, but even so he was able to see that behind him nothing had changed, only that his sister had got up. His last look lingered upon his mother, who was fast asleep.

No sooner was he in his room than the door was pushed shut behind him, and locked and bolted. The sudden noise so alarmed Gregor that his little legs gave way beneath him. It was his sister who had been in such a hurry. She had been already standing on tiptoe, waiting, and had then light-footedly leaped forward. Gregor hadn't even heard her until she cried 'At last!' as she turned the key in the lock.

'What now?' wondered Gregor, and looked around in the dark. He soon made the discovery that he could no longer move. It came as no surprise to him; if anything, it seemed inexplicable that he had been able to get as far as he had on his frail little legs. Otherwise, he felt as well as could be expected. He did have pains all over his body, but he felt they were gradually abating, and would finally cease altogether. The rotten apple in his back and the inflammation all round it, which was entirely coated with a soft dust, he barely felt any more. He thought back on his family with devotion and love. His conviction that he needed to disappear was, if anything, still firmer than his sister's. He remained in this condition of empty and peaceful reflection until the church clock struck three a.m. The last thing he saw was the sky gradually lightening outside his window. Then his head involuntarily dropped, and his final breath passed feebly from his nostrils.

When the charwoman came early in the morning—so powerful was she, and in such a hurry, that, even though she had repeatedly been asked not to, she slammed all the doors so hard that sleep was impossible after her coming—she at first found nothing out of the ordinary when she paid her customary brief call on Gregor. She thought he was lying there immobile on purpose, and was playing at being offended; in her opinion, he was capable of all sorts of understanding. Because she happened to be holding the long broom, she tried to tickle Gregor away from the doorway. When that bore no fruit, she grew irritable, and jabbed Gregor with the broom, and only when she had moved him from the spot without any resistance on his part did she take notice. When she understood what the situation was, her eyes went large and round, she gave a half-involuntary whistle, didn't stay longer, but tore open the door of the bedroom and loudly called into the darkness: 'Have a look, it's gone and perished; it's lying there, and it's perished!'

The Samsas sat up in bed, and had trouble overcoming their shock at the charwoman's appearance in their room, before even beginning to register the import of what she was saying. But then Mr and Mrs Samsa hurriedly climbed out of bed, each on his or her respective side. Mr Samsa flinging a blanket over his shoulders, Mrs Samsa coming along just in her nightdress; and so they stepped into Gregor's room. By now the door from the living room had been opened as well, where Grete had slept ever since the tenants had come: she was fully dressed, as if she hadn't slept at all, and her pale face seemed to confirm that. 'Dead?' said Mrs Samsa, and looked questioningly up at the charwoman, even though she was in a position to check it all herself, and in fact could have seen it without needing to check. 'I should say so,' said the charwoman and, by way of proof, with her broom pushed Gregor's body across the floor a ways. Mrs Samsa moved as though to restrain the broom, but did not do so. 'Ah,' said Mr

Samsa, 'now we can give thanks to God.' He crossed himself, and the three
women followed his example. Grete, not taking her eye off the body, said: 'Look
how thin he had become. He stopped eating such a long time ago. I brought
food in and took it out, and it was always untouched.' Indeed. Gregor's body was
utterly flat and desiccated—only so apparent now that he was no longer up on
his little legs, and there was nothing else to distract the eye.

'Come in with us a bit, Grete,' said Mrs Samsa with a melancholy smile, and,
not without turning back to look at the corpse. Grete followed her parents into
the bedroom. The charwoman shut the door and opened the window as far as
it would go. In spite of the early hour, there was already something sultry in the
morning air. It was, after all, the end of March.

The three tenants emerged from their room and looked around for their
breakfast in outrage; they had been forgotten about. 'Where's our breakfast?'
the middle gentleman sulkily asked the charwoman. She replied by setting her
finger to her lips, and then quickly and silently beckoning the gentlemen into
Gregor's room. They followed and with their hands in the pockets of their
somewhat shiny little jackets stood around Gregor's body in the bright sunny
room.

The door from the bedroom opened, and Mr Samsa appeared in his uniform,
with his wife on one arm and his daughter on the other. All were a little teary:
from time to time Grete pressed her face against her father's arm.

'Leave my house at once!' said Mr Samsa, and pointed to the door, without
relinquishing the women. 'How do you mean:' said the middle gentleman, with
a little consternation, and smiled a saccharine smile. The other two kept their
hands behind their backs and rubbed them together incessantly, as if in the
happy expectation of a great scene, which was sure to end well for them. 'I
mean just exactly what I said,' replied Mr Samsa, and with his two companions, walked straight towards the tenant. To begin with the tenant stood his
ground, and looked at the floor, as if the things in his head were recombining
in some new arrangement. 'Well, I suppose we'd better go then,' he said, and
looked up at Mr Samsa, as if he required authority for this novel humility. Mr
Samsa merely nodded curtly at him with wide eyes. Thereupon the gentleman
did indeed swing into the hallway with long strides: his two friends had been
listening for a little while, their hands laid to rest, and now skipped after him,
as if afraid Mr Samsa might get to the hallway before them, and cut them off
from their leader. In the hallway all three took their hats off the hatstand,
pulled their canes out of the umbrella holder, bowed silently, and left the flat.
Informed by what turned out to be a wholly unjustified suspicion, Mr Samsa
and his womenfolk stepped out on to the landing; leaning against the balustrade, they watched the three gentlemen proceeding slowly but evenly down
the long flight of stairs, disappearing on each level into a certain twist of the
stairwell and emerging a couple of seconds later; the further they descended,
the less interest the Samsa family took in their progress, and when a butcher's
apprentice passed them and eventually climbed up much higher with his tray
on his head, Mr Samsa and the women left the balustrade altogether, and all
turned back, with relief, into their flat.

They decided to use the day to rest and to go for a walk; not only had they
earned a break from work, but they stood in dire need of one. And so they all
sat down at the table, and wrote three separate letters of apology—Mr Samsa

to the board of his bank, Mrs Samsa to her haberdasher, and Grete to her manager. While they were so engaged, the charwoman came in to say she was leaving, because her morning's tasks were done. The three writers at first merely nodded without looking up, and only when the charwoman made no move to leave did they look up in some irritation. 'Well?' asked Mr Samsa. The charwoman stood smiling in the doorway, as though she had some wonderful surprise to tell the family about, but would only do so if asked expressly about it. The almost vertical ostrich feather in her hat, which had annoyed Mr Samsa the whole time she had been working for them, teetered in every direction. 'So what is it you want?' asked Mrs Samsa, who was the person most likely to command respect from the charwoman. 'Well.' replied the charwoman, and her happy laughter kept her from speaking, 'well, just to say, you don't have to worry about how to get rid of the thing next door. I'll take care of it.' Mrs Samsa and Grete inclined their heads over their letters, as if to go on writing; Mr Samsa, who noticed that the woman was about to embark on a more detailed description of everything, put up a hand to cut her off. Being thus debarred from speaking, she remembered the great rush she was in, and, evidently piqued, called out, 'Well, so long everyone', spun round and left the apartment with a terrible slamming of doors.

'I'm letting her go this evening,' said Mr Samsa, but got no reply from wife or daughter, because the reference to the charwoman seemed to have disturbed their concentration, no sooner than it had returned. The two women rose, went over to the window, and stayed there, holding one another in an embrace. Mr Samsa turned towards them in his chair, and watched them in silence for a while. Then he called: 'Well now, come over here. Leave that old business. And pay a little attention to me.' The women came straightaway, caressed him, and finished their letters.

Then the three of them all together left the flat, which was something they hadn't done for months, and took the tram to the park at the edge of the city. The carriage in which they sat was flooded with warm sunshine. Sitting back comfortably in their seats, they discussed the prospects for the future; it turned out that on closer inspection these were not at all bad, because the work of all of them, which they had yet to talk about properly, was proceeding in a very encouraging way, particularly in regard to future prospects. The greatest alleviation of the situation must be produced by moving house; they would take a smaller, cheaper, but also better situated and more practical apartment than their present one, which Gregor had found for them. While they were talking in these terms, almost at one and the same time Mr and Mrs Samsa noticed their increasingly lively daughter, the way that of late, in spite of the trouble that had made her cheeks pale, she had bloomed into an attractive and well-built girl. Falling silent, and communicating almost unconsciously through glances, they thought it was about time to find a suitable husband for her. And it felt like a confirmation of their new dreams and their fond intentions when, as they reached their destination, their daughter was the first to get up, and stretched her nubile young body.

1915

LU XUN

1881–1936

Modern China has produced many talented writers, with the usual division of critical opinion concerning them. There is, however, almost universal agreement on one authentic genius: Lu Xun (also Romanized Lu Hsün), the pen name of Zhou Shuren. Few writers of fiction have gained so much fame for such a small oeuvre. His reputation rests mostly on twenty-five stories released between 1918 and 1926, gathered into two collections: *Cheering from the Sidelines* and *Wondering Where to Turn*. In addition to his fiction, he published a collection of prose poems, *Wild Grass*, and a number of literary and political essays. His small body of stories offers a bleak portrayal of a culture that, despite its failures, continues to capture the modern Chinese imagination. Whether the older culture had indeed failed is less important here than Lu Xun's powerful representation of it and the deep chord of response that his work has touched in Chinese readers. Lu Xun was a controlled ironist and a craftsman whose narrative skill far exceeded that of most of his contemporaries; yet beneath his stylistic mastery the reader senses the depth of his anger at traditional culture.

Born into a Shaoxing family of Confucian scholar-officials, Lu Xun had a traditional education and became a classical scholar of considerable erudition, as well as a writer of poetry in the classical language. Sometimes he displays this learning in his fiction, where it is always undercut with irony. He grew up at a time when the traditional education system, based on the Confucian classics, was giving way, to the approval of Lu Xun and others, to a more modern one; and after the early death of his father in 1896, he joined the many young Chinese intellectuals of the era in traveling abroad for higher education—first in Tokyo, then in Sendai, where he attended a Japanese medical school. (Because it was successfully modernizing a traditional culture, Japan attracted young Chinese intellectuals, who wished the same for their own society.) During his studies, the Russians and Japanese were at war in the former Chinese territory of Manchuria. In a famous anecdote describing his decision to become a writer, Lu Xun tells of seeing a classroom slide of a Chinese prisoner about to be decapitated as a Russian spy. What shocked the young medical student was the apathetic crowd of Chinese onlookers, gathered around to watch the execution. At that moment, he decided that what truly needed healing were not their bodies but their dulled spirits.

Returning to Tokyo, Lu Xun founded a journal in which he published literary essays and Western works of fiction in translation. In 1909, financial difficulties drove him back to China, where he worked as a teacher in Hangzhou and his native Shaoxing. With the arrival of the Republican Revolution of 1911, which overthrew the Qing, or Manchu, dynasty, he joined the Ministry of Education, moving north to Beijing, where he also taught at various universities. The Republican government was soon at the mercy of the powerful armies competing for regional power; during this period, perhaps for self-protection, Lu Xun devoted himself to traditional scholarship. One might have expected this revolutionary to write, as Lu Xun did, a groundbreaking work of scholarship, the first history of Chinese fiction; but he also produced an erudite textual study of the third-century writer Xi Kang, which is still used.

On May 4, 1919, a massive student strike forced the Chinese government not to sign the Versailles Peace Treaty, which would have given Japan effective control over the province of Shandong. The date gave its name to the May Fourth Movement, led by a group of young intellectuals who advocated the use of vernacular Chinese in all writing and the repudiation of classical Chinese literature. Though Lu Xun himself was not an active participant in the political side of the May Fourth Movement, it was during this period (1918–1926) that he wrote all but one of his short stories. In the final decade of his life, he became a political activist and put his satirical talents at the service of the left, becoming one of the favorite writers of the Communist leader Mao Zedong.

"Diary of a Madman" (1918), Lu Xun's earliest story in modern Chinese, opens with a preface in mannered classical Chinese, giving an account of the discovery of the diary. Such ironic use of classical Chinese to suggest a falsely polite world of social appearances had been common in traditional Chinese fiction. Usually its presence suggested, however, the alternative possibility, of immediate, direct, and genuine language, a language of the heart that shows up the language of society. Here,

the diary that follows the preface is indeed immediate, direct, and genuine, but it is also deluded and twisted. The diarist becomes increasingly convinced that everyone around him wants to eat him; after observing this growing circle of cannibals in the present, the diarist then turns to examine old texts, where he discovers that the history of the culture has been one of secret cannibalism. Beneath society's false politeness, the veneer of such decorous forms as the voice in the preface, he detects a brutality lurking, a hunger to assimilate others, to "eat men."

As the diary progresses, it becomes increasingly clear that the diarist, who sees himself as a potential victim, recapitulates the flaws and dangers of the society he describes, assimilating everyone around him into his fixed view of the world. His reading of ancient texts to discover evidence of cannibalism, with its distorting discovery of "secret meanings" that only serve to confirm beliefs already held, works in part as a parody of traditional Confucian scholarship. His is a world closed in on itself, one that survives by feeding on itself and its young. Yet the story opens itself to other interpretations: some see the madman as understanding the truth to which everyone else in the tale is blind, while others have noted that the madman's possible cannibalism undermines his apparent vision and that in any case his account is suspect because he is awaiting appointment to an official position.

Diary of a Madman[1]

There was once a pair of male siblings whose actual names I beg your indulgence to withhold. Suffice it to say that we three were boon companions during our school years. Subsequently, circumstances contrived to rend us asunder so that we were gradually bereft of knowledge regarding each other's activities.

Not too long ago, however, I chanced to hear that one of them had been hard afflicted with a dread disease. I obtained this intelligence at a time when I happened to be returning to my native haunts and, hence, made so bold as to detour somewhat from my normal course in order to visit them. I encountered but one of the siblings. He apprised me that it had been his younger brother who had suffered the dire illness. By now, however, he had long since become sound and fit again; in fact he had already repaired to other parts to await a substantive official appointment.[2]

The elder brother apologized for having needlessly put me to the inconvenience of this visitation, and concluding his disquisition with a hearty smile, showed me two volumes of diaries which, he assured me, would reveal the nature of his brother's disorder during those fearful days.

As to the lapsus calami[3] *that occur in the course of the diaries, I have altered not a word. Nonetheless, I have changed all the names, despite the fact that their publication would be of no great consequence since they are all humble villagers unknown to the world at large.*

Recorded this 2nd day in the 7th year of the Republic.[4]

I

Moonlight's really nice tonight. Haven't seen it in over thirty years. Seeing it today, I feel like a new man. I know now that I've been completely out of things for the last three decades or more. But I've still got to be *very* careful. Otherwise, how do you explain those dirty looks the Zhao family's dog gave me?

I've got good reason for my fears.

2

No moonlight at all tonight—something's not quite right. When I made my way out the front gate this morning—ever so carefully—there was something funny about the way the Venerable Old Zhao looked at me: seemed as though he was afraid of me and yet, at the same time, looked as though he had it in for me. There were seven or eight other people who had their heads together whispering about me. They were afraid I'd see them too! All up and down the street people acted the same way. The meanest looking one of all spread his lips out

---

1. Both selections translated by and with notes adapted from William A. Lyell.
2. When there were too many officials for the number of offices to be filled, a man might well be appointed to an office that was already occupied. The new appointee would go to his post and wait until the office was vacated. Sometimes there would be a number of such appointees waiting their turns.
3. "The fall of the reed [writing instrument]" (literal trans.); hence, lapses in writing.
4. The Qing Dynasty was overthrown and the Republic of China was established in 1911; thus it is April 2, 1918. The introduction is written in classical Chinese, whereas the diary entries that follow are all in the colloquial language.

wide and actually *smiled* at me! A shiver ran from the top of my head clear down to the tips of my toes, for I realized that meant they already had their henchmen well deployed, and were ready to strike.

But I wasn't going to let that intimidate *me*. I kept right on walking. There was a group of children up ahead and they were talking about me too. The expressions in their eyes were just like the Venerable Old Zhao's, and their faces were iron gray. I wondered what grudge the children had against me that they were acting this way too. I couldn't contain myself any longer and shouted, "Tell me, tell me!" But they just ran away.

Let's see now, what grudge can there be between me and the Venerable Old Zhao, or the people on the street for that matter? The only thing I can think of is that twenty years ago I trampled the account books kept by Mr. Antiquity, and he was hopping mad about it too. Though the Venerable Old Zhao doesn't know him, he must have gotten wind of it somehow. Probably decided to right the injustice I had done Mr. Antiquity by getting all those people on the street to gang up on me. But the children? Back then they hadn't even come into the world yet. Why should they have given me those funny looks today? Seemed as though they were afraid of me and yet, at the same time, looked as though they would like to do me some harm. That really frightens me. Bewilders me. Hurts me.

I have it! Their fathers and mothers have *taught* them to be like that!

3

I can never get to sleep at night. You really have to study something before you can understand it.

Take all those people: some have worn the cangue on the district magistrate's order, some have had their faces slapped by the gentry, some have had their wives ravished by *yamen*[5] clerks, some have had their dads and moms dunned to death by creditors; and yet, right at the time when all those terrible things were taking place, the expressions on their faces were never as frightened, or as savage, as the ones they wore yesterday.

Strangest of all was that woman on the street. She slapped her son and said: "Damn it all, you've got me so riled up I could take a good bite right out of your hide!" She was talking to him, but she was looking at me! I tried, but couldn't conceal a shudder of fright. That's when that ghastly crew of people, with their green faces and protruding fangs, began to roar with laughter. Old Fifth Chen[6] ran up, took me firmly in tow, and dragged me away.

When we got back, the people at home all pretended not to know me. The expressions in their eyes were just like all the others too. After he got me into the study, Old Fifth Chen bolted the door from the outside—just the way you would pen up a chicken or a duck! That made figuring out what was at the bottom of it all harder than ever.

---

5. Local government offices. The petty clerks who worked in them were notorious for relying on their proximity to power to bully and abuse the common people. "Cangue": a split board, hinged at one end and locked at the other; holes were cut out to accommodate the prisoner's neck and wrists.

6. People were often referred to by their hierarchical position within their extended family.

A few days back one of our tenant farmers came in from Wolf Cub Village to report a famine. Told my elder brother the villagers had all ganged up on a "bad" man and beaten him to death. Even gouged out his heart and liver. Fried them up and ate them to bolster their own courage! When I tried to horn in on the conversation, Elder Brother and the tenant farmer both gave me sinister looks. I realized for the first time today that the expression in their eyes was just the same as what I saw in those people on the street.

As I think of it now, a shiver's running from the top of my head clear down to the tips of my toes.

If they're capable of eating people, then who's to say they won't eat *me*?

Don't you see? That woman's words about "taking a good bite," and the laughter of that ghastly crew with their green faces and protruding fangs, and the words of our tenant farmer a few days back—it's perfectly clear to me now that all that talk and all that laughter were really a set of secret signals. Those words were poison! That laughter, a knife! Their teeth are bared and waiting—white and razor sharp! Those people are cannibals!

As I see it myself, though I'm not what you'd call an evil man, still, ever since I trampled the Antiquity family's account books, it's hard to say *what* they'll do. They seem to have something in mind, but I can't begin to guess what. What's more, as soon as they turn against someone, they'll *say* he's evil anyway. I can still remember how it was when Elder Brother was teaching me composition.[7] No matter how good a man was, if I could find a few things wrong with him he would approvingly underline my words; on the other hand, if I made a few allowances for a bad man, he'd say I was "an extraordinary student, an absolute genius." When all is said and done, how can I possibly guess what people like *that* have in mind, especially when they're getting ready for a cannibals' feast?

You have to *really* go into something before you can understand it. I seemed to remember, though not too clearly, that from ancient times on people have often been eaten, and so I started leafing through a history book to look it up. There were no dates in this history, but scrawled this way and that across every page were the words BENEVOLENCE, RIGHTEOUSNESS, and MORALITY. Since I couldn't get to sleep anyway, I read that history very carefully for most of the night, and finally I began to make out what was written *between* the lines; the whole volume was filled with a single phrase: EAT PEOPLE!

The words written in the history book, the things the tenant farmer said—all of it began to stare at me with hideous eyes, began to snarl and growl at me from behind bared teeth!

Why sure, *I'm* a person too, and they want to eat *me*!

4

In the morning I sat in the study for a while, calm and collected. Old Fifth Chen brought in some food—vegetables and a steamed fish. The fish's eyes were white and hard. Its mouth was wide open, just like the mouths of those people who wanted to eat human flesh. After I'd taken a few bites, the meat felt so smooth and slippery in my mouth that I couldn't tell whether it was fish or human flesh. I vomited.

---

7. That is, to compose essays in the classical style.

"Old Fifth," I said, "tell Elder Brother that it's absolutely stifling in here and that I'd like to take a walk in the garden." He left without answering, but sure enough, after a while the door opened. I didn't even budge—just sat there waiting to see what they'd do to me. I *knew* that they wouldn't be willing to set me loose.

Just as I expected! Elder Brother came in with an old man in tow and walked slowly toward me. There was a savage glint in the old man's eyes. He was afraid I'd see it and kept his head tilted toward the floor while stealing sidewise glances at me over the temples of his glasses. "You seem to be fine today," said Elder Brother.

"You bet!" I replied.

"I've asked Dr. He to come and examine your pulse today."

"He's welcome!" I said. But don't think for one moment that I didn't know the old geezer was an executioner in disguise! Taking my pulse was nothing but a ruse; he wanted to feel my flesh and decide if I was fat enough to butcher yet. He'd probably even get a share of the meat for his troubles. I wasn't a *bit* afraid. Even though I don't eat human flesh, I still have a lot more courage than those who do. I thrust both hands out to see how the old buzzard would make his move. Sitting down, he closed his eyes and felt my pulse[8] for a good long while. Then he froze. Just sat there without moving a muscle for another good long while. Finally he opened his spooky eyes and said: "Don't let your thoughts run away with you. Just convalesce in peace and quiet for a few days and you'll be all right."

Don't let my thoughts run away with me? Convalesce in peace and quiet? If I convalesce till I'm good and fat, they get more to eat, but what do *I* get out of it? How can I possibly be *all right*? What a bunch! All they think about is eating human flesh, and then they go sneaking around, thinking up every which way they can to camouflage their real intentions. They were comical enough to crack *anybody* up. I couldn't hold it in any longer and let out a good loud laugh. Now *that* really felt good. I knew in my heart of hearts that my laughter was *packed* with courage and righteousness. And do you know what? They were so completely subdued by it that the old man and my elder brother both went pale!

But the more *courage* I had, the more that made them want to eat me so that they could get a little of it for free. The old man walked out. Before he had taken many steps, he lowered his head and told Elder Brother, "To be eaten as soon as possible!" He nodded understandingly. So, Elder Brother, you're in it too! Although that discovery seemed unforeseen, it really wasn't, either. My own elder brother had thrown in with the very people who wanted to eat me!

My elder brother is a cannibal!

I'm brother to a cannibal.

Even though I'm to be the victim of cannibalism, I'm *brother* to a cannibal all the same!

5

During the past few days I've taken a step back in my thinking. Supposing that old man wasn't an executioner in disguise but really was a doctor—well, he'd still be a cannibal just the same. In *Medicinal . . . something or other* by Li

---

8. In Chinese medicine the pulse is taken at both wrists.

Shizhen,[9] the grandfather of the doctor's trade, it says quite clearly that human flesh can be eaten, so how can that old man say that *he's* not a cannibal too?

And as for my own elder brother, I'm not being the least bit unfair to him. When he was explaining the classics to me, he said with his very own tongue that it was all right to *exchange children and eat them.* And then there was another time when he happened to start in on an evil man and said that not only should the man be killed, but his *flesh should be eaten* and *his skin used as a sleeping mat*[1] as well.

When our tenant farmer came in from Wolf Cub Village a few days back and talked about eating a man's heart and liver, Elder Brother didn't seem to see anything out of the way in that either—just kept nodding his head. You can tell from that alone that his present way of thinking is every bit as malicious as it was when I was a child. If it's all right to exchange *children* and eat them, then *anyone* can be exchanged, anyone can be eaten. Back then I just took what he said as explanation of the classics and let it go at that, but now I realize that while he was explaining, the grease of human flesh was smeared all over his lips, and what's more, his mind was filled with plans for further cannibalism.

6

Pitch black out. Can't tell if it's day or night. The Zhao family's dog has started barking again.

Savage as a lion, timid as a rabbit, crafty as a fox . . .

7

I'm on to the way they operate. They'll never be willing to come straight out and kill me. Besides, they wouldn't dare. They'd be afraid of all the bad luck it might bring down on them if they did. And so, they've gotten everyone into cahoots with them and have set traps all over the place so that I'll do *myself* in. When I think back on the looks of those men and women on the streets a few days ago, coupled with the things my elder brother's been up to recently, I can figure out eight or nine tenths of it. From their point of view, the best thing of all would be for me to take off my belt, fasten it around a beam, and hang myself. They wouldn't be guilty of murder, and yet they'd still get everything they're after. Why, they'd be so beside themselves with joy, they'd sob with laughter. Or if they couldn't get me to do that, maybe they could torment me until I died of fright and worry. Even though I'd come out a bit leaner that way, they'd still nod their heads in approval.

9. Lived from 1518 to 1593. *Taxonomy of Medicinal Herbs*, a gigantic work, was the most important pharmacopoeia in traditional China.
1. Both italicized expressions are from the *Zuozhuan* (Zuo commentary to the *Spring and Summer Annals*, a historical work that dates from the 3rd century B.C.E.). In 448 B.C.E., an officer who was exhorting his own side not to surrender is recorded as having said, "When the army of Chu besieged the capital of Song [in 603 B.C.E.], the people exchanged their children and ate them, and used the bones for fuel; and still they would not submit to a covenant at the foot of their walls. For us who have sustained no great loss, to do so is to cast our state away" (translated by James Legge, 5.817). It is also recorded that in 551 B.C.E. an officer boasting of his own prowess before his ruler pointed to two men whom his ruler considered brave and said, "As to those two, they are like beasts, whose flesh I will eat, and then sleep upon their skins" (Legge 5.492).

Their kind only know how to eat dead meat. I remember reading in a book somewhere about something called the *hai-yi-na*.[2] Its general appearance is said to be hideous, and the expression in its eyes particularly ugly and malicious. Often eats carrion, too. Even chews the bones to a pulp and swallows them down. Just thinking about it's enough to frighten a man.

The *hai-yi-na* is kin to the wolf. The wolf's a relative of the dog, and just a few days ago the Zhao family dog gave me a funny look. It's easy to see that he's in on it too. How did that old man expect to fool *me* by staring at the floor?

My elder brother's the most pathetic of the whole lot. Since he's a human being too, how can he manage to be so totally without qualms, and what's more, even gang up with them to eat me? Could it be that he's been used to this sort of thing all along and sees nothing wrong with it? Or could it be that he's lost all conscience and just goes ahead and does it even though he knows it's wrong?

If I'm going to curse cannibals, I'll have to start with him. And if I'm going to *convert* cannibals, I'll have to start with him too.

8

Actually, by now even they should long since have understood the truth of this . . .

Someone came in. Couldn't have been more than twenty or so. I wasn't able to make out what he looked like too clearly, but he was all smiles. He nodded at me. His smile didn't look like the real thing either. And so I asked him, "Is this business of eating people right?"

He just kept right on smiling and said, "Except perhaps in a famine year, how could anyone get eaten?" I knew right off that he was one of them—one of those monsters who devour people!

At that point my own courage increased a hundredfold and I asked him, "Is it right?"

"Why are you talking about this kind of thing anyway? You really know how to . . . uh . . . how to pull a fellow's leg. Nice weather we're having."

"The weather *is* nice. There's a nice moon out, too, but I *still* want to know if it's right."

He seemed quite put out with me and began to mumble, "It's not—"

"Not right? Then how come they're still eating people?"

"No one's eating anyone."

"No one's *eating* anyone? They're eating people in Wolf Cub Village this very minute. And it's written in all the books, too, written in bright red blood!"

His expression changed and his face went gray like a slab of iron. His eyes started out from their sockets as he said, "Maybe they are, but it's always been that way, it's—"

"Just because it's always been that way, does that make it *right*?"

"I'm not going to discuss such things with you. If you insist on talking about that, then *you're* the one who's in the wrong!"

I leaped from my chair, opened my eyes, and looked around—but the fellow was nowhere to be seen. He was far younger than my elder brother, and yet he

---

2. Three Chinese characters are used here for phonetic value only; that is, *hai yi na* is a transliteration into Chinese of the English word *hyena*.

was actually one of them. It must be because his mom and dad taught him to be that way. And he's probably already passed it on to his own son. No wonder that even the children give me murderous looks.

9

They want to eat others and at the same time they're afraid that other people are going to eat them. That's why they're always watching each other with such suspicious looks in their eyes.

But all they'd have to do is give up that way of thinking, and then they could travel about, work, eat, and sleep in perfect security. Think how happy they'd feel! It's only a threshold, a pass. But what do they do instead? What is it that these fathers, sons, brothers, husbands, wives, friends, teachers, students, enemies, and even people who don't know each other *really* do? Why they all join together to hold each other back, and talk each other out of it!

That's it! They'd rather *die* than take that one little step.

10

I went to see Elder Brother bright and early. He was standing in the courtyard looking at the sky. I went up behind him so as to cut him off from the door back into the house. In the calmest and friendliest of tones, I said, "Elder Brother, there's something I'd like to tell you."

"Go right ahead." He immediately turned and nodded his head.

"It's only a few words, really, but it's hard to get them out. Elder Brother, way back in the beginning, it's probably the case that primitive peoples *all* ate some human flesh. But later on, because their ways of thinking changed, some gave up the practice and tried their level best to improve themselves; they kept on changing until they became human beings, *real* human beings. But the others didn't; they just kept right on with their cannibalism and stayed at that primitive level.

"You have the same sort of thing with evolution[3] in the animal world. Some reptiles, for instance, changed into fish, and then they evolved into birds, then into apes, and then into human beings. But the others didn't want to improve themselves and just kept right on being reptiles down to this very day.

"Think how ashamed those primitive men who have remained cannibals must feel when they stand before *real* human beings. They must feel even more ashamed than reptiles do when confronted with their brethren who have evolved into apes.

"There's an old story from ancient times about Yi Ya boiling his son and serving him up to Jie Zhou.[4] But if the truth be known, people have *always* practiced cannibalism, all the way from the time when Pan Gu separated heaven

3. Charles Darwin's (1809–1892) theory of evolution was immensely important to Chinese intellectuals during Lu's lifetime and the common coin of much discourse.
4. An early philosophical text, *Guan Zi*, reports that the famous cook Yi Ya boiled his son and served him to his ruler, Duke Huan of Qi (685–643 B.C.E.), because the meat of a human infant was one of the few delicacies the duke had never tasted. Ji and Zhou were the last evil rulers of the Sang (1776–1122 B.C.E.) and Zhou (1122–221 B.C.E.) dynasties. The madman has mixed up some facts here.

and earth down to Yi Ya's son, down to Xu Xilin,[5] and on down to the man they killed in Wolf Cub Village. And just last year when they executed a criminal in town, there was even someone with T.B. who dunked a steamed bread roll in his blood and then licked it off.

"When they decided to eat me, by yourself, of course, you couldn't do much to prevent it, but why did you have to go and *join* them? Cannibals are capable of anything! If they're capable of eating me, then they're capable of eating *you* too! Even within their own group, they think nothing of devouring each other. And yet all they'd have to do is turn back—*change*—and then everything would be fine. Even though people may say, 'It's always been like this,' we can still do our best to improve. And we can start today!

"You're going to tell me it can't be done! Elder Brother, I think you're very likely to say that. When that tenant wanted to reduce his rent the day before yesterday, wasn't it you who said it couldn't be done?"

At first he just stood there with a cold smile, but then his eyes took on a murderous gleam. (I had exposed their innermost secrets.) His whole face had gone pale. Some people were standing outside the front gate. The Venerable Old Zhao and his dog were among them. Stealthily peering this way and that, they began to crowd through the open gate. Some I couldn't make out too well— their faces seemed covered with cloth. Some looked the same as ever—smiling green faces with protruding fangs. I could tell at a glance that they all belonged to the same gang, that they were all cannibals. But at the same time I also realized that they didn't all think the same way. Some thought *it's always been like this* and that they really should eat human flesh. Others knew they shouldn't but went right on doing it anyway, always on the lookout for fear someone might give them away. And since that's exactly what I had just done, I knew they must be furious. But they were all *smiling* at me—cold little smiles!

At this point Elder Brother suddenly took on an ugly look and barked, "Get out of here! All of you! What's so funny about a madman?"

Now I'm on to *another* of their tricks: not only are they unwilling to change, but they're already setting me up for their next cannibalistic feast by labeling me a "madman." That way, they'll be able to eat me without getting into the slightest trouble. Some people will even be grateful to them. Wasn't that the very trick used in the case that the tenant reported? Everybody ganged up on a "bad" man and ate him. It's the same old thing.

Old Fifth Chen came in and made straight for me, looking mad as could be. But he wasn't going to shut *me* up! I was going to tell that bunch of cannibals off, and no two ways about it!

"You can change! You can change from the bottom of your hearts! You ought to know that in the future they're not going to allow cannibalism in the world anymore. If you don't change, you're going to devour each other anyway. And even if a lot of you *are* left, a real human being's going to come along and eradicate the lot of you, just like a hunter getting rid of wolves—or reptiles!"

5. From Lu's hometown, Shaoxing (1873–1907). After studies in Japan, he returned to China and served as head of the Anhui Police Academy. When a high Qing official, En Ming, participated in a graduation ceremony at the academy, Xu assassinated him, hoping that this would touch off the revolution. After the assassination, he and some of his students at the academy occupied the police armory and managed, for a while, to hold off En Ming's troops. When Xu was finally captured, En Ming's personal body guards dug out his heart and liver and ate them. Pan Gu (literally, "Coiled-up Antiquity") was born out of an egg. As he stood up, he separated heaven and earth. The world as we know it was formed from his body.

Old Fifth Chen chased them all out. I don't know where Elder Brother disappeared to. Old Fifth talked me into going back to my room.

It was pitch black inside. The beams and rafters started trembling overhead. They shook for a bit, and then they started getting bigger and bigger. They piled themselves up into a great heap on top of my body!

The weight was incredibly heavy and I couldn't even budge—they were trying to kill me! But I knew their weight was an illusion, and I struggled out from under them, my body bathed in sweat. I was still going to have my say. "Change this minute! Change from the bottom of your hearts! You ought to know that in the future they're not going to allow cannibals in the world anymore . . ."

11

The sun doesn't come out. The door doesn't open. It's two meals a day.

I picked up my chopsticks and that got me thinking about Elder Brother. I realized that the reason for my younger sister's death lay entirely with him. I can see her now—such a lovable and helpless little thing, only five at the time. Mother couldn't stop crying, but *he* urged her to stop, probably because he'd eaten sister's flesh himself and hearing mother cry over her like that shamed him! But if he's still capable of feeling shame, then maybe . . .

Younger Sister was eaten by Elder Brother. I have no way of knowing whether Mother knew about it or not.

I think she *did* know, but while she was crying she didn't say anything about it. She probably thought it was all right, too. I can remember once when I was four or five, I was sitting out in the courtyard taking in a cool breeze when Elder Brother told me that when parents are ill, a son, in order to be counted as a really good person, should slice off a piece of his own flesh, boil it, and let them eat it.[6] At the time Mother didn't come out and say there was anything wrong with that. But if it was all right to eat one piece, then there certainly wouldn't be anything wrong with her eating the whole body. And yet when I think back to the way she cried and cried that day, it's enough to break my heart. It's all strange—very, very strange.

12

Can't think about it anymore. I just realized today that I too have muddled around for a good many years in a place where they've been continually eating people for four thousand years. Younger Sister happened to die at just the time when Elder Brother was in charge of the house. Who's to say he didn't slip some of her meat into the food we ate?

Who's to say I didn't eat a few pieces of my younger sister's flesh without knowing it? And now it's my turn . . .

Although I wasn't aware of it in the beginning, now that I *know* I'm someone with four thousand years' experience of cannibalism behind me, how hard it is to look real human beings in the eye!

13

Maybe there are some children around who still haven't eaten human flesh. Save the children . . .

1918

6. In traditional literature, stories about such gruesome acts of filial piety were not unusual.

LUIGI PIRANDELLO

1867–1936

"Who am I?" and "What is real?" are the persistent questions that underlie Luigi Pirandello's novels, short stories, and plays. Sometimes in a playful mood, sometimes more anxiously, Pirandello toys with these questions but refuses to answer them definitively. In fact, the term *Pirandellismo*, or "Pirandellism"—coined from the author's name—has come to stand in for the idea that there are as many truths as there are points of view. Yet Pirandello treats such weighty philosophical issues with a combination of humor and pathos that makes them highly entertaining.

Pirandello's great fame came late in life, as a result of his experimental dramas, but he had been an active writer for decades. Born in Girgenti (now Agrigento), Sicily, on June 28, 1867, Pirandello was the son of a sulfur merchant who intended his son to follow him into business. Pirandello preferred language and literature. After studying in Palermo and at the University of Rome, he traveled to the University of Bonn, where he received a doctorate in romance philology with a dissertation on the dialect of his hometown. Soon after completing his doctorate, Pirandello agreed to an arranged marriage with the daughter of a rich sulfur merchant, although he had never met her. They lived for ten years in Rome, where he wrote poetry and short stories, until the collapse of the sulfur mines destroyed the fortunes of both families, and he was suddenly forced to earn a living. To add to his misfortune, his wife developed a jealous paranoia that lasted until her death, in 1918.

Pirandello's early work included short stories and novellas written under the influence of the narrative style *verismo* (realism or naturalism) that he found exemplified in the work of the Sicilian writer Giovanni Verga (1840–1922). Pirandello wrote hundreds of stories of all lengths. He is recognized—in his clarity, realism, and psychological acuteness (often including a taste for the grotesque)—as an Italian master of the story form. His anthology of 1922, *A Year's Worth of Stories*, remains hugely popular in Italy. Not until he was in his fifties, however, did Pirandello write the more experimental plays, such as *Six Characters in Search of an Author* (1921) and *Henry IV* (1922), which established him as a major dramatist.

Despite the intellectualism of his plays, in politics Pirandello favored the irrational appeal of a strong leader. He was drawn toward the Fascist dictator Benito Mussolini and supported his regime at key moments—for example, in the wake of the murder by Fascists of a Socialist member of Parliament, Giacomo Matteotti. As Pirandello's fame spread, he directed his own company (the Teatro d'Arte di Roma) with support from Mussolini's government and toured Europe with his plays. In 1934 he received the Nobel Prize for Literature. His later plays, featuring fantastic and grotesque elements, did not achieve the wide popularity of their predecessors.

Pirandello's plays turn the trappings of the theater itself—the stage, the producer, the author, the actors—into the material for comedy and invention. In their manipulation of ambiguous appearances and tragicomic effects, these plays foreshadow the absurdist theater of **Samuel Beckett** and others. Above all, they insist that "real" life is that which changes from moment to moment, exhibiting a fluidity that renders difficult and perhaps impossible any single formulation of either character or situation. Pirandello's playful treatment of the theatrical enterprise has been dubbed "metatheater," or theater about theater.

SIX CHARACTERS IN SEARCH OF AN AUTHOR

Six Characters in Search of an Author, the selection below, combines the elements of "metatheater" in an extraordinary self-reflexive style. At the beginning of the play, the Stage Hand's interrupted hammering suggests that the audience has chanced on a rehearsal—of still another play by Pirandello—instead of coming to an actual performance. Concurrently, Pirandello's stage dialogue pokes fun at his reputation for obscurity. Just as the Actors are apparently set to rehearse *The Rules of the Game*, six unexpected persons come down the aisle seeking the Producer: they are Characters from an unwritten novel who demand to be given dramatic existence. The play *Six Characters* is continually in the process of being composed: composed as the interwoven double plot we see on stage, composed by the Prompter writing a script in shorthand for the Actors to reproduce, and composed as the inner drama of the Characters finally achieves its rightful existence as a work of art.

The play's initial absurdity emerges when the six fictional Characters arrive with their claim to be "truer and more real" than the "real" Actors who seek to impersonate them. (Of course, to the audience all the figures onstage are equally real.) Each Character represents a particular identity created by the author. Pirandello later had the Characters wear masks to distinguish them from the Actors—not the conventional masks of ancient Greek drama or of the Japanese *Noh* theater that identify the characters' roles, nor the cere-

monial masks, representing spirits in African ritual, that temporarily invest the wearer with the spirit's identity and authority. Instead, they are a theatrical device, a symbol and visual reminder of each Character's unchanging being. The six Characters are incapable of developing outside their roles and are condemned, in their search for existence, painfully to reenact their essential roles.

Conversely, the fictional Characters have more stable personalities than "real" people, including the Actors, who are still "nobody," incomplete, open to change and misinterpretation. Characters can claim to be "somebody" because their natures have been decided once and for all. Yet further complications attend this contrast between fictional characters and real actors: for instance, the Characters feel the urge to play their own roles and are disturbed at the prospect of having Actors represent them incorrectly. All human beings, indicates Pirandello, whether fictional or real, are subject to misunderstanding. We even misunderstand ourselves when we think we are the same person in all situations. "We always have the illusion of being the same person for everybody," says the Father, "but it's not true!"

Pirandello does not hold his audience's attention simply by uttering grand philosophical truths, however. *Six Characters* hums with suspense and discovery, from the moment that the Characters interrupt the rehearsal with its complaining Actors and Stage Manager. The story that the Characters tell about themselves hints of melodrama and family scandal, like headlines from a sensationalist newspaper, that attracts the viewer's interest. Indeed, Pirandello plays with the risqué element by focusing on the characters' repeated attempts to portray one florid scene. Eventually, the pathos of this play within the play comes to overwhelm the more philosophical metatheatrical frame.

Six Characters in Search of an Author underwent an interesting evolution to become the play that we see today. First performed in Rome in 1921, where its unsettling plot and characters already scandalized a traditionalist audience, it was reshaped in more radical form after the remarkable performance produced by Georges Pitoëff in 1923. Pirandello, who came to Paris wary of Pitoëff's innovations (for instance, he had the Characters arrive in a green-lit stage elevator), was soon convinced that the Russian director's stagecraft enhanced the original text. Pitoëff used his knowledge of technical effects to accentuate the relationship of appearance and reality: he extended the stage with several steps leading down to the auditorium (a break in the conventional "fourth wall" concept, in which the actors on stage proceed as if unaware of the audience, that Pirandello was quick to exploit); he underscored the play within a play with rehearsal effects, showing the Stage Hand hammering and the Director arranging suitable props and lighting; he emphasized the division between Characters and Actors by separating the groups on stage and dressing all the Characters (except the Little Girl) in black. Pirandello welcomed these changes and expanded on many of them. To distinguish the Characters even further from the Actors, he proposed contrasting clothing in addition to masks, black for the former and pale for the latter. Most striking, however, is his transformation of Pitoëff's steps into an actual bridge between the world of the stage and the auditorium, a strategy that allows the Actors (and Characters) to come and go in the "real world" of the audience.

In breaking down comfortable illusions of compartmentalized, stable reality, Pirandello revolutionized European stage techniques. In place of the nineteenth century's "well-made play"—with its neatly constructed plot that boxes real life into a conventional beginning, middle, and end, and its safely inaccessible characters on the other side of the footlights—he offers unpredictable plots and ambiguous roles. It is not easy to know the truth about others, he suggests, or to make oneself known behind the "mask" that each of us wears.

Readers might enjoy testing the continued liveliness of Pirandello's dialogue by rehearsing their own selection of scenes—or perhaps by relocating them in a contemporary setting. According to the director Robert Brustein, whose 1988 production of *Six Characters in Search of an Author* set the action in New York and replaced Madame Pace with a pimp, "Pirandello both encourages and stimulates a pluralism in theater because there can be dozens, hundreds, thousands of productions of *Six Characters*, and every one of them is going to be different."

Six Characters in Search of an Author[1]

A Comedy in the Making

THE CHARACTERS	THE COMPANY
FATHER	THE PRODUCER
MOTHER	THE STAGE STAFF
STEPDAUGHTER	THE ACTORS
SON	
LITTLE BOY	
LITTLE GIRL	
MADAME PACE	

Act 1

When the audience enters, the curtain is already up and the stage is just as it would be during the day. There is no set; it is empty, in almost total darkness. This is so that from the beginning the audience will have the feeling of being present, not at a performance of a properly rehearsed play, but at a performance of a play that happens spontaneously. Two small sets of steps, one on the right and one on the left, lead up to the stage from the auditorium. On the stage, the top is off the PROMPTER's *box and is lying next to it. Downstage, there is a small table and a chair with arms for the* PRODUCER: *it is turned with its back to the audience.*

Also downstage there are two small tables, one a little bigger than the other, and several chairs, ready for the rehearsal if needed. There are more chairs scattered on both left and right for the ACTORS *to one side at the back and nearly hidden is a piano.*

When the houselights go down the STAGE HAND *comes on through the back door. He is in blue overalls and carries a tool bag. He brings some pieces of wood on, comes to the front, kneels down and starts to nail them together.*

The STAGE MANAGER *rushes on from the wings.*

STAGE MANAGER   Hey! What are you doing?

STAGE HAND   What do you think I'm doing? I'm banging nails in.

STAGE MANAGER   Now? [*He looks at his watch.*] It's half-past ten already. The Producer will be here in a moment to rehearse.

STAGE HAND   I've got to do my work some time, you know.

STAGE MANAGER   Right—but not now.

STAGE HAND   When?

STAGE MANAGER   When the rehearsal's finished. Come on, get all this out of the way and let me set for the second act of *The Rules of the Game*.[2]

[*The* STAGE HAND *picks up his tools and wood and goes off, grumbling and muttering. The* ACTORS *of the company come in through the door, men and women, first one then another, then two together and so on: there will be*

1. Translated by John Linstrum. In the Italian editions, Pirandello notes that he did not divide the play into formal acts or scenes. The translator has marked the divisions for clarity, however, according to the stage directions.
2. *Il giuoco delle parti*, written in 1918. The hero, Leone Gala, pretends to ignore his wife, Silia's, infidelity until the end, when he takes revenge by tricking her lover, Guido Venanzi, into taking his place in a fatal duel she had engineered to get rid of her husband.

nine or ten, enough for the parts for the rehearsal of a play by Pirandello,
The Rules of the Game, today's rehearsal. They come in, say their "Good-
mornings" to the STAGE MANAGER *and each other. Some go off to the dressing-*
rooms; others, among them the PROMPTER *with the text rolled up under his*
arm, scatter about the stage waiting for the PRODUCER *to start the rehearsal.*
Meanwhile, sitting or standing in groups, they chat together; some smoke,
one complains about his part, another one loudly reads something from
"The Stage." It would be as well if the ACTORS *and* ACTRESSES *were dressed*
in colourful clothes, and this first scene should be improvised naturally and
vivaciously. After a while somebody might sit down at the piano and play a
song; the younger ACTORS *and* ACTRESSES *start dancing.*]

STAGE MANAGER [*Clapping his hands to call their attention.*]   Come on, everybody! Quiet please. The Producer's here.

[*The piano and the dancing both stop. The* ACTORS *turn to look out into the*
theatre and through the door at the back comes the PRODUCER; *he walks*
down the gangway between the seats and, calling "Good-morning" to the
ACTORS, *climbs up one of the sets of stairs onto the stage. The* SECRETARY
gives him the post, a few magazines, a script. The ACTORS *move to one side*
of the stage.]

PRODUCER   Any letters?

SECRETARY   No. That's all the post there is. [*Giving him the script.*]

PRODUCER   Put it in the office. [*Then looking round and turning to the* STAGE
MANAGER.] I can't see a thing here. Let's have some lights please.

STAGE MANAGER   Right. [*Calling.*] Workers please!

[*In a few seconds the side of the stage where the* ACTORS *are standing is bril-*
liantly lit with white light. The PROMPTER *has gone into his box and spread*
out his script.]

PRODUCER   Good. [*Clapping hands.*] Well then, let's get started. Anybody
missing?

STAGE MANAGER [*Heavily ironic.*]   Our leading lady.

PRODUCER   Not again! [*Looking at his watch.*] We're ten minutes late already.
Send her a note to come and see me. It might teach her to be on time for
rehearsals. [*Almost before he has finished, the* LEADING ACTRESS's *voice is*
heard from the auditorium.]

LEADING ACTRESS   Morning everybody. Sorry I'm late. [*She is very expensively*
dressed and is carrying a lap-dog. She comes down the aisle and goes up on to
the stage.]

PRODUCER   You're determined to keep us waiting, aren't you?

LEADING ACTRESS   I'm sorry. I just couldn't find a taxi anywhere. But you
haven't started yet and I'm not on at the opening anyhow. [*Calling the* STAGE
MANAGER, *she gives him the dog.*] Put him in my dressing-room for me will
you?

PRODUCER   And she's even brought her lap-dog with her! As if we haven't
enough lap-dogs here already. [*Clapping his hands and turning to the*
PROMPTER.] Right then, the second act of *The Rules of the Game.* [*Sits in his*
arm-chair.] Quiet please! Who's on?

[*The* ACTORS *clear from the front of the stage and sit to one side, except for*
three who are ready to start the scene—and the LEADING ACTRESS. *She has*
ignored the PRODUCER *and is sitting at one of the little tables.*]

PRODUCER   Are you in this scene, then?

LEADING ACTRESS   No—I've just told you.

PRODUCER [*Annoyed.*]   Then get off, for God's sake. [*The* LEADING ACTRESS *goes and sits with the others. To the* PROMPTER.] Come on then, let's get going.

PROMPTER [*Reading his script.*]   "The house of Leone Gala. A peculiar room, both dining-room and study."

PRODUCER [*To the* STAGE MANAGER.]   We'll use the red set.

STAGE MANAGER [*Making a note.*]   The red set—right.

PROMPTER [*Still reading.*]   "The table is laid and there is a desk with books and papers. Bookcases full of books and china cabinets full of valuable china. An exit at the back leads to Leone's bedroom. An exit to the left leads to the kitchen. The main entrance is on the right."

PRODUCER   Right. Listen carefully everybody: there, the main entrance, there, the kitchen. [*To the* LEADING ACTOR *who plays Socrates.*[3]] Your entrances and exits will be from there. [*To the* STAGE MANAGER.] We'll have the French windows there and put the curtains on them.

STAGE MANAGER [*Making a note.*]   Right.

PROMPTER [*Reading.*]   "Scene One. Leone Gala, Guido Venanzi, and Filippo, who is called Socrates." [*To* PRODUCER.] Have I to read the directions as well?

PRODUCER   Yes, you have! I've told you a hundred times.

PROMPTER [*Reading.*]   "When the curtain rises, Leone Gala, in a cook's hat and apron, is beating an egg in a dish with a little wooden spoon. Filippo is beating another and he is dressed as a cook too. Guido Venanzi is sitting listening."

LEADING ACTOR   Look, do I really have to wear a cook's hat?

PRODUCER [*Annoyed by the question.*]   I expect so! That's what it says in the script. [*Pointing to the script.*]

LEADING ACTOR   If you ask me it's ridiculous.

PRODUCER [*Leaping to his feet furiously.*]   Ridiculous? It's ridiculous, is it? What do you expect me to do if nobody writes good plays any more[4] and we're reduced to putting on plays by Pirandello? And if you can understand them you must be very clever. He writes them on purpose so nobody enjoys them, neither actors nor critics nor audience. [*The* ACTORS *laugh. Then crosses to* LEADING ACTOR *and shouts at him.*] A cook's hat and you beat eggs. But don't run away with the idea that that's all you are doing—beating eggs. You must be joking! You have to be symbolic of the shells of the eggs you are beating. [*The* ACTORS *laugh again and start making ironical comments to each other.*] Be quiet! Listen carefully while I explain. [*Turns back to* LEADING ACTOR.] Yes, the shells, because they are symbolic of the empty form of reason, without its content, blind instinct! You are reason and your wife is instinct: you are playing a game where you have been given parts and in which you are not just yourself but the puppet of yourself.[5] Do you see?

3. Nickname given to Gala's servant, Philip, in *The Rules of the Game*, the play they are rehearsing.
4. The producer refers to the realistic, tightly constructed plays (often French) that were internationally popular in the late 19th century and a staple of Italian theaters at the beginning of the 20th.
5. Leone Gala is a rationalist and an aesthete—the opposite of his impulsive, passionate wife, Silia. By masking his feelings and constantly playing the role of gourmet cook, he chooses his own role and thus becomes his own "puppet."

LEADING ACTOR [*Spreading his hands.*]   Me? No.

PRODUCER [*Going back to his chair.*]   Neither do I! Come on, let's get going; you wait till you see the end! You haven't seen anything yet! [*Confidentially.*] By the way, I should turn almost to face the audience if I were you, about three-quarters face. Well, what with the obscure dialogue and the audience not being able to hear you properly in any case, the whole lot'll go to hell. [*Clapping hands again.*] Come on. Let's get going!

PROMPTER   Excuse me, can I put the top back on the prompt-box? There's a bit of a draught.

PRODUCER   Yes, yes, of course. Get on with it.

> [*The* STAGE DOORKEEPER, *in a braided cap, has come into the auditorium, and he comes all the way down the aisle to the stage to tell the* PRODUCER *the* SIX CHARACTERS *have come, who, having come in after him, look about them a little puzzled and dismayed. Every effort must be made to create the effect that the* SIX CHARACTERS *are very different from the* ACTORS *of the company. The placings of the two groups, indicated in the directions, once the* CHARACTERS *are on the stage, will help this: so will using different coloured lights. But the most effective idea is to use masks for the* CHARACTERS, *masks specially made of a material that will not go limp with perspiration and light enough not to worry the actors who wear them: they should be made so that the eyes, the nose and the mouth are all free. This is the way to bring out the deep significance of the play. The* CHARACTERS *should not appear as ghosts, but as created realities, timeless creations of the imagination, and so more real and consistent than the changeable realities of the* ACTORS. *The masks are designed to give the impression of figures constructed by art, each one fixed forever in its own fundamental emotion; that is, Remorse for the* FATHER, *Revenge for the* STEPDAUGHTER, *Scorn for the* SON, *Sorrow for the* MOTHER. *Her mask should have wax tears in the corners of the eyes and down the cheeks like the sculptured or painted weeping Madonna in a church. Her dress should be of a plain material, in stiff folds, looking almost as if it were carved and not of an ordinary material you can buy in a shop and have made up by a dressmaker.*
>
> *The* FATHER *is about fifty: his reddish hair is thinning at the temples, but he is not bald: he has a full moustache that almost covers his young-looking mouth, which often opens in an uncertain and empty smile. He is pale, with a high forehead: he has blue oval eyes, clear and sharp: he is dressed in light trousers and a dark jacket: his voice is sometimes rich, at other times harsh and loud.*
>
> *The* MOTHER *appears crushed by an intolerable weight of shame and humiliation. She is wearing a thick black veil and is dressed simply in black; when she raises her veil she shows a face like wax, but not suffering, with her eyes turned down humbly.*
>
> *The* STEPDAUGHTER, *who is eighteen years old, is defiant, even insolent. She is very beautiful, dressed in mourning as well, but with striking elegance. She is scornful of the timid, suffering, dejected air of her young brother, a grubby* LITTLE BOY *of fourteen, also dressed in black; she is full of a warm tenderness, on the other hand, for the* LITTLE SISTER (GIRL), *a girl of about four, dressed in white with a black silk sash round her waist.*
>
> *The* SON *is twenty-two, tall, almost frozen in an air of scorn for the* FATHER *and indifference to the* MOTHER: *he is wearing a mauve overcoat and a long green scarf round his neck.*]

DOORMAN   Excuse me, sir.

PRODUCER [*Angrily.*]   What the hell is it now?

DOORMAN   There are some people here—they say they want to see you, sir.

> [*The* PRODUCER *and the* ACTORS *are astonished and turn to look out into the auditorium.*]

PRODUCER   But I'm rehearsing! You know perfectly well that no-one's allowed in during rehearsals. [*Turning to face out front.*] Who are you? What do you want?

FATHER [*Coming forward, followed by the others, to the foot of one of the sets of steps.*]   We're looking for an author.

PRODUCER [*Angry and astonished.*]   An author? Which author?

FATHER   Any author will do, sir.

PRODUCER   But there isn't an author here because we're not rehearsing a new play.

STEPDAUGHTER [*Excitedly as she rushes up the steps.*]   That's better still, better still! We can be your new play.

ACTORS [*Lively comments and laughter from the* ACTORS.]   Oh, listen to that, etc.

FATHER [*Going up on the stage after the* STEPDAUGHTER.]   Maybe, but if there isn't an author here . . . [*To the* PRODUCER.] Unless you'd like to be . . .

> [*Hand in hand, the* MOTHER *and the* LITTLE GIRL, *followed by the* LITTLE BOY, *go up on the stage and wait. The* SON *stays sullenly behind.*]

PRODUCER   Is this some kind of joke?

FATHER   Now, how can you think that? On the contrary, we are bringing you a story of anguish.

STEPDAUGHTER   We might make your fortune for you!

PRODUCER   Do me a favour, will you? Go away. We haven't time to waste on idiots.

FATHER [*Hurt but answering gently.*]   You know very well, as a man of the theatre, that life is full of all sorts of odd things which have no need at all to pretend to be real because they are actually true.

PRODUCER   What the devil are you talking about?

FATHER   What I'm saying is that you really must be mad to do things the opposite way round: to create situations that obviously aren't true and try to make them seem to be really happening. But then I suppose that sort of madness is the only reason for your profession.

> [*The* ACTORS *are indignant.*]

PRODUCER [*Getting up and glaring at him.*]   Oh, yes? So ours is a profession of madmen, is it?

FATHER   Well, if you try to make something look true when it obviously isn't, especially if you're not forced to do it, but do it for a game . . . Isn't it your job to give life on the stage to imaginary people?

PRODUCER [*Quickly answering him and speaking for the* ACTORS *who are growing more indignant.*]   I should like you to know, sir, that the actor's profession is one of great distinction. Even if nowadays the new writers only give us dull plays to act and puppets to present instead of men, I'd have you know that it is our boast that we have given life, here on this stage, to immortal works.

> [*The* ACTORS, *satisfied, agree with and applaud the* PRODUCER].

FATHER [*Cutting in and following hard on his argument.*]   There! You see? Good! You've given life! You've created living beings with more genuine life than people have who breathe and wear clothes! Less real, perhaps, but nearer the truth. We are both saying the same thing.

[*The* ACTORS *look at each other, astonished.*]

PRODUCER   But just a moment! You said before . . .

FATHER   I'm sorry, but I said that before, about acting for fun, because you shouted at us and said you'd no time to waste on idiots, but you must know better than anyone that Nature uses human imagination to lift her work of creation to even higher levels.

PRODUCER   All right then: but where does all this get us?

FATHER   Nowhere. I want to try to show that one can be thrust into life in many ways, in many forms: as a tree or a stone, as water or a butterfly—or as a woman. It might even be as a character in a play.

PRODUCER [*Ironic, pretending to be annoyed.*]   And you, and these other people here, were thrust into life, as you put it, as characters in a play?

FATHER   Exactly! And alive, as you can see.

[*The* PRODUCER *and the* ACTORS *burst into laughter as if at a joke.*]

FATHER   I'm sorry you laugh like that, because we carry in us, as I said before, a story of terrible anguish as you can guess from this woman dressed in black.

[*Saying this, he offers his hand to the* MOTHER *and helps her up the last steps and, holding her still by the hand, leads her with a sense of tragic solemnity across the stage which is suddenly lit by a fantastic light.*

The LITTLE GIRL *and the* (LITTLE) BOY *follow the* MOTHER: *then the* SON *comes up and stands to one side in the background: then the* STEP-DAUGHTER *follows and leans against the proscenium arch: the* ACTORS *are astonished at first, but then, full of admiration for the "entrance," they burst into applause—just as if it were a performance specially for them.*]

PRODUCER [*At first astonished and then indignant.*]   My God! Be quiet all of you. [*Turns to the* CHARACTERS.] And you lot get out! Clear off! [*Turns to the* STAGE MANAGER.] Jesus! Get them out of here.

STAGE MANAGER [*Comes forward but stops short as if held back by something strange.*]   Go on out! Get out!

FATHER [*To* PRODUCER.]   Oh no, please, you see, we . . .

PRODUCER [*Shouting.*]   We came here to work, you know.

LEADING ACTOR   We really can't be messed about like this.

FATHER [*Resolutely, coming forward.*]   I'm astonished! Why don't you believe me? Perhaps you are not used to seeing the characters created by an author spring into life up here on the stage face to face with each other. Perhaps it's because we're not in a script? [*He points to the* PROMPTER'S *box.*]

STEPDAUGHTER [*Coming down to the* PRODUCER, *smiling and persuasive.*]   Believe me, sir, we really are six of the most fascinating characters. But we've been neglected.

FATHER   Yes, that's right, we've been neglected. In the sense that the author who created us, living in his mind, wouldn't or couldn't make us live in a written play for the world of art.[6] And that really is a crime sir, because whoever has the luck to be born a character can laugh even at death.

6. In the 1925 preface to *Six Characters,* Pirandello explains that these characters came to him first as characters for a novel that he later abandoned. Haunted by their half-realized personalities, he decided to use the situation in a play.

Because a character will never die! A man will die, a writer, the instrument of creation: but what he has created will never die! And to be able to live for ever you don't need to have extraordinary gifts or be able to do miracles. Who was Sancho Panza? Who was Prospero?[7] But they will live for ever because—living seeds—they had the luck to find a fruitful soil, an imagination which knew how to grow them and feed them, so that they will live for ever.

PRODUCER   This is all very well! But what do you want here?

FATHER   We want to live, sir.

PRODUCER [Ironically.]   For ever!

FATHER   No, no: only for a few moments—in you.

AN ACTOR   Listen to that!

LEADING ACTRESS   They want to live in us!

YOUNG ACTOR [Pointing to the STEPDAUGHTER.]   I don't mind . . . so long as I get her.

FATHER   Listen, listen: the play is all ready to be put together and if you and your actors would like to, we can work it out now between us.

PRODUCER [Annoyed.]   But what exactly do you want to do? We don't make up plays like that here! We present comedies and tragedies here.

FATHER   That's right, we know that of course. That's why we've come.

PRODUCER   And where's the script?

FATHER   It's in us, sir. [The ACTORS laugh.] The play is in us: we are the play and we are impatient to show it to you: the passion inside us is driving us on.

STEPDAUGHTER [Scornfully, with the tantalising charm of deliberate impudence.]   My passion, if only you knew! My passion for him! [She points at the FATHER and suggests that she is going to embrace him: but stops and bursts into a screeching laugh.]

FATHER [With sudden anger.]   You keep out of this for the moment! And stop laughing like that!

STEPDAUGHTER   Really? Then with your permission, ladies and gentlemen; even though it's only two months since I became an orphan, just watch how I can sing and dance.

[The ACTORS, especially the younger, seem strangely attracted to her while she sings and dances and they edge closer and reach out their hands to catch hold of her.[8] She eludes them, and when the ACTORS applaud her and the PRODUCER speaks sharply to her she stays still quite removed from them all.]

FIRST ACTOR   Very good! etc.

PRODUCER [Angrily.]   Be quiet! Do you think this is a nightclub? [Turns to FATHER and asks with some concern.] Is she a bit mad?

FATHER   Mad? Oh no—it's worse than that.

STEPDAUGHTER [Suddenly running to the PRODUCER.]   Yes. It's worse, much worse! Listen please! Let's put this play on at once, because you'll see that

7. The magician and exiled duke of Milan in Shakespeare's The Tempest. Sancho Panza was Don Quixote's servant in Cervantes' novel Don Quixote (1605–15).

8. Pirandello uses a contemporary popular song, "Chu-Chin-Chow" from the Ziegfeld Follies of 1917, for the Stepdaughter to display her talents.

at a particular point I—when this darling little girl here—[*Taking the* LITTLE GIRL *by the hand from next to the* MOTHER *and crossing with her to the* PRODUCER.] Isn't she pretty? [*Takes her in her arms.*] Darling! Darling! [*Puts her down again and adds, moved very deeply but almost without wanting to.*] Well, this lovely little girl here, when God suddenly takes her from this poor Mother: and this little idiot here [*Turning to the* LITTLE BOY *and seizing him roughly by the sleeve.*] does the most stupid thing, like the half-wit he is,— then you will see me run away! Yes, you'll see me rush away! But not yet, not yet! Because, after all the intimate things there have been between him and me [*In the direction of the* FATHER, *with a horrible vulgar wink.*] I can't stay with them any longer, to watch the insult to this mother through that supercilious cretin over there. [*Pointing to the* SON.] Look at him! Look at him! Condescending, stand-offish, because he's the legitimate son, him! Full of contempt for me, for the boy and for the little girl: because we are bastards. Do you understand? Bastards. [*Running to the* MOTHER *and embracing her.*] And this poor mother—she—who is the mother of all of us—he doesn't want to recognise her as his own mother—and he looks down on her, he does, as if she were only the mother of the three of us who are bastards—the traitor. [*She says all this quickly, with great excitement, and after having raised her voice on the word "bastards" she speaks quietly, half-spitting the word "traitor."*]

MOTHER [*With deep anguish to the* PRODUCER.]   Sir, in the name of these two little ones, I beg you . . . [*Feels herself grow faint and sways.*] Oh, my God.

FATHER [*Rushing to support her with almost all the* ACTORS *bewildered and concerned.*]   Get a chair someone . . . quick, get a chair for this poor widow.

[*One of the* ACTORS *offers a chair: the others press urgently around. The* MOTHER, *seated now, tries to stop the* FATHER *lifting her veil.*]

ACTORS   Is it real? Has she really fainted? etc.

FATHER   Look at her, everybody, look at her.

MOTHER   No, for God's sake, stop it.

FATHER   Let them look?

MOTHER [*Lifting her hands and covering her face, desperately.*]   Oh, please, I beg you, stop him from doing what he is trying to do; it's hateful.

PRODUCER [*Overwhelmed, astounded.*]   It's no use, I don't understand this any more. [*To the* FATHER.] Is this woman your wife?

FATHER [*At once.*]   That's right, she is my wife.

PRODUCER   How is she a widow, then, if you're still alive?

[*The* ACTORS *are bewildered too and find relief in a loud laugh.*]

FATHER [*Wounded, with rising resentment.*]   Don't laugh! Please don't laugh like that! That's just the point, that's her own drama. You see, she had another man. Another man who ought to be here.

MOTHER   No, no! [*Crying out.*]

STEPDAUGHTER   Luckily for him he died. Two months ago, as I told you: we are in mourning for him, as you can see.

FATHER   Yes, he's dead: but that's not the reason he isn't here. He isn't here because—well just look at her, please, and you'll understand at once—hers is not a passionate drama of the love of two men, because she was incapable of love, she could feel nothing—except, perhaps a little gratitude (but not to me, to him). She's not a woman; she's a mother. And her drama—and, believe me, it's a powerful one—her drama is focused completely on these four children of the two men she had.

MOTHER   I had them? How dare you say that I had them, as if I wanted them myself? It was him, sir! He forced the other man on me. He made me go away with him!

STEPDAUGHTER [*Leaping up, indignantly.*]   It isn't true!

MOTHER [*Bewildered.*]   How isn't it true?

STEPDAUGHTER   It isn't true, it just isn't true.

MOTHER   What do you know about it?

STEPDAUGHTER   It isn't true. [*To the* PRODUCER.] Don't believe it! Do you know why she said that? She said it because of him, over there. [*Pointing to the* SON.] She tortures herself, she exhausts herself with worry and all because of the indifference of that son of hers. She wants to make him believe that she abandoned him when he was two years old because the Father made her do it.

MOTHER [*Passionately.*]   He did! He made me! God's my witness. [*To the* PRODUCER.] Ask him if it isn't true. [*Pointing to the* FATHER.] Make him tell our son it's true. [*Turning to the* STEPDAUGHTER.] You don't know anything about it.

STEPDAUGHTER   I know that when my father was alive you were always happy and contented. You can't deny it.

MOTHER   No, I can't deny it.

STEPDAUGHTER   He was always full of love and care for you. [*Turning to the* LITTLE BOY *with anger.*] Isn't it true? Admit it. Why don't you say something, you little idiot?

MOTHER   Leave the poor boy alone! Why do you want to make me appear ungrateful? You're my daughter. I don't in the least want to offend your father's memory. I've already told him that it wasn't my fault or even to please myself that I left his house and my son.

FATHER   It's quite true. It was my fault.

LEADING ACTOR [*To other actors.*]   Look at this. What a show!

LEADING ACTRESS   And we're the audience.

YOUNG ACTOR   For a change.

PRODUCER [*Beginning to be very interested.*]   Let's listen to them! Quiet! Listen!

    [*He goes down the steps into the auditorium and stands there as if to get an idea of what the scene will look like from the audience's viewpoint.*]

SON [*Without moving, coldly, quietly, ironically.*]   Yes, listen to his little scrap of philosophy. He's going to tell you all about the Daemon of Experiment.

FATHER   You're a cynical idiot, and I've told you so a hundred times. [*To the* PRODUCER *who is now in the stalls.*] He sneers at me because of this expression I've found to defend myself.

SON   Words, words.

FATHER   Yes words, words! When we're faced by something we don't understand, by a sense of evil that seems as if it's going to swallow us, don't we all find comfort in a word that tells us nothing but that calms us?

STEPDAUGHTER   And dulls your sense of remorse, too. That more than anything.

FATHER   Remorse? No, that's not true. It'd take more than words to dull the sense of remorse in me.

STEPDAUGHTER   It's taken a little money too, just a little money. The money that he was going to offer as payment, gentlemen.

[*The* ACTORS *are horrified.*]

SON [*Contemptuously to his stepsister.*]   That's a filthy trick.

STEPDAUGHTER   A filthy trick? There it was in a pale blue envelope on the little mahogany table in the room behind the shop at Madame Pace's. You know Madame Pace, don't you? One of those Madames who sell "Robes et Manteaux" so that they can attract poor girls like me from decent families into their workroom.[9]

SON   And she's bought the right to tyrannise over the whole lot of us with that money—with what he was going to pay her: and luckily—now listen carefully— he had no reason to pay it to her.

STEPDAUGHTER   But it was close!

MOTHER [*Rising up angrily.*]   Shame on you, daughter! Shame!

STEPDAUGHTER   Shame? Not shame, revenge! I'm desperate, desperate to live that scene! The room . . . over here the showcase of coats, there the divan, there the mirror, and the screen, and over there in front of the window, that little mahogany table with the pale blue envelope and the money in it. I can see it all quite clearly. I could pick it up! But you should turn your faces away, gentlemen: because I'm nearly naked! I'm not blushing any longer—I leave that to him. [*Pointing at the* FATHER.] But I tell you he was very pale, very pale then. [*To the* PRODUCER.] Believe me.

PRODUCER   I don't understand any more.

FATHER   I'm not surprised when you're attacked like that! Why don't you put your foot down and let me have my say before you believe all these horrible slanders she's so viciously telling about me.

STEPDAUGHTER   We don't want to hear any of your long winded fairy-stories.

FATHER   I'm not going to tell any fairy-stories! I want to explain things to him.

STEPDAUGHTER   I'm sure you do. Oh, yes! In your own special way.

[*The* PRODUCER *comes back up on stage to take control.*]

FATHER   But isn't that the cause of all the trouble? Words! We all have a world of things inside ourselves and each one of us has his own private world. How can we understand each other if the words I use have the sense and the value that I expect them to have, but whoever is listening to me inevitably thinks that those same words have a different sense and value, because of the private world he has inside himself too. We think we understand each other: but we never do. Look! All my pity, all my compassion for this woman [*Pointing to the* MOTHER.] she sees as ferocious cruelty.

MOTHER   But he turned me out of the house!

FATHER   There, do you hear? I turned her out! She really believed that I had turned her out.

MOTHER   You know how to talk. I don't . . . But believe me, sir, [*Turning to the* PRODUCER.] after he married me . . . I can't think why! I was a poor, simple woman.

FATHER   But that was the reason! I married you for your simplicity, that's what I loved in you, believing—[*He stops because she is making gestures of*

9. The implication is that Madame Pace (Italian for "peace") runs a call-girl operation under the guise of selling fashionable "dresses and coats."

contradiction. *Then, seeing the impossibility of making her understand, he throws his arms wide in a gesture of desperation and turns back to the* PRODUCER.] No, do you see? She says no! It's terrifying, sir, believe me, terrifying, her deafness, her mental deafness. [*He taps his forehead.*] Affection for her children, oh yes. But deaf, mentally deaf, deaf, sir, to the point of desperation.

STEPDAUGHTER   Yes, but make him tell you what good all his cleverness has brought us.

FATHER   If only we could see in advance all the harm that can come from the good we think we are doing.

> [*The* LEADING ACTRESS, *who has been growing angry watching the* LEADING ACTOR *flirting with the* STEPDAUGHTER, *comes forward and snaps at the* PRODUCER.]

LEADING ACTRESS   Excuse me, are we going to go on with our rehearsal?

PRODUCER   Yes, of course. But I want to listen to this first.

YOUNG ACTOR   It's such a new idea.

YOUNG ACTRESS   It's fascinating.

LEADING ACTRESS   For those who are interested. [*She looks meaningfully at the* LEADING ACTOR.]

PRODUCER [*To the* FATHER.]   Look here, you must explain yourself more clearly. [*He sits down.*]

FATHER   Listen then. You see, there was a rather poor fellow working for me as my assistant and secretary, very loyal: he understood her in everything. [*Pointing to the* MOTHER.] But without a hint of deceit, you must believe that: he was good and simple, like her: neither of them was capable even of thinking anything wrong, let alone doing it.

STEPDAUGHTER   So instead he thought of it for them and did it too!

FATHER   It's not true! What I did was for their good—oh yes and mine too, I admit it! The time had come when I couldn't say a word to either of them without there immediately flashing between them a sympathetic look: each one caught the other's eye for advice, about how to take what I had said, how not to make me angry. Well, that was enough, as I'm sure you'll understand, to put me in a bad temper all the time, in a state of intolerable exasperation.

PRODUCER   Then why didn't you sack this secretary of yours?

FATHER   Right! In the end I did sack him! But then I had to watch this poor woman wandering about in the house on her own, forlorn, like a stray animal you take in out of pity.

MOTHER   It's quite true.

FATHER [*Suddenly, turning to her, as if to stop her.*]   And what about the boy? Is that true as well?

MOTHER   But first he tore my son from me, sir.

FATHER   But not out of cruelty! It was so that he could grow up healthy and strong, in touch with the earth.

STEPDAUGHTER [*Pointing to the* SON *jeeringly.*]   And look at the result!

FATHER [*Quickly.*]   And is it my fault, too, that he's grown up like this? I took him to a nurse in the country, a peasant, because his mother didn't seem strong enough to me, although she is from a humble family herself. In fact that was what made me marry her. Perhaps it was superstitious of me; but what was I to do? I've always had this dreadful longing for a kind of sound moral healthiness.

[*The* STEPDAUGHTER *breaks out again into noisy laughter.*]

Make her stop that! It's unbearable.

PRODUCER   Stop it will you? Let me listen, for God's sake.

[*When the* PRODUCER *has spoken to her, she resumes her previous position . . . absorbed and distant, a half-smile on her lips. The* PRODUCER *comes down into the auditorium again to see how it looks from there.*]

FATHER   I couldn't bear the sight of this woman near me. [*Pointing to the* MOTHER.] Not so much because of the annoyance she caused me, you see, or even the feeling of being stifled, being suffocated that I got from her, as for the sorrow, the painful sorrow that I felt for her.

MOTHER   And he sent me away.

FATHER   With everything you needed, to the other man, to set her free from me.

MOTHER   And to set yourself free!

FATHER   Oh, yes, I admit it. And what terrible things came out of it. But I did it for the best, and more for her than for me: I swear it! [*Folds his arms: then turns suddenly to the* MOTHER.] I never lost sight of you did I? Until that fellow, without my knowing it, suddenly took you off to another town one day. He was idiotically suspicious of my interest in them, a genuine interest, I assure you, without any ulterior motive at all. I watched the new little family growing up round her with unbelievable tenderness, she'll confirm that. [*He points to the* STEPDAUGHTER.]

STEPDAUGHTER   Oh yes, I can indeed. I was a pretty little girl, you know, with plaits down to my shoulders and my little frilly knickers showing under my dress—so pretty—he used to watch me coming out of school. He came to see how I was maturing.

FATHER   That's shameful! It's monstrous.

STEPDAUGHTER   No it isn't! Why do you say it is?

FATHER   It's monstrous! Monstrous. [*He turns excitedly to the* PRODUCER *and goes on in explanation.*] After she'd gone away [*Pointing to the* MOTHER.] my house seemed empty. She'd been like a weight on my spirit but she'd filled the house with her presence. Alone in the empty rooms I wandered about like a lost soul. This boy here, [*Indicating the* SON.] growing up away from home—whenever he came back to the home—I don't know—but he didn't seem to be mine any more. We needed the mother between us, to link us together, and so he grew up by himself, apart, with no connection to me either through intellect or love. And then—it must seem odd, but it's true— first I was curious about and then strongly attracted to the little family that had come about because of what I'd done. And the thought of them began to fill all the emptiness that I felt around me. I needed, I really needed to believe that she was happy, wrapped up in the simple cares of her life, lucky because she was better off away from the complicated torments of a soul like mine. And to prove it, I used to watch that child coming out of school.

STEPDAUGHTER   Listen to him! He used to follow me along the street; he used to smile at me and when we came near the house he'd wave his hand—like this! I watched him, wide-eyed, puzzled. I didn't know who he was. I told my mother about him and she knew at once who it must be. [MOTHER *nods agreement.*] At first, she didn't let me go to school again, at any rate for a few days. But when I did go back, I saw him standing near the door again—looking ridiculous—with a brown paper bag in his hand. He came close and petted me: then he opened the bag and took out a beautiful straw hat with a hoop of rosebuds round it—for me!

PRODUCER   All this is off the point, you know.

SON [*Contemptuously.*]   Yes . . . literature, literature.

FATHER   What do you mean, literature? This is real life: real passions.

PRODUCER   That may be! But you can't put it on the stage just like that.

FATHER   That's right you can't. Because all this is only leading up to the main action. I'm not suggesting that this part should be put on the stage. In any case, you can see for yourself, [*Pointing at the* STEPDAUGHTER.] she isn't a pretty little girl any longer with plaits down to her shoulders.

STEPDAUGHTER   —and with frilly knickers showing under her frock.

FATHER   The drama begins now: and it's new and complex.

STEPDAUGHTER [*Coming forward, fierce and brooding.*]   As soon as my father died . . .

FATHER [*Quickly, not giving her time to speak.*]   They were so miserable. They came back here, but I didn't know about it because of the Mother's stubbornness. [*Pointing to the* MOTHER.] She can't really write you know; but she could have got her daughter to write, or the boy, or tell me that they needed help.

MOTHER   But tell me, sir, how could I have known how he felt?

FATHER   And hasn't that always been your fault? You've never known anything about how I felt.

MOTHER   After all the years away from him and after all that had happened.

FATHER   And was it my fault if that fellow took you so far away? [*Turning back to the* PRODUCER.] Suddenly, overnight, I tell you, he'd found a job away from here without my knowing anything about it. I couldn't possibly trace them; and then, naturally I suppose, my interest in them grew less over the years. The drama broke out, unexpected and violent, when they came back: when I was driven in misery by the needs of my flesh, still alive with desire . . . and it is misery, you know, unspeakable misery for the man who lives alone and who detests sordid, casual affairs; not old enough to do without women, but not young enough to be able to go and look for one without shame! Misery? Is that what I called it. It's horrible, it's revolting, because there isn't a woman who will give her love to him any more. And when he realises this, he should do without . . . It's easy to say though. Each of us, face to face with other men, is clothed with some sort of dignity, but we know only too well all the unspeakable things that go on in the heart. We surrender, we give in to temptation: but afterwards we rise up out of it very quickly, in a desperate hurry to rebuild our dignity, whole and firm as if it were a gravestone that would cover every sign and memory of our shame, and hide it from even our own eyes. Everyone's like that, only some of us haven't the courage to talk about it.

STEPDAUGHTER   But they've all got the courage to do it!

FATHER   Yes! But only in secret! That's why it takes more courage to talk about it! Because if a man does talk about it—what happens then?—everybody says he's a cynic. And it's simply not true; he's just like everybody else; only better perhaps, because he's not afraid to use his intelligence to point out the blushing shame of human bestiality, that man, the beast, shuts his eyes to, trying to pretend it doesn't exist. And what about woman—what is she like? She looks at you invitingly, teasingly. You take her in your arms. But as soon as she feels your arms round her she closes her eyes. It's the sign of her mission, the sign by which she says to a man, "Blind yourself— I'm blind!"

STEPDAUGHTER   And when she doesn't close her eyes any more? What then? When she doesn't feel the need to hide from herself any more, to shut her eyes and hide her own shame. When she can see instead, dispassionately and dry-eyed this blushing shame of a man who has blinded himself, who is without love. What then? Oh, then what disgust, what utter disgust she feels for all these intellectual complications, for all this philosophy that points to the bestiality of man and then tries to defend him, to excuse him . . . I can't listen to him, sir. Because when a man says he needs to "simplify" life like this—reducing it to bestiality—and throws away every human scrap of innocent desire, genuine feeling, idealism, duty, modesty, shame, then there's nothing more contemptible and nauseating than his remorse—crocodile tears!

PRODUCER   Let's get to the point, let's get to the point. This is all chat.

FATHER   Right then! But a fact is like a sack—it won't stand up if it's empty. To make it stand up, first you have to put in it all the reasons and feelings that caused it in the first place. I couldn't possibly have known that when that fellow died they'd come back here, that they were desperately poor and that the Mother had gone out to work as a dressmaker, nor that she'd gone to work for Madame Pace, of all people.

STEPDAUGHTER   She's a very high-class dressmaker—you must understand that. She apparently has only high-class customers, but she has arranged things carefully so that these high-class customers in fact serve her—they give her a respectable front . . . without spoiling things for the other ladies at the shop who are not quite so high-class at all.

MOTHER   Believe me, sir, the idea never entered my head that the old hag gave me work because she had an eye on my daughter . . .

STEPDAUGHTER   Poor Mummy! Do you know what that woman would do when I took back the work that my mother had been doing? She would point out how the dress had been ruined by giving it to my mother to sew: she bargained, she grumbled. So, you see, I paid for it, while this poor woman here thought she was sacrificing herself for me and these two children, sewing dresses all night for Madame Pace.

[The ACTORS make gestures and noises of disgust.]

PRODUCER [Quickly.]   And there one day, you met . . .

STEPDAUGHTER [Pointing at the FATHER.]   Yes, him. Oh, he was an old customer of hers! What a scene that's going to be, superb!

FATHER   With her, the mother, arriving—

STEPDAUGHTER [Quickly, viciously.]   —Almost in time!

FATHER [Crying out.]   —No, just in time, just in time! Because, luckily, I found out who she was in time. And I took them all back to my house, sir. Can you imagine the situation now, for the two of us living in the same house? She, just as you see her here: and I, not able to look her in the face.

STEPDAUGHTER   It's so absurd! Do you think it's possible for me, sir, after what happened at Madame Pace's, to pretend that I'm a modest little miss, well brought up and virtuous just so that I can fit in with his damned pretensions to a "sound moral healthiness"?

FATHER   This is the real drama for me; the belief that we all, you see, think of ourselves as one single person: but it's not true: each of us is several different people, and all these people live inside us. With one person we seem like this and with another we seem very different. But we always have the illusion of being the same person for everybody and of always being the same person in everything we do. But it's not true! It's not true! We find this out for ourselves very clearly when by some terrible chance we're suddenly stopped in the middle of doing something and we're left dangling there, suspended. We realise then, that every part of us was not involved in what we'd been doing and that it would be a dreadful injustice of other people to judge us only by this one action as we dangle there, hanging in chains, fixed for all eternity, as if the whole of one's personality were summed up in that single, interrupted action. Now do you understand this girl's treachery? She accidentally found me somewhere I shouldn't have been, doing something I shouldn't have been doing! She discovered a part of me that shouldn't have existed for her: and now she wants to fix on me a reality that I should never have had to assume for her: it came from a single brief and shameful moment in my life. This is what hurts me most of all. And you'll see that the play will make a tremendous impact from this idea of mine. But then, there's the position of the others. His . . . [*Pointing to the* SON.]

SON [*Shrugging his shoulders scornfully.*]   Leave me out of it. I don't come into this.

FATHER   Why don't you come into this?

SON   I don't come into it and I don't want to come into it, because you know perfectly well that I wasn't intended to be mixed up with you lot.

STEPDAUGHTER   We're vulgar, common people, you see! He's a fine gentleman. But you've probably noticed that every now and then I look at him contemptuously, and when I do, he lowers his eyes—he knows the harm he's done me.

SON [*Not looking at her.*]   I have?

STEPDAUGHTER   Yes, you. It's your fault, dearie, that I went on the streets! Your fault! [*Movement of horror from the* ACTORS.] Did you or didn't you, with your attitude, deny us—I won't say the intimacy of your home—but that simple hospitality that makes guests feel comfortable? We were intruders who had come to invade the country of your "legitimacy"! [*Turning to the* PRODUCER.] I'd like you to have seen some of the little scenes that went on between him and me, sir. He says that I tyrannised over everyone. But don't you see? It was because of the way he treated us. He called it "vile" that I should insist on the right we had to move into his house with my mother—and she's his mother too. And I went into the house as its mistress.

SON [*Slowly coming forward.*]   They're really enjoying themselves, aren't they, sir? It's easy when they all gang up against me. But try to imagine what happened: one fine day, there is a son sitting quietly at home and he sees arrive as bold as brass, a young woman like this, who cheekily asks for his father, and heaven knows what business she has with him. Then he sees her come back with the same brazen look in her eye accompanied by that little girl there: and he sees her treat his father—without knowing why—in a most ambiguous and insolent way—asking him for money in a tone that leads one to suppose he really ought to give it, because he is obliged to do so.

FATHER   But I was obliged to do so: I owed it to your mother.

SON   And how was I to know that? When had I ever seen her before? When had I ever heard her mentioned? Then one day I see her come in with her, [Pointing at the STEPDAUGHTER.] that boy and that little girl: they say to me, "Oh, didn't you know? This is your mother, too." Little by little I began to understand, mostly from her attitude. [Points to STEPDAUGHTER.] Why they'd come to live in the house so suddenly. I can't and I won't say what I feel, and what I think. I wouldn't even like to confess it to myself. So I can't take any active part in this. Believe me, sir, I am a character who has not been fully developed dramatically, and I feel uncomfortable, most uncomfortable, in their company. So please leave me out of it.

FATHER   What! But it's precisely because you feel like this . . .

SON [Violently exasperated.]   How do you know what I feel?

FATHER   All right! I admit it! But isn't that a situation in itself? This withdrawing of yourself, it's cruel to me and to your mother: when she came back to the house, seeing you almost for the first time, not recognising you, but knowing that you're her own son . . . [Turning to point out the MOTHER to the PRODUCER.] There, look at her: she's weeping.

STEPDAUGHTER [Angrily, stamping her foot.]   Like the fool she is!

FATHER [Quickly pointing at the STEPDAUGHTER to the PRODUCER.]   She can't stand that young man, you know. [Turning and referring to the SON.] He says that he doesn't come into it, but he's really the pivot of the action! Look here at this little boy, who clings to his mother all the time, frightened, humiliated. And it's because of him over there! Perhaps this little boy's problem is the worst of all: he feels an outsider, more than the others do; he feels so mortified, so humiliated just being in the house,—because it's charity, you see. [Quietly.] He's like his father: timid; he doesn't say anything . . .

PRODUCER   It's not a good idea at all, using him: you don't know what a nuisance children are on the stage.

FATHER   He won't need to be on the stage for long. Nor will the little girl—she's the first to go.

PRODUCER   That's good! Yes. I tell you all this interests me—it interests me very much. I'm sure we've the material here for a good play.

STEPDAUGHTER [Trying to push herself in.]   With a character like me you have!

FATHER [Driving her off, wanting to hear what the PRODUCER has decided.]   You stay out of it!

PRODUCER [Going on, ignoring the interruption.]   It's new, yes.

FATHER   Oh, it's absolutely new!

PRODUCER   You've got a nerve, though, haven't you, coming here and throwing it at me like this?

FATHER   I'm sure you understand. Born as we are for the stage . . .

PRODUCER   Are you amateur actors?

FATHER   No! I say we are born for the stage because . . .

PRODUCER   Come on now! You're an old hand at this, at acting!

FATHER   No I'm not. I only act, as everyone does, the part in life that he's chosen for himself, or that others have chosen for him. And you can see that sometimes my own passion gets a bit out of hand, a bit theatrical, as it does with all of us.

PRODUCER   Maybe, maybe . . . But you do see, don't you, that without an author . . . I could give you someone's address . . .

FATHER   Oh no! Look here! You do it.

PRODUCER   Me? What are you talking about?

FATHER   Yes, you. Why not?

PRODUCER   Because I've never written anything!

FATHER   Well, why not start now, if you don't mind my suggesting it? There's nothing to it. Everybody's doing it. And your job is even easier, because we're here, all of us, alive before you.

PRODUCER   That's not enough.

FATHER   Why isn't it enough? When you've seen us live our drama . . .

PRODUCER   Perhaps so. But we'll still need someone to write it.

FATHER   Only to write it down, perhaps, while it happens in front of him—live—scene by scene. It'll be enough to sketch it out simply first and then run through it.

PRODUCER [Coming back up, tempted by the idea.]   Do you know I'm almost tempted . . . just for fun . . . it might work.

FATHER   Of course it will. You'll see what wonderful scenes will come right out of it! I could tell you what they will be!

PRODUCER   You tempt me . . . you tempt me! We'll give it a chance. Come with me to the office. [Turning to the ACTORS.] Take a break: but don't go far away. Be back in a quarter of an hour or twenty minutes. [To the FATHER.] Let's see, let's try it out. Something extraordinary might come out of this.

FATHER   Of course it will! Don't you think it'd be better if the others came too? [Indicating the other CHARACTERS.]

PRODUCER   Yes, come on, come on. [Going, then turning to speak to the ACTORS.] Don't forget: don't be late: back in a quarter of an hour.

[The PRODUCER and the SIX CHARACTERS cross the stage and go. The ACTORS look at each other in astonishment.]

LEADING ACTOR   Is he serious? What's he going to do?

YOUNG ACTOR   I think he's gone round the bend.

ANOTHER ACTOR   Does he expect to make up a play in five minutes?

YOUNG ACTOR   Yes, like the old actors in the commedia dell'arte![1]

LEADING ACTRESS   Well if he thinks I'm going to appear in that sort of nonsense . . .

YOUNG ACTOR   Nor me!

FOURTH ACTOR   I should like to know who they are.

THIRD ACTOR   Who do you think? They're probably escaped lunatics—or crooks.

YOUNG ACTOR   And is he taking them seriously?

YOUNG ACTRESS   It's vanity. The vanity of seeing himself as an author.

1. A form of popular theater beginning in 16th-century Italy; the actors improvised dialogue according to basic comic or dramatic plots and in response to the audience's reaction.

LEADING ACTOR   I've never heard of such a thing! If the theatre, ladies and gentlemen, is reduced to this . . .

FIFTH ACTOR   I'm enjoying it!

THIRD ACTOR   Really! We shall have to wait and see what happens next I suppose.

> [*Talking, they leave the stage. Some go out through the back door, some to the dressing-rooms.*
> *The curtain stays up.*
> *The interval lasts twenty minutes.*]

Act 2

The theatre warning-bell sounds to call the audience back. From the dressing-rooms, the door at the back and even from the auditorium, the ACTORS, *the* STAGE MANAGER, *the* STAGE HANDS, *the* PROMPTER, *the* PROPERTY MAN *and the* PRODUCER, *accompanied by the* SIX CHARACTERS *all come back on to the stage.*

The house lights go out and the stage lights come on again.

PRODUCER   Come on, everybody! Are we all here? Quiet now! Listen! Let's get started! Stage manager?

STAGE MANAGER   Yes, I'm here.

PRODUCER   Give me that little parlour setting, will you? A couple of plain flats and a door flat will do. Hurry up with it!

> [*The* STAGE MANAGER *runs off to order someone to do this immediately and at the same time the* PRODUCER *is making arrangements with the* PROPERTY MAN, *the* PROMPTER, *and the* ACTORS: *the two flats and the door flat are painted in pink and gold stripes.*]

PRODUCER [*To* PROPERTY MAN.]   Go see if we have a sofa in stock.

PROPERTY MAN   Yes, there's that green one.

STEPDAUGHTER   No, no, not a green one! It was yellow, yellow velvet with flowers on it: it was enormous! And so comfortable!

PROPERTY MAN   We haven't got one like that.

PRODUCER   It doesn't matter! Give me whatever there is.

STEPDAUGHTER   What do you mean, it doesn't matter? It was Mme. Pace's famous sofa.

PRODUCER   It's only for a rehearsal! Please, don't interfere. [*To the* STAGE MANAGER.] Oh, and see if there's a shop window, will you—preferably a long, low one.

STEPDAUGHTER   And a little table, a little mahogany table for the blue envelope.

STAGE MANAGER [*To the* PRODUCER.]   There's that little gold one.

PRODUCER   That'll do—bring it.

FATHER   A mirror!

STEPDAUGHTER   And a screen! A screen, please, or I won't be able to manage, will I?

STAGE MANAGER   All right. We've lots of big screens, don't you worry.

PRODUCER [*To* STEPDAUGHTER.]   Then don't you want some coat-hangers and some clothes racks?

STEPDAUGHTER   Yes, lots of them, lots of them.

PRODUCER [*To the* STAGE MANAGER.]   See how many there are and have them brought up.

STAGE MANAGER   Right, I'll see to it.

[*The* STAGE MANAGER *goes off to do it: and while the* PRODUCER *is talking to the* PROMPTER, *the* CHARACTERS *and the* ACTORS, *the* STAGE MANAGER *is telling the* SCENE SHIFTERS *where to set up the furniture they have brought.*]

PRODUCER [*To the* PROMPTER.]   Now you, go sit down, will you? Look, this is an outline of the play, act by act. [*He hands him several sheets of paper.*] But you'll need to be on your toes.

PROMPTER   Shorthand?

PRODUCER [*Pleasantly surprised.*]   Oh, good! You know shorthand?

PROMPTER   I don't know much about prompting, but I do know about shorthand.

PRODUCER   Thank God for that anyway! [*He turns to a* STAGE HAND.] Go fetch me some paper from my office—lots of it—as much as you can find!

[*The* STAGE HAND *goes running off and then comes back shortly with a bundle of paper that he gives to the* PROMPTER.]

PRODUCER [*Crossing to the* PROMPTER.]   Follow the scenes, one after another, as they are played and try to get the lines down . . . at least the most important ones. [*Then turning to the* ACTORS.] Get out of the way everybody! Here, go over to the prompt side [*Pointing to stage left.*] and pay attention.

LEADING ACTRESS   But, excuse me, we . . .

PRODUCER [*Anticipating her.*]   You won't be expected to improvise, don't worry!

LEADING ACTOR   Then what are we expected to do?

PRODUCER   Nothing! Just go over there, listen and watch. You'll all be given your parts later written out. Right now we're going to rehearse, as well as we can. And they will be doing the rehearsal. [*He points to the* CHARACTERS.]

FATHER [*Rather bewildered, as if he had fallen from the clouds into the middle of the confusion on the stage.*]   We are? Excuse me, but what do you mean, a rehearsal?

PRODUCER   I mean a rehearsal—a rehearsal for the benefit of the actors. [*Pointing to the* ACTORS.]

FATHER   But if we are the characters . . .

PRODUCER   That's right, you're "the characters": but characters don't act here, my dear chap. It's actors who act here. The characters are there in the script—[*Pointing to the* PROMPTER.] that's when there is a script.

FATHER   That's the point! Since there isn't one and you have the luck to have the characters alive in front of you . . .

PRODUCER   Great! You want to do everything yourselves, do you? To act your own play, to produce your own play!

FATHER   Well yes, just as we are.

PRODUCER   That would be an experience for us, I can tell you!

LEADING ACTOR   And what about us? What would we be doing then?

PRODUCER   Don't tell me you think you know how to act! Don't make me laugh! [*The* ACTORS *in fact laugh.*] There you are, you see, you've made them laugh. [*Then remembering.*] But let's get back to the point! We need to cast the play. Well, that's easy: it almost casts itself. [*To the* SECOND ACTRESS.] You, the mother. [*To the* FATHER.] You'll need to give her a name.

FATHER Amalia.

PRODUCER But that's the real name of your wife isn't it? We can't use her real name.

FATHER But why not? That is her name . . . But perhaps if this lady is to play the part . . . [*Indicating the* ACTRESS *vaguely with a wave of his hand.*] I don't know what to say . . . I'm already starting to . . . how can I explain it . . . to sound false, my own words sound like someone else's.

PRODUCER Now don't worry yourself about it, don't worry about it at all. We'll work out the right tone of voice. As for the name, if you want it to be Amalia, then Amalia it shall be: or we can find another. For the moment we'll refer to the characters like this: [*To the* YOUNG ACTOR, *the juvenile lead.*] you are The Son. [*To the* LEADING ACTRESS.] You, of course, are The Stepdaughter.

STEPDAUGHTER [*Excitedly.*] What did you say? That woman is me? [*Bursts into laughter.*]

PRODUCER [*Angrily.*] What are you laughing at?

LEADING ACTRESS [*Indignantly.*] Nobody has ever dared to laugh at me before! Either you treat me with respect or I'm walking out! [*Starting to go.*]

STEPDAUGHTER I'm sorry. I wasn't really laughing at you.

PRODUCER [*To the* STEPDAUGHTER.] You should feel proud to be played by . . .

LEADING ACTRESS [*Quickly, scornfully.*] . . . that woman!

STEPDAUGHTER But I wasn't thinking about her, honestly. I was thinking about me: I can't see myself in you at all . . . you're not a bit like me!

FATHER Yes, that's right: you see, our meaning . . .

PRODUCER What are you talking about, "our meaning"? Do you think you have exclusive rights to what you represent? Do you think it can only exist inside you? Not a bit of it!

FATHER What? Don't we even have our own meaning?

PRODUCER Not a bit of it! Whatever you mean is only material here, to which the actors give form and body, voice and gesture, and who, through their art, have given expression to much better material than what you have to offer: yours is really very trivial and if it stands up on the stage, the credit, believe me, will all be due to my actors.

FATHER I don't dare to contradict you. But you for your part, must believe me—it doesn't seem trivial to us. We are suffering terribly now, with these bodies, these faces . . .

PRODUCER [*Interrupting impatiently.*] Yes, well, the make-up will change that, make-up will change that, at least as far as the faces are concerned.

FATHER Yes, but the voices, the gestures . . .

PRODUCER That's enough! You can't come on the stage here as yourselves. It is our actors who will represent you here: and let that be the end of it!

FATHER I understand that. But now I think I see why our author who saw us alive as we are here now, didn't want to put us on the stage. I don't want to offend your actors. God forbid that I should! But I think that if I saw myself represented . . . by I don't know whom . . .

LEADING ACTOR [*Rising majestically and coming forward, followed by a laughing group of* YOUNG ACTRESSES.] By me, if you don't object.

FATHER [*Respectfully, smoothly.*] I shall be honoured, sir. [*He bows.*] But I think, that no matter how hard this gentleman works with all his will and all his art to identify himself with me . . . [*He stops, confused.*]

LEADING ACTOR   Yes, go on.

FATHER   Well, I was saying the performance he will give, even if he is made up to look like me . . . I mean with the difference in our appearance . . . [*All the* ACTORS *laugh.*] it will be difficult for it to be a performance of me as I really am. It will be more like—well, not just because of his figure—it will be more an interpretation of what I am, what he believes me to be, and not how I know myself to be. And it seems to me that this should be taken into account by those who are going to comment on us.

PRODUCER   So you are already worrying about what the critics will say, are you? And I'm still waiting to get this thing started! The critics can say what they like: and we'll worry about putting on the play. If we can! [*Stepping out of the group and looking around.*] Come on, come on! Is the scene set for us yet? [*To the* ACTORS *and* CHARACTERS.] Out of the way! Let's have a look at it. [*Climbing down off the stage.*] Don't let's waste any more time. [*To the* STEPDAUGHTER.] Does it look all right to you?

SON   What! That? I don't recognise it at all.

PRODUCER   Good God! Did you expect us to reconstruct the room at the back of Mme. Pace's shop here on the stage? [*To the* FATHER.] Did you say the room had flowered wallpaper?

FATHER   White, yes.

PRODUCER   Well it's not white: it's striped. That sort of thing doesn't matter at all! As for the furniture, it looks to me as if we have nearly everything we need. Move that little table a bit further downstage. [*A* STAGE HAND *does it. To the* PROPERTY MAN.] Go and fetch an envelope, pale blue if you can find one, and give it to that gentleman there. [*Pointing to the* FATHER.]

STAGE HAND   An envelope for letters?

PRODUCER⎫
FATHER   ⎬Yes, an envelope for letters!

STAGE HAND   Right. [*He goes off.*]

PRODUCER   Now then, come on! The first scene is the young lady's. [*The* LEADING ACTRESS *comes to the centre.*] No, no, not yet. I said the young lady's. [*He points to the* STEPDAUGHTER.] You stay there and watch.

STEPDAUGHTER [*Adding quickly.*]   . . . how I bring it to life.

LEADING ACTRESS [*Resenting this.*]   I shall know how to bring it to life, don't you worry, when I am allowed to.

PRODUCER [*His head in his hands.*]   Ladies, please, no more arguments! Now then. The first scene is between the young lady and Mme. Pace. Oh! [*Worried, turning round and looking out into the auditorium.*] Where is Mme. Pace?

FATHER   She isn't here with us.

PRODUCER   So what do we do now?

FATHER   But she is real. She's real too!

PRODUCER   All right. So where is she?

FATHER   May I deal with this? [*Turns to the* ACTRESSES.] Would each of you ladies be kind enough to lend me a hat, a coat, a scarf or something?

ACTRESSES [*Some are surprised or amused.*]   What? My scarf? A coat? What's he want my hat for? What are you wanting to do with them? [*All the* ACTRESSES *are laughing.*]

FATHER   Oh, nothing much, just hang them up here on the racks for a minute or two. Perhaps someone would be kind enough to lend me a coat?

ACTORS   Just a coat? Come on, more! The man must be mad.

AN ACTRESS   What for? Only my coat?

FATHER   Yes, to hang up here, just for a moment. I'm very grateful to you. Do you mind?

ACTRESSES [*Taking off various hats, coats, scarves, laughing and going to hang them on the racks.*]   Why not? Here you are. I really think it's crazy. Is it to dress the set?

FATHER   Yes, exactly. It's to dress the set.

PRODUCER   Would you mind telling me what you are doing?

FATHER   Yes, of course: perhaps, if we dress the set better, she will be drawn by the articles of her trade and, who knows, she may even come to join us . . . [*He invites them to watch the door at the back of the set.*] Look! Look!

> [*The door at the back opens and* MME. PACE *takes a few steps downstage: she is a gross old harridan wearing a ludicrous carroty-coloured wig with a single red rose stuck in at one side, Spanish fashion: garishly made-up: in a vulgar but stylish red silk dress, holding an ostrich-feather fan in one hand and a cigarette between two fingers in the other. At the sight of this apparition, the* ACTORS *and the* PRODUCER *immediately jump off the stage with cries of fear, leaping down into the auditorium and up the aisles. The* STEPDAUGHTER, *however, runs across to* MME. PACE, *and greets her respectfully, as if she were the mistress.*]

STEPDAUGHTER [*Running across to her.*]   Here she is! Here she is!

FATHER [*Smiling broadly.*]   It's her! What did I tell you? Here she is!

PRODUCER [*Recovering from his shock, indignantly.*]   What sort of trick is this?

LEADING ACTOR [*Almost at the same time as the others.*]   What the hell is happening?

JUVENILE LEAD   Where on earth did they get that extra from?

YOUNG ACTRESS   They were keeping her hidden!

LEADING ACTRESS   It's a game, a conjuring trick!

FATHER   Wait a minute! Why do you want to spoil a miracle by being factual? Can't you see this is a miracle of reality, that is born, brought to life, lured here, reproduced, just for the sake of this scene, with more right to be alive here than you have? Perhaps it has more truth than you have yourselves. Which actress can improve on Mme. Pace there? Well? That is the real Mme. Pace. You must admit that the actress who plays her will be less true than she is herself—and there she is in person! Look! My daughter recognised her straight away and went to meet her. Now watch—just watch this scene.

> [*Hesitantly, the* PRODUCER *and the* ACTORS *move back to their original places on the stage.*
>
> *But the scene between the* STEPDAUGHTER *and* MME. PACE *had already begun while the* ACTORS *were protesting and the* FATHER *explaining: it is being played under their breaths, very quietly, very naturally, in a way that is obviously impossible on stage. So when the* ACTORS' *attention is recalled by the* FATHER *they turn and see that* MME. PACE *has just put her hand under the* STEPDAUGHTER's *chin to make her lift her head up: they also hear her speak in a way that is unintelligible to them. They watch and listen hard for a few moments, then they start to make fun of them.*]

PRODUCER   Well?

LEADING ACTOR   What's she saying?

LEADING ACTRESS Can't hear a thing!

JUVENILE LEAD Louder! Speak up!

STEPDAUGHTER [*Leaving* MME. PACE *who has an astonishing smile on her face, and coming down to the* ACTORS.] Louder? What do you mean, "Louder"? What we're talking about you can't talk about loudly. I could shout about it a moment ago to embarrass him [*Pointing to the* FATHER.] to shame him and to get my own back on him! But it's a different matter for Mme. Pace. It would mean prison for her.

PRODUCER What the hell are you on about? Here in the theatre you have to make yourself heard! Don't you see that? We can't hear you even from here, and we're on the stage with you! Imagine what it would be like with an audience out front! You need to make the scene go! And after all, you would speak normally to each other when you're alone, and you will be, because we shan't be here anyway. I mean we're only here because it's a rehearsal. So just imagine that there you are in the room at the back of the shop, and there's no one to hear you.

[*The* STEPDAUGHTER, *with a knowing smile, wags her finger and her head rather elegantly, as if to say no.*]

PRODUCER Why not?

STEPDAUGHTER [*Mysteriously, whispering loudly.*] Because there is someone who will hear if she speaks normally. [*Pointing to* MME. PACE.]

PRODUCER [*Anxiously.*] You're not going to make someone else appear are you?

[*The* ACTORS *get ready to dive off the stage again.*]

FATHER No, no. She means me. I ought to be over there, waiting behind the door: and Mme. Pace knows I'm there, so excuse me will you: I'll go there now so that I shall be ready for my entrance.

[*He goes towards the back of the stage.*]

PRODUCER [*Stopping him.*] No, no wait a minute! You must remember the stage conventions! Before you can go on to that part . . .

STEPDAUGHTER [*Interrupts him.*] Oh yes, let's get on with that part. Now! Now! I'm dying to do that scene. If he wants to go through it now, I'm ready!

PRODUCER [*Shouting.*] But before that we must have, clearly stated, the scene between you and her. [*Pointing to* MME. PACE.] Do you see?

STEPDAUGHTER Oh God! She's only told me what you already know, that my mother's needlework is badly done again, the dress is spoilt and that I shall have to be patient if I want her to go on helping us out of our mess.

MME. PACE [*Coming forward, with a great air of importance.*] Ah, yes, sir, for that I do not wish to make a profit, to make advantage.

PRODUCER [*Half frightened.*] What? Does she really speak like that? [*All the* ACTORS *burst out laughing.*]

STEPDAUGHTER [*Laughing too.*] Yes, she speaks like that, half in Spanish, in the silliest way imaginable!

MME. PACE Ah it is not good manners that you laugh at me when I make myself to speak, as I can, English, señor.

PRODUCER No, no, you're right! Speak like that, please speak like that, madam. It'll be marvelous. Couldn't be better! It'll add a little touch of comedy to a rather crude situation. Speak like that! It'll be great!

STEPDAUGHTER Great! Why not? When you hear a proposition made in that sort of accent, it'll almost seem like a joke, won't it? Perhaps you'll want to laugh when you hear that there's an "old señor"[2] who wants to "amuse himself with me"—isn't that right, Madame?

MME. PACE   Not so old . . . but not quite young, no? But if he is not to your taste . . . he is, how you say, discreet!

[*The* MOTHER *leaps up, to the astonishment and dismay of the* ACTORS *who had not been paying any attention to her, so that when she shouts out they are startled and then smilingly restrain her: however she has already snatched off* MME. PACE's *wig and flung it on the floor.*]

MOTHER   You witch! Witch! Murderess! Oh, my daughter!

STEPDAUGHTER [*Running across and taking hold of the* MOTHER.]   No! No! Mother! Please!

FATHER [*Running across to her as well.*]   Calm yourself, calm yourself! Come and sit down.

MOTHER   Get her away from here!

STEPDAUGHTER [*To the* PRODUCER *who has also crossed to her.*]   My mother can't bear to be in the same place with her.

FATHER [*Also speaking quietly to the* PRODUCER.]   They can't possibly be in the same place! That's why she wasn't with us when we first came, do you see! If they meet, everything's given away from the very beginning.

PRODUCER   It's not important, that's not important! This is only a first run-through at the moment! It's all useful stuff, even if it is confused. I'll sort it all out later. [*Turning to the* MOTHER *and taking her to sit down on her chair.*] Come on, my dear, take it easy; take it easy: come and sit down again.

STEPDAUGHTER   Go on, Mme. Pace.

MME. PACE [*Offended.*]   Oh no, thank-you! I no longer do nothing here with your mother present.

STEPDAUGHTER   Get on with it, bring in this "old señor" who wants to "amuse himself with me"! [*Turning majestically to the others.*] You see, this next scene has got to be played out—we must do it now. [*To* MME. PACE.] Oh, you can go!

MME. PACE   Ah, I go, I go—I go! Most probably! I go!

[*She leaves banging her wig back into place, glaring furiously at the* ACTORS *who applaud her exit, laughing loudly.*]

STEPDAUGHTER [*To the* FATHER.]   Now you come on! No, you don't need to go off again! Come back! Pretend you've just come in! Look, I'm standing here with my eyes on the ground, modestly—well, come on, speak up! Use that special sort of voice, like somebody who has just come in. "Good afternoon, my dear."

PRODUCER [*Off the stage by now.*]   Look here, who's the director here, you or me? [*To the* FATHER *who looks uncertain and bewildered.*] Go on, do as she says: go upstage—no, no don't bother to make an entrance. Then come down stage again.

[*The* FATHER *does as he is told, half mesmerised. He is very pale but already involved in the reality of his re-created life, smiles as he draws near the back of the stage, almost as if he genuinely is not aware of the drama that is about to sweep over him. The* ACTORS *are immediately intent on the scene that is beginning now.*]

2. Old gentleman.

The Scene

FATHER [*Coming forward with a new note in his voice.*] Good afternoon, my dear.

STEPDAUGHTER [*Her head down trying to hide her fright.*] Good afternoon.

FATHER [*Studying her a little under the brim of her hat which partly hides her face from him and seeing that she is very young, he exclaims to himself a little complacently and a little guardedly because of the danger of being compromised in a risky adventure.*] Ah . . . but . . . tell me, this won't be the first time, will it? The first time you've been here?

STEPDAUGHTER No, sir.

FATHER You've been here before? [*And after the* STEPDAUGHTER *has nodded an answer.*] More than once? [*He waits for her reply: tries again to look at her under the brim of her hat: smiles: then says.*] Well then . . . it shouldn't be too . . . May I take off your hat?

STEPDAUGHTER [*Quickly, to stop him, unable to conceal her shudder of fear and disgust.*] No, don't! I'll do it!

[*She takes it off unsteadily.*

The MOTHER *watches the scene intently with the* SON *and the two smaller children who cling close to her all the time: they make a group on one side of the stage opposite the* ACTORS: *She follows the words and actions of the* FATHER *and the* STEPDAUGHTER *in this scene with a variety of expressions on her face—sadness, dismay, anxiety, horror: sometimes she turns her face away and sobs.*]

MOTHER Oh God! Oh God!

FATHER [*He stops as if turned to stone by the sobbing: then he goes on in the same tone of voice.*] Here, give it to me. I'll hang it up for you. [*He takes the hat in his hand.*] But such a pretty, dear little head like yours should have a much smarter hat than this! Would you like to help me choose one, then, from these hats of Madame's hanging up here? Would you?

YOUNG ACTRESS [*Interrupting.*] Be careful! Those are our hats!

PRODUCER [*Quickly and angrily.*] For God's sake, shut up! Don't try to be funny! We're rehearsing! [*Turns back to the* STEPDAUGHTER.] Please go on, will you, from where you were interrupted.

STEPDAUGHTER [*Going on.*] No, thank you, sir.

FATHER Oh, don't say no to me please! Say you'll have one—to please me. Isn't this a pretty one—look! And then it will please Madame too, you know. She's put them out here on purpose, of course.

STEPDAUGHTER No, look, I could never wear it.

FATHER Are you thinking of what they would say at home when you went in wearing a new hat? Goodness me! Don't you know what to do? Shall I tell you what to say at home?

STEPDAUGHTER [*Furiously, nearly exploding.*] That's not why! I couldn't wear it because . . . as you can see: you should have noticed it before. [*Indicating her black dress.*]

FATHER You're in mourning! Oh, forgive me. You're right, I see that now. Please forgive me. Believe me, I'm really very sorry.

STEPDAUGHTER [*Gathering all her strength and making herself overcome her contempt and revulsion.*] That's enough. Don't go on, that's enough. I ought to be thanking you and not letting you blame yourself and get upset. Don't think any more about what I told you, please. And I should do the same. [*Forcing herself to smile and adding.*] I should try to forget that I'm dressed like this.

PRODUCER [*Interrupting, turning to the* PROMPTER *in the box and jumping up on the stage again.*] Hold it, hold it! Don't put that last line down, leave it out. [*Turning to the* FATHER *and the* STEPDAUGHTER.] It's going well! It's going well! [*Then to the* FATHER *alone.*] Then we'll put in there the bit that we talked about. [*To the* ACTORS.] That scene with the hats is good, isn't it?

STEPDAUGHTER But the best bit is coming now! Why can't we get on with it?

PRODUCER Just be patient, wait a minute. [*Turning and moving across to the* ACTORS.] Of course, it'll all have to be made a lot more light-hearted.

LEADING ACTOR We shall have to play it a lot quicker, I think.

LEADING ACTRESS Of course: there's nothing particularly difficult in it. [*To the* LEADING ACTOR.] Shall we run through it now?

LEADING ACTOR Yes right . . . Shall we take it from my entrance? [*He goes to his position behind the door upstage.*]

PRODUCER [*To the* LEADING ACTRESS.] Now then, listen, imagine the scene between you and Mme. Pace is finished. I'll write it up myself properly later on. You ought to be over here I think—[*She goes the opposite way.*] Where are you going now?

LEADING ACTRESS Just a minute, I want to get my hat—[*She crosses to take her hat from the stand.*]

PRODUCER Right, good, ready now? You are standing here with your head down.

STEPDAUGHTER [*Very amused.*] But she's not dressed in black!

LEADING ACTRESS Oh, but I shall be, and I'll look a lot better than you do, darling.

PRODUCER [*To the* STEPDAUGHTER.] Shut up, will you! Go over there and watch! You might learn something! [*Clapping his hands.*] Right! Come on! Quiet please! Take it from his entrance.

> [*He climbs off stage so that he can see better. The door opens at the back of the set and the* LEADING ACTOR *enters with the lively, knowing air of an age- ing roué.[3] The playing of the following scene by the* ACTORS *must seem from the very beginning to be something quite different from the earlier scene, but without having the faintest air of parody in it.*
>
> *Naturally the* STEPDAUGHTER *and the* FATHER *unable to see themselves in the* LEADING ACTOR *and* LEADING ACTRESS, *hearing their words said by them, express their reactions in different ways, by gestures, or smiles or obvious protests so that we are aware of their suffering, their astonishment, their disbelief.*
>
> *The* PROMPTER's *voice is heard clearly between every line in the scene, telling the* ACTORS *what to say next.*]

LEADING ACTOR Good afternoon, my dear.

FATHER [*Immediately, unable to restrain himself.*] Oh, no!

> [*The* STEPDAUGHTER, *watching the* LEADING ACTOR *enter this way, bursts into laughter.*]

3. Dissipated lover.

PRODUCER [*Furious.*]   Shut up, for God's sake! And don't you dare laugh like that! We're never going to get anywhere at this rate.

STEPDAUGHTER [*Coming to the front.*]   I'm sorry, I can't help it! The lady stands exactly where you told her to stand and she never moved. But if it were me and I heard someone say good afternoon to me in that way and with a voice like that I should burst out laughing—so I did.

FATHER [*Coming down a little too.*]   Yes, she's right, the whole manner, the voice . . .

PRODUCER   To hell with the manner and the voice! Get out of the way, will you, and let me watch the rehearsal!

LEADING ACTOR [*Coming down stage.*]   If I have to play an old man who has come to a knocking shop—

PRODUCER   Take no notice, ignore them. Go on please! It's going well, it's going well! [*He waits for the* ACTOR *to begin again.*] Right, again!

LEADING ACTOR   Good afternoon, my dear.

LEADING ACTRESS   Good afternoon.

LEADING ACTOR [*Copying the gestures of the* FATHER, *looking under the brim of the hat, but expressing distinctly the two emotions, first, complacent satisfaction and then anxiety.*]   Ah! But tell me . . . this won't be the first time I hope.

FATHER [*Instinctively correcting him.*]   Not "I hope"—"will it," "will it."

PRODUCER   Say "will it"—and it's a question.

LEADING ACTOR [*Glaring at the* PROMPTER.]   I distinctly heard him say "I hope."

PRODUCER   So what? It's all the same, "I hope" or "isn't it." It doesn't make any difference. Carry on, carry on. But perhaps it should still be a little bit lighter; I'll show you—watch me! [*He climbs up on the stage again, and going back to the entrance, he does it himself.*] Good afternoon, my dear.

LEADING ACTRESS   Good afternoon.

PRODUCER   Ah, tell me . . . [*He turns to the* LEADING ACTOR *to make sure that he has seen the way he has demonstrated of looking under the brim of the hat.*]   You see—surprise . . . anxiety and self-satisfaction. [*Then, starting again, he turns to the* LEADING ACTRESS.] This won't be the first time, will it? The first time you've been here? [*Again turns to the* LEADING ACTOR *questioningly.*] Right? [*To the* LEADING ACTRESS.] And then she says, "No, sir." [*Again to* LEADING ACTOR.] See what I mean? More subtlety. [*And he climbs off the stage.*]

LEADING ACTRESS   No, sir.

LEADING ACTOR   You've been here before? More than once?

PRODUCER   No, no, no! Wait for it, wait for it. Let her answer first. "You've been here before?"

[*The* LEADING ACTRESS *lifts her head a little, her eyes closed in pain and disgust, and when the* PRODUCER *says "Now" she nods her head twice.*]

STEPDAUGHTER [*Involuntarily.*]   Oh, my God! [*And she immediately claps her hand over her mouth to stifle her laughter.*]

PRODUCER   What now?

STEPDAUGHTER [*Quickly.*]   Nothing, nothing!

PRODUCER [*To* LEADING ACTOR.]   Come on, then, now it's you.

LEADING ACTOR   More than once? Well then, it shouldn't be too . . . May I take off your hat?

> [*The* LEADING ACTOR *says this last line in such a way and adds to it such a gesture that the* STEPDAUGHTER, *even with her hand over her mouth trying to stop herself laughing, can't prevent a noisy burst of laughter.*]

LEADING ACTRESS [*Indignantly turning.*]   I'm not staying any longer to be laughed at by that woman!

LEADING ACTOR   Nor am I! That's the end—no more!

PRODUCER [*To* STEPDAUGHTER, *shouting.*]   Once and for all, will you shut up! Shut up!

STEPDAUGHTER   Yes, I'm sorry . . . I'm sorry.

PRODUCER   You're an ill-mannered little bitch! That's what you are! And you've gone too far this time!

FATHER [*Trying to interrupt.*]   Yes, you're right, she went too far, but please forgive her . . .

PRODUCER [*Jumping on the stage.*]   Why should I forgive her? Her behaviour is intolerable!

FATHER   Yes, it is, but the scene made such a peculiar impact on us . . .

PRODUCER   Peculiar? What do you mean peculiar? Why peculiar?

FATHER   I'm full of admiration for your actors, for this gentleman [*To the* LEADING ACTOR.] and this lady. [*To the* LEADING ACTRESS.] But, you see, well . . . they're not us!

PRODUCER   Right! They're not! They're actors!

FATHER   That's just the point—they're actors. And they are acting our parts very well, both of them. But that's what's different. However much they want to be the same as us, they're not.

PRODUCER   But why aren't they? What is it now?

FATHER   It's something to do with . . . being themselves, I suppose, not being us.

PRODUCER   Well we can't do anything about that! I've told you already. You can't play the parts yourselves.

FATHER   Yes, I know, I know . . .

PRODUCER   Right then. That's enough of that. [*Turning back to the* ACTORS.] We'll rehearse this later on our own, as we usually do. It's always a bad idea to have rehearsals with authors there! They're never satisfied. [*Turns back to the* FATHER *and the* STEPDAUGHTER.] Come on, let's get on with it; and let's see if it's possible to do it without laughing.

STEPDAUGHTER   I won't laugh any more, I won't really. My best bit's coming up now, you wait and see!

PRODUCER   Right: when you say "Don't think any more about what I told you, please. And I should do the same." [*Turning to the* FATHER.] Then you come in immediately with the line "I understand, ah yes, I understand" and then you ask . . .

STEPDAUGHTER [*Interrupting.*]   Ask what? What does he ask?

PRODUCER   Why you're in mourning.

STEPDAUGHTER   No! No! That's not right! Look: when I said that I should try not to think about the way I was dressed, do you know what he said? "Well then, let's take it off, we'll take it off at once, shall we, your little black dress."

PRODUCER   That's great! That'll be wonderful! That'll bring the house down!

STEPDAUGHTER   But it's the truth!

PRODUCER   The truth! Do me a favour will you? This is the theatre you know! Truth's all very well up to a point but . . .

STEPDAUGHTER   What do you want to do then?

PRODUCER   You'll see! You'll see! Leave it all to me.

STEPDAUGHTER   No. No I won't. I know what you want to do! Out of my feeling of revulsion, out of all the vile and sordid reasons why I am what I am, you want to make a sugary little sentimental romance. You want him to ask me why I'm in mourning and you want me to reply with the tears running down my face that it is only two months since my father died. No. No. I won't have it! He must say to me what he really did say. "Well then, let's take it off, we'll take it off at once, shall we, your little black dress." And I, with my heart still grieving for my father's death only two months before, I went behind there, do you see? Behind that screen and with my fingers trembling with shame and loathing I took off the dress, unfastened my bra . . .

PRODUCER   [His head in his hands.]   For God's sake! What are you saying!

STEPDAUGHTER   [Shouting excitedly.]   The truth! I'm telling you the truth!

PRODUCER   All right then. Now listen to me. I'm not denying it's the truth. Right. And believe me I understand your horror, but you must see that we can't really put a scene like that on the stage.

STEPDAUGHTER   You can't? Then thanks very much. I'm not stopping here.

PRODUCER   No, listen . . .

STEPDAUGHTER   No, I'm going. I'm not stopping. The pair of you have worked it all out together, haven't you, what to put in the scene. Well, thank you very much! I understand everything now! He wants to get to the scene where he can talk about his spiritual torments but I want to show you my drama! Mine!

PRODUCER   [Shaking with anger.]   Now we're getting to the real truth of it, aren't we? Your drama—yours! But it's not only yours, you know. It's drama for the other people as well! For him [Pointing to the FATHER.] and for your mother! You can't have one character coming on like you're doing, trampling over the others, taking over the play. Everything needs to be balanced and in harmony so that we can show what has to be shown! I know perfectly well that we've all got a life inside us and that we all want to parade it in front of other people. But that's the difficulty, how to present only the bits that are necessary in relation to the other characters: and in the small amount we show, to hint at all the rest of the inner life of the character! I agree, it would be so much simpler, if each character, in a soliloquy or in a lecture could pour out to the audience what's bubbling away inside him. But that's not the way we work. [In an indulgent, placating tone.] You must restrain yourself, you see. And believe me, it's in your own interests: because you could so easily make a bad impression, with all this uncontrollable anger, this disgust and exasperation. That seems a bit odd, if you don't mind my saying so, when you've admitted that you'd been with other men at Mme. Pace's and more than once.

STEPDAUGHTER   I suppose that's true. But you know, all the other men were all him as far as I was concerned.

PRODUCER [*Not understanding.*]   Uum—? What? What are you talking about?

STEPDAUGHTER   If someone falls into evil ways, isn't the responsibility for all the evil which follows to be laid at the door of the person who caused the first mistake? And in my case, it's him, from before I was even born. Look at him: see if it isn't true.

PRODUCER   Right then! What about the weight of remorse he's carrying? Isn't that important? Then, give him the chance to show it to us.

STEPDAUGHTER   But how? How on earth can he show all his long-suffering remorse, all his moral torments as he calls them, if you don't let him show his horror when he finds me in his arms one fine day, after he had asked me to take my dress off, a black dress for my father who had just died: and he finds that I'm the child he used to go and watch as she came out of school, me, a woman now, and a woman he could buy. [*She says these last words in a voice trembling with emotion.*]

   [*The* MOTHER, *hearing her say this, is overcome and at first gives way to stifled sobs: but then she bursts out into uncontrollable crying. Everyone is deeply moved. There is a long pause.*]

STEPDAUGHTER [*As soon as the* MOTHER *has quietened herself she goes on, firmly and thoughtfully.*]   At the moment we are here on our own and the public doesn't know about us. But tomorrow you will present us and our story in whatever way you choose, I suppose. But wouldn't you like to see the real drama? Wouldn't you like to see it explode into life, as it really did?

PRODUCER   Of course, nothing I'd like better, then I can use as much of it as possible.

STEPDAUGHTER   Then persuade my mother to leave.

MOTHER [*Rising and her quiet weeping changing to a loud cry.*]   No! No! Don't let her! Don't let her do it!

PRODUCER   But they're only doing it for me to watch—only for me, do you see?

MOTHER   I can't bear it, I can't bear it!

PRODUCER   But if it's already happened, I can't see what's the objection.

MOTHER   No! It's happening now, as well: it's happening all the time. I'm not acting my suffering! Can't you understand that? I'm alive and here now but I can never forget that terrible moment of agony, that repeats itself endlessly and vividly in my mind. And these two little children here, you've never heard them speak have you? That's because they don't speak any more, not now. They just cling to me all the time: they help to keep my grief alive, but they don't really exist for themselves any more, not for themselves. And she [*Indicating the* STEPDAUGHTER.] . . . she has gone away, left me completely, she's lost to me, lost . . . you see her here for one reason only: to keep perpetually before me, always real, the anguish and the torment I've suffered on her account.

FATHER   The eternal moment, as I told you, sir. She is here [*Indicating the* STEPDAUGHTER.] to keep me too in that moment, trapped for all eternity, chained and suspended in that one fleeting shameful moment of my life. She can't give up her role and you cannot rescue me from it.

PRODUCER   But I'm not saying that we won't present that bit. Not at all! It will be the climax of the first act, when she [*He points to the* MOTHER.] surprises you.

FATHER   That's right, because that is the moment when I am sentenced: all our suffering should reach a climax in her cry. [*Again indicating the* MOTHER.]

STEPDAUGHTER   I can still hear it ringing in my ears! It was that cry that sent me mad! You can have me played just as you like: it doesn't matter! Dressed, too, if you want, so long as I can have at least an arm—only an arm—bare, because, you see, as I was standing like this [*She moves across to the* FATHER *and leans her head on his chest.*] with my head like this and my arms round his neck, I saw a vein, here in my arm, throbbing: and then it was almost as if that throbbing vein filled me with a shivering fear, and I shut my eyes tightly like this, like this and buried my head in his chest. [*Turning to the* MOTHER.] Scream, Mummy, scream. [*She buries her head in the* FATHER's *chest, and with her shoulders raised as if to try not to hear the scream, she speaks with a voice tense with suffering.*] Scream, as you screamed then!

MOTHER   [*Coming forward to pull them apart.*]   No! She's my daughter! My daughter! [*Tearing her from him.*] You brute, you animal, she's my daughter! Can't you see she's my daughter?

PRODUCER   [*Retreating as far as the footlights while the* ACTORS *are full of dismay.*]   Marvellous! Yes, that's great! And then curtain, curtain!

FATHER   [*Running downstage to him, excitedly.*]   That's it, that's it! Because it really was like that!

PRODUCER   [*Full of admiration and enthusiasm.*]   Yes, yes, that's got to be the curtain line! Curtain! Curtain!

[*At the repeated calls of the* PRODUCER, *the* STAGE MANAGER *lowers the curtain, leaving on the apron in front, the* PRODUCER *and the* FATHER.]

PRODUCER   [*Looking up to heaven with his arms raised.*]   The idiots! I didn't mean now! The bloody idiots—dropping it in on us like that! [*To the* FATHER, *and lifting up a corner of the curtain.*] That's marvellous! Really marvellous! A terrific effect! We'll end the act like that! It's the best tag line I've heard for ages. What a First Act ending! I couldn't have done better if I'd written it myself!

[*They go through the curtain together.*]

Act 3

When the curtain goes up we see that the STAGE MANAGER *and* STAGE HANDS *have struck the first scene and have set another, a small garden fountain.*

From one side of the stage the ACTORS *come on and from the other the* CHARACTERS. *The* PRODUCER *is standing in the middle of the stage with his hand over his mouth, thinking.*

PRODUCER [*After a short pause, shrugging his shoulders.*] Well, then: let's get on to the second act! Leave it all to me, and everything will work out properly.

STEPDAUGHTER This is where we go to live at his house [*Pointing to the* FATHER.] In spite of the objections of him over there. [*Pointing to the* SON.]

PRODUCER [*Getting impatient.*] All right, all right! But leave it all to me, will you?

STEPDAUGHTER Provided that you make it clear that he objected!

MOTHER [*From the corner, shaking her head.*] That doesn't matter. The worse it was for us, the more he suffered from remorse.

PRODUCER [*Impatiently.*] I know, I know! I'll take it all into account. Don't worry!

MOTHER [*Pleading.*] To set my mind at rest, sir, please do make sure it's clear that I tried all I could—

STEPDAUGHTER [*Interrupting her scornfully and going on.*] —to pacify me, to persuade me that this despicable creature wasn't worth making trouble about! [*To the* PRODUCER.] Go on, set her mind at rest, because it's true, she tried very hard. I'm having a whale of a time now! You can see, can't you, that the meeker she was and the more she tried to worm her way into his heart, the more lofty and distant he became! How's that for a dramatic situation!

PRODUCER Do you think that we can actually begin the Second Act?

STEPDAUGHTER I won't say another word! But you'll see that it won't be possible to play everything in the garden, like you want to do.

PRODUCER Why not?

STEPDAUGHTER [*Pointing to the* SON.] Because to start with, he stays shut up in his room in the house all the time! And then all the scenes for this poor little devil of a boy happen in the house. I've told you once.

PRODUCER Yes, I know that! But on the other hand we can't put up a notice to tell the audience where the scene is taking place, or change the set three or four times in each Act.

LEADING ACTOR That's what they used to do in the good old days.

PRODUCER Yes, when the audience was about as bright as that little girl over there!

LEADING ACTRESS And it makes it easier to create an illusion.

FATHER [*Leaping up.*] An illusion? For pity's sake don't talk about illusions! Don't use that word, it's especially hurtful to us!

PRODUCER [*Astonished.*] And why, for God's sake?

FATHER It's so hurtful, so cruel! You ought to have realised that!

PRODUCER What else should we call it? That's what we do here—create an illusion for the audience . . .

LEADING ACTOR With our performance . . .

PRODUCER A perfect illusion of reality!

FATHER Yes, I know that, I understand. But on the other hand, perhaps you don't understand us yet. I'm sorry! But you see, for you and for your actors what goes on here on the stage is, quite rightly, well, it's only a game.

LEADING ACTRESS [*Interrupting indignantly.*] A game! How dare you! We're not children! What happens here is serious!

FATHER   I'm not saying that it isn't serious. And I mean, really, not just a game but an art, that tries, as you've just said, to create the perfect illusion of reality.

PRODUCER   That's right!

FATHER   Now try to imagine that we, as you see us here, [*He indicates himself and the other* CHARACTERS.] that we have no other reality outside this illusion.

PRODUCER   [*Astonished and looking at the* ACTORS *with the same sense of bewilderment as they feel themselves.*]   What the hell are you talking about now?

FATHER   [*After a short pause as he looks at them, with a faint smile.*]   Isn't it obvious? What other reality is there for us? What for you is an illusion you create, for us is our only reality. [*Brief pause. He moves towards the* PRODUCER *and goes on.*] But it's not only true for us, it's true for others as well, you know. Just think about it. [*He looks intently into the* PRODUCER'S *eyes.*] Do you really know who you are? [*He stands pointing at the* PRODUCER.]

PRODUCER   [*A little disturbed but with a half smile.*]   What? Who I am? I am me!

FATHER   What if I told you that that wasn't true: what if I told you that you were me?

PRODUCER   I would tell you that you were mad!
        [*The* ACTORS *laugh.*]

FATHER   That's right, laugh! Because everything here is a game! [*To the* PRODUCER.] And yet you object when I say that it is only for a game that the gentleman there [*Pointing to the* LEADING ACTOR.] who is "himself" has to be "me," who, on the contrary, am "myself." You see, I've caught you in a trap.
        [*The* ACTORS *start to laugh.*]

PRODUCER   Not again! We've heard all about this a little while ago.

FATHER   No, no. I didn't really want to talk about this. I'd like you to forget about your game. [*Looking at the* LEADING ACTRESS *as if to anticipate what she will say.*] I'm sorry—your artistry! Your art!—that you usually pursue here with your actors; and I am going to ask you again in all seriousness, who are you?

PRODUCER   [*Turning with a mixture of amazement and annoyance, to the* ACTORS.]   Of all the bloody nerve! A fellow who claims he is only a character comes and asks me who I am!

FATHER   [*With dignity but without annoyance.*]   A character, my dear sir, can always ask a man who he is, because a character really has a life of his own, a life full of his own specific qualities, and because of these he is always "someone." While a man—I'm not speaking about you personally, of course, but man in general—well, he can be an absolute "nobody."

PRODUCER   All right, all right! Well, since you've asked me, I'm the Director, the Producer—I'm in charge! Do you understand?

FATHER   [*Half smiling, but gently and politely.*]   I'm only asking to try to find out if you really see yourself now in the same way that you saw yourself, for instance, once upon a time in the past, with all the illusions you had then, with everything inside and outside yourself as it seemed then—and not only seemed, but really was! Well then, look back on those illusions, those ideas that you don't have any more, on all those things that no longer seem the same to you. Don't you feel that not only this stage is falling away from under your feet but so is the earth itself, and that all these realities of today are going to seem tomorrow as if they had been an illusion?

PRODUCER So? What does that prove?

FATHER Oh, nothing much. I only want to make you see that if we [*Pointing to himself and the other* CHARACTERS.] have no other reality outside our own illusion, perhaps you ought to distrust your own sense of reality: because whatever is a reality today, whatever you touch and believe in and that seems real for you today, is going to be—like the reality of yesterday—an illusion tomorrow.

PRODUCER [*Deciding to make fun of him.*] Very good! So now you're saying that you as well as this play you're going to show me here, are more real than I am?

FATHER [*Very seriously.*] There's no doubt about that at all.

PRODUCER Is that so?

FATHER I thought you'd realised that from the beginning.

PRODUCER More real than I am?

FATHER If your reality can change between today and tomorrow—

PRODUCER But everybody knows that it can change, don't they? It's always changing! Just like everybody else's!

FATHER [*Crying out.*] But ours doesn't change! Do you see? That's the difference! Ours doesn't change, it can't change, it can never be different, never, because it is already determined, like this, for ever, that's what's so terrible! We are an eternal reality. That should make you shudder to come near us.

PRODUCER [*Jumping up, suddenly struck by an idea, and standing directly in front of the* FATHER.] Then I should like to know when anyone saw a character step out of his part and make a speech like you've done, proposing things, explaining things. Tell me when, will you? I've never seen it before.

FATHER You've never seen it because an author usually hides all the difficulties of creating. When the characters are alive, really alive and standing in front of their author, he has only to follow their words, the actions that they suggest to him: and he must want them to be what they want to be: and it's his bad luck if he doesn't do what they want! When a character is born he immediately assumes such an independence even of his own author that everyone can imagine him in scores of situations that his author hadn't even thought of putting him in, and he sometimes acquires a meaning that his author never dreamed of giving him.

PRODUCER Of course I know all that.

FATHER Well, then. Why are you surprised by us? Imagine what a disaster it is for a character to be born in the imagination of an author who then refuses to give him life in a written script. Tell me if a character, left like this, suspended, created but without a final life, isn't right to do what we are doing now, here in front of you. We spent such a long time, such a very long time, believe me, urging our author, persuading him, first me, then her, [*Pointing to the* STEPDAUGHTER.] then this poor Mother . . .

STEPDAUGHTER [*Coming down the stage as if in a dream.*] It's true, I would go, would go and tempt him, time after time, in his gloomy study just as it was growing dark, when he was sitting quietly in an armchair not even bothering to switch a light on but leaving the shadows to fill the room: the shadows were swarming with us, we had come to tempt him. [*As if she could see herself there in the study and is annoyed by the presence of the* ACTORS.] Go away will you! Leave us alone! Mother there, with that son of hers—me with the little girl—that poor little kid always on his own—and then me with him [*Pointing to the* FATHER.] and then at last, just me, on my own, all on my own, in the shadows. [*She turns quickly as if she wants to cling on to the vision she has of herself, in the shadows.*] Ah, what scenes, what scenes we suggested to him! What a life I could have had! I tempted him more than the others!

FATHER   Oh yes, you did! And it was probably all your fault that he did nothing about it! You were so insistent, you made too many demands.

STEPDAUGHTER   But he wanted me to be like that! [*She comes closer to the* PRODUCER *to speak to him in confidence.*] I think it's more likely that he felt discouraged about the theatre and even despised it because the public only wants to see . . .

PRODUCER   Let's go on, for God's sake, let's go on. Come to the point will you?

STEPDAUGHTER   I'm sorry, but if you ask me, we've got too much happening already, just with our entry into his house. [*Pointing to the* FATHER.] You said that we couldn't put up a notice or change the set every five minutes.

PRODUCER   Right! Of course we can't! We must combine things, group them together in one continuous flowing action: not the way you've been wanting, first of all seeing your little brother come home from school and wander about the house like a lost soul, hiding behind the doors and brooding on some plan or other that would—what did you say it would do?

STEPDAUGHTER   Wither him . . . shrivel him up completely.

PRODUCER   That's good! That's a good expression. And then you "can see it there in his eyes, getting stronger all the time"—isn't that what you said?

STEPDAUGHTER   Yes, that's right. Look at him! [*Pointing to him as he stands next to his* MOTHER.]

PRODUCER   Yes, great! And then, at the same time, you want to show the little girl playing in the garden, all innocence. One in the house and the other in the garden—we can't do it, don't you see that?

STEPDAUGHTER   Yes, playing in the sun, so happy! It's the only pleasure I have left, her happiness, her delight in playing in the garden: away from the misery, the squalor of that sordid flat where all four of us slept and where she slept with me—with me! Just think of it! My vile, contaminated body close to hers, with her little arms wrapped tightly round my neck, so lovingly, so innocently. In the garden, wherever she saw me, she would run and take my hand. She never wanted to show me the big flowers, she would run about looking for the "little weeny" ones, so that she could show them to me; she was so happy, so thrilled! [*As she says this, tortured by the memory, she breaks out into a long desperate cry, dropping her head on her arms that rest on a little table. Everybody is very affected by her. The* PRODUCER *comes to her almost paternally and speaks to her in a soothing voice.*]

PRODUCER   We'll have the garden scene, we'll have it, don't worry: and you'll see, you'll be very pleased with what we do! We'll play all the scenes in the garden! [*He calls out to a* STAGE HAND *by name.*] Hey . . . , let down a few bits of tree, will you? A couple of cypresses will do, in front of the fountain. [*Someone drops in the two cypresses and a* STAGE HAND *secures them with a couple of braces and weights.*]

PRODUCER   [*To the* STEPDAUGHTER.]   That'll do for now, won't it? It'll just give us an idea. [*Calling out to a* STAGE HAND *by name again.*] Hey, . . . give me something for the sky will you?

STAGE HAND   What's that?

PRODUCER   Something for the sky! A small cloth to come in behind the fountain. [*A white cloth is dropped from the flies.*] Not white! I asked for a sky! Never mind: leave it! I'll do something with it. [*Calling out.*] Hey lights! Kill everything will you? Give me a bit of moonlight—the blues in the batten and a blue spot on the cloth . . . [*They do.*] That's it! That'll do! [*Now on the scene there is the light he asked for, a mysterious blue light that makes the* ACTORS *speak and move as if in the garden in the evening under a moon. To the* STEP-DAUGHTER.] Look here now: the little boy can come out here in the garden and hide among the trees instead of hiding behind the doors in the house. But it's going to be difficult to find a little girl to play the scene with you where she shows you the flowers. [*Turning to the* LITTLE BOY.] Come on, come on, son, come across here. Let's see what it'll look like. [*But the* (LITTLE) BOY *doesn't move.*] Come on will you, come on. [*Then he pulls him forward and tries to make him hold his head up, but every time it falls down again on his chest.*] There's something very odd about this lad . . . What's wrong with him? My God, he'll have to say something sometime! [*He comes over to him again, puts his hand on his shoulder and pushes him between the trees.*] Come a bit nearer: let's have a look. Can you hide a bit more? That's it. Now pop your head out and look round. [*He moves away to look at the effect and as the* BOY *does what he has been told to do, the* ACTORS *watch impressed and a little disturbed.*] Ahh, that's good, very good . . . [*He turns to the* STEPDAUGHTER.] How about having the little girl, surprised to see him there, run across. Wouldn't that make him say something?

STEPDAUGHTER   [*Getting up.*]   It's no use hoping he'll speak, not as long as that creature's there. [*Pointing to the* SON.] You'll have to get him out of the way first.

SON   [*Moving determinedly to one of the sets of steps leading off the stage.*]   With pleasure! I'll go now! Nothing will please me better!

PRODUCER   [*Stopping him immediately.*]   Hey, no! Where are you going? Hang on!

[*The* MOTHER *gets up, anxious at the idea that he is really going and instinctively raising her arms as if to hold him back, but without moving from where she is.*]

SON   [*At the footlights, to the* PRODUCER *who is restraining him there.*]   There's no reason why I should be here! Let me go will you? Let me go!

PRODUCER   What do you mean there's no reason for you to be here?

STEPDAUGHTER   [*Calmly, ironically.*]   Don't bother to stop him. He won't go!

FATHER   You have to play that terrible scene in the garden with your mother.

SON [*Quickly, angry and determined.*]   I'm not going to play anything! I've said that all along! [*To the* PRODUCER.] Let me go will you?

STEPDAUGHTER [*Crossing to the* PRODUCER.]   It's all right. Let him go. [*She moves the* PRODUCER'*s hand from the* SON. *Then she turns to the* SON *and says.*] Well, go on then! Off you go!

> [*The* SON *stays near the steps but as if pulled by some strange force he is quite unable to go down them: then to the astonishment and even the dismay of the* ACTORS, *he moves along the front of the stage towards the other set of steps down into the auditorium: but having got there, he again stays near and doesn't actually go down them. The* STEPDAUGHTER *who has watched him scornfully but very intently, bursts into laughter.*]

STEPDAUGHTER   He can't, you see? He can't! He's got to stay here! He must. He's chained to us for ever! No, I'm the one who goes, when what must happen does happen, and I run away, because I hate him, because I can't bear the sight of him any longer. Do you think it's possible for him to run away? He has to stay here with that wonderful father of his and his mother there. She doesn't think she has any other son but him. [*She turns to the* MOTHER.] Come on, come on, Mummy, come on! [*Turning back to the* PRODUCER *to point her out to him.*] Look, she's going to try to stop him . . . [*To the* MOTHER, *half compelling her, as if by some magic power.*] Come on, come on. [*Then to the* PRODUCER *again.*] Imagine how she must feel at showing her affection for him in front of your actors! But her longing to be near him is so strong that—look! She's going to go through that scene with him again! [*The* MOTHER *has now actually come close to the* SON *as the* STEPDAUGHTER *says the last line: she gestures to show that she agrees to go on.*]

SON [*Quickly.*]   But I'm not! I'm not! If I can't get away then I suppose I shall have to stay here; but I repeat that I will not have any part in it.

FATHER [*To the* PRODUCER, *excitedly.*]   You must make him!

SON   Nobody's going to make me do anything!

FATHER   I'll make you!

STEPDAUGHTER   Wait! Just a minute! Before that, the little girl has to go to the fountain. [*She turns to take the* LITTLE GIRL, *drops on her knees in front of her and takes her face between her hands.*]   My poor little darling, those beautiful eyes, they look so bewildered. You're wondering where you are, aren't you? Well, we're on a stage, my darling! What's a stage? Well, it's a place where you pretend to be serious. They put on plays here. And now we're going to put on a play. Seriously! Oh, yes! Even you . . . [*She hugs her tightly and rocks her gently for a moment.*] Oh, my little one, my little darling, what a terrible play it is for you! What horrible things have been planned for you! The garden, the fountain . . . Oh, yes, it's only a pretend fountain, that's right. That's part of the game, my pretty darling: everything is pretends here. Perhaps you'll like a pretends fountain better than a real one: you can play here then. But it's only a game for the others; not for you, I'm afraid, it's real for you, my darling, and your game is in a real fountain, a big beautiful green fountain with bamboos casting shadows, looking at your own reflection, with lots of baby ducks paddling about, shattering the reflections. You want to stroke one! [*With a scream that electrifies and terrifies everybody.*] No, Rosetta, no! Your mummy isn't watching you, she's over there with that selfish bastard! Oh, God, I feel as if all the devils in hell were tearing me apart inside . . . And you . . . [*Leaving the* LITTLE GIRL *and turning to the* LITTLE BOY *in the usual way.*] What are you doing here, hanging about like a beggar? It'll be your fault too, if that little girl drowns; you're always like this, as if I wasn't paying the price for getting all of you into this house. [*Shaking his arm to make him take his hand out of his pocket.*] What have you got there? What are you hiding? Take it out, take your hand out! [*She drags his hand out of his pocket and to everyone's horror he is holding a revolver. She looks at him for a moment, almost with satisfaction: then she says, grimly.*] Where on earth did you get that? [*The* (LITTLE) BOY, *looking frightened, with his eyes wide and empty, doesn't answer.*] You idiot, if I'd been you, instead of killing myself, I'd have killed one of those two: either or both, the father and the son. [*She pushes him toward the cypress trees where he then stands watching: then she takes the* LITTLE GIRL *and helps her to climb in to the fountain, making her lie so that she is hidden: after that she kneels down and puts her head and arms on the rim of the fountain.*]

PRODUCER   That's good! It's good! [*Turning to the* STEPDAUGHTER.] And at the same time . . .

SON [*Scornfully.*]   What do you mean, at the same time? There was nothing at the same time! There wasn't any scene between her and me. [*Pointing to the* MOTHER.] She'll tell you the same thing herself, she'll tell you what happened.

> [*The* SECOND ACTRESS *and the* JUVENILE LEAD *have left the group of* ACTORS *and have come to stand nearer the* MOTHER *and the* SON *as if to study them so as to play their parts.*]

MOTHER   Yes, it's true. I'd gone to his room . . .

SON   Room, do you hear? Not the garden!

PRODUCER   It's not important! We've got to reorganize the events anyway. I've told you that already.

SON [*Glaring at the* JUVENILE LEAD *and the* SECOND ACTRESS.]   What do you want?

JUVENILE LEAD   Nothing. I'm just watching.

SON [*Turning to the* SECOND ACTRESS]   You as well! Getting ready to play her part are you? [*Pointing to the* MOTHER.]

PRODUCER   That's it. And I think you should be grateful—they're paying you a lot of attention.

SON   Oh, yes, thank you! But haven't you realised yet that you'll never be able to do this play? There's nothing of us inside you and you actors are only looking at us from the outside. Do you think we could go on living with a mirror held up in front of us that didn't only freeze our reflection for ever, but froze us in a reflection that laughed back at us with an expression that we didn't even recognize as our own?

FATHER   That's right! That's right!

PRODUCER [*To* JUVENILE LEAD *and* SECOND ACTRESS.]   Okay. Go back to the others.

SON   It's quite useless. I'm not prepared to do anything.

PRODUCER   Oh, shut up, will you, and let me listen to your mother. [*To the* MOTHER.] Well, you'd gone to his room, you said.

MOTHER   Yes, to his room. I couldn't bear it any longer. I wanted to empty my heart to him, tell him about all the agony that was crushing me. But as soon as he saw me come in . . .

SON   Nothing happened. I got away! I wasn't going to get involved. I never have been involved. Do you understand?

MOTHER   It's true! That's right!

PRODUCER   But we must make up the scene between you, then. It's vital!

MOTHER   I'm ready to do it! If only I had the chance to talk to him for a moment, to pour out all my troubles to him.

FATHER [*Going to the* SON *and speaking violently.*]   You'll do it! For your Mother! For your Mother!

SON [*More than ever determined.*]   I'm doing nothing!

FATHER [*Taking hold of his coat collar and shaking him.*]   For God's sake, do as I tell you! Do as I tell you! Do you hear what she's saying? Haven't you any feelings for her?

SON [*Taking hold of his* FATHER.]   No I haven't! I haven't! Let that be the end of it!

[*There is a general uproar. The* MOTHER *frightened out of her wits, tries to get between them and separate them.*]

MOTHER   Please stop it! Please!

FATHER [*Hanging on*]   Do as I tell you! Do as I tell you!

SON [*Wrestling with him and finally throwing him to the ground near the steps. Everyone is horrified.*]   What's come over you? Why are you so frantic? Do you want to parade our disgrace in front of everybody? Well, I'm having nothing to do with it! Nothing! And I'm doing what our author wanted as well—he never wanted to put us on the stage.

PRODUCER   Then why the hell did you come here?

SON [*Pointing to the* FATHER.]   He wanted to, I didn't.

PRODUCER   But you're here now, aren't you?

SON   He was the one who wanted to come and he dragged all of us here with him and agreed with you in there about what to put in the play: and that meant not only what had really happened, as if that wasn't bad enough, but what hadn't happened as well.

PRODUCER   All right, then, you tell me what happened. You tell me! Did you rush out of your room without saying anything?

SON [*After a moment's hesitation.*]   Without saying anything. I didn't want to make a scene.

PRODUCER [*Needling him.*]   What then? What did you do then?

SON [*He is now the centre of everyone's agonised attention and he crosses the stage.*]   Nothing . . . I went across the garden . . . [*He breaks off gloomy and absorbed.*]

PRODUCER [*Urging him to say more, impressed by his reluctance to speak.*]   Well? What then? You crossed the garden?

SON [*Exasperated, putting his face into the crook of his arm.*]   Why do you want me to talk about it? It's horrible! [*The* MOTHER *is trembling with stifled sobs and looking towards the fountain.*]

PRODUCER [*Quietly, seeing where she is looking and turning to the* SON *with growing apprehension.*] The little girl?

SON [*Looking straight in front, out to the audience.*] There, in the fountain . . .

FATHER [*On the floor still, pointing with pity at the* MOTHER.] She was trailing after him!

PRODUCER [*To the* SON, *anxiously.*] What did you do then?

SON [*Still looking out front and speaking slowly.*] I dashed across. I was going to jump in and pull her out . . . But something else caught my eye: I saw something behind the tree that made my blood run cold: the little boy, he was standing there with a mad look in his eyes: he was standing looking into the fountain at his little sister, floating there, drowned.

[*The* STEPDAUGHTER *is still bent at the fountain hiding the* LITTLE GIRL, *and she sobs pathetically, her sobs sounding like an echo. There is a pause.*]

SON [*Continued.*] I made a move towards him: but then . . .

[*From behind the trees where the* LITTLE BOY *is standing there is the sound of a shot.*]

MOTHER [*With a terrible cry she runs along with the* SON *and all the* ACTORS *in the midst of a great general confusion.*] My son! My son! [*And then from out of the confusion and crying her voice comes out.*] Help! Help me!

PRODUCER [*Amidst the shouting he tries to clear a space whilst the* LITTLE BOY *is carried by his feet and shoulders behind the white skycloth.*] Is he wounded? Really wounded?

[*Everybody except the* PRODUCER *and the* FATHER *who is still on the floor by the steps, has gone behind the skycloth and stays there talking anxiously. Then independently the* ACTORS *start to come back into view.*]

LEADING ACTRESS [*Coming from the right, very upset.*] He's dead! The poor boy! He's dead! What a terrible thing!

LEADING ACTOR [*Coming back from the left and smiling.*] What do you mean, dead? It's all make-believe. It's a sham! He's not dead. Don't you believe it!

OTHER ACTORS FROM THE RIGHT Make-believe? It's real! Real! He's dead!

OTHER ACTORS FROM THE LEFT No, he isn't. He's pretending! It's all make-believe.

FATHER [*Running off and shouting at them as he goes.*] What do you mean, make-believe? It's real! It's real, ladies and gentlemen! It's reality! [*And with desperation on his face he too goes behind the skycloth.*]

PRODUCER [*Not caring any more.*] Make-believe?! Reality?! Oh, go to hell the lot of you! Lights! Lights! Lights!

[*At once all the stage and auditorium is flooded with light. The* PRODUCER *heaves a sigh of relief as if he has been relieved of a terrible weight and they all look at each other in distress and with uncertainty.*]

PRODUCER God! I've never known anything like this! And we've lost a whole day's work! [*He looks at the clock.*] Get off with you, all of you! We can't do anything now! It's too late to start a rehearsal. [*When the* ACTORS *have gone, he calls out.*] Hey, lights! Kill everything! [*As soon as he has said this, all the lights go out completely and leave him in the pitch dark.*] For God's sake!! You might have left the workers![4] I can't see where I'm going!

---

4. Working lights.

[*Suddenly, behind the skycloth, as if because of a bad connection, a green light comes up to throw on the cloth a huge sharp shadow of the* CHARACTERS, *but without the* LITTLE BOY *and the* LITTLE GIRL. *The* PRODUCER, *seeing this, jumps off the stage, terrified. At the same time the flood of light on them is switched off and the stage is again bathed in the same blue light as before. Slowly the* SON *comes on from the right, followed by the* MOTHER *with her arms raised towards him. Then from the left, the* FATHER *enters.*

They come together in the middle of the stage and stand there as if transfixed. Finally from the left the STEPDAUGHTER *comes on and moves towards the steps at the front: on the top step she pauses for a moment to look back at the other three and then bursts out in a raucous laugh, dashes down the steps and turns to look at the three figures still on the stage. Then she runs out of the auditorium and we can still hear her manic laughter out into the foyer and beyond.*

After a pause the curtain falls slowly.]

1921

AKUTAGAWA RYŪNOSUKE
1892–1927

Despite his short career—he committed suicide at thirty-five—Akutagawa is considered one of the major writers of early twentieth-century Japan. Most of his work consists of short stories, in both historical and contemporary settings, as well as stories based on his experiences. Marked by literary inventiveness, his work reflects the energy and the anxieties of modern Japan but has also come to epitomize the postmodern questioning of absolute truth and certainty.

From the time he was an infant, Akutagawa's mother suffered from a crippling mental illness; she died when he was ten. In later years he admitted to a lasting fear that he would inherit the disease. Meanwhile, he was raised in the family of his maternal uncle, in a cultivated household that encouraged his youthful passion for literature. His reading included Japanese and Chinese classics, Japanese writers from the 1880s to the turn of the century, especially Natsume Sōseki and Mori Ōgai, and European writers including Guy de Maupassant, Anatole France, August Strindberg, and **Fyodor Dostoyevsky**. Traces of these influences can be found throughout Akutagawa's works. In 1913 he entered the English department of Tokyo Imperial University (now the University of Tokyo), and his translations and original works soon appeared in campus literary magazines.

From the start of his career, Akutagawa set most of his stories in the past, favoring three eras: the twelfth century, a time of widespread strife and disorder when the capital city, Kyoto, was wracked by disasters ranging from epidemics to massive fires; the late sixteenth century, when Christianity was exerting a disruptive force over parts of Japan, contributing to a century of civil war; and the 1870s and 1880s, when Japan's intellectual classes were eager to learn about the cultures of Europe and North America. His interest in the latter two periods may in part reflect his far-flung literary tastes, which likewise combined the East Asian classics, modern Japanese fiction, and the literary and philosophical traditions of Europe. Yet however distant his settings, his characters often suffer from distinctly twentieth-century feelings of social dislocation and individual desperation.

As a writer, Akutagawa is known for drawing upon the works of others. The story that launched his career, "The Nose" (1916), about a Buddhist priest with a fantastically large nose, was inspired partly by a story in a classical collection, and possibly also by "The Nose" (1836), a story by the Russian author Nicolay Gogol (1809–1852). Here and elsewhere, we find Akutagawa stitching together material from sources whose juxtaposition seems unlikely: the unifying element comes from Akutagawa's distinctive sensibilities, which include a fascination with the absurd and grotesque, the contradictions of human motivation, social decay, and modernist narrative techniques.

Starting in the early 1920s, as his reputation grew, Akutagawa labored under the strain of editors' requests for new manuscripts; increasingly he complained of nervous exhaustion and insomnia. Yet he continued to make demands on himself to produce stories displaying a virtuosic manipulation of setting and narrative, to be found in

works of the period such as "In a Bamboo Grove" (1921), the selection here. Even the publication of this story showed virtuosity: it was one of four stories that appeared, almost simultaneously, in the prestigious New Year's issues of four magazines in 1922.

The period in which Akutagawa achieved fame was the Taishō era, in the late 1910s and the 1920s, in many ways a time of high cultural play and experimentation, not unlike the Roaring Twenties in the United States. During these years a tide of mass culture that included recorded music, cinema, mass-circulation magazines, and cheap editions of popular fiction swept aside more traditional forms. The triumph of mass culture prompted writers with literary ambitions to set themselves apart as visibly as they could from popular fiction. Taking up the position of an embattled minority, many serious writers, including Akutagawa, portrayed the pursuit of true art as a sacred but dangerous calling, even demonic in its unworldliness and the force of its demands.

"In a Bamboo Grove" incorporates themes and techniques typical of Akutagawa's work. As popular fiction settled into established genres such as the detective novel, Japanese modernists pushed language and narrative form in unknown directions. Their experiments included the creation of fiction composed solely of sensory perceptions and the use of "concrete" prose styles stressing nouns over verbs as well as shifting points of view, such as those in the selection here. Like so many of Akutagawa's works, this story draws upon others: the situation derives from a vignette in a twelfth-century collection, *Tales of Times Now Past*, about a murder and rape. Akutagawa transforms the source, however, by recounting the central crimes from seven points of view. Rather than present the events from the perspective of an omniscient narrator, he provides transcripts of police interviews and other conversations, from which the reader tries to assemble the truth.

The story's reputation as a touchstone in the use of narrative perspective was secured in 1950 with the premiere of Kurosawa Akira's film *Rashōmon*, which won the first prize at the 1951 Venice film festival. The film uses scenes set at the Rashōmon gate from Akutagawa's story of the same name but is mainly based on "In a Bamboo Grove." It became an example of postmodern questioning of the way that the truth varies according to viewers' perspectives. In the story the classic problem of detective fiction—"Who done it?"—leads not only to the mutual recriminations of the three primary witnesses to the event but also to surprising forms of self-revelation.

In a Bamboo Grove[1]

The Testimony of a Woodcutter under Questioning by the Magistrate

That is true, Your Honor. I am the one who found the body. I went out as usual this morning to cut cedar in the hills behind my place. The body was in a bamboo grove on the other side of the mountain. Its exact location? A few hundred yards off the Yamashina post road. A deserted place where a few scrub cedar trees are mixed in with the bamboo.

The man was lying on his back in his pale blue robe with the sleeves tied up and one of those fancy Kyoto-style[2] black hats with the sharp creases. He had only one stab wound, but it was right in the middle of his chest; the bamboo leaves around the body were soaked with dark red blood. No, the bleeding had stopped. The wound looked dry, and I remember it had a big horsefly sucking on it so hard the thing didn't even notice my footsteps.

Did I see a sword or anything? No, Sir, not a thing. Just a length of rope by the cedar tree next to the body. And—oh yes, there was a comb there, too. Just the rope and the comb is all. But the weeds and the bamboo leaves on the ground were pretty trampled down: he must have put up a tremendous fight before they killed him. How's that, Sir—a horse? No, a horse could never have gotten into that place. It's all bamboo thicket between there and the road.

The Testimony of a Traveling Priest under Questioning by the Magistrate

I'm sure I passed the man yesterday, Your Honor. Yesterday at—about noon, I'd say. Near Checkpoint Hill on the way to Yamashina. He was walking toward the checkpoint with a woman on horseback. She wore a stiff, round straw hat with a long veil hanging down around the brim; I couldn't see her face, just her robe. I think it had a kind of dark-red outer layer with a blue-green lining. The

---

1. Translated by, and with some notes adapted from, Jay Rubin.

2. In the fashion of Kyoto, the Japanese capital at the time of the story.

horse was a dappled gray with a tinge of red, and I'm fairly sure it had a clipped mane. Was it a big horse? I'd say it was a few inches taller than most, but I'm a priest after all. I don't know much about horses. The man? No, Sir, he had a good-sized sword, and he was equipped with a bow and arrows. I can still see that black-lacquered quiver of his: he must have had twenty arrows in it, maybe more. I would never have dreamt that a thing like this could happen to such a man. Ah, what is the life of a human being—a drop of dew, a flash of lightning? This is so sad, so sad. What can I say?

The Testimony of a Policeman under Questioning by the Magistrate

The man I captured, Your Honor? I am certain he is the famous bandit, Tajōmaru. True, when I caught him he had fallen off his horse, and he was moaning and groaning on the stone bridge at Awataguchi. The time, Sir? It was last night at the first watch.[3] He was wearing the same dark blue robe and carrying the same long sword he used the time I almost captured him before. You can see he also has a bow and arrows now. Oh, is that so, Sir? The dead man, too? That settles it, then: I'm sure this Tajōmaru fellow is the murderer. A leather-wrapped bow, a quiver in black lacquer, seventeen hawk-feather arrows—they must have belonged to the victim. And yes, as you say, Sir, the horse is a dappled gray with a touch of red, and it has a clipped mane. It's only a dumb animal, but it gave that bandit just what he deserved, throwing him like that. It was a short way beyond the bridge, trailing its reins on the ground and eating plume grass by the road.

Of all the bandits prowling around Kyoto, this Tajōmaru is known as a fellow who likes the women. Last fall, people at Toribe Temple found a pair of worshippers murdered—a woman and a child—on the hill behind the statue of Binzuru.[4] Everybody said Tajōmaru must have done it. If it turns out he killed the man, there's no telling what he might have done to the woman who was on the horse. I don't mean to meddle, Sir, but I do think you ought to question him about that.

The Testimony of an Old Woman under Questioning by the Magistrate

Yes, Your Honor, my daughter was married to the dead man. He is not from the capital, though. He was a samurai serving in the Wakasa provincial office. His name was Kanazawa no Takehiro, and he was twenty-six years old. No, Sir, he was a very kind man. I can't believe anyone would have hated him enough to do this.

My daughter, Sir? Her name is Masago, and she is nineteen years old. She's as bold as any man, but the only man she has ever known is Takehiro. Her complexion is a little on the dark side, and she has a mole by the outside corner of her left eye, but her face is a tiny, perfect oval.

---

3. 8:00 P.M.

4. One of the Buddha's disciples.

Takehiro left for Wakasa yesterday with my daughter, but what turn of fate could have led to this? There's nothing I can do for my son-in-law anymore, but what could have happened to my daughter? I'm worried sick about her. Oh please, Sir, do everything you can to find her, leave no stone unturned: I have lived a long time, but I have never wanted anything so badly in my life. Oh how I hate that bandit—that, that Tajōmaru! Not only my son-in-law, but my daughter . . . (Here the old woman broke down and was unable to go on speaking.)

Tajōmaru's Confession

Sure, I killed the man. But I didn't kill the woman. So, where did she go? I don't know any better than you do. Now, wait just a minute—you can torture me all you want, but I can't tell you what I don't know. And besides, now that you've got me, I'm not going to hide anything. I'm no coward.

I met that couple yesterday, a little after noon. The second I saw them, a puff of wind lifted her veil and I caught a peek at her. Just a peek: that's maybe why she looked so perfect to me—an absolute bodhisattva[5] of a woman. I made up my mind right then to take her even if I had to kill the man.

Oh come on, killing a man is not as big a thing as people like you seem to think. If you're going to take somebody's woman, a man has to die. When *I* kill a man, I do it with my sword, but people like you don't use swords. You gentlemen kill with your power, with your money, and sometimes just with your words: you tell people you're doing them a favor. True, no blood flows, the man is still alive, but you've killed him all the same. I don't know whose sin is greater—yours or mine. (A sarcastic smile.)

Of course, if you can take the woman without killing the man, all the better. Which is exactly what I was hoping to do yesterday. It would have been impossible on the Yamashina post road, of course, so I thought of a way to lure them into the hills.

It was easy. I fell in with them on the road and made up a story. I told them I had found an old burial mound in the hills, and when I opened it it was full of swords and mirrors and things. I said I had buried the stuff in a bamboo grove on the other side of the mountain to keep anyone from finding out about it, and I'd sell it cheap to the right buyer. He started getting interested soon enough. It's scary what greed can do to people, don't you think? In less than an hour, I was leading that couple and their horse up a mountain trail.

When we reached the grove, I told them the treasure was buried in there and they should come inside with me and look at it. The man was so hungry for the stuff by then, he couldn't refuse, but the woman said she'd wait there on the horse. I figured that would happen—the woods are so thick. They fell right into my trap. We left the woman alone and went into the grove.

It was all bamboo at first. Fifty yards or so inside, there was a sort of open clump of cedars—the perfect place for what I was going to do. I pushed through

---

5. Someone who has attained Buddhist enlightenment but remains in the world to help others; here, a woman whose beauty blesses the world.

the thicket and made up some nonsense about how the treasure was buried under one of them. When he heard that, the man charged toward some scrawny cedars visible up ahead. The bamboo thinned out, and the trees were standing there in a row. As soon as we got to them, I grabbed him and pinned him down. I could see he was a strong man—he carried a sword—but I took him by surprise, and he couldn't do a thing. I had him tied to the base of a tree in no time. Where did I get the rope? Well, I'm a thief, you know—I might have to scale a wall at any time—so I've always got a piece of rope in my belt. I stuffed his mouth full of bamboo leaves to keep him quiet. That's all there was to it.

Once I finished with the man, I went and told the woman that her husband had suddenly been taken ill and she should come and have a look at him. This was another bull's-eye, of course. She took off her hat and let me lead her by the hand into the grove. As soon as she saw the man tied to the tree, though, she whipped a dagger out of her breast. I never saw a woman with such fire! If I'd been off my guard, she'd have stuck that thing in my gut. And the way she kept coming, she would have done me some damage eventually no matter how much I dodged. Still, I *am* Tajōmaru. One way or another, I managed to knock the knife out of her hand without drawing my sword. Even the most spirited woman is going to be helpless if she hasn't got a weapon. And so I was able to make the woman mine without taking her husband's life.

Yes, you heard me: without taking her husband's life. I wasn't planning to kill him on top of everything else. The woman was on the ground, crying, and I was getting ready to run out of the grove and leave her there when all of a sudden she grabbed my arm like some kind of crazy person. And then I heard what she was shouting between sobs. She could hardly catch her breath: "Either you die or my husband dies. It has to be one of you. It's worse than death for me to have two men see my shame. I want to stay with the one left alive, whether it's you or him." That gave me a wild desire to kill her husband. (Sullen excitement.)

When I say this, you probably think I'm crueler than you are. But that's because you didn't see the look on her face—and especially, you never saw the way her eyes were burning at that moment. When those eyes met mine, I knew I wanted to make her my wife. Let the thunder god kill me, I'd make her my wife—that was the only thought in my head. And no, not just from lust. I know that's what you gentlemen are thinking. If lust was all I felt for her, I'd already taken care of that. I could've just kicked her down and gotten out of there. And the man wouldn't have stained my sword with his blood. But the moment my eyes locked onto hers in that dark grove, I knew I couldn't leave there until I had killed him.

Still, I didn't want to kill him in a cowardly way. I untied him and challenged him to a sword fight. (That piece of rope they found was the one I threw aside then.) The man looked furious as he drew his big sword, and without a word he sprang at me in a rage. I don't have to tell you the outcome of the fight. My sword pierced his breast on the twenty-third thrust. Not till the twenty-third: I want you to keep that in mind. I still admire him for that. He's the only man who ever lasted even twenty thrusts with me. (Cheerful grin.)

As he went down, I lowered my bloody sword and turned toward the woman. But she was gone! I looked for her among the cedars, but the bamboo leaves on the ground showed no sign she'd ever been there. I cocked my ear for any sound of her, but all I could hear was the man's death rattle.

Maybe she had run through the underbrush to call for help when the sword fight started. The thought made me fear for my life. I grabbed the man's sword and his bow and arrows and headed straight for the mountain road. The woman's horse was still there, just chewing on grass. Anything else I could tell you after that would be a waste of breath. I got rid of his sword before coming to Kyoto, though.

So that's my confession. I always knew my head would end up hanging in the tree outside the prison some day, so let me have the ultimate punishment. (Defiant attitude.)

Penitent Confession of a Woman in the Kiyomizu Temple

After the man in the dark blue robe had his way with me, he looked at my husband, all tied up, and taunted him with laughter. How humiliated my husband must have felt! He squirmed and twisted in the ropes that covered his body, but the knots ate all the deeper into his flesh. Stumbling, I ran to his side. No—I *tried* to run to him, but instantly the man kicked me down. And that was when it happened: that was when I saw the indescribable glint in my husband's eyes. Truly, it was indescribable. It makes me shudder to recall it even now. My husband was unable to speak a word, and yet, in that moment, his eyes conveyed his whole heart to me. What I saw shining there was neither anger nor sorrow. It was the cold flash of contempt—contempt for *me*. This struck me more painfully than the bandit's kick. I let out a cry and collapsed on the spot.

When I regained consciousness, the man in blue was gone. The only one there in the grove was my husband, still tied to the cedar tree. I just barely managed to raise myself on the carpet of dead bamboo leaves, and look into my husband's face. His eyes were exactly as they had been before, with that same cold look of contempt and hatred. How can I describe the emotion that filled my heart then? Shame . . . sorrow . . . anger . . . I staggered over to him.

"Oh, my husband! Now that this has happened, I cannot go on living with you. I am prepared to die here and now. But you—yes, I want you to die as well. You witnessed my shame. I cannot leave you behind with that knowledge."

I struggled to say everything I needed to say, but my husband simply went on staring at me in disgust. I felt as if my breast would burst open at any moment, but holding my feelings in check, I began to search the bamboo thicket for his sword. The bandit must have taken it—I couldn't find it anywhere—and my husband's bow and arrows were gone as well. But then I had the good luck to find the dagger at my feet. I brandished it before my husband and spoke to him once again.

"This is the end, then. Please be so good as to allow me to take your life. I will quickly follow you in death."

When he heard this, my husband finally began moving his lips. Of course his mouth was stuffed with bamboo leaves, so he couldn't make a sound, but I knew immediately what he was saying. With total contempt for me, he said only, "Do it." Drifting somewhere between dream and reality, I thrust the dagger through the chest of his pale blue robe.

Then I lost consciousness again. When I was able to look around me at last, my husband, still tied to the tree, was no longer breathing. Across his ashen face shone a streak of light from the setting sun, filtered through the bamboo and cedar. Gulping back my tears, I untied him and cast the rope aside. And then—and then what happened to me? I no longer have the strength to tell it. That I failed to kill myself is obvious. I tried to stab myself in the throat. I threw myself in a pond at the foot of the mountain. Nothing worked. I am still here, by no means proud of my inability to die. (Forlorn smile.) Perhaps even Kanzeon,[6] bodhisattva of compassion, has turned away from me for being so weak. But now—now that I have killed my husband, now that I have been violated by a bandit—what am I to do? Tell me, what am I to . . . (Sudden violent sobbing.)

The Testimony of the Dead Man's Spirit Told through a Medium

After the bandit had his way with my wife, he sat there on the ground, trying to comfort her. I could say nothing, of course, and I was bound to the cedar tree. But I kept trying to signal her with my eyes: *Don't believe anything he tells you. He's lying, no matter what he says.* I tried to convey my meaning to her, but she just went on cringing there on the fallen bamboo leaves, staring at her knees. And, you know, I could see she was listening to him. I writhed with jealousy, but the bandit kept his smooth talk going from one point to the next. "Now that your flesh has been sullied, things will never be the same with your husband. Don't stay with him—come and be my wife! It's because I love you so much that I was so wild with you." The bandit had the gall to speak to her like that!

When my wife raised her face in response to him, she seemed almost spellbound. I had never seen her look so beautiful as she did at that moment. And what do you think this beautiful wife of mine said to the bandit, in my presence—in the presence of her husband bound hand and foot? My spirit may be wandering now between one life and the next, but every time I recall her answer, I burn with indignation. "All right," she told him, "take me anywhere you like." (Long silence.)

And that was not her only crime against me. If that were all she did, I would not be suffering so here in the darkness. With him leading her by the hand, she was stepping out of the bamboo grove as if in a dream, when suddenly the color drained from her face and she pointed back to me. "Kill him!" she screamed. "Kill him! I can't be with you as long as he is alive!" Again and again she screamed, as if she had lost her mind, "Kill him!" Even now her words like a windstorm threaten to blow me headlong into the darkest depths. Have such hateful words ever come from the mouth of a human being before? Have such damnable words ever reached the ears of a human being before? Have such— (An explosion of derisive laughter.) Even the bandit went pale when he heard her. She clung to his arm and screamed again, "Kill him!" The bandit stared at her, saying neither that he would kill me nor that he would not. The next thing I knew, however, he sent my wife sprawling on the bamboo leaves with a single

6. Also known as Kannon.

kick. (Another explosion of derisive laughter.) The bandit calmly folded his arms and turned to look at me.

"What do you want me to do with her?" he asked. "Kill her or let her go? Just nod to answer. Kill her?" For this if for nothing else, I am ready to forgive the bandit his crimes. (Second long silence.)

When I hesitated with my answer, my wife let out a scream and darted into the depths of the bamboo thicket. He sprang after her, but I don't think he even managed to lay a hand on her sleeve. I watched the spectacle as if it were some kind of vision.

After my wife ran off, the bandit picked up my sword and bow and arrows, and he cut my ropes at one place. "Now it's my turn to run," I remember hearing him mutter as he disappeared from the thicket. Then the whole area was quiet. No—I could hear someone weeping. While I was untying myself, I listened to the sound, until I realized—I realized that I was the one crying. (Another long silence.)

I finally raised myself, exhausted, from the foot of the tree. Lying there before me was the dagger that my wife had dropped. I picked it up and shoved it into my chest. Some kind of bloody mass rose to my mouth, but I felt no pain at all. My chest grew cold, and then everything sank into stillness. What perfect silence! In the skies above that grove on the hidden side of the mountain, not a single bird came to sing. The lonely glow of the sun lingered among the high branches of cedar and bamboo. The sun—but gradually, even that began to fade, and with it the cedars and bamboo. I lay there wrapped in a deep silence.

Then stealthy footsteps came up to me. I tried to see who it was, but the darkness had closed in all around me. Someone—that someone gently pulled the dagger from my chest with an invisible hand. Again a rush of blood filled my mouth, but then I sank once and for all into the darkness between lives.

1921

PREMCHAND (DHANPAT RAI ŚRIVASTAVA)
1880–1936

In the course of a literary career spanning a little over three decades, Premchand became the most accomplished fiction and prose writer of his time in two languages, Urdu and Hindi. More than twenty years after his death, Urdu would be the national language of Pakistan, and Hindi an official language of India. In the first decade of the twenty-first century, Urdu literature (produced in both countries) as well as Hindi literature (produced only in India) claim

Premchand as their foremost modernist and as an inaugural figure in their respective histories of the novel and the short story. Regarded as a model writer of fiction and prose in two national literatures, Premchand has much wider appeal: a realist and an idealist, he maps the range of human passions and follies with wit and irony, even as he meditates on the rhythms of modern history, colonial politics, and social change.

"Premchand" was the literary pseudonym of Dhanpat Rai Śrivastava, a Hindu of the Kayastha caste (a social class below the brāhmaṇa, the highest) who spent most of his life in what is now the heartland of the Hindi language in northern India. He was born in 1880 in Lamahi village, near Banaras (Varanasi), on the River Ganges. His father was a poorly paid postal clerk; his mother, an invalid, died when he was eight years old. Premchand's early education with a Muslim scholar was in Urdu and Persian. After his father remarried, the family moved for a few years to Gorakhpur, where he attended the Mission School and began reading Urdu literature and translations from English and Sanskrit. Back in Lamahi in 1895, Premchand's father arranged his marriage to an incompatible girl; repelled and disillusioned, the fifteen-year-old boy lived by himself in Banaras, working as a tutor and trying to complete his high school education. When his father died the following year, Premchand was unable to matriculate: he found himself with debts, no income, and wife, sister, stepmother, and two stepsiblings to support. Despite these setbacks, Premchand persisted with his dream of education and immersion in Urdu literature. After working as a schoolteacher, he managed to acquire advanced degrees that qualified him for senior positions in the colonial school system. In 1905 his marriage

disintegrated when his wife attempted suicide and was sent back to her parents; the following year he married a prominent Hindu reformer's daughter, who had been widowed before reaching adulthood.

The early pattern of financial insecurity and personal and domestic hardship persisted over the next three decades. After 1905, Premchand frequently changed jobs in the school system, living in Kanpur, Allahabad, Gorakhpur, and elsewhere, often in friction with his superiors. He also wrote for several newspapers and magazines, and tried his hand at editing journals. In 1921 he resigned from government employment and accepted a series of temporary jobs in private schools, book publishing, and journalism—besides a short stint as a writer in the Bombay film industry—until his untimely death in 1936. But these last fifteen years of his life were his most productive: he built and intermittently managed the Saraswati Press in Lamahi; launched and edited Hans, the most prestigious Hindi literary magazine, which survived until 1953 (and was then revived in his memory in 1986, and continues into the present); and, in his final months, served as the first president of the Progressive Writers Association, a Socialist organization that transformed literature, the arts, intellectual life, and politics across the subcontinent from the 1930s to the 1960s.

Premchand began his writing career in 1903 in Urdu, producing a novella, a novel, and several short stories over the next five years. His first collection of short fiction—a small volume containing five stories—was censored by the British colonial government in 1909 for its "seditious content," and its unsold copies were burned; thereafter, Premchand was required to submit all his writing for clearance before publication. While he continued to write and publish his Urdu fiction, between 1913 and 1915 he gradually switched to Hindi: although the two languages are intimately related in grammar and syntax, they use different scripts and stem from different literary traditions. During the next nine years, he published novels in Urdu, as well as his Hindi translations of his Urdu work, and began translating European literary works into Urdu and Hindi, starting with 23 Russian stories by **Leo Tolstoy** in 1916. In his final decade, he rendered much of his fiction in both languages: by the end of his career, he had written more than 190 short stories.

Within this complex and voluminous bilingual output, Premchand was a prime inventor of realism; his novels and short stories, centered on character and situation, are plotted mostly in the realistic mode. He developed a prose style that is deceptively plain and direct, using it to intricately chart out the society and social codes surrounding his characters. Among nineteenth-century English writers, he admired William Makepeace Thackeray and George Eliot (whose *Silas Marner* he adapted), especially the latter's moral vision. But he defined his style as "idealistic realism," in which "things as they are" will always be colored by "things as they ought to be." Most of his short stories are set in villages and in the countryside, and while they depict rural life as he observed it, they offer a critique of the conventional agrarian way of life in northern India. Premchand is thus a modernist whose fiction and prose—often experimental and subversive in its context—has been a vital element in the transformation of subcontinental society from a traditional to a modern one over the past two centuries.

"The Road to Salvation" (1924), the story represented here, is set in a typical early twentieth-century village in the Hindi heartland. Its central characters are Buddhu, a shepherd, and Jhingur, a small farmer, who are types rather than individuals; their names are common Hindi nouns that serve as epithets for the characters' moral qualities: *buddhu* means fool or idiot; *jhingur* is the word for cockroach or cricket. The action unfolds with Buddhu foolishly and obstinately herding his sheep across Jhingur's field, which is likely to damage the latter's ripening crop; Jhingur then attacks and injures the sheep with a cudgel in thoughtless anger. The altercation starts a cycle of revenge, which closes only when the two men have thoroughly degraded each other and themselves. For Premchand, the ingrained culture of feuding and revenge in the Indian village was one of the chief drawbacks of traditional agrarian society.

But the story stimulates our imaginations well beyond its immediate setting and context. The narrator of "The Road to Salvation," anonymous and omniscient, stands outside the story itself, although he keenly observes Buddhu and Jhingur's world. Despite his detachment, however, he narrates the events in an ironic tone; his analogies, exaggerations, and descriptions all contribute to his mockery of the characters' thoughts and actions. The narrator's carefully modulated attitude pushes us, as readers, to question Buddhu's and Jhingur's decisions at every stage of their conflict; we look at them simultaneously up close and from a distance, understanding their desire for revenge with each new provocation but wanting them to stop and take a different path. At the same time, the narrator's irony pushes the story toward a catastrophe, and we watch the events spin out of control with increasing distress. By the end, Premchand's orchestration of the narrative persuades us to consider some general questions about human behavior. Are decisions made in anger ever in our best interests? Is the desire for revenge, no matter how justifiable it seems, ultimately futile? Once a feud begins, is it wiser to let it run its course, or are we morally obliged to stop it as soon as we can?

At the same time, the story engages us with one of Premchand's universal themes: the causes and consequences of poverty in traditional rural societies. Buddhu and Jhingur are low-caste men trapped in a shrunken village economy that offers no opportunities for mobility and change. When faced with the slightest risk to their livelihoods, they respond like cornered men; when subjected to insults, all they can salvage is their pride—which then fuels their vengeance. Like people anywhere whose world has been sunk in poverty for generations, they reach a moment of resolution only when they have nothing left to lose, not even their pride.

The Road to Salvation[1]

1

The pride the peasant takes in seeing his fields flourishing is like the soldier's in his red turban, the coquette's in her jewels or the doctor's in the patients seated before him. Whenever Jhingur looked at his cane[2] fields a sort of intoxication came over him. He had three *bighas* of land which would earn him an easy 600 rupees.[3] And if God saw to it that the rates went up, then who could complain? Both his bullocks were old so he'd buy a new pair at the Batesar fair. If he could hook on to another two *bighas*, so much the better. Why should he worry about money? The merchants were already beginning to fawn on him. He was convinced that nobody was as good as himself—and so there was scarcely anyone in the village he hadn't quarrelled with.

One evening when he was sitting with his son in his lap, shelling peas, he saw a flock of sheep coming towards him. He said to himself, "The sheep path doesn't come that way. Can't those sheep go along the bank? What's the idea, coming over here? They'll trample and gobble up the crop and who'll make good for it? I bet it's Buddhu the shepherd—just look at his nerve! He can see me here but he won't drive his sheep back. What good will it do me to put up with *this*? If I try to buy a ram from him he actually asks for five rupees, and everybody sells blankets for four rupees but he won't settle for less than five."

By now the sheep were close to the cane-field. Jhingur yelled, "*Arrey*,[4] where do you think you're taking those sheep, you?"

Buddhu said meekly, "Chief, they're coming by way of the boundary embankment.[5] If I take them back around it will mean a couple of miles extra."

"And I'm supposed to let you trample my field to save you a detour? Why didn't you take them by way of some other boundary path? Do you think

---

1. Translated by David Rubin.
2. Sugarcane, an important crop in north India.
3. The currency of India. "*Bigha*": a measure of land equal to one-fifth of an acre.

4. A rough form of address, equivalent to "Hey!" or "Hey you!"
5. A bank or raised stone structure, marking the edge of a field.

I'm some bull-skinning nobody or has your money turned your head? Turn 'em back!"

"Chief, just let them through today. If I ever come back this way again you can punish me any way you want."

"I told you to get them out. If just one of them crosses the line you're going to be in a pack of trouble."

"Chief," Buddhu said, "if even one blade of grass gets under my sheep's feet you can call me anything you want."

Although Buddhu was still speaking meekly he had decided that it would be a loss of face to turn back. "If I drive the flock back for a few little threats," he thought, "how will I graze my sheep? Turn back today and tomorrow I won't find anybody willing to let me through, they'll all start bullying me."

And Buddhu was a tough man too. He owned 240 sheep and he was able to get eight annas[6] per night to leave them in people's fields to manure them, and he sold their milk as well and made blankets from their wool. He thought, "Why's he getting so angry? What can he do to me? I'm not his servant."

When the sheep got a whiff of the green leaves they became restless and they broke into the field. Beating them with his stick Buddhu tried to push them back across the boundary line but they just broke in somewhere else. In a fury Jhingur said, "You're trying to force your way through here but I'll teach you a lesson!"

Buddhu said, "It's seeing you that's scared them. If you just get out of the way I'll clear them all out of the field."

But Jhingur put down his son and grabbing up his cudgel he began to whack into the sheep. Not even a washerman would have beat his donkey so cruelly. He smashed legs and backs and while they bleated Buddhu stood silent watching the destruction of his army. He didn't yell at the sheep and he didn't say anything to Jhingur, no, he just watched the show. In just about two minutes, with the prowess of an epic hero, Jhingur had routed the enemy forces. After this carnage among the host of sheep Jhingur said with the pride of victory, "Now move on straight! And don't ever think about coming this way again."

Looking at his wounded sheep, Buddhu said, "Jhingur, you've done a dirty job. You're going to regret it."

2

To take vengeance on a farmer is easier than slicing a banana. Whatever wealth he has is in his fields or barns. The produce gets into the house only after innumerable afflictions of nature and the gods. And if it happens that a human enemy joins in alliance with those afflictions the poor farmer is apt to be left nowhere. When Jhingur came home and told his family about the battle, they started to give him advice.

"Jhingur, you've got yourself into real trouble! You knew what to do but you acted as though you didn't. Don't you realize what a tough customer Buddhu

6. Sixteen annas made a rupee.

is? Even now it's not too late—go to him and make peace, otherwise the whole village will come to grief along with you."

Jhingur thought it over. He began to regret that he'd stopped Buddhu at all. If the sheep had eaten up a little of his crop it wouldn't have ruined him. The fact is, a farmer's prosperity comes precisely from being humble—God doesn't like it when a peasant walks with his head high. Jhingur didn't enjoy the idea of going to Buddhu's house but urged on by the others he set out. It was the dead of winter, foggy, with the darkness settling in everywhere. He had just come out of the village when suddenly he was astonished to see a fire blazing over in the direction of his cane field. His heart started to hammer. A field had caught fire! He ran wildly, hoping it wasn't his own field, but as he got closer this deluded hope died. He'd been struck by the very misfortune he'd set out to avert. The bastard had started the fire and was ruining the whole village because of him. As he ran it seemed to him that today his field was a lot nearer than it used to be, as though the fallow land between had ceased to exist.

When he finally reached his field the fire had assumed dreadful proportions. Jhingur began to wail. The villagers were running and ripping up stalks of millet to beat the fire. A terrible battle between man and nature went on for several hours, each side winning in turn. The flames would subside and almost vanish only to strike back again with redoubled vigour like battle-crazed warriors. Among the men Buddhu was the most valiant fighter; with his dhoti[7] tucked up around his waist he leapt into the fiery gulfs as though ready to subdue the enemy or die, and he'd emerge after many a narrow escape. In the end it was the men who triumphed, but the triumph amounted to defeat. The whole village's sugarcane crop was burned to ashes and with the cane all their hopes as well.

3

It was no secret who had started the fire. But no one dared say anything about it. There was no proof and what was the point of a case without any evidence? As for Jhingur, it had become difficult for him to show himself out of his house. Wherever he went he had to listen to abuse. People said right to his face, "You were the cause of the fire! You ruined us. You were so stuck up your feet didn't touch the dirt. You yourself were ruined and you dragged the whole village down with you. If you hadn't fought with Buddhu would all this have happened?"

Jhingur was even more grieved by these taunts than by the destruction of his crop, and he would stay in his house the whole day.

Winter drew on. Where before the cane-press had turned all night and the fragrance of the crushed sugar filled the air and fires were lit with people sitting around them smoking their hookas,[8] all was desolation now. Because of the cold people cursed Jhingur and, drawing their doors shut, went to bed as soon as it was dark. Sugarcane isn't only the farmers' wealth; their whole way of life depends on it. With the help of the cane they get through the winter.

---

7. A sheet of cloth wrapped around the waist, worn by men throughout India.

8. A type of clay pipe that has a water reservoir, common all over north India.

They drink the cane juice, warm themselves from fires made of its leaves and feed their livestock on the cuttings. All the village dogs that used to sleep in the warm ash of the fires died from the cold and many of the livestock too from lack of fodder. The cold was excessive and everybody in the village was seized with coughs and fevers. And it was Jhingur who'd brought about the whole catastrophe, that cursed, murdering Jhingur.

Jhingur thought and thought and decided that Buddhu had to be put in a situation exactly like his own. Buddhu had ruined him and he was wallowing in comfort, so Jhingur would ruin Buddhu too.

Since the day of their terrible quarrel Buddhu had ceased to come by Jhingur's. Jhingur decided to cultivate an intimacy with him; he wanted to show him he had no suspicion at all that Buddhu started the fire. One day, on the pretext of getting a blanket, he went to Buddhu, who greeted him with every courtesy and honour—for a man offers the hooka even to an enemy and won't let him depart without making him drink milk and syrup.

These days Jhingur was earning a living by working in a jute-wrapping mill.[9] Usually he got several days' wages at once. Only by means of Buddhu's help could he meet his daily expenses between times. So it was that Jhingur reestablished a friendly footing between them.

One day Buddhu asked, "Say Jhingur, what would you do if you caught the man who burned your cane field? Tell me the truth."

Solemnly Jhingur said, "I'd tell him, 'Brother, what you did was good. You put an end to my pride, you made me into a decent man.'"

"If I were in your place," Buddhu said, "I wouldn't settle for anything less than burning down his house."

"But what's the good of stirring up hatred in a life that lasts such a little while in all? I've been ruined already, what could I get out of ruining him?"

"Right, that's the way of a decent religious man," Buddhu said, "but when a fellow's in the grip of anger all his sense gets jumbled up."

4

Spring came and the peasants were getting the fields ready for planting cane. Buddhu was doing a fine business. Everybody wanted his sheep. There were always a half dozen men at his door fawning on him, and he lorded it over everybody. He doubled the price of hiring out his sheep to manure the fields; if anybody objected he'd say bluntly, "Look, brother, I'm not shoving my sheep on you. If you don't want them, don't take them. But I can't let you have them for a pice[1] less than I said." The result was that everybody swarmed around him, despite his rudeness, just like priests after some pilgrim.

Lakshmi, goddess of wealth, is of no great size; she can, according to the occasion, shrink or expand, to such a degree that sometimes she can contract her most magnificent manifestation into the form of a few small figures printed on paper. There are times when she makes some man's tongue her throne and her size is reduced to nothing. But just the same she needs a lot of elbow-room

---

9. In north and eastern India, jute or hemp fiber is made into a kind of cloth that is used as wrapping material or made into sacks.
1. Coin of the lowest value.

for her permanent living quarters. If she comes into somebody's house, the house should grow accordingly, she can't put up with a small one. Buddhu's house also began to grow. A veranda was built in front of the door, six rooms replaced the former two. In short the house was done over from top to bottom. Buddhu got the wood from a peasant, from another the cowdung cakes for the kiln fuel to make the tiles; somebody else gave him the bamboo and reeds for the mats. He had to pay for having the walls put up but he didn't give any cash even for this, he gave some lambs. Such is the power of Lakshmi: the whole job—and it was quite a good house, all in all—was put up for nothing. They began to prepare for a house-warming.

Jhingur was still labouring all day without getting enough to half fill his belly, while gold was raining on Buddhu's house. If Jhingur was angry, who could blame him? Nobody could put up with such injustice.

One day Jhingur went out walking in the direction of the untouchable tanners'[2] settlement. He called for Harihar, who came out, greeting him with "*Ram Ram!*"[3] and filled the hooka. They began to smoke. Harihar, the leader of the tanners, was a mean fellow and there wasn't a peasant who didn't tremble at the sight of him.

After smoking a bit, Jhingur said, "No singing for the spring festival[4] these days? We haven't heard you."

"What festival? The belly can't take a holiday. Tell me, how are you getting on lately?"

"Getting by," Jhingur said. "Hard times mean a hard life. If I work all day in the mill there's a fire in my stove. But these days only Buddhu's making money. He doesn't have room to store it! He's built a new house, bought more sheep. Now there's a big fuss about his house-warming. He's sent *pan*[5] to the headmen of all the seven villages around to invite everybody to it."

"When Mother Lakshmi comes men don't see so clearly," Harihar said. "And if you see him, he's not walking on the same ground as you or I. If he talks, it's only to brag."

"Why shouldn't he brag? Who in the village can equal him? But friend, I'm not going to put up with injustice. When God gives I bow my head and accept it. It's not that I think nobody's equal to me but when I hear *him* bragging it's as though my body started to burn. 'A cheat yesterday, a banker today.' He's stepped on us to get ahead. Only yesterday he was hiring himself out in the fields with just a loincloth on to chase crows and today his lamp's burning in the skies."

"Speak," Harihar said. "Is there something I can do?"

"What can you do? He doesn't keep any cows or buffaloes just because he's afraid somebody will do something to them to get at him."

"But he keeps sheep, doesn't he?"

"You mean, 'hunt a heron and get a grouse'?"

2. Tanners are treated as untouchable by other Hindus because they handle the carcasses and hides of animals, an activity considered ritually polluting.
3. The name of God is repeated as a greeting

and also as an expression of deep emotion.
4. The festival of Holi, during which villagers engage in riotous, carnivalesque play.
5. The betel leaf: a symbol of invitation to auspicious ceremonies.

"Think about it again."

"It's got to be a plan that will keep him from ever getting rich again."

Then they began to whisper. It's a mystery why there's just as much love among the wicked as malice among the good. Scholars, holy men and poets sizzle with jealousy when they see other scholars, holy men and poets. But a gambler sympathizes with another gambler and helps him, and it's the same with drunkards and thieves. Now, if a Brahman Pandit[6] stumbles in the dark and falls then another Pandit, instead of giving him a hand, will give him a couple of kicks so he won't be able to get up. But when a thief finds another thief in distress he helps him. Everybody's united in hating evil so the wicked have to love one another; while everybody praises virtue so the virtuous are jealous of each other. What does a thief get by killing another thief? Contempt. A scholar who slanders another scholar attains to glory.

Jhingur and Harihar consulted, plotting their course of action—the method, the time and all the steps. When Jhingur left he was strutting—he'd already overcome his enemy, there was no way for Buddhu to escape now.

On his way to work the next day he stopped by Buddhu's house. Buddhu asked him, "Aren't you working today?"

"I'm on my way, but I came by to ask you if you wouldn't let my calf graze with your sheep. The poor thing's dying tied up to the post while I'm away all day, she doesn't get enough grass and fodder to eat."

"Brother, I don't keep cows and buffaloes. You know the tanners, they're all killers. That Harihar killed my two cows, I don't know what he fed them. Since then I've vowed never again to keep cattle. But yours is just a calf, there'd be no profit to anyone in harming that. Bring her over whenever you want."

Then he began to show Jhingur the arrangements for the housewarming. Ghee, sugar, flour and vegetables were all on hand. All they were waiting for was the Satyanarayan ceremony.[7] Jhingur's eyes were popping.

When he came home after work the first thing he did was bring his calf to Buddhu's house. That night the ceremony was performed and a feast offered to the Brahmans. The whole night passed in lavishing hospitality on the priests. Buddhu had no opportunity to go to look after his flock of sheep.

The feasting went on until morning. Buddhu had just got up and had his breakfast when a man came and said, "Buddhu, while you've been sitting around here, out there in your flock the calf has died. You're a fine one! The rope was still around its neck."

When Buddhu heard this it was as though he'd been punched. Jhingur, who was there having some breakfast too, said, "Oh God, my calf! Come on, I want to see her! But listen, I never tied her with a rope. I brought her to the flock of sheep and went back home. When did you have her tied with a rope, Buddhu?"

"God's my witness, I never touched any rope! I haven't been back to my sheep since then."

6. A scholar, a learned *brāhmaṇa*. The *brāhmaṇa* is the highest of the four Hindu caste-groups.
7. A ceremony in which the god Vishnu is worshipped to ensure prosperity. Feasting is an important part of the worship. "Ghee": clarified butter, used in Indian cooking and as an offering in Hindu fire rituals.

"If you didn't, then who put the rope on her?" Jhingur said. "You must have done it and forgotten it."

"And it was in your flock," one of the Brahmans said. "People are going to say that whoever tied the rope, that heifer died because of Buddhu's negligence."

Harihar came along just then and said, "I saw him tying the rope around the calf's neck last night."

"Me?" Buddhu said.

"Wasn't that you with your stick over your shoulder tying up the heifer?"

"And you're an honest fellow, I suppose!" Buddhu said. "You saw me tying her up?"

"Why get angry with me, brother? Let's just say you didn't tie her up, if that's what you want."

"We will have to decide about it," one of the Brahmans said. "A cow slaughterer should be stoned[8]—it's no laughing matter."

"Maharaj,"[9] Jhingur said, "the killing was accidental."

"What's that got to do with it?" the Brahman said. "It's set down that no cow is ever to be done to death in any way."

"That's right," Jhingur said. "Just to tie a cow up is a fiendish act."

"In the Scriptures it's called the greatest sin," the Brahman said. "Killing a cow is no less than killing a Brahman."

"That's right," Jhingur said. "The cow's got a high place, that's why we respect her, isn't it? The cow is like a mother. But Maharaj, it was an accident—figure out something to get the poor fellow off."

Buddhu stood listening while the charge of murder was brought against him like the simplest thing in the world. He had no doubt it was Jhingur's plotting, but if he said a thousand times that he hadn't put the rope on the calf nobody would pay any attention to it. They'd say he was trying to escape the penance.

The Brahman, that divinity, also stood to profit from the imposition of a penance. Naturally, he was not one to neglect an opportunity like this. The outcome was that Buddhu was charged with the death of a cow; the Brahman had got very incensed about it too and he determined the manner of compensation. The punishment consisted of three months of begging in the streets, then a pilgrimage to the seven holy places,[1] and in addition the price for five cows and feeding 500 Brahmans. Stunned, Buddhu listened to it. He began to weep, and after that the period of begging was reduced by one month. Apart from this he received no favour. There was no one to appeal to, no one to complain to. He had to accept the punishment.

He gave up his sheep to God's care. His children were young and all by herself what could his wife do? The poor fellow would stand in one door after another hiding his face and saying, "Even the gods are banished for cow-slaughter!" He received alms but along with them he had to listen to bitter

8. The Hindu veneration of the cow has its origins in the pastoral culture of the Vedic Aryans and the importance of the cow in their religious rituals. As Premchand goes on to show, killing a cow is considered among the most heinous sins.

9. "Lord, Sir, Your Majesty" (Hindi). A respect-ful form of address for men of higher rank than oneself.

1. Various lists are given of the seven holy places of pilgrimage in the Hindu religion. These invariably include Benaras (or Kashi), Hardwar, Ramesvaram, and Gaya.

insults. Whatever he picked up during the day he'd cook in the evening under some tree and then go to sleep right there. He did not mind the hardship, for he was used to wandering all day with his sheep and sleeping beneath trees, and his food at home hadn't been much better than this, but he was ashamed of having to beg, especially when some harridan would taunt him with, "You've found a fine way to earn your bread!" That sort of thing hurt him profoundly, but what could he do?

He came home after two months. His hair was long, and he was as weak as though he were sixty years old. He had to arrange for the money for his pilgrimage, and where's the moneylender who loans to shepherds? You couldn't depend on sheep. Sometimes there are epidemics and you're cleaned out of the whole flock in one night. Furthermore, it was the middle of the hot weather when there was no hope of profit from the sheep. There was an oil-dealer who was willing to loan him money at an interest of two annas per rupee—in eight months the interest would equal the principal. Buddhu did not dare borrow on such terms. During the two months many of his sheep had been stolen. When the children took them to graze the other villagers would hide one or two sheep away in a field or hut and afterwards slaughter them and eat them. The boys, poor lads, couldn't catch a single one of them, and even when they saw, how could they fight? The whole village was banded together. It was an awful dilemma. Helpless, Buddhu sent for a butcher and sold the whole flock to him for 500 rupees. He took 200 and started out on his pilgrimage. The rest of the money he set aside for feeding the Brahmans.

When Buddhu left, his house was burgled twice, but by good fortune the family woke up and the money was saved.

5

It was Savan,[2] month of rains, with everything lush green. Jhingur, who had no bullocks now, had rented out his field to share-croppers. Buddhu had been freed from his penitential obligations and along with them his delusions about wealth. Neither one of them had anything left; neither could be angry with the other—there was nothing left to be angry about.

Because the jute mill had closed down Jhingur went to work with pick and shovel in town where a very large rest-house for pilgrims was being built. There were a thousand labourers on the job. Every seventh day Jhingur would take his pay home and after spending the night there go back the next morning.

Buddhu came to the same place looking for work. The foreman saw that he was a skinny little fellow who wouldn't be able to do any heavy work so he had him take mortar to the labourers. Once when Buddhu was going with a shallow pan on his head to get mortar Jhingur saw him. *"Ram Ram"* they said to one another and Jhingur filled the pan. Buddhu picked it up. For the rest of the day they went about their work in silence.

At the end of the day Jhingur asked, "Are you going to cook something?"

"How can I eat if I don't?" Buddhu said.

2. The fifth month in the Hindu calendar, marking the season of the monsoon rains, which corresponds to July or August in the Western calendar.

"I eat solid food only once a day," Jhingur said. "I get by just drinking water with ground meal in it in the evenings. Why fuss?"

"Pick up some of those sticks lying around," Buddhu said. "I brought some flour from home. I had it ground there—it costs a lot here in town. I'll knead it on the flat side of this rock. Since you won't eat food I cook I'll get it ready and you cook it."[3]

"But there's no frying pan."

"There are lots of frying pans," Buddhu said. "I'll scour out one of these mortar trays."

The fire was lit, the flour kneaded. Jhingur cooked the chapatties,[4] Buddhu brought the water. They both ate the bread with salt and red pepper. Then they filled the bowl of the hooka. They both lay down on the stony ground and smoked.

Buddhu said, "I was the one who set fire to your cane field."

Jhingur said light-heartedly, "I know."

After a little while he said, "I tied up the heifer and Harihar fed it something."

In the same light-hearted tone Buddhu said, "I know."

Then the two of them went to sleep.

1924

3. As a member of a caste somewhat higher in the hierarchy than Buddhu's, Jhingur cannot eat food cooked by Buddhu.

4. Flat unleavened bread made of whole wheat flour, a staple food of north India.

VIRGINIA WOOLF
1882–1941

Virginia Woolf was one of the great modern novelists, on par with **James Joyce, Marcel Proust**, and **Thomas Mann**. Woolf is known for her precise evocations of states of mind—or of mind and body, since she refused to separate the two. She was an ardent feminist who explored—directly in her essays and indirectly in her novels and short stories—the situation of women in society, the construction of gender identity, and the predicament of the woman writer.

Born Adeline Virginia Stephen on January 25, 1882, she was one of the four children of the eminent Victorian editor and historian Leslie Stephen and his wife, Julia, both of whom also had children from earlier marriages. The family actively pursued intellectual and artistic interests, and Julia was admired and sketched by some of the most famous Pre-Raphaelite artists. Following the customs of the day, only the sons, Adrian and Thoby, were sent to boarding school and university; Virginia and her sister, Vanessa (the painter Vanessa Bell), were instructed at home by their parents and depended for further education on their father's immense library. Woolf bitterly resented this unequal treatment and the systematic discouragement of women's intellectual development that it implied.

After her mother's death in 1895, Woolf was expected to take over the supervision of the household, which she did until her father's death in 1904. She worried that women in literary families like hers were expected to write memoirs of their fathers or to edit their correspondence. Woolf did in fact write a memoir of her father, but she later noted that if he had not died when she was relatively young, she never would have become an author. Of fragile physical health after an attack of whooping cough when she was six, Woolf suffered psychological breakdowns after the death of each parent and was frequently hospitalized, especially after a number of suicide attempts. During her lifetime Woolf consulted at least twelve doctors and, consequently, experienced firsthand the developments in medicine for treating the mentally ill, from the Victorian era to the shell shock of the First World War.

Woolf moved to central London with her sister and brother Adrian after their father's death and took a house in the Bloomsbury district. It was a time of shifting social and cultural mores, of which Woolf later claimed: "on or about December, 1910, human character changed." She and her sister, though unmarried, lived with several men (some of them openly homosexual), challenging the social conventions that respectable unmarried women were expected to follow. She and her friends soon became the focus of

what was later called the Bloomsbury Group, a gathering of writers, artists, and intellectuals impatient with conservative Edwardian society who met regularly to discuss ideas and to promote a freer view of culture. It was an eclectic group and included the novelist E. M. Forster, the historian Lytton Strachey, the economist John Maynard Keynes, and the art critics Clive Bell (who married Vanessa) and Roger Fry (who introduced the group to the work of French painters Édouard Manet and Paul Cézanne).

Woolf was not yet writing fiction but contributed reviews to the *Times Literary Supplement*, taught literature and composition at Morley College (an institution with a volunteer faculty that provided educational opportunities for workers), and participated in the adult suffrage movement and a feminist group. In 1912 she married Leonard Woolf, who encouraged her to write and with whom she founded the Hogarth Press in 1917. One of the most respected of the small literary presses, it published works by such major authors as **T. S. Eliot**, Katherine Mansfield, Strachey, Forster, Maxim Gorky, and John Middleton Murry, as well as Woolf's own novels and translations of Sigmund Freud's most significant output. Over the next two decades she produced her best-known work while coping with frequent bouts of physical and mental illness. Already depressed during World War II and exhausted after the completion of her final novel, *Between the Acts* (1941), Woolf sensed the approach of a serious attack of psychosis and the confinement it would entail: in such situations, she was obliged to "rest" and forbidden to read or write. In March 1941 she drowned herself in a river close to her Sussex home.

Woolf is admired for her poetic evocations of the way we think and feel. Like Proust and Joyce, she brings to life the concrete, sensuous details of everyday experience; like them, she explores the structures of consciousness. Championing modern fiction as an alternative to the realism of the preceding generation, she proposed a more subjective and, therefore, more accurate account of experience. Her focus was not so much on the object under observation as on the observers' perception of it: "Let us record the atoms as they fall upon the mind in the order in which they fall, let us trace the pattern, however disconnected and incoherent in appearance, which sight or incident scores upon the consciousness." Such writing, undertaken with a woman's creative vision, would open avenues for literature. Although she was dismayed by what she saw as Joyce's vulgarity, she recognized him as one of the few living writers who achieved the successful rendering of stream of consciousness.

Woolf's writing has been compared with modern painting in its emphasis on the abstract arrangement of perspectives to suggest networks of meaning. After two relatively traditional novels, she developed a more flexible approach that manipulated fictional structure. The unfolding plot gave way to an organization by juxtaposed points of view; the experience of "real," or chronological, time was partially displaced by a mind ranging ambiguously among its memories; and an intricate pattern of symbolic themes connected otherwise unrelated characters. These techniques made unfamiliar demands on the reader's ability to synthesize and re-create a complete picture. In *Jacob's Room* (1922), an understanding of the hero must be assembled from a series of partial points of view. In *The Waves* (1931), the multiple perspectives of several characters soliloquizing on their relationship to the dead Percival are broken by ten interludes that together construct an additional, interacting perspective as they describe the passage of a single day from dawn to dusk. Woolf's novels may expand or telescope the passage of time: *Mrs. Dalloway* (1925) seems to focus on Clarissa Dalloway's preparations for a party that evening, but at the same time calls up—at different times, and according to different contexts—her entire life, from childhood to her present age of fifty. Woolf also concerned herself with the question of women's equality with men in marriage, and she brilliantly evoked the inequality in her parents' marriage in her novel *To the Lighthouse* (1927).

A ROOM OF ONE'S OWN

One of Woolf's major themes is society's different attitudes toward men and toward women. The work presented here, *A Room of One's Own* (1929), examines the history of literature written by women and offers an impassioned plea that women writers be given conditions equal to those available for men: specifically, the privacy of a room in which to write and economic independence. (At the time Woolf wrote, it was unusual for women to have money of their own or to be able to devote themselves to a career.) *A Room of One's Own* does not conform to any fixed form. At once lecture and essay, autobiography and fiction, it originated in a pair of lectures on women and fiction that the author gave at Newnham and Girton Colleges (for women) at Cambridge University in 1928. Woolf warns her audience that, instead of defining either women or fiction, she will use "all the liberties and licenses of a novelist" to approach the matter obliquely and leave her auditors to sort out the truth from the "lies [that] will flow from my lips." She will, she claims, retrace the days (that is, the narrator's days) preceding her visit, and lay bare the thought processes leading up to the lecture itself.

The lecture (or, in its written form, Chapter 1), continues as a meditative ramble through various parts of Oxbridge (an informal verbal linking of *Oxford* and *Cambridge* universities) and London. It includes the famous, and apparently true, anecdote in which Woolf is warned off the university lawn and forbidden entrance to the library because she is a woman, as well as a vivid description of the differences between the food and the living quarters for women and those for men at Oxbridge. By the end of her visit, frustrated, furious, and puzzled, she decides that the subject needs research—and London's British Museum, at least, is open to all.

In Chapter 2 the narrator heads for the British Museum to locate a comprehensive definition of femininity. To her surprise and mounting anger, she discovers that the thousands of books on the subject written by men all define women as inferior animals, useful but somewhat alien in nature. Moreover, those very definitions have become prescriptions for generations of young women who learn to see themselves and their place in life accordingly. Raised in poverty and dependence, such women have neither the material means nor the self-confidence to write seriously or to become anything other than the Victorian "Angel of the House." What they require, asserts the narrator, is the self-sufficiency brought by an annual income of five hundred pounds. (Woolf had recently inherited such a sum.)

Chapter 3 pursues similar themes, adding to the five hundred pounds the need for "a room of one's own" and the privacy necessary to follow out an idea. Moving to history, and focusing on the Elizabethan Age, after a discouraging inspection of the well-known *History of England,* by George Macaulay Trevelyan (1876–1962), Woolf evokes the career of the "terribly gifted" Judith Shakespeare, William's imaginary sister (his actual sister was named Joan). Judith has the same literary and dramatic ambitions as her brother, and she too finds her way to London, but she is blocked at each turn by her identity as a woman. Woolf does not belittle William Shakespeare with this contrast; instead, her narrator remarks meaningfully that his work reveals an "incandescent, unimpeded mind."

The bleak portrayals in these chapters are lightened by satirical wit and humor, often conveyed by calculated historical distortion. Woolf uses her novelist's license to subvert and criticize the patriarchal message she describes. The Reading Room of the British Museum, august repository of masculine knowledge about women, is seen as a (bald-foreheaded) dome crowned with the names of famous men. The narrator's scholarly-seeming list of feminine characteristics is not only amusingly biased but contradictory and incoherent; it implies that the "masculine" passion for lists and documentation is not the best way to learn about human nature. Professor von X.'s portrait is an open caricature linked to suggestions that his scientific disdain hides repressed fear and anger. *A Room of One's Own* is still famous for its vivid, scathing, and occasionally humorous portrayal of women as objects of male definition and disapproval. Its model of a feminine literary history and its hypothesis of a separate feminine consciousness and manner of writing had substantial influence on writers and literary theory in the latter half of the twentieth century.

From A Room of One's Own[1]

CHAPTER I

But, you may say, we asked you to speak about women and fiction—what has that got to do with a room of one's own? I will try to explain. When you asked me to speak about women and fiction I sat down on the banks of a river and began to wonder what the words meant. They might mean simply a few remarks about Fanny Burney; a few more about Jane Austen; a tribute to the Brontës and a sketch of Haworth Parsonage under snow; some witticisms if possible about Miss Mitford; a respectful allusion to George Eliot; a reference to Mrs. Gaskell[2] and one would have done. But at second sight the words seemed not so simple. The title women and fiction might mean, and you may have meant it to mean, women and what they are like; or it might mean women and the fiction that they write; or it might mean women and the fiction that is written about them; or it might mean that somehow all three are inextricably mixed together and you want me to consider them in that light. But when I began to consider the subject in this last way, which seemed the most interesting, I soon saw that it had one fatal drawback. I should never be able to come to a conclusion. I should never be able to fulfil what is, I understand, the first duty of a lecturer—to hand you after an hour's discourse a nugget of pure truth to wrap up between the pages of your notebooks and keep on the mantelpiece for ever. All I could do was to offer you an opinion upon one minor point—a woman must have money and a room of her own if she is to write fiction; and that, as you will see, leaves the great problem of the true nature of woman and the true nature of fiction unsolved. I have shirked the duty of coming to a conclusion upon these two questions—women and fiction remain, so far as I am concerned, unsolved problems. But in order to make some amends I am going to do what I can to show you how I arrived at this opinion about the room and the money. I am going to develop in your presence as fully and freely as I can the train of thought which led me to think this. Perhaps if I lay bare the ideas, the prejudices, that lie behind this statement you will find that they have some bearing upon women and some upon fiction. At any rate, when a subject is highly controversial—and any question about sex is that—one cannot hope to tell the truth. One can only show how one came to hold whatever opinion one does hold. One can only give one's audience the chance of drawing their own conclusions as

1. This essay is based upon two papers read to the Arts Society at Newnham and the Odtaa at Girton in October 1928. The papers were too long to be read in full, and have since been altered and expanded [Woolf's note]. Newnham and Girton are women's colleges at Cambridge University, and Odtaa ("One damn thing after another") is the acronym of a literary society. Woolf's talk was entitled *Women and Fiction*.

2. English novelist Elizabeth Gaskell (1810–1865) was the author of *Cranford* (1853). British writers: Fanny (Frances) Burney (1752–1840),

author of *Evelina* (1778); Jane Austen (1775–1817), author of *Pride and Prejudice* (1813); the three Brontë sisters, who were raised in the Yorkshire parsonage of Haworth—Charlotte (1816–1855), author of *Jane Eyre* (1847); Emily (1818–1848), author of *Wuthering Heights* (1847); and Anne (1820–1849), author of *Agnes Grey* (1847); Mary Russell Mitford (1787–1855), author of the blank-verse tragedy *Rienzi* (1828); George Eliot (pen name of Mary Ann Evans; 1819–1880), author of *Middlemarch* (1871–72).

they observe the limitations, the prejudices, the idiosyncrasies of the speaker. Fiction here is likely to contain more truth than fact. Therefore I propose, making use of all the liberties and licences of a novelist, to tell you the story of the two days that preceded my coming here—how, bowed down by the weight of the subject which you have laid upon my shoulders, I pondered it, and made it work in and out of my daily life. I need not say that what I am about to describe has no existence; Oxbridge[3] is an invention; so is Fernham; "I" is only a convenient term for somebody who has no real being. Lies will flow from my lips, but there may perhaps be some truth mixed up with them; it is for you to seek out this truth and to decide whether any part of it is worth keeping. If not, you will of course throw the whole of it into the wastepaper basket and forget all about it.

Here then was I (call me Mary Beton, Mary Seton, Mary Carmichael or by any name you please—it is not a matter of any importance) sitting on the banks of a river a week or two ago in fine October weather, lost in thought. That collar I have spoken of, women and fiction, the need of coming to some conclusion on a subject that raises all sorts of prejudices and passions, bowed my head to the ground. To the right and left bushes of some sort, golden and crimson, glowed with the colour, even it seemed burnt with the heat, of fire. On the further bank the willows wept in perpetual lamentation, their hair about their shoulders. The river reflected whatever it chose of sky and bridge and burning tree, and when the undergraduate had oared his boat through the reflections they closed again, completely, as if he had never been. There one might have sat the clock round lost in thought. Thought—to call it by a prouder name than it deserved—had let its line down into the stream. It swayed, minute after minute, hither and thither among the reflections and the weeds, letting the water lift it and sink it, until—you know the little tug—the sudden conglomeration of an idea at the end of one's line; and then the cautious hauling of it in, and the careful laying of it out? Alas, laid on the grass how small, how insignificant this thought of mine looked; the sort of fish that a good fisherman puts back into the water so that it may grow fatter and be one day worth cooking and eating. I will not trouble you with that thought now, though if you look carefully you may find it for yourselves in the course of what I am going to say.

But however small it was, it had, nevertheless, the mysterious property of its kind—put back into the mind, it became at once very exciting, and important; and as it darted and sank, and flashed hither and thither, set up such a wash and tumult of ideas that it was impossible to sit still. It was thus that I found myself walking with extreme rapidity across a grass plot. Instantly a man's figure rose to intercept me. Nor did I at first understand that the gesticulations of a curious-looking object, in a cut-away coat and evening shirt, were aimed at me. His face expressed horror and indignation. Instinct rather than reason came to my help; he was a Beadle;[4] I was a woman. This was the turf; there was the path. Only the Fellows and Scholars are allowed here; the gravel is the place for me. Such thoughts were the work of a moment. As I regained the path the arms of the Beadle sank, his face assumed its usual repose, and though turf is better walking than gravel, no very great harm was done. The

---

3. A fictional university combining the names of Oxford and Cambridge.

4. A lower-ranked university officer, assistant to authority.

only charge I could bring against the Fellows and Scholars of whatever the college might happen to be was that in protection of their turf, which has been rolled for 300 years in succession, they had sent my little fish into hiding.

What idea it had been that had sent me so audaciously trespassing I could not now remember. The spirit of peace descended like a cloud from heaven, for if the spirit of peace dwells anywhere, it is in the courts and quadrangles of Oxbridge on a fine October morning. Strolling through those colleges past those ancient halls the roughness of the present seemed smoothed away; the body seemed contained in a miraculous glass cabinet through which no sound could penetrate, and the mind, freed from any contact with facts (unless one trespassed on the turf again), was at liberty to settle down upon whatever meditation was in harmony with the moment. As chance would have it, some stray memory of some old essay about revisiting Oxbridge in the long vacation brought Charles Lamb to mind—Saint Charles, said Thackeray,[5] putting a letter of Lamb's to his forehead. Indeed, among all the dead (I give you my thoughts as they came to me), Lamb is one of the most congenial; one to whom one would have liked to say, Tell me then how you wrote your essays? For his essays are superior even to Max Beerbohm's,[6] I thought, with all their perfection, because of that wild flash of imagination, that lightning crack of genius in the middle of them which leaves them flawed and imperfect, but starred with poetry. Lamb then came to Oxbridge perhaps a hundred years ago. Certainly he wrote an essay—the name escapes me—about the manuscript of one of Milton's poems which he saw here. It was Lycidas perhaps, and Lamb wrote how it shocked him to think it possible that any word in Lycidas could have been different from what it is. To think of Milton changing the words in that poem seemed to him a sort of sacrilege. This led me to remember what I could of Lycidas and to amuse myself with guessing which word it could have been that Milton had altered, and why. It then occurred to me that the very manuscript itself which Lamb had looked at was only a few hundred yards away, so that one could follow Lamb's footsteps across the quadrangle to that famous library[7] where the treasure is kept. Moreover, I recollected, as I put this plan into execution, it is in this famous library that the manuscript of Thackeray's Esmond is also preserved. The critics often say that Esmond is Thackeray's most perfect novel. But the affectation of the style, with its imitation of the eighteenth century, hampers one, so far as I remember; unless indeed the eighteenth-century style was natural to Thackeray—a fact that one might prove by looking at the manuscript and seeing whether the alterations were for the benefit of the style or of the sense. But then one would have to decide what is style and what is meaning, a question which—but here I was actually at the door which leads into the library itself. I must have opened it, for instantly there issued, like a guardian angel barring the way with a flutter of black gown instead of white wings, a deprecating, silvery, kindly gentleman, who regretted in a low voice as he waved me back that ladies are only admitted to the library if accompanied by a Fellow of the College or furnished with a letter of introduction.

5. I.e., William Makepeace Thackeray (1811–1863), whose novels include Vanity Fair (1847–1848) and The History of Henry Esmond, Esq. (1852). Charles Lamb (1775–1834): English essayist and letter writer, author of Essays of Elia (1823), which contains Oxford in the Vacation, mentioned in Woolf's text.
6. English caricaturist and writer (1872–1956).
7. Trinity College Library, in Cambridge, designed by Sir Christopher Wren and built from 1676 to 1684.

That a famous library has been cursed by a woman is a matter of complete indifference to a famous library. Venerable and calm, with all its treasures safe locked within its breast, it sleeps complacently and will, so far as I am concerned, so sleep for ever. Never will I wake those echoes, never will I ask for that hospitality again, I vowed as I descended the steps in anger. Still an hour remained before luncheon, and what was one to do? Stroll on the meadows? sit by the river? Certainly it was a lovely autumn morning; the leaves were fluttering red to the ground; there was no great hardship in doing either. But the sound of music reached my ear. Some service or celebration was going forward. The organ complained magnificently as I passed the chapel door. Even the sorrow of Christianity sounded in that serene air more like the recollection of sorrow than sorrow itself; even the groanings of the ancient organ seemed lapped in peace. I had no wish to enter had I the right, and this time the verger might have stopped me, demanding perhaps my baptismal certificate, or a letter of introduction from the Dean. But the outside of these magnificent buildings is often as beautiful as the inside. Moreover, it was amusing enough to watch the congregation assembling, coming in and going out again, busying themselves at the door of the chapel like bees at the mouth of a hive. Many were in cap and gown; some had tufts of fur on their shoulders; others were wheeled in bath-chairs; others, though not past middle age, seemed creased and crushed into shapes so singular that one was reminded of those giant crabs and crayfish who heave with difficulty across the sand of an aquarium. As I leant against the wall the University indeed seemed a sanctuary in which are preserved rare types which would soon be obsolete if left to fight for existence on the pavement of the Strand.[8] Old stories of old deans and old dons came back to mind, but before I had summoned up courage to whistle—it used to be said that at the sound of a whistle old Professor——— instantly broke into a gallop—the venerable congregation had gone inside. The outside of the chapel remained. As you know, its high domes and pinnacles can be seen, like a sailing-ship always voyaging never arriving, lit up at night and visible for miles, far away across the hills. Once, presumably, this quadrangle with its smooth lawns, its massive buildings, and the chapel itself was marsh too, where the grasses waved and the swine rootled. Teams of horses and oxen, I thought, must have hauled the stone in wagons from far countries, and then with infinite labour the grey blocks in whose shade I was now standing were poised in order one on top of another, and then the painters brought their glass for the windows, and the masons were busy for centuries[9] up on that roof with putty and cement, spade and trowel. Every Saturday somebody must have poured gold and silver out of a leathern purse into their ancient fists, for they had their beer and skittles presumably of an evening. An unending stream of gold and silver, I thought, must have flowed into this court perpetually to keep the stones coming and the masons working; to level, to ditch, to dig and to drain. But it was then the age of faith, and money was poured liberally to set these stones on a deep foundation, and when the stones were raised, still more money was poured in from the coffers of kings and queens and great nobles to ensure that

8. One of the busiest streets in London, the main artery between the city and the West End.
9. Just over one century: King's College Chapel at Cambridge was built from 1446 to 1547. The college guidebook attributes its superb craftsmanship to the work of four master masons: Reginald Ely, John Wolrich, Simon Clerk, and John Wastell.

hymns should be sung here and scholars taught. Lands were granted; tithes were paid. And when the age of faith was over and the age of reason had come, still the same flow of gold and silver went on; fellowships were founded; lectureships endowed; only the gold and silver flowed now, not from the coffers of the king, but from the chests of merchants and manufacturers, from the purses of men who had made, say, a fortune from industry, and returned, in their wills, a bounteous share of it to endow more chairs, more lectureships, more fellowships in the university where they had learnt their craft. Hence the libraries and laboratories; the observatories; the splendid equipment of costly and delicate instruments which now stands on glass shelves, where centuries ago the grasses waved and the swine rootled. Certainly, as I strolled round the court, the foundation of gold and silver seemed deep enough; the pavement laid solidly over the wild grasses. Men with trays on their heads went busily from staircase to staircase. Gaudy blossoms flowered in window-boxes. The strains of the gramophone blared out from the rooms within. It was impossible not to reflect—the reflection whatever it may have been was cut short. The clock struck. It was time to find one's way to luncheon.

It is a curious fact that novelists have a way of making us believe that luncheon parties are invariably memorable for something very witty that was said, or for something very wise that was done. But they seldom spare a word for what was eaten. It is part of the novelist's convention not to mention soup and salmon and ducklings, as if soup and salmon and ducklings were of no importance whatsoever, as if nobody ever smoked a cigar or drank a glass of wine. Here, however, I shall take the liberty to defy that convention and to tell you that the lunch on this occasion began with soles, sunk in a deep dish, over which the college cook had spread a counterpane of the whitest cream, save that it was branded here and there with brown spots like the spots on the flanks of a doe. After that came the partridges, but if this suggests a couple of bald, brown birds on a plate you are mistaken. The partridges, many and various, came with all their retinue of sauces and salads, the sharp and the sweet, each in its order; their potatoes, thin as coins but not so hard; their sprouts, foliated as rosebuds but more succulent. And no sooner had the roast and its retinue been done with than the silent serving-man, the Beadle himself perhaps in a milder manifestation, set before us, wreathed in napkins, a confection which rose all sugar from the waves. To call it pudding and so relate it to rice and tapioca would be an insult. Meanwhile the wineglasses had flushed yellow and flushed crimson; had been emptied; had been filled. And thus by degrees was lit, halfway down the spine, which is the seat of the soul, not that hard little electric light which we call brilliance, as it pops in and out upon our lips, but the more profound, subtle and subterranean glow, which is the rich yellow flame of rational intercourse. No need to hurry. No need to sparkle. No need to be anybody but oneself. We are all going to heaven and Vandyck[1] is of the company—in other words, how good life seemed, how sweet its rewards, how trivial this grudge or that grievance, how admirable friendship and the society of one's kind, as, lighting a good cigarette, one sunk among the cushions in the window-seat.

---

1. The Flemish portrait painter Sir Anthony Van Dyck (1599–1641), who was appointed court painter by Charles I of England in 1632 and painted many portraits of the royal family and the nobility.

If by good luck there had been an ash-tray handy, if one had not knocked the ash out of the window in default, if things had been a little different from what they were, one would not have seen, presumably, a cat without a tail. The sight of that abrupt and truncated animal padding softly across the quadrangle changed by some fluke of the subconscious intelligence the emotional light for me. It was as if some one had let fall a shade. Perhaps the excellent hock was relinquishing its hold. Certainly, as I watched the Manx cat pause in the middle of the lawn as if it too questioned the universe, something seemed lacking, something seemed different. But what was lacking, what was different, I asked myself, listening to the talk. And to answer that question I had to think myself out of the room, back into the past, before the war indeed, and to set before my eyes the model of another luncheon party held in rooms not very far distant from these; but different. Everything was different. Meanwhile the talk went on among the guests, who were many and young, some of this sex, some of that; it went on swimmingly, it went on agreeably, freely, amusingly. And as it went on I set it against the background of that other talk, and as I matched the two together I had no doubt that one was the descendant, the legitimate heir of the other. Nothing was changed; nothing was different save only—here I listened with all my ears not entirely to what was being said, but to the murmur or current behind it. Yes, that was it—the change was there. Before the war at a luncheon party like this people would have said precisely the same things but they would have sounded different, because in those days they were accompanied by a sort of humming noise, not articulate, but musical, exciting, which changed the value of the words themselves. Could one set that humming noise to words? Perhaps with the help of the poets one could. A book lay beside me and, opening it, I turned casually enough to Tennyson.[2] And here I found Tennyson was singing:

> There has fallen a splendid tear
>   From the passion-flower at the gate.
> She is coming, my dove, my dear;
>   She is coming, my life, my fate;
> The red rose cries, "She is near, she is near";
>   And the white rose weeps, "She is late";
> The larkspur listens, "I hear, I hear";
>   And the lily whispers, "I wait."

Was that what men hummed at luncheon parties before the war? And the women?

> My heart is like a singing bird
>   Whose nest is in a water'd shoot;
> My heart is like an apple tree
>   Whose boughs are bent with thick-set fruit;
> My heart is like a rainbow shell
>   That paddles in a halcyon sea;
> My heart is gladder than all these
>   Because my love is come to me.[3]

---

2. Alfred, Lord Tennyson (1809–1892); a passage from his long poem *Maud* (1855) follows.

3. The first stanza of "A Birthday," a short poem by Christina Rossetti (1830–1894).

Was that what women hummed at luncheon parties before the war?

There was something so ludicrous in thinking of people humming such things even under their breath at luncheon parties before the war that I burst out laughing, and had to explain my laughter by pointing at the Manx cat, who did look a little absurd, poor beast, without a tail, in the middle of the lawn. Was he really born so, or had he lost his tail in an accident? The tailless cat, though some are said to exist in the Isle of Man, is rarer than one thinks. It is a queer animal, quaint rather than beautiful. It is strange what a difference a tail makes—you know the sort of things one says as a lunch party breaks up and people are finding their coats and hats.

This one, thanks to the hospitality of the host, had lasted far into the afternoon. The beautiful October day was fading and the leaves were falling from the trees in the avenue as I walked through it. Gate after gate seemed to close with gentle finality behind me. Innumerable beadles were fitting innumerable keys into well-oiled locks; the treasure-house was being made secure for another night. After the avenue one comes out upon a road—I forget its name—which leads you, if you take the right turning, along to Fernham. But there was plenty of time. Dinner was not till half-past seven. One could almost do without dinner after such a luncheon. It is strange how a scrap of poetry works in the mind and makes the legs move in time to it along the road. Those words—

> There has fallen a splendid tear
> From the passion-flower at the gate.
> She is coming, my dove, my dear—

sang in my blood as I stepped quickly along towards Headingley.[4] And then, switching off into the other measure, I sang, where the waters are churned up by the weir:

> My heart is like a singing bird
> Whose nest is in a water'd shoot;
> My heart is like an apple tree . . .

What poets, I cried aloud, as one does in the dusk, what poets they were!

In a sort of jealousy, I suppose, for our own age, silly and absurd though these comparisons are, I went on to wonder if honestly one could name two living poets now as great as Tennyson and Christina Rossetti were then. Obviously it is impossible, I thought, looking into those foaming waters, to compare them. The very reason why the poetry excites one to such abandonment, such rapture, is that it celebrates some feeling that one used to have (at luncheon parties before the war perhaps), so that one responds easily, familiarly, without troubling to check the feeling, or to compare it with any that one has now. But the living poets express a feeling that is actually being made and torn out of us at the moment. One does not recognize it in the first place; often for some reason one fears it; one watches it with keenness and compares it jealously and suspiciously with the old feeling that one knew. Hence the difficulty of modern

---

4. In Leeds (Yorkshire).

poetry; and it is because of this difficulty that one cannot remember more than two consecutive lines of any good modern poet. For this reason—that my memory failed me—the argument flagged for want of material. But why, I continued, moving on towards Headingley, have we stopped humming under our breath at luncheon parties? Why has Alfred ceased to sing

She is coming, my dove, my dear?

Why has Christina ceased to respond

My heart is gladder than all these
Because my love is come to me?

Shall we lay the blame on the war? When the guns fired in August 1914, did the faces of men and women show so plain in each other's eyes that romance was killed? Certainly it was a shock (to women in particular with their illusions about education, and so on) to see the faces of our rulers in the light of the shell-fire. So ugly they looked—German, English, French—so stupid. But lay the blame where one will, on whom one will, the illusion which inspired Tennyson and Christina Rossetti to sing so passionately about the coming of their loves is far rarer now than then. One has only to read, to look, to listen, to remember. But why say "blame"? Why, if it was an illusion, not praise the catastrophe, whatever it was, that destroyed illusion and put truth in its place? For truth . . . those dots mark the spot where, in search of truth, I missed the turning up to Fernham. Yes indeed, which was truth and which was illusion, I asked myself. What was the truth about these houses, for example, dim and festive now with their red windows in the dusk, but raw and red and squalid, with their sweets and their boot-laces, at nine o'clock in the morning? And the willows and the river and the gardens that run down to the river, vague now with the mist stealing over them, but gold and red in the sunlight—which was the truth, which was the illusion about them? I spare you the twists and turns of my cogitations, for no conclusion was found on the road to Headingley, and I ask you to suppose that I soon found out my mistake about the turning and retraced my steps to Fernham.

As I have said already that it was an October day, I dare not forfeit your respect and imperil the fair name of fiction by changing the season and describing lilacs hanging over garden walls, crocuses, tulips and other flowers of spring. Fiction must stick to facts, and the truer the facts the better the fiction—so we are told. Therefore it was still autumn and the leaves were still yellow and falling, if anything, a little faster than before, because it was now evening (seven twenty-three to be precise) and a breeze (from the southwest to be exact) had risen. But for all that there was something odd at work:

My heart is like a singing bird
Whose nest is in a water'd shoot;
My heart is like an apple tree
Whose boughs are bent with thick-set fruit—

perhaps the words of Christina Rossetti were partly responsible for the folly of the fancy—it was nothing of course but a fancy—that the lilac was shaking its flowers over the garden walls, and the brimstone butterflies were scudding hither and thither, and the dust of the pollen was in the air. A wind blew, from what quarter I know not, but it lifted the half-grown leaves so that there was a flash of silver grey in the air. It was the time between the lights when colours undergo their intensification and purples and golds burn in window-panes like the beat of an excitable heart; when for some reason the beauty of the world revealed and yet soon to perish (here I pushed into the garden, for, unwisely, the door was left open and no beadles seemed about), the beauty of the world which is so soon to perish, has two edges, one of laughter, one of anguish, cutting the heart asunder. The gardens of Fernham lay before me in the spring twilight, wild and open, and in the long grass, sprinkled and carelessly flung, were daffodils and bluebells, not orderly perhaps at the best of times, and now wind-blown and waving as they tugged at their roots. The windows of the building, curved like ships' windows among generous waves of red brick, changed from lemon to silver under the flight of the quick spring clouds. Somebody was in a hammock, somebody, but in this light they were phantoms only, half guessed, half seen, raced across the grass—would no one stop her?—and then on the terrace, as if popping out to breathe the air, to glance at the garden, came a bent figure, formidable yet humble, with her great forehead and her shabby dress—could it be the famous scholar, could it be J—— H—— herself?[5] All was dim, yet intense too, as if the scarf which the dusk had flung over the garden were torn asunder by star or sword—the flash of some terrible reality leaping, as its way is, out of the heart of the spring. For youth——

Here was my soup. Dinner was being served in the great dining-hall. Far from being spring it was in fact an evening in October. Everybody was assembled in the big dining-room. Dinner was ready. Here was the soup. It was a plain gravy soup. There was nothing to stir the fancy in that. One could have seen through the transparent liquid any pattern that there might have been on the plate itself. But there was no pattern. The plate was plain. Next came beef with its attendant greens and potatoes—a homely trinity, suggesting the rumps of cattle in a muddy market, and sprouts curled and yellowed at the edge, and bargaining and cheapening, and women with string bags on Monday morning. There was no reason to complain of human nature's daily food, seeing that the supply was sufficient and coal-miners doubtless were sitting down to less. Prunes and custard followed. And if any one complains that prunes, even when mitigated by custard, are an uncharitable vegetable (fruit they are not), stringy as a miser's heart and exuding a fluid such as might run in misers' veins who have denied themselves wine and warmth for eighty years and yet not given to the poor, he should reflect that there are people whose charity embraces even the prune. Biscuits and cheese came next, and here the water-jug was liberally passed round, for it is the nature of biscuits to be dry, and these were biscuits to the core. That was all. The meal was over. Everybody scraped their chairs back; the swing-doors swung violently to and fro; soon the hall was emptied of every sign of food and made ready no doubt for breakfast next morning. Down corridors and up staircases the youth of England went banging and singing.

5. Jane Harrison (1850–1928), English classical scholar, fellow, and lecturer at Newnham College, and author of *Prolegomena to the* *Study of Greek Religion* (1903) and *Ancient Art and Ritual* (1913).

And was it for a guest, a stranger (for I had no more right here in Fernham than in Trinity or Somerville or Girton or Newnham or Christchurch), to say, "The dinner was not good," or to say (we were now, Mary Seton and I, in her sitting-room), "Could we not have dined up here alone?" for if I had said anything of the kind I should have been prying and searching into the secret economies of a house which to the stranger wears so fine a front of gaiety and courage. No, one could say nothing of the sort. Indeed, conversation for a moment flagged. The human frame being what it is, heart, body and brain all mixed together, and not contained in separate compartments as they will be no doubt in another million years, a good dinner is of great importance to good talk. One cannot think well, love well, sleep well, if one has not dined well. The lamp in the spine does not light on beef and prunes. We are all *probably* going to heaven, and Vandyck is, we *hope*, to meet us round the next corner—that is the dubious and qualifying state of mind that beef and prunes at the end of the day's work breed between them. Happily my friend, who taught science, had a cupboard where there was a squat bottle and little glasses—(but there should have been sole and partridge to begin with)—so that we were able to draw up to the fire and repair some of the damages of the day's living. In a minute or so we were slipping freely in and out among all those objects of curiosity and interest which form in the mind in the absence of a particular person, and are naturally to be discussed on coming together again—how somebody has married, another has not; one thinks this, another that; one has improved out of all knowledge, the other most amazingly gone to the bad—with all those speculations upon human nature and the character of the amazing world we live in which spring naturally from such beginnings. While these things were being said, however, I became shamefacedly aware of a current setting in of its own accord and carrying everything forward to an end of its own. One might be talking of Spain or Portugal, of book or racehorse, but the real interest of whatever was said was none of those things, but a scene of masons on a high roof some five centuries ago. Kings and nobles brought treasure in huge sacks and poured it under the earth. This scene was for ever coming alive in my mind and placing itself by another of lean cows and a muddy market and withered greens and the stringy hearts of old men—these two pictures, disjointed and disconnected and nonsensical as they were, were for ever coming together and combating each other and had me entirely at their mercy. The best course, unless the whole talk was to be distorted, was to expose what was in my mind to the air, when with good luck it would fade and crumble like the head of the dead king when they opened the coffin at Windsor.[6] Briefly, then, I told Miss Seton about the masons who had been all those years on the roof of the chapel, and about the kings and queens and nobles bearing sacks of gold and silver on their shoulders, which they shovelled into the earth; and then how the great financial magnates of our own time came and laid cheques and bonds, I suppose, where the others had laid ingots and rough lumps of gold. All that lies beneath the colleges down there, I said; but this college, where we are now sitting, what lies beneath its gallant red brick and the wild unkempt grasses of the garden? What force is behind the plain china off which we dined, and (here it popped out of my mouth before I could stop it) the beef, the custard and the prunes?

6. At the royal residence of Windsor Castle, nine English kings are buried in two chapels serving as royal mausoleums.

Well, said Mary Seton, about the year 1860—Oh, but you know the story, she said, bored, I suppose, by the recital. And she told me—rooms were hired. Committees met. Envelopes were addressed. Circulars were drawn up. Meetings were held; letters were read out; so-and-so has promised so much; on the contrary, Mr. —— won't give a penny. The *Saturday Review* has been very rude. How can we raise a fund to pay for offices? Shall we hold a bazaar? Can't we find a pretty girl to sit in the front row? Let us look up what John Stuart Mill said on the subject. Can any one persuade the editor of the —— to print a letter? Can we get Lady —— to sign it? Lady —— is out of town. That was the way it was done, presumably, sixty years ago, and it was a prodigious effort, and a great deal of time was spent on it. And it was only after a long struggle and with the utmost difficulty that they got thirty thousand pounds together.[7] So obviously we cannot have wine and partridges and servants carrying tin dishes on their heads, she said. We cannot have sofas and separate rooms. "The amenities," she said, quoting from some book or other, "will have to wait."[8]

At the thought of all those women working year after year and finding it hard to get two thousand pounds together, and as much as they could do to get thirty thousand pounds, we burst out in scorn at the reprehensible poverty of our sex. What had our mothers been doing then that they had no wealth to leave us? Powdering their noses? Looking in at shop windows? Flaunting in the sun at Monte Carlo? There were some photographs on the mantel-piece. Mary's mother—if that was her picture—may have been a wastrel in her spare time (she had thirteen children by a minister of the church), but if so her gay and dissipated life had left too few traces of its pleasures on her face. She was a homely body; an old lady in a plaid shawl which was fastened by a large cameo; and she sat in a basket-chair, encouraging a spaniel to look at the camera, with the amused, yet strained expression of one who is sure that the dog will move directly the bulb is pressed. Now if she had gone into business; had become a manufacturer of artificial silk or a magnate on the Stock Exchange; if she had left two or three hundred thousand pounds to Fernham, we could have been sitting at our ease tonight and the subject of our talk might have been archaeology, botany, anthropology, physics, the nature of the atom, mathematics, astronomy, relativity, geography. If only Mrs Seton and her mother and her mother before her had learnt the great art of making money and had left their money, like their fathers and their grandfathers before them, to found fellowships and lectureships and prizes and scholarships appropriated to the use of their own sex, we might have dined very tolerably up here alone off a bird and a bottle of wine; we might have looked forward without undue confidence to a pleasant and honourable lifetime spent in the shelter of one of the liberally endowed professions. We might have been exploring or writing; mooning about the venerable places of the earth; sitting contemplative on the steps of the Parthenon, or going at ten to an office and coming home comfortably at

7. "We are told that we ought to ask for £30,000 at least. . . . It is not a large sum, considering that there is to be but one college of this sort for Great Britain, Ireland and the Colonies, and considering how easy it is to raise immense sums for boys' schools. But considering how few people really wish women to be educated, it is a good deal."—Lady Stephen, *Life of Miss Emily Davies* [Woolf's note].

8. "Every penny which could be scraped together was set aside for building, and the amenities had to be postponed."—R. Strachey, *The Cause* [Woolf's note].

half-past four to write a little poetry. Only, if Mrs Seton and her like had gone into business at the age of fifteen, there would have been—that was the snag in the argument—no Mary. What, I asked, did Mary think of that? There between the curtains was the October night, calm and lovely, with a star or two caught in the yellowing trees. Was she ready to resign her share of it and her memories (for they had been a happy family, though a large one) of games and quarrels up in Scotland, which she is never tired of praising for the fineness of its air and the quality of its cakes, in order that Fernham might have been endowed with fifty thousand pounds or so by a stroke of the pen? For, to endow a college would necessitate the suppression of families altogether. Making a fortune and bearing thirteen children—no human being could stand it. Consider the facts, we said. First there are nine months before the baby is born. Then the baby is born. Then there are three or four months spent in feeding the baby. After the baby is fed there are certainly five years spent in playing with the baby. You cannot, it seems, let children run about the streets. People who have seen them running wild in Russia say that the sight is not a pleasant one. People say, too, that human nature takes its shape in the years between one and five. If Mrs Seton, I said, had been making money, what sort of memories would you have had of games and quarrels? What would you have known of Scotland, and its fine air and cakes and all the rest of it? But it is useless to ask these questions, because you would never have come into existence at all. Moreover, it is equally useless to ask what might have happened if Mrs Seton and her mother and her mother before her had amassed great wealth and laid it under the foundations of college and library, because, in the first place, to earn money was impossible for them, and in the second, had it been possible, the law denied them the right to possess what money they earned. It is only for the last forty-eight years that Mrs Seton has had a penny of her own. For all the centuries before that it would have been her husband's property—a thought which, perhaps, may have had its share in keeping Mrs Seton and her mothers off the Stock Exchange. Every penny I earn, they may have said, will be taken from me and disposed of according to my husband's wisdom—perhaps to found a scholarship or to endow a fellowship in Balliol or Kings,[9] so that to earn money, even if I could earn money, is not a matter that interests me very greatly. I had better leave it to my husband.

At any rate, whether or not the blame rested on the old lady who was looking at the spaniel, there could be no doubt that for some reason or other our mothers had mismanaged their affairs very gravely. Not a penny could be spared for "amenities"; for partridges and wine, beadles and turf, books and cigars, libraries and leisure. To raise bare walls out of the bare earth was the utmost they could do.

So we talked standing at the window and looking, as so many thousands look every night, down on the domes and towers of the famous city beneath us. It was very beautiful, very mysterious in the autumn moonlight. The old stone looked very white and venerable. One thought of all the books that were assembled down there; of the pictures of old prelates and worthies hanging in the panelled rooms; of the painted windows that would be throwing strange globes and crescents on the pavement; of the tablets and memorials and inscriptions; of the fountains and the grass; of the quiet rooms looking across

9. I.e., King's College, Cambridge. "Balliol": Balliol College, Oxford.

the quiet quadrangles. And (pardon me the thought) I thought, too, of the admirable smoke and drink and the deep armchairs and the pleasant carpets: of the urbanity, the geniality, the dignity which are the offspring of luxury and privacy and space. Certainly our mothers had not provided us with anything comparable to all this—our mothers who found it difficult to scrape together thirty thousand pounds, our mothers who bore thirteen children to ministers of religion at St Andrews.[1]

So I went back to my inn, and as I walked through the dark streets I pondered this and that, as one does at the end of the day's work. I pondered why it was that Mrs Seton had no money to leave us; and what effect poverty has on the mind; and what effect wealth has on the mind; and I thought of the queer old gentlemen I had seen that morning with tufts of fur upon their shoulders; and I remembered how if one whistled one of them ran; and I thought of the organ booming in the chapel and of the shut doors of the library; and I thought how unpleasant it is to be locked out; and I thought how it is worse perhaps to be locked in; and, thinking of the safety and prosperity of the one sex and of the poverty and insecurity of the other and of the effect of tradition and of the lack of tradition upon the mind of a writer, I thought at last that it was time to roll up the crumpled skin of the day, with its arguments and its impressions and its anger and its laughter, and cast it into the hedge. A thousand stars were flashing across the blue wastes of the sky. One seemed alone with an inscrutable society. All human beings were laid asleep—prone, horizontal, dumb. Nobody seemed stirring in the streets of Oxbridge. Even the door of the hotel sprang open at the touch of an invisible hand—not a boots was sitting up to light me to bed, it was so late.

CHAPTER 3

It was disappointing not to have brought back in the evening some important statement, some authentic fact. Women are poorer than men because—this or that. Perhaps now it would be better to give up seeking for the truth, and receiving on one's head an avalanche of opinion hot as lava, discoloured as dish-water. It would be better to draw the curtains; to shut out distractions; to light the lamp; to narrow the enquiry and to ask the historian, who records not opinions but facts, to describe under what conditions women lived, not throughout the ages, but in England, say in the time of Elizabeth.[2]

For it is a perennial puzzle why no woman wrote a word of that extraordinary literature when every other man, it seemed, was capable of song or sonnet. What were the conditions in which women lived, I asked myself; for fiction, imaginative work that is, is not dropped like a pebble upon the ground, as science may be; fiction is like a spider's web, attached ever so lightly perhaps, but still attached to life at all four corners. Often the attachment is scarcely perceptible; Shakespeare's plays, for instance, seem to hang there complete by themselves. But when the web is pulled askew, hooked up at the edge, torn in the middle, one remembers that these webs are not spun in mid-air by incorporeal creatures, but are the work of suffering human beings, and are attached to grossly material things, like health and money and the houses we live in.

1. Probably St. Andrew's in Holborn, an old London church rebuilt under the famous architect Sir Christopher Wren during 1683–1695.
2. Queen of England from 1558 to 1603.

I went, therefore, to the shelf where the histories stand and took down one of the latest, Professor Trevelyan's *History of England*.[3] Once more I looked up Women, found "position of," and turned to the pages indicated. "Wife-beating," I read, "was a recognised right of man, and was practised without shame by high as well as low. . . . Similarly," the historian goes on, "the daughter who refused to marry the gentleman of her parents' choice was liable to be locked up, beaten and flung about the room, without any shock being inflicted on public opinion. Marriage was not an affair of personal affection, but of family avarice, particularly in the 'chivalrous' upper classes. . . . Betrothal often took place while one or both of the parties was in the cradle, and marriage when they were scarcely out of the nurses' charge." That was about 1470, soon after Chaucer's[4] time. The next reference to the position of women is some two hundred years later, in the time of the Stuarts.[5] "It was still the exception for women of the upper and middle class to choose their own husbands, and when the husband had been assigned, he was lord and master, so far at least as law and custom could make him. Yet even so," Professor Trevelyan concludes, "neither Shakespeare's women nor those of authentic seventeenth-century memoirs, like the Verneys and the Hutchinsons,[6] seem wanting in personality and character." Certainly, if we consider it, Cleopatra must have had a way with her; Lady Macbeth,[7] one would suppose, had a will of her own; Rosalind, one might conclude, was an attractive girl. Professor Trevelyan is speaking no more than the truth when he remarks that Shakespeare's women do not seem wanting in personality and character. Not being a historian, one might go even further and say that women have burnt like beacons in all the works of all the poets from the beginning of time—Clytemnestra, Antigone, Cleopatra, Lady Macbeth, Phèdre, Cressida, Rosalind, Desdemona, the Duchess of Malfi,[8] among the dramatists; then among the prose writers: Millamant, Clarissa, la-rissa, Becky Sharp, Anna Karenina, Emma Bovary, Madame de Guermantes[9]— the names flock to mind, nor do they recall women "lacking in personality and character." Indeed, if woman had no existence save in the fiction written by men, one would imagine her a person of the utmost importance; very various; heroic and mean; splendid and sordid; infinitely beautiful and hideous in the

3. Published in London in 1926. References are to pages 260–61 and, later, to pages 436–37.
4. Geoffrey Chaucer (1340?–1400), author of *The Canterbury Tales* (1390–1400).
5. The British royal house from 1603 to 1714 (except for the Commonwealth interregnum of 1649–60).
6. F. P. Verney compiled *The Memoirs of the Verney Family during the Seventeenth Century* (1892–1899), and Lucy Hutchinson recounted her husband's life in *Memoirs of the Life of Colonel Hutchinson* (1806).
7. Heroine of Shakespeare's *Macbeth*. Cleopatra (69–30 B.C.E.), queen of Egypt and heroine of Shakespeare's *Antony and Cleopatra*.
8. Doomed heroine of John Webster's *The Duchess of Malfi* (ca. 1613). Clytemnestra is the heroine of Aeschylus's *Agamemnon*

(458 B.C.E.). Antigone is the eponymous heroine of a 442 B.C.E. play by Sophocles. Phèdre is the heroine of Jean Racine's *Phèdre* (1677). Cressida, Rosalind, and Desdemona are heroines of Shakespeare's *Troilus and Cressida*, *As You Like It*, and *Othello*, respectively.
9. A character in Marcel Proust's *Remembrance of Things Past* (*The Guermantes Way*, 1920–21). Millamant is the heroine of William Congreve's satirical comedy *The Way of the World* (1700). Clarissa is the eponymous heroine of Samuel Richardson's seven-volume epistolary novel (1747–48). Becky Sharp appears in William Thackeray's *Vanity Fair* (1847–48). Anna Karenina is the title character in a Leo Tolstoy novel (1875–77). Emma Bovary is the heroine of Gustave Flaubert's *Madame Bovary* (1856).

extreme; as great as a man, some think even greater.[1] But this is woman in fiction. In fact, as Professor Trevelyan points out, she was locked up, beaten and flung about the room.

A very queer, composite being thus emerges. Imaginatively she is of the highest importance; practically she is completely insignificant. She pervades poetry from cover to cover; she is all but absent from history. She dominates the lives of kings and conquerors in fiction; in fact she was the slave of any boy whose parents forced a ring upon her finger. Some of the most inspired words, some of the most profound thoughts in literature fall from her lips; in real life she could hardly read, could scarcely spell, and was the property of her husband.

It was certainly an odd monster that one made up by reading the historians first and the poets afterwards—a worm winged like an eagle; the spirit of life and beauty in a kitchen chopping up suet. But these monsters, however amusing to the imagination, have no existence in fact. What one must do to bring her to life was to think poetically and prosaically at one and the same moment, thus keeping in touch with fact—that she is Mrs. Martin, aged thirty-six, dressed in blue, wearing a black hat and brown shoes; but not losing sight of fiction either—that she is a vessel in which all sorts of spirits and forces are coursing and flashing perpetually. The moment, however, that one tries this method with the Elizabethan woman, one branch of illumination fails; one is held up by the scarcity of facts. One knows nothing detailed, nothing perfectly true and substantial about her. History scarcely mentions her. And I turned to Professor Trevelyan again to see what history meant to him. I found by looking at his chapter headings that it meant—

"The Manor Court and the Methods of Open-field Agriculture . . . The Cistercians and Sheep-farming . . . The Crusades . . . The University . . . The House of Commons . . . The Hundred Years' War . . . The Wars of the Roses . . . The Renaissance Scholars . . . The Dissolution of the Monasteries . . . Agrarian and Religious Strife . . . The Origin of English Sea-power . . . The Armada . . ." and so on. Occasionally an individual woman is mentioned, an Elizabeth, or a Mary; a queen or a great lady. But by no possible means could middle-class women with nothing but brains and character at their command have taken part in any one of the great movements which, brought together, constitute the historian's view of the past. Nor shall we find her in any collection of anecdotes. Aubrey[2] hardly mentions her. She never writes her own life and scarcely keeps a diary; there are only a handful of her letters in existence. She left no plays or poems by

---

1. "It remains a strange and almost inexplicable fact that in Athena's city, where women were kept in almost Oriental suppression as odalisques or drudges, the stage should yet have produced figures like Clytemnestra and Cassandra, Atossa and Antigone, Phèdre and Medea, and all the other heroines who dominate play after play of the 'misogynist' Euripides. But the paradox of this world where in real life a respectable woman could hardly show her face alone in the street, and yet on the stage woman equals or surpasses man, has never been satisfactorily explained. In modern tragedy the same predominance exists. At all events, a very cursory survey of Shakespeare's work (similarly with Webster, though not with Marlowe or Jonson) suffices to reveal how this dominance, this initiative of women, persists from Rosalind to Lady Macbeth. So too in Racine; six of his tragedies bear their heroines' names; and what male characters of his shall we set against Hermione and Andromaque, Bérénice and Roxane, Phèdre and Athalie? So again with Ibsen; what men shall we match with Solveig and Nora, Hedda and Hilda Wangel and Rebecca West?"—F. L. Lucas, *Tragedy*, pp. 114–15 [Woolf's note].

2. John Aubrey (1626–1697), author of *Brief Lives*, which includes sketches of his famous contemporaries.

which we can judge her. What one wants, I thought—and why does not some brilliant student at Newnham or Girton[3] supply it?—is a mass of information; at what age did she marry; how many children had she as a rule; what was her house like; had she a room to herself; did she do the cooking; would she be likely to have a servant? All these facts lie somewhere, presumably, in parish registers and account books; the life of the average Elizabethan woman must be scattered about somewhere, could one collect it and make a book of it. It would be ambitious beyond my daring, I thought, looking about the shelves for books that were not there, to suggest to the students of those famous colleges that they should re-write history, though I own that it often seems a little queer as it is, unreal, lop-sided; but why should they not add a supplement to history? calling it, of course, by some inconspicuous name so that women might figure there without impropriety? For one often catches a glimpse of them in the lives of the great, whisking away into the background, concealing, I sometimes think, a wink, a laugh, perhaps a tear. And, after all, we have lives enough of Jane Austen; it scarcely seems necessary to consider again the influence of the tragedies of Joanna Baillie[4] upon the poetry of Edgar Allan Poe; as for myself, I should not mind if the homes and haunts of Mary Russell Mitford were closed to the public for a century at least. But what I find deplorable, I continued, looking about the bookshelves again, is that nothing is known about women before the eighteenth century. I have no model in my mind to turn about this way and that. Here am I asking why women did not write poetry in the Elizabethan age, and I am not sure how they were educated; whether they were taught to write; whether they had sitting-rooms to themselves; how many women had children before they were twenty-one; what, in short, they did from eight in the morning till eight at night. They had no money evidently; according to Professor Trevelyan they were married whether they liked it or not before they were out of the nursery, at fifteen or sixteen very likely. It would have been extremely odd, even upon this showing, had one of them suddenly written the plays of Shakespeare, I concluded, and I thought of that old gentleman, who is dead now, but was a bishop, I think, who declared that it was impossible for any woman, past, present, or to come, to have the genius of Shakespeare. He wrote to the papers about it. He also told a lady who applied to him for information that cats do not as a matter of fact go to heaven, though they have, he added, souls of a sort. How much thinking those old gentlemen used to save one! How the borders of ignorance shrank back at their approach! Cats do not go to heaven. Women cannot write the plays of Shakespeare.

Be that as it may, I could not help thinking, as I looked at the works of Shakespeare on the shelf, that the bishop was right at least in this; it would have been impossible, completely and entirely, for any woman to have written the plays of Shakespeare in the age of Shakespeare. Let me imagine, since facts are so hard to come by, what would have happened had Shakespeare had a wonderfully gifted sister, called Judith,[5] let us say. Shakespeare himself went, very probably— his mother was an heiress—to the grammar school, where he may have learnt

---

3. Woolf delivered her lectures at Newnham and Girton Colleges for women, part of Cambridge University since 1880 and 1873, respectively.

4. Joanna Baillie (1762–1851) was a poet and dramatist whose *Plays on the Passions* (1798–1812) were famous in her day.
5. The name of Shakespeare's younger daughter.

Latin—Ovid, Virgil and Horace[6]—and the elements of grammar and logic. He was, it is well known, a wild boy who poached rabbits, perhaps shot a deer, and had, rather sooner than he should have done, to marry a woman in the neighbourhood, who bore him a child rather quicker than was right. That escapade sent him to seek his fortune in London. He had, it seemed, a taste for the theatre; he began by holding horses at the stage door. Very soon he got work in the theatre, became a successful actor, and lived at the hub of the universe, meeting everybody, knowing everybody, practising his art on the boards, exercising his wits in the streets, and even getting access to the palace of the queen. Meanwhile his extraordinarily gifted sister, let us suppose, remained at home. She was as adventurous, as imaginative, as agog to see the world as he was. But she was not sent to school. She had no chance of learning grammar and logic, let alone of reading Horace and Virgil. She picked up a book now and then, one of her brother's perhaps, and read a few pages. But then her parents came in and told her to mend the stockings or mind the stew and not moon about with books and papers. They would have spoken sharply but kindly, for they were substantial people who knew the conditions of life for a woman and loved their daughter—indeed, more likely than not she was the apple of her father's eye. Perhaps she scribbled some pages up in an apple loft on the sly, but was careful to hide them or set fire to them. Soon, however, before she was out of her teens, she was to be betrothed to the son of a neighbouring wool-stapler.[7] She cried out that marriage was hateful to her, and for that she was severely beaten by her father. Then he ceased to scold her. He begged her instead not to hurt him, not to shame him in this matter of her marriage. He would give her a chain of beads or a fine petticoat, he said; and there were tears in his eyes. How could she disobey him? How could she break his heart? The force of her own gift alone drove her to it. She made up a small parcel of her belongings, let herself down by a rope one summer's night and took the road to London. She was not seventeen. The birds that sang in the hedge were not more musical than she was. She had the quickest fancy, a gift like her brother's, for the tune of words. Like him, she had a taste for the theatre. She stood at the stage door; she wanted to act, she said. Men laughed in her face. The manager—a fat, loose-lipped man—guffawed. He bellowed something about poodles dancing and women acting—no woman, he said, could possibly be an actress. He hinted—you can imagine what. She could get no training in her craft. Could she even seek her dinner in a tavern or roam the streets at midnight? Yet her genius was for fiction and lusted to feed abundantly upon the lives of men and women and the study of their ways. At last—for she was very young, oddly like Shakespeare the poet in her face, with the same grey eyes and rounded brows—at last Nick Greene[8] the actor-manager took pity on her; she found herself with child by that gentleman and so—who shall measure the heat and violence of the poet's heart when caught and tangled in a woman's body?—

---

6. Roman authors. Publius Ovidius Naso (43 B.C.E.–17 C.E.), author of the *Metamorphoses*. Publius Vergilius Maro (70–19 B.C.E.), author of the *Aeneid*. Quintus Horatius Flaccus (65–8 B.C.E.), author of *Odes* and satires.

7. A dealer in woolen goods, which were a "staple" or established type of merchandise.
8. A fictional character based on Shakespeare's contemporary Robert Greene (1558–1592) and appearing in Woolf's *Orlando*.

killed herself one winter's night and lies buried at some cross-roads where the omnibuses now stop outside the Elephant and Castle.[9]

That, more or less, is how the story would run, I think, if a woman in Shakespeare's day had had Shakespeare's genius. But for my part, I agree with the deceased bishop, if such he was—it is unthinkable that any woman in Shakespeare's day should have had Shakespeare's genius. For genius like Shakespeare's is not born among labouring, uneducated, servile people. It was not born in England among the Saxons and the Britons. It is not born today among the working classes. How, then, could it have been born among women whose work began, according to Professor Trevelyan, almost before they were out of the nursery, who were forced to it by their parents and held to it by all the power of law and custom? Yet genius of a sort must have existed among women as it must have existed among the working classes. Now and again an Emily Brontë or a Robert Burns[1] blazes out and proves its presence. But certainly it never got itself on to paper. When, however, one reads of a witch being ducked, of a woman possessed by devils, of a wise woman selling herbs, or even of a very remarkable man who had a mother, then I think we are on the track of a lost novelist, a suppressed poet, of some mute and inglorious[2] Jane Austen, some Emily Brontë who dashed her brains out on the moor or mopped and mowed about the highways crazed with the torture that her gift had put her to. Indeed, I would venture to guess that Anon, who wrote so many poems without signing them, was often a woman. It was a woman Edward Fitzgerald,[3] I think, suggested who made the ballads and the folk-songs, crooning them to her children, beguiling her spinning with them, or the length of the winter's night.

This may be true or it may be false—who can say?—but what is true in it, so it seemed to me, reviewing the story of Shakespeare's sister as I had made it, is that any woman born with a great gift in the sixteenth century would certainly have gone crazed, shot herself, or ended her days in some lonely cottage outside the village, half witch, half wizard, feared and mocked at. For it needs little skill in psychology to be sure that a highly gifted girl who had tried to use her gift for poetry would have been so thwarted and hindered by other people, so tortured and pulled asunder by her own contrary instincts, that she must have lost her health and sanity to a certainty. No girl could have walked to London and stood at a stage door and forced her way into the presence of actor-managers without doing herself a violence and suffering an anguish which may have been irrational—for chastity may be a fetish invented by certain societies for unknown reasons—but were none the less inevitable. Chastity had then, it has even now, a religious importance in a woman's life, and has so wrapped itself round with nerves and instincts that to cut it free and bring it to the light of day demands courage of the rarest. To have lived a free life in London in the sixteenth century would have meant for a woman who was poet and playwright a nervous stress and dilemma which might well have killed her. Had she survived, whatever she had written would have been twisted and deformed, issuing from

9. A popular London pub. "Cross-roads": suicides were commonly buried at crossroads.
1. Scottish poet (1759–1796).
2. A reference to Thomas Gray's line in *Elegy Written in a Country Churchyard* (1751): "Some mute inglorious Milton here may rest."
3. British author (1809–1883), known for his translation from the Persian of *The Rubáiyát of Omar Khayyám* (1859).

a strained and morbid imagination. And undoubtedly, I thought, looking at the shelf where there are no plays by women, her work would have gone unsigned. That refuge she would have sought certainly. It was the relic of the sense of chastity that dictated anonymity to women even so late as the nineteenth century. Currer Bell, George Eliot, George Sand,[4] all the victims of inner strife as their writings prove, sought ineffectively to veil themselves by using the name of a man. Thus they did homage to the convention, which if not implanted by the other sex was liberally encouraged by them (the chief glory of a woman is not to be talked of, said Pericles,[5] himself a much-talked-of man), that publicity in women is detestable. Anonymity runs in their blood. The desire to be veiled still possesses them. They are not even now as concerned about the health of their fame as men are, and, speaking generally, will pass a tombstone or a signpost without feeling an irresistible desire to cut their names on it, as Alf, Bert or Chas. must do in obedience to their instinct, which murmurs if it sees a fine woman go by, or even a dog, Ce chien est à moi.[6] And, of course, it may not be a dog, I thought, remembering Parliament Square, the Sièges Allée[7] and other avenues; it may be a piece of land or a man with curly black hair. It is one of the great advantages of being a woman that one can pass even a very fine negress without wishing to make an Englishwoman of her.

That woman, then, who was born with a gift of poetry in the sixteenth century, was an unhappy woman, a woman at strife against herself. All the conditions of her life, all her own instincts, were hostile to the state of mind which is needed to set free whatever is in the brain. But what is the state of mind that is most propitious to the act of creation, I asked. Can one come by any notion of the state that furthers and makes possible that strange activity? Here I opened the volume containing the Tragedies of Shakespeare. What was Shakespeare's state of mind, for instance, when he wrote Lear and Antony and Cleopatra? It was certainly the state of mind most favourable to poetry that there has ever existed. But Shakespeare himself said nothing about it. We only know casually and by chance that he "never blotted a line."[8] Nothing indeed was ever said by the artist himself about his state of mind until the eighteenth century perhaps. Rousseau[9] perhaps began it. At any rate, by the nineteenth century self-consciousness had developed so far that it was the habit for men of letters to describe their minds in confessions and autobiographies. Their lives also were written, and their letters were printed after their deaths. Thus, though we do not know what Shakespeare went through when he wrote Lear, we do know what Carlyle went through when he wrote the French Revolution; what Flaubert went through when he wrote Madame Bovary; what Keats[1] was going

---

4. Pseudonyms of Charlotte Brontë, Mary Ann Evans (1819–1880), and Lucile-Aurore Dupin (1804–1876), author of Lélia (1833), respectively.
5. From the Greek leader Pericles' funeral oration (431 B.C.E.). as reported in Thucydides' history of the Peloponnesian War (2.35–46).
6. This dog is mine (French); from the philosopher Blaise Pascal's Thoughts (1657–58). He uses an anecdote about poor children to illustrate a universal impulse to assert property claims.
7. An avenue in Berlin containing statues of Hohenzollern rulers. Parliament Square is in London next to the Houses of Parliament and Westminster Abbey.
8. Ben Jonson's (1572–1637) description of Shakespeare.
9. Jean-Jacques Rousseau (1712–1778), French author of the Confessions (1781).
1. John Keats (1795–1821), British poet. Thomas Carlyle (1795–1881), essayist and historian, translator of Goethe and author of The French Revolution (1837).

through when he tried to write poetry against the coming of death and the indifference of the world.

And one gathers from this enormous modern literature of confession and self-analysis that to write a work of genius is almost always a feat of prodigious difficulty. Everything is against the likelihood that it will come from the writer's mind whole and entire. Generally material circumstances are against it. Dogs will bark; people will interrupt; money must be made; health will break down. Further, accentuating all these difficulties and making them harder to bear is the world's notorious indifference. It does not ask people to write poems and novels and histories; it does not need them. It does not care whether Flaubert finds the right word or whether Carlyle scrupulously verifies this or that fact. Naturally, it will not pay for what it does not want. And so the writer, Keats, Flaubert, Carlyle, suffers, especially in the creative years of youth, every form of distraction and discouragement. A curse, a cry of agony, rises from those books of analysis and confession. "Mighty poets in their misery dead"[2]—that is the burden of their song. If anything comes through in spite of all this, it is a miracle, and probably no book is born entire and uncrippled as it was conceived.

But for women, I thought, looking at the empty shelves, these difficulties were infinitely more formidable. In the first place, to have a room of her own, let alone a quiet room or a sound-proof room, was out of the question, unless her parents were exceptionally rich or very noble, even up to the beginning of the nineteenth century. Since her pin money, which depended on the good will of her father, was only enough to keep her clothed, she was debarred from such alleviations as came even to Keats or Tennyson or Carlyle, all poor men, from a walking tour, a little journey to France, from the separate lodging which, even if it were miserable enough, sheltered them from the claims and tyrannies of their families. Such material difficulties were formidable; but much worse were the immaterial. The indifference of the world which Keats and Flaubert and other men of genius have found so hard to bear was in her case not indifference but hostility. The world did not say to her as it said to them, Write if you choose; it makes no difference to me. The world said with a guffaw, Write? What's the good of your writing? Here the psychologists of Newnham and Girton might come to our help, I thought, looking again at the blank spaces on the shelves. For surely it is time that the effect of discouragement upon the mind of the artist should be measured, as I have seen a dairy company measure the effect of ordinary milk and Grade A milk upon the body of the rat. They set two rats in cages side by side, and of the two one was furtive, timid and small, and the other was glossy, bold and big. Now what food do we feed women as artists upon? I asked, remembering, I suppose, that dinner of prunes and custard. To answer that question I had only to open the evening paper and to read that Lord Birkenhead is of opinion—but really I am not going to trouble to copy out Lord Birkenhead's opinion upon the writing of women. What Dean Inge says I will leave in peace. The Harley Street specialist may be allowed to rouse the echoes of Harley Street[3] with his vociferations without raising a hair on my head. I will quote, however, Mr. Oscar Browning,

2. From Wordsworth's "Resolution and Independence" (1807).

3. A London street known for its many prominent physicians.

because Mr. Oscar Browning was a great figure in Cambridge at one time, and used to examine the students at Girton and Newnham. Mr. Oscar Browning was wont to declare "that the impression left on his mind, after looking over any set of examination papers, was that, irrespective of the marks he might give, the best woman was intellectually the inferior of the worst man." After saying that Mr. Browning went back to his rooms—and it is this sequel that endears him and makes him a human figure of some bulk and majesty—he went back to his rooms and found a stable-boy lying on the sofa—"a mere skeleton, his cheeks were cavernous and sallow, his teeth were black, and he did not appear to have the full use of his limbs. . . .'That's Arthur' [said Mr. Browning]. 'He's a dear boy really and most high-minded.'" The two pictures always seem to me to complete each other. And happily in this age of biography the two pictures often do complete each other, so that we are able to interpret the opinions of great men not only by what they say, but by what they do.

But though this is possible now, such opinions coming from the lips of important people must have been formidable enough even fifty years ago. Let us suppose that a father from the highest motives did not wish his daughter to leave home and become writer, painter or scholar. "See what Mr. Oscar Browning says," he would say; and there was not only Mr. Oscar Browning; there was the *Saturday Review*; there was Mr. Greg[4]—the "essentials of a woman's being," said Mr. Greg emphatically, "are that *they are supported by, and they minister to, men*"—there was an enormous body of masculine opinion to the effect that nothing could be expected of women intellectually. Even if her father did not read out loud these opinions, any girl could read them for herself; and the reading, even in the nineteenth century, must have lowered her vitality, and told profoundly upon her work. There would always have been that assertion—you cannot do this, you are incapable of doing that—to protest against, to overcome. Probably for a novelist this germ is no longer of much effect; for there have been women novelists of merit. But for painters it must still have some sting in it; and for musicians, I imagine, is even now active and poisonous in the extreme. The woman composer stands where the actress stood in the time of Shakespeare. Nick Greene, I thought, remembering the story I had made about Shakespeare's sister, said that a woman acting put him in mind of a dog dancing. Johnson repeated the phrase two hundred years later of women preaching. And here, I said, opening a book about music, we have the very words used again in this year of grace, 1928, of women who try to write music. "Of Mlle. Germaine Tailleferre one can only repeat Dr. Johnson's dictum concerning a woman preacher, transposed into terms of music. 'Sir, a woman's composing is like a dog's walking on his hind legs. It is not done well, but you are surprised to find it done at all.'"[5] So accurately does history repeat itself.

Thus, I concluded, shutting Mr. Oscar Browning's life and pushing away the rest, it is fairly evident that even in the nineteenth century a woman was not encouraged to be an artist. On the contrary, she was snubbed, slapped,

4. William Rathbone Greg (1809–1891), cited from a *Saturday Review* essay entitled "Why Are Women Redundant" (1873).
5. *A Survey of Contemporary Music*, Cecil Gray, p. 246 [Woolf's note]. The statement is originally found in James Boswell's *Life of Johnson* (1791).

lectured and exhorted. Her mind must have been strained and her vitality lowered by the need of opposing this, of disproving that. For here again we come within range of that very interesting and obscure masculine complex which has had so much influence upon the woman's movement; that deep-seated desire, not so much that *she* shall be inferior as that *he* shall be superior, which plants him wherever one looks, not only in front of the arts, but barring the way to politics too, even when the risk to himself seems infinitesimal and the suppliant humble and devoted. Even Lady Bessborough,[6] I remembered, with all her passion for politics, must humbly bow herself and write to Lord Granville Leveson-Gower: ". . . notwithstanding all my violence in politics and talking so much on that subject, I perfectly agree with you that no woman has any business to meddle with that or any other serious business, farther than giving her opinion (if she is ask'd)." And so she goes on to spend her enthusiasm where it meets with no obstacle whatsoever upon that immensely important subject, Lord Granville's maiden speech in the House of Commons. The spectacle is certainly a strange one, I thought. The history of men's opposition to women's emancipation is more interesting perhaps than the story of that emancipation itself. An amusing book might be made of it if some young student at Girton or Newnham would collect examples and deduce a theory—but she would need thick gloves on her hands, and bars to protect her of solid gold.

But what is amusing now, I recollected, shutting Lady Bessborough, had to be taken in desperate earnest once. Opinions that one now pastes in a book labelled cock-a-doodle-dum and keeps for reading to select audiences on summer nights once drew tears, I can assure you. Among your grandmothers and great-grandmothers there were many that wept their eyes out. Florence Nightingale shrieked aloud in her agony.[7] Moreover, it is all very well for you, who have got yourselves to college and enjoy sitting-rooms—or is it only bed-sitting-rooms?—of your own to say that genius should disregard such opinions; that genius should be above caring what is said of it. Unfortunately, it is precisely the men or women of genius who mind most what is said of them. Remember Keats. Remember the words he had cut on his tombstone.[8] Think of Tennyson; think—but I need hardly multiply instances of the undeniable, if very, unfortunate, fact that it is the nature of the artist to mind excessively what is said about him. Literature is strewn with the wreckage of men who have minded beyond reason the opinions of others.

And this susceptibility of theirs is doubly unfortunate, I thought, returning again to my original enquiry into what state of mind is most propitious for creative work, because the mind of an artist, in order to achieve the prodigious effort of freeing whole and entire the work that is in him, must be incandescent, like Shakespeare's mind, I conjectured, looking at the book which lay

---

6. Henrietta, Countess of Bessborough (1761–1821), who corresponded with Lord Granville George Leveson-Gower (1815–1891), British foreign secretary in William Gladstone's administrations and after him the leader of the Liberal Party.
7. See *Cassandra*, by Florence Nightingale, printed in *The Cause*, by R. Strachey [Woolf's note]. Nightingale (1820–1910) was an English nurse and founder of nursing as a profession for women.
8. "Here lies one whose name was writ in water."

open at *Antony and Cleopatra*. There must be no obstacle in it, no foreign matter unconsumed.

For though we say that we know nothing about Shakespeare's state of mind, even as we say that, we are saying something about Shakespeare's state of mind. The reason perhaps why we know so little of Shakespeare—compared with Donne or Ben Jonson or Milton—is that his grudges and spites and antipathies are hidden from us. We are not held up by some "revelation" which reminds us of the writer. All desire to protest, to preach, to proclaim an injury, to pay off a score, to make the world the witness of some hardship or grievance was fired out of him and consumed. Therefore his poetry flows from him free and unimpeded. If ever a human being got his work expressed completely, it was Shakespeare. If ever a mind was incandescent, unimpeded, I thought, turning again to the bookcase, it was Shakespeare's mind.

1929

JORGE LUIS BORGES
1899–1986

In the briefest of short stories, Jorge Luis Borges created convincing fictional worlds: alternate universes that obey their own laws of time and causation and shed light on the peculiarities of our own world. Borges's favorite symbol of these imaginary settings was the labyrinth, and readers the world over have enjoyed being lost in the mazes Borges built from his thought experiments. To read one of Borges's stories is to enter a new reality, imagined with great concreteness as an extension of our own world yet bearing distinctive features of the universes of fantasy and science fiction.

Born in Buenos Aires, Argentina, on August 24, 1899, Borges grew up in a large house whose library and garden were to form an essential part of his imagination. His father, who was half-English, was an unsuccessful lawyer with philosophical and literary interests; he spent much of his son's childhood working on a novel that he eventually published in middle age. Borges's mother also had literary ambitions; she translated works by William Faulkner, **Franz Kafka**, and D. H. Lawrence into Spanish. Her family, which the young Borges idealized, included Argentine patriots who had fought for independence from Spain and in the civil wars of the nineteenth century. At home Borges spoke English with his father, his paternal grandmother, and his tutor. He read widely in English as well as Spanish; his first publication was a Spanish translation of a children's story by Oscar Wilde, which a Buenos Aires newspaper published when he was only nine years old. Later he would translate works by **Walt Whitman**, **James Joyce**, and others. He remained close to his mother all his life and lived with her until her death, when she was ninety-nine and he was seventy-five.

Borges's father suffered from eye troubles and traveled to Europe with his family in 1914 for an operation. The family was caught in Geneva at the outbreak of World War I. Borges attended secondary school in Switzerland, learning French, German, and Latin. After the war the family moved to Spain, where he associated with a group of young experimental poets known as the Ultraists. When he returned to his homeland in 1921, Borges founded the Argentinian Ultraists, and befriended and collaborated with other intellectuals and artists, including the philosopher Macedonio Fernandez and a younger writer, Adolfo Bioy Casares.

Around the time of his father's death, in 1938, Borges got his first job, as a librarian in a small municipal library. His workplace served as the basis for one of the first, and most famous, of his stories, partly inspired by Kafka, "The Library of Babel." Taking the format of an academic essay, it tells of an endless library whose mazelike, interlocking galleries contain not only all books ever written but all possible combinations of letters. Although the library is infinite, the books, many of them meaningless, are shelved at random and therefore useless.

Early in the twentieth century, Argentina was among the wealthiest Latin American countries, but it suffered during the Great Depression and the years of Juan Perón's military dictatorship that followed. Borges openly opposed the Perón regime and its Fascist tendencies, making his political views plain in his speeches and nonliterary writings, some of which circulated privately and were not published until after his death. His attitude did not go unnoticed. When Perón became president in 1946, his government removed Borges from the librarian's post that he had held since 1938 and offered him a job

as a chicken inspector. Borges refused the position and instead began teaching English and North American literature at the University of Buenos Aires. Having inherited weak eyes from his father, Borges suffered from increasingly poor vision in middle age; despite undergoing eight operations, he was forced eventually to dictate his work and to rely on his prodigious memory.

After the fall of Perón's regime in 1955, Borges was given the prestigious post of director of the National Library—in the same year that he became almost totally blind. When Perón's party returned to power, Borges opposed him, eventually supporting the military coup that overthrew the Peronists in 1976. His failure to recognize the autocratic character of the military government was a misjudgment that tarnished his image in his final years. Until his death, Borges lived in his beloved Buenos Aires, the city he had celebrated in his first volume of poetry.

The Garden of Forking Paths (1941), his first major collection, introduced Borges to a wider public as an idealist writer whose short stories subordinate character, scene, plot, and narration to a central concept, which is often a philosophical premise. Borges uses these ideas not didactically but as the starting point of fantastic elaborations that entertain and perplex readers—much like a challenging game or puzzle. In the immense labyrinth, or "garden of forking paths," that is Borges's world, images of mazes and infinite mirroring, of cyclical repetition and recall, leave the reader in a sort of hall of mirrors, unsure of what is reality and what is illusion. In *Borges and I* the author commented on the parallel existence of two Borgeses: the one who exists in his work (the one his readers know) and the warm, living identity felt by the man who sets pen to paper. "Little by little, I am giving over everything to him. . . . I do not know which one of us has written this page." Borges elaborated this notion by spinning out fictional identities and alternate realities. Disdaining the "psychological fakery" of realistic novels (the "draggy novel of characters"), he preferred art that calls attention to its own artificiality. He wrote many of his stories in the style of encyclopedia entries or historical essays, as in "The Garden of Forking Paths." Borges was fond, too, of detective stories (and wrote several of them), in which the search for an elusive explanation, the pursuit of intricately planted clues, matters more than the characters' recognizability. The author contrives an art of puzzles and discovery.

"The Garden of Forking Paths," the selection below, begins as a simple spy story purporting to reveal the hidden truth about a German bombing raid during World War I. Borges alludes to documented facts: the geographic setting of the town of Albert and the Ancre River; a famous Chinese novel that serves as Ts'ui Pên's proposed model; the *History of the World War (1914–1918)* published by B. H. Liddell Hart in 1934. Official history is undermined on the first page, however, both by the recently discovered confession of Dr. Yu Tsun and by his editor's suspiciously defensive footnote, which calls into question the work we are about to read. Although Borges presents the story as a historical document, he warns his readers that it contains interpretive traps. In fact, the story is far from simple—it is a complex labyrinth in which the reader may easily be misled.

Borges executes his detective story with the carefully planted clues traditional to the genre, such as the need to convey the name of a bombing target and the presence of a single bullet in a revolver. Yet halfway through, what started as a conventional spy story takes on bizarre spatial and temporal dimensions. Coincidences—those chance relationships that might well have had different outcomes—introduce the idea of forking paths, or choice between two routes, for history. By inventing an ancient Chinese text modeled on a labyrinth, Borges portrays the universe as a series of alternative versions of experience. An infinite number of worlds opens up—but only one is embodied in this particular story: Yu Tsun faces a dilemma that places his personal loyalties at odds with his military duty. Both the personal and the philosophical ramifications of this choice are at the center of Borges's story.

Just as the "forking paths" present alternative versions of experience, so too has Borges's reputation and influence led in various directions. Perceived by outsiders as a major Argentine writer and a forerunner of the magical realism of successive Latin American generations, he is seen by many Latin Americans as a primarily European writer, a precursor to postmodernism. A favorite of literary intellectuals, he has influenced the development of science fiction. In the labyrinth of contemporary literature, Borges's fictions open up many paths for later writers.

The Garden of Forking Paths[1]

On page 22 of Liddell Hart's *History of World War I* you will read that an attack against the Serre-Montauban line by thirteen British divisions (supported by 1,400 artillery pieces), planned for the 24th of July, 1916, had to be postponed until the morning of the 29th. The torrential rains, Captain Liddell Hart comments, caused this delay, an insignificant one, to be sure.

1. Translated by Donald A. Yates.

The following statement, dictated, reread and signed by Dr. Yu Tsun, former professor of English at the *Hochschule* at Tsingtao,[2] throws an unsuspected light over the whole affair. The first two pages of the document are missing.

". . . and I hung up the receiver. Immediately afterwards, I recognized the voice that had answered in German. It was that of Captain Richard Madden. Madden's presence in Viktor Runeberg's apartment meant the end of our anxieties and—but this seemed, *or should have seemed*, very secondary to me—also the end of our lives. It meant that Runeberg had been arrested or murdered.[3] Before the sun set on that day, I would encounter the same fate. Madden was implacable. Or rather, he was obliged to be so. An Irishman at the service of England, a man accused of laxity and perhaps of treason, how could he fail to seize and be thankful for such a miraculous opportunity: the discovery, capture, maybe even the death of two agents of the German Reich?[4] I went up to my room; absurdly I locked the door and threw myself on my back on the narrow iron cot. Through the window I saw the familiar roofs and the cloud-shaded six o'clock sun. It seemed incredible to me that that day without premonitions or symbols should be the one of my inexorable death. In spite of my dead father, in spite of having been a child in a symmetrical garden of Hai Feng, was I—now—going to die? Then I reflected that everything happens to a man precisely, precisely *now*. Centuries of centuries and only in the present do things happen; countless men in the air, on the face of the earth and the sea, and all that really is happening is happening to me . . . The almost intolerable recollection of Madden's horselike face banished these wanderings. In the midst of my hatred and terror (it means nothing to me now to speak of terror, now that I have mocked Richard Madden, now that my throat yearns for the noose) it occurred to me that that tumultuous and doubtless happy warrior did not suspect that I possessed the Secret. The name of the exact location of the new British artillery park on the River Ancre. A bird streaked across the gray sky and blindly I translated it into an airplane and that airplane into many (against the French sky) annihilating the artillery station with vertical bombs. If only my mouth, before a bullet shattered it, could cry out that secret name so it could be heard in Germany . . . My human voice was very weak. How might I make it carry to the ear of the Chief? To the ear of that sick and hateful man who knew nothing of Runeberg and me save that we were in Stafford shire[5] and who was waiting in vain for our report in his arid office in Berlin, endlessly examining newspapers . . . I said out loud: *I must flee*. I sat up noiselessly, in a useless perfection of silence, as if Madden were already lying in wait for me. Something—perhaps the mere vain ostentation of proving my resources were nil—made me look through my pockets. I found what I knew I would find. The American watch, the nickel chain and the square coin, the key ring with the incriminating useless keys to Runeberg's apartment, the notebook, a letter which I resolved to destroy immediately (and which I did not destroy), a

2. Or Ch'ing-tao; a major port in east China, part of territory leased to (and developed by) Germany in 1898. "Hochschule": university (German).
3. "A hypothesis both hateful and odd. The Prussian spy Hans Rabener, alias Viktor Runeberg, attacked with drawn automatic the bearer of the warrant for his arrest, Captain Richard Madden. The latter, in self-defense, inflicted the wound which brought about Runeberg's death [Editor's note]." This entire note is by Borges as "Editor."
4. Empire (German).
5. County in west-central England.

crown, two shillings and a few pence, the red and blue pencil, the handkerchief, the revolver with one bullet. Absurdly, I took it in my hand and weighed it in order to inspire courage within myself. Vaguely I thought that a pistol report can be heard at a great distance. In ten minutes my plan was perfected. The telephone book listed the name of the only person capable of transmitting the message; he lived in a suburb of Fenton,[6] less than a half hour's train ride away.

I am a cowardly man. I say it now, now that I have carried to its end a plan whose perilous nature no one can deny. I know its execution was terrible. I didn't do it for Germany, no. I care nothing for a barbarous country which imposed upon me the abjection of being a spy. Besides, I know of a man from England—a modest man—who for me is no less great than Goethe.[7] I talked with him for scarcely an hour, but during that hour he was Goethe . . . I did it because I sensed that the Chief somehow feared people of my race—for the innumerable ancestors who merge within me. I wanted to prove to him that a yellow man could save his armies. Besides, I had to flee from Captain Madden. His hands and his voice could call at my door at any moment. I dressed silently, bade farewell to myself in the mirror, went downstairs, scrutinized the peaceful street and went out. The station was not far from my home, but I judged it wise to take a cab. I argued that in this way I ran less risk of being recognized; the fact is that in the deserted street I felt myself visible and vulnerable, infinitely so. I remember that I told the cab driver to stop a short distance before the main entrance. I got out with voluntary, almost painful slowness; I was going to the village of Ashgrove but I bought a ticket for a more distant station. The train left within a very few minutes, at eight-fifty. I hurried; the next one would leave at nine-thirty. There was hardly a soul on the platform. I went through the coaches; I remember a few farmers, a woman dressed in mourning, a young boy who was reading with fervor the *Annals* of Tacitus,[8] a wounded and happy soldier. The coaches jerked forward at last. A man whom I recognized ran in vain to the end of the platform. It was Captain Richard Madden. Shattered, trembling, I shrank into the far corner of the seat, away from the dreaded window.

From this broken state I passed into an almost abject felicity. I told myself that the duel had already begun and that I had won the first encounter by frustrating, even if for forty minutes, even if by a stroke of fate, the attack of my adversary. I argued that this slightest of victories foreshadowed a total victory. I argued (no less fallaciously) that my cowardly felicity proved that I was a man capable of carrying out the adventure successfully. From this weakness I took strength that did not abandon me. I foresee that man will resign himself each day to more atrocious undertakings; soon there will be no one but warriors and brigands; I give them this counsel: *The author of an atrocious undertaking ought to imagine that he has already accomplished it, ought to impose upon himself a future as irrevocable as the past.* Thus I proceeded as my eyes of a man

---

6. In Lincolnshire, a county in east England.
7. Johann Wolfgang von Goethe (1749–1832), German poet, novelist, and dramatist; author of *Faust*; often taken as representing the peak of German cultural achievement.

8. Cornelius Tacitus (55–117). Roman historian whose *Annals* give a vivid picture of the decadence and corruption of the Roman Empire under Tiberius, Claudius, and Nero.

already dead registered the elapsing of that day, which was perhaps the last, and the diffusion of the night. The train ran gently along, amid ash trees. It stopped, almost in the middle of the fields. No one announced the name of the station. "Ashgrove?" I asked a few lads on the platform. "Ashgrove," they replied. I got off.

A lamp enlightened the platform but the faces of the boys were in shadow. One questioned me, "Are you going to Dr. Stephen Albert's house?" Without waiting for my answer, another said, "The house is a long way from here, but you won't get lost if you take this road to the left and at every crossroads turn again to your left." I tossed them a coin (my last), descended a few stone steps and started down the solitary road. It went downhill, slowly. It was of elemental earth; overhead the branches were tangled; the low, full moon seemed to accompany me.

For an instant, I thought that Richard Madden in some way had penetrated my desperate plan. Very quickly, I understood that that was impossible. The instructions to turn always to the left reminded me that such was the common procedure for discovering the central point of certain labyrinths. I have some understanding of labyrinths: not for nothing am I the great grandson of that Ts'ui Pên who was governor of Yunnan and who renounced worldly power in order to write a novel that might be even more populous than the *Hung Lu Meng*[9] and to construct a labyrinth in which all men would become lost. Thirteen years he dedicated to these heterogeneous tasks, but the hand of a stranger murdered him—and his novel was incoherent and no one found the labyrinth. Beneath English trees I meditated on that lost maze: I imagined it inviolate and perfect at the secret crest of a mountain; I imagined it erased by rice fields or beneath the water; I imagined it infinite, no longer composed of octagonal kiosks and returning paths, but of rivers and provinces and kingdoms . . . I thought of a labyrinth of labyrinths, of one sinuous spreading labyrinth that would encompass the past and the future and in some way involve the stars. Absorbed in these illusory images, I forgot my destiny of one pursued. I felt myself to be, for an unknown period of time, an abstract perceiver of the world. The vague, living countryside, the moon, the remains of the day worked on me, as well as the slope of the road which eliminated any possibility of weariness. The afternoon was intimate, infinite. The road descended and forked among the now confused meadows. A high-pitched, almost syllabic music approached and receded in the shifting of the wind, dimmed by leaves and distance. I thought that a man can be an enemy of other men, of the moments of other men, but not of a country: not of fireflies, words, gardens, streams of water, sunsets. Thus I arrived before a tall, rusty gate. Between the iron bars I made out a poplar grove and a pavilion. I understood suddenly two things, the first trivial, the second almost unbelievable: the music came from the pavilion, and the music was Chinese. For precisely that reason I had openly accepted it without paying it any heed. I do not remember whether there was a bell or whether I knocked with my hand. The sparkling of the music continued.

From the rear of the house within a lantern approached: a lantern that the trees sometimes striped and sometimes eclipsed, a paper lantern that had the

9. *The Dream of the Red Chamber* (1791) by Ts'ao Hsüeh-ch'in; the most famous Chinese novel, a love story and panorama of Chinese family life involving more than 430 characters.

form of a drum and the color of the moon. A tall man bore it. I didn't see his face for the light blinded me. He opened the door and said slowly, in my own language: "I see that the pious Hsi P'êng persists in correcting my solitude. You no doubt wish to see the garden?"

I recognized the name of one of our consuls and I replied, disconcerted, "The garden?"

"The garden of forking paths."

Something stirred in my memory and I uttered with incomprehensible certainty, "The garden of my ancestor Ts'ui Pên."

"Your ancestor? Your illustrious ancestor? Come in."

The damp path zigzagged like those of my childhood. We came to a library of Eastern and Western books. I recognized bound in yellow silk several volumes of the Lost Encyclopedia, edited by the Third Emperor of the Luminous Dynasty but never printed.[1] The record on the phonograph revolved next to a bronze phoenix. I also recall a *famille rose*[2] vase and another, many centuries older, of that shade of blue which our craftsmen copied from the potters of Persia . . .

Stephen Albert observed me with a smile. He was, as I have said, very tall, sharp-featured, with gray eyes and a gray beard. He told me that he had been a missionary in Tientsin "before aspiring to become a Sinologist."

We sat down—I on a long, low divan, he with his back to the window and a tall circular clock. I calculated that my pursuer, Richard Madden, could not arrive for at least an hour. My irrevocable determination could wait.

"An astounding fate, that of Ts'ui Pên," Stephen Albert said. "Governor of his native province, learned in astronomy, in astrology and in the tireless interpretation of the canonical books, chess player, famous poet and calligrapher— he abandoned all this in order to compose a book and a maze. He renounced the pleasures of both tyranny and justice, of his populous couch, of his banquets and even of erudition—all to close himself up for thirteen years in the Pavilion of the Limpid Solitude. When he died, his heirs found nothing save chaotic manuscripts. His family, as you may be aware, wished to condemn them to the fire; but his executor—a Taoist or Buddhist monk—insisted on their publication."

"We descendants of Ts'ui Pên," I replied, "continue to curse that monk. Their publication was senseless. The book is an indeterminate heap of contradictory drafts. I examined it once: in the third chapter the hero dies, in the fourth he is alive. As for the other undertaking of Ts'ui Pên, his labyrinth . . ."

"Here is Ts'ui Pên's labyrinth," he said, indicating a tall lacquered desk.

"An ivory labyrinth!" I exclaimed. "A minimum labyrinth."

"A labyrinth of symbols," he corrected. "An invisible labyrinth of time. To me, a barbarous Englishman, has been entrusted the revelation of this diaphanous mystery. After more than a hundred years, the details are irretrievable;

---

1. The Yung-lo emperor of the Ming ("bright") Dynasty commissioned a massive encyclopedia between 1403 and 1408. A single copy of the 11,095 manuscript volumes was made in the mid-1500s; the original was later destroyed, and only 370 volumes of the copy remain today.

2. Pink family (French); refers to a Chinese decorative enamel ranging in color from an opaque pink to purplish rose. *Famille rose* pottery was at its best during the reign of Yung Chên (1723–1735).

but it is not hard to conjecture what happened. Ts'ui Pên must have said once: *I am withdrawing to write a book.* And another time: *I am withdrawing to construct a labyrinth.* Every one imagined two works; to no one did it occur that the book and the maze were one and the same thing. The Pavilion of the Limpid Solitude stood in the center of a garden that was perhaps intricate; that circumstance could have suggested to the heirs a physical labyrinth. Ts'ui Pên died; no one in the vast territories that were his came upon the labyrinth; the confusion of the novel suggested to me that *it* was the maze. Two circumstances gave me the correct solution of the problem. One: the curious legend that Ts'ui Pên had planned to create a labyrinth which would be strictly infinite. The other: a fragment of a letter I discovered."

Albert rose. He turned his back on me for a moment; he opened a drawer of the black and gold desk. He faced me and in his hands he held a sheet of paper that had once been crimson, but was now pink and tenuous and cross-sectioned. The fame of Ts'ui Pên as a calligrapher had been justly won. I read, uncomprehendingly and with fervor, these words written with a minute brush by a man of my blood: *I leave to the various futures (not to all) my garden of forking paths.* Wordlessly, I returned the sheet. Albert continued:

"Before unearthing this letter, I had questioned myself about the ways in which a book can be infinite. I could think of nothing other than a cyclic volume, a circular one. A book whose last page was identical with the first, a book which had the possibility of continuing indefinitely. I remembered too that night which is at the middle of the Thousand and One Nights when Scheherazade[3] (through a magical oversight of the copyist) begins to relate word for word the story of the Thousand and One Nights, establishing the risk of coming once again to the night when she must repeat it, and thus on to infinity. I imagined as well a Platonic, hereditary work, transmitted from father to son, in which each new individual adds a chapter or corrects with pious care the pages of his elders. These conjectures diverted me; but none seemed to correspond, not even remotely, to the contradictory chapters of Ts'ui Pên. In the midst of this perplexity, I received from Oxford the manuscript you have examined. I lingered, naturally, on the sentence: *I leave to the various futures (not to all) my garden of forking paths.* Almost instantly, I understood: 'The garden of forking paths' was the chaotic novel; the phrase 'the various futures (not to all)' suggested to me the forking in time, not in space. A broad rereading of the work confirmed the theory. In all fictional works, each time a man is confronted with several alternatives, he chooses one and eliminates the others; in the fiction of Ts'ui Pên, he chooses—simultaneously—all of them. *He creates,* in this way, diverse futures, diverse times which themselves also proliferate and fork. Here, then, is the explanation of the novel's contradictions. Fang, let us say, has a secret; a stranger calls at his door; Fang resolves to kill him. Naturally, there are several possible outcomes: Fang can kill the intruder, the intruder can kill Fang, they both can escape, they both can die, and so forth. In the work of Ts'ui Pên, all possible outcomes occur; each one is the point of

---

3. The narrator of the collection also known as the *Arabian Nights*, a thousand and one tales supposedly told by Scheherazade to her husband, Shahrayar, king of Samarkand, to postpone her execution.

departure for other forkings. Sometimes, the paths of this labyrinth converge: for example, you arrive at this house, but in one of the possible pasts you are my enemy, in another, my friend. If you will resign yourself to my incurable pronunciation, we shall read a few pages."

His face, within the vivid circle of the lamplight, was unquestionably that of an old man, but with something unalterable about it, even immortal. He read with slow precision two versions of the same epic chapter. In the first, an army marches to a battle across a lonely mountain; the horror of the rocks and shadows makes the men undervalue their lives and they gain an easy victory. In the second, the same army traverses a palace where a great festival is taking place; the resplendent battle seems to them a continuation of the celebration and they win the victory. I listened with proper veneration to these ancient narratives, perhaps less admirable in themselves than the fact that they had been created by my blood and were being restored to me by a man of a remote empire, in the course of a desperate adventure, on a Western isle. I remember the last words, repeated in each version like a secret commandment: *Thus fought the heroes, tranquil their admirable hearts, violent their swords, resigned to kill and to die.*

From that moment on, I felt about me and within my dark body an invisible, intangible swarming. Not the swarming of the divergent, parallel and finally coalescent armies, but a more inaccessible, more intimate agitation that they in some manner prefigured. Stephen Albert continued:

"I don't believe that your illustrious ancestor played idly with these variations. I don't consider it credible that he would sacrifice thirteen years to the infinite execution of a rhetorical experiment. In your country, the novel is a subsidiary form of literature; in Ts'ui Pên's time it was a despicable form. Ts'ui Pên was a brilliant novelist, but he was also a man of letters who doubtless did not consider himself a mere novelist. The testimony of his contemporaries proclaims—and his life fully confirms—his metaphysical and mystical interests. Philosophic controversy usurps a good part of the novel. I know that of all problems, none disturbed him so greatly nor worked upon him so much as the abysmal problem of time. Now then, the latter is the only problem that does not figure in the pages of the *Garden*. He does not even use the word that signifies *time*. How do you explain this voluntary omission?"

I proposed several solutions—all unsatisfactory. We discussed them. Finally, Stephen Albert said to me:

"In a riddle whose answer is chess, what is the only prohibited word?"

I thought a moment and replied, "The word *chess*."

"Precisely," said Albert. "*The Garden of Forking Paths* is an enormous riddle, or parable, whose theme is time; this recondite cause prohibits its mention. To omit a word always, to resort to inept metaphors and obvious periphrases, is perhaps the most emphatic way of stressing it. That is the tortuous method preferred, in each of the meanderings of his indefatigable novel, by the oblique Ts'ui Pên. I have compared hundreds of manuscripts, I have corrected the errors that the negligence of the copyists has introduced, I have guessed the plan of this chaos, I have re-established—I believe I have re-established—the primordial organization, I have translated the entire work: it is clear to me that not once does he employ the word 'time.' The explanation is obvious: *The Garden of Forking Paths* is an incomplete, but not false, image of the universe as Ts'ui Pên conceived it. In contrast to Newton and Schopenhauer,[4] your ancestor did not believe in a uniform, absolute time. He believed in an infinite series of times, in a growing, dizzying net of divergent, convergent and parallel times. This network of times which approached one another, forked, broke off, or were unaware of one another for centuries, embraces *all* possibilities of time. We do not exist in the majority of these times; in some you exist, and not I; in others I, and not you; in others, both of us. In the present one, which a favorable fate has granted me, you have arrived at my house; in another, while crossing the garden, you found me dead; in still another, I utter these same words, but I am a mistake, a ghost."

"In every one," I pronounced, not without a tremble to my voice, "I am grateful to you and revere you for your re-creation of the garden of Ts'ui Pên."

"Not in all," he murmured with a smile. "Time forks perpetually toward innumerable futures. In one of them I am your enemy."

Once again I felt the swarming sensation of which I have spoken. It seemed to me that the humid garden that surrounded the house was infinitely saturated with invisible persons. Those persons were Albert and I, secret, busy and multiform in other dimensions of time. I raised my eyes and the tenuous nightmare dissolved. In the yellow and black garden there was only one man; but this man was as strong as a statue . . . this man was approaching along the path and he was Captain Richard Madden.

"The future already exists," I replied, "but I am your friend. Could I see the letter again?"

Albert rose. Standing tall, he opened the drawer of the tall desk; for the moment his back was to me. I had readied the revolver. I fired with extreme caution. Albert fell uncomplainingly, immediately. I swear his death was instantaneous—a lightning stroke.

The rest is unreal, insignificant. Madden broke in, arrested me. I have been condemned to the gallows. I have won out abominably; I have communicated to Berlin the secret name of the city they must attack. They bombed it yesterday; I read it in the same papers that offered to England the mystery of the learned Sinologist Stephen Albert who was murdered by a stranger, one Yu Tsun. The Chief had deciphered this mystery. He knew my problem was to indicate (through the uproar of the war) the city called Albert, and that I had found no other means to do so than to kill a man of that name. He does not know (no one can know) my innumerable contrition and weariness.

For Victoria Ocampo

1941

---

4. German philosopher (1788–1860), whose concept of will proceeded from a concept of the self as enduring through time. In *Seven Conversations with Jorge Luis Borges*, Borges also comments on Schopenhauer's interest in the "oneiric [dreamlike] essence of life." Newton (1642–1727), English mathematician and philosopher best known for his formulation of laws of gravitation and motion.

ZHANG AILING

1920–1995

In many ways the case of Zhang Ailing embodies the complexities and historical twists of a national literature finding its place in a global community—in this case, the literature of a nation with an immense, intellectually vibrant diaspora. Often acclaimed as the best Chinese writer of the mid-twentieth century, Zhang Ailing was recovered from a period of obscurity by a Chinese professor at Yale University. Zhang's fame then spread to Taiwan and Hong Kong, and at last to China itself. Although the literary work on which her fame rests was written in China and Hong Kong, Zhang Ailing herself lived more than half her life in the United States, and her best-known novel, *The Rice-Sprout Song*, from her second residence in Hong Kong, was written first in English and then rewritten in Chinese.

Zhang Ailing was born in Shanghai into an old family of imperial officialdom, with an irascible, opium-smoking father and a mother who left to study in France when Zhang Ailing was a child; thus the girl's family background combined the decadence and fierce independence of spirit of the Shanghai elite in the 1920s and 1930s. After her parents divorced, Zhang was mistreated by her father and fled his house to live with her mother. When the war in China broke out (1941), she left Shanghai to study at the University of Hong Kong; but after the fall of Hong Kong to the Japanese, Zhang returned to Shanghai, where, under Japanese occupation, she wrote her most famous shorter works. Her marriage, albeit brief, to the collaborator Hu Lancheng and her passive acceptance of Japanese rule made her suspect after the

war, and her family background placed her in an even more uncomfortable position when the Communists took Shanghai and the People's Republic of China was established. In 1952 Zhang went again to Hong Kong, where she put her talent at the service of the anti-Communist passions of the era. There she wrote two novels, both critical of the People's Republic: *The Rice-Sprout Song*, which enjoyed a modest success, and *Naked Earth*, which did not. In 1955 she left for the United States. After remarriage and the death of her second husband, Zhang went to Berkeley as a researcher and at last to Los Angeles, where she lived her last days in bleak austerity.

Far more than her novels, her stories from the 1940s, collected as *Tales* (sometimes translated as *Romances*), form the core of her work. One of the best known, a novella later turned into a novel, *The Golden Cangue*, describes a woman who must choose between love and financial advantage; her choice of the latter eventually destroys her and those around her, including her children. In addition to the stories and novels, Zhang Ailing wrote essays and memoirs that are much admired; she also did scholarly work on the *Story of the Stone* and an annotated translation of a late Qing novel, in Wu dialect, into Mandarin Chinese.

Zhang is sometimes called a postmodern writer, both for her experimental approach toward language and narrative structure and for her interest in unsettling and unmasking the discourses of modernity. Her fiction is infused with an atmosphere of desolation at odds with the optimism of the narratives of progress and revolutionary success. Her persistent focus on the trivial, the private feeling, the humble detail can be understood as a rejection of the nation-building myths that many of her contemporaries strove to develop.

The story selected here, "Sealed Off" (1943), opens in the city of Shanghai, the buzzing center of Chinese commercial life, technology, and urban activity. The images of geometric abstraction, with the parallel lines of the tramcar tracks extending seemingly into infinity, and even the air siren telegraphing a pattern of "cold little dots," suggest a rigid and rationalized world, a glowing plane along which the human tokens move in perfect, unending formation. But in shutting down the city, forcing buildings to seal their doors, the streets to clear of pedestrians, and even the tramcar to loiter on its tracks, the air siren imposes an unexpected calm on the metropolis. (The story takes place during the Second World War, when air sirens were a common feature of city life.) Sitting in enforced quietude, the citizens in the tramcar begin to ruminate, ponder, and dream: a groan of complaint, a meditation on food, a fantasy of romance. The narrative voice, too, enters a heavy, dreamlike mode. When the all-clear finally sounds and the hum of the metropolis resumes,

a central character, who has been venturing a cautious flirtation with another passenger, is jolted into an awareness that the possibilities unfolding "while the city was sealed off" cannot belong to real life. Yet a form of life did surface: however fleetingly, the governing grid was locked in stasis, enabling a different kind of humanity to emerge.

The story's genre is psychological fiction, though not in the usual sense of entering directly into the thoughts of characters (although this does happen). Instead, the emphasis lies on the roiling, sensuous unconscious of the city, where the submerged desires and dreams of Shanghai's populace oppose the ruthlessness of the social order. Readers may detect the influence, through various postwar British writers, of Freud, with his stress on the unconscious and the irrational. Zhang's concern as a writer, she said, was not History with a capital H: "I cannot write what is commonly known as the memorials of the times, and I have no intention of attempting it, because there seems at present no such concentration of subject matter. I only write some little things between men and women; also there are no wars or revolution in my works, for I believe that a man is both simpler and freer when he is in love than when he is in war or revolution."

Sealed Off[1]

The tramcar driver drove his tram. The tramcar tracks, in the blazing sun, shimmered like two shiny eels crawling out of the water; they stretched and shrank, stretched and shrank, on their onward way—soft and slippery, long old eels, never ending, never ending . . . the driver fixed his eyes on the undulating tracks, and didn't go mad.

1. Translated by Karen Kingsbury.

If there hadn't been an air raid,[2] if the city hadn't been sealed, the tramcar would have gone on forever. The city was sealed. The alarm-bell rang. Ding-ding-ding-ding. Every "ding" was a cold little dot, the dots all adding up to a dotted line, cutting across time and space.

The tramcar ground to a halt, but the people on the street ran: those on the left side of the street ran over to the right, and those on the right ran over to the left. All the shops, in a single sweep, rattled down their metal gates. Matrons tugged madly at the railings. "Let us in for just a while," they cried. "We have children here, and old people!" But the gates stayed tightly shut. Those inside the metal gates and those outside the metal gates stood glaring at each other, fearing one another.

Inside the tram, people were fairly quiet. They had somewhere to sit, and though the place was rather plain, it still was better, for most of them, than what they had at home. Gradually, the street also grew quiet: not that it was a complete silence, but the sound of voices eased into a confused blur, like the soft rustle of a straw-stuffed pillow, heard in a dream. The huge, shambling city sat dozing in the sun, its head resting heavily on people's shoulders, its spittle slowly dripping down their shirts, an inconceivably enormous weight pressing down on everyone. Never before, it seemed, had Shanghai been this quiet—and in the middle of the day! A beggar, taking advantage of the breathless, birdless quiet, lifted up his voice and began to chant: "Good master, good lady, kind sir, kind ma'am, won't you give alms to this poor man? Good master, good lady . . ." But after a short while he stopped, scared silent by the eerie quiet.

Then there was a braver beggar, a man from Shandong,[3] who firmly broke the silence. His voice was round and resonant: "Sad, sad, sad! No money do I have!" An old, old song, sung from one century to the next. The tram driver, who also was from Shandong, succumbed to the sonorous tune. Heaving a long sigh, he folded his arms across his chest, leaned against the tram door, and joined in: "Sad, sad, sad! No money do I have!"

Some of the tram passengers got out. But there was still a little loose, scattered chatter; near the door, a group of office workers was discussing something. One of them, with a quick, ripping sound, shook his fan open and offered his conclusion: "Well, in the end, there's nothing wrong with him—it's just that he doesn't know how to act." From another nose came a short grunt, followed by a cold smile: "Doesn't know how to act? He sure knows how to toady up to the bosses!"

A middle-aged couple who looked very much like brother and sister stood together in the middle of the tram, holding onto the leather straps. "Careful!" the woman suddenly yelped. "Don't get your trousers dirty!" The man flinched, then slowly raised the hand from which a packet of smoked fish dangled. Very cautiously, very gingerly, he held the paper packet, which was brimming with oil, several inches away from his suit pants. His wife did not let up. "Do you

2. The Japanese frequently bombed Shanghai during the Second Sino-Japanese War (1937–45), which became part of the Second World War (1939–45).
3. A region in eastern China, located to the north of Shanghai.

know what dry-cleaning costs these days? Or what it costs to get a pair of trousers made?"

Lu Zongzhen, accountant for Huamao Bank, was sitting in the corner. When he saw the smoked fish, he was reminded of the steamed dumplings stuffed with spinach that his wife had asked him to buy at a noodle stand near the bank. Women are always like that. Dumplings bought in the hardest-to-find, most twisty-windy little alleys had to be the best, no matter what. She didn't for a moment think of how it would be for him—neatly dressed in suit and tie, with tortoiseshell eyeglasses and a leather briefcase, then, tucked under his arm, these steaming hot dumplings wrapped in newspaper—how ludicrous! Still, if the city were sealed for a long time, so that his dinner was delayed, then he could at least make do with the dumplings.

He glanced at his watch; only four-thirty. Must be the power of suggestion. He felt hungry already. Carefully pulling back a corner of the paper, he took a look inside. Snowy white mounds, breathing soft little whiffs of sesame oil. A piece of newspaper had stuck to the dumplings, and he gravely peeled it off; the ink was printed on the dumplings, with all the writing in reverse, as though it were reflected in a mirror. He peered down and slowly picked the words out: "Obituaries . . . Positions Wanted . . . Stock Market Developments . . . Now Playing . . ." Normal, useful phrases, but they did look a bit odd on a dumpling. Maybe because eating is such serious business; compared to it, everything else is just a joke. Lu Zongzhen thought it looked funny, but he didn't laugh: he was a very straightforward kind of fellow. After reading the dumplings, he read the newspaper, but when he'd finished half a page of old news, he found that if he turned the page all the dumplings would fall out, and so he had to stop.

While Lu read the paper, others in the tram did likewise. People who had newspapers read them; those without newspapers read receipts, or lists of rules and regulations, or business cards. People who were stuck without a single scrap of printed matter read shop signs along the street. They simply had to fill this terrifying emptiness—otherwise, their brains might start to work. Thinking is a painful business.

Sitting across from Lu Zongzhen was an old man who, with a dull clacking sound, rolled two slippery, glossy walnuts in his palm: a rhythmic little gesture can substitute for thought. The old man had a clean-shaven pate, a reddish yellow complexion, and an oily sheen on his face. When his brows were furrowed, his head looked like a walnut. The thoughts inside were walnut-flavored: smooth and sweet, but in the end, empty-tasting.

To the old man's right sat Wu Cuiyuan, who looked like one of those young Christian wives, though she was still unmarried. Her Chinese gown of white cotton was trimmed with a narrow blue border—the navy blue around the white reminded one of the black borders around an obituary—and she carried a little blue-and-white checked parasol. Her hairstyle was utterly banal, so as not to attract attention. Actually, she hadn't much reason to fear. She wasn't bad-looking, but hers was an uncertain, unfocused beauty, an afraid-she-had-offended-someone kind of beauty. Her face was bland, slack, lacking definition. Even her own mother couldn't say for certain whether her face was long or round.

At home she was a good daughter, at school she was a good student. After graduating from college, Cuiyuan had become an English instructor at her alma mater. Now, stuck in the air raid, she decided to grade a few papers while she waited. The first one was written by a male student. It railed against the evils of the big city, full of righteous anger, the prose stiff, choppy, ungrammatical. "Painted prostitutes . . . cruising the Cosmo . . . low-class bars and dancing-halls." Cuiyuan paused for a moment, then pulled out her red pencil and gave the paper an "A." Ordinarily, she would have gone right on to the next one, but now, because she had too much time to think, she couldn't help wondering why she had given this student such a high mark. If she hadn't asked herself this question, she could have ignored the whole matter, but once she did ask, her face suffused with red. Suddenly, she understood: it was because this student was the only man who fearlessly and forthrightly said such things to her.

He treated her like an intelligent, sophisticated person; as if she were a man, someone who really understood. He respected her. Cuiyuan always felt that no one at school respected her—from the president on down to the professors, the students, even the janitors. The students' grumbling was especially hard to take: "This place is really falling apart. Getting worse every day. It's bad enough having to learn English from a Chinese, but then to learn it from a Chinese who's never gone abroad . . ." Cuiyuan took abuse at school, took abuse at home. The Wu household was a modern, model household, devout and serious. The family had pushed their daughter to study hard, to climb upwards step by step, right to the tip-top . . . A girl in her twenties teaching at a university! It set a record for women's professional achievement. But her parents' enthusiasm began to wear thin and now they wished she hadn't been quite so serious, wished she'd taken more time out from her studies, tried to find herself a rich husband.

She was a good daughter, a good student. All the people in her family were good people; they took baths every day and read the newspaper; when they listened to the wireless, they never tuned into local folk-opera, comic opera, that sort of thing, but listened only to the symphonies of Beethoven and Wagner; they didn't understand what they were listening to, but still they listened. In this world, there are more good people than real people . . . Cuiyuan wasn't very happy.

Life was like the Bible, translated from Hebrew into Greek, from Greek into Latin, from Latin into English, from English into Chinese. When Cuiyuan read it, she translated the standard Chinese into Shanghainese. Gaps were unavoidable.

She put the student's essay down and buried her chin in her hands. The sun burned down on her backbone.

Next to her sat a nanny with a small child lying on her lap. The sole of the child's foot pushed against Cuiyuan's leg. Little red shoes, decorated with tigers, on a soft but tough little foot . . . this at least was real.

A medical student who was also on the tram took out a sketchpad and carefully added the last touches to a diagram of the human skeleton. The other passengers thought he was sketching a portrait of the man who sat dozing across from him. Nothing else was going on, so they started sauntering over, crowding into little clumps of three or four, leaning on each other with their hands behind their backs, gathering around to watch the man sketch from life. The husband who dangled smoked fish from his fingers whispered to his wife: "I can't get used to this cubism, this impressionism, which is so popular these days." "Your pants," she hissed.

The medical student meticulously wrote in the names of every bone, muscle, nerve, and tendon. An office worker hid half his face behind a fan and quietly informed his colleague: "The influence of Chinese painting. Nowadays, writing words in is all the rage in Western painting. Clearly a case of 'Eastern ways spreading Westward.'"

Lu Zongzhen didn't join the crowd, but stayed in his seat. He had decided he was hungry. With everyone gone, he could comfortably munch his spinach-stuffed dumplings. But then he looked up and caught a glimpse, in the third-class car, of a relative, his wife's cousin's son. He detested that Dong Peizhi was a man of humble origins who harbored a great ambition: he sought a fiancée of comfortable means, to serve as a foothold for his climb upwards. Lu Zongzhen's eldest daughter had just turned twelve, but already she had caught Peizhi's eye; having made, in his own mind, a pleasing calculation, Peizhi's manner grew ever softer, ever more cunning.

As soon as Lu Zongzhen caught sight of this young man, he was filled with quiet alarm, fearing that if he were seen, Peizhi would take advantage of the opportunity to press forward with his attack. The idea of being stuck in the same car with Dong Peizhi while the city was sealed off was too horrible to contemplate! Lu quickly closed his briefcase and wrapped up his dumplings, then fled, in a great rush, to a seat across the aisle. Now, thank God, he was screened by Wu Cuiyuan, who occupied the seat next to him, and his nephew could not possibly see him.

Cuiyuan turned and gave him a quick look. Oh no! The woman surely thought he was up to no good, changing seats for no reason like that. He recognized the look of a woman being flirted with—she held her face absolutely motionless, no hint of a smile anywhere in her eyes, her mouth, not even in the little hollows beside her nose; yet from some unknown place there was the trembling of a little smile that could break out at any moment. If you think you're simply too adorable, you can't keep from smiling.

Damn! Dong Peizhi had seen him after all, and was coming toward the first-class car, very humble, bowing even at a distance, with his long jowls, shiny red cheeks, and long, gray, monklike gown—a clean, cautious young man, hard-working no matter what the hardship, the very epitome of a good son-in-law. Thinking fast, Zongzhen decided to follow Peizhi's lead and try a bit of artful nonchalance. So he stretched one arm out across the window-sill that ran behind Cuiyuan, soundlessly announcing flirtatious intent. This would not, he knew, scare Peizhi into immediate retreat, because in Peizhi's eyes he already was a dirty old man. The way Peizhi saw it, anyone over thirty was old, and all the old were vile. Having seen his uncle's disgraceful behavior, the young man would feel compelled to tell his wife every little detail—well, angering his wife was just fine with him. Who told her to give him such a nephew, anyway? If she was angry, it served her right.

He didn't care much for this woman sitting next to him. Her arms were fair, all right, but were like squeezed-out toothpaste. Her whole body was like squeezed-out toothpaste, it had no shape.

"When will this air raid ever end?" he said in a low, smiling voice. "It's awful!"

Shocked, Cuiyuan turned her head, only to see that his arm was stretched out behind her. She froze. But come what may, Zongzhen could not let himself pull his arm back. His nephew stood just across the way, watching him with brilliant, glowing eyes, the hint of an understanding smile on his face. If, in the middle of everything, he turned and looked his nephew in the eye, maybe the little no-account would get scared, would lower his eyes, flustered and embarrassed like a sweet young thing; then again, maybe Peizhi would keep staring at him—who could tell?

He gritted his teeth and renewed the attack. "Aren't you bored? We could talk a bit, that can't hurt. Let's . . . let's talk." He couldn't control himself, his voice was plaintive.

Again Cuiyuan was shocked. She turned to look at him. Now he remembered, he had seen her get on the tram—a striking image, but an image concocted by chance, not by any intention of hers. "You know, I saw you get on the tram," he said softly. "Near the front of the car. There's a torn advertisement, and I saw your profile, just a bit of your chin, through the torn spot." It was an ad for Lacova powdered milk that showed a pudgy little child. Beneath the child's ear this woman's chin had suddenly appeared; it was a little spooky, when you thought about it. "Then you looked down to get some change out of your purse, and I saw your eyes, then your brows, then your hair." When you took her features separately, looked at them one by one, you had to admit she had a certain charm.

Cuiyuan smiled. You wouldn't guess that this man could talk so sweetly—you'd think he was the stereotypical respectable businessman. She looked at him again. Under the tip of his nose the cartilage was reddened by the sunlight. Stretching out from his sleeve, and resting on the newspaper, was a warm, tanned hand, one with feeling—a real person! Not too honest, not too bright, but a real person. Suddenly she felt flushed and happy; she turned away with a murmur. "Don't talk like that."

"What?" Zongzhen had already forgotten what he'd said. His eyes were fixed on his nephew's back—the diplomatic young man had decided that three's a crowd, and he didn't want to offend his uncle. They would meet again, anyway, since theirs was a close family, and no knife was sharp enough to sever the ties; and so he returned to the third-class car. Once Peizhi was gone, Zongzhen withdrew his arm; his manner turned respectable. Casting about for a way to make conversation, he glanced at the notebook spread out on her lap. "Shenguang University," he read aloud. "Are you a student there?"

Did he think she was that young? That she was still a student? She laughed, without answering.

"I graduated from Huaqi." He repeated the name. "Huaqi." On her neck was a tiny dark mole, like the imprint of a fingernail. Zongzhen absentmindedly rubbed the fingers of his right hand across the nails of his left. He coughed slightly, then continued: "What department are you in?"

Cuiyuan saw that he had moved his arm and thought that her stand-offish manner had wrought this change. She therefore felt she could not refuse to answer. "Literature. And you?"

"Business." Suddenly he felt that their conversation had grown stuffy. "In school I was busy with student activities. Now that I'm out, I'm busy earning a living. So I've never really studied much of anything."

"Is your office very busy?"

"Terribly. In the morning I go to work and in the evening I go home, but I don't know why I do either. I'm not the least bit interested in my job. Sure, it's a way to earn money, but I don't know who I'm earning it for."

"Everyone has family to think of."

"Oh, you don't know . . . my family . . ." A short cough. "We'd better not talk about it."

"Here it comes," thought Cuiyuan. "His wife doesn't understand him. Every married man in the world seems desperately in need of another woman's understanding."

Zongzhen hesitated, then swallowed hard and forced the words out: "My wife—she doesn't understand me at all."

Cuiyuan knitted her brow and looked at him, expressing complete sympathy.

"I really don't understand why I go home every evening. Where is there to go? I have no home, in fact." He removed his glasses, held them up to the light, and wiped the spots off with a handkerchief. Another little cough. "Just keep going, keep getting by, without thinking—above all, don't start thinking!" Cuiyuan always felt that when nearsighted people took their glasses off in front of other people it was a little obscene; improper, somehow, like taking your clothes off in public. Zongzhen continued: "You, you don't know what kind of woman she is."

"Then why did you . . . in the first place?"

"Even then I was against it. My mother arranged the marriage. Of course I wanted to choose for myself, but . . . she used to be very beautiful . . . I was very young . . . young people, you know . . ." Cuiyuan nodded her head.

"Then she changed into this kind of person—even my mother fights with her, and she blames me for having married her! She has such a temper—she hasn't even got a grade-school education."

Cuiyuan couldn't help saying, with a tiny smile, "You seem to take diplomas very seriously. Actually, even if a woman's educated it's all the same." She didn't know why she said this, wounding her own heart.

"Of course, you can laugh, because you're well-educated. You don't know what kind of—" He stopped, breathing hard, and took off the glasses he had just put back on.

"Getting a little carried away?" said Cuiyuan.

Zongzhen gripped his glasses tightly, made a painful gesture with his hands. "You don't know what kind of—"

"I know, I know," Cuiyuan said hurriedly. She knew that if he and his wife didn't get along, the fault could not lie entirely with her. He too was a person of simple intellect. He just wanted a woman who would comfort and forgive him.

The street erupted in noise, as two trucks full of soldiers rumbled by. Cuiyuan and Zongzhen stuck their heads out to see what was going on; to their surprise, their faces came very close together. At close range anyone's face is somehow different, is tension-charged like a close-up on the movie screen. Zongzhen and Cuiyuan suddenly felt they were seeing each other for the first time. To his eyes, her face was the spare, simple peony of a watercolor sketch, and the strands of hair fluttering at her temples were pistils ruffled by a breeze.

He looked at her, and she blushed. When she let him see her blush, he grew visibly happy. Then she blushed even more deeply.

Zongzhen had never thought he could make a woman blush, make her smile, make her hang her head shyly. In this he was a man. Ordinarily, he was an accountant, a father, the head of a household, a tram passenger, a store customer, an insignificant citizen of a big city. But to this woman, this woman who didn't know anything about his life, he was only and entirely a man.

They were in love. He told her all kinds of things: who was on his side at the bank and who secretly opposed him; how his family squabbled; his secret sorrows; his schoolboy dreams . . . unending talk, but she was not put off. Men in love have always liked to talk; women in love, on the other hand, don't want to talk, because they know, without even knowing that they know, that once a man really understands a woman he'll stop loving her.

Zongzhen was sure that Cuiyuan was a lovely woman—pale, wispy, warm, like the breath your mouth exhales in winter. You don't want her, and she quietly drifts away. Being part of you, she understands everything, forgives everything. You tell the truth, and her heart aches for you; you tell a lie, and she smiles as if to say, "Go on with you—what are you saying?"

Zongzhen was quiet for a moment, then said, "I'm thinking of marrying again."

Cuiyuan assumed an air of shocked surprise. "You want a divorce? Well . . . that isn't possible, is it?"

"I can't get a divorce. I have to think of the children's well-being. My oldest daughter is twelve, just passed the entrance exams for middle school, her grades are quite good."

"What," thought Cuiyuan, "what does this have to do with what you just said?" "Oh," she said aloud, her voice cold, "you plan to take a concubine."

"I plan to treat her like a wife," said Zongzhen. "I—I can make things nice for her. I wouldn't do anything to upset her."

"But," said Cuiyuan, "a girl from a good family won't agree to that, will she? So many legal difficulties . . ."

Zongzhen sighed. "Yes, you're right. I can't do it. Shouldn't have mentioned it . . . I'm too old. Thirty-four already."

"Actually," Cuiyuan spoke very slowly, "these days, that isn't considered very old."

Zongzhen was still. Finally he asked, "How old are you?"

Cuiyuan ducked her head. "Twenty-four."

Zongzhen waited awhile, then asked, "Are you a free woman?"

Cuiyuan didn't answer. "You aren't free," said Zongzhen. "But even if you agreed, your family wouldn't, right?"

Cuiyuan pursed her lips. Her family—her prim and proper family—how she hated them all. They had cheated her long enough. They wanted her to find them a wealthy son-in-law. Well, Zongzhen didn't have money, but he did have a wife—that would make them good and angry! It would serve them right!

Little by little, people started getting back on the tram. Perhaps it was rumored out there that "traffic will soon return to normal." The passengers got on and sat down, pressing against Zongzhen and Cuiyuan, forcing them a little closer, then a little closer again.

Zongzhen and Cuiyuan wondered how they could have been so foolish not to have thought of sitting closer before. Zongzhen struggled against his happiness. He turned to her and said, in a voice full of pain, "No, this won't do! I can't let you sacrifice your future! You're a fine person, with such a good education . . . I don't have much money, and don't want to ruin your life!"

Well, of course, it was money again. What he said was true. "It's over," thought Cuiyuan. In the end she'd probably marry, but her husband would never be as dear as this stranger met by chance—this man on the tram in the middle of a sealed-off city . . . it could never be this spontaneous again. Never again . . . oh, this man, he was so stupid! So very stupid! All she wanted was one small part of him, one little part that no one else could want. He was throwing away his own happiness. Such an idiotic waste! She wept, but it wasn't a gentle, maidenly weeping. She practically spit her tears into his face. He was a good person—the world had gained one more good person!

What use would it be to explain things to him? If a woman needs to turn to words to move a man's heart, she is a sad case.

Once Zongzhen got anxious, he couldn't get any words out, and just kept shaking the umbrella she was holding. She ignored him. Then he tugged at her hand. "Hey, there are people here, you know! Don't! Don't get so upset! Wait a bit, and we'll talk it over on the telephone. Give me your number."

Cuiyuan didn't answer. He pressed her. "You have to give me your phone number."

"Seven-five-three-six-nine." Cuiyuan spoke as fast as she could.

"Seven-five-three-six-nine?"

No response. "Seven-five-three-six-nine, seven-five . . ." Mumbling the number over and over, Zongzhen searched his pockets for a pen, but the more frantic he became, the harder it was to find one. Cuiyuan had a red pencil in her bag, but she purposely did not take it out. He ought to remember her telephone number; if he didn't, then he didn't love her, and there was no point in continuing the conversation.

The city started up again. "Ding-ding-ding-ding." Every "ding" a cold little dot, which added up to a line that cut across time and space.

A wave of cheers swept across the metropolis. The tram started clanking its way forward. Zongzhen stood up, pushed into the crowd, and disappeared. Cuiyuan turned her head away, as if she didn't care. He was gone. To her, it was as if he were dead.

The tram picked up speed. On the evening street, a tofu-seller had set his shoulder-pole down and was holding up a rattle; eyes shut, he shook it back and forth. A big-boned blonde woman, straw hat slung across her back, bantered with an Italian sailor. All her teeth showed when she grinned. When Cuiyuan looked at these people, they lived for that one moment. Then the tram clanked onward, and one by one they died away.

Cuiyuan shut her eyes fretfully. If he phoned her, she wouldn't be able to control her voice; it would be filled with emotion, for he was a man who had died, then returned to life.

The lights inside the tram went on; she opened her eyes and saw him sitting in his old seat, looking remote. She trembled with shock—he hadn't gotten off the tram, after all! Then she understood his meaning: everything that had happened while the city was sealed was a non-occurrence. The whole of Shanghai had dozed off, had dreamed an unreasonable dream.

The tramcar driver raised his voice in song: "Sad, sad, sad! No money do I have! Sad, sad, sad—" An old beggar, thoroughly dazed, limped across the street in front of the tram. The driver bellowed at her. "You swine!"

1943

MODERN POETRY

odern poets often proclaimed their break with nineteenth-century precursors, notably the Romantics and the symbolists. Romanticism had aspired, according to the English poet **William Wordsworth**, to speak in the "real language of men," but a century later, Romantic reveries about natural beauty or the soul had become, in the eyes of the modernists, just another set of poetic clichés. Wordsworth had also claimed that "all good poetry is the spontaneous overflow of powerful feelings"; the modernists were more skeptical of emotion. They sought, instead, precision and clarity; in place of self-expression, they emphasized the construction of the literary work. Correspondingly, they turned away from ballads and narrative poetry and toward compressed lyrics that often used language in a shocking or an unfamiliar way, far from the everyday language that Wordsworth had praised.

Some modernists likewise saw the late nineteenth-century symbolism of the French poets **Charles Baudelaire** and Stéphane Mallarmé as merely an overwrought kind of Romanticism in which personal vision counted for more than precision and formal innovation. In fact, however, many modernists drew on the symbolist inheritance in their attempts to transform verse. One area of continuity was the role of images and symbols. **William Butler Yeats** and **Constantine Cavafy**, who were already writing poetry during the heyday of symbolism, stress the power of what Yeats called "masterful images"—striking visual creations hermetic or esoteric enough to require challenging acts of interpretation on the reader's part. Both poets found inspiration in the storehouse of images associated with myth and legend to create complex personal mythologies that enriched their poems, even for the reader who might be unaware of the poet's private associations.

Rainer Maria Rilke and **T. S. Eliot** likewise incorporated elements of ancient myth in their poetry, but they were less comfortable with symbolist subjectivity; their aim was to achieve impersonal objectivity. Rilke became known in particular for his "object poems," in which precise observation yields indirect commentary on human society. Eliot used complex metrical play and surprising rhymes to revitalize the resources of English verse. (A parallel movement in Russia, Acmeism, influenced the young **Anna Akhmatova**.) Eliot frequently alluded to or quoted other writers, creating layers of voices or registers that collide uneasily in the poems and keep the reader on edge. Yeats, who (like Cavafy in Greek and Rilke in German) generally relied on traditional stanza forms, used meter to achieve a high formality while evoking the rhythms of spoken English. Both English-language poets were substantially influenced by Ezra Pound, who, in arguing against adherence to the most widely used metrical pattern, iambic pentameter, asserted that poets should "compose in the sequence of the musical phrase, not the sequence of a metronome."

Although the modernists often undertook long poems, these works were seldom narrative epics but, rather, fragmentary collections of lyrics, like Eliot's *The Waste Land* (1922) and *Four Quartets* (1943) or Akhmatova's *Requiem* (1963). Eliot argued that "our civilization comprehends great variety and complexity, and this variety and complexity, playing upon a refined sensibility, must produce various and complex results. The poet must become more and more comprehensive, more allusive, more indirect, in order to force, to dislocate if necessary, language to his meaning." While many poets undertook the dislocation of language through play with traditional forms, rhymes, and meters, the literary avant-gardes—especially the advocates of surrealism—launched a fundamental attack on traditional poetry. Led by André Breton and inspired by Sigmund Freud and Karl Marx, the surrealists tapped into the unconscious and undermined the repressive tendencies of Western society. Many of them, moreover, hoped to transform society through a Communist revolution. In different ways, **Pablo Neruda** and **Octavio Paz** were both influenced by surrealism's quest for political, erotic, and spiritual liberation. To varying degrees they embraced free verse, long and loose poetic lines, and the startling juxtaposition of images. That they came from the developing or colonized world, and spent formative periods in Paris, helps to explain their openness to the surrealist revolution against traditional poetry.

The more politically oriented poets, notably Neruda, often found themselves balancing their interest in literary experiment with a desire to write in a direct, unadorned style that could attract a wide readership. Although **Federico García Lorca** befriended the early surrealists and shared their experimental attitude in his plays, his elegy **"Lament for Ignacio Sánchez Mejías"** (1935) is in many respects a more traditional poem than anything produced by the avant-gardes. His use of repetition and rhetorical techniques intended to move an audience shares something with the work of his friend Neruda, who would later memorialize Lorca himself in **"I'm Explaining a Few Things"** (1937).

Modernist poetry, particularly as exemplified by Eliot's *The Waste Land* and championed in his essays, has been rejected by some critics as elitist. It can certainly be challenging, inviting the reader to engage with untested literary forms and to respond to unexpected meaning. Whether cryptic like some of Yeats's symbols or direct like Neruda's odes, the poetry of the early twentieth century reinvents and reinvigorates language for an age in which words can all too easily lose their meanings and traditional forms their power to structure experience. The selection of modernist poetry that follows suggests the variety and complexity of this rich period in literary history, a period whose implications are still being worked out by poets and readers today.

CONSTANTINE CAVAFY

1863–1933

A private poet who circulated his work in folders to relatives and friends and never offered a book for sale, Constantine Cavafy became, almost in spite of himself, the most influential Greek poet of the twentieth century when a posthumous edition of 154 short poems was published in 1935. His precisely worded, obliquely evocative portraits of historical figures, displayed with their poignant desires and personal tragedies, subtly link the past and the present. The present-day world is present, too: glimpses of contemporary Alexandria spark the recall of erotic memories, and forgotten landscapes resurge with complex emotional and intellectual associations.

Cavafy was born in 1863 to Greek parents living in Alexandria, Egypt. The export-import firm of Cavafy Brothers had once been wealthy, but its fortunes declined and Constantine's father died in 1870. Two years later, Cavafy's mother took the family to England, where the boy's parents had lived in the 1850s and where she hoped they would prosper again. Unfortunately, the boy's two older brothers were inexperienced in business affairs; the rest of their funds vanished, obliging them to return to Alexandria, where they lived in straitened circumstances. During the poet's seven years in England, however, he became bilingual and read widely in English literature. In 1882, Cavafy's mother returned to her father's house outside Constantinople with Cavafy and his two brothers. They remained there for three years, during which time Cavafy discovered his ho-mosexuality and had his first love affair. The young writer—who was now fluent in English, Greek, and French—began to write poems in the three languages. In 1885 the family returned to Alexandria where Cavafy settled for the rest of his life, living with his mother until 1899 and, after her death, sharing quarters with his unmarried brothers. Although he became the greatest of modern Greek poets, he did not visit Greece itself until he was almost fifty.

Cavafy continued to write poetry and essays while working for an Alexandrian newspaper and for the Egyptian Stock Exchange before receiving the position he would hold from then on: special clerk in the Irrigation Service of the Ministry of Public Works. Although Cavafy shared his poetry with friends and relatives, he seems to have had no interest in seeking a wider audience. He had several pamphlets printed privately—an initial booklet of fourteen poems in 1904, enlarged with seven more in 1910—but otherwise restricted himself to folders of poems given to a few readers. In his later years, his reputation spread internationally through the efforts of the British novelist E. M. Forster, who met Cavafy during the First World War in Alexandria and remained a friend for the next twenty years. Cavafy's poem "Ithaka" was published in **T. S. Eliot**'s journal *Criterion*; occasionally, European visitors to Alexandria came to meet its author. He was reportedly a sociable person and a fascinating conversationalist, but he kept to himself and his circle of friends. Forster described him as a Greek gentleman with a straw hat standing "at a slight angle to the universe," and he was virtually unknown in Greece when he died in 1933.

Cavafy's poetry draws his readers into an astonishingly real personal world, establishing a common bond between them and fictional characters in an immense variety of circumstances. The sense of participation comes not merely from the recognition of familiar emotional situations but also from Cavafy's ironic and philosophical perspective that makes subtle demands on the reader's imagination. Cavafy observed that his works could be divided into three broad categories—historical, philosophical, and erotic—and he arranged his folders of poetry in thematic as well as chronological order. It is easy to see how a primary division could be made: of the poems printed here, "Kaisarion" (1918) is historical; "The Next Table" (1919) is erotic; and "Ithaka" (1911) is philosophical. But isn't such compartmentalizing too simple? The young Kaisarion is "good-looking and sensitive," with a "dreamy, an appealing beauty"; "The Next Table" involves memory, self-deception, and a portrait of aging as much as the act of love; and "Ithaka" would not exist without its basis in historical legend. The primary categories are not only broad but (as Cavafy undoubtedly knew) they overlap and leave room for others, whether political allusion ("When the Watchman Saw the Light," 1900), psychological portrait ("The City," 1910, "A Sculptor from Tyana," 1911), or devotion to art ("A Craftsman of Wine Bowls," 1921),

or philosophical evocation of memory ("Evening," 1917).

In these poems history exists on several levels. It is not the better-known Homeric and Periclean ages of Greek history, but rather the Hellenistic period and the Byzantine Empire, whose tangled politics, sophisticated art, social decadence, and vulnerability to invasion have their analogue in twentieth-century Alexandria. Cavafy's Alexandria is a modern metropolis with a glorious past, and the poet searches history for dramatic anecdotes that reveal the texture of life in that turbulent earlier age. It is not merely the murdered Kaisarion—son of Caesar and Cleopatra—who interests him, but John Kantakuzinos, a minor, impoverished ruler forced to decorate his crown with glass jewels; King Dimitrios, who in 288 B.C.E. disguised himself in simple clothes to escape capture after being deserted by his soldiers; and the scheming Anna Komnina, furious at seeing the Byzantine throne slip out of her hands in 1137. Ancient Greece appears primarily as a reference point in the distant past: the home of heroes like Patroklos or the god Hermes, who are both subjects for the vain sculptor of Tyana; of gods who fleetingly appear in the streets of Alexandria or the landscape of Ionia; or of Odysseus, whose epic voyage becomes a lesson that you can't go home again. From whatever era, Cavafy's precisely rendered narratives invite readers to enter, for a moment, the world of his poetic imagination and to draw their own connections to contemporary life.

When the Watchman Saw the Light[1]

Winter and summer the watchman sat on the roof
of the palace of the sons of Atreus and looked out. Now he tells
the joyful news. He saw a fire flare in the distance.[2]
And he is glad, and his labor is over as well.
It is hard work night and day,   5
in heat or cold, to look far off
to Arachnaion[3] for a fire. Now the desired
omen has appeared. When happiness
arrives it brings a lesser joy
than expected.[4] Clearly,   10
we've gained this much: we are saved from hopes
and expectations. Many things will happen
to the Atreus dynasty. One doesn't have to be wise
to surmise this now that the watchman
has seen the light. So, no exaggeration.   15
The light is good, and those that will come are good.
Their words and deeds are also good.
And we hope all will go well. But
Argos can manage without the Atreus family.
Great houses are not eternal.   20
Of course, many will have much to say.
We'll listen. But we won't be fooled
by the Indispensable, the Only, the Great.
Some other indispensable, only, and great
is always instantly found.   25

1900

---

1. All poems in this selection are translated by Aliki Barnstone. This poem was written in 1900 and was not published during the poet's lifetime. The title, a reference to the prologue of Aeschylus's play *Agamemnon*, a speech given by the watchman who is waiting for the signal that announces the king's return to Argos, is a reminder of the hereditary curse on the family: King Atreus was Agamemnon's father, and Atreus himself was supposed to have revenged himself on his brother Thyestes by serving his children to him for dinner.

2. A chain of bonfires that stretched from Troy to Greece had been prepared as a way of announcing the long-awaited return of Agamemnon's ship from the Trojan War.
3. A mountain in the Epidauros (Argeia) region of Greece.
4. A general statement but also a reminder that Agamemnon is coming home to his death at the hands of his wife, Queen Clytemnestra. Just as in Aeschylus's play, the watchman knows that all is not well at home.

Waiting for the Barbarians[1]

—What are we waiting for, gathered in the agora?[2]

The barbarians are arriving today.

—Why is nothing happening in the Senate?
Why do the Senators sit making no laws?

Because the barbarians are arriving today.   5
What laws can the Senators make now?
When the barbarians come, they will make laws.
—Why did our emperor wake up so early,
and, in the city's grandest gate, sit in state
on his throne, wearing his crown?   10

Because the barbarians are arriving today,
and the emperor is waiting to receive
their leader. In fact, he prepared
a parchment to give them, where
he wrote down many titles and names.   15

—Why did our two consuls and the praetors[3]
come out today in their crimson embroidered togas;
why did they don bracelets with so many amethysts
and rings resplendent with glittering emeralds;
why do they hold precious staffs today,   20
beautifully wrought in silver and gold?

Because the barbarians are arriving today,
and such things dazzle barbarians.

—Why don't the worthy orators come as usual
to deliver their speeches and say their piece?   25

Because the barbarians are arriving today
and they are bored by eloquence and harangues.

—Why should this anxiety and confusion
suddenly begin. (How serious faces have become.)

---

1. Written in 1898; published in 1904. The
setting appears to be ancient Rome during the
decadence of the empire, when the city was
sacked by the Visigoth leader Alaric in 410 c.e.
Cavafy has specified that there is no precise
reference, however, noting that the barbarians
are only a symbol and that "the emperor, the
senators and the orators are not necessarily
Roman."
2. A large public area, containing temples,

shops, and buildings; in Rome, the equivalent
would be the forum, which also contained the
Senate building.
3. Judicial officers in Rome who held preliminary hearings before cases were assigned to a
judge. "Consuls": the two chief administrative
officers of the state who presided over the
Senate. They were elected by the people under
the republic but named by the emperor during
the empire.

Why have the streets and squares emptied so quickly,   30
and why has everyone returned home so pensive?

Because night's fallen and the barbarians have not arrived.
And some people came from the border
and they say the barbarians no longer exist.

Now what will become of us without barbarians?   35
Those people were some kind of solution.

1904

The City[1]

You said, "I'll go to another land, I'll go to another sea.
I'll find a city better than this one.
My every effort is a written indictment,
and my heart—like someone dead—is buried.
How long will my mind remain in this decaying state.   5
Wherever I cast my eyes, wherever I look,
I see my life in black ruins here,
where I spent so many years, and ruined and wasted them."

You will not find new lands, you will not find other seas.
The city will follow you. You will roam   10
the same streets. And you will grow old in the same neighborhood,
and your hair will turn white in the same houses.
You will always arrive in this city. Don't hope for elsewhere—
there is no ship for you, there is no road.
As you have wasted your life here,   15
in this small corner, so you have ruined it on the whole earth.

1910

A Sculptor from Tyana[1]

As you may have heard, I'm not a beginner.
Quite a lot of stone has taken shape in my hands.
In my homeland, Tyana, I am well known,
and here senators have commissioned
many statues from me.   5
                    Let me show you
a few right now. Observe this Rhea,[2]

1. Written in 1894 under the title "Once More in the Same City" and listed under "Prisons." It was published with the current title in 1910.
1. First written in June 1893, entitled "A Sculptor's Studio"; published in 1911. Tyana was a city in Cappadocia, a district in Asia Minor, but the scene—in Rome—is imaginary.
2. Daughter of heaven and earth, and mother of the gods on Olympus.

inspiring reverence, full of fortitude, wholly archaic.
Observe Pompey. Marius,
Paulus Aemilius, Scipio Africanus.[3]
Likenesses faithful as I could make them.   10
Patroklos (I'll retouch him a bit).
Near the yellowish marble—
those pieces over there—is Kaisarion.[4]

For some time now I've been working on
a Poseidon.[5] I'm particularly studying   15
his horses, how to form them.
They must be made so light
to show clearly that their bodies, their feet
don't tread on earth, only gallop on water.
But look, here is my work I love most,   20
made with feeling and greatest care.
With him, on a warm summer day,
when my mind was rising to the ideal,
he came to me in a dream, this young Hermes.[6]

                                                        1911

Ithaka[1]

As you set out on the journey to Ithaka,
wish that the way be long,
full of adventures, full of knowledge.
Don't be afraid of Laistrygonians, the Cyclops,
angry Poseidon,[2] you'll never find them on your way   5
if your thought stays exalted, if a rare
emotion touches your spirit and body.
You won't meet the Laistrygonians
and the Cyclops and wild Poseidon,

3. Scipio Africanus the Younger (185–129 B.C.E.) led the army that destroyed Carthage in 146 B.C.E. "Pompey": Gnaeus Pompeius Magnus (106–48 B.C.E.), Roman general and statesman who fled to Egypt after being defeated by Julius Caesar, was assassinated by King Ptolemy. Gaius Marius (157–86 B.C.E.), a popular general, was elected consul seven times. Lucius Aemilius Paulus (228–160 B.C.E.) was a Roman consul whose army was disastrously defeated by Hannibal at the Battle of Cannae (216 B.C.E.).
4. Or Caesarion ("Little Caesar," 47–30 B.C.E.), the son of Cleopatra and Julius Caesar. Co-ruler of Egypt with his mother, he was killed by Octavian (the future emperor Augustus Caesar) for political reasons after her death. "Patroklos": Achilles' friend in Homer's Iliad, killed in battle.
5. Greek god of the sea.
6. Son of Zeus and messenger of the gods, often depicted as a nude youth bearing a herald's wand, or caduceus.
1. Ithaka is Odysseus's island kingdom and the destination of his homeward journey after the Trojan War. An early, different version of this poem was entitled "Second Odyssey."
2. Greek god of the sea. Odysseus encounters both the Laistrygonians (fierce rock-throwing cannibal giants in Odyssey 10) and the Cyclops (one-eyed cannibal giant in Odyssey 9) on his voyage home.

if you don't bear them along in your soul,   10
if your soul doesn't raise them before you.

Wish that the way be long.
May there be many summer mornings
when with such pleasure, such joy
you enter ports seen for the first time;   15
may you stop in Phoenician emporia[3]
to buy fine merchandise,
mother-of-pearl and coral, amber and ebony,
and every kind of sensual perfume,
buy abundant sensual perfumes, as many as you can.   20
Travel to many Egyptian cities
to learn and learn from their scholars.
Always keep Ithaka in your mind.
Arriving there is your destination.
But don't hurry the journey at all.   25
Better if it lasts many years,
and you moor on the island when you are old,
rich with all you have gained along the way,
not expecting Ithaka to make you rich.

Ithaka gave you the beautiful journey.   30
Without her you would not have set out on your way.
She has no more to give you.

And if you find her poor, Ithaka did not betray you.
With all your wisdom, all your experience,
you understand by now what Ithakas mean.   35

                                                    1911

Evening[1]

Anyway, they would not have lasted long. So the experience
of the years shows me. But Fate came
somewhat hastily and stopped them.
The good life was short.
But how strong the perfumes were,   5
how divine the beds where we lay,
to what pleasure we gave our bodies.

An echo of the days of pleasure,
an echo of the days came close to me,

---

3. The Phoenicians (from Phoenicia, in modern Syria and Lebanon) were famous merchants and sailors who established trade routes throughout the Mediterranean.

1. Published in 1917; written in 1916 as "Alexandrian" (a reference to the city of Alexandria, Egypt).

something of our youth's fire, something of the two of us.   10
In my hands was a letter I picked up again,
and I read it again and again until the light was gone.

I went out on the balcony, melancholy—
I went out to change my thoughts, at least to see
a little of the beloved city,   15
a little of the activity in the streets and the stores.

                                                              1917

Kaisarion[1]

In part to verify an era,
in part to pass the time,
last night I chose a collection
of Ptolemaic epigraphs to read.
The extravagant praise and flattery   5
was the same for everybody. All are splendid,
glorious, powerful, and altruistic;
every undertaking very wise.
If you talk about the women of that generation, they, too,
all the Berenikis and Kleopatras,[2] were marvelous.   10

When I succeeded in verifying the era,
I would have put the book down if a small
and unimportant note about King Kaisarion
did not immediately attract my attention.

Ah, here you came with your ambiguous   15
charm. In history only a few
lines about you exist,
and so I created you more freely in my mind.
I created you handsome and sensitive.
My art gives your face   20
a dreamy, amiable beauty.

And I imagine you so fully
that late last night as my light
went out—I let it go out on purpose—
I imagined you came in my room,   25
it seemed to me you stood as before, as you would have
in the vanquished Alexandria,
pale and tired, ideal in your sorrow,

---

1. Kaisarion or Caesarion ("Little Caesar," 47–30 B.C.E.) was the son of Cleopatra and Julius Caesar.
2. Kleopatra or Cleopatra (69–30 B.C.E.) was queen of Egypt and mother of Kaisarion. Bere-niki or Berenice (ca. 273–221 B.C.E.), the sister of Ptolemy III Euergetes (ca. 284–221 B.C.E.), married Antiochus II, king of Syria and, after his death, would have married the emperor Titus if the Romans had not objected.

still hoping they might show you compassion,
the vicious ones—who whispered, "too many Caesars."[3]   30

1918

The Next Table

He[1] must be barely twenty-three years old.
And yet I am sure almost as many
years ago, I enjoyed this same body.

It isn't merely an erotic flush.
I've only been in the casino[2] a little while   5
and haven't even had time to drink a lot.
I enjoyed this same body.

And even if I don't recall where—one lapse of memory means nothing.

Ah, now, there, now that he sits at the next table,
I know each way he moves—and under his clothes,   10
naked, are the loved limbs I see again.

1919

A Craftsman of Wine Bowls[1]

On this wine bowl   made of pure silver
that was made   for the home of Irakleidis[2]
where good taste   prevails supreme—
look, here are elegant flowers   and streams and thyme,
and in the center I have placed   a beautiful young man   5
naked, erotic;   he still dangles one of his calves
in the water.—   Oh, memory, I prayed
to find you my best   helper, so I might make
the face of the young man   I loved, as it was.
It turned out to be   a vast difficulty   10
because almost fifteen years   have passed since the day
he fell, a soldier   in the defeat of Magnesia.[3]

1921

3. The teenage Kaisarion was killed because, as the son of Julius Caesar and Cleopatra, he represented a political threat to the future emperor Augustus (then Octavian). The reason for his execution was given in a sentence modeled on a line from Homer's *Iliad* (2.204): "It is not a good thing to have too many Caesars."
1. The language of the Greek original does not reveal the gender of the person seated at the next table, but this calculated ambiguity is not possible in English translation.
2. Casinos were respectable places of entertainment.
1. Printed in 1921; written in 1903 and twice revised.
2. Treasurer of Antiochus IV Epiphanus (ruled 175–163 B.C.E.).
3. In 190 B.C.E. at the battle of Magnesia, the Romans defeated Antiochus III the Great, the father of Antiochus IV.

WILLIAM BUTLER YEATS

1865–1939

The twentieth century's greatest English-language poet, William Butler Yeats became a major voice of modern, independent Ireland. His captivating imagery and his fusion of history and vision continue to stir readers around the world, and many of his poetic phrases have entered the language. Yeats created a private mythology that helped him come to terms with personal and cultural pain and allowed him to explain—as symptoms of Western civilization's declining spiral—the plight of Irish society and the chaos in Europe in the period surrounding the First World War.

The eldest of four children born to John Butler and Susan Pollexfen Yeats, William came from a middle-class Protestant family. His father, a cosmopolitan Irishman who had turned from law to painting and whose inherited fortune had mostly evaporated, gave his son an unconventional education at home. J. B. Yeats was an argumentative religious skeptic who alternately terrorized his son and fostered the boy's interest in poetry and the visual arts, inspiring rebellion against scientific rationalism and belief in the superiority of art. His mother's ties to her home in County Sligo, where Yeats spent many summers and school holidays with his wealthy grandparents, introduced him to the beauties of the Irish countryside and to the folklore and supernatural legends that appear throughout his work. Living alternately in Ireland and England for much of his youth, Yeats became part of literary society in both countries and—though an Irish nationalist—rejected any narrowly patriotic point of view. Before he turned

fully to literature in 1886, Yeats attended art school and had planned to become an artist. (His brother Jack became a well-known painter.) Yeats's early works show the influence of the Pre-Raphaelite school in art and in literature. Pre-Raphaelitism called for a return to the sensuous representation and concrete details found in Italian painting before Raphael (1483–1520); Pre-Raphaelite poetry evoked a realm of luminous supernatural beauty in allusive, erotic imagery. Yeats combined the Pre-Raphaelite fascination with the medieval with his exploration of Irish legend: in 1889 he published an archaically styled poem describing a traveler in fairyland ("The Wanderings of Oisin") that established his reputation and won the praise of the designer and writer William Morris. The musical style of Yeats's Pre-Raphaelite period is evident in one of his most popular poems, "The Lake Isle of Innisfree" (1890), with its hidden "bee-loud glade" where "peace comes dropping slow" and evening, after the "purple glow" of noon, is "full of the linnet's wings."

In 1887, Yeats's family moved to London, where the writer pursued his interest in mystical philosophy by studying theosophy under its Russian interpreter, Madame Blavatsky. She claimed mystical knowledge from Tibetan monks and preached the doctrine of the Universal Oversoul, individual spiritual evolution through cycles of reincarnation, and the world as a conflict of opposing forces. Yeats was taken with the grandeur of her cosmology, although he inconveniently wished to test it by experiment and analysis and, in 1890, was expelled from the Theosophical

Society. He found a more congenial literary model in the works of **William Blake**, which he coedited in 1893 with F. J. Ellis. The appeal that mysticism had for Yeats later waned but never disappeared; traces may be seen in the introduction he wrote in 1913 for *Gitanjali*, a collection of poems by the Indian author **Rabindranath Tagore**, the preeminent figure in modern Bengali literature.

Several anthologies of Irish folk and fairy tales and a book describing Irish traditions (*The Celtic Twilight*, 1893) demonstrated a corresponding interest in Irish national identity. In 1896 he had met Lady Augusta Gregory, a nationalist who invited him to spend summers at Coole Park, her country house in Galway, and who worked closely with him (and later J. M. Synge) in founding the Irish National Theater (later the Abbey Theater). Along with other participants in the Irish literary renaissance, Yeats aimed to create "a national literature that made Ireland beautiful in the memory . . . freed from provincialism by an exacting criticism." To this end, he wrote *Cathleen ni Houlihan* (1902), a play in which the title character personified Ireland; it became immensely popular with the nationalists. Yeats also established literary societies, promoted and reviewed Irish books, and lectured and wrote about the need for Irish community. Gradually Yeats became embittered by the barriers he believed nationalism was erecting around the free expression of Irish culture. He was outraged at the attacks on Synge's *Playboy of the Western World* (1907) for its supposed derogatory picture of Irish culture, and he commented scathingly in *Poems Written in Discouragement* (1913; reprinted in *Responsibilities*, 1914) on the inability of the middle class to appreciate art or literature.

Except for summers at Coole Park, Yeats in his middle age was spending more time in England than in Ireland. He began *Autobiographies* in 1914 and wrote symbolic plays intended for small audiences on the model of the Japanese Noh theater. His works of this period display a change in tone—a precision and epigrammatic quality that reflects partly his disappointment with Irish nationalism and partly the tastes in poetry promulgated by his friend Ezra Pound and by **T. S. Eliot**. Although Yeats had claimed in a poem just before the First World War that "Romantic Ireland's dead and gone," he found himself drawn again to politics as a subject for poetry and as an arena for action. Shocked by the aftermath of the Easter 1916 uprising against British rule, when sixteen leaders were shot for treason, Yeats wrote that, through their sacrifice, "a terrible beauty is born." The revolutionary figures whom Yeats had known in life took their place in a mythic framework within which he interpreted human history. In the subsequent Anglo-Irish War (1919–21) and Irish Civil War (1922–23), great violence, as Yeats had prophesied, attended the birth of the Irish nation-state. In the Irish Free State, Yeats became a senator from 1922 to 1928, Nobel Prize laureate in 1924, and a "sixty-year-old smiling public man," in the words of "Among School Children" (1926). Much of his best poetry was still to come.

Yeats's marriage in 1917 to Georgie Hyde-Lees provided him with much-needed stability. Intrigued by his wife's experiments with automatic writing (jotting down whatever comes to mind, without correction or rational intent), he viewed them as glimpses into a cosmic order; he gradually evolved his interpretation into a symbolic scheme. He explained the system in *A Vision* (1926): the wheel of history takes 26,000 years to turn; and inside the wheel, civilizations evolve in roughly 2,000-year gyres, spirals expanding outward until they collapse at the onset of a new gyre, which reverses the direction of the old. Within the system human personalities fall into various types, and both gyres and types relate to the phases of the moon. Yeats's later poems in *The Tower* (1928), *The Winding Stair* (1933), and *Last Poems* (1939) are set in the context of this system. His enthusiasms for mythical systems sometimes led him astray, notably when he flirted with the Irish Blue Shirts, a para-Fascist movement in the 1930s. Throughout his life, he affected an aristocratic disdain for the rough-and-tumble of democratic politics; by the end of his life, he had abandoned practical politics and devoted himself to the reality of personal experience inside a mystic view of history. The final poem in his posthumous *Last Poems*, "Politics," suggests that events in Russia, Italy, and Spain (communism, Fascism, and the impending Second World War) held less interest for the poet than a girl standing nearby: "maybe what they say is true / Of war and war's alarms / But O that I were young again / And held her in my arms."

For many readers Yeats's "masterful images" (in the words of another late poem, "The Circus Animals' Desertion," 1939) define his work. From his early use of symbols as metaphors for personal emotions, to the cosmology of his last work, Yeats created a poetry whose power derives from the interweaving of sharp-edged images. Symbols such as the Tower, Byzantium, Helen of Troy, the sun and the moon, birds of prey, the blind man, and the fool recur frequently and draw their meaning not from connections established inside the poem (as is true for the French symbolists) but from an underlying myth based on occult tradition, Irish folklore, history, and Yeats's private experience. Even readers unacquainted with his mythic system will respond to images that express a situa-

tion or state of mind—for example, golden Byzantium for intellect, art, wisdom—all that "body" cannot supply.

The seven poems included here cover the range of Yeats's career, which embraced several styles. A poem from his early, Pre-Raphaelite period, "When You Are Old" (1895), pleads his love for the beautiful actress and Irish nationalist Maud Gonne, whom he met in 1889 and who repeatedly refused to marry him.

In middle age, when Yeats adopted a more political tone, he did so with an element of meditative distance. When he celebrates the abortive nationalist uprisings in "Easter 1916" (1916), it is from a universal, aesthetic point of view: "A terrible beauty is born" in the self-sacrifice that leads even a "drunken, vainglorious lout" (Major John MacBride, Maud Gonne's husband) to be "transformed utterly" by martyrdom. Yeats recognized that the Easter Rebellion, led by radicals whose politics and violence he disapproved, had altered not just the political situation in Ireland but its spiritual state as well.

His early poetry made substantial use of public, straightforward symbols, such as the rose for Ireland. Later on, Yeats employed symbols in a more indirect, allusive way. For example, in "The Second Coming" (1921), the "gyre," or spiral unfolding of history, is represented by the falcon's spiral flight. The sphinxlike beast slouching blank-eyed toward Bethlehem is an enigmatic but terrifying image. Yeats believed that contemporary society was witnessing a transformation similar to that of the fall of Troy or the birth of Christ: "twenty centuries of stony sleep" since Christ's birth are again to be "vexed to nightmare by a rocking cradle," the poem declares; he asks what sort of savior or Antichrist will announce the impending age. This poem demonstrates how Yeats, a master of English meter and rhyme, evolved a loose poetic line with only hints of rhyme. The fourteen lines of the second stanza can be read as an unconventional sonnet.

In form a more conventional sonnet, "Leda and the Swan" (1924) is an erotic retelling of a mythical rape. But it also foreshadows the Trojan War—brute force mirroring brute force. Yeats called the poem's subject "a violent annunciation": as the event that conceives Helen of Troy, Zeus's transformation into a swan and rape of Leda embodies a moment of world-historical change. Once again Yeats draws parallels between the upheavals of history and the catastrophic events of ancient narratives. The poem combines the Shakespearean sonnet in its first two quatrains (the eight lines rhyming *ababcdcd*) with the Petrarchan form in the sestet (the final six lines rhyming *defdef*).

In the two poems on the legendary city of Byzantium, "Sailing to Byzantium" (1926) and "Byzantium" (1930), Yeats admires an artistic civilization that "could answer all my questions" but that was, in fact, only a moment in history. Byzantine art, with its stylized perspectives and mosaics assembled from colored bits of stone, represents the opposite of the tendency of Western art to imitate nature, and it provides a kind of escape for the poet. The idea in "Sailing to Byzantium" of an inhuman, metallic, abstract beauty that art separates "out of nature" expresses a mystic, symbolist quest for an invulnerable world distinct from the ravages of time. This world is to be found in an idealized Byzantium, where the poet's body will be transmuted into artifice.

By the time of the second of these poems, the possibility of achieving such a separation seems problematic: the speaker recognizes, on the one hand, that artistic images remain close to the living, suffering world—"the dolphin's mire and blood"—and, on the other hand, that such images have a life independent of the people who would merge with them—"Those images that yet / Fresh images beget."

In "Lapis Lazuli," the tragic figures of history transcend their roles by the calm "gaiety" with which they accept their fate: the ancient Chinamen carved in the blue stone climb toward a vantage point where they can gaze, without concern, upon the world's tragedies: "Their eyes mid many wrinkles, their eyes, / Their ancient, glittering eyes, are gay."

Yet the world is still there, tragedies still abound, and Yeats's poetry remains aware of the physical and emotional roots from which the words spring. Whatever the wished-for distance, his poems are full of passionate feelings, erotic desire and disappointment, delight in beauty, horror at civil war and anarchy, dismay at degradation and change. By the time of his death, on January 28, 1939, Yeats had rejected his Byzantine identity as the golden songbird and sought out "the brutality, the ill breeding, the barbarism of truth." Yeats's poetry, which draws its initial power from the formal mastery of images and verbal rhythm, resonates in the reader's mind for its attempt to come to terms with reality, to grasp and make sense of human experience in the language of art.

When You Are Old[1]

When you are old and gray and full of sleep,
And nodding by the fire, take down this book,
And slowly read, and dream of the soft look
Your eyes had once, and of their shadows deep;

How many loved your moments of glad grace,   5
And loved your beauty with love false or true,
But one man loved the pilgrim soul in you,
And loved the sorrows of your changing face;

And bending down beside the glowing bars,
Murmur, a little sadly, how Love fled   10
And paced upon the mountains overhead
And hid his face amid a crowd of stars.

1895

Easter 1916[1]

I have met them at close of day
Coming with vivid faces
From counter or desk among grey
Eighteenth-century houses.
I have passed with a nod of the head   5
Or polite meaningless words,
Or have lingered awhile and said
Polite meaningless words,
And thought before I had done
Of a mocking tale or a gibe   10
To please a companion
Around the fire at the club,
Being certain that they and I
But lived where motley is worn:
All changed, changed utterly: 15
A terrible beauty is born.

1. An adaptation of a love sonnet by the French Renaissance poet Pierre de Ronsard (1524–1585), which begins similarly ("Quand vous serez bien vieille") but ends by asking the beloved to "pluck the roses of life today."

1. On Easter Sunday 1916, Irish nationalists began an unsuccessful rebellion against British rule, which lasted throughout the week and ended in the surrender and execution of its leaders.

That woman's[2] days were spent
In ignorant good-will,
Her nights in argument
Until her voice grew shrill.   20
What voice more sweet than hers
When, young and beautiful,
She rode to harriers?
This man had kept a school
And rode our wingèd horse;   25
This other his helper and friend[3]
Was coming into his force;
He might have won fame in the end,
So sensitive his nature seemed,
So daring and sweet his thought.   30
This other man[4] I had dreamed
A drunken, vainglorious lout.
He had done most bitter wrong
To some who are near my heart,
Yet I number him in the song;   35
He, too, has resigned his part
In the casual comedy;
He, too, has been changed in his turn,
Transformed utterly:
A terrible beauty is born.   40

Hearts with one purpose alone
Through summer and winter seem
Enchanted to a stone
To trouble the living stream.
The horse that comes from the road,   45
The rider, the birds that range
From cloud to tumbling cloud,
Minute by minute they change;
A shadow of cloud on the stream
Changes minute by minute;   50
A horse-hoof slides on the brim,
And a horse plashes within it;
The long-legged moor-hens dive,
And hens to moor-cocks call;
Minute by minute they live: 55
The stone's in the midst of all.

Too long a sacrifice
Can make a stone of the heart.

2. Constance Gore-Booth (1868–1927), later
Countess Markiewicz, an ardent nationalist.
3. Patrick Pearse (1879–1916) and his friend
Thomas MacDonagh (1878–1916), both schoolmasters and leaders of the rebellion and both
executed by the British. As a Gaelic poet, Pearse
symbolically rode the winged horse of the Muses,
Pegasus.
4. Major John MacBride (1865–1916), who
had married and separated from Maud Gonne
(1866–1953), Yeats's great love.

O when may it suffice?
That is Heaven's part, our part   60
To murmur name upon name,
As a mother names her child
When sleep at last has come
On limbs that had run wild.
What is it but nightfall?   65
No, no, not night but death;
Was it needless death after all?
For England may keep faith
For all that is done and said.
We know their dream; enough   70
To know they dreamed and are dead;
And what if excess of love
Bewildered them till they died?
I write it out in a verse—
MacDonagh and MacBride   75
And Connolly⁵ and Pearse
Now and in time to be,
Wherever green is worn,
Are changed, changed utterly:
A terrible beauty is born.   80

                                                          1916

The Second Coming¹

Turning and turning in the widening gyre²
The falcon cannot hear the falconer;
Things fall apart; the centre cannot hold;
Mere anarchy is loosed upon the world,
The blood-dimmed tide is loosed, and everywhere   5
The ceremony of innocence is drowned;
The best lack all conviction, while the worst
Are full of passionate intensity.

Surely some revelation is at hand;
Surely the Second Coming is at hand.   10
The Second Coming! Hardly are those words out
When a vast image out of *Spiritus Mundi*³

---

5. James Connolly (1870–1916), labor leader and nationalist executed by the British.
1. The Second Coming of Christ, believed by Christians to herald the end of the world, is transformed here into the prediction of a birth initiating an era and terminating the two-thousand-year cycle of Christianity.

2. The cone pattern of the falcon's flight and of historical cycles, in Yeats's vision.
3. World-soul (Latin) or, as *Anima Mundi* in Yeats's *Per Amica Silentia Lunae*, a "great memory" containing archetypal images; recalls C. G. Jung's collective unconscious.

Troubles my sight: somewhere in sands of the desert
A shape with lion body and the head of a man
A gaze blank and pitiless as the sun,   15
Is moving its slow thighs, while all about it
Reel shadows of the indignant desert birds.
The darkness drops again; but now I know
That twenty centuries of stony sleep
Were vexed to nightmare by a rocking cradle,   20
And what rough beast, its hour come round at last,
Slouches towards Bethlehem to be born?

                                                                    1921

Leda and the Swan[1]

A sudden blow: the great wings beating still
Above the staggering girl, her thighs caressed
By the dark webs, her nape caught in his bill,
He holds her helpless breast upon his breast.

How can those terrified vague fingers push   5
The feathered glory from her loosening thighs?
And how can body, laid in that white rush,
But feel the strange heart beating where it lies?

A shudder in the loins engenders there
The broken wall, the burning roof and tower   10
And Agamemnon dead.[2]
                          Being so caught up,
So mastered by the brute blood of the air,
Did she put on his knowledge with his power
Before the indifferent beak could let her drop?

                                                                    1924

1. Zeus, ruler of the Greek gods, took the form of a swan to rape the mortal Leda; she gave birth to Helen of Troy, whose beauty caused the Trojan War.
2. The ruins of Troy and the death of Agamem-non, the Greek leader, whose sacrifice of his daughter Iphigenia to win the gods' favor caused his wife, Clytemnestra (also a daughter of Leda), to assassinate him on his return.

Sailing to Byzantium[1]

I

That is no country for old men. The young
In one another's arms, birds in the trees
—Those dying generations—at their song,
The salmon-falls, the mackerel-crowded seas,
Fish, flesh, or fowl, commend all summer long   5
Whatever is begotten, born, and dies.
Caught in the sensual music all neglect
Monuments of unageing intellect.

2

An aged man is but a paltry thing,
A tattered coat upon a stick, unless   10
Soul clap its hands and sing, and louder sing
For every tatter in its mortal dress,
Nor is there singing school but studying
Monuments of its own magnificence;
And therefore I have sailed the seas and come   15
To the holy city of Byzantium.

3

O sages standing in God's holy fire
As in the gold mosaic of a wall,
Come from the holy fire, perne in a gyre,[2]
And be the singing-masters of my soul.   20
Consume my heart away; sick with desire
And fastened to a dying animal
It knows not what it is; and gather me
Into the artifice of eternity.

4

Once out of nature I shall never take   25
My bodily form from any natural thing,
But such a form as Grecian goldsmiths make
Of hammered gold and gold enamelling
To keep a drowsy Emperor awake;
Or set upon a golden bough to sing   30
To lords and ladies of Byzantium
Of what is past, or passing, or to come.

1926

1. The ancient name for modern Istanbul, the capital of the Eastern Roman Empire, which represented for Yeats (who had seen Byzantine mosaics in Italy) a highly stylized and perfectly integrated artistic world where "religious, aesthetic, and practical life were one."
2. I.e., come spinning down in a spiral. "Perne": a spool or bobbin. "Gyre": the cone pattern of the falcon's flight and of historical cycles, in Yeats's vision.

Byzantium[1]

The unpurged images of day recede;
The Emperor's drunken soldiery are abed;
Night resonance recedes, night-walkers' song
After great cathedral gong;
A starlit or a moonlit dome[2] disdains   5
All that man is,
All mere complexities,
The fury and the mire of human veins.

Before me floats an image, man or shade,
Shade more than man, more image than a shade;   10
For Hades' bobbin bound in mummy-cloth
May unwind the winding path;[3]
A mouth that has no moisture and no breath
Breathless mouths may summon;
I hail the superhuman;   15
I call it death-in-life and life-in-death.

Miracle, bird or golden handiwork,
More miracle than bird or handiwork,
Planted on the starlit golden bough,
Can like the cocks of Hades crow,[4]   20
Or, by the moon embittered, scorn aloud
In glory of changeless metal
Common bird or petal
And all complexities of mire or blood.

At midnight on the Emperor's pavement flit   25
Flames that no faggot feeds, nor steel has lit,
Nor storm disturbs, flames begotten of flame,
Where blood-begotten spirits come
And all complexities of fury leave,
Dying into a dance,   30
An agony of trance,
An agony of flame that cannot singe a sleeve.

Astraddle on the dolphin's[5] mire and blood,
Spirit after spirit! The smithies break the flood,

1. The holy city of "Sailing to Byzantium"
(p. 1374), seen here as it resists and transforms
the blood and mire of human life into its own
transcendent world of art.
2. According to Yeats's system in *A Vision*
(1925), the first "starlit" phase in which the
moon does not shine and the fifteenth, opposing phase of the full moon represent complete
objectivity (potential being) and complete subjectivity (the achievement of complete beauty).
In between these absolute phases lie the evolving "mere complexities" of human life.

3. Unwinding the spool of fate that leads from
mortal death to the superhuman. "Hades": the
realm of the dead in Greek mythology.
4. To mark the transition from death to the
dawn of new life.
5. A dolphin rescued the famous singer Arion
by carrying him on his back over the sea. Dolphins were associated with Apollo, Greek god
of music and prophecy, and in ancient art they
are often shown escorting the souls of the
dead to the Isles of the Blessed. Here, the
dolphin is also flesh and blood, a part of life.

The golden smithies of the Emperor!   35
Marbles of the dancing floor
Break bitter furies of complexity,
Those images that yet
Fresh images beget,
That dolphin-torn, that gong-tormented sea.   40

                                                                    1930

Lapis Lazuli[1]

For Harry Clifton

I have heard that hysterical women say
They are sick of the palette and fiddle-bow,
Of poets that are always gay,
For everybody knows or else should know
That if nothing drastic is done   5
Aeroplane and Zeppelin will come out,
Pitch like King Billy[2] bomb-balls in
Until the town lie beaten flat.
All perform their tragic play,
There struts Hamlet, there is Lear,   10
That's Ophelia, that Cordelia;[3]
Yet they, should the last scene be there,
The great stage curtain about to drop,
If worthy their prominent part in the play,
Do not break up their lines to weep.   15
They know that Hamlet and Lear are gay;
Gaiety transfiguring all that dread.
All men have aimed at, found and lost;
Black out; Heaven blazing into the head:[4]
Tragedy wrought to its uttermost.   20
Though Hamlet rambles and Lear rages,
And all the drop-scenes drop at once
Upon a hundred thousand stages,
It cannot grow by an inch or an ounce.

On their own feet they came, or on shipboard,   25
Camel-back, horse-back, ass-back, mule-back,

1. A deep blue semiprecious stone. One of Yeats's letters (to Dorothy Wellesley, July 6, 1935) describes a Chinese carving in lapis lazuli that depicts an ascetic and pupil about to climb a mountain: "Ascetic, pupil, hard stone, eternal theme of the sensual east . . . the east has its solutions always and therefore knows nothing of tragedy."
2. A linkage of past and present. According to an Irish ballad, King William III of England "threw his bomb-balls in" and set fire to the tents of the deposed James II at the Battle of the Boyne in 1690. Also a reference to Kaiser Wilhelm II (King William II) of Germany, who sent zeppelins to bomb London during World War I. "Zeppelin": a long, cylindrical airship, supported by internal gas chambers.
3. Tragic figures in Shakespeare's plays.
4. The loss of rational consciousness making way for the blaze of inner revelation or "mad" tragic vision. Also suggests the final curtain and an air raid curfew.

Old civilisations put to the sword.
Then they and their wisdom went to rack:
No handiwork of Callimachus[5]
Who handled marble as if it were bronze,   30
Made draperies that seemed to rise
When sea-wind swept the corner, stands;
His long lamp-chimney shaped like the stem
Of a slender palm, stood but a day;
All things fall and are built again,   35
And those that build them again are gay.
Two Chinamen, behind them a third,
Are carved in Lapis Lazuli,
Over them flies a long-legged bird,[6]
A symbol of longevity;   40
The third, doubtless a serving-man,
Carries a musical instrument.

Every discoloration of the stone,
Every accidental crack or dent,
Seems a water-course or an avalanche,   45
Or lofty slope where it still snows
Though doubtless plum or cherry-branch
Sweetens the little half-way house
Those Chinamen climb towards, and I
Delight to imagine them seated there;   50
There, on the mountain and the sky,
On all the tragic scene they stare.
One asks for mournful melodies;
Accomplished fingers begin to play.
Their eyes mid many wrinkles, their eyes,   55
Their ancient, glittering eyes, are gay.

                                                        1938

---

5. Athenian sculptor (5th century B.C.E.), famous for a gold lamp in the Erechtheum (temple on the Acropolis) and for using drill lines in marble to give the effect of flowing drapery.
6. A crane.

RAINER MARIA RILKE
1875–1926

In his intensely personal quest to understand the "great mysteries" of the universe, Rilke asks questions that we ordinarily think of as religious. Whether his gaze turns toward earth, which he describes with extraordinary clarity and affection, or toward a higher realm whose enigmas remain to be deciphered, he seeks a comprehensive vision of cosmic unity. Rilke's sharply focused yet visionary lyricism made him the best-known and most influential German poet of the twentieth century.

Born in Prague on December 4, 1875, to German-speaking parents who separated when he was nine, Rilke had an unhappy childhood. His mother dressed him as a girl to compensate for the earlier loss of a baby daughter; as a teenager he was sent to military academies, where he was lonely and miserable. After a year in business school, he worked in his uncle's law firm and studied at the University of Prague. His heart was already set on a literary career, however, and between his work and his studies, he stole enough time to publish two books of poetry and write plays, stories, and reviews. In 1897 he moved to Munich and fell in love with the married psychoanalyst Lou Andreas-Salomé, who would be an influence on him throughout his life. Accompanying Andreas-Salomé and her husband to Russia in 1899, Rilke met **Leo Tolstoy** and Boris Pasternak and—swayed by Russian mysticism and the Russian landscape—wrote some of his first successful poems. Rilke met his future wife, the sculptor Clara Westhoff, when the two were living in the artists' colony Worpswede, in northern Germany; they soon separated, and Rilke moved to Paris to begin a book on the sculptor Rodin. In Paris the German poet encountered an unexpected kind of literary and artistic inspiration. In Rodin, who became his friend, Rilke found a dedication to the technical demands of his craft; an intense concentration on visible, tangible objects; and, above all, a belief in art as an essentially religious activity. Rilke was also struck by the poetry of **Charles Baudelaire**. Although he wrote in distress to Lou Andreas-Salomé, complaining of nightmares and a sense of failure, it is at this time (and with her encouragement) that Rilke launched his major work. The anguished, semiautobiographical spiritual confessions of *The Notebook of Malte Laurids Brigge* (1910) date from this period, as do *New Poems* (1907–08), in which the writer develops a symbolic vision focused on objects.

When a patron, Princess Marie von Thurn und Taxis-Hohenlohe, proposed that he stay by himself in her castle at Duino, near Trieste, during the winter of 1911–12, Rilke found the quiet and isolation that he needed as a writer. Walking on the rocks above the sea and puzzling over his answer to a bothersome business letter, Rilke seemed to hear in the roar of the wind the first lines of an elegy: "Who, if I cried out, would hear me among the angels' / hierarchies?" By February he had written two elegies, and when he left Duino Castle in May, he had conceived the cycle and written fragments of four other elegies, which would eventually be published in the sequence of ten poems called the *Duino Elegies* (1923). (An elegy is a mournful lyric poem, usually a lament for loss.) Drafted into the German army during the First World War, Rilke spent his days drawing precise vertical and horizontal lines on paper for the War Archives Office in Vienna. Released from military service in 1916, he produced few poems and feared that he would never be able to complete the Duino sequence. In 1922, however, a friend's purchase of the tiny Château de Muzot in Switzerland gave him a peaceful place to retire to and write. Not only did he complete the *Duino Elegies* in Muzot; he also wrote—as a memorial for the young daughter of a friend—a two-part sequence of fifty-five sonnets, *Sonnets to Orpheus* (1922). Affirming the essential unity of life and death, Rilke closed his two complementary sequences ("the little rust-colored sail of the Sonnets and the Elegies' gigantic white canvas") and wrote little—chiefly poems in French—over the next few years. Increasingly ill with leukemia, he died on December 29, 1926, as the result of an infection after pricking himself on roses he cut for a friend in his garden.

The four selections from *New Poems* (1907–08) printed here demonstrate Rilke's visual imagination of his "thing-poems" (*Dinggedichte*). *New Poems* emphasizes physical reality, the absolute otherness and "thing-like" nature of what is observed—be it fountain, panther, flower, human being, or the "Archaic Torso of Apollo." A letter to Andreas-Salomé describes the poet's sense that ancient art objects take on a peculiar luster once they are detached from history and are seen as "things" in and for themselves: "No subject matter is attached to them, no irrelevant voice interrupts the silence of their concentrated reality . . . no history casts a shadow over their naked clarity—: they *are*. That is all . . . one day one of them reveals itself to you, and shines like a first star." Such "things" are not dead or inanimate but supremely alive, filled with a strange vitality before the poet's glance: the charged sexuality of the marble torso, the caged panther padding around his prison, and the metamorphosis of the Spanish dancer. Faced with a physical presence that transcends words, the viewer is challenged on an existential level. The "archaic torso of Apollo" is not a living being but an ancient Greek sculpture on display in the Louvre Museum in Paris. This headless marble is truly a "thing": a lifeless, even defaced chunk of stone. Yet such is the perfection of its luminous sensuality—derived, the speaker suggests, from the brilliant gaze of its missing head and "ripening" eyes—that it seems alive, and an inner radiance bursts starlike from the marble. The torso puts to shame the observer's puny existence, demanding: "You must change your life."

In his poetry Rilke is haunted by the incompleteness of human experience and by the passage of time. His response is to turn to art to draw objects into a "human" world, infusing them with ideas, emotions, and value. The poet's role, according to Rilke, is to observe with renewed sensitivity "this fleeting world, which in some strange way / keeps calling to us," and to bear witness, by means of language, to the transfiguration of its materiality through human emotions.

From NEW POEMS[1]

Archaic Torso of Apollo[2]

We cannot know his legendary head[3]
with eyes like ripening fruit. And yet his torso
is still suffused with brilliance from inside,
like a lamp, in which his gaze, now turned to low,

gleams in all its power. Otherwise   5
the curved breast could not dazzle you so, nor could
a smile run through the placid hips and thighs
to that dark center where procreation flared.

Otherwise this stone would seem defaced
beneath the translucent cascade of the shoulders   10
and would not glisten like a wild beast's fur:

would not, from all the borders of itself,
burst like a star: for here there is no place
that does not see you. You must change your life.

                                                                              1908

The Panther

In the Jardin des Plantes,[1] Paris

His vision, from the constantly passing bars,
has grown so weary that it cannot hold
anything else. It seems to him there are
a thousand bars; and behind the bars, no world.

---

1. All selections are translated by Stephen Mitchell.
2. The first poem in the second volume of Rilke's *New Poems* (1908), which were dedicated "to my good friend, Auguste Rodin" (the French sculptor, 1840–1917, whose secretary Rilke was for a brief period and on whom he wrote two monographs, in 1903 and 1907). The poem itself was inspired by an ancient Greek statue discovered at Miletus (a Greek colony on the coast of Asia Minor) that was called simply the *Torso of a Youth from Miletus*; since the god Apollo was an ideal of youthful male beauty, his name was often associated with such statues.
3. In a torso, the head and limbs are missing.
1. A zoo in Paris. Rilke also admired, at Rodin's studio, the plaster cast of an ancient statue of a panther.

As he paces in cramped circles, over and over,   5
the movement of his powerful soft strides
is like a ritual dance around a center
in which a mighty will stands paralyzed.

Only at times, the curtain of the pupils
lifts, quietly—. An image enters in,   10
rushes down through the tensed, arrested muscles,
plunges into the heart and is gone.

                                                          1907

The Swan

This laboring through what is still undone,
as though, legs bound, we hobbled along the way,
is like the awkward walking of the swan.

And dying—to let go, no longer feel
the solid ground we stand on every day—   5
is like his anxious letting himself fall

into the water, which receives him gently
and which, as though with reverence and joy,
draws back past him in streams on either side;
while, infinitely silent and aware,   10
in his full majesty and ever more
indifferent, he condescends to glide.

                                                          1907

Spanish Dancer[1]

As on all its sides a kitchen-match darts white
flickering tongues before it bursts into flame:
with the audience around her, quickened, hot,
her dance begins to flicker in the dark room.

And all at once it is completely fire.   5

---

1. The dance described is the flamenco (from *flamear*, "to flame").

One upward glance and she ignites her hair
and, whirling faster and faster, fans her dress
into passionate flames, till it becomes a furnace
from which, like startled rattlesnakes, the long
naked arms uncoil, aroused and clicking.[2]   10

And then: as if the fire were too tight
around her body, she takes and flings it out
haughtily, with an imperious gesture,
and watches: it lies raging on the floor,
still blazing up, and the flames refuse to die—.   15
Till, moving with total confidence and a sweet
exultant smile, she looks up finally
and stamps it out with powerful small feet.

1907

2. The dancer accompanies herself with the rhythmic clicking of castanets (worn on the fingers).

T. S. ELIOT
1888–1965

Thomas Stearns Eliot had a unique role in defining modernist taste and style. As a poet and as a literary critic, he rejected the narrative, moralizing, frequently "noble" style of late Victorian poetry, instead employing highly focused, startling images and an elliptical, ironic voice that has had enormous impact on modern poetry throughout the world. Readers in far-flung regions who know nothing of Eliot's other works are likely to be familiar with *The Waste Land* (1922), a literary-historical landmark representing the cultural crisis in Europe after the First World War. Although Eliot did not consider himself a generational icon, his challenging, quirky, memorable poetry is indissolubly linked with the spiritual and intellectual crises of modernism.

Two countries, England and the United States, claim Eliot as part of their national literature. Although Eliot was born in St. Louis, the Eliots were a distinguished New England family; Eliot's grandfather had gone west to found Washington University in St. Louis. Eliot attended Harvard (where his father's cousin was president of the university) for his undergraduate and graduate education. There he found literary models that would feed his work in future years: the poetry of Dante and John Donne, and the plays of Elizabethan and Jacobean dramatists. In 1908, Eliot read Arthur Symons's *The Symbolist Movement in Literature* and became acquainted with the French Symbolist poets, whose richly allusive images—and highly self-conscious, ironic, and craftsmanlike technique—he would adopt as his own. He began writing poetry while still in college and published his first major work, "The Love Song of J. Alfred Prufrock," in *Poetry* magazine in 1915.

At twenty-two he left for Europe to study at Oxford and the Sorbonne; the outbreak of the First World War prevented him from returning to Harvard, where he intended to continue graduate study in philosophy. Nonetheless, he completed a doctoral dissertation on the philosopher F. H. Bradley, whose examination of private consciousness became a theme of Eliot's later essays and poems. Settling in England, Eliot married, taught briefly, and worked for several years in the foreign department of Lloyd's Bank. Unhappy in his marriage and under pressure in his job at the bank, Eliot suffered from writer's block and then had a breakdown soon after the First World War. He wrote most of *The Waste Land* (1922) while recovering in a sanatorium in Lausanne, Switzerland. It was immediately hailed as one of the most important poems of the modernist movement and an expression of the postwar sense of social crisis. Already well known for his essays, collected in *The Sacred Wood* (1920), and his editorial work for the literary journals *The Egoist* and *The Criterion*, Eliot left Lloyd's for a position with the publishing firm Faber & Faber.

Raised an American Unitarian, Eliot joined the Church of England in 1927 and became a naturalized British sub-ject the same year. He continued to write poetry, and also turned to drama, composing a verse play on the death of the English St. Thomas à Becket (*Murder in the Cathedral*, 1935) as well as more conventional stage plays, *The Family Reunion* (1939), which recasts the Orestes story from Greek tragedy, and *The Cocktail Party* (1949), a drawing-room comedy that explores the search for salvation. During this time, Eliot became increasingly conservative in his political attitudes; the anti-Semitic remarks in his speeches and poems from this period have tarnished his reputation. By the time he received the Nobel Prize for Literature, in 1948, however, Eliot was recognized as a major contemporary writer in English. For such an influential poet, his output was relatively small; but in addition to writing some of the greatest verse of the twentieth century and essays that shaped literary opinion, he nurtured many younger writers as a director at Faber & Faber. Despite his social, political, and religious conservatism, Eliot ushered in the revolution in literary form known as modernism.

The selection here includes two of Eliot's major poems. "The Love Song of J. Alfred Prufrock," begun while Eliot was in college and published in 1915, displays the evocative yet confounding images, abrupt shifts in focus, and combination of human sympathy and ironic wit that would attract and puzzle readers of his later works. Clearly Prufrock's dramatic monologue aims to startle readers—by bidding them, in the opening lines, to imagine the evening spread out "like a patient etherised upon a table," and by shifting focus abruptly among metaphysical questions, drawing-room chatter, imaginary landscapes, and literary and biblical allusions. Tones of high seriousness jar against banal and even singsong speech: "I grow old . . . I grow old . . . / I shall wear the bottoms of my trousers rolled." The stanzas of "Prufrock" are individual scenes, each with a stylistic coherence (for example, the third stanza's yellow fog as a cat). Together, they create a symbolic landscape that unfolds in the narrator's mind as a combination of factual observation and subjective feelings. In its discontinuity, its precise yet evocative imagery, its mixture of romantic and everyday reference, and its formal and conversational speech, as well as in the complex and ironic self-consciousness of its very unheroic hero, "The Love Song of J. Alfred Prufrock" anticipates the modernist traits typical of Eliot's larger corpus. Also anticipating Eliot's later work are the theme of spiritual void and the disoriented protagonist helpless to cope with a crisis that is as much the face of modern Western culture as of his personal tragedy.

Eliot dedicated *The Waste Land* (1922), the next selection, to his friend, fellow poet, and editor Ezra Pound, with a quotation from Dante that praises the "better craftsman." Quotations from, or allusions to, a vast range of sources—including Shakespeare, Dante, **Charles Baudelaire**, Richard Wagner, Ovid, St. Augustine, Buddhist sermons, folk songs, and the anthropologists Jessie Weston and James Frazer—punctuate this lengthy work, to which Eliot added explanatory notes when it appeared in book form. A poem that depicts society in a time of cultural and spiritual crisis, *The Waste Land* juxtaposes images of the fragmentation of modern experience, on the one hand, and references (some in foreign languages) to a more stable heritage, on the other. The classical prophet Tiresias is contrasted to the contemporary charlatan Madame Sosostris; the celebrated lovers Antony and Cleopatra, to a real estate agent's clerk who mechanically seduces a bored typist at the end of her workday; Buddhist sermons and the religious visions of St. Augustine, to a sterile world of rock and dust where "one can neither stand nor lie nor sit." Throughout the poem runs a series of oblique allusions to the legend of a knight passing trials in a Chapel Perilous and healing a Fisher King by asking the right questions about the Holy Grail and the Holy Lance. The implication is that the modern wasteland might be redeemed if its inhabitants learned to answer (or perhaps to ask) the appropriate questions. These and other references that Eliot integrates into the poem constitute, the speaker says, "fragments I have shored against my ruins"—pieces of a puzzle whose resolution might bring "shantih," or the peace that passeth understanding but that remains enigmatically out of reach, as the poem's final lines in a mosaic of foreign languages suggest.

The groundbreaking technical innovation in *The Waste Land* is the deliberate use of fragmentation and discontinuity. Eliot pointedly refused to provide transitional passages or narrative thread, relying on the reader to construct a pattern whose implications would make sense as a whole. The writer's approach represents a direct attack on the conventional experience of the written word; the poem undercuts readers' expectations of linearity by inserting unexplained literary references, sudden shifts in scene or perspective, interpolations of foreign language, and changes of verbal register from lofty diction to slang. Eliot's refusal to fulfill traditional expectations serves several functions: it contributes to the poem's picture of cultural disintegration; it allows Eliot to exploit the Symbolist or allusive powers of language, since the diction rather than the narrative content must carry the burden of meaning; and by drawing attention to itself as a technique, it exemplifies modernist self-reflexive, or self-conscious, style.

Eliot's early essays on literature and literary history helped to bring about a different understanding of poetry, which afterward was no longer seen as the expression of personal feeeling but as a carefully made aesthetic object. Yet much of Eliot's impact was not merely formal but spiritual and philosophical. The search for meaning that pervades his work created a lasting picture of the barrenness of modern culture and of the search for alternatives. But while many later poets rejected Eliot's religious beliefs, they found inspiration in his expression of the dilemmas facing an anxious and infinitely vulnerable modern soul.

The Love Song of J. Alfred Prufrock

> S'io credessi che mia risposta fosse
> a persona che mai tornasse al mondo,
> questa fiamma staria senza più scosse.
> Ma per ciò che giammai di questo fondo
> non tornò vivo alcun, s'i'odo il vero,
> senza tema d'infamia ti rispondo.[1]

Let us go then, you and I,
When the evening is spread out against the sky
Like a patient etherised upon a table;
Let us go, through certain half-deserted streets,
The muttering retreats   5
Of restless nights in one-night cheap hotels
And sawdust restaurants with oyster-shells:
Streets that follow like a tedious argument
Of insidious intent
To lead you to an overwhelming question . . .   10
Oh, do not ask, "What is it?"
Let us go and make our visit.

In the room the women come and go
Talking of Michelangelo.[2]

The yellow fog that rubs its back upon the window-panes,   15
The yellow smoke that rubs its muzzle on the window-panes
Licked its tongue into the corners of the evening,
Lingered upon the pools that stand in drains,
Let fall upon its back the soot that falls from chimneys,
Slipped by the terrace, made a sudden leap,   20

---

1. From Dante's *Inferno* 27.61–66, in which the false counselor Guido da Montefeltro, enveloped in flame, explains that he would never reveal his past if he thought the traveler could report it: "If I thought my reply were meant for one / who ever could return into the world, / this flame would stir no more; and yet, since none— / if what I hear is true—ever returned / alive from this abyss, then without fear / of facing infamy, I answer you."
2. Michelangelo Buonarroti (1475–1564), famous Italian Renaissance sculptor, painter, architect, and poet; here, merely a topic of fashionable conversation.

And seeing that it was a soft October night,
Curled once about the house, and fell asleep.

And indeed there will be time[3]
For the yellow smoke that slides along the street,
Rubbing its back upon the window-panes;   25
There will be time, there will be time
To prepare a face to meet the faces that you meet;
There will be time to murder and create,
And time for all the works and days of hands[4]
That lift and drop a question on your plate;   30
Time for you and time for me,
And time yet for a hundred indecisions,
And for a hundred visions and revisions,
Before the taking of a toast and tea.

In the room the women come and go   35
Talking of Michelangelo.

And indeed there will be time
To wonder, "Do I dare?" and, "Do I dare?"
Time to turn back and descend the stair,
With a bald spot in the middle of my hair—   40
(They will say: "How his hair is growing thin!")
My morning coat, my collar mounting firmly to the chin,
My necktie rich and modest, but asserted by a simple pin—
(They will say: "But how his arms and legs are thin!")
Do I dare   45
Disturb the universe?
In a minute there is time
For decisions and revisions which a minute will reverse.

For I have known them all already, known them all—
Have known the evenings, mornings, afternoons,   50
I have measured out my life with coffee spoons;
I know the voices dying with a dying fall[5]
Beneath the music from a farther room.
    So how should I presume?

And I have known the eyes already, known them all—   55
The eyes that fix you in a formulated phrase,
And when I am formulated, sprawling on a pin,
When I am pinned and wriggling on the wall,
Then how should I begin
To spit out all the butt-ends of my days and ways?   60
    And how should I presume?

3. Echo of a love poem by Andrew Marvell (1621–1678), *To His Coy Mistress*: "Had we but world enough and time."
4. An implied contrast with the more productive agricultural labor of hands in the *Works and Days* of the Greek poet Hesiod (8th century B.C.E.).
5. Recalls Duke Orsino's description of a musical phrase in Shakespeare's *Twelfth Night* (1.1.4): "It has a dying fall."

And I have known the arms already, known them all—
Arms that are braceleted and white and bare
(But in the lamplight, downed with light brown hair!)
Is it perfume from a dress   65
That makes me so digress?
Arms that lie along a table, or wrap about a shawl.
    And should I then presume?
    And how should I begin?

                    •   •   •

    Shall I say, I have gone at dusk through narrow streets   70
And watched the smoke that rises from the pipes
Of lonely men in shirt-sleeves, leaning out of windows? . . .

    I should have been a pair of ragged claws
Scuttling across the floors of silent seas.

                    •   •   •

    And the afternoon, the evening, sleeps so peacefully!   75
Smoothed by long fingers,
Asleep . . . tired . . . or it malingers,
Stretched on the floor, here beside you and me.
Should I, after tea and cakes and ices,
Have the strength to force the moment to its crisis?   80
But though I have wept and fasted, wept and prayed,
Though I have seen my head (grown slightly bald) brought in
      upon a platter,
I am no prophet[6]—and here's no great matter;
I have seen the moment of my greatness flicker,
And I have seen the eternal Footman hold my coat, and snicker,   85
And in short, I was afraid.

    And would it have been worth it, after all,
After the cups, the marmalade, the tea,
Among the porcelain, among some talk of you and me,
Would it have been worth while,   90
To have bitten off the matter with a smile,
To have squeezed the universe into a ball
To roll it toward some overwhelming question,[7]
To say: "I am Lazarus, come from the dead,[8]
Come back to tell you all, I shall tell you all"—   95
If one, settling a pillow by her head,
    Should say: "That is not what I meant at all.
    That is not it, at all."

6. Salome obtained the head of the prophet
John the Baptist on a platter as a reward for
dancing before the tetrarch Herod (Matthew
14.3–11).
7. Another echo of Marvell's "To His Coy Mistress," when the lover suggests rolling "all our
strength and all / our sweetness up into one
ball" to send against the "iron gates of life."
8. The story of Lazarus, raised from the dead,
is told in John 11.1–44.

And would it have been worth it, after all,
Would it have been worth while,   100
After the sunsets and the dooryards and the sprinkled streets,
After the novels, after the teacups, after the skirts that trail along
    the floor—
And this, and so much more?—
It is impossible to say just what I mean!
But as if a magic lantern[9] threw the nerves in patterns on a screen: 105
Would it have been worth while
If one, settling a pillow or throwing off a shawl,
And turning toward the window, should say:
    "That is not it at all,
    That is not what I meant, at all."   110

           • • •

    No! I am not Prince Hamlet, nor was meant to be;
Am an attendant lord, one that will do
To swell a progress,[1] start a scene or two,
Advise the prince; no doubt, an easy tool,
Deferential, glad to be of use,   115
Politic, cautious, and meticulous;
Full of high sentence, but a bit obtuse;
At times, indeed, almost ridiculous—
Almost, at times, the Fool.

    I grow old . . . I grow old . . .   120
I shall wear the bottoms of my trousers rolled.

    Shall I part my hair behind? Do I dare to eat a peach?
I shall wear white flannel trousers, and walk upon the beach.
I have heard the mermaids singing, each to each.

    I do not think that they will sing to me.   125

    I have seen them riding seaward on the waves
Combing the white hair of the waves blown back
When the wind blows the water white and black.

    We have lingered in the chambers of the sea
By sea-girls wreathed with seaweed red and brown   130
Till human voices wake us, and we drown.

                             1915

---

9. A slide projector.
1. A procession of attendants accompanying a
king or nobleman across the stage, as in Elizabethan drama.

The Waste Land[1]

"Nam Sibyllam quidem Cumis ego ipse oculis meis vidi in ampulla
pendere, et cum illi pueri dicerent: Σίβυλλα τί θέλεισ; respondebat
illa: αποθανεῖν θέλω."[2]

For Ezra Pound
il miglior fabbro.[3]

1. The Burial of the Dead[4]

April is the cruellest month, breeding
Lilacs out of the dead land, mixing
Memory and desire, stirring
Dull roots with spring rain.
Winter kept us warm, covering   5
Earth in forgetful snow, feeding
A little life with dried tubers.
Summer surprised us, coming over the Starnbergersee[5]
With a shower of rain; we stopped in the colonnade,
And went on in sunlight, into the Hofgarten,[6]   10
And drank coffee, and talked for an hour.
Bin gar keine Russin, stamm' aus Litauen, echt deutsch.[7]
And when we were children, staying at the arch-duke's,
My cousin's, he took me out on a sled,
And I was frightened. He said, Marie,   15
Marie, hold on tight. And down we went.[8]
In the mountains, there you feel free.
I read, much of the night, and go south in the winter.

What are the roots that clutch, what branches grow
Out of this stony rubbish? Son of man,[9]   20
You cannot say, or guess, for you know only

1. Eliot provided footnotes for *The Waste Land* when it was first published in book form; these notes are included here. A general note at the beginning referred readers to the religious symbolism described in Jessie L. Weston's study of the Grail legend, *From Ritual to Romance* (1920), and to fertility myths and vegetation ceremonies (especially those involving Adonis, Attis, and Osiris) as described in the *The Golden Bough* (1890–1918) by the anthropologist Sir James Frazer.
2. Lines from Petronius's *Satyricon* (ca. 60 C.E.) describing the Sibyl, a prophetess shriveled with age and suspended in a bottle. "For indeed I myself have seen with my own eyes the Sibyl at Cumae, hanging in a bottle, and when those boys would say to her: 'Sibyl, what do you want?' she would reply: 'I want to die.'"
3. The dedication to Pound, who suggested cuts and changes in the first manuscript of *The Waste Land,* borrows words used by Guido Guinizelli to describe his predecessor, the Provençal poet Arnaut Daniel, in Dante's *Purgatorio* (26.117): he is "the better craftsman."
4. From the burial service of the Anglican Church.
5. A lake near Munich.
6. A public park.
7. "I am certainly no Russian, I come from Lithuania and am pure German." German settlers in Lithuania considered themselves superior to the Baltic natives.
8. Lines 8–16 recall *My Past,* the memoirs of Countess Marie Larisch.
9. "Cf. Ezekiel II, i" [Eliot's note]. The passage reads "Son of man, stand upon thy feet, and I will speak unto thee."

A heap of broken images, where the sun beats,
And the dead tree gives no shelter, the cricket no relief,[1]
And the dry stone no sound of water. Only
There is shadow under this red rock,   25
(Come in under the shadow of this red rock),
And I will show you something different from either
Your shadow at morning striding behind you
Or your shadow at evening rising to meet you;
I will show you fear in a handful of dust.   30

       Frisch weht der Wind
       Der Heimat zu
       Mein Irisch Kind,
       Wo weilest du?[2]

"You gave me hyacinths first a year ago;   35
"They called me the hyacinth girl."
—Yet when we came back, late, from the hyacinth garden,
Your arms full, and your hair wet, I could not
Speak, and my eyes failed, I was neither
Living nor dead, and I knew nothing,   40
Looking into the heart of light, the silence.
Oed' und leer das Meer.[3]

    Madame Sosostris,[4] famous clairvoyante,
Had a bad cold, nevertheless
Is known to be the wisest woman in Europe,   45
With a wicked pack of cards.[5] Here, said she,
Is your card, the drowned Phoenician Sailor,
(Those are pearls that were his eyes.[6] Look!)
Here is Belladonna, the Lady of the Rocks,

1. "Cf. Ecclesiastes XII, v" [Eliot's note]. "Also when they shall be afraid of that which is high, and fears shall be in the way, . . . the grasshopper shall be a burden, and desire shall fail."
2. "V. *Tristan und Isolde*, I, verses 5–8" [Eliot's note]. A sailor in Richard Wagner's opera sings, "The wind blows fresh / Towards the homeland / My Irish child / Where are you waiting?" (German)
3. "Id. III, verse 24" [Eliot's note]. "Barren and empty is the sea" (German) is the erroneous report the dying Tristan hears as he waits for Isolde's ship in the third act of Wagner's opera.
4. A fortune-teller with an assumed Egyptian name, possibly suggested by a similar figure in a novel by Aldous Huxley (*Crome Yellow*, 1921).
5. "I am not familiar with the exact constitution of the Tarot pack of cards, from which I have obviously departed to suit my own convenience. The Hanged Man, a member of the traditional pack, fits my purpose in two ways: because he is associated in my mind with the Hanged God of Frazer, and because I associate him with the hooded figure in the passage of the disciples to Emmaus in Part V. The Phoenician Sailor and the Merchant appear later; also the 'crowds of people,' and Death by Water is executed in Part IV. The Man with Three Staves (an authentic member of the Tarot pack) I associate, quite arbitrarily, with the Fisher King himself" [Eliot's note]. Tarot cards are used for telling fortunes; the four suits (cup, lance, sword, and coin) are life symbols related to the Grail legend; and, as Eliot suggests, various figures on the cards are associated with different characters and situations in *The Waste Land*. For example, the "drowned Phoenician Sailor" (line 47) recurs in the merchant from Smyrna (III) and Phlebas the Phoenician (IV). "Belladonna" (line 49)—a poison, hallucinogen, medicine, and cosmetic (in Italian, "beautiful lady"); also an echo of Leonardo da Vinci's painting of the Virgin, *Madonna of the Rocks*—heralds the neurotic society woman amid her jewels and perfumes (II). "The Wheel" (line 51) is the wheel of fortune. "The Hanged Man" (line 55) becomes the sacrificed fertility god whose death ensures resurrection and new life for his people.
6. A line from Ariel's song in Shakespeare's *The Tempest* (1.2.398), which describes the transformation of a drowned man.

The lady of situations.   50
Here is the man with three staves, and here the Wheel,
And here is the one-eyed merchant, and this card,
Which is blank, is something he carries on his back,
Which I am forbidden to see. I do not find
The Hanged Man. Fear death by water.   55
I see crowds of people, walking round in a ring.
Thank you. If you see dear Mrs. Equitone,
Tell her I bring the horoscope myself:
One must be so careful these days.

Unreal City,[7]   60
Under the brown fog of a winter dawn,
A crowd flowed over London Bridge, so many,
I had not thought death had undone so many.[8]
Sighs, short and infrequent, were exhaled,[9]
And each man fixed his eyes before his feet.   65
Flowed up the hill and down King William Street,
To where Saint Mary Woolnoth kept the hours
With a dead sound on the final stroke of nine.[1]
There I saw one I knew, and stopped him, crying: "Stetson!
"You who were with me in the ships at Mylae![2]   70
"That corpse you planted last year in your garden,
"Has it begun to sprout? Will it bloom this year?
"Or has the sudden frost disturbed its bed?
"Oh keep the Dog far hence, that's friend to men,[3]
"Or with his nails he'll dig it up again!   75
"You! hypocrite lecteur!—mon semblable,—mon frère!"[4]

---

7. "Cf. Baudelaire: 'Fourmillante cité, cité pleine de rêves, / Où le spectre en plein jour raccroche le passant'" [Eliot's note]. "Swarming city, city full of dreams, / Where the specter in broad daylight accosts the passerby"; a description of Paris from "The Seven Old Men" in *The Flowers of Evil* (1857).

8. "Cf. *Inferno* III, 55–57: 'si lunga tratta / di gente, ch'io non avrei mai creduto / che morte tanta n' avesse disfatta'" [Eliot's note]. "Behind that banner trailed so long a file / of people—I should never have believed / that death could have unmade so many souls"; not only is Dante amazed at the number of people who have died but he is also describing a crowd of people who were neither good nor bad—non-entities denied even the entrance to hell.

9. "Cf. *Inferno* IV, 25–27: 'Quivi, secondo che per ascoltare, / non avea pianto, ma' che di sospiri, / che l'aura eterna facevan tremare'" [Eliot's note]. "Here, so far as I could tell by listening, there was no weeping but so many sighs that they caused the everlasting air to tremble"; the first circle of hell, or limbo, contained the souls of virtuous people who lived before Christ or had not been baptized.

1. "A phenomenon which I have often noticed" [Eliot's note]. The church is in the financial district of London, where King William Street is also located.

2. An "average" modern name (with business associations) linked to the ancient battle of Mylae (260 B.C.E.), where Rome was victorious over its commercial rival, Carthage.

3. "Cf. the Dirge in Webster's *White Devil*" [Eliot's note]. The dirge, or song of lamentation, sung by Cornelia in John Webster's play (1625), asks to "keep the wolf far thence, that's foe to men," so that the wolf's nails may not dig up the bodies of her murdered relatives. Eliot's reversal of dog for wolf, and friend for foe, domesticates the grotesque scene; it may also foreshadow rebirth since (according to Weston's book), the rise of the Dog Star, Sirius, announced the flooding of the Nile and the consequent return of fertility to Egyptian soil.

4. "V. Baudelaire, Preface to *Fleurs du Mal*" [Eliot's note]. Baudelaire's poem preface, titled "To the Reader," ended "Hypocritical reader!—my likeness!—my brother!" The poet challenges the reader to recognize that both are caught up in the worst sin of all—the moral wasteland of *ennui* ("boredom") as lack of will, the refusal to care one way or the other.

II. A Game of Chess[5]

The Chair she sat in, like a burnished throne,[6]
Glowed on the marble, where the glass
Held up by standards wrought with fruited vines
From which a golden Cupidon peeped out   80
(Another hid his eyes behind his wing)
Doubled the flames of sevenbranched candelabra
Reflecting light upon the table as
The glitter of her jewels rose to meet it,
From satin cases poured in rich profusion.   85
In vials of ivory and coloured glass
Unstoppered, lurked her strange synthetic perfumes,
Unguent, powdered, or liquid—troubled, confused
And drowned the sense in odours; stirred by the air
That freshened from the window, these ascended   90
In fattening the prolonged candle-flames,
Flung their smoke into the laquearia,[7]
Stirring the pattern on the coffered ceiling.
Huge sea-wood fed with copper
Burned green and orange, framed by the coloured stone,   95
In which sad light a carvèd dolphin swam.
Above the antique mantel was displayed
As though a window gave upon the sylvan scene[8]
The change of Philomel,[9] by the barbarous king
So rudely forced; yet there the nightingale[1]   100
Filled all the desert with inviolable voice
And still she cried, and still the world pursues,
"Jug Jug"[2] to dirty ears.
And other withered stumps of time
Were told upon the walls; staring forms   105
Leaned out, leaning, hushing the room enclosed.
Footsteps shuffled on the stair.
Under the firelight, under the brush, her hair

---

5. Reference to a play, *A Game of Chess* (1627)
by Thomas Middleton (1580–1627); see n. 5,
p. 1393. Part II juxtaposes two scenes of modern sterility: an initial setting of wealthy boredom, neurosis, and lack of communication,
and a pub scene in which similar concerns of
appearance, sexual attraction, and thwarted
childbirth are brought out more visibly, and in
more vulgar language.
6. "Cf. *Antony and Cleopatra*, II, ii, 1.190"
[Eliot's note]. A paler version of Cleopatra's
splendor as she met her future lover, Antony:
"The barge she sat in, like a burnished throne, /
Burned on the water."
7. "Laquearia. V. *Aeneid*, 1, 726: dependent
lychni laquearibus aureis incensi, et noctem
flammis funalia vincunt" [Eliot's note]. "Glowing lamps hang from the gold-paneled ceiling,

and the torches conquer night with their
flames"; the banquet setting of another classical love scene, in which Dido is inspired with
a fatal passion for Aeneas.
8. "Sylvan scene. V. Milton, *Paradise Lost*, IV,
140" [Eliot's note]. Eden as first seen by Satan.
9. "V. Ovid, *Metamorphoses*, VI, Philomela"
[Eliot's note]. Philomela was raped by her
brother-in-law, King Tereus, who cut out her
tongue so that she could not tell her sister,
Procne. Later Procne is changed into a swallow and Philomela into a nightingale to save
them from the king's rage after they have
revenged themselves by killing his son.
1. "Cf. Part III, 1.204" [Eliot's note].
2. Represents the nightingale's song in Elizabethan poetry.

Spread out in fiery points
Glowed into words, then would be savagely still.   110

   'My nerves are bad to-night. Yes, bad. Stay with me.
'Speak to me. Why do you never speak. Speak.
  'What are you thinking of? What thinking? What?
'I never know what you are thinking. Think.'

   I think we are in rats' alley[3]   115
Where the dead men lost their bones.

'What is that noise?'
               The wind under the door.[4]
'What is that noise now? What is the wind doing?'
               Nothing again nothing.   120
                      'Do
'You know nothing? Do you see nothing? Do you remember
'Nothing?'

   I remember
Those are pearls that were his eyes.   125
'Are you alive, or not? Is there nothing in your head?'
                        But

O O O O that Shakespeherian Rag—
It's so elegant
So intelligent   130
'What shall I do now? What shall I do?'
'I shall rush out as I am, and walk the street
'With my hair down, so. What shall we do to-morrow?
'What shall we ever do?'
                  The hot water at ten.   135
And if it rains, a closed car at four.
And we shall play a game of chess,[5]
Pressing lidless eyes and waiting for a knock upon the door.

   When Lil's husband got demobbed,[6] I said—
I didn't mince my words, I said to her myself,   140
HURRY UP PLEASE ITS TIME[7]
Now Albert's coming back, make yourself a bit smart.
He'll want to know what you done with that money he gave you
To get yourself some teeth. He did, I was there.
You have them all out, Lil, and get a nice set,   145
He said, I swear, I can't bear to look at you.
And no more can't I, I said, and think of poor Albert,

3. "Cf. Part III, l.195" [Eliot's note].
4. "Cf. Webster: 'Is the wind in that door still?'" [Eliot's note]. From *The Devil's Law Case* (1623), 3.2.162, with the implied meaning "is there still breath in him?"
5. "Cf. the game of chess in Middleton's *Women Beware Women*" [Eliot's note]. In this scene, a woman is seduced in a series of strategic steps that parallel the moves of a chess game, which is occupying her mother-in-law at the same time.
6. Demobilized, discharged from the army.
7. The British bartender's warning that the pub is about to close.

He's been in the army four years, he wants a good time,
And if you don't give it him, there's others will, I said.
Oh is there, she said. Something o' that, I said.   150
Then I'll know who to thank, she said, and give me a straight look.
HURRY UP PLEASE ITS TIME
If you don't like it you can get on with it, I said.
Others can pick and choose if you can't.
But if Albert makes off, it won't be for lack of telling.   155
You ought to be ashamed, I said, to look so antique.
(And her only thirty-one.)
I can't help it, she said, pulling a long face,
It's them pills I took, to bring it off, she said.
(She's had five already, and nearly died of young George.)   160
The chemist[8] said it would be all right, but I've never been the same.
You are a proper fool, I said.
Well, if Albert won't leave you alone, there it is, I said,
What you get married for if you don't want children?
HURRY UP PLEASE ITS TIME   165
Well, that Sunday Albert was home, they had a hot gammon,[9]
And they asked me in to dinner, to get the beauty of it hot—
HURRY UP PLEASE ITS TIME
HURRY UP PLEASE ITS TIME
Goonight Bill. Goonight Lou. Goonight May. Goonight.   170
Ta ta. Goonight. Goonight.
Good night, ladies, good night, sweet ladies, good night, good night.[1]

III. The Fire Sermon[2]

The river's tent is broken: the last fingers of leaf
Clutch and sink into the wet bank. The wind
Crosses the brown land, unheard. The nymphs are departed.   175
Sweet Thames, run softly, till I end my song.[3]
The river bears no empty bottles, sandwich papers,
Silk handkerchiefs, cardboard boxes, cigarette ends
Or other testimony of summer nights. The nymphs are departed.
And their friends, the loitering heirs of city directors;   180
Departed, have left no addresses.
By the waters of Leman I sat down and wept[4] . . .
Sweet Thames, run softly till I end my song,

---

8. The druggist, who gave her pills to cause a miscarriage.
9. Ham.
1. The popular song for a party's end ("Good Night, Ladies") shifts into Ophelia's last words in *Hamlet* (4.5.72) as she goes off to drown herself.
2. Reference to the Buddha's Fire Sermon (see n. 2, p. 555), in which he denounced the fiery lusts and passions of earthly experience. "All things are on fire . . . with the fire of passion . . . of hatred . . . of infatuation." Part III describes the degeneration of even these pas-

sions in the sterile decadence of the modern Waste Land.
3. "V. Spenser, *Prothalamion*" [Eliot's note]. The line is the refrain of a marriage song by the Elizabethan poet Edmund Spenser (1552?–1599) and evokes a river of unpolluted pastoral beauty.
4. In Psalms 137.1, the exiled Hebrews sit by the rivers of Babylon and weep for their lost homeland. "Waters of Leman": Lake Geneva (where Eliot wrote much of *The Waste Land*). A "leman" is a mistress or lover.

Sweet Thames, run softly, for I speak not loud or long.
But at my back in a cold blast I hear[5]   185
The rattle of the bones, and chuckle spread from ear to ear.

A rat crept softly through the vegetation
Dragging its slimy belly on the bank
While I was fishing in the dull canal
On a winter evening round behind the gashouse   190
Musing upon the king my brother's wreck
And on the king my father's death before him.[6]
White bodies naked on the low damp ground
And bones cast in a little low dry garret,
Rattled by the rat's foot only, year to year.   195
But at my back from time to time I hear[7]
The sound of horns and motors, which shall bring[8]
Sweeney to Mrs. Porter in the spring.
O the moon shone bright on Mrs. Porter[9]
And on her daughter   200
They wash their feet in soda water
Et O ces voix d'enfants, chantant dans la coupole![1]

Twit twit twit
Jug jug jug jug jug jug
So rudely forc'd.   205
Tereu[2]

Unreal City
Under the brown fog of a winter noon
Mr. Eugenides, the Smyrna merchant
Unshaven, with a pocket full of currants   210
C.i.f. London: documents at sight,[3]

---

5. Distorted echo of Andrew Marvell's (1621–1678) poem "To His Coy Mistress." "But at my back I always hear / Time's wingèd chariot hurrying near."
6. "Cf. *The Tempest* I.ii" [Eliot's note]. Ferdinand, the king's son, believing his father drowned and mourning his death, hears in the air a song containing the line that Eliot quotes earlier at lines 48 and 125.
7. "Cf. Marvell, 'To His Coy Mistress'" [Eliot's note].
8. "Cf. Day, *Parliament of Bees*: 'When of the sudden, listening, you shall hear, / A noise of horns and hunting, which shall bring / Actaeon to Diana in the spring, / Where all shall see her naked skin'" [Eliot's note]. The young hunter Actaeon was changed into a stag, hunted down, and killed when he came upon the goddess Diana bathing. Sweeney is in no such danger from his visit to Mrs. Porter.
9. "I do not know the origin of the ballad from

which these lines are taken: it was reported to me from Sydney, Australia" [Eliot's note]. A song popular among Allied troops during World War I. One version continues lines 199–201 as follows: "And so they oughter / To keep them clean."
1. "V. Verlaine, *Parsifal*" [Eliot's note]. "And O these children's voices, singing in the dome!" (French); the last lines of a sonnet by Paul Verlaine (1844–1896), which ambiguously celebrates the Grail hero's chaste restraint. In Richard Wagner's opera, Parsifal's feet are washed to purify him before entering the presence of the Grail.
2. Tereus, who raped Philomela (see line 99); also the nightingale's song.
3. "The currants were quoted at a price 'carriage and insurance free to London'; and the Bill of Lading etc. were to be handed to the buyer upon payment of the sight draft" [Eliot's note].

Asked me in demotic French
To luncheon at the Cannon Street Hotel
Followed by a weekend at the Metropole.[4]

At the violet hour, when the eyes and back   215
Turn upward from the desk, when the human engine waits
Like a taxi throbbing waiting,
I Tiresias,[5] though blind, throbbing between two lives,
Old man with wrinkled female breasts, can see
At the violet hour, the evening hour that strives   220
Homeward, and brings the sailor home from sea,[6]
The typist home at teatime, clears her breakfast, lights
Her stove, and lays out food in tins.
Out of the window perilously spread
Her drying combinations touched by the sun's last rays,   225
On the divan are piled (at night her bed)
Stockings, slippers, camisoles, and stays.
I Tiresias, old man with wrinkled dugs
Perceived the scene, and foretold the rest—
I too awaited the expected guest.   230
He, the young man carbuncular, arrives,
A small house agent's clerk, with one bold stare,
One of the low on whom assurance sits
As a silk hat on a Bradford[7] millionaire.
The time is now propitious, as he guesses,   235
The meal is ended, she is bored and tired,
Endeavours to engage her in caresses
Which still are unreproved, if undesired.
Flushed and decided, he assaults at once;
Exploring hands encounter no defence;   240
His vanity requires no response,
And makes a welcome of indifference.
(And I Tiresias have foresuffered all
Enacted on this same divan or bed;
I who have sat by Thebes below the wall   245

4. Smyrna is an ancient Phoenician seaport, and early Smyrna merchants spread the Eastern fertility cults. In contrast, their descendant Mr. Eugenides ("Well-born") invites the poet to lunch in a large commercial hotel and a weekend at a seaside resort in Brighton.
5. "Tiresias, although a mere spectator and not indeed a 'character,' is yet the most important personage in the poem, uniting all the rest. Just as the one-eyed merchant, seller of currants, melts into the Phoenician Sailor, and the latter is not wholly distinct from Ferdinand Prince of Naples, so all the women are one woman, and the two sexes meet in Tiresias. What Tiresias sees, in fact, is the substance of the poem. The whole passage from Ovid is one of great anthropological interest" [Eliot's note]. The passage then quoted from Ovid's Metamorphoses (3.320–38) describes how Tiresias spent seven years of his life as a woman and thus experienced love from the point of view of both sexes. Blinded by Juno, he was recompensed by Jove with the gift of prophecy.
6. "This may or may not appear as exact as Sappho's lines, but I had in mind the 'longshore' or 'dory' fisherman, who returns at nightfall" [Eliot's note]. The Greek poet Sappho's poem describes how the evening star brings home those whom dawn has sent abroad; there is also an echo of Robert Louis Stevenson's (1850–1894) Requiem 1.221: "Home is the sailor, home from the sea."
7. A manufacturing town in Yorkshire that prospered greatly during World War I.

And walked among the lowest of the dead.)[8]
Bestows one final patronising kiss,
And gropes his way, finding the stairs unlit . . .

She turns and looks a moment in the glass,
Hardly aware of her departed lover;   250
Her brain allows one half-formed thought to pass:
'Well now that's done: and I'm glad it's over.'
When lovely woman stoops to folly and[9]
Paces about her room again, alone,
She smoothes her hair with automatic hand,   255
And puts a record on the gramophone.

    'This music crept by me upon the waters'[1]
And along the Strand, up Queen Victoria Street.
O City city,[2] I can sometimes hear
Beside a public bar in Lower Thames Street,   260
The pleasant whining of a mandoline
And a clatter and a chatter from within
Where fishmen lounge at noon: where the walls
Of Magnus Martyr[3] hold
Inexplicable splendour of Ionian white and gold.   265

              The river sweats[4]
              Oil and tar
              The barges drift
              With the turning tide
              Red sails   270
              Wide
              To leeward, swing on the heavy spar.
              The barges wash
              Drifting logs
              Down Greenwich reach   275
              Past the Isle of Dogs.[5]

8. Tiresias prophesied in the marketplace at Thebes for many years before dying and continuing to prophesy in Hades.
9. "V. Goldsmith, the song in *The Vicar of Wakefield*" [Eliot's note]. "When lovely woman stoops to folly / And finds too late that men betray / What charm can soothe her melancholy, / What art can wash her guilt away?" Oliver Goldsmith (ca. 1730–1774), *The Vicar of Wakefield* (1766).
1. "V. *The Tempest*, as above" [Eliot's note, referring to line 191]. Spoken by Ferdinand as he hears Ariel sing of his father's transformation by the sea, his eyes turning to pearls, his bones to coral, and everything else he formerly was into "something rich and strange."
2. A double invocation: the city of London and the City as London's central financial district (see lines 60 and 207). See also lines 375–76,

the great cities of Western civilization.
3. "The interior of St. Magnus Martyr is to my mind one of the finest among Wren's interiors. See *The Proposed Demolition of Nineteen City Churches*: (P. S. King & Son, Ltd)" [Eliot's note]. The architect was Christopher Wren (1632–1723), and the church is located just below London Bridge on Lower Thames Street.
4. "The Song of the (three) Thames-daughters begins here. From line 292 to 306 inclusive they speak in turn. V. *Götterdämmerung* III.i.: the Rhine-daughters" [Eliot's note]. In Wagner's opera *The Twilight of the Gods* (1876), the three Rhine-maidens mourn the loss of their gold, which gave the river its sparkling beauty; lines 277–78 here echo the Rhine-maidens' refrain.
5. A peninsula opposite Greenwich on the Thames.

Weialala leia
Wallala leialala

Elizabeth and Leicester[6]
Beating oars   280
The stern was formed
A gilded shell
Red and gold
The brisk swell
Rippled both shores   285
Southwest wind
Carried down stream
The peal of bells
White towers
    Weialala leia   290
    Wallala leialala

'Trams and dusty trees.
Highbury bore me. Richmond and Kew
Undid me.[7] By Richmond I raised my knees
Supine on the floor of a narrow canoe.'   295
'My feet are at Moorgate,[8] and my heart
Under my feet. After the event
He wept. He promised "a new start."
I made no comment. What should I resent?'

'On Margate Sands.[9]   300
I can connect
Nothing with nothing.
The broken fingernails of dirty hands.
My people humble people who expect
Nothing.'   305
    la la

To Carthage then I came[1]

---

6. "V. Froude, *Elizabeth*, vol. I, ch. iv, letter of De Quadra to Philip of Spain: 'In the afternoon we were in a barge, watching the games on the river. (The queen) was alone with Lord Robert and myself on the poop, when they began to talk nonsense, and went so far that Lord Robert at last said, as I was on the spot there was no reason why they should not be married if the queen pleased" [Eliot's note]. Sir Robert Dudley (1532–1588), the earl of Leicester, was a favorite of Queen Elizabeth and at one point hoped to marry her.

7. "Cf. *Purgatorio*, V, 133: 'Ricorditi di me, che son la Pia; / Siena mi fe', disfecemi Maremma'"

[Eliot's note]. La Pia, in Purgatory, recalls her seduction: "Remember me, who am La Pia. / Siena made me, Maremma undid me." Eliot's parody substitutes Highbury (a London suburb) and Richmond and Kew, popular excursion points on the Thames.

8. A London slum.

9. A seaside resort on the Thames.

1. "V. St. Augustine's *Confessions*: 'to Carthage then I came, where a cauldron of unholy loves sang all about mine ears'" [Eliot's note]. The youthful Augustine is described. Carthage is also the scene of Dido's faithful love for Aeneas, referred to in line 92.

Burning burning burning burning[2]
O Lord Thou pluckest me out[3]
O Lord Thou pluckest   310

burning

IV. Death by Water

Phlebas the Phoenician, a fortnight dead,
Forgot the cry of gulls, and the deep sea swell
And the profit and loss.
                    A current under sea   315
Picked his bones in whispers. As he rose and fell
He passed the stages of his age and youth
Entering the whirlpool.
                    Gentile or Jew
O you who turn the wheel and look to windward,   320
Consider Phlebas, who was once handsome and tall as you.

V. What the Thunder Said[4]

After the torchlight red on sweaty faces
After the frosty silence in the gardens
After the agony in stony places
The shouting and the crying   325
Prison and palace and reverberation
Of thunder of spring over distant mountains
He who was living is now dead[5]
We who were living are now dying
With a little patience   330

Here is no water but only rock
Rock and no water and the sandy road
The road winding above among the mountains
Which are mountains of rock without water
If there were water we should stop and drink   335

2. "The complete text of the Buddha's Fire Sermon (which corresponds in importance to the Sermon on the Mount) from which these words are taken, will be found translated in the late Henry Clarke Warren's *Buddhism in Translation* (Harvard Oriental Studies). Mr. Warren was one of the great pioneers of Buddhist studies in the Occident" [Eliot's note]. The Sermon on the Mount is in Matthew 5–7.
3. "From St. Augustine's *Confessions* again. The collocation of these two representatives of eastern and western asceticism, as the culmination of this part of the poem is not an accident" [Eliot's note]. See also Zechariah 3.2, where the high priest Joshua is described as a "brand plucked out of the fire."

4. "In the first part of Part V three themes are employed: the journey to Emmaus, the approach to the Chapel Perilous (see Miss Weston's book) and the present decay of eastern Europe" [Eliot's note]. On their journey to Emmaus (Luke 24.13–34), Jesus's disciples were joined by a stranger who later revealed himself to be the crucified and resurrected Christ. The *thunder* of the title is a divine voice in the Hindu *Upanishads* (see n. 3, p. 1401).
5. Allusions to stages in Christ's Passion: the betrayal, prayer in the garden of Gethsemane, imprisonment, trial, crucifixion, and burial. Despair reigns, for this is death before the Resurrection.

Amongst the rock one cannot stop or think
Sweat is dry and feet are in the sand
If there were only water amongst the rock
Dead mountain mouth of carious teeth that cannot spit
Here one can neither stand nor lie nor sit   340
There is not even silence in the mountains
But dry sterile thunder without rain
There is not even solitude in the mountains
But red sullen faces sneer and snarl
From doors of mudcracked houses   345
                              If there were water
        And no rock
        If there were rock
        And also water
        And water   350
        A spring
        A pool among the rock
        If there were the sound of water only
        Not the cicada[6]
        And dry grass singing   355
        But sound of water over a rock
        Where the hermit-thrush[7] sings in the pine trees
        Drip drop drip drop drop drop drop
        But there is no water

        Who is the third who walks always beside you?   360
When I count, there are only you and I together[8]
But when I look ahead up the white road
There is always another one walking beside you
Gliding wrapt in a brown mantle, hooded
I do not know whether a man or a woman   365
—But who is that on the other side of you?

        What is that sound high in the air[9]
Murmur of maternal lamentation
Who are those hooded hordes swarming
Over endless plains, stumbling in cracked earth   370
Ringed by the flat horizon only
What is the city over the mountains
Cracks and reforms and bursts in the violet air

---

6. Grasshopper or cricket; see line 23.
7. "The hermit-thrush which I have heard in
Quebec Province. . . . Its 'water-dripping song'
is justly celebrated" [Eliot's note].
8. "The following lines were stimulated by the
account of one of the Antarctic expeditions (I
forget which, but I think one of Shackleton's):
it was related that the party of explorers, at the
extremity of their strength, had the constant
delusion that there was *one more member* than
could actually be counted" [Eliot's note]. See
also n. 4, p. 1399.

9. Eliot's note to lines 367–77 refers to Hermann Hesse's *Blick ins Chaos* (Glimpse into
Chaos) and a passage that reads, translated,
"Already half of Europe, already at least half of
Eastern Europe is on the way to Chaos, drives
drunk in holy madness on the edge of the
abyss and sings at the same time, sings drunk
and hymn-like, as Dimitri Karamazov sang [in
Dostoevsky's *The Brothers Karamazov*]. The
offended bourgeois laughs at the songs; the
saint and the seer hear them with tears."

Falling towers
Jerusalem Athens Alexandria   375
Vienna London
Unreal

   A woman drew her long black hair out tight
And fiddled whisper music on those strings
And bats with baby faces in the violet light   380
Whistled, and beat their wings
And crawled head downward down a blackened wall
And upside down in air were towers
Tolling reminiscent bells, that kept the hours
And voices singing out of empty cisterns and exhausted wells.   385

   In this decayed hole among the mountains
In the faint moonlight, the grass is singing
Over the tumbled graves, about the chapel
There is the empty chapel, only the wind's home.
It has no windows, and the door swings,   390
Dry bones can harm no one.
Only a cock stood on the rooftree
Co co rico co co rico[1]
In a flash of lightning. Then a damp gust
Bringing rain   395

   Ganga was sunken, and the limp leaves
Waited for rain, while the black clouds
Gathered far distant, over Himavant.[2]
The jungle crouched, humped in silence.
Then spoke the thunder   400
DA
Datta: what have we given?[3]
My friend, blood shaking my heart
The awful daring of a moment's surrender
Which an age of prudence can never retract   405
By this, and this only, we have existed
Which is not to be found in our obituaries
Or in memories draped by the beneficent spider[4]
Or under seals broken by the lean solicitor
In our empty rooms   410
DA

1. European version of the cock's crow: *cock-a-doodle-doo*. The cock crowed in Matthew 26.34 and 74, after Peter had denied Jesus three times.
2. A mountain in the Himalayas. "Ganga": the river Ganges in India.
3. "'Datta, dayadhvam, damyata' (Give, sympathise, control). The fable of the meaning of the Thunder is found in the *Brihadaranyaka—Upanishad* 5,1" [Eliot's note]. In the fable, the word *DA*, spoken by the supreme being Prajapati, is interpreted as *Datta* ("to give alms"),

Dayadhvam ("to sympathize or have compassion"), and *Damyata* ("to have self-control") by gods, human beings, and demons respectively. The conclusion is that when the thunder booms DA DA DA, Prajapati is commanding that all three virtues be practiced simultaneously.
4. "Cf. Webster, *The White Devil*, V, vi: '. . . they'll remarry / Ere the worm pierce your winding-sheet, ere the spider / Make a thin curtain for your epitaphs'" [Eliot's note].

Dayadhvam:[5] I have heard the key
Turn in the door once and turn once only
We think of the key, each in his prison
Thinking of the key, each confirms a prison   415
Only at nightfall, aethereal rumours
Revive for a moment a broken Coriolanus[6]
DA
Damyata: The boat responded
Gaily, to the hand expert with sail and oar   420
The sea was calm, your heart would have responded
Gaily, when invited, beating obedient
To controlling hands
                                    I sat upon the shore
Fishing,[7] with the arid plain behind me   425
Shall I at least set my lands in order?
London Bridge is falling down falling down falling down

Poi s'ascose nel foco che gli affina[8]
Quando fiam uti chelidon[9]—O swallow swallow
Le Prince d'Aquitaine à la tour abolie[1]   430
These fragments I have shored against my ruins
Why then Ile fit you. Hieronymo's mad againe.[2]
Datta. Dayadhvam. Damyata.
        Shantih   shantih   shantih[3]

                                                        1922

5. Eliot's note on the command "to sympa-thize" or reach outside the self, cites two descriptions of helpless isolation. The first comes from Dante's *Inferno* 33.46: as Ugolino, imprisoned in a tower with his children to die of starvation, says, "And I heard below the door of the horrible tower being locked up." The second is a modern description by the English philosopher F. H. Bradley (1846–1924) of the inevitably self-enclosed or private nature of consciousness: "My external sensations are no less private to myself than are my thoughts or my feelings. In either case my experience falls within my own circle, a circle closed on the outside; and, with all its elements alike, every sphere is opaque to the others which surround it. . . . In brief, regarded as an existence which appears in a soul, the whole world for each is peculiar and private to that soul" (*Appearance and Reality*).
6. A proud Roman patrician who was exiled and led an army against his homeland. In Shakespeare's play, both his grandeur and his downfall come from a desire to be ruled only by himself.
7. "V. Weston: *From Ritual to Romance;* chapter on the Fisher King" [Eliot's note].
8. Eliot's note quotes a passage in the *Purga-torio* in which Arnaut Daniel (see n. 3, p. 1389) asks Dante to remember his pain. The line cited here, "then he hid himself in the fire

which refines them" (*Purgatorio* 26.148), shows Daniel departing in fire which—in Purgatory—exists as a purifying rather than a destructive element.
9. "V. *Pervigilium Veneris.* Cf. Philomela in Parts II and III" [Eliot's note]. "When shall I be as a swallow?" A line from the *Vigil of Venus,* an anonymous late Latin poem, that asks for the gift of song; here associated with Philomela as a swallow, not the nightingale of lines 99–103 and 203–06.
1. "V. Gerard de Nerval, Sonnet *El Desdi-chado*" [Eliot's note]. The Spanish title means "The Disinherited One," and the sonnet is a monologue describing the speaker as a melan-choly, ill-starred dreamer: "the Prince of Aquit-aine in his ruined tower." Another line recalls the scene at the end of "The Love Song of J. Alfred Prufrock" (p. 1388): "I dreamed in the grotto where sirens swim."
2. "V. Kyd's *Spanish Tragedy*" [Eliot's note]. Thomas Kyd's revenge play (1594) is subtitled *Hieronymo's Mad Againe.* The protagonist "fits" his son's murderers into appropriate roles in a court entertainment so that they may all be killed.
3. "Shantih. Repeated as here, a formal end-ing to an Upanishad. 'The Peace which pass-eth understanding' is our equivalent to this word" [Eliot's note]. The *Upanishads* comment on the sacred Hindu scriptures, the *Vedas.*

ANNA AKHMATOVA
1889-1966

One of the great Russian poets of the twentieth century, Anna Akhmatova expresses herself in an intensely personal, poetic voice, whether as lover, wife, and mother or as a national poet commemorating the mute agony of millions. From the subjective romantic lyrics of her earliest work to the communal mourning of *Requiem*, she conveys universal themes in terms of individual experience, and historical events through the filter of fear, love, hope, and pain. Yet what most distinguishes her work is the way these basic emotions arise from the historical traumas of Akhmatova's native land.

Born Anna Andreevna Gorenko, in a suburb of the Black Sea port of Odessa, she was the daughter of a maritime engineer and an independent woman of revolutionary sympathies. She took the pen name Akhmatova (accented on the second syllable) from her maternal great-grandmother, who was of Tatar descent. Anna attended the local school at Tsarskoe Selo, near St. Petersburg, but completed her degree in Kiev. In 1907 she briefly studied law at the Kiev College for Women before moving to St. Petersburg to study literature. In Tsarskoe Selo, Akhmatova met Nikolai Gumilyov, whom she married in 1910. Gumilyov helped organize the Poets Guild, which became the core of a small new literary movement. Acmeism rejected the romantic, quasi-religious aims of Russian symbolism and valued clarity, concreteness, and closeness to the things of this earth. The Symbolist–Acmeist debate went on inside a lively literary and social life, while the three main figures of the movement—Akhmatova, Gumi-lyov, and Osip Mandelstam—gained a reputation as important poets.

Although Akhmatova and Gumilyov divorced, his arrest and execution for counterrevolutionary activities in 1921 put her status into question. After 1922 she was no longer allowed to publish and was forced into the withdrawal from public activity that Russians call "internal emigration." Officially forgotten, she was not forgotten in fact; in the schools, students who would never hear her name mentioned in class copied out her poems by hand and circulated them secretly. Relying for her living on a meager, irregular pension, Akhmatova prepared essays on the life and works of the Russian author Aleksandr Pushkin (1799–1837) and wrote poems that would not appear until much later. Stalin's "Great Purge" of 1935–38 sent millions of people to prison camps and made the 1930s a time of terror and uncertainty for everyone.

Akhmatova's friend Osip Mandelstam was exiled to Voronezh in 1934 and then sent to a prison camp in 1938, where he died that year. In 1935 her partner, the art critic Nikolai Punin, was arrested briefly and her son Lev Gumilyov, then twenty-three, was imprisoned, an event that inspired the first poems of the cycle that would become *Requiem*. Lev was ultimately imprisoned for a total of fourteen years as the government sought a way to punish his mother for what it perceived as her disloyalty to the regime. Composing *Requiem* was a risky act carried out over several years, and Akhmatova and her friend Lidia Chukovskaya memorized the stanzas in order to preserve the poem in the absence of written copy.

During the Second World War, Akhmatova's interest in larger musical forms motivated her to develop cycles of poems instead of her accustomed individual lyrics. She also began work on *Poem Without a Hero*, a long, complex verse narrative in three parts that sums up many of her earlier themes: love, death, creativity, the unity of European culture, and the suffering of her people. The poet was allowed a partial return to public life, addressing women on the radio during the siege of Leningrad (St. Petersburg) in 1941 and writing patriotic lyrics such as the famous *Courage* (published in *Pravda* in 1942), which rallied the Russian people to defend their homeland (and their national language) from enslavement. Her son was briefly released to serve in the military before being imprisoned again after the war.

Despite her patriotic activities, Akhmatova was subject to vicious official attacks after the war. Because she was considered too independent and cosmopolitan to be tolerated by the authorities, Akhmatova's books were suppressed: they did not fit the government-approved model of literature: they were too "individualistic" and were not "socially useful." After the death of Joseph Stalin, in 1953, however, her collected poems—including poems of the war years and unknown texts written during the periods of enforced silence—brought the range of her work to public attention. *Requiem* was first published "without her consent" in Munich in 1963 (not until 1987 was the complete text published in the Soviet Union). Her death, in 1966, signaled the end of an era in modern Russian poetry, for she was the last of the famous "quartet" that also included Mandelstam, Tsvetaeva, and Boris Pasternak.

Requiem (1940), presented here, is a lyrical cycle, a series of poems written on a theme, but it is also a short epic narrative. The story it tells is acutely personal, even autobiographical, but like an epic it transcends personal significance and describes (as in *The Song of Roland*) a moment in the history of a nation. Akhmatova, who had seen her husband and son arrested and her friends die in prison camps, was only one of millions who had suffered similar losses in the purges of the 1930s. "Instead of a Preface," "Dedication," and two epilogues to *Requiem* constitute a framework examining this image of a common fate, while the core group of numbered poems develops a subjective picture and stages an individual drama. The "Dedication" and "Prologue" establish the context for the poem as a whole: the mass arrests in the 1930s after the assassination on December 1, 1934, of Sergei Kirov, the top Communist Party official in Leningrad. In the inner poems, Akhmatova blends her individual personal losses—husband, son, and friends—to create a single focus: the figure of a mother grieving for her condemned son. The speaker identifies herself with the crowd of women with whom she waited for seventeen months outside the Kresty ("Crosses") prison in Leningrad; at dawn each day they would all arrive, hoping to be allowed to pass their loved ones a parcel or a letter, and fearing that the prisoners would be sentenced to death or exile to the prison camps of Siberia. Instead of experiencing a natural life—one in which "for someone the sunset luxuriates"—these women and the prisoners are forced into a suspended, uncertain existence where all values are inverted and the city itself has become merely the setting for its prisons.

The "I" of the speaker throughout remains anonymous, in spite of the fact that Akhmatova describes her personal emotions in the central poems; her identity is that of a sorrowing mother, and she is distinguished from her fellow sufferers only by the poetic gift that makes her the "exhausted mouth, / Through which a hundred million scream." *Requiem* is at once both public and private: a picture of individual grief linked to the country's disaster, and a vision of community suffering that extends beyond contemporary national tragedy into medieval Russian history and Greek mythology. The poem consistently figures the martyrdom of the Soviet people in religious terms, from the recurrent mention of crosses and Crucifixion to the culminating image of maternal suffering in Mary, the mother of Christ.

With the numbered poems, Akhmatova recounts the growing anguish of a mother as her son is arrested and sentenced to death. The speaker has described her partner's arrest at dawn, in the midst of the family. Her son is arrested later, and in the rest of the poem she relives her numb incomprehension as she struggles against the increasing likelihood that he will be condemned to death. After the sentence is passed, the mother can speak of his execution only in oblique terms, by shifting the image of death onto the plane of the Crucifixion and God's will. It is a tragedy that cannot be comprehended or beheld directly, just as, she suggests, at the Crucifixion "No one glanced and no one would have dared" to look at the grieving Mary.

In the two epilogues, the grieving speaker returns from religious transcendence to Earth and current history. Here she takes on a composite identity, seeing herself not as an isolated sufferer but as the women whose fate she has shared. It is their memory she perpetuates by writing *Requiem*, and it is in their memory that she herself lives on. No longer the victim of purely personal tragedy, she has become a bronze statue commemorating a community of suffering—a figure shaped by circumstances into a monument of public and private grief.

Requiem[1]

1935–1940

No, not under the vault of alien skies,[2]
And not under the shelter of alien wings—
I was with my people then,
There, where my people, unfortunately, were.

1961

Instead of a Preface

In the terrible years of the Yezhov terror,[3] I spent seventeen months in the prison lines of Leningrad. Once, someone "recognized" me. Then a woman with bluish lips standing behind me, who, of course, had never heard me called by name before, woke up from the stupor to which every one had succumbed and whispered in my ear (everyone spoke in whispers there):

"Can you describe this?"

And I answered: "Yes, I can."

1. Translated by Judith Hemschemeyer.
2. A phrase borrowed from *Message to Siberia* by the Russian poet Aleksandr Pushkin (1799–1837).

3. In 1937–38, mass arrests were carried out by the secret police, headed by Nikolai Yezhov.

Then something that looked like a smile passed over what had once been her face.

April 1, 1957
Leningrad[4]

Dedication

Mountains bow down to this grief,
Mighty rivers cease to flow,
But the prison gates hold firm,
And behind them are the "prisoners' burrows"
And mortal woe.   5
For someone a fresh breeze blows,
For someone the sunset luxuriates—
We[5] wouldn't know, we are those who everywhere
Hear only the rasp of the hateful key
And the soldiers' heavy tread.   10
We rose as if for an early service,
Trudged through the savaged capital
And met there, more lifeless than the dead;
The sun is lower and the Neva[6] mistier,
But hope keeps singing from afar.   15
The verdict . . . And her tears gush forth,
Already she is cut off from the rest,
As if they painfully wrenched life from her heart,
As if they brutally knocked her flat,
But she goes on . . . Staggering . . . Alone . . .   20
Where now are my chance friends
Of those two diabolical years?
What do they imagine is in Siberia's storms,[7]
What appears to them dimly in the circle of the moon?
I am sending my farewell greeting to them.   25

March 1940

Prologue

That was when the ones who smiled
Were the dead, glad to be at rest.
And like a useless appendage, Leningrad
Swung from its prisons.
And when, senseless from torment,   5

---

4. The prose preface was written after her son had been released from prison and it was possible to think of editing the poem for publication.
5. The women waiting in line before the prison gates.
6. The large river that flows through St. Petersburg.

7. Victims of the purges who were not executed were condemned to prison camps in Siberia. Their wives were allowed to accompany them into exile, although they had to live in towns at a distance from the camps.

Regiments of convicts marched,
And the short songs of farewell
Were sung by locomotive whistles.
The stars of death stood above us
And innocent Russia writhed   10
Under bloody boots
And under the tires of the Black Marias.[8]

I

They led you away at dawn,
I followed you, like a mourner,
In the dark front room the children were crying,[9]
By the icon shelf the candle was dying.
On your lips was the icon's chill.[1]   5
The deathly sweat on your brow . . . Unforgettable!—
I will be like the wives of the Streltsy,[2]
Howling under the Kremlin towers.

1935

II

Quietly flows the quiet Don,[3]
Yellow moon slips into a home.

He slips in with cap askew,
He sees a shadow, yellow moon.

This woman is ill,   5
This woman is alone,
Husband in the grave,[4] son in prison,
Say a prayer for me.

III

No, it is not I, it is somebody else who is suffering.
I would not have been able to bear what happened,
Let them shroud it in black,
And let them carry off the lanterns . . .
                                            Night.   5

1940

8. Police cars for conveying those arrested.
9. Akhmatova's third husband, the art historian Nikolai Punin, was arrested at dawn while the children (his daughter and her cousin) cried.
1. The icon—a small religious painting—was set on a shelf before which a candle was kept lit. Punin had kissed the icon before being taken away.
2. Elite troops organized by Ivan the Terrible around 1550. They rebelled and were executed by Peter the Great in 1698. Pleading in vain, their wives and mothers saw the men killed under the towers of the Kremlin.
3. The great Russian river, often celebrated in folk songs. This poem is modeled on a simple, rhythmic, short folk song known as a *chastuska*.
4. Akhmatova's first husband, the poet Nikolai Gumilyov, was shot in 1921.

IV

You should have been shown, you mocker,
Minion of all your friends,
Gay little sinner of Tsarskoye Selo,[5]
What would happen in your life—
How three-hundredth in line, with a parcel,   5
You would stand by the Kresty prison,

Your tempestuous tears
Burning through the New Year's ice.
Over there the prison poplar bends,
And there's no sound—and over there how many   10
Innocent lives are ending now . . .

V

For seventeen months I've been crying out,
Calling you home.
I flung myself at the hangman's[6] feet,
You are my son and my horror.
Everything is confused forever,   5
And it's not clear to me
Who is a beast now, who is a man,
And how long before the execution.
And there are only dusty flowers,
And the chinking of the censer, and tracks   10
From somewhere to nowhere.
And staring me straight in the eyes,
And threatening impending death,
Is an enormous star.[7]

1939

VI

The light weeks will take flight,
I won't comprehend what happened.
Just as the white nights[8]
Stared at you, dear son, in prison

So they are staring again,   5
With the burning eyes of a hawk,
Talking about your lofty cross,
And about death.

1939

---

5. Akhmatova recalls her early, carefree, and privileged life in Tsarskoe Selo, outside St. Petersburg.
6. Stalin's. Akhmatova wrote a letter to him pleading for the release of her son.
7. The *star*, the *censer*, the foliage, and the confusion between beast and man recall apocalyptic passages in the Book of Revelation (8.5, 7, 10–11 and 9.7–10).
8. In St. Petersburg, because it is so far north, the nights around the summer solstice are never totally dark.

VII

THE SENTENCE

And the stone word fell
On my still-living breast.
Never mind, I was ready.
I will manage somehow.

Today I have so much to do: 5
I must kill memory once and for all,
I must turn my soul to stone,
I must learn to live again—

Unless . . . Summer's ardent rustling
Is like a festival outside my window.   10
For a long time I've foreseen this
Brilliant day, deserted house.

June 22, 1939[9]
Fountain House

VIII

TO DEATH

You will come in any case—so why not now?
I am waiting for you—I can't stand much more.
I've put out the light and opened the door
For you, so simple and miraculous.
So come in any form you please,   5
Burst in as a gas shell
Or, like a gangster, steal in with a length of pipe,
Or poison me with typhus fumes.
Or be that fairy tale you've dreamed up,[1]
So sickeningly familiar to everyone—   10
In which I glimpse the top of a pale blue cap[2]
And the house attendant white with fear.
Now it doesn't matter anymore. The Yenisey[3] swirls,
The North Star shines.
And the final horror dims   15
The blue luster of beloved eyes.

August 19, 1939
Fountain House

---

9. The date that her son was sentenced to labor camp.
1. A denunciation to the police for imaginary crimes, common during the purges as people hastened to protect themselves by accusing their neighbors.
2. The NKVD (secret police) wore blue caps.
3. A river in Siberia along which there were many prison camps.

IX

Now madness half shadows
My soul with its wing,
And makes it drunk with fiery wine
And beckons toward the black ravine.

And I've finally realized   5
That I must give in,
Overhearing myself
Raving as if it were somebody else.

And it does not allow me to take
Anything of mine with me   10
(No matter how I plead with it,
No matter how I supplicate):

Not the terrible eyes of my son—
Suffering turned to stone,
Not the day of the terror,   15
Not the hour I met with him in prison,

Not the sweet coolness of his hands,
Not the trembling shadow of the lindens,
Not the far-off, fragile sound—
Of the final words of consolation.   20

May 4, 1940
Fountain House

X

CRUCIFIXION

"Do not weep for Me, Mother,
I am in the grave."

1

A choir of angels sang the praises of that momentous hour,
And the heavens dissolved in fire.
To his Father He said: "Why hast Thou forsaken me!"[4]
And to his Mother: "Oh, do not weep for Me . . ."[5]

1940
Fountain House

---

4. Jesus' last words from the Cross (Matthew 27.46).
5. These words and the epigraph refer to a line from the Russian Orthodox prayer sung at services on Easter Saturday: "Weep not for Me, Mother, when you look upon the grave." Jesus is comforting Mary with the promise of his resurrection.

2

Mary Magdalene beat her breast and sobbed,
The beloved disciple[6] turned to stone,
But where the silent Mother stood, there
No one glanced and no one would have dared.

1943
Tashkent

Epilogue I

I learned how faces fall,
How terror darts from under eyelids,
How suffering traces lines
Of stiff cuneiform on cheeks,
How locks of ashen-blonde or black   5
Turn silver suddenly,
Smiles fade on submissive lips
And fear trembles in a dry laugh.
And I pray not for myself alone,
But for all those who stood there with me   10
In cruel cold, and in July's heat,
At that blind, red wall.

Epilogue II

Once more the day of remembrance[7] draws near.
I see, I hear, I feel you:

The one they almost had to drag at the end,
And the one who tramps her native land no more,

And the one who, tossing her beautiful head,   5
Said: "Coming here's like coming home."

I'd like to name them all by name,
But the list[8] has been confiscated and is nowhere to be found.

I have woven a wide mantle for them
From their meager, overheard words.   10

I will remember them always and everywhere,
I will never forget them no matter what comes.

And if they gag my exhausted mouth
Through which a hundred million scream,

6. The apostle John.
7. In the Russian Orthodox Church, a memorial service is held on the anniversary of a death.
8. Of prisoners.

Then may the people remember me   15
On the eve of my remembrance day.

And if ever in this country
They decide to erect a monument to me,

I consent to that honor
Under these conditions—that it stand   20

Neither by the sea, where I was born:
My last tie with the sea is broken,

Nor in the tsar's garden near the cherished pine stump,[9]
Where an inconsolable shade[1] looks for me,

But here, where I stood for three hundred hours,   25
And where they never unbolted the doors for me.

This, lest in blissful death
I forget the rumbling of the Black Marias,

Forget how that detested door slammed shut
And an old woman howled like a wounded animal.   30

And may the melting snow stream like tears
From my motionless lids of bronze,

And a prison dove coo in the distance,
And the ships of the Neva sail calmly on.

March 1940

                                                                       1963

---

9. The gardens and park surrounding the summer palace in Tsarskoe Selo. Akhmatova writes elsewhere of the stump of a favorite tree in the gardens and of the poet Pushkin, whom she describes as walking in the park.

1. A ghost; probably the restless spirit of Akhmatova's executed husband, Gumilyov, who had courted her in Tsarskoe Selo.

FEDERICO GARCÍA LORCA

1898-1936

The poet and playwright Federico García Lorca, the best known writer of modern Spain and perhaps the greatest Spanish author since Cervantes, wrote poignantly about death and would himself suffer an early and infamous death. A member of the "Generation of 1927" who sought to revive the grandeur of Spanish poetry, Lorca is known for the striking imagery and lyric musicality of his work, which was both classical and modern, traditional and innovative, difficult and popular, regional and universal. The poetry and plays that began as personal statements took on larger significance, first as the expression of tragic conflicts in Spanish culture and then as poignant laments for humanity—especially the plight of those who are deprived, by society or simply by death, of the fulfillment that could have been theirs.

Lorca (despite the Spanish practice of using both paternal and maternal names—correctly, "García Lorca"—the author is generally called "Lorca") was born on June 5, 1898, in the small village of Fuentevaqueros, near the Andalusian city of Granada. He studied law at the University of Granada but left in 1919 for Madrid, where he entered the Residencia de Estudiantes, a college that provided a cosmopolitan education for Spanish youth. Madrid, the capital of Spain, was the center of intellectual and artistic ferment, and the Residencia attracted those who would become the most influential writers and artists of their generation (including the artist Salvador Dalí and the film director Luis Buñuel). Although he lived at the Residencia almost continuously until 1928,

he never seriously pursued a degree but spent his time reading, writing, improvising music and poetry with his friends, and producing his first plays.

Lorca's early poems celebrate his home province of Andalusia, a region known for its mixture of Arab and Spanish culture and for a tradition of wandering Gypsy singers who improvised, to guitar accompaniment, rhythmic laments of love and death, often with repetitive refrains such as that in the *Lament for Ignacio Sánchez Mejías*. Impelled by an emotional crisis, Lorca left Spain for New York in 1929 and there wrote a series of poems later published as *Poet in New York* (1940). Along with the familiar themes of doomed love and death is Lorca's tentative exploration of his homosexuality, which he could not reveal in conservative Spanish society and which, in this and later works, announced itself only with hesitation and anxiety. He traveled to Argentina, where he befriended the Chilean poet **Pablo Neruda**. From 1930 to his death, Lorca was active in the theater both as a writer and as a director of a traveling theatrical group (La Barraca) subsidized by the Spanish Republic. After a series of farces that mixed romantically tragic and comic themes, he presented the tragedies for which he is best known: *Blood Wedding* (1933) and *Yerma* (1934). All of Lorca's theater work rejects the conventionally realistic nineteenth-century drama, employing an openly poetic form that suggests musical patterns, with choruses, songs, and stylized movement.

Lorca published his *Lament for Ignacio Sánchez Mejías* in 1935. This long poem commemorates the death of a good friend, a famous toreador who was gored by a bull on August 11, 1934, and died two days later. Lorca's Lament celebrates both his friend and the value of human grace and courage in a world in which death is inevitable.

Lorca's Lament, cast as an elegy (a poem that mourns a death), recalls one of the most famous poems of Spanish literature: the Verses on the Death of His Father, by the medieval poet Jorge Manrique (1440–1479). Yet there is a fundamental difference between the two: while Manrique's elegy stresses religious themes and the prospect of eternal life, Lorca—in grim contrast—rejects such consolation and insists that his friend's death is permanent.

The four parts of the Lament incorporate diverse forms and perspectives, all working together to suggest a progression from the report of death in the first line—"At five in the afternoon"—to the close, where the dead man's nobility and elegance survive in "a sad breeze through the olive trees." The insistent refrain colors the first section, "Cogida and Death," with its throbbing return to the moment of death. The scene in the arena wavers between objective reporting—the boy with the shroud, the coffin on wheels—and the shared agony of the bull's bellowing and wounds burning like suns. In the second section, the speaker refuses to accept his friend's death ("I will not see it!") and requests that images of whiteness cover up the spilled blood; he imagines Ignacio climbing steps in pursuit of a mystic meeting with his true self and instead, bewildered, encountering his broken body.

After paying his friend tribute, the speaker admits what he cannot force himself to envision: the finality of decay as moss and grass invade the bullfighter's buried skull.

At the end of section 3, the speaker accepts physical death ("even the sea dies!") but signals in the rhythmic free verse of the final section that his poetry will preserve a vision of his noble countryman against complete obliteration. In life, Sánchez Mejías was known to his friends for "the signal maturity of your understanding. / Of your appetite for death and the taste of its mouth." These qualities survive in memory. Echoing the pride with which the Latin poet Horace claimed to perpetuate his subjects in a "monument more lasting than bronze," Lorca sings of his friend "for posterity" and captures, in his poem, the death and life of Sánchez Mejías.

On August 16, 1936, shortly after the outbreak of the Spanish Civil War, when right-wing troops led by General Francisco Franco, with support from the Catholic Church, attacked the young Spanish Republic, and almost precisely two years after the death of Sánchez Mejías, Lorca was dragged from a friend's house by a squadron of Franco's Fascist guards; three days later he was killed. Unlike that of his friend Ignacio, his body was never recovered. Lorca's murder, commemorated in Pablo Neruda's poem "I'm Explaining a Few Things," outraged the European and American literary and artistic community; it seemed to symbolize the mindless destruction of humane values that loomed with the approach of World War II.

Lament for Ignacio Sánchez Mejías[1]

1. Cogida[2] and Death

At five in the afternoon.
It was exactly five in the afternoon.
A boy brought the white sheet
at five in the afternoon.
A frail of lime[3] ready prepared
at five in the afternoon.
The rest was death, and death alone
at five in the afternoon.

The wind carried away the cottonwool[4]
at five in the afternoon.
And the oxide scattered crystal and nickel
at five in the afternoon.
Now the dove and the leopard[5] wrestle
at five in the afternoon.
And a thigh with a desolate horn
at five in the afternoon.
The bass-string struck up
at five in the afternoon.
Arsenic bells[6] and smoke
at five in the afternoon.
Groups of silence in the corners
at five in the afternoon.
And the bull alone with a high heart!
At five in the afternoon.
When the sweat of snow was coming
at five in the afternoon.
when the bull ring was covered in iodine[7]
at five in the afternoon.
death laid eggs in the wound
at five in the afternoon.
At five in the afternoon.
Exactly at five o'clock in the afternoon.

A coffin on wheels is his bed
at five in the afternoon.
Bones and flutes resound in his ears[8]

---

1. Translated by Stephen Spender and J. L. Gili.
2. Harvesting (Spanish, literal trans.); the toss when the bull catches the bullfighter.
3. A disinfectant that was sprinkled on the body after death. "Frail": a basket.
4. To stop the blood; the beginning of a series of medicinal, chemical, and inhuman images that emphasize the presence of death.
5. Traditional symbols for peace and violence; they wrestle with one another as the bullfighter's thigh struggles with the bull's horn.
6. Bells are rung to announce a death. The "bass-string" of the guitar strums a lament.
7. A blood-colored disinfectant for wounds.
8. A suggestion of the medieval dance of death.

at five in the afternoon.
Now the bull was bellowing through his forehead
at five in the afternoon.
The room[9] was iridescent with agony
at five in the afternoon.   40
In the distance the gangrene now comes
at five in the afternoon.
Horn of the lily through green[1] groins
at five in the afternoon.
The wounds were burning like suns   45
at five in the afternoon,
and the crowd was breaking the windows[2]
at five in the afternoon.
At five in the afternoon.
Ah, that fatal five in the afternoon!   50
It was five by all the clocks!
It was five in the shade of the afternoon!

2. The Spilled Blood

I will not see it!

Tell the moon to come
for I do not want to see the blood
of Ignacio on the sand.   55
I will not see it!

The moon wide open.
Horse of still clouds,
and the grey bull ring of dreams
with willows in the barreras.[3]   60
I will not see it!

Let my memory kindle![4]
Warn the jasmines[5]
of such minute whiteness!
I will not see it!   65

The cow of the ancient world
passed her sad tongue
over a snout of blood

---

9. The room adjoining the arena where wounded bullfighters are taken for treatment.
1. Gangrene turns flesh a greenish color. "Lily": the shape of the wound resembles this flower.
2. A Spanish idiom for the crowd's loud roar.
3. The barriers around the ring within which the fight takes place and over which a fighter may escape the bull's charge. "Willows": symbols of mourning.
4. My memory burns within me (literal trans.).
5. The poet calls on (*warn* as "notify") the small white jasmine flowers to come and cover the blood.

spilled on the sand,   70
and the bulls of Guisando,[6]
partly death and partly stone,
bellowed like two centuries
sated with treading the earth.
No.   75
I do not want to see it!
I will not see it!

Ignacio goes up the tiers[7]
with all his death on his shoulders.
He sought for the dawn   80
but the dawn was no more.
He seeks for his confident profile
and the dream bewilders him.
He sought for his beautiful body
and encountered his opened blood.   85
Do not ask me to see it!
I do not want to hear it spurt
each time with less strength:
that spurt that illuminates
the tiers of seats, and spills   90
over the corduroy and the leather
of a thirsty multitude.
Who shouts that I should come near!
Do not ask me to see it!

His eyes did not close   95
when he saw the horns near,
but the terrible mothers
lifted their heads.[8]
And across the ranches,[9]
an air of secret voices rose,   100
shouting to celestial bulls,
herdsmen of pale mist.
There was no prince in Seville[1]
who could compare with him,
nor sword like his sword   105
nor heart so true.
Like a river of lions
was his marvellous strength,
and like a marble torso
his firm drawn moderation.   110
The air of Andalusian Rome
gilded his head[2]

6. Carved stone bulls from the Celtic past, a tourist attraction in the province of Madrid.
7. An imaginary scene in which the bullfighter mounts the stairs of the arena.
8. The three Fates traditionally raised their heads when the thread of life was cut.
9. Fighting bulls are raised on the ranches of Lorca's home province of Andalusia.
1. Leading city of Andalusia.
2. The image suggests a statue from Roman times, when Andalusia was part of the Roman Empire.

where his smile was a spikenard[3]
of wit and intelligence.
What a great torero[4] in the ring!   115
What a good peasant in the sierra![5]
How gentle with the sheaves!
How hard with the spurs!
How tender with the dew!
How dazzling in the fiesta!   120
How tremendous with the final
banderillas[6] of darkness!

But now he sleeps without end.
Now the moss and the grass
open with sure fingers   125
the flower of his skull.
And now his blood comes out singing;
singing along marshes and meadows,
sliding on frozen horns,
faltering soulless in the mist,   130
stumbling over a thousand hoofs
like a long, dark, sad tongue,
to form a pool of agony
close to the starry Guadalquivir.[7]
Oh, white wall of Spain!   135
Oh, black bull of sorrow!
Oh, hard blood of Ignacio!
Oh, nightingale of his veins!
No.
I will not see it!   140
No chalice can contain it,
no swallows[8] can drink it,
no frost of light can cool it,
nor song nor deluge of white lilies,
no glass can cover it with silver.   145
No.
I will not see it!

3. The Laid Out Body[9]

Stone is a forehead where dreams grieve
without curving waters and frozen cypresses.

---

3. A small, white, fragrant flower common in Andalusia; by extension, the bullfighter's white teeth.
4. Bullfighter.
5. Mountainous country. Sánchez Mejías is seen as a good *serrano* or "man of the hills."
6. The multicolored short spears that are thrust into the bull's shoulders to provoke him to attack.
7. A great river that passes through all the major cities of Andalusia. The singing stream of the bullfighter's blood suggests both the river and a nightingale.
8. According to a Spanish legend of the Crucifixion, swallows—a symbol of innocence—drank the blood of Christ on the Cross. The "chalice" refers to the legend of the Holy Grail, said to have held Christ's blood after the Crucifixion. The poet is seeking ways of concealing the dead man's blood.
9. Present body (literal trans.); the Spanish expression for a funeral wake, when the body is laid out for public mourning. The title contrasts with that of the next section: *Absent Soul*.

Stone is a shoulder on which to bear Time   150
with trees formed of tears and ribbons and planets.[1]

I have seen grey showers move towards the waves
raising their tender riddled arms,
to avoid being caught by the lying stone
which loosens their limbs without soaking their blood.   155

For stone gathers seed and clouds,
skeleton larks and wolves of penumbra:
but yields not sounds nor crystals nor fire,
only bull rings and bull rings and more bull rings without walls.

Now Ignacio the well born lies on the stone.   160
All is finished. What is happening? Contemplate his face:
death has covered him with pale sulphur
and has placed on him the head of a dark minotaur.[2]

All is finished. The rain penetrates his mouth.
The air, as if mad, leaves his sunken chest,   165
and Love, soaked through with tears of snow,
warms itself on the peak of the herd.[3]

What are they saying? A stenching silence settles down.
We are here with a body laid out which fades away,
with a pure shape which had nightingales   170
and we see it being filled with depthless holes.

Who creases the shroud? What he says is not true![4]
Nobody sings here, nobody weeps in the corner,
nobody pricks the spurs, nor terrifies the serpent.
Here I want nothing else but the round eyes   175
to see this body without a chance of rest.

Here I want to see those men of hard voice.
Those that break horses and dominate rivers;
those men of sonorous skeleton who sing
with a mouth full of sun and flint.   180

Here I want to see them. Before the stone.
Before this body with broken reins.
I want to know from them the way out
for this captain strapped down by death.

1. Traditional funeral imagery carved on gravestones.
2. A monster from Greek myth: half man, half bull.
3. Of the ranch (literal trans).

4. The speaker criticizes the conventional pieties voiced by someone standing close to the shrouded body; he prefers a clear-eyed, realistic view of death.

I want them to show me a lament like a river 185
which will have sweet mists and deep shores,
to take the body of Ignacio where it loses itself
without hearing the double panting of the bulls.

Loses itself in the round bull ring of the moon
which feigns in its youth a sad quiet bull: 190
loses itself in the night without song of fishes
and in the white thicket of frozen smoke.

I don't want them to cover his face with handkerchiefs
that he may get used to the death he carries.
Go, Ignacio; feel not the hot bellowing. 195
Sleep, fly, rest: even the sea dies!

4. Absent Soul

The bull does not know you, nor the fig tree,
nor the horses, nor the ants in your own house.
The child and the afternoon do not know you
because you have died for ever. 200

The back of the stone does not know you,
nor the black satin in which you crumble.
Your silent memory does not know you
because you have died for ever.

The autumn will come with small white snails,[5] 205
misty grapes and with clustered hills,
but no one will look into your eyes
because you have died for ever.

Because you have died for ever,
like all the death of the Earth, 210
like all the dead who are forgotten
in a heap of lifeless dogs.[6]

Nobody knows you. No. But I sing of you.
For posterity I sing of your profile and grace.
Of the signal maturity of your understanding. 215
Of your appetite for death and the taste of its mouth.
Of the sadness of your once valiant gaiety.

It will be a long time, if ever, before there is born
an Andalusian so true, so rich in adventure.
I sing of his elegance with words that groan, 220
and I remember a sad breeze through the olive trees.

1935

5. Horns in the shape of conch shells; the
shepherds' horns that sound in the hills each
fall as the sheep are driven to new pastures.

6. Dogs as an image for undignified, inferior
creatures.

PABLO NERUDA

1904–1973

The son of a railroad worker and a schoolteacher, with both Spanish and Indian ancestry, the Nobel Prize winner Pablo Neruda became Latin America's most important twentieth-century poet, as well as an advocate for social justice and a leading cultural figure on the Communist left. He wrote in a variety of styles (lyrical, polemic, objective, and prophetic) on an array of subjects (love, daily life, the natural world, political oppression), evoking the most elemental levels of human emotion and experience. In the second half of his life, moved especially by the Spanish Civil War, Neruda adopted the role of public poet, putting his writing at the service of the people.

The writer was born Neftalí Ricardo Reyes y Basoalto, on July 12, 1904, in the small town of Parral, in southern Chile. His mother died a month after his birth. Two years later his father moved to Temuco, where he remarried and where Neruda had his early schooling. Temuco was a frontier town, and the boy's father, who disapproved of aesthetic pursuits, did not encourage his love of literature. Neruda was fortunate to find a mentor in the poet Gabriela Mistral, the principal of the girls' school at Temuco, who would herself win the Nobel Prize in Literature in 1945. To encourage the young writer, Mistral loaned him books. He began publishing his poetry at age thirteen. Seeking a pen name that would not be tied to the provinces, he chose the surname of a Czech writer, Jan Neruda, and the given name Pablo, which some critics have associated with Saint Paul the apostle.

After working and studying in poverty in Chile's capital, Santiago, from 1921 to 1927, Neruda was appointed the nation's consul to Rangoon, Burma (now Myanmar). He would serve in Ceylon (now Sri Lanka), Java (in Indonesia), and Singapore, and then, after 1933, in Buenos Aires, Barcelona, Madrid, Paris, and Mexico City. During his residence in Spain, Neruda, influenced by his friends the poets **Federico García Lorca**, Rafael Alberti, and Miguel Hernández, assumed a more activist political stance. In 1936, civil war broke out in Spain between the Republic and the forces of General Francisco Franco. Franco's Fascist guards dragged Neruda's friend Lorca out of a friend's house; he was presumably shot, but his body was never recovered. (Neruda recalls the event in the poem "I'm Explaining a Few Things.") From that point on, Neruda would be a public poet, dedicating his voice to social issues rather than to private feelings and addressing a larger community.

Neruda returned to Chile in 1943, and, within two years, was elected to the Senate, as a representative of the Communist Party. When he criticized Chile's president in a speech on the Senate floor, Neruda's house was attacked, the government ordered his arrest, and he was forced to flee the country. Though he was celebrated internationally, with official honors from Latin America, the Soviet Union, Europe, India, and China, Neruda nonetheless could not return to Chile until 1952. He retained his close association with the Communist Party and even wrote a poem in praise of the Soviet dictator Joseph Stalin.

In 1970, Neruda ran for president of Chile as the Communist candidate, but he withdrew in favor of the Socialist Salvador Allende, who won the election and appointed Neruda ambassador to Paris. In 1971, Neruda received the

Nobel Prize for Literature; the following year he returned to his home in Isla Negra, gravely ill with cancer. The news at home was not good: political tensions were mounting, and Neruda watched television coverage of the rising unrest. On September 11, 1973, President Allende was assassinated in a military coup led by General Augusto Pinochet. Neruda died twelve days later. It was at Neruda's funeral that the first public demonstration against Pinochet's military government took place—a fitting tribute to Chile's national poet and representative of the people.

The selections presented here begin with Neruda's beautiful and popular early love poem "Tonight I Can Write . . ."

(1924), which makes use of couplets, repetition, and chiasmus (rhetorical inversion) to explore the speaker's evolving consciousness of a love affair. While maintaining the lyrical and personal tone of his earlier poetry, "Walking Around" demonstrates Neruda's turn toward public subject matter—here expressed not in the political terms of his later work but as a description of urban life and the sufferings of the poor. In "I'm Explaining a Few Things" (1936), however, Neruda engages explicitly with politics, and his repeated exhortation, "Come and see the blood in the streets!" illustrates the speaker's intention to address his audience directly and to dedicate his voice to public issues rather than private feelings.

Tonight I Can Write . . .[1]

Tonight I can write the saddest lines.

Write, for example, 'The night is shattered
and the blue stars shiver in the distance.'

The night wind revolves in the sky and sings.

Tonight I can write the saddest lines.   5
I loved her, and sometimes she loved me too.

Through nights like this one I held her in my arms.
I kissed her again and again under the endless sky.

She loved me, sometimes I loved her too.
How could one not have loved her great still eyes.   10

Tonight I can write the saddest lines.
To think that I do not have her. To feel that I have lost her.

To hear the immense night, still more immense without her.
And the verse falls to the soul like dew to the pasture.

What does it matter that my love could not keep her.   15
The night is shattered and she is not with me.

This is all. In the distance someone is singing. In the distance.
My soul is not satisfied that it has lost her.

1. Translated by W. S. Merwin.

My sight searches for her as though to go to her.
My heart looks for her, and she is not with me.   20

The same night whitening the same trees.
We, of that time, are no longer the same.

I no longer love her, that's certain, but how I loved her.
My voice tried to find the wind to touch her hearing.

Another's. She will be another's. Like my kisses before.   25
Her voice. Her bright body. Her infinite eyes.

I no longer love her, that's certain, but maybe I love her.
Love is so short, forgetting is so long.

Because through nights like this one I held her in my arms
my soul is not satisfied that it has lost her.   30

Though this be the last pain that she makes me suffer
and these the last verses that I write for her.

                                                                   1924

Walking Around[1]

It happens that I am tired of being a man.
It happens that I go into the tailor's shops and the movies
all shrivelled up, impenetrable, like a felt swan
navigating on a water of origin and ash.

The smell of barber shops makes me sob out loud.   5
I want nothing but the repose either of stones or of wool,
I want to see no more establishments, no more gardens,
nor merchandise, nor glasses, nor elevators.

It happens that I am tired of my feet and my nails
and my hair and my shadow.   10
It happens that I am tired of being a man.

Just the same it would be delicious
to scare a notary with a cut lily
or knock a nun stone dead with one blow of an ear.

It would be beautiful   15
to go through the streets with a green knife
shouting until I died of cold.

I do not want to go on being a root in the dark,
hesitating, stretched out, shivering with dreams,

1. Translated by W. S. Merwin.

downwards, in the wet tripe of the earth,   20
soaking it up and thinking, eating every day.

I do not want to be the inheritor of so many misfortunes.
I do not want to continue as a root and as a tomb,
as a solitary tunnel, as a cellar full of corpses,
stiff with cold, dying with pain.   25

For this reason Monday burns like oil
at the sight of me arriving with my jail-face,
and it howls in passing like a wounded wheel,
and its footsteps towards nightfall are filled with hot blood.

And it shoves me along to certain corners, to certain damp houses,   30
to hospitals where the bones come out of the windows,
to certain cobblers' shops smelling of vinegar,
to streets horrendous as crevices.

There are birds the colour of sulphur, and horrible intestines
hanging from the doors of the houses which I hate,   35
there are forgotten sets of teeth in a coffee-pot,
there are mirrors
which should have wept with shame and horror,
there are umbrellas all over the place, and poisons, and navels.

I stride along with calm, with eyes, with shoes,   40
with fury, with forgetfulness,
I pass, I cross offices and stores full of orthopaedic appliances,
and courtyards hung with clothes on wires,
underpants, towels and shirts which weep
slow dirty tears.   45

                                                                         1933

I'm Explaining a Few Things[1]

You are going to ask: and where are the lilacs?
and the poppy-petalled metaphysics?
and the rain repeatedly spattering
its words and drilling them full
of apertures and birds?   5

I'll tell you all the news.

I lived in a suburb,
a suburb of Madrid,[2] with bells,
and clocks, and trees.

---

1. Translated by Nathaniel Tarn.   2. The capital of Spain.

From there you could look out   10
over Castile's[3] dry face:
a leather ocean.
        My house was called
the house of flowers, because in every cranny
geraniums burst: it was
a good-looking house   15
with its dogs and children.
                Remember, Raúl?
Eh, Rafael?
        Federico,[4] do you remember
from under the ground
my balconies on which
the light of June drowned flowers in your mouth?
                        Brother, my brother!   20

Everything
loud with big voices, the salt of merchandises,
pile-ups of palpitating bread,
the stalls of my suburb of Argüelles with its statue
like a drained inkwell in a swirl of hake:[5]   25
oil flowed into spoons,
a deep baying
of feet and hands swelled in the streets,
metres, litres, the sharp
measure of life,
           stacked-up fish,   30
the texture of roofs with a cold sun in which
the weather vane falters,
the fine, frenzied ivory of potatoes,
wave on wave of tomatoes rolling down to the sea.

And one morning all that was burning,   35
one morning the bonfires
leapt out of the earth
devouring human beings—
and from then on fire,
gunpowder from then on,   40
and from then on blood.
Bandits with planes and Moors,
bandits with finger-rings and duchesses,
bandits with black friars[6] spattering blessings

---

3. Spain.
4. I.e., the poet Federico García Lorca, who was murdered by the Fascists on August 19, 1936. "Rafael": his friend, the poet Rafael Alberti.
5. A fish similar to the cod. "Argüelles": a busy shopping area in Madrid, near the university.
6. "Finger-rings," "duchesses," "friars" imply a collusion of the wealthy, the aristocracy, and the Church to suppress the people. "Bandits": Neruda lists categories of invaders. "Moors": probably an analogy between the early Muslim invaders of Spain and German and Italian pilots who bombed the village of Guernica in April 1937.

came through the sky to kill children   45
and the blood of children ran through the streets
without fuss, like children's blood.

Jackals that the jackals would despise,
stones that the dry thistle would bite on and spit out,
vipers that the vipers would abominate!   50

Face to face with you I have seen the blood
of Spain tower like a tide
to drown you in one wave
of pride and knives!

Treacherous   55
generals:
see my dead house,
look at broken Spain:
from every house burning metal flows
instead of flowers,   60
from every socket of Spain
Spain emerges
and from every dead child a rifle with eyes,
and from every crime bullets are born
which will one day find   65
the bull's eye of your hearts.

And you will ask: why doesn't his poetry
speak of dreams and leaves
and the great volcanoes of his native land?

Come and see the blood in the streets.   70
Come and see
the blood in the streets.
Come and see the blood
in the streets!

                                        1936

OCTAVIO PAZ

1914-1998

A leading Mexican writer of the twentieth century, the Nobel Prize winner Octavio Paz drew on ancient myth to characterize urban life in his native land and around the world. A poet, cultural critic, diplomat, and public intellectual, Paz applied the experimental forms of Latin American and European modernism to the challenge of expressing contemporary Mexican identity.

Paz was born during the chaotic years of the Mexican Revolution. His father, a journalist and lawyer, supported the revolutionary Emiliano Zapata and was exiled from Mexico after Zapata's death in 1919. Although Paz lived briefly with his father in Los Angeles, he grew up mostly in the suburban Mexico City home of his paternal grandfather, a liberal intellectual whose library included great works of Spanish classical literature and Latin American modernism. Paz started writing poetry in his teens and soon became involved in the literary journal *Contemporáneos*, which published translations of many French- and English-language modernists. He particularly admired **T. S. Eliot's** *The Waste Land.* Paz studied law at college before dropping out to teach at a school for peasant children in the Yucatán peninsula.

Inspired by the ideals of social justice espoused by the revolution, Paz became active in international left-wing politics. In 1937, during the Spanish Civil War, he attended the second International Congress of Anti-Fascist Writers in Spain as the guest of the Chilean poet **Pablo Neruda**, whose work Paz admired. "For me," he wrote, "Neruda was the great destructor-creator of His-panic poetry." Like Neruda, Paz entered his country's diplomatic service, first representing Mexico as a cultural attaché in Paris from 1946 to 1951. He had long been interested in surrealism and became friendly with the movement's founder, André Breton. Later he would represent Mexico in Geneva, New York, and India, where he developed an interest in Buddhism and Hinduism.

The writer's most famous work on Mexican history and culture, *The Labyrinth of Solitude* (1950), emphasized the condition of solitude and despair that affected Mexicans but was in some sense universal: "our situation of alienation is that of the majority of people." He saw the Mexican as by nature reserved, enclosed, and isolated. At this time, Paz still acknowledges the legacy of the Mexican Revolution in bringing individuals together as a community. He became disillusioned with Mexican politics and resigned his post as ambassador to India in 1968, however, in protest against the Mexican government massacre of student demonstrators. Paz returned to Mexico City and wrote a series of poems later collected as *Vuelta* (*Return*), which was also the title of a journal he edited from 1975 until his death. In 1990 he celebrated the end of communism in Eastern Europe by hosting a conference of leading writers and intellectuals from East and West in Mexico City. That same year the Nobel committee honored him for his "impassioned writing with wide horizons, characterized by sensuous intelligence and humanistic integrity."

The works selected here span the later stages of Paz's career, when he was at the height of his poetic powers.

They combine intense lyricism with a surrealist-inspired fascination with the irrational and the unconscious. Surrealism, Buddhism, and Hinduism seemed to Paz to offer alternatives to the rationalism of traditional European culture. "Surrealism was not merely an esthetic, poetic and philosophical doctrine," he once said. "It was a vital attitude. A negation of the contemporary world and at the same time an attempt to substitute other values for those of democratic bourgeois society: eroticism, poetry, imagination, liberty, spiritual adventure, vision." Paz's long poem "I Speak of the City" (1976) evokes elements of the Mexican capital, New York City, London, and Rome and draws on the tradition of free verse from Walt Whitman and T. S. Eliot through the surrealists. Another late poem, specifically about New York, "Central Park" (1987) was inspired by a painting by the Belgian artist Pierre Alechinsky and contains the repeated warning (in English in the original) "Don't cross Central Park at night." "Small Variation" (1987), written when the poet was in his seventies, recollects the sorrow of Gilgamesh in the ancient epic and echoes other, later laments to create a moving meditation on human mortality. Throughout these lyrical and imaginative works, Paz uses rhythmic, loose poetic forms, in the tradition of free verse, to present a haunting vision of urban life that is in touch with the deeper, subterranean forces of the human spirit.

I Speak of the City[1]

for Eliot Weinberger

a novelty today, tomorrow a ruin from the past, buried and resurrected every day,

lived together in streets, plazas, buses, taxis, movie houses, theaters, bars, hotels, pigeon coops and catacombs,

the enormous city that fits in a room three yards square, and endless as   5
a galaxy,

the city that dreams us all, that all of us build and unbuild and rebuild as we dream,

the city we all dream, that restlessly changes while we dream it,

the city that wakes every hundred years and looks at itself in the mir-   10
ror of a word and doesn't recognize itself and goes back to sleep,

the city that sprouts from the eyelids of the woman who sleeps at my side, and is transformed,

with its monuments and statues, its histories and legends,

into a fountain made of countless eyes, and each eye reflects the same   15
landscape, frozen in time,

before schools and prisons, alphabets and numbers, the altar and the law:

the river that is four rivers, the orchard, the tree, the Female and Male, dressed in wind—   20

to go back, go back, to be clay again, to bathe in that light, to sleep under those votive lights,

to float on the waters of time like the flaming maple leaf the current drags along,

to go back—are we asleep or awake?—we are, we are nothing more,   25
day breaks, it's early,

we are in the city, we cannot leave except to fall into another city, different yet identical,

I speak of the immense city, that daily reality composed of two words:
the others,   30

and in every one of them there is an I clipped from a we, an I adrift,

I speak of the city built by the dead, inhabited by their stern ghosts, ruled by their despotic memory,

the city I talk to when I talk to nobody, the city that dictates these insomniac words,   35

I speak of towers, bridges, tunnels, hangars, wonders and disasters,

the abstract State and its concrete police, the schoolteachers, jailers, preachers,

the shops that have everything, where we spend everything, and it all turns to smoke,   40

the markets with their pyramids of fruit, the turn of the seasons, the sides of beef hanging from the hooks, the hills of spices and the towers of bottles and preserves,

---

1. Translated by Eliot Weinberger, a frequent translator of Paz's work to whom the poem is dedicated.

all of the flavors and colors, all the smells and all the stuff, the tide of
voices—water, metal, wood, clay—the bustle, the haggling and conniv- 45
ing as old as time,
　　I speak of the buildings of stone and marble, of cement, glass and
steel, of the people in the lobbies and doorways, of the elevators that rise
and fall like the mercury in thermometers,
　　of the banks and their boards of directors, of factories and their man- 50
agers, of the workers and their incestuous machines,
　　I speak of the timeless parade of prostitution through streets long as
desire and boredom,
　　of the coming and going of cars, mirrors of our anxieties, business,
passions (why? toward what? for what?), 55
　　of the hospitals that are always full, and where we always die alone,
　　I speak of the half-light of certain churches and the flickering candles
at the altars,
　　the timid voices with which the desolate talk to saints and virgins in
a passionate, failing language, 60
　　I speak of dinner under a squinting light at a limping table with
chipped plates,
　　of the innocent tribes that camp in the empty lots with their women
and children, their animals and their ghosts,
　　of the rats in the sewers and the brave sparrows that nest in the wires, 65
in the cornices and the martyred trees,
　　of the contemplative cats and their libertine novels in the light of the
moon, cruel goddess of the rooftops,
　　of the stray dogs that are our Franciscans and *bhikkus*,[2] the dogs that
scratch up the bones of the sun, 70
　　I speak of the anchorite and the libertarian brotherhood, of the secret
plots of law enforcers and of bands of thieves,
　　of the conspiracies of levelers and the Society of Friends of Crime, of
the Suicide Club, and of Jack the Ripper,[3]
　　of the Friend of the People, sharpener of the guillotine, of Caesar, De- 75
light of Humankind,[4]
　　I speak of the paralytic slum, the cracked wall, the dry fountain, the
graffitied statue,
　　I speak of garbage heaps the size of mountains, and of melancholy
sunlight filtered by the smog, 80
　　of broken glass and the desert of scrap iron, of last night's crime, and
of the banquet of the immortal Trimalchio,[5]
　　of the moon in the television antennas, and a butterfly on a filthy jar,
　　I speak of dawns like a flight of herons on the lake, and the sun of
transparent wings that lands on the rock foliage of the churches, and the 85
twittering of light on the glass stalks of the palaces,

2. Buddhist monks. "Franciscans": Catholic
monks.
3. Famous serial killer in 19th-century London whose identity was never discovered. The
Society of Friends of Crime is a fictional organization invented by the Marquis de Sade
(1740–1814). The Suicide Club was a similar
organization invented by the Scottish novelist
Robert Louis Stevenson (1850–1894). All three
references concern urban criminality.

4. An epithet of the Roman emperor Titus
(39–81). Caesar was a title associated with
several Roman emperors. The French revolutionary Jean-Paul Marat said that the king
should be "a friend of the people." These references concern the power of a strong leader
to control the mob.
5. Character in *The Satyricon* by Petronius,
famous for throwing ostentatious dinners of
many courses.

I speak of certain afternoons in early fall, waterfalls of immaterial gold, the transformation of this world, when everything loses its body, everything is held in suspense,

and the light thinks, and each one of us feels himself thought by that reflective light, and for one long moment time dissolves, we are air once more, 90

I speak of the summer, of the slow night that grows on the horizon like a mountain of smoke, and bit by bit it crumbles, falling over us like a wave,

the elements are reconciled, night has stretched out, and its body is a powerful river of sudden sleep, we rock in the waves of its breathing, the hour is tangible, we can touch it like a fruit, 95

they have lit the lights, and the avenues burn with the brilliancy of desire, in the parks electric light breaks through the branches and falls over us like a green and phosphorescent mist that illuminates but does not wet us, the trees murmur, they tell us something, 100

there are streets in the half-light that are a smiling insinuation, we don't know where they lead, perhaps to the ferry for the lost islands,

I speak of the stars over the high terraces and the indecipherable sentences they write on the stone of the sky, 105

I speak of the sudden downpour that lashes the windowpanes and bends the trees, that lasted twenty-five minutes and now, up above, there are blue slits and streams of light, steam rises from the asphalt, the cars glisten, there are puddles where ships of reflections sail,

I speak of nomadic clouds, and of a thin music that lights a room on the fifth floor, and a murmur of laughter in the middle of the night like water that flows far-off through roots and grasses, 110

I speak of the longed-for encounter with that unexpected form with which the unknown is made flesh, and revealed to each of us:

eyes that are the night half-open and the day that wakes, the sea stretching out and the flame that speaks, powerful breasts: lunar tide, 115

lips that say *sesame*, and time opens, and the little room becomes a garden of change, air and fire entwine, earth and water mingle,

or the arrival of that moment there, on the other side that is really here, where the key locks and time ceases to flow: 120

the moment of *until now*, the last of the gasps, the moaning, the anguish, the soul loses its body and crashes through a hole in the floor, falling in itself, and time has run aground, and we walk through an endless corridor, panting in the sand,

is that music coming closer or receding, are those pale lights just lit or going out? space is singing, time has vanished: it is the gasp, it is the glance that slips through the blank wall, it is the wall that stays silent, the wall, 125

I speak of our public history, and of our secret history, yours and mine, 130

I speak of the forest of stone, the desert of the prophets, the ant-heap of souls, the congregation of tribes, the house of mirrors, the labyrinth of echoes,

I speak of the great murmur that comes from the depths of time, the incoherent whisper of nations uniting or splitting apart, the wheeling of multitudes and their weapons like boulders hurling down, the dull sound of bones falling into the pit of history, 135

I speak of the city, shepherd of the centuries, mother that gives birth to us and devours us, that creates us and forgets. 140

1976

Small Variation[1]

Like music come back to life—
who brings it from over there, from the other side,
who conducts it through the spirals
of the mind's ear?—
like the vanished   5
moment that returns
and is again the same
presence erasing itself,
the syllables unearthed
make sound without sound: 10
and at the hour of our death, amen.[2]

In the school chapel
I spoke them many times
without conviction. Now I hear them
spoken by a voice without lips,   15
a sound of sand sifting away,
while in my skull the hours toll
and time takes another turn around my night.
I am not the first man on earth—
I tell myself in the manner of Epictetus[3]—   20
who is going to die.
And as I say this
the world breaks down in my blood.

                          The sorrow
of Gilgamesh[4] when he returned   25
from the land without twilight
is my sorrow. On our shadowy earth
each man is Adam:
                    with him the world begins,[5]
with him it ends.   30
                Between after and before—
brackets of stone—
for an instant that will never return I shall be
the first man and I shall be the last.
And as I say it, the instant—   35
bodiless, weightless—
opens under my feet
and closes over me and is pure time.

1987

1. Translated by Mark Strand.
2. The final line of the prayer, "Hail Mary."
3. Greek stoic philosopher who counseled acceptance of fate, including mortality.
4. Protagonist of the Mesopotamian *Epic of Gilgamesh*, who visits the underworld where the dead dwell.
5. Adam was punished with mortality for his disobedience (Genesis 2.17).

Central Park[1]

Green and black thickets, bare spots,
leafy river knotting into itself:
it runs motionless through the leaden buildings
and there, where light turns to doubt
and stone wants to be shadow, it vanishes.   5
Don't cross Central Park at night.[2]

Day falls, night flares up,
Alechinsky draws a magnetic rectangle,
a trap of lines, a corral of ink:
inside there is a fallen beast,   10
two eyes and a twisting rage.
Don't cross Central Park at night.

There are no exits or entrances,
enclosed in a ring of light
the grass beast sleeps with eyes open,   15
the moon exhumes razors,
the water in the shadows has become green fire.
Don't cross Central Park at night.

There are no entrances but everyone,
in the middle of a phrase dangling from the telephone,   20
from the top of the fountain of silence or laughter,
from the glass cage of the eye that watches us,
everyone, all of us are falling in the mirror.
Don't cross Central Park at night.

The mirror is made of stone and the stone now is shadow,   25
there are two eyes the color of anger,
a ring of cold, a belt of blood,
there is a wind that scatters the reflections
of Alice, dismembered in the pond.
Don't cross Central Park at night.   30

Open your eyes: now you are inside yourself,
you sail in a boat of monosyllables
across the mirror-pond, you disembark
at the Cobra dock: it is a yellow taxi
that carries you to the land of flames   35
across Central Park at night.

1987

---

1. Translated by Eliot Weinberger. The poem
was inspired by a painting by Belgian artist
Pierre Alechinsky entitled *Central Park* (1965).

2. This line is in English in the Spanish version of the poem.

VII

Postwar and Postcolonial Literature, 1945–1968

I n the middle of the twentieth century, the two superpowers, the United States and the Soviet Union, having emerged from the bloody, or "hot," wars of the previous decades, found themselves locked in a Cold War: their most powerful weapons, though fired only in tests, would be capable of annihilating the planet. The two sides—the North Atlantic Treaty Organization, representing Western Europe and North America, and the Warsaw Pact, uniting the military forces of Soviet-dominated Eastern Europe—divided most of the globe into spheres of influence. By 1949, with the success of the Communist Revolution in China, led by Mao Zedong, almost half of the world's population lived under communism. The competing blocs, as they were called, understood that if either one launched a nuclear attack, the enemy would retaliate, an unstable balance known as "mutually assured destruction" (producing an ironic acronym).

To avoid planetary disaster, the two sides fought wars by proxy, notably in Korea (1950–53) and Vietnam (1955–75). Within the Communist world, the purges and mass imprisonments initiated by the

A photograph from October 1947 by Margaret Bourke-White (American, 1904–1971) of a refugee camp in Delhi. The picture was taken a month before British-ruled India was partitioned into two nations, India and Pakistan.

Soviet dictator Joseph Stalin were selectively repudiated, after Stalin's death in 1953, by his successor, Nikita Khrushchev. It was during this period of de-Stalinization that the works of the dissident **Alexander Solzhenitsyn** were briefly allowed to be published. The bloody suppression of the Hungarian revolt against communism in 1956, however, showed the limits of de-Stalinization. Stalin's techniques spread, moreover, to Mao's China. The forced collectivization of the Great Leap Forward (1958–59) led to a famine that caused an estimated twenty million deaths, while the Cultural Revolution, which began in 1966 and lasted until Mao's death in 1976, attacked intellectuals and the middle classes, resulting in the destruction of most of the country's functioning institutions.

While the Communist world was undergoing radical transformations, the colonial powers of Western Europe, facing pressure from nationalist movements among their subject peoples, began to relinquish direct political control of their colonies. The process of decolonization, often accompanied by conflicts over redrawn borders, became a major topic for a generation of writers who, though born in the formerly colonized nations, were likely to have been educated in Europe and who sought to give voice to the concerns of their recently independent nations. The initial stages of postcolonial development were frequently marked by internal conflicts, civil wars, and dictatorships, and by jockeying to align newly independent nations with either the United States or the Soviet Union (or to find an alternative, "nonaligned" path). It was also in these years, however, that the basis was laid for the prosperity of what was then known as the "third world" (in contrast to the liberal capitalist democracies of the developed first world and the rapidly industrializing second world of Communist regimes). In particular, the Green Revolution of the 1960s and 1970s improved agricultural methods in the developing world and made it possible to feed a rapidly expanding population, while smallpox was eliminated and other serious illnesses, such as tuberculosis, malaria, and plague, were brought under control. Still, in the poorer countries of Africa and South Asia, it was common for as much as half the population to live in poverty.

In Western Europe, the postwar period saw rapid rebuilding and further industrialization, even as thinkers and writers struggled to comprehend the enormity of the Holocaust. The young Polish journalist **Tadeusz Borowski** shocked his compatriots with his account of life in the Nazi concentration camps, while the Romanian-born Jew **Paul Celan**, writing in German, turned his experiences in the camps into austere and beautiful poetry. In the wake of the Nazi occupation of France (1940–44), the theme of choice became critical to a generation of authors who had had to decide between allegiance to the collaborationist Vichy state or to the Resistance movement. The philosophy of existentialism, derived by Jean-Paul Sartre from the writings of the German philosophers Friedrich Nietzsche and Martin Heidegger, emphasized the role of free choice in human life. Glimpses of existentialism occur in the bleak humor of **Samuel Beckett**'s apocalyptic *Endgame*. Like Beckett, **Albert Camus** had worked for the Resistance. He develops the theme of choice in his account of a schoolteacher's experiences in Algeria in "**The Guest**." In different ways, these writers turned to a stripped-down literary style— either direct and realistic, like Camus and Borowski, or elusive and minimalist, like Celan and Beckett—and thus away from the exuberant modernism of the earlier part of the century.

Partly because it had been incorporated into the French state (unlike British colonies, which tended to be governed locally), Algeria became one

The Algerian writer Albert Camus (1913–1960), on the balcony of his Paris publisher's office in 1955.

of the bloodiest colonial battlefields until its eventual independence in 1962. Elsewhere, decolonization occurred more rapidly. In the immediate aftermath of the war, faced with nationalist pressures in the colonies and with the moral bankruptcy of any claims to racial superiority, many colonial powers began granting independence. At midnight on August 14, 1947, Britain divided its territorial possessions in South Asia into two states, India and Pakistan. The partition took place along religious (or "communal") lines between Hindus and Muslims, but there remained many Muslims in India and Hindus in Pakistan. During the weeks before and after independence, large populations were transferred and an untold number were killed in communal violence—the subject of **Saadat Hasan Manto's** "**Toba Tek Singh**" and later of **Salman Rushdie's** *Midnight's Children*. The following year, under a United Nations mandate, Britain left most of its former territories in Palestine in the hands of the new Jewish state, Israel. Its Arab neighbors attacked the new country

and, during a series of short wars from 1948 to 1968, Israel expanded its national boundaries, at the same time occupying territories inhabited by Arab Palestinians. The continuing Arab-Israeli conflict and the Israeli Occupation are themes in the poetry of **Yehuda Amichai** and **Mahmoud Darwish** in this volume.

Elsewhere in the Middle East and North Africa, a series of military coups created dictatorships, sometimes focused on the Pan-Arabist movement for Muslim unity, at other times oriented more toward socialism. It was in this context that Arabic writers such as **Naguib Mahfouz** combined traditional literary language with the European form of the novel to chronicle the transformations of their cultures. Sub-Saharan Africa also experienced a series of civil wars and dictatorships, as well as ongoing minority rule by the white settler communities in South Africa and Rhodesia, which **Doris Lessing** describes. Despite Africa's hardships, it developed a remarkable literature, typically in the languages of

Egyptian premier Gamal Abdel Nasser Hussein (right) and the prime minister of the Sudan, Ismail Al Azhari, clasp hands among a crowd of supporters in Egypt in July 1954. Nasser, a central figure in the Egyptian revolution of 1952, which overthrew the monarchy of Egypt and Sudan, became Egypt's president in 1956.

the former colonial powers, represented here by **Chinua Achebe, Ngugi Wa Thiong'o**, and **Bessie Head**. Although they sometimes took inspiration from the celebration of African identity typical of the earlier French-speaking writers of the Négritude movement, these anglophone authors typically explore village life as it has been transformed by contact with Europeans and then by the process of establishing independence.

In the United States, too, racial segregation and the disenfranchisement of African Americans were challenged in the civil rights movement, whose landmarks included the Supreme Court decision *Brown v. Board of Education* of 1954, which ended public school segregation, and the Civil Rights Acts of 1964, which banned segregation in public accommodations and outlawed discriminatory voter registration. **James Baldwin** explores the challenges that African Americans faced in the North during and after the Second World War.

Alongside the impetus for African American rights, a renewed consciousness of Native American history and society emerged. As the appeal of the mainstream media, particularly radio, television, and the movies, threatened to silence the Native oral tradition, scholars and others took steps to record what might be a vanishing cultural legacy.

The intersection of oral and written forms points to a distinctive characteristic of world literature in the late twentieth century—its hybridity. With the increasing globalization of literature and the media, writers frequently adapted certain genres, especially the short story and the novel but drama and lyric poetry as well, to local conditions. For example, authors might use the language of a traditional literature (Classical Chinese, Standard Arabic, and biblical Hebrew) to produce a colloquial, contemporary short story. In other cases, writers transformed a historically European genre by introducing elements of local customs and storytelling techniques (examples include magic realism in Latin America; the postcolonial African novel). More broadly, the encounters between indigenous societies and widely accepted literary forms caused writers to rethink the defining characteristics of their homeland; many authors valued hybrid qualities that tended to dismantle claims to cultural uniqueness or homogeneity.

Much of the writing of the postwar period engages in the movement toward "neorealism"—a return to political and social issues, in contrast to the interiority and linguistic inventiveness of the modernists. While sometimes drawing on modernist techniques such as the representation of individual consciousness and intense irony, the realists tended to use the chronological plot, omniscient narrator, and objective description typical of nineteenth-century European works. Such preferences apply equally to postcolonial writers eager to portray the history of their nations and to Western authors grappling with social issues such as civil rights, immigration, and gender relations. There are some notable exceptions, however, to the reinvigorated realism of postwar literature. Many politically oriented writers, such as Mahfouz, Manto, and Solzhenitsyn, wove allegory into their seeming realism, sometimes conveying hidden political messages in apparently straightforward narratives, at other times using allegory openly as a way of commenting on current events. At the same time, writers of all nationalities continued to use language wittily, finding expressiveness in the sounds and unexpected meanings of words.

LÉOPOLD SÉDAR SENGHOR

1906–2001

Léopold Sédar Senghor was a poet, a founder of the Négritude movement, and the first president of independent Senegal. His poetry takes as its central subject the encounter between Africa and Europe. The harsh circumstances of the encounter on both the personal and social levels, the conflict between two races and their conceptions of life, provide the background to his intense exploration of the historical and moral implications of the African and black experience in modern times.

Senghor was born in Joal, a small fishing village in the Sine-Saloum basin in west-central Senegal, then a colony of France. His father, a Serer (the dominant ethnic group of his native region), was a prosperous and influential merchant. His mother was a Peul, one of a pastoral and nomadic people found all over the northern savannah belt of western Africa. This double ethnic ancestry was later to assume a larger meaning for Senghor. As he says in *Prayer of the Senegalese Soldiers*: "I grew up in the heartland of Africa, at the crossroads / Of castes and races and roads." An award-winning student, Senghor originally intended to become a Catholic priest, but he decided instead to continue his education in France, where he attended the prestigious École Normale Supérieure. As the first African student to pass the highly competitive examination for the *agrégation*, he was qualified to pursue a career in the French educational system. He held various teaching positions in France until the outbreak of the Second World War, in 1939, when he was drafted as an officer into the French army. Sen-

ghor served on the northern front, where he was taken prisoner by the Germans in 1940. Two years later, released on medical grounds but confined to Paris, he resumed teaching and in 1944 was appointed professor of African languages at the École Nationale de la France d'Outre-Mer.

Throughout this eventful period, Senghor was writing poetry, inspired by the French symbolists and surrealists and by Marxist theory. From the beginning of his sojourn in France, Senghor found himself at the center of a group of African and Caribbean students and intellectuals who had been influenced by radical currents in Western thought, especially Marxism, and by the militant literature of black American writers associated with the Harlem Renaissance. This group included a fellow student, Aimé Césaire, with whom Senghor struck up an important friendship. It was through their collaboration that the Négritude (or "blackness") movement developed, with its challenge of the colonial order and its passionate concern for the rehabilitation of Africa and the black race. After the war Senghor was active in the effort to launch a cultural journal, *Présence Africaine*, a vehicle for African and black self-affirmation. Senghor also published the historic *Anthologie de la nouvelle poésie nègre et malgache* (1948), which may be said to have launched Négritude as a movement, largely because of the impact of the prefatory essay, "Orphée noir" ("Black Orpheus"), by the eminent French philosopher Jean-Paul Sartre. Sartre provided both a critical review of black poetry and a philosophical exposition of the concept of Négritude. As

Senghor imagined it, Négritude put forth African culture as the source of strengths from which Europe could benefit. In arguing that Africans could teach each other and Europeans about their homeland, rather than merely being beneficiaries of European civilization, Senghor was reacting against his experience of the French colonial educational system.

Meanwhile, with his election in 1946 to the French Constituent Assembly as deputy for Senegal, Senghor had launched his political career, which was to be distinguished by service as an advocate for Africa in the French Parliament and would culminate in his election to the presidency of Senegal at its independence in 1960. Politics and literature thus ran more or less parallel in his career, as complementary aspects of a life devoted to the African cause.

Although he was a controversial figure in African literary and intellectual circles, Senghor was widely respected as both poet and statesman. When he voluntarily gave up the presidency of Senegal in 1980 to return to private life, he left behind an outstanding contribution to the political and social development of Africa and to the continent's cultural and intellectual renaissance. His election to the French Academy in 1983—the first black African to attain this honor—came as a fitting recognition of one of the foremost modern writers in the French language.

The selections from Senghor's poetry printed here represent the range of his career. "Letter to a Poet" (1945), addressed to Aimé Césaire, appeared in Senghor's first volume, *Chants d'ombre* (1945), a kind of mental diary of his experience of cultural exile in Europe. Although the volume came out at the end of the Second World War, many of the poems were composed before the conflict started. The

long, loose verses draw on the cadences of the Bible; although the original French makes use of rhyme, the effect is of free verse. Césaire had by this time returned to his home in Martinique, and Senghor wrote this poem as a letter of praise to his intellectual companion. The next three poems, all from the first volume, draw on Senghor's nostalgia for his homeland. "Night in Sine" (1945) is a love poem addressed to a woman, but the love expressed is also for Africa itself. Likewise, "Black Woman" (1945) celebrates the beauty of an idealized woman who is at once mother, lover, and symbol of a continent. "Prayer to the Masks" (1945) focuses on an element in traditional African religion. While these masks had become a symbol of European fascination with the supposedly primitive (especially after Pablo Picasso used them as the basis for some of his cubist paintings), Senghor understands the faces, in their starkness, as speaking for his ancestors. Here he addresses the challenge of reimagining the relations between Europe and Africa.

Senghor's second collection of poems, *Hosties noires* (*Black Hosts*, 1948), includes many of his wartime poems. "Letter to a Prisoner" (1942) addressed to a friend from Senghor's time in a German prisoner-of-war camp, recalls their homeland in Africa and despairs of the bleached and sterile quality of life in wartime Paris. Through their references to the war, the poems in this volume provide commentary on public events and a judgment on the passions that impelled them. The colonial protest and the critique of Europe are intertwined—a point that the title of the volume conveys, suggesting the sacrifice of Africans to the blind fury of the European war. The association also carries religious overtones: that of the collective passion of the black race, conferring on it the nobility of suffering.

Between 1949 and 1960, Senghor's energies were absorbed by politics and his campaign, through a stream of essays and lectures in France and other parts of Europe, as well as in Africa, for the rehabilitation of the continent and its peoples. In 1956, Senghor's collection *Ethiopiques* represented a new direction in his poetry, one less overtly related to the colonial experience. "The Kaya-Magan" (1956), from this collection, celebrates a legendary African ruler and the bounty of the continent, without reference to European colonialism. From the same volume, "To New York" (1956) begins by admiring the metropolis and associating it with African American jazz, but quickly turns to contrasting the barrenness and artificiality of New York with the authenticity of the African countryside. The speaker finds a sort of synthesis in imagining the "black blood" of Harlem transforming New York and making it more organic and closer to God, imagined here as a jazz saxophonist.

Senghor's later poetry confirms his standing as a lyric poet, as he pursues a deeper exploration of the poetic self and develops a more complex attitude toward the world. The interplay between the elegiac and the lyrical that runs as an undercurrent in the early poems receives, in the later work, an expanded frame of reference. The final two poems in the selection here were published in the collection *Nocturnes* (1961) after Senghor became president of Senegal. "Songs for Signare" (1961) belongs to the pastoral tradition, observing the simple lives of herdsmen, but transfers this tradition from Greece and Western Europe to central Africa. "Elegy of the Circumcised" (1961) celebrates adolescent circumcision as a male rite of passage. Throughout Senghor's later works, the tensions of public life are balanced against the comforts of love, the deaths of individuals and civilizations, and the assurance of rebirth in the stream of life. In his early volumes Senghor portrays an individual predicament as part of a collective historical plight; in the later poetry his vision embraces a wider range of experience. Africa appears in poetic terms, becoming an image of both the racial homeland and humanity's appropriate relation to the universe.

Letter to a Poet[1]

to Aimé Césaire

To my Brother *aimé*,[2] beloved friend, my bluntly fraternal greetings!
Black sea gulls like seafaring boatmen have brought me a taste
Of your tidings mixed with spices and the noisy fragrance of
    Southern Rivers[3]
And Islands.[4] They showed your influence, your distinguished brow,
The flower of your delicate lips. They are now your disciples,   5
A hive of silence, proud as peacocks. You keep their breathless zeal
From fading until moonrise. Is it your perfume of exotic fruits,
Or your wake of light in the fullness of day?
O, the many plum-skin women in the harem of your mind!

1. All selections translated by Melvin Dixon.
2. Beloved (French). The poem pays homage to fellow poet Aimé Césaire.
3. Senghor plays here on the poetic resonance of the French administrative term (*Rivières du Sud*) for the area comprising the former French empire in west and central Africa.
4. The Caribbean, where Césaire was born.

Still charming beyond the years, embers aglow under the ash   10
Of your eyelids, is the music we stretched our hands
And hearts to so long ago. Have you forgotten your nobility?
Your talent to praise the Ancestors, the Princes,
And the Gods, neither flower nor drops of dew?[5]
You were to offer the Spirits the virgin fruits of your garden   15
—You ate only the newly harvested millet blossom
And stole not a petal to sweeten your mouth.
At the bottom of the well of my memory, I touch your face
And draw water to refresh my long regret.
You recline royally, elbow on a cushion of clear hillside,   20
Your bed presses the earth, easing the toil of wetland drums
Beating the rhythm of your song, and your verse
Is the breath of the night and the distant sea.
You praised the Ancestors and the legitimate princes.
For your rhyme and counterpoint you scooped a star from the
    heavens.   25
At your bare feet poor men threw down a mat of their year's wages,
And women their amber[6] hearts and soul-wrenching dance.

My friend, my friend—Oh, you will come back, come back!
I shall await you under the mahogany tree,[7] the message
Already sent to the woodcutter's boss. You will come back   30
For the feast of first fruits[8] when the soft night
In the sloping sun rises steaming from the rooftops
And athletes,[9] befitting your arrival,
Parade their youthfulness, adorned like the beloved.

1945

Night in Sine[1]

Woman, place your soothing hands upon my brow,
Your hands softer than fur.
Above us balance the palm trees, barely rustling
In the night breeze. Not even a lullaby.
Let the rhythmic silence cradle us.   5
Listen to its song. Hear the beat of our dark blood,
Hear the deep pulse of Africa in the mist of lost villages.

Now sets the weary moon upon its slack seabed
Now the bursts of laughter quiet down, and even the storyteller
Nods his head like a child on his mother's back   10

5. The conventions of Western lyricism are contrasted with the more pressing social themes of the black poet.
6. A translucent stone, with a brownish yellow hue.
7. Of royal significance.
8. The harvest festival.
9. Wrestlers, the traditional sporting heroes of Senegal.
1. A river in Senegal. The Serer, Senghor's ethnic group, inhabit the basin formed by the confluence of Sine and Saloum.

The dancers' feet grow heavy, and heavy, too,
Come the alternating voices of singers.

Now the stars appear and the Night dreams
Learning on that hill of clouds, dressed in its long, milky pagne.[2]
The roofs of the huts shine tenderly. What are they saying   15
So secretly to the stars? Inside, the fire dies out
In the closeness of sour and sweet smells.

Woman, light the clear-oil lamp. Let the Ancestors
Speak around us as parents do when the children are in bed.
Let us listen to the voices of the Elissa[3] Elders. Exiled like us   20
They did not want to die, or lose the flow of their semen in the sands.
Let me hear, a gleam of friendly souls visits the smoke-filled hut,
My head upon your breast as warm as tasty *dang*[4] steaming from the fire,
Let me breathe the odor of our Dead, let me gather
And speak with their living voices, let me learn to live   25
Before plunging deeper than the diver[5]
Into the great depths of sleep.

                                                              1945

Black Woman

Naked woman, black woman
Dressed in your color[1] that is life, in your form that is beauty!
I grew up in your shadow. The softness of your hands
Shielded my eyes, and now at the height of Summer and Noon,
From the crest of a charred hilltop I discover you, Promised Land[2]   5
And your beauty strikes my heart like an eagle's lightning flash.

Naked woman, dark woman
Ripe fruit with firm flesh, dark raptures of black wine,
Mouth that gives music to my mouth
Savanna of clear horizons, savanna quivering to the fervent caress   10
Of the East Wind,[3] sculptured tom-tom, stretched drumskin
Moaning under the hands of the conqueror
Your deep contralto voice[4] is the spiritual song of the Beloved.

---

2. Printed cloth (French African); here the Milky Way, with which the moon appears to be robed.
3. A village in Guinea Bissau, south of Senegal, where Senghor's ancestors are buried.
4. A cereal meal.
5. The setting moon.
1. A reference to the green vegetation of the African landscape, to which the black woman is assimilated.

2. The analogy with the Israelites in the Old Testament of the Bible confers a religious note on this poem.
3. The Harmattan, a dry, sharp wind that blows from the Sahara, northeast of Senegal, between November and April.
4. An allusion to the vocal register of Marian Anderson (1897–1993), an African American singer famous for her rendering of Negro spirituals.

Naked woman, dark woman
Oil no breeze can ripple, oil soothing the thighs   15
Of athletes and the thighs of the princes of Mali[5]
Gazelle with celestial limbs, pearls are stars
Upon the night of your skin. Delight of the mind's riddles,
The reflections of red gold from your shimmering skin
In the shade of your hair, my despair   20
Lightens in the close suns of your eyes.

Naked woman, black woman
I sing your passing beauty and fix it for all Eternity
before jealous Fate reduces you to ashes to nourish the roots of life.

                                                                          1945

Prayer to the Masks

Masks![1] O Masks!
Black mask, red mask, you white-and-black masks
Masks of the four cardinal points where the Spirit blows
I greet you in silence!
And you, not the least of all, Ancestor with the lion head.[2]   5
You keep this place safe from women's laughter
And any wry, profane smiles[3]
You exude the immortal air where I inhale
The breath of my Fathers.
Masks with faces without masks, stripped of every dimple   10
And every wrinkle
You created this portrait, my face leaning
On an altar of blank paper[4]
And in your image, listen to me!
The Africa of empires is dying—it is the agony   15
Of a sorrowful princess
And Europe, too, tied to us at the navel.
Fix your steady eyes on your oppressed children
Who give their lives like the poor man his last garment.
Let us answer "present" at the rebirth of the World   20
As white flour cannot rise without the leaven.[5]
Who else will teach rhythm to the world
Deadened by machines and cannons?

5. The ancient empire of the West African savanna.
1. Representatives of the spirits of the ancestors. In African belief, the ancestors inhabit the immaterial world beyond the visible, from there offering protection to their living descendants.
2. The animal totem of Senghor's family. His father bore the Serer name Diogoye ("Lion"). A totem is an animal or plant that is closely associated with a family, sometimes considered to be a member of the family.
3. Ancestral masks are usually kept in an enclosure, a sacred place forbidden to women and uninitiated males. There is also a suggestion here that Senghor will protect them from the patronizing gaze of white people.
4. An ironic reference to Senghor's Western education.
5. An ingredient (for example, yeast) in baked goods that make them rise; also a biblical image.

Who will sound the shout of joy at daybreak to wake orphans and the dead?
Tell me, who will bring back the memory of life   25
To the man of gutted hopes?
They call us men of cotton, coffee, and oil
They call us men of death.
But we are men of dance, whose feet get stronger
As we pound upon firm ground.[6]   30

1945

Letter to a Prisoner

Ngom! Champion of Tyâné![1]

It is I who greet you, I your village neighbor, your heart's neighbor.
I send you my white[2] greeting like the dawn's white cry,
Over the barbed wires of hate and stupidity,
And I call you by your name and your honor.   5
My greetings to Tamsir Dargui Ndyâye, who lives off parchments[3]
That give him a subtle tongue and long thin fingers,[4]
To Samba Dyouma, the poet, whose voice is the color of flame[5]
And whose forehead bears the signs of his destiny,
To Nyaoutt Mbodye and to Koli Ngom, your namesake   10
And to all those who, at the hour when the great arms
Are sad like branches beaten by the sun, huddle at night
Shivering around the dish of friendship.

I write you from the solitude of my precious—and closely guarded—
Residence of my black skin. Fortunate are my friends   15
Who know nothing of the icy walls and the brightly lit
Apartments that sterilize every seed on the ancestors' masks
And even the memories of love.
You know nothing of the good white bread, milk, and salt,
Or those substantial dishes that do not nourish,   20
That separate the refined from the boulevard crowds,
Sleepwalkers who have renounced their human identity
Chameleons[6] deaf to change, and their shame locks you
In your cage of solitude.
You know nothing of restaurants and swimming pools   25
Forbidden to noble black blood

6. A reference to Antaeus, who in Greek mythology drew strength by touching the earth with his feet.
1. A Serer female name. The direct address with which the poem opens is a convention of oral poetry. Ngom, a comrade in the German prisoner-of-war camp, is addressed by his praise name as a champion wrestler, whose exploits in the arena bring honor to his beloved, Tyâné. In the poem, Senghor shares his experience of wartime Paris, to which he has returned after his release from the camp, with the Africans whom he left behind.
2. Wan, melancholic.
3. Implies intellectual and spiritual nourishment. "Tamsir": a title for a learned man, equivalent to "doctor."
4. Of the ascetic man of letters.
5. A reference to Dyouma's golden voice and the passionate content of his lyrics. Oral poets sang or declaimed their compositions.
6. A reference to those French people who collaborated with the German forces of the Occupation.

And Science and Humanity erecting their police lines
At the borders of negritude.[7]
Must I shout louder? Tell me, can you hear me?
I no longer recognize white men, my brothers,   30
Like this evening at the cinema, so lost were they
Beyond the void made around my skin.[8]

I write to you because my books are white like boredom,
Like misery, like death.
Make room for me around the pot so I can take my place   35
Again, still warm.
Let our hands touch as they reach into the steaming
Rice of friendship. Let the old Serer words
Pass from mouth to mouth like a pipe among friends.
Let Dargui share his succulent fruits,[9] the hay   40
Of every smelly drought! And you, serve us your wise words
As huge as the navel[1] of prodigious Africa.
Which singer this evening will summon the Ancestors around us,
Gathering like a peaceful herd of beasts of the bush?
Who will nestle our dreams under the eyelids of the stars?   45

Ngom! Answer me by the new-moon mail.
At the turn in the road, I shall meet your naked, hesitant words.
Like the fledgling emerging from his cage
Your words are put together so naively; and the learned may mock them,
But they bring me back to the surreal   50
And their milk gushes on my face.
I await your letter at the hour when morning lays death low.
I shall receive it piously like the morning ablution,
Like the dew of dawn.

Paris, June 1942

To New York

(for jazz orchestra and trumpet solo)

I

New York! At first I was bewildered by your beauty,
Those huge, long-legged, golden girls.
So shy, at first, before your blue metallic eyes and icy smile,
So shy. And full of despair at the end of skyscraper streets
Raising my owl eyes at the eclipse of the sun.   5
Your light is sulphurous against the pale towers

---

7. Here, a collective term for the black race, in its historical circumstance the world over.
8. A rare report of Senghor's personal experience of racial discrimination.
9. Of his mind, which is well stocked with learning and wisdom.
1. Many African children have large navels. Senghor turns this into a mark of natural strength.

Whose heads strike lightning into the sky,
Skyscrapers defying storms with their steel shoulders
And weathered skin of stone.
But two weeks on the naked sidewalks of Manhattan—   10
At the end of the third week the fever
Overtakes you with a jaguar's leap
Two weeks without well water or pasture all birds of the air
Fall suddenly dead under the high, sooty terraces.
No laugh from a growing child, his hand in my cool hand.   15
No mother's breast, but nylon legs. Legs and breasts
Without smell or sweat. No tender word, and no lips,
Only artificial hearts paid for in cold cash
And not one book offering wisdom.
The painter's palette yields only coral crystals.   20
Sleepless nights, O nights of Manhattan!
Stirring with delusions while car horns blare the empty hours
And murky streams carry away hygenic loving
Like rivers overflowing with the corpses of babies.

II

Now is the time for signs and reckoning, New York!   25
Now is the time of manna and hyssop.[1]
You have only to listen to God's trombones,[2] to your heart
Beating to the rhythm of blood, your blood.
I saw Harlem teeming with sounds and ritual colors
And outrageous smells—   30
At teatime in the home of the drugstore-deliveryman
I saw the festival of Night begin at the retreat of day.
And I proclaim Night more truthful than the day.
It is the pure hour when God brings forth
Life immemorial in the streets,   35
All the amphibious elements shining like suns.
Harlem, Harlem! Now I've seen Harlem, Harlem!
A green breeze of corn rising from the pavements
Plowed by the Dan[3] dancers' bare feet,
Hips rippling like silk and spearhead breasts,   40
Ballets of water lilies and fabulous masks
And mangoes of love rolling from the low houses
To the feet of police horses.
And along sidewalks I saw streams of white rum
And streams of black milk in the blue haze of cigars.   45
And at night I saw cotton flowers snow down
From the sky and the angels' wings and sorcerers' plumes.
Listen, New York! O listen to your bass male voice,

1. An aromatic herb with religious associations. "Manna": the food that came down miraculously from Heaven to feed the Israelites when they were wandering in the desert after leaving Egypt.
2. The title of a book of sermons by James Weldon Johnson, written in the idiom of black preachers. The work has become a classic of African American literature.
3. An ethnic group in Ivory Coast, reputed for the vigor of its dances. These lines establish a racial and cultural connection between Africa and black America.

Your vibrant oboe voice, the muted anguish of your tears
Falling in great clots of blood,   50
Listen to the distant beating of your nocturnal heart,
The tom-tom's rhythm and blood, tom-tom blood and tom-tom.

III

New York! I say New York, let black blood flow into your blood.
Let it wash the rust from your steel joints, like an oil of life
Let it give your bridges the curve of hips and supple vines.   55
Now the ancient age returns, unity is restored,
The reconciliation of Lion and Bull and Tree[4]
Idea links to action, the ear to the heart, sign to meaning.
See your rivers stirring with musk alligators[5]
And sea cows[6] with mirage eyes. No need to invent the Sirens.   60
Just open your eyes to the April rainbow
And your ears, especially your ears, to God
Who in one burst of saxophone laughter
Created heaven and earth in six days,
And on the seventh slept a deep Negro sleep.   65

1956

Songs for Signare[1]

(for flutes[2])

A *hand of light*[3] caressed my dark eyelids and your smile rose
Over the mists floating monotonously on my Congo.[4]
My heart has echoed the virgin song of the dawn birds
As my blood used to beat to the white song of sap in my branching arms.
See the bush flower and the star in my hair   5
And the bandana on the brow of the herdsman athlete.[5]
I will take up the flute and play a rhythm for the peace
Of the herds and sitting all day in the shade of your lashes,
Close to the Fimla Springs[6] I shall graze faithfully the golden
Lowings[7] of your herds. For this morning a hand of light   10
Caressed my dark eyelids, and all day long
My heart has echoed the virgin song of the birds.

1961

---

4. Symbolic of suffering, from the Christian cross. "Lion": a symbol of the black race. "Bull": a symbol of the white race.

5. Held in Serer mythology to conserve the memory of the past.

6. Or manatees, credited by the Serer with being able to see into the future.

1. The name of the woman addressed is also the French word for a mixed-race woman of Portuguese and African descent.

2. Associated with shepherds in the pastoral tradition.

3. That is, of the beloved. This is a love poem based on the Western pastoral convention.

4. A river in central Africa that flows through dense tropical landscape; here, an image of the poet's state of mind.

5. The poet himself.

6. The source of a stream in Sine-Saloum.

7. This association of the sound of the cattle with color is an example of synaesthesia.

Elegy of the Circumcised[1]

Childhood Night,[2] blue Night, gold Night, O Moon!
How often have I invoked you, O Night! while weeping by the road,
Feeling the pain of adulthood. Loneliness! and its dunes all around.
One night during childhood it was a night as black as pitch.
Our backs were bent with fear at the lion's roar,[3] and the shifting   5
Silence in the night bent the tall grass. Branches caught fire
And you were fired with hope! and my pale memory of the Sun
Barely reassured my innocence. I had to die.[4]
I laid my hands on my neck like the virgin who shivers in the throes
Of death. I had to die to the beauty of the song—all things drift   10
Along the thread of death. Look at twilight on the turtledoves' breast,
When blue ringdoves coo and dream sea gulls fly
With their plaintive cries.

Let us die and dance elbow to elbow in a braided garland[5]
May our clothes not impede our steps, but let the gift   15
Of the betrothed girl glow like sparks under the clouds.
Woi![6] The drum furrows the holy silence.
Let us dance, the song whipping the blood, and let the rhythm
Chase away the agony that grabs us by the throat.
Life keeps death away.   20
Let us dance to the refrain of agony, may the night of sex[7]
Rise above our ignorance, above our innocence.
Ah! To die to childhood, let the poem die, the syntax disintegrate,
And all the unimportant words become spoiled.
The rhythm's weight is sufficient, no need for cement words   25
To build the city of tomorrow on rock.
May the Sun rise up from the sea of shadows
Blood![8] The waves are the color of dawn.

But God, I have wailed too much—how many times?
—The transparent childhood nights.   30
The Male-Noon is the time of Spirits, when all form
Gets rid of its flesh, like trees in Europe under the winter sun.
See, the bones are abstract, they obey only the measures
Of the ruler, the compass, the sextant.
Like sand, life slips freely from man's fingers,   35
And snowflakes imprison the water's life,

---

1. The circumcision rite is the essential element in the initiation ceremony that marks the formal passage of the adolescent to adult status. The ceremony involves the confinement of candidates in the bush for a long period, during which they undergo a series of tests and receive instruction in the history and customs of the land. At the end of this period, on a designated night, they are circumcised one after the other.
2. The night of the circumcision.
3. Simulated, as part of the initiation cere-
mony, and intended to develop the virtue of courage in the boys.
4. Initiation is the symbolic death of the child who is reborn an adult.
5. The triumphant dance of the initiates after the ceremony.
6. A chant.
7. Initiation also purifies the adolescent, in preparation for sexuality in its creative function.
8. That shed at circumcision, heralding a new birth.

The water snake[9] glides through the vain hands of the reeds.
Lovely Nights, friendly Nights, childhood Nights
Along the salt flats and in the woods, nights throbbing
With presences and with eyelids, full of wings and breaths   40
And living silence, now tell me how many times
Have I cried for you in the bloom of my age?

The poem withers in the midday sun and feeds upon the evening dew,
The tom-tom beats the rhythm of sap in the smell of ripe fruit.
Master of the Initiates,[1] I know I need your knowledge
    to understand   45
The cipher of things, to be aware of my duties as father and *lamarque*,[2]
To measure exactly the scope of my responsibilities, to distribute
The harvest without forgetting any worker or orphan.
The song is not just a charm, it feeds the woolly heads of my flock.
The poem is a snake-bird,[3] the dawn marriage of shadow and light   50
It soars like the Phoenix![4] It sings with wings spread
Over the slaughter of words.

1961

9. A symbol of wisdom and durability.
1. An elder who supervises the ceremony.
2. A word coined by Senghor from the Wolof *lam* and the Greek *archos*, both meaning "landowner." The line refers to the civic and moral obligations taught to the initiates.
3. Or plumed serpent, which is endowed with

visionary powers. This creature is found in the mythology of many cultures.
4. A mythical bird that is supposed to rise from its own ashes, thus a symbol of regeneration. Like the bird, poetry embodies the force of renewal in nature.

TADEUSZ BOROWSKI

1922–1951

Incarcerated in the extermination camps of Auschwitz-Birkenau, Dautmergen, and Dachau-Allach between the ages of twenty and twenty-two, a tormented suicide by gas at twenty-eight, Tadeusz Borowski wrote stories of life in the camps that have made him the foremost writer of what is called the "literature of atrocity." His fiction is still read for its powerful evocation of the death camps, for its analysis of human relationships under pressure, and for its agonizing portrayal of individuals forced to choose between physical or spiritual survival.

Tadeusz Borowski was born on November 12, 1922, to Polish Catholic parents in Żytomierz, a Soviet-controlled city with Polish, Ukrainian, Jewish, and Russian residents. When he was three years old, his father was sent to a labor camp in Siberia as a suspected dissident. Four years later, his mother was deported as well, and Tadeusz was separated from his twelve-year-old brother. Tadeusz was raised by an aunt and educated in a

Soviet school until a prisoner exchange in 1932 brought his father home; his mother's release in 1934 reunited the family. Money was scarce, however, and the boy was sent away to a Franciscan boarding school where he could be educated inexpensively. Later he commented that he had never had a family life: "Either my father was sitting in Murmansk or my mother was in Siberia, or I was in a boarding school, on my own, or in a camp." The Second World War began when he was sixteen, and—since the Nazis did not permit higher education for Poles—Borowski continued his studies at Warsaw University via illegal underground classes. Unlike his fellow students, he refused to join political groups and did not become involved in the Resistance; he wanted merely to write poetry and continue his literary studies. Polish publications were illegal, however, and his first poetry collection, *Wherever the Earth* (1942)—run off in 165 copies on a clandestine mimeograph machine—was enough to condemn him. *Wherever the Earth* prefigures the bleak perspective of the concentration camp stories: prophesying the end of the human race, it sees the world as a gigantic labor camp and the sky as a "low, steel lid" or "a factory ceiling" (an oppressive image that he may have adapted from **Baudelaire's "Spleen LXXXI"**). In late February 1943, Borowski and his fiancée, Maria Rundo, were arrested; they were sent to Auschwitz two months later. In the meantime, Borowski was able to see, from his cell window, both the Jewish uprising in the Warsaw ghetto and the ghetto's fiery destruction by Nazi soldiers.

On arriving in Auschwitz, Borowski was put to hard labor with the other prisoners. After a bout with pneumonia, he survived by taking a position as an orderly in the Auschwitz hospital—which was not just a clinic but a place where doctors used prisoners as experimental subjects. Rundo had been sent to the women's barracks at the same camp, and he wrote daily letters that were smuggled to her. He got to see her when he was sent to the women's camp to pick up the corpses of infants, and later when he was assigned to repair roofs in the women's camp. Borowski wrote about his camp experiences immediately after the war, when he was living in Munich with two other former Auschwitz prisoners, Janusz Nel Siedlecki and Krystyn Olszewski. The three men were transferred from Dachau-Allach to the Freimann repatriation camp, outside Munich, which they soon left when the Polish artist and publisher Anatol Girs located them and found them jobs. Sharing an apartment in Munich, they published their slightly fictionalized memoirs, including Borowski's "This Way for the Gas, Ladies and Gentlemen," in the 1946 collection *We Were in Auschwitz*. On his return to Poland, Borowski's searing talent was recognized and he became a prominent writer. He married Maria Rundo and was courted by Poland's Stalinist government. At the government's urging, he wrote journalism and weekly stories that followed communist political lines and employed a newly strident tone. The Cold War had begun, and Borowski was persuaded that he had joined a popular revolution that would prevent more horrors like Auschwitz. He went so far as to do intelligence work in Berlin for the Polish secret police in 1949. The revelation of Soviet prison camps, however, as well as the spectacle of political purges in Poland, gradually disillusioned him: once more, he was part of a concentration-camp system and complicit with the oppressors. Although he and his wife had a newborn daughter, he committed suicide by gas on July 1, 1951.

Narrated in an impersonal tone by one of the prisoners, "This Way for the Gas, Ladies and Gentlemen" describes the extermination camp of Birkenau, the largest of three concentration camps at Auschwitz (Polish: *Oświęcim*), an enclosed world of hierarchical authority and desperate struggles to survive. Food, shoes, shirts, underwear: this vital currency of the camp is obtained when prisoners are stripped of their belongings as they arrive in railway cattle cars. The story follows the narrator's first trip to the railroad station with the labor battalion "Canada." The trip will salvage goods from a train bringing fifteen thousand Polish Jews, former inhabitants of the cities Sosnowiec and Będzin. By the end of the day, most of the travelers will be burning in the crematorium, and the camp will live for a few more days on the loot from "a good, rich transport."

Borowski suggests from the beginning the systematic dehumanization of the camps: prisoners are equated with lice, and they mill around by the naked thousands in blocked-off sections. The same gas is used in exterminating lice and humans—who will later be equated with sick horses (the converted stables retain their old signs), lumber and concrete trucked in from the railroad station, and insects whose jaws work away at moldy pieces of bread. Constantly supervised, subject to arbitrary rules and punishment, malnourished and pushed to exhaustion, their identities reduced to numerals tattooed on their arms, the prisoners live in the shadow of a hierarchical authority that is to be both feared and placated. Paradoxically, their common vulnerability leads to alienation and rage at their fellow victims rather than at the executioners. The Nazis have foreseen everything, explains the narrator's friend Henri, including the fact that weakness needs to vent itself on the weaker. The only way to cope is to distance oneself from what is happening, to become a cog

in the machine so that one does not actually experience the events—to suspend, for the moment, one's humanity.

The story's brutal realism and matter-of-fact tone convey as no passionate oratory could the mind-numbing horror of a situation in which systematic slaughter was the background for everyday life. The narrator, Tadeusz, is modeled partly on Borowski, but he is also a composite figure; he has become another part of the concentration-camp system, a survivor. He has a job in the system; assists the Kapos, or senior prisoners who organize the camp; and carries a burden of guilt that his adopted impersonal attitude cannot quite suppress. Borowski's stories shocked their postwar audience with their uncompromising honesty: here were no saintly victims and demonic executioners, but rather human beings—human beings—going about the business of extermination or, reduced to near-animal level, cooperating in the destruction of themselves and others. It is a picture that sorely tests any belief in civilization, common humanity, or divine providence; Borowski's bleak outlook questions everything and does not pretend to offer encouragement.

The narrator's dispassionate tone, as he describes senseless cruelty and mass murder, individual scenes of desperation, or the eccentric emotions of people about to die, continues to shock many readers. Borowski is certainly describing a world of antiheroes, those who survive by accommodating themselves to things as they are and avoiding acts of heroism. Borowski wrote this story after the Nazi defeat, but for its duration the picture is one of a spiritual desolation that not only illustrates a shameful moment in modern history but raises questions about what it means to be civilized, or even human.

This Way for the Gas, Ladies and Gentlemen[1]

All of us[2] walk around naked. The delousing is finally over, and our striped suits are back from the tanks of Cyclone B[3] solution, an efficient killer of lice in clothing and of men in gas chambers. Only the inmates in the blocks cut off from ours by the 'Spanish goats'[4] still have nothing to wear. But all the same, all of us walk around naked: the heat is unbearable. The camp has been sealed off tight. Not a single prisoner, not one solitary louse, can sneak through the gate. The labour Kommandos have stopped working. All day, thousands of naked men shuffle up and down the roads, cluster around the squares, or lie against the walls and on top of the roofs. We have been sleeping on plain boards, since our mattresses and blankets are still being disinfected. From the rear blockhouses we have a view of the F.K.L.—*Frauen Konzentration Lager*;[5] there too the delousing is in full swing. Twenty-eight thousand women have been stripped naked and driven out of the barracks. Now they swarm around the large yard between the blockhouses.

The heat rises, the hours are endless. We are without even our usual diversion: the wide roads leading to the crematoria are empty. For several days now, no new transports have come in. Part of 'Canada'[6] has been liquidated and detailed to a labour Kommando—one of the very toughest—at Harmenz.[7] For there exists in the camp a special brand of justice based on envy: when the rich and mighty fall, their friends see to it that they fall to the very bottom. And Canada, our Canada, which smells not of maple forests but of French perfume, has amassed great fortunes in diamonds and currency from all over Europe.

Several of us sit on the top bunk, our legs dangling over the edge. We slice the neat loaves of crisp, crunchy bread. It is a bit coarse to the taste, the kind that stays fresh for days. Sent all the way from Warsaw[8]—only a week ago my mother held this white loaf in her hands . . . dear Lord, dear Lord . . .

We unwrap the bacon, the onion, we open a can of evaporated milk. Henri, the fat Frenchman, dreams aloud of the French wine brought by the transports from Strasbourg, Paris, Marseille[9] . . . Sweat streams down his body.

'Listen, *mon ami*,[1] next time we go up on the loading ramp, I'll bring you real champagne. You haven't tried it before, eh?'

'No. But you'll never be able to smuggle it through the gate, so stop teasing. Why not try and "organize" some shoes for me instead—you know, the perforated kind, with a double sole,[2] and what about that shirt you promised me long ago?'

---

1. Translated by Barbara Vedder.
2. Inmates in Auschwitz 11, or Birkenau, the largest of the Nazi extermination camps, established in October 1941 near the town of Birkenau, Poland. Its death toll is usually estimated between 1 million and 2.5 million people.
3. Gas used in extermination camps.
4. Crossed wooden beams wrapped in barbed wire.
5. Women's concentration camp (German).
6. The name given to the camp stores (as well as prisoners working there) where valuables and clothing taken from prisoners were sorted for dispatch to Germany. Like the nation of Canada, the store symbolized wealth and prosperity to the camp inmates.
7. One of the subcamps outside Birkenau itself.
8. Capital of Poland; most of its Jewish residents were executed by the Nazis.
9. A large French port on the Mediterranean Sea. Strasbourg is a city in northeast France.
1. My friend (French).
2. A Hungarian style.

'*Patience, patience*. When the new transports come, I'll bring all you want. We'll be going on the ramp again!'

'And what if there aren't any more "cremo"[3] transports?' I say spitefully. 'Can't you see how much easier life is becoming around here: no limit on packages, no more beatings? You even write letters home . . . One hears all kind of talk, and, dammit, they'll run out of people!'

'Stop talking nonsense.' Henri's serious fat face moves rhythmically, his mouth is full of sardines. We have been friends for a long time, but I do not even know his last name. 'Stop talking nonsense,' he repeats, swallowing with effort. 'They can't run out of people, or we'll starve to death in this blasted camp. All of us live on what they bring.'

'All? We have our packages . . .'

'Sure, you and your friend, and ten other friends of yours. Some of you Poles get packages. But what about us, and the Jews, and the Russkis? And what if we had no food, no "organization" from the transports, do you think you'd be eating those packages of yours in peace? We wouldn't let you!'

'You would, you'd starve to death like the Greeks. Around here, whoever has grub, has power.'

'Anyway, you have enough, we have enough, so why argue?'

Right, why argue? They have enough, I have enough, we eat together and we sleep on the same bunks. Henri slices the bread, he makes a tomato salad. It tastes good with the commissary mustard.

Below us, naked, sweat-drenched men crowd the narrow barracks aisles or lie packed in eights and tens in the lower bunks. Their nude, withered bodies stink of sweat and excrement; their cheeks are hollow. Directly beneath me, in the bottom bunk, lies a rabbi. He has covered his head[4] with a piece of rag torn off a blanket and reads from a Hebrew prayer book (there is no shortage of this type of literature at the camp), wailing loudly, monotonously.

'Can't somebody shut him up? He's been raving as if he'd caught God himself by the feet.'

'I don't feel like moving. Let him rave. They'll take him to the oven that much sooner.'

'Religion is the opium of the people,'[5] Henri, who is a Communist and a *rentier*,[6] says sententiously. 'If they didn't believe in God and eternal life, they'd have smashed the crematoria long ago.'

'Why haven't you done it then?'

The question is rhetorical; the Frenchman ignores it.

'Idiot,' he says simply, and stuffs a tomato in his mouth.

Just as we finish our snack, there is a sudden commotion at the door. The Muslims[7] scurry in fright to the safety of their bunks, a messenger runs into the Block Elder's shack. The Elder,[8] his face solemn, steps out at once.

'Canada! *Antreten!*[9] But fast! There's a transport coming!'

---

3. The crematorium.
4. Jews are expected to keep their heads covered while at prayer.
5. A quotation from the German political philosopher Karl Marx (1818–1883).
6. Someone with unearned income, a stockholder (French).

7. Camp nickname for people who had given up, considered the camp pariahs.
8. A Kapo, or senior prisoner in charge of a group of prisoners.
9. Report (German).

'Great God!' yells Henri, jumping off the bunk. He swallows the rest of his tomato, snatches his coat, screams '*Raus*'[1] at the men below, and in a flash is at the door. We can hear a scramble in the other bunks. Canada is leaving for the ramp.

'Henri, the shoes!' I call after him.

'*Keine Angst!*'[2] he shouts back, already outside.

I proceed to put away the food. I tie a piece of rope around the suitcase where the onions and the tomatoes from my father's garden in Warsaw mingle with Portuguese sardines, bacon from Lublin (that's from my brother), and authentic sweetmeats from Salonica.[3] I tie it all up, pull on my trousers, and slide off the bunk.

'*Platz!*'[4] I yell, pushing my way through the Greeks. They step aside. At the door I bump into Henri.

'*Was ist los?*'[5]

'Want to come with us on the ramp?'

'Sure, why not?'

'Come along then, grab your coat! We're short of a few men. I've already told the Kapo,' and he shoves me out of the barracks door.

We line up. Someone has marked down our numbers, someone up ahead yells, 'March, march,' and now we are running towards the gate, accompanied by the shouts of a multilingual throng that is already being pushed back to the barracks. Not everybody is lucky enough to be going on the ramp . . . We have almost reached the gate. *Links, zwei, drei, vier! Mützen ab!*[6] Erect, arms stretched stiffly along our hips, we march past the gate briskly, smartly, almost gracefully. A sleepy S.S.[7] man with a large pad in his hand checks us off, waving us ahead in groups of five.

'*Hundert!*'[8] he calls after we have all passed.

'*Stimmt!*'[9] comes a hoarse answer from out front.

We march fast, almost at a run. There are guards all around, young men with automatics. We pass camp II B, then some deserted barracks and a clump of unfamiliar green—apple and pear trees. We cross the circle of watchtowers and, running, burst on to the highway. We have arrived. Just a few more yards. There, surrounded by trees, is the ramp.

A cheerful little station, very much like any other provincial railway stop: a small square framed by tall chestnuts and paved with yellow gravel. Not far off, beside the road, squats a tiny wooden shed, uglier and more flimsy than the ugliest and flimsiest railway shack; farther along lie stacks of old rails, heaps of wooden beams, barracks parts, bricks, paving stones. This is where they load

---

1. Outside (German).
2. Don't panic (German).
3. Major port city in northeast Greece. Lublin is a city in eastern Poland.
4. Make room (German).
5. What's the matter? (German).
6. Left, two, three, four! Caps off! (German).
7. Abbreviation for *Schutzstaffel* (Protective Echelon, German), the Nazi police system that began as Hitler's private guard and grew, by 1939, to a 250,000-member military and

political organization that administered all state security functions. The SS was divided into numerous bureaucratic units, one of which, the Death's Head Battalions, managed the concentration camps. Selected for physical perfection and (Aryan) racial purity, SS members wore black or gray-green uniforms decorated with silver insignia.
8. A hundred! (German).
9. Right! (German).

freight for Birkenau: supplies for the construction of the camp, and people for the gas chambers. Trucks drive around, load up lumber, cement, people—a regular daily routine.

And now the guards are being posted along the rails, across the beams, in the green shade of the Silesian chestnuts,[1] to form a tight circle around the ramp. They wipe the sweat from their faces and sip out of their canteens. It is unbearably hot; the sun stands motionless at its zenith.

'Fall out!'

We sit down in the narrow streaks of shade along the stacked rails. The hungry Greeks (several of them managed to come along, God only knows how) rummage underneath the rails. One of them finds some pieces of mildewed bread, another a few half-rotten sardines. They eat.

'*Schweinedreck*,'[2] spits a young, tall guard with corn-coloured hair and dreamy blue eyes. 'For God's sake, any minute you'll have so much food to stuff down your guts, you'll bust!' He adjusts his gun, wipes his face with a handkerchief.

'Hey you, fatso!' His boot lightly touches Henri's shoulder. '*Pass mal auf*,[3] want a drink?'

'Sure, but I haven't got any marks,' replies the Frenchman with a professional air.

'*Schade*, too bad.'

'Come, come, Herr[4] Posten, isn't my word good enough any more? Haven't we done business before? How much?'

'One hundred. *Gemacht?*'[5]

'*Gemacht.*'

We drink the water, lukewarm and tasteless. It will be paid for by the people who have not yet arrived.

'Now you be careful,' says Henri, turning to me. He tosses away the empty bottle. It strikes the rails and bursts into tiny fragments. 'Don't take any money, they might be checking. Anyway, who the hell needs money? You've got enough to eat. Don't take suits, either, or they'll think you're planning to escape. Just get a shirt, silk only, with a collar. And a vest. And if you find something to drink, don't bother calling me. I know how to shift for myself, but you watch your step or they'll let you have it.'

'Do they beat you up here?'

'Naturally. You've got to have eyes in your ass. *Arschaugen*.'[6]

Around us sit the Greeks, their jaws working greedily, like huge human insects. They munch on stale lumps of bread. They are restless, wondering what will happen next. The sight of the large beams and the stacks of rails has them worried. They dislike carrying heavy loads.

'*Was wir arbeiten?*'[7] they ask.

'*Niks. Transport kommen, alles Krematorium, compris?*'[8]

---

1. Probably local chestnuts. Silesia, in central Europe, was partitioned among Poland, Czechoslovakia, and Germany after World War I; Germany occupied Polish Silesia in 1939.
2. Dirty pigs (German).
3. See here (German).
4. Mister (German).

5. Done? (German).
6. Eyes on your ass (German; literal trans.).
7. What are we working on? (German).
8. Nothing. Transport coming, everything crematorium, understood? (German; *compris* is French).

'*Alles verstehen*,' they answer in crematorium Esperanto.[9] All is well—they will not have to move the heavy rails or carry the beams.

In the meantime, the ramp has become increasingly alive with activity, increasingly noisy. The crews are being divided into those who will open and unload the arriving cattle cars and those who will be posted by the wooden steps. They receive instructions on how to proceed most efficiently. Motor cycles drive up, delivering S.S. officers, bemedalled, glittering with brass, beefy men with highly polished boots and shiny, brutal faces. Some have brought their briefcases, others hold thin, flexible whips. This gives them an air of military readiness and agility. They walk in and out of the commissary—for the miserable little shack by the road serves as their commissary, where in the summertime they drink mineral water, Sudetenquelle,[1] and where in winter they can warm up with a glass of hot wine. They greet each other in the state-approved way, raising an arm Roman fashion, then shake hands cordially, exchange warm smiles, discuss mail from home, their children, their families. Some stroll majestically on the ramp. The silver squares on their collars glitter, the gravel crunches under their boots, their bamboo whips snap impatiently.

We lie against the rails in the narrow streaks of shade, breathe unevenly, occasionally exchange a few words in our various tongues, and gaze listlessly at the majestic men in green uniforms, at the green trees, and at the church steeple of a distant village.

'The transport is coming,' somebody says. We spring to our feet, all eyes turn in one direction. Around the bend, one after another, the cattle cars begin rolling in. The train backs into the station, a conductor leans out, waves his hand, blows a whistle. The locomotive whistles back with a shrieking noise, puffs, the train rolls slowly alongside the ramp. In the tiny barred windows appear pale, wilted, exhausted human faces, terror-stricken women with tangled hair, unshaven men. They gaze at the station in silence. And then, suddenly, there is a stir inside the cars and a pounding against the wooden boards.

'Water! Air!'—weary, desperate cries.

Heads push through the windows, mouths gasp frantically for air. They draw a few breaths, then disappear; others come in their place, then also disappear. The cries and moans grow louder.

A man in a green uniform covered with more glitter than any of the others jerks his head impatiently, his lips twist in annoyance. He inhales deeply, then with a rapid gesture throws his cigarette away and signals to the guard. The guard removes the automatic from his shoulder, aims, sends a series of shots along the train. All is quiet now. Meanwhile, the trucks have arrived, steps are being drawn up, and the Canada men stand ready at their posts by the train doors. The S.S. officer with the briefcase raises his hand.

'Whoever takes gold, or anything at all besides food, will be shot for stealing Reich property. Understand? *Verstanden?*'

'*Jawohl!*'[2] we answer eagerly.

9. An artificial language, created in 1887 by L. L. Zamenhof, to simplify communication between nationalities. "*Alles verstehen*": Everything understood.
1. Water from the Sudetenland or Sudeten Mountains; a narrow strip of land on the northern and western borders of the Czech Republic. The Sudeten was annexed by Hitler in 1938.
2. Yes! (German). "*Verstanden*": understand? (German).

'*Also los!*[3] Begin!'

The bolts crack, the doors fall open. A wave of fresh air rushes inside the train. People . . . inhumanly crammed, buried under incredible heaps of luggage, suitcases, trunks, packages, crates, bundles of every description (everything that had been their past and was to start their future). Monstrously squeezed together, they have fainted from heat, suffocated, crushed one another. Now they push towards the opened doors, breathing like fish cast out on the sand.

'Attention! Out, and take your luggage with you! Take out everything. Pile all your stuff near the exits. Yes, your coats too. It is summer. March to the left. Understand?'

'Sir, what's going to happen to us?' They jump from the train on to the gravel, anxious, worn-out.

'Where are you people from?'

'Sosnowiec-Będzin.[4] Sir, what's going to happen to us?' They repeat the question stubbornly, gazing into our tired eyes.

'I don't know. I don't understand Polish.'

It is the camp law: people going to their death must be deceived to the very end. This is the only permissible form of charity. The heat is tremendous. The sun hangs directly over our heads, the white, hot sky quivers, the air vibrates, an occasional breeze feels like a sizzling blast from a furnace. Our lips are parched, the mouth fills with the salty taste of blood, the body is weak and heavy from lying in the sun. Water!

A huge, multicoloured wave of people loaded down with luggage pours from the train like a blind, mad river trying to find a new bed. But before they have a chance to recover, before they can draw a breath of fresh air and look at the sky, bundles are snatched from their hands, coats ripped off their backs, their purses and umbrellas taken away.

'But please, sir, it's for the sun, I cannot . . .'

'*Verboten!*'[5] one of us barks through clenched teeth. There is an S.S. man standing behind your back, calm, efficient, watchful.

'*Meine Herrschaften,*[6] this way, ladies and gentlemen, try not to throw your things around, please. Show some goodwill,' he says courteously, his restless hands playing with the slender whip.

'Of course, of course,' they answer as they pass, and now they walk alongside the train somewhat more cheerfully. A woman reaches down quickly to pick up her handbag. The whip flies, the woman screams, stumbles, and falls under the feet of the surging crowd. Behind her, a child cries in a thin little voice 'Mamele!'—a very small girl with tangled black curls.

The heaps grow. Suitcases, bundles, blankets, coats, handbags that open as they fall, spilling coins, gold, watches; mountains of bread pile up at the exits, heaps of marmalade, jams, masses of meat, sausages; sugar spills on the gravel. Trucks, loaded with people, start up with a deafening roar and drive off amidst

---

3. Then get going! (German).
4. Two cities in Katowice province (southern Poland). Będzin was also the site of a concentration camp, and more than ten thousand of

its inhabitants were exterminated.
5. Forbidden (German).
6. Gentlemen (German).

the wailing and screaming of the women separated from their children, and the stupefied silence of the men left behind. They are the ones who had been ordered to step to the right—the healthy and the young who will go to the camp. In the end, they too will not escape death, but first they must work.

Trucks leave and return, without interruption, as on a monstrous conveyor belt. A Red Cross van drives back and forth, back and forth, incessantly: it transports the gas that will kill these people. The enormous cross on the hood, red as blood, seems to dissolve in the sun.

The Canada men at the trucks cannot stop for a single moment, even to catch their breath. They shove the people up the steps, pack them in tightly, sixty per truck, more or less. Near by stands a young, cleanshaven 'gentleman', an S.S. officer with a notebook in his hand. For each departing truck he enters a mark; sixteen gone means one thousand people, more or less. The gentleman is calm, precise. No truck can leave without a signal from him, or a mark in his notebook: *Ordnung muss sein.*[7] The marks swell into thousands, the thousands into whole transports, which afterwards we shall simply call 'from Salonica', 'from Strasbourg', 'from Rotterdam'.[8] This one will be called 'Sosnowiec-Będzin'. The new prisoners from Sosnowiec-Będzin will receive serial numbers 131–2—thousand, of course, though afterwards we shall simply say 131–2, for short.

The transports swell into weeks, months, years. When the war is over, they will count up the marks in their notebooks—all four and a half million of them. The bloodiest battle of the war, the greatest victory of the strong, united Germany. *Ein Reich, ein Volk, ein Führer*[9]—and four crematoria.

The train has been emptied. A thin, pock-marked S.S. man peers inside, shakes his head in disgust and motions to our group, pointing his finger at the door.

'*Rein.*[1] Clean it up!'

We climb inside. In the corners amid human excrement and abandoned wrist-watches lie squashed, trampled infants, naked little monsters with enormous heads and bloated bellies. We carry them out like chickens, holding several in each hand.

'Don't take them to the trucks, pass them on to the women,' says the S.S. man, lighting a cigarette. His cigarette lighter is not working properly; he examines it carefully.

'Take them, for God's sake!' I explode as the women rush from me in horror, covering their eyes.

The name of God sounds strangely pointless, since the women and the infants will go on the trucks, every one of them without exception. We all know what this means, and we look at each other with hate and horror.

'What, you don't want to take them?' asks the pockmarked S.S. man with a note of surprise and reproach in his voice, and reaches for his revolver.

'You mustn't shoot, I'll carry them.' A tall, grey-haired woman takes the little corpses out of my hands and for an instant gazes straight into my eyes.

7. Order in everything (German).
8. Large port city in the Netherlands.
9. One State, One People, One Leader! (the

slogan of Nazi Germany).
1. Clean (German).

'My poor boy,' she whispers and smiles at me. Then she walks away, staggering along the path. I lean against the side of the train. I am terribly tired. Someone pulls at my sleeve.

'*En avant*,[2] to the rails, come on!'

I look up, but the face swims before my eyes, dissolves, huge and transparent, melts into the motionless trees and the sea of people . . . I blink rapidly: Henri.

'Listen, Henri, are we good people?'

'That's stupid. Why do you ask?'

'You see, my friend, you see, I don't know why, but I am furious, simply furious with these people—furious because I must be here because of them. I feel no pity. I am not sorry they're going to the gas chamber. Damn them all! I could throw myself at them, beat them with my fists. It must be pathological, I just can't understand . . .'

'Ah, on the contrary, it is natural, predictable, calculated. The ramp exhausts you, you rebel—and the easiest way to relieve your hate is to turn against someone weaker. Why, I'd even call it healthy. It's simple logic, *compris?*' He props himself up comfortably against the heap of rails. 'Look at the Greeks, they know how to make the best of it! They stuff their bellies with anything they find. One of them has just devoured a full jar of marmalade.'

'Pigs! Tomorrow half of them will die of the shits.'

'Pigs? You've been hungry.'

'Pigs!' I repeat furiously. I close my eyes. The air is filled with ghastly cries, the earth trembles beneath me, I can feel sticky moisture on my eyelids. My throat is completely dry.

The morbid procession streams on and on—trucks growl like mad dogs. I shut my eyes tight, but I can still see corpses dragged from the train, trampled infants, cripples piled on top of the dead, wave after wave . . . freight cars roll in, the heaps of clothing, suitcases and bundles grow, people climb out, look at the sun, take a few breaths, beg for water, get into the trucks, drive away. And again freight cars roll in, again people . . . The scenes become confused in my mind—I am not sure if all of this is actually happening, or if I am dreaming. There is a humming inside my head; I feel that I must vomit.

Henri tugs at my arm.

'Don't sleep, we're off to load up the loot.'

All the people are gone. In the distance, the last few trucks roll along the road in clouds of dust, the train has left, several S.S. officers promenade up and down the ramp. The silver glitters on their collars. Their boots shine, their red, beefy faces shine. Among them there is a woman—only now I realize she has been here all along—withered, flat-chested, bony, her thin, colourless hair pulled back and tied in a 'Nordic'[3] knot; her hands are in the pockets of her wide skirt. With a rat-like, resolute smile glued on her thin lips she sniffs around the corners of the ramp. She detests feminine beauty with the hatred of a woman who is herself repulsive, and knows it. Yes, I have seen her many times before and I know her well: she is the commandant of the F.K.L. She has

---

2. Forward (French).
3. A northern (especially Scandinavian) style

encouraged by the Nazis to establish an image of Teutonic racial purity.

come to look over the new crop of women, for some of them, instead of going on the trucks, will go on foot—to the concentration camp. There our boys, the barbers from Zauna,[4] will shave their heads and will have a good laugh at their 'outside world' modesty.

We proceed to load the loot. We lift huge trunks, heave them on to the trucks. There they are arranged in stacks, packed tightly. Occasionally somebody slashes one open with a knife, for pleasure or in search of vodka and perfume. One of the crates falls open; suits, shirts, books drop out on the ground . . . I pick up a small, heavy package. I unwrap it—gold, about two handfuls, bracelets, rings, brooches, diamonds . . .

'*Gib hier*,'[5] an S.S. man says calmly, holding up his briefcase already full of gold and colourful foreign currency. He locks the case, hands it to an officer, takes another, an empty one, and stands by the next truck, waiting. The gold will go to the Reich.[6]

It is hot, terribly hot. Our throats are dry, each word hurts. Anything for a sip of water! Faster, faster, so that it is over, so that we may rest. At last we are done, all the trucks have gone. Now we swiftly clean up the remaining dirt: there must be 'no trace left of the *Schweinerei*'. But just as the last truck disappears behind the trees and we walk, finally, to rest in the shade, a shrill whistle sounds around the bend. Slowly, terribly slowly, a train rolls in, the engine whistles back with a deafening shriek. Again weary, pale faces at the windows, flat as though cut out of paper, with huge, feverishly burning eyes. Already trucks are pulling up, already the composed gentleman with the notebook is at his post, and the S.S. men emerge from the commissary carrying briefcases for the gold and money. We unseal the train doors.

It is impossible to control oneself any longer. Brutally we tear suitcases from their hands, impatiently pull off their coats. Go on, go on, vanish! They go, they vanish. Men, women, children. Some of them know.

Here is a woman—she walks quickly, but tries to appear calm. A small child with a pink cherub's face runs after her and, unable to keep up, stretches out his little arms and cries: 'Mama! Mama!'

'Pick up your child, woman!'

'It's not mine, sir, not mine!' she shouts hysterically and runs on, covering her face with her hands. She wants to hide, she wants to reach those who will not ride the trucks, those who will go on foot, those who will stay alive. She is young, healthy, good-looking, she wants to live.

But the child runs after her, wailing loudly: 'Mama, mama, don't leave me!'

'It's not mine, not mine, no!'

Andrei, a sailor from Sevastopol,[7] grabs hold of her. His eyes are glassy from vodka and the heat. With one powerful blow he knocks her off her feet, then, as she falls, takes her by the hair and pulls her up again. His face twitches with rage.

---

4. The "sauna" barracks, in front of Canada, where prisoners were bathed, shaved, and deloused.

5. Give it to me (German).

6. The German state.

7. A Soviet (now, Ukrainian) port on the Black Sea.

'Ah, you bloody Jewess! So you're running from your own child! I'll show you, you whore!' His huge hand chokes her, he lifts her in the air and heaves her on to the truck like a heavy sack of grain.

'Here! And take this with you, bitch!' and he throws the child at her feet.

'*Gut gemacht*, good work. That's the way to deal with degenerate mothers,' says the S.S. man standing at the foot of the truck. '*Gut, gut, Russki*.'[8]

'Shut your mouth,' growls Andrei through clenched teeth, and walks away. From under a pile of rags he pulls out a canteen, unscrews the cork, takes a few deep swallows, passes it to me. The strong vodka burns the throat. My head swims, my legs are shaky, again I feel like throwing up.

And suddenly, above the teeming crowd pushing forward like a river driven by an unseen power, a girl appears. She descends lightly from the train, hops on to the gravel, looks around inquiringly, as if somewhat surprised. Her soft, blonde hair has fallen on her shoulders in a torrent, she throws it back impatiently. With a natural gesture she runs her hands down her blouse, casually straightens her skirt. She stands like this for an instant, gazing at the crowd, then turns and with a gliding look examines our faces, as though searching for someone. Unknowingly, I continue to stare at her, until our eyes meet.

'Listen, tell me, where are they taking us?'

I look at her without saying a word. Here, standing before me, is a girl, a girl with enchanting blonde hair, with beautiful breasts, wearing a little cotton blouse, a girl with a wise, mature look in her eyes. Here she stands, gazing straight into my face, waiting. And over there is the gas chamber: communal death, disgusting and ugly. And over in the other direction is the concentration camp: the shaved head, the heavy Soviet trousers in sweltering heat, the sickening, stale odour of dirty, damp female bodies, the animal hunger, the inhuman labour, and later the same gas chamber, only an even more hideous, more terrible death . . .

Why did she bring it? I think to myself, noticing a lovely gold watch on her delicate wrist. They'll take it away from her anyway.

'Listen, tell me,' she repeats.

I remain silent. Her lips tighten.

'I know,' she says with a shade of proud contempt in her voice, tossing her head. She walks off resolutely in the direction of the trucks. Someone tries to stop her; she boldly pushes him aside and runs up the steps. In the distance I can only catch a glimpse of her blonde hair flying in the breeze.

I go back inside the train; I carry out dead infants; I unload luggage. I touch corpses, but I cannot overcome the mounting, uncontrollable terror. I try to escape from the corpses, but they are everywhere: lined up on the gravel, on the cement edge of the ramp, inside the cattle cars. Babies, hideous naked women, men twisted by convulsions. I run off as far as I can go, but immediately a whip slashes across my back. Out of the corner of my eye I see an S.S. man, swearing profusely. I stagger forward and run, lose myself in the Canada group. Now, at last, I can once more rest against the stack of rails. The sun has leaned low over the horizon and illuminates the ramp with a reddish glow; the

---

8. Good, good, Russky (German). "*Gut gemacht*": well done (German).

shadows of the trees have become elongated, ghostlike. In the silence that settles over nature at this time of day, the human cries seem to rise all the way to the sky.

Only from this distance does one have a full view of the inferno on the teeming ramp. I see a pair of human beings who have fallen to the ground locked in a last desperate embrace. The man has dug his fingers into the woman's flesh and has caught her clothing with his teeth. She screams hysterically, swears, cries, until at last a large boot comes down over her throat and she is silent. They are pulled apart and dragged like cattle to the truck. I see four Canada men lugging a corpse: a huge, swollen female corpse. Cursing, dripping wet from the strain, they kick out of their way some stray children who have been running all over the ramp, howling like dogs. The men pick them up by the collars, heads, arms, and toss them inside the trucks, on top of the heaps. The four men have trouble lifting the fat corpse on to the car, they call others for help, and all together they hoist up the mound of meat. Big, swollen, puffed-up corpses are being collected from all over the ramp; on top of them are piled the invalids, the smothered, the sick, the unconscious. The heap seethes, howls, groans. The driver starts the motor, the truck begins rolling.

'Halt! Halt!' an S.S. man yells after them. 'Stop, damn you.'

They are dragging to the truck an old man wearing tails and a band around his arm. His head knocks against the gravel and pavement; he moans and wails in an uninterrupted monotone: '*Ich will mit dem Herrn Kommandanten sprechen*[9]— I wish to speak with the commandant . . .' With senile stubbornness he keeps repeating these words all the way. Thrown on the truck, trampled by others, choked, he still wails: '*Ich will mit dem . . .*'

'Look here, old man!' a young S.S. man calls, laughing jovially. 'In half an hour you'll be talking with the top commandant! Only don't forget to greet him with a *Heil Hitler!*'

Several other men are carrying a small girl with only one leg. They hold her by the arms and the one leg. Tears are running down her face and she whispers faintly: 'Sir, it hurts, it hurts . . .' They throw her on the truck on top of the corpses. She will burn alive along with them.

The evening has come, cool and clear. The stars are out. We lie against the rails. It is incredibly quiet. Anaemic bulbs hang from the top of the high lampposts; beyond the circle of light stretches an impenetrable darkness. Just one step, and a man could vanish for ever. But the guards are watching, their automatics ready.

'Did you get the shoes?' asks Henri.

'No.'

'Why?'

'My God, man, I am finished, absolutely finished!'

'So soon? After only two transports? Just look at me, I . . . since Christmas, at least a million people have passed through my hands. The worst of all are the transports from around Paris—one is always bumping into friends.'

---

9. I want to speak with the commandant (German).

'And what do you say to them?'

'That first they will have a bath, and later we'll meet at the camp. What would you say?'

I do not answer. We drink coffee with vodka; somebody opens a tin of cocoa and mixes it with sugar. We scoop it up by the handful, the cocoa sticks to the lips. Again coffee, again vodka.

'Henri, what are we waiting for?'

'There'll be another transport.'

'I'm not going to unload it! I can't take any more.'

'So, it's got you down? Canada is nice, eh?' Henri grins indulgently and disappears into the darkness. In a moment he is back again.

'All right. Just sit here quietly and don't let an S.S. man see you. I'll try to find you your shoes.'

'Just leave me alone. Never mind the shoes.' I want to sleep. It is very late.

Another whistle, another transport. Freight cars emerge out of the darkness, pass under the lamp-posts, and again vanish in the night. The ramp is small, but the circle of lights is smaller. The unloading will have to be done gradually. Somewhere the trucks are growling. They back up against the steps, black, ghostlike, their searchlights flash across the trees. *Wasser! Luft!*[1] The same all over again, like a late showing of the same film: a volley of shots, the train falls silent. Only this time a little girl pushes herself halfway through the small window and, losing her balance, falls out on to the gravel. Stunned, she lies still for a moment, then stands up and begins walking around in a circle, faster and faster, waving her rigid arms in the air, breathing loudly and spasmodically, whining in a faint voice. Her mind has given way in the inferno inside the train. The whining is hard on the nerves: an S.S. man approaches calmly, his heavy boot strikes between her shoulders. She falls. Holding her down with his foot, he draws his revolver, fires once, then again. She remains face down, kicking the gravel with her feet, until she stiffens. They proceed to unseal the train.

I am back on the ramp, standing by the doors. A warm, sickening smell gushes from inside. The mountain of people filling the car almost halfway up to the ceiling is motionless, horribly tangled, but still steaming.

'*Ausladen!*[2] comes the command. An S.S. man steps out from the darkness. Across his chest hangs a portable searchlight. He throws a stream of light inside.

'Why are you standing about like sheep? Start unloading!' His whip flies and falls across our backs. I seize a corpse by the hand; the fingers close tightly around mine. I pull back with a shriek and stagger away. My heart pounds, jumps up to my throat. I can no longer control the nausea. Hunched under the train I begin to vomit. Then, like a drunk, I weave over to the stack of rails.

I lie against the cool, kind metal and dream about returning to the camp, about my bunk, on which there is no mattress, about sleep among comrades who are not going to the gas tonight. Suddenly I see the camp as a haven of peace. It is true, others may be dying, but one is somehow still alive, one has enough food, enough strength to work . . .

1. Water! Air! (German).   2. Unload! (German).

The lights on the ramp flicker with a spectral glow, the wave of people—feverish, agitated, stupefied people—flows on and on, endlessly. They think that now they will have to face a new life in the camp, and they prepare themselves emotionally for the hard struggle ahead. They do not know that in just a few moments they will die, that the gold, money, and diamonds which they have so prudently hidden in their clothing and on their bodies are now useless to them. Experienced professionals will probe into every recess of their flesh, will pull the gold from under the tongue and the diamonds from the uterus and the colon. They will rip out gold teeth. In tightly sealed crates they will ship them to Berlin.[3]

The S.S. men's black figures move about, dignified, businesslike. The gentleman with the notebook puts down his final marks, rounds out the figures: fifteen thousand.

Many, very many, trucks have been driven to the crematoria today.

It is almost over. The dead are being cleared off the ramp and piled into the last truck. The Canada men, weighed down under a load of bread, marmalade and sugar, and smelling of perfume and fresh linen, line up to go. For several days the entire camp will live off this transport. For several days the entire camp will talk about 'Sosnowiec-Będzin'. 'Sosnowiec-Będzin' was a good, rich transport.

The stars are already beginning to pale as we walk back to the camp. The sky grows translucent and opens high above our heads—it is getting light.

Great columns of smoke rise from the crematoria and merge up above into a huge black river which very slowly floats across the sky over Birkenau and disappears beyond the forests in the direction of Trzebinia.[4] The 'Sosnowiec-Będzin' transport is already burning.

We pass a heavily armed S.S. detachment on its way to change guard. The men march briskly, in step, shoulder to shoulder, one mass, one will.

'*Und morgen die ganze Welt* . . .'[5] they sing at the top of their lungs.

'*Rechts ran!*[6] To the right march!' snaps a command from up front. We move out of their way.

1946

---

3. The capital of Germany.
4. A town west of Auschwitz, near Krakow.
5. And tomorrow the whole world (German): the last line of the Nazi song "The Rotten Bones Are Shaking," written by Hans Baumann. The previous line reads "for today Germany belongs to us."
6. To the right, get going! (German).

PAUL CELAN

1920–1970

A survivor of the Holocaust, Paul Celan wrote spare, hauntingly beautiful lyric poems about suffering and loss. The critic Theodor Adorno famously noted that "to write a poem after Auschwitz is barbaric." Yet Celan, who lost both parents in Nazi prison camps and who himself spent much of the Second World War in a forced labor camp, managed to write poetry that spoke directly about the unspeakable.

Born Paul Antschel in Czernowitz, Romania, Celan came from a religious Jewish family. (Celan is an anagram of the Romanian spelling of his last name, Ancel.) He was raised speaking German, and his mother passed on to him her love of German literature, while his father transmitted his Zionism and concern with the Jewish tradition. Czernowitz was linguistically and ethnically diverse, and Celan quickly learned Yiddish and Romanian, as well as Hebrew; later in life, he learned French, Russian, Ukranian, and English as well.

In 1938, Celan enrolled in a premedical program in Paris, where he was exposed to avant-garde literary movements such as surrealism; he had recently begun writing poetry. Returning home in the summer of 1939, he was trapped in Czernowitz by the outbreak of the Second World War. Under the Hitler-Stalin pact, the Soviet Union occupied Czernowitz in 1940. Distressed by harsh Soviet rule, Celan abandoned his youthful support of communism. After the Nazi invasion of the Soviet Union in the summer of 1941, the Germans took control of Czernowitz, and the Jews of the city were attacked and confined to a ghetto by the Nazi SS (abbreviation for the German word *Schutzstaffel*, the elite security organization) and by Romanian soldiers. Celan was given the task of clearing trash and destroying Russian books. On June 27, 1942, while Celan was away from the house, the Germans seized his parents and deported them to Nazi prison camps in the Ukraine. His father died of typhus later that year, and his mother was shot when she was no longer capable of working. Celan spent the next year and a half in labor camps in German-allied Romania, where, though conditions were severe, he was at less risk of being killed. He continued to write poetry. After the Soviet Red Army reoccupied eastern Romania and the full horror of the concentration camps came to be known, Celan, now released from his prison camp, wrote "Deathfugue," one of the first and most moving poems about the camps, published first in Romanian translation in 1947, then in German in 1952.

Near the end of the war, Celan left Czernowitz for Bucharest, where he worked translating literature, including some of **Franz Kafka**'s parables, into Romanian. For the remainder of his life, he was active as a translator of much modern French, Russian, and English poetry (and also Shakespeare) into German. Celan fled Bucharest in 1947, just before the Soviet takeover, and was smuggled with his poems over the border to Vienna. From there he went on to Paris and the prestigious École Normale Supérieure, where he received his degree and then taught German literature. He visited Germany occasionally, receiving the premier German literary award, the Büchner Prize, in 1960 and later meeting the existential philosopher

Martin Heidegger, whose work had inspired Celan despite the German's support of the Nazi regime. In 1969, Celan visited Israel for the first time.

During the 1960s, however, Celan suffered periods of increasing paranoia, the result of his concerns about anti-Semitism and of false accusations of plagiarism that continually dogged him. He briefly entered a psychiatric clinic in 1965, and remained under psychiatric treatment for the following five years. On April 20, 1970, Celan committed suicide by jumping off a bridge into the Seine, in Paris.

The poems printed here represent the range of Celan's career. They show his use of a restrained and difficult language to bear witness to the horrors suffered by his parents and other victims of the Holocaust. "Deathfugue," his first published poem and eventually his most famous, originally appeared in Romanian translation as "Tangoul Mortii" (Tango of Death). That title refers to the dance music that an SS commander forced prisoners to play during marches and executions at the Janowska camp in L'vov, Ukraine. The poem contrasts the golden hair of the commander's beloved Margareta (a typically German name) with the dark hair of the Jewish Shulamith, a prisoner in the camp. Her hair is described as "ashen," recalling the crematoria where the bodies of concentration camp victims were often burned. Celan re-creates the musical quality of the tango or fugue—two very different musical forms both characterized by rhythmic repetition—in his repetition of short, rhythmic phrases. The fragmentation and absence of punctuation suggest a breakdown of the moral order. The translator, John Felstiner, has left some of the poem in German to give the sense of its original language. Of the German language and why he continued to write in it, Celan once said, "Only in the mother tongue can one speak one's own truth. In a foreign tongue the poet lies."

Many of Celan's early poems have an elegiac tone, grieving for the dead of the Holocaust and the war. Written in the final years of the war, "Aspen Tree" (published in 1948) is a simpler, more direct poem than "Deathfugue." It laments the death of the poet's mother by addressing inanimate objects (the tree, the dandelion, the cloud, the star, the door) that remind him of her absence. "Corona" (1949), a response to a poem by **Rainer Maria Rilke**, tells of two lovers who realize that their love is haunted by the losses in wartime but who also believe that human decency will eventually reassert itself—that "It's time the stone consented to bloom." "Shibboleth" (1955), named after a biblical password, alludes to two incidents in the rise of Nazism and Fascism—the suppression of the Viennese Socialists in 1934 and the Spanish Civil War (1936–1939). While stating Celan's allegiance to the political left, the poem creates a powerful image of the exile who has no homeland but cries out into "homeland strangeness."

Later in life, Celan wrote poems that were less political and often more explicitly religious. The title "Tenebrae" (1959), or "darkness" in Latin, refers to the Crucifixion. Drawing on both the Old and the New Testaments, the poem uses the language of the Psalms and the Lamentations of Jeremiah to commemorate the suffering of victims in the Holocaust, which is likened to Christ's suffering on the cross. Although the poem's speakers ("we") insistently address the Lord, they seem to sense his absence. Indeed, since they are presumably Jewish, they may be praying to a God who is not their own. "Near are we," they cry, but the Lord is nowhere near and appears to have abandoned his people. "Zurich, at the Stork" (1963) recalls Celan's debate with an older poet, Nelly Sachs, about God's existence. Though deeply concerned with Jewish religious teaching, Celan never believed in God in a straightforward sense. And yet, in keeping with certain forms of Jewish mysticism, he believed in God as an absence, to which he prays in "Psalm" (1963).

During the last years of his life, Celan's poetry became increasingly difficult and hermetic. Two brief poems from this period, "You were" (1968) and "World to be stuttered after" (1968), combine the political and religious themes of his earlier works with a more intimate despair. The condensation of the lyrics in these years resembles a darker version of the late work of **Samuel Beckett**, whom Celan never met but of whom he said, late in life, "That's probably the only man here [in Paris] I could have an understanding with." Like Beckett, Celan responded to the calamities and horrors of his time with a restrained, minimalist art that spoke the truth about the unnamable.

Deathfugue[1]

Black milk of daybreak we drink it at evening
we drink it at midday and morning we drink it at night
we drink and we drink
we shovel a grave in the air where you won't lie too cramped
A man lives in the house he plays with his vipers he writes   5
he writes when it grows dark to Deutschland[2] your golden hair
   Margareta[3]
he writes it and steps out of doors and the stars are all sparkling he
   whistles his hounds to stay close
he whistles his Jews into rows has them shovel a grave in the ground
he commands us play up for the dance[4]

Black milk of daybreak we drink you at night   10
we drink you at morning and midday we drink you at evening
we drink and we drink
A man lives in the house he plays with his vipers he writes
he writes when it grows dark to Deutschland your golden hair
   Margareta
Your ashen hair Shulamith[5] we shovel a grave in the air
   where you won't lie too cramped   15

He shouts dig this earth deeper you lot there you others sing up and play
he grabs for the rod in his belt he swings it his eyes are so blue
stick your spades deeper you lot there you others play on for the dancing

Black milk of daybreak we drink you at night
we drink you at midday and morning we drink you at evening   20
we drink and we drink

1. All selections translated from German by John Felstiner.
2. Germany (German).
3. A typically German name.

4. Concentration camp commanders are reported to have forced prisoners to play dance tunes, sometimes while graves were being dug.
5. A typically Jewish name.

a man lives in the house your goldenes Haar[6] Margareta
your aschenes Haar[7] Shulamith he plays with his vipers

He shouts play death more sweetly this Death is a master from
   Deutschland
he shouts scrape your strings darker you'll rise up as smoke to the sky[8]
you'll then have a grave in the clouds where you won't lie too cramped

Black milk of daybreak we drink you at night   25
we drink you at midday Death is a master aus Deutschland
we drink you at evening and morning we drink and we drink
this Death is ein Meister aus Deutschland his eye it is blue
he shoots you with shot made of lead shoots you level and true
a man lives in the house your goldenes Haar Margarete   30
he looses his hounds on us grants us a grave in the air
he plays with his vipers and daydreams der Tod ist ein Meister aus
   Deutschland[9]

dein goldenes Haar Margarete
dein aschenes Haar Sulamith

                                     1947

Aspen Tree

Aspen tree, your leaves glance white into the dark.
My mother's hair never turned white.

Dandelion, so green is the Ukraine.[1]
My fair-haired mother did not come home.

Rain cloud, do you linger at the well?   5
My soft-voiced mother weeps for all.

Rounded star, you coil the golden loop.
My mother's heart was hurt by lead.

Oaken door, who hove you off your hinge?
My gentle mother cannot return.   10

                                     1948

6. Golden hair (German). The translator has left some phrases in the original.
7. Ashen hair (German).
8. Murdered prisoners were burned in crematoria.

9. Death is a Master from Germany (German).
1. Many concentration camps were located in Ukraine; Celan's mother died in one of these.

Corona

Autumn nibbles its leaf from my hand: we are friends.
We shell time from the nuts and teach it to walk:
time returns into its shell.

In the mirror is Sunday,
in the dream comes sleeping,   5
the mouth speaks true.

My eye goes down to my lover's loins:
we gaze at each other,
we speak dark things,
we love one another like poppy and memory,   10
we slumber like wine in the seashells,
like the sea in the moon's blood-jet.

We stand at the window embracing, they watch from the street:
it's time people knew!
It's time the stone consented to bloom,   15
a heart beat for unrest.
It's time it came time.

It is time.

1949

Shibboleth[1]

Together with my stones
wept large
behind the bars,

they dragged me
to the midst of the market,   5
to where
the flag unfurls that I
swore no kind of oath to.

Flute,
double flute of night: 10
think of the dark
twin reddenings
in Vienna and Madrid.[2]

---

1. A password in the Bible (Judges 12). The Ephraimites, who could not pronounce the word, were put to death by their opponents, the Gileadites.
2. Refers to the destruction of Viennese socialism (1934), to the unification of Austria with Nazi Germany (1938), and to the Fascist defeat of the Republic in the Spanish Civil War (1936–39).

Set your flag at half mast,
memory.
At half mast
today and for ever.

Heart:
make yourself known even here,
here in the midst of the market.
Cry out the shibboleth
into your homeland strangeness:
February. No pasaran.[3]

Einhorn:[4]
you know of the stones,
you know of the waters,
come,
I'll lead you away
to the voices
of Estremadura.[5]

                                            1955

Tenebrae[1]

Near are we, Lord,
near and graspable.

Grasped already, Lord,
clawed into each other, as if
each of our bodies were
your body, Lord.

Pray, Lord,
pray to us,
we are near.

Wind-skewed we went there,
went there to bend
over pit and crater.

Went to the water-trough, Lord.
It was blood, it was
what you shed, Lord.

It shined.

3. "They shall not pass" (Spanish). An international leftist slogan during and after the
Spanish Civil War.
4. Erich Einhorn, a friend of Celan's.
5. A region in western Spain where some of

the earliest battles of the Civil War were
fought.
1. "Darkness" (Latin), with special reference
to the Crucifixion.

It cast your image into our eyes, Lord.
Eyes and mouth stand so open and void, Lord.
We have drunk, Lord.
The blood and the image that was in the blood, Lord.   20

Pray, Lord.
We are near.

1959

Zurich, at the Stork[1]

For Nelly Sachs

Our talk was of Too Much, of
Too Little. Of Thou
and Yet-Thou, of
clouding through brightness, of
Jewishness, of   5
your God.

Of
that.
On the day of an ascension, the
Minster stood over there, it came   10
with some gold across the water.

Our talk was of your God, I spoke
against him, I let the heart
I had
hope: 15
for
his highest, death-rattled, his
wrangling word—

Your eye looked at me, looked away,
your mouth   20
spoke toward the eye, I heard:

We
really don't know, you know,
we
really don't know   25
what
counts.

1963

1. A hotel where Celan had a theological conversation with his friend the poet Nelly Sachs
(1891–1970).

DORIS LESSING

born 1919

Conflicts between cultures, between values within a culture, and even between elements of a personality, are fundamental themes in Doris Lessing's work—as is the struggle to integrate these entities into a higher, unified order. The recipient of the 2007 Nobel Prize in Literature, Lessing has spent her life in the midst of such conflicts. A witness to harsh colonial policies toward native subjects in Rhodesia as well as to the sexual and feminist revolutions in Europe, she has used her writing to interrogate both the psychology of the self and the larger relations between the personal and the political.

Lessing was born Doris May Tayler in October 1919 in Persia (now Iran). Her parents were British: her mother was a nurse, and her father a clerk in the Imperial Bank of Persia who had been crippled in World War I; his horrific memories of combat would seep into his daughter's recollections of childhood. In 1925 the family moved to the British colony of Rhodesia (now Zimbabwe), where the colonial government was offering economic incentives to encourage the immigration of white settlers. For ten shillings an acre, the family bought three thousand acres of farmland in Mashonaland, a section of Southern Rhodesia that once had been the home of the Matabele tribe but from which the government had evicted most of the native population. The farm never prospered. Lessing attended a convent school until she was fourteen, but she considers herself largely self-educated, from her avid reading of the classics of European and American literature. Above all, she loved the nineteenth-century novel; realists such as Stendhal,

Tolstoy, and **Dostoyevsky** impressed her, she later said, with "the warmth, the compassion, the humanity, the love of people" that gave impetus and passion to their social criticism. Gradually Lessing became aware of the racial injustice in Southern Rhodesia, and of the fact that she was, as she later put it, "a member of the white minority pitted against a black majority that was abominably treated and still is."

Social awareness is a defining theme of her early work, especially her first novel, *The Grass Is Singing* (1949), and the collection *African Stories* (1964). Arguing that "literature should be committed" to political issues, Lessing was herself politically active in Rhodesia, as well as a member of the British Communist Party from 1952 until 1956, the year of the Soviet intervention in Hungary. Her activism and socially oriented writing made their mark, and in 1956 she was declared a prohibited alien in both Southern Rhodesia and South Africa.

While still in Rhodesia, Lessing worked in several office jobs in Salisbury and made two unsuccessful marriages. (Lessing is the name of her second husband.) In 1949 she moved to England with the son from her second marriage and took a gamble on a literary career: "I was working in a lawyer's office at the time, and I remember walking in and saying to my boss, 'I'm giving up my job and writing a novel.' He very properly laughed, and I indignantly walked home and wrote *The Grass Is Singing*." The novel was a surprising and immediate success, and she was able, from that point, to make a profession of writing. Her next project was the five-volume series, *Children of Violence* (1952–69): the portrait of an era, after the form of the nineteenth-century bildungsroman, or "education novel," *Children of Violence* follows the life of a symbolically named heroine, Martha Quest, while exploring social and moral issues including race relations, the conflict between autonomy and socialization, and the hopes and frustrations of political idealism.

Lessing's most famous novel, *The Golden Notebook* (1962), makes a sharp break with the linear narrative style that *Children of Violence* shares with the bildungsroman tradition. In this work, too, a female protagonist (Anna Wulf) struggles to build a unified identity from the multiple, fragmented elements that constitute her personality; yet the exploratory process by which she pursues this goal takes her story beyond the confines of chronological narrative. Although the book is framed by a conventional short novel called *Free Women*, the governing structure is a series of different-colored notebooks that Anna uses to record the distinct versions of her experience: black for Africa, red for politics, yellow for a fictionalized rendering of herself as a character named Ella, and blue for a factual diary. By analyzing her life from these varying perspectives, Anna learns to understand and reconcile her contradictions—to write, ultimately, the "Golden Notebook," which is "all of me in one book."

During the 1970s and early 1980s, Lessing embarked on a series of science-fiction novels, which she termed "inner-space fiction," extending her interest in psychology and consciousness into speculative and quasi-mystical regions of the imagination. Since then, she has shifted to realistic stories that carry a sharp satiric or symbolic twist, such as *The Good Terrorist* (1985), a satire in which a group of naive British terrorists try to make a homey atmosphere in an empty

house in London while carrying out bombing raids. She has also published collections of essays and interviews that address politics, life, and art in a nonfiction voice. In presenting Lessing with the Nobel Prize in 2007, the committee praised her as an epic poet of "the female experience, who with scepticism, fire and visionary power has subjected a divided civilisation to scrutiny."

"The Old Chief Mshlanga" is one of Lessing's earliest African stories, written during the period, from 1950 to 1958, when she wrote most of her fiction set on that continent. The collection in which the story first appeared, *This Was the Old Chief's Country* (1951), together with *The Grass Is Singing* and *Five* (1953), a group of novellas set in Africa, established Lessing as an important interpreter of the colonial experience in contemporary Africa. The long act of dispossession that underlies "The Old Chief Mshlanga" began with the economic infiltration of the country by white settlers, under the leadership of the Chartered Company, a private firm that ruled the land under a British charter. Company policies soon formalized segregation by dividing land into tracts categorized as "alienated" (owned by white settlers) or "unalienated" (occupied by natives). The Land Apportionment Act of 1930 confirmed this arrangement by dividing the territory into areas called Native and European. In the story the figure of the Old Chief bridges the earlier dispensation, an era fifty years before, when his people owned the country, and the new, when they can be forcibly relocated to a Reserve after disagreeing with a white settler. Yet the Old Chief is not the protagonist here: significantly, his story comes into the foreground only some distance in, when it intrudes on the consciousness of a young white girl. The "vein of richness" that his tribe represents makes itself known only gradually. By the narrative's end, the tribe has disappeared altogether; the girl visits their village to find it disintegrating into the landscape.

Yet in spite of her remark that "there was nothing there," the girl's intimate description of the lush landscape shows that her encounter, however brief, with its former inhabitants has opened her eyes to an African presence that initially she had not been able to see. Nonetheless, the gain is one-sided: even her altered perceptions can bring her no closer to the members of the tribe, only throw light on the ground they occupied. For the Old Chief, there is no advantage: he and his people have disappeared into a symbolic essence, a "richness" that the settlers derive from the land they take over. Lessing's observant young girl has been changed by her encounter with the Old Chief, but the awakening is a bleak one that endows her with a sense of loss and responsibility. Perhaps, one day, she will write about it.

The Old Chief Mshlanga

They were good, the years of ranging the bush over her father's farm which, like every white farm, was largely unused, broken only occasionally by small patches of cultivation. In between, nothing but trees, the long sparse grass, thorn and cactus and gully, grass and outcrop and thorn. And a jutting piece of rock which had been thrust up from the warm soil of Africa unimaginable eras of time ago, washed into hollows and whorls by sun and wind that had travelled so many thousands of miles of space and bush, would hold the weight of a small girl whose eyes were sightless for anything but a pale willowed river, a pale gleaming castle—a small girl singing: "Out flew the web and floated wide, the mirror cracked from side to side . . ."[1]

Pushing her way through the green aisles of the mealie[2] stalks, the leaves arching like cathedrals veined with sunlight far overhead, with the packed red earth underfoot, a fine lace of red starred witchweed would summon up a black bent figure croaking premonitions: the Northern witch, bred of cold Northern forests, would stand before her among the mealie fields, and it was the mealie fields that faded and fled, leaving her among the gnarled roots of an oak, snow falling thick and soft and white, the woodcutter's fire glowing red welcome through crowding tree trunks.

A white child, opening its eyes curiously on a sun-suffused landscape, a gaunt and violent landscape, might be supposed to accept it as her own, to make the msasa trees and the thorn trees as familiars, to feel her blood running free and responsive to the swing of the seasons.

This child could not see a msasa tree,[3] or the thorn, for what they were. Her books held tales of alien fairies, her rivers ran slow and peaceful, and she knew the shape of the leaves of an ash or an oak, the names of the little creatures

1. The child is reciting lines 114–15 of Tennyson's "The Lady of Shalott."
2. Maize; corn.
3. A large tree of central Africa, notable for the vivid colorings (pink through copper) of its spring foliage and for the fragrance of its white flowers.

that lived in English streams, when the words "the veld"[4] meant strangeness, though she could remember nothing else.

Because of this, for many years, it was the veld that seemed unreal; the sun was a foreign sun, and the wind spoke a strange language.

The black people on the farm were as remote as the trees and the rocks. They were an amorphous black mass, mingling and thinning and massing like tadpoles, faceless, who existed merely to serve, to say "Yes, Baas,"[5] take their money and go. They changed season by season, moving from one farm to the next, according to their outlandish needs, which one did not have to understand, coming from perhaps hundreds of miles north or east, passing on after a few months—where? Perhaps even as far away as the fabled gold mines of Johannesburg,[6] where the pay was so much better than the few shillings a month and the double handful of mealie meal twice a day which they earned in that part of Africa.

The child was taught to take them for granted: the servants in the house would come running a hundred yards to pick up a book if she dropped it. She was called "Nkosikaas"—Chieftainess, even by the black children her own age.

Later, when the farm grew too small to hold her curiosity, she carried a gun in the crook of her arm and wandered miles a day, from vlei to vlei, from kopje[7] to kopje, accompanied by two dogs: the dogs and the gun were an armour against fear. Because of them she never felt fear.

If a native came into sight along the kaffir[8] paths half a mile away, the dogs would flush him up a tree as if he were a bird. If he expostulated (in his uncouth language which was by itself ridiculous) that was cheek. If one was in a good mood, it could be a matter for laughter. Otherwise one passed on, hardly glancing at the angry man in the tree.

On the rare occasions when white children met together they could amuse themselves by hailing a passing native in order to make a buffoon of him; they could set the dogs on him and watch him run; they could tease a small black child as if he were a puppy—save that they would not throw stones and sticks at a dog without a sense of guilt.

Later still, certain questions presented themselves in the child's mind; and because the answers were not easy to accept, they were silenced by an even greater arrogance of manner.

It was even impossible to think of the black people who worked about the house as friends, for if she talked to one of them, her mother would come running anxiously: "Come away; you mustn't talk to natives."

It was this instilled consciousness of danger, of something unpleasant, that made it easy to laugh out loud, crudely, if a servant made a mistake in his English or if he failed to understand an order—there is a certain kind of laughter that is fear, afraid of itself.

4. Unenclosed country, open grassland.
5. Boss.
6. The largest city in the Union (now Republic) of South Africa.

7. A small hill (Afrikaans). "Vlei": a shallow pool or swamp (Afrikaans).
8. A black African; usually used disparagingly.

One evening, when I was about fourteen, I was walking down the side of a mealie field that had been newly ploughed, so that the great red clods showed fresh and tumbling to the vlei beyond, like a choppy red sea; it was that hushed and listening hour, when the birds send long sad calls from tree to tree, and all the colours of earth and sky and leaf are deep and golden. I had my rifle in the curve of my arm, and the dogs were at my heels.

In front of me, perhaps a couple of hundred yards away, a group of three Africans came into sight around the side of a big antheap. I whistled the dogs close in to my skirts and let the gun swing in my hand, and advanced, waiting for them to move aside, off the path, in respect for my passing. But they came on steadily, and the dogs looked up at me for the command to chase. I was angry. It was "cheek"[9] for a native not to stand off a path, the moment he caught sight of you.

In front walked an old man, stooping his weight on to a stick, his hair grizzled white, a dark red blanket slung over his shoulders like a cloak. Behind him came two young men, carrying bundles of pots, assegais,[1] hatchets.

The group was not a usual one. They were not natives seeking work. These had an air of dignity, of quietly following their own purpose. It was the dignity that checked my tongue. I walked quietly on, talking softly to the growling dogs, till I was ten paces away. Then the old man stopped, drawing his blanket close.

"Morning, Nkosikaas," he said, using the customary greeting for any time of the day.

"Good morning," I said. "Where are you going?" My voice was a little truculent.

The old man spoke in his own language, then one of the young men stepped forward politely and said in careful English: "My Chief travels to see his brothers beyond the river."

A Chief! I thought, understanding the pride that made the old man stand before me like an equal—more than an equal, for he showed courtesy, and I showed none.

The old man spoke again, wearing dignity like an inherited garment, still standing ten paces off, flanked by his entourage, not looking at me (that would have been rude) but directing his eyes somewhere over my head at the trees.

"You are the little Nkosikaas from the farm of Baas Jordan?"

"That's right," I said.

"Perhaps your father does not remember," said the interpreter for the old man, "but there was an affair with some goats. I remember seeing you when you were . . ." The young man held his hand at knee level and smiled.

We all smiled.

"What is your name?" I asked.

"This is Chief Mshlanga," said the young man.

"I will tell my father that I met you," I said.

The old man said: "My greetings to your father, little Nkosikaas."

"Good morning," I said politely, finding the politeness difficult, from lack of use.

"Morning, little Nkosikaas," said the old man, and stood aside to let me pass.

9. Impudence.
1. Spears.

I went by, my gun hanging awkwardly, the dogs sniffing and growling, cheated of their favourite game of chasing natives like animals.

Not long afterwards I read in an old explorer's book the phrase: "Chief Mshlanga's country." It went like this: "Our destination was Chief Mshlanga's country, to the north of the river; and it was our desire to ask his permission to prospect for gold in his territory."

The phrase "ask his permission" was so extraordinary to a white child, brought up to consider all natives as things to use, that it revived those questions, which could not be suppressed: they fermented slowly in my mind.

On another occasion one of those old prospectors who still move over Africa looking for neglected reefs, with their hammers and tents, and pans for sifting gold from crushed rock, came to the farm and, in talking of the old days, used that phrase again: "This was the Old Chief's country," he said. "It stretched from those mountains over there way back to the river, hundreds of miles of country." That was his name for our district: "The Old Chief's Country"; he did not use our name for it—a new phrase which held no implication of usurped ownership.

As I read more books about the time when this part of Africa was opened up, not much more than fifty years before, I found Old Chief Mshlanga had been a famous man, known to all the explorers and prospectors. But then he had been young; or maybe it was his father or uncle they spoke of—I never found out.

During that year I met him several times in the part of the farm that was traversed by natives moving over the country. I learned that the path up the side of the big red field where the birds sang was the recognized highway for migrants. Perhaps I even haunted it in the hope of meeting him: being greeted by him, the exchange of courtesies, seemed to answer the questions that troubled me.

Soon I carried a gun in a different spirit; I used it for shooting food and not to give me confidence. And now the dogs learned better manners. When I saw a native approaching, we offered and took greetings; and slowly that other landscape in my mind faded, and my feet struck directly on the African soil, and I saw the shapes of tree and hill clearly, and the black people moved back, as it were, out of my life: it was as if I stood aside to watch a slow intimate dance of landscape and men, a very old dance, whose steps I could not learn.

But I thought: this is my heritage, too; I was bred here; it is my country as well as the black man's country; and there is plenty of room for all of us, without elbowing each other off the pavements and roads.

It seemed it was only necessary to let free that respect I felt when I was talking with old Chief Mshlanga, to let both black and white people meet gently, with tolerance for each other's differences: it seemed quite easy.

Then, one day, something new happened. Working in our house as servants were always three natives: cook, houseboy, garden boy. They used to change as the farm natives changed: staying for a few months, then moving on to a new job, or back home to their kraals.[2] They were thought of as "good" or "bad" natives; which meant: how did they behave as servants? Were they lazy, efficient, obedient, or disrespectful? If the family felt good-humoured, the phrase

---

2. Native villages: collections of huts surrounding a central space.

was: "What can you expect from raw black savages?" If we were angry, we said: "These damned niggers, we would be much better off without them."

One day, a white policeman was on his rounds of the district, and he said laughingly: "Did you know you have an important man in your kitchen?"

"What!" exclaimed my mother sharply. "What do you mean?"

"A Chief's son." The policeman seemed amused. "He'll boss the tribe when the old man dies."

"He'd better not put on a Chief's son act with me," said my mother.

When the policeman left, we looked with different eyes at our cook: he was a good worker, but he drank too much at week-ends—that was how we knew him.

He was a tall youth, with very black skin, like black polished metal, his tightly growing black hair parted white man's fashion at one side, with a metal comb from the store stuck into it; very polite, very distant, very quick to obey an order. Now that it had been pointed out, we said: "Of course, you can see. Blood always tells."

My mother became strict with him now she knew about his birth and prospects. Sometimes, when she lost her temper, she would say: "You aren't the Chief yet, you know." And he would answer her very quietly, his eyes on the ground: "Yes, Nkosikaas."

One afternoon he asked for a whole day off, instead of the customary half-day, to go home next Sunday.

"How can you go home in one day?"

"It will take me half an hour on my bicycle," he explained.

I watched the direction he took; and the next day I went off to look for this kraal; I understood he must be Chief Mshlanga's successor: there was no other kraal near enough our farm.

Beyond our boundaries on that side the country was new to me. I followed unfamiliar paths past *kopjes* that till now had been part of the jagged horizon, hazed with distance. This was Government land, which had never been cultivated by white men; at first I could not understand why it was that it appeared, in merely crossing the boundary, I had entered a completely fresh type of landscape. It was a wide green valley, where a small river sparkled, and vivid waterbirds darted over the rushes. The grass was thick and soft to my calves, the trees stood tall and shapely.

I was used to our farm, whose hundreds of acres of harsh eroded soil bore trees that had been cut for the mine furnaces and had grown thin and twisted, where the cattle had dragged the grass flat, leaving innumerable criss-crossing trails that deepened each season into gullies, under the force of the rains.

This country had been left untouched, save for prospectors whose picks had struck a few sparks from the surface of the rocks as they wandered by; and for migrant natives whose passing had left, perhaps, a charred patch on the trunk of a tree where their evening fire had nestled.

It was very silent: a hot morning with pigeons cooing throatily, the midday shadows lying dense and thick with clear yellow spaces of sunlight between and in all that wide green park-like valley, not a human soul but myself.

I was listening to the quick regular tapping of a woodpecker when slowly a chill feeling seemed to grow up from the small of my back to my shoulders, in a constricting spasm like a shudder, and at the roots of my hair a tingling sensation began and ran down over the surface of my flesh, leaving me goose-fleshed and cold, though I was damp with sweat. Fever? I thought; then uneasily, turned to look over my shoulder; and realized suddenly that this was fear. It was extraordinary, even humiliating. It was a new fear. For all the years I had walked by myself over this country I had never known a moment's uneasiness; in the beginning because I had been supported by a gun and the dogs, then because I had learnt an easy friendliness for the Africans I might encounter.

I had read of this feeling, how the bigness and silence of Africa, under the ancient sun, grows dense and takes shape in the mind, till even the birds seem to call menacingly, and a deadly spirit comes out of the trees and the rocks. You move warily, as if your very passing disturbs something old and evil, something dark and big and angry that might suddenly rear and strike from behind. You look at groves of entwined trees, and picture the animals that might be lurking there; you look at the river running slowly, dropping from level to level through the vlei, spreading into pools where at night the bucks come to drink, and the crocodiles rise and drag them by their soft noses into underwater caves. Fear possessed me. I found I was turning round and round, because of that shapeless menace behind me that might reach out and take me; I kept glancing at the files of *kopjes* which, seen from a different angle, seemed to change with every step so that even known landmarks, like a big mountain that had sentinelled my world since I first became conscious of it, showed an unfamiliar sunlit valley among its foothills. I did not know where I was. I was lost. Panic seized me. I found I was spinning round and round, staring anxiously at this tree and that, peering up at the sun which appeared to have moved into an eastern slant, shedding the sad yellow light of sunset. Hours must have passed! I looked at my watch and found that this state of meaningless terror had lasted perhaps ten minutes.

The point was that it was meaningless. I was not ten miles from home: I had only to take my way back along the valley to find myself at the fence; away among the foothills of the *kopjes* gleamed the roof of a neighbour's house, and a couple of hours' walking would reach it. This was the sort of fear that contracts the flesh of a dog at night and sets him howling at the full moon. It had nothing to do with what I thought or felt; and I was more disturbed by the fact that I could become its victim than of the physical sensation itself: I walked steadily on, quietened, in a divided mind, watching my own pricking nerves and apprehensive glances from side to side with a disgusted amusement. Deliberately I set myself to think of this village I was seeking, and what I should do when I entered it—if I could find it, which was doubtful, since I was walking aimlessly and it might be anywhere in the hundreds of thousands of acres of bush that stretched about me. With my mind on that village, I realized that a new sensation was added to the fear: loneliness. Now such a terror of isolation invaded me that I could hardly walk; and if it were not that I came over the crest of a small rise and saw a village below me, I should have turned and gone home. It was a cluster of thatched huts in a clearing among trees. There were neat patches of mealies and pumpkins and millet, and cattle grazed under some trees at a distance. Fowls scratched among the huts, dogs lay sleeping on the grass, and goats friezed a *kopje* that jutted up beyond a tributary of the river lying like an enclosing arm around the village.

As I came close I saw the huts were lovingly decorated with patterns of yellow and red and ochre mud on the walls; and the thatch was tied in place with plaits of straw.

This was not at all like our farm compound, a dirty and neglected place, a temporary home for migrants who had no roots in it.

And now I did not know what to do next. I called a small black boy, who was sitting on a lot playing a stringed gourd, quite naked except for the strings of blue beads round his neck, and said: "Tell the Chief I am here." The child stuck his thumb in his mouth and stared shyly back at me.

For minutes I shifted my feet on the edge of what seemed a deserted village, till at last the child scuttled off, and then some women came. They were draped in bright cloths, with brass glinting in their ears and on their arms. They also stared, silently; then turned to chatter among themselves.

I said again: "Can I see Chief Mshlanga?" I saw they caught the name; they did not understand what I wanted. I did not understand myself.

At last I walked through them and came past the huts and saw a clearing under a big shady tree, where a dozen old men sat crosslegged on the ground, talking. Chief Mshlanga was leaning back against the tree, holding a gourd in his hand, from which he had been drinking. When he saw me, not a muscle of his face moved, and I could see he was not pleased: perhaps he was afflicted with my own shyness, due to being unable to find the right forms of courtesy for the occasion. To meet me, on our own farm, was one thing; but I should not have come here. What had I expected? I could not join them socially: the thing was unheard of. Bad enough that I, a white girl, should be walking the veld alone as a white man might: and in this part of the bush where only Government officials had the right to move.

Again I stood, smiling foolishly, while behind me stood the groups of brightly clad, chattering women, their faces alert with curiosity and interest, and in front of me sat the old men, with old lined faces, their eyes guarded, aloof. It was a village of ancients and children and women. Even the two young men who kneeled beside the Chief were not those I had seen with him previously: the young men were all away working on the white men's farms and mines, and the Chief must depend on relatives who were temporarily on holiday for his attendants.

"The small white Nkosikaas is far from home," remarked the old man at last.

"Yes," I agreed, "it is far." I wanted to say: "I have come to pay you a friendly visit, Chief Mshlanga." I could not say it. I might now be feeling an urgent helpless desire to get to know these men and women as people, to be accepted by them as a friend, but the truth was I had set out in a spirit of curiosity: I had wanted to see the village that one day our cook, the reserved and obedient young man who got drunk on Sundays, would one day rule over.

"The child of Nkosi Jordan is welcome," said Chief Mshlanga.

"Thank you," I said, and could think of nothing more to say. There was a silence, while the flies rose and began to buzz around my head; and the wind shook a little in the thick green tree that spread its branches over the old men.

"Good morning," I said at last. "I have to return now to my home."

"Morning, little Nkosikaas," said Chief Mshlanga.

I walked away from the indifferent village, over the rise past the staring amber-eyed goats, down through the tall stately trees into the great rich green valley where the river meandered and the pigeons cooed tales of plenty and the woodpecker tapped softly.

The fear had gone; the loneliness had set into stiff-necked stoicism; there was now a queer hostility in the landscape, a cold, hard, sullen indomitability that walked with me, as strong as a wall, as intangible as smoke; it seemed to say to me: you walk here as a destroyer. I went slowly homewards, with an empty heart: I had learned that if one cannot call a country to heel like a dog, neither can one dismiss the past with a smile in an easy gush of feeling, saying: I could not help it, I am also a victim.

I only saw Chief Mshlanga once again.

One night my father's big red land was trampled down by small sharp hooves, and it was discovered that the culprits were goats from Chief Mshalanga's kraal. This had happened once before, years ago.

My father confiscated all the goats. Then he sent a message to the old Chief that if he wanted them he would have to pay for the damage.

He arrived at our house at the time of sunset one evening, looking very old and bent now, walking stiffly under his regally-draped blanket, leaning on a big stick. My father sat himself down in his big chair below the steps of the house; the old man squatted carefully on the ground before him, flanked by his two young men.

The palaver was long and painful, because of the bad English of the young man who interpreted, and because my father could not speak dialect, but only kitchen kaffir.

From my father's point of view, at least two hundred pounds' worth of damage had been done to the crop. He knew he could not get the money from the old man. He felt he was entitled to keep the goats. As for the old Chief, he kept repeating angrily: "Twenty goats! My people cannot lose twenty goats! We are not rich, like the Nkosi Jordan, to lose twenty goats at once."

My father did not think of himself as rich, but rather as very poor. He spoke quickly and angrily in return, saying that the damage done meant a great deal to him, and that he was entitled to the goats.

At last it grew so heated that the cook, the Chief's son, was called from the kitchen to be interpreter, and now my father spoke fluently in English, and our cook translated rapidly so that the old man could understand how very angry my father was. The young man spoke without emotion, in a mechanical way, his eyes lowered, but showing how he felt his position by a hostile uncomfortable set of the shoulders.

It was now in the late sunset, the sky a welter of colours, the birds singing their last songs, and the cattle, lowing peacefully, moving past us towards their sheds for the night. It was the hour when Africa is most beautiful; and here was this pathetic, ugly scene, doing no one any good.

At last my father stated finally: "I'm not going to argue about it. I am keeping the goats."

The old Chief flashed back in his own language: "That means that my people will go hungry when the dry season comes."

"Go to the police, then," said my father, and looked triumphant.

There was, of course, no more to be said.

The old man sat silent, his head bent, his hands dangling helplessly over his withered knees. Then he rose, the young men helping him, and he stood facing my father. He spoke once again, very stiffly; and turned away and went home to his village.

"What did he say?" asked my father of the young man, who laughed uncomfortably and would not meet his eyes.

"What did he say?" insisted my father.

Our cook stood straight and silent, his brows knotted together. Then he spoke. "My father says: All this land, this land you call yours, is his land, and belongs to our people."

Having made this statement, he walked off into the bush after his father, and we did not see him again.

Our next cook was a migrant from Nyasaland, with no expectations of greatness.

Next time the policeman came on his rounds he was told this story. He remarked: "That kraal has no right to be there; it should have been moved long ago. I don't know why no one has done anything about it. I'll have a chat with the Native Commissioner next week. I'm going over for tennis on Sunday, anyway."

Some time later we heard that Chief Mshlanga and his people had been moved two hundred miles east, to a proper Native Reserve; the Government land was going to be opened up for white settlement soon.

I went to see the village again, about a year afterwards. There was nothing there. Mounds of red mud, where the huts had been, had long swathes of rotting thatch over them, veined with the red galleries of the white ants. The pumpkin vines rioted everywhere, over the bushes, up the lower branches of trees so that the great golden balls rolled underfoot and dangled overhead: it was a festival of pumpkins. The bushes were crowding up, the new grass sprang vivid green.

The settler lucky enough to be allotted the lush warm valley (if he chose to cultivate this particular section) would find, suddenly, in the middle of a mealie field, the plants were growing fifteen feet tall, the weight of the cobs dragging at the stalks, and wonder what unsuspected vein of richness he had struck.

1951

SAADAT HASAN MANTO

1911–1955

Readers of modern Urdu literature, which is now produced in Pakistan and India as well as the South Asian diaspora in the West, often value it most for its novels and poetry. But if there is one genre in which recent Urdu writing stands out in world literature, it is the short story, which has attracted the greatest imaginative talent and technical skill in the language since **Premchand** set the standard early in the twentieth century. Even in a field crowded with masters, however, Saadat Hasan Manto remains exceptional for his scope and depth. Late in his short life, Manto composed an epitaph for himself that captures the combination of sardonic humor and irony that characterized most of his fiction: "Here lies Saadat Hasan Manto. With him lie buried all the arts and mysteries of short-story writing. Lying under mounds of earth, he wonders which of the two is the greater composer of short stories—God, or he."

Manto was born in 1911 near Ludhiana in Punjab; his family, middle-class Muslims originally from Kashmir, had settled in Amritsar (now near the India-Pakistan border), which became his "home town." Manto was an unsuccessful student; he failed his high-school examination in Urdu, his future literary language; and he dropped out of college after repeating a year in the freshman class. Throughout his teenage years, Punjab was in political turmoil: the 1919 Jallianwallah Bagh massacre in Amritsar, in which British-Indian soldiers fired indiscriminately at Indians gathered for a peaceful political rally, had triggered widespread unrest in the

region. Looking for direction, Manto informally joined a local Socialist group. This association had a greater influence on his writing than on his politics, leading him to read Russian, French, and English literature, to translate works by Victor Hugo and Oscar Wilde into Urdu, and to try writing short stories himself. After an initial literary success, and another failed attempt at higher education (at Aligarh Muslim University), Manto found his first job, with a popular magazine in Lahore, northern India's cultural center in the late colonial period.

This journalistic experience enabled Manto to move to Bombay in 1936, as the editor of an Indian film weekly. He fell in love with the city, and lived there for more than a decade, working for periodicals, film companies, and radio, and writing short stories and film scripts. For Manto, the Partition of the subcontinent at the end of British colonial rule, in August 1947, posed an existential dilemma; his wife, children, and extended family migrated to Pakistan, but he stayed on, because he "found it impossible to decide which of the two countries was now my homeland—India or Pakistan?"

By January 1948, however, Manto could no longer remain in Bombay, because of local retaliation against Muslims. Although he left for Lahore to join his family, the move proved to be disastrous. He witnessed, close-up, the bloodshed among Hindus, Muslims, and Sikhs over land and property, which left at least one million dead and forced the displacement of at least

14 million people across the new national borders, the largest mass migration in history. In Pakistan, the new "homeland" for subcontinental Muslims, Manto's writings were banned by the government, probably because they would have mass appeal, were potentially inflammatory, and might have mobilized further public interest in Socialist causes. In the lonely final months in Bombay, he had begun drinking heavily; in Lahore, his health deteriorated with alcoholism, leading to a painful early death in his forty-fourth year. Nevertheless, the last seven years of his life in Pakistan were his most productive. By 1955 he had published some 250 short stories (in twenty-two collections), one novel, and ten volumes containing radio plays, essays, and sketches and reminiscences.

Approximately half of Manto's short fiction is concerned with the imaginative representation of the history, politics, sociology, psychology, and pathology of Partition. Nearly one hundred of his stories and sketches provide a vivid, unvarnished, yet fully controlled record of the various events, large and small, that unfolded on the subcontinent in 1947 and 1948. Taken together, these spare ("minimalist") narratives provide the most complete literary account we have of what numerous people observed, felt, thought, and did during that period of upheaval.

Manto's primary mode is realism, but he often combines it with a variety of other styles and devices to change the reader's perspectives on mass violence, human brutality, religious bigotry, ethnic prejudice, and greed and hatred. Most of his descriptions, which are like vignettes based on empirical observation, are infused with irony, often revealing something different from what they seem to say; and many of his factual narratives quickly become nightmarish scenarios, in which the reader cannot distinguish easily between physical sensation and hallu-cination, illusion, and reality. Sometimes the characters in his stories resemble types rather than individuals, or appear to be personifications of ideas and abstract qualities; and sometimes his reports of mass violence are steeped in "black humor," laughter in the midst of tragedy that mocks the grotesque elements in human perversity and viciousness. Most of his characters are honest, ordinary people caught in circumstances beyond their control, but their instincts, choices, and actions push them to the edges of morality and reason, life and death.

The selection here, "Toba Tek Singh" (1955), taking a place-name for its title, questions the colonial and nationalist rationalizations of Partition. The action is set mostly in an asylum in Lahore, for patients who have been declared "insane," after the separation of India and Pakistan; and its central figure is Bishan Singh, a Sikh confined mostly among Muslims and Hindus. The story begins with the announcement that the new nations will exchange their asylum inmates, so that patients can be placed in the same country as their families. The inmates then try to understand this exchange—and the underlying division of nations—from their "irrational" perspectives, but actually succeed in exposing the absurd logic of Partition itself. Even the "craziest" patients comprehend that nationalist ideologies are manipulative and that attempts to redraw maps for political purposes cannot alter the deep, often unconscious connections between individual identity and place. During the exchange of patients at the India–Pakistan border, Bishan Singh finally becomes a personification of resistance to ideology: since no one can tell him whether the village of Toba Tek Singh is now situated in Pakistan or in India, he refuses to move from the no-man's-land between the two national borders, and prefers to die there, at one—in his own mind—with the place where he was born and that defines him.

Regarded widely as Manto's greatest short story, "Toba Tek Singh" brings together most of the distinctive features of his style and his most urgent themes. The story displays his characteristic surreal blurring of reason and unreason, as well as his focus on the rich diversity of human perspectives and experiences that the modern nation-state often suppresses. While emphasizing the role of religion and politics in the devastation of innocent lives, the work celebrates the resilience of the individual spirit.

Toba Tek Singh[1]

A couple of years after the Partition of the country,[2] it occurred to the respective governments of India and Pakistan that inmates of lunatic asylums, like prisoners, should also be exchanged. Muslim lunatics in India should be transferred to Pakistan and Hindu and Sikh lunatics in Pakistani asylums should be sent to India.

Whether this was a reasonable or an unreasonable idea is difficult to say. One thing, however, is clear. It took many conferences of important officials from the two sides to come to this decision. Final details, like the date of actual exchange, were carefully worked out. Muslim lunatics whose families were still residing in India were to be left undisturbed, the rest moved to the border for the exchange. The situation in Pakistan was slightly different, since almost the entire population of Hindus and Sikhs had already migrated to India.[3] The question of keeping non-Muslim lunatics in Pakistan did not, therefore, arise.

While it is not known what the reaction in India was, when the news reached the Lahore lunatic asylum, it immediately became the subject of heated discussion. One Muslim lunatic, a regular reader of the fire-eating daily newspaper *Zamindar*, when asked what Pakistan was, replied after deep reflection: 'The name of a place in India where cut-throat razors are manufactured.'

This profound observation was received with visible satisfaction.

A Sikh lunatic asked another Sikh: 'Sardarji,[4] why are we being sent to India? We don't even know the language they speak in that country.'

---

1. Translated by Khalid Hasan. The story takes its title from the name of a small town, primarily known as a Sikh pilgrimage center, now in Pakistan.

2. Most of the Indian subcontinent, or what is now South Asia, was a single political unit in the British-Indian empire. When the British decided to leave in 1947, the continuous mainland was "partitioned" into India and Pakistan, with Nepal and Sri Lanka forming separate nations. Here the narrator refers to the undivided mainland, before decolonization, as "the country."

3. The British decided on the Partition of 1947 mainly in response to the demand by the All-India Muslim League for a separate homeland for the subcontinent's Muslims. In 1947–

48, about 14 million people migrated across the new borders of India and Pakistan, with numerous Muslims moving into Pakistani territory, and comparable numbers of Hindus and Sikhs moving into Indian territory. After independence, Pakistan explicitly defined itself as a Muslim nation, whereas India defined itself as a secular republic.

4. Sikhism emerged as an organized religion in the early sixteenth century but continued to evolve under its first ten gurus (masters) until the eighteenth century. Since then, the Sikh male has often been known as a *sardar* (leader, prince); "Sardarji" is therefore a common term of respectful address.

The man smiled: 'I know the language of the Hindostoras.[5] These devils always strut about as if they were the lords of the earth.'

One day a Muslim lunatic, while taking his bath, raised the slogan 'Pakistan Zindabad'[6] with such enthusiasm that he lost his footing and was later found lying on the floor unconscious.

Not all inmates were mad. Some were perfectly normal, except that they were murderers. To spare them the hangman's noose, their families had managed to get them committed after bribing officials down the line. They probably had a vague idea why India was being divided and what Pakistan was, but, as for the present situation, they were equally clueless.

Newspapers were no help either, and the asylum guards were ignorant, if not illiterate. Nor was there anything to be learnt by eavesdropping on their conversations. Some said there was this man by the name Mohamed Ali Jinnah, or the Quaid-e-Azam, who had set up a separate country for Muslims, called Pakistan.[7]

As to where Pakistan was located, the inmates knew nothing. That was why both the mad and the partially mad were unable to decide whether they were now in India or in Pakistan. If they were in India, where on earth was Pakistan? And if they were in Pakistan, then how come that until only the other day it was India?

One inmate had got so badly caught up in this India–Pakistan–Pakistan–India rigmarole that one day, while sweeping the floor, he dropped everything, climbed the nearest tree and installed himself on a branch, from which vantage point he spoke for two hours on the delicate problem of India and Pakistan. The guards asked him to get down; instead he went a branch higher, and when threatened with punishment, declared: 'I wish to live neither in India nor in Pakistan. I wish to live in this tree.'

When he was finally persuaded to come down, he began embracing his Sikh and Hindu friends, tears running down his cheeks, fully convinced that they were about to leave him and go to India.

A Muslim radio engineer, who had an MSc degree, and never mixed with anyone, given as he was to taking long walks by himself all day, was so affected by the current debate that one day he took all his clothes off, gave the bundle to one of the attendants and ran into the garden stark naked.

A Muslim lunatic from Chaniot, who used to be one of the most devoted workers of the All India Muslim League,[8] and obsessed with bathing himself fifteen or sixteen times a day, had suddenly stopped doing that and announced—his name was Mohamed Ali—that he was Quaid-e-Azam Mohamed Ali Jinnah. This had led a Sikh inmate to declare himself Master

5. A deliberately disrespectful term for "Hindus," used here by a Sikh character.
6. An Urdu-Persian term corresponding to "Long Live Pakistan!"
7. Mohamed Ali Jinnah (1876–1948) was the principal leader of the All-India Muslim League for over three decades; he is credited with creating Pakistan as an independent homeland for subcontinental Muslims, and is known as Quaid-e-Azam, "the great leader," and Baba-e-Qaum, "the father of the nation." He served as Pakistan's first governor-general (1947–48).
8. The principal political organization of Muslims on the Indian subcontinent during the late colonial period.

Tara Singh,[9] the leader of the Sikhs. Apprehending serious communal trouble, the authorities declared them dangerous, and shut them up in separate cells.

There was a young Hindu lawyer from Lahore[1] who had gone off his head after an unhappy love affair. When told that Amritsar[2] was to become a part of India, he went into a depression because his beloved lived in Amritsar, something he had not forgotten even in his madness. That day he abused every major and minor Hindu and Muslim leader who had cut India into two, turning his beloved into an Indian and him into a Pakistani.

When news of the exchange reached the asylum, his friends offered him congratulations, because he was now to be sent to India, the country of his beloved. However, he declared that he had no intention of leaving Lahore, because his practice would not flourish in Amritsar.

There were two Anglo-Indian[3] lunatics in the European ward. When told that the British had decided to go home after granting independence to India, they went into a state of deep shock and were seen conferring with each other in whispers the entire afternoon. They were worried about their changed status after independence. Would there be a European ward or would it be abolished? Would breakfast continue to be served or would they have to subsist on bloody Indian chapati?[4]

There was another inmate, a Sikh, who had been confined for the last fifteen years. Whenever he spoke, it was the same mysterious gibberish: '*Uper the gur gur the annexe the bay dhayana the mung the dal of the laltain.*'[5] Guards said he had not slept a wink in fifteen years. Occasionally, he could be observed leaning against a wall, but the rest of the time, he was always to be found standing. Because of this, his legs were permanently swollen, something that did not appear to bother him. Recently, he had started to listen carefully to discussions about the forthcoming exchange of Indian and Pakistani lunatics. When asked his opinion, he observed solemnly: '*Uper the gur gur the annexe the bay dhayana the mung the dal of the Government of Pakistan.*'

---

9. Tara Singh Malhotra (1885–1967), the primary leader of the Sikhs in the late colonial and early postcolonial periods. In the 1930s and 1940s he opposed Jinnah's demand for Partition because it would permanently displace millions of Sikhs from the western half of the Punjab region (as it did in 1947–48). After independence, Tara Singh led the movement for the statehood of Punjab, the eastern portion of the region that remained in the Republic of India.
1. The premier city of the undivided Punjab region, now in eastern Pakistan, close to the border with India.
2. The holy city of the Sikhs, now in the Indian state of Punjab, close to the border with Pakistan.
3. Common, neutral term in Indian English for a person of racially mixed, Indian and British descent. Subcontinental society categorizes Anglo-Indians as "Europeans," whereas

Europeans classify them as "Indians."
4. Unleavened bread made with whole wheat flour, rolled thin and round and cooked on a griddle; the main form in which wheat is consumed across the Indian subcontinent.
5. A surreal mixture of Hindi, Urdu, Punjabi, English, Persian, and Sanskrit words and phrases that strings them into a meaningless "sentence." The protagonist, Bishan Singh, subsequently repeats it half a dozen times, all except once with variations. A transcription of the first occurrence would be "*Upara di gad gad di* annexe *di be-dhyana di munga di dala* of the *lalataina*," which may be translated in one way as "The porridge of the mung beans of the lantern of the un-conscious of the annexe of the thudding and thundering from above." The first variation on this, for example, replaces "the lantern" with "the Government of Pakistan."

Of late, however, the Government of Pakistan had been replaced by the Government of Toba Tek Singh, a small town in the Punjab[6] which was his home. He had also begun inquiring where Toba Tek Singh was to go. However, nobody was quite sure whether it was in India or Pakistan.

Those who had tried to solve this mystery had become utterly confused when told that Sialkot, which used to be in India, was now in Pakistan. It was anybody's guess what was going to happen to Lahore, which was currently in Pakistan, but could slide into India any moment. It was also possible that the entire subcontinent of India might become Pakistan. And who could say if both India and Pakistan might not entirely vanish from the map of the world one day?

The old man's hair was almost gone, and what little was left had become a part of the beard, giving him a strange, even frightening, appearance. However, he was a harmless fellow and had never been known to get into fights. Older attendants at the asylum said that he was a fairly prosperous landlord from Toba Tek Singh, who had quite suddenly gone mad. His family had brought him in, bound and fettered. That was fifteen years ago.

Once a month, he used to have visitors, but since the start of communal troubles in the Punjab, they had stopped coming. His real name was Bishan Singh,[7] but everybody called him Toba Tek Singh. He lived in a kind of limbo, having no idea what day of the week it was, or month, or how many years had passed since his confinement. However, he had developed a sixth sense about the day of the visit, when he used to bathe himself, soap his body, oil and comb his hair and put on clean clothes. He never said a word during these meetings, except occasional outbursts of '*Uper the gur gur the annexe the bay dhayana the mung the dal of the laltain.*'

When he was first confined, he had left an infant daughter behind, now a pretty young girl of fifteen. She would come occasionally, and sit in front of him with tears rolling down her cheeks. In the strange world that he inhabited, hers was just another face.

Since the start of this India-Pakistan caboodle, he had got into the habit of asking fellow inmates where exactly Toba Tek Singh was, without receiving a satisfactory answer, because nobody knew. The visits had also suddenly stopped. He was increasingly restless, but, more than that, curious. The sixth sense, which used to alert him to the day of the visit, had also atrophied.

He missed his family, the gifts they used to bring and the concern with which they used to speak to him. He was sure they would have told him whether Toba Tek Singh was in India or Pakistan. He also had a feeling that they came from Toba Tek Singh, where he used to have his home.

One of the inmates had declared himself God. Bishan Singh asked him one day if Toba Tek Singh was in India or Pakistan. The man chuckled: 'Neither in India nor in Pakistan, because, so far, we have issued no orders in this respect.'

Bishan Singh begged 'God' to issue the necessary orders, so that his problem could be solved, but he was disappointed, as 'God' appeared to be preoccupied

---

6. Now located in the province of Punjab in Pakistan.
7. The name of the story's protagonist; Sikh men add "Singh" (lion) to their given and family names in order to identify their religion.

with more pressing matters. Finally, he told him angrily: '*Uper the gur gur the annexe the mung the dal of Guruji da Khalsa and Guruji ki fateh . . . jo boley so nihal sat sri akal.*'

What he wanted to say was: 'You don't answer my prayers because you are a Muslim God. Had you been a Sikh God, you would have been more of a sport.'

A few days before the exchange was to take place, one of Bishan Singh's Muslim friends from Toba Tek Singh came to see him—the first time in fifteen years. Bishan Singh looked at him once and turned away, until a guard said to him: 'This is your old friend Fazal Din. He has come all the way to meet you.'

Bishan Singh looked at Fazal Din[8] and began to mumble something. Fazal Din placed his hand on his friend's shoulder and said: 'I have been meaning to come for some time to bring you the news. All your family is well and has gone to India safely. I did what I could to help. Your daughter Roop Kaur[9] . . .'—he hesitated—'She is safe too . . . in India.'

Bishan Singh kept quiet. Fazal Din continued: 'Your family wanted me to make sure you were well. Soon you will be moving to India. What can I say, except that you should remember me to bhai Balbir Singh, bhai Vadhawa Singh and bahain[1] Amrit Kaur. Tell bhai Bibir Singh that Fazal Din is well by the grace of God. The two brown buffaloes he left behind are well too. Both of them gave birth to calves, but, unfortunately, one of them died after six days. Say I think of them often and to write to me if there is anything I can do.'

Then he added: 'Here, I brought you some rice crispies from home.'

Bishan Singh took the gift and handed it to one of the guards. 'Where is Toba Tek Singh?' he asked.

'Where? Why, it is where it has always been.'

'In India or in Pakistan?'

'In India . . . no, in Pakistan.'

Without saying another word, Bishan Singh walked away, murmuring: '*Uper the gur gur the annexe the be dhyana the mung the dal of the Pakistan and Hindustan dur fittey moun.*'

Meanwhile, exchange arrangements were rapidly getting finalised. Lists of lunatics from the two sides had been exchanged between the governments, and the date of transfer fixed.

On a cold winter evening, buses full of Hindu and Sikh lunatics, accompanied by armed police and officials, began moving out of the Lahore asylum towards Wagah,[2] the dividing line between India and Pakistan. Senior officials from the two sides in charge of exchange arrangements met, signed documents and the transfer got under way.

It was quite a job getting the men out of the buses and handing them over to officials. Some just refused to leave. Those who were persuaded to do so began to run pell-mell in every direction. Some were stark naked. All efforts to get

8. A Muslim name; the close friendship between Bishan Singh and Fazal Din works across their religious differences.
9. Sikh women add "Kaur" (princess) to their given names.

1. In Hindi and Punjabi, *bhai* means "brother" and *bahain* means "sister."
2. The main international crossing point between India and Pakistan, at the border near Amritsar and Lahore.

them to cover themselves had failed because they couldn't be kept from tearing off their garments. Some were shouting abuse or singing. Others were weeping bitterly. Many fights broke out.

In short, complete confusion prevailed. Female lunatics were also being exchanged and they were even noisier. It was bitterly cold.

Most of the inmates appeared to be dead set against the entire operation. They simply could not understand why they were being forcibly removed, thrown into buses and driven to this strange place. There were slogans of 'Pakistan Zindabad' and 'Pakistan Murdabad',[3] followed by fights.

When Bishan Singh was brought out and asked to give his name so that it could be recorded in a register, he asked the official behind the desk: 'Where is Toba Tek Singh? In India or Pakistan?'

'Pakistan,' he answered with a vulgar laugh.

Bishan Singh tried to run, but was overpowered by the Pakistani guards who tried to push him across the dividing line towards India. However, he wouldn't move. 'This is Toba Tek Singh,' he announced. *'Uper the gur gur the annexe the be dyhana mung the dal of Toba Tek Singh and Pakistan.'*

Many efforts were made to explain to him that Toba Tek Singh had already been moved to India, or would be moved immediately, but it had no effect on Bishan Singh. The guards even tried force, but soon gave up.

There he stood in no man's land on his swollen legs like a colossus.

Since he was a harmless old man, no further attempt was made to push him into India. He was allowed to stand where he wanted, while the exchange continued. The night wore on.

Just before sunrise, Bishan Singh, the man who had stood on his legs for fifteen years, screamed and as officials from the two sides rushed towards him, he collapsed to the ground.

There, behind barbed wire, on one side, lay India and behind more barbed wire, on the other side, lay Pakistan. In between, on a bit of earth which had no name, lay Toba Tek Singh.

1955

---

3. *"Pakistan Murdabad,"* translatable as "Death to Pakistan," is the semantic opposite of the preceding phrase, "Long Live Pakistan!"

JAMES BALDWIN
1924–1987

A leading African American novelist, James Baldwin was one of the great prose stylists of the twentieth century. He is best known for his remarkable essays that, in poetic rhetoric drawing on both the classics of English literature and the tones of biblical prophecy, combine personal reflection with a wider view of social justice. An icon of the civil rights movement, Baldwin nonetheless felt considerably alienated both from black culture and from white liberal society. He lived much of his life abroad but continually affirmed his American identity as a "native son."

Baldwin grew up in his "father's house"—that is, in the Harlem home of his stepfather, David Baldwin, a preacher whom his mother married when James was two. David Baldwin, a preacher in small black churches, reacted with suspicion when a white teacher, Orilla Miller, took James to plays, including Orson Welles's all-black production of Shakespeare's *Macbeth*. (The elder Baldwin did not approve of theater.) David Baldwin's mother, who had been born in slavery, lived with the family in Harlem. Although his acquaintance with secular literature strained his relationship to the church, James remained affiliated with various churches over the years and preached sermons as a young man.

As the United States mobilized for the Second World War, Baldwin found a job in a defense plant in New Jersey— and hated both the job and the place, where he had his first serious experiences of racial discrimination. When his stepfather died, in 1943, he was expected to move back home and take care of his mother and siblings. Instead, Baldwin moved to Greenwich Village,

in lower Manhattan, to pursue his career as a writer. Here he met older writers, including Richard Wright. "Writing was an act of love," Baldwin would later say, "an attempt to be loved." While living in the Village, he became aware of his homosexuality.

After the war Baldwin left New York for Paris, following in the paths of a generation of famous American writers before him. Of this self-imposed expatriation, he later wrote, "In my own case, I think my exile saved my life." In the years that followed, Baldwin wrote and then suffered writer's block; he was arrested on a false charge of theft; he tried to commit suicide; and he succeeded in finishing *Go Tell It on the Mountain* (1953), his first published novel, an autobiographical story of a deeply religious young man who ultimately leaves the church. For the rest of his life, Baldwin divided his time between New York, Paris, Switzerland, and Turkey. Amid constant interpersonal turmoil (and additional suicide attempts), his literary career was now on the rise: in 1955, *Notes of a Native Son*, a collection of essays that cemented his public voice, was released; a year later, *Giovanni's Room*, a novel about a white American in Paris struggling with his homosexuality, appeared. Despite difficulties in finding a publisher, the work increased Baldwin's fame. Encouraged by the rise of the civil rights movement, he renewed his political engagement; with *The Fire Next Time* (1963), in which he commented on race and American history, he became an international figure.

Like other leading African Americans of the civil rights era, Baldwin was unhappy with the radicalization of movements with which he had been associated. Although he had known the Black Nationalist leader Malcolm X and met Elijah Muhammad of the Nation of Islam, their successors in such groups as the Black Panthers tended to think of Baldwin as a darling of white liberals who was more concerned with cosmopolitan life in Paris than with the plight of ordinary African Americans. Baldwin's generally optimistic, liberal views led him to exhort his readers to work together for change: "If we—and now I mean the relatively conscious whites and the relatively conscious blacks, who must, like lovers, insist on, or create, the consciousness of the others—do not falter in our duty now, we may be able, handful that we are, to end the racial nightmare, and achieve our country, and change the history of the world." In his later years, Baldwin's primary home was a farmhouse in Saint-Paul-de-Vence, a town in southern France, but he continued traveling in the United States, writing essays, and teaching in several colleges. He died in Saint-Paul in 1987.

Baldwin begins "Notes of a Native Son," the essay printed here, with the conjunction of two profound events in his personal life: the death of his father (actually his stepfather) and the birth of his father's youngest child. These personal rites of passage are, however, quickly placed in the context of broader social and political events—namely, the race riots that shook Detroit in June 1943. The protests, in which nearly three dozen people died, were a shocking episode in a series of conflicts between blacks and whites in the wake of the Great Migration between the two world wars. African Americans were leaving the segregated South in search of greater freedom, and work, in northern industrial cities, where they were not always welcomed. Baldwin's father had likewise moved to New York from New Orleans not long before the boy's birth, and Baldwin describes the racial tensions of wartime New York and New Jersey. The juxtaposition of experiences of great personal significance with momentous public events becomes a central issue in the essay.

While it offers a profound meditation on a relationship between a son and a father who was both physically and mentally ill, the essay explains how both men's encounters with racial discrimination contributed to the conflicts in their private lives. Baldwin represents the relationship, and his evolving consciousness of his place in the family and in American society, with subtlety and nuance. Baldwin's style—direct but meditative, confessional but aware of the broader context—gives this classic work its status as one of the most memorable personal meditations published in the twentieth century.

Notes of a Native Son[1]

On the 29th of July, in 1943, my father died. On the same day, a few hours later, his last child was born. Over a month before this, while all our energies were concentrated in waiting for these events, there had been, in Detroit, one of the bloodiest race riots of the century.[2] A few hours after my father's funeral, while he lay in state in the undertaker's chapel, a race riot broke out in Harlem. On the morning of the 3rd of August, we drove my father to the graveyard through a wilderness of smashed plate glass.

1. The title alludes to Richard Wright's novel *Native Son* (1940).
2. Three days of rioting in June 1943, in which 25 African Americans and 9 whites were killed.

The day of my father's funeral had also been my nineteenth birthday. As we drove him to the graveyard, the spoils of injustice, anarchy, discontent, and hatred were all around us. It seemed to me that God himself had devised, to mark my father's end, the most sustained and brutally dissonant of codas. And it seemed to me, too, that the violence which rose all about us as my father left the world had been devised as a corrective for the pride of his eldest son. I had declined to believe in that apocalypse which had been central to my father's vision; very well, life seemed to be saying, here is something that will certainly pass for an apocalypse until the real thing comes along. I had inclined to be contemptuous of my father for the conditions of his life, for the conditions of our lives. When his life had ended I began to wonder about that life and also, in a new way, to be apprehensive about my own.

I had not known my father very well. We had got on badly, partly because we shared, in our different fashions, the vice of stubborn pride. When he was dead I realized that I had hardly ever spoken to him. When he had been dead a long time I began to wish I had. It seems to be typical of life in America, where opportunities, real and fancied, are thicker than anywhere else on the globe, that the second generation has no time to talk to the first. No one, including my father, seems to have known exactly how old he was, but his mother had been born during slavery. He was of the first generation of free men. He, along with thousands of other Negroes, came North after 1919 and I was part of that generation which had never seen the landscape of what Negroes sometimes call the Old Country.[3]

He had been born in New Orleans and had been a quite young man there during the time that Louis Armstrong,[4] a boy, was running errands for the dives and honky-tonks of what was always presented to me as one of the most wicked of cities—to this day, whenever I think of New Orleans, I also helplessly think of Sodom and Gomorrah.[5] My father never mentioned Louis Armstrong, except to forbid us to play his records; but there was a picture of him on our wall for a long time. One of my father's strong-willed female relatives had placed it there and forbade my father to take it down. He never did, but he eventually maneuvered her out of the house and when, some years later, she was in trouble and near death, he refused to do anything to help her.

He was, I think, very handsome. I gather this from photographs and from my own memories of him, dressed in his Sunday best and on his way to preach a sermon somewhere, when I was little. Handsome, proud, and ingrown, "like a toe-nail," somebody said. But he looked to me, as I grew older, like pictures I had seen of African tribal chieftains: he really should have been naked, with war-paint on and barbaric mementos, standing among spears. He could be chilling in the pulpit and indescribably cruel in his personal life and he was certainly the most bitter man I have ever met; yet it must be said that there was something else in him, buried in him, which lent him his tremendous power and, even, a rather crushing charm. It had something to do with his blackness,

---

3. The South. Over a million African Americans left the South for the Midwest and the Northeast after the First World War (1914–18).

4. Armstrong (1901–1971), jazz trumpeter, cornetist, and singer.
5. Biblical cities destroyed by God for their wickedness. See Genesis 18–19.

I think—he was very black—with his blackness and his beauty, and with the fact that he knew that he was black but did not know that he was beautiful. He claimed to be proud of his blackness but it had also been the cause of much humiliation and it had fixed bleak boundaries to his life. He was not a young man when we were growing up and he had already suffered many kinds of ruin; in his outrageously demanding and protective way he loved his children, who were black like him and menaced, like him; and all these things sometimes showed in his face when he tried, never to my knowledge with any success, to establish contact with any of us. When he took one of his children on his knee to play, the child always became fretful and began to cry; when he tried to help one of us with our homework the absolutely unabating tension which emanated from him caused our minds and our tongues to become paralyzed, so that he, scarcely knowing why, flew into a rage and the child, not knowing why, was punished. If it ever entered his head to bring a surprise home for his children, it was, almost unfailingly, the wrong surprise and even the big watermelons he often brought home on his back in the summertime led to the most appalling scenes. I do not remember, in all those years, that one of his children was ever glad to see him come home. From what I was able to gather of his early life, it seemed that this inability to establish contact with other people had always marked him and had been one of the things which had driven him out of New Orleans. There was something in him, therefore, groping and tentative, which was never expressed and which was buried with him. One saw it most clearly when he was facing new people and hoping to impress them. But he never did, not for long. We went from church to smaller and more improbable church, he found himself in less and less demand as a minister, and by the time he died none of his friends had come to see him for a long time. He had lived and died in an intolerable bitterness of spirit and it frightened me, as we drove him to the graveyard through those unquiet, ruined streets, to see how powerful and overflowing this bitterness could be and to realize that this bitterness now was mine.

When he died I had been away from home for a little over a year. In that year I had had time to become aware of the meaning of all my father's bitter warnings, had discovered the secret of his proudly pursed lips and rigid carriage: I had discovered the weight of white people in the world. I saw that this had been for my ancestors and now would be for me an awful thing to live with and that the bitterness which had helped to kill my father could also kill me.

He had been ill a long time—in the mind, as we now realized, reliving instances of his fantastic intransigence in the new light of his affliction and endeavoring to feel a sorrow for him which never, quite, came true. We had not known that he was being eaten up by paranoia, and the discovery that his cruelty, to our bodies and our minds, had been one of the symptoms of his illness was not, then, enough to enable us to forgive him. The younger children felt, quite simply, relief that he would not be coming home anymore. My mother's observation that it was he, after all, who had kept them alive all these years meant nothing because the problems of keeping children alive are not real for children. The older children felt, with my father gone, that they could invite their friends to the house without fear that their friends would be insulted or, as had sometimes happened with me, being told that their friends were in league with the devil and intended to rob our family of everything we owned. (I didn't fail to wonder, and it made me hate him, what on earth we owned that anybody else would want.)

His illness was beyond all hope of healing before anyone realized that he was ill. He had always been so strange and had lived, like a prophet, in such unimaginably close communion with the Lord that his long silences which were punctuated by moans and hallelujahs and snatches of old songs while he sat at the living-room window never seemed odd to us. It was not until he refused to eat because, he said, his family was trying to poison him that my mother was forced to accept as a fact what had, until then, been only an unwilling suspicion. When he was committed, it was discovered that he had tuberculosis and, as it turned out, the disease of his mind allowed the disease of his body to destroy him. For the doctors could not force him to eat, either, and, though he was fed intravenously, it was clear from the beginning that there was no hope for him.

In my mind's eye I could see him, sitting at the window, locked up in his terrors; hating and fearing every living soul including his children who had betrayed him, too, by reaching towards the world which had despised him. There were nine of us. I began to wonder what it could have felt like for such a man to have had nine children whom he could barely feed. He used to make little jokes about our poverty, which never, of course, seemed very funny to us; they could not have seemed very funny to him, either, or else our all too feeble response to them would never have caused such rages. He spent great energy and achieved, to our chagrin, no small amount of success in keeping us away from the people who surrounded us, people who had all-night rent parties[6] to which we listened when we should have been sleeping, people who cursed and drank and flashed razor blades on Lenox Avenue.[7] He could not understand why, if they had so much energy to spare, they could not use it to make their lives better. He treated almost everybody on our block with a most uncharitable asperity and neither they, nor, of course, their children were slow to reciprocate.

The only white people who came to our house were welfare workers and bill collectors. It was almost always my mother who dealt with them, for my father's temper, which was at the mercy of his pride, was never to be trusted. It was clear that he felt their very presence in his home to be a violation: this was conveyed by his carriage, almost ludicrously stiff, and by his voice, harsh and vindictively polite. When I was around nine or ten I wrote a play which was directed by a young, white schoolteacher, a woman, who then took an interest in me, and gave me books to read and, in order to corroborate my theatrical bent, decided to take me to see what she somewhat tactlessly referred to as "real" plays. Theater-going was forbidden in our house, but, with the really cruel intuitiveness of a child, I suspected that the color of this woman's skin would carry the day for me. When, at school, she suggested taking me to the theater, I did not, as I might have done if she had been a Negro, find a way of discouraging her, but agreed that she should pick me up at my house one evening. I then, very cleverly, left all the rest to my mother, who suggested to my

---

6. Parties at which money was collected from the guests to help cover tenants' rent; normally, the parties included hired bands; during Prohibition (1920–33), bootlegged alcohol was served.
7. Major north–south thoroughfare in Harlem.

father, as I knew she would, that it would not be very nice to let such a kind woman make the trip for nothing. Also, since it was a schoolteacher, I imagine that my mother countered the idea of sin with the idea of "education," which word, even with my father, carried a kind of bitter weight.

Before the teacher came my father took me aside to ask *why* she was coming, what *interest* she could possibly have in our house, in a boy like me. I said I didn't know but I, too, suggested that it had something to do with education. And I understood that my father was waiting for me to say something—I didn't quite know what; perhaps that I wanted his protection against this teacher and her "education." I said none of these things and the teacher came and we went out. It was clear, during the brief interview in our living room, that my father was agreeing very much against his will and that he would have refused permission if he had dared. The fact that he did not dare caused me to despise him: I had no way of knowing that he was facing in that living room a wholly unprecedented and frightening situation.

Later, when my father had been laid off from his job, this woman became very important to us. She was really a very sweet and generous woman and went to a great deal of trouble to be of help to us, particularly during one awful winter. My mother called her by the highest name she knew: she said she was a "christian." My father could scarcely disagree but during the four or five years of our relatively close association he never trusted her and was always trying to surprise in her open, Midwestern face the genuine, cunningly hidden, and hideous motivation. In later years, particularly when it began to be clear that this "education" of mine was going to lead me to perdition, he became more explicit and warned me that my white friends in high school were not really my friends and that I would see, when I was older, how white people would do anything to keep a Negro down. Some of them could be nice, he admitted, but none of them were to be trusted and most of them were not even nice. The best thing was to have as little to do with them as possible. I did not feel this way and I was certain, in my innocence, that I never would.

But the year which preceded my father's death had made a great change in my life. I had been living in New Jersey, working in defense plants, working and living among southerners, white and black. I knew about the south, of course, and about how southerners treated Negroes and how they expected them to behave, but it had never entered my mind that anyone would look at me and expect *me* to behave that way. I learned in New Jersey that to be a Negro meant, precisely, that one was never looked at but was simply at the mercy of the reflexes the color of one's skin caused in other people. I acted in New Jersey as I had always acted, that is as though I thought a great deal of myself—I had to *act* that way—with results that were, simply, unbelievable. I had scarcely arrived before I had earned the enmity, which was extraordinarily ingenious, of all my superiors and nearly all my co-workers. In the beginning, to make matters worse, I simply did not know what was happening. I did not know what I had done, and I shortly began to wonder what *anyone* could possibly do, to bring about such unanimous, active, and unbearably vocal hostility. I knew about jim-crow[8] but I had never experienced it. I went to the same self-service restaurant three times and

8. System of laws and customs enforcing segregation of blacks and whites in southern states; some aspects of Jim Crow were also in force in northern states, including New Jersey.

stood with all the Princeton boys before the counter, waiting for a hamburger and coffee; it was always an extraordinarily long time before anything was set before me; but it was not until the fourth visit that I learned that, in fact, nothing had ever been set before me: I had simply picked something up. Negroes were not served there, I was told, and they had been waiting for me to realize that I was always the only Negro present. Once I was told this, I determined to go there all the time. But now they were ready for me and, though some dreadful scenes were subsequently enacted in that restaurant, I never ate there again.

It was the same story all over New Jersey, in bars, bowling alleys, diners, places to live. I was always being forced to leave, silently, or with mutual imprecations. I very shortly became notorious and children giggled behind me when I passed and their elders whispered or shouted—they really believed that I was mad. And it did begin to work on my mind, of course; I began to be afraid to go anywhere and to compensate for this I went places to which I really should not have gone and where, God knows, I had no desire to be. My reputation in town naturally enhanced my reputation at work and my working day became one long series of acrobatics designed to keep me out of trouble. I cannot say that these acrobatics succeeded. It began to seem that the machinery of the organization I worked for was turning over, day and night, with but one aim: to eject me. I was fired once, and contrived, with the aid of a friend from New York, to get back on the payroll; was fired again, and bounced back again. It took a while to fire me for the third time, but the third time took. There were no loopholes anywhere. There was not even any way of getting back inside the gates.

That year in New Jersey lives in my mind as though it were the year during which, having an unsuspected predilection for it, I first contracted some dread, chronic disease, the unfailing symptom of which is a kind of blind fever, a pounding in the skull and fire in the bowels. Once this disease is contracted, one can never be really carefree again, for the fever, without an instant's warning, can recur at any moment. It can wreck more important things than race relations. There is not a Negro alive who does not have this rage in his blood—one has the choice, merely, of living with it consciously or surrendering to it. As for me, this fever has recurred in me, and does, and will until the day I die.

My last night in New Jersey, a white friend from New York took me to the nearest big town, Trenton, to go to the movies and have a few drinks. As it turned out, he also saved me from, at the very least, a violent whipping. Almost every detail of that night stands out very clearly in my memory. I even remember the name of the movie we saw because its title impressed me as being so patly ironical. It was a movie about the German occupation of France, starring Maureen O'Hara and Charles Laughton and called *This Land Is Mine*. I remember the name of the diner we walked into when the movie ended: it was the "American Diner." When we walked in the counterman asked what we wanted and I remember answering with the casual sharpness which had become my habit: "We want a hamburger and a cup of coffee, what do you think we want?" I do not know why, after a year of such rebuffs, I so completely failed to anticipate his answer, which was, of course, "We don't serve Negroes here." This reply failed to discompose me, at least for the moment. I made some sardonic comment about the name of the diner and we walked out into the streets.

This was the time of what was called the "brown-out," when the lights in all American cities were very dim. When we re-entered the streets something happened to me which had the force of an optical illusion, or a nightmare. The streets were very crowded and I was facing north. People were moving in every direction but it seemed to me, in that instant, that all of the people I could see, and many more than that, were moving toward me, against me, and that everyone was white. I remember how their faces gleamed. And I felt, like a physical sensation, a *click* at the nape of my neck as though some interior string connecting my head to my body had been cut. I began to walk. I heard my friend call after me, but I ignored him. Heaven only knows what was going on in his mind, but he had the good sense not to touch me—I don't know what would have happened if he had—and to keep me in sight. I don't know what was going on in my mind, either; I certainly had no conscious plan. I wanted to do something to crush these white faces, which were crushing me. I walked for perhaps a block or two until I came to an enormous, glittering, and fashionable restaurant in which I knew not even the intercession of the Virgin would cause me to be served. I pushed through the doors and took the first vacant seat I saw, at a table for two, and waited.

I do not know how long I waited and I rather wonder, until today, what I could possibly have looked like. Whatever I looked like, I frightened the waitress who shortly appeared, and the moment she appeared all of my fury flowed towards her. I hated her for her white face, and for her great, astounded, frightened eyes. I felt that if she found a black man so frightening I would make her fright worth-while.

She did not ask me what I wanted, but repeated, as though she had learned it somewhere, "We don't serve Negroes here." She did not say it with the blunt, derisive hostility to which I had grown so accustomed, but, rather, with a note of apology in her voice, and fear. This made me colder and more murderous than ever. I felt I had to do something with my hands. I wanted her to come close enough for me to get her neck between my hands.

So I pretended not to have understood her, hoping to draw her closer. And she did step a very short step closer, with her pencil poised incongruously over her pad, and repeated the formula: ". . . don't serve Negroes here."

Somehow, with the repetition of that phrase, which was already ringing in my head like a thousand bells of a nightmare, I realized that she would never come any closer and that I would have to strike from a distance. There was nothing on the table but an ordinary watermug half full of water, and I picked this up and hurled it with all my strength at her. She ducked and it missed her and shattered against the mirror behind the bar. And, with that sound, my frozen blood abruptly thawed, I returned from wherever I had been, I *saw*, for the first time, the restaurant, the people with their mouths open, already, as it seemed to me, rising as one man, and I realized what I had done, and where I was, and I was frightened. I rose and began running for the door. A round, potbellied man grabbed me by the nape of the neck just as I reached the doors and began to beat me about the face. I kicked him and got loose and ran into the streets. My friend whispered, "*Run!*" and I ran.

My friend stayed outside the restaurant long enough to misdirect my pursuers and the police, who arrived, he told me, at once. I do not know what I said to him when he came to my room that night. I could not have said much. I felt, in the oddest, most awful way, that I had somehow betrayed him. I lived it over and over and over again, the way one relives an automobile accident after it has happened and one finds oneself alone and safe. I could not get over two facts, both equally difficult for the imagination to grasp, and one was that I could have been murdered. But the other was that I had been ready to commit murder. I saw nothing very clearly but I did see this: that my life, my *real* life, was in danger, and not from anything other people might do but from the hatred I carried in my own heart.

II

I had returned home around the second week in June—in great haste because it seemed that my father's death and my mother's confinement were both but a matter of hours. In the case of my mother, it soon became clear that she had simply made a miscalculation. This had always been her tendency and I don't believe that a single one of us arrived in the world, or has since arrived anywhere else, on time. But none of us dawdled so intolerably about the business of being born as did my baby sister. We sometimes amused ourselves, during those endless, stifling weeks, by picturing the baby sitting within in the safe, warm dark, bitterly regretting the necessity of becoming a part of our chaos and stubbornly putting it off as long as possible. I understood her perfectly and congratulated her on showing such good sense so soon. Death, however, sat as purposefully at my father's bedside as life stirred within my mother's womb and it was harder to understand why he so lingered in that long shadow. It seemed that he had bent, and for a long time, too, all of his energies towards dying. Now death was ready for him but my father held back.

All of Harlem, indeed, seemed to be infected by waiting. I had never before known it to be so violently still. Racial tensions throughout this country were exacerbated during the early years of the war,[9] partly because the labor market brought together hundreds of thousands of ill-prepared people and partly because Negro soldiers, regardless of where they were born, received their military training in the south. What happened in defense plants and army camps had repercussions, naturally, in every Negro ghetto. The situation in Harlem had grown bad enough for clergymen, policemen, educators, politicians, and social workers to assert in one breath that there was no "crime wave" and to offer, in the very next breath, suggestions as to how to combat it. These suggestions always seemed to involve playgrounds, despite the fact that racial skirmishes were occurring in the playgrounds, too. Playground or not, crime wave or not, the Harlem police force had been augmented in March, and the unrest grew—perhaps, in fact, partly as a result of the ghetto's instinctive hatred of policemen. Perhaps the most revealing news item, out of the steady parade of reports of muggings, stabbings, shootings, assaults, gang wars, and accusations of police brutality, is the item concerning six Negro girls who set upon a white girl in the subway because, as they all too accurately put it, she was stepping on their toes. Indeed she was, all over the nation.

I had never before been so aware of policemen, on foot, on horseback, on corners, everywhere, always two by two. Nor had I ever been so aware of small

---

9. The Second World War (1939–45), which the United States entered on December 8, 1941.

knots of people. They were on stoops and on corners and in doorways, and what was striking about them, I think, was that they did not seem to be talking. Never, when I passed these groups, did the usual sound of a curse or a laugh ring out and neither did there seem to be any hum of gossip. There was certainly, on the other hand, occurring between them communication extraordinarily intense. Another thing that was striking was the unexpected diversity of the people who made up these groups. Usually, for example, one would see a group of sharpies standing on the street corner, jiving the passing chicks;[1] or a group of older men, usually, for some reason, in the vicinity of a barber shop, discussing baseball scores, or the numbers,[2] or making rather chilling observations about women they had known. Women, in a general way, tended to be seen less often together—unless they were church women, or very young girls, or prostitutes met together for an unprofessional instant. But that summer I saw the strangest combinations: large, respectable, churchly matrons standing on the stoops or the corners with their hair tied up, together with a girl in sleazy satin whose face bore the marks of gin and the razor, or heavy-set, abrupt, no-nonsense older men, in company with the most disreputable and fanatical "race" men,[3] or these same "race" men with the sharpies, or these sharpies with the churchly women. Seventh Day Adventists and Methodists and Spiritualists seemed to be hobnobbing with Holyrollers[4] and they were all, alike, entangled with the most flagrant disbelievers; something heavy in their stance seemed to indicate that they had all, incredibly, seen a common vision, and on each face there seemed to be the same strange, bitter shadow.

The churchly women and the matter-of-fact, no-nonsense men had children in the Army. The sleazy girls they talked to had lovers there, the sharpies and the "race" men had friends and brothers there. It would have demanded an unquestioning patriotism, happily as uncommon in this country as it is undesirable, for these people not to have been disturbed by the bitter letters they received, by the newspaper stories they read, not to have been enraged by the posters, then to be found all over New York, which described the Japanese as "yellow-bellied Japs." It was only the "race" men, to be sure, who spoke ceaselessly of being revenged—how this vengeance was to be exacted was not clear—for the indignities and dangers suffered by Negro boys in uniform; but everybody felt a directionless, hopeless bitterness, as well as that panic which can scarcely be suppressed when one knows that a human being one loves is beyond one's reach, and in danger. This helplessness and this gnawing uneasiness does something, at length, to even the toughest mind. Perhaps the best way to sum all this up is to say that the people I knew felt, mainly, a peculiar kind of relief when they knew that their boys were being shipped out of the south, to do battle overseas. It was, perhaps, like feeling that the most dangerous part of a dangerous journey had been passed and that now, even if death should come, it would come with honor and without the complicity of their countrymen. Such a death would be, in short, a fact with which one could hope to live.

It was on the 28th of July, which I believe was a Wednesday, that I visited my father for the first time during his illness and for the last time in his life. The

1. Talking nonsense with the girls passing by. "Sharpies": tricksters or con men.
2. An illegal lottery.
3. Men who emphasized the importance of

African American pride and mutual support.
4. Pentecostalists, who emphasized prophecy, healing, and speaking in tongues.

moment I saw him I knew why I had put off this visit so long. I had told my mother that I did not want to see him because I hated him. But this was not true. It was only that I *had* hated him and I wanted to hold on to this hatred. I did not want to look on him as a ruin: it was not a ruin I had hated. I imagine that one of the reasons people cling to their hates so stubbornly is because they sense, once hate is gone, that they will be forced to deal with pain.

We traveled out to him, his older sister and myself, to what seemed to be the very end of a very Long Island. It was hot and dusty and we wrangled, my aunt and I, all the way out, over the fact that I had recently begun to smoke and, as she said, to give myself airs. But I knew that she wrangled with me because she could not bear to face the fact of her brother's dying. Neither could I endure the reality of her despair, her unstated bafflement as to what had happened to her brother's life, and her own. So we wrangled and I smoked and from time to time she fell into a heavy reverie. Covertly, I watched her face, which was the face of an old woman; it had fallen in, the eyes were sunken and lightless; soon she would be dying, too.

In my childhood—it had not been so long ago—I had thought her beautiful. She had been quick-witted and quick-moving and very generous with all the children and each of her visits had been an event. At one time one of my brothers and myself had thought of running away to live with her. Now she could no longer produce out of her handbag some unexpected and yet familiar delight. She made me feel pity and revulsion and fear. It was awful to realize that she no longer caused me to feel affection. The closer we came to the hospital the more querulous she became and at the same time, naturally, grew more dependent on me. Between pity and guilt and fear I began to feel that there was another me trapped in my skull like a jack-in-the-box who might escape my control at any moment and fill the air with screaming.

She began to cry the moment we entered the room and she saw him lying there, all shriveled and still, like a little black monkey. The great, gleaming apparatus which fed him and would have compelled him to be still even if he had been able to move brought to mind, not beneficence, but torture; the tubes entering his arm made me think of pictures I had seen when a child, of Gulliver,[5] tied down by the pygmies on that island. My aunt wept and wept, there was a whistling sound in my father's throat; nothing was said; he could not speak. I wanted to take his hand, to say something. But I do not know what I could have said, even if he could have heard me. He was not really in that room with us, he had at last really embarked on his journey; and though my aunt told me that he said he was going to meet Jesus, I did not hear anything except that whistling in his throat. The doctor came back and we left, into that unbearable train again, and home. In the morning came the telegram saying that he was dead. Then the house was suddenly full of relatives, friends, hysteria, and confusion and I quickly left my mother and the children to the care of those impressive women, who, in Negro communities at least, automatically appear at times of bereavement armed with lotions, proverbs, and patience, and an ability to cook. I went downtown. By the time I returned, later the same day, my mother had been carried to the hospital and the baby had been born.

---

5. The hero of *Gulliver's Travels* (1726) by the English-Irish writer Jonathan Swift (1667–1745); Gulliver is washed ashore on Lilliput, an island inhabited by tiny people who tie him down with cords while he is sleeping.

III

For my father's funeral I had nothing black to wear and this posed a nagging problem all day long. It was one of those problems, simple, or impossible of solution, to which the mind insanely clings in order to avoid the mind's real trouble. I spent most of that day at the downtown apartment of a girl I knew, celebrating my birthday with whiskey and wondering what to wear that night. When planning a birthday celebration one naturally does not expect that it will be up against competition from a funeral and this girl had anticipated taking me out that night, for a big dinner and a night club afterwards. Sometime during the course of that long day we decided that we would go out anyway, when my father's funeral service was over. I imagine *I* decided it, since, as the funeral hour approached, it became clearer and clearer to me that I would not know what to do with myself when it was over. The girl, stifling her very lively concern as to the possible effects of the whiskey on one of my father's chief mourners, concentrated on being conciliatory and practically helpful. She found a black shirt for me somewhere and ironed it and, dressed in the darkest pants and jacket I owned, and slightly drunk, I made my way to my father's funeral.

The chapel was full, but not packed, and very quiet. There were, mainly, my father's relatives, and his children, and here and there I saw faces I had not seen since childhood, the faces of my father's one-time friends. They were very dark and solemn now, seeming somehow to suggest that they had known all along that something like this would happen. Chief among the mourners was my aunt, who had quarreled with my father all his life; by which I do not mean to suggest that her mourning was insincere or that she had not loved him. I suppose that she was one of the few people in the world who had, and their incessant quarreling proved precisely the strength of the tie that bound them. The only other person in the world, as far as I knew, whose relationship to my father rivaled my aunt's in depth was my mother, who was not there.

It seemed to me, of course, that it was a very long funeral. But it was, if anything, a rather shorter funeral than most, nor, since there were no overwhelming, uncontrollable expressions of grief, could it be called—if I dare to use the word—successful. The minister who preached my father's funeral sermon was one of the few my father had still been seeing as he neared his end. He presented to us in his sermon a man whom none of us had ever seen—a man thoughtful, patient, and forbearing, a Christian inspiration to all who knew him, and a model for his children. And no doubt the children, in their disturbed and guilty state, were almost ready to believe this; he had been remote enough to be anything and, anyway, the shock of the incontrovertible, that it was really our father lying up there in that casket, prepared the mind for anything. His sister moaned and this grief-stricken moaning was taken as corroboration. The other faces held a dark, non-committal thoughtfulness. This was not the man they had known, but they had scarcely expected to be confronted with *him*; this was, in a sense deeper than questions of fact, the man they had not known, and the man they had not known may have been the real one. The real man, whoever he had been, had suffered and now he was dead: this was all that was sure and all that mattered now. Every man in the chapel hoped that when his hour came he, too, would be eulogized, which is to say forgiven, and that all of his lapses, greeds, errors, and strayings from the truth would be invested with coherence and looked upon with charity. This was perhaps the last thing human beings could give each other and it was what they demanded, after all, of the Lord. Only the Lord saw the midnight tears, only He was present when one of His children, moaning and wringing hands, paced up and down the room. When one slapped one's child in anger the recoil in the heart reverberated through heaven and became part of the pain of the universe. And when the children were hungry and sullen and distrustful and one watched them, daily, growing wilder, and further away, and running headlong into danger, it was the Lord who knew what the charged heart endured as the strap was laid to the backside; the Lord alone who knew what one *would* have said if one had had, like the Lord, the gift of the living word. It was the Lord who knew of the impossibility every parent in that room faced: how to prepare the child for the day when the child would be despised and how to *create* in the child—by what means?—a stronger antidote to this poison than one had found for oneself. The avenues, side streets, bars, billiard halls, hospitals, police stations, and even the playgrounds of Harlem—not to mention the houses of correction, the jails, and the morgue—testified to the potency of the poison while remaining silent as to the efficacy of whatever antidote, irresistibly raising the question of whether or not such an antidote existed; raising, which was worse, the question of whether or not an antidote was desirable; perhaps poison should be fought with poison. With these several schisms in the mind and with more terrors in the heart than could be named, it was better not to judge the man who had gone down under an impossible burden. It was better to remember: *Thou knowest this man's fall; but thou knowest not his wrassling.*[6]

While the preacher talked and I watched the children—years of changing their diapers, scrubbing them, slapping them, taking them to school, and scolding them had had the perhaps inevitable result of making me love them, though I am not sure I knew this then—my mind was busily breaking out with a rash of disconnected impressions. Snatches of popular songs, indecent jokes, bits of books I had read, movie sequences, faces, voices, political issues—I thought I was going mad; all these impressions suspended, as it were, in the solution of the faint nausea produced in me by the heat and liquor. For a moment I had the impression that my alcoholic breath, inefficiently disguised with chewing gum, filled the entire chapel. Then someone began singing one of my father's favorite songs and, abruptly, I was with him, sitting on his knee, in the hot, enormous, crowded church which was the first church we attended. It was the Abyssinia Baptist Church on 138th Street.[7] We had not gone there long. With this image, a host of others came. I had forgotten, in the rage of my growing up, how proud my father had been of me when I was little. Apparently, I had had a voice and my father had liked to show me off before the members of the church. I had forgotten what he had looked like when he was pleased but now I remembered that he had always been grinning with pleasure when my solos ended. I even remembered certain expressions on his face when he teased my mother—had he loved her? I would never know. And when had it all

---

6. From the English author John Donne (1572–1631), *Biathanatos* (1608), a defense of suicide. "Wrassling": wrestling.

7. A famous African American church in Harlem.

begun to change? For now it seemed that he had not always been cruel. I remembered being taken for a haircut and scraping my knee on the footrest of the barber's chair and I remembered my father's face as he soothed my crying and applied the stinging iodine. Then I remembered our fights, fights which had been of the worst possible kind because my technique had been silence.

I remembered the one time in all our life together when we had really spoken to each other.

It was on a Sunday and it must have been shortly before I left home. We were walking, just the two of us, in our usual silence, to or from church. I was in high school and had been doing a lot of writing and I was, at about this time, the editor of the high school magazine. But I had also been a Young Minister and had been preaching from the pulpit. Lately, I had been taking fewer engagements and preached as rarely as possible. It was said in the church, quite truthfully, that I was "cooling off."

My father asked me abruptly, "You'd rather write than preach, wouldn't you?"

I was astonished at his question—because it was a real question. I answered, "Yes."

That was all we said. It was awful to remember that that was all we had *ever* said.

The casket now was opened and the mourners were being led up the aisle to look for the last time on the deceased. The assumption was that the family was too overcome with grief to be allowed to make this journey alone and I watched while my aunt was led to the casket and, muffled in black, and shaking, led back to her seat. I disapproved of forcing the children to look on their dead father, considering that the shock of his death, or, more truthfully, the shock of death as a reality, was already a little more than a child could bear, but my judgment in this matter had been overruled and there they were, bewildered and frightened and very small, being led, one by one, to the casket. But there is also something very gallant about children at such moments. It has something to do with their silence and gravity and with the fact that one cannot help them. Their legs, somehow, seem *exposed*, so that it is at once incredible and terribly clear that their legs are all they have to hold them up.

I had not wanted to go to the casket myself and I certainly had not wished to be led there, but there was no way of avoiding either of these forms. One of the deacons led me up and I looked on my father's face. I cannot say that it looked like him at all. His blackness had been equivocated by powder and there was no suggestion in that casket of what his power had or could have been. He was simply an old man dead, and it was hard to believe that he had ever given anyone either joy or pain. Yet, his life filled that room. Further up the avenue his wife was holding his newborn child. Life and death so close together, and love and hatred, and right and wrong, said something to me which I did not want to hear concerning man, concerning the life of man.

After the funeral, while I was downtown desperately celebrating my birthday, a Negro soldier, in the lobby of the Hotel Braddock,[8] got into a fight with a white policeman over a Negro girl. Negro girls, white policemen, in or out of uniform, and Negro males—in or out of uniform—were part of the furniture of

8. Hotel at Eighth Avenue and 126th Street in Harlem.

the lobby of the Hotel Braddock and this was certainly not the first time such an incident had occurred. It was destined, however, to receive an unprecedented publicity, for the fight between the policeman and the soldier ended with the shooting of the soldier. Rumor, flowing immediately to the streets outside, stated that the soldier had been shot in the back, an instantaneous and revealing invention, and that the soldier had died protecting a Negro woman. The facts were somewhat different—for example, the soldier had not been shot in the back, and was not dead, and the girl seems to have been as dubious a symbol of womanhood as her white counterpart in Georgia usually is,[9] but no one was interested in the facts. They preferred the invention because this invention expressed and corroborated their hates and fears so perfectly. It is just as well to remember that people are always doing this. Perhaps many of those legends, including Christianity, to which the world clings began their conquest of the world with just some such concerted surrender to distortion. The effect, in Harlem, of this particular legend was like the effect of a lit match in a tin of gasoline. The mob gathered before the doors of the Hotel Braddock simply began to swell and to spread in every direction, and Harlem exploded.

The mob did not cross the ghetto lines. It would have been easy, for example, to have gone over Morningside Park on the west side or to have crossed the Grand Central railroad tracks at 125th Street on the east side, to wreak havoc in white neighborhoods. The mob seems to have been mainly interested in something more potent and real than the white face, that is, in white power, and the principal damage done during the riot of the summer of 1943 was to white business establishments in Harlem. It might have been a far bloodier story, of course, if, at the hour the riot began, these establishments had still been open. From the Hotel Braddock the mob fanned out, east and west along 125th Street, and for the entire length of Lenox, Seventh, and Eighth avenues. Along each of these avenues, and along each major side street—116th, 125th, 135th, and so on—bars, stores, pawnshops, restaurants, even little luncheonettes had been smashed open and entered and looted—looted, it might be added, with more haste than efficiency. The shelves really looked as though a bomb had struck them. Cans of beans and soup and dog food, along with toilet paper, corn flakes, sardines and milk tumbled every which way, and abandoned cash registers and cases of beer leaned crazily out of the splintered windows and were strewn along the avenues. Sheets, blankets, and clothing of every description formed a kind of path, as though people had dropped them while running. I truly had not realized that Harlem *had* so many stores until I saw them all smashed open; the first time the word *wealth* ever entered my mind in relation to Harlem was when I saw it scattered in the streets. But one's first, incongruous impression of plenty was countered immediately by an impression of waste. None of this was doing anybody any good. It would have been better to have left the plate glass as it had been and the goods lying in the stores.

It would have been better, but it would also have been intolerable, for Harlem had needed something to smash. To smash something is the ghetto's chronic need. Most of the time it is the members of the ghetto who smash each other, and themselves. But as long as the ghetto walls are standing there will

<hr />

9. Baldwin here refers to the origins of many lynchings in the South: allegations that black men had insulted white women.

always come a moment when these outlets do not work. That summer, for example, it was not enough to get into a fight on Lenox Avenue, or curse out one's cronies in the barber shops. If ever, indeed, the violence which fills Harlem's churches, pool halls, and bars erupts outward in a more direct fashion, Harlem and its citizens are likely to vanish in an apocalyptic flood. That this is not likely to happen is due to a great many reasons, most hidden and powerful among them the Negro's real relation to the white American. This relation prohibits, simply, anything as uncomplicated and satisfactory as pure hatred. In order really to hate white people, one has to blot so much out of the mind—and the heart—that this hatred itself becomes an exhausting and self-destructive pose. But this does not mean, on the other hand, that love comes easily: the white world is too powerful, too complacent, too ready with gratuitous humiliation, and, above all, too ignorant and too innocent for that. One is absolutely forced to make perpetual qualifications and one's own reactions are always canceling each other out. It is this, really, which has driven so many people mad, both white and black. One is always in the position of having to decide between amputation and gangrene. Amputation is swift but time may prove that the amputation was not necessary—or one may delay the amputation too long. Gangrene is slow, but it is impossible to be sure that one is reading one's symptoms right. The idea of going through life as a cripple is more than one can bear, and equally unbearable is the risk of swelling up slowly, in agony, with poison. And the trouble, finally, is that the risks are real even if the choices do not exist.

"But as for me and my house," my father had said, "we will serve the Lord." I wondered, as we drove him to his resting place, what this line had meant for him. I had heard him preach it many times. I had preached it once myself, proudly giving it an interpretation different from my father's. Now the whole thing came back to me, as though my father and I were on our way to Sunday school and I were memorizing the golden text: *And if it seem evil unto you to serve the Lord, choose you this day whom you will serve; whether the gods which your fathers served that were on the other side of the flood, or the gods of the Amorites, in whose land ye dwell: but as for me and my house, we will serve the Lord.*[1] I suspected in these familiar lines a meaning which had never been there for me before. All of my father's texts and songs, which I had decided were meaningless, were arranged before me at his death like empty bottles, waiting to hold the meaning which life would give them for me. This was his legacy: nothing is ever escaped. That bleakly memorable morning I hated the unbelievable streets and the Negroes and whites who had, equally, made them that way. But I knew that it was folly, as my father would have said, this bitterness was folly. It was necessary to hold on to the things that mattered. The dead man mattered, the new life mattered; blackness and whiteness did not matter; to believe that they did was to acquiesce in one's own destruction. Hatred, which could destroy so much, never failed to destroy the man who hated and this was an immutable law.

It began to seem that one would have to hold in the mind forever two ideas which seemed to be in opposition. The first idea was acceptance, the acceptance, totally without rancor, of life as it is, and men as they are: in the light of

1. Joshua 24.15.

this idea, it goes without saying that injustice is a commonplace. But this did not mean that one could be complacent, for the second idea was of equal power: that one must never, in one's own life, accept these injustices as commonplace but must fight them with all one's strength. This fight begins, however, in the heart and it now had been laid to my charge to keep my own heart free of hatred and despair. This intimation made my heart heavy and, now that my father was irrecoverable, I wished that he had been beside me so that I could have searched his face for the answers which only the future would give me now.

1955

ALBERT CAMUS
1913–1960

From his childhood among the most disadvantaged in Algiers to his later roles as journalist, Resistance fighter in World War II, iconic literary figure, and winner of the Nobel Prize in Literature, in 1957, Albert Camus was intensely aware of the basic levels of human existence and of the struggles of the poor and the oppressed. "I can understand only in human terms," he said. "I understand the things I touch, things that offer me resistance." He describes the raw experience of life that human beings share, the humble but ineradicable bond between them. Camus kept a sympathetic yet critical eye on the tensions of his day: observing the Soviet Union from afar, and the bloody battles for Algerian independence up-close, led him to examine the way people can respond to oppressive systems without themselves becoming oppressors.

Camus was born on November 7, 1913, into a "world of poverty and light" in Mondavi, Algeria, then a colony of France. He was the second son in a poor family of mixed Alsatian and Spanish descent, and his father died in an early battle of the First World War. Camus's mother was illiterate; an untreated childhood illness had left her deaf and with a speech impediment. The two boys lived together with their mother, uncle, and grandmother in a two-room apartment in the working-class section of the capital city, Algiers. Camus and his brother, Lucien, were raised by their strict grandmother while their mother worked as a cleaning woman to support the family. Images of the Mediterranean landscape, with the sensual appeal of sea and blazing sun, recur throughout his work, as does a profound compassion for those who—like his mother—labor unrecognized and in silence.

A passionate athlete as well as a scholarship recipient, Camus completed his secondary education and enrolled as a philosophy student at the University of Algiers before contracting, at seventeen, the tuberculosis that corroded his health and made him aware of the body's vulnerability to disease and death. Camus eventually finished his degree, but in the meantime his illness had provided a metaphor for the personal and natural events that oppose and limit human fulfillment and happiness: elements he was later to term the "plague," which infects bodies, minds, cities, and society. (*The Plague* is the title of his second novel.)

Camus lived and worked as a journalist and essayist. Then, as later, however, his work extended well beyond journalism. He founded a collective theater, Le Théâtre du Travail (The Labor Theater), for which he wrote and adapted a number of plays. The theater fascinated Camus, possibly because it involved groups of people and spontaneous interaction between actors and audience. Sponsored by the Communist Party, the Labor Theater was designed for the working people, with performances on the docks in Algiers. Like many intellectuals of his day, Camus joined the Communist Party, but he withdrew after a year to protest its opposition to Algerian nationalism. He eventually left the Labor Theater too and, with a group of young Algerians associated with the publishing house Charlot, organized the politically independent Team Theater (Théâtre de l'Équipe). In 1940 he moved to France after his political commentary, including a famous report on administrative mismanagement during a famine among the Berbers (tribal peoples in North Africa), so outraged the Algerian government that his newspaper was suspended and he himself refused a work permit.

Soon after leaving Algeria, Camus published his first and most famous novel, *The Stranger* (1942), the play *Caligula* (1944), and a lengthy essay defining his concept of the "absurd" hero, *The Myth of Sisyphus* (1942). During World War II, Camus worked in Paris as a reader for the publishing firm of Gallimard, a post that he kept until his death, in 1960. At the same time, he took part in the French Resistance and helped edit the underground journal *Combat*. His friendship with the existentialist philosopher Jean-

Paul Sartre began in 1944; after the war he and Sartre were internationally known as uncompromising analysts of the modern conscience. Camus's second novel, *The Plague* (1947), portrays an epidemic in a quarantined city, Oran, Algeria, to symbolize the spread of evil during World War II ("the feeling of suffocation from which we all suffered, and the atmosphere of threat and exile") and to show the struggle against physical and spiritual death in its many forms. He continued, as well, to write plays (*Cross Purposes*, 1944; *The Just Assassins*, 1949). Not content to express his views symbolically in fiction, Camus also spoke out in philosophical essays and political statements. His independent mind and rejection of doctrinaire positions brought him attacks from both the left and the right.

Unlike many intellectuals of his day, Camus did not place a higher value on ideology than on its practical effects: when word emerged about Stalinist labor camps, for instance, he criticized the Soviets rather than defend the Communist ideal, as many of his friends did. Camus's open anti-Communism led to a spectacular break with Sartre, whose magazine, *Les Temps Modernes* (Modern Times), condemned Camus's book-length essay *The Rebel* (1951); the personal and public dispute between the old friends may have been unavoidable. In the bitter struggle over Algeria, Camus supported the claims of French colonists, including his own family, and therefore opposed Algerian independence, while at the same time attacking the violence of the French colonial regime. Camus did not live to witness the end of the Algerian conflict, which led to independence in 1962. After being awarded the Nobel Prize in 1957, he died in a car accident in 1960. His death at the height of his powers contributed to his posthumous fame as an analyst of the tragic elements of the human condition.

Camus is often linked with Sartre as an existentialist writer, and indeed—as novelist, playwright, and essayist—he is widely known for his analysis of two issues fundamental to existentialism: its distinctive assessment of the human condition and its search for authentic beliefs and values. Yet Camus rejected doctrinaire labels, and Sartre himself suggested that Camus was better placed in the tradition of French moralist writers, such as Michel de Montaigne and René Pascal, who observed human behavior within an implied ethical context that had its own standards of good and evil.

A consummate artist as well as a moralist, Camus was well aware of both the opportunities and the illusions of his craft. When he received the Nobel Prize, his acceptance speech emphasized the artificial but necessary "human" order that art imposes on the chaos of immediate experience. Artists are important as *creators*, because they shape a human perspective, allow understanding in human terms, and therefore provide a basis for action. By stressing the gap between art and reality, Camus provides a link between two poles of human understanding. His works juxtapose realistic detail and a philosophical, almost mythical dimension. The symbolism of his titles, from *The Stranger* to the last collection of stories, *Exile and the Kingdom* (1957), indicates the status of outsider, and the feeling of alienation in the world, while suggesting a search for the realm of human solidarity and agency.

The two terms around which Camus's thinking and writing revolve are the nouns *the absurd* and *revolt*. Camus's wartime output established his reputation as a philosopher of the absurd: the impossibility of "making sense" of a world that has no discernible sense. How to live in such an enviroment nevertheless becomes the main object of his philosophical and literary work. *Revolt*, for Camus, is more ethical than political, a rejection of the conventional and the

inauthentic, but also an embrace of a shared humanity. Because the impulse to rebel is a basis for social tolerance and has no patience for master plans that prescribe patterns of thought or action, *revolt* actually opposes revolutionary nihilism.

In the story presented here, "The Guest" (1957), taken from *Exile and the Kingdom*, Camus returns to the landscape of his native Algeria. The colonial context is crucial in this story, not only to explain the real threat of guerrilla reprisal (Camus may be recalling the actual killing of rural schoolteachers in 1954) but to establish the dimensions of a political situation in which the government, police, educational system, and economic welfare of Algeria are all controlled by France. As in the works of **Doris Lessing**, **Naguib Mahfouz**, and **Chinua Achebe**, the colonial (or newly postcolonial) setting generates a charged atmosphere. The beginning of the story illustrates how French colonial education emphasizes French rather than local concerns: the schoolteacher's geography lesson outlines the four main rivers of France. The Arab is led along like an animal behind the gendarme Balducci, who rides a horse (here too, Camus may be recalling a humiliation reported two decades before and used as a way to inspire Algerian nationalists). Within this specific context, however, Camus concentrates on wider issues: freedom, brotherhood, responsibility, and the ambiguity of actions along with the inevitability of choice.

The remote desert landscape establishes a complete physical and moral isolation for the story's events. "No one, in this desert, . . . mattered," and the schoolteacher and his guest must each decide, independently, what to do. When Balducci invades Daru's monastic solitude and tells him that he must deliver the Arab to prison, Daru is outraged to be given involvement in, and indeed responsibility for, another's fate. Cursing both the system that tries to force him into complicity and the Arab who has not had enough sense to get away, Daru tries, in every way possible, to avoid taking a stand. Yet he finds himself confronted with the essential human demand for hospitality, which creates burdens and links between guest and host. The choice that Daru must make leads to a further necessary choice by the Arab prisoner. As possible titles for this story, Camus considered "Cain" and "The Law" before settling on "The Guest": the title word, *l'hôte*, means both "guest" and "host" in French. Joined in their fundamental humanity, both guest and host are obliged to shoulder the ambiguous, and potentially fatal, burden of freedom.

The Guest[1]

The schoolmaster was watching the two men climb toward him. One was on horseback, the other on foot. They had not yet tackled the abrupt rise leading to the schoolhouse built on the hillside. They were toiling onward, making slow progress in the snow, among the stones, on the vast expanse of the high, deserted plateau. From time to time the horse stumbled. Without hearing anything yet, he could see the breath issuing from the horse's nostrils. One of the men, at least, knew the region. They were following the trail although it had disappeared days ago under a layer of dirty white snow. The schoolmaster calculated that it would take them half an hour to get onto the hill. It was cold; he went back into the school to get a sweater.

He crossed the empty, frigid classroom. On the blackboard the four rivers of France,[2] drawn with four different colored chalks, had been flowing toward their estuaries for the past three days. Snow had suddenly fallen in mid-October after eight months of drought without the transition of rain, and the twenty pupils, more or less, who lived in the villages scattered over the plateau had stopped coming. With fair weather they would return. Daru now heated only the single room that was his lodging, adjoining the classroom and giving also onto the plateau to the east. Like the class windows, his window looked to the south too. On that side the school was a few kilometers from the point where the plateau began to slope toward the south. In clear weather could be seen the purple mass of the mountain range where the gap opened onto the desert.

Somewhat warmed, Daru returned to the window from which he had first seen the two men. They were no longer visible. Hence they must have tackled the rise. The sky was not so dark, for the snow had stopped falling during the night. The morning had opened with a dirty light which had scarcely become brighter as the ceiling of clouds lifted. At two in the afternoon it seemed as if the day were merely beginning. But still this was better than those three days when the thick snow was falling amidst unbroken darkness with little gusts of wind that rattled the double door of the classroom. Then Daru had spent long hours in his room, leaving it only to go to the shed and feed the chickens or get some coal. Fortunately the delivery truck from Tadjid, the nearest village to the north, had brought his supplies two days before the blizzard. It would return in forty-eight hours.

1. Translated by Justin O'Brien.
2. The Seine, Loire, Rhone, and Gironde riv- ers. French geography was taught in the French colonies.

Besides, he had enough to resist a siege, for the little room was cluttered with bags of wheat that the administration left as a stock to distribute to those of his pupils whose families had suffered from the drought. Actually they had all been victims because they were all poor. Every day Daru would distribute a ration to the children. They had missed it, he knew, during these bad days. Possibly one of the fathers or big brothers would come this afternoon and he could supply them with grain. It was just a matter of carrying them over to the next harvest. Now shiploads of wheat were arriving from France and the worst was over. But it would be hard to forget that poverty, that army of ragged ghosts wandering in the sunlight, the plateaus burned to a cinder month after month, the earth shriveled up little by little, literally scorched, every stone bursting into dust under one's foot. The sheep had died then by thousands and even a few men, here and there, sometimes without anyone's knowing.

In contrast with such poverty, he who lived almost like a monk in his remote schoolhouse, nonetheless satisfied with the little he had and with the rough life, had felt like a lord with his whitewashed walls, his narrow couch, his unpainted shelves, his well, and his weekly provision of water and food. And suddenly this snow, without warning, without the foretaste of rain. This is the way the region was, cruel to live in, even without men—who didn't help matters either. But Daru had been born here. Everywhere else, he felt exiled.

He stepped out onto the terrace in front of the schoolhouse. The two men were now halfway up the slope. He recognized the horseman as Balducci, the old gendarme he had known for a long time. Balducci was holding on the end of a rope an Arab who was walking behind him with hands bound and head lowered. The gendarme waved a greeting to which Daru did not reply, lost as he was in contemplation of the Arab dressed in a faded blue jellaba, his feet in sandals but covered with socks of heavy raw wool, his head surmounted by a narrow, short *chèche*.[3] They were approaching. Balducci was holding back his horse in order not to hurt the Arab, and the group was advancing slowly.

Within earshot, Balducci shouted: "One hour to do the three kilometers from El Ameur!" Daru did not answer. Short and square in his thick sweater, he watched them climb. Not once had the Arab raised his head. "Hello," said Daru when they got up onto the terrace. "Come in and warm up." Balducci painfully got down from his horse without letting go the rope. From under his bristling mustache he smiled at the schoolmaster. His little dark eyes, deep-set under a tanned forehead, and his mouth surrounded with wrinkles made him look attentive and studious. Daru took the bridle, led the horse to the shed, and came back to the two men, who were now waiting for him in the school. He led them into his room. "I am going to heat up the classroom," he said. "We'll be more comfortable there." When he entered the room again, Balducci was on the couch. He had undone the rope tying him to the Arab, who had squatted near the stove. His hands still bound, the *chèche* pushed back on his head, he was looking toward the window. At first Daru noticed only his huge lips, fat, smooth, almost Negroid; yet his nose was straight, his eyes were dark and full of fever. The *chèche* revealed an obstinate forehead and, under the weathered skin now rather discolored by the cold, the whole face had a restless

---

3. Scarf; here, wound as a turban around the head. "Jellaba": a long hooded robe worn by Arabs in North Africa.

and rebellious look that struck Daru when the Arab, turning his face toward him, looked him straight in the eyes. "Go into the other room," said the schoolmaster, "and I'll make you some mint tea." "Thanks," Balducci said. "What a chore! How I long for retirement." And addressing his prisoner in Arabic: "Come on, you." The Arab got up and, slowly, holding his bound wrists in front of him, went into the classroom.

With the tea, Daru brought a chair. But Balducci was already enthroned on the nearest pupil's desk and the Arab had squatted against the teacher's platform facing the stove, which stood between the desk and the window. When he held out the glass of tea to the prisoner, Daru hesitated at the sight of his bound hands. "He might perhaps be untied." "Sure," said Balducci. "That was for the trip." He started to get to his feet. But Daru, setting the glass on the floor, had knelt beside the Arab. Without saying anything, the Arab watched him with his feverish eyes. Once his hands were free, he rubbed his swollen wrists against each other, took the glass of tea, and sucked up the burning liquid in swift little sips.

"Good," said Daru. "And where are you headed?"

Balducci withdrew his mustache from the tea. "Here, son."

"Odd pupils! And you're spending the night?"

"No. I'm going back to El Ameur. And you will deliver this fellow to Tinguit. He is expected at police headquarters."

Balducci was looking at Daru with a friendly little smile.

"What's this story?" asked the schoolmaster. "Are you pulling my leg?"

"No, son. Those are the orders."

"The orders? I'm not . . ." Daru hesitated, not wanting to hurt the old Corsican.[4] "I mean, that's not my job."

"What! What's the meaning of that? In wartime people do all kinds of jobs."

"Then I'll wait for the declaration of war!"

Balducci nodded.

"O.K. But the orders exist and they concern you too. Things are brewing, it appears. There is talk of a forthcoming revolt. We are mobilized, in a way."

Daru still had his obstinate look.

"Listen, son," Balducci said. "I like you and you must understand. There's only a dozen of us at El Ameur to patrol throughout the whole territory of a small department[5] and I must get back in a hurry. I was told to hand this guy over to you and return without delay. He couldn't be kept there. His village was beginning to stir; they wanted to take him back. You must take him to Tinguit tomorrow before the day is over. Twenty kilometers shouldn't faze a husky fellow like you. After that, all will be over. You'll come back to your pupils and your comfortable life."

Behind the wall the horse could be heard snorting and pawing the earth. Daru was looking out the window. Decidedly, the weather was clearing and the light was increasing over the snowy plateau. When all the snow was melted, the sun would take over again and once more would burn the fields of stone. For days, still, the unchanging sky would shed its dry light on the solitary expanse where nothing had any connection with man.

---

4. Balducci is a native of Corsica, a French island north of Sardinia.

5. French administrative and territorial division; like a county.

"After all," he said, turning around toward Balducci, "what did he do?" And, before the gendarme had opened his mouth, he asked: "Does he speak French?"

"No, not a word. We had been looking for him for a month, but they were hiding him. He killed his cousin."

"Is he against us?"[6]

"I don't think so. But you can never be sure."

"Why did he kill?"

"A family squabble, I think. One owed the other grain, it seems. It's not at all clear. In short, he killed his cousin with a billhook. You know, like a sheep, *kreezk!*"

Balducci made the gesture of drawing a blade across his throat and the Arab, his attention attracted, watched him with a sort of anxiety. Daru felt a sudden wrath against the man, against all men with their rotten spite, their tireless hates, their blood lust.

But the kettle was singing on the stove. He served Balducci more tea, hesitated, then served the Arab again, who, a second time, drank avidly. His raised arms made the jellaba fall open and the schoolmaster saw his thin, muscular chest.

"Thanks, kid," Balducci said. "And now, I'm off."

He got up and went toward the Arab, taking a small rope from his pocket.

"What are you doing?" Daru asked dryly.

Balducci, disconcerted, showed him the rope.

"Don't bother."

The old gendarme hesitated. "It's up to you. Of course, you are armed?"

"I have my shotgun."

"Where?"

"In the trunk."

"You ought to have it near your bed."

"Why? I have nothing to fear."

"You're crazy, son. If there's an uprising, no one is safe, we're all in the same boat."

"I'll defend myself. I'll have time to see them coming."

Balducci began to laugh, then suddenly the mustache covered the white teeth.

"You'll have time? O.K. That's just what I was saying. You have always been a little cracked. That's why I like you, my son was like that."

At the same time he took out his revolver and put it on the desk.

"Keep it; I don't need two weapons from here to El Ameur."

The revolver shone against the black paint of the table. When the gendarme turned toward him, the schoolmaster caught the smell of leather and horseflesh.

"Listen, Balducci," Daru said suddenly, "every bit of this disgusts me, and first of all your fellow here. But I won't hand him over. Fight, yes, if I have to. But not that."

The old gendarme stood in front of him and looked at him severely.

"You're being a fool," he said slowly. "I don't like it either. You don't get used to putting a rope on a man even after years of it, and you're even ashamed— yes, ashamed. But you can't let them have their way."

6. I.e., against the French colonial government.

"I won't hand him over," Daru said again.

"It's an order, son, and I repeat it."

"That's right. Repeat to them what I've said to you: I won't hand him over."

Balducci made a visible effort to reflect. He looked at the Arab and at Daru. At last he decided.

"No, I won't tell them anything. If you want to drop us, go ahead; I'll not denounce you. I have an order to deliver the prisoner and I'm doing so. And now you'll just sign this paper for me."

"There's no need. I'll not deny that you left him with me."

"Don't be mean with me. I know you'll tell the truth. You're from hereabouts and you are a man. But you must sign, that's the rule."

Daru opened his drawer, took out a little square bottle of purple ink, the red wooden penholder with the "sergeant-major" pen he used for making models of penmanship, and signed. The gendarme carefully folded the paper and put it into his wallet. Then he moved toward the door.

"I'll see you off," Daru said.

"No," said Balducci. "There's no use being polite. You insulted me."

He looked at the Arab, motionless in the same spot, sniffed peevishly, and turned away toward the door. "Good-by, son," he said. The door shut behind him. Balducci appeared suddenly outside the window and then disappeared. His footsteps were muffled by the snow. The horse stirred on the other side of the wall and several chickens fluttered in fright. A moment later Balducci reappeared outside the window leading the horse by the bridle. He walked toward the little rise without turning around and disappeared from sight with the horse following him. A big stone could be heard bouncing down. Daru walked back toward the prisoner, who, without stirring, never took his eyes off him. "Wait," the schoolmaster said in Arabic and went toward the bedroom. As he was going through the door, he had a second thought, went to the desk, took the revolver, and stuck it in his pocket. Then, without looking back, he went into his room.

For some time he lay on his couch watching the sky gradually close over, listening to the silence. It was this silence that had seemed painful to him during the first days here, after the war. He had requested a post in the little town at the base of the foothills separating the upper plateaus from the desert. There, rocky walls, green and black to the north, pink and lavender to the south, marked the frontier of eternal summer. He had been named to a post farther north, on the plateau itself. In the beginning, the solitude and the silence had been hard for him on these wastelands peopled only by stones. Occasionally, furrows suggested cultivation, but they had been dug to uncover a certain kind of stone good for building. The only plowing here was to harvest rocks. Elsewhere a thin layer of soil accumulated in the hollows would be scraped out to enrich paltry village gardens. This is the way it was: bare rock covered three quarters of the region. Towns sprang up, flourished, then disappeared; men came by, loved one another or fought bitterly, then died. No one in this desert, neither he nor his guest, mattered. And yet, outside this desert neither of them, Daru knew, could have really lived.

When he got up, no noise came from the classroom. He was amazed at the unmixed joy he derived from the mere thought that the Arab might have fled and that he would be alone with no decision to make. But the prisoner was there. He had merely stretched out between the stove and the desk. With eyes open, he was staring at the ceiling. In that position, his thick lips were particularly noticeable, giving him a pouting look. "Come," said Daru. The Arab got up and followed him. In the bedroom, the schoolmaster pointed to a chair near the table under the window. The Arab sat down without taking his eyes off Daru.

"Are you hungry?"

"Yes," the prisoner said.

Daru set the table for two. He took flour and oil, shaped a cake in a frying-pan, and lighted the little stove that functioned on bottled gas. While the cake was cooking, he went out to the shed to get cheese, eggs, dates, and condensed milk. When the cake was done he set it on the window sill to cool, heated some condensed milk diluted with water, and beat up the eggs into an omelette. In one of his motions he knocked against the revolver stuck in his right pocket. He set the bowl down, went into the classroom, and put the revolver in his desk drawer. When he came back to the room, night was falling. He put on the light and served the Arab. "Eat," he said. The Arab took a piece of the cake, lifted it eagerly to his mouth, and stopped short.

"And you?" he asked.

"After you. I'll eat too."

The thick lips opened slightly. The Arab hesitated, then bit into the cake determinedly.

The meal over, the Arab looked at the schoolmaster. "Are you the judge?"

"No, I'm simply keeping you until tomorrow."

"Why do you eat with me?"

"I'm hungry."

The Arab fell silent. Daru got up and went out. He brought back a folding bed from the shed, set it up between the table and the stove, perpendicular to his own bed. From a large suitcase which, upright in a corner, served as a shelf for papers, he took two blankets and arranged them on the camp bed. Then he stopped, felt useless, and sat down on his bed. There was nothing more to do or to get ready. He had to look at this man. He looked at him, therefore, trying to imagine his face bursting with rage. He couldn't do so. He could see nothing but the dark yet shining eyes and the animal mouth.

"Why did you kill him?" he asked in a voice whose hostile tone surprised him.

The Arab looked away.

"He ran away. I ran after him."

He raised his eyes to Daru again and they were full of a sort of woeful interrogation. "Now what will they do to me?"

"Are you afraid?"

He stiffened, turning his eyes away.

"Are you sorry?"

The Arab stared at him openmouthed. Obviously he did not understand. Daru's annoyance was growing. At the same time he felt awkward and self-conscious with his big body wedged between the two beds.

"Lie down there," he said impatiently. "That's your bed."

The Arab didn't move. He called to Daru:

"Tell me!"

The schoolmaster looked at him.

"Is the gendarme coming back tomorrow?"

"I don't know."

"Are you coming with us?"

"I don't know. Why?"

The prisoner got up and stretched out on top of the blankets, his feet toward the window. The light from the electric bulb shone straight into his eyes and he closed them at once.

"Why?" Daru repeated, standing beside the bed.

The Arab opened his eyes under the blinding light and looked at him, trying not to blink.

"Come with us," he said.

In the middle of the night, Daru was still not asleep. He had gone to bed after undressing completely; he generally slept naked. But when he suddenly realized that he had nothing on, he hesitated. He felt vulnerable and the temptation came to him to put his clothes back on. Then he shrugged his shoulders; after all, he wasn't a child and, if need be, he could break his adversary in two. From his bed he could observe him, lying on his back, still motionless with his eyes closed under the harsh light. When Daru turned out the light, the darkness seemed to coagulate all of a sudden. Little by little, the night came back to life in the window where the starless sky was stirring gently. The schoolmaster soon made out the body lying at his feet. The Arab still did not move, but his eyes seemed open. A faint wind was prowling around the schoolhouse. Perhaps it would drive away the clouds and the sun would reappear.

During the night the wind increased. The hens fluttered a little and then were silent. The Arab turned over on his side with his back to Daru, who thought he heard him moan. Then he listened for his guest's breathing, become heavier and more regular. He listened to that breath so close to him and mused without being able to go to sleep. In this room where he had been sleeping alone for a year, this presence bothered him. But it bothered him also by imposing on him a sort of brotherhood he knew well but refused to accept in the present circumstances. Men who share the same rooms, soldiers or prisoners, develop a strange alliance as if, having cast off their armor with their clothing, they fraternized every evening, over and above their differences, in the ancient community of dream and fatigue. But Daru shook himself; he didn't like such musings, and it was essential to sleep.

A little later, however, when the Arab stirred slightly, the schoolmaster was still not asleep. When the prisoner made a second move, he stiffened, on the alert. The Arab was lifting himself slowly on his arms with almost the motion of a sleepwalker. Seated upright in bed, he waited motionless without turning his head toward Daru, as if he were listening attentively. Daru did not stir; it had just occurred to him that the revolver was still in the drawer of his desk. It was better to act at once. Yet he continued to observe the prisoner, who, with the same slithery motion, put his feet on the ground, waited again, then began to stand up slowly. Daru was about to call out to him when the Arab began to walk, in a quite natural but extraordinarily silent way. He was heading toward the door at the end of the room that opened into the shed. He lifted the latch with precaution and went out, pushing the door behind him but without shutting it. Daru had not stirred. "He is running away," he merely thought. "Good riddance!" Yet he listened attentively. The hens were not fluttering; the guest must be on the plateau. A faint sound of water reached him, and he didn't know what it was until the Arab again stood framed in the doorway, closed the door carefully, and came back to bed without a sound. Then Daru turned his back on him and fell asleep. Still later he seemed, from the depths of his sleep, to hear furtive steps around the schoolhouse. "I'm dreaming! I'm dreaming!" he repeated to himself. And he went on sleeping.

When he awoke, the sky was clear; the loose window let in a cold, pure air. The Arab was asleep, hunched up under the blankets now, his mouth open, utterly relaxed. But when Daru shook him, he started dreadfully, staring at Daru with wild eyes as if he had never seen him and such a frightened expression that the schoolmaster stepped back. "Don't be afraid. It's me. You must eat." The Arab nodded his head and said yes. Calm had·returned to his face, but his expression was vacant and listless.

The coffee was ready. They drank it seated together on the folding bed as they munched their pieces of the cake. Then Daru led the Arab under the shed and showed him the faucet where he washed. He went back into the room, folded the blankets and the bed, made his own bed and put the room in order. Then he went through the classroom and out onto the terrace. The sun was already rising in the blue sky; a soft, bright light was bathing the deserted plateau. On the ridge the snow was melting in spots. The stones were about to reappear. Crouched on the edge of the plateau, the schoolmaster looked at the deserted expanse. He thought of Balducci. He had hurt him, for he had sent him off in a way as if he didn't want to be associated with him. He could still hear the gendarme's farewell and, without knowing why, he felt strangely empty and vulnerable. At that moment, from the other side of the schoolhouse, the prisoner coughed. Daru listened to him almost despite himself and then, furious, threw a pebble that whistled through the air before sinking into the snow. That man's stupid crime revolted him, but to hand him over was contrary to honor. Merely thinking of it made him smart with humiliation. And he cursed at one and the same time his own people who had sent him this Arab and the Arab too who had dared to kill and not managed to get away. Daru got up, walked in a circle on the terrace, waited motionless, and then went back into the schoolhouse.

The Arab, leaning over the cement floor of the shed, was washing his teeth with two fingers. Daru looked at him and said: "Come." He went back into the room ahead of the prisoner. He slipped a hunting-jacket on over his sweater and put on walking-shoes. Standing, he waited until the Arab had put on his *chèche* and sandals. They went into the classroom and the schoolmaster pointed to the exit, saying: "Go ahead." The fellow didn't budge. "I'm coming," said Daru. The Arab went out. Daru went back into the room and made a package of pieces of rusk, dates, and sugar. In the classroom, before going out, he hesitated a second in front of his desk, then crossed the threshold and locked the door. "That's the way," he said. He started toward the east, followed by the prisoner. But, a short distance from the schoolhouse, he thought he heard a slight sound behind them. He retraced his steps and examined the surroundings of the house, there was no one there. The Arab watched him without seeming to understand. "Come on," said Daru.

They walked for an hour and rested beside a sharp peak of limestone. The snow was melting faster and faster and the sun was drinking up the puddles at once, rapidly cleaning the plateau, which gradually dried and vibrated like the air itself. When they resumed walking, the ground rang under their feet. From time to time a bird rent the space in front of them with a joyful cry. Daru breathed in deeply the fresh morning light. He felt a sort of rapture before the vast familiar expanse, now almost entirely yellow under its dome of blue sky. They walked an hour more, descending toward the south. They reached a level height made up of crumbly rocks. From there on, the plateau sloped down, eastward, toward a low plain where there were a few spindly trees and, to the south, toward outcroppings of rock that gave the landscape a chaotic look.

Daru surveyed the two directions. There was nothing but the sky on the horizon. Not a man could be seen. He turned toward the Arab, who was looking at him blankly. Daru held out the package to him. "Take it," he said. "There are dates, bread, and sugar. You can hold out for two days. Here are a thousand francs too." The Arab took the package and the money but kept his full hands at chest level as if he didn't know what to do with what was being given him. "Now look," the schoolmaster said as he pointed in the direction of the east, "there's the way to Tinguit. You have a two-hour walk. At Tinguit you'll find the administration and the police. They are expecting you." The Arab looked toward the east, still holding the package and the money against his chest. Daru took his elbow and turned him rather roughly toward the south. At the foot of the height on which they stood could be seen a faint path. "That's the trail across the plateau. In a day's walk from here you'll find pasturelands and the first nomads. They'll take you in and shelter you according to their law." The Arab had now turned toward Daru and a sort of panic was visible in his expression. "Listen," he said. Daru shook his head: "No, be quiet. Now I'm leaving you." He turned his back on him, took two long steps in the direction of the school, looked hesitantly at the motionless Arab, and started off again. For a few minutes he heard nothing but his own step resounding on the cold ground and did not turn his head. A moment later, however, he turned around. The Arab was still there on the edge of the hill, his arms hanging now, and he was looking at the schoolmaster. Daru felt something rise in his throat. But he swore with impatience, waved vaguely, and started off again. He had already gone some distance when he again stopped and looked. There was no longer anyone on the hill.

Daru hesitated. The sun was now rather high in the sky and was beginning to beat down on his head. The schoolmaster retraced his steps, at first somewhat uncertainly, then with decision. When he reached the little hill, he was bathed in sweat. He climbed it as fast as he could and stopped, out of breath, at the top. The rock-fields to the south stood out sharply against the blue sky, but on the plain to the east a steamy heat was already rising. And in that slight haze, Daru, with heavy heart, made out the Arab walking slowly on the road to prison.

A little later, standing before the window of the classroom, the schoolmaster was watching the clear light bathing the whole surface of the plateau, but he hardly saw it. Behind him on the blackboard, among the winding French rivers, sprawled the clumsily chalked-up words he had just read: "You handed over our brother. You will pay for this." Daru looked at the sky, the plateau, and, beyond, the invisible lands stretching all the way to the sea. In this vast landscape he had loved so much, he was alone.

1957

SAMUEL BECKETT

1906–1989

At once among the grimmest and funniest of modern writers, Samuel Beckett offers in his novels and plays a stark, spare representation of the human condition in its "absurd" emptiness. Beckett's world is haunted by an absence of meaning at the core, yet the absence of meaning becomes the occasion for puns, parodies, and clowning. Filling the void with desperate stagecraft and patter, Beckett's characters live out a hopeless attempt to find or to create meaning for themselves. Often they spend their lives waiting for an explanation that never comes; and yet Beckett makes this predicament a source of intense black humor.

Born near Dublin on April 13, 1906 (Good Friday), to a well-to-do Protestant family, Beckett was educated in Ireland and received a bachelor's degree from Trinity College in 1927. He then taught English for two years at the École Normale Supérieure in Paris, where he met **James Joyce** and was influenced by the older novelist's exuberant and punning use of language. Beckett wrote an essay on the early stages of Joyce's *Finnegans Wake* and later helped in the French translation of some portions of the book. In 1930, Beckett entered a competition for a poem on the subject of time and won first prize with a ninety-eight-line (and seventeen-footnote) dramatic monologue, *Whoroscope*; the poem's speaker is the seventeenth-century French philosopher René Descartes, whose ideas about the dualism between mind and body became an obsession of Beckett's literary work. Beckett returned to Trinity College, where he took a master's degree in 1931, published an essay on **Marcel Proust**,

and briefly taught French. In 1937, after living in England, France, and Germany, Beckett made Paris his permanent home. During the Second World War, Beckett worked for the French Resistance, helping to collate intelligence reports from occupied France. Nearly discovered by the Nazis, he fled south to Roussillon, where he remained for the rest of the war. On a visit to his mother in Dublin after the war, Beckett experienced a revelation, seemingly connected with the concept of nothingness, that he recalled (in his characteristically elliptical way) in the later play *Krapp's Last Tape* (1958). In the scene the main character listens to a tape of his own voice recollecting an earlier vision:

> Spiritually a year of profound gloom and indigence until that memorable night in March, at the end of the jetty, in the howling wind, never to be forgotten, when suddenly I saw the whole thing. The vision, at last. . . . What I suddenly saw then was this, that the belief I had been going on all my life, namely—. . . that the dark I have always struggled to keep under is in reality my most . . .

Before this belief can be revealed, however, Krapp switches off the tape and winds it forward, so that the audience never learns the content of the revelation. Beckett later told his biographer that the missing words were "precious ally." Certainly, in the years after the war, Beckett made darkness his ally.

Although two highly amusing early novels, *Murphy* (1938) and *Watt* (published in 1953), were written in English, during the war Beckett turned to French as his preferred language for composition. In the years after the war, he wrote almost exclusively in French and only later translated the texts (often with substantial changes) into English. He explained his choice of language for creating his works: "in French it is easier to write without style"—without the native speaker's temptation to elegance and virtuoso display. Comparing the French and English versions of Beckett's works often suggests such a contrast, with the French text closer to basic grammatical forms and therefore possessing a harsher, starker focus. Indeed, Beckett claimed to care little about the formalities of language. "Grammar and Style," he wrote: "To me they seem to have become as irrelevant as a Victorian bathing suit or the imperturbability of a true gentleman. A mask. Let us hope the time will come . . . when language is most efficiently used where it is most efficiently misused." He sought a way to achieve a language of darkness, a language suitable to the postwar world in which old proprieties should be discarded in favor of a more austere, less artificial reality. Yet, as if against his will, he infused these dark and minimalist works with the wit and eloquence of his personal idiom. He later compared himself to his old friend Joyce: "The more Joyce knew the more he could. He's tending toward omniscience and omnipotence as an artist. I'm working with impotence, ignorance." The movement toward reductionism and minimalism helped to define postwar literature.

Beckett's first works in the spare style were a trilogy of novels, completed in 1949: *Molloy* (published in 1951), *Malone Dies* (1951), and *The Unnamable* (1953). The narrative perspective moves from a series of related monologues (in which a number of narrators, all of whose names begin with "M," come increasingly to resemble one another) to the ramblings, at the end, of an "unnamable" speaker who seems to represent them all. The reader can never be sure who is speaking, whether what the narrator is saying is true in the fictional world, or what the relationships among the various narrators might be. Beckett's early fiction received admiring attention from the philosopher Jean-Paul Sartre, among others, but Beckett's true fame came suddenly with the production of his first play, *Waiting for Godot* (published in 1952), first in French (1953), then in English (1955). The play's popularity showed that absurdist theater— with its empty, repetitive dialogue, its grotesquely bare yet evidently symbolic settings, and its refusal to build to a dramatic climax—could have meaning even for audiences accustomed to theatrical realism and logical plots. The audiences encountered two clownlike tramps, Vladimir and Estragon (Didi and Gogo), talking, quarreling, falling down, contemplating suicide, and generally filling up time with conversation that ranges from vaudeville patter to metaphysical speculation as they wait under a tree for "Godot," who never comes. Instead, the two are joined by another grotesque pair: the rich Pozzo and his brutally abused servant, Lucky, whom he leads around by a rope tied to the neck. As the first act comes to an end, Vladimir and Estragon agree to give up waiting, to leave; yet as the curtain falls, they stay where they were. A plot summary of the second act would be virtually identical with a summary of the first. As one critic put it, in *Waiting for Godot*, "nothing happens, twice." The popular interpretation of "Godot" as a diminutive for "God," and of the play as a statement of existential anguish at the inexplicable human condition, is scarcely defused by Beckett's caution that "If by Godot I had meant God, I would have said God." Yet identifying Godot is less important than identifying the wretched plight on stage as symbolically our own, and identifying *with* the characters as they express the anxious, often repugnant, but also comic picture of human relationships in an absurd universe. Both *Waiting for Godot* and *Endgame* draw on the full resources of modern theater while stripping the elements of traditional theater—plot, character, setting, dialogue—to a minimum.

After the popular success of *Waiting for Godot*, Beckett wrote *Endgame* (French version performed 1957; English, 1958) and a series of stage plays and brief pieces for the radio. The stage plays have the same bare yet striking settings: *Krapp's Last Tape* presents an old man sitting at a table with his tape recorder, recalling a love affair thirty years past; *Happy Days* (1961) portrays a married couple, with the wife chattering ceaselessly about her possessions, although she is buried in dirt up to her waist in the first act and up to her neck in the second. When he received the Nobel Prize for Literature in 1969, Beckett's wife declared the prize a "catastrophe" and another friend advised him to go into hiding—he was now a world-famous author, much sought after by admirers. In later years he wrote a number of shorter plays and novels, moving in the direction he had identified as distinguishing him from Joyce: toward minimalism, ignorance, and impotence. An unidentified voice in one of his final novellas, *Worstward Ho* (1983), says, "Fail again. Fail better." Beckett continued to produce successful works about failure for the rest of his long life. He died in a nursing home at the age of 83. The Nobel Prize conferred recognition on Beckett as the purest exponent of the twentieth century's chief philosophical dilemma: the notion of the "absurd," or the contradiction between human attempts to discover meaning in life and the simultaneous conviction that no "meaning" exists that we have not created ourselves.

Endgame, the play printed here, often called Beckett's major achievement, is a prime example of this dilemma. When the curtain rises on *Endgame*, the world seems to awaken from sleep. The sheets draping the furniture and central character are taken off, and Hamm sets himself in motion like an actor or a chess pawn: "Me . . . to play." Yet we are also near the story's end, for, as the title implies, nothing new will happen. An "endgame" is the final phase of a chess game, the stage at which the end is predictably in sight although the play must still be completed. Throughout, the theme of "end," "finish," "no more" resounds, even while Hamm notes the passage of time: "Something is taking its course." But time does not lead anywhere; it is either past or present and always barren. The past exists as Nagg's and Nell's memories, as Hamm's story, which may or may not describe Clov's entry into the home, and as a period when Clov once loved Hamm. The present shows four characters dwindling away, alone in a dead world, caught between bleak visions of hell and dreams of life reborn. In one of the biblical echoes that permeate the play, Hamm and Clov repeatedly evoke the final words of the crucified Jesus in the Gospel according to John: "It is finished." But this is not a biblical morality play, and *Endgame* describes a world not of divine creation but of self-creation. It is even possible that Hamm is composing and directing the entire performance: he is a storyteller and playwright with "asides" and "last soliloquy" whose "dialogue" keeps Clov onstage against his will, who (when looking out the window onto a clearly flourishing world) can see only dust and ashes, or a magician presiding over an imaginary kingdom who concludes a personal narrative and hopeless prayer with Prospero's line from Shakespeare's *The Tempest* (4.1.148): "Our revels now are ended." Or perhaps Hamm is simply the only character who is aware of his or her life *as* a performance, without other meaning. (As Shakespeare's passage continues later, "We are such stuff / As dreams are made on, and our little life / Is rounded with a sleep.") By the end of the play, the situation has changed little: it just becomes barer, as Hamm discards his stick, whistle, and dog, "reckoning closed and story ended." Yet as Hamm covers his face after this line, Clov is still waiting to depart rather than actually departing. It is not impossible that the play will resume in precisely the same terms tomorrow.

Like *Waiting for Godot*, *Endgame* has been given a number of interpretations. Some refer to Beckett's love of wordplay: Hamm as Hamm-actor, Hammlet, Hammer. The setting of a boxlike room with two windows is seen as a skull, the seat of consciousness, or (emphasizing the bloody handkerchief and the reference to fontanelles—the soft spot in the skull of a newborn) as a womb. The characters' isolation in a dead world after an unnamed catastrophe (which may be Hamm's fault) suggests the world after atomic holocaust. Or, for those who recall Beckett's fascination with the apathetic figure of Belacqua waiting, in the Purgatory of Dante's *Divine Comedy*, for his punishment to begin, *Endgame* evokes an image of pre-Purgatorial consciousness. The ash cans in which Hamm has "bottled" his parents, and the general cruelty between characters, may represent the dustbin of modern Western civilized values (while they also offer a sort of slapstick humor). Hamm and Clov represent the uneasy adjustment of soul and body, the class struggle of rich and poor, or the master-slave relationship in all senses (including the slave's acceptance of victimization). Clearly Beckett has created a

structure that accommodates all these readings while authorizing none. He himself said to the director Alan Schneider that he was less interested in symbolism than in describing a "local situation," an interaction of four characters in a given set of circumstances, and that the audience's interpretation was its own responsibility.

Beckett both authorized and denied these interpretations. He pruned down an earlier, more anecdotal two-act play to achieve *Endgame*'s skeletal plot and almost anonymous characters, and in doing so, created a structure that immediately elicits the reader's instinct to "fill in the blanks." His puns and allusions point to a further meaning that *may* be contained in the implied reference but may also be part of an infinite regress of meaning—expressing the "absurd" itself. Working against too heavy an insistence on symbolic meanings is the fact that the play is funny—especially when performed on stage. The characters popping out of ash cans; the jerky, repetitive motions with which Clov carries out his master's commands; and the often obscene vaudeville patter accompanied by appropriate gestures—all provide a comic perspective that keeps *Endgame* from sinking into tragic despair. The intellectual distance offered by comedy is entirely in keeping with the more somber side of the play, which rejects pathos and constantly drags its characters' escapist fancies down to the minimal facts of survival: food, shelter, sleep, painkiller. Thus it is possible to say that *Endgame* describes—but only among many other things—what it is like to be alive, declining toward death in a world without meaning.

Endgame[1]

For Roger Blin

CHARACTERS

NAGG
NELL
HAMM
CLOV

Bare interior.
Gray light.
Left and right back, high up, two small windows, curtains drawn.
Front right, a door. Hanging near door, its face to wall, a picture.
Front left, touching each other, covered with an old sheet, two ashbins.
Center, in an armchair on castors, covered with an old sheet, HAMM.
Motionless by the door, his eyes fixed on HAMM, CLOV. *Very red face.*
Brief tableau.

[CLOV *goes and stands under window left. Stiff, staggering walk. He looks up at window left. He turns and looks at window right. He goes and stands under window right. He looks up at window right. He turns and looks at window left. He goes out, comes back immediately with a small step-ladder, carries it over and sets it down under window left, gets up on it, draws back curtain. He gets down, takes six steps (for example) towards window right, goes back for ladder, carries it over and sets it down under window right, gets up on it, draws back curtain. He gets down, takes three steps towards window right, goes back for ladder, carries it over and sets it down under window left, gets up on it, looks out of window. Brief laugh. He gets down, takes one step towards window right, goes back for ladder, carries it over and sets it down under window right, gets up on it, looks out of window. Brief laugh. He gets down, goes with ladder towards ashbins, halts, turns, carries back ladder and sets it down under window right, goes to ashbins, removes sheet covering them, folds it over his arm. He raises one lid, stoops and looks into bin. Brief laugh. He closes lid. Same with other bin. He goes to* HAMM, *removes sheet covering him, folds it over his arm. In a dressing-gown, a stiff toque[2] on his head, a large blood-stained handkerchief over his face, a whistle hanging from his neck, a rug over his knees, thick socks on his feet,* HAMM *seems to be asleep.* CLOV *looks him over. Brief laugh. He goes to door, halts, turns towards auditorium.*]

CLOV [*Fixed gaze, tonelessly.*]   Finished, it's finished, nearly finished, it must be nearly finished. [*Pause.*] Grain upon grain, one by one, and one day, suddenly, there's a heap, a little heap, the impossible heap. [*Pause.*] I can't be punished any more. [*Pause.*] I'll go now to my kitchen, ten feet by ten feet by ten feet, and wait for him to whistle me. [*Pause.*] Nice dimensions, nice proportions, I'll lean on the table, and look at the wall, and wait for him to whistle me.

　　　[*He remains a moment motionless, then goes out. He comes back immediately, goes to window right, takes up the ladder and carries it out. Pause.*

---

1. Translated by the author.
2. A fitted cloth hat with little or no brim, sometimes indicating official status, as with a judge's toque.

HAMM *stirs. He yawns under the handkerchief. He removes the handkerchief from his face. Very red face. Black glasses.*]

HAMM   Me— [*He yawns.*] —to play[3] [*He holds the handkerchief spread out before him.*] Old Stancher![4] [*He takes off his glasses, wipes his eyes, his face, the glasses, puts them on again, folds the handkerchief and puts it back neatly in the breast-pocket of his dressing-gown. He clears his throat, joins the tips of his fingers.*] Can there be misery— [*He yawns.*] —loftier than mine? No doubt. Formerly. But now? [*Pause.*] My father? [*Pause.*] My mother? [*Pause.*] My . . . dog? [*Pause.*] Oh I am willing to believe they suffer as much as such creatures can suffer. But does that mean their sufferings equal mine? No doubt. [*Pause.*] No, all is a— [*He yawns.*] —bsolute, [*Proudly.*] the bigger a man is the fuller he is. [*Pause. Gloomily.*] And the emptier. [*He sniffs.*] Clov! [*Pause.*] No, alone. [*Pause.*] What dreams! Those forests! [*Pause.*] Enough, it's time it ended, in the shelter too. [*Pause.*] And yet I hesitate, I hesitate to . . . to end. Yes, there it is, it's time it ended and yet I hesitate to— [*He yawns.*] —to end. [*Yawns.*] God, I'm tired, I'd be better off in bed. [*He whistles. Enter* CLOV *immediately. He halts beside the chair.*] You pollute the air! [*Pause.*] Get me ready, I'm going to bed.

CLOV   I've just got you up.

HAMM   And what of it?

CLOV   I can't be getting you up and putting you to bed every five minutes, I have things to do. [*Pause.*]

HAMM   Did you ever see my eyes?

CLOV   No.

HAMM   Did you never have the curiosity, while I was sleeping, to take off my glasses and look at my eyes?

CLOV   Pulling back the lids? [*Pause.*] No.

HAMM   One of these days I'll show them to you. [*Pause.*] It seems they've gone all white. [*Pause.*] What time is it?

CLOV   The same as usual.

HAMM   [*Gesture towards window right.*]   Have you looked?

CLOV   Yes.

HAMM   Well?

CLOV   Zero.

HAMM   It'd need to rain.

CLOV   It won't rain. [*Pause.*]

HAMM   Apart from that, how do you feel?

CLOV   I don't complain.

HAMM   You feel normal?

CLOV [*Irritably.*]   I tell you I don't complain.

HAMM   I feel a little queer. [*Pause.*] Clov!

CLOV   Yes.

HAMM   Have you not had enough?

CLOV   Yes! [*Pause.*] Of what?

---

3. Hamm announces that it is his move at the beginning of *Endgame*: the comparison is with a game of chess, of which the "endgame" is the final stage.

4. The handkerchief that stanches his blood.

HAMM   Of this . . . this . . . thing.

CLOV   I always had. [*Pause.*] Not you?

HAMM [*Gloomily.*]   Then there's no reason for it to change.

CLOV   It may end. [*Pause.*] All life long the same questions, the same answers.

HAMM   Get me ready. [CLOV *does not move.*] Go and get the sheet. [CLOV *does not move.*] Clov!

CLOV   Yes.

HAMM   I'll give you nothing more to eat.

CLOV   Then we'll die.

HAMM   I'll give you just enough to keep you from dying. You'll be hungry all the time.

CLOV   Then we won't die. [*Pause.*] I'll go and get the sheet. [*He goes towards the door.*]

HAMM   No! [CLOV *halts.*] I'll give you one biscuit per day. [*Pause.*] One and a half. [*Pause.*] Why do you stay with me?

CLOV   Why do you keep me?

HAMM   There's no one else.

CLOV   There's nowhere else. [*Pause.*]

HAMM   You're leaving me all the same.

CLOV   I'm trying.

HAMM   You don't love me.

CLOV   No.

HAMM   You loved me once.

CLOV   Once!

HAMM   I've made you suffer too much. [*Pause.*] Haven't I?

CLOV   It's not that.

HAMM [*Shocked.*]   I haven't made you suffer too much?

CLOV   Yes!

HAMM [*Relieved.*]   Ah you gave me a fright! [*Pause. Coldly.*] Forgive me. [*Pause. Louder.*] I said, Forgive me.

CLOV   I heard you. [*Pause.*] Have you bled?

HAMM   Less. [*Pause.*] Is it not time for my pain-killer?

CLOV   No. [*Pause.*]

HAMM   How are your eyes?

CLOV   Bad.

HAMM   How are your legs?

CLOV   BAD.

HAMM   But you can move.

CLOV   Yes.

HAMM [*Violently.*]   Then move! [CLOV *goes to back wall, leans against it with his forehead and hands.*] Where are you?

CLOV   Here.

HAMM   Come back! [CLOV *returns to his place beside the chair.*] Where are you?

CLOV   Here.

HAMM   Why don't you kill me?

CLOV   I don't know the combination of the cupboard. [*Pause.*]

HAMM   Go and get two bicycle-wheels.

CLOV   There are no more bicycle-wheels.

HAMM   What have you done with your bicycle?

CLOV   I never had a bicycle.

HAMM   The thing is impossible.

CLOV   When there were still bicycles I wept to have one. I crawled at your feet. You told me to go to hell. Now there are none.

HAMM   And your rounds? When you inspected my paupers. Always on foot?

CLOV   Sometimes on horse. [*The lid of one of the bins lifts and the hands of* NAGG *appear, gripping the rim. Then his head emerges. Nightcap. Very white face.* NAGG *yawns, then listens.*] I'll leave you, I have things to do.

HAMM   In your kitchen?

CLOV   Yes.

HAMM   Outside of here it's death. [*Pause.*] All right, be off. [*Exit* CLOV. *Pause.*] We're getting on.

NAGG   Me pap![5]

HAMM   Accursed progenitor!

NAGG   Me pap!

HAMM   The old folks at home! No decency left! Guzzle, guzzle, that's all they think of. [*He whistles. Enter* CLOV. *He halts beside the chair.*] Well! I thought you were leaving me.

CLOV   Oh not just yet, not just yet.

NAGG   Me pap!

HAMM   Give him his pap.

CLOV   There's no more pap.

HAMM   [*To* NAGG.]   Do you hear that? There's no more pap. You'll never get any more pap.

NAGG   I want me pap!

HAMM   Give him a biscuit. [*Exit* CLOV.] Accursed fornicator! How are your stumps?

NAGG   Never mind me stumps.

[*Enter* CLOV *with biscuit.*]

CLOV   I'm back again, with the biscuit. [*He gives biscuit to* NAGG *who fingers it, sniffs it.*]

NAGG   [*Plaintively.*] What is it?

CLOV   Spratt's medium.[6]

NAGG [*As before.*]   It's hard! I can't!

HAMM   Bottle him!

[CLOV *pushes* NAGG *back into the bin, closes the lid.*]

CLOV [*Returning to his place beside the chair.*]   If age but knew!

HAMM   Sit on him!

CLOV   I can't sit.

HAMM   True. And I can't stand.

CLOV   So it is.

HAMM   Every man his speciality. [*Pause.*] No phone calls? [*Pause.*] Don't we laugh?

5. Food, mush.
6. A common plain cookie.

CLOV [*After reflection.*]   I don't feel like it.

HAMM [*After reflection.*]   Nor I. [*Pause.*] Clov!

CLOV   Yes.

HAMM   Nature has forgotten us.

CLOV   There's no more nature.

HAMM   No more nature! You exaggerate.

CLOV   In the vicinity.

HAMM   But we breathe, we change! We lose our hair, our teeth! Our bloom! Our ideals!

CLOV   Then she hasn't forgotten us.

HAMM   But you say there is none.

CLOV [*Sadly.*]   No one that ever lived ever thought so crooked as we.

HAMM   We do what we can.

CLOV   We shouldn't. [*Pause.*]

HAMM   You're a bit of all right, aren't you?[7]

CLOV   A smithereen.[8] [*Pause.*]

HAMM   This is slow work. [*Pause.*] Is it not time for my pain-killer?

CLOV   No. [*Pause.*] I'll leave you, I have things to do.

HAMM   In your kitchen?

CLOV   Yes.

HAMM   What, I'd like to know.

CLOV   I look at the wall.

HAMM   The wall! And what do you see on your wall? Mene, mene?[9] Naked bodies?

CLOV   I see my light dying.

HAMM   Your light dying! Listen to that! Well, it can die just as well here, *your* light. Take a look at me and then come back and tell me what you think of *your* light. [*Pause.*]

CLOV   You shouldn't speak to me like that. [*Pause.*]

HAMM [*Coldly.*]   Forgive me. [*Pause. Louder.*] I said, Forgive me.

CLOV   I heard you.
[*The lid of* NAGG's *bin lifts. His hands appear, gripping the rim. Then his head emerges. In his mouth the biscuit. He listens.*]

HAMM   Did your seeds come up?

CLOV   No.

HAMM   Did you scratch round them to see if they had sprouted?

CLOV   They haven't sprouted.

HAMM   Perhaps it's still too early.

CLOV   If they were going to sprout they would have sprouted. [*Violently.*] They'll never sprout!
[*Pause.* NAGG *takes biscuit in his hand.*]

HAMM   This is not much fun. [*Pause.*] But that's always the way at the end of the day, isn't it, Clov?

CLOV   Always.

---

7. You're pretty good, aren't you? (British slang).
8. A tiny bit.
9. From Daniel 5.25: "Mene, mene, tekel, upharsin"; words written by a divine hand on the wall during the feast of Belshazzar, king of Babylon. They predict doom and tell the king "Thou art weighed in the balances, and art found wanting" (Daniel 5.27).

HAMM It's the end of the day like any other day, isn't it, Clov?

CLOV Looks like it. [*Pause.*]

HAMM [*Anguished.*] What's happening, what's happening?

CLOV Something is taking its course. [*Pause.*]

HAMM All right, be off. [*He leans back in his chair, remains motionless.* CLOV *does not move, heaves a great groaning sigh.* HAMM *sits up.*] I thought I told you to be off.

CLOV I'm trying. [*He goes to door, halts.*] Ever since I was whelped.
   [*Exit* CLOV.]

HAMM We're getting on.
   [*He leans back in his chair, remains motionless.* NAGG *knocks on the lid of the other bin. Pause. He knocks harder. The lid lifts and the hands of* NELL *appear, gripping the rim. Then her head emerges. Lace cap. Very white face.*]

NELL What is it, my pet? [*Pause.*] Time for love?

NAGG Were you asleep?

NELL Oh no!

NAGG Kiss me.

NELL We can't.

NAGG Try.
   [*Their heads strain towards each other, fail to meet, fall apart again.*]

NELL Why this farce, day after day? [*Pause.*]

NAGG I've lost me tooth.

NELL When?

NAGG I had it yesterday.

NELL [*Elegiac.*] Ah yesterday!
   [*They turn painfully towards each other.*]

NAGG Can you see me?

NELL Hardly. And you?

NAGG What?

NELL Can you see me?

NAGG Hardly.

NELL So much the better, so much the better.

NAGG Don't say that. [*Pause.*] Our sight has failed.

NELL Yes.
   [*Pause. They turn away from each other.*]

NAGG Can you hear me?

NELL Yes. And you?

NAGG Yes. [*Pause.*] Our hearing hasn't failed.

NELL Our what?

NAGG Our hearing.

NELL No. [*Pause.*] Have you anything else to say to me?

NAGG Do you remember—

NELL No.

NAGG When we crashed on our tandem[1] and lost our shanks.
   [*They laugh heartily.*]

NELL It was in the Ardennes.
   [*They laugh less heartily.*]

1. A bicycle built for two.

NAGG On the road to Sedan.[2] [*They laugh still less heartily.*] Are you cold?

NELL Yes, perished. And you?

NAGG [*Pause.*] I'm freezing. [*Pause.*] Do you want to go in?

NELL Yes.

NAGG Then go in. [NELL *does not move.*] Why don't you go in?

NELL I don't know. [*Pause.*]

NAGG Has he changed your sawdust?

NELL It isn't sawdust. [*Pause. Wearily.*] Can you not be a little accurate, Nagg?

NAGG Your sand then. It's not important.

NELL It is important. [*Pause.*]

NAGG It was sawdust once.

NELL Once!

NAGG And now it's sand. [*Pause.*] From the shore. [*Pause. Impatiently.*] Now it's sand he fetches from the shore.

NELL Now it's sand.

NAGG Has he changed yours?

NELL No.

NAGG Nor mine. [*Pause.*] I won't have it! [*Pause. Holding up the biscuit.*] Do you want a bit?

NELL No. [*Pause.*] Of what?

NAGG Biscuit. I've kept you half. [*He looks at the biscuit. Proudly.*] Three quarters. For you. Here. [*He proffers the biscuit.*] No? [*Pause.*] Do you not feel well?

HAMM [*Wearily.*] Quiet, quiet, you're keeping me awake. [*Pause.*] Talk softer. [*Pause.*] If I could sleep I might make love. I'd go into the woods. My eyes would see . . . the sky, the earth. I'd run, they wouldn't catch me. [*Pause.*] Nature! [*Pause.*] There's something dripping in my head. [*Pause.*] A heart, a heart in my head. [*Pause.*]

NAGG [*Soft.*] Do you hear him? A heart in his head! [*He chuckles cautiously.*]

NELL One mustn't laugh at those things, Nagg. Why must you always laugh at them?

NAGG Not so loud!

NELL [*Without lowering her voice.*] Nothing is funnier than unhappiness, I grant you that. But—

NAGG [*Shocked.*] Oh!

NELL Yes, yes, it's the most comical thing in the world. And we laugh, we laugh, with a will, in the beginning. But it's always the same thing. Yes, it's like the funny story we have heard too often, we still find it funny, but we don't laugh any more. [*Pause.*] Have you anything else to say to me?

NAGG No.

NELL Are you quite sure? [*Pause.*] Then I'll leave you.

NAGG Do you not want your biscuit? [*Pause.*] I'll keep it for you. [*Pause.*] I thought you were going to leave me.

NELL I am going to leave you.

NAGG Could you give me a scratch before you go?

---

2. Town in northern France where the French were defeated in the Franco-Prussian War (1870). Ardennes is a forest in northern France, the scene of bitter fighting in both world wars.

NELL   No. [*Pause.*] Where?

NAGG   In the back.

NELL   No. [*Pause.*] Rub yourself against the rim.

NAGG   It's lower down. In the hollow.

NELL   What hollow?

NAGG   The hollow! [*Pause.*] Could you not? [*Pause.*] Yesterday you scratched me there.

NELL   [*Elegiac.*]   Ah yesterday!

NAGG   Could you not? [*Pause.*] Would you like me to scratch you? [*Pause.*] Are you crying again?

NELL   I was trying. [*Pause.*]

HAMM   Perhaps it's a little vein. [*Pause.*]

NAGG   What was that he said?

NELL   Perhaps it's a little vein.

NAGG   What does that mean? [*Pause.*] That means nothing. [*Pause.*] Will I tell you the story of the tailor?

NELL   No. [*Pause.*] What for?

NAGG   To cheer you up.

NELL   It's not funny.

NAGG   It always made you laugh. [*Pause.*] The first time I thought you'd die.

NELL   It was on Lake Como.[3] [*Pause.*] One April afternoon. [*Pause.*] Can you believe it?

NAGG   What?

NELL   That we once went out rowing on Lake Como. [*Pause.*] One April afternoon.

NAGG   We had got engaged the day before.

NELL   Engaged!

NAGG   You were in such fits that we capsized. By rights we should have been drowned.

NELL   It was because I felt happy.

NAGG   [*Indignant.*]   It was not, it was not, it was my story and nothing else. Happy! Don't you laugh at it still? Every time I tell it. Happy!

NELL   It was deep, deep. And you could see down to the bottom. So white. So clean.

NAGG   Let me tell it again. [*Raconteur's voice.*] An Englishman, needing a pair of striped trousers in a hurry for the New Year festivities, goes to his tailor who takes his measurements. [*Tailor's voice.*] "That's the lot, come back in four days, I'll have it ready." Good. Four days later. [*Tailor's voice.*] "So sorry, come back in a week, I've made a mess of the seat." Good, that's all right, a neat seat can be very ticklish. A week later. [*Tailor's voice.*] "Frightfully sorry, come back in ten days. I've made a hash of the crotch." Good, can't be helped, a snug crotch is always a teaser. Ten days later. [*Tailor's voice.*] "Dreadfully sorry, come back in a fortnight, I've made a balls of the fly." Good, at a pinch, a smart fly is a stiff proposition. [*Pause. Normal voice.*] I never told it worse. [*Pause. Gloomy.*] I tell this story worse and worse. [*Pause. Raconteur's voice.*] Well, to make it short, the bluebells are

---

3. A large lake and tourist resort in northern Italy, near the Swiss border.

blowing and he ballockses[4] the buttonholes. [*Customer's voice.*] "God damn you to hell, Sir, no, it's indecent, there are limits! In six days, do you hear me, six days, God made the world. Yes Sir, no less Sir, the WORLD! And you are not bloody well capable of making me a pair of trousers in three months!" [*Tailor's voice, scandalized.*] "But my dear Sir, my dear Sir, look— [*Disdainful gesture, disgustedly.*] —at the world— [*Pause.*] and look— [*Loving gesture, proudly.*] —at my TROUSERS!"

> [*Pause. He looks at* NELL *who has remained impassive, her eyes unseeing, breaks into a high forced laugh, cuts it short, pokes his head towards* NELL, *launches his laugh again.*]

HAMM Silence!

> [NAGG *starts, cuts short his laugh.*]

NELL You could see down to the bottom.

HAMM [*Exasperated.*] Have you not finished? Will you never finish? [*With sudden fury.*] Will this never finish? [NAGG *disappears into his bin, closes the lid behind him.* NELL *does not move. Frenziedly.*] My kingdom for a nightman![5] [*He whistles. Enter* CLOV.] Clear away this muck! Chuck it in the sea!

> [CLOV *goes to bins, halts.*]

NELL So white.

HAMM What? What's she blathering about?

> [CLOV *stoops, takes* NELL's *hand, feels her pulse.*]

NELL [*To* CLOV.] Desert!

> [CLOV *lets go her hand, pushes her back in the bin, closes the lid.*]

CLOV [*Returning to his place beside the chair.*] She has no pulse.

HAMM What was she drivelling about?

CLOV She told me to go away, into the desert.

HAMM Damn busybody! Is that all?

CLOV No.

HAMM What else?

CLOV I didn't understand.

HAMM Have you bottled her?

CLOV Yes.

HAMM Are they both bottled?

CLOV Yes.

HAMM Screw down the lids. [CLOV *goes towards door.*] Time enough. [CLOV *halts.*] My anger subsides, I'd like to pee.

CLOV [*With alacrity.*] I'll go and get the catheter. [*He goes towards door.*]

HAMM Time enough. [CLOV *halts.*] Give me my pain-killer.

CLOV It's too soon. [*Pause.*] It's too soon on top of your tonic, it wouldn't act.

HAMM In the morning they brace you up and in the evening they calm you down. Unless it's the other way round. [*Pause.*] That old doctor, he's dead naturally?

CLOV He wasn't old.

HAMM But he's dead?

---

4. "Bollixes," botches.
5. Parody of Shakespeare's *Richard III*, where the defeated king seeks a horse to escape from the battlefield: "A horse! a horse! My kingdom for a horse!" (5.4.7).

CLOV Naturally. [*Pause.*] *You* ask *me* that? [*Pause.*]

HAMM Take me for a little turn. [CLOV *goes behind the chair and pushes it forward.*] Not too fast! [CLOV *pushes chair.*] Right round the world! [CLOV *pushes chair.*] Hug the walls, then back to the center again. [CLOV *pushes chair.*] I was right in the center, wasn't I?

CLOV [*Pushing.*] Yes.

HAMM We'd need a proper wheel-chair. With big wheels. Bicycle wheels! [*Pause.*] Are you hugging?

CLOV [*Pushing.*] Yes.

HAMM [*Groping for wall.*] It's a lie! Why do you lie to me?

CLOV [*Bearing closer to wall.*] There! There!

HAMM Stop! [CLOV *stops chair close to back wall.* HAMM *lays his hand against wall.*] Old wall! [*Pause.*] Beyond is the . . . other hell. [*Pause. Violently.*] Closer! Closer! Up against!

CLOV Take away your hand. [HAMM *withdraws his hand.* CLOV *rams chair against wall.*] There!

[HAMM *leans towards wall, applies his ear to it.*]

HAMM Do you hear? [*He strikes the wall with his knuckles.*] Do you hear? Hollow bricks! [*He strikes again.*] All that's hollow! [*Pause. He straightens up. Violently.*] That's enough. Back!

CLOV We haven't done the round.

HAMM Back to my place! [CLOV *pushes chair back to center.*] Is that my place?

CLOV Yes, that's your place.

HAMM Am I right in the center?

CLOV I'll measure it.

HAMM More or less! More or less!

CLOV [*Moving chair slightly.*] There!

HAMM I'm more or less in the center?

CLOV I'd say so.

HAMM You'd say so! Put me right in the center!

CLOV I'll go and get the tape.

HAMM Roughly! Roughly! [CLOV *moves chair slightly.*] Bang in the center!

CLOV There! [*Pause.*]

HAMM I feel a little too far to the left. [CLOV *moves chair slightly.*] Now I feel a little too far to the right. [CLOV *moves chair slightly.*] I feel a little too far forward. [CLOV *moves chair slightly.*] Now I feel a little too far back. [CLOV *moves chair slightly.*] Don't stay there, [*i.e., behind the chair*] you give me the shivers.

[CLOV *returns to his place beside the chair.*]

CLOV If I could kill him I'd die happy. [*Pause.*]

HAMM What's the weather like?

CLOV As usual.

HAMM Look at the earth.

CLOV I've looked.

HAMM With the glass?

CLOV No need of the glass.

HAMM Look at it with the glass.

CLOV I'll go and get the glass.

[*Exit* CLOV.]

HAMM   No need of the glass!

[*Enter* CLOV *with telescope.*]

CLOV   I'm back again, with the glass. [*He goes to window right, looks up at it.*] I need the steps.

HAMM   Why? Have you shrunk? [*Exit* CLOV *with telescope.*] I don't like that, I don't like that.

[*Enter* CLOV *with ladder, but without telescope.*]

CLOV   I'm back again, with the steps. [*He sets down ladder under window right, gets up on it, realizes he has not the telescope, gets down.*] I need the glass. [*He goes towards door.*]

HAMM   [*Violently.*]   But you have the glass!

CLOV   [*Halting, violently.*]   No, I haven't the glass!

[*Exit* CLOV.]

HAMM   This is deadly.

[*Enter* CLOV *with telescope. He goes towards ladder.*]

CLOV   Things are livening up. [*He gets up on ladder, raises the telescope, lets it fall.*] I did it on purpose. [*He gets down, picks up the telescope, turns it on auditorium.*] I see . . . a multitude . . . in transports . . . of joy.[6] [*Pause.*] That's what I call a magnifier. [*He lowers the telescope, turns towards* HAMM.] Well? Don't we laugh?

HAMM   [*After reflection.*]   I don't.

CLOV   [*After reflection.*]   Nor I. [*He gets up on ladder, turns the telescope on the without.*] Let's see. [*He looks, moving the telescope.*] Zero . . . [*he looks*] . . . zero . . . [*he looks*] . . . and zero.

HAMM   Nothing stirs. All is—

CLOV   Zer—

HAMM   [*Violently.*]   Wait till you're spoke to! [*Normal voice.*] All is . . . all is . . . all is what? [*Violently.*] All is what?

CLOV   What all is? In a word? Is that what you want to know? Just a moment. [*He turns the telescope on the without, looks, lowers the telescope, turns towards* HAMM.] Corpsed. [*Pause.*] Well? Content?

HAMM   Look at the sea.

CLOV   It's the same.

HAMM   Look at the ocean!

[CLOV *gets down, takes a few steps towards window left, goes back for ladder, carries it over and sets it down under window left, gets up on it, turns the telescope on the without, looks at length. He starts, lowers the telescope, examines it, turns it again on the without.*]

CLOV   Never seen anything like that!

HAMM   [*Anxious.*]   What? A sail? A fin? Smoke?

CLOV   [*Looking.*]   The light is sunk.

HAMM   [*Relieved.*]   Pah! We all knew that.

CLOV   [*Looking.*]   There was a bit left.

HAMM   The base.

CLOV   [*Looking.*]   Yes.

HAMM   And now?

6. Echo of Revelation 7.9–10: "After this I beheld, and, lo, a great multitude, which . . . cried with a loud voice, saying, Salvation."

CLOV [*Looking.*] All gone.

HAMM No gulls?

CLOV [*Looking.*] Gulls!

HAMM And the horizon? Nothing on the horizon?

CLOV [*Lowering the telescope, turning towards* HAMM, *exasperated.*] What in God's name could there be on the horizon? [*Pause.*]

HAMM The waves, how are the waves?

CLOV The waves? [*He turns the telescope on the waves.*] Lead.

HAMM And the sun?

CLOV [*Looking.*] Zero.

HAMM But it should be sinking. Look again.

CLOV [*Looking.*] Damn the sun.

HAMM Is it night already then?

CLOV [*Looking.*] No.

HAMM Then what is it?

CLOV [*Looking.*] Gray. [*Lowering the telescope, turning towards* HAMM, *louder.*] Gray! [*Pause. Still louder.*] GRRAY! [*Pause. He gets down, approaches* HAMM *from behind, whispers in his ear.*]

HAMM [*Starting.*] Gray! Did I hear you say gray?

CLOV Light black. From pole to pole.

HAMM You exaggerate. [*Pause.*] Don't stay there, you give me the shivers.
    [CLOV *returns to his place beside the chair.*]

CLOV Why this farce, day after day?

HAMM Routine. One never knows. [*Pause.*] Last night I saw inside my breast. There was a big sore.

CLOV Pah! You saw your heart.

HAMM No, it was living. [*Pause. Anguished.*] Clov!

CLOV Yes.

HAMM What's happening?

CLOV Something is taking its course. [*Pause.*]

HAMM Clov!

CLOV [*Impatiently.*] What is it?

HAMM We're not beginning to . . . to . . . mean something?

CLOV Mean something! You and I, mean something! [*Brief laugh.*] Ah that's a good one!

HAMM I wonder. [*Pause.*] Imagine if a rational being came back to earth, wouldn't he be liable to get ideas into his head if he observed us long enough. [*Voice of rational being.*] Ah, good, now I see what it is, yes, now I understand what they're at! [CLOV *starts, drops the telescope and begins to scratch his belly with both hands. Normal voice.*] And without going so far as that, we ourselves . . . [*With emotion.*] . . . we ourselves . . . at certain moments . . . [*Vehemently.*] To think perhaps it won't all have been for nothing!

CLOV [*Anguished, scratching himself.*] I have a flea!

HAMM A flea! Are there still fleas?

CLOV On me there's one. [*Scratching.*] Unless it's a crablouse.

HAMM [*Very perturbed.*] But humanity might start from there all over again! Catch him, for the love of God!

CLOV I'll go and get the powder.
    [*Exit* CLOV.]

HAMM A flea! This is awful! What a day!

[*Enter* CLOV *with a sprinkling-tin.*]

CLOV I'm back again, with the insecticide.

HAMM Let him have it!

[CLOV *loosens the top of his trousers, pulls it forward and shakes powder into the aperture. He stoops, looks, waits, starts, frenziedly shakes more powder, stoops, looks, waits.*]

CLOV The bastard!

HAMM Did you get him?

CLOV Looks like it. [*He drops the tin and adjusts his trousers.*] Unless he's laying doggo.

HAMM Laying! Lying you mean. Unless he's *lying* doggo.

CLOV Ah? One says lying? One doesn't say laying?

HAMM Use your head, can't you. If he was laying we'd be bitched.

CLOV Ah. [*Pause.*] What about that pee?

HAMM I'm having it.

CLOV Ah that's the spirit, that's the spirit! [*Pause.*]

HAMM [*With ardour.*] Let's go from here, the two of us! South! You can make a raft and the currents will carry us away, far away, to other . . . mammals!

CLOV God forbid!

HAMM Alone, I'll embark alone! Get working on that raft immediately. Tomorrow I'll be gone for ever.

CLOV [*Hastening towards door.*] I'll start straight away.

HAMM Wait! [CLOV *halts.*] Will there be sharks, do you think?

CLOV Sharks? I don't know. If there are there will be. [*He goes towards door.*]

HAMM Wait! [CLOV *halts.*] Is it not yet time for my pain-killer?

CLOV [*Violently.*] No! [*He goes towards door.*]

HAMM Wait! [CLOV *halts.*] How are your eyes?

CLOV Bad.

HAMM But you can see.

CLOV All I want.

HAMM How are your legs?

CLOV Bad.

HAMM But you can walk.

CLOV I come . . . and go.

HAMM In my house. [*Pause. With prophetic relish.*] One day you'll be blind, like me. You'll be sitting there, a speck in the void, in the dark, for ever, like me. [*Pause.*] One day you'll say to yourself, I'm tired, I'll sit down, and you'll go and sit down. Then you'll say, I'm hungry, I'll get up and get something to eat. But you won't get up. You'll say, I shouldn't have sat down, but since I have I'll sit on a little longer, then I'll get up and get something to eat. But you won't get up and you won't get anything to eat. [*Pause.*] You'll look at the wall awhile, then you'll say, I'll close my eyes, perhaps have a little sleep, after that I'll feel better, and you'll close them. And when you open them again there'll be no wall any more. [*Pause.*] Infinite emptiness will be all around you, all the resurrected dead of all the ages wouldn't fill it, and there you'll be like a little bit of grit in the middle of the steppe. [*Pause.*] Yes, one day you'll know what it is, you'll be like me, except that you won't have anyone with you, because you won't have had pity on anyone and because there won't be anyone left to have pity on. [*Pause.*]

CLOV   It's not certain. [*Pause.*] And there's one thing you forget.

HAMM   Ah?

CLOV   I can't sit down.

HAMM [*Impatiently.*]   Well you'll lie down then, what the hell! Or you'll come to a standstill, simply stop and stand still, the way you are now. One day you'll say, I'm tired, I'll stop. What does the attitude matter? [*Pause.*]

CLOV   So you all want me to leave you.

HAMM   Naturally.

CLOV   Then I'll leave you.

HAMM   You can't leave us.

CLOV   Then I won't leave you. [*Pause.*]

HAMM   Why don't you finish us? [*Pause.*] I'll tell you the combination of the cupboard if you promise to finish me.

CLOV   I couldn't finish you.

HAMM   Then you won't finish me. [*Pause.*]

CLOV   I'll leave you, I have things to do.

HAMM   Do you remember when you came here?

CLOV   No. Too small, you told me.

HAMM   Do you remember your father?

CLOV [*Wearily.*]   Same answer. [*Pause.*] You've asked me these questions millions of times.

HAMM   I love the old questions. [*With fervor.*] Ah the old questions, the old answers, there's nothing like them! [*Pause.*] It was I was a father to you.

CLOV   Yes. [*He looks at* HAMM *fixedly.*] You were that to me.

HAMM   My house a home for you.

CLOV   Yes. [*He looks about him.*] This was that for me.

HAMM [*Proudly.*]   But for me, [*Gesture towards himself.*] no father. But for Hamm, [*Gesture towards surroundings.*] no home. [*Pause.*]

CLOV   I'll leave you.

HAMM   Did you ever think of one thing?

CLOV   Never.

HAMM   That here we're down in a hole. [*Pause.*] But beyond the hills? Eh? Perhaps it's still green. Eh? [*Pause.*] Flora! Pomona! [*Ecstatically.*] Ceres![7] [*Pause.*] Perhaps you won't need to go very far.

CLOV   I can't go very far. [*Pause.*] I'll leave you.

HAMM   Is my dog ready?

CLOV   He lacks a leg.

HAMM   Is he silky?

CLOV   He's a kind of Pomeranian.

HAMM   Go and get him.

CLOV   He lacks a leg.

HAMM   Go and get him! [*Exit* CLOV.] We're getting on.

[*Enter* CLOV *holding by one of its three legs a black toy dog.*]

CLOV   Your dogs are here. [*He hands the dog to* HAMM *who feels it, fondles it.*]

HAMM   He's white, isn't he?

---

7. In Roman mythology, the goddesses of flowers, fruits, and fertility.

CLOV Nearly.

HAMM What do you mean, nearly? Is he white or isn't he?

CLOV He isn't. [*Pause.*]

HAMM You've forgotten the sex.

CLOV [*Vexed.*] But he isn't finished. The sex goes on at the end. [*Pause.*]

HAMM You haven't put on his ribbon.

CLOV [*Angrily.*] But he isn't finished, I tell you! First you finish your dog and then you put on his ribbon! [*Pause.*]

HAMM Can he stand?

CLOV I don't know.

HAMM Try. [*He hands the dog to* CLOV *who places it on the ground.*] Well?

CLOV Wait! [*He squats down and tries to get the dog to stand on its three legs, fails, lets it go. The dog falls on its side.*]

HAMM [*Impatiently.*] Well?

CLOV He's standing.

HAMM [*Groping for the dog.*] Where? Where is he?

　　　[CLOV *holds up the dog in a standing position.*]

CLOV There. [*He takes* HAMM's *hand and guides it towards the dog's head.*]

HAMM [*His hand on the dog's head.*] Is he gazing at me?

CLOV Yes.

HAMM [*Proudly.*] As if he were asking me to take him for a walk?

CLOV If you like.

HAMM [*As before.*] Or as if he were begging me for a bone. [*He withdraws his hand.*] Leave him like that, standing there imploring me.

　　　[CLOV *straightens up. The dog falls on its side.*]

CLOV I'll leave you.

HAMM Have you had your visions?

CLOV Less.

HAMM Is Mother Pegg's light on?

CLOV Light! How could anyone's light be on?

HAMM Extinguished!

CLOV Naturally it's extinguished. If it's not on it's extinguished.

HAMM No, I mean Mother Pegg.

CLOV But naturally she's extinguished! [*Pause.*] What's the matter with you today?

HAMM I'm taking my course. [*Pause.*] Is she buried?

CLOV Buried! Who would have buried her?

HAMM You.

CLOV Me! Haven't I enough to do without burying people?

HAMM But you'll bury me.

CLOV No I won't bury you. [*Pause.*]

HAMM She was bonny once, like a flower of the field. [*With reminiscent leer.*] And a great one for the men!

CLOV We too were bonny—once. It's a rare thing not to have been bonny— once. [*Pause.*]

HAMM Go and get the gaff.[8]

　　　[CLOV *goes to door, halts.*]

---

8. A long stick with a hook, usually for catching fish.

CLOV   Do this, do that, and I do it. I never refuse. Why?

HAMM   You're not able to.

CLOV   Soon I won't do it any more.

HAMM   You won't be able to any more. [*Exit* CLOV.] Ah the creatures, the creatures, everything has to be explained to them.

[*Enter* CLOV *with gaff.*]

CLOV   Here's your gaff. Stick it up. [*He gives the gaff to* HAMM *who, wielding it like a puntpole, tries to move his chair.*]

HAMM   Did I move?

CLOV   No.

[HAMM *throws down the gaff.*]

HAMM   Go and get the oilcan.

CLOV   What for?

HAMM   To oil the castors.

CLOV   I oiled them yesterday.

HAMM   Yesterday! What does that mean? Yesterday!

CLOV [*Violently.*]   That means that bloody awful day, long ago, before this bloody awful day. I use the words you taught me. If they don't mean anything any more, teach me others. Or let me be silent. [*Pause.*]

HAMM   I once knew a madman who thought the end of the world had come. He was a painter—and engraver. I had a great fondness for him. I used to go and see him, in the asylum. I'd take him by the hand and drag him to the window. Look! There! All that rising corn! And there! Look! The sails of the herring fleet! All that loveliness! [*Pause.*] He'd snatch away his hand and go back into his corner. Appalled. All he had seen was ashes. [*Pause.*] He alone had been spared. [*Pause.*] Forgotten. [*Pause.*] It appears the case is . . . was not so . . . so unusual.

CLOV   A madman! When was that?

HAMM   Oh way back, way back, you weren't in the land of the living.

CLOV   God be with the days!

[*Pause.* HAMM *raises his toque.*]

HAMM   I had a great fondness for him. [*Pause. He puts on his toque again.*] He was a painter—and engraver.

CLOV   There are so many terrible things.

HAMM   No, no, there are not so many now. [*Pause.*] Clov!

CLOV   Yes.

HAMM   Do you not think this has gone on long enough?

CLOV   Yes! [*Pause.*] What?

HAMM   This . . . this . . . thing.

CLOV   I've always thought so. [*Pause.*] You not?

HAMM [*Gloomily.*]   Then it's a day like any other day.

CLOV   As long as it lasts. [*Pause.*] All life long the same inanities.

HAMM   I can't leave you.

CLOV   I know. And you can't follow me. [*Pause.*]

HAMM   If you leave me how shall I know?

CLOV [*Briskly.*]   Well you simply whistle me and if I don't come running it means I've left you. [*Pause.*]

HAMM   You won't come and kiss me goodbye?

CLOV   Oh I shouldn't think so. [*Pause.*]

HAMM   But you might be merely dead in your kitchen.

CLOV   The result would be the same.

HAMM   Yes, but how would I know, if you were merely dead in your kitchen?

CLOV   Well . . . sooner or later I'd start to stink.

HAMM   You stink already. The whole place stinks of corpses.

CLOV The whole universe.

HAMM   [*Angrily.*]   To hell with the universe. [*Pause.*] Think of something.

CLOV   What?

HAMM   An idea, have an idea. [*Angrily.*] A bright idea!

CLOV   Ah good. [*He starts pacing to and fro, his eyes fixed on the ground, his hands behind his back. He halts.*] The pains in my legs! It's unbelievable! Soon I won't be able to think any more.

HAMM   You won't be able to leave me. [CLOV *resumes his pacing.*] What are you doing?

CLOV   Having an idea. [*He paces.*] Ah! [*He halts.*]

HAMM   What a brain! [*Pause.*] Well?

CLOV   Wait! [*He meditates. Not very convinced.*] Yes . . . [*Pause. More convinced.*] Yes! [*He raises his head.*] I have it! I set the alarm. [*Pause.*]

HAMM   This is perhaps not one of my bright days, but frankly—

CLOV   You whistle me. I don't come. The alarm rings. I'm gone. It doesn't ring. I'm dead. [*Pause.*]

HAMM   Is it working? [*Pause. Impatiently.*] The alarm, is it working?

CLOV   Why wouldn't it be working?

HAMM   Because it's worked too much.

CLOV   But it's hardly worked at all.

HAMM   [*Angrily.*]   Then because it's worked too little!

CLOV   I'll go and see. [*Exit* CLOV. *Brief ring of alarm off. Enter* CLOV *with alarm-clock. He holds it against* HAMM's *ear and releases alarm. They listen to it ringing to the end. Pause.*] Fit to wake the dead! Did you hear it?

HAMM   Vaguely.

CLOV   The end is terrific!

HAMM   I prefer the middle. [*Pause.*] Is it not time for my pain-killer?

CLOV   No! [*He goes to door, turns.*] I'll leave you.

HAMM   It's time for my story. Do you want to listen to my story.

CLOV   No.

HAMM   Ask my father if he wants to listen to my story.

        [CLOV *goes to bins, raises the lid of* NAGG's, *stoops, looks into it. Pause. He straightens up.*]

CLOV   He's asleep.

HAMM   Wake him.

        [CLOV *stoops, wakes* NAGG *with the alarm. Unintelligible words.* CLOV *straightens up.*]

CLOV   He doesn't want to listen to your story.

HAMM   I'll give him a bon-bon.

        [CLOV *stoops. As before.*]

CLOV   He wants a sugar-plum.

HAMM   He'll get a sugar-plum.

        [CLOV *stoops. As before.*]

CLOV   It's a deal. [*He goes towards door.* NAGG's *hands appear, gripping the rim. Then the head emerges.* CLOV *reaches door, turns.*] Do you believe in the life to come?

HAMM Mine was always that. [*Exit* CLOV.] Got him that time!

NAGG I'm listening.

HAMM Scoundrel! Why did you engender me?

NAGG I didn't know.

HAMM What? What didn't you know?

NAGG That it'd be you. [*Pause.*] You'll give me a sugar-plum?

HAMM After the audition.

NAGG You swear?

HAMM Yes.

NAGG On what?

HAMM My honor.
[*Pause. They laugh heartily.*]

NAGG Two.

HAMM One.

NAGG One for me and one for—

HAMM One! Silence! [*Pause.*] Where was I? [*Pause. Gloomily.*] It's finished, we're finished. [*Pause.*] Nearly finished. [*Pause.*] There'll be no more speech. [*Pause.*] Something dripping in my head, ever since the fontanelles. [*Stifled hilarity of* NAGG.] Splash, splash, always on the same spot. [*Pause.*] Perhaps it's a little vein. [*Pause.*] A little artery. [*Pause. More animated.*] Enough of that, it's story time, where was I? [*Pause. Narrative tone.*] The man came crawling towards me, on his belly. Pale, wonderfully pale and thin, he seemed on the point of— [*Pause. Normal tone.*] No, I've done that bit. [*Pause. Narrative tone.*] I calmly filled my pipe—the meerschaum, lit it with . . . let us say a vesta, drew a few puffs. Aah! [*Pause.*] Well, what is it *you* want? [*Pause.*] It was an extraordinarily bitter day, I remember, zero by the thermometer. But considering it was Christmas Eve there was nothing . . . extra-ordinary about that. Seasonable weather, for once in a way. [*Pause.*] Well, what ill wind blows you my way? He raised his face to me, black with mingled dirt and tears. [*Pause. Normal tone.*] That should do it. [*Narrative tone.*] No, no, don't look at me, don't look at me. He dropped his eyes and mumbled something, apologies I presume. [*Pause.*] I'm a busy man, you know, the final touches, before the festivities, you know what it is. [*Pause. Forcibly.*] Come on now, what is the object of this invasion? [*Pause.*] It was a glorious bright day, I remember, fifty by the heliometer,[9] but already the sun was sinking down into the . . . down among the dead. [*Normal tone.*] Nicely put, that. [*Narrative tone.*] Come on now, come on, present your petition and let me resume my labors. [*Pause. Normal tone.*] There's English for you. Ah well . . . [*Narrative tone.*] It was then he took the plunge. It's my little one, he said. Tsstss, a little one, that's bad. My little boy, he said, as if the sex mattered. Where did he come from? He named the hole. A good half-day, on horse. What are you insinuating? That the place is still inhabited? No no, not a soul, except himself and the child—assuming he existed. Good. I enquired about the situation at Kov, beyond the gulf. Not a sinner. Good. And you expect me to believe you have left your little one back there, all alone, and alive into the bargain? Come now! [*Pause.*] It was a howling wild

9. Literally, a "sun meter." Ordinarily, a telescope used to measure distances between celestial bodies.

day, I remember, a hundred by the anemometer.[1] The wind was tearing up the dead pines and sweeping them . . . away. [*Pause. Normal tone.*] A bit feeble, that. [*Narrative tone.*] Come on, man, speak up, what is you want from me, I have to put up my holly. [*Pause.*] Well to make it short it finally transpired that what he wanted from me was . . . bread for his brat? Bread? But I have no bread, it doesn't agree with me. Good. Then perhaps a little corn? [*Pause. Normal tone.*] That should do it. [*Narrative tone.*] Corn, yes, I have corn, it's true, in my granaries. But use your head. I give you some corn, a pound, a pound and a half, you bring it back to your child and you make him—if he's still alive—a nice pot of porridge, [NAGG *reacts.*] a nice pot and a half of porridge, full of nourishment. Good. The colors come back into his little cheeks—perhaps. And then? [*Pause.*] I lost patience. [*Violently.*] Use your head, can't you, use your head, you're on earth, there's no cure for that! [*Pause.*] It was an exceedingly dry day, I remember, zero by the hygrometer.[2] Ideal weather, for my lumbago. [*Pause. Violently.*] But what in God's name do you imagine? That the earth will awake in spring? That the rivers and seas will run with fish again? That there's manna in heaven still for imbeciles like you? [*Pause.*] Gradually I cooled down, sufficiently at least to ask him how long he had taken on the way. Three whole days. Good. In what condition he had left the child. Deep in sleep. [*Forcibly.*] But deep in what sleep, deep in what sleep already? [*Pause.*] Well to make it short I finally offered to take him into my service. He had touched a chord. And then I imagined already that I wasn't much longer for this world. [*He laughs. Pause.*] Well? [*Pause.*] Well? Here if you were careful you might die a nice natural death, in peace and comfort. [*Pause.*] Well? [*Pause.*] In the end he asked me would I consent to take in the child as well—if he were still alive. [*Pause.*] It was the moment I was waiting for. [*Pause.*] Would I consent to take in the child . . . [*Pause.*] I can see him still, down on his knees, his hands flat on the ground, glaring at me with his mad eyes, in defiance of my wishes. [*Pause. Normal tone.*] I'll soon have finished with this story. [*Pause.*] Unless I bring in other characters. [*Pause.*] But where would I find them? [*Pause.*] Where would I look for them? [*Pause. He whistles. Enter* CLOV.] Let us pray to God.

NAGG   Me sugar-plum!
CLOV   There's a rat in the kitchen!
HAMM   A rat! Are there still rats?
CLOV   In the kitchen there's one.
HAMM   And you haven't exterminated him?
CLOV   Half. You disturbed us.
HAMM   He can't get away?
CLOV   No.
HAMM   You'll finish him later. Let us pray to God.
CLOV   Again!
NAGG   Me sugar-plum!
HAMM   God first! [*Pause.*] Are you right?
CLOV [*Resigned.*]   Off we go.

1. A wind meter.
2. A moisture meter.

HAMM [*To* NAGG.] And you?

NAGG [*Clasping his hands, closing his eyes, in a gabble.*] Our Father which art—

HAMM Silence! In silence! Where are your manners? [*Pause.*] Off we go. [*Attitudes of prayer. Silence. Abandoning his attitude, discouraged.*] Well?

CLOV [*Abandoning his attitude.*] What a hope! And you?

HAMM Sweet damn all! [*To* NAGG.] And you?

NAGG Wait! [*Pause. Abandoning his attitude.*] Nothing doing!

HAMM The bastard! He doesn't exist!

CLOV Not yet.

NAGG Me sugar-plum!

HAMM There are no more sugar-plums! [*Pause.*]

NAGG It's natural. After all I'm your father. It's true if it hadn't been me it would have been someone else. But that's no excuse. [*Pause.*] Turkish Delight,[3] for example, which no longer exists, we all know that, there is nothing in the world I love more. And one day I'll ask you for some, in return for a kindness, and you'll promise it to me. One must live with the times. [*Pause.*] Whom did you call when you were a tiny boy, and were frightened, in the dark? Your mother? No. Me. We let you cry. Then we moved you out of earshot, so that we might sleep in peace. [*Pause.*] I was asleep, as happy as a king, and you woke me up to have me listen to you. It wasn't indispensable, you didn't really need to have me listen to you. [*Pause.*] I hope the day will come when you'll really need to have me listen to you, and need to hear my voice, any voice. [*Pause.*] Yes, I hope I'll live till then, to hear you calling me like when you were a tiny boy, and were frightened, in the dark, and I was your only hope. [*Pause.* NAGG *knocks on lid of* NELL's *bin. Pause.*] Nell! [*Pause. He knocks louder. Pause. Louder.*] Nell! [*Pause.* NAGG *sinks back into his bin, closes the lid behind him. Pause.*]

HAMM Our revels now are ended.[4] [*He gropes for the dog.*] The dog's gone.

CLOV He's not a real dog, he can't go.

HAMM [*Groping.*] He's not there.

CLOV He's lain down.

HAMM Give him up to me. [CLOV *picks up the dog and gives it to* HAMM. HAMM *holds it in his arms. Pause.* HAMM *throws away the dog.*] Dirty brute! [CLOV *begins to pick up the objects lying on the ground.*] What are you doing?

CLOV Putting things in order. [*He straightens up. Fervently.*] I'm going to clear everything away! [*He starts picking up again.*]

HAMM Order!

CLOV [*Straightening up.*] I love order. It's my dream. A world where all would be silent and still and each thing in its last place, under the last dust. [*He starts picking up again.*]

HAMM [*Exasperated.*] What in God's name do you think you are doing?

CLOV [*Straightening up.*] I'm doing my best to create a little order.

HAMM Drop it! [CLOV *drops the objects he has picked up.*]

CLOV After all, there or elsewhere. [*He goes towards door.*]

---

3. A sticky sweet candy.
4. Lines spoken by Prospero in Shakespeare's *The Tempest* 4.1.148.

HAMM [*Irritably.*]   What's wrong with your feet?

CLOV   My feet?

HAMM   Tramp! Tramp!

CLOV   I must have put on my boots.

HAMM   Your slippers were hurting you? [*Pause.*]

CLOV   I'll leave you.

HAMM   No!

CLOV   What is there to keep me here?

HAMM   The dialogue. [*Pause.*] I've got on with my story. [*Pause.*] I've got on with it well. [*Pause. Irritably.*] Ask me where I've got to.

CLOV   Oh, by the way, your story?

HAMM [*Surprised.*]   What story?

CLOV   The one you've been telling yourself all your days.

HAMM   Ah you mean my chronicle?

CLOV   That's the one. [*Pause.*]

HAMM [*Angrily.*]   Keep going, can't you, keep going!

CLOV   You've got on with it, I hope.

HAMM [*Modestly.*]   Oh not very far, not very far. [*He sighs.*] There are days like that, one isn't inspired. [*Pause.*] Nothing you can do about it, just wait for it to come. [*Pause.*] No forcing, no forcing, it's fatal. [*Pause.*] I've got on with it a little all the same. [*Pause.*] Technique, you know. [*Pause. Irritably.*] I say I've got on with it a little all the same.

CLOV [*Admiringly.*]   Well I never! In spite of everything you were able to get on with it!

HAMM [*Modestly.*]   Oh not very far, you know, not very far, but nevertheless, better than nothing.

CLOV   Better than nothing! Is it possible?

HAMM   I'll tell you how it goes. He comes crawling on his belly—

CLOV   Who?

HAMM   What?

CLOV   Who do you mean, he?

HAMM   Who do I mean! Yet another.

CLOV   Ah him! I wasn't sure.

HAMM   Crawling on his belly, whining for bread for his brat. He's offered a job as gardener. Before— [CLOV *bursts out laughing.*] What is there so funny about that?

CLOV   A job as gardener!

HAMM   Is that what tickles you?

CLOV   It must be that.

HAMM   It wouldn't be the bread?

CLOV   Or the brat. [*Pause.*]

HAMM   The whole thing is comical, I grant you that. What about having a good guffaw the two of us together?

CLOV [*After reflection.*]   I couldn't guffaw again today.

HAMM [*After reflection.*]   Nor I. [*Pause.*] I continue then. Before accepting with gratitude he asks if he may have his little boy with him.

CLOV   What age?

HAMM   Oh tiny.

CLOV   He would have climbed the trees.

HAMM   All the little odd jobs.

CLOV   And then he would have grown up.

HAMM   Very likely. [*Pause.*]

CLOV   Keep going, can't you, keep going!

HAMM   That's all. I stopped there. [*Pause.*]

CLOV   Do you see how it goes on.

HAMM   More or less.

CLOV   Will it not soon be the end?

HAMM   I'm afraid it will.

CLOV   Pah! You'll make up another.

HAMM   I don't know. [*Pause.*] I feel rather drained. [*Pause.*] The prolonged creative effort. [*Pause.*] If I could drag myself down to the sea! I'd make a pillow of sand for my head and the tide would come.

CLOV   There's no more tide. [*Pause.*]

HAMM   Go and see is she dead.

[CLOV *goes to bins, raises the lid of* NELL's, *stoops, looks into it. Pause.*]

CLOV   Looks like it.

[*He closes the lid, straightens up.* HAMM *raises his toque. Pause. He puts it on again.*]

HAMM [*With his hand to his toque.*]   And Nagg?

[CLOV *raises lid of* NAGG's *bin, stoops, looks into it. Pause.*]

CLOV   Doesn't look like it. [*He closes the lid, straightens up.*]

HAMM [*Letting go his toque.*]   What's he doing? [CLOV *raises lid of* NAGG's *bin, stoops, looks into it. Pause.*]

CLOV   He's crying. [*He closes lid, straightens up.*]

HAMM   Then he's living. [*Pause.*] Did you ever have an instant of happiness?

CLOV   Not to my knowledge. [*Pause.*]

HAMM   Bring me under the window. [CLOV *goes towards chair.*] I want to feel the light on my face. [CLOV *pushes chair.*] Do you remember, in the beginning, when you took me for a turn? You used to hold the chair too high. At every step you nearly tipped me out. [*With senile quaver.*] Ah great fun, we had, the two of us, great fun. [*Gloomily.*] And then we got into the way of it. [CLOV *stops the chair under window right.*] There already? [*Pause. He tilts back his head.*] Is it light?

CLOV   It isn't dark.

HAMM [*Angrily.*]   I'm asking you is it light.

CLOV   Yes. [*Pause.*]

HAMM   The curtain isn't closed?

CLOV   No.

HAMM   What window is it?

CLOV   The earth.

HAMM   I knew it! [*Angrily.*] But there's no light there! The other! [CLOV *stops the chair under window left.* HAMM *tilts back his head.*] That's what I call light! [*Pause.*] Feels like a ray of sunshine. [*Pause.*] No?

CLOV   No.

HAMM   It isn't a ray of sunshine I feel on my face?

CLOV   No. [*Pause.*]

HAMM   Am I very white? [*Pause. Angrily.*] I'm asking you am I very white!

CLOV   Not more so than usual. [*Pause.*]

HAMM   Open the window.

CLOV   What for?

HAMM   I want to hear the sea.

CLOV   You wouldn't hear it.

HAMM   Even if you opened the window?

CLOV   No.

HAMM   Then it's not worth while opening it?

CLOV   No.

HAMM   [*Violently.*]   Then open it! [CLOV *gets up on the ladder, opens the window. Pause.*] Have you opened it?

CLOV   Yes. [*Pause.*]

HAMM   You swear you've opened it?

CLOV   Yes. [*Pause.*]

HAMM   Well . . . ! [*Pause.*] It must be very calm. [*Pause. Violently.*] I'm asking you is it very calm!

CLOV   Yes.

HAMM   It's because there are no more navigators. [*Pause.*] You haven't much conversation all of a sudden. Do you not feel well?

CLOV   I'm cold.

HAMM   What month are we? [*Pause.*] Close the window, we're going back. [CLOV *closes the window, gets down, pushes the chair back to its place, remains standing behind it, head bowed.*] Don't stay there, you give me the shivers! [CLOV *returns to his place beside the chair.*] Father! [*Pause. Louder.*] Father! [*Pause.*] Go and see did he hear me.

    [CLOV *goes to* NAGG's *bin, raises the lid, stoops. Unintelligible words.* CLOV *straightens up.*]

CLOV   Yes.

HAMM   Both times?

    [CLOV *stoops. As before.*]

CLOV   Once only.

HAMM   The first time or the second?

    [CLOV *stoops. As before.*]

CLOV   He doesn't know.

HAMM   It must have been the second.

CLOV   We'll never know. [*He closes lid.*]

HAMM   Is he still crying?

CLOV   No.

HAMM   The dead go fast. [*Pause.*] What's he doing?

CLOV   Sucking his biscuit.

HAMM   Life goes on. [CLOV *returns to his place beside the chair.*] Give me a rug. I'm freezing.

CLOV   There are no more rugs. [*Pause.*]

HAMM   Kiss me. [*Pause.*] Will you not kiss me?

CLOV   No.

HAMM   On the forehead.

CLOV   I won't kiss you anywhere. [*Pause.*]

HAMM   [*Holding out his hand.*]   Give me your hand at least. [*Pause.*] Will you not give me your hand?

CLOV   I won't touch you. [*Pause.*]

HAMM   Give me the dog. [CLOV *looks round for the dog.*] No!
CLOV   Do you not want your dog?
HAMM   No.
CLOV   Then I'll leave you.
HAMM   [*Head bowed, absently.*]   That's right.
       [CLOV *goes to door, turns.*]
CLOV   If I don't kill that rat he'll die.
HAMM   [*As before.*]   That's right. [*Exit* CLOV. *Pause.*] Me to play. [*He takes out his handkerchief, unfolds it, holds it spread out before him.*] We're getting on. [*Pause.*] You weep, and weep, for nothing, so as not to laugh, and little by little . . . you begin to grieve. [*He folds the handkerchief, puts it back in his pocket, raises his head.*] All those I might have helped. [*Pause.*] Helped! [*Pause.*] Saved. [*Pause.*] Saved! [*Pause.*] The place was crawling with them! [*Pause. Violently.*] Use your head, can't you, use your head, you're on earth, there's no cure for that! [*Pause.*] Get out of here and love one another! Lick your neighbor as yourself![5] [*Pause. Calmer.*] When it wasn't bread they wanted it was crumpets. [*Pause. Violently.*] Out of my sight and back to your petting parties! [*Pause.*] All that, all that! [*Pause.*] Not even a real dog! [*Calmer.*] The end is in the beginning and yet you go on. [*Pause.*] Perhaps I could go on with my story, end it and begin another. [*Pause.*] Perhaps I could throw myself out on the floor. [*He pushes himself painfully off his seat, falls back again.*] Dig my nails into the cracks and drag myself forward with my fingers. [*Pause.*] It will be the end and there I'll be, wondering what can have brought it on and wondering what can have . . . [*He hesitates.*] . . . why it was so long coming. [*Pause.*] There I'll be, in the old shelter, alone against the silence and . . . [*He hesitates.*] . . . the stillness. If I can hold my peace, and sit quiet, it will be all over with sound, and motion, all over and done with. [*Pause.*] I'll have called my father and I'll have called my . . . [*He hesitates.*] . . . my son. And even twice, or three times, in case they shouldn't have heard me, the first time, or the second. [*Pause.*] I'll say to myself, He'll come back. [*Pause.*] And then? [*Pause.*] And then? [*Pause.*] He couldn't, he has gone too far. [*Pause.*] And then? [*Pause. Very agitated.*] All kinds of fantasies! That I'm being watched! A rat! Steps! Breath held and then . . . [*He breathes out.*] Then babble, babble, words, like the solitary child who turns himself into children, two, three, so as to be together, and whisper together, in the dark. [*Pause.*] Moment upon moment, pattering down, like the millet grains of . . . [*He hesitates.*] . . . that old Greek,[6] and all life long you wait for that to mount up to a life. [*Pause. He opens his mouth to continue, renounces.*] Ah let's get it over! [*He whistles. Enter* CLOV *with alarm-clock. He halts beside the chair.*] What? Neither gone nor dead?
CLOV   In spirit only.
HAMM   Which?

---

5. Parody of Jesus' words in the Bible: "Thou shalt love thy neighbor as thyself" (Matthew 19.19).
6. Zeno of Elea, a Greek philosopher active around 450 B.C., known for logical paradoxes that reduce to absurdity various attempts to define *Being*. Aristotle reports that Zeno's paradox on sound questioned: If a grain of millet falling makes no sound, how can a bushel of grains make any sound? (Aristotle's *Physics* 5.250a.19).

CLOV   Both.

HAMM   Gone from me you'd be dead.

CLOV   And vice versa.

HAMM   Outside of here it's death! [*Pause.*] And the rat?

CLOV   He's got away.

HAMM   He can't go far. [*Pause. Anxious.*] Eh?

CLOV   He doesn't need to go far. [*Pause.*]

HAMM   Is it not time for my pain-killer?

CLOV   Yes.

HAMM   Ah! At last! Give it to me! Quick! [*Pause.*]

CLOV   There's no more pain-killer. [*Pause.*]

HAMM [*Appalled.*]   Good . . . ! [*Pause.*] No more pain-killer!

CLOV   No more pain-killer. You'll never get any more pain-killer. [*Pause.*]

HAMM   But the little round box. It was full!

CLOV   Yes. But now it's empty.

     [*Pause.* CLOV *starts to move about the room. He is looking for a place to put down the alarm-clock.*]

HAMM [*Soft.*]   What'll I do? [*Pause. In a scream.*] What'll I do? [CLOV *sees the picture, takes it down, stands it on the floor with its face to the wall, hangs up the alarm-clock in its place.*] What are you doing?

CLOV   Winding up.

HAMM   Look at the earth.

CLOV   Again!

HAMM   Since it's calling to you.

CLOV   Is your throat sore? [*Pause.*] Would you like a lozenge? [*Pause.*] No. [*Pause.*] Pity. [*He goes, humming, towards window right, halts before it, looks up at it.*]

HAMM   Don't sing.

CLOV [*Turning towards* HAMM.]   One hasn't the right to sing any more?

HAMM   No.

CLOV   Then how can it end?

HAMM   You want it to end?

CLOV   I want to sing.

HAMM   I can't prevent you.

     [*Pause.* CLOV *turns towards window right.*]

CLOV   What did I do with that steps? [*He looks around for ladder.*] You didn't see that steps? [*He sees it.*] Ah, about time. [*He goes towards window left.*] Sometimes I wonder if I'm in my right mind. Then it passes over and I'm as lucid as before. [*He gets up on ladder, looks out of window.*] Christ, she's under water! [*He looks.*] How can that be? [*He pokes forward his head, his hand above his eyes.*] It hasn't rained. [*He wipes the pane, looks. Pause.*] Ah what a fool I am! I'm on the wrong side! [*He gets down, takes a few steps towards window right.*] Under water! [*He goes back for ladder.*] What a fool I am! [*He carries ladder towards window right.*] Sometimes I wonder if I'm in my right senses. Then it passes off and I'm as intelligent as ever. [*He sets down ladder under window right, gets up on it, looks out of window. He turns towards* HAMM.] Any particular sector you fancy? Or merely the whole thing?

HAMM   Whole thing.

CLOV   The general effect? Just a moment. [*He looks out of window. Pause.*]

HAMM Clov.

CLOV [*Absorbed.*] Mmm.

HAMM Do you know what it is?

CLOV [*As before.*] Mmm.

HAMM I was never there. [*Pause.*] Clov!

CLOV [*Turning towards* HAMM, *exasperated.*] What is it?

HAMM I was never there.

CLOV Lucky for you. [*He looks out of window.*]

HAMM Absent, always. It all happened without me. I don't know what's happened. [*Pause.*] Do you know what's happened? [*Pause.*] Clov!

CLOV [*Turning towards* HAMM, *exasperated.*] Do you want me to look at this muckheap, yes or no?

HAMM Answer me first.

CLOV What?

HAMM Do you know what's happened?

CLOV When? Where?

HAMM [*Violently.*] When! What's happened? Use your head, can't you! What has happened?

CLOV What for Christ's sake does it matter? [*He looks out of window.*]

HAMM I don't know.

[*Pause.* CLOV *turns towards* HAMM.]

CLOV [*Harshly.*] When old Mother Pegg asked you for oil for her lamp and you told her to get out to hell, you knew what was happening then, no? [*Pause.*] You know what she died of, Mother Pegg? Of darkness.

HAMM [*Feebly.*] I hadn't any.

CLOV [*As before.*] Yes, you had. [*Pause.*]

HAMM Have you the glass?

CLOV No, it's clear enough as it is.

HAMM Go and get it.

[*Pause.* CLOV *casts up his eyes, brandishes his fists. He loses balance, clutches on to the ladder. He starts to get down, halts.*]

CLOV There's one thing I'll never understand. [*He gets down.*] Why I always obey you. Can you explain that to me?

HAMM No. . . . Perhaps it's compassion. [*Pause.*] A kind of great compassion. [*Pause.*] Oh you won't find it easy, you won't find it easy.

[*Pause.* CLOV *begins to move about the room in search of the telescope.*]

CLOV I'm tired of our goings on, very tired. [*He searches.*] You're not sitting on it? [*He moves the chair, looks at the place where it stood, resumes his search.*]

HAMM [*Anguished.*] Don't leave me there! [*Angrily* CLOV *restores the chair to its place.*] Am I right in the center?

CLOV You'd need a microscope to find this— [*He sees the telescope.*] Ah, about time. [*He picks up the telescope, gets up on the ladder, turns the telescope on the without.*]

HAMM Give me the dog.

CLOV [*Looking.*] Quiet!

HAMM [*Angrily.*] Give me the dog!

[CLOV *drops the telescope, clasps his hands to his head. Pause. He gets down precipitately, looks for the dogs, sees it, picks it up, hastens towards* HAMM *and strikes him violently on the head with the dog.*]

CLOV   There's your dog for you!
        [*The dog falls to the ground. Pause.*]
HAMM   He hit me!
CLOV   You drive me mad, I'm mad!
HAMM   If you must hit me, hit me with the axe. [*Pause.*] Or with the gaff, hit
        me with the gaff. Not with the dog. With the gaff. Or with the axe.
        [CLOV *picks up the dog and gives it to* HAMM *who takes it in his arms.*]
CLOV [*Imploringly.*]   Let's stop playing!
HAMM   Never! [*Pause.*] Put me in my coffin.
CLOV   There are no more coffins.
HAMM   Then let it end! [CLOV *goes towards ladder.*] With a bang! [CLOV *gets up
        on ladder, gets down again, looks for telescope, sees it, picks it up, gets up ladder,
        raises telescope.*] Of darkness! And me? Did anyone ever have pity on me?
CLOV [*Lowering the telescope, turning towards* HAMM.]   What? [*Pause.*] Is it
        me you're referring to?
HAMM [*Angrily.*]   An aside, ape! Did you never hear an aside before? [*Pause.*]
        I'm warming up for my last soliloquy.
CLOV   I warn you. I'm going to look at this filth since it's an order. But it's the
        last time. [*He turns the telescope on the without.*] Let's see. [*He moves the
        telescope.*]   Nothing . . . nothing . . . good . . . good . . . nothing . . . goo—
        [*He starts, lowers the telescope, examines it, turns it again on the without.
        Pause.*] Bad luck to it!
HAMM   More complications! [CLOV *gets down.*] Not an underplot, I trust.
        [CLOV *moves ladder nearer window, gets up on it, turns telescope on the
        without.*]
CLOV [*Dismayed.*]   Looks like a small boy!
HAMM [*Sarcastic.*]   A small . . . boy!
CLOV   I'll go and see. [*He gets down, drops the telescope, goes towards door,
        turns.*] I'll take the gaff. [*He looks for the gaff, sees it, picks it up, hastens
        towards door.*]
HAMM   No! [CLOV *halts.*]
CLOV   No? A potential procreator?
HAMM   If he exists he'll die there or he'll come here. And if he doesn't . . .
        [*Pause.*]
CLOV   You don't believe me? You think I'm inventing? [*Pause.*]
HAMM   It's the end, Clov, we've come to the end. I don't need you any more.
        [*Pause.*]
CLOV   Lucky for you. [*He goes towards door.*]
HAMM   Leave me the gaff.
        [CLOV *gives him the gaff, goes towards door, halts, looks at alarm-clock,
        takes it down, looks round for a better place to put it, goes to bins, puts it
        on lid of* NAGG's *bin. Pause.*]
CLOV   I'll leave you. [*He goes towards door.*]
HAMM   Before you go . . . [CLOV *halts near door.*] . . . say something.
CLOV   There is nothing to say.
HAMM   A few words . . . to ponder . . . in my heart.
CLOV   Your heart!
HAMM   Yes. [*Pause. Forcibly.*] Yes! [*Pause.*] With the rest, in the end, the
        shadows, the murmurs, all the trouble, to end up with. [*Pause.*] Clov. . . .

He never spoke to me. Then, in the end, before he went, without my having asked him, he spoke to me. He said . . .

CLOV [*Despairingly.*] Ah . . . !

HAMM Something . . . from your heart.

CLOV My heart!

HAMM A few words . . . from your heart. [*Pause.*]

CLOV [*Fixed gaze, tonelessly, towards auditorium.*] They said to me, That's love, yes, yes, not a doubt, now you see how—

HAMM Articulate!

CLOV [*As before.*] How easy it is. They said to me, That's friendship, yes, yes, no question, you've found it. They said to me, Here's the place, stop, raise your head and look at all that beauty. That order! They said to me. Come now, you're not a brute beast, think upon these things and you'll see how all becomes clear. And simple! They said to me, What skilled attention they get, all these dying of their wounds.

HAMM Enough!

CLOV [*As before.*] I say to myself—sometimes, Clov, you must learn to suffer better than that if you want them to weary of punishing you—one day. I say to myself—sometimes, Clov, you must be there better than that if you want them to let you go—one day. But I feel too old, and too far, to form new habits. Good, it'll never end, I'll never go. [*Pause.*] Then one day, suddenly, it ends, it changes, I don't understand, it dies, or it's me, I don't understand, that either. I ask the words that remain—sleeping, waking, morning, evening. They have nothing to say. [*Pause.*] I open the door of the cell and go. I am so bowed I only see my feet, if I open my eyes, and between my legs a little trail of black dust. I say to myself that the earth is extinguished, though I never saw it lit. [*Pause.*] It's easy going. [*Pause.*] When I fall I'll weep for happiness. [*Pause. He goes towards door.*]

HAMM Clov! [CLOV *halts, without turning.*] Nothing. [CLOV *moves on.*] Clov! [CLOV *halts, without turning.*]

CLOV This is what we call making an exit.

HAMM I'm obliged to you, Clov. For your services.

CLOV [*Turning, sharply.*] Ah pardon, it's I am obliged to you.

HAMM It's we are obliged to each other. [*Pause.* CLOV *goes towards door.*] One thing more. [CLOV *halts.*] A last favor. [*Exit* CLOV.] Cover me with the sheet. [*Long pause.*] No? Good. [*Pause.*] Me to play. [*Pause. Wearily.*] Old endgame lost of old, play and lose and have done with losing. [*Pause. More animated.*] Let me see. [*Pause.*] Ah yes! [*He tries to move the chair, using the gaff as before. Enter* CLOV, *dressed for the road. Panama hat, tweed coat, raincoat over his arm, umbrella, bag. He halts by the door and stands there, impassive and motionless, his eyes fixed on* HAMM, *till the end.* HAMM *gives up.*] Good. [*Pause.*] Discard. [*He throws away the gaff, makes to throw away the dog, thinks better of it.*] Take it easy. [*Pause.*] And now? [*Pause.*] Raise hat. [*He raises his toque.*] Peace to our . . . arses. [*Pause.*] And put on again. [*He puts on his toque.*] Deuce. [*Pause. He takes off his glasses.*] Wipe. [*He takes out his handkerchief and, without unfolding it, wipes his glasses.*] And put on again. [*He puts on his glasses, puts back the handkerchief in his pocket.*] We're coming. A few more squirms like that and I'll call. [*Pause.*] A little poetry. [*Pause.*] You prayed— [*Pause. He corrects himself.*] You CRIED for night; it comes— [*Pause. He corrects himself.*] It FALLS: now cry in darkness. [*He repeats, chanting.*] You cried for night; it falls: now cry in darkness.[7] [*Pause.*] Nicely put, that. [*Pause.*] And now? [*Pause.*] Moments for nothing, now as always, time was never and time is over, reckoning closed and story ended. [*Pause. Narrative tone.*] If he could have his child with him. . . . [*Pause.*] It was the moment I was waiting for. [*Pause.*] You don't want to abandon him? You want him to bloom while you are withering? Be there to solace your last million last moments? [*Pause.*] He doesn't realize, all he knows is hunger, and cold, and death to crown it all. But you! You ought to know what the earth is like, nowadays. Oh I put him before his responsibilities! [*Pause. Normal tone.*] Well, there we are, there I am, that's enough. [*He raises the whistle to his lips, hesitates, drops it. Pause.*] Yes, truly! [*He whistles. Pause. Louder. Pause.*] Good. [*Pause.*] Father! [*Pause. Louder.*] Father! [*Pause.*] Good. [*Pause.*] We're coming. [*Pause.*] And to end up with? [*Pause.*] Discard. [*He throws away the dog. He tears the whistle from his neck.*] With my compliments. [*He throws whistle towards auditorium. Pause. He sniffs. Soft.*] Clov! [*Long pause.*] No? Good. [*He takes out the handkerchief.*] Since that's the way we're playing it . . . [*He unfolds handkerchief.*] . . . let's play it that way . . . [*He unfolds.*] . . . and speak no more about it . . . [*He finishes unfolding.*] . . . speak no more. [*He holds handkerchief spread out before him.*] Old stancher! [*Pause.*] You . . . remain.

> [*Pause. He covers his face with handkerchief, lowers his arms to armrests, remains motionless.*]
>
> [*Brief tableau.*]

Curtain

1957

---

7. Parody of a line from the poem *Meditation*, by Baudelaire: "You were calling for evening; it falls; here it is."

CLARICE LISPECTOR

1920–1977

Reaching for an apple in the dark, claims Brazilian modernist Clarice Lispector, demonstrates the limits of our knowledge: we know that the object is an apple, but little more. Its color and ripeness remain shrouded in obscurity—tantalizingly *there* and *not there* at the same time. The characters in Lispector's novels and short stories live in the constant awareness of this kind of mystery; theirs is a plane of immediate experience and bodily sensations that has little to do with the orderly, daylight world of our shared rationality, where everything has been named and placed within a cognitive or social system. A pivotal figure in modern Brazilian literature, Lispector deploys a simple vocabulary but an unusual syntax; she makes extended use of interior monologues to evoke the immediacy of subjective consciousness.

Lispector was born in December 1920 in Tchetchelik, a small town in Ukraine, as her parents—Russian Jews who had been the victims of pogroms—made the long journey to a new home in Brazil. Upon their arrival, they changed their infant daughter's name from Chaya to Clarice. They settled in Recife, the capital of the northeastern state of Pernambuco, where Lispector received her early schooling, but later moved to Rio de Janeiro. There, Lispector entered law school and became the first woman reporter at the major newspaper *A Noite*. Her first novel, *Close to the Savage Heart*, published in 1943 (the title derives from a line in **James Joyce**'s *A Portrait of the Artist as a Young Man*), won her the Graça Aranha Prize and a reputation as an innovative young Brazilian writer.

Over the next fifteen years, she traveled widely with her husband, a diplo-

mat she married when they were both in law school. They lived in Italy, Switzerland, England, and the United States. Lispector published some further fiction but spent much of her time in Washington, D.C., between 1952 and 1960, writing detailed notes that she would later incorporate into her fiction. Returning to Rio after separating from her husband, she made use of notes she had written during the previous eight years to compose her best-known short-story collection, *Family Ties* (1960), from which the selection here is taken. The collection won the prestigious Jabuti Prize, the foremost literary award in Brazil. Lispector published novels, short stories, chronicles (nonfiction pieces), and children's tales during the remaining years before her death from cancer in 1977.

Lispector is best known as a writer of intense, tightly structured short stories that portray the external world through a character's innermost thoughts and feelings and that emphasize sensuous perception to attain intuitive knowledge beyond words. She has often been compared, in this respect, with **Virginia Woolf**. Lispector's special contribution to literary modernism may lie in her ability to draw connections between bodily sensations, the limits of language, and the mysteries of existence—and to make these connections the unifying structure of her work. Her fluid, lyrical style has been called "feminine writing," because it explores the relationship of immediate bodily experience to language.

The work presented here, "The Daydreams of a Drunk Woman" (1960) is a disturbing tale. The title disposes of the protagonist in a few words: she is an alcoholic, and she imagines things. (The *rapariga* [young woman] of the original title suggests, in Brazilian Portuguese, that she may be promiscuous and possibly of poor immigrant stock.) The narrative's course confirms these descriptions: it begins with the protagonist in bed at home, possibly already drunk, and goes on to show her flying into alcoholic rages and bouts of self-pity. Yet the story reveals deeper possibilities in this woman. Oblique details and brilliant imagery suggest other dimensions to her life: the reasons for her misery and repressed rage, the choices that she has made while seeking security and protection, and the social conditions that foster such pitiable circumstances. From the beginning, when she stares at her reflection in a triple mirror and sees "the intersected breasts of several women," her identity appears fragmented, her self-image either in shards or swollen and unreachable. As she congratulates herself repeatedly on being "protected like everyone who had attained a position in life," and viciously criticizes a more stylish woman she sees in the restaurant, it gradually becomes clearer that she has arrived at her position, and escaped poverty, by exploiting her body to marry a man she neither loves nor respects. While filling in a devastatingly detailed picture of this abject modern figure in her day-to-day delusions, unhappiness, and destructive relationships, Lispector's prose evokes the existential dilemma that the young woman feels and half understands.

The Daydreams of a Drunk Woman[1]

It seemed to her that the trolley cars were about to cross through the room as they caused her reflected image to tremble. She was combing her hair at her leisure in front of the dressing table with its three mirrors, and her strong white arms shivered in the coolness of the evening. Her eyes did not look away as the mirrors trembled, sometimes dark, sometimes luminous. Outside, from a window above, something heavy and hollow fell to the ground. Had her husband and the little ones been at home, the idea would already have occurred to her that they were to blame. Her eyes did not take themselves off her image, her comb worked pensively, and her open dressing gown revealed in the mirrors the intersected breasts of several women.

"Evening News" shouted the newsboy to the mild breeze in Riachuelo Street,[2] and something trembled as if foretold. She threw her comb down on the dressing table and sang dreamily: "Who saw the little spar-row . . . it passed by the window . . . and flew beyond Minho!"[3]—but, suddenly becoming irritated, she shut up abruptly like a fan.

She lay down and fanned herself impatiently with a newspaper that rustled in the room. She clutched the bedsheet, inhaling its odor as she crushed its starched embroidery with her red-lacquered nails. Then, almost smiling, she started to fan herself once more. Oh my!—she sighed as she began to smile. She beheld the picture of her bright smile, the smile of a woman who was still

1. Translated by Giovanni Pontiero.
2. A street in Rio de Janeiro that intersects with Mem de Sá Street. Riachuelo is the name of a large department store; Mem de Sá was a 16th-century Portuguese governor-general of Brazil and the founder of Rio de Janeiro.
3. A river in northwest Portugal.

young, and she continued to smile to herself, closing her eyes and fanning herself still more vigorously. Oh my!—she would come fluttering in from the street like a butterfly.

"Hey there! Guess who came to see me today?" she mused as a feasible and interesting topic of conversation. "No idea, tell me," those eyes asked her with a gallant smile, those sad eyes set in one of those pale faces that make one feel so uncomfortable. "Maria Quiteria, my dear!" she replied coquettishly with her hand on her hip. "And who, might we ask, would she be?" they insisted gallantly, but now without any expression. "You!" she broke off, slightly annoyed. How boring!

Oh what a succulent room! Here she was, fanning herself in Brazil. The sun, trapped in the blinds, shimmered on the wall like the strings of a guitar. Riachuelo Street shook under the gasping weight of the trolley cars which came from Mem de Sá Street. Curious and impatient, she listened to the vibrations of the china cabinet in the drawing room. Impatiently she rolled over to lie face downward, and, sensuously stretching the toes of her dainty feet, she awaited her next thought with open eyes. "Whosoever found, searched," she said to herself in the form of a rhymed refrain, which always ended up by sounding like some maxim. Until eventually she fell asleep with her mouth wide open, her saliva staining the pillow.

She only woke up when her husband came into the room the moment he returned from work. She did not want to eat any dinner nor to abandon her dreams, and she went back to sleep: let him content himself with the leftovers from lunch.

And now that the kids were at the country house of their aunts in Jacarepaguá,[4] she took advantage of their absence in order to begin the day as she pleased: restless and frivolous in her bed . . . one of those whims perhaps. Her husband appeared before her, having already dressed, and she did not even know what he had prepared for his breakfast. She avoided examining his suit to see whether it needed brushing . . . little did she care if this was his day for attending to his business in the city. But when he bent over to kiss her, her capriciousness crackled like a dry leaf.

"Don't paw me!"

"What the devil's the matter with you?" the man asked her in amazement, as he immediately set about attempting some more effective caress.

Obstinate, she would not have known what to reply, and she felt so touchy and aloof that she did not even know where to find a suitable reply. She suddenly lost her temper. "Go to hell! . . . prowling round me like some old tomcat."

He seemed to think more clearly and said, firmly, "You're ill, my girl."

She accepted his remark, surprised, and vaguely flattered.

She remained in bed the whole day long listening to the silence of the house without the scurrying of the kids, without her husband who would have his meals in the city today. Her anger was tenuous and ardent. She only got up to go to the bathroom, from which she returned haughty and offended.

The morning turned into a long enormous afternoon, which then turned into a shallow night, which innocently dawned throughout the entire house.

She was still in bed, peaceful and casual. She was in love. . . . She was anticipating her love for the man whom she would love one day. Who knows, this

---

4. A quiet neighborhood in Rio de Janeiro with a beach where families would gather to picnic.

sometimes happened, and without any guilt or injury for either partner. Lying in bed thinking and thinking, and almost laughing as one does over some gossip. Thinking and thinking. About what? As if she knew. So she just stayed there.

The next minute she would get up, angry. But in the weakness of that first instant she felt dizzy and fragile in the room which swam round and round until she managed to grope her way back to bed, amazed that it might be true. "Hey, girl, don't you go getting sick on me!" she muttered suspiciously. She raised her hand to her forehead to see if there was any fever.

That night, until she fell asleep, her mind became more and more delirious—for how many minutes?—until she flopped over, fast asleep, to snore beside her husband.

She awoke late, the potatoes waiting to be peeled, the kids expected home that same evening from their visit to the country. "God, I've lost my self-respect, I have! My day for washing and darning socks. . . . What a lazy bitch you've turned out to be!" she scolded herself, inquisitive and pleased . . . shopping to be done, fish to remember, already so late on a hectic sunny morning.

But on Saturday night they went to the tavern in Tiradentes Square[5] at the invitation of a rich businessman, she with her new dress which didn't have any fancy trimmings but was made of good material, a dress that would last her a lifetime. On Saturday night, drunk in Tiradentes Square, inebriated but with her husband at her side to give her support, and being very polite in front of the other man who was so much more refined and rich—striving to make conversation, for she was no provincial ninny and she had already experienced life in the capital. But so drunk that she could no longer stand.

And if her husband was not drunk it was only because he did not want to show disrespect for the businessman, and, full of solicitude and humility, he left the swaggering to the other fellow. His manner suited such an elegant occasion, but it gave her such an urge to laugh! She despised him beyond words! She looked at her husband stuffed into his new suit and found him so ridiculous . . . so drunk that she could no longer stand, but without losing her self-respect as a woman. And the green wine[6] from her native Portugal slowly being drained from her glass.

When she got drunk, as if she had eaten a heavy Sunday lunch, all things which by their true nature are separate from each other—the smell of oil on the one hand, of a male on the other; the soup tureen on the one hand, the waiter on the other—became strangely linked by their true nature and the whole thing was nothing short of disgraceful . . . shocking!

And if her eyes appeared brilliant and cold, if her movements faltered clumsily until she succeeded in reaching the toothpick holder, beneath the surface she really felt so far quite at ease . . . there was that full cloud to transport her without effort. Her puffy lips, her teeth white, and her body swollen with wine. And the vanity of feeling drunk, making her show such disdain for everything, making her feel swollen and rotund like a large cow.

Naturally she talked, since she lacked neither the ability to converse nor topics to discuss. But the words that a woman uttered when drunk were like being

5. A square in Rio de Janeiro named after the Brazilian revolutionary patriot; he was executed by the Portuguese in 1792.   6. *Vinho Verde*, literally "green wine," is a soft wine produced in Portugal and often drunk cold before meals.

pregnant—mere words on her lips which had nothing to do with the secret core that seemed like a pregnancy. God, how queer she felt! Saturday night, her every-day soul lost, and how satisfying to lose it, and to remind her of former days, only her small, ill-kempt hands—and here she was now with her elbows resting on the white and red checked tablecloth like a gambling table, deeply launched upon a degrading and revolting existence. And what about her laughter? . . . this outburst of laughter which mysteriously emerged from her full white throat, in response to the polite manners of the businessman, an outburst of laughter coming from the depths of that sleep, and from the depths of that security of someone who has a body. Her white flesh was as sweet as lobster, the legs of a live lobster wriggling slowly in the air . . . that urge to be sick in order to plunge that sweetness into something really awful . . . and that perversity of someone who has a body.

She talked and listened with curiosity to what she herself was about to reply to the well-to-do businessman who had so kindly invited them out to dinner and paid for their meal. Intrigued and amazed, she heard what she was on the point of replying, and what she might say in her present state would serve as an augury for the future. She was no longer a lobster, but a harsher sign—that of the scorpion. After all, she had been born in November.

A beacon that sweeps through the dawn while one is asleep, such was her drunkenness which floated slowly through the air.

At the same time, she was conscious of such feelings! Such feelings! When she gazed upon that picture which was so beautifully painted in the restaurant, she was immediately overcome by an artistic sensibility. No one would get it out of her head that she had really been born for greater things. She had always been one for works of art.

But such sensibility! And not merely excited by the picture of grapes and pears and dead fish with shining scales. Her sensibility irritated her without causing her pain, like a broken fingernail. And if she wanted, she could allow herself the luxury of becoming even more sensitive, she could go still further, because she was protected by a situation, protected like everyone who had attained a position in life. Like someone saved from misfortune. I'm so miserable, dear God! If she wished, she could even pour more wine into her glass, and, protected by the position which she had attained in life, become even more drunk just so long as she did not lose her self-respect. And so, even more drunk, she peered round the room, and how she despised the barren people in that restaurant. Not a real man among them. How sad it really all seemed. How she despised the barren people in that restaurant, while she was plump and heavy and generous to the full. And everything in the restaurant seemed so remote, the one thing distant from the other, as if the one might never be able to converse with the other. Each existing for itself, and God existing there for everyone.

Her eyes once more settled on that female whom she had instantly detested the moment she had entered the room. Upon arriving, she had spotted her seated at a table accompanied by a man and all dolled up in a hat and jewelry, glittering like a false coin, all coy and refined. What a fine hat she was wearing! . . . Bet you anything she isn't even married for all that pious look on her face . . . and that fine hat stuck on her head. A fat lot of good her hypocrisy would do her, and she had better watch out in case her airs and graces proved her undoing! The more sanctimonious they were, the bigger frauds they turned out to be. And as for the waiter, he was a great nitwit, serving her, full of gestures and finesse, while the sallow man with her pretended not to notice. And that pious ninny so pleased with herself in that hat and so modest about her slim waistline, and I'll bet she couldn't even bear her man a child. All right, it was none of her business, but from the moment she arrived she felt the urge to give that blonde prude of a woman playing the grand lady in her hat a few good slaps on the face. She didn't even have any shape, and she was flat-chested. And no doubt, for all her fine hats, she was nothing more than a fishwife trying to pass herself off as a duchess.

Oh, how humiliated she felt at having come to the bar without a hat, and her head now felt bare. And that madam with her affectations, playing the refined lady! I know what you need, my beauty, you and your sallow boy friend! And if you think I envy you with your flat chest, let me assure you that I don't give a damn for you and your hats. Shameless sluts like you are only asking for a good hard slap on the face.

In her holy rage, she stretched out a shaky hand and reached for a toothpick.

But finally, the difficulty of arriving home disappeared; she now bestirred herself amidst the familiar reality of her room, now seated on the edge of the bed, a slipper dangling from one foot.

And, as she had half closed her blurred eyes, everything took on the appearance of flesh, the foot of the bed, the window, the suit her husband had thrown off, and everything became rather painful. Meanwhile, she was becoming larger, more unsteady, swollen and gigantic. If only she could get closer to herself, she would find she was even larger. Each of her arms could be explored by someone who didn't even recognize that they were dealing with an arm, and someone could plunge into each eye and swim around without knowing that it was an eye. And all around her everything was a bit painful. Things of the flesh stricken by nervous twinges. The chilly air had caught her as she had come out of the restaurant.

She was sitting up in bed, resigned and sceptical. And this was nothing yet, God only knew—she was perfectly aware that this was nothing yet. At this moment things were happening to her that would only hurt later and in earnest. When restored to her normal size, her anesthetized body would start to wake up, throbbing, and she would begin to pay for those big meals and drinks. Then, since this would really end up by happening, I might as well open my eyes right now (which she did) and then everything looked smaller and clearer, without her feeling any pain. Everything, deep down, was the same, only smaller and more familiar. She was sitting quite upright in bed, her stomach so full, absorbed and resigned, with the delicacy of one who sits waiting until her partner awakens. "You gorge yourself and I pay the piper," she said sadly, looking at the dainty white toes of her feet. She looked around her, patient and obedient. Ah, words, nothing but words, the objects in the room lined up in the order of words, to form those confused and irksome phrases that he who knows how will read. Boredom . . . such awful boredom. . . . How sickening! How very annoying! When all is said and done, heaven help me— God knows best. What was one to do? How can I describe this thing inside me? Anyhow, God knows best. And to think that she had enjoyed herself so much last night . . . and to think of how nice it all was—a restaurant to her liking— and how she had been seated elegantly at table. At table! The world would exclaim. But she made no reply, drawing herself erect with a bad-tempered click of her tongue . . . irritated . . . "Don't come to me with your endearments" . . . disenchanted, resigned, satiated, married, content, vaguely nauseated.

It was at this moment that she became deaf: one of her senses was missing. She clapped the palm of her hand over her ear, which only made things worse . . . suddenly filling her eardrum with the whirr of an elevator . . . life suddenly becoming loud and magnified in its smallest movements. One of two things: either she was deaf or hearing all too well. She reacted against this new suggestion with a sensation of spite and annoyance, with a sigh of resigned satiety. "Drop dead," she said gently . . . defeated.

"And when in the restaurant . . ." she suddenly recalled when she had been in the restaurant her husband's protector had pressed his foot against hers beneath the table, and above the table his face was watching her. By coincidence or intentionally? The rascal. A fellow, to be frank, who was not unattractive. She shrugged her shoulders.

And when above the roundness of her low-cut dress—right in the middle of Tiradentes Square! she thought, shaking her head incredulously—that fly had settled on her bare bosom. What cheek!

Certain things were good because they were almost nauseating . . . the noise like that of an elevator in her blood, while her husband lay snoring at her side . . . her chubby little children sleeping in the other room, the little villains. Ah, what's wrong with me! she wondered desperately. Have I eaten too much? Heavens above! What *is* wrong with me?

It was unhappiness.

Her toes playing with her slipper . . . the floor not too clean at that spot. "What a slovenly, lazy bitch you've become."

Not tomorrow, because her legs would not be too steady, but the day after tomorrow that house of hers would be a sight worth seeing: she would give it a scouring with soap and water which would get rid of all the dirt! "You mark my words," she threatened in her rage. Ah, she was feeling so well, so strong, as if she still had milk in those firm breasts. When her husband's friend saw her so pretty and plump he had immediately felt respect for her. And when she started to get embarrassed she did not know which way to look. Such misery! What was one to do? Seated on the edge of the bed, blinking in resignation. How well one could see the moon on these summer nights. She leaned over slightly, indifferent and resigned. The moon! How clearly one could see it. The moon high and yellow gliding through the sky, poor thing. Gliding, gliding . . . high up, high up. The moon! Then her vulgarity exploded in a sudden outburst of affection; "you slut," she cried out, laughing.

1960

CHINUA ACHEBE
born 1930

The best-known African writer today is the Nigerian Chinua Achebe, whose first novel, *Things Fall Apart*, exploded the colonialist image of Africans as childlike people living in a primitive society. Achebe's novels, stories, poetry, and essays have made him a respected and prophetic figure in Africa and the West. In Western countries, where he has traveled, taught, and lectured widely, he is admired as a major writer who has given a new direction to the English-language novel. Achebe helped to create the African postcolonial novel with its themes and characters; he also developed a complex narrative voice that questions cultural assumptions with a subtle irony and compassion born from bicultural experience.

Achebe was born in Ogidi, an Igbo-speaking town of Eastern Nigeria, on November 16, 1930. He was the fifth of six children in the family of Isaiah Okafor Achebe, a teacher for the Church Missionary Society, and his wife, Janet. Achebe's parents christened him Albert after Prince Albert, husband of Queen Victoria. Two cultures coexisted in Ogidi: on the one hand, African social customs and traditional religion; on the other, British colonial authority and Christianity. Instead of being torn between the two, Achebe found himself curious about both ways of life and fascinated with the dual perspective that came from living "at the crossroads of cultures."

He attended church schools in Ogidi, where instruction was carried out in English. Achebe read the various books in his father's library, most of them primers or church related, but he also listened eagerly to his mother and sister when they told traditional Igbo stories. Entering a prestigious secondary school in Umuahia, he immediately took advantage of its well-stocked library. Achebe later recalled that when he read books about Africa, he tended to identify with the white narrators rather than the black inhabitants: "I did not see myself as an African in those books. I took sides with the white men against the savages." After graduating in 1948, Achebe entered University College, Ibadan, on a scholarship to study medicine. In the following year he changed to a program in liberal arts that combined English, history, and religious studies. Research in the last two fields deepened his knowledge of Nigerian history and culture; the assigned literary texts, however, brought into sharp focus the distorted image of African culture offered by British colonial literature. Reading Joyce Cary's *Mister Johnson* (1939), a novel recommended for its depiction of life in Nigeria, he was shocked to find Nigerians described as violent savages with passionate instincts and simple minds: "and so I thought if this was famous, then perhaps someone ought to try and look at this from the inside." While at the university, Achebe rejected his British name in favor of his indigenous name Chinua, which abbreviates *Chinualumogu*, or "My spirit come fight for me."

Achebe began writing while at the university, contributing articles and sketches to several campus papers and publishing four stories in the *University Herald*, a magazine whose editor he became in his third year. His first novel, *Things Fall Apart* (1958), was a conscious attempt to counteract the distortions of English literature about Africa by describing the richness and complexity of traditional African society before the colonial and missionary invasion. It was important, Achebe said, to "teach my readers that their past—with all its imperfections—was not one long night of savagery from which the first Europeans acting on God's behalf delivered them." The novel was recognized immediately as an extraordinary work of literature in English. It also became the first classic work of modern African fiction, translated into nine languages, and Achebe became, for many readers and writers, the teacher of a whole generation. His later novels continue to examine the individual and cultural dilemmas of Nigerian society, although their background varies from the traditional religious society of *Arrow of God* (1964) to thinly disguised accounts of contemporary political strife.

Achebe worked as a radio journalist for the Nigerian Broadcasting Service, ultimately rising to the position of director of external services in charge of the Voice of Nigeria. The radio position was more than a merely administrative post, for Achebe and his colleagues were creating a sense of shared national identity through the broadcasting of national news and information about Nigerian culture. Since the end of the Second World War, Nigeria had been torn by intellectual and political rivalries that overlaid the common struggle for independence (achieved in 1960). The three major ethnolinguistic groups—Yoruba, Hausa-Fulani, and Igbo—were increasingly locked in economic and political competition at the same time they were fighting to erase the vestiges of British colonial rule. These problems eventually boiled over in the Nigerian Civil War (1967–70).

It is hard to overestimate the influence of Nigerian politics on Achebe's life after 1966. In January a military coup d'état led by young Igbo officers overthrew the government; six months later a second coup led by non-Igbo officers took power. Ethnic strife intensified: thousands of Igbos were killed and driven out of the north. Soldiers were sent to find Achebe in Lagos; his wife and young children fled by boat to Eastern Nigeria, where after a dangerous and roundabout journey, Achebe joined them, taking up the post of senior research fellow at the University of Nigeria, Nsukka. In May 1967 the eastern region, mainly populated by Igbo-speakers, seceded as the new nation of Biafra. From then until the defeat of Biafra in January 1970, a bloody civil war was waged with high civilian casualties and widespread starvation. Achebe traveled in Europe, North America, and Africa to win support for Biafra, proclaiming that "no government, black or white, has the right to stigmatize and destroy groups of its own citizens without undermining the basis of its own existence." A group of his poems about the war won the Commonwealth Poetry Prize in 1972, the same year that he published a volume of short stories, *Girls at War*, and left Nigeria to take up a three-year position at the University of Massachusetts at Amherst. Returning to Nsukka as professor of literature in 1976, Achebe continued to participate in his country's political life. Badly hurt in a car accident in 1990, Achebe slowly recovered and returned to writing and teaching at Bard College in Annandale-on-Hudson, New York, where he stayed for most of the following two decades. Since then he has taught at Brown University in Providence, Rhode Island. Among many other novels and memoirs, he has published the essay collection *Education of a British Protected Child* (2009).

Achebe is convinced of the writer's social responsibility, and he draws frequent contrasts between the European "art for art's sake" tradition and the African belief in the indivisibility of art and society. His favorite example is the Owerri Igbo custom of *mbari*, a communal art project in which villagers selected by the priest of the earth goddess Ala live in a forest clearing for a year or more, working under the direction of master artists to prepare a temple of images in the goddess's honor. This creative communal enterprise and its culminating festival are diametrically opposed, the writer says, to the European custom of secluding art objects in museums or private collections. Instead, *mbari* celebrates art as a cultural process, affirming that "art belongs to all and is a 'function' of society." Achebe's own practice as novelist, poet, essayist, founder and editor of two journals, lecturer, and active representative of African letters exemplifies this commitment to the community.

"Chike's School Days" (1960), published in the year of Nigerian independence, tells the story of a child with a dual inheritance like Achebe's own. Like Achebe himself, the boy has three names: the Christian John, the familiar Chike, and the more formal African name Obiajulu, meaning "the mind at last is at rest." Yet if Chike is the answer to his parents' prayers for a son, he is also about to enter a transformative experience in a Christian school, where he will master the English language. Achebe's literary language is an English skillfully blended with Igbo vocabulary, proverbs, images, and speech patterns to create a voice embodying the linguistic pluralism of modern African experience. By including Standard English, Igbo, and pidgin in different contexts, Achebe demonstrates the existence of a diverse society that is otherwise concealed behind language barriers. He thereby acknowledges that his primary African audience is composed of younger, schooled readers who are relatively fluent in English, readers like Chike. Chike's story, however, focuses less on the school days of the title than on his background. Chike's education turns out to be the product of his paternal grandmother's conversion to Christianity, and of his father's marriage (following his own new Christian convictions) to an outcaste woman, an *Osu* (a member of the traditional Igbo slave caste). Thus a seemingly simple tale about a boy going to school turns out to be a story of historical change as it affects three generations. Chike's love of English, while it separates him from his neighbors, suggests the potential for a love of literature. Elsewhere, Achebe has written that literature is important because it liberates the human imagination; it "begins as an adventure in self-discovery and ends in wisdom and human conscience."

Chike's School Days

Sarah's last child was a boy, and his birth brought great joy to the house of his father, Amos. The child received three names at his baptism—John, Chike, Obiajulu. The last name means "the mind at last is at rest."[1] Anyone hearing this name knew at once that its owner was either an only child or an only son. Chike was an only son. His parents had had five daughters before him.

Like his sisters Chike was brought up "in the ways of the white man," which meant the opposite of traditional. Amos had many years before bought a tiny bell with which he summoned his family to prayers and hymn-singing first

1. In the Igbo or Ibo language.

thing in the morning and last thing at night. This was one of the ways of the white man. Sarah taught her children not to eat in their neighbours' houses because "they offered their food to idols." And thus she set herself against the age-old custom which regarded children as the common responsibility of all so that, no matter what the relationship between parents, their children played together and shared their food.

One day a neighbour offered a piece of yam to Chike, who was only four years old. The boy shook his head haughtily and said, "We don't eat heathen food." The neighbour was full of rage, but she controlled herself and only muttered under her breath that even an *Osu*[2] was full of pride nowadays, thanks to the white man.

And she was right. In the past an *Osu* could not raise his shaggy head in the presence of the free-born. He was a slave to one of the many gods of the clan. He was a thing set apart, not to be venerated but to be despised and almost spat on. He could not marry a free-born, and he could not take any of the titles of his clan. When he died, he was buried by his kind in the Bad Bush.

Now all that had changed, or had begun to change. So that an *Osu* child could even look down his nose at a free-born, and talk about heathen food! The white man had indeed accomplished many things.

Chike's father was not originally an *Osu*, but had gone and married an *Osu* woman in the name of Christianity. It was unheard of for a man to make himself *Osu* in that way, with his eyes wide open. But then Amos was nothing if not mad. The new religion had gone to his head. It was like palm-wine. Some people drank it and remained sensible. Others lost every sense in their stomach.

The only person who supported Amos in his mad marriage venture was Mr. Brown, the white missionary, who lived in a thatch-roofed, red-earth-walled parsonage and was highly respected by the people, not because of his sermons, but because of a dispensary he ran in one of his rooms. Amos had emerged from Mr. Brown's parsonage greatly fortified. A few days later he told his widowed mother, who had recently been converted to Christianity and had taken the name of Elizabeth. The shock nearly killed her. When she recovered, she went down on her knees and begged Amos not to do this thing. But he would not hear; his ears had been nailed up. At last, in desperation, Elizabeth went to consult the diviner.

This diviner was a man of great power and wisdom. As he sat on the floor of his hut beating a tortoise shell, a coating of white chalk round his eyes, he saw not only the present, but also what had been and what was to be. He was called "the man of the four eyes." As soon as old Elizabeth appeared, he cast his stringed cowries[3] and told her what she had come to see him about. "Your son has joined the white man's religion. And you too in your old age when you should know better. And do you wonder that he is stricken with insanity? Those who gather ant-infested faggots must be prepared for the visit of lizards." He cast his cowries a number of times and wrote with a finger on a bowl of sand, and all the while his *nwifulu*,[4] a talking calabash, chatted to itself. "Shut up!" he roared, and it immediately held its peace. The diviner then muttered a few incantations and rattled off a breathless reel of proverbs that followed one another like the cowries in his magic string.

At last he pronounced the cure. The ancestors were angry and must be appeased with a goat. Old Elizabeth performed the rites, but her son remained insane and married an *Osu* girl whose name was Sarah. Old Elizabeth renounced her new religion and returned to the faith of her people.

We have wandered from our main story. But it is important to know how Chike's father became an *Osu*, because even today when everything is upside down, such a story is very rare. But now to return to Chike who refused heathen food at the tender age of four years, or maybe five.

Two years later he went to the village school. His right hand could now reach across his head to his left ear, which proved that he was old enough to tackle the mysteries of the white man's learning. He was very happy about his new slate and pencil, and especially about his school uniform of white shirt and brown khaki shorts. But as the first day of the new term approached, his young mind dwelt on the many stories about teachers and their canes. And he remembered the song his elder sisters sang, a song that had a somewhat disquieting refrain:

Onye nkuzi ewelu itali piagbusie umuaka.[5]

One of the ways an emphasis is laid in Ibo is by exaggeration, so that the teacher in the refrain might not actually have flogged the children to death. But there was no doubt he did flog them. And Chike thought very much about it.

Being so young, Chike was sent to what was called the "religious class" where they sang, and sometimes danced, the catechism. He loved the sound of words and he loved rhythm. During the catechism lesson the class formed a ring to dance the teacher's question. "Who was Caesar?"[6] he might ask, and the song would burst forth with much stamping of feet.

Siza bu eze Rome
Onye nachi enu uwa dum.[7]

It did not matter to their dancing that in the twentieth century Caesar was no longer ruler of the whole world.

And sometimes they even sang in English. Chike was very fond of "Ten Green Bottles." They had been taught the words but they only remembered the first and the last lines. The middle was hummed and hie-ed and mumbled:

Ten grin botr angin on dar war,
Ten grin botr angin on dar war,
Hm hm hm hm hm
Hm, hm hm hm hm hm,
An ten grin botr angin on dar war.[8]

5. "The teacher took a whip and flogged the pupils mercilessly" (Ibo).
6. Julius Caesar (100–44 B.C.E.), Roman general and political leader whose near-monopoly on power in the late days of the Roman Republic led to the creation of the Roman Empire.
7. "Caesar was the chief of Rome, / the ruler of the whole world" (Ibo).
8. A British children's song, "Ten green bottles hanging on the wall," as pronounced by African children who are learning English.

In this way the first year passed. Chike was promoted to the "Infant School," where work of a more serious nature was undertaken.

We need not follow him through the Infant School. It would make a full story in itself. But it was no different from the story of other children. In the Primary School, however, his individual character began to show. He developed a strong hatred for arithmetic. But he loved stories and songs. And he liked particularly the sound of English words, even when they conveyed no meaning at all. Some of them simply filled him with elation. "Periwinkle" was such a word. He had now forgotten how he learned it or exactly what it was. He had a vague private meaning for it and it was something to do with fairyland. "Constellation" was another.

Chike's teacher was fond of long words. He was said to be a very learned man. His favourite pastime was copying out jaw-breaking words from his *Chambers' Etymological Dictionary*. Only the other day he had raised applause from his class by demolishing a boy's excuse for lateness with unanswerable erudition. He had said: "Procrastination is a lazy man's apology." The teacher's erudition showed itself in every subject he taught. His nature study lessons were memorable. Chike would always remember the lesson on the methods of seed dispersal. According to teacher, there were five methods: by man, by animals, by water, by wind, and by explosive mechanism. Even those pupils who forgot all the other methods remembered "explosive mechanism."

Chike was naturally impressed by teacher's explosive vocabulary. But the fairyland quality which words had for him was of a different kind. The first sentences in his *New Method Reader* were simple enough and yet they filled him with a vague exultation: "Once there was a wizard. He lived in Africa. He went to China to get a lamp." Chike read it over and over again at home and then made a song of it. It was a meaningless song. "Periwinkles" got into it, and also "Damascus." But it was like a window through which he saw in the distance a strange, magical new world. And he was happy.

1960

ALEXANDER SOLZHENITSYN
1918–2008

Like his great predecessors **Tolstoy** and **Dostoyevsky**, Alexander Solzhenitsyn was both a popular writer and a prophetic voice of moral conscience during the last decades of Soviet dictatorship. Solzhenitsyn used the techniques of nineteenth-century realism to explore a distinctively twentieth-century society. Imprisoned by the Stalinist regime, then later expelled from the Soviet Union and stripped of his citizenship, Solzhenitsyn criticized both the political oppression of the East and the materialism of the West, while proclaiming the virtues of an older, religious way of life.

He was born Alexander Isayevich Solzhenitsyn on December 11, 1918, a little more than a year after the Russian Revolution, in Kislovodsk, in the northern Caucasus. His father had died six months earlier, and his mother supported the family in Rostov-on-Don by working as a typist. They were extremely poor, and—although Solzhenitsyn would have preferred studying literature in Moscow—he was obliged, on graduation from high school, to enroll in the local Department of Mathematics at Rostov University. The choice, he later said, was a lucky one, for his double degree in mathematics and physics allowed him to spend four years of his prison-camp sentence in a relatively privileged *sharashka*, or research institute, instead of at hard manual labor. Unlike other writers (such as **Anna Akhmatova** and Boris Pasternak) who had known life before the revolution, Solzhenitsyn grew up a committed Communist, supporting the regime even during the catastrophic famine of 1933, but during the Second World War he became disillusioned with the Soviet leadership.

Soon after graduating from the university, Solzhenitsyn was put in charge of an artillery reconnaissance battery at the front; he served for almost four years before his sudden arrest in February 1945. The military censor had found passages in his letters to a friend that showed him to be—even under a pseudonym—disrespectful of the Soviet dictator Joseph Stalin, and Solzhenitsyn was sentenced to eight years in the prison camps. He worked at first as a mathematician in research institutes staffed by prisoners but in 1950 was taken to a new kind of camp for political prisoners, where he worked as a manual laborer. The hardships he endured there became the material for his most memorable writing, which combined autobiography, fiction, and historical events.

After his sentence was over, an administrative order sent him into permanent exile in southern Kazakhstan, a republic in Central Asia that was then a part of the Soviet Union. Solzhenitsyn spent the years of exile teaching physics and mathematics in a rural school and writing prose in secret. A cancerous tumor that had developed in his first labor camp grew worse, and in 1954 the author received treatment in a clinic in Tashkent (events recalled in the novel *Cancer Ward*, published in 1968). Solzhenitsyn remained in internal exile during the first phases of de-Stalinization, after the dictator's death in 1953, but was rehabilitated in 1957. He moved to Ryazan, in European Russia, where he continued to teach, while secretly writing fiction. The novella *Matryona's Home* and the novel *One Day in the Life of Ivan Denisovich* were composed during this period.

At the age of forty-two, Solzhenitsyn had written a great deal but published nothing. In 1961, however, it looked as though the climate of political censorship might change. Soviet Premier Nikita Khrushchev publicly attacked the "cult of personality" and hero worship that had surrounded Stalin, and the poet and editor Alexander Tvardovsky called on writers to portray "truth," not the idealized picture of Soviet society that Stalin had preferred. Solzhenitsyn was encouraged to submit *One Day in the Life of Ivan Denisovich*, an account of a bricklayer in a Russian concentration camp, beset, from morning to night, by hunger, cold, and brutally demanding work. The novel appeared, with Khrushchev's approval, in the November 1962 issue of Tvardovsky's journal *Novy Mir* (*The New World*) and seemed to announce a more relaxed era in Soviet culture—never before had the prison camps been openly discussed. Solzhenitsyn's matter-of-fact narration of the prisoners' day-to-day struggle to survive and retain their humanity shocked readers in Russia and in the West. In January 1963, Tvardovsky issued *Matryona's Home* and another novella, *An Incident at Krechetovka Station*, but—with the exception of two short stories and an article on style—Solzhenitsyn would not be allowed to publish anything more in his native land for more than twenty-five years. Even the highly praised *One Day in the Life of Ivan Denisovich* was removed from candidacy for the Lenin Prize in 1963.

Khrushchev himself was forced into retirement in October 1964, and the temporary loosening of censorship came to an end. The only means of publishing officially unacceptable works was to convey them to a Western publishing house or to circulate copies of typewritten manuscripts in *samizdat* ("self-publishing") form. Solzhenitsyn made arrangements to have his works, including the novels *Cancer Ward* and *The First Circle*, published in the West, in 1968. Within a year he was expelled from the official Writer's Union; in 1970 he was awarded the Nobel Prize in Literature, which he accepted in absentia because he was afraid that he would not be permitted to reenter the Soviet Union once he left. He continued work on his masterpiece, *The Gulag Archipelago* (1973–75), a three-volume, seven-section account of Stalin's widespread prison camp system, in which up to sixty million people suffered. Solzhenitsyn described the horror of these camps in quasi-anecdotal form, using personal experience, oral testimony, excerpts of documents, written eyewitness reports, and a massive collection of evidence accumulated inside *An Attempt at Artistic Investigation* (the subtitle). In the book there is a tension between the bare facts that Solzhenitsyn transmits and the spiritual interpretation of history into which they are made to fit. The author is overtly present, commenting, guessing intuitively from context when particular facts are missing, and stressing, in his own voice, the theme that has pervaded all his work: the purification of the soul through suffering. Solzhenitsyn tried to keep the work in progress a secret, but the KGB (the Soviet secret police) found a copy of the manuscript as a result of their interrogation of Solzhenitsyn's typist, who subsequently committed suicide. After the publication abroad of the first volume, Solzhenitsyn was arrested and expelled from the country. He went first to Zurich, then to the United States, where he lived in seclusion on a farm in Vermont.

The expulsion remained in effect until 1990, when the president of the Soviet Union, Mikhail S. Gorbachev, offered to restore Solzhenitsyn's citizenship as part of the rehabilitation of artists and writers disgraced during previous regimes. Solzhenitsyn did not accept the offer, though, and refused a prize awarded by the Russian Republic for *The Gulag Archipelago*—noting that the book was not widely available in the Soviet Union and that the "phenomenon of the Gulag" had not been overcome. In September 1991 the old charge of treason was officially dropped, and the writer returned to Russia in May 1994 to widespread public acclaim. The novelist expected, and was expected, to be a prominent voice in contemporary Russian society—for a while, he even had a television program. His moral strictures and nostalgia for a simpler past, however, proved alien to a post-Soviet society intent on prosperity. His massive series of historical novels about the Russian Revolution, *The Red Wheel*, on which he spent some thirty years, was poorly received. Disillusioned by post-Communist Russia, he increasingly supported authoritarian figures, including the Russian President Vladimir Putin.

Since Solzhenitsyn was such a dedicated anti-Communist and anti-Marxist, many Westerners jumped to the conclusion—incorrectly, as it turned out—that he supported the capitalist, democratic system. Instead, he looked back to an earlier, more nationalist and spiritual authoritarianism represented for him by the image of Holy Russia: "For a thousand years Russia lived with an authoritarian order . . . that authoritarian order possessed a strong moral foundation . . . Christian Orthodoxy." In a speech given at Harvard in 1978, "A World Split Apart," he criticized Western democracy's "herd instinct" and "need to accommodate mass standards," its emphasis on "well-being" and "constant desire to have still more things," its "spiritual exhaustion" in which "mediocrity triumphs under the guise of

democratic restraints." He returned to the theme of purification by suffering that permeates his fiction: "We have been through a spiritual training far in advance of Western experience. The complex and deadly crush of life has produced stronger, deeper, and more interesting personalities than those generated by standardized Western well-being."

One of those strong, deep personalities is surely Matryona in *Matryona's Home*, the novella reprinted here. The story, which is probably modeled on the old Russian literary form of the saint's life, is a testimony to Matryona's absolute simplicity, her refusal to possess anything more than the necessities (she will not raise a pig to kill for food), her willingness to help others without promise of reward. The narrator, like Solzhenitsyn an ex-convict and mathematics teacher, has buried himself deep in the country to avoid signs of modern Soviet society and to find—if it still exists—an image of the Old Russia. The town of Talnovo itself is tainted not just by the *kolkhoz* (collective farm) system, which ceases to consider Matryona part of the collective as soon as she becomes ill, but by the laziness, selfishness, and predatory greed of its inhabitants. Although Matryona's life has been filled with disappointment and deprivation, and she remains an outsider in a materialist society that despises her lack of acquisitive instinct, she seems to live in a dimension of spiritual contentment and love that is unknown to those around her. Only the narrator, who has learned to value essential qualities from his experience in the concentration camps, is able finally to recognize her as "the righteous one" (Genesis 18.23–33), one of those whose spiritual merit seems alien to modern society yet is needed to save society from divine retribution.

Matryona's Home[1]

I

A hundred and fifteen miles from Moscow trains were still slowing down to a crawl a good six months after it happened. Passengers stood glued to the windows or went out to stand by the doors. Was the line under repair, or what? Would the train be late?

It was all right. Past the crossing the train picked up speed again and the passengers went back to their seats.

Only the engine drivers knew what it was all about.
The engine drivers and I.

In the summer of 1953 I was coming back from the hot and dusty desert, just following my nose—so long as it led me back to European Russia. Nobody waited or wanted me at my particular place, because I was a little matter of ten years overdue. I just wanted to get to the central belt, away from the great heat, close to the leafy muttering of forests. I wanted to efface myself, to lose myself in deepest Russia . . . if it was still anywhere to be found.

A year earlier I should have been lucky to get a job carrying a hod this side of the Urals.[2] They wouldn't have taken me as an electrician on a decent construction job. And I had an itch to teach. Those who knew told me that it was a waste of money buying a ticket, that I should have a journey for nothing.

But things were beginning to move.[3] When I went up the stairs of the N——— Regional Education Department and asked for the Personnel Section, I was surprised to find Personnel sitting behind a glass partition, like in a chemist's shop, instead of the usual black leather-padded door. I went timidly up to the window, bowed, and asked, "Please, do you need any mathematicians somewhere where the trains don't run? I should like to settle there for good."

They passed every dot and comma in my documents through a fine comb, went from one room to another, made telephone calls. It was something out of the ordinary for them too—people always wanted the towns, the bigger the better. And lo and behold, they found just the place for me—Vysokoe Polye. The very sound of it gladdened my heart.

Vysokoe Polye[4] did not belie its name. It stood on rising ground, with gentle hollows and other little hills around it. It was enclosed by an unbroken ring of forest. There was a pool behind a weir. Just the place where I wouldn't mind living and dying. I spent a long time sitting on a stump in a coppice and wishing with all my heart that I didn't need breakfast and dinner every day but could just stay here and listen to the branches brushing against the roof in the night, with not a wireless anywhere to be heard and the whole world silent.

Alas, nobody baked bread in Vysokoe Polye. There was nothing edible on sale. The whole village lugged its victuals in sacks from the big town.

1. Translated by H. T. Willetts.
2. Mountain chain separating European Russia from (Asiatic) Siberia.
3. Stalin's death, on March 5, 1953, brought a gradual relaxation of the Soviet state's repressive policies.
4. High meadow.

I went back to the Personnel Section and raised my voice in prayer at the little window. At first they wouldn't even talk to me. But then they started going from one room to another, made a telephone call, scratched with their pens, and stamped on my orders the word "Torfoprodukt."

Torfoprodukt? Turgenev[5] never knew that you can put words like that together in Russian.

On the station building at Torfoprodukt, an antiquated temporary hut of gray wood, hung a stern notice, BOARD TRAINS ONLY FROM THE PASSENGERS' HALL. A further message had been scratched on the boards with a nail, *And Without Tickets*. And by the booking office, with the same melancholy wit, somebody had carved for all time the words, *No Tickets*. It was only later that I fully appreciated the meaning of these addenda. Getting to Torfoprodukt was easy. But not getting away.

Here too, deep and trackless forests had once stood and were still standing after the Revolution. Then they were chopped down by the peat cutters and the neighboring kolkhoz.[6] Its chairman, Shashkov, had razed quite a few hectares of timber and sold it at a good profit down in the Odessa region.

The workers' settlement sprawled untidily among the peat bogs—monotonous shacks from the thirties, and little houses with carved façades and glass verandas, put up in the fifties. But inside these houses I could see no partitions reaching up to the ceilings, so there was no hope of renting a room with four real walls.

Over the settlement hung smoke from the factory chimney. Little locomotives ran this way and that along narrow-gauge railway lines, giving out more thick smoke and piercing whistles, pulling loads of dirty brown peat in slabs and briquettes. I could safely assume that in the evening a loudspeaker would be crying its heart out over the door of the club and there would be drunks roaming the streets and, sooner or later, sticking knives in each other.

This was what my dream about a quiet corner of Russia had brought me to—when I could have stayed where I was and lived in an adobe hut looking out on the desert, with a fresh breeze at night and only the starry dome of the sky overhead.

I couldn't sleep on the station bench, and as soon as it started getting light I went for another stroll round the settlement. This time I saw a tiny marketplace. Only one woman stood there at that early hour, selling milk, and I took a bottle and started drinking it on the spot.

I was struck by the way she talked. Instead of a normal speaking voice, she used an ingratiating singsong, and her words were the ones I was longing to hear when I left Asia for this place.

"Drink, and God bless you. You must be a stranger round here?"

"And where are you from?" I asked, feeling more cheerful.

I learnt that the peat workings weren't the only thing, that over the railway lines there was a hill, and over the hill a village, that this village was Talnovo, and it had been there ages ago, when the "gipsy woman" lived in the big house and the wild woods stood all round. And farther on there was a whole countryside full of villages—Chaslitsy, Ovintsy, Spudni, Shevertni, Shestimirovo, deeper

5. A master of Russian prose style (1818–1883), best known for the novel *Fathers and Sons* (1861) and for a series of sympathetic sketches of peasant life published as *A Sportsman's* Sketches (1882). "Torfoprodukt": peat product; a new word made by combining two words of Germanic origin: *torf* ("peat") and *produkt*. **6.** Collective farm.

and deeper into the woods, farther and farther from the railway, up towards the lakes.

The names were like a soothing breeze to me. They held a promise of back-woods Russia. I asked my new acquaintance to take me to Talnovo after the market was over and find a house for me to lodge in.

It appeared that I was a lodger worth having: in addition to my rent, the school offered a truckload of peat for the winter to whoever took me. The woman's ingratiating smile gave way to a thoughtful frown. She had no room herself, because she and her husband were "keeping" her aged mother, so she took me first to one lot of relatives then to another. But there wasn't a separate room to be had and both places were crowded and noisy.

We had come to a dammed-up stream that was short of water and had a little bridge over it. No other place in all the village took my fancy as this did: there were two or three willows, a lopsided house, ducks swimming on the pond, geese shaking themselves as they stepped out of the water.

"Well, perhaps we might just call on Matryona," said my guide, who was get-ting tired of me by now. "Only it isn't so neat and cozy-like in her house, neglects things she does. She's unwell."

Matryona's house stood quite near by. Its row of four windows looked out on the cold backs, the two slopes of the roof were covered with shingles, and a little attic window was decorated in the old Russian style. But the shingles were rotting, the beam ends of the house and the once mighty gates had turned gray with age, and there were gaps in the little shelter over the gate.

The small gate was fastened, but instead of knocking my companion just put her hand under and turned the catch, a simple device to prevent animals from straying. The yard was not covered, but there was a lot under the roof of the house. As you went through the outer door a short flight of steps rose to a roomy landing, which was open, to the roof high overhead. To the left, other steps led up to the top room, which was a separate structure with no stove, and yet another flight led down to the basement. To the right lay the house proper, with its attic and its cellar.

It had been built a long time ago, built sturdily, to house a big family, and now one lonely woman of nearly sixty lived in it.

When I went into the cottage she was lying on the Russian stove[7] under a heap of those indeterminate dingy rags which are so precious to a working man or woman.

The spacious room, and especially the big part near the windows, was full of rubber plants in pots and tubs standing on stools and benches. They peopled the householder's loneliness like a speechless but living crowd. They had been allowed to run wild, and they took up all the scanty light on the north side. In what was left of the light, and half-hidden by the stovepipe, the mistress of the house looked yellow and weak. You could see from her clouded eyes that ill-ness had drained all the strength out of her.

While we talked she lay on the stove face downward, without a pillow, her head toward the door, and I stood looking up at her. She showed no pleasure at getting a lodger, just complained about the wicked disease she had. She was just getting over an attack: it didn't come upon her every month, but when it

7. A large stove built of masonry, used for both heating and cooking.

did, "It hangs on two or three days so as I shan't manage to get up and wait on you. I've room and to spare, you can live here if you like."

Then she went over the list of other housewives with whom I should be quieter and cozier and wanted me to make the round of them. But I had already seen that I was destined to settle in this dimly lit house with the tarnished mirror, in which you couldn't see yourself, and the two garish posters (one advertising books, the other about the harvest), bought for a ruble each to brighten up the walls.

Matryona Vasilyevna made me go off round the village again, and when I called on her the second time she kept trying to put me off, "We're not clever, we can't cook, I don't know how we shall suit. . . ." But this time she was on her feet when I got there, and I thought I saw a glimmer of pleasure in her eyes to see me back. We reached an agreement about the rent and the load of peat which the school would deliver.

Later on I found out that, year in year out, it was a long time since Matryona Vasilyevna had earned a single ruble. She didn't get a pension. Her relatives gave her very little help. In the kolkhoz she had worked not for money but for credits; the marks recording her labor days in her well-thumbed workbook.

So I moved in with Matryona Vasilyevna. We didn't divide the room. Her bed was in the corner between the door and the stove, and I unfolded my camp bed by one window and pushed Matryona's beloved rubber plants out of the light to make room for a little table by another. The village had electric light, laid on back in the twenties, from Shatury. The newspapers were writing about "Ilyich's little lamps," but the peasants talked wide-eyed about "Tsar Light."[8]

Some of the better-off people in the village might not have thought Matryona's house much of a home, but it kept us snug enough that autumn and winter. The roof still held the rain out, and the freezing winds could not blow the warmth of the stove away all at once, though it was cold by morning, especially when the wind blew on the shabby side.

In addition to Matryona and myself, a cat, some mice, and some cockroaches lived in the house.

The cat was no longer young, and was gammy-legged as well. Matryona had taken her in out of pity, and she had stayed. She walked on all four feet but with a heavy limp: one of her feet was sore and she favored it. When she jumped from the stove she didn't land with the soft sound a cat usually makes, but with a heavy thud as three of her feet struck the floor at once—such a heavy thud that until I got used to it, it gave me a start. This was because she stuck three feet out together to save the fourth.

It wasn't because the cat couldn't deal with them that there were mice in the cottage: she would pounce into the corner like lightning and come back with a mouse between her teeth. But the mice were usually out of reach because somebody, back in the good old days, had stuck embossed wallpaper of a greenish color on Matryona's walls, and not just one layer of it but five. The layers held together all right, but in many places the whole lot had come away from the wall, giving the room a sort of inner skin. Between the timber of the

---

8. The newspapers reflect the new order. "Ilyich": i.e., Vladimir Ilyich Lenin (1870–1924), leader of the 1917 Russian Revolution and first head of the new state. The peasants still think in terms of the emperor (*Tsar*, or czar).

walls and the skin of wallpaper the mice had made themselves runs where they impudently scampered about, running at times right up to the ceiling. The cat followed their scamperings with angry eyes, but couldn't get at them.

Sometimes the cat ate cockroaches as well, but they made her sick. The only thing the cockroaches respected was the partition which screened the mouth of the Russian stove and the kitchen from the best part of the room.

They did not creep into the best room. But the kitchen at night swarmed with them, and if I went in late in the evening for a drink of water and switched on the light the whole floor, the big bench, and even the wall would be one rustling brown mass. From time to time I brought home some borax from the school laboratory and we mixed it with dough to poison them. There would be fewer cockroaches for a while, but Matryona was afraid that we might poison the cat as well. We stopped putting down poison and the cockroaches multiplied anew.

At night, when Matryona was already asleep and I was working at my table, the occasional rapid scamper of mice behind the wallpaper would be drowned in the sustained and ceaseless rustling of cockroaches behind the screen, like the sound of the sea in the distance. But I got used to it because there was nothing evil in it, nothing dishonest. Rustling was life to them.

I even got used to the crude beauty on the poster, forever reaching out from the wall to offer me Belinsky, Panferov,[9] and a pile of other books—but never saying a word. I got used to everything in Matryona's cottage.

Matryona got up at four or five o'clock in the morning. Her wall clock was twenty-seven years old and had been bought in the village shop. It was always fast, but Matryona didn't worry about that—just as long as it didn't lose and make her late in the morning. She switched on the light behind the kitchen screen and moving quietly, considerately, doing her best not to make a noise, she lit the stove, went to milk the goat (all the livestock she had was this one dirty-white goat with twisted horns), fetched water and boiled it in three iron pots: one for me, one for herself, and one for the goat. She fetched potatoes from the cellar, picking out the littlest for the goat, little ones for herself and egg-sized ones for me. There were no big ones, because her garden was sandy, had not been manured since the war, and she always planted with potatoes, potatoes, and potatoes again, so that it wouldn't grow big ones.

I scarcely heard her about her morning tasks. I slept late, woke up in the wintry daylight, stretched a bit, and stuck my head out from under my blanket and my sheepskin. These, together with the prisoner's jerkin round my legs and a sack stuffed with straw underneath me, kept me warm in bed even on nights when the cold wind rattled our wobbly windows from the north. When I heard the discreet noises on the other side of the screen I spoke to her, slowly and deliberately:

"Good morning, Matryona Vasilyevna!"

And every time the same good-natured words came to me from behind the screen. They began with a warm, throaty gurgle, the sort of sound grandmothers make in fairy tales.

"M-m-m . . . same to you too!"

And after a little while, "Your breakfast's ready for you now."

9. Fedor Ivanovich Panferov (1896–1960), socialist-realist writer popular in the 1920s, best known for his novel *The Iron Flood*. Vis- sarion Grigoryevich Belinsky (1811–1848), Russian literary critic who emphasized social and political ideas.

She didn't announce what was for breakfast, but it was easy to guess: taters in their jackets or tatty soup (as everybody in the village called it), or barley gruel (no other grain could be bought in Torfoprodukt that year, and even the barley you had to fight for, because it was the cheapest and people bought it up by the sack to fatten their pigs on it). It wasn't always salted as it should be, it was often slightly burnt, it furred the palate and the gums, and it gave me heartburn.

But Matryona wasn't to blame: there was no butter in Torfoprodukt either, margarine was desperately short, and only mixed cooking fat was plentiful, and when I got to know it, I saw that the Russian stove was not convenient for cooking: the cook cannot see the pots and they are not heated evenly all round. I suppose the stove came down to our ancestors from the Stone Age, because you can stoke it up once before daylight, and food and water, mash and swill will keep warm in it all day long. And it keeps you warm while you sleep.

I ate everything that was cooked for me without demur, patiently putting aside anything uncalled-for that I came across: a hair, a bit of peat, a cockroach's leg. I hadn't the heart to find fault with Matryona. After all, she had warned me herself.

"We aren't clever, we can't cook—I don't know how we shall suit. . . ."

"Thank you," I said quite sincerely.

"What for? For what is your own?" she answered, disarming me with a radiant smile. And, with a guileless look of her faded blue eyes, she would ask, "And what shall I cook you for just now?"

For just now meant for supper. I ate twice a day, like at the front. What could I order for just now? It would have to be one of the same old things, taters or tater soup.

I resigned myself to it, because I had learned by now not to look for the meaning of life in food. More important to me was the smile on her roundish face, which I tried in vain to catch when at last I had earned enough to buy a camera. As soon as she saw the cold eye of the lens upon her, Matryona assumed a strained or else an exaggeratedly severe expression.

Just once I did manage to get a snap of her looking through the window into the street and smiling at something.

Matryona had a lot of worries that winter. Her neighbors put it into her head to try and get a pension. She was all alone in the world, and when she began to be seriously ill she had been dismissed from the kolkhoz as well. Injustices had piled up, one on top of another. She was ill, but was not regarded as a disabled person. She had worked for a quarter of a century in the kolkhoz, but it was a kolkhoz and not a factory, so she was not entitled to a pension for herself. She could only try and get one for her husband, for the loss of her breadwinner. But she had had no husband for twelve years now, not since the beginning of the war, and it wasn't easy to obtain all the particulars from different places about his length of service and how much he had earned. What a bother it was getting those forms through! Getting somebody to certify that he'd earned, say, three hundred rubles a month; that she lived alone and nobody helped her; what year she was born in. Then all this had to be taken to the Pension Office. And taken somewhere else to get all the mistakes corrected. And taken back again. Then you had to find out whether they would give you a pension.

To make it all more difficult the Pension Office was twelve miles east of Talnovo, the Rural Council Offices six miles to the west, the Factory District

Council an hour's walk to the north. They made her run around from office to office for two months on end, to get an *i* dotted or a *t* crossed. Every trip took a day. She goes down to the Rural District Council—and the secretary isn't there today. Secretaries of rural councils often aren't here today. So come again tomorrow. Tomorrow the secretary is in, but he hasn't got his rubber stamp. So come again the next day. And the day after that back she goes yet again, because all her papers are pinned together and some cockeyed clerk has signed the wrong one.

"They shove me around, Ignatich," she used to complain to me after these fruitless excursions. "Worn out with it I am."

But she soon brightened up. I found that she had a sure means of putting herself in a good humor. She worked. She would grab a shovel and go off to pull potatoes. Or she would tuck a sack under her arm and go after peat. Or take a wicker basket and look for berries deep in the woods. When she'd been bending her back to bushes instead of office desks for a while, and her shoulders were aching from a heavy load, Matryona would come back cheerful, at peace with the world and smiling her nice smile.

"I'm on to a good thing now, Ignatich. I know where to go for it (peat she meant), a lovely place it is."

"But surely my peat is enough, Matryona Vasilyevna? There's a whole truckload of it."

"Pooh! Your peat! As much again, and then as much again, that might be enough. When the winter gets really stiff and the wind's battling at the windows, it blows the heat out of the house faster than you can make the stove up. Last year we got heaps and heaps of it. I'd have had three loads in by now. But they're out to catch us. They've summoned one woman from our village already."

That's how it was. The frightening breath of winter was already in the air. There were forests all round, and no fuel to be had anywhere. Excavators roared away in the bogs, but there was no peat on sale to the villagers. It was delivered, free, to the bosses and to the people round the bosses, and teachers, doctors, and workers got a load each. The people of Talnovo were not supposed to get any peat, and they weren't supposed to ask about it. The chairman of the kolkhoz walked about the village looking people in the eye while he gave his orders or stood chatting and talked about anything you liked except fuel. He was stocked up. Who said anything about winter coming?

So just as in the old days they used to steal the squire's wood, now they pinched peat from the trust. The women went in parties of five or ten so that they would be less frightened. They went in the daytime. The peat cut during the summer had been stacked up all over the place to dry. That's the good thing about peat, it can't be carted off as soon as it's cut. It lies around drying till autumn, or, if the roads are bad, till the snow starts falling. This was when the women used to come and take it. They could get six peats in a sack if it was damp, or ten if it was dry. A sackful weighed about half a hundred-weight and it sometimes had to be carried over two miles. This was enough to make the stove up once. There were two hundred days in the winter. The Russian stove had to be lit in the mornings, and the "Dutch"[1] stove in the evenings.

---

1. Not a real tiled Dutch stove, but a cheap small stove (probably made from an oil barrel) that provided heat with less fuel than a big Russian stove.

"Why beat about the bush?" said Matryona angrily to someone invisible. "Since there've been no more horses, what you can't have around yourself you haven't got. My back never heals up. Winter you're pulling sledges, summer it's bundles on your back, it's God's truth I'm telling you."

The women went more than once in a day. On good days Matryona brought six sacks home. She piled my peat up where it could be seen and hid her own under the passageway, boarding up the hole every night.

"If they don't just happen to think of it, the devils will never find it in their born days," said Matryona smiling and wiping the sweat from her brow.

What could the peat trust do? Its establishment didn't run to a watchman for every bog. I suppose they had to show a rich haul in their returns, and then write off so much for crumbling, so much washed away by the rain. Sometimes they would take it into their heads to put out patrols and try to catch the women as they came into the village. The women would drop their sacks and scatter. Or somebody would inform and there would be a house-to-house search. They would draw up a report on the stolen peat and threaten a court action. The women would stop fetching it for a while, but the approach of winter drove them out with sledges in the middle of the night.

When I had seen a little more of Matryona I noticed that, apart from cooking and looking after the house, she had quite a lot of other jobs to do every day. She kept all her jobs, and the proper times for them, in her head and always knew when she woke up in the morning how her day would be occupied. Apart from fetching peat and stumps which the tractors unearthed in the bogs, apart from the cranberries which she put to soak in big jars for the winter ("Give your teeth an edge, Ignatich," she used to say when she offered me some), apart from digging potatoes and all the coming and going to do with her pension, she had to get hay from somewhere for her one and only dirty-white goat.

"Why don't you keep a cow, Matryona?"

Matryona stood there in her grubby apron, by the opening in the kitchen screen, facing my table, and explained to me.

"Oh, Ignatich, there's enough milk from the goat for me. And if I started keeping a cow she'd eat me out of house and home in no time. You can't cut the grass by the railway track, because it belongs to the railway, and you can't cut any in the woods, because it belongs to the foresters, and they won't let me have any at the kolkhoz because I'm not a member any more, they reckon. And those who are members have to work there every day till the white flies swarm and make their own hay when there's snow on the ground—what's the good of grass like that? In the old days they used to be sweating to get the hay in at midsummer, between the end of June and the end of July, while the grass was sweet and juicy."

So it meant a lot of work for Matryona to gather enough hay for one skinny little goat. She took her sickle and a sack and went off early in the morning to places where she knew there was grass growing—round the edges of fields, on the roadside, on hummocks in the bog. When she had stuffed her sack with heavy fresh grass she dragged it home and spread it out in her yard to dry. From a sackful of grass she got one forkload of dry hay.

The farm had a new chairman, sent down from the town not long ago, and the first thing he did was to cut down the garden plots for those who were not fit to work. He left Matryona a third of an acre of sand—when there was over a thousand square yards just lying idle on the other side of the fence. Yet when they were short of working hands, when the women dug in their heels and wouldn't budge, the chairman's wife would come to see Matryona. She was from the town as well, a determined woman whose short gray coat and intimidating glare gave her a somewhat military appearance. She walked into the house without so much as a good morning and looked sternly at Matryona. Matryona was uneasy.

"Well now, Comrade Vasilyevna," said the chairman's wife, drawing out her words. "You will have to help the kolkhoz! You will have to go and help cart manure out tomorrow!"

A little smile of forgiveness wrinkled Matryona's face—as though she understood the embarrassment which the chairman's wife must feel at not being able to pay her for her work.

"Well—er," she droned. "I'm not well, of course, and I'm not attached to you any more . . . ," then she hurried to correct herself, "What time should I come then?"

"And bring your own fork!" the chairman's wife instructed her. Her stiff skirt crackled as she walked away.

"Think of that!" grumbled Matryona as the door closed. "Bring your own fork! They've got neither forks nor shovels at the kolkhoz. And I don't have a man who'll put a handle on for me!"

She went on thinking about it out loud all evening.

"What's the good of talking, Ignatich. I must help, of course. Only the way they work it's all a waste of time—don't know whether they're coming or going. The women stand propped up on their shovels and waiting for the factory whistle to blow twelve o'clock. Or else they get on to adding up who's earned what and who's turned up for work and who hasn't. Now what I call work, there isn't a sound out of anybody, only—oh dear, dear—dinner time's soon rolled round—what, getting dark already."

In the morning she went off with her fork.

But it wasn't just the kolkhoz—any distant relative, or just a neighbor, could come to Matryona of an evening and say, "Come and give me a hand tomorrow, Matryona. We'll finish pulling the potatoes."

Matryona couldn't say no. She gave up what she should be doing next and went to help her neighbor, and when she came back she would say without a trace of envy, "Ah, you should see the size of her potatoes, Ignatich! It was a joy to dig them up. I didn't want to leave the allotment, God's truth I didn't."

Needless to say, not a garden could be plowed without Matryona's help. The women of Talnovo had got it neatly worked out that it was a longer and harder job for one woman to dig her garden with a spade than for six of them to put themselves in harness and plow six gardens. So they sent for Matryona to help them.

"Well—did you pay her?" I asked sometimes.

"She won't take money. You have to try and hide it on her when she's not looking."

Matryona had yet another troublesome chore when her turn came to feed the herdsmen. One of them was a hefty deaf mute, the other a boy who was never without a cigaret in his drooling mouth. Matryona's turn came round only every six weeks, but it put her to great expense. She went to the shop to buy canned fish and was lavish with sugar and butter, things she never ate herself. It seems that the housewives showed off in this way, trying to outdo one another in feeding the herdsmen.

"You've got to be careful with tailors and herdsmen," Matryona explained. "They'll spread your name all round the village if something doesn't suit them."

And every now and then attacks of serious illness broke in on this life that was already crammed with troubles. Matryona would be off her feet for a day or two, lying flat out on the stove. She didn't complain and didn't groan, but she hardly stirred either. On these days Masha, Matryona's closest friend from her earliest years, would come to look after the goat and light the stove. Matryona herself ate nothing, drank nothing, asked for nothing. To call in the doctor from the clinic at the settlement would have seemed strange in Talnovo and would have given the neighbors something to talk about—what does she think she is, a lady? They did call her in once, and she arrived in a real temper and told Matryona to come down to the clinic when she was on her feet again. Matryona went, although she didn't really want to; they took specimens and sent them off to the district hospital—and that's the last anybody heard about it. Matryona was partly to blame herself.

But there was work waiting to be done, and Matryona soon started getting up again, moving slowly at first and then as briskly as ever.

"You never saw me in the old days, Ignatich. I'd lift any sack you liked, I didn't think a hundredweight was too heavy. My father-in-law used to say, 'Matryona, you'll break your back.' And my brother-in-law didn't have to come and help me lift on the cart. Our horse was a warhorse, a big strong one."

"What do you mean, a warhorse?"

"They took ours for the war and gave us this one instead—he'd been wounded. But he turned out a bit spirited. Once he bolted with the sledge right into the lake, the men folk hopped out of the way, but I grabbed the bridle, as true as I'm here, and stopped him. Full of oats that horse was. They liked to feed their horses well in our village. If a horse feels his oats he doesn't know what heavy means."

But Matryona was a long way from being fearless. She was afraid of fire, afraid of "the lightning," and most of all she was for some reason afraid of trains.

"When I had to go to Cherusti,[2] the train came up from Nechaevka way with its great big eyes popping out and the rails humming away—put me in a regular fever. My knees started knocking. God's truth I'm telling you!" Matryona raised her shoulders as though she surprised herself.

"Maybe it's because they won't give people tickets, Matryona Vasilyevna?"

"At the window? They try to shove only first-class tickets on to you. And the train was starting to move. We dashed about all over the place, 'Give us tickets for pity's sake.'"

"The men folk had climbed on top of the carriages. Then we found a door that wasn't locked and shoved straight in without tickets—and all the carriages

2. About 100 miles east of Moscow and some 250 miles northwest of Nechaevka.

were empty, they were all empty, you could stretch out on the seat if you wanted to. Why they wouldn't give us tickets, the hardhearted parasites, I don't know. . . ."

Still, before winter came, Matryona's affairs were in a better state than ever before. They started paying her at last a pension of eighty rubles. Besides this she got just over one hundred from the school and me.

Some of her neighbors began to be envious.

"Hm! Matryona can live forever now! If she had any more money, she wouldn't know what to do with it at her age."

Matryona had some new felt boots made. She bought a new jerkin. And she had an overcoat made out of the worn-out railwayman's greatcoat given to her by the engine driver from Cherusti who had married Kira, her foster daughter. The hump-backed village tailor put a padded lining under the cloth and it made a marvelous coat, such as Matryona had never worn before in all her sixty years.

In the middle of winter Matryona sewed two hundred rubles into the lining of this coat for her funeral. This made her quite cheerful.

"Now my mind's a bit easier, Ignatich."

December went by, January went by—and in those two months Matryona's illness held off. She started going over to Masha's house more often in the evening, to sit chewing sunflower seeds with her. She herself didn't invite guests in the evening out of consideration for my work. Once, on the feast of the Epiphany, I came back from school and found a party going on and was introduced to Matryona's three sisters, who called her "nan-nan" or "nanny" because she was the oldest. Until then not much had been heard of the sisters in our cottage—perhaps they were afraid that Matryona might ask them for help.

But one ominous event cast a shadow on the holiday for Matryona. She went to the church three miles away for the blessing of the water and put her pot down among the others. When the blessing was over, the women went rushing and jostling to get their pots back again. There were a lot of women in front of Matryona and when she got there her pot was missing, and no other vessel had been left behind. The pot had vanished as though the devil had run off with it.

Matryona went round the worshipers asking them, "Have any of you girls accidentally mistook somebody else's holy water? In a pot?"

Nobody owned up. There had been some boys there, and boys got up to mischief sometimes. Matryona came home sad.

No one could say that Matryona was a devout believer. If anything, she was a heathen, and her strongest beliefs were superstitious: you mustn't go into the garden on the fast of St. John or there would be no harvest next year. A blizzard meant that somebody had hanged himself. If you pinched your foot in the door, you could expect a guest. All the time I lived with her I didn't once see her say her prayers or even cross herself. But, whatever job she was doing, she began with a "God bless us," and she never failed to say "God bless you," when I set out for school. Perhaps she did say her prayers, but on the quiet, either because she was shy or because she didn't want to embarrass me. There were icons[3] on

---

3. Religious images or portraits, usually painted on wood. A small lamp was set in front of the icons to illuminate them.

the walls. Ordinary days they were left in darkness, but for the vigil of a great feast, or on the morning of a holiday, Matryona would light the little lamp.

She had fewer sins on her conscience than her gammy-legged cat. The cat did kill mice.

Now that her life was running more smoothly, Matryona started listening more carefully to my radio. (I had, of course, installed a speaker, or as Matryona called it, a peeker.)[4]

When they announced on the radio that some new machine had been invented, I heard Matryona grumbling out in the kitchen, "New ones all the time, nothing but new ones. People don't want to work with the old ones any more, where are we going to store them all?"

There was a program about the seeding of clouds from airplanes. Matryona, listening up on the stove, shook her head, "Oh, dear, dear, dear, they'll do away with one of the two—summer or winter."

Once Shalyapin[5] was singing Russian folk songs. Matryona stood listening for a long time before she gave her emphatic verdict, "Queer singing, not our sort of singing."

"You can't mean that, Matryona Vasilyevna—just listen to him."

She listened a bit longer and pursed her lips, "No, it's wrong. It isn't our sort of tune, and he's tricky with his voice."

She made up for this another time. They were broadcasting some of Glinka's[6] songs. After half a dozen of these drawing-room ballads, Matryona suddenly came from behind the screen clutching her apron, with a flush on her face and a film of tears over her dim eyes.

"That's our sort of singing," she said in a whisper.

2

So Matryona and I got used to each other and took each other for granted. She never pestered me with questions about myself. I don't know whether she was lacking in normal female curiosity or just tactful, but she never once asked if I had been married. All the Talnovo women kept at her to find out about me. Her answer was, "You want to know—you ask him. All I know is he's from distant parts."

And when I got round to telling her that I had spent a lot of time in prison, she said nothing but just nodded, as though she had already suspected it.

And I thought of Matryona only as the helpless old woman she was now and didn't try to rake up her past, didn't even suspect that there was anything to be found there.

I knew that Matryona had got married before the Revolution and had come to live in the house I now shared with her, and she had gone "to the stove"

4. The translator is imitating Solzhenitsyn's wordplay. In the original, the narrator calls the speaker *razvedka* ("scout," literal trans: a military term); Matryona calls it *rozetka* (an electric plug).
5. Feodor Ivanovich Shalyapin (or Chaliapin, 1873–1938), Russian operatic bass with an international reputation as a great singer and

actor; he included popular Russian music in his song recitals.
6. Mikhail Ivanovich Glinka (1804–1857), Russian composer who was instrumental in developing a "Russian" style of music, including the two operas *A Life for the Czar* and *Ruslan and Ludmila*.

immediately. (She had no mother-in-law and no older sister-in-law, so it was her job to put the pots in the oven on the very first morning of her married life.) I knew that she had had six children and that they had all died very young, so that there were never two of them alive at once. Then there was a sort of foster daughter, Kira. Matryona's husband had not come back from the last war. She received no notification of his death. Men from the village who had served in the same company said that he might have been taken prisoner, or he might have been killed and his body not found. In the eight years that had gone by since the war Matryona had decided that he was not alive. It was a good thing that she thought so. If he was still alive he was probably in Brazil or Australia and married again. The village of Talnovo and the Russian language would be fading from his memory.

One day when I got back from school, I found a guest in the house. A tall, dark man, with his hat on his lap, was sitting on a chair which Matryona had moved up to the Dutch stove in the middle of the room. His face was completely surrounded by bushy black hair with hardly a trace of gray in it. His thick black moustache ran into his full black beard, so that his mouth could hardly be seen. Black side-whiskers merged with the black locks which hung down from his crown, leaving only the tips of his ears visible; his broad black eyebrows met in a wide double span. But the front of his head as far as the crown was a spacious bald dome. His whole appearance made an impression of wisdom and dignity. He sat squarely on his chair, with his hands folded on his stick, and his stick resting vertically on the floor, in an attitude of patient expectation, and he obviously hadn't much to say to Matryona, who was busy behind the screen.

When I came in, he eased his majestic head round toward me and suddenly addressed me, "Schoolmaster, I can't see you very well. My son goes to your school. Grigoryev, Antoshka."

There was no need for him to say any more. However strongly inclined I felt to help this worthy old man, I knew and dismissed in advance all the pointless things he was going to say. Antoshka Grigoryev was a plump, red-faced lad in 8-D who looked like a cat that's swallowed the cream. He seemed to think that he came to school for a rest and sat at his desk with a lazy smile on his face. Needless to say, he never did his homework. But the worst of it was that he had been put up into the next class from year to year because our district, and indeed the whole region and the neighboring region were famous for the high percentage of passes they obtained; the school had to make an effort to keep its record up. So Antoshka had got it clear in his mind that however much the teachers threatened him they would promote him in the end, and there was no need for him to learn anything. He just laughed at us. There he sat in the eighth class, and he hadn't even mastered his decimals and didn't know one triangle from another. In the first two terms of the school year I had kept him firmly below the passing line and the same treatment awaited him in the third.

But now this half-blind old man, who should have been Antoshka's grandfather rather than his father, had come to humble himself before me—how could I tell him that the school had been deceiving him for years, and that I couldn't go on deceiving him, because I didn't want to ruin the whole class, to become a liar and a fake, to start despising my work and my profession.

For the time being I patiently explained that his son had been very slack, that he told lies at school and at home, that his record book must be checked frequently, and that we must both take him severely in hand.

"Severe as you like, Schoolmaster," he assured me, "I beat him every week now. And I've got a heavy hand."

While we were talking I remembered that Matryona had once interceded for Antoshka Grigoryev, but I hadn't asked what relation of hers he was and I had refused to do what she wanted. Matryona was standing in the kitchen doorway like a mute suppliant on this occasion too. When Faddey Mironovich left, saying that he would call on me to see how things were going, I asked her, "I can't make out what relation this Antoshka is to you, Matryona Vasilyevna."

"My brother-in-law's son," said Matryona shortly, and went out to milk the goat.

When I'd worked it out, I realized that this determined old man with the black hair was the brother of the missing husband.

The long evening went by, and Matryona didn't bring up the subject again. But late at night, when I had stopped thinking about the old man and was working in a silence broken only by the rustling of the cockroaches and the heavy tick of the wall-clock, Matryona suddenly spoke from her dark corner, "You know, Ignatich, I nearly married him once."

I had forgotten that Matryona was in the room. I hadn't heard a sound from her—and suddenly her voice came out of the darkness, as agitated as if the old man were still trying to win her.

I could see that Matryona had been thinking about nothing else all evening.

She got up from her wretched rag bed and walked slowly toward me, as though she were following her own words. I sat back in my chair and caught my first glimpse of a quite different Matryona.

There was no overhead light in our big room with its forest of rubber plants. The table lamp cast a ring of light round my exercise books, and when I tore my eyes from it the rest of the room seemed to be half-dark and faintly tinged with pink. I thought I could see the same pinkish glow in her usually sallow cheeks.

"He was the first one who came courting me, before Efim did—he was his brother—the older one—I was nineteen and Faddey was twenty-three. They lived in this very same house. Their house it was. Their father built it."

I looked round the room automatically. Instead of the old gray house rotting under the faded green skin of wallpaper where the mice had their playground, I suddenly saw new timbers, freshly trimmed, not yet discolored, and caught the cheerful smell of pine tar.

"Well, and what happened then?"

"That summer we went to sit in the woods together," she whispered. "There used to be a woods where the stable yard is now. They chopped it down. I was just going to marry him, Ignatich. Then the German war started. They took Faddey into the army."

She let fall these few words—and suddenly the blue and white and yellow July of the year 1914 burst into flower before my eyes: the sky still peaceful, the floating clouds, the people sweating to get the ripe corn in. I imagined them side by side, the black-haired Hercules with a scythe over his shoulder, and the red-faced girl clasping a sheaf. And there was singing out under the open sky, such songs as nobody can sing nowadays, with all the machines in the fields.

"He went to the war—and vanished. For three years I kept to myself and waited. Never a sign of life did he give."

Matryona's round face looked out at me from an elderly threadbare headscarf. As she stood there in the gentle reflected light from my lamp, her face seemed to lose its slovenly workday wrinkles, and she was a scared young girl again with a frightening decision to make.

Yes . . . I could see it. The trees shed their leaves, the snow fell and melted. They plowed and sowed and reaped again. Again the trees shed their leaves, and the snow fell. There was a revolution. Then another revolution.[7] And the whole world was turned upside down.

"Their mother died and Efim came to court me. 'You wanted to come to our house,' he says, 'so come.' He was a year younger than me, Efim was. It's a saying with us—sensible girls get married after Michaelmas, and silly ones at midsummer. They were shorthanded. I got married. . . . The wedding was on St. Peter's day, and then about St. Nicholas' day[8] in the winter he came back—Faddey, I mean, from being a prisoner in Hungary."

Matryona covered her eyes.

I said nothing.

She turned toward the door as though somebody were standing there. "He stood there at the door. What a scream I let out! I wanted to throw myself at his feet! . . . but I couldn't. 'If it wasn't my own brother,' he says, 'I'd take my ax to the both of you.'"

I shuddered. Matryona's despair, or her terror, conjured up a vivid picture of him standing in the dark doorway and raising his ax to her.

But she quieted down and went on with her story in a sing-song voice, leaning on a chairback, "Oh dear, dear me, the poor dear man! There were so many girls in the village—but he wouldn't marry. I'll look for one with the same name as you, a second Matryona, he said. And that's what he did—fetched himself a Matryona from Lipovka. They built themselves a house of their own and they're still living in it. You pass their place every day on your way to school."

So that was it. I realized that I had seen the other Matryona quite often. I didn't like her. She was always coming to my Matryona to complain about her husband—he beat her, he was stingy, he was working her to death. She would weep and weep, and her voice always had a tearful note in it. As it turned out, my Matryona had nothing to regret, with Faddey beating his Matryona every day of his life and being so tightfisted.

"Mine never beat me once," said Matryona of Efim. "He'd pitch into another man in the street, but me he never hit once. Well, there was one time—I quarreled with my sister-in-law and he cracked me on the forehead with a spoon. I jumped up from the table and shouted at them, 'Hope it sticks in your gullets, you idle lot of beggars, hope you choke!' I said. And off I went into the woods. He never touched me any more."

---

7. The February and the October revolutions (1917).
8. December 19 (December 6, old style).

"Michaelmas": October 12 (September 29, old style). "St. Peter's Day": probably July 12 (June 29, old style), Sts. Peter and Paul's Day.

Faddey didn't seem to have any cause for regret either. The other Matryona had borne him six children (my Antoshka was one of them, the littlest, the runt) and they had all lived, whereas the children of Matryona and Efim had died, every one of them, before they reached the age of three months, without any illness.

"One daughter, Elena, was born and was alive when they washed her, and then she died right after. . . . My wedding was on St. Peter's day, and it was St. Peter's day I buried my sixth, Alexander."

The whole village decided that there was a curse on Matryona.

Matryona still nodded emphatic belief when she talked about it. "There was a *course*[9] on me. They took me to a woman who used to be a nun to get cured, she set me off coughing and waited for the *course* to jump out of me like a frog. Only nothing jumped out."

And the years had run by like running water. In 1941 they didn't take Faddey into the army because of his poor sight, but they took Efim. And what had happened to the elder brother in the First World War happened to the younger in the Second—he vanished without a trace. Only he never came back at all. The once noisy cottage was deserted, it grew old and rotten, and Matryona, all alone in the world, grew old in it.

So she begged from the other Matryona, the cruelly beaten Matryona, a child of her womb (or was it a drop of Faddey's blood?), the youngest daughter, Kira.

For ten years she brought the girl up in her own house, in place of the children who had not lived. Then, not long before I arrived, she had married her off to a young engine driver from Cherusti. The only help she got from anywhere came in dribs and drabs from Cherusti: a bit of sugar from time to time, or some of the fat when they killed a pig.

Sick and suffering, and feeling that death was not far off, Matryona had made known her will: the top room, which was a separate frame joined by tie beams to the rest of the house, should go to Kira when she died.[1] She said nothing about the house itself. Her three sisters had their eyes on it too.

That evening Matryona opened her heart to me. And, as often happens, no sooner were the hidden springs of her life revealed to me than I saw them in motion.

Kira arrived from Cherusti. Old Faddey was very worried. To get and keep a plot of land in Cherusti the young couple had to put up some sort of building. Matryona's top room would do very well. There was nothing else they could put up, because there was no timber to be had anywhere. It wasn't Kira herself so much, and it wasn't her husband, but old Faddey who was consumed with eagerness for them to get their hands on the plot at Cherusti.

He became a frequent visitor, laying down the law to Matryona and insisting that she should hand over the top room right away, before she died. On these occasions I saw a different Faddey. He was no longer an old man propped up by a stick, whom a push or a harsh word would bowl over. Although he was slightly bent by backache, he was still a fine figure; in his sixties he had kept the vigorous black hair of a young man; he was hot and urgent.

9. *Curse/course* reflects wordplay in the Russian original, where a similar misuse of language indicates Matryona's lack of formal education.

1. Lumber was scarce and valuable, and old houses were well built. Moving houses or sections of houses is still common in the country.

Matryona had not slept for two nights. It wasn't easy for her to make up her mind. She didn't grudge them the top room, which was standing there idle, any more than she ever grudged her labor or her belongings. And the top room was willed to Kira in any case. But the thought of breaking up the roof she had lived under for forty years was torture to her. Even I, a mere lodger, found it painful to think of them stripping away boards and wrenching out beams. For Matryona it was the end of everything.

But the people who were so insistent knew that she would let them break up her house before she died.

So Faddey and his sons and sons-in-law came along one February morning, the blows of five axes were heard and boards creaked and cracked as they were wrenched out. Faddey's eyes twinkled busily. Although his back wasn't quite straight yet, he scrambled nimbly up under the rafters and bustled about down below, shouting at his assistants. He and his father had built this house when he was a lad, a long time ago. The top room had been put up for him, the oldest son, to move into with his bride. And now he was furiously taking it apart, board by board, to carry it out of somebody else's yard.

After numbering the beam ends and the ceiling boards, they dismantled the top room and the storeroom underneath it. The living room and what was left of the landing they boarded up with a thin wall of deal. They did nothing about the cracks in the wall. It was plain to see that they were wreckers, not builders, and that they did not expect Matryona to be living there very long.

While the men were busy wrecking, the women were getting the drink ready for moving day—vodka would cost too much. Kira brought forty pounds of sugar from the Moscow region, and Matryona carried the sugar and some bottles to the distiller under cover of night.

The timbers were carried out and stacked in front of the gates, and the engine-driver son-in-law went off to Cherusti for the tractor.

But the very same day a blizzard, or "a blower," as Matryona once called it, began. It howled and whirled for two days and nights and buried the road under enormous drifts. Then, no sooner had they made the road passable and a couple of trucks had gone by, than it got suddenly warmer. Within a day everything was thawing out, damp mist hung in the air and rivulets gurgled as they burrowed into the snow, and you could get stuck up to the top of your jackboots.

Two weeks passed before the tractor could get at the dismantled top room. All this time Matryona went around like someone lost. What particularly upset her was that her three sisters came, with one voice called her a fool for giving the top room away, said they didn't want to see her any more, and went off. At about the same time the lame cat strayed and was seen no more. It was just one thing after another. This was another blow to Matryona.

At last the frost got a grip on the slushy road. A sunny day came along, and everybody felt more cheerful. Matryona had had a lucky dream the night before. In the morning she heard that I wanted to take a photograph of somebody at an old-fashioned handloom. (There were looms still standing in two cottages in the village; they wove coarse rugs on them.) She smiled shyly and said, "You just wait a day or two, Ignatich, I'll just send off the top room there and I'll put my loom up, I've still got it, you know, and then you can snap me. Honest to God!"

She was obviously attracted by the idea of posing in an old-fashioned setting. The red frosty sun tinged the window of the curtailed passageway with a faint pink, and this reflected light warmed Matryona's face. People who are at ease with their consciences always have nice faces.

Coming back from school before dusk I saw some movement near our house. A big new tractor-drawn sledge was already fully loaded, and there was no room for a lot of the timbers, so old Faddey's family and the helpers they had called in had nearly finished knocking together another homemade sledge. They were all working like madmen, in the frenzy that comes upon people when there is a smell of good money in the air or when they are looking forward to some treat. They were shouting at one another and arguing.

They could not agree on whether the sledges should be hauled separately or both together. One of Faddey's sons (the lame one) and the engine-driver son-in-law reasoned that the sledges couldn't both be taken at once because the tractor wouldn't be able to pull them. The man in charge of the tractor, a hefty fat-faced fellow who was very sure of himself, said hoarsely that he knew best, he was the driver, and he would take both at once. His motives were obvious: according to the agreement, the engine driver was paying him for the removal of the upper room, not for the number of trips he had to make. He could never have made two trips in a night—twenty-five kilometers each way, and one return journey. And by morning he had to get the tractor back in the garage from which he had sneaked it out for this job on the side.

Old Faddey was impatient to get the top room moved that day, and at a nod from him his lads gave in. To the stout sledge in front they hitched the one they had knocked together in such a hurry.

Matryona was running about among the men, fussing and helping them to heave the beams on the sledge. Suddenly I noticed that she was wearing my jacket and had dirtied the sleeves on the frozen mud round the beams. I was annoyed and told her so. That jacket held memories for me: it had kept me warm in the bad years.

This was the first time that I was ever angry with Matryona Vasilyevna.

Matryona was taken aback. "Oh dear, dear me," she said. "My poor head. I picked it up in a rush, you see, and never thought about it being yours. I'm sorry, Ignatich."

And she took it off and hung it up to dry.

The loading was finished, and all the men who had been working, about ten of them, clattered past my table and dived under the curtain into the kitchen. I could hear the muffled rattle of glasses and, from time to time, the clink of a bottle, the voices got louder and louder, the boasting more reckless. The biggest braggart was the tractor driver. The stink of hooch floated in to me. But they didn't go on drinking long. It was getting dark and they had to hurry. They began to leave. The tractor driver came out first, looking pleased with himself and fierce. The engine-driver son-in-law, Faddey's lame son, and one of his nephews were going to Cherusti. The others went off home. Faddey was flourishing his stick, trying to overtake somebody and put him right about something. The lame son paused at my table to light up and suddenly started telling me how he loved Aunt Matryona, and that he had got married not long ago, and his wife had just had a son. Then they shouted for him and he went out. The tractor set up a roar outside.

After all the others had gone, Matryona dashed out from behind the screen. She looked after them, anxiously shaking her head. She had put on her jacket and her headscarf. As she was going through the door, she said to me, "Why ever couldn't they hire two? If one tractor had cracked up, the other would have pulled them. What'll happen now, God only knows!"

She ran out after the others.

After the boozing and the arguments and all the coming and going, it was quieter than ever in the deserted cottage, and very chilly because the door had been opened so many times. I got into my jacket and sat down to mark exercise books. The noise of the tractor died away in the distance.

An hour went by. And another. And a third. Matryona still hadn't come back, but I wasn't surprised. When she had seen the sledge off, she must have gone round to her friend Masha.

Another hour went by. And yet another. Darkness, and with it a deep silence had descended on the village. I couldn't understand at the time why it was so quiet. Later, I found out that it was because all evening not a single train had gone along the line five hundred yards from the house. No sound was coming from my radio, and I noticed that the mice were wilder than ever. Their scampering and scratching and squeaking behind the wallpaper was getting noisier and more defiant all the time.

I woke up. It was one o'clock in the morning, and Matryona still hadn't come home.

Suddenly I heard several people talking loudly. They were still a long way off, but something told me that they were coming to our house. And sure enough, I heard soon afterward a heavy knock at the gate. A commanding voice, strange to me, yelled out an order to open up. I went out into the pitch darkness with a torch. The whole village was asleep, there was no light in the windows, and the snow had started melting in the last week so that it gave no reflected light. I turned the catch and let them in. Four men in greatcoats went on toward the house. It's a very unpleasant thing to be visited at night by noisy people in greatcoats.

When we got into the light though, I saw that two of them were wearing railway uniforms. The older of the two, a fat man with the same sort of face as the tractor driver, asked, "Where's the woman of the house?"

"I don't know."

"This is the place the tractor with a sledge came from?"

"This is it."

"Had they been drinking before they left?"

All four of them were looking around, screwing up their eyes in the dim light from the table lamp. I realized that they had either made an arrest or wanted to make one.

"What's happened then?"

"Answer the question!"

"But . . ."

"Were they drunk when they went?"

"Were they drinking here?"

Had there been a murder? Or hadn't they been able to move the top room? The men in greatcoats had me off balance. But one thing was certain: Matryona could do time for making hooch.

I stepped back to stand between them and the kitchen door. "I honestly didn't notice. I didn't see anything." (I really hadn't seen anything—only heard.) I made what was supposed to be a helpless gesture, drawing attention to the state of the cottage: a table lamp shining peacefully on books and exercises, a crowd of frightened rubber plants, the austere couch of a recluse, not a sign of debauchery.

They had already seen for themselves, to their annoyance, that there had been no drinking in that room. They turned to leave, telling each other this wasn't where the drinking had been then, but it would be a good thing to put in that it was. I saw them out and tried to discover what had happened. It was only at the gate that one of them growled. "They've all been cut to bits. Can't find all the pieces."

"That's a detail. The nine o'clock express nearly went off the rails. That would have been something." And they walked briskly away.

I went back to the hut in a daze. Who were "they"? What did "all of them" mean? And where was Matryona?

I moved the curtain aside and went into the kitchen. The stink of hooch rose and hit me. It was a deserted battlefield: a huddle of stools and benches, empty bottles lying around, one bottle half-full, glasses, the remains of pickled herring, onion, and sliced fat pork.

Everything was deathly still. Just cockroaches creeping unperturbed about the field of battle.

They had said something about the nine o'clock express. Why? Perhaps I should have shown them all this? I began to wonder whether I had done right. But what a damnable way to behave—keeping their explanations for official persons only.

Suddenly the small gate creaked. I hurried out on to the landing. "Matryona Vasilyevna?"

The yard door opened, and Matryona's friend Masha came in, swaying and wringing her hands. "Matryona—our Matryona, Ignatich—"

I sat her down, and through her tears she told me the story.

The approach to the crossing was a steep rise. There was no barrier. The tractor and the first sledge went over, but the towrope broke and the second sledge, the homemade one, got stuck on the crossing and started falling apart—the wood Faddey had given them to make the second sledge was no good. They towed the first sledge out of the way and went back for the second. They were fixing the towrope—the tractor driver and Faddey's lame son, and Matryona (heaven knows what brought her there) were with them, between the tractor and the sledge. What help did she think she could be to the men? She was forever meddling in men's work. Hadn't a bolting horse nearly tipped her into the lake once, through a hole in the ice? Why did she have to go to the damned crossing? She had handed over the top room and owed nothing to anybody. The engine driver kept a lookout in case the train from Cherusti rushed up on them. Its headlamps would be visible a long way off. But two engines coupled together came from the other direction, from our station, backing without lights. Why they were without lights nobody knows. When an engine is backing, coal dust blows into the driver's eyes from the tender and he can't see very well. The two engines flew into them and crushed the three people between the tractor and the sledge to pulp. The tractor was wrecked, the sledge was matchwood, the rails were buckled, and both engines turned over.

"But how was it they didn't hear the engines coming?"

"The tractor engine was making such a din."

"What about the bodies?"

"They won't let anybody in. They've roped them off."

"What was that somebody was telling me about the express?"

"The nine o'clock express goes through our station at a good clip and on to the crossing. But the two drivers weren't hurt when their engines crashed, they jumped out and ran back along the line waving their hands, and they managed to stop the train. The nephew was hurt by a beam as well. He's hiding at Klav-ka's now so that they won't know he was at the crossing. If they find out they'll drag him in as a witness. . . .'Don't know lies up, and do know gets tied up.' Kira's husband didn't get a scratch. He tried to hang himself, they had to cut him down. It's all because of me, he says, my aunty's killed and my brother. Now he's gone and given himself up. But the madhouse is where he'll be going, not prison. Oh, Matryona, my dearest Matryona. . . ."

Matryona was gone. Someone close to me had been killed. And on her last day I had scolded her for wearing my jacket.

The lovingly drawn red and yellow woman in the book advertisement smiled happily on.

Old Masha sat there weeping a little longer. Then she got up to go. And suddenly she asked me, "Ignatich, you remember, Matryona had a gray shawl. She meant it to go to my Tanya when she died, didn't she?"

She looked at me hopefully in the half-darkness—surely I hadn't forgotten?

No, I remembered. "She said so, yes."

"Well, listen, maybe you could let me take it with me now. The family will be swarming in tomorrow and I'll never get it then." And she gave me another hopeful, imploring look. She had been Matryona's friend for half a century, the only one in the village who truly loved her.

No doubt she was right.

"Of course—take it."

She opened the chest, took out the shawl, tucked it under her coat, and went out.

The mice had gone mad. They were running furiously up and down the walls, and you could almost see the green wallpaper rippling and rolling over their backs.

In the morning I had to go to school. The time was three o'clock. The only thing to do was to lock up and go to bed.

Lock up, because Matryona would not be coming.

I lay down, leaving the light on. The mice were squeaking, almost moaning, racing and running. My mind was weary and wandering, and I couldn't rid myself of an uneasy feeling that an invisible Matryona was flitting about and saying good-bye to her home.

And suddenly I imagined Faddey standing there, young and black-haired, in the dark patch by the door, with his ax uplifted. "If it wasn't my own brother, I'd chop the both of you to bits."

The threat had lain around for forty years, like an old broad sword in a corner, and in the end it had struck its blow.

3

When it was light the women went to the crossing and brought back all that was left of Matryona on a hand sledge with a dirty sack over it. They threw off the sack to wash her. There was just a mess . . . no feet, only half a body, no left hand. One woman said, "The Lord has left her her right hand. She'll be able to say her prayers where she's going."

Then the whole crowd of rubber plants were carried out of the cottage—these plants that Matryona had loved so much that once when smoke woke her up in the night she didn't rush to save her house but to tip the plants onto the floor in case they were suffocated. The women swept the floor clean. They hung a wide towel of old homespun over Matryona's dim mirror. They took down the jolly posters. They moved my table out of the way. Under the icons, near the windows, they stood a rough unadorned coffin on a row of stools.

In the coffin lay Matryona. Her body, mangled and lifeless, was covered with a clean sheet. Her head was swathed in a white kerchief. Her face was almost undamaged, peaceful, more alive than dead.

The villagers came to pay their last respects. The women even brought their small children to take a look at the dead. And if anyone raised a lament, all the women, even those who had looked in out of idle curiosity, always joined in, wailing where they stood by the door or the wall, as though they were providing a choral accompaniment. The men stood stiff and silent with their caps off.

The formal lamentation had to be performed by the women of Matryona's family. I observed that the lament followed a coldly calculated, age-old ritual. The more distant relatives went up to the coffin for a short while and made low wailing noises over it. Those who considered themselves closer kin to the dead woman began their lament in the doorway and when they got as far as the coffin, bowed down and roared out their grief right in the face of the departed. Every lamenter made up her own melody. And expressed her own thoughts and feelings.

I realized that a lament for the dead is not just a lament, but a kind of politics. Matryona's three sisters swooped, took possession of the cottage, the goat, and the stove, locked up the chest, ripped the two hundred rubles for the funeral out of the coat lining, and drummed it into everybody who came that only they were near relatives. Their lament over the coffin went like this, "*Oh, nanny, nanny! Oh nan-nan!* All we had in the world was you! You could have lived in peace and quiet, you could. And we should always have been kind and loving to you. Now your top room's been the death of you. Finished you off, it has, the cursed thing! Oh, why did you have to take it down? Why didn't you listen to us?"

Thus the sisters' laments were indictments of Matryona's husband's family: they shouldn't have made her take the top room down. (There was an underlying meaning, too: you've taken the top room, all right, but we won't let you have the house itself!)

Matryona's husband's family, her sisters-in-law, Efim and Faddey's sisters, and the various nieces lamented like this, "*Oh poor auntie, poor auntie!* Why didn't you take better care of yourself! Now they're angry with us for sure. Our own dear Matryona you were, and it's your own fault! The top room is nothing to do with it. Oh why did you go where death was waiting for you? Nobody asked you to go there. And what a way to die! Oh why didn't you listen to us?" (Their answer to the others showed through these laments: we are not to blame for her death, and the house we'll talk about later.)

But the "second" Matryona, a coarse, broad-faced woman, the substitute Matryona whom Faddey had married so long ago for the sake of her name, got out of step with family policy, wailing and sobbing over the coffin in her simplicity, "Oh my poor dear sister! You won't be angry with me, will you now? Oh-oh-oh! How we used to talk and talk, you and me! Forgive a poor miserable woman! You've gone to be with your dear mother, and you'll come for me some day, for sure! Oh-oh-oh-oh! . . ."

At every "oh-oh-oh" it was as though she were giving up the ghost. She writhed and gasped, with her breast against the side of the coffin. When her lament went beyond the ritual prescription, the women, as though acknowledging its success, all started saying, "Come away now, come away."

Matryona came away, but back she went again, sobbing with even greater abandon. Then an ancient woman came out of a corner, put her hand on Matryona's shoulder, and said, "There are two riddles in this world: how I was born, I don't remember, how I shall die, I don't know."

And Matryona fell silent at once, and all the others were silent, so that there was an unbroken hush.

But the old woman herself, who was much older than all the other old women there and didn't seem to belong to Matryona at all, after a while started wailing, "Oh, my poor sick Matryona! Oh my poor Vasilyevna! Oh what a weary thing it is to be seeing you into your grave!"

There was one who didn't follow the ritual, but wept straight-forwardly, in the fashion of our age, which has had plenty of practice at it. This was Matryona's unfortunate foster daughter, Kira, from Cherusti, for whom the top room had been taken down and moved. Her ringlets were pitifully out of curl. Her eyes looked red and bloodshot. She didn't notice that her headscarf was slipping off out in the frosty air and that her arm hadn't found the sleeve of her coat. She walked in a stupor from her foster mother's coffin in one house to her brother's in another. They were afraid she would lose her mind, because her husband had to go on trial as well.

It looked as if her husband was doubly at fault: not only had he been moving the top room, but as an engine driver, he knew the regulations about unprotected crossings and should have gone down to the station to warn them about the tractor. There were a thousand people on the Urals express that night, peacefully sleeping in the upper and lower berths of their dimly lit carriages, and all those lives were nearly cut short. All because of a few greedy people, wanting to get their hands on a plot of land, or not wanting to make a second trip with a tractor.

All because of the top room, which had been under a curse ever since Faddey's hands had started itching to take it down.

The tractor driver was already beyond human justice. And the railway authorities were also at fault, both because a busy crossing was unguarded and because the coupled engines were traveling without lights. That was why they had tried at first to blame it all on the drink, and then to keep the case out of court.

The rails and the track were so twisted and torn that for three days, while the coffins were still in the house, no trains ran—they were diverted onto another line. All Friday, Saturday, and Sunday, from the end of the investigation until the funeral, the work of repairing the line went on day and night. The repair gang was frozen, and they made fires to warm themselves and to light their work at night, using the boards and beams from the second sledge, which were there for the taking, scattered around the crossing.

The first sledge just stood there, undamaged and still loaded, a little way beyond the crossing.

One sledge, tantalizingly ready to be towed away, and the other perhaps still to be plucked from the flames—that was what harrowed the soul of black-bearded Faddey all day Friday and all day Saturday. His daughter was going out of her mind, his son-in-law had a criminal charge hanging over him, in his own house lay the son he had killed, and along the street the woman he had killed and whom he had once loved. But Faddey stood by the coffins, clutching his beard, only for a short time, and went away again. His high forehead was clouded by painful thoughts, but what he was thinking about was how to save the timbers of the top room from the flames and from Matryona's scheming sisters.

Going over the people of Talnovo in my mind, I realized that Faddey was not the only one like that.

Property, the people's property, or my property, is strangely called our "goods." If you lose your goods, people think you disgrace yourself and make yourself look foolish.

Faddey dashed about, never stopping to sit down, from the settlement to the station, from one official to another, there he stood with his bent back, leaning heavily on his stick, and begged them all to take pity on an old man and give him permission to recover the top room.

Somebody gave permission. And Faddey gathered together his surviving sons, sons-in-law, and nephews, got horses from the kolkhoz and from the other side of the wrecked crossing, by a roundabout way that led through three villages, brought the remnants of the top room home to his yard. He finished the job in the early hours of Sunday morning.

On Sunday afternoon they were buried. The two coffins met in the middle of the village, and the relatives argued about which of them should go first. Then they put them side by side on an open sledge, the aunt and the nephew, and carried the dead over the damp snow, with a gloomy February sky above, to the churchyard two villages away. There was an unkind wind, so the priest and the deacon waited inside the church and didn't come out to Talnovo to meet them.

A crowd of people walked slowly behind the coffins, singing in chorus. Outside the village they fell back.

When Sunday came the women were still fussing around the house. An old woman mumbled psalms by the coffin, Matryona's sisters flitted about, popping things into the oven, and the air round the mouth of the stove trembled with the heat of red-hot peats, those Matryona had carried in a sack from a distant bog. They were making unappetizing pies with poor flour.

When the funeral was over and it was already getting on toward evening, they gathered for the wake. Tables were put together to make a long one, which hid the place where the coffin had stood in the morning. To start with they all stood round the table, and an old man, the husband of a sister-in-law, said the Lord's Prayer. Then they poured everybody a little honey and warm water,[2] just enough to cover the bottom of the bowl. We spooned it up without bread or anything, in memory of the dead. Then we ate something and drank vodka and the conversation became more animated. Before the jelly they all stood up and sang "Eternal remembrance" (they explained to me that it had to be sung before the jelly). There was more drinking. By now they were talking louder than ever, and not about Matryona at all. The sister-in-law's husband started boasting, "Did you notice, brother Christians, that they took the funeral service slowly today? That's because Father Mikhail noticed me. He knows I know the service. Other times, it's saints defend us, homeward wend us, and that's all."

At last the supper was over. They all rose again. They sang "Worthy Is She." Then again, with a triple repetition of "Eternal Remembrance."[3] But the voices were hoarse and out of tune, their faces drunken, and nobody put any feeling into this "eternal memory."

Then most of the guests went away, and only the near relatives were left. They pulled out their cigarets and lit up, there were jokes and laughter. There was some mention of Matryona's husband and his disappearance. The sister-in-law's husband, striking himself on the chest, assured me and the cobbler who was married to one of Matryona's sisters, "He was dead, Efim was dead! What could stop him coming back if he wasn't? If I knew they were going to hang me when I got to the old place, I'd come back just the same!"

The cobbler nodded in agreement. He was a deserter and had never left the old place. All through the war he was hiding in his mother's cellar.

The stern and silent old woman who was more ancient than all the ancients was staying the night and sat high up on the stove. She looked down in mute disapproval on the indecently animated youngsters of fifty and sixty.

But the unhappy foster daughter, who had grown up within these walls, went away behind the kitchen screen to cry.

Faddey didn't come to Matryona's wake—perhaps because he was holding a wake for his son. But twice in the next few days he walked angrily into the house for discussions with Matryona's sisters and the deserting cobbler.

The argument was about the house. Should it go to one of the sisters or to the foster daughter? They were on the verge of taking it to court, but they made peace because they realized that the court would hand over the house to neither side, but to the Rural District Council. A bargain was struck. One sister took the goat, the cobbler and his wife got the house, and to make up Faddey's share, since he had "nursed every bit of timber here in his arms," in addition to the top room which had already been carried away, they let him have the shed which had housed the goat and the whole of the inner fence between the yard and the garden.

Once again the insatiable old man got the better of sickness and pain and became young and active. Once again he gathered together his surviving sons

<hr />

2. Traditionally Russians have *kutiia*, a wheat pudding with honey and almonds, at funerals and memorial gatherings; the villagers are too poor to have the main ingredients and their honey and water are symbolic of the *kutiia*.

3. Dirges, religious hymns sung to honor the dead. The village still follows religious rituals in time of crisis and does not use the civil ceremony proposed by the Soviet government.

and sons-in-law, they dismantled the shed and the fence, he hauled the timbers himself, sledge by sledge, and only toward the end did he have Antoshka of 8-D, who didn't slack this time, to help him.

They boarded Matryona's house up till the spring, and I moved in with one of her sisters-in-law, not far away. This sister-in-law on several occasions came out with some recollection of Matryona and made me see the dead woman in a new light. "Efim didn't love her. He used to say, 'I like to dress in an educated way, but she dresses any old way, like they do in the country.' Well then, he thinks, if she doesn't want anything, he might as well drink whatever's to spare. One time I went with him to the town to work, and he got himself a madam there and never wanted to come back to Matryona."

Everything she said about Matryona was disapproving. She was slovenly, she made no effort to get a few things about her. She wasn't the saving kind. She didn't even keep a pig, because she didn't like fattening them up for some reason. And the silly woman helped other people without pay. (What brought Matryona to mind this time was that the garden needed plowing, and she couldn't find enough helpers to pull the plow.)

Matryona's sister-in-law admitted that she was warmhearted and straightforward, but pitied and despised her for it.

It was only then, after these disapproving comments from her sister-in-law, that a true likeness of Matryona formed before my eyes, and I understood her as I never had when I lived side by side with her.

Of course! Every house in the village kept a pig. But she didn't. What can be easier than fattening a greedy piglet that cares for nothing in the world but food! You warm his swill three times a day, you live for him—then you cut his throat and you have some fat.

But she had none.

She made no effort to get things round her. She didn't struggle and strain to buy things and then care for them more than life itself.

She didn't go all out after fine clothes. Clothes, that beautify what is ugly and evil.

She was misunderstood and abandoned even by her husband. She had lost six children, but not her sociable ways. She was a stranger to her sisters and sisters-in-law, a ridiculous creature who stupidly worked for others without pay. She didn't accumulate property against the day she died. A dirty-white goat, a gammy-legged cat, some rubber plants. . . .

We had all lived side by side with her and had never understood that she was the righteous one without whom, as the proverb says, no village can stand.[4]

Nor any city.

Nor our whole land.

1963

---

4. See Genesis 18.23–33, the story of Sodom.

NAGUIB MAHFOUZ
1911–2006

The first Arabic novelist to win the Nobel Prize, Naguib Mahfouz traced the roots of his work to the civilization of the ancient Egyptians, over five thousand years ago. Past and present combine in his novels and stories, as he explores the destiny of his people and their often traumatic adjustment to industrial society. To chronicle the rapidly changing culture, Mahfouz adapts the techniques of nineteenth-century European realism and combines them with a mystical outlook and a command of both the literary resources of classical Arabic and the idioms of contemporary speech.

Without Mahfouz, it is said, the turbulent history of twentieth-century Egypt would never be known. Indeed, he lived through almost a century of transition and documented the successive stages of social and political life from the time the country cast off foreign rule and became a postcolonial society. Mahfouz was born in Cairo on December 11, 1911, the youngest of seven children in the family of a civil servant. The family moved from its home in the old Jamaliya district to the suburbs of Cairo when Mahfouz was a young boy. He attended government schools and the University of Cairo, graduating in 1934 with a degree in philosophy. These were not quiet years: Egypt, officially under Ottoman rule, had been occupied by the British since 1883 and was declared a British protectorate at the start of the First World War, in 1914. Mahfouz grew up in the midst of the struggle for national independence that culminated in a violent uprising against the British in 1919 and the negotiation of a constitutional monarchy in 1923. The consistent focus on Egyptian cultural identity that permeates his work may well have its roots in this turbulent period.

While at the university, Mahfouz befriended the Socialist and Darwinian thinker Salama Musa and began to write articles for Musa's journal *Al-Majalla al-Jadida* (*The Modern Magazine*). In 1938 he published his first collection of stories, *Whispers of Madness*, and in 1939 the first of three historical novels set in ancient Egypt. At that time he planned to write a set of forty books on the model of the historical romances written by the British novelist Sir Walter Scott (1771–1832). These first novels contained allegories of modern politics, and readers easily recognized the criticism of the reigning King Farouk in *Radubis* (1943) or the analogy in *The Struggle for Thebes* (1944) between the ancient Egyptian battle to expel Hyksos usurpers and twentieth-century rebellions against foreign rule. In 1945, Mahfouz shifted decisively to the realistic novel and a portrayal of modern society. He focused on the social and spiritual dilemmas of the middle class in Cairo, documenting in vivid detail the life of an urban society that represented Egypt.

The major work of this period, and Mahfouz's masterwork in many eyes, is *The Cairo Trilogy* (1956–57), three volumes depicting the experience of three generations of a Cairo family between 1918 and 1944. Into this story Mahfouz wove a social history of Egypt after the First World War. Mahfouz has been called the "Balzac of Egypt"—a comparison to the French novelist and panoramic chronicler of society Honoré de Balzac (1799–1850)—and he was well acquainted with the nineteenth-century realists. Traditional Arabic literature has many forms of narrative, but the novel is not one of them; Arabic writers like Mahfouz adapted the Western form to their own needs. He made use of familiar nineteenth-century strategies such as a chronological plot, unified characters, the inclusion of documentary information and realistic details, a panoramic view of society including a strong moral and humanistic perspective, and a picture of urban middle-class life. Mahfouz's achievement was recognized in the State Prize for literature in 1956, but he temporarily ceased to write after finishing the *Trilogy* in 1952.

In that year, an officers' coup headed by Gamal Abdel Nasser overthrew the monarchy and instituted a republic that promised democratic reforms, and Mahfouz described the changes in Egyptian society that resulted. Although the author was at first optimistic about the new order, he soon recognized that few improvements had occurred in the lives of the general population. When he started publishing again in 1959, Mahfouz's works included open criticism of the Nasser regime. Three years after *The Cairo Trilogy* brought him international praise, Mahfouz shocked many readers with a new book, *Children of Gebelawi*. An allegory of religious history, *Children of Gebelawi* scandalized orthodox believers by its personification of God and its depiction of the prophets chiefly as social reformers rather than as religious figures. The book was banned throughout the Arab world except in Lebanon, and the Jordan League of Writers attacked Mahfouz as a "delinquent man" whose novels were "plagued with sex and drugs." From this point on, Mahfouz tended to add an element of political or social allegory and subjective mysticism to his literary realism.

Although he had become the best-known writer in the Arab world, his works read by millions, Mahfouz was unable to make a living from his books. Copyright protection was minimal, and without such safeguards, even best-selling authors received only small sums for their books. Until he began writing for motion pictures in the 1960s, he supported himself and his family through various positions in governmental ministries and as a contributing editor for the leading newspaper, *Al-Ahram* (*The Pyramids*). Attached to the Ministry of Culture in 1954, he adapted novels for film and television and later became director-general of the governmental Cinema Organization, overseeing production and also, controversially, censorship. Eventually more than thirty of his stories and novels were made into films. After his retirement from the civil service in 1971, Mahfouz continued to publish articles and short stories in *Al-Ahram*, where most of his novels appeared in serialized form before being issued as paperbacks. When he received the Nobel Prize in Literature, in 1988, at the age of seventy-six, he was still contributing a weekly column, "Point of View," to *Al-Ahram*. Despite his fame, Mahfouz's books were censored and banned in many Arab nations; in his own country, he faced attacks from Islamic fundamentalists. Sheikh Omar Abdel-Rahman (later convicted in the first bombing of the World Trade Center, in New York, in 1993) condemned his work publicly and made death threats against Mahfouz in the early 1990s. In 1994, Mahfouz was stabbed in the neck by an assailant who fled the scene. Although the writer recovered from the attack, he lost most of his sight in old age and became reclusive. He died in Cairo at the age of ninety-four.

"Zaabalawi," the selection here, is a story from Mahfouz's second collection, *God's World* (1963). It contains many of the author's predominant themes and draws on an Islamic mystical tradition whose comprehensive tolerance is far from (and often opposed by) the rigid beliefs of contemporary Muslim fundamentalists. Written two years after *Children of Gebelawi*, it echoes the earlier work's religious symbolism in the mysterious character of Zaabalawi himself. It also demonstrates Mahfouz's shift from an "objective," realistic style toward one emphasizing subjective, mystical awareness. The perceptions of individual characters—here, the narrator—dominate many of his short stories. Mahfouz's later works would include adaptations of folk narratives like the *Arabian Nights*, and there is an element of the folktale in this story, as it draws on Arabic culture and comments, from a broader, often prophetic perspective, on the contemporary scene. Yet this story is also a social document: the narrator's quest for Zaabalawi brings him before various representatives of modern Egyptian society inside a realistically described Cairo. "Zaabalawi," therefore, takes on the character of a social and metaphysical allegory. Its terminally ill narrator seeks to be cured in a quest that implies not only physical healing but religious salvation as well. He has exhausted the resources of medical science and, in desperation, seeks out a holy man whose name he recalls from childhood tales.

Although he is never fully identified, Zaabalawi seems to stand for a spiritual principle of some sort. Zaabalawi's former acquaintances, whom the narrator interviews, form an allegorical portrait of Egyptian society. The bureaucrats who depend on reason, technology, and businesslike efficiency seem least capable of encountering Zaabalawi, while the artists have a closer relationship with him, even if they cannot quickly find him. As the narrator's quest proceeds, he is continually surprised by the difficulty in locating this mystical figure. The story, which combines concreteness with mysticism, the spirit of nineteenth-century realism with that of the *Arabian Nights*, suggests that magic is still possible, even in twentieth-century industrial Cairo.

Zaabalawi[1]

Finally I became convinced that I had to find Sheikh[2] Zaabalawi.

The first time I had heard of his name had been in a song:

> Oh what's become of the world, Zaabalawi?
> They've turned it upside down and taken away its taste.

It had been a popular song in my childhood, and one day it had occurred to me to demand of my father, in the way children have of asking endless questions: "Who is Zaabalawi?"

He had looked at me hesitantly as though doubting my ability to understand the answer. However, he had replied, "May his blessing descend upon you, he's a true saint of God, a remover of worries and troubles. Were it not for him I would have died miserably—"

In the years that followed, I heard my father many a time sing the praises of this good saint and speak of the miracles he performed. The days passed and brought with them many illness, for each one of which I was able, without too

---

1. Translated by Denys Johnson-Davies.
2. A title of respect (originally "old man"), often indicating rulership.

much trouble and at a cost I could afford, to find a cure, until I became afflicted with that illness for which no one possesses a remedy. When I had tried everything in vain and was overcome by despair, I remembered by chance what I had heard in my childhood: Why, I asked myself, should I not seek out Sheikh Zaabalawi? I recollected my father saying that he had made his acquaintance in Khan Gaafar[3] at the house of Sheikh Qamar, one of those sheikhs who practiced law in the religious courts, and so I took myself off to his house. Wishing to make sure that he was still living there, I made inquiries of a vendor of beans whom I found in the lower part of the house.

"Sheikh Qamar!" he said, looking at me in amazement. "He left the quarter ages ago. They say he's now living in Garden City and has his office in al-Azhar Square."[4]

I looked up the office address in the telephone book and immediately set off to the Chamber of Commerce Building, where it was located. On asking to see Sheikh Qamar, I was ushered into a room just as a beautiful woman with a most intoxicating perfume was leaving it. The man received me with a smile and motioned me toward a fine leather-upholstered chair. Despite the thick soles of my shoes, my feet were conscious of the lushness of the costly carpet. The man wore a lounge suit and was smoking a cigar; his manner of sitting was that of someone well satisfied both with himself and with his worldly possessions. The look of warm welcome he gave me left no doubt in my mind that he thought me a prospective client, and I felt acutely embarrassed at encroaching upon his valuable time.

"Welcome!" he said, prompting me to speak.

"I am the son of your old friend Sheikh Ali al-Tatawi," I answered so as to put an end to my equivocal position.

A certain languor was apparent in the glance he cast at me; the languor was not total in that he had not as yet lost all hope in me.

"God rest his soul," he said. "He was a fine man."

The very pain that had driven me to go there now prevailed upon me to stay.

"He told me," I continued, "of a devout saint named Zaabalawi whom he met at Your Honor's. I am in need of him, sir, if he be still in the land of the living."

The languor became firmly entrenched in his eyes, and it would have come as no surprise if he had shown the door to both me and my father's memory.

"That," he said in the tone of one who has made up his mind to terminate the conversation, "was a very long time ago and I scarcely recall him now."

Rising to my feet so as to put his mind at rest regarding my intention of going, I asked, "Was he really a saint?"

"We used to regard him as a man of miracles."

"And where could I find him today?" I asked, making another move toward the door.

"To the best of my knowledge he was living in the Birgawi Residence in al-Azhar," and he applied himself to some papers on his desk with a resolute movement that indicated he would not open his mouth again. I bowed my head in thanks, apologized several times for disturbing him, and left the office, my head so buzzing with embarrassment that I was oblivious to all sounds around me.

---

3. Gaafar Market, an area of shops.
4. An area of Cairo close to the famous mosque and university of al-Azhar.

I went to the Birgawi Residence, which was situated in a thickly populated quarter. I found that time had so eaten at the building that nothing was left of it save an antiquated façade and a courtyard that, despite being supposedly in the charge of a caretaker, was being used as a rubbish dump. A small, insignificant fellow, a mere prologue to a man, was using the covered entrance as a place for the sale of old books on theology and mysticism.

When I asked him about Zaabalawi, he peered at me through narrow, inflamed eyes and said in amazement, "Zaabalawi! Good heavens, what a time ago that was! Certainly he used to live in this house when it was habitable. Many were the times he would sit with me talking of bygone days, and I would be blessed by his holy presence. Where, though, is Zaabalawi today?"

He shrugged his shoulders sorrowfully and soon left me, to attend to an approaching customer. I proceeded to make inquiries of many shopkeepers in the district. While I found that a large number of them had never even heard of Zaabalawi, some, though recalling nostalgically the pleasant times they had spent with him, were ignorant of his present whereabouts, while others openly made fun of him, labeled him a charlatan, and advised me to put myself in the hands of a doctor—as though I had not already done so. I therefore had no alternative but to return disconsolately home.

With the passing of days like motes in the air, my pains grew so severe that I was sure I would not be able to hold out much longer. Once again I fell to wondering about Zaabalawi and clutching at the hope his venerable name stirred within me. Then it occurred to me to seek the help of the local sheikh of the district; in fact, I was surprised I had not thought of this to begin with. His office was in the nature of a small shop, except that it contained a desk and a telephone, and I found him sitting at his desk, wearing a jacket over his striped galabeya.[5] As he did not interrupt his conversation with a man sitting beside him, I stood waiting till the man had gone. The sheikh then looked up at me coldly. I told myself that I should win him over by the usual methods, and it was not long before I had him cheerfully inviting me to sit down.

"I'm in need of Sheikh Zaabalawi," I answered his inquiry as to the purpose of my visit.

He gazed at me with the same astonishment as that shown by those I had previously encountered.

"At least," he said, giving me a smile that revealed his gold teeth, "he is still alive. The devil of it is, though, he has no fixed abode. You might well bump into him as you go out of here, on the other hand you might spend days and months in fruitless searching."

"Even you can't find him!"

"Even I! He's a baffling man, but I thank the Lord that he's still alive!"

He gazed at me intently, and murmured, "It seems your condition is serious."

"Very."

"May God come to your aid! But why don't you go about it systematically?" He spread out a sheet of paper on the desk and drew on it with unexpected speed and skill until he had made a full plan of the district, showing all the various quarters, lanes, alleyways, and squares. He looked at it admiringly and

5. The traditional Arabic robe, over which this modernized district officer wears a European jacket.

said, "These are dwelling-houses, here is the Quarter of the Perfumers, here the Quarter of the Coppersmiths, the Mouski,[6] the police and fire stations. The drawing is your best guide. Look carefully in the cafés, the places where the dervishes perform their rites, the mosques and prayer-rooms, and the Green Gate,[7] for he may well be concealed among the beggars and be indistinguishable from them. Actually, I myself haven't seen him for years, having been somewhat preoccupied with the cares of the world, and was only brought back by your inquiry to those most exquisite times of my youth."

I gazed at the map in bewilderment. The telephone rang, and he took up the receiver.

"Take it," he told me, generously. "We're at your service."

Folding up the map, I left and wandered off through the quarter, from square to street to alleyway, making inquiries of everyone I felt was familiar with the place. At last the owner of a small establishment for ironing clothes told me, "Go to the calligrapher[8] Hassanein in Umm al-Ghulam—they were friends."

I went to Umm al-Ghulam,[9] where I found old Hassanein working in a deep, narrow shop full of signboards and jars of color. A strange smell, a mixture of glue and perfume, permeated its every corner. Old Hassanein was squatting on a sheepskin rug in front of a board propped against the wall; in the middle of it he had inscribed the word "Allah"[1] in silver lettering. He was engrossed in embellishing the letters with prodigious care. I stood behind him, fearful of disturbing him or breaking the inspiration that flowed to his masterly hand. When my concern at not interrupting him had lasted some time, he suddenly inquired with unaffected gentleness, "Yes?"

Realizing that he was aware of my presence, I introduced myself. "I've been told that Sheikh Zaabalawi is your friend; I'm looking for him," I said.

His hand came to a stop. He scrutinized me in astonishment. "Zaabalawi! God be praised!" he said with a sigh.

"He *is* a friend of yours, isn't he?" I asked eagerly.

"He was, once upon a time. A real man of mystery: he'd visit you so often that people would imagine he was your nearest and dearest, then would disappear as though he'd never existed. Yet saints are not to be blamed."

The spark of hope went out with the suddenness of a lamp snuffed by a power-cut.

"He was so constantly with me," said the man, "that I felt him to be a part of everything I drew. But where is he today?"

"Perhaps he is still alive?"

"He's alive, without a doubt. . . . He had impeccable taste, and it was due to him that I made my most beautiful drawings."

"God knows," I said, in a voice almost stifled by the dead ashes of hope, "how dire my need for him is, and no one knows better than you[2] of the ailments in respect of which he is sought."

6. The central bazaar.
7. A medieval gate in Cairo.
8. One who practices the art of decorative lettering (literally "beautiful writing"), which is respected as a fine art in Arabic and Asian cultures.
9. A street in Cairo.
1. God (Arabic).
2. One of the calligrapher's major tasks is to write religious documents and prayers to Allah.

"Yes, yes. May God restore you to health. He is, in truth, as is said of him, a man, and more. . . ."

Smiling broadly, he added, "And his face possesses an unforgettable beauty. But where is he?"

Reluctantly I rose to my feet, shook hands, and left. I continued wandering eastward and westward through the quarter, inquiring about Zaabalawi from everyone who, by reason of age or experience, I felt might be likely to help me. Eventually I was informed by a vendor of lupine[3] that he had met him a short while ago at the house of Sheikh Gad, the well-known composer. I went to the musician's house in Tabakshiyya,[4] where I found him in a room tastefully furnished in the old style, its walls redolent with history. He was seated on a divan, his famous lute beside him, concealing within itself the most beautiful melodies of our age, while somewhere from within the house came the sound of pestle and mortar and the clamor of children. I immediately greeted him and introduced myself, and was put at my ease by the unaffected way in which he received me. He did not ask, either in words or gesture, what had brought me, and I did not feel that he even harbored any such curiosity. Amazed at his understanding and kindness, which boded well, I said, "O Sheikh Gad, I am an admirer of yours, having long been enchanted by the renderings of your songs."

"Thank you," he said with a smile.

"Please excuse my disturbing you," I continued timidly, "but I was told that Zaabalawi was your friend, and I am in urgent need of him."

"Zaabalawi!" he said, frowning in concentration. "You need him? God be with you, for who knows, O Zaabalawi, where you are."

"Doesn't he visit you?" I asked eagerly.

"He visited me some time ago. He might well come right now; on the other hand I mightn't see him till death!"

I gave an audible sigh and asked, "What made him like that?"

The musician took up his lute. "Such are saints or they would not be saints," he said, laughing.

"Do those who need him suffer as I do?"

"Such suffering is part of the cure!"

He took up the plectrum and began plucking soft strains from the strings. Lost in thought, I followed his movements. Then, as though addressing myself, I said, "So my visit has been in vain."

He smiled, laying his cheek against the side of the lute. "God forgive you," he said, "for saying such a thing of a visit that has caused me to know you and you me!"

I was much embarrassed and said apologetically, "Please forgive me; my feelings of defeat made me forget my manners."

"Do not give in to defeat. This extraordinary man brings fatigue to all who seek him. It was easy enough with him in the old days when his place of abode was known. Today, though, the world has changed, and after having enjoyed a position attained only by potentates, he is now pursued by the police on a charge of false pretenses. It is therefore no longer an easy matter to reach him, but have patience and be sure that you will do so."

3. Beans.
4. A quarter for the straw trays made and sold there.

He raised his head from the lute and skillfully fingered the opening bars of a melody. Then he sang:

I make lavish mention, even though I blame myself, of those I love,
For the stories of the beloved are my wine.[5]

With a heart that was weary and listless, I followed the beauty of the melody and the singing.

"I composed the music to this poem in a single night," he told me when he had finished. "I remember that it was the eve of the Lesser Bairam.[6] Zaabalawi was my guest for the whole of that night, and the poem was of his choosing. He would sit for a while just where you are, then would get up and play with my children as though he were one of them. Whenever I was overcome by weariness or my inspiration failed me, he would punch me playfully in the chest and joke with me, and I would bubble over with melodies, and thus I continued working till I finished the most beautiful piece I have ever composed."

"Does he know anything about music?"

"He is the epitome of things musical. He has an extremely beautiful speaking voice, and you have only to hear him to want to burst into song and to be inspired to creativity. . . ."

"How was it that he cured those diseases before which men are powerless?"

"That is his secret. Maybe you will learn it when you meet him."

But when would that meeting occur? We relapsed into silence, and the hubbub of children once more filled the room.

Again the sheikh began to sing. He went on repeating the words "and I have a memory of her" in different and beautiful variations until the very walls danced in ecstasy. I expressed my wholehearted admiration, and he gave me a smile of thanks. I then got up and asked permission to leave, and he accompanied me to the front door. As I shook him by the hand, he said, "I hear that nowadays he frequents the house of Hagg Wanas al-Damanhouri. Do you know him?"

I shook my head, though a modicum of renewed hope crept into my heart.

"He is a man of private means," the sheikh told me, "who from time to time visits Cairo, putting up at some hotel or other. Every evening, though, he spends at the Negma Bar in Alfi Street."

I waited for nightfall and went to the Negma Bar. I asked a waiter about Hagg Wanas, and he pointed to a corner that was semisecluded because of its position behind a large pillar with mirrors on all four sides. There I saw a man seated alone at a table with two bottles in front of him, one empty, the other two-thirds empty. There were no snacks or food to be seen, and I was sure that I was in the presence of a hardened drinker. He was wearing a loosely flowing silk galabeya and a carefully wound turban; his legs were stretched out toward the base of the pillar, and as he gazed into the mirror in rapt contentment, the sides of his face, rounded and handsome despite the fact that he was approaching old age, were flushed with wine. I approached quietly till I stood but a few feet away from him. He did not turn toward me or give any indication that he was aware of my presence.

5. From a poem by the medieval mystic poet Ibn al-Farid, who represents spiritual ecstasy as a kind of drunkenness.

6. A major Islamic holiday, celebrated for three days to end the month's fasting during Ramadan.

"Good evening, Mr. Wanas," I greeted him cordially.

He turned toward me abruptly, as though my voice had roused him from slumber, and glared at me in disapproval. I was about to explain what had brought me to him when he interrupted in an almost imperative tone of voice that was none the less not devoid of an extraordinary gentleness, "First, please sit down, and, second, please get drunk!"

I opened my mouth to make my excuses but, stopping up his ears with his fingers, he said, "Not a word till you do what I say."

I realized I was in the presence of a capricious drunkard and told myself that I should at least humor him a bit. "Would you permit me to ask one question?" I said with a smile, sitting down.

Without removing his hands from his ears he indicated the bottle. "When engaged in a drinking bout like this, I do not allow any conversation between myself and another unless, like me, he is drunk, otherwise all propriety is lost and mutual comprehension is rendered impossible."

I made a sign indicating that I did not drink.

"That's your lookout," he said offhandedly. "And that's my condition!"

He filled me a glass, which I meekly took and drank. No sooner had the wine settled in my stomach than it seemed to ignite. I waited patiently till I had grown used to its ferocity, and said, "It's very strong, and I think the time has come for me to ask you about—"

Once again, however, he put his fingers in his ears. "I shan't listen to you until you're drunk!"

He filled up my glass for the second time. I glanced at it in trepidation; then, overcoming my inherent objection, I drank it down at a gulp. No sooner had the wine come to rest inside me than I lost all willpower. With the third glass, I lost my memory, and with the fourth the future vanished. The world turned round about me and I forgot why I had gone there. The man leaned toward me attentively, but I saw him—saw everything—as a mere meaningless series of colored planes. I don't know how long it was before my head sank down onto the arm of the chair and I plunged into deep sleep. During it, I had a beautiful dream the like of which I had never experienced. I dreamed that I was in an immense garden surrounded on all sides by luxuriant trees, and the sky was nothing but stars seen between the entwined branches, all enfolded in an atmosphere like that of sunset or a sky overcast with cloud. I was lying on a small hummock of jasmine petals, more of which fell upon me like rain, while the lucent spray of a fountain unceasingly sprinkled the crown of my head and my temples. I was in a state of deep contentedness, of ecstatic serenity. An orchestra of warbling and cooing played in my ear. There was an extraordinary sense of harmony between me and my inner self, and between the two of us and the world, everything being in its rightful place, without discord or distortion. In the whole world there was no single reason for speech or movement, for the universe moved in a rapture of ecstasy. This lasted but a short while. When I opened my eyes, consciousness struck at me like a policeman's fist and I saw Wanas al-Damanhouri regarding me with concern. Only a few drowsy customers were left in the bar.

"You have slept deeply," said my companion. "You were obviously hungry for sleep."

I rested my heavy head in the palms of my hands. When I took them away in astonishment and looked down at them, I found that they glistened with drops of water.

"My head's wet," I protested.

"Yes, my friend tried to rouse you," he answered quietly.

"Somebody saw me in this state?"

"Don't worry, he is a good man. Have you not heard of Sheikh Zaabalawi?"

"Zaabalawi!" I exclaimed, jumping to my feet.

"Yes," he answered in surprise. "What's wrong?"

"Where is he?"

"I don't know where he is now. He was here and then he left."

I was about to run off in pursuit but found I was more exhausted than I had imagined. Collapsed over the table, I cried out in despair, "My sole reason for coming to you was to meet him! Help me to catch up with him or send someone after him."

The man called a vendor of prawns and asked him to seek out the sheikh and bring him back. Then he turned to me. "I didn't realize you were afflicted. I'm very sorry. . . ."

"You wouldn't let me speak," I said irritably.

"What a pity! He was sitting on this chair beside you the whole time. He was playing with a string of jasmine petals he had around his neck, a gift from one of his admirers, then, taking pity on you, he began to sprinkle some water on your head to bring you around."

"Does he meet you here every night?" I asked, my eyes not leaving the doorway through which the vendor of prawns had left.

"He was with me tonight, last night and the night before that, but before that I hadn't seen him for a month."

"Perhaps he will come tomorrow," I answered with a sigh.

"Perhaps."

"I am willing to give him any money he wants."

Wanas answered sympathetically, "The strange thing is that he is not open to such temptations, yet he will cure you if you meet him."

"Without charge?"

"Merely on sensing that you love him."

The vendor of prawns returned, having failed in his mission.

I recovered some of my energy and left the bar, albeit unsteadily. At every street corner I called out "Zaabalawi!" in the vague hope that I would be rewarded with an answering shout. The street boys turned contemptuous eyes on me till I sought refuge in the first available taxi.

The following evening I stayed up with Wanas al-Damanhouri till dawn, but the sheikh did not put in an appearance. Wanas informed me that he would be going away to the country and would not be returning to Cairo until he had sold the cotton crop.

I must wait, I told myself; I must train myself to be patient. Let me content myself with having made certain of the existence of Zaabalawi, and even of his affection for me, which encourages me to think that he will be prepared to cure me if a meeting takes place between us.

Sometimes, however, the long delay wearied me. I would become beset by despair and would try to persuade myself to dismiss him from my mind completely. How many weary people in this life know him not or regard him as a mere myth! Why, then, should I torture myself about him in this way?

No sooner, however, did my pains force themselves upon me than I would again begin to think about him, asking myself when I would be fortunate enough to meet him. The fact that I ceased to have any news of Wanas and was told he had gone to live abroad did not deflect me from my purpose; the truth of the matter was that I had become fully convinced that I had to find Zaabalawi.

Yes, I have to find Zaabalawi.

1963

MAHMOUD DARWISH
1941–2008

A poet and an activist, Mahmoud Darwish became a symbol of Palestinian resistance to Israeli rule and a significant figure in Palestinian politics. Although he wrote many lyrical and traditional poems, he is best known for his works in free verse on political themes and as a spokesman for the Palestinian community in exile.

Born in the village of Birweh, near Haifa in Palestine, then ruled by Britain, Darwish was the son of a Sunni Muslim farming family. The United Nations divided Palestine between Israel and its Arab neighbors in 1947, and a series of wars followed as Arab powers attacked the new country, which they saw as an outgrowth of European imperialism. During the Arab-Israeli war of 1948, the forces of the newly created Israeli government occupied and destroyed Birweh. Darwish moved temporarily to Lebanon before returning to school in what was by then northern Israel. As he later recalled of these years, "We lived again as refugees, this time in our own country. It's a collective experience. This wound I'll never forget."

Darwish began publishing his poetry early, completing his first collection,

Sparrows without Wings (1960) at the age of nineteen. After finishing his education, Darwish worked as a journalist in Haifa, where he joined the Communist Rakah Party. His second collection of poetry, Leaves of Olives (1964), contained what would be his most famous poem, "Identity Card," a meditation on living in Israeli-occupied territory. Despite the political tone of his early poetry, however, much of Darwish's later work was concerned with traditional poetic and philosophical matters such as mortality, romantic love, and personal identity. He nonetheless saw his poetry as part of the resistance to Israeli rule and became active in the Palestine Liberation Organization (PLO); he was placed under house arrest by the Israeli government and had his travel restricted. After the Six-Day War, in 1967, when Israel occupied the territories of Gaza and the West Bank, Darwish left Israel, first for Moscow, then for Cairo. He later lived in Beirut and Paris. His poems from this period are nostalgic, focused on trying to recollect the landscape and the people of his childhood; his later works tend to be more abstract and less directly politically engaged, closer to what he called "pure poetry." They also left behind traditional Arabic verse forms (making use, for example of monorhyme—identical or near-identical rhymes for multiple verses) in favor of free verse (without rhymes or regular meters). Among the poets he admired was the Israeli **Yehuda Amichai**.

In 1988, Darwish authored the Palestinian Declaration of Independence, which was adopted by the Palestinian National Council, the legislative body of the PLO. He resigned from the PLO, however, to protest the Oslo Peace Accords with Israel in 1993; he believed that the accords did not guarantee Israeli withdrawal from the Occupied Territories. As relations between the recently formed Palestinian Authority and Israel improved in the following few years, Darwish moved to Ramallah, in the West Bank, the capital of the authority. He also visited Haifa on a temporary government pass. In 2000, however, controversy erupted over the teaching of his poetry in Israeli schools, especially because of a poem written during the first Palestinian Intifada, or uprising, in 1988, "Passing Between Passing Words," in which the writer called for an end to the occupation in

language that suggested an end to the existence of the state of Israel. He denied any such intention and spoke of his relationship to a land where he had not lived for three decades: "I have become addicted to exile. My language is exile. The metaphor for Palestine is stronger than the Palestine of reality." He died of complications following open-heart surgery in Houston, Texas, at the age of sixty-seven and was given a state funeral by the Palestinian Authority in the West Bank city of Ramallah.

"Identity Card" is a short, direct poem about exile and the restrictions on the movements of Palestinians. The speaker addresses an Israeli border guard and speaks of his life, his family, and his efforts to earn a living, while gradually accusing the Israeli of usurping his family's land. The speaker's expression of pride in his humble roots allows him to assert, on behalf of all Palestinians: "I am a name without a family name." The resigned tone of the first stanzas carries with it an undercurrent of rebellion that makes itself felt more fully at the end of the poem. In a broader sense, the poem speaks for all those who have experienced exile and foreign occupation of their land.

Identity Card[1]

Put it on record.
    I am an Arab
And the number of my card is fifty thousand
I have eight children
And the ninth is due after summer.   5
What's there to be angry about?

Put it on record.
    I am an Arab
Working with comrades of toil in a quarry.
I have eight children   10
For them I wrest the loaf of bread,

1. Translated from the Arabic by Denys Johnson-Davies.

The clothes and exercise books
From the rocks
And beg for no alms at your door,
    Lower not myself at your doorstep.   15
    What's there to be angry about?

Put it on record.
    I am an Arab.
I am a name without a title,
Patient in a country where everything   20
Lives in a whirlpool of anger.
    My roots
    Took hold before the birth of time
    Before the burgeoning of the ages,
    Before cypress and olive trees,   25
    Before the proliferation of weeds.
My father is from the family of the plough
    Not from highborn nobles.
And my grandfather was a peasant
    Without line or genealogy.   30
My house is a watchman's hut
    Made of sticks and reeds.
Does my status satisfy you?
    I am a name without a surname.

Put it on record.   35
    I am an Arab.
Colour of hair: jet black.
Colour of eyes: brown.
My distinguishing features:
    On my head the *'iqal* cords over a *keffiyeh*[2]   40
    Scratching him who touches it.
My address:
    I'm from a village, remote, forgotten,
    Its streets without name
    And all its men in the fields and quarry.   45

    What's there to be angry about?

Put it on record.
    I am an Arab.
You stole my forefathers' vineyards
    And land I used to till,   50
    I and all my children,
    And you left us and all my grandchildren
    Nothing but these rocks.
    Will your government be taking them too
    As is being said?   55

---

2. A traditional Palestinian headscarf. "Iqal": two rows of rope made of camel hair that keep the *keffiyeh* in place.

So!
     Put it on record at the top of page one:
     I don't hate people,
     I trespass on no one's property.
And yet, if I were to become hungry   60
     I shall eat the flesh of my usurper.
     Beware, beware of my hunger
     And of my anger!

1964

VIII

Contemporary World Literature

C ertain years in world history stand out in the blaze of a revolution that transforms world politics: 1789 for the French Revolution, 1848 for a series of European revolutions, 1917 for the Russian Revolution. More recently, 1968, a year of student rebellion in Prague, Paris, Mexico City, and elsewhere, seemed at the time to be such a milestone. Challenges to traditional authority shook the 1960s. The subsequent changes to Western culture have shaped all that came after—especially in literature, where the intimate relations among men and women and the tensions between public responsibility and private desire play a central role. Meanwhile, the vision of a post-Communist world that was glimpsed in Prague in the spring of 1968 found its realization in the dismantling of Communist regimes in Eastern Europe in 1989 and the dissolution of the Soviet Union in 1991. The crushing of the Prague Spring led immediately to a period of pessimism and "normalization" (that is, a return to repressive practices) that restricted social movements. The only successful effort to thwart normalization was the Polish trade union Solidarity, which, however, was trampled by the imposition of martial law in 1981. The poet Wisława Szymborska, an ardent Communist in her youth, was one among

A 1965 photograph by Marc Riboud of a street in Beijing as seen from inside an antique dealer's shop.

many writers who sympathized with the attempt to create a civil society outside government control.

In the West, especially in the United States, the focus of protest was the Vietnam War—a conflict the Americans had taken over from the French—in which over half a million (mostly drafted) Americans had failed to defeat a guerrilla insurgency. Communist North Vietnam, backed by the Soviet Union (and for a time by China), eventually reached Saigon, the capital of South Vietnam, in 1975, and unified the country the following year. There were a number of other minor proxy wars between the superpowers during the 1970s and 1980s, but this was the period of détente, or relaxation of hostility, when the Soviet premier Leonid Brezhnev and American presidents including Richard Nixon and Jimmy Carter sought to defuse Cold War tensions and signed a number of treaties on arms control and human rights. Détente, eclipsed by the Soviet invasion of Afghanistan in 1979, was followed by a period of rearmament under President Ronald Reagan, which culminated, sur-

prisingly, in the disarmament agreement with Russian premier Mikhail Gorbachev at Reykjavik, Iceland, in 1986. Seeking to transform the moribund economy and society he had inherited from his Communist predecessors, Gorbachev introduced the principles of glasnost (or openness) and perestroika (or restructuring), intending to make the Soviet system more flexible and accountable. In the end, however, the restructuring went much further than Gorbachev had intended, resulting in the demise of the Communist Party and the dissolution of both the Warsaw Pact military alliance and the Soviet Union itself.

If 1968 marks the high point of the protest movements that would transform contemporary society, 1989 is an equally memorable year, during which the nations of Eastern Europe rebelled against—and finally overthrew—Communist regimes, and the Wall that had separated East and West Berlin fell. Also in 1989, the first steps were taken to dismantle the system of apartheid, or racial segregation and white minority rule in South Africa (white minority rule had ended in Zim-

Young men in Ho Chi Minh City (formerly Saigon, the capital of South Vietnam), in 1975, after "Liberation Day."

babwe, formerly Rhodesia, in 1980). That same year thousands of Chinese students mounted an unsuccessful rebellion against the Communist government of the People's Republic of China; this brief uprising ended with a massacre in Tiananmen Square, in Beijing, the historic center of Chinese politics.

During the 1990s, as the Soviet Union disintegrated and as China moved closer to a capitalist economy, many hoped that humanity's bloodiest century would end with something like the accomplishment of world peace that had been such a bright dream at its beginning. The dictatorships of Latin America, supported by the United States as a bulwark against communism, gave way to democratically elected governments. Peace agreements in Northern Ireland and between Israel and Palestine seemed to confirm such promises. Another date, September 11, 2001, undermined such hopes: on that day, terrorists claiming to act in the name of Islam hijacked four airplanes and flew into the World Trade Center, in New York, and the Pentagon, near Washington, D.C. (one of the planes was forced, by the passengers, to crash in a remote field in Pennsylvania). The wars of the twenty-first century, which began in the aftermath of the terrorist attacks, have chilled the hope that ours would be a uniquely peaceful age. Likewise, the expectation that industrialization would lead inevitably to a more secular world has proved mistaken. Communal violence continues in India, and the Arab-Israeli conflict and Islamic fundamentalism have intensified during the first decades of the twenty-first century, while in much of the world outside Europe, religion is resurgent.

During the past half century or so, even if dreams of world peace have often appeared illusory, great improvement in the living standards of much of the world's still-expanding population has occurred. Four-fifths of the global popu-

Supporters of antiapartheid activist Nelson Mandela gather outside the Victor Verster prison in Cape Town, South Africa, demanding his freedom. After twenty-seven years of confinement, Mandela was finally released in 1990. In 1994 he became South Africa's first black president.

lation now benefits from the fruits of industrialization, even as one-fifth remains in poverty. The years since World War II have been an era of globalization in investment, knowledge, politics, and culture. The information revolution, made possible first by satellite television and then by ever-more-sophisticated computers and the Internet, has unified distant parts of the globe more rapidly than did the telegraph and telephone at the beginning of the twentieth century. Today, a world connected by telecommunications responds more quickly than ever before to news about politics, markets, and even sporting events. It is also a world of increased migration, in which the movements of people from poorer to richer nations have created immense cultural hybridity while sometimes producing tensions in the host countries.

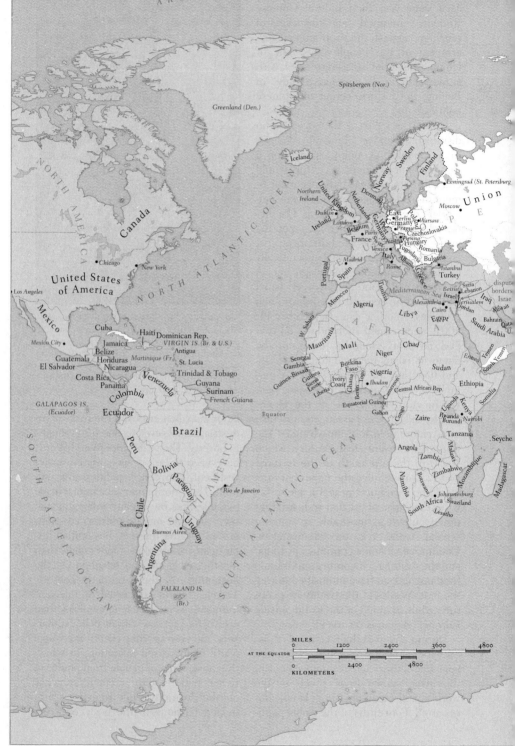

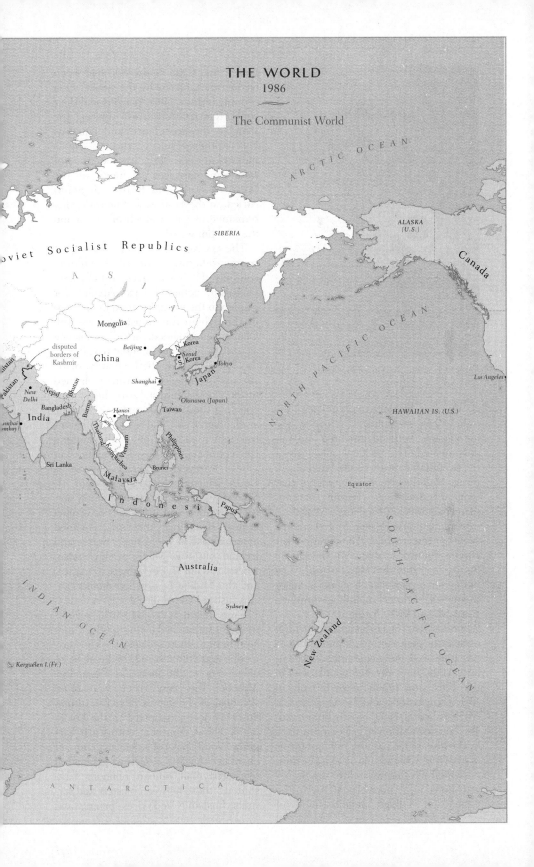

THE WORLD
1986

The Communist World

ARCTIC OCEAN

SIBERIA

...oviet Socialist Republics

A S I ...

Mongolia

disputed
borders of
Kashmir

China

Beijing

N. Korea
Seoul
S. Korea

Japan

Tokyo

Shanghai

Okinawa (Japan)

...akistan

New
Delhi

Nepal Bhutan

Bangladesh

Burma

India

...mbai
...mbay)

Hanoi

Laos

Taiwan

Thailand Kampuchea

Sri Lanka

Vietnam

Philippines

Brunei

Malaysia

I n d o n e s i a

Papua

ALASKA
(U.S.)

Canada

NORTH PACIFIC OCEAN

Los Angeles

HAWAIIAN IS. (U.S.)

Equator

SOUTH PACIFIC OCEAN

Australia

Sydney

INDIAN OCEAN

Kerguélen I. (Fr.)

New Zealand

ANTARCTICA

Speechless, 1996, by Shirin Neshat.

A diverse literature chronicles the experiences of political refugees and immigrants, both documented and un-documented. The political upheavals of the twentieth century created millions of refugees and entrenched conflicts that remain unresolved. Within nations, many migrants left rural areas to move to expanding cities. In search of economic security, meanwhile, immigrants left poorer countries, often in the global South, for the developed world. The immigrant experience became a major theme of writers including **Jamaica Kincaid**, and **V. S. Naipaul**.

Illness, too, travels faster than before; even as the general state of public health has improved, new epidemics, particularly AIDS, have ravaged populations in the West and much more broadly in Africa. In Europe and North America, AIDS at first affected mostly homosexuals. The decimation of gay communities by the disease led to more militant forms of activism, which built on antidiscrimination efforts dating back to the Stonewall uprising. A popular gay bar in the Greenwich Village neighborhood of New York City, Stonewall had been frequently targeted by the police. One evening in June 1969, patrons and their supporters resisted arrest, igniting the struggle for acceptance and equality. Yet another result of the gay rights movement was the introduction of same-sex marriages in much of the West, as well as in Brazil and South Africa. At the same time, homosexuality remained illegal in much of Africa and the Muslim world.

The gay rights movement was one of several outgrowths of 1960s cultural conflicts. The most successful of these, feminism, achieved legal equality for women in the workplace and in the family throughout the industrialized world. Challenges remained, including violence against women and unequal pay, but by the end of the twentieth century, many successful young career women claimed to be "post-feminist." Another factor enabling these transformations was the availability of safe and reliable birth control, which allowed for family planning (the contraceptive pill was introduced in 1960). Works by writers as diverse as **Leslie Marmon Silko** and **Hanan Al-Shaykh** touch on the changes in the status of women and in social norms governing sexuality. Abortion remained controversial in the United States and Ireland but was widely available elsewhere, except Latin America, Africa, and the Middle East, where homosexuality also remained illegal.

Even relatively conservative regions were not untouched by the youth culture born in the 1960s, broadcast by the mass media, and emphasizing the breaking of old taboos and the liberation of sexuality. Although the great writers were often skeptical of the appeal of mass culture, literature too participated in the breaking of taboos. Almost a century ago, **Virginia Woolf** spoke of a change in human character that the modernist generation registered: "All human relations have shifted—those between masters and servants, husbands and wives, parents and

Absence of God, 2007, by Raqib Shaw. Born in Calcutta, raised in Kashmir, and currently working in London, Shaw incorporates imagery from multiple sources—as varied as Renaissance painting, Japanese woodblock prints, and Hindu iconography—into his paintings, creating a dreamlike amalgam of the disparate parts.

children." The literature of the last century has continually reimagined these perpetually shifting relations, and the theme of generational conflict or cultural transmission across the generations plays a prominent role in much contemporary literature.

The literature of the late twentieth century, presented here along with a few works from the twenty-first century, has responded in manifold ways to the period's unprecedented historical transformations. While the cultural hybridity that attends the movement of peoples and the sharing of information sometimes inspires literary innovations, it can also sharpen nostalgia for tradition and the past. Increasingly, writers are conscious of having an audience beyond their nation or region and even beyond their language. Writers with a global readership may feel both responsibility for representing their own people to the world and the need to accommodate their style of writing to the demands of the international marketplace. Indeed, Nobel Prize winners such as V. S. Naipaul, Orhan Pamuk, and **J. M. Coetzee** have often been accused in their homelands of speaking primarily to an international audience. Writers thus find themselves striving to defend and honor the spirit and culture of historically marginalized groups while reaching out to a more elite international audience.

As in the immediate postwar period, many writers seeking to address the need for social change and the elimination of political inequality turn to traditional literary realism or to political allegory. A literary movement emerging in the 1960s, magic realism draws both on the realist tradition of the historical novel and on the inspiration of modernists such as **Franz Kafka**, who depicted his nightmarish worlds in lifelike detail. In various ways, Latin American novelists including **Gabriel García Márquez** and **Isabel Allende**, and the Indian-born **Salman Rushdie**, combine realistic historical narration with fanciful folktales in which individuals and societies seem to be transformed by distinctly nonrealistic events—a character who can fly, perhaps, or a mystical link among people born on the night of Indian independence. The juxtaposition emphasizes the coexistence of modern notions of causality and traditional, prescientific belief in the unexplainable and thus has had its greatest impact in zones of uneven economic development, where educated writers have incorporated the folk wisdom of their rural, sometimes illiterate communities. Toni Morrison has made effective use of such techniques in her writings on African American life. Like the magic realists, Morrison is sometimes described as a postmodernist. In common with an earlier generation inspired by the modernists (Borges, **Beckett**), postmodernists often question the boundary between fiction and history. While treating historical events, such writers as Roberto Bolaño, J. M. Coetzee, and Orhan Pamuk may call attention to the fictionality of their reconstruction of those events—encouraging the reader to keep in mind that stories are the creations of writers who may, by the very act of narration, distort historical reality. These authors tend to present an oblique account of atrocities, whether involving colonization, genocide, or political repression. Both in magic realism and in postmodernism, stories may seem whimsical or fantastical even when they are playing for deadly serious stakes.

The twenty-first century began with reminders of the interconnectedness of a global society linked by industrial capitalism and communications technology but divided by religion and politics. While war, terrorism, and poverty are events that divide us, the greatest world literature suggests, as it always has, what unites us.

YEHUDA AMICHAI

1924–2000

Yehuda Amichai belongs to the first generation of Israeli poets to be fully naturalized into both the language and the landscape of modern Israel. Perhaps more than any other contemporary poet, Amichai established a language of poetry that was independent of the history of Hebrew as a sacred language. By juxtaposing the monumental and the ordinary, Amichai helped to appropriate the language of the epic, biblical struggles of the people of Israel for the mundane realities of the twentieth century.

Hebrew was a spoken language only up to the close of the biblical period in the sixth century B.C.E. For the next 2,500 years, beginning with the exile of the Jews to Babylonia and their long dispersion from the land of Israel and continuing to the present day—a period known as the Diaspora—Hebrew ceased to be a spoken language. During the Diaspora, Hebrew was principally a vehicle for the sacred and the liturgical writings, for biblical commentary, and for official communication, while local Jewish dialects like Yiddish and Ladino served the function of everyday communication. The movement to modernize medieval Hebrew began in the eighteenth century, and by the late nineteenth century, Hebrew had established itself as a vigorous literary language. But it was not revived as a spoken language and adapted to ordinary secular life until the early twentieth century, when European Jews started emigrating to Palestine and reviving Hebrew as a modern, spoken language. Along with other poets of his generation, Amichai sought to create a poetic idiom that was at home with the colloquial rhythms and idiomatic expressions of revived Hebrew.

Amichai was born Ludwig Pfeuffer in Würzburg, Germany, and came to Palestine with his family in 1936, when he was twelve. He had grown up in an Orthodox Jewish home and studied Hebrew since early childhood, however, and like so many other immigrants, he made the transition to modern Hebrew with relative ease. Despite the enforced move from Germany, in his poetry he speaks of his childhood as a time of happiness and peace. His adult life began during the turbulent struggle to establish the State of Israel. Amichai served with the Jewish Brigade in World War II and saw active duty as an infantryman with the elite Jewish army, the Palmach, during the Israeli War of Independence and with the Israeli army in 1956 and 1973.

After completing his studies at Hebrew University, Amichai became a secondary school teacher of Hebrew literature and the Bible, but his career as a teacher soon took second place to his work as a poet. He had begun writing poetry in 1949 and published his first collection, *Now and in Other Days*, in 1955. With his second collection, *Two Hopes Away* (1958), he established himself as a major poet. From the late 1950s until his death, in 2000, Amichai published more than nine volumes of poetry as well as novels—including the one translated as *Not of This Time, Not of This Place* (1968)—short stories, and plays.

At times there is a deceptive simplicity about Amichai's poems. They seem to address ordinary moments and casual encounters. And yet in their simplicity they capture the many, resonating layers of the language and the insistent and contradictory realities of contemporary

Israeli life. The writer's language is despairing, gently ironic, playful and passionate by turns, moving easily between a child's artlessness and the brusque directness of a war-hardened veteran. The scope of his poetry is enormous, but what he brings to each poem is a freshness of vision and metaphors that are rich in unexpected and illuminating juxtapositions—the tomb of the biblical Rachel and the tomb of the modern Zionist leader Theodor Herzl, drying laundry and entrenched enmities, stones and undelivered messages, a lost child and a lost goat, the weariness of the poet who sees soldiers carried home from the hills like so much small change. These metaphors that thrust the deeply historical into the arms of the grittily immediate inspired critics to compare Amichai not with his contemporaries but with Donne and Shakespeare.

Amichai's form of choice was the short lyric, but he composed at least one memorable narrative poem, *The Travels of the Last Benjamin of Tudela*, and he often linked a number of shorter poems into cycles on a single theme. Many of his best poems are love poems, addressed to a woman or to Jerusalem—not as alternatives but as embedded in each other's essence. His poetry evokes with stunning immediacy that ancient city that other peoples and religions besides the Jews know as sacred and claim as home. Jerusalem is "an eternal heart, burning red," the place that must be remembered when all else is forgotten. Until 1967 it was a city divided only by a wall, across which intimate but hostile neighbors could watch each other's laundry drying.

In Israel, Amichai's poems are included in school anthologies and recited on public occasions. In the introduction to *The Selected Poetry of Yehuda Amichai*, Chana Bloch relates an anecdote that gives a more telling sense of the widespread popularity his works enjoy: "Some Israeli students were called up in the 1973 Yom Kippur War. As soon as they were notified, they went back to their rooms at the university, and each packed his gear, a rifle, and a book of Yehuda Amichai's poems" as she points out, despite the fact that his work "isn't patriotic in the ordinary sense of the word, it doesn't cry death to the enemy, and it offers no simple consolation for killing and dying." Amichai was originally brought to the attention of British and American readers by Ted Hughes, who published his work first in the journal *Modern Poetry in Translation* and then collaborated with Amichai in translating a volume of selections from his early poetry, *Amen* (1977). Eight volumes of his poetry have appeared in English translation, and there are numerous translations into other languages as well. It is for his renewal of the Hebrew language, however, that Amichai is best known; more than any other contemporary poet, he liberated Hebrew from the burden of its history.

God Has Pity on Kindergarten Children[1]

God has pity on kindergarten children.
He has less pity on school children.
And on grownups he has no pity at all,
    he leaves them alone,
and sometimes they must crawl on all fours   5
    in the burning sand
to reach the first-aid station
covered with blood.

---

1. Translated by Stephen Mitchell.

But perhaps he will watch over true lovers
and have mercy on them and shelter them   10
like a tree over the old man
sleeping on a public bench.

Perhaps we too will give them
the last rare coins of compassion
that Mother handed down to us,   15
so that their happiness will protect us
now and in other days.

          1956

Jerusalem[1]

On a roof in the Old City[2]
laundry hanging in the late afternoon sunlight:
the white sheet of a woman who is my enemy,
the towel of a man who is my enemy,
to wipe off the sweat of his brow.   5

In the sky of the Old City
a kite.
At the other end of the string,
a child
I can't see   10
because of the wall.

We have put up many flags,
they have put up many flags.
To make us think that they're happy.
To make them think that we're happy.   15

          1963

Tourists[1]

1

So condolence visits is what they're here for,
sitting around at the Holocaust Memorial, putting on a serious face
at the Wailing Wall,[2]
laughing behind heavy curtains in hotel rooms.

They get themselves photographed with the important dead   5
at Rachel's Tomb and Herzl's Tomb, and up on Ammunition Hill.[3]

1. Translated by Stephen Mitchell.
2. The oldest, walled portion of Jerusalem, around which the new city has been built.
1. Translated by Chana Bloch.
2. A remnant of the western wall of the second temple in Jerusalem; a site of pilgrimage, lamentation, and prayer for Jews.
3. The site of a major battle in Israel's War of Independence. Rachel was the second wife of Jacob and mother of Joseph and Benjamin. Theodor Herzl (1860–1904), Hungarian-born founder of Zionism.

They weep at the beautiful prowess of our boys,
lust after our tough girls
and hang up their underwear
to dry quickly   10
in cool blue bathrooms.

2

Once I was sitting on the steps near the gate at David's[4] Citadel and I put down
my two heavy baskets beside me. A group of tourists stood there around their
guide, and I became their point of reference. "You see that man over there with
the baskets? A little to the right of his head there's an arch from the Roman
period. A little to the right of his head." "But he's moving, he's moving!" I said
to myself: Redemption will come only when they are told, "Do you see that
arch over there from the Roman period? It doesn't matter, but near it, a little to
the left and then down a bit, there's a man who has just bought fruit and vegetables for his family."

                                                                    1980

An Arab Shepherd Is Searching for His Goat on Mount Zion[1]

An Arab shepherd is searching for his goat on Mount Zion
and on the opposite mountain I am searching
for my little boy.
An Arab shepherd and a Jewish father
both in their temporary failure.   5
Our voices meet above the Sultan's Pool[2]
in the valley between us. Neither of us wants
the child or the goat to get caught in the wheels
of the terrible *Had Gadya*[3] machine.

Afterward we found them among the bushes   10
and our voices came back inside us, laughing and crying.
Searching for a goat or a son
has always been the beginning
of a new religion in these mountains.

                                                                    1980

4. King David (died ca. 962 B.C.E.), who slew
Goliath and became the second king of Judah
and Israel (after Saul); reputed author of many
psalms.
1. Translated by Chana Bloch. The fortress of
Jerusalem is built on Mt. Zion.

2. Translation of the Hebrew name for a pool
located in the valley just outside the walls of
the Old City of Jerusalem.
3. One kid (Hebrew); alludes to a Passover song
in which "the kid that Daddy bought is eaten by
a cat that is bitten by a dog," and so on.

I Passed a House[1]

I passed a house where I once lived:
A man and a woman are still together in the whispers.
Many years have passed with the silent buzz
of staircase bulbs—on, off, on.

The keyholes are like small delicate wounds   5
through which all the blood has oozed out
and inside people are pale as death.

I want to stand once more as in my
first love, leaning on the doorpost
embracing you all night long, standing.   10
When we left at early dusk the house
started to crumble and collapse
and since then the town
and since then the whole world.

I want once more to have this longing   15
until dark-red burn marks show on the skin.

I want once more to be written
in the book of life, to be written
anew every day
until the writing hand hurts.   20

1977

1. Translated by Yehuda Amichai and Ted Hughes.

DEREK WALCOTT
born 1930

A cosmopolitan poet from a small Caribbean island, a West Indian of mixed African and European ancestry, Derek Walcott depicts the hybridity of Caribbean culture while drawing on the traditions of English literature. In contemplating the violent uprising in Kenya against British colonialism, he wrote in an early poem, "A Far Cry from Africa" (1956), of his dual inheritance: "I who am poisoned with the blood of both / Where shall I turn, divided to the vein?" Yet if he treats his mixed blood as poison, he also makes it a source of strength in his verse, which draws on the rhythms and idioms of Caribbean speech to enliven what he called, in the same poem, "the English tongue I love."

Derek Walcott was born, along with his twin brother, Roderick, on January 23, 1930, in Castries, the capital of the island of St. Lucia, then a British colony. (It had been occupied alternately by the French and the British since the seventeenth century and would not gain its independence from Britain until 1979.) Shortly after their first birthday, the boys' father, who was a government functionary and a talented artist, suddenly died, and the two boys were brought up by their mother, a schoolteacher who later became headmistress of the Methodist elementary school where they began their education. Both inherited their father's creative gift, Derek primarily in language, Roderick in the pictorial arts, and they remained intellectual and artistic companions until Roderick's death, in 1999. Their mother provided an environment in which their talents could be nurtured, an essential factor in Walcott's development as a poet.

Walcott acquired, early on, a sense of his singularity from the fact that he was of mixed ancestry in a predominantly black society (both his grandfathers were white, his grandmothers black). He was also a Protestant and member of the educated middle class in a peasant, Catholic community. Moreover, although he was brought up to speak Standard English as his first language, his exposure to the local French creole reinforced his sense of his ambiguous relation to the communal life around him. Far from unsettling Walcott, these factors of personal history became a source of strength and fascination. He began to write poetry in high school and published his first works as a teenager.

After high school education at St. Mary's College, Walcott studied at the University of West Indies in Jamaica, where he came to understand the Caribbean as a region unified by a common experience and a common historical legacy. His literary studies familiarized him with the great works of Western literature and particularly with the modern English poets **T. S. Eliot, W. B. Yeats**, and W. H. Auden. After his graduation, in 1953, Walcott taught school for a while in Kingston, while doing occasional work in journalism, before moving to Port of Spain, Trinidad, where he became a feature writer for a major local newspaper, the *Sunday Guardian*. In 1957, he was awarded a Rockefeller Fellowship to study theater at New York University. His encounter with the problems of race during his American sojourn gave further definition to his self-awareness as a West Indian; the experience confirmed for him the inescapable connection between race and history with which black people in the New World have to contend. On his return two years later to Port of Spain, he founded the Trinidad Theatre Workshop, to which he devoted his energies for nearly two decades. He was eager to bring the technical knowledge associated with the theater and stagecraft to the West Indies. He became well-known for his plays before he gained an international following for his poetry, which gained an international audience after the publication of his collection *In a Green Night* (1962) in England. Alienated by the Black Power revolts of the 1970s in Trinidad, Walcott resigned from the Trinidad Theatre Workshop and, after winning a MacArthur Fellowship ("genius" grant) in 1981, began teaching regularly at Boston University. Since then, he has divided his time between the United States and St. Lucia. He was awarded the Nobel Prize for Literature in 1992.

All Walcott's poetry flows into *Omeros* (1990), which is best grasped as the imaginative summation of human history as seen from his Caribbean perspective. Its retrospective vision assumes an emotional value for the poet for whom, as he says, "Art is History's nostalgia." In an expansive recollection of his previous themes, *Omeros* sums up the West Indian experience through the adventures of Achille, a humble St. Lucian fisherman, whose travels take him to the points of compass of the West Indian consciousness. Homer's great epics, the *Iliad* and the *Odyssey*, serve as explicit references for the work, and the figure of Homer himself, in his modern Greek rendering of "Omeros," is evoked in a key passage of the poem in which he is represented as the quintessential exile. Moreover, Walcott's use of the blind poet in the character of Seven Seas, modeled on Demodokos in Homer's *Odyssey*, reinforces the importance of this Greek frame of reference. The poem employs some of the standard tropes of the classical epic, such as descent into the underworld and conflict and contest.

Despite these connections, *Omeros* is not a mere rehash of Homer. Although the poem contains stretches of narration, they do not build up to a dramatic progression of events such as we find in the conventional epic. The rivalry between Achille and another local fisherman, Hector, over Helen (who is hardly idealized in the poem and remains, for all her beauty, an ordinary village woman) is presented as part of a strictly local history that features other characters such as the white settler couple, Major Plunkett and his wife, Maud, as well as minor characters who move in and out of the narrative. Thus

the poem does not develop a linear plot, but represents, rather, a vast kaleidoscope, a series of episodes that are woven around its protagonist. Achilles' descent into the underworld recounted in Chapter VIII, for example, renders the sea as the graveyard of history and the site of the turbulent history of the Caribbean. This plunge into a violent past has an obvious connection with the poet's recollection, in Chapter XXXV, of the Native Americans' experience and condition, the pathos of a "tribal sorrow" that originates in the tragic confrontation with the white race.

Walcott's exploration of the African element in Caribbean life, dramatized in Chapter XXV in the dream sequence, takes Achille back to the ancestral homeland. The theme of collective memory and its relation to identity is developed in the dialogue between Achille and his mythic progenitor, Afolabe. *Omeros* reconnects with Africa by emphasizing the continuing tie of the West Indians to the continent of their forbears yet helps its West Indian audience take cultural repossession of their island home. *Omeros* registers both the Afro-Caribbean quest for an established sense of place and of community and, at the same time, the compulsion to move toward the wider horizon of world literature.

OMEROS

From Book One

From *Chapter I*

II

Achille looked up at the hole[1] the laurel had left.
He saw the hole silently healing with the foam
of a cloud like a breaker. Then he saw the swift[2]

crossing the cloud-surf, a small thing, far from its home,
confused by the waves of blue hills. A thorn vine gripped   5
his heel. He tugged it free. Around him, other ships

were shaping from the saw. With his cutlass he made
a swift sign of the cross, his thumb touching his lips
while the height rang with axes. He swayed back the blade,

and hacked the limbs from the dead god,[3] knot after knot,   10
wrenching the severed veins from the trunk as he prayed:
"Tree! You can be a canoe! Or else you cannot!"

The bearded elders endured the decimation
of their tribe without uttering a syllable
of the language they had uttered as one nation,[4]   15

the speech taught their saplings: from the towering babble
of the cedar to green vowels of *bois-campêche*.
The *bois-flot* held its tongue with the *laurier-cannelle*,[5]

the red-skinned logwood endured the thorns in its flesh,
while the Aruacs' patois[6] crackled in the smell   20
of a resinous bonfire that turned the leaves brown

with curling tongues, then ash, and their language was lost.
Like barbarians striding columns they have brought down,
the fishermen shouted. The gods were down at last.

Like pygmies they hacked the trunks of wrinkled giants   25
for paddles and oars. They were working with the same
concentration as an army of fire-ants.[7]

---

1. The opening stanza describes the ritual felling of a laurel tree from which a dugout canoe is to be made. This refers to the hole in the ground where the tree had stood. The section that follows describes the making of the canoe.
2. A small, plainly colored bird, related to the swallow, that serves as a guide to the wandering hero.
3. The laurel tree, venerated as nature.
4. The flora as part of the total living environment.
5. *Bois-campêche, bois-flot, laurier-cannelle*: French for logwood, timber, and laurel, respectively.
6. Dialect. "Aruacs": the original inhabitants of the Caribbean; also Arawaks.
7. Omnivorous ants with powerful stingers in their tails.

But vexed by the smoke for defaming their forest,
blow-darts of mosquitoes kept needling Achille's trunk.
He frotted white rum on both forearms that, at least,   30

those that he flattened to asterisks would die drunk.
They went for his eyes. They circled them with attacks
that made him weep blindly. Then the host retreated

to high bamboo like the archers of Aruacs
running from the muskets of cracking logs,[8] routed   35
by the fire's banner and the remorseless axe

hacking the branches. The men bound the big logs first
with new hemp[9] and, like ants, trundled them to a cliff
to plunge through tall nettles.[1] The logs gathered that thirst

for the sea which their own vined bodies were born with.   40
Now the trunks in eagerness to become canoes
ploughed into breakers of bushes, making raw holes

of boulders, feeling not death inside them, but use—
to roof the sea, to be hulls. Then, on the beach, coals[2]
were set in their hollows that were chipped with an adze.   45

A flat-bed truck had carried their rope-bound bodies.
The charcoals, smouldering, cored the dugouts for days
till heat widened the wood enough for ribbed gunwales.[3]

Under his tapping chisel Achille felt their hollows
exhaling to touch the sea, lunging towards the haze   50
of bird-printed islets, the beaks of their parted bows.

Then everything fit. The pirogues[4] crouched on the sand
like hounds with sprigs in their teeth. The priest
sprinkled them with a bell, then he made the swift's sign.[5]

When he smiled at Achille's canoe, *In God We Troust,*[6]   55
Achille said: "Leave it! Is God' spelling and mine."
After Mass one sunrise the canoes entered the troughs[7]

---

8. Log houses from which white men shot at
the Aruacs.
9. The vine is excellent for making ropes.
1. A plant that stings.
2. They are used to fire the hollowed-out logs.
3. That is, the heat expanded the wood so
that metal strips could be inserted to reinforce
the sides of the boat.

4. French for dugout canoes.
5. The swift's wings are shaped like a cross.
6. The boat's name. The phrase "In God We
Trust" is found on American money.
7. Sea channels.

of the surpliced[8] shallows, and their nodding prows
agreed with the waves to forget their lives as trees;
one would serve Hector and another, Achilles.   60

From *Chapter VIII*

I

In the islet's museum there is a twisted
wine-bottle, crusted with fool's gold[1] from the iron-
cold depth below the redoubt. It has been listed

variously by experts; one, that a galleon
blown by a hurricane out of Cartagena,[2]   5
this far east, had bled a trail of gold bullion

and wine from its hold (a view held by many a
diver lowering himself); the other was nonsense
and far too simple: that the gold-crusted bottle

came from a flagship in the Battle of the Saints,[3]   10
but the glass was so crusted it was hard to tell.
Still, the myth widened its rings every century:[4]

that the *Ville de Paris*[5] sank there, not a galleon
crammed with imperial coin, and for her sentry,
an octopus-cyclops,[6] its one eye like the moon.   15

Deep as a diver's faith but never discovered,
their trust in the relic converted the village,
who came to believe that circling frigates hovered

over the relic, that gulls attacked them in rage.
They kept their faith when the experts' ended in doubt.   20
The galleon's shadow rode over the ruled page

8. The canoes make a lacelike pattern on the water, resembling the surplice worn by Catholic priests at Mass.
1. Pyrite or, by extension, any pyritic material that resembles gold.
2. I.e., Cartagena, a seaport on the northwest coast of Colombia.
3. Naval battle fought off the coast of Martinique on April 12, 1782, between the French fleet commanded by Admiral de Grasset and a British fleet under Admiral Sir George Bridges

Rodney. The French were routed, their fleet annihilated.
4. Like rings on a tree as it ages.
5. The flagship of the French fleet.
6. Here Walcott conflates an octopus—a mollusk that has eight arms, each with two rows of suckers—with Greek mythology's Cyclops, a one-eyed giant who, in Homer's *Odyssey*, holds Odysseus and his men captive until they escape by blinding him.

where Achille, rough weather coming, counted his debt
by the wick of his kerosene lamp; the dark ship
divided his dreams, while the moon's octopus eye

climbed from the palms that lifted their tentacles' shape.   25
It glared like a shilling.[7] Everything was money.
Money will change her, he thought. Is this bad living

that make her come wicked. He had mocked the belief
in a wrecked ship out there. Now he began diving
in a small shallop[8] beyond the line of the reef,   30

with spear-gun[9] and lobster-pot.[1] He had to make sure
no sail would surprise him, feathering the oars back
without clicking the oarlocks. He fed the anchor

carefully overside. He tied the cinder-block
to one heel with a slip-knot[2] for faster descent,   35
then slipped the waterproof bag around his shoulders

for a money-pouch. She go get every red cent,
he swore, crossing himself as he dived. Wedged in boulders
down there was salvation and change. The concrete, tied

to his heel, pulled him down faster than a lead-   40
weighted, canvas-bound carcass, the stone heart inside
his chest added its poundage. What if love was dead

inside her already? What good lay in pouring
silver coins on a belly that had warmed him once?
This weighed him down even more, so he kept falling   45

for fathoms towards his fortune: moidores, doubloons,[3]
while the slow-curling fingers of weeds kept calling;
he felt the cold of the drowned entering his loins.

II

Why was he down here, from their coral palaces.
pope-headed turtles asked him, waving their paddles[4]   50
crusted with rings, nudged by curious porpoises

---

7. An English coin worth one-twentieth of a pound. Its use was discontinued when Britain adopted the decimal currency in 1969.
8. A small boat (from French *chaloupe*).
9. A gun that has a forked end on which fish are speared.
1. A basket for trapping lobsters.

2. A knot that moves along the rope on which it is tied.
3. These are Portuguese and Spanish gold coins, respectively.
4. The turtles propel themselves using their flippers as paddles.

with black friendly skins. Why? asked the glass sea-horses,[5]
curling like questions. What on earth had he come for,
when he had a good life up there? The sea-mosses[6]

shook their beards angrily, like submarine cedars,   55
while he trod the dark water. Wasn't love worth more
than the coins of light pouring from the galleon's doors?

In the corals' bone kingdom his skin calcifies.[7]
In that wavering garden huge fans on hinges
swayed, while fingers of seaweed pocketed the eyes[8]   60

of coins with the profiles of Iberian kings;[9]
here the sea-floor was mud, not corrugating sand
that showed you its ribs; here, the mutating fishes

had goggling eye-bulbs; in that world without sound,
they sucked the white coral, draining it like leeches,   65
and what looked like boulders sprung the pincers of crabs.

This was not a world meant for the living, he thought.
The dead didn't need money, like him, but perhaps
they hated surrendering things their hands had brought.

The shreds of the ocean's floor passed him from corpses   70
that had perished in the crossing, their hair like weeds,
their bones were long coral fingers, bubbles of eyes

watched him, a brain-coral[1] gurgled their words,
and every bubble englobed a biography,
no less than the wine-bottle's mouth, but for Achille,   75

treading the mulch floor of the Caribbean Sea,
no coins were enough to repay its deep evil.
The ransom of centuries shone through the mossy doors

---

5. Small bony fishes that have a horse-shaped
head and the body of a fish with a curved tail
(hence "curling like questions").
6. Any of certain frondlike red algae that look
like moss (and hence "shook their beards").
7. Hardens.

8. Here, covered completely.
9. Relating to Iberia, the peninsula made up
of Spain and Portugal.
1. A reef coral with its surface covered by
ridges and furrows.

that the moon-blind Cyclops counted, every tendril
raked in the guineas[2] it tested with its soft jaws.   80
Light paved the ceiling with silver with every swell.

Then he saw the galleon. Her swaying cabin-doors
fanned vaults of silvery mackerel. He caught the glint
of their coin-packed scales,[3] then the tentacle-shadows

whose motion was a miser's harvesting his mint.   85
He loosened the block[4] and shot up. Next day, her stealth
increased, her tentacles calling, until the wreck

vanished with all hope of Helen. Once more the whelk[5]
was his coin, his bank the sea-conch's.[6] Now, every day
he was clear-headed as the sea, wrenching lace fans   90

from the forbidden reef, or tailing a sting-ray[7]
floating like a crucifix when it sensed his lance,
and saving the conch-shells he himself had drowned.

And though he lost faith[8] in any fictional ship,
an anchor still forked his brow whenever he frowned,   95
for she was a spectre now, in her ribbed shape,

he did not know where she was. She'd never be found.
He thought of the white skulls rolling out there like dice
rolled by the hand of the swell, their luck was like his;

he saw drowned Portuguese captains, their coral eyes   100
entered by minnows,[9] as he hauled the lobster-pot,
bearded with moss, in the cold shade of the redoubt.[1]

2. English coins, supposedly struck from gold
from the Guinea coast in West Africa.
3. The fishes' scales are like silver coins.
4. Concrete (referred to in lines 39–42).
5. A large marine snail with a spiral shell.
6. A large spiral-shelled marine mollusk. Its
shell resonates when blown into; runaway slaves
often sent messages to each other this way.
7. A ray with a flat body and whiplike tail with
spines near its base capable of inflicting severe
wounds.
8. See line 16, above.
9. Tiny fish.
1. A small, usually temporary fort.

From Book Three

Chapter XXV

I

Mangroves,[1] their ankles in water, walked with the canoe.
The swift, racing its browner shadow, screeched, then veered
into a dark inlet. It was the last sound Achille knew

from the other world. He feathered the paddle,[2] steered
away from the groping mangroves, whose muddy shelves   5
slipped warted crocodiles,[3] slitting the pods of their eyes;

then the horned river-horses[4] rolling over themselves
could capsize the keel. It was like the African movies
he had yelped at in childhood. The endless river unreeled

those images that flickered into real mirages: 10
naked mangroves walking beside him, knotted logs
wriggling into the water, the wet, yawning boulders

of oven-mouthed hippopotami. A skeletal[5] warrior
stood up straight in the stern and guided his shoulders,
clamped his neck in cold iron,[6] and altered the oar.   15

Achille wanted to scream, he wanted the brown water
to harden into a road, but the river widened ahead
and closed behind him. He heard screeching laughter

in a swaying tree, as monkeys swung from the rafter
of their tree-house, and the bared sound rotted the sky   20
like their teeth. For hours the river gave the same show

for nothing, the canoe's mouth muttered its lie.
The deepest terror was the mud. The mud with no shadow
like the clear sand. Then the river coiled into a bend.

He saw the first signs of men, tall sapling fishing-stakes; 25
he came into his own beginning and his end,
for the swiftness of a second is all that memory takes.

Now the strange, inimical river surrenders its stealth
to the sunlight. And a light inside him wakes,[7]
skipping centuries, ocean and river, and Time itself.   30

1. Tropical trees that grow in lagoons and
waterways.
2. Turned the oar so that it was horizontal
when lifted from the water at the end of a
stroke. This reduces air resistance.
3. The skin of the crocodiles seems to be covered with hardened protuberances.

4. I.e., hippopotami.
5. Here, ghostly, which is appropriate to the
character of the passage as a dream sequence.
6. Reminiscent of the chains with which
slaves were bound.
7. I.e., awakens ancestral memory.

And God said to Achille, "Look, I giving you permission
to come home. Is I send the sea-swift as a pilot,
the swift whose wings is the sign of my crucifixion.

And thou shalt have no God should in case you forgot
my commandments." And Achille felt the homesick shame   35
and pain of his Africa. His heart and his bare head

were bursting as he tried to remember the name
of the river- and the tree-god in which he steered,
whose hollow body carried him to the settlement ahead.

II

He remembered this sunburnt river with its spindly   40
stakes and the peaked huts platformed above the spindles
where thin, naked figures as he rowed past looked unkindly

or kindly in their silence. The silence an old fence kindles
in a boy's heart. They walked with his homecoming
canoe past bonfires in a scorched clearing near the edge   45

of the soft-lipped shallows whose noise hurt his drumming
heart as the pirogue slid its raw, painted wedge
towards the crazed sticks of a vine-fastened pier.

The river was sloughing[8] its old skin like a snake
in wrinkling sunshine; the sun resumed its empire   50
over this branch of the Congo; the prow found its stake

in the river and nuzzled it the way that a piglet
finds its favourite dug[9] in the sweet-grunting sow,
and now each cheek ran with its own clear rivulet

of tears, as Achille, weeping, fastened the bow   55
of the dugout, wiped his eyes with one dry palm,
and felt a hard hand help him up the shaking pier.

Half of me was with him. One half with the midshipman
by a Dutch canal.[1] But now, neither was happier
or unhappier than the other. An old man put an arm   60

around Achille, and the crowd, chattering, followed both.
They touched his trousers, his undershirt, their hands
scrabbling[2] the texture, as a kitten does with cloth,

8. Shedding.
9. The nipple of a pig from which the young
suck milk.
1. Spoken in the author's own voice, this pas-

sage expresses the split in Walcott's heritage—
half African, half Dutch.
2. Scraping.

till they stood before an open hut. The sun stands
with expectant silence. The river stops talking,   65
the way silence sometimes suddenly turns off a market.

The wind squatted low in the grass. A man kept walking
steadily towards him, and he knew by that walk it
was himself in his father, the white teeth, the widening hands.

III

He sought his own features in those of their life-giver,   70
and saw two worlds mirrored there: the hair was surf
curling round a sea-rock, the forehead a frowning river,

as they swirled in the estuary of a bewildered love,
and Time stood between them. The only interpreter
of their lips' joined babble, the river with the foam,   75

and the chuckles of water under the sticks of the pier,
where the tribe stood like sticks themselves, reversed
by reflection.[3] Then they walked up to the settlement,

and it seemed, as they chattered, everything was rehearsed
for ages before this. He could predict the intent   80
of his father's gestures; he was moving with the dead.

Women paused at their work, then smiled at the warrior
returning from his battle with smoke,[4] from the kingdom
where he had been captured, they cried and were happy.

Then the fishermen sat near a large tree under whose dome   85
stones sat in a circle. His father said:
                    "Afo-la-be,"[5]

touching his own heart.
                    "In the place you have come from

what do they call you?"
                    Time translates.   90
                    Tapping his chest,

the son answers:
            "Achille." The tribe rustles, "Achille."
Then, like cedars at sunrise, the mutterings settle.

---

3. Mirrored upside down in the river.   5. A Yoruba name meaning "born with honor."
4. Of an ordeal, in the dim past.

AFOLABE

Achille. What does the name mean? I have forgotten the one   95
that I gave you. But it was, it seems, many years ago.
What does it mean?

ACHILLE

Well, I too have forgotten.

Everything was forgotten. You also. I do not know.
The deaf sea has changed around every name that you gave   100
us; trees, men, we yearn for a sound that is missing.

AFOLABE

A name means something.[6] The qualities desired in a son,
and even a girl-child; so even the shadows who called
you expected one virtue, since every name is a blessing,

since I am remembering the hope I had for you as a child.   105
Unless the sound means nothing. Then you would be nothing.
Did they think you were nothing in that other kingdom?[7]

ACHILLE

I do not know what the name means. It means something,
maybe. What's the difference? In the world I come from
we accept the sounds we were given. Men, trees, water.   110

AFOLABE

And therefore, Achille, if I pointed and I said, There
is the name of that man, that tree, and this father,
would every sound be a shadow that crossed your ear,

without the shape of a man or a tree? What would it be?
(And just as branches sway in the dusk from their fear   115
of amnesia,[8] of oblivion, the tribe began to grieve.)

ACHILLE

What would it be? I can only tell you what I believe,
or had to believe. It was prediction, and memory,
to bear myself back, to be carried here by a swift,

---

6. African names always have a meaning of   7. I.e., the New World.
great social significance.   8. Loss of memory.

or the shadow of a swift making its cross on water,   120
with the same sign I was blessed with[9] with the gift
of this sound whose meaning I still do not care to know.

AFOLABE

No man loses his shadow except it is in the night,
and even then his shadow is hidden, not lost. At the glow
of sunrise, he stands on his own in that light.   125

When he walks down to the river with the other fishermen
his shadow stretches in the morning, and yawns, but you,
if you're content with not knowing what our names mean,

then I am not Afolabe, your father, and you look through
my body as the light looks through a leaf. I am not here   130
or a shadow. And you, nameless son, are only the ghost

of a name. Why did I never miss you until you returned?
Why haven't I missed you, my son, until you were lost?
Are you the smoke from a fire that never burned?

There was no answer to this, as in life.[1] Achille nodded,   135
the tears glazing his eyes, where the past was reflected
as well as the future. The white foam lowered its head.

From Chapter XXVI

I

In a language as brown[1] and leisurely as the river,
they muttered about a future Achille already knew
but which he could not reveal even to his breath-giver

or in the council of elders. But he learned to chew
in the ritual of the kola nut,[2] drain gourds of palm-wine,[3]   5
to listen to the moan of the tribe's triumphal sorrow

in a white-eyed storyteller[4] to a balaphon's whine,[5]
who perished in what battle, who was swift with the arrow,
who mated with a crocodile,[6] who entered a river-horse

---

9. Baptized as a Christian, with possibly a pun on the French *blessé*, "wounded."
1. Which is filled with unresolved questions.
1. Muddy, alluvial, and therefore fertile.
2. The bitter, caffeine-laden seed of the kola tree; it is chewed on ceremonial occasions.
3. The natural sap of the tropical palm, which, when drawn, ferments and becomes alcoholic.
4. The bard, or griot, whose function was to pre-serve the community's history (see lines 16–20).
5. An African instrument with flat wooden keys like the xylophone that is played to accompany the griot's narrative.
6. In myths, heroes were often said to descend from mixed parentage of humans and animals; in other instances, certain animals are held to be ancestors or relatives of members of the tribe and thus function as their totem.

and lived in its belly, who was the thunder's favourite,   10
who the serpent-god[7] conducted miles off his course
for some blasphemous offence and how he would pay for it

by forgetting his parents, his tribe, and his own spirit
for an albino god,[8] and how that warrior was scarred
for innumerable moons so badly that he would disinherit   15

himself. And every night the seed-eyed, tree-wrinkled[9] bard,
the crooked tree who carried the genealogical leaves[1]
of the tribe in his cave-throated moaning,

traced the interlacing branches of their river-rooted lives
as intricately as the mangrove roots. Until morning   20
he sang, till the river was the only one to hear it.

Achille did not go down to the fishing stakes one dawn,
but left the hut door open, the hut he had been given
for himself and any woman he chose as his companion,

and he climbed a track of huge yams, to find that heaven   25
of soaring trees, that sacred circle of clear ground
where the gods assembled. He stood in the clearing

and recited the gods' names. The trees within hearing
ignored his incantation. He heard only the cool sound
of the river. He saw a tree-hole, raw in the uprooted ground.[2] 30

*   *   *

III

He walked the ribbed sand under the flat keels of whales,
under the translucent belly of the snaking current,
the tiny shadows of tankers passed over him like snails

as he breathed water, a walking fish in its element.
He floated in stride, his own shadow over his eyes   35
like a grazing shark, through vast meadows of coral,

over barnacled[3] cannons whose hulks sprouted anemones[4]
like Philoctete's shin; he walked for three hundred years
in the silken wake like a ribbon of the galleons,

7. The cult of the serpent is central to many African religions and to their derivatives in the New World.
8. Lacking in pigment, white, and therefore an alien god.
9. Gaunt, like an old tree.
1. I.e., the leaves of the family tree.
2. See n. 1, p. 1626.

3. A barnacle is a type of marine crustacean with feathery appendages for gathering food; as adults, they affix themselves permanently to objects.
4. A reference to sea anemones, marine coelenterates whose form, bright colors, and clusters of tentacles resemble flowers.

their bubbles fading like the transparent men-o'-wars   40
with their lilac dangling tendrils, bursting like aeons,[5]
like phosphorous galaxies; he saw the huge cemeteries

of bone and the huge crossbows of the rusted anchors,
and groves of coral with hands as massive as trees
like calcified ferns and the greening gold ingots of bars   45

whose value had outlasted that of the privateers.[6]
Then, one afternoon, the ocean lowered and clarified
its ceiling, its emerald net, and after three centuries

of walking, he thought he could hear the distant quarrel
of breaker with shore; then his head broke clear,[7] and   50
his neck; then he could see his own shadow in the coral

grove, ribbed and rippling with light on the clear sand,
as his fins spread their toes, and he saw the leaf
of his own canoe far out, the life he had left behind

and the white line of surf around low Barrel of Beef[8]   55
with its dead lantern. The salt glare left him blind
for a minute, then the shoreline returned in relief.[9]

He woke to the sound of sunlight scratching at the door
of the hut, and he smelt not salt but the sluggish odour
of river. Fingers of light rethatched the roof's straw.   60

On the day of his feast they wore the same plantain trash
like Philoctete at Christmas. A bannered mitre[1]
of bamboo was placed on his head, a calabash

mask, and skirts that made him both woman and fighter.
That was how they danced at home, to fifes and tambours,   65
the same berries round their necks and the small mirrors

flashing from their stuffed breasts. One of the warriors
mounted on stilts walked like lightning over the thatch
of the peaked village. Achille saw the same dances

that the mitred warriors did with their bamboo stick   70
as they scuttered around him, lifting, dipping their lances
like divining rods turning the earth to music,

---

5. Vast stretches of time.
6. Armed ships and their crew commissioned by governments to attack enemy ships on the open sea.
7. As he resurfaced.
8. A rocky site off the coast of St. Lucia, a prominent landmark on the island.
9. In the double sense of being sharply outlined and of bringing a sense of relief.
1. A ritual headdress, but more usually applied to the liturgical headdress worn by bishops and abbots.

the same chac-chac and ra-ra,[2] the drumming the same,
and the chant of the seed-eyed prophet to the same
response from the blurring ankles. The same, the same.[3]   75

From Book Four

From *Chapter XXXV*

I

"Somewhere over there," said my guide, "the Trail of Tears
started." I leant towards the crystalline creek. Pines
shaded it. Then I made myself hear the water's

language around the rocks in its clear-running lines
and its small shelving falls with their eddies, "Choctaws,"   5
"Creeks," "Choctaws,"[1] and I thought of the Greek revival

carried past the names of towns with columned porches,
and how Greek it was, the necessary evil
of slavery, in the catalogue of Georgia's

marble past, the Jeffersonian ideal[2] in   10
plantations with its Hectors and Achilleses,
its foam in the dogwood's spray, past towns named Helen,

Athens, Sparta, Troy. The slave shacks, the rolling peace
of the wave-rolling meadows, oak, pine, and pecan,
and a creek like this one. From the window I saw   15

the bundles of women moving in ragged bands
like those on the wharf,[3] headed for Oklahoma;
then I saw Seven Seas,[4] a rattle in his hands.

A huge thunderhead[5] was unclenching its bruised fist
over the county. Shadows escaped through the pines   20
and the pecan groves and hounds[6] were closing in fast

---

2. Dance forms in the Caribbean. "Ra-ra" is
derived from a Yoruba genre of chanted poetry.
3. Walcott registers the protagonist's recognition of his cultural connection of Africa.
1. Native American nations expelled from
their original homes and forced to march to
reservations in Oklahoma (see line 17).
2. "Life, liberty and the pursuit of happiness,"
belied by the institution of slavery.
3. Captured Africans waiting to be shipped to
America. This passage establishes a parallel

between the fate of Native Americans and that
of African slaves.
4. A blind poet and singer in St. Lucia who
features prominently in Walcott's play *The
Odyssey*, a stage adaptation of Homer's epic.
5. A large mass of dark cumulus clouds presaging a thunderstorm.
6. Dogs were used to recapture runaway
slaves; they were also set upon black protesters during the civil rights movement.

deep into Georgia, where history happens
to be the baying echoes of brutality,
and terror in the oaks along red country roads,

or the gibbet[7] branches of a silk-cotton tree   25
from which Afolabes hung like bats. Hooded clouds[8]
guarded the town squares with their calendar churches,

whose white, peaked belfries asserted that pastoral
of brooks with leisurely accents. On their verges,
like islands reflected on windscreens, Negro shacks   30

moved like a running wound, like the rusty anchor
that scabbed Philoctete's shin,[9] I imagined the backs
moving through the foam of pods, one arm for an oar,

one for the gunny sack.[1] Brown streams tinkled in chains.
Bridges arched their spines. Led into their green pasture,[2]   35
horses sagely grazed or galloped the plantations.

II

"Life is so fragile. It trembles like the aspens.[3]
All its shadows are seasonal, including pain.
In drizzling dusk the rain enters the lindens

with its white lances, then lindens enclose the rain.   40
So that day isn't far when they will say, 'Indians
bowed under those branches, which tribe is not certain.'

Nor am I certain I lived. I breathed what the farm
exhaled. Its soils, its seasons. The swayed goldenrod,
the corn where summer hid me, pollen on my arm,   45

sweat tickling my armpits. The Plains were fierce as God
and wide as His mind. I enjoyed diminishing,
I exalted in insignificance after

the alleys of Boston, in the unfinishing
chores of the farm, alone. Once, from the barn's rafter   50
a swift or a swallow shot out, taking with it

my son's brown, whirring soul,[4] and I knew that its aim
was heaven. More and more we learn to do without
those we still love. With my father it was the same.

7. Gallows. The reference here is to the lynch-
ing in the Deep South of blacks, usually by
hanging.
8. The Ku Klux Klan.
9. The companion of Achille in his Caribbean
home and, like him, a fisherman.
1. A bag made from coarse, heavy material.
2. Conveying an impression of blessed peace,
but deceptive.
3. A type of poplar tree whose leaves flutter in
the slightest breeze. The speaker here is Catherine Weldon, a historical figure that Walcott
has woven into the poem.
4. Perhaps a reference to an aspect of Native
American beliefs.

The bounty of God pursued me over the Plains 55
of the Dakotas, the pheasants, the quick-volleyed
arrows of finches; smoke bound me to the Indians

from morning to sunset when I have watched its veiled
rising, because I am a widow, barbarous
and sun-cured in the face, I loved them ever since 60

I worked as a hand in Colonel Cody's[5] circus,
under a great canvas larger than all their tents,
when they were paid to ride round in howling circles,

with a dime for their glory, and boys screamed in fright
at the galloping braves. Now the aspens enclosed 65
the lances of rain, and the wet leaves shake with light."

* * *

From Book Six

From *Chapter LII*

II

Provinces, Protectorates, Colonies, Dominions,
Governors-General, black Knights, ostrich-plumed[1] Viceroys,
deserts, jungles, hill-stations, all an empire's zones,

lay spilled from a small tea-chest; felt-footed houseboys
on fern-soft verandahs, hearty Toby-jugged[2] Chiefs 5
of Police, Girl-Guide Commissioners, Secretaries,

poppies on cenotaphs,[3] green-spined Remembrance wreaths,
cornets, kettledrums, gum-chewing dromedaries[4]
under Lawrence,[5] parasols, palm-striped pavilions,

dhows[6] and feluccas,[7] native-draped paddle-ferries 10
on tea-brown rivers, statue-rehearsing lions,
sandstorms seaming their eyes, horizontal monsoons,

5. I.e., William F. Cody, also called Buffalo
Bill (1846–1917), who founded a circus and a
traveling show that featured Native Americans
in various humiliating roles. "A dime for their
glory" (line 64) is an ironic comment on this.
1. The ceremonial uniform of British colonial
governors was topped by a cap with ostrich
feathers.
2. A Toby jug is a small vessel—a mug, for
instance—shaped like a fat man wearing a
cocked hat.

3. Flowers atop tombs or monuments.
4. Camels, which constantly chew their cud.
5. A reference to T. E. Lawrence (1888–
1935), also known as Lawrence of Arabia, who
served as liaison officer between the British
forces and Arab guerrillas fighting against
Turkish rule during the First World War.
6. Arab sailboats.
7. Small, fast sailing vessels common to the
Mediterranean. They are equipped with both
masts and oars.

rank odour of a sea-chest, mimosa memories
touched by a finger, lead soldiers, clopping Dragoons.[8]
Breadfruit hands on a wall. The statues close their eyes.   15

Mosquito nets, palm-fronds, scrolled Royal Carriages,
dacoits,[9] gun-bearers,[1] snarling apes on Gibraltar,[2]
sermons to sweat-soaked kerchiefs, the Rock of Ages[3]

pumped by a Zouave[4] band, lilies light the altar,
soldiers and doxies[5] by a splashing esplanade,   20
waves turning their sheet music, the yellowing teeth

of the parlour piano, *Airs from Erin*[6] played
to the whistling kettle, and on the teapot's head
the cozy's bearskin shako,[7] biscuits break with grief,

gold-braid laburnums,[8] lilac whiff of lavender,
columned poplars marching to Mafeking's relief.[9]   25
Naughty seaside cards, the sepia surrender

of Gordon[1] on the mantel, the steps of Khartoum,
The World's Classics[2] condensed, Clive[3] as brown as India
bathers in Benares,[4] an empire in costume.

His will be done, O Maud, His kingdom come,   30
as the sunflower turns,[5] and the white eyes widen
in the ebony faces, the sloe-eyes, the bent smoke

where a pig totters across a village midden[6]
over the sunset's shambles, Rangoon to Malta,[7]
the regimental button of the evening star.   35

---

8. Heavily armed cavalry unit.
9. A gang of robbers of (Hindi).
1. Armored vehicles.
2. A reference to the Barbary macaques that live in Gibraltar, a British enclave at the southern tip of Spain, long a tourist attraction.
3. A well-known Judeo-Christian hymn.
4. The Zouaves were Algerian infantry units in the French and American Confederate armies.
5. Prostitutes.
6. Ireland.
7. The tea cozy, a cushioned cover draped over a teapot to keep the contents warm, resembles a *shako*, a stiff military hat with a high crown, in this case made from bearskin.
8. A shrub with bright yellow flowers (i.e., "gold-braid").
9. A town in South Africa relieved by British forces after a long siege by Afrikaners during the Boer War.
1. Charles Gordon (1833–1885), British governor-

general in the Sudan who was killed on the steps of his residence at Khartoum during an uprising by the local population.
2. A famous collection of great literature published by Oxford University Press.
3. Robert Clive (1725–1774), an agent of the East India Company considered to have secured India for the British by thwarting the French and by defeating the local Bengali ruler at the Battle of Plassey in 1757.
4. Holy Hindu city situated on the northern bank of the Ganges in India and associated with Buddha.
5. Fragment of an Irish song beginning "Believe me if all those endearing young charms."
6. Rubbish heap.
7. Rangoon is a city in Myanmar (formerly Burma), a former British colony; Malta, an island in the Mediterranean off the Italian coast, was also a British colony.

Solace of laudanum, menstrual cramps, the runnings,
tinkles in the jordan, at dusk the zebra shade
of louvres on the quilt, the maps spread their warnings

and the tribal odour of the second chambermaid.
And every fortnight, ten sharp on Sunday mornings,   40
shouts and wheeling patterns from our Cadet Brigade.[8]

All spilt from a tea-chest, a studded souvenir,
props for an opera, Victoria Regina,[9]
for a bolster-plump Queen the pillbox sentries stamp,

piss, straw and saddle-soap, heaume[1] and crimson feather,   45
post-red double-deckers,[2] spit-and-polished leather,
and iron dolphins leaping round an Embankment[3] lamp.

*   *   *

From Book Seven

From *Chapter LXIV*

I

I sang[1] of quiet Achille, Afolabe's son,
who never ascended in an elevator,
who had no passport, since the horizon needs none,

never begged nor borrowed, was nobody's waiter,
whose end, when it comes, will be a death by water   5
(which is not for this book, which will remain unknown

and unread by him). I sang the only slaughter
that brought him delight, and that from necessity—
of fish, sang the channels of his back[2] in the sun.

I sang our wide country, the Caribbean Sea.   10
Who hated shoes, whose soles were as cracked as a stone,
who was gentle with ropes, who had one suit alone,

---

8. A company of schoolboys selected and groomed to be future officers in the colonial army.
9. I.e., Queen Victoria (Latin): the insignia of Queen Victoria on English coins.
1. Helmet worn by armored men in the Middle Ages.
2. London buses.
3. Area in London where the Houses of Parliament and the main government offices are located.
1. The invocation, usually placed at the beginning of an epic poem, is here put at the end and expressed in the past tense.
2. The ripples of muscles, denoting strength. The human frame represented as a furrowed landscape.

whom no man dared insult and who insulted no one,
whose grin was a white breaker cresting, but whose frown
was a growing thunderhead, whose fist of iron   15

would do me a greater honour if it held on
to my casket's oarlocks[3] than mine lifting his own
when both anchors are lowered in the one island,

but now the idyll dies, the goblet is broken,
and rainwater trickles down the brown cheek of a jar   20
from the clay of Choiseul. So much left unspoken

by my chirping nib![4] And my earth-door lies ajar.
I lie wrapped in a flour-sack sail. The clods thud
on my rope-lowered canoe. Rasping shovels scrape

a dry rain of dirt on its hold, but turn your head   25
when the sea-almond rattles or the rust-leaved grape
from the shells of my unpharaonic pyramid[5]

towards paper shredded by the wind and scattered
like white gulls that separate their names from the foam
and nod to a fisherman[6] with his khaki dog   30

that the skitters from the wave-crash, then frown at his form
for one swift second. In its earth-trough, my pirogue
with its brass-handled oarlocks is sailing. Not from

but with them, with Hector, with Maud[7] in the rhythm
of her beds[8] trowelled over, with a swirling log   35
lifting its mossed head from the swell; let the deep hymn

of the Caribbean continue my epilogue;
may waves remove their shawls as my mourners walk home
to their rusted villages, good shoes in one hand,

passing a boy who walked through the ignorant foam,   40
and saw a sail going out or else coming in,
and watched asterisks of rain[9] puckering the sand.

*   *   *

1990

---

3. At the poet's own funeral.
4. The point of a pen dipped in ink often makes a rasping noise on the paper.
5. Modest, without the monumental grandeur of Egypt's pyramids.
6. I.e., Philoctete.
7. The wife of an English colonial officer, Major Plunkett, whose adventures, intertwined with the life of the St. Lucians, are narrated in earlier passages of the poem. "Hector": rival of Achille who was killed in a car accident.
8. A reference to the flowerbeds tended by Maud. The image evokes her final resting place in the earth.
9. Which is life-giving.

SEAMUS HEANEY
born 1939

Having reached his maturity as a poet during the sectarian violence known as the Troubles in his native Northern Ireland, Seamus Heaney developed a keen awareness of the poet's relationship to history and conflict. A student of the Irish language and of Anglo-Saxon (Old English), he has drawn on the resources of both in reinventing modern English poetry. His verse, alive to historical resonances, explores the ethical commitments of the poet in a world of enduring conflicts.

Born to a Catholic family on a farm in County Derry, Northern Ireland, Heaney was the eldest of nine children. He attended the nearby Anahorish School and then St. Columb's College, a Catholic boarding school in Derry, Northern Ireland's second city, before enrolling in Queen's University, Belfast, where he studied English language and literature. In addition to Anglo-Saxon, he learned Irish and Latin. After briefly teaching middle school, Heaney returned to Queen's in 1966 as an instructor in English literature. In the same year, his first major volume of poems, *Death of a Naturalist,* was released. During the following several years, as tensions heightened in Northern Ireland, Heaney addressed political concerns in his poetry, although often in an indirect fashion that was sometimes criticized for its lack of explicit commitment. In 1972, in a move that was seen at the time as indicating sympathies with the Nationalist cause (unification with the Republic of Ireland), Heaney moved to Dublin. He taught college there for several years, then, as his reputation as a poet grew, began an association with Harvard University,

where he would teach part-time for a quarter of a century. He has also taught at Oxford University, but now lives in Dublin. In 1995, he received the Nobel Prize for Literature.

The late 1960s were a period of intense violence in Northern Ireland, a majority Protestant region that had remained part of the United Kingdom when the rest of Ireland gained its independence. Some members of the substantial Catholic population of Northern Ireland supported the illegal Irish Republican Army, which used violence to promote unification with the Irish Republic (the "Nationalist" position). Catholics often faced hostility and discrimination from Protestant groups, notably the paramilitary Ulster Volunteer Force, that favored continued union with Britain (the "Unionists"). British police and military forces were generally perceived as supporting the Unionists, particularly in the Bloody Sunday massacre of 1972, when thirteen unarmed Catholic protesters were killed by British army forces. The cycle of violence by the IRA, the UVF, and British forces continued until the Good Friday agreement of 1998, which ushered in a period of disarmament and power sharing by Nationalist and Unionist politicians.

"The Tollund Man" (1972) is one of the first of Heaney's poems about the bog people, an ancient folk, related to the Irish, whose bodies were preserved in the wetlands of Jutland, Denmark. In this poem and in "Punishment" (1975), the speaker contemplates the bodies of victims of sacrificial slaughter in the Iron Age society, hinting that such primitive violence is not all that different from the Troubles of Northern Ireland. A more personal poem about that violence, "The Strand at Lough Beg" (1979), is an elegy for the poet's cousin Colum McCartney, a victim of sectarian conflict. Recollecting Dante's visits with the dead in *The Inferno* and *Purgatorio,* Heaney here imagines himself in conversation with his cousin's ghost. He would later criticize the poem, however, for having "whitewashed ugliness."

Heaney is attentive to the formal qualities of his verse, whether in the loose blank verse (unrhymed iambic pentameter) of "The Strand at Lough Beg" or in his characteristic short quatrains (four-line stanzas). Although seldom making use of rhyme, these quatrains recall ballad forms associated with folk tradition, while in other poems (like "The Tollund Man" and "Punishment") they create a melancholy, meditative mood. Heaney frequently uses words of Anglo-Saxon origin, which he seems to associate with the land. Preferring relatively formal poetry rather than experimental verse, Heaney draws heavily on the literary tradition, including Dante, **T. S. Eliot**, and the medieval *Beowulf,* which he has translated into modern English. His work is distinguished by its concreteness and descriptive precision.

The Tollund Man[1]

I

Some day I will go to Aarhus[2]
To see his peat-brown head,
The mild pods of his eyelids,
His pointed skin cap.

In the flat country nearby   5
Where they dug him out,
His last gruel of winter seeds
Caked in his stomach,

Naked except for
The cap, noose and girdle,   10
I will stand a long time.
Bridegroom to the goddess,

She tightened her torc[3] on him
And opened her fen,
Those dark juices working   15
Him to a saint's kept body,

Trove of the turf-cutters'
Honeycombed workings.
Now his stained face
Reposes at Aarhus.   20

---

1. The corpse of a man killed in the 4th century B.C.E, probably a sacrificial victim, preserved in a bog in Jutland, Denmark. Heaney had seen photographs of the Tollund Man and associated Denmark's bogs with those of Northern Ireland.
2. A town in Jutland (the Tollund Man is actually displayed in nearby Silkeborg).
3. An ancient style of metal necklace.

II

I could risk blasphemy,
Consecrate the cauldron bog
Our holy ground and pray
Him to make germinate

The scattered, ambushed   5
Flesh of labourers,
Stockinged corpses
Laid out in the farmyards,

Tell-tale skin and teeth
Flecking the sleepers   10
Of four young brothers,[4] trailed
For miles along the lines.

III

Something of his sad freedom
As he rode the tumbril
Should come to me, driving,   15
Saying the names

Tollund, Grauballe, Nebelgard,[5]
Watching the pointing hands
Of country people,
Not knowing their tongue.   20

Out there in Jutland
In the old man-killing parishes
I will feel lost,
Unhappy and at home.

                                                    1972

Punishment[1]

I can feel the tug
of the halter at the nape
of her neck, the wind
on her naked front.

---

4. The speaker compares the Tollund Man to four Irish nationalist brothers killed by the Protestant Ulster Constabulary Force (forerunner of the Ulster Volunteer Force), in the early 1920s, in Northern Ireland.

5. Other places in Jutland where bog bodies had been found.
1. The speaker contemplates the body, preserved in a bog, of a young woman in ancient Scandinavia, drowned for adultery.

It blows her nipples
to amber beads,
it shakes the frail rigging
of her ribs.

I can see her drowned
body in the bog,
the weighing stone,
the floating rods and boughs.

Under which at first
she was a barked sapling
that is dug up
oak-bone, brain-firkin:[2]

her shaved head
like a stubble of black corn,
her blindfold a soiled bandage,
her noose a ring

to store
the memories of love.
Little adulteress,
before they punished you

you were flaxen-haired,
undernourished, and your
tar-black face was beautiful.
My poor scapegoat,

I almost love you
but would have cast, I know,
the stones of silence.
I am the artful voyeur

of your brain's exposed
and darkened combs,
your muscles' webbing
and all your numbered bones:

I who have stood dumb
when your betraying sisters,
cauled in tar,
wept by the railings,

2. Refers to a head covering on the dead body.

who would connive
in civilized outrage
yet understand the exact
and tribal, intimate revenge.

1975

The Strand at Lough Beg[1]

in memory of Colum McCartney

*All round this little island, on the strand
Far down below there, where the breakers strive,
Grow the tall rushes from the oozy sand*
                    —DANTE, *Purgatorio, I, 100–3*[2]

Leaving the white glow of filling stations
And a few lonely streetlamps among fields
You climbed the hills towards Newtownhamilton
Past the Fews Forest, out beneath the stars—
Along that road, a high, bare pilgrim's track   5
Where Sweeney[3] fled before the bloodied heads,
Goat-beards and dogs' eyes in a demon pack
Blazing out of the ground, snapping and squealing.
What blazed ahead of you? A faked roadblock?
The red lamp swung, the sudden brakes and stalling   10
Engine, voices, heads hooded and the cold-nosed gun?
Or in your driving mirror, tailing headlights
That pulled out suddenly and flagged you down
Where you weren't known and far from what you knew:
The lowland clays and waters of Lough Beg,   15
Church Island's spire, its soft treeline of yew.

There you once heard guns fired behind the house
Long before rising time, when duck shooters
Haunted the marigolds and bulrushes,
But still were scared to find spent cartridges,   20
Acrid, brassy, genital, ejected,
On your way across the strand to fetch the cows.

---

1. I.e., the shore of a lake in Northern Ireland.
Colum McCartney was a cousin of Heaney's,
killed in sectarian violence.
2. Dante writes of the shores of the island on
which stands the mountain of Purgatory, where
the souls of the dead undergo punishment as
they await admission to Paradise.
3. A legendary pagan Irish king who kills a
Christian monk and goes mad.

For you and yours and yours and mine fought shy,
Spoke an old language of conspirators
And could not crack the whip or seize the day: 25
Big-voiced scullions, herders, feelers round
Haycocks and hindquarters, talkers in byres,[4]
Slow arbitrators of the burial ground.

Across that strand of yours the cattle graze
Up to their bellies in an early mist 30
And now they turn their unbewildered gaze
To where we work our way through squeaking sedge
Drowning in dew. Like a dull blade with its edge
Honed bright, Lough Beg half-shines under the haze.
I turn because the sweeping of your feet 35
Has stopped behind me, to find you on your knees
With blood and roadside muck in your hair and eyes,
Then kneel in front of you in brimming grass
And gather up cold handfuls of the dew
To wash you, cousin. I dab you clean with moss 40
Fine as the drizzle out of a low cloud.
I lift you under the arms and lay you flat.
With rushes that shoot green again, I plait
Green scapulars[5] to wear over your shroud.

1979

4. Cow-sheds. "Haycocks": haystacks.
5. Patches of cloth indicating religious devotion, hung from the shoulders.

GABRIEL GARCÍA MÁRQUEZ

(1928–2012)

The best-known novelist of the Latin American "Boom" of the 1960s and 1970s, Gabriel García Márquez embodies, in his work, the mixture of fantasy and actuality known as "magic realism." Again and again García Márquez returns to certain themes: the contrast between dreamlike experiences and everyday reality; the enchanted or inexplicable aspect of fictional creation; and the solitude of individuals in societies that can never quite incorporate them. His fiction, which contains mythic dimensions that are often rooted in local folklore, reimagines regional tales to explore broader social and psychological conflicts. Even those works based in historical fact transform the characters and events into a fictional universe with its own set of laws.

García Márquez was born on March 6, 1928, in the small town of Aracataca, in the "banana zone" of Colombia. The first of twelve children, he was raised by his maternal grandparents until 1936, when his grandfather died. As an adult, he would attribute his love of fantasy to his grandmother, who told him fantastical tales whenever she wanted to shush his incessant questions. His grandfather, meanwhile, passed on a marked interest in politics, having fought on the Liberal side of a civil war early in the century. After receiving his undergraduate degree as a scholarship student at the National Colegio in Zipaquirá, García Márquez studied law at the University of Bogotá in 1947. It was there, he later claimed, that he read **Kafka's** *The Metamorphosis*, in a Spanish translation by **Jorge Luis Borges**. "Shit," he said to himself after reading the first sentence, "that's just the way my grand-mother talked!" The next day he wrote "The Third Resignation," the Kafkaesque tale of a man in his coffin who continued to grow (and retain consciousness) for seventeen years after his death. It was the first of his works to be published. García Márquez found in Kafka the mobile balance of nonrealistic events and realistic detail that—combined with his grandmother's quixotic stories and his grandfather's political concerns—would become the genre known as magic realism. In this mode the narrator treats the subjective beliefs and experiences of the characters, often derived from folklore and supernatural beliefs, as if they were real, even when (to a scientifically minded observer) they seem impossible. Some of García Márquez's early novels also reflected the influence of William Faulkner, whom he later described as "my master"—in particular, Faulkner's representation of subjective experience through stream-of-consciousness technique and the southern writer's depiction of an underdeveloped geographical region beset by a long history of conflict.

In 1950, García Márquez abandoned his legal studies for journalism. As a correspondent for various Latin American newspapers, he traveled to Paris and later to Eastern Europe, Venezuela, Cuba, and New York. After writing several novels, short stories, and film scripts, he gained international fame for his novel *One Hundred Years of Solitude*. Published in 1967, it chronicles the rise and fall of the fortunes of the Buendía family in a mythical town called Macondo (based on the author's hometown of Aracataca). A global best seller, it was soon translated into multiple languages and received prizes in Italy and France. When it was published in English, in 1970, American critics praised it as one of the best books of the year, and it has since become a monument of world literature.

The author's later work was preoccupied with contemporary events, especially the prevalence of dictatorship in Latin American societies. As García Márquez continued to publish successful novels, he also became an advocate for social justice, speaking out for revolutionary governments in Latin America and organizing assistance for political prisoners. There were even rumors of a plot, backed by the Colombian government, to assassinate García Márquez because of his antigovernment activities; in 1981 he sought asylum in Mexico. He lives partly in Mexico City and spends time in Colombia and Europe as well.

The story printed here, "Death Constant Beyond Love" (1970), dates from the author's later, more politically active period. It has a political background, although its protagonist, Senator Onésimo Sánchez, appears chiefly through the lens of his struggles with the existential problem of death. García Márquez presents an essentially satirical portrait of Sánchez, a corrupt politician who accepts bribes and stays in power by helping the local property owners avoid reform. His electoral train is a traveling circus with carnival wagons, fireworks, a ready-made audience of hired Indians, and a cardboard village with imitation brick houses and a painted ocean liner to represent the (shallow) promise of prosperity. Among the citizenry, Sánchez uses carefully placed gifts to encourage support and a feeling of dependence.

Yet the spectacle of the senator's campaign for office, and even the sordid background of poverty and corruption that enables it, fade into insignificance before the broader themes of life and death. Forty-two, happily married, and in

full control, as a powerful politician in mid-career, of the lives of himself and others, he is made suddenly to feel—when told that he will be dead "forever" by next Christmas—helpless, vulnerable, and alone. Theoretically he knows that death is inevitable and that the course of nature cannot be defeated. He has read Marcus Aurelius (121–180 C.E.) and refers to the Stoic philosopher's *Meditations*, which criticizes the delusions of those "who have tenaciously stuck to life" and recommends the cheerful acceptance of natural order, including death.

In this crisis the senator is reduced to basic, instinctual existence, drawing him deeper into García Márquez's recurrent themes of solitude, love, and death. The beautiful Laura provides an opportunity for him to submerge his fear of death in erotic passion. This choice means scandal and the destruction of his political career, but by now Onésimo Sánchez has felt the emptiness of his earlier activities—and has given them up for the hopeless struggle to cheat death. "Death Constant Beyond Love" reverses the ambitious claim of a famous sonnet by the Spanish Golden Age writer Quevedo (1580–1645), according to which there is "Love Constant Beyond Death." Such love is an illusion, for it is death, beyond everything else, that awaits us.

Gabriel García Márquez received the Nobel Prize in Literature in 1982. In his acceptance speech he drew connections between his novels and the sufferings of the peoples of Latin America through dictatorship and civil war. Voicing hope for an end to the nuclear arms race, the writer spoke of a "new and sweeping utopia of life, where no one will be able to decide for others how they die, where love will prove true and happiness be possible, and where the races condemned to one hundred years of solitude will have, at last and forever, a second opportunity on earth."

Death Constant Beyond Love[1]

Senator Onésimo Sánchez had six months and eleven days to go before his death when he found the woman of his life. He met her in Rosal del Virrey,[2] an illusory village which by night was the furtive wharf for smugglers' ships, and on the other hand, in broad daylight looked like the most useless inlet on the desert, facing a sea that was arid and without direction and so far from every-thing no one would have suspected that someone capable of changing the destiny of anyone lived there. Even its name was a kind of joke, because the only rose in that village was being worn by Senator Onésimo Sánchez himself on the same afternoon when he met Laura Farina.

It was an unavoidable stop in the electoral campaign he made every four years. The carnival wagons had arrived in the morning. Then came the trucks with the rented Indians[3] who were carried into the towns in order to enlarge the crowds at public ceremonies. A short time before eleven o'clock, along with the music and rockets and jeeps of the retinue, the ministerial automobile, the color of strawberry soda, arrived. Senator Onésimo Sánchez was placid and weatherless inside the air-conditioned car, but as soon as he opened the door he was shaken by a gust of fire and his shirt of pure silk was soaked in a kind of light-colored soup and he felt many years older and more alone than ever. In real life he had just turned forty-two, had been graduated from Göttingen[4] with honors as a metallurgical engineer, and was an avid reader, although without much reward, of badly translated Latin classics. He was married to a radiant German woman who had given him five children and they were all happy in their home, he the happiest of all until they told him, three months before, that he would be dead forever by next Christmas.

While the preparations for the public rally were being completed, the senator managed to have an hour alone in the house they had set aside for him to rest in. Before he lay down he put in a glass of drinking water the rose he had kept alive all across the desert, lunched on the diet cereals that he took with him so as to avoid the repeated portions of fried goat that were waiting for him during the rest of the day, and he took several analgesic pills before the time prescribed so that he would have the remedy ahead of the pain. Then he put the electric fan close to the hammock and stretched out naked for fifteen minutes in the shadow of the rose, making a great effort at mental distraction so as not to think about death while he dozed. Except for the doctors, no one knew that he had been sentenced to a fixed term, for he had decided to endure his secret all alone, with no change in his life, not because of pride but out of shame.[5]

He felt in full control of his will when he appeared in public again at three in the afternoon, rested and clean, wearing a pair of coarse linen slacks and a floral shirt, and with his soul sustained by the anti-pain pills. Nevertheless, the erosion of death was much more pernicious than he had supposed, for as he

---

1. Translated by Gregory Rabassa.
2. The Rosebush of the Viceroy (governor).
3. People descended from the original inhab-itants of the continent; generally poorer and less privileged than those descended from Spanish or Portuguese colonists.

4. A well-known German university.
5. "Death is such as generation is, a mystery of nature . . . altogether not a thing of which any man should be ashamed" (Marcus Aurelius, *Meditations* 4.5).

went up onto the platform he felt a strange disdain for those who were fighting for the good luck to shake his hand, and he didn't feel sorry as he had at other times for the groups of barefoot Indians who could scarcely bear the hot saltpeter coals of the sterile little square. He silenced the applause with a wave of his hand, almost with rage, and he began to speak without gestures, his eyes fixed on the sea, which was sighing with heat. His measured, deep voice had the quality of calm water, but the speech that had been memorized and ground out so many times had not occurred to him in the nature of telling the truth, but, rather, as the opposite of a fatalistic pronouncement by Marcus Aurelius in the fourth book of his *Meditations.*

"We are here for the purpose of defeating nature," he began, against all his convictions. "We will no longer be foundlings in our own country, orphans of God in a realm of thirst and bad climate, exiles in our own land. We will be different people, ladies and gentlemen, we will be a great and happy people."

There was a pattern to his circus. As he spoke his aides threw clusters of paper birds into the air and the artificial creatures took on life, flew about the platform of planks, and went out to sea. At the same time, other men took some prop trees with felt leaves out of the wagons and planted them in the saltpeter soil behind the crowd. They finished by setting up a cardboard façade with make-believe houses of red brick that had glass windows, and with it they covered the miserable real-life shacks.

The senator prolonged his speech with two quotations in Latin in order to give the farce more time. He promised rainmaking machines, portable breeders for table animals, the oils of happiness which would make vegetables grow in the saltpeter and clumps of pansies in the window boxes. When he saw that his fictional world was all set up, he pointed to it. "That's the way it will be for us, ladies and gentlemen," he shouted. "Look! That's the way it will be for us."

The audience turned around. An ocean liner made of painted paper was passing behind the houses and it was taller than the tallest houses in the artificial city. Only the senator himself noticed that since it had been set up and taken down and carried from one place to another the superimposed cardboard town had been eaten away by the terrible climate and that it was almost as poor and dusty as Rosal del Virrey.

For the first time in twelve years, Nelson Farina didn't go to greet the senator. He listened to the speech from his hammock amidst the remains of his siesta, under the cool bower of a house of unplaned boards which he had built with the same pharmacist's hands with which he had drawn and quartered his first wife. He had escaped from Devil's Island[6] and appeared in Rosal del Virrey on a ship loaded with innocent macaws, with a beautiful and blasphemous black woman he had found in Paramaribo[7] and by whom he had a daughter. The woman died of natural causes a short while later and she didn't suffer the fate of the other, whose pieces had fertilized her own cauliflower patch, but was buried whole and with her Dutch name in the local cemetery. The daughter had inherited her color and her figure along with her father's yellow and astonished eyes, and he had good reason to imagine that he was rearing the most beautiful woman in the world.

6. A former French penal colony off the coast of French Guiana in northern South America.

7. Capital of Suriname (formerly Dutch Guiana) and a large port.

Ever since he had met Senator Onésimo Sánchez during his first electoral campaign, Nelson Farina had begged for his help in getting a false identity card which would place him beyond the reach of the law. The senator, in a friendly but firm way, had refused. Nelson Farina never gave up, and for several years, every time he found the chance, he would repeat his request with a different recourse. But this time he stayed in his hammock, condemned to rot alive in that burning den of buccaneers. When he heard the final applause, he lifted his head, and looking over the boards of the fence, he saw the back side of the farce: the props for the buildings, the framework of the trees, the hidden illusionists who were pushing the ocean liner along. He spat without rancor.

"*Merde,*" he said. "*C'est le Blacamán de la politique.*"[8]

After the speech, as was customary, the senator took a walk through the streets of the town in the midst of the music and the rockets and was besieged by the townspeople, who told him their troubles. The senator listened to them good-naturedly and he always found some way to console everybody without having to do them any difficult favors. A woman up on the roof of a house with her six youngest children managed to make herself heard over the uproar and the fireworks.

"I'm not asking for much, Senator," she said. "Just a donkey to haul water from Hanged Man's Well."

The senator noticed the six thin children. "What became of your husband?" he asked.

"He went to find his fortune on the island of Aruba,"[9] the woman answered good-humoredly, "and what he found was a foreign woman, the kind that put diamonds on their teeth."

The answer brought on a roar of laughter.

"All right," the senator decided, "you'll get your donkey."

A short while later an aide of his brought a good pack donkey to the woman's house and on the rump it had a campaign slogan written in indelible paint so that no one would ever forget that it was a gift from the senator.

Along the short stretch of street he made other, smaller gestures, and he even gave a spoonful of medicine to a sick man who had had his bed brought to the door of his house so he could see him pass. At the last corner, through the boards of the fence, he saw Nelson Farina in his hammock, looking ashen and gloomy, but nonetheless the senator greeted him, with no show of affection.

"Hello, how are you?"

Nelson Farina turned in his hammock and soaked him in the sad amber of his look.

"*Moi, vous savez,*"[1] he said.

His daughter came out into the yard when she heard the greeting. She was wearing a cheap, faded Guajiro Indian[2] robe, her head was decorated with

---

8. Shit. He's the Blacamán of politics (French). Blacamán is a charlatan and huckster who appears in several stories, including *Blacamán the Good, Vendor of Miracles*.
9. Off the coast of Venezuela, famous as a tourist resort.
1. "Oh well, as for me, you know" (French).

2. Inhabitant of the rural Guajira Peninsula of northern Colombia. The figure of Laura Farina is thus connected with the rustic poor, with earthy reality (*farina* means "flour"), and with erotic inspiration. (*Laura* was the beloved celebrated by the Italian Renaissance poet Francis Petrarch, 1304–1374.)

colored bows, and her face was painted as protection against the sun, but even in that state of disrepair it was possible to imagine that there had never been another so beautiful in the whole world. The senator was left breathless. "I'll be damned!" he breathed in surprise. "The Lord does the craziest things!"

That night Nelson Farina dressed his daughter up in her best clothes and sent her to the senator. Two guards armed with rifles who were nodding from the heat in the borrowed house ordered her to wait on the only chair in the vestibule.

The senator was in the next room meeting with the important people of Rosal del Virrey, whom he had gathered together in order to sing for them the truths he had left out of his speeches. They looked so much like all the ones he always met in all the towns in the desert that even the senator himself was sick and tired of that perpetual nightly session. His shirt was soaked with sweat and he was trying to dry it on his body with the hot breeze from an electric fan that was buzzing like a horse fly in the heavy heat of the room.

"We, of course, can't eat paper birds," he said. "You and I know that the day there are trees and flowers in this heap of goat dung, the day there are shad instead of worms in the water holes, that day neither you nor I will have anything to do here, do I make myself clear?"

No one answered. While he was speaking, the senator had torn a sheet off the calendar and fashioned a paper butterfly out of it with his hands. He tossed it with no particular aim into the air current coming from the fan and the butterfly flew about the room and then went out through the half-open door. The senator went on speaking with a control aided by the complicity of death.

"Therefore," he said, "I don't have to repeat to you what you already know too well: that my reelection is a better piece of business for you than it is for me, because I'm fed up with stagnant water and Indian sweat, while you people, on the other hand, make your living from it."

Laura Farina saw the paper butterfly come out. Only she saw it because the guards in the vestibule had fallen asleep on the steps, hugging their rifles. After a few turns, the large lithographed butterfly unfolded completely, flattened against the wall, and remained stuck there. Laura Farina tried to pull it off with her nails. One of the guards, who woke up with the applause from the next room, noticed her vain attempt.

"It won't come off," he said sleepily. "It's painted on the wall."

Laura Farina sat down again when the men began to come out of the meeting. The senator stood in the doorway of the room with his hand on the latch, and he only noticed Laura Farina when the vestibule was empty.

"What are you doing here?"

"C'est de la part de mon père,"[3] she said.

The senator understood. He scrutinized the sleeping guards, then he scrutinized Laura Farina, whose unusual beauty was even more demanding than his pain, and he resolved then that death had made his decision for him.

"Come in," he told her.

Laura Farina was struck dumb standing in the doorway to the room: thousands of bank notes were floating in the air, flapping like the butterfly. But the senator turned off the fan and the bills were left without air and alighted on the objects in the room.

3. "My father sent me" (French).

"You see," he said, smiling, "even shit can fly."

Laura Farina sat down on a schoolboy's stool. Her skin was smooth and firm, with the same color and the same solar density as crude oil, her hair was the mane of a young mare, and her huge eyes were brighter than the light. The senator followed the thread of her look and finally found the rose, which had been tarnished by the saltpeter.

"It's a rose," he said.

"Yes," she said with a trace of perplexity. "I learned what they were in Riohacha."[4]

The senator sat down on an army cot, talking about roses as he unbuttoned his shirt. On the side where he imagined his heart to be inside his chest he had a corsair's tattoo of a heart pierced by an arrow. He threw the soaked shirt to the floor and asked Laura Farina to help him off with his boots.

She knelt down facing the cot. The senator continued to scrutinize her, thoughtfully, and while he was untying the laces he wondered which one of them would end up with the bad luck of that encounter.

"You're just a child," he said.

"Don't you believe it," she said. "I'll be nineteen in April."

The senator became interested.

"What day?"

"The eleventh," she said.

The senator felt better. "We're both Aries,"[5] he said. And smiling, he added: "It's the sign of solitude."

Laura Farina wasn't paying attention because she didn't know what to do with the boots. The senator, for his part, didn't know what to do with Laura Farina, because he wasn't used to sudden love affairs and, besides, he knew that the one at hand had its origins in indignity. Just to have some time to think, he held Laura Farina tightly between his knees, embraced her about the waist, and lay down on his back on the cot. Then he realized that she was naked under her dress, for her body gave off the dark fragrance of an animal of the woods, but her heart was frightened and her skin disturbed by a glacial sweat.

"No one loves us," he sighed.

Laura Farina tried to say something, but there was only enough air for her to breathe. He laid her down beside him to help her, he put out the light and the room was in the shadow of the rose. She abandoned herself to the mercies of her fate. The senator caressed her slowly, seeking her with his hand, barely touching her, but where he expected to find her, he came across something iron that was in the way.

"What have you got there?"

"A padlock,"[6] she said.

"What in hell!" the senator said furiously and asked what he knew only too well. "Where's the key?"

Laura Farina gave a breath of relief.

"My papa has it," she answered. "He told me to tell you to send one of your people to get it and to send along with him a written promise that you'll straighten out his situation."

4. A port on the Guajira Peninsula.
5. Sign in the zodiac; people born between March 21 and April 19 are said to be under the sign of Aries.
6. She is wearing a chastity belt, a medieval device worn by women to prevent sexual intercourse.

The senator grew tense. "Frog[7] bastard," he murmured indignantly. Then he closed his eyes in order to relax and he met himself in the darkness. *Remember, he remembered, that whether it's you or someone else, it won't be long before you'll be dead and it won't be long before your name won't even be left.*[8]

He waited for the shudder to pass.

"Tell me one thing," he asked then. "What have you heard about me?"

"Do you want the honest-to-God truth?"

"The honest-to-God truth."

"Well," Laura Farina ventured, "they say you're worse than the rest because you're different."

The senator didn't get upset. He remained silent for a long time with his eyes closed, and when he opened them again he seemed to have returned from his most hidden instincts.

"Oh, what the hell," he decided. "Tell your son of a bitch of a father that I'll straighten out his situation."

"If you want, I can go get the key myself," Laura Farina said.

The senator held her back.

"Forget about the key," he said, "and sleep awhile with me. It's good to be with someone when you're so alone."

Then she laid his head on her shoulder with her eyes fixed on the rose. The senator held her about the waist, sank his face into woods-animal armpit, and gave in to terror. Six months and eleven days later he would die in that same position, debased and repudiated because of the public scandal with Laura Farina and weeping with rage at dying without her.

1970

7. Epithet for "French."

8. A direct translation of a sentence from Marcus Aurelius's *Meditations* (4.6).

V. S. NAIPAUL

born 1932

Trinidadian Nobel laureate V. S. Naipaul has traveled widely to document the lives of the poor and downtrodden, in essays and novels set on five continents. Of Indian descent, raised in multicultural Trinidad, and educated in England, Naipaul was one of the first writers to gain international prominence for representing the postcolonial world, but he has often riled critics and intellectuals with his controversial views. He has, for example, been critical of postcolonial governments and cultures and displayed an almost nostalgic attitude toward colonial times. His rejection of any political ideology has helped give his observations of the contemporary world their intensity and precision.

Vidiadhar Surajprasad Naipaul was born to Hindu parents on August 17, 1932, in the small town of Chaguanas,

Trinidad. For the first six years of his life, Naipaul lived in the "Lion's Den," a house run with an iron fist by his grandmother and filled with her daughters, sons-in-law, and grandchildren. His father, Seepersad, who would serve as the model for Mr. Biswas in Naipaul's most famous novel, *A House for Mr. Biswas* (1961), was a struggling journalist for the Trinidad *Guardian* and occasional writer of poetry and short stories; he encouraged his son's literary ambitions until his death, in 1953. Depressive and resentful of the domineering influence of his wife and his mother-in-law, Seepersad was a distant but loved figure in Naipaul's early life.

A scholarship student at the elite Queen's Royal College, Naipaul, desperate to escape Trinidad, won one of four scholarships for the entire island in 1949 and left for Oxford the next year, never to see his father again. While at Oxford, Naipaul struggled to publish his work and occasionally felt homesick, even attempting suicide at one point. He met Patricia Hale, an Oxford undergraduate, whom he married in 1955. The two remained unhappily married until Hale's death, in 1996. Naipaul's infidelities and abuses were many and public.

After leaving Oxford and failing to find employment in the civil service or journalism, Naipaul began work, in 1954, as a broadcaster for the BBC's *Caribbean Voices*, reviewing novels and interviewing writers. Later he regularly reviewed books for the *New Statesman*. His first novel, *The Mystic Masseur* (1957), was indebted to his father's comic short stories. His second, more mature novel, *Miguel Street* (1959), written on a BBC typewriter, was a critical success and was soon followed by *A House for Mr. Biswas,* the first of Naipaul's many masterpieces.

Naipaul's work has often been compared with that of **Joseph Conrad,** and many of his novels and travel books deal with the political and psychological implications of exile, colonization, and violence. *A Bend in the River* (1979), in fact, revisits the Congo almost a century after Conrad's experiences there. Naipaul won acclaim as one of the century's greatest travel writers, with books on the West Indies (*The Middle Passage,* 1962), India (*An Area of Darkness,* 1964), and Africa (*A Congo Diary,* 1980). In addition, the writer often used observations gleaned in his travels as the basis for his fiction. His withering criticism of contemporary Islamic movements in Pakistan in *Among the Believers* (1981) brought him notoriety, as has his ambivalent attitude toward Trinidad. He famously said of the country, "I was born there, yes. I thought it was a great mistake." While traveling the world, he has had his permanent home in Britain. In 2001 he was awarded the Nobel Prize for Literature.

Despite his sometimes controversial attitudes toward formerly colonized peoples, and particularly toward those of African descent, Naipaul has been one of the most sympathetic chroniclers of postcolonial life and of migration. In the short story presented here, "One Out of Many" (1971), his setting, unusually for him, is the United States. The title refers to the motto on the Great Seal of the United States, *E pluribus unum,* which originally referred to the union of the states in a federal system. Today, however, the phrase suggests the ideal that, made up of many cultures and races, the United States forms a unified society. In the context of the story, the phrase also reflects the fact that the main character, Santosh, is just one of many immigrants to the United States.

Santosh leaves his wife and children in the hills of India and arrives in Washington, D.C., as servant to an Indian diplomat, only to discover that his unofficial status and low pay seriously restrict his options. Santosh undergoes a number of comic embarrassments as he accustoms himself to the American way of life. Missing his friends and family at home, he meets a sympathetic Indian restaurant owner and several African Americans, whom he describes as *hubshi*, a somewhat demeaning Hindi term for a person of African descent. Santosh has arrived at a time of racial tension, the late 1960s, and feels threatened by riots in Washington (after the assassination of Martin Luther King, Jr.,

in April 1968). Yet he gradually comes to accept his life in his new country.

Naipaul, who once said that modernism had "bypassed" him, achieves his sympathetic portrait of Santosh's situation by means of a precise realism. As the well-rounded first-person narrator tells his story, it is the vivid rendering of his experiences and emotions that gives the work its power.

One Out of Many[1]

I am now an American citizen and I live in Washington, capital of the world. Many people, both here and in India, will feel that I have done well. But.

I was so happy in Bombay. I was respected, I had a certain position. I worked for an important man. The highest in the land came to our bachelor chambers and enjoyed my food and showered compliments on me. I also had my friends. We met in the evenings on the pavement below the gallery of our chambers. Some of us, like the tailor's bearer and myself, were domestics who lived in the street. The others were people who came to that bit of pavement to sleep. Respectable people; we didn't encourage riff-raff.

In the evenings it was cool. There were few passers-by and, apart from an occasional double-decker bus or taxi, little traffic. The pavement was swept and sprinkled, bedding brought out from daytime hiding-places, little oil-lamps lit. While the folk upstairs chattered and laughed, on the pavement we read newspapers, played cards, told stories and smoked. The clay pipe passed from friend to friend; we became drowsy. Except of course during the monsoon, I preferred to sleep on the pavement with my friends, although in our chambers a whole cupboard below the staircase was reserved for my personal use.

It was good after a healthy night in the open to rise before the sun and before the sweepers came. Sometimes I saw the street lights go off. Bedding was rolled up; no one spoke much; and soon my friends were hurrying in silent competition to secluded lanes and alleys and open lots to relieve themselves. I was spared this competition; in our chambers I had facilities.

Afterwards for half an hour or so I was free simply to stroll. I liked walking beside the Arabian Sea, waiting for the sun to come up. Then the city and the ocean gleamed like gold. Alas for those morning walks, that sudden ocean dazzle, the moist salt breeze on my face, the flap of my shirt, that first cup of hot sweet tea from a stall, the taste of the first leaf-cigarette.

Observe the workings of fate. The respect and security I enjoyed were due to the importance of my employer. It was this very importance which now all at once destroyed the pattern of my life.

My employer was seconded by his firm to Government service and was posted to Washington. I was happy for his sake but frightened for mine. He

---

1. Refers to the Latin motto of the United States, *E pluribus unum*.

was to be away for some years and there was nobody in Bombay he could second me to. Soon, therefore, I was to be out of a job and out of the chambers. For many years I had considered my life as settled. I had served my apprenticeship, known my hard times. I didn't feel I could start again. I despaired. Was there a job for me in Bombay? I saw myself having to return to my village in the hills, to my wife and children there, not just for a holiday but for good. I saw myself again becoming a porter during the tourist season, racing after the buses as they arrived at the station and shouting with forty or fifty others for luggage. Indian luggage, not this lightweight American stuff! Heavy metal trunks!

I could have cried. It was no longer the sort of life for which I was fitted. I had grown soft in Bombay and I was no longer young. I had acquired possessions, I was used to the privacy of my cupboard. I had become a city man, used to certain comforts.

My employer said, "Washington is not Bombay, Santosh. Washington is expensive. Even if I was able to raise your fare, you wouldn't be able to live over there in anything like your present style."

But to be barefoot in the hills, after Bombay! The shock, the disgrace! I couldn't face my friends. I stopped sleeping on the pavement and spent as much of my free time as possible in my cupboard among my possessions, as among things which were soon to be taken from me.

My employer said, "Santosh, my heart bleeds for you."

I said, "Sahib,[2] if I look a little concerned it is only because I worry about you. You have always been fussy, and I don't see how you will manage in Washington."

"It won't be easy. But it's the principle. Does the representative of a poor country like ours travel about with his cook? Will that create a good impression?"

"You will always do what is right, sahib."

He went silent.

After some days he said, "There's not only the expense, Santosh. There's the question of foreign exchange. Our rupee[3] isn't what it was."

"I understand, sahib. Duty is duty."

A fortnight later, when I had almost given up hope, he said, "Santosh, I have consulted Government. You will accompany me. Government has sanctioned, will arrange accommodation. But no expenses. You will get your passport and your P form. But I want you to think, Santosh. Washington is not Bombay."

I went down to the pavement that night with my bedding.

I said, blowing down my shirt, "Bombay gets hotter and hotter."

"Do you know what you are doing?" the tailor's bearer said. "Will the Americans smoke with you? Will they sit and talk with you in the evenings? Will they hold you by the hand and walk with you beside the ocean?"

It pleased me that he was jealous. My last days in Bombay were very happy.

I packed my employer's two suitcases and bundled up my own belongings in lengths of old cotton. At the airport they made a fuss about my bundles. They said they couldn't accept them as luggage for the hold because they didn't like

2. Master (Hindi).
3. Indian unit of currency, worth about ten cents at the time of the story.

the responsibility. So when the time came I had to climb up to the aircraft with all my bundles. The girl at the top, who was smiling at everybody else, stopped smiling when she saw me. She made me go right to the back of the plane, far from my employer. Most of the seats there were empty, though, and I was able to spread my bundles around and, well, it was comfortable.

It was bright and hot outside, cool inside. The plane started, rose up in the air, and Bombay and the ocean tilted this way and that. It was very nice. When we settled down I looked around for people like myself, but I could see no one among the Indians or the foreigners who looked like a domestic. Worse, they were all dressed as though they were going to a wedding and, brother, I soon saw it wasn't they who were conspicuous. I was in my ordinary Bombay clothes, the loose long-tailed shirt, the wide-waisted pants held up with a piece of string. Perfectly respectable domestic's wear, neither dirty nor clean, and in Bombay no one would have looked. But now on the plane I felt heads turning whenever I stood up.

I was anxious. I slipped off my shoes, tight even without the laces, and drew my feet up. That made me feel better. I made myself a little betel-nut mixture[4] and that made me feel better still. Half the pleasure of betel, though, is the spitting; and it was only when I had worked up a good mouthful that I saw I had a problem. The airline girl saw too. That girl didn't like me at all. She spoke roughly to me. My mouth was full, my cheeks were bursting, and I couldn't say anything. I could only look at her. She went and called a man in uniform and he came and stood over me. I put my shoes back on and swallowed the betel juice. It made me feel quite ill.

The girl and the man, the two of them, pushed a little trolley of drinks down the aisle. The girl didn't look at me but the man said, "You want a drink, chum?" He wasn't a bad fellow. I pointed at random to a bottle. It was a kind of soda drink, nice and sharp at first but then not so nice. I was worrying about it when the girl said, "Five shillings sterling or sixty cents U.S." That took me by surprise. I had no money, only a few rupees. The girl stamped, and I thought she was going to hit me with her pad when I stood up to show her who my employer was.

Presently my employer came down the aisle. He didn't look very well. He said, without stopping, "Champagne, Santosh? Already we are overdoing?" He went on to the lavatory. When he passed back he said, "Foreign exchange, Santosh! Foreign exchange!" That was all. Poor fellow, he was suffering too.

The journey became miserable for me. Soon, with the wine I had drunk, the betel juice, the movement and the noise of the aeroplane, I was vomiting all over my bundles, and I didn't care what the girl said or did. Later there were more urgent and terrible needs. I felt I would choke in the tiny, hissing room at the back. I had a shock when I saw my face in the mirror. In the fluorescent light it was the colour of a corpse. My eyes were strained, the sharp air hurt my nose and seemed to get into my brain. I climbed up on the lavatory seat and squatted. I lost control of myself. As quickly as I could I ran back out into the comparative openness of the cabin and hoped no one had noticed. The lights

4. A popular, mildly narcotic substance like chewing tobacco, normally chewed and spat out.

were dim now; some people had taken off their jackets and were sleeping. I hoped the plane would crash.

The girl woke me up. She was almost screaming. "It's you, isn't it? Isn't it?"

I thought she was going to tear the shirt off me. I pulled back and leaned hard on the window. She burst into tears and nearly tripped on her sari as she ran up the aisle to get the man in uniform.

Nightmare. And all I knew was that somewhere at the end, after the airports and the crowded lounges where everybody was dressed up, after all those take-offs and touchdowns, was the city of Washington. I wanted the journey to end but I couldn't say I wanted to arrive at Washington. I was already a little scared of that city, to tell the truth. I wanted only to be off the plane and to be in the open again, to stand on the ground and breathe and to try to understand what time of day it was.

At last we arrived. I was in a daze. The burden of those bundles! There were more closed rooms and electric lights. There were questions from officials.

"Is he diplomatic?"

"He's only a domestic," my employer said.

"Is that his luggage? What's in that pocket?"

I was ashamed.

"Santosh," my employer said.

I pulled out the little packets of pepper and salt, the sweets, the envelopes with scented napkins, the toy tubes of mustard. Airline trinkets. I had been collecting them throughout the journey, seizing a handful, whatever my condition, every time I passed the galley.

"He's a cook," my employer said.

"Does he always travel with his condiments?"

"Santosh, Santosh," my employer said in the car afterwards, "in Bombay it didn't matter what you did. Over here you represent your country. I must say I cannot understand why your behaviour has already gone so much out of character."

"I am sorry, sahib."

"Look at it like this, Santosh. Over here you don't only represent your country, you represent me."

For the people of Washington it was late afternoon or early evening, I couldn't say which. The time and the light didn't match, as they did in Bombay. Of that drive I remember green fields, wide roads, many motor cars travelling fast, making a steady hiss, hiss, which wasn't at all like our Bombay traffic noise. I remember big buildings and wide parks; many bazaar areas; then smaller houses without fences and with gardens like bush, with the *hubshi*[5] standing about or sitting down, more usually sitting down, everywhere. Especially I remember the *hubshi*. I had heard about them in stories and had seen one or two in Bombay. But I had never dreamt that this wild race existed in such numbers in Washington and were permitted to roam the streets so freely. O father, what was this place I had come to?

I wanted, I say, to be in the open, to breathe, to come to myself, to reflect. But there was to be no openness for me that evening. From the aeroplane to

5. Mildly derogatory term for a person of African descent (Hindi).

the airport building to the motor car to the apartment block to the elevator to the corridor to the apartment itself, I was forever enclosed, forever in the hissing, hissing sound of air-conditioners.

I was too dazed to take stock of the apartment. I saw it as only another halting place. My employer went to bed at once, completely exhausted, poor fellow. I looked around for my room. I couldn't find it and gave up. Aching for the Bombay ways, I spread my bedding in the carpeted corridor just outside our apartment door. The corridor was long: doors, doors. The illuminated ceiling was decorated with stars of different sizes; the colours were grey and blue and gold. Below that imitation sky I felt like a prisoner.

Waking, looking up at the ceiling, I thought just for a second that I had fallen asleep on the pavement below the gallery of our Bombay chambers. Then I realized my loss. I couldn't tell how much time had passed or whether it was night or day. The only clue was that newspapers now lay outside some doors. It disturbed me to think that while I had been sleeping, alone and defenceless, I had been observed by a stranger and perhaps by more than one stranger.

I tried the apartment door and found I had locked myself out. I didn't want to disturb my employer. I thought I would get out into the open, go for a walk. I remembered where the elevator was. I got in and pressed the button. The elevator dropped fast and silently and it was like being in the aeroplane again. When the elevator stopped and the blue metal door slid open I saw plain concrete corridors and blank walls. The noise of machinery was very loud. I knew I was in the basement and the main floor was not far above me. But I no longer wanted to try; I gave up ideas of the open air. I thought I would just go back up to the apartment. But I hadn't noted the number and didn't even know what floor we were on. My courage flowed out of me. I sat on the floor of the elevator and felt the tears come to my eyes. Almost without noise the elevator door closed, and I found I was being taken up silently at great speed.

The elevator stopped and the door opened. It was my employer, his hair uncombed, yesterday's dirty shirt partly unbuttoned. He looked frightened.

"Santosh, where have you been at this hour of morning? Without your shoes."

I could have embraced him. He hurried me back past the newspapers to our apartment and I took the bedding inside. The wide window showed the early morning sky, the big city; we were high up, way above the trees.

I said, "I couldn't find my room."

"Government sanctioned," my employer said. "Are you sure you've looked?"

We looked together. One little corridor led past the bathroom to his bedroom; another, shorter corridor led to the big room and the kitchen. There was nothing else.

"Government sanctioned," my employer said, moving about the kitchen and opening cupboard doors. "Separate entrance, shelving. I have the correspondence." He opened another door and looked inside. "Santosh, do you think it is possible that this is what Government meant?"

The cupboard he had opened was as high as the rest of the apartment and as wide as the kitchen, about six feet. It was about three feet deep. It had two doors. One door opened into the kitchen; another door, directly opposite, opened into the corridor.

"Separate entrance," my employer said. "Shelving, electric light, power point, fitted carpet."

"This must be my room, sahib."

"Santosh, some enemy in Government has done this to me."

"Oh no, sahib. You mustn't say that. Besides, it is very big. I will be able to make myself very comfortable. It is much bigger than my little cubby-hole in the chambers. And it has a nice flat ceiling. I wouldn't hit my head."

"You don't understand, Santosh. Bombay is Bombay. Here if we start living in cupboards we give the wrong impression. They will think we all live in cupboards in Bombay."

"O sahib, but they can just look at me and see I am dirt."

"You are very good, Santosh. But these people are malicious. Still, if you are happy, then I am happy."

"I am very happy, sahib."

And after all the upset, I was. It was nice to crawl in that evening, spread my bedding and feel protected and hidden. I slept very well.

In the morning my employer said, "We must talk about money, Santosh. Your salary is one hundred rupees a month. But Washington isn't Bombay. Everything is a little bit more expensive here, and I am going to give you a Dearness Allowance. As from today you are getting one hundred and fifty rupees."

"Sahib."

"And I'm giving you a fortnight's pay in advance. In foreign exchange. Seventy-five rupees. Ten cents to the rupee, seven hundred and fifty cents. Seven fifty U.S. Here, Santosh. This afternoon you go out and have a little walk and enjoy. But be careful. We are not among friends, remember."

So at last, rested, with money in my pocket, I went out in the open. And of course the city wasn't a quarter as frightening as I had thought. The buildings weren't particularly big, not all the streets were busy, and there were many lovely trees. A lot of the *hubshi* were about, very wild-looking some of them, with dark glasses and their hair frizzed out, but it seemed that if you didn't trouble them they didn't attack you.

I was looking for a café or a tea-stall where perhaps domestics congregated. But I saw no domestics, and I was chased away from the place I did eventually go into. The girl said, after I had been waiting some time, "Can't you read? We don't serve hippies or bare feet here."

O father! I had come out without my shoes. But what a country, I thought, walking briskly away, where people are never allowed to dress normally but must forever wear their very best! Why must they wear out shoes and fine clothes for no purpose? What occasion are they honouring? What waste, what presumption! Who do they think is noticing them all the time?

And even while these thoughts were in my head I found I had come to a roundabout with trees and a fountain where—and it was like a fulfilment in a dream, not easy to believe—there were many people who looked like my own people. I tightened the string around my loose pants, held down my flapping shirt and ran through the traffic to the green circle.

Some of the *hubshi* were there, playing musical instruments and looking quite happy in their way. There were some Americans sitting about on the grass and the fountain and the kerb. Many of them were in rough, friendly-looking

clothes; some were without shoes; and I felt I had been over hasty in condemning the entire race. But it wasn't these people who had attracted me to the
circle. It was the dancers. The men were bearded, bare-footed and in saffron
robes, and the girls were in saris and canvas shoes that looked like our own
Bata shoes. They were shaking little cymbals and chanting and lifting their
heads up and down and going round in a circle, making a lot of dust. It was a
little bit like a Red Indian dance in a cowboy movie, but they were chanting
Sanskrit words in praise of Lord Krishna.[6]

I was very pleased. But then a disturbing thought came to me. It might have
been because of the half-caste appearance of the dancers; it might have been
their bad Sanskrit pronunciation and their accent. I thought that these people
were now strangers, but that perhaps once upon a time they had been like me.
Perhaps, as in some story, they had been brought here among the *hubshi* as
captives a long time ago and had become a lost people, like our own wandering
gipsy folk, and had forgotten who they were. When I thought that, I lost my
pleasure in the dancing; and I felt for the dancers the sort of distaste we feel
when we are faced with something that should be kin but turns out not to be,
turns out to be degraded, like a deformed man, or like a leper, who from a distance looks whole.

I didn't stay. Not far from the circle I saw a café which appeared to be serving bare feet. I went in, had a coffee and a nice piece of cake and bought a
pack of cigarettes; matches they gave me free with the cigarettes. It was all
right, but then the bare feet began looking at me, and one bearded fellow came
and sniffed loudly at me and smiled and spoke some sort of gibberish, and then
some others of the bare feet came and sniffed at me. They weren't unfriendly,
but I didn't appreciate the behaviour; and it was a little frightening to find,
when I left the place, that two or three of them appeared to be following me.
They weren't unfriendly, but I didn't want to take any chances. I passed a cinema; I went in. It was something I wanted to do anyway. In Bombay I used to
go once a week.

And that was all right. The movie had already started. It was in English, not
too easy for me to follow, and it gave me time to think. It was only there, in the
darkness, that I thought about the money I had been spending. The prices had
seemed to me very reasonable, like Bombay prices. Three for the movie ticket,
one fifty in the café, with tip. But I had been thinking in rupees and paying in
dollars. In less than an hour I had spent nine days' pay.

I couldn't watch the movie after that. I went out and began to make my way
back to the apartment block. Many more of the *hubshi* were about now and I
saw that where they congregated the pavement was wet, and dangerous with
broken glass and bottles. I couldn't think of cooking when I got back to the
apartment. I couldn't bear to look at the view. I spread my bedding in the cupboard, lay down in the darkness and waited for my employer to return.

When he did I said, "Sahib, I want to go home."

"Santosh, I've paid five thousand rupees to bring you here. If I send you back
now, you will have to work for six or seven years without salary to pay me back."

6. Hindu deity, also worshipped by the Hare
Krishnas, mostly white American Hindus sometimes viewed as a cult, who wear traditional
Indian clothes and chant the names of Krishna
in Sanskrit, a classical Indian language.

I burst into tears.

"My poor Santosh, something has happened. Tell me what has happened."

"Sahib, I've spent more than half the advance you gave me this morning. I went out and had a coffee and cake and then I went to a movie."

His eyes went small and twinkly behind his glasses. He bit the inside of his top lip, scraped at his moustache with his lower teeth, and he said, "You see, you see. I told you it was expensive."

I understood I was a prisoner. I accepted this and adjusted. I learned to live within the apartment, and I was even calm.

My employer was a man of taste and he soon had the apartment looking like something in a magazine, with books and Indian paintings and Indian fabrics and pieces of sculpture and bronze statues of our gods. I was careful to take no delight in it. It was of course very pretty, especially with the view. But the view remained foreign and I never felt that the apartment was real, like the shabby old Bombay chambers with the cane chairs, or that it had anything to do with me.

When people came to dinner I did my duty. At the appropriate time I would bid the company goodnight, close off the kitchen behind its folding screen and pretend I was leaving the apartment. Then I would lie down quietly in my cupboard and smoke. I was free to go out; I had my separate entrance. But I didn't like being out of the apartment. I didn't even like going down to the laundry room in the basement.

Once or twice a week I went to the supermarket on our street. I always had to walk past groups of *hubshi* men and children. I tried not to look, but it was hard. They sat on the pavement, on steps and in the bush around their redbrick houses, some of which had boarded-up windows. They appeared to be very much a people of the open air, with little to do; even in the mornings some of the men were drunk.

Scattered among the *hubshi* houses were others just as old but with gas-lamps that burned night and day in the entrance. These were the houses of the Americans. I seldom saw these people; they didn't spend much time on the street. The lighted gas-lamp was the American way of saying that though a house looked old outside it was nice and new inside. I also felt that it was like a warning to the *hubshi* to keep off.

Outside the supermarket there was always a policeman with a gun. Inside, there were always a couple of *hubshi* guards with truncheons, and, behind the cashiers, some old *hubshi* beggar men in rags. There were also many young *hubshi* boys, small but muscular, waiting to carry parcels, as once in the hills I had waited to carry Indian tourists' luggage.

These trips to the supermarket were my only outings, and I was always glad to get back to the apartment. The work there was light. I watched a lot of television and my English improved. I grew to like certain commercials very much. It was in these commercials I saw the Americans whom in real life I so seldom saw and knew only by their gas-lamps. Up there in the apartment, with a view of the white domes and towers and greenery of the famous city, I entered the homes of the Americans and saw them cleaning those homes. I saw them cleaning floors and dishes. I saw them buying clothes and cleaning clothes, buying motor cars and cleaning motor cars. I saw them cleaning, cleaning.

The effect of all this television on me was curious. If by some chance I saw an American on the street I tried to fit him or her into the commercials; and I felt I had caught the person in an interval between his television duties. So to some extent Americans have remained to me, as people not quite real, as people temporarily absent from television.

Sometimes a *hubshi* came on the screen, not to talk of *hubshi* things, but to do a little cleaning of his own. That wasn't the same. He was too different from the *hubshi* I saw on the street and I knew he was an actor. I knew that his television duties were only make-believe and that he would soon have to return to the street.

One day at the supermarket, when the *hubshi* girl took my money, she sniffed and said, "You always smell sweet, baby."

She was friendly, and I was at last able to clear up that mystery, of my smell. It was the poor country weed I smoked. It was a peasant taste of which I was slightly ashamed, to tell the truth; but the cashier was encouraging. As it happened, I had brought a quantity of the weed with me from Bombay in one of my bundles, together with a hundred razor blades, believing both weed and blades to be purely Indian things. I made an offering to the girl. In return she taught me a few words of English. "Me black and beautiful" was the first thing she taught me. Then she pointed to the policeman with the gun outside and taught me: "He pig."

My English lessons were taken a stage further by the *hubshi* maid who worked for someone on our floor in the apartment block. She too was attracted by my smell, but I soon began to feel that she was also attracted by my smallness and strangeness. She herself was a big woman, broad in the face, with high cheeks and bold eyes and lips that were full but not pendulous. Her largeness disturbed me; I found it better to concentrate on her face. She misunderstood; there were times when she frolicked with me in a violent way. I didn't like it, because I couldn't fight her off as well as I would have liked and because in spite of myself I was fascinated by her appearance. Her smell mixed with the perfumes she used could have made me forget myself.

She was always coming into the apartment. She disturbed me while I was watching the Americans on television. I feared the smell she left behind. Sweat, perfume, my own weed: the smells lay thick in the room, and I prayed to the bronze gods my employer had installed as living-room ornaments that I would not be dishonoured. Dishonoured, I say; and I know that this might seem strange to people over here, who have permitted the *hubshi* to settle among them in such large numbers and must therefore esteem them in certain ways. But in our country we frankly do not care for the *hubshi*. It is written in our books, both holy and not so holy, that it is indecent and wrong for a man of our blood to embrace the *hubshi* woman. To be dishonoured in this life, to be born a cat or a monkey or a *hubshi* in the next!

But I was falling. Was it idleness and solitude? I was found attractive: I wanted to know why. I began to go to the bathroom of the apartment simply to study my face in the mirror. I cannot easily believe it myself now, but in Bombay a week or a month could pass without my looking in the mirror; and then it wasn't to consider my looks but to check whether the barber had cut off too much hair or whether a pimple was about to burst. Slowly I made a discovery.

My face was handsome. I had never thought of myself in this way. I had thought of myself as unnoticeable, with features that served as identification alone.

The discovery of my good looks brought its strains. I became obsessed with my appearance, with a wish to see myself. It was like an illness. I would be watching television, for instance, and I would be surprised by the thought: are you as handsome as that man? I would have to get up and go to the bathroom and look in the mirror.

I thought back to the time when these matters hadn't interested me, and I saw how ragged I must have looked, on the aeroplane, in the airport, in that café for bare feet, with the rough and dirty clothes I wore, without doubt or question, as clothes befitting a servant. I was choked with shame. I saw, too, how good people in Washington had been, to have seen me in rags and yet to have taken me for a man.

I was glad I had a place to hide. I had thought of myself as a prisoner. Now I was glad I had so little of Washington to cope with: the apartment, my cupboard, the television set, my employer, the walk to the supermarket, the *hubshi* woman. And one day I found I no longer knew whether I wanted to go back to Bombay. Up there, in the apartment, I no longer knew what I wanted to do.

I became more careful of my appearance. There wasn't much I could do. I bought laces for my old black shoes, socks, a belt. Then some money came my way. I had understood that the weed I smoked was of value to the *hubshi* and the bare feet; I disposed of what I had, disadvantageously as I now know, through the *hubshi* girl at the supermarket. I got just under two hundred dollars. Then, as anxiously as I had got rid of my weed, I went out and bought some clothes.

I still have the things I bought that morning. A green hat, a green suit. The suit was always too big for me. Ignorance, inexperience; but I also remember the feeling of presumption. The salesman wanted to talk, to do his job. I didn't want to listen. I took the first suit he showed me and went into the cubicle and changed. I couldn't think about size and fit. When I considered all that cloth and all that tailoring I was proposing to adorn my simple body with, that body that needed so little, I felt I was asking to be destroyed. I changed back quickly, went out of the cubicle and said I would take the green suit. The salesman began to talk; I cut him short; I asked for a hat. When I got back to the apartment I felt quite weak and had to lie down for a while in my cupboard.

I never hung the suit up. Even in the shop, even while counting out the precious dollars, I had known it was a mistake. I kept the suit folded in the box with all its pieces of tissue paper. Three or four times I put it on and walked about the apartment and sat down on chairs and lit cigarettes and crossed my legs, practising. But I couldn't bring myself to wear the suit out of doors. Later I wore the pants, but never the jacket. I never bought another suit; I soon began wearing the sort of clothes I wear today, pants with some sort of zippered jacket.

Once I had had no secrets from my employer; it was so much simpler not to have secrets. But some instinct told me now it would be better not to let him know about the green suit or the few dollars I had, just as instinct had already told me I should keep my growing knowledge of English to myself.

Once my employer had been to me only a presence. I used to tell him then that beside him I was as dirt. It was only a way of talking, one of the courtesies of our language, but it had something of truth. I meant that he was the man who adventured in the world for me, that I experienced the world through him, that I was content to be a small part of his presence. I was content, sleeping on the Bombay pavement with my friends, to hear the talk of my employer and his guests upstairs. I was more than content, late at night, to be identified among the sleepers and greeted by some of those guests before they drove away.

Now I found that, without wishing it, I was ceasing to see myself as part of my employer's presence, and beginning at the same time to see him as an outsider might see him, as perhaps the people who came to dinner in the apartment saw him. I saw that he was a man of my own age, around thirty-five; it astonished me that I hadn't noticed this before. I saw that he was plump, in need of exercise, that he moved with short, fussy steps; a man with glasses, thinning hair, and that habit, during conversation, of scraping at his moustache with his teeth and nibbling at the inside of his top lip; a man who was frequently anxious, took pains over his work, was subjected at his own table to unkind remarks by his office colleagues; a man who looked as uneasy in Washington as I felt, who acted as cautiously as I had learned to act.

I remember an American who came to dinner. He looked at the pieces of sculpture in the apartment and said he had himself brought back a whole head from one of our ancient temples; he had got the guide to hack it off.

I could see that my employer was offended. He said, "But that's illegal."

"That's why I had to give the guide two dollars. If I had a bottle of whisky he would have pulled down the whole temple for me."

My employer's face went blank. He continued to do his duties as host but he was unhappy throughout the dinner. I grieved for him.

Afterwards he knocked on my cupboard. I knew he wanted to talk. I was in my underclothes but I didn't feel underdressed, with the American gone. I stood in the door of my cupboard; my employer paced up and down the small kitchen; the apartment felt sad.

"Did you hear that person, Santosh?"

I pretended I hadn't understood, and when he explained I tried to console him. I said, "Sahib, but we know these people are Franks and barbarians."

"They are malicious people, Santosh. They think that because we are a poor country we are all the same. They think an official in Government is just the same as some poor guide scraping together a few rupees to keep body and soul together, poor fellow."

I saw that he had taken the insult only in a personal way, and I was disappointed. I thought he had been thinking of the temple.

A few days later I had my adventure. The *hubshi* woman came in, moving among my employer's ornaments like a bull. I was greatly provoked. The smell was too much; so was the sight of her armpits. I fell. She dragged me down on the couch, on the saffron spread which was one of my employer's nicest pieces of Punjabi folk-weaving. I saw the moment, helplessly, as one of dishonour. I saw her as Kali, goddess of death and destruction, coal-black, with a red tongue and white eyeballs and many powerful arms. I expected her to be wild and fierce; but she added insult to injury by being very playful, as though, because I was small and strange, the act was not real. She laughed all the time. I would have liked to withdraw, but the act took over and completed itself. And then I felt dreadful.

I wanted to be forgiven, I wanted to be cleansed, I wanted her to go. Nothing frightened me more than the way she had ceased to be a visitor in the apartment and behaved as though she possessed it. I looked at the sculpture and the fabrics and thought of my poor employer, suffering in his office somewhere.

I bathed and bathed afterwards. The smell would not leave me. I fancied that the woman's oil was still on that poor part of my poor body. It occurred to me to rub it down with half a lemon. Penance and cleansing; but it didn't hurt as much as I expected, and I extended the penance by rolling about naked on the floor of the bathroom and the sitting-room and howling. At last the tears came, real tears, and I was comforted.

It was cool in the apartment; the air-conditioning always hummed; but I could see that it was hot outside, like one of our own summer days in the hills. The urge came upon me to dress as I might have done in my village on a religious occasion. In one of my bundles I had a dhoti-length of new cotton, a gift from the tailor's bearer that I had never used. I draped this around my waist and between my legs, lit incense sticks, sat down crosslegged on the floor and tried to meditate and become still. Soon I began to feel hungry. That made me happy; I decided to fast.

Unexpectedly my employer came in. I didn't mind being caught in the attitude and garb of prayer; it could have been so much worse. But I wasn't expecting him till late afternoon.

"Santosh, what has happened?"

Pride got the better of me. I said, "Sahib, it is what I do from time to time."

But I didn't find merit in his eyes. He was far too agitated to notice me properly. He took off his lightweight fawn jacket, dropped it on the saffron spread, went to the refrigerator and drank two tumblers of orange juice, one after the other. Then he looked out at the view, scraping at his moustache.

"Oh, my poor Santosh, what are we doing in this place? Why do we have to come here?"

I looked with him. I saw nothing unusual. The wide window showed the colours of the hot day: the pale-blue sky, the white, almost colourless, domes of famous buildings rising out of dead-green foliage; the untidy roofs of apartment blocks where on Saturday and Sunday mornings people sunbathed; and, below, the fronts and backs of houses on the tree-lined street down which I walked to the supermarket.

My employer turned off the air-conditioning and all noise was absent from the room. An instant later I began to hear the noises outside: sirens far and near. When my employer slid the window open the roar of the disturbed city rushed into the room. He closed the window and there was near-silence again. Not far from the supermarket I saw black smoke, uncurling, rising, swiftly turning colourless. This was not the smoke which some of the apartment blocks gave off all day. This was the smoke of a real fire.

"The *hubshi* have gone wild, Santosh. They are burning down Washington."[7]

I didn't mind at all. Indeed, in my mood of prayer and repentance, the news was even welcome. And it was with a feeling of release that I watched and heard

7. Refers to riots in 1968 after the assassination of the civil rights leader Martin Luther King, Jr.

the city burn that afternoon and watched it burn that night. I watched it burn again and again on television; and I watched it burn in the morning. It burned like a famous city and I didn't want it to stop burning. I wanted the fire to spread and spread and I wanted everything in the city, even the apartment block, even the apartment, even myself, to be destroyed and consumed. I wanted escape to be impossible; I wanted the very idea of escape to become absurd. At every sign that the burning was going to stop I felt disappointed and let down.

For four days my employer and I stayed in the apartment and watched the city burn. The television continued to show us what we could see and what, whenever we slid the window back, we could hear. Then it was over. The view from our window hadn't changed. The famous buildings stood; the trees remained. But for the first time since I had understood that I was a prisoner I found that I wanted to be out of the apartment and in the streets.

The destruction lay beyond the supermarket. I had never gone into this part of the city before, and it was strange to walk in those long wide streets for the first time, to see trees and houses and shops and advertisements, everything like a real city, and then to see that every signboard on every shop was burnt or stained with smoke, that the shops themselves were black and broken, that flames had burst through some of the upper windows and scorched the red bricks. For mile after mile it was like that. There were *hubshi* groups about, and at first when I passed them I pretended to be busy, minding my own business, not at all interested in the ruins. But they smiled at me and I found I was smiling back. Happiness was on the faces of the *hubshi*. They were like people amazed they could do so much, that so much lay in their power. They were like people on holiday. I shared their exhilaration.

The idea of escape was a simple one, but it hadn't occurred to me before. When I adjusted to my imprisonment I had wanted only to get away from Washington and to return to Bombay. But then I had become confused. I had looked in the mirror and seen myself, and I knew it wasn't possible for me to return to Bombay to the sort of job I had had and the life I had lived. I couldn't easily become part of someone else's presence again. Those evening chats on the pavement, those morning walks: happy times, but they were like the happy times of childhood: I didn't want them to return.

I had taken, after the fire, to going for long walks in the city. And one day, when I wasn't even thinking of escape, when I was just enjoying the sights and my new freedom of movement, I found myself in one of those leafy streets where private houses had been turned into business premises. I saw a fellow countryman superintending the raising of a signboard on his gallery. The signboard told me that the building was a restaurant, and I assumed that the man in charge was the owner. He looked worried and slightly ashamed, and he smiled at me. This was unusual, because the Indians I had seen on the streets of Washington pretended they hadn't seen me; they made me feel that they didn't like the competition of my presence or didn't want me to start asking them difficult questions.

I complimented the worried man on his signboard and wished him good luck in his business. He was a small man of about fifty and he was wearing a double-breasted suit with old-fashioned wide lapels. He had dark hollows below his eyes and he looked as though he had recently lost a little weight. I could see that in our country he had been a man of some standing, not quite the sort of person who would go into the restaurant business. I felt at one with him. He invited me in to look around, asked my name and gave his. It was Priya.

Just past the gallery was the loveliest and richest room I had ever seen. The wallpaper was like velvet; I wanted to pass my hand over it. The brass lamps that hung from the ceiling were in a lovely cut-out pattern and the bulbs were of many colours. Priya looked with me, and the hollows under his eyes grew darker, as though my admiration was increasing his worry at his extravagance. The restaurant hadn't yet opened for customers and on a shelf in one corner I saw Priya's collection of good-luck objects: a brass plate with a heap of uncooked rice, for prosperity; a little copybook and a little diary pencil, for good luck with the accounts; a little clay lamp, for general good luck.

"What do you think, Santosh? You think it will be all right?"

"It is bound to be all right, Priya."

"But I have enemies, you know, Santosh. The Indian restaurant people are not going to appreciate me. All mine, you know, Santosh. Cash paid. No mortgage or anything like that. I don't believe in mortgages. Cash or nothing."

I understood him to mean that he had tried to get a mortgage and failed, and was anxious about money.

"But what are you doing here, Santosh? You used to be in Government or something?"

"You could say that, Priya."

"Like me. They have a saying here. If you can't beat them, join them. I joined them. They are still beating me." He sighed and spread his arms on the top of the red wall-seat. "Ah, Santosh, why do we do it? Why don't we renounce and go and meditate on the riverbank?" He waved about the room. "The yemblems[8] of the world, Santosh. Just yemblems."

I didn't know the English word he used, but I understood its meaning; and for a moment it was like being back in Bombay, exchanging stories and philosophies with the tailor's bearer and others in the evening.

"But I am forgetting, Santosh. You will have some tea or coffee or something?"

I shook my head from side to side to indicate that I was agreeable, and he called out in a strange harsh language to someone behind the kitchen door.

"Yes, Santosh. Yem-*blems*!" And he sighed and slapped the red seat hard.

A man came out from the kitchen with a tray. At first he looked like a fellow countryman, but in a second I could tell he was a stranger.

"You are right," Priya said, when the stranger went back to the kitchen. "He is not of Bharat.[9] He is a Mexican. But what can I do? You get fellow countrymen, you fix up their papers and everything, green card and everything. And then? Then they run away. Run-run-runaway. Crooks this side, crooks that side, I can't tell you. Listen, Santosh. I was in cloth business before. Buy for fifty rupees that side, sell for fifty dollars this side. Easy. But then. Caftan, everybody wants caftan. Caftan-aftan, I say, I will settle your caftan. I buy one thousand, Santosh. Delays India-side, of course. They come one year later.

8. I.e., emblems. 9. India (Hindi).

Nobody wants caftan then. We're not organized, Santosh. We don't do enough consumer research. That's what the fellows at the embassy tell me. But if I do consumer research, when will I do my business? The trouble, you know, Santosh, is that this shopkeeping is not in my blood. The damn thing goes *against* my blood. When I was in cloth business I used to hide sometimes for shame when a customer came in. Sometimes I used to pretend I was a shopper myself. Consumer research! These people make us dance, Santosh. You and I, we will renounce. We will go together and walk beside Potomac[1] and meditate."

I loved his talk. I hadn't heard anything so sweet and philosophical since the Bombay days. I said, "Priya, I will cook for you, if you want a cook."

"I feel I've known you a long time, Santosh. I feel you are like a member of my own family. I will give you a place to sleep, a little food to eat and a little pocket money, as much as I can afford."

I said, "Show me the place to sleep."

He led me out of the pretty room and up a carpeted staircase. I was expecting the carpet and the new paint to stop somewhere, but it was nice and new all the way. We entered a room that was like a smaller version of my employer's apartment.

"Built-in cupboards and everything, you see, Santosh."

I went to the cupboard. It had a folding door that opened outward. I said, "Priya, it is too small. There is room on the shelf for my belongings. But I don't see how I can spread my bedding inside here. It is far too narrow."

He giggled nervously. "Santosh, you are a joker. I feel that we are of the same family already."

Then it came to me that I was being offered the whole room. I was stunned.

Priya looked stunned too. He sat down on the edge of the soft bed. The dark hollows under his eyes were almost black and he looked very small in his double-breasted jacket. "This is how they make us dance over here, Santosh. You say staff quarters and they say staff quarters. This is what they mean."

For some seconds we sat silently, I fearful, he gloomy, meditating on the ways of this new world.

Someone called from downstairs, "Priya!"

His gloom gone, smiling in advance, winking at me, Priya called back in an accent of the country, "Hi, Bab!"

I followed him down.

"Priya," the American said, "I've brought over the menus."

He was a tall man in a leather jacket, with jeans that rode up above thick white socks and big rubber-soled shoes. He looked like someone about to run in a race. The menus were enormous; on the cover there was a drawing of a fat man with a moustache and a plumed turban, something like the man in the airline advertisements.

"They look great, Bab."

"I like them myself. But what's that, Priya? What's that shelf doing there?"

Moving like the front part of a horse, Bab walked to the shelf with the rice and the brass plate and the little clay lamp. It was only then that I saw that the shelf was very roughly made.

1. River in Washington, D.C.

Priya looked penitent and it was clear he had put the shelf up himself. It was also clear he didn't intend to take it down.

"Well, it's yours," Bab said. "I suppose we had to have a touch of the East somewhere. Now, Priya—"

"Money-money-money, is it?" Priya said, racing the words together as though he was making a joke to amuse a child. "But, Bab, how can *you* ask *me* for money? Anybody hearing you would believe that this restaurant is mine. But this restaurant isn't mine, Bab. This restaurant is yours."

It was only one of our courtesies, but it puzzled Bab and he allowed himself to be led to other matters.

I saw that, for all his talk of renunciation and business failure, and for all his jumpiness, Priya was able to cope with Washington. I admired this strength in him as much as I admired the richness of his talk. I didn't know how much to believe of his stories, but I liked having to guess about him. I liked having to play with his words in my mind. I liked the mystery of the man. The mystery came from his solidity. I knew where I was with him. After the apartment and the green suit and the *hubshi* woman and the city burning for four days, to be with Priya was to feel safe. For the first time since I had come to Washington I felt safe.

I can't say that I moved in. I simply stayed. I didn't want to go back to the apartment even to collect my belongings. I was afraid that something might happen to keep me a prisoner there. My employer might turn up and demand his five thousand rupees. The *hubshi* woman might claim me for her own; I might be condemned to a life among the *hubshi*. And it wasn't as if I was leaving behind anything of value in the apartment. The green suit I was even happy to forget. But.

Priya paid me forty dollars a week. After what I was getting, three dollars and seventy-five cents, it seemed a lot; and it was more than enough for my needs. I didn't have much temptation to spend, to tell the truth. I knew that my old employer and the *hubshi* woman would be wondering about me in their respective ways and I thought I should keep off the streets for a while. That was no hardship; it was what I was used to in Washington. Besides, my days at the restaurant were pretty full; for the first time in my life I had little leisure.

The restaurant was a success from the start, and Priya was fussy. He was always bursting into the kitchen with one of those big menus in his hand, saying in English, "Prestige job, Santosh, prestige." I didn't mind. I liked to feel I had to do things perfectly; I felt I was earning my freedom. Though I was in hiding, and though I worked every day until midnight, I felt I was much more in charge of myself than I had ever been.

Many of our waiters were Mexicans, but when we put turbans on them they could pass. They came and went, like the Indian staff. I didn't get on with these people. They were frightened and jealous of one another and very treacherous. Their talk amid the biryanis and the pillaus was all of papers and green cards. They were always about to get green cards or they had been cheated out of green cards or they had just got green cards. At first I didn't know what they were talking about. When I understood I was more than depressed.

I understood that because I had escaped from my employer I had made myself illegal in America. At any moment I could be denounced, seized, jailed, deported, disgraced. It was a complication. I had no green card; I didn't know how to set about getting one; and there was no one I could talk to.

I felt burdened by my secrets. Once I had none; now I had so many. I couldn't tell Priya I had no green card. I couldn't tell him I had broken faith with my old employer and dishonoured myself with a *hubshi* woman and lived in fear of retribution. I couldn't tell him that I was afraid to leave the restaurant and that nowadays when I saw an Indian I hid from him as anxiously as the Indian hid from me. I would have felt foolish to confess. With Priya, right from the start, I had pretended to be strong; and I wanted it to remain like that. Instead, when we talked now, and he grew philosophical, I tried to find bigger causes for being sad. My mind fastened on to these causes, and the effect of this was that my sadness became like a sickness of the soul.

It was worse than being in the apartment, because now the responsibility was mine and mine alone. I had decided to be free, to act for myself. It pained me to think of the exhilaration I had felt during the days of the fire; and I felt mocked when I remembered that in the early days of my escape I had thought I was in charge of myself.

The year turned. The snow came and melted. I was more afraid than ever of going out. The sickness was bigger than all the causes. I saw the future as a hole into which I was dropping. Sometimes at night when I awakened my body would burn and I would feel the hot perspiration break all over.

I leaned on Priya. He was my only hope, my only link with what was real. He went out; he brought back stories. He went out especially to eat in the restaurants of our competitors.

He said, "Santosh, I never believed that running a restaurant was a way to God. But it is true. I eat like a scientist. Every day I eat like a scientist. I feel I have already renounced."

This was Priya. This was how his talk ensnared me and gave me the bigger causes that steadily weakened me. I became more and more detached from the men in the kitchen. When they spoke of their green cards and the jobs they were about to get I felt like asking them: Why? Why?

And every day the mirror told its own tale. Without exercise, with the sickening of my heart and my mind, I was losing my looks. My face had become pudgy and sallow and full of spots; it was becoming ugly. I could have cried for that, discovering my good looks only to lose them. It was like a punishment for my presumption, the punishment I had feared when I bought the green suit.

Priya said, "Santosh, you must get some exercise. You are not looking well. Your eyes are getting like mine. What are you pining for? Are you pining for Bombay or your family in the hills?"

But now, even in my mind, I was a stranger in those places.

Priya said one Sunday morning, "Santosh, I am going to take you to see a Hindi movie today. All the Indians of Washington will be there, domestics and everybody else."

I was very frightened. I didn't want to go and I couldn't tell him why. He insisted. My heart began to beat fast as soon as I got into the car. Soon there were no more houses with gas-lamps in the entrance, just those long wide burnt-out *hubshi* streets, now with fresh leaves on the trees, heaps of rubble on bulldozed, fenced-in lots, boarded-up shop windows, and old smoke-stained signboards announcing what was no longer true. Cars raced along the wide roads; there was life only on the roads. I thought I would vomit with fear.

I said, "Take me back, *sahib.*"

I had used the wrong word. Once I had used the word a hundred times a day. But then I had considered myself a small part of my employer's presence, and the word was not servile; it was more like a name, like a reassuring sound, part of my employer's dignity and therefore part of mine. But Priya's dignity could never be mine; that was not our relationship. Priya I had always called Priya; it was his wish, the American way, man to man. With Priya the word was servile. And he responded to the word. He did as I asked; he drove me back to the restaurant. I never called him by his name again.

I was good-looking; I had lost my looks. I was a free man; I had lost my freedom.

One of the Mexican waiters came into the kitchen late one evening and said, "There is a man outside who wants to see the chef."

No one had made this request before, and Priya was at once agitated. "Is he an American? Some enemy has sent him here. Sanitary-anitary, health-ealth, they can inspect my kitchens at any time."

"He is an Indian," the Mexican said.

I was alarmed. I thought it was my old employer; that quiet approach was like him. Priya thought it was a rival. Though Priya regularly ate in the restaurants of his rivals he thought it unfair when they came to eat in his. We both went to the door and peeked through the glass window into the dimly lit dining-room.

"Do you know that person, Santosh?"

"Yes, sahib."

It wasn't my old employer. It was one of his Bombay friends, a big man in Government, whom I had often served in the chambers. He was by himself and seemed to have just arrived in Washington. He had a new Bombay haircut, very close, and a stiff dark suit, Bombay tailoring. His shirt looked blue, but in the dim multi-coloured light of the dining-room everything white looked blue. He didn't look unhappy with what he had eaten. Both his elbows were on the curry-spotted tablecloth and he was picking his teeth, half closing his eyes and hiding his mouth with his cupped left hand.

"I don't like him," Priya said. "Still, big man in Government and so on. You must go to him, Santosh."

But I couldn't go.

"Put on your apron, Santosh. And that chef's cap. Prestige. You must go, Santosh."

Priya went out to the dining-room and I heard him say in English that I was coming.

I ran up to my room, put some oil on my hair, combed my hair, put on my best pants and shirt and my shining shoes. It was so, as a man about town rather than as a cook, I went to the dining-room.

The man from Bombay was as astonished as Priya. We exchanged the old courtesies, and I waited. But, to my relief, there seemed little more to say. No difficult questions were put to me; I was grateful to the man from Bombay for his tact. I avoided talk as much as possible. I smiled. The man from Bombay smiled back. Priya smiled uneasily at both of us. So for a while we were, smiling in the dim blue-red light and waiting.

The man from Bombay said to Priya, "Brother, I just have a few words to say to my old friend Santosh."

Priya didn't like it, but he left us.

I waited for those words. But they were not the words I feared. The man from Bombay didn't speak of my old employer. We continued to exchange courtesies. Yes, I was well and he was well and everybody else we knew was well; and I was doing well and he was doing well. That was all. Then, secretively, the man from Bombay gave me a dollar. A dollar, ten rupees, an enormous tip for Bombay. But, from him, much more than a tip: an act of graciousness, part of the sweetness of the old days. Once it would have meant so much to me. Now it meant so little. I was saddened and embarrassed. And I had been anticipating hostility!

Priya was waiting behind the kitchen door. His little face was tight and serious, and I knew he had seen the money pass. Now, quickly, he read my own face, and without saying anything to me he hurried out into the dining-room.

I heard him say in English to the man from Bombay, "Santosh is a good fellow. He's got his own room with bath and everything. I am giving him a hundred dollars a week from next week. A thousand rupees a week. This is a first-class establishment."

A thousand chips a week! I was staggered. It was much more than any man in Government got, and I was sure the man from Bombay was also staggered, and perhaps regretting his good gesture and that precious dollar of foreign exchange.

"Santosh," Priya said, when the restaurant closed that evening, "that man was an enemy. I knew it from the moment I saw him. And because he was an enemy I did something very bad, Santosh."

"Sahib."

"I lied, Santosh. To protect you. I told him, Santosh, that I was going to give you seventy-five dollars a week after Christmas."

"Sahib."

"And now I have to make that lie true. But, Santosh, you know that is money we can't afford. I don't have to tell you about overheads and things like that. Santosh, I will give you sixty."

I said, "Sahib, I couldn't stay on for less than a hundred and twenty-five."

Priya's eyes went shiny and the hollows below his eyes darkened. He giggled and pressed out his lips. At the end of that week I got a hundred dollars. And Priya, good man that he was, bore me no grudge.

Now here was a victory. It was only after it happened that I realized how badly I had needed such a victory, how far, gaining my freedom, I had begun to accept death not as the end but as the goal. I revived. Or rather, my senses revived. But in this city what was there to feed my senses? There were no walks to be taken, no idle conversations with understanding friends. I could buy new clothes. But then? Would I just look at myself in the mirror? Would I go walking, inviting passers-by to look at me and my clothes? No, the whole business of clothes and dressing up only threw me back into myself.

There was a Swiss or German woman in the cake-shop some doors away, and there was a Filipino woman in the kitchen. They were neither of them attractive, to tell the truth. The Swiss or German could have broken my back with a slap, and the Filipino, though young, was remarkably like one of our older hill women. Still, I felt I owed something to the senses, and I thought I might frolic with these women. But then I was frightened of the responsibility. Goodness, I had learned that a woman is not just a roll and a frolic but a big creature weighing a hundred-and-so-many pounds who is going to be around afterwards.

So the moment of victory passed, without celebration. And it was strange, I thought, that sorrow lasts and can make a man look forward to death, but the mood of victory fills a moment and then is over. When my moment of victory was over I discovered below it, as if waiting for me, all my old sickness and fears: fear of my illegality, my former employer, my presumption, the *hubshi* woman. I saw then that the victory I had was not something I had worked for, but luck; and that luck was only fate's cheating, giving an illusion of power.

But that illusion lingered, and I became restless. I decided to act, to challenge fate. I decided I would no longer stay in my room and hide. I began to go out walking in the afternoons. I gained courage; every afternoon I walked a little farther. It became my ambition to walk to that green circle with the fountain where, on my first day out in Washington, I had come upon those people in Hindu costumes, like domestics abandoned a long time ago, singing their Sanskrit gibberish and doing their strange Red Indian dance. And one day I got there.

One day I crossed the road to the circle and sat down on a bench. The *hubshi* were there, and the bare feet, and the dancers in saris and the saffron robes. It was mid-afternoon, very hot, and no one was active. I remembered how magical and inexplicable that circle had seemed to me the first time I saw it. Now it seemed so ordinary and tired: the roads, the motor cars, the shops, the trees, the careful policemen: so much part of the waste and futility that was our world. There was no longer a mystery. I felt I knew where everybody had come from and where those cars were going. But I also felt that everybody there felt like me, and that was soothing. I took to going to the circle every day after the lunch rush and sitting until it was time to go back to Priya's for the dinners.

Late one afternoon, among the dancers and the musicians, the *hubshi* and the bare feet, the singers and the police, I saw her. The *hubshi* woman. And again I wondered at her size; my memory had not exaggerated. I decided to stay where I was. She saw me and smiled. Then, as if remembering anger, she gave me a look of great hatred; and again I saw her as Kali, many-armed, goddess of death and destruction. She looked hard at my face; she considered my clothes. I thought: is it for this I bought these clothes? She got up. She was very big and her tight pants made her much more appalling. She moved towards me. I got up and ran. I ran across the road and then, not looking back, hurried by devious ways to the restaurant.

Priya was doing his accounts. He always looked older when he was doing his accounts, not worried, just older, like a man to whom life could bring no further surprises. I envied him.

"Santosh, some friend brought a parcel for you."

It was a big parcel wrapped in brown paper. He handed it to me, and I thought how calm he was, with his bills and pieces of paper, and the pen with which he made his neat figures, and the book in which he would write every day until that book was exhausted and he would begin a new one.

I took the parcel up to my room and opened it. Inside there was a cardboard box; and inside that, still in its tissue paper, was the green suit.

I felt a hole in my stomach. I couldn't think. I was glad I had to go down almost immediately to the kitchen, glad to be busy until midnight. But then I had to go up to my room again, and I was alone. I hadn't escaped; I had never been free. I had been abandoned. I was like nothing; I had made myself nothing. And I couldn't turn back.

In the morning Priya said, "You don't look very well, Santosh."

His concern weakened me further. He was the only man I could talk to and I didn't know what I could say to him. I felt tears coming to my eyes. At that moment I would have liked the whole world to be reduced to tears. I said, "Sahib, I cannot stay with you any longer."

They were just words, part of my mood, part of my wish for tears and relief. But Priya didn't soften. He didn't even look surprised. "Where will you go, Santosh?"

How could I answer his serious question?

"Will it be different where you go?"

He had freed himself of me. I could no longer think of tears. I said, "Sahib, I have enemies."

He giggled. "You are a joker, Santosh. How can a man like yourself have enemies? There would be no profit in it. *I* have enemies. It is part of your happiness and part of the equity of the world that you cannot have enemies. That's why you can run-run-runaway." He smiled and made the running gesture with his extended palm.

So, at last, I told him my story. I told him about my old employer and my escape and the green suit. He made me feel I was telling him nothing he hadn't already known. I told him about the *hubshi* woman. I was hoping for some rebuke. A rebuke would have meant that he was concerned for my honour, that I could lean on him, that rescue was possible.

But he said, "Santosh, you have no problems. Marry the *hubshi*. That will automatically make you a citizen. Then you will be a free man."

It wasn't what I was expecting. He was asking me to be alone forever. I said, "Sahib, I have a wife and children in the hills at home."

"But this is your home, Santosh. Wife and children in the hills, that is very nice and that is always there. But that is over. You have to do what is best for you here. You are alone here. *Hubshi-ubshi,* nobody worries about that here, if that is your choice. This isn't Bombay. Nobody looks at you when you walk down the street. Nobody cares what you do."

He was right. I was a free man; I could do anything I wanted. I could, if it were possible for me to turn back, go to the apartment and beg my old employer for forgiveness. I could, if it were possible for me to become again what I once was, go to the police and say, "I am an illegal immigrant here. Please deport me to Bombay." I could run away, hang myself, surrender, confess, hide. It didn't matter what I did, because I was alone. And I didn't know what I wanted to do. It was like the time when I felt my senses revive and I wanted to go out and enjoy and I found there was nothing to enjoy.

To be empty is not to be sad. To be empty is to be calm. It is to renounce. Priya said no more to me; he was always busy in the mornings. I left him and went up to my room. It was still a bare room, still like a room that in half an hour could be someone else's. I had never thought of it as mine. I was frightened of its spotless painted walls and had been careful to keep them spotless. For just such a moment.

I tried to think of the particular moment in my life, the particular action, that had brought me to that room. Was it the moment with the *hubshi* woman, or was it when the American came to dinner and insulted my employer? Was it the moment of my escape, my sight of Priya in the gallery, or was it when I looked in the mirror and bought the green suit? Or was it much earlier, in that other life, in Bombay, in the hills? I could find no one moment; every moment seemed important. An endless chain of action had brought me to that room. It was frightening; it was burdensome. It was not a time for new decisions. It was time to call a halt.

I lay on the bed watching the ceiling, watching the sky. The door was pushed open. It was Priya.

"My goodness, Santosh! How long have you been here? You have been so quiet I forgot about you."

He looked about the room. He went into the bathroom and came out again. "Are you all right, Santosh?"

He sat on the edge of the bed and the longer he stayed the more I realized how glad I was to see him. There was this: when I tried to think of him rushing into the room I couldn't place it in time; it seemed to have occurred only in my mind. He sat with me. Time became real again. I felt a great love for him. Soon I could have laughed at his agitation. And later, indeed, we laughed together.

I said, "Sahib, you must excuse me this morning. I want to go for a walk. I will come back about tea time."

He looked hard at me, and we both knew I had spoken truly.

"Yes, yes, Santosh. You go for a good long walk. Make yourself hungry with walking. You will feel much better."

Walking, through streets that were now so simple to me, I thought how nice it would be if the people in Hindu costumes in the circle were real. Then I might have joined them. We would have taken to the road; at midday we would have halted in the shade of big trees; in the late afternoon the sinking sun would have turned the dust clouds to gold; and every evening at some village there would have been welcome, water, food, a fire in the night. But that was a dream of another life. I had watched the people in the circle long enough to know that they were of their city; that their television life awaited them; that their renunciation was not like mine. No television life awaited me. It didn't matter. In this city I was alone and it didn't matter what I did.

As magical as the circle with the fountain the apartment block had once been to me. Now I saw that it was plain, not very tall, and faced with small white tiles. A glass door; four tiled steps down; the desk to the right, letters and keys in the pigeonholes; a carpet to the left, upholstered chairs, a low table with paper flowers in the vase; the blue door of the swift, silent elevator. I saw the simplicity of all these things. I knew the floor I wanted. In the corridor, with its illuminated star-decorated ceiling, an imitation sky, the colours were blue, grey and gold. I knew the door I wanted. I knocked.

The *hubshi* woman opened. I saw the apartment where she worked. I had never seen it before and was expecting something like my old employer's apartment, which was on the same floor. Instead, for the first time, I saw something arranged for a television life.

I thought she might have been angry. She looked only puzzled. I was grateful for that.

I said to her in English, "Will you marry me?"

And there, it was done.

"It is for the best, Santosh," Priya said, giving me tea when I got back to the restaurant. "You will be a free man. A citizen. You will have the whole world before you."

I was pleased that he was pleased.

So I am now a citizen, my presence is legal, and I live in Washington. I am still with Priya. We do not talk together as much as we did. The restaurant is one world, the parks and green streets of Washington are another, and every evening some of these streets take me to a third. Burnt-out brick houses, broken fences, overgrown gardens; in a levelled lot between the high brick walls of two houses, a sort of artistic children's playground which the *hubshi* children never use; and then the dark house in which I now live.

Its smells are strange, everything in it is strange. But my strength in this house is that I am a stranger. I have closed my mind and heart to the English language, to newspapers and radio and television, to the pictures of *hubshi* runners and boxers and musicians on the wall. I do not want to understand or learn any more.

I am a simple man who decided to act and see for himself, and it is as though I have had several lives. I do not wish to add to these. Some afternoons I walk to the circle with the fountain. I see the dancers but they are separated from me as by glass. Once, when there were rumours of new burnings, someone scrawled in white paint on the pavement outside my house: *Soul Brother.*[2] I understand the words; but I feel, brother to what or to whom? I was once part of the flow, never thinking of myself as a presence. Then I looked in the mirror and decided to be free. All that my freedom has brought me is the knowledge that I have a face and have a body, that I must feed this body and clothe this body for a certain number of years. Then it will be over.

1971

---

2. An African American man or friend to African Americans, here indicating that Santosh's house should not be vandalized.

LESLIE MARMON SILKO
born 1948

Novelist, poet, memoirist, and writer of short fiction, Leslie Marmon Silko can comfortably alternate between prose and poetry within the confines of a single work, in a manner reminiscent of traditional Native American storytellers. For all its seriousness and lyricism, Silko's work is marked by a touch of irreverence. Well acquainted with the proverbial trickster Coyote, Silko has demonstrated her own wit and versatility as a narrator of Coyote tales. But storytelling is a game with serious ends. "I will tell you something about stories," warns an unnamed voice in one of her novels: "They aren't just entertainment. Don't be fooled."

Silko was born in Albuquerque but grew up in Laguna Pueblo, New Mexico. "I am of mixed-breed ancestry," she has written, "but what I know is Laguna. This place I am from is everything I am as a writer and human being." A Keresan-speaking district, Laguna Pueblo is an old Native community that whites first joined in the mid-nineteenth century when two government employees from Ohio, Walter and Robert Marmon, arrived as surveyors and set down roots. The brothers wrote a constitution for Laguna modeled after the U.S. Constitution; each served a term as governor of the pueblo, an office that no non-Native had held before. They also married Laguna women: Robert Marmon is the great-grandfather of Leslie Marmon Silko. Silko attended Laguna Day School until fifth grade, when she was transferred to Manzano Day School, a small private academy in Albuquerque. Between 1964 and 1969, she studied English at the University of New Mexico, married while still in college, and

gave birth to the older of her two sons, Cazimir Silko. During these years she published her first story, "Tony's Story," a provocative tale of witchery.

Following graduation, Silko stayed on at the university and taught courses in creative writing and oral literature. She studied for a time in the university's American Indian Law Program, with the intention of working in the legal area of Native land claims. In 1971, however, a National Endowment for the Arts Discovery Grant changed Silko's mind about law school, and she quit to devote herself to writing. Seven of her stories, including "Yellow Woman," were published in 1974 in a collection edited by Kenneth Rosen—*The Man to Send Rain Clouds: Contemporary Stories by American Indians*. The novel *Ceremony*, her first large-scale work, appeared in 1977. An enormously complex novel that appeared just after the Vietnam War, *Ceremony* follows a Second World War veteran of mixed ancestry through his struggle for healing. Widely hailed, the novel propelled its author to the front of the growing ranks of indigenous writers in the United States. On the strength of *Ceremony*, Silko was awarded a MacArthur Fellowship (known as the "genius grant") in 1981.

Although much of Silko's work emphasizes the healing of conflicts—between white and Native Americans, between the human and natural worlds, between warring aspects of the self—some of her novels also reveal a more aggressive and despairing tone. Such a novel is *Almanac of the Dead* (1991), which turns a merciless eye on an America that drugs, prostitution, torture, organized crime, and forms of sexual violence have corrupted and deformed. On the map that opens the book read the stern lines: "The Indian Wars have never ended in the Americas. Native Americans acknowledge no borders; they seek nothing less than the return of all tribal lands." Formerly a professor at the University of Arizona, Silko continues to live and write in Tucson.

The story presented here, "Yellow Woman," is one of Silko's shortest and earliest pieces, but it occupies a still-growing place in the canon of short fiction. Often reprinted, it became the subject of a volume of critical essays published in 1993. In traditional Laguna lore, Yellow Woman is either the heroine or a minor character in a wide range of tales. In her earliest incarnations, she might possibly have been a corn spirit—occasionally, Yellow Woman is named together with her three sisters, Blue Woman, Red Woman, and White Woman, thus completing the four colors

of corn—but in Laguna lore she eventually became a kind of Everywoman. A traditional Laguna prayer song, recited at the naming ceremony for a newborn daughter, begins, "Yellow Woman is born, Yellow Woman is born." In narrative lore Yellow Woman most frequently appears in tales of abduction, where she is said to have been captured by a strange man at a stream while she is fetching water. Her captor, who carries her off to another world, is sometimes a kachina, or ancestral spirit; and when at last she returns to her home, she is imbued with power that proves of value for her people. In Silko's version of the tale, traditional elements remain constantly in the foreground. Yet whether the central figures in the story are human or supernatural remains unclear; the story's ambiguity is the source of its fascination. Thus Silko draws on Native tradition to make a major contribution to contemporary American fiction.

Yellow Woman

My thigh clung to his with dampness, and I watched the sun rising up through the tamaracks and willows. The small brown water birds came to the river and hopped across the mud, leaving brown scratches in the alkali-white crust. They bathed in the river silently. I could hear the water, almost at our feet where the narrow fast channel bubbled and washed green ragged moss and fern leaves. I looked at him beside me, rolled in the red blanket on the white river sand. I cleaned the sand out of the cracks between my toes, squinting because the sun was above the willow trees. I looked at him for the last time, sleeping on the white river sand.

I felt hungry and followed the river south the way we had come the afternoon before, following our footprints that were already blurred by lizard tracks and bug trails. The horses were still lying down, and the black one whinnied when he saw me but he did not get up—maybe it was because the corral was made out of thick cedar branches and the horses had not yet felt the sun like I had. I tried to look beyond the pale red mesas to the pueblo. I knew it was there, even if I could not see it, on the sandrock hill above the river, the same river that moved past me now and had reflected the moon last night.

The horse felt warm underneath me. He shook his head and pawed the sand. The bay whinnied and leaned against the gate trying to follow, and I remembered him asleep in the red blanket beside the river. I slid off the horse and tied him close to the other horse, I walked north with the river again, and the white sand broke loose in footprints over footprints.

"Wake up."

He moved in the blanket and turned his face to me with his eyes still closed. I knelt down to touch him.

"I'm leaving."

He smiled now, eyes still closed. "You are coming with me, remember?" He sat up now with his bare dark chest and belly in the sun.

"Where?"

"To my place."

"And will I come back?"

He pulled his pants on. I walked away from him, feeling him behind me and smelling the willows.

"Yellow Woman," he said.

I turned to face him. "Who are you?" I asked.

He laughed and knelt on the low, sandy bank, washing his face in the river. "Last night you guessed my name, and you knew why I had come."

I stared past him at the shallow moving water and tried to remember the night, but I could only see the moon in the water and remember his warmth around me.

"But I only said that you were him and that I was Yellow Woman—I'm not really her—I have my own name and I come from the pueblo on the other side of the mesa. Your name is Silva and you are a stranger I met by the river yesterday afternoon."

He laughed softly. "What happened yesterday has nothing to do with what you will do today, Yellow Woman."

"I know—that's what I'm saying—the old stories about the ka'tsina[1] spirit and Yellow Woman can't mean us."

My old grandpa liked to tell those stories best. There is one about Badger and Coyote who went hunting and were gone all day, and when the sun was going down they found a house. There was a girl living there alone, and she had light hair and eyes and she told them that they could sleep with her. Coyote wanted to be with her all night so he sent Badger into a prairie-dog hole, telling him he thought he saw something in it. As soon as Badger crawled in, Coyote blocked up the entrance with rocks and hurried back to Yellow Woman.

"Come here," he said gently.

He touched my neck and I moved close to him to feel his breathing and to hear his heart. I was wondering if Yellow Woman had known who she was—if she knew that she would become part of the stories. Maybe she'd had another name that her husband and relatives called her so that only the ka'tsina from the north and the storytellers would know her as Yellow Woman. But I didn't go on; I felt him all around me, pushing me down into the white river sand.

Yellow Woman went away with the spirit from the north and lived with him and his relatives. She was gone for a long time, but then one day she came back and she brought twin boys.

"Do you know the story?"

1. Kachina, an ancestral spirit.

"What story?" He smiled and pulled me close to him as he said this. I was afraid lying there on the red blanket. All I could know was the way he felt, warm, damp, his body beside me. This is the way it happens in the stories, I was thinking, with no thought beyond the moment she meets the ka'tsina spirit and they go.

"I don't have to go. What they tell in stories was real only then, back in time immemorial, like they say."

He stood up and pointed at my clothes tangled in the blanket. "Let's go," he said.

I walked beside him, breathing hard because he walked fast, his hand around my wrist. I had stopped trying to pull away from him, because his hand felt cool and the sun was high, drying the river bed into alkali. I will see someone, eventually I will see someone, and then I will be certain that he is only a man—some man from nearby—and I will be sure that I am not Yellow Woman. Because she is from out of time past and I live now and I've been to school and there are highways and pickup trucks that Yellow Woman never saw.

It was an easy ride north on horseback. I watched the change from the cottonwood trees along the river to the junipers that brushed past us in the foothills, and finally there were only piñons, and when I looked up at the rim of the mountain plateau I could see pine trees growing on the edge. Once I stopped to look down, but the pale sandstone had disappeared and the river was gone and the dark lava hills were all around. He touched my hand, not speaking, but always singing softly a mountain song and looking into my eyes.

I felt hungry and wondered what they were doing at home now—my mother, my grandmother, my husband, and the baby. Cooking breakfast, saying, "Where did she go?—maybe kidnapped." And Al going to the tribal police with the details: "She went walking along the river."

The house was made with black lava rock and red mud. It was high above the spreading miles of arroyos and long mesas. I smelled a mountain smell of pitch and buck brush. I stood there beside the black horse, looking down on the small, dim country we had passed, and I shivered.

"Yellow Woman, come inside where it's warm."

He lit a fire in the stove. It was an old stove with a round belly and an enamel coffeepot on top. There was only the stove, some faded Navajo blankets, and a bedroll and cardboard box. The floor was made of smooth adobe plaster, and there was one small window facing east. He pointed at the box.

"There's some potatoes and the frying pan." He sat on the floor with his arms around his knees pulling them close to his chest and he watched me fry the potatoes. I didn't mind him watching me because he was always watching me—he had been watching me since I came upon him sitting on the river bank trimming leaves from a willow twig with his knife. We ate from the pan and he wiped the grease from his fingers on his Levi's.

"Have you brought women here before?" He smiled and kept chewing, so I said, "Do you always use the same tricks?"

"What tricks?" He looked at me like he didn't understand.

"The story about being a ka'tsina from the mountains. The story about Yellow Woman."

Silva was silent; his face was calm.

"I don't believe it. Those stories couldn't happen now," I said.

He shook his head and said softly, "But someday they will talk about us, and they will say, 'Those two lived long ago when things like that happened.'"

He stood up and went out. I ate the rest of the potatoes and thought about things—about the noise the stove was making and the sound of the mountain wind outside. I remembered yesterday and the day before, and then I went outside.

I walked past the corral to the edge where the narrow trail cut through the black rim rock. I was standing in the sky with nothing around me but the wind that came down from the blue mountain peak behind me. I could see faint mountain images in the distance miles across the vast spread of mesas and valleys and plains. I wondered who was over there to feel the mountain wind on those sheer blue edges—who walks on the pine needles in those blue mountains.

"Can you see the pueblo?" Silva was standing behind me.

I shook my head. "We're too far away."

"From here I can see the world." He stepped out on the edge. "The Navajo reservation begins over there." He pointed to the east. "The Pueblo boundaries are over here." He looked below us to the south, where the narrow trail seemed to come from. "The Texans have their ranches over there, starting with that valley, the Concho Valley. The Mexicans run some cattle over there too."

"Do you ever work for them?"

"I steal from them," Silva answered. The sun was dropping behind us and the shadows were filling the land below. I turned away from the edge that dropped forever into the valleys below.

"I'm cold," I said, "I'm going inside." I started wondering about this man who could speak the Pueblo language so well but who lived on a mountain and rustled cattle. I decided that this man Silva must be Navajo, because Pueblo men didn't do things like that.

"You must be a Navajo."

Silva shook his head gently. "Little Yellow Woman," he said, "you never give up, do you? I have told you who I am. The Navajo people know me, too." He knelt down and unrolled the bedroll and spread the extra blankets out on a piece of canvas. The sun was down, and the only light in the house came from outside—the dim orange light from sundown.

I stood there and waited for him to crawl under the blankets.

"What are you waiting for?" he said, and I lay down beside him. He undressed me slowly like the night before beside the river—kissing my face gently and running his hands up and down my belly and legs. He took off my pants and then he laughed.

"Why are you laughing?"

"You are breathing so hard."

I pulled away from him and turned my back to him.

He pulled me around and pinned me down with his arms and chest. "You don't understand, do you, little Yellow Woman? You will do what I want."

And again he was all around me with his skin slippery against mine, and I was afraid because I understood that his strength could hurt me. I lay underneath him and I knew that he could destroy me. But later, while he slept beside me, I touched his face and I had a feeling—the kind of feeling for him that overcame me that morning along the river. I kissed him on the forehead and he reached out for me.

When I woke up in the morning he was gone. It gave me a strange feeling because for a long time I sat there on the blankets and looked around the little house for some object of his—some proof that he had been there or maybe that he was coming back. Only the blankets and the cardboard box remained. The .30-30 that had been leaning in the corner was gone, and so was the knife I had used the night before. He was gone, and I had my chance to go now. But first I had to eat, because I knew it would be a long walk home.

I found some dried apricots in the cardboard box, and I sat down on a rock at the edge of the plateau rim. There was no wind and the sun warmed me. I was surrounded by silence. I drowsed with apricots in my mouth, and I didn't believe that there were highways or railroads or cattle to steal.

When I woke up, I stared down at my feet in the black mountain dirt. Little black ants were swarming over the pine needles around my foot. They must have smelled the apricots. I thought about my family far below me. They would be wondering about me, because this had never happened to me before. The tribal police would file a report. But if old Grandpa weren't dead he would tell them what happened—he would laugh and say, "Stolen by a ka'tsina, a mountain spirit. She'll come home—they usually do." There are enough of them to handle things. My mother and grandmother will raise the baby like they raised me. Al will find someone else, and they will go on like before, except that there will be a story about the day I disappeared while I was walking along the river. Silva had come for me; he said he had. I did not decide to go. I just went. Moonflowers blossom in the sand hills before dawn, just as I followed him. That's what I was thinking as I wandered along the trail through the pine trees.

It was noon when I got back. When I saw the stone house I remembered that I had meant to go home. But that didn't seem important any more, maybe because there were little blue flowers growing in the meadow behind the stone house and the gray squirrels were playing in the pines next to the house. The horses were standing in the corral, and there was a beef carcass hanging on the shady side of a big pine in front of the house. Flies buzzed around the clotted blood that hung from the carcass. Silva was washing his hands in a bucket full of water. He must have heard me coming because he spoke to me without turning to face me.

"I've been waiting for you."

"I went walking in the big pine trees."

I looked into the bucket full of bloody water with brown-and-white animal hairs floating in it. Silva stood there letting his hand drip, examining me intently.

"Are you coming with me?"

"Where?" I asked him.

"To sell the meat in Marquez."

"If you're sure it's O.K."

"I wouldn't ask you if it wasn't," he answered.

He sloshed the water around in the bucket before he dumped it out and set the bucket upside down near the door. I followed him to the corral and watched him saddle the horses. Even beside the horses he looked tall, and I asked him again if he wasn't Navajo. He didn't say anything; he just shook his head and kept cinching up the saddle.

"But Navajos are tall."

"Get on the horse," he said, "and let's go."

The last thing he did before we started down the steep trail was to grab the .30-30 from the corner. He slid the rifle into the scabbard that hung from his saddle.

"Do they ever try to catch you?" I asked.

"They don't know who I am."

"Then why did you bring the rifle?"

"Because we are going to Marquez where the Mexicans live."

The trail leveled out on a narrow ridge that was steep on both sides like an animal spine. On one side I could see where the trail went around the rocky gray hills and disappeared into the southeast where the pale sandrock mesas stood in the distance near my home. On the other side was a trail that went west, and as I looked far into the distance I thought I saw the little town. But Silva said no, that I was looking in the wrong place, that I just thought I saw houses. After that I quit looking off into the distance; it was hot and the wildflowers were closing up their deep-yellow petals. Only the waxy cactus flowers bloomed in the bright sun, and I saw every color that a cactus blossom can be; the white ones and the red ones were still buds, but the purple and the yellow were blossoms, open full and the most beautiful of all.

Silva saw him before I did. The white man was riding a big gray horse, coming up the trail towards us. He was traveling fast and the gray horse's feet sent rocks rolling off the trail into the dry tumbleweeds. Silva motioned for me to stop and we watched the white man. He didn't see us right away, but finally his horse whinnied at our horses and he stopped. He looked at us briefly before he lapped the gray horse across the three hundred yards that separated us. He stopped his horse in front of Silva, and his young fat face was shadowed by the brim of his hat. He didn't look mad, but his small, pale eyes moved from the blood-soaked gunny sacks hanging from my saddle to Silva's face and then back to my face.

"Where did you get the fresh meat?" the white man asked.

"I've been hunting," Silva said, and when he shifted his weight in the saddle the leather creaked.

"The hell you have, Indian. You've been rustling cattle. We've been looking for the thief for a long time."

The rancher was fat, and sweat began to soak through his white cowboy shirt and the wet cloth stuck to the thick rolls of belly fat. He almost seemed to be panting from the exertion of talking, and he smelled rancid, maybe because Silva scared him.

Silva turned to me and smiled. "Go back up the mountain, Yellow Woman."

The white man got angry when he heard Silva speak in a language he couldn't understand. "Don't try anything, Indian. Just keep riding to Marquez. We'll call the state police from there."

The rancher must have been unarmed because he was very frightened and if he had a gun he would have pulled it out then. I turned my horse around and the rancher yelled, "Stop!" I looked at Silva for an instant and there was something ancient and dark—something I could feel in my stomach—in his eyes, and when I glanced at his hand I saw his finger on the trigger of the .30-30 that was still in the saddle scabbard. I slapped my horse across the flank and the sacks of raw meat swung against my knees as the horse leaped up the trail. It was hard to keep my balance, and once I thought I felt the saddle slipping backward; it was because of this that I could not look back.

I didn't stop until I reached the ridge where the trail forked. The horse was breathing deep gasps and there was a dark film of sweat on its neck. I looked down in the direction I had come from, but I couldn't see the place. I waited. The wind came up and pushed warm air past me. I looked up at the sky, pale blue and full of thin clouds and fading vapor trails left by jets.

I think four shots were fired—I remember hearing four hollow explosions that reminded me of deer hunting. There could have been more shots after that, but I couldn't have heard them because my horse was running again and the loose rocks were making too much noise as they scattered around his feet.

Horses have a hard time running downhill, but I went that way instead of uphill to the mountain because I thought it was safer. I felt better with the horse running southeast past the round gray hills that were covered with cedar trees and black lava rock. When I got to the plain in the distance I could see the dark green patches of tamaracks that grew along the river; and beyond the river I could see the beginning of the pale sandrock mesas. I stopped the horse and looked back to see if anyone was coming; then I got off the horse and turned the horse around, wondering if it would go back to its corral under the pines on the mountain. It looked back at me for a moment and then plucked a mouthful of green tumbleweeds before it trotted back up the trail with its ears pointed forward, carrying its head daintily to one side to avoid stepping on the dragging reins. When the horse disappeared over the last hill, the gunny sacks full of meat were still swinging and bouncing.

I walked toward the river on a wood-hauler's road that I knew would eventually lead to the paved road. I was thinking about waiting beside the road for someone to drive by, but by the time I got to the pavement I had decided it wasn't very far to walk if I followed the river back the way Silva and I had come.

The river water tasted good, and I sat in the shade under a cluster of silvery willows. I thought about Silva, and I felt sad at leaving him; still, there was something strange about him, and I tried to figure it out all the way back home.

I came back to the place on the river bank where he had been sitting the first time I saw him. The green willow leaves that he had trimmed from the branch were still lying there, wilted in the sand. I saw the leaves and I wanted to go back to him—to kiss him and to touch him—but the mountains were too far away now. And I told myself, because I believe it, he will come back sometime and be waiting again by the river.

I followed the path up from the river into the village. The sun was getting low, and I could smell supper cooking when I got to the screen door of my house. I could hear their voices inside—my mother was telling my grandmother how to fix the Jell-O and my husband, Al, was playing with the baby. I decided to tell them that some Navajo had kidnaped me, but I was sorry that old Grandpa wasn't alive to hear my story because it was the Yellow Woman stories he liked to tell best.

1974

NGUGI WA THIONG'O
born 1938

As the first successful English-language novelist from East Africa, Ngugi Wa Thiong'o made the surprising decision in middle age to stop writing in English. Believing that Africans should use their native tongues, he began writing in Kikuyu, a language spoken by about six million Kenyans (a quarter of the country's population). At the same time, Ngugi's politics became more radical and he turned from the experimental style of his early fiction to a form of socialist realism and satire in his Kikuyu works. Imprisoned for his criticisms of the Kenyan regime in the late 1970s, Ngugi some became a symbol of the resistance of African writers to the abuse of state power.

Born James Ngugi in 1938 in British-ruled Kenya, the author lived as a youth through the Mau Mau uprising, in which the Mau Mau (a primarily Kikuyu group) rebelled against British laws that gave land to white settlers and forced Africans to work the land for little compensation. His stepbrother was killed in the rebellion; his mother was tortured. The uprising lasted for a decade, until 1963, when Kenya gained its independence. By this time, Ngugi had graduated from Makerere University College in Kampala, the capital of Uganda, and had his first play, *The Black Hermit* (1962), produced by the Uganda National Theatre. Like many African authors of his generation, Ngugi found early inspiration in the modern classics of Western literature, including the works of **Joseph Conrad**. For a brief period he became a Christian.

Shortly after Kenyan independence, Ngugi enrolled at the University of Leeds in England, where he completed three novels. While in England, he became interested in the radical theorists Karl Marx and Frantz Fanon; he would later visit the Soviet Union. In 1967 he was appointed the first African faculty member in the English Department of University College, Nairobi, rising to head of the department within a few years. In the 1970s the author decided to leave behind the name James Ngugi and the English language as his primary vehicle for creative expression. His first experiments with writing in Kikuyu began at this time, although he continued to publish some English-language fiction.

A turning point came in 1977, as he released his first novel in a decade, *Petals of Blood*. His last in English and his most explicitly political novel to date, it focused on Marxist analysis of relations among social classes rather than on the nationalist questions that had concerned the author earlier. In the same year, a play in Kikuyu, *I Will Marry When I Want*, had great success with its criticism of capitalism and Christianity. Its indirect attacks on government policies drew the attention of Daniel arap Moi, then vice president, who ordered Ngugi detained. He was imprisoned for almost a year; during this time Moi became president of Kenya, and when Ngugi was released, he was refused employment as a professor and eventually reimprisoned. His time in confinement led to his being declared a Prisoner of Conscience by Amnesty International; in 1978 an open letter calling for his release was published, signed by many Western authors. While in prison, Ngugi composed the first full-length novel written in Kikuyu, *Devil on the Cross* (1980), using prison toilet paper as stationery.

Shortly after his release, he left Kenya to live in London, and did not return until 2004, after Moi's departure from office.

Ngugi has continued his career as a novelist and a playwright, a journalist and a teacher, and an essayist and a postcolonial theorist. He has argued for the importance of writing in native languages rather than in English and has maintained his Socialist ideological commitments, although he currently lives in the United States, where he is a professor of English and Comparative Literature at the University of California, Irvine.

Like **Chinua Achebe**, Ngugi explores the disastrous consequences for Africans of contact with the British. In the English-language work from the earliest years of his career, Ngugi wrote historical fiction about colonial rule in Kenya. By the middle years of his career, he turned his eye to independent Kenya and his writings became increasingly satirical and critical of Kenyan society and government. In the story included here, "Wedding at the Cross" (1975), Ngugi shows the effects of the previous decades of Kenyan history on a particular married couple and thus chronicles the compromises made by the Westernized middle classes in the pursuit of prosperity. He said of the collection in which it appears, *Secret Lives* (1975), his only collection of stories in English, that it contained his "creative autobiography over the last twelve years," that is, the years since independence.

Christianity plays an ambiguous role in Ngugi's works. On the one hand, it is an antimaterialist religion that exalts the poor; on the other hand, it is the religion of the colonizers and thus potentially a vehicle for social advancement. The story begins with the rebellious and charismatic Wariuki seeking to marry Miriamu, the daughter of a wealthy grocer in the years of colonial rule. Miriamu's father, a Christian who gets along well with the British authorities, opposes the match because of Wariuki's poverty. The young couple elopes, and the initial tone of the story is positive, even romantic. As the narrator relates the history of their marriage, however, it becomes clear that Wariuki's personality has suffered from his rejection by Miriamu's father. He fights for the British during the Second World War, becomes a Christian, and takes an English name, but even as he gains in prosperity, his resentment of Miriamu's father remains. As independence comes and Wariuki benefits from the discriminatory policies of the Kenyan government against his employers (South Asian Kenyans who were expelled from the country in the late 1960s), Miriamu discovers a more authentic, but unofficial, Christianity, the Religion of Sorrows. The conflict between their two views of Christianity leads to the crisis of "Wedding at the Cross." Ngugi's subtle rendering of the tensions between official Christianity and popular religion adds depth to his memorable portrayal of postcolonial African society.

Wedding at the Cross

Everyone said of them: what a nice family; he, the successful timber merchant; and she, the obedient wife who did her duty to God, husband and family. Wariuki and his wife Miriamu were a shining example of what cooperation between man and wife united in love and devotion could achieve: he tall, correct, even a little stiff, but wealthy; she, small, quiet, unobtrusive, a diminishing shadow beside her giant of a husband.

He had married her when he was without a cent buried anywhere, not even for the rainiest day, for he was then only a milk clerk in a settler farm earning thirty shillings a month—a fortune in those days, true, but drinking most of it by the first of the next month. He was young; he did not care; dreams of material possessions and power little troubled him. Of course he joined the other workers in collective protests and demands, he would even compose letters for them; from one or two farms he had been dismissed as a dangerous and subversive character. But his heart was really elsewhere, in his favourite sports and acts. He would proudly ride his Raleigh Bicycle[1] around, whistling certain lines from old records remembered, yodelling in imitation of Jim Rogers,[2] and occasionally demonstrating his skill on the machine to an enthusiastic audience in Molo township. He would stand on the bicycle balancing with the left leg, arms stretched about to fly, or he would simply pedal backwards to the delight of many children. It was an old machine, but decorated in loud colours of red, green and blue with several Wariuki home-manufactured headlamps and reflectors and with a warning scrawled on a signboard mounted at the back seat: Overtake Me, Graveyard Ahead. From a conjurer on a bicycle, he would move to other roles. See the actor now mimicking his white bosses, satirizing their way of talking and walking and also their mannerisms and attitudes to black workers. Even those Africans who sought favours from the whites were not spared. He would vary his acts with dancing, good dancer too, and his mwomboko steps, with the left trouser leg deliberately split along the seam to an inch above the knee, always attracted approving eyes and sighs from maids in the crowd.

That's how he first captured Miriamu's heart.

On every Sunday afternoon she would seize any opportunity to go to the shopping square where she would eagerly join the host of worshippers. Her heart would then rise and fall with his triumphs and narrow escapes, or simply pound in rhythm with his dancing hips. Miriamu's family was miles better off than most squatters in the Rift Valley. Her father, Douglas Jones, owned several groceries and tea-rooms around the town. A God-fearing couple he and his wife were: they went to church on Sundays, they said their prayers first thing in the morning, last thing in the evening and of course before every meal. They were looked on with favour by the white farmers around; the District Officer would often stop by for a casual greeting. Theirs then was a good Christian home and hence they objected to their daughter marrying into sin, misery and poverty: what could she possibly see in that Murebi, Murebi bii-u? They told her not to attend those heathen Sunday scenes of idleness and idol worship. But Miriamu had an independent spirit, though it had since childhood been schooled into inactivity by Sunday sermons—thou shalt obey thy father and mother and those that rule over us—and a proper upbringing with rules straight out of the Rt. Reverend Clive Schomberg's classic: *British Manners for Africans*.[3] Now Wariuki with his Raleigh bicycle, his milkman's tunes, his baggy trousers and dance which gave freedom to the body, was the light that beckoned her from the sterile world of Douglas Jones to a neon-lit city in a far

---

1. A British make of bicycle.
2. American country singer Jimmie Rodgers (1897–1933), known for his yodeling.

3. A work encouraging Africans to imitate a British lifestyle.

horizon. Part of her was suspicious of the heavy glow, she was even slightly revolted by his dirt and patched up trousers, but she followed him, and was surprised at her firmness. Douglas Jones relented a little: he loved his daughter and only desired the best for her. He did not want her to marry one of those useless half-educated upstarts, who disturbed the ordered life, peace and prosperity on European farms. Such men, as the Bwana District Officer[4] often told him, would only end in jails: they were motivated by greed and wanted to cheat the simple-hearted and illiterate workers about the evils of white settlers and missionaries. Wariuki looked the dangerous type in every way.

He summoned Wariuki, 'Our would-be-son-in-law', to his presence. He wanted to find the young man's true weight in silver and gold. And Wariuki, with knees weakened a little, for he, like most workers, was a little awed by men of that Christian and propertied class, carefully mended his left trouser leg, combed and brushed his hair and went there. They made him stand at the door, without offering him a chair, and surveyed him up and down. Wariuki, bewildered, looked alternately to Miriamu and to the wall for possible deliverance. And then when he finally got a chair, he would not look at the parents and the dignitaries invited to sit in judgement but fixed his eyes to the wall. But he was aware of their naked gaze and condemnation. Douglas Jones, though, was a model of Christian graciousness: tea for our—well—our son—well—this young man here. What work? Milk clerk? Ahh, well, well—no man was born with wealth—wealth was in the limbs you know and you, you are so young—salary? Thirty shillings a month?[5] Well, well, others had climbed up from worse and deeper pits: true wealth came from the Lord on high, you know. And Wariuki was truly grateful for these words and even dared a glance and a smile at old Douglas Jones. What he saw in those eyes made him quickly turn to the wall and wait for the execution. The manner of the execution was not rough: but the cold steel cut deep and clean. Why did Wariuki want to marry when he was so young? Well, well, as you like—the youth today—so different from our time. And who 'are we' to tell what youth ought to do? We do not object to the wedding: but we as Christians have a responsibility. I say it again: we do not object to this union. But it must take place at the cross. A church wedding, Wariuki, costs money. Maintaining a wife also costs money. Is that not so? You nod your head? Good. It is nice to see a young man with sense these days. All that I now want, and that is why I have called in my counsellor friends, is to see your savings account. Young man, can you show these elders your post office book?

Wariuki was crushed. He now looked at the bemused eyes of the elders present. He then fixed them on Miriamu's mother, as if in appeal. Only he was not seeing her. Away from the teats and rich udder of the cows, away from his bicycle and the crowd of rich admirers, away from the anonymous security of bars and tea-shops, he did not know how to act. He was a hunted animal, now cornered: and the hunters, panting with anticipation, were enjoying every moment of that kill. A buzz in his head, a blurring vision, and he heard the still gracious voice of Douglas Jones trailing into something about not signing his daughter to a life of misery and drudgery. Desperately Wariuki looked to the door and to the open space.

---

4. Highest-ranking British officer in a locality.
5. About $5 in the period of the story, or around $60 today.

Escape at last: and he breathed with relief. Although he was trembling a little, he was glad to be in a familiar world, his own world. But he looked at it slightly differently, almost as if he had been wounded and could not any more enjoy what he saw. Miriamu followed him there: for a moment he felt a temporary victory over Douglas Jones. They ran away and he got a job with Ciana Timber Merchants in Ilmorog forest. The two lived in a shack of a room to which he escaped from the daily curses of his Indian[6] employers. Wariuki learnt how to endure the insults. He sang with the movement of the saw: kneeling down under the log, the other man standing on it, he would make up words and stories about the log and the forest, sometimes ending on a tragic note when he came to the fatal marriage between the saw and the forest. This somehow would lighten his heart so that he did not mind the falling saw-dust. Came his turn to stand on top of the log and he would experience a malicious power as he sawed through it, gingerly walking backwards step by step and now singing of Demi na Mathathi[7] who, long ago, cleared woods and forests more dense than Ilmorog.

And Miriamu the erstwhile daughter of Douglas Jones would hear his voice rising above the whispering or uproarious wind and her heart rose and fell with it. This, this, dear Lord, was so different from the mournful church hymns of her father's compound, so, so, different and she felt good inside. On Saturdays and Sundays he took her to dances in the wood. On their way home from the dances and the songs, they would look for a suitable spot on the grass and make love. For Miriamu these were nights of happiness and wonder as the thorny pine leaves painfully but pleasantly pricked her buttocks even as she moaned under him, calling out to her mother and imaginary sisters for help when he plunged into her.

And Wariuki too was happy. It always seemed to him a miracle that he, a boy from the streets and without a father (he had died while carrying guns and food for the British in their expeditions against the Germans in Tanganyika[8] in the first European World War), had secured the affections of a girl from that class. But he was never the old Wariuki. Often he would go over his life beginning with his work picking pyrethrum[9] flowers for others under a scorching sun or icy cold winds in Limuru, to his recent job as a milk clerk in Molo:[1] his reminiscences would abruptly end with that interview with Douglas Jones and his counsellors. He would never forget that interview: he was never to forget the cackling throaty laughter as Douglas Jones and his friends tried to diminish his manhood and selfworth in front of Miriamu and her mother.

Never. He would show them. He would yet laugh in their faces.

But soon a restless note crept into his singing: bitterness of an unfulfilled hope and promise. His voice became rugged like the voice-teeth of the saw and he tore through the air with the same greedy malice. He gave up his job with the Ciana Merchants and took Miriamu all the way to Limuru. He dumped Miriamu with his aged mother and he disappeared from their lives. They heard of him in Nairobi, Mombasa, Nakuru, Kisumu and even Kampala.[2] Rumours

6. Indians often worked in Africa as merchants.
7. Mythical Kikuyu (Kenyan) giants.
8. Modern Tanzania, south of Kenya.
9. A relative of the chrysanthemum.

1. A town in western Kenya; Limuru is a town in central Kenya.
2. The capital of Uganda; the other towns listed are in various regions of Kenya.

reached them: that he was in prison, that he had even married a Muganda girl.[3] Miriamu waited: she remembered her moments of pained pleasure under Ilmorog woods, ferns and grass and endured the empty bed and the bite of Limuru cold in June and July. Her parents had disowned her and anyway she would not want to go back. The seedling he had planted in her warmed her. Eventually the child arrived and this together with the simple friendship of her mother-in-law consoled her. Came more rumours: whitemen were gathering arms for a war amongst themselves, and black men, sons of the soil, were being drafted to aid in the slaughter. Could this be true? Then Wariuki returned from his travels and she noticed the change in her man. He was now of few words: where was the singing and the whistling of old tunes remembered? He stayed a week. Then he said: I am going to war. Miriamu could not understand: why this change? Why this wanderlust[4]? But she waited and worked on the land.

Wariuki had the one obsession: to erase the memory of that interview, to lay for ever the ghost of those contemptuous eyes. He fought in Egypt, Palestine, Burma and in Madagascar.[5] He did not think much about the war, he did not question what it meant for black people, he just wanted it to end quickly so that he might resume his quest. Why, he might even go home with a little loot from the war. This would give him the start in life he had looked for, without success, in towns all over Colonial Kenya. A lucrative job even: the British had promised them jobs and money-rewards once the wicked Germans were routed. After the war he was back in Limuru, a little emaciated in body but hardened in resolve.

For a few weeks after his return, Miriamu detected a little flicker of the old fires and held him close to herself. He made a few jokes about the war, and sang a few soldiers' songs to his son. He made love to her and another seed was planted. He again tried to get a job. He heard of a workers' strike in a Limuru shoe factory. All the workers were summarily dismissed. Wariuki and others flooded the gates to offer their sweat for silver. The striking workers tried to picket the new hands, whom they branded traitors to the cause, but helmeted police were called to the scene, baton charged the old workers away from the fenced compound and escorted the new ones into the factory. But Wariuki was not among them. Was he born into bad luck? He was back in the streets of Nairobi joining the crowd of the unemployed recently returned from the War. No jobs no money-rewards: the 'good' British and the 'wicked' Germans were shaking hands with smiles. But questions as to why black people were not employed did not trouble him: when young men gathered in Pumwani, Kariokor, Shauri Moyo[6] and other places to ask questions he did not join them: they reminded him of his old association and flirtation with farm workers before the war: those efforts had come to nought: even these ones would come to nought: he was in any case ashamed of that past: he thought that if he had been less of a loafer and more enterprising he would never have been so humiliated in front of Miriamu and her mother. The young men's talk of processions, petitions and pistols, their talk of gunning the whites out of the country,

3. From a Ugandan ethnic group.
4. Desire for travel (German).
5. Theaters of action in the Second World

War (1939–45).
6. Neighborhoods of Nairobi, Kenya.

seemed too remote from his ambition and quest. He had to strike out on his own for moneyland. On arrival, he would turn round and confront old Douglas Jones and contemptuously flaunt success before his face. With the years the memory of that humiliation in the hands of the rich became so sharp and fresh that it often hurt him into sleepless nights. He did not think of the whites and the Indians as the real owners of property, commerce and land. He only saw the picture of Douglas Jones in his grey woollen suit, his waistcoat, his hat and his walking stick of a folded umbrella. What was the secret of that man's success? What? What? He attempted odd jobs here and there: he even tried his hand at trading in the hawk market at Bahati.[7] He would buy pencils and handkerchiefs from the Indian Bazaar and sell them at a retail price that ensured him a bit of profit. Was this his true vocation?

But before he could find an answer to his question, the Mau Mau war of national liberation broke out. A lot of workers, employed and unemployed, were swept off the streets of Nairobi into concentration camps. Somehow he escaped the net and was once again back in Limuru. He was angry. Not with the whites, not with the Indians, all of whom he saw as permanent features of the land like the mountains and the valleys, but with his own people. Why should they upset the peace? Why should they upset the stability just when he had started gathering a few cents from his trade? He now believed, albeit without much conviction, the lies told by the British about imminent prosperity and widening opportunities for blacks. For about a year he remained aloof from the turmoil around: he was only committed to his one consuming passion. Then he drifted into the hands of the colonial regime and cooperated. This way he avoided concentration camps and the forest. Soon his choice of sides started bearing fruit: he was excited about the prospects for its ripening. While other people's strips of land were being taken by the colonialists, his piece, although small, was left intact. In fact, during land consolidation forced on women and old men while their husbands and sons were decaying in detention or resisting in the forest, he, along with other active collaborators, secured additional land. Wariuki was not a cruel man: he just wanted this nightmare over so that he might resume his trade. For even in the midst of battle the image of D. Jones never really left him: the humiliation ached: he nursed it like one nurses a toothache with one's tongue, and felt that a day would come when he would stand up to that image.

Jomo Kenyatta[8] returned home from Maralal. Wariuki was a little frightened, his spirits were dampened: what would happen to his kind at the gathering of the braves to celebrate victory? Alas, where were the Whites he had thought of as permanent features of the landscape? But with independence approaching, Wariuki had his first real reward: the retreating colonialists gave him a loan: he bought a motor-propelled saw and set up as a Timber Merchant.

For a time after Independence, Wariuki feared for his life and business as the sons of the soil streamed back from detention camps and from the forests: he expected a retribution, but people were tired. They had no room in their hearts for vengeance at the victorious end of a just struggle. So Wariuki

---

7. A neighborhood in Nairobi.
8. Leader of the independence movement and later prime minister and president of Kenya (ca. 1894–1978).

prospered undisturbed: he had, after all, a fair start over those who had really fought for Uhuru.[9]

He joined the Church in gratitude. The Lord had spared him: he dragged Miriamu into it, and together they became exemplary Church-goers.

But Miriamu prayed a different prayer, she wanted her man back. Her two sons were struggling their way through Siriana Secondary School. For this she thanked the Lord. But she still wanted her real Wariuki back. During the Emergency[1] she had often cautioned him against excessive cruelty. It pained her that his singing, his dancing and his easy laughter had ended. His eyes were hard and set and this frightened her.

Now in Church he started singing again. Not the tunes that had once captured her soul, but the mournful hymns she knew so well; how sweet the name of Jesus sounds in a believer's ears. He became a pillar of the Church Choir. He often beat the drum which, after Independence, had been introduced into the church as a concession to African culture. He attended classes in baptism and great was the day he cast away Wariuki and became Dodge W. Livingstone, Jr. Thereafter he sat in the front bench. As his business improved, he gradually worked his way to the holy aisle. A new Church elder.

Other things brightened. His parents-in-law still lived in Molo, though their fortunes had declined. They had not yet forgiven him. But with his eminence, they sent out feelers: would their daughter pay them a visit? Miriamu would not hear of it. But Dodge W. Livingstone was furious: where was her Christian forgiveness? He was insistent. She gave in. He was glad. But that gesture, by itself, could not erase the memory of his humiliation. His vengeance would still come.

Though his base was at Limuru, he travelled to various parts of the country. So he got to know news concerning his line of business. It was the year of the Asian exodus.[2] Ciana Merchants were not Kenya Citizens. Their licence would be withdrawn. They quickly offered Livingstone partnership on a fifty-fifty share basis. Praise the Lord and raise high his name. Truly God never ate Ugali.[3] Within a year he had accumulated enough to qualify for a loan to buy one of the huge farms in Limuru previously owned by whites. He was now a big timber merchant: they made him a senior elder of the church.

Miriamu still waited for her Wariuki in vain. But she was a model wife. People praised her Christian and wifely meekness. She was devout in her own way and prayed to the Lord to rescue her from the dreams of the past. She never put on airs. She even refused to wear shoes. Every morning, she would wake early, take her Kiondo, and go to the farm where she would work in the tea estate alongside the workers. And she never forgot her old strip of land in the Old Reserve. Sometimes she made lunch and tea for the workers. This infuriated her husband: why, oh why did she choose to humiliate him before these people? Why would she not conduct herself like a Christian lady? After all, had she not come from a Christian home? Need she dirty her hands now, he asked her, and with labourers too? On clothes, she gave in: she put on shoes

9. Independence (Swahili).
1. State of emergency during the anticolonial Mau Mau uprising of the 1950s.
2. In 1968–69, under pressure from a nation-
alist Kenyan government, South Asian residents of Kenya fled the country.
3. A type of porridge.

and a white hat especially when going to Church. But work was in her bones and this she would not surrender. She enjoyed the touch of the soil: she enjoyed the free and open conversation with the workers.

They liked her. But they resented her husband. Livingstone thought them a lazy lot: why would they not work as hard as he himself had done? Which employer's wife had ever brought him food in a shamba[4]? Miriamu was spoiling them and he told her so. Occasionally he would look at their sullen faces: he would then remember the days of the Emergency or earlier when he received insults from Ciana employers. But gradually he learnt to silence these unsettling moments in prayer and devotion. He was aware of their silent hatred but thought this a natural envy of the idle and the poor for the rich.

Their faces brightened only in Miriamu's presence. They would abandon their guarded selves and joke and laugh and sing. They gradually let her into their inner lives. They were members of a secret sect that believed that Christ suffered and died for the poor. They called theirs *The Religion of Sorrows*.[5] When her husband was on his business tours, she would attend some of their services. A strange band of men and women: they sang songs they themselves had created and used drums, guitars, jingles and tambourines, producing a throbbing powerful rhythm that made her want to dance with happiness. Indeed they themselves danced around, waving hands in the air, their faces radiating warmth and assurance, until they reached a state of possession and heightened awareness. Then they would speak in tongues strange and beautiful. They seemed united in a common labour and faith: this was what most impressed Miriamu. Something would stir in her, some dormant wings would beat with power inside her, and she would go home trembling in expectation. She would wait for her husband and she felt sure that together they could rescue something from a shattered past. But when he came back from his tours, he was still Dodge W. Livingstone, Jr., senior church elder, and a prosperous farmer and timber merchant. She once more became the model wife listening to her husband as he talked business and arithmetic for the day: what contracts he had won, what money he had won and lost, and tomorrow's prospects. On Sunday man and wife would go to church as usual: same joyless hymns, same prayers from set books; same regular visits to brothers and sisters in Christ; the inevitable tea-parties and charity auctions to which Livingstone was a conspicuous contributor. What a nice family everyone said in admiration and respect: he, the successful farmer and timber merchant; and she, the obedient wife who did her duty to God and husband.

One day he came home early. His face was bright—not wrinkled with the usual cares and worries. His eyes beamed with pleasure. Miriamu's heart gave a gentle leap, could this be true? Was the warrior back? She could see him trying to suppress his excitement. But the next moment her heart fell again. He had said it. His father-in-law, Douglas Jones, had invited him, had begged him to visit them at Molo. He whipped out the letter and started reading it aloud. Then he knelt down and praised the Lord, for his mercy and tender understanding. Miriamu could hardly join in the Amen. Lord, Lord, what has hardened my heart so, she prayed and sincerely desired to see the light.

---

4. Vegetable garden (Kikuyu).
5. Christianity has frequently been called a "religion of sorrow" because of its emphasis on sin and suffering (although it also emphasizes redemption).

The day of reunion drew near. His knees were becoming weak. He could not hide his triumph. He reviewed his life and saw in it the guiding finger of God. He the boy from the gutter, a mere milk clerk . . . but he did not want to recall the ridiculous young man who wore patched-up trousers and clowned on a bicycle. Could that have been he, making himself the laughing stock of the whole town? He went to Benbros and secured a new Mercedes Benz 220S. This would make people look at him differently. On the day in question, he himself wore a worsted woollen suit, a waistcoat, and carried a folded umbrella. He talked Miriamu into going in an appropriate dress bought from Nairobi Drapers in Government Road.[6] His own mother had been surprised into a frock and shoe-wearing lady. His two sons in their school uniform spoke nothing but English. (They affected to find it difficult speaking Kikuyu,[7] they made so many mistakes.) A nice family, and they drove to Molo. The old man met them. He had aged, with silver hair covering his head, but he was still strong in body. Jones fell on his knees; Livingstone fell on his knees. They prayed and then embraced in tears. Our son, our son. And my grandchildren too. The past was drowned in tears and prayers. But for Miriamu, the past was vivid in the mind.

Livingstone, after the initial jubilations, found that the memories of that interview rankled a little. Not that he was angry with Jones: the old man had been right, of course. He could not imagine himself giving his own daughter to such a ragamuffin of an upstart clerk. Still he wanted that interview erased from memory forever. And suddenly, and again he saw in that revelation the hand of God, he knew the answer. He trembled a little. Why had he not thought of it earlier? He had a long intimate conversation with his father-in-law and then made the proposal. Wedding at the cross. A renewal of the old. Douglas Jones immediately consented. His son had become a true believer. But Miriamu could not see any sense in the scheme. She was ageing. And the Lord had blessed her with two sons. Where was the sin in that? Again they all fell on her. A proper wedding at the cross of Jesus would make their lives complete. Her resistance was broken. They all praised the Lord. God worked in mysterious ways, his wonders to perform.[8]

The few weeks before the eventful day were the happiest in the life of Livingstone. He savoured every second. Even anxieties and difficulties gave him pleasure. That this day would come: a wedding at the cross. A wedding at the cross, at the cross where he had found the Lord. He was young again. He bounced in health and a sense of well-being. The day he would exchange rings at the cross would erase unsettling memories of yesterday. Cards were printed and immediately despatched. Cars and buses were lined up. He dragged Miriamu to Nairobi. They went from shop to shop all over the city: Kenyatta Avenue, Muindi Bingu Streets, Bazaar, Government Road, Kimathi Street, and back again to Kenyatta Avenue. Eventually he bought her a snow-white long-sleeved satin dress, a veil, white gloves, white shoes and stockings and of course plastic roses. He consulted Rev. Clive Schomberg's still modern classic on good manners for Africans and he hardly departed from the rules and instructions in the matrimonial section. Dodge W. Livingstone, Jr. did not want to make a mistake.

6. An expensive commercial area in Nairobi.
7. The language of the Kikuyu ethnic group, to which Ngugi belongs.

8. Paraphrase of a hymn by William Cowper (1731–1800), "Light Shining Out of Darkness."

Miriamu did not send or give invitation cards to anybody. She daily prayed that God would give her the strength to go through the whole affair. She wished that the day would come and vanish as in a dream. A week before the day, she was driven all the way back to her parents. She was a mother of two; she was no longer the young girl who once eloped; she simply felt ridiculous pretending that she was a virgin maid at her father's house. But she submitted almost as if she were driven by a power stronger than man. Maybe she was wrong, she thought. Maybe everybody else was right. Why then should she ruin the happiness of many? For even the church was very happy. He, a successful timber merchant, would set a good example to others. And many women had come to congratulate her on her present luck in such a husband. They wanted to share in her happiness. Some wept.

The day itself was bright. She could see some of the rolling fields in Molo: the view brought painful memories of her childhood. She tried to be cheerful. But attempts at smiling only brought out tears: What of the years of waiting? What of the years of hope? Her face-wrinkled father was a sight to see: a dark suit with tails, a waist jacket, top hat and all. She inclined her head to one side, in shame. She prayed for yet more strength: she hardly recognized anybody as she was led towards the holy aisle. Not even her fellow workers, members of the *Religion of Sorrows*, who waited in a group among the crowd outside.

But for Livingstone this was the supreme moment. Sweeter than vengeance. All his life he had slaved for this hour. Now it had come. He had specially dressed for the occasion: a dark suit, tails, top hat and a beaming smile at any dignitary he happened to recognize, mostly MPs,[9] priests and businessmen. The church, Livingstone had time to note, was packed with very important people. Workers and not so important people sat outside. Members of the *Religion of Sorrows* wore red wine-coloured dresses and had with them their guitars, drums and tambourines. The bridegroom as he passed gave them a rather sharp glance. But only for a second. He was really happy.

Miriamu now stood before the cross: her head was hidden in the white veil. Her heart pounded. She saw in her mind's eye a grandmother pretending to be a bride with a retinue of aged bridesmaids. The Charade. The Charade. And she thought: there were ten virgins when the bridegroom came. And five of them were wise—and five of them were foolish—Lord, Lord that this cup would soon be over—over me, and before I be a slave . . .[1] and the priest was saying: 'Dodge W. Livingstone, Jr., do you accept this woman for a wife in sickness and health until death do you part?' Livingstone's answer was a clear and loud yes. It was now her turn; . . . Lord that this cup . . . this cup . . . over meeeee. . . . 'Do you Miriamu accept this man for a husband. . . . She tried to answer. Saliva blocked her throat . . . five virgins . . . five virgins . . . came bridegroom . . . groom . . . and the Church was now silent in fearful expectation.

Suddenly, from outside the Church, the silence was broken. People turned their eyes to the door. But the adherents of the *Religion of Sorrows* seemed unaware of the consternation on people's faces. Maybe they thought the ceremony was over. Maybe they were seized by the spirit. They beat their drums,

9. Members of Parliament.
1. Miriamu is thinking of the parable of the wise and foolish virgins in Matthew 25; the foolish virgins seek oil to light their lamps and thus miss the opportunity to meet the bridegroom.

they beat their tambourines, they plucked their guitars all in a jazzy bouncing unison. Church stewards rushed out to stop them, ssh, ssh, the wedding ceremony was not yet over—but they were way beyond hearing. Their voices and faces were raised to the sky, their feet were rocking the earth.

For the first time Miriamu raised her head. She remembered vaguely that she had not even invited her friends. How had they come to Molo? A spasm of guilt. But only for a time. It did not matter. Not now. The vision had come back . . . At the cross, at the cross where I found the Lord . . . she saw Wariuki standing before her even as he used to be in Molo. He rode a bicycle: he was playing his tricks before a huge crowd of respectful worshippers . . . At the cross, at the cross where I found the Lord . . . he was doing it for her . . . he had singled only her out of the thrilling throng . . . of this she was certain . . . came the dancing and she was even more certain of his love . . . He was doing it for her. Lord, I have been loved once . . . once . . . I have been loved, Lord . . . And those moments in Ilmorog forest and woods were part of her: what a moaning, oh, Lord what a moaning . . . and the drums and the tambourines were now moaning in her dancing heart. She was truly Miriamu. She felt so powerful and strong and raised her head even more proudly; . . . and the priest was almost shouting: 'Do you Miriamu . . .' The crowd waited. She looked at Livingstone, she looked at her father, and she could not see any difference between them. Her voice came in a loud whisper: 'No.'

A current went right through the church. Had they heard the correct answer? And the priest was almost hysterical: 'Do you Miriamu . . .' Again the silence made even more silent by the singing outside. She lifted the veil and held the audience with her eyes. 'No, I cannot . . . I cannot marry Livingstone . . . because . . . because . . . I have been married before. I am married to . . . to . . . Wariuki . . . and he is dead.'

Livingstone became truly a stone. Her father wept. Her mother wept. They all thought her a little crazed. And they blamed the whole thing on these breakaway churches that really worshipped the devil. No properly trained priest, etc. . . . etc. . . . And the men and women outside went on singing and dancing to the beat of drums and tambourines, their faces and voices raised to the sky.

1975

BESSIE HEAD

1937–1986

Bessie Head's works combine myth, legend, and oral tradition with realistic detail to portray the struggles of newly liberated southern Africa. Drawing on folktales, she relates them to modern African life to create a picture of contemporary society that is at once convincing and dreamlike. While suffering from mental illness and the effects of political oppression, Head managed to give voice in her writings to the people of Africa.

Born to a single mother in a South African mental asylum, Bessie Amelia Emery was adopted at birth by Nellie and George Heathcote. She grew up thinking of the Heathcotes as her parents and learned only as a teenager that she had a black father and a white mother; her mother had a history of mental illness and had been committed to the asylum when she became pregnant with a servant's child. The apartheid system of racial classification was formalized during her youth, and her adoptive parents were considered "colored" (that is, mixed race). Educated at St. Monica's Home, an Anglican mission school for colored girls, Head later taught at Clairwood Colored School. There, inspired by the teachings and writings of Mahatma Gandhi, Head developed an interest in Hinduism. "Never have I read anything that aroused my feelings like Gandhi's political statements," she later wrote. "There was a simple and astonishing clarity in the way he summarized political truths, there was an appalling tenderness and firmness in the man. I paused every now and then over his paper, almost swooning with worship because I recognized that this could

only be God as man." She later worked as a court reporter in Cape Town, where she became interested in the Négritude and Pan-Africanist movements and began writing stories about social injustice. In 1960 she started a newspaper, *The Citizen*, focused on the injustices of apartheid. After marrying a fellow journalist, Harold Head, she moved to Serowe, Botswana, taking her infant son with her but leaving her husband behind in South Africa.

In Botswana, which had recently gained its independence from Britain, Head taught high school and continued writing fiction, receiving favorable reviews internationally for her first novel, *When the Rain Clouds Gather* (1969), which concerns a South African political prisoner who flees to Botswana. Around this time, Head began to suffer symptoms of bipolar disorder and schizophrenia. After denouncing the president of Botswana, Seretse Khama, as an assassin, Head was arrested by the police and confined in Lobatse Mental Hospital. As she recovered, she continued to write and in 1977 attended the University of Iowa's International Writing Program. In the next several years, she published a collection of short stories, two novels, an oral history of the village of Serowe, and *A Question of Power* (1974), a combination of fiction, autobiography, and political statement. These works often take up themes of cultural conflict similar to those in the works of her contemporary **Chinua Achebe**. Head traveled frequently to writers' conferences around the world, but after her estranged husband filed for divorce, she began to drink heavily, slipped into a coma, and died at age forty-eight. In one of her last published essays, "Why Do I

Write?" she explained: "I am building a stairway to the stars. I have the authority to take the whole of mankind up there with me. That is why I write."

Head's works, many of which are set in Botswana, depict in realistic detail the lives of the downtrodden. They also have a mythic element. In "The Deep River: A Story of Ancient Tribal Migration," presented here, a traditional tale about the origins of a Botswanan ethnic group inspires a meditation on the conflicts between an imagined communal past and the pull of modern individuality, between a mythic origin in the "deep river" of the people, when individuals

had no identity apart from the group, and a present defined by the sense of self and by notions of romantic love. Although Head narrates the story in a manner sympathetic to the claims of the individual, she laments the passing of what she sees as the unified traditional society. Similarly, while she quotes the opinions of old men about the events in the story, she attends to the concerns of the youngest wife, Rankwana. It is in the balance of these sympathies that Head manages to retell the old tale for a contemporary audience, both celebrating traditional culture and acknowledging its limitations.

The Deep River: A Story of Ancient Tribal Migration

Long ago, when the land was only cattle tracks and footpaths, the people lived together like a deep river. In this deep river which was unruffled by conflict or a movement forward, the people lived without faces, except for their chief, whose face was the face of all the people; that is, if their chief's name was Monemapee, then they were all the people of Monemapee. The Talaote tribe have forgotten their origins and their original language during their journey southwards—they have merged and remerged again with many other tribes—and the name, Talaote,[1] is all they have retained in memory of their history. Before a conflict ruffled their deep river, they were all the people of Monemapee, whose kingdom was somewhere in the central part of Africa.

They remembered that Monemapee ruled the tribe for many years as the hairs on his head were already saying white! by the time he died. On either side of the deep river there might be hostile tribes or great dangers, so all the people lived in one great town. The lands where they ploughed their crops were always near the town. That was done by all the tribes for their own protection, and their day-to-day lives granted them no individual faces either for they ploughed their crops, reared their children, and held their festivities according to the laws of the land.

Although the people were given their own ploughing lands, they had no authority to plough them without the chief's order. When the people left home to go to plough, the chief sent out the proclamation for the beginning of the ploughing season. When harvest time came, the chief perceived that the corn was ripe. He gathered the people together and said:

'Reap now, and come home.'

When the people brought home their crops, the chief called the thanksgiving for the harvest. Then the women of the whole town carried their corn in flat baskets, to the chief's place. Some of that corn was accepted on its arrival, but the rest was returned so that the women might soak it in their own yards. After

1. An ethnic group in central Botswana, originally from Zimbabwe.

a few days, the chief sent his special messenger to proclaim that the harvest thanksgiving corn was to be pounded. The special messenger went around the whole town and in each place where there was a little hill or mound, he climbed it and shouted:

'Listen, the corn is to be pounded!'

So the people took their sprouting corn and pounded it. After some days the special messenger came back and called out:

'The corn is to be fermented now!'

A few days passed and then he called out:

'The corn is to be cooked now!'

So throughout the whole town the beer was boiled and when it had been strained, the special messenger called out for the last time:

'The beer is to be brought now!'

On the day on which thanksgiving was to be held, the women all followed one another in single file to the chief's place. Large vessels had been prepared at the chief's place, so that when the women came they poured the beer into them. Then there was a gathering of all the people to celebrate thanksgiving for the harvest time. All the people lived this way, like one face, under their chief. They accepted this regimental levelling down of their individual souls, but on the day of dispute or when strife and conflict and greed blew stormy winds over their deep river, the people awoke and showed their individual faces.

Now, during his lifetime Monemapee had had three wives. Of these marriages he had four sons: Sebembele by the senior wife; Ntema and Mosemme by the second junior wife; and Kgagodi by the third junior wife. There was a fifth son, Makobi, a small baby who was still suckling at his mother's breast by the time the old chief, Monemapee, died. This mother was the third junior wife, Rankwana. It was about the fifth son, Makobi, that the dispute arose. There was a secret there. Monemapee had married the third junior wife, Rankwana, late in his years. She was young and beautiful and Sebembele, the senior son, fell in love with her—but in secret. On the death of Monemapee, Sebembele, as senior son, was installed chief of the tribe and immediately made a blunder. He claimed Rankwana as his wife and exposed the secret that the fifth son, Makobi, was his own child and not that of his father.

This news was received with alarm by the people as the first ripples of trouble stirred over the even surface of the river of their lives. If both the young man and the old man were visiting the same hut, they reasoned, perhaps the old man had not died a normal death. They questioned the councillors who knew all secrets.

'Monemapee died just walking on his own feet,' they said reassuringly.

That matter settled, the next challenge came from the two junior brothers, Ntema and Mosemme. If Sebembele were claiming the child, Makobi, as his son, they said, it meant that the young child displaced them in seniority. That they could not allow. The subtle pressure exerted on Sebembele by his junior brothers and the councillors was that he should renounce Rankwana and the child and all would be well. A chief lacked nothing and there were many other women more suitable as wives. Then Sebembele made the second blunder. In a world where women were of no account, he said truthfully:

'The love between Rankwana and I is great.'

This was received with cold disapproval by the councillors.

'If we were you,' they said, 'we would look for a wife somewhere else. A ruler must not be carried away by his emotions. This matter is going to cause disputes among the people.'

They noted that on being given this advice, Sebembele became very quiet, and they left him to his own thoughts, thinking that sooner or later he would come to a decision that agreed with theirs.

In the meanwhile the people quietly split into two camps. The one camp said: 'If he loves her, let him keep her. We all know Rankwana. She is a lovely person, deserving to be the wife of a chief.'

The other camp said:

'He must be mad. A man who is influenced by a woman is no ruler. He is like one who listens to the advice of a child. This story is really bad.'

There was at first no direct challenge to the chieftaincy which Sebembele occupied. But the nature of the surprising dispute, that of his love for a woman and a child, caused it to drag on longer than time would allow. Many evils began to rear their heads like impatient hissing snakes, while Sebembele argued with his own heart or engaged in tender dialogues with his love, Rankwana.

'I don't know what I can do,' Sebembele said, torn between the demands of his position and the strain of a love affair which had been conducted in deep secrecy for many, many months. The very secrecy of the affair seemed to make it shout all the louder for public recognition. At one moment his heart would urge him to renounce the woman and child, but each time he saw Rankwana it abruptly said the opposite. He could come to no decision.

It seemed little enough that he wanted for himself—the companionship of a beautiful woman to whom life had given many other attractive gifts; she was gentle and kind and loving. As soon as Sebembele communicated to her the advice of the councillors, she bowed her head and cried a little.

'If that is what they say, my love,' she said in despair, 'I have no hope left for myself and the child. It were better if we were both dead.'

'Another husband could be chosen for you,' he suggested.

'You doubt my love for you, Sebembele,' she said. 'I would kill myself if I lose you. If you leave me, I would kill myself.'

Her words had meaning for him because he was trapped in the same kind of anguish. It was a terrible pain which seemed to paralyse his movements and thoughts. It filled his mind so completely that he could think of nothing else, day and night. It was like a sickness, this paralysis, and like all ailments it could not be concealed from sight; Sebembele carried it all around with him.

'Our hearts are saying many things about this man,' the councillors said among themselves. They were saying that he was unmanly; that he was unfit to be a ruler; that things were slipping from his hands. Those still sympathetic approached him and said:

'Why are you worrying yourself like this over a woman, Sebembele? There are no limits to the amount of wives a chief may have, but you cannot have that woman and that child.'

And he only replied with a distracted mind: 'I don't know what I can do.'

But things had been set in motion. All the people were astir over events; if a man couldn't make up his mind, other men could make it up for him.

Everything was arranged in secret and on an appointed day Rankwana and the child were forcibly removed back to her father's home. Ever since the controversy had started, her father had been harassed day and night by the councillors as an influence that could help to end it. He had been reduced to a state of agitated muttering to himself by the time she was brought before him. The plan was to set her up with a husband immediately and settle the matter. She was not yet formally married to Sebembele.

'You have put me in great difficulties, my child,' her father said, looking away from her distressed face. 'Women never know their own minds and once this has passed away and you have many children you will wonder what all the fuss was about.'

'Other women may not know their minds . . .' she began, but he stopped her with a raised hand, indicating the husband who had been chosen for her. In all the faces surrounding her there was no sympathy or help, and she quietly allowed herself to be led away to her new home.

When Sebembele arrived in his own yard after a morning of attending to the affairs of the land, he found his brothers, Ntema and Mosemme there.

'Why have you come to visit me?' he asked, with foreboding. 'You never come to visit me. It would seem that we are bitter enemies rather than brothers.'

'You have shaken the whole town with your madness over a woman,' they replied mockingly. 'She is no longer here so you don't have to say any longer "I-don't-know-what-I-can-do". But we still request that you renounce the child, Makobi, in a gathering before all the people, in order that our position is clear. You must say: "That child Makobi is the younger brother of my brothers, Ntema and Mosemme, and not the son of Sebembele who rules".'

Sebembele looked at them for a long moment. It was not hatred he felt but peace at last. His brothers were forcing him to leave the tribe.

'Tell the people that they should all gather together,' he said. 'But what I say to them is my own affair.'

The next morning the people of the whole town saw an amazing sight which stirred their hearts. They saw their ruler walk slowly and unaccompanied through the town. They saw him pause at the yard of Rankwana's father. They saw Sebembele and Rankwana's father walk to the home of her new husband where she had been secreted. They saw Rankwana and Sebembele walk together through the town. Sebembele held the child Makobi in his arms. They saw that they had a ruler who talked with deeds rather than words. They saw that the time had come for them to offer up their individual faces to the face of this ruler. But the people were still in two camps. There was a whole section of the people who did not like this face; it was too out-of-the-way and shocking; it made them very uneasy. Theirs was not a tender, compassionate, and romantic world. And yet in a way it was. The arguments in the other camp which supported Sebembele had flown thick and fast all this time, and they said:

'Ntema and Mosemme are at the bottom of all this trouble. What are they after for they have set a difficult problem before us all? We don't trust them. But why not? They have not yet had time to take anything from us. Perhaps we ought to wait until they do something really bad; at present they are only filled with indignation at the behaviour of Sebembele. But no, we don't trust them. We don't like them. It is Sebembele we love, even though he has shown himself to be a man with a weakness . . .'

That morning, Sebembele completely won over his camp with his extravagant, romantic gesture, but he lost everything else and the rulership of the kingdom of Monemapee.

When all the people had gathered at the meeting place of the town, there were not many arguments left. One by one the councillors stood up and condemned the behaviour of Sebembele. So the two brothers, Ntema and Mosemme won the day. Still working together as one voice, they stood up and asked if their senior brother had any words to say before he left with his people.

'Makobi is my child,' he said.

'Talaote,' they replied, meaning in the language then spoken by the tribe— 'all right, you can go'.

And the name Talaote was all they were to retain of their identity as the people of the kingdom of Monemapee. That day, Sebembele and his people packed their belongings on the backs of their cattle and slowly began the journey southwards. They were to leave many ruins behind them and it is said that they lived, on the journey southwards, with many other tribes like the Baphaleng, Bakaa, and Batswapong until they finally settled in the land of the Bamangwato.[2] To this day there is a separate Botalaote ward in the capital village of the Bamangwato, and the people refer to themselves still as the people of Talaote. The old men there keep on giving confused and contradictory accounts of their origins, but they say they lost their place of birth over a woman. They shake their heads and say that women have always caused a lot of trouble in the world. They say that the child of their chief was named, Talaote, to commemorate their expulsion from the kingdom of Monemapee.

FOOTNOTE:
The story is an entirely romanticized and fictionalized version of the history of the Botalaote tribe. Some historical data was given to me by the old men of the tribe, but it was unreliable as their memories had tended to fail them. A re-construction was made therefore in my own imagination; I am also partly indebted to the London Missionary Society's *'Livingstone Tswana Readers'*, *Padiso III*, school textbook, for those graphic paragraphs on the harvest thanksgiving ceremony which appear in the story.

B. HEAD.

1977

2. Ethnic groups in Botswana.

SALMAN RUSHDIE

born 1947

Salman Rushdie, whose extended family lives in India as well as Pakistan, published his fourth novel, *The Satanic Verses*, in England in September 1988. On Valentine's Day 1989, Ayatollah Ruholla Khomeini, then the leader of Shi'a Muslims in Iran, issued a *fatwa*, or religious decree, urging Muslims around the world to murder Rushdie for his acts of blasphemy against Islam in writing the novel. With typical irony, Rushdie called the *fatwa* an unusually harsh "book review." The incident sparked off a global controversy about freedom of expression, modernity, and "Islam versus the West," and Rushdie had to live underground for a decade, with maximum security provided by the British secret service. For many readers ever since, the international fallout from *The Satanic Verses* has been a public measure of its literary value, and a confirmation of Rushdie's status as the world's most important living writer.

Rushdie was born into a wealthy Muslim business family in Bombay in 1947, a few weeks before the end of British colonial rule and the Partition of the subcontinent into the two new nations of India and Pakistan. After early education in the city, Rushdie attended boarding school in England and received his undergraduate and master's degrees from the University of Cambridge, where he studied Islamic history. He worked in advertising in London for several years, and wrote his first book—a science-fiction novel—on the side. With the publication of *Midnight's Children* (1980) and its immense literary and commercial success, however, Rushdie was able to turn to writing full time, contributing to periodicals throughout the anglophone world

in the 1980s while producing his next two novels, *Shame* (1983) and *The Satanic Verses*.

During his retreat from public view for a dozen years after the Ayatollah Khomeini's *fatwa*, Rushdie's "normal" life was seriously interrupted—two of his first three marriages ended—but seemingly the experience did not affect his creativity. In fact, the voluminous, multifarious criticism of his work and the continued threat to his life strengthened his resolve to imagine, write, and speak his mind as freely as possible. Among his important works published during this period were *The Moor's Last Sigh* (1995), the surreal saga of an Indian family of Jewish Portuguese descent, with connections to the last Muslim ruler of Moorish Spain in the fifteenth century, and *The Ground Beneath Her Feet* (1999), a novel about a love triangle interwoven with the Greek myth of Orpheus and Eurydice. Around the end of the millennium, Rushdie eased back into public life by moving to the United States, teaching at various universities as a writer-in-residence, and reading from his work and speaking to large audiences. In the first decade of the twenty-first century, his novels—such as *Shalimar the Clown* (2005) and *The Enchantress of Florence* (2008)—and a book for children, *Luka and the Fire of Life* (2010), have not won as much acclaim as his early work. Rushdie's preeminence among his contemporaries was affirmed when the Booker Prize was awarded to *Midnight's Children* in 1981; the novel's enduring achievement was confirmed by special Booker awards, in 1993 and 2008. As a naturalized British citizen, Rushdie was knighted in 2007; toward the end of the decade, he began to spend time in London again, helping his third (former) wife to raise their son.

Rushdie has frequently described himself as a "historian of ideas," and many of his novels are "novels of ideas" rather than narratives centered on plot or character. He is not a realistic writer; he is the foremost practitioner in English of magic realism. Invented before the middle of the twentieth century by Latin American fiction writers, who popularized the genre in the 1950s and 1960s, magic realism is a mode or style in which "reality" is permeated by supernatural forces, miraculous events, larger-than-life presences, and extraordinary characters who may possess magical powers. In his works of magic realism, Rushdie creates characters, objects, and occurrences that break the rules of everyday logic and causality: a person may be present in two places at once, for example, or a human being may travel in time, or live for centuries. Rushdie's goal is to bring the reader closer to reality, which has its rational or rationally explicable features (as described by science) but is also irrational, unpredictable, and bizarre. If magic realism gives Rushdie's work its dimension of fantasy, his fascination with ideas gives it the quality of abstraction. Many of his characters are allegorical, or personifications of ideas: Saleem Sinai, the protagonist of *Midnight's Children*, for instance, is an embodiment of "the idea of India," with his large nose shaped like the country's peninsula on a map, and his physique threatening to break up into 580 million pieces, as many as India's population at the time of writing. In *The Satanic Verses*, a voice asks one of the novel's characters: "What kind of idea are you?" Unlike realistically represented characters, Rushdie's have inner conflicts not of emotions or passions but of ideas.

Rushdie builds his narratives around conflicting ideas and fantastic charac-ters and events with wit and playfulness, and with precise attention to the sensuous details of everyday life. A significant element of his disorienting realism comes from the use of newspaper reports of current events and historical accounts. *Midnight's Children* and *Shame*, for example, draw extensively on the journalistic record on contemporary India and Pakistan, respectively; much of *The Satanic Verses*, *The Moor's Last Sigh*, and *The Enchantress of Florence* relies on readers' historical knowledge of diverse regions of the world, from Arabia in the seventh century, and Spain and Portugal between the eighth and fifteenth centuries, to Italy in the high Renaissance. These shifts in place and time stem from Rushdie's interest in large-scale flux and transformation in human societies: he is the foremost writer of our times on migration, immigrant communities, diasporas, and cultural mixing, or hybridity.

"The Perforated Sheet," the selection below, reads like a self-contained short story but is actually an excerpt, prepared by Rushdie himself, from the first two chapters of *Midnight's Children*, with a few connecting lines not found in the novel. It introduces us to Saleem Sinai, the protagonist and narrator, and to the story of his life and origins, which constitutes the novel's Protean narrative. Saleem is born at midnight, between August 14 and 15, 1947, the moment at which India and Pakistan became separate nations; as a "child" of that historic hour, he finds that his destiny is entwined with India's fate as a nation, so that his life unfolds as a precise parallel to the country's collective history thereafter. In "The Perforated Sheet" we encounter the beginning of that story as Saleem sees it: the time, almost half a century before his birth, when his grandfather returns from Europe with a medical degree; sets up a practice in his home-town of Srinagar, Kashmir; and meets the woman who is destined to become his wife, thereby launching the cascade of events that will culminate, two generations later, in Saleem's momentous arrival.

In the novel itself, every important event in the history of the Sinai family, from Saleem's grandparents onward, is a funny, farcical echo of every major event in the history of the Indian subcontinent. Thus Saleem's birth coincides with the birth of the nation of India. And, since the twin nations of India and Pakistan (which represent the religions of Hinduism and Islam, respectively) are born at the same moment, the birth of Saleem (a Muslim boy) coincides, as well, with the birth of his hateful "nemesis," Shiva (a Hindu boy). Saleem and Shiva's lives, from infancy to adulthood, then replicate the simultaneous histories of India/Hinduism and Pakistan/Islam. This comical story is complicated by the fact that a poor Christian nurse at the hospital where Saleem and Shiva are born (to different mothers) switches the babies, as an act of impersonal class revenge on their well-to-do parents. Saleem, who grows up in the Sinai family believing that he is a Muslim, is actually the biological son of a Hindu mother, and the reverse is true of Shiva.

A further fictional complication then ensues. During the first hour after the fateful midnight of August 14–15, 1947, exactly 1,001 children are born in India and Pakistan, and all of them—including Saleem and Shiva—possess magical powers. They are, as it were, the Chosen Ones; they are all "Midnight's Children" (hence the novel's title), they can telepathically connect with one another, and their individual destinies are intertwined with their nations' and each other's destinies, down to the last detail. Saleem grows up with an inexplicable "buzzing" in his head, and discovers that it is the buzz of the voices of hundreds of other Midnight's Children, with whom he can communicate directly. The culmination of the narrative is that everything that happens on the Indian subcontinent after 1947 has only one objective: to destroy these gifted children. "The Perforated Sheet" is thus the beginning of a story that is at once comic and tragic, on an epic scale.

The Perforated Sheet[1]

I was born in the city of Bombay . . . once upon a time. No, that won't do, there's no getting away from the date: I was born in Doctor Narlikar's Nursing Home on August 15th, 1947.[2] And the time? The time matters, too. Well then: at night. No, it's important to be more . . . On the stroke of midnight, as a matter of fact. Clock-hands joined palms in respectful greeting as I came. Oh, spell it out, spell it out: at the precise instant of India's arrival at independence, I tumbled forth into the world. There were gasps. And, outside the window, fireworks and crowds. A few seconds later, my father broke his big toe; but his accident was a mere trifle when set beside what had befallen me in that benighted moment, because thanks to the occult tyrannies of those blandly saluting clocks I had been mysteriously handcuffed to history, my destinies

---

1. Excerpted by the author from the first two chapters of *Midnight's Children*, with connecting material not in the original novel.

2. The date is that of India's official independence from British colonial rule.

indissolubly chained to those of my country. For the next three decades, there was to be no escape. Soothsayers had prophesied me, newspapers celebrated my arrival, politicos ratified my authenticity. I was left entirely without a say in the matter. I, Saleem Sinai, later variously called Snotnose, Stainface, Baldy, Sniffer, Buddha and even Piece-of-the-Moon, had become heavily embroiled in Fate—at the best of times a dangerous sort of involvement. And I couldn't even wipe my own nose at the time.

Now, however, time (having no further use for me) is running out. I will soon be thirty-one years old. Perhaps. If my crumbling, over-used body permits. But I have no hope of saving my life, nor can I count on having even a thousand nights and a night. I must work fast, faster than Scheherazade,[3] if I am to end up meaning—yes, meaning—something. I admit it: above all things, I fear absurdity.

And there are so many stories to tell, too many, such an excess of intertwined lives events miracles places rumours, so dense a commingling of the improbable and the mundane! I have been a swallower of lives; and to know me, just the one of me, you'll have to swallow the lot as well. Consumed multitudes are jostling and shoving inside me; and guided only by the memory of a large white bedsheet with a roughly circular hole some seven inches in diameter cut into the centre, clutching at the dream of that holey, mutilated square of linen, which is my talisman, my open-sesame, I must commence the business of remaking my life from the point at which it really began, some thirty-two years before anything as obvious, as *present*, as my clock-ridden crime-stained birth.

(The sheet, incidentally, is stained too, with three drops of old, faded redness. As the Quran tells us: *Recite, in the name of the Lord thy Creator, who created Man from clots of blood*.)

One Kashmiri morning in the early spring of 1915, my grandfather Aadam Aziz[4] hit his nose against a frost-hardened tussock of earth while attempting to pray. Three drops of blood plopped out of his left nostril, hardened instantly in the brittle air and lay before his eyes on the prayer-mat, transformed into rubies. Lurching back until he knelt with his head once more upright, he found that the tears which had sprung to his eyes had solidified, too; and at that moment, as he brushed diamonds contemptuously from his lashes, he resolved never again to kiss earth for any god or man. This decision, however, made a hole in him, a vacancy in a vital inner chamber, leaving him vulnerable to women and history. Unaware of this at first, despite his recently completed medical training, he stood up, rolled the prayer-mat into a thick cheroot, and holding it under his right arm surveyed the valley through clear, diamond-free eyes.

The world was new again. After a winter's gestation in its eggshell of ice, the valley had beaked its way out into the open, moist and yellow. The new grass bided its time underground: the mountains were retreating to their hill-stations for the warm season. (In the winter, when the valley shrank under the ice, the mountains closed in and snarled like angry jaws around the city on the lake.)

3. Shahrazad, the narrator in the *Arabian Nights*, who, night after night, tells stories to Prince Shahrayar, the kingdom's ruler, in order to defer, perhaps indefinitely, her execution.
4. A Muslim name; "Aadam" is the Arabic equivalent of Adam.

In those days the radio mast had not been built and the temple of Sankara Acharya, a little black blister on a khaki hill, still dominated the streets and lake of Srinagar.[5] In those days there was no army camp at the lakeside, no endless snakes of camouflaged trucks and jeeps clogged the narrow mountain roads, no soldiers hid behind the crests of the mountains past Baramulla and Gulmarg.[6] In those days travellers were not shot as spies if they took photographs of bridges, and apart from the Englishmen's houseboats on the lake, the valley had hardly changed since the Mughal Empire,[7] for all its springtime renewals; but my grandfather's eyes—which were, like the rest of him, twenty-five years old—saw things differently . . . and his nose had started to itch.

To reveal the secret of my grandfather's altered vision: he had spent five years, five springs, away from home. (The tussock of earth, crucial though its presence was as it crouched under a chance wrinkle of the prayer-mat, was at bottom no more than a catalyst.) Now, returning, he saw through travelled eyes. Instead of the beauty of the tiny valley circled by giant teeth, he noticed the narrowness, the proximity of the horizon; and felt sad, to be at home and feel so utterly enclosed. He also felt—inexplicably—as though the old place resented his educated, stethoscoped return. Beneath the winter ice, it had been coldly neutral, but now there was no doubt; the years in Germany had returned him to a hostile environment. Many years later, when the hole inside him had been clogged up with hate, and he came to sacrifice himself at the shrine of the black stone god in the temple on the hill, he would try and recall his childhood springs in Paradise,[8] the way it was before travel and tussocks and army tanks messed everything up.

On the morning when the valley, gloved in a prayer-mat,[9] punched him on the nose, he had been trying, absurdly, to pretend that nothing had changed. So he had risen in the bitter cold of four-fifteen, washed himself in the pre-scribed fashion, dressed and put on his father's astrakhan cap; after which he had carried the rolled cheroot of the prayer-mat into the small lakeside garden in front of their old dark house and unrolled it over the waiting tussock. The ground felt deceptively soft under his feet and made him simultaneously uncertain and unwary. 'In the Name of God, the Compassionate, the Merciful . . .'—the exordium, spoken with hands joined before him like a book, comforted a part of him, made another, larger part feel uneasy—'. . . Praise be to Allah, Lord of the Creation . . .'[1]—but now Heidelberg invaded his head; here was Ingrid, briefly his Ingrid, her face scorning him for this Mecca-turned

5. The main city in the Valley of Kashmir, now in the northernmost state of India, Srinagar is set on Lake Dal. In the late classical period (ca. 8th to 11th centuries), Kashmir was a Hindu kingdom famous for its patronage of learning and the arts; Shankara Acharya (ca. 8th century) was the period's most influential Hindu philosopher and theologian.
6. Situated close to the western edge of Kashmir, Baramulla is the second-largest city in the region, after Srinagar. Gulmarg is a famous ski resort near Baramulla.
7. The subcontinent's largest and wealthiest empire, the Mughal Empire lasted from 1526

to 1858. "Mughal" is a variation on "Mongol"; the Mughals were descended matrilineally from the Mongolian conqueror Genghis Khan (late 12th–early 13th centuries).
8. The Mughal emperor Jahangir (ruled 1600–25) called Kashmir "Paradise," and the epithet has been popular ever since.
9. As prescribed for Muslims, Aadam Aziz prays five times a day, kneeling on his prayer mat; his injury occurs during one of his prayers.
1. Aadam Aziz's words of prayer are from the Qur'an, and invoke Allah, the one and only true God in Islam.

parroting; here, their friends Oskar and Ilse Lubin the anarchists, mocking his prayer with their anti-ideologies—'. . . The Compassionate, the Merciful. King of the Last Judgment! . . .'—Heidelberg, in which, along with medicine and politics, he learned that India—like radium—had been 'discovered' by the Europeans; even Oskar was filled with admiration for Vasco da Gama,[2] and this was what finally separated Aadam Aziz from his friends, this belief of theirs that he was somehow the invention of their ancestors—'. . . You alone we worship, and to You alone we pray for help . . .'—so here he was, despite their presence in his head, attempting to re-unite himself with an earlier self which ignored their influence but knew everything it ought to have known, about submission for example, about what he was doing now, as his hands, guided by old memories, fluttered upwards, thumbs pressed to ears, fingers spread, as he sank to his knees—'. . . Guide us to the straight path. The path of those whom You have favoured . . .' But it was no good, he was caught in a strange middle ground, trapped between belief and disbelief, and this was only a charade after all—'. . . Not of those who have incurred Your wrath. Nor of those who have gone astray.' My grandfather bent his forehead towards the earth. Forward he bent, and the earth, prayer-mat-covered, curved up towards him. And now it was the tussock's time. At one and the same time a rebuke from Ilse-Oskar-Ingrid-Heidelberg as well as valley-and-God, it smote him upon the point of the nose. Three drops fell. There were rubies and diamonds. And my grandfather, lurching upright, made a resolve. Stood. Rolled cheroot. Stared across the lake. And was knocked forever into that middle place, unable to worship a God in whose existence he could not wholly disbelieve. Permanent alteration: a hole.

The lake was no longer frozen over. The thaw had come rapidly, as usual; many of the small boats, the shikaras, had been caught napping, which was also normal. But while these sluggards slept on, on dry land, snoring peacefully beside their owners, the oldest boat was up at the crack as old folk often are, and was therefore the first craft to move across the unfrozen lake. Tai's shikara . . . this, too, was customary.

Watch how the old boatman,[3] Tai, makes good time through the misty water, standing stooped over at the back of his craft! How his oar, a wooden heart on a yellow stick, drives jerkily through the weeds! In these parts he's considered very odd because he rows standing up . . . among other reasons. Tai, bringing an urgent summons to Doctor Aziz, is about to set history in motion . . . while Aadam, looking down into the water, recalls what Tai taught him years ago: 'The ice is always waiting, Aadam baba,[4] just under the water's skin.' Aadam's eyes are a clear blue, the astonishing blue of mountain sky, which has a habit of dripping into the pupils of Kashmiri men; they have not forgotten how to look. They see—there! like the skeleton of a ghost, just beneath the surface of Lake Dall—the delicate tracery, the intricate crisscross of colourless lines, the

2. Vasco da Gama (ca. 1460–1524), Portuguese explorer and first European to navigate the sea route from Europe, around Africa, to India, in 1498.
3. Tai operates a ferry boat on Lake Dal in Srinagar.

4. In Hindu and Urdu, "baba" is a term of respect (for a social superior) as well as of affection (for a child, an adult, or an old person); here Tai, an old man, uses it in both senses at once.

cold waiting veins of the future. His German years, which have blurred so much else, haven't deprived him of the gift of seeing. Tai's gift. He looks up, sees the approaching V of Tai's boat, waves a greeting. Tai's arm rises—but this is a command. 'Wait!' My grandfather waits; and during this hiatus, as he experiences the last peace of his life, a muddy, ominous sort of peace, I had better get round to describing him.

Keeping out of my voice the natural envy of the ugly man for the strikingly impressive, I record that Doctor Aziz was a tall man. Pressed flat against a wall of his family home, he measured twenty-five bricks (a brick for each year of his life), or just over six foot two. A strong man also. His beard was thick and red—and annoyed his mother, who said only Hajis, men who had made the pilgrimage to Mecca, should grow red beards. His hair, however, was rather darker. His sky-eyes you know about. Ingrid had said, 'They went mad with the colours when they made your face.' But the central feature of my grandfather's anatomy was neither colour nor height, neither strength of arm nor straightness of back. There it was, reflected in the water, undulating like a mad plantain in the centre of his face . . . Aadam Aziz, waiting for Tai, watches his rippling nose. It would have dominated less dramatic faces than his easily; even on him, it is what one sees first and remembers longest. 'A cyranose,' Ilse Lubin said, and Oskar added, 'A proboscissimus.' Ingrid announced, 'You could cross a river on that nose.' (Its bridge was wide.)

My grandfather's nose: nostrils flaring, curvaceous as dancers. Between them swells the nose's triumphal arch, first up and out, then down and under, sweeping in to his upper lip with a superb and at present red-tipped flick. An easy nose to hit a tussock with. I wish to place on record my gratitude to this mighty organ—if not for it, who would ever have believed me to be truly my mother's son, my grandfather's grandson?—this colossal apparatus which was to be my birthright, too. Doctor Aziz's nose—comparable only to the trunk of the elephant-headed god Ganesh—established incontrovertibly his right to be a patriarch. It was Tai who taught him that, too. When young Aadam was barely past puberty the dilapidated boatman said, 'That's a nose to start a family on, my princeling. There'd be no mistaking whose brood they were. Mughal Emperors would have given their right hands for noses like that one. There are dynasties waiting inside it,'—and here Tai lapsed into coarseness—'like snot.'

Nobody could remember when Tai had been young. He had been plying this same boat, standing in the same hunched position, across the Dal and Nageen Lakes . . . forever. As far as anyone knew. He lived somewhere in the insanitary bowels of the old wooden-house quarter and his wife grew lotus roots and other curious vegetables on one of the many 'floating gardens' lilting on the surface of the spring and summer water. Tai himself cheerily admitted he had no idea of his age. Neither did his wife—he was, she said, already leathery when they married. His face was a sculpture of wind on water: ripples made of hide. He had two golden teeth and no others. In the town, he had few friends. Few boatmen or traders invited him to share a hookah when he floated past the shikara moorings or one of the lakes' many ramshackle, waterside provision-stores and tea-shops.

The general opinion of Tai had been voiced long ago by Aadam Aziz's father the gemstone merchant: 'His brain fell out with his teeth.' It was an impression the boatman fostered by his chatter, which was fantastic, grandiloquent and ceaseless, and as often as not addressed only to himself. Sound carries over water, and the lake people giggled at his monologues; but with undertones of awe, and even fear. Awe, because the old halfwit knew the lakes and hills better than any of his detractors; fear, because of his claim to an antiquity so immense it defied numbering, and moreover hung so lightly round his chicken's neck that it hadn't prevented him from winning a highly desirable wife and fathering four sons upon her . . . and a few more, the story went, on other lakeside wives. The young bucks at the shikara moorings were convinced he had a pile of money hidden away somewhere—a hoard, perhaps, of priceless golden teeth, rattling in a sack like walnuts. And, as a child, Aadam Aziz had loved him.

He made his living as a simple ferryman, despite all the rumours of wealth, taking hay and goats and vegetables and wood across the lakes for cash; people, too. When he was running his taxi-service he erected a pavilion in the centre of the shikara,[5] a gay affair of flowered-patterned curtains and canopy, with cushions to match; and deodorised his boat with incense. The sight of Tai's shikara approaching, curtains flying, had always been for Doctor Aziz one of the defining images of the coming of spring. Soon the English sahibs would arrive and Tai would ferry them to the Shalimar Gardens and the King's Spring, chattering and pointy and stooped, a quirky, enduring familiar spirit of the valley.[6] A watery Caliban, rather too fond of cheap Kashmiri brandy.

The Boy Aadam, my grandfather-to-be, fell in love with the boatman Tai precisely because of the endless verbiage which made others think him cracked. It was magical talk, words pouring from him like fools' money, past his two gold teeth, laced with hiccups and brandy, soaring up to the most remote Himalayas[7] of the past, then swooping shrewdly on some present detail, Aadam's nose for instance, to vivisect its meaning like a mouse. This friendship had plunged Aadam into hot water with great regularity. (Boiling water. Literally. While his mother said. 'We'll kill that boatman's bugs if it kills you.') But still the old soliloquist would dawdle in his boat at the garden's lakeside toes and Aziz would sit at his feet until voices summoned him indoors to be lectured on Tai's filthiness and warned about the pillaging armies of germs his mother envisaged leaping from that hospitably ancient body on to her son's starched white loose-pajamas. But always Aadam returned to the water's edge to scan the mists for the ragged reprobate's hunched-up frame steering its magical boat through the enchanted waters of the morning.

'But how old are you really, Taiji?'[8] (Doctor Aziz, adult, red-bearded, slanting towards the future, remembers the day he asked the unaskable question.) For an instant, silence, noisier than a waterfall. The monologue, interrupted. Slap of oar in water. He was riding in the shikara with Tai, squatting amongst goats, on a pile of straw, in full knowledge of the stick and bathtub waiting for him at

5. A "shikara" is a distinctive, long rowboat used on Lake Dal, similar to a British double skiff used on the Thames. It transports people and goods around Srinagar.
6. The Shalimar Gardens are the modern form of the Mughal-style rose garden first laid near Srinagar for Emperor Jahangir in 1619.
7. The western end of the Himalayas, the world's highest mountain range, wraps around the north of Kashmir.
8. In Hindi and Urdu, the main languages of northern India, the suffix "-ji" is an honorific added to names and epithets, to address elders and superiors. Aadam Aziz addresses the "lowly" boatman as "Taiji" out of respect for the latter's age.

home. He had come for stories—and with one question had silenced the storyteller.

'No, tell, Taiji, how old, *truly?*' And now a brandy bottle, materialising from nowhere: cheap liquor from the folds of the great warm chugha-coat. Then a shudder, a belch, a glare. Glint of gold. And—at last!—speech. 'How old? You ask how old, you little wet-head, you nosey . . .' Tai pointed at the mountains. 'So old, nakkoo!' Aadam, the nakkoo, the nosey one, followed his pointing finger. 'I have watched the mountains being born; I have seen Emperors die. Listen. Listen, nakkoo[9] . . .'—the brandy bottle again, followed by brandy-voice, and words more intoxicating than booze—'. . . I saw that Isa, that Christ, when he came to Kashmir.[1] Smile, smile, it is your history I am keeping in my head. Once it was set down in old lost books. Once I knew where there was a grave with pierced feet carved on the tombstone, which bled once a year. Even my memory is going now; but I know, although I can't read.' Illiteracy, dismissed with a flourish; literature crumbled beneath the rage of his sweeping hand. Which sweeps again to chugha-pocket,[2] to brandy bottle, to lips chapped with cold. Tai always had woman's lips. 'Nakkoo, listen, listen. I have seen plenty. Yara,[3] you should've seen that Isa when he came, beard down to his balls, bald as an egg on his head. He was old and fagged-out but he knew his manners. "You first, Taiji," he'd say, and "Please to sit"; always a respectful tongue, he never called me crackpot, never called me *tu* either. Always *aap.*[4] Polite, see? And what an appetite! Such a hunger, I would catch my ears in fright. Saint or devil, I swear he could eat a whole kid in one go. And so what? I told him, eat, fill your hole, a man comes to Kashmir to enjoy life, or to end it, or both. His work was finished. He just came up here to live it up a little.' Mesmerised by this brandied portrait of a bald, gluttonous Christ, Aziz listened, later repeating every word to the consternation of his parents, who dealt in stones and had no time for 'gas'.

'Oh, you don't believe?'—licking his sore lips with a grin, knowing it to be the reverse of the truth; 'Your attention is wandering?'—again, he knew how furiously Aziz was hanging on his words. 'Maybe the straw is pricking your behind, hey? Oh, I'm so sorry, babaji, not to provide for you silk cushions with gold brocade-work—cushions such as the Emperor Jehangir[5] sat upon! You think the Emperor Jehangir as a gardener only, no doubt,' Tai accused my grandfather, 'because he built Shalimar. Stupid! What do you know? His name meant Encompasser of the Earth. Is that a gardener's name? God knows what they teach you boys these days. Whereas I'. . . puffing up a little here . . .'I knew his precise weight, to the tola! Ask me how many maunds, how many seers! When he was happy he got heavier and in Kashmir he was heaviest of all. I used to carry his litter . . . no, no, look, you don't believe again, that big cucumber in

9. "Nakkoo," literally "nosy" in Hindi and Urdu, is Tai's playful epithet for the large-nosed Aadam Aziz.
1. An apocryphal legend in the Muslim and Hindu worlds is that at the end of his life, as recorded in the Bible, Jesus Christ left Jerusalem, living out his last days in Kashmir.
2. "Chuga" or "choga," the Persian word for a loose, cassocklike garment for Muslim men.

3. "Yara" is the common Urdu term of endearment for friend, buddy, loved one, or close companion.
4. In Hindi and Urdu, *tu* is the intimate or familiar form of "you," whereas *aap* is the formal, respectful form of the pronoun.
5. The fourth ruler in the Mughal dynasty, on the throne from 1600 to 1625.

your face is waggling like the little one in your pajamas! So, come on, come on, ask me questions! Give examination! Ask how many times the leather thongs wound round the handles of the litter—the answer is thirty-one. Ask me what was the Emperor's dying word—I tell you it was "Kashmir". He had bad breath and a good heart. Who do you think I am? Some common ignorant lying pie-dog? Go, get out of the boat now, your nose makes it too heavy to row; also your father is waiting to beat my gas out of you, and your mother to boil off your skin.'

Despite beating and boiling, Aadam Aziz floated with Tai in his shikara, again and again, amid goats hay flowers furniture lotus-roots, though never with the English sahibs,[6] and heard again and again the miraculous answers to that single terrifying question: 'But Taiji, how old are you, *honestly?*'

From Tai, Aadam learned the secrets of the lake—where you could swim without being pulled down by weeds; the eleven varieties of water-snake; where the frogs spawned; how to cook a lotus-root; and where the three English women had drowned a few years back. 'There is a tribe of feringhee women who come to this water to drown,' Tai said. 'Sometimes they know it, sometimes they don't, but I know the minute I smell them. They hide under the water from God knows what or who—but they can't hide from me, baba!' Tai's laugh, emerging to infect Aadam—a huge, booming laugh that seemed macabre when it crashed out of that old, withered body, but which was so natural in my giant grandfather that nobody knew, in later times, that it wasn't really his. And, also from Tai, my grandfather heard about noses.

Tai tapped his left nostril. 'You know what this is, nakkoo? It's the place where the outside world meets the world inside you. If they don't get on, you feel it here. Then you rub your nose with embarrassment to make the itch go away. A nose like that, little idiot, is a great gift. I say: trust it. When it warns you, look out or you'll be finished. Follow your nose and you'll go far.' He cleared his throat; his eyes rolled away into the mountains of the past. Aziz settled back on the straw. 'I knew one officer once—in the army of that Iskandar the Great. Never mind his name. He had a vegetable just like yours hanging between his eyes. When the army halted near Gandhara,[7] he fell in love with some local floozy. At once his nose itched like crazy. He scratched it, but that was useless. He inhaled vapours from crushed boiled eucalyptus leaves. Still no good, baba! The itching sent him wild; but the damn fool dug in his heels and stayed with his little witch when the army went home. He became—what?—a stupid thing, neither this nor that, a half-and-halfer with a nagging wife and an itch in the nose, and in the end he pushed his sword into his stomach. What do you think of that?'

<hr>

6. "Sahib" is the Anglicized form of the Persian *saheb*, a respectful term of address for a rich or powerful man, a ruler or administrator, or a superior; it became the common epithet for British colonial administrators in India.
7. "Iskandar" or "Sikandar" is the Indian equivalent of "Alexander" the Great, whose army reached the subcontinent in 327 B.C.E.

The farthest north Alexander went was to Gandhara, the region now around Peshawar and the Swat Valley in northwest Pakistan. When he turned back, Alexander left behind a Greek colony in Gandhara, which flourished there for several centuries as the eastern outpost of his empire.

Doctor Aziz in 1915, whom rubies and diamonds have turned into a half-and-halfer, remembers this story as Tai enters hailing distance. His nose is itching still. He scratches, shrugs, tosses his head; and then Tai shouts.

'Ohé! Doctor Sahib! Ghani the landowner's daughter is sick.'

. . . The young Doctor has entered the throes of a most unhippocratic excitement at the boatman's cry, and shouts, 'I'm coming just now! Just let me bring my things!' The shikara's prow touches the garden's hem. Aadam is rushing indoors, prayer-mat rolled like a cheroot under one arm, blue eyes blinking in the sudden interior gloom; he has placed the cheroot on a high shelf on top of stacked copies of *Vorwärts* and Lenin's *What Is To Be Done?*[8] and other pamphlets, dusty echoes of his half-faded German life; he is pulling out, from under his bed, a second-hand leather case which his mother called his 'doctori-attaché',[9] and as he swings it and himself upwards and runs from the room, the word HEIDELBERG is briefly visible, burned into the leather on the bottom of the bag. A landowner's daughter is good news indeed to a doctor with a career to make, even if she is ill. No: *because* she is ill.

. . . Slap of oar in water. Plop of spittle in lake. Tai clears his throat and mutters angrily, 'A fine business. A wet-head nakkoo child goes away before he's learned one damn thing and he comes back a big doctor sahib with a big bag full of foreign machines, and he's still as silly as an owl. I swear: a too bad business.'

. . .'Big shot,' Tai is spitting into the lake, 'big bag, big shot. Pah! We haven't got enough bags at home that you must bring back that thing made of a pig's skin that makes one unclean just by looking at it? And inside, God knows what all.' Doctor Aziz, seated amongst flowery curtains and the smell of incense, has his thoughts wrenched away from the patient waiting across the lake. Tai's bitter monologue breaks into his consciousness, creating a sense of dull shock, a smell like a casualty ward overpowering the incense . . . the old man is clearly furious about something, possessed by an incomprehensible rage that appears to be directed at his erstwhile acolyte, or, more precisely and oddly, at his bag. Doctor Aziz attempts to make small talk . . .'Your wife is well? Do they still talk about your bag of golden teeth?'. . . tries to remake an old friendship; but Tai is in full flight now, a stream of invective pouring out of him. The Heidelberg bag quakes under the torrent of abuse. 'Sistersleeping pigskin bag[1] from Abroad full of foreigners' tricks. Big-shot bag. Now if a man breaks an arm that bag will not let the bone-setter bind it in leaves. Now a man must let his wife lie beside that bag and watch knives come and cut her open. A fine business, what these foreigners put in our young men's heads. I swear: it is a too-bad thing. That bag should fry in Hell with the testicles of the ungodly.'

. . .'Do you still pickle water-snakes in brandy to give you virility, Taiji? Do you still like to eat lotus-root without any spices?' Hesitant questions, brushed aside by the torrent of Tai's fury. Doctor Aziz begins to diagnose. To the ferryman, the

---

8. Lenin's small book, first published in 1902, quickly became a classic of Socialist and Communist theory and polemics, outlining a program that culminated in the Bolshevik Revolution of 1917 in Russia.

9. "Doctori-attaché" is an Indianized term for a doctor's satchel or attache case.

1. Muslims and Semitic people consider the pig a polluting animal; a pigskin bag is therefore a proscribed object in this context. "Sistersleeping" is the narrator's playful variation on the most common curse word in Hindi and Urdu.

bag represents Abroad; it is the alien thing, the invader, progress. And yes, it has indeed taken possession of the young Doctor's mind: and yes, it contains knives, and cures for cholera and malaria and smallpox; and yes, it sits between doctor and boatman, and has made them antagonists. Doctor Aziz begins to fight, against sadness, and against Tai's anger, which is beginning to infect him, to become his own, which erupts only rarely, but comes, when it does come, unheralded in a roar from his deepest places, laying waste everything in sight; and then vanishes, leaving him wondering why everyone is so upset . . . They are approaching Ghani's house. A bearer awaits the shikara, standing with clasped hands on a little wooden jetty. Aziz fixes his mind on the job in hand.

The bearer[2] holds the shikara steady as Aadam Aziz climbs out, bag in hand. And now, at last, Tai speaks directly to my grandfather. Scorn in his face, Tai asks, 'Tell me this, Doctor Sahib: have you got in that bag made of dead pigs one of those machines that foreign doctors use to smell with?' Aadam shakes his head, not understanding. Tai's voice gathers new layers of disgust. 'You know, sir, a thing like an elephant's trunk.' Aziz, seeing what he means, replies: 'A stethoscope? Naturally.' Tai pushes the shikara off from the jetty. Spits. Begins to row away. 'I knew it,' he says. 'You will use such a machine now, instead of your own big nose.'

My grandfather does not trouble to explain that a stethoscope is more like a pair of ears than a nose. He is stifling his own irritation, the resentful anger of a cast-off child; and besides, there is a patient waiting.

The house was opulent but badly lit. Ghani was a widower and the servants clearly took advantage. There were cobwebs in corners and layers of dust on ledges. They walked down a long corridor; one of the doors was ajar and through it Aziz saw a room in a state of violent disorder. This glimpse, connected with a glint of light in Ghani's dark glasses, suddenly informed Aziz that the landowner was blind. This aggravated his sense of unease . . . They halted outside a thick teak door. Ghani said, 'Wait here two moments,' and went into the room behind the door.

In later years, Doctor Aadam Aziz swore that during those two moments of solitude in the gloomy spidery corridors of the landowner's mansion he was gripped by an almost uncontrollable desire to turn and run away as fast as his legs would carry him. Unnerved by the enigma of the blind art-lover, his insides filled with tiny scrabbling insects as a result of the insidious venom of Tai's mutterings, his nostrils itching to the point of convincing him that he had somehow contracted venereal disease, he felt his feet begin slowly, as though encased in boots of lead, to turn; felt blood pounding in his temples; and was seized by so powerful a sensation of standing upon a point of no return that he very nearly wet his German woollen trousers. He began, without knowing it, to blush furiously; and at this point a woman with the biceps of a wrestler appeared, beckoning him to follow her into the room. The state of her sari[3] told him that she was a servant; but she was not servile. 'You look green as a fish,' she said. 'You young doctors. You come into a strange house and your liver

2. Common British-Indian colonial-era term for a servant, helper, or waiter.

3. The sari, a full-body wrap, is the most common attire for adult Hindu women.

turns to jelly. Come, Doctor Sahib, they are waiting for you.' Clutching his bag a fraction too tightly, he followed her through the dark teak door.

. . . Into a spacious bedchamber that was as ill-lit as the rest of the house; although here there were shafts of dusty sunlight seeping in through a fanlight high on one wall. These fusty rays illuminated a scene as remarkable as anything the Doctor had ever witnessed: a tableau of such surpassing strangeness that his feet began to twitch towards the door once again. Two more women, also built like professional wrestlers, stood stiffly in the light, each holding one corner of an enormous white bedsheet, their arms raised high above their heads so that the sheet hung between them like a curtain.[4] Mr Ghani welled up out of the murk surrounding the sunlit sheet and permitted the nonplussed Aadam to stare stupidly at the peculiar tableau for perhaps half a minute, at the end of which, and before a word had been spoken, the Doctor made a discovery:

In the very centre of the sheet, a hole had been cut, a crude circle about seven inches in diameter.

'Close the door, ayah.' Ghani instructed the first of the lady wrestlers, and then, turning to Aziz, became confidential. 'This town contains many good-for-nothings who have on occasion tried to climb into my daughter's room. She needs,' he nodded at the three musclebound women, 'protectors.'

Aziz was still looking at the perforated sheet. Ghani said, 'All right, come on, you will examine my Naseem right now. *Pronto.*'

My grandfather peered around the room. 'But where is she, Ghani Sahib?' he blurted out finally. The lady wrestlers adopted supercilious expressions and, it seemed to him, tightened their musculatures, just in case he intended to try something fancy.

'Ah, I see your confusion,' Ghani said, his poisonous smile broadening. 'You Europe-returned chappies forget certain things. Doctor Sahib, my daughter is a decent girl, it goes without saying. She does not flaunt her body under the noses of strange men. You will understand that you cannot be permitted to see her, no, not in any circumstances; accordingly I have required her to be positioned behind that sheet. She stands there, like a good girl.'

A frantic note had crept into Doctor Aziz's voice. 'Ghani Sahib, tell me how I am to examine her without looking at her?' Ghani smiled on.

'You will kindly specify which portion of my daughter it is necessary to inspect. I will then issue her with my instructions to place the required segment against that hole which you see there. And so, in this fashion the thing may be achieved.'

'But what, in any event, does the lady complain of?'—my grandfather, despairingly. To which Mr Ghani, his eyes rising upwards in their sockets, his smile twisting into a grimace of grief, replied: 'The poor child! She has a terrible, a too dreadful stomach-ache.'

'In that case,' Doctor Aziz said with some restraint, 'will she show me her stomach, please.'

---

4. Muslim women are required to be fully "veiled" in the presence of men not belonging to their families or intimate social circles. In this part of the novel, the bedsheet serving as a "curtain" between patient and doctor becomes an elaborate, comical proxy for the traditional Muslim veil.

My grandfather's premonitions in the corridor were not without foundation. In the succeeding months and years, he fell under what I can only describe as the sorcerer's spell of that enormous—and as yet unstained—perforated cloth.

In those years, you see, the landowner's daughter Naseem Ghani contracted a quite extraordinary number of minor illnesses, and each time a shikara-wallah was dispatched to summon the tall young Doctor Sahib with the big nose who was making such a reputation for himself in the valley. Aadam Aziz's visits to the bedroom with the shaft of sunlight and the three lady wrestlers became weekly events; and on each occasion he was vouchsafed a glimpse, through the mutilated sheet, of a different seven-inch circle of the young woman's body. Her initial stomach-ache was succeeded by a very slightly twisted right ankle, an ingrowing toenail on the big toe of the left foot, a tiny cut on the lower left calf. 'Tetanus is a killer, Doctor Sahib,' the landowner said. 'My Naseem must not die for a scratch.' There was the matter of her stiff right knee, which the Doctor was obliged to manipulate through the hole in the sheet . . . and after a time the illnesses leapt upwards, avoiding certain unmentionable zones, and began to proliferate around her upper half. She suffered from something mysterious which her father called Finger Rot, which made the skin flake off her hands; from weakness of the wrist-bones, for which Aadam prescribed calcium tablets; and from attacks of constipation, for which he gave her a course of laxatives, since there was no question of being permitted to administer an enema. She had fevers and she also had subnormal temperatures. At these times his thermometer would be placed under her armpit and he would hum and haw about the relative inefficiency of the method. In the opposite armpit she once developed a slight case of tineachloris and he dusted her with yellow powder; after this treatment—which required him to rub the powder in, gently but firmly, although the soft secret body began to shake and quiver and he heard helpless laughter coming through the sheet, because Naseem Ghani was very ticklish—the itching went away, but Naseem soon found a new set of complaints. She waxed anaemic in the summer and bronchial in the winter. ('Her tubes are most delicate,' Ghani explained, 'like little flutes.') Far away the Great War moved from crisis to crisis, while in the cobwebbed house Doctor Aziz was also engaged in a total war against his sectioned patient's inexhaustible complaints. And, in all those war years, Naseem never repeated an illness. 'Which only shows,' Ghani told him, 'that you are a good doctor. When you cure, she is cured for good. But alas!'—he struck his forehead—'She pines for her late mother, poor baby, and her body suffers. She is a too loving child.'

So gradually Doctor Aziz came to have a picture of Naseem in his mind, a badly-fitting collage of her severally-inspected parts. This phantasm of a partitioned woman began to haunt him, and not only in his dreams. Glued together by his imagination, she accompanied him on all his rounds, she moved into the front room of his mind, so that waking and sleeping he could feel in his fingertips the softness of her ticklish skin or the perfect tiny wrists or the beauty of the ankles; he could smell her scent of lavender and chambeli; he could hear her voice and her helpless laughter of a little girl; but she was headless, because he had never seen her face.

By 1918, Aadam Aziz had come to live for his regular trips across the lake. And now his eagerness became even more intense, because it became clear that, after three years, the landowner and his daughter had become willing to lower certain barriers. Now, for the first time, Ghani said, 'A lump in the right chest. Is it worrying, Doctor? Look. Look well.' And there, framed in the hole, was a perfectly-formed and lyrically lovely . . .'I must touch it,' Aziz said, fighting with his voice. Ghani slapped him on the back. 'Touch, touch!' he cried. 'The hands of the healer! The curing touch, eh, Doctor?' And Aziz reached out a hand . . .'Forgive me for asking; but is it the lady's time of the month?' . . . Little secret smiles appearing on the faces of the lady wrestlers. Ghani, nodding affably: 'Yes. Don't be so embarrassed, old chap. We are family and doctor now.' And Aziz, 'Then don't worry. The lumps will go when the time ends.' . . . And the next time, 'A pulled muscle in the back of her thigh, Doctor Sahib. Such pain!' And there, in the sheet, weakening the eyes of Aadam Aziz, hung a superbly rounded and impossible buttock . . . And now Aziz: 'Is it permitted that . . .' Whereupon a word from Ghani; an obedient reply from behind the sheet; a drawstring pulled; and pajamas fall from the celestial rump, which swells wondrously through the hole. Aadam Aziz forces himself into a medical frame of mind . . . reaches out . . . feels. And swears to himself, in amazement, that he sees the bottom reddening in a shy, but compliant blush.

That evening, Aadam contemplated the blush. Did the magic of the sheet work on both sides of the hole? Excitedly, he envisaged his headless Naseem tingling beneath the scrutiny of his eyes, his thermometer, his stethoscope, his fingers, and trying to build a picture in her mind of *him*. She was at a disadvantage, of course, having seen nothing but his hands . . . Aadam began to hope with an illicit desperation for Naseem Ghani to develop a migraine or graze her unseen chin, so they could look each other in the face. He knew how unprofessional his feelings were; but did nothing to stifle them. There was not much he could do. They had acquired a life of their own. In short: my grandfather had fallen in love, and had come to think of the perforated sheet as something sacred and magical, because through it he had seen the things which had filled up the hole inside him which had been created when he had been hit on the nose by a tussock and insulted by the boatman Tai.

On the day the World War ended, Naseem developed the longed-for headache. Such historical coincidences have littered, and perhaps befouled, my family's existence in the world.

He hardly dared to look at what was framed in the hole in the sheet. Maybe she was hideous; perhaps that explained all this performance . . . he looked. And saw a soft face that was not at all ugly, a cushioned setting for her glittering, gemstone eyes, which were brown with flecks of gold: tiger's-eyes. Doctor Aziz's fall was complete. And Naseem burst out, 'But Doctor, my God, what a *nose!*' Ghani, angrily, 'Daughter, mind your . . .' But patient and doctor were laughing together, and Aziz was saying, 'Yes, yes, it is a remarkable specimen. They tell me there are dynasties waiting in it . . .' And he bit his tongue because he had been about to add, '. . . like snot.'

And Ghani, who had stood blindly beside the sheet for three long years, smiling and smiling and smiling, began once again to smile his secret smile, which was mirrored in the lips of the wrestlers.

1980

JAMAICA KINCAID

born 1949

Born and raised among an extended family of "poor, ordinary people," "banana and citrus-fruit farmers, fishermen, carpenters and obeah women," Jamaica Kincaid rose from humble beginnings to become a successful contemporary writer, well known for her books and magazine articles about the immigrant experience. These works often convey a sense of immediacy through Kincaid's use of first-person narration or imagined dialogue.

Born Elaine Cynthia Potter Richardson in Antigua, a small island in the Caribbean, Kincaid grew up in the island's capital city of St. Johns. Part of the British Leeward Island chain, Antigua was a colony of Britain throughout the writer's childhood and adolescence; it gained political independence in 1981 and now belongs to the British Commonwealth. Kincaid's mother was a homemaker, and her stepfather worked as a carpenter (her biological father, a taxi driver, showed no interest in his children). Though Kincaid and her brothers were raised as Methodists, her mother and grandmother also practiced obeah, West Indian voodoo. Kincaid learned from them how to protect herself against the evil eye, how to appease local spirits, how to use herbs to conjure and heal—a familiarity with the supernatural that she later incorporated into her fiction.

At school, Kincaid was a quick student, taking a special interest in history and botany. Although her family had high aspirations for her three brothers and intended them to enter the professions, because Kincaid was a girl, they placed no value on her gifts: "No one expected anything from me at all," she later said. Her teachers often treated her eagerness in the classroom as a disciplinary problem. At thirteen, when Kincaid was about to take university qualifying examinations, her stepfather fell ill, forcing her to leave school and help raise her siblings. Angry and dispirited, she withdrew into books. Later she said that her passion for reading "saved her life." The island's colonial status meant that the local libraries and bookstores carried almost exclusively British literature, mainly of the nineteenth century. The lack of access to more recent works, or to the West Indian literary canon to which Kincaid would contribute so prominent a voice, prevented her at first from seeing art as more than an escape: "I thought writing was something that people just didn't do anymore, that went out of fashion, like the bustle."

Still, she chafed against her colonial upbringing and looked for ways to enter a wider world. At the age of seventeen she accepted a job as a nanny in the United States, and for four years lived with families in the New York City borough of Manhattan and in suburban Scarsdale. She earned a general equivalency diploma and briefly attended a college in New Hampshire before deciding she was too old. Back in Manhattan, and now determined to write, she started freelancing for magazines and weekly newspapers, including the *Village Voice*. It was during this period that she changed her name. Jamaica refers to the West Indies; Kincaid, to a work by the playwright George Bernard Shaw. She explained that the alteration allowed her to evade her family, who opposed her writing, as well as her broader colonial inheritance: the new name was "a way for me to do things without being the same person who couldn't do them—the same person who had all these weights."

Kincaid's first collection of short stories, *At the Bottom of the River*, appeared in 1983. An autobiographical novel, *Annie John*, followed in 1985; her second and third novels also draw on her own and her family's experiences in Antigua. She has continued to publish books and magazine articles and has won many prestigious awards, including the 2000 French Prix Femina Etranger. In recent years the author has turned her attention to nature writing and to botanical studies of the landscape. Throughout her career, though, Kincaid has retained a strong commitment to issues of identity, colonialism, and the color line. In *A Small Place*, written following Kincaid's first visit to Antigua since her youth, she criticizes what she sees as the island's complicity in its exploitation, carried over from the colonial past.

The story selected here, "Girl" (1978), was the first piece of fiction that Kincaid published. It consists of a single, winding sentence; the speaker is a mother giving instructions to her daughter on the rules and rites of womanhood. (The daughter's replies break into the narration in two passages, both printed in italics.) The setting is Antigua, although this point is never explicitly stated and can only be inferred from the story's details. Some of the instructions refer to folk medicine and obeah; for example, the warning against throwing stones at blackbirds, which might be malicious spirits in disguise. As the speaker discusses with equal matter-of-factness such topics as keeping house, enduring a cruel husband, and aborting unwanted pregnancies, a picture emerges of the harshness of countless women's lives, not just in this setting but throughout history and across the globe. During the lecture, the mother stresses how important it is for a young woman to maintain a sense of sexual propriety: the woman warns her daughter repeatedly that she will look like a "slut" if she does not behave properly. The edict against squatting to play marbles suggests that the listener has not left childhood entirely, but the early reference to washing "your little cloths" indicates that she has reached puberty and that the time when these instructions will come into use is not far off.

Girl

Wash the white clothes on Monday and put them on the stone heap; wash the color clothes on Tuesday and put them on the clothesline to dry; don't walk barehead in the hot sun; cook pumpkin fritters in very hot sweet oil; soak your little cloths[1] right after you take them off; when buying cotton to make yourself a nice blouse, be sure that it doesn't have gum on it, because that way it won't hold up well after a wash; soak salt fish overnight before you cook it; is it true that you sing benna[2] in Sunday school?; always eat your food in such a way that it won't turn someone else's stomach; on Sundays try to walk like a lady and not like the slut you are so bent on becoming; don't sing benna in Sunday school; you mustn't speak to wharf-rat boys, not even to give directions; don't

---

1. Pads for menstruation.
2. Improvised Antiguan folk song with African roots.

eat fruits on the street—flies will follow you; *but I don't sing benna on Sundays at all and never in Sunday school*; this is how to sew on a button; this is how to make a buttonhole for the button you have just sewed on; this is how to hem a dress when you see the hem coming down and so to prevent yourself from looking like the slut I know you are so bent on becoming; this is how you iron your father's khaki shirt so that it doesn't have a crease; this is how you iron your father's khaki pants so that they don't have a crease; this is how you grow okra—far from the house, because okra tree harbors red ants; when you are growing dasheen,[3] make sure it gets plenty of water or else it makes your throat itch when you are eating it; this is how you sweep a corner; this is how you sweep a whole house; this is how you sweep a yard; this is how you smile to someone you don't like too much; this is how you smile to someone you don't like at all; this is how you smile to someone you like completely; this is how you set a table for tea; this is how you set a table for dinner; this is how you set a table for dinner with an important guest; this is how you set a table for lunch; this is how you set a table for breakfast; this is how to behave in the presence of men who don't know you very well, and this way they won't recognize immediately the slut I have warned you against becoming; be sure to wash every day, even if it is with your own spit; don't squat down to play marbles—you are not a boy, you know; don't pick people's flowers—you might catch something; don't throw stones at blackbirds, because it might not be a blackbird at all; this is how to make a bread pudding; this is how to make doukona;[4] this is how to make pepper pot;[5] this is how to make a good medicine for a cold; this is how to make a good medicine to throw away a child before it even becomes a child; this is how to catch a fish; this is how to throw back a fish you don't like, and that way something bad won't fall on you; this is how to bully a man; this is how a man bullies you; this is how to love a man, and if this doesn't work there are other ways, and if they don't work don't feel too bad about giving up; this is how to spit up in the air if you feel like it, and this is how to move quick so that it doesn't fall on you; this is how to make ends meet; always squeeze bread to make sure it's fresh; *but what if the baker won't let me feel the bread?*; you mean to say that after all you are really going to be the kind of woman who the baker won't let near the bread?

1978

---

3. A type of taro, a root vegetable.
4. A pudding made of plantains.

5. A spicy stew.

HANAN AL-SHAYKH

born 1945

Lebanese writer Hanan Al-Shaykh explores the conflicts between tradition and modernity as they affect women in the Arab world. Her feminist critique of Arab culture is intimate, focused less on government oppression and more on the daily choices women must make to assert their freedom in a social system that often constrains them. By examining life through the innocent perspectives of girls and young women, the author provides social commentary while concentrating on the human dimensions of the issues raised.

Born in southern Lebanon, Hanan Al-Shaykh was raised in Beirut by her strict Shiite family. Later, Al-Shaykh would recall that her family's traditional religious practices seemed out of place in the cosmopolitan capital: "we lived in a street full of Beirutis. We were from the south, we always felt like outsiders. The whole street thought my father was mad: he wore a shawl on his head and would wash the stairs of the whole building." Her father, a conservative merchant, and her mother, an illiterate housewife, divorced when she was young, and Al-Shaykh began to write short stories in part as an act of rebellion against the restrictive influences of her father and brothers.

Al-Shaykh attended a traditional Muslim girls' primary school and, later, the more cosmopolitan Ahliyyah School and the American College for Girls in Cairo. After graduating, she worked as a journalist for the magazine *al-Hasna* (*Beautiful Woman*) and for the journal *al-Nahar* (*The Day*), which published her earliest short stories. Her first novel, *Suicide of a Dead Man* (1970),

relates a teenage girl's affair with a middle-age man but, surprisingly, from the man's point of view. It brought comparisons to the work of **Naguib Mahfouz**, particularly for its faithful representation of the spoken language. As Al-Shaykh later explained, "My generation of Arab writers adopted a language between the classical and the spoken dialect. The dialogue is, at times, even colloquial and thus much closer to the way people really speak."

During the Lebanese Civil War (1975–90), Al-Shaykh left the country to live in London and in Saudi Arabia, where she wrote *The Story of Zahra* (1980). She released the novel at her own expense, as no publisher in Lebanon would accept the manuscript, but it became her first international success. The protagonist of the story, Zahra, is a young woman mired in the oppressive and misogynistic milieu of war-torn Lebanon. Trapped in a loveless marriage, she falls in love with a sniper, who at some point turns on her as one of his political targets. Her later novels likewise focus on the life experiences of Arab women, especially during the civil war. *Only in London* (2000) was her first novel set in Europe, although the main figures in it are Middle Eastern immigrants. She has written two experimental plays, performed by the Hampstead Theatre in London. Her frank treatment of such topics as abortion, adultery, homosexuality, prostitution, rape, and transvestism has made her work controversial in the Arab world. She has lived in London since 1983.

The story presented here, "The Women's Swimming Pool" (1982), although it addresses none of these controversial subjects, nonetheless concerns the breaking of taboos. The narrator, accustomed to having to cover her head and wear long-sleeve clothes in the fierce heat of southern Lebanese tobacco fields, wants to visit the sea and to bathe in a swimming pool that her friend has seen in Beirut. With great sensitivity Al-Shaykh portrays the innocent perspective of the narrator, an orphan who simply wants to go swimming but who, because of social customs barring women from displaying their bodies, has never had access to a swimming pool. Her grandmother, hoping to fulfill the little girl's wishes, takes her on a long bus ride from their home village, but she is as bewildered as her granddaughter by the metropolis of Beirut. The girl and the old woman have a close, loving relationship, but, as the story progresses, the narrator sees her grandmother, and indeed the customs of her village, in a new light. Although the narrator says little about her adult life, this recollection of childhood seems to mark a turning point, setting the girl on the path to become the woman who writes stories of liberation and separating her from the grandmother she loves but does not want to emulate.

The Women's Swimming Pool[1]

I am in the tent for threading the tobacco, amidst the mounds of tobacco plants and the skewers. Cross-legged, I breathe in the green odor, threading one leaf after another. I find myself dreaming and growing thirsty and dreaming. I open the magazine: I devour the words and surreptitiously gaze at the pictures. I am exasperated at being in the tent, then my exasperation turns to sadness.

Thirsty, I rise to my feet. I hear Abu Ghalib say, "Where are you off to, little lady?" I make my way to my grandmother, saying, "I'm thirsty." I go out. I make my way to the cistern, stumbling in the sandy ground. I see the greenish-blue water. I stretch out my hand to its still surface, hot from the harsh sun. I stretch out my hand and wipe it across my brow and face and neck, across my chest. Before being able to savor its relative coldness, I hear my name and see my grandmother standing in her black dress at the doorway of the tent. Aloud I express the wish that someone else had called to me. We have become like an orange and its navel: my grandmother has welded me so close to her that the village girls no longer dare to make friends with me, perhaps for fear of rupturing this close union.

I returned to the tent, growing thirsty and dreaming, with the sea ever in my mind. What were its waters like? What color would they be now? If only this week would pass in a flash, for I had at last persuaded my grandmother to go down to Beirut and the sea, after my friend Sumayya had sworn that the swimming pool she'd been at had been for women only.

1. Translated from the Arabic by Denys Johnson-Davies.

My grandmother sat on the edge of a jagged slab of stone, leaning on my arm. Her hand was hot and rough. She sighed as she chased away a fly.

What is my grandmother gazing at? There was nothing in front of us but the asphalt road, which, despite the sun's rays, gave off no light, and the white marble tombs that stretched along the high mountainside, while the houses of upper Nabatieh[2] looked like deserted Crusader castles, their alleyways empty, their windows of iron. Our house likewise seemed to be groaning in its solitude, shaded by the fig tree. The washing line stirs with the wind above the tomb of my grandfather, the celebrated religious scholar, in the courtyard of the house. What is my grandmother staring at? Or does someone who is waiting not stare?

Turning her face toward me, she said, "Child, what will we do if the bus doesn't come?" Her face, engraved in my mind, seemed overcast, also her half-closed eyes and the blue tattoo mark on her chin. I didn't answer her for fear I'd cry if I talked. This time I averted my gaze from the white tombs; moving my foot away from my grandmother's leg clothed in thick black stockings, I began to walk about, my gaze directed to the other side where lay the extensive fields of green tobacco, towering and gently swaying, their leaves glinting under the sun, leaves that were imprinted on my brain, their marks still showing on my hands.

My gaze reached out behind the thousands of plants, then beyond them, moving away till it arrived at the tent where the tobacco was threaded. I came up close to my grandmother, who was still sitting in her place, still gazing in front of her. As I drew close to her, I heard her give a sigh. A sprinkling of sweat lay on the pouches under her eyes. "Child, what do you want with the sea? Don't you know that the sea puts a spell on people?" I didn't answer her: I was worried that the morning would pass, that noonday would pass, and that I wouldn't see the green bus come to a stop by the stone my grandmother sat on, to take us to the sea, to Beirut. Again I heard my grandmother mumbling. "That devil Sumayya . . ." I pleaded with her to stop, and my thoughts rose up and left the stone upon which my grandmother sat, the rough road, left everything. I went back to my dreams, to the sea.

The sea had always been my obsession, ever since I had seen it for the first time inside a colored ball; with its blue color it was like a magic lantern, wide open, the surface of its water unrippled unless you tilted the piece of glass, with its small shells and white specks like snow. When I first became aware of things, this ball, which I had found in the parlor, was the sole thing that animated and amused me. The more I gazed at it, the cooler I felt its waters to be, and the more they invited me to bathe in them; they knew that I had been born amidst dust and mud and the stench of tobacco.

If only the green bus would come along—and I shifted my bag from one hand to the other. I heard my grandmother wail, "Child, bring up a stone and sit down. Put down the bag and don't worry." My distress increased, and I was no longer able to stop it turning into tears that flowed freely down my face, veiling it from the road. I stretched up to wipe them with my sleeve; in this

2. A town in southern Lebanon.

heat I still had to wear that dress with long sleeves, that head covering over my braids,[3] despite the hot wind that set the tobacco plants and the sparse poplars swaying. Thank God I had resisted her and refused to wear my stockings. I gave a deep sigh as I heard the bus's horn from afar. Fearful and anxious, I shouted at my grandmother as I helped her to her feet, turning round to make sure that my bag was still in my hand and my grandmother's hand in the other. The bus came to a stop and the conductor helped my grandmother on. When I saw myself alongside her and the stone on its own, I tightened my grip on my bag in which lay Sumayya's bathing costume, a sleeveless dress, and my money.

I noticed as the bus slowly made its way along the road that my anxiety was still there, that it was in fact increasing: Why didn't the bus pass by all these trees and fallow land like lightning? Why was it crawling along? My anxiety was still there and increased till it predominated over my other sensations, my nausea and curiosity.

How would we find our way to the sea? Would we see it as soon as we arrived in Beirut? Was it at the other end of it? Would the bus stop in the district of Zeytouna,[4] at the door of the women's swimming pool? Why, I wondered, was it called Zeytouna?—were there olive trees there? I leaned toward my grandmother and her silent face and long nose that almost met up with her mouth. Thinking that I wanted a piece of cane sugar, she put her hand to her bosom to take out a small twist of cloth. Impatiently I asked her if she was sure that Maryam at-Taweela knew Zeytouna, to which she answered, her mouth sucking at the cane sugar and making a noise with her tongue, "God will look after everything." Then she broke the silence by saying. "All this trouble is that devil Sumayya's fault—it was she who told you she'd seen with her own eyes the swimming pool just for women and not for men." "Yes, Grandma," I answered her. She said, "Swear by your mother's grave." I thought to myself absently: "Why only my mother's grave? What about my father? Or did she only acknowledge her daughter's death . . .?" "By my mother's grave, it's for women." She inclined her head and still munching the cane sugar and making a noise with her tongue, she said, "If any man were to see you, you'd be done for, and so would your mother and father and your grandfather, the religious scholar— and I'd be done for more than anyone because it's I who agreed to this and helped you."

I would have liked to say to her, "They've all gone, they've all died, so what do we have to be afraid of?" But I knew what she meant: that she was frightened they wouldn't go to heaven.

I began to sweat, and my heart again contracted as Beirut came into view with its lofty buildings, car horns, the bared arms of the women, the girls' hair, the tight trousers they were wearing. People were sitting on chairs in the middle of the pavement, eating and drinking; the trams; the roasting chickens revolving on spits. Ah, these dresses for sale in the windows, would anyone be found actually to wear them? I see a Japanese man, the first-ever member of

---

3. Islamic custom requires girls and women to keep their hair, arms, and legs covered.

4. A cosmopolitan district of Lebanon; the name means "olive."

the yellow races outside of books; the Martyrs' monument; Riad Solh Square.[5] I was wringing wet with sweat and my heart pounded—it was as though I regretted having come to Beirut, perhaps because I was accompanied by my grandmother. It was soon all too evident that we were outsiders to the capital. We began walking after my grandmother had asked the bus driver the whereabouts of the district of Khandaq al-Ghamiq[6] where Maryam at-Taweela lived. Once again my body absorbed all the sweat and allowed my heart to flee its cage. I find myself treading on a pavement on which for long years I have dreamed of walking; I hear sounds that have been engraved on my imagination; and everything I see I have seen in daydreams at school or in the tobacco-threading tent. Perhaps I shouldn't say that I was regretting it, for after this I would never forget Beirut. We begin walking and losing our way in a Beirut that never ends, that leads nowhere. We begin asking and walking and losing our way, and my going to the sea seems an impossibility; the sea is fleeing from me. My grandmother comes to a stop and leans against a lamppost, or against the litter bin attached to it, and against my shoulders, and puffs and blows. I have the feeling that we shall never find Maryam at-Taweela's house. A man we had stopped to ask the way walks with us. When we knock at the door and no one opens to us, I become convinced that my bathing in the sea is no longer possible. The sweat pours off me, my throat contracts. A woman's voice brings me back to my senses as I drown in a lake of anxiety, sadness, and fear; then it drowns me once again. It was not Maryam at-Taweela but her neighbor who is asking us to wait at her place. We go down the steps to the neighbor's outdoor stone bench, and my grandmother sits down by the door but gets to her feet again when the woman entreats her to sit in the cane chair. Then she asks to be excused while she finishes washing down the steps. While she is cursing the heat of Beirut in the summer, I notice the tin containers lined up side by side containing red and green peppers. We have a long wait, and I begin to weep inwardly as I stare at the containers.

I wouldn't be seeing the sea today, perhaps not for years, but the thought of its waters would not leave me, would not be erased from my dreams. I must persuade my grandmother to come to Beirut with Sumayya. Perhaps I should not have mentioned the swimming pool in front of her. I wouldn't be seeing the sea today—and once again I sank back into a lake of doubt and fear and sadness. A woman's voice again brought me back to my senses: it was Maryam at-Taweela, who had stretched out her long neck and had kissed me, while she asked my grandmother: 'She's the child of your late daughter, isn't she?'—and she swore by the Imam[7] that we must have lunch with her, doing so before we had protested, feeling perhaps that I would do so. When she stood up and took the primus stove from under her bed and brought out potatoes and tomatoes and bits of meat, I had feelings of nausea, then of frustration. I nudged my grandmother, who leant over and whispered, "What

---

5. One of the main squares in Beirut's commercial district; the Martyrs' monument commemorates Lebanese nationalists who opposed Ottoman rule in the early 20th century.

6. A well-to-do neighborhood in West Beirut.
7. The Imam Ali (ca. 600–661), cousin and son-in-law of the prophet Mohammed and founder of the Shia branch of Islam.

is it, dear?" at which Maryam at-Taweela turned and asked. "What does your granddaughter want—to go to the bathroom?" My mouth went quite dry and my tears were all stored up waiting for a signal from my heartbeats to fall. My grandmother said with embarrassment, "She wants to go to the sea, to the women's swimming pool—that devil Sumayya put it into her head." To my amazement Maryam at-Taweela said loudly, "And why not? Right now Ali Mousa, our neighbor, will be coming and he'll take you, he's got a car"—and Maryam at-Taweela began peeling the potatoes at a low table in the middle of the room and my grandmother asked, "Where's Ali Mousa from? Where does he live?"

I can't wait, I shan't eat, I shan't drink. I want to go now, now. I remained seated, crying inwardly because I was born in the South, because there's no escape for me from the South, and I go on rubbing my fingers and gnawing at my nails. Again I begin to sweat: I shan't eat, I shan't drink, I shan't reply to Maryam at-Taweela. It was as though I was taking vengeance on my grandmother for some wrong she did not know about. My patience vanished. I stood up and said to my grandmother before I should burst out sobbing, "Come along, Grandma, get up, and let's go." I helped her to her feet, and Maryam at-Taweela asked in bewilderment what had suddenly come over me. I went on dragging my grandmother out to the street so that I might stop the first taxi.

Only moments passed before the driver shut off his engine and said, "Zeytouna." I looked about me but saw no sea. As I gave him a lira I asked him, "Where's the women's swimming pool?" He shrugged his shoulders. We got out of the car with difficulty, as was always the case with my grandmother. To my astonishment the driver returned, stretching out his head in concern at us. "Jump in," he said, and we got in. He took us round and round, stopping once at a petrol station and then by a newspaper seller, asking about the women's swimming pool and nobody knowing where it was. Once again he dropped us in the middle of Zeytouna Street.

Then, behind the hotels and the beautiful buildings and the date palms, I saw the sea. It was like a blue line of quicksilver: it was as though pieces of silver paper were resting on it. The sea that was in front of me was more beautiful than it had been in the glass ball. I didn't know how to get close to it, how to touch it. Cement lay between us. We began inquiring about the whereabouts of the swimming pool, but no one knew. The sea remains without waves, a blue line. I feel frustrated. Perhaps this swimming pool is some secret known only to the girls of the South. I began asking every person I saw. I tried to choke back my tears; I let go of my grandmother's hand as though wishing to reproach her, to punish her for having insisted on accompanying me instead of Sumayya. Poor me. Poor Grandma. Poor Beirut. Had my dreams come to an end in the middle of the street? I clasp my bag and my grandmother's hand, with the sea in front of me, separating her from me. My stubbornness and vexation impel me to ask and go on asking. I approached a man leaning against a bus, and to my surprise he pointed to an opening between two shops. I hurried back to my grandmother, who was supporting herself against a lamppost, to tell her I'd found it. When I saw with what difficulty she attempted to walk, I asked her to wait for me while I made sure. I went through the opening but didn't see the sea. All I saw was a fat woman with bare shoulders sitting behind a table. Hesitating, I stood and looked at her, not daring to step forward. My enthusiasm had vanished, taking with it my courage. "Yes," said the woman. I came forward and asked her, "Is the women's swimming pool here?" She nodded her head and said, "The entrance fee is a lira." I asked her if it was possible for my grandmother to wait for me here and she stared at me and said, "Of course." There was contempt in the way she looked at me: Was it my southern accent or my long-sleeved dress? I had disregarded my grandmother and had taken off my head shawl and hidden it in my bag. I handed her a lira and could hear the sounds of women and children—and still I did not see the sea. At the end of the portico were steps; which I was certain led to the roofed-in sea. The important thing was that I'd arrived, that I would be tasting the salty spray of its waters. I wouldn't be seeing the waves; never mind, I'd be bathing in its waters.

I found myself saying to the woman, or rather to myself because no sound issued from my throat, "I'll bring my grandmother." Going out through the opening and still clasping my bag to my chest, I saw my grandmother standing and looking up at the sky. I called to her, but she was reciting to herself under her breath as she continued to look upward: she was praying, right there in the street, praying on the pavement at the door of the swimming pool. She had spread out a paper bag and had stretched out her hands to the sky. I walked off in another direction and stopped looking at her. I would have liked to persuade myself that she had nothing to do with me, that I didn't know her. How, though? She's my grandmother whom I've dragged with my entreaties from the tobacco-threading tent, from the jagged slab of stone, from the winds of the South; I have crammed her into the bus and been lost with her in the streets as we searched for Maryam at-Taweela's house. And now here were the two of us standing at the door of the swimming pool, and she, having heard the call to prayers,[8] had prostrated herself in prayer. She was destroying what lay in my bag, blocking the road between me and the sea. I felt sorry for her, for her knees that knelt on the cruelly hard pavement, for her tattooed hands that lay on the dirt. I looked at her again and saw the passers-by staring at her. For the first time her black dress looked shabby to me. I felt how far removed we were from these passers-by, from this street, this city, this sea. I approached her, and she again put her weight on my hand.

1982

---

8. The Islamic call to prayer, heard five times a day in Muslim countries but ignored by secular residents of some large cities like Beirut.

ISABEL ALLENDE

born 1942

One of the best known contemporary Latin American writers, the Chilean novelist Isabel Allende brought the tradition of magic realism to bear on women's experience. Drawing on the earlier experiments by **Gabriel García Márquez** and other writers of the Latin American Boom, Allende has portrayed women's spiritual lives in the context of the political world of her childhood and youth, adding a dimension to magic realism while bringing her a wide international audience.

Born in Peru, where her father was a diplomat representing Chile, Allende returned to Chile with her mother at the age of three when her parents divorced. She lived for much of her childhood with her grandparents. Her mother's second husband, also a diplomat, later took the family to Bolivia and Beirut. As a young woman, Allende became involved in international affairs herself, working for the Food and Agriculture Organization of the United Nations, before beginning a career in journalism. In 1973 her father's cousin, Salvador Allende, the first elected Socialist president of Chile, was deposed in a coup led by General Augusto Pinochet. Historians still debate whether he killed himself or was assassinated by Pinochet's forces. In the coup's aftermath, Isabel Allende and her family left Chile for Venezuela, where she continued to work as a journalist. She has said that the departure from Chile made her a serious writer: "I don't think I would be a writer if I had stayed in Chile. I would be trapped in the chores, in the family, in the person that people expected me to be. I was not supposed to be in any way a liberated person. I was a female born in the '40s in a patriarchal family;

I was supposed to marry and make everyone around me happy." Instead, she chose a liberated, cosmopolitan lifestyle, although she would marry and have two children.

When she received news, in 1981, that her ninety-nine-year-old grandfather was dying, Allende began writing him a long letter—which developed, transformed, and expanded to become her first novel, *The House of the Spirits* (1982). This novel chronicles the experiences of a South American family haunted by spirits and torn by political events over several decades of the twentieth century. The subjects and style drew comparisons to the magic realism of García Márquez, whom Allende described as "the great writer of the century." The novel was an international success, and Allende moved to California, where she continues to live, teaching at universities throughout the United States. Her daughter died of a rare illness, porphyria, in 1992, and Allende wrote a moving personal memoir with her in mind, *Paula* (1994).

The story presented here, "And of Clay Are We Created" (1989), belongs to a stage of her career in which Allende chose a more direct, less magic, realism. The title refers to the proverb "we are all made of the same clay," which in turn refers to biblical passages (Psalms 103.14, Job 33.6, and Genesis 2–3), in which humans are said to be created of clay or earth. As God reminds Adam on his expulsion from the Garden of Eden, "dust thou art, and unto dust shalt thou return" (Gen. 3.19). In the context of the soil smothering the victims of a volcanic eruption, this passage reminds us not only of our shared humanity but of our

rope to her that she made no effort to grasp until they shouted to her to catch it; then she pulled a hand from the mire and tried to move, but immediately sank a little deeper. Rolf threw down his knapsack and the rest of his equipment and waded into the quagmire, commenting for his assistant's microphone that it was cold and that one could begin to smell the stench of corpses.

"What's your name?" he asked the girl, and she told him her flower name. "Don't move, Azucena," Rolf Carlé directed, and kept talking to her, without a thought for what he was saying, just to distract her, while slowly he worked his way forward in mud up to his waist. The air around him seemed as murky as the mud.

It was impossible to reach her from the approach he was attempting, so he retreated and circled around where there seemed to be firmer footing. When finally he was close enough, he took the rope and tied it beneath her arms, so they could pull her out. He smiled at her with that smile that crinkles his eyes and makes him look like a little boy; he told her that everything was fine, that he was here with her now, that soon they would have her out. He signaled the others to pull, but as soon as the cord tensed, the girl screamed. They tried again, and her shoulders and arms appeared, but they could move her no farther; she was trapped. Someone suggested that her legs might be caught in the collapsed walls of her house, but she said it was not just rubble, that she was also held by the bodies of her brothers and sisters clinging to her legs.

"Don't worry, we'll get you out of here," Rolf promised. Despite the quality of the transmission, I could hear his voice break, and I loved him more than ever. Azucena looked at him, but said nothing.

During those first hours Rolf Carlé exhausted all the resources of his ingenuity to rescue her. He struggled with poles and ropes, but every tug was an intolerable torture for the imprisoned girl. It occurred to him to use one of the poles as a lever but got no result and had to abandon the idea. He talked a couple of soldiers into working with him for a while, but they had to leave because so many other victims were calling for help. The girl could not move, she barely could breathe, but she did not seem desperate, as if an ancestral resignation allowed her to accept her fate. The reporter, on the other hand, was determined to snatch her from death. Someone brought him a tire, which he placed beneath her arms like a life buoy, and then laid a plank near the hole to hold his weight and allow him to stay closer to her. As it was impossible to remove the rubble blindly, he tried once or twice to dive toward her feet, but emerged frustrated, covered with mud, and spitting gravel. He concluded that he would have to have a pump to drain the water, and radioed a request for one, but received in return a message that there was no available transport and it could not be sent until the next morning.

"We can't wait that long!" Rolf Carlé shouted, but in the pandemonium no one stopped to commiserate. Many more hours would go by before he accepted that time had stagnated and reality had been irreparably distorted.

A military doctor came to examine the girl, and observed that her heart was functioning well and that if she did not get too cold she could survive the night.

"Hang on, Azucena, we'll have the pump tomorrow," Rolf Carlé tried to console her.

"Don't leave me alone," she begged.

"No, of course I won't leave you."

Someone brought him coffee, and he helped the girl drink it, sip by sip. The warm liquid revived her and she began telling him about her small life, about her family and her school, about how things were in that little bit of world before the volcano had erupted. She was thirteen, and she had never been outside her village. Rolf Carlé, buoyed by a premature optimism, was convinced that everything would end well: the pump would arrive, they would drain the water, move the rubble, and Azucena would be transported by helicopter to a hospital where she would recover rapidly and where he could visit her and bring her gifts. He thought, She's already too old for dolls, and I don't know what would please her; maybe a dress. I don't know much about women, he concluded, amused, reflecting that although he had known many women in his lifetime, none had taught him these details. To pass the hours he began to tell Azucena about his travels and adventures as a newshound, and when he exhausted his memory, he called upon imagination, inventing things he thought might entertain her. From time to time she dozed, but he kept talking in the darkness, to assure her that he was still there and to overcome the menace of uncertainty.

That was a long night.

Many miles away, I watched Rolf Carlé and the girl on a television screen. I could not bear the wait at home, so I went to National Television, where I often spent entire nights with Rolf editing programs. There, I was near his world, and I could at least get a feeling of what he lived through during those three decisive days. I called all the important people in the city, senators, commanders of the armed forces, the North American[4] ambassador, and the president of National Petroleum, begging them for a pump to remove the silt, but obtained only vague promises. I began to ask for urgent help on radio and television, to see if there wasn't *someone* who could help us. Between calls I would run to the newsroom to monitor the satellite transmissions that periodically brought new details of the catastrophe. While reporters selected scenes with most impact for the news report, I searched for footage that featured Azucena's mudpit. The screen reduced the disaster to a single plane and accentuated the tremendous distance that separated me from Rolf Carlé; nonetheless, I was there with him. The child's every suffering hurt me as it did him; I felt his frustration, his impotence. Faced with the impossibility of communicating with him, the fantastic idea came to me that if I tried, I could reach him by force of mind and in that way give him encouragement. I concentrated until I was dizzy—a frenzied and futile activity. At times I would be overcome with compassion and burst out crying; at other times, I was so drained I felt as if I were staring through a telescope at the light of a star dead for a million years.

I watched that hell on the first morning broadcast, cadavers of people and animals awash in the current of new rivers formed overnight from the melted snow. Above the mud rose the tops of trees and the bell towers of a church where several people had taken refuge and were patiently awaiting rescue teams. Hundreds of soldiers and volunteers from the Civil Defense[5] were clawing through rubble searching for survivors, while long rows of ragged specters awaited their turn for a cup of hot broth. Radio networks announced that their

4. I.e., United States.
5. A group of trained workers prepared to respond to disasters.

phones were jammed with calls from families offering shelter to orphaned children. Drinking water was in scarce supply, along with gasoline and food. Doctors, resigned to amputating arms and legs without anesthesia, pled that at least they be sent serum and painkillers and antibiotics; most of the roads, however, were impassable, and worse were the bureaucratic obstacles that stood in the way. To top it all, the clay contaminated by decomposing bodies threatened the living with an outbreak of epidemics.

Azucena was shivering inside the tire that held her above the surface. Immobility and tension had greatly weakened her, but she was conscious and could still be heard when a microphone was held out to her. Her tone was humble, as if apologizing for all the fuss. Rolf Carlé had a growth of beard, and dark circles beneath his eyes; he looked near exhaustion. Even from that enormous distance I could sense the quality of his weariness, so different from the fatigue of other adventures. He had completely forgotten the camera; he could not look at the girl through a lens any longer. The pictures we were receiving were not his assistant's but those of other reporters who had appropriated Azucena, bestowing on her the pathetic responsibility of embodying the horror of what had happened in that place. With the first light Rolf tried again to dislodge the obstacles that held the girl in her tomb, but he had only his hands to work with; he did not dare use a tool for fear of injuring her. He fed Azucena a cup of the cornmeal mush and bananas the Army was distributing, but she immediately vomited it up. A doctor stated that she had a fever, but added that there was little he could do: antibiotics were being reserved for cases of gangrene. A priest also passed by and blessed her, hanging a medal of the Virgin around her neck. By evening a gentle, persistent drizzle began to fall.

"The sky is weeping," Azucena murmured, and she, too, began to cry.

"Don't be afraid," Rolf begged. "You have to keep your strength up and be calm. Everything will be fine. I'm with you, and I'll get you out somehow."

Reporters returned to photograph Azucena and ask her the same questions, which she no longer tried to answer. In the meanwhile, more television and movie teams arrived with spools of cable, tapes, film, videos, precision lenses, recorders, sound consoles, lights, reflecting screens, auxiliary motors, cartons of supplies, electricians, sound technicians, and cameramen: Azucena's face was beamed to millions of screens around the world. And all the while Rolf Carlé kept pleading for a pump. The improved technical facilities bore results, and National Television began receiving sharper pictures and clearer sound; the distance seemed suddenly compressed, and I had the horrible sensation that Azucena and Rolf were by my side, separated from me by impenetrable glass. I was able to follow events hour by hour; I knew everything my love did to wrest the girl from her prison and help her endure her suffering; I overheard fragments of what they said to one another and could guess the rest; I was present when she taught Rolf to pray, and when he distracted her with the stories I had told him in a thousand and one nights[6] beneath the white mosquito netting of our bed.

---

6. A reference to the collection of medieval Arabic tales, *The Thousand and One Nights*. In the collection, King Shahryar has killed a series of wives after spending a single night with each. Queen Scheherezade tells the king suspenseful stories each night, leaving the endings for the following night; her husband does not kill her because he wants to hear the endings of the stories.

When darkness came on the second day, Rolf tried to sing Azucena to sleep with old Austrian folk songs he had learned from his mother, but she was far beyond sleep. They spent most of the night talking, each in a stupor of exhaustion and hunger, and shaking with cold. That night, imperceptibly, the unyielding floodgates that had contained Rolf Carlé's past for so many years began to open, and the torrent of all that had lain hidden in the deepest and most secret layers of memory poured out, leveling before it the obstacles that had blocked his consciousness for so long. He could not tell it all to Azucena; she perhaps did not know there was a world beyond the sea or time previous to her own; she was not capable of imagining Europe in the years of the war.[7] So he could not tell her of defeat, nor of the afternoon the Russians had led them to the concentration camp to bury prisoners dead from starvation. Why should he describe to her how the naked bodies piled like a mountain of firewood resembled fragile china? How could he tell this dying child about ovens[8] and gallows? Nor did he mention the night that he had seen his mother naked, shod in stiletto-heeled red boots, sobbing with humiliation. There was much he did not tell, but in those hours he relived for the first time all the things his mind had tried to erase. Azucena had surrendered her fear to him and so, without wishing it, had obliged Rolf to confront his own. There, beside that hellhole of mud, it was impossible for Rolf to flee from himself any longer, and the visceral terror he had lived as a boy suddenly invaded him. He reverted to the years when he was the age of Azucena, and younger, and, like her, found himself trapped in a pit without escape, buried in life, his head barely above ground; he saw before his eyes the boots and legs of his father, who had removed his belt and was whipping it in the air with the never-forgotten hiss of a viper coiled to strike. Sorrow flooded through him, intact and precise, as if it had lain always in his mind, waiting. He was once again in the armoire where his father locked him to punish him for imagined misbehavior, there where for eternal hours he had crouched with his eyes closed, not to see the darkness, with his hands over his ears, to shut out the beating of his heart, trembling, huddled like a cornered animal. Wandering in the mist of his memories he found his sister Katharina, a sweet, retarded child who spent her life hiding, with the hope that her father would forget the disgrace of her having been born. With Katharina, Rolf crawled beneath the dining room table, and with her hid there under the long white tablecloth, two children forever embraced, alert to footsteps and voices. Katharina's scent melded with his own sweat, with aromas of cooking, garlic, soup, freshly baked bread, and the unexpected odor of putrescent clay. His sister's hand in his, her frightened breathing, her silk hair against his cheek, the candid gaze of her eyes. Katharina . . . Katharina materialized before him, floating on the air like a flag, clothed in the white tablecloth, now a winding sheet, and at last he could weep for her death and for the guilt of having abandoned her. He understood then that all his exploits as a reporter, the feats that had won him such recognition and fame, were merely an attempt to keep his most ancient fears at bay, a stratagem for taking refuge behind a lens to test whether reality was more tolerable from that perspective. He took excessive risks as an exercise of courage, training by day to conquer the monsters that tormented him by night! But he had come face to face with the moment of truth; he

7. The Second World War (1939–45).
8. Crematoria in which the Nazis incinerated their victims during the Second World War.

could not continue to escape his past. He *was* Azucena; he was buried in the clayey mud; his terror was not the distant emotion of an almost forgotten childhood, it was a claw sunk in his throat. In the flush of his tears he saw his mother, dressed in black and clutching her imitation-crocodile pocketbook to her bosom, just as he had last seen her on the dock when she had come to put him on the boat to South America.[9] She had not come to dry his tears, but to tell him to pick up a shovel: the war was over and now they must bury the dead.

"Don't cry. I don't hurt anymore. I'm fine," Azucena said when dawn came.

"I'm not crying for you," Rolf Carlé smiled. "I'm crying for myself. I hurt all over."

The third day in the valley of the cataclysm began with a pale light filtering through storm clouds. The President of the Republic visited the area in his tailored safari jacket to confirm that this was the worst catastrophe of the century; the country was in mourning; sister nations had offered aid; he had ordered a state of siege; the Armed Forces would be merciless, anyone caught stealing or committing other offenses would be shot on sight. He added that it was impossible to remove all the corpses or count the thousands who had disappeared; the entire valley would be declared holy ground, and bishops would come to celebrate a solemn mass for the souls of the victims. He went to the Army field tents to offer relief in the form of vague promises to crowds of the rescued, then to the improvised hospital to offer a word of encouragement to doctors and nurses worn down from so many hours of tribulations. Then he asked to be taken to see Azucena, the little girl the whole world had seen. He waved to her with a limp statesman's hand, and microphones recorded his emotional voice and paternal tone as he told her that her courage had served as an example to the nation. Rolf Carlé interrupted to ask for a pump, and the President assured him that he personally would attend to the matter. I caught a glimpse of Rolf for a few seconds kneeling beside the mudpit. On the evening news broadcast, he was still in the same position, and I, glued to the screen like a fortuneteller to her crystal ball, could tell that something fundamental had changed in him. I knew somehow that during the night his defenses had crumbled and he had given in to grief; finally he was vulnerable. The girl had touched a part of him that he himself had no access to, a part he had never shared with me. Rolf had wanted to console her, but it was Azucena who had given him consolation.

I recognized the precise moment at which Rolf gave up the fight and surrendered to the torture of watching the girl die. I was with them, three days and two nights, spying on them from the other side of life. I was there when she told him that in all her thirteen years no boy had ever loved her and that it was a pity to leave this world without knowing love. Rolf assured her that he loved her more than he could ever love anyone, more than he loved his mother, more than his sister, more than all the women who had slept in his arms, more than he loved me, his life companion, who would have given anything to be trapped in that well in her place, who would have exchanged her life for Azucena's, and I watched as he leaned down to kiss her poor forehead, consumed by a sweet, sad emotion he could not name. I felt how in that instant both were saved from despair, how they were freed from the clay, how they rose above the vultures and helicopters, how together they flew above the vast swamp of corruption

9. Many refugees fled to South America during and immediately after the Second World War.

and laments. How, finally, they were able to accept death. Rolf Carlé prayed in silence that she would die quickly, because such pain cannot be borne.

By then I had obtained a pump and was in touch with a general who had agreed to ship it the next morning on a military cargo plane. But on the night of that third day, beneath the unblinking focus of quartz lamps and the lens of a hundred cameras, Azucena gave up, her eyes locked with those of the friend who had sustained her to the end. Rolf Carlé removed the life buoy, closed her eyelids, held her to his chest for a few moments, and then let her go. She sank slowly, a flower in the mud.

You are back with me, but you are not the same man. I often accompany you to the station and we watch the videos of Azucena again; you study them intently, looking for something you could have done to save her, something you did not think of in time. Or maybe you study them to see yourself as if in a mirror, naked. Your cameras lie forgotten in a closet; you do not write or sing; you sit long hours before the window, staring at the mountains. Beside you, I wait for you to complete the voyage into yourself, for the old wounds to heal. I know that when you return from your nightmares, we shall again walk hand in hand, as before.

1989

CHU T'IEN-HSIN
born 1958

Chu T'ien-hsin (whose name can also be transliterated Zhu Tianxin) and her sister, Chu T'ien-wen, are among the best-known authors in contemporary Taiwan. Both began their careers in the 1970s, writing fiction that explores the importance of place and allegiance. The two grew up in a literary family: their mother worked as a translator of Japanese literature, concentrating on the works of modern authors such as Kawabata Yasunari; their father, also a celebrated writer, fled with his family from mainland China in the late 1940s. Much of Chu's mature writing deals with the relationship between China and Taiwan, gradually moving from an emphasis on Chinese identity, express-ing nostalgic longing for a lost home-land, toward a direct engagement with Taiwan.

While studying at Taiwan National University, Chu and her sister started a literary magazine, *Three Three Quarterly*. During those years, Chu later said,

> we really began to develop a highly self-conscious sense of "mission." We didn't want to simply hone the technical skills and techniques of writing, we were aiming toward something more like the concept of *shi*, or traditional Chinese scholar. . . . Back when we were running the *Three Three Quarterly*, we very consciously decided that we didn't want to settle for being

mere writers. After all, what's the big deal about being a novelist? All it's based on is technique. Like the traditional Chinese *shi*, we wanted to develop our understanding of politics, economics, and a whole array of other fields. Living in this world, we wanted to feel involved with what was happening in our country and our society.

Chu's more recent fiction, particularly the stories in the collection *Ancient Capital* (1997), is more stylistically experimental, exploring narrative structures that depart from traditional linear plots in order to explore complex questions of personal and cultural memory. The stories in *Ancient Capital* focus primarily on the history, memory, and cultural traditions of Taipei, a city that has been occupied at various times by the Dutch, the Manchus, the Japanese, and finally the Chinese Nationalists, who fled there after their defeat in the civil war with the Communists. A recipient of many literary honors, including the prestigious *China Times* prize for fiction, Chu is also a prolific screenwriter for the New Taiwan cinema movement, where she often collaborates with the writer-director Hou Hsiao-Hsien.

The story selected here, "Man of La Mancha" (1994), examines memory and identity in ways that are at once penetrating and oblique. Although the narration is in the first person, the speaker is a blurred and mysterious figure; we can guess at a profession (writer), but we cannot determine much else about the speaker. The plot revolves around the preparation for death. Unable to sleep one night, the speaker goes to a coffee shop, where the radio is broadcasting a bulletin about the death of "a second-generation descendant of the *ancien régime*" (the old order that precedes a revolution). Feeling faint, either because

of the news, the stress, or the coffee, the narrator leaves the shop and heads to a Japanese-style medical clinic, and is diagnosed with arrhythmia. After leaving the clinic—and briefly passing out—the narrator imagines what would happen if the fainting spell had lasted longer and a passerby had to search the body for identification. Nothing the narrator is presently carrying would provide a useful clue.

This observation leads to a series of reflections on the life stories that we carry on our persons, in the form of trinkets and small documents. Gradually the speaker's list of preparations for an unexpected death becomes more intricate and even obsessive. The story ends with a quotation alluding to Don Quixote, the fictional country gentleman created by Miguel de Cervantes who sets out—absurdly, since even in the don's own time and place, the adventures of chivalric legend are not literally true—to win lasting honor and fame as a knight-errant.

The central topic that the speaker addresses—the question of how people are remembered after death—has deep roots in Chinese literature—most famously in the works of Sima Qian, a second-century historian who provided important models for the writers who followed. How one is remembered is critical to one's sense of identity, perhaps more critical than many of us would imagine. The story's subtle references to the fading lineage of the ancien régime, to the spread of Japanese institutions through Taiwan, to international travel and culturally specific forms of self-definition link these meditations to issues of cultural memory and Taiwanese identity. How much of the old Taiwan remains available to each generation's memory? And what are we to make of the distance between the generations? In short, what does it mean to be Taiwanese?

Man of La Mancha[1]

Strictly speaking, that was the day I began thinking about making preparations for my own death.

I should probably start from the night before.

Because a short essay of absolutely no importance was due the following noon, my brain, as usual, defied orders and turned itself on, ignoring the lure of the dream world and causing me to stay awake till dawn.

A few hours later, barely making it there before breakfast hours ended, I set to work in a Japanese-style chain coffee shop, effortlessly finishing that short, unimportant essay. It was then that I had the leisure to notice that, in order to fortify myself against the cold blasts from the air conditioner, I'd already downed five or six scalding refills of coffee, which had turned my fingers and toes numb, as if I'd been poisoned. I quietly stretched in my cramped seat, only to discover that my lips were so numb I couldn't open them to yawn. Even more strange was that my internal organs, whose existence had pretty much gone unnoticed over the three decades or so they'd been with me, were now frozen and shrunken, like little clenched fists, hanging tightly in their places inside me. I looked up at the girl who, in her clean, crisply pressed, nurselike uniform and apron, diligently refilled my cup over and over, and just about called out to her for help.

I was anxiously pondering the language to use in seeking help from a stranger— even though this stranger was all smiles and would never refuse requests such as "Please give me another pat of butter," "Let me have another look at the menu," "Where can I make a phone call?" etc. But, "Help me?" "Please call me an ambulance?" "Please help me stand up?". . .

Yet for someone else, obviously, it was too late. The noontime headline news over the coffee shop radio announced that a certain second-generation descendant of the *ancien régime*[2] had been discovered early that morning dead in a hospital examination room, still in the prime of his youth, cause of death unknown, a peaceful look on his face. Which meant he hadn't even had time to struggle or call out for help.

That was all I needed: picking up my essay and bag, I paid and left.

I refused to pass out during the few minutes I spent waiting for a bus or a taxi (whichever came first), but if I'd wanted to, I could have slumped to the pavement and plunged into a deep slumber. Then a series of screams would have erupted around me, mixed with whisperings, and many heads, framed in the light behind them, would have bent down and appeared on the retina of my enlarged iris, as in the camera shot used in all movies for such scenes.

No matter how you looked at it, it would have been a pretty loutish way to go, so I refused to fall or even to rest, though by then the chill from my internal organs was spreading out to my flesh and skin. I forced myself to head toward an old and small nearby clinic. My mind was a blank; I have no idea how long

1. Translated from Chinese by Howard Goldblatt.
2. The old regime (French) of Chinese nationalist politicians who ruled Taiwan from 1949 until the end of the 20th century; a reference to the monarchy before the French Revolution of 1789. The descendant mentioned here is Jiang Xiaowu (1945–1991), grandson of nationalist leader Chiang Kai-shek (1887–1975).

it took me to get there. "I'm going to faint, please help me," I said to the work-study student nurse, who was about the same age as the coffee shop girl who'd served me.

When I came to, I was lying on a narrow examination bed; the gray-haired old doctor, mixing Mandarin and Taiwanese, answered the puzzled look and questions brimming in my eyes with a voice that seemed very loud, very far away, and very slow: "Not enough oxygen to your heart. We're giving you an IV.[3] Lie here a while before you leave. The nurse can help you phone your family, if you want. Don't stay up too late or eat anything that might upset you. Arrhythmia is a serious matter."

With that warning, he went off to see the next patient.

So concise, so precise, he'd pinpointed my problems: insomnia, too much coffee, and arrhythmia. Strange, why was a very, very cold tear hanging in the corner of each of my eyes?

I still felt cold, but it was only the chill of the old Japanese-style clinic, no longer the deadly silent, numbing cold from the gradual loss of vital signs I'd experienced a few minutes earlier. But I hesitated, like a spirit floating in the air, as if I could choose not to return to my body. I missed the body that had nearly slumped to the pavement a few minutes before. The site of the near fall was the bus stop in front of McDonald's, so there would have been young mothers with their children and old men with grandchildren waiting for the bus. The sharp-eyed youngsters would be the first to spot it, then the mothers would vigilantly pull them away or draw them under their wings for protection, instinctively believing that it must be a beggar, a vagrant, or a mental patient, or maybe someone suffering from the effects of the plague, cholera, or epilepsy. But some of the grandpas who'd seen more of the world would come up to check and then, judging from my more or less respectable attire, take me off the list of the aforementioned suspects and decide to save me.

Looking into my wide-open but enlarged irises, they'd shout, "Who are you? Who should we call? What's the number?" They'd also order one of the gawking young women, "Go call an ambulance."

Who am I? Who should I call? What number?

I'd think back to how, on busy mornings, my significant other would lay out his schedule for the day, and I'd promptly forget; it would go something like this: "At ten-thirty I'm going to X's office; at noon I have to be at XX Bank as a guarantor. Do we have bills to pay? In the afternoon I'll go. . . . Want me to get you. . . . Or page me when you decide. . . ."

So I'd give up searching for and trying to recall his whereabouts.

Grandpa would say, "We have no choice, we have to go through his bag."

And, under watchful eyes, so as to avoid suspicion, he'd open my bag. Let's see, plenty of money—coins and bills—some ATM receipts, one or two unused lengths of dental floss, a claim ticket for film developing and a coupon for a free enlargement from the same photo studio; here, here's a business card . . . given to me yesterday by a friend, for a super-cheap London B&B[4] (16 pounds a night), at 45 Lupton Street, phone and fax (071) 4854075. Even though it would have an address and a phone number, it would of course provide no clue

---

3. Intravenous drip.
4. Bed and breakfast (a small, informal hotel).

to my identity. So Grandpa would have to check my pockets; in one he'd find a small packet of facial tissues, in the other, after ordering the onlookers to help turn me over, a small stack of napkins with the name of the Japanese coffee shop I'd just visited printed in the corner. Different from the plain, unprinted McDonald's napkins in their pockets.

Then someone would take out that short, insignificant essay and start to read, but be unable to retrieve, from my insignificant pen name, any information to decipher my identity.

Finally a tender-hearted, timid young mother would cover her sobbing face and cry out, "Please, someone hurry, send him to the hospital."

That's what scared me most. Just like that, I could become a nameless vegetable lying in a hospital for who knows how long; of course, even more likely, I'd become an anonymous corpse picked up on a sidewalk and lie for years in cold storage at the city morgue.

Could all this really result from an absence of identifiable items?

From that moment on, from that very moment on, I began to think about making preparations for my own death—or should I say, it occurred to me that I ought to prepare for unpredictable, unpreventable circumstances surrounding my death?

Maybe you'll say nothing could be easier; all I had to do was start carrying a picture ID or a business card, like someone with a heart condition who's never without a note that says: whoever finds this please send the bearer to a certain hospital, phone the following family members, in the order their numbers appear here, and, most important, take a glycerin pill out of the little bottle in my pocket and place it under my tongue. But no, that's not what I meant. Maybe I should say that was the genesis of my worries but, as my thoughts unfolded, they went far beyond that.

Let me cite a couple of examples by way of explanation.

Not long ago I found a wallet in a phone booth. It was a poor-quality knock-off of a name-brand item. So I opened it without much curiosity, with the simple intention of finding the owner's address in order to, as my good deed for the day, mail it back to him or her—before opening it, I couldn't get a sense of the owner's gender, given its unisex look.

The wallet was quite thick, even though the money inside amounted to a meager 400 NT. In addition to a color photo of Amy Lau, it was all puffed up with over a dozen cards: a phone card, a KTV[5] member discount card, a student card from a chain hair salon, a point-collecting card from a bakery, a raffle ticket stub, a membership exchange card for a TV video game club, an iced tea shop manager's business card, an honor card for nonsmokers, etc.

I probably didn't look beyond the third card before I was confident I could describe the wallet's owner: a sixteen- or seventeen-year-old insipid (in my view) female student. That, in fact, turned out to be the case; my assumption was corroborated by a swimming pool membership card, which included her school and grade, so I could return the wallet to her when I found the time.

Here's another example. I don't know if you've read the autobiography of the Spanish director, Luis Buñuel,[6] but I recall that he said he stopped going on

5. Karaoke TV, a private karaoke studio.
6. Spanish surrealist filmmaker (1900–1983), author of the memoir *My Last Sigh* (1982).

long trips after turning sixty because he was afraid of dying in a foreign land, afraid of the movielike scene of opened suitcases and documents strewn all over the ground, ambulance sirens and flashing police lights, hotel owners, local policemen, small-town reporters, gawkers, total chaos, awkward and embarrassing. Most important, he was probably afraid that, lacking the ability to defend himself, he'd be identified and labeled, whether or not he'd led a life that was serious, complex, worthy.

Here's another related example, although it doesn't concern death, taken from a certain short story that nicely describes the extramarital affair of a graceful and refined lady. When, by chance, she encounters her lover, and sex is on the agenda, she changes her mind. What stops her is surely not morality, nor her loving husband, who treats her just fine, nor the enjoyment-killing idea that there's no time for birth control measures. Rather, it's that she left home that day on the spur of the moment to take a stroll and do some shopping during a time when everything was scarce, and she was wearing ordinary cotton undergarments that were tattered from too many washings.

What would you have done?

Let me put it this way: these examples quickly convinced me that, if death came suddenly and without warning, who could manage to follow the intention of "a dying tiger leaves its skin intact"?

And that's why I envy chronically ill patients and old folks nearing the end of their lives, like Buñuel, for they have adequate time to make their preparations, since death is anticipated. I don't mean just writing a will or making their own funeral arrangements, stuff like that. What I'm saying is: they have enough time to decide what to burn and destroy and what to leave behind—the diaries, correspondence, photographs, and curious objects from idiosyncratic collecting habits they've treasured and kept throughout their lives.

For example, I was once asked by the heartbroken wife of a teacher who had died unexpectedly to go through the effects in his office. Among the mountains of research material on the Zhou[7] dynasty city-state, I found a notebook recording the dates of conjugal bliss with his wife over the thirty years of their marriage. The dates were accompanied by complicated notations that were clearly secret codes, perhaps to describe the degree of satisfaction he'd achieved. I couldn't decide whether to burn it to protect the old man or treat it as a rare treasure and turn it over to his wife.

Actually, in addition to destroying things, I should also fabricate or arrange things in such a way that people would think what I wanted them to think about me. A minor ruse might be to obtain some receipts for charitable donations or copy down some occasional, personal notes that are more or less readable and might even be self-published by the surviving family. Even more delicate was a case I once read about in the health and medical section of the newspaper: a gramps in his seventies who had a penile implant wrote to ask if he should have it removed before emigrating to mainland China, for he was afraid that, after he died and was cremated, his children and grandchildren would discover his secret from the curious object that neither burned nor melted.

So you need to understand that the advance preparations I'm talking about go far beyond passive procedures to prevent becoming a nameless vegetable or

---

7. Dynasty of Chinese rulers (1046–221 B.C.E.).

an anonymous corpse; in fact, they have developed into an exquisite, highly proactive state.

I decided to begin by attending to my wallet.

The first thing I threw away was the sloppy-looking dental floss; then I tossed some business cards I'd taken out of politeness from people whose names I could no longer remember, a few baffling but colorful paper clips, a soft drink pull-tab to exchange for a free can, a book coupon, etc. In sum, a bunch of junk whose only significance was to show how shabby I was.

What then are the things that are both meaningful and fully explanatory, and are reasonably found in a wallet?

First of all, my career does not require business cards, and I had no employee ID card or work permit. I didn't have a driver's license and hadn't joined any serious organization or recreational club, so I had no membership cards. I didn't even have a credit card!

—Speaking of credit cards, they create a mystery that causes considerable consternation. I'm sure you've experienced this: you're in a department store or a large shop or a restaurant, and the cashier asks, "Cash or charge?"

Based on my observations, even though the cashier's tone is usually neutral and quite proper, those who pay cash stammer their response, while those who pay with a credit card answer loud and clear. Isn't that weird? Aren't the credit card users, simply put, debtors? The implication, at least, is: I have the money to pay you, but for now, or for the next few weeks, the credit guarantee system of my bank lets me owe you without having to settle up.

But what about those who pay cash? They are able to hand over the money with one hand and take possession of the goods with the other, with neither party owing the other a thing. Why then should they be so diffident? And what makes those paying with a credit card so self-assured?

Could it be that the latter, after a credit check to prove that they are now and in the future will continue to be productive, can enter the system and be completely trusted? And the former, those who owe nothing to anyone, why are they so irretrievably timid? Is it possible they cannot be incorporated into the control system of an industrial, commercial society because their mode of production or their productivity is regarded as somehow uncivilized, unscientific, and unpredictable, the equivalent of an agricultural-age barter system? Simply put, when you are not a cog with a clearly defined purpose and prerequisite in the system, their trust in you is based on what they can see, and that must be a one-time exchange of money and goods, since there is no guarantee of exchange credit for the next time, or the time after that. You are neither trusted nor accepted by a gigantic, intimidating system, and that is why you are diffident, timid, even though you could well be able and diligent, and are not necessarily poor, at least not a beggar or a homeless person who pays no taxes.

By contrast, those whose wallets are choked with cards of every kind are trusted by organizations, big and small, which vie to admit them and consider them indispensable. They are so complacent, so confident, and all because: "I have credit, therefore I am."

Can a person living in this world be without a name, or a dwelling place?

My wallet was empty, with nothing to fill it up and no way to disguise that, but I didn't want the person who opened it to see at first glance that it belonged to one of life's losers. So I put in a few thousand-NT bills, which I wouldn't use for so long they'd begin to look as if they were part of the wallet itself.

The wallet may have been empty, but since it wouldn't hold a passport, I debated whether to include my ID card to establish my identity—when 20 million ID cards are attached to 20 million people, you see, the meaning is nullified—and I could not follow your suggestion to, in a feigned casual manner, insert a small note with my name and phone number on it. Which meant that putting aside the issue of becoming a nameless vegetable or an anonymous corpse on the sidewalk, this anonymous wallet would, sooner or later, become nonreturnable, even if found by a Samaritan.

Ah! A savorless, flavorless, colorless, odorless wallet. Sometimes I pretended to be a stranger, examining and fondling it, speculating how the Samaritan who found it would sigh emotionally: "What an uninteresting and unimportant person your owner must be!"

After I lost interest in the disguise and the construction of my wallet, for a while I turned my attention to my clothes. Especially my underwear. To be ready for an unexpected sexual encounter—no, I mean for the unannounced visit of death.

Underwear is very important, and it's not enough just to keep it from becoming tattered or turning yellow. On psychological, social, even political levels, it describes its owner more vividly than many other things. Didn't Bill Clinton respond shyly that his underpants weren't those trendy plaid boxers, but were skin-hugging briefs?[8]

And just look at his foreign policy!

Still, I gave serious consideration to changing and washing my underwear religiously, and to the purchase of new sets. For starters, I tossed my black and purple sets, along with my Clinton-style briefs, all of which might have caused undue speculation. After mulling over the replacements, I decided to go to the open-rack garment section of Watson's,[9] where no salesperson would bother me, and picked out several pairs of white Calvin Klein 100 percent cotton underpants, though their yuppie style didn't quite match my antisocial tendencies. My significant other was all but convinced I had a new love interest, and we had a big fight over that. But I didn't reveal the truth. If one day I happened to depart this world before him, then my clear, white underwear would remind that grief-stricken man of what I looked like after my shower on so many nights. Those sweet memories might comfort him, at least a little.

But my preparatory work didn't end there.

On some days, when I had to go to work, I passed the site where I'd nearly fallen, knowing full well that the strength that had sustained me and would not let me fall came from the thought: "I'll not be randomly discovered and identified like this."

Randomly discovered. In addition to the state I was in, the wallet, my clothes, there was also location.

That's right, location. I thought back carefully to the routes I took when I went out and realized that, even though I was in the habit of roaming a bit, there was a

---

8. In April 1994, a student asked U.S. president Bill Clinton what kind of underwear he wore, boxer shorts or briefs; he replied, "usu-ally briefs."
9. A Chinese drugstore chain.

definite sense of order and, in the end, it would be easy for a secret agent, even a neophyte P.I., to follow me. Even so, I strove to simplify my routes, avoiding places that would be hard to explain, even if I was just passing by.

Let me put it this way. An upright, simple, extremely religious, and highly disciplined college classmate of mine died in a fire at a well-known sex sauna last year. The firefighters found him, neatly dressed, dead of asphyxiation, in the hallway. We went to give our condolences to his wife, also a college classmate, and as we warmly recalled all the good deeds he'd performed when alive and said he'd definitely be ushered into heaven, we couldn't completely shake the subtle sense of embarrassment—what exactly was the good fellow, our classmate, doing there?

We could not ask, and she could not answer.

So I was determined to avoid vulgar, tasteless little local temples, shrouded in incense smoke; I didn't want to die in front of a spirit altar, giving my significant other the impression I'd changed religions.

And I didn't want to go to the Ximen-ding[1] area, which I'd pretty much avoided since graduating from college, afraid I'd end up dead in an area honeycombed with dilapidated sex-trade alleys, fall under suspicion, like that good classmate of mine, and be unable to defend myself.

From then on, I quickened my steps whenever I walked by some of my favorite deep-green alleys, with their Japanese-style houses, where time seemed to stand still. I no longer stopped or strolled there, afraid that my significant other would suspect I'd hidden away an illegitimate child or was having a secret rendezvous with an old flame.

I even stopped roaming wherever my feet took me, as I'd done when I was younger, just so I wouldn't be found dead on a beach where people came to watch the sunset. Otherwise, my credit card–carrying significant other would be embroiled in a lifelong puzzle and be mired in deep grief.

After all, death only visits us once in our lifetime, so we should make advance preparations for its arrival.

> Hundreds of years ago, the Man of La Mancha[2]
>   howled at the sky—
> A windblown quest
> Seeking love in steel and rocks
> Using manners with savages

And me, afraid that the handwriting would be eaten away by mites and no longer legible, I wrote this down.

1994

---

1. A shopping district in Taipei, the capital of Taiwan.
2. The nickname for Cervantes' Don Quixote, from the La Mancha region of Spain, who tried to model his life on the knights in chival- ric romances; Man of La Mancha was a play by Dale Wasserman, produced for television in 1959, transformed into a Broadway musical in 1965, and made into a successful feature film in 1972.

J. M. COETZEE

born 1940

One of the most challenging of contemporary novelists, J. M. Coetzee frequently addresses moral and political issues. He does so, however, within complex fictional frameworks that present not a single ethical message but an interplay of competing views, as he hedges his authorial judgments with irony. These qualities have led Coetzee's name to be associated with postmodernism and the questioning of absolutes. Yet the ethical streak in Coetzee's work suggests that, for all his questioning of absolutes, a sense of right and wrong motivates his literary experiments, which compel our attention through their impeccably controlled style.

Born in Cape Town, South Africa, to liberal Afrikaners who opposed the system of segregation and white minority rule known as apartheid, John Maxwell Coetzee learned both Afrikaans and English as a child. He studied English literature and mathematics at the University of Cape Town before leaving for England to take up a position as a computer programmer. Bored with his work at International Business Machines, Coetzee moved to the United States and completed a doctoral degree in English at the University of Texas. There he wrote a dissertation on **Samuel Beckett**, whose spare, minimalist style and dark humor influenced Coetzee's own fiction. After teaching at the State University of New York at Buffalo, where he started his first novel, *Dusklands* (published in 1974), Coetzee was forced to leave the United States when he was denied a green card. Along with forty-five other faculty members, Coetzee had occupied a university building to protest American involvement in the Vietnam War. Coetzee returned to South Africa and took up a position at the University of Cape Town, where he remained for thirty years, witnessing the intensification of the apartheid system, its fall, and the introduction of a democracy not based on race discrimination. He earned a growing reputation from a series of spare and elegant novels, often set in bleak landscapes that recall the semidesert Karoo, where Coetzee spent many summers as a boy. His works may combine imaginary worlds with historical events or with encounters between colonizers and the colonized; they frequently make use of demented or unstable narrators. The writer has paid homage to several revered novelists, notably **Fyodor Dostoyevsky** and **Franz Kafka**, whose works explored the mind on the verge of insanity.

Coetzee often plays with the relationship between fiction and reality. His works of autobiographical fiction, *Boyhood* (1997), *Youth* (2002), and *Summertime* (2010), for example, are written in the third person, leaving open the question of whether the "John" is really an "I." *Disgrace* (1999), about a white professor accused of sexual harassment, was seen by some as a critique of the Truth and Reconciliation Commission, established by the country's first postapartheid president, Nelson Mandela, to help the nation come to terms with the crimes of the apartheid era. The novel portrays a serious crime committed by black characters, which led to accusations of racism from the ruling African National Congress. Shortly after this accusation, Coetzee moved to Australia, and in 2006 he became an Australian citizen. In 2003, he was awarded the Nobel Prize.

"The Novel in Africa" (1999) takes up the relationship between fiction and reality. The protagonist, Elizabeth Costello, is an Australian novelist who shares several characteristics with Coetzee himself (although she is older than her creator and, of course, female). Like Coetzee, she spends a great deal of time giving lectures about literature; also like the famously reclusive Coetzee, she does not relish the small talk that accompanies such assignments. In this story, while on a leisure cruise, she chooses to give a lecture titled "The Future of the Novel," even though she has little faith that the novel as a literary form has a future. Meanwhile, an old acquaintance, the fictional black African novelist Emmanuel Egudu, gives a lecture called "The Novel in Africa," in which he speaks about real African novelists, including Amos Tutuola and Ben Okri. The conflict between the two novelists seems to turn at first on literary politics, then on sexual politics, but it ultimately comes to seem more personal than political.

Elizabeth Costello was to become an alter ego for Coetzee; he later wrote several other stories about her life, including snippets of her lectures on such sensitive topics as animal rights, religion, and the Holocaust, and combined them in an unusual novel, *Elizabeth Costello: Eight Lessons* (2003). "The Novel in Africa" is the second "lesson." By putting controversial views in the mouth of his fictional heroine, Coetzee both challenges what he has criticized as the liberal consensus and creates a vivid, emotional story about a woman approaching old age. In the first lesson, "Realism," Costello discusses the way the traditional realist novel has been superseded: "We used to believe that when the text said, 'On the table stood a glass of water,' there was indeed a table, and a glass of water on it, and we had only to look in the word-mirror of the text to see them," says Costello. "But all that has ended. The word-mirror is broken, irreparably it seems." Coetzee's fiction reassembles the broken bits of the "word-mirror" to reflect a complex, multiform reality.

The Novel in Africa

At a dinner party she meets X, whom she has not seen in years. Is he still teaching at the University of Queensland, she asks? No, he replies, he has retired and now works the cruise ships, travelling the world, screening old movies, talking about Bergman and Fellini to retired people![1] He has never regretted the move. 'The pay is good, you get to see the world, and—do you know what?—people that age actually listen to what you have to say.' He urges her to give it a try: 'You are a prominent figure, a well-known writer. The cruise line I work for will jump at the opportunity to take you on. You will be a feather in their cap. Say but the word and I'll bring it up with my friend the director.'

The proposal interests her. She was last on a ship in 1963, when she came home from England, from the mother country. Soon after that they began to retire the great ocean-going liners, one by one, and scrap them. The end of an era. She would not mind doing it again, going to sea. She would like to call at Easter Island and St Helena, where Napoleon languished.[2] She would like to visit Antarctica—not just to see with her own eyes those vast horizons, that

---

1. Ingmar Bergman (1918–2007), Swedish filmmaker, and Federico Fellini (1920–1993), Italian filmmaker, known for their sophisticated, intellectual films.
2. The French emperor Napoleon Bonaparte (1769–1821) was exiled to Saint Helena in the South Atlantic Ocean after his defeat at the Battle of Waterloo (1815). Easter Island, in the South Pacific, is famous for its monumental statues, carved before 1500 C.E.

barren waste, but to set foot on the seventh and last continent, feel what it is like to be a living, breathing creature in spaces of inhuman cold.

X is as good as his word. From the headquarters of Scandia Lines[3] in Stockholm comes a fax. In December the SS *Northern Lights* will be sailing from Christchurch on a fifteen-day cruise to the Ross Ice Shelf, and thence onward to Cape Town.[4] Might she be interested in joining the education and entertainment staff? Passengers on Scandia's cruise ships are, as the letter puts it, 'discriminating persons who take their leisure seriously'. The emphasis of the on-board programme will be on ornithology and cold-water ecology, but Scandia would be delighted if the noted writer Elizabeth Costello could find the time to offer a short course on, say, the contemporary novel. In return for which, and for making herself accessible to passengers, she will be offered an A-class berth, all expenses paid, with air connections to Christchurch and from Cape Town, and a substantial honorarium to boot.

It is an offer she cannot refuse. On the morning of 10 December she joins the ship in Christchurch harbour. Her cabin, she finds, is small but otherwise quite satisfactory; the young man who coordinates the entertainment and self-development programme is respectful; the passengers at her table at lunchtime, in the main retired people, people of her own generation, are pleasant and unostentatious.

On the list of her co-lecturers there is only one name she recognizes: Emmanuel Egudu, a writer from Nigeria. Their acquaintance goes back more years than she cares to remember, to a PEN conference in Kuala Lumpur.[5] Egudu had been loud and fiery then, political; her first impression was that he was a poseur. Reading him later on, she had not changed her mind. But a poseur, she now wonders: what is that? Someone who seems to be what he is not? Which of us is what he seems to be, she seems to be? And anyway, in Africa things may be different. In Africa what one takes to be posing, what one takes to be boasting, may just be manliness. Who is she to say?

Towards men, including Egudu, she has, she notices, mellowed as she has grown older. Curious, because in other respects she has become more (she chooses the word carefully) acidulous.

She runs into Egudu at the captain's cocktail party (he has come aboard late). He is wearing a vivid green dashiki,[6] suave Italian shoes; his beard is spotted with grey, but he is still a fine figure of a man. He gives her a huge smile, enfolds her in an embrace. 'Elizabeth!' he exclaims. 'How good to see you! I had no idea! We have so much catching up to do!'

In his lexicon, it appears, catching up means talking about his own activities. He no longer spends much time in his home country, he informs her. He has become, as he puts it, 'an habitual exile, like an habitual criminal'. He has acquired American papers; he makes his living on the lecture circuit, a circuit that would appear to have expanded to encompass the cruise ships. This will be

3. An actual shipping service of the 19th century, here presumably a stand-in for Norwegian Cruise Line, a popular cruise operator.
4. The cruise will leave Christchurch, New Zealand, visit the Ross Ice Shelf in Antarctica, and end in Cape Town, South Africa, Coetzee's

hometown.
5. Capital of Malaysia. International PEN is a worldwide association of writers that promotes freedom of expression.
6. Traditional, colorful West African robe.

his third trip on the *Northern Lights*. Very restful, he finds it; very relaxing. Who would have guessed, he says, that a country boy from Africa would end up like this, in the lap of luxury? And he treats her again to his big smile, the special one.

I'm a country girl myself, she would like to say, but does not, though it is true, in part. *Nothing exceptional about being from the country*.

Each of the entertainment staff is expected to give a short public talk. 'Just to say who you are, where you come from,' explains the young coordinator in carefully idiomatic English. His name is Mikael; he is handsome in his tall, blond, Swedish way, but dour, too dour for her taste.

Her talk is advertised as 'The Future of the Novel', Egudu's as 'The Novel in Africa'. She is scheduled to speak on the morning of their first day out to sea; he will speak the same afternoon. In the evening comes 'The Lives of Whales', with sound recordings.

Mikael himself does the introduction. 'The famous Australian writer,' he calls her, 'author of *The House on Eccles Street*[7] and many other novels, whom we are truly privileged to have in our midst.' It vexes her to be billed once again as the author of a book from so far in the past, but there is nothing to be done about that.

'The Future of the Novel' is a talk she has given before, in fact many times before, expanded or contracted depending on the occasion. No doubt there are expanded and contracted versions of the novel in Africa and the lives of whales too. For the present occasion she has chosen the contracted version.

'The future of the novel is not a subject I am much interested in,' she begins, trying to give her auditors a jolt. 'In fact the future in general does not much interest me. What is the future, after all, but a structure of hopes and expectations? Its residence is in the mind; it has no reality.

'Of course, you might reply that the past is likewise a fiction. The past is history, and what is history but a story made of air that we tell ourselves? Nevertheless, there is something miraculous about the past that the future lacks. What is miraculous about the past is that we have succeeded—God knows how—in making thousands and millions of individual fictions, fictions created by individual human beings, lock well enough into one another to give us what looks like a common past, a shared story.

'The future is different. We do not possess a shared story of the future. The creation of the past seems to exhaust our collective creative energies. Compared with our fiction of the past, our fiction of the future is a sketchy, bloodless affair, as visions of heaven tend to be. Of heaven and even of hell.'

The novel, the traditional novel, she goes on to say, is an attempt to understand human fate one case at a time, to understand how it comes about that some fellow being, having started at point A and having undergone experiences B and C and D, ends up at point Z. Like history, the novel is thus an exercise in making the past coherent. Like history, it explores the respective contributions of character and circumstance to forming the present. By doing so, the novel suggests how we may explore the power of the present to produce the future. That is why we have this thing, this institution, this medium called the novel.

7. An allusion to James Joyce's *Ulysses* (1922), whose protagonist, Leopold Bloom, lives at 7 Eccles Street, Dublin.

She is not sure, as she listens to her own voice, whether she believes any longer in what she is saying. Ideas like these must have had some grip on her when years ago she wrote them down, but after so many repetitions they have taken on a worn, unconvincing air. On the other hand, she no longer believes very strongly in belief. Things can be true, she now thinks, even if one does not believe in them, and conversely. Belief may be no more, in the end, than a source of energy, like a battery which one clips into an idea to make it run. As happens when one writes: believing whatever has to be believed in order to get the job done.

If she has trouble believing in her argument, she has even greater trouble in preventing that absence of conviction from emerging in her voice. Despite the fact that she is the noted author of, as Mikael says, *The House on Eccles Street* and other books, despite the fact that her audience is by and large of her generation and ought therefore to share with her a common past, the applause at the end lacks enthusiasm.

For Emmanuel's talk she sits inconspicuously in the back row. They have in the meantime had a good lunch; they are sailing south on what are still placid seas; there is every chance that some of the good folk in the audience—numbering, she would guess, about fifty—are going to nod off. In fact, who knows, she might nod off herself; in which case it would be best to do so unnoticed.

'You will be wondering why I have chosen as my topic the novel in Africa,' Emmanuel begins, in his effortlessly booming voice. 'What is so special about the novel in Africa? What makes it different, different enough to demand our attention today?

'Well, let us see. We all know, to begin with, that the alphabet, the idea of the alphabet, did not grow up in Africa. Many things grew up in Africa, more than you might think, but not the alphabet. The alphabet had to be brought in, first by Arabs, then again by Westerners. In Africa writing itself, to say nothing of novel-writing, is a recent affair.

'Is the novel possible without novel-writing, you may ask? Did we in Africa have a novel before our friends the colonizers appeared on our doorstep? For the time being, let me merely propose the question. Later I may return to it.

'A second remark: reading is not a typically African recreation. Music, yes; dancing, yes; eating, yes; talking, yes—lots of talking. But reading, no, and particularly not reading fat novels. Reading has always struck us Africans as a strangely solitary business. It makes us uneasy. When we Africans visit great European cities like Paris and London, we notice how people on trains take books out of their bags or their pockets and retreat into solitary worlds. Each time the book comes out it is like a sign held up. *Leave me alone, I am reading*, says the sign. *What I am reading is more interesting than you could possibly be.*

'Well, we are not like that in Africa. We do not like to cut ourselves off from other people and retreat into private worlds. Nor are we used to our neighbours retreating into private worlds. Africa is a continent where people share. Reading a book by yourself is not sharing. It is like eating alone or talking alone. It is not our way. We find it a bit crazy.'

We, we, we, she thinks. *We Africans.* It is not *our* way. She has never liked *we* in its exclusive form. Emmanuel may have grown older, he may have acquired the blessing of American papers, but he has not changed. Africanness: a special identity, a special fate.

She has visited Africa: the highlands of Kenya, Zimbabwe, the Okavango[8] swamps. She has seen Africans reading, ordinary Africans, at bus stops, in trains. They were not reading novels, admittedly, they were reading newspapers. But is a newspaper not as much an avenue to a private world as a novel?

'In the third place,' continues Egudu, 'in the great, beneficent global system under which we live today, it has been allotted to Africa to be the home of poverty. Africans have no money for luxuries. In Africa, a book must offer you a return for the money you spend on it. What do I stand to learn by reading this story, the African will ask? How will it advance me? We may deplore the attitude of the African, ladies and gentlemen, but we cannot dismiss it. We must take it seriously and try to understand it.

'We do of course make books in Africa. But the books we make are for children, teaching-books in the simplest sense. If you want to make money publishing books in Africa, you must put out books that will be prescribed for schools, that will be bought in quantity by the education system to be read and studied in the classroom. It does not pay to publish writers with serious ambitions, writers who write about adults and matters that concern adults. Such writers must look elsewhere for their salvation.

'Of course, ladies and gentlemen of the *Northern Lights*, it is not the whole picture I am giving you here today. To give you the whole picture would take all afternoon. I am giving you only a crude, hasty sketch. Of course you will find publishers in Africa, one here, one there, who will support local writers even if they will never make money. But in the broad picture, storytelling provides a livelihood neither for publishers nor for writers.

'So much for the generalities, depressing as they may be. Now let us turn our attention to ourselves, to you and to me. Here I am, you know who I am, it tells you in the programme: Emmanuel Egudu, from Nigeria, author of novels, poems, plays, winner, even, of a Commonwealth Literary Award (Africa Division).[9] And here you are, wealthy folk, or at least comfortable, as you say (I am not wrong, am I?), from North America and Europe and of course let us not forget our Australasian representation, and perhaps I have even heard the odd word of Japanese whispered in the corridors, taking a cruise on this splendid ship, on your way to inspect one of the remoter corners of the globe, to check it out, perhaps to check it off your list. Here you are, after a good lunch, listening to this African fellow talk.

'Why, I imagine you asking yourselves, is this African fellow on board our ship? Why isn't he back at his desk in the land of his birth following his vocation, if he really is a writer, writing books? Why is he going on about the African novel, a subject that can be of only the most peripheral concern to us?

'The short answer, ladies and gentlemen, is that the African fellow is earning a living. In his own country, as I have tried to explain, he cannot earn a living. In his own country (I will not labour the point, I mention it only because it holds true for so many fellow African writers) he is in fact less than welcome. In his own country he is what is called a dissident intellectual, and dissident intellectuals must tread carefully, even in the new Nigeria.

8. In southwestern Africa.
9. An allusion to the Commonwealth Writers Prize, which awards prizes for various regions of the former British Empire.

'So here he is, abroad in the wide world, earning his living. Part of his living he earns by writing books that are published and read and reviewed and talked about and judged, for the most part, by foreigners. The rest of his living he earns from spin-offs of his writing. He reviews books by other writers, for example, in the press of Europe and America. He teaches in colleges in America, telling the youth of the New World about the exotic subject on which he is an expert in the same way that an elephant is an expert on elephants: the African novel. He addresses conferences; he sails on cruise ships. While so occupied, he lives in what are called temporary accommodations. All his addresses are temporary; he has no fixed abode.

'How easy do you think it is, ladies and gentlemen, for this fellow to be true to his essence as writer when there are all these strangers to please, month after month—publishers, readers, critics, students, all of them armed not only with their own ideas about what writing is or should be, what the novel is or should be, what Africa is or should be, but also about what being pleased is or should be? Do you think it is possible for this fellow to remain unaffected by all the pressure on him to please others, to be for them what they think he should be, to produce for them what they think he should produce?

'It may have escaped your attention, but I slipped in, a moment ago, a word that should have made you prick up your ears. I spoke about my essence and being true to my essence. There is much I could say about essence and its ramifications; but this is not the right occasion. Nevertheless, you must be asking yourselves, how in these anti-essential days, these days of fleeting identities that we pick up and wear and discard like clothing, can I justify speaking of my essence as an African writer?

'Around essence and essentialism, I should remind you, there is a long history of turmoil in African thought. You may have heard of the *négritude* movement of the 1940s and 1950s.[1] *Négritude*, according to the originators of the movement, is the essential substratum that binds all Africans together and makes them uniquely African—not only the Africans of Africa but Africans of the great African diaspora in the New World and now in Europe.

'I want to quote some words to you from the Senegalese writer and thinker Cheikh Hamidou Kane.[2] Cheikh Hamidou was being questioned by an interviewer, a European. I am puzzled, said the interviewer, by your praise for certain writers for being truly African. In view of the fact that the writers in question write in a foreign language (specifically French) and are published and, for the most part, read in a foreign country (specifically France), can they truly be called African writers? Are they not more properly called French writers of African origin? Is language not a more important matrix than birth?

'The following is Cheikh Hamidou's reply: "The writers I speak of are truly African because they are born in Africa, they live in Africa, their sensibility is African . . . What distinguishes them lies in life experience, in sensitivities, in rhythm, in style." He goes on: "A French or English writer has thousands of years of written tradition behind him . . . We on the other hand are heirs to an oral tradition."

1. A movement celebrating African heritage (French). Leading figures were Léopold Sédar Senghor (1906–2001) and Aimé Césaire (1913–2008).
2. Senegalese writer (b. 1928), author of *Ambiguous Adventure*.

'There is nothing mystical in Cheikh Hamidou's response, nothing meta-physical, nothing racist. He merely gives proper weight to those intangibles of culture which, because they are not easily pinned down in words, are often passed over. The way that people live in their bodies. The way they move their hands. The way they walk. The way they smile or frown. The lilt of their speech. The way they sing. The timbre of their voices. The way they dance. The way they touch each other; how the hand lingers; the feel of the fingers. The way they make love. The way they lie after they have made love. The way they think. The way they sleep.

'We African novelists can embody these qualities in our writings (and let me remind you at this point that the word *novel*, when it entered the languages of Europe, had the vaguest of meanings: it meant the form of writing that was formless, that had no rules, that made up its own rules as it went along)—we African novelists can embody these qualities as no one else can because we have not lost touch with the body. The African novel, the true African novel, is an oral novel. On the page it is inert, only half alive; it wakes up when the voice, from deep in the body, breathes life into the words, speaks them aloud.

'The African novel is thus, I would claim, in its very being, and before the first word is written, a critique of the Western novel, which has gone so far down the road of disembodiment—think of Henry James, think of Marcel Proust[3]—that the appropriate way and indeed the only way in which to absorb it is in silence and in solitude. And I will close these remarks, ladies and gentlemen—I see my time is running out—by quoting, in support of my posi-tion and Cheikh Hamidou's, not from an African, but from a man from the snowy wastes of Canada, the great scholar of orality Paul Zumthor.[4]

'"Since the seventeenth century," writes Zumthor, "Europe has spread across the world like a cancer, at first stealthily, but for a while now at gathering pace, until today it ravages life forms, animals, plants, habitats, languages. With each day that passes several languages of the world disappear, repudiated, stifled . . . One of the symptoms of the disease has without doubt, from the beginning, been what we call literature; and literature has consolidated itself, prospered, and become what it is—one of the hugest dimensions of mankind—by denying the voice . . . The time has come to stop privileging writing . . . Perhaps great, unfortunate Africa, beggared by our political–industrial imperialism, will, because less gravely affected by writing, find itself closer to the goal than will the other continents."'

The applause when Egudu ends his talk is loud and spirited. He has spoken with force, perhaps even with passion; he has stood up for himself, for his call-ing, for his people; why should he not have his reward, even if what he says can have little relevance to the lives of his audience?

Nevertheless, there is something about the talk she does not like, something to do with orality and the mystique of orality. Always, she thinks, the body that is insisted on, pushed forward, and the voice, dark essence of the body, welling up from within it. *Négritude*: she had thought Emmanuel would grow out of that pseudo-philosophy. Evidently he has not. Evidently he has decided to keep

---

3. French novelist (1871–1922) famed for his exploration of consciousness, as was the Amer-ican novelist Henry James (1843–1928).
4. Noted medievalist (1915–1995).

it as part of his professional pitch. Well, good luck to him. There is still time, ten minutes at least, for questions. She hopes the questions will be searching, will search him out.

The first questioner is, if she is to judge by accent, from the Midwest of the United States. The first novel she ever read by an African, decades ago, says the woman, was by Amos Tutuola, she forgets the title. ('*The Palm Wine Drinkard*,'[5] suggests Egudu. 'Yes, that's it,' she replies.) She was captivated by it. She thought it was the harbinger of great things to come. So she was disappointed, terribly disappointed, to hear that Tutuola was not respected in his own country, that educated Nigerians disparaged him and considered his reputation in the West unmerited. Was this true? Was Tutuola the kind of oral novelist our lecturer had in mind? What has happened to Tutuola? Had more of his books been translated?

No, responds Egudu, Tutuola has not been translated any further, in fact he has not been translated at all, at least not into English. Why not? Because he did not need to be translated. Because he had written in English all along. 'Which is the root of the problem that the questioner raises. The language of Amos Tutuola is English, but not standard English, not the English that Nigerians of the 1950s went to school and college to learn. It is the language of a semi-educated clerk, a man with no more than elementary schooling, barely comprehensible to an outsider, fixed up for publication by British editors. Where Tutuola's writing was frankly illiterate they corrected it; what they refrained from correcting was what seemed authentically Nigerian to them, that is to say, what to their ears sounded picturesque, exotic, folkloric.

'From what I have just been saying,' Egudu continues, 'you may imagine that I too disapprove of Tutuola or the Tutuola phenomenon. Far from it. Tutuola was repudiated by so-called educated Nigerians because they were embarassed by him—embarassed that they might be lumped with him as natives who did not know how to write proper English. As for me, I am happy to be a native, a Nigerian native, a native Nigerian. In this battle I am on Tutuola's side. Tutuola is or was a gifted storyteller. I am glad you like him. Several more books penned by him were put out in England, though none, I would say, as good as *The Palm Wine Drinkard*. And, yes, he is the kind of writer I was referring to, an oral writer.

'I have responded to you at length because the case of Tutuola is so instructive. What makes Tutuola stand out is that he did not adjust his language to the expectations—or to what he might have thought, had he been less naive, would be the expectations—of the foreigners who would read and judge him. Not knowing better, he wrote as he spoke. He therefore had to yield in a particularly helpless way to being packaged, for the West, as an African exotic.

'But, ladies and gentlemen, who among African writers is not exotic? The truth is, to the West we Africans are all exotic, when we are not simply savage. That is our fate. Even here, on this ship sailing towards the continent that ought to be the most exotic of all, and the most savage, the continent with no human standards at all, I can sense I am exotic.'

There is a ripple of laughter. Egudu smiles his big smile, engaging, to all appearances spontaneous. But she cannot believe it is a true smile, cannot

5. A novel by Nigerian writer Amos Tutuola (1920–1997).

believe it comes from the heart, if that is where smiles come from. If being an
exotic is the fate Egudu has embraced for himself, then it is a terrible fate. She
cannot believe he does not know that, know it and in his heart revolt against it.
The one black face in this sea of white.

'But let me return to your question,' Egudu continues. 'You have read
Tutuola, now read my countryman Ben Okri.[6] Amos Tutuola's is a very simple,
very stark case. Okri's is not. Okri is an heir of Tutuola's, or they are the heirs
of common ancestors. But Okri negotiates the contradictions of being himself
for other people (excuse the jargon, it is just a native showing off) in a much
more complex way. Read Okri. You will find the experience instructive.'

'The Novel in Africa' was intended, like all the shipboard talks, to be a light
affair. Nothing on the shipboard programme is intended to be a heavy affair.
Egudu, unfortunately, is threatening to be heavy. With a discreet nod, the
entertainment director, the tall Swedish boy in his light blue uniform, signals
from the wings; and gracefully, easily, Egudu obeys, bringing his show to an
end.

The crew of the *Northern Lights* is Russian, as are the stewards. In fact, everyone but the officers and the corps of guides and managers is Russian. Music on
board is furnished by a balalaika orchestra—five men, five women. The accompaniment they provide at the dinner hour is too schmaltzy for her taste; after
dinner, in the ballroom, the music they play becomes livelier.

The leader of the orchestra, and occasional singer, is a blonde in her early
thirties. She has a smattering of English, enough to make the announcements.
'We play piece that is called in Russian *My Little Dove. My Little Dove*.'[7] Her
dove rhymes with *stove* rather than *love*. With its trills and swoops, the piece
sounds Hungarian, sounds gypsy, sounds Jewish, sounds everything but Russian; but who is she, Elizabeth Costello, country girl, to say?

She is there with a couple from her table, having a drink. They are from
Manchester, they inform her. They are looking forward to her course on the
novel, in which they have both enrolled. The man is long-bodied, sleek, silvery:
she thinks of him as a gannet. How he has made his money he does not say and
she does not enquire. The woman is petite, sensual. Not at all her idea of Manchester. Steve and Shirley. She guesses they are not married.

To her relief, the conversation soon turns from her and the books she has
written to the subject of ocean currents, about which Steve appears to know all
there is to know, and to the tiny beings, tons of them to the square mile, whose
life consists in being swept in serene fashion through these icy waters, eating
and being eaten, multiplying and dying, ignored by history. Ecological tourists,
that is what Steve and Shirley call themselves. Last year the Amazon, this year
the Southern Ocean.

Egudu is standing at the entranceway, looking around. She gives a wave and
he comes over. 'Join us,' she says. 'Emmanuel. Shirley. Steve.'

They compliment Emmanuel on his lecture. 'Very interesting,' says Steve. 'A
completely new perspective you gave me.'

'I was thinking, as you spoke,' says Shirley more reflectively, 'I don't know
your books, I'm sorry to say, but for you as a writer, as the kind of oral writer

6. Nigerian novelist (b. 1959).　　　　7. Popular Russian song of Gypsy origin.

you described, maybe the printed book is not the right medium. Have you ever thought about composing straight on to tape? Why make the detour through print? Why even make a detour through writing? Speak your story direct to your listener.'

'What a clever idea!' says Emmanuel. 'It won't solve all the problems of the African writer, but it's worth thinking about.'

'Why won't it solve your problems?'

'Because, I regret to say, Africans will want more than just to sit in silence listening to a disc spinning in a little machine. That would be too much like idolatry. Africans need the living presence, the living voice.'

The living voice. There is silence as the three of them contemplate the living voice.

'Are you sure about that?' she says, interposing for the first time. 'Africans don't object to listening to the radio. A radio is a voice but not a living voice, a living presence. What you are demanding, I think, Emmanuel, is not just a voice but a performance: a living actor performing the text for you. If that is so, if that is what the African demands, then I agree, a recording cannot take its place. But the novel was never intended to be the script of a performance. From the beginning the novel has made a virtue of not depending on being performed. You can't have both live performance and cheap, handy distribution. It's the one or the other. If that is indeed what you want the novel to be—a pocket-sized block of paper that is at the same time a living being—then I agree, the novel has no future in Africa.'

'No future,' says Egudu reflectively. 'That sounds very bleak, Elizabeth. Do you have a way out to offer us?'

'A way out? It's not for me to offer you a way out. What I do have to offer is a question. Why are there so many African novelists around and yet no African novel worth speaking of? That seems to me the real question. And you yourself gave a clue to the answer in your talk. Exoticism. Exoticism and its seductions.'

'Exoticism and its seductions? You intrigue us, Elizabeth. Tell us what you mean.'

If it were only a matter of Emmanuel and herself she would, at this point, walk out. She is tired of his jeering undertone, exasperated. But before strangers, before customers, they have a front to maintain, she and he both.

'The English novel,' she says, 'is written in the first place by English people for English people. That is what makes it the English novel. The Russian novel is written by Russians for Russians. But the African novel is not written by Africans for Africans. African novelists may write about Africa, about African experiences, but they seem to me to be glancing over their shoulder all the time they write, at the foreigners who will read them. Whether they like it or not, they have accepted the role of interpreter, interpreting Africa to their readers. Yet how can you explore a world in all its depth if at the same time you are having to explain it to outsiders? It is like a scientist trying to give full, creative attention to his investigations while at the same time explaining what he is doing to a class of ignorant students. It is too much for one person, it can't be done, not at the deepest level. That, it seems to me, is the root of your problem. Having to perform your Africanness at the same time as you write.'

'Very good, Elizabeth!' says Egudu. 'You really understand; you put it very well. The explorer as explainer.' He reaches out, pats her on the shoulder.

If we were alone, she thinks, *I would slap him.*

'If it is true that I really understand'—she is ignoring Egudu now, speaking to the couple from Manchester—'then that is only because we in Australia have been through similar trials and have come out at the other end. We finally got out of the habit of writing for strangers when a proper Australian readership grew to maturity, something that happened in the 1960s. A readership, not a writership—that already existed. We got out of the habit of writing for strangers when our market, our Australian market, decided that it could afford to support a home-grown literature. That is the lesson we can offer. That is what Africa could learn from us.'

Emmanuel is silent, though he has not lost his ironic smile.

'It's interesting to hear the two of you talk,' says Steve. 'You treat writing as a business. You identify a market and then set about supplying it. I was expecting something different.'

'Really? What were you expecting?'

'You know: where writers find their inspiration, how they dream up characters, and so forth. Sorry, pay no attention to me, I'm just an amateur.'

Inspiration. Receiving the spirit into oneself. Now that he has brought out the word he is embarrassed. There is an awkward silence.

Emmanuel speaks. 'Elizabeth and I go way back. We have had lots of disagreements in our time. That doesn't alter things between us—does it, Elizabeth? We are colleagues, fellow writers. Part of the great, worldwide writing fraternity.'

Fraternity. He is challenging her, trying to get a rise out of her before these strangers. But she is suddenly too sick of it all to take up the challenge. Not fellow writers, she thinks: fellow entertainers. Why else are we on board this expensive ship, making ourselves available, as the invitation so candidly put it, to people who bore us and whom we are beginning to bore?

He is goading her because he is restless. She knows him well enough to see that. He has had enough of the African novel, enough of her and her friends, wants something or someone new.

Their chanteuse has come to the end of her set. There is a light ripple of applause. She bows, bows a second time, takes up her balalaika. The band strikes up a Cossack dance.[8]

What irritates her about Emmanuel, what she has the good sense not to bring up in front of Steve and Shirley because it will lead only to unseemliness, is the way he turns every disagreement into a personal matter. As for his beloved oral novel, on which he has built his sideline as a lecturer, she finds the idea muddled at its very core. *A novel about people who live in an oral culture,* she would like to say, *is not an oral novel. Just as a novel about women isn't a women's novel.*

In her opinion, all of Emmanuel's talk of an oral novel, a novel that has kept in touch with the human voice and hence with the human body, a novel that is not disembodied like the Western novel but speaks the body and the body's truth, is just another way of propping up the mystique of the African as the last repository of primal human energies. Emmanuel blames his Western publishers and his Western readers for driving him to exoticize Africa; but Emmanuel

8. A folk dance from southern Russia and Ukraine.

has a stake in exoticizing himself. Emmanuel, she happens to know, has not written a book of substance in ten years. When she first got to know him he could still honourably call himself a writer. Now he makes his living by talking. His books are there as credentials, no more. A fellow entertainer he may be; a fellow writer he is not, not any longer. He is on the lecture circuit for the money, and for other rewards too. Sex, for instance. He is dark, he is exotic, he is in touch with life's energies; if he is no longer young, at least he carries himself well, wears his years with distinction. What Swedish girl would not be a pushover?

She finishes her drink. 'I'm retiring,' she says. 'Good night, Steve, Shirley. See you tomorrow. Good night, Emmanuel.'

She wakes up in utter stillness. The clock says four thirty. The ship's engines have stopped. She glances through the porthole. There is fog outside, but through the fog she can glimpse land no more than a kilometre away. It must be Macquarie Island: she had thought they would not arrive for hours yet.

She dresses and emerges into the corridor. At the same moment the door to cabin A-230 opens and the Russian comes out, the singer. She is wearing the same outfit as last night, the port-wine blouse and wide black trousers; she carries her boots in her hand. In the unkind overhead light she looks nearer to forty than to thirty. They avert their eyes as they pass each other.

A-230 is Egudu's cabin, she knows that.

She makes her way to the upper deck. Already there are a handful of passengers, snugly dressed against the cold, leaning against the railings, peering down.

The sea beneath them is alive with what seem to be fish, large, glossy-backed black fish that bob and tumble and leap in the swell. She has never seen anything like it.

'Penguins,' says the man next to her. 'King penguins. They have come to greet us. They don't know what we are.'

'Oh,' she says. And then: 'So innocent? Are they so innocent?'

The man regards her oddly, turns back to his companion.

The Southern Ocean. Poe never laid eyes on it, Edgar Allan,[9] but crisscrossed it in his mind. Boatloads of dark islanders paddled out to meet him. They seemed ordinary folk *just like us*, but when they smiled and showed their teeth the teeth were not white but black. It sent a shiver down his spine, and rightly so. The seas full of things that seem like us but are not. Sea-flowers that gape and devour. Eels, each a barbed maw with a gut hanging from it. Teeth are for tearing, the tongue is for churning the swill around: that is the truth of the oral. Someone should tell Emmanuel. Only by an ingenious economy, an accident of evolution, does the organ of ingestion sometimes get to be used for song.

They will stand off Macquarie until noon, long enough for those passengers who so desire to visit the island. She has put her name down for the visiting party.

The first boat leaves after breakfast. The approach to the landing is difficult, through thick beds of kelp and across shelving rock. In the end one of the sailors has to half help her ashore, half carry her, as if she were an old old woman.

9. American writer (1809–1849).

The sailor has blue eyes, blond hair. Through his waterproofs she feels his youthful strength. In his arms she rides as safe as a baby. 'Thank you!' she says gratefully when he sets her down; but to him it is nothing, just a service he is paid dollars to do, no more personal than the service of a hospital nurse.

She has read about Macquarie Island.[1] In the nineteenth century it was the hub of the penguin industry. Hundreds of thousands of penguins were clubbed to death here and flung into cast-iron steam boilers to be broken down into useful oil and useless residue. Or not clubbed to death, merely herded with sticks up a gangplank and over the edge into the seething cauldron.

Yet their twentieth-century descendants seem to have learned nothing. Still they innocently swim out to welcome visitors; still they call out greetings to them as they approach the rookeries (*Ho! Ho!* they call, for all the world like gruff little gnomes), and allow them to approach close enough to touch them, to stroke their sleek breasts.

At eleven the boats will take them back to the ship. Until then they are free to explore the island. There is an albatross colony on the hillside, they are advised; they are welcome to photograph the birds, but should not approach too closely, should not alarm them. It is breeding season.

She wanders away from the rest of the landing party, and after a while finds herself on a plateau above the coastline, crossing a vast bed of matted grass.

Suddenly, unexpectedly, there is something before her. At first she thinks it is a rock, smooth and white mottled with grey. Then she sees it is a bird, bigger than any bird she has seen before. She recognizes the long, dipping beak, the huge sternum. An albatross.

The albatross regards her steadily and, so it seems to her, with amusement. Sticking out from beneath it is a smaller version of the same long beak. The fledgling is more hostile. It opens its beak, gives a long, soundless cry of warning.

So she and the two birds remain, inspecting each other.

Before the fall, she thinks. *This is how it must have been before the fall. I could miss the boat, stay here. Ask God to take care of me.*

There is someone behind her. She turns. It is the Russian singer, dressed now in a dark green anorak with the hood down, her hair under a kerchief.

'An albatross,' she remarks to the woman, speaking softly. 'That is the English word. I don't know what they call themselves.'

The woman nods. The great bird regards them calmly, no more afraid of two than of one.

'Is Emmanuel with you?' she says.

'No. On ship.'

The woman does not seem keen to talk, but she presses on anyway. 'You are a friend of his, I know. I am too, or have been, in the past. May I ask: what do you see in him?'

It is an odd question, presumptuous in its intimacy, even rude. But it seems to her that on this island, on a visit that will never be repeated, anything can be said.

'What I see?' says the woman.

'Yes. What do you see? What do you like about him? What is the source of his charm?'

---

1. In the southwest Pacific, between New Zealand and Antarctica.

The woman shrugs. Her hair is dyed, she can now see. Forty if a day, probably with a household to support back home, one of those Russian establishments with a crippled mother and a husband who drinks too much and beats her and a layabout son and a daughter with a shaven head and purple lipstick. A woman who can sing a little but will one of these days, sooner rather than later, be over the hill. Playing the balalaika to foreigners, singing Russian kitsch, picking up tips.

'He is free. You speak Russian? No?'

She shakes her head.

'*Deutsch?*'[2]

'A little.'

'*Er ist freigebig. Ein guter Mann.*'[3]

Freigebig, generous, spoken with the heavy *g* of Russian. Is Emmanuel generous? She does not know, one way or the other. Not the first word that would occur to her, though. Large, maybe. Large in his gestures.

'*Aber kaum zu vertrauen,*'[4] she remarks to the woman. Years since she last used the language. Is that what the two of them spoke together in bed last night: German, imperial tongue of the new Europe? *Kaum zu vertrauen*, not to be trusted.

The woman shrugs again. '*Die Zeit ist immer kurz. Man kann nicht alles haben.*' There is a pause. The woman speaks again. '*Auch die Stimme. Sie macht daß man*'—she searches for the word—'*man schaudert.*'[5]

Schaudern. Shudder. The voice makes one shudder. Probably does, when one is breast to breast with it. Between her and the Russian passes what is perhaps the beginning of a smile. As for the bird, they have been there long enough, the bird is losing interest. Only the fledgling, peering out from beneath its mother, is still wary of the intruders.

Is she jealous? How could she be? Still, hard to accept, being excluded from the game. Like being a child again, with a child's bedtime.

The voice. Her thoughts go back to Kuala Lumpur, when she was young, or nearly young, when she spent three nights in a row with Emmanuel Egudu, also young then. 'The oral poet,' she said to him teasingly. 'Show me what an oral poet can do.' And he laid her out, lay upon her, put his lips to her ears, opened them, breathed his breath into her, showed her.

1999

2. German (German).
3. He is generous. A good man (German).
4. But hardly to be trusted (German).

5. Time is always short. One cannot have everything . . . Also his voice. It makes one . . . one shudder (German).

Selected Bibliographies

I. The Enlightenment in Europe and the Americas

Peter Gay, *Age of Enlightenment* (1966) is the classic work on the subject. Two other good historical introductions are Dorinda Outram, *The Enlightenment* (1995; 2nd ed. 2005) and Roy Porter, *The Enlightenment* (2001). See also Porter's *Creation of the Modern World: The Untold Story of the British Enlightenment* (2001). Studies of women in the period include Carla Hesse, *The Other Enlightenment: How French Women Became Modern* (2003), Karen O'Brien, *Women and Enlightenment in Eighteenth-Century Britain* (2009), and M. Williamson, *Raising Their Voices, 1650–1750* (1990). For excellent studies of Enlightenment philosophical thinking, see F. C. Beiser, *The Sovereignty of Reason: The Defense of Rationality in the Early English Enlightenment* (1996); L. Crocker, *An Age of Crisis: Man and World in Eighteenth-Century French Thought* (1959); Knud Haakonssen, *Natural Law and Moral Philosophy: From Grotius to the Scottish Enlightenment* (1996); and Jonathan Israel, *Enlightenment Contested: Philosophy, Modernity, and the Emancipation of Man* (2006). A brilliant survey of literature, art, and history can be found in John Brewer, *The Pleasures of the Imagination: English Culture in the Eighteenth Century* (1998). Useful works for considering the literature of the period include M. Price, *To the Palace of Wisdom: Studies in Order and Energy from Dryden to Blake* (1964); L. Gossman, *French Society and Culture: Background for Eighteenth-Century Literature* (1972); S. Gearhart, *The Open Boundary of History and Fiction: A Critical Approach to the French Enlightenment* (1984); J. Sambrook, *The Eighteenth Century: The Intellectual and Cultural Context of English Literature, 1700–1789* (1986); and T. M. Kavanaugh, *Esthetics of the Moment: Literature and Art in the French Enlightenment* (1996).

Sor Juana Inés de la Cruz

Gerard Flynn's *Sor Juana Inés de la Cruz* (1971) provides a biographical, critical, and bibliographical introduction. Octavio Paz's *Sor Juana; Or, The Traps of Faith* (1988) is a famous study by the Mexican writer and Nobel Prize winner. Other important studies include Pamela Kirk, *Sor Juana Inés de la Cruz: Religion, Art, and Feminism* (1998); Stephanie Merrim, *Early Modern Women's Writing and Sor Juana Inés de la Cruz* (1999); and Frederick Luciani, *Literary Self-Fashioning in Sor Juana Inés de la Cruz* (2004). *Feminist Perspectives on Sor Juana Inés de la Cruz*, ed. Stephanie Merrim (1991), is a useful collection of essays.

Molière

H. Walker, *Molière* (1990), provides a general biographical and critical introduction to the playwright. Useful critical studies include L. Gossman, *Men and Masks: A Study of Molière* (1963); Jacques Guicharnaud, ed., *Molière: A Collection of Critical Essays* (1964); N. Gross, *From Gesture to Idea: Esthetics and Ethics in Molière's Comedy* (1982); J. F. Gaines, *Social Structures in Molière's Theater* (1984); and L. F. Norman, *The Public Mirror: Molière and the Social Commerce of Depiction* (1999). An excellent treatment of Molière in his historical context is W. D. Howarth, *Molière: A Playwright and His Audience* (1984). Harold C.

Knutson, *The Triumph of Wit* (1988) examines Molière in relation to Shakespeare and Ben Jonson. Martin Turnell, *The Classical Moment: Studies of Corneille, Molière, and Racine* (1975) offers useful insight into the French dramatic tradition.

Alexander Pope
The standard edition of Pope's poetry is the eleven-volume *Poems of Alexander Pope*, ed. John Butt et al. (1938–1969). Maynard Mack's *Alexander Pope: A Life* (1985) is a fascinating read, joining insightful criticism of the poetry with the poet's life. Brean Hammond's *Pope Among the Satirists* (2005) provides wonderful contextual material and is concise and well written. Leo Damrosch's *The World of Alexander Pope* (1987) includes perceptive criticism, and for a reading that focuses on the relationship between Pope's work and his disabled body, see Helen Deutsch, *Resemblance and Disgrace* (1996). Pope's relationship to the changing marketplace is brilliantly captured in Catherine Ingrassia's concise essay, "Money," in *The Cambridge Companion to Alexander Pope*, ed. Pat Rogers (2007): 175–85. David Foxon's illustrated *Pope and the Early Eighteenth-Century Book Trade* (1991) gives a rich picture of the complex relationship between Pope and his printers, including questions of typography and design.

Voltaire
Roger Pearson has a lively biography called *Voltaire Almighty: A Life in Pursuit of Freedom* (2005). Theodore Besterman's *Voltaire* (1969) is longer and more detailed. Nicholas Cronk's collection of essays in *The Cambridge Companion to Voltaire* (2009) provides both excellent readings and helpful contextual material. Haydn Mason's *Candide, Optimism Demolished* (1992) considers

the ideas, the reception, and the form of the text. For a series of competing interpretations of the Eldorado section of *Candide*, see Thomas Walsh, ed., *Readings on* Candide (2001).

What Is Enlightenment?
For general introductions to Enlightenment thought, see Ernst Cassirer, *The Philosophy of the Enlightenment*, trans. Fritz Koelln and James Pettegrove (1951); Peter Gay, *The Enlightenment: The Science of Freedom* (1996); and Roy Porter, *The Enlightenment* (2001). *The Portable Enlightenment Reader*, ed. Isaac Kramnick (1995), provides a good range of short readings. Those interested in scientific developments during the period will enjoy Thomas L. Hankins, *Science and the Enlightenment* (1985). For the influence of Enlightenment thinkers on the emerging form of modern democracy, see Jonathan Yisrael, *A Revolution of the Mind* (2009). For a bleaker take on the legacy of Enlightenment power and authority, see Michel Foucault, *Discipline and Punish*, trans. Alan Sheridan (1977). Foucault also responds to Kant in his own essay, "What is Enlightenment?" in *The Foucault Reader*, ed. Paul Rabinow (1984). Robert Darnton's *The Business of Enlightenment: A Publishing History of the Encyclopédie* (1986) tells a fascinating story about the dissemination of the encyclopedia after its initial publication. Emmanuel Chukwudi Eze has published an excellent reader called *Race and the Enlightenment* (1997). There is a lively debate among scholars concerning the relation between Enlightenment thinkers and European imperial expansion. See, for example, Uday Singh Mehta, *Liberalism and Empire* (1999), Sankar Muthu, *Enlightenment against Empire* (2003), and Jennifer Pitts, *A Turn to Empire* (2006).

II. Early Modern Chinese Vernacular Literature

For an introduction to Chinese vernacular literature, including drama, stories, and novels, see the relevant chapters in Victor H. Mair's *The Columbia History of Chinese Literature* (2001) and Stephen Owen and Kang-i Sun Chang's *The Cambridge History of Chinese Literature* (2010). To further explore women's writing in the early modern period, the second half of Wilt Idema and Beata Grant's *The Red Brush: Writing Women of Imperial China* (2004) and the relevant parts of Kang-i Sun Chang and Haun Saussy's *Women Writers of Traditional China: An Anthology of Poetry and Criticism* (1999) are a treasure trove with introductions to major female authors and sample works.

A basic survey of the history of Chinese drama can be found in William Dolby, *A History of Chinese Drama* (1976). C. T. Hsia's *The Classic Chinese Novel: A Critical Introduction* (1968) remains one of the most readable introductions to the major novels. Patrick Hanan, *The Chinese Vernacular Story* (1981) provides an insightful study of the cultural background of vernacular fiction. To explore how writers of China's literary revolution during the first half of the twentieth century discovered vernacular literature and elevated it to its central place in the Chinese literary canon, see the tremendously popular *A Brief History of Chinese Fiction* (1959, originally published 1925) by Lu Xun, one of China's first and foremost modern writers, whose works are included in the last volume of this anthology.

Cao Xueqin

There is a complete translation of *The Story of the Stone* in five volumes (1973–1982), the first three volumes by David Hawkes and the last two by John Minford. Selections of this have also appeared in a bilingual version in 2005. Andrew Plaks, *Archetype and Allegory in the Dream of the Red Chamber* (1976); Anthony C. Yu, *Rereading the Stone: Desire and the Making of Fiction in Dream of the Red Chamber* (1997); and Dore J. Levy, *Ideal and Actual in The Story of the Stone* (1999) are useful studies. C. T. Hsia's *The Classic Chinese Novel: A Critical Introduction* (1968) has chapters on China's great novels. For comparisons of the pursuit of enlightenment and the role of magic stones in *The Story of the Stone* and *The Journey to the West* see Li Qiancheng's *Fictions of Enlightenment: Journey to the West, Tower of Myriad Mirrors, and Dream of the Red Chamber* (2004) and Jing Wang's *Story of Stone: Intertextuality, Ancient Chinese Stone Lore, and the Stone Symbolism in Dream of the Red Chamber, Water Margin, and The Journey to the West* (1992). On the significance of the garden scenes in the novel, see Xiao Chi's *The Chinese Garden as Lyric Enclave: A Generic Study of the Story of the Stone* (2001).

Wu Cheng'en

Arthur Waley's translation *Monkey* (1943) is an abridged adaptation of thirty of the original hundred chapters, but Waley's gifts as a translator and the nature of his abridgement make this version still a delight to read. There is a complete translation in four volumes by Anthony C. Yu, *The Journey to the West* (1977). The translation of the selections here comes from Anthony C. Yu's abridged version *Monkey & the Monk: A Revised Abridgment of The Journey to the West* (2006). There is an excellent chapter on the novel in C. T. Hsia, *The Classic Chinese Novel: A Critical Introduction* (1968). Glen Dudbridge's *The Hsi-yu-chi: A Study of the Antecedents to the Sixteenth-Century Chinese Novel* (1970) examines the development of Xuanzang's story before the novel. For comparisons of the pursuit of enlightenment and the role of magic stones in *The Journey to the West* and *The Story of the Stone*, see Li Qiancheng's *Fictions of Enlightenment: Journey to the West, Tower of Myriad Mirrors, and Dream of the Red Chamber* (2004) and Jing Wang's *Story of Stone: Intertextuality, Ancient Chinese Stone Lore, and the Stone Symbolism in Dream of the Red Chamber, Water Margin, and The Journey to the West* (1992).

III. Early Modern Japanese Popular Literature

For a close-up of Tokugawa culture and society see Andrew C. Gerstle's *Eighteenth-Century Japan: Culture and Society* (1989), Matsunosuke Nishiyama's *Edo Culture: Daily Life and Diversions in Urban Japan 1600–1868* (1997), and Chie Nakane and Shinzaburō Ōishi's *Tokugawa Japan: The Social and Economic Antecedents of Modern Japan* (1991).

To read more of early modern Japanese literature, Haruo Shirane's *Early Modern Japanese Literature: An Anthology 1600–1900* (2002) is a treasure trove of texts with excellent introductions. On Tokugawa wood prints and urban culture see Christine Guth's *Art of Edo Japan: The Artist and the City, 1615–1868* (1996). On the Japanese printing revolution in the context of the development of book culture Peter Kornicki's *The Book in Japan: A Cultural History from the Beginnings to the Nineteenth Century* (1998) is highly recommended. To further explore the pleasure quarters there is Cecilia Segawa's *Yoshiwara: The Glittering World of the Japanese Courtesan* (1993) and Elizabeth Swinton's *The Women of the Pleasure Quarter: Japanese Paintings and Prints of the Floating World* (1995).

Chikamatsu Monzaemon

To explore the world of Japanese puppet theater, Barbara Curtis Adachi's *Backstage at Bunraku: A Behind the Scenes Look at Japan's Traditional Puppet Theater* (1985), Adachi's *The Voices and Hands of Bunraku* (1978), Donald Keene's *Bunraku: The Art of the Japanese Puppet Theatre* (1965), and C. U. Dunn's *The Early Japanese Puppet Drama* (1966) are recommended.

To read other plays by Chikamatsu, see Andrew C. Gerstle's *Chikamatsu: Five Late Plays* (2001), Donald Keene's *Four Major Plays of Chikamatsu* (1969) and his *Major Plays of Chikamatsu* (1961). Gerstle's *Circles of Fantasy: Convention in the Plays of Chikamatsu* (1986) discusses Chikamatsu's art and craft as a playwright.

To read some of the greatest puppet plays by authors other than Chikamatsu, consult Stanleigh H. Jones's *Sugawara and the Secrets of Calligraphy* (1985) (a puppet play revolving around the tenth-century poet-official Sugawara no Michizane), Stanleigh H. Jones's *Yoshitsune and the Thousand Cherry Trees: A Masterpiece of the Eighteenth-Century Japanese Puppet Theater* (1993), and Donald Keene's *Chūshingura: The Treasury of Loyal Retainers* (1971), a play about the forty-seven samurai who avenged the humiliation of their lord and then committed ritual suicide.

The World of Haiku

For compelling introductions into the world of Japanese haiku see Haruo Shirane, *Traces of Dreams: Landscape, Cultural Memory, and the Poetry of Bashō* (1998); Kenneth Yasuda, *The Japanese Haiku: Its Essential Nature, History, and Possibilities in English* (1957); Harold G. Henderson, *An Introduction to Haiku* (1958); Koji Kawamoto's *The Poetics of Japanese Verse:*

Imagery, Structure, Meter (2000); Stephen Addiss, Fumiko Yamamoto, and Akira Yamamoto, *Haiku: An Anthology of Japanese Poems* (2009); and Michael F. Marra's *Seasons and Landscapes in Japanese Poetry: An Introduction to Haiku and Waka* (2009). Nippon Gakujutsu Shinkokai, ed., *Haikai and Haiku* (1958) is a basic reference.

To explore haiku movements beyond Japan, see Bruce Ross's *Haiku Moment: An Anthology of Contemporary North American Haiku* (1993); John Brandi and Dennis Maloney, *The Unswept Path: Contemporary American Haiku* (2005); and Hiroaki Sato's *One Hundred Frogs: From Renga to Haiku in English* (1983). Yoshinobu Hakutani's *Haiku and Modernist Poetics* (2009) explores the impact of haiku on modernist literature in the West.

For Bashō's poetry see Jane Reichhold, *Bashō: The Complete Haiku* (2008); Sam Hamill, *The Essential Bashō* (1999). All five of Bashō's travel journals are found in Nobuyuki Yuasa's *The Narrow Road to the Deep North and Other Travel Sketches* (1966). For Bashō's linked verse see Earl Miner and Hiroko Odagiri, *The Monkey's Straw Raincoat* (1981) and, more generally, Earl Miner's *Japanese Linked Poetry* (1979). The following translations of *Narrow Road of the Interior* are recommended: Cid Corman and Kamaike Susumu, *Back Roads to Far Towns* (1986); Donald Keene, *The Narrow Road to Oku* (1996); Dorothy Britton, *A Haiku Journey: Bashō's "Narrow Road to a Far Province"* (1980). There are two interesting studies of Bashō, both by Makoto Ueda: *Matsuo Bashō* (1982) and *Bashō and His Interpreters* (1991).

On the painter literatus and haiku poet Yosa Buson, see Makoto Ueda's study *The Path of Flowering Thorn: The Life and Poetry of Yosa Buson* (1998) and Yuki Sawa and Eith M. Shiffert's *Haiku Master Buson* (1978).

IV. An Age of Revolutions in Europe and the Americas

The excellent, classic resource for the industrial and political revolutions of the period is E. J. Hobsbawm, *The Age of Revolution, 1789–1848* (1962). Another fine introduction to the upheavals of the period is Charles Breunig, *Age of Revolution and Reaction, 1789–1850* (1977). For the global implications of the industrial revolution, see E. J. Hobsbawm, *Industry and Empire* (1990) and Peter N. Stearns, *The Industrial Revolution in World History* (3rd ed. 2007). Gavin Weightman tells absorbing stories about particular inventors, entrepreneurs, and industrial break-throughs in *The Industrial Revolutionaries* (2010). Good scholarly works on the French Revolution include William Doyle, *The Oxford History of the French Revolution* (2003) and Simon Schama, *Citizens* (1990). Alan Schom's *Napoleon Bonaparte: A Life* (1998) is a lively biography; see also J. Christopher Herold, *The Age of Napoleon* (2002). *Latin American Independence: An Anthology of Sources*, ed. John Chasteen and Sarah C. Chambers (2010), contains fascinating source materials; for a historical overview, see Michael Eakin, *The History of Latin America* (2007). A detailed account of the upheavals of 1848 can be found in Mike Rapport, *1848: Year of Revolution* (2009).

Charles Baudelaire

There have been many English translations of Baudelaire's poetry, including those by the well-known poets included here. The most comprehensive collection is Walter Martin's *Charles Baudelaire: Complete Poems* (2002), which includes juvenilia and poems that have been ascribed to Baudelaire; Keith Waldrop's prose translation of *Flowers of Evil*, with French and English on facing pages, is widely respected (2006). Baudelaire's essays on painting and the other arts, including his studies of Delacroix, Poe, and Wagner, have been considered the beginning of modern criticism: see *The Painter of Modern Life and Other Essays*, trans. Jonathan Mayne (1964). The definitive biography is Claude Pichois and Jean Ziegler, *Charles Baudelaire*, trans. G. Robb (1991). The most famous essays on Baudelaire as a modern writer are Walter Benjamin's *Charles Baudelaire*, trans. Harry Zohn (1973). For useful introductions, see Lois Boe Hyslop, *Charles Baudelaire Revisited* (1992); Laurence Porter, ed., *Approaches to Teaching Baudelaire's Flowers of Evil* (2000); and Rosemary Lloyd, *Baudelaire's World* (2002). Strong readings of individual works include Barbara Johnson's classic deconstructive approach, "Poetry and Its Double: Two *Invitations au voyage*," in *The Critical Difference* (1980), 23–51; Jonathan Culler's introduction to *Charles Baudelaire: The Flowers of Evil* (1993); and the collection of readings in William J. Thompson, ed., *Understanding Les Fleurs du Mal* (1997). For more on the city, see Ross Chambers, "Baudelaire's Paris," in *The Cambridge Companion to Baudelaire*, ed. Rosemary Lloyd (2005), 101–16.

Andrés Bello

The best work on Andrés Bello is Julio Ramos, *Divergent Modernities*, trans. John D. Blance (1999). See also Iván Jaksić's thoughtful introduction to *The Selected Writings of Andrés Bello*, trans. Frances M. López-Morillas (1997); and Iván Jaksić, *Andrés Bello: Scholarship and Nation-Building in Nineteenth-Century Latin America* (2001). For an excellent reading of this poem as a response to Virgil, see *Bello and Bolívar: Poetry and Politics in the Spanish American Revolution* (1992).

William Blake

The standard edition of the works is David V. Erdman's *The Complete Poetry and Prose of William Blake* (rev. 1988). Peter Ackroyd's marvelously well-written biography *William Blake: A Life* (1996) is to be recommended, as is the more scholarly, detailed life by G. E. Bentley Jr., *The Stranger from Paradise* (2003).

Martin K. Nurmi's *William Blake* (1976) is a helpful introduction to the man and his work. For excellent critical and contextual readings, see *The Cambridge Companion to William Blake*, ed. Morris Eaves (2003), which suggests a range of approaches to reading and teaching Blake, including serious attention to Blake's images and processes of image-making. Also helpful are Jacob Brunowski, *William Blake and the Age of Revolution* (1965); W. J. T. Mitchell, *Blake's Composite Art: A Study of the Illuminated Poetry* (1978); and Saree Makdisi, *William Blake and the Impossible History of the 1790s* (2003).

Elizabeth Barrett Browning
The Complete Works of Elizabeth Barrett Browning, ed. Sandra Donaldson et al. (2010), is the only scholarly edition of her works. The standard biography is Margaret Foster's *Elizabeth Barrett Browning* (1989). The story of the Brownings' romance has been retold many times in fiction and film. A particularly appealing version is Virginia Woolf's novel *Flush*, which relates the Brownings' courtship from the perspective of her dog. Helpful critical and contextual commentary can be found in Simon Avery and Rebecca Stott, *Elizabeth Barrett Browning* (2003). For a close reading of "The Cry of the Children," see Caroline Levine, "Strategic Formalism: Toward a New Method in Cultural Studies," in *Victorian Studies* (2006).

Anna Bunina
Wendy Rosslyn's *Anna Bunina (1774–1829) and the Origins of Women's Poetry in Russia* (1997) is a fine critical biography that includes a rich context for thinking about nineteenth-century Russian writers and audiences. Catriona Kelly's *A History of Russian Women's Writing, 1820–1992* (1998) gives a broad history of women's writing in Russia and includes a brief discussion of Bunina.

Rubén Darío
Rubén Darío's work has been translated into English more than once, but the best version remains Lysander Kemp's *Selected Poems* (1965). Also from 1965 is Charles Watland's *Poet-Errant: A Biography of Rubén Darío*, the only book-length biography in English. It is carefully documented and reliable. Keith Ellis offers five different ways of reading Darío— biographical, socio-political, literary historical,

formal, and structural—in *Critical Approaches to Rubén Darío* (1974), and Octavio Paz discusses Darío's work in the title essay of *The Siren and the Seashell* (1970). Cathy Login Jrade in *Rubén Darío and the Romantic Search for Unity* (1983) and Dolores Ackel Fiore in *Rubén Darío in Search of Inspiration* (1963) explore influences on Darío from ancient to contemporary times. A brief review essay by the influential scholar Roberto González Echevarría, called "Master of Modernismo," does a beautiful job of capturing Darío's importance to Spanish American literary history (*The Nation*, January 25, 2006).

Emily Dickinson
R. W. Franklin's three-volume edition of Emily Dickinson's work is carefully comprehensive and preserves as much as possible her spelling and punctuation: *The Poems of Emily Dickinson: The Variorum Edition* (1998). Franklin has also put together a more accessible, one-volume version: *The Poems of Emily Dickinson: Reading Edition* (2005) and a facsimile edition, which allows readers to see her handwritten pages (1981). The classic biography is the award-winning *Life of Emily Dickinson* by Richard B. Sewall (1974). Alfred Habegger has added fresh material and perspectives in *My Wars Are Laid Away in Books: The Life of Emily Dickinson* (2001). The poet Adrienne Rich has a wonderful essay on Dickinson's sense of her own genius in *Critical Essays on Emily Dickinson*, ed. Paul J. Ferlazzo (1984), 175–95. For critical readings, see Sharon Cameron, *Lyric Time: Dickinson and the Limits of Genre* (1979); J. Dobson, *Dickinson and the Strategies of Reticence* (1989); E. Phillips, *Emily Dickinson: Personae and Performance* (1996); Elizabeth A. Petrino, *Emily Dickinson and Her Contemporaries: Women's Verse in America, 1820–85* (1998); and Virginia Jackson, *Dickinson's Misery: A Theory of Lyric Reading* (2005). For Dickinson in context, see *The Emily Dickinson Handbook*, ed. Gudrun Grabher, Roland Hagenbüchle, and Cristanne Miller (1998); Paula Bernat Bennett, "Emily Dickinson and her American Women Poet Peers," in *The Cambridge Companion to Emily Dickinson* (2002), 215–35; and *A Historical Guide to Emily Dickinson*, ed. Vivian R. Pollak (2004).

Frederick Douglass
Douglass himself wrote three autobiographies: not only the *Narrative*, but also *My Bondage*

and My Freedom (1855) and *The Life and Times of Frederick Douglass, Written by Himself* (1892). For a more recent scholarly account, see William S. McFeely's *Frederick Douglass* (1991). Excellent critical and historical studies include *The Cambridge Companion to Frederick Douglass*, ed. Maurice S. Lee (2009); William L. Andrews, *To Tell a Free Story* (1986); Houston A. Baker, *Blues, Ideology, and Afro-American Literature* (1991); Audrey A. Fisch, *American Slaves in Victorian England* (2000); Dwight A. McBride, *Impossible Witnesses: Truth, Abolitionism, and Slave Testimony* (2001); and John Stauffer, *Giants: The Parallel Lives of Frederick Douglass and Abraham Lincoln* (2008). On the question of gender in the narrative, see Deborah E. McDowell, "In the First Place: Making Frederick Douglass and the Afro-American Narrative Tradition," in *Critical Essays on Frederick Douglass*, ed. William L. Andrews (1991), 192–211.

Ghalib

Ghalib's poetry and prose have been translated and discussed widely in English. New poetic translations, with a comprehensive introduction and notes, are found in Vinay Dharwadker, *Ghalib: Ghazals* (2011); Aijaz Ahmad, *Ghazals of Ghalib* (1971) includes translations by American poets, with commentary on individual poems. For historical context, biographical interpretation, and analysis of the Urdu and Persian writings, see Ralph Russell and Khurshidul Islam, *Ghalib: Life and Letters* (1994); and Ralph Russell, *Ghalib: The Poet and His Age* (1997). Daud Rahbar, *Urdu Letters of Mirza Asadu'llah Khan Ghalib* (1987) is a large translated selection; Pavan K. Verma, *Ghalib: The Man, the Times* (1988) is an informative popular biography. Agha Shahid Ali's *Ravishing Disunities: Real Ghazals in English* (2000) collects recent experiments in the form by a large number of British, American, South Asian, and diasporic poets.

Johann Wolfgang von Goethe

Nicholas Boyle's two-volume biography, *Goethe: The Poet and the Age* (1991), is the most recent and one of the most extensive, informative biographies of Goethe and his work. More compact is John R. Williams's *The Life of Goethe: A Critical Biography* (1998), which is divided by genre and thus allows for a good, concise overview of Goethe's dramatic work. A classic study of *Faust* in English is Stuart Atkins's *Goethe's Faust: A Literary Analysis* (1964), a close textual analysis of the play in the tradition of the New Critics. John R. Williams's *Goethe's Faust* (1987) is more varied in its method and includes a useful discussion of the different sources, versions, and revisions that led to the final text. Most attuned to literary form is Benjamin Bennett's *Goethe's Theory of Poetry* (1986), which discusses Goethe's use and interruption of the traditional tragic plot as well as other stylistic devices. Focusing on Goethe's theater practice is Marvin Carlson's *Goethe and the Weimar Theatre* (1978). Goethe's *Faust* has also attracted the attention of philosophers and cultural critics. An early example was the Marxist critic Georg Lukács, whose *Goethe and His Age* (1940, 1969) places Goethe within the history of political and social upheaval. This line of interpretation was later taken up by Marshall Berman, whose powerful *All That Is Sold Melts into Air* (1982) reads *Faust* alongside Marx and Engels's *Communist Manifesto*, written some fifteen years after Goethe's death, as an expression of modernist upheaval and productivity.

Heinrich Heine

Heine has been translated into English many times. The most comprehensive edition is Hal Draper's *The Complete Poems of Heinrich Heine* (1982). The best English-language biography is Jeffrey L. Sammons's *Heinrich Heine* (1979). Hanna Spencer provides a useful introduction to the work in *Heinrich Heine* (1982). For a series of contextualizing essays by leading Heine scholars, see Roger F. Cook, *A Companion to the Works of Heinrich Heine* (2002).

John Keats

Andrew Motion's *Keats* (1999) is a fine biography. William Walsh's *Introduction to Keats* (1981) is a critical biography with strong readings of the poetry. Jack Stillinger's edition of Keats's *Complete Poems* (1978) remains the standard. For a brilliant and sustained reading of the odes, see Helen Vendler, *The Odes of John Keats* (1983); see also Geoffrey Hartman's *The Fate of Reading* (1975), 57–73. William Keach writes about the reception of Keats as a political member of the Cockney School in "Cockney Couplets: Keats and the Politics of Style," *Studies in Romanticism* 25 (summer 1986): 182–96; see also Jeffrey Cox, *Poetry and Politics in the Cockney School* (1998).

Giacomo Leopardi

Ottavio Casale has put together a wonderful collection of selections from Leopardi's poetry and prose, including his diary, woven together to make a critical biography: *A Leopardi Reader* (1981). The only full-length English biography of Leopardi dates from 1935 (revised in 1953): Iris Origo's *Leopardi: A Study in Solitude*. For insightful readings of the poetry, see J. H. Whitfield, *Giacomo Leopardi* (1954) and Daniela Bini, *A Fragrance from the Desert* (1983).

José Martí

Esther Allen's *José Martí: Selected Writings* (2002) features Martí's fine prose as well as his poetry and includes a valuable essay about the poet's life, work, and reception, by renowned Latin American scholar Roberto González Echevarría. *José Martí: Major Poems*, trans. Elinor Randall, ed. Philip S. Foner (1982), provides good translations and a helpful biographical and critical introduction.

Arthur Rimbaud

Graham Robb's *Rimbaud* (2000) recounts Rimbaud's tempestuous life in vivid and persuasive terms. Frederic St. Aubyn's *Arthur Rimbaud* (1988) weaves together a brief biography with readings of the poems. Other useful introductions include Cecil Arthur Hackett, *Rimbaud, a Critical Introduction* (1981) and Harold Bloom, ed., *Arthur Rimbaud* (1988). For a focus on the self in Rimbaud, see James Lawler, *Rimbaud's Theatre of the Self* (1992) and Susan Harrow, *The Material, the Real, and the Fractured Self* (2004). David Evans thinks in intriguing ways about the use of rhythm in Baudelaire, Mallarmé, and Rimbaud in *Rhythm, Illusion, and the Poetic Idea* (2004).

Jean-Jacques Rousseau

Leo Damrosch has written an excellent, lively biography, *Jean-Jacques Rousseau: Restless Genius* (2005). For a study of Rousseau's impact, see Thomas McFarland, *Romanticism and the Heritage of Rousseau* (1995). An appealing and readable account of the relationship between Hume and Rousseau, including a meditation on the ideas of both, can be found in David Edmonds and John Eidinow, *Rousseau's Dog: Two Great Thinkers at War in the Age of Enlightenment* (2006). For classic readings of *The Confessions*, see Jean Starobinski, *Jean-Jacques Rousseau: Transparency and Obstruction*, trans. Arthur Goldhammer (1988); Huntington Williams, *Rousseau and Romantic Autobiography* (1983); and Christopher Kelly, *Rousseau's Exemplary Life: The Confessions as Political Philosophy* (1987). One of the most important works of contemporary French philosophy is Jacques Derrida's reading of *The Confessions* in *Of Grammatology*, trans. Gayatri Chakravorty Spivak (1976). James Olney reads Rousseau as part of the history of autobiography in *Memory and Narrative: The Weave of Life-Writing* (1999). For a look at gender in Rousseau, see Linda Zerilli, *Signifying Women: Culture and Chaos in Rousseau, Burke, and Mill* (1994), and Lynda Lange, ed., *Feminist Interpretations of Jean-Jacques Rousseau* (2002). The distinguished historian Robert Darnton writes about Rousseau's reception in "Readers Respond to Rousseau" in *Jean-Jacques Rousseau: Politics, Art, and Autobiography*, ed. John T. Scott (2006), 303–40.

Alfred, Lord Tennyson

Christopher Ricks has edited *The Poems of Tennyson* (1987). Leonee Ormond's *Alfred Tennyson: A Literary Life* (1993) is a fine biography. For excellent contextual and critical readings, see Alan Sinfield, *Alfred Tennyson* (1986), Herbert F. Tucker, *Tennyson and the Doom of Romanticism* (1988), and Isobel Armstrong, *Victorian Poetry: Poetry, Poetics, and Politics* (1993).

Paul Verlaine

Stefan Zweig's *Paul Verlaine* (1913), trans. O. F. Theis (1980), is the classic biography. A. E. Carter's *Verlaine* (1971) offers a general introduction to his life and work. For critical and historical studies, see Laurence M. Porter, *The Crisis of French Symbolism* (1990) and David Hillery, *Verlaine: Fixing an Image* (1988).

Walt Whitman

The standard scholarly edition of Whitman's works took many years and a number of volumes: *The Collected Writings of Walt Whitman*, ed. Gay Wilson Allen and Sculley Bradley (1961–2004). Whitman's additions and revisions are so extensive that they are difficult to capture in print. An excellent new online edition called *The Walt Whitman Archive*, ed. Kenneth M. Price and Ed Folsom, has the advantage of incorporating multiple texts, including facsimiles of original editions, poems published in periodicals, and editions of *Leaves of Grass* printed outside of the United

States. The best-known scholarly biography is Gay Allen Wilson, *The Solitary Singer* (rev. 1985). Another fine biography is Jerome Loving, *Walt Whitman: The Song of Himself* (1998). David S. Reynolds has brought together a series of essays that contextualize the poet in *A Historical Guide to Walt Whitman* (2000). Ezra Greenspan's *Walt Whitman's Song of Myself: A Sourcebook and Critical Edition* (2005) brings together a rich collection of reviews and critical responses starting in the nineteenth century, and offers a good overview of the historical context for Whitman's work. For critical studies, see Mark Bauerlein, *Whitman and the American Idiom* (1991); Jimmie M. Killingsworth, *Whitman's Poetry of the Body: Sexuality, Politics, and the Text* (1989); Michael Moon, *Disseminating Whitman: Revision and Corporeality in Leaves of Grass* (1991); *Whitman East and West: New Contexts for Reading Walt Whitman*, ed. Ed Folsom (2002); and Susan Belasco, Ed Folsom, and Kenneth M. Price, eds., *Leaves of Grass: The Sesquicentennial Essays* (2007). For a valuable approach to teaching "Out of the Cradle Endlessly Rocking," see Dennis K. Renner, "Reconciling Varied Approaches to 'Out of the

Cradle Endlessly Rocking,'" in *Approaches to Teaching Whitman's "Leaves of Grass,"* ed. Donald D. Kummings (1990), 67–73.

William Wordsworth
The best editions of Wordsworth's poetry are the volumes in "The Cornell Wordsworth" series, ed. Stephen Parrish (1974–2008). A good serious biography of the poet is Stephen Gill's *William Wordsworth: A Life* (1989); for a stunningly sensitive and intelligent reading of Wordsworth's poetry with his politics, see David Bromwich's *Disowned by Memory: Wordsworth's Poetry of the 1790s* (1998). Other fine studies include Geoffrey Hartman's *Wordsworth's Poetry* (1964), Alan Liu's *Wordsworth: A Sense of History* (1989), and Theresa M. Kelley's *Wordsworth's Revisionary Aesthetics* (1988). For a study of Wordsworth's ecological consciousness, see Jonathan Bate, *Romantic Ecology* (1991) and *The Song of the Earth* (2000); for a general look at audiences of Wordsworth's historical moment, see Richard Altick's classic study, *The English Common Reader* (1957), and William St. Clair, *The Reading Nation in the Romantic Period* (2004).

V. Realism Across the Globe

Erich Auerbach's beautiful classic work of criticism, *Mimesis* (1946), explores a number of different attempts to capture reality in the Western tradition, including nineteenth-century realism. Pam Morris's *Realism* (2003) is a fine introduction to the concept, focusing exclusively on French and British literary examples. For a historical understanding of the rise of realism, with a special focus on the visual arts, see Linda Nochlin, *Realism* (1972). György Lukács has been one of the most influential theorists of the realist novel: see his *Theory of the Novel* (1920) and *Studies in European Realism* (1948). For the roots of British realism in eighteenth-century thought and social experience, Ian Watt's *Rise of the Novel* (1957) is a landmark study. An overview of Russian realism can be found in Dmitrij Cizevskij and Dmitrij Tschižewskij, *The History of Nineteenth-Century Russian Literature: The Age of Realism* (1974).

Anton Chekhov
Donald Rayfield's detailed biography *Anton Chekhov: A Life* (2000) is the most substantial in English. Rayfield's *Understanding Chekhov: A Critical Study of Chekhov's Prose and Drama* (1999) brings together biography and criticism. A more popular book on Chekhov is Janet Malcolm's *Reading Chekhov: A Critical Journey*

(2001), which combines travel writing, biography, and criticism in a lively and intelligent—though not scholarly—combination. Three fine collections of essays offer an array of good historical and critical responses to Chekhov's drama: the first is *A Chekhov Companion*, ed. Toby W. Clyman (1985), the second is *Critical Essays on Anton Chekhov*, ed. Thomas A. Eekman (1989), and the third is *The Cambridge Companion to Chekhov*, ed. Vera Gottlieb and Paul Allain (2000). Jean-Louis Barrault's poetic essay "Why *The Cherry Orchard?*" explores the musical structure of the play (collected in *Anton Chekhov's Selected Plays*, ed. Laurence Senelick [2005], 620–28).

Fyodor Dostoyevsky
Written over the course of three decades, Joseph Frank's magisterial five-volume biography of Dostoyevsky is widely hailed as a great achievement (1976–2002). There is a helpfully condensed one-volume version of this, called *Dostoevsky: A Writer in His Time*, ed. Mary Petrusewicz (2009), that focuses mostly on the impact of events on the author's ideas. Mikhail Bakhtin makes his influential argument that Dostoyevsky's work is always multi-voiced—"polyphonic"—in *Problems of Dostoyevsky's Poetics*, trans. Caryl Emerson (1984). The Norton Critical Edition of the text contains many useful critical commentaries, including Joseph Frank's, which considers the two parts of the text as responding to two different historical contexts, the first part concerned with the mid-1860s, the second part looking back to the idealist moment of the 1840s. This edition also includes parodies and imitations of the text by Woody Allen, Ralph Ellison, and Jean-Paul Sartre. See Fyodor Dostoevsky, *Notes from Underground*, ed. Michael Katz (2000).

Gustave Flaubert
Frederick Brown's *Flaubert: A Biography* (2006) is rich in historical detail; Geoffrey Wall's *Flaubert: A Life* (2002) is more psychological in focus. Flaubert's *Selected Letters*, ed. Geoffrey Wall (1998), give access to the writer's feelings and opinions in a way that his literary texts deliberately do not. Victor Brombert offers a classic reading of *A Simple Heart* in *The Novels of Flaubert* (1966). Winifred Woodhull investigates the relationship between private experience and public, historical events in "Configurations of the Family in *Un Coeur Simple*," *Comparative Literature* 39 (1987): 139–61.

Henrik Ibsen
Overall, the best book on Ibsen is Toril Moi's *Henrik Ibsen and the Birth of Modernism* (2006). Among the early reactions to Ibsen was George Bernard Shaw's *The Quintessence of Ibsenism* (1891), which emphasizes Ibsen's concern with pressing social and political issues, while William Archer's essays, collected by Thomas Postlewait in *William Archer on Ibsen: The Major Essays, 1889–1919* (1984), foreground Ibsen's poetic choices and techniques. Charles Lyons's compilation, *Critical Essays on Henrik Ibsen* (1987), includes landmark essays by Ibsen's modernist admirers, including James Joyce, E. M. Forster, and Georg Lukàcs. The wider cultural context of Ibsen's European success, as well as a wealth of personal detail, is captured in Michael Meyer's *Ibsen: A Biography* (1971). Michael Goldman's *Ibsen: The Dramaturgy of Fear* (1999) focuses on subtexts and psychologies. In *Ibsen and Early Modernist Theatre, 1890–1900*, Kirsten Shepherd-Barr situates Ibsen in the context of theater history, and Joan Templeton's *Ibsen's Women* is the first in-depth analysis of Ibsen's construction of female characters, including Hedda Gabler. *The Cambridge Companion to Ibsen*, ed. James McFarlane (1994), provides a good introduction into recent scholarship and contemporary approaches.

Higuchi Ichiyō
The only full-length biography of Ichiyō in English is Robert Lyons Danly's *In the Shade of Spring Leaves* (1981). Donald Keene's *Dawn to the West: Japanese Literature in the Modern Era* (1998) traces Ichiyō's life and career in some detail, locating her in a literary context. For a reading of Ichiyō in the context of other women writers, see Yukiko Tanaka, *Women Writers of Meiji and Taishō Japan: Their Lives, Works, and Critical Reception* (2000); and Rebecca Copeland and Melek Ortabasi, eds., *The Modern Murasaki: Writing by Women of Meiji Japan* (2006).

Machado de Assis
There is no full-length biography of Machado in English, but Helen Caldwell's *Machado de Assis: The Brazilian Master and his Novels* (1970) interweaves details about his life with readings of the novels, and Earl E. Fitz gives an overview of both life and work in *Machado de Assis* (1989). The most famous reading of Machado's literary innovations in their social context is Roberto Schwartz, *A Master on the Periphery of Capitalism*, trans. John Gledson (2001). Helpful and informative essays on Machado can be found in *Machado de Assis: Reflections on a Brazilian Master Writer* (1999).

Orature

For excellent introductions to thinking about oral traditions, see Eric Havelock's classic *Preface to Plato* (1963); Walter J. Ong, *Orality and Literacy* (1982); Isidore Opkewho, *African Oral Literature* (1992); and Ruth Finnegan, *The Oral and Beyond* (2007). Ngugi Wa Thiong'o makes a powerful case for studying orature in order to understand African cultures in *Decolonizing the Mind* (1986). On the Grimms, see Jack David Zipes, *The Brothers Grimm* (2002) and James M. McGlathery, ed., *The Brothers Grimm and Folktale* (1988). For an intriguing study of African American folk heroes, see *From Trickster to Badman* by John W. Roberts (1989). Leonard Fox's *Hainteny* (1990) is the best English-language introduction to Malagasy wisdom poetry. James C. Faris gives a detailed description of the Navajo Night Chant in an essay called "Context and Text" in Philip G. Cohen, ed., *Texts and Textuality* (1997).

Rabindranath Tagore

Amiya Chakravarty, ed., *A Tagore Reader* (1961) and Krishna Dutta and Andrew Robinson, *Rabindranath Tagore: An Anthology* (1997) provide the best overviews of Tagore's career and work in many genres. Dutta and Robinson's *Rabindranath Tagore: The Myriad-Minded Man* (1995) and Krishna Kripalani's *Rabindranath Tagore: A Biography* (1962) offer informative accounts in English of the artist's life. Older translations, prepared under Tagore's own supervision, are still available in *Collected Poems and Plays* (1936). Among important recent translations and accounts of Tagore's work are William Radice's *Rabindranath Tagore: Selected Poems* (1985) and *Rabindranath Tagore: Selected Short Stories* (1991); Ketaki Kushari Dyson's *I Won't Let You Go* (1993), a selection of poetry; and Anand Lal's *Rabindranath Tagore: Three Plays* (2001). Some of the best new translations and critical introductions are contained in the Oxford Tagore Translations series edited by Shukanta Chaudhuri and others, which includes *Selected Short Stories* (2000) and *Selected Writings on Literature and Language* (2001).

Leo Tolstoy

A. N. Wilson's *Tolstoy* (1988) is an entertaining and readable biography. Gary R. Jahn's *Tolstoy's The Death of Ivan Il'ich* (1999) contains a number of fine interpretive essays and an excellent introduction. It also includes a set of notes on connotations of phrases in the original Russian text. For other good critical essays, see R. F. Christian, *Tolstoy: A Critical Introduction* (1969); Edward Wasiolek, ed., *Critical Essays on Tolstoy* (1986); Harold Bloom, ed., *Leo Tolstoy* (1986); *Tolstoy* by John Bayley (1997); and David Holbrook's *Tolstoy, Woman and Death* (1997). The fascinating correspondence between Tolstoy and Gandhi can be found in B. Srinivasa Murthy, ed., *Mahatma Gandhi and Leo Tolstoy: Letters* (1987).

VI. Modernity and Modernism, 1900–1945

Pericles Lewis, *The Cambridge Introduction to Modernism* (2007), offers an overview of developments in England and Europe. Ástráður Eysteinsson and Vivian Lisca, eds., *Modernism*, 2 vols. (2007) provides detailed studies of particular national contexts. Harry Levin, "What Was Modernism?" (1962, repr. in *Refractions*, 1966) is a survey of modernist writers as humanists and inheritors of the Enlightenment. Many of the original critical writings on modern literature and art are collected in Vassiliki Kolocotroni, Jane Goldman, and Olga Taxidoe, eds., *Modernism: An Anthology of Sources and Documents* (1998). Richard Gilman, *The Making of Modern Drama* (1974) treats developments in drama, while Martin Puchner, *Stage Fright: Modernism, Anti-Theatricality, and Drama* (2002) explores the modernists' ambivalence toward theater. H. H. Arnason and Elizabeth Mansfield, *History of Modern Art: Painting, Sculpture, Architecture* (6th ed., 2009, illus.) follows the evolution of the arts in the West, from the nineteenth century to the 1960s. Matei Calinescu, *Five Faces of Modernity* (1987) is an informative collection of essays on the aesthetics of modernism, avant-garde, decadence, and kitsch. Peter Gay, *Modernism: The Lure of Heresy* (2007) places the movement in historical context.

Anna Akhmatova

Eileen Feinstein, *Anna of All the Russias: A Life of Anna Akhmatova* (2007) is a good recent biography. Roberta Reeder, *Anna Akhmatova: Poet and Prophet* (1994) is thorough. David Wells, *Anna Akhmatova: Her Poetry* (1996) is a readable, well-documented study that discusses works in chronological order. Amanda Haight, *Anna Akhmatova: A Poetic Pilgrimage* (1976) and Susan Amert, *In a Shattered Mirror: The Later Poetry of Anna Akhmatova* (1992) are perceptive book-length studies. Ronald Hingley, *Nightingale Fever: Russian Poets in Revolution* (1981) discusses Akhmatova, Pasternak, Tsvetaeva, and Mandelstam in the context of Russian literary history and Soviet politics up to the early years of World War II. Anna Akhmatova, *My Half Century: Selected Prose*, ed. Ronald Meyer (1992), includes autobiographical material, correspondence, short pieces on other writers, and an essay on Akhmatova's prose.

Akutagawa Ryūnosuke

Akutagawa's masterpieces are all works of short fiction. *Rashōmon and Seventeen Other Stories* (2006) collects many, including "Rashōmon," "Hell Screen," "The Nose," "The Spider Thread," "Spinning Gears," and "The Life of a Stupid Man." *Kappa* (1970) is his most treasured longer piece. On the writer's career as a whole, see Yu Beongcheon, *Akutagawa* (1972) and the chapter on the author in Donald Keene, *Dawn to the West* (1984). Seiji M. Lippit devotes a chapter to Akutagawa's late works in *Topographies of Japanese Modernism* (2002).

Jorge Luis Borges

Useful biographies include James Woodall, *The Man in the Mirror of the Book: A Life of Jorge Luis Borges* (1996); James Woodall, *Borges: A Life* (1996); and Jason Wilson, *Jorge Luis Borges* (2006). George R. McMurray, *Jorge Luis Borges* (1980) and Martin S. Stabb, *Borges Revisited* (1991) are general introductions to the man and his work. Jaime Alazraki, ed., *Critical Essays on Jorge Luis Borges* (1987) assembles articles and reviews (including the 1970 *Autobiographical Essay*), four comparative essays, and a general introduction that offer valuable perspectives on Borges's writing as well as his impact on writers and critics in the United States. Edna Aizenberg, ed., *Borges and His Successors: The Borgesian Impact on Literature and the Arts* (1990) is a wide-ranging collection of essays describing Borges as the precursor of postmodern fiction and criticism. Anna Maria Barrenechea, *Borges the Labyrinth Maker* (1965) discusses the writer's intricate style, while Daniel Balderston, *Out of Context: Historical Reference and the Representation of Reality in Borges* (1993) focuses on the texts' manipulation of fictional and historical reality. Fernando Sorrentino, *Seven Conversations with Jorge Luis Borges* (1981) is a series of informal, widely ranging interviews from 1972, with a list of the topics of each conversation. Recent translations into English include *Collected Fictions*, trans. Andrew Hurley (1998) and *Selected Non-Fictions*, ed. Eliot Weinberger (2000).

Constantine Cavafy

Biographical information is available in Peter Bien, *Constantine Cavafy* (1964) and Robert Liddell, *Cavafy: A Critical Biography* (1974, repr. 2000), which contains a bibliography. The best full-length study in English is Edmund Keeley, *Cavafy's Alexandria* (1996). A wide-ranging collection of essays is Denise Harvey, ed., *The Mind and Art of C. P. Cavafy* (1983).

Joseph Conrad

Among the many sources of biographical information are Conrad's *The Mirror of the Sea* (1906) and *A Personal Record* (1912) and Jocelyn Baines, *Joseph Conrad: A Critical Biography* (1960). The best general biography is Zdzislaw Najder, *Joseph Conrad: A Life* (2007). Albert J. Guérard's critical study, *Conrad the Novelist* (1958), is also recommended. The best general critical study, Ian Watt's *Conrad in the Nineteenth Century* (1979), discusses Conrad's impressionist and symbolist techniques. Chinua Achebe's essay "An Image of Africa: Racism in Conrad's *Heart of Darkness*" is published in his *Hopes and Impediments* (1988). J. H. Stape, ed.,

The Cambridge Companion to Joseph Conrad (1996) offers a wide variety of perspectives on Conrad's work, including *Heart of Darkness*; Allan Simmons, *Heart of Darkness: A Reader's Guide* (2007) provides an introduction to the critical themes of the novella. Adam Hochschild, *King Leopold's Ghost: A Story of Greed, Terror, and Heroism in Colonial Africa* (1998) is a detailed and informative study of the Congo setting of Conrad's novella.

T. S. Eliot
Peter Ackroyd, *T. S. Eliot* (1984) and Tony Sharpe, *T. S. Eliot: A Literary Life* (1991) are brief, readable introductions to Eliot's life and works. Lyndall Gordon, *T. S. Eliot: An Imperfect Life* (1998) is a fuller biography. Several volumes of Eliot's correspondence are being published in Valerie Eliot and Hugh Haughton, ed., *The Letters of T. S. Eliot* (2009–). The influence of Eliot's life on his poems is the subject of Ronald Schuchard, *Eliot's Dark Angel: Intersections of Life and Art* (1999). Martin Scofield, *T. S. Eliot: The Poems* (1988) offers a concise, balanced discussion of the evolution of Eliot's poetry. A fine study is Denis Donogue, *Words Alone: The Poet T. S. Eliot* (2000). Useful general collections are Linda Wagner, ed., *T. S. Eliot: A Collection of Criticism* (1974); Ronald Bush, ed., *T. S. Eliot: The Modernist in History* (1991); A. David Moody, ed., *The Cambridge Companion to T. S. Eliot* (1995); and Harold Bloom, ed., *T. S. Eliot* (1999).

James Joyce
Harry Levin, *James Joyce: A Critical Introduction* (1941) is an excellent, readable general introduction. The standard, detailed biography, with illustrations, is Richard Ellmann, *James Joyce* (1982). Morris Beja, *James Joyce: A Literary Life* (1992) includes recent scholarship. Derek Attridge, ed., *The Cambridge Companion to James Joyce* (1990) and Mary T. Reynolds, ed., *James Joyce: A Collection of Critical Essays* (1993) treat various aspects of the work. Daniel R. Schwarz, ed., *The Dead* (1994) is a useful short book that contains the text and contextual material, an account of *Dubliners'* history and criticism from the 1950s, and analyses by several authors using five critical perspectives. John Wyse Jackson and Bernard McGinley, eds., *Joyce's Dubliners: An Illustrated Edition with Annotations* (1995) is a fascinating, copiously illustrated and documented edition that includes allusions to other works and a capsule essay after each story. A valuable recent introduction is David Pierce, *Reading Joyce* (2008). Pierce's earlier *James Joyce's Ireland* (1992) provides contemporary photographs by Dan Harper and uses documents, photographs, and quotations to reconstruct Joyce's biography in historical context.

Franz Kafka
Kafka's life has been the subject of many studies, starting with Max Brod, *Franz Kafka: A Biography* (English trans., 1960). One of the best recent works is Nicholas Murray, *Kafka: A Biography* (2004). Readable introductions to the author's life and work include Klaus Wagenbach, *Kafka* (2003) and Louis Begley, *The Tremendous World I Have Inside My Head: Franz Kafka: A Biographical Essay* (2008). Heinz Politzer, *Franz Kafka: Parable and Paradox* (1962) is an interesting early study concerned with Kafka's symbolism. *Kafka: A Collection of Critical Essays*, ed. Ronald Gray (1962), introduces the main themes of Kafka criticism, while more recent essays, specifically on the selection here, are collected in Harold Bloom, ed., *Franz Kafka's The Metamorphosis* (1988) and Stanley Corngold, ed., *The Metamorphosis* (1996). Kafka's religious background is the subject of Sander Gilman, *Franz Kafka: The Jewish Patient* (1995), while the Czech context is discussed by Scott Spector, *Prague Territories* (2000).

Federico García Lorca
Leslie Stainton, *Lorca: A Dream of Life* (1998) is an extensive biography. Carl W. Cobb, *Federico García Lorca* (1967) is a good general biography, while Gwynne Edwards, *Lorca: Living in the Theatre* (2003) focuses on his dramatic work. Candelas Newton, *Understanding Federico García Lorca* (1995) is a brief discussion of the work; E. Honig, *García Lorca* (1980) provides a critical introduction in literary historical context; and C. B. Morris, *Son of Andalusia: The Lyrical Landscapes of Federico García Lorca* (1997) offers a more specialized view, with illustrations. Federico Bonaddio, ed., *Companion to Federico García Lorca* (2007) is a valuable collection of essays on the poet and his work.

Lu Xun
A valuable and readable biography is David Pollard, *The True Story of Lu Xun* (2002). Leo Ou-fan Lee, *Voices from the Iron House: A Study of Lu Xun* (1987) is an excellent introduction to Lu Xun's work, placing it in the context of his

life and Chinese cultural history; and Lee, *Lu Xun and His Legacy* (1985) is a collection of scholarly articles treating Lu's literary work, his politics, and his influence. William A. Lyell, *Lu Hsün's Vision of Reality* (1976) is also useful.

Thomas Mann

Hermann Kurzke, *Thomas Mann: A Biography* (2002) provides a thorough account of Mann's life. Harold Bloom, ed., *Thomas Mann* (1986) and Ritchie Robertson, ed., *The Cambridge Companion to Thomas Mann* (2001) present essays on different works and brief biographical information. Terence J. Reed, *Thomas Mann: The Uses of Tradition* (2nd ed., 1996), is an excellent, well-written general study incorporating recent material. Richard Winston, *Thomas Mann: The Making of an Artist 1875–1911* (1981), the first volume of an unfinished study, is a detailed and authoritative presentation by the translator of Mann's diaries and letters. Ellis Shookman reviews almost a century's worth of criticism in *Thomas Mann's Death in Venice: A Novella and Its Critics* (2003).

Pablo Neruda

Pablo Neruda, *Memoirs*, trans. Hardie St. Martin (1977) contains much biographical information. A good recent biography in English is Adam Feinstein, *Pablo Neruda: A Passion for Life* (2004). Manuel Duran and Margery Safir, *Earth Tones: The Poetry of Pablo Neruda* (1981) is an excellent thematic study that includes a short biography. *Pablo Neruda*, ed. Harold Bloom (1989), contains nineteen valuable essays and reminiscences by scholars, translators, and those who knew Neruda. John Felstiner, *Translating Neruda: The Way to Macchu Picchu* (1980) describes in detail the process of translating *The Heights of Macchu Picchu* in terms of Neruda's life and perspectives. Louis Poirot, *Pablo Neruda: Absence and Presence* (1990) matches photographs of Neruda, his friends, and his homes with related passages from the poet, his wife, and friends. A recent work is *The Poetry of Pablo Neruda*, trans. Ilan Stavans (2005).

Octavio Paz

Paz discusses the development of his ideas in *Itinerary: An Intellectual Journey*, trans. Jason Wilson (1999). Wilson analyzes the Mexican writer's surrealist poetry in *Octavio Paz: A Study of His Poetics* (1979), while the essays in Harold Bloom, ed., *Octavio Paz* (2002) explore a range of perspectives on his work. Nick Caistor, *Octavio Paz* (2007) provides an overview of the poet's life and works.

Luigi Pirandello

Gaspare Guidice's *Pirandello: A Biography* (1975), trans. Alastair Hamilton provides a good overview of the artist's life. The best essay on Pirandello and metatheater is by Maurizio Grande, "Pirandello and the Theatre-within-the-Theatre: Thresholds and Frames in *Cascuno a suo modo*" (in *Luigi Pirandello: Contemporary Perspectives* [1999]). Roger W. Oliver's *Dreams of Passion: The Theater of Luigi Pirandello* (1979) focuses on Pirandello's theory of humor and applies it to his best-known plays, including *Six Characters*. Ann Hallamore Caesar's *Characters and Authors in Luigi Pirandello* (1998) offers a wide-ranging discussion of Pirandello through the diversity of genres in which he worked, from novels and poetry to drama and film. Pirandello's work in the theater is captured in *Luigi Pirandello in the Theatre: A Documentary Record* (1993), ed. Susan Bassnett and Jennifer Lorch, and in A. Richard Sogliuzzo's *Luigi Pirandello, Director: The Playwright in the Theatre* (1982).

Premchand

An excellent resource is Alok Rai, *The Oxford India Premchand* (2004). David Rubin, *The World of Premchand* (1969), reissued as *The Illustrated Premchand* (2006), provides a good introduction to and translations of the short fiction. Translations of Premchand's novels include Gordon Roadarmal's *The Gift of a Cow* (1968); Alok Rai's *Nirmala* (1999); Snehal Shingavi's *Sevasadan* (2005); and Lalit Srivastava's *Karmabhumi* (2006). The most comprehensive biography is by the writer's son Amrit Rai, *Premchand: His Life and Times* (2002); and an important discussion of Premchand's work appears in Meenakshi Mukherjee, *Realism and Reality* (1985).

Marcel Proust

Roger Shattuck, *Proust's Way* (2001) is a general study including advice on how to read Proust. Malcolm Bowie, *Proust Among the Stars* (2000) offers a slightly more advanced starting point. George D. Painter, in *Marcel Proust: A Biography* (rev. 1996), presents a comprehensive biography. Excellent recent biographies include William C. Carter, *Marcel Proust*

(2000) and Jean-Yves Tadié, *Marcel Proust* (2000). Terence Kilmartin, *A Reader's Guide to Remembrance of Things Past* (1984) is a handbook to Proust's characters, persons referred to in the text, places, and themes, all keyed to the revised translation. René Girard, *Proust: A Collection of Critical Essays* (1962); Harold Bloom, ed., *Marcel Proust's Remembrance of Things Past* (1987); and Barbara J. Bucknall, ed., *Critical Essays on Marcel Proust* (1987) are also recommended.

Rainer Maria Rilke
J. F. Hendry, *The Sacred Threshold: A Life of Rainer Maria Rilke* (1983) and Patricia Pollock Brodsky, *Rainer Maria Rilke* (1988) are brief, readable biographies with numerous citations from Rilke's letters and work. A more recent, comprehensive biography is Ralph Freedman's *Life of a Poet: Rainer Maria Rilke* (1998). Heinz F. Peters, *Rainer Maria Rilke: Masks and the Man* (1977) is a biographical and thematic study of the poet's work and influence. William H. Gass, *Reading Rilke: Reflections on the Problems of Translation* (1999) combines biography, philosophy, and commentary on specific translation problems in the *Duino Elegies*. Judith Ryan, *Rilke, Modernism and Poetic Tradition* (1999) places his work in its literary-historical context.

Virginia Woolf
Hermione Lee's biography, *Virginia Woolf* (1996) is now, and surely for a while to come, the definitive work on Woolf's life. Julia Briggs has also produced a detailed recent biography that pays close attention to the author's works and their creation, *Virginia Woolf: An Inner Life* (2005). Alison Light's study, *Mrs. Woolf and the Servants* (2007), examines Woolf's place amid the shifting social and economic issues of the era through the lens of her relationships with the domestic help. Two valuable collections of essays on Woolf's writing and her position in the modernist tradition are Patricia Clements and Isobel Grundy, eds., *Virginia Woolf: New Critical Essays* (1983) and Margaret Homans, ed., *Virginia Woolf: A Collection of Critical Essays* (1993). S. P. Rosenbaum, ed., *Virginia Woolf: Women and Fiction* (1992) transcribes and edits two draft manuscripts that are the basis for *A Room of One's Own*. Gillian Beer, *Virginia Woolf: The Common Ground* (1996) offers four useful general essays and four discussions of specific novels.

William Butler Yeats
Edward Malins presents a brief introduction with biography, illustrations, and maps in *A Preface to Yeats* (1994). Richard Ellmann, *The Identity of Yeats* (1964) is an excellent discussion of the poet's work as a whole. Norman A. Jeffares has revised his major study, *A New Commentary on the Collected Poems of W. B. Yeats* (1983); a useful reference work is Lester I. Conner, *A Yeats Dictionary: Persons and Places in the Poetry of William Butler Yeats* (1998). The most thorough and balanced biographical study is R. F. Foster, *W. B. Yeats: A Life*, 2 vols. (1997–2003). A major account of Yeats's use of poetic form is Helen Vendler, *Our Secret Discipline: Yeats and Lyric Form* (2007). Essay collections include Harold Bloom, ed., *William Butler Yeats* (1986); Richard J. Finneran, ed., *Critical Essays on W. B. Yeats* (1986); and Marjorie Howes and John Kelly, eds., *Cambridge Companion to W. B. Yeats* (2006).

Zhang Ailing
C. T. Hsia's *A History of Modern Chinese Fiction* (1961) contains the first study of Zhang Ailing's work. *The Rice-Sprout Song* (repr. 1988) has an excellent introduction by David Der-Wei Wang.

VII. Postwar and Postcolonial Literature, 1945–1968

Ihab and Sally Hassan, eds., *Essays in Innovation/Renovation: New Perspectives on the Humanities* (1983) explores change in Western culture in the second half of the twentieth century. Tony Judt, *Postwar: A History of Europe Since 1945* (2005) explores the historical context in Europe, while Michael Howard and William Roger Louis, eds., *The Oxford History of the Twentieth Century* (1998) includes informative essays on other parts of the world. Janheinz Jahn, *Muntu: African*

Culture and the Western World, trans. Marjorie Grene (1990, orig. 1961) is an influential discussion of the interface of two cultures. Anthony Appiah, *In My Father's House: Africa in the Philosophy of Culture* (1992) explores similar issues in a postcolonial context. Marjorie Perloff, ed., *Postmodern Genres* (1989) collects essays on postmodernism in art and literature. Linda Hutcheon, *A Poetics of Postmodernism* (1988) analyzes the movement's literary forms.

Chinua Achebe

A good reference is Ezenwa Ohaeto, *Chinua Achebe: A Biography* (1997). Achebe has written a series of memoirs of his early life, collected as *The Education of a British-Protected Child* (2009). C. L. Innes, *Chinua Achebe* (1990) is a comprehensive study of the writer's work through 1988 that emphasizes his literary techniques and Africanization of the novel. Simon Gikandi, *Reading Chinua Achebe: Language and Ideology in Fiction* (1991) is also recommended. Also of interest is *Conversations with Chinua Achebe* (1997), ed. Bernth Lindfors. Jago Morrison, *The Fiction of Chinua Achebe* (2007) is a guide to criticism that includes discussions of his short fiction.

James Baldwin

David Leeming, who served as Baldwin's personal secretary, later recollected his friend and employer in *James Baldwin: A Biography* (1995). Also recommended is James Campbell, *Talking at the Gates: A Life of James Baldwin* (1991). A collection of essays published near the end of Baldwin's life, Harold Bloom, ed., *James Baldwin: Modern Critical Views* (1986) represents a range of views by Baldwin's contemporaries. A more recent collection, Dwight A. McBride, ed., *James Baldwin Now* (1999) includes a number of essays on race and sexuality.

Samuel Beckett

Beckett's works have been collected in four volumes in the Grove Centenary Edition (2006), ed. Paul Auster. *The Letters of Samuel Beckett* (first vol., 2009) are being published in an edition by Martha Dow Fehsenfeld and Lois More Overbeck. Samuel Beckett, *Endgame: with a Revised Text* (1992), ed. S. E. Gontarski is based on productions directed or supervised by Beckett; the attached theatrical notebooks often clarify situations and settings. Arthur N. Athanason, *Endgame: The Ashbin Play* (1993) is a brief introduction; and Alexander Astro, *Understanding Samuel Beckett* (1990) discusses the complete work with interpretations emphasizing cultural and linguistic aspects. Mark S. Byron, ed., *Samuel Beckett's Endgame* (2007) collects essays on this play. Andrew Kennedy, *Samuel Beckett* (1989) provides a compact, comprehensive overview of Beckett's work, with chapters on the major plays and novels. Richard Begam, *Samuel Beckett and the End of Modernity* (1996) discusses Beckett in the context of postmodernism. Cathleen Culotta Andonian organizes *The Critical Response to Samuel Beckett* (1998) in ten sections that represent the various stages in the reception of his work. Useful biographies are Deirdre Bair, *Samuel Beckett: A Biography* (1993); Anthony Cronin, *Samuel Beckett: The Last Modernist* (1996); Lois G. Gordon, *The World of Samuel Beckett, 1906–1946* (1996); and James Knowlson, *Damned to Fame: The Life of Samuel Beckett* (1996). Hugh Kenner, *Samuel Beckett: A Critical Study* (1974) is an earlier but still valuable discussion of the writer's work. Useful essay collections are Jennifer Birkett and Kate Ince, eds., *Samuel Beckett* (2000) and Steven Connor, ed., *Waiting for Godot and Endgame—Samuel Beckett* (1992), which includes eleven essays, of which seven are wholly or partially on *Endgame*.

Tadeusz Borowski

Brief discussions of Borowski are found in Czeslaw Milosz, *The History of Polish Literature* (1969); and from a different perspective, Sidra DeKoven Ezrahi, *By Words Alone: The Holocaust in Literature* (1980) and James Hatley, *Suffering Witness: The Quandary of Responsibility after the Irreparable* (2000). Jan Kott, "Introduction," *This Way for the Gas, Ladies and Gentlemen* (1976), and Jan Walc, "When the Earth Is No Longer a Dream and Cannot Be Dreamed through to the End," *Polish Review* (1987), combine biography and literary analysis, while Czeslaw Milosz, *The Captive Mind* (1953) analyzes Borowski's later communism in relation to his generation. Selections from the poetry are available in *Selected Poems* (1990), trans. Tadeusz Pióro with Larry Rafferty. Tadeusz Drewnowski, ed., *Postal Indiscretions: The Correspondence of Tadeusz Borowski* (2007), trans. Alicia Nitecki, includes letters written to his family from Auschwitz.

Albert Camus

Germaine Brée, *Albert Camus* (1964) is an excellent general study. Catherine Savage Brosman, *Albert Camus* (2001) is a short introduction and biography. Herbert Lottman, *Albert Camus: A Biography* (1979) and Oliver Todd, *Albert Camus: A Life* (1997) are detailed accounts. English Showalter, *Exiles and Strangers: A Reading of Camus's* Exile and the Kingdom (1984) offers essays on the six stories in Camus's collection and separate comments on translations. For a collection of recent essays on Camus, see Edward J. Hughes, ed., *The Cambridge Companion to Camus* (2007), which contains a bibliography.

Paul Celan

A translator of Celan discusses the poet's life and the challenges that his works pose for translation in John Felstiner, *Paul Celan: Poet, Survivor, Jew* (2001). A friend of the poet and distinguished critic interprets three of his major poems in Peter Szondi, *Celan Studies* (2003). Celan has attracted much commentary from philosophers, notably Hans-Georg Gadamer, *Gadamer on Celan*, ed. and trans. Richard Heinemann and Bruce Krajewski (1997), and Philippe Lacoue-Labarthe, *Poetry as Experience*, trans. by Andrea Tarnowski (1999). Aris Fioretos, ed., *Word Traces: Readings of Paul Celan* (1994) is a valuable collection of essays.

Mahmoud Darwish

The theme of exile in Darwish's work is compared with that of a contemporary novelist in Najat Rahman, *Literary Disinheritance: The Writing of Home in the Work of Mahmoud Darwish and Assia Djebar* (2008). Essays on various aspects of his work are collected in Hala Khamis Nassar and Najat Rahman, eds., *Mahmoud Darwish, Exile as Poet* (2008). Darwish is among fifteen authors interviewed in Runo Isaksen, *Literature and War: Conversations with Israeli and Palestinian Writers* (2008).

Doris Lessing

The most comprehensive biography is Carol Klein, *Doris Lessing* (2000). Ruth Whittaker, *Doris Lessing* (1988) is a concise, informative discussion of the writer's fiction to 1985; it includes biographical contexts and selective bibliography. Two volumes of Lessing's autobiography are published as *Under My Skin* (1995) and *Walking in the Shade* (1997). A good critical study of the novels is Roberta Rubenstein, *The Novelistic Vision of Doris Lessing* (1979). Perspectives on women and literature are the focus of Gayle Greene, *Doris Lessing: The Poetics of Change* (1994).

Clarice Lispector

The best biography is Benjamin Moser, *Why This World: A Biography of Clarice Lispector* (2008). Earl E. Fitz, *Clarice Lispector* (1985), a valuable introduction to her life and work, contains an annotated bibliography. Hélène Cixous, *Reading with Clarice Lispector*, ed., trans., and intro. Verena Andermatt Conley (1990), discusses Lispector's style with reference to three stories and three novels.

Naguib Mahfouz

Roger M. A. Allen, *The Arabic Novel: An Historical and Critical Introduction* (1982) is an authoritative introduction that situates Mahfouz in the context of modern Arabic literature and includes a bibliography of works in Arabic and Western languages. The author's own perspective is given in Najib Mahfuz, *Echoes of an Autobiography*, trans. Denys Johnson-Davies (1997). Sasson Somekh, "Za 'balawi"— Author, Theme and Technique," in *Journal of Arabic Literature* (1970), examines the story as a "double-layered" structure governed by references to Sufi mysticism. Michael Beard and Adnan Haydar, eds., *Naguib Mahfouz: From Regional Fame to Global Recognition* (1993) assembles eleven original essays on themes, individual works, and cultural contexts in Mahfouz's work. Trevor le Gassick, ed., *Critical Perspectives on Naguib Mahfouz* (1991) reprints articles on the writer's work up to the 1970s. Rasheed El-Enany, ed., *Naguib Mahfouz: The Pursuit of Meaning* (1993) is an excellent study that offers biography; analyses of novels, short stories, and plays; and a guide for further reading. Comparative studies include Mona Mikhail, *Studies in the Short Fiction of Mahfouz and Idris* (1992), an introductory work juxtaposing themes in Hemingway, Yusuf Idris, Mahfouz, and Camus, and Samia Mehrez, *Egyptian Writers Between History and Fiction: Essays on Naguib Mahfouz, Sonallah Ibrahim, and Gamal al-Ghitani* (1994). Rasheed

El-Enany discusses the place of religion in Mahfouz's work in "The Dichotomy of Islam and Modernity in the Fiction of Naguib Mahfouz," in John C. Hawley, ed., *The Postcolonial Crescent: Islam's Impact on Contemporary Literature* (1998).

Saadat Hasan Manto

Manto's stories have been translated extensively into English. Khalid Hasan's *Saadat Hasan Manto: A Wet Afternoon* (2001) contains a large, representative selection, though the translations are not always exact. Hamid Jalal's translations in *Black Milk: A Collection of Short Stories by Saadat Hasan Manto* (1997) offer excellent alternatives. Important material on Manto, including the work of translator and commentator M. Asaduddin, has appeared in *The Annual of Urdu Studies*, vol. 11; and several versions of "Toba Tek Singh," with texts and commentary, are available at www.columbia.edu\itc\mealac\pritchett\00urdu\tobateksingh\index.html.

Léopold Sédar Senghor

The selections presented here are taken from *The Collected Poetry* (1991), trans. Melvin Dixon, whose introduction is helpful. Sylvia Washington Bâ's *The Concept of Négritude in the Poetry of Léopold Sédar Senghor* (1973) provides the most comprehensive discussion of the poet's work. An essay collection, Janice Spleth, ed., *Critical Perspectives on Leopold Sedar Senghor* (1993) offers a range of views. For an account of Senghor's life and intellectual development, with incidental comments on his poetry, see Janet G. Vaillant, *Black, French and African: A Life of Léopold Sédar Senghor* (1990). A collection of essays edited by Isabelle Constant and Kahiudi C. Mabana, *Negritude: Legacy and Present Relevance* (2009) analyzes and defends the concept of Négritude.

Alexander Solzhenitsyn

Andrej Kodjak, *Alexander Solzhenitsyn* (1978) provides a biographical and critical introduction up to the writer's deportation from the Soviet Union in 1974; it includes a discussion of Russian terms. Michael Scammell's detailed *Solzhenitsyn: A Biography* (1984) is complemented by Joseph Pearce, *Solzhenitsyn: A Soul in Exile* (1999). Kathryn B. Feuer, ed., *Solzhenitsyn: A Collection of Critical Essays* (1976) and Harold Bloom, ed., *Alexander Solzhenitsyn* (2000) contain a range of essays on aspects and particular works, including *Matryona's Home*. John B. Dunlop, Richard S. Haugh, and Michael Nicholson, eds., *Solzhenitsyn in Exile: Critical Essays and Documentary Material* (1985) offers critical essays and discussions of Solzhenitsyn's reception in several countries. A collection of shorter works is available in Edward E. Ericson Jr., and Daniel J. Mahoney, eds., *The Solzhenitsyn Reader: New and Essential Writings 1946–2005* (2006).

VIII. Contemporary World Literature

Lois Parkinson Zamora and Wendy B. Faris, eds., *Magical Realism: Theory, History, Community* (1997) examines the theoretical and cultural implications of the style in Latin America and elsewhere. Nancy K. Miller, ed., *The Poetics of Gender* (1986) presents essays on various aspects of feminist criticism. Sarah Lawall, ed., *Reading World Literature: Theory, History, Practice* (1994) includes a theoretical introduction to the subject of world literature and twelve essays on specific topics. David Damrosch, *What Is World Literature?* (2003) explores a range of issues in the study of world literature, while Pascale Casanova, *The World Republic of Letters* (2004) offers a sociological view of the development of literary reputations. Accounts of crucial moments in contemporary history include Jeremi Suri, ed., *The Global Revolutions of 1968* (2007); Timothy Garton Ash, *The Magic Lantern: The Revolution of '89 Witnessed in Warsaw, Budapest, Berlin, and Prague* (1993); and Thomas L. Friedman, *The World Is Flat 3.0: A Brief History of the Twenty-First Century* (2007).

Isabel Allende

Interviews are collected in Celia Correas Zapata, *Isabel Allende: Life and Spirits* (2002) and in John Rodden, ed., *Conversations with Isabel Allende* (2004). Harold Bloom offers a critical assessment of Allende's work but collects the best early essays on her in *Isabel Allende* (2003). General introductions are available in Linda Gould Levine, *Isabel Allende* (2002) and Karen Castellucci Cox, *Isabel Allende: A Critical Companion* (2003), which contains a bibliography.

Hanan Al-Shaykh

Several of Al-Shaykh's novels, and her memoir, *The Locust and the Bird: My Mother's Story* (2010), have been translated into English. A lengthy interview by Paula W. Sunderman was published in *Literary Review* in 1997 as "Between Two Worlds: An Interview with Hanan al-Shaykh."

Yehuda Amichai

Glenda Abramson, *The Writing of Yehuda Amichai: A Thematic Approach* (1989) provides a comprehensive overview of the poet's work. Nili Scharf Gold, *Yehuda Amichai: The Making of Israel's National Poet* (2008) treats his work in relation to his biography. Joseph Cohen, *Voices of Israel* (1990) includes a long essay on Amichai as well as an extended interview. Articles by Glenda Abramson, Naomi B. Sokoloff, and Nili Scharf Gold appear in "Amichai at Sixty" (1984), a special issue of *Prooftexts*.

J. M. Coetzee

The best, albeit unreliable, source for information on Coetzee's life is his autobiographical fiction, *Boyhood* (1997), *Youth* (2002), and *Summertime* (2010). Derek Attridge offers a rich interpretation of Coetzee's work in relation to modernism in *J. M. Coetzee and the Ethics of Reading: Literature in the Event* (2005). A more explicitly political approach to the early fiction is David Attwell, *J. M. Coetzee: South Africa and the Politics of Writing* (1993). Graham Huggan and Stephen Watson, eds., *Critical Perspectives on J. M. Coetzee* (1996), with an introduction by Nadine Gordimer, collects essays on various facets of Coetzee's work.

Chu T'ien-Hsin

Essays on Chu T'ien-Hsin and other contemporary Taiwanese writers are collected in David Der-Wei Wang and Carlos Rojas, eds., *Writing Taiwan: A New Literary History*. "Man of La Mancha" is one of five loosely connected chapters in Chu T'ien-Hsin, *The Old Capital: A Novel of Taipei*, trans. Howard Goldblatt (2007).

Gabriel García Márquez

The best biography is Gerald Martin, *Gabriel García Márquez* (2008). A shorter overview is Rubén Pelayo, *Gabriel García Márquez: A Biography* (2009). García Márquez has himself published a remarkable autobiography, *Living to Tell the Tale* (2003). Regina Janes, *Gabriel García Márquez, Revolutions in Wonderland* (1981) is an excellent early study on the author in a Latin American context. Other useful introductions to the writer and his work are George P. McMurray, *Gabriel García Márquez* (1977); Robin W. Fiddian, *García Márquez* (1995); and Joan Mellen, *Gabriel García Márquez* (2000). See also Julio Ortega, ed., *Gabriel García Márquez and the Powers of Fiction* (1988) and Isabel Rodriguez-Vergara, *Haunting Demons: Critical Essays on the Works of Gabriel García Márquez* (1998). Harley D. Oberhelman, ed., *Gabriel García Márquez: A Study of the Short Fiction* (1991) includes a bibliography.

Bessie Head

Gillian Stead Eilerson presents the author's biography in *Bessie Head: Thunder Behind Her Ears, Her Life and Writing* (1995). Some of her letters are collected, with a memoir by a close friend, in Patrick Cullinan, ed., *Imaginative Trespasser: Letters Between Bessie Head and Patrick and Wendy Cullinan, 1963–1977* (2005). Craig MacKenzie provides a helpful overview of her work in *Bessie Head* (1999).

Seamus Heaney

Michael Parker, *Seamus Heaney: The Making of a Poet* (1993) combines biography with literary criticism, while the best overall critical study is Helen Vendler, *Seamus Heaney* (1998), which focuses on Heaney's intellectual and aesthetic experiments. Bernard O'Donoghue, ed., *The Cambridge Companion to Seamus Heaney* (2009) includes several essays on Heaney's relationship to other poets. A number of the poet's interviews are collected in Dennis O'Driscoll, ed., *Stepping Stones: Interviews with Seamus Heaney* (2008).

Jamaica Kincaid
Diane Simmons provides an overview of Kincaid's work, with biographical information, in *Jamaica Kincaid* (1994). Elizabeth Paravisini-Gebert, *Jamaica Kincaid: A Critical Companion* (1999) focuses on the early short stories and the first three novels. A more recent overview is Justin Edwards, *Understanding Jamaica Kincaid* (2007).

V. S. Naipaul
A remarkable, authorized biography is Patrick French, *The World Is What It Is* (2009). Bruce King provides an accessible introduction to Naipaul's work in *V. S. Naipaul* (1993; 2nd ed., 2003). Gillian Dooley, *V. S. Naipaul: Man and Writer* (2006) offers a sympathetic reading of the author's work in relation to his life. Naipaul's memorable correspondence with his father is collected in V. S. Naipaul, *Between Father and Son: Family Letters* (2000), ed. Gillon Aitken.

Ngugi wa Thiong'o
A good overview of Ngugi's works is David Cook and Michael Okenimkpe, *Ngugi wa Thiong'o: An Exploration of His Writings* (2nd ed., 1997). Thorough critical accounts include Simon Gikandi, *Ngugi wa Thiong'o* (2000) and Patrick Williams, *Ngugi wa Thiong'o* (1999). Oliver Lovesey provides a biography with relevant historical context in *Ngugi wa Thiong'o* (2000). The historical background is comprehensively treated in Carol Sicherman, ed., *Ngugi wa Thiong'o: The Making of a Rebel. A Source Book in Kenyan Literature and Resistance* (1990).

Salman Rushdie
Midnight's Children (1980) has been in print since its first publication. Among the many books about Rushdie and his work, particularly helpful and informative are Damian Grant, *Salman Rushdie* (1999), for an overview of much of his career; Jaina C. Sanga, *Salman Rushdie's Postcolonial Metaphors* (2001) and Sabrina Hassumani, *Salman Rushdie* (2002), for analyses of his style and major themes. Discussions of the writer's work in wider literary contexts appear in Timothy Brennan, *Salman Rushdie and the Third World* (1989) and Fawzia Afzal-Khan, *Cultural Imperialism and the Indo-English Novel* (1993). Important documentary sources include Lisa Appignanesi and Sara Maitland, *The Rushdie File* (1990); Michael R. Reder, *Conversations with Salman Rushdie* (2000); and Pradyumna S. Chauhan, *Salman Rushdie Interviews* (2001).

Leslie Marmon Silko
Gregory Salyer, *Leslie Marmon Silko* (1997) is a brief introduction to the author and her work; Brewster E. Fitz offers an updated view of the author's career in *Silko: Writing Storyteller and Medicine Woman* (2004). Helen Jaskoski, *Leslie Marmon Silko: A Study of the Short Fiction* (1998) focuses on the stories. Leslie Marmon Silko, *Sacred Water: Narratives and Pictures* (1994) is an autobiographical narrative. Melody Graulich, ed., *"Yellow Woman": Leslie Marmon Silko* (1993) collects pertinent critical essays. "Yellow Woman" and other works are treated in Louise K. Barnett and James L. Thorson, eds., *Leslie Marmon Silko: A Collection of Critical Essays* (1999). For traditional texts on Yellow Woman and other figures in Laguna mythology, the best source is Franz Boas, *Keresan Texts* (1928); the stories in Boas's volume were obtained in 1919–1921 from several Laguna informants, including Leslie Silko's great-grandfather, Robert Marmon.

Derek Walcott
Derek Walcott, *Another Life* (1973), an autobiography in verse, traces the poet's artistic development. A full biography is Bruce King, *Derek Walcott: A Caribbean Life* (2000). Walcott's collection of essays, *What the Twilight Says* (1998), is an indispensable compendium of his social and aesthetic ideas. Robert Hamner, *Derek Walcott* (1978, rev. 1993), is a comprehensive and accessible full-length study of the writer's work; John Thieme, *Derek Walcott* (1999) is more up-to-date and provides commentaries on the key poems in Walcott's various collections and on the dramatic works. Robert Hamner, *Epic of the Dispossessed* (1997) offers a detailed discussion of *Omeros* that considers its adaptation of epic idiom to the experience and life dilemmas of the common folk. *The Art of Derek Walcott*, ed. Stewart Brown (1991), and *Critical Perspectives on Derek Walcott*, ed. Robert Hamner (1993), are collective volumes that cover Walcott's work up to the dates of their publication.

TIMELINE *for*

I. The Enlightenment in Europe and the Americas

II. Early Modern Chinese Vernacular Literature

III. Early Modern Japanese Popular Literature

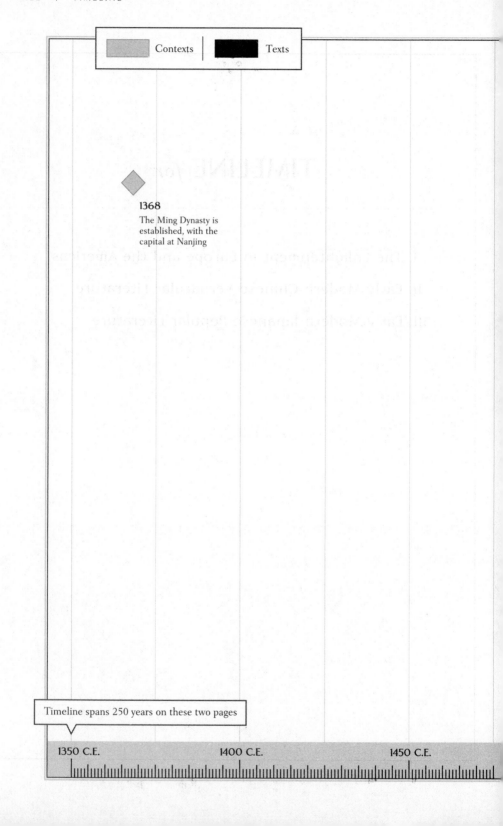

Contexts | Texts

1368
The Ming Dynasty is
established, with the
capital at Nanjing

Timeline spans 250 years on these two pages

1350 C.E.   1400 C.E.   1450 C.E.

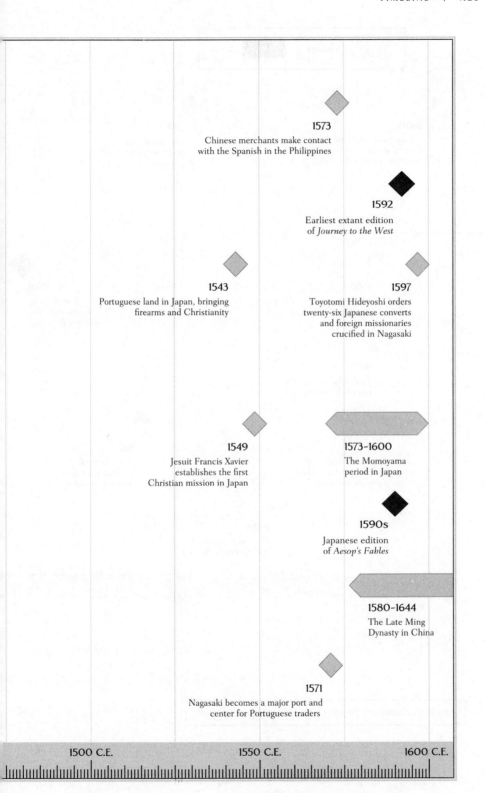

1573

Chinese merchants make contact
with the Spanish in the Philippines

1592

Earliest extant edition
of *Journey to the West*

1543

Portuguese land in Japan, bringing
firearms and Christianity

1597

Toyotomi Hideyoshi orders
twenty-six Japanese converts
and foreign missionaries
crucified in Nagasaki

1549

Jesuit Francis Xavier
establishes the first
Christian mission in Japan

1573-1600

The Momoyama
period in Japan

1590s

Japanese edition
of *Aesop's Fables*

1580-1644

The Late Ming
Dynasty in China

1571

Nagasaki becomes a major port and
center for Portuguese traders

1500 C.E.   1550 C.E.   1600 C.E.

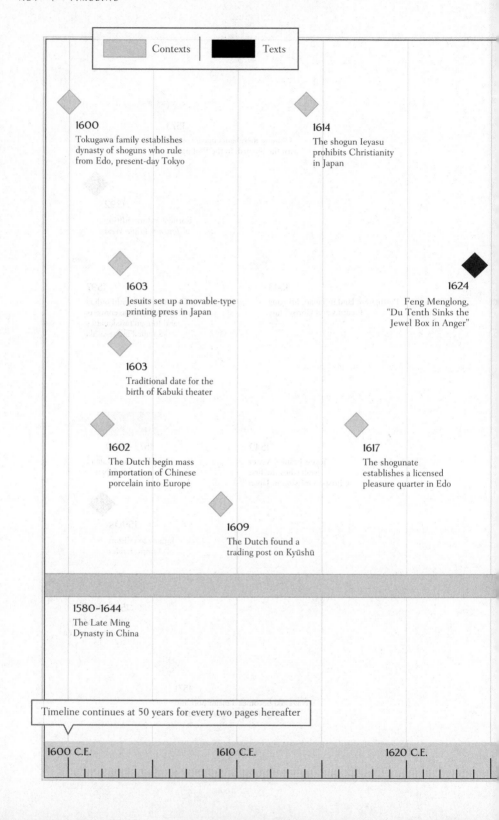

Contexts   Texts

1600
Tokugawa family establishes
dynasty of shoguns who rule
from Edo, present-day Tokyo

1614
The shogun Ieyasu
prohibits Christianity
in Japan

1603
Jesuits set up a movable-type
printing press in Japan

1624
Feng Menglong,
"Du Tenth Sinks the
Jewel Box in Anger"

1603
Traditional date for the
birth of Kabuki theater

1602
The Dutch begin mass
importation of Chinese
porcelain into Europe

1617
The shogunate
establishes a licensed
pleasure quarter in Edo

1609
The Dutch found a
trading post on Kyūshū

1580-1644
The Late Ming
Dynasty in China

Timeline continues at 50 years for every two pages hereafter

1600 C.E.   1610 C.E.   1620 C.E.

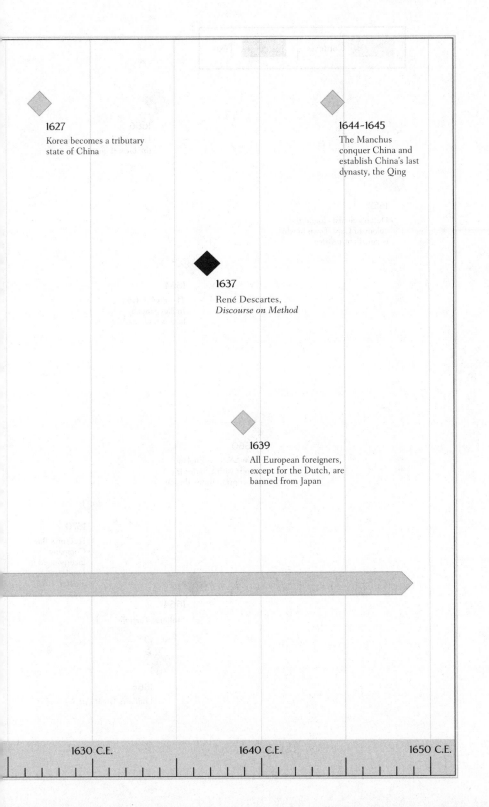

1627
Korea becomes a tributary
state of China

1644-1645
The Manchus
conquer China and
establish China's last
dynasty, the Qing

1637
René Descartes,
Discourse on Method

1639
All European foreigners,
except for the Dutch, are
banned from Japan

1630 C.E.   1640 C.E.   1650 C.E.

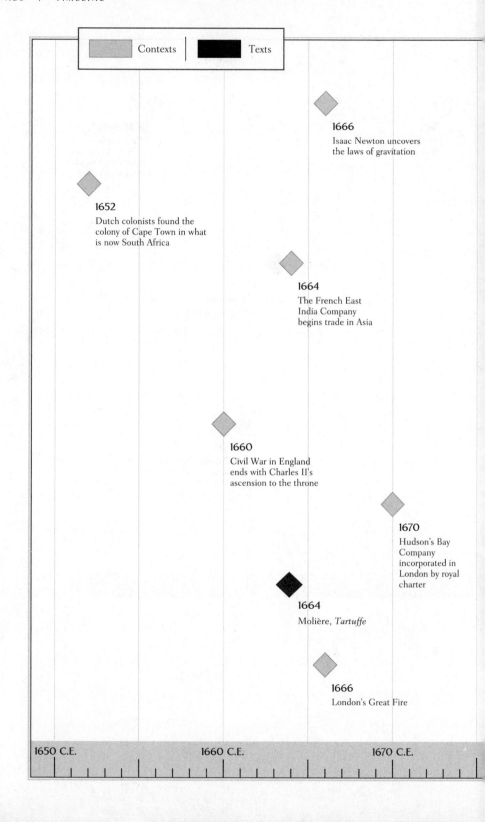

Contexts | Texts

1666
Isaac Newton uncovers
the laws of gravitation

1652
Dutch colonists found the
colony of Cape Town in what
is now South Africa

1664
The French East
India Company
begins trade in Asia

1660
Civil War in England
ends with Charles II's
ascension to the throne

1670
Hudson's Bay
Company
incorporated in
London by royal
charter

1664
Molière, *Tartuffe*

1666
London's Great Fire

1650 C.E.   1660 C.E.   1670 C.E.

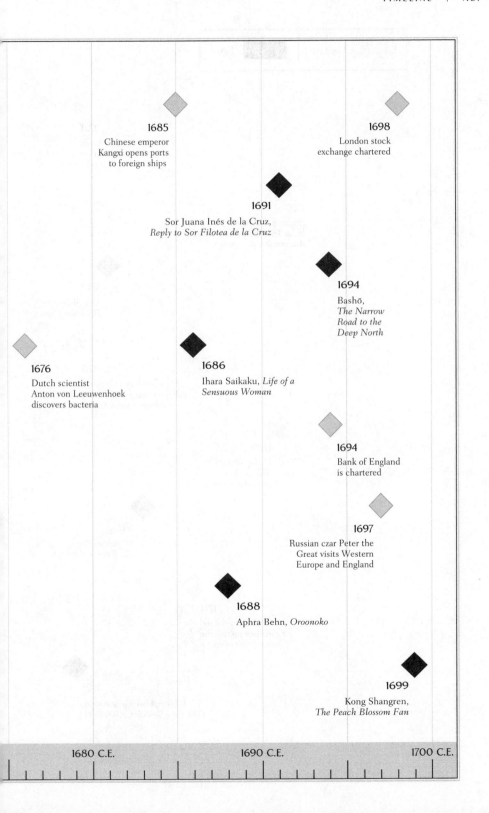

1685
Chinese emperor
Kangxi opens ports
to foreign ships

1698
London stock
exchange chartered

1691
Sor Juana Inés de la Cruz,
Reply to Sor Filotea de la Cruz

1694
Bashō,
*The Narrow
Road to the
Deep North*

1676
Dutch scientist
Anton von Leeuwenhoek
discovers bacteria

1686
Ihara Saikaku, *Life of a
Sensuous Woman*

1694
Bank of England
is chartered

1697
Russian czar Peter the
Great visits Western
Europe and England

1688
Aphra Behn, *Oroonoko*

1699
Kong Shangren,
The Peach Blossom Fan

1680 C.E.   1690 C.E.   1700 C.E.

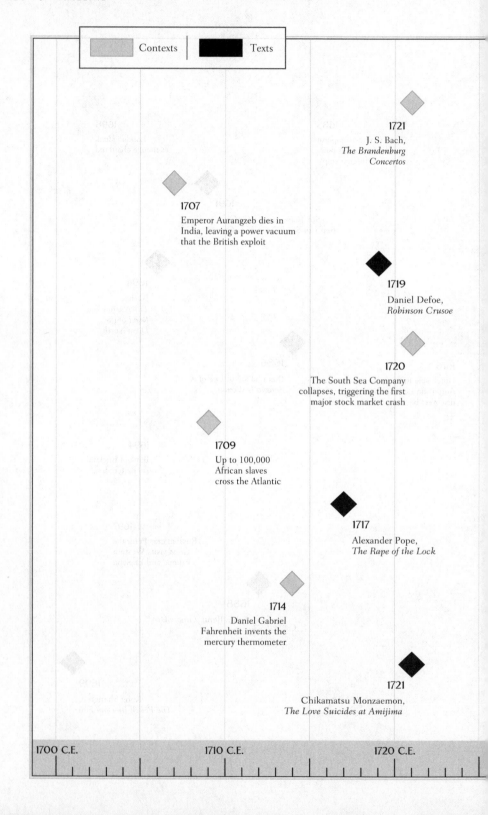

Contexts | Texts

1721
J. S. Bach,
*The Brandenburg
Concertos*

1707
Emperor Aurangzeb dies in
India, leaving a power vacuum
that the British exploit

1719
Daniel Defoe,
Robinson Crusoe

1720
The South Sea Company
collapses, triggering the first
major stock market crash

1709
Up to 100,000
African slaves
cross the Atlantic

1717
Alexander Pope,
The Rape of the Lock

1714
Daniel Gabriel
Fahrenheit invents the
mercury thermometer

1721
Chikamatsu Monzaemon,
The Love Suicides at Amijima

1700 C.E.   1710 C.E.   1720 C.E.

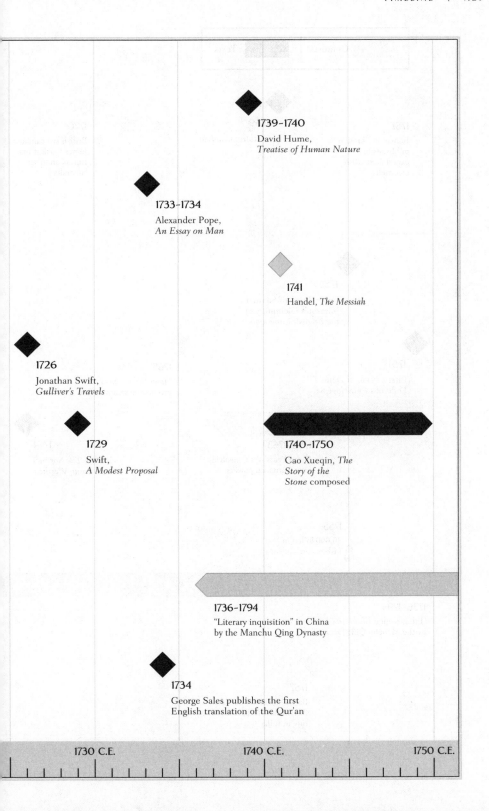

1739-1740
David Hume,
Treatise of Human Nature

1733-1734
Alexander Pope,
An Essay on Man

1741
Handel, *The Messiah*

1726
Jonathan Swift,
Gulliver's Travels

1729
Swift,
A Modest Proposal

1740-1750
Cao Xueqin, *The Story of the Stone* composed

1736-1794
"Literary inquisition" in China
by the Manchu Qing Dynasty

1734
George Sales publishes the first
English translation of the Qur'an

1730 C.E.   1740 C.E.   1750 C.E.

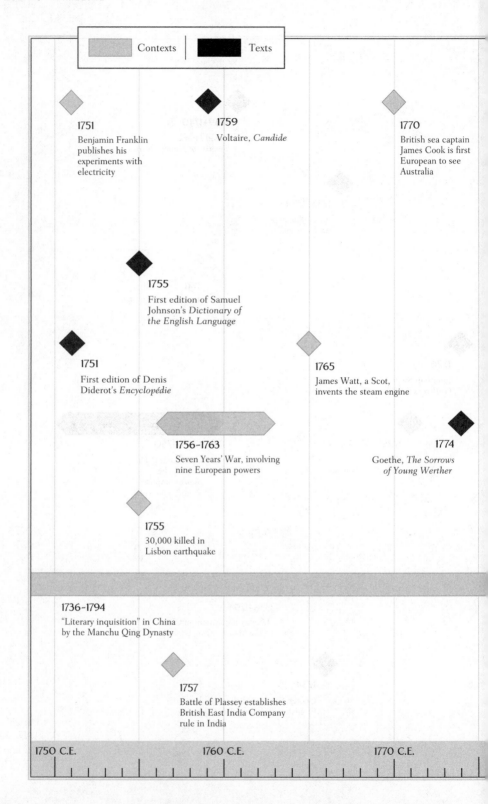

Contexts | Texts

1751
Benjamin Franklin publishes his experiments with electricity

1759
Voltaire, *Candide*

1770
British sea captain James Cook is first European to see Australia

1755
First edition of Samuel Johnson's *Dictionary of the English Language*

1751
First edition of Denis Diderot's *Encyclopédie*

1765
James Watt, a Scot, invents the steam engine

1756–1763
Seven Years' War, involving nine European powers

1774
Goethe, *The Sorrows of Young Werther*

1755
30,000 killed in Lisbon earthquake

1736–1794
"Literary inquisition" in China by the Manchu Qing Dynasty

1757
Battle of Plassey establishes British East India Company rule in India

1750 C.E.   1760 C.E.   1770 C.E.

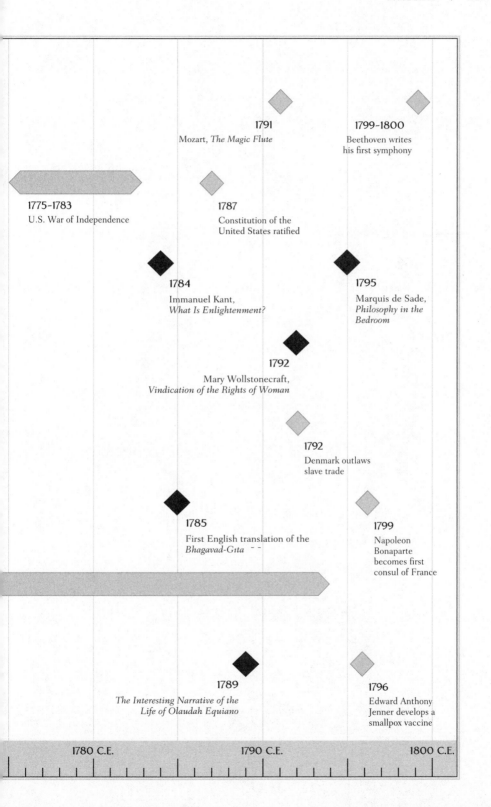

1791
Mozart, *The Magic Flute*

1799-1800
Beethoven writes
his first symphony

1775-1783
U.S. War of Independence

1787
Constitution of the
United States ratified

1784
Immanuel Kant,
What Is Enlightenment?

1795
Marquis de Sade,
*Philosophy in the
Bedroom*

1792
Mary Wollstonecraft,
Vindication of the Rights of Woman

1792
Denmark outlaws
slave trade

1785
First English translation of the
Bhagavad-Gita

1799
Napoleon
Bonaparte
becomes first
consul of France

1789
*The Interesting Narrative of the
Life of Olaudah Equiano*

1796
Edward Anthony
Jenner develops a
smallpox vaccine

1780 C.E.   1790 C.E.   1800 C.E.

TIMELINE *for*

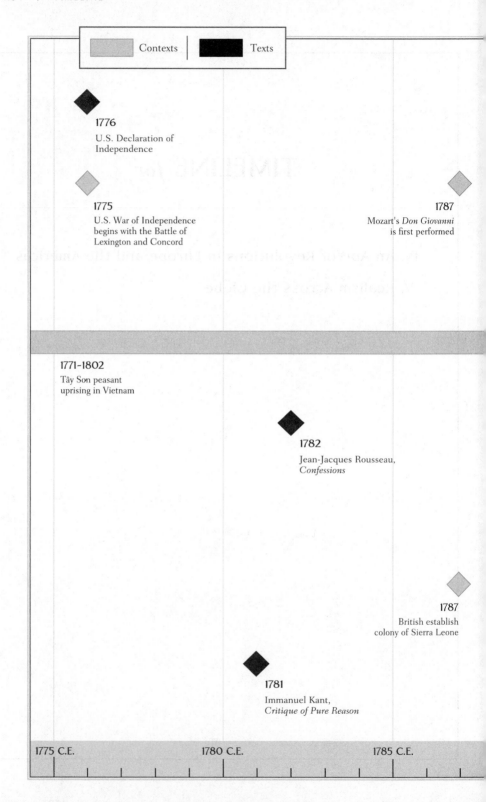

Contexts | Texts

1776
U.S. Declaration of
Independence

1775
U.S. War of Independence
begins with the Battle of
Lexington and Concord

1787
Mozart's *Don Giovanni*
is first performed

1771–1802
Tây Sơn peasant
uprising in Vietnam

1782
Jean-Jacques Rousseau,
Confessions

1787
British establish
colony of Sierra Leone

1781
Immanuel Kant,
Critique of Pure Reason

1775 C.E.   1780 C.E.   1785 C.E.

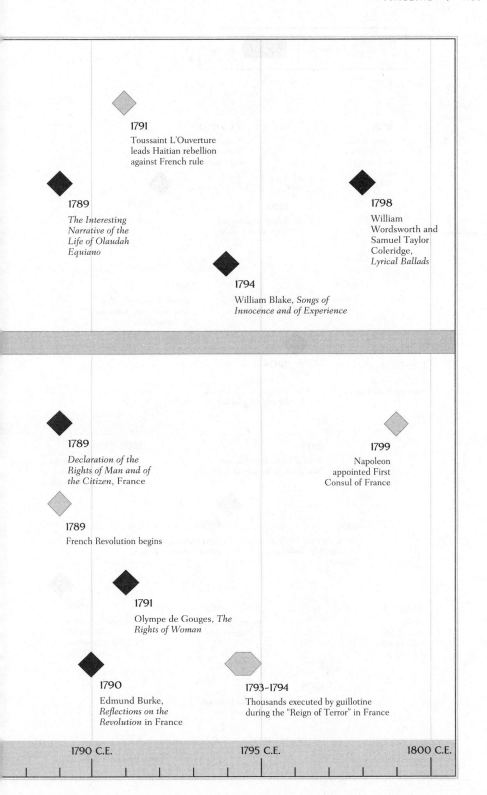

1791

Toussaint L'Ouverture leads Haitian rebellion against French rule

1789

The Interesting Narrative of the Life of Olaudah Equiano

1798

William Wordsworth and Samuel Taylor Coleridge, *Lyrical Ballads*

1794

William Blake, *Songs of Innocence and of Experience*

1789

Declaration of the Rights of Man and of the Citizen, France

1799

Napoleon appointed First Consul of France

1789

French Revolution begins

1791

Olympe de Gouges, *The Rights of Woman*

1790

Edmund Burke, *Reflections on the Revolution* in France

1793-1794

Thousands executed by guillotine during the "Reign of Terror" in France

1790 C.E.   1795 C.E.   1800 C.E.

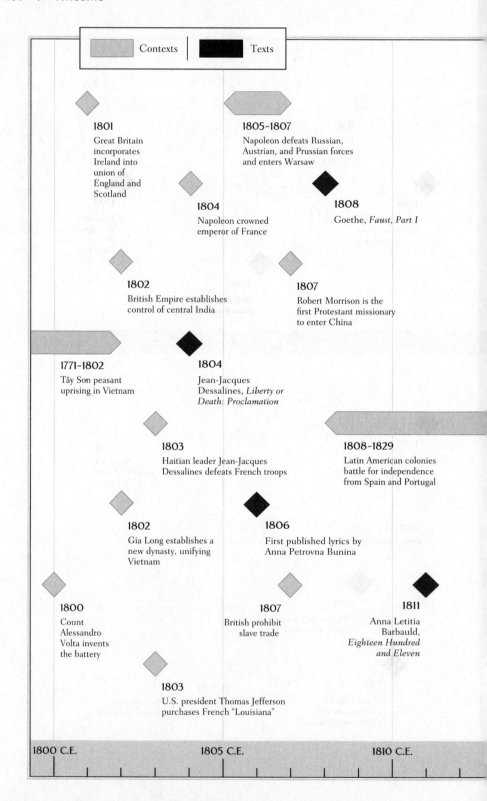

Contexts | Texts

1801
Great Britain incorporates Ireland into union of England and Scotland

1805–1807
Napoleon defeats Russian, Austrian, and Prussian forces and enters Warsaw

1804
Napoleon crowned emperor of France

1808
Goethe, *Faust, Part I*

1802
British Empire establishes control of central India

1807
Robert Morrison is the first Protestant missionary to enter China

1771–1802
Tây Sơn peasant uprising in Vietnam

1804
Jean-Jacques Dessalines, *Liberty or Death: Proclamation*

1803
Haitian leader Jean-Jacques Dessalines defeats French troops

1808–1829
Latin American colonies battle for independence from Spain and Portugal

1802
Gia Long establishes a new dynasty, unifying Vietnam

1806
First published lyrics by Anna Petrovna Bunina

1800
Count Alessandro Volta invents the battery

1807
British prohibit slave trade

1811
Anna Letitia Barbauld, *Eighteen Hundred and Eleven*

1803
U.S. president Thomas Jefferson purchases French "Louisiana"

1800 C.E.   1805 C.E.   1810 C.E.

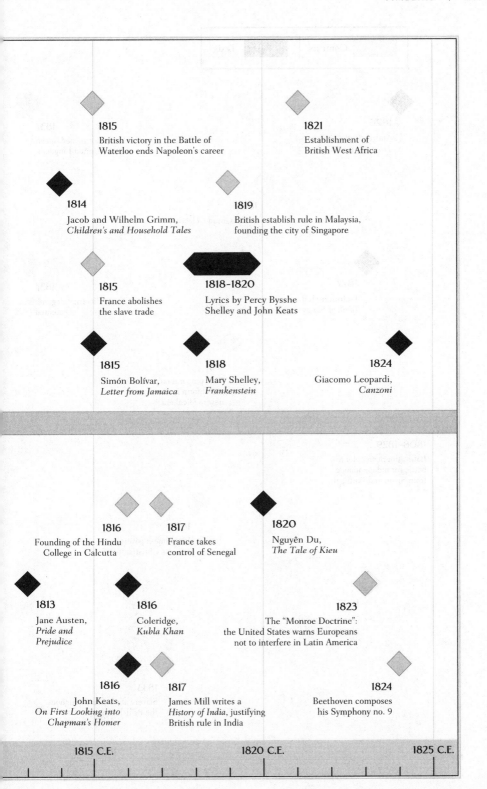

1815

British victory in the Battle of Waterloo ends Napoleon's career

1821

Establishment of British West Africa

1814

Jacob and Wilhelm Grimm, *Children's and Household Tales*

1819

British establish rule in Malaysia, founding the city of Singapore

1815

France abolishes the slave trade

1818–1820

Lyrics by Percy Bysshe Shelley and John Keats

1815

Simón Bolívar, *Letter from Jamaica*

1818

Mary Shelley, *Frankenstein*

1824

Giacomo Leopardi, *Canzoni*

1816

Founding of the Hindu College in Calcutta

1817

France takes control of Senegal

1820

Nguyên Du, *The Tale of Kieu*

1813

Jane Austen, *Pride and Prejudice*

1816

Coleridge, *Kubla Khan*

1823

The "Monroe Doctrine": the United States warns Europeans not to interfere in Latin America

1816

John Keats, *On First Looking into Chapman's Homer*

1817

James Mill writes a *History of India*, justifying British rule in India

1824

Beethoven composes his Symphony no. 9

1815 C.E.   1820 C.E.   1825 C.E.

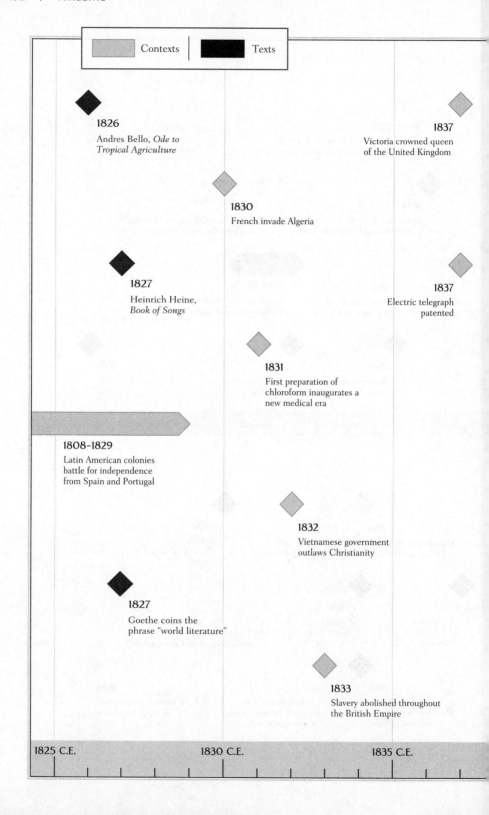

Contexts   Texts

1826
Andres Bello, *Ode to Tropical Agriculture*

1837
Victoria crowned queen of the United Kingdom

1830
French invade Algeria

1827
Heinrich Heine, *Book of Songs*

1837
Electric telegraph patented

1831
First preparation of chloroform inaugurates a new medical era

1808–1829
Latin American colonies battle for independence from Spain and Portugal

1832
Vietnamese government outlaws Christianity

1827
Goethe coins the phrase "world literature"

1833
Slavery abolished throughout the British Empire

1825 C.E.   1830 C.E.   1835 C.E.

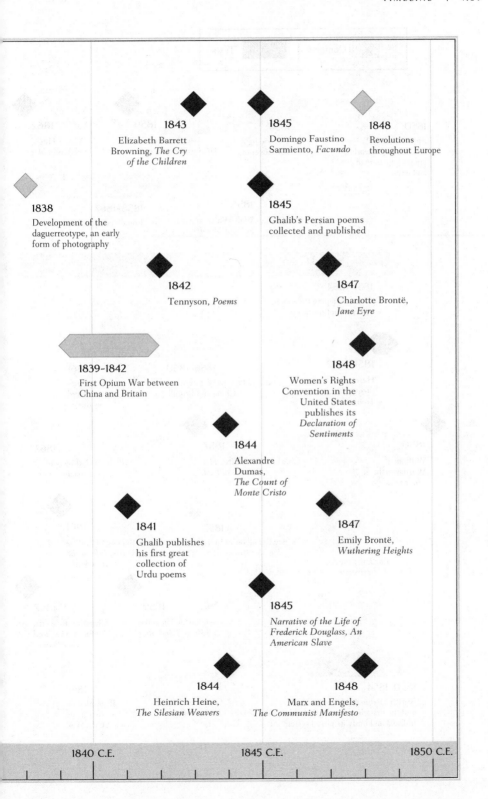

1843
Elizabeth Barrett
Browning, *The Cry
of the Children*

1845
Domingo Faustino
Sarmiento, *Facundo*

1848
Revolutions
throughout Europe

1838
Development of the
daguerreotype, an early
form of photography

1845
Ghalib's Persian poems
collected and published

1842
Tennyson, *Poems*

1847
Charlotte Brontë,
Jane Eyre

1839–1842
First Opium War between
China and Britain

1848
Women's Rights
Convention in the
United States
publishes its
*Declaration of
Sentiments*

1844
Alexandre
Dumas,
*The Count of
Monte Cristo*

1841
Ghalib publishes
his first great
collection of
Urdu poems

1847
Emily Brontë,
Wuthering Heights

1845
*Narrative of the Life of
Frederick Douglass, An
American Slave*

1844
Heinrich Heine,
The Silesian Weavers

1848
Marx and Engels,
The Communist Manifesto

1840 C.E.   1845 C.E.   1850 C.E.

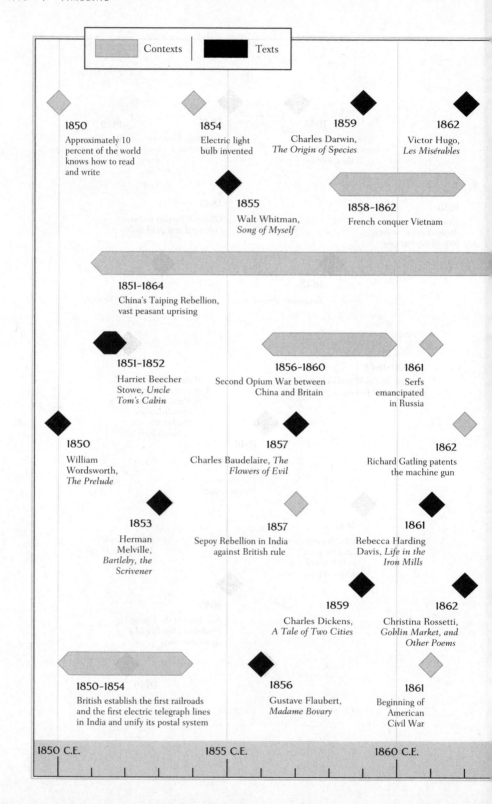

Contexts | Texts

1850
Approximately 10 percent of the world knows how to read and write

1854
Electric light bulb invented

1859
Charles Darwin, *The Origin of Species*

1862
Victor Hugo, *Les Misérables*

1855
Walt Whitman, *Song of Myself*

1858–1862
French conquer Vietnam

1851–1864
China's Taiping Rebellion, vast peasant uprising

1851–1852
Harriet Beecher Stowe, *Uncle Tom's Cabin*

1856–1860
Second Opium War between China and Britain

1861
Serfs emancipated in Russia

1850
William Wordsworth, *The Prelude*

1857
Charles Baudelaire, *The Flowers of Evil*

1862
Richard Gatling patents the machine gun

1853
Herman Melville, *Bartleby, the Scrivener*

1857
Sepoy Rebellion in India against British rule

1861
Rebecca Harding Davis, *Life in the Iron Mills*

1859
Charles Dickens, *A Tale of Two Cities*

1862
Christina Rossetti, *Goblin Market, and Other Poems*

1850–1854
British establish the first railroads and the first electric telegraph lines in India and unify its postal system

1856
Gustave Flaubert, *Madame Bovary*

1861
Beginning of American Civil War

1850 C.E.   1855 C.E.   1860 C.E.

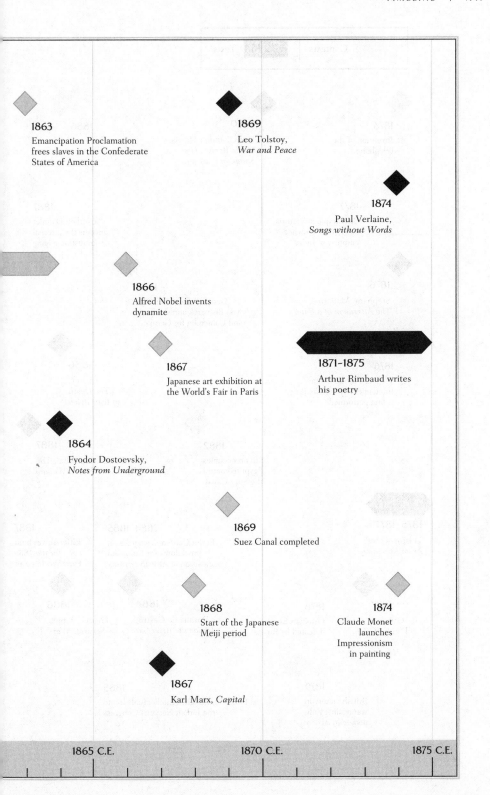

1863
Emancipation Proclamation
frees slaves in the Confederate
States of America

1869
Leo Tolstoy,
War and Peace

1874
Paul Verlaine,
Songs without Words

1866
Alfred Nobel invents
dynamite

1867
Japanese art exhibition at
the World's Fair in Paris

1871–1875
Arthur Rimbaud writes
his poetry

1864
Fyodor Dostoevsky,
Notes from Underground

1869
Suez Canal completed

1868
Start of the Japanese
Meiji period

1874
Claude Monet
launches
Impressionism
in painting

1867
Karl Marx, *Capital*

1865 C.E.   1870 C.E.   1875 C.E.

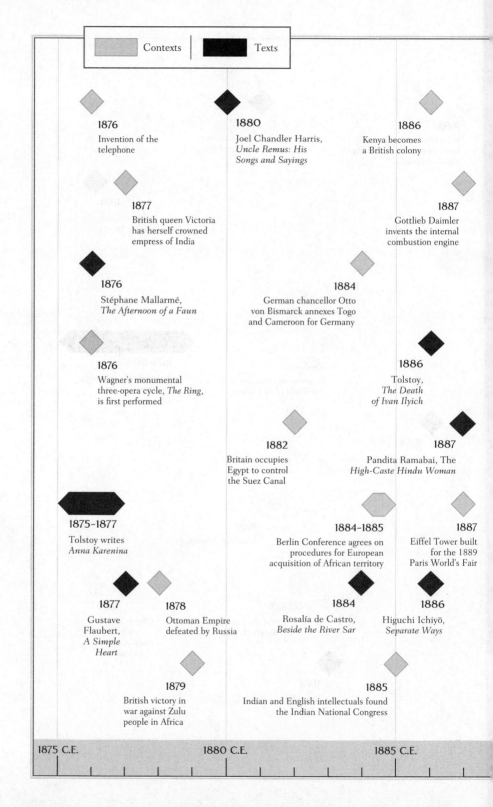

Contexts   Texts

1876
Invention of the
telephone

1880
Joel Chandler Harris,
*Uncle Remus: His
Songs and Sayings*

1886
Kenya becomes
a British colony

1877
British queen Victoria
has herself crowned
empress of India

1887
Gottlieb Daimler
invents the internal
combustion engine

1876
Stéphane Mallarmé,
The Afternoon of a Faun

1884
German chancellor Otto
von Bismarck annexes Togo
and Cameroon for Germany

1876
Wagner's monumental
three-opera cycle, *The Ring*,
is first performed

1886
Tolstoy,
*The Death
of Ivan Ilyich*

1882
Britain occupies
Egypt to control
the Suez Canal

1887
Pandita Ramabai, The
High-Caste Hindu Woman

1875–1877
Tolstoy writes
Anna Karenina

1884–1885
Berlin Conference agrees on
procedures for European
acquisition of African territory

1887
Eiffel Tower built
for the 1889
Paris World's Fair

1877
Gustave
Flaubert,
*A Simple
Heart*

1878
Ottoman Empire
defeated by Russia

1884
Rosalía de Castro,
Beside the River Sar

1886
Higuchi Ichiyō,
Separate Ways

1879
British victory in
war against Zulu
people in Africa

1885
Indian and English intellectuals found
the Indian National Congress

1875 C.E.   1880 C.E.   1885 C.E.

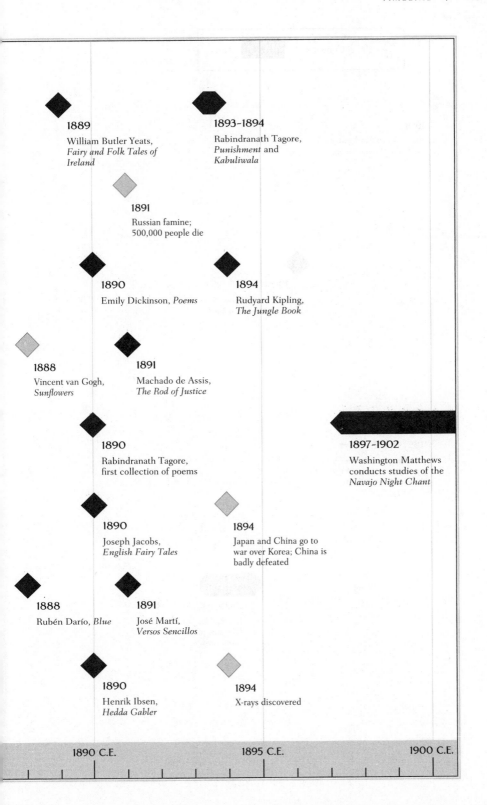

1889

William Butler Yeats,
*Fairy and Folk Tales of
Ireland*

1893-1894

Rabindranath Tagore,
Punishment and
Kabuliwala

1891

Russian famine;
500,000 people die

1890

Emily Dickinson, *Poems*

1894

Rudyard Kipling,
The Jungle Book

1888

Vincent van Gogh,
Sunflowers

1891

Machado de Assis,
The Rod of Justice

1890

Rabindranath Tagore,
first collection of poems

1897-1902

Washington Matthews
conducts studies of the
Navajo Night Chant

1890

Joseph Jacobs,
English Fairy Tales

1894

Japan and China go to
war over Korea; China is
badly defeated

1888

Rubén Darío, *Blue*

1891

José Martí,
Versos Sencillos

1890

Henrik Ibsen,
Hedda Gabler

1894

X-rays discovered

1890 C.E.   1895 C.E.   1900 C.E.

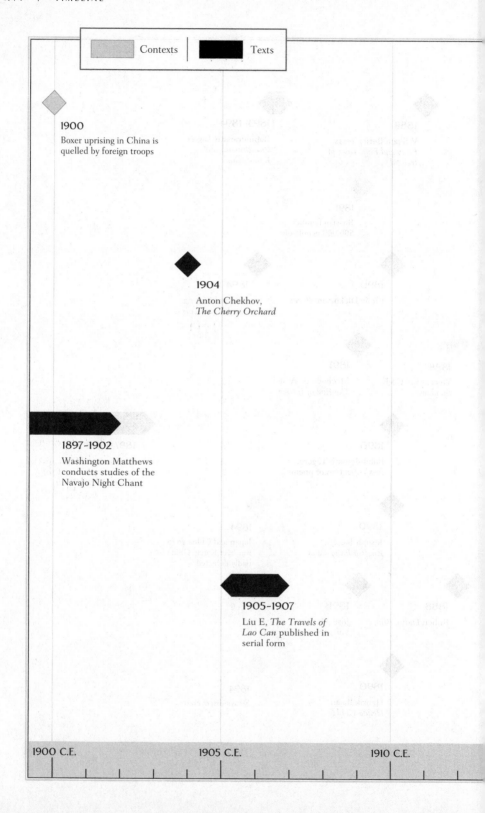

| Contexts | Texts |

1900
Boxer uprising in China is
quelled by foreign troops

1904
Anton Chekhov,
The Cherry Orchard

1897–1902
Washington Matthews
conducts studies of the
Navajo Night Chant

1905–1907
Liu E, *The Travels of
Lao Can* published in
serial form

1900 C.E.   1905 C.E.   1910 C.E.

1915 C.E.

1920 C.E.

1925 C.E.

TIMELINE *for*

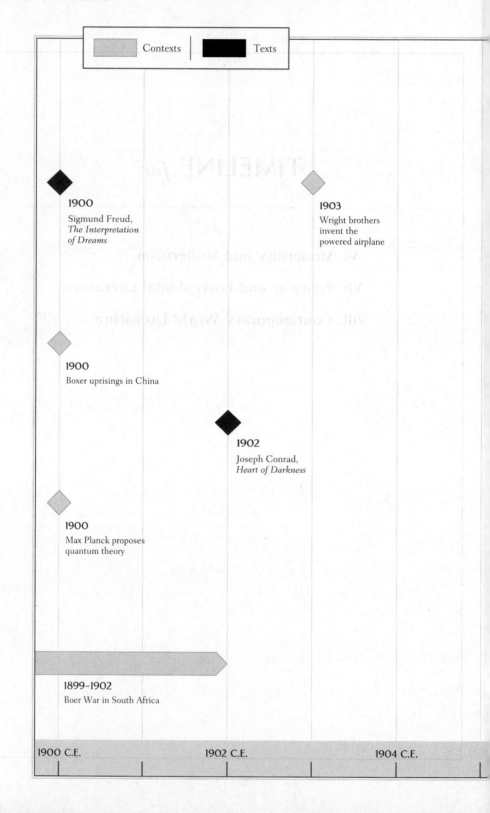

Contexts | Texts

1900
Sigmund Freud,
*The Interpretation
of Dreams*

1903
Wright brothers
invent the
powered airplane

1900
Boxer uprisings in China

1902
Joseph Conrad,
Heart of Darkness

1900
Max Planck proposes
quantum theory

1899–1902
Boer War in South Africa

1900 C.E.   1902 C.E.   1904 C.E.

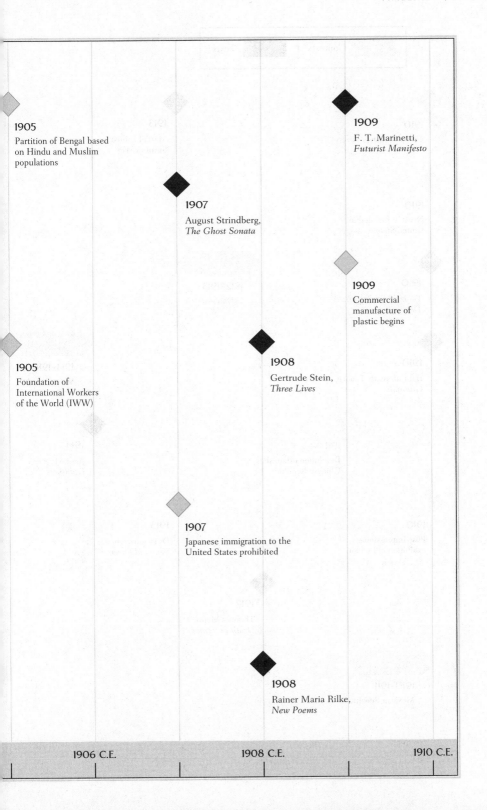

1905
Partition of Bengal based
on Hindu and Muslim
populations

1909
F. T. Marinetti,
Futurist Manifesto

1907
August Strindberg,
The Ghost Sonata

1909
Commercial
manufacture of
plastic begins

1908
Gertrude Stein,
Three Lives

1905
Foundation of
International Workers
of the World (IWW)

1907
Japanese immigration to the
United States prohibited

1908
Rainer Maria Rilke,
New Poems

1906 C.E.   1908 C.E.   1910 C.E.

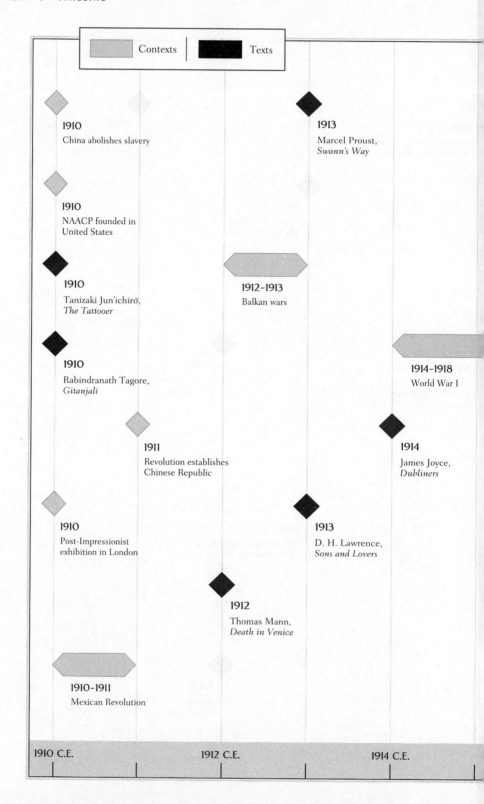

Contexts | Texts

1910
China abolishes slavery

1910
NAACP founded in
United States

1910
Tanizaki Jun'ichirō,
The Tattooer

1910
Rabindranath Tagore,
Gitanjali

1911
Revolution establishes
Chinese Republic

1910
Post-Impressionist
exhibition in London

1910–1911
Mexican Revolution

1913
Marcel Proust,
Swann's Way

1912–1913
Balkan wars

1914–1918
World War I

1914
James Joyce,
Dubliners

1913
D. H. Lawrence,
Sons and Lovers

1912
Thomas Mann,
Death in Venice

1910 C.E.   **1912 C.E.**   **1914 C.E.**

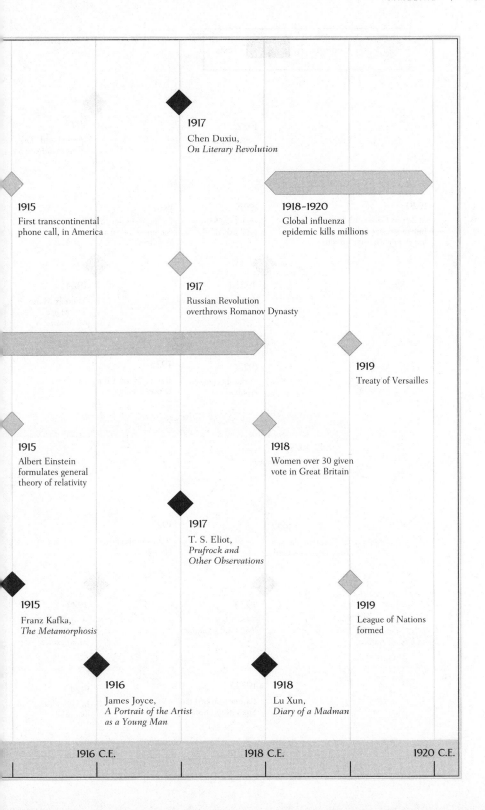

1917
Chen Duxiu,
On Literary Revolution

1915
First transcontinental
phone call, in America

1918–1920
Global influenza
epidemic kills millions

1917
Russian Revolution
overthrows Romanov Dynasty

1919
Treaty of Versailles

1915
Albert Einstein
formulates general
theory of relativity

1918
Women over 30 given
vote in Great Britain

1917
T. S. Eliot,
*Prufrock and
Other Observations*

1915
Franz Kafka,
The Metamorphosis

1919
League of Nations
formed

1916
James Joyce,
*A Portrait of the Artist
as a Young Man*

1918
Lu Xun,
Diary of a Madman

1916 C.E.   1918 C.E.   1920 C.E.

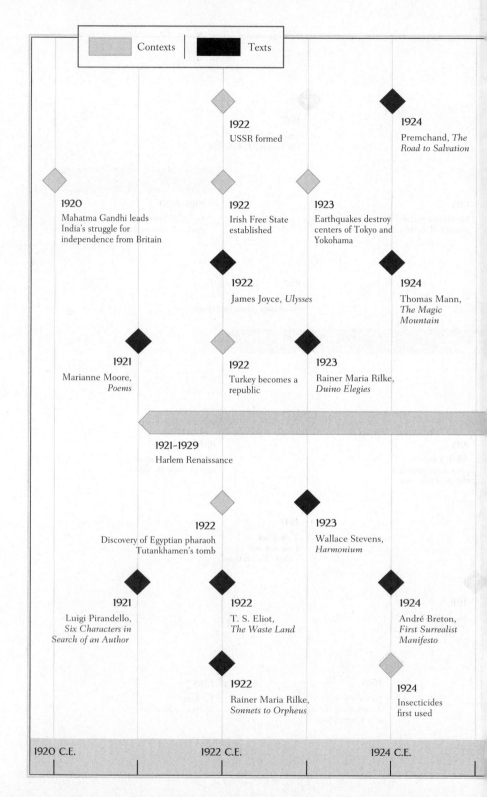

Contexts | Texts

1922
USSR formed

1924
Premchand, *The Road to Salvation*

1920
Mahatma Gandhi leads India's struggle for independence from Britain

1922
Irish Free State established

1923
Earthquakes destroy centers of Tokyo and Yokohama

1922
James Joyce, *Ulysses*

1924
Thomas Mann, *The Magic Mountain*

1921
Marianne Moore, *Poems*

1922
Turkey becomes a republic

1923
Rainer Maria Rilke, *Duino Elegies*

1921–1929
Harlem Renaissance

1922
Discovery of Egyptian pharaoh Tutankhamen's tomb

1923
Wallace Stevens, *Harmonium*

1921
Luigi Pirandello, *Six Characters in Search of an Author*

1922
T. S. Eliot, *The Waste Land*

1924
André Breton, *First Surrealist Manifesto*

1922
Rainer Maria Rilke, *Sonnets to Orpheus*

1924
Insecticides first used

1920 C.E.   1922 C.E.   1924 C.E.

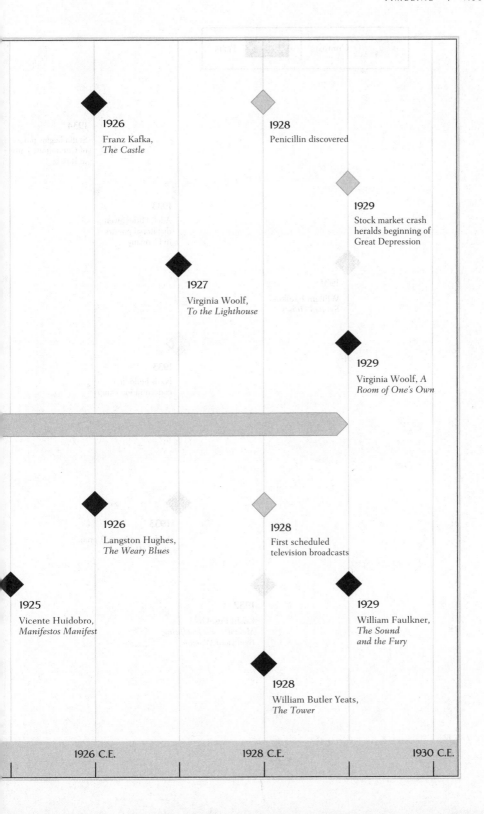

1926

Franz Kafka,
The Castle

1928

Penicillin discovered

1929

Stock market crash
heralds beginning of
Great Depression

1927

Virginia Woolf,
To the Lighthouse

1929

Virginia Woolf, *A
Room of One's Own*

1926

Langston Hughes,
The Weary Blues

1928

First scheduled
television broadcasts

1925

Vicente Huidobro,
Manifestos Manifest

1929

William Faulkner,
*The Sound
and the Fury*

1928

William Butler Yeats,
The Tower

1926 C.E.   1928 C.E.   1930 C.E.

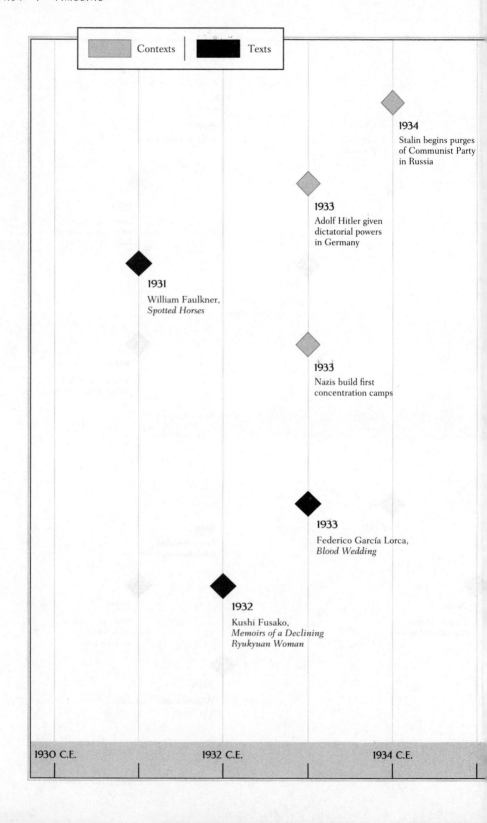

Contexts | Texts

1934
Stalin begins purges
of Communist Party
in Russia

1933
Adolf Hitler given
dictatorial powers
in Germany

1931
William Faulkner,
Spotted Horses

1933
Nazis build first
concentration camps

1933
Federico García Lorca,
Blood Wedding

1932
Kushi Fusako,
*Memoirs of a Declining
Ryukyuan Woman*

1930 C.E.   1932 C.E.   1934 C.E.

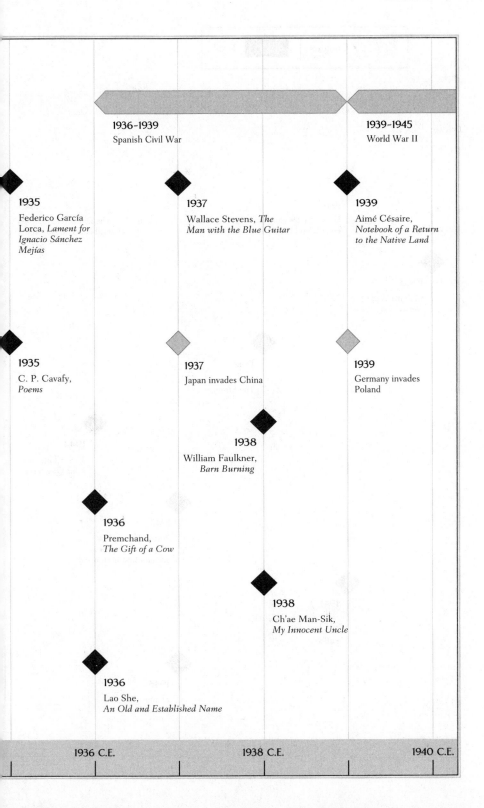

1936–1939
Spanish Civil War

1939–1945
World War II

1935
Federico García
Lorca, *Lament for
Ignacio Sánchez
Mejías*

1937
Wallace Stevens, *The
Man with the Blue Guitar*

1939
Aimé Césaire,
*Notebook of a Return
to the Native Land*

1935
C. P. Cavafy,
Poems

1937
Japan invades China

1939
Germany invades
Poland

1938
William Faulkner,
Barn Burning

1936
Premchand,
The Gift of a Cow

1938
Ch'ae Man-Sik,
My Innocent Uncle

1936
Lao She,
An Old and Established Name

1936 C.E.

1938 C.E.

1940 C.E.

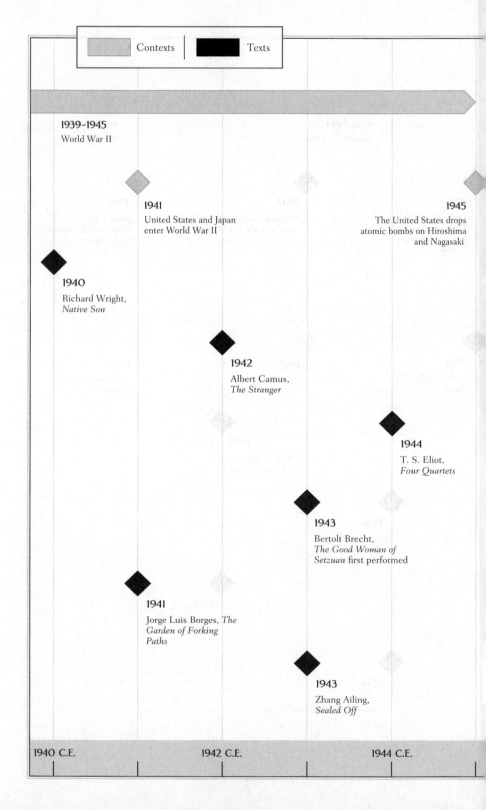

Contexts   Texts

1939-1945
World War II

1941
United States and Japan
enter World War II

1945
The United States drops
atomic bombs on Hiroshima
and Nagasaki

1940
Richard Wright,
Native Son

1942
Albert Camus,
The Stranger

1944
T. S. Eliot,
Four Quartets

1943
Bertolt Brecht,
*The Good Woman of
Setzuan* first performed

1941
Jorge Luis Borges, *The
Garden of Forking
Paths*

1943
Zhang Ailing,
Sealed Off

1940 C.E.   1942 C.E.   1944 C.E.

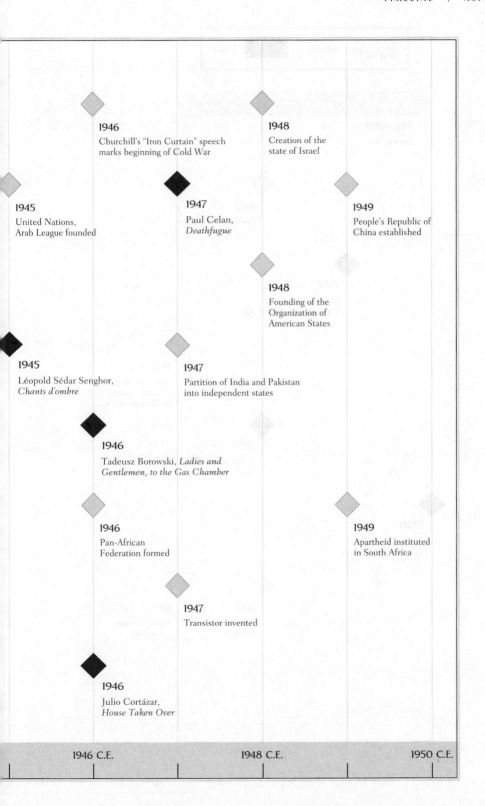

1946
Churchill's "Iron Curtain" speech marks beginning of Cold War

1948
Creation of the state of Israel

1945
United Nations,
Arab League founded

1947
Paul Celan,
Deathfugue

1949
People's Republic of
China established

1948
Founding of the
Organization of
American States

1945
Léopold Sédar Senghor,
Chants d'ombre

1947
Partition of India and Pakistan
into independent states

1946
Tadeusz Borowski, *Ladies and
Gentlemen, to the Gas Chamber*

1946
Pan-African
Federation formed

1949
Apartheid instituted
in South Africa

1947
Transistor invented

1946
Julio Cortázar,
House Taken Over

1946 C.E.   1948 C.E.   1950 C.E.

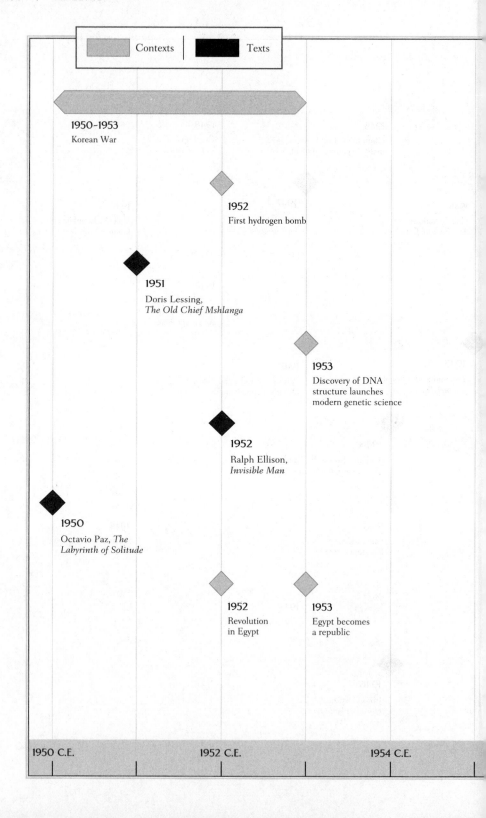

Contexts   Texts

1950–1953
Korean War

1952
First hydrogen bomb

1951
Doris Lessing,
The Old Chief Mshlanga

1953
Discovery of DNA
structure launches
modern genetic science

1952
Ralph Ellison,
Invisible Man

1950
Octavio Paz, *The
Labyrinth of Solitude*

1952
Revolution
in Egypt

1953
Egypt becomes
a republic

1950 C.E.   1952 C.E.   1954 C.E.

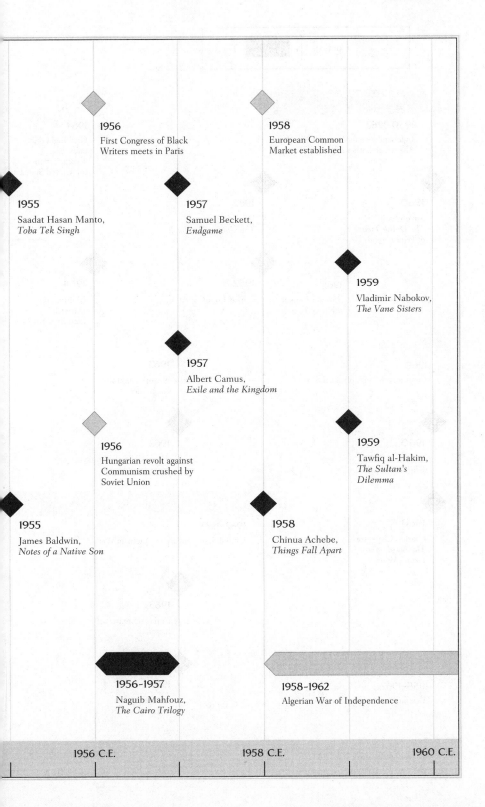

1956
First Congress of Black
Writers meets in Paris

1958
European Common
Market established

1955
Saadat Hasan Manto,
Toba Tek Singh

1957
Samuel Beckett,
Endgame

1959
Vladimir Nabokov,
The Vane Sisters

1957
Albert Camus,
Exile and the Kingdom

1956
Hungarian revolt against
Communism crushed by
Soviet Union

1959
Tawfiq al-Hakim,
*The Sultan's
Dilemma*

1955
James Baldwin,
Notes of a Native Son

1958
Chinua Achebe,
Things Fall Apart

1956-1957
Naguib Mahfouz,
The Cairo Trilogy

1958-1962
Algerian War of Independence

1956 C.E.   **1958 C.E.**   **1960 C.E.**

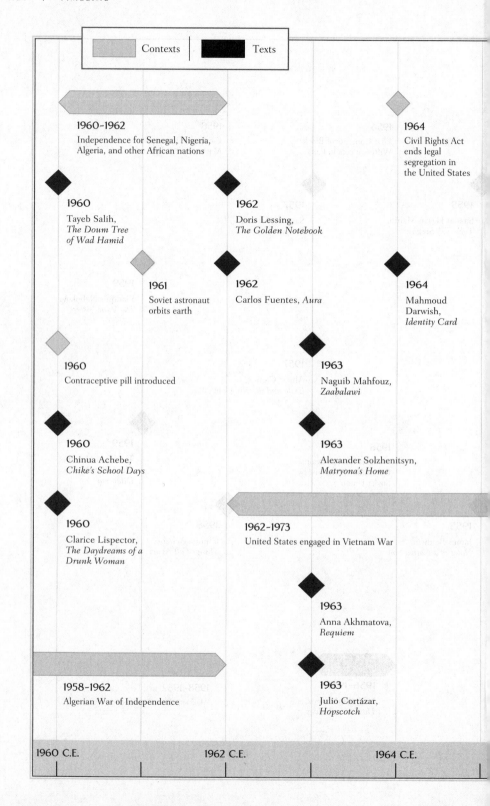

Contexts   Texts

1960–1962
Independence for Senegal, Nigeria, Algeria, and other African nations

1964
Civil Rights Act ends legal segregation in the United States

1960
Tayeb Salih, *The Doum Tree of Wad Hamid*

1962
Doris Lessing, *The Golden Notebook*

1961
Soviet astronaut orbits earth

1962
Carlos Fuentes, *Aura*

1964
Mahmoud Darwish, *Identity Card*

1960
Contraceptive pill introduced

1963
Naguib Mahfouz, *Zaabalawi*

1960
Chinua Achebe, *Chike's School Days*

1963
Alexander Solzhenitsyn, *Matryona's Home*

1960
Clarice Lispector, *The Daydreams of a Drunk Woman*

1962–1973
United States engaged in Vietnam War

1963
Anna Akhmatova, *Requiem*

1958–1962
Algerian War of Independence

1963
Julio Cortázar, *Hopscotch*

1960 C.E.   1962 C.E.   1964 C.E.

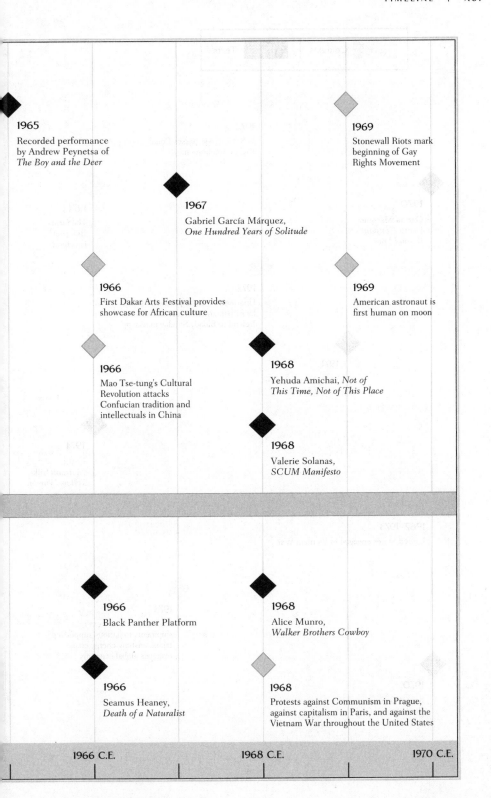

1965
Recorded performance
by Andrew Peynetsa of
The Boy and the Deer

1969
Stonewall Riots mark
beginning of Gay
Rights Movement

1967
Gabriel García Márquez,
One Hundred Years of Solitude

1966
First Dakar Arts Festival provides
showcase for African culture

1969
American astronaut is
first human on moon

1966
Mao Tse-tung's Cultural
Revolution attacks
Confucian tradition and
intellectuals in China

1968
Yehuda Amichai, *Not of
This Time, Not of This Place*

1968
Valerie Solanas,
SCUM Manifesto

1966
Black Panther Platform

1968
Alice Munro,
Walker Brothers Cowboy

1966
Seamus Heaney,
Death of a Naturalist

1968
Protests against Communism in Prague,
against capitalism in Paris, and against the
Vietnam War throughout the United States

1966 C.E.   1968 C.E.   1970 C.E.

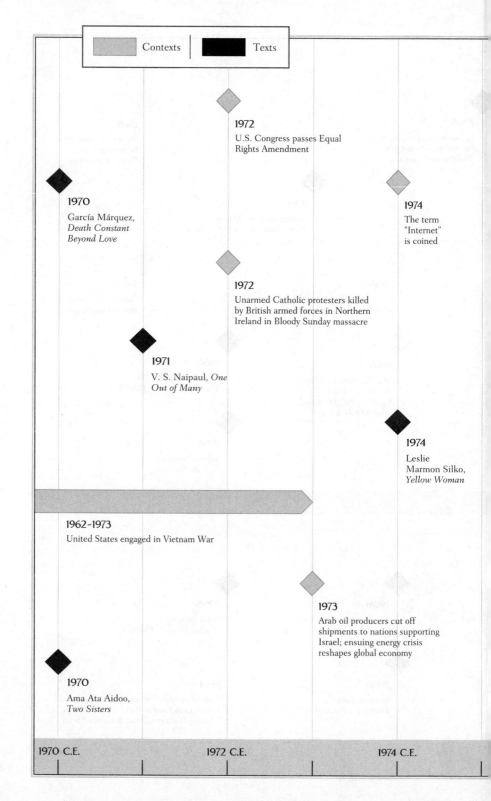

Contexts | Texts

1972
U.S. Congress passes Equal
Rights Amendment

1970
García Márquez,
*Death Constant
Beyond Love*

1974
The term
"Internet"
is coined

1972
Unarmed Catholic protesters killed
by British armed forces in Northern
Ireland in Bloody Sunday massacre

1971
V. S. Naipaul, *One
Out of Many*

1974
Leslie
Marmon Silko,
Yellow Woman

1962–1973
United States engaged in Vietnam War

1973
Arab oil producers cut off
shipments to nations supporting
Israel; ensuing energy crisis
reshapes global economy

1970
Ama Ata Aidoo,
Two Sisters

1970 C.E.   1972 C.E.   1974 C.E.

1976

North and South Vietnam
reunited as a single country

1977

Bessie Head,
Deep River

1975

Wole Soyinka,
*Death and the
King's Horseman*

1979

Soviet invasion
of Afghanistan

1975

Ngugi wa Thiong'o,
Wedding at the Cross

1978

First "test tube baby"
born in England

1976 C.E.   1978 C.E.   1980 C.E.

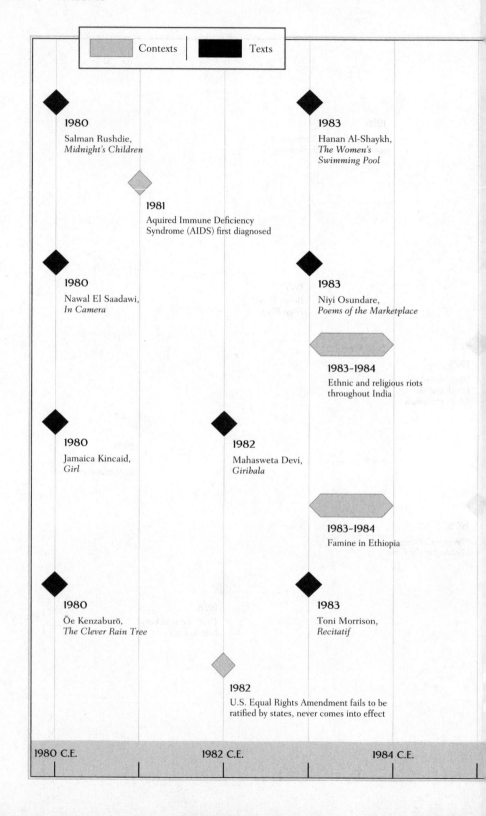

Contexts | Texts

1980
Salman Rushdie,
Midnight's Children

1983
Hanan Al-Shaykh,
*The Women's
Swimming Pool*

1981
Aquired Immune Deficiency
Syndrome (AIDS) first diagnosed

1980
Nawal El Saadawi,
In Camera

1983
Niyi Osundare,
Poems of the Marketplace

1983-1984
Ethnic and religious riots
throughout India

1980
Jamaica Kincaid,
Girl

1982
Mahasweta Devi,
Giribala

1983-1984
Famine in Ethiopia

1980
Ōe Kenzaburō,
The Clever Rain Tree

1983
Toni Morrison,
Recitatif

1982
U.S. Equal Rights Amendment fails to be
ratified by states, never comes into effect

1980 C.E.   1982 C.E.   1984 C.E.

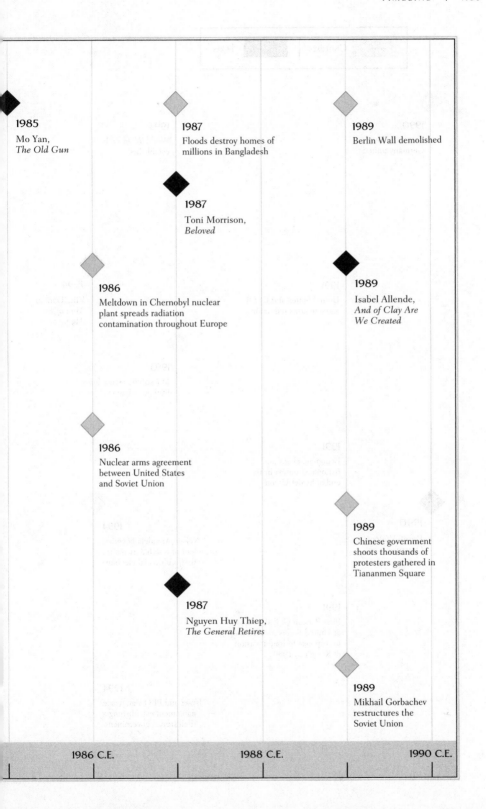

1985

Mo Yan,
The Old Gun

1987

Floods destroy homes of
millions in Bangladesh

1989

Berlin Wall demolished

1987

Toni Morrison,
Beloved

1986

Meltdown in Chernobyl nuclear
plant spreads radiation
contamination throughout Europe

1989

Isabel Allende,
*And of Clay Are
We Created*

1986

Nuclear arms agreement
between United States
and Soviet Union

1989

Chinese government
shoots thousands of
protesters gathered in
Tiananmen Square

1987

Nguyen Huy Thiep,
The General Retires

1989

Mikhail Gorbachev
restructures the
Soviet Union

1986 C.E.   1988 C.E.   1990 C.E.

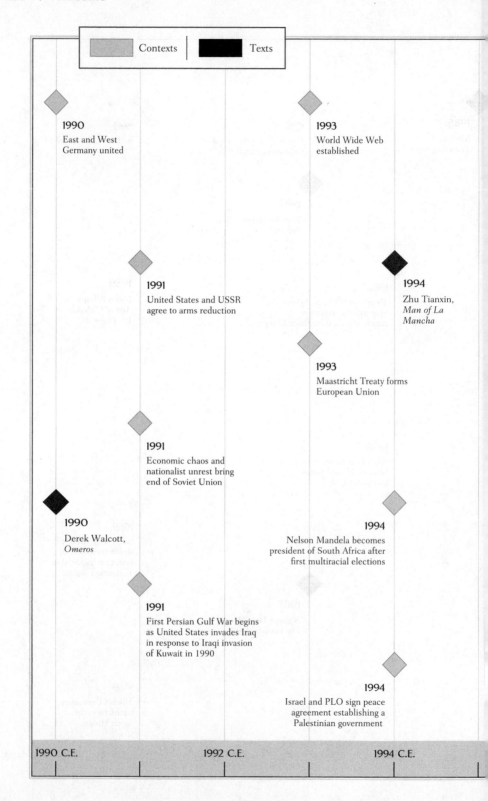

Contexts | Texts

1990
East and West
Germany united

1993
World Wide Web
established

1991
United States and USSR
agree to arms reduction

1994
Zhu Tianxin,
*Man of La
Mancha*

1993
Maastricht Treaty forms
European Union

1991
Economic chaos and
nationalist unrest bring
end of Soviet Union

1990
Derek Walcott,
Omeros

1994
Nelson Mandela becomes
president of South Africa after
first multiracial elections

1991
First Persian Gulf War begins
as United States invades Iraq
in response to Iraqi invasion
of Kuwait in 1990

1994
Israel and PLO sign peace
agreement establishing a
Palestinian government

1990 C.E.   1992 C.E.   1994 C.E.

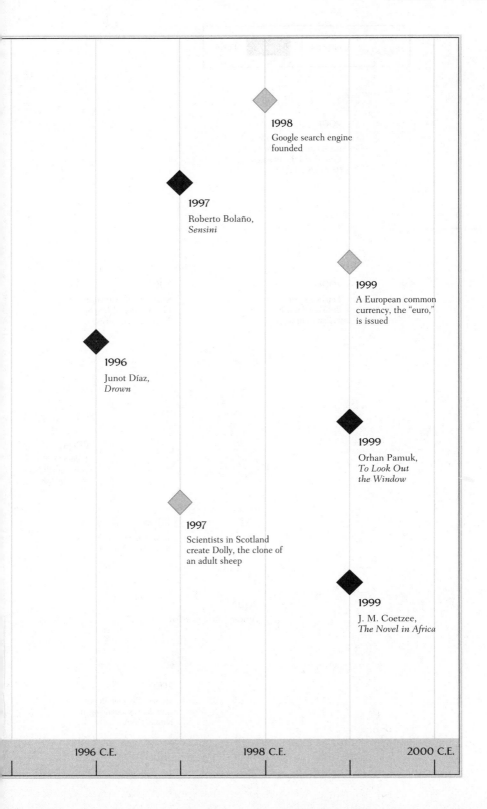

1998
Google search engine
founded

1997
Roberto Bolaño,
Sensini

1999
A European common
currency, the "euro,"
is issued

1996
Junot Díaz,
Drown

1999
Orhan Pamuk,
*To Look Out
the Window*

1997
Scientists in Scotland
create Dolly, the clone of
an adult sheep

1999
J. M. Coetzee,
The Novel in Africa

1996 C.E.   1998 C.E.   2000 C.E.

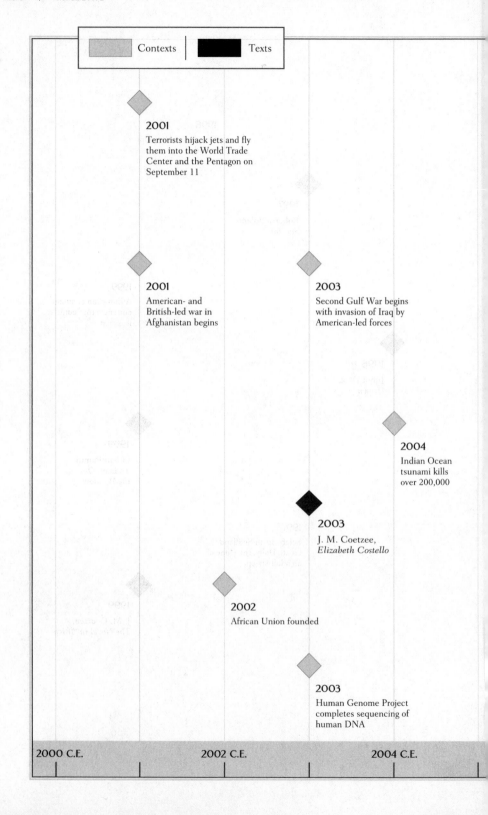

Contexts | Texts

2001
Terrorists hijack jets and fly them into the World Trade Center and the Pentagon on September 11

2001
American- and British-led war in Afghanistan begins

2003
Second Gulf War begins with invasion of Iraq by American-led forces

2004
Indian Ocean tsunami kills over 200,000

2003
J. M. Coetzee, *Elizabeth Costello*

2002
African Union founded

2003
Human Genome Project completes sequencing of human DNA

2000 C.E.   2002 C.E.   2004 C.E.

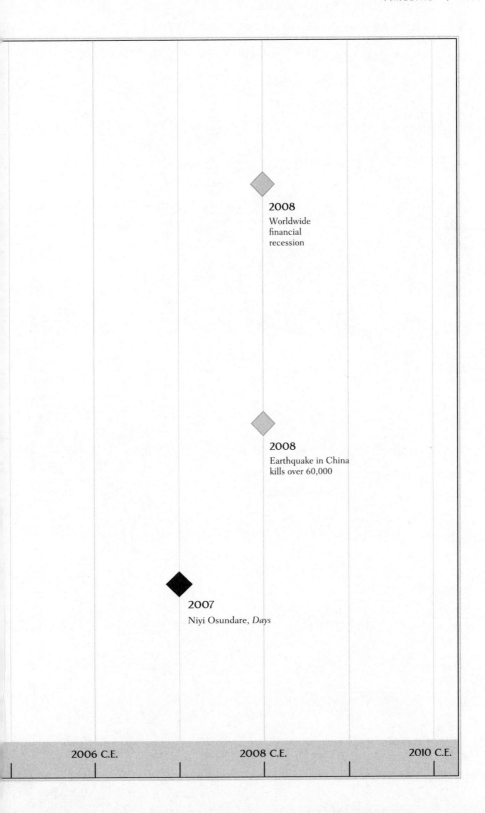

2008
Worldwide
financial
recession

2008
Earthquake in China
kills over 60,000

2007

Niyi Osundare, *Days*

2006 C.E.   2008 C.E.   2010 C.E.

Permissions Acknowledgments

IMAGES

Life Pictures/Getty Images; **1438** © Bettmann/Corbis; **1610–11** Marc Riboud/Magnum Photos; **1612** Jean-Claude LABBE/Gamma-Rapho via Getty Images; **1613** Gallo Images/Oryx Media Archive/Getty Images; **1616** Shirin Neshat; **1617** Andy Johnson.

COLOR INSERT

Dushi Wang. Réuniion des Musée Nationaux/Art Resource, NY; **Calligraphy by Matsuo Basho.** Werner Forman/Art Resource, NY; **The Peddler.** Réuniion des Musée Nationaux/Art Resource, NY; **Commonplace Book.** Wikimedia Commons/Yale University Beinecke Library; **Gulliver's Travels.** The Pierpont Morgan Library/Art Resource, NY; **Daytime in the Gay Quarters.** Brooklyn Museum/Corbis; **Sister Juana Ines de la Cruz.** Schalkwijk/Art Resource, NY; **Wedgewood anti-slavery medallion.** Trustees of the British Museum/Art Resource, NY; **Freedom of the Press.** Reunion des Musees Nationaux /Art Resource, NY; **The store of book dealer Pieter Meijer Warnars.** bpk, Berlin / Art Resource, NY; **Cover: The Pencil of Nature.** SSPL/National Media Museum / Art Resource, NY; **Bust of Patroclus, 1841.** SSPL/National Media Museum / Art Resource, NY; **Hoe's Printing Machine.** Corbis **Swimming Carp.** V&A Images, London / Art Resource, NY; **Street Storyteller in Yokuhama.** Corbis; **Writing ball by Hans Rasmus Mailing-Hansen.** INTERFOTO / Alamy; **Queen Victoria with her Indian servant.** Adoc-photos / Art Resource; **Typing - Photo-Dynamic Futurisim, 1913.** Alinari / Art Resource, NY. **The Reader .** Picasso, Pablo (1881-1973) © ARS, NY. The Reader [Woman in grey]. 1920. CNAC/MNAM/ Reunion des Musees Nationaux /Art Resource, NY. © ARS, NY. **"From darkness into light."** HIP / Art Resource, NY. **"Circe" Chapter of James Joyce's Ulysses.** Lorenzo Ciniglio/Corbis; **Portrait photograph of Virginia Woolf.** The New York Public Library / Art Resource, NY. **Draft notes of Virginia Woolf for her novel Mrs Dalloway.** HIP / Art Resource, NY. **Nigerian author Chinua Achebe.** Eliot Elisofon/Time Life Pictures/Getty Images. **Calligraphy contest in Xian, China.** Imaginechina/Corbis. **T.S.Eliot cover.** © The Touch Press; **T.S.Eliot menu page.** © The Touch Press.

Index